Francis E. J. Valpy

Whittaker's Improved Edition of Valpy's Gradus Ad Parnassum

Greatly amended and enl. with many thousand new articles

Francis E. J. Valpy

Whittaker's Improved Edition of Valpy's Gradus Ad Parnassum
Greatly amended and enl. with many thousand new articles

ISBN/EAN: 9783337406462

Printed in Europe, USA, Canada, Australia, Japan

Cover: Foto ©Andreas Hilbeck / pixelio.de

More available books at **www.hansebooks.com**

WHITTAKER'S

IMPROVED EDITION OF

VALPY'S

GRADUS

AD PARNASSUM.

GREATLY AMENDED AND ENLARGED WITH MANY
THOUSAND NEW ARTICLES.

NEW EDITION.

LONDON:

WHITTAKER AND CO., AVE MARIA LANE.

1860.

LONDON :
GILBERT AND RIVINGTON, PRINTERS,
ST. JOHN'S SQUARE.

PREFACE.

"THE GRADUS," says Dr. Knox, "*proves more pernicious than useful to the young men who use it.*" In consequence of such respectable authority, it has been endeavoured to remedy the evil, by presenting this abridged work to the notice of Schoolmasters. Many indeed have for a long time complained that the Gradus, in its former shape, occasioned not only a considerable loss of time, but was equally prejudicial to the taste, good sense, and fancy of the student.

At each word, he is checked by a multitude of quotations, descriptions, phrases, &c., which not only divert his attention from the subject he is treating, but also present him with such an assemblage of different styles and sentiments, that his imagination is confused and often impeded.

The first effect of the old Gradus, *intended to introduce us to* Parnassus, was to obscure both unity of thought, and clearness of conception, so necessary to those who court the muse.

That work proved still more fatal to fancy, because the young were obliged to adopt the same ideas which bad, as well as good, poets had before imagined.

Such reflections indeed, added to Dr. Knox's just complaint, first created the desire of pruning the Gradus, and offering to the student an improved and concise *Poetical Dictionary*, which should fully enable him to make Latin verse, without those injurious aids, which are entirely destructive of all original composition.

The whole plan, therefore, has been altered; all descriptions and phrases omitted; epithets and synonyms added; and the volume augmented with a *considerable* number of words, which were not noticed in the old edition. It was strange indeed, that a semi-barbarous word should be introduced, because employed by *Prudentius* and *Nemesianus*, while another word of the purest Latinity was neglected, as unemployed by the Latin poets now in use!

The often erroneous prosody has been corrected; obscure or prolix quotations rendered clearer and shorter; *declension* and *conjugation* of verbs observed; and the *English translation* after each Latin term given.

M. NOEL's extensive Dictionary has been consulted, and great obligation to that publication is confessed. In short, the work required only patience and time, which have not been spared, to render it worthy of its destination. This attempt will be well rewarded, if this work should preserve to our country a single poet, and *protect* the first soaring of some vivid and strong imagination, which would have sunk under the weight of the old Gradus.

ADVERTISEMENT TO THE SIXTH EDITION.

In the present edition the work has been further augmented by the addition of some thousands of new articles; and the student may now refer to it, with confidence, for any word occurring in Virgil, Horace, Ovid, and other poets of the best authority, and the safest models for imitation. The prosody has been carefully revised, and the usage of all previous editions, in many instances, departed from, more particularly in the terminations *um, am, em*, which are now invariably marked short, except in cases of crasis or syncope. Also, to remove a difficulty hitherto in the way of young versifiers, tables have been supplied of the quantities of final syllables of nouns and verbs in inflexion.

J. H.

GRADUS

AD

PARNASSUM.

A, *preposition, which has various meanings.—By, after, with, from, from above, near, against, since, of, for, on, hard by, as to.* Dŭlcēs ā fŏntĭbŭs ūndæ, Virg. SYN. Ăb, ăbs, dē, ē, ēx.

Aă, æ, m., *a river of France, famous for a battle between the French and Burgundians.* SYN. Ăgnĭo, Eūnēno. EPITH. Pĭcārdŭs, Bēlgĭcŭs. Vide Fluvius.

Aărŏn, or Aărŏn *dissyllable,* m. indecl., *son of Amram, brother of Moses, and first Jewish high-priest.* Scēptrī gēstāmĕn Aărŏn, Prud. Mōsēs, Aărŏnquĕ săcērdōs, Fort. SYN. Ămrāmĭdēs, *or* Ămrāmĭădēs, æ, m. EPITH. Māgnŭs, pĭŭs, săcĕr, sānctŭs, clārŭs, fācūndŭs, sacrātŭs, īnclўtŭs, ōptĭmŭs, vĕrēndŭs, vĕnĕrābĭlĭs, vĕnĕrāndŭs, sācrĭfĭcŭs, īnfŭlātŭs. V. Pontifex, Sacerdos.

Ăb. V. a.

ăbāctŏr, ōrĭs, m., Apul., *a sheep-stealer.* EPITH. Ŏccūltŭs, scĕlĕrātŭs, nōctūrnŭs. ăbāctŭs, ă, ŭm, pt. (*from* ăbĭgŏr) *carried away.* Mĕdĭo jām nōctĭs ăbūctæ, Virg. SYN. Ăbdūctŭs, āblātŭs, *or* dējēctŭs, ēxpūlsŭs, pūlsŭs, rĕmōtŭs, rējēctŭs, fŭgātŭs; āctŭs, ēxāctŭs. V. Exul.

ăbāctŭs, ūs, m., *action of carrying away.* V. Furtum.

ăbăcŭs, ī, m., *a desk, a board.* Nēc qui ăbăcō nŭmĕrōs, Pers. SYN. Ăbāx, tābŭlă, mēnsā Pўthăgŏrĕă; mēnsā strūctōrĭă. EPITH. Dīvēs, pūlchĕr, nĭtĭdŭs, aūrĕŭs, ĕbūrnĕŭs, ārgēntĕŭs, cælātŭs, mārmŏrĕŭs, ĕlĕphāntĭnŭs, pīctŭs, dĕcōrŭs; Sămĭŭs (*from the Samian Pythagoras*): dōctŭs, nŭmĕrīs īnscrīptŭs; grăvĭs, mădēns, mădĭdŭs; vīnŏlēntŭs.

ăbălĭēno, ās, *to estrange, to cast off.* Nēc ăbălĭēnēt quās ŏpēs āccēpĕrĭt. (Iamb.) SYN. Ălĭēno, dīsjūngo, āvērto, dīstrăho, dīvēllo, vēndo.

Ăbāntēŭs, ă, ŭm, *of Abas.* Nŭpĕr Ăbāntēĭs, Ov.

Ăbāntĭădēs, æ, m., *Perseus, the descendant of Abas.* Vīctŏr Ăbāntĭădēs, Ov. V. Perseus.

Ăbāntĭăs, ădĭs, f., *a name of the island of Eubœa.* Eūrōpēs Mācrīs cōntīngĭt Ăbāntĭăs ōrăm, Prisc. V. Eubœa.

Ăbāntĭŭs, ă, ŭm, *of Eubœa.* Lĭttŭs ăd Aūsŏnĭŭm dēvēxĭt Ăbāntĭă clāssĭs, Stat. SYN. Eūbœŭs, Eūbŏĭcŭs, Chālcĭdĭcŭs.

ăbārcĕo, ŭī, *or* ăbērcĕo, *to remove.* Ĕam ăbērcēt dŏmō, Plaut. SYN. Arcĕo, prŏhĭbĕo, ămŏvĕo, āvērto, ăbĭgo, pēllo, ēxpēllo, fŭgo. V. Arceo.

Ăbărĭs, ĭs, m., *a priest of Apollo.* Caūcăsĕūmque Ăbārĭm Spērchĭŏnĭdēnquĕ, Ov.—2. *A Rutulian.* Hērbēsūmquĕ sŭbĭt, Rhœtūmque, Ăbārĭmquĕ, Virg.

Ăbās, āntĭs, m., *the twelfth king of Argos.—2. The son of Hippothoon and Meleanira, metamorphosed by Ceres into a lizard.—3. The son of Ixion.* Ĕt Ăbās prædātŏr ăprōrŭm, Ov. SYN. Ixĭōnĭdēs. EPITH. Sævŭs, fĕrōx, sŭpērbŭs, sēmĭfĕr. V. Centaurus.—4. *A companion of Æneas.* Ĕt quā vēctŭs Ăbās, Virg. EPITH. Trŏs ŏĭs, Trŏĭŭs, Trŏjānŭs, Dārdănĭŭs, naūfrăgŭs.—5. *A Greek, killed at the siege of Troy.* Clўpĕūm, māgnī gēstāmĕn Ăbāntĭs, Virg.

Ăbătŏs, ī, f., *an island near Memphis.* Hīnc Ăbătŏs quăm, Lucan. EPITH. Ægўptĭă, Mēmphĭtĭcă, pălūdōsă, ĭnāccēssă.

B

ăbăvŭs, ĭ, m., *a great-grandfather's father.* Nōn ăbăvī sōlŭm, sĕd ăvı quŏquĕ jūn-gĕrĕ făscēs, Sidon. Syn. Quārtŭs pătĕr, Virg. Epith. Lōngævŭs, grāndævŭs, cōlēndŭs, vĕnĕrābĭlĭs, vĕnĕrāndŭs, grăvĭs, sĕnĭŏr, vĕtŭstŭs.

|| ābbās, ātĭs, m., *an abbot.* Ō dĕcŭs ābbātŭm, Ser. Syn. Antĭstĕs, præsŭl, pătĕr, cœnŏbĭārchă. Epith. Vĕnĕrāndŭs, rĕlĭgĭōsŭs, pĭŭs, sānctŭs, īnfŭlātŭs, grăvĭs, săcĕr. V. Episcopus.

|| ābbātĭă, æ, f., *an abbey.* Syn. Cœnŏbĭŭm. Epith. Inclўtă, cĕlĕbrĭs, pĭă. ābcēdo. V. Abscedo.

Ābdēră, æ, f., *a town of Thrace, near which was a lake on which nothing would float.* Aŭt tĕ dĕvŏvĕăt fēstĭs Ābdērā dĭēbŭs, Ovid. Syn. Clăzŏmĕnæ. Epith. Bīstŏnĭă, Thrācĭă, Thrēĭcĭă.

Ābdērītæ, ārŭm, m. pl., *a Thracian nation, the frenzy of which Lucian describes.* Epith. Vēsānī, stŏlĭdī, āmentēs.

Ābdērītānŭs, ă, ŭm, *Abderitan,* or *stupid as an Abderitan.* Ābdērītānæ pēctŏră plēbĭs hăbēs, Mart. Syn. Ābdērītĭcŭs.

ābdĭco, ās, *to abdicate, to renounce.* Sī vērsŭs făcĭs, ābdĭcēs pŏētăm (Phal.), Mart. Syn. Ēxŭo, ābjĭcĭo, dēpōno, rējĭcĭo, prīvo, spŏlĭo.

ābdĭco, ĭs, xī, ctŭm, *to refuse, to disapprove.* Crūdēlĕ sŭōs ābdĭcĕre ămōrēs, Ov. Syn. Rējĭcĭo, rĕcūso, reprŏbo, ābnŭo, ābjūdĭco.

ābdĭtŭm, ĭ, n., *a hidden place or thing.* Abdĭtă tĕrræ, Lucr.—Abdĭtă rērŭm, Hor. Syn. Sēcrētŭm ; lŏcŭs ābdĭtŭs; ōccŭltŭs sēcēssŭs; tēctæ lătebræ; ārcānŭm.

ābdĭtŭs, ă, ŭm, *concealed.* Abdĭtă frōndĕ lĕvī, Ov. Syn. Cōndĭtŭs, ōccŭltātŭs, ābscōndĭtŭs, rĕcōndĭtŭs, lătēns, lătĭtāns ; tēctŭs, ōbtēctŭs, cōntēctŭs, ōbdŭctŭs, vēlātŭs, ŏpērtŭs, ădŏpērtŭs, ŏpācŭs, lătebrōsŭs, ōbscūrŭs, ābstrūsŭs, rĕmōtŭs, ĭnāspēctŭs, ārcānŭs, sēcrētŭs.

ābdo, ĭs, ĭdī, ĭtŭm, *to conceal.* Nātŭm frōndōsĭs mōntĭbŭs ābdĭt, Virg. Syn. Cōndo, ābscōndo, rĕcōndo; ōccŭlo, ōccŭlto, ābstrūdo ; tĕgo, ōbtĕgo, cōntĕgo, ōbdūco, vēlo, īnvōlvo, ŏpĕrĭo, cēlo. V. Occulto.

ābdŏr, ĕrĭs, *to be concealed.* Syn. Cōndŏr, ābscōndŏr, rĕcōndŏr, &c. : lătĕo, lătĭto, dēlĭtēsco. V. Lateo.

ābdōmĕn, ĭnĭs, n., *the belly, the paunch.* Vēntĕr ădēst ābdōmĭnĕ tārdŭs, Juv. Syn. Vēntĕr, ālvŭs, pēctŏră, vīscĕră, īlĭă, ădēps, pīnguēdo. Epith. Albŭm, ūnctŭm, tŭmĭdŭm, pīnguĕ, tūrgēns, īnsătŭrābĭlĕ, ĭnēxplētŭm. V. Venter.

ābdūco, xī, ctŭm, *to lead away.* Illōs ābdūcĕrĕ Thēstўlĭs ōrăt, Virg. Syn. Āmŏvĕo, ābstrŭho, aŭfĕro, sŭbdūco, sŭmmŏvĕo, răpĭo, ābrĭpĭo, ăbĭgo, tōllo, āvērto, rĕmŏvĕo, rĕpēllo, rējĭcĭo.

Abĕl, ĕlĭs, *and* Abĕlŭs, ī, m., *the second son of Adam.* Imĭtēntŭr Abēlĕm, Man. Lŭcrō dĭgnīssĭmŭs Abĕl, Victor. Cuī jūnctŭs Abĕlŭs, Cypr. Abĕlō nōtæ quērcŭs, Lebeau. Syn. Căīnī frātĕr. Epith. Sānctŭs, jūstŭs, pĭŭs, īnsōns, īnnŏcŭŭs, hŭmĭlĭs, māctātŭs, bĕnīgnŭs.

Abēllă, æ, f., *a little town in the kingdom of Naples.* Mœnĭa Abēllæ, Virg. Epith. Mălĭfĕră.

ăbĕo, ăbīs, ăbīvī *or* ăbĭī, ăbĭtŭm, ăbĭrĕ, *to go away.* Paŭca ăbĕo, ēt rĕvŏcās nōnō pōst mēnsĕ, Hor. Syn. Dīscēdo, rĕcēdo, ēxcēdo, ābscēdo, ēxĕo, făcēsso, āvōlo, migro, ēgrĕdĭŏr, prŏfĭcīscŏr. V. Fugio, proficiscor.

ăbĕrăm, ăbĕro, &c. *of* absum. Tītўrŭs hīnc ăbĕrăt, Virg. Tēmpŏre ăbēst, ăbĕrĭtquĕ dĭŭ, Ov.

ăbērro, ās, *to wander.* Sōlŭs ăbērrābăt, Cl. Syn. Rĕcēdo, dēflēcto, dēvĭo, ērro, văgŏr, dĕērro. V. Labyrinthus.

ăbēssĕ, *the infinitive of* absum. Vīcīnī quĕrŏr hās ăbēssĕ fūrtō, (Phal.) Mart. Syn. Dīstārĕ, dīsjūngī, dēēssĕ. V. Absum.

ăbfŏrĕ, *the infin. fut. of* absum. Nĭhĭl ābfŏrĕ crēdūnt, Virg.

ăbhīnc, adv., *hence.* Scrīptŏr ăbhīnc ānnōs cēntŭm, Hor. Syn. Ā, ăb ; dĕhīnc.

ăbhōrrĕo, rŭī, *to dislike, to abhor.* Tāntŭm ăbhōrrēt āc mŭtăt, Catull. Syn. Hŭrrĕo, hōrrēsco, ăbhōrrēsco, pĕrhōrrēsco, ăbŏmĭnŏr, dētēstŏr, ōdī, āvērsŏr ārĭs ; fŭgĭo, rĕfŭgĭo ; rēspŭo, fāstĭdĭo, āspērnŏr, dēspĭcĭo, spērno, cōntēmno ; dīscrĕpo, dīffĕro, ābsŭm.

ăbĭcĭo, ĭs, ĕrĕ, *same as* abjicio. Hūnc ăbĭcĭt, Juv.

ābjēctŭs, ă, ŭm, *cast off, thrown out.* Tŭm sŭpĕr ābjēctŭm pŏsĭtō pĕdĕ, Virg. Syn. Prōjēctŭs, rējēctŭs, pŏsĭtŭs, dēpŏsĭtŭs ; vīlĭs, hŭmĭlĭs, dēmīssŭs ; cōntēmptŭs, dēspēctŭs, sprētŭs, nēglēctŭs. V. Jacens.

ăbĭēgnŭs, *or* ābjēgnŭs, ă, ŭm, *made of fir.* Cærŭlă vērrēntēs ăbĭēgnīs æquŏră pālmīs, Catull. Indŭĭt ābjēgnœ cōrnŭă fālsă bŏvĭs, Prop.

ăbĭēns, ăbēūntĭs, *the partic. pres. of* abeo. Dēdĕrātque ăbĕūntĭbŭs hērōs, Virg. V. Abeo.

ăbĭēs, ăbĭĕtĭs, *or* ābjĕtĭs *trisyl.* f., *fir, a tree.* Pōpŭlŭs īn flŭvĭīs, ăbĭēs īn mōntĭbŭs āltīs, Virg. Abjĕtĭbŭs jŭvĕnēs pătrĭīs, Virg. Eᴘɪᴛʜ. Āĕrĭă, āltă, prōcĕră, mōntānă, sūblīmĭs; ŏpācă, ūmbrōsă, crīspă, pătŭlă; ēnōdĭs, vĭrĭdĭs, ămœnă, rĕdŏlēns. V. Arbor, jaculum, trabs, navis.

ăbĭgo, ăbēgī, ăbāctŭm, *to drive away, to expel.* Vēntōs ăbĭgōquĕ vŏcōquĕ, Ov. Sʏɴ. Expēllo, pēllo, fŭgo, ārcĕo, prōpēllo. V. Pello, abduco, abstraho.

ābjĭcĭo, ābjēcī, ābjēctŭm, *to throw away.* Abjĭcĭtō pŏtĭŭs, quăm quō pērfērrĕ jŭbērĭs, Hor. Sʏɴ. Prōjĭcĭo, rējĭcĭo, pŏno, dēpōno, ēxŭo; cōntēmno, spērno, āspērnŏr, dēspĭcĭo, tēmno, nēglĭgo, rēspŭo. V. Contemno, jacio.

ăb īntēgrō, *henceforth, again.* Mägnŭs ăb īntēgrō sēclōrŭm nāscĭtŭr ōrdo, Virg. Sʏɴ. Dēhīnc, pōstĕă, ĭtĕrŭm, dēnŭō.

ăbĭtŭs, ūs, m., *a departure.* Ămphĭtrўōnĭădēs ārmēnta, ăbĭtūmquĕ părābăt, Virg. Sʏɴ. Dīscēssŭs, ēxcēssŭs, rĕcēssŭs.

ābjūngo, ĭs, xī, ctŭm, *to unyoke, to separate.* Mœrēntem ābjūngēns frātērnă mōrtĕ jŭvēncŭm, Virg. Sʏɴ. Dīsjūngo, sējūngo, sēpăro.

ābjūrātŭs, ă, ŭm, *the pass. partic. of* abjuro. Ābjūrātæquĕ răpīnœ, Virg. Sʏɴ. Nĕgātŭs.

ābjūro, ās, *to deny with oath.* Prædās ābjūrăt ĭnĭquās, Sed. Sʏɴ. Nĕgo, pērnĕgo, pērjūrŭs nĕgo; dĕtēstŏr.

|| āblācto, ās, *to wean.*

āblātŭs, ă, ŭm, *the pass. partic. of* aufero. Pēnnīs āblātă rĕfŭgĭt, Virg. Sʏɴ. Sūblātŭs, rāptŭs, ērēptŭs, cāptŭs. V. Aufero.

āblēgo, ās, *to expel.* Ablēgāndœ Tĭbērim ŭltră, Juv. Sʏɴ. Amāndo, ējĭcĭo, pēllo, ēxpēllo. V. Ejicio.

āblĭgŭrĭo, ĭs, īvī, ītŭm, *to spend riotously.* Bŏnĭs sŭĭs quī nŭpĕr āblĭgūrĭtĭs, (Scaz.) Scal. Sʏɴ. Lĭgūrĭo, vŏro, hēllŭŏr. V. Ligurio.

āblūdo, ĭs, sī, sŭm, *to be unlike.* Hæc ā tē nōn mūltum āblūdĭt ĭmāgo, Hor. Sʏɴ. Dīscrĕpo, dīffĕro, ābsŭm.

āblŭo, ĭs, ŭī, ŭtŭm, *to wash away.* Mē flūmĭnĕ vīvō Āblŭĕro, Virg. Sʏɴ. Lăvo, pūrgo, ēlŭo, tērgo, ābstērgo, mūndo.

āblūtŭs, ă, ŭm, *the pass. partic. of* abluo. Sŏcĭōs āblūtă cædĕ rĕmīsĭt, Virg. Sʏɴ. Lăvātŭs, lautŭs (*or* lōtŭs), ēlŭtŭs, tērsŭs, ābstērsŭs, pūrgātŭs, īnspērsŭs, rĕspērsŭs, pērfūsŭs, spārsŭs, rĭgātŭs, īrrōrātŭs, mērsŭs, mădēns.

ābnăto, ās, *to swim away.* Abnătăt, ēt blāndĭs, Stat.

ābnĕgo, ās, *to deny.* Abnĕgăt ēxcīsă vītăm prōdūcĕrĕ Trōjă, Virg. Sʏɴ. Abnŭo, rĕnŭo, rĕcūso, nĕgo, pērnĕgo; ĭmprŏbo. V. Recuso, inficior.

ābnĕpŏs, ōtĭs, m., *a grandchild's grandson.* Nātōs, nĕpōtēs, ābnĕpōtēs ēdĭtōs, (Iamb.) Prud.

ābnōdo, ās, *to clear of knots.* Abnōdăt sīlvās, Colum.

ābnōrmĭs, ĕ, *irregular, unequal.* Rūstĭcŭs, ābnōrmĭs săpĭēns, Hor. Sʏɴ. Enōrmĭs.

ābnŭo, ābnŭī, *to deny by gesture.* Abnŭĭt, ēt tōtŭm nūtū trĕmĕfēcĭt Ōlўmpŭm, Virg. Sʏɴ. Rēnŭo, ābnĕgo, rĕcūso, dēnĕgo, nĕgo. V. Abnego.

ăbŏlĕo, ēvī *and* ŭī, lĭtŭm, *to abolish, take away, consume.* Nĕc ĕdāx ăbŏlērĕ vĕtūstās, Ov. Sʏɴ. Antīquo, rēscīndo, tōllo, dēlĕo, ēxtīnguo.

ăbŏlēsco, ĕrĕ, lēvī, lĭtŭm, *to wither away.* Inquĕ dĭēs prīmōs ăbŏlēscĕrĕ quæquĕ crēātă, Lucr. Sʏɴ. Abŏlĕŏr, āntĭquŏr, rēscīndŏr, ōbsŏlēsco; pĕrĕo, īntĕrĕo.

ăbŏlĭtŭs, ă, ŭm, *abolished, effaced.* Sʏɴ. Antīquātŭs, rēscīssŭs, ōbsŏlētŭs, ēxtīnctŭs.

ăbŏllă, œ, f., *a philosopher's or soldier's garment.* Făcĭnŭs mājōrĭs ăbŏllæ, Juv. V. Vestis.

ăbōmĭnāndŭs, ă, ŭm, *abominable.* Fĕr ăbōmĭnāndăm nūnc ŏpĕm nātō părēns, (Iamb.) Sen. Sʏɴ. Dētēstābĭlĭs, dĕtēstāndŭs, ēxecrābĭlĭs, ēxecrāndŭs, hōrrēndŭs.

ăbōmĭnŏr, ārĭs, *to abominate.* Quŏd ăbōmĭnŏr, ērgo, Ov. Sʏɴ. Execrŏr, dētēstŏr, fŭgĭo, hōrrĕo, ăbhōrrĕo. V. Execror, imprecor.

ăbŏrĭŏr, īrĭs, ăbŏrtŭm, *to be born before the time.* Vōcēmque ăbŏrīrī, Lucr. Sʏɴ. Mănĕ; āntĕ dĭem ŏrĭŏr.

ăbŏrtĭo, ōnĭs, f., *miscarriage.* Ut ăbŏrtĭōni ŏpĕrăm, Plaut.

ăbŏrtīvŭm, ī, m., *a means of causing abortion.* Ăbŏrtīvŏ nŏn ŏpŭs ēst, Juv.

ăbŏrtīvŭs, ă, ŭm, *abortive.* Ăbŏrtīvīs fœcūndŭm Jūlĭă vēntrĕm, Juv.

|| ăbŏrtŭs, ūs, m., *miscarriage.* Hīc nīdŏr ăbŏrtum īmmīttĕrĕ suēvĭt, Lucr. Syn. Immătūrŭs pārtŭs.

ābrādo, sī, sŭm, *to scrape.* Ābrādīt spŏllīsque ūnguēs ēxērcĕt ălĭēnōs, Prud. Syn. Rādo, cōrrādo, dērādo.

Abrăhăm, m., *Abraham the patriarch, the son of Terah.* Ăbrăhăm sānctī mĕrĭtō sŏcĭăndĕ pătrōnĭs, Sed. Pătrēm mūndī sē crēdĭt Ăbrăhăm, Prud. Ēst Ăbrăhăm, cūjŭs gnātōs vōs ēssĕ nĕgătĭs, Tertull. Syn. Abrāmŭs, Abrām, Abrās, Thārĭădēs, Sāræ cōnjŭx. Thārā gĕnĭtŭs or sătŭs. Īsăcī pătĕr, gĕnĭtŏr, părēns. Epith. Sānctŭs, jūstŭs, īnnŏcēns, innŏcŭŭs, bĕnīgnŭs, inclўtŭs, māxĭmŭs, sācrĭfĭcŭs, fīdēlĭs, pĭŭs.

Abrămĭdæ, m. pl., *Abraham's descendants.* O dŏmŭs Abrămĭdŭm, Mill. Syn. Prōlēs Abrăhāmī, Abrăhāmō sătī or nātī. V. Hebræi.

ābrēptŭs, ă, ŭm, *the pass. partic. of* abripio. Ābrēptŭm dīvēllĕrĕ cōrpŭs, Virg. Syn. Abstrāctŭs, rāptŭs, dīrēptŭs, dīvŭlsŭs, dīstrāctŭs, dĕhīscēns.

ābrĭpĭo, pŭī, rēptŭm, *to drag away.* Abrĭpĕre, ēt Dănăăs, St. Syn. Abstrăho, răpĭo, dīrĭpĭo, āvērto, sūrrĭpĭo, tōllo, ērĭpĭo, aūfĕro. V. Rapio; divello, distraho.

ābrōdo, sī, sŭm, *to gnaw off.* Ābrōdēns ăĭt hæc, Pers. Syn. Rōdo, cōrrōdo, ēxĕdo. V. Rodo.

ābrŏgo, ās, *to abolish.* Scrīptīs ābrŏgăt īllĕ mĕīs, Ov. Syn. Rēscīndo, ăbŏlĕo, ăntīquo, ēxpūngo, tōllo; ădĭmo, dētrăho.

ăbrŏtŏnŭm, ī, n., *and* ŭs, ī, m., *the herb southernwood.* Abrŏtŏnum, ēt lōngē, Lucr. Epith. Mĕdĭcŭm. V. Medicamen.

ābrūmpo, rūpī, rūptŭm, *to break off.* Quāmprīmum ābrūmpĕrĕ lūcĕm, Virg. Syn. Rūmpo, dīsrūmpo, frāngo; abscīndo, āvēllo, ābrĭpĭo. V. Rumpo.

ābrūptŭs, ă, ŭm, *broken off.* Abrūptō sīdĕrĕ nīmbŭs, Virg. Syn. Rūptŭs, dīsrūptŭs, frāctŭs; prærūptŭs, præcēps, ārdŭŭs, Ināccēssŭs. V. Præceps.

Absălōn, *and* Abēssălōn, *the son of David and Maacha.* Absălōn cŭm pātre aūsŭs concūrrĕrĕ bēllō, S. Syn. Absălo, Absălōmŭs, Māăchĭdēs, Absălōm. Epith. Pērfĭdŭs, aūdāx, rĕbēllĭs, tĕmĕrārĭŭs, imprūdēns, mĭsĕr, īnfēlīx, dēmēns, scĕlĕrātŭs, īmprŏbŭs, īmpĭŭs.

ābscēdo, cēssī, *to depart.* Nŏn tămĕn ābscēdĭt, Ov. Syn. Rĕcēdo, dīscēdo, dēcēdo, ēxcēdo, cēdo, ăbĕo, ēxĕo. V. Abeo, recedo.

ābscēssŭs, ūs, m., *departure.* Ăt Rŭtŭlŭm ābscēssŭ, Virg. Syn. Dīscēssŭs, rĕcēssŭs, ēxcēssŭs, ēxĭtŭs, ăbĭtŭs. Epith. Trīstĭs, flēbĭlĭs, mœstŭs, ăcērbŭs, dūrŭs, sŭbĭtŭs, ĭnŏpīnŭs, suprēmŭs.—Pro tumore. V. Vomica.

ābscīdo, ābscĭdī, ābscīsŭm, *to cut off; from* abs *and* cædo. Abscīdīt jŭgŭlō pēctŭs, Ov. Syn. Rĕcīdo, rĕsĕco, abscīndo.

ābscīndo, ābscĭdī, ābscīssŭm, *to cut off; from* ab *and* scindo. Tērrīs ābscĭdĭt ūndās, Ov. Syn. Scīndo, rēscīndo, dīscīndo, abscīdo, rĕcīdo, sĕco, rĕsĕco, ēxsĕco, dīssĕco, ămpŭto, ōbtrūnco, ābrūmpo. V. Scindo.

ābscīssŭs, *or* ābscīsŭs, ă, ŭm. *cut off.* Flāvēntēs ābscīssā cŏmās, Virg. Syn. Scīssŭs, rēscīssŭs, rĕcīsŭs, sēctŭs, rĕsēctŭs, ēxsēctŭs, ămpŭtātŭs, trūncŭs.

ābscōndĭtŭs, ă, ŭm, *the pass. partic. of* abscondo. Abscōndĭtă flāmmă, Lucan. Syn. Cōndĭtŭs. V. Abditus.

ābscōndo, ābscōndī, ābscōndĭtŭm, *sometimes* ābscōndĭdī, *to hide, to lose sight of.* Phæācum ābscōndĭmŭs ārcēs, Virg. Syn. Abdo, cōndo, tĕgo, ōbtĕgo, rĕcōndo, cēlo ās. V. Abdo.

ābsēns, *absent.* Absēns absēntem aūdītquĕ vĭdētquĕ, Virg. Syn. Dīssĭtŭs, rĕmōtŭs, dĭsjūnctŭs, ămōtŭs. V. Distans.

*ăbsēntĭă, æ, f., *absence.* Dĕvŏrāvi absēntĭæ, Aus. Epith. Lōngă, brĕvĭs, dūră, trīstĭs, mœstă, grăvĭs, īnfaūstă.

ābsĭlĭo, ĭs, ĭī *and* ŭī, *to leap out.* Aŭt prŏcŭl ăbsĭlĭēbăt, Lucr. Syn. Exĭlĭo, trānsĭlĭo, dīssĭlĭo; sălĭo. V. Salio.

|| ābsĭmĭlĭs, *unlike.* Syn. Dīssĭmĭlĭs, haūd sĭmĭlĭs; dīspār, īmpār.

ābsīnthĭŭm, ĭī, n., *wormwood.* Dēsīnt absīnthĭă Pŏntō, Ov. Epith. Cănŭm, trīstĕ, tetrŭm, grăvĕ, ămărŭm, īngrātŭm, vīrōsŭm, ăcērbŭm, Pōntĭcŭm.

ābsīs, ĭdĭs, *or* ăpsīs, ĭdĭs, f., *the ring of a wheel.* Epith. Cūrvă, īncūrvă, fērvēns. V. Rota.

ăbsīsto, ăbstǐtī, *to depart, to cease.* Absīstāmŭs, ăǐt, Virg. Syn. Dīscēdo, ăbĕo, ăbscēdo; cēsso, dēsǐno, dēsīsto, ābstǐnĕo. V. Abeo, cesso.

ŭbsōlūtŭs, ă, ŭm, *the pass. partic. of* absolvo. Jăcēt ŭbsōlŭtă cāsŭ, (Phal.) Mart.

ŭbsōlvo, vī, ūtŭm, *to acquit, to release.* Absōlvĕs hŏmǐnĕm, Hor. Syn. Pērfǐcǐo, cōnfǐcǐo, pĕrăgo, fīnem ǐmpōno. V. Finio, perficio.

ăbsŏnŭs, ă, ŭm, *harsh in sound, unharmonious.* Fōrtūnīs ābsŏnă dīctă, Hor. Syn. Mălĕ sŏnāns, dīssŏnŭs; nōn cōnsŏnŭs; sŏnō dīscōrs.

ăbsōrbĕo, bŭī *or* psī, ptŭm, *to swallow.* Sǐmŭl ābsōrbērĕ plăcēntās, Hor. Syn. Sōrbĕo, vōro, dēvŏro, haŭrǐo. V. Voro.

ābsquĕ, adv., *without.* Absquĕ crŭōrĕ, Luc. Syn. Sǐnĕ.

ăbstēmǐŭs, ă, ŭm, *abstemious.* Gaŭdētquĕ mĕrīs ābstēmǐŭs ūndīs, Ov. Syn. Sōbrǐŭs.

ăbstērgo, ǐs, ĕrsǐ; *or,* ăbstērgĕo, ēs, ĕrsǐ; sī, sŭm, *to wipe off.* Catull. Syn. Dētērgo, tērgo, pūrgo, ăblŭo, dīlŭo. V. Abluo, tergo.

ăbstērrĕo, ŭī, ǐtŭm, *to frighten from.* Ă cōrǐō nōn ăbstērrēbǐtŭr ūnctō, Hor. Syn. Tērrĕo, tērrōrem ǐncŭtǐo; dētērrĕo, āvōco. V. Terreo, deterreo.

ăbstǐnēns, *abstinent.* Vīndēx ăvārœ fraŭdǐs, ĕt ābstǐnēns, Hor. Syn. Tēmpĕrāns, sōbrǐŭs, mŏdĕrātŭs, pārcŭs.

ăbstǐnēntǐă, *abstinence.* Dīcātă pārcŭs ābstǐnēntǐă, (Iamb.) Prud. Syn. Pārcŭs vīctŭs, mŏdǐcŭs cǐbŭs, sōbrǐă mēnsă, sōbrǐĕtās. Epith. Pārcă, dūră, sānă, lōngă, sānctă, pǐă.

ăbstǐnĕo, ŭī, *to abstain from.* Abstǐnŭīssĕ bŏnīs, Ov. Syn. Tēmpĕro, mē cōntǐnĕo, mē cŏhǐbĕo. V. Jejuno.

ăbsto, ās, sǐtī, *to be distant.* Sī lōngǐŭs ābstēs, Hor. Syn. Dīsto, ābsŭm, lōngē stō.

ăbstrāctŭs, ă, ŭm, *the pass. partic. of* abstraho. Abstrāctœquĕ bŏvēs, Virg.

ăbstrăho, xī, ctŭm, *to drag away.* Abstrăhĕre ǐndĕ pŏtēst, Ov. Syn. Abrǐpǐo, dǐstrăho, āvēllo, rēvēllo, rēscīndo, ābdūco, ămōvĕo, aŭfĕro. V. Rapio.

ăbstrūdo, ǐs, sī, sŭm, *to conceal.* Plaut. Syn. Abdo, ābscōndo, rēcōndo, ŏccūlto. V. Abdo, occulto.

ăbstrūsŭs, *the pass. partic. of* abstrudo. Abstrūsum ēxcūdĕrēt īgnĕm, Virg. Syn. Abdǐtŭs, ābscōndǐtŭs, ōccūltŭs, lătēns. V. Abditus, occultus.

ŭbsŭm, ăbĕs, ābfŭī, ăbēssĕ, *to be absent.* Nūllūm nūmĕn ăbēst, Juven. Syn. Dēsŭm; dīsto; sŭm rēmōtŭs, dīssǐtŭs, dīsjūnctŭs.

ābsūmo, ǐs, psī, ptŭm, *to consume.* Mālīs ābsūmĕrĕ mēnsās, Virg. Syn. Cōnsūmo, cōnfǐcǐo, ēxhaŭrǐo; pērdo, vōro, ābsōrbĕo, lǐgūrǐo. V. Voro, ligurio.

ābsūmptŭs, ă, ŭm, *the pass. partic. of* absumo. Sīn ābsūmptă sălŭs, Virg. Syn. Cōnsūmptŭs, cōnfēctŭs; ēxhaŭstŭs, pērdǐtŭs.

ābsūrdŭs, ă, ŭm, *harsh, absurd.* Ter. Syn. Absōnŭs, ǐnēptŭs, stŭltŭs.

ābsȳnthǐŭm, ǐī, n., *wormwood.* V. Absinthium.

Absȳrtǐs, ǐdǐs, f., Absȳrtǐdēs, ŭm, f. pl., *islands of the Adriatic, near the coast of Istria.* Absȳrtǐs ǐn ūndās, Luc.

Absȳrtŭs, ī, m., *the son of Æetes, and brother of Medea.* Syn. Æĝǐăleŭs, Æētǐădēs. Epith. Infēlīx, mǐsĕr, nǐl tālĕ mĕrēns.

ăbūndāns, āntǐs, *abundant.* Quăm lāctǐs ăbūndāns, Virg. Syn. Fĕrāx, fērtǐlǐs, pīngŭǐs, ūbĕr; dīvēs, ăfflŭēns, plēnŭs, rĕfērtŭs. V. Abundo.

•ăbūndāntǐă, œ, f., *abundance.* Cic. Syn. Cōpǐă, ūbērtās, fērtǐlǐtās, vīs, ăfflŭēntǐă. Epith. Lārgă, dīvēs, lœtă, aūrĕă, ŏpŭlēntă, bĕātă.

ăbūndĕ, adv., *enough.* Fraŭdǐs ăbūndĕ ēst, Virg Syn. Sătǐs, săt; cōpǐōsē, ăffătǐm, ūbērtǐm, ăbūndāntĕr, ăfflŭēntĕr.

ăbūndo, ās, *to overflow.* Rūrsŭs ăbūndābăt flŭǐdŭs lǐquŏr, Virg. Syn. Afflŭo, cīrcūmflŭo, sŭm dīvĕs, ēxŭbĕro, rĕdūndo, ēxūndo: mǐhi ăbūndĕ ēst.

ăbūsquĕ, adv., *from as far as.* Prōspēxǐt ăbūsquĕ Pāchȳnō, Virg. Syn. Ā, ăb, ūsque ā, ūsque ăb.

ăbūtŏr, ĕrǐs, ăbūsŭs sŭm, *to use contrary to the nature of any thing.* Ēt Bācchī nōmǐne ăbūtī, Lucr.

Abȳdēnŭs, ă, ŭm, *Abydenian.* Sēstōn Abȳdēnă sēpărăt ūrbĕ frĕtŭm, Ov.

Abȳdŭs, ī, f., *a town of the Troad.* In spĕcŭlīs ōmnīs Abȳdŏs ĕrăt, Ov. Epith. Hēllēspōntǐăcă, Leāndrǐă, āntīquă, prīscă, nōbǐlǐs.

Abȳlă, œ, f., *a mountain of Mauritania.* Inde Abȳlœ vērtēx, M. Epith. Hērcŭlĕă, Lǐbȳcă, āltă.

ăbўssŭs, ī, f., *a gulf.* Pŭtĕŏ fērvēntĭs ăbўssī, Prud. Syn. Vŏrāgo, gŭrgĕs, hĭātŭs bărathrŭm. Epith. Cœnōsă, prŏfūndă, īmmānĭs, hŏrrēndă, īngēns, hŏrrĭbĭlĭs, ăpērtă, hŏrrĭdă, stŭpēndă, āltă, vāstă, vŏrāx, tērrĭfĭcă, pēstĭfĕră, īmă, īnfērnă, tūrbĭdă, cæcă, ŏpācă, tetră. V. Gurges.

āc, conj., *and.* Ăc ŭbĭ nōn lōngūm spătĭum ēst, Lucr. Syn. Ět, quĕ, ātquĕ, nēcnōn.

Ăcădēmĭă, *or* Ăcădēmĭă, æ, f., *a garden near Athens, where Plato used to teach his disciples.* In Lătĭŭm sprētĭs ăcădēmĭă mīgrăt Ăthēnĭs, Claud. Inque ăcădēmīa ūmbrĭfĕră, Cic. Syn. Gўmnăsĭŭm, Lўcæŭm, schŏlă. Epith. Dōctă, cĕlebrĭs, āntīquă, ūmbrĭfĕră, nĕmŏrōsă.

Ăcădēmŭs, ī, m., *an Athenian, from whom the Academical gardens received their name.* Intēr sўlvās Ăcădēmī, Hor.

Ăcādīnŭs, ī, m., *a fountain of Sicily.* Epith. Dēlĭŭs, Sĭcŭlŭs, săcĕr, vērĭdĭcŭs.

Ăcāmās, āntĭs, *the son of Theseus and Phædra.* Ăcămāsquĕ Thŏāsquĕ, Virg.— 2. *A Thracian warrior slain by Ajax.*

ăcānthĭnŭs, ă, ŭm, *of bears-foot.* V. Acanthus.

ăcānthĭs, *or* ăcălānthĭs, ĭdĭs, f., *a goldfinch.* Lĭttŏrăque hālcўŏnēm rĕsŏnănt, ĕt ăcānthĭdă dūmī, Virg. Syn. Phĭlŏmēlă, lūscĭnĭă.

ăcānthŭs, ī, m., *the herb bears-foot.* Cŏlŏcāsĭă fūndĕt ăcānthō, Virg. Epith. Sĭdŏnĭŭs, mōllĭs, frōndēns, tōrtŭs, rīdēns, vĭrĭdĭs, vĭrēns, īnflēxŭs, lēntŭs, flēxŭs, crŏcĕŭs.

Ăcārnān, ānĭs, *Acarnanian.* Amnĭs Ăcārnānŭm, Ov. Epith. Văgŭs, cōrnĭgĕr, dūrŭs, ăspĕr, cēlsŭs. V. Achelous *and* Pindus.

Ăcārnānĭă, æ, f., *a part of Epirus separated from Ætolia by the river Achelous and the mountain Pindus.*

Ăcāstŭs, ī, m., *son of Pelias, king of Thessaly, the husband of Hippolyte.* Sōlvĭt Ăcāstŭs ăquās, Ov. Epith. Ăcĕr, vēnātŏr, crēdŭlŭs, sævŭs, Thēssălŭs, Æmŏnĭŭs.

Accă, æ, *one of the companions of Camilla.*—2. *The nurse of Romulus.* Pāssīs Accă căpĭllĭs, Ov.

āccānto *or* ādcānto, ās, *to sing to.* Tŭmŭlĭs āccāntŭ măgīstrī, Stat.

āccēdo, ĭs, āccēssī, *to approach.* Blāndīs āccēdĕrĕ dīctĭs, Ov. Syn. Ădvĕnĭo, ādvēnto, vĕnĭo, ădĕo, sŭccēdo, āccūrro, ādvŏlo, prŏpīnquo, ădjūngŏr, āddŏr, trānsĕo. V. Advento.

āccĕlĕro, ās, *to hasten.* Āccĕlĕrēmŭs, ăĭt, Virg. Syn. Cĕlĕro, mātūro, fēstīno, prŏpĕro, āccūrro, ādvŏlo, prĕmo, ūrgĕo. V. Celero.

āccēndo, ĭs, dī, sŭm, *to set on fire.* Mārtēmque āccēndĕrĕ cāntū, Virg. Syn. Incēndo, īnflāmmo, sŭccēndo; ūro: īmpēllo, īncĭto, īnstīgo, ăcŭo, ēxcĭto, ūrgĕo. V. Ignem accendo; incendo; hortor.

āccēnsĕŏr, ērĭs, ērī, pass., *to be of any one's train, to accompany.* Atque āccēnsĕŏr ĭllī, Ov.

āccēnsŭs, ă, ŭm, *the pass. partic. of* accendo. Tālĭbŭs āccēnsī fīrmāntŭr, Virg. Syn. Incēnsŭs, sŭccēnsŭs, īnflāmmātŭs.—Metaph. Impūlsŭs; īrātŭs.

āccēntŭs, ūs, m., *tone, accent.* Dōctīs āccēntĭbŭs ēffĕr, Aus.

āccēptŭs, ă, ŭm, *the pass. partic. of* accipio. Mēnsīs ēt Dīs āccēptă sĕcūndīs, Virg. Syn. Rĕcēptŭs; grātŭs, jūcūndŭs.

āccērsītŭs, ă, ŭm, *the pass. partic. of* accerso. Nōn āccērsītŭs, ĕt hærĕt, Hor. Syn. Vŏcātŭs, āccītŭs, ēxcītŭs.

āccērso, ĭs, ĕrĕ, *or* āccērsĭo, īs, īvī, ītŭm, īrĕ, *to fetch, to call.* Syn. Vŏco, āppēllo ās: ādvŏco, cĭĕo, āccĭo īs; ēxcĭo, ēvŏco, ārcēsso.

‖ āccēssĭo, ōnĭs, f., *an addition, increase; an approaching to.* Quæ tĭbi āccēssĭo ēst, Plaut. Syn. Incrēmēntŭm, ādjēctĭo; āccēssŭs. Epith. Mūltă, āmplă, īngēns, cŭmŭlātă.

āccēssŭs, ūs, m., *an approach.* Pōrtŭs ăb āccēssū vēntōrum īmmōtŭs, Virg. Syn. Advēntŭs, ădĭtŭs. V. Adventus.

āccĭdo, ĭs, ĭdī, *to fall down at; from* ab *and* cado. Āccĭdĭt hæc fēssīs ĕtĭăm fōrtūnă Lătīnĭs, Virg. Syn. Cădo, cōncĭdo: cōntĭngo, ōbtĭngo, ēvĕnĭo, ādvĕnĭo, ōccūrro, vĕnĭo, īntĕrvĕnĭo, fīo: āccēdo.

āccīdo, īdī, īsŭm, *to cut, to weaken; from* ab *and* cædo. Insĭdĭīs āccīdĕrĕ tūrmās, Mill. Syn. Cædo, cōnsūmo, ābsūmo, cīrcūmcīdo. V. Scindo, cædo.

ăccīčo, ēs, īvī, ītŭm, ĭĕrĕ, *to fetch.* Jam ăccĭēbo, Plaut. Syn. Ăccĭo, ĭs; ăccērso. V. Accerso.

ăccĭngo, xī, ctŭm, *to gird to, to prepare for.* Părībŭsque ăccīngĭtŭr ārmīs, Virg. Syn. Cīngo, mŭnĭo, īnstrŭo, ārmo, păro, præpăro, cōmpăro. V. Præparo.

ăccĭno, ĭs, ŭī, *to sing with.* Sȳlvīs rĕpărābĭlĭs ăccĭnĭt ēcho, Pers. Syn. Concĭno, āssŏno, rĕsŭlto, ăccănto.

ăccĭo, ĭs, īvī, ītŭm, īrĕ, *to send for.* Sŏcĭōs sum ăccīrĕ părātŭs, Virg. Syn. Ăccērso, ādvŏco. V. Accerso.

ăccĭpĭendŭs, ă, ŭm, *partic. of* accipio. Vīx ăccĭpĭendā trĭbŭlī, Mart.

ăccĭpĭo, ăccēpī, *to receive.* Accĭpĭēbăt ĭn amplīs, Virg. Syn. Căpĭo, rĕcĭpĭo, sŭscĭpĭo: sŭmo, āssŭmo, prĕhēndo, prēndo, ēxcĭpĭo; aŭdĭo.

ăccĭpĭtĕr, ĭtrĭs, m., *a hawk.* Accĭpĭtrēs, ātque ossĭfrăgæ, Sc. Epith. Răpāx, cĭtŭs, præcēps, fĕrŭs, crūdēlĭs, vēlōx, ācĕr, vŏlucrĭs, aŭdāx, īntrĕpĭdŭs, īmpĭŭs, fĕrōx, trŭx, īmmītĭs, atrōx.

ăccīsŭs, ŭ, ŭm, *the pass. partic. of* ăccīdo. Accīsīs cōgĕt dăpĭbŭs, Virg. Syn. Cīrcŭmcīsŭs, cōnsūmptŭs, ābsūmptŭs.

ăccītŭs, ă, ŭm, *the pass. partic. of* accio, is. Impĕrĭo ăccītōs āltā īntrā līmĭnă cōgĭt, Virg. Syn. Excĭtŭs, vŏcătŭs, ăccērsītŭs.

ăccītŭs, ūs, m., *a sending for.* Rēgĭŭs ăccītū cārī gĕnĭtōrĭs ăd ūrbĕm, Virg. Syn. Impĕrĭŭm.

Accĭŭs, *or* Attĭŭs, ī, *a tragic poet.* Accĭŭs āltī, Hor.

ăcclāmātĭo, ōnĭs, f., *acclamation.* Acclāmātĭŏ sībĭlāns cŏrōnæ, (Phal.) Sidon. Syn. Plaŭsŭs, āpplaŭsŭs. Epith. Sĕcūndā, īngēns, lætā, cănōrā. V. Plausus.

ăcclāmo, ās, *to shout.* Syn. Clāmo, cōnclāmo, plaŭdo, āpplaŭdo, plaŭsūm dŏ. V. Plaudo.

ăcclīnĭs, ĕ, *prone, leaning on.* Arbŏrĭs ăcclīnĭs trūnco, Virg. Syn. Inclīnātŭs, prŏpēnsŭs, prōclīvĭs, prōnŭs, ăcclīvĭs.

ăcclīno, ās, *to lean, to bend.* Sēque ăcclīnāvĭt ăd īllăm, Ov. Syn. Inclīno; prŏpēndĕo, īmpēndĕo.

ăcclīvĭs, ĕ, *or* ăcclīvŭs, ă, ŭm, *steep, up-hill.* Sīn tŭmŭlīs ăcclīvĕ sŏlŭm, Virg. Lēnĭtĕr ăcclīvō cōnstĭtŭērĕ jŭgō, Ov. Syn. Clīvōsŭs, dēclīvĭs, ăcclīnĭs.

ăccŏlă, æ, m., *a borderer.* Accŏlā Vūltūrnī, Virg. Syn. Vīcīnŭs, hăbĭtātŏr, cūltŏr, īncŏlă, cīvĭs, cŏlōnŭs.

ăccŏlo, ŭī, *to live near.* Accŏlĕt īmpĕrĭŭmquĕ pătĕr Rōmānŭs hăbēbĭt, Virg. Syn. Cŏlo, hăbĭto, īncŏlo.

ăccōmmŏdo, ās, *to apply, put to.* Lătĕrīque Argīvum ăccōmmŏdăt ēnsĕm, Virg. Syn. Applĭco, ādjūngo, āpto, rĕfĕro, cōmpōno, cōmpăro. V. Apto.

ăccōmmŏdŭs, ă, ŭm, *apt, suitable.* Vāllēs ăccōmmŏdā fraŭdī, Virg. Syn. Cōmmŏdŭs, ōppōrtūnŭs, āptŭs, āppŏsĭtŭs, ĭdōnĕŭs. V. Aptus.

ăccrēdo, ĭs, ĭdī, *to believe.* Tĭbī nōs ăccrēdĕrĕ pār ēst, Hor. Syn. Crēdo. V. Credo.

ăccrēsco, ĭs, ēvī, *to grow.* Invĭdĭă ăccrēvīt prīvātō, Hor. Syn. Crēsco, aŭgĕŏr.

ăccŭbĭto, ās, *the frequentative of* accubo. Nōstrīs ăccŭbĭtărĕ tŏrīs, Sedul. Syn. Accŭbo, ăccūmbo.

ăccŭbĭtŭs, ūs, m., *a sitting near.* Accŭbĭtū gĕnĭŏquĕ dĕŭs, Stat.

ăccŭbo, ās, ŭī, *to lie down.* Sācrā nĕmŭs ăccŭbĕt ūmbrā, Virg. Syn. Accŭmbo, ādjăcĕo.

ăccūmbo, ĭs, ŭbŭī, *to lie down.* Epŭlīs ăccūmbĕrĕ Dīvŭm, Virg. Syn. Accŭbo, dīscūmbo, rĕcūmbo. V. Epulor.

ăccŭmŭlo, ās, *to accumulate.* Hīs sāltem ăccŭmŭlēm dōnīs, Virg. Syn. Cōngĕro ĭs, āggĕro ās *and* ĭs, ēxāggĕro, ăcērvo, cŏăcērvo, cōmpōno, cōllĭgo, cōgo, cōntrăho, cŭmŭlo, aŭgĕo. V. Cumulo.

|| ăccūrātē, adv., *with care.* Ter. Syn. Sōlĕrtī cūrā, sēdŭlō, stŭdĭōsē.

ăccūrātŭs, ā, ŭm, *the pass. partic. of* accuro. Plaut.

ăccŭro, ās, *to take care of.* Sī quăm rem ăccūrēs, Plaut. Syn. Cūro, prōcūro; vĭgĭlī cūrā pērfĭcĭo, stŭdĭōsē, āssĭdŭē făcĭo.

accūrro, ĭs, ăccūrrī, ăccūrsŭm, *to run to.* Prīmūsque ăccūrrĭt Acēstēs, Virg. Syn. Cūrro, ăccĕlĕro, ādvŏlo, āpprŏpĕro; āfflŭo, cōncŭrro, cōnvŏlo, cŏĕo. V. Curro.

ăccūrsŭs, ūs, m., *a running to.* Accūrsū cŏmĭtŭm, Stat. Syn. Cūrsŭs; cōncūrsŭs.

ăccūsātĭo, ōnĭs, f., *an accusation.* Jūsti ăccūsātĭŏ sūrgēns, Juv. Syn. Scĕlĕrĭs *or* crīmĭnĭs dēlātĭo. Epith. Fālsă, ĭmprŏbă, tēctă, ĭnjūstă.

ăccūsātŏr, ōrĭs, m., *an accuser.* Ăccūsātŏr ĕrĭt, Juv. Syn. Dēlātŏr.

|| ăccūsātŭs, ă, ŭm, *the pass. partic. of* accuso. Syn. Rĕŭs. V. Reus.

ăccūso, ās, *to accuse.* Ăccūsārĕ pŏtēst, Juv. Syn. Incūso, īnsĭmŭlo ; ārgŭo, rĕdārgŭo.

ăcēdĭă, æ, f., *sloth.* Dēlūdĭt ăcēdĭă cūltū, Mant. Syn. Ignăvĭă, ĭnērtĭă, pigrĭtĭă, trīstĭtĭă, tædĭŭm, sŏcōrdĭă. Epith. Tōrpēscēns, lānguĭdă, lēntă, sēgnĭs, tārdă, fāstīdĭōsă, jăcēns.

ăcĕr, ācrĭs, ācrĕ, adj., *sharp, sour.* Stĕtĭt ăcĕr ĭn ārmĭs, Virg. Syn. Ăcūtŭs, īngēns, māgnŭs, vĕhĕmēns, āspĕr ; sōlērs, gnāvŭs; fōrtĭs, vălĭdŭs. V. Fortis.

ăcĕr, ĕrĭs, n., *a maple-tree.* Nūpĕr vīlĕ fŭĭstĭs ăcĕr, Ov. Epith. Dūrŭm. V. Arbor.

ăcērbo, ās, *to sharpen, to heighten.* Fōrmīdĭnĕ crīmĕn ăcērbăt, Virg. Syn. āspĕro, ēxăcērbo, īrrīto, ăcŭo. V. Irrito.

ăcērbŭs, ă, ŭm, *unripe, sour.* Pērsĕphŏnĕ nōstrăs pūlsăt ăcērbă fŭrēs, Ov. Syn. Ăcĕr ; āspĕr ; grăvĭs, dūrŭs, trīstĭs, atrōx, sĕvērŭs, mŏlēstŭs, ĭncōmmŏdŭs, crūdēlĭs.

ăcērnŭs, ă, ŭm, *of maple wood.* Trăbĭbŭs cōntēxtŭs ăcērnĭs, Virg.

ăcĕrōsŭs, ă, ŭm, *full of bran.* Fārre ăcĕrōso, ŏlĕĭ dēcŭmānŏ pānĕ cŏēgĭt, Lucil.

ăcērră, æ, f., *a censer.* Thūrĭs ăcērră fŭĭt, Ov. Syn. Thūrĭbŭlŭm. Epith. Aūrĕă, fūmāns, ŏdōră, āccēnsă, ŏdōrātă, ŏlēns, rĕdŏlēns, plēnă. V. Thus.

Ăcērræ, ārŭm, f. pl., *a town of Campania.* Nōn æquŭs Ăcērrĭs, Virg.

ăcērrĭmŭs, ă, ŭm, *very sharp, very brave.* Pōrtæ cŭstōs, ăcērrĭmŭs ārmĭs, Virg.

ăcērvātĭm, adv., *by heaps.* Cōnfērtōs ĭta ăcērvātĭm mōrs āccŭmŭlābăt, Lucr. Syn. Cŭmŭlātĭm.

ăcērvo, ās, *to heap up.* Nām crīmĕn ăcērvăt, Alcim. Syn. Cŭmŭlo, āccŭmŭlo, cōngĕro. V. Cumulo.

ăcērvŭs, ī, m., *a heap.* Ærĭs ăcērvŭs ĕt aūrī, Hor. Syn. Cōngĕrĭēs, strŭēs, cŭmŭlŭs, cōpĭă. Epith. Ingēns, nŭmĕrōsŭs, mŏdĭcŭs, āltŭs, māgnŭs, grāndĭs, văstŭs.

ăcēsco, ĕrĕ, *to grow sour.* Quōdcūnque īnfūndĭs, ăcēscĭt, Hor. Syn. Ăcĕo, cŏăcēsco ; ăcōrĕm cōntrăho *or* cōncĭpĭo.

Ăcēstă, æ, f., *a town of Sicily.* Nōmĭne Ăcēstăm, Virg.

Ăcēstēs, æ, m., *a king of Sicily.* Dīvīnæ stīrpĭs Ăcēstēs, Virg. Epith. Trŏjānŭs, Dārdănĭŭs, Hēctŏrĕŭs, sĕnĭŏr, bŏnŭs, grăvĭs, clārŭs.

ăcētŭm, ī, n., *vinegar.* Vĕtĕrĭs nōn pārcŭs ăcētī, Pers. Syn. Vīnŭm ăcĭdŭm. Epith. Ăcrĕ, mōrdāx, rŭbēns, sŭbtīlĕ, dūrŭm, mōrĭēns, vīlĕ, frīgēns.

Ăchăb, *or* Ăchăbŭs, ī, m., *a king of Israel, the husband of Jezabel.* Epith. Impĭŭs, crūdēlĭs, ăvārŭs.

Ăchæŭs, ă, ŭm, *Greek.* Œbălĭōsquĕ dŭcēs, ĕt Ăchæă pĕr ŏppĭdă mātrēs, St. Syn. Ăchāĭŭs, Ăchīvŭs, Græcŭs.

Ăchāĭă, æ, *and* Ăchāĭs, ĭdĭs *or* ĭdŏs, f., *a part of the Morea.* Aūxĭlĭŭm prōmīttĕt Ăchāĭă Trōjæ, Ov. Quæ sūnt ĭn Ăchāĭdĕ, dīxĭt, Id. Syn. Græcĭă.

Ăchāĭăs, ădĭs *or* ădŏs, *and* Ăchāĭs, ĭdĭs, f., *Greek.* Intĕr Ăchāĭădăs lōngē, Ov. Pĕr tŏt Ăchāĭdăs ūrbēs, Id.

Ăchāĭcŭs, ă, ŭm, *Greek.* Nāvēs ĕt Ăchāĭcă cāstră, Virg. Syn. Ăchæŭs, Ăchīvŭs, Græcŭs.

Ăchæmĕnēs, æ, m., *the son of Ægeus.* Quæ tĕnŭĭt dīvēs Ăchæmĕnēs, (Asclep.) Hor. Epith. Pŏtēns, dīvēs.

Ăchæmĕnĭdēs, æ, m., *one of the companions of Ulysses.* Līttŏra Ăchæmĕnĭdēs, Virg.

Ăchæmĕnĭŭs, ă, ŭm, *Persian.* Nōn tŏt Ăchæmĕnĭĭs, Luc. V. Persicus.

ăchātēs, æ, m., *a precious stone.* Sĭbī nōn sēgnĭs ăchātēs, Lucan. Epith. Vērsĭcŏlŏr. V. Gemma.

Ăchātēs, æ, m., *a friend of Æneas.* Prīmŭs cōnclāmăt Ăchātēs, Virg. Epith. Fīdŭs, fōrtĭs, māgnănĭmŭs, gĕnĕrōsŭs, aūdāx.—2. *A river of Sicily.* Splēndēntī gūrgĭtĕ Ăchātēn, Sil.

Ăchĕlōĭăs, ădĭs *or* ădŏs, *and* Ăchĕlōĭs, ĭdĭs, f., *of the river Achelous ; daughter of Achelous.* Ăchĕlōĭădŭmquĕ rĕlīnquĭt Sīrēnŭm, Ov. Vōbĭs, Ăchĕlōĭdēs, ūndĕ, Ov.

Ăchĕlōĭŭs, ă, ŭm, *of the river Achelous.* Pōcŭlăque īnvēntīs Ăchĕlōĭă mĭscŭĭt ūvīs, Virg.

Ăchĕlŏŭs, ī, m., *Aspro Potamo, a river in the Morea.* Ăchĕlŏŭs Ĕchīnĭdăs ēxĭt, St. Syn. Ăcārnāu. Epith. Cĕlĕr, văgŭs, cŏrnĭgĕr, tūmēns.

Ăchĕrōn, ōntĭs, m., *a river of hell.* Quæ fert Ăchĕrōntĭs ăd ūndās, Virg. Epith. Imŭs, ădūstŭs, prŏfūndŭs, mœstŭs, fĕrōx, dūrŭs, īnvĭŭs, ătĕr, ŏpācŭs, lāngŭĭdŭs, mĭsĕr, īnfīmŭs, pĭcĕŭs, trīstĭs, mōrtŭŭs, nĭgĕr, īnsătĭābĭlĭs, sīlēns, lāngŭēns, cæcŭs, tĕnebrōsŭs, cœnōsŭs, īrrĕmĕābĭlĭs, ăvĭdŭs, tūrbĭdŭs. Infēlīx, hŏrrĭbĭlĭs, hŏrrēndŭs, tērrĭfĭcŭs, īnfērnŭs, Tārtărĕŭs, Tænărĭŭs. V. Styx, Lethe, Infernus.

Ăchĕrōntĭă, æ, f., *a town of the kingdom of Naples.* Cēlsæ nīdum Ăchĕrōntĭæ, (Alcaic.) Hor. Epith. Appŭlă, cēlsă.

Ăchĕrūsĭă, æ, *or* ĭs, ĭdŏs, f., *a lake of Campania.* Trīstēs Ăchĕrūsĭdŏs ōrās, Val. Flac.

Ăchīllēă, æ, f., *an island in the Euxine sea, where Achilles was buried.* Nūdŭs Ăchīllēā dēstĭtŭārĭs hūmō, Ov. Epith. Pārvă, clāră.

Ăchīllēs, ĭs, ĕŏs *or* eī, m., *the son of Thetis and Peleus, king of Thessaly.* Ătque īmmītĭs, Ăchīllēī, Virg. Syn. Pēlīdēs, Æăcĭdēs. Epith. Phthĭŭs, Lārīssæŭs, Pĕllæŭs, Thĕssălĭcŭs, Dănăŭs, Nērēĭŭs, æquŏrĕŭs; ĭmpĭgĕr, crīstātŭs, sævŭs, măgnŭs, sŭpērbŭs, ănĭmōsŭs, fōrtĭs, ārmĭpŏtēns, īndŏmĭtŭs, māgnănĭmŭs, pūgnāx, fĕrōx, dīrŭs, fătālĭs, ĭmpăvĭdŭs, pŏtēns, īmplācābĭlĭs.

Ăchīllēŭs, ă, ŭm, *of Achilles.* Stīrpĭs Ăchīllēæ făstŭs, Virg.

Ăchīllīdēs, æ, *son of Achilles.* Pŷrrhŭs Ăchīllīdēs, Ov.

Ăchīvī, ōrŭm, m. pl., *the Greeks.* Plēctūntŭr Ăchīvī, Hor. V. Græci.

Ăchīvŭs, ă, ŭm, *Greek; of Greece.* Gēntem ēxsēcrātŭr Ăchīvăm, Ov.

āchrăs, ădŏs *or* ădĭs, f., *a wild pear-tree.* Ăchrădŏs aūt prūnī, Colum.

ăcĭcŭlă, æ, f., *the tongue of a buckle.* Quŏd sērvăt ăcĭcŭlă fīlō, Ser. Epith. Tĕnŭĭs, pūngēns.

Ăcīdălĭŭs, ĭī, m., *a fountain of Bœotia, sacred to Venus.* Mātrĭs Ăcīdălĭæ, Virg.

ăcĭdŭs, ă, ŭm, *sour.* Ătque ăcĭdĭs ĭmĭtāntŭr vītĕā sōrbĭs, Virg. Syn. Ăcĕr, ăcērbŭs.

ăcĭēs, ēī, f., *a sharp edge; the eyes, sight.* Stēllīs ăcĭēs ōbtūsă vĭdĕtŭr, Virg. Syn. Ăcūmēn, cūspĭs, mūcro, ēnsĭs. Epith. Tĕnŭĭs, ācrĭs, ăcūtă, ōbtūsă, hĕbĕs, strīctă, cŏrūscă, nĭtĭdă, pĕnĕtrāns. V. Oculus.

ăcĭēs ingenii, *quickness of apprehension.* Syn. Indūstrĭă, sōlērtĭă, ăcūmēn, īngĕnĭŭm. Epith. Ăcrĭs, pērspĭcāx, sōlērs, prōmptă, vīvāx, săgāx, mīrăbĭlĭs, sūbtĭlĭs, ăcūtă. V. Ingenium.

ăcĭēs militaris, *an army in order of battle.* Rōmānās ăcĭēs ĭtĕrŭm vīdĕrĕ Phĭlīppī, Virg. Syn. Agmĕn, ēxērcĭtŭs, cŏhŏrs, phălānx, tūrmă, lĕgĭo, mănĭplŭs, cătērvă, mīlĭtŭm mănŭs. Epith. Mārtĭă, lūnātă, fūlgĭdă, bēllĭgĕră, mĭsĕră, părātă, crŭēntă, sāngŭĭnĕă, hōstīlĭs, hāstātă, dēnsă, nŭmĕrōsă, mĭnāx, răpāx, răbĭdă, vīctrīx, clŷpĕātă, prædātrīx, fĕrōx, īnhūmānă. V. Exercitus.

ăcīnăcēs, *or* ăcīnăcĭs, ĭs, m., *a Persian scimitar.* Insīgnĭs ăcīnăcĕ dēxtră, Val. Fl. Epith. Pērsĭcŭs, Mēdŭs. V. Ensis.

ăcĭnŭs, ī, m., *and* ŭm, ī, n., *the stone of grapes, mulberries, &c.* Ex pārvīs ăcĭnōs pŏtărĕ săbūcīs, Ser. Ărīdum ĕt ōrĕ fĕrēns ăcĭnŭm, Hor. Syn. Grānŭm, răcēmŭs.

ăcĭpēnsĕr, ĕrĭs, *or* ăcĭpēnsĭs, ĭs, m., *a sturgeon.* Ăcĭpēnsĕrĕ mēnsa īnfāmĭs, Hor. Ăd Pālātīnās ăcĭpēnsĕm mīttĭtĕ mēnsās, Mart. Epith. Nōbĭlĭs, cārŭs.

Ăcĭs, ĭs *or* ĭdĭs, m., *the son of Faunus, loved by Galatea, and metamorphosed into a fountain.* Mēĭs cōmplēxĭbŭs Ăcĭn, Ov. Epith. Pūlchĕr, Sĭcŭlŭs, hērbĭfĕr, lĭmpĭdŭs, vītrĕŭs.

ăclĭs, ĭdĭs, f., *a kind of short dart.* Tĕrĕtēs sūnt ăclĭdēs īllīs, Virg. V. Jaculum.

Ăcmōn, ŏnĭs, m., *one of the companions of Diomed.* Plĕurŏnĭŭs Ăcmōn, Ov.

Ăcmŏnĭdēs, æ, m., *one of the Cyclopes.* Stĕrŏpēs, Ăcmŏnĭdēsquĕ sŏlēnt, Ov.

Ăcœtēs, æ, m., *a poor Mæonian fisherman.* 2. *one of Evander's attendants.* Nōmēn mĭhĭ, dīxĭt, Ăcœtēs, Ov. Epith. Paūpĕr, mĭsĕr, mēndīcŭs. V. Pauper.

ăcŏnītŭm, *or* ŏn, ī, n., *wolfsbane.* Scŷthĭcĭs ăcŏnītŏn ăb ōrĭs, Ov. Fāllūnt ăcŏnītă lĕgēntēs, Virg. Epith. Cērbĕrĕŭm, Stŷgĭŭm, Tārtărĕŭm. V. Venenum.

Ăcōntĕŭs, ĕŏs, ĕī *or* eī, m., *the name of a warrior.* Excūssŭs Ăcōntĕŭs, Virg.

Ăcōntĭŭs, ĭī, *a youth of the island of Cea, the lover of Cydippe.* Tĭbĭ nōmĕn Ăcōntĭŭs ēssĕt, Ov.

ăcŏr, ōrĭs, m., *sharpness, sourness.* Chrīstŭs dēglŭtĭt ăcŏrĕm, Calc. Syn. Acĭdŭs, ācrĭs săpŏr. Epith. Mŏrdāx, ĭngrātŭs.

ācquĭēsco, ēvī, *to rest.* Dēsĭdĕrātŏque ācquĭēscĭmŭs lēctō, (Scaz.) Catul. Syn. Quĭēsco ; ăccŭmbo, ĭnnĭtŏr ; dēlēctŏr, cōntēntŭs sŭm ; āssēntĭo, cōnsēntĭo.

ācquīro, sīvī, sītŭm, *to get, to obtain.* Vīrēsque ācquīrĭt ĕŭndo, Virg. Syn. Adĭpīscŏr, āssēquŏr, cōmpăro, cōncĭllĭo, păro, cōnsēquŏr, ĭnvĕnĭo, ŏbtĭnĕo, cōllĭgo, quæro.

ācquīsītŭs, ă, ŭm, *the pass. partic. of* acquiro. Ācquīsītă mĕō sērvīt tĭbĭ Crētă Mĕtēllō, Sid.

Acrăgās, āntĭs, m., *a mountain and town.* Ardŭŭs ĭnde Acrăgās ōstēntăt, Virg.

ăcrēdŭlă, æ, f., *a nightingale.* Cōmpōnĭt ăcrēdŭlă cāntŭs, Ov. Syn. Lūscĭnĭă, Phĭlŏmēlă. V. Philomela.

Acrĭmōnĭă, æ, f., *sharpness, harshness.* Vălēmŭs ācrĭmōnĭăm, (Iamb.) Prud.

Acrĭsĭōnæŭs, ă, ŭm, *of Acrisione or Danaë, of Argos or of Ardea.* Acrĭsĭōnæĭs Dănăē fūndāssĕ cŏlōnĭs, Virg.

Acrĭsĭōnē, ēs, f., *the daughter of Acrisius, Danaë.* Ĭnăchĭs Acrĭsĭōnē, Virg.

Acrĭsĭōnĭădēs, æ, m., *the son of Danaë, Perseus.* Mēdūsæ Acrĭsĭōnĭădēs, Ov.

Acrĭsĭŭs, ĭī, m., *the king of the Argians, the father of Danaë.* Acrĭsĭŭs sŭpĕrēst, Ov. Syn. Ĭnăchĭdēs.

ăcrĭtĕr, adv., *sharply.* Acrĭtĕr ēlātum ĭngĕnĭŭm, Hor. Syn. Fōrtĭtĕr, vĕhĕmēntĕr, ācrī ănĭmō.

Acrŏcĕraŭnĭă, ōrŭm, n. pl., *high mountains in Epirus.* Hæc Acrŏcĕraŭnĭă vītă, Ov. V. Ceraunia.

Acrŏcŏrīnthŭs, ī, f., *a mountain above Corinthus.* Tōllĭt căpŭt Acrŏcŏrīnthŭs Ĭn aŭrās, St. Epith. Altă, cēlsă, sacră.

Acrōn, ōntĭs, m., *a king of the Ceninians.* Acrōn Hērcŭlĕŭs, Prop. Epith. Cēnīnŭs, Hērcŭlĕŭs.

Acrŏtă, æ, m., *the son of Tiberinus.* Mŏdĕrātĭŏr Acrŏtă fōrtī, Ov.

āctă, æ, f., *a shore.* In sōlă sēcrētæ Trōădēs āctă, Virg. Syn. Rīpă, līttŭs, ōră. V. Littus.

Actæōn, ōnĭs, m., *the son of Aristæus and Autonoë.* Actæōn ĕgŏ sŭm, Ov. Syn. Cădmī nĕpōs. Cădmēĭŭs hērōs. Nātŭs Arīstæī. Aŭtŏnŏēĭŭs hērōs. Fīlĭŭs Aŭtŏnŏēs. Epith. Cădmæŭs, cōrnĭgĕr, vēnātŏr, fŭgĭtīvŭs, sўlvānŭs, mĭsĕr, văgăbŭndŭs, văgŭs, păvĭdŭs, vēlōx, flēbĭlĭs, ērrāns, cēlĕr.

Actæŭs, ă, ŭm, *of Attica.* Actæĭs Phōcĭs ăb ārvĭs, Ov.

Actĭācŭs *and* Actĭŭs, ă, ŭm, *of Actium ; of Apollo.* Actĭācō quæ nūnc, Ov. Actĭāque Ĭlĭācĭs cĕlĕbrāmŭs līttŏră, Virg.

Actĭăs, ădĭs *or* ădōs, *of Attica ; Athenian.* Hēbrŭs ĕt Actĭăs Orīthўĭă, Virg.

ăctĭo, ōnĭs, f., *an action.* Syn. Fāctŭm, fācĭnŭs, āctŭs ūs, ŏpŭs ĕrĭs ; aŭsŭs ūs, aŭsŭm, *i. e.* cœptŭm, ĭncēptŭm, lăbŏr ; āctă ōrŭm, gēstă ōrŭm. Epith. Ĭnsīgnĭs, clāră, præclāră.

āctĭto, ās, *the frequent. of* ago, *to plead often.* Sen. Ctēsўphōntĭs āctĭtărēt, Sid.

Actĭŭm, ĭī, n., *a town and port of Epirus.* Actĭă Jūlēæ Pĕlăgŭs, Prop.

āctŏr, ōrĭs, m., *an actor, doer, pleader.* Trăbēăs āctŏrĕ rŏgāntēs, Hor. Syn. Pērsōnă. Epith. Thĕātrĭcŭs, scēnĭcŭs. V. Histrio.

Actŏr, ōrĭs, *the grandfather of Patroclus.—2. An ancient hero of Ausonia.* Actŏrĭs Aŭrūncī spŏlĭŭm, Virg.

Actŏrĭdēs, æ, *the grandson of Actor, Patroclus.* At nōn Actŏrĭdēs, Ov.

āctŭs, ă, ŭm, *the pass. partic. of* ago. Ērrābănt āctī fātīs, Virg.

āctŭs, ūs, m., *an act, deed.* Adde āctŭs tāntŏs, Lucr. Syn. Actĭo : āctă ōrŭm, fāctŭm. V. Actio.

āctūtŭm, adv., *forthwith.* Actūtŭm pĭŭs Ænēās, Virg. Syn. Cōnfēstĭm, rĕpēntĕ, cĭto, pĭŏtĭnŭs, ēxtēmplō, cōntĭnŭō, ĭllĭcō. V. Statim.

ăcŭlĕātŭs, ă, ŭm, *having a sting.* Plaut. Syn. Ăcŭmĭnātŭs, ăcūtŭs.

ăcŭlĕŭs, ī, m., *a sting.* Mĕŭm ĭllŏ pēctŭs pūngĭt ăcŭlĕŭs, (Iamb.) Syn. Stĭmŭlŭs. Epith. Sŭbtīlĭs, tĕnŭĭs, ēxīlĭs, sævŭs, āspĕr, crŭēntŭs. V. Stimulus, calcar.

ăcūmĕn, ĭnĭs, n., *the edge of any thing.* Cŭrvāntŭr ăcūmĭnĕ crūră, Lucr. Epith. Tĕnŭĕ sūmmŭm.

ăcūmĕn ingenii, *subtilty.* Quæ nōn fōrmīdăt ăcūmĕn, Hor. Syn. Acĭēs, ĭngĕnĭŭm, sōlērtĭă, cĕlĕrĭs ănĭmī vīs, ĭndūstrĭă. Epith. Argūtŭm, sōlērs, sŭbtīlĕ, sāgāx, pĕnĕtrāns, ācrĕ. V. Ingenium *and* Sales.

|| ăcŭmĭno, ās. Syn. Ăcŭo, ĕxăcŭo. V. Acuo.

ăcŭo, ĭs, ăcŭī, ăcūtŭm, *to point.* Vărīisque ăcŭūnt rūmŏrĭbŭs īrās, Virg. Syn.
Exăcŭo, ăcŭmĭno ;· ĕxcĭto, hŏrtŏr, accĕndo, ănĭmo, ĭnflāmmo, pĕllo, ĭmpĕllo.

ăcŭs, ĕrĭs, n., *chaff.* Vēntŭs ăcŭs pălĕāsquĕ, Passerat. Syn. Pălĕă, stĭpŭlă.
Epitii. Tĕnŭĕ, frăgĭlĕ, sīccŭm, lĕvĕ.

ăcŭs, ūs, f., *a needle.* Seŭ pīngēbăt ăcŭ, Ov. Epith. Sŭbtīlĭs, tĕnŭĭs, crīnālĭs,
ăcūtă, mŏrdāx, mŭlĭĕbrĭs : Assўrĭă, Lўdĭă, Mæŏnĭă, Phrўgĭă.

ăcŭs, ī, m., *a sea-fish.* Tĕnŭĕs dūcĕrĕ crēdĭs ăcŏs, Mart.

ăcūtŭs, *the pass. partic. of* acuo, *sharpened, acute.* Cārĭcĕ pāstŭs ăcūtā, Virg.
Syn. Sŭbtīlĭs, tĕnŭĭs : sŏlērs, săgāx, ăcĕr, ĭngĕnĭōsŭs, ārgūtŭs.

ăd, prep., *to, at, near, towards.* Cănēt frŏndātŏr ăd aūrās, Virg. Syn. In ;
ūsquĕ ; jūxtă, prŏpĕ, cīrcā, cīrcŭm ; vērsŭs.

ădāctŭs, *the pass. partic. of* adigo. Vīrĭbŭs ēnsĭs ădāctŭs, Virg.

|| ădæquo, ās, *to equalize.* Syn. Æquo, ēxæquo ; æquălĕ, păr făcĭo, ĕffĭcĭo,
rēddo. V. Æquo.

ădæstŭo, ās, *to boil over.* Illĭsŭs ădæstŭăt āmnĭs, Stat. V. Æstuo.

ădăgĭŭm, ĭī, n., *a proverb.* Plaut. Syn. Prŏvĕrbĭŭm ; sērmo trītŭs, vŭlgātŭs, pĕr-
vŭlgātŭs. Epith. Cŏmmūnĕ, vŭlgărĕ, brĕvĕ, vērŭm, cĕrtŭm.

Adām, *and* Adāmŭs. *The first, and father of mankind.* Prīmŭs Ădām cāptŭs,
Vida. Măcŭlīs sŏrdēntĭbŭs Adăm, Prud. Syn. Prīmŭs hŏmo, prīmævŭs pătĕr.
Epitii. Antīquŭs, lŭtĕŭs, īnfēlīx, rĕŭs, mĭsĕr, ĭmprūdēns, crēdŭlŭs, tērrĭgĕnă,
īncaūtŭs.

Ădămāntĕŭs, ă, ŭm, *of adamant.* Ecce ădămāntēĭs Vŭlcānŭm nārĭbŭs ĕfflānt.
Ov.

ădămāntĭnŭs, ă, ŭm, *hard as adamant.* Imprīmīs ădămāntĭnă sāxă, Lucr. Syn.
Ădāmāntĕŭs, dūrŭs, fīrmŭs, sŏlĭdŭs : ĭnēxŏrābĭlĭs, ĭnēxpūgnābĭlĭs, īnsŭpĕrābĭlĭs,
ĭndŏmĭtŭs, ĭnvīctŭs, īnfrāctŭs, cēdĕrĕ nēscĭŭs.

ădāmās, āntĭs, m., *a diamond.* Sŏlĭdōquĕ ădămāntĕ cŏlŭmnæ, Virg. Epith.
Dūrŭs, pĕrēnnĭs, īnvīctŭs, īnfrāctŭs, rĭgĭdŭs, splēndēns, cŏrŭscŭs, lūcĭdŭs, īn-
cŏrrūptŭs, prĕtĭōsŭs, clārŭs, ætērnŭs, nĭtĭdŭs, mĭcāns, sīdĕrĕŭs, pŭlchĕr, Indĭcŭs,
Indŭs, Eŏŭs, rădĭāns, dīvĕs, trēmŭlŭs. V. Gemma.

Ădămāstŭs, ī, m., *the father of Achæmenides.* Gĕnĭtŏre Ădămāstō, Virg.

Ădămĭcŭs, ă, ŭm, *of Adam.* Ad Elўsĭōs sŏbŏlēs Ădămĭcă cāmpōs, Mant.

Ădămītă, æ, m., *son of Adam.* Chārŭs Ădămītĭs. (Pent.) Syn. Hŏmo, Adāmī
sŏbŏlēs.

ădămo, ās, *to love greatly.* Nŏn ădămāssĕt ĕquŏs, Ov. Syn. Dēpĕrĕo. V. Amo.

ădăpĕrĭo, rĭs, rŭī, ĕrtŭm, *to open, discover.* Syn. Ăpĕrĭo, rĕsĕro, reclūdo, pāndo.
V. Aperio.

ădăpĕrtĭlĭs, adj., *which may be opened.* Hŏc ădăpĕrtĭlĕ taūrī, Ov.

ădăpĕrtŭs, *the pass. partic. of* adaperio. Pārs ădăpĕrtă fŭĭt, Ov. Syn. Hĭāns,
hĭŭlcŭs, ăpĕrtŭs, rĕsĕrātŭs, reclūsŭs, pătĕfāctŭs, pătēns.

|| ădăquo, ās, *to water.* Ădăquărĕ cănālĭbŭs hŏrtŭm, Mart. Syn. Aquŏr, ăd
ăquam dūco, īrrĭgo. V. Aquor *and* irrigo.

*ădaūgĕo, xī, ctŭm, *to increase.* Syn. Aŭgĕo, āccŭmŭlo, cŭmŭlo. V. Augeo.

ădaūgēsco, ĭs, *to be increased.* Nām nĕquĕ ădaūgēscĭt quīcquăm, Lucr. Syn.
Aŭgĕŏr, ădŏlēsco, crēsco, mājŏr fīo, āmplĭfĭcŏr.

ădbĭbo, ĭs, ădbĭbī, *to drink hard, to suck in.* Nūnc ădbĭbĕ pūrō, Hor. Syn.
Bĭbo, haūrĭo. V. Bibo.

ăddĕcĕt, *it behoves, it is right.* Mūtŭm ēsse ăddĕcĕt, Plaut.

ăddēnsĕo, ēs, *and* ăddēnso, ās, *to thicken.* Ēxtrēmī ăddēnsēnt ăcĭēs, Virg. Syn.
Dēnso, stīpo, cōgo.

ăddīco, ĭs, xī, ctŭm, *to ratify, to sell, to submit.* Emptŏr, gaŭdēntēm nŭmmō te
ăddĭcĕrĕ, Hor. Syn. Dēdo, dēstĭno, dŏ ; sŭbmītto.

ăddīsco, ăddĭdĭcī, *to learn.* Ăddĭdĭcī rēgĭmēn dēxtrā, Ov. Syn. Dīsco.

ăddĭtŭs, ă. ŭm, *the pass. partic. of* addo. Mŏx ēt frŭmēntīs lābŏr ăddĭtŭs, Virg.

ăddo, ăddĭdī, ăddĭtŭm, *to add.* Ădĭdĕrāt sŏcĭŭm, Virg. Syn. Admŏvĕo, ădjūngo, ădhĭbĕo, āpplĭco, ānnēcto, jūngo, cŏnnēcto, āppŏno.

ăddŏcĕo, ēs, *to teach in addition.* Addŏcĕt ārtēs, Hor. V. Doceo.

Āddŭă, æ, m., *the Adda, a river of Italy.* Ăddŭă spūmōsŭs, Claud. Epitii.
Cĕlĕr, cærŭlĕŭs, vēlōx, cĭtŭs, cŏncĭtŭs, præcĕps, raŭcŭs, ămœnŭs.

ăddŭbĭto, ās, *to have some doubt.* Nĕcnĕ sĭt, ăddŭbĭtēs, Hor. V. Dubito.

B 6

ăddūco, xī, ctŭm, *to lead to.* Ăddūcĭtquĕ cŭtĕm măcĭĕs, Ov. Syn. Dūco, dēdūco, īnvīto, cōmpello ĭs ; fĕro, āllĭcĭo, pēllĭcĭo, īmpēllo ; cōntēndo, īntēndo, tēndo.

ădēdo, ădēdī, ădēsŭm, *to devour, eat up.* Saepĕ făvōs īgnōtŭs ădēdĭt, Virg. Syn. Exēdo, pĕrēdo, rōdo, ārrōdo, cōnsūmo, vŏro. V. Edo.

ădēmptŭs, *the pass. partic. of* adimo. Thēssălō vīctōre ĕt ădēmptŭs Hēctŏr, (Sapph.) Hor. Syn. Rāptŭs, ērēptŭs. V. Adimo.

ădĕo, īs, ădĭī, ădĭtŭm, *to go to.* Quīn, ădēās vātĕm, Virg. Syn. Cōnvĕnĭo, īnvīso, vīso, vīsĭto, āccēdo. V. Eo, venio ; subeo, suscipio.

ădĕŏ, adv., *so.* Tēque ădĕŏ dĕcŭs hōc aevī, Virg.

ădēps, ĭpĭs, m., *fat.* Cȳgnēōs ădĭpēs hĭlărī mīscētĕ Lȳaeō, Ser. Syn. Pīnguēdo.

ădēptŭs, *the partic. of* adipiscor. Mōns ēst cōgnōmĕn ădēptŭs, Prop. Syn. Acquīsītŭs, pārtŭs.

ădērro, ās, *to wander near.* Dēlphīnĕs ădērrānt, Stat.

ădĕs, *2nd pers. indic. pres. of* adsum. Prīmŭs ădĕs ; sēd nōn, Virg. *2nd pers. imper.* Tūque ădĕs, Id.

ădēsdŭm, *the imperat. of* adsum. Syn. Adsīs ād mē ; hūc ădĕs.

ădēsŭs, ă, ŭm, *the pass. partic. of* adedo. Et pōstĭbŭs haesĭt ădēsīs, Virg. Syn. Rōsŭs, ārrōsŭs, cōrrōsŭs, cōnsūmptŭs, ēxēsŭs.

ădfrīngo, ēgī, *to break against.* Ădfrīngŭnt pōstĭbŭs ūnguēs, Stat. Syn. Frāngo, cōnfrīngo. V. Frango.

ădgĕmo, ŭī, *to sigh at.* Ădgĕmĭt Alcīdēs, Ov. Syn. Gĕmo, cōndŏlĕo.

ădhaec, *besides.* Syn. Praetĕrĕā.

ădhaerĕo, ădhaesī, *to stick to.* Cōgnōmĕn ădhaerĕt, Hor. Syn. Haerĕo, ădjăcĕo, ădjŭngŏr, ădhaerēsco, āpplĭcŏr, cōnjūngŏr ; sŭm īnfīxŭs.

ădhĭbĕo, ŭī, ĭtŭm, *to apply.* Ēst ădhĭbērĕ nĕcēssŭm, Mart. Syn. Adjĭcĭo, ădmŏvĕo, āppōno, ādjūngo, āddo, ōffĕro.

ădhīnnĭo, īs, ĭī, *to neigh after.* Acĕr ădhīnnĭt ĕquŭs, Ser. Syn. Hīnnĭo : hīnnītūm rēddo.

ădhōrrĕo, *or* ădhōrrēsco, rŭī, *to be afraid of.* Tȳbĕrīnŭs ădhōrrŭĭt ūndīs, Ov. V. Horreo.

ădhōrtŏr, ārĭs, *to counsel, to encourage.* Rēs ădhōrtātŭr tŭă, (Iamb.) Ter. Syn. Hōrtŏr, mŏnĕo, ēxhōrtŏr, ădmŏnĕo, īncĭto, īmpēllo, ēxcĭto. V. Hortor.

ădhūc, adv., *hitherto.* Sōlŭs ădhūc ĕgŏ, Ovid. Syn. Rūrsŭs, ĭtĕrŭm ; hāctĕnŭs ; ĕtĭamnŭm, ĕtĭăm nūnc.

ādjăcĕo, ŭī, *to lie contiguous.* Adjăcŭĭtquĕ căvīs, Mant. Syn. Adhaerēsco, ădhaerĕo, ādjŭngŏr, cōujūngŏr ; sŭm vīcīnŭs, prŏpīnquŭs, prōxĭmŭs. V. Vicinus.

ădĭcĭo, ĭs, *same as* adjicio. Nīl ădĭcīt pēnsō, Mart.

ădĭgo, ēgī, āctŭm, *to drive.* Ădĭgāt mē fūlmĭne ăd ūmbrās, Virg. Syn. Cōgo, cōmpēllo, īmpēllo. V. Cogo.

ādjĭcĭo, ādjēcī, ādjēctŭm, *to add to.* Ădjĭcĭām ; făcĭāmque ōmnēs, Virg. Syn. Āddo, ādjūngo, ădhĭbĕo, ădmŏvĕo, āppōno.

ădĭmo, ădēmī, ădēmptŭm, *to take away.* Haūd īmpūnĕ fĕrēs, ădīmām tĭbĭ, Ov. Syn. Răpĭo, ērĭpĭo, căpĭo, aūfĕro, tōllo, sūbtrăho, ābrĭpĭo, ēxtōrquĕo, sūbdūco. V. Furor, aris.

|| ădĭmplĕo, ēvī, ētŭm, *to fill up.* Quōd mēntĕ părārăt, ădīmplĕt, Passer. Syn. Cōmplĕo, replĕo, īmplĕo.

ădĭpātŭm, ī, n., *fat.* Fērvēnt ădĭpātă vĕnēnŏ, Juv.

ădĭpīscŏr, ĕrĭs, *to get, to obtain.* Hānc ădĭpīscūntŭr, cīrcŭm, Lucr. Syn. Acquīro, āssĕquŏr, cōnsĕquŏr, păro, cōmpăro. V. Acquiro.

ădĭtŭs, ūs, m., *a way, an access.* Innŭmĕrōsque ădĭtŭs, Ov. Syn. Vĭă, ĭtĕr, īngrēssŭs. Epith. Mălīgnŭs, făcĭlĭs, dĭffĭcĭlĭs, pătēns, ārdŭŭs, claūsŭs. V. Janua.

ādjūdĭco, ās, *to attribute, to impute.* Itălīs ădjūdĭcăt ārmīs, Hor. Syn. Trĭbŭo, āttrĭbŭo, āddīco.

ādjŭmēntŭm, ī, n., *a help.* Haec quŏquĕ rēs ādjŭmēntŏ, Lucr. Syn. Aŭxĭlĭŭm, lĕvāmĕn, sōlāmĕn. V. Auxilium.

ādjūngo, xī, ctŭm, *to unite.* Ūlmīsque ădjūngĕrĕ vītēs, Virg. Syn. Āddo, cōnjūngo, ādjĭcĭo, āllĭgo, ădmŏvĕo, ădhĭbĕo, āpplĭco, āppōno, ānnēcto. V. Jungo.

ādjūro, ās, *to swear solemnly.* Adjūrō Stȳgĭī căpŭt, Virg. Syn. Sūpplēx ōro, ōbtēstŏr. V. Oro, precor.

ădjŭtŏr, ōrĭs, m., *and* trīx, īcīs, f., *a helper.* Măgnum ădjūtōrēm, pōssēt, Hor.
Ădjūtrīxquĕ vĕnīs, Ov. Syn. Aŭxĭlĭātŏr, faŭtŏr, sŏcĭŭs, ădmĭnīstĕr.

ădjŭvo, jŭvī, jŭtŭm, *to help.* Adjŭvăt īră mănŭs, Ovid. Syn. Jŭvo, aŭxĭlĭŏr, sŭccŭrro, sŭbvĕnĭo, ŏpĕm fĕro. V. Auxilior.

Ădmētŭs, ī, m., *a king of Thessaly, son of Pheres.* Cērnĭs ŭt Admētī cāntētŭr, Ov. Syn. Phĕrētĭădēs. Epith. Thēssălŭs, Thēssălĭcŭs, Æmŏnĭŭs, Æmăthĭŭs, Phĕræŭs.

ădmĭnĭcŭlŭm, ī, n., *a prop.* Plaut. Syn. Fūlcrŭm, fūlcĭmēntŭm, cŏlŭmĕn, sŭbsĭdĭŭm.

|| ădmĭnīstĕr, trī, m., *an assistant.* Syn. Mĭnīstĕr, ădjŭtŏr. Epith. Vĭgĭl, pĕrvĭgĭl, ĭmpĭgĕr.

|| ădmĭnīstro, ās, *to administer.* Syn. Rĕgo; mĭnīstro, sŭppĕdĭto.

ădmīrābĭlĭs, ĕ, *admirable.* Ŏpŭs ădmīrābĭlĕ sæpĕ, Ov. Syn. Mīrābĭlĭs, mīrāndŭs, ădmīrāndŭs, mīrŭs, stŭpēndŭs, mīrĭfĭcŭs.

ădmīrātĭo, ōnĭs, f., *admiration.* Mĭnŏr ădmīrātĭŏ sūmmĭs, Juv.

|| ădmīrātŏr, ōrĭs, m., *an admirer.* Absēntĭs ădmīrātŏr māxĭmŭs, Ph. Syn. Ădmīrāns, mīrāns. Epith. Stŭpĕfāctŭs, āttŏnĭtŭs, pērcŭlsŭs, tăcĭtŭs, cōnfūsŭs.

ădmīrŏr, ārĭs, *to admire.* Sēd tămĕn ădmīrŏr, Hor. Syn. Mīrŏr, dēmīrŏr, stŭpĕo, ŏbstŭpĕo, sūspĭcĭo. V. Miror.

ădmīscĕo, cŭī, stŭm *or* xtŭm, *to mix.* Gāllæ ădmīscĕrĕ săpōrĕm, Mant. Syn. Mīscĕo, cōmmīscĕo, pērmīscĕo. V. Misceo.

ădmīssŭm, ī, n., *a fault.* Gēntīsque ădmīssā dŏlōsæ, Ov.

ădmītto, īsī, īssŭm, *to admit.* Hŏc ădmīsīssēt nēc Cătĭlīnă nĕfās, Mart. Syn. Excĭpĭo, sūscĭpĭo, īndūco, īntrōdūco; prŏbo, āpprŏbo, cōmprŏbo; cōmmītto.

ădmŏdŭlŏr, ārĭs, *to murmur to.* Ādmŏdŭlētŭr ălnīs, Claud.

ădmŏdŭm, adv., *much, very.* Nŭpēr nōtĭtĭa ădmŏdum ēst, Ter.

ădmōlĭŏr, īrĭs, *to heap up.* Plaut. Syn. Mōlĭŏr, ădnītŏr. V. Molior.

ădmŏnĕo, ŭī, ĭtŭm, *to admonish.* Admŏnĕt ēt māgnā, Virg. Syn. Mŏnĕo, cōmmŏnĕo, præcĭpĭo, suādĕo, hŏrtŏr, māndo, jŭbĕo. V. Hortor.

ădmŏnĭtŏr, ōrĭs, m., *an adviser, encourager.* Admŏnĭtŏrque ŏpĕrŭm, Ov.

ădmŏnĭtŭs, ūs, m., *and* ŭm, ī, n., *counsel.* Flēt tămēn ădmŏnĭtū, Ov. Syn. Mŏnĭtŭm, mŏnĭtŭs, hŏrtātŭs, ĭmpŭlsŭs, hŏrtātĭo, præcēptŭm. Epith. Ūtĭlĭs, prūdēns, ămīcŭs, sălūtĭfĕr, dūrŭs, grātŭs.

ădmōrdĕo, sī, sŭm, *to bite hard.* Plaut. Syn. Mōrdĕo.

ădmŏvĕo, ōvī, ōtŭm, *to move, to bring to.* Prŏpĕrāntēs ădmŏvĕt hŏrās, Lucan. Syn. Ăpplĭco, āppōno, ădhĭbĕo, ădjūngo, ădjĭcĭo.

ădmōtŭs, ă, ŭm, *the pass. partic. of* admoveo. Īllĕ sĭbi ădmōtās ā vīrgĭnĕ, Prop.

ădmūgĭo, īs, ĭī, *to low.* Admŭgīt fœmĭnă taŭrō, Ov. Syn. Mūgĭo, mŭgītŭm rēddo.

ădmūrmŭro, ās, *to applaud, or hiss at.* Bŏrĕæque ădmūrmŭrăt Aŭstĕr, Ov. Syn. Mūrmŭro, frĕmo, āpplaŭdo, plaŭdo, ācclāmo, prŏbo, āpprŏbo, cōmprŏbo, ĭmprŏbo, rējĭcĭo. V. Murmuro.

ădmŭtĭlo, ās, *to mutilate.* Quī me ūsque ădmŭtĭlāvīstī ād cŭtĕm, Ter.

ădnīxŭs, ă, ŭm, *the partic. of* adnitor. Sūmmīs ădnīxŭs vīrĭbŭs, Virg. V. Innitor.

ădno, *or* ădnăto, ās, *to swim to.* Vēstrīs ădnāvĭmŭs ōrīs, Virg. V. Nato.

ădnūbĭlo, ās, *to darken.* Vēlīs ădnūbĭlăt aŭrā sĕcūndīs, Stat. Syn. Ŏbscūro. V. Nubes.

ădŏlĕo, ēvī, *to grow, to burn.* Hæc ădŏlēt flāmmīs, Ov. Syn. Crēsco; ūro, cōmbūro, ĭncēndo. V. Uro, thus.

ădŏlēscēns, tĭs, m. f., *a young man or woman.* Ēgo ădŏlēscēns, ēgo ĕphēbŭs, Cat. Syn. Jŭvĕnĭs, ĕphēbŭs, pūbĕr. Epith. Ădūltŭs, lĕvĭs, īncōnstāns, aŭdāx, fōrmōsŭs, prōdĭgŭs, fērvēns, fērvĭdŭs, ĭmpăvĭdŭs, vērnāns, ălăcrĭs, pĕtŭlāns, mălĕsānŭs, ĭncaŭtŭs, āmēns, blāndŭs, mĭnāx, ĭndŏcĭlĭs, cæcŭs, īngĕnĭōsŭs, văgŭs, ēffrænātŭs, ĭmprūdēns, gĕnĕrōsŭs. V. Juvenis.

ădŏlēscēntĭă, æ, f., *youth.* Rĕgēndā măgĭs ēst fērvĭda ădŏlēscēntĭā, (Iamb.) Sen. Syn. Jŭvēntă, jŭvēntŭs, jŭvĕnĭlĭs ætās, pūbērtās, flōs ætātĭs, vēr ætātĭs. Epith. Fērvĭdă, lĕvĭs, īnstăbĭlĭs, ĭmprūdēns, grātă, ămœnă, jŭcūndă, aŭdāx, mōllĭs, ēffrœnĭs. V. Juventus.

ădŏlēscēntŭlŭs, ī, m., *the dimin. of* adolescens. Nōn ēst flāgĭtĭŭm, făcĕre hŏc ădŏlēscēntŭlŭm, Ter.

ădŏlēsco, ădŏlēvī, ădŭltŭm, *to grow, to burn.* Prīmă nŏvīs ădŏlēscīt frŏndĭbŭs aetās, Virg. Syn. Ŭrŏr, īncēndŏr ; aūgĕŏr, crēsco.

Ădōnīă, ōrŭm, n. pl., *festivals in honour of Adonis.* Epith. Trīstĭă, fĕrālĭă.

Ădōnĭs, ĭdĭs, m., *the son of Myrrha and Cinyra, loved by Venus.* Ŏvēs ăd flūmĭnă pāvĭt Ădōnĭs, Virg. Syn. Cĭnўrēĭŭs hērōs or jŭvĕnĭs. Mўrrhae fīlĭŭs or nātŭs. Epith. Fōrmōsŭs, pŭlchĕr, tĕnĕr, blāndŭs, Cўthĕrēĭŭs, pūrpŭrĕŭs, nĭvĕŭs, mōl-lĭs, tĕnēllŭs, vēnātŏr, vĕnŭstŭs, cāndĭdŭs, săgĭttĭfĕr, phăretrātŭs.

ădŏpĕrĭo, ĭs, *to cover all over.* Syn. Ŏpĕrĭo, tĕgo, ābdo, vēlo, ŏccŭlto, ōbtĕgo. V. Occulto.

ădŏpērtŭs, ă, ŭm, *the pass. particip. of* adoperio. Cōmās ădŏpērtŭs ămīctū, Virg.

ădŏpīnŏr, ārĭs, *to conjecture.* Deīnde ădŏpīnāmŭr dē sīgnĭs māxĭmă pārvĭs, Lucr.

ădōptĭo, ōnĭs, f., *adoption.* Ĭmĭtātŭr ădōptĭŏ prōlĕm, Aus. Epith. Fēlīx, grātă, splēndĭdă, nōbĭlĭs. V. Insitio.

ădōptīvŭs, ă, ŭm, *belonging to adoption.* Ĕt fĭt ădōptīvā nōbĭlĭtātĕ tŭŭs, Ov. Syn. Ălĭēnŭs, ădōptātĭtĭŭs.

ădōpto, ās, *to adopt.* Nōmĕn ădōptēs, Mart. Syn. Ŏpto, ēlĭgo.

ădŏr, ŏrĭs, n., *corn.* Mŏx ădŏr ātque ădŏrĭs dē pōllĭnĕ, Aus. Syn. Frūmēntŭm, fār, trītĭcŭm. Epith. Ēlēctŭm, lēctŭm, sēlēctŭm, pūrŭm. V. Frumentum.

ădōrātŭs, ă, ŭm, *the pass. particip. of* adoro. Ārdĕt ădōrātŭm pŏpŭlō căpŭt, Juv.

ădōrĕă, ae, f., *a distribution of corn, by way of reward ; reward ; victory.* Rĕvŏ-cāvĭt ădōrĕă laūrōs, Claud. Syn. Frūmēntă ōrŭm ; ŏpēs, glōrĭă, hŏnŏr, laūs ; vīctōrĭă. Epĭɪʜ. Ālmă.

ădōrĕŭs, ă, ŭm, *made of wheat.* Ĕt ădōrĕă lībă pĕr hērbăm, Virg.

ădōrĭŏr, īrĭs, ōrtŭm, *to attempt, to begin.* Cuĭcūnque ădŏrītŭr, ĕt īnfĭt, Lucr. Aggrĕdĭŏr, ădŏrĭŏr, īncĭpĭo ; lăcēsso, ōppŭgno.

ădōrno, ās, *to adorn.* Cōnŭs ădōrnābăt gălĕăm. Syn. Ōrno, ēxōrno, dĕcŏro, īnstrŭo. V. Orno. Praepăro, cōmpăro, păro. V. Praeparo.

ădōro, ās, *to adore.* Prŏcĕ nūmĕn ădŏrā, Virg. Syn. Ōro, sŭpplēx ōro ; rĕvĕrĕor, cōlo, vĕnĕrŏr. V. Precor, Sacrifico.

ădōrsŭs, ă, ŭm, *the partic. of* adordior. Mājŭs ădōrsă nĕfās, Virg.

ădōrtŭs, ă, ŭm, *the partic. of* adorior. Thălămō dēdūcĕre ădōrtī, Virg.

ădpărĭo, ĭs, ĕrĕ, *to acquire.* Adpărĕrēt spătĭŭm, Lucr.

ădpōsco, ĭs, *to demand in addition.* Sī plūs ădpōscĕrĕ vīsŭs, Hor.

ădrādo, ĭs, rāsī, rāsŭm, *to scrape ; to shave.* Ădrāsŭm quēndăm văcŭā tōnsōrĭs Ĭn ŭmbrā, Hor.

Ădrāstĭă, ae, f., *the goddess of revenge, daughter of Jupiter and Necessity.* Quŏd nēc sĭnĭt Ădrāstĭă, Virg. V. Nemesis.

Ădrāstŭs, ī, m., *king of Argos, the son of Thalaon and Eurynome.* Ĕt Ădrāstī pāllēntĭs ĭmāgo, Virg. Tūnc mītĭs Ădrāstŭs, Stat. Epith. Thălăōnĭŭs, Ĭnāchĭŭs, Achaeŭs, pŏtēns, pōllēns.

ădrēpo, ĭs, rēpsī, *to creep to.* Ădrēpe ōffĭcĭōsŭs, Hor. Syn. Rēpo, īrrēpo, āscēndo, āccedo, āllābŏr, īllābŏr.

Ădrĭă, ae, m., *the Adriatic sea.* Văgŭs Ădrĭă pōntō, Lucan. Nōn ĕgŏ nūnc Ădrĭae, Prop. Epĭɪʜ. Raūcŭs, praecēps, văgŭs, tŭmĭdŭs, mĭnāx, vēntōsŭs.

Ădrĭăcŭs, *and* Ădrĭānŭs, ă, ŭm, *of the Adriatic sea.* Rŭdĭs Ădrĭăcī vĕhŏr, Prop. Sīvĕ mărī lĭbĕt Ădrĭānō, Hor. Syn. Ădrĭătĭcŭs.

ădscīsco, ĭs, īvī, *to associate.* Ădscīscĕt nŏvă, Hor. V. Ascisco.

ădsīcco, ās, *to dry.* Ădsīccātă cŭtĭs, Luc.

ădsĭtŭs, ă, ŭm, *the pass. partic. of* adsero. Pōpŭlŭs ădsĭtă cērtĭs, Hor. Syn. Jūxtă cōnsĭtŭs.

ădsŭm, ădĕs, *to be present.* Quēm quaerĭtĭs ădsŭm, Virg. Syn. Ĭntĕrsŭm, āssīsto, praesēnĕ sŭm, āsto ; ŏpĕm fĕro, aūxĭlĭŏr, jŭvo. V. Auxilior, accedo.

ădvēcto, ās, *the frequent. of* adveho. Ădvēctēt rătĭs, Val. Fl.

ădvĕho, ĭs, ēxī, ctŭm, *to carry to.* Ădvĕhĭtŭr Teūcrōs, Virg. Syn. Vĕho, īnvĕho, fĕro, dēfĕro, īnfĕro.

ădvēlo, ās, *to cover.* Ădvēlāt tēmpŏră laūrō, Virg. Syn. Vēlo ās, ŏpĕrĭo, tĕgo, ābdo, ŏccŭlto, ābscōndo. V. Occulto.

ădvĕnă, ae, m. f., *a stranger.* Jām pŏtĕs ădvĕnă dīcī, Mart. Syn. Hŏspĕs, pĕr-egrīnŭs, ēxtērnŭs, ălĭēnĭgĕnă. Epith. Fēssŭs, sŭpplēx, nŏvŭs, ĭgnōtŭs, văgŭs. V. Hospes.

ădvĕnĕrŏr, ārĭs, *to venerate.* Pŭĕr ădvĕnĕrātŭs ĕūntēs, Sil. V. Veneror.

ădvĕnĭo, ădvēnī, ădvēntŭm, *to come to.* Ădvĕnĭāt vūltŭs, Ov. Tўrĭām qui ādvĕnĕrĭs ūrbĕm, Virg. SYN. Vĕnĭo, āllābŏr, āccēdo, pērvĕnĭo, dēvĕnĭo, ădvēnto ădĕo, pĕto, cōntīngo.

ădvēnto, ās, *the frequent. of* advenio. Sŭb ĭpsŭm Fīnem ādvēntābānt, Virg.

|| ădvēntōrĭŭs, ă, ŭm, *accidental; congratulatory.* Advēntōrĭă cœnă, Mart.

ădvēntŭs, ūs, m., *an arrival.* Phўllĭdĭs ādvēntū, Virg. SYN. Āccēssŭs. EPITH. Jūcūndŭs, lœtŭs, faūstŭs, fēlīx, ōptātŭs, tārdŭs, sērŭs, īnspērātŭs, ĭnŏpīnŭs, sŭbĭtŭs, cĕlĕr.

|| ădvērbĕro, ās, *to beat sore.* Advērbĕrăt ūnguĭbŭs ārmōs, Stat.

ădvērro, ĭs, *to sweep, roll.* Ădvērrēnsquĕ nătāntĭă sāxă, Stat.

ădvērsă, ōrŭm, n. pl.; *affliction, misfortune.* Sī quāndo ādvērsă vŏcārēnt, Virg. SYN. Ærūmnă, căsŭs, clādēs, ēxĭtĭŭm. V. Infortunium.

ădvērsārĭŭs, ī, m., *an enemy.* Ădvērsārĭŭs ēst frātĕr, Hor. SYN. Æmŭlŭs, ādvērsŭs, ōppŏsĭtŭs, ĭnĭmīcŭs, hōstĭs. V. Hostis.

ădvērsŏr, ārĭs, *to oppose.* Nōn ādvērsātă pĕtēntī, Virg. SYN. Rĕpūgno, ōbsīsto, rĕlūctŏr; sŭm hōstĭs, ĭnĭmīcŭs, ādvērsārĭŭs. V. Resisto.

ădvērsŭs, ă, ŭm, *opposite.* Intĕr se ādvērsīs lūctāntŭr, Virg. SYN. Cōntrārĭŭs, ōppŏsĭtŭs, ĭnĭmīcŭs, hōstĭs. V. Hostis.

ădvērsŭs, *or* ādvērsŭm, *against.* Tēndēntem ādvērsŭm pēr grāmĭnă, Virg. SYN. Cōntrā, ĭn.

ădvērto, ĭs, tī, sŭm, *to turn to, to observe.* Advērtĭtĭs æquŏrĕ cūrsŭm, Virg. SYN. Nŏto, ānnŏto, ōbsērvo, ănĭmādvērto, vĭdĕo, cōgnōsco, pērspĭcĭo. V. Observo.

|| ădūlātĭo, ōnĭs, f., *flattery.* SYN. Āssēntātĭo, blāndĭtĭæ, blāndĭmēntă. EPITH. Mēllĕă, blāndă, præblāndă, pērnĭcĭōsă, īnsĭdĭōsă, mēllītă, pērfĭdă, mēndāx, fāllāx, lŏquāx, vērbōsă, īmprŏbă, ōccūltă, ābdĭtă, dŏlōsă. V. Blanditiæ.

ădūlātŏr, ōrĭs, m., *a flatterer.* Cæcŭs ădūlātŏr, Juv. SYN. Āssēntātŏr, gnātho. EPITH. Vīlĭs, pērfĭdŭs, īmprŏbŭs, mēndāx, fāllāx, blāndŭs, blāndĭlŏquŭs, lĕvĭs, pērnĭcĭōsŭs, vērsūtŭs, mēllĕŭs, fīctŭs, sŭbdŏlŭs; fūgĭēndŭs, gārrŭlŭs.

ădūlo, ās, *to caress.* Lŏcă flūmĭne ădūlăt, Tib.

ădūlŏr, ārĭs, *to flatter.* Āgmĕn ădūlāntŭm, Ov. SYN. Blāndĭŏr, āssēntŏr.

ădūltĕr, ĕră, ĕrŭm, *falsified, counterfeit.* Ădūltĕră clāvĭs, Ov.

ădūltĕr, ĕrī, *an adulterer.* Sēcrētŭs ădūltĕr, Juv. SYN. Mœchŭs. EPITH. Tūrpĭs, ōbscœnŭs, nōctūrnŭs, sēcrētŭs, ōccūltŭs, lāscīvŭs, lūbrĭcŭs, īmpūrŭs, nēfāndŭs, īmprŏbŭs, dŏlōsŭs, sōrdĭdŭs. V. Adultero.

ădūltĕră, æ, f., *an adultress.* Cōgnōvĭt ădūltĕră vīrgo, Ov. SYN. Mœchă. EPITH. Tūrpĭs, īmpūră, ōbscœnă, īmpĭă, nēfāndă. V. Adultero.

*ădūltĕrīnŭs, ă, ŭm, *begot in adultery; false,* Cic. SYN. Nŏthŭs, spūrĭŭs.

ădūltĕrĭŭm, ī, n., *adultery.* Quĭque ŏb ădūltĕrĭŭm cæsī, Virg. SYN. Stuprŭm. EPITH. Ārcānŭm, sēcrētŭm, nōctūrnŭm, nēfāndŭm, īmpūrŭm.

ădūltĕro, ās, *to commit adultery* (Plaut.); *or* ădūltĕrŏr, ārĭs. Ădūltĕrētŭr ēt cŏlūmbă mīlvĭō, (Iamb. pur.) Hor. SYN. Mœchŏr, stupro; cōrrŭmpo. V. Adulter.

ădūltŭs, ă, ŭm, *grown up.* Spēm gēntĭs ădūltōs, Virg. V. Adolescens.

ădūmbrātĭm, *faintly, indistinctly,* Sēd quăsi ădūmbrātŭm, Lucr.

ădūmbrātŭs, ă, ŭm, *the pass. partic. of* adumbro. Ārtĭs ădūmbrātæ, Lucr.

*ădūmbro, ās, *to shade, to shadow out,* Cic. SYN. Ēffīngo, dēscrībo, ēxprĭmo.

ădūncŭs, ă, ŭm, *hooked.* Rōstrōque īmmānīs vūltŭr ădūncō, Virg. SYN. Cūrvŭs, rĕpāndŭs, flēxŭs, reflēxŭs, īncūrvŭs.

ădvŏcātŭs, ă, ŭm, *the pass. partic. of* advoco.—2. ī, m., *an advocate.* Nōn bĕne ādvŏcātŭs? (Phal.) Catul. SYN. Caūsĭdĭcŭs, pătrōnŭs. EPITH. Dīsērtŭs, pĕrītŭs, fācūndŭs, dōctŭs. V. Causidicus.

ădvŏco, ās, *to call together.* Advŏcăt ēt rāmĭs, Virg. SYN. Vŏco, āccērso, cōmpēllo ās. V. Voco.

ădvŏlo, ās, *to fly to.* Advŏlăt, haūd ālĭa ēst, Virg. SYN. Vŏlo; fēstīno, prŏpĕro, āccūrro. V. Festino.

ădvŏlo, ĭs, ādvōlvī, ādvōlūtŭm, *to roll to.* Advōlvērĕ fŏcīs ūlmōs, Virg. SYN. Vōlvo, sūbvōlvo, āddūco, trăho.

ădvōlvŏr gĕnĭbŭs, *to prostrate oneself.* Gĕnĭbŭs ādvōlvŏr tŭĭs, Sen. V. Genua flecto.

ādvŏlūtŭs, ă, ŭm, *the pass. partic. of* advolvo.   Flēs ādvŏlūtă, quĭd, (Iamb.) Sen.
ădūrgĕo, ēs, *to press upon, to chase.*   Rēmīs ădūrgēns, Hor.
ădūro, ĭs, ūssī, ūstŭm, *to burn, scorch.*   Pĕnĕtrābĭlĕ frīgŭs ădūrăt, Virg.   SYN.
Ūro, ĕxūro ; sīcco, ĕxsīcco, īndūro.
ădūsquĕ, adv., *even to ; as far as.*   Mĕnĕlāŭs ădūsquĕ cŏlūmnās, Virg.
ădўtŭm, ĭ, n., *the most secret place of thĕ temple.*   Isque ădўtĭs, Virg. SYN. Tĕmplŭm, sacrŭm, săcēllŭm, pĕnetrālĕ, pĕnetrālĭă.   EPITH. Tĕrrĭfĭcŭm, lătēns,
vĕnĕrābĭlĕ, sūblīmĕ, ĭnclўtŭm, grāndĕ, ĭngēns, pīctŭm, aŭgūstŭm, āltŭm, ĕxcēl-
sŭm, aūrĕŭm, sānctŭm, fūlgĭdŭm, sacrātŭm.   V. Templum.
Æ̆ă, *a huntress, metamorphosed into an island.*   In pătrĭīs sēctātŭr mōntĭbŭs Æ̆ăm,
Val. Flacc.   EPITH. Clāră, nōbĭlĭs.
Æ̆ăcĭdēĭŭs, ă, ŭm, *of Æacus.*   Æ̆ăcĭdēĭă rēgnă, Ov.
Æ̆ăcĭdēs, æ, m., *a descendant of Æacus.*   Sævŭs ŭbi Æ̆ăcĭdæ tēlŭ, Virg.
Æ̆ăcŭs, ī, m., *the son of Jupiter and Ægina, one of the infernal Judges.*   Æ̆ăcŭs īn
pœnās, Ovid.   SYN. Jūdĕx, ārbĭtĕr Ōrcī; Asōpĭădēs.   EPITH. Jūstŭs, jūrĭdĭ-
cŭs, Tārtărĕŭs, Stўgĭŭs, trĕmēndŭs, æquŭs, īmmītĭs, mĕtŭēndŭs, vĕnĕrāndŭs,
ātĕr, dīrŭs, sŭpērbŭs, tērrĭbĭlĭs, vĕrēndŭs, tōrvŭs, nĭgĕr, dūrŭs, lēthālĭs, ĭnfĕrŭs,
Āvērnālĭs, sĕvērŭs.
Æ̆æŭs, ă, ŭm, *of Æ̆æ̆ă, or Æ̆æē, an island in the Tyrrhenian sea, which Circe*
inhabited.   Æ̆æ̆æque īnsŭlă Cīrcēs, Virg.
Æ̆ās, āntĭs, m., *a river of Epirus.*   Amphrўsŏs ĕt Æ̆ās, Ov.
ædēs, ĭs, f. sing., *a temple.*   Cūjŭs īn ædĕ sŭmŭs, Ov.—Ædēs, ĭŭm, f. pl., *a house.*
Ædĭbŭs īn mĕdĭīs, Virg.   SYN. Dŏmŭs, tēctŭm, ātrĭă, hōspĭtĭŭm, pĕnātēs, sēdēs,
lărēs, căsă, rēgĭă, līmĕn ; tēmplŭm.   EPITH. Āltă, ārdŭă, ĕxĭmĭă, sŭpērbă,
mägnĭfĭcă.   V. Domus ; templum.
ædĭcŭlă, æ, f., *a little chapel.*   Sĭ quĭs ĭn ædĭcŭlă, Juv.
ædĭfĭcātŏr, ōrĭs, m., *a builder.*   Ædĭfĭcātŏr ĕrăt, Juv.   SYN. Cōnstrŭctŏr, ĕx-
strŭctŏr, cōndĭtŏr.   EPITH. Dīvĕs, sŭpērbŭs, prōvĭdŭs.
ædĭfĭcātŭs, ă, ŭm, *the pass. partic. of* ædifico.   Ædĭfĭcātă mănŭ, Prud.
ædĭfīco, ās, *to build.*   Ædĭfĭcārĕ dŏmōs, Juv.   SYN. Ēxstrŭo, strŭo, cōndo, cōnstrŭo, mōlĭŏr, fabrĭcŏr.
Ædīlĭs, ĭs, m., *an Ædile.*   Sūmmĭs ædīlĭbŭs ālbæ, Juv.   EPITH. Cŭrūlĭs, plēbēĭŭs.
ædĭtŭŭs, ī, *and* ædĭtŭēns, ēntĭs, m., *a churchwarden.*   Quālĕs ædĭtŭŏs hăbĕăt, Hor.
Lŏcă quæ cōmplērănt ædĭtŭēntēs, Lucr.   SYN. Tēmplī cūstōs, ædĭtĭmŭs.
ăĕdōn, ŏnĭs, m., *a nightingale.*   Sĭ dīrŭs ăĕdŏnă būbo, Calph.   EPITH. Suāvĭs,
trīstĭs.   V. Philomela.
Ædōn, ŏnĭs, *of Thrace.*   Ac vĕlŭt Ædōnī Bŏrĕæ, Virg.
Aĕdŏnĭŭs, ă, ŭm, *of a nightingale.*   Sīc ĕt Aĕdŏnĭă sŭpĕrāntŭr, Ov.
Æ̆ētēs, *or* Æ̆ētă, æ, m., *the king of Colchis, son of Apollo and Persa, father of Medea.*
Dīxĕrăt Æ̆ētēs, Ov.   Jŭvĕnēs Æ̆ētă Pĕlāsgŏs, Ov.   EPITH. Sōlĭgĕnă, sōlĕ sătŭs,
Æ̆æŭs ; fĕrŭs ; Phāsĭăcŭs.
Æ̆ētĕŭs, *or* Æ̆ētĭŭs, ă, ŭm, *of Æetes.*   Et fīnēs Æ̆ētĕŏs, Cat.   Æ̆ētĭă Phrўxī,
Val. Fl.
Æ̆ētĭăs, ădĭs, Æ̆ētĭs, ĭdŏs, *or* Æ̆ētīnē, ēs, f., *Medea, daughter of Æetes.*   Æ̆ētĭăs
ĭgnēs, Ov.   Æ̆ētĭdă pērcŭlĭt hōrrŏr, Val. Fl.   Sēd Phāsĭăs Æ̆ētīnē, Ov.
Æ̆gæōn, onĭs, m., *a giant, the son of Earth and Titan.*   Cēntēni Æ̆gæōnĭs ŭmbrăm,
Stat.   Æ̆gæōnă sŭĭs īmmānĭă tērgă lăcērtĭs, Ov.   SYN. Brĭărĕŭs.   EPITH. Cēn-
tĭmănŭs, cēntūmgĕmĭnŭs, īmpĭŭs.   V. Briareus.
æ̆gĕr, æ̆gră, æ̆grŭm, *diseased.*   Quătĭt æ̆gĕr ănhēlĭtŭs ārtŭs, Virg.   SYN. Mōr-
bĭdŭs, æ̆grōtŭs, ĭnvălĭdŭs, ĭnfīrmŭs, lānguĭdŭs, lānguēns.   V. Moribundus,
æ̆groto.
Æ̆gĕrĭă, æ, f., *a nymph, consulted by Numa, and honoured as a goddess.*   Illă ĕt
Æ̆gĕrĭa ēst, Hor.   EPITH. Pōmpĭlĭă, nŏctūrnă, Rōmŭlă.
Æ̆gæŭm, ī, n., *the Ægean sea.*   Āltŏ Īnsŏnăt Æ̆gæŏ, Virg.
Æ̆gæŭs, ă, ŭm, *of the Ægean sea, Ægean.*   Æ̆gæī quōs sūnt pĕnĕs æquŏră
pŏntī, Ov.
Æ̆geūs, ĕŏs, ĕī *or* eī, m., *king of Athens, father of Theseus.*   Æ̆gĕă sīc Thēseŭs,
Ov.   Vēntĭs cōncĕdĕrĕt Æ̆geŭs, Catul.   EPITH. Mĭsĕr, ĭnfēlīx.
Æ̆gĭălē, ēs, f., *daughter of Adrastus, wife of Diomedes.*   Quēstă ēst Æ̆gĭălĕ, Stat.
Æ̆gīdēs, æ, m., *the son of Ægeus, Theseus.*   Tĕ vŏcăt Æ̆gīdēn, Ov.

Ægīnă, æ, f., *daughter of Asopus, loved by Jupiter.* Ægīnæ Asōpĭdŏs Issĕ, Ov.

Ægĭpān, ānĭs, m., *a rural deity.* V. Pan, Satyri.

Ægĭs, ĭdĭs, f., *a shield covered with a goat's skin, and made terrible by a Gorgon's head affixed to it.* Ægĭdă sĕmpĕr hăbē, Ov. Epith. Hŏrrĭdă, sŏnāns, tĕrrĭfĭcă, cruēntă, fūlvă, tĕrrĭbĭlĭs, crūdă, Pāllādĭă, sŭpĕrbă.

Ægĭsŏnŭs, ă, ŭm, *which sounds as the Ægis.* Ægĭsŏnūm pēctŭs, Val. Fl.

Ægīsthŭs, ī, m., *son of Thyestes, murderer of Atreus.* Quærĭtĭs Ægīsthŭs quārē, Ov. Syn. Thўēstĭădēs, Thўēstæ prŏlēs; Thўēstē nātŭs. Epith. Adūltĕr, dēsĭdĭōsŭs.

Æglē, ēs, f., *one of the Naiads.* Æglē, Nāĭădūm pūlchērrĭmă, Virg.

Ægŏcĕrōs, ōtĭs, *or* Ægŏcĕrŭs, ī, m., *the sign Capricorn.* Ægŏcĕrūm cāncrūmquĕ, Juv. E pārtĭbŭs Ægŏcĕrōtĭs, Lucr. Syn. Caprĭcōrnŭs. Epith. Ūdŭs, hūmĭdŭs, frĭgĭdŭs, cĕlĕr, cōrnĭgĕr, nĭvōsŭs. V. Capricornus.

ægrē, adv., *with difficulty.* Ergo ægrē rāstrīs, Virg. Syn. Vīx, mŏlēstē, dĭffĭcūltĕr.

ægrēsco, ĭs, *to grow sick.* Ægrēscītquĕ mĕdēndō, Virg. Syn. Ingrăvēsco. V. Ægroto.

ægrĭmōnĭă, æ, f., *sorrow.* Trīstĭs ægrĭmōnĭă, (Iamb.) Hor.

ægrĭtūdo, ĭnĭs, f., *bodily sickness, anxiety.* Sōlētūr sĕnĭum, ægrĭtūdĭnēmquĕ, (Phal.) Syn. Mōrbŭs, lānguŏr ; V. Morbus. Anxĭĕtās, cūră, sōllĭcĭtŭdo ; V. Cura.

ægrŏr, ōrĭs, m., *sickness.* Pĕcŭbŭs bālāntĭbŭs ægrŏr, Lucr.

ægrŏto, ās, *to be ill.* Dăbĭs ægrōtārĕ tĭmēntī, Hor. Syn. Lānguĕo, dēcūmbo, lānguēsco, dŏlĕo.

ægrōtŭs, ă, ŭm, *sick.* Ægrōtō dŏmĭnī, Hor. Syn. Ægĕr, īnvălĭdŭs, īnfīrmŭs, lānguĭdŭs, lānguēns, mōrbĭdŭs. V. Æger.

Ægўpsŏs, *or* ŭs, ī, f., *or* Ægўssŏs, *a city at the mouth of the Danube.* Nōn nĕgăt Ægўpsŏs, Ov.—2. m., *the founder thereof.* Cāspĭŭs Ægўpsŏs, Id.

Ægўptĭī, ōrūm, m. pl., *Egyptians.* Ægўptĭŭs ātque Arăbārchēs, Juv. Syn. Nīlĭgĕnæ, Phărĭī, Nīlĭcŏlæ. Epith. Ustī, cāllĭdī, īngĕnĭōsī, săgācēs, ātrī, dŏctī, ācūtī, prūdēntēs, vēntōsī, cālvī.

Ægўptĭŭs, *and* Ægўptĭăcŭs, ă, ŭm, *of Egypt.* Ægўptĭă cōnjux, Virg. Quŏs Ægўptĭăcō sĕmpĕr, Calc. Syn. Phărĭŭs, Nīlŏtĭcŭs, Nīlĭăcŭs, Mēmphītĭcŭs.

Ægўptŏs, *or* ŭs, ī, f., *Egypt.* Dīcĭtŭr Ægўptŏs cărŭīssĕ, Ov. Et vīrĭdem Ægўptūm, Virg. Syn. Phărŏs, Cănōpŭs. Epith. Dīvĕs, tŏrrĭdă, fœcūndă, fērtĭlĭs, ĕxūstă, āntīquă, mĕtāllĭfĕră, sĭtĭbūndă, vāstă, ŏpīmă, hŏrrĭdă, cāllĭdă, ārdēns, ūstă, ădūstă, gēmmĭfĕră.

Ægўptŭs, ī, m., *a son of Neptune.* Nēc mĭnŭs Ægўptī, Virg.

Aēllō, ūs, f., *one of the Harpies.* Alĕs Aēllō, Ov. V. Harpyia.—2. *One of Actæon's dogs.* Fōrtĭs Aēllō, Ov.

ælūrŭs, ī, m., *a cat.* Illĭc ælūrōs, Juv. Syn. Fēlĭs.

Æmāthĭă, æ, f. V. Emathia.

Æmĭlĭŭs, ă, ŭm, *of Romania, in Italy.* Æmĭlĭæ gēntēs, Mart.

Æmŏnĭă, æ, f., *Thessaly.* Pēlĭŏn, Æmŏnĭæ mōns ēst, Ov. Syn. Thēssălĭă.

Æmŏnĭdæ, ārŭm, m. pl., *the Thessalians; the Argonauts.* Stănt lĭttŏrĕ fīxī Æmŏnĭdæ, Val. Fl.

Æmŏnĭdēs, æ, m., *the name of a warrior.* Nēc prŏcŭl Æmŏnĭdēs, Virg.

Æmŏnĭŭs, ă, ŭm, *and* Æmŏnĭs, ĭdĭs, f., *Thessalian.* Trāctŭs ăb Æmŏnĭō, Ov.

æmŭlātŏr, ōrĭs, m., *a rival.* Atrōx æmŭlātŏr hŏstĭæ, (Iamb.) Prud. V. Æmulus.

æmŭlŏr, ārĭs, *to endeavour to imitate or excel.* Æmŭlŏr ūmbrās, Pr. Syn. Imĭtŏr ; īnvĭdĕo, sēctŏr. V. Imitor.

æmŭlŭs, ă, ŭm, *emulous, vying with.* Æmŭlŭs ēxcēptūm Trītōn, Virg. Syn. Imĭtātŏr ; īnvĭdŭs, ādvērsārĭŭs, cōntrārĭŭs.

Æmŭs, ī, m., *a mountain.* V. Hæmus.

Ænărĭă, æ, f., *an island, near the Gulf of Naples.* Ænărĭæquĕ lăcŭs, Stat.

Ænĕădæ, ārŭm, *or* ădēs, ŭm, m. pl., *Trojans, Romans.* Quĭs gĕnŭs Ænĕădŭm, Virg.

Ænĕădēs, *or* Æneīdēs, æ, m., *son or descendant of Æneas ; patronymic of Iulus and others.* Fērt lĭbĕr Ænĕădĕn, Ov. Sīt sătĭs, Æneīdē, tēlīs, Virg.

Ænēās, æ, m., *the son of Anchises and Venus, founder of the Roman empire, and celebrated by Virgil.* Ænēās īgnārŭs ăbēst, Virg. Syn. Anchīsĭădēs, Dārdănĭdēs, Lāŏmĕdŏntĭădēs. Dūx, hērōs, Phrўgĭŭs, Ilĭăcŭs, Trōĭŭs, Trōjānŭs, Dārdănĭŭs, Lāŏmĕdŏntĭŭs, Cўthĕrēĭŭs, Vēnērĭs fīlĭŭs, Ănchīsæ sŏbŏlēs, Ănchīsē gĕnĕrātŭs, gĕnĭtŭs, sătŭs. Epith. Māgnănĭmŭs, Dārdănĭŭs, pĭŭs, Trōjānŭs, Trōĭŭs, cāstŭs, prŏfŭgŭs, flūctĭvăgŭs, Phrўx, Phrўgĭŭs, inclўtŭs, fŭgĭtĭvŭs, fōrtĭs, impăvĭdŭs, bēllāx, aūdāx, bŏnŭs, gĕnĕrōsŭs, Dārdănĭdēs, fātālĭs, Cўthĕrēĭŭs, Ilĭăcŭs, Rhœtēĭŭs.

*ænĕātŏr, ōrĭs, m., a trumpeter, Suet.

Ænēĭs, or ēĭs, ĭdŏs, f., a poem of Virgil. Ænēĭdŏs aūctŏr, Ov. Ænēĭdōs sūmmō, Id.

Ænēĭŭs, ă, ŭm, of Æneas. Stābŭnt Ænēĭă pārvō, Virg.

ænĕŭs, ă, ŭm, brazen. Ænĕŭs ūt stēs, Hor. Syn. Ahēnĕŭs. V. Aheneus.

ænīgmă, ătĭs, n., a riddle. Lēgum ænīgmătă sōlvăt, Juv. Epith. Obscūrŭm, dīffĭcĭlĕ, dūbĭŭm, cæcŭm, Thēbānŭm, tĕnebrōsŭm, āncēps, ābdĭtŭm, rĕcōndĭtŭm, ārcānŭm, Œdĭpœŭm, ĭnvŏlūtŭm, lătēns, lătĭtāns, sēcrētŭm.

Æŏlĭă, æ, f., a group of islands between Italy and Sicily; the kingdom of Æolus, according to the poets. Æŏlĭă ēxcītōs, Virg. Epith. Vāstă, nĭmbōsă, cīrcūmflŭă, ūdă, rīgŭă, æquŏrĕă. V. Æolus.

Æŏlĭdæ, ārŭm, m. pl., Æolians, the ancient Thessalians.—2. The sons of Æolus. Æŏlĭdæ Dŏlŏpēsque, Luc.

Æŏlĭdēs, æ, m., son or descendant of Æolus. Mīsēnum Æŏlĭdēn, Virg.

Æŏlĭs, ĭdĭs, f., Æolian, Thessalian. Gēns Æŏlĭs, Ter. Maur.—2. The daughter or granddaughter of Æolus. Æŏlĭs ĭntĕrĕă, Ov.

Æŏlĭŭs, ă, ŭm, of the Æolians and their colonies; Æolian. Æŏlĭăm Pĭtānēn, Ov. —2. Of Lesbos; of Sappho. Æŏlĭīs fĭdĭbŭs, Hor.—3. Of Æolus: of the Æolian islands. Æŏlĭōs Ithăcīs inclūsĭmŭs ūtrĭbŭs eūrōs, Ov.

Æŏlŭs, ī, m., the son of Jupiter and Sergesta; king of the winds. Rēx Æŏlŭs āntrō, Virg. Syn. Hĭppŏtădēs. Epith. Impĕrĭōsŭs, mĭnāx, vēntĭpŏtēns, īnsānŭs, trĕmēndŭs, fūrēns, tūrbĭdŭs, hōrrĭsŏnŭs, frĕmēns, fūrĭōsŭs, trĕmēns, hōrrĭdŭs; sĕnēx, trūx, plŭvĭŭs.

Æpў, n., a town of Messenia. Mōntĭbŭs Æpў, Stat.

Æpўtŭs, ī, m., king of Messenia. Æpўtŭs, Albā, tŭīs, Ov.

*æquăbĭlĭtās, ātĭs, f., equability. De æquăbĭlĭtātĕ mŏvēbŏr, Mant. Syn. Æquālĭtās; cōnstāntĭă, æquă mēns.

æquævŭs, ă, ŭm, of the same age. Ūt rēgem æquævŭm, Virg. Syn æquālĭs.

æquālĭs, ĕ, equal. Æquālī tēcum pūbēscĕrĕt ævō, Virg. Syn. Æquăbĭlĭs, æquŭs, pār, cōmpār, sĭmĭlĭs; æquævŭs.

æquālĭtĕr, adv., equally. Strātăque æquālĭtĕr ūndā, Ov. Syn. Æquē, părĭtĕr. ‖ æquănĭmĭs, ĕ, or æquănĭmŭs, ă, ŭm, of an even temper. Æquănĭmūs fīăm, Aus. Syn. Mŏdĕrātŭs, pătĭēns, tŏlĕrāns.

æquātŏr, ōrĭs, m., the equator. Oltra æquātŏrĕm, Nat. C.

æquē, adv., as well. Æquē jŭvĕnēmquĕ măgĭstrī, Virg. Syn. Părĭtĕr, sĭmĭlĭtĕr, æquālĭtĕr, nōn sĕcŭs, haūd sĕcŭs, nōn ălĭtĕr, haūd ălĭtĕr.

Æquī, m. pl., Æquĭcŏlă, æ, and Æquĭcŏlŭs, ī, m., a people of ancient Italy. Æquōsquĕ Fālīscōs, Virg. Dūrīs Æquĭcŏlă glēbīs, Virg. Æquĭcŏlŭs ācĕr, Ov.

æquĭdĭēs, ēī, m., or æquĭdĭŭm, ī, n., the equinox. Æquĭdĭēmquĕ făcĭt, Archith. Æquĭdĭŭm dŭplēx, Mant. V. Æquinoctium.

*æquĭlĭbrĭŭm, ī, n., an even poise. Sen. ph. Syn. Æquăbĭlĭtās, æquālĭtās. ‖ æquĭmănŭs, ī, m., ambidexter. Cōntēndĭtŭr æquĭmănŭs? Thrāx. Aus.

æquĭnōctĭālĭs, ĕ, of the equinox. Cœlī fŭrŏr æquĭnōctĭālĭs, (Phal.) Catul. * ‖ æquĭnōctĭŭm, ī, n., the vernal or autumnal equinox. Vērĭs æquĭnōctĭālĭs, Aus.

æquĭpār, ărĭs, equal. Cōntĭnĕt æquĭpārēs? Aus. Syn. Pār, nōn impār. ‖ æquĭpărābĭlĭs, ĕ, which may be equalled. Æquĭpărābĭlĕ quīcquăm, Prud. Syn. Cōnfērrī dīgnŭs.

æquĭpăro, as, to equal. Sōlum æquĭpărās, Virg. Syn. Cōmpăro, cōnfĕro ; æquo, ēxæquo, ădæquo. V. Comparo.

æquĭtās, ātĭs, f., equity. Æquĭtātĕ Maūrĭcōs, (Scaz.) Mart. Syn. Æquŭm, jūs. V. Justitia.

æquĭvălĕo, ēs, to be equivalent. Mŏdŭlīs æquĭvălērĕ tŭīs, Ov. Syn. ‖ Æquĭpōllĕo.

æquo, ās, to equal, to level. Pārtĭbŭs æquābăt, Virg. Syn. Ădæquo, ēxæquo ; pār, æquālĕ rēddo, făcĭo, ēffĭcĭo.

æquŏr, ŏrĭs, n., *any plain ; the sea.* Mărĭs æquŏr ărāndŭm, Virg. Syn. Mărĕ, āltŭm, prŏfūndŭm, pōntŭs, frētŭm, sălŭm, cærŭlă, pĕlăgŭs, mārmŏr, ōcĕănŭs Nēptūnĭŭs; Nēptūnĭă ārvă; plānĭtĭēs, cāmpŭs ăpērtŭs, lātŭs. V. Planities, mare.

æquŏrēŭs, ă, ŭm, *of the sea.* Stērnĭt ĕt æquŏrēăs, Ov.

æquŭm, ī, n., *equity.* Nĕc ămāntĭŏr æquī, Virg. Syn. Æquĭtās, jūstĭtĭă.

æquŭs, ă, ŭm, *level, just.* Æquŭs ĭn hōstĕ fŭĭt, Prop. Syn. Jūstŭs. V. Justus, planus, æqualis.

āēr, āĕrĭs *or* āĕrŏs, m., *the air.* Prōxĭmŭs ēst āēr īllī, Ov. Syn. Æthēr, æthrā, văcŭŭm, ĭnānĕ, Jūpĭtĕr, aūră, āstră, dīŭm. Epith. Lĭquĭdŭs, pătēns, īmmēnsŭs, tĕnŭĭs, hūmĭdŭs, tĕnĕr, pūrŭs, spīrābĭlĭs, rōrĭfĕr, mĕābĭlĭs, ăgĭtātŭs, cīrcūmflŭŭs, ūdŭs, rōscĭdŭs, aūrĭcŏmŭs, līmpĭdŭs, īgnĭfĕr, fūlgēns, mūtābĭlĭs, sĕrēnŭs, nīmbōsŭs, rārŭs, prŏcēllōsŭs. V. Cœlum, æthra.

āĕrĕŭs, *or* āĕrĭŭs, ă, ŭm, *airy.* Aĕrēī dīscērpŭnt īrrĭtă vēntī, Cat. Aĕrĭă cēssābĭt tūrtŭr ăb ūlmō, Virg. Syn. Æthĕrĕŭs, sīdĕrĕŭs, cœlēstĭs. V. Altus.

*cĕră, æ, f., *darnel.* Plin.

*cĕrārĭă, æ, f., *a copper-mine.* Plin.

ærārĭŭm, ī, n., *a treasury.* Sācra ærārĭă sērvēnt, Mant. Syn. Ŏpēs pūblĭcæ: fīscŭs.

ærārĭŭs, īī, m., *a copper-smith.* Ærārĭōrŭm mārcŭlī, Mart.

ærātŭs, ă, ŭm, *covered with brass.* Ærātæquĕ mĭcānt, Virg. Syn. Ærĕ tēctŭs, ōbdūctŭs, mūnītŭs, īnstrūctŭs, ārctātŭs, grăvĭs.

ærĕŭs, ă, ŭm, *made of brass.* Mĭcăt ærĕŭs ēnsĭs, Virg. Syn. Ăhēnŭs, ăhēnĕŭs, ærātŭs.

ærĭfĕr, ă, ŭm, *bearing brass.* Ærĭfĕræ cŏmĭtŭm, Ov.

ærĭpēs, ĕdĭs, *brazen-footed.* Fīxĕrĭt ærĭpĕdĕm cērvăm, Virg. Syn. Lĕvĭs, cĕlĕr, vēlōx; fōrtĭs, sŏlĭdŭs.

ærĭsŏnŭs, ă, ŭm, *sounding like brass.* Ærĭsŏnās ŭlŭlārĕ pĕr ūrbĕs, Claud.

Aĕrŏpē, ēs, f., *wife of Atreus, seduced by the brother of her husband.* Aĕrŏpēn frātĕr scĕlĕrātŭs, Ov.

ærūgo, ĭnĭs, f., *rust of brass.* Cūm tōta ærūgĭnĕ fōllĕm, Juv. Syn. Rubīgo. Epith. Scabră, nigră, tūrpĭs, vĭrĭdĭs. V. Rubigo.

ærūmnă, æ, f., *affliction.* Ærūmnĭs lāssŭs, Hor. Syn. Mœrŏr, dŏlŏr; pōndŭs, ŏnŭs. Epith. Grăvĭs, mălă, dūră, lūctĭfĭcă, trīstĭs, crūdēlĭs, lūgubrĭs. V. Mœror, miseria.

ærūmnābĭlĭs, nālĭs, ĕ, *or* nōsŭs, ă, ŭm, *calamitous.* Ærūmnābĭle ĕrăt, Lucr. Ærūmnōsīquĕ Sŏlōnēs, Pers. Syn. Īnfēlix, mĭsĕr, īnfōrtūnātŭs. V. Miser.

æs, ærĭs, n., *brass, money, arms.* Ēphўrēĭăquĕ ærā, Virg. Syn. Ærĭs mĕtāllŭm; V. Metallum. Pĕcūnĭă, nūmmŭs; V. Pecunia. Tŭbă, būccĭnă, lĭtŭŭs, cōrnū clāssĭcŭm; V. Tuba. Lōrīcă, gălĕă, ārmă; V. Arma. Stătŭă, sĭmŭlācrŭm. Epith. Dūrŭm, sŏlĭdŭm, splēndĭdŭm, grăvĕ, Cŏrīnthĭŭm.

Æsăcŭs, ī, m., *the son of Priam and Alexirrhoe, metamorphosed into a sea-fowl.* Æsăcŏn ūmbrōsă fūrtĭm, Ov.

Æsălŏ, ŏnĭs, *or* Æsălŭs, ī, m., *a merlin.* Æsălŏ sīs ălĭĭs, Thuan.

Æsăr, ărĭs, m., *a river of Sicily.* Æsărĭs ūndăs, Ov.

Æsărĕŭs, ă, ŭm, *of the river Æsar.* Īnvēnĭt Æsărēī fātālĭă flūmĭnĭs ōră, Ov.

Æschўlĕŭs, ă, ŭm, *of Æschylus.* Dēsīne ĕt Æschўlĕŏ, Prop.

Æschўlŭs, ī, m., *a tragic poet.* Æschўlŭs ūtĭlĕ fērrēnt, Hor. Epith. Dōctŭs, sōlērs, grāndĭlŏquŭs.

Æscŭlāpĭŭs, ī, m., *the son of Apollo and Coronis ; god of physic.* Săcrātŭs āspĭs Æscŭlāpīī, (Iamb. pur.) Prud. Syn. Ēpĭdaūrĭŭs; Cŏrōnĭdĕ nātŭs; Phœbĭgĕnă. Epith. Sălūtĭfĕr, Phœbēĭŭs, Pērgămĕŭs.

æscŭlētŭm, ī, n., *a grove of beech trees.* Lātĭs ălĭt æscŭlētĭs, (Sapph.) Hor.

æscŭlĕŭs, ă, ŭm, *of beech.* Vīcĕrăt, æscŭlĕæ, Ov. Syn. Quērnŭs, quērcĕŭs, īlĭcĕŭs, īlīgnŭs, rōbŏrĕŭs.

æscŭlŭs, ī, f., m., *beech.* Æscŭlŭs ĭn prīmĭs, Virg. Syn. Quērcŭs, īlēx, rōbŭr. Epith. Glāndĭfĕră, frōndēns, prōcĕră. V. Quercus.

Æsōn, ŏnĭs, m., *the son of Creteus and Tyro, made young by Medea.* Æsŏnĭă ēffœtŭm, Ov.

Æsŏnĭdēs, æ, m., *son of Æson, Jason.* Cuī sīc Æsŏnĭdēs, Ov.

Æsŏnĭŭs, ă, ŭm, *of Æson.* Aūsŭs ĕt Æsŏnĭă, Ov.

Æsŏpēŭs, pĭcŭs, *or* pīŭs, ă, ŭm, *of Æsop.* Quās Æsōpēās, (Iamb.) Phædr.

Æsŏpĭām trĭmĕtrĭăm, (Iamb.) Aus.

Æsŏpŭs, ī, m., *a Phrygian philosopher, author of fables.* Æsōpŭs auctŏr quăm mătĕrĭăm, (Iamb.) Phædr. Epith. Jŏcōsŭs, fĭngĕndī dōctŭs.—2. *A Roman actor.* Quæ grăvĭs Æsōpŭs, Hor.

æstās, ātĭs, f., *summer.* Stābāt nūda æstās, ĕt spĭcĕă sĕrtă gĕrēbăt, Ov. Syn. Æstīvŭm tēmpŭs. Epith. Ignĕă, cālĭdă, fĕrvēns, fĕrvĭdă, sĕrēnă, ĭnĕrs, sĭtĭēns, mŏrbōsă, lāscīvă, fĕrtĭlĭs, lætă, jūcūndă, flōrēns, ūptātă, spērātă, pigră, pēstĭfĕră, flāmmĕă, sīccă, sălūbrĭs.

æstĭfĕr, ă, ŭm, *sultry.* Æstĭfĕræ Lĭbÿēs, Lucan. Syn. Fĕrvĭdŭs, æstīvŭs.

|| æstĭmātĭo, ōnĭs, f., *estimation, price.* Quŏd mē nōn mŏvĕt æstĭmātĭōnĕ, Cat.

æstĭmātŏr, ōrĭs, m., *he who values.* Rĕrum æstĭmātŏr, (Iamb.) Sen. Syn. Jūdēx. Epith. Æquŭs, jūstŭs; ĭnĭquŭs. V. Judex.

æstĭmo, ās, *to value.* Vīrtūtem æstĭmĕt ānnĭs, Hor. Syn. Jūdĭco, ĕxĭstĭmo; cēnsĕo; cōnsĭdĕro; măgnī, părvī făcĭo, pēndo.

æstīvă, ōrŭm, n. pl., *a shade for cattle.* Æstīvā Lÿcæī, Stat.

æstīvo, ās, *to spend the summer.* Jŭvăt æstīvārĕ sŭb Æmō, Stat.

æstīvŭs, ă, ŭm, *of summer.* Æstīvā grātĭŏr ūmbrā, Ov.

æstŭo, ās, *to be very hot, to swelter.* Mŏrĭēntĭbŭs æstŭăt hĕrbĭs, Virg. Syn. Fĕrvĕo, flāgro, ēxæstŭo; flūctŭo, ăgĭtŏr.

æstŭōsē, adv., *hotly.* Ĭnārsĭt æstŭōsĭŭs, Hor.

æstŭōsŭs, ă, ŭm, *very hot.* Grŏgem æstŭōsă tŏrrĕt ĭmpŏtēntĭă, (Iamb.) Hor.

æstŭs, ūs, m., *a scorching heat.* Immĭttĭtŭr æstŭs Āvērnĭs, Virg. Syn. Călŏr, ārdŏr, fĕrvŏr; flūctŭs, mōtŭs. Epith. Flāmmĭfĕr, sīdĕrĕŭs, ūrēns, mălĭgnŭs, fĕrvĭdŭs.

Æsŭlă, æ, f., *a town near Tibur.* Tĭbŭr ĕt Æsŭlæ, Hor.

ætās, ātĭs, f., *age.* Et mŏnĕt ætātĭs spĕcĭē, Ov. Syn. Ævŭm, sæcŭlŭm, ævī spătĭŭm; vītă, ănnī tēmpŭs, vītæ tēmpŭs. Epith. Fŭgĭtīvă, ĭrrĕvŏcābĭlĭs, præcēps, prŏpĕră, cĭtă, ĭnstābĭlĭs, ĭrrĕquĭētă, cădūcă, præpĕs, fāllāx, fŭgĭēns, rĕvŏlūbĭlĭs, lūbrĭcă, prætĕrĭtă. V. Pueritia, adolescentia, juventus, virilis ætas, senectus.

ætātŭlă, æ, f., *diminut. of* ætas. *childhood.* Hūnc ætātŭlăm, (Iamb.) Prud.

ætērnĭtās, ātĭs, f., *eternity.* Ætērnĭtātĭs jānŭăs, (Iamb. Dim.) Prud. Epith. Lōngă, pĕrēnnĭs, ĭmmūtābĭlĭs.

ætērno, ās, *to perpetuate.* Mĕmŏrēsquĕ făstōs ætērnĕt, Hor.

ætērnō *and* ætērnŭm, adv., *for ever.* Scīlĭcĕt ætērnō, Ov. Sĕdĕt ætērnŭmquĕ sĕdĕbĭt, Virg. Syn. Sēmpĕr, pērpĕtŭō, ūsquĕ, nūnquăm nōn; ōmnī tēmpŏrĕ, ævŏ. V. Semper.

ætērnŭŭs, ă, ŭm, *eternal.* Tūm pătĕr ætērnō, Virg. Syn. Pērpĕtŭŭs, pĕrēnnĭs, cōntĭnŭŭs, sēmpĭtērnŭs, ĭmmŏrtālĭs. V. Immortalis; semper; æternitas.

Æthălĭă, æ, *and* Æthălĭs, ĭdĭs, f., *Greek name of the island of Elba.* Æthălĭs Ilvă gĕnĭs, Ov.

Æthălĭōn, ōnĭs, m., *a Tuscan sailor, changed by Bacchus into a dolphin.* Ē quĭbŭs Æthălĭōn, Ov.

Æthălĭŭs, ī, m., *name of an unknown person.* Æthălĭōn vītă spŏlĭāvĭt ŭt Isĭdĭs hōspĕs, Ov.

æthĕr, ĕrĭs, m., *the sky.* Inde æthĕr ĭgnĭfĕr ĭpsĕ, Lucr. Syn. Cœlŭm, pŏlŭs, Ŏlÿmpŭs; V. Cœlum. Aēr, ĭnānĕ; V. Aer. Epith. Lēvĭs, răpĭdŭs, rĕvŏlūbĭlĭs, nĭtĭdŭs, lĭquĭdŭs, sĕrēnŭs, vāstŭs, sĭgnĭfĕr, săcĕr, ĭgnĕŭs, cærŭlĕŭs, stēllātŭs, cūrvŭs, ĭncūrvŭs; ōmnĭpŏtēns, aŭrĕŭs, lūcĭdŭs, lætŭs, cōnspĭcŭŭs, pūrpūrĕŭs, cāndēns, ārdēns, pĭctŭs.

æthĕrĕŭs, *or* rĭŭs, ă, ŭm, *etherial.* Æthĕrĕās tēlŭm, Virg. Mĕdĭum æthĕrĭō cūrsū, Virg. Syn. Aĕrĭŭs; cœlēstĭs.

Æthīōn, ōnĭs, m., *name of a soothsayer.* Æthīōnquĕ săgāx, Ov.

Æthĭŏps, ŏpĭs, m., *and* Æthĭŏpēs, ŭm, m. pl., *an Æthiopian, a negro; a people of Africa.* Æthĭŏpem ālbŭs, Juv. Æthĭŏpŭm vērsēmŭs ŏvēs, Virg. Epith. Nigrī, ūstī, ātrī, tŏrrĭdī, nūdī, hŏrrĭdī, dēfōrmēs, fūscī, văgī, ēxūstī, tōstī, fĕrōcēs.

Æthōn, ōntĭs, m., *one of the four horses of the Sun.* Aŭrōræ nūntĭŭs Æthōn, Claud.

Æthĭŏpĭă, æ, f., *Æthiopia.* Ex Æthĭŏpĭā, Ter.

æthrā, æ, f., *the clear sky.* Aĕs ĭn æthrā. Virg. Syn. Cœlŭm, æthēr, pŏlŭs, Olȳmpŭs; V. Cœlum. Āēr, ĭnānĕ, aūræ; V. Aer.

Æthrā, æ, f., *the daughter of Pittheus; mother of Theseus.* Ūtquĕ nĕpōs Æthræ, Ov. Aĕtĭtēs, *or* œtītēs, æ *and* ēs, m., *the eagle stone.* Hīc Aĕtītēs ēst, Prisc. Epith. Sălūtārĭs, sălūtĭfĕr, pārtŭbŭs ūtĭlĭs.

Ætnă, æ, f., *a volcano of Sicily.* Tŏnăt Ætnă rŭīnīs, Virg. Syn. Mōns Trīnacrĭŭs, Sĭcŭlŭs. Epith. Fērvĭdă, ārdēns, īgnĭfĕră, īgnĭvŏmă, Vŭlcānĭă, Trīnacrĭs, Trīnacrĭă, Sĭcŭlă, Tȳphŏīs, flăgrāns, īgnĕă, sŭlphŭrĕă. hōrrĭfĭcă, tōrrĭdă, fūmāns, flāmmĭvŏmă, rĕsŏnāns, căvă, sŏnāns, călĭdă, fūmōsă, văpŏrĭfĕră, mōnstrĭfĕră, răpĭdă, fĕră.

Ætnœŭs, ă, ŭm, *of Ætna.* Ætnœī Cȳclōpĕs, Virg. Syn. Trīnacrĭŭs, Sĭcŭlŭs.

Ætōlĭă, æ, f., *a country of Achaia.* Ætōlĭă tāntī, Ov.

Ætōlĭŭs *and* Ætōlŭs, ă, ŭm, *and* Ætōlĭs, ĭdĭs, f., *Ætolian; of Ætolia.* Ætōlĭŭs hērōs, Ov. Ætōlĭs ŏnĕrātă plāgĭs, Hor. Pūlsa Ætōlĭdĕ Dēĭānīrā, Ov.

Ætōlŭs, ī, m., *an Ætolian.* Ætōlŭs ĕt Arpī, Virg.

Ævă, æ, f. V. Eva.

ævŭm, ī, n, *a great space of time ; eternity.* Tāntum ævī lōngīnquă, Virg. Syn. Vītă, ætās ; ævī spătĭŭm. Epith. Āngŭstŭm, brĕvĕ, mĭsĕrābĭlĕ, ānnōsŭm, vŏlāns, lūbrĭcŭm, præpĕs, lōngŭm, fŭgĭēns, cădūcŭm, fāllāx, lābĭlĕ, īncērtŭm, flŭĭdŭm, lāmēntābĭlĕ. V. Ætas.

Āfĕr, Afrī, m., Afrī, ōrŭm, m. pl., *an African.* Āfĕr ăgĭt, Virg. Ibĭmŭs Afrōs, Id. Epith. Dīscīnctŭs, rĕbēllĭs, sævŭs, tĕnŭĭs, sĭtĭēns. V. Africa.

affābĭlĭs, ĕ, *affable.* Dīctu affābĭlĭs ūllī, Virg. Syn. Cōmĭs, mītĭs, plăcĭdŭs, bĕnīgnŭs, ūrbānŭs, hūmānŭs.

|| affābrē, adv., *artificially.* Ēlăbŏrāt affābrē sĭbĭ, (Iamb.) Syn. Pūlchrē, sōlērtĕr, bēllē, pĕrītē, ĕlĕgāntĕr.

|| affāmĕn, ĭnĭs, n., *a parley.* Affāmĭnă sēnsĭt, Juvenc.

affānĭæ, ārŭm, f. pl., *trifles.* Vēndĭdĭt affānĭās. V. Nugæ.

affātĭm, adv., *abundantly.* Affātĭm plēnĭs, quĭbŭs ĭmbŭātŭr, (Sapph.) Syn. Ābūndē, lārgē, mūltŭm.

affātŭs, ūs, m., *a speaking to.* Aūdĕăt affātū, Virg. Syn. Āllŏquĭŭm, sērmo.

affātŭs, ă, ŭm, *the partic. of* affor. Trīstēs affātŭs ămīcōs, Hor.

affēctātŭs, ă, ŭm, *the pass. partic. of* affecto. Affēctātă tĭbĭ, Stat.

affēcto, ās, *to affect, follow after.* Vĭāmque affēctăt Ōlȳmpō, Virg. Syn. Cŭpĭo, āppĕto, ēxquīro, āmbĭo, aūcŭpŏr, dēsīdĕro.

affēctŭs, ūs, m., *affection, disposition of the soul.* Hæc dăbĭt affēctŭs, Juv. Syn. Stŭdĭŭm, mōtŭs ănĭmī, mēntĭs, pēctŏrĭs. Epith. Vĕhĕmēns, tūrbĭdŭs, vĭŏlēntŭs.

affēctŭs, ă, ŭm, *the pass. partic. of* afficio. Jūpĭtĕr affēctæ tāndĕm, Prop.

affĕro, āttŭlī, āllātŭm, *to bring.* Affĕrēt ĭmprīmĭs, Hor. Syn. Fĕro, dēfĕro, pōrto, āddūco.

afficĭo, fēcī, fēctŭm, *to affect.* Affĭcĕ mūnĕrĭbŭs, Catul. Syn. Cōmmŏvĕo, mŏvĕo, tūrbo, vēxo, pērtūrbo, afflīgo, tōrquĕo.

affīgo, xī, xŭm, *to fasten.* Rădīcem affīgĕrĕ tērræ, Virg. Syn. Fīgo, īnsĕro, ādnēcto, cōnnēcto, jūngo, ādjūngo, cōnjūngo.

*affīngo, fīnxī, fīctŭm, *to form, to feign.* Affīngĕrĕ nōlī, Lucr. Syn. Fīngo, āssĭmŭlo, sĭmŭlo.

affīnĭs, ĕ, *neighbouring, of kin.* Affīnĭă vīncŭlă, Ovid. Syn. Cŏgnātŭs, cōnsānguĭnĕŭs, āgnātŭs, prŏpīnquŭs, sānguĭnĕ jūnctŭs ; æquālĭs, sĭmĭlĭs ; prŏpīnquŭs, vīcīnŭs.

affīrmo, ās, *to affirm.* Quĭs tămĕn affīrmāt nīl, Juv. Syn. Assĕro, assĕvĕro, ăĭo, (*or* aĭo, dissyl.) cōnfīrmo, jūro.

affīxŭs, ă, ŭm, *the pass. partic. of* affigo. Affīxŭs lătĕrī, Virg.

|| afflāmĕn, ĭnĭs, n., *breath, inspiration.* Afflāmĭnĕ sānctō, Juvenc.

afflātŭs, ă, ŭm, *the pass. partic. of* afflo. Afflāta ēst nūmĭnĕ, Virg.

afflātŭs, ūs, m., *a breathing on.* Frōndēs afflātĭbŭs ārdēnt, Ov. Syn. Flātŭs, īnstīnctŭs, ănhēlĭtŭs, ĭmpĕtŭs.

afflĕo, ēs, *to weep to.* Flēntĭbŭs afflēnt, Hor.

afflīcto, ās, *the frequent. of* affligo, *to afflict.* Fœdo afflīctāntŭr ămōrĕ, Lucr.

afflīctŭs, ă, ŭm, *the pass. partic. of* affligo. Afflīctŭs vītam īn tĕnĕbrīs, Virg. V Infelix.

affīgo, xī, ctŭm, *to cast down, to afflict.* Spŏllīs afflīgĭt ĕgēstās, Claud. Syn. Vēxo, āngo; prōstērno, dēprĭmo, dējĭcĭo, pēssŭndo.

afflo, ās, *to breathe on.* Fŭlmĭnĭs afflāvĭt vēntĭs, Virg. Syn. Inspĭro; ăgĭto, ĭmpēllo; ădhālo.

afflŭo, afflūxī, *to flow on, to abound.* Cŏmĭtum afflūxīssĕ nŏvōrŭm, Virg. Syn. Abūndo; āccūrro, cōncūrro. V. Abundo, concurro.

affōr, affārĭs, *to speak to.* Dĭctīs affātŭr Ămŏrĕm, Virg. Syn. Allŏquŏr, cōm-pēllo ās. V. Alloquor.

affōrĕ, *inf. fut. of* adsum. Affōrĕ tēmpŭs, Virg.

|| affrĕmo, mŭī, mĭtŭm, *to bluster.* Affrĕmĭt ălĭs, Sil. V. Fremo.

|| affrĭco, ās, ŭī, *to rub against.* Lŭtōsŭs affrĭcābĭt, Tib. V. Frico.

affulgĕo, sī, *to shine on.* Affŭlsīt pŏpŭlō, Hor. Syn. Rēfŭlgĕo.

affundo, ūdī, *to pour on.* Ov.

affūsŭs, ă, ŭm, *the pass. partic. of* affundo. Spārgĭtŭr affūsō cōrnŭā, Ov.

Afranĭŭs, ĭī, m., *a Latin comic poet.* Afrānĭī tŏgā, Hor. Agĭtāvĭt Afrānī, Aus. Afrī, *from* Afĕr. V. Afer.

Afrĭcă, æ, f., *one of the four quarters of the world.* Afrĭcă tāntă jăcēs, Prop. Syn. Tērră, tēllūs, plāgă Lĭbўcă, Gætŭlă, Mārmărĭcă, Māssўlă, Maūrŭsĭă, tēllūs Năsămōnĭă, Gărămāntĭcă, Pūnĭcă, Bārbără tēllūs, ōræ Lĭbўcæ, ārvă Pœnōrŭm; Nŏmădŭm tēllūs; Lĭbўæ agrī, dēsērtă, ōræ, rēgnă, ārvă; Lĭbўcŭm līttŭs. Epith. Arĭdă, ūstă, dīvĕs, gēmmĭfĕră, ēxūstă, fĕră, ărēnōsă, ĭncūltă, ĭnhōspĭtă.

Afrĭcānŭs, ĭ, m., *cognomen of Scipio.* Cōgĭs Afrĭcānīs, (Phal.) Mart.

Afrĭcŭs, ă, ŭm, *African, of Africa.* Quōs Afrĭcă tērră, Virg.—2. *Of the wind Africus.* Afrĭcīs vēntŭs prōcēllīs, Hor.

Afrĭcŭs, ĭ, m., *the wind south-west by west.* Afrĭcŭs, ēt vāstōs, Virg. Epith. Præcēps, pēstĭlēns, cĕlĕr, nĭgĕr, hūmĭdŭs, nĭmbōsŭs, cālĭdŭs, pēstĭfĕr, ăquōsŭs, ĭmbrĭfĕr, ĭgnāvŭs, ĭnĕrs, pĭgĕr, ēxĭtĭālĭs, nūbĭlŭs, ūdŭs, plŭvĭŭs.

Agămēmno, *and* mēmnōn, ŏnĭs, m., *the son of Atreus, king of Mycenæ, and supreme chief of the Greeks at the siege of Troy.* Agămēmnŏ vŏlēntēm, Virg. Agă-mēmnŏnă fērrō, Ov. Syn. Tāntālĭdēs, Atrīdēs; dūx Mўcēnæŭs, Argīvŭs. Epith. Græcŭs, strēnŭŭs, gĕnĕrōsŭs, pŏtēns, māgnănĭmŭs, ĭntrĕpĭdŭs, aūdāx, bēllātŏr, vĭgĭl, clўpĕātŭs, tērrĭfĭcŭs, Mārtĭŭs.

Agămēmnŏnĭdēs, æ, m., *son of Agamemnon, Orestes.* Pār Agămēmnŏnĭdæ crīmĕn, Juv.

Agămēmnŏnĭŭs, ă, ŭm, *of Agamemnon.* Rēs Agămēmnŏnĭās, Virg.

Agănīppē, ēs, f., *a fountain sacred to the Muses.* Aŏnĭæ Agănīppēs, Virg. Syn. Hīppocrēnē, fōns Căbāllīnŭs, Agănīppĕŭs, Hēlĭcōnĭŭs, Pērmēssĭŭs; Hўāntæŭs, Hўāntĭŭs; Aŏnĭŭs; Aŏnĭī lătĭcēs; Pēgāsĭŭs fōns; ūndă Agă-nīppēā. Epith. Bœōtĭcă, dōctă, dūlcĭs, grātă, ămœnă, Pērmēssĭă.

Agănīppĕŭs, ă, ŭm, *and* Agănīppĭs, ĭdĭs *or* ĭdŏs, f., *of Aganippe.* Pār Agănīppĕæ, Prop. Fōntēs Agănīppĭdĭs Hīppōcrēnēs, Ov. Syn. Căbāllīnŭs, Aŏnĭŭs.

ăgāso, ōnĭs, m., *a horse-keeper.* Pĕdĕ lāpsŭs frāngăt ăgāsō, Hor. Syn. Agĭtātŏr ăsēllī, ĕquī.

Agăthoclēs, ĭs *and* ĕōs, m., *a tyrant of Sicily.* Agăthōclĕă rēgĕm, Aus.

Agăthŷrsī, ōrŭm, m. pl., *a people of Scythia.* Pīctīque Agăthŷrsī, Virg. Epith. Pīctī, dēpīctī, ĭmmānēs.

Agāvē, ēs, f., *the daughter of Cadmus and Hermione, mother of Pentheus, whom she murdered and dilacerated.* Dēmēns cŭm pōrtăt Agāvē, Hor. Epith. Cādmæă, Thēbānă, pērfĭdă, crŭēntă, fūrēns.

ăgĕ, *the imper. of* ago. *Come on, well.* Dīc ăgĕ, năm, Ov. Syn. Agĕdŭm, ăgēsĭs, ējă ăgĕ.

|| Agĕă, æ, f., *the deck.* Agĕāquĕ lōngă, Enn.

Agĕdŭm, adv., *come on.* En ăgĕdŭm, Prop.

ăgēllŭs, *and* lŭlŭs, ĭ, m., *diminut. of* ager. Pōssēssŏr ăgellī, Virg. Agēllŭlum ħūnc, (Iamb.) Cat. V. Ager.

Agēnŏr, ŏrĭs, m., *king of Phœnicia, father of Cadmus.* Impĕrĭōsŭs Agēnŏr, Stat. Syn. Bēlīdĕs.

Agēnŏrĕŭs, *or* rĭŭs, ă, ŭm, *of Agenor or his descendants.* Dŏmŭmque ĭntrăt Agēnŏrĕăm, Ov.

Agēnŏrĭdēs, æ, m., *son of Agenor, Cadmus.* Vītăt Agēnŏrĭdēs, Ov.

ăgĕr, agrī, m., *a field.* Huīc ăgĕr īllĕ, Virg. Syn. Cāmpŭs, ārvŭm, jūgĕră, tĕrrā, sōlŭm, rūrā, tĕllūs, hŭmŭs, ăgĕllŭs. Epith. Pīnguĭs, dīvĕs, frūgĭfĕr, laetŭs, foecūndŭs, lūxŭrĭōsŭs, fĕrāx, hĕrbōsŭs, vīrēns, ămoenŭs, bĕnīgnŭs, stĕrĭlĭs, īngrātŭs, vēstītŭs, trītĭcĕŭs, ārĭdŭs, vērnāns, lăpĭdōsŭs, grămĭnĕŭs, mōllĭs, pătŭlŭs, hĕrbĭfĕr, hŭmĭdŭs, rĭgŭŭs, īrrĭgŭŭs, ălmŭs, cūltŭs, mădĭdŭs, ūbĕr, fĕrtĭlĭs, bŏnŭs, ŏpĕrōsŭs, ūdŭs, sīccŭs, īncūltŭs, lātŭs, pŭtēns, vĭtĭfĕr, Cĕrĕālĭs, flāvēns, flāvŭs, pūmĭfĕr, sāxōsŭs, spīnōsŭs, flōrēns, ŏlēns, aprīcŭs, ăpĕrtŭs, līmōsŭs, ăquōsŭs. V. Arvum.

ăgĕsĭs, adv., *go to, come on.* Nūnc ăgĕsīs, quŏnĭăm, Luc. Syn. Ăgĕdŭm, ĕjā ăgĕ.

ăggĕmo, ŭī. V. Adgemo.

ăggĕr, ĕrĭs, m., *a heap, a rampart.* Aggĕrĭbŭs sēptăm, Virg. Syn. Vāllŭm, mŭnīmĕn, prōpūgnācŭlŭm; tĕrrā ăggĕstā; tĕrrĕā mōlēs. Epith. Tĕrrĕŭs, hĕrbōsŭs, lăpĭdōsŭs, grămĭnĕŭs, īncūrvŭs, tĕrrēnŭs, fīrmŭs, cērtŭs, sēcūrŭs, ĭnĕxpūgnābĭlĭs, āltŭs, cēlsŭs, ēxcēlsŭs, ārdŭŭs, bēllĭcŭs, Mārtĭŭs, sūblīmĭs, īngēns, vălĭdŭs, īnsŭpĕrābĭlĭs, sŏlĭdŭs. V. Munimen.

|| ăggĕrĕŭs, ă, ŭm, *heaped up.* Aggĕrŏī vēlōx tŭmŭlī, Fulg.

ăggĕro, ās or ĭs, *to heap.* Aggĕrītŭr tŭmŭlō, Virg. Aggĕrăt īrās, Virg. Syn. Cōngĕro, cŭmŭlo, ăgglōmĕro, āccŭmŭlo; aūgĕo. V. Accumulo.

ăgglŏmĕro, ās, *to throng together.* Lătĕri ăgglŏmĕrānt nŏstrō, Virg. Syn. Implīco, ādjūngo.

|| ăgglūtĭno, ās, *to cement.* Plaut. Syn. Glūtĭnĕ nēcto, ādnēcto, jūngo, cōnjūngo, cōnnēcto, cōpŭlo.

ăggrăvēsco, ĭs, *to grow heavy, depressed.* Ter. Syn. Dēprĭmŏr, ăggrăvŏr, ŏpprĭmŏr, ŏbrŭŏr.

ăggrăvo, ās, *to aggravate.* Aggrăvăt, īllā lĕvăt, Ovid. Syn. Dēprīmo, ŏnĕro, grăvo, ŏpprĭmo, ŏbrŭo.

ăggrĕdĭŏr, ĕrĭs, ăggrēssŭs, *to go towards; to accost; to assault.* Aggrĕdĭŏr dīctĭs, Virg. Syn. Invādo, lăcēsso, prŏvŏco, ŏppūgno, prĭŏr īrrŭo, ădŏrĭŏr; V. Irruo. Ordĭŏr, sūscĭpĭo, īncĭpĭo; V. Incipio.

ăggrĕgo, ās, *to gather together.* Aggrĕgăt, ĕt, Claud. Syn. Cōngrĕgo, cōllĭgo, cōgo.

ăgĭlĭs, ĕ, *nimble, brisk.* Lāssābŭnt ăgĭlēs, Ov. Syn. Lĕvĭs, cĕlĕr, prōmptŭs, ēxpĕdītŭs, vēlōx, vŏlŭcĕr, ălăcĕr, pērnīx, cĭtŭs. V. Velox.

Agĭs, ĭdĭs, m., *king of Lacedæmon.* Hŏc Agĭs, hŏc Ăgĭdĭs, Mant. Epith Jūstŭs.

ăgĭtăbĭlĭs, ĕ, *moveable.* Vŏlŭcrēs ăgĭtăbĭlĭs āēr, Ov.

ăgĭtātŏr, ŏrĭs, m., *a driver.* Equŏrum ăgĭtātŏr Achīllēs, Virg.

ăgĭtātŭs, ă, ŭm, *the pass. partic. of* agito. Agĭtātăquĕ rŏbŏră, Ov.

ăgĭto, ās, *to drive; to shake; to stumble.* Lūcĭs ăgĭtăbăt ĭn āltīs, Virg. Syn. Jācto, ăgo, vērso, vĕxo, tūrbo, dīstūrbo.

Aglăĭă, æ, or Aglăĭē, ēs, f., *one of the three Graces.* Bācchŭs ĕt Aglăĭē, Cal. V. Gratiæ.

Aglaūrŏs, ī, f., *the daughter of Ceres, metamorphosed into a stone.* Vīdĕrăt Aglaūrŏs, Ov.

āgmĕn, ĭnĭs, n., *an army marching.* Agmĕn ăgēns, Virg. Syn. Tūrbă, cătĕrvă, ēxērcĭtŭs, cŏhōrs, phălānx, lĕgĭo, mănĭplŭs, mănŭs. Epith. Fŏrtĕ, ārmātŭm, tĕrrĭfĭcŭm, răpĭdŭm, nŭmĕrōsŭm, hōrrēndŭm. V. Acies, Exercitus.

āgnă, æ, f., *an ewe lamb.* Vēllĕrĭs ăgnăm, Virg. Syn. Bĭdēns, ŏvĭs, bălāns. Epith. Lānĭgĕră, tĕnĕră, plăcĭdă, păvĭdă, tĕnēllă, ĭmbēllĭs. V. Ovis.

* || Agnālĭă, ōrŭm, n. pl., *festivals during sheep-shearing.* Fēstŭm prīscīs Agnālĭă dīctŭm, Ov.

* āgnātŭs, ă, ŭm, *related.* Plin. Syn. Cōgnātŭs, āffĭnĭs, cōnsānguĭnĕŭs, prŏpīnquŭs.

āgnīnŭs, ă, ŭm, *of a lamb.* Vīlĭs, ĕt ăgnīnī, Hor.

āgnĭtĭo, ōnĭs, f., *an acknowledgment.* Agnĭtĭōnĕ nŏtās rērŭm, Prud. Syn. Nŏtĭo, cōgnĭtĭo, nŏtĭtĭă.

āgnĭtŭs, ă, ŭm, *the pass. partic. of* agnosco. Agnĭtă naūtĭs, Stat.

āgnōmĕn, ĭnĭs, n., *the third name of a Roman.* Agnōmĭnă Cōttæ, Ov. Syn. Cōgnōmĕn. Epith. Clārŭm, aūgūstŭm. V. Nomen.

āgnōsco, āgnōvī, āgnĭtŭm, *to know, to find out.* Ænēās āgnōvĭt ĕŭm, Virg. Syn. Nōsco, cōgnōsco, pērspĭcĭo, scĭo; fătĕŏr, cōnfĭtĕŏr, ādmītto. V. Cognosco.

āgnŭs, ī, m., *a sucking lamb.* Pāscēntēs vēstĭĕt ăgnōs, Virg. Syn. Bălāns, bĭdēns. Epitii. Mŏllĭs, lānĭgĕr, tĕnĕr, tĕnēllŭs, tĭmĭdŭs, mītĭs, ĭmbēllĭs, blāndŭs. V. Ovis.

Agnŭs, ī, m., *pro* Christo. V. Christus.

ăgo, ēgī, āctŭm, *to drive; to sue; to move.* Pĕlīgnĭs ăgĭtūr vīndēmĭă, Mart. Syn. Gĕro, făcĭo, ēffĭcĭo; ăgĭto; pēllo, dūco; ūrgĕo, pērsĕquŏr; tēnto, mōlĭŏr, āggrĕdĭŏr; trācto, cūro, prŏcūro.

|| ăgōn, ōnĭs, m., *fight.* Vīncĕre ăgōnĕ, Aus. Syn. Cērtāmĕn, lūdŭs, pălæstră.

Agōnālĭs, ĕ, *of or pertaining to the Agonia.* Agōnālī lūcĕ pĭāndŭs, Ov.

Agōnĭă, *festivals in honour of Janus.* Quærĭt Agōnĭă, Ov. V. Ludi.

Agrē, ēs, f., *name of a dog.* Ĕt nārĭbŭs ūtĭlĭs Agrē, Ov.

agrēstĭs, ĕ, *belonging to the country, wild.* Armăt ăgrēstēs, Virg. Syn. Sȳlvēstrĭs, rūrĭcŏlă, agrĭcŏlă, ĭncŏlă rūrĭs; V. Agricola. Inūrbānŭs, ĭncŭltŭs, hōrrĭdŭs, ĭncōndĭtŭs.

agrĭcŏlă, æ, m., *a husbandman.* Agrĭcŏlæ strĭngŭnt, Virg. Syn. Rūrĭcŏlă, ărātŏr, cŏlōnŭs, vīllĭcŭs, rūstĭcŭs, agrēstĭs, fōssŏr. Epith. Avĭdŭs, ăvārŭs, rōbūstŭs, impĭgĕr, pērvĭgĭl, īnsōmnĭs, ĭnūrbānŭs, īrrĕquĭētŭs, īndŏmĭtŭs, hīrsūtŭs, īnfēlīx, pătĭēns, gnāvŭs, ĭncŭltŭs, dēcŏlŏr, dēspēctŭs, rūgōsŭs, vĭgĭl, quĭētŭs, sōlērs, săgāx, ānxĭŭs, lăcērtōsŭs. V. Arator, rusticus.

• agrĭcūltūră, æ, f., *husbandry.* Cic. Syn. Agrōrŭm cūltŭs, V. Arare; rus, ager.

Agrīppă, æ, m., *the son-in-law of Augustus.* Ĕt Dīs Agrīppă sĕcūndīs, Virg. Epith. Fōrtĭs, īnclȳtŭs, clārŭs.

Agrīppīnă, æ, f., *of two sisters of that name, one was mother of Caligula, the other of Nero.* Nŏcēns ĕrĭt Agrīppīnæ, Juv.

Agrĭŭs, ī, m., *the father of Thersites.* Agrĭŭs ōlĭm, Ov.

Agyĭĕŭs, ĕŏs, m., *Apollo, presiding over the streets.* Lævĭs Agyĭeŭ, Hor.

Agyllă, æ, f., *a city of Etruria, the same as Cære.* Nōmĕn Agyllă vĕtŭs, Rutil.

Agyllīnŭs, ă, ŭm, *of Agylla.* Ūrbĭs Agyllīnæ sēdēs, Virg.

Agyrtēs, æ, m, *name of a parricide.* Infāmĭs Agyrtēs, Ov.

āh! interj., *ah! alas!* Ah! ĕgŏ nōn pōssŭm, Ov.

ăhēnĕŭs, *or* ăhēnŭs, ă, ŭm, *brazen.* Mūrŭs ăhēnĕŭs ēsto, Hor. Crātērăs ăhēnōs, Virg. Syn. Ærĕŭs, ēx ære.

ăhēnĭpēs, ĕdĭs, *brazen-footed.* Nārrăt ăhēnĭpĕdēs, Ov.

ăhēnŭm, ī, n., *a cauldron.* Līttŏre ăhēnă lŏcănt, Virg. Syn. Lēbēs, ōllă, căcăbŭs. Epith. Ūndāns, pătŭlŭm, tĕpĭdŭm, călĭdŭm, căvŭm, ārdēns, fērvēns, spūmāns, Amȳclæŭm, Spārtānŭm; Tȳrĭŭm, Sīdonĭŭm, Agēnŏrĕŭm; Assȳrĭŭm; Gætŭlŭm.

1. Ajāx, ācĭs, m., *the son of Telamon and Hesione.* Nēc quīsquam Ajācēm pōssĭt, Ov. Syn. Tĕlămōnĭădēs, Tĕlămōnĕ sătŭs, gĕnĭtŭs, nātŭs. Tĕlămōnĭă prōlēs, Tĕlămōnĭŭs hērōs. Epith. Aūdāx, māgnănĭmŭs, Tĕlămōnĭŭs, īnvīctŭs, fōrtĭs, sŭpērbŭs, gĕnĕrōsŭs, Sălămīnĭŭs; īnsānŭs, fĕrōx.

2. Ajāx, ācĭs, m., *the son of Oïleus, punished by Minerva.* Fūrĭās Ajācĭs Oīleī, Virg. Syn. Oīlīdēs, hērōs Nārȳcĭŭs. Epith. Tūrpĭs, ōbscœnŭs, spūrcŭs, īmpūrŭs, īmprŏbŭs, nĕfāndŭs, aūdāx, sacrĭlĕgŭs, īmpĭŭs, scĕlĕrātŭs, māgnănĭmŭs, fōrtĭs, gĕnĕrōsŭs.

ăĭo, ăĭs, ăĭt; *or* aīo, *to say.* Sōlŏs aīō bĕnĕ vīvĕrĕ, Hor. Dējēcĭt, ŭt aīŭnt, Hor. Syn. Dīco, āssĕro, āffīrmo, lŏquŏr. V. Loquor.

ālă, æ, f., *a wing.* Lūdŭnt strīdēntĭbŭs ālīs, Virg. Syn. Pēnnă. Epith. Lĕvĭs, cĭtă, sŭbĭtă, trĕmŭlă, strīdŭlă, tĕnĕră, ēxtēnsă, ăgĭtătă, pīctă, præcēps, aūdāx, vŏlucrĭs, vēntōsă. V. Volo, as.

ălăbāstrŭm, ī, n., *and* tĕr, ī, *a box of perfume.* Ălăbāstră, fŏcīquĕ, Mart. Epith. Ōlēns, ŏdōrŭm.

ălăcĕr, crĭs, crĕ, *or* ălăcrĭs, ĕ, *brisk.* In dēnsōs ălăcĕr Mēzēntĭŭs, Virg. Ergo ălăcrĭs, cūnctōs, Virg. Syn. Vēlōx, cĕlĕr, lĕvĭs; hĭlărĭs; părātŭs, prōmptŭs, ēxpĕdītŭs.

Alānī, ōrŭm, m. pl., *a people of Sarmatia.* Trānsĭt Alānŭs ĕquō, Mart. Epith. Ārdēntēs, īmplăcātī, fĕrī, dūrī.

ălăpă, æ, f., *a cuff.* Sūstēntāns ălăpās, Sid. Syn. Cŏlăphŭs. V. Colaphus.

Alărĭc, *or* Alărīcŭs, ī, m., *king of the Visigoths, the first king of Spain.* Lēthōque, Alărīcĕ, dĕdīstī, Cl.

Alāstŏr, ōrĭs, m., *one of Pluto's horses.* Sīgnātŭs Alāstŏr, Cl Epith. Stȳgĭŭs, Plūtōnĭŭs, ātĕr.

ălātŭs, ă, ŭm, *winged.* Ŭt prīmum ālātīs tĕtīgĭt, Virg. Syn. Ālĭgĕr.

ălaŭdă, æ, f., *a lark.* Gălĕăque īnsīgnĭs ălaŭdă, Mant. Epith. Mătūtīnă, lēvĭs, trĕmŭlă, lŏquāx, gārrŭlă, dŭlcĭs, blāndă, blāndĭsŏnă, fŭgāx, păvĭdă, cĭtă, præpĕs.

Albă, æ, f., *a town founded by Ascanius.* Vī mūnĭĕt Albăm, Virg. Epith. Ilĭăcă, lōngă, Ascănĭă, Rōmānă, Dārdănĭă, Trōjānă, vĕtŭs, pŏtēns, cēlsă. V. Urbs.

Albānī, ōrŭm, m. pl., *Albans, inhabitants of Alba.* Albānī dŏcŭērĕ sŭōs, Virg.

Albānŭs, ă, ŭm, *Alban, of Alba.* Albānīquĕ pătrēs, Virg.

ālbātŭs, ă, ŭm, *clothed in white.* Albātŭs cĕlĕbrĕt, Hor.

|| ālbēdo, ĭnĭs, f., *whiteness.* Splēndēns ālbēdĭnĕ tēctŭm, Mart. Syn. Cāndŏr. Epith. Nĭvĕă, ārgēntĕă, lāctĕă, ĕburnĕă. V. Candor.

ālbĕo, ŭī, *to be white.* Ossĭbŭs ālbēnt, Virg. Syn. Cāndĕo, cānĕo.

ālbēsco, ĭs, *to grow white.* Ā tērgo ālbēscĕrĕ trāctŭs, Virg. Syn. Albĭco, cāndĕo, ālbĕo, cānēsco.

ālbĭco, ās, *to be white.* Cānīs ālbĭcānt prŭīnīs, Hor.

ālbĭdŭs, ă, ŭm, *whitish.* Cīrcūmflŭĭt ālbĭdă rīctŭs, Ov. Syn. Albŭs.

Albĭnŏvānŭs, ī, m., *a Latin poet.* Albĭnŏvānĕ, mĕæ, Ov.

Albīnŭs, ī, m., *the name of a man.* Fīlĭŭs Albīnī, Hor.

Albĭōn, ōnĭs, m, *England.* Sāxo Albĭōnĭs ŏccŭpātŏr āntīquŭs, (Scaz.) Scal.

Albĭŭs, ĭī, m., *the prænomen of Tibullus.* Albī, nōstrōrŭm, Hor.

Albūcĭŭs, or tĭŭs, ĭī, m., *the name of a man.* Cānĭdĭa Albūtī, Hor.

Albŭlă, æ, m., *a name of the Tiber, a river of Italy.* Albŭlă, quēm Tĭbĕrĭm, Ov. V. Tiberis.

Albŭnĕă, and Albūnă, æ, f., *a fountain and wood, which took their name from the tenth Sibyl.* Albūnă săcrās Tĭbĕrĭs, Tibul. Dŏmŭs Albŭnĕæ rĕsŏnāntĭs, Hor. Epith. Rĕsŏnāns, āltă, ŏpācă.

* ālbūrnŭm, ī, n., *a white sap.* Plin.

Albūrnŭs, ī, m., *a mountain of Lucania.* Plūrĭmŭs Albūrnŭm, Virg.—2. *a little fish.* Nōrĭt, ĕt ālbūrnōs, Aus.

ālbŭs, ă, ŭm, *white.* Sūlphŭrĕă Nār ālbŭs ăquā, Virg. Syn. Cāndĭdŭs, cānŭs, ālbēscēns, cāndēscēns, lāctĕŭs, ĕbūrnĕŭs, ĕbūrnŭs, nĭvĕŭs.

Alcæŭs, ī, m., *the ancestor of Hercules.*—2. *a lyric poet.* Tēmpĕrāt Alcæŭs ; sĕd, Hor. Epith. Lēsbĭŭs, lȳrĭcŭs, brĕvĭs, ăcūtŭs, ēlātŭs.

Alcāndĕr, drī, m., *a Lycian slain by Ulysses.* Alcāndrūmque Hălĭŭmquĕ, Ov.

Alcānŏr, ŏrĭs, m , *the name of a man.* Idæo Alcānŏrĕ crētī, Virg.

Alcăthŏē, ēs, f., *the city of Megara, founded by Alcathoüs.* Tūtŭs ăd Alcăthŏēn, Ov.

Alcăthŏŭs, ī, m., *the son of Pelops.* Et quōs Alcăthŏī, Ov.

ālcē, ēs, or ēs, ĭs, f., *an elk, or wild ass.* Plin.

ālcēdo, ĭnĭs, f., *the king-fisher, a bird which makes her nest during the calm.* Alcēdĭnēs mărīs cīvēs, (Scaz.) Syn. Alcўŏnē. V. Alcyon.

ālcēdŏnĭă, ōrŭm, n. pl., *the time the king-fisher makes her nest.* Syn. Alcўŏnīī dĭēs.

Alcēstĭs, ĭs, and ē, ēs, f., *the wife of Admetus.* Alcēstēn, Juv. Alcēstim, ĕt sĭmĭlĭs, Id. Epith. Thēssălă, Păgăsæă.

Alcĭdămās, āntĭs, m., *the name of an inhabitant of the island of Cea.* Quā pătĕr Alcĭdămās, Ov.

Alcīdēs, æ, m., *a name of Hercules.* Vĕnĕrāt Alcīdēs, Ov. Syn. Alcæī nĕpōs. V. Hercules.

Alcĭmĕdē, ēs, f., *the mother of Jason.* Alcĭmĕdēs plānctŭs, Val. Fl.

Alcĭmĕdōn, ŏntĭs, m., *a famous sculptor.* Ŏpŭs Alcĭmĕdōntĭs, Virg.

Alcĭnŏŭs, ōī, m., *whose gardens are celebrated by Homer.* Alcĭnŏī sȳlvæ, Virg. Epith. Mūnīfĭcŭs, Cōrcȳræŭs, nōbĭlĭs.

Alcīppē, ēs, f., *the name of a woman.* Nĕque ĕgo Alcīppēn, Virg.

Alcĭthŏē, ēs, f., *one of Minyas' daughters.* Ăt nōn Alcĭthŏē, Ov.

Alcmæōn, ŏnĭs, m., *the son of Amphiaraus, and murderer of his mother.* Syn. Amphĭlŏchī frātĕr, Amphĭărāīdēs.

Alcmæōnĭŭs, ă, ŭm, *of Alcmæon.* Aŭt Alcmæōnĭæ, Prop.

Alcmēnă, æ, and nē, ēs, f., *mother of Hercules ; deceived by Jupiter.* Argŏlĭs Alcmēnē, Ov. Alcmēnā mātrĕ crēātŭm, Id. Epith. Argŏlĭs, Hērcŭlĕă, gĕnĕrōsă, īnclўtă, Græcă, clāră, nōbĭlĭs, cōnstāns, fōrtĭs.

C

Alcōn, ōnĭs, m., *the son of Erechtheus, famous for shooting.* Aŭt Alcōnĭs hăbēs, Virg. EPITH. Dēxtĕr, pĭŭs.

ălcўōn, ōnĭs, f., *the king-fisher, which builds her nest during the calm.* Dīlēctæ Thĕtĭdi ălcўōnĕs, Virg. SYN. Alcēdo, Alcўōnē, Cēўcĭs ăvĭs. EPITH. Æquŏrĕă, pārvă, lĕvĭs, dēsērtă, mœstă. V. Alcyone.

Alcўōnē, ēs, f., *the daughter of Æolus ; changed into a sea-bird with her husband Ceyx.* Nīl ŏpĭs, Alcўōnē, nōbīs, Ov. EPITH. Mœstă, gĕmĕbūndă, vĭdŭă, trĭstĭs, dŏlēŭs, mĭsĕră ; sūspīrāns. V. Alcyon.

ălcўōnēŭs, ă, ŭm, *of the king-fisher.*—2. subst., ŭm, ī, n., *a sort of drug for taking out spots or stains.* Alcўōnĕă vŏcānt, Ov.

ālĕă, æ, f., *gaming, danger.* Quĭbŭs ālĕă lūdĭtŭr, ārtēs, Ov. EPITH. Pĕrīcŭlōsă, vĕtĭtă, præcēps, blāndă, fāllāx, dāmnōsă, āncēps, ĭnīquă, tūrpĭs, dŭbĭă, fŭgĭēndă. V. Periculum.

ālĕātŏr, ōrĭs, m., *a gamester.* Ūdŭs ālĕātŏr, (Phal.) Mart. SYN. Ălĕo ; lūsŏr ālĕæ cŭpĭdŭs. EPITH. Tūrpĭs, fāllāx.

Alēbās, āntĭs, m., *a tyrant of Larissa.* Ūt Lārĭssœŭs Ālēbās, Ov.

Ālēctō, ūs, f., *one of the Furies.* Lūctĭfĭcam Ālēctō dīrārŭm, Virg. SYN. Ērīnnўs, Tīsĭphŏnē, Mĕgæră. EPITH. Ātră, fŭrībūndă, trĭstĭs, Stўgĭă, Cōcўtĭă, īnfērnă, crūdēlĭs, tōrvă, īmpĭă, ătrōx. V. Furiæ.

Alēĭŭs, ă, ŭm, *Lycian.* Ĭn Alēĭă dēcĭdĭt ārvă, Ov.

Ălĕmānnī, ōrŭm, m. pl., *the Germans ; a nation of Europe.* Fĕrōx Ălĕmānnĕ, bĭbēbās, Sid. SYN. Gērmānī, Teūtŏnĭcī, Teūtŏnēs, Sĭcāmbrī. EPITH. Trŭcēs, fĕrōcēs, sŭpērbī, aŭdācēs, īmmītēs, sœvī ; īngĕnĭōsī, bēllĭgĕrī, īndŏmĭtī, Mărtīī. V. Germani.

Ălĕmānnĭă, æ, f., *Germany.* Ălĕmānnĭă nōmĕn, Cl. SYN. Gērmānĭă, Sĭcāmbrĭă, Teūtŏnĭă.

Ălēmōn, ōnĭs, m., *the name of a man.* Gĕnĕrātŭs Ălēmŏnĕ quĭdăm, Ov.

Ălēmŏnĭdēs, æ, m., *the son of Alemon.* Sōlvĭt Ălēmŏnĭdēn, Ov.

|| ālĕo, ōnĭs, m., *a dice-player.* Et vŏrāx, ŏt ālĕo, (Iamb.) Cat. SYN. Ālĕātŏr.

ālēs, ĭtĭs, m. f., *any great bird.* Jŏvĭs ālēs ĭn æthrā, Virg. SYN. Ăvĭs, vŏlucrĭs. EPITH. Sўlvēstrĭs, pēnnātŭs, *or* pēnnātă ; quĕrŭlŭs, cănōrŭs, gārrŭlŭs, lŏquāx, strĕpĭtāns, crīstātŭs, vēlōx. V. Avis ; Augurium.

ālēs, ĭtĭs, *winged, swift.* Pāssū vŏlăt ālĭtĕ, Ov. SYN. Vēlōx, cĕlĕr, præcēps ; ālĭgĕr.

|| ălēsco, ĭs, *to grow.* Dōnĕc ălēscēndī, Lucr. SYN. Ădŏlēsco.

Alēthēs, æ, m., *one of the companions of Æneas.* Grāndævŭs Ālēthēs, Virg.

Ălēxāndĕr, drī, m., *the son of Philip, king of Macedon, and conqueror of Persia.* Fōrtĭs Ălēxāndrī, Hor. EPITH. Māgnŭs, aŭdāx, fĕrōx, pŏtēns, bēllĭgĕr, īnsĭgnĭs, īntrĕpĭdŭs, tērrĭbĭlĭs, trĕmēndŭs, māgnănĭmŭs, īnfēlīx, strēnŭŭs.—2. *the tyrant of Pheres.* Jŭgŭlērĭs mŏrĕ Phĕræī, Ov.

Ălēxāndrĭă, æ, f., *a town of Egypt.* Pōrtŭs Ălēxāndrĭă sūpplēx, (Alc.) Hor. EPITH. Părætōnĭă ; īnsĭgnĭs, Lĭbўcă, dīvēs, nōbĭlĭs.

Ălēxāndrīnŭs, ă, ŭm, *of Alexandria.* Nōxĭa Ălēxāndrīnă, dŏlīs, Prop.

Ălēxĭrhŏē, ēs, f., *a nymph, daughter of the river Granicus.* Fērtŭr Ălēxĭrhŏē, Ov.

Ălēxĭs, ĭs, m., *the name of a shepherd.* Ō crūdēlĭs Ălēxĭ, Virg.—2. *a young servant-boy of Virgil.* Mūnŭs Ălēxĭs ĕrăt, Mart.

ālgă, æ, f., *sea-weed.* Rĕfūndĭtŭr ālgă, Virg. EPITH. Mărīnă, ĭnūtĭlĭs, mōllĭs, vĭrĭdĭs, lĭttŏrĕă, hūmĭdă, tōrtĭlĭs, tĕnŭĭs, vīlĭs, æquŏrĕă, flūctĭvāgă, ūndĭvāgă, hūmēns, vĭrĭdāns, vĭrēscēns ; vāgă, putrĭs, prōjēctă.

ālgĕo, ālsī, ālsŭm, *to be chill.* Sūdāvĭt, ĕt ālsĭt, Hor. SYN. Frīgĕo, ālgēsco, frīgēsco, frīgŏrĕ rĭgĕo. V. Frigeo.

ālgĭdŭs, ă, ŭm, *chill with cold.* Ālgĭdŭs hōrrēscĭt, Claud. SYN. Frīgĭdŭs, gĕlĭdŭs. V. Frigidus.—2. *of the mountain Algidus.* Ālgĭdă tērră, tŭĭs, Ov.

Ālgĭdŭs, ī, m., *a mountain near Tusculum.* Nēc gĕlĭdō prōmĭnĕt Ālgĭdō, Hor.

|| ālgŏr, ōrĭs, *and* ālgŭs, ī *or* ŭs, m., *great cold.* Nĕque ĭn īgnī gīgnĭĕr ālgŏr, Lucr. Algōquĕ fămēquĕ, Id.

ălĭās, adv., *at another time.* Hæc, ălĭās jūstŭm, Hor.

ălĭbī, adv., *at another place.* Præsēntēs ălĭbī cōgnōscĕrĕ Dīvŏs, Virg.

ălĭcă, *and* ălĭcŭlă, æ, f., *a liquor made with wheat.* Nōs ălĭcăm, Mart. Ūmbĕr ălĭcŭlām mĭhī, (Scaz.) Id.

ălĭcŭbi, adv., *somewhere,* Ter. SYN. Ūsquăm, ūspĭăm.

ălĭcŭndĕ, adv., *from some place.* Ălĭcŭndĕ vĕnīrĕm, Fort.
ălĭēnĭgĕnă, æ, m. f., *a stranger.* Et nērvōs ălĭēnĭgĕnīs, Lucr. Syn. Extērnŭs, extĕrŭs.
ălĭēno, ās, *to alienate.* Ălĭēnănt mūrmŭră sēnsŭs, Claud. Syn. Tēndo; sēpăro; tŭrho.
ălĭēnŭs, ă, ŭm, *foreign, of another country.* Hīc ălĭēnŭs ŏvēs, Virg. Syn. Avērsŭs, dīstāns, rĕmōtŭs; dīscrĕpāns.
ălĭfĕr, or gĕr, ră, rŭm, *winged.* Trānsĭt, ĕt ălĭfĕrō, Ov. Agmĭnīs ălĭgĕrī, Virg. Syn. Ālātŭs, ālĕs, pēnnātŭs, pēnnīs īnstrŭctŭs.
ălĭmēntŭm, ī, n., *nourishment.* Sŭnt ălĭmēntă vĭcēs, Ov. Syn. Pābŭlŭm, ēscă, cĭbŭs, nūtrīmēntŭm. Epith. Mītĕ; vīlĕ; jūcŭndŭm, suāvĕ, ŭtĭlĕ. V. Cibus.
|| ălĭmōnĭă, æ, f., *aliment.* Pĭcĕăm fērt ălĭmōnĭăm, (Ascl.) Prud. V. Alimentum.
ălĭō, adv., *in another place.* Sătās ălĭō vīdī, Virg.
ălĭōquī or quīn, adv., *otherwise.* Ălĭōquī cāndĭdŭs ŏrbĭs, Lucr.
ălĭōrsŭm, adv., *elsewhither, in another sense.* Nēve ălĭōrsŭm, Ter.
ălĭpēs, ĕdĭs, *wing-footed, swift.* Instrātōs ōstro ălĭpēdēs, Virg. Syn. Ălĭgĕr, ālātŭs, ālĕs, pērnīx, vēlōx.
Ălĭphānă, ōrŭm, n. pl., *vases of Aliphe.* Ălĭphānīs vīnārĭă tōtă, Hor.
ălĭptēs, æ, m., *he that anointed the wrestlers.* Pīctŏr, ălĭptēs, Juv. Epith. Ŭnctŭs.
ălĭquāndo, adv., *sometimes, at length.* Dīc ălĭquāndō mălĕ, Mart. Ălĭquāndō fŭlmĭnă pōnăt, Ov. Syn. Nōnnūnquăm, īntērdŭm, quāndōquĕ; sæpĕ; quōndăm; tāndĕm.
ălĭquāntīspĕr, adv., *a little while.* Hōsque ălĭquāntīspĕr, Ovid.
ălĭquāntŭm, īllŭm, *and* ŭlŭm, adv. Ălĭquāntŭm nōctĭs hăbēbŭnt, Ov. Ălĭquāntīllŭm quŏd, Plaut. Syn. Paŭlŭm, nōnnĭhĭl, lĕvĭtĕr, paŭlīspĕr, ălĭquāntīspĕr.
ălĭquĭd, n., *something.* Aŭde ălĭquĭd, Juv. Syn. Quĭd, quĭppĭăm, nōnnĭhĭl.
ălĭquĭs, quă, quĭd, *some.* Aŭt ălĭquīs lătĕt, Virg. Syn. Quĭs, quĭdăm, nōnnūllŭs, quĭspĭăm.
ălĭquō, adv., *somewhither.* Ălĭquō prōfŭgĭĕt, Ter.
ălĭquŏt, pl. indecl., *some.* Pŏst ălĭquŏt mĕă, Virg. Syn. Quĭdăm, nōnnūllī, ălĭquī.
ălĭtĕr, adv., *otherwise.* Nōn ălĭtĕr vīrēs, Virg. Syn. Sĕcŭs, ălĭās, ălĭă rătĭŏnĕ, ălĭă vĭā.
ălĭtŭs, ă, ŭm, *the pass. partic. of* alo. Nāti ātque ălĭtī, Man.
ălĭŭndĕ, adv., *from some other place.* Sīve ălĭŭndĕ flŭēns, Lucr.
ălĭŭs, ă, ŭd, (Gen. ălĭŭs,) *another.* Aŭt ălĭŭs cāsŭs, Hor. Syn. Altĕr; dīvērsŭs.
āllābŏr, ĕrĭs, *to slide by.* Cūrētum āllābĭmŭr ōrīs, Virg. Syn. Accēdo, ādjŭngŏr, āddŏr, pērtīngo, vĕnĭo. V. Accedo.
āllăboro, ās, *to add by labour.* Nĭhĭl āllăbōrēs, (Sapph.) Hor. Syn. Lăbōro, ēnītŏr, cōnŏr, cōntēndo, mōlĭŏr. V. Laboro.
|| āllambo, ĭs, āllāmbī, *to lick.* Āllāmbĕrĕ lymphīs, Aus. Syn. Lāmbo, lībo, dēgŭsto.
āllāpsŭs, ūs, m., *a sliding by.* Ŭt grĕgĭs āllăpsū, Sil.
āllātro, ās, *to bark at.* Āllātrēs lĭcĕt, (Phal.) Mart. Syn. Lātro, ās; mălĕdīco, cōnvīcĭŏr, ōbstrĕpo.
āllātŭs, ă, ŭm, *the pass. partic. of* affero. Āllātă pŏpĭnīs, Hor.
Āllēdĭŭs, ī, m., *the name of a man.* Āllēdĭŭs īnquĭt, Juv.
āllēgo, ās, *to send, to allege.* Āllēgāntquĕ sŭōs, Stat.
*āllĕgo, ĭs, lēgī, lēctŭm, *to choose, to admit,* Liv. Syn. Lĕgo, ĭs; ēlĭgo, sēlĭgo, dēlĭgo; āscrībo, āddo, jūngo.
|| āllēgŏrĭă, æ, f., *an allegory.* Dīc āllēgŏrĭăm, Desp.
|| Āllēlūĭă, (Hebr.) *praise the Lord!* Āllēlūĭă dīxĭt, (Phal.) Prud.
āllĕvo, ās, *to lift up, to ease.* Cōmplēxĭbŭs āllĕvĕt ārtŭs, Prop. Syn. Lĕvo, sūblĕvo; mītĭgo, mōllĭo, tēmpĕro, lēnĭo; tōllo, ērĭgo.
Allĭă, æ, m., *a river of Italy, famous for the defeat of the Romans.* Intērlŭĭt Allĭă nōmĕn, Virg. Epith. Flēbĭlĭs, grăvĭs, īnfaŭstŭs.
āllĭcĭo, ēxī, ēctŭm, *to allure.* Āllĭcĭŭnt sōmnōs, Ov. Syn. Invīto, căpĭo, căpto, trăho, āttrăho, dūco, īndūco, ēxcĭto, pēllĭcĭo.
āllīdo, ĭs, sī, sŭm, *to dash against.* Flŭctŭs sĭmŭl āllīdēbănt, Catull. Syn. Īllīdo, īmpīngo, frāngo.
āllĭgātŭs, ă, ŭm, *the pass. partic. of* alligo. Lăctĭs āllĭgātī, (Phal.) Mart.

āllīgo, ās, *to bind.* Allīgăt ānchŏră mŏrsŭ, Virg. Syn. Līgo, cōllīgo, vīncĭo, strīngo, ăstrīngo, ŏbstrīngo. V. Vincio.

āllīno, ĭs, ēvī, ĭtŭm, *to anoint.* Allīnĕt ātrŭm, Hor. Syn. Līno, ŭngo.

āllīsŭs, ă, ŭm, *the pass. partic. of* allido. Sŏlĭdīs āllīsă lŏcīs, Lucr.

āllĭŭm, ĭī, n., *garlic.* Allĭă sĕrpȳllŭmquĕ, Virg. Syn. Bŭlbŭs. Epith. Ŏlēns, rĕdŏlēns, ācrĕ, grăveŏlēns.

Allobrŏgĕs, ŭm, pl., *a people of Savoy and Dauphiné.* Infĭdēlĭs Allŏbrŏx, Hor. Sĕquānīs Allŏbrŏgĕs ŏrīs, Aus. Epith. Incŭltī, rŭdēs, infĭdī, bārbărī, mŏntĭcōlæ, mŏntānī.

Allobrŏgĭcŭs, ă, ŭm, *of the Allobroges.* Cūr Allŏbrŏgĭcīs, Juv.

āllŏquĭŭm, ĭī, n., *conversation.* Dūlcĭbŭs āllŏquĭīs, Hor. Syn. Cōllŏquĭŭm, āffātŭs, vērbă, sērmo, ōrātĭo. Epith. Mītĕ, blāndŭm, grātŭm, jūcŭndŭm, bĕnīgnŭm, ŏptātŭm, mūtŭŭm, brĕvĕ, hŏnēstŭm, ūtĭlĕ, mēllītŭm, hūmĭlĕ, ārcānŭm, nĭmĭŭm.

āllŏquŏr, ĕrĭs, *to speak to.* Tămĕn āllŏquŏr hŏrā, Virg. Syn. Cōmpēllo, ās; āffŏr, āffārĭs. V. Loquor.

āllŭbēsco, *to please.* Nĕc āllŭbēscĭt, (Iamb.) Syn. Plăcĕo, sŭm grātŭs, ārrīdĕo.

āllūcĕo, āllūxī, *to shine upon.* Fōrtūna āllūxĭt tĭbi, Plaut. Syn. Lūcĕo, splēndĕo, rĕsplēndĕo, fūlgĕo, mĭco.

āllūcĭnŏr, ārĭs, *to be mistaken.* Ŏcŭlīs āllūcĭnŏr, aŭdĕt, Claud. Syn. Fāllŏr, ērro, dēcĭpĭŏr.

āllūdo, ĭs, sī, *to play with; to allude to.* Allūdēns, ĕă vŏx, Virg. Syn. Dīctă ălĭŏ rĕfĕro; lūdēndŏ blāndĭŏr.

āllŭo, ĭs, ŭī, *to bathe.* Quŏdque āllŭĭt īnfrā, Virg. Syn. Prætērflŭo, cīrcŭmflŭo, āllăbŏr, hŭmēcto, īrrĭgo; āblŭo.

āllŭvĭēs, ĭēī, f., *a land-flood.* Ĕt āllŭvĭē mŏns ēst, Ov. Syn. Āllŭvĭo, āllŭvĭŭm, ē͂ŭvĭēs, ĕlŭvĭo, dīlŭvĭŭm. V. Diluvium.

Almo, ŏnĭs, m., *a sacred rivulet in Rome.* Cūrsŭquĕ brĕvīssĭmŭs Almo, Ov. Epith. Săcĕr, ĭtălŭs, pārvŭs, lūbrĭcŭs, tĕpĭdŭs.

almŭs, ă, ŭm, *nourishing, holy, pure.* Almă Cĕrēs, Virg. Syn. Ālēns, fĕrāx, fœcŭndŭs.

alnŭs, ī, f., *alder-tree.* Flŏrĕăt alnŭs, Virg. Epith. Flūmĭnĕă, prŏcēllŏsă, vĭrēns, Phăĕthōntĕă, frŏndēns, flŭvĭālĭs, āltă, āĕrĭă, vĭrĭdāns, lōngă. V. Navis.

alo, ălŭī, ălĭtŭm *or* āltŭm, *to nourish.* Bīnōs ălĭt ūbĕrĕ fœtŭs, Virg. Syn. Nūtrĭo, pāsco. V. Nutrio, alimentum.

ălŏĕ, ēs, f., *a bitter plant.* Plŭs ălŏēs, Juv. Syn. Amără, āspĕră, trīstĭs, īngrātă.

Ălŏeŭs, ĕŏs, ĕī *or* eī, m., *the name of a giant.* Sŭpĕrīs ĭmmīsĭt Ălŏeŭs, Luc.

Ălŏīdēs, ŭm, m. pl., *sons of Aloeus, two giants.* Hīc ĕt Ălŏīdās, Virg.

ălōsă, æ, f., *a fish.* Ŏbsōnĭă plēbĭs ălŏsās, Aus.

|| Alpēs, ĭs, f., *a high mountain.* Evŏlăt Alpĕm, Luc. V. Mons.

Alpēs, ĭŭm, pl., *the Alps.* Alpēs ĭmmīttăt ăpērtās, Virg. Epith. Aĕrĭæ, nūbĭfĕræ, cĕlsæ, ēxcēlsæ, pătŭlæ, cānæ, vēntōsæ, frŏndōsæ, ăpērtæ, āltæ, sȳlvōsæ, nĭmbōsæ, dēsērtæ, sŭpērbæ, hŏrrēndæ, nūbĭlæ, Bŏrĕæ, hŏrrĭdæ.

alphă, *the first letter of the Greeks; the first.* Alphă pĕnŭlātŏrŭm, (Scaz.) Mart.

alphābētŭm, ī, n., *alphabet.* Pārs ālphābētī fŭĕrĭt, Ov.

Alphēĭās, ădĭs, f., *daughter of the Alpheus; Arethusa.* Alphēĭās ēxtŭlĭt ūndīs, Ov.

Alphēnŏr, ŏrĭs, m., *one of the sons of Niobe.* Adspĭcĭt Alphēnŏr, Ov.

Alphēnŭs, ī, m., *a Roman lawyer.* Ŭt Alphēnŭs văfĕr, ōmnī, Hor.

Alphĕsĭbœă, æ, f., *daughter of the river Phlegeus, and wife of Alcmæon.* Alphĕsĭbœă sŭŏs, Prop.

Alphĕsĭbœŭs, ī, m., *the name of a shepherd.* Dāmōnĭs ĕt Alphĕsĭbœī, Virg.

Alphĕŭs, ēī, m., *a hunter, lover of Arethusa, and who was changed into a river by Diana.* Ŏrtȳgĭam, Alphēŭm fāma ēst, Virg. Epith. Advĕnă, cĕlĕr, răpāx, răpĭdŭs, Græcŭs, ŏccŭltŭs, rĕcōndĭtŭs, fūgāx, ābdĭtŭs.

Alphēŭs, ă, ŭm, *of the Alpheus.* Alphĕă rŏtīs prælābī flūmĭnă Pīsæ, Virg.

|| ălphĭcŭs, ă, ŭm, *troubled with the gravel.* Alphĭcŭs āntĕ fŭĭt, Mart.

Alphĭŭs *or* Alfĭŭs, ĭī, m., *the name of a man.* Fœnĕrātŏr Alphĭŭs, Hor.

Alpīnŭs, ă, ŭm, *of the Alps.* Alpīnăquĕ bēllă, Luc. V. Alpes.

Alpīnŭs, ī, m., *the name of a bad poet.* Tūrgĭdŭs Alpīnŭs, Hor.

|| alsĭŭs, ă, ŭm, *chill.* Alsĭă cōrpŏră, Lucr.

Alsŭs, ī, m., *the name of a shepherd.* Pŏdălīrīŭs Alsŭm Pāstōrĕm, Virg.

āltārĕ, ĭs, n., *an altar.* Āltārīă fūmānt, Virg. Syn. Ār. Epith. Fūmĭdŭm, thūrĕŭm, pīnguĕ, fēstŭm, sacrŭm, cūltŭm, dīvīnŭm, thūrĕ vāpōrātŭm. V. Ara.

āltē, adv., *aloft.* Hæc āltē vŏlŭcrĭs, Ov. Syn. Excēlsē, sŭblīmĕ, prŏfūndē.

āltĕr, ă, ŭm, *gen.* āltĕrīŭs, *another.* Tū cŏmĕs āltĕrīŭs, Mart. Syn. Alīŭs, dīversŭs, dīssĭmĭlĭs, dīspār; sĕcūndŭs.

āltĕr, ĕrĭs. V. Halter.

* āltĕrcātĭo, ōnĭs, f., *strife,* Liv. V. Rixa, lis.

āltĕrco, ās, *and* āltĕrcŏr, ārĭs, *to quarrel.* Āltĕrcāntĕ lībīdĭnĭbŭs, Hor. Syn. Rīxŏr, jūrgŏr, cōntēndo, pŭgno, cērto. V. Rixor.

āltērnĭs, adv., *by turns.* Āltērnĭs dīcĕtĭs, Virg. Syn. Āltērnātĭm, vīcīssĭm, pēr vĭcēs, īnvĭcĕm.

āltērno, ās, *to do by turns.* Āltērnāntquĕ vĭcēs, Virg. Syn. Āltērnĭs ăgo, dīco; vărĭo.

āltĕro, ās, *to disguise, to spoil.* Āltĕrăt ārtĕ, Ov. Syn. Mūto ; pērdo, dēprāvo, cōrrūmpo, vērto īn pējŭs.

āltĕrŭtĕr, tră, ŭm, *gen.* utriŭs, *the one or the other.* Ăb āltĕrŭtrā dētrăxĭt, Luc.

Althæă, æ, f., *the daughter of Thestius, mother of Meleager.* Frātrēs Althæā rĕfērrī, Ov. Epith. Sævă.

āltĭlĭs, ĕ, *fatted.* Laūdō sătŭr āltĭlĭŭm, Hor.

āltĭsōnāns, āntĭs, *and* sŏnŭs, ă, ŭm, *which sounds from above; sublime.* Altĭsōnŭs Māro, Juv.

āltĭtŏnāns, āntĭs, *the thunderer from above.* Nām pătĕr āltĭtŏnāns, Cic. V. Jupiter.

āltĭtūdo, ĭnĭs, f., *height.* Psāllăt āltĭtūdŏ cœlī, (Troch.) Prud. Syn. Căcŭmĕn, ăpĕx, vērtĕx ; fāstīgīŭm. V. Cacumen.

āltĭvōlāns, āntĭs, *and* lŭs, lă, lŭm, *soaring aloft.* Altĭvōlāns pĕtĕrĕt, Lucr. V. Volo, as.

āltŏr, ōrĭs, m., *a nourisher.* Altŏrĕ rĕcēptŏ, Ov.

āltrīnsĕcŭs, adv., *from another side.* Altrīnsĕcŭs āmnĕm, Avien.

āltrīx, īcĭs, f., *a nurse.* Idāque āltrīcĕ rēlīctā, Ov.

āltŭm, ī, n., *heaven, the sea.* Tēllūrĭs īn āltŭm, Virg. Syn. Cœlŭm, āēr ; mărĕ.

āltŭs, ă, ŭm, *high; deep.* Sŏpŏr āltŭs hăbēbăt, Virg. Syn. Cēlsŭs, ēxcēlsŭs, īngēns, præcēlsŭs, sūmmŭs, ēlātŭs, sūblīmĭs, prŏcērŭs, suprēmŭs, ēdĭtŭs, ārdŭŭs, āĕrĭŭs ; prŏfūndŭs, īmŭs ; măgnŭs, ēxcēllēns.

ālvĕārĭŭm, (quadrisyl.) īī ; ālvĕārĕ, (trisyl.) ĭs ; ālvĕăr, ārĭs, *a bee-hive.* Ālvĕārīă vīmĭnĕ tēxtā, Virg. Syn. Alvĕŭs ; ālvĕŭs, (dissyl.) Epith. Ōlēns, rĕdŏlēns, pīnguĕ, ŏdōrīfĕrŭm, ŏdōrŭm, vīmĭnĕŭm, mēllīflŭŭm, liquēns, căpāx, dūlcĕ, Cēcrŏpīŭm, Hÿblæŭm ; ŏpĕrōsŭm, căvŭm.

ālvĕŏlŭs, ī, m., *a little channel.* Cūjŭs ĕt ālvĕŏlōs, Juv.

ālvĕŭs, ālveŭs, (dissyl.) ī, m., *a channel.* Tÿbrĭdĭs ālveō, Virg. Răpĭt ālvĕŭs āmnī, Virg. Epith. Flūĭdŭs, căvŭs, ōblīquŭs, āngūstŭs, sērpēns, ērrătĭcŭs, hūmĭdŭs, ūdŭs, bĭbŭlŭs, ărēnōsŭs, sĭnŭōsŭs.

|| ălūmĕn, ĭnĭs, n., *alum.* Flĕt ălūmĭnĕ līnī, Ov. Epith. Dūrŭm, sālsŭm, ālbŭm.

ălūmnŭs, ī, m., *a pupil'; ă, æ, f., a nurse.* Dīxĭt, ălūmnŭs, Ov. Cōmmūnĭs ălūmnă, Virg. Syn. Āltŏr, faŭtŏr ; dīscĭpŭlŭs.

ălūtă, æ, f., *tanned leather.* Tūmĭdāquĕ sŭpērbŭs ălūtā, Juv. Epith. Albă.

ālvŭs, ī, f., *the belly.* Brĕvĭs ālvŭs, ŏbēsăquĕ tērgă, Virg. Syn. Vēntĕr, ŭtĕrŭs, vīscĕră, ĭlĭă. Epith. Căpāx, dūră. V. Venter.

Alÿăttŭs, *or* Alÿăttīŭs, ă, ŭm, *of Alyattes, king of Lydia.* Mÿgdŏnīī rēgnum Alÿăttī cāmpĭs, Hor.

Alÿmōn, ŏnĭs, m., *father of the Pleiad Sterope.* Cīrcēque ĕt Alÿmŏnĕ nātă, Ov.

Alÿxŏthŏē, ēs, f. V. Alexirhoe.

ămābĭlĭs, ĕ, *amiable.* Cōndĭs ămābĭlĕ cārmĕn, Hor. Syn. Āmāndŭs, bĕnīgnŭs, āffābĭlĭs, blāndŭs, dūlcĭs, grātŭs, jūcūndŭs, suāvĭs.

ămābĭlĭtĕr, adv., *amiably.* Lūsĭt ămābĭlĭtĕr, Hor.

ămābo, interj., *I prithee.* Mărcĕ, dīc ămābo, (Phal.) Mart. Syn. Prĕcŏr, ōro, quæso.

Amālthæă, æ, *and* æē, ēs, f., *the daughter of Melissus, and nurse of Jupiter.* Naĭs Amālthæē, Ov. Syn. Jŏvĭs nūtrīx, ălūmnă.

āmāndo, ās, *to send away.* Lōngĭŭs āmāndăt, Virg. Syn. Ăblēgo, rĕlēgo, pĕllo, ējĭcĭo, ēxpēllo,

ămāns, āntĭs, *a lover.* Spērēmŭs ămāntēs, Virg. Syn. Amātŏr; prŏcŭs. Epith.

Stūltŭs, āmēns, īnsōmnĭs, sōllĭcĭtŭs, lānguēns, trīstĭs, gĕmēns, īnsānŭs, mĭsĕrāndŭs, lānguĭdŭs, īmpătĭēns, īncērtŭs, căptīvŭs, pērvĭgĭl, dĕcōrŭs, īrrĕquīētŭs, pāllĭdŭs, īmprūdēns, pērjūrŭs, ēxcōrs, fĭdēlĭs, mītĭs, dŏlōsŭs, īnsĭdĭōsŭs, fūcātŭs, ūrbānŭs, mēndāx, dēmēns.

ămāns, āntĭs, f., *a lover.* Ēt ămāns ēt fœmĭnă, Ov. Syn. Ămātrīx, dŏmĭnă, ămāsĭă. Epith. Pŭlchră, vĕnūstă, fūcātă, ōrnātă, cōmptă, splēndĭdă, āmbĭtĭōsă, tŭmĭdă, lĕvĭs, sŭpērbă, stŏlĭdă, pĕrēnnĭs, rĕbēllĭs, īngrātă, cāră, sīncĕră, cōnstāns, fĭdēlĭs, mūtābĭlĭs, fīdă.

Āmānŭs, ī, m., *a mountain between Syria and Cilicia.* Nūnc cūltŏr Ămānī, Luc.

ămărăcŭs, ī, m., *the herb marjoram.* Mōllĭs ămărăcŭs, Virg. Syn. Sāmpsūchŭs. Epith. Suāvĭs, nōbĭlĭs, dūlcĭs, ŏlēns, ŏdōrātŭs.

ămărăcĭnŭm, ī, n., *a perfume made with sweet marjoram.* Ūngĭt ămărăcĭnō, Lucr.

ămărānthŭs, ī, m., *everlasting, a flower.* Īllās, ămărānthĕ, mŏrārĭs, Ov. Epith. Īmmōrtālĭs, flōrēns, pūrpŭrĕŭs, ŏlēns, ætērnŭs, pĕrēnnĭs, pērpĕtŭŭs, pūlchĕr, ămœnŭs, grātŭs.

ămărĭtĭēs, ĭēī, f., *bitterness.* Mīscĕt ămărĭtĭĕm, Cat. Syn. Ămārĭtūdo, ămārŏr. Epith. Aspĕră, īngrātă, mŏrōsă.

ămārŏr, ōrĭs, m., *bitterness.* Tōrquēbĭt ămārŏr, Virg. Syn. Ămārĭtĭēs.

ămārŭs, ă, ŭm, *bitter, sad.* Nūnc ĕt ămără dĭēs, Tib. Syn. Ăcērbŭs; mœstŭs, trīstĭs, īngrātŭs, mŏlēstŭs.

Ămārȳllĭs, ĭdĭs, f., *a shepherdess.* Ămărȳllĭdă sȳlvās, Virg. Epith. Fōrmōsă, tĕnĕră, pūlchră, sȳlvēstrĭs, vĕnūstă, sīmplēx, īncōmptă, blāndŭlă, tĭmĭdă, hĭlărĭs, vĕrēcūndă, cāntātrīx, īncūltă.

Ămăsēnŭs, ī, m., *a river of Latium.* Ămăsēnŭs ăbūndāns, Virg.

Ămăsĭs, ĭs, m., *a king of Egypt.* Tŭmūlĭs ēvūlsŭs Ămăsĭs, Luc.

ămāsĭŭs, ĭī, and sĭo, ōnĭs, m., *a suitor.* Ămāsĭŭs mĭhi, Plaut. Ămāsĭōnūm cōmprĭmūntŏr fraudĭbŭs, (Iamb.) Prud. Syn. Ămātŏr. V. Amans.

Ămāstĕr, trī, m., *the name of a warrior.* Hĭs āddĭt Ămāstrŭm, Virg.

Ămāstrĭăcŭs, ă, ŭm, *of Amastris.* Aŭt ŭt Ămāstrĭăcĭs, Ov.

Ămāstrĭs, ĭs, f., *a city of Pontus.* Ămāstrĭ Pōntĭca, ĕt, Cat.

Ămātă, æ, f., *the wife of Latinus.* Mănĕt īnfēlīcĭs Ămātæ, Virg.

ămăthūntĕŭs, and thūsĭŭs, ă, ŭm, *of Amathus.* Ămăthūntēāsquĕ bĭdēntēs, Ov. Ămăthūsĭă cūrăm, Cat.

Ămăthūs, thūntĭs, f., *a town of Cyprus, sacred to Venus.* Ēst Ămăthūs, ēst, Virg. Epith. Mĕtāllĭfĕră, nōbĭlĭs, clāră.

ămātŏr, ōrĭs, m., *a lover.* Vērsăt ămātŏr ĭtĕr, Prop. Syn. Ămāns, ămĭcŭs, stŭdĭōsŭs.

ămātrīx, īcĭs, f., *a she-lover.* Ēt quŏd ămātrīcēs, Mart. Syn. Ămāns, stŭdĭōsă, cŭpĭdă. Epith. Vĕnūstă, ōrnātă, cōmptă, fūcātă, fōrmōsă, blāndŭlă, mălĕsānă, dĕmēns, dĕcōră.

ămātŭs, ă, ŭm, *the pass. particip. of* amo. Ēt ămātă rĕlīnquĕrĕ, Hor.

Ămāzōn. ŏnĭs, f., *an Amazon.* Vīdĭt Ămāzōn, Virg.—2. *a female warrior.* Ēxsūltăt Ămāzōn (*of Camilla*), Virg.

Ămāzŏnĕs, and Ămāzŏnĭdĕs, ŭm, f. pl., *warlike women of Cappadocia.* Bēllāntŭr Ămāzŏnĕs ārmĭs, Virg. Dūcĭt Ămāzŏnĭdŭm, Id. Epith. Sĕcūrĭgĕræ, Māvōrtĭæ, Mārtĭæ, trŭcēs, fĕrōcēs, Scȳthĭcæ, Thrĕĭcĭæ, Thērmōdōntĭăcæ, aŭdācēs, īntrĕpĭdæ, vĭrīlēs, māscŭlæ, mărītæ, crūdēlēs, pēltātæ, pēltĭgĕræ, fōrtēs, fĕræ, īmpăvĭdæ, săgīttĭfĕræ, bēllĭgĕræ, sŭpērbæ, nōbĭlēs, bēllĭcæ, īmmītēs, crŭēntæ, fŭrēntēs, bēllātrīcēs, măgnănĭmæ, īnsĭgnēs, bēllĭcōsæ, āntīquæ, crīstātæ, pŏtēntēs, scūtĭfĕræ, fŭrĭōsæ, phăretrātæ.

Ămāzŏnĭcŭs, and ĭŭs, ă, ŭm, *of the Amazons.* Nōstĕr Ămāzŏnĭcŭs, Mart. Āltĕr Ămāzŏnĭăm, Virg.

āmbāgēs, ŭm, f. pl., *turnings, windings.* Ămbāgĭbŭs ērrānt, Ov. Syn. Ămbāgo, mæāndrī, sīnŭs, flēxŭs, gȳrī, spīræ. Epith. Lōngæ, dĭffĭcĭlēs, ōbscūræ, ōblīquæ, mŏlēstæ, hōrrēndæ, mūltĭvĭæ; lăbȳrīnthĭăcæ, pērplēxæ, flēxæ, īnvĭæ, cæcæ, lūbrĭcæ, fāllācēs, nēxæ, mūltĭfōrmēs, cōnnēxæ, lătebrōsæ. V. Labyrinthus. *Also in the abl. sing.* Vērbōrum āmbāgĕ nŏvōrŭm, Ov.

Ambārvālĭă, ōrŭm, n. pl., *festivals in honour of Ceres.* V. Arvales

‖ ămbēdo, ēdī, ēsŭm, *to eat round about.* Plaut. Syn. Rōdo, ādrōdo, cōrrōdo, cīrcŭmrōdo.

ămbēsŭs, ă, ŭm, *the pass. partic. of* ambedo. Ămbēsă rĕpōnŭnt, Virg.

ămbīgo, ĭs, *to doubt.* Ămbīgĕrēs, rŭpĕrĕt, Aus. Syn. Dŭbīto, ăncēps ănĭmī sŭm. V. Dubito.

ămbīgŭē, adv., *ambiguously.* Ămbīgŭē dīctŭm, Hor. Syn. Dŭbīē, vărīē.

ămbīgŭŭs, ă, ŭm, *doubtful.* In vūlgum ămbīgŭăs, Virg. Syn. Dŭbīŭs, īncērtŭs, ăncēps, vărīŭs.

ămbĭo, ĭs, īvī *and* ĭī, ītŭm, *to go about, encompass.* Ămbīt aūrō, Virg. Syn. Cīrcŭmdo, cīngo; sēctŏr, prēnso, cŭpĭo, aūcŭpŏr.

ămbītĭo, ōnĭs, f., *ambition, pride.* Ămbĭtĭōnĭs, ĕrăm, Ov. Syn. Vānĭtās, fāstŭs, sŭpērbĭă; ămbĭtŭs. Epith. Ĭnānĭs, ĭmpătĭēns, dēmēns, tūrpĭs, īnfēlīx, ārdēns, vēntōsă, tŭmĭdă, mălĕsānă, pērvĭgĭl, īnsōmnĭs, īrrĕquĭētă, īnflātă, trŭcŭlēntă, ēlātă, pērnĭcĭōsă, trūx, fĕră, vănă, īnsānă, ĭnīquă, mĭsĕră, nĕfāndă, prāvă, pēndŭlă, dēgĕnĕr, ĭmpŏtēns, ĭmpĕrĭōsă, aūdāx. V. Superbia.

ămbĭtĭōsŭs, ă, ŭm, *spacious, pompous, proud.* Ămbĭtĭōsă dŏmŭs, Ov. Syn. Vānŭs, sŭpērbŭs, tŭmĭdŭs. V. Superbus.

ămbītŭs, ă, ŭm, *the pass. partic. of* ambio. Jŭssĭt ĕt ămbītæ, Ov.

ămbītŭs, ūs, m., *a going round.* Pĕr ămœnōs ămbĭtŭs āgrōs, Hor. Syn. Cīrcŭĭtŭs; ămbĭtĭo. V. Ambitio.

āmbo, æ, o, *both.* Ămbŏ rĕlūcēntēs, āmbo, Mant. Syn. Dŭo, ŭtērquĕ.

Ămbrăcĭă, æ, f., *a city of Epirus.* Cērtāntēm lītĕ dĕōrŭm Ambrăcĭăm, Ov.

Ămbrăcĭŭs, ă, ŭm, *of Ambracia.* Ōræquĕ mālīgnōs Ambrăcĭæ, Luc.

āmbrŏsĭă, æ, f., *the food of the gods.* Nēctăr ĕt ămbrŏsĭăm, Ov. Epith. Cœlēstĭs, dūlcĭs, ŏdōră, ŏdōrātă, æthĕrĕă, ætērnă, ōptĭmă, ŏdōrĭfĕră, sacră.

āmbrŏsĭŭs, ă, ŭm, *ambrosial.* Ămbrŏsĭæquĕ cŏmæ, Virg. Syn. Immōrtālĭs: dūlcĭs, frāgrāns.

Ambūbāĭæ, ārŭm, f. pl., *female flute-players from Syria.* Ambūbāĭārŭm cōllēgĭă, Hor.

āmbŭlācrŭm, ī, n., *a walk, a gallery.* In ămbŭlācrīs, rīvŭlōs, (Scaz.) Syn. Ārĕă, pōrtĭcŭs. Epith. Amœnŭm, jŭcŭndŭm, grātŭm.

ămbŭlātĭo, ōnĭs, f., *a walking.* Sīmŭl ămbŭlātĭōnĕ, (Phal.) Catull.

ămbŭlātŏr, ōrĭs, m., *a walker.* Trānstĭbĕrīnŭs ămbŭlātŏr, (Phal.) Mart.

ămbŭlo, ās, *to walk.* Ămbŭlăt, ēt sŭbĭtō, Prop. Syn. Ĭnămbŭlo, īncēdo, dĕāmbŭlo, īngrĕdĭŏr, grādĭŏr, spătĭŏr, prōgrĕdĭŏr.

ămbūro, ūssī, ūstŭm, *to burn round.* Plaut. Syn. Ūro, ădūro, ēxūro.

ămbūstŭs, ă, ŭm, *the pass. partic. of* amburo. Ambūstă dĕdĭt, Virg.

ămēllŭs, ī, m., *starwort, a flower.* Cuī nōmĕn ămēllō, Virg.

‖ amēn, (Hebr.) *let it be so.* Vōcĭbŭs āmēn, Vict. Caūsă sălūtĭs ămēn, Fortun.

Ămĕnānŭs, ī, m., *a river of Sicily.* Vōlvēns Ămĕnānŭs ărēnăs, Ov.

āmēns, ēntĭs, *mad.* Cōllĭgĭt āmēntēs, Ov. Syn. Dēmēns, stŭltŭs, stōlĭdŭs, fŭrĭōsŭs, mălĕsānŭs, fŭrēns, īnsānŭs, lỹmphātŭs, fătŭŭs, vēcŏrs, ēxcŏrs, stŭpĭdŭs, īnsĭpĭēns. V. Stultus.

āmēntĭă, æ, f., *madness.* Ănĭmōs āmēntĭă cēpĭt, Virg. Syn. Dēmēntĭă, īnsānĭă, fŭrŏr, stŭltĭtĭă, vēcŏrdĭă. Epith. Præcēps, pĕtŭlāns, cæcă, aūdāx, tĕmĕrārĭă, mălĕsānă, văgă, grăvĭs, fŭrēns, răbĭdă, fŭrĭbūndă.

‖ āmēnto, ās, *to tie.* Lĭbỹs āmēntāvĭt hăbēnă, Lucan.

āmēntŭm, ī, n., *a strap to hold a weapon by.* Arcŭs āmēntăquĕ tōrquēnt, Virg. Syn. Lōrŭm, vīncŭlŭm, lĭgāmēn.

Amĕrĭcă, æ, f., *one of the four parts of the world.* Ămĕrĭca ēxpāndĭt ărēnĭs, Ruœ. Sĕpĭt Ămĕrĭcă crīnēs, De Luc.

ămĕrīnă, ōrŭm, n. pl., *a kind of pear.* Ămĕrīnă nōn pĕrūstĭs, Stat.

Ămĕrīnŭs, ă, ŭm, *of Ameria, a city of Umbria.* Atque Ămĕrīnă părănt, Virg.

ămĕs, ĭtĭs, m., *a small stake to stay up nets.* Aūt ămĭtĕ lævī, (Iamb.) Hor.

ămĕthўstĭnŭs, ă, ŭm, *of an amethyst colour.* Ămĕthўstĭnōs trĭēntēs, (Phal.) Mart. Syn. Pūrpŭrĕŭs.

ămĕthўstŭs, ī, m., *amethyst.* Pūrpŭrĕōs ămĕthўstōs, Ov. Epith. Mĭcāns. V. Gemma.

ămīcă, æ, f., *a sweetheart.* Fōrmōsæ līmĕn ămīcæ, Ov. Epith. Fōrmōsă, mōllĭs, fāllāx, tĕnĕră, dīlēctă, vēnālĭs, blāndă, tūrpĭs, cūltă, lĕvĭs. V. Meretrix.

c 4

ămĭcĭo, ĭs, ŭī, *to wrap up.* Chārtĭs ămĭcītŭr ĭnēptĭs, Hor. Syn. Vēstĭo, tĕgo, ŏpērĭo, ĭnvŏlvo, vēlo.

ămĭcĭtĭă, æ, *and* ēs, ēī, f., *friendship.* Illŭd ămĭcĭtĭæ, Ov. Tŭnc ĕt ăm'cĭtĭæm, Lucr. Syn. Cōncōrdĭă, cōnjūnctĭŏ, fœdŭs, ămŏr. Epith. Sŏcĭālĭs, sănctă, tĕnĕră, sīncēră, pŭdīcă, vēră, fīdēlĭs, hŏnēstă, cōnstāns, frātērnă, pācĭfĭcă, jŭgālĭs, ĭmmōrtālĭs, ĭntĕmĕrātă, pērpĕtŭă, āntīquă, tĕnāx, fīrmă, mūtŭă, ōptātă, fĭdă.

|| ămīco, ās, *to make propitious.* Nūmĕn ămīcăt, Stat.

ămīctŭs, ă, ŭm, *the pass. partic. of* amicio. Cōrpŭs ămīctă sŭă, Ov.

ămīctŭs, ūs, m., *a garment.* Dējēcĭt ămīctŭm, Virg. Syn. Vēstĭs, chlămўs. vēlāmĕn, tēgmĕn, tŭnĭcă, vēstīmēntŭm, tŏgă, pāllĭŭm; pāllă, cărbăsŭs, līnŭm, peplŭm, Epith. Pūrpŭrĕŭs, fūscŭs, nĭvĕŭs, crŏcĕŭs, aŭrātŭs, pŭnĭcĕŭs, nĭtĭdŭs, plēbēĭŭs, sōrdĭdŭs, tĕnŭĭs, pīctŭs. V. Vestis.

ămīcŭlŭs, ī, m., *dimin. of* amicus. Cēnsĕt ămīcŭlŭs, Hor.

ămīcŭs, ī, m., *a friend.* Tŭă mē vīrtŭs tĭbĭ fēcĭt ămīcŭm, Hor. Syn. Cārŭs, dīlēctŭs. Epith. Fīdŭs, mĕmŏr, pūrŭs, cērtŭs, ŭnănĭmĭs, cōnstāns, tĕnāx, fīdēlĭs, ĭmmūtābĭlĭs, cāndĭdŭs, pĕrēnnĭs, cōncōrs, ætērnŭs, sīncērŭs, cārŭs, dūlcĭs, ōffĭcĭōsŭs. V. Amicitia.

ămīcŭs, ă, ŭm, *friendly, favourable.* Pĕr ămīcă sĭlēntĭă Lūnæ, Virg. Syn. Grātŭs, jŭcūndŭs, dīlēctŭs, cārŭs; ūtĭlĭs, āptŭs.

Amīlcăr, ărĭs, m., *the father of Annibal.* Gĕnĕrātŭs Amīlcărĕ sævĭt, Sil.

Amīnēŭs, ă, ŭm, *Aminean, of a district in Italy famous for its wines.* Sŭnt ĕt Amīnēæ vītēs, Virg.

ămīssŭs, *the pass. part. of* amitto. Amīssōs quērĭtŭr fœtŭs, Virg.

ămītă, æ, f., *an aunt by the father's side.* Jăm rēlĭqua ēx ămītĭs, Pers.

Amītērnŭs, ă, ŭm, *of Amiternum, a city of the Sabines.* Amītērnă cŏhōrs, Ov.

ămītto, ămīsī, *to dismiss, to part with.* Amīsĭt ĭnŭltŭs, Virg. Syn. Dīmītto, pērdo, ăbjĭcĭo.

Ammōn, ŏnĭs, m., *a name of Jupiter.* Hīc Ammōnĕ sătŭs, Virg. Syn. Jŭpĭtĕr. Epith. Cōrnĭgĕr, Sŷrtĭcŭs, Gărămāntĭcŭs.

ămmōnĭăcŭs, ă, ŭm, *of Ammoniac* (Ammōnĭăcŭm, Plin.) *an African gum.* Cŭmque ămmōnĭăcŏ māscŭlă thūră sălĕ, Ov.

ămnĭcŏlă, æ, m. f., *dwelling by a river.* Amnĭcŏlæquĕ sĭmŭl, Ov. Syn. Flŭmĭnĭs ĭncŏlă.

ămnĭcŭs, ă, ŭm, *of a river.* Sŭpĕr ămnĭcă tērgă, Aus. Syn. Flūmĭnĕŭs, flŭvĭālĭs.

|| ămnĭgĕnă, æ, m., *bred in rivers.* Amnĭgĕnăs īntĕr pīscēs, Aus.

ămnĭs, ĭs, m., *a river.* Dŭm dēflŭăt ămnĭs, Hor. Syn. Flūmĕn, flŭvĭŭs, rīvŭs, ūndă. Epith. Amœnŭs, ārgēntĕŭs, līmpĭdŭs, pēllūcĭdŭs, văgŭs, præcēps, răpĭdŭs, frīgĭdŭs, tŭmĭdŭs. V. Fluvius.

ămo, ās, *to love.* Nōn ŭt ămēs ōrō, Ov. Syn. Dīlĭgo, ārdĕo, dēpĕrĕo.

|| ămœno, ās, *to enliven.* Jōrdānĭs ămœnăt, Vict. Syn. Recrĕo, rĕlāxo, sōlŏr, cōnsōlŏr.

Amœbeŭs, ĕŏs, m., *an Athenian musician.* Sŭpĕrēs ĕt Amœbĕă cāntū, Ov.

ămœnŭs, ă, ŭm, *pleasant.* Ĕt ămœnă vīrētă, Virg. Syn. Jŭcūndŭs, grātŭs, dēlĭcĭīs plēnŭs.

ămōlĭŏr, īrĭs, *to remove.* Amōlītŭr ŏnŭs, Lucan. Syn. Avērto, ămŏvĕo, rĕmŏvĕo, ārcĕo, prŏhĭbĕo.

ămōmŭm, ī, n., *a shrub of Armenia, famous for its perfume.* Tērgĭt ămōmă cŏmĭs, Ov. Epith. Sŷrĭŭm, frāgrāns, pīnguĕ, Armĕnĭŭm, spīrāns, rĕdŏlēns, grātŭm, crāssŭm, ŏlēns, ŏdōrŭm, Săbæŭm; eŏŭm.

ămŏr, ōrĭs, m., *love.* Sēmpĕr ămōrĭs ĕgēns, Prop. Epith. Dūlcĭs, blāndŭs, jŭcūndŭs, suāvĭs, grātŭs, tĕnĕr, mōllĭs, plăcĭdŭs, māgnŭs, ĭngēns, flāgrāns, ācĕr, fērvĭdŭs, vĕhĕmēns, ĭndŏmĭtŭs, fērvēns, ūrēns, ārctŭs, sōllĭcĭtŭs, sēdŭlŭs, gnāvŭs, tĭmĭdŭs, vĭgĭl, ĭngĕnŭōsŭs, sævŭs, vērŭs, fīctŭs, āntīquŭs; ānxĭŭs, sŏcĭālĭs, sŏcĭŭs, vĭgĭlāns, ăpērtŭs, ĭmpĭgĕr, ōffĭcĭōsŭs, mūtŭŭs, fēstīvŭs, frātērnŭs, sīngŭlārĭs.—2. Amor Deus, *the god of love.* Ālĭgĕrŭm dīctŭs āffātŭr Amōrĕm, Virg. Tĕnĕr, blāndŭs, săgĭttĭfĕr, ālĭgĕr, pēnnātŭs, ārcĭtĕnēns, phărĕtrātŭs, nūdŭs, fōrmōsŭs, dĕcōrŭs, ārrĭdēns. V. Cupido, Amo.—3. Amor honestus, *love of one's country, of one's friends, parents, children, &c.* Nātī sērvă cōmmūnĭs ămōrĕm, Virg. Syn. Stŭdĭŭm, chărĭtās, pĭĕtās, cāstŭs ĭgnĭs. Epith. Sānctŭs, cōnstāns, pĕrēnnĭs, cōncōrs, pācĭfĭcŭs, fīdŭs, sīncērŭs, fīdēlĭs, ĭmmūtābĭlĭs, ætērnŭs, vērŭs, tĕnāx, pūrŭs, suāvĭs, mŭtŭŭs, săcĕr, sŏcĭālĭs. V. Amicitia.—4. Amor lascivus, *unruly or criminal love.* Inde ămŏr ēxĭtĭum ēst, Virg. Syn. Cŭpīdo, lĭbīdo, ārdŏr, rœstŭs, Vĕnŭs. Epith. Ægĕr, īnsānŭs. vēsānŭs, vĭgĭlāns, tŭrpĭs, īmpătĭēns, īrrĕquĭētŭs, ēffrænŭs, īnfēlīx, fāllāx, văgŭs, mălĕsānŭs, īndŏmĭtŭs, spūrcŭs, fœdŭs, mălĕsuādŭs, vĕnēnōsŭs, vūlnĭfĭcŭs, stūltŭs, sōllĭcĭtŭs, dŏlōsŭs, scĕlĕrātŭs, āmēns, dēmēns, īmpĭŭs, īmprŏbŭs, sævŭs, fērvĭdŭs, tŭmĭdŭs, pătĭēns, fœmĭnĕŭs, ăvĭdŭs, călĭdŭs, pēstĭfĕr, crūdēlĭs, sĭmŭlātŭs, mēllītŭs, flāmmĕŭs, sūbdŏlŭs. V. Libido, Amo.

āmōtŭs, ă, ŭm, *the pass. partic. of* amoveo. Sēd tămĕn āmōtō, Hor.

āmŏvĕo, āmōvī, ōtŭm, *to remove.* Āmŏvĕt ætās, Lucr. Syn. Aūfĕro, rĕmŏvĕo.

Ampĕlŏs, *or* ŭs, ī, m., *a youth who gave his name to the vine.* Ampĕlŏn īntōnsŭm, Ov.

Amphĭārāĭdēs, æ, m., *son of Amphiaraus, patronym. of Alcmæon.* Amphĭārāĭdēs Naūpāctĕō Achĕlōō, Ov.

Amphĭāræŭs, ă, ŭm, *of Amphiaraus.* Amphĭārææ nīl prōsŭnt, Prop.

Amphĭārāŭs, ī, m., *a famous necromancer, swallowed up into the earth.* Amphĭārāŭs ĕquīs, Ov. Epith. Aūrĭgĕr, Argŏlĭcŭs, aūgŭr, săcĕr.

āmphĭbĭŭs, ă, ŭm, *who lives either in water or on land.* Amphĭbĭum nūmĕn, Lucr.

Amphĭlŏchŭs, ī, m., *a son of Amphiaraus.* Amphĭlŏchī frătĕr, Ov.

Amphĭmĕdōn, ōntĭs, m., *the name of a Centaur.* Et Lĭbўs Amphĭmĕdōn, Ov.

Amphĭōn, ŏnĭs, m., *the son of Jupiter, who built Thebes by the sound of his lyre.* Dīctŭs ĕt Amphīōn, Hor. Syn. Vātēs Thēbānŭs, Dīrcæŭs. Epith. Cĭthārœdŭs, mūsĭcŭs, fācūndŭs, dūlcĭsŏnŭs, Phœbēŭs, Apōllĭnĕŭs, grātŭs, săcĕr, dŏcĭlĭs, lĕpĭdŭs.

Amphīōnĭŭs, ă, ŭm, *of Amphion.* Aūt Amphīōnĭæ, Prop. Syn. Thēbānŭs.

āmphīsbæna, æ, f., *a serpent which seems to have a head at both ends.* Căpŭt āmphīsbænă, Luc. Epith. Bĭcēps, tōrtĭlĭs. V. Serpens.

Amphīssă, æ, f., *a city of Phocis.* Phōcăĭcās Amphīssă mănŭs, Luc.

Amphīssĭŭs, ă, ŭm, *of Amphissa.* Amphīssĭă rēmīs Sāxă fŭgĭt, Ov.

Amphīssŭs, ī, m., *a son of Apollo.* Āt pŭĕr Amphīssŭs, Ov.

āmphĭthĕātrālĭs, ĕ, *and* trĭcŭs, ă, ŭm, *of an amphitheatre.* Amphĭthĕātrĭcŭs ōrbĭs. Sidon. Amphĭthĕātrālēs īntĕr, Mart.

āmphĭthĕātrŭm, ī, n., *an amphitheatre.* Cēdāt lăbŏr āmphĭthĕātrō, Mart. Epith. Cōnspĭcŭŭm, āltŭm, sūblīmĕ, māgnŭm, præclārŭm, īngēns, rŏtūndŭm.

Amphītrītē, ēs, f., *the daughter of the Ocean, and wife of Neptune.* Pōrrēxĕrăt Amphītrītē, Ov. Epith. Nēptūnĭă, flŭctĭvŏmă, Nērēĭă, cœrŭlĕă, æquŏrĕă, ūndĭvăgă, mărīnă. V. Mare.

Amphītrўo, *or* ōn, ōnĭs, m., *the husband of Alcmena.* Amphītrўōn fŭĕrĭt, Ov. Amphītrўōnĭădēs, ĭs, m., *Hercules.* Amphītrўōnĭădēs ārmēntă, Virg.

āmphŏră, æ, f., *a firkin.* Amphŏră nōn mĕrŭĭt, Mart. Epith. Aūrĕă, ārgēntĕă, căpăx, căvă, cōncăvă, pūlchră, aūrātă, vīnārĭă.

Amphrўsĭăcŭs, *and* Amphrўsĭŭs, ă, ŭm, *of Amphrysus, of Apollo.* Aūt Amphrўsĭăcō pāstŏr, Stat. Fāta ēst Amphrўsĭă vātēs, Virg.

Amphrўsŭs, ī, m., *a river of Thessaly.* Pāstŏr ăb Amphrўsō, Virg. Epith. Lēnĭs, grātŭs, stāgnāns, īrrĭgŭŭs.

āmplēctŏr, ĕrĭs, *to embrace.* Tēllūrem āmplēctĭtŭr ālĭs, Virg. Syn. Amplēxŏr, ārĭs ; cōmplēctŏr. V. Osculor, Amplexus.

āmplēxŭs, ŭs, m., *an embrace.* Cōnjŭgĭs āmplēxŭs, Ped. Syn. Cōmplēxŭs. Epith. Mōllĭs, tĕnāx, fūrtīvŭs, ăvĭdŭs, cārŭs, plăcĭdŭs, mūtŭŭs, cāstŭs, fēlīx, sānctŭs, cōncōrs, ĭtĕrātŭs, grātŭs, sĭmŭlātŭs, vērŭs, fīdēlĭs, fīdŭs, strīctŭs, ōptātŭs.

|| āmplĭfĭcē, adv., *largely.* Amplĭfĭcē vēstĭs, Cat.

āmplĭfĭco, ās, *to amplify.* Amplĭfĭcārĕ mŏrās, Auson. Syn. Aūgĕo, ēxtēndo, ădaūgĕo, dīlāto, dīdūco, prōtrăho, prōdūco, pōrrĭgo.

āmplĭo, ās, *to increase.* Amplĭĕt ūt rĕm, Hor.

āmplĭŭs, adv., *more.* Amplĭŭs ōbjēctăm, Virg. Syn. Măgĭs, plŭs ; īnsŭpĕr ; deīncēps ; pōsthāc.

āmplŭs, ă, ŭm, *large, great.* Spŏlĭa āmplă rĕfērtŭs, Virg. Syn. Lātŭs, māgnŭs. spătĭōsŭs, lātē pătēns.

āmpūllă, æ, f., *a cruet; an oblong vessel; bombast.* Prōjĭcĭt āmpūllās, Hor. Epith. Căvă, tŭmĭdă, căpăx, tūrgĭdă.

āmpŭllŏr, ārĭs, *to use bombastic words.* Ămpŭllātŭr ĭn ārtĕ, Hor. Syn. Tŭmēsco, tŭrgēsco, ĭnflŏr : sŭpērbĭo.

āmpŭto, ăs, *to cut off.* Ămpŭtăt ārtŭs, Sil. Syn. Sĕco, rĕsĕco, scĭndo, rēscĭndo, ābscĭndo, īncĭdo, ēxsĕco. V. Scindo.

Ampўcĭdēs, æ, m., *son of Ampyx, patronym. of Mopsus.* Ămpўcĭdēsquĕ sā-gāx, Ov.

Ampўx, ўcĭs, m., *the father of Mopsus.* Ămpўcă quĭd rĕfĕrăm, Ov.

Āmsānctŭs, ī, m., *a deep and fetid lake in Italy.* Ămsānctī vāllēs, Virg. Epith. Frŏndōsŭs, ŭmbrōsŭs, pēstĭlēns, sūlphŭrĕŭs.

amūlētŭm, ī, n., *an amulet.* Amūlētă gĕrĭt, Mart. Quŏd tĭbi ămūlētŭm, Fill. Syn. Antĭdŏtŭm, phārmăcŭm, mĕdĭcāmĕn. V. Medicamen.

Amūlĭŭs, ĭī, m., *son of Procas, killed by Remus and Romulus.* . Trājēctŭs Ămūlĭŭs ēnsĕ, Ov. Epith. Ămbĭtĭōsŭs, ĭnĭquŭs, ĭnjūstŭs.

ămūrcă, æ, f., *the lees of oil.* Pērfūndĕre ămūrcā, Virg. Epith. Ătră, spĭssă, nigrā, putrĭs.

ămūssĭs, ĭs, f., *a mason's rule.* Dēlīrĕt ămūssĭs, Aus. Syn. Līnĕā rēctā, rēgŭlā. Epith. Rēctă, ēxāctă.

|| ămūssĭtātŭs, ă, ŭm, *nicely wrought, perfect.* Ămūssĭtātum ŏpŭs, Plaut. V. Pŏrfectus.

Amўclæ, ārŭm, *and* clē, ēs, f., *two towns known by that name ; one in Laconia, the other in Campania.* Rēgnāvĭt Ămўclĭs, Virg. Epith. Antīquæ, ărmĭfĕræ, vĭrĭdēs, tĕtrĭcæ, œrĭsŏnæ, Graīæ, Thērăpnĕæ ; Ăpŏllĭnĕæ, Phœbĕæ, Lēdĕæ.

Amўclæŭs, ă, ŭm, *of Amyclæ.* Ămўclæŭmquĕ cănĕm, Virg.

Amўclās, æ, m., *the name of a fisherman.* Cōnsūrgĭt Ămўclās, Luc.

Amўclĭdēs, æ, m., *son of Amyclas, Hyacinthus.* Tē quŏque, Ămўclīdē, Ov.

Amўcŭs, ī, m., *the son of Neptune, who murdered travellers, and was killed by Pollux.* Ămўcŭs pĕnĕtrālĭă, Ov. Epith. Sævŭs, fĕrŭs, prŏdĭtŏr, ĭnfĭdŭs.

Amўdōn, ŏnĭs, f., *a city of Pæonia.* Ămўdōnĕ rĕlĭctā, Juv.

ămўgdălă, ōrŭm, n. pl., *the fruit of the almond tree.* Nĕc ămўgdălă dēsŭnt, Ov. Syn. Vĭrĭdĭs, vĭrēŭs, pătŭlă, frŏndōsă.

ămўgdălĕŭs *and* ĭnŭs, ă, ŭm, *of almond.* Quĭn ĕt ămўgdălĕōs, Pall. Fērtŭr ămўgdălĭnæ, Ser.

Amўmōnē, ēs, f., *one of the Danaids.* Flēvĭt Ămўmōnē, Val. Fl. Syn. Dănăĭs.

Amўntās, æ, m., *a shepherd ; a king of Macedonia.* Făcĭēbăt Ămўntās, Virg.

Amўntĭădēs, æ, m., *son of Amyntas king of Macedonia, Philip.* Aŭt ŭt Ămўntĭădēn, Ov.

Amўntŏr, ŏrĭs, m., *a king of the Dolopes.* Sŭpĕrātŭs Ămўntŏr, Ov.

Amўntŏrĭdēs, æ, m., *son of Amyntor, Phœnix.* Flēvĭt Ămўntŏrĭdēs, Ov.

|| ămўstĭs, ĭdŏs, f., *a way of drinking without fetching the breath or shutting the mouth.* Vīncăt ămўstĭdĕ, Hor.

Amўthāōn, ŏnĭs, m., *the father of Melampus.* Ămўthāōnĕ nātŭs, Ov.

Amўthāōnĭŭs, ă, ŭm, *of Amythaon.* Ămўthāōnĭŭsquĕ Mĕlāmpŭs, Virg.

ăn, adv., *whether.* Quĭs scĭt ăn ădjĭcĭănt? Hor. Syn. Utrŭm, ānnĕ, nŭnquĭd.

|| ănăbathrŭm, ī, n., *a ladder.* Ănăbāthră tĭgĭllō, Juv.

|| ănăchorētă, *or* rītă, æ, m., *a hermit.* Nīl ănăchōrētæ, Prosp. Ănăchŏrētă trĕmĭt, Sid. V. Desertum.

Anacrĕōn, ōntĭs, m., *a lyric poet.* Lŭsĭt Ănăcrĕōn, Hor. Epith. Tĕĭŭs, lўrĭcŭs, vīnōsŭs, cŭpīdĭnĕŭs.

Ănāctŏrĭă, æ, *or* rĭē, ēs, f., *the ancient name of Miletus.* Vīlĭs Ănāctŏrĭē, Ov.

ănădēmă, ătĭs, n., *a head-ornament.* Ănădēmătă, mītræ, Lucr. Syn. Tænĭă, cŏrōnă.

ănaglўphă, *or* ўptă, ōrŭm, n. pl., *embossed vessels of plate.* Ănăglўptă dē pătĕrnĭs, (Phal.) Mart.

ănălēctă, ōrŭm, n. pl., *crumbs and scraps from a table.* Nŭnc ănălēctă dăbŭnt, Mart.

|| ănălēctĭdēs, ŭm, f. pl., *the stuffings of a garment, to make a crooked body appear straight.* Scăpŭlĭs ănălēctĭdēs āltĭs, Ov.

ănăpæstĭcŭs, ă, ŭm, *made up of anapests.* Sīve.ănăpæstĭcŏ, (Choriamb.) Sid.

ănăpæstŭs, ī, m., *a foot of this quantity :* ˇˇˉ. Ănăpæstŭs ĭpsĕ, Sid.

Ănăphē, ēs, f., *an island in the Cretan sea.* Hīnc Ănăphēn, Ov.

Ănāpŭs, ī, m., *a river of Sicily.* Fōntēs lēnĭs Ănăpī, Ov.

ănăthēmă, ătĭs, n., *a gift, an* ex-voto. Ănăthēmă făvillĭs, Prud. EPITH. Pēnsĭlĕ, vōtĭvŭm.

ănăs, ătĭs, m., *a duck.* Et pictĭs ănăs ēnŏtătă pēnnĭs, (Phal.) Petron. EPITH. Flŭvĭālĭs, inglŭvĭŭs, tĭmĭdŭs, ăquōsŭs, lătĭpēs, pălūstrĭs, ūndĭvăgŭs, ăquătĭcŭs, tārdŭs, inglŭvĭōsŭs, flŭctĭvăgŭs, ămnĭcŏlă. V. Avis.

Ănāxăgŏrăs, æ, m., *a philosopher.* Id quŏd Ănāxăgŏrăs sĭbi, Lucr. EPITH. Phȳsĭcŭs, măgnănĭmŭs, Clāzŏmēnĭŭs.

Ănāxārchŭs, ī, m., *a philosopher of Abdera.* Aūt, ŭt Ănāxārchŭs, Ov.

Ănāxărĕtĕ, ēs, f., *a young girl of Salamis, changed into a rock.* Iphĭs Ănāxărētēn, hŭmĭlī dē stirpĕ crēātŭs, Ovid.

Ancæŭs, ī, m., *an Arcadian, killed by the Calydonian boar.* Cōncĭdĭt Ancæŭs, Ovid.

ăncĕps, cĭpĭtĭs, *with two faces ; dubious.* Tūm vēro ăncĭpĭtī, Virg. SYN. Dŭbĭŭs, ămbĭgŭŭs, incērtŭs, ānxĭŭs.

Anchĕmŏlŭs, ī, m., *a son of Rhœtus king of the Marrhubii.* Dē gēntĕ vĕtūstā, Anchĕmŏlŭm, Virg.

Anchĭălŭs, ī, m., *a town of Thrace.* Altă sŭb Anchĭālī, Ov.

Anchīsæŭs, ă, ŭm, *of Anchises.* Addĭtŭr Anchīsæŏ, Virg.

Anchīsēs, æ, m., *son of Capys, loved by Venus, and father of Æneas.* Anchīsēn ăgnōscĭt, Virg. EPITH. Dārdănĭŭs, Trōĭŭs, pĭŭs, măgnănĭmŭs, Phrȳx, Phrȳgĭŭs, grăvĭs, sĕnēx, ānnōsŭs.

Anchīsĭădēs, æ, m., *son of Anchises, patronym. of Æneas.* Trōs Anchīsĭădēs, Virg.

ānchŏră, æ, f., *an anchor.* Anchŏră jām, Ov. SYN. Dēns fērrĕŭs, fērrĕŭs ŭncŭs. EPITH. Mōrdāx, cūrvă, rĕcūrvă, ădūncă, naūtĭcă, mărīnă, grăvĭs, pŏndĕrōsă, æquŏrĕă, mērsă, īmmērsă, fērrĕă.

ăncīlĕ, ĭs, n., *an oval shield.* Ancīlĕ gĕrēbăt, Virg. SYN. Clȳpĕŭs, scūtŭm. EPITH. Sacrŭm, Rōmānŭm, cœlēstĕ, dīvīnŭm.

ăncīllă, æ, f., *a maid-servant.* Părēt ancīllăs, părĕt aūrŭm, Hor. SYN. Fămŭlă, mĭnīstră. EPITH. Fĭdēlĭs, vĭgĭl, sŏllĭcĭtă, insōmnĭs, indĭgă.

‖ ăncīllārĭŏlŭs, ī, m., *who takes up with servant-maids.* Ancīllārĭŏlŭm tŭă tē, Mart.

‖ ăncīllŏr, ārĭs, *to wait servilely.* SYN. Fămŭlŏr, mĭnīstro, sērvĭo. V. Servio.

Ancīllŭlă, æ, f., *the diminut. of* ancilla. Ancīllŭlă fictŭm, Ov.

āncōn, ōnĭs, m., *an angle, pitchfork, gulf, corbel.* Sūstĭnĕt āncōn, Juv.—2. f., *a town of Italy.* Ōbnōxĭă flŭctĭbŭs Ancōn, Luc.

Ancŭs, ī, m., *the fourth king of Rome.* Sēquĭtūr jāctāntĭŏr Ancŭs, Virg.

Andræmōn, ōnĭs, m., *the father of Thoas.* Andræmŏnĕ nātŭs, Ov.

Andrēăs, ēæ, m., *the son of Jonas, the brother of Peter.* Nōbĭlĭs Andrēăm, Fort.

‖ āndrŏdămās, æ, m., *a precious stone.* Andrŏdămāsquĕ fĕrī, Prisc.

Andrŏgĕōs, *or* ŭs, ī, *or* ōn, ōnĭs, m., *the son of Minos.* Andrŏgĕōs ōffĕrt, Virg. Andrŏgĕīquĕ nĕcĕm, Ov. SYN. Mĭnōĭă prōlēs. V. Minos.

āndrŏgȳnŭs, ī, m., *male and female.* Andrŏgȳnum intĕr, Lucr.

Andrŏmăchē, ēs, *or* chă, æ, f., *the wife of Hector, and mother of Astyanax.* Lībābăt cĭnĕri Andrŏmăchē, Virg.

Andrŏmĕdĕ, ēs, *or* dă, æ, f., *the daughter of Cepheus, exposed to a sea-monster, from which she was delivered by Perseus.* Andrŏmĕdē fŭĕrăt, Prop. SYN. Cēphēĭs. EPITH. Fōrmōsă, trīstĭs, vĕnūstă, pūlchră, mœrēns, fāmōsă, Cēphēĭs, infēlix.

Andrŏs, *or* Andrŭs, ī, m., *one of the Cyclades.* Et tŏtĭdēm nātĭs Andrŏs, Ov.

ănēllŭs, ī, m., *a small ring.* Sæpe ēx ănēllĭs, Lucr.

Ănĕmōnē, ēs, *or* ă, æ, f. Părĭŭnt ănĕmōnēs, Ov. Ănĕmōnă prōcēllĭs, Rap.

ănēthŭm, ī, n., *the herb dill.* Bĕne ŏlēntĭs ănēthī, Virg. EPITH. Olēns, ŏdōrĭfĕrŭm, rĕdŏlēns, vĭrĭdĕ, ŏdōrŭm.

ānfrāctŭs, ūs, m., *the winding of a way.* Est cūrvo ānfrāctū vāllĭs, Virg. SYN. Ambāgēs, flēxŭs. EPITH. Ĭnāccēssŭs, lōngŭs, ŏbscūrŭs, cœcŭs, inflēxŭs, ōblīquŭs, dĭffĭcĭlĭs, tōrtŭs, irrĕmĕăbĭlĭs, ambĭgŭŭs.

‖ āngĕlĭcŭs, ă, ŭm, *of an angel.* Angĕlĭcī Chrīstō, Sed.

‖ āngĕlŭs, ī, m., *an angel.* Angĕlŭs īllŭd, Prud. SYN. Ālĕs, nūncĭŭs, cœlēstĭs. EPITH. Æthĕrĕŭs, fōrmōsŭs, cĭtŭs, vĕlōx, præpĕs, aīdĕrĕŭs, pēnnĭgĕr, cĕlĕr, ālĭpēs.

āngīnă, æ, f., *the quinsy.* Vērum āngīnă sĭbi, Ser.

ăngĭpŏrtŭm, ī, n., *or* ŭs, ūs, m., *a narrow passage.* Ět ăngĭpŏrtĭs, Cat. Lĕvĭs, ăngĭpŏrtŭ, (Sapph.) Hor.

Ănglĭă, æ, f., *the daughter of Æetes, and sister of Medea.* Tē nēmŭs Ăngĭtĭæ, Virg. Ănglī, ōrŭm, m. pl., *the English.* Syn. Brĭtănnī. Epith. Æquŏrĕī, bĕllācēs, aūdācēs, mărīnī, ŏccĭdŭī, gĕnĕrōsī. V. Britanni.

Ănglĭă, æ, f., *England.* Ănglĭă cōnvēntŭs, Mant. Syn. Brĭtănnĭă, Ălbĭŏn. Epith. Dīvēs, pŏtēns; sævă, dīră; fœcūndă. V. Britannia.

ăngo, ĭs, ānxī, *to choke, vex.* Ăngĭt ĭnhærēns, Virg. Syn. Tŏrquĕo, vēxo, crŭcĭo.

ăngŏr, ōrĭs, m., *anguish.* Ănxĭŭs ăngŏr, Lucr. Syn. Dŏlŏr, mœrŏr, trīstĭtĭă. Epith. Ănxĭŭs, pērvĭgĭl, trīstĭs, flēbĭlĭs. V. Dolor.

ănguĭcŏmŭs, ă, ŭm, *having snakes for hair.* Gŏrgŏnĭs ănguĭcŏmæ, Ov.

ănguĭfĕr, ă, ŭm, *which has serpents ; speaking of a constellation, the serpent-holder.* Gŏrgŏnĭs ănguĭfĕræ, Prop.

ănguĭllă, æ, f., *an eel.* Vōs ănguĭllā mănĕt, Juv. Epith. Lŭbrĭcă, ŏblōngă, vŏlūbĭlĭs.

ănguĭgĕnă, æ, m. f., *engendered of a snake.* Quĭs fŭrŏr, ănguĭgĕnæ, Ov.

ănguĭmănŭs, ī, m., *an elephant.* Ănguĭmănŏs bĕllī, Lucr. V. Elephas.

ănguĭnĕŭs *and* īnŭs, ă, ŭm, *of or like a snake.* Ănguīnĕō rĕdĭmītă căpĭllō, Cat. Tŏrtāque ĭn ănguīnōs, M.

ănguĭpēs, ĕdĭs, m., *snake-footed.* Injĭcĕre ănguĭpĕdŭm, Ov.

ănguĭs, ĭs, m., *a serpent.* Lătĕt ănguĭs ĭn hērbā, Virg. Syn. Sērpēns, drāco, cŏlŭbĕr, chĕlydrŭs, āspĭs. Epith. Frīgĭdŭs, tōrtĭlĭs, squāmĕŭs, reflēxŭs, lūbrĭcŭs, tŏrtŭs, īntŏrtŭs, īmplĭcĭtŭs, mĭnāx, hōrrĭdŭs, sīnŭōsŭs. V. Serpens.

ăngŭlŭs, lŭlŭs, *(diminut.)* ī, m., *an angle ; a little angle.* Ăngŭlŭs ōmnĭs, Ov. Sĕd măgĭs ăngŭlŭlĭs, Lucr. Epith. Sēcrētŭs, ăbdĭtŭs, ŏccūltŭs, lătēns.

* ăngūstĭæ, ărŭm, f. pl., *narrowness, trouble.* Cic. Syn. Mœrŏr, dŏlŏr, ăngŏr, trīstĭtĭă, ærūmnă. Epith. Grăvēs, īntŏlĕrābĭlēs, sōllĭcĭtæ, quĕrŭlæ. V. Dolor.

ăngūsto, ās, *to straiten.* Quā mărĭs ăngūstăt, Luc.

ăngūstŭs, ă, ŭm, *narrow.* Quăquĕ pĕr ăngūstās, Ov. Syn. Arctŭs, cōntrăctŭs.

ănhēlĭtŭs, ūs, m., *the breath.* Ægĕr ănhēlĭtŭs ārtŭs, Virg. Syn. Hālĭtŭs, spīrĭtŭs, flātŭs. Epith. Lănguĭdŭs, fœtĭdŭs, dĭffĭcĭlĭs, lēntŭs, lēnĭs, tĕpĭdŭs, călĭdŭs, fērvēns, fērvĭdŭs, vīvĭdŭs.

ănhēlo, ās, *to breathe short.* Nūllŭs ănhēlābăt, Ov. Syn. Rēspīro, spīro.

ănhēlŭs, ă, ŭm, *short-winded.* Orĭēns ăfflāvĭt ănhēlĭs, Virg. Syn. Ănhēlāns.

ănĭcŭlă, *or* īclă, æ, f., *a little old woman.* Sĭtĭcŭlōsæ ănīcŭlæ, (Scaz.) Prud.

Ănĭēn, ēnĭs, nĭō, ōnĭs, *and* nĭēnŭs, ī, m., *a river in Italy.* Præcēps Ănĭēn, St. Laūs, Ănĭēnĕ, tŭæ, Pr. Rāmōsĭs Ănĭō quā, Prop.

Ănĭēnŭs, ă, ŭm, *of the Anio.* Ănĭēnă flŭēntă, Virg.

Ănĭgrŭs, *or* ŏs, ī, m., *a river in Thessaly.* Fūndĭt Ănĭgrŏs ăquās, Ov.

ănĭlĭs, ĕ, *of an old woman.* Sōmnŭs ănĭlĕ căpŭt, Ov.

ănĭlĭtās, ātĭs, f., *old age of women.* Cănă tēmpŭs ănĭlĭtās, (Dactyl.) Catul.

ănĭmă, æ, f., *air, the soul.* Inspīrāns ănĭmăm, Virg. Syn. Ănĭmŭs, vītă, spīrĭtŭs ; hālĭtŭs, āĕr, vēntŭs. Epith. Vīvāx, īmmōrtālĭs, dīvīnă, ætērnă, pĕrēnnĭs, mīrābĭlĭs, vĭgĭl, pērvĭgĭl, īrrĕquĭētă, īnsōmnĭs, cœlēstĭs, æthĕrĕă, fŏrtĭs, săgāx, sōlērs, mĕmŏr. V. Animus, Mors.

ănĭmæ, ārŭm, f. pl., *spirits of the dead.* Vōs ănĭmæ tĕnŭēs, Ov. Syn. Ŭmbræ, mănēs. Epith. Lĕvēs, tĕnŭēs, ĭnānēs.

ănĭmădvērto, tī, sŭm, *to observe.* Hĭs ănĭmādvērsĭs, Virg. Syn. Ădvērto, ŏbsērvo, pērspĭcĭo, cōgnōsco, īntēllĭgo, sēntĭo, vĭdĕo ; pūnĭo.

ănĭmăl, ālĭs, n., *a living creature.* Ănĭmālĭă cætĕră tērrăm, Ov. Syn. Ănĭmāns, pĕcŭs ŭdĭs ; brūtŭm, fĕră, bĕllŭă, bēstĭă. Epith. Immānĕ, tērrēstrĕ, sævŭm, fĕrŏx, īndŏmĭtŭm, agrēstĕ, dōmēstĭcŭm, păvĭdŭm, cōrnĭgĕrŭm, sўlvēstrĕ, văgŭm, ērrāns, răpāx, aūdāx. V. Fera, grex.

ănĭmālĭs, ĕ, *having life.* Ănĭmālĕ gĕnŭs, Lucr. Syn. Ănĭmātŭs.

ănĭmāns, āntĭs, m. f. n., *any living creature.* Ănĭmāntĭs mōrĭbŭs ēssēnt, Lucr.

ănĭmātŏr, ōrĭs, m., *who gives life.* Nōvĭt ănĭmātŏr, (Iamb.) Pr.

ănĭmo, ās, *to give life.* Vărĭōs ănĭmāvĭt ĭn ănguēs, Ov. Syn. Incĭto, cōmmŏvĕo, īncēndo, āccēndo, cōmpēllo, ēxcĭto, hŏrtŏr. V. Hortor.

* ănĭmōsē, adv., *valiantly.* Syn. Fōrtĭtĕr, gĕnĕrōsē.

ănĭmōsŭs, ă, ŭm, *courageous.* Frātrēs, ănĭmōsă phălānx, Virg. Syn. Fōrtĭs, aŭdăx, măgnănĭmŭs, gĕnĕrōsŭs, ĭntrĕpĭdŭs, ĭmpăvĭdŭs, ĭntērrĭtŭs, ĭnvĭctŭs, prœstāns ănĭmī. V. Generosus.

|| ănĭmŭlă, œ, f., *the diminut. of* anima. Ănĭmŭlă văgŭlă! Cæs. Hadr. ănĭmŭs, ī, m., *breath, the soul.* Extēmplō tūrbāti ănĭmī, Virg. Syn. Ănĭmă; mēns, rătĭo; fōrtĭtūdo, vīrtŭs, ănĭmī rōbŭr, cōnstāntĭă, vĭgŏr; vīs, ārdŏr. Epitĭi. Impăvĭdŭs, māscŭlŭs, vĭrĭlĭs, nōbĭlĭs, ārdēns; dūrŭs, fĕrrĕŭs, sævŭs, crūdēlĭs, atrōx, crŭēntŭs, sānguĭnĕŭs, ĭnmĭtĭs, ĭmpērtērrĭtŭs; ăbjēctŭs, ĭgnāvŭs, ĭnērs, mōllĭs, lēntŭs; ĭncōncŭssŭs, Hērcŭlĕŭs, bārbărŭs, Mārtĭŭs; sōlērs, mĕmŏr, sŭbtīlĭs, ācĕr, dīvīnŭs, ĭmmōrtālĭs.

Ănĭo, ōnĭs, m. V. Anien.

Ănĭsēnŭs, ă, ŭm, *of the Anisus, a river of Sicily.* Ănĭsēnăquĕ flŭmĭnă, Ov.

ănīsŭm, ī, n., *the herb anise.* Indūcăt ănīsō, Mill. Epitĭi. Frăgrāns, dŭlcĕ.

Ănĭŭs, īī, m., *king of Delos, high-priest of Apollo.* Rēx Ănĭŭs, rēx, Virg. Epith. Dēlĭŭs, clārŭs.

Ānnă, æ, f., *the sister of Dido.* Ānnă, fătēbŏr ĕnĭm, Virg. Syn. Ēlīsæ sŏrŏr.

ānnālēs, ĭŭm, m. pl., *annals.* Annālĭbŭs ērŭtă prīscĭs, Ov. Syn. Hĭstŏrĭæ, scrīptă; vĕtūstātĭs mŏnŭmēntă. Epith. Vērī, āntīquī, mĕmŏrēs, prīscī, ĭmmōrtālēs, vērācēs.

ānnĕ, conj., *whether or no.* Glōrĭĕr, ānnĕ vĭrō, Ov.

ānnēcto, ĭs, xŭī *and* xī, xŭm, *to tie.* Annēctĭt fĭbŭlă vēstēs, Virg. Syn. Nēcto, lĭgo, āllĭgo.

Ānnĭbăl, ălĭs, m., *the son of Amilcar, a general of the Carthaginians.* Pērfrĭngĕrĕt Ānnĭbăl ārcēs, Cl. Annĭbălĭs mīnæ, Hor. Epitĭi. Āfĕr, Pœnŭs, Pūnĭcŭs, Lĭbўcŭs, Bārbărŭs, Năsămōnĭăcŭs, Gætŭlŭs; crŭēntŭs, dūrŭs, dīrŭs, pērfĭdŭs, trūx, bēllĭgĕr, fŭrĭbūndŭs, Ēlīsæŭs, Tўrĭŭs, Sīdonĭŭs, Āgēnŏrĕŭs; văgŭs, ĭnfēstŭs, bārbărŭs, măgnănĭmŭs, crūdēlĭs, atrōx, cāllĭdŭs, ĭmmānĭs.

ānnĭcŭlŭs, ă, ŭm, *of one year's age.* Ānnĭcŭlŭs săcĕr, (Scaz.) Prud.

ānnĭtŏr, ĕrĭs, *to endeavour.* Dēxtrās ānnītĕrĕ cōllēs, Prosp. Syn. Cōnŏr, nītŏr, tēnto, ādmōlĭŏr, ĭnnītŏr. V. Adnixus.

ānnōnă, æ, f., *yearly provision of victuals.* Cāra ēst ānnōnă vĕnēnī, Juv. Épith. Cōpĭōsă, cōmmōdă, ăbūndāns, lārgă, ŭtĭlĭs, mŏdĭcă, ăbscōndĭtă, brĕvĭs, dŏmēstĭcă.

ānnōsŭs, ă, ŭm, *full of years.* Ānnōsă vŏlūmĭnă vătŭm, Hor. Syn. Āntīquŭs, vĕtūstŭs, prīscŭs, lōngævŭs, grāndævŭs. V. Senex.

• ānnŏto, ās, *to mark,* Juv. Syn. Nŏto, ōbsērvo, ănĭmādvērto; ĭnscrībo, rĕfĕro.

ānnŭlŭs, ī, m., *a ring.* Ānnŭlŭs ūsū, Ov. Epith. Lævĭs, aūrĕŭs, prĕtĭōsŭs, jŭgālĭs.

ānnŭmĕro, ās, *to reckon up.* Ānnŭmĕrārĕ tĭbi, Mart. Syn. Ascrībo, āccēnsĕo; ĭn nŭmĕrŭm rĕfĕro, ĭn nŭmĕrō pōno; nŭmĕro, rĕcēnsĕo ĭntĕr. V. Numero.

• ānnūntĭo, ās, *to deliver a message.* Cic. V. Nuntio.

ānnŭo, ĭs, ānnŭī, *to assent by a nod.* Ānnŭīt, ātquĕ dŏlīs, Virg. Syn. Assēntĭŏr, cōncēdo, cōnsēntĭo. V. Consentio, Faveo.

ānnŭs, ī, m., *a year.* Vōlvĭtŭr ānnŭs, Virg. Syn. Tēmpŭs, spătĭŭm ānnī. Epith. Lābēns, lūbrĭcŭs, vērtēns, lābĭlĭs, fŭgāx, vŏlŭcĕr, frăgĭlĭs, vēlōx, præcēps, mōbĭlĭs, prŏpĕrāns, prŏfŭgŭs, ĭrrĕvŏcābĭlĭs, fērtĭlĭs, flōrĭgĕr, pōmĭfĕr, trĭtĭcĕŭs, vīnĭfĕr, frŭgĭfĕr, tăcĭtŭs, fŭgĭēns, vărĭābĭlĭs, rĕvērtēns, rĕdĭēns, rĕcūrrēns.

ānnūto, ās, *the frequent. of* annuo. Sīc ăĭt, ānnūtāns, Mant. V. Annuo.

ānnŭŭs, ă, ŭm, *of a year.* Ānnŭŭs ēxāctĭs, Virg.

|| ānquīnă, æ, f., *the rope of the sail-yard.* Ātque ānquīnă rĕgăt, Cin.

Ānquīro, ĭs, ĕrĕ, *to search, seek.* Ōmnēs ānquīrĕrĕ nīsŭs, Lucr.

ānsă, æ, f., *a handle.* Pēndēbāt cānthărŭs ānsā, Virg. Epith. Pāndă, ārctă, dūră, fērrĕă.

ānsĕr, ĕrĭs, *and* ērcŭlŭs, ī, (*dimin.*) m., *a goose or gander.* Ānsĕrĭs ēt tūtŭm, Prop. Epitĭi. Raŭcŭs, strīdŭlŭs, cănōrŭs, ārgūtŭs, pălūstrĭs, flŭvĭālĭs, grăvĭs, ăquōsŭs, ĭmprŏbŭs, ĕdāx, ĭnglŭvĭōsŭs, clāmōsŭs, sēgnĭs, tārdŭs, ĭnērs, vŏlŭcĕr, tĭmĭdŭs, lātĭpēs, ămnĭcŏlă.

Āntæŭs, ī, m., *a giant, son of Neptune.* Āntæo ērĭpŭī, Ov. Epith. Sŭpērbŭs.

Āntāndrŏs, *or* drŭs, ī, m., *a city and harbour of Phrygia.* Fērtŭr ăb Āntāndrō, Virg.

|| Āntārctĭcŭs, ă, ŭm, *Antarctic.* Āntārctĭcŭs āxĭs, Mart. Syn. Āustrālĭs.

āntĕ, prep. *and* adv., *before.* Āntĕ Jŏvĕm, Virg. Syn. Prŏ, ōb, præ; āntĕă, prĭŭ s.

āntĕă, *or* āntĕā, adv., *before.* Sīcŭt āntĕă, jŭvăt, (Iamb.) Hor.

ānteāctŭs, ă, ŭm, *done before.* Cŭm mĕmŏr, ānteāctōs, Tibul. Syn. Prætĕrĭtŭs, ēlāpsŭs, ēxāctŭs, trānsāctŭs.

āntĕāmbŭlo, *or* āntĕāmbŭlo (*quadrisyl.*), ōnĭs, m., *one who walks before.* Anteāmbŭlōnēs ēt tŏgātŭlōs, (Scaz.) Mart.

‖ Āntĕcănĭs, ĭs, m., *the lesser dog-star.* Āntĕcănēm, Prŏcўon, Cic.

āntĕcāpĭo, cēpī, cāptŭm, *to take before.* Āntĕ lŏcŭm căpĭēs ŏcŭlīs, Virg. Syn. Ŏccŭpo, præŏccŭpo, āntĭcĭpo, prĭŏr ŏccŭpo, căpĭo; āntĕvĕnĭo.

āntĕcēdo, ĭs, ēssī, *to go before.* Cŭrsŏr āntĕcēdĭt, (Phal.) Mart. Syn. Præcēdo, præĕo, āntĕĕo, āntegrĕdĭŏr, āntĕvērto, prævērto, prægrĕdĭŏr, āntĕcēllo.

• āntĕcēllo, ĭs, ŭī, *to excel.* Syn. Āntĕĕo, præsto, ēxcēllo, sŭpĕro, præcēdo.

āntĕĕo, *or* āntĕĕo, ĕīs, *to go before.* Cāndŏrĕ nīvēs āntĕīrēnt, Virg. Syn. Āntĕcēdo, præĕo. V. Antecedo.

āntĕfĕro, tŭlī, *to bring before, to prefer.* Quæ quĭbŭs āntĕfĕrăm? Virg. Syn. Āntĕpōno, præfĕro.

Antehāc, adv., *before, hitherto.* Antehāc īncōgnĭtă, Lucr.

Āntēmnă, æ, f., *and* Āntēmnæ, ārŭm, f. pl., *a town of the Sabines.* Āntēmnăquĕ prīscō, Stat. Tŭrrĭgĕnæ Āntēmnæ, Virg.

āntēnnă, æ, f., *a sail-yard.* Antēnnæ brāchĭă fīŭnt, Ov. Epith. Vēlĭfĕră.

Antēnŏr, ŏrĭs, m., *a Trojan prince, the founder of Padua.* Āntēnŏr pŏtŭĭt, Virg. Epith. Phrўgĭŭs, Trŏjānŭs, prŏfŭgŭs, Māvōrtĭŭs, īnclўtŭs.

• āntĕpōno, pŏsŭī, pŏsĭtŭm, Cic. V. Antefero.

Āntēnŏrĭdēs, æ, m., *son of Antenor.* Trēs Āntēnŏrĭdās, Virg.

āntĕquăm, conj., *before that.* Āntĕquăm tūrpĭs, (Sapph.) Hor. Syn. Prĭūsquăm.

āntĕrĭŏr, ĭŭs, *former.* Āntĕrĭŏr nŭmĕro ēst, Hor.

āntĕrĭs, ĭdĭs, f., *a pillar.* Āntĕrĭdĭs ĭpsĭs, Nocet.

Āntĕrōs, ōtĭs, f., *a kind of amethyst.*—2. m., *the god who punished slighted love.* V. Gemma; Cupido.

āntēs, ĭŭm, m. pl., *the fore ranks of vines.* Vīnĭtŏr āntēs, Virg.

āntĕsīgnānŭs, ī, m., *the soldier who protects the standard.* Vĕlīti āntĕsīgnānō, (Scaz.)

āntēstŏr, ārĭs, *to call one for a witness.* Lĭcĕt āntēstārī, Hor.

āntĕvĕnĭo, ēnī, *to come before.* Āntĕvĕni, ēt sŏbŏlĕm, Virg. Syn. Prævĕnĭo, prævērto, āntĕcēdo, āntegrĕdĭŏr.

āntĕvŏlo, ās, *to fly before.* Tūrnŭs, ŭt āntĕvŏlāns, Virg. Syn. Prævērto, præcŭrro, prævĕnĭo.

Ānthēdōn, ŏnĭs, f, *a medlar-tree; a little town of Bœotia.* Ānthēdŏnĕ grāmĕn, Ov. Ānthēdŏnĕ mēmbrĭs, Id.

Antheūs, ĕŏs *or* ĕī, m., *one of Æneas' companions.* Ānthĕă, Sērgēstŭmquĕ, Virg.

Ānthōrēs, æ, m., *an Argive who followed Hercules into Italy.* Hērcŭlĭs Ānthōrēn, Virg.

‖ ānthrŏpŏphăgŭs, ī, m., *a cannibal.* Plin. Epith. Dīrŭs, crūdēlĭs, ēffĕrŭs.

Āntĭcăto, ōnĭs, m., *a work written by Cæsar, in answer to a eulogy on Cato by Cicero.* Dŭŏ Cæsărĭs āntĭcătōnēs, Juv.

‖ Āntĭchrīstŭs, ī, m., *Antichrist,* Eccles. Extīnctŏr Āntĭchrīstī, (Anacr.) Epith. Immītĭs, tērrĭbĭlĭs, pēssĭmŭs, īmpūrŭs, scĕlĕrātŭs, nĕfārĭŭs.

āntĭcĭpo, ās, *to anticipate.* Āntĭcĭpārĕ dĭēm, Virg. Syn. Præŏccŭpo, āntĕvērto, prĭŏr ŏccŭpo, căpĭo.

āntĭcŭs, ă, ŭm, *belonging to the fore part.* Et sŭpĕr āntĭcōs, Mill. Syn. Āntĕrĭŏr.

Āntĭcўră, æ, f., *an island famous for its hellebore.* Nēscĭo ăn Āntĭcўrăm, Hor.

āntĭdŏtŭm, ī, n., *and* ŭs, ī, f., *a counter-poison.* Āntĭdŏtōs ĭmĭtātŭr hŏnēstās, Scr. Syn. Mĕdĭcāmĕn, amŭlētŭm. Epith. Effĭcāx, præsēns, sălūtārĕ. V. Medicamen.

Āntĭgĕnēs, ĭs, m., *the name of a man.* Nōn tŭlĭt Āntĭgĕnēs, Virg.

Āntĭgŏnē, ēs, f., *the daughter of Œdipus.* Āntĭgŏnē dĕvōtă ĭnălĭs, Stat. Epith. Pĭă, Thēbānă, ănĭmōsă. fōrtĭs, mĭsĕră.—2. *the sister of Priam.* Pīnxĭt ēt Antĭgŏnēn, Ov. Epith. Lăŏmĕdōntĕă, pŭlchră, sŭpērbă.

Āntĭlŏchŭs, ī, m., *the son of Nestor, slain before Troy.* Sīvĕ quĭs Āntĭlŏchŭm, Ov.

Āntĭmăchŭs, ī, m., *a Greek poet.* Gaūdĕăt Āntĭmăchō, Cat.

Āntĭnŏŭs, ī, m., *one of the suitors of Penelope.* Cōgĕrĕt Āntĭnŏō, Prop.

Antĭŏchĭă, æ, f., *the capital of Syria.* Dĕdĭt Antĭŏchĭæ, Fann.

Antĭŏchŭs, ī, m., *the name of several Syrian kings.* Nĕc tămĕn Antĭŏchŭs, Juv.

Antĭŏpă, æ, *and* ē, ēs, f., *a nymph loved by Jupiter.* Tū līcĕt Antĭŏpæ, Prop.

Antĭphătēs, æ, m., *a king of the Læstrygons.* Quĭs nōn Antĭphătēn, Ov. EPITH. Crŭentŭs, trŭx, hŏrrendŭs, fĕrŭs.

|| antĭpŏdēs, ŭm, m. pl., *the inhabitants of any place on the earth directly opposite to ours.* Nōn hīc antĭpŏdăs, (Phal.) Sid.

antĭquārĭŭs, ī, or ă, æ, m., *one studious of antiquity.* Tĕnĕt antĭquārĭă vērsŭs, Juv.

antĭquĭtās, ātĭs, ˙f., *antiquity.* Antĭquĭtātēm, Rōmŭlō, (Iamb.) Prud.   SYN. Vĕtŭstās, sĕnectŭs.

antĭquĭtŭs, adv., *formerly.* Pŏsŭisse antĭquĭtŭs ūrbī, Sil.   SYN. Antīquē, quōn-dăm, ōlĭm, ălĭās.

* antīquo, ās, *to abolish.* Liv.   SYN. Abŏlĕo, rēscīndo, ĭrrĭto, ăbrŏgo.

antīquŭs, ă, ŭm, *ancient.* Hōspĭtĭs antīquī, Ov.   SYN. Prīscŭs, vĕtŭstŭs, lōngævŭs.

Antīssă, æ, f., *a city of Lesbos.* Antīssă Phărōsquĕ, Ov.

antīstĕs, ĭtĭs, m., *a chief priest or man.* Crātĕr antīstĭtĭs aūrō, Prop.   SYN. Săcerdōs, præsŭl, ĕpīscŏpŭs.   EPITH. Dīvīnŭs, săcĕr, cōnspĭcŭŭs, cāstŭs, pĭŭs, vĕnĕrāndŭs, vīttātŭs, īnfŭlātŭs.

antīstĭtă, æ, f., *a priestess.* Antīstĭtă nūmĭnĭs ārās, C. Sev.   EPITH. Sacră.

|| antīsto, ās, *to excel.* Antīstāre aūtĕm, Lucr.   SYN. Præsto.

|| antīthĕtŏn, ī, n., *a rhetorical figure.* Lĭbrăt ĭn antĭthĕtĭs, Pers.

Antĭŭm, ī, n., *a maritime town of Latium.* Quæ rēgĭs Antĭŭm, Hor.

antlĭă, æ, f., *a water-pump.* Antlĭă tōllĭt ăquās, Mart.

Antōnīnŭs, ī, m., *the name of several Roman emperors.* Antōnīnōrŭm nōmĕn, Cæs. Hadr.

Antōnĭŭs, ĭī, m., *the name of several Romans.* Antōnĭŭs ārmĭs, Virg.

antrŭm, ī, n., *a den.* Aspĭce ŭt antrŭm, Virg.   SYN. Spĕcŭs, căvernă, lŭstrŭm, spēluncă, spēlæŭm, lătebĭă, cryptă, fŏvĕă, fōssă.   EPITH. Opācŭm, cæcŭm, ōb-scūrŭm, vāstŭm, dēclīvĕ, cūrvŭm, ārcānŭm, cōncăvŭm, frōndōsŭm, cōnvēxŭm, ūmbrōsŭm, sĭnŭōsŭm, prŏfūndŭm, fŭrtīvŭm, ōccŭltŭm, hŏrrendŭm, căvernōsŭm, pĭcĕŭm, fūscŭm, mōntānŭm, stŭpendŭm, văcŭŭm, ăbdĭtŭm, căpāx, ĭnhōspĭtŭm, vĭrĭdĕ, gĕlĭdŭm, ēffōssŭm, rōrĭdŭm, nigrŭm, nigrāns, vĭrēns, sēcrētŭm, ūdŭm, mūscōsŭm, frīgēns, lătebrōsŭm, rōrāns, nĕmŏrōsŭm.

Ănūbĭs, ĭdĭs, m., *an Egyptian deity.* Pĕr Ănūbĭdĭs ōră, Ov.   EPITH. Vĕrendŭs, lātrātŏr, lātrāns.

ănŭlŭs.   V. Annulus.

ănŭs, ūs, f., *an old woman.* Ecce ănŭs, ĭn mĕdĭĭs, Ov.   SYN. Vĕtŭlă.   EPITH. Trĕmēns, mārcĭdă, sēdŭlă, frĭgĭdă, trīstĭs, rūgōsă, cūrvă, sēgnĭs, mōrbōsă, mŭl-tĭlŏquă, lānguĭdă, dēlīrāns, ēxsānguĭs, sōrdĭdă, pārcă, ārĭdă, dēfōrmĭs, vĭgĭl, sĕvĕră.   V. Senex.

ănŭs, ī, m., *the anus.* Tūrpēs ānŭm sī fōrtĕ păpĭllæ, Ser.   SYN. Pōdēx.

ānxĭĕtās, ātĭs, f., *anxiety.* Ănxĭĕtātĕ cărēns, Luc.   SYN. Cūră, sōllĭcĭtūdo.   EPITH. Trīstĭs, īnfōrmĭs, mōrdāx, mŏlestă, păvĭdă, grăvĭs, stĭmŭlāns, mōrdēns, rōdēns.   V. Cura.

|| ānxĭfĕr, ă, ŭm, *bringing trouble.* Anxĭfĕrās cūrās, Cic.

ānxĭŭs, ŭ, ŭm, *anxious, troubled.* Tĭmŏr ānxĭŭs ūrgĕt, Virg.   SYN. Ambĭgŭŭs, īncertŭs, dŭbĭŭs, ānceps, sōllĭcĭtŭs.   V. Sollicitus.

Ănxŭr, ŭrĭs, m. *and* n., *a maritime town of the Volscians.* Lātē cāndentĭbŭs Ănxŭr, Hor.

Ănxŭrŭs, ī, m., *a name of Jupiter.* Jŭpĭtĕr Ănxŭrŭs ārvĭs, Virg.

Ănȳgrŭs, *or* Ănīgrŭs, ī, m., *a river of Thessaly.* Fūndĭt Ănīgrŭs ăquās, Ov.

Ănȳtŭs, ī, m., *one of Socrates' accusers.* Pȳthăgŏrān, Ănȳtīquĕ, Hor.

Ăŏnĕs, ŭm, m. pl., *inhabitants of Aonia; Aonian, of Aonia.* Ăŏnăs ĭn mōntēs, Virg.

Ăŏnĭă, æ, f., *a part of Bœotia.* Ăŏnĭam, Eūbœāmquĕ, Stat.   V. Parnassus.

Ăŏnĭdēs, ŭm, f. pl., *the Muses.* Lūx rĕdĭt, Ăŏnĭdŭm, Mart.   V. Musæ.

Ăŏnĭŭs, ă, ŭm, *and* Ăŏnĭs, ĭdĭs, f., *Aonian.* Cūm lĕvĭs Ăŏnĭās, Ov.   Tellūs Ăŏnĭs, Stat.   SYN. Hĕlĭcōnĭŭs, Pĭĕrĭŭs, Cāstălĭŭs, Pērmessĭŭs.

|| ăpăgĕ, adv., *away, take away.* Dīxīsse, ăpăge hœc, Cat.

‖ ăpĕllă, æ, m., [sine pelle] *circumcised*. Jūdæŭs ăpĕllă, Hor.

Ăpĕllŭs, ĭs, m., *the famous Greek painter*. Cōŭs pīnxīssĕt Ăpĕllēs, Ov. EPITH. Insignĭs, clārŭs, inclўtŭs, mīrandŭs, fāmōsŭs, illūstrĭs, præclārŭs, nōbĭlĭs, pērĭtŭs, mīrābĭlĭs.

Ăpĕllĕŭs, ă, ŭm, *of Apelles*. Quālĭs Ăpĕllēĭs, Prop.

Ăpĕnnīnĭcŏlă, æ, m. f., *an inhabitant of the Apennines*. Ăpĕnnīnĭcŏlæ bĕllātŏr, Virg.

Ăpĕnnīnĭgĕnă, æ, m. f., *one born on the Apennines*. Ăpĕnnīnĭgĕnĭs cūltăs, Cl.

Ăpĕnnīnŭs, ī, m., *a mountain of Italy*. Căpŭt Ăpĕnnīnŭs, Sil. EPITH. Cĕlsŭs, nūbĭfĕr, gĕlĭdŭs, āĕrĭŭs, nīvālĭs, lŏngŭs, sāxōsŭs, frŏndēns, āspĕr. V. Mons.

ăpĕr, aprī, m., *a wild boar*. Trūx ăpĕr īnsĕquĭtŭr, Ov. SYN. Sūs. EPITH. Spūmĕŭs, mĭnāx, fūrĭbūndŭs, fūrēns, fĕrŭs, tŏrvŭs, fŭlvŭs, fŭlmĭnĕŭs, hīspĭdŭs, vĭŏlēntŭs, fĕrōx, trŭcŭlēntŭs, frēndēns, hīrsūtŭs, fĕrvĭdŭs, vūlnĭfĭcŭs, sānguĭnĕŭs, sōrdĭdŭs, dēntātŭs, hīrtŭs, sētĭgĕr, sētōsŭs, crŭēntŭs, hŏrrĭdŭs, prŏtĕrvŭs, aŭdāx, īmpăvĭdŭs, spūmōsŭs, vāstātŏr, frĕmēns, răbĭdŭs, īnglŭvĭōsŭs, ācĕr, spūmāns, Arcădĭcŭs, Mœnălĭŭs, Mārsŭs.

ăpĕrĭo, īs, ăpĕrŭĭ, pĕrtŭm, *to open*. Īntĕr flūctŭs ăpĕrĭt, Virg. SYN. Pāndo, ēxplĭco, rĕsĕro, reclūdo, rĕtĕgo.

ăpĕrtē, adv., *openly*. Vĕl ăpĕrtē tūtŭs ămărē, Ov. SYN. Pălăm, mănĭfēstē. V. Palam, Ingenue.

ăpĕrtŭs, ă, ŭm, *open*. Īn ăpĕrtă pĕrĭcŭlă, Virg. SYN. Reclūsŭs, rĕsĕrātŭs, pătēns.

ăpēs, *or* ăpĭs, ĭs; ăpēs, ŭm *or* ĭŭm, f., *a bee; bees*. Īnnātŭs ăpēs ămŏr, Virg. EPITH. Mēllĭfĕræ, sĕdŭlæ, flōrĭgĕræ, fŭgăcēs, īngĕnĭōsæ, mēllĭflŭæ, cāstæ, vĭgĭlēs, sōllĭcĭtæ, īnnūbæ, mēllĭtæ, văgæ, pērvĭgĭlēs, pārvæ, grăcĭlēs, īndūstrĭæ, Attĭcæ, Cecrōpĭæ, Hÿblææ.

ăpēx, ĭcĭs, m., *a cap of a conic form; the top*. Jāmquĕ vŏlāns ăpĭcĕm, Virg. SYN. Fāstĭgĭŭm, vērtēx, căcūmĕn, cūlmĕn. EPITH. Āltŭs, ēxcēlsŭs, ārdŭŭs, ăpĕrtŭs, sūmmŭs, sŭpĕrbŭs, cēlsŭs, sūblīmĭs.

Ăphărēĭŭs, ă, ŭm, *of Aphareus*. Prōlēs Ăphărēĭă Lÿncēŭs, Ov.

Ăphăreŭs, ĕŏs, ĕĭ *or* eī, m., *a centaur slain by Theseus*. Ūltŏr ădēst Ăphăreŭs, Ov.

Ăphīdās, æ, m., *the name of a man*. Īnēxpērrēctŭs Ăphīdās, Ov.

Ăphīdnŭs, ī, m, *the name of a warrior*. Tŭm stĕrnĭt Ăphīdnŭm, Virg.

Ăphrŏdītă, æ, f., *a name of Venus*. Nāmque Ăphrŏdītă cŏmēs, Aus.

‖ āphrŏnĭtrŭm, ī, n., *saltpetre*. Dīcŏr ĕt āphrŏnĭtrŭm, Mart.

‖ ăpĭărĭŭs, ă, ŭm, *who keeps bees*. Sērvāns ăpĭārĭŭs āgmĕn, Sil.

ăpĭcātŭs, ă, ŭm, *tufted*. Cōnjŭx ăpĭcātĭ, Ov.

Ăpĭcĭŭs, ĭī, m., *a famous Roman glutton*. Vĕllĕt Ăpĭcĭŭs ūtĭ, Mart. EPITH. Dīvēs, hēllŭo, gŭlōsŭs.

ăpĭcŭlă, æ, f., *diminut. of* apis. Haŭrĭt ăpĭcŭlă, quæ tē, (Scal.) Plaut.

Ăpĭdănŭs, ī, m., *a river of Thessaly, which falls into the Peneus*. Mūltă quŏque Ăpĭdănĭ, Ov.

Ăpĭs, ĭs *and* ĭdĭs, m., *an Egyptian deity*. Cōrnĭgĕr Ăpĭs ĕăt, Ov. EPITH. Săcĕr, Ægÿptĭŭs, Mēmphītĭcŭs. V. Osiris.

‖ ăpīscŏr, *to obtain*. Prægēstĭt ăpīscī, Cat.

ăpĭŭm, ĭī, n., *parsley*. Ēt vĭrĭdēs ăpĭŏ rīpæ, Virg. EPITH. Ămārŭm, vĭrĭdĕ, vĭrēns, vīvāx, ūdŭm, vĭrĭdāns.

aplūstrĕ, ĭs, n., [plur. tră, trĭă,] *gr* āmplūstrĕ, *a ship ornament*. Quærĕrĕ ăplūstră, Cic. Trānquīllŭs ăplūstrĭă flātŭs, Rut. Āmplūstrĕ, Juv.

Ăpōllĭnārĭs, ĕ, *and* ĕŭs, ă, ŭm, *of Apollo*. Aŭsŭs Ăpōllĭnĕŏs, Ov. SYN. Phœbēŭs.

Ăpōllo, ĭnĭs, m., *the god of light, poetry, music, eloquence, physic, and arts*. Fācĭātĭs Ăpōllĭnĕ cārmĕn, Ov. SYN. Phœbŭs, Cÿnthĭŭs, Dēlĭŭs, Pўthĭŭs, Tītān, Sōl. EPITH Arcĭtĕnēns, fōrmōsŭs, pūlchĕr, īntōnsŭs, fācūndŭs, fātĭdĭcŭs, vērĭdĭcŭs, cĭthărœdŭs, pūlchrĭcŏmŭs, laŭrĭgĕr, dōctŭs, crīnītŭs, aŭgŭr, rŏsĕŭs, fătĭcĭnŭs, dīvīnŭs, săgāx, sōlērs, ĕphēbŭs, mūsĭcŭs, mĕdĭcŭs, ŏpĭfĕr, Lātōnĭŭs; Dēlĭŭs, Cÿnthĭŭs, Clārĭŭs, Cÿrrhæŭs, Dēlphĭcŭs, Pătăræŭs, Lÿcĭŭs, Thÿmbræŭs, Smīnthæŭs, Chrÿsæŭs, Thērăpnæŭs, Grÿnæŭs, Hēlĭcōnĭŭs.

‖ ăpŏlŏgŭs, ī, m., *an apologue*. Ăpŏlŏgŏn aŭdĭ, (Iamb.)

Ăpōnŭs, ī, m., *a fountain near Padua*. Cōllĕ sĕdēns Ăpōnŭs, Lucan. EPITH. Călĭdŭs, sălūbrĭs, ămœnŭs.

|| ăpŏstătă, æ, m., *an apostate*. Nŭnc vīlīs ăpŏstătă fāctŭs, Sed.

|| ăpŏstătĭcŭs, ă, ŭm, *of an apostate*. Plēbīs ăpŏstătĭcæ, Sedul.

|| Āpŏstŏlī, ōrŭm, m. pl., *the twelve Apostles*. Dōctŏr Ăpŏstŏlŭs ōmnĕm, Prud

|| Ăpŏstŏlĭcŭs, ă, ŭm, *of an Apostle*. Ōrīs Ăpŏstŏlĭcī, Prud.

ăpŏthēcă, æ, f., *a storehouse, a cellar*. Aūt ăpŏthēcă prōcīs, Hor.

ăppărātŭs, ūs, m., *a preparation*. Ŏdī, pŭĕr, ăppărātŭs, (Sapph.) Hor. Epith. Sŭpērbŭs, māgnĭfĭcŭs.

ăppărĕo, ŭī, *to appear*. Appārēnt rārī nāntēs, Virg. Syn. Vĭdĕŏr, cōmpărĕo, ŏrĭŏr, ĕxŏrĭŏr, sūrgo, ēxsūrgo.

ăppărĭtŏr, ŏrĭs, m., *an apparitor*. Appărĭtōrēs sēd fŭrēntī, (Iamb.) Prud. Syn. Sătēllēs, līctŏr, stĭpātŏr. Epith. Clāmōsŭs, sævŭs, pēllītŭs, trūx, răbĭdŭs, rĭgĭdŭs.

ăppăro, ās, *to prepare*. Dăpēs ĭnēmptās ăppărĕt, Hor. Syn. Păro, cōmpăro, ŏrno, ădōrno, præpăro.

ăppēllo, ās, *to call*. Āsĭæ Brūtum ăppēllăt, Hor. Syn. Vŏco, nōmĭno, cōmpēllo ās. V. Voco.

ăppēllo, ĭs, pŭlī, pūlsŭm, *to drive to*. Nōstrīs Dĕŭs ăppŭlĭt ōrīs, Virg. Syn. Ădmŏvĕo, ăppĭco.

ăppēndīx, ĭcĭs, *and* ĭcŭlă, æ, (*diminut*.) f., *an appendage*. Cic. Epith. Pārvă, lĕvīs.

ăppēndo, ĭs, *to hang by*. Cic. Syn. Sŭspēndo, pŏndĕro.

ăppĕtītŭs, ă, ŭm, *the pass. partic. of* appeto. Syn. Pĕtītŭs, ēxpĕtītŭs, ŏptātŭs.

ăppĕto, tī, tītŭm, *to desire*. Appĕtăt īllă mĕōs, Tib. Syn. Cŭpĭo, ēxŏpto, ēxpĕto, pĕrōpto.

Appĭă, æ, f., [sub. via] *the Appian road*. Appĭă trītă rŏtīs, Ov.

Appĭăs, ădĭs, f.; Appĭădēs, ŭm, f. pl., *Venus, Pallas, Concord, Peace, and Vesta*. Appĭăs ĭpsă prŏbăt, Ov. Appĭădēsquĕ Dĕæ, Id.

ăppīngo, ĭs, *to paint*. Sylvīs ăppīngĭt, Hor.

Appĭŭs, ĭī *or* ī, m., *the name of a noble Roman family*. Appĭŭs, īngĕnŭō, Hor.

ăpplaūdo, *or* ăpplōdo, ĭs. Plaut. V. Plaudo.

ăpplaūsŭs, ūs, m., *a clashing, shock*. Tērrĭbĭle ăpplaūsū cīrcŭm, Stat.

ăpplĭcātŭs, *and* ĭtŭs, ă, ŭm, *the pass. partic. of* applico. Prōxĭmŭs ăpplĭcĭtō, Sil.

ăpplĭco, ās, ŭī, ĭtŭm, *to apply*. Immānĭbŭs ăpplĭcăt ōrīs? Virg. Syn. Jŭngo, ădjŭngo, āddo, āttĕxo, ādmŏvĕo.

ăpplōro, ās, *to lament to*. Quĕrēbăr ăpplōrāns tĭbi, Hor.

ăppōno, pŏsŭī, pŏsĭtŭm, *to put to, near*. Cāptăt, ĕt ăppōnĭt, Hor. Syn. Affīngo, āscrībo, jūngo, ădjŭngo, ādmŏvĕo, jūxtā pōno.

• ăppōrto, *to carry to*. Appōrtānt mōrbōs, Lucr.

ăppŏsĭtŭs, ă, ŭm, *the pass. partic. of* appono. Tē măgīs ăppŏsĭtīs, Hor.

Apprĕcŏr, ārĭs, *to pray to*. Dĕōs prĭŭs ăpprĕcātī, Hor.

ăpprĕhēndo, ăpprēndo, ĭs, *to take hold of*. Nĭsūsque ăpprēndĕrĕ prīmōs, Sil. Syn. Prĕhēndo, prēndo, cōmprēndo, căpĭo, ārrĭpĭo, ăccĭpĭo.

ăpprīmē, *or* mă, adv., *very much*. Flōs ăpprīmă tĕnāx, Virg.

ăpprŏbo, ās, *to approve*. Cŭpīs ăpprŏbārĕ cūnctīs, (Phal.) Mart. Syn. Prŏbo, cōmprŏbo, ānnŭo.

ăpprŏpĕro, ās, *to hasten*. Apprŏpĕrēmŭs, ŭt hŏstīs, Sil. Syn. Prŏpĕro, fēstīno, cĕlĕro, ăccĕlĕro, ādvŏlo, cūrro, mātūro, ăccēdo, grădum ūrgĕo. V. Propero.

• ăpprŏpīnquo, ās, *to approach near*. Cic. Syn. Prŏpīnquo, ăccēdo, ādvēnto. V. Advento.

Aprēs, æ, m., *the name of a warrior*. Jăm saūcĭŭs Aprēn, Virg.

aprĭcŏr, ārĭs, *to bask in the sun*. Ăprīcāntŭr, hŭmŭs, Mant.

aprīcŭs, ă, ŭm, *sunny*. Immīttĭt ăprīcīs, Virg. Dūcĕrĕt ăprīcīs, Id.

Aprīlīs, ĭs, m., *the fourth month*. Ăprīlĕm mĕmŏrănt, Ov.

aprīnŭs, *or* ūgnŭs, ă, ŭm, *of a boar*. Vīscŭs ăprūgnŭm, Lucil.

āpsīs, ĭdĭs. V. Absis.

āptē, adv., *rightly*. Sēmpĕr ĭn hīs āptē, Ov.

āpto, ās, *to make fit*. Āptăt ăd ārmă mănŭs, Ov. Syn. Accŏmmŏdo, cōmpōno, ădāpto, *or* īnstrŭo, ŏrno, păro.

āptŭs, ă, ŭm, *fit*. Naūtīs āptŭs, nōn āptŭs ămāntī, Ov. Syn. Accŏmmŏdātŭs, ăppŏsĭtŭs, cōnvĕnĭēns, cōngrŭēns, cōngrŭŭs, cōnnĕxŭs, cŏhærēns; cōmmŏdŭs, ĭdŏnĕŭs; ōrnātŭs.

ăpŭd, prep., *at.* Cœnās ăpŭd ōmnēs, nūllŭs ăpŭd tē, Mart. Syn. Pĕnĕs, jŭxtā, ĭn.

Apŭlĭă, *or* Appŭlĭă, æ, f., *a part of the kingdom of Naples.* Mōntēs Apŭlĭă nŏtōs, Hor. Epith. Siccă, sĭtĭēns, sĭtĭcŭlōsă.

Apŭlŭs, *or* Appŭlŭs, ă, ŭm, *of Appulia.* Lūcānŭs ăn Apŭlŭs, Hor. || ăpỹrĭnă, ōrŭm, n. pl., *which have no kernel.* Mīttūntŭr ăpỹrĭnă rāmīs, Mart.

ăquă, æ, f., *water.* Quærĭt ăquās ĭn ăquīs, Ov. Syn. Lỹmphă, ūndă, lătēx, hūmŏr, liquŏr, flūmĕn, rīvŭs, flŭvĭŭs, fōns. Epith. Dŭlcĭs, tōrrēns, flŭvĭālĭs, sălĭēns, fōntānă, strĕpēns, æquŏrĕă, prŏpĕrāns, cănōră, vīvă, clără, ămœnă, plăcĭdă, frīgĭdă, gĕlĭdă, flŭēns, liquĭdă, cœnōsă, lŭtōsă, cōrrūptă, dēsĕs, quĭĕtă, pūră, īmmōtă, jăcēns, līmōsă, pălūstrĭs, īrrĭgŭă, lĭmpĭdă, sŏnŏră, prōsĭlĭēns, stăgnāns, răpĭdă, plŭvĭālĭs. V. Lympha, unda.

ăquālĭcŭlŭs, ī, m., *the paunch.* Pīnguĭs ăquālĭcŭlŭs, Pers. Syn. Alvŭs, vēntĕr.

ăquālĭs, ĭs, m., *a ewer.* Quŏque ăquālĭbŭs ūnŭm, Fil. Syn. Pōcŭlŭm, vās.

ăquārĭŭs, ĭī, m., *a waterman.* Vĕnĭēt cōndūctŭs ăquārĭŭs, Juv.—2. *one of the signs in the zodiac.* Vīcīnŭs Ăquārĭŭs ūrgĕt, Man. Syn. Undĕcĭmŭm sīgnŭm, Gănỹmēdēs, ūrnĭgĕr. Epith. Frīgĭdŭs, hūmĭdŭs, rădĭāns, liquēns, gĕlĭdŭs, īrrĭgŭŭs, ūdŭs, trīstĭs, ūrnĭgĕr, nīmbĭfĕr, nīmbōsŭs, plŭvĭōsŭs, hūmēns, frīgēns, pūlchĕr, flŭvĭālĭs.

ăquătĭcŭs, ă, ŭm, *of the water.* Sōlvĭt ăquătĭcŭs Aŭstĕr, Ov.

ăquătĭlĭs, ĕ, *born in the water.* Incŏlāsque ăquătĭlēs, (Iamb.) Prud.

ăquātŏr, ōrĭs, m., *who fetches water.* Indŭs ăquātŏr Ibērŭm, Sil.

ăquĭlă, æ, f., *an eagle.* Ăquĭlă vĕnĭēntĕ, Virg. Syn. Jŏvĭs ārmĭgĕr ālĕs, Jŏvĭs ālĕs ădūncŭs. Epith. Rĕgĭă, præpĕs, fĕrōx, flāmmĭgĕră, fŭlvă, ăltĭvŏlāns, sūblīmĭs, rēgālĭs, prædātrīx, ădūncă, vēnātrīx, bēllātrīx, vēlōx, nūbĭvăgă, gĕnĕrōsă, īmpăvĭdă, cĕlĕrĭs, præcĕps, āĕrĭă, cĭtă, māgnănĭmă.

Aquĭlă Rōmānă, *the Roman banner.* Rōmānæ āccēdūnt ăquĭlæ, Lucan. Epith. Mărtĭă, tērrĭbĭlĭs.

ăquĭlēgĭă, æ, f., *the flower columbine.* Sŭōs ăquĭlēgĭă flōrēs, Rap.

ăquĭlēx, ēgĭs, m., *a conduit-maker.* Ipse ăquĭlēx, cæcīs, Mil. Epith. Dēxtĕr, sōlērs.

ăquĭlīnŭs, ă, ŭm, *of an eagle.* Ĕt ăquĭlīnīs ūngŭlīs, (Iamb.) Plaut. Syn. Uncŭs, ădūncŭs, rĕcūrvŭs.

Aquĭlo, ōnĭs, m., *the north wind.* Māgnīs Aquĭlōnĭbŭs īmbrĕm, Virg. Syn. Bŏrĕās. Epith. Nĭvālĭs, nūbĭlŭs, ĭnĭquŭs, rĭgĭdŭs, sĕrēnĭfĕr, gĕlĭdŭs, glăcĭālĭs, sŏnōrŭs, ālgēns, tērrĭbĭlĭs, mĭnāx, prŏcēllōsŭs, Gĕtĭcŭs, Thrĕĭcĭŭs, Rĭphæŭs, Scỹthĭcŭs, Bŏrĕālĭs, sævŭs, raŭcŭs, ăcūtŭs, hōrrĭfĕr, nĭvōsŭs, īnsānŭs, præcēps, ēffrœnŭs, sălūtĭfĕr, pūrŭs, pēstĭfŭgă. V. Ventus.

Aquĭlōnĭgĕnæ, ārŭm, m. pl., *northern nations.* Aquĭlōnĭgĕnāsque Brĭtānnōs, Aus.

Aquĭlōnĭŭs, ă, ŭm, *of the north wind.* Aquĭlōnĭă prōlēs, Sil.

Aquīnās, ātĭs, m., *of Aquinum.* Nēscĭt Aquīnātĕm, Hor.

Aquīnŭm, ī, n., *a city of Latium, the native place of Juvenal.* Prŏpĕrāntēm rēddĕt Aquīnō, Juv.

Aquĭtānĭă, æ, f., *part of ancient Gaul.* Grĕmĭōque Aquĭtānĭă lātō, Aus.

Aquĭtānĭcŭs, *or* ĭtānŭs, ă, ŭm, *of Aquitania.* Hūnc fŏre Aquĭtānăs, Tib.

ăquŏr, ārĭs, *to fetch or draw water.* Ūrbĭs ăquēntŭr, Virg. Syn. Aquam haŭrĭo, trăho, ēxtrăho; ădăquo; ăd ăquām dūco; pōtŭm dūco; ăquās mĭnĭstro, præbĕo; flŭvĭōs mĭnĭstro.

ăquōsŭs, ă, ŭm, *watery.* Ĕt ăquōsŭs Ōrīōn, Virg. Syn. Hūmĭdŭs, plŭvĭŭs.

āră, æ, f., *an altar.* Ără cŏrōnĭs, Ov. Syn. Āltărĕ, fŏcŭs. Epith. Sŏlēnnĭs, pīnguĭs, flăgrāns, fūmōsă, fŭlgēns, vĕnĕrăbĭlĭs, māgnĭfĭcă, splēndĭdă, ĭnvĭŏlābĭlĭs, sānctă, sacră, pĭă, mărmŏrĕă, ŏdōră, frăgrāns, fūmāns, ērēctă, rŭtĭlă, fēstă, vōtīvă, thūrĭcrĕmă, thūrĭfĕră, sacrĭfĭcă, ārdēns, cŏrōnātă. V. Sacrifico, Victima.

Āræ, ārŭm, f. pl., *three rocky islands near Sicily.* In flŭctĭbŭs, Ārās, Virg.

Ărăbĭă, æ, f., *a part of Asia.* Tē trĕmĭt Ărăbĭæ, Prop. Syn. Pānchăĭă. Epith. Dīvĕs, thūrĭfĕră, pālmĭfĕră; sāxōsă, dēsērtă, fēlīx.

Ărăbĭcŭs *or* Ărăbĭŭs, *or* Ărăbŭs, ă. ŭm, *of Arabia.* Nēc sī qua Ărăbĭō, Prop. Nōn Ărăbō nōstĕr rŏrĕ, Ov. Syn. Pānchæŭs, Săbæŭs, Năthăbæŭs, Pānchăĭŭs, Pānchăĭcŭs.

|| ărābĭllĭs, ĕ, *arable.*

Ārābs, ăbĭs, m., Ārăbēs, ŭm, m. pl., *an Arabian.* Ōmnĭs Ārăbs, Virg. Thūrĭlĕgŏs Ārăbĕs, Ov. Syn. Săbœī. Epith. Mōllēs, ŏdōrātī, pīctī, pālmĭfĕrī, gĕmmĭfĕrī, bārbărī, eōī, dītēs, nigrī, ŏpŭlēntī, ēxtrēmī, fēlīcēs, rĕmōtī, mitrātī. V. Arabia.

Arāchnē, ēs, f., *daughter of Idmon, changed into a spider by Minerva.* Intēndĭt Arāchnēs, Ov. Epith. Ŏpĕrōsă, sōlērs, aūdāx, ănĭmōsă, sŭpērbă, dōctă, Mœŏnĭă, Lӯdă, Lӯdĭă, pĕrĭtă, ămbĭtĭōsă.

ărānĕă, æ, f., *and* ĕŭs, ī, m., *a spider.* Sŭspēndĭt ărānĕă cāssēs, Virg. Nēc cīmēx nĕque ărānĕŭs, Cat. Epith. Văgă, pēndŭlă, sŭblīmĭs, dōctă, ārĭdă, īngĕnĭōsă, ārtĭfēx, ēxĭlĭs, vĕnēnĭfĕră, īndūstrĭă, sŭbdŏlă, ăĕrĭă, sŭspēnsă, pēndēns, tūrpĭs, vĭgĭl, stŭdĭōsă, tŭmĭdă, ŏpĭfēx, pērvĭgĭl. V. Arachne.

ărānĕŏlŭs, ī, m., *a little spider.* Atque ŭt ărānĕŏlī, Virg.

ărānĕōsŭs, ă, ŭm, *full of spider-webs.* Arānĕōsō tūrpĭs, (Iamb.) Cat.

Ărăr, *or* Ărărĭs, ĭs, m., *a river of Gaul.* Aŭt Ărārīm Pārthŭs, Virg. Epith. Sēgnĭs, lēnĭs, tăcĭtŭs, pĭgĕr, tārdŭs, lēntŭs, lōngīnquŭs, fĕrāx, Gāllŭs.

ărātŏr, ōrĭs, m., *a husbandman.* Cūrvŭs ărātŏr, Virg. Syn. Cŏlōnŭs, āgrĭcŏlă, rūrĭcŏlă, rūstĭcŭs, agrēstĭs, cūltŏr ăgēllī, vīllĭcŭs. V. Agricola, Rusticus.

ărātrŭm, ī, n., *a plough.* Āspĭce, ărātră jŭgō, Virg. Syn. Vōmĕr. Epith. Flēxŭm, īncūrvŭm, dēprēssŭm, ōblĭquŭm, ūncŭm, vălĭdŭm, trāctăbĭlĕ, mōrdāx, fērrĕŭm, ūtĭlĕ, ădūncŭm, dūrŭm, prēssŭm, rūstĭcŭm, sōrdĭdŭm. V. Aro.

Arātŭs, ī, m., *a Greek poet and astronomer.* Sēmpĕr Arātŭs ĕrĭt, Ov. Epith. Dōctŭs, săgāx, āstrŏlŏgŭs, āstrĭlŏquŭs.

Arāxēs, ĭs, m., *a river of Armenia.* Indīgnātŭs Arāxēs, Virg. Epith. Bārbărŭs, Armĕnĭŭs, gĕlĭdŭs, văgŭs, īmplācātŭs, răpĭdŭs, nĭvĕŭs, flŭĭtāns, Scӯthĭcŭs, Mēdŭs, fĕrŭs. V. Fluvius.

ārbĭtĕr, itrī, m., *an arbitrator.* Ārbĭtĕr ēs fōrmæ, Ov. Syn. Jūdēx. Epith. Æquŭs, jūstŭs, ămīcŭs, sĕvĕrŭs, ĭnīquŭs, īnjūstŭs. V. Judex.

Ārbĭtrără, æ, f., *a female witness.* Nōn īnfĭdēlēs ārbĭtræ, Hor.

ārbĭtrărĭŭs, ă, ŭm, *arbitrary.* Haŭd ārbĭtrărĭō, (Iamb.) Pl.

ārbitrĭŭm, ĭī, n., *judgment, will.* Pĕnēs ārbĭtrĭŭm ēst, Hor. Syn. Vŏlūntās, jūdĭcĭŭm, sēntēntĭă. Epith. Æquŭm, jūstŭm, ĭnīquŭm, īnjūstŭm, ămīcŭm, sĕvĕrŭm.

ārbitrŏr, ărĭs, *to judge.* Ārbītrābĕrĕ dīvōs, Sil. Syn. Pŭtō, jūdĭco, cēnsĕo, sēntĭo, crēdo, ēxīstĭmo.

ārbŏr, *and* ārbōs, ŏrĭs, f., *a tree.* Āltĭŭs ārbŏr ăgĭt, Ov. Syn. Ārbūstŭm, vīrgūltŭm, rāmŭs, frōndēs. Epith. Sӯlvēstrĭs, ūmbrōsă, ŏpācă, pătŭlă, frūctĭfĕră, frōndēns, flōrēns, vĭrēns, fērtĭlĭs, fĕrāx, fŏlĭātă, āltă, prōcĕră, rāmōsă, āltĭcŏmă, ārdŭă, vĭrĭdĭs, rĭgĭdă, fœtă, cūrvātă, nōbĭlĭs, ŏdōrĭfĕră, vīrēscēns, cūltă, īncūltă, ămbĭtĭōsă, cēlsă, rēdĭvīvă, frūctŭōsă, ămœnă, lūxŭrĭōsă, ānnōsă, cădūcă.

|| ārbŏrētŭm, ī, n., *a plantation of trees.* Sen. Syn. Ārbūstŭm.

ārbŏrĕŭs, ă, ŭm, *of a tree.* Ārbŏrĕī fœtŭs, Virg.

ārbūscŭlă, æ, f., *a shrub.* Explōsa ārbūscŭlă dīxĭt, Hor.

ārbūstŭm, ī, n., *an orchard ; shrub.* Nōn ōmnēs ārbūstă jŭvānt, Virg. Syn. Frŭtēx, vīrgūltŭm. Epith. Lætŭm, ūmbrāns, ōrnātŭm, frūctĭfĕrŭm, vĭrēns, frōndōsŭm, vĭrĭdĕ, dēnsŭm, ŏpācŭm, ūmbrĭfĕrŭm, frōndēns, grātŭm, ămœnŭm, tĕnĕrŭm, vērnŭm, tūrgēscēns, sӯlvēstrĕ, frŭtĭcōsŭm, ūmbrōsŭm.

ārbŭtĕŭs, ă, ŭm, *of the strawberry-tree.* Ārbŭtēĭs tēxŭnt, Virg.

ārbŭtŭm, ī, n., *the fruit of the strawberry-tree.* Dănt ārbŭtă sӯlvæ, Virg.

ārbŭtŭs, ī, f., *a kind of strawberry-tree.* Ārbŭtŭs, ēt lēntæ, Ov. Syn. Vĭrĭdĭs, hōrrĭdă, fœcūndă, ŏpācă, ūmbrōsă, ūmbrĭfĕră, vĭrĭdāns, pătŭlă, sŭpērbă, plēnă, văcŭă, claūsă, ăpērtă, lĭgnĕă, aūrātă, dīvēs, căpāx, pīctă, rĕfērtă.

ārcă, æ, f., *a chest.* Nūllŭs ĭn ārcă, Juv. Syn. Ārcŭlă, căpsă, căpsŭlă, scrīnĭŭm. Epith. Ærātă, fērrātă, lĭgnĕă, aūrātă, pīctă, sŭpērbă, dīvēs, pătŭlă, căpāx, rĕfērtă, plēnă, văcŭă, claūsă, ăpērtă.

Arcădĭă, æ, f., *a country of the Morea.* Prōtĭnŭs Arcădĭæ, Virg. Syn. Tēllŭs Ērӯmānthĭdŏs ūrsæ ; tēllūs Mænălĭă, Nōnācrĭă ; Mænălĭs ōră ; Pārrhăsĭs ōră.

Arcăs, ădĭs *or* ădŏs, m., *Arcadian,* and Arcădēs, ŭm, m. pl., *Arcadians.* Arcăs ĕquēs, Virg. Arcădēs āmbo, Virg. Syn. Arcădĭī, Arcădĭcī, Mænălĭī, Lӯcæī, Pārrhăsĭī. V. Arcadius. Epith. Vĕtĕrēs, āntīquī.

Arcădĭcŭs, *and* ĭŭs, ă, ŭm, *of Arcadia.* Arcădĭcō jŭvēnī, Juv. Arcădĭo īnfēlīx,

Virg. Syn. Mænăllŭs, Lўcæŭs, Nōnăcrĭnŭs, Nōnăcrĭŭs, Cўllēnæŭs, Pārrhăsĭŭs, Tĕgĕæŭs, Clĕōnæŭs, Ērўmănthæŭs. V. Arcadia.

ărcănŭm, ĭ, n., *a secret.* Fātōrum ārcănă mŏvēbo, Virg.

ărcānŭs, ă, ŭm, *secret.* Ūt ārcānās pŏssĭm, Ov. Syn. Sēcrētŭs, ŏccŭltŭs. ābdĭtŭs, ābscōndĭtŭs, lătēns, ābstrūsŭs, ŏpērtŭs, rĕcōndĭtŭs, lătĭtāns. V. Abditus.

Arcēns, ēntĭs, m., *the name of a man.* Arcēntĭs fīlĭŭs ărmĭs, Virg.

ārcĕo, cŭī, *to keep off.* Arcēbāt lōngē, Virg. Syn. Abārcĕo, āmŏvĕo, āvērtⁿ, prŏhĭbĕo, ēxpēllo.

Arcĕsĭlās, æ, m., *a Greek philosopher.* Essĕ quŏd Arcĕsĭlās, Pers.

Arcēsĭŭs, ĭī, m., *the father of Laertes.* Arcēsĭŭs ĭllī, Ov.

ārcēssītŭs, ŭ, ŭm, *the pass. partic. of* arcesso. Arcēssītŭs ŏrĭt, Prop.

ārcēsso, ĭs, ĭvī, ītŭm, *to send for.* Arcēssĕrĕ vītās, Virg. Syn. Vŏco, ādvŏco, āccĭo, āccūso.

|| ārchāngĕlŭs, ĭ, m., *an archangel.* Sūmmŭsque ārchāngĕlŭs ĭllĕ, Alcim.

Archĕtĭŭs, ĭī, m., *the name of a warrior.* Archĕtĭŭm Mnēstheŭs, Virg.

|| ārchĕtўpŭs, ă, ŭm, *original.* Archĕtўpŭm Mўŏs ārgēntŭm, Mart. Syn. Exēmplăr.

Archĭăcŭs, ă, ŭm, *of Archias.* Sī pŏtĕs Archĭăcĭs, Hor.

Archĭgĕnēs, ĭs, m., *a physician.* Ādvŏcăt Archĭgĕnēn, Juv.

Archĭlŏchŭs, ĭ, m., *a Greek poet.* Archĭlŏchī, nōn rēs, Hor. Epith. Spārtănŭs, ōbscœnŭs, ĭmmōrtālĭs.

ārchĭmăgīrŭs, ĭ, m., *the master-cook.* Lībrărĭŭs Archĭmăgīrī, Juv. Syn. Cŏquōrŭm prīncēps.

Archĭmēdēs, ĭs, m., *the Syracusan geometrician.* Epith. Sўrācŭsĭŭs, dōctŭs, cĕlĕbĕr, Ingĕnĭōsŭs, săgāx, sōlĕrs, mīrābĭlĭs, īllŭstrĭs, sōllĭcĭtŭs, pŏtēns, Industrĭŭs.

Archīppŭs, ĭ, m., *a king of Italy.* Archīppī rēgīs mīssū, Virg.

ārchĭtēctŭs, ĭ, m., *an architect.* Vĕl ārchĭtēctŭm, (Phal.) Mart. Syn. Archĭtēctōn, măchĭnātŏr.

Archўtās, æ, m., *a Pythagorean philosopher.* Mĕ crĕăt Archўtæ sŏbŏlēs, Pr. Epith. Tărēntīnŭs, dōctŭs, sōlĕrs.

ārcĭpŏtēns, *and* ārcĭtĕnēns, ēntĭs, *epithets of Apollo.* Arcĭpŏtēns, ādvērtĕ, prĕcŏr, Val. Fl. Quăm pĭŭs ārcĭtĕnēns, Virg. V. Apollo.

ārctē, adv., *narrowly.* Arctĭŭs ātque hĕdĕrā, Hor.

ārctĭcŭs, ă, ŭm, *arctic.* Arctĭcŭs ēst, Ov. Syn. Arctōŭs, Hўpērbŏrĕŭs, Bŏrĕālĭs, Āquĭlōnĭŭs, glăcĭālĭs ; Scўthĭcŭs, Thrācĭŭs, Sīthōnĭŭs, Strўmŏnĭŭs, Cāspĭŭs.

ārcto, ās, *to strain.* Hōs ĕmĕ, quŏs ārctăt, Mart. Syn. Strīngo, cōnstrīngo, cŏārcto, cōmprĭmo.

Arctŏphўlāx, ăcĭs, m., *a constellation.* Nĭtĕt Arctŏphўlāx, īdēmquĕ, Cic. Syn. Bŏōtēs, Arctūrŭs. Epith. Glăcĭālĭs, tārdŭs, pĭgĕr, trīstĭs, rĭgēns, fĕrŭs, frīgēns, frĭgĭdŭs, Scўthĭcŭs, Thrācĭŭs. V. Arcticus, Arctos.

Arctŏs *or* ŭs, ĭ, f., *two constellations near the north pole.* Pārrhăsĭs Arctŏs ĕrăt, Ov. Syn. Ūrsă, Pārrhăsĭs, Hĕlĭcē, Plaŭstrŭm. Epith. Ērўmănthĭs, Mænălĭă, Mænălĭs, Lўcăōnĭă, frĭgēns, gĕlĭdă, ŏpācă, glăcĭālĭs, frŏmēns, vēntōsă, Sīthōnĭă, Scўthĭcă, prŭīnōsă, æthĕrĕă, ālgēns, hўbērnă. V. Arcticus, Ursa.

ārctōŭs, ă, ŭm, *arctic.* Sōlĭbŭs ārctōĭs, Mart. V. Arcticus.

Arctūrŭs, ĭ, m., *a star.* Arctūrī sīdĕră nōbīs, Virg. Syn. Arctŏphўlāx.

ārctŭs, ă, ŭm, *close.* Arctīs cōmpāgĭbŭs hærēnt, Sant. Syn. Angūstŭs, cōntrăctŭs, strīctŭs, cōnstrīctŭs, cōmprēssŭs, ārctātŭs.

ārcŭlă, æ, f., *a small chest.* Arcŭlă sўnthēsĭbŭs, Mart.

ārcŭs, ūs, m., *a bow.* Tōrquēntŭr ĭn ārcŭs, Virg. Syn. Cōrnū, nērvŭs. Epith. Lēthĭfĕr, ĭncērtŭs, cōrnĕŭs, sĭnŭātŭs, ădŭncŭs, flēxĭbĭlĭs, Inīquŭs, tēnsŭs, dŭbĭŭs, hōrrĭsŏnŭs, fūlgēns, lēntŭs, flēxĭlĭs, cūrvŭs, Cўdōnĭŭs, Gōrtўnĭŭs, Lўcĭŭs, Achæmēnĭŭs, Ārmĕnĭŭs, sŏnōrŭs, bēllĭgĕr, săgīttĭfĕr, aūrātŭs, Apōllĭnĕŭs, Hērcŭlĕŭs, ĕbūrnŭs, rĭgĭdŭs, nŏxĭŭs.—2. *to stretch a bow.* Arcŭm cōntēndĕrĕ, Intēndĕrĕ, āddūcĕrĕ, sĭnŭārĕ, cūrvārĕ, flēctĕrĕ, Incūrvārĕ. Arcŭm ŏppŏsĭtō flēctĕrĕ nērvō. Vălĭdīs Inflēctĕrĕ vīrĭbŭs ārcŭm. Arcŭm ŏppŏsĭtō cūrvārĕ gĕnū.—3. *to shoot an arrow.* Arcŭ, nērvō, cōrnū, spīcŭlă, *vel* săgīttās, călămōs, tēlă, mīttĕrĕ, tōrquĕrĕ, dīrĭgĕrĕ, Impēllĕrĕ, cōntōrquĕrĕ.

ārcŭs cœlēstĭs, *the rainbow.* Cōmplēctĭtŭr āĕră gўrō Arcŭs. Syn. Irĭs. Epith. Pīctŭs, plŭvĭŭs, nūbĭlŭs, ĭmbrĭfĕr, pūrpŭrĕŭs, mūltĭcŏlŏr. V. Iris.

ārdĕă, æ, f., *a heron.* Dēplăngĭtŭr ārdĕă pĕnnĭs, Ov. Epith. Tĕnŭĭs, āĕrĭă, āltĭvŏlāns.—2. *an old town of the Rutuli.* Ardĕă sōlstĭtĭŏ, Mart.
ūrdĕllĭo, ōnĭs, m., *a busybody.* Ardĕllĭōnĕ sĕnĕ, Mart.
ārdĕo, ārsī, ārsŭm, *to burn.* Mĕssĭbŭs ārdĕt ăgĕr, Ov. Syn. Crĕmŏr, īncĕndŏr, āccĕndŏr, īnflāmmŏr, flăgro, cōnflāgro, ārdēsco, ēxārdēsco, ŭrŏr, fērvĕo, æstŭŏ, īncāndēsco ; cŭpĭo, dēsīdĕro, ōpto, ēxōpto, āppĕto ; dēpĕrĕo, ămo ; fūlgĕo, splēndĕo, mĭco, splēndēsco.
ārdēsco, ĭs, *the frequentat. of* ardeo. Ardēscītquĕ tŭēndo, Virg. V. Ardeo.
ārdŏr, ōrĭs, m., *a great heat.* Sĭmŭl ārdŏr hăbĕt, Virg. Syn. Æstŭs, călŏr fērvŏr ; ămŏr, dēsīdĕrĭŭm, cŭpīdo. Epith. Flāmmĕŭs, tūrbĭdŭs, Vŭlcānĭŭs, ănhēlŭs, rădĭāns, nŏcŭŭs, æstīvŭs, sĭtĭbūndŭs, fērvĭdŭs, nĭmĭŭs, tōrrēns, fērvēscēns, ūrēns, vĕhĕmēns, sēgnĭs, ĭnērs, īgnāvŭs, rĕpēntīnŭs, dēsĕs, mōrbōsŭs, sōlārĭs, nātīvŭs. V. Calor.
ārdŭŭs, ă, ŭm, *high, difficult.* Ardŭŭs ārmātōs, Virg. Syn. Cēlsŭs, ēxcēlsŭs, sūblīmĭs, āltŭs, dĭffĭcĭlĭs, mŏlēstŭs.
ārĕă, æ, f., *a barn-floor, yard.* Pălĕă tĕrĕt ārĕă cūlmōs, Virg. Syn. Plătĕă. Epith. Lātă, pătēns, brĕvĭs, spătĭōsă, ĭnānĭs, văcŭă, căpāx, măgnă, āmplă, trītĭcĕă.
ārĕfăcĭo, fēcī, *to dry.* Et făcĭt ārĕ, Lucr. Syn. Sīcco, ēxsīcco.
ărēnă, *and* ŭlă, æ, f., *sand, shore.* Dēdŭcĭt ărēnā, Virg. Syn. Săbŭlŭm, līttŭs, cāmpŭs. Epith. Stĕrĭlĭs, fūlvă, flāvēns. grăcĭlĭs, līttŏrĕă, flūmĭnĕă, æquŏrĕă, mōbĭlĭs, mărīnă, āttrītă, līmōsă, mōllĭs, gĕlĭdă, hūmēns, pūlvĕrĕă, ūdă, mădēns, mădĭdă, Lĭbўcă, ārdēns, sīccă, ărĭdă, tōstă, ărēns, tōrrĭdă.
|| ărēnĭvăgŭs, ă, ŭm, *wandering through sands.* Vĭdĭt ărēnĭvăgŭm, Luc.
ărēnōsŭs, ă, ŭm, *sandy.* Līttŭs ărēnōsŭm, Virg. Syn. Ărēnĭs tēctŭs, ōbdūctŭs, crēbĕr.
ārĕo, ēs, ārŭī, *to be dry.* Tāntălŭs ārĕt ăquā, Ov. Syn. Ārēsco, ārĕfīo, sĭccor, ēxsīccor, mārcēsco.
ārĕŏlă, æ, f., *the diminut. of* area. Tĕr cĭrcum ārĕŏlās, Col.
|| Ārĕŏpăgŭs, ī, m., *the famous Athenian tribunal.*
ārēsco, ĭs, *the frequent. of* areo. Exĭgŭĭs ārēscānt sūlphŭrā fūmĭs, Ov. V. Areo.
Ārēstŏrĭdēs, æ, m., *the son of Arestor.* Dōnĕc Ārēstŏrĭdæ, Ov.
|| ărĕtălŏgŭs, ī, m., *a quack philosopher.* Ŭt mēndāx ărĕtălŏgŭs, Juv. Epith. dŏctŭs, mēndāx.
Arēthūsă, æ, f., *the daughter of Nereus and Doris, metamorphosed into a fountain.* Ōre, Ărĕthūsă, tŭō, Virg. Epith. Sĭcŭlă, frĭgĭdă, fūgāx, vēlōx. V. Alpheus.
Arēthūsæŭs, *and* sĭŭs, ă, ŭm, *and* Ărĕthūsĭs, ĭdĭs, f., *of Arethusa.* Quās Ărĕthūsæī lătĭcēs, Claud. Ărĕthūsĭă prōlēs, Sil. Sўrācūsās Ărĕthūsĭdās, Ov.
Ārĕŭs, ĕī, m., *the name of a man.* Lўcĭdās ĕt Ăːĕŭs, Ov.
Argānthōnĭăcŭs, ă, ŭm, *of Arganthonius.* Argānthōnĭăcōs ārmăt, Sil.
Argānthōnĭŭs, ĭī, m., *a king who lived three centuries.* Rēx Argānthōnĭŭs ōrĭs, Sil. Epith. Vĕtŭs, bĕllĭgĕr, dīvĕs, pŏtēns, vīvāx.
Argēī, ōrŭm, m. pl., *places in Rome consecrated by Numa.* Itŭr ăd Argēōs, Ov.
ārgēntārĭă, æ, f., *a banker's office.* Ārgēntārĭă, Pŏllă, (Phal.) Sil.
ārgēntārĭŭs, ă, ŭm, *which belongs to money ; and* ī, m., *a banker.* Mōns ārgēntārĭŭs ăgrōs, Rutil.
ārgēntātŭs, ă, ŭm, *silvered over.* Ārgēntātă, tŭōs, Virg. Syn. Ārgēntō tēctŭs, īndūctŭs, fūlgēns, mĭcāns.
ūrgēntĕŭs, ă, ŭm, *of or as silver.* Nĭtĭdĭs ārgēntĕŭs ūndĭs, Ov. Syn. Ārgēntō făctŭs, grăvĭs, sŏlĭdŭs, mĭcāns ; ālbŭs, cāndĭdŭs, nĭtēns.
ārgĕntŭm, ī, n , *silver.* Ārgēntŭm, Părĭŭsvĕ lăpĭs, Virg. Syn. Ārgēntī mētāllŭm. Epith. Sŏlĭdŭm, clārŭm, dīvĕs, nĭtēns, nĭtĭdŭm, splēndēns, grătŭm, prĕtĭōsŭm, pāllĭdŭm, ālbŭm. V. Pecunia.
Argēstēs, æ, m., *the name of a wind.* Frĭgĭdŭs Argēstēs, Ov.
Argĕŭs, ă, ŭm, *of Argos.* Argĕō pōsĭtŭm cŏlōnŏ, Hor. Syn. Argōŭs.
Argīlētŭm, ī, m., *a district of Rome.* Mōnstrāt nĕmŭs Argīlētī, Virg.
ărgīllă, æ, f., *white clay.* Tĕnŭĭs ŭbi ārgīlla, ĕt, Virg. Epith. Dūlcĭs, ūdă.
Argītĭs, ĭs, f., *a kind of white grapes.* Argītĭsquĕ mĭnŏr, Virg. V. Uva.
Argīvŭs, ă, ŭm, *Greek.* Et jam Argīvă phălānx, Virg. Syn. Argŏlĭcŭs, Argōŭs, Achīvŭs, Achæŭs, Ăchāĭcŭs, Ināchĭŭs, Græcŭs, Pĕlāsgŭs, Grājŭgĕnă. V. Græcus.

Ărgō, ūs, f., *the Argonauts' ship.* Ărgō sāxă păvēns, Ped.—2. *a constellation.* Tūm nōbĭlĭs Ărgō, Manil. Epith. Ărdŭă, vēlōx, lēvĭs, nōbĭlĭs, flŭctĭvăgă, bēllĭgĕră, Thēssălĭcă, Păgăsæă, īmprŏbă. V. Argonautæ.

Ărgŏlĭcŭs, ă, ŭm, *Greek.* Ărgŏlĭcī rēdĭērĕ dŭcēs, Ov. V. Argivus.

Ărgŏlĭs, ĭdĭs, f., *of Argos; a Greek woman.* Ărgŏlĭs Alcmēnē, Ov. Ărgŏlĭdās tĭmŭī, Id. Syn. Pĕlăsgĭs, Pĕlăsgĭăs, Argīvă.

Ărgŏnaūtæ, ārŭm, m. pl., *Grecian heroes, who sailed in the ship Argo.* Sĕd Ărgŏnaūtăs, (Phal.) Mart. Epith. Sēmĭdĕī, Iāsŏnĭī, aūdācēs, Pĕlăsgī, Thēssălī, Æmŏnĭī, Thēssălĭcī, Grāiī, gĕnĕrōsī, īmpăvĭdī, māgnănĭmī, flŭctĭvăgī, clārī, mĭnācēs, fōrtēs, Mārtĭī, īmmōrtālēs, cĕlebrēs. V. Argo.

Ărgŏs, n., [*used in the nom., acc., and voc. sing. ; m. pl.,* Argī.] *a country and town of Greece.* Ăltă pĕr Ărgŏs ĕrăt, Ov. Epith. Nŏbĭlĕ, sŭpērbŭm, Inăchĭŭm, dīvĕs, clārŭm, flōrēns, pŏtēns, pōllēns, īndŏmĭtŭm, āntīquŭm, māgnĭfĭcŭm, cĕlebrĕ.

Ărgŏŭs, ă, ŭm, *of Argos.* Nōn hūc Ărgōŏ, Hor. V. Argivus.

|| ārgūmēntŏr, ārĭs, *to dispute.* Ărgūmēntātŭr vălĭdă, Ser. Syn. Rătĭŏcĭnŏr, dīssĕro, dīspŭto, prŏbo.

ārgūmēntōsŭs, ă, ŭm, *full of argument.* Ărgūmēntōsĭs dăt rētĭă sўllōgīsmĭs, (Spond.) Sidon.

ārgūmēntŭm, ī, n., *argument.* Vōti ārgūmēntă pătēntĭs, Ov. Syn. Sīgnŭm, īndĭcĭŭm, mŏnĭmēntŭm, nŏtă. V. Signum.

ārgŭo, ŭī, ūtŭm, *to show, object, reprove.* Ărgŭĕt āmbĭgŭē, Hor. Syn. Insĭmŭlo, ĭncūso, rĕprĕhēndo, īncrĕpo, āccūso ; ōstēndo, rĕdārgŭo, cōnvīnco. V. Redarguo.

Ărgŭs, ī, m., *the guardian of Io, born with a hundred eyes, deluded by Mercury.* Cēntŭm lūmĭnĭbŭs cīnctŭm căpŭt Ărgŭs hăbēbăt, Ov. Syn. Ărīstŏnĭdēs. Epith. Stēllātŭs, vĭgĭl, vĭgĭlāns, lўncĕŭs, īnsōmnĭs, pērvĭgĭl, pērnōx, fīdŭs, fīdēlĭs, cēntŏcŭlŭs.

|| ārgūtātĭo, ōnĭs, f., *a creaking.* Lēcti ārgūtātĭo, Cat.

ārgŭtĭă, æ, f., *a clear and sharp sound.* Rĕsŏnāns ārgūtĭă vōcĭs, Text.

ārgŭtĭæ, ārŭm, f. pl., *witticisms.* Suāvēs sūnt ārgŭtĭæ, Phædr. Syn. Acūtē dĭctă.

ārgŭtŭs, ă, ŭm, *sharp, shrill.* Cōgŏr ăd ārgūtās, Prop. Syn. Sŭbtīlĭs, sōlērs, īngĕnĭōsŭs, ăcūtŭs.

Ărgўrĭpă, æ, f., *a city of Apulia, also called Arpi.* Ille ūrbem Ărgўrĭpăm, Virg.

Ărĭă, or Ărrĭă, æ, f., *the wife of Pœtus.* Cūm trādĕrĕt Ărĭă Pœtō, Mart.

Ărĭădnă, æ, or nē, ēs, f., *the daughter of Minos, abandoned by Theseus.* Gĕrēns Ărĭădnă fŭrōrēs, Cat. Syn. Gnōsĭăs, Gnōsĭs, Mĭnōĭs. Epith. Gnōsĭă, pŭlchră, īngĕnĭōsă, Crētēnsĭs, Crēssă, fŏrmōsă, dēcēptă, fĭdēlĭs, vĕnūstă. V. Aberro.

Ărĭădnæŭs, ă, ŭm, *of Ariadne.* Ex Ărĭădnæō sīdĕrĕ, Ov.

Ărĭcĭă, æ, f., *a wood and town of Italy.* Nĕmŏrālĭs Ărĭcĭă fāstŏs, Ov.

Ărĭcīnŭs, ă, ŭm, *of Aricia.* Vāllĭs Ărĭcīnæ, Ov.

ārĭdĭtās, ātĭs, f., *dryness.* Cōrrĭpĭt ārĭdĭtās, Manil. Syn. Sīccĭtās. Epith. Fērvĭdă, īgnĕă, flāmmătă. V. Siccitas.

ārĭdŭs, ă, ŭm, *dry.* Ărĭdă lŭmbĭs, Ov. Syn. Mārcĭdŭs, sīccŭs, ărēns, ărēscēns, sīccātŭs. V. Siccus.

ărĭes, ărĭĕtĭs or ărĭĕtĭs (trisyll.), m., *a ram.* Ipse ărĭes ĕtĭăm, Virg. Ărĭĕtĕ cæsō, Id. Epith. Cōrnĭgĕr, pĕtŭlcŭs, pūgnāx, tōrvŭs, lānĭgĕr, pĕtŭlāns, mītĭs, bālāns, cĕlĕr, præcēps.—2. *a sign of the zodiac.* Pīscīque Ărĭēs sŭccēdĭt, Ov. Syn. Sīgnōrŭm prīncēps. Epith. Cœlēstĭs, sŭblīmĭs, æthĕrēŭs, cēlsŭs, ēxcēlsŭs.—3. *a battering-ram.* Pūlsābānt ărĭĕtĕ mūrōs, Virg. Epith. Fērrĕŭs, dūrŭs, fōrtĭs, Vŭlcānĭŭs, mĭnāx, stŭpēndŭs, Māvōrtĭŭs, vălĭdŭs, mūrālĭs, fērrātŭs.—4. *a great fish.* Trūx ărĭes, Claud.

ărĭeto, *to push, to batter.* Ărĭĕtăt īn pōrtās, Virg. Syn. Quătĭo, cōncŭtĭo ; cōrnĭbŭs īmpĕto, vērbĕro, fĕrĭo.

Ărĭmāspī, ōrŭm, m. pl., *a people of Scythia.* Gĕlĭdōsque Ărĭmāspōs, Luc.—2. Ărĭmāspŭs, ī, m., *a river of Scythia.* Sūmmĭs Ărĭmāspŭs ărēnĭs, Lucan. Syn. Aŭrĭfĕr, aŭrĭflŭŭs.

Ărīmīnŭm, ī, n., *a city of Umbria.* Invādĭt Ărīmĭnum ĕt īngēns, Lucr.

ărĭŏlŭs, *sometimes* hărĭŏlŭs, ī, m., *a diviner.* Ărĭŏlŭs, ēxtīspēx, (Scaz.) Syn. Ărūspēx, aŭgŭr, vātēs.

Ărīŏn, ŏnīs, m., *a lyric poet and singer, carried by a dolphin upon the sea.* Quæ nēscīt Ărīŏnă tēllūs ? Ov. Epith. Vŏcālīs, Ăpŏllīnēūs, Phœbēīūs, dōctūs, dūlcīs, cīthārīstă, dūlcīsŏnūs, cănōrūs, cĕlebrīs, blăndūs, īnfēlīx, cĕlebrātūs.

Ărīŏnīūs, ă, ŭm, *of Arion.* Quī pūto, Ărīŏnīăm, Prop.

Ărīsbă, æ, *and* ē, ēs, f., *a city of Troas.* Quæ cēpīt Ărīsbā, Virg.

ărīstă, æ, f., *an ear of corn.* Flāvēscēt cāmpūs ărīstă, Virg. Syn. Spīcă, cūlmūs, sĕgĕs, mēssīs, frūgēs. Epith. Pīnguīs, œstīvă, tĕnĕră, flāvă, grăcīlīs, frăgīlīs, frūgīfĕră, fœcūndă, lœtă, ŏpīmă, Cĕrĕālīs, jĕjūnă, flāvēns, fērtīlīs, aūrātă, aūrĕă, lōngă, grăvīs, dīvĕs, cūrvātă, pāndă, ŏdōră, ŏdōrātă, ŏdōrīfĕră, ēxīlīs, mŏdīcă, ēxĭgŭă, ānnŭă, mūltă, plūrīmă, ēxpēctātă. V. Seges.

Ărīstæūs, ī, m., *the lover of Eurydice.* Pāstŏr Ărīstæūs, Virg. Epith. Arcădīūs, prŏcāx, Ăpŏllīnĕūs, jŭvĕnīs.

Ărīstārchūs, ī, m., *a celebrated critic.* Māgnūs Ărīstārchō, Ov. Epith. Dōctūs, sĕvērūs, săgāx.

Ărīstīdēs, īs *or* æ, m., *an Athenian, famous for his love of justice.* Jūstūs Ărīstīdēs, Aus. Epith. Jūstūs, æquūs, paūpĕr.

ărīstīfĕr, ă, ŭm, *which bears corn.* Dīvĕs ărīstīfĕræ, Prud.

Ărīstīppūs, ī, m., *a Greek philosopher.* Ōmnīs Ărīstīppūm, Hor. Epith. Ōbscœnūs, tūrpīs, Græcūs, Ēpīcūrēūs, Sōcrătīcūs, Cўrēnæūs, Lăcĕdæmŏnīūs.

Ărīstĭūs, ī, m., *a grammarian and orator.* Fūscūs Ărīstĭūs, Hor.

Ărīstŏphănēs, īs, m., *a Greek comic poet.* Crătīnūs Ărīstŏphănēsquĕ pŏĕtæ, Hor. Epith. Mōrdāx, sālsūs, dīsērtūs.

Ărīstŏtĕlēs, īs, m., *a Greek philosopher.* Sī quīs Ărīstŏtĕlĕm, Juv. Syn. Stăgīrītēs, Stăgīræūs sŏphūs, sŏphōrūm prīncēps, dūx. Epith. Dīvīnūs, dōctūs, īngĕnĭŏsūs, mīrābīlīs, sūbtīlīs, săgāx, sōlērs, pĕrītūs, cĕlebrīs, īngrātūs, īmmōrtālīs.

Ărĭūs, ī, m., Ărĭī, ōrŭm, pl., *a people of Scythia.* Hīnc fōrtīs Ărĭūs, Luc.—2. *a famous sectarian.*

ārmă, ōrŭm, n. pl., *arms.* Ărmă vīrūmquĕ căno, Virg. Syn. Fērrūm, ēnsīs, glădīūs, tēlŭm, hāstă, frāxĭnūs, jăcŭlŭm. Epith. Dīscōrdĭă, fūlgēntĭă, īmpĭă, Vūlcānĭă, rădĭāntĭă, grăvĭă, fōrtĭă, pīctă, fūrĭālĭă, īnĭmīcă, nŏcĭtūră, fūnēstă, hōrrĭdă, crŭēntă, călēntĭă, trĕpĭdāntĭă, lēthālĭă, hōstīlĭă, īnsānă, sŏnāntĭă, aūrātă, Māvōrtĭă, bēllĭcă, sānguĭnŏlēntă, crŭēntātă, cāstrēnsĭă, vīctrīcĭă, dīră, crūdēlĭă, īnfēstă, nĕfāndă, Mārtĭă, fūtālĭă, hōrrēntĭă, grāssāntĭă, mīnācĭă, strĕpēntĭă, ăhēnă, īmprŏbă, īnfēlīcĭă, īnfaūstă, trīstĭă, fērrĕă, răbĭdă. V. Armo, Bellum.

ārmāmēntă, ōrŭm, n. pl., *tackle, rigging.* Jŭbĕt ārmāmēntīs, Ov.

ārmāmēntārĭŭm, ĭī, n., *an arsenal, magazine.* Ărmāmēntārĭă cœlī, Juv.

ārmārĭŭm, *and* ōlŭm, ī, n., *a store-house, locker.* Ărmārĭă, cīstăs, Juv. V. Abacus.

ārmātūră, æ, f., *armour.* Lĕvīs ārmātūră mănĭplōs, Luc. V. Arma.

ārmātūs, ă, ŭm, *the pass. partic. of* armo. Tōrrē ārmātūs ŏbūstō, Virg. V. Arma, Bellicosus.

Ărmĕnĭă, æ, f., *a country of Asia.* Ărmĕnĭæ cēlsīs, Alc. Epith. Mōntōsă, hōrrĭdă, hōrrēndă.

Ărmĕnĭūs, ă, ŭm, *Armenian; of Armenia.* Dāphnīs ĕt Ărmĕnĭās, Virg

ārmēntālīs, ĕ, *of a herd.* Ărmēntālīs ĕquæ māmmīs, Virg.

ārmēntārĭūs, ĭī, m., *a herdsman.* Ărmēntārĭūs ŏmnīs, Lucr. Syn. Bŭbūlcūs, pāstŏr.

ārmēntŭm, ī, n., *a herd.* Ărmēntă vŏcābăt, Virg. Syn. Grēx, pĕcūs. Epith. Lœtŭm, dīscŏlŏr, mōntānŭm, lānĭgĕrŭm, pīnguĕ, ērrāns, nŭmĕrōsŭm, cŏāctŭm, spūmāns, fōrtĕ, cōrnĭgĕrŭm, mōntĭvăgŭm, tārdŭm, pĭgrŭm, ĕdāx, ŏbēsŭm. V. Grex.

ārmĭfĕr, ă, ŭm, *bearing armour.* Sīgnĭfĕr, ārmĭfĕrōs, Syl.

ārmĭgĕr, ă, ŭm, *armed.* Hæc ēst ārmĭgĕræ, Ov.

ārmīllă, æ, f., *a bracelet.* Ărmīllīs cāptă Săbīnīs, Ov. Epith. Dīvĕs, gēmmātă. V. Monile.

ārmīllātūs, ă, ŭm, *wearing bracelets.* Atquĕ ārmīllātōs, Prop.

ārmĭpŏtēns, ēntīs, *powerful in arms.* Ărmĭpŏtēntīs Achīllĕī, Virg.

ārmĭsŏnūs, ă, ŭm, *rustling with armour.* Pāllădīs ārmĭsŏnæ, Virg ārmo, ās, *to arm, to furnish.* Sē quīsquĕ rĕcēntĭbŭs ārmăt, Virg. Syn. Armīs Indŭo, cīngo, īnstrŭo, mŭnĭo.

Ārmŏrĭcī, ōrŭm, m. pl., *a people of ancient Gaul.* Epith. Ŏccĭdŭī, naūtæ, nă-vārchī, vēllĭcōsī, fōrtēs, ănĭmōsī, fĕrōcēs, trūcēs.

ārmŭs, ī, m., (*often,* mī, ōrŭm) *the shoulder.* Rĕcūmbĭt ĭn ārmō, Virg. Syn. Hŭmĕrŭs, ārmī. Epith. Lătŭs, vălĭdŭs, hīrtŭs, rĭgĭdŭs.

Arnē, ēs, f., *a nymph metamorphosed into a jackdaw, for her love of money.* Prōdĭdĭt Ārnē, Ov.

Arnŭs, ī, m, *a river of Tuscany.* Ărnŭs ăquīs, Pamphil. Epith. Thūscŭs, Ētrūscŭs, nōbĭlĭs, lūcĭdŭs, frĭgĭdŭs, cĕlĕr, præcēps.

ăro, ās, *to plough.* Līttŭs ărānt, Virg

ărōmă, ătĭs, n., *spice ; sweet odour.* Spīrāmĕn ărōmătĭs ēfflăt, Prud. Syn. Ŏdŏr. Epith. Dūlcĕ, grātŭm, ŏlēns, Săbæūm ; Assўrĭŭm, Indĭcŭm, bālsămĕŭm, Cyprĭŭm. ărōmătĭcŭs, ă, ŭm, *aromatic.* Mēssĭs ărōmătĭcæ, Sedul.

Ărpī, ōrŭm, m. pl., *a city of Apulia.* Ætōlŭs ĕt Ārpī, Virg.

Arpīnās, ātĭs, m., *of Arpinum, a city of the Volscians.* Ārpīnās ālĭŭs, Juv.

ārrēctŭs, ă, ŭm, *the pass. partic. of* arrigo. Ēxtēmplo ārrēctŭs ŭtērquĕ, Virg.

ārrhă, æ, *and* ăbo, ōnĭs, m., *an earnest, a pledge.* Lēno ārrhăbōnĕm, (Iamb.) Plaut.

ārrīdĕo, īsī, *to laugh at, smile.* Hīs Dĕŭs ārrīsĭt, Mant. Syn. Plăcĕo, sūbrīdĕo.

ārrĭgo, ĭs, ēxī, ēctŭm, *to lift up.* Nōn pŏtĕs ārrĭgĕrĕ ? Mart. Syn. Ērĭgo, tōllo, ăttōllo, sūbrĭgo.

ārrĭpĭo, ĭpŭī, ēptŭm, *to seize.* Ărrĭpŭītquĕ lŏcŭm, Virg. Syn. Sūbrĭpĭo, răpĭo, prĕhēndo, prēndo, ăpprĕhēndo.

ārrŏgāns, āntĭs, *arrogant.* Chlŏēn sĕmĕl ārrŏgāntĕm, Hor. V. Superbus.

ārrŏgo, *to arrogate, ascribe.* Nĭhĭl nōn ārrŏgĕt ārmīs, Hor. Syn. Ăssūmo, sŭmo, ăscīsco, vīndĭco, trībŭo.

ārrōsŭs, ă, ŭm, *the pass. partic. of* arrodo. Ārrōsō rōbŏrĕ, Nem. V. Rodo.

ārs, ārtĭs, f., *art, science, power.* Hīc ĕrĭt ārtĭs ŏpŭs, Ov. Syn. Ārtĭfĭcĭŭm, făcūltās, scĭēntĭă, dōctrīnă, stŭdĭŭm : fraūs, dŏlŭs. Epith. Mīră, sălūtărĭs, āptă, dīvīnă ; ŏpĕrōsă, clāră, ĭmĭtātrīx, mīrāndă, nŏvă, ĭngĕnĭōsă, sōlĭcĭtă, nōbĭlĭs, ābjēctă, cĕlebrĭs, dŏlōsă, vērsūtă. V. Dolus.

ārtēs, *liberal arts.* Quī vītam ēxcŏlŭĕrĕ pĕr ārtēs, Virg. Epith. Ingĕnŭæ, ēgrĕgĭæ, præclāræ, dōctæ.

Arsăcĭdæ, ārŭm, m. pl., *kings of the Parthians, and successors of Arsaces ; Par-thians, Persians.* Arsăcĭdŭm dŏmĭnŭs, Lucr.

Arsăcĭŭs, ă, ŭm, *of the Arsacidæ ; of the Persians.* Scīs quĭd ĭn Arsăcĭă, Mart.

Artāxătā, ōrŭm, n. pl., *a town of Armenia.* Vīncūnt Artāxătă mōrēs, Juv.

Artĕmĭsĭă, æ, f., *the wife of Mausolus, king of Caria.* Epith. Cāstă, nōbĭlĭs, fōrtĭs, pŭdīcă, mœstă.

|| ārtĕrĭă, æ, f., *an artery.* Grădĭēns ārtērĭă clāmŏr, Lucr.

|| ārthrītĭs, ĭdĭs, f., *the gout.* Pŏdāgra ĕt ārthrītĭs, Prud.

ārtĭcŭlātĭm, adv., *distinctly.* Discērnīque ārtĭcŭlātĭm, Lucr.

ārtĭcŭlo, ās, *to articulate.* Mōbĭlĭs ārtĭcŭlăt, Lucr.

ārtĭcŭlŭs, ī, m., *a finger.* Nēc prēmĭt ārtĭcŭlōs, Ov. Syn. Dĭgĭtŭs. Epith. Mōllĭs, mōllĭcŭlŭs, tĕnŭĭs, rŏsĕŭs, nĭtĭdŭs, cāndĭdŭs.

ārtĭfēx, ĭcĭs, m., *an artist.* Artĭbŭs, ārtĭfĭcī, Ov. Syn. Ŏpĭfēx. Epith. Clārŭs, pĕrītŭs, mănŭĭtŭs, cĕlebrĭs, vĭgĭl, mătūtīnŭs, ĭngĕnĭōsŭs, nōbĭlĭs, săgāx, sōlērs, præclārŭs, sōlĭcĭtŭs, mīrābĭlĭs.

ārtŏcŏpŭs, ī, m., *a baker.* Sĭt ārtŏcŏpī rĕvĕrēntĭă, Juv. Syn. Pīstŏr.

ārtŏcrĕās, ătĭs, n., *a meat-pie.* Artŏcrĕāsquĕ pŏpēllō, Pers. Epith. Laūtŭm, ŏpīmŭm.

ārtŭs, ŭŭm, ŭbŭs, m. pl., *limbs.* Ēt fīngĭtŭr ārtŭbŭs, (Alcaic.) Hor. Syn. Mēmbră. Epith. Rōbūstī, fōrtēs, cădūcī, frăgĭlēs, mŏrĭbūndī, pūlchrī, vălĭdī, fōrmōsī, fēssī.

ărūndĭfĕr, ă, ŭm, *bearing reeds.* Tĭbrīs ărūndĭfĕrŭm, Ov. Syn. Ărūndĭnĭbŭs frĕquēns, tēctŭs, ŏpērtŭs.

ărūndĭnĕŭs, ă, ŭm, *of a reed.* Pāstŏr ărūndĭnĕŏ, Ov.

ărūndĭnōsŭs, ă, ŭm, *full of reeds.* Cnīdŭmque ărūndĭnōsăm, Catul.

ărūndo, ĭnĭs, f., *a reed.* Ēquĭtāre ĭn ărūndĭnĕ lōngă, Hor. Syn. Ăvēnă, călămŭs cānnă. Epith. Flŭvĭālĭs, ūmbrōsă, ēxĭlĭs, dēfōrmĭs, pălūstrĭs, prōcēră, frăgĭlĭs, lĕvĭs, ăquātĭcă, flūmĭnĕă, ăquōsă, vĭrēscēns, vĭrēns, vĭrĭdĭs, nŏbĭlĭs, ĭncōnstāns, ăgĭtātă, glaūcă.—2. *a flute.* Mĕdĭtābŏr ărūndĭnĕ Mūsăm, Virg. V. Fistula.— 3. *an arrow.* Lēthālĭs ărūndo, Virg. Syn. Săgĭttă, spīcŭlŭm, tēlŭm, jăcŭlŭm. Epith. Lēthālĭs, vŏlāns, vŏlucrĭs, lĕvĭs, pĕnnātă, strīdēns, ăcūtă. V. Sagitta.

Ārūns, ūntĭs, m., *a Tuscan diviner.* Ārūns ĭncŏlŭĭt, Luc.—2. *the name of a warrior.* Sŭpĕrōs Ārūns sīc vŏcĕ prĕcātŭr, Virg.

ărūspēx, ĭcĭs, m., *a soothsayer.* Ăn ărūspĭcĕ nōbĭs? Juv. Syn. Aūgŭr, vātēs. Epith. Thūscŭs, Rōmānŭs, Etrūscŭs; săcĕr, vānŭs, vērŭs, fātĭdĭcŭs, obscūrŭs, Phœbēŭs, tĕrrĭfĭcŭs, sōlērs, săgāx, sēdŭlŭs, prŏvĭdŭs, pĕrītŭs, āncēps, mēndāx, ĭncērtŭs, dŭbĭŭs, dīvīnŭs, lōngævŭs, sānctŭs, vĕnĕrābĭlĭs, prænūncĭŭs, sĭnĭstĕr. V. Augur.

ărūspĭcĭŭm, ī, n., *soothsaying.* Pērsĭcum ărūspĭcĭŭm, Cat. V. Augurium.

Arvālēs, ĭŭm, m. pl., *twelve officers chosen to superintend the sacrifices of Ceres, and disputes about the limits of the fields.* V. Ambarvalia.

ārvīnă, æ, f., *fat, tallow.* Arvīnā pīnguī, Virg. Epith. Mōllĭs, pīnguĭs, tĕnāx.

Arvīrăgŭs, ī, m., *a British king.* Excīdĕt Arvīrăgŭs, Juv.

Arvīsĭŭm, ĭī, n., *a promontory in the island of Chios, famous for good wine.* Călăthīs Arvīsĭā nēctăr, Virg.

ārvŭm, ī, n., *ploughed land.* Sŭbĭgēbānt ārvă cŏlōnī, Virg. Epith. Dūlcĕ, pīnguĕ. V. Ager.

ārx, ārcĭs, f., *a summit, citadel, wall, castle.* Quæ vērtĕrĕt ārcēs, Virg. Syn. Mūnīmēn, vāllŭm, tūrrĭs, cāstrŭm, cāstēllŭm, prŏpūgnācŭlŭm. Epith. Sūmmă, sŭpērbă, āĕrĭă, ēlātă, ĭnēxpūgnābĭlĭs, sūblīmĭs, ārdŭă, āltă, cēlsă, ēxcēlsă, tūrrītă, tūrrĭgĕră, vălĭdă, fōrtĭs, mūnītă, vāllātă, sŏlĭdă, sēcūră; Māvōrtĭă. V. Turris.

ās, āssĭs, m. f., *the Roman pound.* Sē dēmīttĕt ŏb āssĕm, Hor.

ăsărōtŭm, ī, n., *mosaic work.* Nŏvĭs ăsărōtă fĭgūrĭs, Sil.

Asbŏlŭs, ī, *one of Actæon's dogs.* Asbŏlŭs ātrĭs, Ov.

Ascălăphŭs, ī, m., *the son of Acheron, changed into an owl for his indiscretion.* Vīdĕrăt Ascălăphŭs, Ov.

Ascănĭŭs, ĭī, m., *the son of Æneas, founder of Alba.* Syn. Ilŭs, Iūlŭs, Ænĕădēs. Epith. Rēgĭŭs, Dārdănĭŭs, Trŏĭŭs. dŭlcĭs, bīnōmĭnĭs, pūlchĕr, Ālbānŭs.

āscēndo, dī, sŭm, *to mount.* Būthrōtī ăscēndĭmŭs ūrbĕm, Virg. Syn. Scāndo, cōnscēndo. V. Cœlos ascendo.

ăscēnsŭs, ūs, m., *an ascent.* Virg. Syn. Cōnscēnsŭs. Epith. Ardŭŭs, ĭnīquŭs, dĭffĭcĭlĭs; făcĭlĭs, mōllĭs.

* āscĭă, æ, f., *an axe.* Cic. Syn. Sĕcūrĭs, bĭpēnnĭs.

āscīsco, īvī, ītŭm, *to call for.* Cic. Gĕnĕrŭmque āscīvĕrĭt ūrbī, Virg. Syn. Vŏco ādvŏco, cōnvŏco, āccērso, āccĭo; āscrībo, ādjūngo. V. Accerso.

āscītŭs, ă, ŭm, *the pass. partic. of* ascisco. Ascītŭm cōgnōmĕn, Sil. V. Ascisco.

Ascră, æ, f., *a-village of Bœotia, where Hesiod was born.* Vāllĭbŭs, Ascră, tŭĭs, Ov. Epith. Vĕtŭs, Pārnāssĭă, Hĕlĭcōnĭă.

Ascræŭs, ă, ŭm, *of Ascra.* Ascræūmquĕ căno, Virg.

āscrībo, *to write unto, to ascribe.* Rēstăt ŭt āscrībăt, Ov. Syn. Sūbscrībo, āssīgno; trĭbŭo, āttrĭbŭo; ĭmpōno, dō; āscīsco.

ăsēllŭs, ī, m., *and* ă, æ, f., *a young ass.* Dēlāpsŭs ăsēllō, Ov. Tūrpĭs ăsēllă, Ov. V. Asinus.

Asĭă, æ, f., *one of the three divisions of the old world.* Extrēmĭs Asĭæ jăm, Virg. Epith. Māgnă, pŏtēns, dīvĕs, lātă, spātĭōsă, fĕrāx, fœcūndă, ŏpŭlēntă, fērtĭlĭs.

Asĭă, æ, f., *palus, a lake in Mysia.* Asĭā lōngē Pūlsă pălŭs, Virg.

Asĭăcŭs, Asĭănŭs, *and* ĭātĭcŭs, ă, ŭm, *of Asia.* Ecquĭd ŭbī Asĭăcŏs, Ov. Hæc Asĭānōrŭm, Juv. Vĕnĭūnt Asĭātĭcă fœtū, Col.

ăsĭlŭm, ī, n., *or* ŭs, ī, m., *a horse-fly.* Syn. Œstrŭm.

ăsĭnŭs, ī, m., *and* ă, æ, f., *an ass.* Aūrĭcŭlăs ăsĭnī, Pers. Asĭnæquĕ pătērnŭm, Hor. Syn. Asēllŭs, ă. Epith. Tārdŭs, vīlĭs, pĭgĕr, dĕsĕs, ŏnĕrātŭs, ĭnērs, tārdŭs, aūrītŭs, tūrpĭs, sēgnĭs, Arcādĭcŭs, grăvĭs, rŭdĭs, stŏlĭdŭs, ĭgnāvŭs, vīllōsŭs.

Asĭs, ĭdĭs, f., *of Lydia.* Ĭn Asĭdĕ tērrā, Ov.

Asĭŭs, ă, ŭm, *of Lydia, or Mæonia.* Asĭă cīrcŭm, Virg. Asĭă Dēĭŏpeĭă, Id.

Asōpĭădēs, æ, m., *the son or descendant of Asopus, Æacus.* Huĭc Asōpĭădēs, Ov.

D

Asdrŭbăl. ălĭs, m., *a Carthaginian general.* Asdrŭbăl ĭpsĕ sŭĭs, Ov.

Asōpĭs, ĭdĭs, f., *of Asopus, daughter of Asopus.* Asōpĭdă lūsĕrĭt ĭgnĭs, Ov.

Asōpŭs *or* ŏs, ī, m., *a river near Thebes.* Quĭd rĕfĕram Asōpōn, Ov.

āspărăgŭs, ī, m. Mōntāni āspărăgī, Juv.

āspĕcto, ās, *the frequent. of* aspicio. Aspĕctāt dēsŭpĕr ārcēs, Virg. Syn. Spĕcto, āspĭcĭo.

āspēctŭs, ūs, m., *aspect.* Obstŭpŭĭt prīmo āspĕctŭ, Virg. Syn. Făcĭēs, vūltŭs, ŏs, frōns, ŏcŭlī, lūmĭnă; cōnspĕctŭs, ōbtŭtŭs. Epith. Grātŭs, bĕnīgnŭs, ămābĭlĭs, dūlcĭs, rīdēns, sĕrēnŭs, ămīcŭs, hĭlărĭs, blandŭs, plăcĭdŭs, cōmĭs, mītĭs, jūcŭndŭs, lāscīvŭs, tĕrrĭbĭlĭs, fĕrōx, trūx, fĕrŭs, tōrvŭs, mĕtŭēndŭs, mĭnāx, · sĕvērŭs, trŭcŭlēntŭs, hōrrĭdŭs, hōrrĭbĭlĭs, fōrmīdābĭlĭs. V. Aspicio.

āspĕr, ă, ŭm, *rough, harsh.* Aspĕrĭŭs nĭhĭl ēst, Claud. Syn. Scăbĕr; ăcērbŭs, dūrŭs, mŏlēstŭs, ărdŭŭs, dĭffĭcĭlĭs, grăvĭs, īnjūcūndŭs, īngrātŭs; cœlātŭs.

āspērgo, ĭs, sī, sŭm, *to besprinkle.* Aspērgĕ săpōrēs, Virg. Syn. Spărgo, rĭgo, pērfūndo. V. Rigo.

āspērgo, ĭnĭs, f., *a besprinkling.* Spūmānt āspērgĭnĕ caūtēs, Virg.

āspĕrĭtăs, ātĭs, f., *harshness.* Aspĕrĭtātĭs, ĕt īnvĭdĭæ, Hor. Syn. Scabrĭtĭēs; grăvĭtăs. Epith. Agrēstĭs, fērālĭs, hōstīlĭs, flēbĭlĭs, ăcērbă, īntŏlĕrābĭlĭs, dūră, grăvĭs.

āspĕro, ās, *to make rough.* Aspĕrăt ūndās, Virg. Syn. Dūro, īndūro; ăcērbo.

āspērnŏr, ārĭs, *to contemn.* Cūram āspērnăbĕrĕ lēntĭs, Virg. Syn. Spērno, tĕmno, cōntēmno, fāstīdĭo, rēspŭo, nĕglĭgo, ăbjĭcĭo, dēspĭcĭo. V. Contemno.

āspērsŭs, ă, ŭm, *the pass. partic. of* aspergo. Sānĭēque āspērsă nătārēnt, Virg.

Asphāltītĕs, œ, m., *the Dead Sea.* Inque Asphāltītĕ ēst, Till.

āspĭcĭo, ēxī, ēctŭm, *to see.* Sōl āspĭcĭēbăt Ŏlȳmpō, Virg. Syn. Vĭdĕo, tŭĕŏr, īntŭĕŏr, cērno, cōnspĭcĭo, īnspĭcĭo, rēspĭcĭo, spĕcto, āspĕcto. V. Video.

āspīrāmĕn, ĭnĭs, n., *breath.* Blānda āspīrāmĭnă fōrmæ, Val. Fl. Syn. Aspīrātĭo, āfflātŭs, hālĭtŭs.

āspīro, ās, *to breathe.* Aspīrătĕ cănēntī, Virg. Syn. Afflo, spīro; făvĕo, ŏpēm fĕro.

āspĭs, ĭdĭs, f., *an asp.* Aspĭdĕs, īn mĕdĭĭs, Lucan. Syn. Sērpēns, ānguĭs. Epith. Sōmnĭfĕră, Phărĭă; lēthĭfĕră, sīccă, vĕnēnōsă, lūbrĭcă, hōrrĭdă, tūrgĭdă, tŭmēscēns. V. Serpens.

āspōrto, ās, *to carry away.* Aspōrtărĕ Crĕūsăm, Virg. Syn. Aŭfĕro, āvĕho.

āssă, œ, f., *a nurse.* Pōscēntĭbŭs āssœ, Juv.

Assărăcŭs, ī, m., *a son of Tros, and king of Troy.* Ĕt gĕnŭs Assărăcī, Virg.

āssēclă, œ, m., *an attendant.* Vōs hŭmĭli āssēclæ, Juv. Syn. Cŏmĕs, sŏcĭŭs, sēctātŏr.

āssēctŏr, ārĭs, *to accompany.* Cum āssēctārētŭr, Hor. Syn. Sĕquŏr, cōmĭtŏr.

āssĕcūtŭs, ă, ŭm, *the part. of* assequor. Săpĭēntĭam āssĕcūtŭs, (Phal.)

āssēnsŭs, ūs, m., *assent.* Ĕt vōx āssēnsŭ nĕmŏrŭm, Virg. Syn. Cōnsēnsŭs. Epith. Lĭbĕr, ōptātŭs, grātŭs, cōmmūnĭs.

|| āssēntātĭo, ōnĭs, f., *flattery.* V. Adulatio.

āssēntātŏr, ōrĭs, m., *a flatterer.* Assēntātōrēs jŭbĕt, Hor.

|| āssēntĭo, ĭs, *and* ĭŏr, īrĭs, *to assent.* Syn. Cōnsēntĭo, ānnŭo, āstĭpŭlŏr; ăpprŏbo, prŏbo.

|| āssēntŏr, ārĭs, *to flatter.* Syn. Adŭlŏr, blāndĭŏr. V. Adulor.

āssĕquŏr, ĕrĭs, *to obtain.* Assĕquĭtŭr, nĕc ŏpīnāntĕm, Sil. Syn. Cōnsĕquŏr, ·ădĭpīscŏr, ācquīro, păro, cōmpăro. V. Acquiro, Attingo.

āssĕr, ĕrĭs, m., *a pole.* Fĕrĭt āssĕrĕ dūrō, Juv. Syn. Assĭs, āssērcŭlŭs.

āssĕro, ŭī, ērtŭm, *to rescue, to assert.* Scīlĭcĕt āssĕrŭī, Ov. Syn. Affīrmo, āssĕvēro, jūro; vīndĭco.

āssērtŏr, ōrĭs, m., *he who rescues.* Pūblĭcŭs āssērtŏr, Ov.

āssērvo, ās, *to preserve.* Prædam āssērvābānt, Virg. Syn. Sērvo, cōnsērvo, tŭĕŏr, cūstōdĭo.

āssĕvēro, ās, *to affirm.* Assĕvērăbĭt, Scaz. Syn. Affīrmo, āssĕro.

āssĭbĭlo, ās, *to hiss.* Dŏmĭnĭs āssĭbĭlăt ārĭs, Stat. Syn. Sībĭlo, sībĭlă rēddo.

āssĭdĕo, āssēdī, *or* sīdo, sīdī, *to sit by.* Assĭdĕrĕ mātrī, (Phal.) Syn. Sĕdĕo, cōnsīdĕo, cōnsīdo: jūxtă, prŏpĕ sĕdĕo.

āssĭdŭē, adv., *assiduously.* Assĭdŭĕ dūcŭnt, Virg. Syn. Usquĕ, cōntĭnŭŏ, sēmpĕr.

ăssĭdŭŭs, ă, ŭm, *assiduous, continual.* Assĭdŭō lăbŭntūr tĕmpŏră mōtū, Ov. Syn. Pĕrpĕtŭŭs, cōntĭnŭŭs, frĕquēns, dīlĭgēns.

āssĭgno, ās, *to assign.* Cōmpōnŭnt, āgrōs āssĭgnănt, Hor. Syn. Ascrībo, āttrĭbŭo.

āssĭlĭo, ŭī, ŭltŭm, *to leap at.* Cŭm sæpe āssĭlŭĭt, Ov. Syn. Āssŭlto.

āssĭmĭlĭs, ĕ, *very like.* Assĭmĭlēmquĕ sŭī, Ov.

āssĭmĭlo, ās, *to liken, to compare.* Assĭmĭlărĕ lĭcĕt, Ov. Syn. Sĭmĭlo, cōnsĭmĭlo, cōmpăro, cōnfĕro, cōmpōno. V. Similis.

āssĭmŭlo, *to feign.* Assĭmŭlăvĭt ănŭm, Ov. Syn. Fīngo, sĭmŭlo.

āssĭsto, āstĭtī, *to be present, to assist.* Assĭstĭt ĭn ārmīs, Virg. Syn. Adsŭm, īntērsŭm, ăsto.

āssĭtŭs, ă, ŭm, *the pass. partic. of* assero. Vĭrĭdāntĭbŭs āssĭtă prātīs, Aus.

|| āsso, ās, *to roast.* Syn. Tōrrĕo.

āssŏcĭo, ās, *to associate.* Assŏcĭāt pāssŭs, Stat. Syn. Adjūngo, cōnjūngo, āddo, sŏcĭŭm dŏ.

āssŏlĕt, *it is wont.* Ter. Syn. Sŏlĕt, sŏlĭtum ēst, mōs ēst.

āssŏno, ŭī, *to re-echo.* Assŏnăt ēchō, Ov. V. Echo.

* āssŭēfăcĭo, fēcī, fāctŭm, *to accustom.* Cic. Syn. Cōnsuēfăcĭo, dŏcĕo, ēdŭcĕo.

āssŭēsco, ēvī, ētŭm, *to accustom oneself.* Plŭrĭbŭs āssŭēvĭt, M. Syn. Cōnsuēsco, sŏlĕo: mĭhi mōs ēst.

āssŭētŭdo, ĭnĭs, f., *custom.* Nīl āssuētŭdĭnĕ mājŭs, Ov. Syn. Mōs, ŭsŭs, cōn-suētŭdo. Epith. Lōngă, făcĭlĭs, ŭtĭlĭs, tēnāx. V. Assuesco.

āssŭētŭs, ă, ŭm, *the pass. partic. of* assuesco. Cōnjŭgĭs āssuētæ, Ov. V. Assuesco.

āssŭlă, æ, f., *a board.* Assŭlīs stāntĭs, Catul.

āssŭlto, ās, *to assault.* Assŭltārĕ lĕōnēs, Sil. Syn. Assĭlĭo.

āssŭltŭs, ŭs, m., *an assault.* Assŭltĭbŭs īrrĭtŭs ūrgĕt, Virg.

āssūmo, sūmpsī, ptŭm, *to take, choose.* Dīgnōs āssūmĕrĕ, prăvă, Hor. Syn. Căpĭo, āccĭpĭo ; mĭhi trĭbŭo, ārrŏgo.

āssŭo, ŭī, ŭtŭm, *to sew on.* Assŭĭtŭr pānnŭs, Hor. Syn. Cōnsŭo.

āssūrgo, ĭs, āssūrrēxī, *to rise.* Assūrgŭnt tūrrēs, Virg. Syn. Sūrgo, cōnsūrgo ; crēsco, ēxcrēsco, aūgĕŏr ; cēdo.

āssŭs, ă, ŭm, *roasted.* At sĭmŭl āssĭs, Hor. Syn. Assătŭs, tōrrĭdŭs, sĭccŭs.

Assўrĭă, æ, f., *a kingdom of Asia.* Dīvēs ĕt Assўrĭă, Tib. Epith. Pŏtēns, fĕrāx.

Assўrĭŭs, ă, ŭm, *Assyrian.* Albă nĕque Assўrĭō, Virg.

āst, conj., *but.* Ast ŭbĭ, Ov. Syn. At, sĕd.

Astĕrĭă, æ, *or* ē, ēs, f., *the daughter of Ceüs, loved by Jupiter.* Seū nĕmŭs Astĕrĭæ, Virg. Fēcĭt ĕt Astĕrĭēn, Ov.

āstērnŏr, ĕrĭs, *to lie along.* Astērnūntūrquĕ sĕpŭlchrō, Ov.

āsto, ĭtī, *to stand by.* Astĭtĭt ĭmbĕr, Virg. Syn. Stō, ādsŭm, præsēns sŭm, īntērsŭm, āssĭsto.

āstră, ōrŭm, n. pl., *the stars, heaven.* Astră vŏcăt crūdēlĭă, Virg. Syn. Stēllæ, sīdĕră. Epith. Cœlēstĭă, īgnĕă, rădĭāntĭă, lūcĭdă, ārdēntĭă, nĭtĭdă, pūră, rŭtĭlă, pŭlchră, rōrāntĭă, īnsĭgnĭă, cōnspĭcŭă, splēndĭdă, sŭblīmĭă, nŏctĭvăgă, ērrāntĭă, clāră, cœlĭvăgă, pĕrēnnĭă, văgă, aūrĕă, lūcēntĭă, flāmmĭgĕră, flāmmĭvŏmă, æthĕrĕă, trĕmŭlă. V. Stella, Sidus.

Astræă, æ, f., *the goddess of justice.* Tērrās Astræă rĕlīquĭt, Ov. Syn. Jūstĭtĭă. Epith. Æquă, sānctă, īnclўtă, dīvīnă, ēxŭl, cœlēstĭs, prŏfŭgă.

Astræŭs, ī, m., *one of the Titans, father of the winds,* Ov.

Astreŭs, eī, m., *the name of a warrior.* Occĭdĭt Astreŭs, Ov.

āstrīctŭs, ă, ŭm, *the pass. partic. of* astringo. Dŏlōre āstrīctŭm, Ov.

āstrĭfĕr, *and* gĕr, ă, ŭm, *that bears stars.* Tōrquĕt, ĕt āstrĭfĕrōs, St. Cŏmĭnŭs āstrĭgĕrōs, Id. Syn. Stēllĭfĕr, stēllătŭs.

āstrīngo, īnxī, īctŭm, *to tie.* Vēnās āstrīngĭt hĭāntēs, Virg. Syn. Strīngo, cōn-strīngo, lĭgo, cŏārcto, cōgo.

āstrŏlŏgŭs, ī, m., *an astrologer.* Bĕllŭs ĕs āstrŏlŏgŭs, Mart. Epith. Vĭgĭl, præ-săgŭs, fātĭdĭcŭs, dŭbĭŭs, īncērtŭs, mēndāx, nēscĭŭs, īnsōmnĭs, præscĭŭs, pērvĭgĭl, āttēntŭs, vĭgĭlāns, vērāx, săgāx, pĕrĭtŭs, āncēps. V. Philosophus.

|| āstrŏnŏmŭs, ī, m., *an astronomer.* V. Astrologus.

āstrŭm, ī, n., *a star.* V. Astra.

ăstrŭo, *or* ădstrŭo, ŭxī, ŭctŭm, *to build near, to add.* Ădstrŭĕ fŏrn.æ, Ov. SYN.
Cōnstrŭo, ædĭfīco, cōmpōno.
ăstŭpĕo, ēs, uī, ērĕ, *to be astonished at.* Ăstŭpĕt īpsĕ sĭbi, Ov.
ăstŭs, ūs, m., *craftiness.* Ingrēssŭs ĕt āstū, Virg. SYN. Ăstūtĭă, fraŭs, dŏlŭs,
vērsūtĭă, cāllĭdĭtās, fāllācĭă, tēchnæ, īnsĭdĭæ. EPITH. Arcānŭs, lătēns, tăcĭtŭs;
dŏlōsŭs, fāllāx, pērfĭdŭs, sŭbdŏlŭs, vērsūtŭs; īnsĭdĭōsŭs, hōstĭlĭs, ĭnīquŭs, ĭnŏpīnŭs.
ăstūtĭă, æ, f., *craftiness.* Hūmāna āstūtĭă nīsă, Tert. SYN. Ăstŭs, fraŭs, dŏlŭs,
tēchnæ, fāllācĭă, cāllĭdĭtās. EPITH. Păvĭdă, cāllĭdă, dŏlōsă, dētēstāndă, sōlērs,
săgāx, hōstĭlĭs, fĭctă. V. Fallacia, Astus.
ăstūtŭs, ă, ŭm, *cunning.* Căptēs āstūtŭs ŭbīquĕ, Hor. SYN. Vērsūtŭs, văfĕr,
cāllĭdŭs, caŭtŭs, dŏlōsŭs. V. Fallax.
Astўăgēs, ĭs, m., *the king of the Medes, and grandfather of Cyrus.—2. a warrior
changed into a stone.* Dŭm stŭpĕt Astўăgēs, Ov.
Astўănāx, ăctĭs, m., *the son of Hector.* Sŭpĕr Astўănāctĭs ĭmāgo, Virg. EPITH.
Infēlīx.
Astўlŭs, ī, m., *a centaur, and a diviner.* Astўlŭs īlle ĕtĭăm, Ov.
Astўpălæă, æ, f., *one of the Cyclades.* Astўpălæă vădĭs, Ov.
Astўpălœĭŭs, ă, ŭm, *of Astypalæa.* Astўpălæĭă rēgnă, Ov.
Asўlăs, æ, m., *a man's name.* Intērprĕs Asўlăs, Ov.
ăsўlŭm, ī, n., *a sanctuary.* Jūnōnĭs ăsўlō, Virg. EPITH. Infāmĕ, sacrŭm, sē-
cūrŭm, fēlīx, ŏptābĭlĕ, ŏptātŭm, quæsītŭm, trānquĭllŭm.
|| ăsўmbŏlŭs, ă, ŭm, *who pays nothing for his reckoning.* Cœnāvĭt ăsўmbŏlŭs, Ter.
ăt, conj., *but, however.* Dĭxĭt; ăt īllă, Virg. SYN. Ast, sĕd, vērŭm, ăttămĕn.
Ătăbŭlŭs, ī, m., *a wind of Apulia.* Tōrrĕt Ătăbŭlŭs, ēt quōs, Hor.
Ătăcīnŭs, ī, m., Varro, *a Latin poet.* Vārrōne Ătăcīnō, Hor.
Ătălāntă, æ, *or* ē, ēs, f., *the daughter of Schœneus, vanquished by Hippomenes.* Nīl
ŏpŭs ēst, Ătălāntă, tĭbi, Ov. EPITH. Schœnĭs, cĭtă, vēlōx.—2. *the daughter of
Jasius, loved and married by Meleager.* Mœnălĭă Ătălāntă, Ov. EPITH. Fŭgāx,
Cālўdōnĭă, Mĕlĕăgrĭă, Arcădĭă, Nōnăcrĭă.
Ătălāntæŭs, ă, ŭm, *of Atalanta.* Jámque Ătălāntæăs, Stat.
Ătălāntĭădēs, æ, m., *the son of Atalanta, Parthenopæus.* Trūx Ătălāntĭădēs, Stat.
Ătārnītēs, æ, m., *of Atarne a city of Mysia, Hermeas.* Aŭt ŭt Ătārnītēs, Ov.
ătăvŭs, ī, m., *a grandsire.* Ăvīs ătăvīsquĕ pŏtēns, Virg. V. Avus.
ātĕr, tră, trŭm, *black.* Dēmītĭtŭr ătĕr ĭn ūrnăm, Ov. SYN. Nĭgĕr, fŭscŭs,
nĭgrăns, nĭgrēscēns, fūlĭgĭnĕ tēctŭs. V. Niger.
Ăthămān, ānĭs, m., *an inhabitant of Athamania.* Ăthămān ēt nōmĭnĕ prīscō, Luc.
Ăthămānĭă, æ, f., *a province of Ætolia or Epirus.* Ăthămānĭă fraŭdēs, Grat.
Ăthămănĭs, ĭdĭs, f., *of Athamania.* Ăthămănĭs ăquĭs, Ov.
Ăthămāntæŭs, *and* ăntĭcŭs, ă, ŭm, *of Athamas.* Ăthămāntæōsquĕ pĕrērrānt, Ov.
Ăthămāntĭădēs, æ, m., *the son of Athamas.* Ăthămāntĭădēsquĕ Pălæmōn, Ov.
Ăthămāntĭs, ĭdĭs *or* ĭdŏs, f., *the daughter of Athamas.* Ăthămāntĭdŏs Hēllēs, Ov.
Ăthămănŭs, ă, ŭm, *of Athamania.* Ăthămāna ād lĭttŏră, Prop.
Ăthămās, ăntĭs, m., *a king of Thebes, who, excited by Juno, murdered his spurious
children.* Hūnc Ăthămās, hūnc, Ov. EPITH. Infēlīx, tōrvŭs, crŭēntŭs, mĭsĕr,
īnsānŭs, fĕrōx, fŭrēns.
Athēnæ, ārŭm, f. pl., *the famous city of Greece.* Nĭsĭ nōmĕn Ăthēnæ, Ov. EPITH.
Clāræ, bŏnæ, Pāllădĭæ, Cecrŏpĭæ, Ěrēchthēæ, Mōpsŏpĭæ, Thēsēæ, dŏctæ, sŭb-
līmēs, īllūstrēs, vĕtĕrēs, Graĭæ, cĕlebrēs; āltĭlŏquæ, āntīquæ, flŏrēntēs.
Ăthēnæŭs, ă, ŭm, *of Athens.* Ēst ĕt Ăthēnæĭs, Lucr. SYN. Cecrŏpĭŭs, Păn-
dĭōnĭŭs, Pāllădĭŭs. V. Athenæ.
* Ăthēnĭēnsēs, ĭŭm, m. pl., *the Athenians.* SYN. Cecrŏpĭdæ, Thēseĭdæ, Ěrēch-
thēī, Cecrŏpĭī, Attĭcī. EPITH. Fōrtēs, gĕnĕrōsī, dŏctī; lĕvēs; fācŭndī, lŏquācēs;
mēndācēs. V. Athenæ.
Ăthēsĭs, ĭs, m., *a river in Italy.* Rīpĭs, Ăthēsīm seū, Virg.
āthlĕtă, æ, m., *a wrestler, a gladiator.* Nūnc āthlētārŭm stŭdĭĭs, Hor. SYN.
Pŭgĭl, lūctātŏr, glădĭātŏr. EPITH. Gŷmnĭcŭs, lēnĭs, īntrĕpĭdŭs, lăcērtōsŭs,
nērvōsŭs: māgnănĭmŭs, pŏtēns, ŭnctŭs, aŭdāx, rŏbūstŭs, fĕrŭs, sævŭs, ĭmmītĭs,
hōrrēndŭs, sāngŭĭnĕŭs, răbĭdŭs, crŭēntŭs, fĕrōx, atrōx, impērtērrĭtŭs.
Ăthō, ōn, ōnĭs, *or* ōs, ō, m., *a high mountain of Macedonia.* Quŏt lĕpōrēs ĭn Ăthō,
Ov. Ăspĕri Ăthōnēs, Lucil. Quāntŭs Ăthōs, aŭt, Virg. EPITH. Vāstŭs.

Æmŏnĭŭs, prœrūptŭs, sălebrōsŭs, glăcĭālĭs, vēlĭfĭcātŭs, măgnŭs, ēxcēlsŭs, sūb-lĭmĭs.

Athȳs, *or* Ătȳs, ȳdĭs, m., *a companion of Phineus.* Ĕrăt Indŭs Athȳs, Ov.—2. *a companion of Ascanius.* Altĕr Athȳs, Virg.

Ătīnă, æ, f., *a town of Campania.* Ătīnă pŏtēns, Virg.

Ătīnās, æ, m., *the name of a warrior.* Acĕr Ătīnās, Virg.

Atlāntēŭs, ĭăcŭs, ĭcŭs, *and* ĭŭs, ă, ŭm, *of Atlas.* Atlāntēŭsquĕ fīnĭs cōncŭtĭtŭr, Hor. Tālĭs Atlāntĭăcō, Aus. Ætōlōs Atlāntĭcŭs āccōlă, Sil. Atlāntĭă rēgnă, Id.

Atlāntĭădēs, æ, m., *Mercury.* Vēnĭt Atlāntĭădēs, Ov. Syn. Mĕrcŭrĭŭs. V. Mercurius

Atlāntĭdĕs, ŭm, f. pl., *the seven daughters of Atlas.* Mĕtŭānt Atlāntĭdĕs ōrtŭs, Col. Epith. Eōæ, ĭmbrĭfĕræ. V. Pleiades.—2. *the Fortunate Islands were called by the same name.*

Atlāntĭs, ĭdĭs, f., *daughter of Atlas ; of Atlas.* Ătlāntĭdĕ crētŭm, Ov.

Atlās, āntĭs, m., *the son of Jupiter, said to have borne the heavens upon his shoulders.* Mōns făctŭs Atlās, Ov. Claŭsĕrăt Atlās, Id. Epith. Cœlĭfĕr, vălĭdŭs, fōrtĭs, ārdŭŭs, prŭīnōsŭs, gĕlĭdŭs, Maŭrūsĭŭs, Maŭrŭs, Lĭbycŭs, Afrĭcŭs, pĭnĭfĕr, sūb-lĭmĭs, āstrĭfĕr, āspĕr, ōccĭdŭŭs, nūbĭfĕr, măgnŭs, āltŭs. V. Mons.

ătŏmŭs, ī, f., *an atom.* Cōnnēxa ătŏmōrŭm, Aus. Epith. Lĕvĭs, vōlĭtāns, părvă, tĕnŭĭs.

ātquĕ, conj., *and.* Atquĕ Dĕōs, ātque āstră vŏcăt, Virg. Syn. Ac, ĕt, quĕ.

ātquī, conj., *but, and yet.* Atquī nōn Mǎssĭcā Bācchī, Virg. Syn. Sĕd, ăt, ĕt ĕnĭm, sĕd ĕnĭm, āst, vērŭm.

Ătrăcĭdēs, æ, m., *an inhabitant of Thessaly.* Ĕxĭgĭt Ătrăcĭdēs, Ov.

Ătrăcĭs, ĭdĭs, f., *Thessalian.* Ătrăcĭs Hœmŏnĭŏs, Ov.

Ătrăcĭŭs, ă, ŭm, *of the river Atrax ; Thessalian.* Ătrăcĭæ sŭbĭtæ, Virg.

ātrāmēntŭm, ī, n., *ink.* Ātrāmēntă, fĕrē, Hor. Syn. Sēpĭă, sŭccŭs ātĕr. Epith. Nigrŭm, splēndēns.

ātrātŭs, ă, ŭm, *in black, in mourning.* Sōlĭs ĕt ātrātĭs, Propert. Syn. Atĕr; ātrā. vēstĕ ĭndūtŭs.

Ătrĕbătēs, ŭm, m. pl., *the ancient inhabitants of Berkshire.* Ătrĕbătŭm tērrās, Sidon.

Atreŭs, ĕŏs, ĕī *or* eī, m., *the son of Pelops, and brother of Thyestes.* Dīgnum Ātrĕō, Sen. Ătrĕi ĕt Thȳēstæ. Id. Pĕlŏpĕĭŭs Ātreŭs? Ov. Syn. Tāntălĭdēs ; Thȳ-ēstæ frātĕr : Pĕlŏpĕĭŭs hērōs. Epith. Fĕrŭs, dīrŭs, nĕfārĭŭs, bārbărŭs, ĭmmānĭs, trŭcŭlēntŭs, pĕrfĭdŭs, atrōx, sānguĭnĕŭs, sūbdŏlŭs, ĭnsĭdĭōsŭs, ĭnhūmānŭs, hŏr-rēndŭs, crŭēntŭs, crūdēlĭs, fŭrēns, fĕrōx.

Atrĕŭs, ă, ŭm, *of Atreus.* I prĕcŏr, Ātrĕī sī quĭd, St.

ātrĭcŏlŏr, ōrĭs, *black.* Plūmĕŭs, ātrĭcŏlŏr, Ov.

Atrīdēs, *or* dă, æ, m., *the son of Atreus, Agamemnon, or Menelaus.* Pŏpŭlātŏr Ătrīdēs, Ov. Gāvīsŭs Ătrīdă trĭūmpho ēst, Prop. Quĭn ĕt Ătrīdās, Hor. Epith. Gĕmĭnŭs, fōrtĭs, măgnănĭmŭs, gĕnĕrōsŭs, clărŭs, grăvĭs.

ātrĭŭm, *and* Iŏlŭm, (dimin.) ī, n., *a court-yard, hall.* Ătrĭă lūstrăt, Virg. Syn. Pōrtĭcŭs, vēstĭbŭlŭm, līmĕn. Epith. Ærātŭm, mārmŏrĕŭm, pŭlchrŭm, fŭlgĭ-dŭm, sŭblīmĕ, nŏbĭlĕ, lātŭm, spătĭōsŭm, măgnĭfĭcŭm, nĭtĭdŭm, ēxĭmĭŭm, præ-clārŭm, nĭtēns.

atrōcĭtĕr, adv., *cruelly.* Mŏrĭtūram ătrōcĭtĕr ōrĭs, Man. Syn. Crūdēlĭtĕr, fĕrōcĭtĕr.

Ătrŏpŏs, ī, f., *one of the three Parcæ, or Fates.* Ătrŏpŏs ĕt Lăchĕsĭs, Claud. Epith. Ĭmmūtābĭlĭs, dūră, fŭnēstă, crūdēlĭs, ĭmmītĭs, ĭnēxŏrābĭlĭs. V. Parcæ.

atrōx, ocĭs, *cruel, fierce.* Ecce ĭnĭmīcŭs ătrōx, Virg. Ătrōx ĭllă fīdēs, Stat. Syn. Dīrŭs, crūdēlĭs, ĭnĭmītĭs. bārbărŭs, ĭnhūmānŭs, fĕrōx, āspĕr.

Āttă, æ, m., *a Latin poet.* Pĕrāmbŭlĕt Āttæ Fābŭlă, Hor.

āttāctŭs, ūs, m., *a touch.* Vŏlvĭtŭr āttāctū, Virg. Syn. Tāctŭs, cōntāctŭs.

āttăgēn, ēnĭs, m., *and* Āttăgēnă, æ, f., *a kind of pheasant.* Nōn āttăgēn Iŏnĭcŭs, Hor. Gŭstŭs āttăgēnārŭm, Mart.

Āttălĭcŭs, ă, ŭm, *of Attalus ; sumptuous.* Āttălĭcĭs cōndĭtĭōnĭbŭs, Hor. Syn. Pērgămĕŭs.

Āttălŭs, ī, m., *a king of Pergamus, celebrated for his riches.* Nĕque Āttăli ĭgnōtŭs, Hor. Epith. Pērgămĕŭs, dīvĕs, pŏtēns.

āttămĕn, conj., *however.* Făcĭs āttămĕn ōmnĭă bēllĕ, Mart. Syn. Vērŭm, tămĕn, ăt, āst, sĕd.

‖ āttĕgĭæ, ārŭm, f. pl., *huts.* Maŭrōrum āttĕgĭās, Juv.
Āttēllānŭs, ă, ŭm, *of Attella, a town in Campania, where an ancient kind of farces were first played.* Rīsŭm mŏvĕt Āttēllānæ, Juv.
āttēmpĕro, ās, *to make fit.* Āttēmpĕrăt aūrēs, Virg.
āttēndo, dī, tŭm, *to take care, to hear.* Nūllo āttēndēntĕ dĕōrŭm, Sil. Syn.
Intēndo, aūdĭo, ādvērto, aūscūlto. V. Audio.
āttēntĕ, adv., *with care.* Spēctāre āttēntĭŭs, Hor.
āttēnto, ās, *to attempt.* Āttēntārĕ nĕfās, Virg.
āttēntŭs, ă, ŭm, *attentive.* Āspĕr ĕt āttēntŭs quæsītīs, Hor.
āttĕnŭo, ās, *to diminish.* Āttĕnŭārĕ tŭōs, Ov. Syn. Tĕnŭo, ēxtĕnŭo, ĭmmĭnŭo, dīmĭnŭo.
āttĕro, āttrīvī, ītŭm, *to rub against.* Quō măgĭs āttĕrĭtŭr, Prop. Syn. Tĕro, prōtĕro, cōntĕro, cōncūlco, prōcūlco.
* āttĕxo, xŭī, xtŭm, *to knit.* Cæs. Syn. Āddo, ādjūngo, ānnēcto, āpplĭco.
āttēstŏr, ārĭs, ārī, *to call to witness.* Āttēstārĕ dĕōs, Aus.
Ātthĭs, ĭdĭs, f., *the country of Attica.* Ātthĭdĕ tēnlāntŭr, Lucr. Syn. Āttĭcă.—
2. *a nightingale.* Ātthĭdĕs īn nīdĭs, M. V. Philomela.
Āttĭcī, ōrŭm, m. pl., *the inhabitants of Attica.* Epith. Fōrtēs, gĕnĕrōsī, dōctī, lĕvēs, fācūndī, lŏquācēs, mēndācēs. V. Athenæ.
Āttĭcŭs, ă, ŭm, *Attic, Athenian.* Āttĭcă pŏnĭt ăpĭs, Ov.
‖ āttĭgŭŭs, ă, ŭm, *contiguous.* Gūrgĭtĭs āttĭgŭăm, Aus. Syn. Cōntĭgŭŭs, prōxĭmŭs, vīcīnŭs.
Āttĭlā, *and* Ātĭlă, æ, m., *the king of the Huns, who called himself the Scourge of God.* Āttĭlā tūrmīs, Sid. Tārtārĕās Ātĭlăm, Mant. Epith. Dīrŭs, sævŭs, fĕrōx, īmpĭŭs, sacrīlĕgŭs.
āttĭnĕt, *it belongs to.* Tē nĭhĭl āttĭnĕt, (Alcaic.) Hor. Syn. Pērtĭnĕt, spēctăt.
āttīngo, tĭgĭ, āctŭm, *to touch.* Āttĭgĭt hērbăm, Virg. Syn. Tāngo, pērtīngo, vĕnĭo, āccēdo.
Āttĭŭs. · V. Accius.
āttōllo, sūstŭlī, sūblătŭm, *to lift.* Āttōllĭtquĕ glōbōs, Virg. Syn. Erĭgo, ēvĕho, ēffĕro, tōllo, fĕro.
āttōndĕo, ēs, dī, sŭm, *to clip close, to shear.* Dŭm tĕnĕra āttōndēnt. V. Tondeo.
āttŏnĭtŭs, ă, ŭm, *astonished.* Gūttă pĕr āttŏnĭtăs, Ov. Syn. Tērrĭtŭs, pērcūlsŭs, stŭpĕfāctŭs, stŭpēns. V. Territus, Obstupefactus.
āttŏno, ās, ŭī, *to astonish.* Āttŏnŭērĕ sŭō, Ov.
āttrăho, āttrāxī, ctŭm, *to draw to.* Vātēs ūttrāxĕrăt, Ov. Syn. Āllĭcĭo, trăho.
āttrēcto, ās, *to touch.* Āttrēctārĕ nĕfās, Virg. Syn. Trācto, pălpo.
āttrĭbŭo, ŭī, ūtŭm, *to attribute.* Āttrĭbŭīt, lōtŭmquĕ, Man. Syn. Trĭbŭo, āssīgno, āddīco, āscrībo, cōncēdo.
āttrĭbūtŭs, ă, ŭm, *the pass. partic. of* attribuo. Āttrĭbūtŭs ēst ērrŏr, (Scaz.) Cat.
āttrītŭs, ă, ŭm, *the pass partic. of* attero. Ēt grăvĭs āttrītā, Virg. Syn. Trītŭs, prōtrītŭs, cālcātŭs.
Ātŭr, ŭrĭs, m., *a river of France.* Vīctŭs Ātŭr, Cat.
Āttўs *or* Ātўs, ўīs *or* ўŏs, Āttĭs, ĭdĭs, *and* Āttīn, īnĭs, m., *a young man, loved by Cybele, and punished for his inconstancy.* Lūcēntĭbŭs Āttўs, Stat. Fœmĭna ŭt Āttўs, Ov. Bĕrĕcynthĭŭs Āttīn, Pers. Epith. Cўbĕlēĭŭs, Bĕrĕcynthĭŭs; Phrўx, sēmĭvĭr, tĕnĕr, pūlchĕr, vĕnūstŭs, rŏsĕŭs, cāndĭdŭs, lāctĕŭs, dĕcōrŭs.—
2. Ātўs, ўdĭs, m. V. Athys.
ăvārĭtĭă, æ, *or* ăvārĭtĭēs, ēī, f., *avarice.* Fērvĕt ăvārĭtĭă, Hor. Dēnĭque ăvārĭtĭēs, ĕt hŏnōrŭm, Lucr. Epith. Cŭpĭdă, crŭēntă, hĭāns, tābĭdă, trīstĭs, sōllĭcĭtă, tūrpĭs, fœdă, ĭnēxplētă, sĭtĭbūndă, ārdēns, mĭsĕră, lāngŭĭdă, răbĭdă, īndĭgă, īnsōmnĭs, cæcă, fŭrēns, īrrĕquĭētă, vĭgĭl, pērvĭgĭl, răpāx, pārcă, ĕgĕnă, īndīgnă, sævă, trŭx, fĕrōx, mălĕsānă. V. Avarus.
ăvārŭs, ă, ŭm, *covetous, avaricious.* Vēntrī dōnābăt ăvārō, Hor. Syn. Pārcŭs, tĕnāx, sōrdĭdŭs.—2. ŭs, ī, m., *a miser.* Sēmpĕr ăvārŭs ĕgĕt, Hor. Epith. Mēndīcŭs, paūpĕr, vĭgĭl, tūrpĭs, sōrdĭdŭs, sōllĭcĭtŭs, īnsătĭābĭlĭs, cŭpĭdŭs, mĭsĕr, īnfēlīx, lāngŭĭdŭs, īnfāmĭs, dīvēs, răbĭdŭs, sĭtĭbūndŭs, ĕgĕnŭs, ĕgēns, trīstĭs, ĭnēxplētŭs, mĭsĕrāndŭs, pāllĭdŭs, ārdēns.
aūcēps, aūcŭpĭs, m., *a fowler.* Aūcŭpĭs īdĕm, Mart. Epith. Cāllĭdŭs, vērsūtŭs, īnsĭdĭōsŭs, fāllāx, vĭgĭl, vĭgĭlāns, pēllāx, āstūtŭs, prōmptŭs, sōlērs, dŏlōsŭs, ābdĭtŭs, pērvĭgĭl, īmmōtŭs, ăvĭdŭs, īmpĭgĕr, prŏpĕrŭs, sūbdŏlŭs, īnsōmnĭs.

auctĭo, ōnĭs, f., *a sale by auction*. Quŏd auctĭŏ vēndĭt, Juv.

auctŏr, ōrĭs, m. f, *an author, a chief, an adviser*. Nōmĭnĭs auctŏr ĕrĭs, Ov. SYN. Suāsŏr, īmpŭlsŏr, hōrtātŏr ; dōctŏr, măgīstĕr ; căpŭt, prīncēps, dūx.

auctōrĭtās, ātĭs, f., *authority*. Si auctōrĭtātĕm, (Iamb.) SYN. Pŏndŭs, mō-mēntŭm, vīs ; fĭdēs, nōmĕn ; pŏtēstās, īmpĕrĭum.

auctōro, ās, *to engage*. Auctōrātŭs ēās, Hor.

auctŭs, ă, ŭm, *the pass. partic. of* augeo. Et hŏnōrĭbŭs auctōs, Hor.

aucŭpĭŭm, ĭī, n., *birding or fowling*. Sūm Dĕŭs aucŭpĭŏ, Prop. SYN. Avĭŭm vēnātĭo. EPITH. Sūbtīlĕ, dŏlōsŭm, fāllāx, āstūtŭm.

aucŭpŏr, ārĭs, *to go a birding or fowling*. Aucŭpŏr īnfēlīx, Ov.

audācĭă, æ, f., *audaciousness*. Audācĭă mīstă pŭdōrī, Ov. SYN. Impătĭēns, īn-dŏcĭlĭs ănĭmŭs ; īngēntēs ănĭmī ; ārdŏr ănĭmī ; vīrtūs āccēnsă ; audācēs ănĭmī. V. Audeo.

audāctĕr, adv., *boldly*. Et mĭnŭs audāctĕr, Ov. SYN. Audēntĕr ; audācī ănĭmō ; gĕnĕrōsē, fōrtĭtĕr.

audāx, ācĭs, *bold*. Dīcăt ; ĕt audācī, Prop. SYN. Audēns, īntērrĭtŭs, īmpēr-tērrĭtŭs, īntrĕpĭdŭs, īmpăvĭdŭs, gĕnĕrōsŭs, fōrtĭs ; tĕmĕrārĭŭs, īncōnsūltŭs, ănĭmī præcēps. V. Audeo, Fortis, Generosus.

audĕo, ausŭs sŭm, *to dare*. Audĕăt ēsŭrĭēns, Hor. SYN. Audāx sŭm, nōn tĭmĕo, sŭm īntrĕpĭdŭs ; nōn dŭbĭto ; cōnfīdo. V. Pericula adire.

audĭo, īvī *or* ĭī, ītŭm, *to hear*. Audĭăt hæc gĕnĭtŏr, Virg. SYN. Ausculto ; ēx-audĭo ; ŏbēdĭo. V. Attendo.

audĭtŏr, ōrĭs, m., *an auditor*. Excĭtăt audĭtŏr stŭdĭŭm, Ov. SYN. Audĭēns, dīscĭ-pŭlŭs.

audĭtŭs, ă, ŭm, *the pass. partic. of* audio. Crēscĭt ; ĕt audĭtĭs, Ov. V. Audio.

audĭtŭs, ūs, m., *the sense of hearing*. Audĭtū tĕnŭs, Aus.

ăvē, *God save you*. Pōrtăt ĭnēptŭs ăvē, Mart. SYN. Sălvē.

āvēctŭs, ă, ŭm, *the pass. partic. of* aveho. Infŭdĭunt, āvēctāquĕ pārtĭm, Virg.

āvĕho, āvēxī, āvēctŭm, *to carry away*. Plaut. Ter. SYN. Vĕho, dēvĕho.

ăvēllo, vēllī, vŭlsŭm, *to drag away*. Sācrāto ăvēllĕrĕ tēmplŏ, Virg. SYN. Vēllo, cōnvēllo, ēxtīrpo, ābstrăho, aufĕro.

ăvēnă, æ, f., *oats*. Stăbăt ăvēnă sōlŏ, Ov. SYN. Călămŭs, ărūndo, fīstŭlă, cĭcūtă, cūlmŭs. EPITH. Exīlĭs, ēxĭgŭă, grăcĭlĭs, tĕrĕs, ĭnērs, ŭdă, bĭbŭlă, dŏcĭlĭs, ārgŭtă, rĕsŏnāns, āltĭsŏnă, sēptĭfŏrĭs, Phœbĕă, rūstĭcă, sylvēstrĭs. V. Fistula.

Avēntīnŭs, ī, m., *Mount Aventine, one of the hills on which Rome was built.* Cōllĭs Avēntīnī, Virg. EPITH. Cēlsŭs, Rōmānŭs.—2. *a son of Hercules.* Pūlchĕr Avēntīnŭs, Virg.—3. *a king of Alba.* Trādĭt Avēntīnŏ, Ov.—4. ă, ŭm, *of the Aventine.* Cœpĭt Avēntīnă Pāllăs ĭn ārcĕ cŏlī, Ov.

ăvĕo, *to wish*. E quĭbŭs ūnŭs ăvĕt, Hor. SYN. Cŭpĭo, ŏpto, ēxŏpto, vŏlo, dē-sĭdĕro.

Avērnālĭs, ĕ, *of Avernus*. Intĕr Avērnālēs, Ov. SYN. Avērnŭs, ă, ŭm. Avērnĭcŭs, Tārtărĕŭs, Infērnŭs, Stўgĭŭs, Tænărĭŭs, Phlĕgĕthōntæŭs, Achĕrōntĭcŭs.

Avērnŭs, ī, m., ă, ōrŭm, n. pl., *a lake in the territory of Naples ; Hell.* Dēscēnsŭs Avērnī, Virg. SYN. Orcŭs, Infērnŭs, Tārtărŭs. EPITH. Tārtărĕŭs, Stўgĭŭs, Achĕrōntæŭs, ŏlēns, trīstĭs, fœtēns, nĭgĕr, īmmītĭs, lūgēns, sĭlēns, pĭgĕr, tăcĭtŭs, văcŭŭs, pēstĭfĕr, īnvīsŭs, ĭnēxplētŭs, tētĕr, prŏfūndŭs, hōrrĭbĭlĭs, cæcŭs, squā-lēns, lūrĭdŭs, ōbscūrŭs, ŭmbrōsŭs, fœtĭdŭs, putrĭs. V. Infernus.

āvērsābĭlĭs, ĕ, *abominable*. Scĕlŭs āvērsābĭlĕ cūmque ēst, Lucr. SYN. Dētēstābĭlĭs.

āvērsŏr, ārĭs, *to hate, fly from*. Nōn āvērsātŭs hŏnōrĕm, Ov. SYN. Fŭgĭo, rĕfŭgĭo, ōdī, dētēstŏr, ăbŏmĭnŏr, ēxecrŏr.

āvērsŭs, ă, ŭm, *turned away*. Ocŭlōs āvērsă tĕnēbăt, Virg. SYN. Alĭēnŭs, ĭn-ĭmīcŭs, īnfēnsŭs.

āvērto, tī, sŭm, *to turn away*. Lĭbўcās āvērtĕrĕt ōrās, Virg. SYN. Abdūco, āvŏco, ămŏvĕo.

aufĕro, ābstŭlī, āblātŭm, *to take away*. Aufĕrĕt ēxtrēmī, Prop. SYN. Tōllo, ērĭpĭo, ădĭmo, răpĭo, ēxtōrquĕo, ābrĭpĭo. V. Furor, aris.

Aufīdĭŭs, ĭī, m., *the name of a man*. Fūndōs Aufīdĭŏ Lūscŏ, Hor.

Aufīdŭs, ī, m., *a river of Apulia*. Vērbĕrăt Aufīdŭs ūndās, Virg.

aufŭgĭo, aufŭgī, *to fly from*. Aufŭgĕ blāndĭtĭăs, Prop. SYN. Fŭgĭo, dīffŭgĭo, vīto.

augĕo, xī, ctŭm, *to increase*. Altārĭbŭs augĕt, Virg. SYN. Adaugĕo, ēxaugĕo, āmplĭfĭco, ēxtēndo, mūltĭplĭco, cŭmŭlo, āccŭmŭlo. V. Accumulo.

aūgēsco, ĕre, *the frequent.* of augeo. Aūgēscŭnt ăllæ, Lucr. Syn. Aūgĕŏr, crēsco, cŭmŭlŏr, ădŏlēsco.

Aūgīās *and* ēās, æ, m , *a king of Elis, whose stables Hercules cleansed.* Sēptĭmŭs Aūgĭæ stăbŭlŭm, Auson.

aūgmĕn, Ĭnĭs, *or* ēntŭm, ĭ, n., *increase.* Aūgmĭnă nōctēs, Lucr.

aūgŭr, ŭrĭs, m., *a soothsayer.* Aūgŭrĭbŭs Phœbŭs, Ov. Syn. Ărūspēx, vātēs, aūspĕx. Epith. Pērītŭs, prōvĭdŭs, fātĭdĭcŭs, Phœbēĭŭs, præscĭŭs, prænūncĭŭs, vĭgĭl, cērtŭs, săcĕr. V. Aruspex, Vates.

aūgŭrĭŭm, ĭĭ, n., *divination.* NĬ frūstra aūgŭrĭŭm, Virg. Syn. Vātĭcĭnĭŭm, aūspĭcĭŭm. Epith. Fātĭdĭcŭm, trīstĕ, cæcŭm, īnfēlīx, bŏnŭm, mălŭm, cērtŭm, īncērtŭm, prōspĕrŭm, fătālĕ, ădvērsŭm, āncēps, dŭbĭŭm, præsăgŭm, tērrĭfĭcŭm, ōptātŭm, sĭnĭstrŭm.

aūgŭrŏr, ārĭs, *or* o, ās *to presage.* Aūgŭrŏr, ŭxōrĭs, Tib. Mēns aūgŭrăt, ōpto, Virg. Syn. Vātĭcĭnŏr, prædīco, ĭs. V. Prædico, is; Vaticinor.

Aūgūstă, æ, f., *a title of the Roman empresses.* Aūgūstă nŏvŭm, Ov.

Aūgūstīnŭs, [Sanctus,] ĭ, m., *a doctor of the church of Rome.* Aūgūstīnŭs ĕrăt, P. Syn. Aūrēlĭŭs.

Aūgūstŭs, ĭ, m., *the name of the emperor Octavius and his successors.* Tērră sŭb Aūgūstō, Ov. Syn. Cæsăr. Epith. Vīctŏr, fēlīx, īndŏmĭtŭs, gĕnĕrōsŭs, pācĭfĭcŭs, bēllĭgĕr, īnvīctŭs, pĭŭs, mītĭs, fōrtĭs.—2. *August, the eighth month.* Aūgūstŭm mēnsĕm, Aug. Syn. Sēxtĭlĭs. Epith. Spĭcĕŭs, frūgĭfĕr, călĭdŭs, tōrrĭdŭs, ārĭdŭs, ūstŭs, fērvēns, sĭtĭbūndŭs, ĭnĕrs, pĭgĕr, Ĭgnāvŭs, sēgnĭs, pŭl-vĕrŭlēntŭs, trĭtĭcĕŭs.—3. ă, ŭm, *majestic.* Tēctum aūgūstum, īngēns, Virg. Syn. Vĕnĕrāndŭs, vĕnĕrābĭlĭs, cōlēndŭs, sānctŭs, săcĕr, sucrātŭs, rēlĭgĭōsŭs.

- ăvĭă, æ, f.. *a grandame.* Ecce ăvĭa aŭt, Pers.

ăvĭārĭŭm, ĭĭ, n., *an aviary.* Rŭbēnt ăvĭārĭă băccĭs, Virg.

ăvĭdĭtās, ātĭs, f., *avidity.* Plaut. Syn. Cŭpĭdĭtās, cŭpīdo, fămēs, sĭtĭs, ārdŏr, dēsĭdĕrĭŭm.

ăvĭdŭs, ă, ŭm, *eager.* Sævæque ăvĭdīssĭmă cædĭs, Ov. Syn. Cŭpĭdŭs, stŭdĭōsŭs, ămāns, āppĕtēns.

ăvĭs, ĭs, f., *a bird.* Nŭnc ăvĭs īn rāmō, Ov. Syn. Vŏlucrĭs, ālĕs. Epith. Acrĭs, gārrŭlă, ārgūtă, văgă, păvĭdă, lŏquāx, nūbĭvăgă, āĕrĭă, præpĕs, ālĭgĕră, quĕrŭlă, răpĭdă, lēvĭs, tĭmĭdă, cĭtă, fūgĭtīvă, pēnnātă, pēnnĭgĕră, cĕlĕr, vēlōx, fŭgāx, cĭcūrătă. V. Ales, Volucris.

ăvītŭs, ă, ŭm, *left by ancestors.* Cōnsēdĭt ăvītō, Virg. Syn. Pătrĭŭs, pătērnŭs.

- ăvĭŭs, ă, ŭm, *pathless.* Ăvĭă tŭm rĕsŏnănt, Virg. Syn. Invĭŭs, īmpervĭŭs, dē-vĭŭs, āmbĭgŭŭs, āncēps, īncērtŭs, cæcŭs. Phr. Plēnŭs āmbāgĭbŭs; dēcĭpĭēns ērrōrĕ lŏcōrŭm.

aūlă, æ, f., *a hall, a prince's court.* Exĕăt aūlă, Val. Epith. Văcŭă, nĭtĭdă, sŭb-lĭmĭs, pătēns, vĕnĕrābĭlĭs, māgnĭfĭcă, aūgūstă, vărĭă, prædīvĕs, spătĭōsă, pūlchră, splēndĭdă, aūrātă, pīctă, sŭpērbă, clāră, īllūstrĭs, rēgĭă, mārmŏrĕă, părātă, ōrnātă, cōrūscāns, rēgālĭs. V. Domus, Regia.

aūlæă, ōrŭm, n. pl., *hangings, curtains.* Pōrtĭcŭs, aūlæĭs, Prop. Syn. Tăpētēs. Epith. Sŭspēnsă, sŭpērbă, vărĭătă, pēndēntĭă, pīctă, pēndŭlă, īnsĭgnĭă, Băbўlōnĭcă, Tўrĭă, splēndēntĭă; aūrō grăvĭă; spīrāntĭă sīgnĭs. V. Tapes.

Aūlētēs, æ, m., *a king of Etruria.* Ĭt grăvĭs Aūlētēs, Virg.

aūlĭcŭs, ă, ŭm, *court-like.*—2. ĭ, m., *a courtier.* Jŭvĕnŭm, sĕd aūlĭcōrŭm, (Phal.) Sid.

Aūlĭs, ĭdĭs, f., *a part of Bœotia.* Aūlĭdĕ jūrāvī, Virg. Epith. Pīscōsă, Eūbŏĭcă, Bœōtă.

Aūlōn, ōnĭs, m., *a mountain of Calabria.* Fēlīx vītĭbŭs Aūlōn, Mart.

Aūlŭs, ĭ, m., *the name of several Romans.* Tālŏs, Aūlĕ, nŭcēsquĕ, Hor.

Aūnŭs, ĭ, m., *the name of a man.* Fīlĭŭs Aūnī, Virg.

ăvŏco, ās, *to call away.* Mĕlĭŏr sŏnŭs āvŏcĕt aūrēs, Calph. Syn. Āvērto, ābdūco, ābstrăho.

ăvŏlo, ās, *to fly away.* Āvŏlăt īmpĕtĕ mīlĕs, Sil. Syn. Ēvŏlo, aūfŭgĭo, aūfĕrŏr, ēxĕo, fŭgĭo, ăbĕo.

aūră, æ, f., *a breeze.* Spīrāvĭt crīnĭbŭs aūră, Virg. Syn. Āēr, æthēr, vēntŭs, flātŭs, flāmĕn. Epith. Tĕpēns, dĭffūsă, æthĕrĕă, spīrāns, flŭēns, lĭquĭdă, tĕnŭĭs, gĕlĭdă, frīgĭdă, lēvĭs, văgă, mōbĭlĭs, fūmĭdă, cĭtă, hūmĭdă, nūbĭfĕră, mūtābĭlĭs,

circumflŭă, Bŏrĕālĭs, jūcūndă, nōctūrnă, vītālĭs ; æstīvă, aprīcă, tĕnĕră, mītĭs, lēnĭs, fœcūndă, fūrĭōsă, ōptātă, sĕcūndă. V. Aër, Zephyrus.
aŭrārĭŭs, ă, ŭm, *belonging to gold.* Vēnĭăs aŭrārĭă caŭsæ, Var.
aŭrātŭs, ă, ŭm, *gilded.* Aŭrātī bĭs sēx, Virg.
Aŭrēlĭă, æ, f., *the name of a woman.* Aŭrēlĭă vēndăt, Juv.
Aŭrēlĭŭs, ĭī, m., *a Roman orator.* Fŭri ĕt Aŭrēlī, Cat.
aŭrĕŏlŭs, ĭ, m., *a little piece of gold.* Aŭrĕŏlōs ūltrō, Mart.
aŭrĕŭs, ă, ŭm, *of gold.* Aŭrĕŭs ; ēt sĭmĭlī, Virg.
aŭrĭcŏlŏr, ōrĭs, *of a golden colour.* Aŭrĭcŏlōrĭă mălă, Mant. SYN. Aŭrĕŭs, flāvŭs.
aŭrĭcŏmŭs, ă, ŭm, *who has golden locks.* Jăm pŭĕr aŭrĭcŏmō, Sil.
aŭrĭcŭlă, æ, f., *a diminutive of* auris. Aŭrĭcŭlĭs ălĭēnĭs cŏllĭgĭs ēscās, Pers. V. Aures.
aŭrĭcŭlārĭs, ĕ, *which belongs to the ear.* Dĭgĭti aŭrĭcŭlārĭs, Mart.
aŭrĭfĕr, ă, ŭm, *that brings gold.* Fŭlvōs aŭrĭfĕră, Sil. SYN. Aŭrĭgĕr.
aŭrĭfēx, ĭcĭs, m., *a goldsmith.* Ēt dāta ăb aŭrĭfĭcŭm, M.
aŭrīgă, æ, m., *a charioteer, driver.* Cūrrūs aŭrīgă pătĕrnī, Ov. EPITH. Dŏcĭlĭs, īmprŏpĕrŭs, pĕrītŭs, prūdēns, sōllĭcĭtŭs, cĕlĕr, cĭtŭs, vēlōx, fōrtĭs, lăcērtōsŭs, rŏbūstŭs, īmpĭgĕr, clāmōsŭs, īndŏcĭlĭs, īmprūdēns.—2. *a constellation,* Cic.
aŭrīgĕnă, æ, m., *a name given to Perseus.* Hāctĕnŭs aŭrīgĕnæ, Ov.
aŭrīgĕr, ă, ŭm, *that bears gold.* Aŭrīgĕrĭs Dīvŭm, Cic. SYN. Aŭrĭfĕr, aŭrātŭs.
aŭrīlĕgŭs, ă, ŭm, *who collects gold.* Mĕ vŏcēt aŭrīlĕgĭs, T.
aŭrĭs, ĭs, f., *the ear ;* aŭrēs, ĭŭm, f. pl., *the ears.* Sērmōnĭbŭs aŭrĕm, Hor. Aŭrĭbŭs haŭsī, Virg. SYN. Aŭrĭcŭlæ. EPITH. Pătŭlæ, cāvæ, īmmōtæ, ăvĭdæ, vĭgĭlēs, cūrvātæ, tĕnēllæ, ăcūtæ, cŭpĭdæ, prōnæ, plăcĭdæ, ōbsĕrātæ, āttēntæ, ămĭcæ, văcŭæ, făcĭlēs, ārrēctæ, sūrdæ, dēcēptæ. V. Audio.
aŭrītŭs, *and* ītŭlŭs, ă, ŭm, *having ears, long ears.* Aŭrītōsquĕ sĕquī lĕpŏrēs, Virg.
Aŭrōră, æ, f., *the goddess of morning.* Līnquēns Aŭrōră cŭbĭlĕ, Virg. SYN. Ēōs, Pāllāntĭăs, Mātūtă, Leŭcŏthŏē, Tīthōnĭă cōnjūx. EPITH. Pāllĭdă, hŭmĭdă, pūrpŭrĕă, ālmă, rŭtĭlāns, prævĭă, fūlgĭdă, rŏsĕă, clără, mātūră, lūcĭfĕră, fōrmōsă, sĕrēnă, crŏcĕă, vĭgĭl, tārdă, stēllĭfŭgă, rĕdūx.
Aŭrōrĕŭs, ă, ŭm, *of Aurora.* Aŭrōrĕă vūltŭ, Mant.
aŭrŭm, ĭ, n., *gold.* Ārgēntī pōndŭs ĕt aŭrī, Virg. EPITH. Rēgālĕ, cŏrŭscāns, fūlgēns, ōbrŷzŭm, mĭcāns, nĭtĭdŭm, clārŭm, sōlĭdŭm, dīvĕs, rŭtĭlŭm, rădĭāns, pāllĭdŭm, prĕtĭōsŭm. tērsŭm, Dālmătĭcŭm, rŭtĭlāns, īnvĭdĭōsŭm, flāvŭm, fūlvŭm, nōbĭlĕ, fātālĕ, ēxĭtĭālĕ, ōptātŭm, spĕcĭōsŭm, nŏcēns, ōptātŭm, grātŭm, jūcūndŭm, Hīspānŭm, ădōrātŭm, ēxpĕtītŭm, lēntŭm, fūsĭlĕ, cælātŭm. V. Pecunia.
Aŭrūncă, æ, f., *an ancient town of Campania.* Aŭrūŋcæ flēxĭt ălŭmnŭs, Juv.
Aŭrūncī, ōrŭm, m. pl., *ancient inhabitants of Campania.* Aŭrūncī Rŭtŭlīquĕ, Virg.—2. ŭs, ă, ŭm, *of the Aurunci.* Aŭrūncæquĕ mănŭs, Virg.
aŭscŭlto, ās, *to listen.* Jāmdūdum aŭscŭlto, Hor. SYN. Aŭdĭo, ādvērto. V. Attendo.
Aŭsŏn, ŏnĭs, m., *of Ausonia, of Italy.* Aŭsŏnĕ tĕrră, T. Maur.—2. Aŭsŏnĕs, ŭm, m. pl., *Ausonians, Italians.* Aŭsŏnŭm pōrtŭs, Stat.
Aŭsŏnĭă, æ, f., *a part of Italy, Italy.* Aŭsŏnĭæ nĕquĕ Aŭsŏnĭæ, Virg. SYN. Itălĭă, Lătĭŭm. EPITH. Dīvĕs, sŭpērbă, ārmĭpŏtēns, fērtĭlĭs. V. Italia.
Aŭsŏnĭdæ, ārŭm, m. pl., *the Ausonians, Italians.* Aŭsŏnĭdæ Phrŷgĭbŭs, L. SYN. Aŭsŏnĕs, Aŭsŏnĭī, Lătīnī, Lătĭī, Itălī. V. Itali.
Aŭsŏnĭs, ĭdĭs, f., *Ausonian, Italian.* Aŭsŏnĭs ōră sŏnĭs, Ov.
Aŭsŏnĭŭs, ă, ŭm, *Ausonian, Italian.* Aŭsŏnĭă Teŭcrōs cōnsīdĕrĕ tĕrră, Virg.—2. Aŭsŏnĭī, ōrŭm, m. pl., *the same as* Ausonidæ.
aŭspēx, ĭcĭs, m., *a diviner.* Dīs ĕquĭdem aŭspĭcĭbŭs, Virg. SYN. Aŭgŭr. V. Augur, Author, Dux.
aŭspĭcātŭs, ă, ŭm, *lucky.* Nōn aŭspĭcātōs, (Alcaic.) Hor. SYN. Faŭstŭs, prōspĕr, fēlīx, făvēns.
aŭspĭcĭŭm, ĭī, n., *divination.* Aŭspĭcĭīs ĭtĕrŭm, Claud.
aŭspĭcŏr, ārĭs, *to gather from omens, to begin.* Hīnc aŭspĭcārī, (Iamb.) Sen. SYN. Aŭgŭrŏr ; īncĭpĭŏ, sŭscĭpĭŏ. V. Auguror.
aŭstĕr, strī, m., *the south wind.* Tērrŭĭt aŭstĕr ĕŭntēs, Virg. SYN. Nŏtŭs. EPITH. Hŭmĭdŭs, frīgĭdŭs, nŭbĭlŭs, tūrbĭdŭs, vălĭdŭs, plŭvĭŭs, īnsānŭs, præcĕps, hŭmēns, tōrrĭdŭs, mădĭdŭs, īmbrĭfĕr, mădēns, nōxĭŭs, nŏcēns, nŏcŭŭs. V. Ventus, Notus.—2. *the south.* Căprĭcōrnŭs vērsŭs ăd aŭstrŭm, Cic.

aŭstērĭtās, ātĭs, f., *austerity.* Nŭlla aŭstērĭtās, (Iamb. Dim.) Prud. Syn. Aspĕrĭtās, dūrĭtĭēs, grăvĭtās, sĕvērĭtās.

aŭstērŭs, ă, ŭm, *harsh, grave.* Quī vŏlĕt aŭstērŏs, Prop. Syn. Sĕvērŭs, grăvĭs, dūrŭs, āspĕr, ĭmmītĭs.

aŭstrālĭs, ĕ, *southern.* Aŭstrālĭbŭs hūmĭdă nĭmbĭs, Ov.

aŭstrīnŭs, ă, ŭm, *from the south.* Aŭstrīnōs tŭlĕrĭt, Virg.

|| aŭstrŭm, ī, n., *a wheel to draw water with.* Aŭstră vĭdēmŭs, Lucr.

aŭsŭs, ūs, m., *and* aŭsŭm, ī, n., *an adventurous act.* Aŭsĭbŭs Ĭllĭcĭtĭs, Prosp. Ānnŭăt aŭsĭs, Ov. Epith. Impăvĭdŭs, Hērcŭlĕŭs, stŏlĭdŭs, tĕmĕrārĭŭs, gĕnĕrōsŭs, grăndĭs, fŭrĭālĭs, vălĭdŭs, præcēps, cæcŭs, pĕtŭlāns, sŏns, ĭmpĭŭs, mălĕsānŭs, răpĭdŭs, præstāns, nĕfāndŭs, prŏtērvŭs. V. Audax.

aŭt, conj., *or.* Aŭt ārĭs sērvīrĕ sācrĭs, Virg. Syn. Vĕl, seŭ ; sīvĕ, vĕ.

aŭtĕm, conj., *but, nevertheless.* Ille aŭtĕm, Virg. Syn. Ăt, āst, sĕd, vērŭm.

Aŭtŏmĕdōn, ōntĭs, m., *the equerry of Achilles.* Ărmĭgĕr Aŭtŏmĕdōn, Virg.

Aŭtŏlŏlēs, ŭm, *and* æ, ārŭm, m. pl., *a people of Mauritania.* Nēc nōn Aŭtŏlŏlēs, Luc.

Aŭtŏlўcŭs, ī, m., *a son of Mercury, and grandfather of Ulysses.* Nāscĭtŭr Aŭtŏlўcŭs, Ov.

Aŭtŏnŏē, ēs, f., *daughter of Cadmus, and mother of Actæon.* Aŭtŏnŏē, mŏvĕānt ănĭmōs Actæŏnĭs ŭmbræ, Ov.

Aŭtŏnŏēĭŭs, ă, ŭm, *son of Autonoe.* Fŭgĭt Aŭtŏnŏēĭŭs hērōs, Ov.

aŭtŭmnālĭs, ĕ, *of autumn.* Ipsa aŭtŭmnālĭă cōrnă, Ov.

aŭtŭmnŭs, ī, m., *autumn.* Aŭtŭmnŭs ; ĕt āltē, Virg. Epith. Pămpĭnĕŭs, vīnĭfĕr, pōmĭfĕr, grăvĭdŭs, sōrdĭdŭs, pāllēns, fēlīx, frŭgĭfĕr, hūmĭdŭs, fērtĭlĭs, fĕrāx, fœcūndŭs, dīvĕs, mōrbōsŭs, nĭmbōsŭs, ūdŭs, mădēns, plŭvĭŭs, răcēmĭfĕr.

aŭtŭmo, ās, *to think.* Aŭtŭmăt ; hæc pŏpŭlōs, Hor. Syn. Pŭto, ēxīstĭmo, ŏpīnŏr, jūdĭco, cēnsĕo, sēntĭo.

ăvūlsŭs, ă, ŭm, *the pass. partic. of* avello. Cōmplēxu ăvūlsŭs Ĭŭlī, Virg. Syn. Vūlsŭs, dīvūlsŭs.

ăvūncŭlŭs, ī, m., *a mother's brother.* Ēt ăvūncŭlŭs ēxcĭtĕt, Virg.

ăvŭs, ī, m., *a grandfather or ancestor.* Stăt fōrtūnă dŏmŭs, ĕt ăvī, Virg. Syn. Ătăvŭs, prŏăvŭs. Epith. Lōngævŭs, vĕtūstŭs, grăvĭs, sĕnĭŏr, vīvăx, vĕnĕrāndŭs.

aŭxĭlĭārĭs, ĕ, *auxiliary.* Aŭxĭlĭărĭbŭs ŭndĭs, Ov.

aŭxĭlĭātŏr, ōrĭs, m., *a helper.* Īnfīrmŭs aŭxĭlĭātŏr, (Iamb.) Petron. Syn. Adjūtŏr, faŭtŏr.

aŭxĭlĭātrīx, īcĭs, *she who helps.* Aŭxĭlĭātrīcēm clēmēntī, M.

aŭxĭlĭŏr, ārĭs, *to help.* Aŭxĭlĭātŭr ăquīs, Ov. Syn. Jŭvo, ādsŭm, sŭccŭrro, ŏpĭtŭlŏr, sŭbvĕnĭo, sŭblĕvo, ādjŭvo, făvĕo. V. Auxilium.

aŭxĭlĭŭm, ĭī, n., *help.* Aŭxĭlĭō tūtōs, Virg. Syn. Sŭbsĭdĭŭm, sŭppĕtĭæ, ādjūmēntŭm, ŏpĭs, (*gen.*) *and* ŏpĕm, (*accus.*) [ŏps *not used,*] sōlāmēn, præsĭdĭŭm, jŭvāmēn, lĕvāmēn, cōlŭmēn, sōlātĭŭm. Epith. Præsēns, dīvīnŭm, dūlcĕ, grātŭm, mītĕ, ēxpēctātŭm, cŭpītŭm, pĕtītŭm, blāndŭm, făvēns, ămīcŭm, spērātŭm, hūmānŭm, cœlēstĕ, sălūtĭfĕrŭm, mūtŭŭm, sŭbĭtŭm, rĕpēntīnŭm, prōmptŭm, tārdŭm, lēntŭm, ĭnŏpīnŭm, sēgnĕ. V. Auxilior.

āxĭcŭlŭs, ī, m., *the diminut. of* axis. Fŭr vĕlŏt āxĭcŭlō, Calc. V. Axis.

āxĭōmă, ătĭs, n., *an axiom.* Præstĭtŭĭt āxĭōmă, Capet. Syn. Sēntēntĭă, ēffātŭm, mĕmŏrābĭlĕ dīctŭm. Epith. Cērtŭm, vērŭm, dōctŭm, rĕcēptŭm, nōtŭm, brĕvĕ.

āxĭs, ĭs, m., *an axle-tree, around which the wheel turns ; sometimes a cart, or the heavens.* Sŭb āxĕ tŏnāntī, Virg. Epith. Rēctŭs, sŏnŏrŭs, fērvĭdŭs, cĭtŭs, cĭtātŭs. V. Currus, Cœlum.

Ăzān, ānĭs, m., *a mountain of Arcadia.* Æmŭlŭs Ăzān, Stat.

āzўmŭs, ă, ŭm, *without leaven.* Sĭmĭlāgĭnĭs āzўmōn ēssĕ, Prud.

B.

|| BAĂL, (*undecl.*) *or* ăalĭs, m., *an idol.* Tūnc cŏlŭĕrĕ Baăl, Sed. Cōctĭlĕ Baāl, Prud. Dĭdĭcērĕ Baălĭs, Cruc. Căpĭtŭm Baălĭs cōnsūmĕrĕ, Mill.

|| Băbĕl, (*undecl.*) f., Eccles.

Băbўlōn, ōnĭs, f., *the capital of Chaldea, and of the East.* Nēc Băbўlōnă lăbŏr,

Mart. Epith. Sŭpērbă, ăltă, lōngă, rĕbēllĭs, āntīquă, pōrtēntōsă, ŏpŭlēntă, splēndĭdă, cĕlĕbrĭs, māgnĭfĭcă, tūrrītă, Chāldœă, Āssўrĭă, Pērsĕă, pŏtēns, ārdŭă mūrĭs, tūrrĭgĕră, īnclўtă, dīvēs ŏpŭm, pūlchră.

Bābўlōnĭă, œ, f., *Babylonia, Chaldea.* Dē tē, Bābўlōnĭă, nārrēt, Ov.

Bābўlōnĭăcŭs, ĭcŭs, *or* ĭŭs, ă, ŭm, *of Babylon, Babylonian, Chaldean.* Cūm Bābў-lōnĭăcās, Manil. Ut Bābўlōnĭcă, Lucr. Nēc Bābўlōnĭŏs Tēntārīs nŭmĕrōs, Hor. Syn. Āssўrĭŭs, Chāldæŭs.

băccă, æ, f., *a berry.* Băccă trăpĕtŭs, Virg. Epith. Sўlvēstrĭs, sānguĭnĕă, Sĭcў-ōnĭă, Pāllădĭă, bĭcŏlŏr, ămără, tūrgēns, vĭrēns, ārbŏrĕă, pīnguĭs, Īdŭmæă.—2. *a pearl.* Dīlŭĭt īnsīgnēm băccăm, Hor. Syn. Gēmmă, ūnĭo. Epith. Fūlgĭdă, cāndĭdă, īnsīgnĭs, Nērēĭă, lĕvĭs, rŏtūndă. V. Gemma.

băccăr, ărĭs, f., *lady's-glove, a herb.* Cūm băccărĕ tēllūs, Virg. Epith. Frōndēns, vĭrĭdĭs, ŏdōrātă, suāvĭs, bĕnĭgnă, sălūtĭfĕră, grātă, jūcūndă.

băccătŭs, ă, ŭm, *adorned with pearls.* Băccātum īndūtă mŏnīlĕ, Sil. Syn. Gēm-mātŭs.

Bācchæ, ārŭm, f. pl., *priestesses of Bacchus.* Dūm sĕquĭtūr Bācchās, Bācchæ, Ov. Syn. Bācchāntēs, Mœnădēs, Bāssărĭdēs, Thўădēs, Mīmāllŏnĭdēs, Ēlēlēĭdēs, Ēdōnĭdēs, Trĭĕtĕrĭdēs. Epith. Thēbānæ, Cādmēæ, Ogўgĭæ, Thrēĭcĭæ, Ismărĭæ; sævœ, fŭrēntēs, lўmphātæ, fŭrĭōsæ, īnsānæ, mălĕsānæ, thўrsĭgĕræ Mīmāllōnĕæ.

Bācchānālĭă, ŭm *or* ōrŭm, n. pl., *festivals of Bacchus.* Bācchānālĭă vīvŭnt, Juv. Syn. Ōrgĭă. Epith. Sōlēnnĭă, fŭrĭōsă, īnsānă.

bācchātŭs, ă, ŭm, *the partic. of* bacchor. Bācchātă pĕr ūrbēs, Virg. Bācchātă Lăcænĭs, Id. Syn. Fŭrēns, fŭrĭōsŭs, lўmphātŭs, īnsānŭs. V. Furiosus.

Bācchēĭs, f., *and* ēĭŭs, ēŭs, ĭcŭs, ă, ŭm, *of Bacchus.* Ēphўrēs Bācchēĭdŏs āltŭm, St. Bācchēĭă dōnă, Ser. Bācchēā vōcĕ frēmēntĕm, Col. Bācchĭcă săcră, Ov.

Bācchĭădæ, ārŭm, m. pl., *a Corinthian family.* Ēt quā Bācchĭădæ, Ov.

Bācchĭs, ĭdĭs, f., *a female Bacchanal.* Ūtquĕ sŭŭm Bācchĭs, Ov.

Bācchĭŭs, ĭī, m., *the name of a man.* Cūm Bīthō Bācchĭŭs, Hor.

bācchŏr, ārĭs, *to keep the feasts of Bacchus ; to revel, bully.* Bācchātŭr vātēs, Virg. Syn. Fŭro, īnsānĭo. V. Ebrius.

Bācchŭs, ī, m., *the God of wine ; wine.* Bācchŭs ămāt cōllēs, Virg. Syn. Lībĕr, Lўæŭs, Ēvān, Brōmĭŭs, Ĭācchŭs, Lēnæŭs. Epith. Mītĭs, nōctūrnŭs, ārmĭgĕr, gēnĕrōsŭs, răcēmĭfĕr, cāndĭdŭs, fœmĭnĕŭs, ălŭmnŭs, īntōnsŭs, aūdāx, sævŭs, jŭvĕnĭs, nĭtĭdŭs, mōllĭs, bĕnĭgnŭs, Mārtĭŭs, ĭmbērbĭs, blāndŭs, rŭbĭcūndŭs, călēns. Dīrcæŭs, cōrnĭgĕr, lætĭfĭcŭs, spūmāns, ēbrĭŭs, tĭtūbāns. V. Vinum.

băccĭfĕr, ă, ŭm, *bearing berries.* Bācchĭfĕrō nūtrĭtă Săbīnō, Sil.

băcillŭs, ī, m., *a little staff.* Sŭbĕūntĕ băcillō, Juv. Syn. Băcŭlŭm.

Bāctră, ōrŭm, n. pl., *the capital of Bactriana.* Nēc Bāctră nēc Indī, Virg.

Bāctrĭŭs, ă, ŭm, *of Bactriana.* Bāctrĭŭs Hālcўŏnĕŭs, Ov.

Bāctrŏs, *and* ŭs, ī, m., *a river of Bactriana.* Gūrgĭtĕ Bāctrŏs, Luc.

băcŭlŭs, ī, m., *or* ŭm, ī, n., *a stick.* Prætēntēs băcŭlō, Ov. Syn. Fūstĭs, stīpĕs, băcillŭs, ărŭndo. Epith. Nōdōsŭs, ācclīvĭs, dūrŭs, rēctŭs, tĕrēs, agrēstĭs, ācēr-nŭs, quērnŭs, fīrmŭs. V. Palus, i.

|| bætĭcātŭs, ă, ŭm, *of a red brown.* Bætĭcātŭs ātquĕ, Mart.

Bætĭs, ĭs, m., *a river of Spain.* Bætĭs, ĕt īn rīpĭs, Mant. Epith. Hēspĕrĭŭs, Ĭbērŭs, ŏlīvĭfĕr, plăcĭdŭs. V. Fluvius.

Bāgŏŭs, ī, m., *a eunuch.* Sērvāndĭ cūră, Bāgŏĕ, Ov.

Baiæ, ārŭm, f. pl., *a watering-place in the country of Naples.* Hūmĭdă Baĭārŭm, Prop. Epith. Lĭquĭdæ, ămœnæ, tĕpēntēs, călēntēs, fēlīcēs, mōllēs, æstŭāntēs, văpōrĭfĕræ, sălūbrēs.

Baiānŭs, ă, ŭm, *of Baiæ.* Baiānæ pērvĭă cўmbæ, Juv.

bājŭlo, ās, *to carry.* Vīx bājŭlāt ālvŭm, M. Syn. Hŭmĕrīs fĕro, dēfĕro, ēffĕro, gĕro, pōrto.

bājŭlŭs, ī, m., *a porter.* Bājŭlŭs, ĕt cūstōs, Mant.

bălæna, æ, f., *a whale.* Bălæna Brĭtānnĭcă, Juv. Epith. Stŭpēndă, squāmōsă, ūndĭvăgă, māgnă, prædātrīx, mărīnă, văgă, Nēptūnĭă.

|| bălănātŭs, ă, ŭm, *anointed with perfumes.* Bălănātum gaūsăpĕ pēctŭs, Pers.

|| bălănŭs, ī, m., *an odoriferous acorn.* Cōnstăt ĕt ēx bălānō, Mart.

bălātro, ōnĭs, m., *a rogue, rascal.* Mēndīcī, mīmæ, bălātrōnēs, Hor.

bălātŭs, ūs, m., *bleating.* Bălātŭ pĕcŏrŭm, Virg. V. Balo.

Bālbīnŭs, ī, m., *the name of a man.* Vĕlŭtī Bālbīnŭm, Hor.

bălbŭs, ă, ŭm, *stammering.* Quĭd, cūm bălbă fērĭs. Hor.

bălbūtĭo, *to stammer.* Bălbūtĭt scaŭrŭm, Hor. Syn. Lĭnguā hæsĭto, hærĕo.

Bălĕărĭcŭs, ă, ŭm, *or* ĭs, ĕ, *of the Balearic islands.* Bălĕărĭcă plŭmbŭm, Ov. Bălĕărīs vērbĕră fūndæ, Virg.

bălĭstă, æ, f., *a warlike engine to throw stones, &c.* Quăm grăvĕ bălīstæ, Ov. Syn. Cătăpūltă. Epith. Tŏrtă, fērrĕă, bēllĭcă, dūră, Mărtĭă, pŏtēns, Vŭlcānĭă, ĭmmītĭs, vălĭdă, tūrrĭfrăgă, Māvŏrtĭă, trūx, hŏrrĭbĭlĭs, fĕră, hŏrrēns, ēxĭtĭŏsă, ēxĭtĭălĭs.

bălnĕărĭŭs, ă, ŭm, *belonging to baths ; he who waits at a bath.* Ŏptĭmĕ bălnĕărĭ-ŏrŭm, (Phal.) Catul.

bălnĕātŏr, ōrĭs, m., *the master of a bath.* Bălnĕātŏr ēxtīnctă, Mart.

bălnĕŏlŭm, ī, n., *the diminut. of* balneum. Bălnĕŏlŭm Găbĭĭs, Juv.

bălnĕŭm, ī, n., *a bath.* Bălnĕă Grȳllī, Mart. Syn. Thērmæ. Epith. Dūlcĕ, mŭlcēns, sūdāns, călĭdŭm, tĕpĭdŭm, grātŭm, jūcūndŭm, hŭmĭdŭm, fērvĭdŭm, sălūtĭfĕrŭm, ămœnŭm, ŏptātŭm, frĭgēns, ŭdŭm, sălūbrĕ. V. Abluo.

bălo, ās, *to bleat.* Sŭlphŭrĕ bālĕt ŏvĭs, Ov.

bălsămĕŭs, *or* ĭnŭs, ă, ŭm, *balsamic.* Ūnguĭnĕ bălsămĕŏ, Lact. Bălsămĭnūm Jĕrĭchūs, Fil.

bălsămŭm, ī, n., *balsam, balm.* Bălsămă quī sēmpĕr, Mart. Epith. Ŏdōrŭm, rĕdŏlēns. grātŭm, ŏdōrĭfĕrŭm, prĕtĭŏsŭm, pĭnguĕ, ărōmătĭcŭm, ŏdōrātŭm, frā-grāns, mītĕ, gĕnĭălĕ, sălūtārĕ, dūlcĕ.

băltĕŭm, ī, n.. *and* ŭs, ī, m., *a girdle.* Băltĕŭs, ēt tĕrĕtī, Virg. Syn. Cĭngŭlŭm. Epith. Pēndŭlŭs, dīscŏlŏr, sĭgnĭfĕr, aŭrātŭs, aŭrĕŭs, splēndēns, pŭlchĕr, ēnsĭfĕr, pĭctŭs.

Băntīnŭs, ă, ŭm, *of Bantia, a town in Apulia.* Săltŭsquĕ Băntīnŏs, Hor.

|| băptīsmă, ătĭs, n., *or* ŭs, ī, m., *baptism.* Băptīsmătĕ lăbĕm, Prud. Epith. Sānctŭm, sōlēnnĕ, sălūtĭfĕrŭm, sacrŭm, sălūbrĕ.

Băptīstă, æ, m., *St. John the Baptist.* Pāstŭs băptīstă lŏcūstīs, Prud.

|| băptīzātŭs, *the pass. partic. of* baptizo. Băptīzāti ăgĭmŭs, Alcim.

|| băptīzo, ās, *to baptise.* Eccl.

bărăthrŭm, ī, n., *a gulf.* Imō bărăthrī tĕr gŭrgĭtĕ vāstōs, Virg. Immānĕ bărā-thrŭm, Id. Syn. Vŏrāgo, vŏrtēx, gŭrgĕs. Epith. Tārtărĕŭm, cæcŭm, ābrŭptŭm, præcēps, nĭgrŭm, fĕrŭm, lātŭm, ĭrrĕmĕābĭlĕ, īnfērnŭm, fĕrālĕ, Stȳgĭŭm, tĕtrŭm, prŏfūndŭm, ŏpācŭm, cālĭgāns, hŏrrēndŭm, ăpērtŭm, obscūrŭm, hŏrrĭbĭlĕ. V. Hiatus.

bărbă, æ, f., *the beard.* Bărbă cădēbăt, Virg. Epith. Impēxă, fœdă, rĭgĭdă, cūltă, sēnīlĭs, cānă, cāndĭdă, nĭvĕă, rĕnāscēns, hĭrtă, āspĕră, lōngă, prŏlīxă, cōmāns, vĕnĕrāndă.

bărbărĭă, æ, *and* ĭes, ēī, f., *any barbarous country, barbarity, rudeness.* Nōmĭnă bărbărĭæ, Ov. Syn. Crūdēlĭtās, sævĭtĭă, fĕrĭtās, rūstĭcĭtās, sævĭtĭes. Epith. Inhūmānă, fĕrīnă, fŭrēns, hŏrrĭdă, fĕră, scĕlĕrātă, ĭmmānĭs, dīră, crūēntă, atrōx, crūdēlĭs, hŏrrēndă, fĕrōx, răbĭdă, invĭdă, tȳrānnĭcă, fŭrĭŏsă, præcēps, ēffĕră, ēffræn̆ĭs, impătĭēns, tĕmĕrārĭă, mĭnāx, impĭă, ăcērbă, Stȳgĭă, Tārtărĕă, fērvĭdă, ĭnaŭdītă, āspĕră, crūdă, ĭnāmăbĭlĭs. V. Crudelitas, Barbarus.

bărbărĭcŭs, ă, ŭm, *belonging to barbarians.* Bărbărĭcō pōstēs, Virg.

bărbărŭs, ă. ŭm, *outlandish, barbarous.* Bărbărŭs hĭc ĕgŏ sŭm, Ov. Syn. Crū-dēlĭs, ĭmmānĭs, fĕrŭs, ēffĕrŭs, dīrŭs, āspĕr, atrōx, fĕrōx, ĭmmītĭs, trūx ; lōngīn-quŭs, ēxtērnŭs, ălĭēnĭgĕnă. V. Crudelis.

bărbātŭs, ă, ŭm, *bearded.* Bārbātum hæc crēdĕ măgīstrŭm, Pers. Syn. Băr-bĭgĕr.

bărbĭgĕr, ă, ŭm, *having a beard.* Bārbĭgĕrās pĕcŭdēs, Lucr.

bărbĭtŏs, *or* ŭs, ī, m. f., *and* ŏn, ī, n., *a lyre.* Bārbĭtŏs ūllă, Ov. Syn. Tēstūdo, lȳră, cĭthără, chĕlȳs. Epith. Făcĭlĭs, quĕrŭlă, cănŏră, nĭvĕă, mōllĭs, Æōlĭă, aŭrĕă, Aŏnĭă, dūlcĭs, sŏnŏră, ārgūtă. V. Cithara.

Bārcæī, ōrŭm, m. pl., *inhabitants of Barce.* Lātēquĕ fŭrēntĕs Bārcæī, Virg.

Bārcē, ēs, f., *a town of Africa.* Arĭdă Bārcē, Sil.—2. *the nurse of Sichæus.* Tūnī brĕvĭtĕr Bārcēn, Virg.

bărdī, ōrŭm, m. pl., *Celtic poets.* Fūdīstĭs cārmĭnă, bārdī, Luc. V. Poeta.

bărdĭăcŭs, ă, ŭm, *belonging to bards.* Lăssī bārdĭăcŭs, Mart.

bărdŏcŭcŭllātŭs, ă, ŭm, *covered with a cloak.* Bārdŏcŭcŭllātŭs căpŭt, Mart.

bărdŏcŭcŭllŭs, ī, m., *a cloak with a cowl.* Vēstīt tĕ bārdŏcŭcŭllō, Mart.

bārdŭs, ă, ŭm, *stupid.* Bārde, ĕt cōmpēscĕ quĕrēlās, Lucr. Syn. Stŭpĭdŭs, stŏlĭdŭs, hĕbĕs, tārdŭs.

Bărĕăs, æ, m., *the name of a man.* Stōĭcŭs ōccĭdĭt Bărĕăm, Juv.

bărĭs, ĭdĭs *and* ĭdŏs, f., *a boat, a bark.* Bărĭdŏs ēt cōntĭs, Prop.

Bărĭŭm, ĭī, n., *a town of Apulia.* Bărī mœnĭā pĭscōsī, Hor.

bārrĭnŭs, ă, ŭm, *of an elephant.* Bărrĭno ĭn dēntĕ părārĭnt, Claud. Syn. Ĕlĕphăntĭnŭs.

bārrŭs, ī, m., *an elephant.* Dignĭssĭmă bārrĭs, Hor. Syn. Ĕlĕphās, ĕlĕphăntŭs.

bāsĭătĭo, ōnĭs, f., *a kissing.* Ōffĕndĕrĕ bāsĭătĭōnēs, (Phal.) Mart. V. Osculum.

bāsĭătŏr, ōrĭs, m., *a kisser.* Bāssĕ, bāsĭătōrēs, (Scaz.) Mart.

Bāsĭlŭs, ī, m., *the name of a man.* Quāndŏ lĭcēt Bāsĭlŏ, Juv.

bāsĭlĭscŭs, ī, m., *a kind of serpent, to which are ascribed many fabulous properties.* Rēgnăt bāsĭlĭscŭs ărēnā, Lucan. Epith. Mōrtĭfĕr, Lĭbўcŭs, vĕnēnōsŭs, vĕnēnĭfĕr, crĭstātŭs, vūlnĭfĭcŭs, rēgĭŭs, rēgālĭs, dīrŭs, lēthālĭs, pēstĭfĕr, lūbrĭcŭs. V. Serpens.

bāsĭo, ās, *to kiss.* Bāsĭă mūltă bāsĭārĕ, (Phal.) Cat.

bāsĭs, ĭs, f., *a base.* Stăt bāsĭs ōrbă Dĕā, Ov. Syn. Fūndāmēntŭm, fūndāmĕn, fūlcīmēntŭm. Epith. Fōrtĭs, sōlĭdă, ænĕă, ætērnă, pĕrēnnĭs.

bāsĭŭm, ĭī, n., *a kiss.* Bāsĭă rhēdæ. Syn. Ōscŭlŭm, suāvĭŭm; āmplēxŭs. V. Osculum.

Bāssāreŭs, ĕŏs, ĕī *or* eī, m., *a name of Bacchus.* Cāndĭdĕ Bāssāreŭ, Hor.

Bāssārĭcŭs, ă, ŭm, *of Bacchus.* Cīngēt Bāssārĭcās, Prop.

Bāssārĭdĕs, ŭm, f. pl., *female Bacchanals.* Ēt tū Bāssārĭdŭm, (Phal.) Stat. Epith. Insānæ, vēsānæ. V. Bacchæ.

Bāssŭs, ī, m., *the name of a poet, and others.* Bāssŭs quŏquĕ clārŭs ĭambō, Hor.

Bătăvī, ōrŭm, m. pl., *inhabitants of Holland.* Bătāvĭquĕ trŭcēs, Lucan. Dŏmĭĭĭquĕ Bătāvī, Juv. Hōllāndī. Epith. Fĕrōcēs, ĭndŏmĭtī, fōrtēs, gĕnĕrōsī, măgnănĭmī, bēllĭgĕrī, Mārtiī, aūdācēs, ĭmpăvĭdī, cōncōrdēs.

Băthўllŭs, ī, m., *the name of a man.* Dīcŭnt ārsĭssĕ Băthўllō, Hor.

‖ bătĭllŭm, ī, n., *or* ŭs, ī, m., *a fire-shovel, incense-pan.* Prūnæquĕ bătĭllŭm, Hor.

bătĭs, ĭs, f., *a robin red-breast.* Ēt pēctŭs rŭtĭlō bătĭs, (Phal.) Comm.

Băto, ōnĭs, m., *a German chief.* Sūmmă căpŭtquĕ Băto, Ov.

Bāttĭs, ĭdĭs, f., *the name of a woman.* Bāttĭs āmātă sŭō, Ov.

Bāttŭs, ī, m., *a shepherd punished by Mercury for his perfidy.* Bāttŭs ăb ĭpsĕ sŭā, Ov.

Bătŭlŭm, ī, n., *a fortress of Campania.* Bătŭlŭmquĕ tĕnēnt, Virg.

baūbŏr, ārĭs, *to bark.* Baūbāntŭr ĭn ædĭbŭs, Lucr.

Baūcĭs, ĭdĭs, f., *the wife of Philemon.* Pĭă Baūcĭs ănŭs, Ov. Epith. Paūpĕr, vĕtŭlă.

Băvĭŭs, ī, m., *a sorry poet, contemporary with Virgil.* Quī Băvĭŭm nōn ōdĭt,Virg.

bĕātĕ, adv., *happily.* Bĕnĕ āc bĕātĕ, Cat.

● bĕătĭtūdo, ĭnĭs, f., *beatitude.* Cic. Syn. Bĕātĭtās, fēlĭcĭtās.

bĕātŭlŭs, ă, ŭm, *somewhat happy.* Bĕātŭlŭs āltō, Pers.

bĕātŭs, ă, ŭm, *happy.* Bĕātŭs ĭllĕ, (Iamb. pur.) Hor. Syn. Fēlīx, fōrtūnātŭs. V. Felix.

Bēbrўcĭă, æ, f., *a country of Asia, afterwards called Bithynia.* Arvă fŭrēntĭs Bēbrўcĭæ, Val. Fl.

Bēbrўcĭŭs, ă, ŭm, *of Bebrycia, or Bithynia.* Bēbrўcĭă vĕnĭēns, Virg.

Bēbrўx, ўcĭs, m., *a barbarous king of Scythia ; another king of the Pyrenees.* Bēbrўcĭs ēt Scўthĭcī, Val. Fl. Bēbrўcĭs ĭn aŭlā, Sil.

Bēlgæ, ārŭm, m. pl., *a nation of Europe.* Epith. Ārmĭfĕrī, aūdācēs, pūgnācēs, crūdī, prūdēntēs, ĭngĕnĭōsī, fōrtēs.

Bēlgĭcŭs, ă, ŭm, *Belgian.* Bēlgĭcŭs āprōs, Sil.

Bēlĭdĕs, ŭm, f. pl., *the Danaids.* Bēlĭdēs ūndās, Ov. Syn. Dănăĭdĕs, Bēlĭădĕs. Epith. Impĭæ, scĕlēstæ, crŭēntæ, ĭnĭquæ, mĭsĕræ, fĕræ, pērfĭdæ, crūdēlēs, scĕlērātæ, ĭnhūmānæ, ĭmmītēs, vĭgĭlēs, ĭnsōmnēs, ĭnfēlīcēs.—2. Bēlĭdēs, æ, m., *the patronymic name of Palamedes.* Bēlĭdæ nōmēn Pălămēdĭs, Virg.

Bēlĭsārĭŭs, ĭī, m., *a great general of Justinian, said to have died in disgrace.* Bēlĭsārĭŭs ōrbĭs, Mant Epith. Fōrtĭs, ĭnvĭctŭs; mĭsĕr, ēxŭl, ĭnŏps, cæcŭs.

bēllārĭă, ōrŭm, n. pl., *sweetmeats.* Bēllārĭa ădŏrĕă plŭēbānt, (Phal.) Epith. Mēllītă, laūtă, mōllĭă, quæsītă, Āttĭcă.

bĕllātŏr, ōrĭs, m., *a warrior.* Bĕllātŏr ĭn ārmĭs, Juv. SYN. Bĕllĭgĕr, bĕllĭcōsŭs, bĕllĭcŭs, bĕllĭpŏtēns. V. Bellum, arma.

bĕllātrīx, īcĭs, f., *a female warrior.* Vūlnĕrĕ bĕllātrīx, Sil.

bĕllāx, ācĭs, *warlike.* Illīc bĕllācī, Lucan. SYN. Bĕllātŏr, bĕllĭgĕr.

Bĕllĕrŏphŏn, ōntĭs, m., *the son of Glaucus, and vanquisher of the Chimera.* Bĕllĕrŏphōntĕm, Mart. SYN. Bĕllĕrŏphōntēs, æ. EPITH. Cāstŭs, bĕllĭgĕr, pŭdīcŭs, vīctŏr, aūdāx, gĕnĕrōsŭs, mágnānĭmŭs, cōnstāns.

Bĕllĕrŏphōntēŭs, ă, ŭm, *of Bellerophon.* Bĕllĕrŏphōntēī quā flŭĭt, Prop.

bĕllĭcōsŭs, ă, ŭm, *martial.* Quĭd bĕllĭcōsŭs Cāntăbĕr, (Alcaic.) Hor.

bĕllĭcŭs, ă, ŭm, *of war.* Bĕllĭcă lætă Dĕa ēst, Ov. SYN. Mārtĭŭs, Māvōrtĭŭs.

bĕllĭfĕr, *and* gĕr, ă, ŭm, *making war, warlike.* Bĕllĭfĕrām cōmmūnĭbŭs ūrŭnt, Claud. Sīc ĕgŏ bĕllĭgĕrĭs, Ov.

bĕllĭgĕrātŏr, ōrĭs, m., *a soldier.* Bĕllĭgĕrātōrēs nūtrīx, Avien.

bĕllĭgĕro, ās, *to make war.* Bĕllĭgĕrārĕ trĭbŭs, Text. V. Bellum gerere.

bĕllĭpŏtēns, ēntĭs, *powerful in war.* Bĕllĭpŏtēns: āptăt, Virg. V. Bellator.

bĕllĭs, ĭdĭs, f., *a daisy.* Bĕllĭdēs hōrtō, Rap.

bĕllĭsŏnŭs, ă, ŭm, *full of the noise of war.* Sīc mŏdŏ bĕllĭsŏnŏ, Paul. Nolan.

bĕllo, ās, *and* ŏr, ārĭs, *to make war.* Sīvĕ cōmpărĕ bĕllăt, Ov. SYN. Bĕllĭgĕro, pūgno.

Bĕllōnă, æ, f., *the goddess of war.* Sĕquĭtŭr Bĕllōnă flăgĕllō, Virg. SYN. Ĕnȳo. EPITH. Fŭrēns, Tārtărĕă, ātră, hāstātă, vīndēx, īmplăcābĭlĭs, īmpĭă, ārdēns, trīstĭs, fĕrōx, ĭnfērnă, atrōx, sævă, Stȳgĭă, trŭcŭlēntă, sōrdĭdă, răbĭdă, āspĕră, bārbără, .hōrrēndă, fŭrĭbūndă, ĭnhūmănă, dīscōrs, mĭnāx, mĕtŭēndă, hōrrĭdă, īntrĕpĭdă, ĕxĭtĭōsă.

bĕllŭă, æ, f., *a great beast.* Bĕllŭă Lērnæ, Virg. V. Fera.

|| bĕllŭātă tăpētĭă, *tapestry wrought with the figures of beasts,* Pl.

bĕllŭīnŭs, ă, ŭm, *beastly.* Bĕllŭīnĭs faūcĭbŭs, (Iamb.) Prud.

bĕllŭm, ī, n., *war.* Dēfēndĕrĕ bĕllō, Virg. SYN. Prælĭŭm, cērtāmĕn, cōnflīctŭs, pūgnă, Mārs, ārmă, mīlĭtĭă. EPITH. Trĭstĕ, fŭnēstŭm, crūdēlĕ, mōrtĭfĕrŭm, dīrŭm, ĕxĭtĭālĕ, dīscōrs, nĕfāndŭm, īnfāndŭm, īmpĭŭm, fĕrālĕ, īmmānĕ, sævŭm, īnfaūstŭm, crŭēntŭm; Mārtĭŭm, īrrĕquĭētŭm, mĭsĕrābĭlĕ, fērrĕŭm, fōrtĕ, ātrŭm, fērvĭdŭm, fŭrĭbūndŭm, fŭrĭālĕ, rĕdĭvīvŭm, tūrbĭdŭm, răpāx, pērfĭdŭm, hōstĭlĕ, ĕffĕrŭm, sānguĭnĕŭm, lūctĭfĕrŭm, ăcērbŭm, lacrȳmābĭlĕ, flēbĭlĕ, răbĭdŭm, sŭpērbŭm, mĭsĕrŭm, pēstĭfĕrŭm, ăvĭdŭm, lēthālĕ, fūnĕrĕŭm, rĭgĭ.lŭm, aūdāx, trĕmēndŭm, ārmĭsŏnāns, tērrĭbĭlĕ, fŭrĭōsŭm, āncĕps, dŭbĭŭm, īncērtŭm. V. Pugna.

bĕllŭm gĕrĕrĕ, *to make war.* Bĕllŭmque īnfērrĕ, Virg. SYN. Bĕllo, ās; pūgno, cērto, dīmĭco, cōnflīgo, cōngrĕdĭŏr. V. Bellum, bellator.

bĕllŭōsŭs, ă, ŭm, *full of monsters.* Tĕ bĕllŭōsŭs, (Iamb. Hyperc.) Hor.

bĕllŭs, ă, ŭm, *pretty.* Bĕllŭs hŏmo, Mart.

Bēlŭs, ī, m., *a king of Assyria, and father of Ninus.* Ŏrĭgĭnĕ Bēlō, Ov.

Bēnācŭs, ī, m., *a lake in Italy.* Quōs pătrĕ Bēnācō, Virg. EPITH. Vōrtĭcōsŭs, pīscōsŭs, sŏnāns, aūrĕŭs.

bĕnĕ, adv., *well.* Cuī bŏnĕ cēssĭt, hăbĕt, Ov.

bĕnĕdīco, ĭs, *to speak well of.* Dōctŭs bĕnĕdīcĕrĕ lēctŏr, Ov. SYN. Bĕnĕ vŏlo, bĕnĕ cŭpĭo, bĕnĕ prĕcŏr, faūstă prĕcŏr.

bĕnĕfăcĭo, fēcī, *to do good.* Quŏd bĕnĕfēcĕrĭs, (Ascl.) Hor.

bĕnĕfāctŭm, ī, n., *a good action.* Nĕque ĕnĭm bĕnĕfāctă, Ov.

bĕnĕfĭcĭŭm, ĭī, n., *a benefit.* Bĕnĕfĭcĭă plūră rĕcĭpĭt, Publ. SYN. Dōnŭm, mūnŭs, bĕnĕfāctŭm. EPITH. Grātŭm, māgnŭm, māgnĭfĭcŭm, rēgĭŭm, prĕtĭōsŭm, dătŭm, grāndĕ, āmplŭm.

|| bĕnĕfĭcŭs, ă, ŭm, *beneficent.* SYN. Mūnĭfĭcŭs, lībĕrālĭs, lārgŭs, bĕnīgnŭs.

Bĕnĕvēntānŭs, ă, ŭm, *of Beneventum.* Tŭ Bĕnĕvēntānī, Juv.

Bĕnĕvēntŭm, ī, n., *a city of Italy.* Hīnc rēctă Bĕnĕvēntŭm, Hor.

|| bĕnĕvŏlēntĭă, æ, f., *benevolence.* SYN. Stŭdĭŭm, ămōr, ămīcă vŏlūntās.

|| bĕnĕvŏlŭs, ă, ŭm, *well wishing.* Cic. SYN. Bĕnĕvŏlēns, ămāns, ămīcŭs, stŭdĭōsŭs.

bĕnīgnĕ, *or* ĭtĕr, adv., *kindly.* Bĕnīgnĭŭs mē sălūtānt, Phædr.

bĕnīgnĭtās, ātĭs, f., *benignity.* Mē bĕnīgnĭtās tŭă, (Iamb. pur.) Hor. SYN. Bŏnĭtās, lēnĭtās, mānsuētūdo, clēmēntĭă. EPITH. Clēmēns, grātă, mītĭs.

bĕnīgnŭs, ă, ŭm, *benevolent, kind.* Mēntēmquĕ bĕnīgnăm, Virg. SYN. Cōmĭs, ūrbānŭs, făcĭlĭs, blāndŭs, hūmānŭs, mānsuētŭs, lēnĭs, mītĭs, plăcĭdŭs, bŏnŭs.

bĕo, ās, *to make happy.* Mŭsă bĕăt, Hor.

Bĕrĕcynthĭă, æ, f., *a name of Cybele.* Quālīs Bĕrĕcynthĭă mātĕr, Virg. V. Cybele.

Bĕrĕcynthĭăcŭs, ĭŭs, ă, ŭm, *or* ĭădĕs, *of the mountain Berecynthus.* Cŭr Bĕrĕcynthĭăcŭs, Prud. Bĕrĕcythĭŭs hĕrōs, Ov. Sīs Bĕrĕcynthĭădēs, Id.

Bĕrĕnīcē, ēs, f., *queen of Egypt, whose hair was said to have been changed into a constellation.* Et Bĕrĕnīcēs, Juv.

Bĕrŏē, ēs, f., *the nurse of Semele.* Bĕrŏē Sĕmĕlēs, Ov.

bērўllŭs, ī, m., *a precious stone.* Dĭgĭtō bērўllŏn ădēdĕrăt, Prop. EPITH. Vĭrĭdĭs, glaucŭs, ĭnæquālĭs, Indŭs, Indĭcŭs. V. Gemma.

bēs, ēssĭs, m., *the weight of eight ounces.* Bēssēmquĕ bĭbāmŭs, Mart.

Bēssī, ōrŭm, m. pl., *a people of Thrace.* Bēssōsquĕ Gĕtāsquĕ, Ov.

bēstĭă, æ, f., *a beast.* Bēstĭă, nĕc quĭcŭm, Catul. SYN. Ănĭmăl, bēllŭă, fĕră, quadrŭpēs ; pĕcŭs ; brūtŭm. EPITH. Fĕră, sævă, fĕrōx, immānĭs. V. Fera.

bētă, æ, f., *beet, an herb.* Prāndĭă bētæ, Mart. EPITH. Plēbēĭă, tĕnĕră.—2. *the second Greek letter.* Alpha ēt bētă pŭēllæ, Juv.

Bethlĕhĕm *or* Bethlēm *(indecl.)* ; Bethlĕhĕmă *or* Bethlĕmă, æ, f. ; *and* Bethlē, ēs, f., *the place where Jesus Christ was born.* Mĭlle īn Bĕthlĕhĕm, (Iamb.) Sānctă Bĕthlĕm căpŭt ēst, Amœn. Quĭppe īn Bĕthlĕhĕmă, Fil. EPITH. Sacră, sānctă, clără, fēlīx, nōbĭlĭs, īnclўtă, ăngūstă, vĕnĕrāndă, cōlēndă.

Bethlemĭcŭs, ă, ŭm, *of Bethlehem.* Bĕthlēmĭcă cōmpĭtă cædĕ, Juvenc. SYN. Bethlemĭtĭcŭs, Bethlēŭs.

Bētrĭăcŭm, ī, n., *a city of Italy.* Bĕtrĭăci īn cāmpō, Juv.

Bĭānŏr, ŏrĭs, m., *a centaur.*—2. *a son of the Tiber.* Bĭānŏrĭs āltī, Ov.

Bĭās, āntĭs, m., *one of the seven Greek sages.* Prĭēnæĕ Bĭă, Sid. EPITH. Græcŭs ; săpĭēns, prūdēns, fēlīx.

bĭbāx, ācĭs, *who likes drinking.* Tēntărĕ bĭbācēs, Mant. SYN. Pōtātŏr. V. Ebrius.

bĭblĭŏpōlă, æ, m., *a bookseller.* Bĭblĭŏpōlă pŭtăt, Mart.

bĭblĭŏthēcă, æ, f., *a library.* Bĭblĭŏthēcă căpĭt, Mart. EPITH. Dōctă, plēnă.

Bĭblĭs, *or* Bўblĭs, ĭdŏs, f., *daughter of Miletus, changed into a fountain.* Bĭblĭdă quīn rĕfĕrăm ? Ov. SYN. Mĭlētĭs. EPITH. Phœbēĭă.

bĭblŭs, ī, m., *papyrus.* Cōntēmnĕrĕ bĭblōs, Lucr.

bĭbo, ĭs, *to drink.* Săt prătă bĭbērŭnt, Virg. SYN. Pōto, haŭrĭo. V. Poto.

Bĭbŭlă, æ, f., *the name of a woman.* Bĭbŭlæ Sērtōrĭŭs ardĕt, Juv.

Bĭbŭlŭs, ī, *the name of several Romans.* Cēssāntēm Bĭbŭlī.

bĭbŭlŭs, ă, ŭm, *soaking.* Bĭbŭlă dēdŭcĭt ărēnă, Virg. SYN. Bĭbāx, bĭbōsŭs.

bĭcĕps, ĭpĭtĭs, *with two heads.* Nĕc īn bĭcĭpĭtī, (Scaz.) Pers. SYN. Bĭvērtēx, bĭfrōns.

bĭcŏlŏr, ŏrĭs, *of two colours.* Sŭbēst, bĭcŏlōrĭbŭs ōbsĭtă baccīs, Ov. SYN. Gĕmĭnō cŏlōrĕ dīstīnctŭs, clārŭs, īnsĭgnĭs.

bĭcōrnĭgĕr, ă, ŭm, *and* nĭs, ĕ, *with two horns.* Bĭcōrnĭgĕr hāstă, Ov. Fŭrcāsquĕ bĭcōrnēs, Virg.

bĭcōrpŏr, ŏrĭs, *with two bodies.* Fōrmæquĕ bĭcōrpŏrĭs, Mant. SYN. Bĭmēmbrĭs, bĭfōrmĭs.

bĭdēns, ēntĭs, f., *a sheep two years old.* Dē mŏrĕ bĭdēntēs, Virg. EPITH. Mĭtĭs, lānĭgĕră, cāndĭdă, plăcĭdă, mānsuĕtă. V. Ovis.

bĭdēns, ēntĭs, m., *a pitchfork.* Pīnguĕ bĭdēntĕ sŏlŭm, Tib. V. Aro.

bĭdēntăl, ālĭs, n., *a place blasted with lightning.* Ēvĭtāndŭmquĕ bĭdēntăl. EPITH. Sacrŭm, hōrrēndŭm.

bĭdŭŭm, ī, n., *two days.* Hŏc ābs tē bĭdŭŭm, (Iamb.) Plaut.

bĭfārĭăm, adv., *in two parts.* Obsōnĭum hŏc bĭfārĭăm, (Iamb.) Plaut.

bĭfĕrŭs, ă, ŭm, *yielding fruit twice a year.* At quĭbŭs īn bĭfĕrō, M. SYN. Bĭfĕr.

bĭfĭdŭs, ă, ŭm, *cut in two parts.* Bĭfĭdōsquĕ rĕlīnquĭt, Ov. SYN. Fīssŭs, scīssŭs.

bĭfŏrĭs, ĕ, *with two doors.* Bĭfŏrēm dăt tĭbĭă cāntŭm, Virg.

bĭfōrmĭs, ĕ, *with two forms.* Prōlēsquĕ bĭfōrmĭs, Virg. SYN. Bĭmēmbrĭs, bĭcōrpŏr.

bĭfrōns, ōntĭs, *with two faces.* Jānĭquĕ bĭfrōntĭs, Virg. SYN. Bĭfōrmĭs.

bĭfūrcŭs, ă, ŭm, *forked.* Illĕ bĭfūrcŭm, Ov. SYN. Bĭsŭlcŭs, bĭfĭdŭs.

bīgæ, ārŭm, f. pl., *a chariot.* Pŏlŭm bĭgīs sŭbvēctă tĕnēbăt, Virg. SYN. Bĭjŭgēs, bījŭgī cŭrrūs. Epith. Cītæ, cŏncĭtæ, răpĭdæ, spūmāntēs, ālĭpēdēs, vēlōcēs. V. Currus.

bījŭgĭs, ĕ, *or* gŭs, ă, ŭm, *yoked.* Mārtĭs ĕquī bījŭgēs, Virg. Cŏmĭtūm bījŭgŏ cŭrrū, Sil.

bĭlĭbrĭs, ĕ, *of two pounds' weight.* Nūllūmvĕ bĭlībrĕm, Mart.

bĭlīnguĭs, ĕ, *having two tongues.* Tȳrĭōsquĕ bĭlīnguēs, Virg. Syn. Gĕmĭnā hōr-rēns cūspĭdĕ līnguæ ; mēndāx.

bīlĭs, ĭs, f., *bile.* Bīlĕ tūmĕt, Pers. Syn. Irā, īrācūndĭā. Epith. Diffĭcĭlĭs, ămārā, māscŭlā, ārdēscēns, flāvā, āptā, hōrrĭdā, ĭnīquā, pĕrūrēns, crōcĕă, fēr-vĭdă, fĕrōx, răbĭdă, ăcērbă, flāmmātă, ăcūtă, īrācūndă. V. Ira.

bĭlīx, ĭcĭs, *double-platted.* Infīxă bĭlīcĕm, Virg.

bĭlūstrĭs, ĕ, *which lasts ten years [two lustres].* Sŭpĕrātă bĭlūstrī, Ov. Syn. Dĕcēnnĭs.

bĭmārĭs, ĕ, *between two seas.* V. Isthmus.

bĭmātĕr, trĭs, m., *an epithet of Bacchus.* Sōlēmquĕ bĭmātrĕm, Ov.

bĭmēmbrĭs, ĕ, *with two natures.* Invīctĕ, bĭmēmbrēs, Virg. Syn. Bĭcōrpŏr.

bĭmēstrĭs, ĕ, *of two months.* Crūdă bĭmēstrĕ tĕnĕt, Ov.

bĭmūlŭs, *and* mŭs, ă, ŭm, *two years old.* Pŭĕri īnstār bĭmŭlī, Cat. Tūm vĭtŭlŭs, bĭmā cūrvāns, Virg.

bĭnōmĭnĭs, ĕ, *that has two names.* Vīcīnă bĭnōmĭnĭs Istrī, Ov.

bīnŭs, ă, ŭm, *double.* Pōcŭlă bīnă nŏvŏ, Virg. Syn. Gĕmĭnŭs, duplēx.

Bĭōnēŭs, ă, ŭm, *of Bion, the satirical philosopher.* Illĕ Bĭōnēĭs sērmōnĭbŭs, Hor.

bĭpārtītō, adv., *in two parts.* Sēctă bĭpārtītō cŭm, Ov.

bĭpātēns, ēntĭs, *open on two sides.* Ālī bĭpătēntĭbŭs ādsŭnt, Virg. Syn. Bĭfŏrĭs.

bĭpĕdālĭs, ĕ, *two feet long.* Mŏdŭlī bĭpĕdālĭs, Hor.

bĭpēnnĭfĕr, ă, ŭm, *carrying a halberd.* Fātă bĭpēnnĭfĕr Arcăs, Ov.

bĭpēnnĭs, ĭs, f., *a halberd.* Tōnsă bĭpēnnĭbŭs, (Alcaic.) Hor. Syn. Sĕcŭrĭs. Epith. Vălĭdă, sævă, dūră, fūlgēns, ærātă, vūlnĭfĭcă, fērrĕă, crŭēntă, lēthĭfĕră, rĭgĭdă, mĭnāx, nĕfāndă. V. Securis.

bĭpēnnĭs, ĕ, *having two pinions.* Altă bĭpēnnī, Virg.

bĭpēs, ĕdĭs, *having two feet.* Et jūnctŏ bĭpĕdŭm, Virg.

bĭrēmĭs, ĭs, f., *a ship with two banks of oars.* Dē clāssĕ bĭrēmēs, Virg. Syn. Nāvĭs. V. Navis.

bis, adv., *twice.* Tŭm bĭs ăd ōccāsŭm, Ov. Hīc tĭbī bĭs æstās, Id.

Bĭsāltæ, ārŭm, m. pl., *a people of Thrace.* Bĭsāltæ quŏ mŏrĕ, Virg. Epith. Fĕrī, sævī, sānguĭnĕī, crŭēntī, crūdēlēs.

Bĭsāltĭs, ĭdĭs, f., *a nymph beloved by Neptune.* Arĭēs Bĭsāltĭdă fāllĭs, Ov.

bĭsōn, ōntĭs, m., *a bison, buffalo.* Būbălŭs ātquĕ bĭsōn, Mart. Epith. Fĕrŭs, tŭrpĭs, vīllōsŭs.

bĭssēnŭs, ă, ŭm, *twelfth, twelve.* Pŭĕrī bĭssēnī quēmquĕ sĕcūtī, Virg. Syn. Dŭŏdēnŭs, bĭs sēx.

Bīstŏnēs, ŭm, m. pl., *the Thracians.* Bīstŏnēs aŭt mĕdĭæ, Stat.

Bīstŏnĭă, æ, f., *Thrace.* Pēctĭnĕ, Bīstŏnĭæ, Val. Fl.

Bīstŏnĭŭs, ă, ŭm, *and* Bīstŏnĭs, ĭdĭs, f., *Thracian.* Bīstŏnĭā mēmbră, Ov. Bīstŏnĭs ōrā, Id. Bīstŏnĭdūm sĭnĕ fraŭdĕ, Ov.

bĭsŭlcŭs, ă, ŭm, *cloven-footed.* Pĕdĕ pŭlsāvĕrĕ bĭsŭlcō, Ov. Syn. Bĭfūrcŭs, bĭfĭdŭs.

Bĭthȳnĭă, æ, *or* nĭs, ĭdĭs, f., *a country of Asia Minor.* Nūnc Bĭthȳnĭă fērtŭr, Cl. Bĭthȳnĭdĕ dīcĭtŭr ēssĕ, Ov.

Bĭthȳnĭcŭs, *or* Bĭthȳnŭs, ă, ŭm, *and* Bĭthȳnĭs, ĭdĭs, f., *of Bithynia.* Vŏlūsī Bĭthȳnĭcĕ, Juv. Bĭthȳnă nĕgŏtĭă, Hor. In Mĕlĭĕ Bĭthȳnĭdĕ, Ov.

Bĭtĭăs, æ, m., *one of the companions of Æneas.* Pāndărŭs ĕt Bĭtĭăs, Virg.

bĭtūmĕn, ĭnĭs, n., *bitumen.* Incēndĕ bĭtūmĭnĕ laŭrōs, Virg. Epith. Ātrŭm, pīnguĕ, lēntŭm, liquĭdŭm, fūmāns, Sēmĭrāmĭŭm ; nĭgrŭm.

bĭtūmĭnĕŭs, ă, ŭm, *bituminous.* Sīvĕ bĭtūmĭnĕæ, Ov.

bĭvērtēx, ĭcĭs, *having two tops.* Sūmmăquĕ bĭvērtĭcĭs ūmbră, St. Syn. Bĭcēps.

bĭvĭŭm, ĭī, n., *a way having two paths.* Et tŭŭs īn bĭvĭŏ, Ov. Epith. Ancēps, dŭbĭŭm, sēctŭm, scīssŭm.

bĭvĭŭs, ă, ŭm, *having two ways.* Ut bĭvĭăs ārmātō, Virg.

blæsŭs, ă, ŭm, *stammering.* Rēddēbās blæsō, Ov. Syn. Bălbŭs.

blāndē, adv., *charmingly, kindly.*   Blāndĭŭs Ōrphĕō, Hor.   SYN. Suāvĭtĕr, cŏmĭtĕr.

blāndĭcŭlŭs, *the diminut. of* blandus.

blāndĭdĭcŭs, *or* lŏquŭs, ă, ŭm, *speaking sweetly.*   Blāndĭdĭcŭs ēs, Plaut.   Blāndĭlŏquīs ōlĭm, Aus.

blāndĭmēntŭm, ī, n., *an allurement.*   Blāndīmēntă prĕcēsquĕ, Ov.   V. Blanditiæ.

blāndўŏr, īrĭs, *to flatter.*   Mēntīrĭs vānōquĕ tĭbī blāndīrĭs hŏnōrĕ, Mart.   V. Adulor.

blāndĭtĭæ, ārŭm, f. pl., *compliments, flatteries.*   Mīstăquĕ blāndĭtĭīs, Ov.   SYN. Illĕcĕbræ, lēnōcĭnĭă, blāndīmēntă.   EPITH. Mōllēs, ārgūtæ; dŏlōsæ, blāndæ, dūlcēs, mēllītæ, tĕnĕræ, mūlĭēbrēs, sŭbdŏlæ, lŏquācēs, ūxŏrĭæ, mātērnæ, fīctæ.

blāndītŭs, ă, ŭm, *the partic. of* blandior.   Blāndītæquĕ flŭānt, Prop.

blāndītŭs, ūs, m., *an enticing.*   Vĕnĕrĭs blāndītŭm, Luc.

blāndŭs, ă, ŭm, *kind.*   Dōctă prĕcĕ blāndŭs, Hor.   V. Comis.

Blāndŭsĭă, æ, f., *a celebrated spring.*   Fōns Blāndŭsĭæ, Hor.   V. Fons.

|| blāsphēmĭă, æ, f., *blasphemy.*   Blāsphēmĭă mōnstrī, Prud.   EPITH. Impĭă, sacrĭlĕgă, pērjūră.

¶ blāsphēmo, ās, *to blaspheme.*   Blāsphēmās dŏmĭnŭm, Prud.

|| blāsphēmŭs, ī, m., *a blasphemer.*   Jām, blāsphēmĕ, tĭbī ēst, Prud.

blătĕro, ās, *to babble, bray.*   Māgnō blătĕrās clāmōrĕ, Hor.

blătĕro, ōnĭs, m., *a babbler, a talker.*   EPITH. Clāmōsŭs, ĭnēptŭs.

blăttă, æ, f., *a moth, beetle.*   Cŭbīlĭă blāttĭs, Virg.

bŏārĭŭs, ă, ŭm, *of an ox.*   Sāncītĕ bŏārĭă lōngō, Prop.

bŏātŭs, ūs, m., *a lowing.*   Mūgīt spēlūncă bŏātŭ, Mant.   SYN. Mūgītŭs.   EPITH. Hōrrĭfĭcŭs, māgnŭs, cōnfūsŭs, hōrrēndŭs, raūcŭs, īngēns, rĕsŏnāns, hōrrĭsŏnŭs, ĭtĕrātŭs, văgŭs, frēmēns, rĕpĕtītŭs, crēbĕr.   V. Mugitus.

Bŏccăr, ārĭs, m., *king of Mauritania.*   Cūm Bŏccărĕ nēmo, Juv.

Bœbē, ēs, *and* Bœbēĭs, ĭdĭs, f., *a lake or marsh of Thessaly.*   Lĭttŏră Bœbēs, Ov.

Bœōtĭă, æ, f., *a country of Greece.*   Bœōtĭă Dīrcēn, Ov.   SYN. Aŏnĭă, Hўāntĭs, Cādmēĭs, Ōgўgĭă.

Bœōtĭŭs, ĭcŭs, tŭs, ă, ŭm, *of Bœotia.*   Bœōtĭcŭs Hæmōn, Prop.   Bœōtĭăque īllă, Ov.   Bœōtăquĕ tēllŭs, Id.   SYN. Aŏnĭŭs, Hўāntĭŭs, Cādmĕŭs, Ōgўgĭŭs.

Bŏhēmī, ōrŭm, m. pl., *a nation of Germany.*   Frēgĕrĕ Bŏhēmōs, Stroz.   SYN. Albĭcŏlæ.   EPITH. Sævī, ācrēs, īncūltī.

Bŏlă, æ, f., *an ancient city of Latium.*   Bŏlāmquĕ Cŏrāmquĕ, Virg.

Bŏlānŭs, ī, m., *the name of a man.*   Ō tĕ, Bŏlānĕ, Hor.

bŏlētŭs, ī, m., *a mushroom.*   Sūnt tĭbī bŏlētī, Mart.

|| bŏlŭs, ī, m., *a lump, a draught with a net.*   Ĕnŭmĕrāssĕ bŏlōs, Aus.   V. Tormentum.

bŏmbĭlo, ās, *to buzz.*   Bŏmbĭlăt ōrĕ, Ov.

bŏmbŭs, ī, m., *a buzzing.*   Bārbără bŏmbŭm, Lucr.   EPITH. Grăvĭs, raūcĭsŏnŭs, sŏmnĭfĕr, rĕsŏnāns, tŭmĭdŭs, sūrdŭs, cōnfūsŭs, tērrĭfĭcŭs, hōrrĭsŏnŭs.

bŏmbўcĭnŭs, ă, ŭm, *of silk.*   Bŏmbўcĭnŭs ūrĭt, Juv.

bŏmbўx, ўcĭs, m., *a silk-worm.*   Bŏmbўcĕ pŭēllă, Prop.   SYN. Vērmĭs Indĭcŭs.   EPITH. Lānĭfēx, Indĭcŭs, lānĭvŏmŭs, ārtĭfēx, īngĕnĭōsŭs, īndūstrĭŭs, ŏpĭfēx.

bŏnă, ōrŭm, n. pl., *riches.*   Bŏnă tū pērdāsquĕ lūpīnĭs, Hor.   V. Divitiæ.

Bŏnă, æ, f., *a goddess, whose sacrifices were performed by women only.*   Sācră Bŏnæ . . . . nōn ăddŭndă Dĕæ, Tib.

bŏnĭtās, ātĭs, f., *goodness.*   Quī bŏnĭtātĕ sĕnĕm, Mart.   SYN. Prŏbĭtās.   EPITH. Sānctă, pĭă, mītĭs, dūlcĭs, clēmēns, ămābĭlĭs, hūmānă, cāndĭdă, īnnŏcŭă, nātīvă, īnnātă.

bŏnŭs, ă, ŭm, *good.*   Nēc bŏnŭs Eūrўtĭōn, Virg.   SYN. Cāstŭs, prŏbŭs, rēctŭs, īntĕgĕr.

bŏo, ās, *to low.*   Vōcĕ bŏāntĕ fŏrō, Ov.   SYN. Rēbŏo, mūgĭo.

Bŏōtēs, æ, m., *a star.*   Sārrācă Bŏōtæ, Juv.   SYN. Ārctūrŭs, Ārctŏphўlāx.   EPITH. Tārdŭs, Ārctōŭs, Hўpērbŏrĕŭs, Scўthĭcŭs, Cāspĭŭs; V. Arcticus.   Gĕlĭdŭs, sērŭs, rĭgĭdŭs, glăcĭālĭs, fĕrŭs, frĭgĭdŭs, ālgēns, nĭvōsŭs, ālgĭdŭs, īgnāvŭs, hōrrēndŭs, frīgēns.   V. Arctophylax.

bŏrĕālĭs, ĕ, *northern.*   Ārctōs bŏrĕālĭs, Avien.   SYN. Bŏrĕŭs.

Bŏrĕăs, æ. m., *the north wind.*   Aūt Bŏrĕæ pĕnĕtrābĭlĕ, Virg.   SYN. Aquĭlo.   EPITH. Frīgĭdŭs, gĕlĭdŭs, sævŭs, hōrrĭfĕr, præcēps, răpĭdŭs, Ārctōŭs, Cāspĭŭs,

Scŷthĭcŭs, Thrācĭŭs, Thrēĭcĭŭs; V. Arcticus. Hŷbērnŭs, crūdēlĭs, īnsānŭs, sæ-vĭēns, strīdŭlŭs, vŏlŭcĕr, vĭŏlēntŭs, mĭnāx, īmmītĭs, fĕrōx, nĭvōsŭs, prŏcēllōsŭs, nīmbōsŭs, tūrgĭdŭs, sŏnōrŭs, ăcĕrbŭs; V. Aquilo.

Bŏrēŭs, *and* īnŭs, ă, ŭm, *of Boreas, northern.* Sŭb āxĕ Bŏrēō, Ov. Frĕmĭtūsquĕ Bŏrīnī, Luc. Syn. Āquĭlōnĭŭs, Bŏrĕālĭs.

Bŏrŷsthĕnĭŭs, ă, ŭm, *of the river Borysthenes, or Dnieper.* Cūmquĕ Bŏrŷsthĕnĭō, Ov.

Bŏrŷsthĕnĭdæ, ārŭm, m. pl., *people dwelling on the banks of the Borysthenes.* Lātă Bŏrŷsthĕnĭdās, Prop.

bōs, bŏvĭs, m., *an ox.* Quæ bōs ēx hŏmĭnĕ ēst, Ov. Syn. Taūrŭs, jŭvēncŭs. Epith. Cōrnĭgĕr, tārdŭs, pĭgĕr, tŭmĭdŭs, hīrsūtŭs, lăbōrĭfĕr, īndŏmĭtŭs, fĕrōx, săgīnátŭs, ŏpīmŭs, ŏbēsŭs, rūrĭcŏlă, mĭnāx, fĕrŭs, tōrvŭs, trūx, dūrŭs.—2. f., *a 'cow.* Incūstōdītæ lātă pĕr ārvă bŏvēs, Ov. Syn. Vĭtŭlă, jŭvēncă, văccă. Epith. Grăvĭdă, fōrmōsă, pīnguĭs, fœdă, prēgnāns. V. Vacca.

Bōspŏrānī, ōrŭm, *and* ĭdæ, ārŭm, m. pl., *inhabitants of the shores of the Bosporus.* Stŭpŭērĕ Bōspŏrānī, (Phal.) Bōspŏrĭdæ ōbvērsīs, Man.

Bōspŏrĭcŭs, *or* ĭŭs, ă, ŭm, *of the Bosporus.* Bōspŏrĭcōs Thrācēs, Mant. Bōspŏrĭō-quĕ mărī, Ov.

Bōspŏrŭs, ī, m., *two straits, situate on the confines of Europe and Asia.* Bōspŏrŭs ūndās, Luc. Epith. Ĭnērs, Thrāx, reflŭŭs, Thrācĭŭs, Thrēĭcĭŭs, Cīmmĕrĭŭs, ăngŭstŭs.

|| bŏtēllŭs, *and* ŭlŭs, ī, m., *a sausage.* Prēmēns bŏtēllŭs, (Phal.) Mart. Quī vēnĭt bŏtŭlŭs, Id. Syn. Hīllă, tŏmācŭlŭm.

|| botrŭs, ī, *and* rŷōn, ōnĭs, m., *a cluster of grapes.* Cōllēs bōtrĭs, Mant. Tē bŏtrŷōnĕ pŭtăt, Mart. V. Uva.

bŏvīlĕ, ĭs, n., *an ox-stall.* Cērvŭs sē bŏvīlī cōndĭdĭt, Phæd. Syn. Bŭbīlĕ. V. Stabulum.

Bŏvīllæ, ārŭm, f. pl., *an ancient city of Latium.* Fŭĭt Ānnă Bŏvīllĭs, Ov. bŏvīnŭs, ă, ŭm, *of an ox.* Ōră bŏvīnă, N. C. Syn. Bŏvīllŭs, bŭbŭlŭs.

brăbīŭm, bĕŭm, ī, n., *a public prize.* Sōlŭs brăbīī dŭplĭcĭs, Prud. Syn. Cērtā-mĭnĭs, pălæstræ præmĭŭm.

brăcă, *or* brăccă, æ, f., *breeches, trousers.* Brāccă tĕgĭt, Ov. Epith. Lāxă, flŭxă, tŭmĭdă, tŭmēns.

brăcātŭs, *or* ccātŭs, ă, ŭm, *wearing breeches.* Brāccātī mīlĭtĭs ārcŭs, Prop.

brăchĭă, ōrŭm, n. pl., *the arms.* Brāchĭă tōllŭnt, Virg. Syn. Lăcērtī, ūlnæ. Epith. Cāndĭdă, lāctĕă, cāndēntĭă, fōrtĭă, nĭvĕă, pŭlchră, fōrmōsă, vĕnŭstă, fīrmă, vălĭdă, ămĭcă. V. Lacertus.

brăchĭŏlŭm, ī, n., *the diminut. of* brachium. Mĭttĕ brăchĭŏlŭm, Catull.

Brāchmănēs, ŭm, *or* mănæ, ārŭm, m. pl., *Indian philosophers.* Epith. Dōctī, pĕrītī, Indī.

brăctĕă, æ, f., *a leaf of gold or other metal.* Brāctĕă vēntō, Virg. Epith. Aūrĕă, ārgēntĕă, splēndēns, mĭcāns.

* brăctĕātŭs, ă, ŭm, *covered with tinsel.* Sen. Phil. V. Bractea.

brăctĕŏlă, æ, f., *the diminut. of* bractea. Nēptūnī quī brăctĕŏlăm, Juv.

brāssĭcă, æ, f., *cauliflower.* Brāssĭcă vīnctă lĕvī, Prop. Syn. Caūlĭs.

Brēnnŭs, ī, m., *a Gallic conqueror.* Līmĭnă Brēnnŭm, Prop. Epith. Māgnănĭ-mŭs, gĕnĕrōsŭs, fōrtĭs, pŏtēns, tĕmĕrārĭŭs.

brĕvĭ, adv., *shortly.* Rōmănă brĕvī vēntūrŭs ĭn ōră, Hor. Syn. Mōx, mŏdŏ, jāmjăm, brĕvī tēmpŏrĕ, brĕvĭtĕr.

brĕvĭă, ĭŭm, n. pl., *fords.* In brĕvĭa ēt sŷrtēs, Virg.

brĕvĭo, ās, *to shorten.* Sīc brĕvĭāntŭr, Man. Syn. Ābbrĕvĭo, cōntrăho.

brĕvĭs, ĕ, *short.* Brĕvĭs ēst vĭă, Virg. Syn. Pārvŭs, pŭsīllŭs, ēxĭgŭŭs, ăngŭstŭs, cōntrāctŭs, nōn lōngŭs, cōncīsŭs.

brĕvĭtās, ātĭs, f., *shortness.* Dē brĕvĭtătĕ quĕrī, Mart.

brĕvĭtĕr, adv., *shortly.* Ātquĕ mŏdŭs brĕvĭtĕr, Mart. Syn. Āngūstē, cōncīsē, brĕvī, ēxĭgŭē.

Brĭărēŭs, ă, ŭm, *of Briareus.* Brĭărēĭă tūrbă, Claud. Syn. Gÿgāntēŭs.

Brĭărēŭs, ĕŏs, ĕī *or* eī, m., *one of the Titans.* Cēntūmgĕmĭnŭs Brĭărēŭs, Virg. Syn. Ægēōn, gĭgās cēntĭmănŭs. Epith. Vāstŭs, sævŭs, īmmānĭs. V. Gigas.

Brĭgāntēs, ŭm, m. pl., *ancient inhabitants of Northumberland.* Cāstēllă Brĭgāntŭm, Juv.

Brīseïs, ĭdĭs, f., *the daughter of Brises, loved by Achilles.* Brīsēïdă cēpĭt Achĭllēs, Ov. Epith. Trōĭă, sērvă, fōrmōsă, Lȳrnēssĭs, Trōjănă, Phrȳgĭă, pŭlchră.

Brĭtannī, ōrŭm, m. pl., *Britons.* Dīvīsōs ōrbĕ Brĭtānnōs, Virg. Syn. Ănglī. Epith. Flāvī, rĕmōtī, fĕrī, æquŏrēī; vĭrĭdēs, dĭffūsī, ēxtrēmī, pūgnācēs, gĕlĭdī, aūdācēs, ōccĭdŭī, dūrī, Arctōī, sēpŏsĭtī, fĕrōcēs, hōrrĭbĭlēs.

Brĭtānnĭă, æ, f., *Great Britain.* Cāntărĕ Brĭtānnĭă vērsūs, Mart. Syn. Ănglĭă. Brĭtānnĭs, ĭdĭs, f., *a British woman.* Vīctă Brĭtānnĭs ăquă, Cin.

Brĭtānnĭcŭs, *or* nŭs, ă, ŭm, *British.* Bālænă Brĭtānnĭcă, Juv. Essĕdă cælātĭs sīstĕ Brĭtānnă jŭgīs, Prop. Syn. Ănglĭcŭs.

Brĭtŏmārtĭs, ĭdĭs, f., *a Cretan nymph.* Prŏpĕrāt Brĭtŏmārtĭs ăb Idā, Mart. Syn. Dīctȳnnă.

Brĭtŏnēs, ŭm, m. pl., *the inhabitants of Bretagne in France.* Brĭtŏnēs ūnquăm, Juv. Brāccæ Brĭtŏnĭs paūpĕrĭs, Mart. Syn. Armŏrĭcī.

Brŏmĭŭs, ī, m., *a name of Bacchus.* Brŏmĭŭmquĕ Lȳæŭm, Ov. V. Bacchus.

Brŏmŭs, ī, m., *the name of a man.* Stȳphĕlŭmquĕ Brŏmŭmquĕ, Ov.

Brŏntēs, ĭs, m., *one of the Cyclopes.* Brŏntēsquĕ Stĕrŏpēsquĕ, Virg. V. Cyclopes.

Brŏthĕŭs, ī, m., *Vulcan's son.* Quŏdquĕ fĕrūnt Brŏthĕŭm, Ov.

brūchŭs, ī, m., *a caterpillar.* Gērmĭnă brūchŭs, Prud. Epith. Ĕdāx, vŏrāx.

brūnă, æ, f., *winter-solstice, winter.* Brūmă nŏvī, Ov. Syn. Hȳēms. Epith. Intrāctābĭlĭs, frīgĭdă, gĕlĭdă, cānă, nīmbōsă, mădēns, rĭgĭdă, ālgĭdă, rĭgēns, intŏlĕrābĭlĭs, ālbă, ĭnīquă. V. Hyems.

brūmālĭs, ĕ, *winterly.* Brūmālī frĭgŏrĕ vīscŭm, Virg. Syn. Hȳbērnŭs, hȳĕmālĭs.

Brūndĭsĭŭm, *or* Brūndŭsĭŭm, ī, n., *a town and harbour of Calabria, on the Adriatic.* Brūndŭsĭŭm lōngē, Hor.

|| brūtŭm, ī, n., *a wild-beast.* Syn. Ănĭmăl, bēllŭă, fĕră. Epith. Fŭrĭōsŭm, hōrrĭdŭm, răbĭdŭm, păvĭdŭm, mĕtŭēndŭm. V. Animal.

brūtŭs, ă, ŭm, *brute, insensible.* Quŏ brūtă tēllūs, (Alcaic.) Hor.

Brūtŭs, ī, m., *the first consul of Rome.—2. one of the conspirators against Cæsar.* Ūltōrĭs Brūtī, Virg.

būbălŭs, ī, m., *a buffalo.* Būbălŭs ātquĕ bĭsōn, Mart.

Būbāstĭs, ĭs, f., *the Egyptian name of Diana.* Sānctăquĕ Būbāstĭs, Ov.

būbīlĕ, ĭs, n., *an ox-stall.* Syn. Bŏvīlĕ.

būbo, ōnĭs, m. f., *an owl.* Ignāvŭs būbo, Ov. Epith. Sĭnīstĕr, trĕpĭdŭs, fœdŭs, ĭgnāvŭs, prŏfānŭs, fūnĕrĕŭs, Stȳgĭŭs, raūcŭs, dāmnōsŭs, īnfēstŭs, dīrŭs, lūctĭfĕr, mœstŭs, nōctĭcănŭs, nōctūrnŭs, quĕrŭlŭs, raūcĭsŏnŭs, trīstĭs.

būbulcŭs, ī, m., *a herdsman.* Vēnĕrĕ būbŭlcī, Virg. Syn. Ărmēntārĭŭs, pāstŏr. Epith. Ignāvŭs, dūrŭs, vĭgĭl, tārdŭs, ĕgēnŭs, rūstĭcŭs, paūpĕr, īncūltŭs, lābōrĭfĕr, hīrsūtŭs, mĭsĕr, pānnōsŭs, sōrdĭdŭs, īnfēlīx.

būbŭlŭs, ă, ŭm, *of an ox.* Vērŭs ēst, nōn būbŭlŭs. (Iamb.) V. Bovinus.

būccă, æ, f., *the hollow part of the cheek.* Irātŭs būccās īnflăt, Hor. Epith. Tŭmēns, tŭmĭdă, rŭbēns, tūrgēns, tŭmĕfāctă. V. Os.

būccĭnă, æ, f., *a trumpet.* Mŏdŭlātĭs būccĭnă nērvĭs, Luc. Syn. Tŭbă, cōrnū, lĭtŭŭs. Epith. Raūcă, īnflātă, cănŏră, tōrtĭlĭs, sŏnāns, dīră, lūctĭsŏnă, bēllĭcă, clāssĭcă, Mārtĭă, trĕmēndă, clāngēns, rĕsŏnāns, mĕtŭēndă, fĕră, fūnēstă, ănĭmāns, rĕsŏnă, bēllĭgĕră. V. Tuba.

būccŭlă, æ, f., *a little cheek, also a beaver.* Būccŭlă pēndēns, Juv.

Būcĕphălŭs, ī, m., *the horse of Alexander.* Būcĕphălŭs fōrmæ, Ser. V. Equus.

būcĕrĭŭs, *or* rŭs, ă, ŭm, *horned, belonging to beasts.* Būcĕrĭæquĕ grĕgēs, Luc. Ārmēntăquĕ būcĕră păvĭt, Ov.

būcētŭm, ī, m., *a pasture for cattle.* Būcētă Mătīnī, Luc.

būcŏlĭcŭs, ă, ŭm, *pastoral.* Būcŏlĭcīs jŭvĕnĭs, Ov. Syn. Pāstōrālĭs, agrēstĭs, rūstĭcŭs.

būcŭlă, æ, f., *a heifer.* Būcŭlă cāmpō, Virg.

būfo, ōnĭs, m., *a toad.* Invēntūsquĕ căvīs būfo, Virg. Epith. Nŏcŭŭs, cœnōsŭs, tŭmĭdŭs, fœdŭs, fœtĭdŭs, vĕnēnōsŭs, tūrgĭdŭs, tūrpĭs, hōrrĭdŭs, lēthĭfĕr, tŭmĕfāctŭs, pălūstrĭs.

būlbŭs, ī, m., *a scallion.* Būlbŭs, ĕt ēx hōrtō, Ov. Syn. Āllĭŭm. Epith. Sălāx, cāndĭdŭs.

|| būlgă, æ, f., *a leathern purse.* Spēs hŏmĭnĭs būlgă, Lucil.

būllă, æ, f., *a bubble.* Būllă sŭpĕr frōntĕm, Ov. Epith. Tŭmēns, tŭmĭdă.

būllātŭs, ă, ŭm, *adorned with studs, swelling.* Būllātīs ūt mĭhĭ nūgīs, Pers.

bŭllĭo, ĭs, ĭī, *to bubble.* Bŭllĭt ĭn ŭndā, Pers. Syn. Ĕbŭllĭo, fĕrvĕo.

bŭmāstŭs, ī, m., *a kind of raisin.* Tŭmĭdĭs, bŭmāstĕ, răcēmĭs, Virg.

Bŭpālŭs, ī, m., *a sculptor.* Ācēr hŏstĭs Bŭpālō, Hor.

Bŭrdĕgălă, *or* dĭgălă, æ, f., *Bordeaux.* Bŭrdĭgăla ēst, Aus. Epith. Clără, nŏbĭlĭs.

bŭră, æ, *and* ĭs, ĭs, f., *a plough's beam.* In bŭrim, ĕt, Virg. V. Aratrum.

Bŭsĭrĭs, ĭdĭs, m., *a barbarous king of Egypt.* Sævĭŏr ēst trīstī Būsĭrĭdĕ, Ov. Epith. Crŭēntŭs, fĕrŭs, dīrŭs, dūrŭs, Nīlĭācŭs, Mărĕŏtĭcŭs; Afĕr; crūdēlĭs, bărbărŭs, trūx, pērfĭdŭs.

bŭstŭālĭs, ĕ, *and* ārĭŭs, ă, ŭm, *belonging to funeral piles.* Ăntrō bŭstŭālī, (Trochaic Dim.) Prud. Intēr bŭstŭārĭās mœchās, (Scaz.) Mart.

bŭstŭm, ī, n., *a funeral pile.* Ex ăggĕrĕ bŭstŭm, Virg. Syn. Sĕpŭlcrŭm, tŭmŭlŭs, pўră, rŏgŭs. Epith. Hŏrrĭfĭcŭm, ĭnhŏnōrŭm, trīstĕ, căvŭm, dīrŭm, săxĕŭm, gĕlĭdŭm, mūtŭm, mĭsĕrābĭlĕ. V. Sepulcrum.

Bŭtă *and* Būtēs, æ, m., *the name of a warrior.* Ăntīquŭm Būtēn, Virg.

Būthrōtŭm, ī, n., *and* ŭs *or* ŏs, ī, f., *a maritime town of Epirus.* Būthrōti āscĕndĭmŭs ūrbĕm, Virg.

butyrŭm, ī, n., *butter.* Cāsĕŏquĕ sīvĕ būtўrō. (Scaz.) Lāc nĭvĕŭm, bŭtўrŭmquĕ, Valg. Epith. Mŏllĕ, pīnguĕ, nŏvŭm, ŏdōrŭm, liquĭdŭm, liquēns, flāvēns.

bŭxētŭm, ī, n., *a place planted with box-trees.* Tĕpĭdæ bŭxētă rĕcŭrrĭt, Mart.

bŭxĕŭs, ă, ŭm, *of box, of a box colour.* Pĭcĕīquĕ bŭxĕīquĕ, (Hendec.) Mart.

bŭxĭfĕr, ĕră, ĕrŭm, *producing box-trees.* Cўtŏrĕ bŭxĭfĕr, Cat.

bŭxŭs, ī, f., *or* ŭm, ī, n., *box-tree.* Crīspātă căcūmĭnĕ bŭxŭs, Cl. Et dēnsŭm fŏllĭs bŭxŭm, Ov. Epith. Vĭrēns, pāllēns, tōnsĭlĭs, pūllĭdă, crīspă, vĭrĭdĭs, Bĕrĕcўnthĭă; frŏndēns, frŏndōsă, ŏpācă, īncŭltă. V. Fistula, Pecten.

Bўrsă, æ, f., *the citadel of Carthage.* Nŏmĭnĕ Bўrsăm, Virg. Epith. Tўrĭă, Pŭnĭcă, pŏtēns. V. Carthago.

bўssĭnŭs, ă, ŭm, *of linen.* Bўssĭnă vēlă, Mart.

bўssŭs, ī, f., *fine linen.* Pŭrpŭră bўssō, Mart. Syn. Līnŭm. Epith. Tĕnŭĭs, cānēns, ālbŭs, cāndĭdŭs, nītēns, tēxtĭlĭs, tĕrĕs.

Bўzāntĭācŭs, ĭnŭs, *and* ĭŭs, ă, ŭm, *of Byzantium.* Aŭt Bўzāntĭācōs, (Phal.) Stat. Bўzāntīnă Sŏphōs, (Phal.) Sid. Bўzāntĭă pūtrŭĭt ōrcă, Hor.

Bўzāntĭŭm, ĭī, n., *a city of Thrace, now Constantinople.* Syn. Cōnstāntīnŏpŏlĭs. Epith. Sŭpērbŭm, nŏbĭlĕ, īnsīgnĕ, măgnĭfĭcŭm, fōrtĕ, pŏtēns, mūnītŭm, măgnŭm, āltŭm. V. Constantinopolis.

C.

CĂBĂLLĪNŬS, ă, ŭm, *of a horse.* Prŏlŭī căbāllīnō, (Scaz.) Pers.

căbāllŭs, ī, m., *a horse, jade.* Ărārĕ căbāllŭs, Hor. Syn. Ĕquŭs, quadrŭpēs, sŏnĭpēs. Epith. Pĭgĕr, vŏlŭcĕr, sŭpērbŭs. V. Equus.

‖ cācăbo, ās, *to cry as a partridge.* Cācăbăt hīnc pērdīx, Ov.

cācăbŭs, ī, m., *a kettle.* Ătquĕ cācăbōrŭm, (Phal.) Stat.

căcātŭrĭo, ĭs, *to have a mind to go to stool.* Nŏn cācātŭrĭt, Mart.

căchĭnno, ŏnĭs, m., *a great laughter.* Pĕtŭlāntī splēnĕ căchĭnno, Pers.

căchĭnnŏr, ārĭs, *or* no, ās, *to laugh aloud.* Cŏncŭssă căchĭnnĕt, Lucr. Syn. Obgānnĭo, rīdĕo. V. Rideo, derideo.

căchĭnnŭs, ī, m., *laughter, derision.* Nāsō crīspāntĕ căchĭnnōs, Pers. Syn. Rīsŭs, jŏcŭs, gānnītŭs. Epith. Lætŭs, pĕtŭlāns, trĕmŭlŭs, ārgūtŭs, tĕnĕr, mŏllĭcŭlŭs, sŭbsānnāns, mōrdāx, rĭgĭdŭs. V. Risus.

căco, ās, *to go to stool.* Cărĭŭs ērgŏ cācās, Mart.

căcŏēthĕs, ĭs, m., *an evil custom.* Scrībēndī căcŏēthĕs ĕt ægrō, Juv. Syn. Prāvŭs mōs; prūrītŭs.

căcŭlă, æ, m., *a camp-servant.* Cŭm mātre ēt căcŭlĭs, Juv.

căcŭmĕn, ĭnĭs, n., *a peak, a top.* Tēllūrĕ căcŭmĭnă tōllŭnt, Ov. Syn. Cŭlmĕn, vērtēx, ăpēx, fāstīgĭŭm. Epith. Umbrōsŭm, cēlsŭm, mōntānŭm, sŭblīmĕ, ăcūtŭm, frŏndōsŭm, nīmbōsŭm, āltŭm, săxōsŭm, vĭrĭdāns, ārdŭŭm, ăĕrĭŭm, rāmōsŭm, ēxcēlsŭm, ăpērtŭm, sŭpērbŭm, frŏndĭfĕrŭm, ĭnhŏspĭtŭm, vĭrēns, stĕrĭlĕ, ĭnāccēssŭm, scŏpŭlōsŭm, dēclīvĕ, āvĭŭm. V. Culmen, vertex.

căcŭmĭno, ās, *to make sharp.* Sŭmmāsquĕ căcŭmĭnăt aŭrēs, Ov. Syn. Acŭo, ăcŭmĭno.

Cacŭs, ī, m., *the son of Vulcan, a daring robber killed by Hercules.* Cācŭs Avēntīnæ, Ov. Hīc Cācŭs, hŏrrēndŭm, Ov. Epith. Fĕrōx, īmmānĭs, vĭgĭl, pērvĭgĭl, rāptŏr, caūtŭs, cāllĭdŭs.

cădāvĕr, ĕrĭs, n., *a corpse.* Dīlāpsă cădāvĕră tābō, Virg. Epith. Infōrmĕ, mœstŭm, tetrŭm, tūrpĕ, dēfōrmĕ, mĭsĕrābĭlĕ, ĕxānguĕ, fœdŭm, gĕlĭdŭm, crŭēntŭm, flēbĭlĕ, trānslōssŭm, frīgēns, frīgĭdŭm, pāllĭdŭm, pāllēns, hŏrrēndŭm. Cādmēĭs, ĭdĭs, f., *of Cadmus, Theban.* Cādmēĭdĕs ādsŭnt, Ov.

Cādmēĭŭs, *and* mēŭs, ă, ŭm, *of Cadmus, Theban.* Cādmēĭŭs hērōs, St. Cādmĕă jŭvēntŭs, Id.

Cādmŭs, ī, m., *the son of Agenor, and founder of Thebes.* Cādmŭs ĭn ānguĕm, Hor. Syn. Ăgēnŏrĭdēs, Ăgēnŏrĕ nātŭs. Epith. Hўāntĭŭs; dīrŭs, Thēbānŭs, prŏfŭgŭs, Mārtĭŭs, aūdāx, gĕnĕrōsŭs, bēllāx, clārŭs, īnsĭgnĭs, pŏtēns, īmpăvĭdŭs.

cădo, cĕcĭdĭ, cāsŭm, *to fall.* Cĕcĭdērĕ, cădēntquĕ, Hor. Syn. Dēcĭdo, cōncĭdo, ĕxcĭdo, prŏcĭdo, lābŏr, dēlābŏr, prōlābŏr, cōllābŏr, rŭo, cŏrrŭo, præcĭpĭto, prŏcŭmbo. V. Morior.

Cādŭcĕŭs, ĕī, m., *or* ĕŭm, ĕī, n., *Mercury's wand.* Epith. Pācĭfĭcŭs, fēlīx, faūstŭs, pācĭfĕr.

Cādŭcĭfĕr, ī, m., *an epithet of Mercury.* Părĭbŭs Cādŭcĭfĕr ālĭs, Ov. V. Mercurius.

cădŭcŭs, ă, ŭm, *falling.* Tēlă cădŭcă, Prop. Syn. Frăgĭlĭs, īnfīrmŭs, lābāns, pĕrĭtūrŭs, flŭxŭs, dēbĭlĭs; cădēns, lābēns.

cădŭs, ī, m., *a large Roman measure, a cask.* Quæ deīndĕ cădīs ŏnĕrārăt, Virg. Syn. Dōlĭŭm. Epith. Pĭcēātŭs, vĕtŭlŭs, frăgĭlĭs, nĭvĕŭs, nĭgĕr, fūmōsŭs, spūmāns, Fălērnŭs.

* cæcĭgĕnŭs, ă, ŭm, *born blind.* Nŭm cŭm cæcĭgĕnī, Lucr. V. Cæcus.

cæcĭtās, ātĭs, f., *blindness.* In cæcĭtātĕ cōrpŏrĭs, (Iamb.) Paul. Nol.

cæco, ās, *to blind.* Cæcāntŭr stīpĭtĕ sўlvæ, Avien. Syn. Ēxcæco, ŏbcæco.

Cæcŭbŭm, ī, n., *a town of Campania, famous for its wines.*

Cæcŭbŭs, ă, ŭm, *of Cæcubum.* Cæcŭbă vīnă fĕrēns, Hor. Dēprōmĕrĕ Cæcŭbŭm, Id.

Cæcŭlŭs, ī, m., *a son of Vulcan.* Stīrpĕ crēātŭs Cæcŭlŭs, Virg.

cæcŭs, ă, ŭm, *blind.* Aūrī cæcŭs ămōrĕ, Virg. Syn. Ŏbcæcātŭs, ēxcæcātŭs.

cæcūtĭo, īs, īi, *to be blind.* Cæcūtīre ĕtĭăm, Fill.

cædēs, ĭs, f., *slaughter.* Tūnc cædēs hŏmĭnŭm, Tib. Syn. Clādēs, strāgēs, fūnĕră. Epith. Impĭă, dīră, fūrĭālĭs, sānguĭnĕă, fĕră, dūră, mĭsĕrāndă, ăcērbă, fĕrālĭs, īnfaūstă, lēthĭfĕră, crŭēntă, fūnēstă, imprŏbă, īnsānă, atrōx, hŏrrĭfĭcă, crūdēlĭs, mĭsĕră, īnfāndă, nēfāndă, hōrrĭdă, ātră, lūctŭōsă, flēbĭlĭs, trīstĭs, hōstīlĭs, rĕpēntīnă, ēffĕră. V. Occisio, strages.

Cædĭcĭŭs, ī, m., *the name of a judge.* Quās ēt Cædĭcĭŭs, Juv.

cædo, cĕcīdĭ, cæsŭm, *to lash, to cut, to slaughter.* Nŭllă cĕcīdĕrăt ætās, Ov. Syn. Vērbĕro, pērcŭtĭo, fĕrĭo; ōccīdo, īntĕrfĭcĭo, īntĕrĭmo, pĕrĭmo, nĕco. V. Occido, verbero.

cælāmĕn, ĭnĭs, n., *etching in metal.* Clўpĕī cælāmĭnă nŏvĭt, Ov.

cælātŏr, ōrĭs. m., *an engraver.* Cūrvŭs cælātŏr, ĕt āltĕr, Juv.

cælātūră, æ, f., *the skill of engraving.* Gēmmās, cælātūræquĕ mŏnĭlĭs, Fill.

cælātŭs, ă, ŭm, *the pass. partic. of cælo.* Cælātŭs fērrō, Virg.

cælēbs, ĭbĭs, *unmarried.* Nīl cælĭbĕ vītā, Hor. Syn. Iunŭbŭs; īnnŭbă, īnnūptă. V. Castus.

Cælĕs, ĭtĭs, m.; Cælĭtŭs, ŭm, m. pl., *inhabitant or inhabitants of heaven.* Cælĭtĕ fāctă nŏvō, Ov. Cælĭtĭbŭs vīsum ēst, Ov. V. Cælicolæ.

cælēstĭs, ĕ, *heavenly.* Ănĭmīs cælēstĭbŭs īræ, Virg. Syn. Æthĕrĕŭs, āĕrĕŭs, sīdĕrĕŭs, sŭpĕrŭs.

cælĭcŏlæ, ārŭm, m. pl., *inhabitants of heaven.* Nŭllă sŭpĕr nūbēs cōnvīvĭă cælĭcŏlārŭm, Juv. Syn. Cælĭtēs, cælēstēs, sŭpĕrī, Dīvī, Bĕātī.

cælĭcŭs, ă, ŭm, *of heaven.* Cælĭcă tēctă, Mant. V. Cælestis.

cælĭfĕr, ă, ŭm, *upholding heaven.* Cælĭfĕr Atlās, Virg.

cælĭgĕnă, æ, m., *one heaven-born, a god.* Sānguĭnĕ cælĭgĕnăm, Aus.

cælĭtŭs, adv., *in heaven, from heaven.* Cælĭtŭs ĭnsĕrĭtŭr, Er.   Syn. Cælō, ē cælō; dīvīnĭtŭs.

Cælĭŭs, ĭī, m., *one of the seven hills of Rome.* Cælĭŭs ăccĭpĭăt, Ov.

cælo, ās, *to emboss.* Mŭltō cælāvĕrăt aūrō, Virg.   Syn. Scūlpo, ĭncīdo.

cælŭm, ī, n., *heaven.* Vīx cælō nŏctīs dēcēssĕrăt ŭmbră, Virg.   Syn. Æthēr, sīdĕră, āstră, æthră, aūră, āxīs, pŏlŭs, Ŏlўmpŭs.   Epith. Prŏfŭndŭm, cēlsŭm, nĭtĭdŭm, sīdĕrĕum, stēllāns, pŭrŭm, vŏlūbĭlĕ, māgnŭm, plŭvĭŭm, liquĭdŭm, cōnvĕxŭm, fūlgēns, ĭgnĭfĕrŭm, cærūlĕum, sūblīmĕ, cōlōrātŭm, splēndĭdŭm, flāmmĭgĕrŭm, rĕfūlgēns, stēllātŭm, pīctŭm, āstrĭfĕrŭm, vărĭābĭlĕ, bĕātŭm, īn-cūrvŭm, pūlchrŭm, rŭtĭlŭm, oblīquŭm, sĕrēnŭm, ĭmmēnsŭm, cŏrūscŭm, ārdŭŭm, gēmmĕum, rĕcūrvŭm, vērsātĭlĕ, nĭmbōsŭm, nūbĭlŭm, plăcĭdŭm.   V. Aer.—2. *a graving-tool.* Fōrmātŭm Jūlĭă cælō, Mart.   Syn. Scālprŭm.   Epith. Pŏly-clētæum, l'hĭdĭăcŭm, Mēntŏrĕum; lăbŏrĭfĕrŭm, mōrdāx, dūrŭm, ăcūtŭm, fēr-rĕum.

Cœneūs, ĕōs, ĕī *or* eī, m., *and* Cænĭs, ĭdĭs, f., *the daughter of Elatus, metamor-phosed into a man, and afterwards into a bird.* Ov.

Cœnīnă, æ, f., *a city of Latium.* Cŭrēs, Cœnīnăquĕ, Ov.

cœpă, æ, f., *or* ĕ, ĭs, n., *an onion.* Pŏrrum ēt cæpĕ nĕfās, Juv.   Ĕrūtă cæpă mĕīs, Ov.

Cærĕ, n., *undecl.,* and Cærēs, ĭtĭs *or* ētĭs, f., *a city of Etruria.* Prŏpĕ Cærĭtĭs āmnĕm, Virg.

Cærēs, ĭtĭs *or* ētĭs, *of Cære.* Cærĭtĕ cērā dīgnī, Hor.   Quī Cærĕtĕ dŏmō, Virg.

cærĕmōnĭă, æ, f., *ceremony.* Cōnsēcrātĭō cærĕmōnĭārŭm, (Phal.) Sid.

cærŭlă, ōrŭm, n. pl., *the sea.* Cærŭlă vērrŭnt, Virg.   V. Mare.

cærŭlĕus, *or* lŭs, ă, ŭm, *azure.* Ipsăquĕ cærŭlĕīs, Ov.   Cærŭlă cōllă, Id.   Syn. Glaūcŭs, cæsĭŭs, vĭrĭdĭs, mărīnŭs.

Cæsăr, ărĭs, m., *surname of the Julian family at Rome.* Cæsărĭbŭs, cŭm cōnjŭgĕ dĭgnā, Ov.   Epith. Trŏjānŭs, ācĕr, ĭndŏmĭtŭs, crŭēntŭs; Hēspĕrĭŭs, Lātĭŭs, Rōmānŭs, Tārpĕĭŭs; ēgrĕgĭŭs, ĭnvīctŭs, fĕrōx, fĕrŭs, māgnŭs, māgnănĭmŭs, ārmĭsŏnŭs, sŭpĕrbŭs.

Cæsărĕus, *and* ĭānŭs, ă, ŭm, *of Cæsar.* Cæsărĕōs vīdĕō vūltŭs, Ov.

cæsărĭēs, ĭēī, f., *the hair.* Aūrĕă cæsărĭēs ōllīs, Virg.   Syn. Căpīllī, crīnēs, cŏmă.   Epith. Nĭtĭdă, pēndŭlă, rădĭāns, flŭĭtāns, cāndĭdă, gĕnĭālĭs, flāvĭcŏmă, pūlchră, flāvă, dĕcōră, fūlvă.   V. Capilli.

cæsĭŭs, ă, ŭm, *sky-coloured.* Cæsĭō vēnĭam obvĭŭs, (Hendec.) Catul.

cæstŭs, ŭs, m., *a kind of gauntlet, used in boxing.* Indūcĕrĕ cæstŭs, Virg.   Epith. Vălĭdŭs, grăvĭs, ĭngēns, ĭmmānĭs, ærĭsŏnŭs, pīctŭs, plŭmbĕŭs, lēthĭfĕr, lēthālĭs, crŭēntātŭs, crŭēntŭs.

cæsūră, æ, f., *an incision.* Cæsūră tămēn sē, Lucr.   Syn. Cæsĭo, ĭncīsĭo, scīs-sūră.

cætĕră, ō, *and* ŭm, adv., *in other respects.* Cætĕră lætŭs, Hor.   Syn. Dēnĭquĕ, tămēn, āttămēn, dĕīncēps.

cætĕrōquīn, *or* quī, adv., *otherwise.*   Syn. Ălĭōquīn.

Cājētă, æ, f., *Æneas' nurse.* Fāmăm, Cājētă, dĕdīstī, Virg.

Caīn, *or* Caīnŭs, ī, m., *Abel's brother.* Ārvă Caīn, Vict.   Dēsĭnĕ jām, Caīn, Leb.   Tēstĕ Caīnō, Vict.   Epith. Sævŭs, Impĭŭs, crūdēlĭs, ĭnvīsŭs, ĭmmānĭs, ĭnīquŭs, dīrŭs.

Caīnĭgĕnæ, ārŭm, m. pl., *Cain's descendants.* Nāmquĕ Caīnĭgĕnŭm, Vict.

Caĭŭs, Cājŭs, ī, m., *a Roman prænomen.* Caĭŭs ŭt fĭăt, Mart.   Cājŭs ŭtrŭmquĕ, Id.

Călăbrĭă, æ, f., *the remotest part of Italy.* Grātă Călăbrĭæ, Hor.

Călăbĕr, abră, ŭm, *Calabrian.* Ēnnĭŭs ēmĕrŭĭt Călăbrīs, Ov.

Călăĭs, ĭs, m., *son of Boreas.* Călăĭs Zēthēsquĕ, Virg.

Călămĭs, ĭdĭs, m., *the name of a sculptor.* Vīndĭcĕt ŭt Călămĭs, Ov.

* călămīstĕr, *or* trŭm, ī, n., *a crisping-pin.* Cic.   Epith. Ūrēns, crīspāns.

călămīstro, ās, *to curl.* Plaut.

călămĭtŭs, ātĭs, f., *misfortune.* Nēc pērmŏvērī călămĭtătĕ, (Scaz.)   Syn. Ærŭm-nă, mĭsĕrĭă, ægrĭtūdo, mœrŏr, mălă, dŏlōrēs, ādvērsī cāsŭs, fōrtūnă ādvērsă, ĭnfōrtūnĭum, clādēs, străgēs, dāmnŭm, ēxĭtĭŭm, dētrīmēntŭm, ĭncōmmŏdŭm.   V. Malum.

călămĭtōsŭs, ă, ŭm, *calamitous.* In călămĭtōsō, Publ.   V. Miser.

călămăs, ī, m., *a reed, straw, pipe.* Quæ vēllēm călămō, Virg. Syn. Cŭlmŭs, stīpŭlă, ărūndo, ăvēnă; fĭstŭlă. V. Fistula; săgittă, spĭcŭlŭm. V. Sagitta.

Epith. Grăcĭlĭs, lēvĭs, mōllĭs; frăgĭlĭs, tĕnŭĭs, pălŭstĕr; lŏquāx, ārgūtŭs, dūlcĭlŏquŭs, sŏnōrŭs, cănōrŭs.

călăthĭscŭs, ī, m., *the diminut. of* calathus. Cūstōdībănt călăthĭscī, Catul.

călăthŭs, ī, m., *a basket.* Nymphæ călăthĭs, Virg. Syn. Cănĭstrŭm, cĭstă, cĭstŭlă, fĭscĭnă, fĭscēllă. Epith. Vīmĭnĕŭs, nēxŭs, căpāx, īnērs, vīrgātŭs, ĕbūrnŭs, fœmĭnĕŭs, ŏdōrŭs, flōrĭgĕr, frăgrāns, rĕdŏlēns, pătēns. V. Canistrum.

Călaūrĕă, æ, f., *an epithet of Diana.* Indĕ Călaūrĕæ, Ov.

călcānĕŭs, ī, m., *or* nĕŭm, ī, n., *the heel.* Călcănĕă scĭssă rĭgēbănt, Virg. Syn. Călx.

călcăr, ărĭs, n., *a spur.* Fŏdĕrēt călcārĭbŭs ārmōs, Virg. Syn. Stĭmŭlŭs, ăcŭlĕŭs. Epith. Acūtŭm, ærātŭm, dūrŭm, sŭbĭtŭm, rĕpĕtītŭm, pūngēns, pērpĕtŭŭm, ĭmpōrtūnŭm, ādmōtŭm. V. Stimulus.

călcārĭŭs, ă, ŭm, *belonging to lime.* Fōrnāx călcārĭă vāstŏ, Mant.

călcătŏr, ōrĭs, m., *and* trīx, īcĭs, f., *one who treads upon.* Sălĭāt călcătŏr ĭn ūvās, Calph. Călcātrīx mūndī, Prud.

călcĕo, ās, *to shoe.* Căpŭt ēssĕ călcĕātŭm, (Phal.) Mart.

călcĕŏlŭs, ī, m., *the diminut. of* calceus. Călcĕŏlŭm pĕdĭbŭs, Fill.

călcĕŭs, ī, m., *a shoe.* Călcĕŭs ōllĭm, Hor. Epith. Aptŭs, ūtĭlĭs, hăbĭlĭs, lēvĭs.

Călchās, āntĭs, m., *the son of Thestor, a Greek diviner.* Călchās ăttŏllĕrĕ mŏlŏm, Virg. Syn. Thēstŏrĭdēs. Epith. Aŭgŭr, vātēs, vērŭs, vērāx, prŏvĭdŭs. V. Augur.

călcĭtro, ās, *to kick.* Călcĭtrăt, ĕt pŏsĭtās, Ov.

călco, ās, *to trample upon.* Pĕdĭbŭs călcāmŭs ămōrĕm, Ov. Syn. Cōntĕro, ōbtĕro, prōcūlco; cōntĕmno.

‖ călcŭlo, ās, *to cast accounts.* Năm călcŭlāndŏ prīmĭtŭs, (Iamb.) Prud. Syn. Nŭmĕro, sŭppŭto.

călcŭlŭs, ī, m., *a small pebble.* Călcŭlŭs ārvĭs, Virg. Syn. Lăpĭllŭs, ărēnă.

căldŭs, ă, ŭm, *sync. for* calidus. Căldām pōscĭs ăquăm, Mart. Căldĭŏr ēst, Hor.

Călēdŏnĭă, æ, f., *Scotland.*

Călēdŏnĭŭs, ă, ŭm, *Scotch.* Nūdă Călēdŏnĭŏ, Mart.

călĕfăcĭo, călfăcĭo, ĭs, *and* călĕfăcto, ās, *to warm.* Graĭŏs călĕfēcĕrĭt āmnēs, Cl. Călfăcĭt īgnĕ fŏcŭm, Ov. Lignĭs călĕfāctăt ăhēnŭm, Hor.

Călēndæ, ārŭm, f. pl., *the first day of the Roman month.* Hăbŭērĕ călēndās, Ov.

călēndārĭŭm, ĭī, n., *an account book.* Quŏd vŏcănt, călēndārī, (Scaz.)

Călēnŭs, ă, ŭm, *of Cales.* Ēt prælō dŏmĭtăm Călēnŏ, Hor.

călĕo, ŭī, *to grow warm.* Călŭērūnt mōllĭă săxă, Juv. Syn. Călēsco, ārĕo, æstŭo, ārdĕo, fērvĕo, sīccŏr, ēxsiccŏr. V. Sudo.

Călēs, ĭŭm, f. pl., *a small village of Campania.* Sēd prēssŭm Călĭbŭs, Hor.

călēsco, ĭs, *the frequent. of* caleo. Ăgĭtāntĕ călēscĭmŭs īllŏ, Ov.

călĭdŭs, ă, ŭm, *warm.* Illĕ răpĭt călĭdŭm, Virg. Syn. Æstŭōsŭs, ārdēns, ĭgnītŭs, tōrrĭdŭs, fērvĭdŭs, flāmmĕŭs, fērvēns, ārdēscēns, ēxārdēscēns, fērvēscēns.

călĭēndrŭm, ī, n., *false hair, a wig.* Săgănæ călĭēndrŭm, Hor.

călĭgă, æ, f., *a soldier's boot.* Cŏgnōmēn călĭgæ cuī cāstră dĕdĕrūnt, Aus.

călĭgātŭs, ă, ŭm, *booted.* Vĕnĭăm călĭgātŭs ĭn ăgrōs, Juv.

călĭgĭnĕŭs, *and* ōsŭs, ă, ŭm, *foggy.* Vĕl călĭgĭnĕŏ, Grat. Călĭgĭnōsă nōctĕ, (Alcaic.) Hor. Syn. Tĕnĕbrōsŭs, ōbscūrŭs, nĭgĕr, ŏpācŭs.

călĭgo, ĭnĭs, f., *fog.* Ēt călĭgĭnĕ mērsās, Virg. Syn. Tĕnĕbræ, nōx. Epith. Pīcĕă, ōbscūră, dēnsă, ātră, crāssă, tērrĭbĭlĭs, nūbĭlă, ŏpācă, fūmōsă, gĕlĭdă, sōmnĭfĕră, Stўgĭă, Āvērnālĭs, hōrrēns, hōrrĭdă, squālĭdă, nōctūrnă, trīstĭs, tērrĭfică, lūrĭdă. V. Tenebræ, nubes, nox.

călĭgo, ās, *to be dark.* Ēt călĭgāntĕm, Virg. Syn. Ōbscūrŏr, ōbscūrŭs sŭm; cæcūtĭo.

Călĭgŭlă, æ, m., *a Roman emperor.* Epith. Dūrŭs, tўrānnŭs, pērfĭdŭs, scĕlĕrātŭs, nĕfāndŭs, crūdēlĭs.

Călĭstŏ, ūs, f., *the daughter of Lycaon, changed into a she-bear.* Lūmĭnă Călĭstŏ, Catul. Syn. Părrhăsĭs. Epith. Pūlchră, vĕnūstă, fōrmōsă, Tĕgĕæă, Nōnăcrīnă. V. Arctos.

cǎlīx, ĭcĭs, m., *a cup.* Plēbeīŏs cǎlĭcēs, Juv. Syn. Crātēr, pǎtěrǎ. Epith. Pērspĭcŭŭs, fœcūndŭs, gēmmātŭs, aūrātŭs, lūcĭdŭs, aūrěŭs, ārgēntěŭs, crȳstāllīnŭs. V. Poculum.

Cāllǎĭcŭs, ǎ, ŭm, *of Callæcia, a province of Spain.* Tūm sĭbĭ Cāllǎĭcō, Ov.

cāllěo, ŭī, *tc know perfectly.* Dĭgĭīs cāllēmŭs ět aūrě, Hor. Syn. Scĭo.

cāllĭdĭtās, ātĭs, f., *skill, subtilty.* Cāllĭdĭtātě pūto, Ov. Syn. Astūtĭǎ, fraūs, vērsūtĭǎ. Epith. Prŏtērvǎ, vērsūtǎ, āstūtǎ, fāllāx, caūtǎ. V. Astutia, dolus.

cāllĭdŭs, ǎ, ŭm, *skilful, cunning.* Cāllĭdŭs ūsū, Ov. Syn. Caūtŭs, āstūtŭs, sūbdŏlŭs, vērsūtŭs. V. Fallax.

Cāllĭmǎchŭs, ī, m., *a Greek poet.* Et cŭm Cāllĭmǎchō, Ov. Syn. Bātĭĭǎdēs. Epith. Clārŭs, dŏctŭs, pěrītŭs, sōlērs, cūltŭs, fǎcūndŭs.

Cāllĭŏpē, ēs, *and* ǽǎ, æ, f., *one of the Muses.* Quěm měǎ Cāllĭŏpē, Ov. Cāllĭŏpæǎ chŏrīs, Prop. V. Musæ.

Cāllĭrhŏē, ēs, f., *several young princesses were called by that name ; the Calydonian nymph, loved by Coresus ; and the daughters of Achelous, Scamander, and Lycus.* Ā Jŏvě Cāllĭrhŏē, Ov.—2 *a spring near Athens.* Et quŏs Cāllĭrhŏē, Stat.

cāllīs, ĭs, m. f., *a beaten track.* Sěcrētī cēlāut cāllēs, Virg. Syn. Sēmĭtǎ, trāměs.

Epith. Āngūstŭs, ŏccūltŭs, hērbōsŭs, ārctŭs, āmbĭgŭŭs. V. Via, iter.

cāllōsŭs, ǎ, ŭm, *callous, hard.* Hūmĭdǎ cāllōsǎ cŭm, Ov.

cāllŭs, ī, m., *hardness, brawn.* Aūt cāllo, aūt cōrtĭcě, Lucr. Syn. Cāllŭm. Epith. Rĭgĭdŭs, dūrŭs, āspěr, větŭs, āntīquŭs.

cǎlō, ōnĭs, m., *a soldier's drudge.* Cālōnēs ātquě cǎbāllī, Hor.

cǎlōr, ōrĭs, m., *warmth.* Věnĭět trītūrǎ cǎlōrě, Virg. Syn. Ārdŏr, æstŭs, fērvŏr.

Epith. Æstīvŭs, fērvĭdŭs, fērvēns, vǎlĭdŭs, ārĭdŭs, flāmmāns, ĭnērs, ignāvŭs, sēgnĭs, pĭgěr, lēthĭfěr, Phœběŭs, sōlārĭs, Vūlcānĭŭs, īgněŭs, flāmměŭs, ānhēlŭs, nĭmĭŭs, ūrēns, sĭtĭbūndŭs, īnsŏlĭtŭs, īngēns, nătīvŭs, vītālĭs. V. Ardor, æstus, fervor.

Cālpē, ēs, *and* ēs, ĭs, f., *a mountain in Spain.* Ĭbērĭcǎ Cālpē, Avien. Cālpě rělīctǎ, Juv. Epith. Hērcŭlěǎ, Tārtēssĭǎ, Ĭbērǎ, Hēspěrĭǎ; ŏccĭdŭǎ, ēxcēlsǎ, ārdŭǎ. V. Abyla.

Cālpětŭs, ī, m., *an ancient king of Latium.* Cālpětě, fǎctŭs ǎvŭs, Ov.

cālthǎ, æ, f., *the marigold.* Vāccīnĭǎ cālthǎ, Virg. Epith. Lūtěǎ, flāmměŏlǎ, ūstǎ, rūbēns, flōrēns, pūlchrǎ, věnūstǎ, ŏdōrǎ.

cālvĭtĭēs, ēī, f., *or* .vĭtĭŭm, ĭī, n., *baldness.* Cālvĭtĭēmquě sŭīs, Sant. Jām cŭtě cālvĭtĭŭm, Aus.

cǎlūmnĭǎ. æ, f., *calumny.* Spīnōsǎ cǎlūmnĭǎ, Prud. Syn. Injūrĭǎ, cōnvĭcĭŭm. Epith. Ĭnīquǎ, nōxĭǎ, tūrpĭs, fœdǎ, něfārĭǎ. V. Convicium.

cǎlūmnĭātŏr, ōrĭs, m., *a slanderer.* Et cǎlūmnĭātŏr, (Phal.) Mart.

cǎlūmnĭŏr, ārĭs, *to accuse falsely.* Cǎlūmnĭārī sī quĭs, Phædr. Syn. Cōnvĭcĭŏr, dētrǎho. V. Convicior.

cālvǎ. æ, f., *the scalp.* Vērtĭcēmquě cālvæ, Mart.

Cālvīnŭs, ī, m., *the name of a man.* Cālvīně, rěcēntī, Juv.

cālvŭs, ǎ, ŭm, *bald, without hair.* Et grěgě cālvō, Juv.

cālx, cālcĭs, m. f., *the heel.* Cālcēmquě těrīt jām cālcě Dĭōrēs, Virg. Epith. Dūrŭs, văgŭs, ǎgĭlĭs; ūrēns, cāndĭdǎ, fērvēns, těnāx; dūrǎ, fērrātǎ.

cālx, cālcĭs, f., *mortar.* Sōlǎ cŏǎlēscěrě cālcě, Lucr. Epith. Crāssǎ, pīnguĭs, ārdēns.

Cǎlȳbē, ēs, f., *the name of a woman.* Fīt Cǎlȳbē, Virg.

Cǎlȳdnǎ, æ, *or* ē, ēs, f., *an island of the Ægean sea.* Mēllě Cǎlȳdnē, Ov.

Cǎlȳdōn, ōnĭs, *or* ōnǎ, æ, f., *a town of Ætolia.* Quāntŭs ěrāt Cǎlȳdōn, aūt, Mart. Epith. Mělěǎgraěǎ, mōnstrīfěrǎ, Ætōlǎ, īmpĭǎ, pūlchrǎ.

Cǎlȳdōnĭŭs, ǎ, ŭm, *and* Cǎlȳdōnīs, ĭdĭs, f., *of Calydon.* Cǎlȳdōnĭŭs hěrōs, Ov. Cǎlȳdōnĭdēs Ēvēnīnæ, Id.

Cǎlȳpsō, ūs, f., *a nymph who loved Ulysses.* Āmŏrě Cǎlȳpsō, Ov. Epith. Æquŏrěǎ, fāmōsǎ, Atlāntĭs, Atlāntĭǎs.

cǎlȳx, ȳcĭs, m., *a cup of a flower.* Prǽdǎ, nŭcūm cǎlȳcēs, M.

Cāmbȳsēs, æ, m., *son of Cyrus.* Cāmbȳsēs lōngē, Luc.

cǎmēllǎ, æ, f., *a drinking-cup.* Crātērě cǎmēllǎ, Ov.

cǎmēlŭs, ī, m., *a camel.* Tēxtǎ cǎmēlōrŭm, Juv. Epith. Hīrtŭs, dēfōrmĭs, īngēns, vēlōx, cĭtŭs, cělěr, vŏlūcěr, ŏněrārĭŭs, hīrsūtŭs.

cǎměrǎ. æ, f., *a vault.* Nēc cǎměrǎ aūrātǎs, Prop. Syn. Tēstūdo, ārcŭs, fōrnīx.

Epith. Pēndēns, rěpāndǎ, ěbūrnǎ, cūrvǎ, pīctǎ, mārmŏrěǎ, aūrātǎ, splēndĭdǎ, mĭcāns, præclāră, cōnvěxă, pŭlchră, fŭlgĭdă, mĭrābĭlĭs, mŭltĭcŏlŏr, rŭtĭlă, cŏrūscă, cūrvātă, sĭnŭātă.

Cămĕrīnŭs, ī, m., *a Latin poet.* Cămĕrīnŭs ăb Hēctŏrĕ Trōjăm, Ov.

Căměrs, tĭs, m., *the name of a warrior.* Assĭmĭlātă Căměrtī, Virg.

Cămīllă, æ, f., *a famous Amazon, killed by Aruns.* Ală Cămīllæ, Virg. EPITH.

Fōrtĭs, Prĭvērnĭă, Vōlscă, bēllātrīx, Ămāzōn.

Cămīllŭs, ī, m, *a great Roman general.* Rĕfĕrēntēm sĭgnă Cămīllŭm, Virg.
EPITH. Fōrtĭs, fěrŭs, măgnŭs, fātālĭs, tōrquātŭs, īnvīctŭs.

cămīnŭs, ī, m., *a stove.* Expīrārĕ cămīnīs, Virg. SYN. Fōrnāx. EPITH. Avĭdŭs,
flămmĭfěr, rŭtĭlŭs, ĭgnītŭs, ārdēns, ĭgnĭvŏmŭs, ănhēlāns, fūmāns, ātěr. V.
Fornax.

cămmărŭs, ī, m., *a kind of crab-fish.* Cămmărŭs ōvō, Juv.

Cămœnă, æ, f., *a Muse, song, verse.* Sŭmmă dīcēndĕ Cămœnā, Hor.

Cămœnæ, ārŭm, f. pl., *the Muses.* Sīvĕ Cămœnārŭm, Mart. SYN. Mūsæ,
Pĭĕrĭdĕs, Aŏnĭdĕs, Căstălĭdĕs. V. Musæ.

Cămpānĭă, æ, f., *a province in the kingdom of Naples.* Cămpānĭă tērră dărētŭr,
Tibull. EPITH. Dīvĕs, prŏvĭdă, fěrtĭlĭs, fœcŭndă.

Cămpānŭs, ă, ŭm, *of Campania.* Cămpānă sŭpěllēx, Hor.

Cămpēstěr *or* strĭs, m., strĭs, f., strĕ, n., *of a plain, of the plains.* Cămpēstrēs
mēlĭŭs Scўthæ, Hor.—2. *of the Campus Martius.* Cămpēstrĭbŭs ābstĭnĕt ārmĭs,
Hor.

cāmpŭs, ī, m., *a field.* Cămpōrum īn pŭlvěrĕ līnquŭnt, Virg. SYN. Arvŭm,
ăgěr, tēllŭs, rūră, jūgěră, plānĭtĭĕs, cāmpōrŭm æquŏr. EPITH. Fērtĭlĭs, pīnguĭs, vĭrĭdĭs, pătěns, grāmĭněŭs, jăcēns, ăpērtŭs, frōndēns, plānŭs, lātŭs, hērbĭdŭs, lætŭs, spēctābĭlĭs, vĭrēns, stěrĭlĭs, hūmĭdŭs, pălūstěr, pătŭlŭs, ărēnōsŭs,
ūdŭs, flōrēns, ămœnŭs, pŭlvěrěŭs, ăquōsŭs, ārĭdŭs, flōrĭgěr, frūgĭfěr, ŏpīmŭs,
præpīnguĭs, vērnāns, fěrāx. V. Ager.

cămŭrŭs, ă, ŭm, *crooked.* Et cămŭrĭs hīrtæ, Virg.

Cănăcē, ēs, f., *daughter of Æolus.* Nōbĭlĭs ēt Cănăcē, Ov.

Cănāchū, ēs, f., *the name of a dog.* Et Drŏmăs, ēt Cănāchē, Ov.

cănālĭs, ĭs, m. [lĭcŭlă, æ, f., *and* cŭlŭs, ī, m., *dimin.*] *a canal, a waterspout.* Pŏtărĕ cănālĭbŭs, Virg. SYN. Tŭbŭs. EPITH. Plŭmběŭs, lōngŭs, ăngŭstŭs,
flēxŭōsŭs, īrrĭgŭŭs, pătŭlŭs, ōccūltŭs, ărŭndĭněŭs, căvŭs, rĭgŭŭs, cūrvŭs, cūrvātŭs, flēxŭs, īnflēxŭs.

cāncēllī, ōrŭm, m. pl., *lattices.* Cāncēllĭs prīmōs, Ov. EPITH. Těnŭĕs, rārī,
cōnspĭcŭī, pătēntēs.

Căncěr, crī, m., *a sign of the Zodiac.* Sīděrĕ Cāncrī, Virg. EPITH. Tōrrēns,
călĭdŭs, ārdēns, plŭvĭālĭs, ĭgnītŭs, flăgrāns, ădūstŭs, ārĭdŭs, vĭŏlēntŭs, ĭněrs,
sĭtĭēns, sĭtĭbūndŭs, sīccŭs, ūrēns.—2. *a crab-fish.* Urĕ fŏcō cāncrōs, Virg.
EPITH. Līttŏrěŭs, tēstūdĭněŭs, tārdigrădŭs, rŭbĭcŭndŭs, rŭhēns, pĭgěr, tārdŭs,
ĭgnāvŭs, squămměŭs, āmnĭcŏlă.—3. *a canker.* Immědĭcābĭlĕ cāncěr, Ov. EPITH.
Immědĭcābĭlĭs, īnflămmātŭs, mōrdāx, mŏlēstŭs, ăcērbŭs, lānguēns, mōrtĭfěr,
lēthālĭs, crūdēlĭs, īněxplētŭs, rōdēns, vōrāx.

cāndēlă, æ, f., *a candle.* Cāndēlæ, cūjŭs, Juv. SYN. Cěrěŭs, tædă, fāx. EPITH.
Clără, trěmŭlă, rŭtĭlāns, ārdēns, lūcēns, cěrěă, pīnguĭs, mĭcāns, rădĭāns, pērspĭcŭă, flămmĭvŏmă. V. Fax.

cāndēlābrŭm, ī, n., *a candlestick.* Dē cāndēlābrō, Mart.

cāndēo, ŭī, *to be white.* Cāndērēt vēstĭs ěbŭrnŏs, Hor. SYN. Albĕo, ālbēsco,
cāndīco, cānēsco, cānĕo, cāndēsco; ĭgnēsco.

cāndēsco, ĭs, *the frequent. of* candeo. Cāndēscěrĕ sēntĭt, Ov. SYN. Incāndēsco;
ālbēsco.

cāndĭdātŭs, ă, ŭm, *dressed in white; a candidate.* Cāndĭdātĭs præsĭdĕt, (Troch.)
Prud. SYN. Albātŭs, cāndĭdŭs, ālbŭs; āspīrāns, ălŭmnŭs.

cāndĭdŭlŭs, *dimin. of* candidus. Cāndĭdŭlī dīvīnă tŏmăcŭlă, Juv.

cāndĭdŭs, ă, ŭm, *white.* Cāndĭdă bārbă vĭrō, Mart. SYN. Albŭs, nĭvěŭs,
ěbŭrnŭs, ěbŭrněŭs, lāctěŭs, cānŭs, cānēscēns, cāndēscēns, ālbēscēns, ālbēdĭnĕ
tīnctŭs, cāndōrĕ děcōrŭs; sīncěrŭs, īngěnŭŭs; īntěgěr, īnnŏcēns, īnnōxĭŭs,
īnnŏcŭŭs. V. Alhus.

cāndŏr, ōrĭs, m., *shining whiteness.* Quī cāndōrĕ nĭvēs, Virg. SYN. Albēdo.
EPITH. Nĭvālĭs, nĭvěŭs, ālbŭs, pūrŭs, cōnspĭcŭŭs, ārgēntěŭs, lāctěŭs, vĭrgĭněŭs,
mĭrābĭlĭs, ěbŭrněŭs, īntěměrātŭs, pŭēllārĭs, āngělĭcŭs, īnnŏcŭŭs. V. Albedo.

74 CAN

cānĕo, ŭī, *to be white.* Grăvĭdīs cānēbăt ārīstīs, Ov. Syn. Cānēsco, ālbēsco, cāndĭco, ālbĭco. V. Senesco.

cānī, ōrŭm, m. pl., *white locks.* Vērtĭcĕ cānī, Boët.

Cānĭcŭlă, æ, f., *a sign in the heavens.* Sānă Cānĭcŭlă mēssēs, Pers. Syn. Cānĭs, Sīrĭŭs. Epith. Æstĭfĕră, sĭtĭēns, flăgrāns, Icărĭă, æstīvă, ārdēns, sēgnĭs, ĭnērs, pēstĭfĕră, pigră, fŭrēns, ĭgnĭvŏmă, fērvĭdă, sĭtĭbŭndă, ĭgnĕă, ācrĭs, ĭgnītă, ēxĭtĭōsă, lēthālĭs, pērnĭcĭōsă, cālēns, ŭstă, ădŭstă, tōrrĭdă, mōrbōsă, dāmnōsă.

Cānĭdĭă, æ, f., *the name of a sorceress.* Cānĭdĭăm pēdĭbŭs, Hor.

cānīnŭs, ă, ŭm, *of a dog.* Indĕ cănīnă fŏrō, Prud.

cănĭs, ĭs, m., *a dog.* [Domesticus.] Hīnc cănĭbŭs blāndĭs, Virg. Syn. Lўcīscă, Mŏlōssŭs. Epith. Vĭgĭl, ācĕr, lĕvĭsōmnŭs, vōcĭfĕr, cŏmĕs, sōllĭcĭtŭs, fīdŭs, fīdēlĭs, pērnōx, vōcālĭs, pērvĭgĭl, săgāx, cūstōs, impăvĭdŭs, tērrĭbĭlĭs, sēdŭlŭs, āttēntŭs, cĕlĕr, fĕrŭs, īnfēstŭs, cĭtŭs, ăvĭdŭs, aŭdāx, hōrrĭsŏnŭs, aūrītŭs, ŏdōrĭsĕquŭs, prŏpĕrŭs, tērrĭfĭcŭs, mōrdāx, răpĭdŭs, lātrātŏr.—2. [Venaticus.] *a hound.* Epith. Ācĕr, săgāx, īnfēstŭs, prŏpĕrŭs, răpĭdŭs, cĭtŭs, pērnīx, vēlōx, ānhēlāns, āstūtŭs, ăvĭdŭs, răpāx, aūdāx, intrĕpĭdŭs, vōcĭfĕr, mōrdāx, īrrēquĭ-ētŭs, sēdŭlŭs, ŏdōrĭsĕquŭs, hōrrēndŭs, ārmīllātŭs, hīrsūtŭs, raŭcŭs, trūx, fĕrŭs, lĕvĭs, fōrtĭs. V. Venor, Molossus.—3. [Astrum.] *the dog-star.* Fīndĭt Cānĭs æstĭfĕr ārvă, Virg. Epith. Sĭtĭēns, flăgrāns. V. Canicula.

cānĭstrŭm, ī, n., *a basket.* Plēnĭs āppŏnĕ cănĭstrĭs, Virg. Syn. Călăthŭs, cīstă, cīstŭlă. Epith. Pătŭlŭm, grăvĭdŭm, vīmĭnĕŭm. V. Calathus.

cānĭtĭēs, ĭēī, f., *hoariness.* Cānĭtĭēs incŭltă, Virg. Syn. Cānī. Epith. Mōrōsă, sōrdĭdă, sānctă, ālbă, prōlīxă, prīscă, tŭrpĭs, nĭvĕă, cāndēns, incŭltă, vĕnĕrāndă, squālēns, ārĭdă, rără, frīgĭdă, prūdēns, hŏnōrātă, sĕnīlĭs, ānnōsă, săpĭēns, lōn-gævă, īmpēxă, ēffŭsă, squālĭdă. V. Senectus.

cānnă, æ, f., *a cane.* Sŭb ărūndĭnĕ cānnæ, Ov. Syn. Călămŭs, ărŭndo, fīstŭlă. Epith. Pălūstrĭs, vĭrĭdĭs, crāssă, ārgŭtă, lĕvĭs, pălūdĭgĕnă, strīdŭlă, trĕmŭlă.

cānnăbĭs, ĭs, f., *and* ŭm, ī, n., *hemp.* Cānnăbĕ fŭltō, Pers.

Cānnæ, ārŭm, f. pl., *a village of Apulia, where Hannibal defeated the Romans.* Epith. Cĕlĕbrēs, grăvēs, crŭēntātæ, fērālēs, īnsĭgnēs.

căno, cĕcĭnī, cāntŭm, *to sing.* Lætŭs cĕcĭnī, cănŏ trīstĭă, Ov. Syn. Cōncĭno, cānto, mŏdŭlŏr.

canōn, ŏnĭs, m., *rule, precept.* Grāmmătĭcōs cănōnăs, Aus. Syn. Rēgŭlă, nōrmă, lēx. Epith. Rēctŭs.

canōnĭcŭs, ă, ŭm, *regular.* Cānŏnĭcās mŏdŭlĭs, M.

Cănōpēŭs, *and* ĭcŭs, ă, ŭm, *of Canope.* Grătă Cănōpēĭs, Catul. Rēgnă Cănōpĭcă cŭm fŭgĕrĕt, Prud.

Cănōpŭs, ī, m., *a town of Egypt.* Fōrtūnātă Cănōpī, Virg. Epith. Pēllæŭs, Pēlūsĭăcŭs, Phărĭŭs, Isĭăcŭs, Spārtănŭs, Amўclæŭs, Thĕrāpnæŭs; fāmōsŭs, incēstŭs. V. Ægyptus.

cănŏr, ōrĭs, m., *melody.* Strŭctă cănōrĕ lўræ, Ov. Syn. Sŏnŏr, sŏnŭs, cāntŭs.

cănōrŭs, ă, ŭm, *loud, harmonious.* Vīrgŭltă cănōrĭs, Virg. Syn. Sŏnōrŭs, sŏnāns, strĕpēns, strīdēns, strīdŭlŭs.

Cāntăbĕr, brī, m., Cāntăbrī, ōrŭm, m. pl., *a nation of Spain.* Cāntăbĕr Agrīppæ, Hor. Cāntăbrum indōctŭm, Id.

Cāntăbrĭcŭs, ă, ŭm, *of Cantabria.* Ět Cāntăbrĭcă bēllă, Hor.

cāntūmĕn, ĭnĭs, n., *an enchantment.* Cāntāmĭnă Mūsæ, Prop. Syn. Cāntŭs, īncāntāmēntŭm.

cāntātŏr, ōrĭs, m., *a singer.* Cāntātōr cўcnŭs, Mart.

cāntātrīx, īcĭs, f., *a songstress.* Cāntātrīcēsquĕ chŏrēās, Claud.

cānthărĭs, ĭdĭs, f., *the Spanish fly.* Cānthărĭdum sūccōs, Ov.

cānthărŭs, ī, m., *a kind of cup.* Cānthărŭs ānsă, Virg. Syn. Pōcŭlŭm. Epith. Līgnĕŭs, spūmāns, tūrgĭdŭs, dŭlcĭfĕr, grăvĭs.

cānthŭs, ī, m., *the felly of a wheel.* Sēctăbĕrĕ cānthŭm, Pers.

cāntĭcŭm, ī, n., *a ballad.* Cāntĭcă quī nīlī, Mart. Syn. Cārmĕn, cāntŭs, mĕlōs.

cāntĭlēnă, æ, f., *a song.* Tĭbĭ cāntĭlēnă, (Sapph.) Aus.

cāntĭto, ās, *the frequent. of* canto. Hăbēās quīcŭm cāntĭtēs, (Iamb.) Ter. V. Cano.

cānto, ās, *to sing.* Cāntō quæ sōlĭtŭs, Virg. V. Cano.

cāntŏr, ōrĭs, m., *a songster, poet.* Cāntōrĭs mōrtĕ Tĭgēllī, Hor.

cāntŭs, ūs, m., *singing.* Cāntĭbŭs hērbās, Gr. Syn. Cōncēntŭs, cārmĕn, cāntĭo, mŏdŭlāmĕn, Mūsă, Cămœnă, mŏdī, mŏdŭlī, mĕlōs. Epith. Ōrphæŭs, Ăpōllīnĕŭs, Cāstălĭŭs, trĕmŭlŭs, ārgūtŭs, rĕsŏnŭs, lœtŭs, dŭlcĭs, ămbrŏsĭŭs, mĕllĭflŭŭs, sŏnŏrŭs, fēstīvŭs, dŭlcĭsŏnŭs, dōctŭs, ămœnŭs, raucŭs, mātūtīnŭs, blāndĭsŏnŭs, sŏnāns, ăcūtŭs, blāndŭs, grātŭs, bĭllărĭs, plăcĭdŭs, trīstĭs, mœstŭs, gĕmĕbūndŭs, flēbĭlĭs, rūstĭcŭs. V. Cano.

cănŭs, ă, ŭm, *white.* Cānă cōncrētă prŭīnă, Virg. Syn. Cāndĭdŭs, cānēscēns, cāndĕus, ālbŭs.

Cănŭsīnŭs, ă, ŭm, *of Canusium.* Cănŭsī mŏrĕ bĭlīnguĭs, Hor.

Cănŭsĭŭm, īi or ī, n., *a city of Apulia.* Ŏppĭdĭŭs Cănŭsī, Hor.

Căpăneŭs, ĕŏs, ĕĭ or eī, (*trisyl.*) m., *one of the seven Theban chiefs, who braved Jupiter's power, and was struck with thunder by him.* Cŭm cĕcĭdĭt Căpăneŭs sŭbĭtŏ, Ov. Epith. Ārgŏlĭcŭs, māgnănĭmŭs, īmpĭŭs.

căpāx, ācĭs, *capacious, apt.* Pŭtēĭsquĕ căpācĭbŭs, Ov. Syn. Amplŭs, spătĭŏsŭs, lātŭs, lātē pătēns; āptŭs, ĭdŏnĕŭs.

căpĕllă, æ, f., *a kid.* Ītĕ căpĕllœ, Virg. Syn. Capră, caprĕă. Epith. Grăcĭlĭs, hīrsūtă, hīrtă. V. Capra.

Căpēnă, æ, f., *one of the gates of Rome.* Mădĭdāmquĕ Căpēnăm, Juv.—2. *an ancient city of Etruria.*

Căpēnŭs, ă, ŭm, *of Capena.* Lūcōsquĕ Căpĕnōs, Virg.

căpĕr, caprī, m., *a goat.* Căpĕr ŏmnĭbŭs ārĭs, Virg. Syn. Hœdŭs, hīrcŭs, caprĕŏlŭs. Epith. Bārbĭgĕr, bārbātŭs, bĭcōrnĭs, hīrtŭs, sōrdĭdŭs, grăvĭs, fœtĭdŭs, cōrnĭgĕr, sētĭgĕr, hīrsūtŭs, ŏlēns, lāscīvŭs, pĕtŭlāns, cāmpēstrĭs, tĭmĭdŭs, văgăbūndŭs, īmmūndŭs, hīspĭdŭs, sȳlvēstrĭs, īntōnsŭs, pĕtŭlcŭs, tōrvŭs, sālĭēns, ācĕr, fœdŭs. V. Hœdus, bircus.

căpēsso, ĭs, *to undertake, to hold.* Jūssă căpēssĕrĕ fās ēst, Virg. Syn. Căpĭo, ăccĭpĭo, tĕnĕo, ōbtĭnĕo.

Căpĕĭŭs, ī, m., *a king of Alba.* Căpĕtūsquĕ Căpȳsquĕ, Ov.

Căphărēĭŭs, or reŭs, ă, ŭm, *of Caphareus.* Graĭă Căphārēă, Ov. Căphārĕă pūppēs, Prop.

Căphăreŭs, ĕŏs, ĕĭ or eĭ, (*trisyl.*) m., *a promontory in Eubœa.* Ūltŏrquĕ Căphăreŭs, Virg. Epith. Impŏrtūnŭs, dūrŭs, Eŭbŏĭcŭs, āltŭs, prŏcēllōsŭs, fāllāx, dīrŭs, scŏpŭlōsŭs, trīstĭs.

căpīllărĕ, ĭs, n., *oil for the hair.* Paŭpĕrĭs căpīllărĕ, (Scaz.) Mart.

căpīllātŭs, ă, ŭm, *wearing long hair.* Vīllīcŏ căpīllātŏ, (Scaz.) Mart.

căpīllŭs, ī, m., căpīllī, ōrŭm, m. pl., *hair.* Nĭgrōquĕ căpīllŏ, Hor. Sīnĕ lēgĕ căpīllī, Ov. Syn. Crīnēs, cæsărĭēs, cŏmă. Epith. Rŏsĕī, fōrmōsī, cōmptī, nĭtĭdī, nĭgrī, mōllēs, rōrāntēs, crŏcĕī, tĕnŭēs, pūrpŭrĕī, ădōrnātī, mădĭdī, dŭlcēs, tĕnĕrī, pēxī, ūdī, ōrnātī, ēffūsī, nĭvĕī, ămbrŏsĭī, aūrātī, īntōnsī, rĕdŏlēntēs, flāvĭcŏmī, pŭēllārēs, lōngī, spārsī, cōnspĭcŭī, ūndāntēs, flŭĭdī, crīspāntēs, crīspī, vĕnūstī, văgī, văgāntēs, tōrtī, ērrāntēs, sŏlūtī, pēndŭlī, vŏlĭtāntēs, dīffūsī, tĕnŭēs, cūltī, flŭēntēs, squālĭdī, squālēntēs, sōrdĭdī, tūrpēs, īmpēxī, hōrrĭdī, rĭgĭdī, īntōrtī, cōntōrtī. V. Cæsaries, coma, crines.

căpĭo, cēpī, căptŭm, *to take.* Trŏjă căpĭt, Virg. Syn. Accĭpĭo, sūmo, āssūmo, prĕhēndo, prēndo.

căpīstrātŭs, ă, ŭm, *haltered, muzzled.* Inquĕ căpīstrātīs tĭgrĭbŭs, Ov.

căpīstrŭm, ī, n., *a halter.* Ŏră căpīstrīs, Virg. Syn. Frænŭm, hăbēnă. Epith. Nŏdōsŭm, dūrŭm, fērrātŭm, mōllĕ, pūrpŭrĕŭm, strīctŭm, īmpŏrtūnŭm.

căpĭtālĭs, ĕ, *deadly, dangerous.* Īră fŭīt căpĭtālĭs, Hor. Syn. Sŭmmŭs.

Căpĭto, ōnĭs, m., *the name of a man.* Căpĭtōnĕ cŭlīnăm, Hor.—2. *a fish.* Căpĭto īntĕrlūcĕt ărēnŭs, Aus.

Căpĭtōlīnŭs, ă, ŭm, *of the Capitol.* Căpĭtōlīnŭmquĕ Tŏnāntĕm, Ov.

Căpĭtōlĭŭm, īi, n., *the famous Roman citadel.* Căpĭtōlĭă cēlsă, Virg. Epith. Āltŭm, aūrĕŭm, cēlsŭm, Jūlĭŭm, aūrātŭm, Rōmānŭm, sŭblīmĕ, ēxcēlsŭm, sŭpērbŭm, māgnĭfĭcŭm, āntīquŭm, mīrābĭlĕ, ēlātŭm, mārmŏrĕŭm.

căpo, ōnĭs, *and* ŭs, ī, m., *a capon.* Āmārĕ căpōnĕ, Mart. Căpŭs ĕrĭs, Id.

Cāppădŏcŭs, ă, ŭm, *and* Cāppădŏx, ŏcĭs, *of Cappadocia, a province in Asia Minor.* Hæc sŭă Cāppădŏcæ, Col. Cāppădŏcŭm rēx, Hor.

căppărĭs, ĭs, f., *a caper-bush, caper.* Cāppărĭn ēt pūtrī, Mart.

căpră, æ, f., *a she-goat.* Incōgnĭtă căprīs, Virg. Syn. Caprĕă, căpēllă. Epith. Vīllōsă, bārbĭgĕră, sȳlvēstrĭs, sĕquāx, īntōnsă, tĭmĭdă, cŭpĭdă, dūmĭvăgă, păvĭdă, pĕtŭlcă, văgă, fŭgĭtīvă, bārbātă, fŭgāx, hīspĭdă, lūctĭfĭcă, quĕrŭlă. V. Capella, caper.

caprĕă, æ, f., *a roe.* Imbēllēs căprĕæ, Ov. V. Capra.

Căprĕæ, ārŭm, f. pl., *an island of the Tusᵣan sea.* Indĕ lēgīt Căprĕās, Ov.

caprĕŏlŭs, ī, m., *a cheveril.* Căprĕŏlī, spärsĭs, Virg.

Cŭprĭcōrnŭs, ī, m., *one of the zodiacal signs.* Căprĭcōrnŭs ĭn ōrbĕ, Virg. Syn.

Æʒŏcĕrōs. Epith. Rĭgēns, gĕlĭdŭs, frĭgĭdŭs, ătrōx, cōrnĭgĕr, ĭmbrĭfĕr, brū-mālĭs, hȳĕmālĭs, hōrrēndŭs, ūdŭs, nĭmbōsŭs.

caprĭfīcŭs, ī, f., *a wild fig-tree.* Jăm căprĭfīcŭs ĕrĭs, Mart. V. Ficus.

caprĭgĕnŭs, ă, ŭm, *of goat's breed.* Căprĭgĕnŭmquĕ pĕcŭs, Virg.

caprĭmŭlgŭs, ī, m., *a milker of goats.* Căprĭmŭlgŭs aŭt fōssōr, (Scaz.) Cat.

caprīnŭs, ă, ŭm, *of a goat.* Sæpĕ căprīnā, Hor.

caprĭpēs, ĕdĭs, m., *goat-footed.* Căprĭpĕdēs ăgĭtăt, Aus.

Caprĭŭs, ĭī, m., *the name of a man.* Ambŭlăt ĕt Căprĭŭs, Hor.

căpsă, *and* ŭlă, æ. f., *a coffer.* Vērnŭlā căpsæ, Juv. Syn. Căpsŭlă, cĭstă, ārcă. Epith. Căvă, cōncăvă, ămplă, pătŭlă, ærătă, fērrătă, aŭrĕă, ārgēntĕă.

căptātŏr, ōrĭs, m., *he who endeavours to procure.* Ŭt căptātōrĭ, Hor.

|| căptĭvĭtăs, ātĭs, f., *captivity.* Căptĭvĭtăs ĕt cæcĭtăs, (Iamb.) Syn. Sērvĭtŭs.

|| căptīvo, ās, *to take captive.* Căptīvăt ărānĕă mūscās, Tex.

căptīvŭs, ă, ŭm, *captive.* Căptīvŭm pōrtātŭr ĕbŭr, Hor. Syn. Sŭb jŭgă mĭssŭs. Căptŭs ăb hōstĕ. V. Vincula, carcer.

căpto, ās, *to go about to take.* Lăquĕĭs căptārĕ fĕrās, Virg. V. Capio.

căptūră, æ, f., *a catching.* Implēvĭt căptūrā sĭnŭs, Sed. Syn. Prædă.

căptŭs, ūs, m., *understanding.* Prō căptū lēctōrĭs, Ter. Maur.

Căpŭă, æ, f., *a city of the kingdom of Naples.* Dīvēs ărăt Căpŭa, ĕt, Virg. Epith. Sŭblīmĭs, ŏpĭmă, ămplă, dĕcōră, nōbĭlĭs. V. Capys.

căpŭlārĭs, ĕ, *very old.* Dŭm căpŭlārĭs ĕro, Text. Syn. Dĕcrĕpĭtŭs, sĕnēx.

căpŭlŭs, ī, m., *and* ŭm, ī, n., *a handle.* Lătĕrī căpŭlŏ tĕnŭs ăbdĭdĭt, Virg. Epith. Aŭrĕŭs, ĕbŭrnŭs, aŭrātŭs, mĭcāns, splēndēns, splēndĭdŭs, ārgēntĕŭs, ĭnsĭgnĭs, pŭlchĕr, rŭtĭlāns, cōrŭscŭs, gĕmmātŭs.

căpŭt, ĭtĭs, n., *the head.* Thēsaūrŭs căpŭt ēst, prō căpĭtĕ æră pĕtĭt, Nov. Syn. Tēmpŏră, vērtēx, cērvīx, cōllŭm. Epith. Rŭtĭlŭm, cēlsŭm, nĭtĭdŭm, ăm-brŏsĭŭm, rŏsĕŭm, ĭntōnsŭm, cānŭm, grāndĕ, jŭv. ĭlĕ; ĭllūstrĕ, fĭdēlĕ, ĭgnāvŭm, sōllĭcĭtŭm; ĭnsŭpĕrābĭlĕ, hūmānŭm, ăcūtŭm, vĕnĕrābĭlĕ, ērēctŭm, sŭbmĭssŭm, cŏrōnātŭm.

Căpȳs, ȳŏs, m., *a king of the Latins.* Ĕt Căpȳs, hīnc, Virg.

cārbăsĕŭs, *and* ĭnŭs, ă, ŭm, *of fine flax.* Pōst hæc cārbăsĕĭs, Tib. Cārbăsīnum āc spătĭĭs, Fill.

cārbăsŭs, ī, m. f., -băsă, ōrŭm, n. pl., *sails.* Cārbăsă dēdŭcĭt, Ov. Syn. Vēlă, līntĕă. Epith. Flūxă, văgă, spūmāntĭă, căvă, ālbă, ĭnflātă, tēnsă, cūrvă, lātă, tūrgĭdă, sĭnŭōsă, flēxă, ăpērtă, tŭmēntĭă, prōspĕră, sĕcūndă, cĭtă, sŭbĭtă, rĕ-cūrvă, fŭgācĭă, pătēntĭă, plēnă, cōntrāctă. V. Velum navis. V. Vestis.

cārbo, ōnĭs, m., *a coal.* Cārbōnĕ nŏtāstĭ, Pers.

cārbōnārĭŭs, ĭī, m., *a collier.* Tānquăm cārbōnărĭŭm, Plaut.

cārbūncŭlŭs, ī, m., *a carbuncle.* Cārbūncŭlŭs ĭgnĕ, Man. Syn. Pȳrōpŭs. Epith. Ignĭvŏmŭs, flāmmĭvŏmŭs, præfŭlgēns, rădĭāns, splēndĭdŭs, nĭtĭdŭs, mĭcāns, lūcĭdŭs, ārdēns, scĭntĭllāns, rŭtĭlāns, rŭbĕŭs, rŭbēns, rŭbĭcūndŭs, lūcēns, splēndēns, rŭbēscēns. V. Pyropus, gemma.

cārcĕr, ĕrĭs, m., *a prison.* Cārcĕrĕ rēgnăt, Virg. Syn. Cŭstōdĭă, cārcĕrĭs āntrŭm. Epith. Ātĕr, sōllĭcĭtŭs, squālĭdŭs, mœstŭs, pĭcĕns, tĕnĕbrōsŭs, dūrŭs, tētĕr, hōstĭlĭs, ĭnĕrs, ăngūstŭs, sævŭs, fĕrōx, prŏfūndŭs, ĭngrātŭs, ĭnfaŭstŭs, ōbscūrŭs, mœrēns, ŏpācŭs, căvŭs, ĭnvīsŭs, fērrātŭs, squālēns, hōrrēndŭs, nĭgĕr, nĭgrāns, ăbstrūsŭs, trīstĭs, fœtĭdŭs, hōrrĭbĭlĭs, tērrĭfĭcŭs, dīrŭs, crūdēlĭs, mŏlēstŭs, mĕtŭ-ēndŭs, gĕmĕbūndŭs, ĭnămœnŭs, quĕrŭlŭs, căvērnōsŭs.—2. *a barrier.* Cārcĕrĕ prōnŭs, Ov. Syn. Claūstrŭm. V. Captivus.

cārdĭăcŭs, ă, ŭm, *sick at heart.* Cārdĭăcō nūnquăm, Juv.

cārchēsĭŭm, ĭī, n., *a large bowl.* Lībāns cārchēsĭă Bācchō, Virg. V. Poculum.

cārdĭnĕŭs, ă, ŭm, *of a hinge.* Cŭī cārdĭnĕĭ tŭmŭltŭs, Sept.

cārdo, ĭnĭs, m., *the hinge of a gate.* Cārdĭnĕ vēllĭt, Virg. Epith. Fērrātŭs, văgŭs, dūrŭs, ærātŭs, strīdēns, sōlĭdŭs, fērrĕŭs. V. Polus.

cārdŭŭs, ī, m., *a thistle.* Cārdŭŭs ĕt spīnĭs, Virg. Epith. Agrēstĭs, āspĕr, sēgnĭs, ăcūtŭs, mōrdāx, pūngēns, hōrrĭdŭs, ĭnămœnŭs.

cārēctŭm, ī, n., *a place where sedge grows.* Pōst cārēctă lătēbās, Virg.

cărĕo, ŭī, *to want.* Fīnĕ cărērĕ prĕcēs, Ov. Syn. Prīvŏr, ĕgĕo, ĭndĭgĕo, nōn hăbĕo, ŏpŭs hăbĕo, ĕgēns sŭm.

Cărēs, ŭm, m. pl., *the Carians.* Hĭc Lĕlĕgās, Cărăsquĕ, Virg.

cărēx, ĭcĭs, m., *sedge.* Cărĭcĕ pāstŭs, Virg.

cărĭcă, æ, f., *a wild fig.* Cărĭcă pālmĭs, Ov.

cărĭcĕŭs, ă, ŭm, *covered with sedge.* Cărĭcĕæ sŭccĕdĕ căsæ, Mart.

cărĭes, ĭĕī, f., *rottenness.* Ĭn tĕnĕrăm cărĭĕm, Ov. Epith. Sĕnīlĭs, rōdēns, vĕtŭs, ĕdāx. V. Cariosus.

cărīnă, æ, f., *a ship.* Cĕlĕrī vēnīssĕ cărīnā, Ov. Epith. Cŭrvă, păndă, ĭnflēxă, ūnctă, căvă, trĕpĭdă, pīctă, ĭncŭrvă, aŭdāx, vēlĭfĕră, ærătă, bēllātrīx, cĭtă, lĕvĭs, frăgĭlĭs, vēlĭvŏlă. V. Navis.

cărĭōsŭs, ă, ŭm, *rotten.* Cărĭōsă sĕnēctŭs, Ov.

cărĭtăs, ātĭs, f., *love.* Cŏpĭōsă cărĭtătĕ paŭpĕrēs, (Iamb. Trim.) Prud. Syn. Ămŏr, stŭdĭŭm; pĕnūrĭă, ĕgēstăs. Epith. Cœlēstĭs, ĭgnĕă, vīvāx, ănĭmōsă, pătĭēns, sĕrēnă, ĭllūstrĭs, bĕnīgnă, bŏnă, cĕlĕbrātă, clără.

Cărmēlŭs, ī, m., *a mountain of Syria.* Cărmēlŭs săcĕr ēst, Drep. Epith. Ardŭŭs, sacrūtŭs, antīquŭs, pĭŭs, vĕrēndŭs.

cărmĕn, ĭnĭs, n., *verse, a poem.* Cărmĭnĭbŭs vīncĕt, Virg. Syn. Vērsŭs, nŭmĕrī, mŏdī, Mūsă. Epith. Dūlcĕ, nōbĭlĕ, grātŭm, ŏpĕrōsŭm, ămābĭlĕ, Phœbēŭm, Ăpōllĭnĕŭm. Pĭērĭŭm, Cāstălĭŭm, Mæŏnĭŭm, Ăndīnŭm, lēnĕ, vĕnŭstŭm, vōcālĕ, mōllĕ, sūblīmĕ, tĕnĕrŭm, vĭgĭlātŭm, blāndŭm, dōctŭm, jŏcōsŭm, fătĭdĭcŭm, dīvīnŭm, mŏdŭlābĭlĕ, cănōrŭm, ēxcūltŭm, cūltŭm, ămīcŭm, blāndĭsŏnŭm, lætŭm, ætērnŭm, nēctărĕŭm, cŏmpŏsĭtŭm, præclārŭm, gārrŭlŭm, lætĭfĭcŭm, sŏnōrŭm, lĕpĭdŭm, ĭngĕnĭōsŭm, quĕrŭlŭm, mēllĭtŭm, fēstīvŭm, grāndĭsŏnŭm, dēdūctŭm, scēnĭcŭm, grăvĕ, nŭmĕrōsŭm, cōmptŭm, făcūndŭm, dīvĕs, cōncĭnnŭm, cœlēstĕ, ămātŭm, fŭrēns, fŭrĭōsŭm, măcĭlēntŭm, ābjēctŭm, hŭmĭlĕ. V. Veneficium, musa, versus.

Cărmēntă, æ, *or* ēntĭs, ĭs, f., *the mother of Evander.* Cărmēntĭs nўmphæ, Virg. Syn. Nĭcōstrătă. Epith. Ărcădĭă, Pārrhăsĭă, Tĕgĕæă, Mænălĭs; dōctă, fătĭlŏquă, fătĭdĭcă, vērĭdĭcă.

Cărmēntālĭs, *and* tĭs, ĭs, f., *a gate of Rome.* Et Cărmēntālĕm, Virg.

‖ cărmĭno, ās, *to comb wool.* Var. Syn. Pēcto.

Cărnă, æ, f., *the goddess who presided over doors.* Cārnă dătŭr, Ov.

cărnālĭs, ĕ, *of flesh.* Nēc cārnălĕ gĕnŭs, Drac.

cărnărĭŭm, ĭī, n., *butchers' shambles.* Cārnărĭă fŭrtĭm, Lucil.

cărnărĭŭs, ă, ŭm, *who likes flesh.* Cārnărĭŭs sŭm, Mart.

cărnĭfēx, ĭcĭs, m., *an executioner.* Cărnĭfīcēsvĕ mănŭs, Sil. Syn. Tŏrtŏr, līctŏr. Epith. Crŭēntŭs, mĭsĕr, ĭmmītĭs, dīrŭs, sāngŭĭnĕŭs, ĭnhūmānŭs, atrōx, sævŭs, bārbărŭs, trūx, trŭcŭlēntŭs, hōrrēndŭs, fĕrōx, tērrĭfĭcŭs, ātĕr, ĭmpĭŭs, mĕtŭēndŭs, mĭnāx, dūrŭs, ĭnēxōrābĭlĭs, fērrĕŭs, tĕtĕr, sāngŭĭnŏlēntŭs, ĭnfāmĭs, fĕrālĭs, ĭmmānĭs.

‖ cărnĭfīcīnă, æ, f., *a place of execution.* Cărnĭfīcīnă pĕrērrăt, Aus.

cărnĭvŏrŭs, ă, ŭm, *devouring flesh.* Mĭttĕrĕ cărnĭvŏrīs, Mant.

căro, cārnĭs, f., *flesh.* Ægră cărŏ prōdēst, Mant. Epith. Mōrtālĭs, frăgĭlĭs, ĭnfīrmă, rŭbēns, rĕbēllĭs, ĭmmūndă, ægră, sēdĭtĭōsă, vīlĭs, lāngŭĭdă.

Cărpăthĭŭs, ă, ŭm, *of Carpathos, an island of the Ægean sea.* Ēst ĭn Cărpăthĭŏ Nēptūnī gŭrgĭtĕ, Virg.

cārpēntŭm, ī, n., *a chariot.* Cārpēntă vĕhēbānt, Ov. V. Currus.

cărpo, cārpsī, cārptŭm, *to gather.* Cārpēbāt nōctĕ quĭētĕm, Virg. Syn. Căpĭo, dēcērpo, lĕgo, cōllĭgo. V. Colligo.

Cărpŏphŏrŭs, ī, m., *a man's name.* Quāntŭlă Cărpŏphŏrī, Mart.

cārptŏr, ōrĭs, m., *a carver.* Ārchĭmăgīrī, cārptōrēs, Juv.

Cărrīnās, ātĭs, m., *an orator, proscribed by Caligula.* Cārrīnātĭs; ĕt hūnc, Juv.

cărrŭcă, æ, f., *a kind of cart.* Cărrŭcă părătŭr, Mart.

Cărsĕŏlānŭs, ă, ŭm, *of Carseoli.* Cārsĕŏlānă vĕtăt, Ov.

Cārsĕŏlī, ōrŭm, m. pl., *a city of Latium.* Frīgĭdă Cărsĕŏlĭs, Ov.

Cārthæŭs, *or* ēĭŭs, ă, ŭm, *of Carthæa, a town of the island of Cea.* Cārthæă tĕnēntĭbŭs, Ov. Cārthĕĭă mœnĭă Cēæ, Id.

Cārthāgĭnĭēnsēs, ĭŭm, m. pl., *the inhabitants of Carthage.* Ērĭt Cārthāgĭnĭēnsĭs, Enn. Syn. Pœnī, Pūnĭcī, Tўrĭī, Sīdonĭī, Ēlĭsæī. Epith. Āntīquī, sŭpērbī, aŭdācēs, pĕrfĭdī, magnănĭmī, bĕllācēs, pŏtēntēs, fĕrī, ĭmmītēs, fĕrōcēs, crūdēlēs, bārbărī, bĕllĭgĕrī, crŭēntī, Māvŏrtĭī, dīrī, saevī, fŭrĭōsī.

Cārthāgo, ĭnĭs, f., *Carthage*. Nŏvæ Cārthāgĭnĭs ārcĕm, Virg. Syn. Bўrsă.

Epith. Lĭbўcă, Bārbărĭcă, Pūnĭcă, Tўrĭă, Sĭdonĭă, Ăgēnŏrĕă, Ēlĭsæă, fĕră, āltă, magnă, īmpĭă, fĕrōx, pĕrfĭdă, ăcĕrbă, tŭmĭdă, Bўrsĭcă, āntīquă, sŭpĕrbă, splēn-dĭdă, măgnĭfĭcă, bĕllĭgĕră, pŏtēns, dīvĕs.

cārŭs, ă, ŭm, *dear*. Quĭdām, cārīssĭmĕ Jūlī, Mart. Syn. Prĕtĭōsŭs, dīlēctŭs; ămātŭs, jūcūndŭs, grātŭs, ăccēptŭs, suāvĭs.

Cărўă, æ, f., *a name of Diana*. Cărўæ rĕsŏnārĕ Dĭānæ, Stat.

cărўōtă, æ, *and* ŏtĭs, ĭdĭs, f., *a date*. Cărўōtă cŭlēndĭs, Mart.

Cărўstĭŭs, *and* Cărўstŏŭs, ă, ŭm, *of Carystos*. Quăquĕ Cărўstŏĭs, Ov.

Cărўstŏs, *and* tŭs, ī, m., *a city of Eubœa*. Sīvĕ, Cărўstĕ, tŭĭs, Tib.

căsă, æ, f., *a cottage*. Hŭmĭlēs hăbĭtārĕ căsās, Virg. Syn. Măgălĭă, măpālĭă, tŭgŭrĭŭm. Epith. Pārvă, frŏndĕă, ēxĭgŭă, strāmĭnĕă, ĭmmūndă, āngūstă, sŏr-dĭdă, ăgrēstĭs, cāmpēstrĭs, vĭrĭdĭs, lŭtĕă, vīlĭs, rŭdĭs, frīgĭdă, rūrālĭs, grāmĭnĕă, tūrpĭs, paūpĕr, mūltĭfŏrĭs, sēcūră, lăcĕră, tūtă, mŏdĭcă, ĭndĭgă, pācĭfĭcă.

Cāscēllĭŭs, ĭī, m., *the name of a man*. Cāscēllĭŭs Aŭlŭs, Hor.

căsĕŏlŭs, ī, m., *a small cheese*. Cāsĕŏlōsquĕ dĭĕ, V.

căsĕŭm, ī, n., *and* ŭs, ī, m., *a cheese*. Cāsĕŭs ūrbī, Virg. Epith. Pīnguĭs, ŏvīlĭs, mōllĭs, dūlcĭs, cāndĭdŭs, vēnālĭs, prēssŭs, mōllĭcŭlŭs.

căsĭă, æ, f., *a flower that bees delight in*. Tūm căsĭa, ātque āllĭs, Virg. Epith. Mītĭs, hŭmĭlĭs, vĭrĭdĭs, ŏlēns, rŭbēns, flŏrēns, rŭbĕă, ŏdŏră, frāgrāns.

Căsĭŭs, ĭī, m., *a mountain of Egypt*. Nēc tĕnŭīt Căsĭŭm, Luc.

Cāspĕrĭă, æ, f., *a town of the Sabines*. Cāspĕrĭāmquĕ cŏlŭnt, Virg.

Cāspĭŭs, ă, ŭm, *Caspian*. Aŭt mărĕ Cāspĭŭm, Hor.

Cāssāndră, æ, f., *the daughter of Priam, gifted with the knowledge of futurity*. Crīnĭbŭs ā templō Cāssāndră, Virg. Epith. Prĭāmĕĭă, Ilĭăcă, Phrўgĭă, Ilĭă, Pērgămĕă, prænūncĭă, præscĭă, fātĭdĭcă, præsāgă, vērāx, Phœbăs.

cāssēs, ĭŭm, m. pl., *nets*. Cāssĭbŭs īmpŏsĭtĭs, Pr. Syn. Lăquĕī, rētĭă, plāgæ. Epith. Dŏlōsī, lāxī, ārctī, lătēntēs, părātī, fāllācēs, ŏccūltī, sūbdŏlī, mĕtŭēndī, ābdĭtī, pŏsĭtī, ăppŏsĭtī, dīspŏsĭtī, caŭtī, fērrĕī, tĕnācēs, īmpŏrtūnī.

cāssĭdă, æ, f., *a helmet*. Nūdāvīt cāssĭdă frŏntĕm, Prop. V. Cassis.

Cāssĭŏpē, ēs, f., *one of the Muses*. Tālĭă Cāssĭŏpē, Man. Epith. Astrĭgĕră, ĭnfōrtūnātă, fūlgēns, rădĭŏsă, ĭnfēlīx.

cāssĭs, ĭdĭs, f., *a helmet*. Crīstātă cāssĭdĕ pēnnĭs, Ov. Syn. Gălĕă, cāssĭdă. Epith. Fūlvă, ærĕă, aūrĭcŏmă, aūrātă, mĭnāx, nĭtĭdă, tŏrvă, Mārtĭă, ĭnfēstă, hīrsūtă, căvă, fērrĕă, ăhēnă, ærātă, cælātă. V. Galea.

cāssŭs, ă, ŭm, *vain, frivolous*. Nōn cāssa ĭn vŏtă vŏcāvīt, Virg. Syn. Ĭnānĭs, văcŭŭs, frăgĭlĭs, prīvātŭs, ōrbātŭs.

Cāstălĭă, æ, f., *a fountain sacred to the Muses*. Cāstălĭăm mōllī, Virg.

Cāstălĭdĕs, ŭm, f. pl., *the Muses*. Sīlī Cāstălĭdŭm, (Phal.) Mart. V. Musæ.

cāstănĕă, æ, f., *a chestnut*. Cāstănĕāsquĕ nŭcēs, Virg. Epith. Mōllĭs, hīrsūtă.

cāstănīnŭs, *or* nĕŭs, ă, ŭm, *of chestnut*. Nēc tĭbī cāstănĕæ, Ov.

cāstēllŭm, ī, n., *a castle*. Cāstēllă sŭb ārmīs, Virg.

* cāstīgātĭo, ōnĭs, f., *a chastisement*. Syn. Ōbjūrgātĭo, pœnă, mūlctă, cōrrēctĭo. Epith. Jūstă, pĭă, ūtĭlĭs, ămīcă, ămără, dūră, ăcĕrbă. V. Pœna.

‖ cāstīgātŏr, ōrĭs, m., *a corrector*. Cāstīgātōrquĕ mĭnōrŭm, Hor. V. Censor.

cāstīgo, ās, *to chastise*. Ēt cāstīgābĭs ăcĕrbō, Juv. Syn. Ēmēndo, pūnĭo, plēcto, mūlcto, cōrrĭgo, ōbjūrgo, īncrēpo. V. Punio.

cāstĭmōnĭă, æ; *titas, ătĭs*; *and* tĭtūdo, ĭnĭs, f., *chastity*. Cērtō fœdĕrĕ cāstĭtās, Hor. Sērvātĕ cāstĭtūdĭnĕm, (Iamb.) Acc. Syn. Pūrĭtās, ĭntegrĭtās, pŭdīcĭtĭă. Epith. Pūră, cāndĭdă, sānctă, vĕnĕrāndă, īntāctă, pŭdīcă, ĭnnŏcēns, hŏnēstă, īncōrrūptă, vĕrēcūndă, īntĕmĕrātă, vīctrīx, cœlēstĭs, āngĕlĭcă, dīvīnă, ĭngĕnŭă, mĭră. V. Castus.

Cāstŏr, ŏrĭs, m., *the son of Leda, brother of Pollux*. Cāstŏră, nē rĕdĕăt, Mart. Syn. Tўndărĭdēs. Epith. Lēdæŭs, Ămўclæŭs, Œbălĭŭs, Thērăpnæŭs, gĕnĕrōsŭs, Ārgŏnaŭtă, ĭmmōrtālĭs. V. Pollux.

‖ cāstŏr, ŏrĭs, m., *a beaver*. Pŏntĭcĕ cāstŏr, Ov. Syn. Fĭbĕr.

cāstŏrĕŭs, ă, ŭm, *of a beaver*. Cāstŏrĕa, Elĭădŭm, Virg. Syn. Cāstŏrīnŭs, fĭbrīnŭs.

căstră, ōrŭm, n. pl., *a camp; an army.* Căstrōrum, ĕt cămpī, Virg. Syn. Tēntōrĭă; tūrmæ, phălāngēs, cătērvæ, āgmĭnă. Epith. Æstīvă, hībērnă, hōrrĭdă, hŏstīlĭă, ăcērbă, nĕfāndă, Mārtĭă, sævă, ŏpŭlēntă, fīdă, tūtă. V. Agmen.

căstrēnsĭs, ĕ, *of a camp.* Căstrēnsĭă pēnsă, Prop.

căstrŭm, ī, n., *a fortress.* Căstrūmque Ĭnŭī, Virg.

căstŭs, ă, ŭm, *chaste.* Āltārĭă căstīs, Virg. Syn. Pūrŭs, pŭdīcŭs, ĭntĕmĕrātŭs, īllībătŭs, mūndŭs; cælēbs. V. Virgo.

căsŭlă, æ, f., *the diminut. of* casa. Vīvĭtĕ cōntēntī căsŭlīs, Juv. V. Casa.

căsŭs, ŭs, m., *a fall, chance.* Pĕr vărĭōs căsŭs, Virg. Syn. Lāpsŭs, prōlāpsĭo, rŭīnă, ĭntĕrĭtŭs, ēxĭtĭŭm, pērnĭcĭēs, ĭnfōrtūnĭŭm, dāmnŭm, clădēs, strāgēs, ālĕă, pĕrīcŭlŭm. Epith. Sŭbĭtŭs, rĕpēntīnŭs, ĭnŏpīnŭs, præcēps, cĭtŭs, ādvērsŭs, trīstĭs, fūnēstŭs, mœstŭs, dūrŭs, īnsōlĭtŭs, flēbĭlĭs, lāmēntābĭlĭs, lūctŭōsŭs, lūctĭfĭcŭs, īnfāndŭs, īnīquŭs, hōrrēndŭs, ăcērbŭs, īnfaŭstŭs. V. Cado, strages, periculum.

cătăgrăphŭs, ă, ŭm, *adorned with drawings.* Cătăgrăphōsquĕ Thŷnōs, Cat.

|| cătămĭtŭs, ī, m., *an effeminate youth.* Tū cătămītŭs ĕrĭs, Auson.

|| cătăphrăctŭs, ă, ŭm, *armed from top to toe.* Nēc cătăphrāctŭs ĕquō, Prop. V. Armatus.

|| cătăpūltă, æ, f., *a warlike engine.* Tōrquĕt cătăpūltă mŏlārēs, Sid. Syn. Bălīstă, tōrmēntŭm.

|| cătărāctă, *or* tēs, æ, f., *a cataract.* Præcĭpĭtēs cătărāctæ, Lucan. Epith. Āltă, prærūptă.

cătāstă, æ, f., *a cage wherein slaves were exposed to sale.* Fērrĕ cătāstă pĕdēs, Tib. Epith. Bārbărĭcă, ăvāră, ārcānă, ĭnērs, rĭgĭdă, bārbără.

cătējă, *or* eīă, æ, f., *a missile weapon.* Tōrquĕrĕ cătējās, Virg.

cătēllă, æ, f., *diminut. of* catula. Sæpĕ cătēllăm, Hor. V. Catula.

cătēllŭs, ī, m., *diminut. of* catulus. Ēxtă cătēllī, Juv. Syn. Cătŭlŭs; pārvŭs, ēxĭgŭŭs cănĭs. V. Catulus.

cătēnă, æ, f., *a chain.* Trāctæquĕ cătēnæ, Virg. Syn. Vīncŭlŭm, nēxŭs, cōmpēdēs, mănĭcæ, lăquĕŭs, fūnĭs, nōdŭs, lōră, lōrŭm; lĭgāmēn. Epith. Grăvĭs, sævă, nēxă, dūră, ārctă, fērrĕă, ærātă, fērrātă, strīdēns, fērrūgĭnĕă, tĕrēs, sŏlĭdă, nōdōsă, ærĕă, vălĭdă, īmprŏbă, ŏnĕrōsă, pōndĕrōsă, rĭgĭdă, crŭēntă, tĕnāx, fĕră, ăcērbă, ænĕă, ălĭēnă, Vūlcānĭă, sērvīlĭs, probrōsă. V. Vincio.

cătēnātŭs, ă, ŭm, *chained.* Cūræquĕ, cătēnātĭquĕ lăbōrēs, Mart.

cătēnŭlă, æ, f., *diminut. of* catena. Gĕmĭnātă cătēnŭlā, Fill. V. Catena.

cătērvă, æ, f., *a troop.* Stīpāntĕ cătērvā, Virg. Syn. Tūrmă, phălānx, āgmēn, cŏhōrs, mănŭs, lĕgĭo, mănĭplŭs, ēxērcĭtŭs, glŏbŭs. Epith. Flōrēns, fūlgēns, aŭdāx, hōstīlĭs, văgă, īnsānă, ærātă, ārmĭfĕră, spūmāns, trĕpĭdă, trĕpĭdāns, ārmātă. V. Exercitus, turba.

cătērvātĭm, adv., *by bands.* Jāmquĕ cătērvātĭm, Virg. Syn. Tūrmātĭm.

Căthărīnă, æ, (Sānctă) f., *the daughter of Costus, and a martyr.* Vērtĭt Căthărīnă dīsērtōs. Syn. Cōstŭs. Epith. Sānctă, pĭă, dōctă, mārtŷr.

căthēdră, æ, f., *a chair.* Ēt stĕrĭlēs căthĕdrās, Mart. Pænĕ căthēdră, Juv.

căthedrālĭtĭŭs, ă, ŭm, *belonging to chairs; a chairman.* Cūm căthĕdrālĭtĭŭs, Mart.

|| căthŏlĭcŭs, ă, ŭm, *universal, catholic.* Eccles. Cāthŏlīcō īn tēmplō, Prud.

Cătĭēnă, æ, f., *the name of a woman.* Vēl Cătĭēnæ, Juv.

Cătĭlīnă, æ, m., *the conspirator.* Cătīlīnă cădăvĕrĕ tōtō, Juv. Epith. Impĭŭs, sævŭs, mĭnāx, pērfĭdŭs.

cătīllŭs, ī, m., *a small dish.* Cīrcŭmpŏsŭĭssĕ cătīllīs, Hor. Syn. Cătīllŭm.

Cătīllŭs, ī, m., *a son of Amphiaraus.* Cătīllŭsque ăcērquĕ Cŏrās, Virg.

Cătĭnă, æ, *or* nē, ēs, f., *a town of Sicily.* Tūm Cătĭnē, Sil.

cătīnŭs, ī, m., *a dish.* Ūrgĕrĕ cătīnō, Hor. Syn. Cătīnŭm, lānx, dīscŭs. Epith Fīctĭlĭs, căpāx, laŭtŭs.

Cătĭŭs, ĭī, m., *an Epicurean philosopher.* Ēt quō Cătĭŭs, Hor.

Căto, ōnĭs, m., [Porcius,] *the Roman general and censor.* Sĕvĕră Cătōnĭs Frōns, Hor. Epith. Cēnsōrĭŭs, aŭstērŭs, sĕvērŭs, grăvĭs, īntōnsŭs, rĭgĭdŭs, tetrĭcŭs, trīstĭs.—2. [Uticensis.] *the censor's grandson, who killed himself after the battle of Pharsalia.* Sēd vīctă Cătōnī, Luc. Epith. Invīctŭs, dūrŭs, īntōnsŭs, īntĕgĕr, sānctŭs.

Cătōnĭānŭs, ă, ŭm, *of Cato.* Cătōnĭănā. Chrēstĕ, (Scaz.) Mart.

Cătŭllŭs, ī, m., *the Latin poet.* Vērōnă Cătŭllō, Ov. Epith. Dōctŭs, tĕnĕr, fācŭndŭs, ărgūtŭs, suāvĭs, nĭtĭdŭs, mōllĭs, dōctĭlŏquŭs, tĕnŭĭs.

cāttā, æ, f., *a kind of bird.* Ūmbrĭā cāttās, Mart.

Cătŭlŭs, ī, m., *a noble Roman family.* Vīrtūtĕm Cătŭlī, Rut.

cătŭlŭs, ī, m., *and* ā, æ, f., *a little dog.* Dŏmī căŭŭlōrŭm blāndă prŏpāgo, Lucr. Syn. Cătĕllŭs; pārvŭs, ēxĭgŭŭs, tĕnĕr, tĕnēllŭs cănĭs. Epith. Lāctāns, mōllĭs, tĭmĭdŭs, tĕnĕr, blāndŭs, păvĭdŭs, fūgĭtīvŭs, fŭgāx, mōrdāx, păvēns, tĕnēllŭs, dŏcĭlĭs, săgāx.

cătŭs, ā, ŭm, *sharp, sly.* Cătŭs, ēt dĕcōræ, (Sapph.) Hor. Syn. Caŭtŭs, āstūtŭs, cāllĭdŭs, vērsūtŭs.

cătŭs, ī, m., *a cat.* Ac mūrī cătŭs ĭllĕ, Mart. Syn. Fēlĭs. Epith. Astūtŭs, mūrĭbŭs hŏstĭs.

Caŭcăsĕŭs, *or* sĭŭs, ā, ŭm, *of the Caucasus.* Ipsæ Caŭcăsĕō, Virg.

Caŭcăsŭs, ī, m., *a great mountain of Asia.* Caŭcăsŭs, Hўrcānæquĕ, Virg. Syn. Caŭcăsĕæ rūpēs. Epith. Hōrrēns, īngēns, nĭvālĭs, frĭgĭdŭs, āspĕr, glăcĭālĭs, Scўthĭcŭs, ĭnhōspĭtŭs, cēlsŭs, Sārmătĭcŭs. V. Mons.

caŭdă, æ, f., *a tail.* Æquŏră vērrēbānt caŭdīs, Virg. Epith. Lōngă, sĭnŭōsă, vērsĭcŏlŏr, stēllātă.

caŭdēx, ĭcĭs, m., *a stock, the stump of a tree.* Quīn ēt caŭdĭcĭbŭs, Virg. Syn. Trūncŭs, lībĕr.

căvĕ, (*the imper. of* caveo,) *beware.* Lĭgnă, căvē, nē, Hor. Vălē; căvĕ nē tĭtŭbēs, Id. V. Caveo.

căvĕă, æ, f., *a cave, den.* Exŏrĭtūr căvĕĭs, Claud. Syn. Fŏvĕă, fōssă, căvĕrnă, spĕcŭs, āntrŭm. Epith. Ōbscūră, prŏfūndă, īmā.

căvĕo, cāvī, caŭtŭm, *to take care.* Ērgŏ căvĕtĕ, vĭrī, Pr. Syn. Vĭdĕo, prŏvĭdĕo, āntĕvĭdĕo, prŭspĭcĭo, ādvērto, præcăvĕo, ōbsērvo.

căvērnă, æ, f., *a cavern.* Păthĕrĕ căvērnæ, Virg. Syn. Āntrŭm, spĕcŭs, spĕlūncă, spĕlæŭm, lătĕbră, lūstră fĕrārŭm. Epith. Tēctă, cæcă, ōbscūră, ŭmbrĭfĕră, īmă, claŭsă, prŏfūndă, căvă, vāstă, ēxēsă, ēffōssă, ābrūptă, fŭlvă, fōssă, ātră, īmmānĭs. V. Specus, antrum.

căvērnōsŭs, ă, ŭm, *full of caves.* Pērquĕ căvērnōsŏs, Prud. Syn. Căvŭs; căvērnĭs frĕquēns; mūltĭs cōncăvŭs āntrĭs.

* căvīllātĭo, ōnĭs, f., *a cavilling.* Cic. Syn. Jŏcătĭo, jŏcī, jŏcŭs, căvīllŭs, scōmmă. Epith. Tūrpĭs, sŏlūtă, pŭĕrīlĭs, mōrdāx, līvēns, prŏcāx, mīmĭcă, pĕtŭlāns, aŭdāx. V. Risus.

* căvīllātŏr, ōrĭs, m., *a caviller.* Cic. Syn. Jŏcŭlātŏr. V. Cavillatio.

* căvīllŏr, ārĭs, *to cavil.* Cic. Syn. Rīdĕo, īrrīdĕo, lūdo, īllūdo, jōcŏr. V. Derideo.

căvīllŭs, ī, f., *raillery.* Strŏphās căvīllō, (Iamb. Dim.) Prud. V. Cavillatio.

caŭlă, æ, f., *a sheep-cote.* Frĕmĭt ād caŭlās, Virg. Syn. Ŏvīlĕ, stăbŭlŭm; sēptă, ōrŭm. Epith. Claŭsă, tūtă, āngūstă, lātă, pīngŭĭs, ŏpīmă, plēnă, călĭdă, ăpērtă, mūnītă. V. Stabulum.

caŭlĭcŭlŭs, ī, m., *diminut. of* caulis. Nĭgră caŭlĭcŭlŭs, (Phal.) Prud.

caŭlĭs, ĭs, m., *the stalk of a plant.* Caŭlĭbŭs, aŭt pōmĭs, Juv. Epith. Tĕnĕr, nŏvŭs, frăgĭlĭs, trĕmŭlŭs, vĭrĭdĭs, vĭrēns, vērnāns, tūrgēns, pătŭlŭs.

Caŭlōn, ōnĭs, m., *a town of Magna Græcia.* Caŭlōnīsque ārcēs, Virg.

caŭnă, æ, f., *a kind of fig.* Caŭnĭs æmŭlă Chĭĭs, Col.

Caŭnŭs, ī, m., *a son of Miletus.* Fĕrōcĭă Caŭnī, Ov.

căvo, ās, *to hollow.* Sāxă căvāntŭr ăquă, Ov. Syn. Excăvo, cōncăvo, fŏdĭo, ēffŏdĭo, pērfŏro.

caŭpo, ōnĭs, m., *a vintner.* Caŭpōnĭbŭs ātquĕ mălĭgnĭs, Hor. Epith. Bĭbŭlŭs, pērfĭdŭs, mălĭgnŭs, sōrdĭdŭs.

caŭpōnă, æ, f., *a tavern.* Vŏlĕt īn caŭpōnă vīvĕrĕ, Hor. Syn. Pŏpīnă, tăbērnă. Epith. Ăpērtă, cōmmūnĭs, pătēns, īnsīgnĭs, sōrdĭdă.

caŭpōnŏr, ārĭs, *to huckster.* Nēc caŭpōnāntēs bēllŭm, Enn.

caŭrīnŭs, ă, ŭm, *belonging to the west-wind.* Vērum ŭbī caŭrīnō, Juv.

caŭrŭs, (*or* cōrŭs,) ī, m., *the west-wind.* Frīgŏră caŭrī, Virg. Epith. Rĕpēntīnŭs, vĭŏlēntŭs, fŭrēns, sævŭs, grăvĭdŭs, mădĭdŭs, răbĭdŭs, īnsānŭs, īmbrĭfĕr, răpĭdŭs, nīmbōsŭs, āspĕr, īmmītĭs. V. Ventus.

caŭsă, æ, f., *cause.* Lānguŏr ĕnĭm caŭsĭs, Ov. Syn. Prīncĭpĭŭm, fōns, ŏrīgo, căpŭt, rădīx; rătĭo; lĭs, jūdĭcĭŭm. Epith. Occūltă, lătēns, cērtă, sūffĭcĭēns, hŏnēstă, pĭă, bŏnă, mălă, lĕvĭs, dĭffĭcĭlĭs, ōbscūră, īnnŏcŭă.

caŭsĭdĭcŭs, ī, m., *an advocate.* Caŭsĭdĭcŭmquĕ pŭtās, Mart. Syn. Patrōnŭs, ādvŏcātŭs. Epith. Raŭcŭs, dōctŭs, ăvārŭs, pĕrītŭs, fācŭndŭs, dīsĕrtŭs, lŏquāx. V. Orator.

caŭsŏr, āris, *to pretend ; plead as an excuse.* Caŭsātŭr ĭnīquĕ, Hor.

caŭtē, adv., *with caution.* Scrīptă mĭhī caŭtē, Ov.

caŭtēlă, æ, f., *caution.* Hŏmĭnŭm caŭtēlă fŭĭt, Ser. Syn. Caŭtĭo ; vērsūtĭă, āstūtĭă, cāllĭdĭtās, prūdēntĭă.

caŭtēs, ĭs, f., *a rock.* Caŭtēs ŏbnŏxĭă vēntĭs, Tib. Syn. Rūpēs, scŏpŭlŭs, sāxŭm. Epith. Dūră, Mārpēsĭă, crūdă, sŏlĭdă, spīnōsă, āspĕră, sāxōsă, rĭgĭdă, rĭgēns. V. Rupes.

caŭtŭs, ă, ŭm, *cautious, circumspect.* Pārŭm caŭtōs jăm frīgŏră mōrdēnt, Hor. Syn. Prūdēns, prōvĭdŭs, vērsūtŭs. cāllĭdŭs, āstūtŭs, sūbdŏlŭs, văfĕr, dŏlōsŭs.

căvŭs, ă, ŭm, *hollow.* Mōns căvŭs, īgnāvī, Ov. Syn. Căvātŭs, cōncăvŭs, ēffōssŭs, āltŭs, prŏfūndŭs, hĭāns, pătēns.

căvŭs, ī, m., *a hole.* Invēntūsquĕ căvīs, Virg. Syn. Căvŭm, ī ; fōssă, căvērnă, spĕcŭs, āntrŭm.

Căycŭs, *or* Căĭcŭs, ī, m., *a river of Phrygia and Mysia.* Pērfūsă Căycō, Luc. Epith. Teŭthrāntæŭs ; Mўsŭs.

Căystĕr, strī, m., *a river of Lydia.* Prātă Căystrī, Virg. Epith. Gĕlĭdŭs, dūlcĭsŏnŭs, lēnĭs, Lўdŭs, Lўdĭŭs, Mæŏnĭŭs.

Căystrĭŭs, ă, ŭm, *of the Cayster.* Căystrĭŭs ālĕs, Ov.

cĕ, *a syllable which is joined with* hic, hæc, hoc. Hōscĕ sĕcūtŭs, Hor.

Cecrŏpĭdæ, ŭm, m. pl., *or* ĭŭs, ă, ŭm, *or* pĭs, ĭdĭs, f., *of Attica.* Cēcrŏpĭdæ jŭssī, Virg. Cēcrŏpĭăs ĭnnātŭs ăpēs, Id. Cēcrŏpī tērră. Ov. Syn. Ăthēnĭēnsĭs, Āttĭcŭs.

Cĕă, æ, f., *an island of the Ægean sea.* Cuī pīnguĭă Cēæ, Virg.

Cebrēnĭs, ĭdĭs, f., *daughter of Cebren, a river of Troas.* Pătrĭă Cēbrēnĭdă rīpā, Ov.

Cecrōps, ŏpĭs, m., *the first king of Athens.* Nēc nōn ēt Cĕcrŏpĭs, Ov. Epith. Pŏtēns, dīvĕs, īnclўtŭs.

cēdo, cēssī, *to give ground, yield.* Cēdĕ rĕpūgnāntī, Ov. Syn. Dīscēdo, rĕcēdo, fācēsso, ēxĕo, ăbĕo, ēvādo, ēxcēdo ; cōncēdo.

cĕdo, *give, tell me.* Cĕdŏ, sī cōnātă pĕrēgĭt, Juv.

cedrĭnŭs, ă, ŭm, *of cedar.* Ac ĕtĭăm cĕdrĭnām cĕdrĭnĭs, Fil.

cedrŭs, ī, f., *cedar.* Pōssĕ lĭnēndă cĕdrō, Hor. In lūmĭnă cĕdrŭm, Virg. Epith. Ŏdōrātă, ŏdōră, ŏlēns, ēnōdĭs, ætērnă, Lībănĭtĭs, fērālĭs, ĭmmōrtālĭs, frāgrāns, vīrēns, ūmbrōsă, frōndēns, pătŭlă, dēnsă, āltă, frōndōsă, ūmbrĭfĕră, prōcĕră, ŏdōrĭfĕră, pūlchră, ārdŭă, ēxcēlsă, sūblīmĭs, ānnōsă, dūră, īncōrrūptă. V. Arbor.

Cĕlădōn, ōntĭs, *a man slain at the nuptials of Peleus.* Ōccĭdĭt ēt Cĕlădōn, Ov.— 2. *one of the Lapithæ.* Lăpĭthæ Cĕlădōntĭs, Id.

Cĕlænō, ūs, f., *one of the Harpies.* Hārpyĭă Cĕlænō, Virg. Epith. Jējūnă, dīră, hōrrĭdă, ăvĭdă, Tārtărĕă, răpāx, fœdă, ĭmmūndă. V. Harpyiæ.

cĕlĕbĕr, *or* ebrĭs, ĕ, *celebrated, frequented.* Ăquītānæ cĕlĕbĕr, Tib. Syn. Clārŭs, nōbĭlĭs, īllūstrĭs, īnsĭgnĭs, fāmōsŭs, laŭdātŭs, spēctātŭs ; frĕquēns. V. Illustris.

cĕlebrātŏr, ōrĭs, m., *who celebrates.* Cĕlĕbrātŏr stēllă trĭŭmphī, Mart.

cĕlebro, ās, *to celebrate ; to haunt.* Dŏcŭīt cĕlĕbrārĕ Lătīnōs, Virg. Sēquĕ cĕlĕbrārī, Ov. Syn. Laŭdo ; prædīco, ās. V. Laudo, frequento.

Cĕlēnnă, æ, *and* nē, ēs, f., *a city of Campania.* Ārvă Cĕlēnnæ, Virg.

Cĕlĕr, ĕrĭs, m., *an officer who organized the first cavalry of Romulus.* Hōc Cĕlĕr ūrgĕt ŏpŭs, Ov. Cĕlĕrēs, ŭm, pl., *three hundred horsemen instituted by Romulus.* Cĕlĕrēsquĕ Lătīnī, Virg.

cĕlĕr, ĕrĭs, ĕ, *swift, speedy.* Nē dētūr cĕlĕrī, Ov. Syn. Vēlōx, pērnīx, prōmptŭs, ēxpĕdītŭs, cĭtŭs, præpēs, vŏlūcĕr, lĕvĭs, fēstīnŭs, prŏpĕrŭs, cĭtātŭs, prŏpĕrāns, fēstīnāns, haŭd sēgnĭs, īmpĭgĕr, vŏlāns. V. Festino, velox.

* cĕlĕrĭtās, ātĭs, f., *haste.* Cic. Syn. Vēlōcĭtās, lĕvĭtās.

cĕlĕrĭtĕr, adv., *speedily.* Syn. Vēlōcĭtĕr, prōmptē, prŏpĕrē, lĕvĭtĕr, ōcўŭs, cĭto, cōntĭnŭō, ēxtēmplō, quāmprīmŭm, rĕpēntē, mōx, cōnfēstĭm, sūbĭto, haŭd mŏră.

cĕlĕro, ās, *to hasten.* Sēd cĕlĕrārĕ fŭgăm, Virg. Syn. Prŏpĕro, fēstīno, mātūro, āccĕlĕro. V. Festino.

Cĕlĕŭs, ī, m., *the father of Triptolemus.* Prætĕrĕă Cĕlĕī, Virg. Epith. Rēx ărātŏr ; agrĭcŏlă.

‖ cĕleūsmā, *or* eūmă, ătĭs, n., *mariners' cry of exhortation.* Naŭtĭcūm cĕleūsmā, Mart.

cĕllă, æ, f., *a cellar, storehouse, cell.* Cĕllɪs ĭdĕŏ cōntēndĕ Fălērnĭs, Virg. EPITH. Plēnă, rĕfērtă, dīvĕs, văcŭă, āmplă.

cĕllārĭŭm, ĭī, n., *a cellar, a storehouse.* Cĕllārĭă plēnă, Mart. SYN. Cĕllă.

cĕllārĭŭs, ĭī, m., *a butler, steward.* Hīnc cĕllārĭŭs, Mart.

Cĕlmŭs, ī, m., *a man who nursed Jupiter.* Pārvŏ, Cĕlmĕ, Jŏvī, Ov.

cĕlo, ăs, *to conceal.* Sĕd bĕnĕ cēlētūr, bĕnĕ sī cĕlābĭtŭr īndĕx, Ov. SYN. Occŭlo, ŏccŭlto, tĕgo, cōndo, rĕcōndo, ābscōndo, vēlo, ābdo, ōbtĕgo, ŏbŭmbro, prætĕxo. V. Abscondo.

Cĕisŭs, ī, m., *the name of a man.* Quĭd mĭhĭ Cĕlsŭs ăgĭs, Hor.

cĕlsŭs, ă, ŭm, *high.* Cĕlsă Păphŭs, Virg. SYN. Āltŭs, ēxcēlsŭs, sūblīmĭs, ārdŭŭs. V. Altus.

Cĕltæ, ārŭm, m. pl., *a people of Celtic Gaul.* Vănĭlŏquūm Cĕltæ gĕnŭs, Sil.

Cĕltĭbērī, ōrŭm, m. pl., *a people of Spain.* Sălŏ Cĕltĭbĕr ŏrūs, Mart.

Cĕltĭcŭs, ă, ŭm, *of Celtic Gaul.* Pĕr Cĕltĭcă rūră, Sil.

cēmēntārĭŭs, ĭī, m., *a bricklayer.* Făbrōquĕ cēmēntārĭŏ, (Scaz.)

cēmēntŭm, ī, n., *mortar.* Strūctĭlīvĕ cēmēntŏ, (Scaz.) Mart. EPITH. Mōllĕ, tĕnāx.

Cēnœŭs, ī, m., *an epith. of Jupiter.* Āră Cēnæī Jŏvĭs, Ov.

Cēnchræ, ārŭm, f. pl., *a city near Corinth.* Cōgnĭtă Cēnchrĭs, Ov.

Cēnchrēĭs, ĭdĭs, f., *the wife of Cinyras.* Cēnchrēĭs ĭn ĭllă, Ov.

cēnchrĭs, ĭs, m., *a kind of spotted serpent.* Līmĭtĕ Cēnchrĭs, Luc.

cēnsĕo, ŭĭ, *to think.* Cēnsĕbo, ēxērcĕăt ārtĕm, Hor. SYN. Pŭto, sēntĭo, ārbitrŏr, ēxīstĭmo, jūdĭco ; rĕcēnsĕo. V. Sentio.

cēnsŏr, ōrĭs, m., *a censurer.* Ănĭmūm cēnsōrĭs, Hor. EPITH. Rĭgĭdŭs, tetrĭcŭs, sĕvērŭs, trīstĭs, hŏnēstŭs.

Cēnsōrīnŭs, ī, m., *the name of a man.* Cēnsōrīnĕ, mĕīs, Hor.

cēnsōrĭŭs, ă, ŭm, *of a censor.* Quĕm cēnsōrĭă cūm mĕŏ, (Phal.) Mart.

cēnsūră, æ, f., *censure.* Vēxăt cēnsūră cŏlūmbās, Juv. SYN. Jūdĭcĭŭm. EPITH. Sŭpērbă, rĭgĭdă, fāstŭōsă, sĕvēră, īnjūstă, dūră.

cēnsŭs, ūs, m., *a valuation made by the censors ; property, fortune.* Dăt cēnsŭs hŏnōrēs, Ov. SYN. Cēnsĭo, rĕcēnsĭo, rĕcēnsŭs ; bŏnă, ŏpēs, rēs, dīvĭtĭæ.

cēntaūrĕă, æ, f., *and* ēŭm, ī, n., *the herb centaury.* Grăvĕŏlēntĭă cēntaūrĕă, Virg. EPITH. Thēssălŭm, Chīrōnĭŭm.

Cēntaūrĕŭs, *and* ĭcŭs, ă, ŭm, *of a centaur.* Et Cēntaūrĕōs Lăpĭthās, Virg. Cēntaūrĭcă plēctră, Sid.

Cēntaūrī, ōrŭm, m. pl., *Centaurs, half men and half horses.* Cēntaūri ĭn fōrĭbŭs, Virg. SYN. Nūbĭgĕnæ, Ixĭŏnĭdæ. EPITH. Fŭrēntēs, bĭfōrmēs, mĭnācēs, nūbĭgĕnæ, bĭmēmbrēs, răpĭdī, sēmĭhŏmĭnēs, sēmĭvīrī, sēmĭmārēs, sēmĭfĕrī, sævī, trŭcēs, sŭpērbī.

cēntēnŭs, ă, ŭm, *a hundred.* Hīs ĕgŏ cēntēnās, Pr.

cēntēsĭmŭs, ă, ŭm, *the hundredth.* Cēntēsĭmă tūrbæ, Ov.

cēntĭcēps, cĭpĭtĭs, *hundred-headed.* Bēllŭă cēntĭcēps, (Alcaic.) Hor.

cēntĭēs, adv., *a hundred times.* Cēntĭēs āmīcī, Mart.

cēntĭfĭdŭs, ă, ŭm, *divided a hundred ways.* Cēntĭfĭdūm cōnfūndĭt ĭtĕr, Prud.

cēntĭmănŭs, ă, ŭm, *hundred-handed.* Cēntĭmănūmquĕ Gȳgēn, Ov.

cēnto, ōnĭs, m., *a patched garment.* Vĕtĕrī cēntōnĕ lŭpānăr, Juv.

cēntrŭm, ī, m., *the centre.* Sŭb ăcūmĭnĕ cēntrī, Aus.

cēntŭm, (*indecl.*) *a hundred.* Trīvĕrĭt ārĕă cēntŭm, Hor.

cēntūmgĕmĭnŭs, ă, ŭm, *multiplied to the number of a hundred, having a hundred, as hands, gates, &c.* Et cēntūmgĕmĭnūs Brĭărĕŭs, Virg. Et cēntūmgĕmĭnæ cēntēnă nŏvālĭă Thēbēs, Val. Fl.

cēntūmvĭrī, ōrŭm, m. pl., *centumvirs, magistrates at Rome who judged civil causes.* Ăd cēntūmvĭrōs, Phædr. Cēntūmquĕ vĭrī, Mart.

cēntŭplēx, ĭcĭs, *or* plŭs, ă, ŭm, *a hundred-fold.* Cēntŭplĭcēmquĕ fĕrānt, Juv. Præmĭă, cēntŭplŭm, Alcim.

cēntŭrĭă, æ, f., *a company of a hundred men.* Cēntūrĭæ sĕnĭōrum, Hor.

cēntŭrĭo, ōnĭs, m., *the captain of a hundred men.* Cēntŭrĭōnĭbŭs ōrtī, Hor.

cēpĕ, ēs, n., *or* pă, æ, f., *an onion.* Pŏrrum ēt cēpĕ nĕfās, Juv. Hōrtŭs ĕrŭtă cēpă mĕīs, Ov. EPITH. Rŭbēns, mōrdāx, ācrĭs, sōrdĭdă, mœstă, lacrȳmōsă.

Cĕphălŭs, ī, m., *the son of Æolus, loved by Aurora.* Nĕc Cĕphălū ŏ ĕœ, Ov.
Syn. Æŏlĭdēs. Epith. Cūltŭs, fōrmōsŭs, nĕmŏrōsŭs, Æŏlĭdēs.

Cĕphēĭă, æ, *and* Cĕphēĭs, ĭdĭs, f., *daughter of Cepheus, Andromeda.* Cĕphēĭă
Pērseō, Ov. Albīs, Cĕphēĭ, plăcēbās, Id.

Cĕphēĭŭs, *and* Cĕphēŭs, ă, ŭm, *of Cepheus.* Cĕphēam hīc Mĕrŏĕn, Ov. Cĕphēĭă
cōnspĭcĭt ārvă, Id.

Cĕphēŭs, ĕŏs, ĕī *or* eī, *acc.* ĕă, m., *a king of Ethiopia, father of Andromeda.*
Exĭĕrăt Cĕpheŭs, Ov. Syn. Iăsĭdēs.

Cĕphīsĭăs, ădŏs, *and* Cĕphīsĭs, ĭdŏs, f., *of Cephisus.* Cĕphīsĭăs ōră, Ov. Cĕphī-
sĭdăs ūndăs, Id.

Cĕphīsĭŭs, ĭī, m., *son of Cephisus, Narcissus.* Cĕphīsĭŭs ānnŭm, Ov.

Cĕphīsŭs, ī, m., *the name of two rivers, one in Bœotia, and the other in Attica.*
Fătĭdĭcă Cĕphīsŭs ăquā, Lucan.

cĕrŭ, æ, f., *wax.* Est mīhī cĕră tŭŏs, Ov. Epith. Pīnguĭs, liquĭdă, flăvă, ŏdōrātă, flăvēns, dūlcĭs, Attĭcă, Cecrŏpĭă, Hÿblæă. V. Apes. Tĕnŭĭs, mōllĭs, dīvĕs,
tĕnēllă, liquēns, ŏdōră, tŏnĕră, liquēscēns, trāctăbĭlĭs, dūctĭlĭs, ŏdōrĭfĕră, tĕnāx,
lăbōrătă, īmprēssă.

Cĕrāmbŭs, ī, m., *the name of a man.* Lŏcă nōtă Cĕrāmbī, Ov.

cĕrāstēs, æ, m., *a kind of horned serpent.* Lōngŏ strīdōrĕ cĕrāstēn, St. Epith.
Lȳbȳcŭs, văgŭs, ănhēlāns, cōrnĭgĕr, crīstātŭs, lēthĭfĕr. V. Serpens.

cĕrăsŭs, ī, f., *a cherry-tree.* Hīc dūlcēs cĕrăsŏs, Prop. Syn. Cĕrăsŭm. Epith.
Dūlcĭs, suāvĭs, jūcūndă. V. Arbor, fructus.

Cĕrăsūs, ūntĭs, f., *a town in Asia.* Cĕrăsūntĭs ōpēs, Mant.

cĕrātŭs, ă, ŭm, *waxed.* Cærūlă cĕrātăs, Ov.

Cĕraūnĭă, ōrŭm, n. pl., *high mountains of Epirus.* Vīcīnă Cĕraūnĭă jūxtă, Virg.
Syn. Acrŏcĕraūnĭă. Epith. Vĭŏlēntă, āltă, scŏpŭlōsă, prærūptă, ēxcēlsă, īgnĕă,
fūlmĭnĕă, īnfămĭă.

Cĕrbĕrĕŭs, ă, ŭm, *of Cerberus.* Nēmpĕ tĭmēs nĕ Cĕrbĕrĕŏs, Stat.

Cĕrbĕrŭs, ī, m., *the three-headed dog of Avernus.* Trĭă Cĕrbĕrŭs ōră, Virg. Syn.
Cănĭs tērgĕmĭnŭs, Tārtărĕŭs, Stȳgĭŭs, Mĕdūsæŭs; cūstŏs Plūtōnĭŭs. Epith.
Hĭāns, ĭnhĭāns, īmmānĭs, Mĕdūsæŭs, īnsŏmnĭs, īmpăvĭdŭs, pērvĭgĭl, Stȳgĭŭs,
īnfērnŭs, trĭfōrmĭs, tērrĭfĭcŭs, vŏrāx, hōrrĭdŭs, cruēntŭs, īnfĕrŭs, sævŭs, atrōx,
aūdāx, īrrĕquiētŭs, Lēthæŭs, Phlĕgĕthōntæŭs, ăcĕr, ăspĕr, fōrmīdăbĭlĭs, tērrĭbĭlĭs,
dīrŭs, Āvērnālĭs, nĭgĕr, ātĕr, tētĕr, triplēx, hōrrĭfĭcŭs, tūrbĭdŭs.

Cĕrcōpēs, ŭm, m. pl., *the inhabitants of the isle of Pithecusa, metamorphosed into
monkeys.* Cĕrcōpum ēxōsŭs, Ov.

cĕrcŏpĭthēcŭs, ī, m., *a monkey.* Cĕrcŏpĭthēcŭs ĕrăm, Mart. V. Simius.

Cĕrcūrŭs, ī, m., *a kind of fish.* Cĕrcūrŭsquĕ fĕrōx, Ov.

Cĕrcȳōn, ŏnĭs, m., *an Arcadian slain by Theseus.* Cĕrcȳōnĭs lēthŭm, Ov.

Cĕrcȳōnēŭs, ă, ŭm, *of Cercyon.* Cĕrcȳōnĕă mănū, Ov.

Cĕrĕālĭs, ĕ, *belonging to Ceres.* Et Cĕrĕālĕ sōlŭm, Virg. n. pl., Cĕrĕālĭă, ŭm,
festivals of Ceres. Cĕrĕālĭbŭs ālbăs, Ov.

cĕrebrōsŭs, ă, ŭm, *hasty, passionate.* Cĕrĕbrōsŭs prōsĭlĭt ūnŭs, Hor.

cĕrebrŭm, ī, n., *the brains.* Cĕrĕbrŭmquĕ, mĕrŭmquĕ, Ov. Infēctă cĕrĕbrō, Virg.
Epith. Mōllĕ, călĭdŭm, dōctŭm, īngĕnĭōsŭm, tĕnĕrŭm, cālēns.

cĕrĕŏlĭs, ă, ŭm, *dimin. of cereus.* Et cĕrĕŏlĭs, Colum.

Cĕrēs, rĕrĭs, f., *the goddess of agriculture.* Pārvă Cĕrēs āltŏ, Virg. Syn. Mātĕr
Ēleūsīnă, Ēleūsĭs. Epith. Flāvă, mūndă, fālcĭfĕră, aūrĕă, lætă, fœcūndă,
spīcĭfĕră, rŭbĭcūndă, māgnă, Ætnĕă, dīvĕs, ālmă, frūgĭfĕră, ānnōsă, trītĭcĕă,
flāvēns, cūltă, spīcātă, grātă, mūnĭfĭcă, pūlchră, sĭtĭbūndă, aūrĭcōmă, spērātă,
ēxpēctātă, āltrīx, ōptātă, spīcĕă, rūrĭcŏlă, Actæă, Attĭcă, Ēleūsīnă, Ēnnæă,
Sĭcŭlă, Sĭcānă, Ætnæă. V. Panis, seges.

cĕrĕŭs, ă, ŭm, *waxen, of wax.* Cĕrĕŭs īn vĭtĭŭm, Hor. Syn. Cĕrīnŭs, ēx cĕrā,
mōllĭs, trāctăbĭlĭs, dūctĭlĭs, flēxĭbĭlĭs.

cĕrĕŭs, ī, m., *a taper.* Cĕrĕŭs īgnēs, Mart. Syn. Fūnālĭă, cāndēlă, lūcērnă.
Epith. Pīnguĭs, īgnĭfĕr, cŏrūscŭs, flāmmĭvŏmŭs, rŭtĭlāns, ārdēns. V. Candela,
fax.

cĕrīnthĕ, ēs; rīnthă, æ, f., *honeysuckle.* Cĕrīnthæ īgnōbĭlĕ grāmĕn, Virg.

cĕrītŭs, ă, ŭm, *crazed.* Cĕrītŭs fŭĭt, Hor.

cĕrno, ĭs, *to see.* Cĕrnĕrĕ lēthŭm, Virg. Syn. Vĭdĕo, ăspĭcĭo, cōnspĭcĭo, pērspĭcĭo, tŭĕŏr, īntŭĕŏr, rēspĭcĭo. V. Aspicio.

E 6

cĕrnŭŭs, ă, ŭm, *bent forward.* Cĕrnŭŭs ārmō, Virg. SYN. Acclīnĭs, prōnŭs.

cĕrōmă, ătĭs, n., *wrestlers' ointment.* Injēctō cĕrōmătĕ brāchĭă tēndĭs, Mart. SYN. Cĕrōtŭm. EPITH. Pīnguĕ, crāssŭm, lēnĕ, ūnctŭm.

cĕrōmătĭcŭs, ă, ŭm, *anointed with ceroma.* Et cĕrōmătĭcō fērt, Juv.

cĕrōtŭm, ī, n., *a plaster made of wax.* Dēlĭbŭtă cĕrōtō, (Scaz) Mart.

cĕrtāmĕn, ĭnĭs, n., *and* tātŭs, ūs, m., *a battle.* Vŏcăt īn cĕrtāmĭnă Dīvōs, Virg. SYN. Pūgnă, cōnflictŭs, prælĭŭm, bēllŭm, Mārs. EPITH. Fūnēstŭm, Mărtĭŭm, trĕpĭdŭm, ăspĕrŭm, ănhēlŭm, mĭsĕrŭm, lūctŭōsŭm, mĭsĕrābĭlĕ, vălĭdŭm, dūrŭm, ăcērbŭm. māgnŭm, cĕlĕbrĕ, āncēps, dŭbĭŭm, ăcrĕ, sævŭm, īmpĭŭm, ănĭmōsŭm, mĭsĕrāndŭm, ălācrĕ. V. Pugna.

cĕrtātĭm, adv., *with contention.* Cērtātĭmque ōmnēs, Ov.

cĕrtĕ, adv., *certainly.* Hĭs cēr'ē nĕc ămŏr, Virg. SYN. Cērtō, prōfēctō, vērē.

cĕrto, ās, *to fight.* Cērtărĕ părātī, Virg. SYN. Pūgno, cōnflīgo, dīmĭco, cōntēndo, cōngrĕdĭŏr. V. Pugno.

cĕrtŭs, ă, ŭm, *certain.* Ămīcŭs cērtŭs īn re īncērtā, Enn. ap Cic. SYN. Nōn dŭbĭŭs, nōn īncērtŭs, prōmtŭs, fīdŭs, clārŭs, mănĭfēstŭs, īndŭbĭtātŭs.

cĕrvă, æ, f., *a hind.* Ærĭpēdēm cērvăm, Virg. EPITH. Cōrnĭgĕră, ānnōsă, cĕlĕr, ăgĭlĭs, tĭmĭdă, tērrĭtă, fŭgāx.

‖ cĕrūchŭs, ī, m., *the rope attached to the end of a sail-yard.* Arsĕrĕ cĕrūchī, Luc.

cĕrvīcăl, ālĭs, n., *a bolster.* Cervīcăl ōlēbĭt, Mart.

cĕrvīnŭs, ă, ŭm, *of a stag.* Cērvīnă sĕnēctŭs, Juv.

cĕrvīsĭă, æ, f., *beer.* Cĕrvīsĭæ cōctŏr, B. SYN. Zȳthŭm.

cĕrvīx, īcĭs, f., *the neck; head.* Cĕrvīcĭbŭs āltē, Virg. SYN. Cōllŭm, faūcēs. EPITH. Lāctĕă, ĕbūrnĕă, ārgēntĕă, ĕbūrnă, cāndĭdă, nĭtēns, nĭvĕă, āmbrōsĭă, blāndă, mōllĭs, fōrmōsă, ōlōrīnă, ālbă, vĕnŭstă, tŭmēns, tŭmĭdă, tŭmēscēns. V. Collum.

cĕrūssă, æ, f., *ceruse.* Nĕc cĕrūssă tĭbi, Ov. EPITH. Ālbă, cāndĭdă, nĭtēns. V. Fucus.

cĕrūssātŭs, ă, ŭm, *painted with ceruse.* Et cĕrūssātă, Mart. V. Fucatus.

cĕrvŭs, ī, m., *a stag.* Vŏlŭcrēs fōrmīdĭnĕ cērvī, Sil. EPITH. Lĕvĭs, īmbēllĭs, fŭgāx, păvēns, ălĭpēs, ălātŭs, vēlōx, quadrŭpēs, păvĭdŭs, cōrnĭgĕr, trĕpĭdŭs, cĕlĕr, văgŭs, tĭmĭdŭs, ānnōsŭs, vīvāx, lōngævŭs, fŭgĭtīvŭs, cĭtŭs, sȳlvēstrĭs, ăgĭlĭs, văgābūndŭs, pērnīx, ērrāns, præpĕs, tērrĭtŭs, pērtērrĭtŭs.

cēspĕs, ĭtĭs, m., *a turf.* Cēspĭtĭbŭs mēnsăm. Tib. SYN. Glēbă, grāmĕn. EPITH. Grāmĭnĕŭs, crāssŭs, hērbĭfĕr, hūmēns, ŏdōrŭs, gĕlĭdŭs, agrēstĭs, hērbōsŭs, pīnguĭs, vĭrēns, mōllĭs, hūmĭlĭs, vīvŭs, lĕvĭs.

cēssātŏr, ōrĭs, m., *an idler.* Cēssātŏr Dăvŭs, Hor.

cēsso, ās, *to rest, cease.* Sī quĭd cēssărĕ pŏtĕs, Virg. SYN. Dēsīsto, ābsīsto, dēsĭno, quĭēsco. V. Finio, quiesco.

cēstŭs, ī, m., *the girdle of Venus; a marriage-girdle.* Cēstōn dē Vĕnĕrĭs sĭnŭ cālēntĕm, Hor.

cētārĭă, ōrŭm, n. pl., *great fish-ponds.* Cētārĭă crēscēnt, Hor.

cētē, n. pl., *(undecl.) whales.* Ăd mūrmŭr cētē tōtō, Sil. SYN. Cētī, m. pl., cētŭs; bālænă. EPITH. Grāndĭă, hōrrĭdă, scŏpŭlōsă, īmmānĭă.

Cĕthēgŭs, ī, m., *an ancient Roman family.* Exaūdītă Cĕthēgĭs, Hor.

‖ cētră, æ, f., *a Spanish shield.* Ībērĭă cētrās. Luc.

ceū, conj., *as.* Ceū tēmpēstătĕ cŏlŭmbæ, Virg. SYN. Ūt, quăsi, tānquăm, nōn sĕcŭs āc, haŭd sĕcŭs āc, nōn ălĭtĕr.

Cēŭs, ă, ŭm, *of Cea; of Simonides.* Cēæque ĕt Alcæī, Hor.

Cēȳx, ȳcĭs, m., *the husband of Alcyone.* Frăgmĭnă nāvĭgĭī Cēȳx, Ov. EPITH. Trāchĭnĭŭs; Œtæŭs; fōrtĭs, pŏtēns, māgnănĭmŭs, gĕnĕrōsŭs, lūgēndŭs, mĭsĕr, naūfrăgŭs.

Chălcēdōn, ŏnĭs, f., *a city of Asia Minor.* Chălcēdŏnă cūrsū, Luc.

chălcĕŭs, ă, ŭm, *of brass.* Chălcĕă dōnāntī, Mart. SYN. Œnĕŭs, ærĕŭs, ăhēnĕŭs.

Chālcĭdĭcŭs, ă, ŭm, *of Chalcis.* Chālcĭdĭcāquĕ lĕvĭs, Virg.

Chălcĭōpē, ēs, f., *sister of Medea.* Chālcĭōpēquĕ sŏrŏr, Ov.

Chālcĭs, ĭdĭs *and* ĭdōs, f., *a town of Negropont.* Chālcĭdĭs Eŭbŏĭcæ, Luc.

Chāldæī, ōrŭm, m. pl., *Chaldeans, astronomers.* Chāldæĭs sēd mājŏr ĕrĭt, Juv.

Chălўbēs, ŭm, m. pl., *a nation of Spain.* Ăt Chălўbēs nūdī, Virg. EPITH. Dūrī, rōbūstī, fōrtēs, vălĭdī, pĕrītī.

chălўbs, ўbĭs, m., *a kind of hard steel.* Chălўbīs pĕrfēctă mĕtāllō, Sil. Syn.
Fērrŭm. Epith. Dūrŭs, rĭgĭdŭs, lēthĭfĕr, strictŭs.

Chăŏn, ŏnĭs, m., *a son of Priam.* Trōjāno ā Chăŏnĕ dīxĭt, Virg.

Chăŏnĕs, ŭm, m. pl., *inhabitants of Chaonia.* Nŏn Chăŏnăs, Claud.

Chăŏnĭă, æ, f., *a region of Epirus.* Chăŏnĭāmque ŏmnĕm, Virg.

Chăŏnĭŭs, ă, ŭm, *and* Chăŏnĭs, ĭdĭs, f., *of Chaonia.* Chăŏnĭām pīnguī, Virg.
Chăŏnĭs ālĕs, Ov. Syn. Dōdōnēŭs, Dōdōnĭŭs.

chăŏs, n., *a confused heap of matter.* In chăŏs āntīquŭm, Ov. Syn. Māssă, cōngĕrĭēs. Epith. Antīquŭm, vĕtūstŭm, ĭnānĕ, Cĭmmĕrĭŭm, tristĕ, hŏrrēndŭm,
prŏfūndŭm, dūrŭm, ātrŭm, dēfōrmĕ, īnfōrmĕ, ŏbscūrŭm, hŏrrĭfĭcŭm, ŭmbrōsŭm,
ŏmnĭgĕnŭm, cæcŭm, cōnfūsŭm, tĕtrŭm.

* chărāctēr, ĕrĭs, m., *a character or letter.* Col. Syn. Fōrmă, fĭgūră, insĭgnĕ,
sĭgnŭm.

Chărāxŭs, ī, m., *the brother of Sappho.* Mœrōrĕ Chărāxŭs, Ov.

Chărīclō, ūs, f., *the wife of Chiron.* Nўmphă Chărīclō, Ov.

Chărīstĭă, ōrŭm, n. pl., *a family repast.* Chărīstĭă cārī, Ov.

Chărĭtes, ŭm, f. pl., *the three Graces.* Lăcrўmĭs Chărĭtēs; āvērsŭs Apōllo, Prop.
Syn. Grătĭæ. Epith. Dūlcēs, blāndæ, cūltæ, lætæ, dĕcēntēs, grātæ, mĕmōrēs,
jŭvĕnēs. V. Gratia.

Chărōn, ōntĭs, m., *the ferryman of Styx.* Illĕ, Chărōn : hī, quŏs, Virg. Epith.
Hōrrēndŭs, squālĭdŭs, ăvārŭs, pāllĭdŭs, sĕnēx, hŏrrĭdŭs, dīrŭs, dūrŭs, Stўgĭŭs,
Lēthæŭs, trīstĭs, ātĕr, ĭnēxōrābĭlĭs, ĭmmĭtĭs, fĕrōx, īnsătĭăbĭlĭs, sævŭs, trĕ-
mēndŭs, pērvĭgĭl, īrrĕquĭētŭs, vĭgĭl, Avērnālĭs.

Chărōps, ōpĭs, m., *a Trojan slain by Ulysses.* Ēt Chărŏpĕm, Ov.

chārtă, æ, f., *paper.* Chārtă nŏtātă, Ov. Syn. Pápўrŭs. Epith. Albă, pŏlītă,
ĭmmăcŭlātă. V. Papyrus.

Chărўbdĭs, ĭs, f., *a gulf of the Sicilian sea.* Vāstă Chărўbdĭs ăquās, Pr. Syn. Zānclæă vŏrāgo. Epith. Mĕtŭēndă, ātră, Zānclæă, īrrĕquĭētă, ăvĭdă, tōrtă, dīră,
sævă, tōrvă, răpāx, hūmĭdă, Sĭcŭlă, mĭnāx, cōncăvă, trŭx, vĭŏlēntă, răpĭdă, hōrrēndă, prŏcēllōsă, tērrĭbĭlĭs, ăgĭtātă, ūndĭsŏnă, scŏpŭlōsă, īnāccēssă, spūmōsă,
hŏrrĭsŏnă, cærŭlĕă, æquŏrĕă, spūmāns, naŭfrăgă, tūrbĭdă, fĕră, ĭnĭmĭcă.

|| chāsmă, ătĭs, n., *a chasm.* Sen. Syn. Gūrgĕs, vŏrāgo, bărathrŭm, hĭātŭs.
Epith. Hĭāns, lātŭm.

chēlæ, ārŭm, f. pl., *the arms of the scorpion.* Chēlāsquĕ sĕquēntēs, Virg.

chĕlydrŭs, ī, m., *a kind of snake.* Ēt bēllārĕ mănu, ēt chĕlўdrīs, Sil. Mēmbrānă
chĕlўdrī, Ov. Epith. Nĭgĕr, grăvĭs, rĭgĭdŭs, sĭnŭōsŭs, măcŭlōsŭs. V. Serpens.

chĕlўs, ўos, f., *a lyre.* Hīc chĕlўn, hīc flāvŭm, Stat. Syn. Tēstūdo, cĭthără,
lўră. Epith. Aūrātă, cănōră, ĕbūrnă, aūrĕă, tĕnĕră, dōctă, ārgūtă, Phœbēă,
Apōllĭnĕă, Pĭĕrĭă, blāndă, dūlcĭsŏnă. V. Cithara.

Chērsĭdămās, āntĭs, m., *a Trojan slain by Ulysses.* Chērsĭdămāntĕ Thŏŏnă, Ov.

Chĭmæră, æ, f., *a mountain of Lycia, transformed by the poets into a monster, lion-
like in the fore part, dragon-like behind, goat-like in the middle ; because its summit emitted flames, its middle part was abundant in pasture, and its base in serpents.*
Mĕdĭa īpsă Chĭmæră, Luc. Syn. Mōnstrŭm flāmmĭvŏmŭm. Epith. Trĭfōrmĭs,
ĭgnĕă, trĕmēndă, ĭgnĭfĕră, fūrēns, fĕră, răbĭdă, ārdēns, hōrrēndă, hŏrrĭdă, tērrĭbĭlĭs, ĭmmānĭs, fĕrōx, mĕtŭēndă, Lўcĭă.

Chĭmærēŭs, ă, ŭm, *of the Chimæra.* Almă Chĭmærēō Xānthī, Virg.

Chĭmærĭfĕr, ă, ŭm, *producing the Chimæra.* Jāmquĕ Chĭmærĭfĕræ, Ov.

|| Chĭmĕrĭnŭs, ă, ŭm, *winterly, of the winter tropic.* Sĭdĕră, Chĭmĕrĭnŏs, Mart.

Chĭōnē, ēs, f., *a nymph beloved by Apollo.* Ērăt huīc Chĭŏnē, Ov.

Chĭŏnĭdēs, æ, m., *son of Chione.* Āt nōn Chĭŏnĭdēs, Ov.

Chĭŏs, ī, f., *an island of the Archipelago.* Sămŏs ēt Chĭŏs ēt Rhŏdŭs, Hor.

chīragră, æ, f., *gout in the hand.* Pŏdāgră, chīrāgrăquĕ, Mart. Prŏhĭbĕrĕ chīrāgră,
Hor. Epith. Nŏdōsă, dūră, lăpĭdōsă, frĭgĭdă, sævă, mŏlēstă, ăcūtă, vĭŏlēntă,
dīră, āspĕră, crūdēlĭs, īnsŏmnĭs, ăcērbă, ĭmmĕdĭcābĭlĭs, īmpŏrtūnă, rĕdŭx, rĕdĭvīvă, rĕnāscēns, fĕră, clāmōsă, īnmītĭs, quĕrŭlă, vĭgĭl, pērvĭgĭl, trīstĭs.

chīrŏgrăphŭm, ī, n., *a bill, bond.* Dīcŭnt chīrŏgrăphă lignī, Juv.

Chīrōn, ōnĭs, m., *a centaur, the tutor of Achilles.* Gĕmĭnŭm Chīrōnă crĕārĭt, Ov.
Syn. Phĭllўrĭdēs, Phĭlўrēĭŭs hērōs. Epith. Sēmĭvĭr Phĭllўrĭŭs, bĭfōrmĭs,
gĕmĭnŭs, tōrvŭs, lōngævŭs, dōctŭs, Thēssălŭs, jūstŭs, Æmōnĭŭs, mĕdĭcŭs, hĕrbĭ-
pŏtēns, Pēlĭācŭs, săgāx, sōlĕrs, prūdēns.

|| chīrŏnŏmŭs, ī, *and* mŏn, mŏntĭs, m., *using graceful motions with the hands.* `Chĭrŏnŏmŏntă vŏlāntī, Juv.

chīrūrgŭs, ī, m., *a surgeon.* Chīrūrgūs fŭĕrăt, Mart. Epith. Sŏlērs, pĕrītŭs, dēxtĕr.

Chīŭs, ă, ŭm, *of Chios.* Aūt Chīă vīnă, Hor.

chlămўs, ўdĭs, f., *a cloak.* Ēt tŏrtŏ chlămўdēm dĭsfībŭlăt, St. Syn. Vēstĭs, ămīctŭs, tēgmĕn, vēlāmĕn, tŭnīcă, vēstīmēntŭm. Epith. Dēpīctă, Phœnīcĭă, Sārrānă, Tўrĭă; aūrātă, rŭbēns, ŏdōrātă, cŏccīnĕă, pīctă, pūrpŭrĕă, pŭlchră, præclāră, splēndĭdă, mīlĭtārĭs, bēllīcă. V. Vestis.

Chlīdē, ēs, f., *the name of a woman.* Bĭs flāvă Chlīdĕ, Ov.

Chlŏē, ēs, f., *the name of a woman.* Thrēssă Chlŏē rēgĭt, Hor.

Chlŏreŭs, ĕŏs, ĕī *or* eī, m., *a priest of Cybele.* Cўbēlæ Chlŏreŭs, Virg.

Chlōrĭs, ĭdŏs, f., *the goddess of flowers, and wife of Zephyrus.* Chlōrĭdŏs ālĕs. Syn. Flōră, Zĕphўrītă. Epith. Vērnă, cāndĭdă, pŭlchră, flōrĭdă. V. Flora.

|| chŏlĕră, æ, f., *anger.* Sī pĕnĭtūs chŏlĕrăm, Ser. Syn. Īră, bīlĭs, īrăcūndĭă. V. Ira.

Chŏāspēs, ĭs, m., *a river of Media.* Lўmphă, Chŏāspēs, Tib.

Chœrĭlŭs, ī, m., *the name of a bad poet.* Chœrĭlŭs īncūltĭs, Hor.

chŏlĭāmbŭs, ī, m., *a sort of verse.* Dēbĭlĭtărĕ chŏlĭāmbŭm, Mart.

|| chŏrāgĭŭm, ĭī, n., *stage decorations.* Quæ mēntĭŭm chŏrāgĭŭm, (Iamb.)

|| chŏrāgŭs, ī, m., *a setter forth, master of plays.* Gērĭt īpsă chŏrāgŭm, Mart.

|| chŏraūlēs, æ, m., *who plays upon the flute.* Ămbrŏsīūsquĕ chŏraūlēs, Juv.

chŏrdă, æ, f., *the string of a harp.* Syn. Nērvŭs; fīdēs, ĭŭm. Epith. Tĕnŭĭs, tīnnŭlă, sŏnōră, rĕsŏnă, lĕvĭs, Phœbĕă, Ăpōllĭnĕă, Aŏnĭă, Pīĕrĭă, grātă, gārrŭlă, jūcūndă, dūlcĭs, lŏquāx, sŏnāns, rĕsŏnāns. V. Fides, ium.

chŏrĕă, æ, f., *a dance.* Dūxĕrĕ chŏrĕās, Ov. Pĕdĭbŭs plaūdūnt chŏrĕās, Virg. Syn. Chŏrŭs, sāltătĭo. Epith. Lūdēns, pērnīx, fēstă, mōllĭs, cāntātrīx, lĕpĭdă, sŏcĭă, grātă, dūlcĭs, lætă, plăcĭdă, lĕvĭs, făcĭlĭs, plaūsă, hĭlărĭs, ăgĭlĭs, blāndă, rĕvŏlūtă, sāltāns, pŭēllārĭs, nōctūrnă, jūcūndă, sŏnōră, nŭmĕrōsă, cōncŏrs, lāscīvă, lūxŭrĭāns, pūblīcă, īrrĕquĭētă. V. Salto.

Chŏrĭāmbŭs, ī, m., *a metrical foot.* Ēlēgŏs, chŏrĭāmbŭm, Aus.

chŏrŭs, ī, m., *a choir.* Phœbī chŏrŭs āssūrrēxĕrĭt, Virg. Syn. Cœtŭs, cōncĭlĭŭm, tūrbă; chŏrĕă.

Chrēmēs, mĕtĭs *and* mĭs, m., *a personage in comedy.* Dăvŏquĕ Chrēmĕtă, Hor.

Christīădæ, tīcŏlæ, ārŭm, *and* tīānī, ōrŭm, m. pl., *Christians.* Eccl. Epith. Fīdēlēs, sānctī, sŏcĭī, ūnănĭmēs, īngĕnŭī, īncōrrūptī, cōnstāntēs, stăbĭlēs, sīncērī, rēlĭgĭōsī, fīrmātī, īntĕmĕrātī.

CHRISTUS, ī, m., *our Saviour.* Syn. Vērbŭm, Rĕdēmptŏr, Sālvātŏr. Epith. Sălūtĭfĕr, ūnĭgĕnă, ūnctŭs, săcĕr, pŏtēns, ōmnĭpŏtēns, bŏnŭs, jūdēx, dŏmĭnŭs, ætērnŭs, īnclўtŭs, cœlĭpŏtēns, bĕnīgnŭs, sălūtārĭs, mītĭs, pācĭfĭcŭs, pătĭēns, vīndēx, vīctŏr, ădōrāndŭs, trĭūmphāns, clēmēns, vīnctŭs, ŏccīsŭs, plăcābĭlĭs, mūnĭfĭcŭs. V. Jesus.

Chrŏmĭs, ĭs, m., *a centaur.* Vīrtūtĕ Chrŏmĭn, Ov.—2. f., *a sort of fish.* Immūndă chrŏmĭs, Id.

* chrŏnĭcă, ōrŭm, n. pl., *chronicles.* Plin. V. Annales.

Chrўsă, æ, *and* ē, ēs, f., *a city of Mysia.* Tĕnĕdŏn Chrўsēnquĕ, Ov.

chrўsānthŭs, ī, m., *corn-marigold.* Chrўsānthŭsque hĕdĕræquĕ, Virg.

Chrўsēĭs, ĭdĭs *or* ĭdŏs, f., *daughter of Chryses, Astynome.* Chrўsēĭdă vīctŏr, Ov.

chrўsēndĕtă, ōrŭm, n. pl., *vases adorned with gold and diamonds.* Tĕgūnt chrўsēndĕtă mūllī, Mart. V. Vas.

Chrўsēs, æ, m., *a priest of Apollo.* Prŏ nātă Chrўsēn, Ov.

Chrўsĕŭs, ă, ŭm, *of gold.* Chrўsĕă quī dĕdĕrăt, Mart.

Chrўsīppŭs, ī, m., *a stoic philosopher.* Mĕlĭŭs Chrўsīppŏ, Hor.

chrўsŏlĭthŭs, ī, m., *a chrysolite.* Pĕr jŭgă chrўsŏlĭthī, Ov. Epith. Flāvēscēns, aūrĕŭs, rŭtĭlāns, rŭtĭlŭs, splēndĭdŭs, mĭcāns, crŏcĕŭs. V. Gemma.

chrўsophrўs, ўŏs, f., *a sea-fish.* Ēt aūrī Chrўsŏphrўs, Ov.

Chrўsŏstŏmŭs, ī, m., *a Father of the Church.* Trāxĭt Chrўsŏstŏmŭs ōrĕ. Epith. Dĭsērtŭs, fācūndŭs.

Chthŏnĭŭs, ĭī, m., *the name of a warrior.* Chthŏnĭŭs quŏquĕ, Ov.

chўmĭcŭs, ă, ŭm, *chymical.* Chўmĭca ădūltĕrĭă, Mart.

cĭbārĭa, ōrŭm, n. pl., *victuals.* Cōngēstā cĭbārĭā sīcŭt, Hor. Syn. Ālĭmēntă, cĭbī, ēscæ, vīctŭs.

cĭbātŭs, ūs, m., *meat.* Pĕcŭdŭmquĕ cĭbātŭs, Lucr. Syn. Cĭbŭs, ēscă.

cĭbo, ās, *to eat.* Quāquĕ cĭbēntŭr, Lucr. Syn. Nūtrĭo, pāsco, ălo. V. Nutrio.

cĭbōrĭŭm, ĭī, n., *a large drinking-cup, like a sort of Egyptian bean.* Cĭbōrĭa ēxplē, Hor.

cĭbŭs, ī, m., *food.* Hīc cĭbŭs ūtĭlĭs ægrō, Ov. Syn. Escă, dăpēs, ĕpŭlæ, ālĭmēntŭm, vīctŭs. Epith. Săpĭdŭs, dūlcĭs, grātŭs, lætŭs, rēgĭŭs, sōlēnnĭs, ŏpīmŭs, ūtĭlĭs, pārcŭs, vīlĭs, mēndīcātŭs.

cĭcădă, æ, f., *a grasshopper.* Ārbūstă cĭcādæ, Virg. Epith. Raŭcă, ārgŭtă, æstīvă, vōcālĭs, strīdēns, rĕsŏnāns, dūlcĭsŏnă, grăcĭlĭs, dūlcĭs, cāmpēstrĭs, agrēstĭs, ēxīlĭs, cāntātrīx, lŏquāx, gārrŭlă, īmprŏvĭdă, mălĕsānă, văgă, sālĭtātrīx, strīdŭlă, lĕvĭs.

cĭcātrīx, īcĭs, f., *a wound.* Cērnĕ cĭcātrīcēs, Ov. Syn. Ūlcŭs. Epith. Fœdă, mārcĭdă, vĕtŭs, ōbdūctă, tūrpĭs, dēfōrmĭs. V. Vulnus.

cĭcĕr, ĕrĭs, n., *vetches.* Sēpŏsĭtĭ cĭcĕrĭs, Hor. Syn. Cĭcĕră, cĭcērcŭlă.

Cĭcĕro, ōnĭs, m., *the Roman orator.* Cĭcĕrōnĭs hăbĕt, Mart. Syn. Tŭllĭŭs, Ārpīnās. Epith. Dĭsērtŭs, fācūndŭs, dīvīnŭs, dōctŭs, māgnŭs, ēlŏquēns, Rōmānŭs, mēllĭtŭs, mēllĭflŭŭs, aŭdāx, sūbtīlĭs, pŏtēns, fūlmĭnĕŭs, tŏnāns, nŭmĕrōsŭs, cōncīnnŭs, īngĕnĭōsŭs, mīrāndŭs, clārŭs, vērbōsŭs, flēxănĭmŭs, īnsīgnĭs, īllūstrĭs, ămbĭtĭōsŭs, sōlērs, săgāx.

cĭchŏrĕă, æ, f., *and* ŭm, ī, n., *succory.* Mĕ cĭchŏrĕă lĕvēsquĕ mālvæ, Hor. Syn. Intŭbŭs, īntўbŭm.

Cĭcŏnēs, ŭm, m. pl., *a people of Thrace.* Sprētæ Cĭcŏnŭm, Virg.

cĭcōnĭă, æ, f., *a stork.* Crēpĭtāntĕ cĭcōnĭā rōstrō, Ov. Epith. Grăcĭlĭs, pĭă, ālbă.

cĭcŭr, ŭrĭs, ĕ, *tame.* Quī cĭcŭrūm sēnsūs, Man. Syn. Mānsuēfāctŭs, cĭcŭrātŭs, plăcĭdŭs, mītĭs.

cĭcŭro, ās, *to tame.* Rēs cĭcŭrārĕ nĕquĕ, Pac. Syn. Mānsuēfăcĭo, mītĭgo, lēnĭo.

cĭcūtă, æ, f., *a poison.* Epith. Frăgĭlĭs, vĭrĭdĭs, mœstă, cānă, gĕlĭdă, dīră, sævă, frīgĭdă, lēthĭfĕră, lēthālĭs, vēnēnōsă, vēnēnĭfĕră, frīgēns, fūnēstă, mōrtĭfĕră, trīstĭs, ālgĭdă, hōrrēndă, tōrpēns, ēxĭtĭōsă, ēxĭtĭālĭs, nōxĭă, nŏcŭă, īmmĕdĭcābĭlĭs, glăcĭālĭs. V. Fistula.

cĭĕo, cĭvī, cĭtŭm, *to excite.* Vōcĕ cĭĕmŭs, Virg. Syn. Pērcĭĕo, mŏvĕo, ēxcĭto, cōncĭto, ănĭmo, āccēndo, stĭmŭlo, cōmmŏvĕo ; vŏco, āccĭĕo.

Cĭlĭcĭă, æ, f., *a kingdom of Asia.* Syn. Tēllūs, *or* tērră, Cĭlĭssă. Epith. Crŏcīs ăbūndāns, crŏcī fĕrāx.

cĭlĭŭm, ĭī, n., *hair of the eyelids.* Sētĭs, cĭlĭŏvĕ, Pr. V. Supercilium.

Cĭlĭx, īcĭs, m., *and* Cĭlĭssă, æ, f., Cĭlĭcēs, ŭm, m. pl., *of Cilicia ; inhabitants of Cilicia.* Ēt Cĭlĭcēs nīmbīs, Mart. Epith. Fĕrī, văgī, īmmānēs, īmmītēs, īntōnsī, crŏcĕī, fĕrōcēs.

Cĭllă, æ, f., *a city of Troas.* Chrўsēnque ēt Cĭllăm, Ov.

Cĭmbĕr, brī, m., Cĭmbrī, ōrŭm, m. pl., *inhabitants of the banks of the Baltic sea.* Cĭmbrŭmquĕ rŭēntĕm, Lucr. Epith. Bĭbācēs, bēllācēs, bēllĭgĕrī, fŭrēntēs, fŭrĭbūndī, fōrtēs.

*cĭmēx, īcĭs, m., *a kind of fly.* Epith. Fœdŭs, fœtĭdŭs, rōdēns, ĕdāx.

Cĭmīnŭs, ī, m., *a mountain of Etruria.* Ēt Cĭmīnī, Virg.

Cĭmmĕrĭŭs, ă, ŭm ; Cĭmmĕrĭī, ōrŭm, m. pl., *Cimmerian ; the inhabitants of Crimea.* Est prŏpĕ Cĭmmĕrĭōs, Ov. Syn. Scўthæ, Ārctōī pŏpŭlī. Epith. Frīgĭdī, gĕlĭdī, ālgēntēs, ālgĭdī, Hўpērbŏrĕī, Ārctōī, lătĕbrōsī, tĕnĕbrōsī.

Cĭmōlŭs, ī, m., *an island of the Ægean sea.* Rŭră Cĭmōlī, Ov.

cĭnără, æ, *or* cĭnărē, ēs, f., *an artichoke.* Pŏnātŭr cĭnărē, Colum.—2. *the name of a woman.* Sŭb rēgnō Cĭnāræ, Hor.

cīnctūtŭs, ă, ŭm, *wearing a girdle.* Fīngĕrĕ cīnctūtīs, Hor.

cĭnædĭcŭs, ă, ŭm, *rakish.* Cāntātĭō cĭnædĭcă, Plaut.

cĭnædŭs, ī, m., *a rake.* Īmprŏbĭs cĭnædīs, (Phal.) Cat. Epith. Īmpūrŭs, ōbscœnŭs, pĕtŭlāns, prŏcāx, īmprŏbŭs, prŏtērvŭs, īmpŭdēns.

cīnctŭs, ūs, m., *a man's girdle.* Cīnctūquĕ Găbīnō, Virg.

cĭnĕfāctŭs, ă, ŭm, *reduced to ashes.* Hōrrĭfĭcō cĭnĕfāctŭm, Lucr.

cĭnĕrārĭŭs, ĭī, m., *a woman's hair-dresser.* Nūnc tŭŭm cĭnĕrārĭŭs, Cat. Syn. Cĭnīflo.

cĭngo, xĭ, ctŭm, *to tie about.* Cŭm cĭngĕrĕt Albăm, Virg. Syn. Ambĭo, cĭr-cŭmdo, cŏrōno, cĭrcŭmcĭngo, ŏbĕo, ĭnclūdo, sēpĭo, āmplēctŏr, cŏmprĕhēndo, *or* cŏmprēndo.

cĭngŭlă, æ, f., *a girth.* Cĭngŭlă lædăt, Ov.

cĭngŭlŭm, ĭ, n., *a woman's girdle.* Cĭngŭlă būllĭs, Virg. Syn. Bāltĕŭs, zōnă, cĭnctŭs. Epith. Aūrĕŭm, aūrātŭm, prĕtĭōsŭm, pĭctŭm, fŭlgēns, lĕvĕ, hăbĭ.ĕ. V. Balteus.

cĭnĭflo, ōnĭs, m., *a woman's hair-dresser.* Lēctĭcă, cĭnĭflōnēs, Hor. Syn. Cĭnĕrārĭŭs. cĭnĭs, ĕrĭs, m., *ashes.* Fĭdēs cĭnĕrī prōmĭssă, Virg. Epith. Fŭmăns, fērvēns, ēxĭgŭŭs, vērmĭfĕr, ădūstŭs, ĭngrātŭs, ātĕr, tĕpĭdŭs, ĭmmūndŭs, tĕnŭĭs, lĕvĭs, sēpŭlchrālĭs, trĭstĭs, săcĕr. V. Manes.

Cĭnnă, æ, m., *the name of a man.* Nēc dīcĕrĕ Cĭnnă, Virg.

cĭnnămŭm, *or* nămŏn, ĭ, n., *cinnamon.* Cĭnnămă flāmmœ, Ov. Cĭnnămōn, ēx-tērnă, Luc. Epith. Ŏdōrŭm, rĕdŏlēns, ărōmātĭcŭm, ŏdōrātŭm, ŏdōrĭfĕrŭm, grātŭm, frăgrāns, spīrāns, ŏlēns, suāvĕ, dūlcĕ, jūcŭndŭm, āmœnŭm.

Cĭnўphĭŭs, ă, ŭm, *of Libya.* Cĭnўphĭī tŏndēnt, Virg.

Cĭnўrās, æ, m., *king of Cyprus, the father of Myrrha.* Vīrgĭnĕī Cĭnўrās, Ov. cĭo, cĭs, cīvī *and* cĭī, cĭtŭm, *to excite, call.* Sūbĭgēntēs cĭmŭs ăd ōrtŭs, Lucr. V. Cieo.

Cīppŭs, ĭ, m., *a noble Roman.* Cīppŭs ĭn ūndă, Ov.—2. *a tombstone.* Cīppŭs ĭn ăgrŭm, Hor.

circă, adv., *about, around.* Bŏŭm cīrcă māctāntŭr, Virg. Syn. Cīrcŭm, cīrcĭtĕr.

Cīrcă, æ, *and* ē, ēs, f., *daughter of the Sun, and a famous sorceress.* Et Cīrcæ pŏcŭlă, Hor. Cārmĭnĭbŭs Cīrcē sŏcĭōs, Virg. Syn. Tītānĭs ; fīlĭă Pērsēs, Sōlĕ sătă. Epith. Tītānĭă, Phœbĕă, vĕnēfĭcă, cāllĭdă, Dædălă ; măgĭcă, dōctă, pŭlchră, īnsĭdĭōsă.

Cīrceīī, ōrŭm, m. pl., *a city of Latium.* Ōstrĕă Cīrceīīs, Hor.

Cīrcēnsĭs, *of the circus.* Cīrcēnsēs, ĭŭm, m. pl., *(lūdī) games of the circus.* Cīr-cēnsĭbŭs āctĭs, Virg.

Cīrcĕŭs *or* cœŭs, ă, ŭm, *of Circe.* Prōxĭmă Cīrcĕœ, Virg.

cīrcĭno, ās, *to compass around.* Cīrcĭnăt Irĭs, Man.

cīrcĭnŭs, ĭ, m., *a compass.* Cīrcĭnŭs ānnŭm, Aus.

cīrcĭtĕr, adv., *about, nearly.* Cīrcĭtĕr hōrăm, Hor. Syn. Cīrcă, ăd, sŭb (*with an accus.*) ; fĕrĕ, pænĕ, fērmĕ.

Cīrcĭŭs, ĭī, m., *a north-west wind.* Lĭttŏră tūrbăt Cīrcĭŭs, Luc.

cīrcŭĭtŭs, ŭs, m., *a winding, circuit.* Sœvăquĕ cīrcŭĭtū, Ov. Syn. Ambĭtŭs, ōrbĭs, cīrcŭlŭs, gўrŭs.

cīrcŭlātŏr, ōrĭs, m., *a mountebank.* Fālsŭs cīrcŭlātŏr dĕcĭpĭt, (Iamb.) Prud. Syn. Præstīgĭātŏr, hīstrĭo, lūdĭo, lūdĭŭs, mīmŭs.

cīrcŭlātrīx, īcĭs, f., *a strolling woman.* Prŏbră cīrcŭlātrīcĭs, (Scaz.) Mart.

* cīrcŭlo, ās, *and* ŏr, ārĭs, *to compass about, encircle.* Syn. Cīngo, ămbĭo, cīr-cŭmdo.

cīrcŭlŭs, ĭ, m., *a circle.* Cīrcŭlŭs aūrī, Virg. Syn. Ōrbĭs, ōrbĭcŭlŭs, cīrcŭĭtŭs, ămbĭtŭs, gўrŭs. Epith. Flēxĭlĭs, ŏblīquŭs, tōrtĭlĭs, rŏtūndŭs. V. Gyrus.

cīrcŭm, prep. *and* adv., *about, around.* Tēmpŏră cīrcŭm, Virg. Prŏpĕrārī lĭttŏrĕ cīrcŭm, Id.

cīrcŭmăgo, ĭs, ēgī, āctŭm, *to turn around.* Ŏpŭs ēst tē cīrcŭmăgī, Hor. Syn. Cīrcŭmfĕro, cīrcŭmdūco, cīrcŭmvōlvo.

cīrcŭmcīdo, īdī, īsŭm, *to cut about.* Cīrcŭmcīdĕrĕ suētōs, T. Syn. Cīrcŭmsĕco, rĕsĕco, āmpŭto. V. Scindo.

cīrcŭmcīsŭs, ă, ŭm, *the pass. partic. of* circumcido, *circumcised.* Cīrcŭmcīsŭs ădēst, Arat.

cīrcŭmclāmo, ās, *to cry about.* Cīrcŭmclāmătă prŏcēllĭs, Sidon. V. Clamo.

cīrcŭmclūdo, ĭs, sī, sŭm, *to enclose around.* V. Claudo, cingo.

cīrcŭmdătŭs, ă, ŭm, *the pass. partic. of* circumdo. Cīrcŭmdătŭs ālĭs, Tib.

cīrcŭmdo, dĕdī, dătŭm, *to compass about.* Cīrcŭmdĕdĭt ārcēs, Virg. Syn. Ambĭo, cīngo, cŏrōno, sēpĭo, cīrcŭmcĭngo, cīrcŭmvāllo, ŏbĕo. V. Cingo.

cīrcŭmĕo, *or* cīrcŭĕo, ĭs, ĭī, ĭrĕ, *to go around.* Cīrcŭmĭĕrĕ căpŭt, Prop. Cīrcŭĭt, ēt quæ, Virg. Syn. Ŏbĕo, ŏbāmbŭlo, pĕragro, pĕrērro, lūstro, pĕrlūstro ; ămbĭo, cīngo.

cīrcŭmfĕro, tŭlī, lātŭm, *to carry about.* Cīrcŭmtŭlĭt ūndă, Virg. Syn. Cīrcŭm-dūco, cīrcŭmvĕho.

cĭrcŭmflĕcto, ĭs, *to bend about.* Cĭrcŭmflĕctĕrĕ cŭrsŭs, Virg. V. Flecto.

cĭrcŭmflo, ās, *to blow on all sides.* Cĭrcŭmflāntĭbŭs Aŭstrĭs, Stat.

cĭrcŭmflŭo, ĭs, flŭxī, *to flow about.* Cĭrcŭmflŭĭt ŭndă, Mart. Syn. Cĭrcŭmlăbŏr, cĭrcŭmfŭndŏr, cĭrcŭmlŭo, āllŭo.

cĭrcŭmflŭŭs, ă, ŭm, *flowing about.* Cĭrcŭmflŭŭs āmnĭs, Ov. Syn. Cĭrcŭmflŭēns.

cĭrcŭmfŭndo, ĭs, ūdī, ĕrĕ, *to pour around.* Cĭrcŭmfŭndĭmŭr ārmĭs, Virg.

cĭrcŭmfūsŭs, ă, ŭm, *the pass. partic. of* circumfundo. Nām cĭrcŭmfūsō cōnsĭstĭt, Tib.

cĭrcŭmgĕmo, ĭs, *to groan about.* Cĭrcŭmgĕmĭt ūrsŭs ŏvīlĕ, Hor.

cĭrcŭmlātŭs, ă, ŭm, *the pass. partic. of* circumfero. Cĭrcŭmlātă dīū, Mart.

cĭrcŭmlĭgo, ās, *to tie about.* Cĭrcŭmlĭgăt īllă vīnclō, Stat. Syn. Necto, vīncĭo. V. Ligo.

cĭrcŭmlĭno, ĭs, *to anoint all over.* Cĭrcŭmlĭnĭt hȳdrŏs, Ov.

cĭrcŭmlĭtŭs, ă, ŭm, *the pass. partic. of* circumlino. Cĭrcŭmlĭtă sāxă, Hor.

cĭrcŭmpōno, ĭs, *to put around.* Cĭrcŭmpōsŭĭssĕ cătĭllīs, Hor. Syn. Pōno cĭrcŭm, cĭrcŭmfŭndo.

cĭrcŭmpŏsĭtŭs, ă, ŭm, *the pass. partic. of* circumpono. Sēmpĕr ĕnĭm cĭrcŭm-pŏsĭtŭs, Lucr.

cĭrcŭmquāquĕ, adv., *from all sides.* Cĭrcŭmquāquĕ pătēns, Man. Syn. Ŭndĭquĕ, ŭndĭcŭnquĕ.

cĭrcŭmrētĭo, ĭs, *to surround with snares.* Cĭrcŭmrētĭt ĕnĭm, Lucr.

cĭrcŭmrĭgŭŭs, ă, ŭm, *watered around.* Ĕt cĭrcŭmrĭgŭō, Prop.

cĭrcŭmrōdo, ĭs, *to gnaw about, to detract.* Cŭm cĭrcŭmrōdĭtŭr, ēcquĭd, Hor.

cĭrcŭmsālto, ās, *to dance around.* Cĭrcŭmsāltāntĕ chŏrō, Prud.

cĭrcŭmscrībo, ĭs, *to circumscribe.* Quŏt cĭrcŭmscrīpsĕrĭt, Juv. Syn. Cōnclūdo, cōmprēndo, dēfīnĭo, līmĭto.

cĭrcŭmsĭlĭo, ĭs, *to leap around.* Tŭm cĭrcŭmsĭlĭēns, Cat.

cĭrcŭmsĭsto, ĭs, *to stand around.* Ārmātī cĭrcŭmsĭstŭnt, Virg.

cĭrcŭmsŏno, ās, *to sound all about.* Cĭrcŭmsŏnăt ārmĭs, Virg.

cĭrcŭmsŏnŭs, ă, ŭm, *resounding around.* Cĭrcŭmsŏnă tērrĕt, Ov.

cĭrcŭmspēctŭs, ūs, m., *a looking around.* Ĭn cĭrcŭmspēctū, Ov.

cĭrcŭmspĭcĭo, ĭs, spēxĭ, *to look around.* Dīvērsī cĭrcŭmspĭcĭŭnt, Virg. V. Aspicio.

cĭrcŭmstĭpo, ās, *to guard around.* Cĭrcŭmstīpāntĕ cătĕrvā, Sil.

cĭrcŭmsto, stĕtī, *to stand about.* Cĭrcŭmstĕtĭt ŭndă, Virg. Syn. Stŏ cĭrcŭm, cĭrcŭmsĭsto; cĭngo, āmbĭo.

cĭrcŭmtĕgo, ĭs, xĭ, *to cover all over.* Cĭrcŭmtĕgĭt ōmnĭă, Lucr.

cĭrcŭmtēxo, ĭs, *to weave all around.* Ĕt cĭrcŭmtēxtŭm, Virg.

cĭrcŭmtŏno, ās, *to thunder from all sides.* Hŭnc cĭrcŭmtŏnŭĭt, Hor.

cĭrcŭmtrĕmo, ĭs, ŭī, *to tremble around.* Cĭrcŭmtrĕmĕre æthĕră sĭgnĭs, Lucr.

cĭrcŭmvăgŭs, ă, ŭm, *wandering round about.* Cĭrcŭmvăgă flămmæ, Ov.

cĭrcŭmvāllo, ās, *to trench about.* Cĭrcŭmvāllāvĕrăt ōrbĕ, Sil. Syn. Vāllo, ŏb-vāllo. V. Vallo.

* cĭrcŭmvĕho, ĭs, xĭ, *to carry about.* Cæs.; *and* vēcto, ās, [*the frequent.*] Frūstrā cĭrcŭmvĕhŏr, Virg. Cĭrcŭmvēctāmŭr ămŏrĕ, Id.

cĭrcŭmvĕnĭo, ĭs, vēnī, vēntŭm, *to surround.* Mŭltă sēnēm cĭrcŭmvĕnĭŭnt, Hor. Syn. Cĭrcŭmdo, āmbĭo, cĭngo, ŏbsĭdĕo.

cĭrcŭmvērto, ĭs, *to turn round.* Cĭrcŭmvērtĭtŭr āxĕm, Virg.

cĭrcŭmvŏlĭto, ās, *to fly about.* Cĭrcŭmvŏlĭtāvĭt hĭrŭndo, Virg. Syn. Vŏlĭto, vŏlo cĭrcŭm.

cĭrcŭmvŏlo, ās, *to fly around.* Cĭrcŭmvŏlăt ŭmbră, Virg.

cĭrcŭmvŏlvo, ĭs, vī, ĕrĕ, *to roll round.* Sōl cĭrcŭmvŏlvĭtŭr ānnŭm, Virg.

cĭrcŭs, ī, m., *circle, circus.* Cĭrcŭs ădhŭc, Ov. Syn. Cĭrcŭĭtŭs, āmbĭtŭs, cĭrcŭlŭs. Epith. Cĕlĕbĕr, māgnŭs, lōngŭs, căpāx, clāmōsŭs, ōblīquŭs, cūrvŭs, māgnĭĭcŭs, fēstŭs, ăpērtŭs, pătēns, spătĭōsŭs.

cĭrĭs, ĭs, f., *a kind of lark.* Cĭrĭs, ĕt ā tōnsō. V. Scylla.

cĭrrātŭs, ă, ŭm, *having curled hair.* Cĭrrātă cătĕrvā, Mart.

Cĭrrhă, æ, f., *a city near Delphi; the oracle.* Cĭrrhă sĭlĕt, Luc.

cĭrrŭs, ī, m., *a curl, hair in curl.* Cōrnŭă cĭrrō, Juv.

Cĭssēĭs, ĭdĭs, f., *daughter of Cisseus, Hecuba.* Cĭssēĭs prægnāns, Virg.

cĭsĭŭm, ĭī, n., *a two-wheeled chariot.* Vēl cĭsĭō trĭjŭgī, Aus.

cĭstă, æ, f., *a basket.* Cĭstă lĭbēllōs, Juv. Syn. Ārcă, cĭstŭlă, călăthŭs, cănĭstrŭm. Epith. Căvă, tĕxtă, vĭmĭnĕă, cŏncăvă, căpāx, āmplă, pătŭlă, claūsă, lĭgnĕă, pīctă.

cĭstērnă, æ, f., *a cistern.* Sĭt cīstērnă mĭhī, quām vīnĕă, mālŏ, Mart.

cĭstĭfĕr, ă, ŭm, *that carries a basket.* Gēllĭă cīstĭfĕrō, Mart.

cĭtātĭm, adv., *hastily.* Præcūrsĭbŭs āptă cĭtātĭm, Fill.

cĭtātŭs, ă, ŭm, *swift.* Cătŭlīs cĭtătă rāptīs, (Phal.) Mart. Syn. Cĭtŭs, cĕlĕr, vēlōx, prŏpĕrāns.

Cĭthærōn, ōnĭs, m., *one of the tops of Parnassus.* Clāmŏrĕ Cĭthærōn, Virg. V. Cytheron.

cĭthără, æ, f., *a lyre.* Nēc stŭdĭō cĭthăræ, Hor. Syn. Chĕlўs, lўră, bārbĭtŭs, tēstūdo, plēctrŭm, fĭdēs. Epith. Ōrphĕă, Ōrphēĭă, Thrācĭă, Thrēīcĭă, Ōdrўsĭă, Rhŏdŏpēĭă, Ărīōnĭă, Amphīōnĭă, Ăpōllĭnĕă, Dēlĭăcă, Phœbēă, Pĭērĭă, Ăŏnĭă, ĭmbēllĭs, bĭcōrnĭs, rĕsŏnāns, cānŏră, blāndă, vōcālĭs, aūrĕă, ārgūtă, sŏnāns, dūlcĭsŏnāns, quĕrŭlă, ĕbūrnă, ĕbūrnĕă, jūcūndă, tīnnŭlă, dūlcĭsŏnă, grātă, sŏnōră. V. Lyra, fides.

cĭthărīstă, æ, m., *a harper.* Āltērnīs cĭthărīstă tōtō, Paulin. V. Citharœdus.

cĭthărīzo, ās, *to play on the harp.* Ēt cĭthărīzāntēs, Mant. Syn. Cĭthărām pūlso, tāngo. V. Cithara.

cĭthărœdŭs, ī, m., *who plays on the harp.* Dē quā cĭthărœdŭs Ēchīon, Juv. Syn. Cĭthărīstă, cĭthărām pūlsāns ; cĭthăræ pūlsāndæ pĕrītŭs, fĭdĭcĕn. Epith. Insĭgnĭs, blāndŭs, grātŭs, lætŭs, dūlcĭsŏnŭs, Phœbēŭs, Ăpōllĭnĕŭs, mŭlcēns, Ăŏnĭŭs, Pĭērĭŭs.

cĭtĭmŭs, ă, ŭm, *next, nearest.* Quā cĭtĭmŭs līmēs, Fulg. Syn. Prŏxĭmŭs, vīcīnŭs.

cĭtĭŭs, *the compar. of* cito. Sīc ăĭt, ēt dīctō cĭtĭŭs, Virg. Syn. Vēlōcĭŭs. V. Cito.

cĭto, adv., *quickly.* Nām cĭtŏ fāctŭm, Luc. Illĕ cĭtō mŏnĭtŭs, Mant. Syn. Cōnfēstĭm, rĕpēntĕ, sŭbĭtō, mōx, cōntĭnŭō, ēxtēmplō, prōtĭnŭs, haūd mŏră. V. Celeriter.

cĭto, ās, *to summon.* Sī quāndŏ cĭtābĕrĕ, Juv. Syn. Cĭĕo, vŏco ; ūrgĕo.

citrā, prep., *on this side, without.* Cĭtrāquĕ cārnĭs, (Phal.) Quŏs ŭltrā cītrāquĕ nĕquĭt, Hor. Syn. Cĭs, hīnc ; ābsquĕ.

citrĕŭs, ă, ŭm, *of the citron-tree.* Scrībĭtŭr īn cĭtrēĭs, Pers. Syn. Citrĭnŭs.

citrō, adv., *thither.* Ūltrō cītrōquĕ pĕr aūrās, Lucr. Syn. Hūc.

citrŭs, ī, f., *the citron-tree ; and* citrŭm, ī, n., *citron-wood.* Sēd cītrī cōntēntă, Lucan. Pōndĕră rără cĭtrī, Mart. Epith. Maūrūsĭăcă, Aphrŏdīsĭă, Cўthĕrēĭă ; Ădōnĭă, frōndōsă, ŏdōrātă, bārbără, Atlāntĭcă.

cĭtŭs, ă, ŭm, *the pass. partic. of* cieo, *quick.* Sōlvĭtĕ vēlă cĭtī, Virg. Syn. Cĕlĕr, vēlōx, cĭtātŭs, pērnīx, prōmptŭs, præpĕs, vŏlŭcĕr, lĕvĭs, fēstīnŭs, prŏpĕrŭs, vŏlāns. V. Velox, celer.

cĭvĭcŭs, ă, ŭm, *of a city.* Cīvĭcă bēllă, Ov.

cīvīlĭs, ĕ, *belonging to citizens.* Ăd cīvīlĭă vērtĕt, Ov. Syn. Cīvĭcŭs, ūrbānŭs, nĭtĭs, lĕpĭdŭs, cōmĭs, pōlītŭs.

cīvīlĭtĕr, adv., *as a citizen, civilly.* Ōdĭō cīvīlĭtĕr ūsŭs, Ov.

cīvĭs, ĭs, m., *a citizen.* Āt fēssī tāndēm cīvēs, Virg. Syn. Incŏlă. Epith. Clārŭs, nōbĭlĭs, āntĭquŭs, īnsĭgnĭs, cĕlĕbĕr.

cīvĭtās, ātĭs, f., *a city.* Tū cīvĭtātĕm, (Alcaic.) Hor. Syn. Ūrbs, ŏppĭdŭm. Epith. Clără, pūlchră, āntĭquă, sŭpērbă, pŏtēns, bēllĭcă, mūnītă, sēcūră, ĭmpăvĭdă, ĭnăcēssă. V. Urbs.

clādēs, ĭs, f., *slaughter, misfortune.* Clādĭbŭs īrrŭĭmŭs, Lucan. Syn. Cædēs, strāgēs, cāsŭs, fūnĕră. Epith. Tētră, trīstĭs, bēllĭcă mōrtĭfĕră, ăcērbă, īnīquă, ĭmmēnsă, sævă, fūnēstă, āspĕră, mĭsĕră, crŭēntă, sāngŭĭnĕă, crūdēlĭs, nēfāndă, hōrrĭdă, fœdă, īnfāndă, ēxĭtĭōsă, ēxĭtĭālĭs, fŭrĭōsă, lāmēntābĭlĭs, rĕpēntīnă, fĕrālĭs, lūctŭōsă, hōrrēndă, fĕră, dīră, Māvōrtĭă, pērnĭcĭōsă. V. Occisio, strages.

clăm, adv., *secretly.* Clăm fērrō īncaūtŭm, Virg. Syn. Clāncŭlŭm, clāncŭlō.

clămĭto, ās, *the frequent. of* clamo. Quătĕrquĕ clămĭtărĭs, (Phal.) Mart.

clămo, ās, *to cry, proclaim aloud.* Clāmābīs căpĭtī, Prop. Syn. Exclāmo, cōnclāmo, vōcĭfĕrōr. V. Clamor, echo.

clămŏr, ōrĭs, m., *a loud voice.* Vŏcānt clāmōrĭbŭs hōstĕm, Virg. Syn. Vōx, sŏnŭs, sŏnĭtŭs, mūrmŭr, frĕmĭtŭs, strĕpĭtŭs, frăgŏr, plāngŏr, ŭlŭlātŭs, gĕmĭtŭs, lāmēntŭm, quēstŭs, mūgītŭs. Epith. Flēbĭlĭs, dīssŏnŭs, hōrrēndŭs, răbĭdŭs, hōrrĭsŏnŭs, tērrĭfĭcŭs, īngēns, lætŭs, fœmĭnĕŭs, cōnfūsŭs, văgŭs, tērrĭbĭlĭs, frĕmēns, pŏpŭlārĭs, quĕrŭlŭs, īnsānŭs, īnsŏlēns, īnsŏlĭtŭs, mŏlēstŭs, rĕsŏnāns, rĕsŏnŭs, ēĭnīssŭs, tūrbĭdŭs, nĭmĭŭs, mŭlĭēbrĭs, raŭcŭs, sŭbĭtŭs, faŭstŭs, rĕpĕtītŭs, lĭcrātŭs, Ĭnānĭs, trĭŭmphālĭs. V. Clamo, murmur.

clāmōsŭs, ă, ŭm, *clamorous.* Lĕvĭs clāmōsă Mŏlŏssī, Lucan. Syn. Clāmāns, ēxclāmāns, clāmŏrĕ rĕsūltāns, frĕmēns.

clāncŭlārĭŭs, ă, ŭm, *secret, anonymous.* Quĭdăm clāncŭlārĭŭs spārgĭt, Mart.

clāncŭlŭm, adv., *secretly.* Intĕr sē clāncŭlŭm, Ter. V. Clam.

clāndēstīnŭs, ă, ŭm, *clandestine.* Ceū clāndēstīnō, Sil. Syn. Ārcānŭs, sēcrētŭs, ŏccŭltŭs.

clāngo, ĭs, xī, ĕrĕ, *to sound, resound.* Hōrrĭdă clāngūnt, Virg.

clāngŏr, ōrĭs, m., *the sound of a trumpet; a cry, scream.* Quătĭūnt clāngōrĭbŭs ālās, Virg. Syn. Tūbārūm sŏnŭs, strĕpĭtŭs. Epith. Raŭcŭs, lūctĭfĭcŭs, saevŭs, Mārtĭŭs, rĕsŏnāns, tĕrrĭfĭcŭs, aerĭsŏnŭs, hŏrrĭsŏnŭs, trĕmŭlŭs, mĭuāx, crĕbĕr, hōrrēndŭs, sŏnāns, rĕsŏnŭs, strīdēns, frĕmēns, trīstĭs, Māvōrtĭŭs, bĕllĭcŭs, hōrrēns, hōrrĭdŭs. V. Classicum, tuba.

Clănĭs, ĭs, m., *the name of a warrior.* Jăcŭlŭm Clănĭs, Ov.—2. *a river of Etruria.* Ĕt Clănĭs, Sil.

Clănĭŭs, ĭī, m., *a river of Campania.* Ĕt văcŭĭs Clănĭŭs, Virg.

clārĕo, ŭī, *to shine.* Glŏrĭă clārĕt, Enn. Syn. Clārēsco, ēnĭtĕo. V. Luceo.

clārēsco, ĭs, ĕrĕ, *to become bright or clear.* Clārēscānt ātrĭă vĭllĭs, Virg.

‖ clārĭsŏnŭs, ă, ŭm, *sounding clear.* Clārĭsŏnās īmō, Cat.

clārĭtăs, ātĭs, f., *clearness, brightness.* Cūm clārĭtātĭs vēnĕrĭs, (Iamb.) Laber. Syn. Splēndŏr, lūx, lūmĕn, (V. Lux,) hŏnŏr, fāmă, nŏmĕn. V. Honor.

Clārĭŭs, ă, ŭm, *of Claros.* Clārĭō Dēlŏs, Ov.—2. m., *Apollo.* Clārĭī laūrŏs, Virg.

clāro, ās, *to clear, make famous.* Clārābĭt pŭgĭlĕm, Hor. Syn. Illūstro; nŏmĕn, fāmăm dō, cōnfĕro.

Clārŏs, ī, f., *an island of the Ægean sea.* Ĕt Clărŏs ēt Tĕnĕdŏs, Ov. Epith. Phœbĕă, Ăpŏllĭnĕă, Dēlĭă, fācŭndă.

clārŭs, ă, ŭm, *clear, famous.* Clārŭs ēt ŏstrō, Virg. Syn. Pērspĭcŭŭs, dīlūcĭdŭs, pēllūcĭdŭs, lūcĭdŭs, splēndĭdŭs, nĭtĭdŭs; V. Lucidus. Ēvĭdēns, ăpērtŭs, mănĭfēstŭs, nŏtŭs, nŏtīssĭmŭs, nŏn ŏbscūrŭs; cĕlēbrĭs, īnsīgnĭs, īllūstrĭs, ēxĭmĭŭs, ēgrĕgĭŭs, praestāns. V. Illustris.

clāssĭcŭm, ī, n., *the blast of trumpets; a trumpet.* Clāssĭcă jāmquĕ sŏnānt, Virg. Syn. Tūbă, būccĭnă, cōrnŭ; tŭbārūm frĕmĭtŭs, strĕpĭtŭs, clāngŏr. Epith. Fĕrālĕ, Mārtĭŭm, fĕrŭm, tūrbĭdŭm, Māvōrtĭŭm. V. Tuba.

clāssĭcŭs, ă, ŭm, *belonging to a fleet.* Clāssĭcă bēllă, Prop. Syn. Nāvālĭs.

clāssĭs, ĭs, f., *a fleet.* Clāssĭbŭs hīc lŏcŭs, Virg. Epith. Ærātă, lūnātă, prŏfŭgă, vŏlucrĭs, vēlĭvŏlă, flūmĭnĕă, ārmātă, quāssātă, æquŏrĕă, fŭgāx, cĭtă, dēnsă, Mārtĭă, flūctĭvăgă, bēllĭcă. V. Nuvis.

clāthrātŭs, ă, ŭm, *latticed.* Sēptĭs clāthrātŭs ăhēnĭs, Mart. Syn. Sēptŭs, claŭsŭs, cāncēllātŭs.

clāthrŭs, ī, m., *or* rŭm, ī, n., *a lattice.* Frāngĕrĕ clāthrŏs, Hor. Syn. Cāncēllī, claŭstră, sēptă.

clāvă, æ, f., *a club.* Ipsă căpĭt clāvāmquĕ grăvĕm, Ov. Syn. Stīpĕs Hērcŭlĕă. Epith. Trīnōdĭs, dŏmitrīx, trăbālĭs, Hērcŭlĕă, dūră, trĕmēndă, hōrrēndă, crŭēntă, lĕtĭfĕră, rĕcūrvă, vīctrīx, īmmītĭs, vŭlnĭfĭcă, pōndĕrōsă.

Claudĭă, æ, f., *the name of a Vestal.* Claudĭă quīntă gĕnŭs, Ov.

Claudĭŭs, ĭī *or* ī, m., *the name of several noble Romans.* Ābstŭlĭt ārmĭs Claudĭŭs.

claudĭco, ās, *to be lame.* Claudĭcăt īllĕ, Ov.

claudo, sī, sŭm, *to shut.* Claudĕrĕt āgnŏs, Virg. Syn. Ōcclūdo, īnclūdo, īntērclūdo, cīrcŭmclūdo, ōbstrŭo, ōbscĕro; ŏccŭlto, ābscōndo. V. Occulto, carcer.

Claudĭŭs, ă, ŭm, *of the Claudian family.* Nĭl Claudĭæ nŏn ēffĭcĭēnt, Hor.

claudŭs, ă, ŭm, *lame.* Pārs vŭlnĕrĕ claudă, Virg.

clāvĭcŭlă, æ, f., *a vine's tendril.* Sŭbĭgĭt clāvĭcŭlă dēntĕs, G. Epith. Tĕnĕră. V. Vitis.

clāvĭcŭlŭs, ī, m., *the diminut. of* clavus. Clāvĭcŭlō mĕdĭăm, Mant. V. Clavus.

clāvĭgĕr, ŭ, ŭm, *bearing a club.* Clāvĭgĕrŭm vērbĭs, Ov. Syn. Armātŭs. V. Hercules, Janus.

clāvĭs, ĭs, f., *a key.* Nĕc prŏhĭbēnt clāvēs, Tib. Syn. Fērrĕă, ærātă, strīdēns, ăhēnĕă, ærĕă.

claŭstrŭm, ī, n., *an inclosure.* Cīrcŭm claŭstră frĕmūnt, Virg. Syn. Vālvæ, fŏrēs,

jānŭă, pōrtă, ŏbēx. Epith. Fērrĕŭm, tĕnāx, ăhēnŭm, ōbscūrŭm, strīctŭm, ōb-
stāns, ĭnēxpŭgnābĭlĕ, rēlĭgĭōsŭm, sĭlēns, quĭētŭm.

clāvŭs, ī, m., *a nail.* Mīllĭă clāvōrŭm, Juv. Epith. Fērrĕŭs, ærĕŭs, ăcūtŭs,
hŏrrĭdŭs, trăbālĭs, dūrŭs, vălĭdŭs, fīrmŭs, ăhēnŭs.—2. *a helm.* Vīrōs, clāvumque
ād līttŏră, Ov. Syn. Gŭbērnācŭlŭm, gŭbērnāclŭm, tēmo, hăbēnæ. Epith.
Fīrmŭs, fīdŭs, naŭtĭcŭs, pēndēns, flēxĭlĭs, flŭĭtāns, lĕvĭs, fŭgāx, prŏpĕrŭs.—3. *a*
purple stud, which distinguished the senators' robes. Clāvī mēnsūră cōācta ēst, Ov.
Epith. Nŏbĭlĭs.

Clāzŏmĕnæ, ārŭm, f. pl., *a city of Ionia.* Clāzŏmĕnĭs; ĕtĭăm, Hor.

clēmēns, ēntĭs, *mild, merciful.* Prīmō clēmēntĭŏr ævō, Claud. Syn. Mītĭs, cōmĭs,
bĕnīgnŭs, hūmānŭs, mānsuētŭs, lēnĭs, bŏnŭs, plăcĭdŭs, făcĭlĭs. V. Comis.

clēmēntĭă, æ, f., *kindness, compassion.* In Aŭgŭstō clēmēntĭă, Ov. Syn. Bŏnĭtās,
lēnĭtās, mānsuētūdo, mītĭs ănĭmŭs. Epith. Hĭlărĭs, bĕnīgnă, făcĭlĭs, cōmĭs,
hūmānă, pācĭfĭcă, æquă, mītĭs, grātă, rēgĭă. V. Clemens.

Clĕōnæ, ārŭm, m. pl., *a city near the Nemean forest.* Hŭmĭlēsquĕ Clĕōnæ, Ov.

Clĕŏpātră, æ, f., *a queen of Egypt.* Pŏtŭĭt Clĕŏpātră vĕnēnĭs, Lucan. Syn.
Ptŏlĕmāĭs rēgīnă, Ægȳptĭă. Epith. Fĕrōx, scĕlĕrātă, īncēstă, mĕretrīx, Phărĭă,
fōrmōsă, pŭlchră, aŭdāx, nĕfāndă, ōbscœnă, Ægȳptĭă, Ptŏlĕmāĭs.

clēpsȳdră, æ, f., *an hour-glass.* Clēpsȳdră mēntītŭr, Ov. Sēptēm clēpsȳdrās,
Mart.

|| clērĭcŭs, ī, m., *a clergyman.* Clērĭcī nēquĭd, (Sapph.) Sid.

clērŭs, ī, m., *the clergy.* Clērŭs hīnc tāntŭm, (Sapph.) Prud.

clĭbănŭs, ī, m., *a furnace, an oven.* Clĭbănŭs īgnĕ, Mant. Syn. Cŭcŭmēllă,
fūrnŭs.

clĭēns, ntĭs, m., *a client, retainer.* Mānĕ clĭēns, ēt jăm, Hor. Epith. Quĕrŭlŭs,
sōllĭcĭtŭs, mĭsĕr, āssĭdŭŭs.

clĭēntēlă, æ, f., *patronage.* Prōlĕ clĭēntēlĭs, Mart. Syn. Tūtēlă, patrōcĭnĭŭm.

|| clīmă, ătĭs, n., *a clime.* Clīmătĕ mūndī, Tert. Syn. Rēgĭo.

|| clīnĭcŭs, ī, m., *a physician attending the bedridden.* Clīnĭcŭs ēssĕ, Mart.

clīno, ās, ārĕ, *to incline, bend.* Paŭlŭm clīnărĕ nĕcēsse ēst, Lucr.

Clīō, ūs, f., *one of the Muses.* Vīsæ Clīō, Clīūsquĕ sŏrōrēs, Ov. V. Musæ.

clītēllæ, ārŭm, f. pl., *a pack-saddle.* Clītēllās fĕrŭs, Hor

Clītŏrĭŭs, ă, ŭm, *of the Clitor, a fountain of Arcadia.* Clītŏrĭŏ quīcŭnquĕ, Ov.

Clĭtūmnŭs, ī, m., *a river of Umbria.* Hīnc ālbī, Clĭtūmnĕ, Virg.

clīvōsŭs, ă, ŭm, *steep.* Sŭpērcĭlĭō clīvōsī trāmĭtĭs, Virg. Syn. Dēclīvĭs, ācclīvĭs.

clīvŭs, ī, m., *a cliff.* Ōrbĭtă clīvō, Virg. Syn. Cōllĭs, mōns. Epith. Præcēps,
ŏpācŭs, sāxōsŭs, ārdŭŭs, pēndēns, vĭrĭdĭs, mōllĭs, hērbĭdŭs, grāmĭnĕŭs, vīrēns,
hērbōsŭs, mōntānŭs, scŏpŭlōsŭs, pāndŭs, ămœnŭs, īncūltŭs, pătēns, ĭnūtĭlĭs,
sŭpīnŭs, frōndōsŭs. V. Mons.

clŏācă, æ, f., *a sink.* Tōrrēntĕ clŏācă, Juv. Syn. Lătrīnă. Epith. Immūndă,
fœdă, sōrdĭdă, tūrpĭs. V. Mephitis.

Clœlĭă, æ, f., *a Roman heroine.* Clœlĭă rūptĭs, Virg. Epith. Fōrtĭs, aŭdāx, nōbĭlĭs.

Clŏānthŭs, ī, m., *one of the companions of Æneas.* Cōrtēmquĕ Clŏānthŭm, Virg.

Clŏdĭŭs, ĭī, m., *an enemy of Cicero.* Clōdĭŭs āccūsĕt, Juv.

Clŏnĭŭs, ĭī, m., *one of the companions of Æneas.* Ĭtȳn Clŏnĭŭmquĕ, Virg.

Clŏthō, ūs, f., *one of the three Fates.* Clōthō dūră lăcŭs, Sil. Epith. Grāndævă,
īmprŏbă, crūdēlĭs, sævă, sēdŭlă, īmmītĭs. V. Parcæ.

Clŭēntĭŭs, ĭī, m., *a noble Roman family.* Rōmānĕ Clŭēntī, Virg.

* || clŭĕo, *to be called, to appear to be.* Rēs ōppōrtūnă clŭēbĭt, Lucr

clūnēs, ĭŭm, m. f. pl., *the buttocks.* Quŏd pŭlchræ clūnēs, Hor. Syn. Nătēs.

Clŭsīnŭs, ă, ŭm, *of Clusium.* Aŭdēnt Clŭsīnĭs, Hor.

Clŭsĭŭm, ĭī, ī, n., *a city of Etruria.* Quī mœnĭă Clŭsī, Virg.

Clŭsĭŭs, ĭī, m., *a name of Janus.* Clŭsĭŭs ŏrĕ, Ov.

Clȳmĕnæŭs or ēĭŭs, ă, ŭm, *of Clymene.* Clȳmĕnēĭă līmĭtĕ, Ov.

Clȳmĕnē, ēs, f., *a daughter of Oceanus and Tethys.* Nēc fālsă Clȳmĕnē, Ov.

Clȳmĕnŭs, ī, m., *a name of Pluto.* Āt Clȳmĕnŭs Clōthōquĕ, Ov.

clȳpĕātŭs, ă, ŭm, *armed with a shield.* Quŏtĭēs clȳpĕātŭs, ēt aŭrō, Claud. Syn.
Scūtātŭs. V. Armatus.

clȳpĕŭs, ī, m., *or* ŭm, ī, n., *a shield.* Ēt tōtŭm clȳpĕī, Virg. Syn. Scūtŭm,
pārmă, pēltă, ūmbo, ægĭs, cētră. Epith. Sānguĭnĕŭs, fūlgēns, dūrŭs, cŏrŭscāns,
ærātŭs, īngēns, căvŭs, crŭēntŭs, dīrŭs, aŭrātŭs, fērrĕŭs, splēndĭdŭs, crŭēntātŭs,

āhēnŭs, tērrĭbĭlĭs, mĭnāx, rŭtĭlāns, nĭtēns, cŏrŭscŭs, ōppŏsĭtŭs, rŭtĭlŭs, tērrĭfĭcŭs, pĕrēnnĭs, cūrvātŭs, lĕvĭs, hăbĭlĭs, sēptēmplēx, aūrĕŭs.

Clȳtēmnēstrā, æ, f., *the wife of Agamemnon, whom she murdered.* Mănĕ Clȳtēm-
nēstrăm, Juv. Cŭm Clȳtēmnēstrā nĕcĕt, Auson. Syn. Ăgămēmnŏnĭs ūxŏr.
Epith. Sævă, fōrmōsă, crŭēntă, pērfĭdă, scĕlĕrātă, ădŭltĕră.

Clȳtĭă, æ, *or* ĭē, ēs, f., *daughter to the king of Babylon, metamorphosed into a sun-
flower.* Tŭōs, Clȳtĭē, quămvĭs, Ov.

Clȳtĭŭs, ĭī, m., *one of the Argonauts.* Clȳtĭŭmquĕ Clănīnquĕ, Ov.

Clȳtŭs, ī, m., *a centaur.* Phlĕgȳămquĕ Clȳtŭmquĕ, Ov.

Cnĭdŏs *or* Cnĭdŭs, ī, f., *a town of Caria, where Venus had a temple.* Vĕnŭs, rēgīnă
Cnĭdī, Hor.

cŏăcērvo, ās, *to heap.* Pĕr cŏăcērvātŏs, Ov. Syn. Ăcērvo, cōngĕro, āccŭmŭlo,
āggĕro, cŭmŭlo, cōllĭgo.

cŏācto, ās, *to constrain.* Mēmbră cŏāctāns, Lucr. V. Cogo.

cŏæquālĭs, ĕ, *equal.* Ŭnă cŏæquālī, Man. Syn. Æquālĭs.

|| cŏætērnŭs, ă, ŭm, *coëternal.* Illĕ cŏætērnŭs, Prud.

cŏāgŭlŭm, ī, n., *rennet.* Cŭm lāctĕ cŏāgŭlă, Ov.

cŏălēsco, lŭī, *to grow united.* Ŭt cŏălēscĕrĕ pōssĭt, Sil. Syn. Cŏĕo, cōnvĕnĭo,
cōncūrro, cŏhærĕo, cōncrēsco.

cŏārcto, ās, *to straiten.* Nōxquĕ cŏārctăt ĭtĕr, Ov. Syn. Prĕmo, cōmprĭmo,
strīngo, cōnstrīngo, āstrīngo.

cŏārgŭo, ĭs, ŭī, *to convince.* Cŏārgŭĭt aūrēs, Ov. V. Arguo.

cŏăxo, ās, *to croak.* Rānă cŏăxăt ăquĭs, Ov.

Cŏcălŭs, ī, m., *a king of Sicily.* Cŏcălŭs ārmĭs, Ov.

Cŏcceĭŭs, ī, m., *a friend of Augustus.* Cŏcceĭŭs, mĭssī, Hor.

cŏccĭnātŭs, ă, ŭm, *arrayed in scarlet.* Quī cŏccĭnātŏs nōn pŭtăt, (Scaz.) Mart.

cŏccĭnŭm, ī, n., *a scarlet robe.* Cŏccĭnă quĭd făcĭĕnt? Mart. Syn. Cŏccĭnĕă
vēstĭs. V. Purpura.

cŏccĭnŭs, *and* ĕŭs, ă, ŭm, *of scarlet.* Cŏccĭnă lænă, Juv. Cŏccĭnĕās ārmĭs, Mant.
Syn. Cŏccĭnātŭs.

cŏccŭs, ī, m., *and* ŭm, ī, n., *scarlet.* Rŭbro ŭbī cŏccō, Hor. Syn. Mŭrēx, pŭrpŭră, ōstrŭm. Epith. Sāngŭĭnĕŭs, rŭbĕr, ārdēns, pŭrpŭrĕŭs, rŭbēns, rŏsĕŭs.
V. Purpura.

cochlĕă, æ, f., *a snail, a snail's shell.* Sŭm cŏchlĕĭs hăbĭlĭs, Mart. Ŭdă cŏchlĕ-
ārŭm, (Phal.) Stat. Epith. Flŭvĭālĭs, cūrvă, rēptĭlĭs, nēxĭlĭs, Afră.

cochlĕār *and* ārĕ, ĭs, n., *a spoon.* Vĕl cŏchlĕārĕ mĭhi, Mart.

cōclĕs, ĭtĭs, m., *born with one eye.* Cŏclĭtĭs ābscĭssōs, Prop. Syn. Lūscŭs.

cōctănă, ōrŭm, n. pl., *a sort of fig.* Cōctănă, fĭcŭs ĕrās, Mart.

cōctĭlĭs, ĕ, *baked.* Cōctĭlĭbŭs mūrĭs, Ov. Syn. Cŏctŭs.

Cōcȳtŭs, ă, ŭm, *of Cocytus.* Cŏcȳtĭă vīrgo, Virg.

Cŏcȳtŭs, ī, m., *an infernal river.* Cŏcȳtī stăgnă āltă, Virg. Epith. Ătĕr, ĭnămœnŭs, ĭnērs, nĭgĕr, pălŭstĕr, Tārtărĕŭs, īmŭs, prŏfūndŭs, mœstŭs, dūrŭs, lānguĭdŭs.

cōdēx, ĭcĭs, m., *the stock of a tree, a book.* Cōdĭcĕ quī mĭssō, Ov. Syn. Caūdēx,
trūncŭs, lĭbĕr.

cōdĭcĭllŭs, ī, m., *the diminut. of* codex. Tĕnŭēsquĕ cōdĭcĭllōs, (Phal.) Syn.
Lĭbēllŭs, tăbŭlæ.

Cōdrŭs, ī, m., *a king of Athens, who devoted himself to his country.* Jūrgĭă Cōdrī,
Virg. Epith. Fōrtĭs, illūstrĭs.

|| cœmētērĭŭm, ĭī, n., *a cemetery.* Syn. Sĕpŭlcrētŭm.

cŏĕmo, ēmī, ēmptŭm, *to buy.* Cōndŭctĭs cŏĕmēns ōbsōnĭă, Hor. Syn. Ĕmo.

cŏēmptŏr, ōrĭs, m., *a buyer.* Pĭpĕrĭsquĕ cŏēmptŏr, Juv.

cœnă, *and* ŭlă, æ, f., *a supper.* Fāstīdĭă cœnă, Hor. Epith. Sĕră, cōncīnnă,
nōctūrnă, laūtă, sūmptŭōsă, ŏpīmă, dīvĕs, gĕnĭālĭs, mōllĭs, lūxŭrĭōsă. V. Convivium.

cœnācŭlŭm, ī, n., *an upper room.* Ĭn cœnācŭlă mīlĕs, Juv.

cœnātĭo, ōnĭs, f., *a dining-room.* Cērnĭs? cœnātĭŏ pārvă, Mart. Syn. Cœnācŭlŭm.

cœnātōrĭŭm, ĭī, n., *a dress to wear at supper.* Cœnātōrĭă mĭttĭt, (Phal.) Mart.

cœnătŭrĭo, ĭs, *to have an appetite for supper.* Cœnātūrĭt Văcērră, (Iamb.) Mart.

cœnātŭs, ă, ŭm, *the pass. part. of* cœno. Tŏtĭdēm cœnātŭs, Hĕtrūscī, Hor.

cœno, ās, *to sup.* Cœnāvīt nŏctĕ, nĕc īllōs, Juv. V. Epulor.

cœnōsŭs, ă, ŭm, *dirty.* Syn. Sŏrdĭdŭs.

cœnŭnı, ī, n., *dirt, mire.* Aŭt ŭbi ŏdŏr cœnī grăvĭs, Virg. Syn. Sŏrdēs, lŭtŭm. Epith. Crāssŭm, tĕnāx, sŏrdĭdŭm, pălūstrĕ, īnfēctŭm, vīrĭdāns.

cŏĕo, īs, īvī *and* iī, ĭtŭm, īrĕ, *to come together.* Cŏīĕre īn prœlĭă văccā, Nem. Syn. Cōnvĕnĭo, cōngrĕdĭŏr, cōncūrro, jūngŏr.

cœpī, īstī, īssĕ, *to begin.* Sīc pēctŏrĕ cœpĭt, Virg.

cœpto, ās, *to begin.* Cœptēs dīffĭdĕrĕ dīctīs, Lucr.

cœptŭm, ī, n., *an enterprise.* Cœptĭs īmmānĭbŭs, Virg. Syn. Cōnsĭlĭŭm, īncēptŭm, aŭsŭm, prŏpŏsĭtŭm, ŏrsŭm.

cœptŭs, ă, ŭm, *begun.* Cœptī fīdūcĭă bēllī, Virg.

Cœrănŏs *or* ŭs, ī, m., *the name of a man.* Cœrănōn Iphĭtĭdēmquĕ, Ov.

cŏĕrcĕo, ŭī, *to restrain.* Lītŭrā cŏĕrcŭĭt ătquĕ, Hor. Syn. Cōntĭnĕo, rĕtĭnĕo, cŏhĭbĕo, reprĭmo, cōmprĭmo, frœno ; cāstīgo.

cŏĕrcĭtŭs, ă, ŭm, *the pass. partic. of* coerceo. Grăvĭbŭsquĕ cŏĕrcĭtă vīnclĭs, Ov.

cœtŭs, ūs, m., *an assembly.* Līttŏrā cœtū, Virg. Syn. Cōnvēntŭs, cōncĭlĭŭm, tūrbă frĕquēns. Epith. Lœtŭs, vŭlgārĭs, nŭmĕrōsŭs, ĭnnŭmĕrŭs, cīrcūmstāns, cīrcūmvāllāns. V. Turba.

Cœŭs, ī, m., *a giant.* Cœŭmque Iăpĕtŭmquĕ, Virg.

cōgĭtătĭo, ōnĭs, f., *thinking.* Sĭnĕ cōgĭtătĭŏnĕ, (Phal.) Mart. Syn. Méns, sēntēntĭă, cōnsĭlĭŭm.

cōgĭto, ās, *to think.* Mălĕ cōgĭtăt ŏdī, Ov. Syn. Pŭto, rĕpŭto, vērso, ăgĭto, mĕdĭtŏr.

cōgnātĭo, ōnĭs, f., *kindred.* Tĭbī cōgnātĭŏ mŭnŭs, Mart. Syn. Affĭnĭtās, cōnsānguĭnĭtās. Epith. Cāră, grātă, ămīcă.

cōgnātŭs, ă, ŭm, *allied, akin.* Cōgnātĭquĕ pătrēs, Virg. Syn. Affĭnĭs, cōnsānguĭnĕŭs, āgnātŭs; sānguĭnĕ jūnctŭs.

cōgnĭtĭo, ōnĭs, f., *knowledge.* Cōgnĭtĭŏnĕ pĕrāctā, Juv. Syn. Nŏtĭtĭă, nŏtĭo. Epith. Cērtă, vēră, dŭbĭă, fāllăx, clără.

cōgnĭtŏr, ōrĭs, m., *a judge.* Cōgnĭtŏr ŏrĕ lĕgăt, Ov.

cōgnĭtŭs, ă, ŭm, *the pass. partic. of* cognosco. Cōgnĭtŭs ūrbĭs, Virg.

cōgnōmĕn, ĭnĭs, n., *the surname.* Idŭs cōgnōmĭnĕ vīctŏr, Ov. Syn. Cōgnōmēntŭm, āgnōmĕn. Epith. Clārŭm, āntĭquŭm, ōbscūrŭm, hŭmĭlĕ, nŏvŭm. V. Nomen.

cōgnōmĭnĭs, ĕ, *of the same name.* Cōgnōmĭnĕ tērrā, Virg.

cōgnōmĭno, ās, *to give a surname.* Māgnŭs cōgnōmĭnăt Ātlās, Man.

cōgnōsco, nōvī, ĭtŭm, *to know.* Flētŭs cōgnōvĭt ĭnānēs, Virg. Syn. Nōsco, āgnōsco, īntēllĭgo, pērcĭpĭo, nōvī. V. Agnosco.

cōgo, cŏēgī, cŏāctŭm, *to collect.* Cōgŏr ĕt ēxēmplĭs, Prop. Syn. Cōmpēllo, īmpēllo, ădĭgo; cōngrĕgo, cōnvŏco; āccŭmŭlo, cŏăcērvo, cōllĭgo.

cŏhærĕo, sī, sŭm, *to stick together.* Dēfīxā cŏhæsĕrăt hārŭm, Ov. Syn. Cŏhærēsco, hærĕo, ădhærĕo, ădhærēsco, nēctŏr, ānnēctŏr, cŏnnēctŏr, cōnjūngŏr.

cŏhærēs, ēdĭs, m., *a joint heir.* Fŏrtĕ cŏhærēdŭm, Hor.

cŏhĭbĕo, ŭī, *to keep close, contain.* Aŭrō cŏhĭbĕrĕ lăcērtōs, Ov. Syn. Ārcĕo, frœno, tĕnĕo, rĕtĭnĕo, cōntĭnĕo, reprĭmo, cŏĕrcĕo, refrœno, cōmprĭmo. V. Fræno.

cŏhĭbĭtŭs, ă, ŭm, *the pass. partic. of* cohibeo. Plaut.

cŏhōrs, tĭs, f., *a regiment.* Lōngă cŏhōrtēs, Virg. Syn. Cătērvă, tūrmă, āgmĕn, phălānx, ēxērcĭtŭs, cŭnĕŭs, cōpĭæ, ăcĭēs, mănŭs, lĕgĭo, mănĭplŭs. Epith. Nŭmĕrōsă, ārmĭgĕră, bēllātrīx, vălĭdă, ārmătă, ārmĭsōnă, mĭnăx, clўpĕātă, scŭtātă, fūnēstă, trĕmēndă, săgĭttĭfĕră. V. Caterva, turba.—2. *a yard.* Illă cŏhōrtĭs ăvēs, Mart.

* cŏhōrtŏr, ārĭs, *to exhort.* Cic. V. Hortor.

cŏīnquĭno, ās, *to soil.* Mŏnŭmēntă cŏīnquĭnăt ārtĭs, Hor. Syn. Inquĭno, măcŭlo, fœdo, dēfōrmo, pōllŭo, tūrpo. V. Maculo.

cŏītŭs, ūs, m., *a coming together.* Pērquĕ sŭōs cŏītŭs, Ov. Syn. Cŏītĭo, cōncŭbĭtŭs.

cŏlăphŭs, ī, m., *a buffet.* Nōs cŏlăphum īncŭtĭmŭs, Juv. Syn. Ălăpă, īctŭs. Epith. Grăvĭs, dūrŭs, sŏnōrŭs, ăcērbŭs, vĭŏlēntŭs, vălĭdŭs. V. Alapa.

Cŏlchī, ōrŭm, m. pl., *a nation of Asia.* Phăsĭănă Cōlchōrŭm, (Scaz.) Mart. Syn. Phrўxæī. Epith. Trŭcēs, sævī, fĕrōcēs, ālgēntēs, īmpĭī, vĕnēfĭcī.

Cŏlchĭācŭs, chĭcŭs, *and* chŭs, ă, ŭm, *of Colchos.* Cŏlchĭs Cŏlchĭācĭs, Prop. Pĕr-vĕnĭt ĭn Cŏlchās, Ov.

Cŏlchĭs, ĭdĭs, *and* ŏs, ĭ, f., *a country of Asia.* Cŏlchĭdĭs hŏspĭtĭs ōræ, Virg. Epith. Impĭă ; vĕnēnōrūm fĕrāx.

cŏlīphȳŭm, ĭī, n., *wrestler's diet.* Cŏmĕdūnt cŏlīphĭă paūcæ. Juv.

cŏllăbĕfācĭo, fĕcī, fāctŭm, *and* fūcto, ās, *to enfeeble.* Cŏllăbĕfāctăt ŏnŭs, Ov.

cŏllăbŏr, ĕrĭs, lāpsŭs, lābī, *to fall.* Exānguĭs cŏllābĭtŭr, āc vĕlŭt ĭpsŭm, Prud. Syn. Cŏncĭdo, cădo, lābŏr. V. Cado.

cŏllărĕ, ĭs, n., *a collar.* Fĕrrātīs cŏllārĭbŭs ārmānt, Mart. Syn. Tōrquēs ; tōr-quĭs.

Cŏllātĭă, æ, f., *a small town near Rome.* Cŏllātĭă nōmĕn, Ov.

Cŏllātīnŭs, ă, ŭm. *of the Collatine mountain.* Hī Cŏllātīnās, Virg.

cŏllātŭs, ă, ŭm, *the pass. part. of* confero. Quī tĭbĭ cŏllātŭs, Mart. V. Comparo.

cŏllaūdo, ās, *to praise.* Vōcēm cŏllaūdăt, Ov.

cŏllāxo, ās, *to relax.* Omnĭă cīrcūm cŏllāxăt, Lucr.

cŏllēctŭs, ūs, m., *a mass.* Cŏllēctŭs ăquæ, Lucr.

cŏllēgă, æ, f., *a fellow-companion.* Āt Nŏvĭŭs cŏllēgă grădū, Hor.

cŏllēgĭŭm, ĭī, n., *a college.* Quæ sīnt cŏllēgĭă fātīs, Manil. Syn. Gȳmnăsĭŭm, schŏlă ; cœtŭs, cōnvēntŭs. V. Schola.

cŏllĭbĕt, ŭĭt, *it pleases.* Sī cŏllĭbŭĭssĕt, Hor.

cŏllĭcŭlŭs, ī, m., *the diminut. of* collis. Crēdīt cŏllĭcŭlīs, Mart. Syn. Jŭgŭm. V. Collis.

cŭllīdo, īsī, sŭm, *to bruise together.* Prīmō cŏllīdĭtŭr aūrŭm, Ov. Syn. Frāngo, cōntĕro, āttĕro, cōnstrĭngo.

cŏllĭgo, ās, *to tie together.* Cŏllĭgăt ārctă, Tib. Syn. Lĭgo, cōnstrĭngo, vĭncĭo, rĕvĭncĭo. V. Vincio.

cŏllĭgo, ĭs, lēgī, lēctŭm, *to assemble together.* Cŏllĭgĭt ĭgnēs, Virg. Syn. Cōgo, āggrĕgo, cōngrĕgo, cŏngĕro ; lĕgo, cārpo, dēcĕrpo.

cŏllĭno, ĭs, *to anoint, besmear.* Crīnēs pŭlvĕrĕ cŏllĭnēs, Hor.

cŏllīnŭs, ă, ŭm, *of a hill.* Quĭppe ĕt cŏllīnās, Prop. Syn. Mŏntānŭs, clīvōsŭs.

cŏllĭs, ĭs, m., *a hill.* Invīdīt cŏllĭbŭs ūmbrās, Virg. Syn. Mōns, jŭgŭm, clīvŭs, ăpēx, vērtēx. Epith. Āpērtŭs, sŭpīnŭs, pătŭlŭs, ūmbrōsŭs, cēlsŭs, spătĭōsŭs, dūmōsŭs, vĭrĭdĭs, frīgĭdŭs, hērbĭfĕr, fœcūndŭs, flōrĭfĕr, vĭrĭdāns, sălebrōsŭs, aprīcŭs, vērnŭs, scŏpŭlōsŭs, frŏndōsŭs, ābrŭptŭs, ācclīvĭs, flōrēns, vĭrēns, tŭ-mĭdŭs, āĕrĭŭs, frūgĭfĕr, sūrgēns, īncūltŭs.

cŏllīsŭs, ă, ŭm, *the pass. part. of* collido. Lēntō cŏllīsă dŭĕllō, Hor.

cŏllŏco, ās, *to place.* Cŏllŏcăt, ĭpsă prŏcŭl, Virg. Syn. Pōno, stătŭo, cōnstĭtŭo, dēpōno, cōmpōno.

cŏllŏquĭŭm, ĭī, n., *a parley.* Cŏllŏquĭŭmquĕ vŏcēs, Ov. Syn. Āllŏquĭŭm, sērmo, cōngrēssŭs. Epith. Mītĕ, blāndŭm, dūlcĕ, grātŭm, jūcūndŭm, bĕnīgnŭm, ŏp-tātŭm, hŏnēstŭm, mūtŭŭm.

cŏllŏquŏr, ĕrĭs, cŏllŏcūtŭs, *to talk together.* Syn. Āllŏquŏr ; āffŏr, āffārĭs ; cōm-pēllo, ās. V. Loquor.

cŏllūcĕo, xī, ĕre, *to shine.* Tōtŭs cŏllūcēns, Virg. Syn. Rĕfūlgĕo, cŏrūsco. V. Luceo.

cŏllūdo, sī, sŭm, *to play together.* Cŏllūdĕrĕ plūmās, Virg. V. Ludo.

cŏllŭm, ī, n., *the neck.* Cŏllŏquĕ pĕpēndĭt, Virg. Syn. Cērvīx. Epith. Nĭ-vĕŭm, ĕbūrnŭm, cāndĭdŭm, ārgēntĕŭm, tĕnĕrŭm, vĕnūstŭm, cāndēns, āltŭm, pŭlchrŭm, tŭmĭdŭm.

cŏllŭo, lŭī, lūtŭm, *to wash.* Cŏllŭĕrānt fōntēs, Ov. V. Rigo.

cŏllūsŏr, ōrĭs, m., *a playfellow.* Cŏllūsŏrĕ cătēllō, Juv.

cŏllūstro, ās, *to look around, to make clear.* Omnĭă cŏllūstrāns, Virg. Syn. Lūstro, cīrcūmspĭcĭo ; īllūstro. V. Circumspicio.

cŏllŭvĭēs, ĭēī, f., *filth.* Cŏllŭvĭēs ĭn mājŭs ăbĭt, Man. Syn. Cŏllŭvĭo, ēlŭvĭēs, dīlŭvĭŭm. Epith. Sōrdĭdă, cœnōsă, putrĭdă, fœdă, tūrpĭs, fœtēns.

cŏllȳrĭă, ōrŭm, n. pl., *a medicine for the eyes.* Mĕīs cŏllȳrĭă lĭppŭs, Hor.

cŏlo, ĭs, ŭī, cūltŭm, *to cultivate, inhabit, revere.* Quī cŏlŭĕrĕ, cŏlūntŭr, Ov. Syn. Incŏlo, hăbĭto ; vĕnĕrŏr, hŏnōro, ădōro. V. Adoro.

cŏlo, ās, *to strain.* Et cŏlārĕ vāgŏs, Manil. Syn. Pērcŏlo.

cŏlŏcāsĭă, æ, f., *or* ăsĭŭm, ĭī, n., *an Egyptian bean.* Cŏlŏcāsĭă fūndĕt, Virg. Epith. Nĭlĭăcŭm ; lēntŭm, mŏllĕ.

cŏlōnă, æ, f., *a female peasant.* Cŏlōnă nŭcēs, Ov.

cŏlōnĭă, æ, f., *a colony.* Quārtă cŏlōnĭă pōnī, Aus. V. Villa.

cŏlōnĭcŭm, ī, n., *a peasant's hut.* Lăcrўmōsă cŏlōnĭcă fŭmō, Aus. V. Casa.

cŏlōnĭcŭs, ă, ŭm, *of a colony.* Ŏvīsquĕ cŏlōnĭcă, Ov.

cŏlōnŭs, ī, m., *a husbandman, peasant.* Arvă cŏlōnī, Ov. SYN. Agrĭcŏlă, ărātŏr, rūstĭcŭs. agrēstĭs, vīllĭcŭs, cūltŏr agrī. EPITH. Fōrtĭs, paŭpĕr, ĭnŏps, mĭsĕr, lăcērtōsŭs, ăvĭdŭs, dūrŭs, rūdĭs, sīmplēx, sōllĭcĭtŭs, īncūltŭs, pērvĭgĭl, sōlērs. V. Agricola.

Cŏlŏphŏn, ōnĭs, f., *a town of Ionia.* Smўrnă quĭd, ēt Cŏlŏphŏn? Hor.

Cŏlŏphōnĭăcŭs, *and* ĭŭs, ă, ŭm, *of Colophon.* Quæ Cŏlŏphōnĭăcō, Virg. Huĭc Cŏlŏphōnĭŭs Icmōn, Ov.

cŏlŏr, ōrĭs, m., *a colour.* Quăm prātă cŏlōrĭbŭs, ăntĕ, Virg. EPITH. Grātŭs, vīvŭs, splēndēns, lūcĭdŭs, pūlchĕr, nĭtēns, vărĭŭs, mĭcāns, cŏrūscāns, rŭtĭlāns, vĭrĭdĭs, rŭbēns, rŭbĕr, rŭbĭcūndŭs, pūrpŭrĕŭs, rŏsĕŭs, nĭgĕr, ātĕr, pĭcĕŭs, fūscŭs, ŏbscūrŭs, flāvŭs, crŏcĕŭs, lūtĕŭs, aŭrĕŭs, ālbŭs, cāndĭdŭs, nĭvĕŭs, lāctĕŭs, ōlōrĭnŭs, cœrŭlĕŭs, vĭŏlācĕŭs.

cŏlōrātŭs, ă, ŭm, *the pass. partic. of* coloro. Ūsquĕ cŏlōrātīs, Virg.

cŏlōro, ās, *to color.* Rŭbră cŏlōrăt ĕquīs, Prop. SYN. Pīngo.

cŏlōssĕŭs, ă, ŭm, *like a colossus.* Atquĕ cŏlōssēŭm, Mart.

cŏlōssŭs, ī, m., *a colossus.* Gĕmĭnātă cŏlōssō, Stat. EPITH. Mārmŏrĕŭs, grāndĭs, sīdĕrĕŭs, sūblīmĭs, āltŭs, īngēns, hōrrēndŭs, cēlsŭs, ēxcēlsŭs, īmmānĭs, prŏcērŭs, ēnōrmĭs, vāstŭs, stŭpēndŭs, ārdŭŭs, ēlātŭs, ēdĭtŭs, mīrāndŭs, sŭmmŭs, ăhēnŭs, Rhŏdĭŭs. V. Statua.

cŏlŭbĕr, ubrī, m., *and* ubră, æ, f., *a serpent.* Assuētŭs cŏlŭbĕr sŭccēdĕrĕ, Virg. SYN. Sĕrpēns, ānguĭs, drăco. EPITH. Lōngŭs, tŭmĭdŭs, lubrĭcŭs, hīrsūtŭs, nōxĭŭs, vĕnēnātŭs, tērrĭfĭcŭs, sævŭs, cœrŭlĕŭs, Mĕdūsæŭs, Gōrgŏnĕŭs; squāmōsŭs, tōrtŭs, ātĕr, dĭrŭs, lēthĭfĕr, sĭnŭātŭs, mōrdēns, măcŭlōsŭs, tōrtĭlĭs, nĭgĕr, vĕnēnōsŭs, flēxŭs, īmmānĭs. V. Serpens.

cŏlŭbrĭfĕr, ă, ŭm, *with snaky tresses.* Tōrvă cŏlŭbrĭfĕrī, Ov.

cŏlŭbrīnŭs, ă, ŭm, *of a serpent.* Pōrrĭgīt cŏlŭbrīnă, (Scaz.)

cŏlŭm, ī, n., *a strainer.* Cōlăquĕ prælōrŭm, Virg.

cŏlŭmbă, æ, f, *and* bŭs, ī, m., *a dove.* Jūngūntŭr sæpĕ cŏlŭmbæ, Ov. SYN. Pălūmbēs. EPITH. Mōllĭs, ĭmbēllĭs, āĕrĭă, blāndă, tĭmĭdă, tōrquātă, tĕnĕră, nĭvĕă, lāctĕă, mītĭs, ālbă, pūlchră, sīmplēx, cĕlĕr, trĕpĭdă, călĭdă, Cўthĕrēĭă, Idălĭă, Cyprĭă; Dōdōnæă; păvĭdă, raŭcă, văgă, vēlōx, văgăbūndă, præpĕs, mānsuētă.

cŏlŭmbīnŭs, ă, ŭm, *of a dove.* Vīnă, cŏlŭmbīnō, Hor.

cŏlŭmbŭlŭs, ī, m., *the diminut. of* columbus. Ūt ālbŭlŭs cŏlŭmbŭlŭs, Cat.

cŏlŭmĕn, ĭnĭs, n., *a support.* Pōstēs cŏlŭmĕn īmprēssŭm, (Iamb.) Mart. SYN. Tūtēlă, dēfēnsĭo, tūtāmĕn.

cŏlŭmnă, æ, f., *a column.* Pārvă cŏlŭmnă nŏtæ, Ov. SYN. Fūlcrŭm, cŏlŭmĕn. EPITH. Fērrĕă, sūblīmĭs, cēlsă, ēxcēlsă, fērrātă, vălĭdă, sŏlĭdă, fīrmă, nĭtĭdă, fūlgĭdă, pūlchră, mārmŏrĕă, aŭrātă, lōngă, ārdŭă, ēlātă, ērēctă, pĕrēnnĭs, ætērnă, sŭpērbă, măgnĭfĭcă, sŭppŏsĭtă. V. Abyla, Calpe.

cŏlŭmnārĭs, ĕ, *of a column.* Lūcĕ cŏlŭmnārī, Prud.

cŏlūrnŭs, ă, ŭm, *of hazel.* Extă cŏlūrnīs, Virg.

cŏlŭs, ī *and* ūs, f., *a distaff.* Ēt cŏlŭs, ēt fūsŭs, Ov. EPITH. Fœmĭnĕă, frăgĭlĭs, ĭmbēllĭs, lānĭgĕră, Lўdă; Pāllădĭă; ēxĭlĭs, lævĭs, lōngă, mŭlĭebrĭs, tĕrĕs, plēnă, rŏtūndă. V. Neo.

cŏmă, æ, f., *the hair.* Mātrĕ jŭbēntĕ cŏmæ, Ov. SYN. Cæsărĭēs, căpĭllī, crīnēs. EPITH. Ūnctă, nĭtĭdă, prŏlīxă, flāvēns, dīffūsă, dīvĭdŭă, fōrmōsă, ŏdōrātă, ōrnātă, āmbrŏsĭă, mōllĭs, dĕcōră, flēxĭlĭs, flāvă, pēxă, splēndĭdă, tĕnĕră, cūltă, ŏdōră, ēffūsă, hīrsūtă, aŭrĕă, flŭēns, cānă, flēxă, tōrtă, pēndŭlă, rŭtĭlă, aŭrātă, pūlchră, tĕpēxă, cōmptă, lōngă. V. Capilli, crines.

cŏmāns, āntĭs, *having long hair.* Crīstāsquĕ cŏmāntēs, Virg. SYN. Cŏmātŭs, crīnītŭs; frōndōsŭs.

cŏmātŭs, ă, ŭm, *having hair.* Ĕrĭs cŏmātŭs, (Phal.) Mart. SYN. Căpīllātŭs, crīnītŭs.

cŏmbĭbo, bĭbī, *to drink up.* Cŏmbĭbĕ sōlēs, Mart. SYN. Bĭbo, ēbĭbo, haŭrĭo.

cŏmbĭbo, ōnĭs, m., *a pot-companion.* Tūrbă cŏmbĭbōnŭmquĕ, (Scaz.) SYN. Mēnsæ, caŭpōnæ sŏcĭŭs; cŏmĕs; cŏmpŏtŏr.

cōmbūro, ūssī, ūstŭm, *to burn up.* Tūrbĭnĕ vēntōrŭm cōmbūrēns, Lucr. Syn. Ūro, ēxūro, crĕmo, ădūro, īncēndo ; flāmmīs cōnsūmo, ābsūmo. V. Uro, incendo.

cŏmĕdo, ēdī, ēsŭm, *to eat up.* Pŏrcīs cŏmĕdēndă rĕlīnquēs, Hor. Syn. Édo, pāsco, māndūco, māndo. V. Edo.

cŏmĕs, ĭtĭs, m., *a companion.* Dūx cŏmĭtī : tū cŏmĕs īpsă dŭcī, Ov. Syn. Cŏmĭtāns, cŏmĭtātŭs, sŏcĭŭs, sŏcĭātŭs, sŏdālĭs, āssĕclă. Epith. Fīdŭs, fīdēlĭs. V. Comitor, sodalis.

cōmēssātĭo, ōnĭs, f., *a revelling.* Sīt cōmēssātĭŏ tāntī, Mart. Epith. Laūtă, fœdă, tūrpĭs.

cōmēssātŏr, ōrĭs, m., *a reveller.* Nēc cōmēssātŏr hăbērī, Mart. Syn. Hēllŭo. V. Gulosus.

cōmēssŏr, ārĭs, *to revel.* Cōmēssābĕrĕ Māxĭmī, (Glycon.) Hor. Syn. Ēpŭlŏr, cōnvīvŏr.

cŏmēsŭs, ă, ŭm, *the pass. partic. of* comedo. Dē nōbĭlĭtātĕ cŏmēsā, Juv. Syn. Esŭs, ădēsŭs, ēxēsŭs, cōnsūmptŭs.

cŏmētă, *or* ēs, æ, m., *a blazing star.* Ārsērĕ cŏmētæ, Virg. Syn. Stēllă crīnītă. Epith. Dīrŭs, crīnītŭs, sānguĭnĕŭs, cāndĭdŭs, fătālĭs, præcēps, trīstĭs, fŭlgēns, flāmmāns, lūcēns, īnfēlīx, hōrrĭfĭcŭs, rŭbĭcūndŭs, īgnĭfĕr, clārŭs, rŭbēscēns, īgnītŭs, hōrrēndŭs, fūnēstŭs, mĭnāx, sævŭs, crŭēntŭs, flāmmĕŭs, īgnĕŭs, mĕtŭēndŭs, vĕrēndŭs, īnfaūstŭs, pēstĭfĕr, sĭnīstĕr, ēxĭtĭōsŭs, pērnĭcĭōsŭs, căpĭllātŭs, ēxĭtĭālĭs, prænūncĭŭs.

cōmĭcŭs, ă, ŭm, *belonging to comedy.* Rēs cōmĭcă nōn vūlt, Hor.

cōmĭnŭs, adv., *hand to hand.* Cōmĭnŭs ēnsĕ, Ov. Syn. Prŏpĕ, prŏpĭŭs, haūd prŏcŭl.

cōmĭs, ĕ, *courteous, gentle.* Tĭbĭ cōmĭs ănŭs, Ov. Syn. Hūmānŭs, cōmmŏdŭs, făcĭlĭs, bĕnīgnŭs, ūrbānŭs, blāndŭs, mānsuētŭs, mītĭs, lēnĭs, plăcĭdŭs. V. Clemens, mitis.

cōmĭtās, ātĭs, f., *gentleness.* Nērvās cōmĭtātĕ Drūsōnēs, (Scaz.) Mart. Syn. Bĕnīgnĭtās, hūmānĭtās, ūrbānĭtās.

cōmĭtātŭs, ūs, m., *a retinue.* Cūm sēmĭvĭrō cōmĭtātū, Virg. Syn. Cœtŭs, cŏhōrs, cătērvă, tūrbă, cŏmĭtēs, clĭēntēs. V. Turba.

cōmĭtĕr, adv., *gently.* Cōmĭtĕr ēxcĭpĭtŭr, Ov. Syn. Hūmānē, hūmānĭtĕr, bĕnĭgnē.

cōmĭtĭŭm, ĭī, n., *a public assembly.* In cōmĭtĭo ēstōte ōbvĭăm, (Iamb.) Syn. Cōnvēntŭs, cōncĭlĭŭm.

cōmĭtŏr, ārĭs, *or* to, ās, *to accompany.* Cŏmĭtābŏr ŏvāntēs, Virg. Cŏmĭtārēm cāstră pŭēllæ, Prop. Syn. Sŏcĭo, sēctŏr, sĕquŏr ; stĭpo, āssēctŏr.

cōmmăcŭlo, ās, *to soil.* Cōmmăcŭlārĕ mănūs, Virg. Syn. Măcŭlo, fœdo, īnquĭno. V. Maculo.

cōmmĕdĭtŏr, ārĭs, *to meditate upon.* Chārtārŭm cōmmĕdĭtātŭr, Lucr.

* cōmmĕmŏrābĭlĭs, ĕ, *worth remembering.* Cic. Syn. Cōmmĕmŏrāndŭs, mĕmŏrābĭlĭs.

cōmmĕmŏro, ās, *to recount, mention.* Cōmmĕmŏrārĕ jŭvăt, Ov. Syn. Mĕmŏro ; mĕmĭnī, cōmmĕmĭnī. V. Memini.

cōmmēndātĭo, ōnĭs, f., *a commendation.* Mūtă cōmmēndātĭo ēst, (Iamb.) Syn. Laūs.

cōmmēndo, ās, *to commend, commit.* Ĭtă cōmmēndārĕ dīcācēs, Hor. Syn. Laūdo, cĕlebro ; cōmmītto, trādo, crēdo, dĕpōno ; māndo, ās.

* cōmmēntārĭŭs, ĭī, m., *a commentary.* Cic. Syn. Cōmmēntārĭŭm.

cōmmēntŏr, ōrĭs, m., *an inventor.* Ūvæ cōmmēntŏr hăbēbăt, Ov.

cōmmēntŏr, ārĭs, *to meditate.* Plaut. Syn. Cōgĭto, ēxcōgĭto, ădīnvĕnĭo, rĕpĕrĭo, fīngo, cōmmĭnīscŏr ; ēxplāno, trācto, dīspŭto.

cōmmēntŭm, ī, n., *a fiction.* Cōmmēntă rĕtēxĭt, Ov. Syn. Fīctĭo, făbŭlă.

cōmmĕo, ās, *to go to and fro, to move.* Ĭn ūrbēm cōmmĕăt, (Iamb.) Ter.

cōmmērcĭŭm, ĭī, n., *commerce.* Bēllī cōmmērcĭă Tūrnŭs, Virg.

cōmmĕrĕo, ŭī, *to deserve.* Cōmmĕrŭīssĕ părŭm, Ov. Syn. Cōmmĕrĕŏr, mĕrĕo, mĕrĕŏr.

cōmmigro, ās, *to go from one place to another.* Ter. Syn. Migro, ēmigro, dīscēdo, ēxĕo.

F

cŏmmīlĭtĭŭm, ĭī, n., *fellowship in war.* Ět cŏmmīlĭtĭī, Ov.

cŏmmīlĭto, ōnĭs, m., *a fellow-soldier.* Cŏmmīlĭtŏ nŏn tĭmĕt ēnsĕm, Prud. V Miles.

cŏmmĭngo, ĭs, *to bepiss.* Cŏmmĭnxĭt lēctŭm, Hor.

cŏmmĭnīscŏr, mēntŭs sŭm, *to invent, feign.* Cŏmmĭnīscĭtŭr lĭbrōs, (Scaz.) V. Commentor.

cŏmmĭnŭo, ŭī, ūtŭm, *to break.* Cŏmmĭnŭĕrĕ mĕī, Ov. SYN. Mĭnŭo, ĭmmĭnŭo, frāngo, cōntĕro.

‖ cŏmmīscĕo, mīscŭī, mīstŭm, *to mix together.* Gĕmĭtū cŏmmīstă quĕrēlă, Lucr. SYN. Mīscĕo, pērmīscĕo, ādmīscĕo, ĭmmīscĕo, cōnfūndo.

cŏmmĭsĕrŏr, ārĭs, *to pity.* Cŏmmĭsĕrāns hŏmĭnŭm, Cic.

cŏmmīssŭm, ī, n., *a fault committed.* Cŏmmīssă tăcĕrĕ, Hor. SYN. Errŏr, dēlīctŭm, crīmĕn, sēcrētŭm.

cŏmmītto, ĭsī, ĭssŭm, *to commit.* Cŏmmīsĭt sēmĭnă tērræ, Tib. SYN. Ādmītto, patro, făcĭo ; crēdo, cōnfīdo, cŏmmēndo, trādo ; ēxpōno, ōbjĭcĭo.

cŏmmŏdē, adv., *conveniently, handsomely.* Hōc ĕgŏ cŏmmŏdĭŭs, Hor. SYN. Āptē, ŏppōrtūnē.

cŏmmŏdĭtās, ātĭs, f., *commodity.* Cŏmmŏdĭtātĕ frŭī, Ov. SYN. Ūtĭlĭtās, ōccāsĭo, cŏmmŏdă tēmpŏră.

cŏmmŏdo, ās, *to serve, to lend.* Cŏmmŏdĕt aūrĕm, Hor. SYN. Accŏmmŏdo, mūtŭŭm dō, præbĕo.

cŏmmŏdŭm, ī, n., *an advantage.* Cŏmmŏdă sēcŭm, Hor. SYN. Ūtĭlĭtās, ēmŏlŭmēntŭm.

cŏmmŏdŭs, ă, ŭm, *convenient, opportune.* Cŏmmŏdă mīllĕ prĕcŏr, Ov. SYN. Accŏmmŏdŭs, ūtĭlĭs, ŏppōrtūnŭs, āptŭs, tēmpēstīvŭs, ĭdōnĕŭs.

cŏmmōlĭŏr, ĭrĭs, *to attempt, invent.* Cŭm cŏmmōlīrī, Lucr. SYN. Mōlĭŏr, nītŏr, ādnītŏr, cōnnītŏr.

* cŏmmŏnĕfăcĭo, fēcī, *and* cŏmmŏnĕo, ŭī, *to warn, advise.* SYN. Ādmŏnĕo, mŏnĕo.

cŏmmŏnĭtŭs, ă, ŭm, *the pass. partic. of* commoneo. Cŏmmŏnĭtŭs ădĭt, (Glyc.)

* cŏmmŏrŏr, ārĭs, *to stop.* Plaut. SYN. Mŏrŏr, mănĕo, cōnsīsto.

cŏmmōtŭs, ă, ŭm, *the pass. partic. of* commoveo. Ērgo ŭbĭ cŏmmōtā fērvĕt, Pers.

cŏmmŏvĕo, mōvī, tŭm, *to move.* Cŏmmŏvĕt ālās, Virg. SYN. Mŏvĕo, pērtūrbo, tērrĕo, āffĭcĭo, ēxcĭto, cōncĭto, īncĭto.

cŏmmūnĭco, ās, *to communicate.* Cŏmmūnĭcăt āctă, Ov. SYN. Cōnfĕro, crēdo, pārtĭŏr, ĭmpērtĭŏr, pārtĭcĭpēm făcĭo.

‖ cŏmmūnĭo, ĭs, *to fortify.* Cæs. SYN. Mūnĭo, vāllo. V. Munio.

cŏmmūnĭs, ĕ, *common.* Cŏmmūnĭbŭs ōbsto, Virg. SYN. Vŭlgārĭs, pŏpŭlārĭs, plēbēĭŭs, pērvŭlgātŭs, trītŭs, nōn rārŭs, frĕquēns.

* cŏmmūnĭtās, ātĭs, f., *community.* Cic. SYN. Cŏmmūnĭo, cŏmmērcĭŭm, fœdŭs, sŏcĭĕtās. EPITH. Sŏcĭă, fĭdă, suāvĭs.

cŏmmūnĭtĕr, adv., *in common.* Căpĭtŭr cŏmmūnĭtĕr hērbă, Ser. SYN. Vŭlgo, pāssĭm, ŭbīquĕ ; sæpĕ, sæpĭŭs, crēbro, plērūmquĕ, frĕquēntĕr.

cŏmmūrmŭro, ās, *to murmur together.* Cŏmmūrmŭrăt ŏrĕ, Sil.

cŏmmūto, ās, *to change.* Ĭn cŏmmūtātŭm vĕnĭūnt, Lucr. SYN. Mūto, pērmūto, cōnvērto, īnvērto. V. Muto.

cōmo, ĭs, cōmpsī, mptŭm, *to comb, adorn.* Cōmăt vīrgĭnĕās, Ov. SYN. Pēcto, dēpēcto, ōrno, ădōrno.

cōmœdĭă, æ, f., *comedy.* Vōcĕm cōmœdĭă tōllĭt, Hor.

cōmœdŭs, ī, m., *a comedian.* Hæc dē cōmœdīs, Juv.

cōmpāgēs, ĭs, f., *a close joining.* Cūrvăm cōmpāgĭbŭs ālvŭm, Virg. SYN. Cōmpāgo, cŏmmīssūră, vīncŭlŭm. EPITH. Sŏlĭdă, vălĭdă, fērrĕă, dūră, rĭgĭdă, fīrmă, sēcūră, tĕnăx, īncōncūssă. V. Vinculum.

cōmpāgo, ĭnĭs, f., *a joint.* Călămĭs cōmpāgĭnĕ cēræ, Ov. V. Compages.

cōmpār, ărĭs, *equal, like.* Cōmpārĭbŭs frēnĭs, Ov. SYN. Pār, sĭmĭlĭs, æquālĭs.

cōmpār, ărĭs, m. f., *a husband or wife.* Mūnĭă cōmpārĭs, Hor.

cōmpārātŭs, ă, ŭm, *the pass. partic. of* comparo. Cŭm cōmpărātă, (Scaz.) Mart.

cōmpārĕo, ēs, *to appear.* Nŭllī cōmpārŭĭt ōrbĕ, Ov. SYN. Appārĕo, vĭdĕŏr, ādsŭm, ēxsto.

cŏmpăro, ās, *to compare, prepare*. Sē mǐhǐ cŏmpărăt Ājăx, Ov. Syn. Coŭfĕro, āssǐmǐlo, āpto, cōmpōno, æquo, cŏæquo ; păro, āssĕquŏr, cōnsĕquŏr, ācquǐro, ădǐpīscŏr, ōbtǐnĕo, cōllǐgo. V. Simǐlis.—*The usual formulæ of comparison are :* Nōn sĕcŭs āc. Haŭd sĕcŭs āc. Nōn ălǐtĕr. Haŭd ălǐtĕr. Ceŭ. Vĕlŭt. Vĕl-ŭtī. Ac vĕlŭt. Ac vĕlŭtī. Ŭt. Ŭtī. Sīcŭt. Sīcŭtī. Instăr. Ŭt sōlĕt. Nōn sĕcŭs ātque ōlǐm. Ŭt quōndăm.

cōmpĕdēs, dŭm, f. pl., *shackles for the feet*. Sēd nĕquĕ cōmpĕdǐbŭs, Ov. Syn. Cătēnæ, vīncŭlă, lăquĕŭs. Epith. Dūræ, pērdūræ, sævæ, tĕnācēs, fīrmæ, sēr-vīlēs, pōndĕrōsæ, vălǐdæ, tārdæ, grăvēs, fērrĕæ, mŏlēstæ. V. Catena.

cōmpĕdītŭs, ă, ŭm, *tied, chained*. Tŭm cōmpĕdītī jānŭăm, (Iamb.) Sen. Syn. Cōmpĕdǐbŭs vīnctŭs, lǐgātŭs.

cōmpēllo, ās, *to call on, speak to*. Cōmpēllărăt, ĕt hās, Virg. Syn. Vŏco, ădvŏco, āllŏquŏr.

cōmpēllo, ǐs, pŭlī, pŭlsŭm, *to push, force*. Vǐrǐdī cōmpēllĕre hǐbīscō, Virg. Syn. Pēllo, ūrgĕo, ădǐgo, cōgo, ǐmpēllo.

cōmpēndǐŭm, ī, n., *gain*. Cōmpēndǐă tērrīs, Tib.

cōmpēnsātǐo, ōnǐs, f., *a compensation*. Hæc cōmpēnsātǐŏ rūpǐt, Sid. Syn. Mērcēs, præmǐŭm.

cōmpēnso, ās, *to recompense*. Cŭm mĕă cōmpēnsĕt, Hor. Syn. Pēnso, mūnĕrŏr, rĕmūnĕro.

cōmpĕrǐo, ĕrī, ērtŭm, *to discover, know*. Ŭnde hōc cōmpĕrĕrǐm, Ov. Syn. Dē-prĕhēndo, scǐo, nŏvī.

cōmpēs, ĕdǐs, f., *a chain, shackle*. Sōlātŭr cōmpĕdĕ vīnctŭm, Tib. V. Com-pedes.

cōmpēsco, ǐs, ŭī, *to repress*. Cōmpēscĕrĕt ǐnfĕrǐōrĕm, Hor. Syn. Cŏhǐbĕo, rĕtǐnĕo, cōntǐnĕo, cŏērcĕo, fræno, refræno, cōmprǐmo.

¦ cōmpĕto, ǐs, *to be convenient*. Ŭbǐ cōmpĕtĕt ætās, Sil. Syn. Cōnvĕnǐo, cōn-grŭo, dĕcĕo.

cōmpīlo, ās, *to plunder*. Cōmpīlărĕ Cǐlīx, (Phal.) Mart. Syn. Ēxpīlo, dīrǐpǐo, ērǐpǐo, fūrŏr, prædŏr.

cōmpīngo, ǐs, *to compact, thrust in*. Cōmpāctă cǐcūtīs, Virg. Syn. Cōmpēllo, dētrūdo, ădǐgo, ūrgĕo ; cōmpōno, cōnjūngo.

cōmpǐtālǐă, ŭm or ōrŭm, n. pl., *festivals in honour of the household gods*. Ŭnctă cōmpǐtālǐă, Virg.

cōmpǐtŭm, ī, n., *a cross-way*. Cōmpǐtă grātă cănī, Ov. Syn. Vǐă, ǐtĕr, vīcŭs, plătĕă. V. Via.

cōmplăcĕo, ēs, *to please*. Cōmplăcŭǐssĕ vǐrŭm, Ped. Syn. Plăcĕo, ārrīdĕo.

cōmplāno, ās, *to level*. Cōmplānāndă dŏmŭs, Fill. Syn. Æquo, ădæquo, ēx-æquo ; sōlō æquo, ēvērto.

cōmplēctŏr, ĕrǐs, ēxŭs sŭm, *to embrace*. Grĕmǐŏ cōmplēctǐtŭr ōssă, Virg. Syn. Āmplēctŏr, cōmplēxū tĕnĕo, fŏvĕo. V. Amplector.

cōmplĕo, ēvī, ētŭm, *to fill*. Cōmplētŭr mēnsǐbŭs ōrbǐs, Virg. Syn. Implĕo, ădǐmplĕo ; pērfǐcǐo, ābsōlvo, fīnǐo. cōnfǐcǐo, ǐmpōno fīnĕm.

cōmplēxŭs, ūs, m., *an embrace*. Nōstrīs cōmplēxǐbŭs ārcĕt, Virg. Syn. Am-plēxŭs. Epith. Ăvǐdŭs, tĕnāx, mōllǐs, nēxǐlǐs, ārctŭs, mūtŭŭs, dūlcǐs, tĕnĕr, plăcǐdŭs. V. Amplexus.

cōmplǐco, ās, ăvī or ŭī, *to fold*. Rŭdēntēm cōmplǐco, Plaut. Syn. Plǐco, cōn-vōlvo, īnvōlvo, cōntrăho.

cōmplōro, ās, *to bewail*. Chārmē cōmplōrăt ănīlī, Virg.

cōmplūrēs, ǐŭm, m. pl., *several, many*. Cōmplūrēs ălǐŏs, Hor. Syn. Mūltī, pēr-mūltī, plūrēs, plūrǐmī.

cōmpōno, ǐs, *to put together, compare*. Pārvīs cōmpōnĕrĕ māgnă, Virg. Syn. Cōmpăro, cōnfĕro, āpto, āssǐmǐlo, æquo, ēxæquo, ădæquo, cŏæquo ; cōnjūngo, cōmmītto ; scrībo.

cōmpōrto, ās, *to convey*. Ēmptās cōmpōrtĕt ǐn ūnŭm, Hor.

cōmpŏs, ŏtǐs, *possessing*. Vīx mēntǐs cōmpŏs, Ov.

cōmpŏsǐtō, adv., *on purpose*. Cōmpŏsǐtō rūmpǐt, Virg. Syn. Cōnsūltō.

cōmpŏsǐtŏr, ōrǐs, m., *one who puts things together*. Cōmpŏsǐtŏrĕ sŭō, Ov.

cōmpŏsǐtŭs, ă, ŭm, *the pass. partic. of* compono. Mōllǐă cōmpŏsǐtă, Prop.

* cōmpŏtŏr, ōrǐs, m., *a pot-companion*. Syn. Cōmbǐbo.

F 2

cŏmprĕhēndo, cŏmprēndo (*trisyl.*), dī, sŭm, *to seize.* Lōngīs cŏmprēndĕrĕ crīnĭbŭs ĭgnĕm, Virg. Syn. Ăccĭpĭo, căpĭo, ăpprĕhēndo, ăssĕquŏr ; cŏncĭpĭo, Intēllĭgo, pērcĭpĭo.

cŏmprĭmo, prēssī, *to compress.* Cŏmprĭmĕ grēssŭm, Virg. Syn. Tĕnĕo, rĕtĭnĕo, cŏērcĕo, cŏhĭbĕo, cŏmpēsco, sīsto, rĕtārdo ; prĕmo, ŏpprĭmo.

cŏmprŏbo, ās, *to approve.* Cŏmprŏbĕt ōmĕn, Ov. Syn. Prŏbo, ăpprŏbo, laŭdo.

cŏmptŭs, ă, ŭm, *the pass. partic. of* como. Cŏmptōs dē mŏrĕ căpĭllōs, Virg.

cŏmpŭto, ās, *to score.* Cŏmpŭtăt ārtĭcŭlīs, Ov. Syn. Nŭmĕro, cēnsĕo ; pŭto.

cŏmputrēsco, rŭī, *to wax rotten.* Cŏnquĕ pŭtrēscŭnt, Lucr. V. Putresco.

Cŏmŭs, ī, m., *the god of festivity.* Sălēs Cŏmŭs spārgĭt, Mill.

cŏnāmĕn, ĭnĭs, n., *an endeavour.* Fūnĕm cŏnāmĭnĕ trāxĭt, Ov. V. Conatus.

cŏnātŭs, ŭs, m., *and* ŭm, ī, n., *an endeavour, essay.* Fātŭm cŏnātĭbŭs ōbstăt, Ov. Cŏnātă pĕrēgĭt, Juv. Syn. Cŏnāmĕn, tēntāmĕn, mōlīmĕn, nīsŭs, vīs. Epith. Măgnŭs, cōnstāns, aŭdāx, gĕnĕrōsŭs, fōrtĭs, māgnănĭmŭs, laŭdābĭlīs, īngēns, vălĭdŭs, sūmmŭs, gĕmĭnātŭs, ēxĭgŭŭs, cŭpĭdŭs, mŏdĭcŭs.

Cŏncănŭs, ī, m., *a Cantabrian people.* Sāngŭĭnĕ Cŏncănŭm, Hor.

‖ cŏncăvĭtās, ătĭs, f., *concavity.* Cŏncăvĭtās rēgnī, Mant.

cŏncăvo, ās, *to make hollow.* Cŏncăvăt ārcŭs, Ov. Syn. Căvo, ēxcăvo.

cŏncăvŭs, ă, ŭm, *hollow.* Aŭt ŭbĭ cŏncăvă pŭlsŭ, Virg. Syn. Căvŭs, căvātŭs, ēxcăvātŭs, īmŭs, prŏfūndŭs.

cŏncēdo, cēssī, *to depart, yield.* Cŏncēdĭtŭr ŭtī, Hor. Syn. Dōno, dō, lārgĭŏr, trĭbŭo, pērmītto, cēdo ; fătĕŏr, nōn nĕgo, nōn rĕpūgno, nōn rĕcūso, nōn ābnŭo ; āccēdo, trānsĕo.

cŏncĕlebro, ās, *to celebrate, to people.* Cŏncĕlĕbra, ēt mūltō, Tib. V. Celebro.

cŏncēntŭs, ŭs, m., *a concert of voices.* Cŏncēntŭs ĭn ăgrīs, Virg. Syn. Cŏncōrs, cāntŭs. Vōcŭm dīscōrdĭā cŏncōrs. Epith. Grātŭs, dūlcīs, ārgūtŭs, blāndŭs. V. Cantus.

‖ cŏncēptăcŭlŭm, ī, n., *a receptacle.* Pēr cŏncēptăcŭlă sēsĕ, Prud.

cŏnchă, æ, f., *a shell-fish, shell.* Cŏnchārŭm tīnctă cŏlōrĕ, Lucr. Epith. Squālēns, căvă, prĕtĭōsă, vīlīs, dētrītă, mărīnă, tĕnŭĭs, tōrtă, æquŏrĕă, tōrtĭlīs, lūcĭdă, ădūncă, nērvōsă, Īndă, Īndĭcă, Eŏă, gēmmĭfĕră, gēmmātă, squāmōsă, squālĭdă, Sārrānă, Tўrĭă, Sĭdonĭă. V. Ostreum, testa, tuba.

cŏnchĭs, ĭs, f., *a bean unshaled.* Cŏnchĕ tūmēs, Juv.

cŏnchўlĕ, ĭs, *or* lĭŭm, ĭī, n., *a shell-fish, used to dye purple with.* Cŏnchўlī pūrpŭră fūcō, Cat. Implēnt cŏnchўlĭă Lūnæ, Hor. V. Murex.

cŏncīdo (cædo), cīdī, cīsŭm, *to cut in pieces.* Scrŏbĭbŭs cŏncīdĕrĕ mōntēs, Virg. Syn. Cædo, scīndo.

cŏncĭdo (cădo), cĭdī, *to fall.* Cŏncĭdĭt Īllĭă tēllŭs, Virg. Syn. Cădo, dēcĭdo, cōrrŭo, rŭo, lābŏr. V. Cado.

cŏncĭĕo, ēs, ĭvī, ĭtŭm, ĭĕrĕ, *and* cŏncĭo, īs, īvī *or* ĭī, ĭtŭm ĭrĕ, *to stir up, assemble, excite.* Cŏncĭĕt æstŭm, Lucr. Mūrmŭră cŏncĭt, Id.

cŏncĭlĭo, ās, *to join, conciliate.* Cŏncĭlĭāvĭt ămŏr, Mart. Syn. Cōnjūngo, dēvīncĭo ; ācquīro, păro, cŏmpăro.

cŏncĭlĭŭm, ĭī, n., *an assembly.* Ille ē cŏncĭlĭō, Virg. Syn. Cœtŭs, cōnvēntŭs.

cŏncīnno, ās, *to arrange, prepare, produce.* Cŏncīnnăt ămōrĕm, Lucr.

cŏncīnnŭs, ă, ŭm, *neat, elegant.* Quĭd cŏncīnnă Sămŏs, Hor.

cŏncĭno, ĭs, ŭī, *to sing together.* Cŏncĭnŭīssĕ fŏrēs, Ov. Syn. Căno, cănto ; cŏncēntum ĕdo : cāntŭ rēspōndĕo, rēspōnso, āccĭno.

*cŏncĭo, ōnĭs, f., *an assembly, an harangue.* Cic. Syn. Cŏncĭlĭŭm, cœtŭs, ōrātĭo, sērmo.

cŏncĭo, īs, ĭvī. V. Concieo.

cŏncĭpĭo, ĭs, *to conceive, comprehend.* Pīngŭĭă cŏncĭpĭŭnt, Virg. Syn. Pērcĭpĭo, nōsco, cōgnōsco, ăssĕquŏr, Intēllĭgo, căpĭo.

cŏncīsŭs, ă, ŭm, *the pass. partic. of* concīdo. Cŏncīsăquĕ cōnstrŭĭt āltĕ, Ov. V. Scissus.

cŏncĭtātŭs, ă, ŭm, *the pass. partic. of* concito. Sī cŏncĭtātă fērvĕănt, (Iamb.)

cŏncĭto, ās, *to excite.* Cŏncĭtăt ōmnĕ nĕmŭs, Ov. Syn. Ēxcĭto, mŏvĕo, sōllĭcĭto, stĭmŭlo, īncēndo, ăgo, pēllĭcĭo, ăcŭo.

cŏncĭtŭs, ă, ŭm, *the pass. partic. of* concieo. Cŏncĭtŭs ā læsō, Ov.

cŏncĭtŭs, ă, ŭm, *the pass. partic. of* concio. Tāntīs cŏncĭtă fŭrōrĭbŭs, Ov.

cōnclāmātŭs, ă, ŭm, *the pass. partic. of* conclamo. Cōnclāmătă jăcēnt, Luc.

cōnclāmo, ās, *to call aloud.* Prīmŭs cōnclāmăt Ăchātēs, Virg. Syn. Clāmo, ĕxclāmo, vōcīfĕrŏr.

cōnclāvĕ, Ys, n., *a room.* Cōnclāvĕ măgīsquĕ, Hor. Syn. Intĭmă ; sēcrētă, ōrŭm.

cōnclūdo, Ys, *to inclose.* Ĕt cōnclūdĕrĕ sŭlcō, Virg. Syn. Claŭdo, īnclūdo, cōl-līgo, īnsĕro ; ăbsŏlvo, pērfĭcĭo.

cōnclūsŭs, ă, ŭm, *the pass. partic. of* concludo. Rĕsŏnāt cōnclūsŭs, Hor.

cōncŏlŏr, ōrĭs, *of the same colour.* Cōncŏlŏr ālbō, Virg.

cōncŏquo, Ys, *to boil, digest.* Pŭlchrē cōncŏquĭtĭs, (Phal.) Cat.

Cōncōrdĭă, æ, f., *a goddess, the daughter of Jupiter and Themis: concord.* Fēlīx cōncŏrdĭă bĕllō, Prop. Syn. Păx. Epith. Dŭlcĭs, mĭtĭs, fēlīx, cāndĭdă, ĭnnŏcŭă, ālmă. V. Pax.

cōncōrdĭtĕr, adv., *peaceably.* Tōtōs cōncōrdĭtĕr ānnōs, Mant.

cōncŏrdo, ās, *to agree.* Cōncōrdārĕ sŏnōs, Ov.

cōncrĕbrēsco, Ys, bŭī, *to increase.* Cōncrĕbŭĭt eŭrō, Virg.

cōncrēdo, Ys, *to confide, entrust.* Cōncrēdĕrĕ mūrōs, Virg.

cōncrĕmo, ās, *to burn.* Ŭt cōncrĕmārĕm, (Iamb.) Sen. Syn. Cōmbūro, ūro, ĭncēndo, crĕmo, ădūro, ēxūro. V. Uro.

cōncrĕpĭto, ās, *the frequent. of* concrepo. Cōncrĕpĭtārĕ frăgŏr, Prud. Syn. Cōncrĕpo.

cōncrĕpo, ās, *to make a noise.* Cōncrĕpŭĕrĕ Dĕō, Ov. Syn. Crĕpo, crĕpĭto, cōncrĕpĭto, strīdĕo, strĕpĭto, strĕpo.

cōncrēsco, ēvī, ētŭm, *to grow, congeal.* Mŭndī cōncrēvĕrĭt ōrbĭs, Virg. Syn. Cōnflŏr, cŏĕo, cōmmīscĕŏr, cōndēnsŏr, dēnsŏr, cōgŏr, īndūrŏr.

cōncrētŭs, ă, ŭm, *the pass. partic. of* concresco. Mŭltă dĭū cōncrētă mŏdĭs, Virg.

cōncŭbīnŭs, ī, m., *and* ă, æ, f., *a catamite, a concubine.* Prŏcŭlīnă, cōncŭbīnō, (Phal.) Mart. Cōncŭbīnă flăbēllō, Id. Syn. Mœchŭs, ădŭltĕr, lŭxŭrĭōsŭs.

cōncŭbĭtŭs, ūs, m., *lying together.* Cōncŭbĭtū vĕtĭtō, Ov. Syn. Cŏĭtŭs. Epith. Nĕfāndŭs, īmpūrŭs, nōctūrnŭs, scĕlĕrātŭs, sōns, vĕtĭtŭs, īmprŏbŭs, dŏlōsŭs.

cōncŭbĭŭs, ă, ŭm, *when people are in bed.* Nāmque ŭbĭ cōncŭbĭæ, M.

cōncŭlco, ās, *to trample on.* Vīrūm cōncŭlcăt ĕquīnĭs, Ov. Syn. Cālco, tĕro, prŏtĕro, cōntĕro, prŏcŭlco.

cōncŭmbo, Ys, *to lie together.* Cōncŭbŭīssĕ vĭrĭs, Ov. Syn. Cōncŭbo.

cōncŭpīsco, Ys, *to wish for passionately.* Dŏmĭnĭquĕ cōncŭpīscŭnt, (Phal.) Mart. Syn. Cŭpĭo, cōncŭpĭo, ōpto, pĕrōpto, āppĕto.

cōncŭrro, Ys, cŭrrī, cūrsŭm, *to run together.* Cōncūrrĕrĕ prællă vĭdī, Virg. Syn. Accūrro, ādvŏlo, cōnvŏlo, cŏĕo, cōnflŭo.

cōncŭrso, ās, *the freq. of* concurro. Īgnēs cōncūrsānt, Lucr.

cōncūrsŭs, ūs, m., *a running together.* Cōncūrsŭs ăd īpsă, Virg. Syn. Accūrsŭs. Epith. Māgnŭs, īngēns, cĕlĕbrĭs, frĕquēns.

cōncūssŭs, ă, ŭm, *the pass. partic. of* concutio. Cōncūssō vērtĭcĕ nŭtăt, Virg.

cōncŭtĭo, tĭs, ūssī, *to shake.* Ægĭdă cōncŭtĕrĕt, Virg. Syn. Quătĭo, mŏvĕo, cōmmŏvĕo, ăgĭto, cōncĭto, jācto.

cōndĕcŏro, ās, *to adorn.* Pīctūrĭs cōndĕcŏrārī, Ulp. Syn. Dĕcŏro, hŏnēsto, ōrno, ēxōrno, ădōrno.

* cōndēmno, ās, *to condemn.* Cic. Syn. Dāmno.

‖ cōndēnso, as, *and* co, ēs, *to condense.* Cōndēnsăt āĕr, Lucr. Syn. Cōgo, spīsso, dēnso, īndūro, dūro.

cōndīco, Ys, *to promise, appoint.* Plaut. Syn. Sīgnĭfĭco, dēnūncĭo, cōnstĭtŭo.

cōndīmēntŭm, ī, n., *a seasoning.* Tŭndētūr cōndīmēntō, (Spond.) Ser. Syn. Cōndītĭo, cōndĭtūra. Epith. Suāvĕ, dŭlcĕ, grātŭm.

cōndĭo, īvī *and* ĭī, ītŭm, *to season.* Cōndīrĕ gŭlōsŭm, Juv.

cōndīscĭpŭlŭs, ī, m., *and* ă, æ, f., *a school-fellow.* Ĕt cōndīscĭpŭlī, Mart. Hāc cōndīscĭpŭlă, Mart.

cōndīsco, Ys, *to learn together.* Crīmēn cōndīscĭtŭr, Ov. V. Disco.

cōndĭtĭo, ōnĭs, f., *a condition.* Cōndĭtĭōnĕ mălă, Mart. Syn. Lēx, păctŭm, mŏdŭs ; fōrtūnă, sōrs, stătŭs. Epith. Mĭsĕră, cōmmŏdă, dĭffĭcĭlĭs, ĭnīquă, dūră.

* cōndĭtĭo, (*from* cōndĭo,) ōnĭs, f., *a seasoning.* Syn. Cōndīmēntŭm, cōndĭtūră. Epith. Suāvĭs, dŭlcĭs, grātă.

‖ cōndĭtŏr, ōrĭs, (*from* cōndĭo,) m. V. Coquus.

cŏndĭtŏr, ōrĭs, (*from* cōndo,) m,, *a founder.* Rōmānæ cŏndĭtŏr ārcĭs, Virg. SYN. Extrūctŏr, fabrĭcātŏr, fūndātŏr.

cŏndītŭs, ă, ŭm, *the pass. partic. of* condio. Mălĕ cŏndītūm jūs, Hor. SYN. Mīstŭs, āspērsŭs.

cŏndītŭs, ă, ŭm, *the pass. partic. of* condo. Præcŏrdĭă cŏndĭtă Lībĕr, Hor. SYN. Ābscōndĭtŭs, ābdĭtŭs, ŏccūltŭs, lătēns ; cōnstrūctŭs.

cōndo, ĭs, *to conceal, build.* Cŏndĭdĭmŭs tērrā, Virg. SYN. Ābscōndo, ōccŭlo, ŏccūlto, tĕgo, ōbtĕgo ; cōnstrŭo, cōmpōno, cōllĭgo, cŏăcērvo. V. Occulto, ædifico.

cŏndŏlĕo, ēs, *to condole.* Ăt sī cŏndŏlŭĭt, Hor. SYN. Dŏlĕo, īndŏlĕo, mœrĕo.

|| cōndōno, ăs, *to give, to pardon.* Cōndōnăt ŏpēs, Claud. SYN. Dōno ; rĕmītto, pārco, īgnōsco.

cŏndūcĭbĭlĭs, ĕ, *useful.* Cōndūcĭbĭle, ātquĕ bĕātĕ, Sidon. SYN. Cōmmŏdŭs, āptŭs, ūtĭlĭs.

cōndūco, xī, *to be useful, conduct, hire.* Prŏpŏsĭtō cōndŭcăt, ĕt hærĕăt, Hor. SYN. Dūco ; sūm cōmmŏdŭs, ūtĭlĭs, āptŭs ; cōnvĕnĭo ; rĕdĭmo, lŏco.

cōndūctŏr, ōrĭs, m., *a contractor.* Ōmnĭă cōndūctŏr, Ov.

cōndŭplĭco, ăs, *to double.* Quī cōndŭplĭcănt, Lucr.

cōndŭro, ăs, *to harden.* Cōndūrăt ăb īgnĕ, Lucr.

cōndўlŭs, ī, m., *a joint in the knee, finger, &c.* Cōndўlī sŏnābĭt, (Phal.) Mart.

cōnfābŭlŏr, ārĭs, *to speak with.* Cōnfābŭlŏr ūsū, Mant. V. Colloquor.

cōnfēctŭs, ă, ŭm, *the pass. partic. of* conficio. Cōnfēctī cūrsūs, Virg.

cōnfĕro, tŭlī, lātŭm, *to bring.* Cōnfĕr, ăĭt, Ov. SYN. Fĕro ; cōmpăro ; cōngĕro, cōnjĭcĭo ; prōsŭm.

cōnfērtŭs, ă, ŭm, *crowded, filled full.* Quōs ŭbī cōnfērtōs, Virg.

cōnfērvĕo, ēs, bŭī, *to boil.* Cōnfērbŭĭt īrā, Hor.

cōnfēstĭm, adv., *immediately.* Ŭt tē cōnfēstĭm, Hor. SYN. Cōntĭnŭō, stătĭm.

cōnfĭcĭo, fēcī, *to do, to finish.* Cōnfĭcĭt, ēt tĕnĕbrīs, Virg. SYN. Făcĭo, ēffĭcĭo, ābsōlvo, ēxpĕdĭo, pērfĭcĭo ; ābsūmo, pēssūmdo, āttĕro ; ōccīdo, īntērfĭcĭo, pĕrĭmo.

cōnfĭdēns, ēntĭs, *confident.* Jŭvĕnūm cōnfĭdēntĭssĭmĕ, nōstrās, Virg. SYN. Fīdēns, fīsŭs, cōnfīsŭs, aūdāx.

cōnfīdo, īdī, īsŭm, *to trust in.* Quīsquām cōnfīdĕrĕ rēbŭs, Cl. SYN. Fīdo, fīdĕm hăbĕo ; crēdo, cōmmītto. V. Fido.

cōnfīgo, īxī, īxŭm, *to stick, pierce.* Ipsăm cōnfīgĭtĕ mātrĕm, Juv. SYN. Fīgo, trānsfīgo, vūlnĕro, cōnfŏdĭo, saūcĭo.

cōnfĭndo, ĭs, *to cleave.* Cōnfīndĭtŭr ærĕ, Tib.

cōnfīnĕ, ĭs, n., *and* cōnfīnĭŭm, ĭī, n., *the limit, confine.* Ăd cōnfīnĕ māmĭllæ, Virg. Cōnfīnĭă nōctĭs, Ov.

cōnfīngo, īnxī, īctŭm, *to form, feign.* Cōnfīngĭs ĕquŏrŭm, Val. Fl. SYN. Fīngo, ēxcōgĭto, cōmmīnīscŏr, cōmmēntŏr.

cōnfīnĭs, ĕ, *next to.* Dūbĭæ cōnfīnĭă nōctĭs, Ov. SYN. Āffīnĭs, vīcīnŭs, prŏpīnquŭs, fīnītĭmŭs, cōntērmĭnŭs.

cōnfīo, ĭs, *to be done.* Cōnfīĕrī pōssĭt, Virg.

cōnfīrmo, ăs, *to strengthen.* Prīncēps cōnfīrmăt ĭtūrōs, Claud. SYN. Āssĕro, āssĕvĕro, āffīrmo.

cōnfīsŭs, ă, ŭm, *trusting in.* Pĕlāgō cōnfīsĕ sĕrēnō, Virg. SYN. Fīsŭs, fīdēns, cōnfīdēns, aūdāx.

cōnfĭtĕŏr, ērĭs, *to confess.* Cōnfĭtĕārĕ tŭī, Ov. SYN. Fătĕŏr, āgnōsco.

* cōnflagro, ăs, *to burn.* Cic. SYN. Flagro, ārdĕo, crĕmŏr, ūrŏr, cōmbūrŏr, ārdēsco, ēxārdēsco, īncēndŏr. V. Ardeo.

|| cōnflātĭlĭs, ĕ, *cast.* Jūpĭtēr cōnflātĭlĭs, (Iamb.) Prud. SYN. Cōnflātŭs.

cōnflātŭs, ă, ŭm, *the pass. partic. of* conflo. Fōrmæ cōnflātŭs ămōrĕ, Lucr.

* cōnflīctŭs, ūs, m., *the dashing against.* Liv. SYN. Pūgnă, prælĭŭm, cērtāmĕn, cōngrēssŭs. V. Certamen, luctus.

cōnflīgo, īxī, īctŭm, *to fight.* Pōssĕt cōnflīgĕrĕ rēbŭs, Cl. SYN. Pūgno, cōngrĕdĭŏr, cērto, dīmĭco. V. Certo, pugno, luctor.

cōnflo, ăs, *to blow, to form.* Cōnflāvĭt ĭmāgĭnĭs aūrŭm, Prop. SYN. Fabrĭcŏr, fabrĭco ; (ēx ærĕ, aūrō,) fūndo, cūdo, ēxcūdo, lăbōro, cōnfĭcĭo.

cōnflŭo, xī, xŭm, *to flow together.* Sōlērtĭā cōnflŭăt ōrbĕ, Ov. SYN. Cōnvĕnĭo, cōncūrro, cŏĕo.

cŏnflŭvĭum, ĭī, n., *the place where two rivers meet.* Dōnēc cŏnflŭvĭŏ, Sev. Syn. Cŏnflūxŭs, cŏnflŭvĭes.

cŏnfŏdĭo, fŏdī, fŏssŭm, *to dig, stab.* Tĕlăquĕ cŏnfŏdĭŭnt, Val. Fl. Syn. Fŏdĭo, dĕfŏdĭo; fĕrĭo, pĕrcŭtĭo.

* cōnfōrmo, ās, *to form.* Cōnfōrmătă cămĭnīs, Stat. Syn. Assĭmĭlo; cōmpōno, fōrmo, ĭnfōrmo, fĭgūro.

cōnfōssŭs, ă, ŭm, *the pass. partic. of* confodio. Prōjēcĭt ămīcŭm Cōnfōssŭs, Virg.

cōnfrăgōsŭs, and gŭs, ă, ŭm, *rough, craggy.* Cōnfrăgōsa ūt lēnĭbŭs, (Iamb.) Prud. Et cōnfrăgă dēnsĭs, Luc. Syn. Aspĕr, scăbĕr, sălebrōsŭs, scrŭpĕŭs, petrōsŭs, lăpĭdōsŭs, sāxōsŭs, ĭnăccēssŭs.

cōnfrĕmo, ĭs, ŭī, *to murmur together.* Cōnfrĕmŭēre ōmnēs, Ov. V. Fremo.

cōnfrīngo, frēgī, frāctŭm, *to break.* Prīmŭs cōnfrīngĕrĕ claūstră, Luc. Syn. Frāngo, ĭnfrīngo.

cōnfŭgĭo, gĭs, fŭgī, *to fly for shelter.* Ad tē cōnfŭgĭo, Virg. Syn. Fŭgĭo, diffŭgĭo. V. Fugio.

cōnfŭgĭum, ĭī, n., *a refuge.* Cōnfŭgĭŭmquĕ rătī, Ov. Syn. Pĕrfŭgĭŭm, ăsȳlŭm, tūtēla.

cōnfūndo, fūdī, fūsŭm, *to confound.* Sĭcŭlĭs cōnfūndĭtŭr ūndīs, Virg. Syn. Mīscĕo, pĕrmīscĕo, tŭrbo, pērtŭrbo.

cōnfūsŭs, ă, ŭm, *the pass. partic. of* confundo. Vărĭă cōnfūsŭs ĭmăgĭnĕ, Virg.

cōnfūto, ās, *to confute.* An cōnfūtābūnt nārēs? Lucr. Syn. Rĕfūto, rĕfēllo, rŭjĭcĭo, ēxplōdo, dīlŭo, ĭnfīrmo, cŏārgŭo, dīssōlvo, frāngo.

cōngĕlo, ās, *to congeal.* Cōngĕlăt hȳbērnī, Val. Fl. Syn. Cōnglăcĭo, gĕlo. V. Gelo.

cōngĕmĭno, ās, *to redouble.* Cōngĕmĭnāt, vūlnŭs, Virg. Syn. Gĕmĭno, dŭplĭco, cōndŭplĭco.

cōngĕmo, ŭī, *to groan.* Cōngĕmŭīt, trāxītquĕ, Virg. Syn. Gĕmo, īngĕmo, ādgĕmo.

cōngĕnĭtŭs, ă, ŭm, *born together.* Cīvēs cōngĕnĭtōs, Prud. Syn. Ingĕnĭtŭs, īnsĭtŭs, īnnātŭs, nātīvŭs.

cōngĕr and cōngrŭs, ī, m., *a conger eel.* Immītīsquĕ sŭæ cōngĕr, Ov.

cōngĕrĭes, ĭēī, f., *a heap.* Cōngĕrĭem sĕcŭĭt, Ov. Syn. Acērvŭs, strŭēs, cŭmŭlŭs, cŏpĭă. V. Acervus.

cōngĕro, ĭs, *to heap.* Cōngĕrĕre ārbŏrĭbŭs, Virg. Syn. Aggĕro, cōllĭgo, ăcērvo, āccŭmŭlo, aūgĕo, ādaūgĕo, cōnglŏmĕro, cŏārcērvo, āgglŏmĕro, glŏmĕro, strŭo, ēxtrŭo. V. Accumulo.

cōngēstŭs, ūs, m., *a heaping together.* Cōngēstŭs ărēnæ, Lucr

cōngēstŭs, ă, ŭm, *the pass. partic. of* congero. Cōngēstīs ūndĭquĕ sāccīs, Hor.

cōngĭārĭŭm, ĭī, n., *a largess given to the people.* Cōngĭārĭŭm lāssī, (Scaz.) Mart.

cōnglăcĭo, ās, *to freeze.* Cōnglăcĭāntŭr ăquæ, Albinov.

cōnglŏbo, ās, *to gather into a lump.* Cōnquĕ glŏbātă, Lucr.

cōnglŏmĕro, ās, *to heap into a ball.* Sī pōssĭt cōnglŏmĕrārī, Lucr. Syn. Glŏmĕro, āgglŏmĕro, cŏăcērvo. V. Congero.

‖ cōnglūtĭno, ās, *to join.* Ter. Syn. Agglūtĭno, jūngo, cōpŭlo, cōnjūngo, glūtĭnĕ nēcto.

* cōngrătŭlŏr, ārĭs, *to congratulate.* Plaut.

cōngrĕdĭŏr, ĕrĭs, grēssŭs, *to meet together.* Sī cōngrĕdĭāmŭr, hăbēmŭs, Virg. Syn. Cōnflīgo, pūgno, cērto, dēcērto, dīmĭco. V. Luctor, pugno.

cōngrĕgātĭm, adv., *together.* Cōngrĕgātĭm mœnĭă, St. Syn. Acērvātĭm, cŏăcērvātĭm, ūnā, sĭmŭl.

cōngrĕgo, ās, *to assemble.* Cōngrĕgāt, ēt lōngŭm, St. Syn. Cōngĕro, ăcērvo, cŏăcērvo, cōgo, cōllĭgo, cōntrăho, āggĕro, cōnjūngo, glŏmĕro, āgglŏmĕro.

cōngrēssŭs, ūs, m., *a meeting.* Cōngrēssŭquĕ nĕcī, Virg.

cōngrŭo, ĭs, *to agree, to suit.* Cōngrŭĕrĕt tĭtŭlō, Prop. Syn. Cōnvĕnĭo, quadro, cōnsŏno, cōnsēntĭo.

cōngrŭŭs, ă, ŭm, *convenient.* Cōngrŭă tēmpŏră, Cl. V. Commodus.

cōnĭfĕr and cōnĭgĕr, ă, ŭm, *bearing cone-like fruit.* Cōnĭfĕræ cȳpărīssī, Virg. Cōnĭgĕrăm sūdāntī, Cat.

‖ cōnisco, ās, *to butt with the head.* Blāndēquĕ cōnīscănt, Lucr.

cōnjēctūră, æ, f., *a conjecture.* Et cōnjēctūră fŭtūrī, Ov. Syn. Aūgŭrĭŭm, ŏpĭnĭo, sēntēntĭă, sŭspĭcĭo, dīvīnātĭo.

cōnjēctŭs, ŭs, m., *a throwing, heaping together.* Cŏnjēctū mătĕrĭăī, Lucr.

cōnjĭcĭŏ, cĭs, jēcī, *to throw, to conjecture.* Cŏnjĭcĕ săxă, Virg. SYN. Aŭgŭrŏr, dīvīno, sŭspĭcŏr, cōnjēcto, jăcĭo, īnjĭcĭo.

cōnjŭgālĭs, *and* ĭālĭs, ĕ, *belonging to marriage.* Dī cōnjŭgālĕs, (Iamb.) Nēc cōnjŭgĭālĭă jŭră, Ov. SYN. Jŭgālĭs, sŏcĭālĭs, mărītālĭs.

cōnjŭgĭŭm, ĭī, n., *marriage.* Nī dărĕ cōnjŭgĭŭm, Virg. SYN. Cŏnnubĭŭm, nŭptĭæ, Hўmĕnæī. EPITH. Stăbĭlĕ, fīdŭm, sŏcĭălĕ, sānctŭm, fīrmŭm, sacrŭm, sōllĭcĭtŭm, pĕrēnnĕ, fīdēlĕ, gĕnĭālĕ, faŭstŭm, fēlīx, cāstŭm, pŭdīcŭm, sŏcĭŭm, cŏncŏrs, ămīcŭm, sŏlēnnĕ.

cōnjŭgŭs, ă, ŭm, *joined.* Cōnjŭgă pērmīsĭt, Fill.

cōnjūngo, ĭs, *to join.* Cĕră cōnjūngĕrĕ plūrēs, Virg. SYN. Jūngo, ădjūngo, ădnēcto, cŏpŭlo.

cōnjūrātŭs, ă, ŭm, *the pass. partic. of* conjuro. Cōnjūrātă tŭăs, Hor.

cōnjūro, ās, *to conjure.* Ēt cōnjūrăt ămīcē, Hor. SYN. Cōnspīro, ĭnsĭdĭŏr; jūro.

cōnjūx, jŭgĭs, f., *a wife.* Bŏnæ cōnjŭgĭs ēsto, Ov. SYN. Ŭxŏr, spōnsă. EPITH. Pŭlchră, vĕnūstă, fōrmōsă, pŭdīcă, chără, fīdă, fīdēlĭs, grătă, ămātă, ămīcă, dīlēctă, cāstă, sōllĭcĭtă.—2. m., *a husband.* Cōnjŭgĭs aŭdīssĕt, Mart. SYN. Spōnsŭs, mărītŭs, vĭr. EPITH. Fīdŭs, chărŭs, fīdēlĭs, ămātŭs, dīlēctŭs, cāstŭs, sŏcĭŭs, sōllĭcĭtŭs.

cōnlāxo, ās, *to slacken.* Cōnlāxāt rārĕquĕ, Lucr.

cōnnēcto, nēxŭī *or* xī, *to tie.* Vēstēs cōnnēxŭĭt ānguĕ, Claud. SYN. Nēcto, jūngo, ădjūngo, cōnjūngo, ădnēcto, āddo, cōpŭlo, īllĭgo, cōmpōno.

cōnnītŏr, ĕrĭs, nīsŭs *or* xŭs, *to endeavour, to lean.* Tōtō cōnnīxŭs, Virg. SYN. Īnnītŏr, cōnŏr.

cōnnīvĕo, īvī *or* xī, *to wink.* Cōnnīvēns ŏcŭlīs, Sil. SYN. Dīssĭmŭlo; īndŭlgĕo, pārco.

cōnnubĭālĭs, ĕ, *belonging to marriage.* Ŭbĭ cōnnŭbĭālĭă jŭră? Ov.

cōnnubĭŭm, ĭī, n., *marriage.* Cōnnŭbĭŏ jūngăm, Virg. Pўrrhīn cōnnŭbĭă sērvās, Id. V. Conjugium.

Cŏnōn, ŏnĭs, m., *a mathematician of Samos.* Dŭŏ sīgnă : Cŏnōn, Virg.

cōnōpeŭm, eī, n., *a veil, pavilion.* Tărpeĭŏ cōnōpĕă tēndĕrĕ săxō, Prop. Lēntŭlĕ, cŏnōpēō, Juv.

cōnŏr, *to strive.* Cŏnŏr ădīrĕ tŏrō, Prop. SYN. Tēnto, nītŏr, ēnītŏr, cōntēndo, mōlĭŏr, īncŭmbo, āggrĕdĭŏr, cōnnītŏr, ānnītŏr.

cōnquāsso, ās, *to shake, harass.* Cōnquāssātŭr ĕnĭm, Lucr.

cōnquĕrŏr, ĕrĭs, quēstŭs, *to complain.* Cōnquĕrŏr, ĭte ā mē, Tib. SYN. Quĕrŏr. V. Queror.

cōnquĭēsco, ĭēvī, *to repose.* SYN. Quĭēsco, rĕquĭēsco, cēsso, dēsĭno. V. Quiesco.

cōnquĭro, sīvī *or* sĭī, sītŭm, *to seek about.* Vŭlgō cōnquīrĕre ămāntēs, Pr. SYN. Quæro, scrūtŏr, īnvēstīgo, vēstīgo. V. Quæro.

cōnquĭsītŭs, ă, ŭm, *the pass. partic. of* conquiro. Cōnquīsītă dĭŭ, Lucr. SYN. Quæsītŭs.

cōnsānguĭnĕŭs, ă, ŭm, *of the same kindred.* Tūm cōnsānguĭnĕŭs, Virg. SYN. Cōgnātŭs, prŏpīnquŭs, āffīnĭs.

cōnsānguĭnĭtās, ātĭs, f., *kindred by blood.* Cōnsānguĭnītātĕ lĭgāvĭt, St.

cōnscĕlĕrātŭs, ă, ŭm, *the pass. partic. of* conscelero. Cōnscĕlĕrātă pĭă, Ov. V. Sceleratus.

cōnscĕlĕro, ās, *to soil.* Ŏcŭlōsquĕ vĭdēndō Cōnscĕlĕro, Ov. V. Scelero.

cōnscēndo, dī, sŭm, *to mount.* Cōnscēndēbăt ĕquŏs. SYN. Scāndo, āscēndo ; sŭpĕro.

cōns.ĭēntĭă, æ, f., *conscience.* Vĕĭă cōnscĭēntĭă, (Iamb.) Hor. EPITH. Mōrdāx, mōrdēns, stĭmŭlāns, crŭcĭāns, dūră, rĕmōrdēns, tōrquēns.

cōnscīndo, ĭs, *to tear.* Cōnscīndŭnt hŏmĭnĕm, Lucr. SYN. Scīndo, lăcĕro, dīscērpo, dīlănĭo.

cōnscĭo, ĭs, īvī, *to feel oneself culpable.* Nīl cōnscīrĕ sĭbi, Hor. SYN. Cōnscĭŭs sŭm ; tēstĭs mĭhi sŭm.

* cōncīsco, īvī, ītŭm, *to vote by common consent.* Liv. SYN. Dēcērno, īnfĕro.

cōnscĭŭs, ă, ŭm, *conscious, witness of.* Cōnscĭŭs aŭdācĭs făctī, Virg. SYN. Pārtĭcēps, sŏcĭŭs, tēstĭs ; rĕŭs, nŏcēns.

‖ cōnscrĭbīllo, ās, *to write down.* Flăgĕllă cōnscrĭbīllĕnt, Cat.

cōnscrībo, ĭs, psī, *to write, enroll.* Cōnscrībi īn sæcŭlă cīvĭs, Sed. SYN. Scrībo, īnscrībo, cōmpōno; cōllĭgo, cōgo.

cōnsĕco, ās, *to cut.* Cōnsĕcŭīssĕ, sŭī, Ov. V. Scco.

cōnsecro, ăs, *to consecrate.* Pōst fătă cōnsĕcrātŭs, (Iamb.) Sen. SYN. Sacro, dō, dīco, dēdĭco.

cōnsēctŏr, ārĭs, *to pursue.* Cōnsēctăbāntŭr sȳlvēstrĭă sēclă, Lucr. SYN. Sēctŏr, pērsĕquŏr, sĕquŏr, cōnsĕquŏr, aŭcŭpŏr, cāpto.

cōnsĕcūtŭs, ă, ŭm, *the partic. of* consequor. Extērnă cōnsĕcūtŭs, (Iamb.) Sen.

cōnsĕnēsco, nŭī, *to grow old.* Măcēsco, cōnsĕnēsco, (Iamb.) SYN. Sĕnēsco, sĕnēx fīo.

cōnsēnsŭs, ūs, m., *a consent.* Grăvĭŏr cōnsēnsŭs ĕrăt, Claud. SYN. Assēnsŭs; cōncōrdĭă. EPITH. Lībĕr, ămīcŭs, ōptātŭs, grātŭs, quæsītŭs, făcĭlĭs. V. Consentio.

cōnsēntānĕŭs, ă, ŭm, *convenient.* Nōn cōnsēntānĕă brūmæ, Mart. SYN. Cōnsēntĭēns, cōnvĕnĭēns, āptŭs, æquŭs.

cōnsēntĭo, sī, sŭm, *to agree.* Cōnsēntīrĕ sŭĭs stŭdĭĭs, Hor. SYN. Cōnvĕnĭo, āssēntĭo, āssēntĭŏr, ānnŭo, cōngrŭo.

• cōnsēpĭo, sēpsī, sēptŭm, *to hedge in.* Cōnsēptă tĕnēbrĭs, Man. SYN. Sēpĭo, mūnĭo, claŭdo, prætēndo sēpĕm.

cōnsĕquŏr, ĕrĭs, *to follow, emulate, obtain.* Cōnsĕquŏr, hīc ūt mē, Mart. SYN. Sĕquŏr; ădĭpīscŏr, ăcquīro, păro, cōmpăro, āssĕquŏr; V. Acquiro. Æmŭlŏr, ĭmĭtŏr.

cōnsĕro, sēvī, sĭtŭm, *to sow.* Queĭs cōnsēvĭmŭs āgrōs, Virg. SYN. Sĕro, īnsĕro, sēmĭno, plānto.

cōnsĕro, ŭī, sertŭm, *to join, to fight close.* Prælĭă nōctĕm Cōnsĕrĭmŭs, Virg. SYN. Mīscĕo, īmmīscĕo, cōnjūngo, cōnnēcto, cōnfĕro; pūgno, mănŭs cōnsĕro.

cōnsērvo, ās, *to preserve.* Cōnsērvābăt ŏpēs, Petr. SYN. Cūstōdĭo, tŭĕŏr, tūtŏr, sērvo, āssērvo.

cōnsērvŭs, ă, ŭm, *a fellow-slave.* Dūrăquĕ cōnsērvæ, Ov.

cōnsēssŭs, ūs, m., *an assembly.* Pōstquăm cōnsēssŭm, Virg. SYN. Cōnsēssĭo, cōncĭlĭŭm, cœtŭs, cōrōnă, frĕquēntĭă.

cōnsīdĕo, sēdī, sēssŭm, *to sit together.* Cōnsēdērĕ dŭcēs, Ov. SYN. Assĭdĕo, āssĭdo, ūnā sĕdĕo, quĭēsco, mŏrŏr, cōmmŏrŏr, cōnsīsto, cōnsīdo.

cōnsīdĕro, ās, *to consider.* Vēsŭīs cōnsīdĕrăt aŭrŭm, Juv. SYN. Pŭto, rĕpŭto, cōgĭto, cōntēmplŏr, mĕdĭtŏr, pōndĕro, ēxpēndo; V. Cogito. Aspĭcĭo, cōnspĭcĭo, spēcto, īntŭĕŏr. V. Aspicio.

cōnsīdo, ĭs, *to sit down.* Părĭtĕr cōnsīdĕrĕ rēgnĭs, Virg. V. Consideo.

‖ cōnsīgno, ās, *to send, register.* Nōs cōnsīgnēmŭs, Plaut. SYN. Ōbsīgno; īnscrībo.

cōnsĭlĭŏr, ārĭs, *to give advice.* Cōnsĭlĭātŭr ămīcĭs, Hor.

cōnsĭlĭŭm, ĭī, n., *advice.* Cōnsĭlĭŭm vūltŭ tĕgĭt, Virg. SYN. Sēntēntĭă, mēns, sēnsŭs, jūdĭcĭŭm, ănĭmŭs. EPITH. Arcānŭm, prūdēns, prōvĭdŭm, sălūtārĕ, ūtĭlĕ, fīdēlĕ, ămīcŭm, quæsītŭm, sēcrētŭm, cæcŭm, mātūrŭm, sălūtĭfĕrŭm.

cōnsĭmĭlĭs, ĕ, *like, similar.* Tædĭă cōnsĭmĭlī, Ov.

cōnsĭsto, ĭs, stĭtī, *to stop, stand fast, be, exist.* Cōnstĭtĭt Anchīsā sătŭs, Virg. Cōnsīstĕrĕ rēctŭm, Hor.

cōnsĭtŏr, ōrĭs, m., *a planter.* Cōnsĭtŏr ūvæ, Ov.

cōnsĭtŭs, ă, ŭm, *planted, sown, covered.* Cōnsĭtăquc ārbŏrĭbŭs, Ov.

cōnsōbrīnŭs, ī, m., *and* ă, æ, f., *a cousin-german.* Cōnsōbrīnĕ mĕĭs, Aus. SYN. Agnātŭs, cōgnātŭs, āffīnĭs, prōpīnquŭs.

cōnsŏcĭo, ās, *to join.* Cōnsŏcĭārĕ ămănt, (Asclep.) Hor. SYN. Jūngo, cōnjūngo, sŏcĭo.

• cōnsōlātĭo, ōnĭs, f., *consolation.* Cic. SYN. Sōlāmĕn, sōlātĭo, sōlātĭŭm. V. Solatium.

cōnsōlŏr, ārĭs, *to comfort.* Hīs mē cōnsōlŏr, Hor. SYN. Sōlŏr, lĕvo. V. Solor.

cōnsŏno, ās, *to sound, to echo.* Cōnsŏnăt ōmnĕ nĕmŭs, Virg. SYN. Sŏno, rĕsŏno, pērsŏno; cōnsēntĭo, cōnvĕnĭo.

cōnsŏnŭs, ă, ŭm, *of the same sound.* Vōx cōnsŏnă līnguæ, Sil.

cōnsōpĭo, īvī or ĭī, ītŭm, *to lull asleep.* Cōnsōpĭt ĭbīdĕm, Lucr. SYN. Sōpĭo, sŏpōro.

cōnsōrs, ōrtĭs, m. f., *a consort, partaker.* Cōnsōrtĕ cărēbăt, Ov. Syn. Pārtĭcēps, sŏcĭŭs.

‖ cōnsōrtĭŭm, ĭĭ, n., *partnership.* Cōnsōrtĭă tērræ, Sil. Syn. Sŏcĭă vītă. Sŏcĭŭs lăbŏr. Cōnsōrtĭă tēctă. Cōnsōrs stŭdĭŭm.

cōnspēctŭs, ūs, m., *the sight.* Syn. Ăspēctŭs, prōspēctŭs, vīsŭs.

cōnspērgo, sī, sŭm, *to besprinkle.* Cōnspērgŭnt ārăs, Lucr. Syn. Ăspērgo, pērfŭndo, spārgo.

cōnspĭcĭo, ēxī, ēctŭm, *to see, behold.* Cōnspĭcĭārĕ sēnēx, Ped. Syn. Ăspĭcĭo, cōnspĭcŏr, cōnsīdĕro, vĭdĕo, īntŭĕŏr. V. Aspicio.

cōnspĭcŏr, ārĭs, *to look at.* Mē cōnspĭcŏr ĭpsĕ, Ov. V. Conspicio.

cōnspĭcŭŭs, ă, ŭm, *conspicuous.* Cōnspĭcŭŭmquĕ pŏlŭm, Ov. Syn. Cōnspĭcĭēndŭs, clārŭs, pērspĭcŭŭs, ĭllŭstrĭs.

cōnspĭro, ās, *to blow together, to conspire.* Cōnspīrănt cōrnŭă raŭcō, Virg. Syn. Cōnjūro, cōnsēntĭo, cōnvĕnĭo.

cōnspŭo, *to spit upon.* Cōnspŭĕt Alpēs, Hor.

cōnstāns, ntĭs, *steady.* Cōnstāns īn lĕvĭtătĕ sŭa ēst, Ov. Syn. Fīrmŭs, īmmōtŭs, īmmōbĭlĭs, tĕnāx.

cōnstāntĕr, adv., *steadily.* Nĭmĭŭm cōnstāntĕr ĭnĭquŏs, Ov.

cōnstāntĭă, æ, f., *constancy.* Tē cōnstāntĭă lōngæ, Ov. Syn. Grăvĭtās. Epith. Impĕnetrābĭlĭs, īmmōtă, īnvīctă, fīrmă, īntrĕpĭdă, sēcūră, fōrtĭs, aŭdāx, gĕnĕrōsă, māgnănĭmă, vīrīlĭs, stăbĭlĭs, īmmōbĭlĭs, īmpăvĭdă, pērpĕtŭă, īmpērtērrĭtă, māgnă, īncōncŭssă, īmpătĭēns, īntērrĭtă, stŭpēndă, īnēxpŭgnābĭlĭs.

Cōnstāntīnōpŏlĭs, ĭs, f., *the capital of Turkey.* Cōnstāntīnōpŏlĭs, Rhĕtŏrĕ tē, vĭgŭĭt, Aus. Syn. Bȳzāntĭŭm. Epith. Āltă, māgnă, āmplă, pŏtēns, mūnītă. V. Byzantium.

cōnstērno, ĭs, strāvī, *to strew.* Cōnstērnŭnt tērrăm, Virg. Syn. Effŭndo, stērno, spārgo, cōnspērgo.

cōnstērno, ās, *to terrify.* Cōnstērnāntŭr ĕquī, Ov.

cōnstĭpo, ās, *to cram close.* Ēt cōnstīpātă sĕdēbăt, Prud. Syn. Stīpo, dēnso, cōndēnso, cōgo.

cōnstĭtŭo, ŭī, ūtŭm, *to put, dispose.* Taūrūm cōnstĭtŭăm, Virg. Syn. Stătŭo, dēcērno, dēlībĕro, cōgĭto, dēsīgno ; pōno, cōllŏco.

cōnsto, cōnstĭtī, *to stand.* Āddūctō cōnstĭtĭt ārcŭ, Virg. Syn. Stō, pērsto, pērsĕvēro.

cōnstrīngo, strīnxī, strīctŭm, *to tie strait.* Gălĕăm cōnstrīngĭt Ĭāsōn. Syn. Ārcto, cŏārcto, cōmprĭmo, āstrīngo, lĭgo. V. Vincio.

cōnstrŭo, xī, ctŭm, *to build.* Sĭbĭ cōnstrŭĭt ōrĕ, Ov. Syn. Cōndo, strŭo, ædĭfĭco, āccŭmŭlo. V. Ædifico.

cōnsuēfăcĭo, fēcī, făctŭm, *to accustom.* Cōn brăchĭă suēfăcĭŭnt, Lucr. Syn. Assuēfăcĭo.

cōnsuēsco, ēvī, ētŭm, *to be accustomed.* Cōnsuēvērĕ jŏcōs, Mart. Syn. Assuēsco, sŏlĕo, āssŏlĕo. V. Assuesco.

cōnsuētūdo, ĭnĭs, f., *custom.* Cōnsuētūdŏ mălī, Juv. Syn. Mōs, ūsŭs, āssuētūdo. Epith. Āntīquă, vĕtŭs, nŏvă, bŏnă, mălă, pēssĭmă, ūtĭlĭs. V. Assuesco.

cōnsuētŭs, ă, ŭm, *accustomed.* Cŭm Prŏteŭs cōnsuĕtă pĕtēns, Virg. Syn. Assuētŭs, āssuēfăctŭs.

cōnsŭl, ŭlĭs, m., *a Roman magistrate.* Cōnsŭlĭs āltă mĕĭ, Mart. Epith. Vĭgĭl, ānxĭŭs, sōllĭcĭtŭs, æquŭs, jŭstŭs, pŏtēns.

cōnsŭlārĭs, ĕ, *of a consul.* Nĕquĕ cōnsŭlārĭs, (Sapph.) Hor.

cōnsŭlātŭs, ūs, m., *consulship.* Pēr cōnsŭlātŭm, (Iamb.)

cōnsŭlo, ŭī, ŭltŭm, *to consult.* Cōnsŭlĕre, ĕt mōx, Hor. Syn. Prŏvĭdĕo, prōspĭcĭo ; cōnsĭlĭo, ās ; cōnsĭlĭŭm dō, pĕto, căpĭo, āccĭpĭo. V. Consilium.

cōnsŭltē, *and* tō, adv., *advisedly, deliberately.* Īllĕ quī cōnsŭltē, Plaut. Extĕnŭāntĭs ĕās cōnsŭltō, Hor. .

cōnsŭlto, ās, *to consult.* Ămāntēs cōnsŭltēnt, Tib.

cōnsŭltŏr, ōrĭs, m., *who asks or gives counsel.* Cōnsŭltŏr ŭbĭ ōstĭă pŭlsăt, Hor.

cōnsŭltŭm, ī, n., *a decision, decree.* Quī cōnsŭltă pătrŭm, Hor.

cōnsŭltŭs, ă, ŭm, *the pass. partic. of* consulo. Cōnsŭltŭs ērrō, Hor.

cōnsŭmmo, ās, *to complete.* Cŭm cōnsŭmmāvĕrĭs ædēm, Alcim. Syn. Cōnfĭcĭo, ābsōlvo, pĕrăgo. V. Finio.

cōnsūmo, psī, ptŭm, *to consume.* Dăpĭbŭs cōnsūmĕrĕ mēnsās, Virg. Syn. Tĕro, cōntĕro, ābsūmo, īmpēndo, ēxhaūrĭo, dīssĭpo, cōnfĭcĭo, pērdo.

‖ cōnsŭo, ŭī, ūtŭm, *to stitch up.* Plaut. Syn. Sŭo, cōnjŭngo, cōnnēcto, cōntēxo fĭlō.

Cōnsŭs, ī, m., *the god of counsel, in honour of whom the Consualia were celebrated.* Fēstă pără Cōnsō, Ov.

cōnsūtŭs, ă, ŭm, *the pass. partic. of* consuo. Cōnsūtō vūlnĕrĕ, cāssŭm, Juv.

cōntābĕfăcĭo, fēcī, *to waste, consume.* Cūră cōntābĕfăcĭt, (Iamb.) Plaut. Syn. Tăbĕfăcĭo, tābĕ ēxĕdo, pĕrĕdo, cōnfĭcĭo.

• cōntābēsco, bŭī, *to waste away.* Syn. Tăbēsco.

cōntāctŭs, ūs, m., *touch, contact.* Cōntāctūque ōmnĭă fœdānt, Virg.

cōntāgēs, ĭs ; ĭo, ĭōnĭs ; f., *and* ĭŭm, ĭī, n., *contagion.* Quæ cōntāgĕ sŭă, Lucr. Hānc cōntāgĭŏ lābĕm, Juv. Cōntāgĭă lædēnt, Virg. Syn. Lŭēs, pēstĭs. Epith. Mălŭm, dīrŭm, sōrdĭdŭm, fœdŭm, pūtĭdŭm, mōrbĭdŭm, fūnēstŭm, mōrtĭfĕrŭm, īnfēstŭm, nōxĭŭm, lēthālĕ, hōrrēndŭm. V. Pestis.

cōntāmĭno, ās, *to soil.* Cōntāmĭnăt ūnctō, Mart. Syn. Fœdo, īnquĭno, cŏīnquĭno, pōllŭo, īnfĭcĭo, măcŭlo, cōmmăcŭlo. V. Macula.

cōntĕgo, tēxī, tēctŭm, *to cover.* Cōntĕgăr ēxŭl hŭmō, Ov. Syn. Tĕgo, cōndo, ābscōndo, ōccūlto. V. Occulto.

cōntĕmĕro, ās, *to violate.* Cōntĕmĕrărĕ mănŭs, Mart. Syn. Tĕmĕro, vĭŏlo, cōrrūmpo.

cōntĕmno, mpsī, mptŭm, *to despise.* Cōntēmnĕre hŏnōrēs, Hor. Syn. Tēmno, fāstīdĭo, rēspŭo, spērno, āspērnŏr, dēspĭcĭo, cōncūlco, ābjĭcĭo, rējĭcĭo, nēglĭgo; pārvī, nĭhĭlī dūco, făcĭo, æstĭmo, pēndo, pŭto ; nōn cūro. V. Asperno.

cōntēmplātŭs, ūs, m., *contemplation.* Ā cōntēmplātū, Ov.

cōntēmplŏr, ārĭs, *to contemplate.* Nūmmōs cōntēmplŏr ĭn ārcā, Hor. Syn. Ănĭmō lūstro, cōnsīdĕro, mĕdĭtŏr, cōgĭto ; vĭdĕo, pērspĭcĭo, cōnspĭcĭo, spēcto, āspĭcĭo, īntŭĕŏr. V. Cogito, Aspicio.

cōntēmptŏr, ōrĭs, m., trīx, īcĭs, f., *a despiser.* Lūcĭs cōntēmptŏr, Virg. Cōntēmptrīx sŭpĕrum, Ov. V. Contemno.

cōntēmptŭs, ă, ŭm, *the pass. partic. of* contemno. Cōntēmptă rĕlīnquŏr, Ov. V. Abjectus.

cōntēmptŭs, ūs, m., *contempt.* Cōntēmptū nĕcĭs ārmăt, Sil. Syn. Fāstīdĭŭm. Epith. Sŭpērbŭs, ēlātŭs, tŭmēns, tŭmĭdŭs, grăvĭs.

cōntēndo, dī, sŭm *or* tŭm, *to stretch, to contend.* Mālĭt cōntēndĕrĕ bēllō, Virg. Syn. Cōnŏr, nītŏr, ēnītŏr, mōlĭŏr ; V. Conor. Intēndo, āddūco ; rīxŏr, jūrgŏr, āltērcŏr. V. Rixor.

• cōntēntĭo, ōnĭs, f., *a straining, strife.* Cōntēntĭŏ nācta ēst, Aus. Syn. Lĭs, rīxă ; cōnātŭs. Epith. Inĭquă, ămātă, mŏlēstă, vănă, răbĭōsă, clāmōsă, vēsānă, sānguĭnĕă, tūrpĭs, īmprŏbă. V. Rixa.

cōntēntŭs, ă, ŭm, *content, satisfied.* Pārvō cōntēntă părātū, Cl.

cōntērmĭnŭs, ă, ŭm, *bordering, near.* Cōntērmĭnă rīpæ, Ov.

cōntĕro, trīvī, trītŭm, *to bruise small.* Cōntĕrĭt ūnă trĭbŭs, Mart. Syn. Tĕro, āttĕro, prōtĕro, cālco, cōncūlco, prĕmo, prōcūlco ; cōnsūmo, ābsūmo, cōnfĭcĭo.

cōntērrĕo, ŭī, *to frighten.* Cōntērrērĕ mĕtū, Lucr. Syn. Tērrĕo, tērrĭto, ēxtērrĕo.

cōntēxo, ĭs, ŭī, *to weave.* Lĭlĭă cōntēxĕre ămārānthĭs, Tib.

cōntĭcĕo, cŭī, *to be silent.* Cōntĭcŭēre ōmnēs, Virg. Syn. Cōntĭcēsco, tăcĕo, sĭlĕo. V. Sileo.

cōntĭcĭnĭŭm, ĭī, n., *the dead of night.* In cōntĭcĭnĭō, vĕl, (Scaz)

cōntĭgŭŭs, ă, ŭm, *contiguous.* Hūnc ŭbī cōntĭgŭŭm, Virg. Syn. Prōxĭmŭs, prōpīnquŭs, vīcīnŭs, prŏpĭŏr, jūnctŭs, ādjūnctŭs.

cōntĭnēns, ntĭs, *chaste.* Cōntĭnēntĭs lĕgĭmŭs, (Iamb.) Avien. V. Castus.

cōntĭnēntĕr, adv., *continently, continually.* Ād cōntĭnēntĕr, (Scaz.) Catull. Syn. Cōntĭnŭē, pērpĕtŭō, āssĭdŭē.

cōntĭnēntĭă, æ, f., *chastity.* Tērrēntĕ cōntĭnēntĭā, (Iamb.) Paulin. Syn. Abstĭnēntĭă. V. Castitas.

cōntĭnĕo, ēs, *to hold together.* Cōntĭnŭērĕ dĭŭ, Ov. Syn. Cōmprĕhēndo, īnclūdo, cōmplēctŏr ; cŏhĭbĕo, frœno, cŏērcĕo, cōmprĭmo, refrœno, cōmpēsco.

cōntīngo, ĭgī, āctŭm, *to touch.* Cōntīngĕrĕ gaūdēnt, Virg. Syn. Tāngo, āttīngo, āttrēcto ; ēvĕnĭo, āccĭdo.

cŏntĭnŭo, ās, *to go on.* Cŏntĭnŭātquĕ dăpēs, Hor. SYN. Pērgo, pērsĕvēro, nōn ābsĭsto, nōn dēsĭsto, nōn cēsso, nōn dēsĭno.

cŏntĭnŭō, adv., *immediately.* Cŏntĭnŭō vēntĭs, Virg. SYN. Sēmpĕr, pērpĕtŭō, rĕpēntĕ, mōx, sŭbĭtō, prŏtĭnŭs, ēxtēmplō, haŭd mŏră, ĭlĭcĕt, ōcўŭs, cŏntĭnŭĕ, stătĭm, cōnfēstĭm.

cŏntĭnŭŭs, ă, ŭm, *continual.* Sēd quăm cŏntĭnŭĭs, Juv. SYN. Pērpĕtŭŭs, pĕrēnnĭs, cŏntĭnŭātŭs.

cŏntŏrquĕo, ōrsī, ōrtŭm, *to turn, to hurl.* Spīcŭlă cōntŏrquēnt, Virg. SYN. Tŏrquĕo. ĭntŏrquĕo, flēcto, īnflēcto ; vibro, jăcŭlŏr, ēmītto, cōnjĭcĭo.

cŏntōrtŭs, ă, ŭm, *the pass. partic. of* contorqueo. Mōllĭă cōntōrtĭs, Prop.

cōntrā, prep., *against, opposite.* Ităllĭăm cŏntrā, Virg. SYN. In (*with the accus.*); ādvērsŭs, ādvērsŭm.—2. adv., *contrariwise.* SYN. Vĭcīssĭm ; ēx ādvērsō, ē rĕgĭŏnĕ.

cŏntrăho, xī, ctŭm, *to draw together.* Cŏntrăhĭt ārdēns, Virg. SYN. Cōngrĕgo, cōllĭgo, cōgo.

cŏntrārĭŭs, ă, ŭm, *contrary.* Fātĭs cŏntrārĭă nōstrĭs Fātă, Virg. SYN. Ādvērsārĭŭs, æmŭlŭs, ĭnĭmīcŭs, ōppŏsĭtŭs, ādvērsŭs, pūgnāns, rĕpūgnāns, īnfēstŭs.

cŏntrēcto, ās, *to touch often.* Cōntrēctātŭs ŭbi, Hor.

cŏntrĕmīsco, ĭs, trĕmŭī, *to tremble.* Cōntrĕmŭīt nĕmŭs, Virg. SYN. Trĕmo, īntrĕmo, trĕpĭdo. V. Tremo.

cŏntrĭbŭo, ŭī, ŭtŭm, *to contribute.* Cŏntrĭbŭēre ălĭquĭd, Ov. SYN. Cōnfĕro, trĭbŭo.

cŏntrīsto, ās, *to make sorry, dark.* Cŏntrīstăt Ăquārĭŭs ānnŭm, Man.

cŏntrītŭs, ă, ŭm, *the pass. partic. of* contero. Ōmnĭă quŏd cŏntrītă, quŏd, Lucr.

cōntrōvērsĭă, æ, f., *a debate.* Dēclāmātĭō cōntrōvērsĭārŭm, (Phal.) Sidon. SYN. Dĭscēptātĭo, cōntēntĭo, dĭscrīmĕn, pūgnă, lĭs. V. Lis.

cōntrōvērsŭs, ă, ŭm, *disputed.* Sī cōntrōvērsŭm, Aus. SYN. Ămbĭgŭŭs, dŭbĭŭs, īncērtŭs, āncēps.

cŏntrūdo, sī, sŭm, *to push violently.* Vēntī cōntrūdĭt, ĕt ĭpsă, Lucr. SYN. Cōmpēllo, īmpēllo, cōmpĭngo.

cŏntŭbērnālĭs, ĭs, m., *a companion.* Vōsquĕ cōntŭbērnālēs, (Scaz.) Catul. SYN. Dŏmēstĭcŭs, fămĭlĭārĭs, cōnvīctŏr, sŏcĭŭs, sŏdālĭs.

cŏntŭbērnĭŭm, ĭi, n., *a living together, cohabitation.* Tŭrpĕ cōntŭbērnĭŭm, Virg. (Catal.)

|| cŏntŭĕŏr, ērĭs, *to see.* Cŏntŭĭmŭr mĭrās, Lucr.

* cŏntŭmācĭă, æ, f., *stubbornness, resolution.* Cic. SYN. Sŭpērbĭă, fāstŭs, ōbstĭnātĭo, mēntĭs ōbfīrmātæ sŭpērbĭă.

cŏntŭmāx, ācĭs, *headstrong.* Ēssĕ cōntŭmācĕm, (Phal.) Mart. SYN. Pērtĭnāx, ōbfīrmātŭs, sŭpērbŭs, rĕbēllĭs.

cŏntŭmēlĭă, æ, f., *an outrage.* Fērrĕ cōntŭmēlĭās, (Iamb.) Prud. SYN. Cōnvīcĭŭm, īnjūrĭă, călŭmnĭă. EPITH. Grăvĭs, mălīgnă, īnfāndă, dīră, nĕfāndă. V. Convicium.

cŏntŭmēlĭōsŭs, ă, ŭm, *contumelious.* Bārbără cōntŭmēlĭōsī, (Phal.) Mart.

cŏntŭmŭlo, ās, *to inter, bury.* Cŏntŭmŭlāvĭt hŭmō, Mart.

cŏntŭndo, tŭdī, *to beat, bruise.* Cōntŭdĕrīt vĭtēs, Hor. SYN. Tŭndo, ōbtĕro, cōmmĭnŭo, frăngo, pērcŭtĭo, vērbĕro.

cōntŭrbo, ās, *to trouble.* Cōntŭrbābĭmŭs īllă, Catul. SYN. Tŭrbo, pērtŭrbo, mīscĕo, cōnfŭndo, cōmmīscĕo.

cŏntŭs, ī, m., *a pole to gauge water, a javelin.* Ăcŭtā cūspĭdĕ cōntōs, Virg. SYN. Sŭdēs ; hăstă. EPITH. Fērrātŭs, pūgnāx, trăbālĭs, dūrŭs, lōngŭs, ăhēnŭs, fērrĕŭs.

cŏntūsŭs, ă, ŭm, *the pass. partic. of* contundo. Nūllō cōntūsŭs ărātrō, Catul.

cŏnvălĕo, *and* ēsco, lŭī, *to recover health.* Mĕ Nŭmă, cōnvălŭīt, Mart. SYN. Vălĕo ; ēx mōrbō recrĕŏr.

cōnvāllĭs, ĭs, f., *a valley.* Claŭdūnt cōnvāllĭbŭs ŭmbræ, Virg. SYN. Vāllĭs. EPITH. Căvă, dēprēssă, ōbscūră, vĭrēns, ăbrūptă, ŭmbrōsă, sāxōsă, ŭmbrĭfĕră, præcēps, īmă, cŭrvă. V. Vallis.

cōnvēcto, ās, *and* vĕho, ĭs, *to convey.* Cōnvēctărĕ jŭvăt, Virg. SYN. Vĕho, trānsvĕho, trānspŏrto, dēfĕro.

cōnvēllo, vŭlsī, vŭlsŭm, *to pull up.* Pŏtĕrĭs cōnvēllĕrĕ fērrō, Virg. SYN. Vēllo, āvēllo, rĕvēllo, ēvēllo.

cōnvēnæ, ārŭm, m. f., pl., *people assembled together.* Făcĕrēm cōnvēnās, (Iamb.) Plaut.

cōnvĕnĭēns, ēntĭs, *suitable.* Nōn bĕnĕ cōnvĕnĭēns, Prop. SYN. Āptŭs, cōnsŏnŭs, cōngrŭēns, dĕcēns, cōnsēntānĕŭs, ĭdōnĕŭs.

cōnvĕnĭēntĕr, adv., *conveniently.* Sī cōnvĕnĭēntĕr ŏpōrtĕt, Hor. SYN. Aptē, dĕcēntĕr.

cōnvĕnĭo, ĭs, ēnī, *to come together, to agree.* Cōnvĕnĭŭnt pīctīs, Ov. SYN. Adĕo, īnvīso, vīso, vīsĭto ; cŏĕo, cōncŭrro, cōnflŭo, cōngrĕgŏr, cōnsēntĭo, cōnsŏno, cōngrŭo.

cōnvĕnĭt, *it is agreed upon.* Cōnvĕnĭt Ēvāndrī, Virg. SYN. Dĕcĕt, cōngrŭĭt, ēxpĕdĭt, cōndūcĭt ; ēst pār, cōnvĕnĭēns, cōnsŏnŭm, cōngrŭŭm ; cōnstăt, cērtum ēst.

cōnvēntŭm, ī, n., *a compact, contract.* Cōnvēntŭm tămĕn, Juv.

cōnvēntŭs, ūs, m., *an assembly.* Cōnvēntŭs trăhĭt, Virg. SYN. Cœtŭs, cōnsĭlĭŭm, tūrbă.

cōnvērto, tī, sŭm, *to turn.* Cōnvērtĕrĕ Nȳmphās, Virg. SYN. Vērto, mŭto, cōmmŭto, vērso, cīrcŭmăgo.

cōnvēstĭo, ĭs, *to clothe all over.* Cōnvēstīrĕ sŭă, Lucr. V. Vēstĭo, Ōrno.

cōnvĕxŭs, ă, ŭm, *crooked, vaulted.* Aspĭcĕ cōnvĕxō, Virg.

cōnvīcĭātŏr, ōrĭs, m., *a railer.* Cōnvīcĭātŏr sēntĭăt, (Iamb.) Prud. SYN. Călŭmnĭātŏr, mălĕdĭcŭs.

cōnvīcĭŭm, ĭī, n., *loud noise, reproach.* Cōnvīcĭă fūndĕrĕ līnguæ, Ov. SYN. Probrŭm, ōpprobrĭŭm, mălĕdīctŭm, călŭmnĭă. EPITH. Injūrĭōsŭm, văgŭm, rūstĭcŭm, āspĕrŭm, fœdŭm, tūrpĕ, pŭdēndŭm.

cōnvīctŏr, ōrĭs, m., *a daily guest.* Ille ĕgŏ cōnvīctŏr, Hor.

cōnvīctŭs, ūs, m., *living together.* Cōnvīctŭs făcĭlĭs, Mart. SYN. Mēnsæ sŏdālĭtĭŭm. Sŏcĭŭs vīctŭs.

cōnvīnco, ĭs, *to convince.* Cōnvīncĕrĕ fālsŭm, Lucr.

cōnvīso, ĭs, *to see.* Cōnvīsĕrĕ pōssĭs, Lucr. SYN. Intrōspĭcĭo.

cōnvīvă, æ, m., *a guest.* Trēs mĭhī cōnvīvæ, Hor. SYN. Cōnvīctŏr ; cōmpōtŏr, cōmbĭbo ; mēnsæ sŏcĭŭs. EPITH. Avĭdŭs, lætŭs, cōmĭs, ēbrĭŭs, prŏcāx, făcētŭs, īnsānŭs, hĭlărĭs, vŏcātŭs, ādmīssŭs, ōptātŭs, īmpōrtūnŭs, ēxpēctātŭs.

cōnvīvālĭs, ĕ, *belonging to banquets.* Cōnvīvālĕ călēntĭs, Prud.

cōnvīvātŏr, ōrĭs, m., *one who gives a banquet.* Sēd cōnvīvātōrĭs, ŭtī dŭcĭs, Hor. SYN. Părŏchŭs, hĕrŭs, dŏmĭnŭs. EPITH. Scītŭs, laŭtŭs, bĕātŭs.

cōnvīvĭŭm, ĭī, n., *a banquet.* Lætī cōnvīvĭă cūrānt, Virg. SYN. Ēpŭlæ, dăpēs, mēnsă. EPITH. Dūlcĕ, vīnōsŭm, lætŭm, laŭtŭm, sūmptŭōsŭm, cĕlĕbrĕ, māgnĭfĭcŭm, pīnguĕ, bŏnŭm, fœcūndŭm, splēndĭdŭm, sōlēnnĕ, rēgĭŭm, părātŭm, fēstīvŭm, dēlĭcĭōsŭm, nūptĭălĕ, cōnjŭgālĕ, gĕnĭălĕ, rēgālĕ, īnstrūctŭm, ŏpīmŭm, suāvĕ, rĕpĕtītŭm. V. Convivor.

cōnvīvo, ĭs, *to live together.* Nōn cōnvīvĕrĕ, nĕc, (Phal.) Mart. SYN. Sĭmŭl, ūnā vīvo, dēgo.

cōnvīvŏr, ārĭs, *to banquet.* Quōd cōnvīvārīs sĭnĕ mē, Mart. SYN. Ēpŭlŏr. V. Epulor.

cōnvŏcātŭs, ă, ŭm, *the pass. partic. of* convoco. Sēd cōnvŏcātŭs vōcĭs, (Iamb.) Senec.

cōnvŏco, ās, *to call together.* Mĕdĭcōsquĕ cōnvŏcārĕ, (Phal.) Catul. SYN. Vŏco, ādvŏco, āccĭo, āccērso, cōngrĕgo.

cōnvŏlo, ās, *to run together.* Pŏpŭlūs cōnvŏlăt, (Iamb.) Ter. SYN. Ādvŏlo, cōnvĕnĭo, cōncŭrro.

cōnvōlvo, ĭs, *to wrap about.* Cōnvōlvīt lūbrĭcă tērgă, Virg.

cōnvŏmo, ĭs, *to vomit.* Cōnvŏmĭt hæc īntĕr, Juv.

cōnŭm, ī, n., *and* ŭs, ī, m., *the crest of a helmet.* Ēt cōnum īnsīgnĭs, Virg. SYN. Gălĕæ crīstātŭs ăpēx. EPITH. Insīgnĭs, mĭcāns, tērrĭfĭcŭs.

* cŏŏpĕrĭo, ĭs, ŭī, ērtŭm, *to cover.* Liv. SYN. Ŏpĕrĭo, tĕgo, ōbtĕgo, cōntĕgo, ābscōndo, ōccŭlo, ōccūlto. V. Occulto, abscondo.

cŏŏpĕrtŭs, ă, ŭm, *the pass. partic. of* cooperio. Lŭpō cŏŏpĕrtō vērsĭbŭs, Hor.

cŏŏrĭŏr, ōrtŭs sŭm, *to arise as a storm.* Cōmmīsĕrăt ūndă cŏŏrtĭs, Ov.

cŏpă, æ, f., *a hostess.* Cōpă Sȳrīscă, Virg.

|| cŏphĭnŭs, ī, m., *a twig basket.* Ille lŏcŭm cŏphĭnō, fœnŏquĕ, Juv. EPITH. Vĭmĭnĕŭs, tēxtĭlĭs, nēxŭs, vīrgātŭs, căpāx.

cŏpĭă, æ, f., *plenty*. Cŏpĭă mājŏr ĕrĭt, Ov. Syn. Jūs, pŏtēstās, făcūltās; ăbūn-dāntĭă, ūbērtās, vīs, cŭmŭlŭs, ăcĕrvŭs. Epith. Ăfflūēns, fāstīdĭōsă, dīvĕs, lārgă, bŏnă, bĕātă. V. Abundantia.

cŏpĭæ, ārŭm, f. pl., *troops*. V. Exercitus, agmen.

cŏpĭōsŭs, ă, ŭm, *abundant, rich*. Lĭquŏr ĕt cŏpĭōsŭs, Ph.

¶ cŏptă, æ, f., *a kind of hard biscuit*. Clără Rhŏdōs cŏpiăm, Mart.

cŏpŭlă, æ, f., *a tie*. Cŏpŭlă dūră, Ov. Syn. Vīncŭlŭm, lĭgāmĕn, nēxŭs. Epith. Dūră, ĭrrūptă, tĕnāx, ārctă, strīctă.

cŏpŭlo, ās, *to tie, unite*. Quīnquĕ cŏpŭlēntŭr, (Phal.) Mart. Syn. Jūngo, cŏn-jŭngo, ădjŭngo, lĭgo. āllĭgo, nĕcto, cŏnnĕcto.

cŏquīnŭs, ă, ŭm, *of the kitchen*. Fŏrŭm cŏquīnŭm quī vŏcānt, Plaut.

cŏquo, xī, ctŭm, *to cook*. Pŭlvĕrŭlēntă cŏquăt, Virg.

cŏquŭs, ī, m., *a cook*. Sēd cŏquŭs īngēntĕm, Mart. Epith. Sævŭs, pīnguĭs, ātĕr, nĭgĕr, ūnctŭs, sōrdēns, sōrdĭdŭs, clāmōsŭs, sōllĭcĭtŭs.

cor, cōrdĭs, n., *the heart*. Mŏllĕ cŏr ēssĕ mĭhi, Ov. Lĕvĭbŭs cŏr ēst vĭŏlābĭlĕ tēlīs, Ov. Syn. Pēctŭs, præcōrdĭă. Epith. Călēns, ăvĭdŭm, pŭrpŭrĕŭm, cālĭdŭm, fērvēns.

cŏrăcīnŭs, ī, m, *a fish found in the Nile*. Cŏrăcīnĕ, măcēllī, Mart.

corallĭŭm, ĭī, n., *coral*. Nūnc quŏquĕ cŏrāllĭs, Ov. Rŭbră cŏrāllĭă nūdă, Aus. Epith. Frăgĭlĕ, pŭnĭcĕŭm, liquĭdŭm, rŭbĕŭm, rŭbēns, rāmōsŭm, rŭbĭcūndŭm, tĕnĕrŭm, sōlĭdŭm, æquŏrĕŭm, mărīnŭm, dūrŭm.

Cŏrāllĭ, ōrŭm, m. pl., *a people of Mysia*. Scrīptă Cŏrāllīs, Ov.

cŏrăm, adv., *and* prep., *before, in the presence of*. Āīt; cŏrăm, quēm quærĭtĭs, Virg. Syn. Antĕ, īn ŏcŭlīs, āntĕ ŏcŭlōs, ānte ōră, īn cōnspēctū; pălăm, ăpērtĕ.

› Cŏrānŭs, ī, m., *the name of a man*. Nāsīcă Cŏrānō, Hor.

Cŏrās, æ, m., *the brother of Tibur*. Cūm frātrĕ Cŏrās, Virg.

cŏrbĭs, ĭs, m., *a basket*. Cŏrbĭs ŭt īmpŏsĭtī, Prop. V. Calathus.

cŏrbŭlă, æ, f., *the diminut. of* corbis. Ēscăm cŏrbŭlīs, (Iamb.) Plaut.

Cŏrbŭlo, ōnĭs, m., *a Roman general*. Cŏrbŭlŏ vīx fērrĕt, Juv.

Cŏrcȳră, æ, f., *an island of the Adriatic Sea*. Cōrcȳră, sīnŭsquĕ, Luc. Syn. Phæācĭă.

Cŏrcȳræŭs, ă, ŭm, *of Corcyra*. Tĕ Cŏrcȳræŭm, Ov.

cŏrdātŭs, ă, ŭm, *wise, prudent*. Cōrdātă jŭvēntŭs, Mart. Syn. Prūdēns, săpĭēns, sōlērs, īngĕnĭōsŭs.

‖ cŏrdŏlĭŭm, ī, n., *grief of heart*, Plaut.

Cŏrdŭbă, æ, f., *a town in Spain*. Cōrdŭbă tērræ, Sil. Epith. Fācūndă, dōctă, dīvĕs, fœcūndă.

cŏrdȳlă, æ, f., *a fish*. Nĕ tŏgă cŏrdȳlīs, Mart.

Cŏrīnnă, æ, f., *a poetess of Bœotia*. Dīctă Cŏrīnnă mĭhi, Ov.

Cŏrīnthĭăcŭs, *and* ĭŭs, ă, ŭm, *of Corinth*. Jāmquĕ Cŏrīnthĭācī, Ov. Rēgnă Cŏrīnthĭī, Sen.

Cŏrīnthŭs, ī, f., *a town of Achaia*. Ădīrĕ Cŏrīnthŭm, Hor. Syn. Ēphȳrĕ. Epith. Nōbĭlĭs, clără, Graĭă, Ēphȳræă, bĭmărĭs, āltă, vĕtŭs, prīscă, āntīquă, cĕlebrĭs, æquŏrĕă, māgnĭfĭcă, tūrrītă, pŏtēns, vāllātă, ĭnāccēssă, īnsīgnĭs.

cŏrīscŭs, ī, m., *a light arrow*. Cŏrīscīquĕ lĕvēs, Virg.

cŏrĭŭm, ĭī, n., *and* ĭŭs, ĭī, m., *leather*. Ūt cănĭs ā cŏrĭŏ, Hor. Epith. Pīnguĕ, fŭscŭm, lævĕ.

Cŏrnēlĭŭs, ĭī or ī, Cŏrnēlĭă, æ, f., *name of several noble Romans*. Cŏrnēlĭă, mātĕr, Juv. Cŏrnēlī, quĕrĕrĭs, Mart.

cŏrnĕŭs, ă, ŭm, *of horn*. Cŏrnĕă, quā vērĭs, Virg.—2. *of the cornel-tree*. Quā cŏrnĕă sūmnĭŏ, Id.

cŏrnĭcĕn, ĭnĭs, m., *he who blows a horn*. Illīnc cŏrnĭcĭnēs, Juv.

cŏrnīcŏr, ārĭs, *to chatter*. Grăvĕ cŏrnīcārĭs ĭnēptĕ, Pers.

cŏrnīcŭlă, æ, f., *the diminut. of* cornix. Mŏvĕăt cŏrnīcŭlă rīsŭm, Hor.

Cŏrnīfĭcĭŭs, ĭī, m., *the name of a man*. Et lĕvĕ Cŏrnīfĭcī, Ov.

cŏrnĭgĕr, ă, ŭm, *horned*. Cŏrnĭgĕr Hēspĕrĭdŭm, Virg. Syn. Cŏrnū, cŏrnŭă gĕrēns, cŏrnĭbŭs hōrrēns.

cŏrnĭpēs, pĕdĭs, *with horny hoofs*. Cŏrnĭpĕdēs ārcēntŭr ĕquī, Virg.

cŏrnīx, īcĭs, f., *a rook*. Cŏrnīcum ūt sēclă vĕtūstă, Lucr. Epith. Præsāgă, raucă, ānnōsă, vīvāx, lōngævă, ātră, nĭgră, vĕtŭlă, grātă, lŏquāx, sāgă.

cŏrnŭ, n., *a horn.* Cŏrnūque īnfēnsā tětēndĭt, Virg. Syn. Būccĭnă, tŭbă, lĭtŭūs, V. Tuba. Ārcŭs; V. Arcus, ungula. Epith. Dūrŭm, ăcūtŭm, flēxŭm, cūrvŭm, rěcūrvŭm, tŏrvŭm, tŏrtŭm, prōmĭnēns, prōcērŭm, īntŏrtŭm, pătŭlŭm, lūnărě, flēxĭlě, rĭgĭdŭm, īnflēxŭm, ădūncŭm, cūrvātŭm, tērrĭfĭcŭm, hōrrĭsŏnŭm, dīstŏrtŭm, quěrŭlŭm, raūcĭsŏnŭm, mĭnāx, aūdāx, pūgnāx, fěrŭm, sævŭm, gěmĭnŭm, fŏrtě, vălĭdŭm, rāmōsŭm. V. Abundantia.

cŏrnŭm, ī, n., *a cornel.* Lăpĭdōsăquě cŏrnă, Virg.

cŏrnŭs, ūs *and* ī, f., *the cornel-tree.* Bēllīs āccŏmmŏdă cŏrnŭs, Virg. Epith. Nōdōsă, dūră, āltă, prōcēră. V. Hasta, sagitta.

cŏrnūtŭs, ă, ŭm, *horned.* Cŏrnūto ārdōrě pětītŭs, Mart. Syn. Cŏrnĭgěr.

Cŏrœbŭs, ī, m., *a warrior slain at the siege of Troy.* Fŭrĭātā mēntě Cŏrœbō, Virg.

cŏrōllă, æ, f., *the diminut. of* corona. Frōntě cŏrōllās, Prop.

cŏrōnă, æ, f., *a crown, a garland, a circle.* Cŏmă prēssă cŏrōnă, Virg. Syn. Cŏrōllă, vīttă, sērtŭm; tūrbă, cœtŭs. Epith. Aūrěă, gēmmĭfěră, pīctă, nēxă, nēxĭlĭs, sūtĭlĭs, nĭtĭdă, frōndēns, stēllātă, gēmměă, īmplĭcĭtă, fūlgēns, īnsīgnĭs, flōrĭdă, fēstă, splēndĭdă, rēgĭă, clāră, nōbĭlĭs, gēmmātă, prětĭōsă, děcŏră, trĭūmphālĭs, laūrěă, cŏrŭscă, pūlchră, nĭtēns, spēctābĭlĭs, flōrĭcŏmă, ŏdōrĭfěră, sacră, rēgālĭs. V. Turba.—2. *A constellation.* Părĭtěrquě Cŏrōnă,·Auson. Epith. Arĭadnæă, Gnōsĭă, Gnōsĭăcă.

cŏrōnātŭs, ă, ŭm, *the pass. partic. of* corono. Sæpě cŏrōnātĭs, Ov. Syn. Cīnctŭs, āmbītŭs, cīrcūmdātŭs.

Cŏrōneūs, ěī, m., *the father of the nymph Coronis.* Tēllūrě Cŏrōneūs, Ov.

Cŏrōnĭdēs, æ, m., *son of Coronis, Esculapius.* Nūllă Cŏrōnĭdēs, Ov.

|| cŏrōnĭs, ĭdĭs, f., *the top.* Sērăquě cŏrōnĭdě lōngŭs, Mart. Syn. Ăpēx, fīnĭs.— 2. *The mother of Esculapius.* Lārīssæă Cŏrōnĭs, Ov.

cŏrōno, ās, *to crown, surround.* Vīnă cŏrōnănt, Virg. Syn. Cīrcūmdo, cīngo, āmbĭo.

|| cŏrpŏrālĭs, ě, *and* ěŭs, ă, ŭm, *belonging to the body.* Cŏrpŏrālī ērgāstŭlō, (Iamb.) Prud. Cŏrpŏrěæ ēxcēdŭnt, Virg.

|| cŏrpŭlēntŭs, ă, ŭm, *corpulent,* Plaut. Syn. Pīnguĭs, crāssŭs, ŏbēsŭs.

cŏrpŭs, ŏrĭs, n., *the body.* Cŏrpŏrĭs ēxĭgŭī, Hor. Syn. Mēmbră, ārtŭs. Epith. Těněrŭm, fōrmōsŭm, pūlchrŭm, cāndĭdŭm, ēgrěgĭŭm, nĭtĭdŭm, īnfīrmŭm, mŏrbĭdŭm, putrĭdŭm, cădūcŭm, děbĭlě, fŏrtě, rŏbūstŭm, lăcērtōsŭm, věgětŭm, sānŭm, fīrmŭm, mŏrtālě, lānguĭdŭm, ægrŭm, mŏrbōsŭm, frăgĭlě.

cŏrpūscŭlŭm, ī, n., *the diminut. of* corpus. Pěnĭtŭs cŏrpūscŭlă, Lucr.

cŏrrādo, sī, sŭm, *to scrape, collect.* Dīctīs cŏrrāděrě nōstrīs, Lucr. Syn. Rādo, ābrādo; cōllĭgo.

cŏrrēctŏr, ōrĭs, m., *a corrector.* Cŏrrēctŏr āspěrĭtātĭs, Hor. Syn. Cēnsŏr.

cŏrrēpo, ĭs, *to creep.* Cŏrrēpsĭt īn ālnŭm, Luc.

cŏrrīděo, ēs, *to laugh, or smile.* Omnĭă cŏrrīdēnt, Lucr.

cŏrrĭgo, ēxī, *to correct.* Cŏrrĭgěrě āt rēs, Ov. Syn. Ēmēndo.

cŏrrĭpĭo, ŭī, rēptŭm, *to take hold of.* Cŏrrĭpŭěrě vĭăm, Virg. Syn. Pūnĭo, plēcto, cāstīgo, ārgŭo, rědārgŭo, ōbjūrgo; āccĭpĭo, căpĭo, cōmprěhēndo.

cŏrrŏbŏro, ās, *to strengthen.* Těněrōs cŏrrŏbŏrāt ārtŭs, Mart. Syn. Fīrmo, rŏbŏro.

cŏrrōdo, sī, sŭm, *to gnaw.* Cŏrrōdēt sănĭēs, Calph. Syn. Rōdo, ărrōdo, cīrcūmrōdo.

cŏrrŏgo, ŭs, *to ask eagerly, to assemble.* Cŏrrŏgăt aūrās, Corn. Sev. Syn. Rŏgo, pěto, pōstŭlo, quæro; cōngrěgo.

cŏrrōsŭs, ă, ŭm, *the pass. partic. of* corrodo. Cŏrrōsĭs ōssĭbŭs ēdĭt, Juv.

cŏrrūgĭs, ě, *wrinkled.* Cŏrrūgēsquě sĭnŭs, Nemes. Syn. Cŏrrūgātŭs, rūgōsŭs.

cŏrrūgo, ās, *to wrinkle.* Cŏrrūgēt nārēs, Hor.

cŏrrūmpo, rūpī, *to corrupt.* Cŏrrūpěrĭt, ūt sŏlět, (Phal.) Mart. Syn. Vĭtĭo, dēprăvo, cōntāmĭno, dēstrŭo.

cŏrrŭo, ŭī, *to fall.* Cŏrrŭĭt, ēt multăm, Ov. Syn. Rŭo, cădo, lābŏr, cōncĭdo, cōllābŏr. V. Cado.

cŏrrūptēlă, æ, f., *corruption.* Cŏrrūptēlă pŭtrīs, Prud.

cŏrrūptŏr, ōrĭs, m., *a corrupter.* Nŭrūs cŏrrūptŏr ăvāræ, Juv.

Cŏrsĭcă, æ, f., *an island on the coast of Italy.* Cŏrsĭcă mŏntēs, Rutil.

Cŏrsĭcŭs *and* Cŏrsŭs, ă, ŭm, *of Corsica.* Cŏrsĭcă mĭsĭt ăpĭs, Ov

cŏrtĕx, ĭcĭs, m., *a rind.* Ŏrăquĕ cŏrtĭcĭbŭs, Virg. Syn. Lĭbĕr. Epith. Pīnguĭs, căvātŭs, sīccŭs, rūgōsŭs, rīmōsŭs, tūrgĭdŭs, ārbŏrĕŭs, tĕnĕr, tĕnŭĭs, mŏllĭs, rĭgēns.

cŏrtĭcĕŭs, ă, ŭm, *of bark.* Dūcīt cŏrtĭcēĭs, Aus.

cŏrtīnă, æ, f., *Apollo's tripos.* Cŏrtīnă rĕclūsĭs, Virg. Epith. Ăpŏllĭnĕă, Dēlphĭcă, Phœbēă, fātĭdĭcă, prænūnciă, præsāgă, vērĭdĭcă, tērrĭfĭcă, vĕnĕrāndă.

Cŏrtȳnă, *or* Gŏrtȳnă, æ, f., *an ancient town of Crete.* Cērtēt Cŏrtȳnă săgīttĭs, Sil.

cŏrvīnŭs, ă, ŭm, *of a raven.* Cŏrvīnŭs pătrĭĭs, Hor.—2. ī, m., *the name of several Romans.* Cŏrvīnōsquĕ sĭmŭl, Luc.

Cŏrŭs. V. Caurus.

cŏrŭsco, ās, *to shine.* Pēnnīsquĕ cŏrŭscănt, Virg. Syn. Lūcĕo, splēndēsco, splēndĕo, rēsplēndĕo, mĭco, fŭlgĕo, rĕfŭlgĕo, nĭtĕo, ʼrădĭo; vibro, īntŏrquĕo. V. Luceo, vibro.

cŏrŭscŭs, ă, ŭm, *bright.* Lūcĕ cŏrŭscŭs, Virg. Syn. Lūcĭdŭs, fŭlgĭdŭs, rŭtĭlŭs, nĭtĭdŭs, lūcēns, fŭlgēns, rŭtĭlāns, nĭtēns, ārdēns, mĭcāns, rĕlūcēns, splēndĭdŭs, splēndēns, cŏrŭscāns, rădĭāns. V. Lucidus.

cŏrvŭs, ī, m., *a raven.* In crŭcĕ cŏrvōs, Hor. Epith. Nĭgĕr, gārrŭlŭs, crŏcĭtāns, lŏquāx, vōcālĭs, raŭcŭs, vīvĭdŭs, ānnōsŭs, fĕrālĭs, vŏrāx, lŏngævŭs, sĭnĭstĕr, tūrpĭs, ōbscœnŭs, fātĭdĭcŭs, fūnĕrĕŭs, prænūnciŭs, īnfaŭstŭs, mălŭs.

Cŏrȳbāntĕs, ŭm, m. pl., *the priests of Cybele.* Hŏc Cŏrȳbāntĕs ŏpŭs, Ov. Epith. Cȳbĕlēī, clāmōsī, ārmĭgĕrī, īnsānī, ŭlŭlāntēs, fŭriōsī, dēmēntēs, fŭrĭbūndī, mălĕsānī, trŭcēs, Idæī.

Cŏrȳbāntĭăcŭs, *or* tĭŭs, ă, ŭm, *of the Corybantes.* Est Cŏrȳbāntĭăcī, Mart. Cŏrȳbāntĭăque æră, Virg.

Cŏrȳcĭs, ĭdĭs, *and* ciŭs, ă, ŭm, *of Corycus, a promontory of Candia.* Cŏrȳcĭdās nymphās, Ov. Insŭlă Cŏrȳcĭĭs, Ov.

Cŏrȳdōn, ōntĭs, m., *the name of a shepherd.* Pāstŏr Cŏrȳdōn, Virg.

cŏrȳlētŭm, ī, n., *a hazel-grove.* Intĕr cŏrȳlētă jăcēbăt, Ov.

cŏrȳlŭs, ī, f., *the hazel-tree.* Phyllĭs ămăt cŏrȳlōs, Virg. Epith. Dūră, frăgĭlĭs, sylvēstrĭs, flēxĭlĭs, dēnsă.

cŏrȳmbĭfĕr, ă, ŭm, *bearing berries.* Fēstă cŏrȳmbĭfĕrī, Ov.

cŏrȳmbŭs, ī, m., *a bunch, a cluster.* Vēstīt pāllēntĕ cŏrȳmbōs, Virg. Epith. Dīffūsŭs, grăvĭdŭs, cōmāns, tĕnĕr, Bācchæŭs, Nȳsæŭs; tēxtĭlĭs, bĭcŏlŏr, crŏcĕŭs, trĕmŭlŭs, vĭrĭdĭs, mŏllĭs, nĭgĕr, frōndēns, frōndōsŭs, ămœnŭs, răcēmĭfĕr, spīssŭs, hĕdĕrōsŭs.

Cŏrȳnæŭs, ī, m., *the name of a warrior.* Cŏrȳnæŭs ălhēnō, Virg.

Cŏrȳthŭs, ī, m., *a city of Etruria.* Cŏrȳthūm tērrāsquĕ, Virg.

|| cŏrȳtŭs, ī, m., *a quiver.* Cŏrȳtĭquĕ lĕvēs, Virg. Epith. Săgīttĭfĕr. V. Pharetra.

cŏs, cōtĭs, f., *a whetstone.* In cōtĕ sĕcūrēs, Virg. Epith. Dūră, trītă, āspĕră, ēxĭgŭă, tĕnŭĭs, lōngă, mōrdāx, ĕdāx.

Cōsæ, ārŭm, f., *a town of Calabria.* Līquĕrĕ Cōsās, Virg.

|| cōsmētă *and* es, æ, *a groom.* Cōsmētæ tŭnĭcās, Juv.

|| cōsmĭcŭs, ă, ŭm, *perfumed.* Cōsmĭcŭs ēssĕ tĭbi, Mart.

cōstă, æ, f., *a rib.* Dīrĭpĭūnt cōstĭs, Virg.

cōstŭm, ī, n., *and* ŭs, ī, f., *zedoary, an odoriferous herb.* Cōstŭm mŏllĕ dătĕ, Prop.

Cōsȳră, æ, f., *a small island between Sicily and Africa.* Vīcīnă Cōsȳræ, Ov.

cŏthūrnātŭs, ă, ŭm, *wearing buskins.* Illă cŏthūrnātās, Ov.

cŏthūrnŭs, ī, m., *a buskin.* Vīncīrĕ cŏthūrnō, Virg. Epith. Sŏphoclēŭs, Æschȳlĕŭs; grāndĭs, trăgĭcŭs, grăvĭs, grātŭs, āltŭs, pĭctŭs, Lȳdĭŭs; tērrĭfĭcŭs, mägnĭlŏquŭs, ăcĕr, prīscŭs, āltĭsŏnŭs, hĕrōĭcŭs, sŭpērbŭs, sŭblīmĭs, āntīquĭ pūrpŭrĕŭs, Cecrŏpĭŭs.

Cŏtīso, ōnĭs, m., *a king of the Dacians.* Cŏtīsŏnĭs āgmĕn, Hor.

cŏtūrnīx, ĭcĭs, f., *a quail.* Eccĕ cŏtūrnīcēs īntĕr, Ov. Epith. Pĭă, pĕrĕgrīnă, ādvĕnă.

Cŏtȳs, yŏs *or* ȳĭs, m., *the name of several kings of Thrace.* O Cŏtȳ, prŏgĕnĭēs, Ov.

Cŏtȳttĭă, ōrŭm, n. pl., *the mysteries of Cotytto, the goddess of unchastity.* Tŭ rĭsĕrĭs Cŏtȳttĭă, Hor.

cŏvīnŭs, ī, m., *a chariot armed with hooks, used in war.* Bĕlgă cŏvīnī, Luc.

Cŏŭs, ă, ŭm, *of the island of Cos.* Sī Vĕnĕrēm Cŏŭs, Ov.

cŏxă, æ, *or* xĕndīx, ĭcĭs, f., *the hip.* Gĕmĭnās cŏxēndĭcĭs ūmbrās, Ser.

crabro, ōnĭs, m., *a hornet.* Aŭt āspĕr crăbro ĭmpărĭbŭs, Virg. EPITH. Fĕrŭs, fĕrōx, āspĕr, dīrŭs.

‖ crămbē, ēs, f., *a kind of colewort.* Crămbē rĕpĕtītă, Juv.

Crūnē, ēs, f., *a nymph beloved by Janus.* Crānēn dīxĕrĕ, Ov.

Crăntŏr, ŏrĭs, m., *a brother of Phœnix.* Grātīssĭmĕ Crăntŏr, Ov.

‖ crăpŭlă, æ, f., *drunkenness.* Sī crăpŭlă sævĭĕt ēscĭs, Ser. SYN. Ēbrĭĕtās.

EPITH. Grăvĭs, fœdă, ĭnērs, ōbscœnă, tĭtŭbāns, fūrēns, mălĕsănă, īnsănă, dēmēns, āmēns, tūrpĭs, fūrĭōsă, aŭdāx, ĭmpăvĭdă, fŭgĭēndă, pērnĭcĭōsă, hŏrrĭdă, ēxĭtĭōsă. V. Ebrietas.

crăs, adv., *to-morrow.* Dīc mĭhĭ, crăs īstŭd, Mart.

crăssē, adv., *thickly.* Crăssē cŏmpŏsĭtŭm, Hor.

crăssĭtĭēs, ĭēi, f., *thickness.* SYN. Crăssĭtūdo, pīnguēdo, dēnsĭtās.

crăssŭs, ă, ŭm, *thick.* Bœōtum ĭn crăssō, Hor. SYN. Dēnsŭs, ŏpācŭs, pīnguĭs, spīssŭs.

Crassŭs, ī, m., *an opulent Roman.* EPITH. Dīvĕs, cŭpĭdŭs.

crăstĭnŭs, ă, ŭm, *of to-morrow.* Crăstĭnă fāllĕt, Virg.

crātĕr, ērĭs, m., *a cup.* Vērtŭnt crătērăs ăhēnōs, Virg. SYN. Pătĕră, călīx.

EPITH. Ăhēnŭs, aŭrātŭs, ĭnaŭrātŭs, ĭmprēssŭs, aŭrĕŭs, ārgēntĕŭs, prŏfŭndŭs, lātŭs, pŭlchĕr, splēndēns, grătŭs, mĭcāns, sĭgnĭfĕr, cælātŭs, căpāx, ŭndāns, lætŭs. V. Poculum, patera.

crātĕră, æ, f., *a cup.* Vīnă crătēræ, (Sapph.) Hor. V. Crater.

Crătĕrŭs, ī, m., *a Roman physician.* Crătĕrŭm dīxīssĕ pŭtāto, Hor.

Crătēs, ĭs, m., *a river of Africa.* Hȳpănīsquĕ Crătēsquĕ, Ov.

crātēs, ĭs, f., *a hurdle of rods.* Arbŭtĕæ crătēs, Virg. EPITH. Vīmĭnĕă, dēnsātă, tēxtă, frāxĭnĕă.

Crăthĭs, ĭs *or* ĭdĭs, m., *a river of Calabria.* Crăthĭs ĕt hīnc Sȳbărĭs, Ov.

crātĭcŭlă, æ, f., *a roaster.* Cūrvă crătĭcŭlă sŭdĕt, Mart. EPITH. Fērrĕă, ārdēns, cāndēns, fērvēns, āccēnsă, ĭgnītă, sŭppŏsĭtă, ātră, nĭgră.

Crătĭnŭs, ī, m., *a Greek comic poet.* Dōctĕ, Crătĭnō, Hor. EPITH. Prīscŭs, cŏmpŏtŏr, aŭdāx.

‖ crĕāmĕn, ĭnĭs, n., *the creation.* Flūxōquĕ crĕāmĭnĕ, Prud.

crĕātŏr, ŏrĭs, m., trĭx, ĭcĭs, f., *he or she who creates.* Illĕ crĕātŏr, Lucr. Nātūră crĕātrīx, Lucr.

‖ crĕātūră, æ, f. *a creature.* Quīntă crĕātūrās, Sid. SYN. Rēs crĕătă.

crĕātŭs, ă, ŭm, *the pass. partic. of* creo. Stīrpĕ crĕātī, Ov.

crĕbĕr, bră, ŭm, *thick, frequent.* Crēbĕr, ăgēns hȳĕmĕm, Virg. SYN. Frĕquēns, dēnsŭs, rĕpĕtītŭs, mūltŭs, plūrĭmŭs.

crĕbrēsco, bŭi, *to grow thick, to wax common.* Crēbrēscŭnt ŏptātæ, Virg. SYN. Incrēbrēsco, crēsco, aŭgĕŏr; vūlgŏr, dīvūlgŏr.

crĕbrō, adv., *frequently.* Pūrgātăm crēbrō quī pērsŏnĕt, Hor. SYN. Sæpĕ, sæpĭŭs, frĕquēntĕr, nōn rārō.

crēdĭbĭlĭs, ĕ, *credible.* Crēdĭbĭle ēst cæcōs, Ov.

crēdĭtŏr, ŏrĭs, m., *a creditor.* Sēxtĕ, crēdĭtŏrī, (Phal.) Manil.

crēdĭtŭs, ă, ŭm, *the pass. partic. of* credo. Crēdĭtă rēs, Virg. V. Credo.

crēdo, ĭs, dĭdĭ, dĭtŭm, *to believe.* Nīl mĭhĭ crēdĭdĕrĭs, Ov. SYN. Fīdo, cōnfīdo, cŏmmĭtto; fīdĕm dō, hăbĕo, ădhĭbĕo. V. Fido.

crēdŭlĭtās, ātĭs, f., *credulity.* Crēdŭlĭtātĕ frŭăr, Mart.

crēdŭlŭs, ă, ŭm, *credulous.* Crēdŭlă rēs ămŏr, Ov.

Crĕmĕră, æ, f., *a river of Etruria.* Crĕmĕrām tĕtĭgĕrĕ, Ov.

crĕmo, ās, *to burn.* Mēmbră crĕmāndă pȳræ, Ov. SYN. Ūro, ēxūro, cŏmbūro, ĭncēndo, ădūro, īnflămmo.

Crĕmōnă, æ, f., *a town of Italy.* Vīcīnă Crĕmōnæ, Virg. EPITH. Cūltă, pŭlchră, frūmēntĭfĕră, tūrrītă, dīvĕs; mĭsĕră.

crĕmŏr, ŏrĭs, m., *juice.* Infŭndĕ crĕmōrĕm, Ov.

Crēnæŭs, ī, m. *a centaur.* Crēnæĕ, tŭlīstī, Ov.

crĕo, ās, *to create.* Immēnsă crĕăvĕrĭt ōrbĭs, Prud. SYN. Prōcrĕo, gīgno, prŏdūco.

Crĕŏn, ŏntĭs, m, *a tyrant of Thebes, killed by Theseus.* Nătă Crĕŏntĕ sĕrānt, Ov. EPITH. Sævŭs, ĭmmānĭs, dūrŭs, dīrŭs, fērrĕŭs, mĭsĕr, ĭnhūmānŭs, bărbărŭs.

crĕpĕrŭs, ă, ŭm, *dubious.* Sŭnt crĕpĕrī cērtāmĭnă bĕllī, Lucr. Syn. Dŭbĭŭs, āncēps, īncērtŭs.

crĕpĭdă, æ, f., *a slipper.* Sēd tālēs crĕpĭdăs, (Phal.) Syn. Sŏlĕă.

crĕpīdo, ĭnĭs, f., *a creek, a margin.* Cōnjūnctă crĕpīdĭnĕ sāxī, Virg. Syn. Ōră, mārgo, căcūmĕn, ăpēx.

crĕpĭtācŭlŭm *and* bŭlŭm, ī, n., *a timbrel.* Quāssāt crĕpĭtācŭlă pālmīs, Nemes. Syn. Tīntīnnābŭlŭm ; cāmpānă.

crĕpīto, ās, *to clatter.* Crĕpĭtābāt brāctĕă vēntō, Virg. Syn. Strĕpĭto, strīdĕo, sŏno, crēpo.

crĕpĭtŭs, ūs, m., *a rustling noise.* Invērsō crĕpĭtūm dĕdĭt, Juv. Syn. Strĕpĭtŭs, sŏnŭs, sŏnĭtŭs, frăgŏr. Epith. Sŏnōrŭs, hōrrĭsŏnŭs. V. Sonitus.

crĕpo, ŏī, ĭtŭm, *to make a shrill noise.* Et crĕpĕt īn mĕdĭīs, Ov. Syn. Sŏno, pērcrĕpo, crĕpĭto.

crĕpūndĭă, ōrŭm, n. pl., *toys.* Pŭĕrīquĕ crĕpūndĭă, Prud. Epith. Pŭĕrīlĭă, pārvă.

crĕpūscŭlŭm, ī, n., *the twilight.* Ăd prīmă crĕpūscŭlă lūstră, Ov. Epith. Ŏpācŭm, ōbscūrŭm, nōctĭfĕrŭm, ŏccĭdŭŭm, crŏcĕŭm, rŭbĭcūndŭm, rĕdūx, nigrŭm, vēspērtīnŭm. V. Vesper, Aurora.

Crēs, ētĭs, m, *of Crete.* Crētēs ĕrŭnt, Ov. V. Cressius.

crēsco, ĕvī, *to increase.* Crēvĕrāt hērbă, Prop. Syn. Aūgĕŏr, ădaūgĕŏr, aūgēsco, ēxtēndŏr, āccrēsco.

Crēssă, æ, *and* Crētĭs, ĭdĭs, f. *of Crete.* Crēssă gĕnŭs, Virg. Fĕrūntūr Crētĭdēs, Ov. Syn. Crēssĭă, Crētĭcă, Crētæă. V. Cressius.

Crēssĭŭs, ă, ŭm, *of Crete.* Nĕmŏra īntēr Crēssĭă fīxĭt, Virg. Syn. Crētĭcŭs, Crētæŭs, Crētēnsĭs.

crēssŭs, ă, ŭm, *of white clay.* Crēssă nē cărĕăt, Hor.

Crētă, æ, *and* ē, ēs, f., *the largest island of the Mediterranean sea.* Crētă Jŏvĭs, Virg. Syn. Mīnōĭă tēllūs, ārvă Mīnōĭă, Gōrtўnĭă, Gnōsĭă, Dīctæă, Ŏāxĭă. Tērră Cūrētĭs, ĭdĭs.

crētă, æ, f., *white clay, chalk.* Illă prĭūs crētă, Fill. Epith. Ălbă, tĕnāx, putrĭs, Cĭmōlĭă.

crētăcĕŭs, ă, ŭm, *of white clay.* Crētăcĕăm dăbĭs, Ser.

Crētæŭs, ă, ŭm, *of Crete.* Strătăquĕ Crētæăm, Ov. V. Cressius.

crētātŭs, ă, ŭm, *chalked.* Quăm crētātă tĭmĕt, (Phal.) Mart. Syn. Crēta ōbdūctŭs, cōlōrātŭs, fūcātŭs.

Crēteŭs, ĕŏs, m., *a Greek warrior.* Fōrtīssĭmĕ Crēteū, Virg.

Crētheŭs, ĕŏs, ĕī *or* eī, m., *a son of Æolus.*—2. *a Trojan warrior.* Crēthĕă mūsĭs, Virg.

Crētĭcŭs, ă, ŭm, *of Crete.* In mărĕ Crētĭcŭm, (Alcaic.) Hor. Syn. Gnōsĭăcŭs, Dīctæŭs, Mīnōĭŭs. V. Creta.

crētōsŭs, ă, ŭm, *full of clay.* Mўcōnōn, crētōsăquĕ rūră, Ov.

crētŭs, ă, ŭm, *born.* Sānguĭnĕ crētŭm, Virg. Syn. Crĕātŭs, ōrtŭs, gĕnĭtŭs, sătŭs, nātŭs.

Crĕūsă, æ, f., *the second wife of Jason.* Ēphўrēæ flāmmă Crĕūsæ, Ov.—2. *Æneas' wife.* Ūmbră Crĕūsæ, Virg. Epith. Dārdănĭs, Trōjānă, pūlchră, fōrmōsă.

crībrŭm, ī, n., *a sieve.* Sŭb pōndĕrĕ crībrī, Ov.

crīmĕn, ĭnĭs, n., *a crime.* Crīmĭnĕ crīmĕn hăbĕt, Ov. Syn. Scĕlŭs, nĕfās, dēlīctŭm, mălŭm, pĭācŭlŭm, pēccātŭm, nōxă, vĭtĭŭm, cūlpă, făcĭnŭs, flăgĭtĭŭm, ērrātŭm, cōmmīssŭm. Epith. Nōxĭŭm, sævŭm, crūdēlĕ, tūrpĕ, trīstĕ, nĕfāndŭm, fœdŭm, prāvŭm, īnjūstŭm, īnfāndŭm, dīrŭm, dŏlōsŭm, dāmnābĭlĕ, impĭŭm, pērfĭdŭm, ŏccŭltŭm, īnaūdītŭm, īnēxcūsābĭlĕ. V. Scelus.

crīmĭnātŏr, ōrĭs, m., *an accuser.* Crīmĭnātōrēm mĕŭm, (Iamb.) Plaut. Syn. Ăccūsātŏr.

crīmĭnŏr, ārĭs, *to accuse.* Nē crīmĭnĕrĭs impĭŏs, (Iamb. Dim.) Paulin. V. Accuso.

crīmĭnōsŭs, ă, ŭm, *outrageous.* Quĕm crīmĭnōsĭs, (Alcaic.) Hor. Syn. Dāmnāndŭs, scĕlēstŭs.

crīnālĕ, ĭs, n., *a bodkin.* Cūrvŭm crīnălĕ căpīllōs, Ov. Syn. Căpīllārĕ.

crīnālĭs, ĕ, *belonging to the hair.* Sōlvĭtĕ crīnālēs vīttās, Virg. Syn. Căpīllārĭs.

crīnĭgĕr, ă, ŭm, *wearing much hair.* Crīnĭgĕrōs bĕllĭs, Luc. Syn. Crīnītŭs, cŏmātŭs.

crīnĭŏr, īrĭs, *to be covered with hair.* Crīnītūr frōndĭbŭs ārbōs, Sil.

crīnĭs, ĭs, *a hair, and* crīnēs, ĭum, m. pl., *the hair.* Vērtĭcĕ crīnĕm, Virg. Crīnĭbŭs aūră, Id. Syn. Căpĭllī, cŏmă, cæsărĭēs. Epith. Pēndŭlī, flāvĭcŏmī, flāvī, văgī, flāvēntēs, nĭtĭdī, cōnnēxī, hīrsūtī, rĕtŏrtī, aūrātī, cŏmāntēs, dĕcŏrī, dĕcēntēs.

Crīnĭsŭs, ī, m., *a Trojan prince metamorphosed into a river.* Trōĭă Crīnīsō, Virg.

crīnītŭs, ă, ŭm, *hairy.* Crīnītās ānguĕ sŏrōrēs, Ov. V. Comatus.

Crīspīnŭs, ī, m., *the name of several Romans.* Nē mē Crīspīnī, Hor.

crīspo, ās, *to curl, to brandish.* Crīspāns hāstīlĭă fērrō, Virg. Syn. Ūndo, flūctŭo ; vibro, quătĭo, quāsso.

crīspŭs, *and* ŭlŭs, ă, ŭm, *crisped.* Crīspāmque īnvōlvĕrĕ vīsa ēst, Sil. Syn. Cīrrātŭs.

crīstă, æ, f., *a crest.* Excūssīt vērtĭcĕ crīstās, Virg. Epith. Cŏmāns, rŭtĭlă, tērrĭfĭcă, āltă, cŏrūscă, hōrrēns, ūndāns, mĭcāns, ēlătă, mĭnāx, splēndĭdă, rĕfūl-gēns, ēffūsă, sūrgēns, tērrĭbĭlĭs, fōrmīdābĭlĭs, mīlĭtārĭs.

crīstātŭs, ă, ŭm, *tufted.* Crīstātæquĕ sŏnānt, Mart.

crĭtĭcŭs, ī, m., *a critic.* Ŭt crĭtĭcī dīcŭnt, Hor. Syn. Jūdēx, cēnsŏr.

Crŏcălē, ēs, f., *daughter of the river Ismenus.* Ismēnīs Crŏcălē, Ov.

crŏcĕŭs, *and* ĭnŭs, ă, ŭm, *like saffron.* Invītēnt crŏcĕīs, Virg. Fūlgēbāt crŏcĭnā, Catull. Syn. Rŭtĭlŭs, lūtĕŭs, flāvŭs.

crŏcīto, ās, *to croak.* Ēt crŏcītăt cōrvŭs, Ov.

crŏcŏdĭlŭs, ī, m., *the crocodile.* Crŏcŏdīlŏn ădŏrăt, Juv. Epith. Nīlĭăcŭs, Nĭlĭ-cŏlă, Ægȳptĭŭs, Phărĭŭs, vŏrāx, āquātĭcŭs, īngēns, hōrrēndŭs, cāllĭdŭs, āstūtŭs, fĕrŭs, fōrmīdābĭlĭs, mĕtŭēndŭs, mĭnāx, crūdēlĭs, īmmītĭs, īmmānĭs, tērrĭfĭcŭs, īmprŏbŭs, lēthĭfĕr, ēxĭtĭōsŭs.

crŏcŭs, ī, m., *or* ŭm, ī, n., *saffron.* Īllĕ crŏcūm sĭmŭlăt, Ov. Epith. Rŭbēns, aūrĭcŏmāns, pūrpŭrĕŭs, rĕdŏlēns, spīrāns, flāvŭs, flāvēns, lūtĕŭs, fūlvŭs, tĕnĕr, pāllēns, pāllĭdŭs, aūrĕŭs, mōllĭs, Sĭcŭlŭs, Sĭcānĭŭs, Cĭlīx, Cȳlīssŭs, Cŏrȳcĭŭs ; Tȳrĭŭs ; tĕnŭĭs, ŏdōrātŭs, hālāns, grātŭs, āmœnŭs.

Crœsŭs, ī, m., *a king of Lydia.* Crœsŭs ĕrăt, Ov. Epith. Lȳdŭs, māgnŭs, dīvĕs, sŭpērbŭs.

Crŏmȳōn, ŏnĭs, m., *a town near Corinth.* Crŏmȳŏnă cŏlōnŭs, Ov.

crŏtălīstrĭă, æ, f., *a woman who plays upon cymbals.* Crŏtălīstrĭă Phȳllĭs, Prop.

crŏtălŭm, ī, n., *a cymbal, castanet.* Crīspūm sŭb crŏtălō, Virg. Syn. Cȳmbălŭm.

Crŏtōn, *or* ō, ōnĭs, *Crotona, a city of Magna Grœcia.* Āltă Crŏtōn pŏrtăs, Sil.

crŭcĭātŭs, ūs, m., *and* āmĕn, ĭnĭs, n., *torment.* Pēr crŭcĭāmĭnă lēthī, Prud. Lătĕrĭs crŭcĭātĭbŭs ŭrŏr, Ov. Syn. Pœnă, sūpplĭcĭŭm, tōrmēntŭm. Epith. Sævŭs, atrōx, mœstŭs, dīrŭs, Sĭsȳphĭŭs ; dūrŭs, ăcērbŭs, fĕrŭs, trīstĭs, crūdēlĭs, hōrrĭdŭs, sĕvērŭs, īmmānĭs, ămārŭs. V. Supplicium, dolor.

crŭcĭfigo, xī, xŭm, *to crucify.* Crŭcĭfīgĕ, cĭtō crŭcĭfīgĕ, Cal.

crŭcĭo, ās, *to torment.* Quāntūm sīc crŭcĭăt, Prop. Syn. Tōrquĕo, vēxo, ăgĭto, prĕmo, āngo, măcto, āfflīcto, cōnfĭcĭo. V. Affligo.

crūdēlĭs, ĕ, *cruel.* Ēst crūdēlĭŏr īn nōs, Hor. Syn. Sævŭs, atrōx, fĕrŭs, fĕrōx, trūx, dīrŭs, bārbărŭs, dūrŭs, ĭnhūmānŭs, trŭcŭlēntŭs, fērrĕŭs, ăcērbŭs, īm-mānĭs, crŭēntŭs, ēffĕrŭs, tētĕr, īmmītĭs, fŭrēns, īnclēmēns, ăspĕr, ĭmprŏbŭs, sānguĭnĕŭs.

crūdēlĭtās, ātĭs, f., *cruelty.* Crūdēlĭtātĕ, nōn mĕtū, (Iamb.) Prud. Syn. Fĕrĭtās, īmmānĭtās, bārbărĭēs, sævĭtĭă, sævĭtĭēs, īnclēmēntĭă, dūrĭtĭēs, ăspĕrĭtās, fĕrōcĭă, ăcērbĭtās, atrōcĭtās. Epith. Ĭnhūmānă, fĕrīnă, fŭrēns, sævă, crŭēntă, īmmānĭs, hōrrēndă, īnsānă, bārbără, īmmītĭs, răbĭdă, Scȳthĭcă, dūră, īnvĭdă, cæcă, fŭrĭōsă, præcēps, fĕră, atrōx, scĕlĕrātă, ĭnaūdītă, sānguĭnŏlēntă, fŭrĭbūndă, īmpătĭēns, tērrĭbĭlĭs, ŏdĭōsă.

crūdēlĭtĕr, adv., *cruelly.* Nĭmĭŭm crūdēlĭtĕr ūsī, Mart.

crūdēsco, dŭī, *to grow fiercer.* Cœpīt crūdēscĕrĕ mōrbŭs, Virg. Syn. Recrūdēsco, īngrăvēsco, aūgĕŏr.

crūdŭs, ă, ŭm, *raw, cruel.* Seū crūdō fĭdĭs, Virg. Syn. Immātūrŭs, dūrŭs, crūdēlĭs.

crŭēnto, ās, *to make bloody.* Mōrsūquĕ crŭēntăt, Prop.

crŭēntŭs, ă, ŭm, *bloody.* Cædĕ crŭēntŭs, Virg.

crŭmēnă, æ, f., *a purse.* Dēfĭcĭēntĕ crŭmēnă, Hor. Syn. Mārsŭpĭŭm, lŏcŭlī. Epith. Plēnă, rĕfērtă, grăvĭs, dīvĕs.

crŭŏr, ōrĭs, m., *gore.* Vŏmĭt ŏrĕ crŭōrĕm, Virg. Syn. Sănĭēs, sānguĭs. Epith. Flŭĭdŭs, ōbscœnŭs, tētĕr, călĭdŭs, ātĕr, rŭtĭlŭs, rŏsĕŭs, pīnguĭs, fūsŭs, fœdŭs, nĭgĕr, cōrrŭptŭs, putrĭs, ēffūsŭs. V. Sanguis.

crūs, crūrĭs, n., *the leg.* Crūs ŭbĭ cŏmmīsĭt, Ov. Et crūrŭm tĕnŭs, Virg.
crūscŭlŭm, ī, n., *the diminut. of* crus. Crūscŭlŭmquĕ fŏrmīcæ, Mart.
|| crūsmă, ătĭs, n., *a timbrel.* Bætĭcă crūsmătă, Mart.
crŭstă, æ, f., *a crust.* Īn flūmĭnĕ crŭstæ, Virg. Epith. Cŏctă, dūră, prædūră,
   frăgĭlĭs.
crŭstŭlă, æ, f., ŭlŭm, *and* ŭm, ī, n., *a crust, cake.* Crūstŭlă prōmĭt, Hor. Dānt
   mātrēs, crūstŭlă, Hor. Fātālĭs crūstī, Virg.
Crŭstŭmĕrī, ōrŭm, m. pl., *a city of Italy.* Ārdĕă, Crŭstŭmĕrī, Virg.
Crūstŭmĭŭm, ī, n., *a small town near Rome.* Crūstŭmĭŏ prĭŏr, Sil.
Crūstŭmĭŭs, ă, ŭm, *of Crustumium.* Crūstŭmīīs Sȳrīīsvĕ, Virg.
crŭx, crŭcĭs, f., *a cross.* Præbŭĭt īllă crŭcēs, Ov. Syn. Trābs, līgnŭm, trūncŭs,
   stīpēs, ārbŏr, rōbŭr, pătĭbŭlŭm. Epith. Dūră, sævă, hŏrrēndă, rĭgĭdă, crŭēntă,
   ātră, trīstĭs, ămāră, mĭsĕră, lūrĭdă, fūnĕrĕă, fūnēstă, lūctŭōsă, ăcērbă, sălŭtĭfĕră.
|| crȳptă, æ, f., *a cave, a vault.* Mĕdĭæ crȳptăm pĕnĕtrārĕ, Juv. Syn. Āntrŭm,
  - spĕcŭs, fōssă, fŏvĕă.
crȳstāllĭnŭs, ă, ŭm, *of or like crystal.* Crȳstāllĭnă māxĭmă rūrsŭs, Juv.
crȳstāllŭs, ī, f., *and* lŭm, ī, n., *crystal.* Crȳstāllŭsquĕ tŭās, Prop. Nĭvĭbŭs crȳstāllă
   gĕlārī, Stat. Epith. Cāndĭdă, glăcĭālĭs, gĕlĭdă, lĭquĭdă, splēndēns, nĭtĭdă, pūră,
   clāră, lūcĭdă, splēndĭdă, Indă, Eŏă, mĭcāns, lūcēns, frăgĭlĭs.
cŭbĭcŭlŭm, ī, n., *a bed-room.* Sĕd ā cŭbĭcŭlō lēctŭlōquĕ jāctātăm, (Scaz.) Mart.
   Epith. Vāstŭm, ārcānŭm, dīvĕs, ōrnātŭm. V. Domus.
cŭbīlĕ, ĭs, n., *a bed.* Sæpĕ cŭbīlĭbŭs āltĭs, Virg. Syn. Lēctŭs, thălămŭs, tŏrŭs,
   strātŭm. Epith. Cōnjŭgālĕ, mōllĕ, quĭētŭm, sŏcĭŭm, ārcānŭm, plăcĭdŭm,
   pūrŭm, lătebrōsŭm, dūlcĕ, rŏsĕŭm, plŭmōsŭm, tĕnĕrŭm, ŏccŭltŭm, grātŭm, tĕnebrōsŭm. V. Lectus.
cŭbĭtăl, ālĭs, n., *a cushion.* Fāscĭŏlās, cŭbĭtăl, Hor.
cŭbĭtŭs, ī, m., *and* tŭm, ī, n., *the elbow.* Āttŏllēns, cŭbĭtōque ānnīxă, Virg. Epith.
   Flēxŭs, reflēxŭs.
cŭbo, ās, ŭī, ĭtŭm, *to lie down.* Sōlă cŭbărĕ tŏrō, Ov. Syn. Jăcĕo, stērnŏr, prōstērnŏr, rĕcŭmbo, rĕcŭbo, quĭēsco, prōcŭmbo, rĕquĭēsco. V. Jaceo.
cŭbŭs, ī, m., *a cube.* Āddĕ cŭbŭm, Ov.
cŭcŭbo, ās, *to whoop like an owl.* Cŭcŭbăt īn tĕnĕbrīs, Ov. Syn. Ŭlŭlo.
cŭcŭllŭs, ī, m., *a hood.* Vēlās ădŏpērtă cŭcŭllō, Juv. Epith. Vĕnĕtŭs. Sānc-
   tŏnĭcŭs.
cŭcŭlŭs, ī, m., *a cuckoo, dolt.* Vōcĕ cŭcŭlŭm, Hor.
cŭcŭmă, æ, f., *a tin, a hut.* Cŭcŭmăm fēcĭt, Mart.
cŭcŭmĭs, ĭs, *or* cŭmĕr, ĕrĭs, m., *a cucumber.* In vēntrēm cŭcŭmĭs, Virg. Epith.
   Tōrtŭs, īntōrtŭs, cœrŭlĕŭs, lĭvĭdŭs, frĭgĭdŭs, agrēstĭs.
cŭcŭrbĭtă *and* ŭlă, æ, f., *a gourd.* Tŭmĭdōquĕ cŭcŭrbĭtă vēntrĕ, Prop. Epith.
   Grăvĭs, prægnāns, vĭrĭdĭs, sĭlvēstrĭs, ŭncă.
cŭcŭrĭo, ĭs, *to crow like a cock.* Cŭcŭrīrĕ sŏlĕt, Ov.
cūdo, ĭs, cūdī, cūsŭm, *to strike.* Fūlmēn cūdēbăt ĭn āntrīs, Man. Syn. Ēxcūdo,
   prōcūdo. V. Procudo.
cŭdo, ŏnĭs, m., *a cap made of raw skin.* Cūdŏnĕ cŏmāntēs, Sil. Epith. Tūtŭs,
   dūrŭs, hŏrrēns.
cŭi, (dissyl.) *or* cuī, (monosyl.) *the dat. of* qui *or* quis. Sĕd nōrŭnt cŭī sērvĭānt,
   (Phal.) Mart. Cuī lūx prīmă săcrī, Id.
cŭĭcŭnquĕ, *or* cuĭcŭnquĕ, *the dat. of* quicunque. Dōnĕt cŭĭcŭnquĕ tērră, (Sapph.)
   Ŭt cuĭcŭnque ēst, Ov.
cŭĭquăm, *or* cuĭquăm, *the dat. of* quisquam. Tĕ fāllĕrĕ cuĭquăm, Virg.
cŭĭquĕ, *or* cuĭquĕ, *the dat. of* quisque. Nōmĭnă cuīquĕ, Mart. Pĕtēndă cŭīquĕ,
   Mant.
cuĭvĭs, *the dat. of* quivis. Nōn cuĭvĭs hŏmĭnī, Hor.
cūjŭs, [gen.] *whose.* Cūjŭs ĕbŭr, Ov.
cūjŭs, ă, ŭm, *whose.* Cūjŭm pĕcŭs, Virg.
cŭlcĭtă, æ, f., *a bed.* Cēssārēt cŭlcĭtă lēctō, Juv. Syn. Pūlvīnŭs, lēctŭlŭs. Epith.
   Făcĭlĭs, pīctă, lĕvĭs, plŭmĕă, mōllĭs.
cŭlĕŭs, ī, m., *a leather-bag.* Cŭlĕŭs ūnŭs, Juv.
cŭlēx, ĭcĭs, m., *a small fly.* Quæ īn nōstrō cŭlĭcēs, Lucr. Epith. Mălŭs, īnfōrmĭs, rŏtŭndŭs, tĕnŭĭs, lĕvĭs, ēxīlĭs, ăĕrĭŭs, vŏlĭtāns, īmpŏrtūnŭs, văgŭs,
   mŏlēstŭs, văgăbŭndŭs, mōrdāx, ēxĭgŭŭs, pārvŭs.

cŭlīnă, æ, f., *a kitchen.* Pŭtăt illĕ cŭlīnæ, Juv. Epitii. Nigră, pŭtĭdă, ūnctă, crāssă, pīngŭĭs, āngūstă, fœtĭdă, fūmōsă.

cūlmĕn, ĭnĭs, n., *the top of any thing.* Sōlăquĕ cūlmĭnĭbŭs, Virg. Syn. Apēx, vērtēx, fāstīgĭŭm. Epith. Ardŭŭm, aērĭŭm, sŭblīmĕ, ŭmbrōsŭm, mōntānŭm, āltŭm, sŭmmŭm, cēlsŭm. V. Cacumen.

cūlmŭs, ī, m., *a straw.* Strīngĕrĕt hōrdĕă cūlmō, Virg. Syn. Călămŭs, stĭpŭlă, ăvēnă. Epitii. Lĕvĭs, Cĕrēālĭs, ūdŭs, vĭrĭdĭs, tĕnĕr, lăctāns, flāvēns, spīcĕŭs, tĕnŭĭs, flāvŭs, flāvēscēns, crŏcĕŭs, frūgĭfĕr, vērnāns, spīcātŭs, trītĭcĕŭs, fĕrāx, fœcūndŭs, aūrĕŭs.

cūlpă, æ, f., *a fault.* Sūdānt præcōrdĭă cūlpā, Juv. Syn. Nŏxă, dēlīctŭm, vĭtĭŭm, crīmĕn, scĕlŭs, pēccātŭm. Epitii. Tūrpĭs, tăcĭtă, sōrdĭdă, hōrrēns, ŏpērtă, lătēns, nŏxĭă, mĭsĕrāndă, lĕvĭs. V. Crimen, scelus.

cūlpo, ās, *to blame.* Cūlpātŭr ăb īllĭs, Hor. Syn. Accūso, īncūso, īnsĭmŭlo. V. Accuso.

cūltĕr, trī, *and* tēllŭs, ī, m., *a knife.* Cūltrīs ābrūmpĕrĕ cārmĕn, Juv. Cūltēllō prŏprĭōs, Hor. Syn. Glădĭŭs. Epith. Acūtŭs, strīctŭs, fūlgēns, crŭēntŭs, mĭnāx. V. Gladius.

cūltŏr, ōrĭs, m., *and* trīx, īcĭs, f., *a tiller, an inhabitant.* Dŏmĭtŭm cūltōrĭbŭs ŏrbĕm, Virg. Nĕmŏrŭm cūltrīx, Phæd.

cūltŭră, æ, f., *culture.* Cūltŭră pŏtēntĭs ămīcī, Hor.

cūltŭs, ūs, m., *attire.* Cūltŭs dēcŏrōs, (Iamb.) Syn. Ōrnātŭs. Epith. Rēgălĭs, vānŭs, sōlēnnĭs, māgnĭfĭcŭs, rēgĭŭs, splēndĭdŭs, nītĭdŭs, nĭtēns, gēmmātŭs, mŭlĭebrĭs, nōbĭlĭs, fēstŭs, īnsŏlĭtŭs, trĭūmphālĭs, īnsĭgnĭs, ĭnānĭs.—2. *worship, honour.* Dĕō, cūltŭs ēxŏsă prĭōrēs, Prud. Syn. Hŏnŏr, rĕvĕrēntĭă. Epith. Sŭpplēx, dēbĭtŭs, mĕrĭtŭs, dĭgnŭs, hŭmĭlĭs, pĭŭs. V. Honor, Adoro.

cŭlŭllŭs, ī, m., *a kind of cup.* Ūrgĕrĕ cŭlŭllĭs, Hor.

cŭm, prep., *with.* Rĕmō cŭm frātrĕ, Virg.

cŭm, conj., *when, as.* Cŭm sĕmĕl, Ov,

Cūmæ, ārŭm, f. pl., *and* Cūmē *or* Cȳmē, ēs, f., *a town of Campania.* Cūmārŭm āllābĭtŭr ōrīs, Virg.

Cūmæŭs, *or* Cūmānŭs, ă, ŭm, *of Cumæ.* Cūmææm āccēssĕrĭs ūrbĕm, Virg.

|| cŭmĕră, æ, f., *a large basket.* Plūs laūdēs cŭmĕrīs, Hor.

cŭmīnŭm, ī, n., *cummin.* Exānguĕ cŭmīnŭm, Hor.

cŭmŭlātĭm, adv., *by heaps.* Dăpĭbŭs cŭmŭlātĭm āggēstă rĕdūndānt, Prud. Syn. Acērvātĭm.

cŭmŭlo, ās, *to heap.* Aūrī cŭmŭlārĕt ăcērvōs, Avien. Syn. Acērvo, āccŭmŭlo, āggĕro, cōngĕro, cōllĭgo, cōngrĕgo, cŏgo, cōmpōno. V. Accumulo.

cŭmŭlŭs, ī, m., *a heap.* Īnsĕquĭtŭr, cŭmŭlōsquĕ rŭĭt, Virg. Syn. Acērvŭs, cōngĕrĭēs, strŭēs, vīs, cŏpĭă. Epith. Ingēns, māgnŭs, nŭmĕrōsŭs, cōpĭōsŭs, grāndĭs, nĭmĭŭs. V. Acervus.

cūnābŭlă, ōrŭm, n. pl., *a cradle.* Fūndēnt cūnābŭlă flōrēs, Virg. Syn. Incūnābŭlă, cūnæ.

cūnæ, ārŭm, f. pl., *a cradle.* Cūnārŭm lăbŏr ēst, Ov. Syn. Cūnābŭlă, īncūnābŭlă. Epitii. Tĕnĕræ, tĕpĭdæ, dūlcēs, sŏpŏræ, sōmnĭfĕræ, mōllēs, pŭĕrīlēs, sŏpōrĭfĕræ, plăcĭdæ, ĭnērtēs, quĭētæ, flēbĭlēs, prīmæ, lacrȳmōsæ.

cūnctātĭo, ōnĭs, f., *delay.* Cūnctātĭŏ lōngă ēst, Juv. V. Mora.

cūnctātŏr, ōrĭs, m., *a delayer.* Nōn cūnctātŏr ĭnīquī, Stat. Syn. Cūnctāns, cūnctābūndŭs.

cūnctŏr, ārĭs, *to delay.* Cūnctārĭs ănĭmĕ, (Iamb.) Sen. Syn. Mŏrŏr, hærĕo, sūbsīsto. V. Moror.

cūnctŭs, ă, ŭm, *all.* Cūnctă tērrārŭm, Hor. Syn. Ōmnĭs, tōtŭs.

cŭnĕātŭs, ă, ŭm, *wedged.* Cŭnĕātŭs ăcūmĭnĕ lōngō, Ov

cŭnĕŭs, ī, m., *a wedge.* Prīmī cŭnĕĭs scīndēbānt, Virg. Epitii. Fērrĕŭs, līgnĕŭs. V. Findo, exercitus.

cŭnīcŭlōsŭs, ă, ŭm, *full of rabbits.* Cŭnīcŭlōsæ Cēltĭbērĭæ, (Scaz.) Cat.

cŭnīcŭlŭs, ī, m., *a rabbit.* Hăbĭtārĕ cŭnīcŭlŭs āntrīs, Mart.

cŭpă, æ, f., *a cup.* Lūdŭs ĕrāt cŭpā, Hor.

cŭpēdĭă, æ, f.; *and* ă, ōrŭm, n. pl., *dainties.* Mŏrŏr cŭpēdĭă, Plaut.

Cŭpīdĭnĕŭs, ă, ŭm, *of Cupid.* Mōllĕ, Cŭpīdĭnĕĭs, Ov.

Cŭpīdo, ĭnĭs, m., *the son of Venus, and God of Love.* Pĕrīĕrĕ Cŭpīdĭnĭs ārcŭs, Ov. Epitii. Cæcŭs, nūdŭs, ālātŭs, ălĭgĕr, ārcĭtĕnēns, săgĭttĭfĕr, phărĕtrātŭs, præpĕs, vŏlŭcĕr, pĕnnĭgĕr, vĕnŭstŭs, fŏrmōsŭs, blăndŭs, ŏbscœnŭs, lăscīvŭs, impŭrŭs, flămmĭgĕr, lēvĭs, vēlōx, crūdēlĭs, aŭdāx, ignĭfĕr, pŭlchĕr, văgŭs, vēsānŭs, trūx, insĭdĭōsŭs, sŭbdŏlŭs, fĕrvĭdŭs, sōrdĭdŭs, dŭlcĭs, immītĭs, ĭmpĭgĕr, cāllĭdŭs, imprŏbŭs, atrōx, sævŭs, pĕnnātŭs, cŭltŭs, ārmĭgĕr, dīrŭs, fĕrōx, fĕrŭs; Păphĭŭs, Idălĭŭs, Gnўdĭŭs, Cўthĕrēĭŭs. V. Venus.—2. f., ardent wish. Tăm cæcă cŭpīdo ēst, Ov. SYN. Cŭpĭdĭtās, ārdŏr, lĭbīdo, dēsīdĕrĭŭm, ămŏr. EPITH. Vĭgĭl, ăvĭdă, cæcă, mĭsĕră, jējūnă, fŭrĭōsă, imprŏbă, ĭnŏps, dīră, scĕlĕrātă, mălĕsănă, insānă, nĕfāndă, tūrpĭs, prŏnă, immŏdĕrātă, vĕhĕmēns, ĭngēns, vĭŏlēntă, pērvĭgĭl, insōmnĭs, ĕffrænātă, indŏmĭtă, sōllĭcĭtă, ānxĭă, ĭnēxplēbĭlĭs, ĭnēxplētă. V. Desiderium, Amor.

cŭpĭdŭs, ă, ŭm, desirous. Itĕ prŏcŭl, cŭpĭdĭs, Tib. SYN. Avĭdŭs, ămāns, āppĕtēns.

cŭpĭo, ĭs, īvī or ĭi, ītŭm, ĕrĕ, to wish for. Trŏjă cŭpĭērĕ rĕlĭctă, Virg. SYN. Vŏlo, ŏpto, ēxŏpto, dēsīdĕro, āppĕto, ăvĕo. V. Desidero.

cŭpītŭs, ă, ŭm, the pass. partic. of cupio. Pŏtĭtŭrquĕ cŭpītă, Ov.

|| cŭprēssĭfĕr, ă, ŭm, bearing cypress. Ipsă cŭprēssĭfĕrī, Alc.

cŭprēssĭnŭs, ă, ŭm, of cypress. Pāssĭsquĕ cŭprēssĭnă quŏrŭm, Prud.

cŭprēssŭs, ī and ūs, f., a cypress-tree. Lēctūră, cŭprēssŭs, Cl. SYN. Cўpărīssŭs; sĕpŭlchrālĭs ārbŏr. EPITH. Mœstă, fŭnĕrĕă, ŏdōrātă, trīstĭs, fūnēstă, flēbĭlĭs, infaŭstă, infēlīx, Stўgĭă, fūnebrĭs, vīrēns, vĭrĭdāns, frŏndōsă, ūmbrĭfĕră, dēnsă, āltă, pătŭlă, prŏcĕră, cēlsă, ēxcēlsă, Idæă; ārdŭă, āĕrĭă, sŭblīmĭs, lūgŭbrĭs, lacrўmābĭlĭs, sĕpŭlchrālĭs, dēplōrātă.

cūr, adv., why. Vĕnīt? cūr hæc cērtāmĭnă vītăt, Ov.

cūră, æ, f., care. Ō cūrās hŏmĭnŭm, Pers. SYN. Sōllĭcĭtūdo, ānxĭĕtās. EPITH. Trīstĭs, insōmnĭs, mŏlēstă, sēdŭlă, dīlĭgēns, ĕdāx, vĭtĭōsă, ātră, sĕquāx, păvĭdă, ăcērbă, ācrĭs, vĭgĭlāns, grăvĭs, lōngă, ămără, lănguĭdă, mĕmŏr, dāmnōsă, āttŏnĭtă, mœstă, ægră, ăvără, ārcānă, infāndă, dēsēs, sōllĭcĭtă, pērvĭgĭl, tūrpĭs, irrĕquĭĕtă, pāllēns, pāllĭdă, ūrgēns, implăcĭdă, fūnēstă, sĕvĕră, flăgrāns, ānxĭă, ĭnīquă, tetrĭcă, prĕmēns, tūrbĭdă, ingrātă, nŏxĭă, pērnĭcĭōsă, tăcĭtă, nŏcēns, rōdēns, crŭcĭāns, dīră, impŏrtūnă.

cūrābĭlĭs, ĕ, which may be cured. Vĭdēns cūrābĭlĕ vĕnī, Mant. SYN. Sānābĭlĭs.

cūrātŏr, ōrĭs, m., he who takes care of. Cūrātōrĭs ĕgĕt, Juv.

cūrcŭlĭo, ōnĭs, m., a mite. Fārrĭs ăcērvŭm Cūrcŭlĭō, Virg. EPITH. Ēdāx, rōdēns, imprŏbŭs.

Cūrēs, ĭŭm, m. pl., an ancient people of Italy. Cūrĭbŭsquĕ sĕvērĭs, Virg.

Cūrētēs, ŭm, m. pl., the first inhabitants of Crete. Cūrētŭm sŏnĭtŭs, Virg. V. Creta.

Cūrētĭs, ĭdĭs, f., of Crete. Cūrētĭdă tērrăm, Ov.

cūrĭă, æ, f., a ward, the senate. Cūrĭă paŭpĕrĭbŭs, Ov.

cūrĭo, ōnĭs, m., the priest of a ward. Cūrĭō lēgĭtĭmĭs, Ov.—2. a surname of several Romans. Cūrĭō crīstă, Sil.

cūrĭōsŭs, ă, ŭm, curious, careful. Nōstī cūrĭōsŭs, (Iamb.) Hor.

Cūrĭŭs, ĭi, m., a Roman hero. Paŭpĕr ĕrăt Cūrĭŭs, Hor. EPITH. Paŭpĕr, pūgnāx, gĕnĕrōsŭs, fōrtĭs, illūstrĭs.

cūro, ās, to take care of. Sī cūrās ēssĕ quŏd aŭdĭs, Hor. SYN. Lăbōro, stŭdĕo; mĕdĕŏr, sāno. V. Cura.

cūrrĭcŭlŭm, ī, n., a course, a race, a chariot. Cūrrĭcŭlō grăvĭs ēst, Ov. SYN. Cūrsŭs; spătĭŭm, spătĭă, stădĭŭm.

cūrro, cŭcūrrī, cūrsŭm, ĕre, to run. Bĭsquĕ cŭcūrrĭt hўēms, Ov. SYN. Fēstīno, prŏpĕro, vŏlo, ādvŏlo, fŭgĭo. V. Festino.

cūrrŭcă, æ, f., a hedge-sparrow. Nūnc cūrrŭcă, plăcēs, Juv.

cūrrŭs, ūs, m., a chariot. Vīctŏr in cūrrū stĕtĭt, (Iamb.) SYN. Plaŭstrŭm; āxĭs, tēmo, rŏtă, (often taken for the whole chariot.) EPITH. Præcēps, vŏlŭcĕr, răpāx, cĭtātŭs, cĭtŭs, ālēs, sŏnāns, vŏlāns, quădrĭjŭgŭs, cĕlĕr, cōncĭtŭs, prŏpĕrŭs, sŭbĭtŭs, insĭgnĭs, trĭŭmphālĭs, ŏvāns, pīctŭs, aŭrātŭs. (Currus Solis.) EPITH. Ignĭfĕr, flămmĭgĕr, aŭrĕŭs, ignĭvŏmŭs, flămmĭvŏmŭs.

cūrso and ĭo, ās, the freq. of curro, to run to and fro. Cūrsĭtăt hōspĕs, Hor.

cūrsŏr, ōrĭs, m., a runner. Cūrsōrēm sēxtă, Mart.

cūrsŭs, ūs, m., a course. Cūrsĭbŭs mōtæ cĭtĭs, (Iamb.) EPITH. Răpĭdŭs, præcēps, cĕlĕr, sŭbĭtŭs, dēclīvĭs, văgŭs, ĕffrænŭs, vīvāx, cōncĭtŭs, fŭrĭōsŭs, ĕffrænātŭs, ănhēlŭs, vŏlŭcĕr, prŏpĕrŭs, cĭtātŭs, pērnīx, fūlmĭnĕŭs, præpĕs, ăvĭdŭs, ăgĭlĭs, ălăcĕr, ālĕs, aŭdāx, īncītŭs, īrrĕquĭētŭs, ārdēns, ēffūsŭs, vēlōx, āmēns, prærăpĭdŭs, rĕpēntīnŭs, vŏlāns, ālĭgĕr, fŭgāx. V. Curro.

Cūrtīllŭs, ī, m., *the name of a man.* Cūrtīllŭs ĕchīnōs, Hor.

Cūrtŭs, ī, m., *a Roman hero.* Epith. Rōmānŭs, nōbĭlĭs, ănĭmōsŭs, fōrtĭs, gĕnĕrōsŭs, clārŭs, īllūstrĭs.

cūrto, ās, *to shorten.* Sūmmæ cūrtābĭt quīsquĕ, Hor. Syn. Trūnco, mĭnŭo.

cūrtŭs, ă, ŭm, *short.* Cūrtă sŭpēllēx, Pers. Syn. Āngūstŭs, brĕvĭs, ēxĭgŭŭs, pārvŭs.

cūrūlĭs, ĕ, *belonging to the chair of state.* Ērĭpĭētquĕ cūrūlĕ, Hor.

cūrvāmĕu, ĭnĭs, n., *and* tūrā, æ, f., *a bowing, bending.* Lātō cūrvāmĭnĕ līmĕs, Ov. Cūrvātūrā rŏtæ, Ov. Syn. Flēxŭs, sĭnŭs, ōrbĭs.

cūrvo, ās, *to bend, to crook.* Cūrvātŭr ĭn ārcŭm, Virg. Syn. Incūrvo, flēcto, īnflēcto, sĭnŭo, inclīno, rĕcūrvo, cămĕro, tōrquĕo, īntōrquĕo.

cūrvŭs, ă, ŭm, *crooked, bent.* Intĕrĭt, ēt cūrvīs, Virg. Syn. Cūrvātŭs, īnflēxŭs, rĕcūrvŭs, sīnŭātŭs.

cūspĭs, ĭdĭs, f., *a point, a sharp weapon.* Dăt ăcūtæ cŭspĭdĭs hāstăm, Ov. Syn. Spīcŭlŭm, tēlŭm, fērrŭm, hāstă, mŭcro. Epith. Aūrātă, vūlnĭfĭcă, ærātă, aūrĕă, fĕră, sævă, dīră, fūlgēns, īnfēstă, vălĭdă, vĭōlēntă, rĭgēns, ăhēnă, trĕmēndă. V. Hasta.

cūstōdĭă, æ, f., *custody, a prison.* Cēcĭdīt cūstōdĭă sōrtī, Virg. Syn. Ēxcūbĭæ, vĭgĭlĭæ, præsĭdĭŭm ; tūtēlă ; cārcĕr. V. Carcer. Epith. Vĭgĭl, pērvĭgĭl, sōlĕrs, dūră, ārmātă, ārmĭgĕră, sēdŭlă, āttēntă, īnsōmnĭs, īrrĕquĭētă, fīdă, fĭdēlĭs, văgă, nōctūrnă.

cūstōdĭo, īs, īvī, ītŭm, *to keep, to defend.* Cūstōdīte ănĭmās, Juv. Syn. Sērvo, āssērvo, tŭĕōr. V. Vigilo.

cūstōdītŭs, ă, ŭm, *the pass. partic. of* custodio. Spēm cūstōdītă fĕfēllĭt, Virg.

cūstōs, ōdĭs, m., *a keeper.* Sūmmæ cūstōdĭbŭs ārcĭs, Virg. Epith. Vĭgĭl, vĭgĭlāns, sēdŭlŭs, ānxĭŭs, īnsōmnĭs, īrrĕquĭētŭs, fĭdēlĭs, āttēntŭs, nōctūrnŭs, sŏlĕrs, ārmĭgĕr, ārmātŭs, sōllĭcĭtŭs, pērvĭgĭl.

cŭtĭs, ĭs, *and* tĭcŭlă, æ, f., *the rind.* Quæ tĕgăt ōssă, cŭtĕm, Ov. Cōntrāctă, cŭtĭcŭlă sōlĕm, Juv. Syn. Pēllĭs. Epith. Tĕnĕră, tĕnēllă, lāctĕă, tĕnŭĭs, cāndĭdă, ārĭdă, clāră, mōllĭs, dūră, pĭlōsă, hīrtă, hīrsūtă, rūgōsă, cāllōsă, fŭcātă.

Cўānē, ēs, f., *a nymph of Sicily.* Intĕr Sĭcĕlĭdăs Cўānē pūlchērrĭmă, Ov.

Cўānĕæ, ārŭm, f. pl., *rocks in the Euxine sea.* Cўānēăs cērtŭs, Val. Fl. Syn. Sўmplēgădēs. Epith. Instābĭlēs, pătŭlæ, ērrāntēs, præcĭpĭtēs, fūrēntēs.

Cўānĕĕ, ēs, f., *the mother of Byblis and Caunus.* Cōgnĭtă Cўānēĕ, Ov.

cўānŭs, ī, f., *a turquois.* Epith. Cœrŭlĕă, clāră, mĭcāns. V. Gemma.

cўāthŭs, ī, m., *a cup.* In Prĭāmī cўāthīs, Mart. Syn. Călīx, crātĕr, pătĕră, scўphŭs, pōcŭlŭm. Epith. Cōmmŏdŭs, căpāx, ūtĭlĭs. V. Patera, poculum.

Cўbēlē, ēs, f., *the wife of Saturn, and mother of the gods.* Cўbēlēs pīctō, Mart. Syn. Rhĕă, Ops, Vēstă, Dīndўmēnē. Epith. Tūrrītă, tūrrĭgĕră, Phrўgĭă, vĕnĕrāndă, tōrvă, grāndævă, Idæă, fœcūndă, ālmă, prīscă, āntīquă, vĕnĕrābĭlĭs, pŏtēns.

Cўbēlēĭŭs, ă, ŭm, *of Cybele.* Cўbēlēĭă frænă lĕōnēs, Ov. Syn. Bĕrĕcўnthĭŭs.

Cўclădēs, ŭm, f. pl., *islands of the Archipelago.* Quō Cўclădăs āspĭcĭt ōmnēs, Ov. Epith. Ægĕæ, nĭtēntēs, āltæ, spūrsæ, vădōsæ.

cўclăs, ădĭs, f., *a woman's gown.* Cўclădĕ vērrĭt, Prop. Epith. Lōngă, dĕcōră, pūrpŭrĕă, aūrātă.

cўclĭcŭs, ă, ŭm, *circular.* Cўclĭcŭs, ōlĭm, Hor.

Cyclōpĕŭs, ă, ŭm, *of the Cyclops.* Ēt Cўclōpĕă sāxă, Virg.

Cyclōps, ōpĭs, m., Cyclōpĕs, ŭm, m. pl., *giants of Sicily, assistants of Vulcan.* Vāstō Cўclōpĕs ĭn āntrō, Virg. Epith. Ætnæī, Sĭcŭlī, gĭgāntæī, īnfāndī, vāstī, agrēstēs, ærĭsŏnī, răbĭdī, pōrtēntōsī, crūēntī, sānguĭnĕī, fĕrōcēs, lăcērtōsī, nigrī, īmmānēs, hōrrēndī, tērrĭbĭlēs, ānhēlāntēs, lāssī, nūdī, pŏtēntēs, crūdēlēs, trūcēs, bārbārī, trŭcŭlēntī, tērrĭgĕnī, ātrī, fūlvī, ĭgnĭtī, flāmmĕī, sŭpērbī.

cўcnēŭs or gnēŭs, *and* nĕĭŭs, ă, ŭm, *of a swan.* Jām mĕă cўgnēās, Ov. Ēt cўgnēĭă Tēmpĕ, Ov. Syn. Ŏlōrīnŭs.

cycnŭs or cygnŭs, ī, m.. *a swan.* Ēxĕquĭālĭă cўgnnī, Ov. Dōnātūră cўcnī, (Chor.) Hor. Syn. Ŏlōr. Epith. Cāndĭdŭs, ālbŭs, nĭvĕŭs, raūcŭs, flūmĭnĕŭs, mōllĭs, nĭtēns, văgŭs, blāndŭs, Idālĭŭs, mītĭs, dūlcĭs, cănōrŭs, sŏnōrŭs, flŭvĭālĭs, ăquōsŭs, pălūstrĭs, īmbēllĭs, păvĭdŭs, āmnĭcŏlă, sēgnĭs, tārdŭs.

Cўdīppē, ēs, f., *a virgin beloved by Acontius.* Littĕră Cўdīppēn, Ov.

Cўdnŭs, ī, m., *a river of Cilicia.* At tē, Cўdnĕ, cănăm, Tib.

Cўdōn, ōnĭs, m., *a town of Crete : an inhabitant thereof.* Pārthŭs sīvĕ Cўdōn, Virg.

Cўdōnēŭs *or* ĭŭs, ă, ŭm, *of Cydon.* Eccĕ Cўdōnēā, Sil. Cўdōnĭă cōrnŭ, Virg.

cўdōnĭŭm, ĭī, n., *quiddany.* Nātūrā cўdōnĭă, Ov.

cўlīndrŭs, ī, m., *a roller.* Æquāndā cўlīndrō, Virg. Epith. Tĕrĕs, lōngŭs.

Cyllărŭs, ī, m., *a centaur.* Tŭă, Cўllărĕ, fōrmā, Ov.

Cyllēnæŭs, ă, ŭm, *of Cyllene ; of Mercury.* Vērtĭcĕ Cўllēnæō, Ov.

Cўllēnē, ēs, f., *a mountain of Arcadia.* Cўllēnēs gĕlĭdō, Virg.

Cўllēnĕs, ĭdĭs, f., *of Mercury.* Cўllēnĭdĕ cōnsōdĭt hārpē, Ov.

Cўllēnĭŭs, ă, ŭm, *of Cyllene : of Mercury.* Cўllēnĭŭs, ĭī, m., *an epithet of Mercury.* Cўllēnĭŭs ālīs, Virg. V. Mercurius.

cўmbā, æ, f., *a boat.* Cōrpŏră cўmbā, Virg. Syn. Nāvĭcŭlă, lēmbŭs, phăsēlŭs, līntĕr, nāvīgĭŭm, scăphă. Epith. Ādūncă, cĕlĕr, cōncăvă, căpāx, īnstăbĭlĭs, căvă, frăgĭlĭs, nătāns, cūrvā, fŭgāx, flŭvĭālĭs, ēxĭgŭă, naŭfrăgă, āncēps, pārvă, vēlīvŏlă, cĭtă, sŭbĭtă ; æquŏrĕā, āngūstă, prŏpĕră, ērrātĭcă, căpāx. V. Navis.

cўmbălŭm, ī, n., *a cymbal.* Quătĕ cўmbălă cīrcūm, Virg. Epith. Cōncăvŭm, Cŏrўbāntĭŭm, Īdæŭm, Bĕrĕcўnthĭŭm, ærĕŭm, sŏnōrŭm, tīnnĭēns.

cўmbĭŭm, ĭī, n., *a kind of cup.* Spūmāntĭă cўmbĭă lāctĕ, Virg. V. Poculum.

Cўmŏdŏcē, ēs, *and* ĕă, ēæ, f., *a nymph of the sea.* Thălĭăquĕ Cўmŏdŏcēquĕ, Virg. Dōctīssĭmă Cўmŏdŏcēă, Id.

Cўmŏthŏē, ēs, f , *a nymph.* Cўmŏthŏē sĭmŭl, Virg. V. Nympha.

Cўnāpēs, ĭs, m., *a river falling into the Euxine sea.* Vōlvēns sāxă Cўnāpēs, Ov.

Cўnĭcŭs, ī, m., *a Cynic.* Et quī nēc Cўnĭcōs, Juv.

Cўnŏsūră, æ, f., *a constellation.* Quārūm Cўnŏsūră pĕtātŭr, Ov. V. Arctos.

Cўnthĭă, æ, f., *an epithet of Diana.* Mŏdĕrātrīx Cўnthĭă nōctĭs, Virg. V. Diana, Luna.

Cўnthĭŭs, ĭī, m., *an epithet of Apollo.* Cўnthĭŭs aūctŏr, Virg. V. Apollo, Sol, Phœbus.

Cўnthŭs, ī, m., *a mountain of Delos.* Epith. Āltŭs, āĕrĭŭs, Apŏllĭnĕŭs.

cўpărīssĭfĕr, ă, ŭm, *wearing cypress.* Nōn cўpărīssĭfĕr Lўcĕŭs, (Phal.) Sid.

cўpărīssŭs, ī, f., *a cypress-tree.* Cōnĭfĕræ cўpărīssī, Virg. V. Cupressus.

Cyprĭs, ĭdĭs, f., *Venus.* Dēcēns, Cўprĭdīs quī māxĭmă cūra ĕs, Cl. Cўprĭdă quīdăm, Mart. V. Venus.

Cyprĭŭs, ă, ŭm, *of Cyprus.* Nĕ Cўprĭæ Tўrĭævĕ, (Dactyl.) Hor. Ŏt trăbĕ Cўprĭă, (Asclep.) Id.

Cyprŭs, ī, f., *an island of the Mediterranean sea.* Dīvă tēnēs Cўprŭm, (Alcaic.) Hor. Ēmēnsŭs Cўprī scŏpŭlōs, Lucan. Epith. Fērtĭlĭs, Īdălĭă ; Cўthĕrēĭă ; Nēptūnĭă ; Cўnāræă, Cўnārēĭă ; scŏpŭlōsă, cīrcūmflŭă, fœcūndă, ŏpĭmă.

Cўrēnæ, ārŭm, f. pl., *and* Cўrēnē, ēs, f., *a town of Africa, founded by Cyrene.* Dōctăvĕ Cўrēnē, Stat.

Cўrēnē, ēs, f., *the mother of Aristæus.* Mātĕr, Cўrēnē, mātĕr, Virg.

Cўrrhă, æ, f., *a town of Phocis.* Scŏpŭlōsăquĕ Cўrrhă, Lucr. Epith. Ŏpăcă, cēlsă, dōctă, Pārnāssĭs, Phœbēă, Pārnāssĭă.

Cўrŭs, ī, m, *the son of Cambyses, a conqueror.* Luc. Epith. Fōrtĭs, pŏtēns, māgnănĭmŭs, gĕnĕrōsŭs, ănĭmōsŭs, īnclўtŭs ; trūx, fĕrōx, dīrŭs, īmmītĭs crūdēlĭs.

Cўthĕră, æ, f., *a town of Cyprus.* Epith. Lætă, fēlīx.

Cўthĕră, ōrŭm, n. pl., *an island sacred to Venus.* Āltă Cўthĕră, Virg.

Cўthĕrē, ēs, Cўthĕrēă, æ, *and* eĭs, ĭdĭs, f., *Venus.* Nēc nūdā Cўthĕrē, Aus. Pārcĕ mĕtū, Cўthĕrēă, mănēnt, Virg. Dīvă Cўthĕrēĭdĕ nātŭm, Ov. Syn. Vĕnŭs.

Cўthĕrēŭs, ēĭŭs, *and* ĭăcŭs, ă, ŭm, *of Cythera.* Mōtă Cўthĕrēā, Ov. Cўthĕrēĭŭs hērōs, Ov. Sūmĕ Cўthĕrĭăcō, Mart.

Cўthĕrēĭă, ădĭs, f., *of Cythere, of Venus.* Jŏvĭs, Cўthĕrēĭădāsquĕ cŏlūmbās, Ov.

Cўthĕrōn, ōnĭs, m., *a mountain of Bœotia.* Īndĕ Cўthĕrōnĭs. Epith. Mārcĭdŭs, gĕlĭdŭs, āltŭs, cēlsŭs, ēlātŭs, săcĕr, nōctūrnŭs.

cўtĭsŭs, ī, m., *the slender willow.* Flōrēntēm cўtĭsūm, sĕquĭtŭr, Virg. Epith. Flōrēns, vĭrĭdĭs, agrēstĭs, tĕnŭĭs.

Cўtŏrĭăcŭs *and* Cўtŏrĭŭs, ă, ŭm, *of Cytorus.* Sæpĕ Cўtŏrĭăcō, Ov.

Cўtŏrŭs, ī, m., *a mountain of Paphlagonia.* Spēctărĕ Cўtŏrŭm, Virg.

Cўzĭcŭs, ī, m., *a city of the Propontis.* Cўzĭcŏn ōrĭs, Ov.

D.

DĀCI, ōrŭm, m. pl., *the ancient inhabitants of Transylvania, Moldavia, and Wallachia.* Tĕ Dācŭs āspĕr, Hor. SYN. Dācæ. EPITH. Trŭcēs, fĕrōcēs, lĕvēs, atrōcēs, sȳlvĭcŏlæ, spārsī, īmmānēs.

Dācĭcŭs, ă, ŭm, *conqueror of Dacia.* Dācĭcŭs, ĕt scrīptō, Juv.

Dācĭŭs, *and* cŭs, ă, ŭm, *of Dacia.* Dācĭŭs ōrbĕ, l'ed. Dācŭs ăb Istrō, Virg.

|| dāctȳlĭōthēcă, æ, f., *a jewel-box.* Dāctȳlĭōthēcăm nōn hăbĕt, (Iamb. Dim.) Mart.

dāctȳlŭs, ī, m., *a metrical foot.* Dāctȳlŭs īndĕ măgĭs, Ter. Maur.

Dædăleŭs, ă, ŭm, *of Dædalus.* Ŏpĕ Dædălēā, (Sapph.) Hor. Dædălĕŭm līnō, Prop.

Dædălĭŏn, ōnĭs, m., *the son of Lucifer.* Cūm sē Dædălĭŏn, Ov.

Dædălŭs, ī, m., *the celebrated artist.* Dædălŭs īpsĕ dōlōs, Virg. EPITH. Ingĕnĭōsŭs, făbĕr, dōctŭs, cāllĭdŭs, vŏlŭcĕr, mălīgnŭs, Cecrŏpĭŭs; Lăbȳrīnthæŭs, Crētēnsĭs; īndūstrĭŭs.

dædālŭs, ă, ŭm, *skilful, handsomely made.* Dædălă fīngĕrĕ tēctă, Virg.

|| Dæmōn, ŏnĭs, m., *a Dæmon.* Dæmŏnăs āc tălĕm, Sed. SYN. Căcŏdæmōn, dĭăbŏlŭs. EPITH. Mălīgnŭs, pērvērsŭs, vĭŏlēntŭs, răbĭdŭs, tētĕr, hōrrĭdŭs, hōrrēndŭs, īnfērnŭs, tōrvŭs, pērfĭdŭs, sævŭs, pērvĭgĭl, fĕrōx, fœdŭs, dīrŭs, mălŭs, hōrrĭfĭcŭs, cāllĭdŭs, fāllāx, vĭgĭl, rĕbēllĭs, sŭpērbŭs, īnfēstŭs, Stȳgĭŭs, crūdēlĭs, nĕfāndŭs, āstūtŭs, dŏlōsŭs, sŭbdŏlŭs, īnsĭdĭātŏr.

dæmŏnĭcŭs, ă, ŭm, *of a Dæmon.* Dæmŏnĭcō cŭnĕātă, Sed.

dæmŏnĭŭm, ĭī, n., *a Dæmon.* Prīncēps dæmŏnĭōrŭm, Juvenc.

Dăhæ *or* Dăæ, ārŭm, m. pl., *a people of Scythia.* Indŏmĭtīquĕ Dăhæ, Virg.

Dālmătă, æ, m. f., *an inhabitant of Dalmatia.* Dālmătă sŭpplēx, Ad Liv.

Dālmătĭă, æ, f., *a part of Illyria.* Brāchĭă Dālmătĭæ, Ov. EPITH. Ardŭă, frōndēns, vĭrēns, ŏpācă, fēlīx, bĕātă, aŭrĭfĕră.

Dālmătĭcŭs, ă, ŭm, *of Dalmatia.* Illīnc Dālmătĭcĭs, Luc.

dāmă, æ, m. f., *a doe.* Vēnăbĕrĕ dāmăs, Virg. EPITH. Tĭmĭdŭs, păvĭdŭs, mōllĭs, agrēstĭs, păvēns, tērrĭtŭs, īmbēllĭs, prōnŭs, lĕvĭs, fŭgāx, fŭgĭtīvŭs, văgŭs, cĕlĕr.

Dămălĭs, ĭdĭs, f., *name of a woman.* Ōmnēs īn Dămălĭn, Hor.

Dămāscēnŭs, ă, ŭm, *of Damascus.* Āltă Dămāscēnæ, Sidon.

Dămāscŭs, ī, f., *the capital of Syria.* Clārā Dămāscŭs, Ser. EPITH. Pĭă, cĕlĕbrĭs, aŭgūstă, āntīquă, pĕregrīnă, prūnĭfĕră, cūltă, fœcūndă, āmplă, prīscă, ămœnă.

Dămāsīchthŏn, ŏnĭs, m., *a son of Niobe.* Dămāsīchthŏnă vūlnŭs, Ov.

Dămāsīppŭs, ī, *name of a man.* Dămāsīppŭs ēmēndo, Hor.

Dāmœtās, æ, m., *name of a shepherd.* Dīxĭt Dāmœtās, Virg.

dāmnātĭo, ōnĭs, f., *a condemnation.* Quĭd dāmnātĭŏ cōnfĕrt, Juv.

dāmnātŭs, ă, ŭm, *the pass. partic. of* damno. Fālsō dāmnātĭ crīmĭnĕ, Virg.

dāmno, ās, *to condemn.* Scĕlĕrĭs dāmnăbĭs ĕŭndĕm, Hor. SYN. Cōndēmno, mūlcto; īmprŏbo, ārgŭo. V. Condemno.

dāmnōsē, adv., *hurtfully.* Dāmnōsē bĭbĕrĕ, Hor.

dāmnōsŭs, ă, ŭm, *hurtful.* Dāmnōsŭs pĕcŏrī, Ov. SYN. Nŏxĭŭs, nŏcŭŭs, nŏcīvŭs, nŏcēns, īncōmmŏdŭs, īnfēstŭs.

dāmnŭm, ī, n., *harm.* Mē dāmnĭs ūrgĕrĕ, Cl. SYN. Ēxĭtĭŭm, pērnĭcĭēs, nŏxă, dētrīmēntŭm, jāctūră, dīspēndĭŭm, īncōmmŏdŭm. EPITH. Fātălĕ, fĕrālĕ, flēbĭlĕ, ăcērbŭm, īrrĕpărābĭlĕ, īntŏlĕrābĭlĕ, crŭēntŭm, hōstĭlĕ, vĭŏlēntŭm, mœstŭm, grăvĕ, mŏlēstŭm, fūnēstŭm, īngēns, sŭbĭtŭm, ĭnŏpīnŭm. V. Noceo.

Dănăē, ēs, f., *the mother of Perseus, loved by Jupiter.* Quĭd Dănăēn Dănăēsquĕ, Ov. SYN. Ācrĭsĭōnēĭs. EPITH. Pūlchră, fōrmōsă, dĕcēptă, īnclūsă, dĕcŏră, Ācrĭsĭōnēă.

Dănăēĭŭs, ă, ŭm, *of Danae.* Dănăēĭŭs hērōs, Ov.

Dănăī, ōrŭm, m. pl., *the Greeks.* Tĭmĕŏ Dănăŏs, Virg. V. Græci.

Dănăĭdēs, ŭm, f. pl., *the daughters of Danaus, who murdered their husbands.* Frūstrā Dănăĭdēs plēnās, (iamb.) Sen. SYN. Bēlĭdēs. EPITH. Īmpĭæ, scĕlēstæ, mĭsĕræ, ĭnīquæ, crŭēntæ. V. Belides.

G

Dănăŭs, ĭ, m., *a king of Argos.* Mānc ĕrăt, ĕt Dănăŭs, Ov. Syn. Iăsĭdēs,
Bēlĭdēs.—2. -ŭs, ă, ŭm, *Greek.* Prōdĕrĕ rēm Dănăăm, Ov.
Dănĭēl, clĭs, m., *the prophet.* In fŏvĕām Dănĭēl, Sedul.
Dănŭbĭŭs, ĭī, m., *a river of Germany.* Cēdĕrĕ Dănŭbĭŭs, Ov. Syn. Istĕr.
Epitii. Prŏfŭndŭs, căpāx, vēlōx, răpĭdŭs, răpāx, fĕrōx, tĭmĭdŭs, rĕtōrtŭs,
Scȳthĭcŭs, flāvŭs. V. Fluvius.
dăpālĭs, ĕ, *sumptuous.* Mēnsāsquĕ dăpālēs, M.
dăpēs, ŭm, f. pl., *dainties.* Explētŭs dăpĭbŭs, Virg. Syn. Cĭbŭs, ĕpŭlæ, pābŭ-
lŭm, ēscă. Epitii. Ŏpīmæ, laŭtæ, sŭpĕrbæ, grātæ, vīvĭfĭcæ, nēctārĕæ, fēstæ,
sōclæ, āmbrōsĭæ, mēllĭflŭæ, lætæ. V. Cibus, Epulæ, Convivium.
Dăphnē, ēs, f., *loved by Apollo, and changed into a laurel-tree.* Dăphnē Pēnēĭă,
quĕm nōn, Ov. Syn. Fīlĭă Pēnēī, Pēnēĭă nȳmphă, Phœbēĭă vīrgo, nȳmphă
Pēnēĭs, (ĭdŏs.) Epitii. Thēssălĭs, Apŏllĭnĕa, Phœbēă, Pēnēĭs, Pēnēĭă, fŭgĭtĭvă,
fŭgāx, cāstă, pŭdĭcă, ĭnnŭbă. V. Laurus.
Dăphnĭs, ĭdĭs, m., *the son of Mercury.* Otĭă Dăphnĭs, Virg. Epith. Fōrmōsŭs,
pŭlchĕr, dĕcōrŭs, jŭvĕnĭs.
‖ dăphnŏōn, ōnĭs, m., *a laurel-grove.* Dĭspŏsŭīt dăphnŏōnă sŭō, Mart.
dăpsĭlĭs, ĕ, *sumptuous.* Dăpsĭlĭs ēxcēpĭt, Fill. Syn. Ābŭndāns, māgnĭfĭcŭs,
laŭtŭs, ŏpĭpărŭs.
dăpsĭlĭtĕr, adv., *abundantly.* Dăpsĭlĭŭs sē, Lucil. Syn. Laŭtē, māgnĭfĭcĕ.
Dārdănĭă, æ, f., *Troy.* Dārdănĭāmquĕ pĕtĭt, Cat.
Dārdănĭdæ, ārŭm, m. pl., *Trojans.* Dārdănĭdæ īnfēnsī, Virg. V. Trojani.
Dārdănĭŭs, *and* nŭs, ă, ŭm, *or* nĭs, ĕ, *of Troy.* Isque ŭbĭ Dārdănĭōs, Virg.
Dārdănă sŭscĭtăt ārmă, Id. Dārdănĭdēs mātrēs, Id. Syn. Trōjānŭs,
Trōĭŭs.
Dārdănŭs, ĭ, m., *the founder of Troy.* Dārdănŭs aŭctŏr, Virg. Epith. Prŏfŭgŭs,
fŭgāx, crŭēntŭs, crūdēlĭs, īmmītĭs, dūrŭs, fōrtĭs, pŏtēns, gĕnĕrōsŭs, prīscŭs, āntī-
quŭs, aŭdāx.
Dărēs, ĕtĭs, m., *an athlete.* Nōstră Dărēs hæc, Virg. Epith. Sŭpĕrbŭs, Phrȳ-
gĭŭs, aŭdāx, tĕmĕrārĭŭs, īnfēlīx.
Dārĭŭs, ĭī, m., *a king of Persia.* Dārĭum fămŭlĭs, Claud.
dătŏr, ōrĭs, m., *a giver.* Bācchŭs dătŏr, ĕt bŏnă Jūno, Virg. Syn. Dōnătŏr,
lārgītŏr.
dătŭs, ă, ŭm, *the pass. partic. of* do. Is dătŭs ā vōbĭs, Ov.
Dāvīd, Dāvidĭs, m., *the prophet.* Ŭt gĕnŭīt Dāvīd, ălĭăs, Prud. Est Dāvīdĭs
ŏrīgĭnĕ clāră, Juv. Dāvīdĭs ēssĕ pătrĕm, Nem. Syn. Jēssīdēs, Jēssĭădēs,
Jēssēĭă prōlēs. Jēssĕŭs vātēs. Rēx psāltēs; psālmĭcĕn. Epith. Sānctŭs,
pĭŭs, mŭsĭcŭs, cănōrŭs, ārgŭtŭs, fātĭdĭcŭs, săpĭēns, mītĭs, clēmēns, fōrtĭs, gĕnĕ-
rōsŭs.
Dāvīdĭcŭs, ă, ŭm, *of David.* Et Dāvīdĭcă rēgnă, Prud. Cūr ĕgŏ Dāvĭdĭcīs,
Sedul.
Daŭlĭăs, ădĭs, *or* lĭs, ĭdĭs, f., *of Daulis, a town of Phocis.* Daŭlĭăs ālĕs, Ov.
Daŭnĭă, æ, f., *Apulia, so called from Daunus.* Daŭnĭa ĭn lātĭs, Hor.
Daŭnĭŭs, ă, ŭm, *of Apulia.* Daŭnĭæ, dēfēndĕ dĕcŭs, Hor.
Daŭnŭs, ĭ, m., *grandfather of Turnus.* Daŭnī dēĭertŭr ăd ŭrbĕm, Virg.
Dāvŭs, ĭ, m., *name of a slave in comedy.* Dāvōquĕ Chrēmētă, Hor.
dē, prep., *from.* Dē cœlō tāctās, Virg. Syn. Ē, ēx; ăb; sŭpĕr.
Dĕă, æ, f., *a Goddess.* Dēlūbră Dĕārŭm, Virg. Syn. Dīvă. Epith. Fōrmōsă,
cœlēstĭs, æthĕrĕă, vĕnĕrāndă, pŏtēns, mĕtŭēndă, ālmă, ĭnclȳtă, vĕrēndă, ădōrāndă. V. Deus.
* dĕāmbŭlo, ās, *to walk about,* Cic. Syn. Āmbŭlo, īncēdo, prōcēdo, vādo, ĕo,
prōgrĕdĭŏr, spătĭŏr, grădĭŏr. V. Ambulo.
dēbācchŏr, ārĭs. *to rage, to rave.* Pārtĕ dēbācchēntŭr īgnēs, (Iamb. cum Syll.)
Hor. Syn. Bācchŏr, fūro. V. Bacchor.
dēbēllātŏr, ōrĭs, m., *vanquisher, subduer.* Dēbēllātŏrque fĕrārŭm, Virg.
dēbēllo, ās, *to subdue by arms.* Et dēbēllārĕ sŭpĕrbōs, Virg. Syn. Vīnco,
sŭpĕro, dŏmo, sŭbĭgo. V. Vinco.
dēbĕo, ŭī, *to owe.* Tĭbĭ nōs dēbērĕ fătēmŭr, Ov. Syn. Tĕnĕŏr, ŏblĭgŏr.
dēbĭlĭs, ĕ, *weak.* Cōrpŏră dēbĭlĭbŭs, Sil. Syn. Invălĭdŭs, īnfīrmŭs, fēssŭs, dēfēssŭs, frāctŭs, īnfrāctŭs, ĭnērs, lānguĭdŭs, frăgĭlĭs, ĭmbēllĭs, lāssŭs, dēfĭcĭēns,
ēffœtŭs, mōllĭs.

dēbĭlĭtās, ātĭs, f., *weakness.* Dēbĭlĭtātĕ cărēbĭs, Juv. SYN. Infirmĭtās, lānguŏr.
EPITH. Infirmă, ĭnērs, grăvĭs, lēntă, mŏlēstă, trīstĭs, quĕrŭlă, ĭnvălĭdă. V.
Languor.

dēbĭlĭtātŭs, ă, ŭm, *the pass. partic. of* debilito. Dēbĭlĭtātă mălĭs, Ov. V. Debilis.

dēbĭlĭto, ās, *to weaken.* Dēbĭlĭtābĭt ŏnŭs, Ov. SYN. Infirmo, ēnērvo.
dēbĭtŏr, ōrĭs, m., *a debtor.* Dēbĭtŏr hūjŭs, Ov.
dēbĭtŭs, ă, ŭm, *the pass. partic. of* debeo. Dēbĭtŭs ūrbĭs, Ov. SYN. Mĕrĭtŭs,
dignŭs; āddīctŭs.

dēblătĕro, ās, *to blab.* Dēblătĕrās māgnō clāmōrĕ, Hor.
dēcāntātŭs, ă, ŭm, *the pass. partic. of* decanto. Et dēcāntātă Cămĭllĭs, Hor.
dēcānto, ās, *to sing, celebrate.* Dēcāntāre ēlĕgōs, Hor.
dēcēdo, cēssī, *to retire.* Invītēt dēcēdĕrĕ rīpă, Virg. SYN. Ăbĕo, ēxĕo, rēcēdo,
discēdo, migro, ēgrēdĭŏr, ēxcēdo; V. Abeo. Mŏrĭŏr, īntĕrĕo, ōccŭmbo, cădo,
ōccĭdo; V. Morior.

dĕcĕm, *ten.* Līsquĕ dĕcĕm dĕcĭēs, Ov. SYN. Bĭs quīnquĕ.
Dĕcēmbĕr, brĭs, m., *the twelfth month of the year.* Illă Dĕcēmbĕr hăbĕt, Ov.
EPITH. Gĕlĭdŭs, fūmōsŭs, rĭgĭdŭs, cānŭs, frĭgĭdŭs, hōrrĭdŭs, atrōx, brūmālĭs,
pĭgĕr, strĭngēns, hўbērnŭs, fēstŭs.

Dĕcēmbrălĭs, *and* brĭs, ĕ, *of December.* Ălbă Dĕcēmbrălēs, Mant. Lībērtātĕ
Dĕcēmbrī, Hor.

dĕcēmpĕdă, æ, f., *a measure of ten feet.* Nūllă dĕcēmpĕdĭs, Hor.
dĕcēnnālĭs, *and* nĭs, ĕ, *of ten years.* Ătquĕ dĕcēnnālī, Mart. Lŭbrĭcŭm dĕcēnnī,
(Phal.) Mart.

dĕcēnnĭŭm, ĭī, n., *a period of ten years.* Pĕr mūltă dĕcēnnĭă vītăm, Mart.
dĕcēns, ēntĭs, *decent.* Cŏecă dĕcēntĭŏr, (Phal.) Mart. SYN. Ăptŭs, cōnvĕnĭēns,
cōngrŭēns, cōnsŏnŭs, dĕcōrŭs, cōnsēntānĕŭs, ăppŏsĭtŭs, cōngrŭŭs.

dĕcēntĕr, adv., *decently.* Lăcrўmārĕ dĕcēntĕr, Ov.
dĕcēptŏr, ōrĭs, m., *a deceiver.* Dĕcēptŏr dŏmĭnī Mўrtĭlŭs, Sen.
dĕcēptŭs, ă, ŭm, *the pass. partic. of* decipio. Tŏtĭēs dĕcēptŭs fraŭdĕ sĕrēnī,
Virg.

dēcērno, crēvī, *to discern.* Et nōn dēcērnĭs, Mart. SYN. Stătŭo, cōnstĭtŭo;
dēfīnĭo, jūdĭco, cēnsĕo; sāncĭo.

dēcērpo, psī, ptŭm, *to pluck.* Pōmūm dēcērpĕrĕ rāmō, Ov. SYN. Lĕgo, cŏll go,
cārpo, dētrăho, dēlībo, aŭfĕro, ēxcērpo, ăvēllo. V. Colligo.

dēcērto, ās, *to fight.* Ăgmĭnă dēcērtānt, Stat. SYN. Pūgno, prælĭŏr, dīmĭco,
cōnflīgo, cērto, cōngrĕdĭŏr. V. Bellum gero, Pugno.

dĕcĕt, cŭĭt, *it becomes.* Tūnc dĕcŭĭt, Virg. SYN. Cōnvĕnĭt, cōngrŭĭt, jŭvăt,
quădrăt, ēxpĕdĭt.

dēcīdo, cīdī, cīsŭm, [*from* cædo] *to cut down.* Vĕtĕrēs dēcīdĕrĕ fālcĭbŭs, Lucr.
SYN. Sĕco, rĕsĕco, scĭndo, ābscĭndo, rēscĭndo. V. Scindo.

dēcĭdo, cĭdī, [*from* cado] *to fall.* Dēcĭdĭt ĭn cāssēs, Ov. SYN. Cădo, ēxcĭdo,
lābŏr, cōllābŏr, cōncĭdo, rŭo, cōrrŭo, prōlābŏr, dēlābŏr, præcĭpĭto, prōcŭmbo.
V. Cado.

dēcīdŭŭs, ă, ŭm, [*from* cædo] *cut down.* Dēdīt dēcīdŭă quērcŭs, Ov. SYN.
Cædŭŭs, cæsŭs.

dēcĭdŭŭs, ă, ŭm, [*from* cado] *fallen, subject to fall.* Dēcĭdŭăm frŭgĕm, Mart.
SYN. Cădūcŭs, cădēns, lăbāns, flūxŭs.

dĕcĭēs, adv., *ten times.* Ūnō dĕcĭēs aŭt, Mart.
Dĕcĭī, ōrŭm, m. pl., *three Roman heroes.* Dĕcĭōs pŭlchrōs, Cl. EPITH. Fōrtēs,
gĕnĕrōsī, ănĭmōsī, īmpăvĭdī, īmpērtērrĭtī, pĭī, aŭdācēs.

dĕcĭmŭs, ă, ŭm, *the tenth.* Hæsĭt ĕt ĭn dĕcĭmŭm, Virg. SYN. Dēnŭs, bĭs quīnŭs,
āltĕr ā nōnō.

dĕcĭpĭo, cēpī, cēptŭm, *to deceive.* Năm nĕquĕ dĕcĭpĭtŭr, Mart. SYN. Făllo, cīrcŭmvĕnĭo, dēlūdo, ēlūdo. V. Fallo.

dĕcĭpŭlă, æ, f., *a snare.* Dēcĭpŭlă mūrī, (Iamb.) Anon.
dēcīsŭs, ă, ŭm, *the pass. partic. of* decido. Quērcŭm dēcīsīs ūndĭquĕ rāmīs, Virg.
dēclāmātĭo, ōnĭs, f., *a declamation.* Et dēclāmātĭō fīās, Juv.
dēclāmātŏr, ōrĭs, m., *a declaimer.* Dēclāmātōrĭs Mŭtĭnēnsĭs, Juv. EPITH. Scītŭs,
ĭnēptŭs, clāmōsŭs.

dēclāmo, *and* mĭto, ās, *to declaim.* Dēclāmārĕ dŏcēs, Juv. SYN. Clāmo.

Jĕclāro, ās, *to declare.* Dēclārāt, vīrĭdī, Virg. SYN. Sĭgnĭfĭco, dēnŭncĭo, ăpĕrĭo, vūlgo, dīvūlgo, rĕvēlo, ēxpōno, mănĭfēsto, ēxprōmo, ēxplĭco, ĭndĭco, ās. V. Manifesto.

dĕclīno, ās, *to decline.* Dēclīnāmŭs ĭtĕm, Lucr. SYN. Dēflēcto, fūgĭo, vīto, ēvīto.

dĕclīvĭs, ĕ, *bending downwards.* Cīnxĭt dēclīvĭă rīpĭs, Ov. SYN. Inflēxŭs, Inclīnātŭs, dēvēxŭs.

dĕcŏctŏr, ōrĭs, m., *a spendthrift.* Dēcŏctŏrĭs ămīcă, Cat.

dĕcŏlŏr, ōrĭs, *discoloured.* Dēcŏlŏr ætās, Virg. SYN. Pāllēns, pāllĭdŭs.

dĕcŏlōro, ās, *to discolour, tarnish.* Nōn dēcŏlōrāvērĕ cædēs, Hor.

dĕcŏquo, xī, ctŭm, *to boil down.* Dēcŏquērētŭr ŏlŭs, Hor. SYN. Cŏquo, ēxcŏquo; rĕm prōdĭgo, ēffŭndo, dīspērdo, pērdo, dīssĭpo, dēvŏro, ābsŭmo, cōnsūmo.

dĕcŏr, ōrĭs, m., *comeliness.* Mīră dĕcŏrĕ pĭŏ, Stat. SYN. Pŭlchrĭtūdo, vĕnūstās fōrmă, spĕcĭēs, dĕcŭs, cūltŭs, ŏrnātŭs. EPITH. Cōnspĭcŭŭs, rŏsĕŭs, mŏllĭs, rēgālĭs, grātŭs, pŭrpŭrĕŭs, lĕpĭdŭs, tĕnĕr, dīvīnŭs, ēxīmĭŭs, īnsĭgnĭs, pĕrēnnĭs, ămābĭlĭs, nĭvĕŭs, lāctĕŭs, pŭēllārĭs. V. Decorus.

dĕcŏro, ās, [*from* decor] *to adorn.* Dēlūbră dĕcŏrānt, Sil. SYN. Ōrno, ēxōrno V. Orno.

dĕcŏro, ās, [*from* decus] *to adorn, grace.* Dĕcŏrārī vērsĭbŭs ōpto, Hor. SYN. Hŏnēsto, laūdo, ōrno.

dĕcŏrŭs, ă, ŭm, *graceful.* Vērtĕ, dĕcŏrŭs ĕro, Prop. SYN. Pŭlchĕr, fōrmŏsŭs, dĕcēns, cōnvĕnĭēns, hŏnēstŭs, clārŭs, īnsĭgnĭs, cōnspĭcŭŭs, cōnspĭcĭēndŭs, cōncĭnnŭs. V. Pulcher.

dēcrĕpĭtŭs, ă, ŭm, *decrepit.* Sīc cĭtŏ dēcrĕpĭtŭs, Tib. SYN. Ēffœtŭs, sĕnēx, vĕtŭlŭs, grāndævŭs, ānnōsŭs, lōngævŭs. V. Senex.

dēcrēsco, crēvī, crētŭm, *to decrease.* Dēcrēscŭnt ēffōssō, Ov.

dēcrētŭm, ī, n., *a statute.* Sīc dēcrētōrŭm, Vict. SYN. Cōnsĭlĭum.

dēcūlco, ās, *to tread down.* Dĕcūlcārĕ gĕnĭs, Stat.

dēcŭmbo, cŭbŭī, *to lie down.* Dēcŭbŭīssĕ sĕnĕm, Ped. SYN. Rĕcūmbo, cŭbo, rĕcŭbo, quĭēsco, rĕquĭēsco, jăcĕo. V. Cubo, Jaceo.

dĕcŭrĭă, æ, f., *a company of ten.* Ex hāc dĕcŭrĭă, Pl.

dēcūrro, ĭs, *to run down.* Sūmmā dēcūrrĭt ăb ārcĕ, Virg. SYN. Cūrro; pērcūrro.

dēcūrsŭs, ūs, m., *a running down.* Măgnŭs dēcūrsŭs ăquārŭm, Lucr. SYN. Cūrsŭs, īncūrsŭs, īmpĕtŭs.

dĕcŭs, ŏrĭs, n., *grace, honour.* Vĕtĕrŭm dĕcŏra āltă, Virg. SYN. Pŭlchrĭtūdo, vĕnūstās, dĕcŏr; cūltŭs, ŏrnātŭs, ŏrnāmēntŭm; laŭs, glŏrĭă, hŏnŏr, dĭgnĭtās, splēndŏr, nōmĕn. V. Honor. EPITH. Rēgālĕ, ēgrĕgĭŭm, sŭpērbŭm, āltŭm, īmmōrtālĕ, ēxĭmĭŭm, īndēlēbĭlĕ.

dĕcūssĭs, ĭs, m., *the number ten, or the figure* X. Cōnstĭtĭt dĕcūssī, (Phal.) Stat.

dĕcŭtĭo, ūssī, ūssŭm, *to shake down.* Dēcŭtĭāt rōrĕm, Virg. SYN. Ēxcŭtĭo, dējĭcĭo, dētūrbo.

dēdĕcĕt, *it does not become.* Dēdĕcŭĭt chŏrĭs, Hor. SYN. Nōn dĕcĕt, nōn cōnvĕnĭt; tūrpe ēst.

dēdĕcŏr, ōrĭs, *disgraceful.* Dēdĕcŏrem āmplēxī, Stat. SYN. Tūrpĭs, ĭnhŏnōrŭs, probrōsŭs. V. Turpis, Infamis.

dēdĕcŏro, ās, *to disgrace.* Dēdĕcŏrārĕ bŏvĕ, Prop. SYN. Dētūrbo, fœdo, măcŭlo, īnfāmo.

dēdĕcŭs, ŏrĭs, n., *disgrace.* Nōn ĕgŏ dēdĕcŏrī, Ov. SYN. Ōpprŏbrĭŭm, probrŭm, īnfāmĭă, ĭgnōmĭnĭă, măcŭlă, nŏtă, lābēs. EPITH. Tūrpĕ, pŭdēndŭm, īnfāmĕ. V. Infamia.

dēdĭco, ās, *to dedicate.* Dēdĭcăt ārās, Ov. SYN. Dĭco, ās; sacro, cōnsecro, vŏvĕo, dēvŏvĕo, ŏffĕro.

dēdignŏr, ārĭs, *to disdain.* Dēdīgnātă mărītōs, Virg. SYN. Nōn dīgnŏr, āspērnŏr. V. Aspernor.

dēdīsco, dēdĭdĭcī, *to unlearn.* Dēdĭdĭcīssĕ dătăm, Prop. SYN. Ōblīvīscŏr.

dēdĭtĭo, ĭōnĭs, f., *a surrender.* Dēdĭtĭō paūcĭs, Cl. EPITH. Lībĕră, cŏāctă, tūrpĭs.

dēdĭtŭs, ă, ŭm, *the pass. partic. of* dedo. Dēdĭtă fāmă, Virg.

dēdo, ĭs, ĭdī, ĭtŭm, *to give, yield.* Dēdĭdĭt ūrbĕm, Fill. SYN. Dŏ, trādo; trĭbŭo, āddĭco.

¶ dēdŏcĕo, dŏcŭī, *to unteach.* Dēdŏcĕt ūtī, Hor. Syn. Dēsuēfācĭo.

dēdŏlĕo, ŭī, *to cease mourning.* Dēdŏlŭĭtquĕ sĕmĕl, Ov.

dēdūco, xī, ctŭm, *to bring down.* Nŏstrā dēdūcĭt ŏrīgĭnĕ, Virg. Syn. Abdūco, rĕdūco, rĕvŏco, rĕtrăho, rĕmŏvĕo ; dūco, prōsĕquŏr, cŏmĭtŏr.

dēerro, *or* dĕerro, (*dissyl.*) ās, *to wander.* Vāllĕ dĕērrăt, Man. Cŭpĕr deērrāvĕrăt, ātque ĕgo, Virg. Syn. Erro, ăbērro, dēflēcto, dēvĭo. V. Vagor.

¶ dēfătīgo. V. Fatigo.

dēfēctŭs, ūs, m., *a defect, want.* Dēfēctŭs sōlĭs, Virg.

dēfēndo, dī, sŭm, *and so,* sās, *to defend.* Mūrōs dēfēndĕrĕ bēllō, Virg. Syn. Tŭĕŏr, tūtŏr, tĕgo, prōtĕgo, prōpūgno, sērvo, aŭxĭlĭŏr, cūstŏdĭo. V. Auxilior.

• dēfēnsĭo, ōnĭs, f., *a defence.* Cic. Syn. Tūtēlā, pătrŏcĭnĭŭm ; aŭxĭlĭŭm.

dēfēnsŏr, ōrĭs, m., *a defender.* Nēc dēfēnsōrĭbŭs īstīs, Virg. Syn. Cūstŏs, tūtāmĕn, tūtēlă, sērvātŏr, cūstōdĭă, aŭxĭlĭŭm, cŏlŭmĕn, prōpūgnātŏr, tūtŏr, patrōnŭs. Epith. Fīdŭs, fīdēlĭs, fōrtĭs, măgnănĭmŭs, gĕnĕrōsŭs, ămīcŭs, aŭdāx, īntrĕpĭdŭs, īntērrĭtŭs. V. Auxilium.

dēfĕro, tŭlī, lātŭm, *to bring, announce, accuse.* Dēfĕrĭmŭs, sævō, Virg. Syn. Affĕro ; ōffĕro, trādo, trĭbŭo, cōncēdo ; nūncĭo, sīgnĭfĭco ; āccūso.

• dēfērvĕo, ēs, bŭī, *and* vo, ĭs, vī, *to grow cool.* Lātĕ dēfērvĕrĕ cāmpō, Stat. Syn. Dēfērvēsco, rēsĭdo.

dēfēssŭs, ă, ŭm, *tired.* Pāndĭtĕ dēfēssīs, Prop. Syn. Fēssŭs, dēfătīgātŭs, fătīgātŭs, ēxhaŭstŭs, lānguēscēns, lānguĭdŭs, frāctŭs, dēbĭlĭtātŭs, ēnērvātŭs, dēbĭlĭs, lāssŭs.

dēfĭcĭo, fēcī, *to decay, fail, recede.* Dēfĭcĕrēnt sȳlvæ, Virg. Syn. Dēbĭlĭtŏr, īnfīrmŏr, ēnērvŏr, ēxhaŭrĭŏr, frāngŏr, īnfrīngŏr, lānguēsco ; dēsŭm ; dēsĭno ; rēcēdo, rēbēllo, dēsēro, dēscīsco.

dēfīgo, xī, xŭm, *to fix, plant.* In tē dēfīxĭt ŏcēllōs, Ov. Syn. Fīgo, īnfīgo, plānto, īmmītto, cōllŏco, pōno.

¶ dēfīngo, nxī, *to form.* Dēfīngĭt Rhēnī, Hor.

dēfīnĭo, īs, īī, *to limit.* Cērtō dēfīnĭt līmĭtĕ, Mant. Syn. Fīnĭo, cīrcūmscrībo, tērmĭno, dēscrībo.

dēfīt, *is wanting.* Dēfīt ămŏr, Prop. Syn. Dĕēst, *or* deēst, dēfĭcĭt.

dēflagro, ās, *to burn.* Sīc dēflăgārĕ mĭnācēs, Lucan. Syn. Flagro, ārdĕo, ŭrŏr, ēxŭrŏr, cōmbŭrŏr, ārdēsco, ēxārdēsco, cōnflagro, īnflāmmŏr, dēfērvēsco, lānguēsco.

dēflēcto, ĭs, xī, xŭm, *to bend.* Quĭd răpĭdŭm dēflēctĭs ĭtĕr, Luc. Syn. Dētŏrquĕo, flēcto, dēvĭo, ăbērro.

dēflĕo, ēvī, ētŭm, *to weep.* Dēflēvĕrĕ Nŭmăm, Ov. Syn. Flĕo, dēplōro, lūgĕo. V. Fleo, lacrymor.

dēflētŭs, ă, ŭm, *the pass. partic. of* defleo. Tŏrō dēflētă rĕpōnŭnt, Virg.

dēflōrĕo, ēs, *and* ēsco, ĭs, rŭī, *to fade away.* Cārptŭs dēflōrŭĭt ūnguī, Catul. Syn. Flōrem āmītto, flāccēsco, mārcēsco.

dēflōro, ās, *to spoil.* Dēflōrāt frūctŭs, Dracon. Syn. Cōnspūrco, cōntāmĭno, pōllŭo, vĭtĭo. V. Maculo.

dēflŭo, flūxī, flūxŭm, *to flow down.* Dēflŭĭt āmnī, Virg. Syn. Flŭo, lābŏr, dēlābŏr, cādo, ēxcĭdo, dēcĭdo.

¶ dēflŭŭs, ă, ŭm, *flowing down.* Dēflŭă cæsărĭēs, Prud. Syn. Flūxŭs, cădŭcŭs.

dēfŏdĭo, fŏdī, fōssŭm, *to dig, inter.* Dēfŏdĭēt cōndĕtquĕ, Hor.

dēfōrmĭs, ĕ, *deformed.* Făcĭēm dēfōrmĭs ămīcī, Juv. Syn. Tūrpĭs, īnfōrmĭs, fœdŭs, squālĭdŭs, tētĕr, hōrrēndŭs, hōrrĭbĭlĭs.

dēfōrmo, ās, *to disfigure.* Dēfōrmāt măcĭēs, Virg. Syn. Dētūrpo, fœdo, măcŭlo, īnquĭno. V. Maculo.

dēfōssŭs, ă, ŭm, *the pass. partic. of* defodio. In dēfōssĭs spēcŭbŭs, Virg.

dēfraŭdo, ās, *to deceive.* Ter. V. Fallo, decipio.

dēfrēnātŭs, ă, ŭm, *unbridled.* Et dēfrēnātō, Ov.

dēfrĭco, ăī, ctŭm, *to rub hard.* Urbēm dēfrĭcŭĭt, Hor.

dēfrīngo, frēgī, frāctŭm, *to break.* Sūmmās dēfrīngĕrĕ, Virg. V. Frango.

dēfrŭtŭm, ī, n., *a confection of grapes.* Dēfrŭtă vēl Psȳthĭā, Virg.

dēfūnctŭs, ă, ŭm, *partic. of* defungor. Pēlāgī dēfūnctĕ pērĭclīs, Virg. V. Mortuus.

dēfūndo, fūdī, ūsŭm, *to pour down.* Făcĭlī dēfūndĭtŭr haŭstū, Juv. V. Fundo.

• dēfūngŏr, ĕrĭs, *to be rid of.* Syn. Fūngŏr, pērfūngŏr ; lībĕrŏr, ēxĭmŏr.

dēgĕnĕr, ĕrĭs, *degenerate.* Dēgĕnĕrēs ănĭmōs, Virg.

dēgĕnĕro, ās, *to degenerate.* Dēgĕnĕrārĕ tămĕn, Virg. Syn. Dēfīcĭo, dēscīsco, dēflēcto, sūm dēgĕnĕr.

|| dēglūtĭo, īs, īvī *and* ĭī, *to swallow.* Dēglūtīrĕ vīrŭm, Alc. Syn. Sōrbĕo, ābsōrbĕo, haūrĭo, ēxhaūrĭo.

dēgo, gī, *to do, lead, live.* Dēgĕrĕt ævŭm, Luc. Syn. Hăbĭto, ăgo, vīvo.

dēgrāndĭnăt, *it hails.* Dūm dēgrāndĭnăt, ōbsĭt, Ov.

dēgrăvo, ās, *to weigh down.* Dēgrăvăt ūlmŭm, Ov.

dēgūsto, ās, *to taste.* Cĕlĕrī dēgūstāt sīngŭlă, Claud. Syn. Gūsto, dēlībo, āttīngo.

dĕhīnc, *or* dehīnc, (*monosyll.*) adv., *henceforward.* Sūbnēctĕ ; dĕhīnc, ŭbi, Virg. Vŏcāt, dehīnc tālĭă fātŭr, Virg. Syn. Deīndĕ, ēxĭn, deīncēps, pōstĕă.

dĕhīsco, ĭs, *to gape.* Rĕgĭŏnĕ dĕhīscĕrĕ cœpĭt, Ov. Syn. Dīscēdo, hĭo, fīndŏr, ăpĕrĭŏr.

dēhōrtŏr, ārĭs, *to dissuade.* Pēctŏrĕ dēhōrtātŭr, Enn. Syn. Dīssuādĕo, dētērrĕo.

Dēĭănīră, æ, f., *the daughter of Œneus, loved by Hercules.* Dēĭănīră mŏrī, Ov. Epith. Călўdōnĭs ; īmplĭă, pūlchră, fōrmōsă, dĕcŏră, īnfēlīx, mīsĕră.

Dēĭdămīă, æ, f., *daughter of Lycomedes, beloved by Achilles.* Vīdŭŏ Dēĭdămīă tŏrō, . Prop.

dējēctŭs, ūs, m., *a throwing down.* Dējēctūquĕ grăvī, Ov.

dējēctŭs, ă, ŭm, *the pass. partic. of* dejicio. Ŏcŭlōs dējēctă dĕcŏrōs, Virg.

dējĕro, ās, *to swear.* Mĭhī dējĕrāre hīs mēnsĭbŭs, Ter. V. Juro.

dējĭcĭo, jēcī, jēctŭm, *to cast down.* Dējĭcĭt īn tērrās, Virg. Syn. Stērno, prōstērno, dēstrŭo, ēvērto, dīrŭo ; dētūrbo, dēpēllo, ēxtūrbo, ēxpēllo. V. Everto.

dĕīn, *or* deīn, adv., *afterwards, from henceforth.* Deīn ūsque āltĕră, (Phal.) Cat. Syn. Dēindĕ, *or* deīndĕ ; ēxĭn, ēxīndĕ ; dĕhīnc, *or* dehīnc ; deīncēps.

Dēĭŏpēă, æ, f., *the name of a nymph.* Pūlchērrĭmă, Dēĭŏpēăm, Virg.

Dēĭŏtărŭs, ī, m., *a king of Galatia.* Dēĭŏtărum, ĕt gĕhĭdæ, Luc.

Dēĭŏnĭdēs, æ, m., *son of Deione.* Dēĭŏnĭdēnquĕ jŭvēntæ, Ov.

Dēĭphŏbē, ēs, f., *the daughter of Glaucus, a Sibyl.* Dēĭphŏbē Glaūcī, Virg. Epith. Cūmānă, Cūmæă, dōctă, Chălcĭdĭcă, Eūbŏĭcă ; lōngævă.

Dēĭphŏhŭs, ī, m., *the son of Priam, murdered by Ulysses and Menelaus.* Dēĭphŏbūm . vīdĭt, Virg.

|| Dēĭtās, ātĭs, f., *Deity.* Frōntēm Dēĭtātĭs ădīrī, Prud. Epith. Ădōrāndă, vĕnĕrāndă.

dējŭgĭs, ĕ, *sloping.* Nūnc dējŭgĕ dōrsō, Aus.

dēlābŏr, ĕrĭs, lāpsŭs, *to sink down.* Scĭlĭcĕt īn tērrām dēlābī, Lucr. Syn. Lābŏr, . dēcĭdo, cădo. V. Cado.

dēlāmēntŏr, ārĭs, *to deplore.* Dēlāmēntātŭr ădēmptăm, Ov.

dēlāpsŭs, ă, ŭm, *the pass. partic. of* delabor. Mĕdĭōs dēlāpsŭs ĭn hōstēs, Virg.

dēlāsso, ās, *to weary.* Dēlāssārĕ vălēnt, Hor.

dēlātŏr, ōrĭs, m., *an informer.* Ēt dēlātŏr hăbĕt, Mart. Syn. Āccūsātŏr.

dēlātŭs, ă, ŭm, *the pass. partic. of* defero. Sĭcŭlām dēlātŭs ăd Ætnăm, Ov.

dēlēbĭlĭs, ĕ, *that may be erased.* Nūllīs dēlēbĭlĭs āŭnīs, Mart. Syn. Dēlēndŭs, dēlērī făcĭlĭs.

dēlēcto, ās, *to delight.* Nĭmĭŏ dēlēctāvĕrĕ sĕcūndæ, Hor. Syn. Ōblēcto, recrĕo, rĕlāxo, rĕfĭcĭo ; căpĭo, dūco, trăho.—Dēlēctŏr, [*the pass.*] Hīc dēlēctātŭr ĭāmbĭs, Hor. Syn. Căpĭŏr, trăhŏr, dūcŏr, răpĭŏr, tĕnĕŏr, gaūdĕo. V. Voluptas.

dēlēctŭs, ūs, m., *a choice.* Idēm dēlēctŭs ēquīnō, Virg.

* dēlēgo, ās, *to send on an embassy.* Syn. Lēgo, ās.

dēlĕo, lēvī, lētŭm, *to blot out.* Pōssīt dēlĕrĕ vĕtūstās, Ov. Syn. Ēxpūngo, tōllo, ădĭmo, ābstērgo ; ēvērto, dēstrŭo, vāsto, pērdo, dīrŭo, ēxtīnguo ; V. Everto. Cōrrĭgo, ēmēndo ; V. Corrigo.

dēlētŭs, ă, ŭm, *the pass. partic. of* deleo. Dēlētās Vūlscōrŭm, Virg. V. Deleo.

Dēlĭă, æ, f., *a name of Diana born at Delos.* Dēlĭă nōstrĭs, Ov.

Dēlĭăcŭs, ă, ŭm, *of Delos.* Quăm cŭm Dēlĭăcō, (Phal.) Syn. Dēlĭŭs.

dēlībĕrātŭs, ă, ŭm, *the pass. partic. of* delibero. Dēlībĕrātă mōrtĕ, (Alcaic.) Hor.

dēlībĕro, ās, *to deliberate.* Dē quō dēlībĕrăt, ān pĕtăt ūrbĕm, Juv. Syn. Stătŭo, cōnstĭtŭo, dēcērno, cōnsūlto. V. Cogito.

dēlībo, ās, *to touch lightly.* Dēlībāssĕ cĭbōs, Cl. Syn. Lĕvĭtĕr āttīngo, gūsto, pērstrīngo.

• dēlibro, ās, *to peel.* Dēlĭbrăt ōrnōs, Mant. Syn. Dēcŏrtĭco.

dēlĭbūtŭs, ă, ŭm, *anointed.* Hōc dēlĭbūtĭs, (Iamb.) Hor. Syn. Ōnctŭs, pĕr-ūnctŭs, Ĭnūnctŭs, ōblĭtŭs, ĭmbūtŭs, pērfūsŭs, spārsŭs.

dēlĭcātŭs, ă, ŭm, *delicate.* Et dēlĭcātæ, (Scaz.) Mart. Syn. Dēlĭcĭārum ămāns; dēlĭcĭĭs dēdĭtŭs; laūtŭs.

dēlĭcĭæ, ārŭm, f. pl., *pleasures.* Dēlĭcĭæ pŏpŭlī, Mart. Syn. Gaūdĭŭm, vŏlūptās. Epithi. Flŭēntēs, blāndæ, mōllēs, ămœnæ, dūlcēs, grātæ, jūcūndæ, fūgācēs, ōptātæ, quæsītæ, ætērnæ, pŏtēntēs. V. Voluptas.

dēlĭcĭōsŭs, ă, ŭm, *delightful.* Dēlĭcĭōsă flŭĭt, Arat. Syn. Suāvĭs, dūlcĭs, jūcūn-dŭs, grātŭs.

dēlĭcĭŭm, ĭī, n., *a darling object.* Dēlĭcĭŭm pārvŏ, Mart.

dēlĭctŭm, ī, n., *a fault.* Et prŏ dēlĭctĭs, Ov. Syn. Errŏr, crīmĕn, cūlpă, scĕlŭs, ērrātŭm, pēccātŭm, nōxă, pĭācŭlŭm. Epith. Nĕfāndŭm, tūrpĕ, ĭndĭgnŭm, grāndĕ, lĕvĕ. V. Peccatum, Culpa.

dēlĭgo, lēgī, lēctŭm, *to pluck, choose.* Dēlĭgĕre ūnguĕ rōsăm, Ov. Syn. Lĕgo, cārpo; ēlĭgo, sēlĭgo.

dēlīnīmēntŭm, ī, n., *a mitigation.* Nūllă dēlīnīmēnta ĭnvĕnĭt, (Iamb.) Afran. Syn. Blāndĭtĭæ, blāndīmēntă, lēnōcĭnĭŭm.

dēlīnĭo, īs, īvī, ītŭm, *to soften.* Lōngŭm dēlīnītūră lăbōrĕm, Aus. Syn. Lēnĭo, mūlcĕo, dēmūlcĕo, blāndĭŏr, ădūlŏr.

dēlĭnquo, līquī, līctŭm, *to fail.* Paūlŭm dēlĭquĭt ămīcŭs, Hor. Syn. Pēcco, ērro. V. Pecco.

dēlĭquēsco, ĭs, cŭī, *to melt.* Flēndŏ dēlĭcŭĭt, Ov.

dēlĭquĭŭm, ĭī, n., *a failing.* Sēntīt dēlĭquĭŏ, Prud. Syn. Dēfēctĭo, dēfēctŭs. Epith. Pĕrīcŭlōsŭm, ēxĭtĭălĕ, mĕtŭēndŭm.

dēlīrāmēntŭm, ī, n., *a doting foolishness.* Bārbātī dēlīrāmēntă Plătōnĭs, Prud. Syn. Dēlīrĭŭm.

dēlīro, ās, *to dote.* Quĭcquĭd dēlīrānt rēgēs, Hor. Syn. Dēsĭpĭo, ĭnsānĭo; dēvĭo, ērro, ăbērro.

dēlīrŭs, ă, ŭm, *doting, silly.* Mērcātūrĭs, dēlīrŭs ĕt āmēns, Hor. Syn. Stūltŭs, ĭnsānŭs, dēmēns. V. Demens.

dēlĭtĕo, ēs, *or* ēsco, ĭs, tŭī, *to be concealed.* Dēlĭtŭĭssĕ Jŏvĕm, Ov. Syn. Lătĕo, lătĭto, ăbdŏr, ābscōndŏr, ōccūltŏr.

dēlĭtĭgo, ās, *to babble, to dispute.* Tŭmĭdŏ dēlĭtĭgăt ōrĕ, Hor. V. Lis.

Dēlĭŭs, ă, ŭm, *of Delos.* Dēlĭŭs ĭnspīrāt vātēs, Virg.—2. -ĭŭs, ĭī, m., *Apollo.* Dēlĭŭs aūrēs, Hor. V. Apollo.

Dēlōs *and* ŭs, ī, f., *an island of the Ægean sea.* Dēlŏs ŭbi, Tib. Epith. Lātōnĭă, Ăpōllĭnĕă, Ortўgĭă; ērrātĭcă, cāndĭdă, ĭnstābĭlĭs, cīrcūmflŭă, văgă.

Dēlphī, ōrŭm, m. pl., *a town of Bœotia.* Vĕl Ăpōllĭnĕ Dēlphōs, Hor. Epith. Ăpōllĭnĕī, Phœbæī, sōrtĭlĕgī.

Dēlphĭcŭs, ă, ŭm, *of Delphi.* Dēlphĭcă laūrŭs, Cl. Syn. Dēlphĭtĭcŭs.

dēlphīn, īnĭs, *and* īnŭs, ī, m., *a dolphin.* Dēlphīnŭm sўlvĭs, Hor. Intĕr dēl-phīnăs Ărīōn, Virg. Syn. Dēlphīs. Epith. Cūrvŭs, pāndŭs, blāndŭs, æquŏ-rĕŭs, vīrĭdĭs, lĕvĭs, cĕlĕr, squāmōsŭs, pīnnĭfĕr, vēlōx, fūgāx, squāmmĕŭs, lāscī-vŭs, lūdēns.

dēlūbrŭm, ī, n., *a sanctuary, temple.* Ad dēlūbră vĕnĭt, Virg. Syn. Fānŭm, tēmplŭm, ædēs dĕōrŭm. Epith. Sānctŭm, rēlĭgĭōsŭm, præclārŭm, dīvēs, cān-dĭdŭm, āltŭm, māgnĭfĭcŭm, sacrŭm. V. Templum.

dēlūdo, sī, sŭm, *to deceive.* Sōpītŏs dēlūdŭnt sōmnĭă, Virg. Syn. Lūdo, ĭllūdo, rīdĕo, ĭrrīdĕo, dērīdĕo, dēcĭpĭo, cīrcŭmvĕnĭo. V. Decipio, fallo.

‖ dēlŭmbĭs, ĕ, *weak, wanton.* Sūmmă dēlŭmbĕ sălīvă, Pers.

dēlūsŭs, ă, ŭm, *the pass. partic. of* dcludo. Cĭbō dēlūsŭm gūttŭr, Ov.

dēmădĕo, ŭī, *to be wet.* Dēmădŭīssĕ sīnūs, Ov. V. Madeo.

‖ dēmāno, ās, *to flow down.* Flāmmă dēmānăt, (Sapph.) Cat. V. Defluo.

dēmēns, ēntĭs, *mad.* Dēmēns ēt cāntū, Virg. Syn. Āmēns, fūrĭōsŭs, ĭnsānŭs, mălĕsānŭs, fŭrēns, lўmphātŭs, stūltŭs, fătŭŭs, vēcŏrs. V. Stultus.

dēmēntĕr, adv., *madly.* Illŏ dēmēntĕr ămōrĭbŭs, Ov. Syn. Stūltē.

dēmēntĭă, æ, f., *madness.* Tē dēmēntĭă cēpĭt, Virg. Syn. Āmēntĭă, ĭnsānĭă, stūl-tĭtĭă, fŭrŏr. Epith. Spūmĕă, vēsānă, frēndēns, răbĭdă, spūmāns, fĕră, præcēps, cæcă, ĭnsānābĭlĭs, mălĕsānă. V. Stultitia.

dēmĕrĕo, ŭī, *and* ĕŏr, ērĭs, *to deserve.* Dēmĕrŭīssĕ mĕŏ, Ov.

dēmērgo, sī, sŭm, *to immerse.* Tŏtīdēm dēmērsērĭt ōrbēs, Ov. Syn. Mērgo, īmmērgo, ōbrŭo.

dēmērsŭs. ă, ŭm, *the pass. partic. of* demergo. Dēmērsīs æquŏrĕ rōstrīs, Virg.

dēmĕto, mēssŭī, mēssŭm, *to reap.* Dēmĕtīt ārvă, Cat. Syn. Lĕgo, cōllĭgo, mĕto. V. Meto, colligo.

dēmigro, ās, *to change place.* Dēmīgrānt Hēllĭcōnĕ, Stat. Dēmīgrăt ōrīs, Id. Syn. Migro, ēxĕo, rĕcēdo, ăbĕo, ēxcēdo, dīscēdo. V. Exeo, abeo.

* dēmīrŏr, ārīs. V. Miror, obstupeo.

dēmīssē, adv., *humbly.* Vŏlāt dēmīssĭŭs, Ov.

dēmītto, īsī, īssŭm, *to cast down.* Dēmīsērĕ nĕcī, Virg. Syn. Inclīno, dēprīmo, ăbjĭcĭo.

dēmo, dēmpsī, dēmptŭm, *to take away.* Dēmīt ĕquīs, Ov. Syn. Tōllo, aŭfĕro, ădĭmo, dētrăho.

Dēmŏcrĭtŭs, ī, m., *the philosopher.* Dēmŏcrĭtŭs, bŏnă pārs, Hor. Epith. Rīdēns, jŏcōsŭs, săpĭēns, Abdērītēs.

dēmōlĭŏr, īrīs, *to pull down.* Ævī, dēmōlītŭrquĕ prīōrīs, Ov. Syn. Dētūrbo, dējĭcĭo, dēstrŭo, ēvērto. V. Everto.

Dēmŏphŏōn, ōntīs, m., *the son of Theseus.* Hōspĭtă, Dēmŏphŏōn, Ov. Epith. Infīdŭs, Āttĭcŭs.

dēmōrdĕo, dī, sŭm, *to bite off.* Dēmōrsōs săpīt ūnguēs, Pers. V. Mordeo.

dēmŏrŏr, ārīs, *to retard.* Dēmŏrŏr Aŭstrōs, Virg. V. Moror.

Dēmōsthĕnĕs, ĭs, m., *the Greek orator.* Fāmām Dēmōsthĕnīs aŭt Cĭcĕrōnīs, Juv. Epith. Dĭsērtŭs, caŭsīdĭcŭs, dōctŭs, pĕrītŭs, fācūndŭs. V. Eloquens, orator.

dēmŏvĕo, mōvī, mōtŭm, *to move away.* Littŏrĕ dēmŏvĕt, Hor.

|| dēmūgĭo, īs, *to low.* Dēmūgītæquĕ pălūdēs, Ov. V. Mugio.

dēmŭm, adv., *at last.* Sīc dēmŭm sŏcĭōs, Virg. Syn. Tāndĕm, dēnĭquĕ, pōstrēmo.

dēmūrmŭro, ās, *to murmur.* Māgĭcō dēmūrmŭrăt ōrĕ, Ov.

dēnārĭŭs, īī, m., *a Roman coin.* Tŏtā dēnārĭŭs ārcā, Mart.

dēnārro, ās, *to relate.* Mātrī dēnārrăt ŭt ĭngēns, Hor. V. Narro.

dēnăto, ās, *to swim.* Dēnătăt ălvĕō, (Glycon.) Hor. Syn. Năto, nō. V. Nato.

dēnĕgo, ās, *to deny.* Dēnĕgăt hōc gĕnĭtŏr, Ov. Syn. Nĕgo, ăbnĕgo, ābnŭo, rĕnŭo, rĕcūso. V. Recuso, abnego.

dēnī, æ, ă, *ten.* Bīs dēnās Ĭtălō, Virg.

dēnĭquĕ, adv., *at last.* Dēnĭquĕ fīnēs, Hor. Syn. Tāndĕm, dēmŭm, pōstrēmo.

dēnōmĭno, ās, *to denominate.* Dēnōmĭnātōs, ĕt nĕpōtŭm, (Iamb. cum Syll.) Hor. Syn. Vŏco, ăppēllo, nōmĭno, dīco.

dēnōrmo, ās, *to disfigure.* Nūnc dēnōrmăt ăgēllŭm, Hor.

* dēnŏto, ās. Cic. V. Noto.

dēns, ēntīs, m., *a tooth, tusk;* dēntēs, ĭŭm, m. pl., *teeth.* Dēntēmque īn dēntĕ fătīgăt, Ov. Spūtăquĕ pēr dēntēs, Prop. Epith. Răbĭdī, dūrī, vălĭdī, cāndēntēs, ālbī, vūlnĭfīcī, ūncī, spūmōsī, mĭnācēs, nĭvĕī, cāndĭdī, prædūrī, mōrdācēs, ăcūtī, mŏlārēs, gĕnūīnī, sērrātī, fœdī, putrĭdī, sōrdĭdī. V. Mordeo.

dēnsĕo, ēs, *and* dēnso, ās, *to thicken.* Dēnsēt, ĕrānt quæ rāră, Virg. Dēnsātĕ cătērvās, Id. Syn. Cōndēnso, stīpo, cōgo, spīsso.

dēnsŭs, ă, ŭm, *thick.* Dēnsīs ēxērcĭtŭs ālīs, Virg. Syn. Dēnsātŭs, cōndēnsātŭs, cōmpāctŭs, crāssŭs, spīssŭs.

dēntālĕ, ĭs, n., *a ploughshare.* Āptāntūr dēntālĭă dōrsō, Virg. V. Aratrum.

dēntātŭs, ă, ŭm, *having teeth.* Sī dēntătă tĭbi, (Phal.) Mart.

dēntĭscālpĭŭm, īī, n., *a tooth-picker.* Et dēntĭscālpĭă sēptĕm, Mart.

dēntōsŭs, ă, ŭm, *armed with teeth.* Nōn mĭhī dēntōsă crīnĕm, Ov.

|| dēnūbo, psī, ptŭm, *to marry.* Dēnūpsīt thălămōs, Ov. V. Nubo.

dēnūdo, ās, *to make bare.* Dēnūdăt ārtŭs, (Iamb.) Sen. Syn. Nūdo, ēxŭo, spŏlĭo.

dēnūncĭo, ās, *to denounce.* Trīstēs dēnūncĭăt īrās, Virg. Syn. Nūncĭo, sĭgnĭfĭco, dēclāro, ĭndĭco, ās; prædīco, ĭs.

dēnŭo, adv., *again.* Dēnŭŏ, quī mĭhī dĕt, Mant. Syn. Rūrsŭm, rūrsŭs, ĭtĕrŭm.

Dĕōīs, ĭdīs, f., *daughter of Ceres, Proserpine.* Intēr chŏrĕās Dĕōĭdă răptăm, Aus.

Dĕōĭŭs, ă, ŭm, *of Ceres.* Dĕōĭă quērcŭs, Ov.

dĕōrsŭm, *or* deōrsŭm, (*dissyl.*) adv., *down.* Pēr ĭnānĕ dĕōrsŭm, Lucr. Pōndĕră deōrsŭm, Id.

dĕōscŭlŏr, arĭs, *to kiss.* Hōs dĕōscŭlātŭr, (Phal.) Mart. V. Osculor.

dēpāsco, pāvī, pāstŭm, *or* scŏr, pāstūs sŭm, *to feed, to eat up.* Tĕnĕrā dēpāscĭt ĭn hērbā, Virg. Artūs dēpāscĭtŭr ārĭdā fĕbrĭs, Id. SYN. Pāsco, pāscŏr, ĕdo; dēmĕto, mĕto.

dēpēcto, xŭī, ēxŭm, *to comb.* Ut sōlĭs dēpēctānt, Virg.

dēpēllo, pŭlĭ, pūlsŭm, *to expel.* Dēpŭllĭt, ēt cœlō, Virg. SYN. Pēllo, ēxpēllo, rĕpēllo, prōpūlso, prōpēllo, dējĭcĭo, dētūrbo, ēxtūrbo. V. Pello.

dēpēndĕo, ēs, *to hang down.* Ātrĭā; dēpēndēnt, Virg. SYN. Pēndĕo, sūspēnsūs sŭm.

dēpēndo, dī, sŭm, *to pay.* Dēpēndīssĕ căpŭt, Luc. V. Solvo.

dēpērdĭtŭs, ă, ŭm, *the pass. partic. of* deperdo. Ēst dēpērdĭtŭs Iō, Pr.

dēpērdo, ĭs, *to lose.* Vītālēm dēpērdĕrĕ sēnsŭm, Luc. SYN. Pērdo, āmītto.

dēpĕrĕo, ĭs, *to perish.* Quœ dēpĕrĭt īpsăm, Enn. Dēpĕrĭtūrā fŭĭt, Ov. SYN. Pĕrĕo, dīspĕrĕo, īntĕrĕo, ōccĭdo.

dēpīngo, īnxī, īctŭm, *to paint.* Ōbscœnās dēpīnxĭt, Prop. SYN. Pīngo, pīctūro, ădūmbro.

dēplāngo, ĭs, xī, *to deplore.* Dēplānxĕrĕ dŏmŭm, Ov.

dēplĕo, ēs, *to drain, empty.* Dēplēvĭmŭs haūstū, Stat.

dēplōro, ās, *to lament.* Ēt dēplōrātæ, Ov. SYN. Lāmēntŏr, lūgĕo, flĕo, plāngo, quĕrŏr, cōnquĕrŏr, gĕmo, dŏlĕo.

dēpōno, pŏsŭī, pŏsĭtŭm, *to lay down.* Quīcquăm dēpōnĕrĕ tēcŭm, Virg. SYN. Pōno, rĕpōno, ābjĭcĭo, dīmītto, ēxŭo, rĕlīnquo; cōmmītto, crēdo; pīgnŏrĕ cērto.

dēpŏpŭlŏr, ārĭs, *to waste.* Dēpŏpŭlēntŭr ăvēs, Ov. SYN. Vāsto, pŏpŭlŏr, dēprædŏr. V. Vasto.

dēpōrto, ās, *to transport.* Dēpōrtānt ēssĕdā Tibŭr, Prop.

dēpōsco, ĭs, *to ask.* Infēctō dēpōscĭt, Prop. SYN. Pōsco, pĕto, pōstŭlo, ēxpōsco, rĕpōsco.

dēpŏsĭtŭs, ă, ŭm, *the pass. partic. of* depono. Ille, ūt dēpŏsĭtī, Virg.

dēpræl̆ĭŏr, ārĭs, *to fight.* Æquŏrĕ fĕrvĭdō dēprælĭāntēs, Hor. V. Pugno.

dēprāvo, ās, *to deprave.* Dēprāvārĕ fĭdĕm, Sil. SYN. Cōrrūmpo, vĭtĭo, ădūltĕro.

dēprĕcŏr, ārĭs, *to entreat, to refuse.* Dēprĕcŏr īdĕm, Ov. SYN. Prĕcŏr, rŏgo, sūpplĭco; rĕcūso. V. Precor.

dēprĕhēndo *or* dēprēndo, dī, sŭm, *to catch, to discover.* Dēprēndās ănĭmī, Juv. SYN. Cōmprĕhēndo, āgnōsco, cōmpĕrĭo, ādvērto, ănĭmādvērto.

dēprĭmo, prēssī, ēssŭm, *to keep down.* Ēt nē dēprĭmĕrĕt, Ov. SYN. Cōmprĭmo, āfflīgo, āttĕro, prōtĕro, cōntĕro, cōncūlco, dējĭcĭo, dēmītto, dēpēllo.

dēprōmo, mpsī, mptŭm, *to draw out.* Phărētrā dēprōmĕ săgīttăm, Virg. SYN. Prōmo, ēxprōmo, prōfĕro, ēxpōno, ērŭo, ēxtrāho.

dēprōpĕro, ās, *to hasten.* Dēprŏpĕrārĕ ăpĭo, Hor.

dēpŭdĕt, ŭĭt, *it gives no shame.* Dēpŭdŭĭt, prōfŭgŭs, Ov.

dēpūgno, ās, *to fight.* Māgnănĭmō dēpūgnăt, Mart. SYN. Pūgno, cērto, dēcērto, dīmĭco, cōnflīgo, cōngrĕdĭŏr.

dēpūlsŭs, ă, ŭm, *the pass. partic. of* depello. Hūmōr, dēpūlsīs ārbŭtŭs hædīs, Virg.

dēpūngo, ĭs, *to mark with a point.* Dēpūngĕ, ŭbĭ sīstăm, Pers.

dēpŭto, ās, *to judge, to send.* Dēpŭtăt ūmbrās, Ov. SYN. Pŭto, stătŭo, cōnstĭtŭo, dēstĭno; lēgo, ās.

dēpȳgĭs, ĕ, *having no haunches.* Dēpȳgĭs, nāsūtă, Hor.

dērādo, ĭs, *to wipe off.* Dērādĕrĕ līmŭm, Pers.

dērīdĕo, sī, sŭm, *to laugh at.* Dērīdēnt stŏlĭdī, Ov. SYN. Rīdĕo, īrrīdĕo, lūdo, īllūdo, dēlūdo. V. Jocus, irrideo.

dērīdĭcŭlŭs, ă, ŭm, *ridiculous.* Dērīdĭcŭlŭm ēssĕ, Lucr.

dērĭpĭo, ŭī, *to take off.* Dērĭpĭt, ēx hŭmĕrīs, Ov. SYN. Ērĭpĭo.

dērīsŏr, ōrĭs, m., *a railer.* Spēctās, dērīsōrēmquĕ Lătīnŭm, Mart.

dērīvo, ās, *to convey water.* Dērīvārĕ quĕŭnt, Lucr. SYN. Aquăm, rĭvŭm dēdūco.

* dērŏgo, ās, *to derogate.* Pārcă nūtrīx dĕrŏgăt, Prud. SYN. Dētrăho, aūfĕro; ābrŏgo.

dēsævĭo, īs, ĭī, *to cease from anger, to be appeased.* Dŭm dēsævĭăt īră, Lucan. SYN. Mĭtĭgŏr, plācŏr, mītēsco.

dēscēndo, dī, sŭm, *to descend.* Dēscēndĕrĕ mōntĕ, Virg. Syn. Lăbŏr, dēlābŏr, īllābŏr, dēmīttŏr, dēsīlĭo, ād tērrăm fĕrŏr, vōlvŏr, rŭo.

dēscĭo, ĭvī, *to abandon.* Dēscīvērĕ făvīs, Cl.

dēscrībo, psī, ptŭm, *to describe.* Dēscrībĭtŭr ārcŭs, Hor. Syn. Ēxscrībo, ēxăro, scrībo, cōnscrībo, trānscrībo; dēsĭgno, dēlĭnĕo.

dēsĕco, cŭī, ctŭm, *to cut.* Dēsĕcŭīssĕt ămŏr, Ov. Syn. Sĕco, scīndo.

dēsĕctŭs, ă, ŭm, *the pass. partic. of* deseco. Gōrgōnă dēsĕctō, Virg.

dēsĕro, ŭī, tŭm, *to quit, abandon.* Līttŏră dēsĕrŭērĕ, Virg. Syn. Dēsŭm, lĭnquo, rĕlīnquo, nēglĭgo, ōmītto, mītto, prætērmītto; dēstĭtŭo, prōdo.

dēsērtŏr, ōrĭs, m., *a deserter.* Dēsērtōrem Āsĭæ, Virg. Syn. Pērfŭgă.

dēsērtŭm, ī, n., *a desert.* Lĭbȳæ dēsērtă pĕrāgro, Virg. Syn. Ērēmŭs, sōlĭtūdo, rĕcēssŭs, āvĭă. Epith. Ardŭŭm, lōngŭm, īncūltŭm, trīstĕ, mœstŭm, āvĭŭm. V. Antrum.

dēsērtŭs, ă, ŭm, *the pass. partic. of* desero. Dēsērtīs ōlĭm, Prop.

dēsērvĭo, ĭs, *to do service to.* Quī dēsērvĭăt ānnōs, Ov.

dēsēs, ĭdĭs, *slothful.* Dēsĭdĭs ātrĭă Sōmnī, Stat. Syn. Dēsĭdĭōsŭs, ĭnērs, īgnāvŭs, sēgnĭs, ēnērvĭs, lānguēns, tōrpēns, tārdŭs, pĭgĕr. V. Piger.

dēsĭdĕo, ēdī, *to remain idle.* Dēsĭdĕt, ātque ălĭquă, Mart. Syn. Dēsĭdo, rĕsĭdĕo; sŭm dēsĕs.

dēsīdĕrātŭs, ă, ŭm, *the pass. partic. of* desidero. Dēsīdĕrātōquĕ, (Scaz.)

dēsīdĕrĭŭm, ĭī, n., *a desire, a regret.* Sŭbĭt, dēsīdĕrĭŭmquĕ, Ov. Syn. Vōtŭm, cŭpīdo, ămŏr, ārdŏr; sĭtĭs, fămēs. Epith. Ardēns, flagrāns, īmmēnsŭm, vĕhĕmēns, īngēns, vēsānŭm, nĭmĭŭm, dīrŭm. V. Cupido.

dēsīdĕro, ās, *to desire, to need.* Fœtŭs dēsīdĕrăt ārbŏrĕ, Ov. Syn. Cŭpĭo, ōpto, ēxōpto, quæro, vŏlo, āspīro, ārdĕo, lĭbĕt, plăcĕt, cōrdi ēst. V. Desiderium, opto.

dēsīdĭă, æ, f., *laziness.* Dēsīdĭæ cōrdī, Virg. Syn. Pigrĭtĭă, tōrpŏr, sēgnĭtĭēs, īgnāvĭă, ĭnērtĭă. Epith. Imprŏbă, ĭnānĭs, mōllĭs, īmbēllĭs, tōrpēns, sōrdĭdă, ĭnērs, mŭlă, trīstĭs, fāstĭdĭōsă. V. Pigritia.

dēsīdĭōsĕ, adv., *lazily.* Ætātēm dēsīdĭōsĕ, Lucr.

dēsīdĭōsŭs, ă, ŭm, *lazy.* Dēsīdĭōsŭs ĕrăt, Ov. Syn. Dēsĕs, ĭnērs, pĭgĕr.

dēsīdo, ēdī, *to sink.* Cŭr vădă dēsīdānt, Stat. Syn. Dēsĭdĕo, rēsĭdo, rĕsĭdĕo.

dēsīgnātŏr, ōrĭs, m., *a master of ceremonies.* Dēsīgnātōrĕm dĕcŏrăt, Hor.

dēsīgno, ās, *to point out.* Hŭmĭlī dēsīgnăt mœnĭă, Virg. Syn. Nŏto, dēnŏto, dēmōnstro, ōstēndo, dēscrībo, dēfīnĭo.

dēsīlĭo, ĭs, ĭī *and* ŭī, *to leap down.* Dēsĭlŭīt Tūrnŭs, Virg. Syn. Dēscēndo, ēxĭlĭo, cădo.

dēsĭno, ĭs, sĭvī, *to cease.* Vīvĕrĕ dēsĭnĭmŭs, Max. Syn. Cēsso, fīnĭo, īntērmītto, dēsĭsto, ōmītto, sĭno.

dēsĭpĭo, ĭs, ŭī, *to rave.* Dēsĭpĭt, ēxtēntăt, Lucr. Syn. Dēlīro, īnsănĭo.

dēsĭsto, ĭs, dēstĭtī, *to desist.* Dēstĭtĭt ēxtīnctŏs, Cat. Syn. Intērmītto, dēsĭno, cēsso.

dēsĭtŭs, *the pass. partic. of* desino. Dēsĭtă nĕ, Fill.

dēsōlātŭs, ă, ŭm, *the pass. partic. of* desolo. Dŭcēs, dēsōlātĭquĕ mănĭplī, Virg.

dēsōlo, ās, *to lay waste.* Ēt dēsōlāvĭmŭs āgrōs, Virg. Syn. Vāsto, dēpŏpŭlŏr.

dēspēcto, ās, *to look down.* Dēspēctăt dēsŭpĕr ārcēs, Virg.

dēspēctŭs, ă, ŭm, *the pass. partic. of* despicio. Dēspēctŭs tĭbĭ sŭm, Virg. V. Abjectus.

dēspērātĭo, ōnĭs, f., *despair.* Ēt dēspērātĭŏ bārbæ, Juv. Syn. Spēs ăbjēctă.

dēspēro, ās, *to despair.* Nēc quĭă dēspērēs, Hor. Syn. Dīffīdo.

dēspĭcābĭlĭs, ĕ, *contemptible.* Jŭrĕ dēspĭcābĭlĭs, (Iamb.) Syn. Dēspĭcĭēndŭs, āspērnābĭlĭs, cōntēmnēndŭs, āspērnāndŭs, cōntēmptŭs, vīlĭs, ābjēctŭs.

dēspĭcĭo, ēxī, ēctŭm, *and* pĭcŏr, ārĭs, *to despise.* Dēspĭcĭāntŭr ŏpēs, Tib. Syn. Spērno, āspērnŏr, tēmno, cōntēmno, nēglĭgo, rēspŭo, fāstĭdĭo, pōsthăbĕo, nōn cŭro. V. Contemno, aspernor.

dēspŏlĭo, ās, *to spoil.* Dēspŏlĭēs tāntă, Mart.

dēspōndĕo, ēs, *to promise in marriage.* Flāvām dēspōndĕt Ĭānthĕm, Ov.

dēspūmo, ās, *to scum.* Tĕpĭdī dēspūmăt ăhēnī, Virg.

dēstērto, ĭs, *to cease snoring.* Pōstquām dēstērtŭīt, Pers.

dēstĭno, ās, *to design, to appoint.* Dēstĭnăt Īmpĕrĭŏ, Ov. Syn. Trĭbŭo, āttrĭbŭo, āssĭgno, dēcērno, cōnstĭtŭo.

dēstĭtŭo, ŭī, ūtŭm, *to leave destitute.* Dŭstĭtŭīssĕ quĕrŏr, Ov. Syn. Dĕsĕro, līnquo, rĕlīnquo, dērĕlīnquo.

dēstrŭo, xī, ctŭm, *to destroy.* Dēstrŭăt, aūt cāptŭm, Virg. Syn. Ēvērto, dīrŭo. V. Everto.

dēsūdo, ās, *to sweat.* Dēsūdārĕ cămīnīs, Stat.

dēsuēsco, ēvī, ētŭm, *to disuse oneself.* Pātrŭm dēsuēscĭt hŏnōrī, Sil.

dēsuētŭs, *the pass. partic. of* desuesco. Jăm dēsuētă trĭumphīs, Virg.

dēsūltŏr, ōrĭs, m., *a vaulter, inconstant.* Dēsūltŏr ămōrĭs, Ov.

dēsŭm, dēfŭī, *to be wanting.* Dēsŭmŭs, ēccĕ, St. Syn. Absŭm, dĕfĭcĭo, dēsĭdĕrŏr.

dēsūmo, psī, ptŭm, *to pick out.* Dēsūmpsĭt Āthēnās, Hor.

dēsŭpĕr, adv., *from above.* Dēsŭpĕr ūrbī, Virg. Syn. Āb āltō.

dēsūrgo, sūrrēxī, *to rise.* Dēsūrgāt dŭbĭă, Hor. V. Surgo.

dĕtĕgo, xī, ctŭm, *to detect.* Dĕtĕgĭs īmbēllēs, Lucan. Syn. Āpĕrĭo, păndo, rĕsĕro, ōstēndo, rĕtĕgo, reclūdo, ēxplĭco.

dētērgo, sī, sŭm, *and* gĕo, ēs, *to wipe.* Fœdō dētērgīs sēcŭlă vīctū, Cl. Syn. Abstērgo, tērgo, mūndo. V. Abluo.

dētĕrĭŏr, ōrĭs, *worse.* Dētĕrĭōrĭs hĕrī, Catull. Syn. Pējŏr.

dētērmĭno, ās, *to determine.* Tēlī dētērmĭnĕt īctŭs, Lucr. Syn. Tērmĭno, dēfīnĭo, mētĭŏr.

dētĕro, trīvī, ītŭm, *to bruise.* Mănĭbŭs dētrīvĕrăt ūsŭs, Pr. Syn. Āttĕro, cōntĕro, tĕro, ābsūmo.

dētērrĕo, ŭī, ĭtŭm, *to deter.* Fœdō dētērrŭĭt Ōrpheŭs, Hor. Syn. Dĕhōrtŏr, āvŏco, rĕvŏco, dēdūco, āmŏvĕo, āvērto, ābdūco; tērrĕo.

dētērrĭmŭs, ă, ŭm, *very bad.* Ūt dētērrĭmŭs ērrŏr, Prud. Syn. Pēssĭmŭs.

dētērrĭtŭs, *the pass. partic. of* deterreo. Ēst dētērrĭtă nūnquăm, Tib.

dĕtēstăbĭlĭs, ĕ, *detestable.* Tăm dĕtēstăbĭlĕ sēxū, Juv. Syn. Dĕtēstāndŭs, ēxecrāndŭs, execrăbĭlĭs, hōrrēndŭs.

dĕtēstātĭo, ōnĭs, f., *detestation.* Dīră dĕtēstātĭo, Hor.

dĕtēstŏr, ārĭs, *to detest.* Dĕtēstātă; mănĕt, (Asclep.) Hor. Syn. Ābŏmĭnŏr, ēxecrŏr, ăbhōrrĕo, fūgĭo, āvērsŏr, hōrrĕo.

dētēxo, xŭī, xtŭm, *to weave.* Pārās dētēxĕrĕ jūncō, Virg. V. Texo.

dētĭnĕo, nŭī, dētēntŭm, *to detain.* Dētĭnŭĕrĕ tŭōs, Ov. Syn. Tĕnĕo, rĕtĭnĕo, mŏrŏr, dēmŏrŏr.

dētōndĕo, ēs, dī, sŭm, *to shear off, strip.* Dētōnsæ frīgŏrĕ, Ov.

dētŏno, ās, *to thunder loudly.* Dŭm dētŏnĕt, ōmnĕm, Virg.

dētōrquĕo, sī, tŭm, *to turn aside.* Cōrnŭă dētŏrquēntquĕ, Virg. Syn. Dēflēcto, āvērto.

dētrăho, trāxī, ctŭm, *to draw off.* Dētrăhĕt īdĕm, Hor. Syn. Mĭnŭo, dĕrŏgo, aūfĕro, dĕcērpo, tōllo.

dētrēcto, ās, *to refuse.* Vērbĕră dētrēcto, Tib. Syn. Vīto, ēvīto, fūgĭo, rĕcūso, dēvīto, ābnŭo, dēclīno.

dētrīmēntŭm, ī, n., *detriment.* Dētrīmēntă fŭgās, Hor. Syn. Dāmnŭm, nŏxă, ĭncōmmŏdŭm.

dētrītŭs, *the pass. partic. of* detero. Ōmnĭă dētrītō, Prop.

dētrūdo, sī, sŭm, *to throw down.* Jŏvĕm dētrūdĕrĕ rēgnīs, Virg. Syn. Dēpēllo, dējĭcĭo, ēxpēllo, ēxtūrbo, dētūrbo.

dētrūnco, ās, *to cut off, lop.* Dētrūncātquĕ căpŭt, Ov.

dētŭmĕo or ēsco, mŭī, *to cease to swell.* Dētŭmŭēre ănĭmī, Stat. Syn. Dēprĭmŏr, sŭbsīdo, dēsīdo, rĕsīdo, sŭbdūcŏr.

dētūrbo, ās, *to throw down.* Pŭppī dētūrbăt ăb āltā, Virg. Syn. Dēpēllo, dējĭcĭo, ēxtūrbo. V. Dejicio.

* dētūrpo, ās, *to defile.* Dētūrpāt pŭlvĕrĕ crīnēs, Virg. (Ciris.) Syn. Tūrpo, măcŭlo.

dēvāsto, ās, *to lay waste, destroy.* Dēvāstātă mĕō, Ov.

Deūcălĭŏn, ōnĭs, m., *the son of Prometheus.* Deūcălĭōnĭs ăquās, Ov. Syn. Prŏmēthīdēs. Epith. Pĭŭs, jūstŭs, æquŭs, prŏbŭs.

Deūcălĭōnēŭs, ă, ŭm, *of Deucalion.* Deūcălĭōnēās ēffŭgĭt, Ov.

dēvĕho, ēxī, ēctŭm, *to carry away.* Dēvĕhŏr āstră, Prop. Syn. Dēfĕro, vĕho.

dēvēllo, lī, ūlsŭm, *to pull off.* Sŭō dēvēllĕrĕ trūncō, Ov. V. Vello.

dēvēlo, ās, *to unveil.* Ōrăquĕ dēvēlăt, Ov. Syn. Rĕvēlo, dĕtĕgo, rĕtĕgo, ăpĕrĭo.

dĕvĕnĕrŏr, ārĭs, *to worship.* Dĕvĕnĕrātă fŏcĭs, Ov.

dĕvĕnĭo, vēnī, vēntŭm, *to arrive.* Dĕvĕnĭēnt ; ădĕro, Virg. Syn. Pĕrvĕnĭo, ăccēdo, ādvĕnĭo. V. Advenio.

dĕvēxŭs, ă, ŭm, *declining.* Flŭĭt dĕvēxō pŏndĕrĕ, Virg. Syn. Dēclīvĭs, prŏnŭs.

dĕvīctŭs, *the pass. partic. of* devinco. Fātūr dĕvīctŭs ámŏrĕ, Virg.

* dĕvīncĭo, ĭs, xī, nctŭm, *to chain,* Plaut. Ter. Syn. Ŏbstrīngo, vīncĭo, lĭgo. V. Vincio.

dĕvīnctŭs, *the pass. partic. of* devincio. Mē sīt dĕvīnctĭŏr ăltĕr, Hor. Syn. Vīnctŭs, rĕvīnctŭs, lĭgātŭs.

dĕvīto, ās, *to avoid.* Quāntō dĕvītēs ănĭmī, Hor. Syn. Vīto, ēvīto, dēclīno, fŭgĭo, ēffŭgĭo, dētrēcto.

dĕvĭŭs, ă, ŭm, *out of the way.* Lūstră văgāntĕm, Ov. Syn. Ērrāns, ăbērrāns ; ăvĭŭs. V. Avius.

dĕvŏco, ās, *to call down.* Dĕvŏcărĕ sīdĕră, Hor.

dĕvŏlo, ās, *to fly down.* Dĕvŏlăt īn tērrās, Lucr. V. Volo.

dĕvōlvo, ĭs, vōlvī, vŏlūtŭm, *to roll down.* Vērbă dĕvōlvĭt, (Sapph.) Hor.

dĕvŏro, ās, *to devour.* Dĕvŏrăt, ĕt claūsŭm, Ov. Syn. Vŏro, ăbsōrbĕo, V. Voro.

dĕvōtĭo, ōnĭs, f., *devotion.* Tānta ēst dĕvōtĭŏ lēgŭm, Vict. Syn. Rēlĭgĭo, pĭĕtās. V. Pietas.

dĕvōtŭs, ă, ŭm, *the pass. partic. of* devoveo. Pēstī dĕvōtă fŭtūræ, Virg. Syn. Vōtŭs, āddīctŭs, dēstīnātŭs.

dĕvŏvĕo, vōvī, vōtŭm, *to vow.* Dĕvŏvĕt ārĭs, Virg. Syn. Vŏvĕo, cōnsecro, dĭco, ās : āddīco, ĭs ; dēstīno.

Dĕŭs, ī, m., *God.* Impĕrĭum ēst Dĕī, Hor. Syn. Nūmĕn. Epith. Omnĭpŏtēns, ætērnŭs, ĭmmōrtālĭs, clēmēns, vīndĕx, ŭltŏr, prŏvĭdŭs, cælĭpŏtēns, āstrĭpŏtēns, ĭmmōtŭs, ĭmmūtābĭlĭs, māgnŭs, ĭnāccēssŭs, trĕmēndŭs, mĕtŭēndŭs, ĭmmēnsŭs, īnfīnītŭs, jūstŭs, æquŭs, ădōrāndŭs, vĕrēndŭs, sūblīmĭs, īnvīctŭs, vĕnĕrāndŭs, tērrĭbĭlĭs.

dĕxtĕr, tĕră, tĕrŭm, *or* tră, trŭm, *dexterous, lucky.* Dēxtĕrĭŏrĕ prĕmĭt, Mart. Syn. Ingĕnĭōsŭs, sāgāx, sōlērs, īndūstrĭŭs, ăcūtŭs ; sĕcūndŭs, prōspĕr, faūstŭs, fēlīx, fōrtūnātŭs.

dĕxtĕră *or* tră, æ, f., *the right hand.* Dēxtĕră pĕr fērrŭm, Ov. In dēxtrā tēlă fŭĕrĕ mănū, Id. Epith. Pŏtēns, īndŏmĭtă, fōrtĭs, ārtĭfĕx. V. Manus.

dĕxtĕrē, adv., *dexterously.* Dēxtĕrĭŭs, nēmo, Hor.

dĕxtĕrĭtās, ātĭs, f., *dexterity.* Dēxtĕrĭtātĕ bŏnōrŭm, Varr. Syn. Sōlērtĭă, īndūstrĭă.

dĕxtrōrsŭm, sŭs, *and* trŏvērsŭm, adv., *on the right hand.* Hīc dēxtrōrsum ăbĭt, Hor. Dēxtrŏvērsūm cēnsĕo, Plaut.

Dĭă, æ, f., *the island of Naxos.* Dĭă fĕrītŭr ăquĭs, Ov.

|| dĭăbŏlŭs, ī, m., *the devil.* Fŭrvŭm dĭăbŏlī nōmĕn, (Iamb.) Prud. V. Dæmon.

dĭădēmă, ătĭs, n., *a diadem.* Dĭădēmătĕ vīrtŭs, Mart. Syn. Cŏrōnă. Epith. Insīgnĕ, cōnspĭcŭŭm, rēgālĕ, nĭtĭdŭm, cŏrūscŭm, pūnĭcĕŭm, dīvĕs, prĕtĭōsŭm, dĕcōrŭm, clārŭm, splēndĭdŭm, gēmmĭfĕrŭm, rŭtĭlāns.

dĭălēctĭcŭs, ă, ŭm, *logical.* Cērtăt dĭălēctĭcă tūrbă, Aus.

Dĭālĭs, ĕ, *of Jupiter.* Dĭālĭs ĕrăt, Ov.

Dĭānă, æ, f., *the goddess of hunting ; Phœbe in heaven, Diana in the woods, and Hecate in hell.* Lūcŭsquĕ Dĭānæ, Virg. Exērcēt Dĭānă chŏrōs, Id. Syn. Lātōnĭă, Dēlĭă, Cŷnthĭă ; Dīctŷnnă ; Lūnă, Trĭvĭă, Hĕcătĕ, Lūcīnă. Epith. Cāstă, trĭfōrmĭs, hŏnēstă, sūccīnctă, phărĕtrātă, tōrvă, jăcŭlātrīx, ăgĭlĭs, ănĭmōsă, sānctă, vĕrēcūndă, pūlchră, vēnātrīx, īnnūptă, nĕmŏrālĭs, mītĭs, nĭvĕă, mōntĭvăgă, clāră, lūcĭfĕră, cāndĭdă, ālbă, văgă, cĕlĕr, sŷlvĭcŏlă, tērgĕmĭnă, phărĕtrĭgĕră, īntĕmĕrātă, Scŷthĭcă.

Dĭānĭŭs, ă, ŭm, *of Diana.* Tūrbă Dĭānĭă fūrēs, Ov.

dĭărĭŭm, ĭī, n., *a day's provision.* Urbānă dĭărĭă, Hor.

* dĭcācĭtās, ātĭs, f., *drollery, sarcasm.* Rīsŭs, sērĭĕtās, dĭcācĭtātēs, (Phal.) Sid. Syn. Lŏquācĭtās, gārrŭlĭtās.

dĭcāx, ācĭs, *witty, satirical.* Dĭcācēs Cōnvĕnĭĕt, Hor.

dĭco, ās, *to dedicate.* Prŏprĭāmquĕ dĭcābo, Virg. Syn. Dēdĭco, cōnsecro, sacro, nūncŭpo, vŏvĕo, dĕvŏvĕo ; dēstīno ; āddīco, ĭs.

dīco, ĭs, xī, ctŭm, *to say.* Dīcĕrĕt: hæc mĕă sūnt, Virg. SYN. Lŏquŏr, ĕlŏquŏr, fārī, ūflārī, prŏfārī, pāndo, nārro, ēnārro, rĕfĕro, mĕmŏro. V. Loquor.
Dictæŭs, ă, ŭm, *of Mount Dicte, of Crete.* Dīctæō cœlī rĕgĕm, Virg.
Dĭctāmnŭm, ī, n., *and* ŭs, ī, m., *the herb dittany.* Dīctāmnŭm gĕnĭtrīx, Virg.
dīctātŏr, ōrĭs, m., *a dictator.* Cūm dīctātŏrĕ mägĭstrōs, Juv.
dīctātūră, æ, f., *dictatorship.* Dīctātūram ĭndŭĭt, Pers.
dīctērĭŭm, ĭī, n., *a scoff.* Dīctērĭă dīcĭs, Mart.
dīctĭto, ās, *the freq. of* dico. Dīctĭtĕt Albānō, Hor.
dīcto, ās, *to dictate.* Dīctābĭtŭr hærēs, Juv.
dīctŭm, ī, n., *a saying.* Vĕnĕrēm Sātūrnĭă dīctīs, Virg.
Dīctўnnă, æ, f., *a name of Diana.* Dīctўnnă, rĕcēssŭs, Ov.
Dīctўs, ўĭs *or* ўŏs, m., *the name of a centaur.* Dīctўs Hĕlōpsquĕ, Ov.
dīdĭtŭs, *the pass. partic. of* dido. Dīdĭtă fāmă, Virg.
Dīdĭŭs, ĭī, m., *a Roman consul.* Dīdĭŭs hōstīlēs, Ov.
dīdo, dīdĭdī, dīdĭtŭm, *to distribute.* Mūnĭă dīdĭt, Hor. SYN. Dīvĭdo, dīstrĭbŭo.
Dīdō, ūs *or* ōnĭs, f., *the founder of Carthage, who killed herself to avoid the marriage of Iarbas.* Mĭsĕrāmquĕ rĕlĭnquĕrĕ Dīdō, Ov. Cāstæ Dīdōnĭs hŏnōrĕm, Mant.
SYN. Ēlĭsă, Phœnīssă; Sīdonĭă rēgĭnă; Sĭchælă cōnjūx. EPITH. Pūlchră, ĕffĕră, dīvĕs, īnfēlīx, cāndĭdă, mĭsĕră, mĭsĕrābĭlĭs, prŏfŭgă, ādvĕnă, Tўrĭă, fŭrĭătă, āmēns, dēmēns, īnsānă, mălĕsānă, dēcēptă, dēlŭsă, rĕlīctă, dēsērtă, cōncīnnă, pūlchērrĭmă.
dīdūco, xī, ctŭm, *to divide.* Ănĭmŭs dīdūcĭtŭr ōmnĕs, Virg. SYN. Dīstrăho, dīrĭmo.
Dĭdŭmāōn, ŏnĭs, m., *a skilful artificer.* Dĭdŭmāŏnĭs ārtēs, Virg.
dĭēs, dĭēĭ, m. f., *and* dĭēcŭlă, æ, f., *a day.* Ēgērĕ dĭēbŭs, Virg. SYN. Lūx, sōl, lūmĕn, Aŭrōră. EPITH. Lætĭfĭcŭs, clārŭs, nĭtĭdŭs, lūcĭdŭs, vŏlŭcĕr, ālmŭs, cāndĭdŭs, fōrmōsŭs, splēndēns, īnstābĭlĭs, prōnŭs, răpĭdŭs, Phœbĕŭs, cĕlĕr, vĕlōx, nĭtēns, sĕrēnŭs, sĕrēnātŭs, fŭgĭtīvŭs, fŭgāx, flŭēns, brĕvĭs, spērātŭs, grātŭs, ōptātŭs, fēlīx, ēxpēctātŭs.
Dĭēspĭtĕr, trĭs, m., *Jupiter.* Dĭēspĭtĕr īnfāns, Prud. V. Jupiter.
dīffāmo, ās, *to defame.* Dīffāmātūmquĕ pārēntī, Ov.
dīffĕrēntĭă, æ, *or* rĭtăs, ātĭs, f., *difference.* Dīffĕrĭtāsque ēst, Lucr.
dīffĕro, dīstŭlī, dīlātŭm, *to scatter, to differ ; to put off, to defer.* Dīffĕrăt, ĕt præsēns, Hor. SYN. Dīssēntĭo, dīscrĕpo; tārdo, cūnctŏr, mŏrŏr, prōcrāstĭno.
|| dīffĭbŭlo, ās, *to ungird.* Chlāmўdēm dīffĭbŭlăt aŭrō, St.
dīffĭcĭlĭs, ĕ, *difficult.* Heŭ! quăm dīffĭcĭle ēst, Ov. SYN. Ārdŭŭs, ŏpĕrōsŭs, lăbōrĭōsŭs ; mŏrōsŭs, quĕrŭlŭs.
dīffĭcūltās, ātĭs, f., *difficulty.* Plaut. SYN. Nĕgōtĭŭm, mŏlēstĭă, lăbŏr.
dīffĭcŭltĕr, adv., *uneasily.* Haŭd dīffĭcŭltĕr, (Iamb.) Prud. SYN. Dīffĭcīlē, ægrē, vīx, mŏlēstē.
dīffīdēntĭă, æ, f., *diffidence.* Quĕm dīffīdēntĭă nūtrĭt, Ov.
dīffīdo, fĭsŭs sŭm, fĭsŭm, *to distrust.* Lætīs dīffĭdĕrĕ rēbŭs, Sil. SYN. Nōn fĭdo, nōn cōnfĭdo, dēspēro. V. Despero.
dīffīndo, fĭdī, fīssŭm, *to cleave.* Dīffĭdĭt, āc mūltă, Virg. V. Findo.
dīffīngo, xī, ctŭm, *to paint, dissemble, deny.* Dīffīngīt Rhēnī, Hor. V. Fingo, destruo, nego.
dīffĭtĕŏr, ērĭs, *to deny.* Dīffĭtēātŭr ŏpŭs, Ov. SYN. Nĕgo, ābnĕgo.
dīfflŭo, xī, *to flow away.* Dīfflŭĕre hŭmōrĕm, Lucr. SYN. Ēfflŭo, lĭquēsco; lĭquŏr, ĕrĭs.
dīffŭgĭo, ūgī, *to fly away.* Dīffŭgīmŭs vīsū, Virg. SYN. Fŭgĭo, aŭfŭgĭo. V. Fugio.
dīffūndo, ūdī, ūsŭm, *to overspread.* Ambrŏsĭæ dīffūdĭt ŏdōrĕm, Virg. SYN. Ēffūndo, prŏfūndo, fūndo, dīspērgo, dīssĭpo.
dīffūsĭlĭs, ĕ, *which may be diffused.* Dīffūsĭlĭs æthĕr, Lucr.
dīffūsŭs, *the pass. partic. of* diffundo. Dīffūsōs hĕdĕră, Virg.
dīgĕro, gēssī, stŭm, *to distribute.* Dīgĕrĭt īn nŭmĕrŭm, Virg. SYN. Ōrdĭno, dīstīnguo, dīstrĭbŭo, dīspōno; cŏquo, cōncŏquo.
dīgēstŭs, *the pass. partic. of* digero. Sīt dīgēstă pĕr ăgrōs, Virg.
dĭgĭtī, ōrŭm, m. pl., *the fingers.* Ēt dĭgĭtōs dĭgĭtīs, Ov. SYN. Ārtĭcŭlī. EPITH. Cāndĭdī, ĕbūrnī, rŏsĕī, nĭvĕī, mōllēs, mōllĭcŭlī, rŭbēntēs, dŏcĭlēs, fōrmōsī, tĕrĕtēs.
dīgnē, adv., *worthily.* Crŭcĕ dīgnĭŭs, Hor.
dīgnĭtās, ātĭs, f., *dignity.* Dīgnĭtās ĕquēstrĭs, (Phal.) Mart. SYN. Hŏnēstās,

hŏnŏr, splĕndŏr, dĕcŏr, dĕcŭs, ŏrnāmēntŭm. Epith. Insīgr.ĭs, ēxĭmĭă, ŏptātă, mĕrĭtă.

dīgnŏr, ārĭs, ātŭs, *to think, or be thought worthy.* Dŏmĭnōs dīgnābĕrĕ Teūcrōs, Virg. Syn. Haūd dēdīgnŏr.

dīgnōsco, ĭs, *to distinguish, discern.* Dīgnōscĕrĕ rēctŭm, Hor.

dīgnŭs, ă, ŭm, *worthy.* Dīgnĭŏr ætās, Virg. Syn. Mĕrĭtŭs, prōmĕrĭtŭs.

dīgrĕdĭŏr, ĕrĭs, *to retire.* Dīgrĕdĭĕrĕ sĭmŭl, Mant. Syn. Discēdo, ăbĕo, ēxĕo, migro, dēmigro, ēxcēdo, rēcēdo. V. Abeo.

dīgrēssŭs, ūs, m., *a departure.* Dīgrēssŭ mœstă sŭprēmō, Virg.

Dĭĭ, *or* Dī, gen. Dĕōrŭm *and* Dĕŭm, dat. abl. Dĭĭs *and* Dīs, acc. Dĕōs, pl. of Deus, *the heathen gods.* Sē deēssĕ Dĭĭs, Luc. Nōn ĕgŏ tē Dīs, Virg. Syn. Sŭpĕrī, Dīvī, Nūmĭnă, Cœlĭcŏlæ, Cœlēstēs, Cœlĭtēs. Epith. Fālsī, fīctī, ĭnānēs, vānī. V. Deus.

dījūdĭco, ās. *to discern.* Quī dījūdĭcĕt īstŭc, Lucil. Syn. Jūdĭco, dīscēpto, dīscērno, dīstĭnguo.

dīlābŏr, ĕrĭs, *to steal away.* Cŭm pācĕ dīlābēntĭs, Hor. Syn. Ēlābŏr, lābŏr.

dīlăcĕro, ās, *to tear in pieces.* Dīlăcĕrātŭs ēquīs, Prud. Syn. Lăcĕro, dīscērpo, dīlănĭo, lănĭo, dīssĕco. V. Lacero.

dīlănĭo, ās, *to mangle.* Dīlănĭātă fŏrās, Lucr. Syn. Dīlăcĕro, dīspērgo, lăcĕro, lănĭo, dīssĕco.

dīlăpĭdo, ās, *to dissipate.* Grāndĭnĕ dīlăpĭdāns, Colum. Syn. Dīspērdo, cōnsūmo. V. Lapido.

dīlāpsŭs, *the pass. partic. of* dilabor. Fŏrmă dīlāpsŭs ămo, Cl.

dīlātĭo, ōnĭs, f., *a deferring.* Jūstæ dīlātĭŏ pœnæ, Vict. Syn. Mŏră.

dīlāto, ās, *to extend.* Ipsăquĕ dīlātānt, Ov. Syn. Explĭco, ēxtēndo, prŏpāgo.

dīlātŏr, ōrĭs, m., *a delayer.* Dīlātŏr, spē lēntŭs, Hor.

dīlātŭs, *the pass. partic. of* differo. Fātŏ dīlātŭs ĭn ævŭm, Hor.

dīlēctĭo, ōnĭs, f., *love.* Est dīlēctĭŏ nōstrī, Prop. Syn. Ămŏr, stŭdĭŭm.

dīlēctŭs, *the pass. partic. of* diligo. Lūcĕ măgĭs dīlēctă sŏrōrī, Virg.

dīlēctŭs, ūs, m., *a choice.* Cætĕră dīlēctū, Ov. V. Delectus.

dīlĭgēns, ēntĭs, *diligent.* Aūrĕ dīlĭgēntī, (Phal.) Mart. Syn. Impĭgĕr, sēdŭlŭs, stŭdĭōsŭs, Indūstrĭŭs, sŏlērs, gnāvŭs, vĭgĭlāns, āssĭdŭŭs, āttēntŭs.

dīlĭgēntĕr, adv., *diligently.* Rŭfĕ, dīlĭgēntĕr, (Phal.) Mart. Syn. Stŭdĭōsē, sēdŭlo, gnāvĭtĕr, āssĭdŭē.

dīlĭgēntĭă, æ, f., *diligence.* Māgnă dīlĭgēntĭă, (Iamb.) Pl. Syn. Stŭdĭŭm, sēdŭlĭtās, Indūstrĭă, sŏlērtĭă, cūră. Epith. Laūdātă, nōbĭlĭs, prŏvĭdă, sŏlērs, ōffĭcĭōsă, sēdŭlă, gĕnĕrōsă, fōrtĭs, aūdāx, ūtĭlĭs, bŏnă.

dīlĭgo, ēxī, ēctŭm, *to cherish.* Dīlĭgĭtūr nēmo, Ov. Syn. Ămo, dēpĕrĕo, ārdĕo. V. Amo.

dīlūcĕo, ūxī, *to shine.* Tĭbĭ dīlūxīssĕ sŭprēmŭm, Hor. Syn. Illūcĕo, lūcĕo, splēndĕo.

dīlūcĭdē, adv., *clearly.* Dīlūcĭdē ēxpĕdĭvī, (Iamb.) Ter.

dīlūcĭdŭs, ă, ŭm, *clear, bright.* Rērŭm dīlūcĭdŭs ōrdo, Mant. Syn. Lūcĭdŭs, clārŭs, nĭtĭdŭs, pērspĭcŭŭs, cōnspĭcŭŭs, mănĭfēstŭs, ăpērtŭs, nōtŭs.

dīlūcŭlŭm, ī, n., *the first dawn.* Pŭdŏr sĭt ŭt dīlūcŭlŭm, (Iamb. Dim.) Ambros. Syn. Aūrōră, mānĕ. Epith. Clārŭm, nĭtĭdŭm, pērspĭcŭŭm, cōnspĭcŭŭm, rŏsĕŭm, splēndēns, rubrŭm, ālbŭm. V. Aurora, mane.

dīlūdĭŭm, ĭī, m., *repose.* Dīlūdĭă pōsco, Hor.

dīlūdo, *to elude.* Sāltū dīlūdĭt ĭnŭltŭs, Ov.

dīlŭo, ŭī, ŭtŭm, *to wash away.* Dīlŭĕrēntŭr ăquā, Prop. Syn. Ēlŭo, ăblŭo, tērgo, ābstērgo, lævo ; cōnfūto, rĕfūto.

dīlūtŭs, *the pass. partic. of* diluo. Dīlūtās quĕrĭtŭr, Pers.

dīlūvĭēs, ĭēī, f., *an inundation.* Ad dīlūvĭēm rĕvŏcātŭr, Lucr. Syn. Dīlūvĭŭm, ēlŭvĭēs.

dīlūvĭŭm, ĭī, n., *a deluge, inundation.* Dīlūvĭo ēx ĭllō, Virg. Syn. Illŭvĭēs, Inūndāntĭă. Epith. Ŭndāns, hōrrēndŭm, văgŭm, răpĭdŭm, fūrēns, tērrĭbĭlĕ, răpāx, stŭpēndŭm, trīstĕ, ĭmmītĕ, fŭrĭōsŭm, præcēps, sŭbĭtŭm, rĕpēntīnŭm, Inŏpīnŭm, Ingēns.

dīmădĕo, ēs, *to melt away.* Dīmădŭĕrĕ nĭvēs, Luc.

dīmāno, ās, *to flow away.* Ex ŏcŭlĭs lăcrўmæ dīmānānt, Sil. Syn. Māno, prōmāno, flŭo, ēmāno, dīfflŭo, prŏfĭcīscŏr.

dĭmĕtĭŏr, īrĭs, mēnsŭs, *to measure.* Nŭmĕrīs dīmēnsă vĭārŭm, Virg. Syn. Mĕtĭŏr, mēnsūro, dēfīnĭo.

dīmĭco, ās, cŭī, *to fight.* Dīmĭcĕt hāstā, Ov. Syn. Pūgno, cērto, dēcērto, cōnflīgo, cōngrĕdĭŏr. V. Pugno.

dīmĭdĭātŭs, ă, ŭm, *divided into two parts.* Vās vīnī dīmĭdĭātŭm, Enn. Syn. Mĕdĭŭs.

dīmĭdĭŭm, iī, n., *a half.* Dīmĭdĭŭm cūræ, Ov.

dīmĭdĭŭs, ă, ŭm, *half.* Cŭrĭŏs jăm dīmĭdĭŏs, Juv.

dīmĭnŭo, ŭī, ūtŭm, *to diminish.* Dīmĭnŭī sī quā, Ov. Syn. Mĭnŭo, ĭmnŭĭnŭo, ăttĕnŭo, ĕxtĕnŭo, dētrăho, tōllo, rĕsĕco, dēmo, aūfĕro.

dīmĭnūtŭs, ă, ŭm, *the pass. partic. of* diminuo. Grĕgĕ dīmĭnūtō, (Sapph.) Hor. Syn. Mĭnūtŭs, mĭnŏr.

dīmītto, īsī, īssŭm, *to send away.* Dīmīsītque ănĭmăm, Mart. Syn. Mītto, ēmītto, āmītto, rĕmītto, dēpōno.

dīmŏvĕo, mōvī, tŭm, *to move away.* Dīmŏvĕt aūrās, Virg. Syn. Pēllo, dēpēllo, pūlso, rĕmŏvĕo, dīsjĭcĭo.

Dĭndȳmă, ōrŭm, n. pl., *and* Dĭndȳmŭs, ī, m., *a mountain of Phrygia.* Pĕr āltă Dĭndȳmă, Virg. Dĭndȳmŭs, ĕt săcræ, Prop.

Dĭndȳmēnē, ēs, f., *Cybele.* Săcră Dĭndȳmēnēs, (Phal) Mart. V. Cybele.

dĭnŭmĕro, ās, *to number.* Tēmpŏră dĭnŭmĕrāns, Virg. Syn. Nŭmĕro, ēnŭmĕro, rĕcēnsĕo, pērcēnsĕo.

Dĭŏgĕnēs, ĭs, m., *the Cynic.* Dĭŏgĕnēs Crœsŭm, Comm. Epith. Dōctŭs, pĕrītŭs, ĭnŏps, paūpĕr, mēndīcŭs, cōnstāns.

Dĭŏmēdēs, ĭs, m., *the king of Ætolia.* Nūnc quālēs Dĭŏmēdĭs ĕquī, Virg. Syn. Tȳdīdēs, Œnīdēs. Epith. Fōrtĭs, ĭmpĭŭs, atrōx, Ætōlŭs, Ætōlĭŭs, Călȳdōnĭŭs.— 2. *the king of Thrace, vanquished by Hercules.* Crūdī Dĭŏmēdĭs ĭmăgo, Ov. Epith. Thrāx, Thrēĭcĭŭs, Gĕtĭcŭs, Bīstŏnĭŭs ; trūx, crūdŭs, sāngŭĭnĕŭs, crŭēntŭs, ĭmmānĭs, ĭmmītĭs, ĭmpĭŭs, āspĕr.

Dĭŏmēdēŭs, ă, ŭm, *of Diomedes.* Ět Dĭŏmēdēōs, Ov.

Dĭŏnæŭs, ă, ŭm, *of Venus.* Eccĕ Dĭŏnæī, Virg.

Dĭŏnē, ēs, f., *Venus.* Tēmplă Dĭŏnēs, St. V. Venus.

Dĭŏnȳsĭŭs, iī, m., *the name of some Syracusan tyrants.* Epith. Impĭŭs, dīrŭs, crūdēlĭs, bārbărŭs, atrōx, trūx, sacrĭlĕgŭs, Sĭcŭlŭs.

Dĭŏnȳsŭs, ī, m., *a name of Bacchus.* Dĭŏnȳsōn Indī, Aus.

Dĭŏrēs, ĭs, m., *the name of a warrior.* Dē stīrpĕ Dĭŏrēs, Virg.

|| dĭōtă, æ, f., *a jar with two ears.* Mĕrŭm dĭōtă, Hor.

Dĭŏxīppŭs, ī, m., *the name of a warrior.* Dĭŏxīppūm, Prŏmŏlūmquĕ, Virg.

dīpsăs, ădĭs, f., *a kind of serpent.* Dīpsădăs ĭmmēnsīs, Sil. Epith. Vĕnēnōsă, mōrdāx, ārĭdă, răpĭdă, tōrtă, tōrrĭdă, ūrēns, ăquătĭcă. V. Serpens.

Dīræ, ārŭm, f. pl., *the Furies.* Ăt prŏcŭl ŭt Dīræ, Virg. V. Furiæ.

Dīrcæŭs, ă, ŭm, *of Dirce, Theban.* Ămphīōn Dīrcæŭs, Virg.

Dīrcē, ēs, f., *a fountain near Thebes.* Āggĕrĕ Dīrcēs, Stat. Epith. Sŏnŏră, cærŭlă, Aŏnĭă, Cādmēĭă, Cādmæă, Ismēnĭs.

dīrēctŭs, ă, ŭm, *the pass. partic. of* dirigo. Mŏdŏ dīrēctō cōntēndĕrĕ pāssŭ, Tib.

dīrēptŭs, ă, ŭm, *the pass. partic. of* diripio. Dīrēptīsquĕ cŏmīs, Prop.

dīrĭgĕo, ŭī, *to grow stiff.* Dīrĭgŭīt vīsū, Virg. Syn. Rĭgĕo, rĭgēsco, ōbrĭgĕo, hōrrĕo.

dīrĭgo, ēxī, ēctŭm, *to direct.* Dīrĭgĭt īctū, Virg. Syn. Rĕgo, ōrdĭno, cōmpōno, dīspōno ; tēndo.

dĭrĭmo, ēmī, ēmptŭm, *to interrupt.* Cærŭlĕŭm dĭrĭmēbăt, Pers. Syn. Dīvĭdo, dīstrăho, sēpăro, dēcīdo.

dĭrĭpĭo, pŭī, rēptŭm, *to plunder.* Dīrĭpŭĕrĕ Nŏtī, Prop. Syn. Răpĭo, prædŏr, dēprædŏr, pŏpŭlŏr, dēpŏpŭlŏr, vāsto. V. Prædor.

dīrŭo, ŭī, ŭtŭm, *to throw down.* Dīrŭīt, ædĭfĭcăt, Hor. Syn. Dērĭpĭo, pērdo, ēvērto, dēstrŭo. V. Everto.

dīrŭs, ă, ŭm, *cruel.* Dīrŭs Ŭlȳssēs, Virg. Syn. Crūdēlĭs, sævŭs, dūrŭs, atrōx.

dīrŭtŭs, ă, ŭm, *the pass. partic. of* diruo. Dīrŭtă sūnt ălĭīs, Ov.

Dīs, Dītĭs, m., *Pluto.* Jānŭă Dītĭs, Virg. V. Pluto.

dĭs, dĭtĭs ; dītĭŏr, tīssĭmŭs, *rich.* Dēspĭcĭăm dītēs, Tib. Dītĭŏr ; aūrō, St. Hūmānī dītīssĭmŭs ævī, Sil. V. Dives.

dīscēdo, ssī, ssŭm, *to go away.* Sī tŭ dīscēdĕrĕ pŏssīs, Ov. SYN. Ăbĕo, ĕxĕo, cēdo, rĕcēdo, ēxcēdo, fŭgĭo, ēffŭgĭo, migro, dēmigro, dēcēdo. V. Abeo.

dīscēpto, ās, *to debate.* Cic. SYN. Dīspŭto, dēcērto, cōntēndo, cērto.

dīscērnĭcŭlŭm, ī, n., *a bodkin.* Dīscērnĭcŭlŭmquĕ, Lucil.

dīscērno, crēvī, crētŭm, *to distinguish.* Tēlās dīscrēvērăt aūrō, Virg. SYN. Dījŭdĭco, dīstīnguo, īntērnōsco, dīvĭdo, dīscrīmĭno.

dīscērpo, psī, ptŭm, *to pluck into pieces.* Dīscērpĭtŭr aūrŭm, Lucr. SYN. Dīlănĭo, dīssĕco, dīscīndo, lănĭo, lăcĕro. V. Lacero.

dīscēssŭs, ūs, m., *a departure.* Dīscēssŭ fērrĕ dŏlōrĕm, Virg.

dīscĭdĭŭm, ĭī, n., *a division.* Dīscĭdĭŭm părĕrĕ, Lucr.

dīscīndo, cĭdī, cīssŭm, *to cut asunder.* Vīdĕō dīscīndĕrĕ cœlŭm, Virg. SYN. Scīndo, sĕco, dīscērpo, dīvēllo. V. Scindo.

dīscīngo, xī, ctŭm, *to ungird.* Scȳthĭcō dīscīnxĭt Ămāzŏnă, Mart.

dīscĭplīnă, æ, f., *discipline, science.* Mŭnĕră dīscĭplīnæ, (Sp.) Aus. Dīscĭplīna īnfāntĭæ ēst, Prud. SYN. Dōctrīnă, ārs, scīĕntĭă. V. Artes.

dīscĭpŭlŭs, ī, m., ă, æ, f., *a pupil.* Dūc ăgĕ dīscĭpŭlōs, Ov. SYN. Aŭdītŏr.

dīsclŭdo, sī, sŭm, *to open, to separate.* Ēt dīsclŭdĕrĕ Nērĕă pōntŏ, Virg. SYN. Dīsjūngo, sēpăro, reclŭdo.

dīsco, dĭdĭcī, *to learn.* Jăm dĭdĭcī Gĕtĭcĕ, Ov. SYN. Ēdīsco, āddīsco, pērdīsco, pērcĭpĭo, cōgnōsco. V. Studeo.

dīscŏlŏr, ōrĭs, *of various colours.* Dīscŏlŏr hŏstĕ, Mart. SYN. Cŏlōrĕ dīspār, vărĭŭs, dīssĭmĭlĭs, dīvērsŭs.

dīscōnvĕnĭo, vēnī, vēntŭm, *to disagree.* Dīscōnvĕnĭt ōrdĭnĕ tōtŏ, Hor.

dīscōrdĭă, æ, f., *discord.* Cŏmĭs dīscōrdĭă rēgnĭs, Stat. SYN. Dīssēnsŭs, dīssēnsĭo, dīssĭdĭŭm, cērtāmĕn, cōntēntĭo, rīxă, præ1ĭŭm, līs, sēdĭtĭo, pūgnă. EPITH. Dēmēns, fĕrŏx, ēxĭtĭālĭs, flagrāns, pērnĭcĭōsă, īnvĭdă, crūdēlĭs, sævă, præcēps, bārbără, crŭēntă, āmēns, īnsānă, lītĭgĭōsă, īmmītĭs, fĕră, ēffrēnĭs, bēllĭcă, cæcă, fŭnēstă, trŭcŭlēntă, hōrrĭdă, ātră, īnhŭmānă, īmmānĭs, fĕrālĭs. V. Seditio.

dīscōrdo, ās, *to disagree.* Dīscōrdēt pārcŭs ăvārŏ, Hor.

dīscōrs, ōrdĭs, *jarring, discordant.* Dīscōrdĭbŭs ārmĭs, Virg. SYN. Dīssŏnŭs, ādvērsŭs, cōntrārĭŭs, īnfēnsŭs.

dīscrĕpĭto, ās, *freq. of* discrepo. Dīscrĕpĭtānt rēs, Lucr.

dīscrĕpo, ās, pŭī, *to give a different sound, to dissent.* Dīscrĕpăt īpsŏ, Mart. SYN. Dīssēntĭo, dīssĭdĕo, dīsto, ābsŭm; dīffĕro, sŭm dīssĭmĭlĭs, dīspār.

dīscrētŭs, ă, ŭm, *the pass. partic. of* discerno. Hīc ŭbĭ dīscrētăs, Ov.

dīscrīmĕn, ĭnĭs, n., *difference, danger.* Dīscrīmĕn ĕrĭt, dīscrīmĭnă laūdă, Ov. SYN. Dīssĭdĭŭm; pērĭcŭlŭm. EPITH. Sævŭm, dūrŭm, ăncēps, lēthălĕ, dīrŭm. V. Periculum.

dīscrīmĭno, ās, *to distinguish.* Vēstēs dīscrīmĭnăt aūrō, Lucr. SYN. Dīstīnguo, dīscērno.

dīscrŭcĭo, ās, *to torment.* Vērtĭcĕ dīscrŭcĭŏr, Cat. SYN. Crŭcĭo, tōrquĕo, vēxo. V. Crucio, Affligo.

dīscŭmbo, ŭbŭī, *to lie down.* Dīscŭmbĭtŭr ōstrŏ, Virg. SYN. Ăccŭmbo.

dīscŭpĭo, ĭs, īvī *or* ĭī, ĕrĕ, *to wish for.* Vēndĕrĕ dīscŭpĕrĕ, Cat.

dīscūrro, cūrrī, cūrsŭm, *to run to and fro.* Tōtă dīscūrrĭtŭr ūrbĕ, Virg. SYN. Ăccūrro, cōncūrro, cūrro. V. Curro.

dīscūrso, ās, *freq. of* discurro. Dīscūrsăt ărānĕă tēlă, Mart.

dīscŭs, ī, m., *a quoit.* Fīndĕrĕt āĕră dīscŏ, Stat.

dīscŭtĭo, ūssī, ūssŭm, *to shake, discuss.* Dīscŭtĭāmŭs ĕŏrŭm, Paul. SYN. Dīspēllo, rĕmŏvĕo, tōllo; ēxcŭtĭo, ăgĭto, quătĭo, quāsso; ēxămĭno.

dīsērtŭs, ă, ŭm, *copious, eloquent.* Lĭcĕt ēssĕ dĭsērtŏ, Ov. SYN. Făcūndŭs, ēlŏquēns. V. Eloquens.

dīsjēcto, ās, *freq. of* disjicio. Dīsjēctārĕ sŏlĕt, Lucr.

dīsjĭcĭo, jēcī, jēctŭm, *to scatter.* Dīsjĭcĭt, ēt spārsŏ, Virg. SYN. Dīssĭpo, spārgo, dīvĭdo, dīspērgo.

dīsjūngo, xī, nctŭm, *to put asunder.* Lōngĕ dīsjūngĭmŭr ōrĭs, Virg. SYN. Ăbjūngo, dīvĭdo, sēpăro.

|| dīspāndo, ĭs, dī, sŭm, *to extend.* Vēstēs dīspānsæ, Lucr.

dīspār, ărĭs, *different.* Ēst mĭhĭ dīspărĭbŭs, Virg. V. Dissimilis.

dīspărĭtās, ātĭs, f., *disparity.* Dīspărĭtās ănĭmĭs, Mart. SYN. Dīssĭmĭlĭtŭdo, vărĭĕtās.

dispăro, ās, *to sever.* Ĭn ăllĭam dĭspărăt, (Iamb.) Sen. Syn. Dīsjŭngo, sējŭngo, sēpăro.

dispĕllo, pŭlī, pŭlsŭm, *to dispel.* Dīspŭlĕrăt pĕnĭtŭs,Virg. Syn. Dīscŭtĭo, dīsjĭcĭo, pĕllo, ēxpēllo.

dispēndĭŭm, īī, n., *damage.* Dīspēndĭă tāntī, Virg. Syn. Dāmnŭm, dētrī-mēntŭm, ĭncōmmŏdŭm. V. Damnum.

dispēnsātŏr, ōrĭs, m., *a dispenser.* Dīspēnsātŏrĕ vĭdēbĭs, Juv.

dispēnso, ās, *to distribute.* Tŭm quœ dispēnsānt, Ov.

dispērdo, ĭs, *to dissipate.* Stĭpŭlā dīspērdĕrĕ cārmĕn, Virg.

dispērĕo, īs, īī, *to die.* Dīspĕrīt ōmnĭs, Luc. Syn. Pĕrĕo.

dispērgo, pērsī, sŭm, *to scatter.* Vītăm dīspērgĭt ĭn aūrās, Virg. Syn. Spārgo, dīssēmĭno, dīffūndo, ēffūndo, prōjĭcĭo.

dispērtĭo, īs, *and* ĭor, ĭrĭs, *to distribute.* Dīspērtītŭr ŭt hōrrŏr, Lucr.

dispĭcĭo, spēxī, ctŭm, *to look about.* Dīspĭcīt ōmnĕ, Ov.

displĭcĕo, cŭī, *to displease.* Dīsplĭcŭīssĕ vĭrō, Ov. Syn. Nōn plăcĕo, nōn ārrīdĕo, sum ŏdĭōsŭs, ĭngrātŭs, ĭnjūcŭndŭs.

displōdo, sī, sŭm, *to break with a noise.* Năm dīsplōsă sŏnăt, Hor.

dispōno, pŏsŭī, sĭtŭm, *to dispose.* Tŏtŭs dīspōnĭtŭr ōrbĭs, Tib. Syn. Cōmpōno, dīrĭgo, ōrdĭno.

dispŭdĕt, *to be ashamed of.* Dīspŭdŭīssĕ fĕrŭnt, Ov.

dispŭtātĭo, ōnĭs, f., *a dispute, debate.* Dōctă dīspŭtātĭo, (Iamb.) Calph. Syn. Cōntēntĭo, lĭs, pūgnă.

dispŭto, ās, *to debate.* Dīspŭtăt cōnvīvĭŭm, (Iamb.) Mart. Syn. Dīscēpto, cōn-tēndo, rīxŏr; dīssēro.

disquīro, īs, sīvī *and* sĭī, sĭtŭm, *to search.* Mēcŭm dīsquīrĭtĕ, cŭr hŏc, Hor. Syn. Quœro, īnquīro, scrūtŏr, īnvēstĭgo.

dissēco, ās, cŭī, ctŭm, *to cut asunder.* Dīssĕcārēnt ŭvĭdī, · (Iamb.) Syn. Sĕco, lănĭo, dīlănĭo, dīscērpo, scĭndo, dīscĭndo. V. Lacero.

* dissēmĭno, ās, *to sow, spread, publish.* Syn. Sēmĭno, spārgo, dīspērgo ; dīssĭpo ; vŭlgo, dīvūlgo.

dissēnsĭo, ōnĭs, f., *and* sŭs, ŭs, m., *a dissent.* Dīssēnsŭsque ălĭtŭr, Cl. Syn. Dīs-cōrdĭă, dīssĭdĭŭm. V. Discordia.

dissēntĭo, īs, sī, sŭm, *to dissent.* Dīssēntīrĕ vĭdēntŭr, Hor. Syn. Dīscrēpo, dīssĭdĕo, vărĭo.

dissēpĭo, īs, psī, ptŭm, *to separate, divide.* Āēr dīssēpĭt cōllēs, Lucr.

dissēptŭm, ī, n., *an inclosure, wall.* Dīssēptă dōmōrŭm, Lucr.

dissēro, ŭī, *to discourse.* Dīssĕrĕ quālēs, Prud. Syn. Lŏquŏr, nārro, ēnārro, dīco, ēdīssēro ; dīspŭto, dīscēpto.

dissērpo, ĭs, ĕrĕ, *to spread.* Dīssērpŭnt īndĕ trĕmōrēs, Lucr.

dissĭdĕo, ēdī, *to disagree.* Dīssĭdĕt īllĕ, Ov. Syn. Dīssēntĭo, dīscrēpo, dīscōrdo.

dissĭdĭŭm, īī, n., *a dissent.* Dīssĭdĭŭm nōn ēst, Mart. V. Discordia.

dissĭlĭo, īs, īī *and* ŭī, sŭltŭm, *to leap here and there.* Dīssĭlŭīssĕ fĕrŭnt, Virg. Syn. Dīssŭlto ; dīscēdo.

dissĭmĭlĭs, ĕ, *different.* Illĭs dīssĭmĭlēs, Juv. Syn. Nōn sĭmĭlĭs, ābsĭmĭlĭs, dīs-pār, īmpār, dīvērsŭs, vărĭŭs, dīscrēpăns, ĭnœquălĭs.

dissĭmĭlāntĕr, adv., *dissemblingly.* Dīssĭmĭlāntĕr ădī, Ov.

dissĭmŭlātŏr, ōrĭs, m., *a dissembler.* Dīssĭmŭlātŏr ĕrĭs, Mart. Syn. Sĭmŭlātŏr, fīctŏr, fāllāx.

dissĭmŭlo, ās, *to dissemble.* Dīssĭmŭlārĕ ĕtĭăm, Virg. Syn. Fīngo, sĭmŭlo, ōccūlto, cōnnīvĕo.

dissĭpo, ās, *to dissipate.* Dīssĭpăt ōrĕ, Ov. Syn. Spārgo, dīspērgo, dīsjĭcĭo, cōnsūmo, ābsūmo, pērdo, prŏfūndo.

dissĭtŭs, ă, ŭm, *set far distant.* Dīssĭtă cōrpŭs, Lucr. Syn. Rĕmōtŭs, dīsjūnctŭs, dīstāns.

dissŏcĭābĭlĭs, ĕ, *which may be separated.* Ōcĕānŏ dīssŏcĭābĭlī, Hor.

dissŏcĭo, ās, *to disjoin.* Dīssŏcĭātă lŏcĭs, Ov. Syn. Dīsjŭngo, sēpăro, sēpōno, sēgrēgo.

dissōlvo, sōlvī, sŏlūtŭm, *to dissolve.* Dīssōlvĕ frīgŭs, Hor. Syn. Sōlvo, dīlŭo, rĕsōlvo ; ăpĕrĭo, reclūdo ; ēxpēdĭo.

dissŏlūtŭs, ă, ŭm, *the pass. partic. of* dissolvo. Dīssŏlūtĭs prīstĭnōrŭm, (Trocb.) Prud.

dīssŏnŭs, ă, ŭm, *dissonant.* Dīssŏnă vŭlgī, Lucr. Syn. Absŏnŭs, nōn cōnsŏnŭs, dīscōrs.

dīssuădĕo, suāsī, sŭm, *to dissuade.* Hīnc dīssuādĕt ămŏr, Ov. Syn. Dēhŏrtŏr, dētērrĕo.

dīssūlto, ās, *to break asunder.* Dīssūltānt crĕpĭtŭs, Virg. Syn. Dīssĭlĭo, rĕsūlto ; dīscēdo.

dīssŭo, ĭs, *to unstitch.* Altĕră dīssūtŏ, Ov.

|| dīstāntĭă, æ, f., *distance.* Quædăm dīstāntĭă fŏrmīs, Lucr. Syn. Spătĭŭm, dīscrīmĕn.

dīstāns, āntĭs, *distant, remote.* Dīstāntĭbŭs īllīs, Ov.

dīstēndo, ĭs, dī, sŭm, *to extend.* Dūlcī dīstēndūnt nēctărĕ cēllās, Virg. Syn. Extēndo ; replĕo.

dīstērmĭno, ās, *to bound, separate.* Dīstērmĭnăt ārvă, Lucr.

dīstĭchŏn, ī, n., *a distich.* Dīstĭchă paŭcă, Mart.

dīstīllo, ās, *to distil.* Tēmpŏră dīstīllānt, Tib. Syn. Stillo.

dīstĭnĕo, ŭī, *to detain.* Dīstĭnĕt hŏstĕm, Virg. Syn. Tĕnĕo, rĕtĭnĕo, dētĭnĕo, tārdo, mŏrŏr, rĕmŏrŏr ; īmpĕdĭo, ōccŭpo.

dīstīnguo, xī, ctŭm, *to distinguish.* Vērŏ dīstīnguĕrĕ fālsŭm, Hor. Syn. Dīscērno, dīscrīmĭno : sēpăro ; vărĭo.

dīsto, ās, *to be distant.* Īntĕr sē dīstărĕ fĭgūrīs, Lucr. Syn. Absŭm, sēpărŏr, sēmŏvĕŏr, sējūngŏr, sŭm rĕmŏtŭs, dīssĭtŭs ; dīscrĕpo, dīffĕro.

dīstŏrquĕo, sī, tŭm, *to wrest aside.* Dīstŏrquēns ŏcŭlōs, Hor. Syn. Īntŏrquĕo, rĕtŏrquĕo, tŏrquĕo.

dīstrāctŭs, ă, ŭm, *the pass. partic.* of distraho. Ac dīstrāctĭŏr īntŭs, Lucr.

dīstrăho, xī, ctŭm, *to pull asunder.* Dīstrăhĭtūr măgĭs, Lucr. Syn. Sēpăro, sējūngo, dīsjūngo, dīvēllo, dīdūco, ābstrăho.

dīstrĭbŭo, ŭī, ūtŭm, *to distribute.* Dīstrĭbŭēndă pĭos, M. Syn. Dīvĭdo, pārtĭŏr, dīspērtĭŏr, trĭbŭo.

dīstrīngo, xī, ctŭm, *to strain, to graze.* Sūmmūm dīstrīnxĭt, Ov.

* dīstūrbo, ās, *to throw down,* Plaut. Syn. Dīsjĭcĭo, ēvērto, dīrŭo.

dītēsco, ĭs, *to grow rich.* Ēt dītēscĕrĕ prædă, Lucr.

dīthȳrāmbŭs, ī, m., *a dithyramb.* Nŏvă dīthȳrāmbōs, (Sapph.) Hor.

dĭtĭo, ōnĭs, f., *power.* Ōmnī dĭtĭŏnĕ tĕnērēnt, Virg. Syn. Pŏtēstās, īmpĕrĭŭm.

dīto, ās, *to enrich.* Hŏmĭnūm dītărĕ cătērvās, Cl.

dĭū, adv., *a long time.* Phœbĕ, dĭū, Virg.

dīvă, æ, f., *a goddess.* Dīvă pŏtēns, Hor. Syn. Dĕă.

dīvēllo, vŭlsī, sŭm, *to tear away.* Āmplēxū dīvēllĕrĕr ūsquăm, Virg.

dīvērbĕro, ās, *to strike.* Vŏlŭcrēs dīvērbĕrăt aŭrās, Virg. V. Verbero.

dīvērbĭŭm, ĭī, n., *a parley.* Mĕmŏrēm dīvērbĭă cŏgĕ, Aus.

dīvērsōrĭŭm, ĭī, n., *an inn.* Ēt dīvērsōrĭă nŏtă, Hor. Syn. Hŏspĭtĭŭm, dŏmŭs.

dīvērsŭs, ă, ŭm, *different.* Dīvērsōs ŭbī sēnsĭt, Virg. Syn. Dīssĭmĭlīs, dīspār, vărĭŭs, dīscrĕpāns, ălĭŭs.

dīvērtĭcŭlŭm, ī, n., *a turning.* Ā dīvērtĭcŭlŏ, Juv. Syn. Dīvērsōrĭŭm ; sēmĭtă, trāmĕs.

dīvērto, tī, sŭm, *to turn aside.* Mōllī dīvērtĭtūr ōrbĭtă clīvŏ, Virg. Syn. Dē *or* ex vĭā dēflēcto : ălĭo ĭtĕr flēcto, fĕro ; ălĭŏ fĕrŏr. V. Hospitor.

dīvĕs, ĭtĭs, *rich.* Dīvĕs ŏpŭm, Virg. Syn. Lŏcŭplēs, ŏpŭlēntŭs, dītīssĭmŭs, prædīvĕs.

dīvĭtĭŏr, ŭs, *compar.* of dives. Dīvĭtĭŏră mĕī, Ov.

dīvĭdo, vīsī, sŭm, *to divide.* Dīvĭdĭmŭs mūrōs, Virg. Syn. Sēpăro, dīsjūngo, dīstrăho, dīstīnguo, pārtĭŏr, dīspērtĭŏr, dīstrĭbŭo īn pārtēs, sēco, dīssēco, frāngo. dīvĭdŭŭs *or* dŭs, ă, ŭm, *divided.* Ēt mĭhī dīvĭdŭŏ, Hor. Dīvĭdă rūră, Ov.

Dīvīnĭtās, ātĭs, f., *godhead.* Dīvīnĭtātĭs vīm cŏrŭscāntĕm, (Iamb.) Prud. Syn. Dĕĭtās ; dīvīnūm nūmĕn : Dĕī mājēstās.

dīvīnĭtŭs, adv., *from God.* Sīt dīvīnĭtŭs īllīs, Virg. Syn. Ēx Dĕō, cælĭtŭs.

dīvīno, ās, *to foretel.* Ūt dīvīnātŭs, Ovid. Syn. Vātĭcĭnŏr, aŭgŭrŏr, cōnjĭcĭo, prædīco, ĭs ; hărĭŏlŏr. V. Auguror.

dīvīnŭs, ă, ŭm, *heavenly.* Cănĭt dīvīno ēx ŏrĕ săcērdōs, Virg. Syn. Dīvŭs, æthĕrĕŭs, cælēstĭs.—2. -nŭs, ī, m., *and* -nă, æ, f., *a diviner.* Nŏn sŭm dīvīnŭs, Mart. Īmbrĭŭm dīvīna ăvĭs, Hor.

dīvīsŭs, ă, ŭm, *the pass. partic. of* divido. Tŏtŏ dīvīsōs ōrbĕ Brĭtānnōs, Virg. V. Divido.

dīvĭtĭæ, ārŭm, f. pl., *riches.* Dīvĭtĭīs hŏmĭnēs, Hor.   Syn. Ŏpēs, fŏrtūnæ, cōpĭæ, gāzæ, nūmmī, thēsaūrī, pĕcūnĭă, aūrŭm, ārgēntŭm.   Epith. Improbæ, mĭsēræ, rēgālēs, pŏtēntēs, īnvĭdĭōsæ, ŏpĕrōsæ, măgnæ, īngēntēs, prētĭōsæ, sŭpērbæ, vānæ, fŭgĭtīvæ, fŭgācēs, pĕrĭtūræ, flūxæ, cădūcæ, mōllēs, blāndæ, grātæ, nĕfāndæ.   V. Potentia *and* regius.

dĭŭm, ī, n., *the open air.*   Sŭb dīō mŏrērĭs, (Iamb. cum Syll.) Hor.

dīvōrtĭŭm, ī, n., *a dissent, a passage.*   Spārgīt dīvōrtĭă pōntī, Luc.   Syn. Dīscōrdĭă, dīssēnsĭo, dīssĭdĭŭm, līs ; dīvērtĭcŭlŭm, sēmĭtă.

dĭūrnŭs, ă, ŭm, *lasting a day.*   Fātă dĭūrnă, Ov.

|| dĭŭs, ă, ŭm, *heavenly.*   Sĭbĭ dĭă Cămīllă, Virg.   Syn. Dīvīnŭs; gĕnĕrōsŭs, īllūstrĭs.

dĭūtĭnŭs, *and* ŭtūrnŭs, ă, ŭm, *long, continued.*   Văpōr dĭūtĭnŭs, (Iamb. Dim.) Prud.   Dĭūtūrnĭōr ēssĕt, Ov.

dīvūlgo, ās, *to publish.*   Dīvūlgātă vĕtŭs, Lucr.   Syn. Vūlgo, ēvūlgo, pērvūlgo, spārgo.

dīvūlsŭs, ă, ŭm, *the pass. partic. of* divello.   Et dīvūlsă rĕpēntĕ, Lucr.

Dīvŭs, ī, m., *a God.*   Nŭmĕrŭm Dīvōrum āltārĭbŭs aūgĕt, Virg.   Syn. Dĕŭs, nūmĕn.—2. ă, ŭm, *divine.*   Syn. Dīvīnŭs.

dŏ, dĕdī, dătŭm, dărĕ, *to give.*   Sīc ĕgŏ dō pœnās, Ov.   Syn. Dōno, præbĕo, trĭbŭo, lārgĭōr, īmpērtĭo ; īmpērtĭōr ; trādo ; sŭppĕdĭto ; pērmītto, cōncēdo.   V. Dono, as.

dŏcĕo, cŭī, ctŭm, *to teach.*   Adhĭbĕtĕ, dŏcēbo, Virg.   Syn. Ēdŏcĕo, ōstēndo, mōnstro, īndĭco ; īnstrŭo, ērŭdĭo.

dŏcĭlĭs, ĕ, *apt to learn.*   Dŏcĭlēs ĭmĭtāndĭs, Juv.   Syn. Dīscĭplīnæ, dōctrīnæ căpāx ; āptŭs ăd ārtēs ; făcĭlĭs, trāctābĭlĭs, mītĭs.

dŏctē, adv., *learnedly.*   Dŏctĭŭs ūnctĭs.   Syn. Scītē, pĕrītē.

dŏctĭlŏquŭs, ă, ŭm, *eloquent.*   Dŏctĭlŏquī mŏrĭētŭr, Aug.   V. Doctus, eloquens.

dŏctŏr, ōrĭs, m., *a teacher, a doctor.*   Dŏctŏr ārgūtæ, (Sapph.) Hor.   Syn. Măgīstĕr, præcēptŏr.   Epith. Pĕrītŭs, sēdŭlŭs, īmpĭgĕr,· sĕvērŭs, rĭgĭdŭs, āspĕr, dūrŭs, blāndŭs, īnsīgnĭs, cēlĕbĕr.   V. Magister.

dŏctrīnă, æ, f., *learning, doctrine.*   Dŏctrīnæ prĕtĭŭm, Ov.   Syn. Ērŭdĭtĭo, scĭēntĭă, dŏcŭmēntŭm, præcēptŭm, dīscĭplīnă, ārs.   Epith. Sĕnīlĭs, lăbōrĭōsă, hŏnōrāndă, ūtĭlĭs, pūlchră, īnsīgnĭs, præclāră, īngĕnĭōsă, nōbĭlĭs.

dŏctŭs, ă, ŭm, *learned.*   Dŏctŭs ĭtĕr, Hor.   Syn. Ērŭdītŭs, pĕrītŭs, haūd īgnārŭs, nōn nēscĭŭs.

dŏcŭmĕn, ĭnĭs, *or* mēntŭm, ī, n., *a precept.*   Dŏcŭmēn mōrtālĭbŭs ācrĕ, Lucr.   Et dŏcŭmēntă dămŭs, Ov.   Syn. Præcēptŭm, præscrīptŭm, mŏnĭtŭm.

Dōdōnă, æ, *and* ē, ēs, f., *a town and forest of Epirus.*   Vīctŭm Dōdōnă nĕgārĕt, Virg.   Epith. Fĕrāx, glāndĭfĕră, cēlsă, vĕtŭs, sacră.

Dōdōnæŭs. dōnĭŭs, ă, ŭm, *or* dōnĭs, f., *of Dodona.*   Ārgēntŭm, Dōdōnæōsquĕ lĕbētās, Virg.   Invēntīs Dōdōnĭă quērcŭs, Cl.   Dōdōnĭdă quērcŭm, V. Fl.   Syn. Chāonĭŭs.

dōgmă, ătĭs, n., *a decree.*   Dōgmātă sīc sĕquĕrĭs, Mart.   Syn. Plăcĭtŭm, dēcrētŭm, sēntēntĭă, scītŭm.   Epith. Cērtŭm, clārŭm, pērspĭcŭŭm, cōnstāns, rĕcēptŭm, trītŭm, vūlgārĕ, nōbĭlĕ, āntīquŭm.

|| dōgmătĭcŭs, ă, ŭm, *dogmatical.*   Dōgmătĭcās ăgĭtăt, Aus.

dōdrāns, āntĭs, *three-fourths of a sum.*   Sōlvĕrĕ dōdrāntĕm, Mart.

dŏlābră, æ, f., *a chip-axe.*   Cāstră dŏlābrā, Juv.   Syn. Āscĭă, sĕcūrĭs.

dŏlēntĕr, adv., *sorrowfully.*   Vīdīssĕ dŏlēntĭŭs īgnēs, Ov.   Syn. Mœstē, trīstĭŭs, cŭm gĕmĭtū.

dŏlĕo, ŭī, *to be in pain, to grieve.*   Aūt dŏlŭīt mĭsĕrāns, Virg.   Syn. Indŏlĕo, gĕmo, īngĕmo.   V. Queror, dolor.

Dŏlĭchŏs, ī, m., *a man's name.*   Cāstŏr scĭăt ān Dŏlĭchŏs, Hor.

dōlĭŭm, ī, n., *a tub.*   Dōlĭă Bācchō, Prop.   Syn. Cădŭs.   Epith. Ĭnānĕ, spūmāns, dūlcĕ, fictĭlĕ, căvŭm, rīmōsŭm, āmplŭm, căpāx, prŏfūndŭm, pĭcātŭm.   V. Cadus.

dŏlo, ās, *to cut smooth.*   Frăgĭlī dŏlātŭs ūlmō, (Phal.) Mart.   Syn. Lævīgo, cælo, scŭlpo.

dŏlo, ōnĭs, m, *a sword concealed in a stick.*   In bēllă dŏlōnēs, Virg.   Epith. Tĕrēs, dūrŭs, sævŭs, vălĭdŭs.

• Dŏlōn, ōnĭs, m., *a Trojan spy, slain by Ulysses and Diomed.* Præclărā Dŏlōnĭs, Virg. Epith. Cĕlĕr, vēlōx, pērnix, āntīquŭs, ĭmbēllĭs, fŭgāx.

Dŏlōpēs, ŭm, m. pl., *a people of Thessaly.* Hīc Dŏlŏpŭm mănŭs, Virg.

dŏlŏr, ōrĭs, m., *pain, anguish.* Vērīsquĕ dŏlōrĭbŭs ādsĭt, Hor. Syn. Mœrŏr, āngŏr, trīstĭtĭă, crŭcĭātŭs, ærŭmnă. Epith. Crūdēlĭs, grăvĭs, sævŭs, ācērbŭs, ĭntŏlĕrābĭlĭs, quĕrŭlŭs, mœstŭs, ĭnfēlix, sōllĭcĭtŭs, fĕrŭs, āltŭs, ŏccūltŭs, ŭlŭlāns, răbĭdŭs, ægĕr, dīrŭs, mĭsĕr, ācērbŭs, āspĕr, ĭntēstīnŭs, mălŭs, ārdēns, crūdŭs, ăcūtŭs, ĭngrātŭs, ĭnsānŭs, vēsānŭs, ămārŭs, ĭndŏmĭtŭs, vĭŏlēntŭs, trīstĭs, atrōx, gĕmĕbūndŭs, flēbĭlĭs, ĭmpătĭēns, pērvĭgĭl, ānxĭŭs, fūnĕrĕŭs, ĭrrĕquĭētŭs, vĭgĭl. V. Luctus.

dŏlōsŭs, ă, ŭm, *cunning.* Fōrtĕ dŏlōsă, Hor. Syn. Fāllāx, āstūtŭs, cāllĭdŭs, caūtŭs, văfĕr.

dŏlŭs, ī, m., *artifice.* Nĕ quā scīrĕ dŏlōs, Virg. Syn. Fraūs, āstŭs, fāllācĭă, āstūtĭă, ĭnsĭdĭæ. Epith. Tŭrpĭs, mălŭs, ŏccūltŭs, cāllĭdŭs, caūtŭs, hōstīlĭs, cōmpŏsĭtŭs, scĕlēstŭs, fīctŭs, ĭnfīdŭs, ĭnŏpīnŭs, vērsūtŭs, tăcĭtŭs, tēctŭs, ābdĭtŭs, mĕtŭēndŭs, ĭmplēxŭs, pērvĭgĭl, văfĕr, sēcrētŭs, fālsŭs, fāllāx, vărĭŭs, lāscīvŭs, bĭlīnguĭs, nōctūrnŭs, lătēns, sōlērs, săgāx, ĭnsĭdĭōsŭs. V. Fraus, fallacia.

dŏmābĭlĭs, ĕ, *easy to be subdued.* Dŏmābĭlĕ flāmmă, Ov.

dŏmātŏr, ōrĭs, m., *one who subdues.* Tērgă dŏmātŏr, Tib. Syn. Dŏmĭtŏr, dēbēllātŏr, vīctŏr.

dŏmēstĭcŭs, ă, ŭm, *domestic.* Dēnsōquĕ dŏmēstĭcŭs ūsŭ, Ov.

dŏmĭnă, æ, f., *a lady, mistress.* Dŏmĭnāmquĕ rŭēntĕm, Virg. Syn. Grātă, sŭpērbă, pŭlchră ; fāllāx, pŏtēns.

dŏmĭnātĭo, ōnĭs, f., *and* ŭs, ūs, m., *power.* Sīmplēx dŏmĭnātĭŏ rērŭm, Prud. Āstrōrŭm dŏmĭnātŭs ăgĭt, Aus. Syn. Dĭtĭo, pŏtēstās, ĭmpĕrĭŭm, rēgnŭm. V. Imperium.

dŏmĭnātŏr, ōrĭs, m., *and* trīx, trīcĭs, f., *one who rules.* Pōstquăm dŏmĭnātŏr Ōlȳmpī, Prop. Dŏmĭnātrīx quŏs vĕgĕtāt mēns, Aus. Syn. Dŏmĭnŭs.

dŏmĭnŏr, ārĭs, *to rule.* Vīctĭs dŏmĭnābĭtŭr Ārgĭs, Virg. Syn. Impĕro, rēgo, præsŭm. V. Impero.

dŏmĭnŭs, ī, m., *a lord.* Rōmānōs rērŭm dŏmĭnōs, Virg. Syn. Rēctŏr, hĕrŭs. Epith. Sŭpērbŭs, mītĭs, pŏtēns, mĕtŭēndŭs, trĕmēndŭs, atrōx, fĕrōx.

dŏmĭnŭs, ă, ŭm, *of a lord or ruler.* In dŏmĭnŭm sērvă vŏcātă tŏrŭm, Ov.

dŏmĭto, ās, *the freq. of* domo. Prēnsōs dŏmĭtărĕ bŏvēs, Virg. V. Domo.

dŏmĭtŏr, ōrĭs, m., *and* trīx, trīcĭs, f., *one who subdues.* Dŏmĭtōrquĕ fĕrārŭm, Virg. Clāvă dŏmĭtrīcĕ fĕrārŭm, Ov. Syn. Vīctŏr, dēbēllātŏr, dŏmātŏr. V. Victor.

dŏmĭtŭs, ă, ŭm, *the pass. partic. of* domo. Crēscĕrĕ jām dŏmĭtĭs, Virg.

dŏmo, ās, ŭī, ĭtŭm, *to subdue.* Nōn ānnī dŏmŭĕrĕ dĕcĕm, Virg. Syn. Vīnco, sŭpĕro, sŭbĭgo, dēbēllo, dēvīnco. V. Vinco, debello.

dŏmŭs, ūs *or* ī, *and* ŭncŭlă, æ, f., *a house, a small house.* Hīc dŏmŭs Ænēæ, Virg. Tēctă dŏmōrŭm, Id. Syn. Tēctă, ædēs, ātrĭă, līmĕn, pōrtĭcŭs, aūlă, sēdēs, Pĕnātēs, lăr, lărēs, pĕnetrālĭă, hōspĭtĭŭm. Epith. Sŭpērbă, āltă, cōnspĭcŭă, mārmŏrĕă, ēxĭmĭă, ārdŭă, āntīquă, ĭngēns, āmplă, ēxīlĭs, ēxĭgŭă, māgnă, pŭlchră, rēgĭă, splēndĭdă, spătĭōsă, māgnĭfĭcă, pīctă, aūrātă, ārdŭă, ēxcēlsă, pārvă, ābjēctă, hŭmĭlĭs, sōrdĭdă, vīlĭs, dēsērtă, ĭncūltă.

dŏnārĭŭm, ĭī, n., *a gift.* Mănĭbŭs dŏnārĭă pūrĭs, Ov. V. Donum

dōnātĭo, ōnĭs, f., *a donation.* Cūlpæ dŏnātĭŏ mītĕm, Man. Syn. Dōnŭm, mūnŭs ; cōndōnātĭo.

dōnātŭs, ă, ŭm, *the pass. partic. of* dono. Nōn dōnātŭs ăbībĭt, Virg.

dōnĕc, conj., *till, as long as.* Dōnĕc ĕrĭs fēlix, Ov. Syn. Dŭm, quāmdĭŭ ; quŏăd, quŏūsquĕ.

dōno, ās, *to bestow, present.* Scēptrī dōnāvĭt hŏnōrĕ, Virg. Syn. Dŏ, trĭbŭo, lārgĭŏr, ĭmpērtĭŏr, ēlārgĭŏr. V. Donum, præmium, liberalis.

dōnŭm, ī, n., *a gift.* Dōnă lĭcēbĭt, Ov. Syn. Mūnŭs, mūnūscŭlŭm, præmĭŭm. Epith. Hŏnēstŭm, grātŭm, ăccēptŭm, dīvĕs, ŏpŭlēntŭm, lārgŭm, māgnĭfĭcŭm, rēgālĕ, splēndĭdŭm, sōlēnnĕ, vīlĕ, ēxĭgŭŭm, rēgĭŭm, prĕtĭōsŭm. V. Dono.

Dŏnūsă, æ, f., *one of the Cyclades.* Pārvămquĕ Dŏnūsăm, Virg.

dŏrcās, ădĭs, f., *a doe.* Dōrcădă nātō, Mart.

Dōrceūs, ĕŏs, ĕī *or* eī, m., *a man's name.* Et Dōrceūs, ĕt Ŏrībăsŭs, Ov.

Dōrĭcŭs, *and* ĭŭs, ă, ŭm, *Dorian, Grecian.* Dōrĭcă cāstră, Virg. Hāc Dōrĭŭm, īllĭs bārbărŭm, Hor.

Dŏrĭs, ĭdĭs, f., *mother to the Nereids.* Dŏrĭdáque ēt nātăs, Ov. Epith. Amătă, cœrŭlă, spūmōsă, glaūcă, dĭffūsă, Nēptūnĭă, fŏrmōsă, grāndævă, văgāns, hūmĭdă, æquŏrĕă.

dŏrmĭo, ĭs, īvī *or* ĭī, ītŭm, *to sleep.* Fēssŭs dŏrmīrĕ vĭātŏr, Hor. Syn. Quĭēsco, rĕquĭēsco, dŏrmīto. V. Somnus.

dŏrmīto, ās, *to be sleepy.* Aūt dŏrmītābo, aūt, Hor. Syn. Dŏrmĭo ; ōtĭŏr.

dŏrmītŏr, ōrĭs, m., *a long sleeper.* Quīd tĭbĭ dŏrmītŏr, Mart. Syn. Sōpītŭs ; sōmnŏlēntŭs.

dŏrsŭm, ī, n., *the back.* Impŏsĭtī dōrsō, Virg. Syn. Tērgŭm, tērgŭs ; căcūmĕn.

dōs, dōtĭs, f., *a dowry.* In dŏtĕ trĭūmphōs, Mart. Epith. Pătērnă, mātērnă, grāndĭs, jŭgālĭs, dīvĕs, āmplă.

Dōssēnŭs, ī, m., *a Latin poet.* Sīt Dōssēnŭs ĕdācĭbŭs, Hor.

dōtālĭs, ĕ, *of a dowry.* Fœcūndŭs dōtālĭbŭs hŏrtŭs, Ov.

dōto, ās, *to endow.* Rŭtŭlō dōtābĕrĕ vīrgo, Virg. Syn. Dōtĕ dōno.

Dōtō, ūs, f., *one of the Nereids.* Nērēĭă Dōtō, Virg.

drăchmă, æ, f., *a drachm.* Quīngēntĭs ēmptō drāchmĭs, Hor.

drăco, ōnĭs, m., *a dragon.* Eccĕ drăcō squāmĭs, Ov. Syn. Sērpēns, ānguĭs. Epith. Squāmōsŭs, īmmānĭs, īnsŏpītŭs, sævŭs, tŏrtŭs, tŏrtĭlĭs, ālĭgĕr, măcŭlōsŭs, flēxŭs, vĕnēnōsŭs, lēthĭfĕr, hŏrrĭdŭs, fĕrŭs, pērvĭgĭl, dīrŭs, crūdēlĭs, tŭmēns, atrōx, trūx, ātĕr, crīstātŭs, cœrŭlĕŭs, tērrĭbĭlĭs, fŏrmīdābĭlĭs. V. Serpens.

drăcōnĭgĕnă, æ, m. f., *born of a dragon.* Inquĕ drăcōnĭgĕnăm, Ov. Syn. Sērpēntĭgĕnă.

drămă, ătĭs, n., *the action of a play.* Drāmătă făbēllārŭm, Aus. V. Tragœdia, comœdia.

Drāncēs, ĭs, m., *one of Latinus' councillors.* Crīmĭnĕ Drāncēs, Virg.

Drĕpănŭm, ī, n., *a town in Sicily.* Hīnc Drĕpānī mē pōrtŭs, Virg.

|| drŏmăs, ădĭs, f., *a kind of camel.* Strĕpītū gēntĭs, drōmădūmquĕ părātū, Prud. —2. f., *the name of a dog.* Et Drōmăs, ēt Cănăchĕ, Ov.

|| drŏpāx, ācĭs, m., *a kind of perfume.* Et drŏpăcĕ cālvăm, Mart.

Drŭĭdæ, ārŭm, *or* dĕs, ŭm, m. pl., *the Druids.* Săcrōrŭm Drŭĭdæ, Lucan. Epith. Sĕvērī, sȳlvĭvăgī, pĕrītī, dŏctī, sacrī.

Drūso, ōnĭs, m., *a man's name.* Ŭt Drūsōnēm crēdĭtŏr ærĭs, Hor.

Drūsŭs, ī, m., *the name of several illustrious Romans.* Drūsō Gērmānĭă fēcĭt, Ov.

Drȳăs, ădĭs, f., Drȳădĕs, ŭm, f. pl., *the nymphs of the woods.* Nĕc Drȳădās, nĕc Ov. Syn. Hămādrȳădĕs. Epith. Sēmĭdĕæ, cŭltæ, fŏrmōsæ, rūstĭcæ, prŏcācēs, sȳlvēstrēs, sȳlvĭcŏlæ, ērrāntēs, vĕnūstæ, cŏmptæ, pŭdĭcæ, īntāctæ, cāstæ, vĕrēcūndæ, nĕmŏrōsæ, īncūltæ, trĕpĭdæ, lætæ, hĭlărēs. V. Napææ, Oreades.

Drȳăs, āntĭs, m., *one of the Lapithæ.* Dēxtră Drȳāntĭs, Ov.

Drȳŏpē, ēs, f., *the daughter of Eurytus, changed into a lotus.* Et quærŭnt Drȳŏpēn, Ov.

Drȳŏps, ŏpĭs, m., Drȳŏpēs, ŭm, m. pl., *a people of Epirus.* Thĭŏdămāntă Drȳŏps, Ov. Drȳŏpēsquĕ frĕmūnt, Virg.

dŭbĭē, adv., *doubtfully.* Nĕc dŭbĭē vīrēs, Ov.

dŭbĭtābĭlĭs, ĕ, *which may be doubted.* Ĕrīt dŭbĭtābĭlĕ vērŭm, Ov. V. Dubius.

dŭbĭto, ās, *to doubt.* Et dŭbĭtāmŭs ădhŭc, Virg. Syn. Ambĭgo, flūctŭo, hærĕo.

dŭbĭŭs, ă, ŭm, *doubtful.* Sæpĕ mĭhī dŭbĭăm, Claud. Syn. Incērtŭs, ambĭgŭŭs, āncēps, vărĭŭs, sūspēnsŭs, ānxĭŭs. V. Dubito.

dŭcēntī, æ, ă, *two hundred.* Sæpĕ dŭcēntōs, Hor. Syn. Bīs cēntŭm.

dŭcēntĭēs, adv., *two hundred times.* Dŭcēntĭēs āccēpĭt, (Scaz.) Mart.

dŭcēnŭs, ă, ŭm, *two hundred.* Quīnquĭēs dŭcēnă, (Phal.) Mart.

dūco, xī, ctŭm, *to lead.* Dūcĭtĕ Dāphnĭn, Virg. Syn. Dēdūco, āddūco, ăgo ; ēdūco, cōgĭto.

dūctĭlĭs, ĕ, *easy to be drawn.* Dūctĭlĕ flūmĕn, Mart. Syn. Făcĭlĭs, lēntŭs ; dūctŭs.

dūctŏr, ōrĭs, m., *a leader.* Præcĭpŭōs dūctōrĭbŭs āddĭt, Virg. V. Dux.

dūctŭs, ūs, m., *a leading.* Sĕd ēst dūctŭ, Ov.

dūdŭm, adv., *lately, heretofore, long since.* Ipsa ĕgŏmĕt dūdŭm, Virg. Syn. Jāmdūdŭm, jāmprīdĕm, jāmdĭū.

dŭēllĭcŭs, ă, ŭm, *warlike.* Pūgnă dŭēllĭcă pĕr sē, Fill.

dŭēllŭm, ī, n., *a combat.* Lēntō cōllīsă dŭēllō, Hor. Syn. Pūgnă, cērtāmĕn, běllŭm. Epith. Fŏrtě, īncērtŭm, sāngŭīněŭm, răbĭdŭm, īnsānŭm, dīrŭm, fŭrĭōsŭm.

dŭlcě, ĭtěr, adv., *sweetly.* Dŭlcě rīdēntěm, Hor.

dŭlcēdo, ĭnĭs, f., *sweetness.* Prætēr sŏlĭtŭm dŭlcēdĭně lætĭ, Virg. Syn. Suāvĭtās.
Epith. Māgnă, grātă, jūcŭndă, mīră, blāndă, suāvĭs, mēllītă, nēctărěă.

dŭlcĭārĭŭs, ĭī, m., *a confectioner.* Mart.

dŭlcĭlŏquŭs, ă, ŭm, *sweet in words.* Mŏllīt dŭlcĭlŏquă, (Phal.) Sid. Syn. Blāndĭlŏquŭs, blāndŭs, fācŭndŭs.

dŭlcĭs, ě; ĭcŭlŭs, ă, ŭm, *sweet.* Dŭlcĭbŭs īn stāgnĭs, Virg. Syn. Suāvĭs, mēllěŭs, mītĭs, nēctărěŭs, jūcŭndŭs, grātŭs, chārŭs, ămœnŭs.

dŭlcĭsŏnŭs, ă, ŭm, *sweetly-sounding.* Dŭlcĭsŏnŭm quătĭtŭr, Sid.

dŭm, adv., *while, until, so that.* Dŭm cŏnděrět ūrběm, Virg. Syn. Dōněc; quāndo; dŭmmŏdŏ, mŏdŏ.

dūmětŭm, ī, n., *a place full of bushes.* Tŏndēnt dūmětă jŭvēncī, Virg. Syn. Spīnētŭm, vēprētŭm, rŭbētŭm. Epith. Hŏrrēndŭm, hŏrrĭdŭm, dēnsŭm, āspěrŭm, āvĭŭm, īmpērvĭŭm, flōrēns. V. Dumus.

dūmĭcŏlă, æ, ψ. f., *one who lives among bushes.* Dūmĭcŏlās Ārĭēnōs, Av.

dŭmmŏdŏ, adv.,.*provided that.* Dŭmmŏdŏ pūgnāndo, Ov. Syn. Dŭm, mŏdŏ, ŭt; sī tāměn.

dūmōsŭs, ă, ŭm, *full of.bushes.* Dūmōsă pēnděrě prŏcŭl, Virg. Syn. Spīnōsŭs, spīnĭfěr. V. Spinosus.

dūmŭs, ī, m., *a bush.* Ēt ămāntēs ārdŭă dūmōs, Virg. Syn. Rŭbŭs, dūmětŭm, sēntēs, vēprēs, spīnœ. Epith. Hŏrrĭdŭs, hŏrrēns, dēnsŭs, pīnguĭs, āspěr, āvĭŭs, ūmbrōsŭs, spīnōsŭs, sȳlvēstrĭs, vĭrēns, vĭrĭdĭs, rĭgĭdŭs, īmpērvĭŭs, spīnĭfěr, hīrsūtŭs, ăcūtŭs. V. Rubus.

dŭntāxăt, adv., *only.* Dŭntāxăt ăd hŏc, Hor. Syn. Sōlŭm, tāntŭm:

dŭo, æ, o, *two.* Vēl sīmŭlācră dŭŏ, fŏrsān dŭŏ, Mart. Cœnă dŭōbŭs, Mart. Syn. Duplēx, bīnī, gěmĭnī, āmbo.

dŭŏděcĭm, *twelve.*

dŭŏděcĭmŭs, *or* dŭŏděcĭmŭs, ă, ŭm, *the twelfth.* Dŭŏděcĭmō Tūrnŭs, Virg.

dŭŏdēnŭs, ă, ŭm, *twelve.* Pēr dŭŏdēnă rěgĭt, Virg. Syn. Bīssēnī.

duplēx, ĭcĭs, *double.* Ēt dūplĭcēm gēmmĭs, Virg. Syn. Gěmĭnŭs, āmbo.

duplĭcĭtěr, adv., *doubly.* Dūplĭcĭtěr, nām vĭs, Lucr.

duplĭco, ās, *to double.* Mōbĭlĭtās dūplĭcātŭr, ět, Lucr. Dīscēdēns dūplĭcăt ūmbrās, Virg. Syn. Addūplĭco, cōndūplĭco, gěmĭno, āggěmĭno, cōngěmĭno.

dūrăbĭlĭs, ě, *durable.* Rěquĭě, dūrăbĭlě nōn ēst, Ov. Syn. Dĭŭtŭrnŭs, stăbĭlĭs, mănēns, pērmănēns, cōnstāns.

dūrāmĕn, ĭnĭs, n., *a hardening.* Māgnŭm dūrāmĕn ăquārŭm, Lucr.

dūrē, ĭtěr, adv., *hardly.* Dūrĭtěr ēt dūrō, Lucr.

dūrēsco, rŭī, *to become hard.* Hīc dūrēscĭt ĕt hæc, Virg. Syn. Indūrēsco, Indŭrŏr, cōncrēsco, āstrīngŏr, prěmŏr, rĭgěo. V. Gelo.

dūrĭtās, ātĭs; tĭă, æ; tĭēs, ēī, f., *hardness.* Dūrĭtĭă pēllĭs, Ov. Pōněrě dūrĭtĭěm, Id. Syn. Rĭgŏr, sævĭtĭēs, crūdēlĭtās, bārbărĭēs. Epith. Ădămāntĭnă, ăcērbă, fērrěă.

dūro, ās, *to harden.* Dūrāvĭtque ănĭmŭm, Ov. Syn. Indūro, āstrīngo, cōnstrīngo, prěmo, gělo, fīrmo; stŏ, măněo, dĭū măněo, stăbĭlĭs, dĭŭtŭrnŭs sŭm.

dūrŭs, ă, ŭm, *hard.* Dūrŭs ūtěrquě, Virg. Syn. Sŏlĭdŭs, fīrmŭs, fērrěŭs, ădămāntĭnŭs, mārmŏrěŭs; mŏlēstŭs, īngrātŭs, īnjūcŭndŭs; sěvērŭs, rĭgĭdŭs, crūdēlĭs. V. Crudelis.

dŭx, dŭcĭs, m. f., *a leader.* Cōnsěděrě dŭcēs, Ov. Syn. Dūctŏr. Epith. Crŭēntŭs, bēllĭgěr, bēllĭcŭs, fŏrtĭs, aŭdāx, Mārtĭŭs, māgnănĭmŭs, īndŏmĭtŭs, gěněrōsŭs, prūdēns, săgāx, sŏlērs, prōvĭdŭs, vĭgĭl, pērvĭgĭl, Māvōrtĭŭs, tērrĭfĭcŭs, mětŭēndŭs, trūx, atrōx, fěrŭs, crīstātŭs, īnsīgnĭs, præclārŭs, māgnŭs, trěmēndŭs, fěrōx, ācěr, cāllĭdŭs, āstūtŭs, caŭtŭs, vērsūtŭs, fĭdēlĭs, pŏtēns, sēdŭlŭs, strēnŭŭs, mĭnāx, īmpērtērrĭtŭs, īnvīctŭs. V. Bellicosus.

Dȳmāntĭs, ĭdĭs, f., *daughter of Dymas, Hecuba.* Lātrāssě Dȳmāntĭdă, Ov.

Dȳmās, āntĭs, m., *the father of Hecuba.* Euĭxă Dȳmāntĭs, Ov.

Dȳrāspēs, ĭs, m., *a river of Scythia.* Amně Dȳrāspēs, Ov.

Dȳrrhăchĭŭm, ĭī, n., *a town of Albania.* Dȳrrhăchĭī præcēps, Luc. Epith. Clārŭm, nōbĭlě.

E.

Ē, prep., *from, after, according to.* Tū quŏd ĕs, ē pŏpŭlō, Mart. Syn. Ex, dē; jŭxtā, ăd.

ĕă, f., *she.* Infēlīx, ĕă nĕc, Virg.

ĕā, adv., *that way.* Cŏrpŭs ĕā nōn ēst, Lucr. Syn. Hāc.

ĕădĕm, (*from* idem,) Ov.

ĕădĕm, *or* eādĕm (*dissyl.*), *the abl. f.* of idem. Sēmpĕr ŏbērrăt ĕādĕm, Hor. Hāc eādēm rūrsŭs, Prop.

ĕātĕnŭs, *so far.* Insŏmnĭs ĕātĕnŭs āltŭm, Mant. Syn. Hāctĕnŭs.

ĕbĕnŭm, ī, n., *and* ŭs, ī, f, *ebony.* Fērt ĕbĕnŭm, Virg. Epith. Dūră, splēndĭdă, splēndēns, ātră, nĭtēns, nĭtĭdă, fūscā, nigră, Indă, Indĭcă, Eŏă, Mărĕŏtĭcă, i. e. Ægyptĭă; pŏlītă, ēnōdĭs.

ēbĭbo, ĭs, *to drink up.* Ēbĭbăt hærēs, Hor. V. Bibo.

ēbrĭĕtās, ātĭs, f., *drunkenness.* Ēbrĭĕtās ēst, Ov. Syn. Crāpŭlă, tēmŭlēntĭă. Epith. Tūrpĭs, āmēns, īmprŏvĭdă, fœdă, ĭnērs, stŭpĭdă, īnsānă, ŏbscœnă, lŏquāx, gārrŭlă, trĕmŭlă, tĭtŭbāns, grăvĭs, fūrēns, mălĕsānă, ēxĭtĭŏsă, pĕrnĭcĭŏsă.

ēbrĭŏsŭs, ă, ŭm, *given to drinking.* Ebrĭŏsa ăcĭna, (Phal.) Cat. Syn. Bĭbāx, pŏtŏr, pōtātŏr, vīnōsŭs.

ēbrĭŭs, ă, ŭm, *drunken.* Ebrĭŭs ōlĭm, Hor. Syn. Ebrĭŏsŭs, tēmŭlēntŭs, vīnōlēntŭs.

ēbullĭo, ī, ītŭm, *to boil.* Ēbullīt pătrŭī, Pers.

ĕbŭlŭm, ī, n., *the dwarf-elder.* Sănguĭnēĭs ĕbŭlī, Virg.

ĕbŭr, ŏrĭs, n., *ivory.* Pŏrtāntēs aūrīque ĕbŏrĭsque, Virg. Epith. Indŭm, Indĭcŭm, cāndēns, Assўrĭŭm; nĭvĕŭm, splēndĭdŭm, liquĭdŭm, nĭtĭdŭm, pŏlītŭm. V. Elephas, cithara.

ĕbŭrnĕŭs, *or* nŭs, ă, ŭm, *of ivory.* Cīngāntŭr ĕbŭrnĕă mūrĭs, Ov. Cūrrŭs ĕbŭrnŭs ĕquīs, Tib. Syn. Ĕlĕphāntĭnŭs.

Ēbŭsŭs, ī, m., *an island in the Mediteranean.* Jāmque Ēbŭsŭs, Sil. Cōnsūrgĭt Ēbŭsŭs, Avien. Epith. Cīrcūmflŭă, dīvĕs, ŏpīmă, īnnŏcŭă, irrĭgŭă, rĭgŭă, mădĭdă, mădēns.

ēccĕ, interj., *lo, see!* Ecce Dĭōnæī, Virg. Syn. En.

ēcclēsĭă, æ, f, *a church, congregation.* Sūmēns ecclēsĭă cŏrpŭs, Victor. Syn. Tēmplŭm, dēlūbrŭm, fānŭm, ædēs. V. Templum.

ĕchĕnēĭs, ĭs, f., *a small fish.* Pārva ĕchĕnēĭs ădēst, Ov. Syn. Rēmŏră.

ĕchĭdnă, æ, f., *a viper.* Sănguĭs ĕchĭdnæ, Ov. Epith. Tūmĭdă, fēră, dīră, răbĭdă, fŭrĭālĭs, lēthĭfĕră, vĕnēnōsă, vĕnēnĭfĕră, tŭmēns, hŏrrĭdă. V. Hydra.

Ēchīnādĕs, ŭm, f. pl., *nymphs changed into islands.* Ăchĕlōŭs Ēchīnādăs ēxĭt, St.

ĕchīnŭs, ī, m., *an urchin.* Mōllĭs ĕchīnŭs ĕrĭt, Mart. Epith. Rŭbĕr, hĭrtŭs, vŏlūbĭlĭs, æquŏrĕŭs, sўlvēstrĭs, caūtŭs, spīnōsŭs.

Ēchīōn, ŏnĭs, m., *a companion of Cadmus.* Cŏrpŭs Ēchīōn, Ov.

Ēchīŏnīdēs, æ, m., *the son of Echion, Pentheus.* Spērnĭt Ēchīŏnĭdēs, Ov.

Ēchīŏnĭŭs, ă, ŭm, *of Echion.* Nōmĕn Ēchīŏnĭŭm, Virg.

Ēchō, ūs, f., *a nymph changed into echo by the jealousy of Juno.* Āssŏnăt Echō, Pers. Syn. Vōx rĕpērcūssă. Epith. Gārrŭlă, cănōră, văgă, clāră, rĕflēxă, rĕdĭtūră, lŏquāx, rĕsŏnāns, pērcūssă, ĭmĭtātrīx, rēspōnsūră, rĕcōndĭtă, lātēns, vĭgĭl, pērvĭgĭl.

ēclīpsĭs, ĭs, f., *an eclipse.* Syn. Dēfēctŭs, dēlĭquĭŭm. Epith. Mĭnāx, fātālĭs, fūnēstă, trīstĭs, īnfēlīx, hŏrrēndă, mĕtŭēndă, nigră, ātră. V. Sol, luna.

ēclŏgă, æ, f., *an eclogue.* Cārmĭnĭs ēclŏgās, (Asclep.) Sid. Epith. Tĕnŭĭs, dīdūctă, fēstīvă.

ēcquāndo, adv., *ever.* Dīc prĕcŏr, ēcquāndo, Ov.

ēcquĭs, quă, quŏd *or* quĭd, *who, what.* Ecquĭs ĕrĭt, Virg.

ĕcŭlĕŭs, ī, m.,; ă, æ, f., *a colt, a filly; a sort of punishment.* Ĕcŭlĕo ēmĭnŭs, (Iamb.) Prud. V. Equus, supplicium.

ĕdācĭtās, ātĭs, f., *gluttony.* Sēd sŏcŏrs ĕdācĭtās, (Iamb.) Prud. Syn. Vŏrācĭtās, īnglŭvĭēs, gŭlă.

ĕdāx, ācĭs, *gluttonous.* Tēmpŭs ĕdāx, Ov. Syn. Vŏrāx, gŭlōsŭs, hēllŭo. V. Gulosus.

ēdēntŭlŭs, ă, ŭm, *toothless.* Ēdēntŭlārūm cāntĭlēnæ, (Iamb.) Prud. SYN.
Ēdēntātŭs.

ēdīco, ĭs, xī, ctŭm, *to declare, order.* Mēnti ēdīcĕrĕ dōnīs, Prud. SYN. Dēnūncĭo, sīgnĭfĭco, dīco, præmŏnĕo ; stătŭo, cōnstĭtŭo, dēcērno, sāncĭo, jŭbĕo.

ēdīctŭm, ī, n., *a command.* Āddĕ quŏd ēdīctŭm, Ov. SYN. Dēcrētŭm, stătūtŭm,
lēx.

ēdīsco, ēdĭdĭcī, *to learn.* Jūssītque ēdīscĕrĕ laŭrōs, Virg. SYN. Dīsco, pērdīsco,
pērcĭpĭo, cōncĭpĭo. V. Disco.

ēdīssĕro, ĭs, *to rehearse.* Hæc ēdīssĕrĕ vērā, Virg.

ēdĭtŏr, ōrĭs, m., *who produces, announces.* Ēdĭtŏr ūrcĭs, Luc. SYN. Aŭctŏr,
nūncĭŭs.

ēdĭtŭs, *the pass. partic. of* ēdo. Ēdĭtă fōrtĕ, Ov.

ĕdo, ēdī, ēsŭm, *to eat.* Pĕcŭs ēdĭt ăgēllōs, Hor. SYN. Cŏmĕdo, māndūco, mando,
pāscŏr, vēscŏr. V. Manduco.

ēdo, ēdĭdī, ēdĭtŭm, *to produce.* Ēdĕrĕ raŭcŭm, Ov. SYN. Făcĭo ; prŏfĕro,
dīvūlgo, ēmītto, ēxprōmo.

ēdŏcĕo, ŭī, ctŭm, *to instruct.* Ēdŏcĕāt mŭltās, Virg. SYN. Dŏcĕo ; nūncĭo.

ēdŏmo, ăs, ŭī, *to tame.* Ēdŏmăt īnvălĭdīs, Prop. SYN. Dŏmo, dŏmĭto.

Ēdŏnīs, ĭdĭs, f., *Thracian.* Ēdŏnĭdăs ōmnĕs, Ov. Ēdŏnĭs Ōgy̆gĭo, Luc.

Ēdŏnŭs, ă, ŭm, *Thracian.* Āc vĕlŭt Ēdŏnī, Bŏrĕæ, Virg. -ī, ōrŭm, m. pl., *the*
Thracians. Bācchăbŏr Ēdŏnīs, Hor.

ēdōrmĭo, ĭs, ĭī, *to sleep out.* Cum Ilĭŏnam ēdōrmĭt, Hor. SYN. Dōrmĭo ; ēxpēr-
gēfĭo.

ēdŭco, ās, *to feed, form.* Ēdŭcăt ūvās, Ov. SYN. Nūtrĭo, ălo ; īnstĭtŭo, īnfōrmo.
V. Nutrio.

ēdūco, ĭs, *to draw from.* Cælōque ēdūcĕrĕ cērtănt, Virg. SYN. Ēxtrăho, lībĕro,
sōlvo, ēxpĕdĭo, ēxĭmo, trăho, ēmītto.

ĕdūlĭs, ĕ, *eatable.* Sēmpĕr ĕdūlēs, Hor.

ēdūrŭs, ă, ŭm, *very hard.* Ēdūrāmquĕ py̆rūm, Virg. SYN. Dūrŭs, sŏlĭdŭs.

Ēĕtĭōn, ōnĭs, m., *the father of Andromache.* Ēĕtĭōnĭs ŏpēs, Ov.

Ēĕtĭōnēŭs, ă, ŭm, *of Eetion.* Ēĕtĭōnēās īmplēvī, Ov.

ēffārī, *to speak.* Incĭpĭt ēffārī, Virg. SYN. Fārī, lŏquī, ēlŏquī, dīcĕrĕ, prŏfērrĕ.
V. Loquor.

ēffātŭs, *the partic. of* ēffārī. Ōre ēffātŭs ămīcō, Virg.

ēffēctŭs, ūs, m., *effect, execution.* Nōn cărĕt ēffēctū, Ov.

ēffĕro, ēxtŭlī, ēlātŭm, *to carry•forth.* Āltĭŭs ēffērt, Virg. Ēxtŭlĭt ūrbēs, Id.
SYN. Tōllo, ēvĕho, prōvĕho ; laŭdo.

ēffĕro, ās, *to make wild.* Quĭd te ēffĕrārĭt, (Iamb.) Sen. SYN. Ăcērbo, īrrīto.

ēffērvĕo, ēs, ērĕ *or* ĕrĕ, *and* ēsco, ĕrĕ, *to boil over.* Rŭptīs ēffērvĕrĕ cōstīs, Virg.
SYN. Fērvēsco, fērvĕo, ēbūllĭo.

ēffĕrŭs, ă, ŭm, *wild, distracted.* Ēffĕră Dīdō, Virg. SYN. Fĕrŭs, īndŏmĭtŭs,
sævŭs, crūdēlĭs. V. Crudelis.

ēffētŭs, ă, ŭm. V. Effœtus.

ēffĭcāx, ācĭs, *effectual.* Jāmjam ēffĭcācī, (Iamb.) Hor. SYN. Pŏtēns, ūtĭlĭs.

ēffĭcĭo, fēcī, *to effect.* Nōn ēffĭcĭēnt mănŭs, (Alcaic.) Hor. SYN. Făcĭo, pērfĭcĭo,
pĕrăgo, præsto, ēxĕquŏr.

ēffĭgĭēs, ĭĕī, f., *an image.* Ēffĭgĭēs īntĕr, Juv. SYN. Ĭmāgo, sĭmŭlācrŭm, spĕcĭēs,
sīgnŭm. EPITH. Pīctă, dĕcōră, pūlchră, aŭrĕă. V. Statua.

ēffīngo, īnxī, īctŭm, *to imitate.* Cāsūs ēffīngĕre ĭn aŭrō, Virg. SYN. Ēxprĭmo,
fōrmo, īnfōrmo.

ēfflāgĭto, ās, *to crave.* Ēfflāgĭtăt ēnsĕm, Virg. SYN. Flāgĭto, pĕto, pōsco, ēxpōsco, pōstŭlo.

ēfflo, ās, *to breathe out.* Nārĭbŭs ēfflănt, Ov.

ēfflōrĕo, ŭī, *to blow as a flower.* SYN. Ēfflōrēsco, splēndĕo, splēndēsco ; māno,
ēmāno.

ēffluo, xī, *to flow out.* Ēffluăt īllă tŭīs, Ov. SYN. Flŭo, ēlābŏr, ēffūndŏr, ēxcĭdo,
ăbĕo, ēvānēsco.

ēffŏdĭo, ōdī, ōssŭm, *to dig out.* Ēffŏdĭūntŭr ŏpēs, Ov. SYN. Ērŭo, ēvēllo, ēxtrăho, fŏdĭo.

ēffœtŭs, ă, ŭm, *worn out, exhausted.* Frīgēntque ēffœtæ, Virg. SYN. Infīrmŭs,
dēbĭlĭs, īnvălĭdŭs, ægĕr.

effrēnātŭs, ă, ŭm, *unbridled.* Effrēnātōrum mŏdĕrāmĭnĕ, Prud. Syn. Effrēnĭs, effrēnŭs, præcēps, ĭndŏmĭtŭs.

effrēno, ās, *to unbridle, let loose.* In prœlĭă cāmpīs Effrēnăt, Sil.

effrēnŭs, ă, ŭm, *unbridled, unrestrained.* Gēns effrēnā vīrūm, Virg. Syn. Effrēnĭs, præcēps, ĭndŏmĭtŭs, īmpŏtēns.

effrĭngo, frēgī, frāctŭm, *to break.* Sŭbtrăhĭt effrāctō, Ov.

effŭgĭo, fūgī, *to fly away.* Effŭgĕrēnt ălĭquā, Prop. Syn. Fŭgĭo, ēvādo, ēlābŏr, vīto, dēvīto, dēclīno, ēvīto.

effŭgĭŭm, ĭī, n., *a flight.* Effŭgĭŭm præclūdĕre ĕūntī, Lucr. Syn. Fŭgă.

effŭlgĕo, sī, gērĕ *and* gĕrĕ, *to shine forth.* Lūx ŏcŭlīs effŭlsĭt, Virg. Effŭlgērĕ flūctŭs, Virg. Syn. Fŭlgĕo, ēmĭco, mĭco, cŏrūsco, splēndĕo, ēlūcĕo.

effŭndo, ūdī, sŭm, *to pour on.* Cērvīce effŭdĭt ĕquīnā, Virg. Syn. Fŭndo, profŭndo, ēmītto, spārgo.

effūsŭs, ă, ŭm, *the pass. partic. of* effundo. Effūsŭs ĭn ūndīs, Virg.

effŭtĭo, īs, ĭī, ītŭm, *to prate.* Effŭtīrĕ lĕvēs, Hor. Syn. Gārrĭo.

ĕgĕlĭdŭs, ă, ŭm, *lukewarm.* Egĕlĭdūmquĕ Nŏtŭm, Ov. Syn. Gĕlĭdŭs.

ĕgēnŭs, ă, ŭm, *wanting, destitute.* Omnĭum ĕgēnōs, Virg. Syn. Ĕgēns, ĭndĭgēns, ĭndĭgŭs, paūpĕr, ĭnŏps, mēndīcŭs. V. Pauper.

ĕgĕo, ēs, *to want.* Accērsās, ĕt ĕgērĕ vĕtēs, Hor. Syn. Indĭgĕo, cărĕo, ŏpŭs hăbĕo, ŏpŭs ēst mĭhi, paūpĕr sŭm.

Egĕrĭă, æ, f., *a nymph whom Numa pretended to consult.* Ēdūctum Egĕrĭæ lūcīs, Virg.

ĕgĕro, ssī, stŭm, *to bear out.* Egĕrĭtūrquĕ dŏlŏr, Ov. Syn. Expēllo, ējĭcĭo, dējĭcĭo, aūfĕro, rĕmŏvĕo, ārcĕo.

ĕgēstās, ātĭs, f., *poverty.* In rēbŭs ĕgēstās, Virg. Syn. Paūpērtās, paūpĕrĭēs, ĭnŏpĭă, pēnūrĭă. Epith. Sōrdĭdă, grăvĭs, tūrpĭs, crūdēlĭs, dūră, īmmītĭs, īnfēlīx, mĭsĕră, pānnōsă, prædūră, mŏlēstă, lāngŭĭdă, ūrgēns, cōntēmptă, dēspectă, hūmĭlĭs, dīră, ăcērbă, lăcĕră. V. Paupertas.

ĕgo, *I.* Ille ĕgŏ quī, Virg. Aŭsŭs ĕgŏ prīmŭs, Catull.

ĕgŏmĕt, *I myself.* Vīdi ĕgŏmĕt, Virg. Syn. Ipsĕ.

ĕgrĕdĭor, ĕrĭs, *to go out.* Egrĕdĭtūr, fērrō, Virg. Syn. Exĕo, ēxcēdo, dīscēdo, ābĕo. V. Exeo, abeo.

ēgrĕgĭē, adv., *excellently.* Egrĕgĭē fāctŭm, Hor.

ēgrĕgĭŭs, ă, ŭm, *excellent.* Egrĕgĭŏ dĕcŭs, Virg. Syn. Insīgnĭs, ēxĭmĭŭs, ēxcēllēns, præstāns.

ēgrēssŭs, ŭs, m., *a going out.* Pătĕt ēgrēssŭs pĕlăgī, Cat.

ēheū, interj., *alas.* Eheū! quĭd vŏlŭī? Virg. Syn. Heū, prŏh!

ējă, interj., *oh! well.* Eja ăgĕ, Virg. Ejā pĕr ĭpsŭm, Val. Fl.

ējăcŭlŏr, ārĭs, *to shoot off.* Ejăcŭlātŭr ăquās, Ov. V. Jaculor.

ējēcto, ās, *freq. of* ejicio. Ōre ējēctāntĕm, Virg.

ējĭcĭo, jēcī, *to throw away.* Tūrpĭŭs ējĭcĭtŭr, Ov. Syn. Pēllo, ēxpēllo, dējĭcĭo, dētrūdo, ēxtrūdo, dētūrbo. V. Pello.

ējŭlātĭo, ōnĭs, f, *and* tŭs, ūs, m., *a wailing.* Vīrīlĭs ējŭlātĭo, (Iamb.) Hor. Hūnc ējŭlātŭm, (Iamb.) Sen. Syn. Ūlŭlātŭs, lāmēntŭm, lūctŭs.

ējŭlo, ās, *to wail.* Sīc ējŭlāntēs, (Iamb.) Prud. Syn. Lāmēntŏr, ŭlŭlo, lūgĕo, flĕo, dēplōro.

ējūro, ās, *to abjure, renounce.* Saŭcĭŭs ējūrăt, Ov.

ēlābŏr, ĕrĭs, *to slide.* Sĭnŭōso ēlābĭtŭr āngŭĭs, Virg. Syn. Ēvādo, ēxcēdo ; effŭgĭo ; lābŏr, ēxcĭdo.

ēlăbōrātŭs, ă, ŭm, *the pass. partic. of* elaboro. Nōn ēlăbōrātŭm, (Iamb. Dim.) Hor.

ēlăbōro, ās, *to work, labor.* Dŭlcem ēlăbōrābŭnt săpōrĕm, (Iamb. cum syll.) Hor. Syn. Excŏlo, ēxōrno, ēxpŏlĭo ; lābŏro, ēnītŏr.

ēlānguĕo, *or* ēlānguēsco, gŭī, *to languish.* Dŭbĭĭsque ēlāngŭĭt ālĭs, Val. Fl. Sīc ēlānguēscēns, Sil. Syn. Lānguēsco.

ēlāpsŭs, ă, ŭm, *the pass. partic. of* elabor. Pānthēūs ēlāpsŭs Achīvūm, Virg.

ēlārgĭor, īrĭs, *to give largely.* Quāntum ēlārgīrī dĕcĕăt, Pers. Syn. Lārgĭor.

Ēlătēĭŭs, ă, ŭm, *of Elatus.* Cēneūs Ēlătēĭŭs īctŭs, Ov.

ēlātŭs, ă, ŭm, *high.* Cōntra ēlātā mărī, Virg. V. Altus.

Ēlēctră, æ, f., *a nymph.* Ēlēctra, ŭt Graiī pĕrhĭbēnt, Virg. Syn. Atlāntĭs.

ēlēctrĭfĕr, ĕră, ĕrŭm, *bearing amber.* Pădŭs ēlēctrĭfĕrīs, (Choriamb.) Cl.

ēlēctrŭm, ī, n., *amber.* Sūdēnt ēlēctră mўrīcæ, Virg. Syn. Sŭccĭnŭm. Epith.

H

Pīnguĕ, lacrȳmōsŭm, rōscĭdŭm, pāllēns, pāllĭdŭm, præfŭlgēns, liquĭdŭm, flāvŭm, splēndēns, mĭcāns, lūcĭdŭm.

ēlēctŭs, ūs, m., *choice.* In nĕcĭs ēlēctū, Ov.

ēlĕgāns, āntĭs, *elegant.* Nĭmĭs ēlĕgāntĕ līnguā, (Phal.) Cat. Syn. Cōncīnnŭs, pōlītŭs, vĕnūstŭs ; ēlŏquēns; ēxīmĭŭs.

ēlĕgīă, gēīă, æ, f., *or* gŭs, ī, m., *an elegy.* Pĕtŭlāns ēlĕgīā prŏpīnquăt, Stat. Ēlĕgēīă cāntĕt, Ov. Hīc ēlĕgōs, Juv. Epith. Flēbĭlĭs, trīstĭs, mœstă, īnfēlīx, mĭsĕrābĭlĭs, quĕrŭlă, gĕmĕbūndă, mōllĭs, lēnĭs, īmbēllĭs, ăcūtă, pārvă, blāndă, pĕtŭlāns.

ēlĕgīdĭŏn, ī, m., *a small elegy.* Ēlĕgīdĭă crūdī, Pers.

Ēlēī, ōrŭm, m. pl., *a people of Elis.* Virg.

Ēlĕlĕȳs, ĭdĭs, f., *a bacchante.* Fŭrĭīs Ēlĕlĕȳdĕs āctæ, Ov.

Ēlĕleūs, ī, m., *one of the names of Bacchus.* Nȳctēlȳūsque Ēlĕleūsquĕ, Ov. V. Bacchus.

ēlĕmēntă, ōrŭm, n. pl., *the elements.* Mōs ĕlĕmēntōrŭm, Sid.

ēlēnchŭs, ī, m., *a kind of pearl.* Cōmmīsĭt ēlēnchōs, Juv.

|| ēlĕphāntĭnŭs, ă, ŭm, *of an elephant.* Syn. Bārrīnŭs.

ēlĕphās, āntĭs, *or* āntŭs, ī, m., *an elephant.* Sīve ēlĕphās, ālbŭs, Hor. Syn. Bārrŭs. Epith. Indĭcŭs, Indŭs, Eŏŭs; Afĕr, Lĭbȳcŭs, Gētūlŭs, Mārmărĭcŭs ; fōrtĭs, lăcērtōsŭs, īmmānĭs, pŏtēns, rōbūstŭs, dŏcĭlĭs, bēllĭcŭs, vāstŭs, īngēns, mītĭs, clēmēns, sōlērs, īndūstrĭŭs.

ēlēvo, ās, *to lift up.* Ēlĕvĕt aūrā, Prop. Syn. Lĕvo, tōllo ; ēxtōllo ; mĭnŭo, dīmĭnŭo.

Ēlĕŭs, ă, ŭm, *and* Ēlīăs, ădĭs, f., *of Eles.* Ăd Ēlēī mĕtās, Virg. Ēlĭădŭm pālmās, Id.

Ēleūsĭs *and* īn, ĭnĭs, f., *a city of Attica, famous for the mysteries of Ceres.* Inĭta ēst Cĕrĕălĭs Eleūsīn, Ov.

Ēleūsīnŭs, ă, ŭm, *of Eleusis.* Tārdăque Ēleūsīnæ, Virg.

Ēlīās, æ, m., *the prophet.* Cōnvĕnĭt Ēlĭā mĕrĭtō, Sedul.

ēlĭcĭo, hī, *to draw out.* Ēlĭcĭt : īllă cădēns, Virg. Syn. Allĭcĭo, āttrăho, ēxtrăho, ēdūco.

ēlĭcĭtŭs, ă, ŭm, *the pass. partic. of* elicio.

Ēlĭcĭŭs, ī, m., *a surname of Jupiter.* Ēlĭcĭŭmquĕ vŏcānt, Ov.

ēlīdo, sī, sŭm, *to dash.* Ēlīdĭt gĕmĭnōs, Mart. Syn. Frāngo, īncīdo ; ēlĭcĭo.

ēlĭgo, ēgī, *to choose.* Ēlĭgĭtŭr lŏcŭs, Virg. Syn. Lĕgo, dēlĭgo, sēlĭgo, ōpto.

ēlīmĭno, ās, *to turn out.* Fŏrās ēlīmĭnĕt, ūt cŏĕăt pār, Hor. Syn. Ejĭcĭo, ēxpēllo, pēllo, ēxclūdo.

ēlīmo, ās, *to polish.* Ēlīmāt ; nōn īllŭd, Ov. Syn. Pŏlĭo, ēxpŏlĭo, pērpŏlĭo, ēxcŏlo.

ēlīnguĭs, ĕ, *dumb.* Ēlīnguĭs ōrĭs ōrgănŭm, (Iamb.) Prud. Syn. Mūtŭs.

ēlĭquo, ās, *to sweeten.* Plōrābĭlĕ sī quĭd Ēlĭquăt, Pers.

Ēlĭs, ĭdĭs, f., *a town of Peloponnesus.* Ēlĭdĭs āmnĕm, Virg. Epith. Nōbĭlĭs, Ōlȳmpĭăcă.

Ēlīsă, *or* Ēlīssa, æ, f., *a name of Dido.* Mĕmĭnīssĕ pĭgēbĭt Ēlīsæ, Virg.

Ēlīseūs, eī, m., *the prophet.*

ēlīsŭs, ă, ŭm, *the pass. partic. of* elido. Tĕr spūmam ēlīsăm, Virg.

ēlīxŭs, ă, ŭm, *boiled.* Mīscŭĕrĭs ēlīxă sĭmŭl, Hor. Syn. Līxăīŭs, ēlīxātŭs.

ēllĕbŏrŭs, ī, m.; *and* ŭm, ī, n., *the herb hellebore.* Ēllĕbŏrōsquĕ grăvēs, Virg. Epith. Grăvĭs, trīstĭs.

ēlŏgĭŭm, ĭī, n., *praise.* Ēlŏgĭŭm tăcĭtă, Virg. V. Laus.

* ēlŏquēns, ēntĭs, *eloquent.* Tŭlĭt ēlŏquēns cŏrōnăm, Sid. Syn. Fācūndŭs, dĭsērtŭs. V. Causidicus.

ēlŏquēntĭă, æ, f., *eloquence.* Cūjŭs ēlŏquēntĭā, Aus. Syn. Fācūndĭă, ēlŏquĭŭm. Epith. Nēctărĕă, fācūndă, āmbrŏsĭă, dōctă, flēxănĭmă, dūlcĭs, mēllītă, ōrnātă, pŏtēns, dīvīnă, cūltă, ēxcūltă, fūlmĭnĕă, fāllāx, dŏlōsă, cāllĭdă, īnsĭdĭōsă, blāndă, vĕnūstă, mēllĭflŭă.

ēlŏquĭŭm, ĭī, n., *eloquence.* Quī lĭcĕt ēlŏquĭō, Ov. V. Eloquentia.

ēlŏquŏr, ĕrĭs, *to speak.* Ēlŏquăr, ān sĭlĕăm, Virg. Syn. Dīco, prŏfĕro, rĕnūncĭo, ēxprĭmo. V. Loquor.

Elpēnŏr, ŏrĭs, m., *one of Ulysses' companions.* Elpēnŏră pōrcĭs, Juv.

ēlūcĕo, ēlūxī, *to shine forth.* Ēlūcēnt ăllĭæ, Virg. Syn. Lūcĕo, ēnĭtĕo, ēmĭco, āppārĕo, ēmĭnĕo ; ēxcēllo.

ēlūctŏr, ārĭs, *to struggle.* Aqua ēlūctābĭtŭr ōmnĭs, Virg. Syn. Lūctŏr, ērūmpo.

ēlūdo, sī, *to elude, deceive.* Quā văfĕr ēlūdī, Hor. Syn. Lūdo, ārrīdĕo, fāllo, dēcĭpĭo.

ēlŭo, ŭī, ūtŭm, *to wash out.* Iufēctum ēlŭĭtŭr, Virg. Syn. Lăvo, dīlŭo, tērgo, ābstērgo, dēlĕo. V. Purgo.

ēlūsŭs, ă, ŭm, *the pass. partic. of* eludo. Mōrsūque ēlūsŭs ĭnānī, Virg.

ēlūtŭs, ă, ŭm, *the pass. partic. of* eluo. Nīl ēst ēlūtĭŭs hōrtō, Hor.

ēlŭvĭēs, ĭēī, f., *a deluge.* Ēlŭvĭē mōns ēst, Ov. Syn. Dīlŭvĭŭm, āllŭvĭŭm, dīlŭvĭēs, āllŭvĭēs. V. Diluvium.

Elўsĭŭm, ĭī, n., *Paradise.* Mĭttĭmŭr Elўsĭŭm, Virg. Epith. Āmplŭm, lætŭm, quĭētŭm, fēlīx, āmœnŭm.

Elўsĭŭs, ă, ŭm, *of Elysium.* Cōllĕ sŭb Elўsĭō, Ov.

ēmăcŭlo, ās, *to wash out spots.* Ēmăcŭlātūrŭm spŏndĕt, Cl. Syn. Pūrgo, măcŭlās tērgo, ābstērgo, dēlĕo, tōllo, aūfĕro, ēlŭo, dīlŭo.

ēmāncĭpātŭs, ă, ŭm, *the pass. partic. of* emancipo. Ēmāncĭpātŭs fœmĭnæ (Iamb. Dim.) Hor.

ēmāncĭpo, ās, *to set at liberty.* Ēmāncĭpāvīt fīlĭŭm, Sen.

ēmāno, ās, *to flow out.* Ēmānārīt, ŭtī, Lucr. Syn. Māno, dīmāno, prōmāno, ēfflŭo, ēxĕo ; ŏrĭŏr.

Ēmāthĭă, æ, f., *a country of Macedonia; Macedonia, Thessaly.* Ēmāthĭam, ēt lātōs Hæmī, Virg.

Ēmāthĭōn, ōnĭs, m., *the name of a warrior.* Ēmāthĭōnă Lĭgĕr stērnĭt, Virg.

Ēmāthĭŭs, ă, ŭm, *and* Ēmāthĭs, ĭdĭs, f., *Macedonian, Thessalian.* Quæ dŭcĭs Ēmāthĭī, Ov. Tēllūs Ēmāthĭs, Luc.

ēmātūrēsco, ĭs, *to grow full ripe.* Ēmātūrŭĕrīt Cæsărĭs īră, Ov.

ĕmāx, ācĭs, m., *a great buyer.* Pōssĭs ĕmācī, Pers.

ēmblēmă, ătĭs, n., *an emblem.* Ātque ēmblēmătĕ vērmĭcŭlātō, Lucil. Epith. Dīvĕs, mĭnūtŭm.

ēmēndo, ās, *to correct.* Ēmēndātūrŭs, sī lĭcŭĭssĕt, Ov. Syn. Cōrrĭgo, mēndīs pūrgo. V. Corrigo.

ēmēnsŭs, ă, ŭm, *the pass. partic. of* emetior. Hōc ētĭam ēmēnsō, Virg.

ēmēntĭŏr, īrĭs, *to lie.* Ēmēntītŭs ĕrăt, Ov. Syn. Mēntĭŏr, fīngo, cōnfīngo.

ēmĕrĕo, ēs ; ĕŏr, ĕrĭs, *to deserve.* Ēt tămĕn ēmĕrŭī, Prop.

ēmērgo, sī, *to swim, to emerge.* Haūd făcĭle ēmērgŭnt, Juv. Syn. Ēxĕo ; ēvādo ; ēxsūrgo.

ēmĕrĭtŭs, ă, ŭm, *the pass. partic. of* emereo ; *a soldier who has completed his time.* Ēmĕrĭtōs Mūsĭs, Mart. Syn. Mūnĕrĕ fūnctŭs ; mĕrĭtŭs.

ēmētĭŏr, īrĭs, *to measure.* Tānto ēmētĭrĭs ācērvō, Hor. Syn. Mētĭŏr, mēnsūro.

ēmēto, ĭs, ĕrĕ, *to reap.* Dŏtālĭbŭs ēmētăt ārvĭs, Hor.

ēmĭco, cŭī, *to shine forth.* Ēmĭcăt ārdēns, Virg. Syn. Mĭco, lūcĕo, splēndĕo, ēffūlgĕo, lūcēsco, ēnĭtĕo ; ēxūlto.

ēmigro, ās, *to remove from.* Ŭt ēmīgrāvĭmŭs, (Iamb.) Syn. Migro, dēmigro, dīscēdo, ēxcēdo, ēxĕo.

ēmĭnĕo, ēs, *to be higher.* Ēmĭnĕt āmbās, Ov. Syn. Ēxto, āppārĕo, ēxcēdo, sŭpĕro, ēxcēllo.

ēmĭnŭs, adv., *far off.* Ēmĭnŭs ĭpsĕ, Ov. Syn. Lōngē, lōngĭŭs, prŏcŭl.

ēmīrŏr, ārĭs, *to admire.* Ēmīrābĭtŭr īnsōlēns, Hor. V. Miror.

ēmīssŭs, ă, ŭm, *the pass. partic. of* emitto. Ēt sēmĕl ēmīssŭm, Hor.

ēmītto, īsī, īssŭm, *to send forth.* Dŏmĭtōs ēmīttĕrĕ vōcĕm, Tib. Syn. Mītto, dīmītto ; ējĭcĭo.

ĕmo, ēmī, ptŭm, *to buy.* Hæc ĕmĭs, hīrsūtō, Juv. Nēc pŭdŏr ēst ēmīssĕ pălăm, Ov. Syn. Păro, cōmpăro.

ēmŏdĕrŏr, ārĭs, *to moderate.* Ēmŏdĕrāndŭs ĕrĭt, Ov. V. Moderor.

ēmŏdŭlŏr, ārĭs, *to warble.* Ēmŏdŭlāndă pĕdēs, Ov.

ēmōllĭo, īvī *and* ĭī, ītŭm, *to soften.* Ēmōllīt mōrēs, Ov. Syn. Mōllĭo ; plăco, mītĭgo, mūlcĕo, cōlĭbĕo.

ēmŏlo, ĭs, ĕrĕ, *to grind.* Ēmŏlĕ ; quĭd mĕtŭās, Pers.

ēmŏlŭmēntŭm, ī, n., *profit.* Ēmŏlŭmēntă nŏtēmŭs, Juv. Syn. Ŭtĭlĭtās, lucrŭm, cōmmŏdŭm.

ēmŏrĭŏr, ĕrĭs, *to die.* Ānte, ăĭt, ēmŏrĭăr, Ov. V. Morior.

ēmōtŭs, ă, ŭm, *the pass. partic. of* emoveo. Jānŭa ĕt ēmōtī, Virg.

ēmŏvĕo, ōvī, *to move.* Ēmŏvĕt, ēt fīdŭm, Virg. Syn. Mŏvĕo; ēdūco, sūbdūco.

Empĕdŏclēs, ĭs, m., *the philosopher.* Empĕdŏclēs, ārdēntĕm, Hor. Epith. Agrĭgēntīnŭs, Sĭcŭlŭs.

ēmpŏrĭŭm, ĭī, n., *a fair.* Pīsārum ēmpŏrĭŏ, Rutil. V. Forum.

ēmptŏr, ōrĭs, m., *a buyer.* Emptōrem īnvītăt, Hor.

ēmūgĭo, ĭī, ītŭm, *to bellow out.* Lōngās ēmūgīt būccīnă vōcēs, C. Sever.

ēmūndo, ās, *to cleanse.* Syn. Mūndo, pūrgo, ēlŭo.

ēmūngo, xī, ctŭm, *to wipe.* Emūnctæ nārĭs, Hor. Syn. Mūngo.

ēmūnĭo, ĭī, īrĕ, *to fence.* Fūltōsque ēmūnīīt ōbjīcĕ, Virg.

ēn, interj., *lo, see.* Călămōs, ēn āccīpĕ, Virg. Syn. Eccĕ.

Ēnæsĭmŭs, ī, m., *the name of a warrior.* Effūgīt Ēnæsīmŭs, Ov.

ēnārrābĭlĭs, ĕ, *that may be related.* Nōn ēnārrābīlĕ tēxtŭm, Virg. Syn. Effābĭlĭs.

ēnārro, ās, *to declare.* Fŏrās ēnārrĕt īn āĕrĭs aūrās, Lucr. Syn. Nărro, ēxplāno, mĕmŏro, cōmmĕmŏro, rĕfĕro.

ēnāscŏr, ĕrĭs, *to be born.* V. Nascor.

ēnăto, ās, *to swim out.* Ēnătăt ēxspēs, Hor. Syn. Năto, nō. V. Nato.

ēnāvĭgo, ās, *to sail out.* Ēnāvĭgăndă, sīvĕ, (Iamb. cum syll.) Hor. V. Nāvigo.

Encĕlădŭs, ī, m., *a giant struck with thunder by Jupiter.* Fāma ēst, Encĕlădī, Virg. Syn. Gĭgās cēntĭpēs. Epith. Jăcŭlātŏr, fĕrōx, trŭx, atrōx, Trīnacrĭŭs, Sĭcŭlŭs, cēntĭpēs.

ēndrŏmĭs, ĭdĭs, f., *a thick mantle.* Ēndrŏmĭdās Tȳrĭās, Juv. Epith. Tȳrĭă, pĕregrīnă, vīllōsă, hīrsūtă.

Endȳmĭōn, ōnĭs, m., *a Thessalian shepherd, loved by Diana.* Prōdĕrĭt Ēndȳmĭōn, Mart. Epith. Lātmĭŭs dōrmītŏr, vēnātŏr; tĕnĕr, dŭlcĭs, fōrmōsŭs, dīlēctŭs, pūlchĕr, blāndŭs, cōmĭs, vĕnūstŭs, ămābĭlĭs, dĕcōrŭs, Thēssălŭs.

ēnĕco, cŭī, ctŭm, *to kill.* Ēnĕcăt, ēt nūllā, Lucan. Syn. Nĕco, ōccīdo, pĕrĭmo, īntĕrfĭcĭo. V. Occido.

ēnērvĭs, ĕ, *weak.* Frāctīque ēnērvī cōrpŏrĕ grēssŭs, Pet. Syn. Enērvŭs, īmbēllĭs, dēbĭlĭs.

ēnērvo, ās, *to enervate.* Ut Vĕnŭs ēnērvăt, Virg. Syn. Dēbĭlĭto, īnfīrmo.

ĕnĭm, conj., *for.* Prōgĕnĭēm sĕd ĕnĭm, Virg. Syn. Năm, nāmquĕ, ĕtĕnĭm.

Ēnīpeūs, ī, m., *a river in Thessaly.* Tūrbĭdŭs īlĭt Ēnīpeūs, Luc. Epith. Lēntŭs, tŭmĭdŭs, ūndāns, pūlchĕr, ăltŭs, Æmŏnĭŭs, Thēssălĭcŭs.

ēnītĕo, *and* ēsco, tŭī, *to shine.* Ēnītĕt ōrĕ, Virg. Syn. Nītĕo, mĭco, ēmĭco, lūcĕo, splēndĕo, cŏrūsco, ēlūcĕo, ēlūcēsco, fūlgēsco, effūlgēsco.

ēnītŏr, ĕrĭs, xŭs, *to strive.* Nēc sīc ēnītăr, Hor. Syn. Nītŏr, cōnŏr, mōhŏr, cōntĕndo; părĭo.

Ennă, æ, f., *a town in Sicily.* Ennă părēns flōrŭm, Cl.

Ennæŭs, ă, ŭm, *of Enna.* Haūd prŏcŭl Ennæĭs lăcŭs ēst ā mœnĭbŭs, Ov.

Ennĭŭs, ĭī, m., *the ancient poet.* Grăvĭs Ennĭŭs, ōrĕ, Ov. Epith. Grăvĭs, dōctŭs, măgnŭs, rŭdĭs, īngĕnĭōsŭs, ălūmnŭs, Pătĕr.

Ennŏmŭs, ī, m., *a prince of Mysia.* Ennŏmōn āctŭm, Ov.

ēno, ās, *to swim out.* Gĕlĭdās ēnāvĭt ăd Arctōs, Virg.

ēnōdĭs, ĕ, *without knots.* Aūt rūrsum ēnōdēs trŭncī, Virg. Syn. Lævĭs, nōdīs cărēns.

ēnōrmĭs, ĕ, *out of rule, huge.* Lūsĭt ĕt ēnōrmēs, Stat. Syn. Immēnsŭs, īmmānĭs, īngēns.

Enōs, *or* ōch, m., *the patriarch.* Prōdīīt Ēnōs, Vict. Syn. Enōchŭs, Jărīdēs. Epith. Sānctŭs, pīŭs, jūstŭs, lōngævŭs, prīscŭs, āntīquŭs, vĕtŭs.

ēnsĭfĕr, ă, ŭm, *bearing a sword.* Ensĭfĕr Orīōn, Ov.

ēnsĭs, ĭs, m., *a sword.* Ensĭbŭs æră, Virg. Syn. Fērrŭm, glădĭŭs, mūcro, cūspĭs. Epith. Rĭgĭdŭs, dīstrīctŭs, nĕfāndŭs, fērvĭdŭs, īnfīdŭs, cōrūscŭs, fătĭfĕr, dĕcōrŭs, Mārtĭŭs, fērrĕŭs, bēllĭcŭs, fĕrŭs, lēthālĭs, ăcūtŭs, ĭmprŏbŭs, ĭmpĭŭs, īnfaūstŭs, vūlnīfĭcŭs, sānguĭnĕŭs, crŭēntŭs, crŭēntātŭs, īnfēstŭs, mĭnāx, īmmītĭs, pūgnāx, hōrrēndŭs, īnsānŭs, aūrātŭs, vălĭdŭs, hōstĭcŭs, bārbărŭs, Māvōrtĭŭs, crūdēlĭs, sānguĭnŏlēntŭs.

Entēllŭs, ī, m., *a Trojan who founded a city near the Crinisus in Sicily.* Stăt grăvĭs Entēllŭs, Virg.

ēnŭclĕo, ās, *to take out the kernel, explain.* Ĕnŭclĕārĕ mŏlēstŭm, Mart. Syn.
Expōno, pāndo, ĕxplĭco, ēnārro, ăpĕrĭo.
ēnŭmĕro, ās, *to enumerate.* Ĕnŭmĕrāt mīlĕs, Prop.   Syn. Nŭmĕro, rĕcēnsĕo,
dīnŭmĕro, pērcēnsĕo.
* ‖ ēnūncĭo, ās, *to pronounce.* Cic.   Syn. Prōnūncĭo, ēlŏquŏr, prōfĕro, ēxprĭmo,
nūncĭo.
‖ ēnūtrĭo, īī *and* īvī. Ĕnūtrīvĕrĕ sŭb āntrīs. V. Nutrio.
Ĕnўō, ūs, f., *a name of Bellona.* Cīvīlīs Ĕnўō, Mart. Syn. Bĕllōnă. Epitii.
Sævă, Mārtĭă, nāvālīs, fŭrĭālīs, dīrā, fĕrālīs, crūdēlīs. V. Bellona.
ĕo, īvī, ītŭm, *to go.* Deīnde ĕō dŏrmītŭm, Hor. Syn. Incēdo, grădĭŏr, prōgrĕdĭŏr, tēndo, vādo, prŏfīcīscŏr, fĕrŏr, prōcēdo, pērgo, pĕto. V. Abeo.
ĕō, adv., *there.* Ibīt ĕō, quō vīs, Hor. Syn. Hūc ; tāntō.
Eōs, f., *the morning.* Præmīsĕrīt Eōs, Ov. V. Aurora.
Eōŭs, ă, ŭm, *Eastern.* Pōrtŭs ăb Eōō, Virg. Ăpĕrīmŭs Eōās, Lucan. V. Oriens.
Eōŭs, ī, m., *Lucifer ; one of the horses of the Sun.* Cēdēbăt Eōō, Sil. Pўrŏīs,
Eōŭs ŏt Æthōn, Ov. Epith. Ardēns, ācĕr.
Ĕpăphŭs, ī, m., *a son of Jupiter and Io.* Hīnc Ĕpăphŭs māgnī, Ov.
Ĕpēŭs, ī, m., *a Greek who constructed the Trojan horse.* Dŏlī făbrĭcătŏr Ĕpēŭs, Virg.
ĕphēbŭs, ī, m., *a youth.* Ămāntīs ĕphēbī, Hor. Syn. Ădŏlēscēns, jŭvĕnīs. Epith.
Gĕnĕrōsŭs, fōrtīs, aūdāx, fōrmōsŭs, pŭlchĕr, dĕcōrŭs. V. Adolescens.
ĕphēmĕrīs, ĭdīs, f., *a journal.* Cērnīs ĕphēmĕrīdās, Juv.
Ĕphĕsŭs, ī, m., *a city of Ionia.* Aūt Ĕphĕsŭm, Hor.
ĕphīppĭŭm, īī, n., *a saddle.* Ōptăt ĕphīppĭă bōs, Hor. Epith. Strătŭm.
Ĕphўră, æ, *or* rē, ēs, *an ancient name of Corinth.* Hīc Ĕphўrēn bĭmărĕm, Ov.
Ĕphўrœŭs, *and* rēĭŭs, ă, ŭm, *of Corinth.* Ĕphўrœœ Lāĭdŏs ædēs, Prop. Ĕphў-
rēĭăque œră, Virg.
Ĕpĭchārmŭs, ī, m., *a comic poet.* Sĭcŭlī prŏpĕrāre Ĕpĭchārmī, Hor.
Ĕpīctētŭs, ī, m., *the philosopher.* Epith. Paūpĕr, sērvŭs, ĭnŏps, pĕrītŭs, dōctŭs,
ĭngĕnĭōsŭs, săpĭēns, Stōĭcŭs ; claūdŭs.
Ĕpĭcūrēŭs, *and* ĭŭs, ă, ŭm, *of Epicurus.* Ast Ĕpĭcūrēōs, Sid   Ut crēdās Ĕpĭcūrĭŏs,
(Phal.)
Ĕpĭcūrŭs, ī, m., *the Athenian philosopher.* Ĕpĭcūrī dē grĕgĕ pōrcŭm, Hor. Epith.
Lāscīvŭs, mōllīs, dōctŭs, Cўnĭcŭs.
ĕpĭcŭs, ă, ŭm, *epic.* Quōd tū sīve ĕpĭcō, (Phal.) Syn. Hērōĭcŭs.
Ĕpĭdaūrĭŭs, ă, ŭm, *of Epidaurus.* Aūt sērpēns Ĕpĭdaūrĭŭs, Hor.
Ĕpĭdaūrŭs, ī, m., *a city of Achaia.* Dōmĭtrīx Ĕpĭdaūrŭs ĕquōrŭm, Virg.
ĕpĭgrāmmă, ătīs, n, *an epigram.* Hēxămĕtrīs ĕpĭgrāmmă făcīs, Mart. Epitii.
Blāndŭm, ĭngĕnĭōsŭm, ārgūtŭm, sŭbtīlĕ, lĕpĭdŭm, fēstīvŭm, brĕvĕ, vīvĭdŭm,
grātŭm.
ĕpĭrhēdĭŭm, īī, n., *a kind of chariot.* Trăhŭnt ĕpĭrhēdĭă cōllō, Juv.
Ĕpīrŭs, ī, f., *a country of ancient Greece.* Pālmās Ĕpīrŭs ĕquārŭm, Virg. Syn.
Chāŏnĭă. Epitii. Mōntānă, sўlvōsă, ăspĕră, pŏtēns, fĕrāx. -
‖ ĕpīscŏpŭs, ī, m., *a bishop.* Plēbīs ĕpīscŏpŭs, (Glycon.) Prud. Syn. Præsŭl,
āntīstĕs. Epith. Vĕnĕrāndŭs, săcĕr, pĭŭs, īnclўtŭs, lōngævŭs, vīttātŭs, rēlĭgĭōsŭs, vĕrēndŭs, pūrŭs, sānctŭs, īntĕgĕr.
ĕpīstŏlă, æ, f., *and* ĭŭm, īī, n., *a letter.* Vĭŏlārīt ĕpīstŏlă nōstrōs, Ov. Mīttīs
ĕpīstŏlĭŭm, Cat. Syn. Līttĕră, chārtă, lĭbēllŭs. Epitii. Nūncĭă, īntērnūncĭă,
mīssă, cōmmīssă, vērbōsă, brĕvīs. V. Litteræ.
‖ ĕpĭtăphĭŭm, īī, n., *an epitaph.*
Ĕpōpeŭs, ĕī, m., *a man's name.* Hōrtātŏr Ĕpōpeŭs, Ov.
ĕpōps, ŏpīs, m., *a lapwing.* Nōmĕn ĕpōps vŏlŭcrī, Ov.
ĕpŏs, ī *and* ŏdŏs, *or* ŭs, ī, m., *a poem.* Fōrte ĕpŏs ăcĕr, Hor. Dŭlcēm sŭbnēctĭt
ĕpōdŏn, Ter. M. V. Carmen.
ĕpōto, ās, *to drink up.* Tōtĭēs ĕpōtāvĕrĕ lăcērnæ, Mart. Syn. Pōto, haūrĭo,
ēxhaūrĭo.
ĕpōtŭs, ă, ŭm, *drunk up, absorbed.* Hīc vŏmĭt ĕpōtās, Ov.
ĕpŭlæ, ārŭm, f. pl., *and* ĕpŭlŭm, ī, n., *food, a feast, banquet.* Tūrgĭdŭs hīc ĕpŭlīs,
Pers. Atque ĕpŭlum ārbĭtrĭo, Hor. Syn. Dăpēs, cĭbī ; cōnvīvĭŭm. Epitii.
Dūlcēs, rēgālēs, sŭpērbæ, sŏlūtæ, suāvēs, ūnctæ, lætæ, fūmāntēs. V. Epulor.
ĕpŭlo, ōnīs, m., *a guest.* Lūrcōnum, ĕpŭlōnŭm, Mart. Syn. Cōnvīvă.—2. *the
name of a warrior.* Ĕpŭlōnem ōbtrūncăt Achātēs, Virg.

ĕpŭlŏr, ārĭs, *to banquet.* Dăpĭbūsque ĕpŭlămŭr ŏpīmīs, Virg. Syn. Cŏnvīvŏr
V. Convivor.

Ĕpўtĭdēs, æ, m., *the son of Epytus, preceptor of Iulus.* Ĕpўtĭdēn vŏcăt, Virg.

Ĕpўtŭs, ī, m., *the armour-bearer of Anchises.* Māxĭmŭs ārmīs Ĕpўtŭs, Virg.

ĕquă, æ, f., *a mare.* Ĕpīrŭs ĕquārŭm, Virg. Epith. Armēntālĭs, lāscīvă.

ĕquĕs, ĭtĭs, m., *a knight, a horseman.* Făcĭănt ĕquĭtēs Asīānī, Juv. Epith.
Sēvērŭs, clārŭs ; bēllātŏr, sŭpērbŭs, hāstātŭs, cēlsŭs, ēgrĕgĭŭs. V. Equito.

ĕquĕstĕr, *or* strĭs, ĕ, *belonging to a horse.* Annŭlo ĕquĕstrī, Hor.

Ĕquĭcŏlŭs, *or* ŭlŭs, ī, m., *the name of a warrior.* Ĕquĭcŏlŭs ărmīs, Virg.

ĕquĭdĕm, *myself indeed.* Pēr me ĕquĭdĕm, Pers. Syn. Ĕgŏmĕt, *or* cērtē.

ĕquīnŭs, ă, ŭm, *of a horse.* Pīctŏr ĕquīnăm, Hor.

ĕquīrĭă, ōrŭm, n. pl., *horse-races, instituted by Romulus.* Pērmānsĭt ĕquīrĭă
nŏmĕn, Ov.

ĕquĭtātŭs, ūs, m., *cavalry.* Pŏrtīs ĕquĭtātŭs ăpērtīs, Virg. Syn. Ĕquĭtēs.

ĕquĭto, ās, *to ride on horseback.* Lævōs ĕquĭtāvĭt īn ŏrbēs, Virg. V. Equus *and*
eques.

ĕquŭlĕŭs, ī, m. V. Eculeus.

ĕquŭs, ī, m., *a horse.* Ille ĕquŭs, illĕ, Prop. Syn. Cŏrnĭpēs, quadrŭpēs, sŏnĭpēs.
Epith. Bēllātŏr, ārdŭŭs, ārdēns, fŏrtĭs, spūmāns, cĭtātŭs, frĕmēns, fĕrŏx, īmpĭgĕr, vēlŏx, mōrdāx, ănĭmōsŭs, ănhēlŭs, cĭtŭs, răpĭdŭs, āspĕr, nōbĭlĭs, tērrĭbĭlĭs,
vŏlŭcĕr, lĕvĭs, præcēps, īgnĭpēs, īntrĕpĭdŭs, bēllĭcŭs, aūdāx, pūgnāx, pērnīx,
ălăcĕr, gĕnĕrōsŭs, Mārtĭŭs, Thrācĭŭs, īmpăvĭdŭs, phălĕrātŭs, sŭpērbŭs, fŭrēns,
fŭrĭbūndŭs, cŏmāns, jŭbātŭs, crīnītŭs, sūmāns, sūdāns, īntērrĭtŭs, īmpērtērrĭtŭs,
stērnāx.—2. *horses of the Sun.* Epith. Ignĭvŏmī, īgnĭpĕdēs, flāmmĭpĕdēs, flām-
mĭgĕrī, ālĭpĕdēs, vŏlucrēs, lūcēntēs, pŭrpŭrēī.

ērādīco, ās, *to root up.* Dī te ērādīcēnt, Ter. Syn. Avēllo, cōnvēllo, ēxtīrpo,
ēvēllo.

ērādo, sī, sŭm, *to scrape off.* Ērādēndă Cŭpīdĭnĭs, (Choriamb.) Hor. Syn.
Rādo, ēxpūgno.

Ĕrăsīnŭs, ī, m., *a river of Arcadia.* Ingēns Ĕrăsīnŭs ĭn āgrīs, Ov.

Ĕrătō, ūs, *one of the Muses.* Quī rēgēs, Ĕrătō, quæ tēmpŏră, Virg. V. Musæ.

Ĕrĕbĕŭs, ă, ŭm, *belonging to Erebus.* Ŭnxērūnt Ĕrĕbĕæ, Ov.

Ĕrĕbŭs, ī, m., *hell.* Ēt māgnōs Ĕrĕbī, Virg. V. Infernus.

Ĕrēchtheŭs, ĕŏs, ĕī *or* eī, m., *a king of Athens.* Mŏdĕrāmĕn Ĕrēchtheŭs, Ov.

Ĕrēchthĕŭs, ă, ŭm, *belonging to Athens.* Quālĭs Ĕrēchthēĭs, Virg.

Ĕrēchthĭdæ, ārŭm, m. pl., *the Athenians.* Nūllŭs Ĕrēchthīdāĕ, Ov. V. Attici.

Ĕrēchthĭs, ĭdĭs, f., *the daughter of Erechtheus.* Ĕrēchthĭdă Thrācēs, Ov.

ērēctŭs, ă, ŭm, *the pass. partic. of* erigo. Ērēctăs īn tērgă sŭdēs, Juv.

|| ĕrēmŭs, ī, f., *a wilderness.* Vērsāntŭr ĕrēmō. ' Syn. Dēsērtŭm. Epith. Sŏlă.

ērēpo, ĭs, *to creep out.* Ērēpĕt gĕnĭbŭs, Juv.

ērēptŭs, ă, ŭm, *the pass. partic. of* eripio. Nŏmĕn ĕt ērēptī, Ov.

Ĕrētŭs, ī, m., *a city of the Sabines.* Ĕrĕtī mănŭs ŏmnĭs, Virg.

ērgă, prep., *towards.* Quĭd trīstĭbŭs ērgă Fīlĭŏlŭm, Juv.

ērgāstŭlŭm, ī, n., *a workhouse.* Tūsca ērgāstŭlă mīttăs, Juv. Syn. Cārcĕr.

ērgo, adv., *then.* Ērgŏ părēs, Mart. Ērgŏ jūssă părăt, Virg.

Ĕrīchthō, ōnĭs, f., *one of the Furies.* Fŭrĭālĭs Ĕrīchthō, Ov. Epith. Ēffĕră,
Thēssălĭs, vĕnēfĭcă, trīstĭs, prŏfānă.

Ĕrīchthŏnĭŭs, ĭī, m., *a king of Athens.* Prīmŭs Ĕrīchthŏnĭŭs, Virg.

Ĕrīdănŭs, ī, m., *a river in Italy.* Plūrĭmŭs Ĕrĭdānī, Virg. Syn. Pădŭs. Epith.
Aūrātŭs, sŭpērbŭs, Phăēthōntēŭs, māxĭmŭs, tūrbĭdŭs, ēxūndāns, vĭŏlēntŭs, fĕrŭs,
răpāx, văgŭs, nōbĭlĭs, ĭngēns, cŏrnĭgĕr, ĭnūndāns, Vĕnĕtŭs; rĭgŭŭs, īrrĭgŭŭs,
fœcūndŭs, fērtĭlĭs. V. Fluvius.

ērĭgo, rēxī, ctŭm, *to erect, build.* Ērĭgĭt ālnōs, Virg. Syn. Ēxtōllo, ēxcĭto,
ēvĕho, ēffĕro, ēlĕvo, āttōllo.

Ĕrĭgŏnē, ēs, f., *the daughter of Icarus.* Ĕrĭgŏnēn fālsă, Ov. Epith. Icărĭs, Icărĭă,
flēbĭlĭs, pĭă.

Ĕrĭgŏnēĭŭs, ă, ŭm, *of Erigone.* Cănĭs Ĕrĭgŏnēĭŭs ēxĭt, Ov.

Ĕrīnnўs, ўŏs, f., *one of the Furies.* Fērtĭs Ĕrīnnўēs ātræ, Ov. Epith. Trīstĭs,
fĕrālĭs, īnsānă, crūdēlĭs, nōctūrnă, flāmmĭfĕră, tŏrvă, sævă, mĭnāx, ānguĭfĕră,
fŭrĭālĭs, Stўgĭă, īnfērnă, dīră, īmpătĭēns, fūnēstă, răbĭdă, scĕlĕrātă, dīscŏrs, īnfēlīx, īmprŏbă, vēsānă, ānguĭcŏmă. V. Furiæ.

Erĭph̄ylē, ēs, or ȳlă, æ, f., *wife to Amphiaraus.* Epitii. Pērfīdă, nĕfāndă, ĭmpĭă, ĭmprŏbă, scĕlĕrātă, ăvārā, mœstă.

ērĭpĭo, pŭī, ēptŭin, *to snatch.* Erĭpĭt hærēntēs, Hor. Syn. Răpĭo, prærĭpĭo, aŭfĕro, ădĭmo, ēxtōrquĕo, tōllo.

Erĭsīchthōn, ŏnĭs, m., *a Thessalian king, who devoured his own flesh.* Pœnāmque Erĭsīclithōnĭs ōrānt, Ov. Epitii. Sacrĭlĕgŭs, prŏfānŭs, ĭmpĭŭs, nĕfāndŭs, ăvĭdŭs, Trȳŏpēĭŭs. V. Famelicus.

* ĕrŏgo, *to bestow.* Apul. Syn. Lārgĭŏr, dō, dīstrĭbŭo, dōno, ēxpēndo.

ērrābūndŭs, ă, ŭm, *vagrant.* Errābūndă bŏvĭs, Virg. Syn. Văgăbūndŭs, văgŭs, ērrāns, ăbērrāns.

ērrătĭcŭs, ă, ŭm, *wandering.* Vīx ērrătĭcă Dēlŏs, Ov. Syn. Errābūndŭs; vŏlātĭlĭs.

ērrătŭm, ī, n., *an error, fault.* Errātĭs īngĕmŭīssĕ mēĭs, Ov.

ērrātŭs, ūs, m., *a wandering.* Lōngīsque ērrātĭbŭs āctŭs, Ov.

ērro, ās, *to wander.* Cæcīs ērrāmŭs ĭn ūndīs, Virg. Syn. Văgŏr, dēflēcto, ăbērro, dēvĭo; V. Aberro, vagor. Pēcco, lābŏr, dēlīnquo, ōffēndo, cŭlpæ sŭccŭmbo; V. Pecco.

ērro, ōnĭs, m., *a wanderer.* Atque ĭtĕrum ērrōnĕm, Tib.

ērrŏr, ōrĭs, m., *a maze, a wandering.* Errōrēs ēxŭĭt ōmnēs, Juv. Syn. Errŏr vĭæ; ērrātŭm, pēccātŭm, cōmmīssŭm, cŭlpă, mēndŭm. Epitii. Dŭbĭŭs, mălŭs, vānŭs, grăvĭs, tĕmĕrārĭŭs, pērplēxŭs, prāvŭs, cæcŭs, tūrpĭs, ūvĭŭs, dēvĭŭs, văgŭs, vĕrēcūndŭs, īndēlēbĭlĭs, ĭnēxtrīcābĭlĭs. V. Peccatum.

ērŭbēsco, bŭī, *to blush.* Erŭbŭīssĕ rŏsĭs, Ov. Syn. Rŭbĕo.

ērūcă, æ, f., *the herb rocket.* Erŭcās vĭrĭdēs, Hor. Epitii. Călĭdă, sălāx, ūrēns, vĭrēns.

ērūcto, ās, *to belch.* Erĭgĭt ērūctāns, Virg. V. Ejicio.

ērŭdĭo, ĭī, ītŭm, *to instruct.* Erŭdĭt ārtēs, Ov. Syn. Instĭtŭo, īnstrŭo. V. Doceo.

ērŭdĭtŭs, ă, ŭm, *learned.* Erŭdītŭsque ēst, (Phal.) Mart. Syn. Dōctŭs, pĕrītŭs. V. Doctus.

ērūmpo, ūpī, *to burst out.* Sŭbĭto ērūmpŭnt, Virg. Syn. Exĕo, ēgrĕdĭŏr, ăbĕo, ēvādo; cŭm sŏnĭtu ēgrĕdĭŏr; vi ēxĕo. V. Abeo.

ērŭo, rŭī, rŭtŭm, *to root up.* Cōrnĭcum ĭmmĕrĭtās ērŭĭt, Prop. Syn. Vēllo, ēvēllo, ēxtīrpo, ēffŏdĭo; dīrŭo, ēvērto. V. Everto.

ērŭtŭs, ă, ŭm, *the pass. partic. of* eruo. Erŭtă pīnŭs, Virg.

ērvŭm, ī, n., *a lentil, pulse.* Tĕnŭī sōlābĭtŭr ērvŏ, Hor.

Erȳcīnă, æ, f., *a name of Venus.* Hūnc Erȳcīnă văgāntĕm, Ov. V. Venus.

Erȳcīnŭs, ă, ŭm, *of mount Eryx.* Erȳcĭuo ĭn vērtĭcĕ sēdēs, Virg.

Erȳmānthĕŭs, or ĭŭs, ă, ŭm, *of Erymanthus.* Quīque Erȳmānthēī, V. Fl. Erȳmānthĭă pēstĭs. Sil.

Erȳmānthĭs, ĭdŏs, f., *of Arcadia.* Sȳlvās Erȳmānthĭdăs, Ov.

Erȳmānthŭs, ī, m., *a mountain in Arcadia.* Aūt Erȳmānthī sȳlvīs, Hor. Epith. Altŭs, sūblīmĭs, ārdŭŭs, prærūptŭs, rĭgĭdŭs, gĕlĭdŭs, cūprēssĭfĕr, mōnstrĭfĕr.

Erȳmās, āntĭs, m., *a Trojan warrior.* Tŭm Mĕrŏpem ātque Erȳmāntă, Virg.

Erȳthĕă, or ĭă, æ, *an island near Spain, where Geryon dwelt.* Egĕrăt ē stăbŭlīs, O Erȳthĕā, tŭīs, Prop.

Erȳthĕŭs, ă, ŭm, *and* Erȳthĕĭs, f., *of Erythea.* Erȳthĕā ăd līttŏră Gādēs, Sil. Erȳthēĭdă prædăm, Ov.

Erȳthīnŭs, ī, m., *a fish.* Erȳthīnŭs ĭn ūndā, Ov.

Erȳthræŭs, ă, ŭm, mărĕ, *the Red Sea.* Quīcquĭd Erȳthræā, Mart. *Indian.* Cūrrŭs, Erȳthræīs, quĭs nŭpēr vīctŏr ăb ōrīs, Stat.

Erȳx, ȳcĭs, m., *a mountain in Sicily.* Sēmpĕr ăpērtŭs Erȳx, Ov. Epitii. Altŭs, cēlsŭs, sūblīmĭs, īnvĭŭs, nĭmbōsŭs, Sĭcŭlŭs.

ĕs, *of the verb* sum, *thou art.* Quīsquĭs ēs, Virg.

Esăĭăs, or Esājās, æ, m., *the prophet.* Esājās lŏcŭplēs, Tert. Epitii. Sānctŭs, săcĕr, dīvīnŭs, fātĭdĭcŭs, prænūncĭŭs, præscĭŭs, præsăgŭs, vērŭs, vērāx.

ēscă, æ, f., *nourishment.* Escă tĭbi, Ov. Syn. Cĭbŭs, dăpēs, ălĭmēntŭm, pābŭlŭm. V. Cibus.

ēscārĭŭs, ă, ŭm, *belonging to meat.* Et mīlle ēscārĭă, Juv.

ēscŭlēntŭs, ă, ŭm, *good to eat.* Nĕc ēscŭlēntă, Mart.

ēscŭlŭs, ī, m. V. Æsculus

Ésquĭlĭæ, ārŭm, f. pl., *a district of Rome situated on the Esquiline hill.* Quæ nŭnc Ésquĭlĭīs, Ov.

Ésquĭlĭŭs, *and* ĭnŭs, ă, ŭm, *Esquiline, of the Esquiline hill.* Mŏntĕ sŭb Ésquĭlĭŏ, Ov. Ésquĭlĭnī pŏntĭfĕx vĕnĕfĭcī, Hor.

ĕssĕdŭm, ī, n., *a Gallic chariot.* Essĕdă cōllō, Virg. Epith. Bĕlgĭcŭm, strīdĕns, mŭltĭsŏnŭm, Brĭtānnŭm, cūrvŭm. V. Currus.

ĕsŭrĭēs, ĭēī, f., *hunger.* Esŭrĭēs ignōtă, Alcim. V. Fames.

ĕsŭrĭo, īs, īī, *to be hungry.* Sŭstŭlĭt ĕsŭrĭēns, Hor. V. Fames.

* || ĕsŭs, ūs, m., *an eating.* Dēpŏnĭtŭr ēsŭs, Alcim.

ĕt, conj., *and.* Nātŭs ĕt īpsĕ, Virg. Syn. Ac, ătquĕ, quĕ.

ĕtĕnĭm, adv., *for.* Nŭlla ĕtĕnĭm, Hor. Syn. Ēnĭm, năm.

Étĕŏclēs, *or* thĭoclēs, ĭs *or* ĕŏs, m., *the brother of Polynices.* Nĕfās Étĕŏclĭs ăcĕrvăt, Stat. Sævŭs Éthĭoclēs, Id. Epith. Dūrŭs, ĭnfāndŭs, nĕfāndŭs, Cādmæŭs, Thēbānŭs. V. Polynices.

Étēsĭæ, ārŭm, f. pl., *the periodical north-east winds.* Étēsĭæ īn vădă pōntī, Cic.

Étēsĭŭs, ă, ŭm, *of the Etesian winds.* Étēsĭă flābră, Lucr.

Éthēmōn, ŏnĭs, m., *the name of a warrior.* Nābăthæŭs Éthēmōn, Ov.

ĕtĭăm, conj., *also, yes.* Nŭnc ĕtĭăm pĕcŭdēs, Virg. Syn. Ét, āc, quŏquĕ, părĭtĕr, sĭmĭlĭtĕr.

Etrūscŭs, ă, ŭm, *Etrurian, Tuscan.* Insēdĭt Étrūscīs, Virg. Tĭbrĭ, pĕr Étrūscōs, Ov. Syn. Tūscŭs, Tўrrhēnŭs.

Etrūrĭă, æ, f., *a part of Italy.* Sōlērs Etrūrĭă, Cl. Fōrtĭs Etrūrĭă crēvĭt, Virg.

ĕtsī, conj., *though.* Syn. Lĭcĕt, quāmvĭs, quānquăm.

Évă, æ, f., *Adam's wife.* Trāxĕrăt Évă vĭrŭm, Prud. Epith. Antīquă, nŏcēns, vānă, crēdŭlă.

ĕvăcŭo, ās, *to empty.* Évăcŭāt quŏd, Ar. Syn. Văcŭo.

Évādnē, ēs, f., *the wife of Capaneus, who burnt herself on his funeral pile.* Nēc fīda Évādnē, nĕc, Prop. Epith. Iphĭăs, Căpănēĭă, aūdāx, gĕnĕrōsă.

ĕvādo, sī, sŭm, *to get out of.* Sўlvāque ēvādĭt ŏpācă, Virg. Syn. Fīo ; ĕxĕo, ăbĕo, fūgĭo, aūfūgĭo, ĕxcēdo, ērŭmpo ; ēffūgĭo, vīto, ēvīto, dēclīno. V. Abeo.

|| ĕvăgŏr, ārĭs, *to ramble.* V. Vagor.

Évāgrŭs, ī, m., *one of the Lapithæ.* Vĭctŏr ăd Évāgrŭm, Ov.

Évān, ĭn., indecl., *a name of Bacchus.* Ét Ĭacchŭs ĕt Évān, Ov. Syn. Bācchŭs, Lўæŭs. Epith. Thўrsĭgĕr, ūvĭfĕr. V. Bacchus.

Évāndĕr, *and* drŭs, drī, m., *a king of Arcadia.* Pāllās, Évāndĕr, ĭn ĭpsīs, Virg Évāndrŭs hăbēbăt, Id. Epith. Exŭl Pălătīnŭs.

Évāndrĭŭs, ă, ŭm, *of Evander.* Évāndrĭŭs ăbstŭlĭt ēnsĭs, Virg.

ĕvānēsco, nŭī, *to vanish away.* Ócŭlīs ēvānŭĭt aūrăm, Virg. Syn. Vānēsco, ĕxĕo, ĕxcēdo.

ĕvānĭdŭs, ă, ŭm, *fading.* Ăbĕŭnt ēvānĭdă rīvōs, Ov. Syn. Vānēscēns, vānŭs.

|| ĕvāngĕlĭcŭs, ă, ŭm, *of the Gospel.* Aūt ēvāngĕlĭcī, Prud.

|| ĕvāngĕlīstă, æ, m., *an Evangelist.* Évāngĕlīstă scrīpsĭt, (Iamb.) Prud.

|| ĕvāngĕlĭŭm, īī, n., *the Gospel.* Clāra ēvāngĕlĭī, Al.

Eūbĭŭs, īī, m., *the name of a historian.* Eūbĭŭs īmpĭræ, Ov.

Eūbœă, æ, f., *an island in Greece.* Eūbœă dŭăbŭs, Ov. Epith. Cīrcŭmflŭă, rĭgŭă.

Eūbŏĭcŭs, ă, ŭm, *of Eubœa.* Ét tāndem Eūbŏĭcīs, Virg.

|| Eūchărīstĭă, æ, f., *the Eucharist,* Eccl.

ĕvēctŭs, *the pass. partic. of* eveho. Mĕrĭtīs ēvēctŭs ăd aūrās, Ov.

ĕvĕho, vēxī, ctŭm, *to carry out, extol.* Évĕhăt āmnĭs, Tib. Syn. Éxtōllo, ĕffĕro, āttōllo, prōmŏvĕo.

ĕvēllo, ēllī *or* ŭlsī, sŭm, *to pluck up.* Cŭpĭēns ēvēllĕrĕ plāntăm, Hor. Syn. Vēllo, cōnvēllo, ĕffŏdĭo, ēruo, ĕxtīrpo, ēxtrăho. V. Vello.

Évēnīnŭs, ă, ŭm, *of the Evenus.* Călўdŏnĭdēs Évēnīnæ, Ov.

ĕvĕnĭt, (ēnĭt, in perf.) *it happens.* Évĕnĭt, īnquīrānt, Hor. Syn. Cōntĭngĭt; ŏbtīngĭt, fīt, āccĭdĭt.

ĕvēntŭs, ūs, m., *an event, chance.* Quĭsquĭs ăb ēvēntū, Ov Syn. Cāsŭs, ĕxĭtŭs, sŏrs.

Ēvēnŭs, ī, m., *a river of Ætolia.* Vĕnĕrăt Ēvĕnī răpĭdās. Ov.

ēvĕrbĕro, ās, *to beat, buffet.* Clўpĕūmque ēvĕrbĕrăt ālīs, Virg.

ēvērsŏr, ōrĭs, m., *a subverter.* Rēgnōrum ēvērsŏr Ăchillēs, Virg.

ēvērsŭs, *the pass. partic. of* everto. Hūnc sāltem ēvērsō, Virg.

ēvērto, tī, sŭm, *to subvert.* Dīsjēcītquĕ rŭtēs, ēvērtītque, Virg. Syn. Vērto, īnvērto, pērvērto, sūbvērto, dēstrŭo, dīrŭo, dēmōlĭŏr, vāsto, pŏpŭlŏr, dēpŏpŭlŏr; vī frāngo, stērno, prōstērno, dējĭcĭo, quătĭo, cōncŭtĭo. V. Vasto, dejicio.

ēvēstīgūtŭs, ā, ŭm, *sought out.* Ēvēstīgātă prĭōrŭm, Ov.

eūgĕ, interj., *well done.* Eūgĕ pŭĕr, Pers. V. Hortor.

Ēvĭās, ădĭs, f., *a Bacchante.* Exsōmnīs stŭpĕt Ēvĭās, Hor.

Ēūĭŭs, *or* Ēvĭŭs, ĭī, m., *a name of Bacchus.* Dīssĭpăt Ēvĭŭs cūrās, Hor.

• ēvĭdēns, tĭs, *evident,* Cic. Syn. Clārŭs, pērspĭcŭŭs, cōnstāns, mănĭfēstŭs, cērtŭs, ăpērtŭs, nōn dŭbĭŭs.

ēvĭgĭlo, ās, *to wake.* Ēvĭgĭlāvĭt ĭdĕm, Ov. Syn. Expērgĕfăcĭo; expērgīscŏr, ēxcĭtŏr; vĭgĭlo, īnvĭgĭlo.

ēvīncĭo, nxī, nctŭm, *to tie.* Sūrās ēvīnctă cŏthūrnō, Virg. Syn. Vīncĭo, lĭgo, āllĭgo, cōllĭgo, strīngo, ādstrīngo, cōnstrīngo.

ēvīnco, īcī, īctŭm, *to vanquish.* Ŏppŏsĭtāsque ēvīcĭt, Virg. Syn. Sŭpĕro, vīnco, dēbēllo, ēxpūgno. V. Vinco.

ēvīro, ās, *to geld.* Et cōrpŭs ēvĭrāstĭs, Cat. Cūm sīs ēvĭrātĭŏr (*from* eviratus), (Scaz.) Mart.

ēvīscĕro, ās, *to embowel.* Pĕdĭbūsque ēvīscĕrăt ūncīs, Virg.

ēvītābĭlĭs, ĕ, *that may be avoided.* Nōn ēvītābĭlĕ tēlŭm, Ov. Syn. Vītābĭlĭs, vītāndŭs.

ēvīto, ās, *to avoid.* Ēvītārĕ, bŏnăm, Hor. Syn. Vīto, dēvīto, fŭgĭo, ēffŭgĭo, dēclīno.

Eūmēdēs, ĭs, m., *the father of Dolon.* Nōn fŏrēt Eūmēdēs, Ov.

Eūmēlŭs, ī, m., *a king of Patras.* Eūmēlĭquĕ dŏmŭm, Ov.

Eūmĕnĭdĕs, ŭm, f., *the Furies.* Eūmēnĭdŭm thălămī, Virg. Syn. Fŭrĭæ, Dīræ. Epith. Tūrbĭdæ, lœvæ, fērālēs, crŭēntæ, trŭcēs, Tārtărĕæ, āuguĭcŏmæ, hōrrēndæ, fŭrēntēs. V. Furiæ.

Eūmōlpŭs, ī, m., *a son of Neptune.* Cēcrŏpĭŏ Eūmōlpŏ, Ov.

Eūnæŭs, ī, m., *the name of a man.* Eūnæŭm Clўtĭŏ prīmūm pătrĕ, Virg.

eūnūchŭs, ī, m., *a eunuch.* Eūnūchum īpsĕ făcĭt, Juv. Epith. Mōllĭs, īmbēllĭs, rūgōsŭs, tĕnĕr.

ēvŏco, ās, *to call out.* Ēvŏcăt āntīquīs, Ov. Syn. Vŏco, āccĭo, ēxcĭo, āccērso, clĕo; ēxcĭto, ēxsūscĭto.

Ēvŏhĕ, adv., *the Bacchanalian acclamation.* Ēvŏhĕ Bācchĕ, Virg. Syn. Ēvœ.

ēvŏlo, ās, *to fly out.* Ēvŏlăt ālīs, Ov. Syn. Āvŏlo, fŭgĭo, ēffŭgĭo, ēxĕo, ēxcēdo, ērūmpo.

ēvōlvo, vōlvī, vŏlūtŭm, *to roll out.* Ōrās ēvōlvĭtĕ bēllī, Virg. Syn. Vōlvo, pērvōlvo, pēndo, pērpēndo, dīscŭtĭo; ēxplĭco, ēxpōno.

ēvŏlūtŭs, ā, ŭm, *the pass. partic. of* evolvo. Dūm trĭbŭs ēvŏlūtīs, (Sapph.) Prud.

ēvŏmo, ŭī, ĭtŭm, *to vomit up.* Ēvŏmĭt īnvōlvĭtquĕ, Virg. Syn. Vŏmo, ēmītto, ējĭcĭo, ēgĕro, ērūcto. V. Vomo.

Eūpălămōn, ŏnĭs, m., *the name of a man.* Fērtŭr ĕt Eūpălămōn, Ov.

Eūphōrbŭs, ī, m., *the name of a Trojan, assumed by Pythagorus.* Pānthŏïdēs Eūphōrbŭs ĕrăm, Ov.

Eūphrātēs, ĭs, m., *a river.* Eūphrātēs īllīnc, Virg. Epith. Āltŭs, fērtĭlĭs, vāgŭs, tŭmĭdŭs, cĕlĕr, flēxŭōsŭs, præcēps, răpĭdŭs, cĭtŭs, fœcūndŭs, Āssўrĭŭs.

Eūphrŏsўnă, æ, *or* nē, ēs, f., *one of the Graces.* Nōbĭlĭs Eūphrŏsўnē, Anth.

Eūpŏlĭs, ĭdĭs, m., *a poet of the ancient Greek comedy.* Eūpŏlĭs ātquĕ Crătīnŭs, Hor.

Eūrīpĭdēs, ĭs, m., *a celebrated tragic poet.* Făbŭlă sīc Eūrīpĭdĭs īnclўtă mōnstrăt, T. Maur.

Eūrīpŭs, ī, m., *a frith in Bœotia.* Eūrīpŭsquĕ trăhĭt, Luc. Epith. Eūbŏĭcŭs, fŭgāx, vāgŭs, vărĭŭs, tĕnŭĭs, īnstābĭlĭs, lŭbrĭcŭs, īncōnstāns, vēlōx.

Eūrōpă, æ, *or* pē, ēs, f., *Agenor's daughter, loved by Jupiter.* Nōn gĕnĭtrīx Eūrōpă tĭbi, Ov. Sīc ĕt Eūrōpē nĭmĭŭm, Hor. Syn. Ăgēnŏrĭs; Sĭdŏnĭs. Epith. Tўrĭă, Sĭdŏnĭă, pŭlchră, fŏrmōsă, vĕnūstă, răptă.

H 5

Eŭrōpă, æ, f., *one of the parts of the world.* Eŭrōpæ ătque Asĭæ fătĭs, Virg. Syn. Dīvĕs, pŏtēns, fērtĭlĭs, fĕrāx, Mărtĭā, bĕllĭgĕră, ŏpŭlēntă, fœcŭndă, præclără, cŭltă, dŏctă, făcŭndă.

Eŭrōpæŭs, ă, ŭm, *of Europe.* Dŭcĭs Eŭrōpæī, Ov.

Eŭrōtās, æ, m., *a river in Laconia.* Quālĭs ĭn Eŭrōtæ rīpĭs, Virg. Epith. Frīgĭdŭs, gĕlĭdŭs, ăspĕr, ŏlīvĭfĕr, Lăcĕdæmŏnĭŭs, Spărtānŭs, vĭrĭdĭs, vĭrēns.

Eŭrŭs, ī, m., *the east wind.* Nŭbĭfĕr Eŭrŭs, Ov. Syn. Vŭltŭrnŭs. Epith. Eoŭs, Phœbĕŭs, Năbăthæŭs; īnsānŭs, răpĭdŭs, fĕrōx, nŭbĭfĕr, vĭŏlēntŭs, trŭx, sævŭs, præcēps, nĭmbōsŭs. V. Ventus.

Eŭrўălŭs, ī, m., *a young Trojan, a friend of Nisus.* Tūtātŭr făvŏr Eŭrўălŭm, Virg.

Eŭrўbătēs, ĭs, m., *a Grecian herald.* Eŭrўbătī dătă sŭm, Ov.

Eŭrўdĭcē, ēs, f., *the wife of Orpheus.* Eŭrўdĭcē sŭpĕrās, Virg. Epith. Răptă, mĭsĕră, īnfēlīx, pŭlchră, nĭvĕă, fōrmōsă, dĕcōră, Thrēĭcĭă, Thrācĭă.

Eŭrўlŏchŭs, ī, m., *one of Ulysses' companions.* Vīdĭmŭs Eŭrўlŏchŭm, Ov.

Eŭrўmăchŭs, ī, m., *one of Penelope's suitors.* Eŭrўmăchīque ăvĭdās, Ov.

Eŭrўmĭdēs, æ, m., *son of Eurymus.* Tēlĕmŭs Eŭrўmĭdēs, Ov.

Eŭrўnŏmē, ēs, f., *a nymph, the daughter of Oceanus and Tethys.* Edĭdĭt Eŭrў-nŏmē, Ov.

Eŭrўpўlŭs, ī, m., *a famous diviner.* Eŭrўpўlŭm scĭtātŭm, Virg.

Eŭrўstheŭs, ĕŏs, ĕĭ or eī, m., *the son of Sthenelus and king of Mycenæ, who imposed upon Hercules his twelve labours.* Eŭrўsthĕā dūrŭm, Virg.

Eŭrўtĭŏn, ŏnĭs, m., *one of Æneas' companions.* Nēc bŏnŭs Eŭrўtĭŏn, Virg.

Eŭrўtĭs, ĭdĭs, f., *the daughter of Eurytus, Iole.* Eŭrўtĭdĭs lăcrĭmās, Ov.

Eŭrўtŭs, ī, m., *a king of Œchalia, slain by Hercules.* Nāmque hŏc pătĕr Eŭrўtŭs īllī, Ov.

Eŭtērpē, ēs, f., *one of the Muses.* Călămōs Eŭtērpē flātĭbŭs īmplĕt. V. Musæ.

Eŭtrăpĕlŭs, ī, m., *the name of a man.* Eŭtrăpĕlŭs tŏnsŏr, Mart.

* ēvŭlgo, ās, *to publish.* Syn. Vŭlgo, dīvŭlgo, pāndo. V. Explico, vulgo.

ēvŭlsŭs, ă, ŭm, *the pass. partic.* of evello. Ēvŭlsīsquĕ trŭncīs, Hor.

Eŭxīnŭs pŏntŭs, m., *the Euxine sea.* Eŭxīnī līttŏră pŏntī, Ov.

ĕxāctŭs, *the pass. partic. of* exigo. Annŭŭs ĕxāctīs, Virg.

ĕxăcŭo, ŭī, ū:ŭm, *to sharpen.* Ĕxăcŭūnt ălī, Virg. Syn. Ăcŭo, ăcŭmĭno; V. Acuo. Ăspĕro, ĕxăspĕro, ĕxăcĕrbo; ĕxcĭto, ăccēndo, īncĭto, īmpēllo.

ĕxæquo, ās, *to make smooth.* Ĕxæquătăquĕ sŭnt, Lucr. Syn. Æquo, ădæquo.

ĕxæstŭo, ās, *to boil up.* Fŭndōque ĕxæstŭăt īmō, Virg. Syn. Æstŭo, flagro, ārdĕo, ĕxārdĕo, ārdēsco; ĕxŭndo.

* ĕxăggĕro, ās, *to heap up.* Syn. Amplĭfĭco, ĕxtōllo; ăggĕro, cōngĕro, cŏăcĕrvo.

ĕxăgĭto, ās, *to move.* Ĕxăgĭtĕt nŏstrōs, Prop. Syn. Agĭto, vēxo, dīvēxo, īn-sēctŏr, ĕxērcĕo, jācto.

* ĕxālto, ās, *to lift up.* Syn. Extōllo, ēffĕro.

ĕxāmĕn, ĭnĭs, n., *a swarm of bees.* Fŭgĭănt ĕxămĭnă tŭxōs, Virg. Syn. Agmĕn ăpŭm. Epith. Fŭgāx, văgŭm, strīdēns. V. Apes.—2. *a balance; examination.* Dŭās æquăto ĕxămĭnĕ lāncēs, Virg. Syn. Dīscŭssĭo. Epith. Jŭstŭm, æquŭm, īnjŭstŭm, ĭnīquŭm, sĕvērŭm.

ĕxāmĭno, ās, *to examine.* Vērum ĕxāmĭnăt ōmnĭs, Hor. Syn. Pērpēndo, ĕx-pēndo, pōndĕro, dīscŭtĭo, ĕxquīro, ănĭmō vŏlvo, agĭto.

ĕxānguĭs, ĕ, *lifeless.* Lābĭtŭr ĕxānguĭs, Virg. Syn. Pāllĭdŭs, pāllēns; mŏrtŭŭs. V. Mortuus.

ĕxānĭmĭs, ĕ, *and* ŭs, ă, ŭm, *astonished, dead.* Ĕxănĭmēs pŏssŭnt, Virg. Ĕxănĭmĭs ēt bēllī, Id. Syn. Ĕxănĭmātŭs, ĕxānguĭs, mŏrtŭŭs. V. Mortuus.

ĕxănĭmo, ās, *to kill.* Quĕrēlĭs ĕxănĭmās tŭĭs, (Alcaic.) Hor. Syn. Ēnĕco, ōccīdo.

ĕxārdĕo, sī, *to be on fire.* Ĕxārsēre īgnēs, Virg. Syn. Ĕxārdēsco, īnflāmmŏr, ārdēsco, ārdĕo.

* ĕxārĕo, ēs, *to be dry.* Syn. Ārĕo, ārēsco, ĕxārēsco, mārcĕo, mārcēsco.

ĕxārmo, ās, *to disarm.* Prælĭă prīma ĕxārmānt, Luc.

ĕxāro, ās, *to inscribe, to plough up.* Ĕxārăt īllă, Ov. Syn. Pīngo, scrībo; ăro.

ĕxāspĕro, ās, *to irritate.* Mŏtĭs ĕxāspĕrăt ŭndĭs, Ov. Syn. Aspĕro, ĕxăcĕrbo; ĕxăcŭo.

ĕxaŭctŏro, ās, *to dismiss out of service.* Măgĭstrātŭs ĕxaŭctŏrārĕ vĕtŭstōs, Mart. Syn. Dīmītto.

ĕxaŭdĭo, īvī *and* iī, *to hear.* Plānĕ ĕxaŭdīrī, Lucr. Syn. Ănnŭo.

ĕxnŭdītŭs, *the pass. partic. of* exaudio. Nōn ĕxaŭdītŭs, ŭt īllĕ, Hor.

ĕxcœco, ās, *to make blind.* Vēnās ĕxcœcăt īn ūndīs, Ov. Syn. Cæco.

ĕxcālcĕātŭs, ă, ŭm, *unshod.* Ĕxcālcĕātŭs īrĕ cœpĭt, Mart.

ĕxcānto, ās, *to enchant.* Scĭŭt ĕxcāntārĕ pŭēllās, Prop.

* ĕxcăvo, ās, *to make hollow,* Mart. V. Fodio.

ĕxcēdo, cēssī, *to go out.* Dāmnātum ĕxcēdĕrĕ tērrā, Man. Syn. Dīscēdo, rēcēdo, ăbĕo, fŭgĭo, āvŏlo; mŏrĭŏr; sŭpĕro.

ĕxcēllo, ŭī, *to be high, surmount.* Vŏlŭīsti ĕxcēllĕrĕ rēbŭs, Lucr. Syn. Sŭpĕro, prætĕrĕo, ĕxsŭpĕro, sŭpĕrēmĭnĕo, præsto, ēmĭnĕo.

ĕxcēlsŭs, ă, ŭm, *high.* Dīvŭs, ăb ĕxcēlsā, Ov. V. Altus.

ĕxcēpto, ās, *the frequent. of* excipio. Ĕxcēptāntquĕ lĕvēs, Virg.

ĕxcērpo, īs, *to pick out.* Quīd cūm Pīcēnīs ĕxcērpĭs, Hor.

ĕxcĭdĭŭm, iī, n., *a ruin.* Vīdĭmŭs ĕxcĭdĭa, Virg. Syn. Rŭīnă, clādēs, strāgēs.
Epith. Mĭsĕrābĭlĕ, nĕfāndŭm, trīstĕ, hōrrēndŭm, crūdēlĕ, īmmītĕ, sævŭm, lāmēntābĭlĕ, flēbĭlĕ, mœstŭm, lūctĭfĭcŭm, fūmāns, ĭnhūmānŭm, ăcērbŭm, cōmmūnĕ, dīrŭm, īgnĕŭm, īmmĕrĭtŭm. V. Ruina, Cædes.

ĕxcĭdo, īs, (*from* cado,) *to fall away.* Ĕxcĭdĕt aŭt, Virg. Syn. Lābŏr, cōllābŏr, prōcŭmbo, dēĭ̆cĭo.

ĕxcĭdo, īs, (*from* cædo,) *to cut out.* Rūpĭbŭs ĕxcĭdūnt, Virg. Syn. Scīndo, sĕco, ĕxsĕco, ĕxscīndo. V. Scindo, cædo.

ĕxcĭo, īs, īvī, *to call out.* Ĭmīs ĕxcīrĕ sĕpŭlcrīs, Virg. V. Evoco.

ĕxcĭpĭo, ēpī, *to receive.* Intĕr ĕt ĕxcĭpĕrĕt, Virg. Syn. Accĭpĭo, rĕcĭpĭo; sĕquŏr.

ĕxcīsŭs, *the pass. partic. of* excido. Ĕxcīsum Eŭbŏĭcæ, Virg.

ĕxcĭto, ās, *to excite.* Ĕxcĭtăt ārās, Virg. Syn. Ădhōrtŏr, īncĭto, āccēndo, cōncĭto, stĭmŭlo, cōmmŏvĕo; ĕxpērgĕfăcĭo, sŭscĭto.

ĕxcīto, ās, *the frequent. of* excio, *to provoke.* Ĕxcītēt Tўrĭŭs, Sil. Syn. Ĕxcĭo, ēvŏco.

ĕxcītŭs, *the pass. partic. of* excio. Strātīs ĕxcĭtă jŭvēntŭs, Luc.

ĕxcītŭs, *the pass. partic. of* excieo, [*rare.*] Ĕxcĭtă cūrīs, Ov.

ĕxclāmo, ās, *to exclaim.* Tū mĭsĕr ĕxclāmās, Juv. Syn. Clāmo, prōclāmo, cōnclāmo, vōcĭfĕrŏr. V. Clamo.

ĕxclūdo, īs, sī, *to exclude.* Crēdĭt ĕt ĕxclūdĭt, Hor. Syn. Ārcĕo, ăbārcĕo, prōhĭbĕo, ĕxpēllo, ējĭcĭo.

ĕxclūsŭs, *the pass. partic. of* excludo. Mœnĭbŭs ĕxclūsōs, Virg.

ĕxcōgĭto, ās, *to think.* Ĕxcōgĭtāvĭt hŏmo, Mart. Syn. Cōgĭto, mĕdĭtŏr, māchĭnŏr, fīngo, ĭnvĕnĭo.

ĕxcŏlo, cŏlŭī, cūltŭm, *to cultivate.* Vītam ĕxcŏlŭĕrĕ pĕr ārtēs, Virg. Syn. Cŏlo, ĕxōrno, ĕxpŏlĭo, pērpŏlĭo, āccūro.

ĕxcŏquo, cōxī, cōctŭm, *to boil away.* Ĕxcŏquĭtŭr vĭtĭum, Virg. Syn. Cŏquo, pērcŏquo.

* ĕxcŏrĭo, ās, *to excoriate.*

ĕxcōrs, dīs, *heartless.* Ăn măgĭs ĕxcōrs, Hor. Syn. Vēcōrs, stūltŭs, āmēns, īnsĭpĭēns, stŏlĭdŭs.

ĕxcrēsco, īs, *to grow out.* Lēnīque ĕxcrēvĭt īn āltŭm, Lucan. V. Cresco.

ĕxcrŭcĭo, ās, *to torment.* Amplĭŭs ĕxcrŭcĭēs, Cat. Syn. Crŭcĭo, tōrquĕo, vēxo, āngo, cōnfĭcĭo.

ĕxcŭbĭæ, ārŭm, f. pl., *watch and ward.* Intĕrĕā vĭgĭlum ĕxcŭbĭīs, Virg. Syn. Cūstōdēs. Epith. Pērvĭgĭlēs, nōctūrnæ, mūrālēs, āttēntæ, sōllĭcĭtæ, fīdēlēs, ĭmpăvĭdæ, īnsōmnēs, fīdæ. V. Vigilo.

ĕxcŭbĭtŏr, ōrĭs, m., *a sentinel.* Ĕxcŭbĭtōrquĕ dĭēm, Virg. Syn. Vĭgĭl, cŭstōs, ĕxplōrātŏr.

ĕxcŭbo, ās, *to keep watch.* Āntĕ dŏmum ĕxcŭbŭī, Ov. Syn. Vĭgĭlo; ĕxcŭbĭās ăgo; sum īn ĕxcŭbĭīs. V. Vigilo.

ĕxcūdo, ūdī, ūsŭm, *to beat, stamp.* Ĕxcūdēnt ăliī, Virg. Syn. Cūdo, prōcūdo; cōmpōno, ēlūcubro; ēlĭcĭo, ĕxcūtĭo.

ĕxcūrro, īs, *to rush out.* Ĕxcūrrĭt īn æquŏră, Ov.

ĕxcūrsŭs, ūs, m., *an excursion.* Ĕxcūrsŭsquĕ brĕvēs tēntānt, Virg.

ĕxcūsābĭlīs, ĕ, *excusable.* Pārs ĕxcūsābĭlīs ēssĕt, Ov.

ĕxcūso, ās, *to excuse.* Ĕxcūsārĕ lăbōrĕm, Hor.

ĕxcŭtĭo, cŭssī, ssŭm, *to shake off.* Ĕxcŭtĭăt Teŭcrōs, Virg. Syn. Dīscŭtĭo, ăgĭto, quāsso, quătĭo, dējĭcĭo, ēlĭcĭo, ĕxcūdo.

H 6

ēxcrētŭs, ă, ŭm, *pass. part. of* excresco, *grown up.* Excrētŏs prŏhĭbēnt ă mātr" bŭs hœdōs, Virg.

ēxecrābĭlĭs, ĕ, *detestable.* Incēstĭfĭcŭs, ēxēcrābĭlĭs, (Iamb.) Sen. SYN. Execrāndŭs, dētēstāndŭs, hōrrēndŭs.

ēxecrŏr, ārĭs, *to curse, detest.* Sævi ēxēcrāmŭr Ūlyssĭs, Virg. SYN. Dētēstŏr, ăbhōrrĕo, ăbōmĭnŏr, dāmno, fŭgĭo, hōrrĕo.

ēxĕdo, ēdī, sŭm, *to eat up, consume.* Ēxĕdĭt ārtŭs, Ser. SYN. Ēdo, ābsūmo, rōdo, cōrrōdo, cīrcūmrōdo, cōnsūmo, cōnfĭcĭo.

ēxēmplăr, ārĭs, n., *a model.* Nōbĭs ēxēmplăr Ūlyssĕm, Hor. SYN. Exēmplŭm, ĭmāgo, spĕcĭēs. EPITH. Ĭmĭtābĭlĕ, vērŭm.

ēxēmplŭm, ī, n., *a model, copy, example.* Hōmĭnŭmque ēxēmplă mănēmŭs, Ov.

ēxĕo, īvī *and* ĭī, *to go out.* Mēĭs ēxīrēt vīctĭmă sēptĭs, Virg. SYN. Ēgrĕdĭŏr, ābscēdo, ēxcēdo, ăbĕo, dīscēdo. V. Abeo.

ēxĕquĭālĭs, ĕ, *belonging to funerals.* Dēflēnt ēxĕquĭālĭbŭs, (Alcaic.) Pr. SYN. Fūnebrĭs, fūnĕrĕŭs, fērālĭs, fūnēstŭs.

ēxĕquĭæ, ārŭm, f. pl., *funerals.* Fūnĕrĭs ēxĕquĭæ, Ov. SYN. Fūnĕră, Infĕrĭæ, jŭstă. EPITH. Trīstēs, mœrēntēs, plæ, mœstæ, mĭsĕræ. V. Funus.

ēxĕquŏr, ĕrĭs, *to execute.* Ēxĕquĭtūr, clāssēmquĕ, Virg. SYN. Pērfĭcĭo, cōnfĭcĭo, pĕrăgo, ābsōlvo, fīnĭo.

ēxērcĕo, ŭī, ĭtŭm, *to exercise.* Cēnsēbo, ēxērcĕăt ārtĕm, Hor. SYN. Fătīgo, vēxo ; trādo, prōfĭtĕŏr.

ēxērcĭtātŭs, *the pass. partic. of* exercito, *the frequent. of* exerceo. Ēxērcĭtātās aŭt pĕtĭt, (Iamb.) Hor.

ēxērcĭtŭs, ūs, m., *an army.* Dŏlŏpūmque ēxērcĭtŭs ōmnĭs, Virg. SYN. Ācĭēs, cŏhōrs, tūrmă, phălānx, āgmĕn. EPITH. Infēstŭs, fōrtĭs, nŭmĕrōsŭs, hōrrēndŭs, trēmēndŭs, dūrŭs, sævŭs, mĭnāx, crŭēntŭs, tērrĭfĭcŭs, Inĭmīcŭs, pŏtēns, vălĭdŭs. V. Agmen.

ēxĕro, ĭs, ērtŭm, *to draw out.* Ēxĕrĭt āltŭm, Ser. SYN. Ēdūco, ĭs ; ēxsērto, ās.

ēxērro, ās, *to wander abroad.* Dēxtĕrque ēxērrăt Ārĭōn, Stat.

ēxērto, ās, *the freq. of* exero. Ora ēxērtāntĕm, Virg.

ēxēsŭs, ă, ŭm, *the pass. partic. of* excdo. Cāvĭs, ēxēsæque ārbŏrĭs āntrō, Virg.

ēxhærēdo, ās, *to disinherit.* Ēxhærēdāvīt tē, Mart.

ēxhālo, ās, *to exhale.* Sævāmque ēxhālăt ŏpācă, Virg. SYN. Ēmītto, ēffūndo, spīro, hālo.

ēxhaŭrĭo, īs, *to empty, to dig up.* Exhaŭrĭēbăt Ingēmēns, (Iamb.) Hor. SYN. Haŭrĭo, văcŭo, ēvăcŭo, ēxsĭcco, ēbĭbo.

ēxhĭbĕo, ēs, *to show, produce.* Ēxhĭbŭĭt pūlsō, Ov. SYN. Prōfĕro, ōstēndo, prōdo, ēdo.

ēxhĭbĭtŭs, ă, ŭm, *the pass. partic. of* exhibeo. Præstĭtĭt ēxhĭbĭtŭs, Mart.

ēxhĭlăro, ās, *to rejoice.* Ēxhĭlărēnt ĭpsōs, Mart. SYN. Hĭlăro, recrĕo, ōblēcto. V. Recreo.

ēxhōrrĕo, ēs, *or* ēsco, ĭs, *to dread.* Ēxhōrrŭĭt æquŏrĭs Instăr, Ov. SYN. Hōrrĕo, rĭgĕo, ōbrĭgĕo.

ēxhōrtŏr, ārĭs, *to exhort.* Gnātum ēxhōrtārĕr, Virg. SYN. Hōrtŏr, ădhōrtŏr, ēxcĭto, Incĭto, āccēndo, ăcŭo. V. Hortor.

ēxĭgo, ēgī, āctŭm, *to drive out, exact.* Ēxĭgăt ēt pŭlchră, Virg. SYN. Pĕto, pōsco, rĕpōsco ; ēxclūdo, ējĭcĭ, ēxpēllo ; pĕrăgo, ābsōlvo, cōnfĭcĭo.

ēxĭgŭŭs, ă, ŭm, *small.* Ēt quāmvĭs īgni ēxĭgŭō, Virg. SYN. Ēxĭlĭs, pārvŭs, tĕnŭĭs, grăcĭlĭs.

ēxĭlĭo, īs, ŭī *and* ĭī, ŭĭtŭm, *to jump.* Ēxĭlĭt, Indĕ, Hor. SYN. Sălĭo, prŏsĭlĭo, ēmīco. V. Salto, sálio.

ēxĭlĭs, ĕ, *lean.* Ēxīlēs dĭgĭtī, Ov. SYN. Pārvŭs, tĕnŭĭs, ēxĭgŭŭs, grăcĭlĭs.

ēxĭlĭŭm, ĭī, n., *exile.* Ēxĭlĭōquĕ dŏmōs, Virg. EPITH. Dūrŭm, lōngŭm, mĭsĕrŭm, flēbĭlĕ, ăcērbŭm, văgŭm, tūrpĕ, Infēlīx, Infaŭstŭm, lānguĭdŭm, ămārŭm, mœstŭm, Infămĕ, ānxĭŭm, sōllĭcĭtŭm, quĕrŭlŭm, tædĭōsŭm. V. Exul, exulo.

ēxĭmĭŭs, ă, ŭm, *select.* Quālŭŏr ēxĭmĭōs, Virg. SYN. Ēgrĕgĭŭs, ēxcēllēns, præstāns, præclārŭs, Insĭgnĭs, nōbĭlĭs.

ēxĭmo, ēmī, ēmptŭm, *to take out.* Vōs ēxĭmĕt ævō, Virg. SYN. Lībĕro, sōlvo, ēxpĕdĭo, ērĭpĭo, aŭfĕro.

ēxĭn, *or* ēxĭndē, adv., *from thence.* Ēxĭndĕ pĕr āmplŭm, Virg. SYN. Dēĭn, *or* deīn ; dĕīndĕ, *or* deīndĕ ; hĭnc, Indĕ

ĕxīstĭmo, ās, *to think.* Cum hæc ĕxīstĭmās, (Iamb.) Syn. Pŭto, sĕntĭo, cēnsĕo, jūdĭco.

ĕxīsto, ĕxtĭtī, *to exist.* Ĕxīstūnt mōntes, O*t*. Syn. Ēmĭnĕo, ĕxsūrgo, prōdĕo, āppārĕo, ĕxŏrĭŏr ; sŭm.

ĕxĭtĭābĭlĭs, ālĭs, ĕ, *and* ōsŭs, ă, ŭm, *fatal.* Ĕxĭtĭābĭlĕ tēlŭm, Ov. Dōnum ĕxĭtĭālĕ Mĭnērvæ, Virg. Ĕxĭtĭōsĕ, vĭdĕ, Mart. Syn. Pērnĭcĭōsŭs, fūnēstŭs, fătālĭs.

ĕxĭtĭŭm, ĭĭ, n., *ruin, death.* Immĭnĕt ĕxĭtĭō, Ov. Syn. Clādēs, strāgēs, pērnĭcĭēs. Epith. Dūrŭm, fŭrĭālĕ, crŭdēlĕ, trīstĕ, īnfāndŭm, mĭsĕrābĭlĕ, grăvĕ, flēbĭlĕ, ācĕrbŭm. V. Ruina.

ĕxĭtŭs, ūs, m., *egress, the issue.* Exĭtŭs īngēns, Virg. Syn. Ăbĭtŭs, dīscēssŭs, rĕcēssŭs ; fīnĭs ; mōrs ; cāsŭs, ēvēntŭs.

ĕxlēx, ēgĭs, *lawless.* Ĕt pōtŭs, ĕt ĕxlēx, Hor.

ĕxōdĭŭm, ĭĭ, n., *a farce.* Ŭrbĭcŭs ĕxōdĭō rīsūm mŏvĕt, Juv.

ĕxŏlēsco, ēvī, *to grow old.* Săcĕr ĕxŏlēscĕt ævō, (Phal.) Stat. Syn. Ōbsŏlēsco, ăbŏlĕŏr, āntīquŏr.

ĕxŏlētŭs, ă, ŭm, *grown old.* Stăt ĕxŏlētŭs, (Scaz,) Mart. Syn. Obsŏlētŭs, āntīquātŭs, dēsuētŭs.

ĕxŏlvo, ōlvī, ŏlŭtŭm, *to untie.* Mīttĭt, ĕt ĕxŏlvĭt, Lucr. Syn. Sŏlvo, ĕxpĕdĭo, lībĕro.

ĕxŏnĕro, ās, *to discharge.* Ĕxŏnĕrārĕ fŭgăm, Ov. Syn. Lĕvo, sŭblĕvo.

ĕxŏptābĭlĭs, ĕ, *wished for.* Fŭgĭt ĕxŏptābĭlĕ tēmpŭs, Sil.

ĕxŏpto, *to wish.* Rēm strŭĕre ĕxŏptās, Pers. Syn. Ŏpto, pĕrŏpto, cŭpĭo, dēsīdĕro, vŏlo. V. Opto.

ĕxŏrābĭlĭs, ĕ, *easy to be entreated.* Nōn ĕxōrābĭlĭs aūrō, Hor.

ĕxōrdĭŏr, īrĭs, ĕxōrsŭs, *to begin.* Sŭă cuĭque ĕxōrsă lăbōrĕm, Virg. Syn. Ordĭŏr, īncĭpĭo, īnchŏo, aūspĭcŏr.

ĕxōrdĭŭm, ĭĭ, n , *the beginning.* Ĕxōrdĭōrum ēst, (Iamb.) Syn. Ĕxōrsŭs, prīncĭpĭŭm ; ĕxōrsă, ōrŭm.

ĕxŏrĭŏr, īrĭs *and* ĕrĭs, *to rise.* Ĕxŏrĭāre ălĭquĭs, Virg. Syn. Orĭŏr, ēgrĕdĭŏr, nāscŏr, ēmērgo, ĕxsūrgo.

ĕxōrno, ās, *to adorn.* Lĭcĕt vĕtĕrēs ĕxōrnēnt, Juv. Syn. Orno, ădōrno, āppăro, īnstrŭo, dĕcŏro.

ĕxōro, ās, *to get by entreaty.* Ĕxōrăt pācĕm, Virg. Syn. Plāco, sēdo, mītĭgo, lēnĭo, ōro.

ĕxōs, ōssĭs, *without bones.* Ĕxōs ĕt ĕxāngŭĭs, Lucr.

ĕxōsŭs, ă, ŭm, *hating.* Nōndum ĕxōsŭs ăd ūnŭm, Virg. Syn. Pĕrōsŭs, ādvērsātŭs.

ĕxpāllĕo, ēs, *and* ēsco, ĭs, *to grow pale.* Tōtōque ĕxpāllŭĭt ōrĕ, Ov.

ĕxpāndo, dī, sŭm, *to extend.* Nātūram ĕxpāndĕrĕ dīctĭs, Lucr. Syn. Pāndo, ĕxplĭco, ĕxpōno, ăpĕrĭo.

ĕxpăvēsco, ĭs, *or* vĕo, ēs, *to be affrighted.* Frātrem ĕxpăvēscăt frătĕr, (Iamb.) Sen. Syn. Tĭmĕo, mĕtŭo, păvĕo, vĕrĕŏr.

ĕxpēcto, ās, *to expect.* Rūstĭcŭs ĕxpēctăt, Hor. Syn. Ŏppĕrĭŏr ; mănĕo, cūnctŏr, mŏrŏr, hærĕo, stō ; spēro. V. Desidero, spero.

ĕxpĕdĭo, ĭs, īvī, *to free.* Ĕxpĕdĭūnt fēssī, Virg. Syn. Sŏlvo, lībĕro, ĕxĭmo.

ĕxpĕdītĭo, ōnĭs, f., *an expedition.* Pērsĭdĭs ĕxpĕdītĭŏnĕm, (Phal.) Sid. Epith. Bēllĭcă, Mārtĭă.

ĕxpĕdītŭs, ă, ŭm, *the pass. partic. of* expedio. Văgŏr ĕxpĕdītŭs, (Sapph.) Hor.

ĕxpēllo, ĕxpŭlī, ŭlsŭm, *to chase.* Equĭs ; ĕxpēllĕrĕ tēndūnt, Virg. Syn. Pēllo, ĕjĭcĭo, ĕxĭgo, dējĭcĭo, dētūrbo. V. Pello.

ĕxpēndo, dī, *to weigh.* Pœnās ĕxpēndĭmŭs ōmnēs, Virg. Syn. Pōndĕro ; ĕxsōlvo.

ĕxpērgĕfāctŭs, ă, ŭm, *the pass. partic. of* expergefacio. Ĕxpērgĕfāctĭquĕ sĕquūntŭr, Lucr.

ĕxpērgo, pērrēxī, *and* ĕxpērgīscŏr, ĕrĭs, pērrēctŭs sŭm, *to awake.* Ĕxpērgĭtĕ pēctŏră tārdă, Accius. Nōn ĕxpērgīscĕrĭs, Hor. Syn. Ĕxpērgĕfăcĭo ; ĕxcĭto, sūscĭto. V. Excito.

ĕxpĕrĭēntĭă, æ, f., *experience.* Ĕxpĕrĭēntĭă cēpĭt, Virg. Syn. Ŭsŭs. Epith. Dōctă, lōngă, măgīstră.

ĕxpĕrīmēntŭm, ī, n., *an experiment.* Ĕt ĕxpĕrīmēntŭm căpĕ, (Iamb. Dim.) Prud. Syn. Tēntāmĕn, tēntāmēntŭm.

ĕxpĕrĭŏr, īrĭs, *to attempt.* Ĕxpĕrīĕrĕ mĕtŭs, Prop. Syn. Tēnto, āggrĕdĭŏr.

ĕxpērs, tĭs, *destitute of.* Thălămīque ĕxpērtĕm, Virg. Syn. Cārēns, ĕgēns, ĭnŏps.

ĕxpēs, *or* spēs, *hopeless.* Ĕnătăt ĕxspēs, Hor.

ĕxpĕtītŭs, ă, ŭm, *the pass. partic. of* expeto. Rēdde ĕxpĕtītōs, (Iamb.) Sen.

ĕxpĕto, ĭs, īvī *or* ĭī, *to wish ardently.* Ĕxpĕtītŭr cōnjŭx, Ov. Syn. Ŏpto, ĕxŏpto, cŭpĭo, dēsīdĕro. V. Opto.

ĕxpĭlo, ās, *to plunder.* Ĕxpīlātquĕ gēnĭs, Ov. Syn. Dīrĭpĭo, spŏlĭo.

ĕxpĭo, ās, *to expiate.* Părātŭs ĕxpĭārĕ, (Iamb. pur.) Hor. Syn. Pĭo, pūrgŏr, dēlĕo.

ĕxpīro, ās, *to breathe forth.* Ĕxpīrāvĭt ăpĕr, Juv. Syn. Ĕxhālo, spīro; mŏrĭŏr.

ĕxplāno, ās, *to make smooth.* Ter. Syn. Ĕxplĭco.

ĕxplĕo, plēvī, tŭm, *to fill.* Explēbō nŭmĕrŭm, Virg. Syn. Implĕo, ădīmplĕo; pērfĭcĭo, ābsŏlvo, pĕrăgo; sătŭro, sătĭo.

ĕxplētŭs, ă, ŭm, *the pass. partic. of* expleo. Ĕxplētŭs dăpĭbŭs, Virg.

ĕxplĭcĭtŭs, ă, ŭnĭ, *the pass. partic. of* explico. Vērsĭbŭs ĕxplĭcĭtŭm, Mart.

ĕxplĭco, ŭī, ātŭm *or* ĭtŭm, *to unfold.* Ĕxplĭcŭīt vīnō, Hor. Syn. Prōmo, pāndo, ĕvŏlvo, ĕxpōno, ăpĕrĭo, ĕxplāno, ĭntērprĕtŏr.

ĕxplōdo, sī, sŭm, *to expel with contempt.* Nōctem ĕxplōdēntĭbŭs ālīs, Lucr. Syn. Plaŭdo; rējĭcĭo.

ĕxplōrātŏr, ōrĭs, m., *a sentinel, spy.* Ĕxplōrātōrēs ĕquĭtŭm, Virg. Syn. Ĕxcŭbĭtŏr, vĭgĭl.

ĕxplōro, ās, *to view diligently.* Ĕxplōrārĕ lăbŏr, Virg. Syn. Inquīro, ĕxquīro, lūstro, scrūtŏr, rīmŏr.

ĕxplōsŭs, ă, ŭm, *the pass. partic. of* explodo. Ĕxplōsa Ārbŭscŭlă dīxĭt, Hor.

ĕxpŏlĭo, īs, *to polish.* Nūnc ārtēs ĕxpŏlĭūntŭr, Lucr. Syn. Pŏlĭo, pērpŏlĭo, ĕxcŏlo, ĕxōrno, ăccŭro.

ĕxpŏlītŭs, ă, ŭm, *the pass. partic. of* expolio. Pūmĭce ĕxpŏlītŭm, Catull.

ĕxpōno, ĭs, *to set forth.* Vērsĭbŭs ĕxpōnī trăgĭcĭs, Hor. Syn. Ŏbjĭcĭo; ĕxplĭco, ĕxprōmo.

ĕxpōrto, ās, *to carry out or away.* Ĕxpōrtănt tēctĭs, Virg. Syn. Ĕffĕro, ēdūco, aŭfĕro, ābdūco.

ĕxpōsco, ĭs, *and* pōstŭlo, ās, *to ask eagerly.* Ĕxpōscūnt; mīttīquĕ vĭrōs, Virg. Syn. Pōsco, pĕto, pōstŭlo; quĕrŏr, cōnquĕrŏr.

ĕxpŏsĭtŭs, ă, ŭm, *the pass. partic. of* expono. Quī nĭhĭl ĕxpŏsĭtŭm, Juv.

ĕxprĭmo, prēssī, prēssŭm, *to express.* Ĕxprĭmĕt, ēt mŏllēs, Hor. Syn. Ĕlĭcĭo; ĕxpōno, ĕxplĭco, ĕxpāndo; ēffĭngo, ĭmĭtŏr, repræsēnto.

ĕxprobro, ās, *to reproach.* Mĕrĭtum ĕxprŏbrārĕ vŏlŭptās, Ov. Syn. Ŏbjĭcĭo, ŏppōno, ōbjēcto.

ĕxprōmo, mpsī, mptŭm, *to draw out.* Mœstās ĕxprōmĕrĕ vōcēs, Virg. Syn. Prōmo, prŏfĕro, ĕxpōno, dēprōmo.

ĕxpūgnābĭlĭs, ĕ, *to be vanquished.* Ĕxpūgnābĭlĕ rŏbŭr, Stat.

ĕxpūgnātŏr, ōrĭs, m., *one who takes by storm.* Lŭpŭs ĕxpūgnātŏr ŏpīmī, Stat.

ĕxpūgno, ās, *to take by storm.* Ĕxpūgnābĭs, ĕt ēst, Hor. Syn. Vīnco, sŭpĕro, dēbēllo, ōccŭpo. V. Debello.

ĕxpūlsŭs, ă, ŭm, *the pass. partic. of* expello. Fīnĭbŭs ĕxpūlsŭm pătrĭīs, Virg.

ĕxpūngo, xī, ctŭm, *to prick.* Ĕxpūngăm, nāmque ēst, Pers. Syn. Dēlĕo, tōllo; pūngo.

ĕxpŭo, ĭs, *to spit.* Ĕxpŭĭt ūndĭs, Cat.

ĕxpūrgo, ās, *to cleanse, purify.* Ĕxpūrgārĕ cĭcūtæ, Hor.

Ĕxquĭlĭæ, ārŭm, f. pl. V. Esquiliæ.

ĕxquīro, sīvī, *to search into.* Ŭmbrōsam ĕxquīrĕrĕ vāllĕm, Virg. Syn. Quæro, ĭnquīro, pērquīro, scrūtŏr.

• ĕxquīsītŭs, *the pass. partic. of* exquiro, Plin. Syn. Præstāns, ĕxcēllēns, præclārŭs, ĕxĭmĭŭs, ĕgrĕgĭŭs.

ĕxsătĭo, *and* ĕxsătŭro, ās, *to satisfy.* Ĕxsătĭātă dŏmŭs, Ov. Ĕxsătŭrārĕ dŏlōrĕm, Stat. Syn. Sătŭro, sătĭo, ĕxplĕo.

ĕxscīndo, scĭdī, scīssŭm, *and* sĕco, cŭī, *to cut off.* Trōjānam ĕxscīndĕrĕ gēntĕm,

Virg. Exsĕcăt, ătquĕ, Hor. Syn. Excīdo, sĕco, scīndo; ēvērto, dīrŭo, dēlĕo.

ēxscrĕo, ŭs, *to spit out.* Exscrĕăt, ēt fīctă, Ov. V. Spuo.

ēxsĕco, ās, ĕcŭī, ēctŭm, *to cut out or away.* Exsĕcăt, ătquĕ, Hor.

ēxsībĭlo, ās, *to hiss out or forth.* Exsībĭlăt ōrĕ, Sil.

ēxsīcco, ūs, *to dry up, drain.* Exsīccēt cŭlŭllīs, Hor.

ēxsŏmnĭs, ĕ, *sleepless.* Vēstĭbŭlum ēxsŏmnīs sērvăt, Virg.

ēxsŏrbĕo, ūs, ŭī, *to suck, or swallow up.* Pēctŏrăque ēxsŏrbēnt, Ov.

ēxsŏrs, ōrtĭs, *without a share, deprived.* Dūlcīs vītæ ēxsŏrtēs, Virg.

ēxspătĭŏr, ārīs, *to wander abroad.* Exspătĭāntŭr ĭn aūrās, Sil. Syn. Spătĭŏr, ērro, văgŏr, dīvăgŏr, āmbŭlo.

ēxspērgo, ĭs, *to besprinkle.* Sănĭēque ēxspērsă nătārēnt, Virg. V. Spargo.

ēxspŏlĭo, ās, *to despoil, rob.* Exspŏlĭātquĕ gēnās, Ov.

ēxstērno, ūs, *to frighten, madden.* Exstērnătă fūgăm, Ov.

ēxstĭmŭlo, ās, *to spur on.* Exstĭmŭlārĕ vĭrŭm, Ov. Syn. Stĭmŭlo, ēxcĭto.

ēxsūdo, ās, *to sweat out.* Exsūdăt ĭnūtĭlĭs hŭmŏr, Virg.

ēxsūgo, xī, ctŭm, *to suck dry.* Exsūctă mĕdūllīs, Juv.

ēxsŭpĕrābĭlĭs, ĕ, *which may be surpassed.* Exsŭpĕrābĭlĕ sāxŭm, Virg.

ēxsŭpĕro, ās, *to surpass.* Exsŭpĕrānt ūndās, Virg. Syn. Sŭpĕro, præsto, vīnco.

ēxsūrdo, ās, *to make deaf.* Exsūrdānt vīnă pălātŭm, Hor.

ēxsūrgo, ĭs, sūrrēxī, *to rise up.* Exsūrgītquĕ făcem āttŏllēns, Virg

|| ēxsūscĭto, ās, *to raise up.* Syn. Sūscĭto, ēxcĭto.

ēxtă, ōrŭm, n. pl., *the bowels.* Cōnsŭlīt ēxtă, Virg. Syn. Vīscĕră, Intēstīnă. Epith. Pīnguĭă, lūbrĭcă, tŭmĭdă, fŭmāntĭă, călēntĭă, mōllĭă, ĭntĭmă, călĭdă, tĕpĭdă, tĕpēntĭă. V. Viscera.

ēxtēmplō, adv., *immediately.* Extēmplō, Tūrnī, Virg. Syn. Cōntĭnŭō, prōtĭnŭs, sŭbĭto, haŭd mŏră, rĕpēntĕ, ōcўŭs, cōnfēstĭm, īlĭcĕt, āctŭtŭm.

ēxtēmpŏrālĭs, ĕ, *sudden.* Extēmpŏrālīs făctŭs, (Scaz.) Mart. Syn. Sŭbĭtŭs, rĕpēntīnŭs.

ēxtēndo, dī, sŭm, *to extend.* Ingēns ēxtēndĭtŭr āntrō, Virg. Syn. Tēndo, pāndo, ēxpāndo, dīffŭndo, pōrrĭgo, ēxplĭco; prŏpāgo.

ēxtĕnŭo, ās, *to grind small.* Extĕnŭāndă mŏră, Ov. Syn. Tĕnŭo, āttĕnŭo, mĭnŭo, ĭmmĭnŭo.

ēxtĕrĭŏr, ōrĭs, *outward.* Tū cŏmĕs ēxtĕrĭŏr, Hor. Syn. Sŭmmŭs, ēxtērnŭs.

ēxtērmĭno, ās, *to banish, to destroy.* Paŭlŭs hĭnc ēxtērmĭnăt, (Iamb. Dim.) Syn. Ăbŏlĕo; ējĭcĭo; ēxpēllo, pēllo, ăbĭgo.

ēxtērnŭs, *and* rŭs, ă, ŭm, *outward.* Extērnīs āffŏre ăb ōrĭs, Virg. Extĕră quærĕrĕ rēgnă, Virg. Syn. Extrānĕŭs.

ēxtĕro, ĭs, *to tread under foot.* Extĕrĕt īllĕ nĭvēs, Ov.

ēxtērrĕo, ēs, *to frighten.* Mŭgītū nĕmŏră ēxtērrĕt, Sil.

ēxtērrĭtŭs, *the pass. partic. of* exterreo. Sŭbĭtīs ēxtērrĭtŭs ŭmbrīs, Virg.

ēxtĭmēsco, *and* ĕo, ŭī, *to be much afraid.* Extĭmŭĭtquĕ măgĭstrŭm, Hor. Syn. Tĭmĕo.

ēxtīnguo, xī, ctŭm, *to extinguish.* Flāmmās ēxtīnguĭtĕ Vēstæ, Ov. Syn. Rēstīnguo; ăbŏlĕo, pērdo, dĕlĕo, ēvērto; ōccīdo, ĭntērfĭcĭo, pĕrĭmo, ĭntĕrĭmo.

ēxtīrpo, ās, *to extirpate.* Extīrpā, mĭhĭ crēdĕ, Mart. Syn. Vēllo, ēvēllo, ērŭo, ērādīco, āvēllo. V. Evello.

ēxto, ās, *to be, to subsist.* Clārĭŭs ēxtăt ŏpŭs, Ov.

ēxtōllo, tŭlī, ēlātŭm, *to lift up.* Atque ēxtōllĕrĕ vīrēs, Virg. Syn. Ēffĕro, ēdūco, ĭs; laŭdo; prædĭco, ās; cĕlebro.

ēxtōrquĕo, rsī, rtŭm, *to wrench.* Tēndūnt ēxtōrquērĕ pŏēmătă, Hor. Syn. Aūfĕro, răpĭo, ērĭpĭo.

ēxtōrrĭs, ĭs, m. f., *an exile.* Fīnĭbŭs ēxtōrrĭs, Virg.

ēxtră, prep., *out of.* Nĭl ēxtră nŭmĕrŭm, Hor.

ēxtrăho, ăxī, āctŭm, *to draw out of.* Extrăhăt ālvō, Hor. Syn. Exprōmo, ēlĭcĭo.

ēxtrānĕŭs, ă, ŭm, *strange, foreign.* Indŏmĭtă ĭn strāto ēxtrānĕŏ, (Iamb.) Petr. Syn. Extērnŭs, ēxtĕrŭs.

ēxtrēmŭs, ă, ŭm, *extreme.* Extrēmōs cūrrĭt, Hor. Syn. Ultĭmŭs, suprēmŭs; sŭmmŭs.

ĕxtrīco, ās, *to disengage*. Ŭnde ĕxtrīcăt, ămārās, Hor. SYN. Ĕxpĕdĭo, sōlvo, lībĕro.

ĕxtrīnsĕcŭs, adv., *on the outside*. Ĕxtrīnsĕcŭs īntrăt, Pers.

ĕxtrūdo, sī, sŭm, *to thrust out*. Quī vŭlt ĕxtrūdĕrĕ mĕrcēs, Hor. SYN. Dētrūdo, dētŭrbo, pēllo, ĕxpēllo, ējĭcĭo.

ĕxtrŭo, xī, ctŭm. Ĕxtrŭĭs, heŭ rēgnī, Virg. V. Ædĭfĭco.

ĕxtūbĕro, ās, *to swell*. Vērbĕrāta ĕxtūbĕrĕt, (Iamb.) Prud. SYN. Ĕxtŭmēsco, tŭrgĕo, tŭmēsco, īnflŏr, prŏtūbĕro.

ĕxtūndo, ĭs, ŭdī, ŭsŭm, *to beat*. Mĕdĭtāndo ĕxtūndĕrĕt ārtēs, Virg. SYN. Ēlīdo, ĕxprĭmo, ĕlīcĭo; ĕxcūdo.

ĕxtūrbo, ās, *to drive out*. Ĕxtūrbāre ănĭmās, Ov.

ĕxūbĕro, ās, *to abound*. Fŏlĭŏrum ĕxūbĕrăt ūmbră, Virg. SYN. Ăbūndo, ăfflŭo.

ĕxŭl, ĕxŭlĭs, m. f., *an exile*. Ĕxŭl ăb ōctāvā, Juv. SYN. Ĕxpūlsŭs, ējĕctŭs, prŏfūgŭs, ĕxtōrrĭs. EPITH. Văgŭs, mĭsĕr, văgăbūndŭs, flēbĭlĭs, trīstĭs, mœstŭs, sōllĭcĭtŭs, īnsōmnĭs, lānguĭdŭs, ănxĭŭs, mœrēns, īncōgnĭtŭs. V. Exulo.

|| ĕxŭlcĕro, ās, *to make sore*. SYN. Ăspĕro, ĕxāspĕro, ĕxăcĕrbo; crŭcĭo, tōrquĕo, ĕxcrŭcĭo.

ĕxŭlo, ās, *to be banished*. Ĕxŭlăt ōrĭs, Virg. V. Exul, exilium.

ĕxŭlto, ās, *to leap about*. Mŏx ĕxūltăbĭmŭs ōmnēs, Sedul. SYN. Gēstĭo, lætŏr, gaŭdĕo, trĭūmpho.

ĕxŭlŭlo, ās, *to howl*. Ĕxŭlŭlārĕ cŏmĭs, Ov. SYN. Ŭlŭlo, vōcĭfĕrŏr. V. Ululo.

ĕxūndo, ās, *to overflow*. Ĕxūndāt pĕlăgŭs, Sil. SYN. Ŭndo, ăbūndo, ĕfflŭo.

ĕxŭo, ŭī, ŭtŭm, *to put off*. Ĕxŭĭt ārmĭs, Virg. V. Nudo.

ĕxūro, ssī, stŭm, *to burn out*. Aŭt ĕxūrĭtŭr īgnī, Virg. SYN. Ŭro, ădūro, crĕmo, īncēndo, ăccēndo, īnflāmmo. V. Uro.

ĕxŭvĭæ, ārŭm, f. pl., *spoils*. Quī rŏdĭt ĕxŭvĭās, Virg. SYN. Spŏlĭă, prædă. EPITH. Dītēs, ŏpīmæ, crŭēntæ, hōstīlēs.

F.

FĀBĂ, æ, f., *a bean*. Ĕt făbă făbrōrŭm, Colum. EPITH. Dūră, pāllēns, pīnguĭs, pīctă, vēntōsă.

făbālĭs, ĕ, *of a bean*. Stĭpŭlāsquĕ făbālēs, Ov.

Fābărĭs, ĭs, m., *a river of the Sabines*. Fābărīmquĕ bĭbūnt, Virg.

făbēllă, æ, f., *a short fable or tale*. Fābēllām sūrdō, Hor.

făbĕr, fabrī, m., *a workman*. Cīrcă lūdŭm făbĕr, ĭmŭs, Hor. SYN. Ărtīfĕx, ŏpīfĕx. EPITH. Fērrārĭŭs, līgnārĭŭs, ærārĭŭs, īndūstrĭŭs, rōbūstŭs, fōrtĭs. V. Procudo.

făbĕr, bră, ŭm, *of a workman*. Fābræ cĕlĕbērrĭmŭs ārtĭs, Ov.

Fābĭŭs, ĭī, m., *the name of a Roman family*. Ŭnă dĭēs Fābĭōs ād bēllŭm, Ov.

fabrĭcă, æ, f., *a shop or workhouse*. Dēnĭque ŭt īn făbrĭcă, Lucr. SYN. Fabrīle ŏpŭs: ŏffĭcīnă.

fabrĭcātŏr, ōrĭs, m., *a framer*. Dŏlī făbrĭcātŏr Ĕpēŭs, Virg. SYN. Ărtīfĕx, ŏpīfĕx, strūctŏr, ĕxstrūctŏr, făbĕr.

Fabrĭcĭŭs, ĭī, m., *a Roman consul*. Fābrĭcĭŭm? vĕl tē, Virg. EPITH. Grăvĭs, paŭpĕr, rĭgĭdŭs, trīstĭs, Rōmānŭs, fĭdēlĭs, fōrtĭs, gĕnĕrōsŭs, īncōrrūptŭs, īnvīctŭs.

fabrĭcŏr, ārĭs, or co, ās, *to make, frame*. Pŏst făbrĭcāvĕrăt ūsŭs, Hor. SYN. Făcĭo, ĕffĭcĭo, cōndo, ĕxstrŭo, ædĭfĭco, mōlĭŏr, cūdo, ĕxcūdo. V. Procudo, Ædifico.

fabrīlĭs, ĕ, *of a workman*. Fābrīlēs ŏpĕrās, Sev.

fabrīlĭtĕr, adv., *as a workman*. Ŏpīfĕx făbrīlĭtĕr āptāns, Prud.

făbŭlă, æ, f., *a fable*. Fābŭlă nūllă fŭĭt, Ov. SYN. Cōmmēntŭm, fĭgmēntŭm. EPITH. Ănīlĭs, mēndāx, vānă, gărrŭlă, fīctă, ĭnānĭs, īngĕnĭōsă, sōlĕrs, pĕrītă, mōnstrōsă, vŭlgārĭs, pŏētĭcă, lætă, āntīquă, dōctă, dēlīră.

făbŭlŏr, ārĭs, *to talk*. Dūm făbŭlāmūr ĭnīlĭbŭs, (Scaz.) Mart. SYN. Cōllŏquŏr, fābŭlās nārro.

făbŭlōsŭs, ă, ŭm, *fabulous*. Quæ lŏcă făbŭlōsŭs, (Sapph.) Hor. SYN. Fīctŭs, fīctĭtĭŭs, ĕffīctŭs, vānŭs, ĭnānĭs.

fac, *do, suppose*. Nōn pōssŭnt, făc ĕnĭm, Lucr. Hōs făc Ārmĕnĭōs, Ov.

făcēsso, ĭs, *to accomplish*. Præcēptă făcēssĭt, Virg. SYN. Făcĭo; ămŏvĕo.

făcētiœ, ārŭm, f. pl., *merry conceits.* Pŭĕr āc făcētiārŭm, (Phal.) Cat. Syn. Jŏcī, sălēs, lĕpōrēs, fēstīvĭtās.

făcētŭs, ă, ŭm, *facetious.* Quēmquŏ făcētŭs ădōptā, Hor. Syn. Lĕpĭdŭs, fēstīvŭs, sălsŭs, jŏcōsŭs, ūrbānŭs, ārgūtŭs.

făciēs, iēī, f., *the face.* Extēmplŏ făciēs ēt mēntis, Ov. Syn. Ōs, vūltŭs, frōns.

Epith. Pūlchră, nĭtēns, dĕcōră, cāndĭdă, ēgrēgiă, hŏnēstă, sĕrēnă, īnsīgnis, fōrmōsă, grātă, blāndă, vĕrēcūndă, bĕnīgnă, īngĕnŭă, vĕnūstă, rŏsĕă, mŏdēstă, hĭlārĭs, jŭvĕnīlĭs, vĕnĕrāndă, vĕnĕrābĭlĭs, sūbrīdēns, lœtă, sĕvĕră, mĭnāx, cōntrāctă, ōblīquă, tŏrvă, fĕră, tērrĭfĭcă, hōrrēndă, mĕtŭēndă, fōrmīdābĭlĭs, sōrdĭdă, fœdă, rūgōsă. V. Os, oris.

făcĭle, adv., *easily.* Nēc tēmpĕrārī făcĭlĕ nēc rĕprĭmī pŏtēst, (Iamb.) Sen. Ingĕnĭŏ făcĭlĕ cōncĭliāntĕ, Ov.

făcĭlĭs, ĕ, *easy.* Et făcĭlēs mōtŭs, Ov. Syn. Haŭd dĭffĭcĭlĭs; mōbĭlĭs; āptŭs, hăbĭlĭs; mītĭs, lēnĭs.

făcĭnŭs, ŏrĭs, n., *a great action ; a crime.* Pēr mĕōrŭm făcĭnōrŭm laŭdĕm, (Iamb.) Syn. Actĭo, ŏpŭs, fāctŭm; scĕlŭs, crīmĕn, flāgĭtĭŭm. Epith. Ēgrēgiŭm, īnsīgnĕ, gĕnĕrōsŭm, prœclārŭm; mălŭm, ātrōx, ōbscœnŭm, hōrrēndŭm, nĕfāndŭm, tētrŭm, mālīgnŭm. V. Scelus.

făcĭo, fĕcī, fāctŭm, *to do.* Nŭcĭbŭs făcĭmŭs quœcūnquĕ, Pers. Syn. Effĭcĭo, cōnfĭcĭo, pērfĭcĭo, ēxĕquŏr, ăgo, pĕrăgo, mōlĭŏr, ŏpĕrŏr, patro, pērpetro.

făctĭto, ās, *freq. of* facio. Cūr vērsŭs făctĭtĕt, Hor.

făctŭm, ī, n., *a deed, action.* Et făctă părēntĭs, Virg.

făcŭltās, ātĭs, f., *easiness, aptness.* Est ōblātă făcŭltās, Virg. Syn. Pŏtēstăs, vīs. făcūndĭă, œ, f., *eloquence.* Nēc făcūndiă dĕsĕrĕt hūnc, Hor.

făcūndŭs, ă, ŭm, *eloquent.* Nūnc făcūndŭs Ulyssēs, Ov. V. Eloquens.

fœcŭlă, œ, f., *dim. of* fœx, *lees, dregs.* Fœcŭlă Cŏă, Hor.

fœcŭlēntŭs, ă, ŭm, *dreggy.* Et fœcŭlēntōs gūrgĭtēs, (Iamb.) Syn. Cœnōsŭs; crāssŭs, fœx, fœcĭs, f., *dregs.* Ĕgŏ fœcĕm prīmŭs, Hor. Syn. Cœnŭm. Epith. Liquĭdă, vīnōsă, crāssă, lēntă, fœtĭdă, īmă, sĕdēns.

fāgĭnĕŭs *and* nŭs, ă, ŭm, *of a beech-tree.* Illīc fāgĭnĕŭs, Ov. Fāgĭnŭs āxis, Virg. fāgŭs, ī, f., *a beech-tree.* Fāgŭs ēt Arcădĭŏ, Prop. Epith. Pătŭlă, ārdŭă, ēxcēlsă, āltă, ūmbrōsă, frōndōsă, dēnsă.

fălœ, ārŭm, f. pl., *wooden towers; elevated pillars in the circus.* Cōnsŭlĭt āntĕ fălās, Juv.

fălărĭcă, œ, f., *a javelin armed with lighted tow.* Cōntōrtă fălărĭcă vēnĭt, Virg.

fālcātŭs, ă, ŭm, *hooked.* Fālcātī cōmĭnŭs ēnsēs, Virg. Syn. Fālcĭbŭs ārmātŭs; cūrvātŭs.

fālcĭfĕr *and* gĕr, ă, ŭm, *bearing a hook.* Nām sī fālcĭfĕrī, Mart.

fālco, ōnĭs, m., *a hawk.* Sĕcăt āĕră fālco. Epith. Răpāx, răpĭdŭs, vŏrāx, fĕrŭs, atrōx, ăvĭdŭs, rāptŏr, crŭēntŭs. V. Accipiter.

Fălērnŭs, ă, ŭm, *Falernian, of Falernum, a mountain in Campania famous for its wines.* Cēllīs ĭdĕŏ cōntēndă Fălērnīs, Virg. Fălērnŭm, ī, n., *sc.* vinum, *Falernian wine.* Lĭquĭdī mĕdĭă dē nōctĕ Fălērnī, Hor. Mūstă Fălērnă, Mart. Syn. Vīnŭm. Epith. Fūmōsŭm, īndŏmĭtŭm, vĕtŭlŭm, ācrĕ, mōrdāx, suāvĕ, Cāmpănŭm, Sūrrēntīnŭm. V. Vinum.

Fălīscī, ōrŭm, m. pl., *a people of Etruria.* Æquōsquĕ Fălīscōs, Virg.

Fălīscŭs, ă, ŭm, *of the Falisci.* Hērbă Fălīscă, Ov.

fāllācĭă, œ, f., *deceit.* Rĕpĕrīt fāllāciă, vīctŭs, Virg. Syn. Dŏlŭs, fraŭs, āstŭs, āstŭtĭă, cāllĭdĭtās, vafrĭtiēs, īnsĭdĭœ. Epith. Inīquă, mălă, ōccūltă, mēndāx, mālīgnă, pērfĭdă, scĕlĕrātă, īmprŏbă, tēctă, īmplēxă. V. Dolus.

fāllācĭtĕr, adv., *deceitfully.* Fāllācĭtĕr ōmnĭă trānsĭt, Ov. Syn. Dŏlōsē, āstū.

fāllāx, ācĭs, *deceitful.* Fāllācī pērfĕrĕt Aŭnō, Virg. Syn. Mēndāx, dŏlōsŭs, pērfĭdŭs.

fāllo, fĕfēllī, fālsŭm, *to deceive.* Quīs fāllĕrĕ pōssĭt, Virg. Syn. Dēcĭpĭo, fraŭdo, dēlūdo, ēlūdo. V. Decipio.

fālsĭdĭcŭs, *and* lŏquŭs, ă, ŭm, *speaking falsely.* Fālsĭdĭcŭs cōnfīdēnsquĕ, (Iamb.) Syn. Mēndāx.

fālsĭpărēns, ēntĭs, *who owns a wrong father.* Aŭdĭt fālsĭpărēns, Cat.

fālsō, *or* ē, adv., *falsely.* Invĭdĭă ēst fālsō, Tib.

fālsŭs, ă, ŭm, *false.* Dīcĕrĕ fālsŭm. Virg.

fālx, cĭs, f., *a scythe.* Hūc ēt fālcĭs hŏnōs, Virg. Epith. Cūrvă, prŏcūrvă, ŏbtūsă, ăcūtă, ădūncă, fĕrrĕă, dūră, æstīvă, pāndă, rĕpāndă, fœnīsĕcă, lōngă, mŏrdāx, cămpēstrĭs, Cĕrĕālĭs.

Fāmă, æ, f., *the goddess Fame ; honour, infamy.* It Fāmă pĕr ūrbēs, Virg. Syn. Rūmŏr, mūrmŭr, sērmo ; glōrĭă, laūs, nōmĕn, dĕcŭs, hŏnŏr. Epith. Pēnnātă, vŏlĭtāns, mēndāx, văgă, īncērtă, gārrŭlă, tūrbĭdă, sŭpērstĕs, mĕmŏr, vĕlōx, pĕrēnnĭs, mălīgnă, prŏcāx, prænūncĭă, vīvāx, cĕlĕr, vērbōsă, pŏtēns, præpĕs, pērnīx, sŭbĭtă, rĕpēntīnă.

fămēlĭcŭs, ă, ŭm, *hungry.* Lāssōquĕ fămēlĭcă cōllō, Juv. Syn. Impāstŭs.

fămēs, ĭs, f., *hunger.* Et mălĕsuādă Fămēs, āc, Virg. Syn. Ēsŭrĭēs. Epith. Răbĭdă, mălĕsuādă, īnsānă, sævă, mĭsĕră, jējūnāns, āmbĭtĭōsă, stĭmŭlāns, dūră, ĭnŏps, ātră, crūdēlĭs, ūrgēns, vŏrāx, ăcērbă, īmpōrtūnă, āspĕră, ægră, prædūră, ăvĭdă, pāllĭdă, lānguĭdă, fŭrĭbūndă, vĭŏlēntă; ĭnĕrs, īmpătĭēns, quĕrŭlă, vĭgĭl, īnsōmnĭs, īrrĕquĭētă, grăvĭs, rĕdūx, rĕdĭvīvă.

fămĭlĭă, æ, f., *a family.* Pătĕr fămĭlĭæ vĕrŭs, (Scaz.) Mart. Syn. Agnātĭo, cōg-nātĭo, stīrps, gĕnŭs.

fămĭlĭārĭs, ĕ, *of the same family.* Sŭm fămĭlĭārĭs, ēx, (Iamb.) Plaut. Syn. Dŏ-mēstĭcŭs.

fāmōsŭs, ă, ŭm, *notorious.* Lăquĕŭm fāmōsō cārmĭnĕ nēctĭt, Hor. Syn. Insīgnĭs, præclārŭs ; fāmă sŭpĕr æthĕră nōtŭs ; tūrpĭs, īnfāmĭs.

fămŭlārĭs, ĕ, *of a servant.* Fămŭlārĭă jūră dătūrŭs, Ov.

fămŭlātŭs, ūs, m., *service.* Ērgāstŭlă quōs fămŭlātū, Prud. Syn. Sērvĭtŭs.

fămŭlŏr, ārĭs, *to serve.* Bŏnĭs, fămŭlēmŭr ŭt ĭllī, Ar. Syn. Sērvĭo.

fămŭlŭs, ī, m., *and* ă, æ, f., *a servant.* Intĕrĭmām fămŭlŭm, Ov. Intŭs fămŭlæ, quĭbŭs ōrdĭnĕ lōngō, Virg. Syn. Mĭnīstĕr, sērvŭs, pŭĕr. Epith. Prōmptŭs, cĕlĕr, fīdŭs, sūccīnctŭs, gnāvŭs, sōlērs, săgāx, fĭdēlĭs. V. Servus.

fămŭlŭs, ă, ŭm, *servile, subject.* Fămŭlōs vērtĭcĕ fērrĕ pĕdĕm, Ov.

fănātĭcŭs, ă, ŭm, *fanatical, mad.* Fănātĭcŭs ērrŏr, Hor.

fānŭm, ī, n., *a temple.* Hăbĭtāndăquĕ fānă, Hor. Syn. Tēmplŭm, dēlūbrŭm. Epith. Sacrŭm, vĕtūstŭm, āntīquŭm. V. Templum.

fār, fārrĭs, n., *corn, flour.* Făr ĕrăt, Ov. Syn. Frūmēntŭm, trītĭcŭm.

fārcĭo, ārsī, ārtŭm, *to stuff, cram.* Fārtūs păpўrō, Mart.

fārī, *to speak.* Ĭtă fātŭr ămīcīs, Virg. Syn. Ēffārī, prŏfārī, lŏquī.

fărīnă, æ, f., *meal.* Fŭĕrīnt cōnfūsă fărīnæ, Ov. Epith. Trītĭcĕă, ădōrĕă, pūl-tĭfĭcă, cāndĭdă, lĕvĭs, āttrītă.

fārrāgo, ĭnĭs, f., *a mixture.* Māgnŭm fārrāgĭnĕ cōrpŭs, Virg. Epith. Mīxtă, crāssă.

fārtŭm, ī, n., *a hash.* Ŏpīmō vīncĕrĕ fārtō, Pers.

fās, n., (*indecl.*) *right, equity.* Fās ēt jūră sĭnūnt, Virg. Syn. Jūs, æquŭm, lĭcĭtŭm, jūstĭtĭă, æquĭtās.

fāscĭă, æ, f., *a bandage.* Dēnsō fāscĭă lībrō, Juv. Epith. Tĕnŭĭs, grăcĭlĭs, sĭnŭōsă, mōllĭs, pūrpŭrĕă, pēndēns, pēndŭlă.

fāscĭātŭs, ă, ŭm, *bandaged.* Nēc fāscĭātō naūfrăgŭs, Mart.

fāscĭcŭlŭs, ī, m., *a small bundle.* Fāscĭcŭlŭm pōrtĕs, Hor. Syn. Fāscĭs.

fāscĭno, ās, *to bewitch.* Mĭhĭ fāscĭnăt āgnōs, Virg. V. Veneficium, magia.

fāscĭnŭm, ī, n., *a bewitching.* Fāscĭnă pāssŭs, Mart.

fāscĭŏlă, æ, f., *a small bandage.* Fāscĭōlăs, crūrĭbŭs pĕdĭtāl), Hor.

fāscēs, ĭum, m. pl., *bundles of rods carried by the lictors, the insignia of the chief magistrates at Rome.* Prīmōs āttōllĕrĕ fāscēs, Virg.

fāscĭs, ĭs, f., *a fagot, bundle of sticks.* Sŭb fāscĕ dĕdĕrĕ, Virg.

fāstī, ōrŭm, m. pl., *Roman calendars.* Tēmpŏră fāstōs, Ov.

fāstīdĭo, īs, īvī *or* ĭī, *to spurn.* Hīc fāstīdĭt, Alēxĭm, Virg. Syn. Ābhōrrĕo, āvērsŏr, rĕfŭgĭo, cōntēmno, āspērnŏr. V. Contemno, aspernor.

fāstīdĭōsŭs, ă, ŭm, *disdainful.* Fāstīdĭōsă trīstĭs, (Iamb.) Hor.

fāstīdĭŭm, ĭī, n., *disdain.* Tŭlĕrīnt fāstīdĭă mēnsēs, Virg. Syn. Tædĭŭm, naūsĕă, cōntēmptŭs. Epith. Lēntŭm, dĭffĭcĭlĕ, mōrōsŭm, lōngŭm, trīstĕ, grăvĕ, īn-grātŭm.

fāstīgĭŭm, ĭī, n., *the top.* Sĕquăr fāstīgĭă rērŭm, Virg. Syn. Cūlmĕn, vērtēx, ăpēx, căcūmĕn. Epith. Sūmmŭm, āltŭm, cēlsŭm, ēxcēlsŭm. V. Cacumen.

fāstōsŭs, ă, ŭm, *haughty.* Jăcēs fāstōsæ līmĭnă mœchæ, Mart. Syn. Sŭpērbŭs, fāstū tŭmēns, tŭmĭdŭs.

fāstŭs, ūs, m., *pride.* Fāstŭs āssūmĭs ămōrĕ, Prop. Syn. Sŭpērbĭă, āmbĭtĭo.

Epith. Tŭrnĭdŭs, prŏtĕrvŭs, ĭnīquŭs, ĭnānĭs, sŭpĕrbŭs, tŭmēns, mălīgnŭs, grăvĭs, tūrgĭdŭs, ĭmpĕrĭōsŭs, ēlātŭs.

fāstŭs (dies), *a day in which courts of law were open.* Fāstŭs ĕrĭt, Ov.

fătālĭs, ĕ, *fatal.* Aŭt fīnītĕ mĕtŭm fātālĭs, Ov. Syn. Fūnĕstŭs; cērtŭs, rătŭs.

fătālĭtĕr, adv., *fatally.* Prīmŭs fătālĭtĕr hāstā, Ov. Syn. Fātō, fătālī lēgĕ.

fătĕŏr, ērĭs, *to confess.* Ipsĕ fătēbātŭr, Virg. Syn. Cōnfĭtĕŏr, nōn nĕgo; cōncēdo.

fătīdĭcŭs, cănŭs, cīnŭs, lŏquŭs, ă, ŭm, *foretelling.* Vātīs fātĭdĭcă, Virg. Syn. Præsāgŭs, prænūncĭŭs, vātēs.

fătĭfĕr, ă, ŭm, *destructive.* Fātĭfĕrūmque ēnsĕm, Virg. Syn. Fūnĕstŭs, lēthĭfĕr.

fătīgo, ās, *to tire.* Tĕrgă fătīgāmŭs, Virg. Syn. Lăsso, ūrgĕo, prĕmo.

fătĭlĕgŭs, ă, ŭm, *gathering what is fatal.* Tōxĭcă fătĭlĕgī, Luc.

fătīsco, ĭs, *to chap.* Vīctă fătīscăt, Virg. Syn. Sŭccŭmbo; dĕhīsco.

fātŭm, ī, n., *destiny.* Stăbĭlī fātōrūm nūmĭnĕ, Virg. Syn. Fōrs, fŏrtūnă; mōrs, fūnŭs, lēthŭm. Epith. Ĭnēxōrābĭlĕ, ĭnēlūctābĭlĕ, crūdēlĕ, mĭsĕrŭm, ăcĕrbŭm, īncĕrtŭm, mĭsĕrābĭlĕ, trīstĕ, æmŭlŭm, cæcŭm, sōllĭcĭtŭm, ōccŭltŭm, dēflēndŭm, mĭnĭtāns, īnvĭdŭm, dūrŭm, dŭbĭŭm, ēxĭtĭālĕ, īnsōlābĭlĕ, prŏpĕrāns, īmmōtŭm, mălīgnŭm, pērnĭcĭōsŭm, lāmēntābĭlĕ, tērrĭbĭlĕ, fērrĕŭm, fūnĕrĕŭm, ămārŭm, īmmōbĭlĕ, flēbĭlĕ, īmmānĕ, īnstāns, rĕpēntīnŭm.

fătŭŭs, ă, ŭm, *foolish.* Dīcĭtŭr ēt fătŭīs, Catull. Syn. Stŭltŭs, stŏlĭdŭs, vēcōrs, īnsānŭs. V. Stultus.

faŭcēs, ĭŭm, f. pl., *the chaps.* Faŭcĭbŭs ēxŭpĕrăt, Pers. Syn. Jŭgŭlŭm, gŭttŭr, ōrā. Epith. Ōbscūræ, ăvĭdæ, āngūstæ, pătŭlæ.

făvĕo, făvī, faŭtŭm, *to favour.* Cāstă făvē, Virg. Syn. Āspīro, ādsŭm. V. Auxilior, aspiro.

făvīllă, æ, f., *a hot ember.* Vŏlĭtārĕ făvīllăm, Virg. Syn. Scīntīllă, cĭnĭs. Epith. Cāndēns, lĕvĭs, călēns, fērvēns, tĕnŭĭs, ārdēns, fūmāns, īncēnsă, călĭdă, vŏlāns, tĕpĭdă, īgnĕă, bĭbŭlă, spārsă, cānă, vānă, rŭtĭlă, mōbĭlĭs, trĕmŭlă, āltĭvŏlă, crēpĭtāns, vŏlucrĭs, flāmmāns, tōrrēns. V. Ignis.

Faŭnī, ōrŭm, m. pl., *Sylvan Deities.* In nŭmĕrŭm Faŭnōsquĕ, Virg. Syn. Sătyrī, Sylvānī. Epith. Sylvĭcŏlæ, agrēstēs, bĭcōrnēs, caprĭpĕdēs, Mænălĭī, Lўcæī, Arcădĭcī; rūrĭcŏlæ, nōctĭvāgī, cōrnĭgĕrī, mōntĭcŏlæ, prŏcācēs, lāscīvī. V. Satyri.

Făvōnĭŭs, ĭī, m., *the west wind.* Vērĕ Făvōnĭī, (Choriamb.) Hor. Syn. Zĕphўrŭs. Epith. Spīrāns, cāndĭdŭs, tĕnŭĭs, lĭquĭdŭs, lĕvĭs, flōrĭfĕr, plăcĭdŭs, flōrĭdŭs. V. Zephyrus.

făvŏr, ōrĭs, m., *favour.* Ūnctæ dēt făvŏr ārbĭtĕr, (Phal.) Mart. Syn. Stŭdĭŭm, grătĭă. Epith. Dūlcĭs, bĕnīgnŭs, prŏpēnsŭs, sĕcūndŭs.

faūstĭtās, ātĭs, f., *happiness.* Ālmăquĕ faūstĭtās, (Asclep.) Hor.

Faūstŭlŭs, ī, m., *a peasant who reared Romulus and Remus.* Faūstŭlĕ paŭpĕr, ŏpēs, Ov.

faūstŭs, ă, ŭm, *happy.* I pĕdĕ faūstō, Hor. Syn. Fēlīx, fōrtūnātŭs, bĕātŭs. V. Felix.

faūtŏr, ōrĭs, m., *and* trīx, trīcĭs, f., *a favourer.* Hīc ŭbī nēquĭtĭæ faūtōrĭbŭs, Hor. Syn. Făvēns, stŭdĭōsŭs, prōtēctŏr, dēfēnsŏr, ādjūtŏr, āmīcŭs.

făvŭs, ī, m., *honeycomb.* Mēllă făvīs, Virg. Syn. Mĕl. Epith. Prēssŭs, mēllītŭs, flāvŭs, pūrŭs, dūlcĭs, Hўblæŭs, Sĭcŭlŭs; nēctărĕŭs, āmbrŏsĭŭs, grătŭs, ŏlēns, Cecrŏpĭŭs; ŏdōrŭs, ŏdōrĭfĕr, ŏdōrātŭs, pīnguĭs, cœlēstĭs, āĕrĭŭs. V. Mel.

făx, ăcĭs, f., *a torch.* Sīc ēffātă făcĕm, Virg. Syn. Tædă, lāmpăs, lūx, lūmĕn. Epith. Cŏrūscă, fūmĭdă, lūcēns, flāmmĭfĕră, fērvēns, fūmāns, rŭtĭlă, ārdēns, flāmmāns, lūcĭdă, lūcĭfĕră, flāmmĕă, īgnĭvŏmă, splēndĭdă, trĕmŭlă, fērvĭdă, mīcāns, īgnītă, flāmmĭvŏmă, nōctūrnă, grātă, cŏrŭscāns, sīdĕrĕă, cœlēstĭs, Phœbēĭă, clāră, fūnĕrĕă.

febrīcĭto, ās, *to be feverish.* Febrīcĭtāntēm bāsĭābĭt, (Scaz.) Mart.

febrīcŭlōsŭs, ă, ŭm, *feverish.* Nēscĭŏ quīd fĕbrīcŭlōsī, (Phal.) Catull.

febrĭs, ĭs, *and* brīcŭlă, æ, f., *fever.* Ărĭdă fĕbrĭs, Virg. Syn. Febrīlĭs æstŭs, ārdŏr, īgnĭs. Epith. Ărĭdă, ăvĭdă, ōccŭltă, călĭdă, flăgrāns, ārdēns, ănhēlă, mălīgnă, mŏlēstă, dīră, ăcĕrbă, īnsānă, ămără, grăvĭs, trĕmŭlă: ĭnĕrs, fērvēns, rĕcĭdīvă, vĭŏlēntă, vĭgĭl, sēgnĭs, sūrēns, ăcūtă, pāllĭdă, cōrrōdēns, ĕdāx, dēpāscēns, fŭrĭbŭndă, răpĭdă, sĭtĭbŭndă, tōrrēns, rĕcŭrrēns, lēntă, rĕdĭvīvă, rĕdŭx, ēxūrēns, ădūrēns, rĕnāscēns, gĕlĭdă, frīgĭdă, mūtābĭlĭs. V. Febricito.

Fēbrŭā, ōrŭm, n. pl., *sacrifices for the dead.* Fēbrŭā Rōmānī, Ov.
Fēbrŭārĭŭs, ĭī, m., *February.* Jānŭs, Fēbrŭārĭŭs, ātquĕ, Aus. Epith. Brŭ-mālĭs, fērālĭs, plŭvĭŭs, ĭmbrĭfĕr, nĭvōsŭs, brĕvĭs, frĭgĭdŭs, gĕlĭdŭs.
fĕl, fĕllĭs, n.; *bitterness.* Sīvĕ fĕl ūrsīnŭm, Seren. Epith. Ātrŭm, vīpĕrĕŭm, mordāx, ămārŭm, vĭrĭdĕ, vīrōsŭm, mălŭm, trīstĕ, cærŭlĕŭm.
fēlīcĭtās, ātĭs, f., *happiness.* Tēmpŏrĭs fēlīcĭtās, (Iamb.) Senec. Syn. Prōspĕ-rĭtās. Epith. Fōrtūnātă, prōspĕrā, sĕcūndă. V. Felix.
fēlīcĭtĕr, adv., *happily.* Ēt fēlīcĭtĕr audĕt, Hor. Syn. Fōrtūnātĕ, bĕātĕ, faŭstĕ.
fēlĭs *and* lēs, ĭs, m., *a cat.* Fēlĕ sŏrŏr Phœbī, Ov. Syn. Ælūrŭs, cătŭs. Epith. Callĭdŭs.
fēlīx, īcĭs, *happy.* Pōst dĕcĭmām fēlīx, Virg. Ămĭtērnŭs ăgēr fēlīcĭbŭs, Mart. Syn. Bĕātŭs, fōrtūnātŭs : prōspĕr, faŭstŭs, sĕcūndŭs ; cŏmmŏdŭs, ūtĭlĭs, ōppōr-tūnŭs.
fēmĕn, ĭnĭs, n., *the inside of the thigh.* Āc fĕmĭnūm pĕdĭbŭs, Lucr.
fĕmŭr, ŏrĭs, n., *the thigh.* Rōstrō fĕmŭr haŭsĭt, Ov. Syn. Crŭs, fĕmĕn. Epith. Tĕnĕrŭm, hīrsūtŭm, trĕmŭlŭm, mollĕ, tŭmĭdŭm, tĕnĕllŭm, cāndēns, nĭvĕŭm, fīrmŭm, rōbūstŭm, fōrtĕ, vălĭdŭm, lāctĕŭm, hīrtŭm, tĭtūbāns.
fĕnēstră, *and* ĕstēllă, æ, f., *a window.* Īntōrquērĕ fĕnēstrās, Virg. Epith. Căvă, ăngūstă, pătēns, ăpērtă, pătŭlă, sŭblīmĭs, bĭfŏrĭs, claūsă, līgnĕă, vĭtrĕă.
fĕră, æ, f., *a wild beast.* Spĕlæă fĕrārŭm, Virg. Syn. Bēstĭă, brūtŭm. Epith. Hōrrĭbĭlĭs, ĭmmānĭs, sævĭēns, rĭgĭdă, hīrsūtă, sævă, răbĭdă, crūdēlĭs, răpāx, ĭmmītĭs, ācrĭs, hōrrĭdă, ĭnhūmānă, aūdāx, mĭnāx, văgă, atrōx, ērrāns, sўlvēstrĭs, fŭrĭōsă, fĕrōx, ĭmpăvĭdă, frĕmēns, dīră, ĭntērrĭtă, ĭmpērtērrĭtă, sān-guĭnŏlēntă, cōncĭtă, hōrrēns, fōrmīdābĭlĭs. V. Venor.
fĕr, *the imperat. of* fero. Fāctĭs fĕr ăd æthĕră, Virg.
Fērālĭă, ĭŭm, n. pl., *sacrifices to the dead.* Dīxērĕ Fērālĭă lūcĕm, Ov.
fērālĭs, ĕ, *deadly.* Cŭlmĭnĭbŭs fērālī cārmĭnĕ būbo, Virg. Syn. Fūnēstŭs, dīrŭs, ēxĭtĭālĭs.
fĕrāx, ācĭs, *fertile.* Tērră fĕrāx Cĕrĕrĭs, Ov. Syn. Ūbĕr, fœcūndŭs, fērtĭlĭs, ăbūndāns. V. Fertilis.
fērcŭlŭm, ī, n., *a dish.* Fērcŭlă cœnā, Hor. Syn. Ēscă, dăpēs, ĕpŭlæ, cĭbŭs. Epith. Laūtŭm, ŏpĭmŭm, suāvĕ, dūlcĕ, rēgālĕ, sŭpērbŭm, tĕnŭĕ. V. Epulæ.
fĕre, adv., *almost.* Tēcŭm fĕrĕ tōtŭs, Aus. Jāmquĕ fĕrĕ sīccŏ, Virg. Syn. Prŏpĕ, fērmē, pĕnĕ.
Fĕrēntīnŭm, ī, n., *a town of Etruria.* Caūpōnă Fĕrēntīnŭm, Hor.
Fĕretrĭŭs, ĭī *or* ī, m., *a name of Jupiter.* Hīnc Fĕrĕtrī dīctă, Prop. Caūsās ăpĕrīrĕ Fĕrĕtrī, Id.
fĕretrŭm, ī, n., *a coffin.* Fĕrĕtrō Pāllāntă rĕpōstō, Virg. Sŭbĭērĕ fĕrĕtrō, Id. Syn. Sĕpūlcrŭm, tŭmŭlŭs. Epith. Mĭsĕrŭm, trīstĕ, mœstŭm, flēbĭlĕ, fătālĕ, fūnĕrĕŭm, căvŭm, lūgŭbrĕ, ātrŭm, ōbscūrŭm.
fērĭæ, ārŭm, f. pl., *festivals.* Sŭb Stўgĕ fērĭæ, (Choriamb.) Prud. Syn. Fēstă ; ōtĭă.
fērĭātŭs, ă, ŭm, *unemployed.* Mălĕ fērĭātōs, (Sapph.) Hor. Syn. Fēstŭs ; ōtĭōsŭs, quĭētŭs.
fĕrīnŭs, ă, ŭm, *of a wild beast.* Lāctĕ fĕrīnō, Virg. Syn. Bēllŭīnŭs.
fĕrĭo, ĭs, *to strike.* Sŭblīmī fĕrĭăm, (Choriamb.) Hor. Syn. Cædo, pērcŭtĭo, vērbĕro, tūndo, pūlso.
fĕrĭtās, ātĭs, f., *wildness.* Plŭs fĕrĭtātĭs hăbēnt, Ov. Syn. Fĕrōcĭă, bārbărĭēs, crūdēlĭtās. Epith. Tōrvă, sævă, Scўthĭcă, ĭmmānĭs, ĭndŏcĭlĭs. V. Crudelitas, barbaries.
fērmē, adv., *almost.* Ēst fērmē nātŭră mălōrŭm, Juv. Syn. Fĕre, pĕnĕ, prŏpĕ.
fērmēntŭm, ī, n., *leaven.* Fērmēnto ātque ăcĭdīs, Virg.
fĕro, tŭlī, lātŭm, *to carry.* Quŏd fĕrār ĭn pārtēs, Prop. Syn. Pōrto, tōllo, sūs-tĭnĕo, gēsto, gĕro ; sūffĕro, pătĭor, pătĭŏr ; āffĕro ; aūfĕro ; dūco.
fĕrōcĭă, æ, *and* cĭtās, ātĭs, f., *ferocity.* Dŏmĭnæquĕ fĕrōcĭă Caūnī, Ov. Syn. Fĕrĭtās, sævĭtĭēs. V. Barbaries.
fĕrōcĭo, ĭs, ĭī, *to be fierce.* Mŏrĕ fĕrōcĭt ĕquī, Ov. Syn. Ēffĕrŏr, sævĭo. V. Furo.
fĕrōcĭtĕr, adv., *fiercely.* Ēssĕ fĕrōcĭtĕr aūsŭm, Mart. Syn. Crūdēlĭtĕr, ĭmmānĭtĕr

Fĕrōnĭă, æ, f., *a Sylvan goddess.* Gaŭdēns Fĕrōnĭă lūcō, Virg.

fĕrōx, ōcĭs, *fierce.* Ægīs fĕrōcēs ōrĕ, (Iamb.) Sĕnec. SYN. Fĕrŭs, ĕffĕrŭs, bārbărŭs, trŭcŭlēntŭs, crūdēlĭs, atrōx. V. Crudelis, barbarus.

fĕrrāmēntŭm, ī, n., *an instrument of iron.* Crās fĕrrāmēntă Thēānŭm, Hor.

fĕrrĕŭs, ă, ŭm, *of iron.* Fērrĕŭs hāstĭs, Virg.

fĕrrūgĭnĕŭs, ă, ŭm, *of the colour of rusty iron.* Et fĕrrūgĭnĕōs hўăcīnthōs, Virg. SYN. Nigrĭcāns, rŭbēns.

fĕrrūgo, ĭnĭs, f., *rust.* Nĭtĭdūm fĕrrūgĭnĕ tĕxĭt, Virg. SYN. Rubīgo. EPITH. Atră, scabră, ōbscūră, ŏpācă, pĭcĕă, pāllēns, pīctă. V. Rubigo.

fĕrrŭm, ī, n., *iron.* Cōntĭnŭō fĕrrō, Virg. SYN. Ensĭs, glădĭŭs, mŭcro. EPITH. Dūrŭm, vălĭdŭm, sŏlĭdŭm, rĭgĭdŭm, grăvĕ, strīdēns, fōrtĕ, mōrdāx, nŏcēns, ăcūtŭm, mōrtĭfĕrŭm, sævŭm, crŭēntŭm, īnfēstŭm, trīstĕ, fătălĕ, rĭgēns, mīssĭlĕ, vūlnĭfĭcŭm, sānguĭnĕŭm, lēthălĕ, strīctŭm. V. Ensis, telum.

fĕrtĭlĭs, ĕ, *fertile.* Fĕrtĭlĭs æstīvă, Tibull. SYN. Fœcūndŭs, fĕrāx, dīvĕs, ăbūndāns, ūbĕr, grăvĭs, pīnguĭs, ŏpīmŭs. V. Fructuosus.

fĕrtĭlĭtās, ātĭs, f., *fertility.* Fĕrtĭlĭtātĭs hŏnōrĕm, Ov. SYN. Fœcūndĭtās, ūbērtās, fĕrăcĭtās, ūbĕr, ăbūndāntĭă. EPITH. Abūndāns, măgnă, fēlīx, lætă, ŏptātă, ŏpŭlēntă, dīvĕs, grātă, spērātă, īngēns, Cĕrĕālĭs. V. Abundantia.

fĕrtŭm, ī, n., *a cake.* Vīncĕrĕ fĕrtō, Pers.

|| fĕrvĕfăcĭo, fēcī, făctŭm, *to make boil,* Plaut. SYN. Călĕfăcĭo, āccēndo.

fĕrvĕo, bŭī, vērĕ, *or* vo, vī, vĕrĕ, *to be hot.* Fĕrvēbĭt sæpĕ, Pers. SYN. Fĕrvēsco, æstŭo, ēxæstŭo, ārdĕo, būllĭo, ĕbūllĭo.

fĕrvĭdŭs, ă, ŭm, *hot.* Fĕrvĭdŭs īmplĕt, Virg. SYN. Fĕrvēns, ārdēns, īgnĕŭs, æstŭāns; ăgĭtātŭs.

fĕrvŏr, ōrĭs, m., *heat.* Mĕdĭĭs fĕrvōrĭbŭs ācrĭŏr, Virg. SYN. Ārdŏr, æstŭs, călŏr. EPITH. Æstīvŭs, călĭdŭs, sīccŭs, īgnĕŭs, răbĭdŭs, vĕhĕmēns. V. Siccitas, æstus, æstas, calor.

fĕrŭlă, æ, f., *fennel, a rod.* Mănŭm fĕrŭlæ sūbdūxĭmŭs, Juv. EPITH. Mĭnāx, trīstĭs, īnvīsă, dūră.

fĕrŭs, ă, ŭm, *wild.* Fĕrŭs ŏmnĭă Jūpĭtĕr, Virg. SYN. Ĕffĕrŭs, crūdēlĭs, bārbărŭs, īmmānĭs, īunmītĭs, fĕrōx, trŭcŭlēntŭs. V. Crudelis.

Fēscēnnīnŭs, ă, ŭm, *of Fescennia, an ancient city of Etruria.* Fēscēnnīnās ăcĭēs, Virg. — ŭs, ī, m., *and* nă, ōrŭm, n. pl., *Fescennine verse, a sort of licentious satire.* Fēscēnnīnă pĕr hūnc, Hor.

fēssŭs, ă, ŭm, *tired.* Et stătŭīt fēssōs fēssŭs, Prop. SYN. Dēfēssŭs, lāssŭs, fătĭgātŭs, frăctŭs, lānguēns, lānguĭdŭs.

fēstĭno, ās, *to hasten.* Fēstīnătĕ vĭrī, Virg. SYN. Prŏpĕro, mātūro, cĕlĕro, āccĕlĕro, vŏlo, ādvŏlo. V. Curro.

fēstīnŭs, ă, ŭm, *speedy.* Cānĭtĭĕs fēstīnă vĕnĭt, Claud. SYN. Vēlōx, cĭtŭs, cōncĭtŭs, cĭtātŭs, lĕvĭs, pērnīx, prŏpĕrŭs, vŏlŭcĕr, răpĭdŭs. V. Velox, celer.

fēstīvŭs, ă, ŭm, *festive.* Ārdŭă fēstīvō, Text. SYN. Lĕpĭdŭs, făcētŭs, ūrbānŭs; lætŭs, jŏcōsŭs, hĭlărĭs.

fēstūcă, æ, f., *the shoot of a tree.* Nōn īn fēstūcă līctŏr, Pers.

fēstŭm, ī, n., *a holiday.* Tūrbāntēs fēstă Mĭnērvæ, Ov. EPITH. Insīgnĕ, sŏlēnnĕ, ānnŭŭm, lætŭm.

fēstŭs, ă, ŭm, *festal.* Tēmpŏrĕ fēstō, Hor.

fĭbĕr, ibrī, m., *a beaver.* Fĭbĕr, ăvĭŭs hōstĕ, Sil. SYN. Cāstŏr.

fĭbră, æ, f., *an entrail.* Ăn quĭă nōn fībrĭs ŏvĭŭm, Pers. EPITH. Vītālĭs, tĕnĕră, spīrāns, ārcānă, tĕnŭĭs, ōccūltă.

fĭbŭlă, æ, f., *a clasp.* Fĭbŭlă vēstĕīn, Virg. EPITH. Răsĭlĭs, mōrdāx, ĕbūrnĕă, aŭrĕă, ārgēntĕă, fĕrrĕă, ænĕă, dūră, tĕnāx, cūrvă, ădūncă.

fĭcēdŭlă, æ, f., *a fig-pecker.* Lūcĕt fĭcēdŭlă lŭmbō, Mart. Mĕrgĕrĕ fĭcēdŭlās dīdĭcĭt, Juv. EPITH. Vĭrĭdĭs, nătāns, pīnguĭs.

fĭcētŭm, ī, n., *a fig-plantation; body covered with ulcers.* Nīl nĭsĭ fĭcētŭm, Mart.

fĭctĭlĭs, ĕ, *made of earth.* Fīctĭlĭbŭs crēvĕrĕ Dĕĭs, Prop. SYN. Fĭglīnŭs.

fīctŏr, ōrĭs, m., *a feigner, impostor.* Fāndī fīctŏr Ŭlўssēs, Virg.

fĭcŭlnĕŭs, *and* nŭs, ă, ŭm, *of a fig-tree.* Trūncŭs ĕrăm fīcŭlnŭs, Hor.

fĭcŭs, ūs *or* ī, f., *the fig-tree.* Cŭm mĕ fĭcŭs ălăt, Mart. EPITH. Pīnguĭs, vīrēscēns, lāctĕă, lāctēns, mūnĭfĭcă, nēctărĕă, dūlcĭs, suāvĭs, fœcūndă, mōllĭs, tĕnĕră.

fīdēlĭă, æ, f., *an earthen vessel.* Cŏctā fīdēlĭā līmō, Pers. Syn. Tēstă, fĭglīnŭm. Epith. Cŏctĭlĭs, lŭtĕă.

fīdēlĭs, ĕ, *faithful.* Nătā fīdēlĭbŭs hŏrā, Pers. Syn. Fīdŭs, ămīcŭs. V. Constans.

fīdēlĭtĕr, adv., *faithfully.* Cōmmīssă fīdēlĭtĕr aūrēs, Hor. Syn. Fīdē, cōnstāntĕr.

fīdēns, ēntĭs, *the pres. partic. of* fido. Tŭŏ fīdēntēm præsĭdĭŏ, quī, Hor. Syn. Fīsŭs, cōnfīdēns, cōnfīdēntīssĭmŭs, cōnfī-ŭs, frētŭs. V. Audax.

Fīdēs, ĕī, f., *the goddess Faith; faith, fidelity.* Cānă Fīdēs, ēt Vēstă, Virg. Ēn hæc prōmīssă fīdēs ēst, Id. Syn. Fīdūcĭă. Epith. Sānctă, pĭă, pūră, tĕnāx, sŏlĭdă, īmpŏllūtă, jŭrātă, cōnstāns, pāctă, rēctă, sŏcĭālĭs, īntāctă, rēlĭgĭōsă, vērāx, fīrmātă, sĭncēră, īncōrrūptă, īngĕnŭă, sŏcĭă, ŭnănĭmīs, stăbĭlĭs, īmmōtă, pĕrēnnĭs, ĭnvĭŏlātă. V. Fido, fidelis.

fīdĭcĕn, ĭnĭs, m., *a harper.* Rŏmānæ fīdĭcēn lўræ, (Glyconic.) Hor. Syn. Lў-rĭcĕn, cĭthărœdŭs, cĭthărīstă. Epith. Dōctŭs, sōlĕrs, pĕrĭtŭs. V. Citharœdus.

fīdĭcŭlă, æ, f., *a small lyre; an instrument of punishment.* Fĭdĭcŭlæ lĭcĕt cōgănt, Mart. Sŭbdūctā fĭdĭcŭlă tōrquĕt, Ov.

Fīdĭŭs, ĭī, m., *a son of Jupiter.* Sāncŏ Fĭdĭŏnĕ rĕfērrĕm, Ov.

fĭdĭs, ĭs, f. *and* fĭdēs, ĭŭm, f. pl., *a stringed instrument, lyre.* Sŏnĭtŭm fĭdĭs, Hor. Cĭthărā, fĭdĭbŭsquĕ cănōrĭs, Virg. Syn. Cĭthără, chĕlўs, bārbĭtŭs, lўră, tēstūdo; chŏrdæ, nērvī, fīlă. Epith. Dūlcĭsŏnæ, jŏcōsæ, ārgūtæ, dŏctæ, quĕrŭlæ, sŏnāntēs, blāndæ; Aŏnĭæ; dūlcēs, tēstūdĭnĕæ. V. Cithara.

fīdo, dī *and* sŭs sŭm, *to trust.* Fīdĭtĕ dē pĕdĭbŭs, Virg. Syn. Cōnfīdo, fīdem hăbĕo, crēdo. V. Fiducia.

fīdūcĭă, æ, f., *confidence.* Tĕnŭĭt fīdūcĭă, vēstrī, Virg. Syn. Cōnfīdentĭă, aūdācĭă, aŭsŭs. Epith. Aūdāx, sŭpērbă, fīrmă, cērtă, cōnstāns, īntrĕpĭdă, īmmōtă, tĕmĕrārĭă, fāllāx. V. Audacia, spes.

fīdŭs, ă, ŭm, *faithful.* Fŏrtūnātă dŏmŭs, mŏdŏ sīt tĭbĭ fīdŭs ămĭcŭs, Prop. Syn. Fīdēlĭs. V. Fidelis.

fīglīnŭm, ī, n., *a vessel made of earth.* Fīglīnĭs cœnāssĕ fĕrŭnt, Aus. Syn. Fīctĭlĕ.

fīgo, xī, xŭm, *to stick.* Fīgĕrĕ pūgnăt, Ov. Syn. Affīgo, dēfīgo, īnfīgo, præfīgo; fĕrĭo, vūlnĕro; īmmītto, plānto, cōndo, fŏdĭo; fīrmo, rŏbŏro, stătŭo.

fĭgŭlŭs, ī, m., *a potter.* Sīcănĭæ fīgŭlŏ, Auson. Syn. Fīctŏr, ārgīllæ fabrĭcātŏr, tēstārum ŏpĭfēx. V. Artifex.

fĭgūră, æ, f., *a form.* Rĕpĕrīrĕ fīgūrārŭm tŏt nŏmĭnă, Lucr. Syn. Fŏrmă, spĕcĭēs, ĭmago, făcĭēs. Epith. Rēctă, vărĭă, cērtă, āptă, cĕrĕă.

fĭgūro, ās, *to form.* Pŏctă fīgūrăt, Hor. Syn. Fŏrmo, fīngo, ēffīngo, cōmpōno, quadro.

fīlātĭm, adv., *thread by thread.* Fīlātĭm cūm dĭstrăhĭtŭr, Lucr.

fīlĭă, *dim.* fīlĭŏlă, æ, f., *a daughter.* Vēl fīlĭă născĭtŭr, Juv. Fīlĭŏlæ tūrpĕm, Juv. Syn. Nătă, sŏbŏlēs, prŏlēs. Epith. Pūlchră, vĕnūstă, vĕrēcūndă, pŭdīcă, nūbĭlĭs, cāstă.

fīlĭŭs, *dim.* fīlĭŏlŭs, ī, m., *a son.* Fīlĭŭs, ōmnēs, Hor. Quŏd tĭbĭ fīlĭŏlŭs, Juv. Syn. Nătŭs, prŏlēs, sŏbŏlēs, prŏgĕnĭēs, pŭĕr, sătŭs, crĕātŭs, gĕnĭtŭs; sānguĭs. Epith. Chārŭs, dīlēctŭs, vĕnūstŭs, īngĕnŭŭs, blāndŭs, suāvĭs, dūlcĭs.

fīlīx, ĭcĭs, f., *fern.* Istă fīlīx ūllŏ, Pers. Epith. Vĭrēns, vĭrĭdĭs, nŏcēns, nŏxĭă, īnvīsă.

fīlŭm, ī, n., *a thread.* Nŏtās fīlīs īntēxŭĭt ālbĭs, Ov. Syn. Stāmĕn, līnŭm, fīlī stāmĕn. Epith. Grăcĭlĕ, tĕnŭĕ, sŭbtīlĕ, lĕvĕ, tĕrĕs, sērĭcŭm, tēxtĭlĕ, nōdōsŭm. V. Neo.

‖ fīmbrĭă, æ, f., *a fringe.* Syn. Lăcīnĭă, īnstĭtă, līmbŭs, vēstĭs ŏră.

fīmŭs, ī, m., *dung.* Nē sătūrārĕ fīmŏ, Virg. Syn. Lŭtŭm, cœnŭm, stērcŭs. Epith. Pīnguĭs, īmmūndŭs, ūdŭs, tĕnāx, putrĭs, fœtēns, fœtĭdŭs, vīlĭs. V. Stercus.

fīndo, fĭdī, fīssŭm, *to cleave.* Fīndĭt īn āmbās, Virg. Syn. Dīffīndo, scīndo, prōscīndo, sĕco, dīvĭdo. V. Scindo.

fīnēs, ĭŭm, m. pl., *the limits.* Fīnĭbŭs ōmnēs, Virg. Syn. Cōnfīnĭă.

fīngo, xī, īctŭm, *to feign.* Fīngĭtquĕ pŭtāndo, Virg. Syn. Effīngo; sĭmŭlo, dīssĭmŭlo; crĕo, fŏrmo, ēffōrmo, īnfōrmo; ĭmĭtŏr, ēxprĭmo; ēxcōgĭto.

fīnĭo, īī *or* īvī, *to finish.* Sī bēllŭm fīnīrĕ mănŭ, Virg. Syn. Cōnfĭcĭo, pĕrfĭcĭo, ābsŏlvo, cōnclūdo; fīnĕm făcĭo, dŏ, pōno, īmpōno; līmĭto, tĕrmĭno. V. Finis.

fĭnĭs, ĭs, m. f., *the end, a limit.* Núllănĕ fĭnĭs ĕrĭt, Prop.   Syn.   Exĭtŭs, tĕrmĭnŭs, mĕtă, līnĕs, ēvĕntŭs, sŭccēssŭs, ĕffēctŭs.   V. Finio.

fĭnĭtĭmŭs, ă, ŭm, *near to.*   Fĭnĭtĭmās ĭn bēllă fĕrăm, Virg.   Syn. Vīcīnŭs, prŏpĭnquŭs, prōxĭmŭs.

fĭnītŏr, ōrĭs, m., *a finisher.*   Lĭbўcæ fīnītŏr cĭrcŭlŭs ōræ, Luc.

fĭnītŭs, ă, ŭm, *the pass. partic. of* fĭnio.   Nĕc dŭm fīnītŭs Ŏrēstēs, Juv.

fĭo, fĭs, fĭt, *to become.*   Ŏmnĭă jăm fĭŭnt, fĭĕrī quæ, Ov.   Syn.   Ēvādo; ēvĕnĭo.

fĭrmāmĕn, ĭnĭs, *and* mēntŭm, ī, n., *a foundation.*   Lōngī fĭrmāmĭnă trŭncī, Ov.   Syn.   Fŭlcrŭm, cŏlŭmĕn, fŭlcīmĕn.

fĭrmĭtĕr, adv., *firmly.*   Fĭrmĭtĕr ēssēnt, Lucr.   Syn.   Immōtē; cōnstāntĕr.

fĭrmo, ās, *to strengthen.*   Fĭrmārĕt aŭctŏr, Hor.   Syn.   Rōbŏro, cōrrŏbŏro, cōnfīrmo, stăbĭlĭo, mūnĭo.

fĭrmŭs, ă, ŭm, *firm.*   Cōrpŏrĕ fĭrmĭŏr, (Alc.) Hor.   Syn.   Cōnstāns, īmmōtŭs, īmmōbĭlĭs, cērtŭs, stăbĭlĭs, fīxŭs.

fĭscēllă, ĭnă, æ, f., *and* ēllŭm, ī, n., *a small basket of twigs.*   Tēxātŭr fĭscĭnă vīrgă, Virg.   Syn.   Cīstă, cīstŭlă, cănīstrŭm, călăthŭs.   Epith.   Vīmĭnĕă, frăgĭlĭs, tĕnŭĭs, tēxtĭlĭs.

fĭssĭlĭs, ĕ, *easy to be cleft.*   Fĭssĭlĕ lĭgnŭm, Virg.   Syn.   Scīssŭs, rīmōsŭs.

fĭssĭpēs, pĕdĭs, *cloven-footed.*   Tērtĭă fĭssĭpĕdēs, Aus.

fĭstŭlă, æ, f., *a pipe.*   Mĕrŭīssēt fĭstŭlă căprŭm, Virg.   Syn.   Ăvēnă, călămŭs, tībĭă, ărūndo, cānnă, cĭcūtă, būxŭs.   Epith.   Argŭtă, dūlcĭs, suāvĭs, lĕvĭs, tĭnnŭlă, raŭcă, strīdēns, īndōctă, cănōră, agrēstĭs, jūcŭndă, grātă, ămœnă, lætă, sўlvēstrĭs.

flăbēllŭm, ī, n., *a fan.*   Vēntōs mōvīssĕ flăbēllō, Ov.   Caŭdæ flăbēllă sŭpērbæ, Prop.   Epith.   Lĕvĕ, vēntōsŭm, tĕnŭĕ, pīctŭm, dĕcŏrŭm.   V. Ventilo.

flăbrŭm, ī, n., *a blast of wind.*   Hōrrēscŭnt flăbrīs, Virg.   Syn.   Flāmēn, flātŭs, aŭră, vēntŭs; flăbēllŭm.   Epith.   Tĕnŭĕ, vēntōsŭm, ănĭmōsŭm, sævŭm.   V. Flatus.

flăccĭdŭs, ă, ŭm, *faint.*   Flăccĭdĭōrĕ ĕtĭăm quāntō, Lucr.

Flăccŭs, ī, m., *a Roman surname.*   Sī quĭd ĭn Flăccō, Hor.

flăgēllo, ās, *to scourge.*   Mōllēsquĕ flăgēllēnt, Mart.   Syn.   Cædo, pērcŭtĭo, vērbĕro.

flăgēllŭm, ī, n., *a whip.*   Ūltrīx āccīnctă flăgēllō, Virg.   Syn.   Flagrŭm, vērbĕr, vīrgă, lōrŭm, scŭtĭcă.   Epith.   Crŭēntŭm, ātrŭm, hōrrĭsŏnŭm, dūrŭm, grăvĕ, ātrōx, dīrŭm, sævŭm, crūdēlĕ, spīnōsŭm, rĭgĭdŭm, trīstĕ, vŭlnĭfĭcŭm, hōrrēndŭm, sānguĭnĕŭm, mĭnāx, vĭndēx, ăcērbŭm, fŭrĭālĕ, tōrtŭm, cōntōrtŭm, nōdōsŭm, mĕtŭēndŭm, crŭēntŭm, rēsŏnāns, īmmĭtĕ, crēbrŭm.   V. Flagello.

flăgĭtātŏr, ōrĭs, m., *one who importunes.*   Mŏlēstŭs flăgĭtātŏr, Aus.

‖ flăgĭtĭōsŭs, ă, ŭm, *heinous.*   Syn.   Scĕlĕrātŭs, scĕlēstŭs.

flăgĭtĭŭm, ĭī, n., *a scandalous crime.*   Vīvĕrĕ flăgĭtĭō, Prop.   Syn.   Scĕlŭs, crīmĕn.   Epith.   Dētēstābĭlĕ, tŭrpĕ, ĭnaŭdītŭm, īnfāndŭm.   V. Crimen.

flăgĭto, ās, *to ask eagerly.*   Flăgĭtăt ĭn mōrsŭs, Hor.   Syn.   Pĕto, pōstŭlo, pōsco, prĕcŏr.   V. Precor.

flagro, ās, *to burn.*   Crīnēmquĕ flăgrāntĕm, Virg.   Syn.   Dēflagro, ārdĕo, ēxārdĕo, īncēndŏr.   V. Ardeo.

flagrŭm, ī, n., *a whip.*   Flāgră Quĭrītēs, Juv.   Sŭă mēmbră flăgrīs, Damas.   V. Flagellum.

flāmĕn, ĭnĭs, n., *a blast.*   Cŭm flāmĭnĕ pōrtānt, Virg.   Syn.   Vēntŭs, flātŭs, aŭră, spīrĭtŭs.   Epith.   Spīrāns, sŏnōrŭm, lēnĕ.   V. Flatus.

Flāmĕn, ĭnĭs, m., *the priest of particular gods.*   Flāmĕn ăd hæc, Ov.   Syn.   Săcērdōs.   Epith.   Sacrĭfĭcŭs, Dĭālĭs, Quĭrīnŭs, săcĕr, vĕnĕrāndŭs.   V. Sacerdos.

flāmĭnĭca, æ, f., *the wife of a flamen.*   Ipsĕ ĕgŏ flāmĭnĭcăm, Ov.

Flāmĭnĭŭs, ĭī, m., *the name of several noble Romans.*   Sīnt tĭbĭ Flāmĭnĭŭs, Ov.

flāmmă, æ, f., *a flame.*   Ōrdĭnĕ flāmmārum, ĕt, Virg. .   Syn.   Ignĭs, făx, Vŭlcānŭs.   Epith.   Crĕpĭtāns, cŏrŭscă, tōrrēns, ācrĭs, cĕlĕr, călĭdă, Ignĕă, vŏlāns, vēlōx, ăvĭdă, rŭtĭlă, vīvă, răpĭdă, fērvĭdă, rŏgālĭs, lūcēns, rŭtĭlāns, rŏsĕă, mĭcāns, rădĭāns, clāră, cŏrŭscāns, ăgĭlĭs, fērvēns, răpāx, īmpĭă, vŏrāx, tōrrĭdă, ārdēns, ēxārdēns, Ætnæă, īgnĭtă, cŏmāns, mōbĭlĭs, sĕquāx, fŭlgēns, aŭdāx, fūmōsă, fūrēns, pŏpŭlātrīx, vāstātrīx, fĕră, crūdēlĭs.   V. Ignis, incendium.

flāmmĕŏlŭm, ī, n., *a veil of a flame colour.*   Flāmmĕŏlō Tўrĭŭsquĕ, Juv.   Syn.   Flāmmĕŭm.

flămmĕŏlŭs, ă, ŭm, *of a flame colour*. Prēssăquĕ flămmĕŏlă, Col.

flămmēsco, ĭs, *to take fire*. Flămmēscĕrĕ cœlŭm, Lucr. Syn. Ignēsco, āccēndŏr, īncēndŏr, īnflāmmŏr.

flămmĕŭs, ă, ŭm, *flaming*. Tūm flămmĕă tōrquēns, Virg. Syn. Flăınmātŭs, īgnĕŭs, īgnītŭs, āccēnsŭs, ūrēns, flagrāns, flăınmĭvŏmŭs, flāmmĭfĕr, īgnĭfĕr, īgnĭvŏmŭs.

flămmĭfĕr, *and* gĕr, ĕră, ĕrŭm, *bringing flames*. Flāmmĭfĕrĭs īmplēnt, Ov. V. Flămmĕŭs.

flătŭs, ūs, m., *a breath*. Flātĭbŭs Eūrī, Virg. Syn. Flāmĕn, flābrŭm, vēntŭs, aūră, spīrĭtŭs. Epit . Lēnĭs, lĕvĭs, tĕnŭĭs, răpĭdŭs, sŏnōrŭs, vēntōsŭs, ănĭmōsŭs, sævŭs, văgŭs. V. Ventus.

flăvĕo, ĕs, *and* ēsco, ĭs, *to grow yellow*. Paŭlātīm flāvēscēt cāmpŭs, Virg.

Flāvīnĭŭs, ă, ŭm, *of Flavina, a town of Etruria*. Flāvīnĭăque ārvă, Virg.

flăvŭs, ă, ŭm, *yellow*. Ět crīnēs flăvōs, Virg. Syn. Rŭtĭlŭs, crŏcĕŭs, lūtĕŭs, flāvēns, aūrĕŭs.

flēbĭlĭs, ĕ, *doleful*. Flēbĭlĭs āntĕ, Tib. Syn. Lacrýmābĭlĭs, dēflēndŭs, lūgubrĭs, lāmēntābĭlĭs, trīstĭs, mœstŭs, fūnēstŭs.

flēcto, xī, xŭm, *to bend*. Sī flēctĕrĭs ūllĭs, Virg. Syn. Inflēcto, tōrquĕo, cōntōrquĕo, cūrvo. V. Curvo; plăco, mŏvĕo.

flĕo, ēvī, ētŭm, *to weep*. Flēbăt ĕt ābdūctās, Mart. Syn. Dēflĕo, lūgĕo, lacrýmŏr, lāmēntŏr, cōnquĕrŏr, quĕrŏr, dŏlĕo, gĕmo, sūspĭro. V. Lacrymæ.

flētŭs, ūs, m., *a weeping*. Flētĭbŭs hōrrŏr, Prop. Syn. Lacrýmæ, lāmēntŭm, lūctŭs, gĕmĭtŭs, quēstŭs. Epith. Trīstĭs, ăcērbŭs, mĭsĕr, ămārŭs, rōrāns, tĕnĕr, plŭs, largŭs, īmmēnsŭs, ūbĕr, mădēns, mădĭdŭs, stĭllāns, mūltŭs, nĭmĭŭs, āssĭdŭŭs, fāllāx, īnsĭdĭōsŭs, flŭēns, mānāns, hūmēns, lūctĭsŏnŭs, gĕmĕbūndŭs, quĕrŭlŭs, mĭsĕrāndŭs, ēffūsŭs, crēbĕr, lūgubrĭs, sŭpplēx, ĭnēxplētŭs. V. Lacrymæ.

flētŭs, ă, ŭm, *the pass. partic. of* fleo. Mūltūm flēti ād sŭpĕrōs, Virg.

flēxănĭmŭs, ă, ŭm, *bending the mind*. Quæ tĭbī flēxănĭmō, Catul.

flēxĭbĭlĭs *and* xĭlĭs, ĕ, *flexible*. Flēxĭbĭlēs cūrvāntŭr, Ov. Flēxĭlĭs ōbtōrtī, Virg. Syn. Lēntŭs, făcĭlĭs; lēnĭs.

flēxĭpēs, pĕdĭs, *with twisted feet*. Flēxĭpēdēs hĕdĕræ, Ov.

flēxūră, æ, f., *a bending*. Flēxūră prædĭtă nōstrī, Lucr.

flēxŭs, ă, ŭm, *the pass. partic. of* flecto. Tūm vălĭdĭs flēxōs īncūrvānt, Virg.

flēxŭs, ūs, m., *a winding*. Ět lōngōs sŭpĕrānt flēxūs, Virg. Syn. Sĭnŭs, gýrŭs, spīră, cīrcŭĭtŭs. Epith. Văgŭs, ŏblīquŭs, lūnātŭs, sĭnŭātŭs, mūltĭvăgŭs, sŭpīnŭs. V. Gyrus.

flĭctŭs, ūs, m., *shock, collision*. Dānt sŏnĭtūm flĭctū, Virg.

flīgo, ĭs, xī, ctŭm, *to collide*. Ōbvĭă quūm flīxĕrĕ, Lucr.

flo, ās, *to blow*. Flābăt ădhūc Eūrŭs, rĕdĭtūrăquĕ vēlă tĕnēbăt, Ov. Syn. Spĭro, āspīro. V. Venti.

• flŏccŭs, ī, m., *a lock of wool*. Varr.

Flōră, æ, f., *the goddess of flowers*. Flōră vŏcŏr, Ov. Syn. Chlōrĭs, Zĕphýrītĭs, ĭdĭs. Epith. Rūstĭcă, fōrmōsă, ŏlēns, rĕdŏlēns, lætă, jūcūndă, suāvĭs, cāndĭdă, vērnă, ŏdōrĭfĕră, ŏdōrātă, bĕnīgnă, cōmptă, vĕnūstă, fœcūndă, ămœnă, mītĭs, dūlcĭs, mūltĭcŏlŏr, cūltă, rĕnāscēns, rĕdĭvīvă.

Flōrālĭs, ĕ, *of Flora*. Fēstūm Flōrălĕ călēndăs, Ov.—2. -lĭă, ĭŭm, n. pl., *the festival of Flora*. Flōrālĭă lætă thĕātrī, Aus.

Flōrēntĭă, æ, f., *a town of Italy*. Epith. Mārtĭă, pŏtēns, ōrnātă, nōbĭlĭs, īnclýtă.

flōrĕo, ēs, *and* ēsco, ĭs, *to flourish*. Flōrĕăt, īrrĭgŭŭm, Virg. Syn. Flōrēsco.

flōrĕŭs *and* ĭdŭs, ă, ŭm, *flowery*. Flōrĕă rūră, Virg. Flōrĭdă sērtă, Tibull. Syn. Flōrēns, flōrĭgĕr.

flōrĭfĕr *and* gĕr, ă, ŭm, *bearing flowers*. Flōrĭgĕrĭs nūnquăm, Virg.

flōrĭlĕgŭs, ă, ŭm, *that gathers flowers*. Flōrĭlĕgæ nāscūntŭr ăpēs, Ov. Syn. Flōrēs lĕgēns, cārpēns.

Flōrŭs, ī, m., *the name of a man*. Jūlī Flōrĕ, Hor.

flōs, ōrĭs, m., *a flower*. Flōrĕ cŏmāntĕm, Virg. Syn. Sērtŭm; flōscŭlŭs, (dimin.) Epith. Blāndŭs, lætŭs, ŏdōrŭs, ŏlēns, rĕdŏlēns, mōllĭs, ŏdōrātŭs, nĭvĕŭs, suāvĭs, dūlcĭs, mĭcāns, vērnŭs, æstīvŭs, cāndĭdŭs, ŏdōrĭfĕr, nēctărĕŭs, nĭtĭdŭs, grātŭs, frāgrāns, dĕcōrŭs, pūrpŭrĕŭs, crŏcĕŭs, hālāns, vērnālĭs, nāscēns, ămœnŭs, vēr sĭcŏlŏr, pīctŭs, vărĭŭs, rŭtĭlŭs, gēmmāns. V. Floreo.

flōscŭlŭs, ī, m., *the dimin. of* flos. Flōscŭlŭs āngūstæ, Juv. Epith. Tĕnĕr, nŏvŭs, blāndŭs.

flūctĭfrăgŭs, ă, ŭm, *breaking the waves.* Dēnĭquĕ flūctĭfrăgō, Lucr.

flūctĭsŏnŭs, ă, ŭm, *resounding with waves.* Insŭlă flūctĭsŏnō, Sil.

flūctĭvăgŭs, ă, ŭm, *sailing over the waves.* Flūctĭvăgī naūtæ, Stat. Syn. Ūndĭvăgŭs, æquŏrĕŭs.

flūctŭo, ās, *and* ŏr, ārĭs, *to rise in waves.* Flūctŭăt æstŭ, Virg. Cōr flūctŭātŭr, (Iamb.) Sen. Syn. Flŭĭto, æstŭo, ŭndo; flūctĭbŭs, æstŭ jāctŏr, ăgĭtŏr, ĭmpēllŏr; ŭndĭs ĭnnăto, sŭpērnăto; dŭbĭto, văcĭllo; tĭtŭbo. V. Fluctus.

flūctŭs, ūs, m., *a wave.* Flūctĭbŭs īn mĕdĭĭs, Hor. Syn. Æstŭs. Epith. Tŭmĭdŭs, tŭmēns, cānŭs, mărīnŭs, spūmāns, prŏcēllōsŭs, sŏnōrŭs, răpĭdŭs, trĕmŭlŭs, mĭnāx, nĭmbōsŭs, sævŭs, ăgĭtāns, spūmōsŭs, sāxifrăgŭs, vēsānŭs, hōrrĭsŏnŭs, văgŭs, ŭndōsŭs, sălĭēns, frĕmēns, ărēnōsŭs, ērrāns, prŏfūndŭs, vălĭdŭs, spūmĭfĕr, insănŭs, ŭndāns. V. Tempestas, fluctuo.

flŭēntĭsŏnŭs, ă, ŭm, *resounding with waves.* Nāmquĕ flŭēntĭsŏnō, Cat.

flŭēntŭm, ī, n., *a stream.* Ānĭēnă flŭēntă, Virg. Syn. Flŭvĭŭs, flūmĕn, ămnĭs.

flŭĭdŭs, ă, ŭm, *liquid.* Flŭĭdŭm lăvĭt īndĕ, Virg. Syn. Flŭēns, flŭxŭs, lābĭlĭs, liquĭdŭs, dēflŭŭs.

flŭĭto, ās, *to flow.* Ēt flŭĭtāntĭă trānstră, Virg. Syn. Flūctŭo, ŭndo.

flūmĕn, ĭnĭs, n., *a river.* Flūmĭnĭbŭs sălĭcēs, Virg. Syn. Flŭvĭŭs, āmnĭs, flŭēntŭm. V. Fluvius, torrens.

flūmĭnĕŭs, ă, ŭm, *of a river.* Nē sŭă flūmĭnĕă, Ov. Syn. Flŭvĭālĭs.

flŭo, flŭxī, xŭm, *to flow.* Lēnī flŭĭt āgmĭnĕ, Virg. Syn. Dēflŭo, īnflŭo, prōflŭo, lābŏr, āllăbŏr, dēcūrro. V. Inundatio, fluvius.

flŭvĭālĭs, ĕ, *of a river.* Rīpĭs flŭvĭālĭs ărŭndo, Virg. Syn. Flūmĭnĕŭs, ăquātĭcŭs.

flŭvĭŭs, iī, m., *a river.* Pōpŭlŭs īn flŭvĭĭs, Virg. Syn. Flūmĕn, āmnĭs, flŭēntŭm, tōrrēns, pălŭs, rīvŭs. Epith. Văgŭs, sŏnōrŭs, lābēns, cĭtŭs, cōncĭtŭs, ēffūsŭs, răpĭdŭs, spŭmĕŭs, spūmōsŭs, tŭmĭdŭs, ŭndāns, ēxūndāns, vēlōx, tōrrēns, frīgĭdŭs, gĕlĭdŭs, tūrbĭdŭs, lĭmōsŭs, sĭnŭōsŭs, dēclīvĭs, ŏblīquŭs, rĕfŭgŭs, sĭnŭāns, flēxŭs, īnflēxŭs, lubrĭcŭs, prŏpērāns, vĭŏlēntŭs, præcēps, hērbōsŭs, prŏfūndŭs, cĭtātŭs, vitrĕŭs, vĭrĭdāns, ămœnŭs, pūrŭs, glaūcŭs, cœrŭlĕŭs, lēntŭs, tōrpēns, pĭgĕr, dūctĭlĭs, rĭgŭŭs, īrrĭgŭŭs. V. Rivus.

*flŭxŭs, ūs, m., *a flowing.* Cels. Syn. Cūrsŭs, dēcūrsŭs, īnflŭxŭs, lāpsŭs, flŭēntŭm.

fōcălĕ, ĭs, n., *a woollen cravat.* Hōc fōcălĕ tŭăs, Mart.

fŏcŭs, *and* ŭlŭs, ī, m., *a fire, hearth.* Ādvōlvĕrĕ fŏcīs, Virg. Būccā fŏcŭlum ēxcĭtăt, Juv. Epith. Călēns, călĭdŭs, fūmōsŭs, ārdēns, āccēnsŭs, fērvēns, flāmmĭvŏmŭs; thūricrĕmŭs, săcĕr, ŏdōrātŭs. V. Caminus, ignis.

fŏdĭco, ās, *to prick.* Quī fŏdĭcēt lătŭs, Hor. Syn. Fŏdĭo, tŭndo, trānsfŏdĭo.

fŏdĭnă, æ, f., *a mine.* Ŏrĭchālcă fŏdĭnīs, Fil.

fŏdĭo, fŏdī, fōssŭm, *to dig.* Ēquī fŏdĕrēt cālcārĭbŭs ārmōs, Virg. Syn. Ēffŏdĭo, fŏdĭco, cōnfŏdĭo, dēfŏdĭo; căvo, ēxcăvo, pērfŏro; fērĭo. V. Aro.

*fœcūndĭtăs, ātĭs, f., *fertility.* Syn. Fērtĭlĭtăs, ŭbērtās.

fœcūndo, ās, *to fertilise.* Fœcūndāvĭt ămŏr, Prud. Syn. Ŭbĕro.

fœcūndŭs, ă, ŭm, *fruitful.* Tēllŭs fœcūndă, sŭb ĭpsŭm, Virg. Syn. Fērtĭlĭs, fĕrāx. V. Fertilis.

fœdē, adv., *foully.* Jŭvĕnŭm fœdĕ, thălămī, Virg.

fœdo, ās, *to pollute.* Fœdāvĭt vūltŭs, Virg. Syn. Măcŭlo, īnquĭno, cŏīnquĭno, cōmmăcŭlo, cōntămĭno, pōllŭo. V. Maculo.

fœdŭs, ĕrĭs, n., *a compact.* Tēstātŭs fœdĕrĭs ārās, Virg. Syn. Pāctŭm, pāctĭo, cōncōrdĭă. Epith. Sŏcĭālĕ, jŭgālĕ, plăcĭdŭm, ætērnŭm, fīrmŭm, īncōrrūptŭm, tăcĭtŭm, cōncōrs, sŏcĭŭm, ămīcŭm, stăbĭlĕ, lætŭm, jūrātŭm, pācĭfĭcŭm, grătŭm, mūtŭŭm, pērpĕtŭŭm, rūptŭm, vĭŏlātŭm, fīctŭm, mēndāx, dŏlōsŭm, fāllāx, īnsĭdĭōsŭm, ōptātŭm, pĕrēnnĕ, cōnjūrātŭm, lēgĭtĭmŭm.

fœdŭs, ă, ŭm, *foul.* Vēstīgĭă fœdă rĕlīnquŭnt, Virg. Syn. Fœdātŭs, sōrdĭdŭs, tūrpĭs, ōbscœnŭs. V. Turpis.

fœmĭnă, æ, f., *a woman.* Fœmĭnă vīctă, Virg. Syn. Mŭlĭĕr. Epith. Cūltă, cōmptă, pēxă, cāndĭdă, lætă, ĭmbēllĭs, cāllĭdă, mōllĭs, mōbĭlĭs, lŏquāx, īnsĭdĭōsă, prōdĭgă, cōncīnnă, vĕnūstă, pūlchră; vānă, sŭpērbă, īnvĭdă, mēndāx, īncōnstāns,

I

ĭncērtă, gārrŭlă, mŭtābĭlĭs, frăgĭlĭs, lĕvĭs, fāllāx, vărĭābĭlĭs, mălĕsānă, ĭmprŭdēns, vērbōsă, pērfĭdă, ĭnfĭdēlĭs, bĭlĭnguĭs, fūcātă; lĭtĭgĭōsă, fŭgĭēndă.

fœmĭnĕŭs, ă, ŭm, *of a woman.* Et dē fœmĭnĕō, Ov. Syn. Mŭlĭĕbrĭs.

fœnĕrătŏr, ōrĭs, m., *an usurer.* Lŏcūtŭs, fœnĕrătŏr Alphĭŭs, (Iamb.) Hor. Epith. Avārŭs, ĭnjūstŭs, ăvĭdŭs, cŭpĭdŭs, ĭmpĭŭs, sōrdĭdŭs.

fœnĕro, ās, *or* ŏr, ārĭs, *to lend on usury.* Fœnĕrăt ūnă Dĕōs, Mart.

fœnīlĕ, ĭs, n., *a hay-loft.* Claūdēs fœnīlĭă brūmā, Virg.

fœnīsĕcă, æ, m., *a mower.* Fœnīsĕcæ crāssō, Pers.

fœnŭm, ī, n., *a cock of hay.* Fœnum hăbĕt ĭn cōrnū, Hor. Syn. Hērbă, grāmĕn. Epith. Rĭgēns, rĭgĭdŭm, ăspĕrŭm, vīlĕ, vĭrĭdĕ, tĕnŭĕ, grātŭm, vērnāns, ŏdōrŭm, ămœnŭm, ārĭdŭm, aūtūmnālĕ, hērbōsŭm.

fœnŭs, ōrĭs, n., *usury.* Fœnŏrĕ tārdŭs, Prop. Syn. Lucrŭm, ūsūră. Epith. Grāndĕ, fœcūndŭm, ĭnēxplētŭm, ēxĭtĭālĕ, ĕdāx, vŏrāx. V. Fœnero.

fœtĕo, ēs, *to stink.* Hēstērnō ĭœtērĕ mĕrō, Mart. Syn. Pūtĕo. V. Odor, oleo.

fœtĭdŭs, ă, ŭm, *stinking.* Pōrcō fœtĭdō vŏlūtābrŭm, (Scaz.) Syn. Pūtĭdŭs, ĭœtēns, pūtēns, măle ŏlēns, tētĕr, grăvĭs, pēstĭfĕr.

fœtūră, æ, f., *the breeding of cattle.* Sī fœtūrā grĕgĕm, Virg. Syn. Fœtŭs, ūs.

fœtŭs, ūs, m., *the child in the womb, the fœtus.* Fœtĭbŭs ārvă, Virg. Pārtŭs; prōlēs; frūctŭs.

fœtŭs, ă, ŭm, *big ; big with child.* Ergo ăpĭbŭs fœtĭs, Virg. Syn. Plēnŭs, grăvĭdŭs, grăvĭs; grăvĭdă, prægnāns, (mulier.)

fŏlĭŭm, ĭī, n., *a leaf.* Spārgĭte hūmŭm fŏlĭĭs, Virg. Syn. Frōns; chārtă; brāctĕă. Epith. Mōllĕ, tĕnŭĕ, tĕnĕrŭm, crīspŭm, mōbĭlĕ, ŏpācŭm, ŏdōrātŭm, lĕvĕ, cōmāns, vĭrēns, flēxĭlĕ, trĕmŭlŭm, trĕmĕfāctŭm, cădūcŭm, glaūcŭm, vērnŭm, vĭrĭdāns. V. Frondes.

fŏllēs, ĭŭm, m. pl., *bellows.* Fŏllĭbŭs aūrās, Virg. Syn. Vēntōsæ pēllēs. Epith. Vēntōsī, taūrīnī, trĕmēntēs, căvī, īnflātī, tŭmĭdī, Ætnæī, Sĭcŭlī.

fŏllĭcŭlŭs, ī, m., *the dimin. of* follis. Fŏllĭcŭlōs ūt nūnc, Lucr. Syn. Săccŭlŭs, lŏcŭlŭs.

fŏllĭs, ĭs, m., *a leathern ball.* Fŏllĕ dĕcŏt, Mart. Epith. Pŭgĭllātōrĭŭs, tŭmĭdŭs, īnflātŭs, vŏlĭtāns, mīssĭlĭs, ăgĭtābĭlĭs.

fōmēntŭm, ī, n., *a fomentation.* Cūrārŭm fōmēntă rĕlīnquĕrĕ, Hor. Syn. Lēnīmĕn, lĕvāmĕn, mĕdēlă.

fōmĕs, ĭtĭs, m., *fuel.* Syn. Fōmēntŭm, nūtrīmēntŭm, nūtrīmĕn; ārĭdă, pīnguĭs mātĕrĭēs; sūlphŭr, bĭtūmĕn.

fōns, ōntĭs, m., *a spring, or fountain.* Fōntĭs ŏgēns, Ov. Syn. Lătēx, flŭēntŭm. Epith. Līmpĭdŭs, gĕlĭdŭs, īrrĭgŭŭs, mŭndŭs, mōntānŭs, săcĕr, lārgŭs, pŭtĕālĭs, ămœnŭs, lārgĭflŭŭs, frĭgĭdŭs, dūlcĭs, īllīmĭs, ārgēntĕŭs, fœcūndŭs, văgŭs, cærŭlĕŭs, lūtōsŭs, præcēps, văpōrōsŭs, grāmĭnĕŭs, rĭgŭŭs, sŏnāns, āltŭs, pĕrēnnĭs, vĭrēns, raŭcŭs, gārrŭlŭs, grātŭs, clārŭs, crȳstāllīnŭs, sŭsūrrāns, cūrrēns, sălĭēns, fŭgĭēns, ūndāns, ērrāns, cĕlĕr, vēlōx, prŏpĕrāns, tūrbĭdŭs, sĭnūōsŭs, ōblīquŭs, dēflŭŭs, lēntŭs, pēllūcĭdŭs, ŭmbrōsŭs, vĭtrĕŭs, mūscōsŭs, ŏpācŭs, pūmĭcĕŭs.

fōntānŭs, ă, ŭm, *of a spring.* Fōntānā spārgĭtŭr ūndă, Ov.

Fōntēĭŭs, ī, m., *a man's name.* Fōntēĭŭs ăd ūnguĕm, Hor.

fōntĭcŭlŭs, ī, m., *the dimin. of* fons. Fōntĭcŭlō tāntŭndĕm, Hor.

fŏrābĭlĭs, ĕ, *that can be pierced.* Nūllōquĕ fŏrābĭlĭs īctŭ, Ov.

fŏrāmĕn, ĭnĭs, n., *a hole.* Sĭmplēxquĕ fŏrāmĭnĕ paūcō, Hor. Syn. Mĕātŭs căvŭs, āntrŭm, rīmă, fīssūră, spīrāmēntŭm. Epith. Căvŭm, ăpērtŭm; pătēns, hĭāns, tĕnŭĕ, āngūstŭm. V. Rima.

fŏrās, adv., *out of doors.* Dīctă fŏrās ēlīmĭnĕt, Hor.

fōrcēps, ĭpĭs, m., *nippers.* Fōrcĭpĭbŭs glădĭōs, Juv. Syn. Fōrfēx; vŭlsēllă. Epith. Tĕnāx, cūrvă, ădūncă, ăhēnă, bĭfĭdă, mōrdāx, hăbĭlĭs, ăcūtă, bĭsūlcă.

fŏrĕ, fŏrĕm, ēs, ĕt, *from sum.* Hīnc fŏrĕ dūctōrēs, Virg. A stīrpĕ fŏrēs, Id.

fŏrēnsĭs, ĕ, *belonging to the forum.* Grăvĭtātĕ fŏrēnsī, Ov.

Fŏrēntŭm, ī, n., *a town of Campania.* Hŭmĭlĭs Fŏrēntī, Hor.

fŏrēs, ĭŭm, f. pl. *and* fŏrĭs, ĭs, f., *a door, gate.* Lăxōs īn fŏrĭbŭs, Virg. Exclūsŭs fŏrĕ, Hor. Syn. Jānŭă, ōstĭă, ădĭtŭs, vēstĭbŭlŭm. Epith. Aspĕræ, rōbŭstæ, rĭgĭdæ, dĭffĭcĭlēs, sūrdæ, pīctæ, quĕrŭlæ, cælătæ, ærĕæ, fērrĕæ, fōrtēs, ōrnātæ. V. Porta, janua.

fŏrfĕx, ĭcĭs, f., *scissors.* Fŏrfīcĕ læsă, Cat. Syn. Fŏrcĕps. Epith. Bīfīdă, bĭsŭlcă, ăcūtă.

fŏrī, ōrŭm, m. pl., *the decks of a ship.* Dētŭrbāt lāxātquĕ fŏrōs, Virg. Syn. Trănstră; ālvĕŭs, ālvĕārĕ.

fŏrĭcæ, ārŭm, f. pl., *a privy.* Cōndūcŭnt fŏrĭcās, Juv.

fŏrīs, *and* rīnsĕcŭs, adv., *outward.* Bĭbĕrīs dīlūtă; fŏrīs ēst, Hor. Syn. Extrā.

fŭrmă, æ, f., *form.* Āt mĭhĭ, quŏd fōrmās ūnŭs, Prop. Syn. Fĭgūră, ēffĭgĭēs, ĭmāgo; ēxēmplăr, tўpŭs; pŭlchrĭtūdo, vĕnŭstās, dĕcŏr, spĕcĭēs. Epith. Exĭmĭă, sŭpĕrbă, dĕcēns, gĕnĕrōsă, ēgrĕgĭă, hŏnēstă, ăncēps, fŭgāx, vēlōx, brĕvĭs, cādūcă, flŭxă, frăgĭlĭs, cāndĭdă, dĕcōră, splēndĭdă, vĕnŭstă, præstāns, pŏtēns, lætă, vānă, mūtābĭlĭs, īnstābĭlĭs, īnsĭgnĭs, nōbĭlĭs, laūtă. V. Pulchritudo.

Fōrmĭæ, ārŭm, f. pl., *a city of the Volscians.* Quī Fōrmĭārŭm mœnĭă, Hor.

Fōrmĭānŭs, ă, ŭm, *of Formiæ.* Fōrmĭānī Pōcŭlă cōllēs, Hor.

fŏrmīcă, æ, f., *an ant.* Măgnī fŏrmīcă lăbōrĭs, Hor. Epith. Impigră, sōlērs, răpāx, sōllĭcĭtă, frūgĭlĕgă, prūdēns, prōvĭdă, īngĕnĭōsă, vĭgĭl, prōmptă, ēxĭlĭs, pārvă, pārvŭlă, tĕnŭĭs, lăbōrĭōsă, āvără, pārcă, sēdŭlă.

fŏrmīdābĭlĭs, ĕ, *formidable.* Nĕc fŏrmīdābĭlĕ lūmĕn, Ov. Syn. Trĕmēndŭs, tērrĭbĭlĭs, hōrrĭbĭlĭs, hōrrēndŭs, fŏrmīdāndŭs, tĭmēndŭs, mĕtŭēndŭs.

fŏrmīdo, ās, *to dread.* Nōn fŏrmīdăt ăcūmĕn, Hor. Syn. Mĕtŭo, tĭmĕo, păvĕo, rĕfŏrmīdo, pērtĭmēsco. V. Timeo.

fŏrmīdo, ĭnĭs, f., *fear.* Tē fŏrmīdĭnĕ pœnæ, Hor. Syn. Păvŏr, mĕtŭs, tĭmŏr, trĕmŏr, hōrrŏr. Epith. Ancēps, ānxĭă, trĕpĭdă, ēxsānguĭs, gĕlĭdă, sēgnĭs, sōllĭcĭtă, vĭgĭl, īnsōmnĭs, pāllĭdă, hōrrĭdă, ægră, dŭbĭă, frīgĭdă, sŭbĭtă; ĭnŏpīnă, rĕpēntīnă, ĭmbēllĭs, păvēns. V. Timor.

fŏrmīdŏlōsŭs, ă, ŭm, *terrible.* Fŏrmīdŏlōsæ dūm lătēnt, Hor.

fōrmo, ās, *to form.* Sĭmĭlī fŏrmătă vĭdēbānt, Lucr. Syn. Ēffōrmo, fīngo, ēffīngo, cōmpōno.

fōrmōsŭs, ă, ŭm, *handsome.* Pōsĭtīs fŏrmōsŭs ămōrĕ, Mart. Syn. Pŭlchĕr, dĕcōrŭs, vĕnŭstŭs. V. Pulcher.

fŏrmŭlă, æ, f., *a set form.* Jūrāndī fŏrmŭlă jūrĭs, Ov.

Fōrnācālĭs, ĕ, dĕă, *the goddess Fornax.* Ēt Fōrnācālī, Ov.—2. -ālĭă, ĭŭm, n. pl., *the festival of Fornax.* Nūnc Fōrnācālĭă vērbīs, Hor.

fōrnācŭlă, æ, f., *a little furnace.* Măgnă ēst fōrnācŭlă, Juv.

fōrnāx, ācĭs, f., *a furnace.* Rūptīs fōrnācĭbŭs Ætnăm, Virg. Syn. Cămīnŭs. Epith. Căpāx, cūrvă, văpōrĭfĕră, ārdēns, cāndēns, ănhēlāns, fūrēns, flăgrāns, ĭgnĕă, ĭgnĭvŏmă, flāmmĭvŏmă, rŭtĭlă, ĭgnītă, Ætnæă, ātră, fūmāns, fūmĭfĕră, Sĭcŭlă, vŏrāx, āvĭdă, nĭgră, pĭcĕă, ærārĭă, cālcārĭă, mĕtāllĭcă.—2. *the goddess who presided over the baking of bread.* Lætī Fōrnācĕ cŏlōnī, Ov.

fōrnīx, ĭcĭs, f., *a vault.* In fōrnĭcĕ nātī, Juv. Syn. Cămĕră, tēstūdo, ārcŭs, thŏlŭs. Epith. Căvŭs, cōncăvŭs, cūrvŭs, īnflēxŭs, pēndēns, pēnsĭlĭs, ŏpācŭs.

fŏro, ās, *to bore.* Plaut. V. Fodio.

fōrs, tĭs, f., *chance.* Fōrtĕ sŭă, Virg.

fōrsăn, rsĭtăn, rĭāssĕ, rtāssĭs, rtĕ, adv., *perhaps.* Fōrsăn ĕt hæc, Virg. Fōrsĭtăn ēxŭlĭs ōrĭs, Mart. Ănĭmŭm fōrtāssĕ fĕrēbăt, Virg. Cāstūs fōrtāssĭs ămātŏr, Sed. Fōrtĕ sŭb ārgūtă, Virg.

fōrtĭs, ĕ, *magnanimous.* Quăm fōrtī pēctŏrĕ, Virg. Syn. Măgnănĭmŭs, gĕnĕrōsŭs, ănĭmōsŭs, īnvīctŭs, aūdāx. V. Bellator, generosus.—2. *stout.* Fōrtĭs ăd ārmă, Ov. Syn. Rōbŭstŭs, vălĭdŭs, vīrĭbŭs īnsĭgnĭs, pŏtēns, ācĕr. V. Robustus.

fōrtĭtĕr, adv., *bravely.* Fōrtĭtĕr, āddăm, Hor. Syn. Ănĭmōsĕ, cōnstāntĕr; vălĭdĕ, nērvōsĕ.

* fōrtĭtūdo, ĭnĭs, f., *strength, courage.* Cic. Syn. Rōbŭr, vīrēs, vĭgŏr, ănĭmŭs. Epith. Fīrmă, vălĭdă, prævălĭdă, fōrtĭs, sŏlĭdă, dūră, īnvīctă, rĭgĭdă, īndŏmĭtă, ĭnēxpŭgnābĭlĭs, nērvōsă. V. Robur, animus.

* fōrtŭĭto, adv., *casually.* Syn. Cāsū, fōrtĕ, fōrtūnă.

fōrtŭĭtŭs, ă, ŭm, *accidental.* Nĕc fōrtŭĭtŭm spērnĕrĕ, (Alcaic.) Hor. Fōrtŭĭtōs ōrtŭs, Manil.

Fōrtūnă, æ, f., *the goddess Fortune; fortune.* Fōrtūnă sævŏ, Hor. Stăt fōrtūnă dŏmūs, Virg. Syn. Cāsŭs, fōrs, sōrs, fātŭm, Rhāmnūsĭă, Rhāmnūsĭă, Prænēstīnă Dĕă. Epith. Sŭpĕrbă, impĕrĭōsă, lĕvĭs, īncērtă, vŏlūbĭlĭs, īnfĭdă, ăncēps, dŭbĭă, īmprŏbă, mīnāx, īnsĭdĭāns, caūtă, văgă, fāllāx, fătālĭs, vēlōx, răpĭdă, īmpŏtēns, lābāns, mūtābĭlĭs, āmbĭgŭă, mălīgnă, īllūdēns, īnsĭdĭōsă, cădūcă, fŭgāx, fŭgĭtīvă, præcēps, jŏcāns, jŏcōsă, īnsānă, vērsūtă, ĭnānĭs, vānă, mōbĭlĭs, dēcēptrīx, mēndāx, īncōnstāns, īnstăbĭlĭs, īngrătă, crūdēlĭs, ĭnēlūctābĭlĭs, ōmnĭpŏtēns. V. Infortunium.

fŏrtūnātē, adv., *luckily.* Fŏrtūnātĭŭs ārtĕ, Hor. Syn. Fēlīcĭtĕr, bĕātē, faŭstē. V. Feliciter.

fŏrtūnātŭs, ă, ŭm, *happy.* Fŏrtūnātŭs, ĕt ĭllĕ, Virg. Syn. Fēlīx, bĕātŭs; prōspĕr, faŭstŭs. V. Felix.

fŏrtūno, ās, *to make happy.* Tĭbī fŏrtūnāvĕrĭt hŏrăm, Hor. Syn. Bĕo, prōspĕro, fēlīcĭto, sĕcūndo, făvĕo, vōtīs ānnŭo.

fŏrŭlī, ŏrŭm, m. pl., *shelves.* Ēt fŏrŭlōs mĕdĭāmquĕ, Juv.

fŏrŭm, ī, n., *a market-place.* In mĕdĭō plaŭstră fŭĕrĕ fŏrō, Ov. Syn. Plătĕă, ārĕă, cōmpĭtă, mĕrcātŭs, măcēllŭm, nūndĭnæ. Epith. Sŏlēnnĕ, frĕquēns, vēnālĭ, vēnālĭtĭŭm.—2. *a place where courts are kept.* Insānŭmquĕ fŏrŭm, Virg. Syn. Cūrĭă, Sēnātŭs, rōstră. Epith. Clāmōsŭm, frēmēns, tūrbĭdŭm, vērbōsŭm, trīstĕ, ārgūtŭm, dŏlōsŭm, lēgĭfĕrŭm, raŭcŭm, sĕvērŭm, sānctŭm, īnjūstŭm.

fōssă, æ, f., *a ditch.* Ingēntēsquĕ tēnēnt fōssās, Virg. Syn. Fŏvĕă, lăcūnă, scrōbs, vāllŭm. Epith. Præruptă, pătŭlă, hĭāns, īmă, prŏfūndă, ōbscūră, ātră, pătēns, ăpērtă, āltă, hūmĭlĭs, ōbscœnă, căvă.

fōssŏr, ōrĭs, m., *a digger.* Jūgĕră fōssŏr, Virg. V. Arator.

fŏvĕă, æ, f., *a ditch.* Ac fŏvĕīs ābscōndĕrĕ dīscānt, Virg. Syn. Fōssă.

fŏvĕo, fōvī, fōtŭm, *to warm.* Grĕmĭō fŏvĕt īnscĭă, Virg. Syn. Călĕfăcĭo, ălo, tĕgo mūlcĕo, tŭĕŏr, tŭtŏr, dēfēndo.

frāctŭs, ă, ŭm, *the pass. partic. of* frango. Mĭsĕrābĕrĕ frāctās, Virg.

fræno, ās, *to bridle.* Cūrsŭs frænārĕt ăquārŭm, Virg. Syn. Infræno; cŏērcĕo, cōntĭnĕo, rĕtĭnĕo, sŭbĭgo, dŏmo, mŏdĕrŏr. V. Habena.

frænŭm, ī, n., *a bridle.* Frænă fĕrōx spūmāntĭă māndĭt, Virg. Syn. Hăbēnæ, lōră, lŭpātŭm, căpīstrŭm, lŭpī, rĕtĭnācŭlŭm, vīncŭlă; frænī, ŏrŭm, m. Epith. Ārctŭm, strīctŭm, sŭbstrīctŭm, tōrtŭm, sŏnāns, spūmāns, flēxĭlĕ, ēffūsŭm, lāxŭm, vălĭdŭm, lēntŭm, rĭgĭdŭm, hūmēns, ūdŭm, dūrŭm, īmmīssŭm, dĭffĭcĭlĕ, mōbĭlĕ, văgŭm.

frăgă, ōrŭm, pl. n., *strawberries.* Nāscēntĭă frăgă, Virg. Epith. Mōntānă, mōllĭă, rŭtĭlāntĭă, rŭbēntĭă, rĕdŏlēntĭă.

frăgĭlĭs, ĕ, *brittle, perishable.* Annī frăgĭlēs, ĕt, Ov. Syn. Tĕnŭĭs, tĕnĕr, cădūcŭs, dēbĭlĭs, īnfīrmŭs.

frăgmĕn, ĭnĭs, *and* frăgmēntŭm, ī, n., *a fragment.* Frăgmĭnĕ mōntĭs, Virg. Frăgmēntă cărīnæ, Lucr. Syn. Sēgmēntŭm, frūstŭm. Epith. Pārvŭm, ēxĭgŭŭm, ēxĭlĕ, tĕnŭĕ, mĭnūtŭm.

frăgŏr, ōrĭs, m., *a noise.* Omnĕ frăgŏrĕ, Virg. Syn. Sŏnĭtŭs, sŏnŭs, stĕpĭtŭs, strīdŏr, mūrmŭr. Epith. Hōrrĭsŏnŭs, hōrrēndŭs, grăvĭs, raŭcŭs, rĕsŏnŭs, răbĭdŭs, mŏlēstŭs, māgnŭs, sŭbĭtŭs, rĕpēntĭnŭs, vĕhĕmēns, rĕsŏnāns, rĕsŭltāns, văstŭs, præcēps. V. Murmur.

frăgōsŭs, ă, ŭm, *noisy.* Mĕdĭōquĕ frăgōsŭs, Virg. Syn. Sŏnōrŭs, strīdēns; ăspĕr.

frăgro, ās, *to smell sweetly.* Frăgrāt ăcērbŭs, Valer. Frăgrāntĭă mēllă, Virg. Syn. Rĕdŏlĕo, suāvĭtĕr ŏlĕo, spīro. V. Oleo.

Frāncĭă, æ, f., *France.* Frāncĭă rēgēs, Claud. V. Gallia.

frāngo, ēgī, āctŭm, *to break.* Impăvĭdŭs frāngĭt, Virg. Syn. Infrīngo, cōnfrīngo, ēffrīngo, rūmpo, pērrūmpo, pērfrīngo, cōmmĭnŭo, cōntūndo, ēlīdo; īn fĭrmo, fătīgo, dēbĭlĭto.

frātĕr, trĭs, *and* tērcŭlŭs, ī, m., *a brother.* Frātĕr ŭt Ænēās, Virg. Mālīm frātĕrcŭlŭs ēssĕ, Juv. Syn. Gērmānŭs. Epith. Chārŭs, ămātŭs, dīlēctŭs, dūlcĭs, ūnănĭmĭs, fīdŭs, fīdēlĭs.

frātērnŭs, ă, ŭm, *fraternal, kindred.* Frātērnăquĕ pēctŏră, Virg.

frātrĭcīdă, æ, m., *a killer of his brother.* Quĭd frātrĭcīdă, quĭd, (Iamb.)

fraŭdātŏr, ōrĭs, m., *a rogue.* Fraŭdātŏr ĕs, Mart.

fraŭdo, ās, *to deceive.* Mōrsū fraŭdātŭs ăcētī, Mart. Syn. Frūstro, ās; frŭstrŏr ărĭs; fāllo, dēcĭpĭo. V. Fallo, decipio.

fraŭdŭlēntŭs, ă, ŭm, *fraudulent.* Ēt dŭcĕ fraŭdŭlēntō, (Dact. T.) Hor. Syn. Dŏlōsŭs, fāllāx, pērfĭdŭs.

fraŭs, aŭdĭs, f., *deceit.* Fraŭdĭs, ăbūndĕ, Virg. Syn. Dŏlŭs, tēchnæ, fāllācĭă, præstĭgĭæ, āstūtĭă, āstŭs, īnsĭdĭæ. Epith. Occūltă, mălĭgnă, īnsĭdĭōsă, scĕlĕrātă, nĕfāndă, dŏlōsă, mălă, dīră, īnfīdă, tăcĭtă, hōstīlĭs, caŭtă, īmpĭă, īnvīsă,

Inĭquă, vērsūtă, āstūtă, tēctă, hōrrĭdă, ĭngĕnĭōsă, lătēns, fīctă, sŭbdŏlă, mēndāx.
V. Dolus, fallacia.

frāxĭnĕŭs and nŭs, ă, ŭm, *ashen*. Frāxĭncæquĕ trăbēs, Virg.

frāxĭnŭs, ĭ, f., *an ash-tree*. Frāxĭnŭs ĭn sŷlvĭs, Virg. EPITH. Āltă, ĭngēns, prōcēră, ācrĭă, ŭmbrōsă.—2. *a javelin*. Frāxĭnŭs ĭrĕt, Claud. EPITH. Crŭēntă, bēllĭcă, sævă, fātālĭs, fērrātă, mīssĭlĭs.

frĕmĕbŭndŭs, ă, ŭm, *roaring*. Cŭrrŭ frĕmĕbŭndŭs ăb āltŏ, Ov. SYN. Frĕmēns, frēndēns.

frĕmĭtŭs, ūs, m., *a roaring noise*. Cĭrcŭmstānt frĕmĭtŭ dēnsŏ, Virg. SYN. Strĕpĭtŭs. EPITH. Hōrrĭsŏnŭs, raūcŭs, sŏnōrŭs, grăvĭs, trĕpĭdŭs, flēbĭlĭs, trĭstĭs. V. Murmur, fremo.

frĕmo, ŭĭ, ĭtŭm, *to roar*. Frĕmĕt hōrrĭdŭs ŏrĕ, Virg. SYN. Ĭnfrĕmo, strīdĕo, frēndĕo, mūrmŭro ; ĭndĭgnŏr.

frēndĕo, ŭĭ, *to gnash the teeth*. Et grăvĭtĕr frēndēns, Virg. SYN. Ĭnfrēndĕo, frĕmo, fŭro.

frĕquēns, ēntĭs, *frequent*. Tēlīsquĕ frĕquēntĭbŭs īnstānt, Virg. SYN. Crēbĕr, nŭmĕrōsŭs, mūltŭs, plūrĭmŭs ; cĕlĕbĕr, frĕquēntātŭs ; āssĭdŭŭs.

frĕquēntĕr, adv., *frequently*. Ēlĕphāntă frĕquēntĕr, Mart. SYN. Crēbrŏ,˙ sæpĕ, nōn rārŏ ; āssĭdŭē, cōntĭnŭŏ.

frĕquēntĭă, æ, f., *a great company*. Crīmĭnŭm frĕquēntĭăm, (Iamb.) ˙SYN. Mūltĭtūdo, tūrbă, cōpĭă.

frĕquēnto, ās, *to frequent*. Sēcrētă frĕquēntānt, Virg. SYN. Cĕlebro.

frētŭm, ĭ, n., *the sea*. Lēgĭmŭs frētă cōnsĭtă tērrĭs, Virg. SYN. Mărĭs āngūstĭæ, faūcēs ; mărĕ. EPITH. Tŭmēns, ăpērtŭm, ūndāns, tōrrēns, naūfrăgŭm, spūmōsŭm, mĭnāx, sălĭēns, tŭmĭdŭm, frĕmēns. V. Mare.

frētŭs, ă, ŭm, *trusting to*. Queīs ĕgŏ frētŭs ămo, Prŏp. SYN. Fīdēns, fīsŭs, cōnfīsŭs.

frĭco, ŭĭ, tŭm, *to rub*. Tērrām, frĭcăt ārbŏrĕ cōst, Virg. SYN. Pērfrĭco ; ūngo, ŏblĭno.

frĭgĕo, ŭĭ, *to be cold*. Lăvānt frĭgēntĭs ĕt ūn, Virg. SYN. Algĕo, frīgēsco. V. Frĭgus.

frĭgĕro, ās, *to make cold*. Frīgērāns Ăgănīpp at.

frĭgēsco, ĭs, *to grow cold*. Jŭvāt frīgēscĕrĕ l, Val.

‖ frĭgĭdĭtās, ātĭs, f., *coldness*. Frĭgĭdĭtātĕ făcĭt, Mart. SYN. Frīgŭs, gĕlū.

frĭgĭdŭs, and dŭlŭs, ă, ŭm, *cold*. Frīgĭdŭs ĭn prātĭs, Virg. Frīgĭdŭlōs ūdŏ Cat. SYN. Frĭgēns, gĕlĭdŭs, ālgĭdŭs, ālgēns. V. Frigeo.

frĭgĭllă, ĭngīllă, ĭnguīllă, æ, f., *a chaffinch*. Ĭnōpēs frīgĭllārūmquĕ quĕrēlās, Mart.

frīgŭs, ŏrĭs, n., *cold*. Frīgŏrĭbŭs pārtŏ, Virg. SYN. Gĕlū. EPITH. Cōncrētŭm, cōntrāctŭm, hÿĕmālĕ, brūmālĕ, glăcĭālĕ, Scÿthĭcŭm, tōrpēns, ăcērbŭm, rĭgĭdŭm, ācrĕ, ĭmmītĕ, hōrrēndŭm, dūrŭm, ĭnērs, Ārctōŭm, mălĭgnŭm, Rĭphæum, Bŏrēālĕ, ĭnĭquŭm, Hÿpērbŏrĕŭm, ăcūtŭm, hÿbērnŭm, gĕlĭdŭm.

frĭtĭnnĭo, īs, īre, *to chirp, trill*. Cĭcădă frĭtĭnnĭt, Auct. Phil.

frĭtĭllŭs, ĭ, m., *a dice-box*. Mōtŏ spēctārĕ frĭtĭllŏ, Mart.

frĭvŏlŭs, ă, ŭm, *vain, trifling, worthless*. Frĭvŏlă fāmæ, Prud.

frōndătŏr, ŏrĭs, m., *a wood-lopper*. Cănĕt frōndătŏr ăd aūrās, Virg. SYN. Pŭtātŏr.

frōndĕo, ēs, and frōndēsco, ĭs, *to bear leaves*. Sēmpĕr frōndēntĭs ăcānthī, Virg. Frōndēscĭt vīrgă mētāllŏ, Id. V. Frons.

frōndĕŭs, dĭfĕr, and dōsŭs, ă, ŭm, *leafy*. Frōndĕă sēmpĕr, Virg. Frōndĭfĕrāsquĕ dŏmŏs, Lucr. Frōndōsă vītĭs ĭn ūlmŏ, Virg.

frōns, dĭs, f., *a leaf*. Frōndĭs ĭnŭmbrānt, Virg. SYN. Fŏlĭŭm, ārbŏrĕæ cŏmæ, crīnēs. EPITH. Vĭrĭdĭs, āltă, pătŭlă, tĕnĕră, tĕnŭĭs, crīspă, ārbŏrĕă, grāmĭnĕă, trĕmŭlă, cŏmāns, ŭmbrōsă, vērnāns, mōllĭs, vĭrĭdāns, crīspāns, lætă, ŏdŏrātă, ŏdŏrĭfĕră, dēnsă, rĕdĭvīvă, dēcĭdŭă, cădūcă, flāvēscēns, ŏpācă, mōbĭlĭs. V. Frondeo.

frōns, tĭs, f., *the forehead*. Frōntĭs, ŭt ārtĕ, Hor. SYN. Ōs, vūltŭs, făcĭēs. EPITH. Tĕnĕră, dĕcŏră, hŏnēstă, sĕrēnă, nĭtĭdă, lūcĭdă, vĕnūstă, nĭvĕă, plăcĭdă, cāndĭdă, hĭlărĭs, vĕnĕrāndă, rūgōsă, mŏdēstă, rĕmĭssă ; ēlātă, mĭnāx, aūdāx, fĕrōx, tōrvă, ōbscœnă, sĕvĕră, ōbdūctă, sĕnĭlĭs.

‖ frūctĭfĭco, ās, *to fructify*. Laūrŭs frūctĭfĭcăt, Calp. SYN. Frūctŭs părĭo, fĕro, prōmo, fūndo, ēdo, pārtŭrĭo, prōfĕro.

frūctŭōsŭs, ă, ŭm, *fruitful.* Sătŭrnālĭă frŭctŭōsĭōră, (Phal.) Mart. SYN. Frŭctĭfĕr, frūgĭfĕr, fērtĭlĭs, ūtĭlĭs. V. Frugifer.

frūctŭs, ūs, m., *fruit.* Frūctŭs ămīcĭtĭæ, Juv. SYN. Pōmă, fœtŭs, pārtŭs, ūtĭlĭtās. EPITH. Tĕrrēstrĭs, sylvēstrĭs, ămœnŭs, dūlcĭs, grātŭs, nŏvŭs, dēlĭcĭōsŭs, cōrrūptŭs, æstīvŭs, suāvĭs, ānnŭŭs, tĕnĕr, mātūrŭs, præcōx, ūbĕr, dīvĕs, jūcūndŭs, tēmpēstīvŭs. V. Fructuosus.

frūgālĭs, ĕ, *frugal.* Nŏvī frūgālĭŭs; hōc, Juv. SYN. Frūgī, bŏnæ frūgĭs, sōbrĭŭs, mŏdĕrātŭs, mŏdēstŭs, tēmpĕrāns, tēmpĕrātŭs, ābstĭnēns, prūdēns.

frūgālĭtās, ātĭs, f., *sobriety.* Frūgālĭtātĭs lēgĕ, (Scaz.) Petr. SYN. Sōbrĭĕtăs, mŏdēstĭă.

frūgālĭtĕr, adv., *soberly.* Pārcē, frūgālĭtĕr, ātquĕ, Hor.

frūgēs, ŭm, f. pl., *fruits, corn, &c.* Frūgĭbŭs ūmbræ, Virg. SYN. Sĕgĕs, mēssĭs, frūmēntŭm. EPITH. Lætæ, ămœnæ, nĭtĭdæ, tĕnĕræ, nŏvæ, fĕrācēs, ŏpīmæ, ūbĕrēs, fœcūndæ, grăvĭdæ, cūltæ, mātūræ, Cĕrĕālēs, aūrĕæ, flāvæ, flāvēntēs, spīcĕæ, trītĭcĕæ, tōstæ. V. Seges.

|| frūgēsco, ĭs, *to bear fruit.* Stĕrĭlēs frūgēscĕrĕ pārcĭŭs āgrōs, Prud.

frūgī, (indecl.) *temperate, honest.* Tām frūgī Jūno, Mart. SYN. Prŏbŭs.

frūgĭfĕr, ă, ŭm, *and* ĕrēns, ntĭs, *bearing fruit.* Frūgĭfĕr ūndĭs, Porph. SYN. Frūctĭfĕr, frūctŭōsŭs.

frūgĭlĕgŭs, ă, ŭm, *gathering corn.* Hīc nōs frūgĭlĕgās, Ov. SYN. Frūgēs lĕgēns.

frūmēntŭm, ī, n., *corn.* Ingēntēm frūmēntī sēmpĕr, Hor. SYN. Frūgēs, Cĕrēs, sĕgĕs, mēssĭs, trītĭcŭm. EPITH. Pūrŭm, flāvēscēns, æstīvŭm, aūrĕŭm, Cĕrĕālĕ, grăvĕ, lūctēns, grāndĕ, lætŭm. V. Fruges.

frŭŏr, ĕrĭs, *to enjoy.* Pōssĕ frŭī ; frŭăr ō, Prop. SYN. Pŏtĭŏr, ūtŏr, tĕnĕo ; pŏssĭdĕo.

frūstātĭm, adv., *in pieces.* Frūstātĭm sĕcŭĭt, Mant. SYN. In frūstă, mĭnūtātĭm, mēmbrātĭm.

frūstrā, adv., *in vain.* Frūstrā mŏrĭtūră rĕlīnquăt, Virg. SYN. Incāssŭm, nēquīcquăm, ĭnānĭtĕr, ĭnūtĭlĭtĕr.

frūstro, ās, *and* ŏr, ārĭs, *to frustrate.* Spē frūstrābŏr ĭnānī, Arator. Clāmōr frūstrātŭr hĭāntēs, Virg. SYN. Fraūdo, fāllo, dēcĭpĭo.

frūstŭm, ī, n., *a fragment.* Exĭgŭæ frūstĭs ĭmbūtŭs, Juv. SYN. Frūstŭlŭm, pārtĭcŭlă, sēgmēntŭm, frāgmĕn, frāgmēntŭm, mĭnūtăl. EPITH. Exĭgŭŭm, tĕnŭĕ, pārvŭm, ēxīlĕ, mĭnūtŭm.

frŭtētŭm, *and* tĭcētŭm, ī, n., *a shrubbery.* Eccĕ frŭtētĭs, Prud. Lătĭtāntēm frŭtĭcētō, Hor.

frŭtēx, ĭcĭs, m., *a shrub.* Sylvārŭm frŭtĭcŭmquĕ vĭrĕt, Virg. SYN. Ārbūstŭm, ārbūscŭlŭm, vīrgŭltŭm. EPITH. Rāmōsŭs, ārbŏrĕŭs, pārvŭs, ūmbrōsŭs, tĕnĕr, hŭmĭlĭs, ābjēctŭs, lætŭs, dēnsŭs, crīspŭlŭs, ŏpācŭs, vĭrĭdĭs, frōndōsŭs, vĭrēns, vĭrĭdāns. V. Arbustum.

frŭtĭco, ās, *or* cŏr, ārĭs, *to sprout.* Pālmās frŭtĭcārĕ lăcērtĭs, Sid. SYN. Frŭtĭcēsco, pŭllŭlo, gērmĭno. V. Germino.

frŭtĭcōsŭs, ă, ŭm, *shrubby.* Illĭs frŭtĭcōsă lĕgēbānt, Ov.

fūcātŭs, *the pass. partic. of* fuco. Sătŭrō fūcātă cŏlōrĕ, Virg.

Fūcĭnŭs, ī, m., *a lake in Italy.* Tē Fūcĭnŭs ūndā, Virg.

fūco, ās, *to colour.* Ăssyrĭō fūcātŭr lānā vĕnēnō, Virg. SYN. Infūco.

fūcŭs, ī, m., *a dye, deceit.* Fūcōque ēt flōrĭbŭs ōrās, Virg. SYN. Cērūssă, pīgmēntŭm ; ūngŭēntŭm ; fraūs, dŏlŭs. EPITH. Vānŭs, fāllāx, ĭnānĭs, rŏsĕŭs, cŏlōrātŭs, fœmĭnĕŭs, pīctŭs, nĭtēns, ŏdōrŭs, ŏdōrātŭs, splēndēns, pĕrēgrīnŭs. V. Fuco.

—2. *a drone.* Ăd pābŭlă fūcŭs, Virg. SYN. Vēspă. EPITH. Ignāvŭs, ĭnērs, sēgnĭs, stĕrĭlĭs.

Fūfĭdĭŭs, ĭī, m., *a man's name.* Fūfĭdĭŭs vāppæ, Hor.

Fūfĭŭs, ĭī, m., *a man's name.* Fūfĭŭs ēbrĭŭs ōlĭm, Hor.

fŭgă, æ, f., *flight.* Lōngūmquĕ fŭgæ, Virg. SYN. Effŭgĭŭm. EPITH. Fūrtīvă, trĕpĭdātă, præcēps, cĕlĕr, pērnīx, ēffūsă, cĭtă, păvĭdă, văgă, tūrpĭs, tĭmĭdă, trīstĭs, tūtă, āstūtă, probrōsă, vēlōx, rĕpēntīnă, prŏpĕră, lēvĭs, nōctūrnă, ōccūltă, fēstīnă, prŏvĭdă, hŏnēstă, sōllĭcĭtă. V. Fugio.

fŭgāx, ācĭs, *fugitive, fleet, fleeting.* Pĕdĭbūsquĕ fŭgācĭbŭs, Virg. SYN. Tĭmĭdŭs, ĭgnāvŭs, mōllĭs, ĭnērs ; ăd fŭgăm pĕdĕ fērvĭdŭs ; fŭgĭēns, fŭgĭtīvŭs, prŏfūgŭs ; cĕlĕr, vēlōx, pērnīx ; cădūcŭs, frăgĭlĭs, flūxŭs, brĕvĭs.

fŭgĭo, fŭgī, *to fly.* Quī nōs fŭgĭātĭs ămīcōs, Virg. SYN. Ĕffŭgĭo, aŭfŭgĭo, dīffŭgĭo; ōdī, vīto, căvĕo; ēvānēsco.

fŭgĭtīvŭs, ă, ŭm, *fugitive.* Vīctōrēm fŭgĭtīvŭs ăgĭt, Sidon. V. Fugax.

fŭgĭo, ăs, *freq. of* fugio. Ŏcŭlī fŭgĭtānt, Lucr.

fŭgo, ăs, *to put to flight.* Trāns pōntūm fŭgăt, ĕt, Virg. SYN. Pĕllo, rĕpĕllo, ēxpĕllo, prōpŭlso, ăbĭgo. V. Fugio.

fŭlcīmĕn, ĭnĭs, *or* mēntŭm, ī, n., *a prop.* Nūllō fŭlcīmĭnĕ nīxă, Ov. SYN. Cŏlŭmĕn, fŭlcrŭm.

fŭlcĭo, īs, *to prop.* Māgnī fŭlcīrĕ rŭīnăm, Luc. SYN. Sŭffŭlcĭo, sŭstĭnĕo, sŭstĕnto, fĕro. V. Fero.

fŭlcrŭm, ī, n., *a prop.* Fŭlcră tŏrīs, Virg. SYN. Fŭlcīmĕn, fŭlcīmēntŭm, cŏlŭmĕn, ādmĭnĭcŭlŭm. EPITH. Sŭppŏsĭtŭm, fōrtĕ, vălĭdŭm, tūtŭm.

fŭlgĕo, fŭlsī, ērĕ, *and* go, ĕrĕ. Indŭctō fŭlgēbăt, Prop. Fŭlgĕrĕ cērnĭs, Virg. SYN. Ĕffŭlgĕo, rĕfŭlgĕo, fŭlgŭro, splēndĕo, lūcĕo, nĭtĕo, cŏrūsco, mĭco.

fŭlgĭdŭs, ă, ŭm, *shining.* Fŭlgĭdă præsērtĭm, Lucr. SYN. Fŭlgēns, cŏrūscŭs, lūcĭdŭs, rŭtĭlŭs, splēndĭdŭs, mĭcāns.

fŭlgŏr, ōrĭs, m., *brightness.* Illĕ nōtăm fŭlgŏrĕ dĕdĭt, Ov. SYN. Splēndŏr, lūx, nĭtŏr. EPITH. Nĭtĭdŭs, cŏrūscŭs, aūrĕŭs, rŏsĕŭs, rădĭāns, vīvŭs, splēndĭdŭs, nĭvālĭs, gēmmĕŭs, flāmmĕŭs.

fŭlgŭr, ŭrĭs, n., *lightning.* Fŭlgŭrĭs īctŭm, Juv. SYN. Fŭlgetrŭm. EPITH. Răpĭdŭm, mĭcāns, clārŭm, rŭtĭlŭm, sŭbĭtŭm, ignītŭm, flagrāns, flāmmĕŭm, rĕpēntīnŭm, ignĭfĕrŭm, ārdēns, vēlōx, mĭnāx, hŏrrĭfĭcŭm, fōrmīdābĭlĕ, vānēscēns, rădĭāns, cŏrūscŭm. V. Fulmen, tonitru, fulguro.

* fŭlgŭrăt, *it lightens.* V. Fulmen.

fŭlgŭro, ăs, n., *to lighten, flash, glitter.* Fŭlgŭrăt aūrō, Stat. SYN. Fŭlgŭr jăcĭo, jăcŭlŏr, vibro, ēxcŭtĭo, ēmītto, spārgo.

fŭlĭcă, æ, f., *a sea-fowl.* Lūdūnt fŭlĭcæ, Virg. SYN. Fŭlīx. EPITH. Mărīnă, pălūstrĭs, pārvă, văgă.

* fŭlīgĭnōsŭs, ă, ŭm, *sooty.* Fŭlīgĭnōsō thŭrĕ, (Iamb.) Prud. SYN. Ătĕr, nĭgĕr, pĭcĕŭs. Fŭlīgĭnĕ tētĕr, squālēns, nĭgĕr.

fŭlīgo, ĭnĭs, f., *soot.* Pōstēs fŭlīgĭnĕ nĭgrī, Virg. EPITH. Pĭcĕă, ātră, tētrā, ŏbscūră, mădĭdă.

fŭllo, ōnĭs, m., *a fuller of cloth.* Fŭllō tĭbi, Mart.

fŭlmĕn, ĭnĭs, n., *thunder.* Fŭlmĕn ĕrăt, Virg. EPITH. Hŏrrēndŭm, ignĭfĕrŭm, īnfēstŭm, tōrtŭm, īnēvītābĭlĕ, Ætnæŭm, cŏrūscŭm, hŏrrĭdŭm, ātrŭm, răpĭdŭm, hŏrrĭfĭcŭm, rŭtĭlŭm, vĭŏlēntŭm, īntōrtŭm, ōblīquŭm, fŭgăx, lævŭm, vălĭdŭm, mĭssĭlĕ, æthĕrĕŭm, hŏrrĭsŏnŭm, cŏrūscāns, cœlēstĕ, sŭlphŭrĕŭm, ignĭvŏmŭm, trĕmēndŭm, mĕtŭēndŭm, flāmmāns, rĕpēntīnŭm, fŭrēns, tērrĭbĭlĕ, vibrātŭm, pĕnĕtrābĭlĕ, trĭfĭdŭm, præsăgŭm. V. Fulgur, tonitru, fulmino.

fŭlmĭnăt, *it thunders.* Cŭm fŭlmĭnăt, Virg. V. Fulmino.

fŭlmĭnĕŭs, ă, ŭm, *of or like thunder.* Īctū fŭlmĭnĕō, Hor. SYN. Vĭŏlēntŭs, ācĕr, ārdēns.

fŭlmĭno, ăs, *to strike with thunder.* Fŭlmĭnăt Eŭphrātēn, Virg. V. Fulminat, fulgur

fŭltūră, æ, f., *a propping.* Stŏmăchō fŭltūră rŭēntī, Hor.

fŭltŭs, ă, ŭm, *the pass. partic. of* fulcio. Nĭvĕī fŭltŭm Pāllāntĭs, Virg.

fŭlvŭs, ă, ŭm, *of a tawny colour.* Ăt fŭlvæ nĭmbŭs, Virg. SYN. Flāvŭs, rŭtĭlŭs, crŏcĕŭs, aūrĕŭs.

fŭmĕŭs, mĭdŭs, mĭfĕr, mĭfĭcŭs, ă, ŭm, *smoky.* Fŭmĕă Māssĭlĭæ, Mart. Fŭmĭdŭs ātque āltĕ spūmĭs ēxŭbĕrăt āmnĭs, Virg. Fŭmĭfĕrām nōctĕm, Virg. Fŭmĭfĭcĭsquĕ lŏcŭm, Ov.

* fŭmĭgo, ăs, *to perfume.* V. Odoro.

fŭmo, ăs, *to smoke.* Crŭŏr fŭmăbăt ăd ārās, Virg.

fŭmōsŭs, ă, ŭm, *smoky.* Prælōrūm fŭmōsĭs, Virg. SYN. Fŭmĕŭs, fŭmĭfĕr, fŭmĭfĭcŭs, fŭmĭdŭs.

fŭmŭs, ī, m., *smoke.* Pŭlvĕrĕ fŭmŭm, Virg. SYN. Fŭlīgo, cālīgo. EPITH. Ătĕr, nĭgĕr, sōrdĭdŭs, tētĕr, vŏlūcĕr, sĕquāx, tĕnŭĭs, vŏlāns, cālĭdŭs, pīnguĭs, pĭcĕŭs, grăvĭs, ārēns, tĕnebrōsŭs, ūndāns, īnānĭs, lĕvĭs, văpōrōsŭs, āĕrĭŭs, vānēscēns, tūrbĭdŭs, ămārŭs, sŭlphŭrĕŭs, ignītŭs.

fūnālĕ, ĭs, n., *a torch.* Flāmmĭs fūnālĭă vīncŭnt, Virg. SYN. Făx, tædă, lāmpăs.

fūnālĭs, (sc. equus) *a trace-horse.* Fūnālĕmquĕ Thŏēn, Stat.

fūnāmbŭlŭs, ī, m., *a rope-dancer.* Fūnāmbŭli ĕŏdĕm, Mart. Epith. Sŏlĕrs, lĕvĭs, ăgĭlĭs.

fūndă, æ, f., *a sling.* Vĕrbĕră fūndæ, Virg. Epith. Bălĕārĭs, Bălĕārĭcă; cĭtă, tōrtă, vŏlūtă, vŏlūbĭlĭs, āĕrĭă, lĕvĭs, flĕxă, vălĭdă, pŭĕrĭlĭs, vērsātĭlĭs, ĕxcūssă, īntōrtă, sŏnāns.

fūndāmĕn, ĭnĭs, *and* mēntŭm, ī, n., *a foundation.* Fūndāmĭnă; deīndĕ, Virg. Fūndāmēntă lŏcānt, Id. Syn. Sŏlŭm, stăbĭlīmĕn, stăbĭlīmēntŭm. Epith. Āltŭm, stăbĭlĕ, fīrmŭm, sŏlĭdŭm, mānsūrŭm, tūtŭm, sūppŏsĭtŭm.

Fūndānĭŭs, ī, m., *a man's name.* Ūnŭs vīvōrŭm, Fūndānī, Hor.

Fūndānŭs, ă, ŭm, *of Fundi.* Māxĭmă Fūndānī, Ov.

fūndātŏr, ōrĭs, m., *a founder.* Prænēstīnæ fūndātŏr, Virg. Syn. Cōndĭtŏr.

Fūndī, ōrŭm, m. pl., *a city of Campania.* Fūndōs Aūĭĭdĭŏ, Hor.

fūndĭtŏr, ōrĭs, m., *a slinger.* Ēt fūndĭtŏrī, (Scaz.) Scal.

fūndĭtŭs, adv., *utterly.* Fūndĭtŭs ōmnēs, Virg. Syn. Stīrpĭtŭs, rādīcĭtŭs; pĕnĭtŭs, prōrsŭs, ōmnīnō.

fūndo, ās, *to found, establish.* Fūndātŭr Vĕnĕrī, Virg. Ænēān fūndāntem ārcēs, Id. Syn. Fūndāmēntă, fūndāmĭnă pŏno, jăcĭo, lŏco, mŏlĭŏr; cōndo, cōnstĭtŭo, stătŭo, ædĭfĭco, strŭo, ēxstrŭo. V. Ædifico.

fūndo, fūdī, fūsŭm, *to pour.* Fūndĭtŭr, ĕt, Virg. Syn. Ēffūndo, spārgo, dīspērgo, prōjĭcĭo, ēmītto; dīssĭpo, prōstērno; lŏquŏr.

fūndŭs, ī, m., *land.* Cŭm lărĕ fūndŭs, Hor.

fūnebrĭs, ĕ, *and* ĕrĕŭs, ă, ŭm, *belonging to funerals, doleful, lamentable.* Fūnĕbrĕ bēllŭm, Hor. Fūnĕrĕāsque īnfērrĕ făcēs, Virg. Syn. Fērālĭs, fūnēstŭs.

fūnĕro, ās, *to bury.* Prŏpĕ fūnĕrātŭs, Hor.

fūnēsto, ās, *to pollute, afflict.* Mēntĕ, dŏœ, fūnēstăt, Cat.

fūnēstŭs, ă, ŭm, *fatal, belonging to death.* Lūmĭnă fūnēstī, Ov. Syn. Fūnebrĭs, fūnĕrĕŭs; lēthālĭs; trīstĭs, mœstŭs.

fūngīnŭs, ă, ŭm, *of a mushroom.* Fūngīnŏ gĕnĕrĕ, Plaut.

fūngŏr, ĕrĭs, ctŭs, *to discharge an office.* Fūngăr ĭnānī, Virg. Syn. Dēfūngŏr, pērfūngŏr, præsto, ēffĭcĭo, ēxērcĕo, ēxĕquŏr, ŏbĕo.

fūngŭs, ī, m., *a mushroom.* Ōptĭmă fūngĭs, Hor. Syn. Bōlētŭs. Epith. Ālbŭs, frĭgĭdŭs, hūmĭdŭs, hūmēns, ūdŭs, fœdŭs, sōrdĭdŭs, plŭvĭālĭs.

fūnĭs, ĭs, *and* nĭcŭlŭs, ī, m., *a rope.* Fūnĭs ărēnă, Prop. Syn. Rēstĭs, lōrŭm, rūdēns, rētĭnācŭlă, stŭpĕă vīncŭlă, cătēnă. Epith. Tōrtŭs, īntōrtŭs, vŏlūtŭs, dūrŭs, nōdōsŭs, rĭgĭdŭs, tēnsŭs, ēxtēnsŭs, cōntēntŭs, ōblōngŭs, naŭtĭcŭs, mărīnŭs, dūctārĭŭs, sāltātōrĭŭs; stŭpĕŭs, cānnăbīnŭs, līnĕŭs, lōrĕŭs, spārtĕŭs. V. Catena.

fūnŭs, ĕrĭs, n., *a funeral.* Fūnĕrĭs ūnă, Prop. Syn. Ēxĕquĭæ, īnfĕrĭæ, jūstă. Epith. Crūdēlĕ, trīstĕ, mĭsĕrābĭlĕ, mœstŭm, lāmēntābĭlĕ, flēbĭlĕ, ēxtrēmŭm, ămārŭm, jūstŭm, pĭŭm, gĕmĕbūndŭm, ĭnĭquŭm, lūgubrĕ, ăcērbŭm, mĭsĕrāndŭm, lacrўmōsŭm, crŭēntŭm, suprēmŭm, sŏlēnnĕ, fēlīx, præclārŭm, hŏnēstŭm, dēbĭtŭm, īllūstrĕ, cōnspĭcŭŭm. V. Exequiæ, sepelio.—2. *a corpse.* Ēt fūnŭs lăcĕrŭm, Virg.

fūr, ūrĭs, m., *a robber.* Fūrĭs ĕt īmplăcĭdās, Prop. Syn. Latro, prædo, prædātŏr, pŏpŭlātŏr, rāptŏr, ērēptŏr, ăbāctŏr. Epith. Răpāx, nōctūrnŭs, văgāns, tăcĭtŭs, ōccūltŭs, pērvĭgĭl, ăvārŭs, crūdēlĭs, īngĕnĭōsŭs, caŭtŭs, āstūtŭs, sŏlērs, vērsūtŭs, īnsĭdĭōsŭs, scĕlĕrātŭs, īmprŏbŭs, nĕfārĭŭs, ērrāns, īnsōmnĭs, ābdĭtŭs, rĕcōndĭtŭs, āncēps, trĕpĭdŭs, ārmātŭs, mĭnāx, nōctĭvăgŭs, sōllĭcĭtŭs. V. Furor, aris.

fūrāx, ācĭs, *thievish.* Fūrācēs mŏnĕo, (Phal.) Mart. Syn. Răpāx, rāptŏr. V. Fur.

fūrcă, æ, *dimin.* fūrcīllă, f., *a fork.* Vāllōs fūrcāsquĕ bĭcōrnēs, Virg. Epith. Fērrĕă, lignĕă, fīrmă, bĭfĭdă, bĭcūspĭs, trĭcōrnĭs, trĭcūspĭs.—2. *a gibbet.* Brāchĭĭs fūrca ēmĭnŭs, (Iamb.) Prud.

fūrcĭfĕr, ī, m., *a rogue.* Fūrcĭfĕr, ād tē, Hor. V. Fur.

fūrēns, *the pres. partic. of* furo. Spēctārĕ fūrēntĕm, Hor. V. Fŭrĭōsŭs.

fŭrĭă, æ, f., *fury;* Fŭrĭæ, ārŭm, f. pl., *the Furies.* Hānc fŭrĭăm, Hor. Nēscĭă sē Fŭrĭīs, Prop. Syn. Dīræ, Eūmĕnĭdĕs, Ērīnnўĕs. Epith. Infērnæ, Stўgĭæ, Tārtărĕæ, crīnītæ, īmmānēs, hōrrēndæ, Ăchĕrōntĭdĕs, ārdēntēs, dēfōrmēs, squālĭdæ, crūdēlēs, ātræ, nōctĭgĕnæ, sĕvēræ, fĕræ, sævæ, dīræ, īmmītēs, fĕrōcēs, fūrēntēs, ignĭfĕræ, flāmmĭgĕræ, tōrvæ, trŭcēs, scĕlĕrātæ, īmplācābĭlēs, vĕnēnōsæ, fŭrĭōsæ, mĭnācēs, dīscōrdēs, Ăvērnālēs, mĕtŭēndæ, crŭēntæ, lūctĭfĕræ.

fŭrĭālĭs, ĕ, *furious.* Sērpēntĭs fŭrĭălĕ mălŭm, Virg. Syn. Fŭrĭōsŭs, fŭrēns; răbĭdŭs.

fŭrĭālĭtĕr, adv., *furiously.* Fŭrĭālĭtĕr ŏdĭt, Ov. Syn. Fŭrĭōsē, fŭrĭātā mĕntĕ.

fŭrĭātŭs, ĭbŭndŭs, *and* ĭōsŭs, ă, ŭm, *furious.* Fŭrĭātā mĕntĕ Cŏrœbŭs, Virg. Mārtĕm fŭrĭbŭndā cĕcĭdĭ, Mart. Tŭŏ, fŭrĭōsĕ; mĕŏ, Hor. Syn. Fŭrēns.

fŭrĭo, ās, *to render furious.* Mātrēs fŭrĭāre ĕquŏrŭm, Hor.

Fŭrĭŭs, ĭĭ, m., *a Roman prænomen.* Fŭrĭŭs āntīquŭm, Hor.

fŭrnŭs, ĭ, m., *an oven.* Mart.

fŭro, ĭs, *to be furious.* Quĭd fŭrĭs? aŭt, Virg. Syn. Insānĭo, bācchŏr, īrāscŏr. V. Furor, irascor.

fŭrŏr, ōrĭs, m., *fury.* Fŭrŏr ārmă mĭnīstrăt, Virg. Syn. Insānĭă, āmēntĭă, dēmēntĭă, vēsānĭă, fŭrĭæ, răbĭēs, īră. Epith. Impĭŭs, āmēns, ārdēns, īgnĕŭs, dīrŭs, præcēps, ĕffrēnŭs, răbĭdŭs, pērtĭnāx, vēsānŭs, ĭmmĭtĭs, ĭmmānĭs, ĕxĭtĭōsŭs, crŭēntŭs, bārbărŭs, văgŭs, fĕrrĕŭs, īnsānŭs, īmpătĭēns, flagrāns, īndŏmĭtŭs, īnflammātŭs, āccēnsŭs, vēcŏrs, mălĕsānŭs, īmplăcābĭlĭs, crūdēlĭs, scĕlĕrātŭs, nĕfāndŭs, fōrmīdābĭlĭs, sŭbĭtŭs, vĭŏlēntŭs, nōxĭŭs, hōstīlĭs, dīscŏrs, bēllĭcŭs, Mārtĭŭs, Māvōrtĭŭs, īmpŏtēns, vīndēx, atrōx, hōrrĭdŭs, sævŭs, sānguĭnĕŭs, ārmātŭs. V. Furor, rabies, Furiæ.

fŭrŏr, ărĭs, *to steal.* Ŏcŭlōs fŭrārĕ lăbōrī, Virg. Syn. Răpĭo, ābrĭpĭo, dīrĭpĭo, ērĭpĭo, sŭrrĭpĭo, pŏpŭlŏr, cōmpĭlo, ēxpĭlo, sŭbtrăho, āvērto, sŭbdūco, aŭfĕro, tōllo. V. Prædor.

fŭrtĭm, adv., *furtively.* Quĕm fŭrtĭm māndārăt, Virg. Syn. Clăm, clāncŭlŭm.

fŭrtīvŭs, ă, ŭm, *made by surprise, stolen.* Fŭrtīvīs nūdātă cŏlōrĭbŭs, Hor. Syn. Răptŭs, ērēptŭs, ŏccŭltŭs.

fŭrtŭm, ĭ, n., *theft.* Vŏlŭcrēs fŭrtŭmquĕ Prŏmētheī, Virg. Syn. Prædă, răpīnă, răptŭm; latrōcĭnĭŭm. Epith. Păvĭdŭm, nōctūrnŭm, tăcĭtŭm, tūrpĕ, ĭnīquŭm, nĕfāndŭm, lătebrōsŭm, sacrĭlĕgŭm, īnfāmĕ.

fŭrvŭs, ă, ŭm, *dark.* Quăm pænĕ fŭrvæ, Hor. Syn. Fūscŭs, ōbscūrŭs, nĭgĕr, ātĕr. V. Niger.

fŭscātŏr, ōrĭs, m., *one that darkens.* Cælĭ fŭscātŏr ĕŏĭ, Lucr.

fŭscĭnă, æ, f., *a trident.* Fŭscĭnā dēntĕ, Mart. Syn. Trĭdēns, Nēptūnĭ scēptrŭm. Epith. Sævă, ădūncă, Nēptūnĭă.

fŭsco, ās, *to darken.* Fŭscābătquĕ dĭĕm, Ov. Syn. Infūsco, ōbscūro, fūscō cŏlōrĕ tīngo, ĭnfĭcĭo.

fŭscŭs, ă, ŭm, *dark.* Ālbă dĕcēnt fŭscās, Ov. Syn. Nigrĭcāns, sŭbnĭgĕr, ōbscūrŭs.

fūsĭlĭs, ĕ, *that may be melted.* Fūsĭlĕ pēr rīctŭs, Ov. Syn. Dūctĭlĭs, fūsŭs.

fŭstĭs, ĭs, m., *a club.* Fŭstēs hūc, Juv. Syn. Băcŭlŭs, băcŭlŭm, stĭpĕs, sŭdēs, cōntŭs. V. Baculus.

fŭsŭs, ĭ, m., *a spindle.* Dŭm fūsĭs mōllĭă pēnsă, Virg. Epith. Grăvĭdŭs, vērsātŭs, prægnāns, lĕvĭs, tōrtŭs, pŭellārĭs, vērsātĭlĭs, vŏlŭbĭlĭs, sōlērs, sŭccĭnctŭs. V. Neo.

fŭsŭs, *the pass. partic. of* fundo. Vīrēs, fūsīquĕ pĕr hērbăm, Virg.

fŭtĭlĭs, ĕ, *foolish.* Fūtĭlĭs aŭctŏr, Virg. Syn. Gārrŭlŭs, lŏquāx; lĕvĭs, vānŭs, ĭnānĭs, īrrĭtŭs.

fŭtūrŭs, ă, ŭm, *which will be.* Ignārā fŭtūrī, Virg. Syn. Vēntūrŭs, pōstĕrŭs. V. Posteritas, successus.

G.

GĂBĀTĂ, æ, f., *a bowl.* Sīc īmplēt găbătās, Mart.

Găbĭĭ, ōrŭm, m. pl., *a nation in Italy.* Ēt Găbĭōs, ŭrbēmquĕ, Virg.

Găbīnŭs, ă, ŭm, *of Gabii.* Cīnctŭquĕ Găbīnō, Virg.

Gabrĭēl, ēlĭs, m., *the Archangel.* Găbrĭēl Pătrĭs ēx sŏlĭŏ, Prud. Hānc Găbrĭēl vŏcĭtăt, Fort. Epith. Cœlēstĭs, vĕnŭstŭs, fēlīx. V. Angelus.

Gādēs, ĭŭm, f. pl., *Cadiz.* Gādĭbŭs ŭsquĕ, Juv. Epith. Hērcŭlĕæ, ōccĭdŭæ, Hēspĕrĭæ, rĕmōtæ, ēxtrēmæ, Tўrĭæ, Ērўthrææ.

Gādītānŭs, ă, ŭm, *of Cadiz.* Quī Gādītānā sŭsŭrrăt, Mart.

Gætūlĭă, æ, f., *a country of Libya.* Gætūlĭā cāmpĭs, Claud.

Gætūlŭs, ă, ŭm, *Gætulian.* Gætūlæ ŭrbēs, Virg.

Gălānthĭs, ĭdĭs, f., *a servant-maid of Alcmene, changed by Juno into a weasel.* Rīsĭssĕ Gălānthĭdă fāma ēst, Ov.

Gălătă, æ, m., *a Galatian.* Gălătăquĕ Sўrĭquĕ, Luc.

I 5

Gălătĕă, æ, f., *a nymph.* Ō Gălătĕă, quĭs ēst, Virg. Syn. Nērēĭs, Nērīnē.
Epith. Prŏcāx, vĭrĭdĭs, cāndĭdă, fŏrmōsă.

Gălătĭă, œ, f., *a province of Asia Minor.* Hūnc Gălătĭă vĭgēns, Stat.

gălbănĕŭs, ă, ŭm, *of galbanum.* Hīnc jăm gălbănĕŏs, Virg.

gălbănŭm, ī, n., *a fragrant gum.* Gălbănă sūdānt, Luc.

gălbĭnātŭs, ă, ŭm, *clothed in galbinum.* Gălbĭnātŭs īn lēctō, Mart.

gălbĭnŭm, ī, n., *a sort of cloth.* Ēt gălbĭnă răsă, Juv.

gălbĭnŭs, ă, ŭm, *of galbinum, effeminate.* Gălbĭnōs hăbēt mōrēs, Mart.

gălbŭlă, æ, f., *a bird.* Gălbŭlă dēcĭpĭtŭr călămĭs, Mart.

gălĕă, æ, f., *a helmet.* Hāc gălĕă cōntēntŭs, Virg. Syn. Cāssĭs, cāssĭdă, cūdo.
Ăpēx, cōnŭs, crīstă, jŭbæ, pēnnæ. Epith. Cōmāns, crīnītă, tērrĭbĭlĭs, dĕcōră,
nĭtēns, ærĕă, fūlgēns, cŏrŭscă, fērrĕă, mĭnāx, ăhēnă, rĭgēns, ærātă, mĭnĭtāns,
crīstātă, ārdēns, lūcēns, pēnnĭcōmă, Mārtĭă; aūrātă, hōrrēns, hōrrĭfĭcă, Măvōrtĭă.

gălĕātŭs, ă, ŭm, *wearing a helmet.* Tŭbă, gălĕātŭm, Prop. Syn. Gălĕa ārmātŭs.
V. Galea.

gălĕrŭs, ī, m., *and* rŭm, ī, n., *a hat.* Dē pēllĕ gălĕrōs, Virg. Syn. Pĭlĕŭs,
pĕtăsŭs. V. Pileus.

Gălēsŭs, ī, m., *a river in Calabria.* Cūltă Gălēsŭs, Virg. Epith. Lăcĕdæmŏnĭŭs, Spārtānŭs, Thērāpnæŭs; ūmbrōsŭs, pĭgĕr, lēntŭs; Œbălĭŭs, liquĭdŭs,
ālbŭs.—2. *the name of a man.* Sēnĭōrquĕ Gălēsŭs, Virg.

Gălilœă, œ, f., *a part of Palestine.* Fōrtĕ Gălīlæĭs, Prud. Tērrās Gălīlæ, Juven.
Epith. Fēlīx, īllūstrĭs, nōbĭlĭs.

gāllă, æ, f., *a gall-nut.* Ēt tūnsūm gāllæ, Virg.

Gāllī, ōrŭm, m. pl., *priests of Cybele.* Trīstĭă Gāllī, Lucan. Syn. Cŏrȳbāntĕs.
Epith. Phrȳgēs, sānguĭnĕĭ, rĕsŭpīnătĭ, sacrĭfĭcĭ, sēctĭ, sēmĭvĭrĭ.—2. *the Gauls,*
Frenchmen. Syn. Frāncī, Frāncĭgēnæ, Cēltæ. Epith. Gĕnĕrōsī, bēllĭcōsī,
fōrtēs, māgnănĭmī, īndŏmĭtī, fŭrĭōsī, bēllĭgĕrī, Mārtĭī, aūdācēs, īntrĕpĭdī, ēffĕrī,
ārdēntēs, fĕrōcēs, cūltī, hūmānī, mānsuĕtī, bĕnīgnī, dōctī, fācūndī, īngĕnĭōsī,
ācrēs, cōmēs, sōlērtēs, săgācēs.

Gāllĭă, œ, f., *France.* Gāllĭă fērt ācrēs ănĭmōs, ĕt ĭdōnĕă bēllō, Mart. Syn.
Frāncĭă. Epith. Ănĭmōsă, fĕrōx, dīvēs, ărmĭpŏtēns, fērtĭlĭs, pīnguĭs, fœcūndă,
fĕrāx, ŏpīmă, clāră, nōbĭlĭs, īnsĭgnĭs, īnclȳtă, sŭpērbă, pŏtēns, īntrĕpĭdă, īmpăvĭdă, Mārtĭă, bēllĭcă, Măvōrtĭă, īndŏmĭtă, aūdāx, māgnĭfĭcă, gĕnĕrōsă,
fŭrĭōsă.

Gāllĭcānŭs, *and* cŭs, ă, ŭm, *French.* Gāllĭcă quī Phrȳgĭŭm, Ov.

gāllīnă, æ, f., *a hen.* Nēc gāllīnă mălŭm, Hor. Epith. Crīstātă, strēnŭă, sēdŭlă,
sōlĕrs, sōllĭcĭtă, vĭgĭl.

Gāllĭo, ōnĭs, m., *a man's name.* Gāllĭŏ, crīmĕn ĕrĭt, Ov.

Gāllōnĭŭs, ĭī, m., *a man's name.* Gāllōnĭ præcōnĭs ĕrĭt, Hor.

gāllŭs, ī, n., *a cock.* Ăvŏlāvĭt gāllŭs gāllīnācĕŭs, (Iamb.) Titin. Syn. Gāllīnācĕŭs.
Epith. Tītānĭŭs, vĭgĭl, sŭpērbŭs, īnsōmnĭs, pērvĭgĭl, cănōrŭs, sŏnōrŭs, Mārtĭŭs,
bēllĭgĕr.

gănĕo, ōnĭs, m., *a rioter.* Gănĕŏ, pŭltēs, Juv. Epith. Tūrpĭs, ēbrĭŭs.

Gāngărĭdœ, ārŭm, m. pl., *a people on the Ganges.* Pŭgnām Gāngărĭdŭm, Virg.

Gāngēs, ĭs *or* ētĭs, m., *a river in India.* Gāngētīsquĕ rĕplĕt, Virg. Epith. Cōrnĭgĕr, Īndĭcŭs, Īndŭs, Eōŭs, răpĭdŭs, ūndāns, dīvēs, aūrĭfĕr, tōrrēns, māgnŭs,
gēmmĭfĕr, flāvŭs.

Gāngētĭcŭs, ă, ŭm, *and* tĭs, ĭdĭs, *of the Ganges.* Gāngētĭcă tēllŭs, Lucan. Gān-
gētĭdĭs ōræ, Av. Syn. Īndŭs, Īndĭcŭs.

gānnĭo, *to bark, whisper.* Gānnĭt īn aūrēm, Pers. Syn. Gārrĭo, ōbstrĕpo.

gānnītŭs, ūs, m., *a whining.* Ēt gānnītĭbŭs īmprŏbĭs, (Phal.) Mart. Epith.
Strĕpēns, trĕmŭlŭs.

Gănȳmēdēs, ĭs, m., *the cupbearer of Jupiter.* Gănȳmēdĭs hŏnōrēs, Virg. Syn.
Īllădēs. Epith. Pūlchĕr, ūrnĭgĕr, vĕnūstŭs, fōrmōsŭs, cāndĭdŭs, lāctĕŭs, rŏsĕŭs,
nĭvĕŭs, dĕcōrŭs, blāndŭs, flāvŭs, rēgĭŭs, nōbĭlĭs.

Gănȳmēdĕŭs, ă, ŭm, *of Ganymede.* Ēt Gănȳmēdēō, Mart.

Gărāmās, āntĭs, m., Gărămāntĕs, ŭm, m. pl., *a nation of Africa.* Rhŏdōpē, aūt
ēxtrēmī Gărămūntĕs, Virg. Epith. Nūdī, ūstī, pĕrŭstī, īncūltī, sævī, vēlōcēs,
ĭnōpēs, văgī, ărēnĭvăgī, īnfēlīcēs, ātrī, fĕrōcēs, trŭcēs, ădūstī, săgĭttĭfĕrī, tēlĭgĕrī,
phăretrătī.

Gărămăntĭcŭs, ă. ŭm, *and* tĭs, ĭdĭs, f., *of the Garamantes.* Gărămăntĭcŭs ĭncŏlă lūcĭs, Sil. Gărămăntĭdĕ nymphā, Virg.

Gărgūnŭs, ī, m., *a mountain in Apulia.* Vīctŏr Gārgānī, Virg. Syn. Mŏns Apŭlŭs, Iāpyx. Epith. Ardŭŭs, sŭblimĭs, săcĕr.

Gărgăphĭē, ēs, f., *a valley near Platæa.* Nōmĭnĕ Gărgăphĭē, Ov.

Gārgărŭs, ī, m., *the summit of Mount Ida.* Epith. Ardŭŭs, Phrygĭŭs, Idæŭs, fēlīx, flāvēscēns, cūltŭs, fœcŭndŭs.

Gŭrgĭlĭŭs, ī, m., *a man's name.* Gărgĭlĭŭs quī mānĕ, Hor.

gărrĭo, īs, īvī *or* ĭī, *to chatter.* Gărrĭs ĭn aurĕm, Mart. Syn. Gārrītum ēdo nūgŏr. V. Garrulus.

gărrŭlĭtăs. ātĭs, f., *prattling.* Gărrŭlĭtātĕ sŭī, Mart. Syn. Vērbōsĭtăs, lŏquācĭtăs. Epith. Ŏdĭōsă, īnsānă, ācrĭs, īntēmpēstīvă, īmpōrtūnă, mēndāx, mŏlēstă, fœmĭnĕă, prŏcāx, lōngă, nĭmĭă, lītĭgĭōsă.

gărrŭlŭs, ă, ŭm, *talkative.* Gārrŭlŭs ĭdem ēst, Hor. Syn. Lŏquāx, nūgāx, dīcāx, vānĭlŏquŭs. V. Garrio.

gărŭm, ī, n., *a sort of pickle.* Prēssīt cēllă gărŏ, Hor.

Gărūmnă, æ, f., *a river in France.* Ūndă Gărūmnæ, Cl. Epith. Æquŏrĕŭs, vălĭdŭs, vēlĭvŏlŭs, răpĭdŭs, cĕlĕr, māgnŭs, āmœnŭs, grătŭs, præcēps, sĭnŭōsŭs. V. Fluvius.

gaudĕo, gāvīsŭs sŭm, *to rejoice.* Gaudēntquĕ tŭēntēs, Virg. Syn. Lætŏr, ŏvo, ēxŭlto, gēstĭo.

gaudĭŭm, ĭī, n., *joy.* Gaudĭă fāllūnt, Ov. Syn. Lætĭtĭă, vŏlŭptās, ōblēctāmēntŭm, jŏcŭs, plausŭs. Epith. Lætŭm, dūlcĕ, fēstīvŭm, bĕātŭm, sēcūrŭm, blāndŭm, spērātŭm, vērŭm, rĕpēntīnŭm, brĕvĕ, fŭgāx, fāllāx, fŭgĭtīvŭm, īnstăbĭlĕ, ēffūsŭm, nĭmĭŭm, ōptātŭm, trĭŭmphālĕ, īnsŏlĭtŭm, pĭŭm, nŏvŭm, sōlēnnĕ, prŏfānŭm.

gāvīsŭs, ă, ŭm, *the partic. of* gaudeo. Dārdănĭō gāvīsŭs Ātrīdă, Prop.

Gaūrŭs, ī, m., *a mountain in Italy.* Vīnētă mădēntĭă Gaūrī, Stat.

gaūsăpă, æ, f., *and* ŭpĕ, ĭs, n., *a shaggy cloth.* Gaūsăpĕ pūrpŭrĕŏ, Hor.

gāză, æ, f., *treasure.* Nōbĭlĭbŭs gāzīs, Cl. Syn. Dīvĭtĭæ, thēsaūrī, ŏpēs, pĕcūnĭă. Epith. Dīvēs, prētĭōsă, pĕregrīnă, Eŏă, Pērsĭcă, Asĭătĭcă. V. Divitiæ.

Gĕhēnnă, æ, f., *hell.* Dāmnētquĕ Gĕhēnnæ, Prud. Epith. Ōbscūră, hōrrĭdă, tētră, mĕtŭēndă, căvă.

Gĕlās, *or* Gĕlă, æ, m., *a river and city of Sicily.* Īmmānĭsquĕ Gĕlā, Virg.

gĕlăsĭnŭs, ī, m., *a dimple.* Cuī gĕlăsĭnŭs ăbēst, Mart.

gĕlĭdē, adv., *coldly.* Gĕlĭdēquĕ mĭnīstrăt, Hor.

gĕlĭdŭs, ă, ŭm, *chilly.* Sēd gĕlĭdŭm Bŏrĕān, Ov. Syn. Gĕlātŭs, cōngĕlātŭs frĭgĭdŭs. V. Frigidus.

gĕlo, ās, *to freeze.* Păvĭdōquĕ gĕlāntŭr, Juv. Syn. Cōngĕlo, cōnglăcĭo, īndūro, dūrēsco, gĕlāsco. V. Frigeo, hyems.

Gĕlōnī, ōrŭm, m. pl., *a people of Thrace.* Pīctōsquĕ Gĕlōnōs, Virg. Epith. Ācrēs, săgĭttĭfĕrī, vŏlucrēs, sævī, flāvī, īmpĕrĭōsī, dīspērsī, fĕrōcēs, īmmītēs, fōrtēs, lăcērtōsī. V. Bisaltæ.

gĕlū, n., *(indecl.) frost.* Rūră gĕlū tŭm, Virg. Syn. Glăcĭēs, frĭgŭs. Epith. Glăcĭālĕ, hyĕmālĕ, pigrŭm, ārctŭm, āstrīctŭm, cōncrētŭm, cānēus, cānŭm, sævŭm, mārmŏrĕŭm, nĭvālĕ, hōrrēns, dēnsŭm. V. Gelo, frigus.

gĕmĕbūndŭs, ă, ŭm, *sighing.* Tōtăm gĕmĭbūndŭs ōbāmbŭlăt, Cl. Syn. Gĕmēns. V. Gemo.

gĕmēllī, ōrŭm, m. pl., *(fratres,) twins.* Nāmquĕ gĕmēllōs, Virg. Syn. Gĕmĭnī.

gĕmēllĭpără, æ, f., *mother of twins.* Cūrvă gĕmēllĭpāræ, Ov.

gĕmēllŭs, ă, ŭm, *twin.* Prōlēmquĕ gĕmēllăm, Ov.

Gĕmĭnī, ōrŭm. m. pl., *Castor and Pollux.* Tyndărĭdæ Gĕmĭnī, Ov. V. Castor.

gĕmĭno, ās, *to double.* Lăbŏr gĕmĭnāvĕrăt æstŭm, Ov. Syn. Ingĕmĭno, cōngĕmĭno, duplĭco, cōndŭplĭco, cōmbīno ; rĕpĕto, ĭtĕro.

gĕmĭnŭs, ă, ŭm, *double, two, twin.* Ēt trĭpŏdăs gĕmĭnōs, Virg. Syn. Gĕmēllŭs, gĕmĭnātŭs, duplēx, dŭo, bīnī.

gĕmĭtŭs, ŭs, m., *a groan.* Extrēmōsquĕ cĭēt gĕmĭtŭs, Virg. Syn. Lūctŭs, sūspīrĭă, plānctŭs, plāngŏr, lāmēntŭm, flētŭs, quĕrēlă, quēstŭs, clāmŏr, ŭlŭlātŭs. Epith. Trīstĭs, mœstŭs, ăcērbŭs, frĕmēns, sævŭs, dūrŭs, ămārŭs, grăvĭs, mœrēns, lacrymābĭlĭs, ægĕr, mĭsĕrāndŭs, atrōx, lōngŭs, tūrbĭdŭs, quĕrŭlŭs, fœmĭnĕŭs, rĕsŏnāns, crēbĕr, ĭtĕrātŭs, pērpĕtŭŭs, fīctŭs, ēxōsŭs. V. Gemo.

gĕmmă, æ, f., *a precious stone.* Sæpĕ vĕlŭt gĕmmās, Tib. SYN. Lăpĭllŭs; cŏnchă, băcchă; Ăchātēs, Ădămās, Ămĕthўstŭs, Bērўllŭs, Chrўsŏlĭthŭs, Cўănŭs, Hўăcīnthŭs, Iāspĭs, Mārgărītă, *or* Unĭo; Ŏnўx, Sārdŏnўx, Sāpphīrŭs, Smărāgdŭs, Tŏpāzŭs, Pўrōpŭs. EPITH. Cŏlōrătă, tŭmēns, nēxĭlĭs, lūcĭdă, nĭtĭdă, rŭtĭlă, mĭcāns, rădĭāns, scīntīllāns, Indĭcă, dīvĕs, īgnĕă, Gărămāntĭs, pērspĭcŭă, fūlgēns, ārdēns, Iāspĭdĕă, prĕtĭōsă, cūltă, rădĭōsă, fūlgĭdă, clāră, Scўthĭcă, stēllāns, pūră, flāmmātă, Eŏă, nĭtēns, cŏrūscă; Indă, sīdĕrĕă, pēllūcĭdă, vĭrĭdĭs, pĕregrīnă, Ěrythrǽă, Gāngĕtĭcă, tĕrĕs. V. Orno.—2. *a young bud.* In pālmĭtĕ gĕmmæ, Virg. SYN. Gērmĕn, ŏcŭlŭs, sūrcŭlŭs.

gĕmmāns, āntĭs, *glittering with gems.* Gĕmmāntĭă dēxtrā, Ov.

gĕmmātŭs, ă, ŭm, *set with precious stones.* Tĕrĕtĭ gĕmmātă mŏnīlĭă cōllō, Ov. SYN. Gĕmmīs ōrnātŭs, rădĭāns, cŏrūscŭs, ŏnĕrātŭs, ŏnūstŭs, dīstīnctŭs, mĭcāns.

gĕmmĕŭs, ă, ŭm, *of a precious stone.* Gĕmmĕă tēctă, Mart.

gĕmmĭfĕr, ă, ŭm, *wearing precious stones.* Ět frĕtă gĕmmĭfĕrī, Prop.

gĕmmo, ās, *to bud.* Gĕmmāvĭt pāmpĭnŭs ūvĭs, Enn.

gĕmo, ŭĭ, ĭtŭm, *to groan.* Ět gĕmŭĭt; gĕmĭtŭs, Ov. SYN. Ingĕmo, gĕmīsco, lūgĕo, sūspīro, quĕrŏr, plāngo. V. Gemitus, fleo.

gĕnæ, ārŭm, f. pl., *the cheeks.* Pēndēntēsquĕ gĕnās, Juv. SYN. Mălæ. EPITH. Pūlchræ, pūrpŭrĕæ, āmbrŏsĭæ, nĭtĭdæ, ĕbūrnĕæ, nĭvĕæ, rŏsĕæ, dĕcōræ, cāndēntēs, cŏlōrātæ, ālbēntēs, nĭvōsæ, rŭbēntēs, jŭvĕnīlēs, vĕrēcūndæ, vĕnūstæ, rŭbēscēntēs, tĕnēllæ, blāndæ, tŭmĭdæ, sĕnīlēs, rūgōsæ, hīrsūtæ, ērāsæ, sĕvēræ; tābēntēs, mœstæ, pāllēntēs, hūmēntēs, mădĭdæ, ūdæ.

Gĕnaūnī, ōrŭm, m. pl., *a people of Vindelicia.* Drūsŭs Gĕnaūnōs.

|| gĕnĕālŏgŭs, ī, m., *a writer of genealogies.* Ăĭt gĕnĕālŏgŭs īdĕm, Prud.

gĕnĕr, ĕrī, m., *a son-in-law.* Sĭnŭnt: gĕnĕrōs ēxtērnīs, Virg.

gĕnĕrālĭs, ĕ, *universal.* Măcŭlās gĕnĕrālēs, Lucr.

gĕnĕrāsco, ĭs, *to breed.* Ævō gĕnĕrāscŭnt ingĕnĭōquĕ, Lucr.

gĕnĕrātĭm, adv., *generally.* Ō prŏprĭōs gĕnĕrātĭm, Virg.

|| gĕnĕrātĭo, ōnĭs, f., *a generation.* Quŏnĭăm gĕnĕrātĭŏ nōn ēst, Prud. SYN. Prōdūctĭo; prŏgĕnĭēs, prŏpāgo, gĕnŭs.

gĕnĕrātŏr, ōrĭs, m., *a producer.* Gĕnĕrātŏr ĕquōrŭm, Virg. SYN. Sătŏr, părēns.

gĕnĕrātŭs, *the pass. partic. of* genero. Trōjā gĕnĕrātŭs Ăcēstēs, Virg.

gĕnĕro, ās, *to beget.* Dĕŏ gĕnĕrārĕt ŭt ēssĕt, Alcim. SYN. Prōgĕnĕro, gīgno, prōgĭgno, crĕo, prōcrĕo, prōdūco; părĭo. V. Pario.

gĕnĕrōsŭs, ă, ŭm, *noble, generous.* Nēmō gĕnĕrōsĭŏr ēst tē, Hor. SYN. Nōbĭlĭs; fōrtĭs, aūdāx, māgnănĭmŭs, īntrĕpĭdŭs, ănĭmōsŭs, īmpăvĭdŭs, īntērrĭtŭs. V. Fortis.

gĕnĕsĭs, ĭs, f., *birth, nativity.* Gĕnĕsĭs tŭă, Juv

gĕnĭālĭs, ĕ, *cheerful, pleasant.* Lūcēnt gĕnĭālĭbŭs āltĭs, Virg. SYN. Gĕnĭŏ săcĕr, fēstŭs; lætŭs, fēstīvŭs, dēlĭcĭōsŭs, ămœnŭs, dāpsĭlĭs, laūtŭs.

gĕnĭālĭtĕr, adv., *pleasantly.* Fēstŭm gĕnĭālĭtĕr ĕgĭt, Ov.

gĕnĭstă, æ, f., *broom.* Lēntæquĕ gĕnĭstæ, Virg. SYN. Spārtŭm. EPITH. Hŭmĭlĭs, vĭrĭdĭs, lēntă, flēxĭlĭs.

gĕnĭtābĭlĭs, *and* tālĭs, ĕ, *serving to engender.* Vĭgĕt gĕnĭtābĭlĭs aūră, Lucr. Dīs gĕnĭtālĭbŭs ævŭm, Prop.

gĕnĭtŏr, ōrĭs, m, *a father.* Pĕnēī gĕnĭtōrĭs ăd ūndăm, Virg. SYN. Gĕnĕrātŏr, prōgĕnĭtŏr, sătŏr, pārēns, pătĕr. V. Pater.

gĕnĭtrīx, īcĭs, f., *a mother.* Mīrāns gĕnĭtrīcĭs, ĕt, Virg. SYN. Pārēns, mātĕr. V. Mater.

gĕnĭtŭs, ă, ŭm, *the pass. partic. of* gigno. Dīs quānquăm gĕnĭtī, Virg.

Gĕnĭŭs, ĭī, m., *a tutelary deity, genius, inclination.* Māgnĕ Gĕnī, căpĕ, Virg. Indūlgē gĕnĭō, Ov. SYN. Tūtēlārĭs Dĕŭs; vŏlūptātĭs Dĕŭs. EPITH. Dēxtĕr, bŏnŭs, faūstŭs, sĕcūndŭs, fēlīx, faūtŏr, ămīcŭs, fīdŭs, cōmĕs, dūx, nātālĭs, hĭlărĭs, lætŭs, jūcūndŭs, fēstīvŭs.

gēns, ēntĭs, f., *a race.* Gēntĭbŭs īn nōstrīs, Juv. SYN. Sŏbŏlēs, prŏgĕnĭēs, prōlēs, gĕnŭs, stīrps, sānguĭs, prŏpāgo; pŏpŭlŭs, nātĭo.

gēntīlĭs, ĕ, *of the same house.* Nĕc nōn gēntīlĭă tўmpănă, Juv.

gĕnū, n., (*indecl.*) *the knee.* Ět gĕnŭa āmplēxŭs, Virg. SYN. Poplĕs. EPITH. Prōcĭdŭŭm, sūccĭdŭŭm, hŭmĭlĕ, cūrvātŭm, flēxŭm, īmmīssŭm, īncūrvŭm, sūpplēx, lābāns, trĕmēns, fīrmŭm, cērtŭm, tĭtŭbāns, dūrŭm.

gĕnŭālĭă, ŭm, n. pl., *a kind of hose to cover the knees.* Pīctō gĕnŭālĭă līmbō, Ov.

* gĕnŭīnŭs, ă, ŭm, *natural.* Syn. Nātīvŭs.—2. ŭs, ī, m., *the jaw-tooth.* Quī gĕnŭīnum ăgĭtēnt, Juv.

gĕnŭs, ĕrĭs, n., *a kindred, sort.* Nām gĕnŭs, ĕt prŏăvōs, Ov. Syn. Gēns, gēntī-lĭtās, ōrtŭs, ŏrīgo, stīrps, sānguĭs; prŏpāgo, prŏgĕnĭēs; stēmmă. Epith. Nŏbĭlĕ, āntīquŭm, clārŭm, īllūstrĕ, vĕtŭs, rēgĭŭm, præclārŭm, nōtŭm, rēgālĕ, īgnŏbĭlĕ, ăbjēctŭm, vīlĕ, hŭmĭlĕ, sōrdĭdŭm, īgnōtŭm. V. Nobilis, ignobilis.

gĕōmĕtră, æ, *or* trēs, *and* geōmetrēs, *(trisyl.)* ĭs, m., *a geometrician.* Rhētōr, geō-mētrēs, pīctōr, Juv.

Gērmānī, ōrŭm, m. pl., *the Germans.* Syn. Ălĕmānnī, Teūtŏnī *or* nĕs; Sĭcāmbrī. Epith. Invīctī, pŏtēntēs, fĕrōcēs, bēllācēs, aūdācēs, fōrtēs.

Gērmānĭă, æ, f., *Germany.* Aūt Gērmānĭă Tīgrĭm, Virg. Syn. Ălĕmānnĭă, Epith. Aūdāx, fĕrōx, pŏtēns, dīvĕs, bārbără, hōrrĭdă, ĕffĕră, fĕră; dīră, bēllā-trīx, bēllĭcōsă, pērfĭdă, frīgĭdă, pūgnāx, atrōx, fōrtĭs.

Gērmānĭcŭs, *and* ānŭs, ă, ŭm, *of Germany.* Quĕm Gērmānĭcŭs ōrĕ, Mart. Gēr-mānĭs īnfĭcĭt hĕrbīs, Ov. Syn. Teūtŏnĭcŭs.

gērmānŭs, ī, m., *brother;* ă, æ, f., *sister.* Tÿrī gērmānŭs hăbēbăt, Virg. Syn. Frātĕr; ăgnātŭs.—2. ă, ŭm, *true.* Gērmānō nōmĭnĕ, Pl. Syn. Vērŭs. V. Verus.

gērmĕn, ĭnĭs, n., *a sprout.* Ārbŏrĕ gērmĕn, Virg. Syn. Sēmĕn, stīrps. Epith. Mōllĕ, tūrgēns, ŏdōrŭm, flōrĭfĕrŭm, āmbrŏsĭŭm, fœcūndŭm, gĕnĭtālĕ, pūbēns. V. Germino.

gērmĭno, ās, *to bud.* Gērmĭnăt, ĕt nūnquām făllēntīs tērmĕs ŏlīvæ, Hor. Syn. Prŏgērmĭno, pūllŭlo, gēmmo. V. Frutico.

gĕro, ēssī, ēstŭm, *to bear, to do.* Āspĕră sī gĕrĭtĭs, Mart. Syn. Făcĭo; ădmĭ-nīstro; pōrto, gēsto, fĕro.

gĕro, ōnĭs, *and* ŭlŭs, ī, m., *a porter.* Mŭlīs gĕrŭlīsquĕ, Hor. Syn. Bājŭlŭs.

Gērÿōn, ŏnĭs, *and* ŏnēs, æ, m., *a giant with three bodies.* Tērgĕmĭnī nĕcĕ Gērÿŏnĭs, Virg. Gērÿōn trĭplēx, Cl. Epith. Trĭcōrpŏr, trĭfōrmĭs, vāstŭs, fĕrŭs, fĕrōx, īmmānĭs, mĭnāx, fōrtĭs, aūdāx, crūdēlĭs, hŏrrēndŭs, Ībĕrŭs.

gēstāmĕn, ĭnĭs, n., *anything worn.* Māgnī gēstāmĕn Ăbāntĭs, Virg.

gēstātĭo, ōnĭs, f., *a carrying.* Gēstātĭō, făbŭlæ, Mart.

gēstātŏr, ōrĭs, m., *a porter.* Gēstātōr pătĕt, Mart.

gēstĭo, īs, īvī, *to exult.* Incāssŭm gēstīrĕ lăvāndī, Virg. Syn. Exūlto, lætŏr, gaūdĕo. V. Gaudeo.

gēsto, ās, *the frequent. of* gero. Ădĕō gēstāmŭs pēctŏră, Virg. Syn. Gĕro, pōrto, fĕro.

gēstŭs, ūs, m., *a gesture.* Īllă plăcĕt gēstŭ, Ov. Syn. Āctĭo, mōtŭs. Epith. Lŏquēns, pĕtŭlāns, grātŭs, mōllĭs, sŏlūtŭs, dĕcōrŭs, hŏnēstŭs, scēnĭcŭs.

gēsŭm, gēssŭm, *or* gæsŭm, ī, n., *a kind of dart used by the Gauls.* Fūndĕrĕ gēsă rŏtĭs, Prop.

Gĕtă, *and* Gĕtēs, æ, m., Gĕtæ, ārŭm, m. pl., *people of Scythia.* Dēsērtă Gĕtārŭm, Virg. Epith. Hÿbērnī, āstūtī, rĭgĭdī, īnfēstī, squālĭdī, dūrī, ĭnhūmānī, hīrsūtī, trŭcēs, fĕrī, fĕrōcēs, īndŏmĭtī, īntōnsī, bārbărĭcī, phărĕtrātī, Thrācĭī, Thrēĭcĭī.

Gĕtĭcŭs, ă, ŭm, *of the Getæ.* Hānc tŭŭs ē Gĕtĭcō, Ov.

gĭbbă, æ, f.; bĕr, ĕrĭs, *and* bŭs, bī, m., *a bunch.* Gĭbbōquĕ tŭmēntĕm, Juv. Gĭbbĕrĕ nāsŭs, Ov.

gĭgāntēs, ŭm, m. pl., *giants.* Tōrmēntă gĭgāntŭm, Prop. Syn. Tītānēs, tērrĭ-gĕnæ. Epith. Īmmānēs, hōrrēndī, sŭpērbī, aūdācēs, vāstī, tŭmĭdī, fĕrī, fŭ-rēntēs, īmpăvĭdī, crūdēlēs, bārbărī, pŏtēntēs, sævī, mĕtŭēndī, hōrrĭbĭlēs, fŭrĭōsī, dīrī, tērrĭfĭcī, īntērrĭtī, mĭnācēs, trŭcŭlēntī, tĕtrī, ăcērbī, nĕfāndī, īmmītēs, scĕlĕrātī, īmpĭī, ānguĭpĕdēs, Ætnæī; Phlĕgræī.

gĭgāntēŭs, ă, ŭm, *gigantic.* Sīvĕ gĭgāntēă, Prop.

gīgno, gĕnŭī, gĕnĭtŭm, *to beget.* Tālĕm gĕnŭĕrĕ părēntēs, Virg. V. Genero.

gīlvŭs, ă, ŭm, *of an ash-colour.* Et gīlvō, Virg.

gīngīvă, æ, f., *the gum of a tooth.* Mĭsĕrō gīngīvă pānĭs ĭnērmī, Juv.

glăbĕr, bră, brŭm, *bald.* Crūrĕ glăbĕr, Mart.

glăcĭālĭs, ĕ, *frozen.* Ēt glăcĭālĭs hÿēms, Ov. Syn. Gĕlĭdŭs, prŭīnōsŭs, ālgĭdŭs, frīgĭdŭs.

glăcĭēs, lēī, f., *ice.* Nĕ tĕnĕrās glăcĭēs sĕcĕt, Virg. Epith. Āspĕră, nĭvālĭs, cōncrētă, sōlĭdă, rĭgēns, dūrātă, Ālpīnă; Rīphæă; dūră, lūcĭdă, frăgĭlĭs. V. Gelu.

glăcĭo, ăs, *to freeze.* Ot glăcĭēt nĭvēs, (Choriamb.) Hor. Syn. Cōnglăcĭo, gĕlo, cōngĕlo.

glădĭātŏr, ōrĭs, m., *a gladiator.* Mĕdĭām glădĭātŏr ărēnăm, Juv. Syn. Pūgĭl, lūctātŏr, lănīstă. Epith. Fŏrtĭs, rŏbūstŭs, nūdŭs, tŭnĭcātŭs. V. Athleta.

glădĭŭs, ĭī, m., *a sword.* Prīmĭ glădĭōs ēxtēndĕrĕ, Juv. Syn. Ensĭs, fĕrrŭm, pūgĭo, sĭcă, mūcro, cūspĭs, ăcĭēs. Epith. Fūlgēns, mĭnāx, fĕrrĕŭs, āncēps. V. Ensis.

glāndĭfĕr, ĕră, ŭm, *bearing acorns.* Glāndĭfĕrās īntĕr, Lucr.

glāndĭŭm, ĭ, n., *and* ŭlă, œ, *a neck of pork.* Pārtītŭr āprĭ glāndŭlās, Mart.

glāns, āndĭs, f., *an acorn.* Glāndĭbŭs īngēns, Stat. Epith. Dūră, sỹlvēstrĭs, ēxcūssă, vīrēns, agrēstĭs, hỹbērnă, vĕtŭs, cădūcă, quērnă, ĭlĭgnă, æscŭlă, Chāŏnĭă. —2. *a bullet.* Epith. Plūmbĕă, fērrĕă, ăhēnă, mĭssă, vŏlāns, vŏlucrĭs, mĭssĭlĭs, Ignĕă, vūlnĭfĭcă.

glăphĭrŭs, ă, ŭm, *polished.* Plaūdĕrĕ nēc glăphĭrō, Mart.

glārĕă, æ, f., *gravel.* Glārĕă rūrĭs, Virg. Syn. Ărēnă. Epith. Flăvă, jējūnă, dūră, stĕrĭlĭs.

glaūcŭs, *and* cĭnŭs, ă, ŭm, *of a sea-green colour.* Lūmĭnĕ glaūcō, Virg. Glaūcĭnă, Cōsmĕ, Mart. Syn. Cœrŭlŭs, cœrŭlĕŭs, vĭrĭdĭs, vĭrēns, cæsĭŭs, prăsĭnŭs.

Glaūcŭs, ĭ, m., *a sea-god; name of several persons.* Glaūcĭ Pōtnĭādēs, Virg. —2. *a fish.* Cōnspēctŭs tēmpŏrĕ glaūcŭs, Ov.

glēbă, æ, *dimin.* glēbŭlă, f., *a clod.* Sē glēbă rĕsŏlvĭt, Virg. Syn. Cēspĕs. Epith. Jăcēns, ĭnērs, pĭnguĭs, sĭccă, fœcūndă, mădĭdă, fērtĭlĭs, hūmēns, cāmpēstrĭs, ēffōssă, fĕrāx, spĭcĕă. V. Arare.

glĭs, glīrĭs, m., *a dormouse.* Pŏrrĭgĭt glīrēs, (Scaz.) Mart. Syn. ᾿Mūs Ālpīnŭs. Epith. Inērs, pĭgĕr, hỹbērnŭs, sŏpōrātŭs, dōrmītŏr, brĕvĭs, Ālpīnŭs.

glĭsco, ĭs, *to grow.* Glīscĭt vĭŏlēntĭă Tūrnō, Virg. Syn. Crēsco, āccrēsco, aūgēsco, īnvălēsco.

glŏbōsŭs, ă, ŭm, *round as a globe.* Ēssĕ glŏbōsă tămĕn, Lucr. Syn. Rŏtūndŭs, ōrbĭcŭlātŭs.

glŏbŭs, ĭ, m., *a globe.* Quĭs glŏbŭs, ō cīvēs, Virg. Syn. Sphœră, ōrbĭs. Epith. Rŏtūndŭs, lævĭs, dēnsŭs, tōrnātĭlĭs. V. Turbo, turba, glans.

glŏmĕrāmĕn, ĭnĭs, n., *a heap.* Fōrmæ glŏmĕrāmĕn ĭn ūnŭm, Lucr. Syn. Gỹrŭs; cōngĕrĭēs.

glŏmĕro, ăs, *to heap.* Pārvōs glŏmĕrābĭs ĭn ōrbēs, Stat. Syn. Ăgglŏmĕro, āggĕro, cōnvĕho, āccŭmŭlo. V. Accumulo.

glŏrĭă, æ, f., *glory.* Glōrĭă lēthĭ, Stat. Syn. Laūs, hŏnŏr, dĕcŭs; nōmĕn, fāmă, splēndŏr. Epith. Inclỹtă, ārdŭă, ĭnānĭs, vēntōsă, frăgĭlĭs, nōbĭlĭs, fŭgĭtīvă, brĕvĭs, mūtābĭlĭs, ōptātă, dēbĭtă, mĕrĭtă, īnsĭgnĭs, măgnă, pĕrēnnĭs, sūmmă, trĭūmphālĭs, īnvĭdĭōsă, cēlebrĭs, ŏpĕrōsă, ĭnmōrtālĭs, vīvāx, āmbĭtĭōsă, fēlīx. V. Nomen.

glŏrĭŏr, ārĭs, *to boast.* Pĕdĭbūsquĕ glŏrĭārĭ, (Phal.) Mart. Syn. Ōstēnto, jăcto, jăctĭto. V. Superbio.

glŏrĭōsŭs, ă, ŭm, *glorious.* Glōrĭōsă tālĭ, Mart. Syn. Clārŭs, īnclỹtŭs, īnsĭgnĭs, cōnspĭcŭŭs.

glōs, ōrĭs, f., *a sister-in-law.* Āndrŏmăchē glōs, Aus.

glūtĕn, ĭnĭs, n., *glue.* Glūtĭnĕ mātĕrĭēs, Lucr. Syn. Glūtĭnŭm, vīscŭs, vīscŭm. Epith. Tĕnāx, fōrtĕ, vălĭdŭm, strĭngēns, lēntŭm, vīscōsŭm.

glūtĭnĕŭs, *and* nōsŭs, ă, ŭm, *clammy.* Quæ pĕdĕ glūtĭnĕō, Rut. Syn. Vīscōsŭs.

glūtĭno, ăs, *to glue.* Glūtĭnăt āmbās, Pr. Syn. Cōnglūtĭno, āgglūtĭno.

glūtĭo, ĭs, *to swallow.* Ipsŭm glūtĭssĕ pŭtāmŭs, Juv.

glūto, ōnĭs, m., *a glutton.* Crēdĭt glūtōnĕm, Anthol.

glūtŭs, ĭ, m., *the gullet.* Nēc glūtō sōrbĕrĕ, Pers.

Glỹcĕră, æ, *and* rē, ēs, *the name of a woman.* Mĕ Glỹcĕræ nĭtŏr, Hor.

Glỹcōn, ōnĭs, m., *a famous athlete.* Invĭctĭ mēmbră Glỹcōnĭs, Hor.

gnārŭs, ă, ŭm, *skilful.* Ărātŏr gnārŭs ēst, (Iamb.) Stat. Syn. Pĕrītŭs, sōlērs, ēxpērtŭs, scĭēns, dōctŭs, gnāvŭs, prūdēns.

gnātŭs, ĭ, m., *a son.* Gnātum ēxhōrtārĕr, Virg. Syn. Nātŭs, fīlĭŭs.

gnāvĭtĕr, adv., *lustily.* Gnāvĭtĕr īd quŏd, Hoɪ Sʏɴ. Förtĭtĕr, aūdāctĕr, sōlērtĕr.

gnāvŭs, ă, ŭm, *lusty.* Gnāvūs mānĕ fŏrŭm, Hor. Sʏɴ. Gnārŭs, sōlērs, strēnŭŭs, förtĭs, aūdāx, gĕnĕrōsŭs.

gnōmōn, ŏnĭs, m., *the pin of a dial.* Gnōmŏnās ībăt, Cl. Sʏɴ. Nōrmā, rĕgŭlā ; īndēx, stÿlŭs, ăcŭs.

Gnōssĭăcŭs, ssĭŭs, *and* ssŭs, ă, ŭm, *of Gnossus, a town of Crete.* Gnōssĭăcūm rēgnŭm, Stat. Gnōssĭăque ārdēntĭs, Ov. Gnōssās ăgĭtărĕ phărētrās, Luc.

Gnōssĭăs, ădĭs, *and* Gnōssĭs, ĭdĭs, f., *of Gnossus, of Crete.* Gnōssĭăs ūxŏr, Ov. Gnōssĭdă Bācchŭs, Id.

gōbĭo, ōnĭs, *or* bĭŭs, ĭī, m., *a gudgeon.* Gōbĭŭs ēssĕ, Mart. Eᴘɪᴛʜ. Căpĭtātŭs, pīngŭĭs, ŏpīmŭs, flŭvĭālĭs, āmnĭcŏlă.

Gŏlĭās, æ, *and* iāth, m., *a giant killed by David.* Anĭmīsquĕ Gŏlĭăm, Prud. Sʏɴ. Gŏliāthŭs. Eᴘɪᴛʜ. Sŭpērbŭs, mĭnāx, gĭgās, prōcērŭs, Phĭlīstæŭs.

Gŏrgē, ēs, f., *the daughter of Œneus.* Gērmānăquĕ Gŏrgē, Ov.

Gŏrgo *and* Gŏrgōn, ŏnĭs, f., *the name of the three daughters of Phorcus.* Gŏrgŏnĕ bĭs cēntŭm, Ov. Sʏɴ. Phōrcĭs, (ĭdĭs,) Phōrcÿs, Phōrcÿnĭs. Eᴘɪᴛʜ. Sævă, āspĕră, rĭgĭdă, tērrĭfĭcă, dūră, crŭēntă, hōrrēndă, hōrrĭbĭlĭs, fĕră, mĕtŭēndă, förmĭdābĭlĭs, bārbără, hōrrĭdă, sāxĭfĭcă, atrōx. V. Medusa.

Gŏrgŏnĕŭs, ă, ŭm, *of a Gorgon.* Exīn Gŏrgŏnēĭs, Virg. Sʏɴ. Mĕdū-sæŭs.

Gŏrtÿnă *and* nē, ēs, f., *a city of Crete.* Cērtăt Gŏrtÿnă săgĭttĭs, Stat.

Gŏrtÿnĭăcŭs *and* nĭŭs, ă, ŭm, *and* Gŏrtÿnĭs, ĭdĭs, f., *of Gortyna.* Nēc Gŏrtÿnĭăcō, Ov. Stăbŭla ād Gŏrtÿnĭă, Virg. Gŏrtÿnĭs ărūndo, Lucr.

Gŏthī, ōrŭm, m. pl., *the Goths.* Indĕ rĕfērrĕ Gŏthōs, Auson. Eᴘɪᴛʜ. Sævī, īmmānēs, dūrī, crūdēlēs, īnfrænēs, fĕrī, crūēntī, atrōcēs, ēffĕrī, fŭrĭōsī, scĕlĕrātī, Mārtĭī, Māvōrtĭī, ārmĭpŏtēntēs.

grăbātŭs, *and* tŭlŭs, ī, m., *a couch.* Spŏndă grăbātī, Mart. Sʏɴ. Cŭbĭlĕ, tŏrŭs, thălămŭs, strātŭm, lēctŭs. Eᴘɪᴛʜ. Tĕnŭĭs, mōllĭs, nōctūrnŭs, spūmōsŭs, plăcĭdŭs, vīlĭs. V. Lectus.

Grăcchŭs, ī, m., *the name of an illustrious Roman family.* Quīs tŭlĕrīt Grăcchōs, Juv.

grăcĭlēntŭs, ă, ŭm, *and* cĭlĭs, ĕ, *slender.* Fīlō grăcĭlēntō, Enn. Ĕt grăcĭlīs strūctōs, Ov. Sʏɴ. Exīlĭs, măcĭlēntŭs, tĕnŭĭs, pārvŭs, exĭgŭŭs.

grăcŭlŭs, ī, m., *a jackdaw.* Grăcŭlŭs aūctŏr, Ov.

grădātĭm, adv., *by degrees.* Dāmnărĕ grădātĭm, Prud. Sʏɴ. Sēnsĭm, paūlātĭm, pĕdĕtēntĭm.

grădĭŏr, ĕrĭs, *to walk.* Ipse ūnō grădĭtŭr, Virg. Sʏɴ. Incēdo, ĕo, vādo, āmbŭlo, tēndo, dīrĭgo, fĕro, tŏrquĕo, mŏlĭŏr. V. Incedo.

Gradīvŭs, ī, m., *a name of Mars.* Grādīvūmquĕ pătrĕm, Virg. Mīnāsquĕ Grădīvī, Val. V. Mars.

grădŭs, ūs, m., *a step.* Cōntră grădĭbūs sŭblīmĭă, Ov. Sʏɴ. Grēssŭs, pāssŭs, īncēssŭs. Eᴘɪᴛʜ. Cĕlĕr, præcēps, cĭtātŭs, vēlōx, præpĕs, văgŭs, prŏpĕrŭs, tārdŭs, lēntŭs, sēgnĭs, ĭnērs, dŭbĭŭs, cērtŭs, fīrmŭs, tĭtŭbāns, trĕmŭlŭs, răpĭdŭs, fŭgāx, sŭbĭtŭs, īncērtŭs, ănhēlŭs, sŭccĭdŭŭs, lābāns, fēssŭs, ægĕr, cŏmpŏsĭtŭs, sūspēnsŭs, sūblīmĭs, sŭpērbŭs. V. Gradior.—2. *a stair.* Eᴘɪᴛʜ. Sūrgēns, scānsĭlĭs, āssūrgēns.

Græcī, ōrŭm, m. pl., *the Greeks.* Quŏd rŭdĭs ēt Græcĭs, Hor. Sʏɴ. Graiī, Grājŭgĕnæ, Argīvī, Pĕlāsgī, Ăchīvī, Achæī, Ăchāĭcī, Argŏlĭcī, Dănāī, Ināchĭī, Dōrĭcī. Eʀɪᴛʜ. Fācūndī, lŏquācēs, mēndācēs, fāllācēs, ārmĭgĕrī, pŏtēntēs, pūg-nācēs, bēllācēs, aūdācēs, sōlērtēs, săgācēs, vānī.

Græcĭă, æ, f., *Greece.* Græcĭă mēndāx, Juv. Sʏɴ. Hēllăs, Ăchāĭă. Eᴘɪᴛʜ. Fāllāx, vīndēx, sōlērs, dōctă, ūltrīx, vānă, vĕtŭs, gārrŭlă, lŏquāx, dĭsērtă, fā-cūndă, fērtĭlĭs, īngĕnĭōsă.

Græcīnŭs, ī, m., *the name of a man.* Græcīnĕ, fătērī, Ov.

græcŏr, ārĭs, *to live as the Greeks.* Assuētŭm græcārī, Hor.

Græcŭlŭs, ī, m., *and* ŭlă, æ, f., *a Greek.* Græcŭlŭs ĕsŭrĭēns, Juv.

Græcŭs, ă, ŭm, *Greek.* Līttĕră Græcă sŏnō, Ov.

Grājŭgĕnæ, ŭm, m. pl., *the Greeks.* Grājŭgĕnūmquĕ dŏmōs, Virg.

Graiŭs, ĭī, m., *a Greek.* Fās mĭhī Graiōrŭm, Virg. V. Græci.—2. ŭs, ă, ŭm, *Grecian, Greek.* Graiă cărīnă nŏtĕt, Ov. Sʏɴ. Græcŭs.

grāmĕn, ĭnĭs, n., *grass*. Grāmĭnĭis āttĭgĭt hērbăm, Virg. Syn. Hērbă. Epith.
Lætŭm, tĕnĕrŭm, tĕnāx, mŏllĕ, mōntānŭm, fērtĭlĕ, ŏdōrŭm, vērnāns, frŏndēns,
tĕnēllŭm, pīctŭm, mĭcāns, fœcūndŭm, vĭrēns, flōrēns, flōrĭgĕrŭm, hērbōsŭm,
hālāns, hūmĭdŭm, rĕdĭvĭvŭm, rīdēns, ămœnŭm, mădĭdŭm, rĭgŭŭm, īrrĭgŭŭm,
jūcūndŭm, rōscĭdŭm. V. Herba.

grāmĭnĕŭs, *and* nōsŭs, ă, ŭm, *grassy*. Grāmĭnĕō rīpæ, Virg. Syn. Hērbōsŭs,
hērbĭdŭs.

|| grā'nmătĭcă, æ, *and* cē, ēs, f., *grammar*. Epith. Dōctă, pĕrītă, nōbĭlĭs, mă-
gīstră, āptă, īngĕnĭōsă, Pălæmōnĭă.

grămmătĭcŭs, ă, ŭm, *belonging to grammar*. Grămmătĭcās āmbīrĕ trĭbŭs, Hor.—
2. ī, m., *a grammarian*.

grānārĭŭm, ĭī, n., *a granary*. Cŭmĕrīs grānārĭā nōstrīs, Hor. Syn. Hōrrĕŭm.
Epith. Căpāx, ămplŭm, dīvĕs, trītĭcĕŭm, Cĕrĕālĕ, rĕfērtŭm.

grāndævŭs, ă, ŭm, *very old*. Quā grāndævŭs Alētēs, Virg. Syn. Lōngævŭs, ăn-
nōsŭs, sĕnēx. V. Senex.

grāndēsco, ĭs, *to grow up*. Grāndēscĕrĕt ārvĭs, Lucr.

grāndĭlŏquŭs, ă, ŭm, *speaking loftily*. Intĕr grāndĭlŏquŏs, Ar. Syn. Măgnĭlŏ-
quŭs, sŏnōrŭs. V. Eloquens.

grāndĭnĕŭs, *and* nōsŭs, ă, ŭm, *of hail*. Grāndĭnĕŭm flāmmīs, Alcim.

grāndĭo, īs, *to enlarge, make to grow*. Nĕc grāndīrī frūgŭm, Lucr.

grāndĭs, ĕ, *big, large, full-grown, old*. Līlĭă grāndĭă quāssāns, Virg. Grāndĭŏr
ætās, Ov.

grāndo, ĭnĭs, f., *hail*. Grāndĭnĕ nīmbŭm, Virg. Epith. Sāxĕă, dīră, hōrrrĭdă,
hȳbērnă, hȳĕmālĭs, pērnĭcĭōsă, ĕxĭtĭōsă, sævă, ĭnĭmĭcă, brūmālĭs, cānă, mĭnāx,
Arctŏă, Hȳpĕrbŏrĕă, Bŏrĕālĭs, dēnsă, grăvĭs, cōncrĕtă, spīssă, crĕpĭtāns, ēffūsă,
sălĭēns, glăcĭālĭs, nĭvālĭs.

Grānē, ēs, f., *the name of a nymph*. Pērvĕnĭt ād Grānēn, Ov.

Grānĭcŭs, ī, m., *a river of Phrygia*. Grānĭcō nātă bĭcōrnī, Ov.

grānĭfĕr, ĕră, ŭm, *bearing grains of corn*. Grānĭfĕrŭmque āgmēn, Ov.

grānŭm, ī, n., *a grain*. Grănă păpāvĕr, Ov. Epith. Pārvŭm, lāctēns, flāvēscēns, Cĕrĕālĕ, tŭmēns.

grăphĭārĭŭm, ĭī, n., *a case for writing-pencils*. Grăphĭārĭă fērrō, Mart.

grăphĭŭm, ĭī, n., *a style or pencil for writing*. Grăphĭō lāssărĕ, Ov.

grāssātŏr, ōrĭs, m., *a robber*. Sŭbĭtŭs grāssātŏr ăgĭt rĕm, Juv. Syn. Pŏpŭlātŏr,
latro, fūr. V. Fur.

grāssŏr, ārĭs, *to go*. Fērrō grāssātŭr, Juv. Syn. Fŭrŏr; pŏpŭlŏr; īnvādo; dīffūndo, spārgo.

grātēs, f. pl., *thanks*. Grātēs ăgo, Sen.

grātĭă, æ, f., *elegance, a benefit*. Grātĭă fāctī, Virg. Syn. Lĕpŏr, vĕnūstăs,
pūlchrĭtūdo; ămŏr, stūdĭŭm, pĭĕtās, făvŏr, dōnŭm, mūnŭs, ōffĭcĭŭm, grātŭs
ănĭnŭs, grātă mĕmŏrĭă, grātă vŏlūntās.—2. *the grace of God*. Epith. Rŏbūstă,
vălĭdă, vīctrīx, ēffĭcāx, fōrtĭs, pŏtēns, ōmnĭpŏtēns, īmmĕrĭtă, suāvĭs, blāndă,
dīvīnă, aūrĕă, dĭă.

Grātĭă, æ, f., *and* Grātĭæ, ārŭm, f. pl., *the Graces*. Grātĭă, cŭm nȳmphĭs, Hor.
Grātĭæ dĕcēntēs, Hor. Syn. Chărĭtēs. Epith. Mītēs, dūlcēs, cōmptæ, blāndæ,
cōmēs, pūlchræ, fōrmōsæ, vĕnūstæ, vĕrēcūndæ, dĕcōræ, cūltæ, lætæ, jŭvĕnēs, rī-
dēntēs, suāvēs, hĭlărēs. V. Charites.

grātĭfĭcŏr, ārĭs, *to gratify*. Grātĭfĭcătă flŭēntēs, Aus. Syn. Făvĕo, mŭnĕro,
dōnĭs ŏbstrīngo, ōffĭcĭīs dēvīncĭo.

grātĭs, adv., *for nothing*. Dăt grātĭs, ūltrō, Mart. Syn. Ūltrō, grātŭĭtō.

Grātĭŭs, ĭī, m., *a man's name*. Grātĭŭs ārmă dărĕt, Ov.

grātŏr, ārĭs, *to congratulate*. Grātātŭr rĕdūcēs, Virg. V. Gratulor.

grātŭĭtŭs, ă, ŭm, *gratuitous*. Grātŭĭtŭm cădĭt, Stat. Syn. Grātĭs; ūltrō dătŭs,
ōblātŭs.

grātŭlātĭo, ōnĭs, f., *a congratulation*. Īn īpsīs grātŭlātĭōnĭbŭs, (Iamb.) Publ. S.
Epith. Lætă, ămĭcă.

grātŭlātŏr, ōrĭs, m., *one who congratulates*. Rōmă, grātŭlātōrī, Mart.

grātŭlŏr, ārĭs, *to congratulate*. Grātŭlŏr īngĕnĭŭm, Ov. Syn. Cōngrătŭlŏr,
grātŏr. V. Plaudo, gratias ago.

grātŭs, ă, ŭm, *pleasing*. Grātĭŏr ūllă, Virg. Syn. Jūcūndŭs, āccēptŭs, dŭl-

cĭs, suāvĭs, ămātŭs ; mĕmŏr ŏffĭcĭī, nōn ĭngrātŭs, nōn ĭmmĕmŏr.   V.
Grates.

grăvātĭm, adv., *grievously.* Plērŭmquĕ grăvātĭm, Lucr. Syn. Grăvĭtĕr, ægrē.

grăvēdo, ĭnĭs, f., *heaviness of the head.* Hīc mē grăvēdo, (Scaz.) Cat.

grăvĕŏlēns, (*trisyll.*) ntĭs, *stinking.* Faūcēs grăvĕŏlēntĭs Āvērnī, Virg. Syn.
Grăvĭtĕr ŏlēns, fœtēns, fœtĭdŭs.

grăvēsco, ĭs, *to grow heavy.* Ōmnĕ grăvēscĭt, Virg. Syn. Grăvŏr, ŏnĕrŏr.

grăvĭdo, ās, *to load, impregnate.* Sŏlŭm grăvĭdărĕ nŏvālēs, Help. Syn. Ŏnĕro ;
fœtu ĭmplĕo.

grăvĭdŭs, ă, ŭm, *weighty.* Bīs grăvĭdōs cōgŭnt, Virg. Syn. Grăvĭs, ŏnĕrōsŭs,
ŏnūstŭs.—Grăvĭdă, f., *big with child, or with young.* Syn. Prægnāns, fœtă.

grăvĭs, ĕ, *heavy.* Aūt grăvĭbŭs rāstrīs, Virg. Syn. Pŏndĕrōsŭs, ŏnĕrōsŭs, grăvĭdŭs ; mŏlēstŭs, ācērbŭs, dĭffĭcĭlĭs ; aūstērŭs, sĕvērŭs. V. Gravitas.

Grăvīscœ, ārŭm, f. pl., *a city of Etruria.* Intēmpēstæquĕ Grăvīscæ, Virg.

grăvĭtās, ātĭs, f., *heaviness.* Nēquĕŭnt grăvĭtātĕ mŏvērī, Ov. Syn. Pŏndŭs,
ŏnŭs, mōlēs. Epith. Ingēns, ŏnĕrōsă.—2. *gravity.* Syn. Mājēstās, aūstērĭtās,
tetrĭcĭtās, sĕvērĭtās. Epith. Tetrĭcă, sĕvēră, tristĭs, sĕnīlĭs, mātūră, vĕrēndă,
ĭmmōtă, dĕcēns, sĕrēnă, lætă, dĕcōră, spēctābĭlĭs, ĭnsĭgnĭs.

grăvĭtĕr, adv., *heavily.* Ipsĕ grăvĭs grăvĭtĕr, Virg. Syn. Ægrē ; pŏndĕrĕ
vāstō ; sĕvērĕ.

grăvo, ās, *to load.* Illĕ grăvărĕ mănŭs, Prop. Syn. Prægrăvo, ŏnĕro, prĕmo,
ŏpprĭmo, ōbrŭo.

grăvŏr, ārĭs, *to suffer impatiently.* Dŏmĭnōsquĕ grăvāntŭr, Luc.

grĕgālĭs, ĕ, *of the same flock.* Plēbs grĕgālĭs ēxcŏlăt, (Iamb. Dim.) Prud. Syn.
Armēntālĭs.

grĕgātĭm, adv., *by flocks.* Grĕgātĭm fērrĕ mănŭs, St.

grĕgo, ās, *to assemble.* Cælōquĕ dŏmōquĕ grĕgātī, Stat.

grĕmĭŭm, ĭī, n., *the bosom.* Ūt cūm tĕ grĕmĭŏ, Virg. Syn. Sĭnŭs, pēctŭs.
Epith. Dūlcĕ, pērdūlcĕ, āmœnŭm, grātŭm, jūcūndŭm. V. Sinus.

grēssŭs, ūs, m., *a step.* Grēssĭbŭs ĭmprēssĭs, Prop. Syn. Ingrēssŭs, grădŭs.
V. Gradus.

grēx, ēgĭs, m., *a flock.* Ūt grĕgĭbŭs taūrī, Virg. Syn. Pĕcŭs, pĕcŭdēs, pĕcŏră,
pĕcŭārĭă, ārmēntŭm. Epith. Lānĭgĕr, ērrāns, ĭmmūndŭs, hĭrsūtŭs, hĭrtŭs,
văgŭs, pīnguĭs, văgăbūndŭs, păvĭdŭs, pĕtŭlāns, dūmĭvăgŭs, ērrātĭcŭs, pĕtŭlcŭs,
ăvĭdŭs, ĕdāx, ŏpīmŭs, ŏpŭlēntŭs, fœcūndŭs, cōrnĭgĕr. V. Pastor, pasco.

grĭllŭs, ī, m., *a cricket.* Ēt grĭllŭs grĭllăt, Ov.

Grōsphŭs, ī, m., *a man's name.* Ŭtĕrĕ Pŏmpeĭō Grōsphō, Hor.

grūndĭo, *and* nnĭo, īs, *to grunt like a hog.* Grūnnīsse Ēlpēnŏră, Juv.

grūs, gruĭs, f., *a crane.* Tūnc grūĭbŭs pĕdīcă, Virg. Epith. Āĕrĭă, hȳbērnă,
quĕrŭlă, ādvĕnă, brūmālĭs, præsāgă, vĭgĭl, Strȳmŏnĭă, Bĭstŏnĭă.

Grȳnœŭs, ă, ŭm, *an epithet of Apollo.* Grȳnœŭs Ăpōllo, Virg.

Grȳneūs, ĕī *or* eī, m., *the name of a centaur.* Cūmquĕ sŭīs Grȳneūs, Ov.

grȳps, ȳpĭs, m., *a griffin.* Grȳpēs ĕquĭs, Virg. Epith. Indĭcī, Hȳpērbŏrēī,
ŏbūncī, ăvĭdī, ālātī, răpācēs, fĕrōcēs, ĭmpăvĭdī, fŭrĭōsī, fĕrī, aūdācēs, mĭnācēs,
trŭcēs, crūdēlēs, hōrrēndī.

gŭbērnācŭlŭm, *or* clŭm, ī, n., *the rudder of a ship.* Ipsĕ gŭbērnāclŏ, Virg. Syn.
Clāvŭs, tēmo, nāvĭs, mŏdĕrāmĕn, rēgĭmĕn, hăbēnœ ; tēmo, gŭbērnātĭo, ādmĭnĭs-
trātĭo, ĭmpĕrĭum, mūnŭs, ŏffĭcĭŭm. Epith. Naūtĭcŭm, flŭĭtāns, prŏpĕrŭm,
fĭdŭm, pēndēns, flēxĭlĕ. V. Clavus navalis.

gŭbērnātŏr, ōrĭs, m , *a pilot.* Ipsĕ gŭbērnātŏr pūppī, Virg. Syn. Rēctŏr, mŏdĕrātŏr. Epith. Prōvĭdŭs, sŏlērs, vĭgĭl, pērvĭgĭl, sōllĭcĭtŭs.

gŭbērno, ās, *to govern.* Quĭd quī gŭbērnăt āstră, (Iamb.) Prud. Syn. Rĕgo,
dīrĭgo, dūco, mŏdĕrŏr, dŏmĭnŏr, ĭmpĕro. V. Impero.

gŭlă, æ, f, *a gullet, gluttony.* Ēst gŭlă, quœ, Juv. Syn. Faūcēs, jŭgŭlŭm,
gūttŭr ; inglŭvĭēs, ēdācĭtās, vŏrācĭtās. Epith. Ăvĭdă, fœdă, ĭmpătĭēns, ĭnsătĭā-
bĭlĭs, vŏrāx, tūrpĭs, ĭnēxplēbĭlĭs, ĭnēxplētă, răbĭdă, hĭāns, ĭmplăcātă, nēfāndă,
indĭgă, ĭnŏps, vēsānă, ĭmmēnsă, lūxŭrĭōsă, ārdēns, ĭngĕnĭōsă, nŏcēns. V. Fames.

gŭlōsŭs, ă, ŭm, *gluttonous.* Nĭmĭŭm lēctŏrĕ gŭlōsō, Mart. Syn. Hēllŭo, gŭlo,
lūrco. V. Famelicus.

gŭrgĕs, ĭtĭs, m., *a gulf.* Gūrgĭtĭbŭs mīrĭs, Juv. Syn. Vŏrāgo, bărathrŭm, ăbȳs-
sŭs, hĭātŭs. Epith. Præcĕps, līmōsŭs, cœnōsŭs, cūrvŭs, tōrtŭs, sĭnŭātŭs, āltŭs,

prŏfūndŭs, spūmĕŭs, ūndōsŭs, răpĭdŭs, raūcŭs, tŭmĭdŭs. V. Hiatus; Charybdis; fluvius; mare.

gŭsto, ās, *to taste.* Gūstārēmŭs, vĕlŭt īllĭs, Hor. Syn. Dēgūsto, lībo, dēlībo.

gūstŭs, *and* tātŭs, ūs, m., *the taste.* Intĕrĕā gūstŭs ĕlĕmēntă, Juv. Syn. Săpŏr. Epith. Dūlcĭs, grātŭs, suāvĭs, jūcūndŭs, săpĭdŭs, nēctărĕŭs. V. Sapor.

gūttă, *and* tŭlă, æ, f., *a drop.* Sānguĭnĕæ gūttæ, Ov. Syn. Stīllă. Epith. Mānāns, tūrgēns, dēcĭdŭă, prōcĭdŭă, flŭĭtāns, liquĭdă, rĭgŭă, nĭtĭdă, lūcĭdă, tĕrĕs, stīllāns, cădēns, liquēns.

gūttātĭm, adv., *by drops.* Lăcrȳmæ gūttātĭm cădŭnt, (Iamb.) Syn. Stīllātĭm.

gūttātŭs, ă, ŭm, *spotted.* Nŭmĭdĭcæquĕ gūttātæ, Mart.

gūttŭr, ŭrĭs, n., *the throat.* Gūttŭră pāndēns, Virg. Syn. Jŭgŭlŭm, faūcēs. Epith. Căvŭm, pătŭlŭm, pătēns, hĭāns, ăpērtŭm, raūcŭm, tĕnŭĕ, cănōrŭm, sŏnōrŭm, blāndĭsŏnŭm.

gūttŭs, ī, m., *a cruet.* Līntĕă gūttō, Juv. Syn. Ūrcĕŭs, ūrcĕŏlŭs. Epith. Āmbrŏsĭŭs, fāgĭnŭs, Sāmĭŭs, căvŭs, cōncăvŭs, căpāx.

Gȳără, æ, *and* rŭs, ī, f., *a small island in the Archipelago.*

Gȳās, æ, m., *one of the Giants.* Quĭd grăvĭŭs, vīctōrĕ Gȳă, Ov.—2. *one of Æneas'* companions. Fōrtēmquĕ Gȳān, Virg.

Gȳgēs, æ, m., *a man's name.* Sūccīsō pōplĭtĕ Gȳgēn, Virg.

gȳmnăs, ădĭs, f., *wrestling.* Gȳmnădĕ Pōllūx, Juv. V. Palæstra.

gȳmnāsĭŭm, īī, n., *a place of exercise.* Gȳmnāsĭīs ădĕrĭt, Luc. Syn. Pălæstră; schŏlă, cōllēgĭŭm.

gȳpsātŭs, ă, ŭm, *plastered.* Bārbără gȳpsātōs, Tib.

gȳpsŭm, ·ī, n., *plaster.* Plēna ōmnĭă gȳpsō, Juv. Epith. Albŭm, tĕnāx, crāssŭm.

gȳrŭs, ī, m., *a circle.* Sēptem īngēns gȳrōs, Virg. Syn. Ōrbĭs, cīrcŭĭtŭs, cīrcŭlŭs, āmbĭtŭs, nēxŭs, ārcŭs, vŏlūmĕn, flēxŭs, sīnŭs, spīră, rŏtātŭs, glŏmĕrāmĕn. Epith. Sĭnŭātŭs, vŏlūtŭs, ōblīquŭs, ārctŭs, cūrvŭs, rŏtūndŭs, lōngŭs, spătĭōsŭs, vāstŭs, cūrvātŭs, īngēns, căpāx, āltērnŭs, flēxŭs, īntōrtŭs, īnflēxŭs.

H.

HABĒNĂ, æ, f., *the rein of a bridle.* Căpŭt ēgĭt hăbēnā, Virg. Syn. Lōrŭm, frænŭm, rĕtĭnācŭlŭm, căpīstrŭm. Epith. Vălĭdă, āngūstă, strīctă, lāxă, tĕnāx, rĕtēntă, ārctă, flēxĭlĭs, tĕrĕs, ūndāns, făcĭlĭs. V. Fræno, frænum.

hăbĕo, ŭī, *to have.* Fīnēs ălĭquāndo hăbŭĕrĕ Lătīnōs, Virg. Syn. Pŏssĭdĕo, ōbtĭnĕo, tĕnĕo; sērvo, cōnsērvo; pŭto, æstĭmo.

hăbĭlĭs, ĕ, *convenient.* Dē mōre hăbĭlēm sūspēndĕrăt, Virg. Syn. Āptŭs, cōnvĕnĭēns, cōmmŏdŭs, āccōmmŏdŭs; ălăcĕr, ăgĭlĭs, dēxtĕr, sōlērs.

hăbĭtābĭlĭs, ĕ, *habitable.* Sōl hăbĭtābĭlēs, (Alcaic.) Hor. Syn. Cūltŭs, hăbĭtātŭs.

hăbĭtācŭlŭm, ī, n., *a habitation.* Căvīs hăbĭtācŭlă dīgnă, Alc. Syn. Hăbĭtătĭo, sēdēs, dŏmŭs. V. Domus.

hăbĭtātŏr, ōrĭs, m., *and* trīx, īcĭs, f., *an inhabitant.* Nĕmŏrīsque hăbĭtātŏr ămœnī, Claud. V. Incola.

hăbĭto, ās, *to inhabit.* Lūcīs hăbĭtāmŭs ŏpācīs, Virg. Syn. Cŏlo, īncŏlo, tĕnĕo, frĕquēnto.

hăbĭtŭs, ūs, m., *air, countenance.* Ōs hăbĭtūmquĕ, Virg. Syn. Fōrmă, cūltŭs, gēstŭs. Epith. Dēcēns, dĕcōrŭs, hŏnēstŭs, mūndŭs, nĭtĭdŭs, cūltŭs; sōrdĭdŭs, tūrpĭs, fœdŭs; rēgĭŭs, sŭpērbŭs, præstāns.

hăc, adv., *this way.* Hāc ĭtĕr, Virg.

hāctĕnŭs, adv., *hitherto.* Hāctĕnŭs ārvōrŭm, Virg. Syn. Hūc ūsquĕ.

* hæmōrrhŏĭs, ĭdĭs, f., *a serpent.* Hæmōrrhŏĭs ēxplĭcăt ōrbēs, Luc.

Hæmŭs, *or* Æmŭs, ī, m., *a mountain in Thrace.* Nūbĭfĕr Hæmŭs, Claud. Epith. Thrācĭŭs, Thrēĭcĭŭs, Gĕtĭcŭs, Œāgrĭŭs; gĕlĭdŭs, ūmbrōsŭs, nĭvālĭs, nĭvĕŭs, vĭrēns, vĭrĭdĭs, ārdŭŭs, lātŭs, squālēns, nūbĭgĕr, Ōrphæŭs, vāstŭs, spēctābĭlĭs. V. Mons.

hærēdĭtās, ātĭs, f., *also* dĭŭm *and* dĭŏlŭm, ī, n., *an heritage.* Hærĕdĭtātī tĭbi, (Scaz.) Mart. Syn. Patrĭmōnĭŭm, patrĭæ ŏpēs, bŏnă, prædĭă, fōrtūnæ.

hærĕo, hæsī, *to stick.* Hærĕăt āptē, Hor. Syn. Ădhærĕo, cŏhærĕo, dŭbĭto, hæsīto.

hærēs, ēdĭs, m., f., *an heir.* Edēnt hærēdēs, Mart. Syn. Succēssŏr. Epith. Ăvĭdŭs, sollĭcĭtŭs, dīvĕs.

hærēsĭārchă, æ, m., *the chief of a sect.* Hærēsĭārchārūm clāvā, Mant.

bærēsĭs, ĭs *or* ĕōs, f., *heresy.* Hærēsĭs hŏrrĭdă mēmbrĭs, Prosp. Epith. Impĭă, scĕlĕrātă, īnfāndă, scĕlēstă, ēxĭtĭōsă, atrōx, fērālĭs, dīră, hŏrrĭdă, dētēstāndă, sŭpērbă, ēffrænĭs, audāx, īnfēstă, īnsānă, probrōsă, fāllāx, mēndāx, dŏlōsă, pērfĭdă.

hærĕtĭcŭs, ă, ŭm, *heretical.* Cŭm tămĕn hærĕtĭcă, Arat. Syn. Nŏvātŏr, fĭdeī hōstĭs. Epith. Impĭŭs, scĕlĕrātŭs, &c. V. Hæresis.

hæsīto, ās, *to hesitate.* Hæsītăt īgnĭs, Lucr. Syn. Frĕquēns hærĕo, sæpĕ hærĕo ; tĭtŭbo, văcīllo, dŭbĭto.

Hāgna, æ, f., *a woman's name.* Pŏlўpŭs Hāgnæ, Hor.

Hālcўōnē. V. Alcyone.

hālēc, ēcĭs, f., n. ; -ēx, ēcĭs ; *and* ēcŭlă, æ ; f., *a herring.* Prīmŭs ĕt hālēc, Hor.

Hālēsŭs, ī, m., *a river in Sicily.* Flōrēs lēgīstĭs Hālēsī, Col. Epith. Sĭcănĭŭs, Sĭcŭlŭs, præcēps, flŭēns, flŭĭdŭs, ămœnŭs.—2. *the name of a man.* Virg.

hālĭæĕtŭs, ī, m., *a falcon.* Fŭlvĭs hālĭæĕtŭs ālĭs, Ov. Syn. Fălco.

hālĭtŭs, ūs, m., *breath.* Sŭpĕr hālĭtŭs ērrăt, Virg. Syn. Spīrĭtŭs, ănhēlĭtŭs. V. Spiritus.

Hālĭŭs, ī, m., *a man's name.* Ălcāndrūmque Hālĭŭmquĕ, Ov

hālo, ās, *to breathe.* Crŏcēĭs hālāntēs flōrĭbŭs hōrtī, Virg. Syn. Ŏlĕo, spīro. V. Oleo.

hāltēr, ērĭs, m., *a balance for rope-dancers.* Hāltērēm făcĭlī, Mart. Epith. Rĭgĭdŭs.

Hālўs, ўŏs, m., *a river in Anatolia.* Tōrtŭs Hālўs, Ov. Epith. Tūrbĭdŭs, fătālĭs, tōrtŭs, sĭnŭōsŭs, flēxŭs, reflēxŭs.

hămă, *and* ŭlă, æ, f., *a water-bucket.* Prædīvĕs hămĭs, Juv.   Hăbĭlēm lўmphĭs hămŭlăm, Col.

Hāmadrўădĕs, ŭm, f. pl., *nymphs of the woods.* Jām nĕque Hămādrўădĕs, Virg. V. Dryades.

hāmātŭs, ă, ŭm, *hooked.* Pārs cădĭt hāmātĭs, Ov.

hāmo, ās, *to harpoon.* Indūctĭs hāmātūr lāmĭnă mēmbrĭs, Cl.

hāmŭs, ī, m., *a hook.* Fūgĕrĭt hāmō, Hor. Syn. Hāmŭlŭs, ŭncŭs, ŭncīnŭs, hārpăgo. Epith. Cūrvŭs, rĕcūrvŭs, ŭncŭs, ădūncŭs, tōrtŭs, fērrĕŭs, cōnnēxŭs, tĕnāx, īnsĭdĭōsŭs, sŭbdŏlŭs, lēthālĭs, mērsŭs, īmmērsŭs, ĭnēscātŭs, īllēx (ĭcĭs), fāllāx, lĕvĭs. V. Piscari.

hără, æ, f., *a hog-sty.* Cūră fĭdēlĭs hāræ, Ov. Syn. Suīlĕ, stăbŭlŭm. Epith. Fœtĭdă, sōrdĭdă, tūrpĭs, fœdă, ŏlēns, ōbscœnă.

hārmŏnĭă, æ, f., *harmony.* Hārmŏnĭăm Graiī, Lucr. Syn. Cōncēntŭs, mĕlŏs, cōncōrdĭă vōcŭm. Epith. Suāvĭs, jūcūndă, mūsĭcă, dōctă, rĕsŏnāns.

hārpăgo, ōnĭs, m., *a hook.* Caulĭum hārpăgōnĭbŭs, (Iamb.) Syn. Hārpāx, ŭncŭs. Epith. Fērrĕŭs, ŭncŭs, ădūncŭs, ăcūtŭs, rĕcūrvŭs, tĕnăx, mōrdāx.

Hārpălўcē, ēs, f., *a queen of the Amazons.* Hārpălўcē, vŏlŭcrēmquĕ, Virg.

Hārpălўcŭs, ī, m., *a Trojan warrior.*

Hārpălŭs, ī, m., *the name of a dog.*

Hārpāstŭm, ī, n., *a large ball for play.* Sīve hārpāstă mănū, Mart.

hārpē, ēs, f., *a scimitar.* Sūstŭlĭt hārpēn, Lucan. Epith. Fălcātă, īncūrvă, ŭncă, cūrvă, Cўllēnĭs, Cўllēnĭă.

Hārpocrātēs, ĭs, m., *the God of silence.* Hārpŏcrătēs dĭgĭtō, Vet. Poët. Epith. Ægўptĭŭs, Phărĭŭs, Mēmphĭtĭcŭs, Nĭlĭăcŭs, Isĭăcŭs.

Hārpyĭæ. (trisyll.) ārŭm, f. pl., *monsters, sprung from Typhoeus and the Earth.* Hārpyīs gŭlă dīgnă, Hor. Syn. Stўmphālĭdĕs, Tўphōĭdēs. Epith. Răpācēs, ăvĭdæ, pălūstrēs, īnfēstæ, īmmūndæ, crūdēlēs, dīræ, fœdæ, ōbscœnæ, hōrrēndæ, tūrpēs, trŭcēs, ālĭgĕræ, Ărcădĭæ, Phīnēæ.

hărūspēx, ĭcĭs, m., *a soothsayer.* V. Aruspex, augur.

hāstă, æ, f., *a lance.* Hōrruĭt hāstĭs, Virg. Syn. Lăncĕă, spĭcŭlŭm, hāstīlĕ, cūspĭs, tēlŭm, jăcŭlŭm, fērrŭm, frāxĭnŭs, ăbĭēs, pīnŭs. Epith. Mārtĭă, lōngă, grăvĭs, ĭmmĭtĭs, bēllĭcă, ăcŭtă, vălĭdă, saevă, trăbālĭs, ĭnĭnăx, ŏblōngă, trĕmĕ-bŭndă, sānguĭnĕă, crŭēntă, Māvŏrtĭă, fĕrōx, fūnēstă, fātālĭs, fŏrtĭs, vūlnĭfĭcă, āmēntātă, fĕrrātă, frāxĭnĕă, rĭgĭdă, tĕrĕs, mĭssĭlĭs, trĕmēns, vibrāns, vibrātă, ĭn-tōrtă, cōntōrtă, scĕlĕrātă, ĭnfēstă, strīdēns. V. Jaculum.

hāstātŭs, ă, ŭm, *bearing a lance.* Māvŏrs hāstătāquĕ pūgnae, Stat.

hāstĭlĕ, ĭs, n., *a halbert.* Crīspāns hāstĭlĭă fērrō, Virg. EPITH. Lōngŭm, dūrŭm, vălĭdŭm, lēntŭm, tĕrĕs, rĭgĭdŭm, sānguĭnĕŭm. V. Hasta.

haŭd, adv., *not.* Haŭd ŏbscūră cădēns, Virg.

haŭdquāquăm, adv., *by no means.* Dīvĭdĭt: haŭdquāquăm, Virg. SYN. Haŭd, nōn, mĭnĭmē, nĕquāquăm.

haŭrĭo, īs, haŭsī, haŭstŭm, *to draw.* Haŭrĭăt hŭnc, Virg. SYN. Ēxhaŭrĭo, trăho, āttrăho, ēxtrăho, ēdūco, sōrbĕo, ābsōrbĕo, vŏro. V. Poto.

haŭstŏr, ōrĭs, m., *a drinker.* Ūltĭmŭs haŭstŏr āquae, Luc.

haŭstră, ōrŭm, n. pl, *buckets.* Rŏtās ātque haŭstră vĭdēmŭs, Lucr.

haŭstŭs, ūs, m., *a draught.* Haŭstŭs āquae, Ov. SYN. Pōtŭs. EPITH. Ăvĭdŭs, grātŭs.

hēbdŏmăs, ădĭs, f., *a week.* Sēptĭmŭs hēbdŏmădī, Prud. V. Dies.

Hēbē, ēs, f., *the goddess of youth.* Hērcŭlĭs Hēbēn, Prop. EPITH. Nōbĭlĭs, fōrmōsă, pūlchră, vĕnŭstă, rŏsĕă, caelēstĭs, sīdĕrĕă, cāndĭdă, lāctĕă, cōmptă, cōncīnnă, Hērcŭlĕă, Jūnōnĭă, laetă, ălācrĭs.

hĕbĕo, ēs, *and* ēsco, ĭs, *to grow blunt.* Sānguĭs hĕbĕt, Virg. SYN. Hĕbēsco, hĕbĕtŏr, tōrpĕo.

hĕbĕs, ĕtĭs, *blunt.* Jăm glădĭŏs hĕbĕtēs, Ov. SYN. Ōbtūsŭs, rĕtūsŭs, hĕbēns, hĕbēscēns, hĕbĕtēscēns, hĕbĕtātŭs, ăcūmĭnĭs ēxpērs; stŭpĭdŭs, pĭgĕr, sēgnĭs.

hĕbĕto, ās, *to blunt.* Tērrēnĭque hĕbĕtānt, Virg. SYN. Ōbtūndo, rĕtūndo.

hĕbĕtūdo, ĭnĭs, f., *bluntness.* SYN. Ōbtūsă, rĕtūsa ăcĭēs; pigrĭtĭēs, tōrpŏr, stŭpĭdĭtās.

Hēbraeī, ōrŭm, m. pl., *the Hebrews, or Jews.* Gēns Hēbraeōrŭm, Prud. V. Judaei.

Hēbrŭs, ī, m., *a river in Thrace.* Praevērtĭtŭr Hēbrŭm, Virg. EPITH. Ărēnōsŭs, cōrnĭgĕr, spūmĭfĕr, spūmāns, răpĭdŭs, văgŭs, ŭndāns, nĭtĭdŭs, dīvĕs, aŭrĭfĕr; Thrācĭŭs, Rhŏdŏpēĭŭs, Ōdrўsĭŭs, Œagrĭŭs, Ōrphēŭs.

Hĕcălĕ, ēs, f., *a poor woman who received Theseus into her cottage.* Cūr nēmo ēst Hĕcălēn, Ov.

Hĕcătĕ, ēs, f., *a name of Diana.* Prīmōs Hĕcătĕ văpōrēs, (Sapph.) SYN. Lūnă; Diānă; Prōsērpĭnă. EPITH. Trĭcēps, nōctūrnă. V. Luna.

Hĕcătēĭŭs, ă, ŭm, *and* Hĕcătēĭs, ĭdŏs, f., *of Hecate.* Hĕcătēĭă cārmĭnă, Ov. Hĕcătēĭdŏs hērbae, Id.

hĕcătōmbē, ēs, f., *a sacrifice of a hundred victims.* Quī prōmĭttānt hĕcătōmbēn, Juv.

Hēctŏr, ŏrĭs, m., *the son of Priam and Hecuba.* Hēctŏră mūrōs, Virg. SYN. Prĭămĭdēs. EPITH. Phrўgĭŭs, Trōjānŭs, Trōĭŭs, fĕrōx, īnclўtŭs, īmpĭgĕr, fŏrtĭs, māgnŭs, bēllĭgĕr, Māvŏrtĭŭs, Mārtĭŭs, saevŭs, bārbărŭs, ăcĕr, aŭdāx, ātrōx, fĕrŭs, ārmĭpŏtēns.

Hēctŏrĕŭs, ă, ŭm, *of Hector.* Hēctŏrĕōs āmnēs, Virg.

Hĕcŭbă, ae, *or* bē, ēs, f., *the daughter of Cisseus, and wife of Priam.* Hīc Hĕcŭba ēt nātae, Virg. SYN. Cĭssēĭs, mătēr Hēctŏrĭs; Prĭămēĭă cōnjūx. EPITH. Foecūndă, ĭnfēlīx, āmēns, fūrēns, īnsānă, trīstĭs, cāptīvă, ānnōsă, lōngaevă, Trōjānă.

hĕdĕră, ae, f., *ivy.* Nūnc hĕdĕrae sĭne hŏnōrĕ, Ov. EPITH. Ērrāns, pāllēns, lĭgāns, sērpēns, vĭrēns, lāscīvă, vĭgēns, nēxĭlĭs; īntōrtă, vĭrĭdĭs, frōndōsă, tōrtĭlĭs, flēxĭlĭs, frōndēns, cōmāns, sĕquāx, tĕnāx, lēntă, vīvāx, Bācchĭcă, crīnālĭs, dĕcŏră, vīctrīx.

hĕdĕrĭgĕr, ă, ŭm, *bearing ivy.*

hĕdĕrōsŭs, ă, ŭm, *full of ivy.* Fēlīx hĕdĕrōsŏ, Prop.

hēlcĭărĭŭs, ĭī, m., *one who tows a boat.* Vălĕt hēlcĭărĭōrŭm, Mart.

Hĕlĕnă, ae, *or* nē, ēs, f., *the daughter of Jupiter and Leda.* Quōs Hĕlĕnē nūdĭs, Prop. SYN. Tўndărĭs, Lăcaenă, Œbălĭs. EPITH. Lēdĕă, Argīvă, Pĕlāsgă, Ămўclaeă, Thĕrāpnaeă, Spārtānă, Taenărĭă, Œbālĭă; fōrmōsă, dĕcŏră, vĕnŭstă, ădŭltĕră, īnfāmĭs, īnĭquă, pērfĭdă, lāscīvă, īmpŭdĭcă, răptă, sŭpērbă, ēxĭtĭōsă, pērnĭcĭōsă.

Hĕlēnŏr, ŏrĭs, m., *the name of a warrior.* Vīx ūnŭs Hĕlēnŏr, Virg.
Hĕlĕnŭs, ĭ, m., *the son of Priam and Hecuba.* Priămīdēn Hĕlĕnŭm, Virg. EPITH.
Trōĭŭs, Dārdănĭŭs, praesciŭs, prōvĭdŭs, praenūnciŭs, vātēs.
Hĕlērnŭs, ĭ, m., *a wood on the banks of the Tiber.* Ov.
Hĕlĭădĕs, ŭm, f. pl., *the daughters of the Sun and Clymene.* Hĕlĭădēs lūgēnt, Ov.
SYN. Clȳmĕnēïdĕs, Phăĕthōntĭădĕs, Phăĕthōntĭdĕs. EPITH. Pōpŭlĕæ, frōndōsæ,
mœstæ, mĭsĕræ, gĕmĕbūndæ.
Hĕlĭcē, ēs, f., *a constellation.* Ad flātūs Hĕlĭcēs, Gr. V. Ursa, Arctos.
Hĕlĭcōn, ōnĭs, m., *a mountain in Bœotia, sacred to Apollo and the Muses.* Dăs
Hĕlĭcōnĕ lŏcŭm, Sid. EPITH. Săcĕr, ămœnŭs, cănōrŭs, Aŏnĭŭs, Phœbēŭs,
Pĭērĭŭs; laūrĭfĕr, vīrgĭnĕŭs, dōctŭs. V. Paruassus.
Hĕlĭcōnĭădĕs, *and* ĭdĕs, ŭm, f. pl., *a name of the Muses.* Dūctōs Hĕlĭcōnĭdŭm
lĭquōrēs, (Phal.) Sid. Adde Hĕlĭcōnĭădŭm, Lucr. V. Musæ.
Hĕlĭcōnĭŭs, ă, ŭm, *of Mount Helicon.* Cŏhōrs Hĕlĭcōnĭă Phœbī, Sil. SYN. Pār-
nāssĭŭs, Aŏnĭŭs.
Hĕlĭmŭs, ĭ, m., *the name of a centaur.* Ov.
Hĕlĭŏdōrŭs, ĭ, m., *a rhetorician.* Cōmĕs Hĕlĭŏdōrŭs, Hor.
Hĕllăs, ădĭs, f., *Greece.* Hĕllădĕ pērcūssā, Hor. V. Græcia.
Hĕllē, ēs, f., *the daughter of Athamas.* EPITH. Ăthāmāntĭs, Phrȳxæă, Æŏlĭă;
păvĭdă, flēbĭlĭs, trĕpĭdă, īnfēlīx, trĕpĭdāns. SYN. Nĕphĕlēĭăs.
Hĕllēspōntĭăcŭs, *and* tĭŭs, ă, ŭm, *of the Hellespont.* Hĕllēspōntĭăcī sērvĕt, Virg.
Hĕllēspōntŭs, ĭ, m., *a strait which separates Europe from Asia.* EPITH. Răpĭdŭs,
fŭrēns, sævŭs, lōngŭs, Leāndrĭŭs.
Hĕlōrŭs, ĭ, m., *a river in Sicily.* Stāgnāntĭs Hĕlōrī, Virg. EPITH. Stāgnāns,
clāmōsŭs, præcēps, cĭtŭs, cōncĭtŭs, ămœnŭs, grātŭs.
Hĕlvĕtī, ōrŭm, m. pl., *the Swiss.* Hĕlvĕtī tĭbi, Mant. EPITH. Fĕrī, armĭ-
pŏtēntēs, sævī, trŭcēs; gĕnĕrōsī, māgnănĭmī, bĕllĭgĕrī, bĕllācēs, dūrī, immītēs,
impăvĭdī, fōrtēs, rōbūstī, lăcērtōsī.
hēlŭo, ōnĭs, m. V. Gulosus.
hĕlŭŏr, ārĭs, *to gormandise.* Părum hĕlŭātŭs ēst, (Iamb. Pur.) Cat.
Hēnĭŏchŭs, ă, ŭm, *of the Heniochi, a people of Sarmatia.* Hēnĭŏchæ naūtĭs plŭs
nŏcŭĕrĕ rătēs, Ov.
hēpăr, ătĭs, n., *the liver.* V. Jecur.
hĕră, æ, f., *a mistress.* Pēnsă rĕpēndĭs hĕræ, Ov. SYN. Dŏmĭnă.
hĕrbă, æ, f., *an herb, the grass.* Quīquĕ frĕquēns hērbĭs, ĕt, Virg. SYN. Grāmĕn,
cēspĕs. EPITH. Grāmĭnĕă, ŏdōră, vērnāns, vĭrēns, vĭrĭdĭs, vĭrēscēns, mōllĭs,
tĕnĕră, tĕnĕllă, flōrēns, laetă, gēmmāns, pūbēns, pruīnōsă, ŏdōrātă, fērtĭlĭs, ūdă,
tĕnŭĭs, rōscĭdă, rōrāns, flŭvĭālĭs, bĭbŭlă, sȳlvēstrĭs, ărēnōsă, frāgrāns, flōrĭdă,
hālāns, suāvĭs, rĕdŏlēns, sĭtĭēns, săpĭdă, irrĭgŭă, trĕmŭlă, ārēns, ămāră, nŏcēns,
vĕnēnātă, mĕdĭcă, sălūbrĭs, Phœbĕă, Pæŏnĭă, Māchāŏnĭă, sānă, pŏtēns, māgĭcă,
fūnēstă, cāntātă, lēthālĭs, ŏpĕrōsă, Cīrcæă, Mēdēĭs, Hĕcātēĭs. V. Gramen.
hērbĭdŭs, bĭfĕr, bĭgĕr, *and* bōsŭs, ă, ŭm, *grassy.* Hērbĭdă taūrōs, Ov. Hērbĭfĕrī
mōntēs, Id. Nĭvĕōs hērbōsō flŭmĭnĕ cȳcnōs, Virg.
Hērcŭlēs, ĭs, m., *the son of Jupiter and Alcmena, who immortalised himself by his*
labours. Hērcŭlĭs Anthōrĕn, Virg. SYN. Alcīdēs, Tīrȳnthĭŭs, Amphitrȳōnĭădēs.
EPITH. Œtæŭs, Thēbānŭs, Amphitrȳōnĭŭs, cælĭgĕr, gĕnĕrōsŭs, īnvīctŭs, īndŏmĭtŭs, vīctŏr, trĕmēndŭs, mĕtŭēndŭs, hōrrĭdŭs, fōrmĭdăbĭlĭs, impĕrtērrĭtŭs,
strēnŭŭs, mĭnāx, ācĕr, bēllĭcōsŭs, bēllĭpŏtēns, īnsīgnĭs, māgnŭs, clārŭs, cĕlĕbĕr,
ēxĭmĭŭs, pŏtēns, ēgrĕgĭŭs, fŭrvĭdŭs, vĭŏlēntŭs, fĕrōx, fŭrĭōsŭs, fŭrēns, impĭgĕr,
lăbōrĭfĕr, prŏfŭgŭs, văgŭs.
Hērcŭlĕŭs, ă, ŭm, *of Hercules.* Addĭt ĕt Hērcŭlĕōs, Juv.
hĕrĕ, *and* hĕrī, adv., *yesterday.* Hĕrī mĭnās, (Iamb.) Ter.
hĕrīfŭgă, æ, m. f., *a runaway.* Hĕrīfŭgæ fămŭlī, Cat.
hĕrīlĭs, ĕ, *of a master.* Mēnsæque āssuĕtŭs hĕrīlī, Virg.
Hĕrīlŭs, ĭ, m., *an ancient king of Præneste.* Hāc Hĕrīlŭm dēxtrā, Virg.
Hērmăphrŏdītŭs, ĭ, m., *the son of Mercury and Venus.* Cōrpŏrĭs Hērmăphrŏdītŭs,
Aus. EPITH. Bĭfōrmĭs.
Hērmĭnĭŭs, ĭī, m., *the name of a warrior.* Dējĭcĭt Hērmĭnĭŭm, Virg.
Hērmĭŏnē, ēs, f., *the daughter of Menelaus.* Allŏquŏr Hērmĭŏnē, Ov. EPITH.
Fōrmōsă, pūlchră, dĕcōră, vĕnūstă, Lēdæă, Spārtānă.
Hērmŏgĕnēs, ĭs, m., *a man's name.* Quŏd ĕt Hērmŏgĕnēs, Hor.

Hĕrmŭs, ī, m., *a river in Anatolia.* Tŭrbĭdŭs Hĕrmŭs, Virg. EPITH. Tŭrbĭdŭs,
 Lȳdĭŭs, sōrdĭdŭs, fēlīx, dīvĕs, mĕtāllĭfĕr, Lȳdŭs, văgŭs, flāvŭs, ŏpŭlēntŭs.
hĕrnĭă, æ, f., *a rupture.* Hĕrnĭă sācrĭs, Juv. SYN. Entĕrŏcēlē.
Hĕrō, ūs, f., *a priestess of Venus at Sestos, loved by Leander.* EPITH. Sēstĭăs, Sēstă,
 vĕnŭstă, fōrmōsă, spēctābĭlĭs.
Hĕrōdēs, ĭs, m., *the son of Antipater, and king of Judea.* EPITH. Mălŭs, bărbărŭs,
 crūdēlĭs, Ĭdūmæŭs, trūx, crŭēntŭs, fĕrōx, fĕrŭs, tŭrbĭdŭs, īmpĭŭs, īnsānŭs.
hĕrōĭcŭs, ă, ŭm, *heroic, epic.* Rēgēs hĕrōĭcă cārmĭnă laŭdānt, Ov. SYN. Hĕrōŭs.
hĕrōīnă, æ, *and* hĕrōĭs, ĭdĭs, f., *a heroine.* Blāndĭŏr hĕrōīnĭs, (Spond.) Prop.
 Sānctās hĕrōĭdăs īntĕr, Ov.
hĕrōs, ōĭs, m., *a hero.* Hĕrōs Æsŏnĭŭs, Ov. EPITH. Măgnănĭmŭs, ănĭmōsŭs,
 īllūstrĭs, māgnŭs, īngēns, īnsīgnĭs, pŏtēns, fōrtĭs, gĕnĕrōsŭs, clārŭs, īnclȳtŭs.
 V. Illustris.
hĕrōŭs, ă, ŭm, *heroic.* Cārmĭnĭs hĕrōī, Prop.
Hērsē, ēs, f., *a daughter of Cecrops.* Ov.
Hērsĭlĭă, æ, f., *the wife of Romulus.* Hērsĭlĭăm jūssĭs, Ov.
hĕrŭs, ī, m., *a master.* Hīc hĕrŭs Ālbānŭm, Hor. SYN. Dŏmĭnŭs. EPITH.
 Pŏtēns, mĕtŭēndŭs, fĕrōx. V. Dominus.
Hēsĭŏdŭs, ī, m., *a Greek poet.* EPITH. Āscræŭs, Bœōtĭŭs, agrĭcŏlă Hĕlĭcōnĭŭs.
Hēsĭŏnē, ēs, f., *a daughter of Priam.* Hēsĭŏnēn Tĕlămōn, Ov.
Hēspĕrĭă, æ, f., *Italy or Spain.* Sēd quĭs ăd Hēspĕrĭæ, Virg. SYN. Itălĭă,
 Hĭspānĭă.
Hēspĕrĭdēs, ŭm, f. pl., *the daughters of Hesperus.* Cōrnĭgĕr Hēspĕrĭdŭm, Virg.
 EPITH. Vĭgĭlēs, pērvĭgĭlēs, īnsōmnēs, sōllĭcĭtæ, īrrĕquĭĕtæ, sŭgācēs, sōlērtēs,
 ānxĭæ, āttēntæ, hōrtŭlānæ, pōmĭcŏlæ.
Hēspĕrĭŭs, ă, ŭm, *and* Hēspĕrĭs, ĭdĭs, f., *of Hesperia.* Hēspĕrĭŭs scōmbrī, Mart.
 SYN. Itălŭs; Hĭspānŭs; ōccĭdŭŭs.
Hēspĕrŭs, ī, m., *the son of Atlas.* Vĕnĭt Hēspĕrŭs, ītĕ, Virg. SYN. Hēspĕr, vēs-
 pĕr. EPITH. Nōctĭfĕr, ōccĭdŭŭs, ŭmbrĭfĕr, rŭbēns, rōscĭdŭs, frīgĭdŭs. V. Vesper.
hēstērnŭs, ă, ŭm, *of yesterday.* Īnflātum hēstērnō vēnās, Virg.
heū, interj., *alas !* Heū ŭbī pāctă, Ov.
heūs, adv., *ho.* Heūs, īnquĭt, jŭvĕnēs, Virg. SYN. Ēja ăgĕ, ēja ăgĭtĕ.
hēxămĕtĕr, *or* trŭs, ī, *a hexameter verse.* Hēxămĕtrĭs ĕpĭgrămmă, Mart.
Hĭārbās, æ, m., *a king of Getulia.* Dēspēctŭs Hĭārbās, Virg. EPITH. Gætŭlŭs,
 Lĭbўcŭs, Maŭrŭs, prŏcāx, sprētŭs, nĕglēctŭs, fĕrōx, fŭrēns.
hĭātŭs, ūs, m., *a gaping.* Trāxĭt hĭātŭs ăquăm, Prop. SYN. Rīmă; vŏrāgo,
 gŭrgĕs, bărathrŭm, ăbўssŭs. EPITH. Vāstŭs, pătŭlŭs, tērrĭfĭcŭs, pătēns, căvĕr-
 nōsŭs, căvŭs, prŏfūndŭs. V. Gurges, vorago.
hĭbērnă. V. Hyberna.
Hibērnĭă, æ, *and* nē, ēs, f., *Ireland.* Hībērnĭs Hībērnĭă nōmĕn, Mant. Glăcĭālĭs Hĭbērnē, Cl.
hĭbīscŭs, ī, m., *marsh mallows.* Cōmpēllĕre hĭbīscō, Virg. EPITH. Vĭrĭdĭs,
 tĕnŭĭs, vĭrēns, grăcĭlĭs.
hic, hæc, hŏc, *this.* Hīc vĭr hĭc ēst, Virg.
hīc, adv., *here.* Hīc ŏrĭtŭr, Virg. SYN. Hūc.
Hĭcĕtāŏnĭŭs, ă, ŭm, *of Ilicetaon.* Virg.
hĭēms. V. Hyems.
Hĭĕră, æ, f., *an island sacred to Vulcan.* EPITH. Æŏlĭă, Vūlcānĭă, fūmōsă.—
 2. -ēră, æ, f., *a nymph.* Sȳlvēstrĭs Hĭĕră, Virg.
Hĭĕrŭsălĕm, *or* Jĕrūsălĕm, (*indecl.*) f., *the capital of Judea.* SYN. Sŏlўmă, Hĭĕrŭ-
 sŏlўmă. EPITH. Ŏpŭlēntă, māgnĭfĭcă, dīvĕs, īnclўtă, nōbĭlĭs, sānctă, cūltă, vĕnĕrāndă, vĕnĕrābĭlĭs.
Hĭlărĭă, ōrŭm, n. pl., *feasts in honour of Cybele.* EPITH. Fēstă, lætă.
hĭlărĭs, ĕ, *merry.* Ŏdērŭnt hĭlărĕm, Hor. SYN. Hĭlărŭs, lætŭs, gaŭdēns, ălăcĕr,
 ŏvăns, gĕnĭālĭs, fēstīvŭs, jŏcōsŭs, făcētŭs.
* hĭlărĭtās, ātĭs, f., *mirth.* SYN. Lætĭtĭă, gaŭdĭŭm, fēstīvĭtās, ălacrĭtās. V. Gaudium, lætitia.
hĭlăro, ās, *to make merry.* Vōx hĭlărāvĕrăt ŏrĕ, Ov. SYN. Ēxhĭlăro, ōblēcto,
 lætĭfĭco, recrĕo. V. Gaudeo.
hĭlărŭs, ă, ŭm, *merry.* Vĭdēs hĭlărō grāndēscĕre ădaŭctū, Lucr.
hīllă, æ, f., *a sausage.* Āc măgĭs hīllĭs, Hor

hĭlŭm, ĭ, n., *a very nothing.* Pŏndĕrĭs hīlŭm, Lucr.

Hīmĕră, ōrŭm, n. pl., *a city of Sicily.* Hīmĕrăque ēt Dĭdўmēn, Ov. hīnc, adv., *hence.* Hīnc īllæ, Ter.

* hĭnnĭo, ĭs, ī̄, ītŭm, *to neigh.* Cŏncūssĭs ārtŭbŭs hĭnnīt, Lucr. hĭnnītŭs, ūs, m., *a neighing.* Nōn hĭnnītŭs ĭtĕnı, Lucr. SYN. Ĕquōrŭm frĕmĭtŭs, clămōr. EPITH. Sŏnōrŭs, ăcūtŭs, ācĕr, trĕmŭlŭs, hōrrĭfĭcŭs.

hĭnnŭlĕŭs, ĭ, m., *a fawn.* Vītās hĭnnŭlĕō mē sĭmĭllĭs, Hor. hĭo, ūs, *to gape, yawn.* Saŭcĭă tīgrĭs hĭăt, Virg. Gaŭdĕt hĭāns, Id. Hĭppăsĭdēs, æ, m., *the son of Hippasus.* Hĭppăsŭs, ĭ, m., *a centaur.* Hĭppăsŏn, ēt sūmmĭs, Ov. Hĭppŏcŏōn, ōntĭs, m., *a man's name.* Ēt quōs Hĭppŏcŏōn, Ov. Hĭppocrēnē, ēs, f., *a fountain in Bœotia.* Ăgănĭppĭdŏs Hĭppŏcrēnēs, Hor. Fāma ēst Hĭppŏcrēnē, Aus. SYN. Ăgănīppē. EPITH. Pĕgăsĕă, Ăŏnĭă, Hĕlĭcōnĭs, Ăgănĭppĭs, sacră, pēllūcĭdă, clără. V. Aganippe. Hĭppŏdămās, āntĭs, m., *the father of Perimele.* Quōd pătĕr Hĭppŏdămās, Ov. Hĭppŏdămē, ēs, *or* mĭă, æ, f., *the daughter of Œnomaus.* EPITH. Pīsæă, Ēlæă, vĕlōx, cĭtă, cŏncĭtă, præpĕs, vŏlucrĭs.—2. *A name of Briseis.* EPITH. Lўrnēsĭs, Lўrnēssĭă. Hĭppŏlўtē, ēs, f., *the queen of the Amazons.* Seŭ cīrcum Hĭppŏlўtēn, Virg. EPITH. Fĕrōx, vīrāgo, fēlīx, Thrēĭcĭă. EPITH. Mægnēsĭă, lāscĭvă, ădūltĕră. Hĭppŏlўtŭs, ĭ, m., *the son of Theseus.* Ibăt ĕt Hĭppŏlўtī, Virg. SYN. Thēsīdēs. EPITH. Pūdīcŭs, cāstŭs, ĭnsōns, vĕrēcūndŭs, fōrmōsŭs, vĕnūstŭs, mĭsĕr, ĭnfēlīx. hĭppŏmănēs, (*indecl.*) n., *a piece of flesh on the forehead of a colt newly foaled.* Hĭppŏmănēs quŏd sæpĕ mălæ, Virg.

Hĭppŏmĕnēs, ĭs, m., *the husband of Atalanta.* Hĭppŏmĕnēn ădĭī, Ov. Hĭppŏnă, æ, f., *the tutelary goddess of horses.* Hĭppŏnam ēt fācĭēs, Juv. Hĭppŏtădēs, ĭs, m., *the son of Hippotes, Æolus.* Claŭsĕrăt Hĭppŏtădēs, Ov. Hĭppŏthŏŭs, ĭ, m., *one of the hunters of the Calydonian boar.* Ov. hĭppūrŭs, ĭ, m., *a fish.* Hĭppūrī cĕlĕrēs, Ov. hĭrcīnŭs, ă, ŭm, *of a goat.* Īllĕ sĕd hĭrcīnō, Ov. SYN. Caprīnŭs. hircōsŭs, ă, ŭm, *goatish.* Hīrcōsō prĕmīt ōscŭlŏ, Mart. bīrcŭs, *and* quŭs, ĭ, m., *a goat.* Cērtāvīt ŏb hīrcŭm, Hor. SYN. Hœdŭs, căpĕr, EPITH. Cōrnĭgĕr, sētĭgĕr, hīrsūtŭs, ĭmbēllĭs, văgŭs, sălĭēns, prōcāx. V. Caper. Hīrpīnŭs, ĭ, m., *a man's name.* Hīrpīnī vĕtĕrēs, Hor. hīrsūtŭs, *and* hīrtŭs, ă, ŭm, *rough.* Hīrsūtŭmquĕ sŭpērcĭlĭŭm, Virg. Stĕtĭt hīrtă căpīllĭs, Ov. SYN. Hīspĭdŭs, vīllōsŭs, pĭlōsŭs, sētōsŭs. hĭrūdo, ĭnĭs, f., *a horse-leech.* Plēnă crŭōrĭs hĭrūdo, Hor. EPITH. Pălūstrĭs, mōrdāx, tĕnāx. hĭrūndĭnĭnŭs, ă, ŭm, *of a swallow.* Sĕgĕs ēst hĭrūndĭnīnō, Mart. hĭrūndo, ĭnĭs, f., *a swallow.* Cīrcūmvŏlĭtāvīt hĭrūndo, Virg. SYN. Prŏgnē, Daŭlĭăs. EPITH. Ārgŭtă, gărrŭlă, nĭgră, văgă, pĕregrīnă, quĕrŭlă, văgăbūndă, lŏquāx, Cecrŏpĭă, Pāndĭōnĭă, Thrēĭcĭă. V. Progne. hĭsco, ĭs, *to gape.* Vōcĭbŭs hīsco, Virg. SYN. Hĭo ; ōs dīdūco, ăpĕrĭo. Hīspānī, ōrŭm, m. pl., *the Spaniards.* Hīs Hīspānŭs ăgĕr, Aus. SYN. Hēspĕrĭī, Ĭbĕrī. EPITH. Fĕrōcēs, pūgnācēs, aŭdācēs, vānī, sŭpērbī, dūrī. Hīspănĭă, æ, f., *Spain.* Ēst Hīspānĭă, Gāllĭcŭs āxĭs, Juv. SYN. Hēspĕrĭă, Ĭbĕrĭă. EPITH. Pŏpŭlōsă, fērtĭlĭs, dīvĕs, fĕrāx, nōbĭlĭs, pūgnāx. hĭspĭdŭs, *and* dōsŭs, ă, ŭm, *bristly.* Bārba hĭspĭdă mēntō, Sil. V. Hirsutus. hĭstŏrĭă, æ, f., *history.* Prīmŭs ĭn hĭstŏrĭā, Mart. SYN. Ănnālēs. EPITH. Vĕtŭs, prīscă, ăntīquă, mĕmŏrābĭlĭs, cĕlebrĭs, nōbĭlĭs, ārgŭtă, nŏvă, rĕcēns, mægĭstră. hĭstŏrĭcŭs, ĭ, m., *an historian.* Quĭs dăbĭt hĭstŏrĭcŏ, Juv. ¶ hīstrĭo, ōnĭs, m., *a stage-player.* SYN. Mĭmŭs, gēstĭcŭlātŏr, lŭdĭo, cīrcŭlātŏr, præstĭgĭătŏr, cōmœdŭs. EPITH. Hĭlărĭs, fēstīvŭs, lætŭs, fāllāx, gārrŭlŭs, dŏlōsŭs, vĕrbōsŭs, lŏquāx, lĕvĭs, mēndāx; sŭbdŏlŭs, rĭdĭcŭlŭs, jŏcŭlārĭs, ārgūtŭs, prŏtērvŭs, pĕtŭlāns, ĭnēptŭs, ĭndŭstrĭŭs, gnāvŭs, scĕnĭcŭs. hĭŭlcŭs, ă, ŭm, *gaping.* Hŏc, ŭbi hĭŭlcă sĭtĭ, Virg. SYN. Hĭāns, pătēns, hĭscēns, dĕhīscēns, ăpĕrtŭs, rīmōsŭs, fīssŭs, fătīscēns. hŏdĭē, adv., *to-day.* Ēst hŏdĭē, crās, Ov. SYN. Hŏc dĭē ; nūnc, mŏdŏ. hŏdĭērnŭs, ă, ŭm, *of to-day.* Hŏdĭērnæ crāstĭnă sūmmæ, Hor. hœdīnŭs, ă, ŭm, *of a kid.* Hœdīnā tĭbĭ pēllĕ, Mart.

hœdŭlŭs, ī, m., *a little kid.* Hœdŭlŭs ĕt tōtō, Juv.

hœdŭs, ī, m., *a kid.* Cōrnĭbŭs hœdī, Virg. V. Caper.

hŏlŏcaŭstŭm, ī, n., *a burnt-sacrifice.* Hŏlŏcaŭstă rŭīnæ, Prud. Syn. Sacrĭfĭcĭŭm, lībāmĕn. Epith. Sōlĕnnĕ, pīnguĕ, ŏdōrātŭm, pĭŭm, cāstŭm, pūrŭm, sacrŭm. V. Victima.

Hŏmērĭcŭs, ă, ŭm, *of Homer.* Grādīvŭs Hŏmērĭcŭs, aŭdīs, Juv.

Hŏmērŭs, ī, m., *the celebrated Greek poet.* Dōrmītăt Hŏmērŭs, Hor. Syn. Mæŏnĭdēs. Epith. Cōlŏphōnĭăcŭs, Sălămīnĭăcŭs, Ăchæŭs; māgnŭs, vīnōsŭs, īnsĭgnĭs, ætērnŭs, āntīquŭs, cæcŭs, săpĭēns, dīvīnŭs, dōctŭs, săcĕr, grăvīs, grāndĭs, sūblīmĭs, jūcūndŭs, sōlĕrs, ĭmmōrtālĭs.

hŏmĭcīdă, æ, m., *a murderer.* Sīc hŏmĭcīdă Mīlōnī, Juv. Syn. Sævŭs, crŭēntŭs, fĕrōx.

hŏmĭcīdĭŭm, ĭī, n., *a murder.* Hŏmĭcīdĭă lūdăt, Prud. Epith. Sævŭm, crŭdēlĕ.

hŏmo, ĭnĭs, m. f., *a man or woman.* Illĕ mălīs hŏmĭnŭm, Virg. Syn. Mōrtālĭs, tērrĭgĕnă; vĭr. Epith. Frăgĭlĭs, cădŭcŭs, vĭlĭs, mĭsĕr, īnfēlīx, ærŭmnōsŭs, īmbĕcīllŭs, īncaŭtŭs, sōlĕrs, prōvĭdŭs, prūdēns, mēndāx, fāllāx, ĭnōps.

Hŏmōlē, ēs, f., *a mountain of Thrace.* Hŏmōlēn Ōthrȳnquĕ, Virg.

hŏmūllŭs, ŭlŭs, ūncŭlŭs, ī; *and* ūncĭo, ōnĭs, m., *dimin. of* homo. Hŏmūncĭŏ quāntŭs, Juv.

hŏnēstās, ātĭs, f., *honesty.* Cūrăt hŏnēstātĕm, Mant. Syn. Hŏnēstŭm, dĕcŭs, dĕcōrŭm, vīrtŭs.

hŏnēsto, ās, *to adorn.* Vŭltŭs hŏnēstăt, Claud.

hŏnēstŭs, ă, ŭm, *honest.* Fēcĭt hŏnēstī, Juv. Syn. Dĕcōrŭs, dĕcēns; laŭdābĭlĭs, vĕnĕrābĭlĭs, vĕnĕraŭdŭs, laŭdātŭs, hŏnōrātŭs, hŏnōrāndŭs, laŭdāndŭs, cōlēndŭs.

hŏnŏr, *or* ōs, ōrĭs, m., *honour.* Plēnī quĭd hŏnōrĭbŭs ānnī, Cor. Sev. Ăquīlō dēcŭssĭt hŏnōrĕm, Virg. Syn. Glōrĭă, laŭs, fāmă, dĕcŭs, nōmĕn; dĭgnĭtās; rĕvĕrēntĭă, cŭltŭs. Epith. Ēgrĕgĭŭs, sōlēnnĭs, exĭmĭŭs, cōnspĭcŭŭs, mūndānŭs, tērrēnŭs, tŭmĭdŭs, grātŭs, pŏpŭlārĭs, vānŭs, mĕrĭtŭs, ætērnŭs, īncērtŭs, āmbĭtĭōsŭs, quæsītŭs, ōptātŭs. V. Gloria.

hŏnōrātŭs, ă, ŭm, *the pass. partic. of* honoro. Cūjŭs hŏnōrātīs, Prop. V. Celeber.

hŏnōrĭfĭcŭs, ă, ŭm, *doing honour.* Sī quĭd hŏnōrĭfĭcŭm, Mart.

hŏnōro, ās, *to do honour.* Mīlĕs hŏnōrăt, Mart. Syn. Cŏlo, vĕnĕrŏr. V. Adoro, laudo.

hŏnōrŭs, ă, ŭm, *honourable.* Hŏnōrā Arcŭĕrīm fāmā, Stat.

hŏră, æ, f., *an hour.* Crēscĭt ĭn hŏrās, Virg. Epith. Fŭgāx, cĕlĕr, īrrĕvŏcābĭlĭs, prōpĕrāns, fŭgĭēns, vēlōx, mōbĭlĭs, lĕvĭs, sŭbĭtă, răpĭdă, mūtābĭlĭs, præcēps, ăgĭlĭs, flŭēns, lūgĭtīvă, cĭtă. V. Tempus.

Hŏrātĭŭs, ĭī, m., *the Roman poet.* Nŭmĕrōsŭs Hŏrātĭŭs aŭrēs, Ov. Syn. Flāccŭs. Epith. Dōctŭs, ācĕr, nŭmĕrōsŭs, lȳrĭcŭs, mōrdāx, Călăbĕr.—2. ă, ŭm, *of the three Horatii, who fought against the Curiatii.* Ēt Hŏrātĭă pīlă, Prop.

hŏrdĕŭm, ĕī, n., *barley.* Māndāvīmŭs hŏrdĕă sŭlcĭs, Virg.

hŏrīzōn, ōntĭs, m., *the horizon.* Mĕmŏrātŭr hŏrīzōn, Man.

hōrnŭs, ă, ŭm, *of this year.* Dēnŭntĭăt hōrnĭs, Hor.

hŏrrēndŭs, ă, ŭm, *dreadful.* Clāmōrēs sĭmŭl hŏrrēndōs, Virg. V. Horridus.

hŏrrĕo, *and* ēsco, ĭs, rŭī, *to be rough, to shiver, dread.* Ā tērgo hŏrrēbĭs, Virg. Hŏrrēsco rĕfĕrēns, Id. Syn. Ēxhŏrrĕo, ēxhŏrrēsco, ĭnhŏrrĕo, pĕrhŏrrĕo, trĕmo, rĭgĕo, tĭmĕo. V. Horror, tremo, timeo.

hŏrrĕŭm, ĕī, n., *a barn.* Hŏrrĕă mōssēs, Virg. Syn. Grānārĭŭm. Epith. Cĕrĕālĕ, dīvĕs, plēnŭm, trītĭcĕŭm, căpāx, văcŭŭm, rĕfĕrtŭm, stīpātŭm, āltŭm, pēnsĭlĕ.

hŏrrĭbĭlĭs, ĕ, *horrible.* Hŏrrĭbĭlī vīsū, Virg. Syn. Hŏrrĭdŭs, hŏrrēndŭs.

hŏrrĭdŭs, *and* dŭlŭs, ă, ŭm, *rugged.* Hŏrrĭdŭs ĭn jăcŭlīs, Virg. Syn. Hŏrrĭbĭlĭs, hŏrrēndŭs, hŏrrĭfĭcŭs, hŏrrĭbĭlĭs, mĕtŭēndŭs, trĕmēndŭs, stŭpēndŭs, tērrĭfĭcŭs, hĭspĭdŭs, hīrsūtŭs, āspĕr.

hŏrrĭfĭco, ās, *to make one afraid.* Hŏrrĭfĭcānt; ăgĭt ĭpsĕ, Virg. Syn. Tērrĭfĭco, tērrĕo.

hŏrrĭfĭcŭs, *and* fĕr, ă, ŭm, *terrible.* Hŏrrĭfĭcīs jūxtă, Virg. V. Horridus.

hŏrrĭsŏnŭs, ă, ŭm, *making a dreadful noise.* Tŭm dēmum hŏrrĭsŏnō, Virg.

hŏrrŏr, ōrĭs, m., *a shivering, horror.* Ingrŭĭt hŏrrŏr, Virg. Syn. Frĕmĭtŭs, trĕmŏr; tĕrrŏr, fŏrmīdo. Epith. Dīrŭs, ăcĕrbŭs, trĕmŭlŭs, lūrĭdŭs, fĕrŭs, ēxānguĭs, tĕrrĭfĭcŭs, Mārtĭŭs, sērvīlĭs, ĭmplācābĭlĭs, ēxĭtĭālĭs, ātĕr, sŏnōrŭs. V. Timor.

hŏrtāmĕn, ĭnĭs, n. : mēntŭm, ī, n. ; tātĭo, ōnĭs, f. ; and tātŭs, ūs, m., counsel, exhortation. Nōrĭnt hŏrtāmĭnă vōcĭs, Luc. Dăbăt hŏrtāmēntă săcĕrdōs, Mant. Blāndĭs hŏrtātĭbŭs ĭmplĕt, Sil. Syn. Impūlsŭs, mŏnĭtŭs ; stĭmŭlī. Epith. Vĕhĕmēns, grăvĭs, fōrtĭs, ācrĭs, ūrgēns, fĭdēlĭs, dīsērtŭs, fācūndŭs.

hŏrtātŏr, ōrĭs, m., an adviser. Hŏrtātŏr scĕlĕrŭm, Virg. Syn. Suāsŏr, aūctŏr. Hŏrtēnsĭŭs, ĭī, m., a celebrated orator, the rival of Cicero. Nēc mĭnŭs Hŏrtēnsī, Ov.

Hŏrtĭnŭs, ă, ŭm, of Horta, a city of Etruria. Hŏrtīnæ clāssēs, Virg.

hŏrtŏr, ārĭs, to exhort. Hŏrtāmūr fārī, Virg. Syn. Exhŏrtŏr, ădhŏrtŏr, ăcŭo, sūscĭto, stĭmŭlo, ĭncēndo, āccēndo, īnflāmmo, īnstīgo, sōllĭcĭto, īncĭto, cōncĭto, pēllo, ĭmpēllo, fĕro, mŏnĕo, suādĕo, ēxăcŭo, ēxstĭmŭlo.

hŏrtŭs, and tŭlŭs, ī, m., a garden. Prætēxĭtŭr hŏrtĭs, Stat. Syn. Vĭrĭdārĭŭm, vĭrētŭm, pōmārĭŭm. Epith. Pīnguĭs, fĕrāx, mōllĭs, rĭgŭŭs, īrrĭgŭŭs, hĭlārĭs, cūltŭs, ēxcūltŭs, pōmōsŭs, fēlīx, pōmĭfĕr, rĕdŏlēns, frāgrāns, ŏdōrātŭs, hālāns, vīrĭdĭs, plăcĭdŭs, ămœnŭs, gĕnĭālĭs, jūcūndŭs, pīctŭs, sēptŭs, flōrĭcŏmŭs, grātŭs, ūmbrōsŭs, rīdēns, lætŭs, frūctĭfĕr, flōrĭdŭs, flōrēns, frōndēns, fērtĭlĭs, vĭrēns, sŭbūrbānŭs.

hōspĕs, ĭtĭs, m., a guest. Hōspĕs ăb hōspĭtĕ tūtŭs, Ov.—2. a host. Ămābĭlĭs hōspĕs, Hor. Epith. Dūlcĭs, grātŭs, ămīcŭs, jūcūndŭs, ūrbānŭs, mūnĭfĭcŭs, bĕnīgnŭs, fācĭlĭs.—3. a stranger. Syn. Advĕnă, pĕregrīnŭs. Epith. Cārŭs, ēxtērnŭs, văgŭs, mōbĭlĭs, nŏvŭs, īgnōtŭs, sūpplēx, ămīcŭs, fătīgātŭs, ĭnūrbānŭs, prŏcāx.

hōspĭtă, æ, f., a hostess. Hōspĭtă Dēmŏphŏōn, Ov.

hōspĭtālĭs, ĕ, of a guest. Ūmbram hōspĭtālĕm, Hor.

hōspĭtālĭtās, ātĭs, f., and hōspĭtĭŭm, ĭī, n., hospitality. Hōspĭtālĭtātĕ dŏmŭs, Mart. Hōspĭtĭum āntīquŭm, Virg. Hōspĭtĭŏ prŏpĕrăt, Id. Epith. Mītĕ, pĭŭm, dūlcĕ, ămœnŭm, bĕnīgnŭm, grātŭm, quæsītŭm, ōptātŭm, cōmĕ, ăpērtŭm, pătēns, părātŭm.

hōspĭtŭs, ă, ŭm, foreign. Hōspĭtă nāvĭs. Syn. Pĕregrīnŭs.

hōstĭă, æ, f., a victim. Hōstĭă blāndă, Ov. Syn. Vīctĭmă, pĭācŭlŭm. Epith. Plācābĭlĭs, mȳstĭcă, pĭă, īnsōns, sacră. V. Victima.

hōstĭcŭs, ă, ŭm, and īlĭs, ĕ, hostile. Hōstĭcŭs aūfĕrĕt ēnsĭs, Hor. Hōstīlīque āggĕrĕ sēptŭs, Virg. Syn. Ĭnĭmīcŭs.

hōstīlĭtĕr, adv., in a hostile manner. Spērnītque hōstīlĭtĕr ōmnēs, Ov. Syn. Crūdēlĭtĕr, fĕrōcĭtĕr.

hōstĭs, ĭs, m. and f., an enemy. Hōstĭs hăbēt mūrōs, Virg. Syn. Ĭnĭmīcŭs, ădvērsārĭŭs. Epith. Ādvērsŭs, īnfēnsŭs, īnfēstŭs, sævŭs, ĭmpĭŭs, crŭēntŭs, fĕrŭs, bārbārŭs, sŭpērbŭs, pērfĭdŭs, ĭnĭquŭs, ăcērbŭs, īnvīsŭs, trŭcŭlēntŭs, pērnĭcĭōsŭs, pūgnāx, sānguĭnŏlēntŭs, fĕrōx, mĭnāx, īnsĭdĭōsŭs, vĕrēndŭs, crūdēlĭs, caūtŭs, īmmītĭs, ĭnhŭmānŭs, aūdāx, vēsānŭs, fŭrĭbūndŭs, prædātŏr, ĭmpătĭēns, fŏrmīdābĭlĭs, āmēns, vērsūtŭs, īntērrĭtŭs, ĭmpērtērrĭtŭs, vĭgĭl, pērvĭgĭl. V. Invado.

hūc, adv., hither. Hūc ădēs, ō, Virg.

hūccĭnĕ, interj., what hither ? Hūccĭnĕ rērŭm, Pers.

huĭc, or hŭĭc, hūjŭs, from hic. Huĭc ūnī fōrsăn, Virg. Lætŭs hŭĭc, Stat. Cŏrpŏrĭs hūjŭs, Ov.

hūmānĭtās, ātĭs, f., humanity. Hūmānĭtātī quī sē, Phæd. Syn. Cōmĭtās, ūrbānĭtās, bĕnīgnĭtās, clēmēntĭă, lēnĭtās.

hūmānĭtĕr, adv., courteously. Syn. Hūmānē.

hūmānĭtŭs, adv., as a man. Mī fŭĕrīt hūmānĭtŭs, ŭt tĕnĕātĭs, Enn.

hūmānŭs, ă, ŭm, human. Nōn hæc hūmānĭs, Virg. Syn. Cōmĭs, ūrbānŭs, mītĭs, āffābĭlĭs, grātŭs, trāctābĭlĭs, bĕnīgnŭs, lēnĭs, clēmēns. V. Comis.

hŭmātŏr, ōrĭs, m., one who buries. Pœnŭs hŭmātŏr, Luc.

hŭmēcto, ās, to moisten. Quā nĭgĕr hŭmēctăt, Virg. Syn. Mădĕfăcĭo, īrrĭgo, ĭrrōro, ĭmbŭo, rĭgo, ăquĭs spārgo.

hūmēns, ntĭs, damp. Hūmēntēmque Aūrōră pŏlō, Virg.

hūmĕo, ēs, ŭī, to be damp. Hūmĕt ărēnă, Ov.

hŭmĕrī, ōrŭm, m. pl., shoulders. Infēlīx hŭmĕrōs, Prop. Syn. Scăpŭlæ ; ārmī.

K

Epith. Lātī, nĭvĕī, tĕrĕtēs, ĕbūrnī, cāndĭdī, ālbēntēs, rōbūstī, vālĭdī, nērvōsī, fŏrtēs.

hŭmēsco, ĭs, *to grow moist.* Hūmēscŭnt spŭmīs, Virg.

hŭmī, adv., *on the ground.* Prŏcŭmbĭt hŭmī, Virg.

hŭmĭdŭs, *and* ĭdŭlŭs, ă, ŭm, *damp.* Nōx hūmĭdă cælō, Virg. Syn. Hūmēns, mădĭdŭs, mădēns, ūdŭs.

hŭmĭfĕr, *and* fĭcŭs, ă, ŭm, *moistening.* Nārĭbŭs hūmĭfĕrŭm, Cl. Syn. Hūmĭdŭs.

hŭmĭlĭs, ĕ, *low, humble.* Ātque hŭmĭlēs hăbĭtārĕ căsās, Virg. Syn. Dēmīssŭs, sŭbmīssŭs ; vīlĭs, ābjēctŭs, cōntēmptŭs, ĭgnōbĭlĭs.

hŭmo, ās, *to bury.* Mœstŭs hŭmābăt, Lucr. Syn. Ĭnhŭmo, tŭmŭlo. V. Sepelio.

hŭmŏr, ōrĭs, m., *moisture.* Sūdānt hŭmōrĕ lăcūnæ, Virg. Syn. Hūmĭdĭtās, mădŏr ; ăquă, liquŏr. Epith. Tĕnĕr, ăquătĭlĭs, plŭvĭŭs, ēxūndāns, liquĭdŭs, dūlcĭs, spūmĕŭs, fūmĭdŭs, līvĭdŭs, rōscĭdŭs, frīgĭdŭs, ăquātĭcŭs, pīnguĭs, tĕnāx, mădĭdŭs, lēntŭs, spārsŭs.

hŭmŭs, ĭ, f., *the earth, the ground.* Spārgĭte hŭmŭm fŏllĭs, Virg. Syn. Tērră, tēllŭs, ăgĕr, cāmpŭs. V. Terra, jaceo.

Hŭnnī, ōrŭm, m. pl., *a people of Scythia.* Epith. Fĕrōcēs, tōrvī, bēllĭgĕrī, bēllācēs, fĕrī.

Hўăcīnthĭă, ōrŭm, n. pl., *festivals in honour of Hyacinthus.* Rĕdĕūnt Hўăcīnthĭă pōmpā, Ov.

hўăcīnthĭnŭs, ă, ŭm, *of a violet colour.* Cīrcum hŭmĕrōs hўăcīnthĭnă lænă, Pers.

Hўăcīnthŭs, ĭ, m., *the son of Pierus and Clio, metamorphosed into a hyacinth.* Fērrūgĭnĕōs hўăcīnthōs, Virg. Epith. Rŭbēns, vĕnūstŭs, pūlchĕr, dĕcōrŭs, rŏsĕŭs, mōllĭs, flŏrēns, cāndĭdŭs, lūtĕŏlŭs, nĭtēns.—2. *a precious stone.* Epith. Vĭŏlācĕŭs, fūlgĭdŭs, mĭcāns. V. Gemma.

Hўădēs, ŭm, f. pl., *a constellation.* Ārctūrŭm plŭvĭāsque Hўădās, Virg. Syn. Plēĭădēs, Atlāntĭdēs. Epith. Plŭvĭæ, nīmbōsæ, ūdæ, trīstēs, īmbrĭfĕræ, nŭbĭlæ, plŭvĭōsæ. V. Pleiades.

hўænă, æ, f., *an hyena.* Mīrāmŭr hўēnăm, Ov.

Hўălē, ēs, f., *a nymph of Diana's train.* Ov.

hўălŭs, ĭ, f., *glass ; green colour.* Cārpēbānt hўālī, Ov.

Hўāntĕŭs, *and* ĭŭs, ă, ŭm, *Bœotian.* Exŭl Hўāntĕōs, Stat. Hўāntĭŭs ōrĕ, Ov.

Hўās, āntĭs *or* æ, m., *the son of Atlas.* Mātĕr Hўān, Ov. Sīdŭs Hўāntĭs ĕrĭt, Id.

hўbērnă, *and* nācŭlă, ōrŭm, n. pl., *winter-quarters.* Rŭtŭlīs hўbērnă sŭbāctīs, Virg. Nōn hўbērnācŭlă sēgnēs, Claud.

hўbērno, ās, *to winter.* Hўbērnātquĕ mĕŭm, Pers. Syn. Hўĕmo.

hўbērnŭs, ă, ŭm, *belonging to winter.* Ūvĭdŭs hўbērnā, Virg. Syn. Hўĕmālĭs.

Hўblă, æ. *or* ē, ēs, f., *a town and mountain in Sicily.* Pāscăt ĕt Hўblă, Mart. Epith. Crŏcĕă, Trīnacrĭs, Sĭcŭlă, fērtĭlĭs, ŏlēns, rŏdŏlēns, mēllĭfŭă, flŏrēns, dĭvĕs.

Hўblæŭs, ă, ŭm, *of Hybla.* Hўblæĭs ăpĭbŭs, Virg. Syn. Sĭcŭlŭs, Trīnacrĭŭs.

hўbrĭdă, æ, *and* hўbrĭs, ĭdĭs, m. f., *a mongrel creature.* Hўbrĭdă sŭm, Mart. Hўbrĭdă quō pāctō, Hor.

Hўdāspēs, ĭs, m., *a river in India.* Mēdŭs Hўdāspēs, Virg. Epith. Gēmmĭfĕr, aŭrĭfĕr, dĭvĕs, clārŭs, tŭmĭdŭs, gēmmĕŭs, ŏpŭlēntŭs, Mēdŭs, Indŭs, Nўsæŭs ; Eōŭs, Năbăthæŭs, săbŭlōsŭs.

hўdră, æ, f., *a water-serpent.* Hўdră fĕrĭs, Mart. Syn. Ěchīdnă. Epith. Rĕnāscēns, ĭmmānĭs, dīră, ĭmprŏbă, nŏcēns, fĕrōx, fĕră, hŏrrēndă, sēptēmplēx, rĕdĭvīvă, pŭllŭlāns, tŭmēns, squālēns, fœcūndă, sævă, vĕnēnōsă, fōrmīdābĭlĭs, crūdēlĭs, hŏrrĭdă, hŏrrēns, Lērnæă, Hērcŭlĕă.

• hўdrĭă, æ, f., *a water-pot.* V. Vas, poculum.

hydrŏpĭcŭs, ă, ŭm, *dropsical.* Cūrēs hўdrŏpĭcŭs, Hor. Epith. Tūrgĭdŭs, ĭnflātŭs, tŭmĭdŭs, ægĕr, lānguĭdŭs, ăquōsŭs, pāllĭdŭs, sĭtĭēns.

• hydrŏps, ōpĭs, m., *dropsy.* Dīrŭs hўdrŏps, Hor. Crēscĭt hўdrŏps, Ser. Sam. Syn. Ăqua ĭntērcŭs.

hўdrŭs, ĭ, m., *a water-serpent.* Āntĕ pĕdēs hўdrŭm, Virg. Epith. Vĕnēnōsŭs,

nĭgĕr, tŏrvŭs, strīdēns, răbīdŭs, līvēns, sævŭs, Nīlĭgĕnă, Lĭbўcŭs, Gŏrgŏnĕŭs.
V. Serpens, hydra.

hўĕmālĭs, ĕ, *winterly.* Nĭmbĭs hўĕmālĭbŭs aŭctŭs, Ov. Syn. Hўbērnŭs, brŭ-
mālĭs, glăcĭālĭs, gĕlĭdŭs, frīgĭdŭs; plŭvĭālĭs, ăquōsŭs.

hўĕmo, ās, *to winter.* Pīscēs hўĕmāt mărĕ, Hor. Syn. Hўbērno.

hўēms, ĕmĭs, f., *winter.* Nŏctem hўĕmēmquĕ, Virg. Syn. Brŭmă. Epith.
Frīgĭdă, glăcĭālĭs, āspĕră, īnfōrmĭs, gĕlĭdă, plŭvĭōsă, ăquōsă, sævă, fĕră, vēntōsă,
īmbrĭfĕră, īnmītĭs, fērrĕă, dŭră, tŭrbĭdă, ŭndōsă, mălīgnă, stĕrĭlĭs, fĕrōx, nĭvōsă,
nīmbōsă, cānă, ăcērbă, dīră, ālgēns, īntŏlĕrābĭlĭs, pĭgră, sēgnĭs, īgnāvă, Bŏrĕālĭs,
Ăquĭlōnĭă, hŏrrĭdă, cōncrētă, brŭmālĭs. V. Glacies, gelu, nix, frigus, bruma,
gelo.

Hўgēă, æ, f., *the goddess of health.* Nōn quŏd Hўgēă pŏtēst, Mart.

Hўlāctŏr, ŏrĭs, m., *the name of a dog.* Ăcŭtæ vōcĭs Hўlāctŏr, Ov.

Hўlæŭs, ī, m., *a centaur slain by Theseus.* Ēt māgno Hўlæŭm, Virg.

Hўlăs, æ, m., *the son of Theodamas, stolen by nymphs.* Aŭt mŭltŭm quæsītŭs
Hўlăs, Juv. Epith. Thĕŏdămāntæŭs, pārvŭs, pŭlchĕr, fōrmōsŭs.

Hўlāx, āctĭs, m., *the name of a dog.* Hўlāx īn līmĭnĕ lātrăt, Virg.

Hўlēs, æ, m., *the name of a centaur.* Ov.

Hўleŭs, ĕĭ or ĕŏs, *one of the hunters of the Calydonian boar.*

Hymēn, *or* Hўmĕnæŭs, ī, m., *the god of marriage.* Vŭlgŭs Hўmēn Hўmĕnæĕ
vŏcăt, Ov. Hўmēn, ō Hўmĕnæĕ, Catull. Epith. Fōrmōsŭs, mītĭs, dŭlcĭs,
fēstŭs, blāndŭs, cāstŭs, hŏnēstŭs.

Hўmēttĭŭs, ă, ŭm, *of Hymettus.* Hўmēttĭă mēllă Fălērnō, Ov.

Hўmēttŭs, ī, ni., *a mountain in Attica.* Pāscăt Hўmēttŭs ăpēs, Mart. Epith.
Flōrēns, dŭlcĭs, ŏlēns, vērnŭs, vĭrĭdĭs, ŏdōrĭfĕr, mēllĭflŭŭs, Āttĭcŭs.

hўmnĭfĕr, ă, ŭm, *singing hymns.* Hўmnĭfĕrōs īnhĭăt, Ov.

hўmnŭs, ī, m., *a hymn.* Hўmnĭs cōntĭnŭĕt, Prud. Epith. Săcĕr, ălăcĕr,
dŭlcĭs, fēstĭvŭs, dīvīnŭs, blāndĭsŏnŭs, grātŭs, hĭlărĭs, lætŭs, rĕsŏnŭs. V.
Cantus.

Hўpæpă, ōrŭm, n. pl., *a small city of Lydia.* Hăbĭtăbăt Hўpæpīs, Ov.

Hўpănĭs, ĭdĭs, m., *a river in Scythia.* Ēt Scўthĭcīs Hўpănĭs, Ov.

Hўpērbŏrĕŭs, ă, ŭm, *northern.* Tālĭs Hўpērbŏrĕō, Virg. Syn. Bŏrĕālĭs, Ăquĭ-
lōnĭŭs, Ārctōŭs, glăcĭālĭs.

Hўpĕrīōn, ĭŏnĭs, m., *the Sun.* Rădĭīs Hўpĕrīŏnă cīnctŭm, Ov. V. Sol.

Hўpĕrīŏnĭs, ĭdĭs, f., *daughter of the Sun, Aurora.* Hўpĕrīŏnĭs āstrĭs, Ov.

Hўpĕrīŏnĭŭs, ă, ŭm, *of the Sun.* Lūx Hўpĕrīŏnĭō, Av. Syn. Phœbēŭs,
sōlārĭs.

Hўpērmnēstră, æ, *and* trē, ēs, f., *one of the Danaids, who saved her husband.* Mīttĭt
Hўpērmnēstrē, Ov.

hўpocrĭsĭs, ĭs, f., *hypocrisy.* Quŏd hўpocrĭsĭs ōrnăt, Calc. Syn. Fīctă prŏbĭtās,
vīrtŭs, rēlĭgĭo, pĭĕtās. Vānă ōstēntātĭo. Vīrtŭtĭs fāllāx sĭmŭlātĭo. Epith.
Fīctă, mēndāx, fāllāx, īnfĭdă, sŭbdŏlă, spĕcĭōsă, āmbĭtĭōsă, sŭpērbă, fŭcātă,
fraŭdŭlēntă, ĭnīquă.

hўpocrĭtă, *and* tēs, æ, m., *a hypocrite.* Dēfōrmĭs hўpōcrĭtă, mōrbŭm, Prud.
Epith. Fīctŭs, fāllāx, mēndāx, fūcātŭs, spĕcĭōsŭs. V. Hypocrisis.

Hўpsĕă, æ, f., *wife of Æetes.* Hўpsĕă cæcĭōr īllă, Hor.

Hўpseŭs, ĕĭ or ĕŏs, m., *the name of a warrior.* Hўpseŭs, Hўpsĕă Lўncīdēs, Ov.

Hўpsĭpўlæŭs, ă, ŭm, *of Hypsipyle, Lemnian.* Hўpsĭpўlæă cŏllĭt, Ov.

Hўpsĭpўlē, ēs, f., *the daughter of Thoas.* Fōrmōsa Hўpsĭpўlē, Val. Epith.
Thŏāntĭs, (-ĭdĭs,) Thŏāntĭăs, pŭlchră, Lēmnĭăs, Lēmnĭă.

Hўrcānĭă, æ, f., *a province of Asia.* Hўrcānĭă sўlvĭs, Luc.

Hўrcānŭs, ă, ŭm, *of Hyrcania.* Caŭcăsŭs, Hўrcānæ, Virg.

Hўrĭē, ēs, f., *a country of Bœotia.* Īndĕ lăcŭs Hўrĭēs, Ov.

Hўrĭeŭs, ĕĭ or ĕŏs, m., *an old Bœotian labourer, who entertained Jupiter, Neptune,
and Mercury.* Fŏrtĕ sĕnēx Hўrĭeŭs, Ov.

Hўrĭeŭs, ă, ŭm, *of Hyrieus.* Prōlēs Hўrĭēă lăcērtōs, Ov.

Hўrtăcŭs, ī, m., *a Trojan warrior.* Pătĕr Hўrtăcŭs ārĭs, Virg.

hўssōpŭs, ī, f., *hyssop.* Hўssōpūm, vălĭdăm, Ser. Epith. Vĭrēns, ămāră.

hўstrīx, ĭcĭs, m., *a porcupine.* Spīnōsĭŏr hўstrĭcĕ bārbă, Calp. Epith. Hĭrtŭs,
hĭrsūtŭs, hŏrrēns. V. Sus.

к 2

I

I, *the imperat. of* eo. I sŏrŏr, Virg. Syn. Vădĕ, văde ăgĕ.
Iacchŭs, ī, m., *one of the names of Bacchus.* Vītĭs Iăcchō, Virg.
jăcēns, *the pres. partic. of* jaceo. Vīdērĕ jăcēntĕm, Virg. Syn. Rĕsŭpīnŭs.
    V. Jaceo.
jăcĕo, ŭī, *to lie along.* Fūsă jăcēbānt, Virg. Syn. Cŭbo, rĕcŭbo, īncŭbo, rĕ-
    cŭmbo, prōcŭmbo, dīscŭmbo, stērnŏr, prōstērnŏr, ēxtēndŏr.
jăcĭo, jēcī, *to throw.* Dē prōrā jăcĭtŭr, Virg. Syn. Jăcto, prōjĭcĭo, cōnjĭcĭo,
    ējĭcĭo, mītto, ēmītto, fŭndo, ēffŭndo. V. Jaculor.
• jăctāntĭă, æ, f., *boasting.* Syn. Jăctātĭo, ōstēntātĭo, fāstŭs, sŭpērbĭă.
jăctātĭo, ōnĭs, f., *and* tātŭs, ūs, m., *a tossing.* Tōllīt jăctātĭō mēntĭs, Juv. Quārūm
    jăctātĭbŭs ōmnĭs, Ov.
jăctātŏr, ōrĭs, m., *a boaster.* Stīrpĭs jăctātŏr Ăgȳlleŭs, Stat.
jăcto, *and* tĭto, ās, *to throw, to boast.* Lăpĭdēs jăctāvīt īn ōrbĕm, Virg. Jăctĭtăt
    īgnāvæ, Claud. Syn. Ōstēndo, prædĭco, glōrĭŏr ; jăcĭo, vibro.
jăctūră, æ, f., *a loss.* Făcĭlĭs jăctūră sĕpŭlchrī, Virg. V. Damnum.
jăctŭs, ă, ŭm, *the pass. partic. of* jacio. Lăpĭdēs Pȳrrhæ jāctōs, Virg.—2. -us, ūs,
    m., *a throw.* Ēxĭgŭī jāctū, Virg.
jăcŭlābĭlĭs, ĕ, *which may be thrown.* Tēlūm jăcŭlābĭlĕ nōstrī, Ov.
jăcŭlātŏr, ōrĭs, m., *and* trīx, trīcĭs, f., *one who throws.* Māxĭmŭs, ēt jăcŭlātŏr,
    Juv. Jăcŭlātrīcēmquĕ Dĭānăm, Ov.
jăcŭlo, ās, *and* lŏr, ārĭs, *to throw.* Lūcōs jăcŭlātŭr ĕt ārcēs, Ov. Syn. Ējăcŭlŏr,
    jăcĭo, tŏrquĕo, īntōrquĕo, cōntōrquĕo, cōnjĭcĭo, mītto, ēmītto, vibro, spărgo, ēx-
    cŭtĭo, dēfīgo. V. Jaculum.
jăcŭlŭm, ī, n., *a javelin.* Nĕque ēnĭm jăcŭlō, Virg. Syn. Tēlŭm, spīcŭlŭm,
    mīssĭlĕ, pīlŭm, săgĭttă. Epith. Ăcūtŭm, vŏlāns, vēlōx, strīdēns, īntōrtŭm, trĕ-
    mŭlŭm, ālĕs, cŏrŭscŭm, lēthĭfĕrŭm. V. Telum, Hasta.
jăcŭlŭs, ī, m., *a kind of serpent.* Jăcŭlīquĕ vŏlŭcrēs, Luc. V. Serpens.
Iălȳsĭŭs, ă, ŭm, *of Ialysus, an ancient name of Rhodes.* Ēt Iălȳsĭōs Tēlchīnăs, Ov.
jăm, adv., *already.* Jăm mŏdŏ, Hor.
Iămbēŭs, *and* ĭcŭs, ă, ŭm, *iambic.* Jūssīt Iămbēīs, Hor. Hūnc vŏcānt Iămbĭcŭm,
    Ter. M.
Iāmbŭs, ī, m., *a foot in prosody.* Răbĭēs ārmāvīt Iāmbō, Hor. Epith. Mōrdāx,
    răbĭdŭs, trăgĭcŭs, lībĕr, fĕrōx, cĕlĕr, cĭtŭs, pūgnāx, ūltŏr, fĕrŭs, trīstĭs, lāscīvŭs,
    vūlnĭfĭcŭs, lacrȳmōsŭs, hōrrēndŭs, răbĭōsŭs, trūx.
jāmdūdŭm, *and* prīdĕm, adv., *long ago.* Æneās jāmdūdŭm, Virg. Jămprīdĕm
    rĕsīdēs, Id. Syn. Dūdŭm, prīdĕm.
Jānālĭs, ĕ, *of Janus.* Vīrgăquĕ Jānālĭs, Ov.
Jānĭcŭlŭm, ī, n., *one of the seven hills of Rome.* Jānĭcŭlŭm huīc, ĭllī, Virg.
Jānĭgĕnă, æ, m. f., *a child of Janus.* Dūm mīhī Jānĭgĕnăm, Ov.
jānĭtŏr, ōrĭs, m., *a porter.* Jānĭtŏr Ōrcī, Virg. Syn. Pōrtæ cūstōs. Epith.
    Vĭgĭl, pērvĭgĭl, āssĭdŭŭs, fīdŭs.
Iānthē, ēs, f., *the wife of Iphis.* Dēspōndĕt Iānthēn, Ov.
Iānthĭnă, ōrŭm, n. pl., *a violet-coloured cloth.* Iānthĭnă mœchæ, Mart.
jānŭă, æ, f., *a door.* Pătĕt ĭstī jānŭă lētŏ, Virg. Syn. Pōrtă, ōstĭŭm, līmĕn,
    fŏrēs, pōstēs, vālvæ, vēstĭbŭlŭm, īngrēssŭs, ădĭtŭs. Epith. Dūră, ærĕă, fērrĕă,
    līgnĕă, strīdēns, ăpērtă, spătĭōsă, vălĭdă, āngŭstă, lāxă, pătēns, clausă, lātă, īn-
    gēns, sŭpērbă, sŭblīmĭs.
• Jānŭārĭŭs, ĭī, m., *January.* Cic. Epith. Brūmālĭs, stĕrĭlĭs, frĭgĭdŭs, gĕlĭdŭs,
    tōrpēns, glăcĭālĭs, nĭvĕŭs, trīstĭs, īgnāvŭs, ĭnērs, īnfōrmĭs, nīmbōsŭs, pĭgĕr,
    hōrrĭdŭs.
Jānŭs, ī, m., *a Roman god.* Mīrāndŭs ĭmāgĭnĕ Jānŭs, Ov. Syn. Clūsĭŭs,
    Pătūlcĭŭs. Epith. Clāvĭgĕr, āntīquŭs, gĕmĭnŭs, săcĕr, pācĭfĭcŭs, bĭcĕps,
    bifrōns, bĭfōrmĭs, āncĕps.
Jăpĕtīdēs, *and* Iăpĕtĭōnĭdēs, æ, m., *the son of Iapetus.* Tū quŏquĕ, Jăpĕtĭdĕ, Ov.
    Iăpĕtĭōnĭdēs Ātlās fŭĭt, Ov.
Iăpĕtŭs, ī, m., *the son of Uranus.* Cœŭmque Iăpĕtŭmquĕ, Virg. Epith. Dīrŭs,
    trūx, sævŭs, īmmānĭs, pŏtēns, scĕlĕrātŭs.
Iāpĭs, ĭdĭs, m., *a celebrated physician.* Dīlēctŭs Iāpĭs, Virg.

Iăpўgĭă, æ, f., *a district of Apulia.* Inquĭt Iăpўgĭăm, Ov.
Iăpўs, ўdĭs, m., *of Iapydia.* Iăpўdĭs ōrā Tĭmāvī, Virg.
Iăpŷx, ўgĭs, m., *a west wind.* Ět Iăpўgĕ fěrrī, Virg. V. Caurus.
Iārbĭtās, æ, ĭn., *a man's name.* Rūpĭt Iārbĭtās, Hor.
Iārdănĭs, ĭdĭs, f., *the daughter of Iardanus, Omphale.*
Iāsĭdēs, æ, m., *son or descendant of Iasius.* Iāsĭdē Pălĭnūrĕ, fěrūnt, Virg.
Iāsĭŏn, ŏnĭs, *and* Iāsĭŭs, ĭī, m., *the son of Corytus and Electra, slain by his brother
Dardanus.* In Cěrěreın Iāsĭŏn, Ov. Iāsĭūsquĕ pătĕr, Virg.
Iāsŏn, ŏnĭs, m., *the son of Æson, loved by Medea.* Tāngăt Iāsŏnĭs ætūs, Ov. SYN.
Æsŏnĭdēs. EPITH. Æsŏnĭŭs, clārŭs, sŭpērbŭs, măgnănĭmŭs, prædo, ācĕr, ŭn-
dĭvăgŭs, fōrtĭs, aūdāx, gěněrōsŭs, Mārtĭŭs, bēllĭgĕr, Pělāsgŭs, Æmŏnĭŭs, Păgă-
sæŭs ; fōrmōsŭs, fāllāx, pērfĭdŭs, pērjūrŭs.
Iāsŏnĭŭs, ă, ŭm, *belonging to Jason.* Jăm tĭbi Iāsŏnĭā, Prop.
Iāspĭs, ĭdĭs, f., *a precious stone.* Fēcĭt Iāspĭdĭbŭs, Mart. EPITH. Fŭlvă, rŭtĭlă,
ěffulgēns, clāră, præclārā, rŭtĭlāns, vĭrĭdĭs, vĭrēns, tĕrĕs, Eŏă, Ĭndĭcă. V. Gemma.
Iāzŷx, ўgĭs, ın. Iāzўgēs, *or* Jāzўgēs, ŭm, m. pl., *a people near the mouth of the
Danube.* Ŭt dŭcăt Iāzŷx, Ov. Jāzўgēs ēt Cōlchī, Id.
Ĭbēr, ērĭs, m., *a Spaniard.* Quōs nĕc Ĭbĕr, Val. Fl.
Ĭbērĭă, æ, f., *Spain.* Cŭmŭlăvĭt Ĭbērĭā dīvĕs, Av. EPITH. Pŏpŭlōsă, dūră,
ınăgnă, āmplă, spătĭōsă, fěrāx. V. Hispania.
Ĭbērĭcŭs, *and* bĕrŭs, ă, ŭm, *Spanish.* Pŏntŭs Ĭbērĭcŭs ĭllĭnc, Av. Clārŭs Ĭbērā,
Virg. V. Hispanus.
Ĭbi, adv., *there.* Aŭt Ĭbĭ flāvă, Virg. Tēr cōnātŭs ĭbi, Ib. SYN. Illīc, hīc.
Ĭbīdĕm, adv., *in the same place.* Incērtŭs ĭbīdĕm, Virg.
Ĭbĭs, ĭdĭs, f., *a bird of Egypt.* Ĭbĭdĕ dīcăr, Ov. EPITH. Ægyptĭă, Nĭlĭăcă.
Ĭbўcŭs, ī, m., *a man's name.* Ŭxŏr paŭpĕrĭs Ĭbўcī, Hor.
Icărĭŏtĭs, ĭdĭs, f., *Penelope ; of Penelope.* Nĭl Icārĭŏtĭdĕ tēlă, Ov.
Icărĭs, ĭdŏs, f., *daughter of Icarius, Penelope.* Icărĭdōs fāınŭlæ, Ov.
Icărĭŭs, ĭī, m., *the son of Œbalus.* Mē pătĕr Icărĭŭs, Ov.
Icărĭŭs, ă, ŭm, *of Icarius, of the dog-star.* Ět mĭcĕt Icărĭī, Ov.—2. *of Icarus.*
Icărŭs, Icărĭīs, Id. Icărĭŭm, ĭī, n., *the Icarian sea.* Icărĭŭmquĕ lĕgĭt, Id.
Icărŭs, ī, m., *the son of Dædalus.* Icărŭs, Icărĭīs, Ov. EPITH. Dædăleŭs, těmě-
rārĭŭs, aūdāx, ĭnfēlīx, āmēns, dēmēns, sŭpērbŭs, ālĭgĕr, pēnnātŭs, ālātŭs, pēn-
nĭgĕr, ĭmprūdēns, ĭmprŏvĭdŭs, naūfrăgŭs, mērsŭs, sŭbmērsŭs.
Iccĭŭs, ĭī, m., *the name of a man.* Iccī, běātŭs, Hor.
Icĕlŭs, ī, m., *a son of Somnus.* Hūnc Icĕlŏn sŭpĕrī, Ov.
ichneūmŏn, ŏnĭs, m., *a rat of Egypt.* Pērnĭcĭōsŭs ĭchneūmŏn, Mart. EPITH.
Sŏlērs, caŭtŭs, pūgnāx, prŏvĭdŭs, ăgĭlĭs.
Ichnŏbătēs, æ, m., *the name of a dog.* Ichnŏbătēsquĕ săgāx.
Ĭco, Ĭcī, Ĭctŭm, *to beat.* Icĭmŭr ĭctū, Lucr. SYN. Fěrĭo, vērběro, pěrcŭtĭo,
cædo, lædo. V. Percutio.
Ictěrĭcŭs, ă, ŭm, *sick of the jaundice.* Cōnsŭlĭt ĭctěrĭcæ, Juv.
Ictŭs, ūs, ın., *a blow.* Trěmĭt ĭctĭbŭs ærĕă pūppĭs, Virg. SYN. Pērcŭssĭo, pēr-
cŭssŭs, ūs ; vērběr, plăgă, vŭlnŭs. EPITH. Vălĭdŭs, věhěmēns, dūrŭs, lēthālĭs,
rěsŏnŭs, hōrrĭfĭcŭs, sŏnōrŭs, ăcērbŭs, grăvĭs, fōrtĭs, ĭngēns, crěpĭtāns, crŭēntŭs,
ĭnnŭmĕrŭs. V. Percutio, verbero.
Ĭd, n., *that.* Quĭcquĭd ĭd ēst, Virg. SYN. Hōc, ĭllŭd.
Ĭdă, æ, f., *a mountain in Phrygia, and in Crete.* Fōntĭbŭs Ĭdā, Ov. Dīctæā
cārpĭt ăb Ĭdā, Virg. EPITH. Aquōsă, hūmĭdă, ūmbrōsă, ārdŭă, ŏpācă, clīvōsă,
něınōrōsă, gělĭdă, fœcūndă, frōndĭfěră, cuprēssĭfěră, frōndōsă, pīnĭfěră, Phrygĭă,
Dārdănĭă, Dārdănă.
Ĭdæŭs, ă, ŭm, *of mount Ida.* Ĭdæŭmquĕ nĕmŭs, Ov.
Ĭdălĭē, ēs, f., *Venus.* Dūră pěrōsăm Ĭdălĭēn, Ov.
Ĭdălĭŭm, ĭī, n., *and* ă, æ, f., *a mountain of Cyprus.* Aŭt sŭpĕr Ĭdălĭŭm, Virg.
Ĭdălĭŭs, ă, ŭm, *of Idalium.* Vēnāntem Ĭdălĭŏ, Prop. SYN. Cyprĭŭs.
Ĭdās, æ, m., *one of the Argonauts.* Ět frātĕr ĕt Ĭdās, Ov.
Ĭdcīrcō, conj., *therefore.* Idcĭrcŏnĕ rŏgo, Prud. SYN. Ĭdĕŏ.
Ĭdĕm, ěădĕın, Ĭdĕm, *the same.* Amŏr ŏmnĭbŭs īdĕm, Virg. Lædĕrĕ pŏssĭt
Ĭdĕm, Ov.
Ĭdēntĭdĕm, adv., *now and then.* Ădvērsŭs ĭdēntĭdĕm tē, (Sapph.) Cat.
Ĭdĕŏ, adv., *therefore.* Nē cēllĭs Ĭdĕŏ cōntēndĕ Fălērnĭs, Virg. SYN. Idcĭrcŏ.

Idmōn, ŏnĭs, m., *a man's name.* Idmŏnăque audācĕm, Ov.
Idmŏnĭŭs, ă, ŭm, *of Idmon.* Idmŏnĭæ frŏntĕm, Ov.
īdōlŭm *or* lŏn, ī, n., *an idol.* Dĕōs, Idōlăquĕ mūltă, Vict. Syn. Sĭmŭlācrŭm.
Epith. Vānŭm, frăgĭlĕ, prŏfānŭm, fīctĭlĕ.
Idŏmĕneŭs, ĕī *or* eī, ĕŏs *and* ĕōs, m., *the son of Deucalion, and king of Crete.*
Līctĭŭs Idŏmĕneŭs, Virg. Idŏmĕnĕā dūcĕm, Id.
Idōnĕŭs, ă, ŭm, *convenient.* Pătrĭæ sĭt Idōnĕŭs, Juv. Syn. Āptŭs, cōmmŏdŭs,
ŏppōrtūnŭs, ūtĭlĭs.
Idūmæŭs, ă, ŭm, *of Idumea.* Prīmŭs Idūmææs, Virg.
Idūmē, ēs, f., *a town and country in Palestine.* Dīvĕs Idūmē, Lucan. Epith.
Pālmĭfĕră, dīvĕs, ămœnă.
⨍ Idŭs, ŭŭm, m. pl., *the ides.* Idĭbŭs œră, Hor.
jĕcŭr, ŏrĭs, n., *the liver.* Măgnō jĕcŭr ānsĕrĕ, Mart. Syn. Hēpăr. Epith.
Călĭdŭm, pălpĭtāns, fĕrvēns, ārdēns, sānguĭfĭcŭm.
jējūnĭŭm, ĭī, n., *fasting.* Inŏpī jējūnĭā vīctū, Ov. Syn. Ābstĭnēntĭă. Epith.
Lānguēns, trīstĕ, dūrŭm, lōngŭm, ăcērbŭm, mŏlēstŭm, măcĭlēntŭm, ĭnērs, ĭgnā-
vŭm; pĭŭm, sānctŭm, cāstŭm.
jējūno, ās, *to fast.* Cōrdĕ jējūnāvĕrĭt, (Iamb.) Prud.
jējūnŭs, ă, ŭm, *hungry.* Pārĭtĕr jējūnĭs dēntĭbŭs ācĕr, Hor. V. Famelicus.
jēntācŭlŭm, ī, n., *breakfast.* Vŏlēs jēntācŭlă sūmĕrĕ frūgī, Mart. Epith.
Pārcŭm, laūtŭm.
JĒSŪS (*dissyl.*) *or* Ĭēsŭs (*trisyl.*), ū, m., *Christ.* Nōmĭnĕ Jēsŭm, Sed. Tūmŭ-
lātŭm nūpĕr Ĭēsŭm, Alc. Epith. Sălvātŏr, sērvātŏr, sălūtĭfĕr, pācĭfĭcŭs, bĕnīgnŭs, mītĭs, pătĭēns, clēmēns, ămăbĭlĭs. V. Christus.
✝ Ĭgĭtŭr, adv., *therefore.* Āltērnīs Ĭgĭtŭr, Virg. Syn. Ērgo, Ĭtăquĕ.
ĭgnārŭs, ă, ŭm, *ignorant.* Rērūmque ĭgnārŭs ĭmăgĭnĕ, Virg. Syn. Inscĭŭs,
nēscĭŭs, Indŏctŭs, īmpĕrītŭs, rŭdĭs. V. Indoctus.
ĭgnāvĕ, *and* ĭtĕr, adv., *idly.* Cārpĕntem ĭgnāvĭŭs ūmbrās, Virg.
ĭgnāvĭă, æ, f., *idleness.* Ănĭmīs ĭgnāvĭă vēnĭt, Virg. Syn. Ĭnērtĭă, dēsĭdĭă,
vēcōrdĭă. Epith. Tōrpēns, dĕsĕs, tŭrpĭs, lānguĭdă, tĭtŭbāns, ĭnērs. V.
Pigritia.
ĭgnāvŭs, ă, ŭm, *idle.* Ĭgnāvŭm fūcōs pĕcŭs, Virg. Syn. Dĕsĕs, vēcōrs, ēnērvĭs,
ĭnērs, dēsĭdĭōsŭs, pĭgĕr. V. Piger.
ĭgnēsco, ĭs, *to take fire.* Ĭgnēscūnt īræ, Virg. Syn. Ārdēsco, ārdĕo, flagro, ēxārdēsco, incēndŏr, īnflāmmŏr. V. Ardeo.
ĭgnĕŭs, ă, ŭm, *burning.* Ĭgnĕŭs Eūrōs, Virg. Syn. Flāmmĕŭs, flāmmātŭs, āccēnsŭs, ĭgnītŭs, incēnsŭs, fērvĕns, ārdēns, cāndēns, ĭgnĭfĕr, flāmmĭfĕr, ĭgnĭvŏmŭs.
ĭgnĭcōmŭs, ă, ŭm, *with flaming tresses.* Tĕnĕt ĭgnĭcŏmŭs sōl, Aus. Syn. Ĭgnĕ
cōmāns.
ĭgnĭcŭlŭs, ī, m., *the diminut. of* ignis. Ĭgnĭcŭlŭm brūmæ, Juv.
ĭgnĭfĕr, ĕră, ŭm, *bearing fire.* Ĭgnĭfĕr ĭpsĕ, Lucr. Syn. Ĭgnĭvŏmŭs, flāmmĭfĕr;
stēllĭfĕr.
ĭgnĭflŭŭs, ă, ŭm, *flowing with fire.* Ĭgnĭflŭæquĕ căvērnæ, Claud.
Ĭgnĭgĕnă, æ, m., *a name of Bacchus.* Ĭgnĭgĕnāmquĕ, sătŭmque, Ov.
ĭgnĭpēs, ĕdĭs, *having fiery feet.* Ĭgnĭpĕdŭm vīrēs, Ov.
Ĭgnĭpŏtēns, ntĭs, *a name of Vulcan.* Haūd sēcŭs Ĭgnĭpŏtēns, Virg. Syn. Vŭlcānŭs.
ĭgnĭs, ĭs, m., *fire.* Ădōlēscŭnt ĭgnĭbŭs āræ, Virg. Syn. Flāmmă, īncēndĭă, făcēs,
Vŭlcānŭs, Mūlcĭbĕr, rŏgŭs. Epith. Tōrrĭdŭs, rŭtĭlŭs, ăvĭdŭs, cŏrŭscŭs, cĕlĕr,
æstĭfĕr, călĭdŭs, trēmŭlŭs, vŏlāns, flāmmĕŭs, lĕvĭs, ătĕr, dāmnōsŭs, răpĭdŭs, Vŭlcānĭŭs, fērvĭdŭs, vŏlŭcĕr, văgŭs, lūcĭdŭs, splēndĭdŭs, flagrāns, fūmōsŭs, flāmmĭvŏmŭs, scīntĭllāns, tōrrēns, fĕrvēns, vŏrāx. V. Flamma, incendium.
ĭgnītŭs, ă, ŭm, *on fire.* Cōllă vĕl ĭgnītĭs, Prud. Syn. Ārdēns, flāmmāns, cāndēns,
flāmmātŭs, flāmmĕŭs, ĭgnĭvŏmŭs.
ĭgnōbĭlĭs, ĕ, *unknown.* Flōrēntem ĭgnōbĭlĭs ōtī, Virg. Syn. Ignōtŭs, hŭmĭlĭs,
ōbscūrŭs, dēspēctŭs, inglōrĭŭs, vīlĭs, ābjēctŭs.
ĭgnōbĭlĭtās, ātĭs, f., *low birth.* Est ĭgnōbĭlĭtātĕ vĭrōrŭm, Ov.
ĭgnōmĭnĭă, æ, f., *dishonour.* Mūltă gĕmēns, ĭgnōmĭnĭăm, Virg. Syn. Infāmĭă,
dēdĕcŭs, măcŭlă, lābēs, probrŭm. V. Infamia.
ĭgnōmĭnĭōsŭs, ă, ŭm, *dishonourable.* Crĕpĕnt ĭgnōmĭnĭōsăquĕ dīctă, Hor. Syn.
Infāmĭs, probrōsŭs.

Ignŏrăntĭă, æ, f., *ignorance.* Ignōrāntĭă caŭsārŭm, Lucr. Syn. Inscĭtĭă, Ignō-rătĭo, impĕrītĭă. Epith. Rŭdĭs, tŭrpĭs, nŏxĭă.

Ignŏro, ās, *to be ignorant of.* Nĕve Ignŏrātĕ Lătīnōs, Virg. Syn. Nēscĭo. Mĕ lătĕt; sŭm nēscĭŭs *or* Inscĭŭs.

Ignōsco, nōvī, nōtŭm, *to pardon.* Syn. Pārco, Indŭlgĕo, cŏndōno, vĕnĭăm dō.

Ignōtŭs, ă, ŭm, *unknown.* Rără pĕr Ignōtōs, Virg. Syn. Incōgnĭtŭs, ābdĭtŭs, ārcānŭs; Ignōbĭlĭs.

Ilĕrdă, æ, f., *a town of Spain.* Vīnctŭs mīttĕrĭs Ilĕrdăm, Hor.

īlēx, Icĭs, f., *an oak-tree.* Ilĭcĭs ālveō, Virg. Epith. Căvă, frŏndēns, ŏpācă, lĭt-tŏrĕă, nōdōsă, vĭrĭdĭs, rāmōsă, cŭrtă, āltă, hīrsūtă, pătŭlă, frōndōsă, prōcĕră. V. Quercus.

īlĭă, ĭŭm, n. pl., *the small guts.* Ilĭă Cōdrō, Virg. Syn. Lătĕră; vīscĕră. Epith. Crāssă, vēntōsă, īntĭmă.

Ilĭă, æ, f., *the mother of Romulus and Remus.* Epith. Rōmānă, Mārtĭă, Tĭbĕrīnă, Trōĭcă, Dārdănă. Syn. Rhĕă.

Ilĭăcŭs, *and* Iĭŭs, ă, ŭm, *of Troy, Trojan.* Vĭdĕt Ilĭăcās, Virg. Ilĭă tēllūs, Id. Syn. Trōjānŭs, Trōĭŭs.

Ilĭădēs, æ, m., *the son or descendant of Ilus.* Abrĭpĭt Ilĭădēn, Ov.—2. *the son of Ilia.* Rōmŭlŭs Ilĭădēs, Ilĭădēsquĕ Rĕmŭs, Id.

Ilĭăs, ădĭs, f., *a Trojan woman.* Ilĭădŭm tŭrbă, Virg. Syn. Trōăs.—2. *a poem of Homer.* Nāscĭtŭr Ilĭădĕ, Prop. Epith. Lōngă, Mæŏnĭă.

Ilĭcĕt, adv., *immediately.* Ilĭcĕt Ignĭs, Virg. Syn. Illĭco, stătĭm.

Ilĭcētŭm, ī, n., *a grove of holm-oaks.* Cŭltŭs Ilĭcētī, Mart.

Ilĭcĕŭs, Ignĕŭs, *and* Ignŭs, ă, ŭm, *of oak.* Ilĭcĕæquĕ trăbēs, Stat. Cŭrrēntem Ilĭgnĭs, Virg.

Ilĭŏnă, æ, *and* Ilĭŏnē, ēs, f., *the eldest daughter of Priam.* Ilĭŏnam ēdōrmĭt, Hor. Ilĭŏnē quŏd gēssĕrăt āntĕ, Virg.

Ilĭŏneŭs, ĕī, eī, ĕŏs *or* ĕōs, m., *one of the companions of Æneas.* Māxĭmŭs Ilĭŏneŭs, Virg. Ilĭŏnĕă pĕtĭt dēxtră, Id.

Ilĭthyĭă, æ, f., *the goddess who presided over child-birth.* Părĭentĭbŭs Ilĭthyīăm, Ov.

Ilĭŭm, lĭŏn, ĭī, n., *or* Iĭŏs, ī, f., *Troy.* Ilĭŏn ēt Tĕnĕdōs, Ov. Syn. Trōjă; Pĕr-gămă, ōrŭm. Epith. Sŭpērbŭm, pŏtēns, āltŭm, inclĭtŭm, Ingēns, ūstŭm, ēvēr-sŭm, dīrŭtŭm.

illăbĕfāctŭs, ă, ŭm, *unshaken.* Mănĕănt illăbĕfāctă prĕcŏr, Ov.

illābŏr, ĕrĭs, illāpsŭs, *to rush in.* Mīnāns illābĭtŭr ŭrbī, Virg. Syn. Incĭdo, īrrŭo, Influo.

illacrўmābĭlĭs, ĕ, *not to be moved with pity.* Plăcēs illăcrўmābĭlĕm, (Alcaic.) Hor. Syn. Inēxōrābĭlĭs, dūrŭs.

illacrўno, ās, *to weep over.* Illăcrўmāt tēmplĭs, Virg. V. Lacrymor.

illæsŭs, ă, ŭm, *uninjured.* Brūmăque illæsă cŭprēssŭs, Ov.

illætābĭlĭs, ĕ, *sad.* Illætābĭlĕ mūrmŭr, Virg. Syn. Mœstŭs, trīstĭs, flēbĭlĭs.

illăquĕo, ās, *to take in a net.* Illăquĕănt dŭcēs, (Glyconic.) Hor. Syn. Irrĕtĭo, Impĕdĭo, Implĭco, Intrĭco, Illĭgo, Invōlvo, cīrcŭmrētĭo.

illātro, ās, *to bark at.* Mănĭbŭs illātrăt, Luc.

illaudābĭlĭs, ĕ, *not to be praised.* Jŭvăt illaudābĭlĕ cārmĕn, St. Syn. Illaudātŭs.

illaudātŭs, ă, ŭm, *not praised.* Aŭt illaudātī, Virg.

illĕ, ă, ŭd, *he, she, that.* Sīc Jŭpĭtĕr Illĕ, Virg. Syn. Is, hic.

illĕcebræ, ārŭm, f. pl., *allurements.* Illĕcĕbrĭs ĕrăt, Hor. Syn. Blandĭtĭæ, Irrītā-mēntă, Invītāmēntă, lēnōcĭnĭŭm, stĭmŭlŭs. Epith. Dŭlcēs, blandæ, fāllācēs, dŏlōsæ, mōllēs, Inānēs, vānæ, mītēs, fœmĭnĕæ, ārgūtæ, lēnēs, fōrtēs, pŏtēntēs.

illĕcebrōsŭs, ă, ŭm. Illĕcĕbrōsŭs ĕnĭm, Prud. Syn. Blandŭs, fāllāx.

illĕpĭdē, adv., *without grace.* Cōmpōsĭtum Illĕpĭdēvĕ, Hor.

illĕpĭdŭs, ă, ŭm, *without grace.* Dēlĭcĭæ illĕpĭdæ, Cat. Syn. Insūlsŭs, Inēptŭs, stŏlĭdŭs.

illēx, *or* illīx, Icĭs, f., *allurement.* Illĭcĕ căptŭs, Mant. Syn. Blandŭs.

illĭbātŭs, ă, ŭm, *untouched.* Illĭbātă tŏrī, Lucan. Syn. Pūrŭs, Intĕmĕrātŭs, In-tāctŭs, Intĕgĕr, illæsŭs, Incōrruptŭs, Intāmĭnātŭs.

illic, adv., *there.* Illic ōffĭcĭănt, Virg. Syn. Ibi.

illĭcĭo, lēxī, lēctŭm, *to allure.* Illĭcĕre ŭt cŭpĕrēnt, Lucr. Syn. Allĭcĭo, pēllĭcĭo, āttrăho, căpto, Inĕsco.

Illĭcĭtŭs, ă, ŭm, *unlawful.* Illĭcĭtās tēntārĕ, Virg.   Syn. Vĕtĭtŭs, nōn lĭcĭtŭs, Inĭquŭs.

Illĭco, adv., *immediately.* Illĭcŏ mūndānŭm, Buch.   Syn. Stătĭm, cōntĭnŭŏ, prō-tĭnŭs, ōcўŭs, cōnfēstĭm, ēxtēmplŏ, cĭto, nēc mŏrā.

Illĭdo, sĭ, sŭm, *to dash against.* Illĭdĭtquĕ vādĭs, Virg.   Syn. Allĭdo, cōllĭdo, frāngo, Infrĭngo, Impĭngo, cōnfrĭngo, ŏffēndo, ŏbtĕro, cōntĕro.

Illĭgo, ās, *to tie.* Jŭvēncĭs illĭgātă plūrĭbŭs, (Iamb.) Hor.   Syn. Lĭgo, vīncĭo, Implĭco, Irrētĭo, illăquĕo, Intēxo, Innēcto, Imĭnīscĕo.

Illĭmĭs, ĕ, *clear.* Fōns ĕrăt Illĭmĭs, Ov.   Syn. Lĭmpĭdŭs, pūrŭs, nĭtĭdŭs.

Illĭnc, adv., *thence.* Illĭnc Gērmānĭă bēllŭm, Virg.

Illĭno, ĭs, lĭnĭ, lĭvī, *and* lēvī, Iĭtŭm, *or* nĭo, īs, *to anoint.* Illĭnĕt ăgrĭs, Hor.   Syn. Lĭno, ŏblĭno, cīrcŭmlĭno, ūngo, Inŭngo, pĕrūngo, Indūco.

Illĭsŭs, ūs, m., *a shock.* Illĭsū scŏpŭlŭs trĕmĭt, Sil.

Illĭtĕrātŭs, ă, ŭm, *unlearned.* Illĭtĕrātī nūm mĭnŭs, (Iamb.) Hor.   Syn. Indōctŭs, Ignārŭs, Impĕrītŭs.

Illĭtŭs, *the pass. partic. of* illino.   Vēstĭbŭs Illĭtŭm, (Alcaic.) Hor.

Illĭŭs, *from* ille.   Illĭŭs ārās, Virg.   Quăm nōstro Illĭŭs, Id.

Illōtŭs, ă, ŭm, *unwashed.* Illōtă tŏrāllă vēstēs, Hor.   Syn. Sōrdĭdŭs, tūrpĭs, Illūtŭs.

Illūc, adv., *thither.* Hūc căpŭt, ātque Illūc, Virg.   Syn. Ĕō.

Illūcĕo, lūxī, *to shine upon.* Illūcĕrĕ sōlēnt, Mart.   Syn. Illūcēsco, Irrādĭo.   V. Luceo.

Illŭd, *that.* Illŭd Yn hīs, Lucr.   Syn. Id, hōc.

Illūdo, sĭ, sŭm, *to mock.* Cērtāntque Illūdĕrĕ căptō, Virg.   Syn. Lūdo, dēlūdo, rīdĕo, Irrīdĕo.   V. Derideo.

Illūmĭno, ās, *to enlighten.* Dĭēs Illūmĭnăt, ōmnĕ, Ar.   Syn. Illūstro, cōllūstro.   V. Lumen.

Illūnĭs, ĕ, *moonless.* Illūnēm nāctī, Sil.   Syn. Ŏbscūrŭs, ŏpācŭs, tĕnebrōsŭs.

Illūstrĭs, ĕ, *illustrious, clear.* Cōncŭtĭēns Illūstrĕ căpŭt, Ov.   Syn. Lūcĭdŭs, cŏrūscŭs, clārŭs; Insĭgnĭs, cōnspĭcŭŭs, spēctāndŭs, præcēllēns, fāmōsŭs, Inclўtŭs, præstāns, ēxĭmĭŭs, cĕlebrĭs, spēctāndŭs, nōbĭlĭs.   V. Celeber.

Illūstro, ās, *to illustrate.* Græcōrum Illūstrārĕ rĕpērtă, Lucr.   V. Illumino, decoro.

Illūsŭs, *the pass. partic. of* illudo.   Artem Illūsŭs ōmīttăs, Hor.

Illūtŭs, ă, ŭm, *unwashed.* Incŏquĕre Illūtōs, Hor.   Syn. Illōtŭs.

Illŭvĭēs, ĭēĭ, f., *dirt.* Illŭvĭēquĕ pĕrēsă, Virg.   Syn. Cōllŭvĭēs, sōrdēs, squālŏr.   Epith. Fœdă, Immūndă, ōbscœnă, sōrdĭdă, lŭtōsă, fœtĭdă, crāssă.   V. Sordes.

Illўrĭă, æ, *and* rĭs, Idĭs, f.; *or* rĭcŭm, ī, n., *a part of the Macedonian kingdom.* Vĭlŏr Illўrĭă, Prop.   Epith. Dīvĕs.

Illўrĭcŭs, ă, ŭm, *of Illyria.* Illўrĭcī lēgĭs æquŏrĭs, Virg.

Illўrĭs, Idĭs, f., *of Illyria.* Illўrĭs ōră, Ov.

Ilvă, æ, f., *an island in the Etrurian sea.* Ilvă trēcēntōs, Virg.

Ilŭs, ī, m., *the son of Tros and Callirrhoe.* Ilŭs ĕrăt, Virg.

Imāgĭnōsŭs, ă, ŭm, *that sees phantoms.* Sŏlĕt hæc Imāgĭnōsŭm, Cat.

Imāgo, Inĭs, f., *an image.* Fāllĭt Imāgĭnĭbŭs, Tib.   Syn. Effĭgĭēs, spĕcĭēs, ēxēmplăr, fĭgūră, Icōn, sĭmŭlācrŭm, stătŭă, sĭgnŭm.   Epith. Aŭrātă, fīctă, pīctă, ēxcūltă, sŭpērbă, dĕcōră, lūcĭdă, ērēctă, scūlptĭlĭs, ēxprēssă, fīctĭlĭs, ădūmbrātă, scūlptă, æněă, cērĕă, spīrāns.   V. Statua.

Imāōn, ŏnĭs, m., *the name of a warrior.* Tēxĭt Imāŏna Hălēsŭs, Virg.

Imbēcīllĭs, lĕ, *and* lŭs, ă, ŭm, *weak.* Imbēcīllŭs, Inērs, Hor.   Syn. Dēbĭlĭs, Infīrmŭs.   V. Infirmus.

Imbēllĭs, ĕ, *unfit for war.* Eūnŭchi Imbēllēs, Juv.   Syn. Ignāvŭs, tĭmĭdŭs; Infīrmŭs.

Imbĕr, brĭs, m., *rain, a shower.* Imbĕr ătrōx, Stat.   Syn. Plŭvĭă.   Epith. Dēnsŭs, lārgŭs, ūndāns, hўbērnŭs, gĕlĭdŭs, grăvĭs, vēntōsŭs, Insānŭs, rĕpēntīnŭs, sævŭs, sŏnōrŭs, nĭvōsŭs, äquōsŭs, Imbōsŭs, crēbĕr, brūmālĭs, hōrrēndŭs, strīdēns, tērrĭfĭcŭs, ātĕr, ēffŭsŭs, fœcūndŭs, fērtĭlĭs.   V. Pluvia.

Imbērbĭs, ĕ, *or* bŭs, ă, ŭm, *beardless.* Imbērbĭs jŭvĕnĭs, Hor.   Syn. Impūbĭs, Impūbĕr.   V. Adolescens, lanugo.

Imbĭbo, bĭbī, *to drink in.* Imbĭbĕrăt dīrŭm, Alcim.   Syn. Bĭbo, cōmbĭbo, haŭrĭo; cōncĭpĭo.

Imbrăsĭdēs, æ, m., *son of Imbrasus.* Asĭŭs Imbrăsĭdēs, Virg.

Imbrĕŭs, ĕī *or* ĕŏs, m., *the name of a centaur.* Ov.

imbrēx, ĭcĭs, m., *a gutter tile.* Imbrĭcĕ tēctī, Virg. EPITH. Cūrvŭs, dūrŭs, ăltŭs.

imbrĭfĕr, ă, ŭm, *bringing rain.* Imbrĭfĕr ārcŭs, Tibull. SYN. Plŭvĭālĭs, plŭvĭŭs.

Imbrĭŭs, ă, ŭm, *of Imbros, an island near Thrace.* Imbrĭă tērră, Ov.

imbŭo, ŭī, ūtŭm, *to dye, to wet.* Cŭm sĕmĕl imbŭĕrĭt, Hor. SYN. Rĭgo, tĭngo, pĕrfŭndo, lĭno ; īnstrŭo.

imbūtŭs, *the pass. partic. of* imbuo. Quŏ sĕmĕl ēst imbūtă, Hor.

imĭtābĭlĭs, ĕ, *that may be imitated.* Nōn imĭtābĭlĕ fŭlmĕn, Virg.

imĭtāmĕn, ĭnĭs, n., *or* tātĭo, ōnĭs, f., *an imitation.* Prīscĭque imĭtāmĭnă făctī, Ov. Sŭmmōs imĭtātĭŏ fāscēs, Rutil.

imĭtātŏr, ōrĭs, m., *and* trīx, īcĭs, f., *an imitator.* Dēsĭlĭēs imĭtātŏr ĭn ārctŭm, Hor. SYN. Æmŭlŭs. Imĭtātrīx ālĕs ăb ōrĭs, Ov.

imĭtātŭs, *the partic. of* imitor. Sŏnĭtŭs imĭtātă tŭbārŭm, Virg.

imĭtŏr, ārĭs, *to imitate.* Mōllēs imĭtābĭtŭr ærĕ, Hor. SYN. Æmŭlŏr, sĭmŭlo, ăssĭmŭlo.

immăcŭlātŭs, ă, ŭm, *unspotted.* Quānquam immăcŭlātă părēntĭs, Paul. SYN. Intĕmĕrātŭs, īntāctŭs, īllĭbātŭs, pūrŭs.

immădĕo, ēs, *to grow wet.* Gĕnæ immădŭĕrĕ prŏfūsīs, Ov. SYN. Mădĕo, mădēsco, rĭgŏr.

immānĭs, ĕ, *cruel, extraordinary.* Cœptīs immānĭbŭs ēffĕră, Virg. SYN. Immītĭs, crūdēlĭs, fĕrŭs, bārbărŭs, fĕrōx ; īngēns, īmmēnsŭs.

inmānĭtās, ātĭs, f., *cruelty.* Fĕrīna immānĭtās, (Iamb. Dim.) Prud. SYN. Fĕrĭtās, crūdēlĭtās.

immānsuētŭs, ă, ŭm, *cruel.* Immānsuētŭmquĕ fĕrŭmquĕ, Ov. SYN. Nĕscĭŭs mĭtēscĕrĕ.

|| immārcēsco, ĭs, *to grow stale.* Nēmpe immārcēscŭnt, Hor. (*Others read* inămārēscŭnt.)

immātūrŭs, ă, ŭm, *premature, unripe.* Fīlĭŭs immātūrŭs ŏbīssĕt, Hor. SYN. Præmātūrŭs, īntēmpēstĭvŭs, præcēps.

immĕdĭcābĭlĭs, ĕ, *incurable.* Immĕdĭcābĭlĕ cāncĕr, Ov. SYN. Īnsānābĭlĭs.

immĕmŏr, ōrĭs, *forgetful.* Immĕmŏr hērbārŭm, Virg. SYN. Oblītŭs.

immĕmŏrābĭlĭs, ĕ, *not to be remembered.* Vērsūs immĕmŏrābĭlēs, Plaut.

immĕmŏrātŭs, ă, ŭm, *unheard of.* Immĕmŏrātă fĕrēntĕm, Hor.

immēnsŭs, ă, ŭm, *immense.* Immēnsīs ōrbĭbŭs āngŭēs, Virg. SYN. Ingēns, vāstŭs, īmmānĭs.

immĕrēns, ntĭs, *undeserving.* Quĭd immĕrēntēs, (Iamb.) Hor. SYN. Immĕrĭtŭs.

immērgo, sī, sŭm, *to plunge into.* Immērgītquĕ mănŭs, Ov. SYN. Mērgo, dēmērgo, sŭbmērgo. V. Mergo.

immĕrĭtŭs, ă, ŭm, *who has not deserved.* Ĕt răpĭt immĕrĭtās, Mart. SYN. Indīgnŭs.

immērsābĭlĭs, ĕ, *that cannot be sunk.* Rērum immērsābĭlĭs ūndīs, Hor.

immētātŭs, ă, ŭm, *without limits.* Immētātă quĭbŭs, Hor.

immigro, *to come to.* Pōst immĭgrāvī, (Iamb.) SYN. Migro, cōmmigro, ăbĕo.

immĭnēns, *the pres. partic. of* imminieo. Immĭnēns vīllæ, Hor.

immĭnĕo, ŭī, *to hang over.* Immĭnĕt, ēt lēntæ, Virg. SYN. Insto, īmpēndĕo, īngrŭo.

immĭnŭo, ŭī, ūtŭm, *to lessen.* Sē dŏlŏr immĭnŭĭt, Ov. SYN. Mĭnŭo, dīmĭnŭo, ēxtĕnŭo.

immĭnūtŭs, *the pass. partic. of* imminuo. Ăt se immĭnūtī, Prud.

immīscĕo, scŭī, stŭm *or* xtŭm, *to mix.* Rŭtĭlo immīscĕrĭĕr īgnī, Virg. SYN. Mīscĕo, cōmmīscĕo, pērmīscĕo, ădmīscĕo, cōnfūndo.

immĭsĕrābĭlĭs, ĕ, *not exciting pity.* Pĕrīrĕt immĭsĕrābĭlĭs, Hor.

immītĭs, ĕ, *unkind, sour.* Nĭdīs immītĭbŭs ēscăm, Virg. SYN. Bārbărŭs, fĕrŭs, dīrŭs, crūdēlĭs, ĭnhūmānŭs. V. Crudelis.

immītto, mīsī, mīssŭm, *to throw in.* Immīttĭt sylvīs, Virg. SYN. Mītto, īmpēllo, īnjĭcĭo, īnfĕro.

immōbĭlĭs, ĕ, *immoveable.* Căpĭtōli immōbĭlĕ sāxŭm, Virg. SYN. Immōtŭs, fīxŭs, hærēns, fīrmŭs, cōnstāns, stăbĭlĭs, īncōncūssŭs. V. Constans.

K 5

Immŏdĕrātŭs, ă, ŭm, *immoderate*. Tāntum ĭmmŏdĕrātŭm, Lucr. SYN. Immŏ-dēstŭs, ĭntēmpĕrāns ; ĭmmŏdĭcŭs.

Immŏdĭcŭs, ă, ŭm, *excessive*. Immŏdĭcŭs pārĭtĕr, Ov. SYN. Nĭmĭŭs.

Immŏdŭlātŭs, ă, ŭm, *not measured*. Immŏdŭlātă pŏēmătă, Hor.

Immŏlātŏr, ōrĭs, m., *one who immolates*. Nāti ĭmmŏlātŏr ŭnĭcĭ, Prud.

Immŏlātŭs, ă, ŭm, *the pass. partic. of* immolo. Avĕt ĭmmŏlātŏ, Hor.

Immŏlo, ās *to immolate*. Ēt ĭmmŏlāmŭs, (Iamb.) Paul. SYN. Mācto, lĭto, sacrĭ-fĭco. V. Sacrifico.

Immŏrĭŏr, ĕrĭs, *to die upon*. Ĭmmŏrĭtūr stŭdĭĭs, Hor.

Immŏrtālĭs, ĕ, *immortal*. Fāctæ, ĭmmŏrtālĕ cărīnæ, Virg. SYN. Pērpĕtŭŭs, pĕr-ēnnĭs, ætērnŭs.

Immŏrtālĭtās, ātĭs, f., *immortality*. Sūmpsĭt ĭmmŏrtālĭtās, (Iamb.) Prud. SYN. Pērpĕtŭŭm, ætērnŭm, ĭmmŏrtālĕ, mānsŭrŭm, ævŭm, tēmpŭs. Vīta ĭmmŏrtālĭs, ĭmmūnĭs lēthī. Immŏrtālĕ jūs, fās.

Immŏrtŭŭs, ă, ŭm, *dead*. Strĭctĭs ĭmmŏrtŭŭ nērvĭs, Luc.

Immōtŭs, ă, ŭm, *unmoved*. Mēns ĭmmōtă mănĕt, Virg. SYN. Ĭmmōbĭlĭs, fīxŭs, fīrmŭs.

Immūgĭo, ĭs, ĭī, *to bellow, to roar*. Immūgĭĭt Ætnă, Virg. SYN. Mūgĭo, rēbŏo.

Immūlgĕo, ēs, *to milk in*. Tĕnĕrĭs ĭmmūlgēns ūbĕră lābrĭs, Virg.

Immūndŭs, ă, ŭm, *dirty*. Nēc pĭgĕr ĭmmūndŏ, Hor. SYN. Fœdŭs, spŭrcŭs, sōrdĭdŭs, ĭmpūrŭs, tūrpĭs.

Immūnĭs, ĕ, *exempt*. Cūrvīque ĭmmūnĭs ărātrī, Ov. SYN. Lĭbĕr, văcāns, văcŭŭ, sŏlūtŭs, ēxpērs.

Immūnītŭs, ă, ŭm, *unfortified*. Immūnītāmquĕ frĕquēntāt, Ov.

Immūrmŭro, ās, *to murmur in*. Sўlvĭs ĭmmūrmŭrăt Aūstĕr, Virg. V. Murmuro.

Immūtābĭlĭs, ĕ, *immutable*. Immūtābĭlĕ mătĕrĭæ, Lucr. SYN. Cōnstāns, mūtārĭ nēscĭŭs. V. Immobilis.

Immūtātŭs, *the pass. partic. of* immuto. Immūtātă lĭcĕt, Prop.

ımmūto, ās, *to change*. Immūtātquĕ mĕăm, Ov. SYN. Mūto, pērmūto, vărĭo.

īmō, *or* ĭmnĭō, adv., *even*. Fœnĕrăt īmō, Mart. SYN. Quīn, quĭn ĕtĭăm.

Impācātŭs, ă, ŭm, *unappeased*. Aūt ĭmpācātŏs, Virg. SYN. Implācātŭs, crū-dēlĭs.

Impāllĕo, ēs, *and* ēsco, ĭs, *to grow pale*. Jŭbĕt ĭmpāllēscĕrĕ chārtĭs, Pers.

Impār, ărĭs, *unequal*. Crēbro ĭmpărĭbŭs sĕ, Virg. SYN. Inæquālĭs, dĭssĭmĭlĭs ; nōn pār, nōn æquŭs.

Impărātŭs, ă, ŭm, *unprepared*. Ēgo ĭmpărātŭs quæ lŏquāntŭr, (Iamb.) Prud. SYN. Immĕdĭtātŭs ; ĭncautŭs.

Impărĭtĕr, adv., *unequally*. Vērsĭbŭs ĭmpărĭtĕr jūnctĭs, Hor.

Impāstŭs, ă, ŭm, *hungry*. Impāstŭs ceū plēnă lĕo, Virg. SYN. Jējūnŭs, fămē-lĭcŭs.

Impătĭēns, ntĭs, *impatient*. Mōllĭs ĕt ĭmpătĭēns, Ov. SYN. Pătī nēscĭŭs, ĭndŏ-cĭlĭs. Dŏlōrī, fōrtūnæ ĭmpār ; fŭrĭōsŭs, præcēps.

Impăvĭdŭs, ă, ŭm, *fearless*. Impăvĭdŭs frāngĭt, Virg. SYN. Intrĕpĭdŭs, aūdāx. V. Audax.

Impĕdīmēntŭm, ĭ, n., *an obstacle*. Impĕdīmēntŭm cōmæ, (Iamb.) Paul. SYN. Ōbēx ; ōbjēx, mŏră.

Impĕdĭo, ĭī, ītŭm, *to hinder*. Impĕdĭūnt tĕnĕrōs, Ov. SYN. Prŏhĭbĕo, ĭnhĭbĕo, vĕto, ōbsto, ōbsŭm, ōbsīsto, rēsīsto.

Impĕdītŭs, ă, ŭm, *the pass. partic. of* impedio. Aūt ĭmpĕdītăm, Mart.

Impēllo, pŭlī, pūlsŭm, *to thrust*. Vēla, ĭmpēllĭtĕ rēmōs, Virg. SYN. Pēllo, ĭnjĭcĭo, ĭnfēro, ĭndūco, ĭncĭto, cōncĭto, ūrgĕo, prēmo, cōgo. V. Pello, cogo.

Impēndĕo, ēs, *to hang over*. Plŭvĭa ĭmpēndēntĕ, rĕcēdŭnt, Virg.

Impēndĭŭm, ĭī, n., *expense, tribute*. Impēndĭă mūndī, Stat.

Impēndo, dī, sŭm, *to spend, bestow*. Atque ĭmpēndĕrĕ cūrăm, Virg. SYN. Ex-pēndo, cōnsūmo, ĭnsūmo, sūmptŭs făcĭo ; cōnfēro, cōllŏco.

Impĕnetrābĭlĭs, ĕ, *impenetrable*. Mēns ĭmpĕnĕtrābĭlĭs īræ, Sil. SYN. Impērvĭŭs, ĭnvĭŭs, ĭnāccēssŭs, ĭnscrūtābĭlĭs, ārcānŭs.

Impēnsă, æ, f., *and* sŭm, ĭ, n., *expense*. Impēnsāquĕ sŭī, Ov. Impēnsō prāndĕrĕ cŏāctăs, Hor. SYN. Impēndĭŭm, sūmptŭs.

Impĕrātŏr, ōrĭs, m., *an emperor.* Impĕrătŏr ūnĭcĕ, (Iamb.) Cat. Syn. Rēx ; dūx.

Impĕrcēptŭs, ă, ŭm, *unremarked.* Impĕrcēptă pĭā, Ov.

impĕrcūssŭs, ă, ŭm, *unstricken.* Ātque impĕrcūssōs, Ov.

impĕrdĭtŭs, ă, ŭm, *not lost.* Graĭs impĕrdĭtă cōrpŏră, Virg.

impĕrfēctŭs, ă, ŭm, *imperfect.* Pārs impĕrfēctă mănēbăt, Virg.

impĕrfōssŭs, ă, ŭm, *unpierced.* Mănēt impĕrfōssŭs, Ov.

impĕrĭōsŭs, ă, ŭm, *proud, powerful.* Impĕrĭōsā trăhĭt, Hor. Syn. Sŭpērbŭs; pŏtēns.

impĕrĭto, ās, *to command.* Quĭs pĕcŏri impĕrĭtĕt, Virg. Syn. Impĕro, dŏmĭnŏr.

impĕrītŭs, ă, ŭm, *unskilful, ignorant.* Hŏmĭne impĕrītō, (Iamb.) Ter. Syn. Indōctŭs, Ignārŭs, rŭdĭs, Illītĕrātŭs.

impĕrĭŭm, ĭī, n., *empire.* Impĕrĭum ōcĕānō, Virg. Syn. Jūssŭm, præcēptŭm, mandātŭm ; rēgnŭm, pŏtēstăs, dītĭo, dŏmĭnātŭs, dŏmĭnātĭo, mŏdĕrāmĕn, scēptrŭm. Epith. Dūrŭm, vĭŏlēntŭm, sŭpērbŭm, sōlēnnĕ, aūdāx, ĭnīquŭm, mŏlēstŭm, immītĕ, intŏlĕrābĭlĕ, dūlcĕ, suāvĕ, bĕnīgnŭm, ămīcŭm, blāndŭm, grātŭm, fēlīx, pŏtēns.

impērjūrātŭs, ă, ŭm, *that is never falsely sworn by.* Impērjūrātæ lăbĕrĭs, Ov.

impērmīssŭs, ă, ŭm, *prohibited.* Dōnēt impērmīssă, Hor. Syn. Vĕtĭtŭs.

impĕro, ās, *to command, rule.* Atque impĕrăt ārvĭs, Virg. Syn. Præcĭpĭo, præscrībo, jŭbĕo, māndo, ēdīco, dŏmĭnŏr, rēgno, præsŭm. V. Regno.

impērtērrĭtŭs, ă, ŭm, *fearless.* Mănĕt impērtērrĭtŭs īllĕ, Virg. Syn. Intērrĭtŭs, intrĕpĭdŭs, aūdāx, impăvĭdŭs.

impērtĭo, īs, *or* ĭŏr, īrĭs, *to impart.* Mēmbrĭs impērtītūrā mĕdēlās, Dracon. Syn. Dō, trĭbŭo, præbĕo, ēlārgĭŏr. V. Do.

impērtūrbātŭs, ă, ŭm, *not troubled.* Impērtūrbātō bĭbĭt, Ov.

impērvĭŭs, ă, ŭm, *impassable.* Impērvĭŭs āmnĭs, Ov. V. Invius.

impĕto, ĭī *or* īvī, ītŭm, *to attack.* Impĕtĭtō fēlīx, Cl. Syn. Invādo, īrrŭo, impūgno, āggrĕdĭŏr, ădŏrĭŏr.

impeto, ās, *to obtain.* Impĕtrăt ēt păcĕm, Hor. Syn. Ēxōro, ōbtĭnĕo, ēxĭgo, cōnsĕquŏr.

impĕtŭs, ūs, m., *an attack, force, impetuosity.* Fērt impĕtŭs ĭpsĕ, Virg. Syn. Vīs, vĭŏlēntĭā, incūrsĭo, incūrsŭs. Epith. Răpĭdŭs, vĭvĭdŭs, cĕlĕr, cĭtātŭs, ācĕr, vălĭdŭs, mĭnāx, fŭrĭōsŭs, vĕhĕmēns, fŭrĭbūndŭs, fĕrŭs, sævŭs, āmēns, dēmēns, ēffrænĭs, vĭŏlēntŭs, īrātŭs, fŭrĭālĭs, hōstīlĭs, fērvēns, pŏtēns, cæcŭs, ārdēns, văgŭs.

impēxŭs, ă, ŭm, *uncombed.* Impēxīs indūrŭĭt hōrrĭdā bārbīs, Virg.

impĭĕtās, ātĭs, f., *impiety.* Implĕtātĭs hăbĕt, Ov. Syn. Nĕfās, crīmĕn, scĕlŭs, crūdēlĭtās. Epith. Aūdāx, tĕmĕrārĭā, sacrĭlĕgă, fĕră, dīră, ēffrænĭs, pĕtŭlāns, bārbără, īnsānă, crūdēlĭs, stūltă, dēmēns.

impĭgĕr, ă, ŭm, *active.* Impĭgĕr ēxtrēmōs, Hor. Syn. Dīlĭgēns, āssĭdŭŭs, sēdŭlŭs, strēnŭŭs, ācĕr.

impīngo, ēgī, āctŭm, *to throw against.* Impīngĕrēt āgmĭnă mūrīs, Virg.

impĭŭs, ă, ŭm, *impious.* Impĭăque ætērnŭm, Virg. Syn. Scĕlēstŭs, scĕlĕrātŭs, nĕfārĭŭs, nĕfāndŭs; crūdēlĭs.

implācābĭlĭs, ĕ, *implacable.* Nōn implācābĭlĭs īră, Ov. Syn. Inēxōrābĭlĭs. V. Crudelis.

implācātŭs, ă, ŭm, *unappeased.* Lævum implācātă Chărybdĭs, Virg. Syn. Implācābĭlĭs ; tūrbātŭs.

implăcĭdŭs, ă, ŭm, *cruel.* Implăcĭdŭm gĕnŭs, (Alc.) Hor. Syn. Implăcātŭs, fĕrōx, āspĕr, dūrŭs.

implĕo, ēvī, ētŭm, *to fill.* Implēvī māgnī, Mart. Syn. Cōmplĕo, ădīmplĕo, replĕo, cŭmŭlo.

implēxŭs, ă, ŭm, *entwined.* Implēxæ crīnĭbŭs ānguēs, Virg.

implĭcĭtŭs, *and* cĭtŭs, ă, ŭm, *the pass. partic. of* implico. Brĕvĭbŭs implĭcătă vīpĕrĭs, (Iamb.) Hor. Implĭcĭtăsque ērrōrĕ, Lucan. Syn. Implēxŭs.

implĭco, ās, ŭī, ātŭm *and* ĭtŭm, *to wrap, to involve.* Implĭcŭĭt bēllō, Virg. Syn. Illăquĕo, īrrētĭo, cīrcūmrētĭo, invōlvo, impĕdĭo.

implōro, ās, *to implore.* Cœlēstēs implōrăt ăquās, Hor. Syn. Invŏco, ēxpōsco, ōbtēstŏr, prĕcŏr ŏpĕm, tēstŏr, āppēllo.

implūmĭs, ĕ, *featherless.* Ōbsērvāns nīdo implūmēs, Virg.

Īmplŭo, ŭī, *to rain upon.* Sȳlvās īmplŭĭt, Ov. V. Pluo.

* Īmpŏlītŭs, ă, ŭm, *unpolished.* Cic. Syn. Aspĕr, rŭdĭs, ĭnōrnātŭs.

Īmpŏllūtŭs, ă, ŭm, *unstained.* Īmpŏllūtă fĭdēs, Sil. Syn. Ĭntĕmĕrātŭs, pūrŭs.

Īmpōno, sŭī, sĭtŭm, *to put on.* Cŭm dōna īmpōnĕrĕt ārīs, Virg. Syn. Addo, sŭpĕrāddo, sŭpērpōno, āggĕro; īnjŭngo, māndo, īmpĕro; fāllo, dēcĭpĭo, īllŭdo.

Īmpŏrto, ās, *to bring in.* Ōdĭum īmpŏrtārĕ lībĕllīs, Hor.

Īmpŏrtūnŭs, ă, ŭm, *importunate.* Cănĭt īmpŏrtūnă pĕr ŭmbrās, Virg. Syn. Īncōmmŏdŭs, nŏcēns, nŏcŭŭs, nŏxĭŭs, īnfēstŭs, mŏlēstŭs.

* Īmpŏs, ŏtĭs, *unable.* Syn. Nōn cōmpŏs, ēxpĕrs; īmpŏtēns.

Īmpŏsĭtŭs, *and* ōstŭs, ă, ŭm, *the pass. partic. of* impono. Īmpŏsĭtīquĕ rŏgīs, Virg. Īmpŏstă Tȳphŏeō, Id.

Īmpōssĭbĭlīs, ĕ, *impossible.* Ēst īmpōssĭbĭlĕ, Prud. Syn. Vīrĭbŭs, cōnātĭbŭs mājŏr. Nūnquam fŭtūrŭm. V. Nunquam.

Īmpŏtēns, ēntĭs, *impotent.* Dēpĕrĭt īmpŏtēntĕ āmŏrĕ, (Phal.) Catull. Syn. Īmbēcīllīs, īnfīrmŭs, dēbĭlīs, īnvălĭdŭs; īmpŏs.

Īmpŏtēntĭă, æ, f., *impotence.* Tōrrĕt īmpŏtēntĭă, (Iamb. pur.) Hor. Syn. Dēbĭlĭtās; vĭŏlēntĭă.

Īmprānsŭs, ă, ŭm, *that has not dined.* Īmprānsī mēcŭm, Hor.

Īmprĕcŏr, ārĭs, *to curse.* Īmprĕcŏr ārmă, Virg.

Īmprīmīs, adv. V. Inprimis.

Īmprĭmo, ĭs, *to impress.* Īmprĭmĭt ōssă, Pers. Syn. Sĭgno, ōbsĭgno, īnscrĭbo, īnfōrmo, fĭgo, īnfĭgo.

Īmprŏbĭtās, ātĭs, f., *wickedness.* Īmprŏbĭtās īpsōs, Nem. Syn. Scĕlŭs, crīmĕn, īmpĭĕtās.

Īmprŏbo, ās, *to disavow.* Īmprŏbăt hās, Ov. Syn. Rējĭcĭo, dămno, crīmĭnŏr, ārgŭo.

Īmprŏbŭs, *dimin.* ŭlŭs, ă, ŭm, *wicked.* Īmprŏbĕ, dīxĭt, Ov. Syn. Mălŭs, mălīgnŭs, scĕlĕrātŭs.

Īmprŏpĕrātŭs, *or* rŭs, ă, ŭm, *slow.* Īmprŏpĕrātă rĕfĕrt, Virg. Syn. Lēntŭs, tārdŭs.

Īmprōvĭdŭs, ă, ŭm, *imprudent.* Ātque īmprōvĭdă pēctŏră, Virg. Syn. Incaūtŭs, īmprūdēns; īmprōvīsŭs.

Īmprōvīsŭs, ă, ŭm, *unprovided.* Īmprōvīsŭs ăĭt, Virg. Syn. Ĭnŏpīnŭs, ĭnŏpīnātŭs, rĕpēntīnŭs, ĭnēxpēctātŭs, īnspērātŭs, sŭbĭtŭs.

Īmprūdēns, ēntĭs, *imprudent.* Nūnquam īmprūdēntĭbŭs īmbĕr, Virg. Syn. Īmprōvĭdŭs, īncaūtŭs, īnscĭŭs, īgnārŭs.

Īmprūdēntĭă, æ, f., *imprudence.* Quĭd ĕnim īmprūdēntĭă prŏdēst? Ser. Epith. Cæcă, præcēps, tĕmĕrārĭă.

Īmpūbēs, ĭs, *not arrived at puberty.* Dīvĭdĭt, īmpūbēs, Virg. Syn. Īmpūbĕr, īmbērbĭs.

Īmpŭdēns, ēntĭs, *impudent.* Īmpŭdēns lĭquī, (Sapph.) Hor. Syn. Ēffrōns, īnvĕrēcŭndŭs, prŏcāx, prŏtērvŭs, aūdāx, tĕmĕrārĭŭs.

Īmpŭdēntĕr, adv., *impudently.* Nōn īmpŭdēntĕr, (Iamb.) Syn. Prŏcācĭtĕr, prŏtērvē, aūdāctĕr.

* Īmpŭdēntĭă, æ, f., *impudence.* Cic. Syn. Īnvĕrēcŭndĭă.

Īmpŭdīcŭs, ă, ŭm, *unchaste.* Nĕc īmpŭdīcă Cōlchĭs, (Iamb. pur.) Syn. Tūrpĭs, īmpūrŭs, īnfāmĭs, lāscīvŭs, lĭbīdĭnōsŭs. V. Libidinosus.

Īmpūgno, ās, *to attack.* Īmpūgnāntĕ fĭdēmquĕ, Ov.

Īmpūlsĭo, ōnĭs, f., *and* sŭs, ŭs, m., *a pushing.* Īmpūlsū quŏ, Virg.

Īmpūnĕ, adv., *without danger.* Rāmōs īmpūnĕ vĭdēmŭs, Virg.

Īmpūnītŭs, ă, ŭm, *unpunished.* Quī tu īmpūnītĭŏr īllā, Hor. Syn. Inūltŭs.

Īmpūrŭs, ă, ŭm, *impure.* Sĕd quæ se īmpŭrŏ, Catull. Syn. Īmmūndŭs, fœdŭs, spūrcŭs, ōbscœnŭs, sōrdĭdŭs, tūrpĭs.

Īmpŭtātŭs, ă, ŭm, *unpruned.* Ēt īmpŭtātă, Hor.

Īmpŭto, ās, *to impute.* Īmpŭtĕt īpsĕ, Mart. Syn. Trĭbŭo, āttrĭbŭo, ārrŏgo, āscrĭbo, sūppŭto, nŭmĕro.

Īmŭs, *dimin.* ŭlŭs, ă, ŭm, *the lowest.* Gĕmĭtŭs īmō dē pēctŏrĕ dūcēns, Virg. Syn. Īnfĭmŭs, ēxtrēmŭs, prŏfūndŭs, īntĭmŭs.

Ĭn, prep., *in, into.* Pōnĭs ĭn ārmīs, Virg. Cārmĕn dēdŭcĭs ĭn āctŭs, Hor.

Ĭnābrūptŭs, ă, ŭm, *unbroken.* Jūnxĭt ĭnābrūptā, Stat.

Ĭnāccēssŭs, ă, ŭm, *inaccessible.* Dīvĕs ĭnāccēssŏs, Virg. Syn. Invĭŭs, īmpērvĭŭs, ĭnhōspĭtŭs.

Ĭnăcēsco, ĭs, *to become sour.* Pĕr tŏtōs ĭnăcēscănt, Ov.

Ĭnăchĭă, æ, f., *Argolis.* Est lŏcŭs Ĭnăchĭæ, Stat.—2. *a woman's name.* Ĭnăchĭā
lănguēns, Hor.

Ĭnăchĭdēs, æ, m., *the son or descendant of Inachus.* Nōn tŭlĭt Ĭnăchĭdēs, Ov.

Ĭnăchĭs, ĭdŏs, f., *of the race of, or daughter of Inachus.* Ĭnăchĭdŏs vūltŭs, Ov.

Ĭnăchĭŭs, ă, ŭm, *of Inachus, of Io, of Argos.* Lītŭs pĕr Ĭnăchĭŭm, Virg.

Ĭnăchŭs, ī, m., *king of Argos, and father of Io.* Nātŭs ăb Ĭnăchō, Hor.

Ĭnădūstŭs, ă, ŭm, *unburnt.* Ĭnădūstō cōrpŏrĕ taūrōs, Ov.

Ĭnæquālĭs, ĕ, *unequal.* Haūd bĕne ĭnæquālēs, Ov. Syn. Impār, nōn æquŭs.

Ĭnæquātŭs, ă, ŭm, *not made even.* Quālĭs ĭnæquātŭm, Tib.

Ĭnæstŭo, ās, *to boil up.* Mĕīs ĭnæstŭĕt præcōrdĭīs, (Iamb.) Hor. Syn. Æstŭo,
fērvĕo.

Ĭnămābĭlĭs, ĕ, *unamiable.* Fĕrĭtās ĭnămābĭlĭs ĭstōs, Ov. Syn. Invīsŭs, ŏdĭōsŭs,
mŏlēstŭs.

Ĭnămbĭtĭōsŭs, ă, ŭm, *unambitious.* Mōntēs ĕt ĭnămbĭtĭōsă cŏlēbăt, Ov. Syn.
Mŏdēstŭs, mŏdĕrātŭs.

Ĭnămœnŭs, ă, ŭm, *unpleasant.* Adĭīt ĭnămœnăquĕ rēgnă, Ov. Syn. Ingrātŭs,
mœstŭs, trīstĭs, ĭnjūcūndŭs.

Ĭnănĭo, ĭs, *to empty.* Hōc ŭbĭ ĭnānītŭr, Lucr. V. Vacuo.

Ĭnănĭs, ĕ, *empty.* Văcŭās ĕt ĭnănĭă rēgnă, Virg. Syn. Văcŭŭs, văcŭātŭs; vānŭs,
ĭrrĭtŭs.

Ĭnănĭtĕr, adv., *in vain.* Dē rēbŭs ĭnānĭtĕr ŭllīs, Aus. Syn. Frūstrā, ĭncāssŭm.

Ĭnăpērtŭs, ă, ŭm, *unopened.* Fraūdīque ĭnăpērtă sĕnēctŭs, Virg. Syn. Claūsŭs.

Ĭnărātŭs, ă, ŭm, *unploughed.* Est ĭnărātæ, Virg. Syn. Incūltŭs.

Ĭnārdēsco, ĭs, *to take fire.* Sōlĭs ĭnārdēscīt rădĭīs, Virg. Syn. Inārdĕo, ĭncēndŏr,
ĭncāndĕo, ĭncāndēsco, ārdĕo.

Ĭnărĭmē, ēs, f., *an island in the Gulf of Naples.* Ĭnărĭmē Jŏvĭs, Virg.

Ĭnăspēctŭs, ă, ŭm, *unseen.* Sēdĭs ĭnăspēctōs, Stat. Syn. Invīsŭs.

Ĭnăssuētŭs, ă, ŭm, *unaccustomed.* Lūmĕn ĭnăssuētī, Ov. Syn. Insŏlĭtŭs, ĭnsuētŭs.

Ĭnăttĕnŭātŭs, ă, ŭm, *undiminished.* Sĕd ĭnăttĕnŭătă mănēbăt, Ov.

Ĭnaūdāx, ācĭs, *wanting boldness.* Fŭgĭēs ĭnaūdāx, (Sapph.) Hor. V. Timidus.

Ĭnaūgŭro, ās, *to divine, consecrate.* Tībrĭs ĭnaūgŭrăt, ănnŭs, Claud. Syn. Aūgŭrŏr; cōnsecro, sacro, ūngo.

Ĭnaūrĭs, ĭs, f., *an ear-ring.* Gēmmĭs ĕt ĭnaūrĭbŭs, Fill. Syn. Băccă, ĕlēnchŭs,
Epith. Gēmmĕă, gēmmātă, pēndŭlă.

Ĭnaūro, ās, *to gild.* Rīvŭs ĭnaūrĕt, Hor. Syn. Dĕaūro, aūrō dĕcŏro, ōrno,
ēxōrno, ĭllūstro, dīto, tĕgo, ōbdūco, ĭndūco, ăllūdo, ĭllĭno.

Ĭnaūspĭcātŭs, ă, ŭm, *unlucky.* Pĕr ĭnaūspĭcātŭm, (Iamb.) Sen. Syn. Infēlix,
ădvērsŭs, sĭnīstĕr, ĭnfaūstŭs, lævŭs.

Ĭnaūsŭs, ă, ŭm, *unattempted.* Līnquĕre ĭnaūsŭm, Virg. Syn. Intēntātŭs.

Ĭncædŭŭs, ă, ŭm, *uncut.* Mūltīs ĭncædŭŭs ănnĭs, Ov.

Ĭncălēsco, ĭncălŭī, *to grow warm.* Incălŭīt quŏtĭēs, Mart. Syn. Călĕfĭo, ĭnārdēsco, ĭnflāmmŏr.

Ĭncălfăcĭo, fēcī, făctŭm, *to warm.* Incălfăcĭt hōstĭă cūltrōs, Ov.

Ĭncānēsco, nŭī, *to wax hot.* Spūmĭs ĭncānŭīt ūndă, Cat. Syn. Cānēsco,
ālbēsco.

‖ Ĭncāntātĭo, ōnĭs, f., *an enchantment.* Syn. Incāntāmĕn, ĭncāntāmēntŭm, cāntā-
mĕn, făscĭnātĭo. V. Magia, veneficium.

Ĭncānto, ās, *to charm.* Incāntātă lăcērtĭs, Hor.

Ĭncānŭs, ă, ŭm, *hoary.* Crīnēs ĭncānăquĕ mēntă, Virg. Syn. Cānŭs, ālbŭs.

Ĭncāssŭm, adv., *in vain.* Tūrnĕ, tŏt ĭncāssŭm, Virg.

Ĭncāstīgātŭs, ă, ŭm, *uncorrected.* Dīmīttēs ĭncāstīgātŭm, Hor.

Ĭncaūtŭs, ă, ŭm, *unwary.* Dīră pĕr ĭncaūtŭm, Virg. Syn. Incōnsūltŭs, ĭmprō-
vĭdŭs, ĭmprūdēns.

Ĭncēdo, ssĭ, ssŭm, *to walk.* Gaūdēns ĭncēdĭt Iūlī, Virg. Syn. Ĕo, vādo, āmbŭlo,
grădĭŏr.

Ĭncĕlĕbrĭs, ĕ, *unrenowned.* Incĕlĕbrī mīsērŭnt, Sil. V. Ignobilis.

Ĭncēndĭŭm, ĭī, n., *a fire.* Fĕrēns ĭncēndĭă vēntŭs, Virg. Syn. Ignĭs, flāmmă,
rŏgŭs, Vūlcānŭs. Epith. Văgŭm, Vūlcānĭŭm, dīrŭm, sævŭm, fūrēns, fūrĭbūn-
dŭm, trīstĕ, lēthālĕ, vŏrāx, fūmāns, fŭmōsŭm, fŭmĭdŭm, răpĭdŭm.

Incēndo, dĭ, sŭm, *to burn.* Frăgĭlēs īncēndĕ bĭtūmĭnĕ, Virg. Syn. Sŭccēndo, Infāmmo, ūro, ēxūro, ădūro, cŏmbūro, crēmo; incĭto, cōncĭto, prōvŏco, impēllo, hörtŏr. V. Uro.

Incēptŭm, ĭ, n., *a beginning.* Quălĭs ăb incēptō, Hor.

Incēro, ās, *to cover with wax.* Gĕnŭa incērārĕ dĕŏrŭm, Hor.

Incērtŭs, ă, ŭm, *uncertain.* Incērtī quō fātă fĕrānt, Virg. Syn. Ancēps, dūbĭŭs, nōn cērtŭs, āmbĭgŭŭs, ānxĭŭs, dūbĭtāns.

Incēsso, ĭs, *to come.* Rēgĭbŭs incēssĭt, Virg.

Incēssŭs, ūs, m., *a march.* Ēt vēra incēssŭ, Virg.

Incēsto, ās, *to defile.* Tōtămque incēstăt, Virg. Syn. Incēstŭ pōllŭo, vĭŏlo, cōnspūrco, măcŭlo, vĭtĭo, tĕmĕro, foedo, īnquĭno, cōrrŭmpo.

Incēstŭm, ĭ, n., *or* tŭs, ūs, m., *incest.* Cūjŭs incēstŭ, Sen. Epith. Impūrŭm, nĕfāndŭm, scĕlĕrātŭm, ārcānŭm, impĭŭm.

Incēstŭs, ă, ŭm, *unchaste.* Ēt incēstōs āmŏrēs, Hor. Syn. Incēstŭōsŭs.

Inchŏo, ās, *to begin.* Mēns inchŏăt, ēn ăgĕ, Virg. Syn. Incĭpĭo, āggrĕdĭŏr.

Incĭdo, cĭdī, (*from* cădo) *to fall into.* Incĭdĭt in cāssēs, Ov. Syn. Lābŏr, cădo, dēcĭdo; cōntĭngo, ēvĕnĭo.

Incĭdo, cĭdī, (*from* caedo) *to cut.* Vītēs incīdĕrĕ fālcĕ, Virg. Syn. Caedo, praecīdo, scīndo, sĕco, āmpŭto, īnscŭlpo, scŭlpo, caelo. V. Scindo.

Incīdŭŭs, ă, ŭm, *uncut.* Incīdŭă sўlvă, Ov. Syn. Incaedŭŭs.

|| Incīlo, ās, *to blame.* Incrĕpĕt incīlētquĕ, Lucr.

Incīngo, xī, ctŭm, *to gird.* Incīngĕrĕ moenĭbŭs ūrbĕm, Ov.

Incĭno, ŭĭ, *to sing.* Incīnĭt ŏrĕ, Prop.

Incĭpĭo, cēpī, ptŭm, *to begin.* Ēt fŭrēre incĭpĭăs, Juv. Syn. Ōrdĭŏr, ēxōrdĭŏr, Inchŏo; coepī, āggrĕdĭŏr; sūscĭpĭo, īngrĕdĭŏr. V. Initium.

Incīsŭs, ă, ŭm, *the pass. partic. of* incīdo. Nōn incīsă nŏtŭs, (Choriamb.) Stat. V. Incīdo.

Incĭto, ās, *to excite.* Incĭtăt īrās, Virg. Syn. Sŭscĭto, cōncĭto, ăcŭo, ēxăcŭo, incēndo, cŏhōrtŏr, stĭmŭlo, impēllo, ūrgĕo, īnstīgo, prōvŏco. V. Hortor.

Incĭtŭs, ă, ŭm, *moved.* Incĭtă sŭmmŭm, Virg. Syn. Cōncĭtŭs, cĭtŭs, cĕlĕr.

Inclāmo, *and* ĭto, ās, *to call to.* Fīt sŏnŭs, inclāmăt, Ov. Syn. Clāmo, ēxclāmo; vōco, ădvŏco, āccērso.

|| Inclēmēns, ntĭs, *unmerciful.* Inclēmēns hīrsūtĭ, Sil. Syn. Immītĭs, ĭnhūmānŭs, ĭmplācābĭlĭs, crūdēlĭs, ĭnmānĭs, saevŭs, dūrŭs, āspĕr.

Inclēmēntĭă, æ, f., *inclemency, harshness.* Răpĭt inclēmēntĭă mōrtŭs, Virg. Syn. Crūdēlĭtās, saevĭtĭă.

Inclīno, ās, *to bend.* Sūnt, inclīnĕt ămārī, Hor. Syn. Inflēcto, incūrvo; prōpēndĕo, impēndĕo, vērgo.

Inclūdo, sī, sŭm, *to include.* Pĕcŭs inclūdātŭr ŏvīlī, C. Syn. Claudo, cōnclūdo, āmbĭo, cīrcŭmdo, cīngo, sēpĭo, āmplēctŏr.

Inclūsŭs, ă, ŭm, *the pass. partic. of* includo. Mōrs tămĕn inclūsŭm, Prop. Syn. Clausŭs, cīrcŭmdătŭs, cīnctŭs.

Inclўtŭs, ă, ŭm, *famous.* Inclўtĕ Māvōrs, Virg. Syn. Clārŭs, nōbĭlĭs, īnsīgnĭs, īllūstrĭs.

Incoeptĭo, ōnĭs, f.; ŭm, ĭ, n.; *and* ŭs, ūs, m., *an enterprise.* Nōstra incoeptă sĕcūndēnt, Virg.

Incōgĭto, ās, *to meditate.* Pŭĕrōve incōgĭtăt ŭllăm, Hor. V. Cogito.

Incōgnĭtŭs, ă, ŭm, *unknown.* Nōbīsque incōgnĭtă scrīpsĭt, Aus. Syn. Ignōbĭlĭs, ōbscūrŭs, īgnōtŭs.

Incŏlă, æ, m. f., *an inhabitant.* Nŏvŭs incŏlă tērrae, Ov. Syn. Hōspĕs, cīvĭs, cŏlōnŭs, āccŏlă.

Incŏlo, ŭī, *to inhabit.* Incŏlŭīstĭs ăvī, Tibull. Syn. Cŏlo, hăbĭto, ĭnhăbĭto, mănĕo.

Incŏlŭmĭs, ĕ, *safe.* Grātŭlŏr incŏlŭmī, Ov. Syn. Sālvŭs, īntĕgĕr, īllaesŭs, sōspĕs, tūtŭs, sēcūrŭs, sānŭs.

Incŏmĭtātŭs, ă, ŭm, *unaccompanied.* Incŏmĭtātă bŏnĭs, Ov. Syn. Sŏlŭs.

Incōmmēndātŭs, ă, ŭm, *uncommended.* Incōmmēndātăquĕ tēllŭs, Ov.

Incōmmŏdŭm, ĭ, n., *an inconvenience.* Mĭsĕrāntem incōmmŏdă nōstră, Virg. Syn. Dāmnŭm, nōxă, dētrīmēntŭm. V. Damnum.

Incōmmŏdŭs, ă, ŭm, *inconvenient.* Aŭt incōmmŏdŭs āngăt, Hor.

Incōmpŏsĭtŭs, ă, ŭm, *disordered.* Dĕt mōtŭs incōmpŏsĭtōs, Virg. Syn. Incōmptŭs, incŭltŭs.

ĭncōmptŭs, ă, ŭm, *neglected.* Ĭncōmptīs brĕvĭŏr, Ov. Syn. Ĭncūltŭs.

ĭncōncēssŭs, ă, ŭm, *unallowed.* Ĭncōncēssōsque hўmĕnæōs, Virg.

ĭncōncĭnnŭs, ă, ŭm, *ungraceful.* Nōn ĭncōncĭnnŭs ūtrāmquĕ, Hor.

ĭncōncūssŭs, ă, ŭm, *unshaken.* Hўlărēs ĭncōncūssīquĕ pĕnātēs, Stat. Syn. Fīrmŭs, stăbĭlĭs, ĭmmōtŭs.

ĭncōndĭtŭs, ă, ŭm, *out of order.* Hæc ĭncōndĭtă sōlŭs, Virg. Syn. Ĭncōmpŏsĭtŭs.

ĭncōnfēssŭs, ă, ŭm, *not confessed.* Ĭncōnfēssă quĭd ēssĕt, Ov.

ĭncōnsōlābĭlĭs, ĕ, *inconsolable.* Mœrēns, ĭncōnsōlābĭlĕ vūlnŭs, Ov. Syn. Ĭnsōlābĭlĭs.

ĭncōnstāntĕr, adv., *inconstantly.* Mēmbra ĭncōnstāntĕr, Ov. Syn. Lĕvĭtĕr; ægrē.

ĭncōnstāntĭă, æ, f., *inconstancy.* Rērum ĭncōnstāntĭă vērsăt, Ov. Syn. Lĕvĭtăs, mōbĭlĭtăs. V. Fortuna, inconstans.

ĭncōnsuētŭs, ă, ŭm, *unaccustomed.* Stŭpĕt ĭncōnsuētŭs ŏpīmæ, Sil.

ĭncōnsūltŭs, ă, ŭm, *inconsiderate, unadvised.* Ĭncōnsūlti ăbĕŭnt, Virg.

ĭncōnsūmptŭs, ă, ŭm, *unconsumed.* Pārs ĭncōnsūmptă rĕpērtă, Ov.

ĭncōntĭnēns, ntĭs, *incontinent.* Ĭncōntĭnēntēs ĭnjĭcĭăt mănŭs, (Alc.) Hor.

ĭncŏquo, ōxī, ōctŭm, *to boil in.* Ĭncŏquĕ Bācchō, Virg. Syn. Cŏquo; ĭgnĕ cŏquo.

ĭncōrrēctŭs, ă, ŭm, *uncorrected.* Nōn ĭncōrrēctŭm pŏpŭlī, Ov.

ĭncōrrūptŭs, ă, ŭm, *uncorrupted.* Ĭncōrrūptă Fĭdēs, Hor. Syn. Ĭnvĭŏlātŭs, ĭntĕmĕrātŭs, ĭntĕgĕr, pūrŭs, sānŭs, sĭncērŭs, cāstŭs.

ĭncrēbrēsco, būī, *to increase.* Lătĭo ĭncrēbrēscĕrĕ nōmĕn, Virg. Syn. Crēbrēsco, crēsco, aūgĕŏr; vūlgŏr.

ĭncrēdĭbĭlĭs, ĕ, *incredible.* Hīc ĭncrēdĭbĭlĭs, Virg.

ĭncrēdŭlŭs, ă, ŭm, *unbelieving.* Sīc ĭncrēdŭlŭs ōdī, Hor. Syn. Nōn crēdŭlŭs; ōbstĭnātŭs.

ĭncrēmēntŭm, ī, n., *increase.* Jŏvĭs ĭncrēmēntŭm, (Spond.) Virg. Syn. Accēssĭo, aūgmēntŭm. Epith. Māguŭm, āmplŭm, īngēns, mīrāndŭm.

ĭncrĕpo, *and* pĭto, ās, *to rattle, reproach.* Ĭncrĕpŭĕrĕ mănŭs, Prop. Ămārĕ, quĭd ĭncrĕpĭtās, Virg. Syn. Crĕpo, ĭnstrĕpo; ārgŭo, ōbjūrgo, ĭncūso.

ĭncrēsco, ēvī, *to grow.* Jăcŭlīs ĭncrēvĭt ăcūtīs, Virg. V. Cresco.

ĭncrŭēntātŭs, *and* ēntŭs, ă, ŭm, *bloodless.* Ĭnquĕ crŭēntātŭs Cœneŭs, Ov. Rŭĭt ĭncrŭēntă dāmnō, Mart.

ĭncrūsto, ās, *to cover with a hard crust.* Vās ĭncrūstărĕ, Hor.

ĭncŭbo, būī, *to lie upon.* Ĭncŭbŭĕrĕ mărī, Virg. Syn. Ĭncumbo, ĭndōrmĭo; fŏvĕo.

ĭncūlcātŭs, ă, ŭm, *inculcated.* Ĭncūlcātă vĭrīs, Luc.

ĭncrētŭs, ă, ŭm, *mingled.* Cūm sălĕ nĭgrō Incrētŭm, Hor.

ĭncūlpātŭs, ă, ŭm, *blameless.* Ĭncūlpātă fĭdēs, Ov.

ĭncūltŭs, ă, ŭm, *unpolished.* Nam ĭncūltă vĭdĕt, Virg. Syn. Ĭncōmptŭs, ĭnōrnātŭs, ĭnūrbānŭs, ĭncōncĭnnŭs, ĭncōmpŏsĭtŭs, hōrrĭdŭs, squālĭdŭs; stĕrĭlĭs.

ĭncumbo, cŭbŭī, *to lie upon.* Ūrgēnti ĭncumbĕrĕ vēllĕt, Virg. Syn. Ĭncŭbo, ĭunītŏr; stŭdĕo, ĭnvĭgĭlo, văco, ĭntēndo.

ĭncūnābŭlă, ōrŭm, n. pl., *a cradle.* Jŏvĭs ĭncūnābŭlă Crētēn, Ov. Syn. Cūnābŭlă, cūnæ. V. Cunæ.

ĭncūrĭă, æ, f., *negligence.* Quăs aūt ĭncūrĭă fūdĭt, Hor. Syn. Pĭgrĭtĭă. Epith. Tārdă, lēntă, sēgnĭs, dēsĕs. V. Pigritia.

ĭncūrro, ĭs, *and* rso, ās, *to run upon.* Dēnsĭs ĭncūrrĭmŭs ārmīs, Virg. Syn. Cūrro ĭn; ĭncĭdo.

ĭncūrsŭs, ūs, m., *an invasion.* Ĭncūrsŭs ōmnī, Ov.

ĭncūrvo, ās, *to crook.* Vălĭdīs ĭncūrvănt, Virg. V. Curvo.

ĭncūrvŭs, ă, ŭm, *crooked.* Ĭncūrvă cărīnă, Ov. V. Curvus.

ĭncŭs, ūdĭs, f., *an anvil.* Ĭmpŏsĭtīs ĭncūdĭbŭs Ætnă, Virg. Epith. Hōrrĭsŏnă, rĭgĭdă, dūră, fērrĕă, grăvĭs, sŏnāns, rĕsŏnāns, Ætnæă, Vūlcānĭă, Æŏlĭă, Sĭcŭlă. V. Procudo.

ĭncūso, ās, *to accuse.* Quĕm nōn ĭncūsāvī, Virg. Syn. Accūso, dāmno, ārgŭo, ĭncrĕpo. V. Accuso.

ĭncūstōdĭtŭs, ă, ŭm, *unguarded.* Ĭncūstōdĭtŭs ĕt ăpērtĭs, Mart. Syn. Ĭndēfēnsŭs, ĭntūtŭs, rĕlīctŭs.

ĭncūsŭs, ă, ŭm, *stamped.* Ĭncusum, aūt ātræ, Virg. Syn. Cūsŭs. V. Cudo.

Incŭtĭo, ĭs, ŭssī, ŭssŭm, *to strike*. Incŭtĕ vīm, Virg. Syn. Quătĭo, Inflīgo, Impĭngo ; Injĭcĭo, Immĭtto.

• Indăgo, ās, *to seek*. Cic. Syn. Indăgĭnĕ cīngo, lūsiro, pērquīro, scrūtŏr, Investīgo. V. Venor ; quæro.

Indăgo, ĭnĭs, f., *nets*. Sāltūsque Indăgĭnĕ cīngŭnt, Virg. Syn. Rĕtĕ, cāssēs, Indăgātĭo, pērscrūtātĭo. Epith. Vĭgĭl, sŏlĕrs, sŏllĭcĭtă, ānxĭă, săgāx, strēnŭă, lōngă, cōnstāns.

Indĕ, adv., *thence, then*. Indĕ tŏrō, Virg. Syn. Hīnc ; pōst, deīndĕ.

Indēbĭtŭs, ă, ŭm, *not due*. Nōn Indēbĭtă pōsco, Ov. Syn. Nōn dēbĭtŭs, Indignŭs, Immĕrĭtŭs.

Indĕcēns, ntĭs, *indecent*. Spēctăt Indĕcēns ūnō, (Scaz.) Mart.

Indĕcēntĕr, adv., *indecently*. Phĭlēnĭs Indĕcēntĕr, (Phal.) Mart. Syn. Tŭrpĭtĕr, dēfōrmĭtĕr.

Indēclīnātŭs, ă, ŭm, *firm*. Indēclīnātæ mūnŭs ămĭcĭtĭæ, Ov. V. Constans.

Indĕcŏr, ŏrĭs, ĕ, *disgraceful*. Rēgno Indĕcŏrēs, nĕc, Virg.

Indĕcŏrŭs, ă, ŭm, *unbecoming*. Nōn Indĕcŏrō pūlvĕrĕ, (Alc.) Hor. Syn. Inhōnēstŭs, Inglōrĭŭs, tūrpĭs, dēfōrmĭs, Infāmĭs.

Indēfēnsŭs, ă, ŭm, *undefended*. Indēfēnsă rĕcēpĭt, Sil.

Indēfēssŭs, ă, ŭm, *unwearied*. Răpĭt Indēfēssă bĭpēnnĕm, Virg.

Indēflētŭs, ă, ŭm, *unlamented*. Indēflētæquĕ văgāntŭr, Ov. Syn. Indēplōrātŭs, Inflētŭs.

Indējēctŭs, ă, ŭm, *not cast down*. Indējēctă mălō, Ov.

Indēlēbĭlĭs, ĕ, *indelible*. Indēlēbĭlĕ nōstrŭm, Ov.

Indēlībātŭs, ă, ŭm, *untouched*. Indēlībātās cūnctă, Ov. Syn. Illībātŭs, Intāctŭs, Intĕgĕr. ·

Indēplōrātŭs, ă, ŭm, *unbewailed*. Indēplōrātūm bārbără, Ov. V. Indefletus.

Indēprēnsŭs, ă, ŭm, *untaken*. Indēprēnsŭs ĕt īrrĕmĕăbĭlĭs ērrŏr, Virg. Syn. Cæcŭs, lătēns.

Indēsērtŭs, ă, ŭm, *unforsaken*. Indēsērtă mĕō, Ov. Syn. Nōn dēsērtŭs ; tūtŭs, dēfēnsŭs.

Indēspēctŭs, ă, ŭm, *unseen from above*. Indēspēctă tĕnĕt, Luc.

Indētōnsŭs, ă, ŭm, *unshaven*. Indētōnsūsquĕ Thȳŏneŭs, Ov.

Indēvītātŭs, ă, ŭm, *inevitable*. Indēvītātō trājēcĭt, Ov.

Indēvŏrātŭs, ă, ŭm, *not devoured*. Indēvŏrātō căpĭtĕ, (Scaz.) Mart.

Indēx, ĭcĭs, m., *a discoverer*. Nōn ēxōrābĭlĭs Indēx, Ov.

Indī, ŏrŭm, m. pl., *the Indians*. Ægȳptŭs ĕt Indī, Virg. Epith. Cŏlōrātī, sĭtĭēntēs, dēpēxī, ŏdōrātī, thŭrĭfĕrī, gēmmĭfĕrī, ārdēntēs, pīctī, ūstī, grăcĭlēs, ōbscūrī, ātrī, fūscī, ēxūstī, ādūstī, ēxtrēmī, lōngīnquī, lōngævī, Mēmnŏnĭī, Eōī, Hȳdāspæī, Gāngētĭcī. · V. India.

Indĭă, æ, f., *India*. Indĭă mīttĭt, Virg. Epith. Tōstă, gēmmĭfĕră, aūrĭfĕră, rĕmōtă, ēxtrēmă, ĕbūrnĕă, dīvēs, ŏpŭlēntă.

Indĭcĭŭm, ĭī, n., *a sign*. Indĭcĭūm tēctæ, Ov. Syn. Indēx ; sīgnŭm, ārgŭmēntŭm, nŏtă, Insīgnĕ, spĕcĭmĕn ; vēstīgĭŭm.

Indĭco, ās, *to disclose*. Indĭcăt ēt nŏmĕn, Tib. Syn. Ōstēndo, mōnstro, sīgnĭfĭco, ăpĕrĭo. ·

Indīco, ĭs, *to declare*. Tēmplĭs Indīcĭt hŏnōrĕm, Virg. Syn. Ēdīco, dēnūncĭo, prōmūlgo.

Indĭcŭs, ă, ŭm, *of India*. Indĭcă quōs, Mart. Syn. Gāngētĭcŭs, Eōŭs.

Indĭgĕnă, æ, m. f., *a native*. Sūspĭcĭt, Indĭgĕnæ, Ov. Syn. Cīvĭs, Incŏlă.

Indĭgĕo, ŭī, *to want*. Quōrum Indĭgĕt ūsŭs, Virg. Syn. Ēgĕo, cărĕo, ŏpŭs hăbĕo.

Indĭgēstŭs, ă, ŭm, *undigested*. Rŭdĭs Indĭgēstăquĕ mōlēs, Ov. Syn. Incōmpŏsĭtŭs ; cōnfūsŭs.

Indĭgēs, ĕtĭs, m., Indĭgētēs, ŭm, m. pl., *Gods peculiar to any country*. Indĭgĕtem Ænēăn, Virg. Dī pătrĭī, Indĭgētēs, Id.

Indīgnātĭo, ōnĭs, f., *indignation*. Făcĭt Indīgnātĭō vērsŭm, Juv. Syn. Iră. Epith. Præcēps, sŭbĭtă, rĕpēntīnă, sævă, cæcă, dēmēns, mīnāx. V. Ira.

Indīgnātŭs, *the partic. of* indignor. Ălĭquem Indīgnātŭs ăb ūmbrīs, Virg.

Indīgnŏr, ārĭs, *to scorn, to be angry*. Mēcum Indīgnābăr ămīcī, Virg. Syn Irāscŏr, sŭccēnsĕo, stŏmăchŏr. V. Irascor.

Indīgnŭs, ă, ŭm, *unworthy*. Pērcŭlĭt Indīgnōs, Ov. Syn. Innŏcēns, Immĕrĭtŭs, Immĕrens, Innŏcŭŭs.

Ĭndĭgŭs, ă, ŭm, *needing.* Ŏpĭsque haūd ĭndĭgă nŏstræ, Virg. Syn. Ĕgēnūs, ĕgēns, ĭnŏps, paūpĕr.

Ĭndĭscrētŭs, ă, ŭm, *undistinguished.* Ĭndĭscrētă sūīs, Virg. Syn. Ĭndĭstĭnctŭs, sĭmĭllĭmŭs.

Ĭndĭstĭnctŭs, ă, ŭm, *confused.* Ĭndĭstĭnctĭsquĕ cŏrōllĭs, Cat.

Ĭndĭstrĭctŭs, ă, ŭm, *unwounded.* Ĭndĭstrĭctŭs ăbībo, Ov.

Ĭndĭvĭdŭŭs, ă, ŭm, *not to be divided.* Mŏrs ĭndĭvĭdŭa ēst, (Choriamb.) Sen.

Ĭndĭvīsŭs, ă, ŭm, *undivided.* Ĭndĭvīsŭs hŏnŏs, Sil. Syn. Cōnjūnctŭs.

Ĭndo, dĭdī, *to put in.* Ĭndĕrĕ tēnto, Ov.

Ĭndŏcĭlĭs, ĕ, *that cannot be taught.* Gĕnŭs ĭndŏcĭle āc dīspērsŭm, Vīrg. Syn. Rŭdĭs, agrēstĭs.

Ĭndŏctŭs, ă, ŭm, *ignorant.* Trĭvĭīs, ĭndŏctĕ, sŏlēbās, Virg. Syn. Ĭmpĕrītŭs, ĭgnārŭs, ĭllĭtĕrātŭs, rŭdĭs. V. Ignarus.

Ĭndŏlĕo, ēs, ŭī, *to be grieved.* Ĭndŏlŭīt fāctō, Ov. Syn. Dŏlĕo, ĭngĕmo.

Ĭndŏlēs, ĭs, f., *natural disposition.* Ĭndŏlĕ dīgnŭm, Virg. Syn. Ĭngĕnĭŭm, nātūră. Epith. Ĕgrĕgĭă, gĕnĕrōsă, nŏbĭlĭs, ĭngĕnŭă, præstāns, ămābĭlĭs, cūltă. V. Ingenium.

Ĭndŏmĭtŭs, ă, ŭm, *untamed.* Lāssŭs ăb ĭndŏmĭtō, Hor. Syn. Ĭnvīctŭs, ĭnsŭpĕrābĭlĭs, fŏrtĭs.

Ĭndōrmĭo, īs, *to sleep upon.* Sāccīs ĭndōrmīs, Hor. V. Dormio.

Ĭndōtătŭs, ă, ŭm, *unendowed.* Ĭndōtātă mĭhī sŏrŏr, Ov.

Ĭndŭbĭtātŭs, ă, ŭm, *undoubted.* Ĭndŭbĭtātă fĭdēs, Aus. Syn. Cērtŭs, nōn dŭbĭŭs.

Ĭndŭbĭto, ās, *to distrust.* Vīrĭbŭs ĭndŭbĭtārĕ tŭīs, Virg.

Ĭndŭcĭæ, ārŭm, f. pl., *a truce.* Ĭnĭmīcĭtĭæ, ĭndŭcĭæ, (Iamb.) Ter. Epith. Pāctæ, jūrātæ, fīctæ; brĕvēs.

Ĭndŭco, xī, ctŭm, *to introduce.* Vārĭās ĭndŭcĕrĕ plūmās, Hor. Syn. Addŭco, ădmītto, ĭntrŏdūco; ĭmpēllo, ădĭgo, ŏpĕrĭo.

Ĭndŭlgēns, ntĭs, *indulgent.* Crēscĭt ĭndŭlgēns sĭbi, Hor.

Ĭndŭlgēntĭă, æ, f., *indulgence.* Cœli ĭndŭlgēntĭă tērrās, Virg. Syn. Lēnĭtās, clēmēntĭă, pĭĕtās, vĕnĭă, rĕmīssĭo. Epith. Blāndă, mītĭs, plăcĭdă, ămīcă, făcĭlĭs, grātă.

Ĭndŭlgĕo, sī, tŭm, *to indulge.* Jŭvăt ĭndŭlgĕrĕ dŏlōrī, Virg. Syn. Ĭgnōsco, cōndōno, pārco; cōncēdo, pērmītto. V. Parco.

Ĭndūmēntŭm, ĭ, n., *a garment.* Ĭndūmēntă pĕdŭm, (Phal.) Syn. Ămīctŭs, vēstĭs. V. Vestis.

Ĭndŭo, dŭī, dŭtŭm, *to put on.* Ĭndŭĕrāt tŏtĭdĕm, Virg. Syn. Vēstĭo, ămīcĭo, ŏpĕrĭo, tĕgo. V. Vestio.

Ĭndŭpĕrātŏr, ōrĭs, m., *an emperor, a commander.* Bārbărŭs ĭndŭpĕrātŏr, Juv. Syn. Ĭmpĕrātŏr, dūx.

Ĭndūrēsco, ĭs, *to grow hard.* Vēxātum ĭndūrŭĭt ūsŭ, Ov. Syn. Dūrēsco, ĭndūrŏr.

Ĭndūro, ās, *to harden.* Ĭndūrōquĕ nĭvēs ēt tērrās, Ov.

Ĭndŭs, ă, ŭm, *Indian.* Ĭndūm sānguĭnĕŏ, Virg. Syn. Ĭndĭcŭs, Gāngĕtĭcŭs, Eōŭs.

Ĭndūstrĭă, æ, f., *industry.* Vīrēs ĭndūstrĭă fīrmăt, Virg. Syn. Sŏlērtĭă, ārs, dēxtĕrĭtās, ĭngĕnĭŭm. Epith. Sŏlērs, sēdŭlă, vĭgĭl, ācrĭs, cāllĭdă, săgāx, aŭdāx, ĭngĕnĭōsă, ārtĭfēx, dīvīnă, præstāns.

Ĭndūstrĭŭs, ă, ŭm, *active.* Ārmīs ĭndūstrĭŭs; ăt tū, Juv. Syn. Sŏlērs, ĭngĕnĭōsŭs, săgāx, vĭgĭl, ăcĕr, dēxtĕr.

Ĭndŭtŭs, ă, ŭm, *the pass. partic. of* induo. Ĕxŭvĭās ĭndūtŭs Achīllĭs, Virg. Syn. Vēstītŭs, ămīctŭs, tŭnĭcātŭs, tŏgātŭs, ŏpērtŭs, tēctŭs.

Ĭnēbrĭo, ās, *to make drunk.* Vīnōsŭs ĭnēbrĭĕt aūrĕm, Juv. V. Ebrius.

* Ĭnēdĭă, æ, f., *hunger.* Cic. Syn. Fămēs. V. Fames.

Ĭnēdĭtŭs, ă, ŭm, *unpublished.* Ĭnēdĭtă caūsa ēst, Ov.

* Ĭnēffābĭlĭs, ĕ, *ineffable.* Plin. Syn. Ĭnēnārrābĭlĭs.

Ĭnēffĭcāx, ācĭs, *without force.* Dĭi ĭnēffĭcācēs, Sen.

Ĭnēlĕgāns, ntĭs, *without grace.* Ĭllĕpĭdæ ătque ĭnēlĕgāntēs, (Phal.) Cat.

Ĭnēlūctābĭlĭs, ĕ, *unavoidable.* Ĕt ĭnēlūctābĭlĕ tēmpŭs, Virg. Syn. Ĭnsŭpĕrābĭlĭs, ĭnvīctŭs.

Ĭnēmptŭs, ă, ŭm, *unbought.* Ŏnĕrābăt ĭnēmptīs, Virg. Syn. Vīlĭs.

Ĭnēnārrābĭlĭs, ĕ, *inexpressible.* Ĕt ĭnēnārrābĭlĕ mŭnŭs, Mart. SYN. Nōn ēnārrā-
bĭlĭs; ĭnsŏlĭtŭs.
Ĭnĕo, ĭs, ĭī, ĭtŭm, *to go into.* Prīmă lĕvēs ĭnĕŭnt, Virg. SYN. Ădĕo; ĭncĭpĭo.
Ĭnēptē, adv., *foolishly.* Mōlītŭr Ĭnēptē, Hor.
Ĭnēptĭă, æ, f. *and* æ, ārŭm, f. pl., *foolishness.* Dūcēbăt ĭnēptĭă vūlgī, Prud. SYN.
Dēlīrĭă, stŭltĭtĭă, īnsānĭă.
Ĭnēptŭs, ă, ŭm, *foolish.* Quīcquĭd ĭnēptŭs ămŏr, Tibull. SYN. Stŭpĭdŭs, īnsūlsŭs,
fătŭŭs, stŭltŭs, hĕbĕs, stŏlĭdŭs.
Ĭnērmĭs, ĕ, *and* mŭs, ă, ŭm, *unarmed.* Hōstĭs ĭnērmĭs, Prop.
Ĭnērro, ās, *to wander up and down.* Ignĭs ĭnērrăt, Stat.
Ĭnērs, ērtĭs, *lazy.* Rĕspēxĭt ĭnērtĕm, Virg. SYN. Pĭgĕr, ĭgnāvŭs, sēgnĭs, tārdŭs,
lēntŭs, dēsĭdĭōsŭs, sōcŏrs. V. Piger.
Ĭnērtĭă, æ, f., *sloth.* Nōs ēxērcĕt ĭnērtĭă, Hor. SYN. Ĭgnāvĭă, dēsĭdĭă, sēg-
nĭtĭēs, pigrĭtĭă. EPITH. Mōllĭs, stŏlĭdă, lāscīvă, dēgĕnĕr, lānguĭdă, tārdă. V.
Pigritia.
Ĭnēsco, ās, *to entrap.* Nēscĭs ĭnēscāre hŏmĭnĕm, Ter.
Ĭnēvītābĭlĭs, ĕ, *unavoidable.* Ĕt ĭnēvītābĭlĕ fūlmĕn, Ov. SYN. Ĭnēlūctābĭlĭs, nōn
ēvītābĭlĭs, nōn fŭgĭēndŭs, nōn vītāndŭs, nōn dēclīnāndŭs.
Ĭnēvŏlūtŭs, ă, ŭm, *not unfolded.* Rĕdĕăs ĭnēvŏlūtŭs, (Phal.) Mart.
Ĭnēxcītŭs, ă, ŭm, *unprovoked.* Ārdĕt ĭnēxcīta Aūsŏnĭa, Virg.
Ĭnēxcūsābĭlĭs, ĕ, *inexcusable.* Ĕt ĭnēxcūsābĭlĭs ābsĭs, Hor. SYN. Nōn ēx-
cūsāndŭs.
Ĭnēxhaūstŭs, ă, ŭm, *inexhaustible.* Īnsŭla ĭnēxhaūstĭs, Virg. SYN. Ĭnfīnĭtŭs;
plēnŭs.
Ĭnēxōrābĭlĭs, ĕ, *inexorable.* Ĕt ĭnēxōrābĭlĕ fātŭm, Virg. SYN. Nōn ēxōrābĭlĭs,
ĭmplācābĭlĭs, crūdēlĭs.
Ĭnēxpēctātŭs, ă, ŭm, *unexpected.* Ĕt ĭnēxpēctātŭs ĭn ārmĭs, Ov.
Ĭnēxpērrēctŭs, ă, ŭm, *not awakened.* Ĕt ĭnēxpērrēctŭs Ăphȳdnās, Ov.
Ĭnēxpērtŭs, ă, ŭm, *untried, inexperienced.* Dūlcĭs ĭnēxpērtĭs, Hor. SYN. Ĭn-
tēntātŭs; īnsuētŭs.
Ĭnēxplētŭs, ă, ŭm, *unsatisfied.* Cērnĕre ĭnēxplētō, Varr. Atrac. SYN. Ĭnsătŭrātŭs,
īnsătŭrābĭlĭs, ĭnēxsătŭrābĭlĭs.
Ĭnēxplĭcĭtŭs, ă, ŭm, *not explained.* Zēnōnăs ĭnēxplĭcĭtōsquĕ Plātōnēs, Mart.
Ĭnēxpūgnābĭlĭs, ĕ, *impregnable.* Nĕc ĭnēxpūgnābĭlĕ ămōrī, Ov. SYN. Nōn ēx-
pūgnābĭlĭs, īnsŭpĕrābĭlĭs, ĭndŏmĭtŭs, ĭnvīctŭs, nōn ēxsŭpĕrābĭlĭs. V. Invictus.
Ĭnēxsătŭrābĭlĭs, ĕ, *not to be satisfied.* Ĕt ĭnēxsătŭrābĭlĕ pēctŭs, Virg. SYN. Ĭn-
sătŭrābĭlĭs, īnsătŭrātŭs, ĭnēxplētŭs.
Ĭnēxtīnctŭs, ă, ŭm, *inextinguishable.* Ignĭs ĭnēxtīnctŭs, Ov. SYN. Pĕrēnnĭs,
pērpĕtŭŭs.
Ĭnēxtrīcābĭlĭs, ĕ, *inextricable.* Ĕt ĭnēxtrīcābĭlĭs ērrŏr, Virg. SYN. Ĭmplēxŭs,
ĭrrĕmĕābĭlĭs.
Īnfabrē, adv., *rudely.* Scūlptum īnfābrē, Hor.
Īnfabrĭcātŭs, ă, ŭm, *unwrought.* Īnfābrĭcātă fĕrŭnt, Virg.
Īnfăcētĭæ, ārŭm, f. pl., *poor jests.* Tēne īnfăcētĭārŭm, Cat.
Īnfăcētŭs, ă, ŭm, *unpolished.* Nĕc īnfăcētŭm, (Phal.) Mart.
Īnfāmĭă, æ, f., *infamy.* Mēndāx īnfāmĭă tērrĕt, Hor. SYN. Dēdĕcŭs, probrŭm,
ŏpprobrĭŭm, ĭgnŏmĭnĭă; cōnvīcĭŭm. EPITH. Măcŭlōsă, tŭrpĭs, pŭdēndă, pro-
brōsă, sūmmă, īngēns, pĕrēnnĭs.
Īnfāmĭs, ĕ, *infamous.* Hūnc īnfāmĭs ămŏr, Prop. SYN. Ĭnhŏnēstŭs, fāmōsŭs,
tŭrpĭs, probrōsŭs.
Īnfāmo, ās, *to decry.* Pārcĭŭs īnfāmānt, Prop. SYN. Dēdĕcŏro.
Īnfāndŭs, ă, ŭm, *not to be said.* Īnfāndūm rēgīnă, Virg. SYN. Nĕfāndŭs, dē-
tēstāndŭs, scĕlēstŭs, nĕfārĭŭs, īllĭcĭtŭs; nōn dīcēndŭs, tăcēndŭs.
Īnfāns, āntĭs, m. f., *an infant.* Lūdĕrĕt īnfāns, Hor. SYN. Īnfāntŭlŭs. EPITH.
Tĕnēllŭs, pārvŭlŭs, blāndŭs, flēbĭlĭs, pārvŭs, tĕnĕr. V. Puer.
Īnfāntārĭă, æ, f., *fond of infants.* Īnfāntārĭă nōn ēst, Mart.
Īnfāntĭă, æ, f., *infancy.* Mădĭdīque īnfāntĭă nāsī, Juv. SYN. Incūnābŭlă, cūnæ.
EPITH. Tĕnĕră, rŭdĭs, blāndă.
Īnfaūstŭs, ă, ŭm, *unhappy.* Quōsquĕ sĕcāns īnfaūstŭm, Virg. SYN. Ĭnaūspĭcātŭs,
sĭnīstĕr, lævŭs, īnfēlīx.

Infēctŭs, ă, ŭm, *not done.* Infēctŭm vŏlĕt ēssĕ, Hor.

Infēcŭndŭs, ă, ŭm, *unfruitful.* Infēcŭndă quĭdĕm, Ov. V. Sterilis.

Infēlīcĭtās, ātĭs, f., *unhappiness.* Ter. V. Infortunium.

Infēlīx, īcĭs, *unhappy.* Quōsdam infēlīcēs, Prop. Syn. Mĭsĕr, Infōrtūnātŭs, ærŭmnōsŭs, mĭsĕrābĭlĭs, infaustŭs, sĭnĭstĕr, lævŭs. V. Infortunium.

Infēnsŭs, ă, ŭm, *displeased, hostile.* Dīctĭs infēnsŭs ămārĭs, Stat. Syn. Irātŭs, Infēstŭs, Inĭmīcŭs.

Infĕrī, ōrŭm, m. pl., *the shades below.* Cănĭs infĕrōrŭm, (Sapph.) Ser. V. Infernus.

Infĕrĭæ, ārŭm, f. pl., *sacrifices for the dead.* Vīvēntēs răpĭt, infĕrĭās, Virg. Syn. Exĕquĭæ, fūnĕră, jūstă.

Infĕrĭŏr, ōrĭs, *inferior.* Pœnīs cōmpēscĕrĕt infĕrĭōrĕm, Hor. Syn. Mĭnŏr; hŭmĭlĭs, ăbjēctŭs.

Infērnālĭs, ĕ, *and* nŭs, ă, ŭm, *infernal.* Infērnālĭs ăquæ, Man. Infērnă sēdĕ rĕcēptŭs, Ov. Syn. Infĕrŭs.

Infērnŭs, ī, m., *hell.* Pœnă, sĕd infērnīs, Juv. Syn. Ōrcŭs, Ävērnŭs, Tārtărŭs, Ěrĕbŭs. Epith. Ŏpācŭs, ātĕr, prŏfŭndŭs, hōrrēndŭs, ĭmmānĭs, căvērnōsŭs, trīstĭs, squālĭdŭs, mœstŭs, trĕmēndŭs, fōrmīdābĭlĭs, mĕtŭēndŭs, lūrĭdŭs, squālēns, tēnebrōsŭs, ōbscūrŭs, cæcŭs, tētĕr, Stўgĭŭs.

Infĕro, intŭlī, illātŭm, *to bring in.* Infĕrăt ēt pūlchrăm, Virg. Syn. Indūco, Intrūdo, invĕho; āffĕro.

Infĕrŭs, ă, ŭm, *that is below.* Infĕră sŭb tērră, Ov.

Infērvĕo, ēs, bŭī, *to boil.* Sēctĭs infērbŭĭt hērbīs, Hor.

Infēsto, ās, *to plague.* Quăs Scўlla infēstĕt, Ov. Syn. Vēxo, ăngo, tōrquĕo, ēxăgĭto.

Infēstŭs, ă, ŭm, *hostile.* Illum ārdēns infēstō, Virg. Syn. Infēnsŭs, Inĭmīcŭs, mŏlēstŭs, nōxĭŭs, īrātŭs.

Infĭcĭo, fēcī, fāctŭm, *to corrupt, to dye.* Sævæ infēcērĕ nŏvērcæ, Virg. Syn. Cōrrŭmpo, dēprāvo, vĭŏlo, vĭtĭo, pērdo, măcŭlo, tĕmĕro; tĭngo, ĭmbŭo.

Infĭcĭātŏr, ōrĭs, m., *one who denies.* Atque infĭcĭātŏr, ĕāmŭs, Mart.

Infĭcĭŏr, ārĭs, *and* Infĭcĭās ĕo, īs, īrĕ, *to deny.* Infĭcĭābŏr hăbēns, Prop. Quĭque Infĭcĭās nōn ĕăt, Plaut. Syn. Nĕgo, pērnĕgo, dĭnĕgo, ăbnŭo.

Infĭdēlĭs, ĕ, *and* ĭdŭs, ă, ŭm, *faithless.* Rēbŭs infĭdēlĭs Allōbrŏx, (Iamb. pur.) Hor. Flēxĭt ēt infĭdōs, Virg. Syn. Pērfĭdŭs, fāllāx; ĭdōlŏlatră.

Infīgo, xī, xŭm, *to fix upon.* Infĭgĭmŭs ŏscŭlă pōrtĭs, Rutil. Syn. Fīgo, dēfīgo, cōnfīgo.

Infĭmŭs, ă, ŭm, *the lowest.* Sīdŭs ăb infĭmīs, (Choriamb.) Hor. Syn. Imŭs, pōstrēmŭs, ūltĭmŭs.

Infindo, ĭdī, ssŭm, *to cleave.* Tēllūri infĭndĕrĕ sūlcōs, Virg.

Infīnītŭs, ă, ŭm, *infinite.* Ex infīnītō, Lucr. Syn. Intērmĭnātŭs; Innŭmĕrŭs, Innŭmĕrābĭlĭs. V. Innumerabilis.

*Infīrmo, ās, *to weaken.* Syn. Dēbĭlĭto, ēnērvo, frāngo, infrĭngo, āttĕnŭo, ēxtĕnŭo, cōnfĭcĭo.

Infīrmŭs, ă, ŭm, *weak.* Sēmpĕr ĕt infīrmī, Juv. Syn. Dēbĭlĭs, imbēllĭs, ēnērvĭs, ēnērvātŭs, invălĭdŭs, lāngŭĭdŭs, frāctŭs, mōllĭs. V. Debilis, æger.

Infĭt, *begins.* Ită tūrbĭdŭs infĭt, Virg.

Inflāmmo, ās, *to set on fire.* Ănĭmum inflāmmāvĭt ămōrĕ, Virg. Syn. Ūro, cōmbūro, incēndo; hōrtŏr, incĭto. V. Uro, incendo.

Inflēcto, xī, xŭm, *to bend.* Sōlŭs hīc inflēxĭt, Virg. Syn. Flēcto, tōrquĕo, intōrquĕo, cōntōrquĕo, cūrvo, incūrvo.

Inflētŭs, ă, ŭm, *unbewailed.* Inhŭmāta inflētăquĕ, Virg.

Inflēxŭs, ūs, m., *a turning, winding.* Vīcōrum inflēxū, Juv.

Inflīgo, xī, ctŭm, *to strike, to inflict.* Inflīgītquĕ vĭrō, Ov. Syn. Imprĭmo, infĕro, impĭngo, incŭtĭo.

Inflo, ās, *to blow in.* Inflāvĭt cŭm pīnguĭs ĕbŭr, Virg. Syn. Inspīro.

Inflŭo, ĭs, *to flow in.* Inflŭĭt āmnĭs, Virg. V. Fluo, illabor.

Infŏdĭo, fŏdī, fōssŭm, *to dig into.* Ungŭĭbŭs infŏdĭŭnt, Virg. Syn. Fŏdĭo, dēfŏdĭo.

Infōrmĭs, ĕ, *mis-shapen.* Hōrrēndum, infōrme, Virg.

Infōrmo, ās, *to form.* Clўpĕum infōrmānt, Virg. Syn. Fĭngo, ēffĭngo, fĭgūro; imbŭo, ērŭdĭo; expŏlĭo.

Infōrtūnātŭs, ă, ŭm, *unhappy.* Ter. V. Infelix.

Infōrtūnĭŭm, ĭī, n., *misfortune.* Me infōrtūnĭă lædēnt, Hor. Syn. Infēlīcĭtās, ærŭmnă, călămĭtās, mălŭm; ĕxĭtĭŭm, clădēs. EPITH. Trĭstĕ, grăvĕ, crūdēlĕ, dūrŭm, ĭnfāndŭm, ăcĕrbŭm. V. Infelix, miseria.

Infrā, adv., *under, below*. Cōgēbānt Infrā, Lucr.

Infrăgĭlĭs, ĕ, *not to be broken*. Sĭ vōx Infrăgĭlĭs, Ov.

Infrĕmo, ŭī, *to roar*. Ăcrĭŭs infrĕmŭĭt, Sil. SYN. Frĕmo, frēndĕo, Infrēndĕo; mĭnŏr, Indĭgnŏr, Irāscŏr.

Infrēndĕo, ēs, *or* do, ĭs, *to gnash the teeth*. Dēntĭbŭs infrēndēns, Virg.

Infrēnĭs, ĕ, *or* nŭs, ă, ŭm, *unbridled*. Illum Infrēnĭs ĕquī, Virg. Nŭmĭdæ Infrēnī, Virg. SYN. Ēffrēnĭs.

Infrēno, ās, *to bridle*. Infrēnānt ălĭī, Virg. V. Freno.

Infrĕquēns, ntĭs, *unfrequent*. Cūltŏr ĕt Infrĕquēns, (Alcaic.) Hor. SYN. Rārŭs; Insuētŭs.

Infrĭngo, frēgī, frāctŭm, *to bruise*. Ĕt Infrēgī lătŭs, Hor. SYN. Frāngo, cōnfrĭngo.

Infrŏus *or* ŏndĭs, ŏndĭs, *leafless*. Hīc cāmpi Infrōndēs, Ov.

Infŭlă, æ, f., *a fillet*. Infŭlă tēxĭt, Virg. SYN. Mitră. EPITH. Sacră, ēxĭmĭă, splēndĭdă, mĭcāns, lūcēns, gēmmātă, aŭrĕă, Insignĭs.

Infŭlātŭs, ă, ŭm, *wearing a fillet*. Dŏmŭs Infŭlātă, (Sapph.) Prud.

Infŭndo, fūdī, fūsŭm, *to pour in*. Fōrmātæ Infŭndĕrĕ tĕrræ, Ov. SYN. Fŭndo, Instīllo, Ingĕro, Immĭtto, Injĭcĭo.

Infūsco, ās, *to blacken*. Sānĭe Infūscātŭr ărēnă, Virg.

Infūsŭs, ă, ŭm, *the pass. partic. of* infundo. Hŭmĕrōs Infūsă tĕgĭt, Virg.

Ingĕmĭnātŭs, ă, ŭm, *the pass. partic. of* ingemino. Ingĕmĭnātă rĕmūgĭt, Virg.

Ingĕmĭno, ās, *to double*. Ingĕmĭnāns īctŭs, Virg. SYN. Gĕmĭno, cōngĕmĭno, duplĭco, Ĭtĕro.

Ingĕmĭsco *and* mo, mŭī, *to groan*. Ingĕmīscĭt ignĭs, (Iamb.) Sen. Ingĕmĭt, ēt dŭplĭcēs, Virg. V. Gemo.

Ingĕnĕro, ās, *to engender*. Sēmpĕr Ingĕnĕrārī, Cat.

Ingĕnĭōsŭs, ă, ŭm, *ingenious*. Ingĕnĭōsŭs ĕrăm, Ov. SYN. Sŭbtīlĭs, sāgāx, sōlērs, pērspĭcāx.

Ingĕnĭtŭs, ă, ŭm, *innate*. Ingĕnĭtŭs gĕnĭtŭsquĕ, Prud. SYN. Innātŭs, Insĭtŭs, Ingĕnĕrātŭs.

Ingĕnĭŭm, ĭī, n., *genius, character*. Ingĕnĭŭm quŏndăm, Ov. SYN. Nātŭră, Indŏlēs; sŭbtīlĭtās, sāgācĭtās, Indūstrĭă, sōlērtĭă. EPITH. Sōlērs, vēlōx, ăcūtŭm, præstāns, pērspĭcāx, ācrĕ, āstūtŭm, vērsātĭlĕ, sāgāx, mōbĭlĕ, vĕgĕtŭm, dŏcĭlĕ, cūltŭm, vīvāx, fērtĭlĕ, prōmptŭm, sŭbtĭlĕ, mīrābĭlĕ, căpāx, ŭbĕr, dīvīnŭm; rŭdĕ, dūrŭm, ōbtūsŭm, crāssŭm, tārdŭm, Inērs, hĕbĕs.

Ingēns, ēntĭs, *great*. Hŏrrēndum, Infōrme, Ingēns, Virg. SYN. Māgnŭs, āltŭs, prŏcērŭs.

Ingĕnŭŭs, ă, ŭm, *noble*. Aŭt pŭdŏr Ingĕnŭŭs, Prop. SYN. Lībĕrālĭs, hŏnēstŭs, nōbĭlĭs, cāndĭdŭs, sĭncērŭs, prŏbŭs.

Ingĕro, gēssī, gēstŭm, *to throw in*. Ingĕrĭt hāstās, Virg. SYN. Infĕro, Intrūdo, Injĭcĭo, Infūndo.

Ingĭgno, gĕnŭī, *to engender*. Nātŭra Ingĕnŭĭt, Ov. SYN. Ingĕnĕro.

Inglŏmĕro, ās, *to heap upon*. Inglŏmĕrāt nŏctĕm, Stat. SYN. Glŏmĕro, cŭmŭlo, āccŭmŭlo, cōngĕro.

Inglŏrĭŭs, ă, ŭm, *inglorious*. Pārmăque Inglŏrĭŭs ālbă, Virg. SYN. Ignōbĭlĭs, Indĕcōrŭs, Inhŏnōrŭs, ābjēctŭs, vīlĭs, Incōgnĭtŭs, sĭnĕ nōmĭnĕ, nōmĭnĭs ēxpērs.

Inglŭvĭēs, ĭēī, f., *the throat*. Inglŭvĭē rĕm, Hor. SYN. Gŭlă. EPITH. Vŏrāx, ēbrĭă, fœdă, Inēxplēbĭlĭs, Inēxplētă. V. Gula.

Ingrātĭs, adv., *by constraint*. Ingrātĭs hærĕt, Lucr. SYN. Invītĕ, cŏāctĕ.

Ingrātŭs, ă, ŭm, *unpleasant, ungrateful*. Ingrātĭs ōffĕr, Virg. SYN. Injūcŭndŭs, mŏlēstŭs, Immĕmŏr. V. Obliviscor.

• Ingrăvēsco, ĭs, *to grow heavy*. Cæs. SYN. Grăvŏr; recrūdēsco, crūdēsco, Incrūdēsco, ægrēsco.

Ingrăvo, ās, *to make heavy*. Ingrăvăt hæc, Virg. SYN. Grăvo, āggrăvo, prĕmo, ŏpprĭmo, ŏbrŭo; ēxāggĕro.

Ingrĕdĭŏr, ĕrĭs, *to go in, enter*. Ĭtĕr Ingrĕdĭĕtŭr, Juv. SYN. Intro, Intrŏĕo, Inĕo, sŭbĕo.

Ingrēssŭs, ŭs, m., *a going in, entrance*. Ingrēssūs hŏmĭnŭm, Virg. SYN. Ădĭtŭs; līmĕn, vēstĭbŭlŭm; grēssŭs.

Ingrŭo, ŭī, *to assail.* Ingrŭĭt Æneās, Virg. Syn. Irrŭo, ĭrrŭmpo, ĭmmĭnĕo, ĭnsto.

Inguĕn, ĭnĭs, n., *the groin.* Inguĭnă mōnstrīs, Virg. Epith. Lŭtōsŭm, ōbscœnŭm, tŭmĭdŭm, crāssŭm, ŭdŭm.

Ingŭrgĭto, ās, *to devour.* Ŭt ingŭrgĭtăt ĭmpūra ĭn sē, (Iamb.) Plaut. Syn. Absōrbĕo, vŏro.

Ingŭstātŭs, ă, ŭm, *untasted.* Ingŭstātă mĭhi, Hor.

Inhærĕo, ēs, hæsī, *to adhere.* Amplēxŭs ĭnhæsĭt, Virg. Syn. Inhærēsco, hærĕo, ĭnsĭdĕo.

Inhālo, ās, *to breathe, to inhale.* Nĕc ĭnhālăt ŏdōrēs, Luc. Syn. Exhālo, expīro, inspīro, afflo, rēspīro.

Inhĭbĕo, ŭī, *to hinder.* Tēla ĭnhĭbētĕ, Lătīnī, Virg. Syn. Cŏhĭbĕo, prŏhĭbĕo, ĭmpĕdĭo.

Inhĭo, ās, *to gape after.* Dēfīxīs ĭnhĭānt, Prud. Syn. Hĭo; ăvĭdē cŭpĭo.

Inhŏnēsto, ās, *to disparage.* Pālmās ĭnhŏnēstĕt ădēptŭs, Ov. Syn. Dēdĕcŏro, infāmo, dētŭrpo, fœdo, măcŭlo.

Inhŏnēstŭs, ă, ŭm, *dishonest.* Nōn ĭnhŏnēstŭs ĕrĭt, Prop. Syn. Tŭrpĭs, infāmĭs, probrōsŭs, sōrdĭdŭs, ōbscœnŭs, ĭmpūrŭs, pŭdēndŭs.

Inhŏnōrātŭs, *and* rŭs, ă, ŭm, *without honour.* Quæque ĭnhŏnōrātæ, Ov. Făcĭēs ĭnhŏnōrā sĭnĭstrīs, Sil. Syn. Inglōrĭŭs.

Inhŏrrēsco, rŭī, *to quake.* Ĕt ĭnhŏrrŭĭt ūndă, Virg. Syn. Hŏrrĕo, exhŏrrĕo, ĭnhŏrrĕo, tĭmĕo.

Inhōspĭtālĭs, ĕ, *and* pĭtŭs, ă, ŭm, *inhospitable.* Pĕr ĭnhōspĭtālĕm, (Sapph.) Hor. Cīngŭnt, ĕt ĭnhōspĭtā Sȳrtĭs, Virg. Syn. Nōn hăbĭtābĭlĭs, ĭnhăbĭtābĭlĭs, dēsērtŭs, incŭltŭs, ĭnāccēssŭs.

Inhūmānŭs, ă, ŭm, *inhuman.* Lēctŏr, ĭnhūmānā, Mart. Syn. Crūdēlĭs, ĭnūrbānŭs, fĕrŭs, ĭmmītĭs.

Inhŭmātŭs, ă, ŭm, *unburied.* Sŏcĭōs ĭnhŭmātăquĕ cōrpŏră, Virg.

Injēcto, ās, *freq. of* injicio. Injēctārĕ mănŭm, Luc.

Injēctŭs, ūs, m., *a throwing in or upon.* Injēctū mōlĭs ăhēnæ, Stat.

Injĭcĭo, ĭs, jēcī, jēctŭm, *and* ĭnĭcĭo, ĭs, *to throw in.* Injĭcĭŭnt ĭpsĭs, Virg. Ĭnĭcĭt vēlāmĭnă, Stat. Syn. Jăcĭo, ĭmmītto, infĕro.

Inĭmīcĭtĭă, æ, f., *enmity.* Sŭnt ĭnĭmīcĭtĭæ, Mart. Syn. Dīssēnsĭo, dīssĭdĭŭm, ŏdĭŭm, sĭmŭltās. Epith. Hōstīlĭs, crūdēlĭs, fūnēstă, grăvĭs, trŭx, ăcĕrbă, dīră, effĕră, hōrrēndă, atrōx, sævă, ĭmmītĭs, ĭmplācābĭlĭs, ĭmprŏbă. V. Discordia.

Inĭmīco, ās, *to make hostile.* Hōstīlēs ĭnĭmīcēnt, Stat. V. Alieno.

Inĭmīcŭs, ī, m., *an enemy.* Ecce ĭnĭmīcŭs ătrōx, Virg. Syn. Hōstĭs, ădvērsārĭŭs. Epith. Atrōx, ĭmpĭŭs, sævŭs, bārbărŭs, infēstŭs, crŭēntŭs, dīrŭs, bēllĭgĕr, infēnsŭs, lēthĭfĕr, fāllāx, pērnĭcĭōsŭs. V. Hostis.

Inĭmīcŭs, ă, ŭm, *unfriendly.* Gēns ĭnĭmīcă mĭhi, Virg. Syn. Infēnsŭs, infēstŭs, ăvērsŭs, ălĭēnŭs, īrātŭs.

Inīquŭs, ă, ŭm, *unjust.* Pŭlvēre ĭnīquŭs ămōr, Prop. Syn. Injūstŭs.

Inĭtĭŭm, ĭī, n., *a beginning.* Syn. Prīncĭpĭŭm, exōrdĭŭm, prīmōrdĭŭm, exōrsŭs, ingrēssŭs, cœptŭm, incœptŭm, căpŭt, ŏrīgo, tȳrōcĭnĭŭm, rŭdīmēntŭm.

Inĭtŭs, ă, ŭm, *the pass. partic. of* ineo. Quō nōbīs ĭnĭta ēst, Ov. Syn. Ădĭtŭs, incœptŭs.

Inĭtŭs, ūs, m., *copulation.* Pērquĕ sŭōs ĭnĭtŭs, Ov.

* Injūcŭndŭs, ă, ŭm, *unpleasant.* Syn. Ingrātŭs, insuāvĭs, mŏlēstŭs.

Injūrātŭs, ă, ŭm, *unsworn.* Injūrāto plŭs crēdĕt, Plaut.

Injūrĭă, æ, f., *injustice, an injury.* Ēst injūrĭă, lōngæ, Virg. Syn. Injūstĭtĭă, Inĭquĭtās; dīssēnsĭo, cōnvīcĭŭm, probrŭm, ōpprobrĭŭm, mălĕdīctŭm, nōxă, dāmnŭm. Epith. Grăvĭs, atrōx, inīquă, dīră, mŏlēstă, sævă, intŏlĕrābĭlĭs. V. Convicium.

Injūrĭōsŭs, *and* rĭŭs, ă, ŭm, *hurtful.* Injūrĭōsīs ārĭdŭs, (Iamb.) Hor. Syn. Inīquŭs, dāmnōsŭs, nŏcīvŭs, nŏcŭŭs, nōxĭŭs.

Injŭssŭs, ă, ŭm, *unbidden, of one's own accord.* Injŭssă vīrēscŭnt.

Injūstŭs, ă, ŭm, *unjust.* Ēst injūstă nŏvērcă, Virg. Syn. Inīquŭs, injūrĭōsŭs. V. Iniquus.

Innābĭlĭs, ĕ, *that cannot be swum in or upon.* Pălūs, innābĭlĭs ūndă, Ov.

Innăto, *and* no, ās, *to swim in or upon.* Innătĕt ūndă, Ov. Innārĕt Clœlĭă rŭptĭs, Virg. Syn. Sŭpērnăto, năto.

Innātŭs, ă, ŭm, *the partic. of* innascor. Cēcrŏpĭās Innātŭs āpēs, Virg.

Innĕcto, ĭs, nĕxŭm, *to tie with.* Innĕctŭnt tēmpŏră sĕrtĭs, Ov.

Innītŏr, ĕrĭs, Innīxŭs, *to rely on.* Innītēns băcŭlō, Ov. SYN. Nītŏr, fŭlcĭŏr, Incŭmbo.

Innŏcēns, ntĭs, *innocent.* Hīc Innŏcēntĭs, (Alcaic.) Hor. SYN. Insōns, Innŏxĭŭs, Innŏcŭŭs. V. Pius.

* Innŏcēntĭă, æ, f., *innocence.* Cōrdĭs Innŏcēntĭăm, (Iamb.) Prud. SYN. Integrĭtās.

Innŏcŭŭs, ă, ŭm, *harmless.* Innŏcŭĭs vērbĭs, Mart. SYN. Innŏxĭŭs; Innŏcēns; Inŏffēnsŭs, illæsŭs, intĕgĕr.

Innōtēsco, tŭī, *to become known.* Nōstrĭs Innōtŭĭt Illă, Ov. SYN. Cĕlebrŏr.

Innōxĭŭs, ă, ŭm, *harmless.* Nōn Innōxĭă vērbă, Virg.

Innŭbă, æ, f., *a virgin.* Innŭbă pērmănĕo, Ov. SYN. Innŭptă, cœlēbs, vīrgo.

Innūbĭlŭs, ă, ŭm, *and* bĭs, ĕ, *without clouds.* Innūbĭlŭs æthĕr, Lucr. Quālĭs Innūbĭs dĭēs, (Iamb.) Sen. SYN. Sĭnĕ nŭbĕ, pūrŭs, sĕrēnŭs.

Innŭbo, psī, *to take a husband.* Pătĭăre Innŭbĕrĕ nōstrĭs, Ov.

Innŭmĕrābĭlĭs, *aud* rālĭs, ĕ, *and* rŭs, ă, ŭm, *innumerable.* Aŭt Innŭmĕrābĭlĭs, (Chor.) Hor. Nŭmĕrō māgĭs Innŭmĕrālī, Lucr. Innŭmĕræ gēntēs, Virg. SYN. Infīnītŭs. V. Infinitus.

Innŭmĕrābĭlĭtĕr, adv., *without number.* Innŭmĕrābĭlĭtĕr prĭvās, Lucr.

Innŭo, ŭī, *to nod with the head.* Innŭăt, ătquĕ, Juv. SYN. Annŭo, nūtū cōncēdo, cōnsēntĭo.

Innŭptă, æ, f., *unmarried.* Pŭĕri Innŭptæquĕ pŭĕllæ, Virg. SYN. Cœlēbs, Innŭbă, vīrgo.

Inō, ūs, f., *the daughter of Cadmus and Hermione.* Flēbĭlĭs Inō, Hor. SYN. Cādmēĭs, Leŭcŏthŏĕ, Mātŭtă. EPITH. Cādmēĭă, Cādmæă, Thēbānă, flēbĭlĭs.

Inōblītŭs, ă, ŭm, *that has not forgotten.* Sēmpĕr Inōblĭtă, Ov.

Inōbrŭtŭs, ă, ŭm, *not swallowed up.* Effŭgĭt Inōbrŭtŭs ūndăs, Ov.

Inōbsĕquēns, ēntĭs, *stubborn.* Inōbsĕquēntēs prōtĭnŭs, (Iamb.) Sen. SYN. Indŏcĭlĭs.

Inōbsērvābĭlĭs, ĕ, *that cannot be observed.* Inōbsērvābĭlĭs ērrŏr, Cat.

Inōbsērvātŭs, ă, ŭm, *unobserved.* Inōbsērvātŭs In hērbĭs, Ov.

Inōccĭdŭŭs, ă, ŭm, *that never lies down.* Spēctăt Inōccĭdŭĭs, Stat.

Inŏdōrŭs, ă, ŭm, *without odour.* Ōssa Inŏdōră dăbĭt, Pers. SYN. Nōn ŏdōrŭs; ināle ŏlēns.

Inŏffēnsŭs, ă, ŭm, *unoffended.* Dētŭr Inōffēnsæ, Ov. SYN. Illæsŭs, intĕgĕr.

Inŏlēns, ntĭs, *without odour.* Nātūra Inŏlēntĭs ŏlīvī, Lucr.

Inŏlēsco, lŭī, *to grow upon.* Mērsĭs Inŏlēscĕrĕ rāmĭs, Sil. SYN. Crēsco, ădŏlēsco, incresco.

Inŏmĭnātŭs, ă, ŭm, *fatal.* Inŏmĭnātă pērprĭmăt, (Iamb.) Hor.

Inŏpĭă, æ, f., *poverty.* Inŏpĭă dēpērdĭtŭs, Phædr. SYN. Paŭpērtās, ĕgēstās, pĕnūrĭă.

Inŏpīnātŭs, *and* Inŭs, ă, ŭm, *unexpected.* Făcĭēs Inŏpīnăvĕ sŭrgĭt, Virg. SYN. Imprŏvīsŭs, Inēxpēctātŭs, Insperātŭs, rĕpēntĭnŭs, sŭbĭtŭs.

Inŏps, ŏpĭs, *poor.* Tŭrpĭs Inŏpsquĕ, Virg. SYN. Paŭpĕr, ĕgēnŭs, ĕgēns, Indĭgŭs. V. Pauper.

Inōpŭs, ī, m., *a river of Delos.* Fĭdŭs, ŏt Inŏpī, Virg.

Inōrnātŭs, ă, ŭm, *unadorned.* Quīsquĭs Inōrnătŭm, Tib. SYN. Incōndĭtŭs, Incōmptŭs, hōrrĭdŭs.

Inōŭs, ă, ŭm, *of Ino.* Ēt Inōō Mĕlĭcērtæ, Virg.

Inprīmĭs, adv., *first of all.* Inprīmĭs vĕnĕrārĕ dĕōs, Virg. SYN. Præsērtĭm, præcĭpŭĕ, māxĭmĕ.

Inquăm, quĭs, quĭt, *say I, sayest thou, says he.* Ut nūnc ēst, Inquam, ēt cŭpĭo, Hor. Nĕ făcĭam, Inquĭs, Id. Quō vīncŭlă nēctĭtĭs, Inquĭt, Virg.

Inquĭēs, ētĭs, *and* ētŭs, ă, ŭm, *restless.* Dūx Inquĭētī tŭrbĭdŭs Adrĭæ, Hor. SYN. Irrĕquĭētŭs, tŭrbātŭs, pērtŭrbătŭs, tŭrbĭdŭs, sōllĭcĭtŭs, mōbĭlĭs, Impătĭēns mŏræ.

Inquĭlīnŭs, ī, m., *and* ă, æ, f., *a tenant.* Vĕl Inquĭlīnŭs, (Phal.) Mart. V. Hospes.

Inquĭno, ās, *to defile.* Inquĭnăt ĕgrĕgĭōs, Claud. SYN. Cōinquĭno, fœdo, tĕmĕro, cōntāmĭno, pōllŭo, dēfōrmo, măcŭlo.

Inquīro, sīvī, sītŭm, *to seek.* Evĕnĭt, Inquīrānt, Hor. SYN. Quæro, ēxquīro, rĕquīro, pērquīro, Invēstīgo, scrūtŏr, pērscrūtŏr.

Inquīsītŏr, ōrīs, m., *an inquirer.* Inquīsītōrēs ăgĕrēnt, Juv. SYN. Quæsītŏr, scrūtātŏr.

Insălūtātŭs, ă, ŭm, *unsaluted.* Inquĕ sălūtātăm, Virg.

Insānăbĭlīs, ĕ, *incurable.* Căpŭt Insānābĭlĕ nūnquăm, Hor. SYN. Immĕdĭcābĭlīs.

Insānĭă, œ, f., *madness.* Scĕlĕrāta Insānĭă bēllī, Virg. SYN. Fŭrŏr, răbĭēs, āmēntĭă, dēmēntĭă. EPITH. Præcēps, fŭrĭbūndă, tŭrpĭs, tĭtŭbāns, crŭcĭāns, răbĭdă, cæcă, āmēns, vĭŏlēntă, lævă, ārdēns, ēffrænĭs. V. Furor, stultitia.

Insānĭo, ĭī, *to be mad.* Cūnctum Insānīrĕ dŏcēbo, Hor. SYN. Fŭro, sævĭo, dēsĭpĭo.

Insānŭs, ă, ŭm, *mad.* Tūnc Insānŭs ĕrĭs, Hor. SYN. Fŭrēns, āmēns, dēmēns; stūltŭs.

Insătĭābĭlīs, *and* tŭrăbĭlīs, ĕ, *insatiable.* Insătĭābĭlĕ vōtŭm, Juv. Insătŭrābĭlīs ālvŭs, Ser. SYN. Inēxplēbĭlīs, Inēxplētŭs, ăvĭdŭs, vŏrāx, gŭlōsŭs.

Insătĭābĭlĭtĕr, adv., *insatiably.* Insătĭābĭlĭtĕr dēflēbĭmŭs, Lucr.

Insătĭātŭs, ă, ŭm, *insatiate.* Insătĭātŭs ĕūndī, Stat.

Inscĭēntĭă, *and* cītĭă, œ, f., *ignorance.* Quæcūnque Inscītĭă vērī, Hor. SYN. Ignŏrāntĭă, Ignōrātĭo, Impĕrĭtĭă. EPITH. Rŭdīs, tūrpĭs.

Inscītŭs, ă, ŭm, *ignorant.* Inscītĕ măgĭstĕr, Aus. SYN. Ignārŭs, Indōctŭs.

Inscĭŭs, ă, ŭm, *ignorant.* Inscĭŭs āltŏ, Virg. SYN. Nēscĭŭs, Ignārŭs, Ignōrāns, Indōctŭs. V. Ignarus.

Inscrībo, psī, *to inscribe.* Pūlvīs Inscrībĭtŭr hāstā, Pr. SYN. Scrībo, nŏto, Imprĭmo.

Insculpo, psī, *to engrave.* Insculpĕrĕ sāxŏ, Hor.

Insēctŏr, ārĭs, *the frequent. of* insequor. Tērram Insēctābĕrĕ rāstrīs, Virg. SYN. Sēctŏr, cōnsēctŏr, sĕquŏr, Insĕquŏr, pērsĕquŏr.

Insēctŭs, ă, ŭm, *cut in.* Insēctŏ pēctĭnĕ dēntēs, Ov.

Insĕcūtŭs, ă, ŭm, *the partic. of* insequor. Tĕmĕre Insĕcūtæ, Hor.

Insĕdābĭlĭtĕr, adv., *so as not to be quieted.* Insĕdābĭlĭtĕr sĭtĭs, Lucr.

Insĕnēsco, nŭī, *to grow old.* Insĕnŭīssĕ mālĭs, Ov. V. Senesco.

Insēnsĭlīs, ĕ, *senseless.* Ex Insēnsĭlĭbŭs, Lucr.

Insĕquŏr, ĕrĭs, *to pursue.* Insĕquŏr ēt caūsās, Virg. SYN. Sĕquŏr, Insēctŏr, cōnsĕquŏr; pērgo.

Insĕpūltŭs, ă, ŭm, *unburied.* Pŏst Insĕpūltă mēmbră, (Iamb.) Hor. SYN. Intŭmŭlātŭs.

Insĕrēnŭs, ă, ŭm, *cloudy.* Hўăs Insĕrēnă, (Iamb.) Stat. V. Nubilus.

Insĕro, sēvī, sĭtŭm, *to sow, implant.* Insĕrĕ, Dāphnĭ, Virg. SYN. Cōnsĕro, Insēmĭno.

Insĕro, sĕrŭī, sērtŭm, *to put in, to insert.* Insĕrŭīssĕ mēĭs, Prop. SYN. Immĭtto, Insĭnŭo, Immīscĕo.

Insĕrpo, ĭs, *to creep in.* Insērpĭt cūrīs, Hor. V. Serpo.

Insērtĭm, adv., *by way of insertion.* Insērtĭm fūndŭnt, Lucr.

Insĕrto, ās, *the frequent. of* insero. Insērtābam āptāns, Virg.

Insērvĭo, īs, *to serve.* Insērvĭt hŏnōrī, Hor.

Insērvo, ās, *to guard in.* Dēdĭt Insērvārĕ vŏlūcrēs, Stat.

Insībĭlo, ās, *to whistle into.* Trūx Insībĭlăt Eūrŭs, Ov. SYN. Sībĭlo, sībĭlă dŏ, vibro.

Insīcco, ās, *to dry.* Insīccātă crŭŏrĕ, Stat. V. Sicco.

Insĭdĕo, sēdī, *to sit upon.* Insĭdĕăt quāntŭs, Virg. SYN. Hærĕo, ădhærĕo, Inhærĕo, sŭpērsĕdĕo.

Insĭdĭæ, ārŭm, f pl., *snares.* Excĭpĕre Insĭdĭīs, Virg. SYN. Rētĭă, dŏlī. EPITH. Ŏccūltæ, lătēntēs, tăcĭtæ, fāllācēs, nōctūrnæ, caūtæ, hōstīlēs, dŏlōsæ, Inīquæ, sævæ, nĕfāndæ, tūrpēs, vānæ, Inānēs. V. Insidior.

Insĭdĭātŏr, ōrĭs, m., *he who prepares an ambuscade.* Insĭdĭātōrĕm prærōsŏ, Hor. EPITH. Fĕrŭs, ōccūltŭs.

Insĭdĭātŭs, ă, ŭm, *the partic. of* insidior. Insĭdĭātŭs ŏvīlī, Virg.

Insĭdĭŏr, ārĭs, *to lie in ambush.* Insĭdĭābĕrĕ plāntīs, Vict. V. Decipio.

Insĭdĭōsŭs, ă, ŭm, *crafty.* Lēnōnĭs ŭt Insĭdĭōsī, Hor.

Insĭdo, ĭs, sēdī, *to light upon.* Flōrĭbŭs Insĭdŭnt, Virg. SYN. Insĭdĕo.

Insīgnĕ, ĭs, n., *a mark, ornament, banner.* Dănăūmque Insīgnĭă nōbīs, Virg. SYN. Sīgnŭm, Indĭcĭŭm, nŏtă; stēmmă, ōrnāmēntŭm; sīgnŭm, vēxīllŭm.

Insīgnĭo, ĭs, ĭī, ītŭm, *to signalise.* Aūro Insīgnĭbăt, Virg. SYN. Dĕcŏro, cōndĕcŏro, ōrno, ēxōrno, īllūstro.

Insignis, ĕ, *remarkable.* Aciēs insignibŭs ālīs, Virg. Syn. Illūstrĭs, ĕxĭmĭŭs, ĕgrĕgĭŭs, inclўtŭs, nōbĭlĭs.

Insĭlĕ, ĭs, n., *the treadle of a loom.* Insĭlĭa āc fūsī, Lucr.

Insĭlĭo, lūī *or* lĭī, insultŭm, *to jump upon.* Insĭlĭāt, sīt jŭs, Hor. Syn. Irrŭo, sāltu inĕo, sālĭo in.

Insĭmŭlo, ās, *to accuse, to feign.* Insĭmŭlassĕ vĭrŭm, Ov. Syn. Accūso, crĭmĭnŏr, ārgŭo, rĕdārgŭo.

Insincērŭs, ă, ŭm, *corrupted.* Insincērŭs ăpēs, Virg.

Insĭnŭo, ās, *to put in, to insinuate.* Insĭnŭēntŭr ōpēs, Prop. Syn. Immītto, indo, indūco, insĕro, immiscĕo.

Insĭpĭēns, ntĭs, *foolish.* Ō sæclum insĭpĭēns, Cat. Syn. Stūltŭs, insānŭs, excōrs, āmēns, dēmēns.

Insisto, instĭtī, *to* ░░░ *to urge.* Instĭtĕrāt, jăcŭlō, Virg. Syn. Cōnsisto ; insto, ūrgĕo ; pērgo.

Insĭtĭo, ōnĭs, f., *and* tŭs, ūs, m., *a grafting.* Vēnĕrĭt insĭtĭo, Ov. Epith. Vērnă, nŏva, fēlīx.

Insĭtīvŭs, ă, ŭm, *grafted.* Insĭtīvă dēcērpēns pўră, Hor.

Insĭtŏr, ōrĭs, m., *a grafter.* Insĭtŏr hic, Prop. Syn. Sătŏr.

Insĭtŭs, ă, ŭm, *the pass. partic. of* insero. Insĭtă mălă, Virg. Syn. Innātŭs, ingĕnĭtŭs, ingĕnĕrātŭs, inhærēns.

Insōlābĭlĭs, ĕ, *inconsolable.* Insōlābĭlĕ pēctŭs, Paulin. Syn. Incōnsōlābĭlĭs, nĭmĭŭs.

Insōlābĭlĭtĕr, adv., *inconsolably.* Dŏlēntĭs Insōlābĭlĭtĕr, Hor.

Insŏlēns, ntĭs, *unaccustomed.* Lūdum insŏlēntĕm, (Alcaic.) Hor. Syn. Insŏlĭtŭs, insuētŭs, inēxpērtŭs ; sŭpērbŭs, tĕmĕrārĭŭs.

Insŏlēntĭă, æ, f., *insolence.* Mēæque tērrā cĕdĕt insŏlēntĭæ, Hor.

Insŏlĭdŭs, ă, ŭm, *feeble.* Tūrgĕt ĕt insŏlĭda ēst, Ov.

Insŏlĭtŭs, ă, ŭm, *unwonted.* Aūdĭĭt, insŏlĭtīs, Virg. Syn. Insuētŭs, inaūdītŭs, nŏvŭs, inēxpērtŭs, intēntātŭs.

Insōmnĭs, ĕ, *sleepless.* Vēstĭbŭlum insōmnĭs, Virg. Syn. Vĭgĭl, pērvĭgĭl.

Insōmnĭum, ĭī, n., *a dream.* Mittūnt insōmnĭă mānēs, Virg. Syn. Sōmnĭum, vīsŭm ; dēlīrĭum. Epith. Vānŭm, fāllāx, fūlsŭm, inānĕ, mēndāx, nŏctūrnŭm. V. Somnium.

Insŏno, ŭī, *to make a noise.* Insŏnŭĕrĕ căvæ, Virg. Syn. Sŏno, rĕsŏno, pērsŏno, instrĕpo.

Insōns, ntĭs, *guiltless.* Ēt mēcum insōntīs căsŭm, Virg.

Insōpītŭs, ă, ŭm, *sleepless.* Fĕrōs insōpītūmquĕ drăcōnĕm, Ov. Syn. Insōmnĭs, pērvĭgĭl.

Inspēcto, ās, *freq. of* inspicio. Inspēctānt nūmĭnă tērrās, Stat.

Inspērātŭs, ă, ŭm, *unhoped for.* Inspērātă tŭæ, (Chor.) Hor. Syn. Inēxpēctātŭs, inŏpīnŭs.

Inspērgo, sī, sŭm, *to sprinkle on.* Ēgrĕgĭo inspērsōs, Hor. V. Aspergo.

Inspĭcĭo, spēxī, spēctŭm, *to inspect.* Inspĭcĭs, inspĭcĕrĭs, Sid. Syn. Aspĭcĭo, spēcto, inspēcto, intŭĕŏr.

Inspīco, ās, *to sharpen.* Făcēs inspīcăt ăcūtō, Virg. Syn. Acŭo.

Inspīro, ās, *to breathe upon, to inspire.* Dēlŭs inspīrăt, Virg. Syn. Spīro, exspīro, inhālo, exhālo, afflo ; immītto, insĭnŭo, indo.

Inspŏlĭātŭs, ă, ŭm, *not spoiled.* Inspŏlĭātă fĕrăm, Ov.

Inspŭo, ĭs, *to spit upon.* Nāscēntĭbŭs inspŭĭt, hērbās, Lucr.

Instābĭlĭs, ĕ, *unstable.* Instābĭlēs ănĭmōs, Virg. Syn. Mōbĭlĭs, lĕvĭs, mūtābĭlĭs, incōnstāns. V. Inconstans.

Instăr, (*indecl.*) *as, like.* Instăr in ipsō, Virg. Syn. Ŭt, rītū, mŏrĕ.

Instaūro, ās, *to renew.* Ērgo instaūrāmŭs, Virg. Syn. Rēstĭtŭo, rēstaūro, rĕpăro, rĕnŏvo. V. Reparo.

Instērno, strāvī, strātŭm, *to spread upon.* Instērnŏr pēllĕ lĕōnĭs, Virg.

Instīgo, ās, *to excite.* Vārīisque instīgāt vōcĭbŭs, Virg. Syn. Instĭmŭlo, incĭto, cōncĭto ; pēllo, impēllo, sōllĭcĭto, ăcŭo, ēxăcŭo, hōrtŏr.

Instīllo, ās, *to instil.* Faūstōs instīllăt in ignēs, Ov.

Instĭmŭlo, ās, *to incite.* Instĭmŭlāt fĭctĭs, Ov. V. Stimulo.

Instīnctŭs, ă, ŭm, *inspired.* Vōtīs instīnctă pătērnīs, Stat.

Instīnctŭs, ūs, m., *inspiration.* Instīnctū sŭpĕrŭm, Stat.

īnstītā̆, æ, f., *a fringe, lace.*   Tĕgăt īnstītā̆ vēstĕ, Hor.   SYN. Fīmbrīā̆.

īnstītŏr, ōrĭs, m., *a huckster.*   Īnstītŏr īn tŭnĭcīs, Prop.   EPITH. Dīvĕs, ăvārŭs.

īnstītŭo, ŭī, ūtŭm, *to establish.*   Īnstītŭĕrĕ pĕdēs, Virg.   SYN. Stătŭo, cōnstītŭo, dēcĕrno ; dŏcĕo, ērŭdīo.

īnstītūtŭs, ā̆, ŭm, *the pass. partic. of* īnstītŭo.   Bĭbĕre īnstītūtæ, Hor.

īnsto, stĭtī, *to urge, persist.*   Īnstāntĭbŭs ērĭpĕ fātīs, Virg.   SYN. Īnsīsto, ūrgĕo, prĕmo, īrrŭo ; īncŭmbo, văco ; īmmĭnĕo, īmpēndĕo, ādvēnto, prŏpe ādsŭm ; pērgo, pērsto.

īnstrātŭs, ā̆, ŭm, *the pass. partic. of* īnsterno.   Īnstrātōs ōstro, Virg.

īnstrĕpo, ŭī, *to creak.*   Īnstrĕpăt, ēt jūnctōs, Virg.   SYN. Strĕpo, pērstrĕpo, īnsŏno.

īnstrīdēns, ēntĭs, m., *hissing in.*   Īnstrīdēns pĕlăgō, Sil.

īnstrūmēntŭm, ī, n., *an instrument.*   Ābjēcto īnstrūmēnto, ██   EPITH. Hă̆bĭlĕ, āptŭm.

īnstrŭo, strūxī, strūctŭm, *to set in order.*   Īnstrŭĭt ārmīs, Virg.   SYN. Pă̆ro, ăppă̆ro, ōrdĭno, cōmpōno, ōrno : dŏcĕo, ērŭdīo.

īnsuāvĭs, ĕ, *unpleasant.*   Hă̆bēāre īnsuāvĭs, ăcērbŭs, Hor.   SYN. Īnjŭcūndŭs, īngrātŭs, mŏlēstŭs, ăcērbŭs.

īnsūdo, ās, *to sweat at.*   Queīs mănŭs īnsūdĕt, Hor.   SYN. Sūdo, dēʋūdo, īncŭmbo, āllă̆bōro.

īnsuēsco, īnsuēvī, ētŭm, *to accustom.*   Īnsuēvīt pătĕr, Hor.   SYN. Āssuēsco, cōnsuēsco.

īnsuētŭs, ā̆, ŭm, *unaccustomed.*   Ārcădăs īnsuētōs, Virg.   SYN. Īnsŏlĭtŭs, īnsŏlēns ; īmpĕrītŭs.

īnsŭlā̆, æ, f., *an island.*   Īnsŭlă̆ dīvĕs, Virg.   EPITH. Nĕmŏrōsā̆, dīvĕs, sāxōsā̆, fērtĭlĭs, fĕrāx, fœcūndā̆, ōptĭmā̆, cīrcūmflŭā̆, lā̆tā̆, spătĭōsā̆, ūbĕr, ŭdā̆, mădēns, mădĭdā̆, rĭgŭā̆, īrrĭgŭā̆.

īnsūlsŭs, ā̆, ŭm, *unsavoury.*   Sæpe īnsūlsō cœnāndā̆, Pers.   SYN. Īncōndĭtŭs, ābsūrdŭs, īncūltŭs, ĭnēptŭs.

īnsūlto, ās, *to leap upon, to insult.*   Īnsūltārĕ sŏlo, Virg.   SYN. Sæpe īnsĭlĭo, īrrŭo, īrrūmpo : īllūdo, rīdĕo, ēxăgĭto, vēxo, īnsēctŏr.

īnsŭm, ĭnĕs, *to be in.*   Sēd tĭbĭ tāntŭs ĭnēst, Mart.

īnsūmo, psī, ptŭm, *to consume.*   Quo īnsūmĕrĕ pōssīs, Hor.   SYN. Īmpēndo, cōnsūmo.

īnsŭo, ŭī, ūtŭm, *to stitch.*   Cōrpŏrĭs īnsŭĕrĭt, Lucr.   SYN. Āssŭo, jūngo.

īnsŭpĕr, adv., *moreover.*   Īnsŭpĕr, ĭd cāmpī, Virg.   SYN. Ādhūc, ūltĕrĭŭs, prætĕrĕā̆.

īnsŭpĕrābĭlĭs, ĕ, *invincible.*   Īnsŭpĕrābĭlĕ bēllō, Virg.   SYN. Nōn ēxsŭpĕrābĭlĭs, ĭnēxpūgnābĭlĭs, ĭnēlūctābĭlĭs, īndŏmĭtŭs, īnvīctŭs.

īnsūrgo, rēxī, *to rise up.*   Tĕnĕbrās īnsūrgĕrĕ cāmpīs, Virg.   SYN. Sūrgo, cōnsūrgo ; ōbsīsto.

īnsūscēptŭs, ā̆, ŭm, *unreceived.*   Vōta īnsūscēptă̆ rēlĭquĭt, Ov.

‖ īnʋūsūrro, ās, *to whisper, to buzz.*   SYN. Īmmūrmŭro.

īnsūtŭs, ā̆, ŭm, *the pass. partic. of* īnsuo.   Plūmbo īnsūtō fērrōquĕ, Virg.

īntābēsco, bŭī, *to waste away.*   Vīrtūtēm vĭdĕānt, īntābēscāntquĕ rĕlīctā̆, Pers.   SYN. Tābēsco, cōntābēsco, īntŭs tābēsco.

īntāctĭlĭs, ĕ, *that cannot be touched.*   Sīn īntāctĭle ĕrĭt, Lucr.

īntāctŭs, ā̆, ŭm, *untouched.*   Ēt īntāctă̆ tŏtĭdĕm, Virg.   V. Intaminatus.

īntāmĭnātŭs, ā̆, ŭm, *undefiled.*   Īntāmĭnātĭs fūlgĕt, (Alcaic.) Hor.   SYN. Intāctŭs, īmpōllūtŭs, īnvĭōlātŭs, īncōrrūptŭs, īntĕmĕrātŭs, īntĕgĕr, pūrŭs, cāstŭs.

īntĕgĕr, ēgrā̆, grŭm, *entire, uncorrupted.*   Īntĕgĕr āmbĭgŭæ, Juv.   SYN. Īntāctŭs, īntāmĭnātŭs ; īncōrrūptŭs, pērfēctŭs, tōtŭs ; īncŏlŭmĭs.

īntĕgo, tēxī, ctŭm, *to cover.*   Īntĕgĭt, Ārcădĭī, Sil.   SYN. Tĕgo, cōntĕgo.

īntegrāsco, ĭs, *to begin afresh.*   Īntĕgrāscīt mălŭm, Ter.

īntegrātĭo, ōnĭs, f., *a renewing.*   Ămōrĭs īntĕgrātĭo ēst, (Iamb.) Ter.

* īntegrĭtās, ātĭs, f., *purity.*   Cic.   SYN. Cāstĭtās, īnnŏcēntĭā̆.

īntegro, ās, *to renew.*   Īntĕgrăt, ēt mœstīs, Virg.   SYN. Īnstaūro, īnnŏvo, rĕnŏvo.

* īntēllēctŭs, ūs, m., *the understanding.*   SYN. Mēns, ănĭmŭs, rătĭo.

* īntēllĭgēntĭā̆, æ, f., *knowledge.*   Cic.   SYN. Cōgnĭtĭo, scĭēntĭā̆, prūdēntĭā̆.

L

Intĕllĭgo, lēxī, lēctŭm, *to understand.* Nīmīrum intĕllĭgĭt ūnŭs, Hor. Syn. Pērcĭpĭo, cōncĭpĭo, căpĭo, āccĭpĭo, āgnōsco, cōgnōsco. V. Attendo.

Intĕmĕrātŭs, ă, ŭm, *undefiled.* Intĕmĕrātă fĭdēs, Virg. Syn. Intāmĭnātŭs, intĕgĕr, pūrŭs, cāstŭs.

Intĕmpēstă nŏx, *the dead of night.* Nŏx intĕmpēstă tĕnĕbăt, Virg.

Intĕmpēstīvŭs, ă, ŭm, *unseasonable.* Intĕmpēstīvŭs dēscēndĭt, Hor. Syn. Immātūrŭs; incōmmŏdŭs.

Intēndo, dī, tŭm, *to stretch.* Intēndŭnt; scāndĭt, Virg. Syn. Tēndo, ēxtēndo, pōrrĭgo; cōntēndo, āddūco; cōgĭto, mĕdĭtŏr, spēcto; āpplĭco, ādmŏvĕo.

Intēntātŭs, ă, ŭm, *unattempted.* Nĭl intēntātŭm, Hor.

Intēnto, ăs, *to stretch out.* Hæc intēntātă mănĕbăt, Virg. Syn. Sæpĭŭs intēndo; mĭnĭtŏr, mĭnŏr.

Intēntŭs, ă, ŭm, *the pass. partic.* of intendo. Intēntāquĕ brāchĭă rēmīs, Virg.

Intĕpĕo, ŭī, *to grow warm.* Intĕpĕt Ūmbĕr, Prop. Syn. Tĕpĕo, tĕpēsco.

Intĕr, prep., *between.* Cănĭt intĕr ŏpŭs, Tibull.

Intērcēdo, ssī, *to intercede, oppose.* Syn. Intērvĕnĭo; intērsŭm; ōbsto, ādvērsŏr, rĕlūctŏr, rĕsīsto.

* Intērcīdo, ĭdī, *to cut asunder.* Cœs. Syn. Dīvĭdo, scīndo, sĕco.

‖ Intērcĭdo, ĭdī, *to perish.* Quŏd si intērcĭdĕrĭt, Hor. Syn. Intĕrĕo, pĕrĕo, cădo.

Intērcĭno, ĭs, *to sing between.* Mĕdĭōs intērcĭnăt āctŭs, Hor. Syn. Căno intĕr.

Intērcĭpĭo, cēpī, cēptŭm, *to intercept.* Rhœteŭs intērcĭpĭt, ŏptĭmĕ, Virg. Syn. Occŭpo.

Intērclūdo, sī, sŭm, *to shut in.* Intērclūsĭt hўēms, Virg. Syn. Claūdo, ōcclūdo; prŏhĭbĕo, vĕto, īmpĕdĭo.

Intērcūrro, ĭs, *freq.* cūrso, ās, *to run between.* Quīn intērcūrrăt, Lucr.

Intērcŭs, ŭtĭs, *between the skin and flesh.* Intērcŭtĭbŭs vĭtĭs, Sen.

Intērdīco, xī, ctŭm, *to forbid.* Ōrbe intērdīxĭt, Ov. Syn. Prŏhĭbĕo, vĕto.

Intērdŭm, adv., *sometimes.* Intērdum, aūt hĕdĕræ, Virg. Syn. Ălĭquāndo, nōnnūnquăm.

Intĕrĕă, adv., *in the meanwhile.* Pāndĭtŭr intĕrĕă, Virg. Syn. Intĕrīm, tŭm, hæc intĕr.

Intĕrēmptŭs, ă, ŭm, *the pass. partic.* of interimo. Asdrŭbăle intĕrēmptŏ, Hor.

Intĕrĕo, ĭī, *to die.* Intĕrĕūnt sĕgĕtĕs, Virg. Syn. Mŏrĭŏr, ōccĭdo, pĕrĕo.

Intĕrērro, ās, *to wander among.* Ŭtĭnam intĕrērrĕm, Hor.

Intĕrēst, *it concerns.* Nĭl intĕrēst, ăn, (Alcaic.) Hor. Syn. Dīffērt; rēfērt.

Intērfātŭs sŭm, *I spoke between.* Sīc intērfātă dŏlōrĕ, Virg.

Intērfĭcĭo, fēcī, fēctŭm, *to kill.* Ātque intērfĭcĕ mēssēs, Virg. Syn. Occīdo, nĕco, ēnĕco, pĕrĭmo, intĕrĭmo. V. Occido.

Intērfīo, ĭs, *to be consumed.* Aūt flămmīs intērfīăt mālīsvĕ, Lucr.

Intērflŭŭs, ă, ŭm, *flowing between.* Intērflŭă mănĭbŭs, Stat.

Intērfŏdĭo, ĭs, *to dig between or among.* Pūpīllās intērfŏdĭūnt, Lucr.

Intērfūro, ĭs, *to rage through or among.* Măvŏrs intērfŭrĭt ōrbĕm, Stat.

Intērfūsŭs, ă, ŭm, *spread between.* Stўx intērfūsă cŏērcĕt, Virg. Syn. Infūsŭs.

Intērjăcĕo, ŭī, *to lie in the middle.* Intērjăcēt Ārgŏs, Stat.

Intērjĭcĭo, jēcī, *to throw between or among.* Intērjēctāquĕ sūnt, Lucr. Syn. Injĭcĭo, intērpōno.

Intĕrĭm, adv., *in the meanwhile.* Intĕrīm dūm tū, (Sapph.) Hor. Syn. Intĕrĕă, hæc intĕr.

Intĕrĭmo, ēmī, ēmptŭm, *to kill.* Ŭxōrem intĕrĭmĭs, Hor. Syn. Intērfĭcĭo, pĕrĭmo, nĕco, ōccīdo.

Intĕrĭŏr, ŭs, g. ōrĭs, *inner.* Āt dŏmŭs intĕrĭŏr, Virg. Syn. Intĭmŭs, īmŭs, pĕnetrālĭs.

Intĕrĭtŭs, ūs, m., *death.* Scīlĭcĕt intĕrĭtū, Prop. Syn. Mŏrs, ēxĭtĭŭm, ēxcĭdĭŭm.

Intĕrĭŭs, adv., *within.* Intĕrĭŭsquĕ rĕcōndăt, Virg.

Intērjūngo, ĭs, *to unyoke.* Lāssŏs intērjūngĭt ĕquŏs, Mart.

Intērlābēns, ēntĭs, m., *gliding between.* Intērlābēntĭbŭs ūmbrās, Stat.

Intērlābŏr, ĕrĭs, *to glide between.* Intĕr ĕnĭm lābēntŭr ăquæ, Virg.

Intērlĕgo, ĭs, *to gather between.* Frōndēs, intērquĕ lĕgēndæ, Virg.

Intērlĭgo, ās, *to bind between.* Măcŭlās intērlĭgăt ōstrŏ, Stat.

Intĕrlūcĕo, lūxī, *to shine between or among.* Ăcĭēs, intĕrlūcĕīquĕ cŏrōnā, Virg. SYN. Intērmĭco, īntērnĭtĕo.

Intĕrlūdo, ĭs, *to sport between.* Intĕrlūdēntēs, ēxāmĭnā, Aus.

Intĕrlūnĭum, ĭī, n., *the change of the moon.* Sŭb īntĕrlūnĭā vēntō, Hor.

Intĕrlŭo, ŭĭs, *to flow between or among.* Āngŭsto īntĕrlŭĭt æstū, Virg.

intērmănĕo, ēs, *to stay among.* Mĕdĭĭs īntērmănĕt ăgrīs, Lucan.

intērmĭco, ās, *to shine among.* Squāmmĭs īntērmĭcăt aŭrŭm, Cl. V. Interluceo.

intērmĭnātŭs, ă, ŭm, *forbidden with threats.* Intērmĭnātō cūm sĕmĕl, (Iamb.) Hor.

intērmĭnŭs, ă, ŭm, *unbounded.* Fēlīcĭtāte īntērmĭnā, Aus.

intērmīscĕo, ēs, *to intermingle.* Nōn īntērmīscĕăt ūndăm, Virg. V. Misceo.

intērmītto, īsī, īssŭm, *to throw in, to discontinue.* Intērmīttŭntquĕ lăbōrĕm, Ov. SYN. Intērjĭcĭo, īmmītto; ŏmītto, cēsso.

intērmŏrĭŏr, ĕrĭs, *to die among.* Rēs īntērmŏrtŭă pænē, Ov. V. Morior.

* intērnĕcĭo, ōnĭs, f., *slaughter.* Cic. SYN. Occīsĭo, īntĕrĭtŭs, strāgēs, cædēs.

intērnĕcto, xŭī, *to knit together.* Aŭro īntērnēctăt, Virg.

intērnigrāns, ntĭs, *blackish.* Măcŭlĭs īntērnĭgrāntĭbŭs ālbæ, Stat.

Intērnōdĭŭm, ĭī, n., *the space between two knots or joints.* Făcĭt īntērnōdĭă pŏplĕs, Ov.

intērnōsco, ĭs, *to distinguish.* Sī scĭĕt īntērnōscĕrĕ, Hor. V. Discerno.

intērnŭs, ă, ŭm, *internal.* Ōccĭdĭt īntērnās, Ov. V. Interior.

intērpēllo, ās, *to interrupt a speech.* Intērpēllāndī lŏcŭs, Hor.

intērplĭco, ās, *to knit together.* Intērplĭcăt īnfŭlā crīsĭās, Stat.

intērpōno, pŏsŭī, pŏsĭtŭm, *to place between or among.* Intērpōnĭs ăquăm, Mart. SYN. Intērjĭcĭo, īntērsĕro, īntērmīscĕo.

intērprēs, ĕtĭs, m. f., *an interpreter.* Dīvūmque īntērprēs Ăsŷlās, Virg. EPITH. Fĭdŭs, fēlīx.

* intērprĕtŏr, ārĭs, *to explain.* Cic. SYN. Explĭco, ēxpōno, ēxplāno.

intērrĭtŭs, ă, ŭm, *fearless.* Ad sŭpĕrās īntērrĭtŭs ēxtŭlĭt, Virg. SYN. Intrĕpĭdŭs, sēcūrŭs, īmpērtērrĭtŭs, aŭdāx. V. Audax.

intērrŏgo, ās, *to ask.* Plŭs īntērrŏgŏ, sĕd quĭd, Juv. SYN. Quæro, īnquīro, scīscĭtŏr, ăllŏquŏr.

intērrūmpo, ūpī, *to interrupt.* Pīas īntērrūmpēntĕ quĕrēlās, Ov.

intērsĕco, cŭī, ēctŭm, *to divide by cutting.* Intērsĕcāntŭr hīc, (Iamb.) Av. SYN. Abscīndŭ, sĕco.

intērsĕro, ĭs, *to intermingle.* Intērsĕrĭt ōscŭlā vērbĭs, Ov. V. Insero.

intērsŏno, ās, *to sound between.* Intērsŏnăt Ōrphĕŭs, Stat.

intērstīnctŭs, ă, ŭm, *distinguished.* Spătĭa īntērstīnctă cŏlūmnĭs, Stat.

intērstīnguo, ĭs, *to extinguish.* Făcĭunt ĭgnēs īntērstīngui, Lucr.

intērstrĕpo, ŭī, *to make a noise among.* Ārgŭtōs īntērstrĕpĕre ānsĕr, Virg.

intērstrŭo, ūxī, *to join together.* Intērstrŭĭt ārĭŭs, Stat.

intērsŭm, fŭī, *to be present among.* Intērsīntquĕ pătrĭs, Virg. SYN. Adsŭm, præsēus sŭm.

intērtēxo, ŭī, *to interweave.* Intērtēxti hĕdĕrĭs, Ov. V. Texo.

intērvāllŭm, ī, n., *a space.* Prōxĭmŭs īntērvāllō, Virg. SYN. Intērstĭtĭŭm, spătĭŭm.

intērvĕnĭo, vēnī, *to come suddenly.* Vērbōque īntērvĕnĭt ōmnī, Ov. SYN. Imprōvĭsŭs ādsŭm; īntērsŭm, īntērcēdo.

intērvĭrĕo, ēs, *to be green among other colours.* Intērvĭrĕt hūmĭdă, Claud.

intērvŏlo, ās, *to fly amidst.* Fūscās īntērvŏlăt aŭrās, Stat.

intērvŏmo, ĭs, *to vomit amidst.* Intērvŏmĭt ūndās, Lucr.

intēstābĭlĭs, ĕ, *that cannot be attested; detestable.* Intēstābĭlĭs ēt săcĕr, Hor.

intēstātŭs, ă, ŭm, *intestate.* Intēstātŭs ĕăs, Juv.

intēstīnŭs, ă, ŭm, *inward.* Mĕăque īntēstīnā pĕrūrēns, Cat. SYN. Intĕrĭŏr, ĭntĭmŭs; dŏmēstĭcŭs, cīvīlĭs.

intēxo, ŭī, ēxtŭm, *to knit, interweave.* Lætĭs īntēxĭt vītĭbŭs, Virg.

intēxtŭs, ă, ŭm, *the pass. partic. of* intexo. Pūrpŭrĕă īntēxtī, Virg.

intĭmŭs, ă, ŭm, *most inward.* Intĭmă mōrĕ, Virg. SYN. Intērnŭs, īntĕrĭŏr, ĭmŭs; cārīssĭmŭs, dīlēctīssĭmŭs.

intīngo, nxī, nctŭm, *to dye.* Nūtrĭăt īntīnctōs. V. Tingo.

Intŏlĕrābĭlĭs, ĕ, *insufferable.* Intŏlĕrābĭlĭbŭsquĕ mălīs, Lucr. Syn. Intŏlĕrāndŭs, grăvīs, mŏlēstŭs.

Intŏnātŭs, ă, ŭm, *the perf. part. of* intono. Ēŏīs Intŏnātă flŭctĭbŭs, Hor.

Intŏno, ŭī, *to thunder.* Intŏnŭĕrĕ pŏlī, Virg. Syn. Tŏno, Insŏno, pērsŏno.

Intōnsŭs, ă, ŭm, *unshaven.* Intōnsīs căpŭt ēst, Ov.

Intōrquĕo, sī, rtŭm, *to wrest, to hurl.* Scĕlĕrātam Intōrsĕrĭt hāstăm, Virg. Syn. Tōrquĕo ; Immĭtto, jăcŭlŏr.

Intrā, prep., *within.* Intrā cāstrōrŭm, Luc. Syn. In; Intŭs.

Intrāctābĭlĭs, ĕ, *unmanageable.* Gĕnŭs Intrāctābĭlĕ bēllō, Virg. Syn. Indŏmĭtŭs, fĕrōx.

Intrāctātŭs, ă, ŭm, *unattempted.* Aŭt Intrāctātŭm, Virg.

Intrĕmo, *and* mīsco, mŭī, *to tremble.* Gĕnŭa Intrĕmŭĕrĕ tĭmōrĕ, Ov. Syn. Trĕmo, trĕmīsco, trĕpĭdo.

Intrĕpĭdŭs, ă, ŭm, *undaunted.* Ătque ădĕo Intrĕpĭdī, Sil. Syn. Intērrĭtŭs, Impērtērrĭtŭs, Impăvĭdŭs, aŭdāx.

Intrīco, ās, *to enfold.* Intrīcānt mănĭbŭs, Catull. Syn. Illăquĕo, Irrētĭo, implīco, impĕdĭo.

Intrīnsĕcŭs, adv., *on the inside.* Faŭcēs Intrīnsĕcŭs ātræ, Lucr. Syn. Intrā.

Intrō, adv., *within.* Mĭttĕrĕt ăd se Intrō, Catull.

Intro, ās, *to go in.* Pŏrtŭsque Intrārĕ lĭcēbĭt, Virg. Syn. Ĭnĕo, Ingrĕdĭŏr, sŭbĕo.

Intrŏdūco, xī, *to introduce.* Ănĭmăs Intrŏdūxērŭnt, Lucr. Syn. Intrōmĭtto, Indūco, ădmĭtto.

Intrŏĕo, īvī, *to go in, enter,* Quŏd Intrŏĭbŭnt, Aus. Syn. Ingrĕdĭŏr, Intrŏgrĕdĭŏr, Intro.

Intrōgrĕdĭor, ĕrĭs, *to enter.* Pŏstquam Intrōgrēssī, Virg.

Intrŏĭtŭs, ūs, m., *an entrance.* Intrŏĭtŭs ĕt, Pers. Cŭjŭs In Intrŏĭtŭ, Ov. Syn. Līmĕn, ădĭtŭs, Ingrēssŭs.

Intrōrsŭm *and* sŭs, adv., *within.* Lăcrўmăs Intrōrsŭs ŏbŏrtās, Ov.

Intrūdo, sī, *to thrust in.* Syn. Intrōdūco, Impēllo, Injĭcĭo.

Intŭbŭs, *or* tўbŭs, ī, f., *and* Intŭbŭm, *or* tўbŭm, ī, n., *endive.* Intŭbă fībrīs, Virg. Epith. Hōrtēnsĭs, agrēstĭs, vĭrĭdĭs, ămără.

Intŭĕŏr, ĕrĭs, *to look in or on.* Me Intŭĕrĭs, aŭt ŭtī, (Iamb. Pur.) Hor. Syn. Vĭdĕo, cērno, Inspĭcĭo, ăspĭcĭo, spēcto, cōntēmplŏr. V. Aspicio.

Intŭĭtŭs, ūs, m., *a view.* Pāndĭtŭr Intŭĭtŭ, Aus.

Intŭmco, *and* ēsco, mŭī, *to swell.* Intŭmŭīssĕ gĕnās, Ov. Nĕque Intŭmēscĭt āltă, Hor. Syn. Tŭmĕfĭo, Inflŏr, tŭmĕo, tūrgēsco.

Intŭmŭlātŭs, ă, ŭm, *not buried.* Intŭmŭlātă tŭīs, Ov. Syn. Insĕpūltŭs.

Intŭs, adv., *within.* Intŭs ăquæ, Virg. Syn. Intrā.

Invādo, sī, *to invade.* Invādŭnt ŭrbĕm, Virg. Syn. Ădŏrĭŏr, Impĕto, āggrĕdĭŏr, lăcēsso, prōvŏco, ōppūgno, Irrŭo In, fĕrŏr, Invŏlo, Insĭlĭo, Irrūmpo, vīm făcĭo. V. Irruo.

Invălĕo, ŭī, *to grow strong.* Inquĕ vălēbŭnt, Lucr. Syn. Invălēsco, cōrrŏbŏro, vīrēs rĕsūmo.

Invălĭdŭs, ă, ŭm, *weak.* Dētĕrĕt Invălĭdōs, Tibull. Syn. Infīrmŭs, dēbĭlĭs, Imbēcīllĭs, dēbĭlĭtātŭs. V. Ægrotus.

Invĕhŏr, ĕrĭs, *to be carried upon.* Invĕhĭtŭr māgnă, Virg. Syn. Vĕhŏr, Impōrtŏr, Infĕrŏr ; Insēctŏr, ĕxăgĭto, crīmĭnŏr.

Invĕnĭo, vēnī, *to find, invent.* Invĕnĭt Ignēs, Ov. Syn. Rĕpĕrĭo, cōmpĕrĭo, nāncīscŏr ; ădInvĕnĭo, ĕxcōgĭto, cōmmĭnīscŏr.

Invēntŏr, ōrĭs, m., trĭx, trĭcĭs, f., *a discoverer.* Invēntŏr Ulўssēs, Virg. Mĭnērva Invēntrīx, Virg.

Invēntŭs, ă, ŭm, *the pass. partic. of* invenio. Invēntăquĕ flūmĭnă, Virg.

Invĕnūstŭs, ă, ŭm, *ungraceful, indecent.* Ēt Invĕnūsta ēst, (Phal.) Cat. Syn. Incōmptŭs, sōrdĭdŭs.

Invĕrēcūndŭs, ă, ŭm, *shameless.* Invĕrēcūndŭs Dĕŭs, (Iamb.) Hor. Syn. Ēffrōns, Impŭdēns. V. Impudens.

Invērgo, ĭs, *to incline towards.* Tŭm sŭpĕr Invērgēns, Ov.

Invērto, tī, *to turn in.* Ipsăs Invērtĭmŭs, ātquĕ, Hor. Syn. Vērto, cōnvērto, pērvērto, Immūto, In cōntrārĭă vērto.

Invēstīgo, ās, *to search.* Invēstīgātō fōntĕ, Rut. Syn. Indāgo, Inquīro, ĕxquīro, pērquīro, scrūtŏr, pērscrūtŏr.

Invĕtĕrāsco, ĭs, *and* ro, ūs, *to grow old.* Invĕtĕrāscĭt ălēndo, Lucr.

Invĕtĭtŭs, ă, ŭm, *not forbidden.* Invĕtĭtūm sāltŭs pĕnĕtrăt, Sil.

Invĭcĕm, adv., *alternately.* Cāntābĭmŭs invĭcĕm, (Glycon.) Hor. Syn. Vĭcīssĭm, āltērnĭs, mūtŭō.

Invictŭs, ă, ŭm, *invincible.* Gĕnĭti ātque invictī, Virg. Syn. Indŏmĭtŭs, insŭpĕrābĭlĭs, ĭnēxpūgnābĭlĭs, ĭnfrāctŭs, ĭnēxsŭpĕrābĭlĭs.

Invĭdĕo, vīdī, *to envy.* Nōn invĭdĕt ārmĭs, Virg. Syn. Æmŭlŏr. V. Invidus.

Invĭdĭă, æ, f., *envy.* Invĭdĭā Sĭcŭlī, Hor. Syn. Lĭvŏr. Epith. Oblīquă, ācrĭs, nŏxĭă, ēxĭtĭālĭs, prāvă, ægră, ĭnfēlīx, ĭnhūmānă, mĭnāx, fŭrēns, ĭnīquă, trĭstĭs, dēgĕnĕr, cæcă, pāllĭdă, mōrdāx, lĭvēns, măcĭlēntă, fŭrĭōsă, lānguĭdă, ēxsānguĭs, īnsōmnĭs, ĭrrĕquĭētă, tētră, tābĭfĭcă, ŏpĕrtă, glīscēns. V. Invideo, livor.

Invĭdĭōsŭs, ă, ŭm, *envious.* Invĭdĭōsă vĕtŭstās, Ov. Syn. Invĭdŭs ; invīsŭs.

Invĭdŭs, ă, ŭm, *envious.* Invĭdŭs, īrăcūndŭs, Hor. Syn. Lĭvĭdŭs, æmŭlŭs, Zŏĭlŭs. V. Invideo.

Invĭgĭlo, ās, *to watch strictly.* Invĭgĭlātĕ, vĭrī, Col. Syn. Vĭgĭlo ; āttēndo.

Invĭŏlābĭlĭs, ĕ, *inviolable.* Invĭŏlābĭlĕ pīgnŭs, Virg. Syn. Invĭŏlātŭs, săcĕr.

Invĭŏlātŭs, ă, ŭm, *unviolated.* Invĭŏlātă văcăt, Virg. Syn. Intĕmĕrātŭs, ĭntĕgĕr, cāstŭs.

* || Invīsĭbĭlĭs, ĕ, *invisible.* Est Invīsĭbĭlĭs, Prud.

Invīso, sī, *to visit.* Gĕlĭdōs invīsĕrĕ fīnēs, Virg. Syn. Vīso, ădĕo, cōnvĕnĭo.

Invīsŭs, ă, ŭm, *unseen.* Arĭs invīsă sĕdēbăt, Virg. Syn. Ŏdĭōsŭs, ĭnāspēctŭs.

Invīto, ās, *to invite, allure.* Invītēnt crŏcĕĭs, Virg. Syn. Vŏco, ădvŏco ; āllĭcĭo.

Invītŭs, ă, ŭm, *unwilling.* Invītŭs, rēgīnă, tŭō, Virg. Syn. Rĕpūgnāns, cŏāctŭs, nōn lĭbēns, nōlēns.

Invĭŭs, ă, ŭm, *impassable.* Invĭă tērrĭs, Virg. Syn. Impērvĭŭs, ĭnāccēssŭs.

Inŭltŭs, ă, ŭm, *unpunished, unrevenged.* Mŏrĭēmŭr ĭnŭltī, Virg. Syn. Impūnītŭs ; nōn ŭltŭs.

Inŭmbro, ās, *to overshadow.* Frōndĭs ĭnŭmbrānt, Virg. V. Umbro.

Inūnctŭs, ă, ŭm, *anointed.* Cōnchĭs ĭnūnctă, Mart. Syn. Ūnctŭs, ĭllĭtŭs.

Inūndo, ās, *to overflow.* Ēt Inūndānt, Virg. Syn. Ēxūndo, dīfflŭo, ēffūndŏr.

Inūngo, xī, ctŭm, *to anoint.* Lĭppŭs ĭnūngī, Hor. Syn. Ūngo, ĭllĭno.

Invŏco, ās, *to call for.* Invŏcăt ēt dŭplĭcēs, Virg. Syn. Rŏgo, prĕcŏr, implōro, pōsco, ēxpōsco.

Invŏlĭto, ās, *to wave about.* Invŏlĭtānt cŏmæ, Hor. V. Volito.

Invŏlo, ās, *to fly into.* Invŏlĕt ārtŭs, Luc.

Invŏlŭcĕr, ucrĭs, ĕ, *unfledged.* Invŏlŭcĕr pūllŭs, Cat.

Invŏlucrŭm, ī, n., *a wrapper.* Cōntēntum invŏlŭcrĭs, (Asclep.)

Invŏlvo, vī, lūtŭm, *to wrap.* Invōlvĭtquĕ dŏmŭm, Virg. Syn. Illăquĕo, īrrētĭo, ĭntrīco, ĭmplĭco ; ābrĭpĭo, dīrŭo.

Inŭrbānŭs, ă, ŭm, *uncivil.* Scīmŭs ĭnŭrbānŭm, Hor. Syn. Rūstĭcŭs, ĭllĕpĭdŭs.

Inūro, ssī, stŭm, *to mark with a hot iron.* Gēntĭs ĭnūrŭnt, Virg. Syn. Imprĭmo, īnflĭgo, nŏto, īnscrībo.

Inŭsĭtātŭs, ă, ŭm, *unusual.* Inŭsĭtātūm fērrĕ, (Iamb.) Syn. Insŏlĭtŭs, rārŭs, īnsŏlēns, nŏvŭs.

Inūstŭs, *the pass. partic. of* inuro. Ictŭs, ĕt ĭnŭstă. Lucr.

Inūtĭlĭs, ĕ, *useless.* Et sĭbi ĭnūtĭlĭŏr, Ov. Syn. Vānŭs, ĭnānĭs.

Ĭō, interj., *a cry of joy.* Dīcĭte Ĭō Pœān, Ov.

Ĭō, ūs, f., *the daughter of Inachus, turned into a cow.* Jūssĕrĭt Ĭō, Juv. Caŭsă fūgæ, quĭd Ĭō frĕtă, Ov. Syn. Isĭs, Inăchĭs, Phŏrōnĭs. Epith. Văgă, Inăchĭă, Phărĭă, Mēmphītĭs, Nīlĭăcă ; Argīvă, Argŏlĭcă. V. Isis.

S. Jŏānnēs, ĭs, m., *the Baptist.* Epith. Sānctŭs, pūrŭs, ĭntĕgĕr, sĕvērŭs, aŭstērŭs, ĭntĕmĕrātŭs, prænūncĭŭs, præsāgŭs, fătĭdĭcŭs, vātēs.—*2. the Evangelist.*

jŏcŏr, ārĭs, *to speak in jest.* Quĭd lŭbēt jŏcārī, (Phal.) Syn. Rīdĕo, īrrīdĕo, lūdo, ĭllūdo, căvĭllŏr.

jŏcōsŭs, ă, ŭm, *witty, merry.* Fīnīrĕ jŏcōsăm, Mart. Syn. Făcētŭs, fēstīvŭs, lĕpĭdŭs.

jŏcŭlārĭs, ĕ, *and* ārĭŭs, ă, ŭm, *jocular.* Quī jŏcŭlārĭă rīdēns, Hor. Syn. Fēstīvŭs hĭlărĭs, lætŭs.

jŏcŭs, ī, m., *a joke.* Jŭvĕnēs ăgĭtārĕ jŏcōs, Pers. Syn. Rīsŭs, lūdŭs, lūsŭs, sălēs, căvĭllātĭo, căvĭllŭs, scōmmă. Epith. Rĭdĭcŭlŭs, jūcūndŭs, lætŭs, fēstīvŭs, hǐlārǐs, blāndŭs, grātŭs, plăcǐdŭs, lěpǐdŭs, pŭěrīlǐs, sŏlūtŭs, věnūstŭs, ǎlǎcěr, vānŭs, ǐnānǐs, lāscīvŭs, tūrpǐs, īnfāmǐs. V. Sales.

Ǐŏlāŭs, āī, m., *the son of Iphiclus : Hercules restored him to health and youth.* Fātǐs Ǐŏlāŭs ǐn ānnōs, Ov.

Ǐŏlcǐācŭs, ǎ, ŭm, *of Iolcos.* Vīctŏr Ǐŏlcǐācōs, Ov.

Ǐŏlcŏs, ī, f., *a city of Thessaly.* Quās Ǐŏlcŏs ātque Ǐběrǐǎ, Hor.

Ǐŏlē, ēs, f., *the daughter of Eurytus.* Dūmquě rěfěrt Ǐŏlē, Ov.

Ǐōn, ōnǐs, m., Ǐōněs, ŭm, m. pl., *inhabitants of Ionia.* Quæ cōndǐt, Ǐōnăs, Claud.

Ǐōnǐǎ, æ, f., *a country in Asia.* Præbět Ǐōnǐǎ dīvěs, Ov. EPITH. Mōllǐs, fœcūndǎ, ŏpīmǎ, cūltǎ.

Ǐōnǐācŭs, ǐcŭs, *and* Ǐōnǐŭs, ǎ, ŭm, *Ionian.* Intěr Ǐōnǐācās, Ov. Gaūdět Ǐōnǐcōs, (Alcaic.) Hor. Nōssě quŏt Ǐōnǐī, Virg.

Ǐōnǐăs, ădǐs, *and* Ǐōnǐs, ǐdǐs, f., *Ionian.* Intěr Ǐōnǐădās, Ov.·

Ǐōpās, æ, m., *a minstrel at Dido's court.* EPITH. Crīnītŭs, pūlchěr, fŏrmōsŭs, děcōrŭs, věnūstŭs, Lǐbǐcŭs.

Jŏrdānǐs, ǐs, m., *a river in Palestine.* Plăcǐdām Jŏrdānǐs ǎd ūndǎm, Ser. V. Fluvius.

Jŏsěph, *or* Yūsěph, m., *(indecl.) the son of Jacob and Rachel, sold by his brothers, accused by the wife of Potiphar, and preserved by the hand of God.* S. Jŏsěphŭs, ī, m., *the husband of the Virgin Mary.*

Iphǐăs, ădǐs, f., *the daughter of Iphis.* Iphǐăs ǐn mědǐōs, Ov.

Iphǐgěnǐǎ, æ, f., *the daughter of Agamemnon.* Iphǐgěnǐǎ mŏrǎ, Prop. SYN. Iphǐănāssǎ, Mўcēnǐs. EPITH. Ăgāměmnŏnǐǎ, Pělŏpēǐǎ.

Iphǐnŏŭs, ī, m., *a centaur.* Ēmǐnŭs; Iphǐnŏŭm, Ov.

Iphǐs, ǐs, m., *a man's name.* Iphǐs Ānāxǎrětēn, Ov.

Iphǐs, ǐdǐs, f., *a daughter of Lygdus.* Fœmǐnǎ vŏvěrǎt Iphǐs, Ov.

Iphǐtŭs, ī, m., *the name of a warrior.* Iphǐtŭs ēt Pělǐǎs, Ov.

Ipsě, ǎ, ŭm, *one's-self.* Ipsī tē fōntēs, īpsa hæc ārbūstǎ, Virg.

Īrǎ, æ, f., *wrath.* Māgnōque īrārūm flūctŭǎt æstū, Virg. SYN. Fŭrŏr, răbǐēs, īrācūndǐǎ. EPITH. Ăcērbǎ, vǐŏlēntǎ, ěffěrǎ, răbǐdǎ, sævǎ, sānguǐněǎ, ācrǐs, atrōx, īmpǐǎ, īmprŏbǎ, aūdāx, īnsānǎ, dīscōrs, īmmānǐs, cōmmōtǎ, ǐndŏmǐtǎ, lītǐgǐōsǎ, tūmǐdǎ, cæcǎ, ăccēnsǎ, fūlmǐněǎ, præcěps, crūdēlǐs, ārdēns, fŭrēns, frěmēns, vīvāx, mǐnāx, hōrrǐdǎ, vǐtǐōsǎ, īnfrænǐs, īmpătǐēns, flāmmātǎ, fērvēns, nŏcēns, ǐnǐquǎ, spūmāns, Tārtǎrěǎ. V. Furor, irascor; Parco, placo.

īrācūndǐǎ, æ, f., *an inclination to anger.* Prŏbǐ hŏmǐnǐs īrācūndǐǎ, (Iamb.) SYN. Īrǎ.

īrācūndŭs, ǎ, ŭm, *angry.* Impǐgěr, īrācūndŭs, ǐněxōrābǐlǐs, Hor. SYN. Irrǐtābǐlǐs.

īrāscŏr, ěrǐs, *to be angry.* Ātque īrāsci ǐn cōrnŭǎ dīscǐt, Virg. SYN. Sŭccēnsěo, īndīgnŏr. V. Iratus, furor.

īrātŭs, ǎ, ŭm, *angry.* Aūt ūnde īrātŭs sўlvǎm, Virg. SYN. Răbǐdŭs, fŭrēns.

Irǐs, ǐdǐs, f., *the messenger of Juno.* Irim dē cœlō, Virg. SYN. Thaūmāntǐs, Thaūmāntǐās. EPITH. Jūnōnǐǎ, āěrǐǎ, īmbrǐfěrǎ, cūrvātǎ, ūdǎ, rōscǐdǎ, hūmǐdǎ, nǐmbōsǎ, plŭvǐǎ, ǎquōsǎ, æthěrěǎ, pīctǎ, cŏlōrātǎ, cŏrūscǎ, děcōrǎ, dīscŏlŏr.

īrrădǐo, ās, *to shine upon.* Irrădǐārě dǐēs, Sedul. SYN. Rădǐo, lūcěo, īllūmǐno, īllūstro. V. Radio.

īrrědūx, dŭcǐs, ě, *irremeable.* Irrědūcēmquě vǐǎm, Lucan.

īrrělǐgātŭs, ǎ, ŭm, *untied.* Irrělǐgātǎ cŏmās, Ov. SYN. Sŏlūtŭs.

īrrěměābǐlǐs, ě, *admitting no return.* Ēt īrrěměābǐlǐs ērrŏr, Virg.

īrrěpărābǐlǐs, ě, *irreparable.* Fūgǐt īrrěpărābǐlě tēmpŭs, Virg.

īrrěpērtŭs, ǎ, ŭm, *that has not been found.* Aūrum īrrěpērtum, Hor.

īrrěpo, psī, *to creep in.* Nōn īrrěpěrě sācrǐs, Mart. SYN. Rěpo, ōbrěpo, ādrěpo, sērpo.

īrrěprěhēnsŭs, ǎ, ŭm, *blameless.* Irrěprěhēnsǎ fŭǐt, Ov.

īrrěquǐēs, ētǐs, *and* ětŭs, ǎ, ŭm, *restless.* Irrěquǐětǎ gěrǐs, Ov. SYN. Inquǐětŭs, cōntūrbātŭs, tūrbŭlēntŭs, sōllǐcǐtŭs, pērvǐgǐl, īnsōmnǐs.

īrrěsēctŭs, ǎ, ŭm, *not cut.* Hīc īrrěsēctūm sævǎ, Hor.

īrrěsŏlūtŭs, ǎ, ŭm, *not loosed.* Irrěsŏlūtǎ mǎnět, Ov.

īrrěstīnctŭs, ǎ, ŭm, *unextinguished.* Irrěstīnctǎ fŏcǐs, Sil.

īrrětǐo, rētǐī, īvī, rětītŭm, *to entangle.* Irrētīrě plăgīs, Prud. SYN. Implǐco, īllăquěo.

īrrětōrtŭs, ǎ, ŭm, *not averted.* Ŏcŭlo īrrětōrtō, Hor.

ĭrrĕvŏcābĭlĭs, ĕ, *and* ūndŭs, ă, ŭm, *irrevocable.* Irrĕvŏcābĭlĕ vĕrbŭm, Hor. Irrĕvŏcāndŭs ĕăt, Cl.

ĭrrĕvŏcātŭs, ă, ŭm, *not called back, not checked.* Irrĕvŏcātŭs ăb ācrī, Ov.

ĭrrĕvŏlūtŭs, ă, ŭm, *not unfolded.* Rĕdĕās ĭrrĕvŏlūtŭs, Mart.

ĭrrīdĕo, sī, sŭm, *to laugh at.* Irrīdēns vātĕm, Virg. SYN. Rīdĕo, dērīdĕo, ĭllūdo, īnsūlto, jŏcŏr, căvīllŏr, lūdĭfīco, lūdĭfĭcŏr. V. Derideo.

ĭrrĭgo, ās, *to water.* Irrĭgăt ārtŭs, Virg. SYN. Rīgo, āspērgo, hūmēcto, īrrōro. V. Rigo.

ĭrrĭgŭŭs, ă, ŭm, *wet.* Flōrĕăt ĭrrĭgŭŭm, Virg. SYN. Rĭgŭŭs, ūdŭs.

ĭrrīsŏr, ōrĭs, m., *a mocker.* Irrīsŏr ămōrēs, Prop. SYN. Dērīsŏr, căvīllātŏr, scūrră.

ĭrrītābĭlĭs, ĕ, *quickly moved to anger.* Gĕnŭs ĭrrītābĭlĕ vātŭm, Hor. SYN. Irācūndŭs.

ĭrrītāmĕn, ĭnĭs, *and* mēntŭm, ī, n., *an incitement.* Ănĭmi ĭrrītāmĕn ăvārī, Ov. Irrītāmēntă mălōrŭm, Id. SYN. Invītāmēntŭm, īllĕcebræ, stĭmŭlī.

ĭrrīto, ŭs, *to incite.* Sēgnĭŭs ĭrrītānt, Hor. SYN. Prŏvŏco, lăcēsso, ēxāspĕro.

ĭrrĭtŭs, ă, ŭm, *vain.* Irrĭtŭs ūrgĕt, Virg. SYN. Vānŭs, ĭnānĭs, ĭnūtĭlĭs, cāssŭs.

ĭrrŏgo, ās, *to ordain.* Irrŏgĕt æquās, Hor. Impōno, dēcērno.

ĭrrōro, ās, *to bedew.* Tērrās ĭrrōrăt Ĕōŭs, Virg. SYN. Rōro, rĭgo, ĭrrĭgo.

ĭrrŭbĕo, ŭī, *to grow red.* Irrŭbŭĭt, Stat.

ĭrrūgo, ās, *to wrinkle, plait.* Nōdīs ĭrrūgăt Ĭbērĭs, Stat.

ĭrrūmpo, ĭs, *to break in.* Prīmi ĭrrūpērĕ pătēntēs, Virg. V. Irruo.

ĭrrŭo, ŭī, *to rush upon.* Irrŭĭmŭs dēnsīs, Virg. SYN. Rŭo, īncūrro, ĭrrūmpo, īnsĭlĭo, fĕrŏr; mē fĕro, īnfĕro, īnjĭcĭo; mē dŏ ĭn; īnvādo, āggrĕdĭŏr. V. Invado.

ĭrrūptŭs, ă, ŭm, *unbroken.* Quōs ĭrrūptă tĕnĕt cŏpŭlă, Hor.

Irŭs, ī, m., *a beggar.* Irŭs ĕt ēst sŭbĭtō, Ov. EPITH. Paūpĕr, ĕgēnŭs, mĭsĕr, ĭnōps, mēndīcŭs.

Ĭs, ĕă, ĭd, pron., *that.* Prætŏr, ĭs īntēstābĭlĭs, Hor. SYN. Hic, ĭstĕ.

Isĭācŭs, ă, ŭm, *of Isis.* Aūt ăpŭd Isĭācœ, Juv.

Isĭs, ĭs *or* ĭdĭs, f., *an Egyptian goddess.* Isĭdĭs āntīquō, Juv. V. Io.

Ismărĭcŭs, *and* rĭŭs, ă, ŭm, *Thracian.* Ismărĭcĭquĕ rĭgĕt, Ov. Ismărĭæ cĕlĕbrānt, Id.

Ismărŭs, ī, m., *and* ă, ōrŭm, n. pl., *a mountain in Thracia.* Ismărŭs Ōrpheă, Virg. Et pātrĭa Ismără mĭttĭt, Id. EPITH. Āspĕr, rĭgĭdŭs, dūrŭs, nīmbōsŭs, gĕlĭdŭs, nĭvĕŭs, fœcŭndŭs, fērtĭlĭs, fĕrāx, cūltŭs, vīrēns, āmœnŭs.

Ismēnē, ēs, f., *the daughter of Œdipus.* Inchŏăt Ismēnē, Stat.

Ismēnĭŭs, ă, ŭm, *and* Ismēnĭs, ĭdĭs, f., *of the Ismenus, Theban.* Thērsēs Ismēnĭŭs ōrĭs, Ov. Ismēnĭdĕs ārăs, Id.

Ismēnŭs *or* ŏs, ī, m., *a river of Bœotia.* Ismēnŏn ăcērvō, Stat.

Issē, ēs, f., *a daughter of Macareus, beloved by Apollo.* Lŭsĕrĭt Issēn, Ov.

ĭssĕ, ĭssĕm, *for* ĭvīssĕ, ĭvīssĕm. Sĕmĕl ĭssĕ pĕr āmnĕs, Ov.

ĭstĕ, ă, ŭd, gen. iŭs, *that.* Istĭŭs ĭngĕnĭĕm, Ov. Istĭŭs pŭĕrī, Mart.

Istĕr, trī, m., *the Danube.* Istĕr ărēnās, Virg.

Isthmĭācŭs, *and* mĭŭs, ă, ŭm, *of the Isthmus of Corinth.* Tālĭs ĭn Isthmĭācōs, Stat. Nōn lăbŏr Isthmĭŭs, Hor. —mĭă, ōrŭm, n. pl., *games celebrated every five years at Corinth, in honour of Neptune.* Isthmĭă dēfūnctō, Aus.

Isthmŭs, ī, m., *a narrow strait, usually the Isthmus of Corinth.* Spēctāntŭr ăb ĭsthmō, Ov. EPITH. Bĭmărĭs, æquŏrĕŭs, cīrcūmflūŭs, brĕvĭs, lātŭs, ēxtēnsŭs; tĕnŭĭs, ēxĭlĭs.

ĭstīc, ĭstīnc, adv., *there, thence.* Istīc ōblīquō, Hor. Jam ĭstīnc ĕt, Virg.

ĭstūc, adv., *thither.* Tāmĕn ĭstūc mēns, Hor.

ĭtă, adv., *so.* Ērŭĕrēnt; ĭtă tūrbĭnĕ, Virg. SYN. Sīc; nōn ălĭtĕr, haūd sĕcŭs; nōn sĕcŭs.

Ĭtălī, ōrŭm, m. pl., *the Italians.* Pōst Ĭtălī flŭvĭŭm, Virg. SYN. Aūsŏnĭī, Lătīnī, Lătĭī, Œnotrĭī, Aūsŏnĭdæ. EPITH. Fōrtēs, gĕnĕrōsī, bēllācēs, ĭndŏmĭtī, ĭnvīctī, sŭpērbī, pŏtēntēs, ĭngĕnĭōsī.

Ĭtălĭă, æ, f., *Italy.* Ĭtălĭăm fātō, Virg. SYN. Aūsŏnĭă, Œnotrĭă, Hēspĕrĭă, Lătĭŭm. EPITH. Dīvĕs, sŭpērbă, nōbĭlĭs, īllūstrĭs, Mārtĭă, bēllĭcă, gĕnĕrōsă, fĕrāx, fērtĭlĭs, fœcūndă, pŏtēns, ŏpŭlēntă.

Ĭtălĭcŭs, ă, ŭm, *of Italy.* Ĭtălĭcīs aūctŏr, Ov. SYN. Ĭtălŭs, Aūsŏnĭŭs, Lătĭŭs, Lătīnŭs.

Ĭtălĭs, ĭdĭs, f., *an Italian woman.* Ĭtălĭdēs, quās īpsă dēcŭs, Virg. SYN. Ĭtălă, Aūsŏnĭs.

Ĭtălŭs, ă, ŭm, *Italian.* Ĭtălāsnĕ căpēssērĕt ōrās, Virg. Quĭbŭs Ĭtălă jūm tŭm, Id. V. Italicus.

Ĭtăquĕ, adv., *therefore.* Nūnc ĭtăque ēt vērsŭs, Hor. SYN. Ĭgĭtŭr, ērgo, quārē, quăprōptĕr, quāmŏbrĕm, ĭdĕŏ, ĭdcīrcō, ātque ădĕŏ.

Ĭtĕm, adv., *also.* Cōntēmplātŏr ĭtĕm, Virg. SYN. Insŭpĕr, prætĕrĕā, ădhūc, rūrsŭs, rūrsŭm, ĭtĕrŭm.

Ĭtĕr, ĭtĭnĕrĭs, n., *a journey.* Ērgo ĭtĕr incœptŭm, Virg. SYN. Sēmĭtă, vĭă, cāllĭs, trāmĕs, ădĭtŭs, spătĭŭm. V. Via.

Ĭtĕro, ās, *to do again.* Sīc ĭtĕrāt vōcēs, Hor. SYN. Gĕmĭno, īngĕmĭno, duplĭco, īntegro, rĕdīntegro, rĕpĕto, rĕsūmo.

Ĭtĕrŭm, adv., *again.* Ĭtĕrūmque ĭtĕrūmquĕ mŏnēbo, Virg. SYN. Rūrsŭm, rūrsŭs, prætĕrĕā, īnsŭpĕr, ădhūc.

Ĭthăcă, æ, f., *an island in the Ionian sea.* Sūm pătrĭa ēx Ĭthăcā, Virg. EPITH. Aspĕră, īncūltă, mōntānă, scŏpŭlōsă.

Ĭthăcēnsĭs, ĕ, *and* Ĭthăcŭs, ă, ŭm, *of Ithaca.* Ĭthăcēnsĭs Ūlȳsseī, Hor. Æŏlĭŏs, Ĭthăcīs, Ov. SYN. Ĭthăcēsĭs.—2.-cŭs, ī, m, *Ulysses.* Hōc Ĭthăcŭs vĕlĭt, Virg.

Ĭthōmē, ēs, f, *a mountain and fortress of Messina.* Nūtrĭt Ĭthōmē, Stat.

Ĭtĭdĕm, adv., *equally.* Ōmnĭă nōs ĭtĭdĕm, Lucr. SYN. Părĭtĕr.

Ĭtūræi, ōrŭm, n. pl., *inhabitants of Ituræa, a province of Cœle-Syria.* Tūnc ĕt Ĭtūræī, Luc.—2.-ŭs, ă, ŭm, *Ituræan.* Cōrnŭs, Ĭtūræōs, Virg.

Ĭtūrŭs, ă, ŭm, *the fut. partic. of* eo. Ăd lūmĕn ĭtūrăs, Virg.

Ĭtȳs, ȳŏs, m., *the son of Tereus and Procne.* Caūsă dŏlōrĭs Ĭtȳs, Ov. Prŏsĭlĭĭt, Ĭtȳōsquĕ căpŭt, Id.

jūbă, æ, f., *the mane of a horse.* Dēnsă jŭba, ĕt, Virg. SYN. Cŏmă, crīnĭs. EPITH. Flŭēns, ūndāns, cŏmāns, pēxă, lōngă, flāvă, ēffūsă, crīspāns, văgă, spārsă, cōmptă, dīffūsă, rŭtĭlă, ĕquīnă, lĕŏnīnă.

Jŭbă, æ, m., *a king of Mauritania.* Nēc Jŭbæ tēllūs, Hor. EPITH. Maūrŭs, Cīnȳphĭŭs, māgnănĭmŭs, fōrtĭs, pŏtĕn, īnfēlīx.

jŭbăr, ărĭs, n., *a sunbeam.* It pōrtĭs jŭbăre ēxōrtō, Virg. SYN. Fāx, lūmĕn, splēndŏr, fūlgŏr, lūx, rădĭī. V. Fax, lumen.

jŭbātŭs, ă, ŭm, *having a mane.* Ēst cērvīcĕ jŭbātŭs, Salm. SYN. Crīnītŭs, cŏmātŭs.

jŭbčo, jŭssī, jŭssŭm, *to command.* Neū Trōās fĭĕrī jŭbĕās, Virg. SYN. Impĕro, māndo, præcĭpĭo. V. Impero.

jŭcŭndŭs, ă, ŭm, *agreeable.* Hōc jŭcŭndŭs ămīcŭs, Hor. SYN. Grātŭs, suāvĭs, āccēptŭs, dūlcĭs, ămœnŭs, lætŭs, hĭlărĭs, fēstīvŭs, lĕpĭdŭs, jŏcōsŭs.

Jūdæă, æ, f., *a country in Syria.* Hæc, Jūdæă, tŭās, Rut. SYN. Pălæstīnă, Ĭdūmœă, Chănăăn; Chănănæă. EPITH. Infīdă, pērfĭdă, rĕbēllĭs, dīră, pērjūră, sŭpērbă.

Jūdæī, ōrŭm, m. pl., *the Jews.* Cūrtĭs Jūdæĭs, Hor. SYN. Pălæstīnī, Isăcĭdæ, Ĭdūmœī, Hēbræī. EPITH. Infīdī, pērfĭdī, fĕrōcēs, sŭpērbī, rĕbēllēs, prŏfānī.

Jūdæŭs, ă, ŭm, *a Jew, Jewish.* Crēdăt Jūdæŭs Ăpēllă, Hor.

Jūdăĭcŭs, ă, ŭm, *Jewish.* Jūdăĭcum ēdīscŭnt, Juv.

Jūdās, æ, m., *the son of Jacob.*—2. *The Apostle.* Ăstrīctŭm Jūdās ŭt, Sed. SYN. Iscărĭōtēs. EPITH. Prŏdĭtŏr, nĕfāndŭs, īmpĭŭs, ăvārŭs. V. Apostoli.

jŭdēx, ĭcĭs, m., *a judge.* Jūdĭcĭs ārgūtŭm, Hor. SYN. Ărbĭtĕr. EPITH. Æquŭs, jūstŭs, īncōrrūptŭs, īntĕgĕr, sĕvērŭs, grăvĭs, sānctŭs, săgāx, prūdēns; īnīquŭs, īnjūstŭs, cōrrūptŭs, sævŭs, īmmītĭs.

jūdĭcĭālĭs, ĕ, *and* ĭārĭŭs, ă, ŭm, *belonging to judges.* Fŏră jūdĭcĭālĭă pōnŭnt, Ov. SYN. Fŏrēnsĭs.

jūdĭcĭŭm, ĭī, n., *a judgment, a decision.* Jūdĭcĭŭm Părĭdĭs, Virg. SYN. Ărbĭtrĭŭm, sēntēntĭă; prūdēntĭă. EPITH. Rēctŭm, jūstŭm, æquŭm, prūdēns, grăvĕ, vērŭm, īnīquŭm, īnjūstŭm, īmprūdēns.

jūdĭco, ās, *to judge.* Jŏvĕ jūdĭcĕt æquŏ, Hor. SYN. Stătŭo, dījūdĭco, dēcērno, cōnstĭtŭo, ēxīstĭmo, ārbĭtrŏr, cēnsĕo; jūs dīco.

jŭgă, ōrŭm, n. pl., *seats for rowers in a ship.* Pĕr jŭgă lōngă, Virg.

jŭgālĭs, ĕ, *pertaining to a yoke.* Ăd pāscŭă nŏtă jŭgālēs, Claud.

jūgĕr, ĕrĭs, *and* ĕrŭm, ī, n., *an acre of ground.* Jūgĕrĭbŭs paŭcĭs, Hor. Jūgĕră fōssŏr, Virg.

jŭgĭs, ĕ, *perpetual.* Jŭgĭs ăquœ fŏns, Hor. Syn. Pĕrĕnnĭs, pĕrpĕtŭŭs, cŏntĭnŭŭs, ăssĭdŭŭs.

jŭgĭtĕr, adv., *continually.* Hŏspĕs jŭgĭtĕr, Aus. Syn. Cŏntĭnŭŏ.

jŭgo, ās, *to join, yoke.* Prīmīsquĕ jŭgārăt, Virg. Syn. Jŭngo; mărīto.

jŭgŏsŭs, ă, ŭm, *hilly.* Rĕgnārĕ jŭgōsīs.

jŭgŭlo, ās, *to kill.* Ŭt jŭgŭlēnt hŏmĭnēs, Hor. Syn. Jŭgŭlūm rĕsŏlvo; făŭcēs rĕsĕco, sĕco, fŏdĭo, īncīdo; ŏccīdo, pĕrĭmo. V. Occido.

jŭgŭlŭs, ī, m., *and* ŭm, ī, n., *the throat.* Jŭgŭlōs ăpĕrīrĕ sŭsūrrō, Sil. Syn. Făŭcēs, gŭttŭr; cŏllŭm.

jŭgŭm, ī, n., *a yoke.* Ārva āllĕnā jŭgō, Virg. Epith. Grăvĕ, mŏlēstŭm, tūrpĕ, trīstĕ, sĕrvīlĕ, ăcĕrbŭm, īntŏlĕrābĭlĕ, mĭsĕrŭm, ēxĭtĭălĕ, ĭnīquŭm, ŏdĭōsŭm; dūlcĕ, suāvĕ, mītĕ, grātŭm.—2. *the top of a mountain.* Hŏc sŭpĕrătĕ jŭgŭm, Virg. V. Cacumen.

Jŭgūrthă, œ, m., *a king of Numidia.* Rĕttŭlĭt īnfĕrĭās Jŭgūrthœ, Hor. Epith. Trĭŭmphātŭs, īmmānīs, pĕrfĭdŭs, trūx, crūdēlĭs, īmmītĭs, īnfēlīx, mĭsĕr, tĕrrĭbĭlĭs.

Jŭgūrthīnŭs, ă, ŭm, *of Jugurtha.* Illĕ Jŭgūrthīnō, Ov.

Ĭŭlēŭs, ă, ŭm, *of Iulus, Roman.* Gēntĭs Ĭŭlēœ nō[...], Ov.—2. *of July.* Tēmpŭs Ĭŭlæīs crās ēst nātālĕ călēndīs, Id.

Jūlĭă, æ, f., *the name of a woman.* Jūlĭă nūmĕn ĕrĭt, Ov.

Jūlĭŭs, ī, m., *the name of the family of Cæsar.* Jūlĭŭs ā măgnō, Virg.— 2. adj., -ŭs, ă, ŭm, *of Cæsar, of his ancestors or descendants.* Ĭn Jūlĭă tēmplă vŏcātī, Ov.

Jūlĭŭs, ī, m., *the seventh month, so named from Julius Cæsar.* Jūlĭŭs ēt sĕgĕtēs, Aus. Epith. Æstīvŭs, sĕrēnŭs.

Ĭŭlŭs, ī, m., *the son of Æneas.* Cōgnōmĕn Ĭŭlō, Virg.

jŭmēntŭm, ī, n., *a labouring beast.* Plăgĭs jŭmēntă cănēsquĕ, Hor. Epith. Mŭtŭm, rōbŭstŭm.

jŭncĕŭs, ă, ŭm, *made of bulrushes.* Jŭncĕ vīnclă, Ov.

jŭncōsŭs, ă, ŭm, *producing bulrushes.* Jŭncōsăquĕ līttŏră, Ov.

jŭnctūră, æ, f., *a joining.* Jŭnctūrās tăbŭlătă, Virg. Syn. Cŏmmīssūră. Epith. Vălĭdă, fīrmă, pŏlītă, lævĭs.

jŭncŭs, ī, m., *a bulrush.* Dētĕxĕrĕ jŭncō, Virg. Syn. Ărūndo, scīrpŭs: jŭncī vīmĕn. Epith. Mŏllĭs, tĕnŭĭs, tĕnĕr, lĕvĭs, ăcūtŭs, pălūstrĭs; līmōsŭs, flŭvĭālĭs, flŭmĭnĕŭs, ūdŭs, ūvĭdŭs.

jŭngo, xī, ctŭm, *to join.* Jŭngĭtŭr ārtĕ, Tib. Syn. Cōnjŭngo, ādjŭngo, nĕcto, cōnnĕcto, ādnĕcto, lĭgo, āllĭgo, cōpŭlo, cōmmītto; āddo, ādmŏvĕo, ādjĭcĭo, āpplĭco.

jŭnĭpĕrŭs, ī, m., *the juniper-tree.* Jŭnĭpĕrī grăvĭs, Virg. Epith. Vĭrĭdĭs, vĭrēns, ŏlēns, pĕrēnnĭs.

Jūnĭŭs, ī, m., *the sixth month in the year.* Jūnĭŭs ēst jŭvĕnŭm, Ov. Epith. Blāndŭs, ămœnŭs, sūdŭs, bĕnīgnŭs, flōrĭdŭs, rīdēns, ŏdōrŭs, lūxŭrĭāns, gĕnĭālĭs, sĕrēnŭs, grātŭs, plăcĭdŭs, fœcūndŭs, fērtĭlĭs, flōrēns, vĭrēns.

jŭnīx, īcĭs, f., *a heifer.* Jūnīcum ōmēntă, Pers.

Jūno, ōnĭs, f., *the daughter of Saturn, sister and wife of Jupiter.* Mĕmŏrēm Jūnōnĭs ŏb īrām, Virg. Syn. Lūcīnă, Sātūrnĭă. Epith. Rēgĭă, prōnŭbă, ōmnĭpŏtēns, māxĭmă, ālmă, pŏtēns, æthĕrĕă, cœlēstĭs, scēptrĭgĕră, sacră.

Jūnōnālĭs, ĕ, *and* Jūnōnĭŭs, ă, ŭm, *of Juno.* Jūnōnălĕ lēgēs, Ov. Jūnōnĭă vĕrtānt Hōspĭtĭă, Virg.

Jūnōnĭcŏlă, æ, m. f., *that worships Juno.* Jūnōnĭcŏlāsquĕ Fălīscōs, Ov.

Jūnōnĭgĕnă, æ, m., *son of Juno, Vulcan.* Jūnōnĭgĕnæquĕ mărītō, Ov.

Jŭpĭtĕr, Jŏvĭs, m., *the son of Saturn and Ops, king of the Gods, sovereign of Earth and Heaven.* Jŭpĭtĕr Argōs, Virg. Syn. Sātūrnĭŭs, Tŏnāns. V. Deus.— 2. *the air.* Sŭb Jŏvĕ frīgĭdō, Hor. Epith. Vērnŭs, plŭvĭŭs, sĕrēnŭs, pūrŭs, hūmĭdŭs, hōrrĭdŭs Aūstrīs. V. Aēr.—3. *a planet.* Sŭb Jŏvĕ tēmpĕrĭēs, Luc. Epith. Fēlīx, fœcūndŭs, plŭvĭŭs, cŏrūscāns, sīdĕrĕŭs.—4. [Jŭpĭtĕr æquŏrĕŭs.] V. Neptunus.—5. [Jŭpĭtĕr Stўgĭŭs.] V. Pluto.

jūrāmēntŭm, ī, *and* jūsjŭrāndŭm, jūrĭsjŭrāndī, n., *an oath.* Jūrāmēntă pătrī, Æm. Jūrĕjūrāndō sŭăm, Sen. Jūrĕ tŭĕrī Jūrāndō, Juv. Syn. Sacrāmēntŭm.

jūrātŭs, ă, ŭm, *having sworn; sworn by.* Ēt līquĭdō jūrātŭs, Ov.

jūrgĭŭm, ĭī, n., *a quarrel.* Jūrgĭă jāctās, Virg. Syn. Rīxă, cōntēntĭo, pūgnă, discŏrdiă, lis. Epith. Clāmōsŭm, insānŭm, āspĕrŭm, imprŏbŭm, vĕsānŭm, dūrŭm, litigiōsŭm. V. Rixa.

jūrgo, ās, *and* ŏr, āris, *ta quarrel.* Jūrgātūr vĕrbis, Hor. Syn. Rixŏr, āltĕrcŏr, litigo, cōntēndo, cērto. V. Itixor.

jūridicŭs, ă, ŭm, *belonging to law.* Sēptēm jūridicis, Fill.

jūro, ās, *to swear.* Di, cūjŭs jūrārĕ timēnt, Virg. Syn. Adjūro, tēstŏr, āttēstŏr.

jūs, ūris, n., *right.* Dŏminæ jŭs ēssĕ, Hor. Syn. Æquŭm, fās, rēctŭm, jūstŭm; jūstitiă, æquitās. Epith. Sānctŭm, sacrŭm, inviŏlātŭm, ālmŭm ; litigiōsŭm, āncēps, clāmōsŭm; ārctŭm, sĕvērŭm, rigidŭm, inviŏlābilĕ, fīrmŭm. V. Justitia. —2. *an oath.* Syn. Jūrāmēntŭm, sacrāmēntŭm, fidēs, rēligiŏ. Epith. Sŏlēnnĕ, sacrātŭm, sānctŭm, inviŏlābilĕ, tĕnāx. V. Juramentum.—3. *broth.* Ligūrierit jŭs, Hor. Syn. Jūscŭlŭm, sŭccŭs.

jŭssŭm, i, n., *a command.* Jŭssā făcēssŭnt, Virg. Syn. Jŭssŭs, impĕriŭm, māndātŭm, præcēptŭm.

jūstificŭs, ă, ŭm, *doing justice.* Jŭctificām nōbis mēntĕm, Cat.

jūstitiă, æ, f., *justice.* Jŭstitiænĕ priŭs, Virg. Syn. Æquitās; jūs, æquŭm ; Thĕmis, Āstrœă. Epith. Sacră, sānctă, æquă, divină, cōnstāns, sĕvĕră, pŏtēns, piă, fidēlis.

jūstŭs, ă, ŭm, *just.* Mirāntūr jūstiquĕ sĕnēs, Ov. Syn. Æquŭs, rēctŭs ; piŭs, innŏcŭŭs ; mĕritŭs, dēbitŭs, lēgitimŭs. V. Jus.

Jūtūrnă, æ, f., *sister of Turnus.* Jūtūrnă, dŏlōrĕm, Virg.

|| jŭvāmĕn, inis, n., *help.* Sæpĕ jŭvāmĕn, Man. V. Auxilium.

Jŭvĕnālis, is, m., *the Roman satirist.* Cŭm Jŭvĕnălĕ mĕŏ, Mart. Epith. Fācŭndŭs, disērtŭs, tūrgidŭs, Aquīnās, mōrdāx.

jŭvēncă, æ, f., *a heifer.* Mirātă jŭvēncă, Virg. Syn. Bōs, būcŭlă, văccă, vitŭlă, jŭvēncŭlă. Epith. Cōrnigĕră, pīnguis, tĕnĕră, pĕtŭlāns, pĕtŭlcă, fœcŭndă.

jŭvēncŭs, *and* ŭlŭs, i, m., *a young bullock.* Prōscīndĕ jŭvēncis, Virg. Syn. Bōs, taūrŭs, vitŭlŭs. Epith. Tĕnĕr, lāscivŭs, pĕtŭlāns, pĕtŭlcŭs, indŏmitŭs, fortis. V. Bos.

jŭvĕnēsco, is, *to grow young.* Lārgis jŭvĕnēscit hērbis, Hor. Syn. Adŏlēsco.

jŭvĕnilis, *and* ālis, ĕ, *youthful.* Jŭvĕnilibŭs ārmis, Virg.

jŭvĕnilitĕr, adv., *youthfully.* Jŭvĕnilitĕr irĕ sŏlēbăm, Ov.

jŭvĕnis, is, m. f., *a young man or woman.* Mŏx jŭvĕnēs, Pers. Syn. Pŭbĕr, adŏlēscēns, ĕphēbŭs. Epith. Adūltŭs, ălacris, audāx, fortis, ănimōsŭs, fērvidŭs, impăvidŭs, fōrmōsŭs, ēgrĕgiŭs, dŏcilis, indŏcilis. V. Adolescens.

jŭvĕnŏr, āris, *to play the young man.* Jŭvĕnēntŭr vērsibŭs, Hor.

jŭvĕntă, æ, f., *and* tūs, ūtis, f., *youth.* Mēmbră dĕcŏră jŭvĕntæ, Virg. Sævitquĕ jŭvēntūs, Id. Syn. Pūbērtās. Epith. Prīmă, prīmævă, virēns, viridis, vērnāns, flōrēns, rŏsĕă, tĕnĕră ; pūbēscēns, hilāris, jŭcŭndă, blāndă, mōllis, ămœnă, fērvidă, ignĕă, vălidă, gnāvă, gĕnĕrōsă, impăvidă, audāx, dŏcilis, facilis, mitis, pĕtŭlāns, pĕtŭlcă, ēffrænis, præcēps, indŏmită, insūnă, văgă, cæcă, incōnstāns, mōbilis, incaută, imprūdēns.

Jŭvēntās, ātis, f., *the goddess of youth.* Sinĕ tē Jŭvēntās, Hor.

jŭvo, ās, *to help.* Opibŭsquĕ jŭvābo, Virg. Syn. Adjŭvo, aŭxiliŏr. V. Auxilior.

jŭxtā, prep., *near.* Āră fŭit jŭxtā, Virg. Syn. Ad, prŏpĕ, prŏptĕr, sĕcŭndŭm.

Ixiŏn, ŏnis, m., *a king of Thessaly, who attempted to violate Juno, and was cast into hell by Jupiter for his presumption.* Tēntāre Ixiŏnis aŭsi, Tib. Ixiŏnă, Pirithŏŭmquĕ, Virg. Epith. Thēssălŭs, pērfidŭs, impiŭs, lāscivŭs.

Ixiŏniŭs, ă, ŭm, *of Ixion.* Atque Ixiŏnii, Virg.

L.

LĀBĀNS, āntis, *the pres. partic. of* labo. Sŭmmă lăbāntēs, Virg.

Lābdăcidēs, æ, m., *a descendant of Labdacus, Theban.* Hōrtātibŭs implēt Lābdăcidās, Stat.

Lābdăcŭs, i, m., *king of Thebes.* Lābdăcŭs hōc rēgnī, Stat.

lăbĕfăciŏ, fēci, făctŭm, *to shake.* Ēt lăbĕfāctă mŏvēns, Virg. Syn. Lăbĕfācto, cōrrŭmpo, distūrbo, quătiŏ, cōncŭtiŏ, diruŏ, ēvērto, disjiciŏ, pērfrīngo, dissōlvo, dēstrŭo, pērvērto, sŭbvērto.

lăbĕllŭm, ī, n., *a small lip.* Trīvīssĕ lăbĕllŭm, Virg. Syn. Lăbĭŭm.

Lăbĕo, ōnĭs, m., *a man's name.* Lăbĕōne īnsănĭŏr īntĕr, Hor.

Lăbĕrĭŭs, ĭī, m., *the author of mimes.* Ět Lăbĕrī mīmōs, Hor.

lābēs, ĭs, f., *stain, ruin.* Prīmă mălī lābēs, hīnc, Virg. Syn. Măcŭlă, nŏtă, sŏrdēs ; næ- vŭs ; dĕdĕcŭs, īnfāmĭă ; pēstĭs, cōntăgĭo, lŭēs ; ĕxĭtĭŭm, rŭīnă, clădēs. V. Macula.

Lăbīcŭm, ī, n., *a city of Latium.* Ārvă Lăbīcī, Sil.

Lăbīcī, ōrŭm, m. pl., *inhabitants of Labicum.* Pīctī scŭtă Lăbīcī, Virg.

lăbīlĭs, ĕ, *slippery.* Sī lābīlĭs ŏrbĭs, Lact. Syn. Cădūcŭs, flŭxŭs, lăbāns.

lăbĭŭm, ĭī, n., *a lip.* Īntĕr sīngŭltŭs, lăbīsquĕ trĕmēntĭbŭs, Sil. Syn. Labrŭm.

lābo, ās, *and* āsco, ĭs, *to totter.* Lăbăt ārĭĕtĕ crĕbrō, Virg. Syn. Văcīllo, nūto ; īn cāsŭm vērgo, cāsŭm mĭnŏr ; lābŏr, cŭrrŭo, cădo.

lābŏr, ĕrĭs, lāpsŭs sŭm, *to fall, slip.* Tēmpŏră lābūntŭr, Ov. Syn. Prōlābŏr, cădo, cōncĭdo, prōcĭdo, rŭo, cŏrrŭo, prōcŭmbo ; fāllŏr, ērro, dēcĭpĭŏr. V. Cado.

lābŏr *or* ōs, ōrĭs, m., *labour.* Lăbŏr āctŭs īn ōrbĕm, Virg. Syn. Ŏpŭs, ŏpĕră, sŭdŏr ; īncōmmŏdŭm ; cūră, dŏlŏr ; cōntēntĭo, cōnātŭs. Epith. Āssĭdŭŭs, ācĕr, dūrŭs, vĭgĭl, mŏlēstŭs, grăvĭs, pērtĭnāx, ānxĭŭs, īnsōmnĭs, pērvĭgĭl, sŏllĭcĭtŭs, lōngŭs, ăcĕrbŭs, rĭgĭdŭs, ærŭmnōsŭs, ŏpĕrōsŭs, Hērcŭlĕŭs, cōntĭnŭŭs, īndēfēssŭs, īrrĕquĭētŭs, nōn īntērmīssŭs, īmpĭgĕr, sōlērs, sēdŭlŭs, īngēns, īmmānĭs, īm- mēnsŭs, nĭmĭŭs, ūtĭlĭs, fēlīx, īnūtĭlĭs, vānŭs, īrrĭtŭs, īngrātŭs, stĕrĭlĭs, īnfēlīx ; pērdĭŭs, pērnōx. V. Laboro, finio.

lăbōrĭfĕr, ă, ŭm, *industrious.* Nămquĕ lăbōrĭfĕrī, Ov. Syn. Lăbōrĭōsŭs.

lăbōrĭōsŭs, ă, ŭm, *laborious.* Lăbōrĭōsī rēmĭgēs, (Iamb.) Hor. Syn. Dūrŭs ; lăbōrĭs pătĭēns, lăbōri āssŭĕtŭs, lăbōrĭbŭs īnvīctŭs. V. Laboro.

lăbōro, ās, *to work.* Lūnă lăbōrĕt ĕquīs, Prop. Syn. Ēlăbōro, ŏpĕrŏr ; nītŏr, cōnŏr, cōntēndo. V. Laboriosus, labor.

Labrōs, ī, m., *the name of a dog.* Ov.

labrŭm, ī, n., *a brim, a lip.* Lăbră mŏvĕt, Hor. Sæpĕ lăbrō călămōs, Lucr. Syn. Lăbĭŭm, lăbĕllŭm. Epith. Pūrpŭrĕŭm, tĕnĕrŭm, rŭbēns, rŏsĕŭm, tĕnēllŭm, suāvĕ, blāndŭm, dĕcōrŭm, fōrmōsŭm, āmbrŏsĭŭm, vīrgĭnĕŭm, fācūndŭm, dĭ- sērtŭm.

lābrūscă, æ, f., *wild vine.* Spārsīt lābrūscă răcēmīs, Virg. Epith. Sўlvēstrĭs, stĕrĭlĭs, vĭrēns, dēnsă.

lăbўrīnthæŭs, ă, ŭm, *belonging to a labyrinth.* Nĕ lăbўrīnthæīs, Catull. Syn. Lăbўrīnthĭācŭs.

Lăbўrīnthŭs, ī, m., *the Labyrinth.* Fērtŭr lăbўrīnthŭs īn āltă, Virg. Epith. Cūrvŭs, īrrĕmĕābĭlĭs, īnēxtrĭcābĭlĭs, fāllāx, cæcŭs, dŭbĭŭs, āncēps, īnflēxŭs, dīffĭcĭlĭs, āmbĭgŭŭs, mūltĭplēx, sēcrētŭs, īngĕnĭōsŭs, ŏblīquŭs, Dædălĕŭs, Crētēnsĭs.

lāc, lāctĭs, n., *milk.* Lāc ăsĭnæ, Ser. Epith. Cāndĭdŭm, suāvĕ, tĕpĭdŭm, dūlcĕ, cāndēns, nēctărĕŭm, grātŭm, tĕpēns, nĭvĕŭm, nŏvŭm, rĕcēns, pīnguĕ, pūrŭm, cōncrētŭm, prēssŭm, cŏāctŭm.

Lăcæně, æ, f., *a Spartan woman.* Făcĭēs īnvīsă Lăcænæ, Virg.

Lăcĕdæmōn, ŏnĭs, f., *the capital of Laconia.* Cūm Lăcĕdæmŏnă clāssĕ, Ov. Syn. Spārtă. Epith. Prīscă, clāră, sĕvĕră, pŏtēns.

Lăcĕdæmŏnĭī, ōrŭm, m. pl., *the Spartans.* Syn. Spārtānī, Tўndărĭdæ. V. Lacones.

Lăcĕdæmŏnĭŭs, ă, ŭm, *Lacedæmonian.* Lăcĕdæmŏnĭŭmquĕ Tărēntŭm, Ov.

lăcĕr, ră, rŭm, *torn.* Lăcĕr ūndĭquĕ mēmbrīs, Lucr. Syn. Lăcĕrātŭs, dīlăcĕrātŭs, scīssŭs, lănĭātŭs, dīlănĭātŭs, dīscērptŭs, cōnscīssŭs, lăcĕrŭs.

lăcĕrābĭlĭs, ĕ, *that can be torn.* Cōrpŭs lăcĕrābĭlĕ mōrbīs, Aus.

lăcērnă, æ, f., *a cloak.* Nūdă lăcērnā, Hor. Epith. Tўrĭă, pūrpŭrĕă, fūlgēns, pīnguĭs.

lăcērnātŭs, ă, ŭm, *cloaked.* Ipsĕ lăcērnātæ, Juv. Syn. Pænŭlātŭs.

lăcĕro, ās, *to rend.* Cūm lăcĕrāvīt Ĭtўn, Mart. Syn. Dīlăcĕro, dīscērpo, scīndo, dīscīndo, cōnscīndo, ābscīndo, lănĭo, dīlănĭo, sēco, dīssĕco, frāngo, rŭmpo, dīs- rŭmpo. V. Voro.

lăcĕrtōsŭs, ă, ŭm, *robust.* Dūră lăcērtōsī, Ov. Syn. Tŏrōsŭs, nērvōsŭs, rŏbūstŭs.

lăcērtŭs, ī, m., *the arm.* Vērsă lăcērtīs, Virg. Syn. Tŏrŭs, nērvī, brăchĭŭm ; rŏbŭr. Epith. Fōrtĭs, vălĭdŭs, tĕrĕs, nĭvĕŭs, mōllĭs, nērvōsŭs, rŏbūstŭs.

lăcērtŭs, ī, m., *and* tă, æ, f., *a lizard.* Tērgă lăcērtī, Virg. Mēnsūră lăcērta.

Ov. Epith. Vĭrĭdĭs, vērsĭcŏlŏr, ĕxĭlĭs, tĕnŭĭs, grăcĭlĭs, vĭrēns, măcŭlōsŭs, trĕpĭdŭs, nōxĭŭs, vĕnēnōsŭs.

lăcēssītŭs, ă, ŭm, *the pass. partic. of* laçesso. Sōlĕ lăcēssīta, Virg.

lăcēsso, ĭs, īvī, ĭī, *and* ssī, ītŭm, *to provoke, weary.* Vōcĕ lăcēssās, Virg. Syn. Irrīto, ĕxăspĕro, ĕxăcērbo, prōvŏco, āggrĕdĭŏr, ădŏrĭŏr, ōppūgno, pĕto, āppĕto, īnvādo.

Lăchĕsĭs, ĭs, f., *one of the Fates.* Ō dūrām Lăchĕsĭn, Ov. Epith. Immītĭs, fērrĕă, īnvĭdă, īmmānĭs, sĕvēră, trīstĭs, fĕrōx, rĭgĭdă, dīră. V. Parca.

Lăchnē, ēs, f., *the name of a dog.* Hĭrsūtăquĕ cōrpŏrĕ Lăchnē, Ov.

lăcīnĭă, æ, f., *the fold of a gown.* Sūmĕ lăcīnĭăm, Plaut. Syn. Fĭmbrĭă, rūgæ.

Lăcīnĭă, æ, f., *a surname of Juno.* Prætērquĕ Lăcīnĭă tēmplŏ, Ov.

lăcīnĭōsŭs, ă, ŭm, *full of plaits.* Nūdūs, lăcīnĭōsŭs, (Scaz.) Syn. Dīscīssŭs; rūgōsŭs.

Lăcīnĭŭs, ă, ŭm, *of the promontory Lacinium, where there was a temple of Juno.* Lăcīnĭă lĭttŏră, Virg.

Lăco *and* Lăcōn, ōnĭs, m., *a Lacedæmonian.* Rēgnătă Lăcōnī, Hor. Dē plēbĕ Lăcōnŭm, Stat. Syn. Œbălĭī, Thĕrāpnæī, Ămÿclæī, Tænărĭī.

Lăcōnĭă, æ, f., *a part of Peloponnesus.* Syn. Œbălĭă, Lăcĕdæmŏnĭă.

Lăcōnĭcŭs, ă, ŭm, *of Laconia.* Nēc Lăcōnĭcăs, Hor.

Lăcōnĭs, ĭdĭs, f., *of Laconia.* Mātrĕ Lăcōnĭdĕ nātī, Ov.

lacrÿmābĭlĭs, ĕ, *to be wept for.* Nīl lăcrÿmābĭlĕ cērnĭt, Ov. Syn. Flēbĭlĭs, lūgubrĭs.

lacrÿmæ, ārŭm, f. pl., *tears.* Ire ĭtĕrum īn lăcrÿmās, Virg. Syn. Flētŭs, lūctŭs, plōrātŭs, gūttæ. Epith. Mănāntēs, ēffūsæ, flŭēntēs, rōrāntēs, cădēntēs, trīstēs, ūdæ, ămāræ, hūmēntēs, mœstæ, mădĭdæ, tĕpēntēs, tĕpĭdæ, grāvēs, stīllāntēs, liquēntēs, fūnēstæ, ăcērbæ, āssĭdŭæ; sūpplĭcēs, pĭæ, fĭdēlēs; fāllācēs, dŏlōsæ, īnsĭdĭōsæ. V. Lacrymor, fletus.

lacrÿmŏr, ārĭs, *or* mo, ās, *to weep.* Dīscūnt lăcrÿmārĕ dĕcēntĕr, Ov. Syn. Illacrÿmo, flĕo, plōro, lūgĕo.

* lacrÿmōsē, adv., *lamentably.* Plin. V. Lugeo, fleo.

lacrÿmōsŭs, ă, ŭm, *full of tears.* Hīnc bēllūm lăcrÿmōsŭm, (Choriamb.) Hor. Syn. Lacrÿmāns; lacrÿmābĭlĭs.

lacrÿmŭlă, æ, f., *the dimin. of* lacryma. Gaŭdĭă lăcrÿmŭlīs, Catull. V. Lacrÿmæ.

lāctāns, āntĭs, *having milk.* Ăvĭdī lāctāntĭă nātī, Ov.

lāctēns, ēntĭs, *sucking, milky.* Lūctēntēs vĭtŭlī, Ov. Stĭpŭlā lāctēntĭă tūrgēnt, Virg.

lāctĕŭs, ă, ŭm, dimin. ĕŏlŭs, *milky.* Lāctĕă crīnēs, Virg. Syn. Cāndĭdŭs, cāndēns, ālbŭs, nĭvĕŭs.

lāctĭto, ās, *to feed with milk.* Lāctĭtĕt, ēdăm, Mart. V. Lac.

lācto, ās, *to suck, suckle.* Infāns lāctāvĭt, Aus.

lāctūcă, æ, f., *a lettuce.* Năm lāctūca īnnătăt, Hor. Epith. Frōndēns, sÿlvēstrĭs, vĭrĭdĭs, vĭrēns, mōllĭs.

lăcūnă, æ, f., *a ditch.* Sūdānt hūmōrĕ lăcūnæ, Virg. Syn. Fōssă. Epith. Vāstă, ūdă, īnūndāns, līmōsă, bĭbŭlă, ĭnērs, tĕpēns, crāssă, fœdă, pigră; ăquĭs, tĕpĭdo hūmōrĕ plēnă. V. Lacus.

lăcūnăr, ārĭs, n., *a fretted beam.* Spēctărĕ lăcūnăr, Juv. V. Laquear.

lăcūno, ās, *to ornament with fret-work.* Sūmmă lăcūnăbānt, Ov.

lăcŭs, ūs, m., *a lake.* Et lăcŭs æstīvĭs. Prop. Syn. Stăgnŭm, pălŭs. Epith. Līmōsŭs, prŏfūndŭs, căvŭs, āltŭs, īmŭs, pĭgĕr, sēgnĭs, tōrpēns, plăcĭdŭs, pīscōsŭs, stăgnāns, lēntŭs, vāstŭs, trānquīllŭs, sĭlēns, quĭētŭs, spătĭōsŭs, rĭgŭŭs, cœnōsŭs, īllīmĭs, vitrĕŭs, līmpĭdŭs. pērspĭcŭŭs, trānquīllŭs, hūmēns, cœrŭlĕŭs, lātŭs, gĕlĭdŭs, nĭtĭdŭs, flūmĭnĕŭs, ūlvōsŭs.

Lădōn, ōnĭs, m., *a river in Arcadia.* Plăcĭdūm Lădōnĭs ăd āmnĕm, Ov. Epith. Ărēnōsŭs, răpāx, Ăpōllĭnĕŭs, cāstŭs, Ărcădĭŭs.

læd
 o, læsī, læsŭm, *to hurt.* Cārmĭnĕ læsă mĕŏ, Mart. Syn. Ōffēndo, vĭŏlo, nŏcĕo, vŭlnĕro.

Lælāps, ăpĭs, m., *the name of a dog.* Cūm Lælăpĕ Thērōn, Ov.

Lælĭŭs, ĭī, m., *a friend of Scipio.* Săpĭēntĭă Lælī, Hor.

lænă, æ, f., *a kind of cloak.* Mūrĭcĕ lænă, Virg. V. Vestis, pallium.

Lāertēs, æ, m., *a king of Ithaca.* Lāertēsquĕ sĕnēx, Ov. Epith. Fōrtĭs.

Lāērtĭădēs, æ, m., *son of Laertes, Ulysses.* Vīm Lāērtĭădæ, Ov.

Lāērtĭŭs, ă, ŭm, *of Laertes.* Lāērtĭă rēgnă, Virg.

Læstrȳgŏnēs, ŭm, m. pl., *a nation of Italy.* Nōbīs Læstrȳgŏnĭs īmpĭă, Ov.
Epith. Dūrī, īncūltī, īmmānēs, fĕrōcēs, īmmītēs, sævī, bārbărī, crūdēlēs, sānguĭnĕī.

Læstrȳgŏnĭŭs, ă, ŭm, *of the Læstrygons.* Læstrȳgŏnĭă Bācchŭs, Hor.

lætābĭlĭs, ĕ, *gladsome.* Mĕŭm lætābĭlĕ fāctŭm, Ov. Syn. Lætŭs, jūcŭndŭs.

lætātŭs, ă, ŭm, *the part. of lætor.* Sŭm lætātŭs ĕūntĕm, Virg. Syn. Gaūdēns, ŏvāns.

lætĭfĭco, ās, *to make glad.* Lætĭfĭcāt māgnī, Lucan. Syn. Hĭlăro, ōblēcto, recrĕo, dēlēcto.

lætĭfĭcŭs, ă, ŭm, *making glad.* Lætĭfĭcōs nĕquĕăt, Lucr.

lætĭtĭă, æ, f., *joy.* Ādsīt lætĭtĭæ Bācchŭs, Virg. Syn. Gaūdĭŭm. Epith.
Blāndă, fēstīvă, fēstă. V. Gaudium.

lætŏr, ārĭs, *to rejoice.* Lætātŭr gĕmĭnā, Mart. Syn. Gaūdĕo, ēxūlto. V.
Gaudeo.

lætŭs, ă, ŭm, *joyful.* Quī lætĭŏr ēssĕt, Virg. Syn. Hĭlărĭs, ălăcĕr, gaūdēns, ŏvāns. V. Hilaris, gaudens.

lœvă, æ, f., *the left hand.* Dēxtrā lævăquĕ Sĕrēstŭm, Virg. Syn. Sĭnīstră.

lævīgo *and* vo, ās, *to smooth.* Syn. Pŏlĭo, pērpŏlĭo, cōmplāno, æquo, ēxæquo.

lævĭs, ĕ, *smooth.* Ēt lævĭă pōcŭlă sērpēns, Virg. Syn. Pŏlītŭs; nĭtĭdŭs; plānŭs, æquŭs.

lævŭs, ă, ŭm, *left; unlucky.* Bādīt ĭtēr lævŭm, Virg. Syn. Sĭnīstĕr; īnfaūstŭs, īnfēlīx, mălŭs.

lăgănŭm, ī, n., *a sort of pastry.* Lăgănīquĕ cătīnŭm, Hor.

lăgēnă, *and* gŭncŭlă (*the dimin.*), æ, f., *a bottle.* Nōn īnsānīrĕ lăgēnæ, Hor.
Syn. Amphŏră. Epith. Căpāx, pătŭlă, spūmāns, căvă, plēnă, fīctĭlĭs, frăgĭlĭs, dūlcĭs.

lăgĕōs, ī, f., *a kind of raisin.* Tĕnŭīsquĕ lăgĕōs, Virg.

lăgŏĭs, ĭdĭs, f., *a fish.* Pĕrĕgrīnā jŭvărĕ lăgŏĭs, Hor.

Lăĭădēs, æ, m., *the son of Laius, Œdipus.* Carmĭnā Lăĭădēs, Ov.

Lăĭs, ĭdĭs, f., *a celebrated courtesan.* Lăĭs ămātă vĭrĭs, Ov.

Lăĭŭs, ĭī, m., *the son of Labdacus, killed by his son Œdipus.* Lăĭŭs ēxtīnctŭm, Stat.

Lălăgē, ēs, f., *a woman's name.* Lălăgēn ămābo, Hor.

lălĭsĭo, ōnĭs, m., *a young wild ass.* Sōlăquĕ lălĭsĭŏ mātrĕ, Mart.

lăllo, ās, *to sing lullaby.* Lāllărĕ rĕcūsās, Pers.

lāllŭs, ī, m., *or* ŭm, ī, n., *a lullaby.* Lāllīquĕ sŏmnĭfĕrōs, Aus.

lāmă, æ, f., *a ditch.* Flūmĭnă, lāmās, Hor.

lāmbo, bī, *to lick.* Sĭbĭlă lāmbēbānt, Virg. Syn. Āllāmbo, līngo.

lāmēntābĭlĭs, ĕ, *lamentable.* Ēt lāmēntābĭlĕ rēgnŭm, Virg. Syn. Lacrȳmābĭlĭs, lūgēndŭs, lūgŭbrĭs, trīstĭs, fūnēstŭs.

lāmēntātĭo, ōnĭs, f., tātŭs, ŭs, m., *and* mēntŭm, ī, n., *lamentation.* Vāstă lāmēntātĭo, (Iamb.) Lāmēntĭs gĕmĭtūquĕ, Virg. Syn. Lūctŭs, flētŭs, plānctŭs, quēstŭs. V. Fletus, queror.

lāmēntŏr, ārĭs, *to lament.* Cŭm lāmēntāmŭr, Hor. Syn. Quĕrŏr, plōro, lūgĕo, flĕo, gĕmo, dŏlĕo. V. Fleo.

Lămĭă, æ, f., *a hag.* Neū prānsæ Lămĭæ, Hor. Epith. Fĕră, lāscīvă.

lămĭnă *and* mnă, æ, f., *a plate.* Lămĭnă mōllĭs ădhūc, Ov. Lāmnā cāndēntĕ, Hor.

lāmpăs, ădĭs, f., *a lamp.* Phœbēæ lāmpădĭs īnstăr, Virg. Syn. Lȳchnŭs, lūcērnă, făx, tædă, lūmĕn, tēstă. Epith. Clāră, cŏrŭscă, rădĭāns, lūcēns, nĭtĭdă, pēndŭlă, pēndēns, nōctūrnă, ārdēns, īgnĭfĕră, īgnĕă, trĕmŭlă, fūmāns, pīnguĭs, rŭtĭlāns, fūmĭfĕră, rŭtĭlă, cāndēns, splēndēns, călēns, nĭtēns, fūlgĭdă. V. Fax.

Lāmpĕtĭē, ēs, f., *a daughter of the Sun.* Fīlĭă Lāmpĕtĭē, Prop.

Lāmpsăcŭs, ī, m., *a city of Asia Minor.* Lāmpsăcĕ tūtă dĕo, Ov.

lāmpȳrĭs, ĭdĭs, f., *a glow-worm.* Mĭcānt lāmpȳrĭdĕs, ălĭs, Mant.

Lāmŭs, ī, m., *a king of the Læstrygons.* Indĕ Lămī vĕtĕrĕm, Ov.

lămȳrŭs, ī, m., *a sort of fish.* Lămȳrūsquĕ smărīsquĕ, Ov.

lānă, æ, f., *wool.* Lānăquĕ mōllĭs, Ov. Syn. Vēllŭs. Epith. Cāndĭdă,

nĭvĕă, bĭbŭlă, ālbă, dīscŏlŏr, măcŭlōsă, pŭlchră, tĕnŭĭs, tīnctă, tĕxtĭlĭs, dīvĕs, Āttălĭcă.
lāncĕă, æ, f., *a lance.* Lāncĕă cōnsĕquĭtŭr, Virg. SYN. Hāstă, hāstīlĕ, jăcŭlŭm. V. Hasta.
lāncĭno, ās, *to tear.* Quĭdquĭd lāncĭnāmŭr, nōn dŏlĕt, (Iamb.) Prud. SYN. Stĭmŭlo, pūngo. V. Pungo.
lānĕŭs, ă, ŭm, *woolly.* Lānĕŭs Eūgănĕī, Mart. SYN. Vīllōsŭs.
lānguĕo, ēs, *and* guēsco, ĭs, *to languish.* Lānguēbānt cōrpŏră mōrbō, Virg. Lānguēscĭt mŏrĭēns, Virg. SYN. Tōrpĕo, tōrpēsco, mārcēsco.
lānguĭdŭs, *dimin.* dŭlŭs, ă, ŭm, *faint.* Lānguĭdă prēssĭt, Virg. SYN. Lānguēns, tōrpēns, tārdŭs, īnfīrmŭs, dēbĭlĭs, dēbĭlĭtātŭs, ægĕr, mōrbĭdŭs, īnvălĭdŭs. V. Infirmus, æger.
lānguŏr, ōrĭs, m., *faintness.* Lānguōrĕ sŏlūtŭm, Ov. SYN. Tōrpŏr, vĕtērnŭs, mōrbŭs, ĭnērtĭă, sĕgnĭtĭēs, ĭgnāvĭă, sōcōrdĭă, pigrĭtĭēs. EPITH. Pĭgĕr, grăvĭs, lēntŭs, sēgnĭs, ăcērbŭs, frĭgĭdŭs, lēthĭfĕr, nōxĭŭs, trīstĭs.
lānĭātŭs, ūs, m., *a tearing.* Mēmbră lānĭātū ēffĕro, (Iamb.) Sen.
lānĭcĭŭm, ĭī, n., *wool-trade.* Lānĭcĭŭm cūræ, Virg. V. Lanificium.
lānĭēnă, æ, f., *flesh-shambles.* Lānĭēnă quāndo, (Iamb.) Prud. EPITH. Fĕră, sævă, crūdēlĭs.
lānĭfĭcĭŭm, ĭī, n., *working of wool.* SYN. Lānĭcĭŭm.
lānĭfĭcŭs, ă, ŭm, *who works wool.* Sī mĭhĭ lānĭfĭcæ, Mart.
lānĭgĕr, ă, ŭm, *bearing wool.* Lānĭgĕrōs ăgĭtărĕ grĕgēs, Virg. SYN. Lānĭfĕr.
lānĭo, ās, *to tear away.* Dīscīssōs nūdīs lānĭābānt, Virg. SYN. Lăcĕro, dīlăcĕro, dīscērpo, dīssĕco. V. Lacero.
lănĭo, ōnĭs, *and* ŭs, ī, m., *a butcher.* Crūdēlīs lănĭŭs, Mart.
lănīstă, æ, m., *a fencing-master.* Jŭvĕnēsquĕ lănīstæ, Juv. EPITH. Pĕrītŭs, sōlērs.
lānūgo, ĭnĭs, f., *soft hairs.* Sōrdēnt lānūgĭnĕ vŭltŭs, Mart. EPITH. Mōllĭs, tĕnŭĭs, rŏsĕă, rīdēns. V. Juvenis, adolescens.
Lānŭvīnŭs, ă, ŭm, *of Lanuvium.* Lŭpă Lānŭvīnŏ, Hor.
Lānŭvĭŭm, ĭī, n., *a city of Latium.* Lānŭvĭŭmquĕ mĕŭm, Ov.
lānx, lāncĭs, f., *a dish.* Lāncĭbŭs ārūs, Virg. SYN. Stătĕră, trŭtĭnă, lībră, bīlānx; scŭtŭlă, scŭtēllă, cătīnŭs, părōpsĭs, pătĭnă. EPITH. Æquă, jūstă, cērtă, pāndă, rĕpāndă, æquālĭs, pēndŭlă, pēndēns.
Lāŏcŏōn, ōntĭs, m., *a son of Priam.* Lāŏcŏōn ārdēns, Virg.
Lāŏdămĭă, æ, f., *the daughter of Acastus; died in embracing the shadow of her husband.* Lāŏdămĭă sīnŭs, Ov.
Lāŏdĭcē, ēs, f., *the daughter of Priam.* Flāvăquĕ Lāŏdĭcē, Ov.
Lāŏmĕdŏn, ōntĭs, m., *the king of Troy.* Lāŏmĕdōntĭs ŏpēs, Prop. SYN. Trōjæ cōndĭtŏr, Prĭămī pătĕr. EPITH. Īdæŭs, pērjūrŭs, fraudŭlēntŭs, īmpĭŭs, sacrĭlĕgŭs, īnfīdŭs.
Lāŏmĕdōntēŭs, *and* tĭŭs, ă, ŭm, *of Laomedon, Trojan.* Lāŏmĕdōntēæ lŭĭmŭs, Virg. Lāŏmĕdōntĭŭs hĕrōs, Id.
Lāŏmĕdōntĭădēs, æ, m., *the son or descendant of Laomedon.* Lāŏmĕdōntĭădēm Prĭāmŭm, Virg.
lăpăthŭs, ī, m., *or* ŭm, ī, n., *a sort of sorrel.* Lăpăthī, grăvĭs hērbă, Hor.
|| lăpĭdārĭŭs, ă, ŭm, *stony.* Plaut. SYN. Lăpĭdōsŭs.
|| lăpĭdĕŭs, ă, ŭm, *of stone.* Plaut. SYN. Sāxĕŭs.
|| lăpĭdo, ās, *to kill with stones.* Ōlīm lăpĭdātŭs Āthēnīs, Aus.
lăpĭdōsŭs, ă, ŭm, *stony.* Prūnīs lăpĭdōsă rŭbēscĕrĕ cōrnă, Virg. SYN. Sāxōsŭs, petrōsŭs, scrūpĕŭs.
lăpīllŭs, ī, m., *a small stone.* Sæpĕ lăpīllōs, Virg. SYN. Cālcŭlŭs, scrūpŭs, gĕmmă. EPITH. Vĭrĭdĭs, tĕrēs, pīctŭs, pĕregrīnŭs, Īndĭcŭs, Eōŭs, pērlūcēns, cŏlōrātŭs, nĭtĭdŭs, nĭtēns, prĕtĭōsŭs, lūcēns. V. Gemma.
lăpĭs, ĭdĭs, m., *a stone.* Jām lăpĭs īstĕ mĭnās, Mart. SYN. Sāxŭm, sĭlēx. EPITH. Grăvĭs, dūrŭs, rŭdĭs, āspĕr, mūcōsŭs, ădēsŭs, mōntānŭs, īnfōrmĭs, rĭgĭdŭs, scăbĕr.
Lăpĭthæ, ārŭm, m. pl., *a people of Thessaly.* Īllīsĭt frōntī Lăpĭthæ, Ov. EPITH. Cēntaurēī, sēmĭfĕrī, sævī, sўlvēstrēs, Pĕlēthrōnĭī; trŭcēs, īmmānēs, fĕrōcēs, dīrī, mōntĭvăgī.
Lăpĭthæŭs, *and* ēĭŭs, ă, ŭm, *of the Lapithæ.* Lăpĭthææ glōrĭă gēntĭs, Ov. Lăpĭthēĭă mŏvĭt Præēĭă, Id.

lāppă, æ, f, *a bur.* Lūppæquĕ trībŭlīque, Virg. Epitii. Tĕnāx, rĭgĭdă, āspĕră, vĭrĭdĭs, vĭrēns.

lāpso, ās, *to slip.* Mūltŏ lāpsāntēm sānguĭiuĕ, Virg.

lāpsŭs, ūs, m., *a fall.* Āt gĕmĭiuĭ lāpsū, Virg. Syn. Cāsŭs, īllūpsŭs, ūllāpsŭs.

lăquĕārĕ *or* ăr, ārĭs, n., *a roof.* Fĕrīt lăquĕārĭă tēctĭ, Virg. Syn. Lăcūnăr, lăquĕārĭŭm, tăbŭlātŭm. Epitii. Pīctŭm, cælātŭm, aūrātŭm, căvŭm, fūlgēns, mĭcāns, splēndĭdŭm, mārmŏrĕŭm, măgnĭfĭcŭm, cŏrūscāns, gēmmĭfĕrŭm, cēlsŭm, āltŭm, āmplŭm.

lăquĕātŭs, ă, ŭm, *fretted.* Lăquĕātă cīrcūm tēctă, Hor.

lăquĕo, ās, *to take in a net.* Dēxtrī lăquĕāvĕrĭt ērrŏr. Syn. Illăquĕo, īrrētĭo.

lăquĕŭs, ī, m., *a net.* Ēt lăquĕĭs, cāptărĕ, Virg. Syn. Vīncŭlŭm, rētĕ; dŏlŭs. V. Strangulo.

lārdŭm, ī, n., *bacon.* Sēmēsăquĕ lārdī frūstă, Hor.

Lărēs, ĭŭm, m. pl., *the household gods.* Pătrīī sērvātĕ Lărĕs, Tibull. Syn. Pĕnātēs, dŏmŭs, fŏcŭs. Epitii. Sācrī, fĭdēlēs, fīdī, cārī, bĕnīgnī, sānctī, vĕnĕrāndī, vĕrēndī. V. Domus.

lārgē, *or* ĭtĕr, adv., *abundantly.* Lārgē rĕpōnēns, Hor. Lārgĭtĕr ēt mŏrbī, Lucr. Syn. Ūbērtĭm, cŏpĭōsē.

lārgĭfĭcŭs, ă, ŭm, *abundant.* Lārgĭfĭcă stĭpĕ dītāntēs, Lucr.

lārgĭflŭŭs, ă, ŭm, *flowing copiously.* Lārgĭflŭŭm fōntĕm, Lucr.

lārgĭŏr, ĭrĭs, *to bestow.* Mātūrōs lārgīmŭr hŏnōrēs, Hor. Syn. Dŏ, dōno, īmpērtĭo, īmpērtĭŏr, dīstrĭbŭo.

lārgĭtĭo, ōnĭs, f., *a largess.* Jām tŭm lārgītĭŏ pūră, Vict. Syn. Lībĕrālĭtās, lārgă mănŭs.

lārgītŏr, ōrĭs, m., *one who gives lavishly.* Lārgītŏr ŏpŭm, Stat. Syn. Lārgŭs, lībĕrālĭs.

lārgŭs, ă, ŭm, *abundant.* Lārgŭs ŏpum, Virg. Syn. Āmplŭs, lātŭs; lībĕrālĭs; dīvĕs.

Lără, æ, f., *a nymph of the Tiber.* Nāĭs Lără nōmĭnĕ, Ov.

Lărīdēs, æ, m., *the name of a warrior.* Daŭcĭă Lărīdĕ, Virg.

Lărīnŭs, ă, ŭm, *and* nās, ātĭs, *of Larinum, a city on the confines of Apulia.* Lărīnăquĕ vīrgo, Virg. Lărīnās āccŏlă pōntī, Sil.

Lărīssă, æ, f., *a town in Thessaly.* Nēc tăm Lărīssæ, Hor. Epith. Fōrtĭs, pŏtēns, nōbĭlĭs, īnclўtă.

Lărīssæŭs, ă, ŭm, *of Larissa.* Nēc Lărīssæŭs Ăchīllēs, Virg.

Lărĭŭs, ĭī, m., *a lake in upper Italy.* Tĕ, Lārī māxĭmĕ, Virg.

lărīx, ĭcĭs, f., *a larch-tree.* Ēt lărĭcēs, fūmō, Lucr. Epith. Dūră, lōngævă, pĕrēnnĭs.

lārvă, æ, f., *a mask, a ghost.* Nīl īllī lārvā, Hor. Syn. Pērsōnă. Epith. Fāllāx, mēndāx, īnsĭdĭōsă, fālsă, prŏcāx, dēfōrmĭs, hōrrĭdă, dŏlōsă, tērrĭfĭcă, lūdicră, vānă, ŭmbrātĭlĭs, īnānĭs. V. Spectra, manes.

lārvālĭs, ĕ, *ghostly.* Lārvālĭbŭs ēxŭĭt ārtŭs, Arat. Syn. Fīctŭs, mēntītŭs, fālsŭs.

lăsănŭm, ī, n., *a chamber-pot.* Pŭĕrī lăsănŭm pōrtāntēs, Hor.

lāscīvĭă, æ, f., *wantonness.* Lāscīvĭă lætă, Lucr. Syn. Lĭbīdo.

lāscīvĭo, īs, īī, *to sport.* Lāscīvītquĕ fūgă, Ov. Syn. Lāscīve ēxūlto; lūxŭrĭo.

lāscīvŭs, ă, ŭm, *frolicsome.* Lūxŭrĭăm lāscīvŭs hăbĕt, Arat. Syn. Pĕtŭlāns, prŏcāx, sălāx, mōllĭs, lūxŭrĭōsŭs, lĭbīdĭnōsŭs. V. Libidinosus.

lăsĕr, ĕrĭs, n., *a species of gum.* Ēt lăsĕr ālgēns, Marc.

lāssĭtūdo, ĭnĭs, f., *weariness.* Căvĕ lāssĭtŭdo, (Iamb.) Syn. Dēbĭlĭtās, lānguŏr.

lāsso, ās, *to tire, fatigue.* Lāssāvĭmŭs ārtŭs, Ov.

lāssŭs, *and* ātŭs, ă, ŭm, *fatigued.* Lāssōvĕ păpāvĕră cōllō, Virg. In mărĕ lāssātĭs, Ov. Syn. Fătīgātŭs, fēssŭs, dēfēssŭs.

lătĕbră, æ, f., *a hiding-place.* Tŭm lătĕbrās ănĭmœ, Virg. Præbērĕ lătĕbrās, Virg. Syn. Lătĭbŭlŭm, căvērnă, spĕcŭs, āntrŭm, spēlūncă, spēlæŭm. Epith. Tēctă, ōbscūră, ābdĭtă, rĕcōndĭtă, ābscōndĭtă, lātēns, cālīgāns, rĕmōtă, sĭlēns, īmă, squālĭdă, ēffōssă, dēmīssă, cæcă, sāxōsă, tūrpĭs, vīlĭs, ōccūltă, nĭgră, căvă, ātră, īrrĕmĕābĭlĭs. V. Specus.

lătĕbrōsŭs, ă, ŭm, *full of coverts.* Dūlcĕs lătĕbrōso īn pūmĭcĕ nīdī, Virg. Syn. Ōbscūrŭs, tĕnĕbrōsŭs, cæcŭs, lătēns, ōccūltŭs. V. Obscurus.

lătĕo, ŭī, *to be concealed.* Nēc lătŭĕrĕ dŏlī, Virg. Syn. Lătēsco, dēlĭtēsco, lătĭto, ābscōndŏr, ābdŏr, ōccūltŏr.

lătĕr, ĕrĭs, m., *a brick.* Cōnstrīngŭnt īgnī lătĕrēs, Vict. Epitii. Cōctŭs, dūrŭs, dūrātŭs.

lātĕrnă, æ, f., *a lantern.* Dūx lātĕrnă vĭæ, Mart. Syn. Făx, lўchnŭs. Epith. Nŏctūrnă, Ignĭfĕră. V. Fax.

lătĕx, ĭcĭs, m., *liquor.* Sēcūrōs lătĭcēs, Virg. Syn. Hūmŏr, liquŏr, ăquă. V. Aqua, fons.

Lătĭālĭs, ĕ, *of Latium.* Lătĭūlĭs hăbēnās, Ov.

lătĭbŭlŭm, ī, n., *a lurking-place.* Intĕr lătĭbŭlă, (Iamb.) V. Latebra.

Lătīnē, adv., *in Latin.* Nōn dīctă Lătīnē, Ov.

Lătīnŭs, ă, ŭm, *Latin.* Ārvă Lătīnŭs, Virg. Syn. Lătĭŭs, Aŭsŏnĭŭs, Itălŭs.

Lătīnŭs, ī, m., *the king of Latium.* Ipsĕ Lătīnŭs, Virg.

lătīto, ās, *the frequent. of* lateo. Fŭlvō lătĭtārĕt ĭn aŭrō, Pen. Syn. Lătĕo, dēlĭtēsco.

Lătĭŭm, ĭī, n., *a part of Italy.* Dīctă quŏque ēst Lătĭŭm, Ov. Epith. Hēspĕrĭŭm, fŏrtĕ, āntīquŭm, agrēstĕ, pūlchrŭm, nōbĭlĕ, īnclўtŭm.

Lătĭŭs, ă, ŭm, *of Latium.* Lătĭōs Ēvāndĕr ĭn āgrōs, Ov. V. Latinus.

Lătmĭŭs, ă, ŭm, *of mount Latmos.* Lātmĭŭs hērōs, Ov.

Lătōĭs, ĭdĭs, *and* tōnĭă, æ, f., *Diana.* Sævæ Lătōĭdĭs īrăm, Ov. Nĕmŏrŭm Lătōnĭă cūstōs, Virg.

Lătōĭŭs, ă, ŭm, *of Latona, of Apollo.* Lătōĭă vēstrō, Ov.

Lătōnă, æ, f., *the mother of Apollo and Diana.* Lătōnæ, tăcĭtŭm, Virg. Syn. Tītānĭs, Tītānĭă.

Lătōnĭgĕnă, æ, m. f., *born of Latona.* Lătōnĭgĕnīsquĕ dŭōbŭs, Ov.

Lătōnĭŭs, ŏĭŭs, *and* ŏŭs, ă, ŭm, *of Latona.* Lătōnĭă prōlēs, Ov. Nēc stīrps Lătōĭă vēstrō, Ov. Lătōŭs ărūndĭnĕ vīctŭm, Ov.

lătŏr, ōrĭs, m., *a bearer.* Lătōrĕm frūstră, Mant. V. Fero.

lātrātŏr, ōrĭs, m., *a barker.* Cēssānt, lātrātōrēsquĕ Mŏlōssī, Mart. Syn. Lātrāns.

lātrātŭs, ūs, m., *a barking.* Ēt lātrātĭbŭs īnstăt, Virg. Epith. Ăcūtŭs, cānōrŭs, raŭcŭs, hŏrrĭbĭlĭs, vĭgĭl, tērrĭbĭlĭs, īngēns, clārŭs, sævŭs, hŏrrĭsŏnŭs.

Lătreŭs, ĕī *or* eī, m., *one of the centaurs.* Mēmbrĭs ēt cōrpŏrĕ Lātreŭs, Ov.

lătrīnă, æ, f., *a privy.* Vŏmĭt lātrīnă clōācĭs, Claud. Epith. Fœdă, tūrpĭs, ĭmmūndă, ŏlēns, ŏlĭdă.

lātro, ās, *to bark.* Pēllēm lātrāvĭt ĭn aŭlă, Hor. Syn. Ēdo, mītto lātrātŭm.

lătro, ōnĭs, m., *a robber.* Dē nŏctĕ lătrōnēs, Hor. Syn. Fūr, prædo. Epith. Răpāx, ārmātŭs, vĭgĭl, īnsĭdĭōsŭs. V. Fur.

latrōcĭnĭŭm, ĭī, n., *a robbery.* Fūrtă lătrōcĭnĭĭs, Hor. Syn. Fūrtŭm, răpīnă, prædă. V. Furtum.

latrōcĭnŏr, ārĭs, *to plunder.* Plaut. V. Furor, prædor.

lātŭs, ă, ŭm, *broad.* Nēc lātĭs aŭdāx, Virg. Syn. Amplŭs, spătĭōsŭs, pătŭlŭs.

lătŭs, ĕrĭs, n., *a side.* Impŭlĭt ĭn lătŭs, āc, Virg. Syn. Cōstæ. Epith. Dēxtrŭm, sĭnīstrŭm, lævŭm, mŏllĕ, tĕnĕrŭm.

lăvācrŭm, ī, n., *a bath.* Splēndĕrĕ lăvācrĭs, Claud. V. Balneum.

laŭdābĭlĭs, ē, *commendable.* Fĭĕrĕt laŭdābĭlĕ cārmĕn, Hor. Syn. Laŭdāndŭs, hŏnōrāndŭs, cŏlēndŭs, cĕlebrāndŭs, mĕmŏrābĭlĭs, ēgrĕgĭŭs, īllūstrĭs.

laŭdātŏr, ōrĭs, m., *and* trīx, ĭcĭs, f., *a commander.* Plūs laŭdātŏrĕ mŏvētŭr, Hor. Laŭdātrīx Vĕnŭs ēst, Ov. Syn. Laŭdūm præco. Epith. Ingĕnĭōsŭs, pĕrītŭs, dōctŭs, īndūstrĭŭs, īnsĭgnĭs, cĕlĕbĕr, īllūstrĭs.

laŭdo, ās, *to praise.* Pācĕm laŭdātĕ sĕdēntēs, Virg. Syn. Cĕlebro, prædīco, ās.

Lăvērnă, æ, f., *the goddess of robbers.* Pŭlchră Lăvērnă, Hor

Lavīnĭă, æ, f., *the daughter of Latinus.* Dūcēndă Lăvīnĭă Teŭcrĭs, Virg. Sērŭm Lăvīnĭă cōnjŭx, Id.

Lavīnĭŭm, *and* Lavīnŭm, ī, n., *a city of Latium founded by Æneas.* Prōmīssă Lăvīnī, Virg. Lăvīnĭūmquĕ mĕŭm, Ov.

Lavīnĭŭs, *and* Lavīnŭs, ă, ŭm, *of Lavinium.* Lăvīnĭă rēspĭcĭt ārvă, Virg. Lăvīnăquĕ vēnĭt Lĭttŏră, Id.

lăvo, lāvī, lăvātŭm, lōtŭm, laŭtŭm, *to bathe.* Lŭdō, lăvŏ, cœno, Mart. Syn. Ablŭo. V. Abluo.

laŭrĕă, *and* cŏlă, æ, f., *a garland of laurel.* Laŭrĕă pāndĭt, Prop. Tēmpŏră laŭrĕŏlă, Sev.

Laŭrēns, ēntĭs, *of Laurentum.* Laŭrēntem āttīngĕrĕ Tībrĭm, Virg.

Laŭrēntālĭă, ōrŭm, *a festival in honour of Laurentia.* Laŭrēntālĭă dīcăm Ov.

Laŭrēntĭă, æ, f., *the nurse of Romulus.* Laŭrēntĭă, gēntĭs, Ov.

Laŭrēntīnŭs, *and* tīŭs, ă, ŭm, *of Laurentum.* Pălŭs Laŭrēntīă, Virg.

laŭrĕŭs, *or* īnŭs, ă, ŭm, *of laurel.* Laŭrĕă sĕrtă, Ov.

laŭrĭcŏmŭs, ă, ŭm, *shaded with laurels.* Laŭrĭcŏmōs ūt sī, Lucr. SYN. Laŭrĭgĕr, laŭrō cŏmāns.

laŭrĭfĕr, *and* gĕr, ă, ŭm, *wearing laurels.* Laŭrĭfĕrōs nŭllō, Lucan. Cūm tū laŭrĭgĕrīs, Mart.

laŭrŭs, ī *and* ūs, f., *a laurel tree.* Laŭrŭs ădŭstă sŏnō, Ov. EPITH. Vīrĭdĭs, vīrēns, vīrĭdāns, tĕnĕră, ŏpācă, rĕdŏlēns, frŏndōsă, ŏdōră, ŏdōrātă, frŏndēns vīrēscēns, cŏmāns, pătŭlă, cāstă, īnnŭbă, Phœbĕă, Ăpŏllĭnĕă, Dēlphĭcă, Pār-nāssīă, Āŏnīă, Pĭĕrĭă; sacră, vĭctrīx, trĭŭmphālĭs, fātĭdĭcă, vēntūrī præscĭă.

laŭs, aŭdĭs, f., *praise.* Laŭdĭbŭs īmmŏdĭcīs, Mart. SYN. Glōrīă, hŏnŏr, dĕcŭs, fāmă, nōmĕn, præcōnĭŭm, ēncōmĭŭm, laŭdātĭo. EPITH. Māgnĭfĭcă, illŭstrĭs, īnsĭgnĭs, sŭpērbă, pĕrēnnĭs, ætērnă, īmmŏrtālĭs, īngēns, splēndĭdă.

Laŭsŭs, ī, m., *son of Mezentius.* Laŭsŭs ĕquŭm dŏmĭtŏr, Virg.

* laŭtĭtĭă, æ, f., *daintiness.* Cic. SYN. Cŭltŭs, splēndŏr.

laŭtŭs, ă, ŭm, *dainty.* Ēt laŭtīs mūgīrĕ cărīnīs, Luc. SYN. Splēndĭdŭs, cōncīn-nŭs, pŭlchĕr, ēxcŭltŭs, māgnĭfĭcŭs, dīvĕs, ŏpŭlēntŭs.

lāxo, ās, *to loosen.* Quĭēs lāxăvĕrăt ārtŭs, Virg. SYN. Rĕlāxo, rĕmītto; dīlāto, ēxtēndo, dīdūco, prŏdūco, prōtrăho.

lāxŭs, ă, ŭm, *loose.* Ēt lāxăs scīrĕt, Virg.

lĕă, *and* ænă, æ, f., *a lioness.* Fŭlvā cērvīcĕ lĕænă, Virg. EPITH. Tōrvă, gĕnĕ-rōsă, fĕră, Gētŭlă, Lĭbўcă, īrātă, fŭlvă, sævă, aŭdāx, fĕrōx. V. Leo.

Lĕāndĕr, *and* drŭs, drī, m., *the lover of Hero.* Quŏndăm, Lĕāndrĕ, fŭīssĕt, Ov. EPITH. Ăbўdēnŭs, aŭdāx, naŭfrăgŭs, pŭlchĕr, fŏrmōsŭs, dĕcŏrŭs, īnfēlīx, mĭsĕr.

Lĕārchēŭs, ă, ŭm, *of Learchus.* Mœstă Lĕārchēăs, Ov.

Lĕārchŭs, ī, m., *the son of Athamas, killed by his father.* Pārvă Lĕārchŭm, Ov. EPITH. Pārvŭs, īnfēlīx.

Lĕbēdŭs, ī, f., *a city of Ionia.* Ăn Lĕbēdŭm, Hor.

lĕbēs, ētĭs, m., *a cauldron.* Ēx ærĕ lĕbētēs, Ov. SYN. Cācăbŭs, ōllă, ăhēnŭm. EPITH. Cūrvŭs, cōncăvŭs, īngēns. V. Ahenum.

lēctĭcă, (*dimin.* cŭlă,) æ, f., *a litter.* Lēctĭcă, cĭnĭflōnēs, Hor. Lēctĭcŭlă sŏmnōs, Mart. EPITH. Fŭlgēns, lĕvĭs.

lēctĭcărĭŏlă, æ, f., *a common slut.* Lēctĭcārĭŏla ēst, Mart.

lēctĭto, ās, *the frequent. of* lego. Lēctĭtārĕ īn Ălpĭbŭs, (Iamb.) SYN. Ēvŏlvo, pērlĕgo.

lēctŏr, ōrĭs, m., *a reader.* Lēctōrĕm dēlēctāndō, Hor. EPITH. Stŭdĭōsŭs, vĭgĭl, vĭgĭlāns, dōctŭs, īngĕnŭŭs.

lēctŭlŭs, ī, m., *a small bed.* Lēctŭlŭs ŭndæ, Mart. SYN. Grăbātŭs.

lēctŭs, ī, m., *a bed.* Frīgĭdă lēctō, Ov. SYN. Thălămŭs, tŏrŭs, strātŭm, cŭbīlĕ, grăbātŭs. EPITH. Mōllĭs, quĭētŭs, plăcĭdŭs, grătŭs, sŏcĭŭs, sŏcĭālĭs, jŭgālĭs, sēgnĭs, sŏpōrĭfĕr, ĭnērs, cāstŭs, pŭdĭcŭs, gĕnĭālĭs, ignāvŭs, nōctŭrnŭs, plŭmĕŭs, ĕbŭrnŭs. V. Surgo.

Lēdă, æ, *and* dē, ēs, f., *the wife of Tyndarus, loved by Jupiter.* Fēcĭt ŏlōrīnĭs Lēdăm, Ov. Quālĭs ĕrăt Lēdē, Id. EPITH. Pūlchră, fœcŭndă, fŏrmōsă, cāndĭdă.

Lēdæŭs, ă, ŭm, *of Leda.* Lēdæāmque Hĕlĕnăm, Virg.

lēgālĭs, ĕ, *lawful.* Tăbŭlĭs lēgālĭbŭs īndĭtă, Mamerc.

lēgātŭm, ī, n., *a legacy.* Lēgātum ōmnĕ căpĭt, Juv.

lēgātŭs, ī, m., *an ambassador.* Lēgātī rēspōnsă fĕrŭnt, Virg. SYN. Ŏrātŏr; vĭcărĭŭs, vĭcēm gĕrēns.

lēgĭfĕr, ă, ŭm, *making laws.* Lēgĭfĕræ Cĕrĕrī, Virg. SYN. Lēgĭslātŏr.

lĕgĭo, ōnĭs, f., *a legion.* Fāscēs, lĕgĭōnēs, Juv. SYN. Cŏhŏrs, cătĕrvă, phălānx. EPITH. Mārtĭă, bēllātrīx, hŏstīlĭs, ārmĭsŏnă, ārmĭfĕră, nŭmĕrōsă, bēllĭgĕră, ārmātă, ærātă, mĭnāx, hāstātă, pūgnāx. V. Caterva, agmen, acies.

lēgĭtĭmŭs, ă, ŭm, *lawful.* Cōrpŏră lēgĭtĭmĭs, Ov. SYN. Jūstŭs, rēctŭs, æquŭs, dēbĭtŭs, mĕrĭtŭs.

lēgo, ās, *to delegate.* Lēgārăt Tădĭŭs, Pers. SYN. Dēlēgo, mītto, māndo.

lĕgo, ĭs, ī, ctŭm, *to read, to gather.* Quī lĕgĭtīs flōrēs, Virg. SYN. Lēctĭto, pēr-lĕgo, vŏlvo, ēvŏlvo, ŏcŭlīs pērcŭrro, lŭstro, pērlŭstro, ēxcŭtĭo, lĕgēndō lŭstro; ēlĭgo, dēlĭgo, sēlĭgo; cōllĭgo, cārpo, ēxcērpo, dēcērpo.

lĕgūmĕn, ĭnĭs, n., *pulse.* Sĭlĭquā quāssāntĕ lĕgūmĕn, Virg.

Lĕlĕgēĭs, ĭdĭs, f., *and* Lĕlĕgēĭŭs, ă, ŭm, *of the Leleges.* Lĕlĕgēĭdĕs ŭlnĭs, Ov
Lĕlĕgēĭă līttŏră, Id.

Lĕlĕgĕs, ŭm, m. pl., *a pastoral people near Caria.* Hīc Lĕlĕgăs, Virg.

Lĕlĕx, ĕgĭs, m., *a man's name.* Hērōs Pārtĕ Lĕlēx, Ov.

Lĕmānŭs, ī, m., *a lake in Switzerland.* Fīxă Lĕmānō, Lucan. EPITH. Gĕlĭdŭs, ōstrĭfĕr, līmpĭdŭs, vitrĕŭs, plăcĭdŭs, pīscōsŭs, nĭvālĭs.

lĕmbŭs, ī, m., *a boat.* Vīx flŭmĭnĕ lĕmbŭm, Virg.

Lĕmnĭăs, ădĭs, f., *a Lemnian woman.* Lĕmnĭăsīn glădĭŏs, Ov.

Lĕmnĭcŏlă, æ, m., *inhabitant of Lemnos, Vulcan.* Lĕmnĭcŏlæ stīrpĕm, Ov.

Lĕmnĭŭs, *or* ĭăcŭs, ă, ŭm, *of Lemnos.* Lĕmnĭăcăm cōntrā, Ov. Lĕmnĭŭs ĕx-tĕmplō, Id.

Lĕmnŏs, ī, f., *an island in the Archipelago.* Expŏsĭtŭm Lĕmnŏs, Ov. EPITH. Vŭlcānĭă, æquŏrĕă, fŭmĭdă, călēns.

Lĕmŭrēs, ŭm, m. pl., *ghosts.* Tūnc nīgrī lĕmŭrēs, Pers. SYN. Lārvæ, ŭmbræ, spēctră, mānēs. EPITH. Ātrī, văgī, ērrāntēs, pāllēntēs, tērrĭfĭcī, īnfēstī, nōctūrnī.

Lĕmūrĭă, ŏrŭm, n. pl., *festivals for the dead.* Nōctūrnă Lĕmūrĭă, săcrī, Ov.

lēnă, æ, f., *a bawd.* Vēndĕrĕ lēnă tŏrōs, Mart. EPITH. Tŭrpĭs, nĕfāndă, īnsĭdĭōsă.

lēnĕ, adv., *softly.* Ollīs, lēnĕ mŏvēns, Prop. V. Leniter.

Lēnæŭs, ī, m., *a name of Bacchus.* Pătĕr ō Lēnæĕ, Virg.

lēnīmĕn, ĭnĭs, n., *assuagement.* Hōc quŏquĕ lēnīmĕn, Ov. SYN. Lĕvāmĕn, fōmēntŭm, rĕmĕdĭŭm, mĕdēlă, sōlāmĕn, sōlātĭŭm. EPITH. Blāndŭm, dūlcĕ, grātŭm, jūcūndŭm, mōllĕ, suāvĕ, ămīcŭm.

lēnĭo, īs, īvī *and* ĭī, *to mitigate.* Lēnībānt tăcĭtō, Prop. SYN. Plāco, mītĭgo, flēcto, sēdo. V. Placo, solor.

lēnĭs, ĕ, *gentle.* Lēnĭŏr īră, Sed. SYN. Mītĭs, clēmēns, mōllĭs, īndūlgēns, făcĭlĭs, hūmānŭs, mānsuētŭs, cōmĭs, plăcĭdŭs, blāndŭs, bĕnīgnŭs.

* lēnĭtăs, ātĭs, f., *gentleness.* SYN. Clēmēntĭă ; bĕnīgnī, plăcĭdī mōrēs.

lēnĭtĕr, adv., *gently.* Lēnĭtĕr ādmŏvēntŭr, (Phal.) Mart. SYN. Clēmēntĕr, bĕnīgnē, plăcĭdē, blāndē.

lēno, ōnĭs, m., *a pimp.* Attēntī, lēnōnĭs ŭt, Hor. EPITH. Tŭrpĭs, ăvārŭs, īmpūrŭs, ōbscœnŭs, sōrdĭdŭs, nĕfāndŭs, scĕlēstŭs, īmpĭŭs.

lēnōcĭnĭŭm, ĭī, n., *enticement.* Et lēnōcĭnĭŭm vītæ, Man. SYN. Ars lēnōnĭs ; blāndītĭæ, blāndīmēntă, īllĕcebræ.

* lēnōcĭnŏr, ārĭs, *to entice, cajole.* SYN. Blāndĭŏr, ădūlŏr.

lēns, lēntĭs, m., *lentil.* Cūram ăspērnābĕrĕ lēntĭs, Virg. EPITH. Tĕrĕs, Nĭlĭăcă, Pēlūsĭăcă.

lēntē, adv., *slowly.* Lēntē grădĭēntĭs ăsēllī, Ov.

lēntēsco, ĭs, *to become clammy.* Ad dĭgĭtōs lēntēscĭt, Virg.

lēntīscĭfĕr, ă, ŭm, *planted with mastic-trees.* Lēntīscĭfĕrŭmquĕ tĕnēntŭr, Ov.

lēntīscŭm, ī, n., *a grove of mastic-trees.* Lēntīscŭm mĕllĭŭs, Mart.

lēntīscŭs, ī, f., *a mastic-tree.* Quīn ēt lēntīscŭs ămără, Avien.

lēnto, ās, *to bend.* Lēntāndŭs rēmŭs ĭn ūndă, Virg.

lēntŭs, ă, ŭm, *slow, pliant.* Lēntŭs ĭn ūmbrā, Virg. SYN. Tārdŭs, sēgnĭs, pĭgĕr ; ēffœtŭs, lānguĭdŭs ; plăcĭdŭs, lēnĭs, mŏdĕrātŭs.

lĕo, ōnĭs, m , *a lion.* Ōră lĕōnĭs hăbēs, Mart. EPITH. Mārtĭŭs, măgnănĭmŭs, fūlvŭs, răbĭdŭs, fĕrŭs, īndŏmĭtŭs, āspĕr, răpāx, fĕrōx, rūgĭēns, vălĭdŭs, vĭŏlēntŭs, īrācūndŭs, ăvĭdŭs, tōrvŭs, trūx, ănĭmōsŭs, prædātŏr, fūlmĭnĕŭs, fŭrēns, hōrrĭdŭs, fōrtĭs, gĕnĕrōsŭs, īmmānĭs, īntērrĭtŭs, fŭrĭōsŭs, īmpăvĭdŭs, īntrĕpĭdŭs, vīllōsŭs, jŭbātŭs, hīrsūtŭs, Gētūlŭs, Lĭbўcŭs, Māssўlŭs, Pœnŭs, Mārmărĭcŭs ; Armĕnĭŭs, Hīrcānŭs.

lĕōnīnŭs, ă, ŭm, *of a lion.* Mōllĕ lĕōnīnīs, Prop.

lĕpĭdŭs, ă, ŭm, *witty, pleasant.* Est lĕpĭdīssĭmă cōnjūx, Cat. SYN. Făcētŭs, fēstīvŭs, hĭlărĭs, jŏcōsŭs, ūrbānŭs, ārgūtŭs, cōncīnnŭs.

lĕpŏr, *and* ōs, ōrĭs, m., *mirth, wit.* Dīstīnctă lĕpōrĕ, Lucr. SYN. Vĕnūstās, grātĭă, fēstīvĭtās, ūrbānĭtās, ēlĕgāntĭă, sălēs. EPITH. Ūrbānŭs, blāndŭs, grātŭs, dūlcĭs, jūcūndŭs, vĕnūstŭs, suāvĭs, mēllītŭs, īnsĭdĭōsŭs, scūrrīlĭs, jŏcōsŭs, făcētŭs, tĕnĕr, ārgūtŭs

lĕpŏrīnŭs, ă, ŭm, *of a hare.* Lĕpŏrīnă lŭstrānt, (Iamb.)

lēpră, æ, f., *the leprosy.* Mūndāvītquĕ lĕprās, Tert. SYN. Ēlĕphās. EPITH.

Lūrĭdă, ĕdăx, ĭmprŏbă, fœdă, putrĭdă, dĕfŏrmĭs, sŏrdĭdă, fœtĭdă, mŏlēstă, ăcērbă, ēxĭtĭōsă, ēxĭtĭālĭs, pērnĭcĭōsă, trīstĭs, lēthălĭs, lēthĭfĕră, ĭmmĕdĭcābĭlĭs.
leprōsŭs, ă, ŭm, *leprous.* Nĭl tăm lĕprōsum aūt, (Iamb. Dim.) Prud.
lĕpŭs, ŏrĭs, m., *a hare.* Fœcūndī lĕpŏrĭs, Hor. Epith. Aūrĭtŭs, păvĭdŭs, vēlŏx, fŭgăx, tĭmĭdŭs, lĕvĭs, ălacrĭs, agrēstĭs, sȳlvēstrĭs, fŭgĭtīvŭs, præpĕs, pērnīx, cĕlĕr, răpĭdŭs, prōnŭs. V. Venor.
Lērnæŭs, ă, ŭm, *of Lerne.* Lērnæūs lăbŏr, Ov.
Lērnē, ēs, *or* nă, æ, f., *a lake in Achaia.* Pāscŭă Lērnæ, Virg. Epith. Cœrŭlă, nŏcēns, fœcūndă, stăgnāns, Āchāĭcă, Graĭă, līmōsă.
Lēsbĭăcŭs, bĭŭs, *and* bŏŭs, ă, ŭm, *Lesbian.* Jūnctō Lēsbĭăcō, Sid. Lēsbĭă vīnă, Hor. Lēsbōŭm rĕfŭgĭt, Id.
Lēsbĭăs, ădŏs, *and* Lēsbĭs, ĭdŏs, f., *a Lesbian woman.* Nēc mē Lēsbĭădŭm, Ov. Lēsbĭdĕs æquŏrēæ, Id.
Lēsbŏs, ī, f., *an island in the Ægean sea.* Dē pālmĭtĕ Lēsbŏs, Virg. Epith. Mēthȳmnæă.
Lēthæŭs, ă, ŭm, *of Lethe.* Ūrŭnt Lēthæō pērfūsă, Virg. Syn. Ōblīvĭōsŭs.
lēthālĭs, ĕ, *deadly.* Lătĕrī lēthālĭs ărūndo, Virg. Syn. Lēthĭfĕr, ēxĭtĭōsŭs, mōrtĭfĕr.
lēthārgĭcŭs, ă, ŭm, *lethargic.* Ūt lēthārgĭcŭs hic, Hor.
lēthārgŭs, ī, m., *lethargy.* In nīgrās lēthārgī, Lucr.
lēthātŭs, ă, ŭm, *killed.* Intrāvīt, lēthātăquĕ cōrpŏră, Ov.
Lēthē, ēs, f., *the river of oblivion in hell.* Quăm jūxtă Lēthēs tăcĭtŭs, Luc. Epith. Stȳgĭă, īnfērnă, Tārtărĕă, sŏpŏrĭfĕră, quĭētă, tōrpēns, ōblīvĭōsă, ĭmmĕmŏr, īrrĕmĕābĭlĭs, prŏfūndă, ātră.
lēthĭfĕr, *and* fĭcŭs, ă, ŭm, *deadly.* Lēthĭfĕr ānnŭs, Virg. Syn. Lēthālĭs.
lēthŭm, ī, n., *death.* Tūm cōnsănguĭnĕŭs lēthī sŏpŏr, Virg. V. Mors.
lĕvāmĕn, ĭnĭs, *and* mēntŭm, ī, n., *comfort.* Căsūsquĕ lĕvāmĕn, Virg. Syn. Lēnīmĕn, sōlātĭŭm, aūxĭlĭŭm.
Leūcădĭŭs, ă, ŭm, *of Leucadia, of Leucates.* Leūcădĭŭmquĕ vŏcānt, Ov.
Leūcās, ădĭs, f., *a city on the promontory Leucates.* Leūcădă cōntĭnŭăm, Ov. Syn. Leūcădĭă, Leūcātēs.
Leūcāspĭs, ĭdĭs, m., *one of Æneas' companions.* Leūcāspim ēt Lȳcĭæ, Virg.
Leūcātēs, æ, m., *a promontory of Acarnania.* Mŏx ēt Leūcātæ, Virg.
Leūcīppĭs, ĭdĭs, f., *daughter of Leucippus.* Gĕmĭnās Leūcīppĭdăs, Ov.
Leūcīppŭs, ī, m., *a Messenian.* Leūcīppō fĭĕrī pāctŭs, Ov.
Leūcōn, ŏnĭs, m., *a king of Pontus.* Quā cĕcĭdīt Leūcōn, Ov.
Leūcŏnŏē, ēs, f., *a woman's name.* Dīcĕrĕ Leūcŏnŏē, Ov.
Leūcŏsĭă, æ, f., *an island of the Tuscan sea.* Leūcŏsĭămquĕ pĕtĭt, Ov.
Leūcŏthĕă, æ, *and* ĕē, ēs, f., *a name of Ino.* Leūcŏthĕē Graĭĭs, Ov.
Leūcŏthŏē, ēs, f., *a daughter of Orchamus, beloved by Apollo.* Bĭs sēx Leūcŏthŏēn fămŭlās, Ov.
lĕvĭs, ĕ, *and* vĭcŭlŭs, ă, ŭm, *light.* Āntĕ lĕvēs ērgo, Virg. Syn. Grăvĭtātĕ cărēns, ēxpērs grăvĭtātĭs, sĭnĕ pōndĕrĕ, nĭl grăvĭtātĭs, pōndĕrĭs hăbēns ; ăgĭlĭs, ălacrĭs, cĕlĕr ; mōbĭlĭs, īncōnstāns ; pārvŭs, ēxĭgŭŭs, tĕnŭĭs, vīlĭs. V. Celer, inconstans.
lĕvĭsōmnŭs, ă, ŭm, *sleeping lightly.* Ēt lĕvĭsōmnă cănŭm, Lucr.
lĕvĭtās, ātĭs, f., *lightness.* In lĕvĭtātĕ sŭă, Ov. Syn. Mōbĭlĭtās, cĕlĕrĭtās, īncōnstāntĭă.
lĕvĭtĕr, adv., *lightly.* Lēnĭtĕr ēt lĕvĭtĕr, Cat. Syn. Ălacrĭtĕr, mōbĭlĭtĕr ; părŭm, paūlŭm.
lĕvo, ās, *to lift up.* Cūrāquĕ lĕvārĭt, Hor. Syn. Ērĭgo, tōllo, ēxtōllo, ēffĕro ; jŭvo, sōlŏr.
lēx, lēgĭs, f., *a law.* Ōmnĭă sŭb lēgēs, Ov. Syn. Jūs, mōs, īnstĭtūtŭm, īmpērĭŭm, māndātŭm, præcēptŭm, ēdīctŭm, dēcrētŭm, scītŭm, plăcĭtŭm. Epith. Sānctă, æquă, jūstă, sacră, īnjūstă, īmpĕrĭōsă, sĕvēră, dūră, īmmānĭs, āspĕră, rĭgĭdă, īnvĭŏlābĭlĭs, grăvĭs, ăcērbă, īnīquă, īmpĭă.
lībāmĕn, ĭnĭs, *or* mēntŭm, ī, n., *a libation.* Dūcŭnt lībāmĭnă nōmĕn, Ov. Syn. Lĭtāmĕn.
Lĭbănŭs, ī, m., *a mountain between Phœnicia and Syria.* Ōdŏr, Lĭbănī ceū mōntĭs, Aus. Epith. Tĕpēns, cedrĭfĕr, ŏdōrātŭs, ēxcēlsŭs, ārdŭŭs, sūblīmĭs, āĕrĭŭs, vīrēns, vĭrĭdĭs, grātŭs, ămœnŭs.

Lībăs, ădĭs, f., *a woman's name.* Tēr Lībăs ŏffĭcĭŏ, Ov.

lībēllă, æ, f., *a small balance, a level.* Ēt lībēlla, ălĭquā, Lucr.

lībēllŭs, ī, m., *the dimin. of* liber. Cædĕ lībēllŭs ĕrĭt, Ov. Syn. Exĭgŭŭs lībĕr, cōdĕx.

lībēns, ntĭs, *willing.* Scĭt ŭtērquĕ lībēns, Hor. Syn. Lūbēns, vŏlēns, nōn ĭnvītŭs.

lībēntĕr, adv., *willingly.* Pătĭăr dēlīctă lībēntĕr, Hor. Syn. Lūbēntĕr, spōntĕ, ūltrō.

Lībĕr, ĕrī, m., *a name of Bacchus.* Lībĕr, ĕt ālmă, Virg. V. Bacchus.

lībĕr, librī, m., *a book.* Vērtūmnŭm Jānūmquĕ, lībĕr, Hor. Hăbĕăs cūm scrīnĭă lībrīs, Mart. Syn. Cōrtĕx; vŏlūmĕn, chărtæ, cōdĕx, lībēllŭs̄. Epith. Dōctŭs, lăbōrātŭs, lĕpĭdŭs, ārgūtŭs, cūltŭs, ēxcūltŭs, ūtĭlĭs, ĭngĕnĭōsŭs, fācūndŭs, præclārŭs, ēxĭmĭŭs, aūrātŭs, pĭctŭs.

lībĕr, ă, ŭm, *free.* Sīvĕ quŏd ēs lībĕr, Ov. Syn. Sŏlūtŭs, ĭmmūnĭs, ēxpĕdītŭs, lībĕrātŭs, ĭngĕnŭŭs, sŭī jūrĭs.

Lībĕră, æ, f., *a name of Ariadne.* Lībĕră nōmĕn ĕrĭt, Ov.

lībĕrālĭs, ĕ, *noble, liberal.* Prŏdĭgŭs ātquĕ lībĕrālĭs, (Phal.) Mart. Syn. Lārgŭs, mūnĭfĭcŭs, māgnĭfĭcŭs, bĕnĕfĭcŭs. V. Do.

lībĕrālĭtās, ātĭs, f., *liberality.* Sȳnĭstră lībĕrālĭtās, (Iamb. pur.) Cat. Syn. Mūnĭfĭcēntĭă, mūnĭfĭcă nātūră, ĭndŏlēs.

lībĕrē, adv., *freely.* Ōmnĭă lībĕrĭŭs, Virg.

lībĕrī, ōrŭm *or* ŭm, *children.* Pĕr lībĕrōs tē, Hor. V. Proles.

lībĕro, ās, *to deliver.* Pœdăgōgō lībĕrātŭs ĕt cūjŭs, (Scaz.) Mart. Syn. Sŏlvo, ēxpĕdĭo, ēxĭmo, vīndĭco. V. Solvo.

lībērtă, æ, f., *a freed-woman.* Ăt hūnc lībērtă sĕcūrī, Hor.

lībērtās, ātĭs, f., *liberty.* Nēc spēs lībērtātĭs ĕrăt, Virg. Epith. Grātă, dūlcĭs, ămīcă, blāndă, lætă, cără, ōptātă, ămātă, spērātă, prĕtĭōsă, suāvĭs, ēxpēctātă, cŭpītă, fēlīx, cāndĭdă, aūrĕă.

lībērtīnŭs, ă, ŭm, *born of a freed-man.* Et lībērtīnăs, Mart.

lībērtŭs, ī, m., *a freed-man.* Scīs dărĕ lībērtōs, Juv.

lĭbĕt, lĭbŭĭt, *it pleases.* Mīrārī lĭbĕt, ō. Syn. Plăcĕt, jŭvăt, lŭbĕt.

Lībēthră, æ, f., *a fountain sacred to the Muses.*

Lībēthrĭdĕs, ŭm, f. pl., *the Muses.* Nōstĕr ămōr, Lībēthrĭdĕs, Virg.

lĭbīdĭnŏr, ārĭs, *to be lecherous.* Cūm lĭbīdĭnātŭr, (Phal.) Mart. V. Libidinosus.

lĭbīdĭnōsŭs, ă, ŭm, *lustful.* Lĭbīdĭnōsŭs ĭmmŏlābĭtŭr, (Iamb. pur.) Hor. Syn. Lāscīvŭs, ĭmpŭdīcŭs, ĭmpūrŭs, ōbscœnŭs, prŏtērvŭs, prŏcāx. V. Adultĕr.

lĭbīdo, ĭnĭs, f., *will, lust.* Ebrĭĕtās gēmĭnātă lĭbīdĭnĕ rēgnăt, Ov. Syn. Cŭpīdo, vŏlūntās, ārbĭtrĭŭm; lāscīvĭă, lūxŭrĭĕs. Epith. Tūrpĭs, vēsānă, īnsānă, fūrĭōsă, cœcă, dāmnōsă, scĕlĕrātă, probrōsă, pĕtŭlāns, prŏcāx, ĭmprŏbă, ĭmpĭă, nĕfāndă, ĭndŏmĭtă, dīră, ĭllĭcĭtă, prāvă, pērnĭcĭōsă, sĕgnĭs, fœdă. ēffrœnātă, vēcŏrs, īnfāmĭs, fūrēns, blāndă, ĭmpūră, fāllāx, pērfĭdă. V. Libidinosus, amor, cupido, luxuria, voluptas.

Lĭbĭtīnă, æ, f., *the goddess of funerals.* Lĭbĭtīnæ quœstŭs ăcērbæ, Hor. Epith. Trīstĭs, dīră. V. Mors.

lĭbĭtŭm, ī, n., *will, liking.* Sī lĭbĭtŭm tĭbi, Prop. V. Libet.

lībo, ās, *to make a libation.* Lībăt hŏnōrĕm, Virg. Syn. Cōnsecro, dīco, dēdĭco, līto, sacrĭfĭco; dēlībo, gūsto.

Lībo, ōnĭs, m., *a noble Roman family.* Pŭtĕālquĕ Lībōnĭs, Hor.

lībră, æ, f., *a pound, a balance.* Lībrārūm cœnæ, Mart. Syn. Pōndo, lānx, bĭlānx, trŭtĭnă, stătēră. Epith. Æquă, æquălĭs, cērtă, āncĕps, pāndă, rĕpāndă, pēndŭlă, pēndēns. V. Libro.—2. *one of the twelve signs.* Lībră dĭĕ sōmnĭquĕ pārēs, Virg. Syn. Æquātŏr. V. Æquinoctium.

lībrārĭŭs, ī̄, m., *(from* liber) *a copyist.* Lībrārĭŭs ūsquĕ, Hor. Syn. Scrībă.—2. lībrārĭŭs, ī̄, m., *(from* libra) *a dispenser of tasks.* Lībrārĭŭs, ārchĭmăgīrī, Juv.

lībro, ās, *to balance.* Lībrāvīt dēxtră, Virg. Syn. Trŭtĭno, pōndĕro; trŭtĭnă pēndo, āppēndo, ēxāmĭno; ăgĭto, jācto, vērso.

lībŭm, ī, n., *a holy cake.* Ānnŭă lībo, Juv. Epith. Dūlcĕ, suāvĕ, Cĕrĕălĕ.

lĭbūrnŭm, ī, n., *a litter.* Sŭpĕr ōră lĭbūrnō, Juv.

Lĭbūrnŭs, ī, m., *a Liburnian.* Rēgnă Lĭbūrnōrŭm, Virg.

Lĭbȳă, æ, *or* ē, ēs, f., *a part of Africa.* Ēgēns Lĭbȳæ dēsērtă pĕrăgrāns, Virg. Epith. Vāstă, dēsērtă, scŏpŭlōsă, sāxōsă, stĕrīlĭs, ārdēns, flagrāns, ārĭdă. V. Africa.

Lĭbўcŭs, *and* bўstĭnŭs, ă, ŭm, *and* Lĭbўs, ўŏs, m., *of Libya.* Tē Lĭbўcæ gēntēs, Virg. Hīnc Lĭbўs, hīnc Mērŏē, Ov. Mōntĭbŭs Lĭbўstĭnĭs, Cat. Syn. Āfrĭcŭs. Lĭbўstĭs, ĭdĭs, Lĭbўssă, æ, f., *of Libya.* Pēllē Lĭbўstĭdĭs ūrsæ, Virg. Syn. Lĭbўcă. lĭcēntĕr, adv., *licentiously.* Scrībāmquĕ lĭcēntĕr, Hor. Syn. Impūnītē, īnūltē, impūnē, lībĕrē, aūdāctĕr.

lĭcēntĭă, æ, f., *licence, licentiousness.* Invēctă lĭcēntĭă mōrĕm, Hor. Syn. Lībērtās, vēnĭă, pŏtēstās ; făcūltās, lĭbīdo. Epith. Ēffrēnă, ēffrēnātă, īndŏmītă, ēffūsă, văgă, sŏlūtă, lāscīvă, nōxĭă, dāmnōsă, pērnĭcĭōsă, vēsānă, fŭrĭbūndă, aūdāx, tĕmĕrārĭă, præcēps.

lĭcĕŏr, ērĭs, *to bid money for a thing.* Cēntūssĕ lĭcētŭr, Pers. Syn. Æstĭmo, lĭcĭtŏr.

lĭcĕt, ŭĭt, *it is allowed.* Cuī lĭcĕt ūt vŏlŭĭt, Pers. Syn. Fās ēst, lĭcĭtum ēst, pērmīssum ēst, dătŭr.

lĭcĕt, conj., *though.* Āccĭpĭŏ, lĭcĕt īllŭd ĕt, Pers. Syn. Ētsī, tămētsī, quānquăm, quāmvīs.

Lĭchās, æ, m., *a servant of Hercules, thrown into the sea by him.* Ēccĕ Lĭchān trĕpĭdŭm, Ov.

Lĭcĭnĭŭs, ĭī, m., *a man's name.* Vīvēs, Lĭcĭnī, nĕque āltŭm, Hor.

Lĭcĭnŭs, ī, m., *a freedman of Augustus.* Tōnsōrī Lĭcĭnō, Hor.

lĭcĭtŏr, ārĭs, *to cheapen.* Intēr sē lĭcĭtāntŭr, Ennius. Syn. Lĭcĕŏr, æstĭmo.

lĭcĭtŭs, ă, ŭm, *allowed.* Ædĭbŭs, ēt lĭcĭtō, Virg. Syn. Cōncēssŭs, pērmīssŭs, jūstŭs, lēgĭtĭmŭs.

lĭcĭŭm, ĭī, n., *the woof.* Lĭcĭă tēlĭs, Luc. Syn. Fīlŭm, stāmĕn, līnŭm.

līctŏr, ōrĭs, m., *a beadle.* Līctōrĭs ăbĭgĕt, (Scaz.) Mart. Syn. Āppārĭtŏr, sătēllĕs ; cārnĭfēx. Epith. Sævŭs, atrōx, trŭcŭlēntŭs, dūrŭs, mĭnāx, trŭx. V. Carnifex.

lĭgāmĕn, ĭnĭs ; *and* mēntŭm, ī, n., *a bandage.* Dēmpsĭssĕ lĭgāmĭnă vīnclĭs, Ov. Prop. Syn. Nēxŭs, nōdŭs, cătēnă, vīncŭlŭm.

Lĭgĕă, *or* ĭă, æ, f., *a nymph.* Lĭgĕăquĕ Phĭlŏdŏcēquĕ, Virg.

Lĭgĕr, *or* gĕrĭs, ĭs, m., *a river in France.* Sē Lĭgĕr āntĕfĕrĕt, Aus. Epith. Cĭtŭs, cōncĭtŭs, ēffūsŭs, răpĭdŭs, dēclīvĭs, ārēnōsŭs, ōblīquŭs, prŏpĕrāns, prŏfūndŭs, tŭmĭdŭs, pīscōsŭs, fœcūndŭs, ēxūndāns, āmœnŭs.

lignĕŭs, ă, ŭm, *wooden.* Lĭgnĕă, cōntŭlĕrăt, Ov. Syn. Rŏbŏrĕŭs, ārbŏrĕŭs.

lignŭm, ī, n., *wood.* Dănt ŭtĭlĕ lĭgnŭm, Virg. Syn. Stĭpĕs, rŏbŭr, sŭdēs, trăbs, ărbŏr, sўlvă. Epith. Dūrŭm, rŏbŏrĕŭm, vĭrĭdĕ, ārĭdŭm, sēctĭlĕ, rāmōsŭm, tōnsĭlĕ, tōrnātĭlĕ, vĕtūstŭm, ēxēsŭm, cārĭōsŭm.

lĭgo, ās, *to bind.* Ănĭmōsă lĭgāvĭt, Ov. Syn. Āllĭgo, rēllĭgo, vīncĭo, rĕvīncĭo, nēcto, ādnēcto, cōnnēcto, strīngo, cōnstrīngo. V. Vincio.

lĭgo, ōnĭs, m., *a spade.* Pūrgārĕ lĭgōnĭbŭs ārvă, Ov. Epith. Dūrŭs, īncūrvŭs, ōbtūsŭs, āttrītŭs, flēxŭs, grăvĭs, ēxēsŭs, ădūncŭs, fērrĕŭs, ăcūtŭs. V. Aratrum.

lĭgŭlă, æ, f., *a latchet.* Ēt lĭgŭlās dīmĭttĕrĕ, Juv. Syn. Lōrŭm.

Lĭgŭr *and* Lĭgŭs, ŭrĭs, m., Lĭgŭrēs, ŭm, m. pl., *the inhabitants of Liguria.* Et nūnc, tōnsĕ Lĭgŭr, Luc. Vānĕ Lĭgŭs, Virg. Nōn ĕgŏ tē Lĭgŭrŭm, Id. Epith. Vānī, tŭmĭdī, sŭpērbī, Ālpīnī, īndŏmĭtī, fĕrōcēs, īmmītēs, trūcēs.

Lĭgŭrĭă, æ, f., *a part of Italy.* Epith. Mōntānă, hōrrĭdă, īnfōrmĭs, stĕrĭlĭs, sāxōsă, vīrēns, vĭrĭdĭs, sŭpērbă.

Lĭgŭrīnŭs, ī, m., *a man's name.* Hor.

lĭgŭrĭo, ĭs, ĭī, *to eat ravenously.* Dūm fūrtă lĭgŭrĭt, Hor. Syn. Ablĭgūrĭo, vŏro, dĕvŏro, sōrbĕo, ābsōrbĕo, hēllŭŏr, cōnsūmo, ābsūmo.

lĭgŭstrŭm, ĭ, n., *privet.* Ālbă lĭgūstră cădūnt, Virg. Epith. Cāndĭdŭm, vĭrēns, vērnāns, ārgēntĕŭm, cāndēns, lāctĕŭm, fōrmōsŭm, nĭvĕŭm, ŏdōrŭm, ŏdōrātŭm, rŭdōlēns, grătŭm, ămœnŭm, flōrēns, frăgrāns, hālāns, spīrāns, ŏdōrĭfĕrŭm, rōscĭdŭm, īrrĭgŭŭm.

lĭlĭŭm, ĭī, n., *a lily.* Lĭlĭă lŭtĕŏlĭs. Epith. Cāndĭdŭm, vĭrēns, vērnāns, cānēns, ālbŭm, lāctĕŭm, ālbēscēns, nĭvĕŭm, ārgēntĕŭm, cāndēns, pīctŭm, mōllĕ, fūlgēns, ālbĭcōmŭm, hĭāns, flōrēns, vērnŭm, frăgrāns, fōrmōsŭm, īntāctŭm, lūcĭdŭm, rīdēns, ŏdōrŭm, ŏdōrātŭm, ŏdōrĭfĕrŭm, rŭdōlēns, grătŭm, ămœnŭm, hālāns, spīrāns.

Lĭlўbæŭm, ī, n., *a promontory of Sicily.* Lĭlўbæŏn ĕt Ārctŏn, Ov.

Lĭlўbæŭs *and* bēĭŭs, ă, ŭm, *of Lilybæum.* Lĭlўbæŏ līttŏrĕ, Luc. Sāxīs Lĭlўbēĭă cæcīs, Virg.

līmă, æ, f., *a file*. Ultĭmă līmă mĕīs, Ov. Syn. Aspĕră, dĕntātă, fĕrrĕă, ĕdāx, rōdēns. V. Limo.

līmāx, ācĭs, m., *a snail*. Implĭcĭtūs cōnchæ līmāx, Col. Epith. Pĭgĕr, tārdŭs, lēntŭs, tārdigrădŭs, spūmōsŭs, rēpēns, rēptĭlĭs, cōrnĭgĕr.

līmbūs, ī, m., *a fringe*. Cīrcūmdătă līmbō, Virg. Syn. Fīmbrĭă. Epith.

Mæŏnĭŭs, vīllōsŭs, aūrātŭs, pīctūrātŭs, băccātŭs, īnŭs, īnfīmŭs.—2. *a place of happiness for children who die unbaptized*. Syn. Elўsĭŭm.

līmĕn, ĭnĭs, n., *the threshold*. Līmĭnĭbūs pēccās, Mart. Syn. Ostĭŭm, pōrtă, fŏrēs, ātrĭŭm, vēstĭbŭlŭm, jānŭă. Epith. Fĕrrĕŭm, dūrŭm, trītŭm, strīdēns, āltŭm, āngūstŭm, mārmŏrĕŭm, māgnĭfĭcŭm. V. Janua.

līmĕs, ĭtĭs, m., *a boundary*. Pēllītĕ līmĭtĭbŭs, Tib. Syn. Tērmĭnŭs, fīnĭs, mētă, sēmĭtă, vĭă. Epith. Sānctŭs, săcĕr, īmmōbĭlĭs, īmmōtŭs, fīxŭs, rēctŭs, jăcēns.

līmĭto, ās, *to bound, to limit*. Syn. Tērmĭno, fīnĭo, dēfīnĭo, claŭdo, cīrcūmscrībo, dētērmĭno.

līmo, ās, *to file*. Līmāt nōn ŏdĭo, Hor. Syn. Elīmo, līmā tĕro, āttĕro, scālpo, pŏlĭo, ēxpŏlĭo, lævĭgo.

līmōsŭs, ă, ŭm, *muddy*. Līmōsōquĕ lăcū, Virg. Syn. Lŭtŭlēntŭs, lŭtōsŭs.

līmpĭdŭs, ă, ŭm, *clear, transparent*. Līmpĭdī lăcūs ūndæ, (Scaz.) Cat. Syn. Lūcĭdŭs, pēllūcĭdŭs, nĭtĭdŭs, pūrŭs, clārŭs, īllīmĭs, vitrĕŭs, crўstāllīnŭs.

līmŭs, ă, ŭm, *oblique*. Nām mĕmĭnī līmīs, Ov. Syn. Oblīquŭs, trānsvērsŭs.

līmŭs, ī, m., *mud*. Līmŭs ŭt hic, Virg. Syn. Lŭtŭm, fæx, cœnŭm. V. Lutum. —2. *a gown*. Vēlātī līmō, Virg.

Līmўră, æ, *and* rē, ēs, f., *a city of Lycia*. Et Līmўrēn, Ov.

līnĕă, æ, f., *a line*. Ultĭmă līnĕă rērŭm, Hor. Epith. Lōngă, rēctă, tĕnŭĭs, cūrvă, ōblīquă.

līnĕŭs, ă, ŭm, *flaxen*. Vīncŭlă līnĕă rŭpĭt, Virg.

līngo, ĭs, *to lick*. Plaut. Syn. Lāmbo, dēgūsto, āllāmbo.

līnguă, æ, f., *a tongue*. Līnguĭs ănĭmīsquĕ făvēntĕs, Juv. Epith. Lŏquāx, gārrŭlă, blāndă, prŏcāx, prŏtērvă, clāmōsă, īmprŏbă, mōrdāx, mēndāx, pĕtŭlāns, ēffrēnĭs, dūlcĭs, vŏlūbĭlĭs, pŏtēns, aūrĕă, mēllĭflŭă, dōctă, dĭsērtă. V. Loquor.

līnĭgĕr, ă, ŭm, *clothed with linen*. Līnĭgĕră cŏlĭtŭr, Ov.

līnĭo, ĭs, ī, nītŭm, *and* no, ĭs, lītŭm, *to anoint*. Mĕdæ līnĭāntŭr, Prop. Spīrāmēntă līnŭnt, Virg. Syn. Illīno, ūngo, ĭnūngo.

līnquo, līquī, *to leave*. Nōstrī līquerĕ pŏētæ, Hor. Syn. Rĕlīnquo, dēsĕro, dēstĭtŭo, ŏmītto.

līntĕă, ōrŭm, n. pl., *sails*. Dărĕ līntĕă vēntō, Virg. V. Carbasa.

līntĕŏlŭm, ī, n., *the dimin. of* linteum. Sūccŭm līntĕŏlō, (Choriamb.) Prud.

līntĕr, trĭs, m. f., *a small boat*. Līntĕr ăquæ, Tibull. Syn. Lĕmbŭs, scăphă, cўmbă.

līntĕŭm, ī, n., *a veil*. Līntĕă fūllō, Mart. Epith. Cāndĭdŭm, lĕvĕ. V. Velum.

līnŭm, ī, n., *flax*. Cāmpŭm līnī sĕgĕs, Virg. Epith. Tĕnŭĕ, mōllĕ, sŭbtĭlĕ, grăcĭlĕ, cāndēns, ālbŭm, cāndĭdŭm, nĭtēns, tĕrĕs, lōngŭm, lævĕ, Pēlūsĭăcŭm, tēxtĭlĕ.

Līnŭs, ī, m., *a Thracian musician*. Ŭt Līnŭs hæc, Virg. Epith. Thrācĭŭs, Thrēĭcĭŭs, vōcālĭs, Apōllĭnĕŭs, blāndŭs, mēllĭflŭŭs, dūlcĭsŏnŭs, sŏnōrŭs, cănōrŭs.

Līpără, æ, *or* ē, ēs, f., *one of the Æolian islands*. Erĭgĭtŭr Līpărēn, Virg. Epith. Fūmōsă, Æŏlĭă, Vūlcānĭă, tĕpĭdă, tĕtră, hōrrĭdă, fŭrēns.

Līpăræŭs, ă, ŭm, *of Lipara*. Līpăræă nĭgră tăbērnă, Juv.

līppŭs, ă, ŭm, *blear-eyed*. Ocŭlīs mălă līppŭs ĭnūnctĭs, Hor.

līquĕfăcĭo, fēcī, făctŭm, *to melt*. Călōr līquĕfāctă rĕmīttĭt, Virg. Syn. Līquo, ēlīquo, sōlvo, rĕsōlvo, dīssōlvo, mōllĭo.

līquĕfīo, fīs ; ēsco, ĭs ; *and* līquŏr, ĕrĭs, *to become dissolved*. Pērpĕtŭĭs līquĕfīŭnt, Virg. Fōrnācĕ līquĕscĭt, Virg. Līquĭtŭr ŭt glăcĭēs, Ov. Syn. Līquĕo, cōllīquĕsco, līquŏr (ārĭs), sōlvŏr, rĕsōlvŏr, dīssōlvŏr. V. Liquor, eris.

līquēns, ēntĭs, *liquid*. Vīnă līquēntĭă, Virg. Quŭm līquēntĭă, Id.

līquĕt, impers., *it is manifest*. Măgĭs ŭt līquĕăt, Ov. Syn. Cērtum ēst, pătĕt, cōnstăt.

līquĭdŭs, ă, ŭm, *liquid*. Cōnvĕnĭunt līquĭdĭs ēt līquĭdă crāssĭs, Lucr. Syn. Liquēns, hūmĭdŭs, flŭĭdŭs, dēflŭŭs, flūxŭs, mōllĭs, lābĭlĭs, līquĕfāctŭs, sŏlūtŭs, rĕsŏlūtŭs, līquātŭs.

līquo, ās, *to dissolve*. Tēlă līquāvĭt, Luc. Syn. Līquĕfăcĭo.

lĭquŏr, ārĭs, *and* lĭquŏr, ĕrĭs, *to melt.* Mĕllā lĭquătā, Ov. Lĭquĭtŭr ĕt, Virg.
Syn. Lĭquĕsco, lĭquĕffo. sŏlvŏr.

liquŏr, ōrĭs, m., *a liquid.* Pōtŭrā lĭquŏrēs, Ov. Lĭquŏr ăquāī, Lucr.   Syn.
Hūmŏr, lătĕx, ăquă, ŭndă.   V. Aqua.

Līrĭŏpē, ēs, f., *the mother of Narcissus.* Cœrŭlā Līrĭŏpē, Ov.

Līrĭs, ĭs, m., *a river of Campania.* Nōs Līrĭs ănŭt, Mart.

lĭs, lĭtĭs, f., *a law-suit, a quarrel.* Et lĭtĕ mŏrārĭs, Hor.   Syn. Lītĭgĭum, cōntĕntĭo,
rīxă, ăltĕrcātĭo, dĭscōrdĭă, dĭscēptătĭo, cōntrōvĕrsĭă, dĭssēnsĭo, dĭssī-
dĭŭm, jūrgĭŭm, cērtāmĕn, pūgnă.   Epith. Mŏlēstă, ĭnīquă, ĭnjūstă, æquă, jūstă,
ăcĕrbă, sŏllĭcĭtă, dĭffĭcĭlĭs, fŏrēnsĭs, ămbĭgŭă, dŭbĭă, impōrtūnă, dīră, ĕxĭtĭālĭs,
fūnēstă, ĭnsānă, āncēps, ĭnfēstă, vēsānă. trīsĭs.   V. Rixa.

lītāmĕn, ĭnĭs, n., *a sacrifice.* Cūjūs lītāmĕn sōrdĕt, Prud.   Syn. Lībāmĕn.

Lītērnŭm, ī, n., *a port of Campania.* Tĕnētŭr Lītērnŭm, Ov.

lītĭgĭōsŭs, ă, ŭm, *litigious.* Nĭsĭ lītĭgĭōsŭs, Hor.   Syn. Lītĭs ămāns, lītĭbŭs ĭn-
cŭmbēns.

lītĭgĭŭm, ĭī, n., *strife.* Lītĭgĭum ēst cum ūxŏrĕ, Plaut.   V. Lis.

lītĭgo, ās, *to quarrel.* Lītĭgăt, ĕt pŏdăgrā, Mart.   Syn. Dĭscēpto, cōntēndo,
rīxŏr, ăltērcŏr, cērto, pūgno.   V. Rixor.

lĭto, ās, *to offer a sacrifice.* Thūrĕ lĭtābĭs, Pers.   Syn. Sacrĭfĭcĭo ēxōro, ĭm-
petro; sacrĭfĭco, lĭbo.

littĕră, *dimin.* lĭttĕrŭlă, æ, f., *a letter or character in writing.* Littĕrŭlĭs Græcĭs,
Hor.   Littĕră fēcĭt, ămo, Ov.   Syn. Chărāctĕr, nŏtă.

littĕræ, ārŭm, f. pl., *a letter, epistle.* Epith. Mĭssæ, scrīptæ, cōmmĭssæ, vēr-
bōsæ, ārcānæ.   Syn. Ēpĭstŏlă, ĕpĭstŏlĭŭm, chărtă, lĭbēllŭs.   V. Studia.

littĕrātŏr, ōrĭs, m., *a pedant.* - Sȳllă littĕrātŏr, (Phal.) Cat.   Epith. Dōctŭs,
pĕrītŭs.

Lĭvĭă, æ, f., *a woman's name.* Lĭvĭă rēstĭtŭĭt, Ov.

littŏrālĭs, ĕ, *and* rĕŭs, ă, ŭm, *belonging to the shore.* Littŏrĕās ăgĭtăbăt, Virg.

lĭttŭs, ōrĭs, n., *the shore.* Littŏrĭs ōrăm, Virg.   Syn. Rīpă, ōră, ăctă.   Epith.
Ărēnōsŭm, spūmāns, cūrvŭm, prōcūrvŭm, vĭrĭdĕ, sāxōsŭm, văgŭm, ūdŭm, bĭbŭ-
lŭm, spūmōsŭm, sĭnŭōsŭm; ŭndōsŭm, naŭfrăgŭm, prŏcēllōsŭm, reflŭŭm, æquŏrĕŭm, ēxtrēmŭm, rĕsŏnāns, aprīcŭm, sĭnŭāĭŭm, tūtŭm, ŏptātŭm, sēcūrŭm.
V. Ripa.

lĭtūră, æ, f., *a blot.* Ūnă lĭtūră pŏtēst, Mart.   Epith. Fœdă, tūrpĭs, ātră,
dōctă.

lĭtŭŭs, ŭī, m., *a clarion.* Et lĭtŭō pūgnās, Virg.   Epith. Ūncŭs, ădūncŭs, tŏrtĭlĭs, sŏnōrŭs, ærĕŭs.   V. Tuba.—2. *an augur's staff.* .V. Pedum.

lĭvĕo, ēs, *or* ēsco, ĭs, *to be livid, to envy.* Enĭm lĭvēscĕrĕ făs ēst, Claud.   Syn.
Lĭvĭdŭs sŭm; ĭnvĭdĕo.

lĭvĭdŭs, *and* dŭlŭs, ă, ŭm, *pale, envious.* Lĭvĭdă cōllă, Ov.   Lĭvĭdŭlŭs sĭs, Juv.
Syn. Lĭvēns, plŭmbĕŭs, cōntūsŭs; ĭnvĭdŭs.   V. Invideo.

Lĭvĭŭs, ĭī, m., *a Roman name.* Lĭvī scrīptŏrĭs ăb ævō, Hor.

lĭvŏr, ōrĭs, m., *paleness, envy.* Cōmpāctă lĭvōrĕm dūcĭt ăb ūvā, Juv.   Syn.
Lĭvĭdŭs cŏlŏr; ĭnvĭdĭă.   Epith. Ēdāx, ānxĭŭs, ĭnērs, mălŭs, ātĕr, mōrdāx, ēxsānguĭs, oblīquŭs, tābĭfĭcŭs, mălīgnŭs, prōcāx, pāllĭdŭs, Tārtărĕŭs, ūrēns,
tōrvŭs.   V. Invidia.

lŏcārĭŭs, ĭī, m., *a man who kept and sold places at shows.* Dīvĭtĭæ lŏcārĭōrŭm,
Mart.

lŏco, ās, *to place.* Vīrōs lŏcăt īpsĕ, Virg.   Syn. Cōllŏco, pōno, rĕpōno, stătŭo,
cōnstĭtŭo.

Locrī, ōrŭm, m. pl., *a people of Greece.* Mœnĭă Lōcrī, Virg.

lŏcŭlĭs, *and* cēllŭs, ī, m., *a small bag, a purse.* Dē flāvā lŏcŭlōs, Mart.   Syn.
Crŭmēnă, mārsūpĭŭm, pēră, sæccŭlŭs.   Epith. Dīvĕs, tūrgēns, tūmēns, tŭrgĭdŭs, plēnŭs, căpāx, tŭmĭdŭs, ĭnānĭs.

lŏcŭplēs, ētĭs, *rich.* In lŏcŭplētĕ pĕnū, Pers.   Syn. Dīvĕs, ŏpŭlēntŭs.   V.
Dives.

lŏcŭplēto, ās, *to enrich.* Syn. Dīto; dīvĭtĭĭs, ŏpĭbŭs aŭgĕo.

lŏcŭs, ī, m., *a place.* Pĕr ŏpācă lŏcōrŭm, Virg.   Syn. Sēdēs, spătĭŭm, intervāllŭm;
rĕgĭo, tērră, occāsĭo, făcŭltās.   Epith. Căpāx, āmplŭs, ĭngēns, plēnŭs, ēxĭgŭŭs,
văcŭŭs, vīcīnŭs, rĕmōtŭs.

locŭstă, æ, f., *a locust.* Crūrĕ lŏcŭstă, Alc.   Lūcām părĭĕt lŏcŭstă, Enn.   Syn.

Brŭchŭs. Epith. Tĕnŭĭs, lĕvĭs, ēxĭlĭs, grăcĭlĭs, vĭrĭdĭs, pārvă, gārrŭlă, strīdŭlă, lŏquāx, æstīvă, strīdēns, pīctă, văgă, ĕdāx, sāltāns, sălĭēns.

lŏcūtĭo, ōnĭs, f., an expression. Fēscēnnīnă lŏcūtĭo, (Choriamb.) Cat. V. Sermo.

lōdīx, īcĭs, f., a blanket. Lōdīcēs mīttĕt, Mart.

lōlīgo, īgĭnĭs, f., a fish, envy. Sŭccŭs lōlīgĭnĭs, Hor. Syn. Ærūgo.

lōlĭŭm, īī, n., tares. Infēlīx lōlĭŭm, Virg. Syn. Æră; zīzănĭă, æ, ōrŭm. Epith. Stĕrĭlĕ, nŏcīvŭm, nŏxĭŭm, ămārŭm.

Lōllĭŭs, īī, m., a man's name. Quō dūxīt Lōllĭŭs ānnō, Hor.

lōngævŭs, ă, ŭm, old. Cōnjūx lōngævă Dŏrўclī, Virg. Syn. Sĕnēx, sĕnĭōr, grāndævŭs

|| lōngănĭmĭs̄ ̶ ̶g-suffering. V. Patiens.

Lōngārēnŭ ̶ ̶m., a man's name. Lōngārēnŭs fŏrĕt ĭntŭs, Hor.

lōngē, ad̵ ̶r off. Lōngē sŏnăt ŭndă, Virg. Syn. Prŏcŭl, ēmĭnŭs.

lōngīnquŭs, ă, ŭm, at a great distance. Lōngīnquă vĕtŭstās, Virg. Syn. Rĕmōtŭs, dīstāns, dīssĭtŭs, dīsjūnctŭs, ēxtĕrŭs, pĕregrīnŭs; dĭŭtūrnŭs.

lōngĭtūdo, ĭnĭs, f., length. Lōngĭtūdĭnĭs mŏdō, (Iamb.) Avien.

lōngŭs, ă, ŭm, long. Flāmmārŭm lōngōs, Virg. Syn. Ōblōngŭs, prōlīxŭs, prō-dūctŭs; dĭŭtūrnŭs; prŏcĕrŭs, āltŭs, māgnŭs.

lŏquācĭtās, ātĭs, f., talkativeness. Lătĭcīs lŏquācĭtātĕm, (Phal.) Sid. Syn. Gārrŭlĭtās. V. Garrulitas.

lŏquācĭtĕr, adv., pratingly. Fōrmă lŏquācĭtĕr ēt sĭtŭs, Hor. Syn. Vērbōsē.

lŏquācŭlŭs, ă, ŭm, a little talkative. Ōdĭōsă, lŏquācŭlă, Lucr.

lŏquāx, ācĭs, talkative. Rānīsquĕ lŏquācībŭs, Virg. Syn. Vērbōsŭs, gārrŭlŭs, mūltĭlŏquŭs.

lŏquēlă, æ, f., language. Ēx ōrĕ lŏquēlās, Lucr. V. Sermo, vox.

lŏquŏr, ĕrĭs, to speak. Ōbvĭŭm lŏquāmŭr, (Phal.) Syn. Ēlŏquŏr, dīco, fārī, āffārī, prŏfārī.

lōrĕŭs, ă, ŭm, made of leather. Lōrĕă flāgră, Prud. Syn. Ēx lōrō.

lōrīcă, æ, f., a coat of mail. Ēt lōrīcārŭm, Alcim. Syn. Thōrāx. Epith. Grăvĭs, ærātă, ăhēnă, nēxĭlĭs, ænĕă, fērrĕă, dūră, splēndĭdă, aūrātă, squāmmātă, splēndēns, cŏrŭscă, cŏrŭscāns, mĭcāns, trĭlīx, īmpērvĭă, squāmmĭfĕră, sānguĭnĕă, crŭēntă. V. Thorax.

lōrĭpēs, ĭpĕdĭs, bow-legged. Lōrĭpĕdĕm rēctŭs, Juv.

lōrŭm, ī, n., a thong of leather. Dāt lōră sĕcūndō, Virg. Epith. Ārctŭm, tĕnāx, strīctŭm, lōngŭm, vălĭdŭm, dūrŭm, rĭgĭdŭm. V. Habena; flagellum.

Lōtĭs, ĭdĭs, f., a nymph changed into the lote-tree. Lōtĭs ĭn hānc, Ov.

lōtōs, and tŭs, ī, f., the lote-tree. Cўtĭsŭm, lōtōsquĕ frĕquēntēs, Virg. Epith. Impĭă, ăquătĭcă, ăquātĭlĭs, ămāră, Mўgdŏnĭă, Phrўgĭă, Pāllădĭă.

lōtŭs, ă, ŭm, the pass. partic. of lavo. Lōtŭs ēt Hēspĕrĭă, Prosp. Syn. Lăvātŭs, ăblūtŭs.

lŭbēntĕr, adv., willingly. Lŭbēntēr cūrrĕrĕ, (Iamb.) Syn. Lĭbēntĕr, spōntĕ, ūltrō.

lŭbĕt, it pleases. Nōn tĭbī lŭbĕăt, (Phal.) Cat. V. Libet.

lŭbrĭco, ās, to make slippery. Lŭbrĭcĕt ōrbĕm, Juv.

lŭbrĭcŭs, ă, ŭm, slippery. Lŭbrĭcă cōnvōlvĭt, Virg. Syn. Lābĭlĭs, mōbĭlĭs, fŭgĭēns, fāllēns, flŭxŭs, præcēps, pĕrīcŭlōsŭs.

lŭcā-bōs, lŭcæ-bŏvĭs, m , an elephant. Indĕ bŏvēs lūcās, Lucan.

Lūcāgŭs, ī, m., the name of a warrior. Infērt sē Lūcāgŭs ālbĭs, Virg.

Lūcānĭă, æ, f., a province of Italy. Lūcānĭă bēllŭm, Hor.

lūcānĭcă, æ, f., a sausage. Vĕnĭo lūcānĭcă pōrcæ, Mart.

Lūcānŭs, ī, m., the poet; a native of Spain, but early removed to Rome. Jăcĕăt Lūcānŭs ĭn hōrtĭs, Juv. Epith. Dōctĭlŏquŭs, ārdēns, Ĭbērŭs, Hīspānŭs.

lŭcēllŭm, ī, n., the diminut. of lucrum. Ăn dūlcĕ lŭcēllŭm, Hor. V. Lucrum.

lūcĕo, ēs, lūxī, and ēsco, ĭs, to shine. Lūcĕăt ĭgnĕ, Tib. Stŭpĕănt lŭcēscĕrĕ sōlĕm, Virg. Syn. Illūcēsco, īllūcĕo, cōllūcĕo, splēndĕo, fūlgĕo, ēffūlgĕo, rĕfūlgĕo, ēmīco, nĭtĕo, rŭtĭlo, cōrŭsco, rădĭo, ĭrrădĭo. V. Splendor, lumen.

Lŭcērēs, ŭm, m. pl., the third century of knights instituted by Romulus and Tatius. Lŭcērēsquĕ cŏlōnī, Prop. Lŭcērĭbŭsquĕ dĕdĭt, Ov.

Lūcĕrĭă, æ, f., a city of Apulia. Tōnsæ Lūcĕrĭăm, Hor.

lŭcērnă, æ, f., a lamp. Ūnă lŭcērnă vŏcŏr, Mart. Syn. Lўchnŭs, lāmpăs, tædă, fāx. Epith. Vĭgĭl, vīvă, clără, lūcĭdă, fērvēns, mĭcāns, pīnguĭs, nŏctūrnă, ĭgnĭvŏmă, nŏctĭfŭgă, mātūtīnă. V. Lampas.

Lūcētĭŭs, iī, m., *a man's name.* Lūcētĭŭm pōrtæ, Virg.

lūcĭdŭs, ă, ŭm, *bright.* Lūcĭdŭs ōrdo, Hor. Syn. Lūcēns, splēndĭdŭs, splēndēns, fŭlgĭdŭs, fŭlgēns, nĭtĭdŭs, nĭtēns, rŭtĭlŭs, rŭtĭlāns, cŏrŭscŭs, cŏrŭscāns, rādĭāns, mĭcāns. V. Splendidus.

lūcĭfĕr, ă, ŭm, *bearing light.* Lūcĭfĕrĭs pŭĕrĭs, Ov.

Lūcĭfĕr, ĕrī, m., *the morning-star.* Lūcĭfĕr ēxĭt, Ov. Syn. Phōsphŏrŭs. Epith. Ālbŭs, rŏsĕŭs, sĕrēnŭs, aūrĕŭs, lūcĭdŭs, mātūtīnŭs, clārŭs, pūrŭs, pūrpŭrĕŭs. V. Diluculum, Aurora, mane.

lūcĭfŭgŭs, ă, ŭm, *avoiding light.* Stēllĭŏ, lūcĭfŭgīs, Virg. Syn. Nōctĭvăgŭs, nŏctūrnŭs.

Lūcīlĭŭs, iī, m., *a Roman satirical poet.* Lūcīlĭŭs ūrbĕm, H

Lūcīnă, æ, f., *the name of Diana and Juno.* Lūcēm, Lūcīṉ ēdīstī, Ov. V. Juno, Diana, Luna.

lūcĭŭs, iī, m., *a pike.* Lūcĭŭs ōbscūrās, Aus. Epith. Vŏrāx, răpāx, āspĕr.

Lucrētĭă, æ, f., *the wife of Tarquinius Collatinus ; she was violated by the son of Tarquinius Superbus, and slew herself.* Cāstō Lŭcrētĭă fērrō, Claud. Epith. Pŭdĭcă, cāstă, cōnstāns, gĕnĕrōsă, fōrmōsă, māgnănĭmă, vĕnūstă, īnfēlīx, Rōmānă, Cōllātīnă.

Lucrētĭlĭs, ĭs, m., *a mountain of the Sabines.* Sæpĕ Lŭcrētĭlĕm, Hor.

Lucrētĭŭs, iī, m., *the Roman poet.* Tūnc sūnt pĕrĭtūră Lŭcrētī, Ov. Epith. Dōctŭs, ēlĕgāns, ārdŭŭs, dīffĭcĭlĭs.

Lucrīnŭs, ī, m., *a lake near Baiæ.* Lūcrīnōque āddĭtă claūstră, Virg. Stāgnă Lūcrīnī, Mart.—2. -ŭs, ă, ŭm, *of the Lucrine lake.* Stāgnō sătūrātă Lŭcrīnō, Mart.

lucrŏr, ārĭs, *to gain.* Intĕrfēctă lŭcrāndī, Prud. Syn. Lŭcrĭfăcĭo.

lucrōsŭs, ă, ŭm, *advantageous.* Tĭbĭ sīt lŭcrōsă vŏlŭptās, Ov. Syn. Quæstŭōsŭs, ūtĭlĭs.

lucrŭm, ī, n., *gain.* Spērnĕ lŭcrŭm, Val. Mălŭm lŭcrĭquĕ cŭpīdo, Ov. Syn. Quæstŭs, cŏmmŏdŭm. Epith. Māgnŭm, ēxĭgŭŭm, tĕnŭĕ, tŭrpĕ, ĭnhŏnēstŭm, pŭdēndŭm, dūlcĕ, ōptātŭm.

lūctă, æ, *and* tātĭo, ōnĭs, f. ; *and* tāmĕn, ĭnĭs, n., *a wrestling.* Nĕ quīs cērtāmĭnĕ lūctæ, Aus. Rēmo ūt lūctāmĕn ăbēssĕt, Virg. Syn. Lūctātŭs, cērtāmĕn, pūgnă, pălæstră. V. Luctor.

lūctātŏr, ōrĭs, m., *a wrestler.* Ūt jăcĕt Aōnĭŏ lūctātŏr ăb hōspĭtĕ, Ov. V. Athleta.

lūctĭfĕr, *and* fĭcŭs, ă, ŭm, *mournful.* Lūctĭfĭcŭs păvŏr, Sil. Syn. Lūctŭōsŭs.

lūctĭsŏnŭs, ă, ŭm, *having a mournful sound.* Ēt lūctĭsŏnō mūgītū, (Spondaic.) Ov. Syn. Flēbĭlĭs, lāmēntābĭlĭs.

lūctŏr, ārĭs, *to wrestle.* Lūctātūr ărūndĭnĕ tēlŭm, Virg. Syn. Ōblūctŏr, cōntrā cōnŏr, cērto, īnsto, nītŏr, ōbnītŏr, cōntēndo.

lūctŭōsŭs, ă, ŭm, *doleful.* Hēspĕrĭæ mālă lūctŭōsæ, (Dact. Troch.) Hor. Syn. Fūnēstŭs, mĭsĕr, īnfēlīx, flēbĭlĭs, lacrўmābĭlĭs, lūgŭbrĭs, trīstĭs, mœstŭs.

lūctŭs, ūs, m., *sorrow.* Lūctŭs ŭt īn Drūsō, Pedo. Syn. Flētŭs, gĕmĭtŭs, lacrў-mæ, quēstŭs, plānctŭs, lāmēntŭm. Epith. Mœstŭs, trīstĭs, ægĕr, ămārŭs, ĕdāx, ăcērbŭs, ātrōx, tūmĭdŭs, sævŭs, sēgnĭs, mĭsĕr, ĭnērs, ăvĭdŭs, līvĭdŭs, ātĕr, ăcĕr, ūrgēns, hōrrĭfĭcŭs, īnfōrmĭs, quĕrŭlŭs, rĭgĭdŭs, fātālĭs, rĕsŏnāns, ŭndāns, mœrēns. V. Lugeo, lacrymæ, fletus.

lūcubro, ās, *to work in the night.* Nōx lūcŭbrātă Cămœnĭs, Mart. Syn. Ēlū-cubro, lăbōro.

lūcŭlēntē, *aud* tĕr, adv., *clearly.* Lūcŭlēntĕr dīssĕrĕt, (Iamb.) Prud. Syn. Clārē, nĭtĭdē.

lūcŭlēntŭs, ă, ŭm, *clear.* Mĭhĭ lūcŭlēntŭs Ātўs, (Phal.) Mart. Syn. Clārŭs, nĭtĭdŭs.

Lūcŭllŭs, ī, m., *a celebrated Roman.* Chlămўdēs Lūcŭllŭs, Hor.

lūcŭs, ī, m., *a wood.* Cērtă dŏmŭs, lūcĭs, Virg. Syn. Sўlvă, nĕmŭs, sāltŭs. Epith. Săcĕr, sacrātŭs, sĭlēns, īncĭdŭŭs, vĕrēndŭs, hōrrēns, tĕnĕbrōsŭs. V. Sylva.

lūdĭă, æ, f., *a female dancer.* Lūdĭă sūmpsĕrĭt ūnquăm, Juv.

lūdĭbrĭŭm, iī, n., *a mockery.* Mĭsĕræ lūdĭbrĭă chārtæ, Mart. Lūdĭbrĭŭm nĕcĭs, Sil. Syn. Lūdŭs.

M

lŭdĭbŭndŭs, ă, ŭm, *sportive.* Hæc lŭdĭbŭndŭs dīxĕrăt, (Iamb. Dim.) Prud. Syn. Jŏcāns ; ērrābŭndŭs, văgŭs.

lūdĭcĕr, *and* icrŭs, ă, ŭm, *ludicrous.* Aŭt lūdĭcră pĕtūntŭr, Virg. Vălĕăt rēs lūdĭcră, Hor. Syn. Jŏcōsŭs.

lūdicrŭm, ī, n., *a farce.* Cætĕră lūdĭcră, Hor. Syn. Jŏcī.

lūdĭfīco, ās, *and* cŏr, ārĭs, *to mock.* Imprŏvĭdă lūdĭfīcētŭr, Stat. Syn. Illūdo, dērīdĕo, fāllo.

lūdĭŭs, ī̄, m., *a dancer, actor.* Lūdĭŭs æquātăm, Ov.

lūdo, lūsī, *to play.* Lūdēbăm tŭtŭs, Mart. Syn. Văco, īndūlgĕo ; īllūdo, rīdĕo, īrrīdĕo ; dēlūdo, fāllo, dēcĭpĭo.

lūdŭs, ī, m., *a play, sport.* Lūdŭs ĕnĭm, Hor. Syn. Lūsŭs ; jŏcŭs ; gўmnāsĭŭm. Epith. Jŏcōsŭs, lætŭs, jūcūndŭs, mōllĭs, grātŭs, lĕpĭdŭs, īnnŏcŭŭs, blāndŭs, fēstŭs, plăcĭdŭs, ămœnŭs, pŭĕrīlĭs, lĕvĭs, īnānĭs, dūbĭŭs, ăncĕps, fāllăx, vĕtŭŭs, īllĭcĭtŭs. V. Ludo.—2. Lūdī pūblĭcī, *public spectacles.* Cĕlĕbrī cĕrtāmĭnĕ lūdōs, Virg. Syn. Spēctācŭlă. Epith. Sŏlēnnĕs, cĕlebrēs, thĕātrālēs, sacrī, fēstī.

lŭēlă, æ, f., *punishment.* Scĕlĕrīsquĕ lŭēlă, Lucr.

lŭēs, ĭs, f., *a contagion.* Arbŏrĭbŭsquĕ sătīsquĕ lŭēs, Virg. Syn. Pēstĭs, cōntāgĭēs, cōntāgĭo, cōntāgĭă.

Lūgdūnŭm, ī, n., *a town in France.* Lūgdūnŭmquĕ tŭŭm, Sid. Epith. Nŏbĭlĕ, dīvĕs, āntīquŭm, flōrēns, sŭpērbŭm, īnsīgnĕ, pŏpŭlōsŭm, clārŭm, māgnĭfīcŭm.

lūgĕo, lūxī, *to bewail.* Vērsĭs lūgĕrĕt, Virg. Syn. Flĕo, gĕmo, plāngo, lacrў-mŏr, lāmēntŏr, quĕrŏr, dŏlĕo, plŏro. V. Luctus, tristis.

lūgubrĭs, ĕ, *mournful.* Lŭgūbrĕ bēllŭm, Hor. Sāngŭĭnĕī lūgūbrĕ rŭbēnt, Virg. Syn. Lūctŭōsŭs, lāmēntābĭlĭs.

lŭmbŭs, ī, m., lŭmbī, ōrŭm, m. pl., *the loins.* Fĭcēdŭlă lŭmbō, Mart. Pĕr lŭmbōs spīnă, Virg. Epith. Călĭdī, lāscīvī, sălācēs.

lŭmĕn, ĭnĭs, n., *light, an eye, &c.* Lūmĭnĭbŭs flāmmæ, Virg. Syn. Lŭx, fŭlgŏr, splēndŏr, nĭtŏr, jŭbăr, făx ; dĭēs ; ŏcŭlŭs. Epith. Ignĕŭm, flāmmĕŭm, clārŭm, fŭlgĭdŭm, cŏrŭscŭm, rădĭāns, trĕmŭlŭm, nĭtĭdŭm, mĭcāns, īrrădĭāns, sīdĕrĕŭm, ālmŭm, ōptātŭm, pūrŭm, sĕrēnŭm, rŭtĭlāns, splēndĭdŭm, flāmmāns, văgŭm, ērrāns, œthĕrĕŭm, Phœbĕŭm. V. Luceo, illumino, splendor.

Lūnă, æ, f., *the moon.* Vărĭōs lūnæquĕ lăbōrēs, Virg. Syn. Phœbē, Diănă, Lātōnĭă, Lūcīnă, Cўnthĭă, Dēlĭă, Hĕcătĕ, Trĭvĭă. Epith. Mēnstrŭă, trĕmŭlă, lūcĭdă, bĭcōrnĭs, aūrĕă, nĭvĕă, fōrmōsă, glŏbōsă, hūmĭdă, rōscĭdă, cōrnĭgĕră, gĕlĭdă, frīgĭdă, pāllĭdă, clārā, sĕrēnă, crēscēns, dēcrēscēns, sĕnēscēns, mūtābĭlĭs, īnstābĭlĭs, văgă, ērrāns, pērnŏx, nōctūrnă, sĭlēns, tācĭtă.

lūnārĭs, ĕ, *of the moon.* Lūnārī sūbjēctă glŏbō, Claud.

lūnātŭs, ă, ŭm, *horned like the moon.* Ămăzŏnĭdŭm lūnātĭs āgmĭnă, Virg. Syn. Cūrvātŭs, rĕcūrvŭs.

lŭno, ās, *to bend like a half moon.* Lūnāvītquĕ gĕnū, Ov. V. Curvo.

lŭo, ĭs, lŭī, *to atone, pay.* Tāndĕm lŭĭtŭră prŏĭūndō, Claud. Syn. Sōlvo, pēr-sōlvo, ēxsōlvo, pēndo ; lăvo, ēlŭo.

lŭpă, æ, f., *a she-wolf, a harlot.* Trādĭs ŏvĭlĕ lŭpæ, Ov. Epith. Fĕrŏx, trŭx, ĭn-hūmānă, fŭrēns, ōbscœnă, lāscīvă. V. Meretrix.

lŭpānăr, ārĭs, n., *a brothel, a harlot.* Cēntŏnĕ lŭpānăr, Juv. Syn. Prōstĭbŭlŭm, lūstrŭm. Epith. Spūrcŭm, ĭmpūrŭm, tūrpĕ, ĭmmūndŭm, fœdŭm, ōbscœnŭm, prŏbrōsŭm.

lŭpātŭm, ī, n., *a sharp bit for a horse.* Pārĕrĕ lŭpātĭs, Virg. Syn. Frænŭm, hăbēnă. V. Frænum.

Lŭpērcăl, ālĭs, n., *a place at the foot of Mount Palatine, dedicated to Pan.* Sŭb rūpĕ Lŭpērcăl, Virg.

Lŭpērcālĭă, ŭm or ōrŭm, n. pl., *festivals of the Luperci.* Ov.

Lŭpērcī, ōrŭm, m. pl., *the priests of Pan.* Nūdōsquĕ Lŭpērcōs, Virg. Epith. Sŭccīnctī, ăgĭlēs, văgī, văgāntēs.

lŭpī, ōrŭm, m. pl., *a bit.* Accĭpĭt ŏrĕ lŭpōs, Ov.

lŭpīnŭs, ī, m., *and* nŭm, ī, n., *a kind of bitter pulse.* Trīstĭsquĕ lŭpīnī, Virg.

lŭpīnŭs, ă, ŭm, *of a wolf.* Fĭbră lŭpīnī, Ser.

lŭpŭs, ī, m., *a wolf.* Tōrvă lĕænă lŭpŭm, Virg. Epith. Ŭlŭlāns, răptŏr, ācĕr, răpāx, āspĕr, ăvĭdŭs, sævŭs, sāngŭĭnĕŭs, crŭēntŭs, răpĭdŭs, fĕrŭs, răbĭdŭs, vŏrăx, trŭx, fĕrōx, tĕrrĭbĭlĭs, ĭmĭnītĭs, crūdēlĭs, prædo, hīrtŭs, ĭngēns, ĭnfēstŭs, ĭnsĭdĭātŏr, nŏctūrnŭs.

lūrĭdŭs, ă, ŭm, *ghastly.* I.ūrĭdă tĕrrĭbĭlēs, Ov. Syn. Pāllĭdŭs, pāllēns.

lŭrŏr, ōrĭs, m., *paleness.* Lŭrōrĭs dē cŏrpŏre ĕōrŭm, Lucr. V. Pallor.

lŭscīnĭă, æ, f., *a nightingale.* Lŭscĭnĭæ tūmŭlŭm, Mart. Syn. Phĭlōmēlă. V. Philomela.

lūscŭs, ă, ŭm, *blind of one eye.* Lūscŭs ŭtrōquĕ, vīdĕt, Ov.

lŭsĭto, ās, *the frequent. of* ludo. Dēntĕ lūsĭtāntĕ fīmbrĭăm, (Iamb.) V. Ludo.

lŭsŏr, ōrĭs, m., *a deceiver.* Pērdĕrĕ lŭsŏr, Ov.

lŭstrālĭs, ĕ, *belonging to purification.* Ĕt lŭstrālĭbŭs ēxtīs, Virg. Syn. Lŭstrĭcŭs.

lŭstro, ās, *to purify.* Mœnĭă lŭstrăt ĕquō, Ov. Syn. Pĕragro, vīso, ĭnvīso, pĕrērro, ŏbĕo, cīrcŭmĕo; ēxpĭo, pūrgo; cīrcŭmspĭcĭo, ēxămĭno.

lŭstrŭm, ī, n., *a den; the purification of a city by sacrifices.* Lŭstră fĕrārŭm, Virg. Syn. Antrŭm, căvērnă, spēcŭs, fĕrārŭm cŭbĭlĕ, lătĭbŭlŭm; lŭpănăr; lŭstrālĕ sacrĭfĭcĭŭm, sacrŭm; quīnquĕnnĭŭm, Ōlŷmpĭăs.

lŭsŭs, ūs, m., *sport.* Mōllĭbăt lŭsūquĕ sŭō, Ov. Syn. Lūdŭs, jŏcŭs. V. Ludus, jocus.

lŭtĕŏlŭs, ă, ŭm, *yellowish.* Mōllĭă lŭtĕŏlă, Virg. V. Luteus.

lŭtēsco, ĭs, *to become dirty.* Tērră lŭtēscĭt, Fur. Syn. Sōrdēsco, ĭn lŭtŭm cōgŏr.

Lŭtētĭă, æ, f., *Paris, the capital of France.* Pŏpŭlōsă Lŭtētĭă gēntĭs, Sc. Syn. Pārīsĭī. Epith. Māgnă, ĭmmēnsă, rēgĭă, nōbĭlĭs, inclŷtă, dŏctă, pŏtēns, fēlīx, vīctrīx, sŭpērbă, clāră, fămōsă, cĕlēbrĭs.

lŭtĕŭs, ă, ŭm, *yellow.* Lŭtĕă bīgĭs, Virg. Syn. Flāvŭs, flāvēns.

lŭtĕŭs, ă, ŭm, *of clay.* Rhēnī lŭtĕŭm căpŭt, Hor. Syn. Lŭtōsŭs.

lŭto, ās, *to spot, daub.* Nē lŭtĕt īnmūndŭm, Mart. V. Lino.

lŭtŭlēntŭs, ă, ŭm, *muddy.* Vărĭōs lŭtŭlēntă, Hor. Syn. Cœnōsŭs, līmōsŭs, lŭtōsŭs.

lŭtŭm, ī, n., *mud.* Ămīcă lŭtō sŭs, Hor. Syn. Līmŭs, cœnŭm, sōrdēs, fæx, ĭllŭvĭēs. Epith. Tūrpĕ, ūdŭm, sōrdĭdŭm, fœtĭdŭm, grăvĕŏlēns (*trisyl.*); pălūstrĕ, crăssŭm, pīnguĕ, tĕnāx, īnfēctŭm.

lŭtŭm, ī, n., *a yellow herb.* Vēllĕră lŭtō, Virg. Syn. I.ŭtĕă. Epith. Crŏcĕŭm.

lŭx, lūcĭs, f., *light.* In lūcĕ rĕfulsīt, Virg. Syn. Lūmĕn, splēndŏr, fŭlgŏr, nĭtŏr, jŭbăr, fāx; dĭēs. Epith. Ignĕă, flāmmĕă, ălmă, sĕrēnă, rădĭāns. V. Lumen, splendor.

lūxŭrĭă, æ, *or* ĭēs, ĭēī, f., *luxury.* Lūxŭrĭăm prēmĕrĕt, Mart. Syn. Lūxŭs; lāscīvĭă, lĭbīdo. Epith. Prōdĭgă, blāndă, pĕtŭlāns, mĭscră, mōllĭs, dēsĕs, ĭnērs, ĭgnāvă, sēgnĭs, tūrpĭs, ĭnhŏnēstă, nŏcīvă, nōxĭă, dēsĭdĭōsă, ēffūsă, īnsānă, cæcă, ēffrænĭs. V. Libido.

lūxŭrĭo, ās, *and* ŏr, ārĭs, *to be wanton.* Lūxŭrĭānt ănĭmī, Ov. Lūxŭrĭātŭr ăgrō, Id. Syn. Lūxŭrĭŏr, lĭbīdĭnŏr, lāscīvĭo; ăbūndo.

lūxŭrĭōsŭs, ă, ŭm, *luxurious.* Lūxŭrĭōsŭs ŏpēs, Mart. Syn. Lāscīvŭs, lĭbīdĭnōsŭs; prōdĭgŭs; ăbūndāns.

lūxŭs, ūs, m., *luxury, magnificence.* Nĕ lūxu ōbtūsĭŏr ūsŭs, Virg. Syn. Lūxŭrĭēs, lūxŭrĭă; pōmpă, fāstŭs. Epith. Rēgālĭs, splēndĭdŭs, rēgĭfĭcŭs, mōllĭs, mălŭs, Achæmēnĭŭs, nŏcēns, fœdŭs, fœmĭnĕŭs, ēffūsŭs, sēgnĭs, īnfrænĭs, ēxlēx, īnsānŭs, cæcŭs, tūrpĭs. V. Luxuria.

I.ÿæŭs, ī, m., *a name of Bacchus.* Pătrĭquĕ Lÿæō, Virg. V. Bacchus.

Lÿcābās, āntĭs, m., *an Etrurian changed into a dolphin.* Dē nŭmĕrō Lÿcăbās, Ov.

Lÿcæŭs, ī, m., *a mountain of Arcadia.* Dē mŏrĕ Lÿcæī, Virg. Epith. Oĭmbrōsŭs, gĕlĭdŭs, pīnĭfĕr, Pārrhăsĭŭs; ăngūstŭs, āltŭs, frĭgĭdŭs, nĭvĕŭs.

Lÿcāmbēs, æ, m., *a Theban lampooned by Archilochus.* Quālĭs Lÿcāmbæ, Hor.

Lÿcāōn, ŏnĭs, m., *a cruel king of Arcadia, changed by Jupiter into a wolf.* Sŏcĕrŭmquĕ Lÿcăŏnă sūmĭt, Ov. Epith. Ārcădĭŭs, sævŭs, ĭmmānĭs, fĕrōx, crūdēlĭs, dīrŭs, ĭmpĭŭs, ĕffĕgĕŭs.

Lÿcāŏnĭs, ĭdĭs, f., *the daughter of Lycaon.* Pērjŭră Lÿcāŏnĭ, Ov.

Lÿcāŏnĭŭs, ă, ŭm, *of Lycaon.* Eccĕ Lÿcāŏnĭæ, Ov.

I.ÿcē, ēs, f., *a woman's name.* Aŭdīvĕrĕ, I.ÿcē, Hor.

I.ÿcēŭm, ī, n, *the school of Aristotle, near Athens.* Vīsīssĕ Lÿcēŭm, Hor.

lÿchnŭs, ī, m., *a lamp.* Dēpēndēnt lÿchnī, Virg. Syn. Lāmpăs, lūcērnă. V. Lampas.

I.ÿcĭă, æ, f., *a part of Asia Minor.* Lÿcĭæ quŏquĕ fērtĭlĭs ăgrĭs, Ov.

Lўcĭdās, æ, m., *a centaur.* Eūrўnŏmŏs, Lўcĭdās, Ov.
Lўcīmnĭă, æ, f., *the wife of Mæcenas.* Mūsă Lўcīmnĭæ, Hor.
lўcīscă, æ, f., *a mongrel.* Cŭm frātrĕ lўcīscā, Ov.
Lўcīscŭs, ī, m., *a man's name.* Hor.
Lўcīŭs, ă, ŭm, *Lycian.* Lўclŏ Gōrtўnĭā cōrnū, Virg.
Lўcŏmēdēs, ĭs, m., *the king of Scyros.* Nūpĕr Lўcŏmēdĭs ĭn aūlā, Stat. EPITH.
Scўrĭŭs, pĭŭs.
Lўcōrĭăs, ădĭs, f., *a Naiad.* Ēt flāvă Lўcōrĭăs, Virg.
Lўcōrĭs, ĭdĭs, f., *a freed-woman, beloved by the poet Gallus.* Lĕgăt īpsă Lўcōrĭs,
Virg.
Lўcōrmās, æ, m., *a river of Ætolia.* Flāvūsquĕ Lўcōrmās, Ov.
Lўcōtās, æ, m., *a centaur.* Jăcŭlātŏrēmquĕ Lўcōtān, Ov.
Lўctĭŭs, ă, ŭm, *of Lyctus, a city of Crete.* Lўctĭŭs Ĭdŏmĕneŭs, Virg.
Lўcūrgĭdēs, æ, m., *the son of Lycurgus.* Quīquĕ Lўcūrgĭdēn. Ov.
Lўcūrgŭs, ī, m., *a king of Thrace, made mad by Bacchus.* Bĭpēnnĭfĕrŭmquĕ Lў-
cūrgŭm, Ov. EPITH. Ācĕr, Thrāx, māgnănĭmŭs, sĕcūrĭgĕr, īmpĭŭs, vēsānŭs.—
2. *the Spartan lawgiver.* EPITH. Fōrtĭs, lēgĭfĕr, Ămўclæŭs, Thĕrāpnæŭs, Lăcĕ-
dæmŏnĭŭs, jūstŭs, æquŭs, prūdēns.
Lўcŭs, ī, m., *a centaur.* Cĕcĭdīssĕ Lўcŭm, Ov.
Lўdē, ēs, f., *the wife of Antimachus.* Lўdē dīlēctă pŏētæ, Ov.
Lўdĭă, æ, f., *a part of Asia Minor.* Lўdĭă thўrsōs, Claud. SYN. Mæŏnĭă. EPITH.
Dīvĕs, prĕtĭōsă, aūrĕă.
Lўdĭŭs, ă, ŭm, *of Lydia.* Ŭbī Lўdĭŭs ārvă, Virg.
Lўdŭs, ī, m., *a Lydian.* Lўdōrŭmquĕ mănŭm, Virg. SYN. Mæŏnĭŭs.
lўmphă, æ, f., *water.* Dē gūrgĭtĕ lўmphās, Virg. SYN. Āquă, ūndă. V. Aqua.
lўmphātŭs, ă, ŭm, *insane.* Fŭrĭt lўmphātă pĕr ūrbĕm, Virg. SYN. Lўmphātĭcŭs,
fŭrēns, răbĭdŭs, īnsānŭs, dēmēns.
lўmpho, ās, *to madden.* Lўmphāvĕrăt ūrbĕm, V. Flac.
lўncĕŭs, ă, ŭm, *of a lynx.* Ōptĭmă lўncĕĭs, Hor.
Lўncĕŭs, ĕĭ, eī, *or* ĕŏs, m., *one of the Argonauts.* Āphărēĭă Lўncĕŭs, Ov. EPITH.
Fōrtĭs, ācĕr.—2. adj., -cĕŭs, ă, ŭm, *of Lynceus.* Lўncĕŏ Cāstŏr ăb ēnsĕ, Ov.
Lўncīdēs, æ, m., *the son of Lynceus or Lyncus.* Nārrăt Lўncīdēs, Ov.
Lўncŭs, ī, m., *a king of Scythia, changed into a lynx by Ceres.* Lўncŭs ĕrăt, Ov.
EPITH. Pĕrfĭdŭs, īmmānĭs.
Ỹux, lўncĭs, f., *a lynx, an ounce.* Lўncĭbŭs ăd cœlŭm, Prop. EPITH. Măcŭlōsă,
vărĭă, vērsĭcŏlŏr, vēlōx, cĭtă, fŭgāx, Scўthĭcă, tĭmĭdă, ăcŭtă.
lȳră, æ, f., *a lyre.* Pōllĭcĕ fīlă lȳræ, Ov. SYN. Cĭthără, fĭdēs (ĭum), tēstŭdo.
EPITH. Īmbēllĭs, ĕbūrnă, Æmŏnĭă, Phœbēă, Ăpōllĭnĕă, Cāstălĭă, Aŏnĭă, Pĭĕrĭă,
cănōră, blāndă, ārgūtă, vōcālĭs, sŏnōră, suāvĭs, Ăgānĭppēă; Ōrphæă, Ōrphēĭă,
Thrācĭă, Bīstŏnĭă, Bīstŏnĭs, Rhŏdŏpēĭă; Ărĭŏnĭă, Āmphĭŏnĭă, Cўllēnĭă. V.
Fides, ium; Cithara.
lўrĭcĕn, ĭnĭs, m., *one who plays on the lyre.* V. Fidicen.
lўrĭcŭs, ă, ŭm, *lyric.* Ēt lўrĭcī vātēs, Aus.
Lўrnēssĭs, ĭdĭs, f., *of Lyrnessus.* Lўrnēssĭdĕ trīstĭs, Ov.
Lўrnēssĭŭs, ă, ŭm, *of Lyrnessus.* Lўrnēssĭă mœnĭă vīdī, Ov.
Lўrnēssŏs, *or* ŭs, ī, m., *a city of Troas.* Pārvă Lўrnēssŏs, Sen.
Lўsīppŭs, ī, m., *a great sculptor.* Ālĭŭs Lўsīppŏ, Hor. EPITH. Sŏlērs, dēxtĕr,
pĕrĭtŭs, īnclўtŭs, nōbĭlĭs.

M.

MĂCĂRĒĬS, ĭdĭs, f., *the daughter of Macareus.* Măcărēĭdă lŭsĕrĭt, Ov.
Măcăreŭs, ĕĭ *or* eī, (trisyl.) m., *the son of Æolus.* Vēctĕ Pĕlēthrŏnĭŭm Măcăreŭs
īn pēctŭs, Ov. EPITH. Æŏlĭdēs.
Măcĕdo, ŏnĭs, m., *a Macedonian.* Intāctŭm Măcĕdo, Claud.
Măcĕdŏnĭă, æ, f., (*sometimes* cēdŏnĭă, *by licence,*) *a kingdom of Greece.* SYN.
Ēmăthĭă, Æmŏnĭă. EPITH. Pūgnāx, fĕrōx, vīctrīx, īndŏmĭtă, aūdāx, nōbĭlĭs,
clără, fōrtĭs.
Măcĕdŏnĭŭs, ă, ŭm, *Macedonian.* Măcĕdŏnĭăquĕ sărīssă, Ov.
măcēllŭm, ī, n., *and* ŭs, ī, m., *a market-place, shambles.* Mīllĭă tērnă măcēllŏ,
Hor. SYN. Fŏrŭm.

măcĕo, ĕs, ērĕ, *to be lean.* Ĭtă cūrā măcĕt, Plaut.

măcĕr, macră, crŭm, *lean.* Pīnguī măcĕr ēst, Virg. Syn. Măcĭlēntŭs, grăcĭlĭs, grăcĭlēntŭs. Epith. Măcĭē cōnfēctŭs, tĕnŭătŭs, āttĕnŭātŭs, tĕnŭĭs, pĕrēsŭs, hŏrrĭdŭs, dēfŏrmātŭs, tŭrpĭs, īnfŏrmĭs, ēxēsŭs, squālĭdŭs, ōbdūctŭs, ēnēctŭs, āttrītŭs, dēfīcĭēns, lānguēns, lānguĭdŭs, tābēns, tābĭdŭs.

măcĕrĭă, æ, *and* ĭēs, ĭēī, f., *a wall.* Quāmvīs măcĕrĭēs, Prop.

măcĕro, ās, *to make soft by steeping.* Măcĕrŏr ĭntĕrdŭm, Ov. Syn. Cōnfĭcĭo, ēxtĕnŭo, āttĕro, ēxēdo, tābĕfăcĭo.

măcēsco, *and* măcrēsco, ĭs, *to grow lean.* Āltĕrĭŭs măcrēscĭt rēbŭs, Hor.

Māchāōn, ŏnĭs, m., *son of Esculapius.* Dīmīttĕ Māchāŏnăs ōmnēs, Mart. Epith. Dōctŭs, pĕrītŭs, prūdēns, fīdŭs, fĭdēlĭs, ĭngĕnĭōsŭs, īndūstrĭŭs, sōlērs. V. Medicus.

Māchāŏnĭŭs, ă, ŭm, *of Machaon.* Illĕ Māchāŏnĭă, Ov. Syn. Mĕdĭcŭs.

măchĭnă, æ, f., *device, a machine.* Māchĭnă mūrōs, Virg. Syn. Ars, ārtĭfĭcĭŭm, dŏlŭs, āstūtĭă, fraŭs ; mōlēs, īnstrūmēntŭm, tŏrmēntŭm bēllĭcŭm, bālīstă, ărĭēs, bōmbārdă. Epith. Strīdēns, mūrālĭs, sævă, īngĕnĭōsă, īngēns, fūlmĭnĕă, mĭnāx, stŭpēndă, īmmānĭs ; æquātă cælō, sāxă rŏtāns, mūrōs quătĭēns ; dŏlōsă, scĕlĕrātă, dĭră, lătēns. V. Tormentum bellicum ; dolus, fraus.

măchĭnātŏr, ōrĭs, m., *an engineer.* Ō māchĭnātŏr fraūdĭs, (Iamb.) Sen. Syn. Fabrĭcātŏr, ārtĭfēx.

măchĭnŏr, ārĭs, *to frame.* Māchĭnŏr, ĭnvĕnĭāmquĕ, Lucr. .Syn. Mōlĭŏr, ēxcō- gĭto, mĕdĭtŏr, strŭo, ēxtrŭo, fabrĭco, fabrĭcŏr.

măcĭēs, ĭēī, f., *leanness.* Ē sȳlvīs măcĭē, Virg. Syn. Tābēs. Epith. Hōrrĭdă, tŭrpĭs, īnfēlīx, mĭsĕră, īnfŏrmĭs, dēcŏlŏr, jējūnă, squālĭdă, pāllĭdă, dēfŏrmĭs, trīstĭs, ĭnērs, pāllēns, ārĭdă, līvĭdă. V. Macer.

măcĭlēntŭs, ă, ŭm, *lean.* Plaut. V. Macer.

māctĕ, adv., *go on, advance.* Māctĕ nŏvā vīrtūtĕ, Virg.

mācto, ās, *to slay, to sacrifice.* Ĭngēntēm māctābăt ăd ārās, Virg. V. Occĭdo, sacrifico.

măcŭlă, æ, f., *a stain.* Rējĭcĕ, nē măcŭlĭs, Virg. Syn. Nŏtă, lābēs ; dēdĕcŭs, īnfāmĭă. Epith. Tŭrpĭs, ōbscœnă, sōrdĭdă, ātră, īmmūndă, īmpūră, fœdă, dēfŏrmĭs, pŭdēndă. V. Sordes.

măcŭlo, ās, *to stain.* Lūcēns măcŭlātŭr ămīctŭ, Sil. Syn. Cōmmăcŭlo, īnquĭno, cōĭnquĭno, fœdo, pōllŭo, cōntămĭno, cōnspūrco, tūrpo, dētūrpo, dēfŏrmo ; măcŭ- lĭs āspērgo, nŏto, vărĭo, dīstīnguo, pīngo, lĭno, ōblĭno, īllĭno.

măcŭlōsŭs, ă, ŭm, *stained.* Nŏtæ, măcŭlōsŭs ĕt aūrō, Virg. Syn. Măcŭlātŭs, īnquĭnātŭs, sōrdĭdŭs, măcŭlĭs īnfēctŭs ; măcŭlīs pīctŭs, āspērsŭs, vărĭātŭs, īllĭtŭs.

mădĕfăcĭo, fēcī, *to wet.* Mădĕfēcĕrăt hērbās, Virg. Syn. Hūmēcto, īrrĭgo, īrrŏro, ăblŭo.

mădĕfīo, fīs, fīt, *to be made wet.* Ĭtĕrŭm mădĕfīēnt, Virg. Syn. Mădēsco, mădĕo, īmmădĕo, hūmēctŏr.

mădĕo, ēs, *to be wet.* Spārsă crŭŏrĕ mădĕt, Ov. V. Humeo.

mădēsco, ĭs, *to grow wet.* Plŭvĭōquĕ mădēscĭt, Ov. Syn. Mădĕfīo, mădĕo, īmmădĕo.

mădĭdo, ās, *to wet.* Illĕ nŏvō mădĭdāntēs, Claud. V. Madefacio.

mădĭdŭs, ă, ŭm, *wet.* Ĕt sīccāt mădĭdās, Claud. Syn. Mădēns, hūmĭdŭs, hūmēns, ūdŭs, ūvĭdŭs.

mădŏr, ōrĭs, m., *humidity.* Aūstrō cēssāntĕ, mădōrēs, Fill. Syn. Hūmŏr. Epith. Flŭĭdŭs, rōscĭdŭs, rĭgŭŭs, īrrĭgŭŭs.

Mæāndĕr, drōs, *or* drŭs, drī, m., *a river of Anatolia.* Mæāndĕr ĭn ūndīs, Ov. Epith. Sĭnŭōsŭs, ērrāns, văgŭs, tōrtŭs, rĕcūrvŭs, īntōrtŭs, reflŭŭs, sĭbi ōbvĭŭs, īncērtŭs, āmbĭgŭŭs, ōblīquŭs, fāllāx, ămœnŭs, īnflēxŭs.

Mæāndrĭŭs, ă, ŭm, *of the Mæander.* Jŭvĕnīs Mæāndrĭŭs, Ov.

Mæcēnās, ātĭs, m., *the minister of Augustus.* Ex quō Mæcēnās, Hor. Epith. Dōctŭs, īllūstrĭs, mūnīfĭcŭs, clārŭs, ămīcŭs.

Mænă, æ, f., *an anchovy.* Fœcūndūmquĕ gĕnŭs, mænæ, Ov.

Mænădĕs, ŭm, f. pl., *the Bacchantes.* Mænădĕs, ō quāntŭs, Ov. Syn. Bācchæ, Bācchāntĕs, Bāssărĭdĕs. V. Bacchæ.

Mænălĭŭs, ă, ŭm, *and* lĭs, ĭdĭs, f., *of Mænalus, Mænalian, Arcadian.* Incĭpĕ Mæ- nălĭŏs, Virg. Mænălĭs ĕrŏs, Ov.

Mænălŭs, ī, m., *a mountain of Arcadia.* Mænălŭs ārgūtŭm, Virg. Syn. Mænălă. Epith. Altŭs, sŭblīmĭs, ārdŭŭs, pīnĭfĕr, vĭrēns, frōndēns, ūmbrāns, hōrrĭdŭs.

Mænàs, ădĭs, f., *a Bacchante, a Bacchanalian woman.* Mænădĭs ēffūsĭs, Ov. V. Mænades.

Mænĭŭs, ĭi, *a man's name.* Mænĭŭs ābsēntĕm, Hor.

Mæŏnĭă, æ, f., *a name of Lydia.* Pātrĭă Mæŏnĭa ēst, Ov.

Mæŏnĭdēs, æ, m., *a name of Homer.* Mæŏnĭdēs nūllās, Ov. V. Homerus.

Mæŏnĭs, ĭdĭs, f., *and* ĭŭs, ă, ŭm, *Mæonian.* Mæŏnĭs Assўrĭŭm, Ov. Pērlĕgĕ Mæŏnĭŏ, Mart. Syn. Lўdŭs, Lўdĭŭs.

Mæōtĭs, ĭdĭs, f., *a lake in Scythia.* Mæōtĭdĕ clārŭs, Ov. Epith. Gĕlĭdă, pigră, lōngīnquă, Bŏrĕālĭs, Arctĭcă.

Mæōtĭŭs, *and* tĭcŭs, ă, ŭm, *of the lake Mæotis.* Mæōtĭăquc ūndă, Virg.

Mæră, æ, f., *a woman changed into a dog.* Quōs Mæră nŏvō, Ov.

Mævĭŭs, ĭi, m., *a bad poet.* Tŭă cārmĭnă, Mævī, Virg.

mágă, æ, f., *a sorceress.* Ārtēsquĕ mágārŭm, Ov. Syn. Incāntātrīx, vĕnēfĭcă, lămĭă, săgă. Epith. Thēssălă, Æmŏnĭă; Æeă, Cōlchĭcă; īmprŏbă, dīră, ēxĭtĭōsă, tūrpĭs, impĭă, ĭnhūmānă, fĕrōx, scĕlĕrātă, īnfāmĭs, sacrĭlĕgă, scĕlēstă, mĭnāx, vānă, fāllāx, Tārtărĕă, Stўgĭă, īnfērnă, tērrĭbĭlĭs. V. Venefica.

mägālĭă, ōrŭm, n. pl., *Numidian cottages.* Ænēās mägālĭă quōndăm, Virg. Syn. Măpālĭă, căsă, tŭgŭrĭŭm. V. Casa.

mägĕ, *more.* Nŭm mägĕ sīt nōstrŭm, Virg. Syn. Măgĭs, plūs.

Măgī, ōrŭm, m. pl., *the Magi.* V. Magus. Epith. Pĭi, Eōi.

mägĭă, æ, f., *sorcery.* Illĕ mägĭæ, Prud. Syn. Vĕnēfĭcĭŭm, incāntātĭo. V. Incantatio, veneficium.

mägĭcŭs, ă, ŭm, *magical.* Hīc mägĭcōs āffērt, Juv. Syn. Cīrcēŭs, Ææŭs, Thēssälĭcŭs. V. Magia.

mägĭs, *more, rather.* Jăm mägĭs ātquĕ mägĭs, Lucan. Syn. Pŏtĭŭs.

mägīstĕr, trī, m., *a master.* Sæpĕ mägīstĕr ĕrăm, Ov. Syn. Præcēptŏr, dōctŏr, mŏdĕrātŏr. Epith. Dōctŭs, mītĭs, bĕnīgnŭs, ămīcŭs, mānsuĕtŭs, indūstrĭŭs, vĭgĭl, sēdŭlŭs, impĭgĕr, pĕrītŭs, īnsīgnĭs, sĕvērŭs, rĭgĭdŭs, āspĕr, mōrōsŭs, clāmōsŭs, grăvĭs, ăcērbŭs. V. Doceo.

mägīstĕrĭŭm, ĭi, n., *the profession of teaching.* Vănă mägīstĕrĭă, Tib. Syn. Mŏdĕrāmĕn, rĕgĭmĕn.

mägīstrātŭs, ūs, m., *a magistrate, the office of a magistrate.* Jŭră mägīstrātūsquĕ, Virg. Syn. Pŏpŭlī mŏdĕrātŏr; prŏcĕrēs, prīmātēs; mägīstrātŭs ōffĭcĭŭm, mūnŭs, fāscēs, sĕcūrēs. Epith. Grăvĭs, prūdēns, săpĭēns, prŏvĭdŭs, cĕlebrĭs, pŏtēns, sŭpērbŭs, ūrbānŭs.

magnănĭmĭs, ĕ, *and* mŭs, ă, ŭm, *magnanimous.* Mägnănĭmum Ænĕăm, Virg. Syn. Gĕnĕrōsŭs, fōrtĭs, ănĭmōsŭs.

mägnātēs, ŭm, m. pl., *the nobility.* Mägnātēs dărĕ, M. Syn. Prŏcĕrēs, prīmātēs.

mägnēs, ētĭs, m., *a magnet.* Quĕm mägnĕtă vŏcănt, Lucr. Epith. Dēcŏlŏr, ōbscūrŭs, nĭgĕr, ătĕr, mīrābĭlĭs, pŏtēns.

Mägnēssă, æ, *and* ētĭs, ĭdĭs, f., *of Magnesia.* Mägnēssam Hīppŏlўtēn, Hor. Mägnētĭdă vīdĭmŭs Ārgō, Ov.

Mägnētēs, ŭm, m. pl., *people of Magnesia.* Mägnētăs ădĭt, Ov.

mägnētĭcŭs, ă, ŭm, *magnetic.* Vĕnĕrēm mägnētĭcă gēmmă, Claud.

* mägnĭfĭcēntĭă, æ, f., *magnificence.* Syn. Pōmpă, splēndŏr, mūnĭfĭcēntĭă, lībĕrālĭtās.

mägnĭfĭcŭs, ă, ŭm, *magnificent.* Tĕ quŏquĕ mägnĭfĭcă, Ov. Syn. Splēndĭdŭs, lautŭs, rēgĭŭs, lībĕrālĭs.

mägnĭlŏquŭs, ă, ŭm, *high-flown, boasting.* Quæ tū mägnĭlŏquŭs, Mart. Syn. Grāndĭlŏquŭs; lŏquāx, vērbōsŭs.

mägnĭpēndo, *to esteem much.* Nōn mägnĭpēndĭs, Hor.

mägnŏpĕrĕ, adv., *much.* Mägnŏpēre ā vērā, Lucr. Syn. Vāldē, mūltŭm, mūltă, plūrĭmă.

mägnŭs, ă, ŭm, *great.* Āggrĕdĕre ō mägnōs, Virg. Syn. Grāndĭs, īngēns, āmplŭs, vāstŭs, īmmēnsŭs, īmmānĭs, māxĭmŭs, nĭmĭŭs, nōn pārvŭs, nōn ēxĭgŭŭs, nōn tĕnŭĭs, nōn mĕdĭocrĭs, prŏcĕrŭs, āltŭs. V. Altus.

mägŭs, ī, m., *a magician.* Mēdĭcŭs, mägŭs, ōmnĭă, Juv. Syn. Vĕnēfĭcŭs, incāntātŏr. V. Maga, veneficus.—2. adj., -ŭs, ă, ŭm, *magical.* Illĕ mägās ārtēs, Ov. V. Magicus.

Mähŏmētĭcŭs, ă, ŭm, *of Mahomet.* Vāllŭm Mähŏmētĭcă cōntră, Mant.

Mähŏmētŭs, ī, m., *Mahomet.* Fīt Mähŏmētŭs ătrōx, Mant. Epith. Nĕfāndŭs, atrōx, Ārăbs, nĕfārĭŭs, impĭŭs, pērfĭdŭs, ēxecrāndŭs.

Maĭă, æ, f., *the mother of Mercury.* Almæ fīlĭŭs Maĭœ, Hor. Epitu. Atlāntĭs, Atlāntĭācă, Atlāntœă, Atlāntĭăs, Plēĭăs, lūcĭdă, Eŏă, fŏrmōsă.

mājēstās, ātĭs, f., *majesty.* Mājēstās, ētsī, Juv. Syn. Grăvĭtās, splēndŏr, pōmpă. Epitu. Grăvĭs, ĭmpĕrĭōsă, rēgĭă, rēgālĭs, vĕnĕrāndă, aūgūstă, sūblīmĭs, cēlsă, trĕmēndă.

mājŏr, ōrĭs, *the compar. of* magnus. Tē mājōrĭbŭs īrĕ, Virg. Syn. Ingēntĭŏr, grāndĭŏr, āmplĭŏr.

mājōrēs, ŭm, m. pl., *ancestors.* Dēlīctă mājōrum, Hor. Syn. Patrēs, āntīquī, vĕtĕrēs, prīscī, ăvī, prŏăvī. Epitu. Prīscī, āntīquī, pĭī, vĕnĕrāndī, cōlĕndī.

Maĭŭs, ĭī, m., *the fifth month.* Vŏcăbŭlă Maĭō, Ov. Epitu. Vĭrĭdĭs, vērnāns, vĭrēns, hūmĭdŭs, ĭmbrĭfĕr, fœcūndŭs, flōrĭdŭs, nĭmbōsŭs, lūxŭrĭāns, ămœnŭs, grātŭs, blāndŭs, lætŭs, hĭlărĭs, fēstīvŭs.

mălæ, ārŭm, f. pl., *cheeks.* Sŭb vūlnĕrĕ mălæ, Virg. Syn. Gĕnæ.

Mălchīnŭs, ī, m., *a man's name.* Mălchīnŭs tūnĭcĭs, Hor.

mălĕ, adv., *wickedly; scarcely.* Cūrvĭs mălĕ tēmpĕrăt, Virg. Syn. Prăvē, pĕrvērsē, vĭtĭōsē, ĭmprŏbē, nĕfărĭē, nēquĭtĕr, nōn bĕnĕ.

Măleă, æ, f., *a promontory of Laconia.* Iŏnĭŏquĕ mărī, Mălēæquĕ, Virg. Undă Mălēæ, Stat. Epitu. Cūrvă, spūmāns, raūcă, sævă, rĕcūrrēns, trŭcŭlēntă, hōrrĭdă, Spārtānă, Œbălĭă, ūndĭsŏnă.

mălĕdīco, xī, *to rail at.* Vēl quŏd mălĕdīcŭnt, Hor. Syn. Cōnvīcĭŏr, ĭmprĕcŏr. V. Imprecor.

mălĕdīctŭm, ī, n., *railing.* Tŏt mălĕdīctă tŭæ, Prop. Syn. Cōnvīcĭŭm, probrŭm, ōpprobrĭŭm, călūmnĭă, ĭnjūrĭă, ĭmprĕcătĭō, dīræ līnguæ vĕnēnŭm. Epitu. Insānŭm, hōrrēndŭm, atrōx. V. Convicium, injuria.

mălĕdīcŭs, ă, ŭm, *one who rails.* Syn. Injūrĭŭs, ĭnjūrĭōsŭs, ōbtrēctātŏr. V. Invidus.

mălĕfĭcŭs, ă, ŭm, *one who does harm.* Astū mălĕfĭcæ, (Iamb.) Sen. P. Syn. Nŏxĭŭs, nŏcēns, ĭnfēstŭs.

mălĕfīdŭs, ă, ŭm, *not to be trusted.* Stătĭō mălĕfīdă cărīnĭs, Virg. Syn. Infīdŭs, nōn fīdŭs, părŭm fīdŭs.

mălĕsānŭs, ă, ŭm, *insane.* Pōstquăm mălĕsānă sŭpērbĭă, Prud. Syn. Insānŭs, fŭrēns, āmēns, dēmēns.

mălĕsuădŭs, ă, ŭm, *persuading to do wrong.* Et mălĕsuādă fămēs, Virg. Syn. Imprŏbŭs, mălŭs.

mălĕvŏlŭs, ă, ŭm, *bearing ill-will.* Quīn sīt mălĕvŏlŭs, (Iamb.) Syn. Invĭdŭs, ĭnĭmīcŭs, hōstĭs.

mălĭfĕr, ĕră, ĕrŭm, *bearing apples.* Et quŏs mālĭfĕræ, Virg.

mălīgnē, adv., *spitefully.* Bĕnĕfāctă mălīgnē, Ov.

mălīgnĭtās, ātĭs, f., *ill-nature.* Mălīgnĭtātŭm vūlnĕră, (Iamb. Dim.) Prud. Syn. Mălĭtĭă, ĭmprŏbĭtās, pērvērsĭtās, nēquĭtĭă, āstūtĭă, fāllācĭă. Epitu. Scĕlĕrātă, nĕfāndă, dīră, prăvă, dŏlōsă, sŭbdŏlă.

mălīgnŭs, ă, ŭm, *malicious.* Fāmă mălīgnă mĕō, Ov. Syn. Imprŏbŭs, mălŭs, scĕlĕrātŭs ; fāllāx, dŏlōsŭs, āstūtŭs ; dĭffĭcĭlĭs.

mallĕātŏr, ōrĭs, m., *one who works with a hammer.* Pălūdĭs mallĕātŏr Hīspānæ, Mart.

mallĕŭs, ī, m., *a hammer.* Syn. Tŭdēs, mallĕŏlŭs. Epitu. Fērrĕŭs, dūrŭs, grăvĭs, pōndĕrōsŭs, ārtĭfēx, vălĭdŭs, rĭgĭdŭs, rĭgēns.

mălo, māvĭs, mālŭī, *to like better.* Mālŏ mănŭm, Mart.

mālŏbăthrŭm, ī, n., *a tree yielding a perfume.* Mālŏbăthrō Sўrĭō, Hor.

mālvă, æ, f., *the herb mallows.* Grăvī mālvæ sălūbrēs, Hor. Epitu. Flōrēns, vĭrĭdĭs, vĭrēns, mōllĭs, tĕnĕră, lĕvĭs.

mālŭm, ī, n., *an apple.* Mālŏ mē Gălătĕă pĕtĭt, Virg. V. Pomum.

mălŭm, ī, n., *an evil.* Aūt Dĕŭs īllĕ mălĭs, Virg. Syn. Incōmmŏdŭm, dāmnŭm, dētrīmēntŭm, ēxĭtĭŭm, clādēs, străgēs, pērnĭcĭēs ; mĭsĕrĭă, călāmĭtās, ĭnfōrtūnĭŭm ; pĕrīclŭm ; dŏlŏr ; scĕlŭs, crīmĕn. Epitu. Fĕrālĕ, trĭstĕ, lūgŭbrĕ, sævŭm, crūdēlĕ, nĕfāndŭm, mœstŭm, flēbĭlĕ, lūctŭōsŭm, lacrўmābĭlĕ, fūnēstŭm, grāndĕ, ĭngēns, īnfāndŭm, ăcērbŭm, grăvĕ, dūrŭm. V. Infortunium, miseria.

mălŭs, ă, ŭm, *evil.* Tērră mălōs hŏmĭnēs, Juv. Syn. Imprŏbŭs, pērvērsŭs, nēquăm, scĕlĕrātŭs, mălīgnŭs. V. Sceleratus.

mălŭs, ī, f., *an apple-tree.* Plătănī mălōs gĕssērĕ, Virg. V. Pomum.—2. m., *a mast.* Quō tēndănt fērrūm, mălō, Virg. Epith. Tĕrĕs, sŭblīmĭs, trĕmŭlŭs, ĕxcēlsŭs, ērēctŭs, prōcĕrŭs, īngēns, rĭgĭdŭs.

mămmă, *dimin.* mămīllă, *and* mămmŭlă, œ, f., *the pap.* Exsērtœ cīngŭlă mămmœ, Virg. Strīctīsquĕ mămīllĭs, Juv. Syn. Ūbĕr, păpīllă. Epitii. Āltrīx, mātērnă, tŏnĕră, nĭvĕă, pēndŭlă, tĕrĕs, mōllĭs, īrrĭgŭă, pēndēns, fœcūndă, tūmēns, nēctărĕă, lāctāns, tŭmĭdă, tūrgĭdă; lāctĕ plēnă, dīstēntă, tūmēns. V. Lacto.

mămmōsŭs, ă, ŭm, *having large breasts.* Et mămmōsă Cĕrĕs, Lucr.

Māmurŭs, ī, m., *a famous smith.* Māmŭrĭŭs mŏrŭm, Ov. Hīc tĭbĭ, Māmūrī, Prop. Māmūrrœ, ārŭm, m. pl., *a noble family of Formiœ.* Māmūrrārŭm lāssī, Hor.

mānābĭlĭs, ĕ, *which may flow.* Itĕm mānābĭlĕ frĭgŭs, Lucr.

māncĭpĭŭm, ĭī, n., *a slave.* Vītăquĕ māncĭpĭō, Lucr. Syn. Sērvĭtŭs; sērvŭs, căptīvŭs, fămŭlŭs. Epith. Mĭsĕrŭm, vīlĕ, ēmptŭm, vēnălĕ. V. Servus.

māncĭpo, ās, *to alienate.* Māncĭpăt ūsŭs, Hor. Syn. Dō māncĭpĭō; ălĭēno, ābdĭco, ōblĭgo, dēvŏvĕo.

māncŭs, ă, ŭm, *maimed.* Māncŭs ĕrĭt, Ov.

māndātŭm, ī, n., *a command.* Cĕlĕrĕs māndātă pĕr aūrās, Virg. Syn. Jūssŭm, jūssŭs, īmpĕrĭŭm, prœscrīptŭm, prœcēptŭm; cōmmīssŭm. Epith. Ămīcŭm, lœtŭm, dŭlcĕ, bĕnīgnŭm, grăvĕ, dūrŭm, sœvŭm, trīstĕ, ăcērbŭm. V. Imperium.

Māndēlă, œ, f., *a Sabine town.* Quĕm Māndēlă bĭbĭt, Hor.

māndo, ās, *to order.* Māndāvī, dīcēs, Juv. Syn. Impĕro, jŭbĕo, prœscrībo; cōmmītto.

māndo, ĭs, *to chew.* Māndĭt hŭmŭm, Virg.

māndūco, ās, *to eat.* Quōd māndūcāmŭr ĭn ŏrĕ, Lucil. Syn. Edo, cŏmĕdo, ĕxĕdo, vŏro; māndo, ĭs; pāscŏr, vēscŏr. V. Edo, voro.

mānĕ, n., *morning.* Mānĕ nŏvŭm, Virg. V. Lucifer, Aurora, diluculum.

mănĕo, mānsī, *to remain.* Arx āltă mănērĕs, Virg. Syn. Mŏrŏr, pērmănĕo, rĕmănĕo, hœrĕo, stō, rēsto, pērsto, rĕsīsto; hăbĭto, cōmmŏrŏr, vērsŏr.

mānēs, ĭŭm, m. pl., *spirits of the dead.* Imīs mānēs ēxcīrĕ sĕpŭlcrīs, Virg. Syn. Dēfūnctōrum, sĭlēntum ănĭmœ; Gĕnĭī; Lĕmŭrēs; lārvœ, ūmbrœ, spēctră. Epith. Nōctūrnī, nigrī, ātrī, Stȳgĭī, īmī, mœstī, ōbscūrī, dīrī, Tārtărĕī, prōfūndī, īnfērnī, Lēthœī, Ēlȳsĭī, trīstēs, sĭlēntŭs, mūtī, ērrāntēs, văgī, pāllēntēs, ĭnānēs, Phlĕgĕthōntœī, tērrĭfĭcī, īnfēstī, ăcērbī, mĭsĕrī, pĭī, fēlīcēs, bĕātī.

māngo, ōnĭs, m., *a seller of slaves.* Mĕ māngŏ pŏpōscĭt, Mart.

mănĭcă, œ, f., *a sleeve.* Et tŭnĭcœ mănĭcās, Virg. Syn. Mănŭŭm vīnclŭm, lăquĕī, cătēnă. Epitii. Dūră, rĭgĭdă, fērrĕă, tĕnāx, tĕrĕs, ārctă, cōnstrīctă, œrĕă, vălĭdă, ăcērbă, œnĕă, ăhēnă, sœvă, grăvĭs. V. Catena.

mănĭfēstĕ, adv., *openly.* Mănĭfēstĭŭs ĭpsī, Virg.

mănĭfēsto, ās, *to manifest.* Prōdĕt, mănĭfēstābĭtquĕ lătēntĕm, Ov. Syn. Dēclāro, pătĕfăcĭo, ăpĕrĭo, pāndo, rĕsĕro, rĕvēlo, prōdo, dŏcĕo; īndĭco, ās; rĕtĕgo, ĕxprōmo, ēxplĭco, ēxpōno.

mănĭfēstŭs, ă, ŭm, *manifest.* Tŭm vērō mănĭfēstă fĭdēs, Virg. Syn. Clārŭs, pērspĭcŭŭs, ăpērtŭs, vūlgātŭs, ēvĭdēns, cērtŭs, nōn dŭbĭŭs, nōtŭs, cōgnĭtŭs.

mănĭpŭlārĭs, *or* iplārĭs, ĕ, *of a band.* Indĕ mănĭplārĭs, Ov.

mănĭpŭlŭs, *or* iplŭs, ī, m., *a bundle.* Lōngă mănĭplōs, Ov. Syn. Mērgĕs.—2. *a band, a troop.* Dēsōlātīquĕ mănĭplī, Virg. V. Acies, miles.

Mānlĭŭs, ĭī, m., *a name of several illustrious Romans.* Tārpeĭœ Mānlĭŭs ārcĭs, Virg.

|| mānnă, œ, f., *and* n., indecl., *a kind of honey-dew.* Epith. Dūlcĕ, mēllĕŭm, mēllītŭm, grātŭm, mătūtīnŭm.

mānnŭs, *dimin.* ŭlŭs, ī, m., *a nag.* Impŏsĭtŭs mānnīs, Hor.

māno, ās, *to flow.* Lătĭcēs mānārĕ pĕrēnnēs, Lucr. Syn. Dīstīllo, dīmāno, flŭo, *mānsuēfăctŭs, ă, ŭm, *tamed.* Plin. Mānsuēfāctŭm pătrĭs, Prud. Syn. Mānsuētŭs, cĭcŭr.

mānsuēfĭo, ĭs, *and* ēsco, ĭs, *to grow tame.* Mānsuēvērĕ Gĕtœ, Prud. Syn. Mītēsco, mītĭgŏr, plăcŏr; cĭcŭrŏr.

mānsuētūdo, ĭnĭs, f., *mildness.* Quōd mānsuētūdŏ cŏrōnăt, Juv. Syn. Lēnĭtās, bĕnīgnĭtās, clēmēntĭă.

mānsuētŭs, ă, ŭm, *mild.* Cārmĭnă mānsuētŭs, Prop. Syn. Hūmānŭs, făcĭlĭs, lēnĭs, mītĭs, cōmĭs, plăcĭdŭs, bĕnīgnŭs, clēmēns, ūrbānŭs, āffăbĭlĭs. V. Comis măntĭcă, æ, f., *a wallet.* Măntică tērgŏ, Pers.

măntīlĕ, ĭs, u., *a table-cloth.* Fĕrūnt măntīlĭă vīllīs, Virg. EPITH. Nĭtĭdŭm, mŭndŭm.

Mántŏ, ūs, f., *a fortune-teller so named.* Fătĭdĭcæ Mántūs, Virg. EPITH. Phœbĕā, ĭnclўtă, præsclă, Ōgўglă ; Cādmēlă, *or* Thēbănă.

Mántŭă, æ, f., *a town of Italy.* Mántŭă nōmĕn, Virg. EPITH. Vĕtŭs, pŏtēns, āntīquă, nōbĭlĭs, ĭnclўtă, pŏpŭlōsă, cĕlebrĭs, clără, dīvĕs, Mārtĭă, măgnă, āltă, sŭpērbă.

mănūbrĭŭm, ĭī, n., *a handle.* Ipsă mănūbrĭă, Juv.

mănŭs, ūs, *f.*, *the hand, a band of soldiers.* Ět mănŭs īn grĕmĭŏ, Ov. SYN. Dēxtră, sĭnīstră, lævă ; pālmă, dĭgĭtī ; tūrbă, cătērvă, lĕgĭo, cŏhōrs, mănĭpŭlŭs, mănĭplŭs. EPITH. Tĕnĕră, nĭvĕă, cāndĭdă, lāctĕă, cāndēns, ālbēus, rŏsĕă, pŭlchră, fŏrmōsă, dĕcōră, vălĭdă, fŏrtĭs, dūră, Mārtĭă, vīndēx, pŏtēns, răpāx, ăvără, ūncă, ădŭncă, sōrdĭdă, crŭēntă, sacrĭlĕgă, īmpĭă, mūnĭfĭcă, pūră, cāstă, pĭă, fīdă, ārtĭfēx, dōctă, sōlērs, dēbĭlĭs, trĕmēns, sŭpplēx. V. Caterva.

măpālĭă, ōrŭm, n. pl., *Numidian cottages.* Hăbĭtātă măpālĭă tēctĭs, Virg. SYN. Măgālĭă, cāsæ. V. Casa.

măppă, æ, f., *a towel.* Sōrdĭdă măppă, Hor. EPITH. Ălbă, cāndĭdă, nĭvĕă, cāndēns, crētătă. V. Mantile.

Mărăthōn, ōnĭs, f., *a plain of Attica, celebrated for the victory of Miltiades over the Persians.* Mīrāta ēst Mărăthōn, Ov.

mărathrŭm, ī, n., *fennel.* Prŏfŭīt ēt mărăthrŭm, Ov.

Mārcēllŭs, ī, m., *the name of several noble Romans.* Mārcēllŭs ŏpīmĭs, Virg.

mārcĕo, ēs, *and* cēsco, ĭs, *to wither.* Mārcēscŭnt pĕr ĭnērtēs. Sўlvă cŏmīs mārcĕt, Stat. SYN. Putrēsco, lānguĕo, cōrrŭmpo.

Mārcĭă, æ, f., *the wife of Regulus.* Mārcĭă pĭgnŭs, Sil.

mārcĭdŭs, ă, ŭm, *withered.* Mārcĭdă vīnă, (Phal.) Stat. SYN. Mārcēns, flāccĭdŭs, putrĭdŭs ; lānguĭdŭs.

Mārcĭŭs, ĭī, m., *a Roman prætor who caused a supply of very pure water to be conveyed to Rome : it was hence called Marcia.* Mārcĭă lўmphă, Tib.

mārcŭlŭs, ī, m., *a hammer.* Ærārĭōrŭm mārcŭlī, Mart.

mărĕ, ĭs, n., *the sea.* Jăm mărĭs īmmēnsī, Virg. SYN. Æquŏr, āltŭm, prŏfūndŭm, pōntŭs, frētŭm, sălŭm, pĕlăgŭs, mārmŏr ; æquŏră, frĕtă, cœrŭlă, mārmŏră ; Ōcĕănŭs, Ămphītrītē, Nēreŭs, Nēptūnŭs, Tēthўs, Thĕtĭs. EPITH. Răpĭdŭm, vēlĭvŏlŭm, prōnŭm, hūmĭdŭm, tŭmĭdŭm, tŭmēns, āltŭm, Nēptūnĭŭm, reflŭŭm, vāstŭm, ĭncērtŭm, ĭncōnstāns, īnfĭdŭm, ēffūsŭm, trĕmŭlŭm, lĭquĭdŭm, lātŭm, căvŭm, vădōsŭm, sālsŭm, rĕfŭgŭm, vitrĕŭm, glaūcŭm, cœrŭlĕŭm, scŏpŭlōsŭm, săxōsŭm, īnquĭētŭm, prŏcēllōsŭm, ărēnōsŭm, cōmmōtŭm, ŭndōsŭm, tūrbātŭm, tūrbĭdŭm, sōlĭcĭtŭm, cōncĭtŭm, mĭnāx, spūmōsŭm, spūmĕŭm, spūmāns, sævŭm, ĭnīquŭm, naūfrăgŭm, tŭmŭltŭōsŭm, vēntōsŭm, īnfēstŭm, ăspĕrŭm, īrātŭm, īnsānŭm, īmmītĕ, īndŏmĭtŭm, cæcŭm, ăgĭtātŭm, plăcĭdŭm, plăcātŭm, pācātŭm, quĭētŭm, trānquĭllŭm, cōmpŏsĭtŭm, plānŭm, ēffūsŭm, sĕrēnŭm, tūtŭm.

Mărĕōtĭs, ĭdĭs, f., *of the lake Mareotis.* Mărĕōtĭdēs albæ, Virg.

mārgo, ĭnĭs, m. f., *a brink.* Mārgĭnĕ tērrārŭm, Ov. SYN. Crĕpīdo, ōră, lābrŭm ; rīpă. EPITH. Ēxtrēmŭs, sŭmmŭs.

Mărĭă, æ, f., *the mother of Jesus.* Prŏpĕrātă Mărĭæ, Sedul. Illĕ nĭtŏr Mărĭæ, Id. EPITH. Cāstă, īntĕmĕrātă, īmmăcŭlātă, pūră, pĭă, īnclўtă, sānctă, aūgŭstă, vĕnĕrābĭlĭs.

Mărīcă, æ, f., *the wife of Faunus.* Laūrēntĕ Mărīcă, Virg. EPITH. Cāndĭdă, dĕcōră, nĭvĕă, flāvă.

mărīnŭs, ă, ŭm, *of the sea.* Ăbĭĕs vīsūră mărīnōs, Virg. SYN. Æquŏrĕŭs, mārmŏrĕŭs, Nēptūnĭŭs.

mărīscă, æ, f., *a kind of fig.* Fătŭāsquĕ mărīscās, Mart.

mărītă, æ, f., *a wife.* Nēc sīt mărītă quæ, Hor.

mărītālĭs, ĕ, *of marriage.* Lūsă mărītālī, Ov. SYN. Cōnjŭgĭālĭs ; mărītŭs, ă, ŭm.

mărĭtĭmŭs, ă, ŭm, *belonging to the sea.* Plaut. SYN. Mărīnŭs.

mărīto, ās, *to marry.* Jūstă mărītāndī, F. V. Conjugium, nubilis

mărītŭs, ī, m., *a husband.* Cōmpōs mărītŭs, (Iamb.) Sen. SYN. Vĭr, spōnsŭs, cōnjūx. V. Conjux.

mărītŭs, ă, ŭm, *of marriage.* Hæcnĕ mărītă fīdēs, Prop. SYN. Mărītālĭs, cōnjŭgĭālĭs.

Mărĭŭs, ĭi, m., *the Roman consul.* Cōnspēxĭt Mărĭŭs, Cic. Epith. Fĕrōx, ācĕr, fōrtĭs, grăvĭs, sĕvērŭs.

Mărmărĭdă, æ, m., *an inhabitant of Marmarica, a country of Libya.* Cŭspĭdĕ Mărmărĭdæ, Ov.

mărmŏr, ŏrĭs, n., *marble.* Dē mărmŏrĕ tēmplŭm, Virg. Epith. Lævĕ, cāndēns, pĭctŭm, pĭctūrātŭm, prĕtĭōsŭm, nōbĭlĕ, dūrŭm, gĕlĭdŭm, sŭpĕrbŭm, vērsĭcŏlŏr, frĭgĭdŭm, rĭgĭdŭm, măcŭlōsŭm, splēndĭdŭm, lūcēns, nĭtēns, āntĭquŭm, cŏrŭscŭm, dĭscŏlŏr, Phrўgĭŭm, Mўgdŏnĭŭm, Idæŭm, Spārtănŭm, Thĕrăpnæŭm, Amў-clæŭm; Lĭbўcŭm.

mărmŏrātŭs, ă, ŭm, *covered with marble.* Mărmŏrātă dōrsō, Stat.

mărmŏrĕŭs, ă, ŭm, *of marble.* Mărmŏrĕō rĕfĕrŭnt, Virg. Syn. Părĭŭs; mărīnŭs.

Măro, ōnĭs, m., *a name of Virgil.* Pŏnĕ Mărōnĭs ŏpŭs, Mart. V. Virgilius.

Mărpēssĭŭs, ă, ŭm, *of mount Marpessus.* Mărpēssĭă caŭtēs, Virg.

mărră, æ, f., *a kind of spade.* Mărræ ēt sārcŭlă dēsĭnt, Juv.

Mărrŭbĭŭs, ă, ŭm, *of Marrubium.* Quĭn ēt Mărrŭbĭă vĕnĭt, Virg.

Mărs, Mārtĭs, m., *the god of war.* Et mājŏr Mārtĭs jam, Virg. Syn. Māvōrs, Grădīvŭs. Epith. Gĕtĭcŭs, Thrēĭcĭŭs, dūrŭs, ĭmpĭŭs, sævŭs, īnsānŭs, ārmĭ-pŏtēns, crŭēntŭs, sānguĭnĕŭs, fūnēstŭs, nĕfāndŭs, tōrvŭs, rĭgĭdŭs, fĕrōx, ĭmpăvĭ-dŭs, fĕrŭs, tērrĭbĭlĭs, īnfaūstŭs, ārmĭgĕr, trīstĭs, tūrbĭdŭs, īnfēstŭs, vĭŏlēntŭs, āspĕr, gĕnĕrōsŭs, fōrtĭs, măgnănĭmŭs, ĭndŏmĭtŭs, hōrrēndŭs, trŭcŭlēntŭs, īnvīctŭs, răbĭdŭs, ĭmprŏbŭs, fērrĕŭs, pŏtēns, īnclўtŭs, ācĕr, hōstĭlĭs, ātrōx, fūlmĭnĕŭs, hōrrĭdŭs, vēsānŭs, fūrēns, īmmānĭs, aūdāx, trūx, ēffĕrŭs, ācĕrbŭs, ĭnĭquŭs, ādvērsŭs, cæcŭs, īncōnstāns, āmbĭgŭŭs, dŭbĭŭs, īncērtŭs, āncēps.

Mārsæŭs, ī, m., *a man's name.* Quōndăm Mārsæŭs ămātŏr, Hor.

Mārsī, ōrŭm, m. pl., *a people of Latium.* Mārsŭs ēt Apŭlŭs, Hor. Adj. —ŭs, ă, ŭm, *Marsian.* Mārsī mĕmŏrēm dŭēllī, Hor.

Mārsўă, *or* ās, æ, m., *the satyr flayed by Apollo.* Mārsўă vīctŭs, Juv. Epith. Dōctŭs, cănōrŭs, suāvĭs, tĕmĕrārĭŭs, sŭpĕrbŭs, aūdāx, ĭmpĭŭs, mĭsĕr, īnfēlīx, Phrўgĭŭs, Cēlænæŭs.

Mārtĭălĭs, ĭs, m., *the Latin poet.* Ĭn ōrbĕ Mārtĭălĭs, Mart. Epith. Dōctŭs, dĭsērtŭs, mōrdāx, īngĕnĭōsŭs, Bĭlbĭlĭcŭs; ārgūtŭs, lĕpĭdŭs, obscœnŭs.

Mārtĭcŏlă, æ, m. f., *that worships Mars.* Mārtĭcŏlāmquĕ Gĕtēn, Ov.

Mārtĭgĕnă, æ, m. f., *offspring of Mars.* Ĭn quā Mārtĭgĕnæ, Ov.

Mārtĭŭs, ĭi, m., *the third month.* Epith. Nŏvŭs, plăcĭdŭs, ūdŭs, tĕpĭdŭs, bĕnīg-nŭs, blāndŭs, mădĭdŭs, nĭmbōsŭs, īmbrĭfĕr, flōrēns, vĭrēns, fērtĭlĭs, fœcūndŭs.

‖ mārtўrēs, ŭm, m. pl., *martyrs.* Mārtўrĭbŭs rēgīnă fīdēs, P. Epith. Sānctī, īnclўtī, gĕnĕrōsī, fōrtēs, măgnănĭmī, ĭmpăvĭdī, īntērrĭtī, īllūstrēs, clārī, cōn-stāntēs.

‖ mārtўrĭŭm, ĭi, n., *martyrdom.* Sānguĭnĕ mārtўrĭī, (Dactyl.) Prud. Epith. Crŭēntŭm, ātrōx, clārŭm, īllūstrĕ, fōrtĕ.

măs, mărĭs, *and* scŭlŭs, ă, ŭm, *male.* Măs ēssĕ cēssăt īllĕ, (Iamb.) Prud. Mās-cŭlŭs, ēt tōtŭm, Prop.

māssă, æ, f., *a mass.* Aūt ātræ māssăm pĭcĭs, Virg. Epith. Dūră, plŭmbĕă, fērrĕă, grăvĭs, vălĭdă. V. Pondus.

Māssăgĕtæ, *or* tēs, æ, m., *a people of Scythia.* Māssăgĕtās, Ărābēsquĕ, Hor. Epith. Bārbărŭs, fĕrŭs, fĕrōx, trūx, īnhūmānŭs, īmmītĭs, aūdāx, văgŭs, prædo, fūrēns, pērfĭdŭs, īnfĭdŭs.

Māssĭcŭs, ī, m., Māssĭcă, ōrŭm, n. pl., *a mountain in Campania.* Māssĭcă quī rāstrĭs, Virg. Epith. Ūvĭfĕr, vĕtŭs, fēlīx, cūltŭs, fœcūndŭs, fērtĭlĭs.

Māssĭlĭă, æ, f., *a town of France.* Fūmĕă Māssĭlĭæ, Mart. Epith. Cĕlēbrĭs, clără, īnclўtă, dōctă, āntīquă, prīscă, nōbĭlĭs.

Māsĭnīssă, æ, m., *a Numidian king.* Sŭpĕrăt Māsĭnīssă Sўphăcĕm,·Ov.

Māssўlī, ōrŭm, m. pl., *an African people.* Māssўlīquĕ rŭŭnt, Virg.

mătēllă, æ, f., *a chamber-pot.* Præstārĕ mătēllām, Mart. Syn. Mătēllĭō *or* tŭlă.

mătĕr, mātrĭs, (*dimin.* tercŭlă, æ,) f., *a mother.* Mătĕr ĭn ōrĕ, Prop. Syn. Gĕnĭ-trīx, părēns. Epith. Almă, cără, blāndă, sōllĭcĭtă, ānxĭă, vĭgĭl, dīlēctă, fīdă, pĭă, bĕnīgnă, ămātă.

mătĕrĭă, æ, f., *or* ĭēs, ēī, f., *matter.* Mătĕrĭēm sŭpĕrābăt ŏpŭs, Ov. Epith. Amplă, dīffūsă, fœcūndă, dīvĕs.

mătērnŭs, ă, ŭm, *motherly.* Dēvōlvŭnt, ĭtĕrŭm mătērnās, Virg.

mātērtĕră, æ, f., *a mother's sister.* Mĕæ mătērtĕră dīcī, Ov.

măthēmătĭcŭs, ī, m., *a mathematician.* Nēmŏ măthēmătĭcŭs, Juv.

Mătīnŭs, ă, ŭm, *of Mount Matinus.* Āpĭs Mătīnæ, Hor.

mătrālĭă, ŭm, n. pl., *festivals of the Roman matrons.* Vēstrūm mătrālĭă fēstŭm, Ov.

mătrĭmōnĭŭm, ĭī, n., *marriage.* Īre īn mătrĭmōnĭŭm, (Iamb.) SYN. Cōnjŭgĭŭm, cōnnūbĭŭm. V. Conjugium.

mātrōnă, æ, f., *a matron.* Māgnī mătrōnă Tŏnāntĭs, Ov. EPITH. Pŭlchră, fōrmōsă, cāndĭdă, dĕcōră, cāstă.

Mātrŏnă, æ, m., *a river in France.* Mātrŏnă nōn Gāllīs, Aus. EPITH. Cĭtŭs, ămœnŭs.

mătrōnālĭs, ĕ, *of a lady.* Ēt mātrōnālēs, Ov.

mattă, æ, f., *a mat.* Scīrpĕă mattă fŭĭt, Ov. SYN. Tĕgĕs.

mătūrē, adv., *maturely.* Mătūrē rĕdĕăt, Hor.

mătūrēsco, rŭī, *to ripen.* Plēnō mătūrŭĭt ānnō, Ov. V. Maturo.

mătūrĭtās, ātĭs, f., *maturity.* Cŏquăt mătūrĭtās, (Iamb. Dim.) P. EPITH. Plēnă, ūltĭmă.

mătūro, ās, *to make ripe.* Mătūrātĕ fŭgăm, Virg. SYN. Mătūrĭtātēm dŏ, āffĕro, cōncŏquo; āccĕlĕro, prŏpĕro, fēstīno, ūrgĕo.

mătūrŭs, ă, ŭm, *ripe.* Cŏquăt mătūrīs sōlĭbŭs æstās, Virg. SYN. Cŏctŭs, cōncŏctŭs, tēmpēstīvŭs; ōppōrtūnŭs, āptŭs; ĭdōnĕŭs, cōmmŏdŭs; cĭtŭs, sŭbĭtŭs, fēstīnŭs.

Mātūtă, æ, f., *a name of Aurora.* Mātūtă vŏcābĕrĕ nōstrīs, Ov.

mătūtīnŭs, ă, ŭm, *of the morning.* Ēt mătūtīnīs ŏpĕrātŭr, Juv. V. Mane.

Māvŏrs, ōrtĭs, m., *a name of Mars.* Cūm cāssĭdĕ Māvŏrs, Ov. SYN. Mārs. V. Mars.

Māvŏrtĭŭs, ă, ŭm, *of Mars.* Lævæ Māvŏrtĭŭs ūmbo, P. SYN. Mārtĭŭs; bēllĭcōsŭs.

Maurī, ōrŭm, m. pl., *inhabitants of Africa.* Nōn ĕgĕt Maurī jăcŭlīs, Hor. EPITH. Lĕvēs, ōccĭdŭī, Lĭbўcī, nĭgrī, ădūstī, fūscī, tērrĭfĭcī, ātrōcēs, rĕfŭgī, trŭcēs, cĕlĕrēs, bārbărī, hōrrēndī, ūstī, ēxūstī, tōrrĭdī.

Maurŭs, ūsĭăcŭs, *and* ūsĭŭs, ă, ŭm, *of the Moors.* Ŭbĭ Maură sēmpĕr, Hor. Ēt Maurūsĭăcī, Mart.

Mausōlēŭm, ĭī, n., *the tomb which Artemisia built in honour of her husband.* Nēc Mausōlēī dīvēs, Prop. EPITH. Māgnĭfĭcŭm, sŭpērbŭm, dīvēs, nōbĭlĕ, īnclўtŭm, trīstĕ, flēbĭlĕ, fūnĕrĕŭm, fātălĕ.

Mausōlŭs, ī, m., *the king of Caria, and husband of Artemisia.* Mausōlī sāxīs, Mart. EPITH. Dīvēs, sŭpērbŭs.

māxīllă, æ, f., *the cheek-bone.* Tū cūm māxīllīs, Pers. SYN. Mălă, gĕnă. V. Gena.

|| māxĭmĭtās, ātĭs, f., *greatness.* Immānī māxĭmĭtātĕ, Lucr.

māxĭmŭs, ă, ŭm, *the superl. of* magnus. Māxĭmŭs Īlĭōnĕŭs, Virg. SYN. Ingēns, prŏcērŭs, āltŭs, ārdŭŭs.

māzŏnŏmŭs, ī, m., *a large dish.* Māzŏnŏmō pŭĕrī, Hor.

mĕātŭs, ūs, m., *a passage, movement.* Cœlīquĕ mĕātŭs, Virg. SYN. Fŏrāmĕn, ădĭtŭs; cănālĭs; cūrsŭs.

Mēdĕă, æ, f., *the famous sorceress, daughter of Æetes.* Pŏpŭlō Mēdĕă trŭcīdĕt, Hor. SYN. Æētĭs, Æētĭă, Cōlchĭs, Phăsĭăs, Phăsĭs. EPITH. Bārbără, fĕrōx, īmpŭdīcă, cāllĭdă, īmpĭă, ădūltĕră, dīră, crŭēntă, īnfāmĭs, fŭrēns, fŭrĭōsă, fŭrĭbūndă, fĕră, īnsānă, crūdēlĭs, nōxĭă, scĕlĕrātă, sævă, trūx, āmēns, īmmānĭs, hōrrēndă, sānguĭnĕă, īmprŏbă, sāgă, īncāntātrīx, vĕnēfĭcă. V. Venefica, maga, Jason, Æson, Creüsa.

Mēdēĭs, ĭdĭs, f., *of Medea.* Ămōr, Mēdēĭdēs hērbæ, Ov.

mĕdēlă, æ, f., *a remedy.* Fōrmă mĕdēlæ, Ser. SYN. Mĕdĭcāmĕn, mĕdĭcīnă, rĕmĕdĭŭm. EPITH. Sălūbrĭs, præsēns, ōptātă, prōmptă.

mĕdĕŏr, ērĭs, *to cure.* Cūră mĕdērī, Virg. SYN. Cūro, sāno.

mĕdĭcābĭlĭs, ĕ, *that may be cured, medicinal.* Ēst mĕdĭcābĭlĭs hērbīs, Ov. SYN. Sănābĭlĭs.

Mēdĭă, æ, f., *Media, Persia.* Mēdĭă fĕrt trīstēs, Virg.

mĕdĭāstīnŭs, ī, m., *a slave of the worst condition.* Tū mĕdĭāstīnŭs, Hor.

mĕdĭcă, æ, f., *sainfoin, a plant.* Tĕ quŏquĕ mĕdĭcă, pŭtrēs, Virg.

mĕdĭcāmĕn, ĭnĭs, *and* mēntŭm, ī, n.; cătŭs, ūs, m., *and* cīnă, æ, f., *medicine.* Tŏt mĕdĭcāmĭnĭbŭs, Ov. Dŏctīs mĕdĭcātĭbŭs īgnēs, Id. Tēmpŏrĭbŭs mĕdĭcīnā vălĕt, Id. Syn. Rĕmĕdĭŭm, mĕdēlă, fōmēntŭm, lĕvāmĕn, lēnīmĕn, phārmācŭm.

Epith. Sălūbrĕ, sălūtĭfĕrŭm, vălĭdŭm, sălūtārĕ, præsēns, pŏtēns, ūtĭlĕ, dūlcĕ, ămārŭm, ōptātŭm, præscrīptŭm, ēxpēctātŭm, prōmptŭm, suāvĕ, grātŭm, ēffĭcāx.

mĕdĭco, ās, (*more frequently* mĕdĭcŏr, ārĭs,) *to cure.* Dārdănĭæ mĕdĭcārī, Virg. Syn. Mĕdĕŏr; līno, tīngo, īmbŭo, īnfĭcĭo, fūco. V. Medeor.

mĕdĭcŭs, ī, m., că, æ, f., *a physician.* Accēdŭnt mĕdĭcī, Mart. Syn. Mĕdēns.

Epith. Dōctŭs, pĕrītŭs, sōlērs, săgāx, īndūstrĭŭs, īngĕnĭōsŭs, īllūstrĭs, sōllĭcĭtŭs, fĭdŭs, fĭdēlĭs, prūdēns, caūtŭs, scĭēns, pŏtēns.

mĕdĭcŭs, ă, ŭm, *belonging to medicine.* Dŭm mĕdĭcās ădhĭbĕrĕ mănŭs, Virg. Syn. Ŏpĭfĕr, sălūtĭfĕr, Ăpōllĭnĕŭs, Phœbēŭs, Māchāŏnĭŭs, Pæōnĭŭs.

Mĕdĭcŭs, ă, ŭm, *Median, Persian.* Mĕdĭcă rūră, Lucr.

mĕdĭocrĭs, ĕ, *middling.* Sī mĕdĭōcrĭs ĕrĭt, Juv. Syn. Mŏdĭcŭs, pārvŭs, paūcŭs, ēxĭgŭŭs.

mĕdĭocrĭtās, ātĭs, f., *mediocrity.* Quīsquīs mĕdĭōcrĭtātĕm, (Sapph.) Hor Syn. Mŏdŭs, mŏdēstĭă. V. Modus.

mĕdĭocrĭtĕr, adv., *moderately.* Rērŭm mĕdĭōcrĭtĕr ūtĭlĭŭm spēs, Hor. Syn. Mŏdĭcē, părŭm; mŏdēstē.

Mĕdĭōlānŭm, ī, n., *Milan, in Italy.* Et Mĕdĭōlānī mĭra, Aus. Epith. Cĕlĕbrĕ, māgnŭm, āmplŭm, pŏpŭlōsŭm, māgnĭfĭcŭm, clārŭm, āntīquŭm, īnsīgnĕ, ĭnēxpūgnābĭlĕ, īnvīctŭm.

mĕdĭtŏr, ārĭs, *to meditate.* Rēgīnām mĕdĭtŏr, Virg. Syn. Cōgĭto, cōnsīdĕro; căno. V. Cogito.

mĕdĭŭs, ă, ŭm, *middle.* Pĕr mĕdĭōs īnstāns, Virg.

mĕdūllă, æ, f., *marrow.* Văcŭīs ēxhaūstă mĕdūllīs, Juv. Epith. Tĕnŭĭs, tĕnĕră, ĭntĭmă, īmă, ōccūltă, mōllĭs, īntērnă, pīnguĭs, tēctă.

mĕdūllĭtŭs, adv., *to the very marrow.* Īllĕ mĕdūllĭtŭs ōmnēs, Prud.

Mēdŭs, ī, m., *a Mede, Persian.* Mĕdŭs īnfēstŭs, Hor. Sēd nĕquĕ Mēdōrŭm, Virg. —2. adj., -ŭs, ă, ŭm, *Median, Persian.* Mēdŭs ăcīnācĕs, Hor.

Mĕdūsă, æ, f., *the daughter of Phorcus, endowed with the power of changing those who looked at her into stones.* Ārvă Mĕdūsæ, Lucan. Syn. Phōrcŷs, Phōrcŷnĭs, Gōrgōn. Epith. Gōrgŏnĕă, vīpĕrĕă, sāxĭfĭcă, hōrrēndă, ĭuvīsă, sævă, ăngŭĭcŏmă, tērrĭfĭcă, āspĕră.

Mĕdūsæŭs, ă, ŭm, *of Medusa.* Ipsă Mĕdūsææ, Mart. Syn. Gōrgŏnĕŭs.

Mĕgæră, æ, f., *one of the Furies.* Nōx īntēmpēstă Mĕgærăm, Virg. Epith. Tōrvă, dīră, īmprŏbă, scĕlĕrātă, vīpĕrĕă, īnfērnă, īmmānĭs, ūltrīx, crŭēntă, crūdēlĭs, ăngŭĭcŏmă, ātră, răbĭdă, fĕrōx, vīrŭlēntă, sævă, vĕnēnōsă. V. Furiæ.

Mĕgălēsĭă, ōrŭm, n. pl., *festivals in honour of Cybele.* Mĕgălēsĭă lūdī, Ov. Syn. Mĕgălēnsēs lūdī.—2. adj., -sĭŭs *and* sĭăcŭs, ă, ŭm, *of the same.* Īntĕrĕă Mĕgălēsĭăcæ, Juv.

Mĕgără, ōrŭm, n. pl., *a city near Corinth.* Ăn vĕnĭăt Mĕgărĭs, Ov.

Mĕgăreŭs, ĕŏs or ĕī, m., *the son of Onchestus.* Gĕnĭtŏr Mĕgăreŭs, Ov.

Mĕgărĕŭs, *and* rēĭŭs, ă, ŭm, *of Megareus.* Mĕgărĕĭŭs hērōs, Ov.—2. *of Megara.* Mĕgărĕăquĕ, Id.

Mĕgīllă, æ, f., *a woman's name.* Frātĕr Mĕgīllæ, Hor.

meīo, ĭs, *to discharge urine.* Meīĕrĕ fās ēst. Syn. Mīngo, cōmmeīo.

ınĕl, mēllĭs, n., *honey.* Quīs mĕl Ārīstæō, Ov. Syn. Făvŭs. Epith. Rōscĭdŭm, āĕrĭŭm, dūlcĕ, spūmāns, liquēns, liquĭdŭm, pūrŭm, flāvŭm, rĕdŏlēns, frāgrāns, flāvēns, nēctărĕŭm, suāvĕ, grātŭm, ŏdōrŭm, Hŷblæŭm, Sĭcŭlŭm; Hŷmēttĭŭm, Cēcrŏpĭŭm, Āttĭcŭm. V. Apes.

Mĕlāmpŭs, pŏdĭs, m., *a physician.* Ămŷthāŏnĭŭsquĕ Mĕlāmpŭs, Virg.

Mĕlānchætēs, æ, m., *the name of a dog.* Ov.

Mĕlāneŭs, ĕŏs or ĕī, m., *a centaur.* Ov.

Mĕlānīră, æ, f., *a woman's name.* Mātĕr Mĕlānīră vŏcātŭr, Ov.

Mĕlānthĭŭs, ī, m., *the keeper of Ulysses' flocks.* Pĕcōrīsquĕ Mĕlānthĭŭs, Ov.

Mĕlānthō, ūs, f., *a daughter of Proteus.* Dēlphīnă Mĕlānthō, Ov.

Mĕlās, æ, m., *a river of Sicily.* Săcrōrūmquĕ Mĕlān, Ov.

Mĕlĕăgĕr, *or* grŭs, grī, m., *the son of Œneus and Althea.* Quīd sī mē, Mĕlĕăgrĕ Ov. Syn. Œnīdēs, Thēstĭădēs. Epith. Fĕrŭs, fĕrōx, Mārtĭŭs, Călŷdōnĭŭs.

Mĕlĕăgrĭdĕs, ŭm, f. pl., *sisters of Meleager.* Ov.

Mĕlĕsĭgĕnēs, æ, m., *a name of Homer.* V. Homerus.

Mĕlĭbœŭs, ă, ŭm, *of Meliboea, a city of Thessaly.* Mĕlĭbœă cŭcŭrrĭt, Virg.—2. -ŭs, ī, m., *the name of a shepherd.* Ō Mĕlĭbœĕ, dĕŭs, Id.

Mĕlĭcērtă, æ, m., *a sea deity.* Nūdīs, Mĕlĭcērtă, lăcĕrtīs, Ov. EPITH. Infēlīx, mĭsĕr, Inŏŭs. V. Palæmon.

mĕlĭcŭs, ă, ŭm, *lyric.* Et mĕlĭcōs lўrĭcōsquĕ, Aus. SYN. Mūsĭcŭs, cănōrŭs.

mĕlĭmēlă, ōrŭm, n. pl., *sweet apples.* Dŏcŭĭt mĕlĭmēlă rŭbērĕ, Hor.

mĕlĭŏr, ōrĭs, *better.* Fāmæ mĕlĭōrĭs ămāntēs, Virg. SYN. Præstāntĭŏr, pŏtĭŏr.

mĕlīsphўllŭm, ī, n., *mint.* Trītă mĕlīsphўllă, Virg.

Mĕlīssŭs, ī, m., *a comic poet.* Mūsă, Mĕlīssĕ, lēvĭ, Ov

Mĕlĭtă, æ, *or* tē, ēs, f., *the island of Malta.* Fērtĭlĭs ēst Mĕlĭtē, Ov. EPITH. Cīrcūmflŭă, fĕrāx, nōbĭlĭs, pŏtēns, Mārtĭă, īndŏmĭtă, īnvīctă, tūrrītă, vāllātă, ārmĭpŏtēns, sāxōsă.

mĕlĭŭs, adv., *better.* Ōrābŭnt caūsās mĕlĭŭs, Virg.

Mĕllă, æ, f., *a river of Cisalpine Gaul.* Flūmĭnă Mĕllæ, Virg.

Mĕllē, ēs, f., *the daughter of Oceanus.* Ināchŭs īn Mĕllē, Ov.

|| mĕllĕŭs, ă, ŭm, *honeyed.* SYN. Mĕllītŭs, dŭlcĭs.

mĕllĭfĕr, ă, ŭm, *bearing honey.* Mĕllĭfĕr ēlēctīs, Claud.

mĕllĭfĭco, ās, *to make honey.* Mĕllĭfĭcātĭs ăpēs, Virg. SYN. Mĕl cōnfĭcĭo, cōgo, fĭgo, stīpo.

mĕllītŭs, ă, ŭm, *honeyed.* Pāne ĕgĕo jām mĕllītĭs, Hor.

mĕlŏs, n., *melody.* Lōngŭm Cāllĭŏpē mĕlŏs, (Alcaic.) Hor. SYN. Cōncēntŭs, cāntŭs, mŏdŭlātĭo, mŏdŭlāmĕn, mŏdŭlī. EPITH. Suāvĕ, dūlcĕ, grātŭm, cănōrŭm, blāndŭm, lætŭm, fēstīvŭm, ămœnŭm, tĕnĕrŭm, dūlcĭsŏnŭm, plăcĭdŭm, cœlēstĕ, Aŏnĭŭm, Cāstălĭŭm. V. Musica.

Mĕlpŏmĕnē, ēs, f., *one of the Muses.* Cāntŭs Mĕlpŏmĕnē, Hor.

mēmbrānă, æ, f., *a membrane.* Mēmbrānĭs īntŭs, Hor. EPITH. Tĕnŭĭs, mŏllĭs. V. Cutis.

mēmbrātĭm, adv., *in pieces.* Mēmbrātĭm vītālĕm, Lucr. SYN. Pĕr pārtēs, īn mēmbră.

mēmbrŭm, ī, n., *a limb.* Mēmbrōrum ārtŭs, Virg. SYN. Ārtŭs, (plur.) EPITH. Ārgēntĕŭm, cāndĭdŭm, dĕcōrŭm, tĕnēllŭm, cālēns, lānguĭdŭm, cădūcŭm, lāctĕŭm, vītālĕ, mōrbĭdŭm, mŏrĭbūndŭm, vĭgēns, vălĭdŭm, fōrtĕ. V. Artus.

mĕmĭnī, *I recollect.* Cāntūndō mĕnĭnī, Virg. SYN. Rĕcōrdŏr, rĕmĭnīscŏr.

Mēmmĭŭs, ĭī, m., *the name of a Roman family.* Ā quō sānguĭnĕ Mēmmī, Virg.

Mēmnōn, ŏnĭs, m., *the son of Tithonus and Aurora.* Mēmnŏnă sĭ mātĕr, Ov. EPITH. Nĭgĕr, cŏlōrātŭs, nōctĭcŏlŏr, Æthĭōps.

Mēmnŏnĭdēs, ŭm, f. pl., *birds that sprung out of the ashes of Memnon.* Mēmnŏnĭdēs dīctæ, Ov.

Mēmnŏnĭŭs, ă, ŭm, *of Memnon.* Mēmnŏnĭō cўcnōs, Ov.

mĕmŏr, ŏrĭs, *who remembers.* Sævæ mĕmŏrēm Jūnōnĭs, Virg. SYN. Nōn īmmĕmŏr, nōn ŏblītŭs.

mĕmŏrābĭlĭs, ĕ, *and* āndŭs, ă, ŭm, *to be remembered.* Mĕmŏrābĭlĕ nōmĕn, Virg. Tĕ mĕmŏrāndĕ cănēmŭs, Virg.

mĕmŏrātŏr, ōrĭs, m., *he who records.* Cāsŭs mĕmŏrātŏr Hŏmērŭs, Prop.

mĕmŏrĭă, æ, f., *memory.* Rĕdĭt mĕmŏrĭă tĕnŭĕ, (Iamb.) Sen. *Syn. Mnemosyne*

mĕmŏro, ās, *to remember.* Et mĕmŏrārĕ pŏtēstĭs, Virg. V. Memini.

Mēmphĭs, ĭs, f., *a town of Egypt.* Mēmphĭs ămăt, Pr. EPITH. Ægўptĭă, bārbără, tōrrĭdă, tūrrītă, sŭpērbă, clără, dīvĕs, cĕlĕbrĭs, ŏpŭlēntă, flōrēns, pŏtēns.

Mēmphītĭcŭs, ă, ŭm, *and* ītĭs, ĭdĭs, f., *of Memphis.* Mēmphītĭcă sācră jŭvēncæ, Ov. Mēmphītĭdŏs ārās, Id.

Mĕnālcās, æ, m., *the name of a shepherd.* Ipsĕ Mĕnālcās, Virg.

Mĕnāndĕr, drŭs, *or* drŏs, ī, m., *a celebrated comic poet.* Cōnvēnīssĕ Mĕnāndrō, Hor.

mēndă, æ, f., *a blemish.* Mēndă fŭĭt, Ov. SYN. Nævŭs. V. Vitium.

mēndācĭŭm, ĭī, n., *a deceit.* Pĭă mēndācĭă fraūdĕ, Ov. SYN. Cōmmēntŭm. EPITH. Vānŭm, cāllĭdŭm, īmpŭdēns, fāllāx, dŏlōsŭm, ănīlĕ, tūrpĕ, pŭdēndŭm, mŭlĭĕbrĕ, fīctŭm.

mendāx, ācĭs, *lying.* Mēndōsum ēt mēndācĕm, Hor. Syn. Vānŭs, pērjŭrŭs, sĭmŭlāns.

Mēndēsĭŭs, ă, ŭm, *of Mendes, a city of Egypt.* Cĕlădōn Mēndēsĭŭs, Ov.

mēndīcĭtās, ātĭs, f., *beggary.* Mēndīcĭtātēm cui ōbtŭlīstī, (Iamb.) Pl. V. Paupertas.

mēndīco, ās, *to beg.* Trĕmēns mēndīcăt ĭn aūrĕm, Juv. Syn. Ēmēndīco.

mēndīcŭs, ī, m., *a beggar.* Mēndīcī, mĭmī, Hor.—2. adj., -ŭs, ă, ŭm, *beggar-like.* Nēc mēndīcă fĕrăt, Mart. Syn. Paūpĕr, ĕgēns, ĭnŏps, ĕgēnŭs. V. Pauper.

mēndōsŭs, ă, ŭm, *full of blemishes.* Quēm nĭsĭ mēndōsŭm, Hor. Syn. Vĭtĭōsŭs, cōrrŭptŭs.

‖ mēndŭm, ī, n., *a fault.* V. Menda.

Mĕnĕlāŭs, ī, m., *the brother of Agamemnon.* Prōteī Mĕnĕlāŭs ăd ūsquĕ, Virg. Syn. Atrīdēs, Tāntălīdēs. Epith. Fōrtĭs, gĕnĕrōsŭs, māgnănĭmŭs, grăvĭs. V. Helena.

Mĕnēnĭŭs, ī, m., *a noble Roman family.* In gēntĕ Mĕnēnī, Hor.

Mĕnēphrōn, ŏnĭs, m., *a man's name.* Cūm mātrĕ Mĕnēphrōn, Ov.

Mĕnēstheŭs, ĕŏs, ĕī *or* ĕī, m., *a man's name.* Nēc frātrĕ Mĕnēstheō, Virg.

Mĕnœtēs, œ, m., *a man's name.* Cōmpēllāt vōcĕ Mĕnœtēn, Virg.

Mĕnœtĭădēs, æ, m., *son of Menœtius.* Ipsĕ Mĕnœtĭădēs, Ov.

mēns, ntĭs, f., *understanding, soul.* Mēntĭbŭs āddūnt, Virg. Syn. Ănĭmŭs, rătĭo, ĭntēllēctŭs, ĭngĕnĭŭm ; cōgĭtātĭo, jūdĭcĭŭm, sēntēntĭă, prōpŏsĭtŭm, cōnsĭlĭŭm, vŏlūntās. V. Animus.

mēnsă, æ, f., *a table.* Mēnsās ūt strŭĕrēs. Epith. Laūtă, pīnguĭs, ōrnātă, pīctă, ăcērnă, tĕrĕs, fāgĭnĕă, nĭtĭdă, citrĕă, māgnĭfĭcă, splēndĭdă, ŏpīmă, ŏnūstă, rēgĭă, ŏpŭlēntă, ăvāră, gēmmātă, hĭlārĭs, dūlcĭs, mōllĭs, fēstīvă.

mēnsĭs, ĭs, m., *a month.* Vōlvēndīs mēnsĭbŭs ōrbēs, Virg. Epith. Fŭgāx, cĕlĕr, flŭēns, fŭgĭtīvŭs, Lūnārĭs.

mēnsŏr, ōrĭs, m., *a measurer.* Līmĭtĕ mēnsŏr, Ov.

mēnstrŭālĭs, ĕ, *and* strŭŭs, ă, ŭm, *monthly.* Mēnstrŭālēm ..ēstrŭĕt, (Iamb.) Prud.

mēnsūră, æ, f., *a measure.* Mēnsūrăquĕ rōbŏrĭs ūlnās, Ov.

mēnsūro, ās, *to measure.* Sŭās mēnsūrăt ŏpēs, Ov. V. Metior.

mēnthă, æ, f., *the herb mint.* Vērtĕrĕ mēnthās, Ov. Epith. Vĭrēns, tōrtă, sўlvēstrĭs, rūctātrīx, ŏdōră, frāgrāns, suāvĭs.

mēntĭo, ōnĭs, f., *mention.* Mēntĭō sī quă, Hor.

mēntĭŏr, īrĭs, *to lie.* Quō tē mēntīrĭs, Achīllēs, Virg. Syn. Fālsă dīco, mĕmŏro, lŏquŏr, nārro ; vānă, fālsă cōmmĭnīscŏr, sĭmŭlo ; ēmēntĭŏr, sĭmŭlo, ĭmĭtŏr.

mēntŭm, ī, n., *the chin.* Incānăquĕ mēntă, Virg. Epith. Sētōsŭm, hīspĭdŭm, ăcūtŭm, pŭlchrŭm, dĕcŏrŭm, nĭvĕŭm, incānŭm.

mĕo, ās, *to flow, circulate.* In dīvērsă mĕāns, Lucr.

Mĕphītĭs, ĭs, f., *the goddess of fetid smells.* Ēxhālăt ŏpācă Mĕphītĭm, Virg. Syn. Pūtŏr, fœtŏr. Epith. Pūtĭdă, grăvĕŏlēns, grăvĭs, sŭlphŭrĕă, sōrdēns, trīstĭs.

mĕrācŭs, ă, ŭm, *pure.* Mōrbūmquĕ mĕrāco, Hor.

mĕrcābĭlĭs, *and* mĕrcālĭs, ĕ, *which may be bought or hired.* Cērtō mĕrcābĭlĭs ærĕ, Hor.

mĕrcātŏr, ōrĭs, m., *a merchant.* Cūrrĭs mĕrcātŏr ăd Indōs, Hor. Syn. Nĕgōcĭātŏr, vēndĭtŏr, īnstĭtŏr, ēmptŏr. Epith. Văgŭs, vĭgĭl, sōllĭcĭtŭs, pĕregrīnŭs, dīvĕs, prōvĭdēns, īnsōmnĭs, īrrĕquĭētŭs, sūbdŏlŭs, ĭnīquŭs. V. Mercor, avarus.

mĕrcātūră, æ, f., *commerce.* Āvērsŭs mĕrcātūrĭs, Hor. Syn. Cōmmērcĭŭm.

mĕrcātŭs, ă, ŭm, *having bought.* Mĕrcātīquĕ sŏlŭm, Virg.

mĕrcēnārĭŭs, ă, ŭm, *hired.* Mĕrcēnārĭŭs ăgrŭm, Hor.

mĕrcēs, ēdĭs, f., *wages, recompense.* Tālŏs, mĕrcēdĕ dĭūrnă, Hor. Syn. Præmĭŭm, prĕtĭŭm, mūnŭs. Epith. Lārgă, āmplă, māgnĭfĭcă, īnsīgnĭs, ēxĭmĭă, dēbĭtă, æquă, jūstă, grātă. V. Præmium.

mĕrcēs, ĭŭm, f. pl., *goods.* Mērcĭbŭs hīc Ĭtălĭs, P. Epith. Vēnālēs, pĕregrīnæ, quæsītæ, Ēŏæ, Āttălĭcæ, ēxtērnæ, dīvĭtēs, ŏpŭlēntæ, prĕtĭōsæ.

mercŏr, ārĭs, *to buy.* Paŭlātĭm mercārĭs ŭgrŭm, Hor. SYN. Ĕmo, cŏĕmo, nŭn-dĭnŏr. V. Mercator.

Mercŭrĭālĭs, ĕ, *of Mercury.* Frĕquēntĭă Mercŭrĭālī, Hor.

Mercŭrĭŭs, ĭi, m., *Mercury, the son and messenger of Jupiter.* Ōmnĭă Mercŭrĭō, Virg. SYN. Mājŭgēnă, Atlāntĭădēs, cādŭcĭfĕr, Hērmēs. EPITH. Fācŭndŭs, vŏlŭcĕr, ālĭgĕr, sŏlēr, fūr, văfĕr, fūrāx, dŏctŭs, cāllĭdŭs, caŭtŭs, vērsūtŭs, āstūtŭs, præpĕs, ālātŭs, ālĭpĕs, pēnnĭgĕr, Ārcădĭŭs, Cȳllēnĭŭs, Tēgĕæŭs; cādŭ-cĭfĕr.

merdă, æ, f., *ordure.* Mērdĭs căpŭt ĭnquĭnĕr, Hor. V. Stercus.

mĕrĕo, ēs, *to serve in war.* In plēbĕ mĕrēbăt, Lucan. SYN. Mĭlĭto.

mĕrĕŏr, ērĭs, *or* ĕo, ēs, *to deserve.* Quĕm nōn mĕrĕārĭs ămōrĕm, Hor. SYN. Prōmĕrĕŏr, dĭgnŭs sŭm.

mĕrĕtrĭcĭŭs, ă, ŭm, *of a courtesan.* Mĕrĕtrĭcĭă lūdōs, Ov.

mĕretrīx, ĭcĭs, *dimin.* ĭcŭlă, æ, f., *a courtesan.* Tŭrpī mĕrĕtrīcĭs ămōrĕ, Hor. Mĕrĕtrīcŭlă Dūvŭm, Id. SYN. Pēllēx, lŭpă, scōrtŭm, prōstĭbŭlŭm. EPITH. Infāmĭs, lāscīvă, impūră, tŭrpĭs, fāmōsă, obscœnă, sōrdĭdă, sălāx, ăvāră, Ĭn-hŏnēstă, ădŭltĕră, pūblĭcă, āstūtă, pērnĭcĭōsă, lūxŭrĭōsă, mĭsĕră, pĕtŭlāns, ĭn-vĕrēcūndă, aŭdāx, ēffrōns, răpāx, ĭnfēlīx, blāndă, cōmptă, pērfĭdă, scĕlĕrātă, impĭă.

mērgēs, ĭtĭs, m., *a handful of corn.* Mērgĭtĕ cŭlmī, Virg. SYN. Mănĭpŭlŭs, mănĭplŭs.

mergo, sī, sŭm, *to plunge under water.* Mērgĕrĕ vēllĕ, Mart. SYN. Immērgo, mērso, submērgo, dēmērgo. V. Abluo.

mērgŭs, ī, m., *a cormorant.* Ex æquŏrĕ mērgī, Virg. EPITH. Præpĕs, fŭgāx, pērnĭx, cănōrŭs, aprĭcŭs, mărĭnŭs, pīscāns, ăquātĭcŭs, ĕdāx, tŭrpĭs, vŏrāx.

mĕrīdĭānŭs, ă, ŭm, *of noon-tide.* Ĕquōs mĕrīdĭānă, (Phal.) Mart.

mĕrīdĭēs, ĭēī, m., *noon.* Pōst mĕrīdĭēm būxōs, (Scaz.) Mart. EPITH. Mădĭdŭs, hūmēns, plŭvĭŭs, imbrĭfĕr.

Mērĭŏnēs, æ, m., *a Cretan warrior.* Nĭgrŭm Mērĭŏnĕm, Hor.

mĕrĭtō, adv., *deservedly.* Sĕd fŭgĕrĕm mĕrĭtō, Ov. SYN. Dĭgnē.

mĕrĭtōrĭă, ōrŭm, n. pl., *hired chambers.* Mĕrĭtōrĭă sōmnŭm, Juv.

mĕrĭtŭm, ī, n., *a reward.* Lātūrŭs mĕrĭtōrŭm, Hor. SYN. Prōmĕrĭtŭm; bĕnĕ-fĭcĭŭm; vĭrtŭs.

mĕrĭtŭs, ă, ŭm, *the partic. of* mereo *and* -or. Sīc fātŭs mĕrĭtōs, Virg.

Mērmĕrŭs, ī, m., *a centaur.* Mērmĕrŭs āccēptō, Ov.

Mĕrŏē, ēs, f., *an island of Nubia.* Ā Mĕrŏē pōrtābĭt, Juv. EPITH. Fœcūndă, dīvĕs, fērtĭlĭs, Cĕphēă; nĭgră, fūscă, ūstă, ădūstă, ŏdōrātă, suāvĭs, frāgrāns, aŭrĭfĕră, cīrcūmflŭă, Nĭlĭăcă.

Mĕrŏpē, ēs, f., *one of the Pleiades.* Mōrtālī Mĕrŏpē, Ov.

mĕrŏps, ŏpĭs, m., *a tom-tit.* Mĕrŏpēs ālĭæquĕ vŏlŭcrēs, Virg.

mērso, ās, *to dip in.* Flŭvĭō mērsārĕ sălūbrī, Virg.

mĕrŭlă, æ, f., *a blackbird.* Sī vĕlŭtī mĕrŭlīs, Hor.

mĕrŭm, ī, n., *pure wine.* Nōctūrnō cērtārĕ mĕrō, Hor. V. Vinum.

mĕrŭs, ă, ŭm, *pure.* Quăm sī mĕră vīnă, Ov. SYN. Sīncērŭs, vērŭs; pūrŭs, lĭquĭdŭs.

mērx, cĭs, f., *merchandise.* V. Merces, ium.

Mĕsēmbrĭăcŭs, ă, ŭm, *of Mesembria.* Indĕ Mĕsēmbrĭăcōs, Ov.

Mēssālă, æ, m., *the surname of the Valerian family.* Mēssālāsquĕ pătērnōs, Ov.

Mēssālīnă, æ, f., *the wife of Claudius.* Mēssālīnæ ŏcŭlīs, Juv.

Mēssālīnŭs, ī, m., *a man's name.* Hānc, Mēssālīnĕ, sălŭtĕm, Ov.

Mēssānă, æ, f., *a city of Sicily.* Mēssānă sŭpērbŭm, Ov.

Mēssānĭŭs, ă, ŭm, *of Messina.* Mēssānĭă lĭttŏră, Ov.

Mēssāpĭŭs, ă, ŭm, *of Messapia.* Mēssāpĭăque ārvă, Ov.

Mēssāpŭs, ī, m., *a son of Neptune.* Mēssāpŭs ĕquŭm dŏmĭtŏr, Virg.

Mēssēnĕ, ēs, f., *a city of the Peloponnesus.* Mēssēnēquĕ fĕrōx, Ov.

Mēssēnĭŭs, ă, ŭm, *of Messene.* Mēssēnĭă mœnĭă, Ov.

mēssĭs, ĭs, f., *a harvest.* Mēssĭbŭs ūstă, Mart. SYN. Frūgēs, sĕgĕs, Cĕrēs, ărīstæ, spīcæ. EPITH. Trītĭcĕă, Cĕrĕālĭs, spīcĕă, dīvĕs, ŏpīmă, ūbĕr, frūgĭfĕră, fērtĭlĭs, cānă, grăvĭdă, cōpĭōsă, lārgă, āmplă, mātūră, flāvă, lætă, fœcūndă, aŭrĕă, ăbūn-dāns, plēnă, flāvēscēns, ārĭdă, sīccă, pŭlchră, ŏdōră, ēxpēctātă, cōllēctă, scīssă. V. Seges, meto.

Messĭŭs, ĭī, m., *a man's name.* Messĭŭs: accĭpĭo, Hor.

messŏr, ōrĭs, m., *a reaper.* Fessĭs messŏrĭbŭs æstŭ, Virg. EPITH. Rūstĭcŭs, dūrŭs, sūdāns, ūstŭs cūrvŭs, cūrvātŭs, impĭgĕr, sēdŭlŭs, indēfēssŭs, ădūstŭs, mātūtīnŭs, īnsōmnĭs, tōrrĭdŭs.

mētă, æ, f., *a goal or limit.* Hic vĕl ăd Elœī mētās, Virg. SYN. Līmĕs, fīnĭs, termĭnŭs. V. Limes.

Mĕtăbŭs, ī, m., *the father of Camilla.* Antīquā mĕtăbŭs, Virg.

mĕtāllĭcŭs, ă, ŭm, *of metal.* E mĕtāllĭcā vēnā, (Scaz.)

mĕtāllĭfĕr, ĕră, ŭm, *producing metal.* Pārtă mĕtāllĭfĕrĭs, Sil.

mĕtāllŭm, ī, n., *metal.* Gĕnĕrōsă mĕtāllĭs, Virg. EPITH. Rŭtĭlŭm, flāvŭm, grăvĕ, fūlvŭm, fūlgēns, crŏcĕŭm, sŏlĭdŭm, rĭgĭdŭm, nĭtĭdŭm, splēndēns, prĕtĭōsŭm.

mĕtămōrphōsĭs, ĭs, f., *a transformation.* Hāc mĕtămōrphōsī, Mant. SYN. Trānsfōrmātĭo, mūtātĭo.

Mĕtănīră, æ, f., *the mother of Triptolemus.* Mĕtănīră vŏcătŭr, Ov.

mētātŏr, ōrĭs, m., *a measurer.* Vĕnĭăm mētātŏr ĭu āgrōs, Lucan. EPITH. Sŏlērs, æquŭs.

Mĕtaurŭs, ī, m., *or* ŭm, ī, n., *a river in Italy.* Tēstĭs Mĕtaurŭm, Hor. EPITH. Văgŭs, sŏnāns.

Mĕtēllă, æ, f., *a woman's name.* Ex aūrĕ Mĕtēllæ, Hor

Mĕtēllŭs, ī, m., *the name of an illustrious Roman family.* Dŏlŭĕrĕ Mĕtēllō, Hor.

Mĕtĕrĕă, æ, f. tŭrbă, *a people on the banks of the Danube.* Mĕtĕrĕăquĕ tūrbă, Ov.

Mēthĭōn, ŏnĭs, m., *a man's name.* Mēthĭŏnĕ Phōrbăs, Ov.

Mĕthȳmnă, æ, *or* mnē, ēs, f., *a town in the island of Lesbos.* Quŏt hăbēt Mĕthȳmnă. răcēmōs, Ov. EPITH. Cūltă, fĕrāx, fērtĭlĭs, fœcūndă, sacră, dīvĕs, Lēsbĭă.

Mĕthȳmnæŭs, ă, ŭm, *and* nĭăs, ădĭs, *of Methymne.* Et Mĕthȳmnœī, Ov. Mĕthȳmnĭădēsquĕ pŭēllæ, Id.

mĕtĭcūlōsŭs, ă, ŭm, *timorous.* Plaut. V. Timidus.

mētĭŏr, īrĭs, ītŭs, *to measure.* Cūrrū mētītŭr ĕquŏrŭm, Virg. SYN. Mēnsūro, dīmētĭŏr, pōndĕro; æstĭmo.

Mĕtīscŭs, ī, m., *Turnus' charioteer.* Et ārmă Mĕtīscī, Virg.

Mĕtĭŭs, *or* Mēttŭs, ī, m., *a general of the Albans.* Mĕtĭum īn dīvērsă, Virg.

mĕto, mēssŭī, mēssŭm, *to reap.* Pūrpŭrĕōsquĕ mĕtŭnt, Virg. SYN. Dēmĕto.

mētŏr, ārĭs, *to measure.* Cāmpōs mētātŭr ăpērtōs, Nemes. SYN. Mētĭŏr, līmĭto, termĭno, dēfīnĭo. V. Limito.

mĕtrētă, æ, f., *a measure of oil or wine.* Illĕ mĕtrētăm, Juv.

mĕtŭo, ĭs, *to be afraid of.* Id mĕtŭēns, vĕtĕrĭs, Virg. SYN. Tĭmĕo, hōrrĕo, vĕrĕŏr, fōrmīdo, păvĕo. V. Horreo, timeo.

mĕtŭs, ūs, m., *fear.* Spēmquĕ mĕtūmque īntĕr, Virg. SYN. Tĭmŏr, tērrŏr, păvŏr. V. Horror, timor.

mĕŭs, ă, ŭm, *mine.* Illĕ mĕās ērrārĕ bŏvēs, Virg.

Mĕzēntĭŭs, ĭī, m., *a cruel king of the Tyrrhenians.* Dīvŭm Mĕzēntĭŭs, Virg. EPITH. Fĕrŭs, fĕrōx, ĭnhūmānŭs, impĭŭs, dīrŭs, Tȳrrhēnŭs, ācĕr, immānĭs.

mīcă, æ, f., *a crumb.* Mīcă sălĭs, Mart. EPITH. Tĕnŭĭs.

mīco, ŭī, *to shine.* Crēbrĭs mīcăt ignĭbŭs, Virg. SYN. Splēndĕo, fūlgŭro, cŏrŭsco, splēndēsco, nĭtēsco, fūlgĕo, rădĭo, īrrădĭo, rĕfūlgĕo. V. Splendeo, luceo.

mīctūrĭo, ĭs, *to have a desire to make water.* Mīctŭrĭūnt hīc, Lucr. SYN. Mēĭo.

Mīdās, æ, m., *a king of Phrygia, who preferred Pan to Apollo; for which his ears were changed into those of an ass.* Bārbărĭcōquĕ Mīdān, Ov. EPITH. Aūrītŭs, dīvĕs, ăvārŭs, mĭsĕr, stŏlĭdŭs, fămēlĭcŭs, imprūdēns, Mȳgdŏnĭŭs, Phrȳgĭŭs.

mĭgro, ās, *to depart.* Vĕtĕrēs mĭgrătĕ cŏlōnī, Virg. SYN. Dēmigro, ēmigro, cōmmigro, dīscēdo, ăbĕo, ēxĕo. Sŏlŭm vērto, mūto. V. Abeo, discedo.

Mīlănĭōn, ŏnĭs, m., *the husband of Atalanta.* Mīlănĭōnă fĕrūnt, Ov.

mīlĕs, ĭtĭs, m., *a soldier.* Mīlĭtĭs āntĕ fŭī, Mart. SYN. Bēllātŏr. EPITH. Bēllĭgĕr, fōrtĭs, gĕnĕrōsŭs, aūdāx, Mārtĭŭs, Māvōrtĭŭs, indŏmĭtŭs, strēnŭŭs, dūrŭs, rŏbūstŭs, sævŭs, ācĕr, ăcērbŭs, ăvārŭs, fĕrōx, crŭēntŭs, sānguĭnĕŭs, īntrĕpĭdŭs, fĕrŭs, impĭgĕr, crūdēlĭs, vălĭdŭs, fŭrēns, răpāx, scĕlĕrātŭs, impĭŭs, pūgnāx, nŏbĭlĭs, trūx, immītĭs, bārbărŭs, mĭnāx, hōrrēndŭs, ĭnhūmānŭs, clȳpĕātŭs, scūtātŭs, crīstātŭs, phălĕrātŭs. V. Bellator, acies militaris.

Mīlēsĭŭs, ă, ŭm, *of Miletus.* Mīlēsĭă măgnō, Virg.

Milētĭs, ĭdĭs, f., *of Miletus.* Mīlētĭdă sōspēs ăd ŭrbĕm, Ov.

Milētŭs, ī, m., *the son of Apollo.* Mīlētŭ, tuā, Ov.—2. *a city of Ionia, founded by Miletus.* Mīlētō mĭssī, Id.

mīlĭtārĭs, ĕ, *warlike.* Tūrpĕ mīlĭtārĭă, (Iamb.) Hor. Syn. Bĕllĭcŭs, Mārtĭŭs, Māvōrtĭŭs.

mīlĭtĭă, æ, f., *warfare.* Præmĭă mīlĭtĭæ, Ov. Syn. Ars bĕllĭcă; bĕllī, Mārtĭs ŏpŭs; mĭlĭtĭæ lăbŏr; ōffĭcĭŭm. V. Bellum.

mīlĭto, ās, *to serve in war.* Ēt 'mīlĭtāvī nōn sĭnĕ, (Alcaic.) Hor. Syn. Mĕrĕo; bĕllo, ās.

mīlĭŭm, ĭī, n., *millet.* Ēt mīlĭŏ vēnĭt, Virg.

mīllĕ, n., *a thousand.* Mīllĕ mĕæ Sĭcŭlīs, Virg. Syn. Bĭs quīngēntī.

mīllēsĭmŭs, ă, ŭm, *the thousandth.* Cōnjŭx mīllēsĭmă lēctō, Lucan.

Mīlo, ōnĭs, m., *an athlete of Crotona.* Flētquĕ Mīlō sĕnĭŏr, Ov. Epith. Fŏrtĭs, vălĭdŭs, rōbŭstŭs, nērvōsŭs, pŏtēns, dūrŭs, ācĕr.

Mīlōnĭŭs, ă, ŭm, *a man's name.* Sāltāt Mīlōnĭŭs, Hor.

mīlvīnŭs, ă, ŭm, *of a kite.* Nĭsī mīlvīnĭs aŭt ăquĭlīnĭs, (Iamb.) Pl.

mīlvŭs, ī, *or* vĭŭs, ĭī, m., *a kite.* Mīlvĭŭs hāmŭm, Hor. Epith. Răpāx, ăvĭdŭs, răptŏr, ĕdāx, cĕlĕr, præpĕs, vĕlōx, cārnĭvŏrŭs, pērnīx, äĕrĭŭs, cĭtŭs, vŏlŭcĕr, prædātŏr, crūdēlĭs, fĕrōx. V. Accipiter.

Mīmāllŏnĕs, *and* lŏnĭdĕs, f. pl., *Bacchanals.* Scīssōsquĕ Mīmāllŏnĕs ūrsōs, Stat. Eccĕ Mīmāllŏnĭdĕs, Ov.

Mīmās, āntĭs, m., *a giant.* Părĭdīsquĕ Mīmāntă, Virg. Epith. Sævŭs, fĕrōx, īmmānĭs, rĕbēllĭs, vāstŭs, vălĭdŭs.

mīmĭcē, adv., *as an actor.* Tūrpe Incēdĕrĕ mīmĭcē, Cat.

* mīmĭcŭs, ă, ŭm, *like an actor, mimic.* Syn. Cōmĭcŭs; rĭdĭcŭlŭs.

Mīmnērmŭs, ī, m., *an elegiac poet.* Mīmnērmŭs ĕt ōptĭvō, Hor.

mīmŭs, ī, m., mă, æ, f, *a player.* Tūrpĭă mīmōs, Ov. Syn. Gēstĭcŭlātŏr, hīstrĭo, cōmĭcŭs, scēnĭcŭs; æmŭlŭs, ĭmĭtātŏr. V. Histrio.

mĭnācĭtĕr, *and* nāntĕr, adv., *threateningly.* Prēssōquĕ mĭnācĭtĕr ōrĕ, Mant. Mūltā mĭnāntĕr ăgānt, Ov.

mĭnæ, ārŭm, f. pl., *threats.* Frōntĕ mĭnæ, Ov. Syn. Mīnātĭo. Epith. Tŭmĭdæ, sævæ, rĭgĭdæ, grăvēs, trīstēs, tērrĭbĭlēs, fĕrōcēs, sĕvēræ, atrōcēs, sŭpērbæ, aŭdācēs, vānæ, răbĭdæ, dīræ, crūdēlēs, hōstĭlēs, jūstæ, īnjūstæ.

mĭnāx, ācĭs, *threatening.* Tēntārĕ mĭnācēs, Virg. Syn. Mīnĭtāns; ăspĕr.

Mīncĭŭs, ĭī, m., *a river in Italy.* Mīncĭŭs ĕquĕ sācrā, Virg. Epith. Inflēxŭs, tārdŭs, ămœnŭs.

Mīnērvă, æ, f., *the goddess of wisdom and science.* Ignără Mīnērvæ, Virg. Syn. Pāllăs; Trītōnĭă, Trītōnĭs. Epith. Cāstă, īnnŭptă, pŭdĭcă, īnnŭbă; făcŭndă, dŏctă, ĭngĕnĭōsă; ārmĭpŏtēns, bēllĭcă, bēllātrīx, ārmĭgĕră, pūgnāx, fĕrōx, ārmātă, pŏtēns, tērrĭbĭlĭs, gĕnĕrōsă, īmpăvĭdă, fŏrtĭs; Attĭcă, Cecrŏpĭă; lānĭfĭcă, ŏpĕrōsă.

mĭnĭmē, adv., *not at all.* Quōd mĭnĭmē rērĭs, Virg. Syn. Nēquāquăm, nŏn.

mĭnĭmŭs, ă, ŭm, *the superl. of* parvus. Cōgĭt mĭnĭmăs, Juv.

Mīnĭo, ōnĭs, m., *a river of Etruria.* Mīnĭōnĭs ĭn ārvĭs, Virg.

mĭnĭstĕr, trī, m.; trā, æ, f., *an attendant.* Cōmĭtātă mĭnĭstrīs, Virg. Bēllīquĕ mĭnĭstrās, Virg. Syn. Fămŭlŭs, sērvŭs, sătēllĕs. V. Servus.

mĭnĭstĕrĭŭm, ĭī, n., *attendance.* Mēquĕ mĭnĭstĕrĭō, Virg.

mĭnĭstro, ās, *to wait on.* Cœnă mĭnĭstrātŭr, Hor. Syn. Sŭppĕdĭto, sŭffĭcĭo; sērvĭo, fămŭlŏr.

mĭnĭtŏr, ārĭs, *to threaten.* Rēm mĭnĭtātŭr, Lucr. V. Minor.

mĭnĭŭm, ĭī, n., *vermilion.* Mīnĭōquĕ rŭbēntĕm, Virg. Epith. Pūrpŭrĕŭm, rŭbĕŭm, rŭbēns, rŏsĕŭm, rŭtĭlŭm, mĭcāns, nĭtēns, dīlūtŭm, Ibērŭm, Hīspānŭm. V. Fucus.

Mīnŏĭs, ĭdĭs, f., *the daughter of Minos.* Mīnŏĭdă Thēseŭs, Ov.

Mīnŏĭŭs, *and* ōŭs, ă, ŭm, *of Minos.* Mīnŏĭă rēgnă, Virg. Mīnōō nātă Thŏāntĕ, Id.

mĭnŏr, ŭs, ōrĭs, *the compar. of* parvus. Nōn mĭnŏr ēst, Ov.

mĭnŏr, ārĭs, *to threaten.* Quōdcŭnquĕ mĭnābĭtŭr ārcŭs, Hor. Syn. Mīnĭtŏr, cōmmĭnŏr, īntēnto.

Mīnōs, ōĭs, m., *a king of Crete, appointed one of the judges of the dead.* Māgnī

Mĭnŏïs, ŭt aĭunt, Prop. Epith. Gnōssĭăcŭs, Gnōssĭŭs, Gŏrtўnĭŭs, Dictæŭs; Agēnŏrēŭs; quæsītŏr, lēgĭfĕr, rĭgĭdŭs, sĕvērŭs, jūstŭs, īmmītĭs, ĭnēxōrābĭlĭs.
Mīnōtaūrŭs, ī, m., a monster, half man and half bull. Mīnōtaūrŭs ĭnēst, Virg.
Epith. Infōrmĭs, tūrpĭs, hōrrēndŭs, tērrĭbĭlĭs, Crēssĭŭs, Crētēnsĭs, Gnōssĭŭs, Gŏrtўnĭŭs, Dīctæŭs, sævŭs, dīrŭs, īndŏmītŭs. Lābўrīnthæŭs.
Mīntūrnæ, ārŭm, f. pl., a city of Campania. Intēr Mīntūrnās, Hor.
Mĭnŭcĭŭs, ĭī, m., a noble Roman family. Brūndŭsĭŭm Mĭnŭcī, Hor.
mĭnŭo, ŭī, ūtŭm, to lessen. Mĭnŭēntŭr ārtĕ, (Sapph.) Hor. Syn. Dīmĭnŭo, īmmĭnŭo, ēxtēnŭo, āttēnŭo, ēlĕvo, dēbĭlĭto, dētrăho, dēlībo, ēxhaūrĭo.
mĭnŭs, adv., less. Crās mĭnŭs āptŭs, Ov.
mĭnūtăl, ālĭs, n., minced meat. Sērvārĕ mĭnūtăl, Juv.
mĭnūtātĭm, ūtē, ūtĭm, adv., piecemeal. Ossă mĭnūtātĭm, Virg. Syn. Mēmbrātĭm; sēnsĭm.
mĭnūtŭs, ă, ŭm, the partic. of minuo; small. Frūgēs quŏquĕ sæpĕ mĭnūtās, Lucr. Syn. Exĭgŭŭs, tĕnŭĭs, ēxĭlĭs.
Mĭnўæ, ārŭm, m. pl., a nation of Thessaly. Dīrĭgŭĕrĕ mĕtū Mĭnўæ, Ov. Epith. Fōrtēs, māgnănĭmī, gĕnĕrōsī, ănĭmōsī, aūdācēs, bēllācēs, pŏtēntēs.
Mĭnўēĭăs, ădĭs, and ēĭs, ĭdĭs, f., daughter of Minyas, king of Orchomenus. Mĭnўēĭăs ōrgĭă cēnsĕt, Ov. Nŏvīs Mĭnўēĭdăs ālīs, Id.
Mĭnўēĭŭs, ă, ŭm, of Minyos. Adhūc Mĭnўēĭă prōlēs, Ov.
mĭrābĭlĭs, ĕ, wonderful. Sēctīs, mīrābĭlĕ dīctū, Virg. Syn. Mīrŭs, mīrāndŭs, ādmīrābĭlĭs, ādmīrāndŭs, stŭpēndŭs, mīrĭfĭcŭs.
mīrābūndŭs, ă, ŭm, marvellous. Mīrābūndă tămĕn, Mant. Syn. Admīrăns, stŭpĕfăctŭs, ōbstŭpĕfăctŭs.
mīrācŭlŭm, ī, n., a wonder. In mīrācŭlă rērŭm, Virg. Syn. Mīrāclŭm, pōrtēntŭm, prōdĭgĭŭm. Epith. Insīgnĕ, stŭpēndŭm, īnsŏlēns, īnsuētŭm, cĕlebrĕ, nŏvŭm, īnsŏlĭtŭm, ĭnaūdītŭm, īngēns.
mīrātŏr, ōrĭs, m., an admirer. Mīrātŏr vĕtĕrŭm, (Phal.) Mart. Syn. Admīrātŏr.
mīrē, and rĭfīcē, adv., wonderfully. Mīrē săgācēs, (Alcaie.) Hor. Mīrĭfīce ēst ā tē, Cat.
mīrĭfīcŭs, ă, ŭm, wonderful. Quŏd sī mīrĭfĭcăm, Mant. Syn. Mīrābĭlĭs, mīrŭs, stŭpēndŭs.
mīrmĭllo, ōnĭs, m., a kind of gladiator. Mīrmĭllōnĭs ĭn ārmīs, Juv.
mīrŏr, ārĭs, to admire. Mīrāntŭr dōna Ænēæ, Virg. Syn. Admīrŏr, dēmīrŏr, sūspĭcĭo, stŭpĕo, stŭpēsco, ōbstŭpĕo. V. Obstupeo.
mīrŭs, ă, ŭm, marvellous. Crēdēbăt mīrōs, Hor. Syn. Mīrāndŭs; ādmīrābĭlĭs, mīrābĭlĭs, ādmīrāndŭs, stŭpēndŭs.
miscēllānĕă, ōrŭm, n. pl., varieties. Ad mīscēllānĕă lūdī, Juv.
miscĕo, scŭī, stŭm, to mix. Fōrtī mīscēbăt, Hor. Syn. Immīscĕo, ādmīscĕo, pērmīscĕo, cōmmīscĕo, īntērmīscĕo, tēmpĕro, āttēmpĕro, cōnfūndo, tūrbo, pērtūrbo.
Mīsēnŭs, ī, m., Æneas's trumpeter. Mīsēnum Æŏlĭdēn, Virg.
mĭsĕr, and sēllŭs. ă, ŭm, wretched. Sī mĭsĕrŭm fōrtūnă, Virg. Syn. Mĭsĕrābĭlĭs, mĭsĕrāndŭs, călămĭtōsŭs, ærŭmnōsŭs, īnfēlīx, īnfōrtūnātŭs, āfflīctŭs, paūpĕr, ĕgēns. V. Infelix, pauper.
mĭsĕrābĭlĭs, ĕ, wretched. Nēc sīs mĭsĕrābĭlĭs ūllī, Ov.
mĭsĕrātĭo, ōnĭs, f., compassion. Frēndēns mĭsĕrātĭŏ cāmpŭm, Prud. Syn. Mĭsĕrīcōrdĭă, clēmēntĭă, pĭētās, bĕnīgnĭtās.
mĭsĕrē, adv., wretchedly. Hāmătĭs mĭsĕrē cōnfīxă, Ov. Syn. Infēlīcĭtĕr.
mĭsĕrĕŏr, ērĭs, ērĭtŭs or ērtŭs, and rēsco, ĭs, to pity. Ō vīrgō, mĭsĕrērĕ, mĕī, Ov. Et mĭsĕrēscĭmŭs ultrō, Virg. Syn. Mĭsĕrŏr, mĭsĕrēt mē.
mĭsĕrĕt, ĕrŭĭt, ĕrĭtŭm or ērtŭm ēst, impers., to pity. Nēc tē mĭsĕrēt nătĭquĕ tŭīquĕ, Virg.
mĭsĕrĭă, æ, f., misfortune. Xvărŭs ĭpsĕ mĭsĕrĭæ, (Iamb.) P. Syr. Syn. Călămĭtās, ærŭmnă, īnfōrtūnĭŭm. V. Paupertas, infortunium.
mĭsĕrĭcōrdĭă, æ, f., compassion. Illa ēst mĭsĕrĭcōrdĭă, (Iamb.) Ter. Syn. Mĭsĕrātĭo, pĭētās, bĕnīgnĭtās, bŏnĭtās, clēmēntĭă. V. Clementia.
mĭsĕrĭcōrs, ōrdĭs, compassionate. Mōrtēm mĭsĕrĭcōrs, (Iamb.) Sen. Syn. Clēmēns, bĕnīgnŭs, prŏpĭtĭŭs, pĭŭs, mītĭs. V. Clemens.

mĭsĕrŏr, ārĭs, ātŭm, *to pity.* Cāsūs mĭsĕrāri, Virg. V. Miseror.

mĭssĭlĕ, ĭs, n., *an arrow, dart.* Mĭssĭlĭbūs lōnge, Virg. Syn. Tēlŭm, jăcŭlŭm; săgīttă.

mĭssĭlĭs, ĕ, *that may be thrown.*

mĭssŭs, ūs, m., *a sending, mission.* Rēgĭs mīssū, Virg.

mītēsco, ĭs, *to grow mild.* Quī nōn mītēscĕrĕ pōssĭt, Hor. Syn. Mānsuēsco, mānsuēfĭo, flēctŏr, plācŏr.

Mĭthrĭdātēs, ĭs, m., *third king of Pontus.* Mĭthrĭdātēs sæpĕ vĕnēnō, Mart. Epith. Fōrtĭs, pŏtēns, crūdēlĭs, īnfēlīx, Pōntĭcŭs.

Mĭthrĭdātēŭs, *and* tĭcŭs, ă, ŭm, *of Mithridates.* Mĭthrĭdātēīsquĕ tŭmēntĕm, Ov. Mĭthrĭdātĭcūmquĕ bēllŭm, Mart.

mītīgo, ās, *to soften.* Mītĭgĕt ăgrŭm, Hor. Syn. Plāco, lēnĭo, flēcto, sēdo, mōllĭo. V. Placo.

mītĭs, ĕ, *gentle.* Mītĭs ĭn āprīcīs, Virg. Syn. Lēnĭs, clēmēns, plăcĭdŭs, făcĭlĭs, mānsuētŭs, cōmĭs, bĕnĭgnŭs.

mitră, æ, f., *a turban.* Ŭt mītră cæsărĭĕm, Prud. Syn. Infŭlă. Epith. Aūrĕă, aūrātă, īllūstrĭs, gēmmātă, rŭtĭlă, dĕcŏră, cŏrūscă. bĭvērtēx.

mĭtto, mīsī, *to send.* Āltĕră mīttăm, Virg. Syn. Emĭtto, jăcĭo, jăcŭlŏr, ĭmmĭtto, vibro, īmpēllo, tōrquĕo, īntōrquĕo, dīrĭgo; ăblēgo, āmāndo; ōmĭtto, prætĕrĕo.

mītŭlŭs, *or* ўlŭs, ī, *a muscle.* Mītŭlŭs ēt vīlĕs, Hor.

Mĭtўlēnē, ēs, f., *the capital city of Lesbos.* Rhŏdŏn aūt Mĭtўlēnēn, Hor.

mīxtūră, æ, f., *a mixture.* Mĭxtūră dĭcĕrĕ cāllēnt, Lucr.

mīxtŭs, ă, ŭm, *the pass. partic. of* misceo. Hæc lăcĕrāt mīxtōs, Juv.

Mnāsўlŭs, ī, m., *the name of a shepherd.* Mnāsўlŭs ĭn āntrō, Virg.

Mnēstheŭs, ĕī *or* eī, m., *one of Æneas's companions.* Mnēsthĕă Sērgēstūmquĕ, Virg.

mōbĭlĭs, ĕ, *moveable.* Mōbĭlĭbūs dĭgĭtĭs, Lucr. Syn. Lĕvĭs, vŏlūbĭlĭs, mŭtăbĭlĭs, vărĭŭs, īrrĕquĭētŭs, īncērtŭs, flūxŭs, cădūcŭs, īncōnstāns; cĕlĕr, vēlōx.

mōbĭlĭtās, ātĭs, f., *mobility.* Mōbĭlĭtātĕ vĭgĕt, Virg. Syn. Lĕvĭtās, īncōnstāntĭă, vēlōcĭtās. Epith. Lūbrĭcă. ăgĭlĭs, īnfīdă, præcēps, cĭtă, cōncĭtă.

mōbĭlĭto, ās, *to render moveable.* Ōmnĭă mōbĭlĭāntŭr, Lucr.

mŏdĕrābĭlĭs, ĕ, *moderate.* Mŏdĕrābĭlĕ suādēnt, Ov.

mŏdĕrāmĕn, ĭnĭs, n., *management.* Ālĭŭs mŏdĕrāmĭnă, dīxī, Ov. Syn. Rĕgĭmĕn.

mŏdĕrāntĕr, ātĕ, ātĭm, adv., *with moderation.* Ēst mŏdĕrātē, Ov. Mŏdĕrātĭm crēscĕrĕ, Lucr.

mŏdĕrātŏr, ōrĭs, m., *a governor.* Sĕdĕt mŏdĕrātŏr hăbēnĭs, Tib. Syn. Rēctŏr, gŭbērnātŏr.

mŏdĕrātŭs, ă, ŭm, *moderated.* Jāctāntŭr mŏdĕrātĭs, Ov. Syn. Pācātŭs, plăcĭdŭs, mŏdēstŭs.

mŏdĕrŏr, ārĭs, *to rule.* Quī nōn mŏdĕrābĭtŭr īræ, Hor. Syn. Ādmŏdĕrŏr, tēmpĕro, cōntĭnĕo, rĕtĭnĕo, cŏērcĕo, cŏhĭbĕo, ĭnhĭbĕo, cōmpēsco, rĕprĭmo, cōmprĭmo, fræno, refræno, rĕgo, gŭbērno. V. Modum servo.

mŏdēstē, adv., *moderately.* Pĕtĕrĕrĕ mŏdēstē.

mŏdēstĭă, æ, f., *temperance, modesty.* Mĭnŭĭtquĕ mŏdēstĭă crīmĕn, Ov. Syn Mŏdĕrātĭo, pŭdŏr. Epith. Blāndă, plăcĭdă, grātă, ămăbĭlĭs, īnsīgnĭs, hŭmĭlĭs.

mŏdēstŭs, ă, ŭm, *moderate.* Plērūmquĕ mŏdēstŭs, Hor. Syn. Mŏdĕrātŭs, hŏnēstŭs, pācātŭs, plăcĭdŭs.

mŏdĭcŭs, ă, ŭm, *little.* Ŭtăr, ĕt ēx mŏdĭcō, Hor. Syn. Pārvŭs, mŏdĕrātŭs.

mŏdĭŭs, ĭī, m., *a bushel.* Mĭllĕ făbæ mŏdĭĭs, Hor.

mŏdŏ, adv., *just now.* Annēllĭs, mŏdŏ lævā, Hor. Syn. Mŏx, stătĭm, sŭbĭto, nūnc; dŭmmŏdo, sī tămĕn.

mŏdŭlāmĕn, ĭnĭs, n., *harmony.* Prēssō mŏdŭlāmĭnĕ pārcŭs, Prud. Syn. Mŏdŭlātĭo, cāntŭs, cārmĕn, mŏdī, mŏdŭlī, mēlŏs, cōncēntŭs. Epith. Dōctŭm, sŏnōrŭm, dūlcĕ, cănōrŭm, ămœnŭm, plăcĭdŭm, quĕrŭlŭm, lēnĕ, mūlcēns, blāndŭm, dūlcĭsŏnŭm, cōnsōrs, āltĭsŏnŭm, cœlēstĕ, Āŏnĭŭm, Cāstălĭŭm. V. Cantus.

mŏdŭlātŏr, ōrĭs, m., *a tuner.* Ōmnĭsŏnæ mŏdŭlātŏr, Hor. Syn. Cāntŏr.

mŏdŭlŏr, ārĭs, *to sing, to set to a tune.* Sĭcŭlī mŏdŭlābŏr ăvēnā, Virg. Syn. Cāno, cōncĭno, cānto. V. Canto.

mŏdŭlŭs, ī, m., *a measure of proportion.* Pōndĕrĭbŭs mŏdŭlīsquĕ, Hor.

mŏdŭs, ī, m., *a proportion.* Quĭs mŏdŭs ārgēntō, Pers. Syn. Rătĭo; mŏdĕrātĭo, mĕdĭocrĭtās; mŏdēstĭă, sōbrĭĕtās. Epith. Pŭlchĕr, ūtĭlĭs, aūrĕŭs, ōptātŭs, rēctŭs, hŏnēstŭs.

mœchŏr, ārĭs, *to commit adultery.* Quī mœchātŭr, ăt hīc sī, Hŏr. V. Adulteror.

mœchŭs, ī, m., chă, æ, f., *an adulterer, adultress.* Clōdĭŭs āccūsēt mœchōs, Juv. V. Adulter.

mœnĭă, ĭŭm, n. pl., *walls of fortification.* Sŭb mœnĭbŭs āltīs, Virg. Syn. Mūrŭs, părĭēs, āggĕr, mūnīmēntă. Epith. Tūrrītă, mūnītă, ārdŭă, sŭblīmĭă, ēxcēlsă, tūrrĭgĕră, sŭpērbă, ĭnāccēssă, ēlātă, ēdĭtă, āĕrĭă, tūtă, sēcūră, īngēntĭă, vāllātă, cŏctĭlĭă, fōrtĭă. V. Murus.

mœrĕo, ēs, *to be sad.* Ălĭō mœrēbĭs āmōrēs, Hor. Syn. Trīstŏr, dŏlĕo, gĕmo.

Mœrĭs, ĭdĭs, m., *a king of Egypt.—2. the name of a shepherd.* Quō tē, Mœrĭ, pĕdēs, Virg.

mœrŏr, ōrĭs, m., *grief.* Mœrŏr ĭn ūrbĕ, Pedo. Syn. Mœstĭtĭă, dŏlŏr, trīstĭtĭă. V. Tristitia.

mœstŭa, ă, ŭm, *mournful.* Ēt mœstās ēxprōmĕrĕ vōcēs, Virg. Syn. Trīstĭs, āfflīctŭs, dŏlēns, mœrēns. V. Tristis.

mŏlă, æ, f., *a mill-stone.* Dīgnīquĕ mŏlăm vērsārĕ, Juv. Epith. Rĭgĭdă, vērsātĭlĭs, vŏlūbĭlĭs, dūră, scabră, pūnĭcĕă, rūstĭcă, fōrtĭs.—2. *a holy cake.* Ōblīquōquĕ mŏlās, Luc.

mŏlārĭs, ĕ, *pertaining to a mill-stone.* Vāstīsquĕ mŏlārĭbŭs, Virg.

mŏlēs, ĭs, f., *bulk.* Mūndī mŏlēs ŏpĕrōsă, Ov. Syn. Pōndŭs, ŏnŭs, māssă, māchīnă. Epith. Sāxĕă, ŏnĕrōsă, ŏpĕrōsă, grăvĭs, īnsōlĭtă, ārdŭă, sŭblīmĭs, cēlsă, ēxcēlsă, āltă, stŭpēndă, ādmīrāndă, īngēns.

* mŏlēstĭă, æ, f., *trouble.* Cic. Syn. Ĭncŏmmŏdŭm, cūră, dŏlŏr.

mŏlēstŭs, ă, ŭm, *troublesome.* Lītēs cūm rēgĕ mŏlēstās, Hor. Syn. Grăvĭs, dūrŭs, īncŏmmŏdŭs, īmpōrtūnŭs, ŏdĭōsŭs, dĭffĭcĭlĭs, ŏpĕrōsŭs.

mŏlīmĕn, ĭnĭs, n., *an attempt.* Dīvīnī mōlīmĭnĭs, ĭpsĕ, P. E. Syn. Cōnāmĕn, cōnātŭs, nīsŭs, tēntāmĕn. V. Conatus.

mŏlĭŏr, īrĭs, ītŭs, *to build, attempt.* Ōptātæ mŏlĭŏr ūrbĭs, Virg. Syn. Ādmŏlĭŏr, strŭo, ædĭfĭco, cōnstrŭo, fabrĭco; nītŏr, ēnītŏr, tēnto, lăbōro. V. Conor; cogito, meditor, machinor.

mŏlītŏr, ōrĭs, m., *a constructor.* Rătĭs mŏlītŏr Ĭāsōn, Ov.

mŏllēsco, ĭs, *to grow soft.* Tēntātŭm mŏllēscĭt ĕbŭr, Ov. Syn. Mŏllēfĭo, mŏllĭŏr; mītēsco.

mŏllĭo, ĭs, īvī and ĭī, ītŭm, *to make soft.* Dūrăquĕ mŏllĭĕrănt, Ov. Syn. Ēmŏllĭo, lēnĭo, sŭbĭgo, flēcto, tēmpĕro, mītĭgo, plāco.

mŏllĭs, ĕ, *soft.* Mŏllĭbŭs ūtĕrĕ mālvĭs, Mart. Syn. Tĕnĕr, făcĭlĭs, flēxĭbĭlĭs, trāctābĭlĭs; rēmīssŭs, plăcĭdŭs, lēnĭs; suāvĭs, jūcūndŭs, grātŭs, blāndŭs; ămœnŭs; ēffœmĭnātŭs, ĭnērs.

mŏllĭtĕr, adv., *softly.* Mŏllĭtĕr ōssă, Virg. Syn. Lēnĭtĕr, suāvĭtĕr; făcĭlē.

mŏllĭtĭă, æ, or ĭēs, ēī, f., *softness.* Mŏllĭtĭēm, seū, Hor. Syn. Flēxĭlĭtās, lēnĭtās; ĭnērtĭă; lūxŭrĭēs.

mŏllītŭs, ă, ŭm, *the pass. partic. of* mollio. Ēt pēr mŏllītōs, Petr.

mŏlo, lŭī, *to grind.* Grānă mŏlĭt tŏtĭdĕm, Petr. Syn. Ēmŏlo, cōmmŏlo.

Mŏlōrchŭs, ī, m., *a shepherd of Arcadia, for whom Hercules killed the Nemean lion.* Lūcōsquĕ Mŏlōrchī, Virg. Epith. Paūpĕr, ĭnŏps, Ārcădĭŭs, Clĕōnæŭs.

Mŏlōssŭs, ī, m., *a dog of Molossia.* Ācrēmquĕ Mŏlōssŭm, Virg. Epith. Lĕvĭs, īnsānŭs, latrātŏr, mōrdāx, trūx, fōrtĭs, vălĭdŭs, latrāns, ārmĭllātŭs. V. Canis.

Mŏlpeūs, ĕī or eī, m., *the name of a warrior.* Mŏlpĕă trājēctī, Ov.

mŏlў, n., indecl., *a species of garlic.* Mōlў vōcănt sŭpĕrī, Ov.

mŏmēntŭm, ī, n., *movement, an instant.* Mōmēntō cĭtă mōrs, Hor. Syn. Pūnctŭm tēmpŏrĭs, tēmpŭs ēxĭgŭŭm; pōndŭs, vĭs, aūctōrĭtās. Epith. Răpĭdŭm, lĕvĕ, īnstābĭlĕ, brĕvĕ, pārvŭm, mĭnĭmŭm.

Mŏmŭs, ī, m., *the god of mirth.* Epith. Ĭnērs, prōcāx.

Mŏnæsēs, or nēsēs, ĭs, m., *a Parthian king.* Jām bĭs Mŏnæsēs, Hor.

mŏnēdŭlă, æ, f., *a jackdaw.* Vēlātă mŏnēdŭlă pēnnĭs, Ov.

mŏnĕo, ēs, *to advise.* Jūpĭtĕr ĭpsĕ mŏnēbăt, Virg. Syn. Ādmŏnĕo, cōmmŏnĕo, nūncĭō, ĭndĭco, ās; suādĕo, hōrtŏr, ēxcĭto, præcĭpĭo.

mŏnētă, æ, f., *coin.* Dŏmĭnōs nŏvæ mŏnētæ, (Phal.) Mart. Syn. Nŭmmŭs, nŭmïsmă, pĕcūnïă. Epitii. Flāvă, ŏpŭlēntă, fŭlvă, ænĕă, aūrĕă, ārgēntĕă, ūtĭlĭs, prĕtĭōsă. V. Pecunia.

Mŏnētă, æ, f., *a surname of Juno.* Altă Mŏnētă grădŭs, Ov.

mŏnīlĕ, ĭs. n., *a necklace.* Lōngă mŏnīlĭă cōllō, Ov. Syn. Tŏrquĭs, tŏrquēs. Epitii. Prĕtĭōsŭm, bāccātŭm, aūrĕŭm, fŭlvŭm, īnsīgnĕ, splēndēns, fŭlgēns, dĕcōrŭm, dīvĕs, gēmmĕŭm, mĭcāns, nōbĭlĕ, cŏrŭscŭm, rŭtĭlŭm, splēndĭdŭm.

mŏnĭmēntŭm, ī, n., *a monument.* Dĕdĕrāt mŏnĭmēntŭm, Virg. Syn. Sīgnŭm, īndĭcĭŭm, ārgūmēntŭm, nŏtă, tēstĭmōnĭŭm. V. Signum, monumentum.

mŏnĭtŏr, ōrĭs, m., *an adviser.* Flēctī, mŏnĭtōrĭbŭs āspĕr, Hor. Syn. Admŏnĭtŏr, suāsŏr.

mŏnĭtŭm, ī, n., *and* tŭs, ūs, m., *advice.* Mŏnĭtĭs ĭmmōtă tĕnēbăt, Virg. Mŏnĭtū Trītōnĭdĭs, Ov.

mŏnĭtŭs, ă, ŭm, *the pass. partic. of* moneo. Jūstĭtĭăm mŏnĭti, Virg.

Mŏnœcŭs, ī, m., *a city of Liguria.* Ārcĕ Mŏnœcī, Virg.

mōns, ntĭs, m., *a mountain.* Rōmānī mōntēs, Prop. Syn. Cōllĭs, jŭgŭm, ăpēx, vērtēx, cūlmēn, căcūmēn. Epitii. Altŭs, prærūptŭs, ēxcēlsŭs, āĕrĭŭs, præcēps, sūblīmĭs, āspĕr, clīvōsŭs, dēvēxŭs, ĭnāccēssŭs, sŭpĭnŭs, āvĭŭs, ēlātŭs, nĕbŭlōsŭs, ābrūptŭs, īngēns, sŭpērbŭs, nĭmbōsŭs, nĕmŏrōsŭs, ūmbrōsŭs, ăpērtŭs, aprīcŭs, sāxōsŭs, scŏpŭlōsŭs, īncūltŭs, rĭgĭdŭs, nĭvōsŭs, dūmōsŭs, spătĭōsŭs, căvērnōsŭs, āmbĭtĭōsŭs, tŭmĭdŭs, vĭrĭdĭs, frōndōsŭs, ŏpācŭs, hērbōsŭs, īntōnsŭs. V. Altus.

mōnstrātŏr, ōrĭs, m., *a discoverer.* Pŭĕr mōnstrātŏr ărātrī, Virg.

mōnstrĭfĕr, ĕră, ŭm, *bringing forth monsters.* Mōnstrĭfĕrōs ăgĭt ūndă, Lucan. Syn. Mōnstrōrŭm fĕrāx.

mōnstrĭfĭcŭs, ă, ŭm, *doing wonders.* Mōnstrĭfĭcī vūltŭs, M. Syn. Mōnstrōsŭs.

mōnstrĭgĕnŭs, ă, ŭm, *born of a monster.* Mōnstrĭgĕnĭs hōstĕm, Avien. Syn. Mōnstrōsŭs.

mōnstro, ās, *to show, point out.* Tālĭă mōnstrābăt, Virg. Syn. Dēmōnstro, cōmmōnstro, ōstēndo; īndĭco, ās; mănĭfēsto. V. Ostendo.

mōnstrōsŭs, ă, ŭm, *monstrous.* Mōnstrōsīque hŏmĭnŭm, Lucan. Syn. Prōdĭgĭōsŭs, pōrtēntōsŭs.

mōnstrŭm, ī, n., *a monster.* Jūra īnsĭtă mōnstrĭs, Stat. Syn. Prōdĭgĭŭm, pōrtēntŭm, ōstēntŭm. Epith. Īnfāndŭm, īmmānĕ, fātālĕ, ēxecrābĭlĕ, dīrŭm, tūrpĕ, dēfōrmĕ, mīrābĭlĕ, stŭpēndŭm, nŏvŭm, tērrĭbĭlĕ, sævŭm, trūx, atrōx, ēxĭtĭālĕ, fĕrālĕ, mīrŭm, tērrĭfĭcŭm, prōdĭgĭōsŭm; dīctū, vīsū mīrābĭlĕ, Gōrgŏnĕŭm.

mōntānŭs, ă, ŭm, *belonging to a mountain.* Aŭt răpĭdŭs mōntānō, Virg.

mōntĭcŏlă, æ, m. f., *a mountaineer.* Mōntĭcŏlæ Sŷlvānī, Virg.

mōntĭvăgŭs, ă, ŭm, *wandering on mountains.* Mōntĭvăgō gĕnĕrī, Lucr.

mōntōsŭs, ă, ŭm, *mountainous.* Mōntōsæ mĭsērĕ, Virg. Syn. Mōntānŭs, scŏpŭlōsŭs, clīvōsŭs, ācclīvĭs, ārdŭŭs, ābrūptŭs.

mŏnŭmēntŭm, ī, n., *a monument.* Quæ mŏnŭmēntă mĕārŭm, Virg. Syn. Mŏnĭmēntŭm, sīgnŭm; sĕpŭlcrŭm, tŭmŭlī īnscrīptĭo.

Mōpsŏpĭŭs, ă, ŭm, *of Attica.* Rēddĭtă Mōpsŏpĭă, Ov.

Mōpsŭs, ī, m., *one of the Argonauts.* Ampŷcĭdēn Mōpsŭm, Ov.

mŏră, æ, f., *delay.* Mŏră lōngă lābōrĭs, Ov. Syn. Cūnctātĭo, tārdĭtās, sēgnĭtĭēs. Epith. Tārdă, lēntă, ĭgnāvă, ĭnērs, lānguĭdă, dēsĕs, ōtĭōsă, ānnōsă.

mŏrātŭs, ă, ŭm, *part. of* moror, *having stayed.* Haūd mūltă mŏrātŭs, Virg

mŏrātŭs, ă, ŭm, *regulated as to morals.* Mŏrātăquĕ rēctĕ, Hor.

mōrbĭdŭs, *and* ōsŭs, ă, ŭm, *sickly.* Fĭt mōrbĭdŭs āēr, Lucr. Mōrbōsī părĭtĕr, Cat. Epith. Mōrbĭs ŏbnōxĭŭs, lānguĭdŭs, ægrōtŭs.

mōrbŭs, ī, m., *a disease.* Mōrbōrŭm quŏquĕ tē, Virg. Syn. Lānguŏr, febrĭs, lŭēs, cōntăgĭŭm. Epith. Trīstĭs, pătĭēns, pēstĭfĕr, lēthĭfĕr, ăcūtŭs, ĭnērs, ēxsānguĭs, mŏrōsŭs, fœdŭs, pērnĭcĭōsŭs, crūdēlĭs, dīrŭs, īmpătĭēns, grăvĭs, pērĭcŭlōsŭs, īnsānābĭlĭs, īmmĕdĭcābĭlĭs, lătēns, lēthālĭs, vĭŏlēntŭs, ācērbŭs, quĕrŭlŭs, ācĕr, tĕtĕr, mălīgnŭs, īnsōmnĭs, mŏlēstŭs, lānguĭdŭs, sōllĭcĭtŭs, păllĭdŭs, mōrtĭfĕr, āspĕr, īntŏlĕrābĭlĭs, lēntŭs, tābĭfĭcŭs, grāssāns, dēspērātŭs, atrōx, putrĭs, ēxĭtĭālĭs, lōngŭs. V. Ægroto, febris, pestis, hydrops, languor, æger.

mōrdāx, ācĭs, *biting.* Mōrdācĕs ălĭtĕr, (Choriamb.) Hor. Syn. Ēdāx; dēntātŭs.

mŏrdĕo, mŏmŏrdī, mŏrsŭm, *to bite.* Mŏrdĕbĭtquĕ tŭŏs, Mart. Syn. Obmŏrdĕo, ādmŏrdĕo. V. Manduco.

mŏrdĭcŭs, adv., *bitingly.* Mŏrdĭcŭs āgnăm, Hor.

mŏrētŭm, ī, n., *a kind of salad.* Pŏsŭīssĕ mŏrētŭm, Ov. Syn. Lībŭm. Epith. Dŭlcĕ, mŏllĕ, cōctŭm.

mŏrĭbŭndŭs, ă, ŭm, *dying.* Mĕ mŏrĭbŭndām dēsĕrĭs, Virg. Syn. Sēmiănĭmĭs, mŏrĭēns, lānguēns.

mŏrĭgĕro, ās, *and* ŏr, ārĭs, *to humour.* Mŏrĭgĕrāri ŏpŏrtŭĭt, Ter.

mŏrĭgĕrŭs, ă, ŭm, *complaisant.* Seŭ tĭbĭ mŏrĭgĕră, Ter.

Mŏrīnī, ōrŭm, m. pl., *a people of Gaul.* Extrēmĭque hŏmĭnŭm Mŏrīnī, Virg.

mŏrĭo, ōnĭs, m., *a fool.* Ūsquĕ mŏrĭōnĕm, Mart.

mŏrĭŏr, ĕrĭs, *to die.* Dūm mŏrĭtūr, nūm quĭd, Mart. Syn. Ēmŏrĭŏr, ŏbĕo, ŏccŭmbo, cădo, ōccĭdo, īntĕrĕo, ēxspīro, pĕrĕo. V. Mors.

mŏrmȳr, ȳrĭs, f., *a sea-fish.* Mŏrmȳrēs ĕt aūrī, Ov.

mŏrŏr, ārĭs, *to stay.* Quĭd vītăm mŏrŏr īnvīsăm, Virg. Syn. Immŏrŏr, dēmŏrŏr, cūnctŏr, tārdo, dīffĕro, prōcrāstĭno, cēsso, hærĕo; dĕtĭnĕo, rĕtĭnĕo, sīsto, tārdo, rĕtārdo, īmpĕdĭo; sūbsĭsto, stō, hærĕo, cōnsĭsto.

mŏrōsŭs, ă, ŭm, *morose.* Mŏrōsum ŏffēndĕt, Hor. Syn. Dĭffĭcĭlĭs, trīstĭs, ānxĭŭs, mŏlēstŭs.

Mŏrpheŭs, ĕŏs, ĕī, *or* eī, m., *the god of sleep.* Hīs vŏcēm Mŏrpheŭs. Epith. Sŏmnĭfĕr, lĕvĭs, nŏctūrnŭs, vŏlŭcĕr, fīctŏr, sĭmŭlātŏr, plăcĭdŭs.

mŏrs, tĭs, f., *death.* Mŏrtĭs ăpērtă vĭa ēst, Tib. Syn. Fūnŭs, lēthŭm, īntĕrĭtŭs, fātŭm, ŏbĭtŭs, nēx, Lībĭtīnă. Epith. Frīgĭdă, răpĭdă, ăcērbă, nigră, crūdēlĭs, sævă, cērtă, vĭŏlēntă, dūră, crŭēntă, fĕră, mĭsĕră, flēbĭlĭs, gĕlĭdă, īmmātūră, prŏpĕrātă, īmpŏrtūnă, āspĕră, sŭbĭtă, mătūră, præcŏx, īmprŏvīsă, īnēxpēctātă, rĕpēntīnă, īmmītĭs, răpāx, īnvĭdă, sūrdă, īmprŏbă, īntēmpēstīvă, cŏmmūnĭs, īnēxŏrābĭlĭs, īnēxplētă, īnsătĭābĭlĭs, præcēps, cæcă, rĭgĭdă, trūx, ēxsānguĭs, tērrĭbĭlĭs, trŭcŭlēntă, bārbără, plăcĭdă, bĕātă, dĕcŏră, īnclȳtă, fēlīx, ŏbscūră, pŭdēndă, tūrpĭs, ĭgnŏbĭlĭs, īnfēlīx. V. Moribundus.

mŏrsŭm, ī, n., *a piece bitten out.* Hærēbānt mŏrsă lăbēllĭs, Cat.

mŏrsŭs, ūs, m., *a bite.* Mŏrsĭbŭs īnsĕquĭtŭr, Ov. Epith. Avĭdŭs, răbĭdŭs, ĕdāx, dīrŭs, īmmānĭs, crŭēntŭs, crūdēlĭs, tĕnāx, rĕpĕtītŭs, ĭtĕrātŭs, mŏrtĭfĕr, vĕnēfĭcŭs, vĕnēnōsŭs, vīpĕrĕŭs. V. Mordeo.

mŏrtālĭs, ĕ, *mortal.* Mĭsĕrĭs mŏrtālĭbŭs ævī, Virg. Syn. Mŏrti ŏbnŏxĭŭs; hŭmānŭs; hŏmo.

mŏrtārĭŭm, ĭī, n., *a mortar.* Sānānt mŏrtārĭă cæcōs, Juv.

mŏrtĭfĕr, ă, ŭm, *deadly.* Gaŭdĭă, mŏrtĭfĕrūmque, Virg. Syn. Lēthālĭs, fātālĭs, lēthĭfĕr, fūnēstŭs, ēxĭtĭōsŭs, pērnĭcĭōsŭs.

mŏrtŭŭs, ă, ŭm, *dead.* Mŏrtŭŭs ēssēs, Virg. Syn Exănĭmĭs, ĕxănĭmātŭs, fūnctŭs, dēfūnctŭs, ēxsānguĭs, ēxtīnctŭs. V. Morior, cadaver, manes.

mŏrŭm, ī, n., *a mulberry.* Mŏră cŏlŏrĕ, Ov. Epith. Nigrŭm, ātrŭm, dŭlcĕ, sānguĭnĕŭm, pūrpŭrĕŭm, crŭēntŭm, nigrāns, suāvĕ, cŏlōrātŭm.

mŏrŭs, ī, f., *the mulberry tree.* Ardŭă mŏrŭs ĕrăt, Ov. Epith. Tārdă, lēntă, frūctĭfĕră, fērtĭlĭs, fĕrāx. V. Arbor.

mōs, mōrĭs, m., *custom.* Mŏrĕ, bŏnŭs sānĕ, Hor. Syn. Cōnsuētūdo, ăssuētūdo, ūsŭs. Epith. Vĕtŭstŭs, prīscŭs, ăntīquŭs, cōnsuĕtŭs, ăssuētŭs, pătrĭŭs, sōlēnnĭs, īnsuētŭs.

mōrēs, ŭm, *manners, morals.* Nŏvi hŏmĭnĭs mŏrēs, Mart. Syn. Affēctŭs, īngĕnĭŭm, nātūră, īndŏlēs. Epith. Prŏbī, plăcĭdī, mŏdēstī, hŏnēstī, rēctī, æquī, cāstī, pūrī, pŭdīcī, ēgrĕgĭī, mītēs, īngĕnŭī, gĕnĕrōsī, fĕrī, mălīgnī, ŏbscœnī, prāvī, cŏrrūptī, pērvērsī, īnfāndī.

Mŏschŭs, ī, m., *a rhetorician of Pergamus.* Hor.

Mōsēs, ĭs, m., *the son of Amram, lawgiver to the Hebrews.* Jăcēt Mōsēs, Aārōnquĕ. Syn. Mŏȳsēs, Amrāmĭdēs. Epith. Clārŭs, lēgĭfĕr, fătĭdĭcŭs, săcŏr, pŏtēns.

mōto, ās, *the freq. of* moveo. Rĭgĭdās mōtārĕ căcŭmĭnă quērcŭs, Virg. V. Moveo.

mōtŏr, ōrĭs, m., *a mover.* Cūnārŭm fŭĕrās mōtŏr, Mart. Epith. Agĭtātŏr, īmpŭlsŏr.

mōtŭs, ūs, m., *movement.* Trĕmŭērūnt mōtĭbŭs Alpēs, Virg. Syn. Agĭtatĭo, mōtĭo, cōmmōtĭo, pūlsŭs, īmpŭlsŭs, īmpĕtŭs; tŭmŭltŭs. Epith. Tārdŭs, lēntŭs, vēlŏx, cĕlĕr, cŏncĭtŭs, cĭtātŭs, răpĭdŭs, vĭŏlēntŭs, præcĕps, āssĭdŭŭs, trĕmŭlŭs, lĕvĭs, ĭncērtŭs, vānŭs, ĭrrĕquīētŭs, crēbĕr, vărĭŭs.

mŏtŭs, ă, ŭm, *the pass. partic. of* moveo. Sēd mōtŏs præstăt, Virg.

mŏvĕo, mōvī, mōtŭm, *to move.* Fătōrum ārcānă mŏvēbo, Virg. Syn. Cŏm-mŏvĕo, pērmŏvĕo, mōto, quătĭo, quāsso, cŏncŭtĭo, ăgĭto, pēllo, īmpēllo, vērso, ăgo ; flēcto, āfflĭcĭo, cĭĕo, ēxcĭto ; tŭrbo, pērtŭrbo, mōtŭ mīscĕo.

mŏx, adv., *soon.* Mōx frŭmēntă dătŭrŭs, Hor. Syn. Actŭtŭm, cĭto, cŏnfēstĭm, īllĭcĕt, prŏpĕrē.

mūcĭdŭs, ă, ŭm, *mouldy.* Mūcĭdă cærŭlēī pānĭs, Juv.

mūcro, ōnĭs, m., *a sharp point, a sword.* Ăcĭēs mūcrōnĕ cŏrūscō, Virg. Syn. Cūspĭs, ăcĭēs ; ēnsĭs, glădĭŭs, fērrŭm. Epith. Strĭctŭs, fērrĕŭs, mōrtālĭs, āspĕr, ăcūtŭs, āncēps, īnfēstŭs, Mārtĭŭs, fūlgēns, fĕrŭs, brĕvĭs, fŭrēns, crŭēntŭs, dīs-trĭctŭs, dūrŭs, rŭtĭlŭs, fūlgĭdŭs, ārdēns, nĭtĭdŭs, mĭnāx, tērrĭfĭcŭs, sævŭs. V. Cuspis, ensis.

mūcŭs, ī, m., *snot.* Mūcŭsque ēt mălă, Catul.

mūgĭo, īs, īī, *to bellow.* Mūgĭīt, ēt Cācī, Virg. Syn. Bŏo, īmmūgĭo.

mūgītŭs, ūs, m., *a bellowing.* Rūmpĕrĕ mūgītŭ, Tib. Syn. Bŏātŭs. Epith. Tērrĭfĭcŭs, hōrrēndŭs, raŭcŭs, quĕrŭlŭs, trĕmēndŭs, rĕbŏāns, māgnŭs, rĕpĕtītŭs, ĭtĕrātŭs, fĕrōx, frĕmēns, mūltĭplēx, īngēns, tērrĭbĭlĭs, mĭnāx.

mūlă, æ, f., *a she-mule.* Ŭngŭlă mūlæ, Juv. V, Mulus.

mūlcĕo, mŭlsī, *to soothe.* Mūlcēbātque īrās, Virg. Syn. Dēmūlcĕo, pērmūlcĕo, dēlīnĭo, tītīllo, recrĕo, rĕfĭcĭo, rĕlāxo, dēlēcto, āllĭcĭo, āllēcto, căpto, blāndĭŏr, ădŭlŏr ; lēnĭo, mītĭgo, plāco. V. Placo.

Mūlcĭbĕr, ĕrĭs *and* ibrī, m., *Vulcan.* Mūlcĭbĕr īllīc, Ov. V. Vulcanus.

mūlctă, æ, f., *a fine of money, a punishment.* Prōdĭtă mūlctăm, Cat.

mūlcto, ās, *to fine, punish.* Trīstī mūlctātăm mŏrtĕ, Virg. Syn. Pūnĭo, cāstīgo, plēcto, dāmno. V. Punio.

mūlctră, æ, f. ; trālĕ, ĭs, *and* trŭm, ī, n., *a milk-pail.* Vĕnĭt ăd mūlctrăm, Virg. Implēbūnt mūlctrālĭă vāccæ, Id. Ăd mūlctră căpēllæ, Id.

mūlgĕo, mūlsī *or* lxī, *to milk.* Mūlgēt ĭn hōră, Virg.

mūlĭĕbrĭs, ĕ, *of a woman.* Dĭēs, mūlĭēbrĭbŭs ārmĭs, Virg. Syn. Fœmĭnĕŭs.

mūlĭĕbrĭtĕr, adv., *like a woman.* Nēc mūlĭēbrĭtĕr, (Alcaic.) Hor. Syn. Fœnī-nĕum ĭn mōrĕm ; tĭmĭdē, ĭgnāvē.

mūlĭĕr, ĕrĭs, f., *a woman.* In pīscēm mūlĭĕr, Hor. V. Fœmina.

mūlĭērcŭlă, æ, f., *the dimin. of* mulier. Fōrmă mūlĭērcŭla ămĕtŭr, Lucr.

mūlīnŭs, ă, ŭm, *of a mule.* Dēclāmātōrĭs mūlīnŏ cōrdĕ, Juv.

mūlĭo, ōnĭs, m., *a muleteer.* Mūlĭŏ vīrgā, Juv.

mūllŭs, ī, m., *a mullet.* Mūllŭmvĕ bīlĭbrĕm, Mart.

mūlsŭm, ī, n., *honeyed wine.* Præcōrdĭă mūlsŏ, Hor.

mūltĭcăvŭs, ă, ŭm, *with many holes.* Pūmĭcĕ mūltĭcăvŏ, Ov. Syn. Mūltĭfŏrĭs.

mūltĭcĭă, ōrŭm, n., *a sort of brocade.* Quŭm tū mūltĭcĭă sūmăs, Juv.

mūltĭcŏlŏr, ōrĭs, *and* ŭs, ă, ŭm, *of many colours.* Mūltĭcŏlŏr fūcŭs, Prud. Syn. Vărĭŭs, vērsĭcŏlŏr.

mūltĭfĭdŭs, ă, ŭm, *having many clefts.* Mūltĭfĭdāsquĕ făcēs, Ov.

mūltĭfŏrĭs, ĕ, *with many holes.* Lōngāvĕ mūltĭfŏrĭs, Ov. Syn. Mūltĭcăvŭs.

mūltĭlŏquŭs, ă, ŭm, *talkative.* Mūltĭlŏquŏs ōdī, Ov. Syn. Lŏquāx, gārrŭlŭs.

mūltĭmŏdŭs, ă, ŭm, *various.* Mūltĭmŏdī quăm sīnt, Lucr.

mūltĭplēx, ĭcĭs, *manifold.* Hæc tūm mūltĭplĭcī, Virg. Mūltĭplēxquĕ lŏcī, Lucr. Syn. Vărĭŭs, dīvērsŭs ; mūltŭs, plūrĭmŭs.

mūltĭplĭco, ās, *to multiply.* Mūltĭplĭcāvĭt ŏpĭs, Rut. Syn. Aŭgĕo ; vărĭo.

mūltĭsŏnōrŭs, ă, ŭm, *sounding loudly.* Mūltĭsŏnōră trăhūnt, Claud. Syn. Mūltĭ-sŏnŭs, sŏnōrŭs.

mūltĭsŏnŭs, ă, ŭm, *sounding much.* Mūltĭsŏnā fērvĕt, Mart. Syn. Rĕsŏnŭs, mŭl-tĭsŏnōrŭs.

mūltĭvăgŭs, ă, ŭm, *very wandering.* Nūntĭă mŭltĭvāgō, St.

mūltŏ, tŭm, tă, adv., *much.* Mūltŏ pārs māxĭmă, Hor. Mūltă mŏrātŭs, Virg.

mūltŏtĭēs, adv., *many times.* Mūltŏtĭēs ŏffēnsă, Mart. Syn. Sæpĕ, sæpĭŭs, frĕ-quēntĕr.

mūltŭs, ă, ŭm, *many.* Nēc mūltŏs ădhĭbĕt, Juv. Syn. Plūrĭmŭs, nŭmĕrōsŭs, crēbĕr, frĕquēns, cŏpĭōsŭs, nĭmĭŭs, dēnsŭs, lōngŭs, prŏlīxŭs, āmplŭs, mūltĭplēx, īnfīnītŭs, īnnŭmĕrŭs, nōn paŭcŭs, haŭd mŏdĭcŭs.

mŭlŭs, ī, m., mŭlă, æ, f., *a mule.* Mŭlŭs ăprŭm, Hor. Epitii. Cĕlĕr, vēlōx.
cĭtŭs, ăgĭlĭs, pērnīx, pērvĭcāx, stērnāx, īndŏcĭlĭs, strĭgōsŭs, bĭfŏrmĭs, Hīspānŭs.
Mūnātĭŭs, ĭī, m., *a man's name.* Cōnvĕnĭāt, Mūnātĭŭs, Hor.
mūndānŭs, ă, ŭm, *of the world.* Mūndāni ĭnvŏlvăt, P.
mūndĭtĭă, æ, *or* ēs, ēī, f., *neatness.* Tālēs mūndĭtĭæ, Mart. Syn. Cūltŭs.
‖ mūndo, ās, *to clean.* V. Purgo.
mūndŭs, *and* ŭlŭs, ă, ŭm, *neat.* Mūnda hāctĕnŭs, Hor. Mūndŭlōs ămāsĭōs,
(Iamb.) Plaut. Syn. Pūrŭs, tērsŭs, laŭtŭs, pōlītŭs, cŭltŭs, nĭtĭdŭs.
mūndŭs, ī, m., *the world.* Pŭblĭcă mūndī, Ov. Syn. Ōrbĭs. Epith. Cōnvēxŭs,
glŏbōsŭs, tĕrēs, rŏtūndŭs, spătĭōsŭs, āmplŭs, vāstŭs, căpāx, īngēns, mīrābĭlĭs.
mūnĕro, ās, *and* ŏr, ārĭs, *to recompense.* Mŭnĕrăt, ēt laŭrō, Ov. Quā mŭnĕrētŭr
tē, Hor. Syn. Dōno, dŏ, mūnĕre āffĭcĭo, cŭmŭlo, dĕcŏro, ŏrno, ŏnĕro ; mūnĕră,
dŏnă dŏ, cōnfĕro. V. Dono.
mūnĭă, ĭum, n. pl., *public functions.* Mūnĭă rēctæ, Hor. Syn. Offĭcĭŭm, mūnŭs.
mūnĭcĕps, cĭpĭs, *having the privileges of a city.*
mūnĭcĭpālĭs, ĕ, *of a municipal city.* Mūnĭcĭpālĭs ĕquĕs, Juv.
mūnĭfĭcēntĭă, æ, f., *munificence.* Mūnĭfĭcēntĭă nūmmōs, Alc. V. Liberalitas.
mūnĭfĭco, ās, *to give liberally.* Mūnĭfĭcăt tăcĭtā, Lucr. Syn. Mūnĕro, lārgĭŏr.
mūnĭfĭcŭs, ă, ŭm, *munificent.* Vīs tē mūnĭfĭcŭm, Mart. Syn. Lībĕrālĭs.
mūnīmĕn, ĭnĭs, *and* mēntŭm, ī, n., *a rampart.* Ēffūsōs mūnīmĕn ăd ĭmbrēs, Virg.
Mūnīmēntă tŏgæ, Juv. Syn. Vāllŭm, āggĕr, prŏpūgnācŭlă, mūrī. Epith.
Tūtŭm, sēcūrŭm, fŏrtĕ, vălĭdŭm, lōngŭm, tūrrĭgĕrŭm, ĭnēxpūgnābĭlĕ. V.
Turris.
mūnĭo, īs, ĭī, ītŭm, *to fortify.* Et mūnīrĕ făvōs, Virg. Syn. Fīrmo, cōnfīrmo,
vāllo. V. Vallo.
mūnītŏr, ōrĭs, m., *a fortifier.* Trōjæ mūnītŏr ămāvĭt, Ov.
mūnītŭs, ă, ŭm, *the pass. partic. of* munio. Incūrvō mūnītōs, Ov. V. Munio.
mūnŭs, ĕrĭs, n., *a gift, function.* Mūnĕrĭbŭs cŭmŭlăt, Virg. Syn. Dōnŭm, præmĭŭm, mūnŭscŭlŭm ; offĭcĭŭm. Epith. Ŏpŭlēntŭm, præclārŭm, ēgrĕgĭŭm,
mĕmŏrābĭlĕ, īngēns, dīvĕs, māgnĭfĭcŭm, hŏnēstŭm. V. Donum.
mūnŭscŭlŭm, ī, n., *the dimin. of* munus. Nūllō mūnŭscŭlă cŭltū, Virg.
Mŭnўchĭŭs, ă, ŭm, *of Munychia, a harbour of Athens.* Mŭnўchĭōsquĕ vŏlāns,
Ov.
mūrænă, æ, f., *a lamprey.* Intēr mūrænă nătāntēs, Hor.
mūrālĭs, ĕ, *of a wall.* Intōrquēt! mūrālī, Virg.
Mūrēnās, æ, m., *a man's name.* Mūrēnă præbēntĕ dŏmŭm, Hor.
mūrēx, ĭcĭs, m., *a shell-fish, from which the Tyrian purple was obtained.* Mūrĭcĕ
vēstĭs, Virg. Syn. Cōnchўlĕ, cōnchўlĭŭm, ōstrŭm, pŭrpŭră. Epith. Rŭbēns,
rădĭātŭs, Tўrĭŭs, Sīdonĭŭs, Āssўrĭŭs, stēllāns, rŭtĭlŭs, aūrātŭs, ārdēns, pŭrpŭrĕŭs, pūnĭcĕŭs, flagrāns. V. Purpura.
mūrĭă, æ, f., *brine.* Mērō mūrĭāquĕ dĕcēbĭt, Hor.
mūrmŭr, ŭrĭs, n., *a murmur.* Mūrmŭrĭs aūræ, Virg. Syn. Strĕpĭtŭs, sŏnĭtŭs,
sŏnŭs, frăgŏr, strīdŏr, sŭsŭrrŭs, clāmŏr, tŭmūltŭs. Epith. Strīdēns, răpĭdŭm,
frăgōsŭm, quĕrŭlŭm, rĕbŏans, lŏquāx, hōrrĭfĭcŭm, sŏnōrŭm, īnsānŭm, clāmōsŭm,
hōrrēndŭm, cōnfūsŭm, trĕmēndŭm, răbĭdŭm, sævŭm, grăvĕ, īngēns, dēnsŭm,
trĕmŭlŭm, crēbrŭm, flŭvĭālĕ, ārgūtŭm, gārrŭlŭm, lēnĕ, tĕnŭĕ, mōllĕ, blāndŭm,
sōmnĭfĕrŭm, sŏpŏrĭfĕrŭm. V. Clamor.
mūrmŭro, ās, *to murmur.* Mūrmŭrăt ūndă, Virg. Syn. Immūrmŭro, strĕpo,
strĕpĭto, sŏno, strīdĕo, frĕmo, sŭsūrro. V. Clamo, susurro.
Mūrrānŭs, ī, m., *a Latin chief.* Mūrrānŭm hīc, ătăvōs, Virg.
mūrŭs, ī, m., *a wall.* Ingĕnĭō mūrōs, Prop. Syn. Părĭēs, mœnĭă, āggĕr, vāllŭm,
prŏpūgnācŭltŭm, mūnīmĕn, mūnīmēntŭm. Epith. Āltŭs, ārdŭŭs, sūblīmĭs, ēxcēlsŭs, ēlātŭs, ēdĭtŭs, āĕrĭŭs, prōcērŭs, tūrrītŭs, mūnītŭs, vāllātŭs, tūrrĭgĕr,
ăhēnĕŭs, ĭnēxpūgnābĭlĭs, ĭnāccēssŭs, tūtŭs, sēcūrŭs, īngēns, sŭpērbŭs.
mūs, mŭrĭs, *and* scŭlŭs, ī, m., *a mouse.* Cārmĭnă mūrēs, Juv. Syn. Sōrēx.
Epith. Exĭgŭŭs, pārvŭs, ēxīlĭs, grăcĭlĭs, tĕnŭĭs, ĕdāx, trĕpĭdŭs, fŭgāx, păvĭdŭs,
tĭmĭdŭs.
Mūsæ, ārŭm, f. pl., *the nine Muses.* Lŏquĭtŭr Mūsārŭm păgĭnă rēgēs, Cl. Syn.
Cămœnæ, Pīĕrĭdĕs, Ăŏnĭdĕs, Cāstālĭdĕs, Hēlĭcōnĭădĕs, Pārnāssĭdĕs, Ăgănīppĭ-
dĕs, Pēgăsĭdĕs, Thēspĭădĕs, Pīmplæĭdĕs, Lībēthrĭdĕs, Mæŏnĭdĕs. Epith. Dŏctæ, cănŏræ, blāndæ, sacræ, făcūndæ, dūlcēs, vĕnŭstæ, īngĕnĭōsæ, cāstæ, pŭdīcæ,

cōmptæ, vōcālēs, dĭsērtæ, ārgūtæ, gĕnĭālēs, sōlērtēs, laŭrĭgĕræ, Cāstălĭæ, Āŏnĭæ, Pĭĕrĭæ, Ăgănīppēæ, Hĕlĭcōnĭæ, Pīmplææ. Sing. —să, æ, f., *a Muse; a song, verse.* Mūsă, mĭhī caŭsās, Virg. Mĕdĭtābŏr ărūndĭnĕ mūsăm, Id. V. Carmen.

Mūsæŭs, ă, ŭm, *of the Muses.* Ět quăsī mūsæŏ, Lucr.

Mūsæŭs, ī, m., *a Greek poet.* Mūsæŭm ānte ōmnēs, Virg.

mūscŭ, æ, f., *a fly.* Mūsca īn tēmōnĕ, Phæd. EPITH. Lĕvĭs, grăcĭlĭs, ēxĭgŭă, pārvă, mŏlēstă, păvĭdă, fūgāx, āĕrĭă, vŏlĭtāns.

mūscōsŭs, ă, ŭm, *mossy.* Mūscōsī fōntēs, Virg. SYN. Mūsco ŏpērtŭs, vĭrēns, squālēns, squālĭdŭs, vĭrĭdĭs, vĭrĭdāns.

mūscŭlŭs, ī, m., *a muscle.* Mūscŭlŭs ōmnĭs, Luc.

mūscŭs, ī, m., *moss.* Flūmĭnă; mūscŭs ŭbi, Virg. EPITH. Tĕnāx, tĕnĕr, tĕnŭĭs, hūmĭdŭs, ūdŭs, mădĭdŭs, vĭrēns.

mūsĭcă, æ, *or* cē, ēs, f., *music.* Mūsĭcă trĭplēx, Aus. SYN. Ars mūsĭcă, cănēndi ārs; cōncēntŭs, mēlŏs, mŏdŭlātĭo, mŏdŭlāmĕn, cāntŭs. EPITH. Dūlcĭs, suāvĭs, blāndă, lætă, cănŏră, ămœnă, cœlēstĭs, plăcĭdă, fēstīvă, dūlcĭsŏnă, dōctă, rĕsŏnă, trĕmŭlă, Ăpōllĭnĕă, Āŏnĭă, mēllĭflŭă, sŏnŏră. V. Cantus.

‖ mūsĭcŭs, ī, m., *a musician.* SYN. Cāntŏr. EPITH. Pĕrītŭs, cănŏrŭs, dŏctŭs, ārgūtŭs, fēstīvŭs.

mūsso, *and* sīto, ās, *to mutter.* Mœstī mūssāntquĕ pătrēs, Virg. V. Murmuro.

mūstăcĕŭm, ī, n., *a kind of cake.* Ět mūstăcĕă pērdās, Juv.

mūstēlă, æ, f., *a weasel.* Cuī mūstēlă prŏcŭl, Hor

mūstĕŭs, ă, ŭm, *juicy, new.* Mūstĕŭs ēst; prŏpĕrā, Mart.

mūstŭm, ī, n., *must, new wine.* Pīnguĭă mūstă, Mart. V. Vinum.

mŭtābĭlĭs, ĕ, *changeable.* Lăbŏr mŭtābĭlĭs ævī, Virg. SYN. Mōbĭlĭs, vărĭābĭlĭą, īnstăbĭlĭs, īncērtŭs, lĕvĭs, īncōnstāns, mūtārī făcĭlĭs. V. Inconstans.

mŭtābĭlĭtās, ātĭs, f., *inconstancy.* Sēnsŭs mŭtābĭlĭtātĕ, Lucr. SYN. Mōbĭlĭtās, lĕvĭtās, īncōnstāntĭă.

mŭtātĭo, ōnĭs, f., *a changing.* Ter. SYN. Cōnvērsĭo, cōmmūtātĭo, pērmūtātĭo, mŏtŭs. EPITH. Sūbĭtă, rĕpēntīnă, crēbră, īncōnstāns, īnstăbĭlĭs, fēlīx. V. Metamorphosis.

mŭtĭlo, ās, *to mangle.* Mŭtĭlātæ caŭdă cŏlŭbræ, Ov. SYN. Trūnco; ābscīndo, āmpŭto.

mŭtĭlŭs, ă, ŭm, *mangled.* Sīc mŭtĭlŭs mĭnĭtārĭs, Hor. SYN. Trūncātŭs, trūncŭs mŭtĭlātŭs.

Mŭtĭnă, æ, f., *a city of Italy.* Vīctă pĕtēnt Mŭtĭnæ, Ov.

Mŭtĭnēnsĭs, ĕ, *of Mutina.* Hāc Mŭtĭnēnsĭă Cæsăr, Ov.

mŭtĭo, īs, *to grumble.* Mĕn' mŭtīrĕ nĕfās? Pers. SYN. Mūsso, mūssĭto.

mŭto, ās, *to change.* Jām crŏcĕŏ mŭtābĭt, Virg. SYN. Immŭto, cōmmŭto, vērto cōnvērto, vărĭo, trānsfōrmo; nŏvo, īnnŏvo. V. Metamorphosis.

‖ mŭtŭē, mŭtŭŏ, adv., *mutually.* SYN. Vĭcīssĭm, īnvĭcĕm.

‖ mŭtŭo, ās, *to lend.* SYN. Cōmmŏdo, āccōmmŏdo; mŭtŭŭm præbĕo, trādo, trībŭo.

mŭtŭŏr, ārĭs, *to borrow.* Ūsquĕ mŭtŭārĭs, (Phal.) Mart. SYN. Mŭtŭŭm, mŭtŭo āccĭpĭo, căpĭo, sūmo; ūtēndum āccĭpĭo.

mŭtŭs, ă, ŭm, *dumb.* Mōllĕ pĕcŭs, mŭtŭmquĕ, Virg. SYN. Ēlinguĭs, sĭlēns, tăcēns, tăcĭtŭs. V. Obmutesco.

Mŭtŭscă, æ, f., *a Sabine town.* Ōlīvĭfĕræquĕ Mŭtŭscæ, Virg.

mŭtŭŭs, ă, ŭm, *mutual.* Mŭtŭăque īntēr sē, Virg. SYN. Mŭtŭo dătŭs, āccēptŭs; pār, rĕcĭprŏcŭs, āltērnŭs.

Mўcălē, ēs, f., *a promontory of Ionia.* Dīndўmăque ēt Mўcălē, Ov.

Mўcēnæ, ārŭm, f. pl., *a town of Argolis.* Dītēsquĕ Mўcēnās, Hor. EPITH. Ăgămēmnŏnĭæ, Thўēstēæ, māgnæ, vĕtĕrēs, fōrtēs, clāræ, Ināchĭæ; Lăcĕdæmŏnĭæ.

Mўcēnæŭs, ă, ŭm, *and* nĭs, ĭdĭs, f., *of Mycenæ.* Ipsĕ Mўcēnæŭs, Virg. Mŭtāssĕ Mўcēnĭdă cērvă, Ov.

Mўcŏnŭs, ī, f., *one of the Cyclades Islands.* Ērrāntēm Mўcŏnō, Virg.

Mўgdŏnĭdēs, æ, m., *the son of Mygdon.* Cŏrœbŭs Mўgdŏnĭdēs, Ov.

Mўgdŏnĭŭs, ă, ŭm, *and* dŏnĭs, ĭdĭs, f., *of Mygdonia.* Tībĭă Mўgdŏnĭīs, Prop. Mўgdŏnĭdēsquĕ nŭrŭs, Ov.

mўrīcă, æ, f., *a tamarisk.* Hūmĭlēsquĕ mўrīcæ, Virg. EPITH. Ābjēctă, hūmĭlĭs, tĕnŭĭs, frăgĭlĭs, ēxĭlĭs, tĕnĕră, stĕrĭlĭs, pārvă, vĭrĭdĭs, sўlvēstrĭs.

Mўrmĭdŏnēs, ŭm, m. pl., *a people of Thessaly, fabled to have been changed into ants.*

N

Mўrŏn, ŏnĭs, m., *a famous sculptor.* Văccă, Mўrŏnĭs ŏpŭs, Ov.
Mўrrhă, æ, f., *the daughter of Cinyras, changed into myrrh.* Elĭgĕ Mўrrhă tĭbi, Ov. Epith. Pīnguĭs, ŏlēns, rĕdŏlēns, fūlvă, stīllāns, ŏdōrātă, Săbææ, Ărăbs; Eŏă, Assўrĭă, Ŏrŏntææ.
mўrrhēŭs, ă, ŭm, *scented with myrrh.* Mўrrhēŭm nōdō, Hor.
Mўrtălē, ēs, f., *a woman's name.* Cŏmpĕdĕ Mўrtălē, Hor.
mўrtētŭm, ī, n., *a myrtle-grove.* Līttŏră mўrtētīs, Virg.
mўrtěŭs, ă, ŭm, *of myrtle.* Mўrtĕă sērtă, Tib.
Mўrtĭlŭs, ī, m., *the charioteer of Œnomaus.* Mўrtĭlŭs āxĕm, Claud.
Mўrtōŭs, ă, ŭm, *Myrtoan.* Mўrtōŭm păvĭdŭs, Hor.
Mўrtŭm, ī, n., *a myrtle-berry.* Crŭēntăquĕ mўrtă, Virg.
mўrtŭs, ī *and* ūs, f., *myrtle.* Hŏrrĭdă mўrtŭs, Virg. Epith. Pāllĭdă, vĭrĭdĭs, bĭcŏlŏr, frŏndōsă, crīspă, ŏdōră, frăgrāns, pătŭlă, ŏpācă, līttŏrĕă, tĕnĕră, Cyprĭă, Cўthĕrĕă, Cўthĕrĕĭs, Păphĭă, Dĭōnææ, Idălĭă.
Mўscĕlŭs, ī, m., *the founder of Crotona.* Mўscĕlŭs īllĭŭs, Ov.
Mўsĭă, æ, f., *a country of Asia.* Mўsĭă plaūstrīs, Claud.
mўstă *and* tēs, æ, m., *one initiated into the mysteries.* Tēmpŭs hăbēnt mўstæ, Ov.
mўstērĭŭm, ĭī, n., *a mystery.* Vĕnĕrīs mўstērĭă cīstīs, Ov. Epith. Dīvīnŭm, sacrŭm, sānctŭm, vĕrēndŭm, vĕnĕrāndŭm, cŏlēndŭm, ădŏrāndŭm, ārcānŭm, ābdĭtŭm, ŏccūltŭm, sēcrētŭm.
mўstĭcŭs, ă, ŭm, *mystical.* Mўstĭcă vānnŭs, Virg. Syn. Ărcānŭs; săcĕr
Mўsŭs, ă, ŭm, *Mysian.* Mўsŭsquĕ Cāīcŭs, Virg.

N.

NABĀTHÆŬS, ă, ŭm, *of the Nabathæ, a nation of Arabia.* Dĕpŏsŭīt Năbăthæō, Juv.
nāblĭă, ōrŭm, n. pl., *a musical instrument.* Nāblĭă pālmā, Ov.
nāctă, æ, m., *a low artisan.* Vīvĕrĕ nāctæ? Pers. Epith. Immūndŭs, tūrpĭs, mōllĭs, lūxŭrĭōsŭs, īnfāmĭs.
nænĭă, æ, f., *or* nĭæ, ārŭm, f. pl., *a dirge.* Nænĭă, quæ rēgnŭm, Hor. Epith. Flēbĭlĭs, fērālĭă, fūnĕrĕă, fūnebrĭs, lūgŭbrĭs, fūnēstă, mĭsĕră, mœstă, trīstĭs.
Nævĭŭs, ĭī, m., *a dramatic poet.* Nævĭŭs īn mănĭbŭs, Hor.
nævŭs, ī, m., *a spot, blemish.* Cŏrpŏrĕ nævōs, Hor. Syn. Măcŭlă, mēndă.
Nălădĕs, *or* Nāĭădĕs, Năĭădĕs, ŭm, f. pl., *Naiads.* Năĭădĕs, īndĭgnō, Virg. Ægle Năĭădŭm, Virg. Epith. Æquŏrĕæ, ūndōsæ, cærŭlĕæ, ūdæ, fŏrmōsæ, blāndæ, dĕcōræ, vĕnūstæ, fŏntĭcŏlæ. V. Nympha.
Nāĭăs, ădĭs, *or* Nāĭs, ĭdĭs, f., *a Naiad.* Nāĭăs ūnă fŭĭt, Ov. Nāĭs ĕt ĭmplĭcĭtōs, Calph.
năm, nāmquĕ, conj., *for.* Năm quĭs tĕ, Virg. Nāmquĕ cănēbăt, Id. Syn. Ĕnĭm, quĭppĕ.
nāncīscŏr, ĕrĭs, nāctŭs, *to find.* Nāncīscētŭr ĕnĭm, Hor. Syn. Invĕnĭo, rĕpĕrĭo, ācquīro.
nānŭs, ī, m., *a dwarf.* Insīgnĭs nānŭm, Juv. Syn. Pūmĭlĭo, pўgmæŭs.
Năpææ, ārŭm, f. pl., *nymphs of the woods.* Vĕnĕrārĕ Năpææs, Virg. Syn. Drўădĕs. Epith. Vīrĭdĕs, hĭlărēs, nĕmŏrōsæ, ălacrēs, sўlvēstrēs.
Năpē, ēs, f., *a woman's name.* Rēstĭtĭt īctă Năpē, Ov.
Năr, Nărĭs, m., *a river in Italy.* Sūlphŭrĕă Năr ālbŭs ăquā, Virg. Epith. Præcēps, vĭtrĕŭs, ămœnŭs, lŏquăx, quĕrŭlŭs, rĕsŏnāns, gārrŭlŭs, ērrāns, sūlphŭrĕŭs, vĭtĭātŭs.
Nārbo, ŏnĭs, m., *a French town.* Nārbŏ, sĭlĕbĕrĕ, Aus. Syn. Nārbōnă. Epith. Pŏtēns, clārŭs, āntīquŭs, nōbĭlĭs, bēllĭcŭs, Indŏmĭtŭs, īnvīctŭs, Māvŏrtĭŭs.
Nārcīssŭs, ī, m., *a young man who loved himself to despair, and was changed into a daffodil.* Nārcīssŭmquĕ vŏcăt, Ov. Syn. Cēphīsĭŭs. Epith. Tĕnĕr, blāndŭs, pūlchĕr, fŏrmōsŭs, vĕnūstŭs, aūrĭcŏmŭs, nĭvĕŭs; cœlēbs.—2. *The flower daffodil.* Pūrpŭrĕŏ nārcīssŏ, Virg. Epith. Cŏmāns, vērnāns, crŏcĕŭs, flāvēscēns, lūtĕŭs, aūrĕŭs, flāvŭs, suāvĭs, rŭbēns. V. Flos.
nārdŭs, ī, m., *or* ŭm, ī, n., *spikenard.* Pērfūndī nārdŏ, Hor. Epith. Rĕdŏlēns, dīvĕs, frăgrāns, grātă, ŏlēns, suāvĭs, ŏdŏrĭfĕră, Eŏă, ŏdōrātă, Iudĭcă, Ărăbs, Sўrĭă, Assўrĭă; Ăchæmĕnĭă.

nărĭs, ĭs, f., nărēs, ĭŭm, f. pl., *the nostrils, nose.* Nărĭbŭs ĕfflänt, Virg. Nēc nărĭs ŏbēsæ, Hor. Syn. Năsŭs. Epith. Ăpērtæ, spīräntēs, căvæ, pătēntēs, ūncæ, pĭlōsæ, rōräntēs, mădĭdæ, săgŭcēs.

nărrăbĭlĭs, ĕ, *which can be related.* Nărrăbĭlĕ quīcquăm, Ov. Syn. Mĕmŏrăbĭlĭs.

nărrătĭo, ōnĭs, f., *and* tŭs, ūs, m., *a narration.* Fŭndēt nărrătĭŏ lingŭās, Hel. Nărrătĭbŭs hōră, Ov. Epith. Brĕvĭs, grătă.

nărro, ās, *to relate.* Prĭămō nărrăbĭs Achĭllĕm, Virg. Syn. Ēnărro, mĕmŏro, cōmmĕmŏro, rĕfĕro, ēxpōno, dēclāro, dīco, pāndo, ăpĕrĭo, ēxplĭco, ēlŏquŏr, rĕcēnsĕo.

Nărÿcĭă, æ, f., *a small village of Bœotia, the native place of Ajax.* Nărÿcĭămquĕ, Ov. Adj.—ŭs, ă, ŭm, *Narycian.* Nărÿcĭæquĕ pĭcĭs, Virg

Năsămōnĕs, ŭm, m. pl., *a nation in Africa.* Năsămōnĕs hăbēnt, Luc. Epith. Paŭpĕrēs, ĭnŏpēs, dūrī, pŏpŭlătōrēs, æquŏrĕī, bēllătōrēs, ălacrēs, răpācēs, ĭmprŏbī.

născŏr, ĕrĭs, *to be born.* Hīs născătŭr ĭn ōrĭs, Mart. Syn. Ēnāscŏr, ŏrĭŏr.

Năsīcă, æ, m., *the surname of Scipio.* Năsīca ăccēpĭt, Ov.

Năsĭdĭēnŭs, ī, m., *a man's name.* Năsĭdĭēnŭs ăd hæc, Hor.

Năso, ōnĭs, m., *a name of Ovid.* Nōrāt Năsōnĕm, Mart. V. Ovidius.

năsŭs, ī, m., *the nose.* Sŭspēndĕrĕ năsō, Pers. V. Nares.

năsūtŭs, ă, ŭm, *having a great nose.* Năsūtŭs sīs, Mart.

nătă, æ, f., *a daughter.* Ēst mĭhĭ nătă, Virg. Syn. Fīlĭă.

nătālēs, ĭŭm, m. pl., *lineage.* Ănĭmŭm nătălĭbŭs æquās, Luc. Syn. Gĕnŭs, ŏrīgo.

nătālĭs, ĕ, *native.* Quā nătălĕ sŏlŭm, Ov.

nătălĭs, ĭs, m., *a birth-day.* Mĕŭs ēst nătălĭs, Virg.

nătālĭtĭŭs, ă, ŭm, *belonging to a birth-day.* Ēt nătālĭtĭŭm, Juv.

nătătĭlĭs, ĕ, *swimming.* Rēptĭlēs, nătătĭlēs, (lamb.) Prud. Syn. Nătāns.

nătătŏr, ōrĭs, m., *a swimmer.* Irĕ nătātŏr ăquās, Ov.

nătātŭs, ūs, m., *a swimming.* Gălătæă, nătātū, Claud. Syn. Nătătĭo. Epith. Vŏlŭcĕr, cĭtŭs, cĕlĕr, vēlōx, præcēps, ălăcĕr, ĭrrĕquĭētŭs, aŭdāx.

nătēs, ĭŭm, f. pl., *buttocks.* Illă nătēs, Mart. Epith. Crāssæ, dūræ, tŏrōsæ.

nătĭo, ōnĭs, f. *a nation.* Fāctă, nătĭōnēs, (Phal.) Cat. Syn. Gēns, pŏpŭlŭs, gĕnŭs.

nătīvŭs, ă, ŭm, *native.* Lĭttŏră nătīvīs, Prop. V. Naturalis.

năto, ās, *to swim.* Mārcĕ, nătărĕ tŭō, Mart. Syn. Nŏ, ĭnno, ĭnnăto.

natrīx, ĭcĭs, f., *a kind of serpent.* Sī nătĭbŭs nătrĭcem, L. Ēt nātrīx vĭŏlātŏr, Lucan. Epith. Ĭnvīsă, vĕnēnōsă, nŏxĭă, lēthĭfĕră.

Nāttă, æ, m., *a man's name.* Nāttă lŭcērnīs, Hor.

nătū, *abl. of the obsol.* nătŭs, ūs, *by birth.* Māxĭmă nătū, Virg.

nătūră, æ, f., *nature.* Nŭnc ăgĕ, nătūrās, Virg. Syn. Innătă vīs, ĭngĕnĭŭm, rērŭm părēns. Epith. Ingĕnĭōsă, Dædălă, săpĭēns, prōvĭdă, fœcŭndă, mūnĭfĭcă, ŏffĭcĭōsă, sōlērs, ōmnĭpărēns, sēdŭlă, săgāx, pŏtēns, bĕnīgnă, ĭndŭstrĭă, cāllĭdă.

nătūrālĭs, ĕ, *natural.* Nătūrālĭs ăpēx, Pr. Syn. Insĭtŭs, ĭnnătŭs, ĭndĭtŭs, ĭngĕnĭtŭs, ĭngĕnĕrătŭs, nătīvŭs, gĕnŭĭnŭs, gērmānŭs, nōn fūcătŭs, nōn sĭmŭlătŭs, nōn fīctŭs.

nătŭs, ī, m., *a son.* Nēc dŭlcēs nātōs, Virg. Syn. Fīlĭŭs.

nătŭs, ă, ŭm, *the pass. partic. of* nascor. Nătŭs, ĕt ĭndŏmĭtās, Tib. V. Nascor.

năvălĕ, ĭs, n., *and* lĭă, ŭm, n. pl., *a port, docks.* Năvălĕ tĕnĕrĕt, Ov. Rătēs ălīī năvălĭbŭs, Virg.

năvălĭs, ĕ, *naval.* Nīlum āc năvălī, Virg.

năvārchŭs, ī, m., *the captain of a ship.* Năvārchŭs ĭpsĕ, (Iamb.) Paul. Nol. Syn. Naŭclērŭs.

naŭclērĭăcŭs, rĭcŭs, *and* rĭŭs, ă, ŭm, *of the master of a ship.* Naŭclērĭco ĭpse ōrnātū, (Iamb.) Pl.

naŭfrăgĭŭm, ĭī, n., *a shipwreck.* Naŭfrăgĭă, ātque īmās, Mant. Epith. Fūnēstŭm, flēbĭlĕ, ăcērbŭm, trīstĕ, dāmnōsŭm, mĭsĕrăbĭlĕ, mĭsĕrāndŭm, ĭnfēlīx, ĭnfaŭstŭm.

naŭfrăgŏr, ārĭs, (*better,* go, ās,) *to be shipwrecked.* Naŭfrăgăt ŭndīs, Alcim. V. Tempestas.

naŭfrăgŭs, ă, ŭm, *shipwrecked.* Naŭfrăgŭs ĭntĕrĭĭt, Ov.

nāvĭcŭlă, æ, f., *a little ship.* Mŭnĕră nāvĭcŭlā, Hel. Cin. SYN. Cӯmbă, phăsēlŭs, scăphă, nāvĭgĭŭm.

nāvĭfrăgŭs, ă, ŭm, *causing shipwrecks.* Nāvĭfrăgūm Scӯlăcæŭm, Virg. SYN. Naŭfrăgŭs.

nāvĭgăbĭlĭs, ĕ, *navigable.* Făcĭlē nāvĭgăbĭlĭs, (Iamb.) Av.

nāvĭgĕr, ă, ŭm, *bearing ships.* Prīmō nāvĭgĕr, (Iamb.) Av.

nāvĭgĭŭm, ĭī, n., *a ship.* Aŭt ŭbĭ nāvĭgĭĭs, Virg. V. Navis.

nāvĭgo, ās, *to navigate.* Nāvĭgăt æquŏr, Virg.

nāvĭs, ĭs, f., *a ship.* Nāvĭs ăb īgnĭbŭs, Hor. SYN. Nāvĭgĭŭm, phăsēlŭs, rătĭs, cărīnă, cӯmbă, lĭntĕr, lēmbŭs, bĭrēmĭs, clāssĭs; pŭppĭs, prōră, trăbs căvă, pīnŭs, ālnŭs, ăbĭēs. EPITH. Flŭctĭvăgă, vēlĭfĕră, cĕlĕrĭs, lĕvĭs, vēlōx, ăgĭlĭs, fŭgāx, văgă, frăgĭlĭs, vŏlucrĭs, ŭndĭvăgă, æquŏrĕă, naŭfrăgă, cūrvă, pīctă, văgābūndă, rōstrātă, căpāx, ŭnctă, căvă, ærātă, pōntĭvăgă, ŏnĕrārĭă, vēctŏrĭă, bĕllĭcă, bĕllā-trīx. V. Navigo.

nāvĭtă, æ, m., *a sailor.* Nāvĭtă pōntō, Virg.

nāvĭtĕr, adv., *diligently.* Nāvĭtĕr ēxstăt, Lucr. SYN. Sŏlērtĕr, fŏrtĭtĕr, strēnŭē.

naŭlŭm, ī,.n., *and* ŭs, ī, m., *fare, passage-money.* Pērdĕrĕ naŭlŭm, Juv.

naŭmăchĭă, æ, f., *a sea-fight.* Sæcŭlă naŭmăchĭăm, Mart.

nāvo, ās, *to perform diligently.* Nāvĕt ŏpŭs, Flav. SYN. Lăbōro, ādjŭvo.

Naŭpāctŏŭs, ă, ŭm, *of Naupactus.* Naŭpāctŏō Āchĕlōō, Ov.

Naŭpāctŭs, ī, m., *a city of Ætolia.*

naŭsĕă, æ, f., *sickness.* Naŭsĕām cŏērcĕăt, Hor. SYN. Fāstīdĭŭm. EPITH. Ăcērbă, trīstĭs, mŏlēstă.

naŭsĕo, ās, *to be sick.* Æquē naŭsĕăt ăc lŏcŭplēs, Hor.

naŭtă, æ, m., *a sailor.* Hæc īntĕr naŭtās, Juv. SYN. Nāvĭtă, rēmēx. EPITH. Vĭgĭl, sōllĭcĭtŭs, aŭdāx, ĭmpăvĭdŭs, flŭctĭvăgŭs, văgŭs, æquŏrĕŭs, pōntĭvăgŭs, săgāx, cāllĭdŭs, sōlērs, sēcūrŭs, ăvārŭs, pĕrītŭs, rŭdĭs, præscĭŭs, prōvĭdŭs, trĕ-pĭdŭs, mĭsĕr. V. Navigo.

Naŭtēs, æ, m., *a Trojan priest.* Tŭm sĕnĭŏr Naŭtēs, Virg.

naŭtĭcŭs, ă, ŭm, *of a sailor.* Naŭtĭcŭs ēxōrĭtŭr, Virg. SYN. Mărīnŭs.

nāvŭs, ă, ŭm, *diligent.* Nāvŭs ăbīrĕ, Sil. SYN. Gnāvŭs, strēnŭŭs, sōlērs, ĭndūs-trĭŭs, dīlĭgēns, stŭdĭōsŭs, ĭmpĭgĕr.

Nāxŏs, ī, f., *an island of the Archipelago.* Bācchātāmquĕ jŭgīs Nāxŏn, Virg. SYN. Strōngӯlē *or* lŏs. EPITH. Thēsĕă; gĕnĭāllĭs, vītĭgĕnă, bācchātă, Bāc-chĭcă.

Nāzără, æ, *or* rĕth, f., *the village where Christ was born.* Nāzărĕth ĭndĭgĕnăm, C. EPITH. Fēlīx, īnclӯtă, sacră, sānctă, ĭllūstrĭs.

nĕ, conj., *not, lest.* Nē fŭgĭtĕ hŏspĭtĭŭm, Virg. SYN. Quō mĭnŭs, ŭt nōn, ŭt nĕ.

nĕ, interrog, *whether.* Jūstĭtĭænĕ prĭŭs, Virg. SYN. Ăn, ānnĕ, utrŭm.

Nĕæră, æ, f., *a woman's name.* Ĭpsĕ Nĕærăm, Virg.

Nĕæthŭs, ī, m., *a river of Calabria.* Sālēntīnŭmquĕ Nĕæthŭm, Ov.

Nĕālcēs, ĭs, m., *a man's name.* Sălĭŭmquĕ Nĕālcēs, Ov.

Nĕāpŏlĭs, ĭs, f., *Naples.* Crēdĭdĭt Nĕāpŏlĭs, Hor. EPITH. Cūmæă, sĭnŭōsă, dōctă, nōbĭlĭs, dīvēs, āmplă, tūrrītă.

Nĕārchŭs, ī, m., *a man's name.* Rĕpĕtēns Nĕārchŭm, Hor.

nēbrĭs, ĭdĭs, f., *a deer-skin.* Nēbrĭdăs ēt frăgĭlēs, Stat. EPITH. Măcŭlōsă, hĭr-sūtă, vīllōsă.

Nēbrŏphŏnŭs, ī, m., *the name of a dog.* Nēbrŏphŏnŭsquĕ vălēns, Ov.

nĕbŭlă, æ, f., *a cloud.* Ēt mūltō nĕbŭlæ, Virg. V. Nubes.

nĕbŭlo, ōnĭs, m., *a scoundrel.* Pēnĕlŏpēs, nĕbŭlōnēs, Hor. SYN. Tĕnebrĭo, nŭgātŏr, nĕquăm.

nĕbŭlōsŭs, ă, ŭm, *cloudy.* Hӯbērnōs nĕbŭlōsŭs ĭmbrēs, (Sapph.) SYN. Nūbĭlŭs, nīmbōsŭs, tĕnebrōsŭs, ōbscūrŭs, ŏpācŭs. V. Nubilus.

nĕc, conj., *nor.* Pārvĕ, nĕc īnvĭdĕō, Ov. SYN. Nĕquĕ.

nĕcēssārĭŭs, ă, ŭm, *necessary.* Tŭm nĕcēssărĭō sē, (Iamb.) V. Opus. SYN. Ĭnēvĭtābĭlĭs, ĭnēlūctābĭlĭs.

nĕcēssĕ, n., *necessary.* Chārtă nĕcēsse ēst, Aus.

nĕcēssĭtās, ātĭs, f., *necessity.* Dīră nĕcēssĭtās, (Chor.) Hor. SYN. Fātŭm, sŏrs, vīs. EPITH. Sævă, ăcērbă, vĭŏlēntă, ĭnĭmīcă, ĭnvīsă, ūrgēns, prĕmēns, dūră, rĭgĭdă, ĭnēlūctābĭlĭs, ĭnsŭpĕrābĭlĭs.

ñĕcnōn, conj., *also, too.* Nēcnōn gālbănĕōs, Virg.

nĕco, ās, *to kill.* Mōrtĕ nĕcābăt, Virg. Syn. Occīdo, cædo. V. Occīdo, cædo.

nĕcŏpīnāns, āntĭs, *and* ĭnŭs, ă, ŭm, *unawares, unexpected.* Ēt nĕcŏpīnāntī mōrs, Lucr. Nĕcŏpīnā pērdĕrĕ mōrtĕ, Ov. Syn. Iımprūdēns, īncaūtŭs; īmprŏvīsŭs.

nĕctăr, ărĭs, n., *the drink of the gods.* Nēctărĭs īmbŭĭt, (Choriamb.) Hor. Syn. Ambrŏsĭă. ˷Epith. Cœlēstĕ, ŏdōrŭm, dīvīnŭm, īmmōrtālĕ, sacrŭm, dūlcĕ, suāvĕ.

nēctărĕŭs, ă, ŭm, *of nectar.* Āttĭcă nēctărĕŭm, Mart. Syn. Dūlcĭs, suāvĭs.

nĕcto, xŭī *or* xī, xŭm, *to tie.* Vīncŭlă nēctĭtĭs, Virg. Syn. Lĭgo, vīncĭo, strīngo, nōdo, cōnnēcto; cōllĭgo, ās; jūngo, cōnjūngo, cōnstrīngo.

nĕcŭbi, adv., *(for* nē ălĭcŭbi) *lest in any place.* Nĕcŭbī sūpprēssŭs, Luc.

nēdŭm, adv., *much less.* Nēdŭm sērmōnŭm, Hor.

nĕfāndŭs, ă, ŭm, *impious.* Ēnsēsquĕ nĕfāndī, Virg. Syn. Infāndŭs, scĕlēstŭs, scĕlĕrātŭs; tētĕr. V. Malus.

nĕfārĭŭs, ă, ŭm, *abominable.* Ēxtă nĕfārĭŭs Ātreŭs, Hor.

nĕfās, n., *(indecl.) impiety, villany.* Grāndĕ nĕfās, ĕt, Juv. Syn. Scĕlŭs, crīmĕn, flāgĭtĭŭm. V. Crimen.

nĕfāstŭs, ă, ŭm, *inauspicious.* Īllĕ nĕfāstŭs ĕrĭt, Ov.

nēglēctŭs, ūs, m., *neglect.* Plaut. Syn. Cōntēmptŭs.

nēglēctŭs, ă, ŭm, *the pass. partic. of* negligo. Æquĕ nēglēctŭm, Hor.

nēglĭgēns, ntĭs, *negligent.* Ēssĕ nēglĭgēntĕm, (Phal.) Cat. Syn. Vēcōrs, ĭnērs, ĭgnāvŭs, pĭgĕr.

nēglĭgēntĕr, adv., *negligently.* Nēglĭgēntĕr aŭdīs, (Phal.) Mart.

nēglĭgēntĭă, æ, f., *negligence.* Ter. Syn. Incūrĭă, ĭgnāvĭă, ĭnērtĭă, dēsĭdĭă, pigrĭtĭēs.

nēglĭgo, glēxī, ctŭm, *to neglect.* Nēglĭgĭt, aŭt hōrrĕt, Hor. Syn. Nōn cūro, dēsĕro, prætērmĭtto, ōmĭtto, āspērnŏr, spērno, tēmno, cōntēmno, dēspĭçĭo.

nĕgo, ās, *to deny.* Rēddĕrĕ pōssĕ nĕgābăt, Virg. Syn. Dēnĕgo, pērnĕgo, ābnŭgo, īnfĭcĭŏr, rĕpūgno, ābnŭo, rĕcŭso, rĕnŭo.

nĕgōtĭātŏr, ōrĭs, m., *a merchant.* Ēt nĕgōtĭātŏr, (Phal.) V. Mercator.

nĕgōtĭŏr, ārĭs, *to deal in.* Quæ nĕgōtĭātŭr, (Phal.) Mart.

nĕgōtĭōsŭs, ă, ŭm, *busy, troublesome.* Nĕgōtĭōsĭs rēbŭs, (Scaz.) Mart. Syn. Ŏpĕrōsŭs, dĭffĭcĭlĭs.

nĕgōtĭŭm, iī, n., *business.* Ălĭēnă nĕgōtĭă cūro, Hor. Syn. Rēs, ŏpŭs, ŏpĕră, lăbŏr; cūră, mūnŭs, prōvīncĭă. Epith. Ānxĭŭm, vĭgĭl, sōllĭcĭtŭm, īmpōrtūnŭm, grăvĕ, mŏlēstŭm, ăcĕrbŭm.

Nēlēĭŭs, *and* ēŭs, ă, ŭm, *of Neleus.* Nēlēĭă Nēstŏrĭs, Ov. Nēlēī sānguĭnĭs, Id.

Nēleŭs, ĕŏs, ĕĭ *or* eī, m., *king of Pylos, and father of Nestor.* Hērbōsăquĕ păscŭă Nēleī, Ov.

Nēlīdēs, æ, m., *the son of Neleus.* Bīs sēx Nēlīdæ fŭĕrīnt, Ov.

Nĕmĕă, æ, *or* ĕē, ēs, f., *a forest in Achaia.* Ēt vāstūm Nĕmĕæ, Virg. Epith. Frōndēns, frōndōsă, sȳlvōsă, frōndĭfĕră, vĭrēns, vĭrĭdĭs, sacră, sacrātă, Clĕōnææ.

Nĕmæĕŭs, ă, ŭm, *Nemean.* Quĭd Nĕmæĕŭs ĕnĭm, Lucr.

Nĕmĕsĭs, ĭs, f., *one of the infernal deities, whose office it was to inflict vengeance on the wicked, and to reward the good.* Ārgūtī Nĕmĕsĭs, Mart. Syn. Rhāmnŭsĭs, Rhāmnŭsĭă. Epith. Irātă, trūx, ārdēns, fūrēns, pŏtēns, dūră, ăcĕrbă, sævă, fĕrōx, vīndēx, ūltrīx. V. Furiæ, ultio.

nēmo, ĭnĭs, m. f., *nobody.* Nēmŏ quătĕr mīssōs, Mart. Syn. Nūllŭs, nōn ūllŭs, nūllŭs hŏmo.

nĕmŏrālĭs *and* ēnsĭs, ĕ, *of a wood.* Nĕmŏrālĭbŭs ūmbrĭs, Ov. Nĕmŏrēnsĭs ăb ūndā, Prop.

nĕmŏrĭvăgŭs, ă, ŭm, *wandering in the woods.* Ăpĕr nĕmŏrĭvăgŭs, Cat.

nĕmŏrōsŭs, ă, ŭm, *woody.* Nĕmŏrōsă Zăcȳnthŏs, Virg. Syn. Sȳlvōsŭs, ūmbrōsŭs, ŏpācŭs.

nēmpĕ, adv., *surely, however.* Nēmpĕ tŭō, fŭrĭōsĕ, Hor. Syn. Scīlĭcĕt, vĭdēlĭcĕt, nīmīrŭm, quīppĕ.

nĕmŭs, ŏrĭs, n., *a wood.* Nĕmŭs īmmĭnĕt, Virg. Syn. Sȳlvă, sāltŭs, lūcŭs. V Sylva.

nĕo, nēvī, *to spin.* Quæquĕ fŭtūră nĕēnt, Tib.

Nĕŏbūlē, ēs, f., *a woman's name.* Stŭdĭum aūfĕrt Nŏŏbūlē, Hor.

Nĕoclīdēs, æ, m., *the son of Neocles, Themistocles.* Armă Nĕŏclīdēs, Ov.

Nĕŏptŏlĕmŭs, ī, m., *a name of Pyrrhus.* Dēgĕnĕrēmquĕ Nĕŏptŏlĕmŭm, Virg. **V.** Pyrrhus.

nĕpă, æ, m., *a scorpion.* Sēsē nĕpă lūcĭbŭs ēffĕrt, Arat.

Nĕphĕlēĭăs, ădĭs, *and* lēĭs, ĭdĭs, f., *the daughter of Nephele.* Nĕphĕlēĭăs ābstŭlĭt Hēllē, Luc. Nĕphĕlēĭdŏs Hēllēs, Ov.

nĕpōs, ōtĭs, m., *a grandson.* Istĕ nĕpōs ōlĭm, Pers. **V.** Filius.

nĕpōtēs, ŭm, m. pl., *descendants.* Fāctūră nĕpōtĭbŭs ūmbrăm, Virg. Syn. Mĭnōrēs, pōstĕrī, nātī, pōstĕrĭtās. Epith. Sērī, vēntūrī, tārdī. **V.** Posteri.

nĕptĭs, ĭs, f., *a grand-daughter.* Nĕptĭs hăbēbăt, Ov.

Nēptūnīnē, ēs, f., *the daughter of Neptune.* Pūlchērrĭmă Nēptūnīnē, Cat.

Nēptūnĭŭs, ă, ŭm, *of Neptune.* Nēptūnĭă prōlēs, Virg. Syn. Mărīnŭs, æquŏrĕŭs, Nērēĭŭs.

Nēptūnŭs, ī, m., *the god of the sea.* Sēnsīt Nēptūnŭs, ĕt īmīs, Virg. Epith. Prŏcēllōsŭs, ūdŭs, hūmĭdŭs, īncērtŭs, īnstăbĭlĭs, spūmāns, spūmĕŭs, fŭrēns, atrōx, mĭnāx, īmmītĭs, sævŭs, tūrbĭdŭs, plăcĭdŭs, trānquīllŭs, sĭlēns, quĭētŭs, mītĭs. **V.** Mare.

nēquā, (vĭā, *underst.*) adv., *lest any way.* Nēquā scīrĕ dŏlōs, Virg.

nēquăm, *(indecl.) wicked.* Armă vĭrī; nēquăm, Hor. Syn. Imprŏbŭs, scĕlēstŭs. **V.** Sceleratus.

nēquāquăm, adv., *by no means.* Nēquāquăm sătĭs, Hor. Syn. Haūdquāquăm, nōn.

nēquĕ, conj., *nor.* Quīd făcĕrēm? nēquĕ sērvĭtĭō, Virg. Syn. Nĕc, nōn. **V.** Non.

nĕquĕo, ĭs, ĭt, *to be unable.* Cūm nĕquĕo, M. Syn. Nōn quĕo, nōn pōssŭm, nōn vălĕo, nōn ēvălĕo.

nēquīcquăm, adv., *in vain.* Nēquīcquăm sērōs, Virg. Syn. Frūstrā, īncāssŭm.

nēquĭŏr, ōrĭs, *the compar. of* nequam. Nōs nēquĭōrēs, mōx, (Iamb. cum syll.) Hor. **V.** Nequam.

nēquĭtĭēs, ĭēī, *or* ă, æ, f., *wickedness.* Nēquĭtĭēs, aūt, Hor. Nēquĭtĭæ āddĭtŭs, Id. Syn. Imprŏbĭtās.

Nērĕĭs, ĭdĭs, f, Nērĕĭdĕs, ŭm, f. pl., *nymphs of the sea.* Nērĕĭs īngrĕdĭtŭr, Ov. Nērĕĭdĕ, sēd quī, Id. Nērĕĭdēs sўlvāsquĕ, Id. Nērĕĭdēs īncrĕpĭtārēnt, Prop. Epith. Cærŭlēæ, vĭrĭdēs, æquŏrĕæ, ūndĭvāgæ, flūctĭvāgæ, mărīnæ, ūdæ, glaūcæ, hūmĭdæ, fōrmōsæ, vāgæ, vāgăbūndæ, vĕnūstæ, pīctæ. Nērĕī, Dōrĭdĭs nātæ. Ocĕānī, Thĕtĭdĭs, Tēthуōs puēllæ; Nўmphæ. Æquŏrĕæ, cærŭlēæ Dĕæ, Nўmphæ. Nērĕĭă tūrbă, prōlēs, prōpăgo. Nērĕĭdūm chŏrŭs. **V.** Naiades.

Nērēĭŭs, ă, ŭm, *of Nereus.* Quālīs Nērēĭă Dōtō, Virg.

Nēreŭs, ĕī, eī, *or* ĕŏs, m., *a deity of the sea, father of the Nereids.* Nērĕă Pōntō, Virg. Epith. Grāndævŭs, lōngævŭs, spūmāns, spūmĕŭs, vēntōsŭs, glaūcŭs, cærŭlŭs, cærŭlĕŭs, vĭrĭdĭs, ūdŭs, hūmĭdŭs, vāgŭs. **V.** Neptunus, mare.

Nērīnē, ēs, f., *a Nereid.* Nērīnē Gălătæă, Virg.

Nērĭtĭŭs, ă, ŭm, *of Neritus.* Nērĭtĭāsquĕ dŏmōs, Ov.

Nērĭtŭs, *or* ŏs, ī, f., *an island near Ithaca.* Ēt Nērĭtŏs ārdŭă, Virg.

Nĕrĭŭs, ĭī, m., *a man's name.* Scrībĕ dĕcĕm Nĕrĭō, Hor.

Nĕro, ōnĭs, m., *a Roman emperor.* Rōmă, Nĕrōnĭbŭs, (Alcaic.) Hor. Epith. Impĭŭs, īngrātŭs, mātrĭcĭdă, īncēstŭs, scĕlēstŭs, scĕlĕrātŭs, nĕfāndŭs, crūdēlĭs, fĕrŭs, dīrŭs, sānguĭnĕŭs, sŭpērbŭs, īnvīsŭs.

nērvōsŭs, ă, ŭm, *strong.* Pāllădĭŭm nērvōsa ĕt, Juv. Syn. Lăcērtōsŭs, tŏrōsŭs, rŏbūstŭs, vălēns, vĭgēns, vălĭdŭs. **V.** Robustus.

nērvŭs, ī, m., *a nerve.* Ŏdōr nērvīs ĭnĭmīcŭs, Hor. Epith. Vălĭdŭs, fīrmŭs, pŏtēns, fōrtĭs, rŏbūstŭs, dūrŭs, ălăcĕr, tūrgēns. **V.** Robur; chorda; arcus.

Nĕsææ, ēs, f., *a nymph.* Nĕsææ, Spĭōquĕ, Virg.

nescĭo, īs, īvī *and* ĭī, *to be ignorant.* Nescĭō quis tĕnĕrōs, Virg. Syn. Ignōro, sŭm nescĭŭs, īgnārŭs, īnscĭŭs, rŭdĭs; mē fŭgĭt, lătĕt, prætĕrĭt.

Nēssēŭs, ă, ŭm, *of Nessus.* Illĭtă Nēssēō, Ov.

Nēssŭs, ī, m., *the Centaur who was killed by Hercules, and left him the contagious tunic.* Nēssŭs călĭdō, Ov.

Nēstŏr, ŏrĭs, m., *the king of Pylos, the oldest chief in the army of Agamemnon.*

Nĕstŏrĭs ætās, Mart. Epith. Annōsŭs, grāndævŭs, lōngævŭs, mātūrŭs, dīsērtŭs, făcūndŭs, prūdēns, fōrtĭs, bēllātŏr.

Nĕstŏrēŭs, ă, ŭm, *of Nestor.* Fīnēm Nĕstŏrĕæ, Stat.

nēvĕ, conj., *nor.* Nēvĕ tĭbi ād sōlŭm, Virg. Syn. Neū, aūt nē, vēl nē.

neŭtĕr, tră, trŭm, *neither of the two.* Neŭtri ēst fĭdūcĭă, Stat.

neŭtĭquăm, adv., *not at all.* Cărīnĕ, neŭtĭquăm, Ter.

nēx, nĕcĭs, f., *violent death.* Quăm nĕcĭs ārtĭfĭcēs, Ov. Syn. Mŏrs, cædēs, lūthŭm. V. Mors.

nēxĭlĭs, ĕ, *easy to tie.* Nēxĭlĭs āntĕ fŭĭt, Lucr. Syn. Nēxŭs, īnnēxŭs.

nēxo, ās, *the freq. of* necto. Nēxāntēm nōdōs, Virg.

nēxŭs, ūs, m., *a knot.* Nēxĭbŭs ōrbēs, Ov. V. Nodus, catena.

nēxŭs, ă, ŭm, *the pass. partic. of* necto. Mănĭbūs nēxĭs ēx ōrdĭnĕ, Ov.

nī, conj., *unless.* Nī tĕnĕānt, Virg. Syn. Nĭsĭ : sī nōn.

nīcto, ās, *to wink.* Nūtēt, nīctēt, ānnŭăt, (Iamb.) Plaut.

nīctŏr, ārĭs, *to strive.* Hīc ūbĭ nīctārī, Lucr. V. Nitor.

nīdĭfīco, ās, *to build a nest.* Nīdĭfĭcātĭs, ăvēs, Virg. Syn. Nīdŭlŏr.

nīdŏr, ōrĭs, m., *the smell of any thing burnt.* Nīdōrēmque āmbūstă dĕdĭt, Virg. Epith. Fœtĭdŭs, īngrātŭs, grātŭs, frāgrāns, fūmĭfĭcŭs, mŏlēstŭs, jūcūndŭs.

nīdŭs, ī, m., *a nest.* Ōrĕ fĕrūnt dūlcēm nīdĭs, Virg. Epith. Lūtĕŭs, pārvŭs, căvŭs, cōncăvŭs, căvātŭs, lĕvĭs, cēlsŭs, ārdŭŭs, pēndŭlŭs, lŏquāx, gārrŭlŭs, quĕrŭlŭs, mōllĭs, tĕpĭdŭs, vērnŭs, ēxcēlsŭs, āltŭs, pēndēns, tēxtĭlĭs. V. Nidifico.

nĭgĕr, igră, ŭm, *dimin.* ēllŭs, ă, ŭm, *black.* Dēnsīsquĕ nĭgērrĭmŭs Aūstrĭs, Virg. Syn. Nigrāns, nigrēscēns, ātĕr, fūscŭs, fūrvŭs, pūllŭs, ōbscūrŭs, cālīgĭnōsŭs, pĭcĕŭs. V. Nubilus.

nigrēdo, ĭnĭs, f., *blackness.* Syn. Nigrŏr, nigrĭtĭēs, ātrŏr. Epith. Pĭcĕă, dēfōrmĭs, ōbscūră, ātră, tĕnebrōsă, tūrpĭs, ōpācă.

nigrĕfāctŭs, ă, ŭm, *made black.* Fūmāt nĭgrĕfāctŭs ăb Ætnā, An. Syn. Nigrāns, nĭgĕr.

nigrĕo, ēs ; ēsco, ĭs ; *and* īco, ās, *to grow black.* Lĭcĕāt nĭgrēscĕrĕ vēstēs, Cl. Syn. Nigrĕo, nigrĕfīo.

nigro, ās, *to be or make black.* Cūm sæpĕ nĭgrāntĕm, Virg. Nīgrāntī pĭcĕă, Id. Syn. Dēnigro, nigrĕfăcĭo, fūsco, īnfūsco.

nĭhĭl, n., *nothing.* Dē nĭhĭlō nĭhĭl, Pers.

nĭhĭlōmĭnŭs, adv., *nevertheless.* Nĭhĭlōmĭnŭs, ēt mănŭs, ēt pēs, Lucr.

nĭhĭlŭm, *and* nīlŭm, ī, n., *nothing.* Stūltĭtĭāne ērrēt, nĭhĭlŭm, Hor. Rĕdĕānt ād nīlŭm, Lucr.

nīl, n., *nothing.* Tē sīnĕ nīl āltŭm, Virg.

Nīleŭs, ĕŏs *or* ĕī, m., *the son of the Nile.* Āt Nīleŭs quī sē, Ov.

Nīlĭăcŭs *and* lōtĭcŭs, ă, ŭm, *of the Nile.* Nīlĭăcō rĕdĕăs, Mart. Impūrō Nīlŏtĭcă rūră, Luc. Syn. Ægȳptĭŭs, Mēmphĭtĭcŭs.

Nīlĭădēs, ŭm, f. pl., *nymphs of the Nile.* Nīlĭădēs jăcŭlāntŭr, Petr.

Nīlĭgĕnă, æ, m. f., *produced in the Nile.* Heū fŭgĕ Nīlĭgĕnæ, Ov.

Nīlŏtĭs, ĭdĭs, f., *of the Nile.* Tūnĭcă Nīlōtĭdĕ Maūrī, Mart. Syn. Nīlĭăs.

Nīlŭs, ī, m., *a river of Egypt.* Flūmĭnĕ Nīlŭs, Virg. Epith. Sēptēmplēx, sēptēmflŭŭs, stāgnāns, răpāx, cōncĭtŭs, fērtĭlĭs, ūndāns, ēxūndāns, fœcūndŭs, văgŭs, lĭmōsŭs, pīnguĭs, īrrĭgŭŭs, fĕrāx, dīvĕs, păpȳrĭfĕr, tōrrēns, ūndōsŭs, Ægȳptĭŭs, Phărĭŭs ; Mēmphĭtĭcŭs.

nīmbĭfĕr, ĕră, ĕrŭm, *bearing clouds.* Ăd Stȳgă nīmbĭfĕrō, Ov. Syn. Nūbĭfĕr.

nīmbōsŭs, ă, ŭm, *cloudy, rainy.* Flūctū nīmbōsŭs Ōrīōn, Virg. Syn. Imbrĭfĕr, plŭvĭālĭs, nūbĭfĕr.

nīmbŭs, ī, m., *rain, a cloud.* Mĕdĭă nīmbōrŭm īn nōctĕ, Virg. Syn. Imbĕr, plŭvĭă, prŏcēllă. Epith. Nigrāns, ōbscūrŭs, æthĕrĕŭs, nĭgĕr, vŏlāns, rĭgāns, hȳĕmālĭs, Aūstrālĭs, sŭbĭtŭs, tōrrēns, ātĕr, pĭcĕŭs, tĕnŭĭs, præcēps, hĭŭlcŭs, vibrātŭs, hȳbērnŭs, ūndāns, trūx, hōrrĭsŏnŭs, gĕlĭdŭs, glăcĭālĭs, lĕvĭs, stīllāns, ālgēns. V. Imber, pluvia.

nīmīrŭm, adv., *surely.* Sŭă nīmīrum ēst ŏdĭō, Hor. Syn. Nēmpĕ, scīlĭcĕt, quīppĕ, vĭdēlĭcĕt.

nĭmĭs, mĭē, mĭō, *and* mĭŭm, adv., *excessively.* Vĭdĕār nĭmĭs ăcĕr, Hor. Nĭmĭŭm mĭhĭ dūră, Ov. Syn. Īmmŏdĕrātē, īmmŏdĭcē ; ēxtră, prætĕr, suprā mŏdŭm ; plŭs æquō, jūstō.

nĭmĭŭs, ă, ŭm, *excessive.* Quī nĭmĭŏs ŏptābăt, Juv. Syn. Ĭmmŏdĕrātŭs, ĭmmŏdĭcŭs; mŏdum ēxcēdēns; nĭmĭs māgnŭs; æquŏ, jūstŏ mājŏr.

nĭngĭt, *it snows.* Āĕrĕ nĭngĭt, Virg. Syn. Nĭvēs *or* nĭvĭbŭs plŭĭt. V. Nix.

Nĭnŭs *or* ŏs, ī, m., *a king of Assyria.* Būstă Nĭnī, Ov. Dēlĭcĭās Nĭnī, Mart.

Nĭŏbæŭs, ă, ŭm, *of Niobe.* Prŏlēs Nĭŏbæā māgnæ, Hor.

Nĭŏbē, ēs, f., *a queen of Thebes. Her pride caused Apollo and Diana to slaughter all her sons and daughters ; she was changed into a stone.* Eccĕ vĕnĭt cōmĭtūm Nĭŏbēs, Ov. Syn. Tāntălĭs. Epith. Sŭpērbă, aŭdāx, tĕmĕrārĭă, āmēns, īnsānă, tŭmēns, mălĕsānă, īnfēlīx, mœstă, ōrbă, pŭlchră, fōrmōsă, fœcūndă, sāxĕă, āmbĭtĭōsă, sacrĭlĕgă.

Nĭphæŭs, ī, m., *a warrior.* Quīn ēccĕ Nĭphæī, Virg.

Nĭphātēs, ĭs, m., *a mountain of Assyria.* Pūlsūmquĕ Nĭphātēn, Virg. Epith. Ārdŭŭs, ēxcēlsŭs, sūblīmĭs, āltŭs, āĕrĭŭs, nĭvōsŭs, rĭgĭdŭs, nĭvĭfĕr.

Nĭphē, ēs, f., *a nymph of Diana.* Nĭphēque Hўălēquĕ, Ov.

Nīreŭs, ĕī, eī, *or* ĕŏs, *accus.* ĕă, m., *a king of Naxos, famous for his beauty.* Nīrĕă nōn făcĭēs, Prop. Epith. Cāndĭdŭs, nĭvĕŭs, dĕcōrŭs, pŭlchĕr, fōrmōsŭs, pĭctŭs, dīvīnŭs.

Nīsă, æ, f., *a woman's name.* Mōpsō Nīsă dătŭr, Virg.

Nīsēĭs, ĭdĭs, f., *the daughter of Nisus, Scylla.* Nīsēĭdĕ nāvĭtă, Ov.

Nīsēĭŭs, *and* ĕŭs, ă, ŭm, *of Nysus, of Scylla.* Ēt vōs Nīsæī, Ov.

nĭsĭ, conj., *unless.* Quŏd nĭsī mē, Virg. Syn. Sī, sī nōn.

Nīsĭădĕs, ŭm, f. pl., *women of Megara.* Nīsĭădēs mātrēs, Ov.

nĭsŭs, ūs, m., *an effort.* Ēntēllŭs, nĭsūque, Virg. Syn. Cōntēntĭo, cōnātŭs; lăbŏr. V. Conatus.

Nīsŭs, ī, m., *a king of Megara, changed into an ospray.* Insĕquĭtŭr Nīsŭs, Virg.

nĭtēlă, *or* llă, æ, f., *a squirrel.* Aŭrĕāmquĕ nītēllăm, Mart.

nĭtĕo, ēs, *and* ēsco, ĭs, *to shine.* Ēt nĭtĕt īndūctŏ, Virg. Syn. Splēndĕo, splēndēsco, fŭlgĕo, mĭco, rădĭo. V. Splendeo.

nĭtĭdŭs, ă, ŭm, *shining.* Pūrŏ nĭtĭdīssĭmŭs ōrbĕ, Ov. Syn. Nĭtēns, splēndĭdŭs, fŭlgēns, mĭcāns, rădĭāns ; cūltŭs, ēxcūltŭs, pŭlchĕr, fōrmōsŭs. V. Splendidus.

nĭtŏr, ōrĭs, m., *brightness.* Vĭrĭdūmquĕ nĭtōrĕm, Lucr. Syn. Splēndŏr, fūlgŏr, lūx, lūmēn, rădĭŭs. V. Splendor.

nītŏr, ĕrĭs, nīxŭs *and* sŭs, *to strive.* Nītĭmŭr īn vĕtĭtŭm, Ov. Syn. Cōnnītŏr, ēnītŏr, ādnītŏr, cōntēndo, lăbŏro, mōllĭŏr; īncūmbo, īnnītŏr, fūlcĭŏr, fīrmŏr, sŭstēntŏr. V. Conor.

nitrātŭs, ă, ŭm, *mixed with nitre.* Nītrātā vĭrĭdĭs, Mart.

nitrŭm, ī, n., *nitre.* Adjūnctŏquĕ nītrŏ, Seren.

nĭvālĭs, ĕ ; vĕŭs, *and* vōsŭs, ă, ŭm, *snowy, of snow.* Mīscērĕ nĭvālĭbŭs ūndīs, Mart. Aggĕrĭbŭs nĭvĕĭs, Virg. Illĕ nĭvōsă, Ov. Syn. Glăcĭālĭs, Bŏrĕālĭs, Hўpērbŏrĕŭs, Bīstŏnĭĭs. V. Albus.

nīx, nĭvĭs, f., *snow.* Tērrīs nĭvĭs ātquĕ, (Sapph.) Hor. Epith. Ālbă, cāndĭdă, cāndēns, cānă, glăcĭālĭs, hўbērnă, hўĕmālĭs, frīgĭdă, ālgĭdă, ālgēns, ĭnērs, āspĕră, mōntānă, liquēscēns, mădēns, lābēns, cădūcă, dēflŭă, dēcĭdŭă, Hўpērbŏrĕă, Rīphæă ; Scўthĭcă, Bīstŏnĭă ; Thrĕĭcĭă.

nŏ, ās, *to swim.* Nărĕ pĕr æstātĕm, Virg. Syn. Năto, ĭnnăto. V. Nato.

nōbĭlĭs, ĕ, *noble.* Nōbĭlĭs ēst Cănăcē, Ov. Syn. Illūstrĭs, īnsĭgnĭs, clārŭs, ēxĭmĭŭs, ēgrĕgĭŭs, īnclўtŭs. gĕnĕrōsŭs.

nōbĭlĭtās, ātĭs, f., *nobility, fame.* Nōbĭlĭtās ĕădĕm, Ov. Epith. Ingĕnŭă, gĕnĕrōsă, āntīquă, vĕtŭs, cĕlebrĭs, cĕlebrātă, īllūstrĭs, īnsĭgnĭs, clără, ăvītă, pătērnă, vĕră, ēxĭmĭă.

nōbĭlĭto, ās, *to ennoble.* Pōcŭlă Mēntŏrĕā nōbĭlĭtātă mănū, Mart. Syn. Illūstro, ōrno, dĕcŏro, īnsĭgnĭo, cĕlebro. V. Nobilis.

nōbīscŭm, *with us.* Nōbīscūm vīvĭt, Hor.

nŏcēns, ntĭs, *noxious.* Tāxĭquĕ nŏcēntēs, Virg. Syn. Nŏcīvŭs, nŏcŭŭs, nŏxĭŭs, īnfēstŭs, īncōmmŏdŭs, īnĭmīcŭs, mŏlēstŭs, īmpōrtūnŭs, grăvĭs. V. Reus.

nŏcĕo, cŭī, *to injure.* Rēgnă nŏcērēnt, Virg. Syn. Ōbsŭm, ōbsto, ōffĭcĭo, īncōmmŏdo.

nŏcīvŭs, *or* cŭŭs, ă, ŭm, *noxious.* Ēt sĭbĭ nŏcīvŭm, Phædr. V. Nocens.

nŏctēscĭt, *it begins to be night.* V. Vesper, Hesperus.

nŏctĭcŏlă, æ, m. f., *living in darkness.* Vēndăt nŏctĭcŏlæ spūrcīs, Prud. Syn. Nŏctūrnŭs, nŏctĭvăgŭs.

nŏctĭcŏlor, ōrĭs, *of the colour of night.* Nŏctĭcŏlŏr Stӯx, Auṣ.
nŏctĭfĕr, ă, ŭm, *bringing night.* Nŏctĭfĕr īgnĭs, Catull. Syn. Sērŭs, tĕnebrōsŭs;
Hĕspĕrŭs.
nŏctĭlūcă, æ, f., *the moon.* Făcă nŏctĭlūcăm, Hor.
nŏctĭvăgŭs, ă, ŭm, *wandering in the night.* Nŏctĭvăgæquĕ făcēs, Lucr. Syn.
Nŏctūrnŭs, lūcĭfŭgŭs.
nŏctū, adv., *by night.* Dūm nŏctū stērtĭs, Hor.
nŏctŭă, æ, f., *an owl.* Nŏctŭă cāntŭs, Virg. Syn. Ŭlŭlă, būbo. Epith. Nŏctūrnă, nŏctĭvăgă, nŏctĭvĭgĭl, īmprŏbă, fĕră, fătālĭs, fĕrālĭs, fūnēstă, sĭnĭstră,
Pāllădĭă. V. Bubo.
nŏctūrnŭs, ă, ŭm, *of the night.* Strĕpĭtŭs nŏctūrnŏs, Hor. V. Noctivagus.
nōdo, ās, *to tie in a knot.* Crīnēs nōdāntŭr ĭn aūrŭm, Virg. Syn. Innōdo, cōn-
nōdo, nĕcto, nēxo, lĭgo, vīncĭo, rĕvīncĭo. V. Ligo, vincio.
nōdōsŭs, ă, ŭm, *knotty.* Nōdōsā cōrpŭs, Hor.
nōdŭs, ī, m., *a knot.* Nēctĕ trĭbŭs nōdĭs, Virg. Syn. Vīncŭlŭm, nēxŭs, lĭgāmĕn,
vīnclŭm. Epith. Strīctŭs, ārctŭs, vălĭdŭs, dĭffĭcĭlĭs, tōrtŭs, īntōrtŭs, cōntēxtŭs, nēxŭs, tōrtĭlĭs, flēxĭlĭs, īrrĕsŏlūbĭlĭs, ăhēnŭs, ærātŭs, tĕnāx, cæcŭs,
lătēns, ārcānŭs.
Noē, ēs, m., *the patriarch.* Tēmpŏrĭbŭs cōnstrūctă Nŏē, Arat. Prŏăvŭs Nŏē sŭb,
Vict. Syn. Lāmĕchĭdēs, Noă, Noēmŭs, vītĭsătŏr. Epith. Jūstŭs, sānctŭs,
pĭŭs.
Nŏēmōn, ŏnĭs, m., *a warrior.* Hălĭūmquĕ Nŏēmŏnăquĕ, Virg.
Nŏlă, æ, f., *an ancient city of Campania.* Vĕsēvŏ Nōlă jŭgō, Virg.
nōlo, lŭī, *to be unwilling.* Nōlŭĭt ēssĕ, Prop. Syn. Abnŭo, rĕcūso. V. Volo.
Nŏmădēs, ŭm, m. pl., *wandering nations.* Nŏmădūmquĕ tӯrānnī, Virg.
nōmĕn, ĭnĭs, n., *a name.* Nōmĭnĭs īndēx, Prop. Syn. Agnōmĕn, cōgnōmĕn;
fāmă, hŏnŏr, glōrĭă, nōbĭlĭtăs. Epith. Aūgŭstŭm, mĕmŏrābĭlĕ, nōtŭm, īllūstrĕ,
īnsĭgnĕ, cĕlĕbrĕ, ēgrĕgĭŭm, clārŭm ; tūrpĕ, fœdŭm, ĭgnōtŭm, obscūrŭm, īnfāmĕ,
dīrŭm. V. Laus.
nōmēnclātŏr, ōrĭs, m., *an attendant on candidates for popularity, whose office it was
to remind his employer of the names of the citizens, that he might salute them with
familiarity.* Nōmēnclātŏr pŭgĭlĕm, (Scaz.) Mart.
Nōmēntānŭs, ī, m., *a man's name.* Nōmēntānŏquĕ nĕpōtī, Hor.
Nōmēntŭm, ī, n. *and* ŭs, ī, m., *a city of the Latins.* Hī tĭbī Nōmēntŭm, Virg.
nōmĭno, ās, *to name.* Nōmĭnăt ūnăm, Ov. Syn. Vŏco, āppēllo, nūncŭpo, dīco,
prŏfĕro.
nōn, adv., *not.* Dē grĕgĕ nōn aūsĭm, Virg. Syn. Haŭd, haŭdquăquăm, nĕquāquăm, nĕquīcquăm, nĕc, nĕquĕ, nĭhĭl, nīl, mĭnĭmĕ, nūnquăm, nūsquăm.
Nōnăcrīnŭs, *and* crĭŭs, ă, ŭm, *of Mount Nonacris, Arcadian.* In vīrgĭnĕ Nōnā-
crīnā, Ov. Nōnăcrĭŭs hērŏs, Id.
nōnæ, f. pl., *the nones of every month in the Roman calendar.* Sēx Maīŭs nōnās.
nōnāgēsĭmŭs, ă, ŭm, *the ninetieth.* Nōnāgēsĭmā nōstră, Aus.
nōnāgīnta, (indecl.) *ninety.* Nōnāgīntă dĭēs, Aus.
Nōnārĭă, æ, f., *a Roman courtesan.* Pĕtŭlāns Nōnārĭă, Pers.
nōndŭm, adv., *not yet.* Nōndŭm Ilĭŭm ĕt ārcēs, Virg.
nōnnĕ, adv., *is it not ?* Nōnnĕ fŭīt sătĭŭs, Virg.
nōnnĭhĭl, n., *something.* Nōnnĭhĭl ēst, quŏd, Mart. Syn. Alĭquĭd.
nōnnūnquăm, adv., *sometimes.* Nōnnūnquam īrāscĕrĕ, Ov. Syn. Alĭquāndo,
īntērdŭm.
nōnŭs, ă, ŭm, *the ninth.* Pōst ŭbī nōnă sŭōs, Virg. Syn. Tēr trīnŭs.
Nōrĭcŭs, ă, ŭm, *of the Norici.* Et Nōrĭcă sī quĭs, Virg.
nōrmă, æ, f., *a rule.* Nōrmă lŏquēndī, Hor. Syn. Rēgŭlă, lēx. Epith. Cērtă,
rēctă, jūstă, fāllāx.
nōs, pron., *we.* Nōs ănĭmæ, Virg.
nōsco, ōvī, ōtŭm, *to know.* Quī nōvĭt ăgrēstēs, Virg. V. Cognosco.
nŏstĕr, tră, trŭm, *our.* Vīndēmĭă nŏstrīs, Virg.
* nōstrās, ātĭs, *of our country.* Cic.
nŏtă, æ, f., *a mark.* Cuī tērgă nŏtæ, Virg. Syn. Sīgnŭm, īnsĭgnĕ, spĕcĭmĕn,
ārgūmēntŭm, īndĭcĭŭm, mŏnŭmēntŭm, vēstĭgĭŭm ; lābēs, măcŭlă, dēdĕcŭs.
Epith. Mănĭfēstă, cērtă, īncērtă, ăpērtă, fīctă, occūltă ; tūrpĭs, īnfāmĭs, obscœnă, pŭdēndă, ātră, fœdă. V. Macula.

N 5

nŏtābĭlĭs, ĕ, *remarkable*. Căndŏrĕ nŏtābĭlĭs ĭpsō, Ov. SYN. Insĭgnĭs, nōbĭlĭs.

nŏtārĭŭs, ĭī, m., *a short-hand writer*. Aūt nŏtārĭŭs vēlōx, Mart.

nŏtēsco, tŭī, *to become known*. Nŏstrī nŏtēscĕt, Pr. SYN. Innŏtēsco, clārēsco.

nŏthŭs, ĭ, m., *an illegitimate child*. Mātrĕ nŏthōs, Virg.

nŏtĭfĭco, ās, *to make known*. Nŏtĭfĭcārĕ mĕæ, Ov.

nŏtĭtĭă, æ, *and* ēs, ēī, f., *knowledge*. Nŏtĭtĭăm pārs ēst, Ov.

nŏto, ās, *to mark*. Dīctă nŏtă, Ov. SYN. Ōbsērvo, ădnŏto, sīgno, ōbsīgno, ănĭmādvērto.

nŏtŭs, ă, ŭm, *known*. Sīc nōtŭs Ūlyssēs, Virg. SYN. Cōgnĭtŭs, ăgnĭtŭs, pĕrspēctŭs, nōn īgnōtŭs ; īnsīgnĭs, cōnspĭcŭŭs, cĕlĕbĕr, clārŭs, īllūstrĭs.

Nŏtŭs, ĭ, m., *the south-wind*. Mădĭdĭs Nŏtŭs ēvŏlăt, Ov. SYN. Aūstĕr. EPITH. Præpĕs, ātĕr, răpĭdŭs, ūdŭs, fŭrēns, tērrĭbĭlĭs, prŏcēllōsŭs, nūbĭfĕr, mădĭdŭs, trīstĭs, sævŭs, plŭvĭŭs, ācĕr, īnsānŭs, dūrŭs, īrātŭs, āĕrĭŭs, nīmbōsŭs, tūrbĭdŭs, vēlōx, īmbrĭfĕr, sŏnōrŭs, fŭgāx, vŏlŭcĕr, īnflātŭs, cĕlĕr, tĕpĭdŭs, strīdēns, raūcŭs, sūrdŭs, hūmēns, vĭŏlēntŭs. V. Auster.

nŏvācŭlă, æ, f., *a razor*. Pēndēns īn nŏvācŭlă, Phædr. EPITH. Ăcūtă, lēvĭs, sævă.

nŏvālĭs, ĭs, f., *and* lĕ, ĭs, n., *fallow ground*. Cēssārĕ nŏvālēs, Virg. Cūltă nŏvālĭă mĭlĕs, Id. V. Ager.

nŏvātŏr, ōrĭs, m., *and* trīx, īcĭs, f., *a renewer*. Rērūmquĕ nŏvātrīx, Ov.

nŏvēllŭs, ă, ŭm, *the dimin. of* novus. Fālcĕ nŏvēllās, Virg. SYN. Nŏvŭs, tĕnēllŭs.

nŏvĕm, (*indecl.*) *nine*. Ēpŭlātă nŏvĕm, Virg. SYN. Nŏvēnī.

Nŏvēmbĕr, brĭs, m., *the eleventh month*. Tŏtŏquĕ Nŏvēmbrī, Auson. EPITH. Trīstĭs, īmbrĭfĕr, nīmbōsŭs, plŭvĭŭs, mădĭdŭs, īgnāvŭs, ĭnĕrs, nīmbĭfĕr, ūdŭs, hūmĭdŭs.

nŏvēndĭālĭs, ĕ, *of nine days*. Nŏvēndĭālēs dīssĭpārĕ, Hor.

nŏvēnŭs, ă, ŭm, *the ninth*. Rĕpĕtītă nŏvēnĭs, Ov.—2. *nine*. Tērgă nŏvēnă bŏŭm, Ov. V. Novem.

nŏvērcă, æ, f., *a step-mother*. Injūstă nŏvērcă, Virg. EPITH. Inīquă, sævă, trūx, dīră, fĕrōx, tērrĭbĭlĭs, īnvĭdă, īmmītĭs, bārbără, fŭrēns. fŭrĭbūndă, fĕră, crūdēlĭs, tērrĭfĭcă, clāmōsă, fōrmīdābĭlĭs, trŭcŭlēntă, fŭrĭōsă, ĭnēxōrābĭlĭs.

nŏvērcālĭs, ĕ, *of a step-mother*. Stat.

nŏvĭēs, adv., *nine times*. Ēt nŏvĭēs Stўx, Virg.

nŏvīssĭmŭs, ă, ŭm, *the last*. Dīxītquĕ nŏvīssĭmă vērbă, Virg. SYN. Ēxtrēmŭs, ūltĭmŭs, pōstrēmŭs, nŭpĕrŭs.

nŏvĭtās, ātĭs, f., *newness*. Ēt rēgnī nŏvĭtās, Virg.

nŏvĭtĭŭs, ă, ŭm, *new, ignorant*. Tĕtrūmquĕ nŏvĭtĭŭs hōrrĕt, Juv. SYN. Tўro, rŭdĭs, īndŏctŭs ; īgnārŭs, īmpĕrītŭs ; hōspĕs, pĕregrīnŭs.

nŏvo, ās, *to renew*. Mĕrĭtōsquĕ nŏvāmŭs, Virg. SYN. Innŏvo, īnstaūro, rĕnŏvo.

nŏvŭs, ă, ŭm, *new*. Pōstŭlăt ēssĕ nŏvōs, Mart. SYN. Rĕcēns ; ĭnaūdītŭs, īnsŏlĭtŭs, īnsuētŭs.

nŏx, nŏctĭs, f., *the night*. Nōctĭbŭs hīs văcŭī, Prop. SYN. Tĕnĕbræ, cālīgo. EPITH. Nigră, nigrāns, cālīgāns, ātră, cœcă, ōbscūră, tĕnĕbrōsă, squālĭdă, pāllĭdă, ŏpācă, squālēns, hōrrēndă, ūmbrōsă, pāllēns, trīstĭs, lūrĭdă, sōmnĭfĕră, sŏpōrĭfĕră, mūtă, sĕgnĭs, quĭētă, tăcĭtă, plăcĭdă, sĭlēns, īllūnĭs, sĕgnĭs, īgnāvă, ĭnĕrs, lānguĭdă, stēllātă, stēllĭfĕră, hūmēns, frīgĭdă, ūdă, rōscĭdă, rōrĭfĕră, nūbĭlă, hōrrĭdă, hōrrĭbĭlĭs, trānquīllă, tērrĭbĭlĭs, tērrĭfĭcă, īntēmpēstă, ōblĭvĭōsă, lōngă, tetrĭcă, ămīcă, pĭcĕă, hўbērnă, prŭīnōsă, ārcānă, sīdĕrĕă, Tārtărĕă, Stўgĭă.

nŏxă, æ, f., *damage*. Sĭnĕ nŏxā lūcĕ bĭbūntŭr, Ov. SYN. Crīmĕn, cūlpă; dāmnŭm, pērnĭcĭēs.

nŏxĭŭs, ă, ŭm, *hurtful*. Nŏxĭă cōrdă, Ov. V. Nocens, reus.

nūbēs, ĭs, *and* ēcŭlă, æ, f., *a cloud*. Nūbĭbŭs æthĕr, Ov. SYN. Nĕbŭlă, nīmbŭs, nūbĭlă. EPITH. Imbrĭfĕră, hūmĭdă, ăquōsă, nīmbōsă, ūndāns, dēnsă, ōbscūră, ŏpācă, cœcă, nigrāns, tūrbĭdă, liquĭdă, squālēns, squālĭdă, æthĕrĭă, āĕrĭă, lēvĭs, prŏcēllōsă, vēntōsă, cœlĭvăgă, vŏlŭcrĭs, tĕnĕbrōsă, ūdă, văgābūndă, pēndēns, pēndŭlă, vŏlāns, cærŭlĕă, gĕlĭdă, pĭcĕă, grăvĭdă, hūmēns, hōrrēndă, hўbērnă, ūmbrōsă, fŭgāx, pāllĭdă, ārdŭă, vērsĭcŏlŏr, cærŭlă, āltă.

nūbĭfĕr, ă, ŭm, *bringing clouds*. Nūbĭfĕr æquŏrĕ, rūbrī, Aus. SYN. Nīmbōsŭs, nūbĭlŭs ; āltŭs, nūbĭbŭs æquŭs.

nūbǐfŭgŭs, ă, ŭm, *that chases away the clouds.* Nēc tām nūbǐfŭgŏ, Colum.

nūbǐgĕnă, æ, m. f., *born of the clouds.* Nūbǐgĕnās īnvīctĕ, Ov. V. Ixion.

nūbǐlă, ōrŭm, n. pl., *clouds.* Nūbǐlă tōrquēŭs, Sil.

nūbǐlǐs, ĕ, *of age to be married.* Plēnīs nūbǐlǐs ānnīs, Virg. SYN. Cōnnubǐŏ, cōn-jŭgǐŏ, nŭptǐīs āptŭs, ǐdōnĕŭs, mātūrŭs, tēmpēstīvŭs, vīcīnŭs tŏrŏ. Āptă vīrŏ. Tēmpēstīvă vīrŏ. V. Nubo.

nūbǐlŭs, ă, ŭm, *cloudy.* Nūbǐlă, sōlŭs ĕrǐs, Ov. SYN. Nūbǐlōsŭs, nīmbōsŭs, ōbscūrŭs, cālǐgǐnōsŭs, tĕnebrōsŭs, nǐgĕr, nigrāns, ātĕr, cæcŭs, ŏpācŭs, pǐcĕŭs.

nūbo, nūpsī, *to take a husband.* Nūbǐt āmīcŭs, H. SYN. Mărītŏr. V. Conjugium.

nuclĕŭs, ī, m., *a kernel.* Mēllă dărī nŭclĕōsquĕ, Mart. EPITH. Dūrŭs, tĕnŭĭs, tĕrĕs.

nūdo, ās, *to strip naked.* Ādvērsæ nūdārĕ sŏlēnt, Hor. SYN. Dēnūdo, spŏlǐo, ĕxŭo, dēvēlo.

nūdŭs, ă, ŭm, *naked.* Nūdŭs ără, Virg. SYN. Nūdātŭs, ĕxūtŭs, spŏlǐātŭs.

nūgæ, ārŭm, f. pl., *trifles.* Hās nūgās hŭmǐllǐs, Juv. SYN. Nūgāmēntă. EPITH. Lĕvĕs, ǐnēptæ, pŭĕrīlĕs, vānæ, ǐnānēs, ănīlĕs, lætæ, hǐlărĕs, jŏcōsæ, fictæ, fīctǐtǐæ, vānǐlŏquæ, fœmǐnĕæ, fūtǐlĕs.

nūgātŏr, ōrǐs, m., *a trifler.* Cēssās nūgātŏr, Pers. SYN. Nūgāx, scūrră. EPITH. Lŏquāx, gārrŭlŭs, lĕvǐs, fūtǐlǐs, vānŭs, vānǐlŏquŭs, ǐnānǐs, vēntōsŭs.

nūgŏr, ārǐs, *to trifle.* Intērdŭm nūgārǐs, Hor.

nūllŭs, ă, ŭm; lǐŭs, lī, *none, worthless.* Nūllǐŭs āddīctŭs, Hor. Nūllǐŭs ăvārī, Id.

nŭm, adv., *whether.* Nŭm lăcrўmās, Virg. SYN. Nŭnquǐd, nōnnĕ, ăn, ānnĕ.

Nŭmă, æ, m., *the second king of the Romans.* Pārvă Nŭmæ, Ov. EPITH. Sānctŭs, jūstŭs, æquŭs, pǐŭs, rēlǐgǐōsŭs, pācǐfǐcŭs, fātǐdǐcŭs.

Nŭmāntǐă, æ, f., *a town of Spain.* Bēllă Nŭmāntǐæ, Hor.

Nŭmāntīnŭs, ă, ŭm, *of Numantia.* Illĕ Nŭmāntīnă, Ov.

Nŭmānŭs, ī, m., *the name of a warrior.* Fūdīssĕ Nŭmānŭm, Virg.

nūmĕn, ǐnǐs, n., *a deity.* Nŭmǐnĕ dīvŭm, Virg. EPITH. Aŭxǐlǐārĕ, ĕxōrābǐlĕ, ǐnēxōrābǐlĕ, īmmōrtālĕ, īnvǐŏlābǐlĕ, plăcābǐlĕ, sacrŭm, prŏpǐtǐŭm, ădōrāndŭm. V. Deus.

nŭmĕrābǐlǐs, ĕ, *that may be numbered.* Pŏpŭlŭs nŭmĕrābǐlǐs, Hor.

nŭmĕro, ās, *to number.* Dīvŭm nŭmĕrābăt ămōrēs, Virg. SYN. Ēnŭmĕro, dīnŭmĕro, cēnsĕo, rĕcēnsĕo, pērcēnsĕo, sūppŭto, cōmpŭto.

nŭmĕrōsŭs, ă, ŭm, *numerous.* Nŭmĕrōsŭs Hŏrātǐŭs, Ov. SYN. Plūrǐmŭs, frĕquēns, cōpǐōsŭs, mŭltŭs, mŭltǐplēx, vărǐŭs, dēnsŭs, cōnfērtŭs.

nŭmĕrŭs, ī, m., *number.* Nŭmĕrŏ Dĕŭs īmpărĕ gaŭdĕt, Virg. SYN. Vīs, cōpǐă, ăbūndāntǐă, mūltǐtūdo, cŭmŭlŭs, tūrbă. EPITH. Immēnsŭs, īnfīnītŭs, pārvŭs, ĕxǐgŭŭs, īngēns.

Nŭmīcǐŭs, *and* īcŭs, ī, m., *a small river of Latium.* Nŭmīcǐŭs ūndīs, Ov. Stāgnă Nŭmīcī, Virg.

Nŭmīdæ, ārŭm, *or* Nŏmădēs, ŭm, m. pl., *an African people.* Nŭmīdāsquĕ rĕbēllĕs, Ov. EPITH. Iufræni, văgī, fŭgācēs, Maŭrūsǐī, īndŏmǐtī, bēllǐgĕrī, fĕrōcēs.

nŭmīsmă, ătǐs, n., *a piece of money.* Rēgālĕ nŭmīsmă, Phǐlīppŏs, Hor. SYN. Mŏnētă, æs, pĕcūnǐă.

Nŭmītŏr, ōrǐs, m., *king of Alba, dethroned by his brother Amulius.* Et Căpўs ēt Nŭmītŏr, Virg.

nŭmmārǐŭs, ă, ŭm, *relating to money.* Līs fŭĕrīt nŭmmārǐă, Aus.

nŭmmātŭs, ă, ŭm, *a monied man.* Et bĕnĕ nŭmmātŭm, Hor. V. Dives.

nŭmmŭlārǐŭs, īi, m., *a money-changer.* Nŭmmŭlārǐŭs māssă, Mart.

nŭmmŭs *or* nŭmŭs, ī, m., *a piece of money.* Sŭmmām nŭmmōrŭm, Hor. SYN. Pĕcūnǐă, æs, aŭrŭm, ārgēntŭm. EPITH. Vērŭs, fālsŭs, ădūltĕrīnŭs, dŏlōsŭs, īmprŏbŭs, ĕxǐtǐālǐs, aŭrĕŭs, ārgēntĕŭs, prĕtǐōsŭs, pērnǐcǐōsŭs, ĕxǐtǐōsŭs. V. Divitiæ.

nūnc, *now.* Nūnc scǐo. SYN. Jăm, mŏdŏ, jăm nūnc, jāmjăm, mōx; hōc tēmpŏrĕ.

nūncǐo, ās, *to bring tidings.* Nūncǐĕt, āc, Virg. SYN. Ānnūncǐo, dēnūncǐo; rĕnūncǐo, rĕfĕro, rĕpōrto, mŏnĕo, sīgnǐfǐco; īndǐco, ās; scrībo.

nūncĭŭs, ĭī, m., *and* ĭŭm, ĭī, n., *news, tidings.* Nūncĭŭs ārmōrŭm, Luc. Nŭncĭă sōrtĭs, Tib.

nūncĭŭs, ĭī, m., *and* cĭă, æ, f., *a messenger.* Nūncĭŭs āstră, Claud. SYN. Tăbēl-lārĭŭs. EPITH. Cĕlĕr, vŏlŭcĕr, vŏlucrĭs, cĭtŭs, sŭbĭtŭs, fĭdŭs, fĭdēlĭs, ĭnfĭdŭs, ĭn-fĭdēlĭs, faŭstŭs, fēlīx, ĭnfēlīx, lætŭs, trīstĭs, mēndāx, vērāx, cērtŭs, ĭncērtŭs, ōptātŭs, ēxpēctātŭs, mīssŭs.—Adj., -ŭs, ă, ŭm, *bearing tidings.* Nūncĭă vērbă mĕī, Ov. V. Nuncio.

nūncŭpo, ās, *to name.* Nūncŭpăt hæc, Ov. V. Nomino.

nŭndĭnă, æ, f., *and* æ, ārŭm, f. pl., *a fair, a market.* Nūndĭnă mūndī, Alcim.

nūndĭnŏr, ārĭs, *to buy or sell publicly.* Cĭtārī nūndĭnātŭm, (Iamb.) Prud.

nūnquăm, adv., *never.* SYN. Nōn ūnquăm. V. Impossibile.

nūnquĭs, quă, quĭd, *is there any ?* Nūnquĭd dăbĭs, Ov.

nūpĕr, adv., *lately.* Infōrmĭs, nūpĕr me, Virg. SYN. Haŭd prĭdĕm, nēc dūdŭm.

nūpĕrŭs, ă, ŭm, *recent.* Nūpĕrum ēt nŏvĭtĭŭm, (Iamb.) SYN. Rĕcēns, nŏvŭs.

nūptă, æ, f., *a bride.* Nŏvă nūptă vĕnēnĭs, Ov. V. Uxor.

nūptĭæ, ārŭm, f. pl., *nuptials.* Nūptĭārum ēxpērs, (Sapph.) Hor. SYN. Hȳmĕnæī, cōnjŭgĭŭm, cōnnubĭŭm. V. Conjugium.

nūptĭālĭs, ĕ, *nuptial.* Ēt nūptĭālēs ĭmpĭī, (Iamb.) Sen. SYN. Cōnnubĭālĭs, jŭgālĭs.

|| nūptŭrĭo, ĭs, *to long to be married.* Nūptŭrĭŭnt mūltæ, Apul.

nūptŭs, ŭs, m., *marriage.* Nūptŭmquĕ prĭŏr, Stat.

Nūrsæ, ārŭm, f. pl., *a city of the Æqui.* In prælĭă Nūrsæ, Virg.

Nūrsĭă, æ, f., *a city of the Sabines.* Frĭgĭdă mīsĭt Nūrsĭă, Virg.

nŭrŭs, ūs, f., *a daughter-in-law.* Mĭsĕræquĕ nŭrŭs, hic, Virg.

nŭsquăm, adv., *nowhere.* Nŭsquăm tūtă fĭdēs, Virg

nūtāmĕn, ĭnĭs, n., *a poising.* Trĕmŭlō nūtāmĭnĕ pēnnæ, Sil.

nŭto, ās, *to nod, to shake.* Vērtĭcĕ nūtānt, Virg. SYN. Văcĭllo, lăbo, tĭtŭbo, lă-bāsco. V. Nutus.

nŭtrīcŭlă, æ, f., *the dimin. of* nutrix. Dūlcī nŭtrīcŭlă mājŭs, Hor.

nūtrīmēntŭm, ī, *and* īmĕn, ĭnĭs, n., *nourishment.* Nŭtrīmēntă dĕdĭt, Virg. Nŭ-trīmēn deērĭt ĕdācī, Ov. SYN. Cĭbŭs, cĭbārĭŭm, ēscă, ălĭmēntŭm, păbŭlŭm. V. Cibus, alimentum.

nūtrĭo, ĭs, īvī *and* ĭī, ītŭm, *and* ŏr, īrĭs, *to nourish.* Nūtrībāt tĕnĕrĭs, Virg. Nūtrītŭr ŏlīvăm, Id. SYN. Ălo, pāsco, ēdŭco, -ās, ēdūco, -ĭs.

nūtrītŏr, ōrĭs, m., *a breeder.* Stăbŭlī nūtrītŏr Ĭbērī, Mart. SYN. Ăltŏr, ălŭm-nŭs.

nūtrītŭs, *the pass. partic. of* nutrio. Rīpā nūtrītŭs ĭn ĭllā, Juv.

nūtrīx, īcĭs, f., *a nurse.* Fūlvō nūtrīcĭs tĕgmĭnĕ, Virg. SYN. Ălūmnă, āltrīx. EPITH. Sōllĭcĭtă, sēdŭlă, ānxĭă, lāctāns, vĭgĭl, ĭnsōmnĭs, blāndă, fĭdă, mītĭs, pēr-vĭgĭl, pērnōx, ĭrrĕquĭĕtă, ōffĭcĭōsă.

nŭtŭs, ŭs, m., *a nod.* Ad nūtŭs āptŭs, Hor. EPITH. Făcĭlĭs, blāndŭs, lŏquāx, tăcĭtŭs, grăvĭs, hĕrĭlĭs.

nŭx, nŭcĭs, f., *a nut.* Pārcă cŏrōnă nŭcēs, Ov. EPITH. Vĭrĭdĭs, nŏcēns, dūră.

Nȳctĕlĭŭs, ĭī, m., *a name of Bacchus.* Ŭt fĕră Nȳctĕlĭī, Virg.

Nȳctĭmĕnē, ēs, f., *a daughter of Epops, changed into an owl.* Nȳctĭmĕnē nōstrō, Ov.

Nȳmphæ, ārŭm, f. pl., *nymphs.* Gĕnĭtŏr Nȳmphārŭm, Cat. SYN. Ōcĕănĭtĭdĕs. EPITH. Tĕnĕræ, nĭvĕæ, Nērēĭæ, glaŭcæ, cærŭlĕæ, dūlcēs, făcĭlēs, vĕnŭstæ, flūctĭgĕnæ, hūmēntēs, fŏrmōsæ, nĭtĭdæ, dĕcōræ, nĭtēntēs, lætæ, vitrĕæ, flōrĭlĕgæ, cōmptæ, ĭmbēllēs, păvĭdæ, vĕrēcŭndæ, rŏsĕæ, ĭntāctæ, cāstæ.

Nȳsă, æ, f., *a mountain and city of India sacred to Bacchus.* Cēlsō Nȳsæ dē vēr-tĭcĕ tīgrēs, Virg.

Nȳsæŭs, *and* ēĭŭs, ă, ŭm, *of Nysa, of Bacchus.* Indĭcă Nȳsæĭs, Prop. Brŏmĭŏ Nȳsēĭă, quāre, Luc.

Nȳsēĭs, ĭdĭs, *and* sĭăs, ădĭs, f., *of Nysa.* Nȳmphæ Nȳsēĭdĕs āntrĭs, Ov. Nȳ-sĭădēs nȳmphæ, Id.

Nȳseŭs, ĕŏs *or* ĕī, m., *a name of Bacchus.* Addĭtŭr hīs Nȳseŭs, Ov.

O.

O, interj., long before a consonant; common before a vowel. O mĭsĕrās, Lucr.
Ŏ ŭtĭnăm, Ov.   Tē Cŏrўdōn, ŏ Alēxĭ, Virg.
Ŏărĭŏn, ōnĭs, m., *Orion.*   Fūlgĕrĕt Ŏărĭŏn, Cat.
Ŏāxĭs, ĭs, m., *a river in Crete.*   Vēnlēmŭs Ŏāxĕm, Virg.
ŏb, prep., *on account of.*   Cūnctŭs ŏb Ĭtălĭăm, Virg.   SYN. Prŏptĕr; āntĕ.
ŏbămbŭlo, ās, *to walk about.*   Frĕmŏbūndŭs ŏbāmbŭlăt Ætnăm, Ov.   SYN. Ŏbĕo,
    cĭrcum āmbŭlo, īncēdo, spătĭŏr, ĕo.   V. Ambulo.
ŏbārdĕo, ēs, rsī, *to flame before.*   Mĕtŭēndŭs ŏbārsĭt Lūcĕ Drўăs, Stat.
ŏbārmo, ās, *to arm.*   Sĕcūrī dēxtrās ŏbārmĕt, Hor.
ŏbbrūtēsco, ĭs, *to grow brutish.*   Pārtĭbŭs ŏbbrūtēscăt, Lucr.
ŏbcæco, ās, *to blind.*   Obcæcāvĕrăt ārtŭs, Virg.   SYN. Cæco, ēxcæco.   V.
    Cæco.
ŏbdo, dĭdī, *to shut up.*   Obdĕ fŏrēs, Ov.   V. Claudo.
ŏbdūco, ĭs, *to cover.*   Pălūs ŏbdūcăt pāscŭă, Virg.   SYN. Cōndo, tĕgo, ŏpĕrĭo,
    cōntĕgo, ōccūlto.   V. Tego, occulto.
ŏbdūrēsco, ĭs, and ro, ās, *to grow hard.*   Fŭĭt ŏbdūrēscĕrĕ vūltū, Prop.   Pērsta,
    ātque ŏbdūrā; seū, Hor.   SYN. Indūrēsco, īndūrŏr, rĭgēsco, dūrēsco.
ŏbēdĭo, ĭs, *to obey.*   Ēs dīcto ŏbēdĭēns, (Iamb.) Pl.   SYN. Pārĕo, ŏbtēmpĕro, ŏb-
    sĕquŏr, sĕquŏr, aūdĭo.
ŏbĕlīscŭs, ī, m., *an obelisk.*   Sūrgēns ŏbĕlīscŭs ĭn aūrās, Mant.   V. Pyramis.
ŏbĕlŭs, ī, m., *a spit.*   Pōne ŏbĕlōs ĭgĭtŭr, Aus.   V. Veru.
ŏbĕo, ĭs, ŏbīvī and ĭī, *to go round.*   Insīgnĭs ŏbībăt, Virg.   SYN. Cīrcŭmĕo,
    ŏbāmbŭlo, pĕrērro, pĕragro, lūstro, pērlūstro, īnvīso; cīngo, cīrcŭndo; ēx-
    ĕquŏr, pērfīcĭo; mŏrĭŏr.
ŏbērro, ās, *to wander about.*   Sēmpĕr ŏbērrăt, Hor.   SYN. Ērro; pĕrērro, văgŏr,
    pērvăgŏr.
ŏbēsŭs, ă, ŭm, *fat.*   Vēnĭt ŏbēsŭs, Mart.   V. Pinguis.
ŏbēx, or ŏbjēx, ĭcĭs, m., *an obstacle.*   Cērtānt ŏbĭcēs ārcēssĕrĕ, Sil.   Objĭcĕ
    pōntŭs, Virg.   SYN. Obstăcŭlŭm, īmpĕdīmēntŭm, rĕpăgŭlŭm, mŏră.   EPITH.
    Fōrtĭs, vălĭdŭs, ōppŏsĭtŭs, ŏbjēctŭs, pŏtēns, fīrmŭs, tūtŭs.
ŏbhærĕo, sī, *to adhere.*   In flūmĭne ŏbhærĕt, Lucr.
ŏbjăcĕo, ēs, *to lie in the way.*   Objăcĕt āltō, Stat.
ŏbĭcĭo, ĭs, ĕrĕ, *same as* ŏbjĭcĭo.   Cūr ŏbĭcĭs Māgnō tŭmŭlum, Luc.
ŏbjēcto, ās, *the freq. of* objicio.   Ēt rūrsŭs căpŭt ŏbjēctărĕ pĕrĭclīs, Virg.
ŏbjēctŭs, ūs, m., *an interposition.*   Ēffĭcĭt ŏbjēctū, Virg.
ŏbjēctŭs, ă, ŭm, *the pass. partic. of* objicio.   Ĭllĕ tămĕn clўpĕo ŏbjēctō, Virg.
ŏbjĭcĭo, jēcī, ctŭm, *to throw in the way.*   Objĭcĭs hōstī, Virg.   SYN. Oppōno, ŏb-
    jēcto, īntērjĭcĭo, ŏbtrūdo; ŏffĕro, ēxprobro.
ŏbĭtĕr, adv., *by the way, slightly.*   Aŭt ŏbĭtĕr lĕgĕt, Juv.
ŏbĭtŭs, ūs, m., *death.*   Ānte ŏbĭtūm nēmo, Ov.   SYN. Ĭntĕrĭtŭs, mŏrs, fātŭm.
    V. Mors.
ŏbĭtŭs, ă, ŭm, *the pass. partic. of* obeo.   Mōrte ŏbĭtā, Virg.   SYN. Dēfūnctŭs.
* ŏbjūrgātĭo, ōnĭs, f., *a chiding.*   Blānda ŏbjūrgātĭŏ vōcĕm, Aus.   SYN. Reprĕ-
    hēnsĭo, īncūsātĭo, cāstĭgātĭo.
ŏbjūrgo, ās, *to scold.*   Pŭĕr, ŏbjūrgăbĕrĕ rūbrā, Pers.   SYN. Incrĕpo, ārgŭo,
    īncūso.   V. Redarguo.
ŏblātro, ās, *to bark at.*   Ŏblātrātquĕ sĕnātŭm, Sil.
ŏblātŭs, ă, ŭm, *the pass. partic. of* offero.   Ŏblātō gaūdēns, Virg.
ŏblēctāmĕn, ĭnĭs, n., *delight.*   Cĭrcum ŏblēctāmĭnă vītæ, Stat.   SYN. Ŏblēctā-
    mēntŭm, ŏblēctātĭo, dēlēctāmēntŭm, dēlēctātĭo, vŏlŭptās, lŭdŭs.
ŏblēcto, ās, *to delight.*   Ăn măgĭs ŏblēctănt, Juv.   SYN. Dēlēcto, recrĕo,
    ēxhĭlăro.
ŏblĭgo, ās, *to bind up.*   Sĭmŭl ŏblĭgāstī, (Sapph.) Hor.   SYN. Cīrcŭmlĭgo, lĭgo,
    ŏbnēcto, cōnstrĭngo, dēvīncĭo.
ŏblĭmo, ās, *to smear over.*   Sūlcōs ŏblīmĕt ĭnērtēs, Virg.
ŏblĭno, ĭs, lēvī, lĭtŭm, *to anoint.*   Ŏblĭnăt ātrīs, Hor.   SYN. Ŏblĭnĭo, cīrcŭm-
    lĭno, ĭnūngo, īllĭno, ūngo, īmbŭo, īnfĭcĭo, tĭngo, ŏbdūco.

ŏblīquo, ās, *to turn obliquely.* Ŏblīquātquĕ sīnūs, Virg. SYN. Ĭn ŏblīquūm flĕcto, sīnŭo, dūco; Ĭncūrvo.

ŏblīquŭs, ă, ŭm, *oblique.* Ā vēntĭs ŏblīquā lūcĕ, Virg. SYN. Trānsvērsŭs, līmŭs, Ĭncūrvŭs.

ŏblītĕro, ās, *to erase.* Nĕc ūlla ŏblītĕrĕt ætās, Cat. SYN. Dēlĕo, ăbŏlĕo.

ŏblītŭs, *the pass. partic.* of oblino. Ŏblītŭs ā dŏmĭnæ, Ov.

ŏblītŭs, ă, ŭm, *the part.* of obliviscor. Cōrda ŏblītā lăbōrŭm, Virg. SYN. Im-mĕmŏr, nōn mĕmŏr.

ŏblīvĭo, ōnĭs, f., *and* vĭă, ōrŭm, n. pl., *forgetfulness.* Māgna ŏblīvĭŏ rērŭm, Juv. Sōllĭcĭtæ jūcŭnda ŏblīvĭă vītæ, Hor. EPITH. Ĭnĕrs, pigră; dēsĕs, lōngă, Ĭngrātă, Lēthæā.

ŏblīvĭōsŭs, ă, ŭm, *that makes one forget.* Ŏblīvĭōsŏ lævĭă, (Alcaic.) Hor. SYN. Lēthæŭs.

ŏblīvīscŏr, ĕrĭs, *to forget.* Jam ŏblīvīscĕrĕ Graiōs, Ov. SYN. Nōn mĕmĭnĭ, nōn rĕcōrdŏr.

ŏblŏquŏr, ĕrĭs, *to speak against.* Ŏblŏquītūr nŭmĕrĭs, Virg. SYN. Rĕpūgno, ŏbsĭsto; ōccĭno, căno.

ŏblūctŏr, ārĭs, *to struggle against.* Ŏblūctŏr ărēnæ, Virg.

ŏbmūrmŭro, ās, *to murmur against.* Ŏbmūrmŭrăt ĭpsĕ, Ov. SYN. Ŏbstrĕpo, cōntrā mūrmŭro.

ŏbmūtēsco, tŭĭ, *to be silent.* Prēssŏque ŏbmūtŭĭt ōrĕ, Virg. SYN. Mūtēsco, Ĭmmūtēsco, sĭlĕo, tăcĕo, cōntĭcĕo, rĕtĭcĕo. V. Mutus, sileo.

ŏbnītŏr, ĕrĭs, *to strive against.* Nĕc nōs ŏbnītī, Virg. SYN. Ŏblūctŏr, rĕnītŏr; cōntrā nītŏr, rĕsĭsto.

ŏbnīxŭs, *or* nīsŭs, ă, ŭm, *the pass. partic.* of obnītŏr. Ŏbnīxūs lātĭs hŭmĕrĭs, Virg.

ŏbnōxĭŭs, ă, ŭm, *culpable, obnoxious.* Ŏbnōxĭă fāctō, Tib.

ŏbnūbo, ĭs, psī, ptŭm, *to veil.* Cōmās ŏbnūbĭt ămĭctū, Virg. SYN. Ŏbvēlo, tĕgo.

ŏbŏrĭŏr, īrĭs *and* ĕrĭs, īrī, *to arise.* Dīmōvĭt ŏbōrtĭs, Lucr. SYN. Ŏrĭŏr, ēxsūrgo, nāscŏr, ăppārĕo.

ŏbrēpo, psī, ptŭm, *to creep upon.* Ēst ŏbrēpĕrĕ sōmnŭm, Hor. SYN. Irrēpo, rēpo.

ŏbrīgĕo, ŭī, *to be stiff.* Ŏbrīgŭĭt vīttă, Ov. SYN. Rīgĕo, dīrīgĕo.

ŏbrŭo, rŭī, rŭtŭm, *to overwhelm.* Ŏbrŭĭt Aūstĕr, Virg. SYN. Ŏpprĭmo, prĕmo; ŏnĕro, tĕgo, ŏpĕrĭo. V. Lapido.

ŏbrŭtŭs, ă, ŭm, *the pass. partic.* of obruo. Ŏbrŭtŭs ĭnsānĭs, Ov.

ŏbscœnŭs, ă, ŭm, *filthy.* Ŏbscœnĭquĕ cănēs, Virg. SYN. Fœdŭs, Ĭmpūrŭs, sōr-dĭdŭs, tūrpĭs, Ĭmmūndŭs.

ŏbscūrĭtās, ātĭs, f., *obscurity.* Mŏx ŏbscūrĭtās, (Iamb. Dim.) Prud. SYN. Cālīgo, tĕnebræ. V. Tenebræ.

ŏbscūro, ās, *to obscure.* Ŏbscūrānt pēnnĭs, Virg. SYN. Ĭnōbscūro, ŏbūmbro, Ĭnūmbro, ŏbnūbĭlo. V. Tenebræ, nox.

ŏbscūrŭs, ă, ŭm, *obscure.* Mīgrĕt Ĭn ŏbscūrās, Hor. SYN. Tĕnebrōsŭs, nĭgĕr, nigrāns, ătĕr, ŏpācŭs, cālīgĭnōsŭs, nūbĭlŭs. V. Tenebrosus, abditus.

ŏbsecro, ās, *to entreat.* Ŏbsēcro ĕt ŏbtēstŏr, Hor. SYN. Ŏbtēstŏr, prĕcŏr, ōro, rŏgo.

ŏbsĕquĭŭm, ĭī, n., *obsequiousness.* Ŏbsĕquĭŭm vēntrĭs, Hor. SYN. Ŏbēdĭēntĭă, mĭnĭstĕrĭŭm; cōmĭtās. EPITH. Blāndŭm, ūrbānŭm, mītĕ, ŏffĭcĭōsŭm.

ŏbsĕquŏr, ĕrĭs, *to comply with.* Ŏbsĕquĭtūr quōcūmquĕ, Hor. SYN. Ŏbēdĭo, pārĕo, ŏbtēmpĕro.

ŏbsĕro, ās, *to shut up.* Ŏbsĕrăt hērbōsōs, Prop.

ŏbsērvāntĭă, æ, f., *observation, care.* Plăcĕt ŏbsērvāntĭă cūnctĭs, Prud. SYN. Hŏnŏr, vĕnĕrātĭo.

ŏbsērvo, ās, *to observe.* Ŏbsērvātă sĕquŏr, Virg. SYN. Ănĭmādvērto, ādvērto, nŏto, ēxplōro, spĕcŭlŏr, aūcŭpŏr; vĕnĕrŏr, cŏlo, vĕrĕŏr, rĕvĕrĕŏr.

ŏbsĕs, ĭdĭs, m., *a hostage.* Ŏbsĭdĭs ūnīŭs, Ov. SYN. Præs, vas [vădĭs], pĭgnŭs, spōnsŏr.

ŏbsēssŏr, ōrĭs, m., *a besieger.* Vīvārum ŏbsēssŏr ăquārŭm, Ov.

ŏbsĭdĕo, *or* sīdo, sēdī, sēssŭm, *to besiege.* Ŏbsēdēre ăllī, Virg. Ārmātō ŏbsīdăm, Virg. SYN. Ŏppūgno.

ŏbsĭdĭo, ōnĭs, f., *a siege.* Ŏbsĭdĭōnĕ prĕmēbānt, Virg. SYN. Ŏppūgnātĭo, ŏbsĭ-dĭŭm, ŏbsēssĭo. EPITH. Ārctă, strīctă, lōngă, dūră, ānxĭă, sēdŭlă, mŏlēstă, sōllĭcĭtă, saevă, trūx, fĕră, sănguĭnĕă, crŭēntă, crūdēlĭs, ăcērbă, tērrĭbĭlĭs, fōrmĭdābĭlĭs, trīstĭs, ĭnĭmīcă, hōstīlĭs. V. Obsideo.

ŏbsīgno, ās, *to seal up.* Illŭd ĭn hĭs ŏbsīgnătŭm, Lucr.

ŏbsīsto, stĭtĭ, *to oppose.* Ŏbsīstūnt vēntĭs, Ov.

ŏbsĭtŭs, ă, ŭm, *the pass. partic. of* obsero. Ŏbsĭtŭs aevŏ, Virg.

ŏbsŏlētŭs, ă, ŭm, *obsolete.* Ŏbsŏlētă sōrdĭbŭs, (Iamb.) Hor. SYN. Ĭnsŏlĭtŭs, ĭnsuētŭs, vĕtŭs.

ŏbsōnĭŭm, ĭī, n., *victuals.* Cŏēmēns ŏbsōnĭă nūmmĭs, Hor. SYN. Fērcŭlŭm, dăpēs, cĭbĭ, laūtĭtĭæ.

ŏbsŏno, ās, ŭĭ, *to interrupt by making a noise.* Huĭc ŏbsŏnăt, Plaut. SYN. Ŏbstrĕpo, ŏbgānnĭo.

ŏbstācŭlŭm, ī, n., *an obstacle.* Cūncta ŏbstācŭlă rūmpūnt, Prud. V. Obex.

ŏbstetrīx, īcĭs, f., *a midwife.* Crŭōrĕ rūbrōs ŏbstĕtrīx pānnōs, Hor. Ægӯpte ŏbstētrīcĭbŭs īmpĕrăt, Alcim.

ŏbstĭnātĭo, ōnĭs, f., *obstinacy.* Prædūrăt ŏbstĭnātĭo, (Iamb. Dim.) Prud. SYN. Ŏbstĭnātă *or* ŏbdūrātă mēns.

ŏbstĭnātŭs, ă, ŭm, *obstinate.* Quĭbŭs ŏbstĭnātăs, (Sapph.) Hor. SYN. Pērtĭnāx, pērvĭcāx. V. Constans.

ŏbstĭpŭs, ă, ŭm, *stiff, who carries his head stiffly.* Stēs căpĭte ŏbstĭpŏ, Hor.

ŏbsto, ās, stĭtĭ, *to oppose.* Fāmam ŏbstārĕ fŭrōrī, Virg. SYN. Ŏbsīsto, rĕnītŏr, ŏbnītŏr, rĕlūctŏr, rĕsīsto, ŏbsŭm, īmpĕdĭo. V. Resisto, impedio.

ŏbstrĕpo, ĭs, *to make a noise at or against.* Ŏbstrĕpĭt ārbŏr, Prop. V. Strepo.

ŏbstrīngo, īnxī, īctŭm, *to tie hard.* Jūrāndo ŏbstrīngăm, Hor. SYN. Ăstrīngo, cōnstrīngo, dēvīncĭo, ŏblīgo.

ŏbstrŭo, ūxī, ūctŭm, *to stop up.* Ŏbstrŭĭt aūrēs, Virg. SYN. Ŏbsēpĭo, ŏbtūro, ŏbtĕgo, præclūdo. V. Claudo.

ŏbstŭpĕfăcĭo, fēcī, *to amaze.* Ŏbstŭpĕfēcĭt ănŭs, Ov. SYN. Stŭpĕfăcĭo, tērrĕo.

ŏbstŭpĕfāctŭs, ă, ŭm, *astonished.* Lānguēntĭbŭs ŏbstŭpĕfāctī, Prop. SYN. Ăttŏnĭtŭs, cōntērrĭtŭs, ēxtērrĭtŭs, tērrĭtŭs, stŭpĕfāctŭs, cōnfūsŭs, tūrbātŭs, stŭpēns, păvĭdŭs.

ŏbstŭpĕo, *and* pēsco, pŭī, *to be amazed.* Ŏbstŭpŭĭt prīmo, Virg. SYN. Stŭpēsco, stŭpĕo, mīrŏr.

ŏbsŭm, ŏbĕs, ŏbfŭī, ŏbēssĕ, *to hinder.* Ăn ŏbēst quŏquĕ, Ov.

ŏbtĕgo, ĭs, ēxī, ctŭm, *to cover.* Ĭllĭcĕt ŏbtĕgĭtŭr. SYN. Tĕgo, cōntĕgo, ŏpĕrĭo. V. Tego.

ŏbtēmpĕro, ās, *to obey.* Ŏbtēmpĕrăt Indă, Ov. SYN. Pārĕo, ŏbsĕquŏr. V. Obedio.

ŏbtēndo, ĭs, *to spread before.* Vēntōs ŏbtēndĕre ĭnānēs, Virg.

ŏbtēntŭs, ă, ŭm, *the pass. partic. of* obtendo. Ŏbtēntă dēnsāntŭr nōctĕ tĕnēbræ, Virg.

ŏbtēntŭs, ūs, m., *a spreading before.* Ŏbtēntū frōndĭs ĭnūmbrānt, Virg.

ŏbtĕro, trīvī, trītŭm, *to tread under foot.* Ŏbtĕrĕt hōstĕm, Lucan. Ŏbtrītĭs ōssĭbŭs, Id. SYN. Cōntĕro, tĕro, āttĕro.

ŏbtēstŏr, ārĭs, *to call to witness, to conjure.* Ipsum ŏbtēstēmŭr, Virg. SYN. Tēstŏr, āppēllo, īnvōco ; obsecro, ōro, īmplōro, rŏgo, prĕcŏr.

ŏbtēxo, xŭī, ctŭm, *to cover.* Vēlōrum ŏbtēxĭtŭr ŭmbrā, Stat.

ŏbtĭcĕo, cŭī, *to be silent.* Nēc prĭŭs ŏbtĭcŭĭt, Ov. V. Taceo.

ŏbtĭnĕo, ēs, *to obtain.* Scēptra ŏbtĭnēntŭr, (Iamb.) SYN. Ăssĕquŏr, cōnsĕquŏr, ădĭpīscŏr, impetro.

ŏbtīngĭt, *it happens to.* Ŏbtĭgĭt mĭhi, Hor. SYN. Ŏbvĕnĭt, ādvĕnĭt, cōntĭngĭt, ēvĕnĭt, āccĭdĭt.

ŏbtōrquĕo, rsī, *to wrest round.* Prōrāmque ŏbtōrquĕt, Stat.

ŏbtōrtŭs, ă, ŭm, *the pass. partic. of* obtorqueo, *twisted.* Ŏbtōrtī pēr cōllŭm cīrcŭlŭs aūrī, Virg.

ŏbtrēcto, ās, *to disparage.* Ĭnvĭdĭă ŏbtrēctāns, Sil. SYN. Dētrăho, călŭmnĭŏr, cōnvīcĭŏr, vĭtŭpĕro, mălĕdīco. V. Convicior.

ŏbtrūnco, ās, *to cut off the head or limbs.* Cōmĭnŭs ŏbtrūncānt, Virg. SYN. Trūnco, mŭtĭlo ; ōccīdo. V. Occido.

ŏbtūrgēsco, ĭs, *to swell.* Ŏbtūrgēscĭt ĕnĭm, Lucr. V. Turgeo.

ŏbtūro, ās, *to stop up.* Ŏbtūrēm pătŭlās, Hor. SYN. Ŏbstrŭo, præclūdo, claūdo.

ŏbtūsŭs, ă, ŭm, *blunted.* Vŏmĕrĭs ŏbtūsī, Virg. Lūxu ŏbtūsĭŏr ūsŭs, Id. Syn. Hĕbĕs, rĕtūsŭs, hĕbĕtātŭs.

ŏbtūtŭs, ŭs, m., *a steadfast look.* Dūm stŭpĕt, ŏbtūtū, Virg. Syn. Ăspēctŭs, vīsŭs. V. Aspectus.

ŏbvērsŏr, ārĭs, *to be present before.* Obvērsātūr ăd aūrēs, Lucr.

ŏbvērto, ĭs, *to turn towards.* Ŏbvērtŭnt pĕlăgō, Virg.

ŏbvĭŭs, ă, ŭm, *meeting, in the way.* Obvĭŭs ŏrbēs, Virg. Syn. Ŏccūrrēns; ŏppŏsĭtŭs, ādvērsŭs; ēxpŏsĭtŭs.

ŏbūmbro, ās, *to overshadow.* Ŏlĕāstĕr ŏbūmbrĕt, Virg. Syn. Ūmbro, ĭnūmbro, ŏbtĕgo, ŏbscūro.

ŏbūncŭs, ă, ŭm, *hooked.* Vūltūr ŏbūncō, Virg.

‖ ŏbūndo, ās, *to overflow.* Spērchĭŭs ŏbūndăt, Stat.

ŏbvŏlvo, ĭs, *to envelope.* Ŏbvŏlvās vĭtĭŭm, Hor. V. Involvo.

ŏbūstŭs, ă, ŭm, *burnt around.* Armātŭs ŏbūstō, Virg.

ŏccāllĕo, ēs, *and* ēsco, ĭs, lŭī, *to grow hard.* Pāndo ŏccāllēscĕrĕ rōstrō, Ov.

ŏccāsĭo, ōnĭs, f., *opportunity.* Paūcīs ŏccāsĭŏ nŏtă, Aus. Epith. Irrĕvŏcābĭlĭs, mŏbĭlĭs, fŭgĭtĭvă, vŏlūbĭlĭs, fŭgāx, ĭdōnĕă, ŏppōrtūnă, ŏptātă, fēlīx, cŏmmŏdă.

ŏccāsŭs, ūs, m., (sōlĭs,) *sunset.* Ĭbĭt ăd ŏccāsŭm, Ov. Syn. Sŏlĭs ŏbĭtŭs; sōl ŏccĭdēns. Epith. Sērŭs, ūmbrĭfĕr, frĭgĭdŭs, rŭbēns, nŏctĭfĕr. V. Sol occidens.

ŏccĭdēns, ēntĭs, m., *the west.* Vĕl ŏccĭdēntĭs, Hor.

ŏccĭdo, ĭs, ŏccĭdī, (*from* cădo,) *to die, to fall.* Ŏccĭdĭt āstrō, Virg. Syn. Ŏccūmbo, īntĕrĕo, cădo, pĕrĕo, mŏrĭŏr.

ŏccīdo, ĭs, ŏccīdī, (*from* cædo,) *to kill.* Me ŏccīdĭstĭs, ămīcī, Hor. Syn. Nĕco, ēnĕco, pĕrĭmo, īntĕrĭmo, īntērfīcĭo, trŭcīdo, ŏbtrūnco, cædo, măcto, jūgŭlo, ēxtīnguo. V. Occisio, strages, morior.

ŏccĭdŭŭs, ă, ŭm, *western, declining.* Vēspĕr, ĕt ŏccĭdŭō, Ov. V. Caducus.

ŏccĭno, ĭs, *to sing inauspiciously.* Ŏccĭnēntĕs āllītĕs, Cat.

ŏccĭpĭo, ĭs, ēpī, *to begin.* Ŏccĭpĭt ēt mŏllī, Lucr.

ŏccĭpŭt, ĭtĭs, n., *the back part of the head.* Ŏccĭpĭtī cæcō, Pers.

● ŏccīsĭo, ōnĭs, f., Cic. *slaughter.* Syn. Cædēs, strāgēs, fūnĕră.

ŏccīsŭs, ă, ŭm, *the pass. partic. of* occido. Hĭnc ălĭī spŏlĭa ŏccīsīs, Virg. V. Morior, occido.

ŏcclūdo, ĭs, *to shut up.* Vēllēnt ŏcclūdĕrĕ glēbīs, Mart. Syn. Ŏbstrŭo, claūdo, præclūdo. V. Claudo.

ŏcco, ās, *to harrow.* Ŏcca, ēt sĕgĕs, Pers.

ŏccŭbo, ās, ŭī, *to lie dead in or at.* Ŏccŭbăt ūmbrīs, Virg. Syn. Ŏccūmbo, cădo.

ŏccŭlo, ŭī, *and* lto, ās, āvī, *to conceal.* Sāxo ŏccūltābăt ŏpăcō, Virg. Ŏccŭlĕ tērrā, Virg. Syn. Cōndo, rĕcōndo, ābscōndo, ābdo, ŏpĕrĭo, tĕgo, cōntĕgo, ŏbtĕgo, ŏbdūco, ŏcclūdo, ābstrūdo, vēlo, cēlo.

ŏccūltē, adv., *secretly.* Lăbĭtūr ŏccūltē, Ov. Syn. Clăm, fūrtĭm.

ŏccūltŭs, ă, ŭm, *concealed.* Æstŭăt ŏccūltīs, Juv. Syn. Ŏccūltātŭs, ābdĭtŭs, cōndĭtŭs, ābscōndĭtŭs, tēctŭs, ŏbtēctŭs, cōntēctŭs, ŏpērtŭs, ădŏpērtŭs, cŏŏpērtŭs, ŏbdūctŭs, ābstrūsŭs, ŏcclūsŭs, vēlātŭs, lătēns, lătĭtāns, ŏbscūrŭs, ŏpăcŭs, lătebrōsŭs, ārcānŭs. V. Abditus.

ŏccūmbo, cŭbŭī, *to fall, to die.* Ŏccŭbŭīssĕ sĕnēs, Ov. Syn. Ŏccĭdo, cădo, mŏrĭŏr. V. Morior.

ŏccŭpātĭo, ōnĭs, f., *occupation, employment.* Rĕŏr ŏccŭpātĭŏnĕm, (Phal.) Sid. Syn. Nĕgŏtĭŭm, cūră.

ŏccŭpātŭs, ă, ŭm, *the pass. partic. of* occupo. Nāmque ĕt ŏccŭpātŭs, (Phal.) Mart.

ŏccŭpo, ās, *to take hold of, to possess.* Ŏccŭpĕt ŏrbĕm, Virg. Syn. Præ rĭpĭo, ārrĭpĭo, īnvādo; prævērto; dīstĭnĕo; tĕnĕo, pōssĭdĕo.

ŏccūrro, rrī, *and* rso, ās, *to run to, to meet.* Ŏccūrrāmŭs ăd ūndăm, Virg. Ŏccūrsārĕ căprō, Id. Syn. Ŏffĕro mē, ādsŭm; ŏbvĭŭs ĕo, prōdĕo, vĕnĭo, prōcēdo. V. Obvius.

ŏccūrsŭs, ūs, m., *a meeting.* Stĭpĭtĭs ŏccūrsū, Ov.

Ŏcĕănĭtĭs, ĭdĭs, f., *the daughter of Oceanus.* Ŏcĕănītĭdēs āmbæ, Virg. V. Nereides.

Ŏcĕănŭs, ī, m., *the ocean.* Ŏcĕănō prŏpĕrēnt, Virg. Syn. Tēthўŏs cōnjūx. V. Mare.

ŏcēllŭs, ī, m., *a dimin. of* oculus. Sūbrēpĭt ŏcēllīs, Ov. V. Oculus.

ŏcĭŏr, ōrĭs, *swifter.* Ocĭŏr ālīs, Virg. Syn. Pērnĭcĭŏr, lĕvĭŏr, vēlōcĭŏr. V. Cĕler, velox.

ōcĭŭs, adv., *more swiftly.* Ocĭŭs ōmnēs, Virg. Syn. Prŏpĕrē, răpĭdē. V. Statim.

Ŏcnŭs, ī, m., *the son of Tiber and Manto, and founder of Mantua.* Clĕt Ŏcnŭs ăb ōrĭs, Virg.

ŏcrĕă, æ, f., *a boot, greaves.* Tūm lœvēs ŏcrĕās, Virg. Epith. Hăbĭlĭs, āptă, aūrātă, mĭcāns, œnĕă, fērrĕă, fūlgĭdă.

ŏcrĕātŭs, ă, ŭm, *booted.* Dŏrmĭs ŏcrĕātŭs, ŭt āprŏs, Hor.

Ocrīsĭă, œ, f., *a slave, the mother of Servius Tullius.* Ŏcrīsĭă mātĕr, Ov.

Ŏctāvĭŭs, ĭī, m., *a name of Augustus.* Ŏctāvĭŭs ĭdĕm, Aus.

ŏctāvŭs, ă, ŭm, *the eighth.* Săpĭēntum ŏctāvŭs ămīcŏ, Hor.

ŏctĭēs, adv., *eight times.* Ŏctĭēs ĭn ānnŏ, (Phal.) Mart. Syn. Bĭs quătĕr, quătĕr bĭs.

ŏctĭpēs, ĕdĭs, *eight-footed.* Ŏctĭpĕdĭs frūstrā, Ov.

ŏcto, indecl., *eight.* Ŏctŏ vĭdēs, Mart.

Ŏctōbĕr, brĭs, abl. brī, m., *the tenth month.* Tē tăcĕo, Ŏctōbĕr, Aus. Epith. Imbrĭfĕr, mădĭdŭs, hūmēns, nīmbōsŭs, plŭvĭŭs.

ŏctōgēsĭmŭs, ă, ŭm, *the eightieth.* Ātque ŏctōgēsĭmă vĭdĭt, Juv.

ŏctōgīnta, *eighty.* Ānnŏs ŏctōgīnta ēt quătŭŏr, Plaut.

ŏctōnī, æ, ă, *eighty.* Ibānt ŏctōnĭs, Hor.

ŏctŏphŏrŭm, ī, n., *a litter carried by eight servants.* Ŏctŏphŏrŏ sănŭs, Mart.

ŏctŭssĭs, ĭs, m., *a piece of money worth eight-pence.* Ērgo ŏctŭssĭbŭs. Eheū, Hor.

ŏcŭlātŭs, ă, ŭm, *who has good eyes.* Ŏmnēs ŏcŭlātŭs ĕt ūllō, Mart. Syn. Pērspĭcāx, ăcūtŭs.

ŏcŭlŭs, ī, m., *the eye.* Lŏcŭm căpĭēs ŏcŭlīs, Virg. Syn. Lūmĕn, ŏcēllŭs. Epith. Mĭcāns, cærŭlĕŭs, fŏrmōsŭs, vĕnŭstŭs, sĕrēnŭs, plăcĭdŭs, rădĭāns, clārŭs, rŭtĭlāns, vĕrēcūndŭs, ăcūtŭs, ārgūtŭs, sŭbtīlĭs, scintīllāns, tērrĭbĭlĭs, sŭpērbŭs, mălīgnŭs, hŏstīlĭs, sānguĭnĕŭs, tŏrvŭs, sĕvērŭs, ŏblīquŭs, mĭnāx, ārdēns, ĭgnītŭs, flāmmĭfĕrŭs, lāscīvŭs, văgŭs, ērrāns, trūx, fĕrōx, fĕrŭs, cāstŭs, pŭdīcŭs, mŏdēstŭs, rīdēns, bĕnīgnŭs, lȳncĕŭs, lacrȳmāns, mădēns, grăvĭs, hūmēns, līvēns, vĭgĭl, īnsōmnĭs, fēssŭs. V. Circumspicio, aspicio.

ōcȳŏr, ōcȳŭs. V. Ocior, ocius.

Ocȳrhŏē, ēs, f., *a nymph, the daughter of Chiron and Chariclo.*

ōdă, æ, *or* ē, ēs, f., *an ode, a song.* Cōncĭnĭt ŏdīs, Ov. Syn. Cārmĕn, cāntŭs. Epith. Lætă, dūlcĭs, fēstīvă, Lȳrĭcă.

Ŏdēssŏs, *or* ŭs, ī, f., *a city of Mœsia, on the Euxine sea.* Ĕt Ŏdēssŏn ĕt ārcēs, Ov.

ōdī, īstī, īssĕ, *I hate.* Nŏn ōdī, Cīnnă, nĕgāntĕm, Mart. V. Odium.

ŏdĭōsŭs, ă, ŭm, *hateful.* Ŏdĭōsăs āflĕrăt aūrēs, Ov. Syn. Invīsŭs, ēxŏsŭs, ĭnfēnsŭs, invĭdĭōsŭs, mŏlēstŭs; ŏdĭŏ dīgnŭs, flagrāns.

Ŏdītēs, æ, m., *the name of a Centaur.* Tēntāvĭt Ŏdītēs, Ov.

ŏdĭŭm, ĭī, n., *hatred.* Quĭbŭs aūt ŏdĭŭm, Virg. Syn. Sĭmūltās, īră, răbĭēs, fŭrŏr. Epith. Inĭmīcŭm, nĕfāndŭm, pērtĭnāx, ĭmprŏbŭm, ăcērbŭm, crŭēntŭm, ŏccūltŭm, ĭmmītĕ, īnsānŭm, mălĕsānŭm, dĭūtūrnŭm, ĭmplăcābĭlĕ, ĭmplăcātŭm, ĭmmōrtālĕ, ēxĭtĭālĕ, dūrŭm, cæcŭm, pūgnāx, ĭnēxōrābĭlĕ, lēthālĕ, atrōx. V. Odi.

ŏdŏr, ōrĭs, m., *smell.* Tmōlŭs ŏdōrēs, Virg. Syn. Hălĭtŭs, aūră; frăgrāntĭă; sŭffīmĕn; nīdŏr. Epith. Suāvĭs, jūcūndŭs, mōllĭs, grātŭs, frăgrāns; bĕnĕŏlēns, tētĕr, fœtĭdŭs, ĭngrātŭs, grăvĭs, pēstĭfĕr, mŏlēstŭs, īnjūcūndŭs, īnsuāvĭs, dīrŭs, dūlcĭs, spīrāns, ămbrŏsĭŭs, gĕnĭālĭs, mȳrrhœŭs, thūrĕŭs; Sȳrĭŭs, Assȳrĭŭs, Ărăbs, Ărăbŭs, Săbœŭs, Pānchæŭs; Achæmĕnĭŭs. V. Oleo.

* ŏdōrātŭs, ŭs, m., *the sense of smelling.* Syn. Ōlfāctŭs, nārēs.

ŏdōrātŭs, ă, ŭm, *and* rĭfĕr, ră, rŭm, *odoriferous.* Ŭrĭt ŏdōrātăĭn, Virg. Ĕt ŏdōrĭfĕrām pănăcĕăm, Virg.

ŏdōro, ās, *to perfume.* Ŭrĭt ŏdōrātăm, Virg. Syn. Inŏdōro, sŭffĭo, fūmĭgo.

ŏdōrŏr, ārĭs, *to smell.* Ŭnŭs ŏdŏrŏr, Hor. Syn. Ōlfăcĭo.

ŏdōrŭs, ă, ŭm, *of a sweet smell.* Ĕquĭtēs, ĕt ŏdŏră, Virg. Syn. Bĕnĕŏlēns, suāvĕŏlēns, rĕdŏlēns, frăgrāns; suāvĭtĕr hālāns, spīrāns. V. Oleo.

Odrȳsæ, ārŭm, *and* Odrȳsĭī, ōrŭm, m. pl., *a people of Thrace, at the source of the Hebrus.* Dā căpŭt Ŏdrȳsĭīs, Val. Fl. Rēx Ŏdrȳsĭŭs, Ov

Ŏdўssēă, æ, f., *a poem of Homer.* Pĕrlĕge Ŏdўssēăm, Aus.

Œagrĭŭs, ă, ŭm, *of Œagrus, of Orpheus, Thracian.* Œagrĭŭs Hēbrŭs, Virg.

Œagrŭs, *or* Œăger, grī, m., *a king of Thrace, the father of Orpheus.* Quăm sēnĭs Œăgri, Ov.

Œbălĭă, æ, f., *Tarentum, a Lacedemonian colony.* Nāmquĕ sŭb Œbălĭæ, Virg.

Œbălĭdēs, æ, m., *the son of Œbalus, Hyacinthus.* Lābĕrĭs, Œbălĭdē, Ov.—2. *Lacedemonian, Castor and Pollux.* Effŭgĕre Œbălĭdæ, Id.

Œbălĭs, ĭdĭs, f., *Lacedemonian ; Sabine.* Œbălĭ nȳmphă, tŭās, Ov.

Œbălĭŭs, ă, ŭm, *of Œbalus ; Lacedemonian.* Sī nōn Œbălĭā, Ov.

Œbălŭs, *or* ŏs, ī, m., *one of the first kings of Laconia, the father of Hyacinthus ; a king of the Teleboæ.* Œbălĕ, quēm gĕnŭissĕ Tĕlōn, Virg

Œchălĭă, æ, f., *a city of Eubœa, destroyed by Hercules.* Trōjāmque Œchălĭāmquĕ, Virg.

Œchălĭs, ĭdĭs, f., *Œchalian.* Œchălĭdūm Drўŏpē, Ov.

Œclīdēs, æ, m., *the son of Œcleus, Amphiaraus.* Sī scĕlĕre Œclīdēs, Ov.

Œdĭpŏdĭŏnĭdēs, æ, m., *the son of Œdipus.* Œdĭpŏdĭŏnĭdēn vāstīsque hōrrēndă cănēntĭs, Stat.

Œdĭpŏdĭŏnĭŭs, ă, ŭm, *of Œdipus.* Œdĭpŏdĭŏnĭæ quĭd sŭnt, Ov.

Œdĭpŭs, ī, *or* pūs, ŏdĭs, *and* Œdĭpŏdēs, æ, m., *the son of Laius ; he killed his father, and married his mother.* Dāvŭs sŭm, nōn Œdĭpŭs, Ter. Nŏctĕ pŭdōrĕm Œdĭpŏdēs, Stat. Afĕr, ĕt Œdĭpŏdăs, Mart. EPITH. Mĭsĕr, īmpĭŭs, cæcŭs, īnsaŭstŭs, pārrīcīdă.

Œnēĭŭs, *and* Œnēŭs, ă, ŭm, *of Œneus, of Calydon.* Œnēĭŭs hērōs, Stat. Œnēōs ūltōrēm sprētă pĕr āgrōs, Ov.

Œneŭs, ĕŏs, ĕī *or* eī, m., *the king of Ætolia.* Œnĕă nāmquĕ, Ov. EPITH. Sŭpērbŭs, Călўdōnĭŭs.

Œnīdēs, æ, m., *the son of Œneus, Meleager, Tydeus.* Āt mănŭs Œnīdæ, Ov.

Œnŏmăŭs, ī, m., *the king of Elis, and father of Hippodamia ; he was killed in a chariot-race with Pelops through the treachery of his servant Myrtilus.* Māvŏrtĭŭs āxĭs Œnŏmāī, Stat.

Œnōnē, ēs, f., *a nymph loved by Paris.* Œnōnē pŏtĕrĭt, Ov. EPITH. Pēgăsĭs, Phrўgĭă, fōrmōsă.

œnŏphŏrŭm, ī, n., *a vessel to carry wine in.* Œnŏphŏrŭm sĭtĭēns, Juv.

Œnŏpĭă, æ, f., *an ancient name of Ægina.* Œnŏpĭăm vĕtĕrēs, Ov.

Œnŏpĭŭs, ă, ŭm, *of Ægina.* Clāssĭs ăb Œnŏpĭīs, Ov.

Œnōtrĭă, æ, f., *an ancient name of Italy.* Pōst hās Œnōtrĭă lēntĭs, Claud.

Œnōtrĭŭs, ă, ŭm, *of Œnotria.* Ōmnīsque Œnōtrĭă tēllŭs, Virg. Œnōtrī cŏlŭĕrĕ vĭrī, Id.

œstrŭm, ī, n., *and* ŭs, ī, m., *inspired fury.* Fānātĭcŭs œstrō, Juv. SYN. Fŭrŏr, răbĭēs, īnsānĭă. EPITH. Cæcŭm, præcĕps, vĭŏlēntŭm, răbĭdŭm, laūrĭgĕrŭm, sacrŭm, dīvīnŭm, Apŏllīnĕŭm, Phœbĕŭm, Aŏnĭŭm. V. Furor.

œsўpŭm, ī, n., *the oil or grease of wool, greasy wool.* Œsўpă quĭd rĕdŏlēnt, Ov.

Œtē, ēs, *or* tă, æ, f, *a mountain between Thessaly and Macedon.* Vōcĭbŭs Œtăm, Ov. EPITH. Hērcŭlĕă, nĕmŏrōsă, ārdŭă, āĕrĭă, frŏndōsă, frŏndēns, vĭrēns, gĕlĭdă, Æmŏnĭă, Thēssălă.

ŏfēllă, æ, f., *a little bit of flesh, a steak.* Sūdĕt ŏfēllă, Mart.

Ŏfēllŭs, ī, m., *the name of a man.* Hūnc ĕgŏ pārvŭs Ŏfēllŭm, Hor.

ŏffă, æ, f., *a cake.* Frŭgĭbŭs ōffăm, Virg.

ŏffēndo, dī, *to hit, to offend.* Cœnāntēs ŏffēndĕrĕ, Hor. SYN. Incŭrro, īnvĕnĭo ; īmpīngo, āllīdo ; lædo, nŏcĕo ; pēcco, ērro, fāllŏr.

• ŏffēnsă, æ, *and* sĭo, ōnĭs, f., *a stumble, hurt.* Cic. SYN. Ŏffēnsă, dāmnŭm ; īncŭrsŭs ; cūlpă.

ŏffēnso, ās, *the freq. of* offendo. Cōgĭtŭr ŏffēnsāre ĭgĭtŭr, Lucr.

ŏffēnsŭs, ūs, m., *a meeting, shock.* Pĕr ŏffēnsŭs rāmōrŭm, Stat.

ŏffĕro, ōbtŭlī, *to offer.* Ōbtŭlĭt, ĕt pūră, Virg. SYN. Dō, præbĕo, dēfĕro, ēxhĭbĕo.

ŏffīcīnă, æ, f., *a workhouse.* Vĕnēnĭs ŏffĭcīnă Cōlchĭcīs, (Iamb.) Hor.

ŏffĭcĭo, fēcī, *to oppose.* Ŏffĭcĭŭnt ōbstāntquĕ, Lucr. SYN. Ōbsto, ōbsŭm, īmpĕdĭo ; nŏcĕo. V. Noceo, impedio.

offĭcĭōsŭs, ă, ŭm, *obliging.* Offĭcĭōsāquĕ sēdŭlĭtās, Hor. SYN. Obsĕquĭōsŭs, ŭrbānŭs, cōmĭs, bĕnīgnŭs. V. Comis.

offĭcĭŭm, ĭī, n., *duty, office.* Mīlĭtĭs offĭcĭŭm, Ov. SYN. Mūnŭs, pārtēs; mĭnĭstērĭŭm, obsĕquĭŭm. EPITH. Dĭffĭcĭlĕ, ārdŭŭm, ămīcŭm, suāvĕ, grātŭm, pĭŭm, dūrŭm, īnjūcŭndŭm, mŏlēstŭm.

offulgĕo, ēs, ērĕ, *to shine before.* Offulsĭt cōnātĭbŭs ōmĕn, Sil.

‖ offūsco, ās, *to obscure.* SYN. Infūsco, ŏbscūro, nigro, ŏbŭmbro, ōbnūbĭlo.

Ogȳgēs, ĭs, m., *the founder of Thebes, in Bœotia.*

Ogȳgĭŭs, ă, ŭm, *Ogygian, Theban.* Quālĭs ăb Ogȳgĭō, Ov.

ŏh, *and* ohē, *oh.* Ŏh prŏbŭs, Plaut. Insĕrĭs, ŏhē, Hor. Ŏhē jăm sătĭs ēst, ŏhē lĭbēllĕ, Mart.

Oīclŭs, ī, m., *the name of a Centaur.* Quī quādrŭpētāntĭs Oīclī, Ov.

Oīleūs, ĕŏs, ĕī *or* eī, m., *the king of the Locrians.* Ēt fŭrĭās Ajācĭs Oīleī, Virg.

ŏlĕă, æ, f., *the olive-tree.* Sēd trūncĭs ŏlĕæ, Virg. SYN. Ŏlīvă. EPITH. Vĭrēns, vĭrĭdĭs, vĭrĭdāns, frŏndēns, nŏbĭlĭs, cānēns, ālbēns, pāllĭdă, pāllēns, ūmbrōsă, tĕrĕs, vīvāx, mītĭs, dūlcĭs, pācătă, pācālĭs, pācĭfĭcă, fēlīx, lætă, plăcĭtă pācī, ætērnŭm vĭrēns; Attĭcă, Pāllădĭă, Sĭcȳōnĭă.

ŏlĕāgĭnŭs, *and* nĕŭs, ă, ŭm, *of the olive-tree.* Rādīx ŏlĕāgĭnă trūncō, Virg.

ŏlĕāstĕr, strī, m., *the wild olive-tree.* Sūrgēns ŏlĕāstĕr ĕōdĕm, Virg. EPITH. Agrēstĭs.

Ŏlĕnĭŭs, ă, ŭm, *of Olenus, Achæan.* Nāscĭtŭr Ŏlĕnĭæ, Ov.

Ŏlĕnŏs *or* Ŏlĕnŭs, ĭ, f., *a city of Achaia, where Jupiter was brought up with the milk of the goat Amalthea.* Prŏvŏcăt Idăm, Ŏlĕnŏs, Stat.—2. m., *the son of Jupiter, who was changed into a rock.* Ŏlĕnŭs ēssĕ nŏcēns, Ov.

ŏlĕo, ēs, *to smell of.* Cērvīcăl ŏlēbĭt, Mart. SYN. Hālo, spīro, rĕdŏlĕo; suāvĭtĕr ŏlĕo. Fœtĕo, pūtĕo, grăvĭtĕr ŏlĕo, rĕdŏlĕo, hālo, spīro.

ŏlētŭm, ī, n., *a dunghill.* Fĕcĭt ŏlētŭm, Pers.—2. * *an olive-yard,* Cato.

ŏlĕŭm, ī, n., *oil.* Scīntĭllāre ŏlĕŭm, Virg. SYN. Ŏlīvŭm, Pāllăs. EPITH. Pīnguĕ, lĭquĭdŭm, vĭrĭdĕ, lēntŭm, crāssŭm, ūnctŭm, lēnĕ, dūlcĕ, ŏdōrātŭm, lābēns, Pāllădĭŭm; Sȳrĭŭm, Āssȳrĭŭm. V. Odor.

ŏlfăcĭo, fēcī, *to smell.* Ŏlfăcĭēs dĕŏs, (Phal.) SYN. Ŏdōrŏr.

ŏlfāctŭs, ūs, m., *the sense of smelling.* Ŏlfāctŭm nārĭs ĕt ōrĭs hăbĕt, Aus. SYN. Ŏdōrātŭs, nārēs.

Ŏlĭărŏs *or* ŭs, *and* Ŏlĕărŏs, ĭ, f., *one of the Cyclades.* Ŏlĭărŏn nĭvĕāmquĕ Părŏn, Virg.

ŏlĭdŭs, ă, ŭm, *having a strong smell.* Hīc ŏlĭdăm clāmōsŭs, Mart. SYN. Ŏlēns; grăvĕŏlēns.

ŏlĭm, adv., *long since; hereafter.* Ŏlĭm trūncŭs ĕrăm, Hor. SYN. Quŏndăm, ălĭquāndo.

ŏlĭtŏr, ōrĭs, m., *a gardener.* Ĕrĭt, aŭt ŏlĭtōrĭs ăgĕt, Hor. SYN. Hōrtŭlānŭs. EPITH. Indūstrĭŭs, sēdŭlŭs, īmpĭgĕr, gnāvŭs, sōlērs, paŭpĕr, vĭgĭl, vĭgĭlāns, rūstĭcŭs. V. Agricola.

* ŏlĭtōrĭŭs, ă, ŭm, *of a gardener.* Plin.

ŏlīvă, æ, f., *the olive-tree.* Prætēndĭt ŏlīvæ, Virg.

ŏlīvētŭm, ĭ, n., *a grove of olives.* Spārgĕnt ŏlīvētĭs ŏdŏrĕm, Hor.

ŏlīvĭfĕr, ră, rŭm, *bearing olives.* Bœtĭs ŏlīvĭfĕră, Mart.

ŏlīvŭm, ĭ, n., *oil of olives.* Ūsŭs ŏlīvī, Virg. V. Oleum, olea.

ŏllă, æ, f., *a pot.* Ŏllă lĕgĭt, Cat. SYN. Ăhēnŭm, lĕbēs. EPITH. Fīctĭlĭs, frăgĭlĭs, fērvēns. V. Ahenum.

ŏllārĭs, ĕ, *of a pot.* Cōllŏcāntŭr ŏllārēs, (Scaz.) Mart.

ŏlŏr, ōrĭs, m., *a swan.* Ānsĕr ŏlōrēs, Virg. SYN. Cȳcnŭs. V. Cycnus.

ŏlōrīnŭs, ă, ŭm, *of a swan.* Cūjŭs ŏlōrīnæ, Virg. SYN. Cȳcnĕŭs.

ŏlŭs, ĕrĭs, n., *vegetables.* Ŏlŭs ōmnĕ pătēllā, Hor. EPITH. Agrēstĕ, vīlĕ, rĭgĭdŭm, săpĭdŭm, vĭrĭdĕ, vĭrēns, lætŭm, ŏdōrātŭm, ŏpācŭm, mōllĕ.

ŏlŭscŭlă, ōrŭm, n. pl., *small herbs.* Pōnēntŭr ŏlŭscŭlă lārdō, Hor.

Ŏlȳmpĭă, ōrŭm, n. pl., *the Olympic games.* Cĕlĕbrābăt Ŏlȳmpĭă lūdĭs, Stat.

Ŏlȳmpĭă, æ, f., *a place in Elis where the Olympic games were celebrated.* Ăd lūdōs Ŏlȳmpĭæ, Plaut.

Ŏlȳmpĭăcŭs, ĭcŭs, *and* ĭŭs, ă, ŭm. Seŭ quĭs Ŏlȳmpĭăcæ, Virg. Pūlvĕrem Ŏlȳmpĭcŭm, (Asclep.) Hor. Sērtŭm cŏrōnæ præfĕrēns Ŏlȳmpĭæ, Aus.

Ŏlўɪɒpĭăs, ădĭs, f., *the space of five years.* Vĭdĭt Ŏlўmpĭădăs, Mart. Syn. Lŭs-trŭm, quīnquēnnĭŭm.

Ŏlўmpŭs, ī, m., *a mountain of Greece ; sometimes heaven itself.* Ŏmnĭpŏtēntĭs Ŏlўmpī, Virg. Epith. Altŭs, sūmmŭs, cēlsŭs, æthĕrĕŭs, sŭblīmĭs, stēllĭgĕr, ārdŭŭs, prūīnōsŭs ; āstrīs, cœlō vīcīnŭs. V. Cœlum.

Ŏlўnthŭs, ī, f., *a town of Thrace.* Emptŏr Ŏlўnthī, Juv.

ŏmāsŭm, ī, n., *the fat part of the belly, tripe.* Tēntŭs ŏmāsō, Hor. Syn. Ab-dōmēn.

ŏmēn, ĭnĭs, n., *a token of good or bad fortune.* Ŏmĭnĭbŭs, sēd rēgnă, Virg. Syn. Aūgŭrĭŭm, aūspĭcĭŭm, sīgnŭm. Epith. Fēlīx, faūstŭm, lœtŭm, bŏnŭm, prō-spĕrŭnɪ, ŏptātŭm, dēxtrŭm, cērtŭm, īncērtŭm, īnfēlīx, īnfaūstŭm, mălŭm, sīnīstrŭm, ādvērsŭm, trīstĕ, mĭsĕrāndŭm, fūnēstŭm.

ŏmēntŭm, ī, n., *the membrane that envelopes the intestines, tripe.* Tūnĭcum ŏmēntă līquēscŭnt, Pers.

ŏmĭnātŏr, ōrĭs, m., *an augur.* Ŏmēn ŏmĭnātŏr, (Iamb.) Plaut.

ŏmĭnŏr, ārĭs, *to presage.* Măle ŏmĭnātĭs, Hor. Syn. Aūgŭro, cōnjĭcĭo. V. Auspicor.

ŏmīssŭs, ă, ŭm, *the pass. partic.* of omitto. Rēbŭs ŏmīssĭs, Hor.

ŏmītto, īsī, īssŭm, *to pass over.* In tēmpŭs ŏmīttăt, Hor. Syn. Mītto, prætēr-mītto, prætĕrĕo, līnquo, rĕlīnquo, sŭpērsĕdĕo.

ŏmnĭfĕr, ră, rŭm, *producing all things.* Ŏmnĭfĕrōs cōllō, Ov.

ŏmnĭgĕnŭs, ă, ŭm, *of all kinds.* Ŏmnĭgĕnōs gīgnŭnt, Lucr.

ŏmnĭmŏdō, *and* dīs, adv., *in all ways.* Ŏmnĭmŏdo ēxpērtŭs, Lucr. Nēc tămĕn ŏmnĭmŏdīs, Id.

ŏmnīnō, adv., *quite.* Nōn ēquĭdem ŏmnīnō, Virg. Syn. Prōrsŭs, pĕnĭtŭs, plānē.

ŏmnĭpărēns, ntĭs, *bringing forth all things.* Ŏmnĭpărēntĭs ălŭmnŭm, Virg

ŏmnĭpŏtēns, ntĭs, *almighty.* Aūdīt ŏmnĭpŏtēns, Virg.

ŏmnĭs, ĕ, *all.* Ŏmnĭs ămŏr, Tĭb. Syn. Quīsquĕ, cūnctŭs, tōtŭs.

ŏmnĭtŭēns, ēntĭs, *that sees all things.* Quĭbŭs ŏmnĭtŭēntĕs, Lucr.

ŏmnĭvŏlŭs, ă, ŭm, *covetous of all things.* Nōscēns ŏmnĭvŏlī, Cat.

Ŏmphălē, ēs, *and* lă, æ, f., *a queen of Lydia, loved by Hercules.* Ŏmphăle ĕt īn tāntŭm, Prop. Epith. Mæŏnĭă, Lўdĭă, fōrmōsă.

* ŏmphălŏs, *or* lŭs, ī, m., *the navel, the middle.* Sēcērnĭtŭr ŏmphălŏs īdĕm, Aus.

ŏnăgĕr, *or* agrŭs, agrī, m., *a wild ass.* Pūlchĕr ădēst ŏnăgĕr, Mart. Agĭtăbĭs ŏnăgrōs, Virg. Epith. Sўlvēstrĭs, tĭmĭdŭs. V. Asinus.

Ŏnchēstŭs, ă, ŭm, *of Onchestus.* Mĕgărĕŭs Ŏnchēstĭŭs, Ov.

Ŏnchēstŭs, ī, f., *a city of Bœotia.—2.* m., *the name of a man.* Ŏnchēstī Nēptūnĭă prōlēs, Stat.

ŏnĕrārĭŭs, ă, ŭm, *serving for carriage.* E nāvi ēxĕŭntem ŏnĕrārĭă, Plaut.

ŏnĕro, ās, *to load.* Gērmānă, mălĭs ŏnĕrās, Virg. Syn. Grăvo, prĕmo.

ŏnĕrōsŭs, ă, ŭm, *weighty.* Est ŏnĕrōsĭŏr īgnĕ, Ov. Syn. Pŏndĕrōsŭs, grăvĭs, māgnī pōndĕrĭs.

ŏnocrŏtălŭs, ī, m., *a pelican.* Gūttŭr ŏnŏcrŏtălī, Mart.

ŏnŭs, ĕrĭs, n., *a burden.* Cēdēntĕs ŏnĕrī rāmŏs, Mart. Syn. Pŏndŭs, mōlēs, sārcĭnă, grăvĭtăs, grăvāmĕn. Epith. Grăvĕ, dūrŭm, mŏlēstŭm, īngēns, grāndĕ, īntŏlĕrābĭlĕ, īnīquŭm, văstŭm, sŏlīdŭm, īmmānĕ, prēmēns, ēxĭgŭŭm. V. Onero.

ŏnŭstŭs, ă, ŭm, *loaded.* Ŏrĭēntĭs ŏnŭstŭm, Virg. Syn. Ŏnĕrātŭs, grăvātŭs, grăvĭs.

Ŏnўtēs, ĭs, m., *the name of a warrior.* Mīttĭs Ŏnўtĕm, Virg.

ŏnўx, ўchĭs, m., *a precious stone.* Lūcĕt ŏnўx, Mart. Epith. Cāndĭdŭs, lævĭs, mĭcāns, lūbrĭcŭs, crāssŭs, cāndĭcāns, ālbēns, nĭtĭdŭs, rădĭāns, fūlgĭdŭs, ɪnȳrrhĕŭs. V. Gemma.

ŏpāco, ās, *to shadow.* Dīvĕs ŏpācăt, Virg. Syn. Ŏbumbro, ŏbscūro, tĕgo, cōn-tĕgo, ŏpĕrĭo.

ŏpācŭs, ă, ŭm, *dusky, thick.* Fĕrĭmūr pĕr ŏpācă, Virg. Syn. Umbrōsŭs, ŏb-scūrŭs, tēctŭs, ŏpērtŭs, dēnsŭs. V. Obscurus.

ŏpĕ, *the abl. of* ops. Syn. Aūxĭlĭō, ŏpĕrā, sŭbsĭdĭō. V. Ops.

ŏpĕră, *and* ŏpēllă, æ, f., *labour.* Impŏrtēs ŏpĕrā, Hor. Syn. Ŏpŭs, lăbŏr, cūră, stŭdĭum. V. Labor.

ŏpĕrĭo, rĭs, rŭī, *to cover.* Nŏx ŏpĕrĭt, Virg.   SYN. Tĕgo, cŏntĕgo, ŏbūmbro, ŏpāco.

ŏpĕrŏr, ārĭs, *to work.* Mātūtīnīs ŏpĕrāntŭr, Juv.   SYN. Lăbŏro.   V. Laboro.

ŏpĕrōsŭs, ă, ŭm, *difficult.* Mōlēs ŏpĕrōsă lăbōrĕt, Ov.   SYN. Diffĭcĭlĭs.

ŏpĕrtŭs. ă. ŭm. *the pass. partic. of* operio.   Dūxĭt ŏpĕrtă, Prop.

ŏpes, ŭm, *f.* pl., *riches, power.* Hūmānīs ŏpĭbŭs, Virg.   SYN. Bŏnă, ŏpŭlentĭă, fōrtūnæ; sŭbsĭdĭŭm, aŭxĭlĭŭm.   V. Divitiæ.

Ŏphĭăs, ădĭs, f., *the daughter of Ophius, Combe.*   Ŏphĭăs effūgĭt, Ov.

Ŏphīon, ōnĭs, m., *a giant dethroned by Saturn; a centaur.*   Rāmōs exūtŭs Ŏphīon, Claud.

Ŏphīŏnĭdēs, æ, m., *the son of the centaur Ophion, Amycus.*   Prīmŭs Ŏphīŏnĭdēs, Ov.

ŏphītēs, æ, m., *a sort of green-spotted talc, of which kettles were made.*   Tĕnŭī călent ŏphītæ, Mart.

Ŏphĭūsă, æ, f., *the ancient name of Rhodes and Cyprus.*

Ŏphĭūsĭŭs, ă, ŭm, *of Ophiusa.*   Ūrbēs Ŏphĭūsĭăque ārvă părăbăt, Ov.

Ŏpĭcŭs, ă, ŭm, *of the Opici, a people of Italy, near the Volscians; barbarous, filthy.*   Ŏpĭcæ cāstĭgăt ămīcæ, Juv.

ŏpĭfĕr, ĕră, ĕrŭm, *helping.*   Ĭn sōmnīs ŏpĭfĕr, Ov.   SYN. Adjŭtŏr, aŭxĭlĭătŏr.

ŏpĭfex, ĭcĭs, m., *a workman.*   Est ŏpĭfex sōlŭs, Hor.   V. Artifex.

Ŏpĭlĭo, *or* Ūpĭlĭo, ōnĭs, m., *the name of a shepherd.*   Vēnĭt et Ŏpĭlĭo, Virg.

ŏpīmē, adv., *abundantly.*   Plaut.

ŏpīmo, ās, *to fatten.*   Mārĭs æstŭs ŏpīmăt, Aus.

ŏpīmŭs, ă, ŭm, *fat, abundant.*   Laŭdābŏr ŏpīmīs, Virg.   SYN. Pĭnguĭs, ŏbēsŭs, ŏpŭlentŭs, ăbūndāns, dīvēs.

ŏpīnĭo, ōnĭs, f., *and* nātŭs, ūs, m., *opinion.*   Quĭd ŏpīnĭŏ vūlgī, Aus.   Prŏptĕr ŏpīnātŭs ănĭmī, Lucr.   SYN. Sententĭă, cōnsĭlĭŭm, mēns, ănĭmŭs.   EPITH. Certă, ĭncertă, săpĭens, stūltă, ūtĭlĭs, pernĭcĭōsă, prūdens, ĭmprūdens, nŏvă, rĕcens.

ŏpīnŏr, ārĭs, *to think.*   Ūltŭs, ŏpīnŏr, Hor.   SYN. Pŭto, exīstĭmo, ārbĭtrŏr, jūdĭco, sentĭo, censĕo, rĕŏr, aŭtŭmo.

ŏpīnŭs, ă, ŭm, *thought of.*   Occūltă nĕc ŏpīnŭm, Ov.

ŏpĭpărŭs, ă, ŭm, *sumptuous.*   Ŏpĭpărĭsque ŏpsōnĭīs, (Iamb.) Pl.   SYN. Ŏpŭlentŭs, măgnĭfĭcŭs, laŭtŭs, cŏpĭōsŭs.

Ŏpĭs, ĭs, f., *a nymph, the companion of Diana.*   Ĭn sēdĭbŭs Ŏpĭm, Virg.

ŏpĭtŭlŏr, ārĭs, *to help.*   Ter.   SYN. Sŭccŭrro, sŭbvĕnĭo, aŭxĭlĭŏr, jŭvo, ădjŭvo, sŭblĕvo, ādsŭm.   V. Auxilior.

ŏpŏbālsămŭm, ī, n., *balsam, balm.*   Spīrănt ŏpŏbālsămă cōllō, Juv.

ŏpŏrtĕt, tŭĭt, *it is requisite.*   Pāscĕre ŏpŏrtĕt ŏvēs, Virg.   SYN. Nĕcesse est, ŏpŭs est, cōnvĕnĭt, æquum est, pār est.

ŏppēdo, ĭs, *to treat contemptuously.*   Jūdæīs ŏppēdĕrĕ, Hor.   V. Irrideo.

ŏppĕrĭŏr, īrĭs, *to expect.*   Nĕc tārdum ŏppĕrĭŏr, Hor.   SYN. Expēcto, præstŏlŏr, mănĕo.

ŏppēto, ĭs, ĭī, *to die.*   Cōntĭgĭt ŏppĕtĕre, Virg.   SYN. Mŏrĭŏr.   V. Morior.

Ŏppĭdĭŭs, ĭī, m., *the name of a man.*   Sērvĭŭs Ŏppĭdĭŭs, Hor.

ŏppĭdŭlŭm, ī, n., *the dimin. of* oppidum.   Mānsūri ŏppĭdŭlō, Hor.

ŏppĭdŭm, ī, n., *a town.*   Ŏppĭdă cœpērūnt, Hor.   SYN. Vīcŭs, pāgŭs.   V. Civitas, urbs.

ŏppīgnĕro, ās, *to pawn.*   Ŏppĭgnĕrāvīt Claŭdīī, (Scaz.) Mart.

|| ŏppīlo, ās, *to stop up.*   Advērsīs ŏppīlāre ōstĭă cōntrā, Lucr.

ŏpplĕo, ēs, *to fill up.*   Vōcĭbŭs ŏpplent, Lucr.

ŏppōno, pŏsŭī, pŏsĭtŭm, *to oppose.*   Ŏppōnĭtĕ pēctŏră rēbŭs, Hor.   SYN. Objĭcĭo, objēcto, ŏbtrūdo; exprobro.

ŏppōrtūnĭtās, ātĭs, f., *convenience.*   Nōn fŭĕrĭt ŏppōrtūnĭtās, Aus.   SYN. Cōmmŏdĭtās, ŏccāsĭo, tempŭs, ūtĭlĭtās.   V. Occasio.

ŏppōrtūnŭs, ă, ŭm, *commodious.*   Dŏmŭs ŏppōrtūnă vŏlūcrŭm, Virg.   SYN. Cōmmŏdŭs, āccōmmŏdŭs, tempēstīvŭs, ĭdōnĕŭs, āptŭs, ūtĭlĭs.

ŏppŏsĭtŭs, ūs, m., *an opposing.*   Et ŏppŏsĭtū membrōrŭm, Sil.

ŏppŏsĭtŭs, ă, ŭm, *the pass partic. of* oppono.   Et mĭsĕr ŏppŏsĭtīs, Virg.

ŏppressŭs, ūs, m., *an oppressing.*   Ŏppressū vălĭdō, Lucr.

ŏpprĭmo, prĕssī, ĕssŭm, *to oppress.* Ŏpprĭmĕrĕt, mĕtŭĕbăt, Hor. Syn. Prĕmo, ŏbrŭo, ŏnĕro; sŭbĭgo, cōnfĭcĭo; ōccīdo.

ŏpprŏbrĭŭm, ī, n., *shame.* Nēc fŭĭt ŏpprŏbrĭŏ, Ov. Fŭgĭēns ŏpprŏbrĭă cūlpæ, Hor. Syn. Probrŭm, dēdĕcŭs, cōnvĭcĭŭm, scŏmmă, mălĕdīctŭm, ĭnjūrĭă, ĭnfāmĭă, ĭgnōmĭnĭă. Epith. Infāmĕ, īngēns, ĭnīquŭm, fœdŭm, tūrpĕ; pŭdēndŭm. V. Infamia, convicium.

ŏppūgno, ās, *to attack.* Fēssam ŏppūgnārĕ cărīnăm, Ov. Syn. Impūgno, īnvādo, lăcēsso; cōntra ārmă fĕro. V. Obsideo.

Ōps, Ŏpĭs, f., *the wife of Saturn.* Ex Ŏpĕ Jūnōnĕm, Ov. Syn. Cўbĕlē, Rhĕă, Tĕllūs. V. Cybele.

ōps, (*obsol. in the nom.*) ŏpĭs, ŏpĕm, ŏpĕ, f., *power, means, resources, help.* Nōn ŏpĭs ēst nŏstræ, Virg. Dīxĭt ŏpēmquĕ dĕī, Id. Hīnc ŏpĕ bārbărĭcā, Id. Syn. Vīs, făcūltās; ŏpĕră, aūxĭlĭŭm, sŭbsĭdĭŭm; ŏpēs, vīrēs. ŏpsōnĭŭm. V. Obsonium.

ŏptābĭlĭs, ĕ, *to be wished.* Ecce ŏptābĭlĕ tēmpŭs, Ov. Syn. Ŏptāndŭs.

ŏptātō, adv., *according to the wish.* Ac vĕlŭt ŏptātō, Virg.

ŏptātŭs, ă, ŭm, *the pass. partic. of* opto. Ŏptātĭs ĕpŭlĭs, (Choriamb.) Hor.

*ŏptĭmātēs, ŭm, m. pl., *men of the highest rank.* Cic. Syn. Măgnātēs, prīmī, prīmōrēs, prŏcĕrēs, dўnāstæ, nōbĭlĭtās. V. Proceres.

ŏptĭmŭs, ă, ŭm, *the superl. of* bonus. Dēstĭnăt ŏptĭmŭs hic, Juv. Syn. Faūstīssĭmŭs, īntĕgērrĭmŭs, lēctīssĭmŭs. V. Bonus.

ŏptĭo, ōnĭs, f., *choice.* Cōncēdĭtŭr ŏptĭŏ nōbĭs, Aus. Syn. Dēlēctŭs, ēlēctŭs.

ŏptĭvŭs, ă, ŭm, *adopted.* Ŏptĭvŏ cōgnōmĭnĕ crēscĭt, Hor.

ŏpto, ās, *to choose.* Ŏptārēnt tĭbi, (Phal.) Mart. Syn. Ĕxŏpto, pĕrŏpto, dēsīdĕro, cŭpĭo, ārdĕo. V. Desidero.

ŏpŭlēntĭă, æ, f., *opulence.* Trŏjæve ŏpŭlēntĭă deĕrĭt, Virg. V. Divitiæ.

ŏpŭlēnto, ās, *to make rich.* Băccīs ŏpŭlēntĕt ŏlīvæ, Hor. V. Dito.

ŏpŭlēntŭs, ă, ŭm, *wealthy.* Dōnīs ŏpŭlēntŭm, Virg. Syn. Dīvĕs, ŏpĭbŭs ăbūndāns; dīvĕs ŏpŭm. V. Dives.

Ŏpūntĭŭs, ă, ŭm, *of Opus.* Dīcăt Ŏpūntĭæ Frātēr Mĕgīllæ, Hor.

Ŏpūs, ūntĭs, f., *the capital city of the Locrians.* Pātrŏclŭs Ŏpūntă, Ov

ŏpŭs (est), *there is need of.* Nūnc ănĭmīs ŏpŭs, Virg. Syn. Ĕgĕo, ĭndĭgĕo, nĕcēsse ēst.

ŏpŭs, ĕrĭs, n., *a work, labour.* Instāns ŏpĕrī, Virg. Syn. Fāctŭm; ŏpĕră, lăbŏr, stŭdĭŭm; dĭffĭcūltās, nĕgŏtĭŭm. Epith. Dūrŭm, māgnŭm, īngēns, dĭffĭcĭlĕ, ārdŭŭm, mŏlēstŭm, pĕrīcŭlōsŭm; ĭllūstrĕ, mĕmŏrāndŭm, mĕmŏrābĭlĕ, clārŭm, īnsīgnĕ, nōbĭlĕ, mīrābĭlĕ, ætērnŭm, sŭpērstĕs, vīctūrŭm, ĭmmŏrtālĕ; īngĕnĭōsŭm, pērfēctŭm, fabrīlĕ, scūlptĭlĕ, cœlātŭm, mārmŏrĕŭm.

ŏpūscŭlŭm, ī, n., *the dim. of* opus. Ingrātŭs ŏpūscŭlă lēctŏr, Hor.

ōră, æ, f., *a coast, edge, brim.* Ingēntēs ōrās, Virg. Syn. Fīnĭs, ēxtrēmŭm, līmĕs, mārgo; līttŭs, rīpă; rĕgĭo, plăgă, lŏcŭs, tērră, tĕllūs. Epith. Ēxtrēmă, ūltĭmă, rĕmōtă.

ōrācŭlŭm, *or* clŭm, ī, n., *an oracle.* Nĕfās ōrācŭlă suādēnt, Ov. Epith. Dīvīnŭm, sacrŭm, sānctŭm, cērtŭm, vērĭdĭcŭm, fătĭdĭcŭm, præscĭŭm, prænūncĭŭm, vērāx, præsāgŭm, fāllāx, āmbĭgŭŭm, vănŭm, āncēps, īncērtŭm, fēlīx, īnfēlīx, lætŭm, trīstĕ, Phœbĕŭm, Ăpōllĭnĕŭm, Dēlphĭcŭm, Pўthĭcŭm.

ōrātĭo, ōnĭs, f., *language, a speech, prayer.* Vōtīs ōrātĭŏ præstăt, Sil. Syn. Sērmo, cōncĭo, prĕcēs, vōtŭm. V. Preces, sermo.

ōrātŏr, ōrĭs, m., *an orator, ambassador.* Cēntum ōrātōrēs, Virg. Syn. Rhētŏr; lēgātŭs. Epith. Elŏquēns, dīsērtŭs, pŏtēns, suāvĭs, făcūndŭs, sūbtĭlĭs, dōctŭs, īngĕnĭōsŭs, săcĕr, vĕhĕmēns, māgnŭs, pĕrītŭs. V. Eloquens.

ōrbātŏr, ōrĭs, m., *he who deprives one of any possession.* Nōstrīque ōrbātŏr Achīllēs, Ov.

ōrbātŭs, ă, ŭm, *the pass. partic. of* orbo. Lāctēntĕ ōrbātă lĕænă, Ov.

Ōrbĭlĭŭs, ĭī, m., *the preceptor of Horace.* Ōrbĭlĭŭm dīctārĕ, Hor.

ōrbĭs, ĭs, m., *and* bĭcŭlŭs, ī, m., *a circle.* Ōrbĭbŭs, ēt tăm, Juv. Syn. Cīrcŭlŭs, gўrŭs, glŏbŭs. Epith. Rŏtūndŭs, glŏbōsŭs, īnflēxŭs, sĭnŭōsŭs. V. Gyrus.

ōrbĭtă, æ, f., *the track of a wheel.* Ōrbĭtă clīvō, Virg. Syn. Rŏtæ sīgnă, vēstīgĭă, ĭtĕr; rŏtæ cūrvātūră, cūrvāmĕn, ōrbĭs. Epith. Trītă; vŏlūbĭlĭs, cūrvă. V. Rota.

ŏrbĭtās, ātĭs, f., *the being deprived of children or parents.* Ŏrbĭtās ōmnī, Stat. Epith. Trīstĭs, œgrā, ăcĕrbă.

ŏrbo, ās, *to deprive, bereave.* Ŏrbātūră pătrēs, Ov.

ŏrbŭs, ă, ŭm, *deprived of.* Fūnĕrăque ŏrbă, Stat. Syn. Ŏrbātŭs, prīvātŭs; ŏrphănŭs.

ŏrcă, œ, f., *a jar.* Bўzăntĭă pūtrŭĭt ŏrcă, Her.

Ŏrchămŭs, ī, m., *a king of Assyria, who caused his daughter Leucothoe to be buried alive.* Pătĕr Ŏrchămŭs, īsquĕ, Ov.

ŏrchăs, ădĭs, f., *a kind of olive.* Ŏrchădĕs ĕt rādĭī, Virg.

ŏrchēstră, œ, f., *a space between the stage and common seats.* Ŏrchēstram ĕt pŏpŭlŭm, Juv.

Ŏrchŏmĕnŏs, *or* ŭs, ī, f., *a city of Arcadia.* Ūsquĕ sŭb Ŏrchŏmĕnŏn, Ov

Ŏrcīnĭānŭs, ă, ŭm, *of hell.* Ŏrcīnĭānă quī fĕrūntŭr īn spōndā, Mart.

Ŏrcŭs, ī, m., *hell.* Nĕc sătēllĕs Ŏrcī, Hor. Nīl mĭsĕrāntĭs Ŏrcī, Id. Syn. Dīs, Plūtō; īnfĕrnŭs.

ōrdĭno, ās, *to settle.* Ŏrdĭnăt īnvērsīs, Ov. Syn. Dīspōno, cōmpōno, dīgĕro.

ōrdĭŏr, īrĭs, sŭs *and* dītŭs, *to begin.* Ŏrdītŭr ăb ŏvō, Hor. Hăbĭlēs ŏrdītă, nŏvūmquĕ, Mart. Syn. Ēxŏrdĭŏr, īnchŏo, ăggrĕdĭŏr, īncĭpĭo. V. Incipio.

ōrdĭŭm, iī, n., *the beginning.* In ŏrdĭă prīmă, Lucr. V. Primordium.

ōrdo, ĭnĭs, m., *order.* Indūlge ŏrdĭnĭbŭs, Virg. Syn. Sĕrĭēs, rătĭo. Epith. Immūtābĭlĭs, lōngŭs, ŏptĭmŭs, fīxŭs, cōmpŏsĭtŭs, rēctŭs, pūlchĕr, āptŭs, grātŭs.

Ŏrĕăs, ădĭs, f., Ŏrĕădĕs, ŭm, f. pl., *nymphs of the mountains.* Cōmpēllăt Ŏrĕădă dīctīs, Ov. Glŏmĕrāntŭr Ŏrĕădĕs; īllă, Virg. Epith. Agrēstĕs, fōrmōsæ, vĕnūstœ, lĕvĕs, sălĭēntĕs. V. Nymphœ.

Ŏrĕsītrŏphŏs, ī, m., *the name of a dog.* Ov.

Ŏrēstĕs, ĭs, m., *the son of Agamemnon and Clytemnæstra. He killed his mother, to revenge the death of his father.* Agĭtātŭs Ŏrēstĕs, Virg. Syn. Agămēmnŏnĭdĕs. Epith. Scĕlĕrātŭs, fŭrĭōsŭs, mātrīcīdă, īnsānŭs, dēmēns, mĭsĕr, fĕrōx, fĕrŭs, crūdēlĭs, sævŭs, īmprŏbŭs, bārbărŭs, Argīvŭs, Agămēmnŏnĭŭs, fīdŭs, ămīcŭs.

Ŏrēstĕŭs, ă, ŭm, *of Orestes.* Sācrăquc Ŏrēstĕæ gĕmĭtŭ, Ov.

ŏrēxĭs, ĭs, f., *appetite.* Făctūrŭs ŏrēxĭm, Juv.

ōrgănă, ōrŭm, n. pl., *musical instruments.* Ŏrgănă sēmpĕr, Juv. Epith. Sŏnōră, ārgūtă, cănōră, lætă, rĕsŏnāntĭă, suāvĭă, blāndă, căvă, dūlcĭă, raŭcă, īnflātă.

ōrgănĭcŭs, ă, ŭm, *harmonious, musical.* Nōmĕn ăb ŏrgănĭcō, Lucr.—2. ī, m., *a musician.* Mūltă, mŏdo ŏrgănĭcī, Id.

ōrgĭă, ōrŭm, n. pl., *festivals of Bacchus.* Ŏrgĭă cĭstīs, Cat. Syn. Bācchānālĭă. Epith. Mălēsānă, fŭrĭōsă, īnsānă, fœmĭnĕă, mŭlĭebrĭă, Bācchœă, Bācchĭcă, nŏctūrnă, ŏbscūră, Thēbānă. V. Bacchanalia.

Ŏrībăsŭs, ī, m., *the name of a dog.* Ēt Ŏrībăsŭs, Arcădĕs ōmnēs, Ov.

ŏrĭchālcŭm, ī, n., *brass.* Albōque ŏrĭchālcō, Virg. Spārsa ŏrĭchālcă, Stat. Epith. Nĭtĭdŭm, nĭtēns, rĕnīdēns, splēndĭdŭm, fūlvŭm, rŭtĭlŭm, cŏrūscŭm, mĭcāns, dūrŭm, grăvĕ, rĭgĭdŭm.

Ŏrĭcĭŭs, ă, ŭm, *of Oricum.* Aŭt Ŏrĭcĭă tĕrĕbīnthŏ, Virg.

Ŏrĭcŏs, *or* ŭs, ī, f., *and* ŭm, ī, n., *a city of Epirus.* Illĕ nŏtĭs āctŭs ăd Ŏrĭcŭm, Hor.

Ŏrĭēns, ntĭs, m., *the east.* Spŏlĭīs Ŏrĭēntĭs ŏnŭstŭm, Virg.—2. Ŏrĭēns sōl, *the rising sun.* Syn. Sōl, Phœbŭs, Tītān rĕnāscēns, rĕdīvīvŭs. Epith. Rŏsĕŭs, rŭtĭlŭs, nĭtĭdŭs, pūrpŭrĕŭs, clārŭs, sĕrēnŭs. V. Mane, sol.

ŏrĭgo, ĭnĭs, f., *origin.* Trōjānŭs ŏrĭgĭnĕ Cæsăr, Virg. Ŏrtŭs, ēxŏrdĭŭm, prīmōrdĭŭm, ĭnĭtĭŭm, prīncĭpĭŭm, stīrps, sēmĕn, gĕnĕrĭs cūnābŭlă; caŭsă, aŭctŏr, căpŭt, scătūrīgo, fōns. Epith. Prīmă, bŏnă, mălă, vĕtŭs, cērtă, īncērtă, lătēns, cĕlĕbrĭs. V. Causa, genus, fons.

Ŏrīōn, ŏnĭs, m., *a giant sprung from the urine of Jupiter, Neptune, and Mercury.* Strīctūmquc Ŏrīōnĭs ēnsĕm, Ov. Inclīnăt Ŏrīōn, Stat. Cīrcŭmspĭcĭt Ŏrīōnă, Virg. Epith. Ēnsĭfĕr; nūbĭlŭs, trīstĭs, ŏbscūrŭs, mădĭdŭs, hŭmĭdŭs, īmbrĭfĕr, hūmēns, plŭvĭŭs, nīmbōsŭs, ūdŭs, ăquōsŭs, sævŭs, Nēptūnĭŭs, atrōx.

ŏrĭŏr, ĕrĭs, ŏrīrī, *to arise, to be born.* Quæque ŏrītūrquĕ cădĭtquĕ, Ov. Syn. Ēxŏrĭŏr, nāscŏr, ēnāscŏr, ŏbŏrĭŏr, prōcēdo; prōdĕo, ēxsūrgo, ēmāno, ēfflŭo, ēxĕo, prōmāno, dīmāno, dērīvŏr, prŏfīcīscŏr. V. Nascor.

Ŏrīthyĭă, (*quadrisyll.*) æ, f., *the daughter of Erechtheus, loved by Boreas.* Dĕcŭs dĕdĭt Ŏrīthyĭă, Virg. Epith. Răptă, Āttĭs, Āttĭcă, Ērĕchthĭs.

ŏrĭūndŭs, ă, ŭm, sprung from. Stīrpe ŏrĭūndī, Lucr. Syn. Ŏrtŭs, gĕnĭtŭs, sătŭs, nātŭs.

Ŏrĭŭs, or ŏs, ī, m., the name of one of the Lapithæ. Brŏtĕān ĕt Ŏrīŏn; Ŏrīō, Ov.

Ŏrmĕnĭs, ĭdĭs, f., the daughter of Ormenius, Astydamia. Ŏrmĕnĭ nȳmphă, tŭŏs, Ov.

ōrnāmēntŭm, ī, n., an ornament. Ŏrnāmēntă părŭm, Hor. Syn. Ŏrnātŭs cūltŭs.

ōrnātrīx, īcĭs, f., a waiting-maid. Tūtă sĭt ōrnātrīx, Ov.

ōrnātŭs, ūs, m., ornament. Ŏrnātŭs dīvēs, Mart. Syn. Ŏrnāmēntŭm, cūltŭs, dĕcŭs, dĕcŏr, dīgnĭtās, hŏnŏr, īnsīgnĕ, lūmĕn, splēndŏr. Epith. Măgnĭfĭcŭs, ēxĭmĭŭs, īnsīgnĭs, rēgĭŭs, dĕcōrŭs, hŏnēstŭs, cōnvĕnĭēns, cōnspĭcŭŭs, īllūstrĭs, nĭtēns, splēndĭdŭs, prĕtĭōsŭs, sŭpērbŭs, āmbĭtĭōsŭs, nōbĭlĭs, īnsŏlĭtŭs, fēstŭs, trĭūmphālĭs, vānŭs, īnānĭs. V. Cultus.

ōrnātŭs, ă, ŭm, the pass. partic. of orno. Crīnēs ōrnātŭs ămārō, Virg. Syn. Splēndĭdŭs, nĭtĭdŭs, nĭtēns, mĭcāns. V. Orno.

Ŏrnēŭs, ī, m., the name of a Centaur. Fūgĭt ĕt Ŏrnēŭs, Ov.

Ŏrnītŭs, or ȳtŭs, ī, m., the name of a warrior. Prŏcŭl Ŏrnĭtŭs ārmīs, Virg.

ōrno, ās, to adorn. Părĭbūsque ōrnāvĕrăt ārmīs, Virg. Syn. Ădōrno, ēxōrno, dĕcŏro, hŏnēsto, ēxpŏlĭo, lŏcuplēto, īnstrŭo, dīstīnguo, cōmo, ēxcŏlo. V. Fuco, gemma, monile.

ōrnŭs, ī, f., the wild ash. Mōntĭbŭs ōrnŭm, Virg. Epith. Aĕrĭă, ārdŭă, vĭrēns, frŏndēns, stĕrĭlĭs, mōntānă, sŭblīmĭs, ēxcēlsă, dūră, cōmāns.

ōro, ās, to entreat. Tālĭbŭs ōrābăt, Virg. Syn. Rŏgo, prĕcŏr, ōbsecro, ōbtēstŏr, dēprĕcŏr, īnvŏco. V. Adoro, precor.

Ŏrōdēs, æ, m., the name of a warrior. Jăcĕt āltŭs Ŏrōdēs, Virg.

Ŏrōntēs, ĭs, m., a river in Scythia. Dēflūxĭt Ŏrōntēs, Juv. Epith. Cĕlĕr, præcēps, cĭtŭs, cōncĭtŭs, răpĭdŭs, Băbȳlōnĭŭs, Sȳrĭŭs, Eŏŭs.

|| ŏrphănŭs, ī, m., an orphan. Syn. Ŏrbŭs.

ōrphăs, ădĭs, f., a kind of fish. Ŏrphăs ĕt hērbōsā, Colum.

Orpheŭs, ĕŏs, ĕī, or eī, m., the son of Apollo, a famous musician. Īnfĕrĭās Ŏrpheī mīttĭt, Virg. Epith. Thrācĭŭs, Thrēĭcĭŭs, Ŏdrȳsĭŭs, Ŏthrȳsĭŭs, Œagrĭŭs, Rhŏdŏpēĭŭs, Īsmărĭŭs, Bīstŏnĭŭs; cănōrŭs, īnsīgnĭs, cĕlĕbrĭs, dōctŭs, cĭthārœdŭs, dūlcĭsŏnŭs, Aŏnĭŭs, fācūndŭs, vōcālĭs, blāndŭs, pŏtēns, săcĕr.

Ŏrpheŭs, ă, ŭm, of Orpheus. Cērbĕrŭs Ŏrphēō, Lucan. Syn. Thrēĭcĭŭs, Ŏdrȳsĭŭs.

Ŏrphnē, ēs, f., the mother of Ascalaphus. Quōndām dīcĭtŭr Ŏrphnē, Ov.

ōrsă, ōrŭm, n. pl., an enterprise, work, discourse. Quī pŏtĕs, ōrsă rĕflēctās, Virg.

Ŏrsēs, æ, m., the name of a warrior. Prædūrŭm vīrĭbŭs Ŏrsēn, Virg.

Ŏrsĭlŏchŭs, ī, m., the name of a warrior. Prŏtĭnŭs Ŏrsĭlŏchum ēt Būtēn, Virg.

ōrsŭs, ă, ŭm, the partic. of ordior, having begun. Mājōrēmque ōrsă fŭrōrĕm, Virg.

ōrtŭs, ūs, m., origin, birth. Nōbĭlĭs hōc ōrtū, Sil. Syn. Ēxōrtŭs, ŏrīgo, prīncĭpĭŭm, nātīvĭtās.—2. Ortŭs sōlĭs, sunrise. Syn. Phœbēŭs, Eōŭs, mātūtīnŭs ōrtŭs. Epith. Pūrpŭrĕŭs, pūnĭcĕŭs, crŏcĕŭs, rŏsĕŭs, lūcĭdŭs, prīmŭs, nāscēns, pŭrŭs, sĕrēnŭs, ālmŭs, tĕpĭdŭs, rŏscĭdŭs, nĭtĭdŭs, splēndēns. Lūx prīmă dĭĕī. V. Oriens sol, aurora.

ōrtŭs, ă, ŭm, the part. of orior. Lūcĭfĕr ōrtŭs ĕrăt, Ov.

Ŏrtȳgĭă, æ, f., a name of the island Delos. Ŏrtȳgĭæ pōrtŭs, Virg.

Ŏrtȳgĭŭs, ă, ŭm, of Delos. Bŏvēs Ŏrtȳgĭæ, Ov. V. Delius.

ŏrȳx, ȳgĭs, m., an antelope. Et Gætūlŭs ŏrȳx, Juv.

ŏrȳză, æ, f., rice. Pŭsănārĭum ŏrȳzæ, Hor.

ōs, ōrĭs, n., the mouth, face. Ŏrĭbŭs ōră, Virg. Syn. Vūltŭs, făcĭēs, frōns; cōnspēctŭs, præsēntĭă. Epith. Pūrpŭrĕŭm, fōrmōsŭm, rŏsĕŭm, pūlchrŭm; dĕcōrŭm, vĕnūstŭm, plăcĭdŭm, sĕrēnŭm, ēgrĕgĭŭm, nĭtĭdŭm, blāndŭm, mŏdēstŭm; īmpŭdēns, aūdāx, prŏtērvŭm; āmbrŏsĭŭm, dōctŭm, dīsērtŭm, ārgūtŭm, fācūndŭm, sātĭdĭcŭm, pĭŭm, dīvīnŭm; mēndāx, īnfīdŭm, hĭāns, īmmānĕ, pătŭlŭm, spūmāns, crŭēntŭm, tūrbātŭm, ăvĭdŭm, clāmōsŭm, vōcālĕ.

ŏs, ōssĭs, n., a bone. Ex ōssĭbŭs ūltŏr, Virg. Epith. Dūrŭm, ālbŭm, vălĭdŭm, fīrmŭm, sŏlĭdŭm, nōdōsŭm, cānŭm, cāndĭdŭm, īngēns, sīccŭm, ārĭdŭm, căvŭm.

ōscēn, ĭnĭs, m., any bird of omen. Ōscĭnēm cōrvŭm, Hor.

Oscī, ōrŭm, m. pl., *an ancient people between the Volscians and Campania.* Oscŏrŭmquĕ mănŭs, Virg.

ŏscĭllŭm, ī, n., *a small image offered to Saturn and Bacchus, as an expiatory victim.* Oscilla ex altā sūspēndūnt, Virg.

ŏscĭtātĭo, ōnĭs, f., *gaping, yawning.* Sĕnĭs ŏscĭtātĭōnēs, (Phal.) Stat.

ŏscĭto, ās, *to yawn.* Ŏscĭtăt ēxtĕmplō, Lucr.

ŏscŭlātĭo, ōnĭs, f., *kissing.* Nōstræ sĕgĕs ŏscŭlātĭōnĭs, Catul.

ŏscŭlŏr, ārĭs, *to kiss.* Ŏscŭlŏr ārmă, Prop.   V. Amplector.

ŏscŭlŭm, ī, n., *a kiss.* Ŏsculă dăt, Ov.   Syn. Suāvĭŭm, bāsĭŭm, āmplēxŭs; ŏscĭllŭm, pārvum ŏs.   Epith. Dūlcĕ, mōllĕ, blāndŭm, mītĕ, grātŭm, ămīcŭm, cārŭm, lætŭm, mūtŭŭm, suāvĕ, fīdŭm, fīdēlĕ, mātērnŭm, mēllītŭm, jūcūndŭm; tūrpĕ, lāscīvŭm, ĭnhŏnēstŭm; cāstŭm, pŭdīcŭm, hŏnēstŭm.   V. Osculor.

Osīnĭŭs, ĭī, m., *a king of Clusium and ally of Æneas.* Advēctŭs Osīnĭŭs ōrĭs, Virg.

Osīrĭs, ĭs or ĭdĭs, m., *a great deity of the Egyptians.* Fēcĭt Osīrĭs, Tib.   Syn. Apĭs, Sĕrāpĭs.   Epith. Phărĭŭs, Ægyptĭŭs, Mēmphītĭcŭs, frūgĭfĕr, cōrnĭgĕr.

* || ŏsŏr, ōrĭs, m., *a hater.* Ŏsŏr ĭnīquī, Mamert.   Syn. Ēxōsŭs, pĕrōsŭs, ōsŭs, īnfēnsŭs.

Ossă, æ, f., *a mountain of Thessaly.* Pēlĭŏn Ossæ, Ov.   Epith. Pīnĭfĕră, ārdŭă, Thēssălă, nĭvālĭs, Arctŏă, frōndēns, nĕmŏrōsă, āĕrĭă, ābrūptă.

Ossœŭs, ă, ŭm, *of Ossa.* Fūsŭs ĭn Ossœæ, Ov.

ossĕŭs, ă, ŭm, *bony.* Ossĕă Maurī, Juv.

ossĭfrăgă, æ, f., *an ospray.* Ossĭfrăgæ, mērgīquĕ, Lucr.

ōstēndo, tēndī, sŭm, *to show.* Aŭrōra ōstēndĕrĭt ōrtŭs, Virg.   Syn. Mōnstro, dēmōnstro, dēclāro, ĭndĭco, mănĭfēsto, pāndo, rĕtĕgo, dētĕgo, ăpĕrĭo, ēxpōno, rĕvēlo, pătĕfăcĭo, ārgŭo, dŏcĕo, sĭgnĭfĭco.   V. Manifesto.

ōstēntātŏr, ōrĭs, m., *one who makes a show.*   Inde ōstēntātŏr, Aus.

ōstēnto, ās, *the freq. of ostendo.* Făcĭem ōstēntābăt, ĕt ūdō, Virg.   Syn. Jācto, jāctĭto, vēndĭto, glōrĭŏr.   V. Superbio.

ōstēntŭm, ī, n., *a prodigy.* Vīctŭs ĕt ōstēntĭs, Ov.   V. Prodigium.

ōstĭŭm, ĭī, n., *a door, entrance.* Ŏstĭă sāxō, Virg.   Syn. Jānŭă, līmĕn, ădĭtŭs, fŏrēs, pōrtă.   V. Janua.

ōstrĕă, æ, f., *and ĕŭm, ī, n., an oyster.* Ŏstrĕă mŏrdĕt, Juv.   Ŏstrĕăque ĭn cōnchīs tūtă fŭĕrĕ sŭĭs, Ov.

ōstrĕōsŭs, ă, ŭm, *abounding in oysters.* Ŏstrĕōsĭŏr ōră, Cat.

ōstrĭfĕr, ră, rŭm, *producing oysters.* Pōntŭs, ĕt ōstrĭfĕrī, Virg.

ōstrīnŭs, ă, ŭm, *of purple colour.* Ostrīnōs præbĕt, Prop.   Syn. Tyrĭŭs, pūrpŭrĕŭs.

Ōstrŏgŏthī, ōrŭm, m. pl., *the East-Goths.* Ōstrŏgŏthīs cŏlĭtŭr, Claud.

ōstrŭm, ī, n., *purple colour.* Sŭblīmĭs ĭn ōstrō, Ov.   Syn. Mūrēx, pūrpŭră, cŏccŭs.   V. Purpura.

ōsŭs, ă, ŭm, *the partic. of* odi.   Sēmpĕr ōsă sŭm, (Iamb.) Plaut.   Syn. Ēxōsŭs, pĕrōsŭs.

Ŏthō, ōnĭs, m., *a Roman emperor.* Gēstāmĕn Ŏthōnĭs, Juv.   Epith. Mōllĭs, lāscīvŭs, tūrpĭs.

Ŏthryădēs, æ, m., *the son of Othrys.* Pānthŭs Ŏthryădēs, Virg.

Ŏthrys, ўŏs, m., *a mountain of Thessaly.* Sŭbmŏvĕt Ŏthrys, Tib.   Epith. Nĕmŏrōsŭs, nĭvōsŭs, Hypērbŏrĕŭs, glăcĭālĭs, gĕlĭdŭs, rĭgĭdŭs, āspĕr, pīnĭfĕr, Æmăthĭŭs, Thēssălĭcŭs, nūbĭfĕr, nūbĭlŭs.

ōtĭŏr, ārĭs, *to be at leisure.* Dŏmēstĭcŭs ōtĭŏr, Hor.   Syn. Văco, fērĭŏr, quĭēsco.   V. Quiesco.

ōtĭōsŭs, ă, ŭm, *at leisure.* Hăbĕt ōtĭōsĭŏrĕm, (Phal.) Mart.   Syn. Văcŭŭs, fērĭātŭs, lēntŭs, sēgnĭs, ĭnērs, ĭgnāvŭs, ōtĭōsŭs.   V. Piger, otior.

ōtĭŭm, ĭī, n., *sloth, leisure.* Hæc ōtĭă fēcĭt, Virg.   Syn. Quĭēs, ĭnērtĭă, dēsĭdĭă, lānguŏr, tōrpŏr, ĭgnāvĭă, sēgnĭtĭēs.   Epith. Pigrŭm, ĭnērs, tūrpĕ, lēntŭm, ĭgnāvŭm, sēgnĕ, dēsĭdĭōsŭm, dēlĭcĭōsŭm, mōllĕ, fœdŭm, ĭgnōbĭlĕ, mārcĭdŭm; sēcūrŭm, quĭētŭm, trānquĭllŭm, suāvĕ, grātŭm, ămœnŭm.   V. Pigritia, quies, otior.

ŏvātŭs, ūs, m., *a shout of victory.* Glŏmĕrāntŭr ŏvātŭs, Val. Fl.

Ŏvĭdĭŭs, ĭī, m., *the Roman poet.*   Syn. Nāso.   Epith. Ingĕnĭōsŭs, dōctŭs;

O

lāscīvŭs, ĭmpŭrŭs, ŏbscœnŭs; făcŭndŭs, ĭndŭstrĭŭs, sōlērs, dīvīnŭs.—2. *a friend*
of Martial. Nŭllĭs, Ŏvĭdī, tăcēndĕ, Mart.

ŏvīlĕ, Ĭs, n., *a sheep-fold.* Cāptăt ŏvīlĕ, Ov. Syn. Caŭlă, stăbŭlŭm: sēptă,
ōrŭm. Epith. Claŭsŭm, tŭtŭm, sēcŭrŭm, ăpērtŭm, pātēns, fœcŭndŭm, plēnŭm,
ŏpīmŭm, tĕnĕrŭm.

ŏvīllŭs, *and* īnŭs, ă, ŭm, *of sheep.* Hærĕt ŏvīnĭs, Ser.

ŏvĭpărŭs, ă, ŭm, *producing eggs.* Ŏvĭpără cōngēstĭŏr ālvō, Aus.

ŏvĭs, Ĭs, f., *a sheep.* Cŭrăt ŏvēs, ŏvĭŭmquĕ, Virg. Syn. Bālāns, bĭdēns, ăgnă.
Epith. Imbēllĭs, mōllĭs, plăcĭdă, lānĭgĕră, păvĭdă, tĭmĭdă, mānsuētă, mītĭs,
blāndă, tĕnĕră, tĕnēllă, fŭgāx, sălĭēns. V. Grex.

ŏvo, ās, *to triumph, to rejoice.* Tūrnŭs ŏvăt, Virg. Syn. Trĭŭmpho; gēstĭo, ĕxŭlto, lætŏr. V. Triumpho, gaudeo.

ŏvŭm, ī, n., *an egg.* Ordītŭr ăb ŏvō, Hor. Epith. Tĕrĕs, lævĕ, nŏvŭm, rĕcēns,
sălŭbrĕ.

P.

* PABŬLŎR, ārĭs, *to feed.* Prōdīmŭs păbŭlātŭm, Pl. Syn. Frŭmēntŏr; păscŏr.
păbŭlŭm, ī, n., *food for cattle.* Păbŭlă gŭstāssēnt, Virg. Syn. Păscŭă; pāstŭs,
ēscă. Epith. Pīnguĕ, ŏpīmŭm, lætŭm, ămœnŭm, grămĭnĕŭm, vĭrĭdĕ. V.
Pascua.
păcālĭs, ĕ, *belonging to peace.* Săcērdōtĕs păcālĭbŭs āddĭtĕ flāmmĭs, Ov.
păcātŏr, ōrĭs, m., *a peace-maker.* Fĕrārum ŏrbĭsquĕ păcātŏr, Sen.
păcātŭs, ă, ŭm, *the pass. partic. of* paco. Păcātŭmquĕ rĕgĕt, Virg. Syn. Quĭētŭs,
trānquīllŭs, sēdātŭs, plăcĭdŭs, tēmpĕrātŭs.
Pāchўnŭs, ī, m., *a cape in Sicily.* Lūstrārĕ Pāchўnī, Virg. Epith. Sĭcŭlŭs,
āĕrĭŭs, sŭblīmĭs, ārdŭŭs.
păcĭfĕr, ĕră, ĕrŭm; *and* fĭcŭs, ă, ŭm, *peace-making.* Păcĭfĕræquĕ mănū, Virg.
Păcĭfĭcō sērmōnĕ, Lucan. Syn. Mītĭs, lēnĭs, trānquīllŭs.
păcĭfĭco, ās, *to appease.* Păcĭfĭcāns dīvōs, Sil. V. Placo.
păcĭscŏr, ĕrĭs, păctŭs, *to covenant.* Prō laŭdĕ păcīscī, Virg. Syn. Cōnvĕnĭo, cōntrăho, prōmītto. V. Fœdus; pax.
păco, ās, *to appease.* Incŭltæ păcāntŭr, Hor. Syn. Sēdo, mītĭgo, tēmpĕro, lēnĭo,
mōllĭo, flēcto, plăco, mŏdĕrŏr, mŭlcĕo, cōmpōno, cōncīlĭo.
Pācŏrŭs, ī, m., *a king of the Parthians.* Ĕt Pācŏrī mănŭs, Hor.
Pāctōlĭs, ĭdĭs, f., *of the Pactolus.* Nўmphæ Pāctōlĭdĕs ŭndās, Ov.
Pāctōlŭs, ī, m., *a river of Lydia, with golden sand.* Hīc cērtānt, Pāctōlĕ, tĭbi,
Sil. Epith. Dīvĕs, aŭrĭfĕr, aŭrātŭs, aŭrĭflŭŭs, rŭbēns, mĕtāllĭfĕr, Lўdĭŭs. V.
Flumen.
păctŭm, ī, n., *a covenant.* Păctă lĭgāt, păctĭs ĭpsă fŭtŭră cŏmĕs, Prop. Syn.
Fœdŭs, cōnvēntŭm, cōnvēntŭs, cōndĭtĭo, lēx; păctă fĭdēs. V. Fœdus.
păctŭs, ă, ŭm, *the partic. of* paciscor. Păctō prō mœnĭbŭs aŭrō, Ov. Syn. Prō-
mĭssŭs.—2. *of* pango. Āncŏră păctă sŭĭt, Id.
Pācŭvĭŭs, ĭī, m., *a Roman poet.* Pācŭvĭŭsquĕ, ĕt, Pers.
Pădŭă, æ, f., *a town of Italy.* Ānnālēs Pădŭăm, Cat. Syn. Pătăvĭŭm.
Pădŭs, ī, m., *a river in Italy.* Plēnō Pădŭs ŏrĕ, Lucan. V. Eridanus.
Pădŭsă, *the southernmost mouth of the Po.* Ămnĕ Pădŭsæ, Virg. Epith. Ūlvĭpără, ·
Phăëthōntĕă.
Pæān, ānĭs, m., *a hymn to the gods.* Dīcĭte ĭŏ Pæān, Ov. Epith. Lætŭs, săcĕr,
fēstīvŭs, hĭlărĭs, cănōrŭs, Ăpōllĭnĕŭs, Phœbēŭs.
pædăgōgŭs, ī, m., *a teacher.* Scēptră pædăgōgōrŭm, (Scaz.) Mart.
pædŏr, ōrĭs, m., *dirtiness.* In cārcĕrĕ pædŏr, Lucr.
Pæōn, ŏnĭs, m., *a celebrated physician.*
Pæŏnĕs, ŭm, m. pl., *a people of Macedonia.* Pæŏnăs, āddĕ quĭētī, Ov.
Pæŏnĭs, ĭdĭs, f., *of Pæonia.* Pæŏnĭs Ēvĭppæ, Ov.
Pæŏnĭŭs, ă, ŭm, *Pæonian.*—2. *of Pæon, medicinal.* Pæŏnĭĭs rĕvŏcātŭm hērbĭs,
Virg.
Pæstānŭs, ă, ŭm, *of Pæstum.* Cālthăquĕ Pæstānās, Ov.
Pæstŭm, ī, n., *a city of Lucania.* Bĭfĕrīquĕ rŏsārĭă Pæstī, Virg.
pætŭs, ă, ŭm, *squinting.* Āppēllāt pætŭm, Hor.

pāgănĭcŭs, *and* nŭs, ă, ŭm, *of countrymen.* Cŭm păgănă mădĕnt, Prop. Syn.
Rŭstĭcŭs, agrēstĭs.

pāgănŭs, ī, m., *a countryman.* Păgănūm pŏssĭs, Juv.

Păgăsă, æ, f., *a maritime city of Thessaly, where the ship Argo was built.* Păgăsœ
năvălĭbŭs Argō, Prop.

Păgăsŭs, ă, ŭm, *of Pagasa, of the Argonauts.* Mīnўœ Păgăsææ clāssĕ sēcābânt,
Ov.

Păgăsŭs, ī, m., *a Phrygian warrior slain by Camilla.* Tūm Līrĭm Păgăsūmquĕ,
Virg.

pāgĭnă, æ, f., *a page.* Păgĭnă nōmĕn, Virg.

păgŭr, ŭrĭs, m., *a fish.* Ĕt rŭtĭlūs păgŭr, ĕt fūlvī, Ov.

păgŭs, ī, m., *a village.* Păgŭs ăgăt, Ov.

pālă, æ, f., *a spade, shovel.* Vērsētŭr rōbŏrĕ pālæ, Colum.

Pălæmōn, ŏnĭs, m., *the son of Athamas.* Lĭnguă Pălæmŏnă dīcĕt, Ov. Syn.
Athămāntĭădēs, Pŏrtūmnŭs, Mĕlĭcērtēs. Epith. Æquŏrĕŭs, naŭfrăgŭs, præcēps,
fŭgāx ; īnfēlīx, Inŏŭs, Thēbānŭs.

Pălæstīnī, ōrŭm, m. pl., *the inhabitants of Palestine.* Stāgnă Pălæstīnī, Ov.—2.
-ŭs, ă, ŭm, *of Palestine.* Inquĕ Pălæstīnæ, Id.

pălæstră, æ, f., *wrestling, a place for wrestling.* Ŏlĕŏ lābēntĕ pălæstrās, Virg.
Syn. Lūctă, gўmnăsĭŭm. Epith. Grāmĭnĕă, ūnctă, dūră, vălĭdă, rōbūstă, sævă,
āspĕră, cĕlebrĭs, sōlēnnĭs, ăgĭlĭs, Ŏlŷmpĭăcă.

pălæstrītă, æ, m., *an athlete.* Quīnquĕ pălæstrītæ, Pers.

pălăm, adv., *publicly.* Tūrbă pălăm, Ov. Syn. Mănĭfēstĕ, ăpērtĕ, ĭn ŏcŭlĭs, ĭn
cōnspēctū, ĭn ŏrĕ, ānte ŏră, vŭlgō.

Pălămēdēs, ĭs, m., *the son of Nauplius, the inventor of weights and measures, chess,*
&c. Infēlīx Pălămēdēs, Ov.

Pălātīnŭs, m., *and* Ĭŭm, n., ī, *the largest of the seven hills on which Rome was built.*
Nĕmŏrōsă Pălātĭă, Ov.

Pălātīnŭs, ă, ŭm, *of Mount Palatine.* Scrīptă Pălātīnŭs, Hor. Ăd Pălātīnās
ăcĭpēnsĕm, Mart.

pălātĭŭm, ĭī, n., *a palace.* Dīxīssĕ pălătĭă cœlī, Ov. Pĕtĭs pălătĭă clīvō, Mart.
V. Regia.

pălātŭm, ī, n., *the palate.* Dīvērsă pălātō, Hor. Epith. Tĕnĕrŭm, mŏllĕ, ăvĭdŭm,
vŏrāx, căvŭm, pătŭlŭm, hĭāns, ūdŭm, ăpērtŭm, pătēns.

pălĕă, æ, f., *straw.* Ăd zĕphŷrŭm pălĕæ, Virg. Syn. Călămŭs, cŭlmŭs, stĭpŭlă.
Epith. Lĕvĭs, ĭnānĭs, ēxīlĭs, tĕnŭĭs, frăgĭlĭs, ārĭdă, sīccă, vŏlăus, vŏlĭtāns,
trītĭcĕă.

pălĕārĭă, n. pl., *dewlaps.* Pălĕārĭă pēndēnt, Virg. Epith. Lōngă, crāssă.

Pălēs, ĭs, f., *the goddess of shepherds.* Măgnă Pălēs, ĕt, Virg. Syn. Pāstōrūm
dĕă. Epith. Rŭstĭcă, sŷlvēstrĭs, agrēstĭs, sacră, grāndævă, fōrmōsă, ālmă, vĕnĕrāndă, fœcūndă.

Pălīcī, ōrŭm, m. pl., *twin brothers, sons of Jupiter and Thalia : they were honoured*
as gods in Sicily, where their temple was an asylum for fugitive slaves. Plăcābĭlĭs
āră Pălīcī, Virg.

Pălīlĭă, ōrŭm, n. pl., *festivals in honour of Pales.* Fūmōsă Pălīlĭă fœnō, Pers.
Epith. Fūmĭdă, pŏĕrīllă, prīscă, āntīquă, sacră.

Pălīnūrŭs, ī, m., *the pilot of the ship of Æneas, who fell into the sea.* Līttŭs, Pălī-
nŭrĕ, tŭŭm, Lucan.

pălĭūrŭs, ī, m., *a sort of thorn.* Sŭrgĭt pălĭūrŭs ăcūtĭs, Virg. Epith. Āspĕr,
ăcūtŭs, spīnōsŭs.

pāllă, æ, f., *a long gown.* Păllă crŏcō, Ov. V. Vestis.

Pāllădĭŭm, ĭī, n., *a statue of Minerva.* Pāllădĭŭm, cæsĭs, Virg.

Pāllădĭŭs, ŭm, *of Pallas.* Pāllădĭă gaŭdēnt sŷlvă, Ov.

Pāllāntēŭm, ī, n., *a city founded by Evander on the Palatine hill.* Pāllāntĭs prŏăvī
dē nōmĭnĕ Pāllāntēŭm, Virg.—2. adj., -ŭs, ă, ŭm, *of Pallanteum.* Ĕt mœnĭă
Pāllāntĕă, Id. Syn. Pălātīnŭs.

Pāllāntĭăs, ădĭs, *and* tĭs, ĭdĭs, f., *the daughter of the giant Pallas, Aurora.* Pāllāntĭăs īnfīcĭt ōrbĕm, Ov. Sēxtō Pāllāntĭdŏs ōrtū, Id.

Pāllāntĭŭs, ă, ŭm, *descended from Pallas, Evander.* Pāllāntĭŭs hērōs, Ov.

Pāllăs, ădĭs, f., *a name of Minerva.* Pāllădĭs ĕt, Mart. Syn. Mĭnērvă, Trītōnĭă,
dĕă bēllātrīx. V. Minerva.

Păllās, ăntĭs, m., *one of the Titans.* Pāllāntă rĕfōrmăt, Claud.—2. *the son of Evander.* Fŭltūm Pāllāntĭs ĕt ōrǎ, Virg.

Pāllēnē, ēs, f., *a city of Macedonia, near the Thermaic gulf.* Pătrĭāmquĕ rĕvīsĭt Pāllēnēn, Virg.

pāllĕo, ēs, *and* ēsco, ĭs, *to grow pale.* Pāllĕăt ōmnĭs, Ov. Pāllēscĕt sŭpĕr, Hor. SYN. Ēxpāllēsco, ēxālbēsco. V. Macer.

pāllĭdŭlūs, ǎ, ŭm, *a little pale.* Pāllĭdŭlūm mānāns āblŭĭt ŭndǎ pĕdĕm, Cat.

pāllĭdŭs, ǎ, ŭm, *pale.* Pāllĭdǎ mōrtĕ, Virg. SYN. Pāllēns, dēcŏlŏr. V. Palleo.

pāllĭŭm, *dimin.* ĭŏlŭm, ī, n., *a cloak.* Cūltām pāllĭŏlō, Juv. Pāllĭǎ jăctăt, Id. V. Vestis.

pāllŏr, ōrĭs, m. *paleness.* Pāllŏr ămāntĭŭm, (Chor.) Hor. EPITH. Lūrĭdŭs, ālbŭs, mārcĭdŭs, ēxānguĭs, dēfōrmĭs, lānguĭdŭs, līvĭdŭs, plūmbĕŭs, frīgĭdŭs, trīstĭs, ēxănĭmĭs, tērrĭbĭlĭs, sĕpŭlcrālĭs, hōrrĭdŭs, tūrpĭs. V. Palleo.

pālmǎ, æ, f., *a palm-tree.* Ēlĭădūm pālmās, Virg. EPITH. Ŏlўmpĭăcǎ, Ēlæǎ ; ārdǔǎ, nōbĭlĭs, īnsīgnĭs, ēgrĕgĭǎ, vĭrĭdĭs, vĭrēns, vĭrĭdāns, ămœnǎ, glōrĭŏsǎ, Mārtĭǎ, vīctrīx, trĭūmphālĭs, lætǎ, quæsītǎ, pārtǎ, Ĭdūmæǎ.

pālmǎ, æ, f., *the palm of the hand.* Făcĭĕm cōntūndĕrĕ pālmǎ, Juv. Pēctŏrǎ pālmĭs, Ov. SYN. Mănŭs. EPITH. Dŭplĭcēs, gĕmĭnæ, sŭpplĭcēs, bīnæ.

pālmātŭs, ǎ, ŭm, *adorned with palms.* Pālmātæquĕ dŭcĕm, Mart.

pālmĕs, ĭtĭs, m., *the shoot of a vine.* Pālmĭtĕ gēmmǎ, Ov. EPITH. Vĭrĭdĭs, lēntŭs, frōndōsŭs, ŭvĭfĕr, răcĕmĭfĕr, vērnŭs, rĕnāscēns, ŭbĕr, fĕrāx, fœcūndŭs. V. Ramus.

pālmētūm, ī, n., *a place planted with palms.* Hĕrōdĭs pālmētĭs, Hor.

pālmĭfĕr, rǎ, rŭm, *bearing palms.* Pālmĭfĕrōs Ărăbǎs, Ov.

pālmōsŭs, ǎ, ŭm, *abounding in palms.* Vēntĭs, pālmōsǎ Sĕlīnŭs, Virg.

pālmŭlǎ, æ, f., *the dimin. of* palma, *an oar.* Strīngăt sĭnĕ pālmŭlǎ caūtēs, Virg SYN. Pālmǎ. V. Remus.

pālŏr, ārĭs, *to wander.* Fœmĭnǎ pālāntēs, Virg. SYN. Ērro, văgŏr, fŭgĭo.

pālpebrǎ, æ, f., *the eyelid.* Pālpĕbræquĕ cădŭnt, Lucr.

pālpĭto, ās, *to pant, tremble.* Pālpĭtĕt : ăt tū, Juv. SYN. Trĕmo, mĭco, ēxĭlĭo.

pālpo, ās, *and* pŏr, ārĭs, *to stroke.* Mūnĕrĕ pālpăt, Juv. Pālpĕrĕ, rĕcālcĭtrăt, Hor. SYN. Tāngo, trācto, āttrēcto. V. Tango.

pālpo, ōnĭs, m., *a flatterer.* Jūs hăbĕt ĭllĕ sŭī pālpō, quī, Pers.

pălūdātŭs, ǎ, ŭm, *clad in the paludamentum or military cassock.* Cūmquĕ pălū-dātĭs dŭcĭbŭs, Juv.

pălūdōsŭs, ǎ, ŭm, *marshy.* Ĭllĕ pălūdōsōs, Prop. SYN. Pălŭstrĭs, stāgnāns.

pălūmbēs, ĭs, f., *also* ŭs, ī, m., *a wood-pigeon.* Tŭǎ cūrǎ, pălūmbēs, Virg. Gĕmĭt hīnc pălūmbŭs, Mart. SYN. Cŏlūmbǎ. EPITH. Aĕrĭǎ, tĕnĕrǎ, præpĕs, vēlōx, păvĭdǎ, fŭgāx. V. Columba.

pălūs, ūdĭs, f., *a marsh.* Tārdăquĕ pălūs ĭnămăbĭlĭs, Virg. SYN. Lăcŭs, stāgnŭm. EPITH. Crāssǎ, plăcĭdǎ, pigrǎ, tōrpēns, līmōsǎ, spūrcǎ, putrĭdǎ.

pălūs, ī, m., *a post.* Tĕnĕrām pālīs ādjūngĕrĕ, Tib. SYN. Sŭdēs, stīpĕs, trūncŭs, vāllŭs. EPITH. Līgnĕŭs, tĕrĕs, dūrŭs, vălĭdŭs, rōbūstŭs, fīrmŭs.

pǎlūstrĭs, ĕ, *marshy.* Fœtǎ pălūstrĭbŭs ūlvĭs, Ov. SYN. Pălūdōsŭs, stāgnāns.

Pāmphăgŭs, ī, m., *the name of a dog.* Pāmphăgŭs ĕt Dōrceŭs, Ov.

Pāmphўlĭǎ, æ, f., *a country of Asia Minor.* Tĭmŭĭt Pāmphўlĭǎ mēssēs, Stat.

Pāmphўlĭŭs, *and* lŭs, ǎ, ŭm, *of Pamphylia.* Pāmphўlĭǎ pūppī Ōccūrrĭt tēllŭs, Luc. Pāmphўlūmquĕ lătŭs, Prisc.

pāmpĭnĕŭs, ǎ, ŭm, *of vine leaves.* Nēc quī pāmpĭnĕĭs, Virg.

pāmpĭnŭs, ī, m. *or* f., *a vine leaf.* Pāmpĭnŭs Aŭstrōs, Virg. EPITH. Tĕnĕr, vĭrĭdĭs, frōndōsŭs, lēntŭs, ūmbrōsŭs, ŏpācŭs.

Pān, ānŏs, m., *the god of shepherds.* Pān ŏvĭŭm cūstōs, Virg. EPITH. Prŏtēr-vŭs, prŏcāx, pĕtŭlāns, bĭcōrnĭs, cōrnĭgĕr, rūstĭcŭs, cĕlĕr, vēlōx, mōntĭvăgŭs, sўlvēstrĭs, agrēstrĭs, sēmĭfĕr, caprĭpēs, hīrtŭs, hīrsūtŭs, vīllōsŭs ; hōrrĭbĭlĭs, dē-fōrmĭs, mōntānŭs, Arcădĭŭs, Mænālĭdēs, Mænālĭŭs, Lўcæŭs ; Tĕgĕæŭs.

pănăcĕǎ, æ, *also* pănāx, ăcĭs, f., *an herb said to cure all diseases.* Ēt pănăcĕǎ pŏtēns, Luc. Mĕdĭcǎ pănăcēm lăcrўmǎ, Colum. EPITH. Ŏdōrĭfĕrǎ, sălūtĭfĕrǎ.

Pănætĭŭs, ĭi, m., *a Stoic philosopher.* Lĭbrōs Pănætī, Hor.

pănārĭŭm, *dimin.* ārĭŏlŭm, ī, n. *a bread-basket.* Hī pānārĭǎ cāndĭdāsquĕ, Stat. Cŭm pānārĭŏlīs Mart.

Pănchœŭs, chăīcŭs, *and* chăīŭs, ă, ŭm, *of Panchaia.*   Pănclæīs ădŏlēscūnt īgnī-
bŭs, Virg.   Pănchăīcă tēllūs, Ov.   Pănchăīă cīnnămă, Claud.
Păndărŭs, ī, m., *one of Æneas' companions.*   Păndărŭs ēt Bĭtīăs, Virg.
Păndīōn, ŏnīs, m., *a king of Athens, father of Progne and Philomela.*   Gĕnītăs
Pāndīōnĕ fūrrō, Ov.
Pāndīōnīŭs, ă, ŭm, *of Pandion.*   Quīd Pāndīōnīæ rēstănt, Ov.
pāndo, īs, *to open.*   Pāndĭmŭs ūrbīs, Virg.   Syn.   Ăpĕrīo, rĕsĕro, pătĕfăcīo ;
ēxplīco, mănīfēsto, dēclāro, īndīco.   V. Aperio, janua.
Pāndrŏsŏs, ī, m., *the son of Cecrops.*   Pāndrŏsŏs ātque Hīrsē, Ov.
pāndŭs, ă, ŭm, *bent, crooked.*   Lāncībŭs ēt pāndīs, Virg.
pănēgўrĭcŭs, ă, ŭm, *laudatory.*   Sīvĕ pănēgўrĭcōs, Aus.
Pānēs, ŭm, m. pl., *gods of the woods.*   Nūmĭnă Pānēs, Ov.   Epith.   Mŏntĭcŏlæ,
sўlvānī, rūrĭcŏlæ.
Pāngæa, ōrŭm, n. pl., *a promontory on the confines of Thrace and Macedonia.*
Āltăquĕ Pāngæa ēt Rhēsī, Virg.—Adj. -ŭs, ă, ŭm, *of Pangæa.*   Pāngææ Bŏrĕăs, Id.
pāngo, pĕpĭgī *or* pānxī, pāctŭm, *to fix, compose.*   Pŏĕmătă pāngo, Hor.   Syn.
Fĭgo, plānto ; cōmpōno.
pānīs, īs, m., *bread.*   Cærŭlēī pānīs, Juv.   Syn.   Cĕrēs.   Epith.   Trītīcĕŭs, fūr-
fŭrĕŭs, ūtīlīs, dūlcīs, lætŭs, ōptātŭs, cōctŭs, suāvīs, fērmēntātŭs.
Pānnŏnĭă, æ, f., *the modern Hungary.*   Aūt jŭgă Pānnŏnīæ, Stat.
Pānnŏnĭcŭs, ă, ŭm, *of Pannonia.*   Pānnŏnīcăs nōbīs, Mart.
Pānnŏnīī, ōrŭm, m. pl., *the Hungarians.*   Pānnŏnīūsquĕ fĕrōx, Stat.   Epith.
Trŭcēs, bēllācēs, bēllĭgĕrī.
Pānnŏnīs, īdīs, f., *of Pannonia.*   Pānnŏnīs haūd ălītĕr, Luc.
pānnōsŭs, *or* nŭcĕŭs, ă, ŭm, *ragged.*   Pānuōsăm fæcĕm, Pers.   Pānnūcĕă Baūcīs,
Pers.   Syn.   Lăcĕr, nūdŭs.
pānnŭs, *and* ĭcŭlŭs, m., *and* ŭm, n., ī, *cloth, rags.*   Fīdēs vēlātă pānnō, Hor.   Dē-
līcīăs ēt pānnĭcŭlăs, Juv.   Epith.   Tēxtīlīs, lăbōrātŭs, pīctŭs, prĕtīŏsŭs,
sērīcŭs, īntēxtŭs, tēxtŭs, vīllōsŭs, ăspĕr, squālēns.
pănōmphœŭs, ă, ŭm, *worshipped in all languages, an epith. of Jupiter.*   Ără pănōm-
phæō vētŭs ēst, Ov.
Pănŏpē, ēs, *and* pĕă, æ, f., *one of the Nereids.*   Pănŏpĕăquĕ vīrgo, Virg.   Pănŏpē
flŭvīālīs ămīcăs, Aus.
Pănŏpeŭs, ĕŏs *or* ĕī, m., *the name of a man.*   Lēlēx Pănŏpeŭs, Hўleūsquĕ, Ov.
Pănōrmŏs *and* ŭs, ī, f., *a city of Sicily.*   Fēcūndă Pănōrmŭs, Sil.
Pāntăgīăs *and* gĭēs, æ, m., *a small river near Syracuse.*   Pāntăgīæ, Mĕgărōsquĕ
sīnŭs, Virg.   Mĕgărĕăquĕ Pāntăgīēnquĕ, Ov.
pāntēx, ĭcīs, m., *the intestines, belly.*   Quŏd cūm pāntĭcībŭs, Mart.
pānthēră, æ, f., *or* ĕr, ērīs, m., *a panther.*   Gĕnŭs pānthēră cămēlō, Hor.   Epith.
Pīctă, fĕrōx, vērsĭcŏlŏr, ŏdōră, măcŭlōsă, cĕlĕr, vĕlōx.
Pānthŏīdēs, æ, m., *the son of Panthus.*   Pānthŏīdēs Eūphōrbŭs ĕrăm, Ov.
Pānthŭs, ŭs, voc. ū, m., *the son of Othrys, and priest of Apollo.*   Pānthŭs Ŏthrўădēs,
Virg.
Pāntīlĭŭs, īī, m., *the name of a man.*   Mĕn' mŏvĕăt cīmēx Pāntīlĭŭs ? Hor.
Pāntŏlăbŭs, ī, m., *the name of a man.*   Pāntŏlăbŭm scūrrăm, Hor.
* ‖ Pāpă, æ, m., *the Pope.*   Ŏptĭmĕ Pāpă, Prud.
păpæ, interj., *a cry of admiration.*   Dāmă! Pāpæ! Pers.
păpāvĕr, ĕrīs, n., *a poppy.*   Mīstă păpăvĕrībŭs, Prop.   Epith.   Sŏmnīfĕrŭm,
Lēthæŭm, vēscŭm, Cĕrĕălĕ ; frĭgĭdŭm, tŏrpēns, grăvĭdŭm, fœcūndŭm.
păpăvĕrĕŭs, ă, ŭm, *of a poppy.*   Īllă păpăvĕrĕăs, Ov.
Păphāgēs, īs, m., *a king of Ambracia, devoured by a lioness.*—Adj. -ēŭs, ĕă, ĕŭm,
of Paphages.   Sīīquĕ Păphāgēæ, Ov.
Pāphĭŭs, ă, ŭm, *of Paphos.*   Sŏlĭdō Pāphĭŭs, Ov.
Pāphŏs, ī, f., *a town of Cyprus.*   Ēst Pāphŏs Idălĭūmquĕ, Virg.   Epith.   Cyprĭă,
cēlsă, ārdŭă, flōrĭfĕră.
Pāphŭs, ī, m., *the son of the sculptor Pygmalion, who gave his name to the island of
Paphos.*   Īllă Pāphŭm gĕnŭīt, Ov.
pāpīlĭo, ōnīs, m., *a butterfly.*   Pāpīlĭōnĭbŭs mŏlēstī, (Phal.) Mart.   Epith. Lĕvīs,
vŏlītāns, ălĭgĕr, ālātŭs.
păpīllă, æ, f., *a nipple of the breast.*   Pērlătă păpīllăm, Virg.   V. Mamma.
păppās, æ, m., *a servant to bring up children.*   Pōcŭlă păppās, Juv.

pāppo, ās, *to eat pap.* Pŭĕrīs pāppārĕ mĭnūtŭm, Pers.

pāppŭs, ī, m., *thistle-down.* Pāppōsquĕ vŏlāntēs, Lucr.—2. *a grandfather.* Pāppŏs ăvīāsquĕ trĕmēntēs, Aus.

pāpŭlă, æ, f., *a pimple.* Ārdēntēs pāpŭlæ, Virg.

păpȳrĭfĕr, rŭ, rŭm, *bearing papyrus.* Pērquĕ păpȳrĭfĕrī, Ov.

păpȳrĭŭs, ă, ŭm, *of the papyrus.* Mūsă, păpȳrĭŭm, Aus.

păpȳrŭs, ī, f., *a shrub growing in Egypt, from which paper was made.* Dāmnōsă păpȳrŏ, Juv. Syn. Chārtă. Epith. Lævĭs, tĕnŭĭs, frăgĭlĭs, dōctă, sacră, fīdă, bĭbŭlă, pălūstrĭs, Nīlĭăcă, Ægȳptĭă.

pār, ărĭs, *even, equal.* Lūdĕrĕ pār īmpār, Hor. Syn. Cōmpār, sūppār, nōn īmpār, părĭlĭs, sĭmĭlĭs, æquālĭs.—2. subst. n., *a couple.* Pārvĕ cŏlūmbārŭm, Ov.

părābĭlĭs, ĕ, *easy to obtain.* Hor. Syn. Pārātū *or* īnvēntū făcĭlĭs.

părădă, æ, f., *a curtain.* Sŭbtĕr părădās, lēctōquĕ jăcēntĕm, Aus.

Părădīsŭs, ī, m., *Paradise.* Circūmstānt Părădīsī, Sidon. Epith. Flōrēns, ămœnŭs, fōrtūnātŭs, bĕātŭs, fēlīx, lætŭs, cœlēstĭs, săcĕr. V. Cælum.

Părætŏnĭŭm, ĭĭ, n., *a city of Marmarica, not far from Alexandria.* Isĭ, Părætŏnĭŭm, Mărĕōtĭcăque ārvă, Phărōnquĕ, Ov.

părăsītă, æ, *and* tŭs, ī, m., *a parasite.* Cīnĭflōnēs, părăsītæ, Hor. Syn. Ădūlātŏr, āssēntātŏr. Epith. Blāndŭs, blāndŭlŭs, tūrpĭs, blāndĭlŏquŭs, ĭnānĭs, īmpūrŭs, fīctŭs, sūbdŏlŭs.

părātŭs, *the pass. partic. of* paro. Sēdēsquĕ părātăs, Virg.

părātŭs, ūs, m., *a preparation.* Nūllīsquĕ părātĭbŭs ōrānt, Ov.

Pārcă, æ, f., Pārcæ, ārŭm, f. pl., *the Fates, daughters of Night and Erebus.* Pārcă nōn mēndāx, Hor. Pārcārūmquĕ dĭēs, Virg. Epith. Dūræ, crūdēlēs, sævæ, fĕrōcēs, trŭcēs, īmmītēs, īmmānēs, cōncōrdēs, ĭnĭquæ, diræ, lānĭfĭcæ, ĭnvĭdæ, sĕvēræ, Stȳgĭæ, răpācēs, trīstēs, ĭnēxōrābĭlēs, ăcērbæ, atrōcēs, bārbăræ, īmpĭæ, ĭnhūmānæ.

pārcē, adv., *sparingly.* Vīvĕrĕ pārcē, Lucr. Syn. Ăvārē, sōrdĭdē, mŏdĭcē.

pārcĭtās, ātĭs, f., *sparingness.* Pārcĭtātēm sōbrĭăm, (Iamb.) Prud. Syn. Pārsĭmōnĭă, frūgālĭtās, mŏdĕrātĭo.

pārco, pārsī, (*oftener* pĕpērcī,) *to spare.* Pārcĕrĕ sŭbjēctīs, Virg. Syn. Ignōsco, cōndōno, rĕmĭtto, īndūlgĕo. V. Placo, preces.

pārcŭs, ă, ŭm, *thrifty.* Tānquām pārcŭs hŏmo, Juv. Syn. Sōrdĭdŭs, cŭpĭdŭs, ăvārŭs, abstĭnēns. V. Avarus.

pārdŭs, ī, m., *a panther.* Pārdŭs hĭātū, Juv. Epith. Cĕlĕr, vŏlūcĕr, pērnīx, lĕvĭs, fŭlmĭnĕŭs, vŏrāx, cāllĭdŭs, măcŭlōsŭs, vērsĭcŏlŏr, pīctŭs, īmmītĭs, īmmānĭs.

părēăs, œ, m., *a sort of serpent.* Caudă sūlcărĕ părēăs, Luc.

părēns, ntĭs, m. f., *a father or mother.* Grātūsquĕ părēntĭbŭs ērrŏr, Virg. V. Pater, mater.

părēntālĭs, ĕ, *belonging to parents.* Fāmă părēntālī, Ov.

părēnto, ās, *to perform the funeral rites of dead relations.* Vēnĕrĕ, părēntānt, Lucr. V. Sepelio.

părĕo, ŭī, *to obey.* Pārēbĭt prāvī, Hor. Syn. Ōbsĕquŏr, aūscūlto, mōrēm gĕro. V. Obedio.

părĭēs, rĭĕtĭs, m., *a wall.* Quăm fīxăm părĭēs ĭllōs, Virg. Pārĭĕtĭbŭs scālæ, Virg. V. Murus.

Părīlĭă, ŭm, n. pl., *festivals in honour of Pales.* Fēstīsquĕ Părīlĭbŭs ūrbĭs, Ov. Syn. Pălīlĭă.

părĭlĭs, ĕ, *equal.* Ārtĕ sŭŭm părĭlī, Ov. V. Par, similis.

părĭo, pĕpĕrī, pārtŭm, *to beget.* Nŏvĭēs părĭtūră vŏcāvĭt, Ov. Syn. Pārtŭrĭo, gīgno, gĕnĕro, prōcrĕo, ēnītŏr. V. Genero.

Părĭs, ĭdĭs, m., *the son of Priam, who carried away Helen, and occasioned the downfall of Troy.* Jūdĭcĭŭm Părīdĭs, Virg. Syn. Ălēxāndĕr. Epith. Ădūltĕr, pērfĭdŭs, lāscīvŭs, fōrmōsŭs, fătālĭs, tĕmĕrārĭŭs, īnsānŭs, Idæŭs, Ilĭăcŭs, Phrȳgĭŭs, Trōjānŭs, Trōĭcŭs, Dārdănĭŭs, Dārdănĭdēs, Prĭămēlŭs, Prĭămĭdēs.

Părīsĭăcŭs, ă, ŭm, *of Paris, Parisian.* Ipsĕ Părīsĭăcă prŏpĕrăt Dĭŏnȳsĭŭs ūrbĕ, Sant.

Părīsĭī, ōrŭm, m. pl., *the inhabitants of Paris; Paris.* Gĕnĕrătă Părīsĭŭs ūrbĕ, Fort. Syn. Părīsĭăcī, Părīsĭădæ. V. Lutetia.

părĭtĕr, adv., *equally.* Infīndūnt părĭtĕr, Virg. Syn. Æquē; nōn sĕcŭs, haūd ălĭtĕr.

Părĭŭs, ă, ŭm, *of Paros.* Hærĕt ŭt ē Părĭō, Ov.

pārmă, æ, f., *a buckler.* Tĕgmĭnă pārmœ, Sil. Syn. Clўpĕŭs, scūtŭm, ūmbo, pĕltă. V. Clypeus.

pārmŭlă, æ, f., *the dimin. of* parma. Nŏn bĕnĕ pārmŭlă, (Alc.) Hor.

Pārnāssĭs, ĭdĭs, f., *of Parnassus.* Laŭrō Pārnāssĭdĕ vīnctŭs, Ov

Pārnāssĭŭs, ă, ŭm, *of Parnassus.* Gaŭdēt Pūrnāssĭă rūpēs, Virg. Syn. Ăpŏl-lĭnĕŭs, Phœbēŭs.

Pūrnāssŭs, ī, m., *a mountain in Bœotia, sacred to the Muses.* Nōmĭnĕ Pūrnāssŭs, Ov. Epitii. Ărdŭŭs, āltŭs, ĕxcēlsŭs, sūblīmĭs, Ăpŏllĭnĕŭs, Phœbēŭs, ămœnŭs, laŭrĭgĕr, săcĕr, dōctŭs, sacrātŭs, ūmbrōsŭs, aĕrĭŭs, bĭcēps, gĕmĭnŭs, vīrgĭnĕŭs, cănōrŭs, nĭvālĭs. V. Helicon, Pindus, Pierius.

păro, ās, *to prepare.* Māgnī pārērĕ părābăt, Virg. Syn. Ăppăro, cōmpăro, īnstrŭo, īnstĭtŭo, ădōrno, me āccīngo; cōmpăro, ācquīro, cōnsĕquŏr, āssĕquŏr. V. Acquiro.

părŏchŭs, ī, m., *he who gives an entertainment.* Tŭm părŏchī făcĭĕm, Hor.

părōpsĭs, ĭdĭs, f., *a plate.* Ancīllă părŏpsĭdĕ nīgrā, Hor.

Părŏs, ī, f., *an island in the Archipelago.* Nĭvĕāmquĕ Părōn, Virg. Epitii. Mār-mŏrĕă, cāndēns, rĭgĭdă, Dēlphĭcă, nĭvĕă.

părră, æ, f., *a bird of evil omen, probably the screech owl.* Pārræ rĕcĭnēntĭs ōmĕn, Hor

Pārrhāsĭs, ĭdĭs, f., *Arcadian.* Pārrhāsĭs ūrsă pŏlō, Ov.—2. subst., *Callisto.* Pār-rhāsĭs ērŭbŭĭt, Id.

Pārrhāsĭŭs, ă, ŭm, *of Parrhasia, a city of Arcadia; Arcadian.* Pārrhāsĭŏ dīctūm Pānŏs dē mōrĕ Lўcæī, Virg.—2. subst., m., *a celebrated painter of Ephesus.* Cūm Pārrhāsĭī tăbŭlĭs, Juv.

pārrĭcīdă, æ, m. f., *a parricide.* Quĭs pārrĭcīdă, quĭs, Prud.

pārs, pārtĭs, f., *a part.* Pārtĭbŭs æquābăt, Virg. Syn. Pōrtĭo; ălĭī, nōnnūllī, quĭdăm, hī, īllī.

pārsĭmōnĭă, *or* cĭmōnĭă, æ, f., *frugality.* Chrīstĕ, pārsĭmōnĭĭs, (Iamb.) Prud. Syn. Pārcĭtās, frūgālĭtās.

pārtēs, ĭŭm, f. pl., *a charge, office.* Māndēntŭr jŭvĕnī pārtēs, Hor. Syn. Mŭnĭă, mŭnŭs, ŏfficĭŭm.

Pārthāōn, ŏnĭs, m., *the father of Œneus.* Dīxī, Pārthāŏnĕ nātĕ, Ov.

Pārthāŏnĭŭs, ă, ŭm, *of Parthaon, Ætolian.* Quās, Pārthāŏnĭæ, Ov.

pārthĕnĭcĕ, ēs, f., *the plant pellitory.* Ālbă pārthĕnĭcĕ, Catul.

Pārthĕnĭŭs, ī, m., *a mountain of Arcadia.*—2. *a river of Paphlagonia.* Pārthĕnĭŭs-quĕ răpāx, Ov.—3. *one of Æneas' companions.* Pārthĕnĭŭmquĕ Răpō, Virg.—4. adj., -ŭs, ă, ŭm, *of the mountain Parthenius.* Pārthĕnĭōs căŭĭbŭs, Id.

Pārthĕnŏpæŭs, ī, m., *the son of Meleager and Atalanta, famous for his exploits in the Theban war.* Pārthĕnŏpæŭs, ĕt, Virg. Epith. Arcăs, Ĕrўmānthĭŭs, Tĕ-gēæŭs, aŭdāx.

Pārthĕnŏpē, ēs, f., *one of the Syrens.*—2. *Naples.* Nātăm Pārthĕnŏpēn, Ov. Epith. Ĕgrĕgĭă, īnclўtă, dĕcōră, sŭpērbă.

Pārthĕnŏpēĭŭs, ă, ŭm, *of Parthenope or Naples.* Et Pārthĕnŏpēĭă dēxtrā, Ov.

Pārthī, ōrŭm, m. pl., *a nation of Persia.* Præĭĭă Pārthī, Virg. Epith. Lĕvēs, pūgnācēs, ănĭmōsī, fĕrōcēs, rĕfŭgī, fŭgācēs, Mārtĭī, trŭcēs, vŏlucrēs, pŏtēntēs, cĕlĕrēs, flūxī, săgĭttĭfĕrī, īmmānēs.

Pārthĭă, æ, f., *a country of Asia.* Pārthĭă mōrēs, Claud.

Pārthĭcŭs, *and* thŭs, ă, ŭm, *Parthian.* Pārthĭcă quæ tāntĭs, Claud. Pŭrthāsquĕ săgĭttās, Ov.

pārtĭcēps, ĭpĭs, m. f., *a partaker.* Quārĕ pārtĭcĭpĕm, Lucr. Syn. Cōnsŏrs, cōm-pŏs, sŏcĭŭs, cōnscĭŭs, nōn ēxpērs, nōn ēxsŏrs.

pārtĭcĭpo, ās, *to take a share of.* Sēnsŭ pārtĭcĭpēntŭr, Lucr.

pārtĭcŭlă, æ, f., *the diminut. of* pars. Dīvĭnæ pārtĭcŭlam aūræ, Hor.

pārtĭcŭlātĭm, adv., *one by one.* Mŏrĭbŭndī pārtĭcŭlātĭm, Lucr.

pārtĭm, adv., *in part.* Pārtĭm sŏrbēntŭr, Ov.

pārtĭŏr, īrĭs, *to divide.* Sŏcĭŏs pārtītŭr ĭn ōmnēs, Virg. Syn. Dīvĭdo, dīstrĭbŭo.

pārtŭrĭo, īs, ĭī, *to be in labour.* Pārtŭrĭūnt mŏntēs, Hor. V. Gravida.

pārtŭs, ūs, m., *the act of bringing forth.* Tŭm pārtŭ tērrā nĕfāndō, Virg. Syn. Pŭĕrpĕrĭŭm. Epith. Dĭfficĭlĭs, dūrŭs, ăcērbŭs, sævŭs, mŏlēstŭs, grăvĭs, mœstŭs, faŭstŭs, īnfaŭstŭs, fēlīx, trīstĭs, vĭŏlēntŭs, quĕrŭlŭs, flēbĭlĭs, lŭthĭfĕr, ānxĭŭs, mātūrŭs. V. Pario.—2. *production, fruit.* Nēc pārtŭm grātĭă tālĕm,

o 4

Virg. Syn. Fœtŭs, sŏbŏlēs, prōlēs, prōgĕnĭēs, prōpāgo. Epith. Tĕnĕr, nōbĭlĭs, illūstrĭs. V. Soboles.

părŭm, adv., *little.* Nāsŏ părŭm prūdēns, Ov. Syn. Paŭlīspĕr, lĕvĭtĕr, paŭlŭm, paŭlō, mŏdĭcŭm.

părŭmpĕr, adv., *for a little time.* Pŭlsūsquĕ părŭmpĕr, Virg. Syn. Ălĭquāntŭm, ălĭquā.

pŭrvŭlŭs, ă, ŭm, *the diminut. of* parvus. Pārvŭlŭs aŭlā, Virg.

pārvŭs, ă, ŭm, *little.* Pārvŭs ŏlīvō, Pers. Syn. Pārvŭlŭs, ĕxĭgŭŭs, grăcĭlĭs, tĕnŭĭs, ĕxĭlĭs, mĭnūtŭs, āngūstŭs, pŭsĭllŭs, mĭnĭmŭs, cōntrāctŭs, mŏdĭcŭs, brĕvĭs, nōn măgnŭs.

pāsco, pāvī, *to feed.* Rēgēm pāvērĕ sŭb āntrō, Virg. Syn. Pāscŏr, pābŭlŏr, ĕdo, vēscŏr; nūtrĭo, ălo; recrĕo, dēlēcto. V. Gregem pasco.

pāscŭă, ōrŭm, n. pl., *pastures.* Pāscŭă vērsŭ, Virg. Syn. Pābŭlă, pāstŭs. Epith. Laetă, hērbōsă, pīngŭĭă, fœcūndă, vĭrēntĭă, hērbĭdă, grāmĭnĕă, hūmĭdă, āmœnă, mădĭdă, ŏpīmă, rōscĭdă. V. Herba, pratum, pasco.

pāscŭŭs, ă, ŭm, *proper for pasturage.* Et pāscŭă rēddĕrĕ rūră, Lucr.

Pāsĭphăē, ēs, f., *daughter of the Sun, mother of the Minotaur.* Nēc prŏbă Pāsĭphăē, Prop. Epith. Mīnŏă, Mīnŏĭă, Gnōssĭă, mōnstrĭfĕră, dīră, ădūltĕră, tūrpĭs, ĭnfāmĭs, ĭmpūră, ĭmpŭdīcă.

Pāsĭphăēĭă, æ, f., *the daughter of Pasiphae.* Mē Pāsĭphăēĭă quōndăm, Ov.

pāssĕr, ĕrĭs, m., *a sparrow.* Pāssĕr, dēlĭcĭæ, Cat. Epith. Ārgūtŭs, aĕrĭŭs, ĕxĭgŭŭs, ĕxĭlĭs, tĕnŭĭs, văgŭs, vŏlŭcĕr, sălāx, sŏlĭvăgŭs.

pāssĭm, adv., *everywhere.* Strătă jăcēnt pāssĭm, Virg. Syn. Ŭbĭquĕ, ŭndĭquĕ, hūc ĭllŭc, tĕmĕrĕ, sīnĕ lēgĕ, dīscrīmĭnĕ nūllō.

pāssŭs, ă, ŭm, *the part. pass. of* pando, *stretched.* Pāssīs dē lĭttŏrĕ pālmīs, Virg. —2. *the part. of* patior, *having suffered.* Ŏ pāssī grăvĭōră, Id.

pāssŭs, ŭs, m., *a step.* Pāssĭbŭs æquīs, Virg. Syn. Grēssŭs, grădŭs. V. Gradus.

pāstĭllŭs, ī, m., *a small scented pill.* Pāstĭllŭm Rŭfīllŭs ŏlĕt, Hor.

pāstŏr, ōrĭs, m., *a shepherd.* Incaŭtīs pāstŏrĭbŭs ēxcĭdĭt, Virg. Syn. Ārmēntārĭŭs, ŭpĭlĭo, bŭbūlcŭs. Epith. Rŭstĭcŭs, agrēstĭs, sўlvēstrĭs, sēdūlŭs, vĭgĭl, sōllĭcĭtŭs, ānxĭŭs, fĭdŭs, fĭdēlĭs, văgŭs, ērrāns, dūrŭs, paŭpĕr, ĭnōps, ĕgēnŭs, mĭsĕr, vĭgĭlāns, mātūtīnŭs, ĭnsōmnĭs, ĭncūltŭs, squālĭdŭs, laetŭs. V. Grex.

pāstōrālĭs, ĕ, *and* tōrĭŭs, ĭă, ĭŭm, *pastoral, belonging to shepherds.* Pāstōrālĕ cănĭt, Virg. Pāstōrĭă pēllĭs, Ov. Syn. Agrēstĭs, rūstĭcŭs.

pāstŭs, ŭs, m., *the act of feeding, pasturage.* In pāstŭs ārmēntăquĕ, Virg.

Pătără, æ, f., *a town of Lycia, celebrated for an oracle of Apollo.*—2. adj., -ræŭs, ă, ŭm, *of Patara.* Pătăræăquĕ rēgĭă sērvĭt, Ov.

Pătărcŭs, ĕŏs *or* ĕī, m., *a surname of Apollo, worshipped at Patara.* Dēlĭŭs ēt Pătărcŭs Ăpōllo, Hor.

Pătăvĭŭm, ĭī *or* ĭ, n., *Padua, a city of Venetia.* Pătăvī sēdēsquĕ lŏcăvĭt, Virg.

pătĕfăcĭo, fēcī, făctŭm, *to open.* Lāssōs pătĕfēcĭt ŏcēllōs, Prop. Ătquĕ pătĕfēcĭt quōs, Lucr. Syn. Mōnstro, ĭndĭco, ōstēndo, mănĭfēsto, ăpĕrĭo, rĕsĕro. rēclūdo, rēsĭgno, pāndo; dēclāro, rĕtĕgo, rĕvēlo, dīvūlgo.

pătĕfĭo, fĭĕrī, făctŭs, *to be opened.* Dŏmĭnæ pătĕfĭānt, Prop.

pătēllă, æ, f., *a dish.* Cœnă pătēllā, Juv. Epith. Pīngŭĭs, ŏpīmă, ŏnūstă, ūnctă, frăgĭlĭs, pūră.

pătēns, ntĭs, *open, extended.* Cāmpōsquĕ pătēntēs, Virg. Syn. Ăpērtŭs; pătŭlŭs, lātŭs; mănĭfēstŭs, vūlgātŭs.

pătĕo, ŭī, *to be open.* Trīstĕ pătĕrēt ĭtĕr, Mart. Syn. Pătēsco, pătĕfĭo, āppărĕo, rĕtĕgŏr, dĕtĕgŏr, reclūdŏr, nūdŏr, pāndŏr, rĕvēlŏr.

pătĕr, pătrĭs, m., *a father.* Et pătrĭbŭs dăt, Virg. Syn. Părēns, gĕnĭtŏr, sătŏr. Epith. Cārŭs, dīlēctŭs, vĕrēndŭs, hŏnōrāndŭs, cōlēndŭs, sōllĭcĭtŭs, pĭŭs, vĕnĕrāndŭs, mădĭdă, ŏpīmă, făcĭlĭs, rĭgĭdŭs, grāndævŭs.

pătĕră, æ, f., *a cup, a goblet.* Fŭndēbăt pătĕrĭs, Virg. Syn. Scŷphŭs, călīx, crātĕr, pōcŭlŭm. Epith. Aŭrĕă, aŭrātă, ārgēntĕă, cælātă, gēmmāns, gēmmātă, spūmāns, pătēns, căpāx, mĭcāns. V. Poculum.

pătērnŭs, ă, ŭm, *of a father.* Jūră pătērnă, Mart.

pătēsco, ĭs, *to be open.* Pōrtŭsquĕ pătēscĭt, Virg.

pătĭbŭlŭm, ī, n., *a gibbet.* Est nōn pătĭbŭlŭm, (Iamb.) Syn. Crŭx, găbălŭs, fŭrcă. Epith. Ĭnfāmĕ, ĭnhŏnēstŭm, trīstĕ, nĕfāndŭm, dūrŭm, probrōsŭm, hŏrrēndŭm, mœstŭm, tĕrrībīlĕ, fūnĕrĕŭm, īnfaūstŭm, ăcĕrbŭm, ērēctŭm, părātŭm, fătālĕ. V. Crux.

pătĭēns, ntīs, *patient.* Tē pătĭēntĕ, mĕæ, Prop. SYN. Tŏlĕrāns. V. Constans.

pătĭēntĕr, adv., *patiently.* Tūlĭmŭs pătĭēntĭŭs āntĕ, Ov. SYN. Plăcīdĕ, fortĭtĕr, cōnstāntĕr. V. Patior.

pătĭēntĭă, æ, f., *patience.* Pānnō pătĭēntĭă vēlăt, Hor. SYN. Tŏlĕrāntĭă. EPITH. Invīctă, plăcīdă, īmmōtă, trānquīllă, mītīs, īnfrāctă, lēntă, fōrtīs.

pătĭnă, æ, f., *a hollow dish.* In pătĭnă pōrrēctā, Hor. SYN. Cătīnŭs, cătīllŭs, părōpsīs, lānx.

pătĭŏr, tĕrīs, *to suffer.* Fātă mĕīs pătĕrēntŭr, Virg. SYN. Fĕro, tŏlĕro, pērfĕro, pērpĕtĭŏr, sŭbĕo, sūstĭnĕo ; sĭno, pērmītto.

Pātræ, ārŭm, f. pl., *an ancient city of Achaia.* Pātræque, hŭmīlēsquĕ Clĕōnæ, Ov.

patrĭă, æ, f., *one's country.* Nōs pătrĭæ fīnēs, Virg. EPITH. Dīlēctă, dūlcīs, ămābīlīs, cāră, ōptātă, grātă, ămœnă, cōmmūnīs, nūtrīx, vĕtŭs.

patrĭcīdă, æ, m. f., *a parricide.* Gĕnŭīt pătrĭcīdăm, Prud.

Patrĭcĭŭs, ă, ŭm, *belonging to the Patricians.* Ōrăquĕ Pătrĭcĭŭs, Claud.

patrĭmōnĭŭm, īī, n., *a paternal estate.* Cōmĕdŭnt pătrĭmōnĭă mēnsā, Ov. SYN. Hærēdĭtās ; cēnsŭs. EPITH. Āmplŭm, laūtŭm, dīvēs, īngēns, māgnŭm, pārvŭm, ēxīgŭŭm, tĕnŭĕ, ēxīlĕ. V. Divitiæ.

patrĭŭs, ă, ŭm, *paternal.* Ēt pătrĭăs aūdītĕ, Virg. SYN. Pătērnŭs, ăvītŭs.

patro, ās, *to accomplish.* Cōnātă pătrāntŭr, Lucr. SYN. Făcĭo, pērpetro, ădmītto, cōmmītto.

patrōcĭnĭŭm, īī, n., *patronage.* Caūsă pătrōcĭnĭō, Ov. SYN. Dēfēnsĭo, tūtēlă, tūtāmĕn, præsĭdĭŭm. EPITH. Fīdēlĕ, vălĭdŭm, sălūtĭfĕrŭm, grātŭm, ēxpēctātŭm.

patrōcĭnŏr, ārīs, *to patronise.* Pătrōcĭnāntem ŭbī, Turpil. SYN. Tŭĕŏr, tūtŏr, cūstōdĭo, dēfēndo, sērvo, tĕgo, prōtĕgo ; sŭm tūtēlă, sūscĭpĭo patrōcĭnĭŭm. V. Tueor.

Patrōclŭs, ī, m., *the friend of Achilles.* Fāctă Pātrōclŭs Ōpūntă, Ov. EPITH. Graĭŭs, fortīs, aūdāx, tĕmĕrārĭŭs. SYN. Mĕnœtĭădēs, Āctŏrīdēs.

Patrōn, ōnīs, m., *one of the companions of Evander.* Sĭmŭl ēt Pātrōn, Virg.

patrōnă, æ, f., *a protectress.* Nūllī nōn tŭă præfĕrāt pătrōnă, Mart.—2. Adj., Ūt vōcem mĭhī cōmmŏdēs pătrōnăm.

patrōnŭs, ī, m., *a protector, an advocate.* Quŏvĕ pătrōnō, Hor. SYN. Caūsĭdĭcŭs, ōrātŏr. EPITH. Sōllĭcĭtŭs, fīdēlīs, fīdŭs, fācūndŭs, dīsērtŭs, dōctŭs, īngĕnĭōsŭs, sūbtīlīs, sōlērs. V. Causidicus.

patrŭēlīs, ĕ, *belonging to a brother's children.* Pătrŭēlĭă rēgnă, Ov.

patrŭēlīs, īs, m., *a father's brother's son.* Lēthŭm pătrŭēlĭbŭs aūsæ, Ov.

patrŭŭs, ī, m., *a father's brother.* Ērgŏ trĭbŭs pătrŭīs, Juv.

patrŭŭs, ă, ŭm, *of a father's brother.* Pătrŭæ vērbĕră līnguæ, Hor.

Pătŭlcĭŭs, īī, m., *a surname of Janus.* Nāmquĕ Pătŭlcĭŭs īdĕm, Ov.

pătŭlŭs, ă, ŭm, *opened.* Hūjŭs dŭm pătŭlōs, Mart. SYN. Pătēns, ăpērtŭs, dīffūsŭs.

paucī, *or* cŭlī, æ, ă, *few.* Cōntēntŭs paucīs, Hor. SYN. Paūcŭlī, ălĭquŏt, ălĭquī, nōnnūllī, pērpaūcī, rārī.

paucŭs, ă, ŭm, *few, small.* Sīmplēxquĕ fŏrāmĭnĕ paūcō, Hor.

păvĕfăctŭs, ă, ŭm, *terrified.* Păvĕfāctŭs īnfāns, (Iamb.) Sen. SYN. Tērrĭtŭs, ēxtērrĭtŭs.

păvĕo, pāvī, *also* ēsco, īs, *to be afraid, fear.* Ĭtĕrŭm păvĕŭs, Hor. Tŭ lætă păvēscĕ, Sil. SYN. Tīmĕo, mĕtŭo, vĕrĕŏr, fōrmīdo, rĕfōrmīdo, hōrrĕo, hōrrēsco, trĕmo, trĕpīdo. V. Timeo.

păvĭdŭs, ă, ŭm, *timid.* Stānt păvĭdæ īn mūrīs, Virg. SYN. Păvēns, tĭmĭdŭs, trĕpĭdŭs ; tērrĭtŭs, ēxtērrĭtŭs. V. Timidus.

păvīmēntŭm, ī, n., *pavement.* Vērrĕ păvīmēntŭm, Juv. SYN. Strātŭm. EPITH. Mārmŏrĕŭm, nītĭdŭm, mĭcāns, tērsŭm, mūndŭm, māgnĭfĭcŭm.

păvĭto, ās, *the freq. of* paveo. Prōsĕquĭtŭr pătrĭŭs, Virg.

paulātĭm, adv., *by little and little.* Dōnĕc paŭlātĭm, Virg. SYN. Sēnsĭm.

paŭlīspĕr, adv., *a little while.* Ipse ĕgŏ paŭlīspĕr, Virg.

paulō, lŭm, *and* lŭlŭm, adv., *a little.* Paūlō mājŏră cănāmŭs, Virg. Paūlum āspēctū cōntērrĭtŭs, Id. SYN. Pārŭm.

S. Paulŭs, ī, m., *Paul the apostle.* Epith. Sānctŭs, fācūndŭs, dōctŭs, pĭŭs, dīvīnŭs, īgnĕŭs.

pāvo, ōnĭs, m., *a peacock.* Ĕt crūdūm pāvōnĕm, Juv. Epith. Pīctŭs, sŭpērbŭs, vērsĭcŏlŏr, splēndĭdŭs, pŭlchĕr, īnsīgnĭs, gēmmĕŭs, gēmmātŭs, splēndēns, sīdĕrĕŭs, stēllātŭs, stēllīfĕr ; Jūnōnĭŭs, Sāmĭŭs.

pāvŏr, ōrĭs, m., *fear.* Strāvīt pāvŏr īllĕ, Virg. Syn. Tīmŏr, mĕtŭs, tērrŏr. V. Formido, timor.

paūpĕr, ĕrĭs, *poor.* Paūpĕrĭs ēt tŭgŭrī, Virg. Syn. Ĕgēnŭs, ĕgēns, īndĭgŭs, ĭnŏps, mēndīcŭs.

paūpērcŭlŭs, ă, ŭm, *very poor.* Paūpērcŭlă mātĕr, Hor.

paūpĕrĭēs, ĭēī, f., *poverty.* Nūnc ēt paūpĕrĭēm, Virg. V. Paupertas.

paūpĕro, ās, *to deprive of.* Cāssā nŭcĕ paūpĕrĕt, Hor. V. Privo.

paūpērtās, ātĭs, f., *poverty.* Paūpērtās, ātquĕ, Juv. Syn. Paūpĕrĭēs, ĕgēstās, ĭnŏpĭă, pēnūrĭă, īndĭgēntĭă. Epith. Sōrdĭdă, tūrpĭs, īncūltă, īmmūndă, īgnōbĭlĭs, dūră, āspĕră, sævă, īmpōrtūnă, īnfēlīx, īnfaūstă, ārctă, cōntrāctă, āugūstă, hŭmĭlĭs, pānnōsă, īnfēstă, ĭnĭmīcă, mălīgnă, ĭnvīdă, īndĭgă, ĭnŏps, jējūnă, sōbrĭă.

paūsă, æ, f., *a stop.* Vītæ paūsă, Lucr.

paūsĭă, æ, f., *a kind of olive.* Ēt ămārā paūsĭā bāccă, Virg.

Paūsĭăcŭs, ă, ŭm, *of Pausias, a celebrated Greek painter.* Paūsĭăcā tōrpēs, īnsānĕ, tăbēllā, Hor.

paūxĭllŭs, ă, ŭm, *very little.* Paūxĭllă mĭnūtăquĕ, Lucr.

pāx, pācĭs, f., *peace.* Ĕgrĕgĭæ pācĭs, Claud. Syn. Cōncōrdĭă, fœdŭs, ămīcĭtĭă ; quĭēs, ōtĭŭm. Epith. Trānquīllă, quĭētă, tūtă. cōncŏrs, cāndĭdă, cērtă, ālmă, lætă, gĕnĭālĭs, īnnōxĭă, īnnŏcŭă ; aūrĕă, blāndă, fēlīx, faūstă, bĕātă, sānctă, ămīcă, dūlcĭs, ămœnă, ōptātă, ōptābĭlĭs, mītĭs, ætērnă, lōngă, ēxpēctătă, tōgātă, fœcūndă, sīncēră, cōmpŏsĭtă, pērpĕtŭă, fīrmă, stăbĭlĭs.

pēccātŏr, ōrĭs, m., *a sinner.* Dēt pēccātōrī vĕnĭăm, Prosp. Syn. Nŏcēns, sōns. Epith. Tūrpĭs, fœdŭs, trīstĭs, nĕfāndŭs, nĕfārĭŭs, pērvērsŭs, mĭsĕr, īnīquŭs, āmēns, scĕlĕrātŭs.

pēccātŭm, ī, n., *a sin, a fault.* Nōctēm pēccātĭs, Hor. Syn. Dēlīctŭm, nōxă, cūlpă, crīmĕn, scĕlŭs, flāgĭtĭŭm, vĭtĭŭm, pĭācŭlŭm, nĕfās, ērrŏr, ērrātŭm, mălŭm. Epith. Nĕfāndŭm, tūrpĕ, fœdŭm, grăvĕ, īnēxcūsābĭlĕ, dētēstābĭlĕ, ēxecrābĭlĕ, īnfāndŭm, dīrŭm, grāndĕ, īngēns, nōxĭŭm, īmpĭŭm, atrōx. V. Crimen.

pēcco, ās, *to sin, to err.* Ămēt pēccārĕ tĭmēntēs, Hor. Syn. Dēlīnquo, ērro.

pĕcŏrōsŭs, ă, ŭm, *abundant in sheep.* Grĕgēm pĕcŏrōsō, Stat.

pēctĕn, ĭnĭs, m., *a comb.* Pēctĭnĭbŭs pătŭlĭs, Hor. Epith. Ĕbūrnŭs, ĕbūrnĕŭs, aūrĕŭs, rārŭs, dēntātŭs, mūltīfīdŭs, būxĕŭs, sēctŭs.—2. *a wool-card.* Pērcūrrīt pēctĭnĕ tēlās, Virg.—3. *a stick to play on an instrument with.* Pēctĭnĕ pūlsăt, Virg. Syn. Plēctrŭm. Epith. Cānōrŭs, blāndŭs, mōllĭs, Phœbēŭs, Aōnĭŭs, Apōllĭnĕŭs, ĕbūrnŭs, dūlcĭs, lēnĭs, aūrātŭs, rĕsŏnāns, vōcālĭs. V. Cithara.

pēcto, pēxūī *or* pēxī, pēxŭm, *to comb.* Pēctĕbātquĕ fĕrŭm, Virg.

pēctŭs, ŏrĭs, n., *the breast.* Pēctŏrĭs ēgīt, Prop. Syn. Cor. Epith. Nĭvĕŭm, cāndĭdŭm, lāctĕŭm, gŭnĕrōsŭm, măgnănĭmŭm, fōrtĕ, ĕbūrnŭm, pūlchrŭm, cāndēns, dĕcōrŭm, tĕnĕrŭm ; călĭdŭm.

pĕcŭārĭŭs, ă, ŭm, *of a flock.* Pĕcŭārĭă, ōrŭm, n. pl., *flocks.* In Vĕnĕrēm pĕcŭārĭă prīmŭs, Virg.

pĕcūlĭārĭs, ĕ, *of private possession, singular.* Lūcĕ nĭtēt ĕcūlĭārī, (Phal.) Mart.

pĕcūlĭŭm, ĭī, n., *private possession.* Cūră pĕcūlī, Virg. Epith. Pārvŭm, tĕnŭĕ, mŏdĭcŭm.

pĕcūnĭă, æ, f., *money.* Rēgīnă pĕcŭnĭă dŏnăt, Hor. Syn. Nūmmŭs, ŏpēs, dīvĭtĭæ, æs, aūrŭm, ārgēntŭm. Epith. Prētĭōsă, dīlēctă, fŭgāx, flūxă, pērnĭcĭōsă, īnsĭdĭōsă, īmprŏbă, scĕlĕrātă, pŏtēns, īngēns, pārvă, mŏdĭcă. V. Divitiæ, avaritia.

pĕcūnĭōsŭs, ă, ŭm, *rich.* Vūlt pĕcūnĭōsās, (Phal.) Mart. Syn. Ŏpŭlēntŭs, dīvēs, ārgēntī dīvēs ēt aūrī.

pĕcŭs, ŏrĭs, n., *and* cŭs, ŭdĭs, f., *sheep, cattle.* Quăm dīvēs pĕcŏrĭs, Virg. Pĕcŭdēs pīctæquĕ vŏlŭcrēs, Id. Syn. Armēntŭm, grēx. Epith. Immūndŭm, ērrāns, văgābūndŭm, mūtŭm, pĕtŭlāns, pĕtūlcŭm, lānĭgĕrŭm, vīllōsŭm, tĭmĭdŭm, păvĭdŭm, lāscīvŭm, ēffœtŭm, stŏlĭdŭm, plăcĭdŭm. V. Armentum, grex.

Pĕdănŭs, ă, ŭm, *of Pedum, a city near Rome.* In rĕgĭōnĕ Pĕdānā, Hor.

pĕdĕs, ĭtĭs, m., *a foot-soldier.* Cāmpō pĕdĕs īrĕ, Stat. Syn. Pĕdēstĕr. V. Miles.

pĕdēstĕr, trĭs, *going on foot.* Infĕrrĕ pĕdēstrēs, Virg.

pĕdĕtĕntĭm, adv., *step by step.* Est pĕdĕtēntĭm, Lucr.

Pĕdĭātĭă, æ, f., *Julius Pediatius, ironically called Pediatia.* Frăgĭlĭs Pĕdĭātĭă fūrquĕ, Hor.

pĕdĭcă, æ, f., *a fetter, snare.* Tūm grŭĭbūs pĕdĭcăs, Virg. Syn. Lăquĕŭs, rĕtĕ.

pĕdĭcŭlōsŭs, ă, ŭm, *lousy.* Dŏmĭnŭs pĕdĭcŭlōsī, (Phal.) Mart.

pĕdīssĕquŭs, ī, m., *and ă, æ, f., a footman, waiting-maid.* In pŏpĭnām pĕdīssĕquī, Plaut.

pĕdĭtātŭs, ūs, m., *infantry.* Ăt pĕdĭtātūs rĕlĭquĭæ, Plaut. Syn. Pĕdĭtēs.

Pĕdĭŭs, ĭī, m., *the name of a man.* Quŭm Pĕdĭŭs caūsăs, Hor.

Pĕdo, ōnĭs, m., *a Latin poet.* Cūr sīnt nārrātă Pĕdōnī, Hor. Syn. Albĭnŏvānŭs.

pĕdŭm, ī, n., *a sheep-hook.* Sūmĕ pĕdŭm, Virg. Epith. Pāstōrālĕ, ĭncūrvŭm, ĭnflēxŭm, fōrmōsŭm.—2. *a prelate's staff.* Syn. Lĭtŭŭs. Epith. Incūrvŭm, aūrātŭm, aūrĕŭm, ĕbūrnŭm, īnsĭgnĕ, gēmmāns.

Pēgăsĕŭs, *and* sĭŭs, *und* ēĭŭs, ă, ŭm, *of Pegasus.* Pēgăsēŭm gūrgĭtĕm, M. Cap. Pēgăsĭō fĕrăr, Cat. Pēgăsēĭŭm mĕlŏs, Pers.

Pēgăsĭs, ĭdĭs, f., *of Pegasus.* Hōc ĕgŏ Pēgăsĭdăs, Ov. Pēgăsĭdĕs, ŭm, f. pl., *the Muses.* Ăt mĭhī Pēgăsĭdĕs, Id. Syn. Mūsæ.

Pēgăsŭs, ī, m., *the winged horse which Bellerophon mounted.* Pēgăsŭs ībăt, Ov. Epith. Præpĕs, vēlōx; cĕlĕr, vŏlŭcĕr, āĕrĭŭs, ālĭgĕr, ālātŭs, pēnnātŭs, lēvĭs, vŏlāns.

pēgmă, ătĭs, n., *a scaffold on the stage.* Ĕt pēgma, ēt pŭĕrōs, Juv.

pējĕro, ās, *to violate an oath.* Pējĕrăt hўbērnī, Prop. Syn. Fālsē jūro.

pējŏr, ōrĭs, *worse.* Sĭt pējŏrĭbūs ōrtŭs, Hor. Syn. Dētĕrĭŏr, nēquĭŏr.

Pĕlăgo, *or* ōn, ōnĭs, m., *the name of a man.* Eūpălĕmōn Pĕlăgōnăquĕ, Ov.

pĕlăgŭs, ī, n., *the sea.* Ŭt pĕlăgŭs tĕnŭĕrĕ, Virg. Syn. Æquŏr, mărĕ, frĕtŭm, gūrgĕs, pōntŭs, sāl, āltŭm, prŏfūndŭm, ŏcĕănŭs. Epith. Pătēns, spūmāns, spūmōsŭm, īnsānŭm, tŭmĭdŭm. V. Mare.

pĕlămĭs, ĭdĭs, f., *a young thunny-fish.* Aūt vās pĕlămĭdŭm, Juv.

Pĕlāsgī, ōrŭm, m. pl., *the Greeks.* Prōdĭtĭŏnĕ Pĕlāsgī, Virg. V. Græci.—Adj. -ŭs, ă, ŭm, *Grecian.* Ēt ārtĕ Pĕlāsgā, Virg.

Pĕlāsgĭăs, ădĭs, *and* gĭs, ĭdĭs, f., *Grecian.* Fāmă Pĕlāsgĭădăs, Ov. Pĕlāsgĭdă Sāpphō, Id. Syn. Pĕlāsgă, Graīă, Ăchāĭs.

Pĕlātēs, æ, m., *the name of a man.* Cĭnўphĭŭs Pĕlătēs, Ov.

Pĕlēthrŏnĭī, ōrŭm, m. pl., *the inhabitants of a town in Thessaly.* Frænă Pĕlēthrŏnĭī, Virg. V. Lapithæ.

Pēleŭs, ĕŏs, ĕĭ *or* eī, m., *the father of Achilles.* Tĕlămōn, Pēleŭs, ĕt, Ov. Epith. Æmŏnĭŭs, Thēssălŭs, fōrtĭs.

Pĕlĭăcŭs, ă, ŭm, *of mount Pelion.* Trŏăquĕ Pĕlĭăcæ, Ov.

Pĕlĭăs, ădĭs, f., *of Pelion.* Pĕlĭăs ārbŏr ŏvĕm, Ov.—Subst., *the spear of Achilles.* Pĕlĭăs ēssĕ pŏtēst, Id.

Pĕlĭās, æ, m., *a king of Thessaly, put to death by his own daughters.* Prīmīs Pĕlĭās frænābăt ăb ārmĭs, V. Fl.

pĕlĭcānŭs, ī, m., *a pelican.* Mœrĕt pĕlĭcănŭs ăd ārcēs, Lud.

Pĕlīdēs, æ, m., *the son of Peleus, Achilles.* Aūsŭs Pĕlīdæ prētĭŭm, Virg.

Pĕlīgnī, ōrŭm, m. pl., *a people of Italy.* Pĕlīgnīs nātŭs ăquōsīs, Ov.

Pĕlĭŏn, ĭī, m., *a mountain in Thessaly.* Pĕlĭŏn hīnnītŭ, Virg. Epith. Āltŭs, ūmbrōsŭs, gĕlĭdŭs, Æmŏnĭŭs, Thēssălĭcŭs, Thēssălŭs, ŭmbrĭfĕr, āspĕr, vērnāns, vĭrēns.

Pēllă, æ, f., *a town of Macedon.* Prōvīncĭă Pēllæ, Lucan.

pēllācĭă, æ, f., *cunning, perfidy.* Plăcĭdī pēllācĭă pōntī, Ov.

Pēllæŭs, ă, ŭm, *of Pella, Macedonian.* Pēllæĭs dīvĕs ĭn ārvĭs, Ov.

pēllāx, ācĭs, *wheedling.* Pōstquăm pēllācīs Ŭlўsseī, Virg.

pēllēx, ĭcĭs, f., *a courtesan.* Pēllĭcĕ saŭcĭŭs, (Chor.) Hor. V. Meretrix.

pēllĭcĭo, lēxī, lēctŭm, *to allure.* Pēllĭcĕre ĭn fraūdĕm, Lucr. Syn. Āllĭcĭo, Āllēcto, prōlēcto, dēlīnĭo, īndūco, īmpēllo, ēxcĭto. V. Allicio.

o 6

pēllĭcŭlă, *diminut. of* pellis. Pēllĭcŭlā, cērdŏ, Mart. Epith. Tĕnŭĭs, tĕnĕră.

pĕllĭs, ĭs, f., *skin.* Pēllĭbŭs hāstās, Virg. Syn. Cŭtĭs; cŏrĭŭm, tēgmĕn; ĕxŭvĭæ, vēllŭs. Epith. Hīrsūtă, vīllōsă, dūră, măcŭlōsă, ālbă, nĭvĕă, lāctĕă, cāndēns, tĕnĕră, mōllĭs, lĕvĭs, tĕnŭĭs, pĭlōsă, rūgōsă.

pēllītŭs, ă, ŭm, *covered with a skin.* Pēllītŏs hăbŭĭt, Prop. V. Pellis. ·

pēllo, pĕpŭlī, pūlsŭm, *to drive away.* Pēllĭtĕ cūrās, Hor. Syn. Dēpēllo, ēxpēllo, propēllo, pūlso, propūlso, dētūrbo, ēxtūrbo, dētrūdo, ējĭcĭo, dējĭcĭo, ārcĕo; rēlēgo, āmāndo; īmpēllo, ăgĭto. V. Exulo.

pēllūcĕo, ēs, *to be transparent.* Sūppŏsĭtĭs pēllūcĕnt, Mart. Syn. Pērlūcĕo, trānslūcĕo, rēlūcĕo.

pēllūcĭdŭlŭs, ă, ŭm, *the dimin. of* pellucidus. Aŭt pēllūcĭdŭlī, Catul.

pēllūcĭdŭs, ă, ŭm, *transparent.* Māgĭs pēllūcĭdă gēmmă, Ov. Syn. Pēllūcĭdŭs, lūcĭdŭs, līmpĭdŭs.

Pĕlŏpēă, æ, f., *the daughter of Thyestes.* Sī quŏd Pĕlŏpēā Thўēstæ, Ov.

Pĕlŏpēĭăs, ădĭs, *and* pēĭs, ĭdĭs, f., *of Pelops.* Spārtē, Pĕlŏpēĭădēsquĕ Mўcēnæ, Ov. Dēxtrā Pĕlŏpēĭdăs ūndās, Id. Syn. Pĕlŏpēă, Pĕlŏpēĭă.

Pĕlŏpēŭs, *or* ēĭŭs, ă, ŭm, *of Pelops.* Stāt Pĕlŏpēā dŏmŭs, Ov. Mē Pĕlŏpēĭă Pĭttheŭs, Pr.

Pĕlŏpōnnēsŭs, ī, f., *the Morea.* In Pĕlŏpōnnēsō, Lucr.

Pĕlōps, ŏpĭs, m., *the son of Tantalus, killed by his father.* Flēssĕ Pĕlōps, hŭmĕrō, Ov. Epith. Tāntălĭdēs, Dārdănŭs, Phrўgĭŭs, pērjūrŭs.

pĕlōrĭs, ĭdĭs, f., *a large oyster.* Mēlĭŏr Lūcrīnă pĕlōrĭs, Hor.

Pĕlōrŭs, ī, m., *also* rĭăs, ădĭs, *and* rĭs, ĭdĭs, f., *a cape in Sicily.* Claŭstră Pĕlōrī, Virg. Jāmquĕ Pĕlōrĭădĕm, Ov. Cēlsā Pĕlōrĭs, Avien. Epith. Pĭscōsŭs, āngūstŭs, Sĭcŭlŭs, Sĭcănĭŭs, cēlsŭs, tŭmĭdŭs, āltŭs.

pēltă, æ, f., *a small buckler.* Āgmĭnă pēltīs, Virg. Syn. Clўpĕŭs, scūtŭm, ūmbo, pārmă. Epith. Lūnātă, ærātă, Thērmōdōntĭăcă, Āmăzōnĭă; hōrrĭdă, fālcātă.

pēltāstēs, ĭs; tātŭs, *and* tĭfĕr, ă, ŭm, *armed with a buckler.* Pēltātăm Scўthĭcō, Ov.

pēlvĭs, ĭs, f., *a vessel to wash in.* Pēlvĭs ŏlĕt, Juv. Syn. Pēllŭvĭŭm, cătīnŭs.

Epith. Căvă, āmplă, pătŭlă, căpāx, nītēns, mĭcāns, ăhēnă, ænĕă, āquārĭă.

Pēlūsĭŭm, ĭī, n., *a city and harbour of Egypt.* Sŭb Căsĭŏ Pēlūsī, Prisc.—Adj. sĭăcŭs *and* sĭŭs, ă, ŭm, *of Pelusium, Pelusian.* Nēc Pēlūsĭăcæ, Virg. Pēlūsĭă tīnxĕrĭt ōră, Luc.

pĕnātēs, ŭm, m. pl., *household gods.* Pŏpŭlārĕ pĕnātēs, Virg. Syn. Dĭī patrĭī, dĭī dŏmēstĭcĭ. Epith. Fīdī, cārī, sacrī, vĕnĕrāndī, cūstōdēs. V. Lares.

pĕnātĭgĕr, ĕră, ĕrŭm, *carrying his household goods.* Pĕnātĭgĕrō Ænēæ, Ov.

pĕndĕo, pĕpēndī, *to hang.* Pēndĕt ăb ōrĕ, Ov. Syn. Dēpēndĕo. V. Strangulo.

pēndo, ĭs, *to weigh.* Pēndĕrĕ pœnās, Virg. Syn. Ēxpēndo, pōndĕro; lŭo; sŏlvo; æstĭmo.

pēndŭlŭs, ă, ŭm, *hanging down.* Pēndŭlŭs hōræ, Hor. Syn. Pēndēns, dēpēndēns, sūspēnsŭs, pēnsĭlĭs.

pĕnĕ, adv., *almost.* Pĕnĕ sĭmŭl, Virg. Syn. Fērmē, fĕrĕ, prŏpĕ.

Pēnēĭs, ĭdĭs, f., *of the Peneus.* Spēctāns Pēnēĭdăs ūndās, Ov.

Pēnēĭŭs, ă, ŭm, *of the Peneus.* Pēnēĭă Tēmpē, Virg.—2. Subst. - ēĭă, æ, f., *the daughter of Peneus, Daphne.* Răpĭdō Pēnēĭă cūrsū, Ov.

Pēnĕlŏpē, ēs, f., *the wife of Ulysses.* Hānc tŭă Pēnĕlŏpē, Ov. Syn. Icărĭs, Icărĭŏtĭs. Epith. Icărĭă, pŭdīcă, cāstă, pĭă, fĭdēlĭs, fīdă, fōrmōsă, dĕcōră, Ārgŏlĭcă.

Pēnĕlŏpēŭs, ă, ŭm, *of Penelope.* Pēnĕlŏpēă fīdēs, Ov.

pĕnēs, prep, *in the power of.* Mē pĕnēs ēst ūnŭm, Ov.

pĕnetrābĭlĭs, ĕ, *piercing.* 'Bŏrēæ pĕnĕtrābĭlĕ frīgŭs, Virg. Syn. Ăcūtŭs.

pĕnetrālĕ, ĭs, n., *the inmost part.* Vĕtĕrŭm pĕnĕtrālĭă rēgŭm, Virg. Syn. Ădўtŭm, sacrārĭŭm. Epith. Arcānŭm, sēcrētŭm, sacrŭm, rĕcōndĭtŭm, ōbscūrŭm, īntĭmŭm, īntĕrĭŭs.

pĕnetrālĭs, ĕ, *inmost.* Ădўtīs ēffērt pĕnĕtrālĭbŭs ūrbĕm, Virg.

pĕnetro, ās, *to penetrate.* Illўrĭcōs pĕnĕtrārĕ sĭnūs, Virg. Syn. Pērvādo, pērmĕo, sŭbĕo, īrrēpo, īllābŏr, me īnsĭnŭo.

Pēnēŭs, ēī, *or* Pēnĕŭs, eī, *(dissyll.)* m., *a river of Thessaly.* Xānthō, Pēnēĕ, Crēūsăm, Ov. Ărīstæŭs, Pēneī gĕnĭtŏrĭs, Virg. Epith. Stāgnāns, Thēssălŭs, cănōrŭs, ămœnŭs.

pĕnĭcīllŭm, n., *and* ŭs, m., ī, *a pencil.* Quīn pĕnĭcīllō, quō, (Scaz.) EPITH. Sŏlērs, dŏctŭm, aŭdāx.

pĕnīnsŭlă, æ, f., *almost an island.* Pĕnīnsŭlārŭm Sīrmĭo, (Scaz.) Cat.

pĕnĭtŭs, adv., *to the bottom.* Ēt caūsās pĕnĭtŭs, Virg. SYN. Ăltē; ăd īmŭm; ĭn īmă.

Pĕnĭŭs, ĭī, m., *a river discharging itself into the Euxine.* Săgărīs, Pĕnĭŭsquĕ, Ov

pĕnnă, æ, f., *a feather.* In sȳlvăm pĕnnīs, Virg. SYN. Ălă. V. Ala.

pĕnnĭgĕr, *and* nātŭs, ă, ŭm, *winged.* Nēc nōs pĕnnĭgĕrīs, Ov. SYN. Ălātŭs, ālĭgĕr.

pĕnnĭpēs, pĕdĭs, *having wings at the feet.* Pĕnnĭpēsvĕ Pērseŭs, Cat.

pĕnnĭpŏtēns, ntĭs, *having a strong wing.* Cōrpŏră pĕnnĭpŏtēntŭm, Lucr.

pēnsĭlĭs, ĕ, *hanging.* Pēnsĭlĭs ŭvă, Hor. SYN. Pĕndŭlŭs, pēndēns, sŭspēnsŭs.

pēnsĭo, ōnĭs, f., *payment, rent.* Sēd pēnsĭō clāmăt, Juv.

pēnso, ās, *to weigh exactly.* Trŭtĭnă pēnsāntŭr ĕădĕm, Hor.

pēnsŭm, ī, n., *a task.* Rĕvŏlūtăquĕ pēnsă, Virg. SYN. Stāmĕn.

Pēnthĕsĭlĕă, æ, f., *the queen of the Amazons.* Pēnthĕsĭlĕă rĕfĕrt, Virg. EPITH. Fŭrēns, Mārtĭă, fĕră, fŭrĭbūndă, bēllātrīx, fōrtĭs, pŏtēns, gĕnĕrōsă, ănĭmōsă.

Pēntheŭs, (*dissyll.*) ĕŏs, ĕĭ *or* eī, m., *a king of Thebes, torn to pieces by the Bac-chantes.* Agmĭnă Pēntheŭs, Virg. SYN. Ēchĭŏnĭdēs. EPITH. Sŭpērbŭs, īmpĭŭs, mĭsĕr, īnfēlix, lănĭātŭs.

Pēnthĕŭs, *and* ēĭŭs, ă, ŭm, *of Pentheus.* Pēnthĕā cædĕ sătīsquĕ, Ov. Pēnthēĭă mātĕr, Sid.

Pēnthīdēs, æ, m., *the son of Pentheus.* Ēt quæ Pēnthīdēs, Ov.

pĕnŭlă, æ, f., *a thick mantle.* Pĕnŭlă sōlstĭtĭō, Hor. EPITH. Ŏnĕrōsă, grăvĭs, tŭtă, ŭtĭlĭs, dēpīctă, pīctă, scōrtĕă.

pĕnŭlātŭs, ă, ŭm, *covered with a thick mantle.* Alphă pĕnŭlātōrŭm, (Scaz.) Mart.

pĕnŭrĭă, æ, f., *indigence.* In Cĕrĕrĕm pēnŭrĭa ădēgĭt, Virg. SYN. Ēgēstăs, paŭpērtās.

pĕnŭs, ī *and* ŭs, m. *and* f.; *or* pĕnŭs, ŏrĭs, n., *victuals.* Cūră pĕnŭm, Virg SYN. Vīctŭs, ānnōnă, ălĭmēntă, cĭbārĭă. EPITH. Cōpĭōsă, ăbūndāns, lārgă, ŭtĭlĭs, cōmmŏdă, mŏdĭcă, brĕvĭs, ăbscōndĭtă, dŏmēstĭcă.

Pĕpărēthŏs, *or* ŭs, ī, f., *a small island in the Ægean sea.* Fĕrax Pĕpărēthŏs ŏlīvæ, Ov.

peplŭm, ī, n. *and* ŏs *or* ŭs, ī, m., *a veil.* Pāssĭs, pēplŭmquĕ, Virg. Pēplŭmquĕ fluēntĕm, Aus. Ēxŭïtŭr nūdātă pĕplō, Prud. EPITH. Pēndēns, ālbŭm, cān-dĭdŭm, nĭvĕŭm, pūrpŭrĕŭm, ēffūsŭm, fluēns, lōngŭm, tĕnŭĕ, ōrnātŭm, dĕcōrŭm, gēmmātŭm, aūrātŭm, ĭnaūrātŭm.

pĕr, prep, *by, through.* Trānstră pĕr ēt rēmŏs, Virg. SYN. Intĕr.

pĕră, æ, f., *a bag.* Pĕră rŏgăt, Mart. SYN. Pĕrŭlă, săccŭlŭs.

pĕrăcūtŭs, ă, ŭm, *very sharp.* Pĕrăcūtă fălcĕ sĕcărĕ, Mart.

pĕrăgo, ēgī, āctŭm, *to finish.* Sīc pĕrăgāmŭs ĭtĕr, Prop. SYN. Ăgo, pērfĭcĭo, cōnfĭcĭo, ēxĕquŏr, ābsōlvo.

pĕragro, ās, *to ramble over.* Pĭĕrĭdŭm pĕrăgro, Lucr. SYN. Lūstro, pĕrērro, ŏbĕo, pērcūrro, pērlūstro. V. Peregrinor.

pĕrāmbŭlo, ās, *to go through.* Flōrēsquĕ pĕrāmbŭlĕt, Hor. SYN. Ŏbāmbŭlo, ŏbĕo, pĕrērro.

Pĕrānnă, æ, f., *a Roman goddess.* Nĕmŭs Pĕrānnæ, (Phal.) Mart.

pĕrăro, ās, *to plough over.* Rūgīs pĕrărāvĭt, Ov.

pērbĭbo, bĭbī, *to drink up.* Pērbĭbĭt īmĭs, Ov. V. Bibo.

* pērbrĕvĭs, ĕ, *very short.* Pērbrĕvĭs ævī, Liv.

pērcă, æ, f., *a fish, perch.* Pērcæquĕ trăgīquĕ, Ov.

pērcălĕfāctŭs, ă, ŭm, *quite warm.* Pērcălĕfāctă vīdēs, Lucr.

pērcălĕo, ēs, *to grow quite warm.* Pērcălŭīt sōlĭs, Ov.

pērcēllo, cŭlī, ŭlsŭm, *to strike down.* Pērcŭlīt ēt fūlvā, Virg.

pērcēnsĕo, ēs, *to reckon up.* Pērcēnsŭīt ōrbĕm, Ov.

pērcĭĕo, ēs, ērĕ, *and* cĭo, īs, īrĕ, *to move, agitate.* Quăm rēs sē pērcĭĕt ŭllă, Lucr. Făx sūbdĭtă pērcĭt, Id.

pērcĭpĭo, cēpī, cēptŭm, *to understand, reap.* Pērcĭpĭănt ănĭmī, Hor.

pērcĭtŭs, ă, ŭm, *the pass. part. of* percieo, *moved.* Pērcĭtŭs ācrī, Lucr. SYN. Ēx-cĭtŭs, pērcŭlsŭs, pērmōtŭs, ābrēptŭs, cōntāctŭs, īrātŭs. V. Iratus.

pērcolo, ās, *to filter.* Pēr tērrās crēbrĭŭs īdĕm Pērcōlātŭr, Lucr.

pērcōntātŏr, ōrĭs, m., *an inquisitive person.* Pērcōntātōrĕm fŭgĭto, Hor.

pērcōntŏr, ārĭs, *to question.* Pērcōntābĕrĕ dūctŭs, Hor. SYN. Scīscĭtŏr, quæro, īnquīro, pĕto, pōsco, rŏgĭto, pōstŭlo, īntērrŏgo.

pērcŏquo, quĭs, xĭ, *to cook thoroughly.* Pērcŏquĭt ūvās, Ov.

pērcūrro, rsŭm, *to run over.* Pērcūrrīssĕ pŏlŭm, Hor.

pērcūssŭs, ûs, m., *a stroke.* Pērcūssū crēbrō, Ov.

pērcŭtĭo, ŭssī, ŭssŭm, *to strike.* Pērcŭtĭāt lăpĭs, Luc. Syn. Vērbĕro, fĕrĭo, tŭndo, pŭlso. V. Verbero.

pērdēlīrŭs, ă, ŭm, *stark mad.* Pērdēlīrum ēssĕ vĭdētŭr, Lucr.

pērdēspŭo, ĭs, *to detest.* Pătrŭī pērdēspŭĭt īpsăm, Cat. V. Contemno.

pērdīsco, dĭdĭcī, *to learn.* Nătūræ pērdīscĕrĕ mŏrēs, Prop.

pērdĭtŭs, ă, ŭm, *the pass. part. of* perdo, *lost.* Pērdĭtŭs īn quādăm, Prop. Syn. Amīssŭs.

pērdĭŭs, ă, ŭm, *during the day.* Pērdĭŭs ēt pērnōx, Col.

pērdīx, īcĭs, *a partridge.* Pērdīcĭs părĭlī, Ser. Epith. Gārrŭlă, pīctă, Dædălă, fāllāx, tĭmĭdă, fŭgāx, pēnnĭgĕră, agrēstĭs. V. Avis.

pērdo, dĭdī, dĭtŭm, *to lose.* Pērdĭdĭt, īnquĭt, Hor. Syn. Dēpērdo, āmītto. V. Amitto.

pērdŏcĕo, ēs, *to learn.* Pērdŏcŭērĕ Dĕæ, Ov.

pērdŏctŭs, ă, ŭm, *very learned.* Pērdŏctī quŏd sŭmŭs āntĕ, Lucr.

pērdŏmĭtŏr, ōrĭs, *a conqueror.* Mōrtĭs pērdŏmĭtŏr, Prud. Syn. Dŏmĭtŏr, vīctŏr, sŭpĕrātŏr.

pērdŏmĭtŭs, ă, ŭm, *the pass. partic. of* perdomo. Pērdŏmĭtās ōmnēs, Lucan.

pērdŏmo, ās, ŭī, *to conquer.* Pērdŏmŭīssĕ fĕrās, Mart. Syn. Dŏmo, vīnco, sŭpĕro.

pērdūco, xī, ctŭm, *to lead through.* Dūm tū pērdūcĭs Āchīllĕm, Hor. Syn. Ābdūco, dūco.

pērdūro, ās, *to persevere.* Lōngŭm pērdūrăt ĭn ævŭm, Ov. Syn. Dūro, pērsto, mănĕo.

pĕrĕdo, ēdī, ēsŭm, *to eat away.* Sāxă pĕrĕdĭt ăquā, Tibull. Syn. Ēxĕdo, ĕdo, cōnsūmo.

pĕrĕgrē, adv., *in a foreign country.* Dūm pĕrĕgre ēst, Hor. Syn. Lōngē.

* pĕrĕgrīnŏr, ārĭs, *to travel.* Cic.

pĕrĕgrīnŭs, ă, ŭm, *foreign.* Vērtĭt pĕrĕgrīnăm, Ov. Prīmă pĕrĕgrīnōs, Juv. Syn. Ādvĕnă, hōspĕs, ălĭēnŭs, ēxtērnŭs, ēxtĕrŭs, ēxtrānĕŭs.

pĕrēmptŏr, ōrĭs, m., *a murderer.* Ēt quĭs pĕrēmptŏr, (Iamb.) Sen. Syn. Īntērfēctŏr, pērcūssŏr.

pĕrēmptŭs, ă, ŭm, *the pass. partic. of* perimo. Quāquĕ pĕrēmptă fĕră, Mart.

pĕrēndĭē, adv., *the day after to-morrow.* Pĕrēndĭē fŏrās fĕrātŭr, (Iamb. pur.) Plaut.

pĕrēndĭnŭs, ă, ŭm, *of the day after to-morrow.* Tu īn pĕrēndĭnŭm, Plaut.

pĕrēnnĭs, ĕ, *eternal.* Mŏnŭmēntă pĕrēnnĭă fāctī, Ov. Syn. Pērpĕtŭŭs, ætērnŭs, jūgĭs, cōntĭnŭŭs, āssĭdŭŭs, nōn īntērmīssŭs.

pĕrēnno, ās, *to last for ever.* Ārtĕ pĕrēnnăt, Ov.

pĕrĕo, ĭs, ĭī, *to die.* Părĭtĕr pĕrĕātĭs, ăvārī, Pers. Syn. Dīspĕrĕo, īntĕrĕo, cădo, ōccĭdo; pērdŏr.

pĕrērro, ās, *to wander over.* Tōtămquĕ pĕrērrăt, Virg. Syn. Ōbērro, ērro, cīrcŭmērro.

pĕrēsŭs, ă, ŭm, *the pass. partic. of* peredo. Īllŭvĭĕquĕ pĕrēsă, Virg.

pērfăcĭlĭs, ĕ, *very easy.* Pērfăcĭle ēst ănĭmī, Lucr.

pērfătŭŭs, ă, ŭm, *very foolish.* Heŭ quăm pērfătŭæ sŭnt, Mart.

pērfĕro, tŭlī, *to endure.* Pērfĕrĕt Aŭnō, Virg. Syn. Pătĭŏr, sŭstĭnĕo, ēxāntlo; ēxhaŭrĭo; tŏlĕro. V. Patior, tolero.

pērfĭcĭo, fēcī, fēctŭm, *to finish.* Pērfĭcĭt ānnōs, Hor. Syn. Pĕrăgo, ābsōlvo, cōnfĭcĭo, ēxĕquŏr, ēxplĕo, ēxĭgo; pōlĭo, pērpŏlĭo. V. Finio.

pērfĭcŭs, ă, ŭm, *perfecting.* Pērfĭcă fīnĕm, Lucr.

pērfĭdĭă, æ, f., *perfidy.* Pērfĭdĭæ cŭmŭlŭm, Ov. Syn. Fraŭs, dŏlŭs. Epith. Ōccūltă, dŏlōsă, ēxĭtĭōsă, dētēstābĭlĭs, dētēstāndă, īmpĭă, ēxecrāndă, fāllāx, ārcānă, tēctă, hōrrēndă, nĕfāndă, īnfāndă, tūrpĭs, fœdă, scĕlĕrātă, Pœnă, Pūnĭcă. V. Fraus.

pērfĭdŭs, ă, ŭm, *deceitful, perfidious.* Pērfĭdĕ, tāntŭm, Virg. Syn. Pērfĭdĭōsŭs, īnfĭdŭs, dŏlōsŭs, mălĕfĭdŭs, pērjūrŭs. V. Mendax, fallax, fraus.

pērfĭgo, ĭs, xī, *to pierce.* Tēlĭs pērfīxă văpōrĭs, Lucr.

pērfĭnĭo, ĭs, *to accomplish.* Nēc rēs pērfīnĭĕt ūllă, Lucr.

pērflo, ās, *to blow violently upon.* Tūrbĭnĕ pērflănt, Virg.

‖ pĕrflŭctŭo, ās, *to float over.* Tūmĭdōs pĕrflŭctŭăt ārtŭs, Lucr.

pĕrflŭo, ūxī, *to flow over.* Hāc ĕt illāc pĕrflŭo, (Iamb.) Ter.

pĕrfŏdĭo, fŏdī, fossŭm, *to dig through.* Pĕrfŏdĭunt ălĭī, Sil. SYN. Fŏdĭo, cōnfŏdĭo, trānsfŏdĭo, pĕrfŏro, pĕrfrīngo, ăpĕrĭo; ĭntĕrĭŏrā rīmŏr.

‖ pĕrfōrmīdātŭs, ă, ŭm, *much feared.* Sil.

pĕrfŏro, ās, *to bore through.* Pĕrfŏrăt ĭngēns, Virg. SYN. Fŏro, fŏdĭo, ăpĕrĭo.

pĕrfrīco, ās, ŭī, *to rub.* Pĕrfrīcŭīt dēntēs, Ov.

pĕrfrīgĕo, xī, *to be quite cold.* Pĕrfrīxīssĕ tŭŭs, Mart. V. Frigeo.

pĕrfrīngo, ēgī, āctŭm, *to break through.* Lētĭfĕrā pĕrfrīngĕrĕ cōllă, Val. SYN. Ēffrīngo, rūmpo, frāngo. V. Frango.

pĕrfrŭŏr, ĕrĭs, *to enjoy thoroughly.* Amplēxū pĕrfrŭītūrquĕ tŭŏ, Ov.

pĕrfŭgĭŭm, ĭī, n., *an asylum.* Pĕrfŭgĭŭmquĕ, Lucr. SYN. Prōfŭgĭŭm, rĕfŭgĭŭm, pōrtŭs, ăsȳlŭm, sōlātĭŭm. EPITH. Tūtŭm, sēcūrŭm, quĭētŭm, plăcĭdŭm, faŭstŭm, fēlīx, ōptābĭlĕ.

pĕrfūlcĭo, sī, tŭm, *to support.* Pĕrfūlcīrĕ sĕuātŭm, Ov.

pĕrfūndo, fūdī, fūsŭm, *to pour all over.* Ănĭmōs pĕrfūdĕrăt ārdēns, Juv. SYN. Aspērgo, spārgo, īrrĭgo, rĭgo, īrrōro. V. Rigo.

pĕrfūngŏr, ĕrĭs, *to execute fully.* Ōmnĭă pĕrfūnctŭs, Lucr.

pĕrfūro, ĭs, *to be in a rage.* Pĕrfūrĭt āc mūltăm, Virg. V. Furo.

pĕrfūsŭs, ă, ŭm, *poured all over, wetted.* Cōcȳtā pĕrfūsŭs ăquā, Pet. Arb.

Pērgămă, ōrŭm, n. pl., *the citadel of Troy.* Pērgămă dēxtrā, Virg. EPITH. Āltă, Nēptūnĭă, Phœbēă, Dārdănă, ārdŭă. V. Troja.

Pērgămĕŭs, ă, ŭm, *of Troy.* Ārcēs Pērgămĕæ, Virg.

pērgo, pērrēxī, *to go on.* Pērgĭtĕ, Pĭĕrīdĕs, Virg. SYN. Pērsĕvēro, pērsto, pērsīsto, nōn cēsso, nōn ĭntērmītto, cōntĭnŭo ; ĕo, tēndo.

pērgrātŭs, ă, ŭm, *very agreeable.* Vēnĭēt pērgrātā vŏlŭptās, Ov.

pērgŭlă, æ, f., *a balcony.* Juv. EPITH. Tēctă, ăpērtă, aprīcă, sōlārĭs.

Pērgŭs, ī, m., *a lake in Sicily.* Nōmĭnĕ Pērgŭs ăquæ, Ov.

pērhĭbĕo, ēs, *to relate.* Quŏd pērhĭbēs, Virg. SYN. Dīco, nārro, rĕfĕro, mĕmŏro, cōmmĕmŏro. V. Dico, narro.

pērhĭlŭm, ī, n., *very little.* Imā pērhīlŭm, Lucr.

pērhŏrrĕo, ēs, or ēsco, ĭs, ŭī, *to be horror-struck.* Quŭmquĕ pērhōrrērĕt, Ov. Jūrĕ pērhōrrŭī, (Chor.) Hor. V. Timeo, horreo.

‖ pērhōspĭtŭs, ă, ŭm, *very hospitable.*

Pĕrĭāndēr, or drŭs, ī, m., *one of the seven wise men of Greece.* Hūc Pĕrĭāndēr prōdĕo, Aus.

Pĕriclēs. ĭs or ī, m., *a celebrated Athenian.* Māgnī pŭpīllĕ Pĕrĭclī, Pers.

pĕrĭclītŏr, ārĭs, *to be in danger.* Pĕrĭclītātūr căpĭtĕ, (Scaz.) Mart. SYN. Explōro, tēnto, prŏbo. V. Periculum.

Pĕrĭclȳmĕnŭs, ī, m., *the brother of Nestor.* Mīră Pĕrĭclȳmĕnī mŏrs ēst, Ov.

pĕrīcŭlōsŭs, ă, ŭm, *dangerous.* Vītĭŭm pĕrīcŭlōsŭm ēst, (Phal.) Mart.

pĕrīcŭlŭm, and clŭm, ī, n., *a danger.* Pĕr tāntă pĕrīcŭlă cāsŭs, Virg. Căpŭt ōbjēctārĕ pĕrīclīs, Id. SYN. Dīscrīmĕn, ălĕă, cāsŭs. EPITH. Sævŭm, dŭbĭŭm, āncēps, fūnēstŭm, ēxĭtĭālĕ, hōrrēndŭm, præsēns, tĭmēndŭm, sĭnīstrŭm, flēbĭlĕ, trīstĕ, ĭngēns, ĭnēxtrīcābĭlĕ, īmpēndēns, ĭnēvītābĭlĕ, exhaŭstŭm, cērtŭm, ăpērtŭm.

Pĕrīllă, æ, f., *the name of a woman.* Dīssĭmŭlātă Pĕrīllæ, Ov.

Pĕrīllĕŭs, ă, ŭm, *of Perillus.* Ipsĕ Pĕrīllĕō Phălărĭs, Ov.

Pĕrīllŭs, ĭī, m., *the name of a man.* Mĭhī crēdĕ, Pĕrīllī, Hor.

Pĕrīllŭs, ī, m., *the fabricator of the brazen bull for Phalaris.* Mēmbră Pĕrīllī, Ov. EPITH. Vĭōlēntŭs, ĭnfēlīx, sævŭs, dīrŭs, fĕrŭs, fĕrōx, ĭngĕnĭōsŭs, mĭsĕr. V. Phalaris.

Pĕrĭmĕlē, ēs, f., *the daughter of Hippodamas, changed into an island.* Insŭlă grātă mĭhī, Pĕrĭmĕlēn nāvĭtă dīcĭt, Ov.

pĕrĭmo, ēmī, ēmptŭm, *to kill.* Sācrĭlĕgæ pĕrĭmŭnt, Ov. SYN. Intĕrĭmo, īntĕrfĭcĭo, ōccīdo, nĕco. V. Occīdo, [*from* cædo.]

pĕrĭndĕ, adv., *equally.* Mŏrĭēnsquĕ pĕrĭndĕ, Mart. SYN. Părĭtĕr, æquē.

Pĕrĭphās, āntĭs, m., *one of the Lapithæ.* Gĕmĭnī Pĕrĭphāntă Pȳrētī, Ov.

pĕrīscĕlĭs, ĭdĭs, f., *a garter.* Sæpĕ pĕrīscĕlĭdĕm, Hor.

pĕrītĭă, æ, f., *experience.* Nŏcĭtūră pĕrītĭā frŭctŭ, Anon. SYN. Prūdēntĭă, scĭēntĭă, ārs.

pĕrītŭs, ă, ŭm, *experienced.* Sōlī căntārĕ pĕrītī, Virg. Syn. Dōctŭs, scīēns, gnārŭs, haŭd īgnārŭs, prūdēns. V. Doctus.

pērjūrātŭs, ă, ŭm, *violated by perjury.* Ēt pērjūrātōs, Ov. Syn. Pējĕrātŭs.

pērjŭrĭŭm, ĭī, n., *perjury.* Lŭīmŭs pērjŭrĭă Trōjæ, Virg. Epith. Impĭŭm, hōrrēndŭm, fœdŭm, tūrpĕ, dŏlōsŭm, ēxecrāndŭm. V. Perfidia, mendacia, fraus.

pērjŭro, ās, *to forswear one's self.* Tū pērjŭrārĕ tĭmēto, Ov. Syn. Pējĕro, mēntĭŏr.

pērjŭrŭs, ă, ŭm, *perjured.* Pērjŭrīque ārtĕ Sĭnōnĭs, Virg. V. Perfidus.

pērlābŏr, ĕrĭs, *to slip away.* Pērlābĭtŭr ūndās, Virg.

pērlĕgo, ēgī, *to read through.* Nēc quōs pērlĕgăt, (Phal.) Mart.

pērlibro, ās, *to level.* Jăcŭlŭm pērlībrăt ăd ōssă, Sil.

pērlūcĕo, xī, *to be transparent.* Nătīvīs pērlūcēnt, Ov.

pērlūcĭdŭs, ă, ŭm, *transparent.* Tĕnŭī pērlūcĭdŭs ūndā, Ov.

pērlūdo, ĭs, sī, *to play in.* Tŭcĭtŭm pērlŭdĕrĕ cāmpīs, Prop. V. Ludo.

pērlŭo, ĭs, ŭī, *to wash all over.* Pērlŭĭt ūndā, Ov. V. Lavo.

pērlūstro, ās, *to view all over.* Tōtŭm pērlūstrăt, Virg. V. Percurro.

pērmădēsco, ĭs, *to be quite damp.* Pērmădŭīssĕ crŏcō, Mart.

pērmāgnŭs, ă, ŭm, *very great.* Pērmāgnă nĕgōtĭă, Hor. V. Magnus.

pērmănĕo, mānsī, *to stay to the end.* Pērmănĕt aŭră, Prop. Syn. Mănĕo, pērsto.

pērmāno, ās, *to flow through.* Pērmānāre ănĭmăm, Lucr. Syn. Māno, īnflŭo, pērvādo.

pērmātūrēsco, ĭs, *to grow ripe.* Ūbĭ pērmātūrŭĭt, ātĕr, Ov. V. Maturesco.

pērmĕo, ās, *to pass through.* Pērmĕăt ānnŭs, Ov.

pērmĕrĕo, ēs, *to deserve.* Pērmĕrŭĭt jūrātă mănŭs, Sil.

Pērmēssŭs, ī, m., *and* ĭs, ĭdĭs *or* ĭdŏs, f, *a river of Bœotia, sacred to the Muses.* Ērrāntēm Pērmēssī, Virg. Cŭm Pērmēssĭdŏs ūndā, Mart. Lārgō Pērmēssĭdă pōssĕt, Id.

pērmētĭŏr, īrĭs, mēnsŭs sŭm, *to measure.* Ēt dūrŭm pērmēnsŭs ĭtĕr, Stat.

pērmĕtŭo, ĭs, *to fear much.* Irās pērmĕtŭēns, Virg. V. Timeo.

pērmiscĕo, scŭī, xtŭm *or* stŭm, *to mingle.* Pĕlăgō pērmĭscŭĭt Eūrŭs, Virg. V. Misceo.

pērmītto, mīsī, mīssŭm, *to permit.* Cæsār pērmīsĭt ĕphēbō, Mart. Syn. Cōncēdo, sĭno, pătĭŏr, dō, īndŭlgĕo. V. Licet.

pērmōtŭs, ă, ŭm, *very much moved.* Cŭm mărĕ pērmōtŭm, Lucr.

pērmŏvĕo, mōvī, mōtŭm, *to move very much.* Pērmŏvĕt ūndās, L. Syn. Mŏvĕo, cŏmmŏvĕo, ăgĭto.

pērmūlcĕo, sī, *to caress.* Pērmūlsĭt ĕŭm, Ov. Syn. Mūlcĕo, mītĭgo, mōllĭo, lēnĭo, plāco.

pērmūltĭ, æ, ă, *very many.* Pērmūltă jŏcātŭs, Hor.

pērmūtātĭo, ōnĭs, f., *a change.* Pērmŭtātĭō dĕtŭr, Juv.

pērmūto, ās, *to change.* Fāllāx pērmūtĕt ŏdŏrĕ, Mart. Syn. Mūto, cōmmūto.

pērnă, æ, f., *a gammon.* Cŭm pĕdĕ pērnæ, Hor.

pērnĕgo, ās, *to deny absolutely.* Pērnĕgăt īllă, Tib.

pērnĕo, ēs, *to spin out.* Lăchēsīs pērnĕvĕrĭt ānnōs, Mart.

pērnĭcĭālĭs, ĕ, *pernicious.* Sĭnĕ pērnĭcĭālī Dīscĭdĭō, Lucr.

pērnĭcĭēs, ĭēī, f., *ruin.* Pērnĭcĭēs, ĕt, Hor. Syn. Ēxĭtĭŭm, dētrĭmēntŭm, dāmnŭm, clādēs, rŭīnă. Epith. Grăvĭs, trīstĭs, ēxĭtĭōsă, mĕtŭēndă, flēbĭlĭs, lacrȳmābĭlĭs, lāmēntābĭlĭs, īngēns, īnfāndă, ăcērbă, dūră. V. Damnum.

pērnĭcĭōsŭs, ă, ŭm, *destructive.* Pērnĭcĭōsŭs ēst: cūr, Hor. Syn. Dāmnōsŭs, ēxĭtĭōsŭs, ēxĭtĭālĭs, ēxĭtĭābĭlĭs, fātālĭs.

pērnĭcĭtĕr, adv., *quickly.* Ŭt pērnĭcĭtĕr ēxĭlŭĕrĕ, Catull. Syn. Prŏpĕrē, ōcўŭs, cĭto.

pērnīx, īcĭs, *swift.* Ēt pērnīcĭbŭs ālīs, Virg.

pērnōcto, ās, *to spend the night.* Prō mē pērnōctĕt, Ov.

pērnōsco, nōvī, *to know entirely.* Pērnōscĕrĕ jūrĭs, Hor.

pērnōx, ctĭs, *lasting all night.* Lūnā pērnōctĕ prŭīnās, Ov.

pērnŭmĕro, ās, *to count over.* Quæ nēc pērnŭmĕrārĕ, Cat.

pēro, ōnĭs, m., *boots worn by country people.* Āltĕră pēro, Virg. Epith. Albŭs, vīlĭs, ābjēctŭs, rūstĭcŭs, sōrdĭdŭs.

pĕrŏlĕo, lŭī, *to smell strong.* Răncĭdă quō pĕrŏlēnt, Lucr.

pĕrōnātŭs, ă, ŭm, *wearing boots or gaiters.* Sĭbĭ pĕrōnātŭs ărătŏr, Pers.

pĕrōro, ās, *to finish a speech.* Cūm pĕrōrāssēnt sŭăm, Phæd.

pĕrōsŭs, ă, ŭm, *hating thoroughly.* Lūcēmquĕ pĕrōsī, Virg. Syn. Ōsŭs, ēxōsŭs, ăvērsātŭs.

pērpărvŭs, ă, ŭm, *very small.* Pērpārvĭs ēssĕ nĕcēsse ēst, Lucr.

pērpaūcī, œ. ă, *very few.* Pērpaūcă lŏquēntĕm, Hor.

pērpēndĭcŭlŭm, ī, n., *a perpendicular.* Ad pērpēndĭcŭlŭm, Aus.

pērpĕs, ĕtĭs, *entire, continued.* Pērpĕtēm crēdēntĭbŭs, Prud. Syn. Īntĕgĕr; pēr-pĕtŭŭs.

pērpĕtĭŏr, ĕrĭs, *to suffer patiently.* Tēlŭm pērpĕtĭŭntŭr, Lucr. Syn. Pătĭŏr, pērfĕro, tŏlĕro, fĕro. V. Patior.

pērpetro, ās, *to perform.* Syn. Patro, ādmītto, cŏmmītto, făcĭo.

pērpĕtŭō, adv., *continually.* Pērpĕtŭōquĕ vĭrēns, Ov. Syn. Sēmpĕr. V. Semper.

pērpĕtŭŭs, ă, ŭm, *perpetual.* Ad mĕă pērpĕtŭŭm, Ov. Syn. Pērpĕs, pĕrēnnĭs, œtērnŭs, jūgĭs, cōntĭnŭŭs, āssĭdŭŭs. V. Æternus.

pērplēxŭs, ă, ŭm, *perplexed.* Pērplēxum ĭtĕr ōmnĕ, Virg. Syn. Invŏlūtŭs, īm-plĭcĭtŭs, dŭbĭŭs, āncēps. V. Dubius.

pērplĭcātŭs, ă, ŭm, *the pass. partic. of the obsol.* perplico, *entangled.* Intēr sē pērquĕ plĭcātĭs, Lucr.

pērpōto, ās, *to drink up.* Intĕrĕā pērpōtĕt ămārŭm, Lucr.

pērprĕmo, *and* ĭmo, ēssī, *to press hard.* Pērprĭmăt cŭbīlĭă, Hor. V. Premo.

pērquīro, ĭs, sīvī, *to make strict search for.* Nātăm pērquīrĕrĕ Cādmō, Ov. V. Quæro.

pērrārō, adv., *very rarely.* Pērrāro hæc ălĕă fāllĭt, Hor. V. Raro.

pērrēpo, psī, *to creep through.* Gĕnĭbŭs pērrēpĕrĕ sūpplēx, Tib.

Pērrhæbī, ōrŭm, m. pl., *a people on the confines of Macedonia and Thrace.* Pēr-rhæbūm Cænĕă vīdī, Ov.

pērrīdĭcŭlŭs, ă, ŭm, *very ridiculous.* Rēs pērrīdĭcŭla ēst, Mart.

pērrūmpo, rūpī, rūptŭm, *to break through or in pieces.* Acĭēm pērrūmpĕrĕ, Virg. Syn. Rūmpo, frāngo; vĭŏlo. V. Frango.

Pērsæ, ārŭm, m. pl., *the Persians.* Pērsārūm stătŭĭt, Prop. Syn. Arsăcĭdæ, Achēmĕnĭī. Epith. Phăretrātī, āntīquī, pŏtēntēs, fōrtēs, măgnănĭmī, săgĭttĭ-fĕrī, fāllācēs, vănĭlŏquī, Eōī.

pērsæpĕ, adv., *very often.* Pērsæpĕ căvă, Virg.

Pērsæŭs *and* eĭŭs, ă, ŭm, *of Perses.* Mōnstrō Pērsæă bĭfōrmī, Virg.

pērscīndo, scĭdī, *to cleave.* Mēmbrĭs pērscīndĕrĕ vēstĕm, Tib. V. Scindo.

pērscrībo, psī, *to write out.* Vērsŭm pērscrībĕrĕ vērbĭs, Hor.

pērscrūtŏr, ārĭs, *to search thoroughly.* Nēc pērscrūtārī, Lucr. Syn. Scrūtŏr; pērquīro.

Pērsēĭs, ĭdĭs, f., *the daughter of Perses, Hecate.—Adj., of Hecate.* Pērsēĭdĕs hērbæ, Ov.

pērsēntĭo, sī, *to feel.* Māgnō pērsēntĭt pēctŏrĕ, Virg.

Pērsēphŏnē, ēs, f., *a name of Proserpine.* Pērsēphŏnē dĭgna ēst, Ov.

pērsēquŏr, ĕrĭs, sĕcūtŭs, *to pursue.* Pērsēquĭtŭr vĭtĕm, Virg. Syn. Īnsĕ-quŏr, īnsēctŏr, cōnsēctŏr, ūrgĕo, īnsto; prōgrĕdĭŏr, pērgo, pērsīsto. V. Pergo.

Pērsēs, œ, m., *the son of Sol, and father of Hecate.* Pērsēs bārbărĭcăs, V. Fl.

pērsĕvēro, ās, *to persevere.* Tūmŭlūmquĕ pērsĕvērĕt, (Phal.) Mart. Syn. Pērsto, pērsīsto, pērgo. V. Pergo.

Pērsēŭs, *and* eĭŭs, ă, ŭm, *of Perseus.* Sēctăquĕ Pērsēā, Prop. Pērsēĭă rēgnă sĕcūtŭs, Ov.

Pērsēŭs, (dissyll.) ĕī, ĕŏs, *or* eī, acc. ĕă, m., *the son of Jupiter and Danaë, deliverer of Andromeda.* At mĭhī quās Pērsēŭs, Ov. Pērsĕŏs aĕrĭī, V. Fl. Epith. Aūrĭgĕnă, aūrĕŭs, cĕlĕr, Inăchĭŭs, fĕrōx, fūlgēns, pēnnĭfĕr, præpĕs, pēnnĭpĕs, ālĕs, ālātŭs, īnclўtŭs. Syn. Inăchĭdēs, Ābāntĭădēs; Acrīsĭōnĭădēs.

Pērsĭă, œ, *and* sĭs, ĭdĭs, f., *a country in Asia.* Ūsque ē Pērsĭă, Pl. V. Persis.

pērsĭcŭm, ī, n., *a peach.* Pērsĭcă cără sūmŭs, Mart.

Pērsĭcŭs, ă, ŭm, *of Persia.* Pērsĭcōs ōdī, Hor.

pērsīdĕo, sēdī, *to stay, penetrate.* Ad vīvum pērsēdĭt, Virg.

pērsĭmĭlĭs, ĕ, *very like.* Lĭbrŭm pērsĭmĭlĕm, Hor.

Pērsĭs, ĭdĭs, f., *Persian.* Pērsĭdăs ĭndūxĭt, Ov.—Subst., *Persia* Vĭcĭnĭă Pērsĭdĭs ūrgĕt, Virg.

|| pērsĭsto, stĭtī, *to persevere.* Prŏhĭbēt pērsīstĕrĕ bĕssĕm, Aus. V. Persevero.

Pērsĭŭs, ĭī, m., *a satirical Roman poet.* Mĕmŏrātūr Pērsĭŭs ūnō, Mart.

pērsŏlĭdo, ās, *to render very solid.* Pērsŏlĭdāt Bŏrēās, Lucr.

pērsŏlvo, ĭs, ŏlvī *and* ŏlūī, *to pay all.* Grātēs pērsŏlvĕrĕ dīgnās, Virg. Pērsŏlŭĕrĕ mĭhi, Ov. SYN. Sōlvo, pĕndo, rĕddo.

pērsōnă, æ, f., *a mask.* Pērsōnăm căpĭtī, Mant. SYN. Lārvă. EPITH. Vānă, fālsă, fāllāx, mēndāx, īnsĭdĭōsă, dŏlōsă, dēfōrmĭs, hōrrĭdă, tērrĭbĭlĭs, tērrĭfĭcă, ūmbrātĭlĭs.

pērsōnātŭs, ă, ŭm, *disguised.* Quō pērsōnātŭs pāctō, Hor. SYN. Lārvātŭs; pērsōna īndūtŭs.

pērsŏno, ās, sŏnŭī, *to resound.* Pērsŏnĕt aūrĕm, Hor. SYN. Sŏno, rĕsŏno, cōnsŏno, īnsŏno, sŏnum ēdo, ēmītto, īngĕmĭno; rĕmūgĭo, rĕbŏo.

pērspĭcĭo, spĕxī, spĕctŭm, *to perceive thoroughly.* Pērspĭcĭēmŭs, ĕt ūndĕ, Lucr. SYN. Inspĭcĭo, āspĭcĭo, āgnōsco, ōbsērvo. V. Aspicio.

pērspĭcŭŭs, ă, ŭm, *perspicuous.* Prōdăt pērspĭcŭŭs, Mart. SYN. Ăpērtŭs, mănĭfēstŭs, clārŭs, līmpĭdŭs, pēllūcĭdŭs, vitrĕŭs, nĭtĭdŭs.

pērsto, ās, stĭtī, *to persevere.* Pērsta ātque ōbdūră, Hor. SYN. Pērsĭsto, pērgo; stō, hærĕo.

pērstrĕpo, pŭī, *to make a noise.* Pērstrĕpĭt aūlă, Stat. SYN. Strĕpo, strĕpĭto.

pērstrīngo, xī, *to bind close, to astound.* Pērstrīngĭs aūrēs, Hor.

pērsuādĕo, suāsī, *to persuade.* Quĭs tĭbĭ pērsuāsĭt, Mart. SYN. Suādĕo; ĕxcĭto, īmpēllo, īndūco.

pērsūlco, ās, *to furrow.* Pērsūlcātă gĕnās, Claud.

pērsūlto, ās, *to jump about.* Lĕvĭbŭs pērsūltăt ĕquĭs, Sil.

pērtædĕt, æsum ēst, *to be tired of.* Sī nōn pērtæsŭm, Virg.

pērtēnto, ās, *to try thoroughly.* Trĕmōr pērtēntĕt ĕquōrŭm, Virg.

pērtērgĕo, ēs, sī, *and go,* ĭs, sī, *to wipe over.* Mēnsăm pērtērgĭt, Hor.

pērtērrĭcrĕpŭs, ă, ŭm, *making a dreadful noise.* Tūm pērtērrĭcrĕpō, Lucr.

pērtērrĭtŭs, ă, ŭm, *frightened.* Vĕlūtī pērtērrĭtă cērvă, Ov. SYN. Tērrĭtŭs, āttŏnĭtŭs, stŭpĕfāctŭs.

pērtēxo, ĭs, *to weave throughout, to set forth completely.* Cœptūm pērtēxĕrĕ dīctīs, Lucr.

pērtĭcă, æ, f., *a pole.* Pērtĭcă dăt, Ov. SYN. Stīpĕs, băcŭlŭs. EPITH. Lōngă, ōblōngă, tĕrĕs, dūră, fīrmă, nōdōsă, rēctă.

pērtĭcātŭs, ă, ŭm, *carrying a pole.* Frōntĕ pērtĭcātă, Mart.

pērtĭmēsco, mŭī, *to fear much.* Pērtĭmŭīssĕ vĭās, Mart.

pērtĭnācĭă, æ, f., *obstinacy.* Tū pērtĭnācĭam ēssĕ, (Iamb.) Acc. SYN. Pērvĭcācĭă, ōbstīnātĭo.

pērtĭnāx, ācĭs, *obstinate.* Frōntĕ pērtĭnācī, (Phal.) Mart. SYN. Obstĭnātŭs, pērvĭcāx, tĕnāx, cōnstāns, īmmōtŭs, īmmōbĭlĭs.

pērtĭnĕo, ēs. *to belong to.* Quōrsūm pērtĭnŭĭt, Hor. SYN. Āttĭnĕo, spēcto; pērtīngo, pērvādo.

pērtīngo, ĭs, *to reach.* Lūx ŏcŭlōs pērtīngĕt, Lucr. SYN. Pērvādo, pērvĕnĭo.

pērtŏlĕro, ās, *to endure to the end.* Ōmnĭă pērtŏlĕrānt, Lucr. V. Patior.

pērtōrquĕo, sī, *to twist about.* Fœdō pērtōrquĕnt, Lucr.

pērtrācto, ās, *to touch, treat.* Pērtrāctāns vūlnĕră vīsū, Sil.

pērtūndo, tŭdī, *to break through.* Gūttæ pērtūndūnt, Lucr. V. Foro, terebro.

pērtūrbo, ās, *to disturb.* Pērtūrbātūr ĭbī, Lucr. SYN. Tūrbo, cōmmŏvĕo, cōnfūndo, mĭscĕo.

pērvādo, ĭs, sī, *to pass through.* Ætātĭs pērvādĕrĕ flōrĕm, Lucr. SYN. Ăccēdo, pērtīngo, cōntīngo.

pērvăgŭs, ă, ŭm, *wandering.* Pērvăgŭs ōrbĕ, Ov. V. Vagus.

pērvĕho, ĭs, xī, *to carry along.* Pērvēctă cĭtō, Sil. V. Veho.

pērvēllo, ĭs, *to excite.* Pērvēllūnt stŏmăchŭm, Hor.

pērvĕnĭo, vēnī, *to come to.* Pērvĕnĭt, ĕt vīctŏr, Mart. SYN. Dēvĕnĭo, tāngo, āttīngo, pērtīngo, āccēdo, tĕnĕo. V. Advenio.

pērvērsŭs, ă, ŭm, *untoward.* Ōmnĭă pērvērsă, Lucr. SYN. Īmprŏbŭs, pērdĭtŭs, nēquăm. V. Sceleratus.

pĕrvĭcāx, ācĭs, *obstinate.* Fās pĕrvĭcācŭs ēst, (Alcaic.) Hor. Syn. Pērtĭnāx. V. Pertinax.

pĕrvĭdĕo, ēs, *to see clearly.* Cūm tŭă pĕrvĭdĕŭs, Hor. V. Video.

pĕrvĭgĭl, ĭlĭs, *watchful.* Pĕrvĭgĭl ānguĭs, Ov. Syn. Vĭgĭl, vĭgĭlāns, sēdŭlŭs, ācĕr.

pĕrvĭgĭlo, ās, *to watch continually.* Pĕrvĭgĭlărĕ grăvĕ, Mart.

pĕrvinco, ĭs, vīcī, *to triumph.* Vīs ănĭmī pĕrvĭcĭt, Lucr. V. Vinco, evinco.

pĕrvĭŭs, ŭ, ŭm, *passable.* Pĕrvĭă vēntŏ, Ov. Syn. Pĕnetrābĭlĭs, ăpĕrtŭs, pătēns.

pĕrŭngo, xī, *to anoint all over.* Tōtă pĕrŭngĕ mănū, Ov.

pĕrvŏlo, *and freq.* pĕrvŏlĭto, ās, *to fly through or about.* Ăgĭtātĭs pĕrvŏlăt ālĭs, Virg.   Ōmnĭă pĕrvŏlĭtăt, Id.   Syn. Cīrcŭmvŏlĭto, lūstro, ēxplōro.

pĕrvŏlvo, *and by diær.* ŏlŭo, ĭs, *to roll through.* Sæcŭlă pĕrvŏlŭent, Catul.

pĕrūro, ĭs, ūssī, ūstŭm, *to burn entirely.* Vălĭdōquĕ pĕrūrĭmŭr æstū, Ov. Syn. Exūro, ūro.

pĕrvūlgo, ās, *to disseminate. divulge.* Pĕrvūlgātūră Fălērnī, Sil.

pēs, pĕdĭs, m., *a foot.* Pēs ĕtĭam, ēt cămŭrĭs, Virg. Ac pĕdĕ, vērum ēst, Hor. Syn. Plāntă.   Epith. Tĭtūbāns, văcĭllāns, tĕnĕr, vēlōx, tārdŭs, lēntŭs, fīrmŭs, ăgĭlĭs, cĕlĕr, vŏlucrĭs.

pēssĭmŭs, ă, ŭm, *the superl. of* malus. Pēssĭmŭs mărĭtŭs, (Phal.) Mart.

pēssŭlŭs, ī, m., *a bolt.* Ōbdĕrĕ pēssŭlŭm, Ter.

pēssūmdo, ās, *to ruin.* Quærēntī pēssūmdărĕ cūnctă, Ov.

pēstĭfĕr, ă, ŭm, *and* pēstĭlēns, ntĭs, *pestilent.* Hīnc pēstĭfĕr āēr, Claud.   Nēc pēstĭlēntĕm sēntĭĕt, (Alcaic.) Hor. Syn. Cŏrrŭptŭs, vĭtĭātŭs, lēthălĭs.

pēstĭlēntĭă, æ, *and* pēstĭs, ĭs, f., *a pestilence.* Tĕ pēstĭlēntĭă pŏssĭt, (Scaz.) Mart. Pēstĭs ĕt īră Dĕūm, Virg.   Syn. Lŭēs, cōntāgĭă, -ōrŭm, cōntāgĭo ; pērnĭcĭēs, ēxĭtĭŭm, lābēs, rŭīnă.   Epith. Ignĕă, fērvĭdă, Stўgĭă, trīstĭs, ăcērbă, dīră, lēthālĭs, mōrtĭfĕră, fœdă, Lēthœă, crūdēlĭs, răbĭdă, nōxĭă, īnfēstă, ĭnĭmīcă, mālĭgnă, tērrĭbĭlĭs, mĕtŭēndă, grāssāns, sērpēns, īmmĕdĭcābĭlĭs, pērnĭcĭōsă, ēxĭtĭōsă, ārdēns, līvĭdă, lūrĭdă, tĕtră, cōntăgĭōsă, flŭĭdă, sævă, mŏlēstă, īmpōrtūnă.

pĕtăso, ōnĭs, m., *a gammon.* Sĭt pĕtăsōnĕ nĭhĭl, Mart.

pĕtăsūncŭlŭs, ī, m., *the dimin. of* petaso. Sĭccŭs pĕtăsūncŭlŭs, ēt vās, Juv. Syn. Pērnă.

pĕtaūrŭm, ī, n., *a dancing-rope.* Jăctātă pĕtaūrŏ, Juv.

Pĕtēlĭă, *or* ĭlĭă, ōrŭm, n. pl., *a city in Bruttium.* Sŭbnīxă Pĕtēlĭă mūrŏ, Virg.

Pĕtĭlĭŭs, ĭī, m., *the name of a man.* Sĭt caūsă Pĕtĭlī, Hor.

pĕtīsco, ĭs, *the frequent. of* peto. Cædēsquĕ pĕtīscĭt, Lucr.

pĕtĭtĭo, ōnĭs, f., *and* ĭtŭm, ī, n., *a petition.* Făcta ēst ūtrīŭsquĕ pĕtītī, Cat.

pĕtītŏr, ōrĭs, m., *a demander.* Stēllă pĕtītŏr ăquæ, Mart.

pĕtītŭs, ă, ŭm, *the pass. partic. of* peto. Ĭpsă pĕtītă lăcū, Prop.

pĕtītŭs, ūs, m., *desire.* Tērræquĕ pĕtītŭs, Lucr.

pĕto, ĭs, īvī *and* ĭī, ītŭm, *to ask.* Extērnă pĕtītŭr, Virg.   Syn. Pōstŭlo, pōsco, ēxpōsco, dēpōsco, quæro, rŏgo, flāgĭto, ēfflāgĭto, ēxĭgo, vērbĕro, cædo, pērcŭtĭo ; ĕo, vădo, prŏfĭcīscŏr; scīscĭtŏr, pērcōntŏr.   V. Oro, precor, posco.

pĕtōrĭtŭm, ī, n., *a sort of four-wheeled carriage.* Pĭlēntă, pĕtōrĭtă, nāvēs, Hor.

Pĕtŏsīrĭs, ĭdĭs, m., *an Egyptian astrologer.* Quăm dēdĕrĭt Pĕtŏsīrĭs, Juv.

petră, æ, f., *a rock.* Frētŭs ămōrĕ pĕtræ, Prud. Syn. Sāxŭm, rūpēs.

Pĕtrœŭs, ī, m., *one of the Centaurs.* Cōstīs īmmīssă Pĕtræī, Ov.

|| petrĭcōsŭs, ă, ŭm, *stony, difficult.* Rēs pĕtrĭcōsa ēst, Mart. Syn. Petrōsŭs.

Pĕtrīnŭm, ī, n., *a hill and villa in Campania.* Sĭnŭēssānŭmquĕ Pĕtrīnŭm, Hor.

S. Petrŭs, ī, m., *the Apostle.* Epith. Ĭdūmæŭs, hămĭgĕr, sānctŭs, pŏtēns, făcūndŭs, dĭsērtŭs.

Pĕttălŭs, ī, m., *the name of a warrior.* Pĕttălŭs īrrīdēns, Ov.

pĕtŭlāns, ntĭs, *insolent, saucy.* Pĕtŭlāntī splēnĕ căchĭnnō, Pers. Syn. Pĕtŭlcŭs, prŏtērvŭs, lāscīvŭs ; īmpŭdēns, aūdāx.

pĕtŭlāntĭă, æ, f., *insolence.* Læsĭt pĕtŭlāntĭă līnguæ, Prop. Syn. Prŏtērvĭă, prŏcācĭtās.

pĕtŭlcŭs, ă, ŭm, *striking with the horns.* Hœdīquĕ pĕtŭlcī, Virg. Syn. Pĕtŭlāns.

Peŭcĕtĭī, ōrŭm, m. pl., *the inhabitants of Peucetia, a part of Apulia.* Peŭcĕtĭōsquĕ sĭnūs, Ov.

pēxātŭs, ă, ŭm, *having a new and smooth-napped dress.* Pēxātŭs pūlchrĕ, Mart.

pēxŭs, ă, ŭm, *the pass. part. of* pecto, *combed.* Prŏptĕr cōnvĭvĭă pēxī, Juv.

Phæācĭă, æ, f., *the ancient name of Corcyra.* Phæācĭă tērrĭs, Tib.—2. adj., -cĭŭs and cŭs, ă, ŭm, *Phæacian.* Phæācĭă tĕllūs, Id. Nēc mĕă Phæācās, Prop.

Phæācĭs, ĭdĭs, f., *the Phæacian, title of a poem of Tuticanus.* Dīgnām Mæōnĭĭs Phæācĭdă cōndĕrĕ chārtĭs, Ov.

Phæāx, ācĭs, m. ; Phæācĕs, ŭm, m. pl., *the ancient inhabitants of Corcyra.* Pŏpŭlŭm Phæācă pŭtăvĭt, Juv. Phæācum ābscōndĭmŭs ārcēs, Virg.

phæcăsĭŭm, ĭī, n., *a sort of shoe.*—2. adj., -ānŭs *or* ătŭs, ă, ŭm, *shod with the phæcasium.* Phæcăsĭātōrūm vĕtĕra ōrnāmēntă dĕōrŭm, Juv.

Phædĭmŭs, ī, m., *one of the sons of Niobe.* Phædĭmŭs īnfēlīx, Ov.

Phædră, æ, f., *the wife of Theseus, and false accuser of Hippolytus.* Hīs Phædrām, Prōcrĭnquĕ, Virg. EPITH. Scĕlĕrātă, Crētēnsĭs, Mīnōĭă, Gnōssĭăcă; Thēsēă, fūnēstă, īncēstă. V. Hippolytus.

Phædŏcōmēs, æ, m., *one of the Centaurs.*

Phæstĭăs, ădĭs, f., *and* ĭŭs, ă, ŭm, *of Phæstus, a city of Crete.* Intēr Phæstĭădăs, Ov. Phæstĭă rēgnă, Id.

Phăĕthōn, ōntĭs, m., *a son of Apollo, who presumed to drive the solar chariot, and thereby set the world on fire.* Aŭrōrām Phăĕthōntĭs ĕquī, Virg. SYN. Clўmēnēĭŭs, Clўmĕnēs pŭĕr. EPITH. Tĕmĕrārĭŭs, māgnănĭmŭs, īnfēlīx, aŭdāx, āmēns, stūltŭs, īnsānŭs, mălĕsānŭs, Hўpĕrīōnĭŭs, dēvĭŭs, āmbūstŭs, ēxūstŭs, cōmbūstŭs, īgnārŭs, īmpĕrītŭs, mĭsĕr, īmprūdēns, īncōnsūltŭs.

Phăĕthōntĕŭs, *and* tĭŭs, ă, ŭm, *of Phaethon.* Dūm Phăĕthōntĕā, Mart. Cēdāt Phăĕthōntĭă vūlgī, Sil.

Phăĕthōntĭădĕs, ŭm, f. pl., *the sisters of Phaethon.* Tūm Phăĕthōntĭădĕs, Virg. V. Heliades.

Phăĕthōntĭs, ĭdĭs, f., *of amber.* Lūcēt Phăĕthōntĭdĕ cōndĭtă gūttă, Mart.

Phăĕthūsă, æ, f., *one of the sisters of Phaethon.* Queĭs Phăĕthūsă sŏrōrŭm, Ov.

Phălāntŭs, ī, m., *the leader of a Lacedemonian colony which settled at Tarentum.* Lăcōnī rūră Phălāntō, Hor.

phălānx, āngĭs, f., *a squadron.* Ăgămēmnŏnĭæquĕ phălāngēs, Virg. SYN. Lēgĭo, āgmĕn, mănĭplŭs, cŏhōrs, cătĕrvă. V. Acies militaris, cohors.

phălărĭcă, æ, f., *a kind of javelin, with wildfire in it, shot from an engine.* Cōntōrtă phălārĭcă vēnĭt, Virg. EPITH. Vībrātă, mĕtŭēndă, cōntōrtă, lōngă, mĭssĭlĭs, tĕrēs, fērrātă, ārdēns, flāmmĕă, flāmmātă.

Phălărĭs, ĭdĭs, m., *the tyrant of Agrigentum.* Ūtquĕ fĕrōx Phălărĭs. EPITH. Sĭcŭlŭs, trūx, crūdēlĭs, fĕrōx, bārbărŭs, īmmītĭs, fĕrŭs, dīrŭs, īmmānĭs, atrōx, āspĕr, sævŭs, crŭēntŭs.

phălĕræ, ārŭm, f. pl., *trappings for a horse.* Ūt lætī phălĕrĭs, Juv. SYN. Ēphīppĭă, ōrŭm. EPITH. Nĭtēntēs, ĕquēstrēs, fūlgēntēs, aŭrātæ, ĭnaŭrātæ, gēmmātæ, cŏrūscæ, splēndĭdæ, nōbĭlēs, ōrnātæ, dĕcōræ, rŭtĭlæ.

‖ phălĕrātŭs, ă, ŭm, *harnessed.* Ter.

Phānæŭs, ī, m., *of Phanæ, a maritime town in the island of Chio, famous for its vines.* Ēt rēx īpsĕ Phānæŭs, Virg.

phānātĭcŭs, ă, ŭm, *furious.* Aŭt phānātĭcŭs ērrōr, Hor. V. Furiosus.

phāntāsmă, ătĭs, n., *a phantom.* Vānō phāntāsmătĕ tāctŭs, Alcim. SYN. Vīsŭm, spēctrŭm, fōrmă, spĕcĭēs, ĭmāgo. EPITH. Nōctūrnŭm, mĕtŭēndŭm, hōrrēndŭm, ĭnānĕ, fāllāx, ūmbrātĭlĕ, văgŭm, pāllēns, pāllĭdŭm. V. Somnium.

phāntăsōs, ī, m., *a dream.*

Phăōn, ōnĭs, m., *a Lesbian, loved by Sappho.* Ārvă Phăōn cĕlĕbrăt, Ov. Ēt fāstīdītă Phăōnī, Aus. EPITH. Pūlchĕr, fōrmōsŭs.

Phărăō, ōnĭs, m., *a surname of the kings of Egypt.* Vīctō Phărăōnĕ chŏrēās, Paul. SYN. Phărĭŭs tўrānnŭs. EPITH. Sŭpērbŭs, dīrŭs, cæcŭs, īmpĭŭs, ĭnhūmānŭs, crūdēlĭs, īmmītĭs, sævŭs, bārbărŭs, dūrŭs, ĭnēxōrābĭlĭs, mērsŭs, dēmērsŭs, sŭbmērsŭs, naŭfrăgŭs, Phărĭŭs, Ægўptĭŭs.

Phărăōnĭăcŭs, ă, ŭm, *of Pharaoh.* Ēt Phărăōnĭăcĭs, Mant.

phăretră, æ, f., *a quiver.* Lævēs hŭmĕrō phărĕtrās, Virg. Vēnātrīcēmquĕ phărētrăm, Claud. SYN. Cōrўtŭs. EPITH. Insīgnĭs, pīctă, căpāx, sŏnāns, rĕsŏnāns, lĕvĭs, pēndēns, hăbĭlĭs, dĕcŏră, aŭrātă, grăvĭdă, Ămāzŏnĭă, sævă, grăvĭs, pēndŭlă, gēmmātă, vēnātrīx, ĕbūrnă, nĭtēns, Ăpōllĭnĕă, Crēssă, Gnōssĭă, Gōrtўnĭă, Cўdōnĭă, Scўthĭcă, Lўcĭă, Gĕtĭcă.

phărĕtrātŭs, *and* ĭgĕr, ă, ŭm, *wearing a quiver.* Pūgnæ phărĕtrātă Cămīllă, Virg. Clādĕ phărĕtrĭgĕrī, Sil.

PHA PHI 309

Phărĭŭs, ă, ŭm, *of Pharos in Egypt.* Ălĭī sīgnŭm Phărĭăm, Ov.

phārmăcŏpōlă, æ, m., *an apothecary.* Cōllēgĭă, phărmăcŏpōlæ, Hor.

phārmăcŭm, ī, n., *a medicine or drug.* Phărmăcă Sīmŏn, M. V. Medicamen.

Phărŏs, ī, f., *an island of Egypt.* Pālmĭfĕrŭmquĕ Phărŏn, Ov. Epith. Clāră, ĕxcēlsă, nŏctūrnă, Ptŏlĕmæă, nūdă.

Phārsālĭă, æ, f., *a district of Thessaly.* Phārsālĭă sēntĭĕt īllŭm, Ov.

Phārsālĭcŭs, *and* līŭs, ă, ŭm, *of Pharsalus.* Phārsālĭcă cāstră, Luc. Phārsālĭă rūră, Claud.

Phārsālŏs, *or* lŭs, ī, m., *a city of Thessaly, where Pompey was vanquished by Cæsar.* Rēgnŭm Phársālŏs Āchīllĭs, Luc.

phăsēlŭs, ī, m., *a long-boat.* Rūră phăsēlĭs, Virg. Syn. Lēmbŭs, cўmbă. V. Cymba, navis.

Phăsīăcŭs, ă, ŭm, *of the river Phasis, Colchian.* Tūrbăquĕ Phăsīăcăm, Ov.

Phăsīānŭs, ă, ŭm, *of the Phasis.* Epith. Scўthĭcŭs, lēvĭs, Cōlchŭs, pĕregrīnŭs, vŏlāns, pēnnĭgĕr, pēnnĭpŏtēns.

Phăsĭăs, ădĭs, *and* āsĭs, ĭdĭs, f., *of the Phasis, Medea.* Phăsĭăs ūltă sŭŏs, Ov. Phăsīdă pūppĕ tŭlĭt, Id.

Phăsĭs, ĭs *or* ĭdĭs, m. f., *a river of Colchis.* Dītīssĭmă Phăsĭs, Lucan. Epith. Pŏntĭcŭs; līmōsŭs, nĭvōsŭs, fĕrŭs, hŏrrĭdŭs, gĕlĭdŭs, răpĭdŭs, Scўthĭcŭs, cœnōsŭs, bārbărŭs, āltŭs, āspĕr.

Phēgeĭŭs, ă, ŭm, *of Phegeus.* Phēgeĭŭs haŭsĕrăt ēnsĭs, Ov.

Phēgeŭs, eŏs, ĕĭ *or* eī, m., *a king of Thessaly; the name of a warrior.* Cōnfīxā Phēgĕă pārmă, Virg.

Phēgĭs, ĭdĭs, f., *the daughter of Phegeus, Alphesibœa.* Nē Phēgĭdă sēmpĕr ămārĕt, Ov.

Phēmĭŭs, ĭī, m., *a musician, the preceptor of Homer.* Phēmĭŭs aūrēs, Ov.

Phēnĕŭs, ī, m., *a lake in Arcadia.* Ārcădĭæ, Phēnĕŭm, Ov.

Phĕræŭs, ă, ŭm, *of Pheræ, a city of Thessaly, Thessalian.* Cūltŏrĕ Phĕræī, Virg.

Phĕreclēŭs, ă, ŭm, *of Phereclus, the builder of Paris's ship.* Lōngă Phĕreclēā.

Phĕrētĭădēs, æ, m., *the son of Pheres, Admetus.* Fātă Phĕrētĭădæ, Ov.

phĭălă, æ, f., *a phial.* Vīrrŏ tĕnēt phĭālās, Juv.

Phĭălē, ēs, f., *one of the nymphs of Diana.* Ov.

Phĭdĭăcŭs, ă, ŭm, *of Phidias.* Phĭdĭăcŭs sīgnō, Prop.

Phĭdĭăs, æ, m., *a famous sculptor.* Phĭdĭæ pŭtāvī, (Phal.) Mart. Epith. Clārŭs, pĕrītŭs, īllūstrĭs, īnclўtŭs, sōlērs.

Phĭdўlē, ēs, f., *the name of a woman.* Rūstĭcă Phĭdўlē, Hor.

Phĭlāmmōn, ŏnĭs, m., *a famous musician.* Cĭthārăquĕ Phĭlāmmōn, Ov.

Phĭlēmōn, ŏnĭs, m., *the husband of Baucis.* Tĭmĭdŭsquĕ Phĭlēmōn, Ov.

Phĭlēnī, ōrŭm, m. pl., *two Carthaginian brothers who sacrificed their lives for their country.* Pŏsŭĕrĕ Phĭlēnī, Sil.

Phĭlētās, æ, m., *a Greek poet.* Sācră Phĭlētæ, Prop. Epith. Cŏŭs, Sămĭŭs; dŏctŭs, pĕrītŭs, făcūndŭs, dŏctĭlŏquŭs, dūlcĭcănēns, tĕnŭĭs, lĕvĭs.

Phĭlīppī, ōrŭm, m. pl., *a city of Macedonia, where Brutus and Cassius were vanquished.* Ĭtĕrŭm vīdĕrĕ Phĭlīppī, Virg.

Phĭlīppĭcă, ōrŭm, n. pl., *speeches of Demosthenes against Philip.* Dīvīnă Phĭlīppĭcă, Juv.

Phĭlīppŭs, ī, m., *king of Macedon, father of Alexander the Great.* Mŏnĭmēntă Phĭlīppī, Ov. Epith. Ănĭmōsŭs, gĕnĕrōsŭs, fōrtĭs, pŏtēns, Æmăthĭŭs.

Phĭlōctētēs, ētĭs *or* ētæ, m., *the companion of Hercules.* Quĭdvĕ Phĭlōctētēs īctŭs, Ov. Syn. Pœāntĭădēs, Pœāntĭŭs. Epith. Fōrtĭs, māgnănĭmŭs, pŏtēns, ægĕr, saŭcĭŭs.

Phĭlŏdēmŭs, *or* ēmŭs, ī, m., *the name of a man.* Phĭlŏdēmŭs ăĭt, Hor.

Phĭlŏmēlă, æ, f., *daughter of Pandion, changed into a nightingale.* Dīvĕs Phĭlŏmēlă părātŭ, Ov. Syn. Lūscĭnĭă, acrēdŭlă, Āttĭs. Epith. Gărrŭlă, flēbĭlĭs, vōcālĭs, ārgūtă, cănōră, quĕrŭlă, Āttĭcă, Cecrŏpĭă; Thrācĭă, Thrēĭcĭă, Gētĭcă; Ismărĭă, Daŭlĭăs.

phĭlŏsŏphŭs, ī, m., *a philosopher.* Dīcăt ălĭquĭs phĭlŏsŏphŭs, Varr. Prīmōrdĭă phĭlŏsŏphōrŭm, Sid. Syn. Sŏphŭs. Epith. Dŏctŭs, prūdēns, sōlērs, pĕrītŭs. V. Astrologus, prudens.

phĭltră, ōrŭm, n. pl., *love-charms.* Phĭltră nŏcēnt, Ov. Epith. Pāllēntĭă, īgnĕă, sævă, mōrbĭdă, tābĭdă, Thēssălă; ĭmpĭă, lāscīvă, dīră, fŭrĭōsă.

phĭlўrā, æ, f., *the linden-tree.* Ēbrўŭs ĭncīnctĭs phĭlўrā, Ov.

Phĭlўræŭs, *and* rēĭŭs, ă, ŭm, *of Philyrus.* Phĭlўræăquĕ tēctă, Ov. Phĭlўrēĭŭs hērōs, Id.

Phĭlўrĭdēs, *and poet.* Phĭllўrĭdēs, æ, m., *the son of Philyrus, Chiron.* Phĭllўrĭdēs Chīrōn, Virg.

Phīnēĭŭs, *and* ēŭs, ă, ŭm, *of Phineus.* Phīnēĭă pōstquăm, Virg. Phīnēă cĕcĭdĕrĕ mănū, Ov.

Phīneŭs, ĕŏs, ĕĭ *or* eī, m., *a king of Arcadia, killed by Hercules.* Phīneŭs vīsŭs ĕrăt, Ov. EPITH. Ăgēnŏrēŭs, fātĭdĭcŭs, sævŭs, dūrŭs, crūdēlĭs, ĭmmītĭs, bārbărŭs, fœdŭs, mĭsĕr, ĭnfēlīx.

Phīnīdes, æ, m., *the son of Phineus.* Ūt dŭŏ Phīnīdæ, Ov.

Phlĕgĕthŏn, ōntĭs, m., *a river of Hell.* Tārtărēŭs Phlĕgĕthŏn, Virg. EPITH. Ardēns, ĭgnītŭs, sūlphŭrēŭs, răpĭdŭs, vĭŏlēntŭs, ĭnfērnŭs, răpāx, nĭgĕr, ĭrrĕmĕăbĭlĭs, fūmĭdŭs, flāmmĕŭs, ĭgnĕŭs, trīstĭs, Stўgĭŭs. V. Acheron, Cocytus.

Phlĕgĕthōntēŭs, ă, ŭm, *of the Phlegethon.* Et Phlĕgĕthōntēŏ sūb gūrgĭtŭ, Prud.

Phlĕgŏn, ōntĭs, m., *one of the horses of the Sun.* Quārtūsquĕ Phlĕgōn, Ov.

Phlĕgrā, æ, *or* grē, ēs, f., *a valley in Thessaly.* Ārgāntĭ Phlĕgrē sūb, Prop. EPITH. Thēssălă, tŭmĭdă, vĕtŭs.

Phlĕgræŭs, ă, ŭm, *of Phlegra.* Spārsăquĕ Phlĕgræĭs, Ov.

Phlĕgўās, æ, m., *a son of Mars.* Īnfēlīx Thēseŭs, Phlĕgўāsquĕ, Virg.

Phlīāsĭŭs, ă, ŭm, *of Phlius, a city near Sicyon.* Phlīāsĭă rēgnă, Ov.

Phŏbĕtŏr, ŏrĭs, m., *one of the children of Morpheus.* Mōrtālĕ Phŏbĕtŏră vūlgŭs, Ov. phŏcæ, ārŭm, f. pl., *sea-calves.* Gūrgĭtĕ phŏc.ŭs, Virg. EPITH. Dēfōrmēs, ĭmmānēs, hōrrēndæ, æquŏrēæ, mărīnæ, ūndĭvăgæ, tērrĭbĭlēs, fĕrōcēs.

Phŏcæī, ōrŭm, m. pl., *the inhabitants of Phocæa, a city in Ionia.* Phŏcæōrŭm Vŏlŭt prŏfūgĭt, Hor.

Phŏcăĭcŭs, ă, ŭm, *of Phocæa in Ionia.* Idmōn Phŏcăĭcō, Ov.—2. *of Phocis.* Phŏcăĭcă clārŭs tēllūrĕ, Id.

Phŏcēŭs, ă, ŭm, *of Phocis.* Phŏcēăquĕ mīlĭtĕ rūră, Ov.

Phŏcĭs, ĭdŏs, f., *a country of Greece.* Phŏcĭdŏs ārcēs, Lucan. EPITH. Aŏnĭă, dōctă, Pĭĕrĭă, Phœbēă.

Phŏcŭs, ī, m., *the son of Æacus, slain by his brother Peleus.* In līmĭnĕ Phŏcŭs, Ov.

Phœbăs, ădĭs, f., *a priestess of Apollo.* Cōnsīstĕrĕ Phœbăs, Luc. EPITH. Ēffrēnă, fātĭdĭcă.

Phœbē, ēs, f., *the moon.* Cōrnŭă Phœbē, Ov. SYN. Lūnă, Diānă; Phœbī sŏrŏr. V. Luna.

Phœbēĭŭs, *and* bēŭs, ă, ŭm, *of Apollo.* Săcrīs Phœbēĭă Cīrcē, P. A. Phœbēæ lāmpădĭs īnstăr, Virg. SYN. Sōlārĭs, Ăpōllĭnēŭs.

Phœbĭgĕnă, æ, m. f., *a son or daughter of Phœbus.* Fūlmĭnĕ Phœbĭgĕnăm, Virg.

Phœbŭs, ī, m., *Apollo.* Phœbŭs Ăpōllo, Virg. SYN. Ăpōllo, Sōl, Tītān, Dēlĭŭs, Cўnthĭŭs. V. Sol, Apollo.

Phœnīcēs, ŭm, m. pl., *the Phœnicians.* Pŏpŭlĭs Phœnīcĭbŭs ērgo, Luc. SYN. Tўrīī, Sīdonĭī. EPITH. Clārī, dōctī, pĕrītī, sōlērtēs, săgācēs, māgnănĭmī.

Phœnīcēŭs, cĭŭs, *or* ssŭs, ă, ŭm, *of Phœnicia.* Phœnīcĭă tēllŭs, Drac. Phœnīssă Tўrŏs, Ov. Sīdonĭŭs, Tўrĭŭs.

Phœnīcōptĕrŭs, ī, m., *a species of crane, flamingo.* Phœnīcōptĕrŭs ĭngēns, Juv.

Phœnīx, ĭcĭs, m., *the son of Agenor and brother of Cadmus.*—2. *the son of Amyntor and preceptor of Achilles.* Crētŭs Ămўntŏrĕ Phœnīx, Ov.—3. *a fabulous bird, said to revive from its own ashes.* Et vīvāx Phœnīx, Ov. EPITH. Ūnĭcŭs, nōbĭlĭs, lōngævŭs, rĕdĭvīvŭs, rĕnāscēns, rĕpărābĭlĭs, ĭnmōrtālĭs, pĕrēnnĭs, ætērnŭs, vīvāx, crīstātŭs, vērsĭcŏlŏr, Tītānĭŭs, Phœbēĭŭs; Săbæŭs, Pānchæŭs, Ărābs; Assўrĭŭs, Sўrĭŭs, Phărĭŭs, Īndŭs, Gāngētĭcŭs, Eŏŭs, fābŭlōsŭs.

Phŏlŏē, ēs, f., *a mountain of Arcadia.* Ipsă pĕtĭt Phŏlŏēm, Lucr. EPITH. Opācă, nĕmŏrōsă, vĭrĭdĭs, frōndōsă, āĕrĭă.

Phŏlŭs, ī, m., *a centaur, the son of Ixion.* Hўlæūmquĕ Phŏlŭmquĕ, Virg.

Phŏnŏlĕnĭdēs, æ, m., *the son of Phonolenus.*

Phōrbās, āntĭs, m., *a son of Priam, slain by Menelaus.* Phōrbāntĭ sĭmĭlĭs, Virg.

Phōrcĭs, ĭdŏs, *and* Phōrcўnĭs, ĭdŏs, f., *the daughter of Phorcus.* Phōrcĭdŏs ōră, Prop. Phōrcўnĭdă trānstŭlĭt ĭllăm, Ov.

Phōrcŭs, ī, *or* cўs, ўŏs, *and* cўn, ўnŏs, m., *an ancient king of Corsica, father of the Gorgons and Scylla.* Phōrcīque ēxērcĭtŭs ōmnĭs, Virg.

Phŏrōnĭs, ĭdĭs, f., *the daughter of Inachus; Io, or Isis.* Phŏrōnĭdĭs ūltrā, Ov.
Phŏsphŏrŭs, ī, m., *the morning-star.* Phŏsphŏrĕ, rĕddĕ, Mart. Syn. Lūcĭfĕr. V.
Lucifer.
Phrăātēs, æ, m., *a king of the Parthians.* Impĕrĭūmquĕ Phrăātēs, Hor.
phrĕnĕsĭs, ĭs, f., *a phrenzy.* Mănĭfĕstă phrĕnĕsĭs, Mart. V. Furor.
phrĕnētĭcŭs, ă, ŭm, *frantic.* Cōrdĕ phrĕnētĭcŭs ægĕr, Prop.
Phrўgĕs, ŭm, m. pl., *Phrygians.* Nĕque ĕŭīm Phrўgĕs, Virg.
Phrўgĭă, æ, f., *a country of Asia Minor.* Idæās Phrўgĭæ, Virg.
Phrўgĭŭs, ă, ŭm, *Phrygian.* Bīs dēnīs Phrўgĭŭm, Virg.—2. *of Cybele.* Phrўgĭōs
sūbjūnctă lĕōnēs, Id.
Phrўx, ўgĭs, m., *Phrygian : Æneas, &c.* Phrўx plŭs ūsŭs ĕrăt, Ov.
Phrўxĕŭs, ă, ŭm, *of Phryxus.* Jăm Tўrĭŭs Phrўxĕī, Hor.
Phrўxŭs, ī, m., *the son of Athamas, king of Thebes.* Ēt sŏrŏr, ēt Phrўxŭs, Ov.
Epith. Nūbĭgĕnă, æquŏrĕŭs, prŏfŭgŭs, Graīŭs, Æŏlĭŭs.
Phthĭă, æ, f., *a city of Thessaly.* Assărăcī Phthĭām clārāsquĕ Mўcēnās, Virg.
Phthĭās, ădĭs, f., *of Phthia.* Nŏn ĕgŏ sūm Phthĭās măgnīsquĕ, Ov.
Phthĭōtĭcŭs, *and* Phthĭŭs, ă, ŭm, *of Phthiotis.* Līnquūnt Phthĭōtĭcă Tēmpē, Cat.
Phthĭŭs Achīllēs, Hor.
phthĭsĭcŭs, ă, ŭm, *consumptive in the lungs.* Quăm quæ dē phthĭsĭcō, Mart.
phthĭsĭs, ĭōs, f., *a consumption of the lungs.* Ēt phthĭsĭs ēt vŏmĭcæ, Juv.
Phўācēs, æ, m., *the name of a man or of a people.* Cўclōps fĕrĭtătĕ Phўācēn,
Ov.
Phўlăcē, ēs, f., *a city of Thessaly.* Quæ tĕtĭgīt Phўlăcē, Luc.—2. adj., -cēĭŭs, ă,
ŭm, *and* cēĭs, ĭdĭs, f., *of Phylace.* Cōnjūx Phўlăcēĭă, cūjŭs, Ov.
Phўlăcĭdēs, *poet.* Phўllăcĭdēs, æ, m., *descended from Phylacus, Protesilaus.* Phўllăcĭdēs ăbĕrăt, Ov.
Phўllĭs, ĭdĭs, f., *the daughter of Lycurgus, king of Thrace ; she hanged herself, and
was changed into an almond-tree.* Epith. Rhŏdŏpēĭă, Thrēĭcĭă, dīvĕs, mĭsĕră,
īmpătĭēns. V. Demophoon.
Phўllĭŭs, īī, m., *a Bœotian, the friend of Cycnus.*
Phўllŏdŏcē, ēs, f., *one of the Nereids.* Lĭgēăquĕ Phўllŏdŏcēquĕ, Virg.
pĭābĭlĭs, ĕ, *that may be expiated.* Tērrĕrĕ, pĭābĭlĕ fūlmĕn, Ov. Syn. Pĭāndŭs.
pĭācŭlŭm, ī, *and* āmĕn, ĭnĭs, n., *a crime, an atonement.* Prīmă pĭācŭlă sūnto, Virg.
Dīxĕrĕ pĭāmĭnă pātrēs, Ov. Syn. Crīmĕn, scĕlŭs ; vīctĭmă.
pīcă, æ, f., *a magpie.* Pīcă lŏquăx, Mart. Epith. Imprŏbă, gārrŭlă, quĕrŭlă,
clāmōsă, cănōră, dῐsĕrtă, sălūtātrīx, vērsĭcŏlŏr, pīctă.
pīcātŭs, ă, ŭm, *stopped up with pitch.* Vēnīssĕ pīcātă Vĭēnnă, Mart.
pīcĕă, æ, f., *and* ĕăstĕr, trī, m., *the pitch-tree.* Nīgrāntī pīcĕă trăbĭbūsquĕ, Virg.
pīcĕātŭs, ă, ŭm, *covered with pitch.* Tăm pīcĕātă mănŭs, Mart.
Pīcēntīnŭs, *and* cēnŭs, ă, ŭm, *of Picenum, a country of Italy.* Pīcēntīnă Cĕrēs,
Mart. Quīd ? quŭm Pīcēnīs, Hor.
pīcĕŭs, *and* cĭnŭs, ă, ŭm, *like pitch.* Pīcĕīquĕ būxĕīquĕ, (Phal.) Mart. Syn.
Ātĕr ; vīscōsŭs.
pictŏr, ōrĭs, m., *a painter.* Pīctōrĭbŭs ătquĕ pŏētīs, Hor. Epith. Pĕrītŭs, dōctŭs,
īndūstrῐŭs, īnsīgnῐs, pērfēctŭs, cĕlĕbrῐs, clārŭs, ēgrēgĭŭs, præclārŭs.
pīctūră, æ, f., *painting.* Ŭt pīctūră pŏēsĭs, Hor. Epith. Nōbĭlῐs, mīrābĭlῐs, ăd-
mīrāndă, āntīquă, lætă, hōrrῐdă, īnsīgnῐs, Apēllĕă.
pīctūro, ās, *to paint.* Fērt pīctūrātās, Virg. V. Pingo.
pīctŭs, ă, ŭm, *the pass. partic. of* pingo. Pīctŭs ŏbērrĕt, Pers.
Pīcŭs, ī, m., *a king of Latium.* Pīcŭs ῐn Aūsŏnῐīs, Ov.
pĭē, adv., *piously.* Ŭltă pĭē, Ov.
Pĭĕrĭdĕs, ŭm, f. pl., *the Muses.* Dīcĭtĕ, Pĭĕrĭdĕs, Virg. V. Musæ.
Pĭĕrĭŭs, ă, ŭm, *of Pieria.* Nēc vīr Pĭĕrĭă, (Choriamb.) Hor.
Pĭĕrŭs, ī, m., *the father of nine daughters who were changed into magpies.* Pĭĕrŭs
hās gĕnŭĭt, Ov.
pĭĕtās, ātĭs, f., *piety, affection.* Īnsīgnēm pĭĕtūtĕ vῐrŭm, Virg. Syn. Rĕlῐgῐo,
bĕnῐgnĭtās. Epith. Sānctă, sacră, vēră, ῐllūstrῐs, īnsῐgnῐs, spĕctātă, ēgrēgĭă,
clēmēns, ōffĭcĭōsă.
pĭgĕr, pῐgră, grŭm, *sluggish.* Sĕd pῐgĕr, ēt, Mant. Syn. Ignāvŭs, ῐnĕrs, sōcŏrs,
vēcŏrs, dēsĕs, lānguῐdŭs, sēgnῐs, dēsῐdῐōsŭs, lēntŭs. V. Otiosus, otior.
pῐgĕt, *it is irksome.* Nōn pῐgĕt ῐrĕ, Mart. Syn. Tœdĕt.

pĭgnēro, ās, *to pawn.* Pĭgnĕrăt Ātreŭs, Stat. Syn. Ŏppĭgnēro, ŏppōno.
pĭgnĕrŏr, ārĭs, *to take a pledge.* Quŏd dās mĭhĭ, pĭgnĕrŏr ōmĕn, Ov.
pĭgnŭs, ŏrĭs, n., *a pledge.* Pĭgnŏră cără, Virg. Epith. Ĕxĭmĭŭm, laūtŭm, dīvĕs, prĕtĭōsŭm, măgnĭfĭcŭm, pŭlchrŭm, ămīcŭm.
pĭgrĭtĭă, æ, f., *sluggishness.* Pĭgrĭtĭa ēst, Mart. Syn. Pĭgrĭtĭēs, ĭgnāvĭă, ĭnērtĭă, sōcōrdĭă, vēcōrdĭă, dēsĭdĭă, lāngŭŏr, sēgnĭtĭēs, tŏrpŏr, vĕtērnŭs, ōtĭŭm. Epith. Ignāvă, ĭnērs, lēntă, lāngŭĭdă, lāngŭēns, ĭmbēllĭs, tŏrpēns, fœdă, tūrpĭs, sēgnĭs, ĭmprŏbă, dēsĕs, mōllĭs, sōmnĭfĕră. V. Otium:
pĭgrŏr, ārĭs, *to be idle.* Quŏd sī pĭgrārĭs, Lucr.
pĭlă, æ, f., *a ball to play with.* Indōctŭsquĕ pĭlæ, Hor. Epith. Rŏtūndă, lĕvĭs, vŏlūbĭlĭs, vŏlāns, sŏnāns, strīdēns, cĭtă, cōncĭtă.
pĭlă, æ, f., *a mole.* Sāxĕă pĭlă, Virg. Syn. Mōlēs. Epith. Căvă, āltă.—2. *a pilaster.* Pĭlă lĭbēllōs, Hor. Syn. Cŏlŭmnă.
pĭlānŭs, ī, m., *a lancer.* Tŏtĭdēm pĭlānŭs hăbēbăt, Ov.
pĭlātŭs, ă, ŭm, *bald.* Atquĕ pĭlātă rĕdĭt, Mart.
pĭlātŭs, ă, ŭm, *armed with a javelin.* Pĭlātăquĕ plēnĭs Āgmĭnă, Virg.
pĭlēātŭs, ă, ŭm, *wearing a hat.* Prŏcŭl ītĕ pĭlēātōs, (Phal.) Mart.
pĭlēntŭm, ī, n., *a covered chariot for ladies.* Pĭlēntĭs mātrēs, Virg.
pĭlĕŭs, ī, m., ŭm, ī, *and* ĕŏlŭm, ī, n., *a hat, bonnet.* Pĭlĕă dōnānt, Pers. Pĭlĕŏlŭm nĭtĭdīs, Ov. Syn. Gălērŭs, pĕtăsŭs. Epith. Tēxtĭlĭs, lăbōrātŭs, ūtĭlĭs, cŏmmŏdŭs, făcĭlĭs, lĕvĭs, ōrnātŭs, cŏmpŏsĭtŭs, lānĕŭs, vīllōsŭs.
pĭlo, ās, *to deprive of the hair.* Quā pĭlāntŭr ŭxōrēs, Mart.
pĭlōsŭs, ă, ŭm, *hairy.* Tūrpĕ pĭlōsĭs, Mart. Syn. Vīllōsŭs.
pĭlŭm, ī, n., *a javelin.* Pĭlă mĭnāntĭă pĭlīs, Lucan. V. Telum.
Pīlŭmnŭs, ī, m., *the son of Jupiter, and king of Daunia.* Cuī Pīlŭmnŭs ăvŭs, Virg.
pĭlŭs, ī, m., *a hair.* Sēd frŭtĭcāntĕ pĭlo, Juv. V. Capillus.
Pīmplă, æ, f., *a mountain of Thrace, sacred to the Muses.* Epith. Vĭrēns, vĭrĭdĭs, frŏndōsă, nĕmŏrōsă, Pīērĭă, Āŏnĭă.
Pīmplēĭdĕs, ŭm, *or* plœæ, ārŭm, f. pl., *a name of the Muses.* V. Musæ.
Pīnārĭī, ōrŭm, m. pl., *an ancient family of Latium, consecrated to the worship of Hercules.* Ēt dŏmŭs Hērcŭlēī cŭstōs Pīnārĭī săcrī, Virg.
Pīndărĭcŭs, ă, ŭm, *of Pindar.* Pīndărĭcī fōntĭs, Hor.
Pīndărŭs, ī, m., *the lyric poet.* Pīndărŭm quīsquĭs, Hor. Epith. Thēbānŭs, lўrĭcŭs, dōctŭs, pĕrītŭs, Āŏnĭŭs, Pīĕrĭŭs, făcūndŭs, suāvĭs, dīvīnŭs, Āpōllĭnĕŭs, Phœbēŭs, cĕlĕbrĭs, nōbĭlĭs, ĭngĕnĭōsŭs. V. Vates.
Pīndŭs, ī, m., *a mountain in Thessaly, sacred to the Muses.* Năm nĕquĕ Pīndī, Virg. Epith. Āltŭs, ārdŭŭs, săcĕr, Āpōllĭnĕŭs, pīnĭfĕr, nĭvālĭs. V. Parnassus.
pīnētŭm, ī, n., *a place planted with pine-trees.* Cædūnt pīnētă sĕcūrēs, Ov.
pīnĕŭs, ă, ŭm, *of pine-tree.* Pīnĕă sўlvă, Virg.
pingo, pīnxī, pīctŭm, *to paint.* Pīngĕrĕt aūt ăllŭs, Hor. Syn. Dēpīngo, pīctūro, ădūmbro. V. Pictor.
pīnguēdo, ĭnĭs, f., *fatness.* Dīră pīnguēdĭnĕ tēllŭs, Alcim. Syn. Ādēps ; crāssĭtĭēs.
pīnguēsco, ĭs, *to grow fat.* Pīnguēscĕrĕ cŏrpŏrĕ cŏrpŭs, Ov.
pīngŭĭărĭŭs, ă, ŭm, *who likes fat.* Pīngŭĭārĭŭs nōn sŭm, Mart.
pīngŭĭs, ĕ, *fat.* Sāngŭĭnĕ pīngŭĭŏr, (Alcaic.) Hor. Syn. Ŏbēsŭs, ŏpīmŭs, crāssŭs ; rŭdĭs, hĕbĕs, tārdŭs.
pīnĭfĕr, ă, ŭm, *producing pines.* Pīnĭfĕr ānnōs, Virg.
pīnĭgĕr, ă, ŭm, *carrying or crowned with pine.* Pīnĭgĕrŭm Faūnī, Ov.
* pīnnă, *and* ŭlă, æ, f., *a fin or large feather.* Col.—2. *the battlements of a wall.* Pīnnīs ātque āggĕrĕ cīngĭt, Virg.
pīnnātŭs, *and* pīnnĭgĕr, ă, ŭm, *having fins, or winged.* Tēmpŏră pīnnātĭs, Prud. Syn. Crūrăquĕ pīnnĭgĕrō, Ov.
Pīnnĭrăpŭs, ī, m., *the gladiator who combated with the Samnite ; so called, because he had to knock down the peacock's feather which adorned the crest of his antagonist.* Pīnnĭrăpī cŭltōs jŭvĕnēs, Juv.
pīnso, ĭs, suī, sĭtŭm *or* stŭm, *to grind.* Pīnsĕrĕt hōrrĕă, Ov. Syn. Tĕro, cōntĕro, ōbtĕro, tūndo, cōntŭndo, mĭnŭo.
pīnŭs, ī *and* ūs, f., *a pine-tree.* Pīnŭs ĭn hōrtīs, Virg. Epith. Āltă, prŏcēră, ārdŭă, vĭrēns, ŏdŏră, ŏdŏrĭfĕră, naūtĭcă, Pōntĭcă, sўlvēstrĭs, hīrsūtă, ăcūtă, căvă, căpīllātă, Bĕrĕcŷnthĭcă, Cўbĕlēĭă, Idœă, cōnĭfĕră, nūtāns, pīngŭĭs.

pĭo, ās, *to expiate.* Trīstĕ pĭārĕt, Virg. Syn. Expĭo, lŭo, pūrgo.

pĭpĕr, ĕrĭs, n., *pepper.* Rŭgōsūm pĭpĕr ĕt, Juv. Epith. Mōrdāx, ŏdōrŭm, ācrĕ, nigrŭm, ŏdōrĭfĕrŭm, Eōŭm.

pĭpĭlo, ās, *and* pĭpĭo, īs, *to chirp.* Ūsquĕ pĭpĭlābăt, (Phal.) Cat.

Pīræeŭs, ĕŏs, *and* œŭs, ī, m., æïs, ĕŏs, f., *and* œǎ, ōrŭm, n. pl., *the port of Athens* Stăbĭlēm Pīrœĕǎ naūtĭs, Stat. Inde ŭbĭ Pīræīs, Prop. Pīrœăquĕ tūtǎ, Ov.

Pīræŭs, ǎ, ŭm, *of Piræeus.* Pīrœăquĕ līttŏrǎ tāngĭt, Ov.

pīrātǎ, æ, m., *a pirate.* Pĕlăgī pīrātǎ rĕlĭquĭt, Lucan. Syn. Naŭtĭcŭs prædo, latro.

pīrātĭcŭs, ǎ, ŭm, *of a corsair.* Pōst pīrātĭcǎ dāmnǎ, (Phal.) Sid.

Pīrĭthŏŭs, ŏī, m., *the son of Ixion, and friend of Theseus.* Pīrĭthŏŭs, vălĭdǎ, Ov.

Pīsǎ, æ, f., *and* sæ, ūrŭm, f. pl., *a city of Elis.* Prælābī flūmĭnǎ Pīsæ, Virg.

Pīsāndĕr, drī, m., *one of Penelope's suitors.* Ārcădǎ pīscōsæ, Virg.

pīscātŏr, ōrĭs, m., *a fisherman.* Ĕdīcīt, pīscātŏr ŭtī, Hor. Epith. Æquŏrĕŭs, sōlērs, sēdŭlŭs, paŭpĕr, hāmĭfĕr, flūctĭvăgŭs, pătĭēns, vĭgĭl. V. Piscor.

Pīscēs, ĭŭm, m. pl., *a constellation.* Aŭxĭlĭō Pīscēs sŭbĭĕrĕ, Ov.

pīscīnǎ, æ, f., *a fish-pond.* Pīscīnǎ rhōmbŭm, Mart. Epith. Căvǎ, fĕrāx. V. Stagnum.

pīscĭs, īs, m., *a fish.* Pīscĭbŭs ēscǎ nătǎt, Prop. Epith. Ăquōsŭs, flŭvĭālĭs, mūtŭs, mărīnŭs, pīnnĭfĕrŭs, flūctĭvăgŭs, ūndĭvăgŭs, squāmmĭgĕr, squāmmĕŭs, squāmmōsŭs, æquŏrĕŭs.

pīscŏr, ārĭs, *to fish.* Nōn clāssĭbŭs pīscāmŭr, (Iamb.)

pīscōsŭs, ǎ, ŭm, *full of fishes.* Pīscōsæ, Virg.

Pīsēnŏr, ōrĭs, m.. *the name of a man.* Ĕt cŭm Pīsēnŏrĕ Cæneŭs, Ov.

Pīso, ōnĭs, m., *the name of a Patrician family at Rome.* Crēdĭtĕ Pīsōnĕs, Hor.

pīstŏr, ōrĭs, m., *a baker.* Pīstōrī tōtĭĕs, Mart.

pīstrīnŭm, ī, n., *a bakehouse.* Ĕt nōn pīstrīnō, Cat.

Pīstrĭs, V. Pristis.

Pĭtănǎ, æ, *and* nē, ēs, f., *a city of the Æolians.* Æŏlĭăm Pĭtănēn, Ov.

Pĭthēcūsǎ, æ, f., *and* sæ, ārŭm, f. pl., *two islands opposite Naples.* Cōllĕ Pĭthēcūsās, Ov.

Pīthō, ūs, f., *the goddess of persuasion.* Epith. Făcūndǎ, dĭsērtǎ, dōctǎ, sōlērs, īngĕnĭōsǎ.

Pĭthŏlĕōn, ōntĭs, m., *a bad poet of Rhodes* Rhŏdĭō quŏd Pĭthŏlĕōntī, Hor.

Pīttheŭs. ĕŏs *or* ĕī, m., *a king of Trœzene.*—Adj., -theŭs, *and* -theīŭs, ǎ, ŭm, *and* -theīs, ĭdĭs, f., *of Pittheus, of Trœzene.* Pīttheām prŏfūgŏ, Ov. Pīttheīǎ rēgnǎ, Id. Nōn tū Pīttheīdŏs Æthræ, Id.

pĭtuītǎ, *or* pĭtuītǎ, (*tris.*) æ, f., *phlegm.* Mălǎ pĭtuītǎ nāsī, (Phal.) Cat. Cŭm pĭtuītǎ mŏlēsta ēst, Hor. Sŏmnĭǎ pĭtuītǎ quī, Pers.

pĭŭs, ǎ, ŭm, *pious.* Plăcĭdī sērvătĕ pĭŏs, Virg. Syn. Rĕlĭgĭōsŭs, jūstŭs, sānctŭs.

pīx, ĭcĭs, f., *pitch.* Sĕd pĭcĭs īn mŏrĕm, Virg. Epith. Nigrǎ, ātrǎ, pīnguĭs, crāssǎ, liquĭdǎ, tĕnāx, Idæǎ, Illўrĭcǎ, Nārўcĭǎ.

plăcābĭlĭs, ĕ, *easy to appease.* Ĕst plăcābĭlĭs īrǎ, Ov. Syn. Exōrābĭlĭs, mītĭs, clēmēns.

plăcāmĕn, mĭnĭs, n., *that which appeases.* Dūrō plăcāmĭnǎ Dītī, Sil.

plăcātŭs, *the pass. partic. of* placo. Plăcātō cōnvērsǎ fŭrōrĕ, Lucr.

plăcēns, ēntĭs, *pleasing.* Ĕt plăcēns Ūxŏr, Hor. Syn. Jūcŭndŭs, dūlcĭs, cārŭs.

plăcēntǎ, æ, f., *a cake.* Quādrǎ plăcēntæ, Mart. Epith. Mēllītǎ.

plăcĕo, cŭī, cĭtŭs, *to please.* Dŏtĕ plăcēbăm, Ov. Syn. Jūcūndŭs, grātŭs, ăccēptŭs sŭm, ārrīdĕo, prŏbŏr.

plăcĕt, *it pleases.* Syn. Stăt, lĭbĕt, jŭvăt, sĕdĕt.

plăcĭdĕ, adv., *quietly.* Plăcĭdĕ āmplēctī, Virg.

plăcĭdŭlŭs, ǎ, ŭm, *the dimin. of* placidus. Cĭnĭs ŭtī plăcĭdŭlǎ, Aus.

plăcĭdŭs, ǎ, ŭm, *quiet.* Ŭt sāltēm plăcĭdĭs, Virg. V. Placatus.

plăcĭtŭs, ǎ, ŭm, *pleasing.* Ĕst vīrtŭs plăcĭtŭs, Ov. Syn. Grātŭs, jūcūndŭs.

plăco, ās, *to appease.* Vĕl bŏvĕ plăcăt, Hor. V. Moveo, parco.

plăgǎ, æ, f., *a net.* Rētĭǎ rārǎ, plăgæ, Virg. Syn. Rĕtĕ, lăquĕī, cāssēs, līnǎ. V. Rete.—2. *a country.* Dīrĭmĭt plăgǎ sōlĭs, Virg. Syn. Rĕgĭo, trāctŭs, ōrǎ.

P

plāgă, æ, f., *a wound.* Ŏbstrŭĭtŭr; plăgīsquĕ pĕrēmptŏ, Virg. Syn. Vŭlnŭs, īctŭs. V. Vulnus.

plăgĭārĭŭs, ĭī, m., *a plagiary.* Impōnēs plăgĭārĭŏ, (Phal.) Mart.

plăgōsŭs, ă, ŭm, *who likes to strike.* Plăgōsūm mĭhī pārvŏ, Hor.

plānctŭs, ūs, m., *lamentation.* Pēctŏrĕ plānctŭs, Stat. Syn. Lūctŭs, ējŭlātŭs, dŏlŏr, gĕmĭtŭs. Epith. Illīsŭs, īngēns, āssĭdŭŭs, ăcērbŭs, trīstĭs, fœmĭnĕŭs, flēbĭlĭs, quĕrŭlŭs, āmēns. V. Plangor.

Plāncŭs, ī, m., *the name of a Roman family.* Cōnsŭlĕ Plāncŏ, Hor.

plānē, adv., *plainly.* Cŏmmūnī sēnsū plānē cărĕt, Hor. Syn. Prōrsŭs, ŏm-nīno.

plănētă, æ, m., *and* tēs, æ, f., *a planet.* Quīsquĕ plănētă dăbo, Ov. Epith. Ērrāns, ērrātĭcŭs, văgŭs, splēndĭdŭs, mĭcāns, clārŭs, cŏrūscŭs, rŭtĭlŭs.

plāngo, ānxī, ctŭm, *to beat.* Lĭttŏră plāngūnt, Virg. V. Lugeo.

plāngŏr, ōrĭs, m., *a great outcry, a yelling.* Căvæ plāngŏrĭbŭs ædēs, Virg. Syn. Plānctŭs, gĕmĭtŭs, ŭlŭlātŭs. Epith. Sævŭs, trīstĭs, pērvĭgĭl, sēgnĭs, īllīsŭs, fœmĭnĕŭs, flēbĭlĭs, fœdŭs, quĕrŭlŭs. V. Luctus, fletus.

plānĭpēs, pĕdĭs, m., *a buffoon, or actor in low comedy, whose shoe was not elevated like the sock or cothurnus.* Plānĭpĕdēs audīt Făbĭŏs, Juv.

plānĭtĭēs, ĭēī, f., *a level surface.* Plānĭtĭem ād spĕcŭlī, Lucr. Syn. Cāmpŭs, æquŏr. Epith. Spătĭōsă, pătēns, āmplă, vāstă, īngēns, ăpērtă, grāmĭnĕă, vĭrĭdĭs, flōrĭdă, pīctă, vērsĭcŏlŏr, rīdēns, āmœnă. V. Campus.

plāntă, æ, f., *a plant.* Fīgăt hŭmŏ plāntăs, Virg. Syn. Ārbŏr. Epith. Tĕnĕră, tĕnēllă, ēxīlĭs, pārvă, fĕrāx, ŏdōrātă, fœcūndă, fērtĭlĭs, vīrēns, vĭrĭdĭs, lūxŭrĭāns. V. Planto, arbor, flos, herba.—2. *the sole of the foot.* Fīgēns vēs-tīgĭă plāntă, Juv. Epith. Tĕnĕră, mōllĭs, tĕnēllă, tērsă, lēvĭs, cĭtă.

plāntārĭs, ĕ, *belonging to the sole of the foot.* Plāntārĭbŭs ūllĭgăt ālĭs, Stat.

plāntārĭūm, ĭī, n., *the plant of trees or herbs.* Sŭă plāntārĭă tērrā, Virg. V. Seminarium.

* plānto, ās, *to plant.* Plin. V. Insero.

plānŭs, ă, ŭm, *even.* Ŭt nĕquĕ plānĭs, Hor. Syn. Æquŭs, lēvĭs, cāmpēstrĭs, æquālĭs; clārŭs.

plānŭs, ī, m., *an impostor.* Crŭrĕ plănūm līcĕt, Hor.

plătānŭs, ī, f., *a plane-tree.* Nūtāntī plătănŏ, Catul. Epith. Stĕrĭlĭs, īnsīgnĭs, ūmbrāns, prōcēră, āltă, sȳlvēstrĭs, ārdŭă, sūblīmĭs, lātă, frōndēns, cŏmāns, ūm-brĭfĕră, nūtāns, ŏpācă.

plătĕă, æ, f., *a street.* Pūræ sūnt plătĕæ, Hor. Epith. Pŏpŭlōsă, lātă, āmplă, căpăx, īngēns. V. Via.

plătēssă, æ, f., *a fish, plaice.* Mōllēsquĕ plătēssæ, Aus.

Plāto, ōnĭs, m., *the philosopher.* Dōctūmquĕ Plătōnă, Hor. Epith. Cecrŏpĭŭs; dīvīnŭs, dōctŭs, īngĕnĭōsŭs, sōlērs, săgăx, ăcūtŭs, īnsīgnĭs, cĕlebrĭs, fācūndŭs, dĭsērtŭs.

plaudo, sī, *to applaud.* Plausērĕ thĕātră, Mart. Syn. Applaudo, cōmplaudo; ēxplōdo. V. Gaudeo.

plausŏr, ōrĭs, m., *an applauder.* Sī plausōrĭs ĕgēs, Hor.

plaustrŭm, ī, n., *a chariot.* Nēc plaustrĭs cēssānt, Virg. Syn. Cūrrŭs, āxĭs. Epith. Vōlvēns, grăvĕ, trĕmēns, tārdŭm, quĕrŭlŭm, gĕmēns, sŏnōrŭm, strīdŭ-lŭm, raucŭm, lēntŭm, rōbūstŭm.

plausŭs, ūs, m., *applause.* Ōmnĭă plausū, Virg. Syn. Applausŭs, ācclāmātĭo, clāmŏr, mūrmŭr, stŭdĭŭm pŏpŭlī. Epith. Lætŭs, ălăcĕr, hĭlărĭs, sōlēnnĭs, cănōrŭs, māgnŭs, trĭūmphālĭs, fēstīvŭs, cōnfūsŭs, ēffūsŭs, pūblĭcŭs, thĕātrālĭs, sĕcūndŭs, pŏpŭlārĭs. V. Plaudo.

Plautīnŭs, ă, ŭm, *of Plautus.* Plautīnōs nŭmĕrōs, Hor.

Plautŭs, ī, m., *the comic poet.* Plautŭs ăd ēxēmplăr, Hor. Epith. Jŏcōsŭs, dĭsērtŭs, fācūndŭs, īngĕnĭōsŭs, āntīquŭs.

plēbēcŭlă, æ, f., *the common people.* Fērvĕt plēbēcŭlă bĭlĕ, Pers.

plēbeĭŭs, or ēĭŭs, ă, ŭm, *of the common people.* Quærŏ plēbeĭŭs, ĕt æquăm, M. Syn. Vŭlgārĭs.

plēbēs, *and* plēbs, ēbĭs, f., *the common people.* Plēbĭs, ĕt īdĕm, Hor. Syn. Plēbēcŭlă, vŭlgŭs, pŏpŭlŭs. Epith. Ignără, rŭdĭs, īndōctă, īncōnstāns, tĕmĕ-rărĭă, lēvĭs, mŭtābĭlĭs, īmprūdēns, lŏquāx, clāmōsă, crēdŭlă, īnēptă, türbĭdă, stŭltă, āmēns, īnsānă, mălĕsānă, ăvĭdă, hŭmĭlĭs, ĭmă, īnfīmă, vīlĭs, īnglōrĭă, cœcă, audax, mĭsĕră, ĕgēnă, prŏcāx, prŏtĕrvă, sēdĭtĭōsă, tŭmŭltŭōsă, īncaūtă, īmprŏvĭdă. V. Vulgus.

plēbīscītŭm, ī, n., *a statute made by the people.* Ĕt plēbīscītă cōăctă, Luc.

plŭcto, xī and xŭī, *to punish, to twist.* Plēctŭntŭr Ăchīvī, Hor.

plēctrŭm, ī, n., *a quill to play on instruments with.* Ăltĕră plēctrŭm, Ov. SYN. Pēctĕn. EPITH. Sŏnāns, rĕsŏnāns, mŏdŭlāns, īnsīgnĕ, Ăŏnĭŭm, Ăpŏllĭnĕŭm, Phœbēŭm, lēnĕ, tŭmŭltŭōsŭm, vōcālĕ, dūlcĕ, blāndŭm, rădĭāns, aūrātŭm, fācŭndŭm, sŏnōrŭm, lĕpĭdŭm, cănōrŭm, lŏquāx, gārrŭlŭm, quĕrŭlŭm, grātŭm, ĕbūrnŭm.

Plēĭădĕs, Plĕĭădĕs, *or* Plĭădĕs, ŭm, f. pl., *a constellation of seven stars.* Plēĭădēs făcĭŭnt, Prop. Plĭădūmquĕ nĭvōsŭm, Stat. SYN. Vērgĭlĭæ, Atlāntĭdĕs. EPITH. Imbrĭfĕræ, nĭmbōsæ, ūndōsæ, prŏcēllōsæ, ūdæ, mădĭdæ, mădēntēs, hūmĭdæ, nūbĭlæ, mœstæ, trīstēs, vērnæ, lūcĭdæ, Atlāntææ.

Plĕĭăs, *or* Plĕĭăs, (*dissyll.*) ădĭs, f., *a Naiad.* Plēĭăs ēnīxa ēst, Ov. Plĕĭăs, ĕt Ŏcĕănī, Virg.

Plēĭŏnē, ēs, f., *a nymph.* Plēĭŏnēsquĕ nĕpōs, Ov.

Plēmmўrĭŭm, ĭī, n., *a promontory near Syracuse.* Plēmmўrĭum ūndōsŭm, Virg.

plēnē, adv., *entirely.* Ŭt fōrtŭnātăm plēnē, Hor. SYN. Cŭmŭlātē.

plēnŭs, ă, ŭm, *full, complete.* Plēnĭŏr ūt sī, Hor. SYN. Cōnfērtŭs, ăbūndāns, frĕquēns, āfflŭēns, cŭmŭlātŭs, replētŭs ; īntĕgĕr, pērfēctŭs.

plērīquĕ, æquĕ, ăquĕ, *the greatest part.* Ŭt plērīquĕ sŏlēnt, Hor. SYN. Mūltī, nŏnnūllī, nōn paūcī, māxĭmă pārs, plūrĭmī.

plērŭmquĕ, adv., *mostly.* Ăgrĭcŏlæ plērŭmquĕ frŭūntŭr, Virg. SYN. Sæpĕ, sæpĭŭs, frĕquēntĕr, crēbrō.

Pleūrōn, ōnĭs, m., *a city of Ætolia.* Ădjăcĕt hīs Pleūrōn, Ov.

plĭco, ās, *to knit, fold.* Mēmbră plĭcāntĕin, Virg. SYN. Cōmplĭco, replĭco, cōllĭgo, īntōrquĕo, cōnvōlvo.

Plīnĭŭs, ĭī, m., *the name of two celebrated Roman writers.* Plīnĭŭs Ăndrŏgўnŭm, Aus. Făcŭndō mĕă Plīnĭŏ Thălĭă, Mart.

Plīsthĕnĭŭs, ă, ŭm, *of Plisthenes.* Illăm Plīsthĕnĭŏ, Ov.

plōrăbĭlĭs, ĕ, *to be deplored.* Plŏrăbĭlĕ sī quĭd, Pers. V. Tristis.

plōrătŏr, ōrĭs, m., *a mourner.* Sī quĭs plōrătŏr, Mart.

plōrātŭs, ūs, m., *a wailing.* Plŏrātŭs, mōrtīs cŏmĭtēs, Lucr. SYN. Flētŭs, lacrўmæ, lūctŭs.

plōro, ās, *to lament.* Plŏrātŭr lăcrўmīs, Juv. V. Fleo, lacrymor, lugeo.

Plŏtĭŭs, ĭī, m., *the name of a man.* Plŏtĭŭs ēt· Vărĭŭs, Hor.

plŭĭt, *it rains.* Dŭm plŭĭt, īn tērrīs, Virg. V. Imber, grando

plŭmă, æ, f., *a feather.* Pēnsĭlĭbŭs plŭmīs, Juv. SYN. Pēnuă. EPITH. Lĕvĭs, mōllĭs, tĕnĕră, pĭctă, mĭcāns. V. Ala.

plŭmătĭlĭs, ĕ, *of feathers.* Vărĭŏ plŭmātĭlĭs ōrsŭ, Anon.

plŭmbĕŭs, ă, ŭm, *leaden.* Plŭmbĕŭs Aūstĕr, Hor.—Plŭmbĕă glāns, *a bullet.* EPITH. Lēthĭfĕră, lēthālĭs, fātālĭs, fŭlmĭnĕă, ēmīssă.

plŭmbŭm, ī, n., *lead.* Lĭcĭă plŭmbō, Luc. EPITH. Liquĭdŭm, līquēns, līvēns, grăvĕ, flēxĭlĕ, trāctābĭlĕ, sōlĭdŭm, vŭlnĭfĭcŭm.

plŭmĕŭs, ă, ŭm, *full of feathers.* Plūmĕă tēlīs, Prud.

plŭmĭpēs, ĕdĭs, *feather-footed.* Ădde hūc plūmĭpēdēs, Cat.

plŭmōsŭs, ă, ŭm, *full of feathers.* Sīc plŭmōsă nŏvĭs, Ov. SYN. Plūmĭgĕr; plūmă tēctŭs, ŏpērtŭs.

plŭo, ĭs, *to rain.* V. Pluvia.

plūrēs, ă, *more, many.* Plūrĭbŭs ăssĕrŭĭt, Hor. SYN. Mūltī, plūrĭmī, plērīquĕ, frĕquēntēs.

plūrĭmŭm, adv., *much.* Plūrĭmum ŏbēssĕ sŏlēnt, Ov.

plūrĭmŭs, ă, ŭm, *very much.* Plūrĭmŭs ūrbī, Virg. SYN. Mūltŭs; lōngŭs, māxĭmŭs.

plūrĭs, *more, dearer.* Plūrĭs ĕmŭntŭr, Juv. SYN. Măgĭs ; cărĭŭs.

plūs, ūrĭs, n., *more.* Plūs ĕrăt īn glădĭō, Ov. SYN. Măgĭs.

plŭtĕŭm, ī, n., *a bedstead.* Nāmquĕ pŭĕr plŭtĕŏ, Mart.

plŭtĕŭs, ī, m., *a book-case, a desk.* Nēc plŭtĕŭm cædĭt, Pers. EPITH. Dōctŭs; librīs ŏpērtŭs.

Plūto, *and* ōn, ōnĭs, m., *the brother of Jupiter, and god of the infernal regions.* Pătĕr Plūtōn, ōdĕrĕ, Virg. SYN. Dīs. EPITH. Immītĭs, sævŭs, dīrŭs, tŏrvŭs, tētĕr,

fĕrōx, ăvĭdŭs, ăvārŭs, hŏrrĭdŭs, ūmbrōsŭs, plăcĭdŭs, sŭpĕrbŭs, trĕmēndŭs, īmpĭŭs, fĕrŭs, crūdēlīs, bārbărŭs, fērrĕŭs, sĕvērŭs, īnĕxōrābĭlīs, prŏfūndŭs, ātĕr, nĭgĕr, pāllēns, pāllĭdŭs, squālĭdŭs, Stȳgĭŭs, Tārtărĕŭs, Lēthæŭs, Phlĕgĕthōntæŭs, īnfērnŭs, īmŭs, Sātŭrnĭŭs.
Plūtōnĭŭs, ă, ŭm, *of Pluto.* Dŏmŭs ēxīlīs Plūtōnĭă, Hor. SYN. Tārtărĕŭs, īnfērnŭs.
＊ Plūtŭs, ī, m., *the god of riches.*
plŭvĭă, æ, f., *rain.* Cœrŭlĕŭs plŭvĭăm, Virg. SYN. Imbĕr, nīmbŭs. V. Imber, ros; pluit.
plŭvĭālīs, ĕ, *and* vĭŭs, ă, ŭm, *rainy.* Vēnĭēns plŭvĭālĭbŭs hœdĭs, Virg. Plŭvĭŭs dēscrībĭtŭr ārcŭs, Hor. SYN. Plŭvĭōsŭs, īmbrĭfĕr; nūbĭlŭs.
pōcŭlŭm, ī, n., *a cup.* Pōcŭlă sī quāndō. SYN. Scȳphŭs, călīx, crātĕr, crātēră, pătēră, cārchēsĭŭm.· EPITH. Spūmāns, aūrĕŭm, ārgēntĕŭm, lūcĭdŭm, mĭcāns, căndĭdŭm, ăhēnŭm, æuĕŭm, făgĭnŭm, cælătŭm.
pŏdăgĕr, agrĭcŭs, *or* ōsŭs, ă, ŭm, *gouty.* Stărĕ pŭtāt pŏdăgĕr, Claud.
pŏdagră, æ, f., *the gout.* Tŭrpēsquĕ pŏdăgrās, Virg. Lĭtĭgăt, ēt pŏdăgrā, Mart. EPITH. Tŭrpĭs, īmmītĭs, dīră, sēgnĭs, īgnāvă, ĭnērs, lăpĭdōsă, crūdēlĭs, mŏlēstă, ăcērbă, īmpōrtūnă, īnsōmnĭs, ācrĭs, īmmĕdĭcābĭlīs, quĕrŭlă. V. Chiragra.
Pŏdălīrĭŭs, ĭī, m., *a famous physician, the son of Æsculapius.* Dănăōs Pŏdălīrĭŭs ārtĕ, Ov.
pŏdēx, ĭcĭs, m., *the fundament.* Pŏdĭcĕ lævī, Juv.
pŏdĭŭm, ĭī, n., *a balcony.* Ōmnĭbŭs ād pŏdĭŭm, Juv.
Pœāntĭădēs, æ, m., *the son of Pœas, Philoctetes.* Nēc Pœāntĭădĕm, Ov.
Pœāntĭŭs, ă, ŭm, *of Pœas.* Pœāntĭă prōlēs, Ov.
Pœās, āntĭs, m., *a Thessalian of Melibœa, the father of Philoctetes.* Fērrĕ jŭbēs Pœāntĕ sătŭm, Ov.
pŏēmă, ătĭs, n., *a poem.* Dūlcĕ pŏēmă săcrĭs, Rutil. SYN. Cārmĕn. EPITH. Pŭlchrŭm, făcētŭm, dīvīnŭm, făcūndŭm, sacrŭm, Āŏnĭŭm, Pīĕrĭŭm, dūlcĕ. V. Carmen, poëta.
Pœmĕnĭs, ĭdĭs, f., *the name of a dog.*
pœnă, æ, f., *punishment.* Nē pœnās ēxĭgăt Ajāx, Juv. SYN. Sŭpplĭcĭŭm; crūcĭātŭs, dŏlōr, lăbŏr. EPITH. Mĭsĕrāndă, dūră, mĭsĕrābĭlĭs, trīstĭs, fūnēstă, sævă, ātră, crūdēlĭs, crŭēntă, dēfōrmĭs, ăcērbă, dīră, īnfāmĭs, mĭsĕră, hōrrĭbĭlĭs, tūrpĭs, īmmānĭs, atrōx, īmpĭă, ĭnīquă, grăvĭs, ămără, īmmītĭs, suprēmă, vĕhĕmēns, īntŏlĕrābĭlĭs, vĭŏlēntă, ĭnaūdītă. V. Punio, labor, dolor, supplicium.
Pœnī, ōrŭm, m. pl., *the Carthaginians.* Pŏnūntquĕ fĕrōcĭă Pœnī, Virg. V. Carthaginiensis.
pœnĭtēntĭă, æ, f., *repentance.* Adēstŏ pœnĭtēntĭæ, Hilar. EPITH. Trīstĭs, mœrēns, dŏlēns, ămără, quĕrŭlă, ŭlŭlāns, frēndēns, īntēstīnă, īmpătĭēns, pērvĭgĭl, īrrĕquĭĕtă, sălūtĭfĕră, ŭtĭlĭs.
pœnĭtĕt, ŭĭt, *to repent of.* Nēc tē pœnĭtĕāt călămō, Virg. SYN. Pĭgĕt.
pŏēsĭs, ĭs *or* ĕŏs; ētĭcă, æ, *and* tĭcĕ, ēs, f., *poetry.* Ŭt pīctūră pŏēsĭs ĕrĭt, Hor. EPITH. Dīvīnă, dōctă, sacră, blāndă, gĕnĕrōsă, pŏtēns, cĕlebrĭs, īnclȳtă, nōbĭlĭs, īngĕnĭōsă.
pŏētă, æ, m., *a poet.* Rēgŭmquĕ pŏētæ, Ov. SYN. Vātēs. EPITH. Sōlērs, dōctŭs, cĕlebrĭs, nōbĭlĭs, făcūndŭs, dĭsērtŭs, dīvīnŭs, īllūstrĭs, săcĕr, īngĕnĭōsŭs, īndŭstrĭŭs, lŏquāx, lāscīvŭs, nūgāx, ēxĭmĭŭs, clārŭs, vīlĭs, ābjēctŭs, īgnārŭs, Pīĕrĭŭs, Āŏnĭŭs, Phœbēŭs, Ăpōllĭnĕŭs.
pŏētĭcŭs, ă, ŭm, *poetical.* Mānărĕ pŏētĭcă mēllă, Hor. SYN. Ăpōllĭnĕŭs, Pīĕrĭŭs.
pŏētrĭă, æ, f., *a poetess.* Pŏētrĭă pĭcă, Pers.
pŏl, adv., *a brief mode of swearing by Pollux.* Nēc pŏl hŏmo, Enn.
Pŏlĕmōn, ōnĭs, m., *an Athenian philosopher, the disciple of Xenocrates.* Mūtātŭs Pŏlĕmōn, Hor.
pŏlēntă, æ, f., *barley-flour dried at the fire.* Pāstă pŏlēntă, Pers.
pŏlĭo, īs, īvī *or* ĭī, *to polish.* Aŭrōquĕ pŏlībānt, Virg. SYN. Pērpŏlĭo, ēxpŏlĭo, lævĭgo, cōmplāno, ēxōrno, ēxcŏlo, ōrno, ădōrno, rādo, ābrādo.
Pŏlītēs, æ, m., *one of the sons of Priam, slain by Pyrrhus.* Dē cædĕ Pŏlītēs, Virg.
pŏlītŭs, ă, ŭm, *the pass. partic. of* polio. Īndŏ quōd dēntĕ pŏlītŭm, Catull. SYN. Ēxpŏlītŭs, lævĭs; ōrnātŭs, nĭtĭdŭs.
pōllĕo, ēs, *to be able, strong.* Ēt pĕtĕ quā pōllēs, Prop.

pōllēx, ĭcĭs, m., *the thumb.* Lædērĕ pŏllĭcĭbŭs, Prop. Epith. Mŏllĭs, tĕnĕr, dŏctŭs. V. Digitus.

pŏllĭcĕŏr, cĭtŭs sŭm, *to promise.* Pŏllĭcĭtŭs, quæ tē, Virg. Syn. Pŏllĭcĭtŏr, prŏmĭtto, spŏndĕo. V. Promitto.

pŏllĭcĭtŭm, ī, n., *a promise.* Fāc mŏdŏ pŏllĭcĭtī, Ov. Syn. Prŏmĭssŭm.

pŏllīnctŏr, ōrĭs, m., *an embalmer.* Jām pŏllīnctŏrĕ părātō, Mart.

Pŏllĭo, ōnĭs, m., *a poet of the Augustan age.* Pŏllĭo ămāt nōstrŭm, Virg.

pŏllŭo, ĭs, ŭī, *to pollute, defile.* Pŏllŭīt ŏrĕ dăpēs, Virg. Syn. Cŏntămĭno, ĭnquĭno, cŏĭnquĭno, vĭŏlo, măcŭlo, tĕmĕro, dēfōrmo, fœdo, tūrpo. V. Maculo.

pŏllūtŭs, ă, ŭm, *the pass. partic.* of polluo. Pŏllūtă păcĕ, Lătīnŭm, Virg.

Pŏllŭx, ūcĭs, m., *son of Jupiter, brother of Castor.* Cŭm Pŏllŭcĕ mŏlēstō, Mart. V. Castor.

pŏlŭs, ī, m., *the pole.* Intŏnŭĕrĕ pŏlī, Virg. Syn. Axĭs ; cœlŭm, æthēr, Ŏlympŭs. Epith. Frīgĭdŭs, ālgēns, glăcĭālĭs, ĭnhōspĭtŭs, ĭnăccēssŭs, nĭvōsŭs. V. Cœlum.

Pŏlўbētēs, æ, m., *the name of a man.* Cĕrĕrīque sācrŭm Pŏlўbētēn, Virg.

Pŏlўbŭs, ī, m., *a king of Corinth.*—2. *one of the suitors of Penelope.* Quĭd tĭbĭ Pīsāndrŭm Pŏlўbūmquĕ, Ov.

Pŏlyclētŭs, ī, m., *a famous sculptor.* Ēt, Pŏlўclētĕ, tŭās, Mart. Epith. Dōctŭs, pĕrītŭs.

Pŏlўdæmōn, ŏnĭs, m., *an Assyrian warrior, the foe of Perseus.* Pŏlўdæmŏnă sānguĭnĕ crētŭm, Ov.

Pŏlўdāmās, āntĭs, m., *a Trojan prince.* Nĕquĕ Pŏlўdāmāntă, nĕque ĭpsŭm, Ov.

Pŏlўdēctēs, æ, m., *a king of the island of Seripho, changed into a rock.* Rēctŏr, Pŏlўdēctă, Sĕrīphī, Ov.

Pŏlўdōrĕŭs, ă, ŭm, *of Polydorus.* Ēt Pŏlўdōrĕō, Ov.

Pŏlўdōrŭs, ī, m., *a son of Priam, confided to Polymnestor, king of Thrace, who murdered him.* Pŏlўdōrum ōbtrūncăt, ĕt aŭrō, Virg.

Pŏlўhўmnĭă, Pŏlўmnĭă, *or* mnēĭă, æ, f., *one of the Muses.* Eūtērpē cŏhĭbēt, nēc Pŏlўhўmnĭă, Hor. V. Musæ.

Pŏlўmēstŏr, *and* mnēstŏr, ōrĭs, m., *a king of Thrace, murderer of Polydorus.* Thrācĭs Pŏlўmnēstŏrĭs aŭrō, Prop. Epith. Impĭŭs, pērfĭdŭs, ĭnfĭdŭs, ĭmmītĭs, crūdēlĭs, bārbărŭs, ăvārŭs, Thrāx.

Pŏlўnīcēs, ĭs, m., *the son of Œdipus.* Stat. Epith. Thēbānŭs, Cādmēĭŭs, Cādmæŭs ; Ārgīvŭs, ĭnfāndŭs, dīrŭs, sævŭs, nĕfāndŭs, atrōx, Œdĭpŏdiŏnĭdēs.

Pŏlўpēmōn, ŏnĭs, m., *the father of Procrustes.* Ēt dē Pŏlўpēmŏnĕ nātŭs, Ov.

Pŏlўphēmŭs, ī, m., *a giant, or Cyclops.* Căvŏ Pŏlўphēmŭs ĭn āntrō, Virg. Epith. Trūx, bārbărŭs, ĭmmānĭs, ĭmmītĭs, fĕrŭs, tērrĭbĭlĭs, dīrŭs, răpāx, cæcŭs, Ætnæŭs, Sĭcŭlŭs, Nēptūnĭŭs.

pŏlўpŭs, ī, m., *a kind of fish.* Pŏlўpŭs ēx ōmnī, Ov.—2. *a disease in the nose.* Pŏlўpŭs ān grăvĭs, Hor.

Pŏlўxĕnă, æ, f., *the daughter of Hecuba and Priam, beloved by Achilles.* Scīssāquĕ Pŏlўxĕnă pāllā, Juv. Epith. Fōrmōsă, cāstă, pŭdīcă, fōrtĭs, māgnănĭmă, ĭnnūbă, Phrўgĭă, Ĭlĭăcă, Dārdănĭă, Trōjānă.

pōmārĭŭm, ĭī, n., *an orchard.* Plēnĭs pōmārĭă cārpĕrĕ rāmĭs, Ov. Syn. Pōmētŭm, hōrtŭs. Epith. Fœcūndŭm, frāgrāns, ŏlōrŭm.

pōmārĭŭs, ĭī, m., *a fruiterer.* Pīscătŏr ūtī, pōmārĭŭs, aūcĕps, Hor.

Pŏmĕtĭī, ōrŭm, m. pl., *the inhabitants of Pometia, a city of the Volscians.* Pŏmĕtĭī cāstrūmque Ĭnŭī, Virg.

pōmĭfĕr, ă, ŭm, *bearing fruit.* Pōmĭfĕr ĭncŭbăt ārvĭs, Prop.

pōmœrĭŭm, ĭī, n., *a space about the walls of a town.* Ēxtrēmōs pōmœrĭă cīngĕrĕ fīnēs, Lucan.

Pōmōnă, æ, f., *the goddess of fruit-trees.* Hōc Pōmōnă fŭīt, Ov. Epith. Lætă, fēlīx, dīvĕs.

pōmōsŭs, ă, ŭm, *of fruit.* Sōlvīt pōmōsă, Prop.

pŏmpă, æ, f., *pomp.* Pŏmpă căpŭtquĕ, Mart. Epith. Sōlēnnĭs, dīvĕs, sŭpĕrbă, trĭūmphālĭs, rēgālĭs, māgnă, ınāgnĭfĭcă, fēstă, āmbĭtĭōsă, ĭngēns, ĭllūstrĭs, ĭnsĭgnĭs, laūrĭgĕră, vănă, ĭnānĭs, fūnĕbrĭs, fūnĕrĕă. V. Triumphus.

Pŏmpēĭānŭs, ă, ŭm, *of Pompey.* Quæ Pŏmpēĭānĭs, Luc. Syn. Pŏmpēĭŭs.

Pŏmpēĭŭs, *or* ējŭs, ī, m., *Pompey, surnamed the Great, the rival of Cæsar. He was vanquished at Pharsalus, and assassinated in Egypt.* Pŏmpeīum ēmptīquĕ clĭēntēs, Luc.

Pŏmpeĭŭs, *or* ējŭs, ă, ŭm, *of Pompey.* Indĕ dŏmŭs nōbīs Pŏmpeĭă pĕtātŭr, Ov.

Pŏmpĭlĭŭs, ĭĭ, m., *the surname of Numa.* Pŏmpĭlĭŭs mēnsēs, Ov. V. Numa.— Adj., -ŭs, ă, ŭm. Vōs ō Pŏmpĭlĭŭs sănguĭs, Hor.

pŏmpīlŭs, ī, m., *a sea-fish.* Sĕquĕrīs, pŏmpīlĕ, nĭtēntēs, Ov.

Pŏmpōnĭŭs, ĭĭ, m., *the name of a poet, and others.* Nŭmquīd Pŏmpōnĭŭs īstīs, Hor.

Pŏmptīnă, *or* Pōmtīnă, æ, f., *the Pomptine marsh in Campania.* Ĕt Pŏmptīnă pălŭs, Juv.

pŏmŭm, ī, n., *an apple, fruit.* Caŭlĭbŭs aŭt pōmīs, Juv. SYN. Mālŭm. EPITH. Rŏtŭndŭm, rŭbēns, dūlcĕ, mātūrŭm, mītĕ, agrēstĕ, dūrŭm, ăcērbŭm, putrĕ, pēndŭlŭm, frāgrāns, ŏdōrŭm, ŏdōrātŭm, rĕdŏlēns, Neŭstrĭăcŭm. V. Fructus.

pōmŭs, ī, f., *an apple-tree.* Insĭtă pōmŭs, Tib. SYN. Mālŭs. EPITH. Fœcūndă, fĕrāx, fērtĭlĭs, frŏndēns, ămœnă, stĕrĭlĭs, agrēstĭs, Neŭstrĭăcă. V. Arbor.

pŏndĕro, ās, *to weigh.* Pūgnōs pŏndĕrăt, Pl. SYN. Pēndo, ēxpēndo, āppēndo, pērpēndo, lĭbro; dīscŭtĭo, ēxcŭtĭo ; ēxămĭno, æstĭmo.

pŏndŭs, ĕrĭs, n., *weight.* Pŏndĕrĭbŭsquĕ sŭīs, Lucr. SYN. Ŏnŭs, grăvĭtās, sārcĭnă, mōlēs ; mōmēntŭm, vīs, aŭctōrĭtās. EPITH. Grăvĕ, lĕvĕ, īngēns, dūrŭm, ūrgēns, prōnŭm, ĭnĭquŭm, ŏnĕrōsŭm. V. Onus.

pŏnĕ, adv., *behind.* Pŏnĕ sŭbĭt, Virg. SYN. Pōst, ā tērgō, retrō, pōst tērgă.

pŏno, pŏsŭī, pŏsĭtŭm, *to put, to place.* Mīnăs pŏnēbăt ĭnănēs, Lucr. SYN. Dēpōno, rĕpōno, cōllŏco, lŏco, stătŭo, cōnstĭtŭo ; īnsŭmo, īnpētŭdo.

pōns, ntĭs, m., *a bridge.* Pŏntĭbŭs ūt crēbrīs, Virg. EPITH. Vălĭdŭs, fīrmŭs, sŏlĭdŭs, āltŭs, cēlsŭs, ēxcēlsŭs, sŭblīmĭs, ēlātŭs, cămĕrātŭs, tūtŭs, sēcūrŭs, flŭvĭālĭs, strŭctŭs, sŭbstrŭctŭs, līgnĕŭs, sāxĕŭs, mārmŏrĕŭs, pēnsĭlĭs.

pŏntĭcŭlŭs, ī, m., *the dimin. of* pons, *a little bridge.* Catul.

Pŏntĭcŭs, ă, ŭm, *of Pontus in Asia Minor.* Pŏntĭcă tērră mĕŏs, Ov.—Subst. -ŭs, ī, m., *a man's name.* Pŏntĭcŭs hērŏō, Id.

pŏntĭfex, ĭcĭs, m., *a high-priest.* Dīcĭtĕ, pŏntĭfĭcēs, Pers. SYN. Āntīstēs, săcērdōs, flāmĕn, præsēs, præsŭl. EPITH. Rĕlĭgĭōsŭs, pĭŭs, sānctŭs, vĕnĕrāndŭs, vĕrēndŭs, māxĭmŭs, lōngævŭs.

pŏntĭfĭcālĭs, ĕ, *of a high-priest.* Pŏntĭfĭcālĭs hŏnōs, Ov.

pŏntŭs, ī, m., *the sea.* Pŏntŭs hăbĕt, Ov. V. Mare.

Pŏntŭs, ī, m., *a country of Asia Minor.* Plūrĭmă Pŏntō, Virg.

pŏpă, æ, m., *the priest who killed the victim.* Sācră pŏpæ, Prop.

pŏpănŭm, ī, n., *a cake for an offering.* Ĕt tĕnŭī pŏpănŏ, Juv.

pŏpēllŭs, ī, m., *a dimin. of* pŏpulus. Cūrārĕ pŏpēllī, Mart. V. Plebs.

pŏpīnă, æ, f., *a tavern.* Unctă pŏpīnă, Hor. SYN. Gănĕă, cŭlīnă. EPITH. Immūndă, sōrdĭdă, fūmāns, tĕpĭdă, pīnguĭs, tētră, īnfāmĭs.

pŏplĕs, ĭtĭs, m., *the knee.* Pŏplĭtĕ Tūrnŭs, Virg. Cădūnt pŏplĭtēsquĕ, Lucr. SYN. Gĕnū. EPITH. Trĕmēns, trĕmĕbūndŭs, trĕmŭlŭs, ægĕr, lăbāns, fīrmŭs, cērtŭs, fŏrtĭs, vălĭdŭs, rōbūstŭs, nērvōsŭs, nōdōsŭs, cūrvŭs, īncūrvŭs, sŭccĭdŭŭs. V. Genu.

Pŏplĭcŏlă, *or* Pŭblĭcŏlă, æ, m., *the surname of the consul Valerius, colleague of the first Brutus, and others.* Pŏplĭcŏla ātquĕ, Hor.

Pŏppæānă, ōrŭm, n. pl., *a sort of perfume.* Pīnguĭă Pŏppæānă, Juv.

pŏpŭlābĭlĭs, ĕ, *that may be devastated.* Pŏpŭlābĭlĕ flāmmă, Ov.

pŏpŭlārĭs, ĕ, *of the people.* Gaŭdēns pŏpŭlārĭbŭs aūrĭs, Virg. SYN. Plēbeĭŭs.

pŏpŭlārĭtĕr, adv., *with the favour of the people.* Ŏccĭdūnt pŏpŭlārĭtĕr, Juv.

pŏpŭlātŏr, ōrĭs, m. ; trīx, īcĭs, f., *a ravager.* Trōjæ pŏpŭlātŏr Ăchīllēs, Ov. Pŏpŭlātrīcēsquĕ cătērvæ, Cl.

pŏpŭlātŭs, ūs, m., *a ravaging.* Sævīs pŏpŭlātĭbŭs āgrī, Lucr.

pŏpŭlĕŭs, ă, ŭm, *belonging to a poplar.* Pŏpŭlĕĭs ādsūnt, Virg. V. Pŏpŭlŭs.

pŏpŭlĭfĕr, ă, ŭm, *bearing poplar-trees.* Pŏpŭlĭfĕr Pădŭs, Virg.

pŏpŭlo, ās, *and* ŏr, ārĭs, *to devastate.* Lĭbўcōs pŏpŭlārĕ pĕnātēs, Virg. SYN. Dēpŏpŭlŏr, vāsto, răpĭo, prædŏr.

Pŏpŭlōnĭă, æ, f., *a maritime city of Etruria.* Dēdĕrăt Pŏpŭlōnĭă mātĕr, Virg.

pŏpŭlōsŭs, ă, ŭm, *populous.* Cūrătŭr pŏpŭlōsŭm. SYN. Pŏpŭlo īngēntī cĕlēbrĭs, cĕlēbrātŭs ; pŏpŭlĭs frĕquēns.

pŏpŭlŭs, ī, m., *the people, a nation.* Aŭrōræ pŏpŭlīs, Virg. SYN. Gĕns, nātĭo, plĕbs, vŭlgŭs. EPITH. Dīvĕs, nŭmĕrōsŭs, fŏrtĭs, bĕllĭcŭs, bĕllātŏr, Mārtĭŭs, Māvōrtĭŭs, pŏtēns, ārmĭpŏtēns, aŭdāx, ĭgnāvŭs, ĭmbĕllĭs, ĭnērs, ĭncōnstāns, lĕvĭs, tĭmĭdŭs, fŭgāx, mōllĭs, hĕbĕs, stŏlĭdŭs, cĕlĕbrĭs, clārŭs, ūrbānŭs, cōmĭs, hŏnēstŭs, cŭltŭs, ĭncŭltŭs, bārbārŭs, fĕrōx, fĕrŭs, crūdēlĭs. V. Plebs.

pŏpŭlŭs, ī, f., *a poplar-tree.* Pŏpŭlŭs ĭn flŭvĭīs, Virg. EPITH. Bĭcŏlŏr, ālbă, glaŭcă, vĭrĭdĭs, āltă, prōcēră, ārdŭă, vĭrēns, frōndēns, stăbĭlĭs, lacrў̆mōsă, flūvĭālĭs.

Pōrcĭŭs, ĭī, m., *the name of a man.* Pōrcĭŭs ĭnfrā, Hor.

pōrcŭs, ī, m.; ă, œ, f., *a hog, a sow.* Hæc pōrcīs hŏdĭē, Hor. SYN. Sūs. EPITH. Sōrdĭdŭs, hōrrĭdŭs, sētĭgĕr, spūmĭgĕr, vūlnĭfĭcŭs, hīspĭdŭs, ōbscœnŭs, spūrcŭs, clāmōsŭs, glāndĭlĕgŭs, ūdŭs, ĭgnāvŭs, cœnōsŭs.

Pōrphў̆rĭōn, ŏnĭs, m., *the name of a giant.* Quīd mĭnācī Pōrphў̆rĭōn stătū, Hor.

pōrrĭcĭō, īs, *to offer as a sacrifice.* Pōrrĭcĭam ĭn flūctŭs, Virg.

pōrrĭgo, ĭnĭs, f., *scurf.* Ēt pōrrĭgĭnĕ pōrcī, Hor.

pōrrĭgo, ēxī, ēctŭm, *to stretch.* Pōrrĭgĭtūr ; rōstrō, Virg. SYN. Ēxpōrrĭgo, tēndo, ĭntēndo, ēxtēndo, prōtēndo, ēxpāndo.

Pōrrĭmă, æ, f., *the sister or companion of Carmenta.* Pōrrĭmă plācātŭr, Ov.

pōrro, adv., *moreover.* Nēc pōrrŏ rērŭm, Lucr. Pōrrŏ vĭdēs, Juv. SYN. Dēmŭm.

pōrrŭm, ī, n., *a leek.* Pīscēs, seŭ pōrrŭm, Hor. EPITH. Sēctīvŭm, sēctĭlĕ, ŏlēns, ŏlĭdŭm, sălāx, grăvĕ, căpĭtātŭm, Tărēntīnŭm.

Pōrsēnă, *or* sēnnă, æ, m., *a king of Etruria.* Ētrūscă Pōrsēnæ mănŭs, Hor. Pōrsēnnă jŭbēbăt, Virg. EPITH. Mĭnāx, măgnănĭmŭs, gĕnĕrōsŭs, fŏrtĭs, sŭpērbŭs, pŏtēns, Thūscŭs ; Ētrūscŭs rēx, tў̆rānnŭs.

pōrtă, æ, f., *a door.* Pōrtārŭm vĭgĭlēs, Virg. SYN. Jānŭă, vālvæ, fŏrēs, ōstĭŭm, līmēn, ădĭtŭs, pōstēs, vēstĭbŭlŭm, pōrtĭcŭs. EPITH. Ærātă, vāllātă, fērrĕă, stăbĭlĭs, ăhēnă, strīdēns, vălĭdă, claūsă, fīrmă, līgnĕă, dūră, ăpērtă, pătēns, ōcclūsă, ænĕă, ærĕă, ārdŭă, māgnĭfĭcă, sŭpērbă, ădămāntĭnă, rōbūstă. V. Janua.

pōrtēndo, dī, tŭm, *to portend.* Gĕnĕrī pōrtēndĕrĕ dēbĭtă, Virg. V. Prædico, is.

pōrtēntĭfĭcŭs, ă, ŭm, *producing great wonders.* Prævĭtĭăt pōrtēntĭfĭcĭs, Ov.

pōrtēntŭm, ī, n., *a wonder.* Quālĕ pōrtēntŭm, Hor. SYN. Prōdĭgĭŭm, mōnstrŭm, ōmĕn. EPITH. Hōrrēndŭm, tērrĭbĭlĕ, stŭpēndŭm. V. Monstrum.

pōrtĭcŭs, ūs, f., *a porch.* Ĭllōs pōrtĭcĭbŭs, Virg. SYN. Vēstĭbŭlŭm, atrĭŭm, līmĕn. EPITH. Sŭpērbă, splēndĭdă, māgnĭfĭcă, spătĭōsă, āmplă, pŭlchră, pīctă, aūrātă, mārmŏrĕă, nōbĭlĭs, āntīquă, ēxcēlsă, sŭblīmĭs, cămĕrātă, ĭngēns.

pōrtĭo, ōnĭs, f., *a portion.* Brĕvīssĭmă vītæ Pōrtĭo, Juv. V. Pars.

pōrtĭtŏr, ōrĭs, m., *a boatman.* Pōrtĭtŏr hās, Virg. SYN. Nāvĭtă, rēctŏr.

pōrto, ās, *to carry.* Sŭspēnsōs pōrtābăt, Ov. SYN. Gĕro, gēsto, fĕro, ēffĕro, sūstĭnĕo, tōllo. V. Tollo.

Pōrtūmnŭs, *or* ūnŭs, ī, m., *a sea-god who presided over harbours, the same as Melicerta or Palæmon.* Māgnā Pōrtūmnŭs ĕūntĕm, Virg. SYN. Pălæmōn, Mĕlĭcērtă.

pōrtŭs, ūs, m., *a haven.* Nōstræ pōrtŭs rĕquĭēsquĕ, Mart. SYN. Lĭttŭs, rīpă, ōră ; stătĭo, ōstĭă, pērfŭgĭŭm, lŏcŭs tūtŭs. EPITH. Tūtŭs, sēcūrŭs ; quĭētŭs ; plăcĭdŭs, trānquīllŭs, ămœnŭs, ōptātŭs, quæsītŭs, căpāx, sĭnŭōsŭs, cūrvŭs, rĕcūrvŭs.

Pŏrŭs, ī, m., *a king of India, vanquished by Alexander.* Rēgĭă Pōrī, Claud. EPITH. Indĭcŭs ; Eōŭs, fūscŭs, āltŭs.

pōsco, pŏpōscī, *to demand, to exact.* Aŭrōquĕ pŏpōscĭt, Virg. SYN. Pĕto, pŏstŭlo, flăgĭto, ēfflāgĭto, rŏgo, ēxpōsco, dēpōsco ; scīscĭtŏr, quæro. V. Sciscitor, oro.

pŏsĭtŏr, ōrĭs, m., *he who places.* Tēmplōrŭm pŏsĭtŏr, Ov.

pŏsĭtūră, æ, f., *position.* Sīt pŏsĭtūră dĕī, Prop.

pŏsĭtŭs, ūs, m., *situation.* Mœnĭbŭs ēt pŏsĭtū, Ov.

pŏsĭtŭs, ă, ŭm, *the pass. partic. of* pono. Āgrō pŏsĭtŭs, lītĕm, Virg.

pōssēssŏr, ōrĭs, m., *a possessor.* Nōstrī pōssēssŏr ăgēllī, Virg.

pōssĭbĭlĭs, ĕ, *possible.* Pōssĭbĭlĕ ēst jūs, Sed. V. Possum.

pōssĭdĕo, sēdī, sēssŭm, *and* sīdo, ĭs, *to possess.* Pōssĭdĕt aūră, Prop. Pōssĭdăt ĭnānĕ, Lucr. SYN. Tĕnĕo, hăbĕo, pŏtĭŏr, frŭŏr.

pŏssŭm, pŏtĕs, pŏtŭī, *to be able.* Pŏssŭmŭs ōmnēs, Virg. SYN. Quĕo, vălĕo, ēvălĕo. V. Licet, potestas.

pŏst, adv. *and* prep., *behind, after.* Tŭ pŏst cārēctă, Virg.

pŏstĕa, adv., *afterwards.* Pŏstĕā mīrābăr, Ov. SYN. Dĕīn *or* deīn, dĕīndĕ *or* deīndĕ, tŭm, prætĕrĕā, Indĕ, ēxīndĕ.

pŏstĕaquăm, conj., *after.* Pŏstĕaquăm rūrsŭs, Virg. SYN. Pŏstquăm.

pŏstĕrĭtās, ātĭs, f., *posterity.* Pŏstĕrĭtās; ĕădĕm, Juv. SYN. Pŏstĕrī, vēntūrī, fŭtūrī, nĕpŏtēs, mĭnōrēs. EPITH. Tārdă, sēră, vēntūră. V. Immortalis, gloria.

pŏstĕrŭs, ă, ŭm, *following, future.* Pŏstĕră Phœbĕā, Virg. SYN. Sĕquēns, vēntūrŭs; fŭtūrŭs.

pŏstfĕro, fērs, *to esteem less.* Nĕc rēgnīs pŏstfērtĕ fĭdĕm, Sil.

pŏstgĕnĭtŭs, ă, ŭm, *born after.* Clārŭs pŏstgĕnĭtīs, Hor.

pŏsthăbĕo, ēs, ŭī, *to esteem less.* Pŏsthăbŭī tămĕn, Virg. SYN. Pŏstpōno, nēglĭgo.

pŏsthăbĭtŭs, ă, ŭm, *the pass. partic. of* posthabeo. Pŏsthăbĭtā cŏlŭīssĕ, Virg.

pŏsthāc, *and* hæc, adv., *for the future.* Măgnŭs pŏsthāc ĭnĭmĭcĭs, Hor. SYN. Pŏstĕa, deīndĕ, ēxīndĕ.

pŏsthīnc, adv., *afterwards.* Pŏsthīnc ād nāvēs, Virg.

pŏstĭcŭm, ī, n., *a back-door.* Sĕrvāntĕm pŏstĭcō, Hor.

pŏstĭcŭs, ă, ŭm, *belonging to the back part.* Pŏstĭcæ ŏccūrrĭtĕ sānnæ, Pers.

pŏstĭs, ĭs, m., pŏstēs, ĭŭm, m. pl., *a doorpost, door.* Clўpĕŭm dē pŏstĕ rĕvūlsŭm, Virg. Fērrātōs pŏstēs, Hor. SYN. Lĭmĕn, vēstĭbŭlŭm. EPITH. Dūrī, rĭgĭdī, ærātī, mārmŏrĕī, fūltī, ăhēnī, fērrātī, nĭtĭdī, strīdēntēs, raŭcī. V. Limen, janua.

pŏstmŏdŏ, adv., *afterwards.* Pŏstmŏdŏ quæ vōtīs, Tib.

pŏstpōno, pŏsŭī, pŏsĭtŭm, *to esteem less.* Ignāvŭs pŏstpōnĭtŭr āmbĭtŭs, Ser. SYN. Pŏsthăbĕo, nēglĭgo, spērno.

pŏstpŏsĭtŭs, ă, ŭm, *the pass. partic. of* postpono. Pŏstpŏsĭtō făctă, Ov.

pŏstquăm, conj., *after.* Pŏstquam ēxēmptă fămēs, Virg. SYN. Pŏstĕaquăm, ŭbi, ŭt, stătĭm āc.

*•pŏstrēmo, adv., *lastly.* Cic. SYN. Dēnĭquĕ, dēmŭm, tāndĕm.

pŏstrēmŭs, ă, ŭm, *last.* Hōc pŏstrēmŭs ōmīttās, Hor. SYN. Ūltĭmŭs, ēxtrēmŭs, nŏvīssĭmŭs, suprēmŭs.

pŏstrĭdĭĕ, adv., *the day after.* Pŏstrĭdĭe ăd ănŭm, (Iamb.) Ter. SYN. Dĭēs pŏstĕră.

pŏstscēnĭŭm, ĭī, n., *the place behind the stage.* Vītæ pŏstscēnĭă cēlānt, Lucr.

pŏstŭlī, conj., *after.* Pŏstŭlĭ jām călămīs, Virg. V. Postquam.

Pŏstvērtă, æ, f., *a Latin nymph who presided at difficult labours.* Pŏrrĭmă plăcātŭr Pŏstvērtăquĕ, Ov.

pŏstŭlo, ās, *to ask.* Pŏstŭlĕt ĭrĕ, Hor. SYN. Pĕto, rŏgo, prĕcŏr, ōro. V. Posco.

Pŏstŭmĭŭs, ĭī, m., *the name of a man.* Pŏstŭmĭŏ Lēnās, Ov.

pŏstŭmŭs, ă, ŭm, *superl. formed from* post, *the last.* Tŭă pŏstŭmă prōlēs, Virg. Pŏstŭmŭs, ī, m., *the name of a man.* Heŭ, heŭ! fŭgācēs, Pŏstŭmĕ, Pŏstŭmĕ, Hor.

pŏtābĭlĭs, ĕ, *that may be drunk.* Mĕdĭcō pŏtābĭlĭs haūstŭ, Aus.

pŏtātĭo, ōnĭs, f., *drinking.* Pŏtātĭōnēs plūrĭmæ, (Iamb.) Plaut. SYN. Cŏmpōtātĭo; cōnvĭvĭŭm.

pŏtātŏr, ōrĭs, m., *a drunkard.* Ātquĕ pŏtātōrēs māxĭmī, (Iamb.) Plaut. SYN. Pŏtŏr, bĭbāx.

pŏtēns, ntĭs, *powerful.* Rōmă pŏtēns ŏpĭbŭs, Ov. SYN. Vălēns, vălĭdŭs, pŏllēns.

pŏtēntĕr, adv., *powerfully.* Lēctă pŏtēntĕr ĕrĭt, Hor. SYN. Vălĭdĕ.

pŏtēntĭă, æ, *and* ēstās, ātĭs, f., *power.* Dīvīnă pŏtēntĭă rēbŭs, Ov. Scīrĕ pŏtēstātēs, Virg. SYN. Pŏtēntĭă; Impĕrĭŭm, dĭtĭo; făcūltās, cōpĭă, lĭcēntĭă, lībērtās; vīs, vīrtūs. EPITH. Sūmmă, fīrmă, Indŏmĭtă, vălĭdă, Invīctă, āmplă, īnsŭpĕrābĭlĭs, Impĕrĭōsă.

pŏtĭo, ōnĭs, f., *drinking, a potion.* Vārĕ, pŏtĭōnĭbŭs, (Iamb.) Hor.

pŏtĭŏr, ōrĭs, *better.* Hæc āltērnāntī pŏtĭŏr, Virg. SYN. Mĕlĭŏr, præstāntĭŏr, prĭŏr, cārĭŏr.

pŏtĭŏr, īrĭs, pŏtītŭs, *to enjoy, to gain possession of.* Nōn pŏtĭātŭr ămātŭ, Ov. SYN. Frŭŏr, hăbĕo, tĕnĕo, pŏssĭdĕo; ŏccŭpo.

pŏtĭs, ĕ, *able.* Nĕc pŏtĭs, Cat.

pŏtīssĭmŭs, ă, ŭm, *best, strongest.* Cūră pŏtīssĭmă, Stat.   Syn. Ŏptĭmŭs; vălĭdīs-sĭmŭs.

Pŏtītĭŭs, ĭī, m., *the name of an ancient Latin family, consecrated to the worship of Hercules.* Prīmŭsquĕ Pŏtītĭŭs aūctŏr, Virg.

pŏtītŭs, ă, ŭm, *the partic. of* potior.   Gaūdētquĕ pŏtītŭs, Virg.

pŏtĭŭs, adv., *rather.*   Dēnsōs pŏtĭŭs ĕt, (Ianıb.) Ser.   Syn. Mĕlĭŭs; măgĭs.

Pŏtnĭădēs, ŭm, f. pl., *of Potnia, a city of Bœotia, near Thebes.*   Pŏtnĭădēs mālĭs, Virg.

pŏto, ās, *to drink.*   Sī nōn pŏtārēs, Mart.   Syn. Bĭbo, pērpŏto, haūrĭo.   V Haurio, ebrius.

pŏtŏr, ōrĭs, m., *a drunkard.*   Pŏtōrēs bĭbŭlī, Hor.   Syn. Bĭbăx; pŏtătŏr.

pŏtŭs, ă, ŭm, *drunk.*   Pōmpă, sĕnēm pŏtŭm, Ov.   Syn. Pŏtātŭs; ēbrĭŭs.

pŏtŭs, ūs, m., *a drink, beverage.*   Quī pŏtŭs dŭbĭum ēst, Ov.   Syn. Pŏtĭo, pōcŭlŭm, haūstŭs, liquŏr.

præ, prep., *before, in comparison with.*   Cūnctăquĕ præ cāmpŏ, Hor.

prædācūtŭs, ă, ŭm, *very sharp.*   Vīdērūnt, prædăcūtæ cūspĭdĭs, Ov.   Syn. Ăcūtŭs, tĕnŭĭs.

præbĕo, ēs, *to afford.*   Præbēbānt cæsī, Prop.   Syn. Dŏ, trĭbŭo, pŏrrĭgo, ŏffĕro, lārgĭŏr; sūppĕdĭto, mĭnĭstro, ĕxhĭbĕo.

præcānŭs, ă, ŭm, *prematurely grey-headed.*   Cōrpŏrĭs ĕxĭgŭī, præcānŭm, Hor.

præcēdo, cēssī, *to go before.*   Nĕc præcēdēntĭbŭs īnsto, Hor.   Syn. Āntĕcēdo, prævērto, āntĕĕo; præcūrro, prægrĕdĭŏr, præĕo.

præcĕlĕr, ĕrĭs, ĕrĕ, *very swift or quick.*   Ad præınĭă cūrsū Præcĕlĕrēs, Stat.

præcĕlĕro, ās, *to run before.*   Præcĕlĕrāntquĕ dŭcĕm, St.   Syn. Præcūrro.

præcĕllo, ĭs, ŭĭ, *to excel.*   Præcĕllĕrĕ rŏbŏrĕ, Sil.

præcēlsŭs, ă, ŭm, *very high.*   Rūpēs præcēlsă, Virg.   V. Altus, excelsus.

præcēps, cĭpĭtĭs, *headlong.*   Præcĭpĭtēs ŭt, Juv.   Syn. Præcĭpĭtāns, rŭēns, cădēns; ārdŭŭs; prærūptŭs, ābrūptŭs; præāltŭs; tĕmĕrārĭŭs, īncōnsŭltŭs, ĭmprūdēns.

præcēptŏr, ōrĭs, m., *a teacher.*   Nĕc præcēptŏrĭs hăbēnās, Aus.   Epith. Dōctŭs, sŏlērs, sŏllĭcĭtŭs, ămīcŭs, sĕvērŭs.   V. Magister.

præcēptŭm, ī, n., *an order.*   Præcēptă sĕcūtī, Virg.   Syn. Māndātŭm, jŭssŭm, jŭssŭs, jūs, īmpĕrĭŭm, plăcĭtŭm, mŏnĭtŭm, præscrīptŭm.   Epith. Dūrŭm, trīstĕ, mŏlēstŭm, grăvĕ, ămīcŭm, grātŭm, sălūtārĕ, sălūtĭfĕrŭm, sānctŭm, vĕnĕrāndŭm, vĕrēndŭm.   V. Imperium, decalogus.

præcērpo, ĭs, *to cut beforehand or before.*   Nōstrās præcērpĕrĕ mēssēs, Ov.

præcīdo, cīdī, sŭm, *to cut off.*   Bēllī præcīdĕrĕ caūsăm, Hor.   Syn. Sĕco, rĕsĕco, scīndo, cædo, īncīdo, āmpŭto, ēxsĕco, dīscīndo, rĕvēllo.   V. Scindo.

præcīngo, xī, ctŭm, *to begird.*   Caūtŭs præcīngĭtŭr ēnsĕ, Ov.

præcīno, ĭs, ŭī, *to sing before, to prophesy.*   Præcĭnŭīssēt ănŭs, Tib.   Syn. Cāntum īnchŏo; prædīco, ĭs.

præcĭpĭo, ēpī, *to take before.*   Præcĭpĭēs ēstŏ, Hor.   Syn. Māndo, jŭbĕo, īmpĕro, præscrībo, ĭnjūngo, ēdīco.   V. Jubeo.

præcĭpĭtāntĕr, adv., *with great speed.*   Ad vīllam hīc præcĭpĭtāntĕr, Lucr.

præcĭpĭto, ās, *to throw headlong.*   Præcĭpĭtāt, suādēntquĕ, Virg.   Syn. Dētūrbo, dējĭcĭo, dētrūdo, ēxcŭtĭo, ēxtūrbo, prōjĭcĭo, rŭo, cădo, cōrrŭo, prōlābŏr, cōncĭdo.   V. Mergo, sterno, ruo.

præcĭpŭĕ, adv., *especially.*   Præcĭpŭĕ fŭgĭăm, Juv.   Syn. Præsērtīm, īmprīmīs, pŏtīssĭmŭm.

præcĭpŭŭs, ă, ŭm, *particular, principal.*   Ipsĭs præcĭpŭōs, Virg.   Syn. Māxĭmŭs, ēxĭmĭŭs, præclārŭs.

præcīsŭs, ă, ŭm, *the pass. partic. of* præcido.   Præcīsĭs ūndĭquĕ sāxĭs, Virg.

præclārŭs, ă, ŭm, *illustrious.*   Quĭd mē præclārā, Virg.   Syn. Ēxĭmĭŭs, īnsīgnĭs, præstāns, clārŭs, cōnspĭcŭŭs, īllūstrĭs, īnclўtŭs.

præclūdo, sī, sŭm, *to shut up.*   Ēffŭgĭŭm præclŭdĭt, Lucr.   Syn. Claūdo, īntĕr-clūdo, ōcclūdo, ōbstrŭo.

præclūsŭs, ă, ŭm, *the pass. partic. of* præcludo.   Lēthī præclūsa ēst, Lucr.

præco, ōnĭs, m., *a common crier.*   Māgnā præcōnĭs vōcĕ, Virg.   Syn. Būccĭnātŏr, ēdīctŏr; laūdātŏr.

‖ præcōmpŏsĭtŭs, ă, ŭm, *prepared beforehand.*   Cŭm præcōmpŏsĭtŏ, Ov.

] ræcōnĭŭm, iī, n., *the crier's office, praise.* Pĕrăgŭnt præcōnĭă rērŭm, Ov. Syn. Encōmĭŭm, laŭs.

] ræcōnsūmo, ĭs, mpsī, *to consume beforehand.* Præcōnsūmĕrĕ vīrēs, Ov.

] ræcōntrēcto, ās, *to touch beforehand.* Præcōntrēctātquĕ vĭdēndo, Ov.

] ræcōquo, ĭs, *to ripen before.* Et quās præcŏquĭt, Stat.

præcŏquŭs, ă, ŭm, *early ripe.* Præcŏquā rāmĭs, Mart.

præcŏrdĭă, ŭm, n. pl., *the diaphragm, the mind.* Rĕdĭt īn præcŏrdĭă vīrtūs, Virg. Syn. Vīscĕră; Ĭntĭmă cōrdĭs, pēctŏrĭs. V. Cor.

præcōrrūmpo, ūpī, *to corrupt beforehand.* Præcōrrūmpĕrĕ dōnĭs, Ov.

præcōx, ŏcĭs, *early ripe.* Insĭtă præcŏcĭbŭs, Calph. Syn. Præmātūrŭs, præcŏquŭs, īmmātūrŭs, crūdŭs.

] ræcūltŭs, ă, ŭm, *much adorned.* Sācrō præcūltă sŭpērvēnĭt aŭrō, Stat.

] ræcūrro, cŭcūrrī and cūrrī, *to run before.* Pĕrēnnĭs præcŭcūrrĭt, (Iamb.) Prud. Syn. Cūrrēndo præĕo, āntĕĕo, præcēdo.

præcŭtĭo, ĭs, *to shake before.* Hӯmĕnæŭs Amōrquĕ Præcŭtĭŭnt, Ov.

prædă, æ, f., *booty.* Cōnvēctārĕ jŭvăt prædās, Virg. Syn. Exŭvĭæ, spŏlĭă; răpīnă, fūrtŭm. Epith. Dīvĕs, ŏpŭlēntă, ĭngēns, ŏpīmă, ŏptātă, spērātă, răptă, nōctūrnă, pārtă, ŭcquīsĭtă, vĭŏlēntă, bēllĭcă, hōstīlĭs, crŭēntă, sōrdĭdă, ăvĭdă, tūrpĭs, nĕfāndă, dīră. V. Prædor, furtum, triumphus.

prædătŏr, ōrĭs, m., and trīx, īcĭs, f., *a plunderer.* Et Abās prædātŏr ĕquōrŭm, Ov. Hӯlæ prædātrīx, Ov. V. Prædo.

prædēlūsso, ās, *to tire before.* Prædēlāssārĕt ăquārŭm, Ov.

prædĭco, ās, *to celebrate, publish.* Prædĭcăt ūndĕ, Prud. Syn. Cĕlebro, mĕmŏro, cōmmĕmŏro, laŭdo, jāctĭto. V. Laudo, concionor.

prædĭco, xī, ctŭm, *to foretel.* Mĕmĭnī prædĭcĕrĕ quērcŭs, Virg. Syn. Præñūncĭo, vātĭcĭnŏr, præcĭno, āntĕmŏnĕo, præmŏnĕo. V. Auguror.

prædĭctĭo, ōnĭs, f., and tŭm, ī, n., *a prophecy.* Vātŭm prædĭctă prĭōrŭm, Virg. Syn. Ōrācŭlŭm, præsāgĭŭm, mŏnĭtŭm, vātĭcĭnĭŭm.

prædisco, dĭdĭcī, *to learn before.* Cœlī prædĭscĕrĕ mōrĕm, Virg. V. Disco.

prædĭtŭs, ă, ŭm, *endowed.* Prædĭtă sēnsū, Lucr. Syn. Cōmpŏs, cŭmŭlātŭs, ōrnātŭs, aūctŭs, dĕcŏrātŭs, īnsĭgnĭs, īllūstrĭs, præstāns, pōllēns, mūnītŭs.

prædīvĕs, ĭtĭs, *very rich.* Tēctĭs prædīvĭtĭs ūrbĕ, Virg. Syn. Dīvĕs, ŏpŭlēntŭs. V. Dives.

prædĭŭm, iī, n., *a farm, an estate.* Prædĭă dīvĕs, Hor. Syn. Vīllă, fūndŭs, pōssessĭo, ăgĕr. Epith. Cūltŭm, ōmnĭfĕrŭin, fŏrāx, fērtĭlĕ, fœcūndŭm, ēxcūltŭm, prĕtĭōsŭm, ēxĭmĭŭm, dīvĕs. V. Ager.

] rædo, ōnĭs, m., *a plunderer.* Prædōnĭbŭs, ūt sācră nōbĭs, P. Syn. Prædătŏr, fūr, latro, grāssātŏr. Epith. Insĭdĭōsŭs, scĕlĕrātŭs, īnfēstŭs, fūnēstŭs, grāssāns. V. Fur.

prædŏr, ārĭs, *to plunder.* Prædārĭquĕ lŭpōs, Virg. Syn. Fŭrŏr, dĕprædŏr, spŏlĭo, pŏpŭlor, dĕpŏpŭlŏr, dīrĭpĭo, răpĭo, ĕrĭpĭo, cōmpĭlo, ēxpĭlo. V. Præda, furor, -aris, vasto, rapio.

prædūco, xī, *to lead before.* Cāstrīs prædūcĕrĕ fōssăm, Tib.

prædūlcĭs, ĕ, *very sweet.* Lūxūrĭēs, prædūlcĕ mălŭm, Claud. V. Dulcis.

prædūrŭs, ă, ŭm, *very hard.* Nūdăt prædūră pălœstră, Virg.

præĕo, ĭs, īvī or iī, *to go before.* Prĭŏr præĕūntĕ cărīnā, Virg. V. Præcedo.

præfārī, *to say before, recite, invoke.* Præfātŭs dīvōs, Virg. Syn. Prælŏquŏr; īnvŏco.

præfātĭo, ōnĭs, f., *a preface.* Est præfātĭŏ, faŭcēs, Mart. V. Exordium.

præfēctūră, æ, f., *the office of prefect, a government.* Præfēctūră dŏmŭs, Juv.

præfēctŭs, ă, ŭm, *the pass. partic. of* præficio, *set over.* Sācrĭs præfēctă mărītĭs, Ov.

præfĕro, tŭlī, lātŭm, *to prefer, to carry, to put before.* Præfĕrĭmŭs mănĭbŭs, Virg. Syn. Præpōno, āntĕfĕro.

præfĕrōx, ŏcĭs, *very fierce or warlike.* Præfĕrōcēs prælĭŏ, Aus.

|| præfēstīno, ās, *to make great haste.* Præfēstīnātō mūnŭs, Ov.

præfĭcĭo, fēcī, ctŭm, *to put at the head.* Præfĭcĭtūr lătĕrī, Cl. Hĕcătē præfēcĭt Avērnĭs, Virg. Syn. Præpōno.

præfīgo, ĭs, xī, xŭm, *to fix before.* Præfīgĕrĕ pŭppĭbŭs ārmă, Virg. Syn. Affīgo, fīgo. V. Figo.

præflŭo, ĭs, *to flow before or near.* Quæ Tībŭr ăquæ fērtĭlĕ præflŭūnt, Hor

SYN. Prætērflŭo, prætērlăbŏr, prælăbŏr, prænăto, āllŭo, lămbo, prælămbo, āllămbo.

præsŏco, ās, *to strangle.* Præsŏcēnt ănĭmæ, Ov

præsŏdĭo, ĭs, *to dig before.* Præsŏdĭūnt ălĭī, Virg.

præfōrmo, ās, *to form beforehand.* Atque hīs præfōrmāt dīctīs, Sil.

præfrāctŭs, ă, ŭm, *the pass. partic. of* præfringo, *broken before.* Pĭnūm præfrāctūm mīsĭt ĭn hŏstĕm, Ov.

præfrĭgĭdŭs, ă, ŭm, *very cold.* Præfrĭgĭdŭs Aŭstĕr, Ov.

præfŭlgĕo, sī, *to shine much.* Pēllĭs præfŭlgēns, Virg. V. Fulgeo.

præfŭlgŭro, ās, *to lighten, make bright.* Vĭās præfŭlgŭrăt ēnsĕ, Val. Fl.

præfŭro, ĭs, *to be very furious.* Præfŭrĭs; ĭn mĕdĭōs, Stat. V. Perfuro.

prægĕlĭdŭs, ă, ŭm, *very cold.* Quōs ĭn prægĕlĭdīs, Sil.

prægēstĭo, ĭs, *to be glad beforehand.* Ănĭmŭs prægēstĭt ăpīscī, Cat.

prægnāns, ntĭs, f., *pregnant with child.* Cīssēĭs prægnāns, Virg. SYN. Grăvĭdă, fœtă, grăvĭs. V. Gravida.

prægrāndĭs, ĕ, *very large.* Prægrāndī cūm sēnĕ pāllēs, Pers.

prægrăvĭdŭs, ă, ŭm, *and* grăvĭs, ĕ, *very heavy.* Mōlĭs prægrăvĭdæ, Stat. Prægrăvĭs ūndă, Mart. V. Gravis.

prægrăvo, ās, *to make heavy.* Prægrăvăt ūnă, Hor.

prægrĕdĭŏr, ĕrĭs, ēssŭs sŭm, *to go before.* Fāmā dĭēm prægrēssă, Stat. V. Præcedo.

prægūsto, ās, *to taste first or before.* Quŏd prægūstāvĕrĭt ĭllĕ, Ov.

prælăbŏr, ĕrĭs, *to flow, glide before or near.* Prælābī flūmĭnă Pīsæ, Virg. V. Præfluo.

prælămbo, ĭs, *to taste before or first.* Prælāmbēns ōmnĕ quŏd āffērt, Hor.

prælārgŭs, ă, ŭm, *very large.* Prælārgŭs ănhēlĕt, Pers.

prælātŭs, ă, ŭm, *the pass. partic. of* præfero. Prælāto ĭnvīdĭt, Virg. SYN. Præpŏsĭtŭs.

prælēgo, ĭs, *to choose before, read before.* Quæ prælĕgăt ĭn schŏlă, Mart.

prælībo, ās, *to taste before.* Quī prælībārĕ vĕrēndŭm, Stat.

prælĭŭm, ĭī, n., *a battle.* Prælĭă caŭsæ, Luc. SYN. Cērtāmĕn, pūgnă, cōnflīctŭs. EPITH. Hŏrrĭdŭm, sævŭm, fĕrŭm, dīrŭm, scĕlĕrātŭm, īnfāndŭm, tūrbĭdŭm, vĭŏlēntŭm. V. Pugna.

prælōngŭs, ă, ŭm, *very long.* Gaŭdērĕt, prælōngă sĕnĕx, Lucr.

prælūcĕo, xī, *to shine before, outshine.* Prælūxĕrĕ fācēs, Mart.

prælūdĭŭm, ĭī, n., *a prelude, preamble.* Tĭmĭdæ prælūdĭă prīmă, Polit.

prælūdo, ĭs, sī, sŭm, *to prelude.* Ăd pūgnām prælūdĭt ărēnā, Virg. SYN. Præcĭno; vīrēs tēnto.

prælŭm, ī, n., *a press.* Cōlăquĕ prælōrŭm, Virg. EPITH. Spūmāns, mădĭdŭm, ēbrĭŭm; Fălērnŭm, Cāmpānŭm, Pēlīgnŭm.

prælūstrĭs, ĕ, *very bright.* Pŏtēs, prælūstrĭă vītă, Ov. V. Illustris.

præmātūrŭs, ă, ŭm, *ripe before due time.* Nōn præmātūrī cĭnĕrēs, Juv. SYN. Præcōx, præcŏquŭs.

præmĕdĭcātŭs, ă, ŭm, *previously medicated.* Præmĕdĭcātŭs ĭn ĭgnēs, Ov.

|| præmēnsŭs, ă, ŭm, *measured before.* Tib.

præmĕtŭo, ĭs, *to anticipate with fear.* Præmĕtŭēns ădhĭbĕt, Lucr.

præmĭnĕo, ēs, *to rise above, excel.* Præmĭnēant gĕnĭtĭs, Aus. SYN. Sŭpĕrĕmĭnĕo.

præmītto, ĭs, *to send before.* Răpĭdum ād nāvēs præmīttĭt Ăchātēn, Virg.

præmĭŭm, ĭī, n., *a recompense.* Mĕrĭtæque ēxpĕctēnt, Virg. SYN. Mērcēs, prĕtĭŭm, mūnŭs, dōnŭm, frūctŭs. EPITH. Māgnĭfĭcŭm, īnsĭgnĕ, āmplŭm, ēxĭmĭŭm, lārgŭm, ŏpŭlēntŭm, dīvĕs, prĕtĭōsŭm, īngēns, mĕmŏrābĭlĕ, præclārŭm, jūstŭm, mĕrĭtŭm, sŏlēnnĕ, rēgĭŭm; vīlĕ, pārvŭm.

præmŏnĕo, ŭī, *to forewarn.* Præmŏnŭĭssĕ nĕfās, Ov.

præmōnstro, ās, *to foreshow.* Stat. V. Doceo.

præmōrdĕo, ēs, *to bite before.* Cūstŏs præmōrdĕt, Juv.

præmŏrĭŏr, ĕrĭs, *to die before a certain time.* Præmŏrĭār, prīmō, Ov.

prænăto, ās, *to swim before.* Prænătăt āmnĕm, Virg. SYN. Prætērflŭo.

Prænēstĕ, ĭs, f., *a town of Italy.* Ăltŭm Prænēstĕ vĭrī, Virg.

Prænēstīnŭs, ă, ŭm, *of Præneste.* Nĕc Prænēstīnæ, Virg.

prænĭtĕo, ēs, *to surpass in brightness.* Prænĭtĕāt fĭdĕ, Hor.

prænōmĕn, ĭnĭs, n., *the first name.* Prænōmĭnĕ mŏllĕs, Hor.

prænŏsco, ŏvī, *to know before.* Vēntūrūm prænŏssĕ lăbŏrĕm, Stat.

prænūbĭlŭs, ă, ŭm, *very obscure.* Dēnsā prænūbĭlŭs ārbŏrĕ, Ov. V. Obscurus.

prænūntĭŭs, ă, ŭm, *foreboding.* Prænūntĭă lūctūs, Virg. SYN. Nūntĭŭs, præsăgŭs.

præŏpto, ās, *to prefer.* Thēseī præŏptārĭt ămŏrĕm, Catul.

præpāndo, ĭs, *to spread open.* Præpāndĕrĕ lūmĭnă mēntī, Lucr.

præpăro, ās, *to prepare.* Præpărăt ūlmōs, Hor. SYN. Păro, āppăro, cōmpăro, īnstrŭo, ōrno, ădōrno, ōrdĭno, cōmpōno.

præpĕdĭo, īs, *to embarrass.* Præpĕdĭt ōssă, Ov. V. Impedio.

præpēndĕo, *to hang before.* Præpēndēt mēntō, Mart.

præpĕs, ĕtĭs, *swift.* Præpĕtĭs ōmĭnă pēnnæ, Virg. SYN. Cĕlĕr, vēlōx, cĭtŭs, pērnīx, cōncĭtŭs. V. Celer.

præpīnguĭs, ĕ, *very fat.* Præpīnguĕ sōlŭm, Virg.

præpōndĕro, ās, *to weigh.* Præpōndĕrăt ēxŭl, Stat.

præpōno, pŏsŭī, pŏsĭtŭm, *to place before, prefer.* Frōndī præpōnĕre ŏlīvăm, Hor. SYN. Præfĕro, āntĕfĕro.

præpōrto, ās, *to carry before.* Frōns ēxpīrāutĭs præpōrtăt, Cat. SYN. Præfĕro.

præpŏsĭtŭs, ă, ŭm, *the pass. partic. of* præpono. Ăt pŭtŏ præpŏsĭta ēst, Ov.

præpōstĕrŭs, ă, ŭm, *preposterous.* Exīstāt præpōstĕrŭs ōrdo, Lucr. SYN. Præprŏpĕrŭs, pērvērsŭs, præmātūrŭs, præcōx, īntēmpēstīvŭs. V. Impossibilis.

¶ præpŏtēns, ntĭs, *very powerful.* Mŏdŏ præpŏtēntēm cērnăt, (Iamb.) Sen.

præprŏpĕrāntĕr, *and* pĕrē, adv., *very hastily.* Cērtārēquĕ præprŏpĕrāntĕr, Lucr.

‖ præprŏpĕrŭs, ă, ŭm, *very hasty.* Præprŏpĕrŏ nīsū, Sil. V. Celer.

præpūtĭŭm, ĭī, n., *the prepuce.* Ēt præpūtĭă pōnūnt, Juv.

præquēstŭs, ă, ŭm, *who has complained before.* Mūltăquĕ præquēstŭs, Ov.

prærădĭo, ās, *to cause to shine bright.* Prærădĭăt stēllĭs, Ov.

prærăpĭdŭs, ă, ŭm, *very rapid.* Prærăpĭdă pŏtŭĕrĕ fŭgā, Sil.

prærĭpĭo, ĭs, rĭpŭī, rēptŭm, *to carry off.* Līttŏră prærĭpĕre, ĕt, Virg. SYN. Răpĭo, aūfĕro; ōccŭpo.

prærōdo, ĭs, sī, *to gnaw before.* Prærōsŏ fŭgĕrĭt hāmŏ, Hor.

prærūmpo, ūpī, *to break off.* Prærūpĭt Phrȳgĭæ, Ov.

præs, ædĭs, m., *bail, security.* Quĭs dăbĭtūr? Præs, Aus.

præsăgĭo, īs, īvī *or* ĭī, *to foretel.* Mĕlĭŭs præsăgĭt năvĭtă, Prop. SYN. Præsēntĭo, præsēntīsco, prævĭdĕo, aūgŭrŏr, vātĭcĭnŏr, prædīco.

præsăgĭŭm, ĭī, n., *an omen.* Tīmĭdæ præsăgĭă mēntĭs, Ov. SYN. Aūgŭrĭŭm, ōmĕn.

præsăgŭs, ă, ŭm, *divining.* Mēns præsăgă fŭtūrī, Claud. SYN. Præscĭŭs, prænūncĭŭs, vātēs, aūgŭr. V. Augur.

præscĭo, īs, īī *and* īvī; *or* scīsco, ĭs, *to know beforehand.* Lōngē præscīscĕrĕ, Virg.

præscĭŭs, ă, ŭm, *knowing the future.* Præscĭă vēntūrī, Virg. SYN. Præsăgŭs, prænūncĭŭs, vātēs, aūgŭr.

præscribo, psī, ptŭm, *to determine, ordain.* Præscrībĕ; quĭēscās, Hor. SYN. Dēfīnĭo, præfīnĭo, dēsīgno; stătŭo, māndo, jŭbĕo, īmpĕro, præcĭpĭo

præsĕco, ās, *to cut off.* Præsĕcŭīssĕ mănŭ, Ov.

‖ præsĕgmĕn, ĭnĭs, n., *a paring.* Ūnguĭŭm præsĕgmĭnă, (Iamb.) Plaut.

præsēns, ntĭs, *present, ready.* Quĭd præsēntĭŭs aūdēs, Virg. SYN. Spēctāns, spēctātŏr, tēstĭs, ārbĭtĕr; īnstāns, īmmĭnēus; prōmptŭs, ălăcĕr; īntrĕpĭdŭs, īmmōtŭs.

præsēntĭă, æ, f., *presence.* Mĭnŭīt præsēntĭă fāmăm, Claud.

præsēntĭo, īs, sī, *to foresee.* Præsēnsīt mōtŭs, Virg. SYN. Præsăgĭo, aūgŭrŏr, præscĭo, prævĭdĕo.

præsēpĕ, ĭs, *and* pĭŭm, ĭī, n., *a stable.* In præsēpĭbŭs āltĭs, Virg. SYN. Stăbŭlŭm. V. Stabulum.

præsērtĭm, adv., *principally.* Præsērtim īncērtĭs. SYN. Imprīmĭs.

præsĕs, ĭdĭs, m. f., *a president.* Præsĭdĭs ĭpsă, Mart. SYN. Prīncĕps.

præsĭdĕo, sēdī, *to preside.* Præsĭdĕt ēt vĭrĭdī, Virg. SYN. Præsŭm, īmpĕro, dŏmĭnŏr.

præsĭdĭŭm, ĭī, n., *a garrison, protection.* Præsĭdĭŏ quī, Hor. SYN. Cūstōdĭă, mīlĭtŭm lēgĭo, cŏhōrs, stătĭo; prōpūgnācŭlŭm, mūnĭmēntŭm, tūtēlă, sŭbsĭdĭŭm, aŭxĭlĭŭm. EPITII. Tūtŭm, sălūtărĕ, mūnītŭm, vălĭdŭm, vāllātŭm, tūrrītŭm. V. Auxilium.

prœsīgnĭs, ĕ, *very conspicuous.* Præsīgnĭs ăvŭncŭlŭs, Stat.

prœspērgo, ĭs, *to scatter before, strew.* Prœspērgēns ăntĕ vĭāi, Lucr.

prœstābĭlĭs, ĕ, *and* stāns, ntĭs, *excellent.* Ŏ prœstāns ănĭmī, Virg. V. Insignis.

prœstĕr, ērĭs, m., *a serpent whose bite caused a raging thirst.* Cœlŏ prœstĕra ĭmĭtĕtŭr, Lucr. EPITII. Tŏrrĭdŭs, ăvĭdŭs, vĕnēnōsŭs, lēthĭfĕr, tŭmēns, nŏcŭŭs, fĕrŭs, āspĕr, dīrŭs.

prœstĕrno, ĭs, *to spread before, strew.* Prœstērnĕrĕ flōrēs, Stat.

prœstĕrno, strāvī, *to prepare before.* Quœ sĭbĭ prœstērnăt, Stat.

prœstĕs, stĭtĭs, m., *a chief, a prelate.* Prœstĭtĭbŭs Maĭœ, Ov. SYN. Præsĕs.

prœstīgĭœ, ārŭm, f. pl., *tricks, delusions.* Pătĕnt prœstīgĭœ, (Iamb.) Pl. SYN. Incāntātĭo, vĕnēfĭcĭŭm, măgĭă. EPITII. Fāllācēs, dŏlōsœ, nēfāndœ, măgĭcœ, ārcānœ, vānœ, ĭnānēs, invālĭdœ, scĕlĕrātœ, crūdēlēs, dīrœ, infāndœ, vĕnēfĭcœ, scĕlēstœ, hōrrēndœ, tērrĭbĭlēs, Thēssālĭcœ, Tārtărĕœ, Stўgĭœ. V. Magia.

prœstīgĭātŏr, ōrĭs, m., *a juggler.* SYN. Măgŭs; cīrcŭlātŏr, hīstrĭo.

prœsto, stĭtī, *to excel.* Prœstĭtĕrīt, tŏtĭdĕm, Virg. SYN. Ēxcēllo, præcēllo, sŭpĕro, ēxsŭpĕro, vīnco, prœĕo, ăntĕĕo, prœvērto, sŭm prœstāntĭŏr; ēxĕquŏr, ēffĭcĭo, pĕrăgo; prōmĭtto, pōllĭcĕŏr.

prœstŏ, adv., *at hand.* Paŭpĕr ĕrĭt prœstŏ, Tib. SYN. Cŏrăm; præsēns.

|| prœstŏlŏr, ārĭs, *to wait for.* Quĕm præstŏlārĕ, (Iamb.) Ter.

|| prœstrīngo, xī, *to bind fast, dazzle.* Lūx ŏcŭlōs præstrīngĭt, Claud.

prœstrŭo, ĭs, *to build before, block up.* Prœstrūxĕrăt ōbjĭcĕ mōntĭs, Ov. SYN. Ōbstrŭo, &c.

præsūdo, ās, *to sweat before.* Præsūdārĕ părăt, Stat.

præsŭl, ŭlĭs, m., *a prelate.* Præsŭlĕ măgnŏ, Mant. SYN. Āntīstĕs, pōntĭfĕx. V. Antistes.

præsŭm, præĕs, *to be at the head.* Præfŭĕrăt tēmplŏ, Ov. SYN. Prœsĭdĕo, ĭmpĕro, dŏmĭnŏr.

præsūmo, psī, *to take before, anticipate.* Spĕ præsūmĭtĕ bēllŭm, Virg.

præsŭo, ĭs, *to sew before.* Quœ fŏlĭĭs præsūtă nŏtăm, Ov.

prœtēgo, ĭs, *to cover before.* Bāltĕŭs aŭrŏ Prœtĕgĭt, Ov.

prœtēndo, dĭs, *to stretch before.* Sĕgĕtī prœtēndĕrĕ sēpĕm, Virg.

prœtĕnĕr, ă, ŭm, *very tender.* Vīscĕrĕ prœtĕnĕrŏ, Aus.

prœtēnto, ās, *to try before.* Ēt pĕdĭbŭs prœtēntăt ĭtĕr, Tib.

prœtĕnŭĭs, ĕ, *very slight.* Prœtĕnŭĭs mĕrĭtī, Aus.

prœtĕpĕo, ēs, *and* ēsco, ĭs, *to warm beforehand.* In quāvīs prœtĕpŭĭssĕt ămŏr, Ov.

prœtĕr, prep., *except, beyond, near, before.* Prœtĕr Apēllĕm, Hor.

prœtĕrăgo, ēgī, *to lead by or over.* Prœtĕrăgēndŭs ĕquŭs, Hor.

prœtĕrĕā, *moreover, besides.* Prœtĕrĕā vătŭm, Virg. SYN. Insŭpĕr, ĕtĭăm, ādhūc, ăd hœc, tŭm, deĭn, deĭndĕ, quĭnĕtĭăm.

prœtĕrĕo, īs, ĭī, ĭtŭm, *to pass by, go beyond, omit.* Prœtĕrĭt ĭngēns, Virg. SYN. Prœtērgrĕdĭŏr; trānsĕo, prœĕo, āntĕĕo, prœcūrro; ŏmĭtto, mītto, lĭnquo, prœtērmĭtto, mīssŭm făcĭo, tăcĕo, rĕtĭcĕo, sĭlĕo, cōntĭcĕo.

prœtērfĕrŏr, lătŭs sŭm, *to be carried past, pass by.* Prœtērlătă pĕrĭt, Lucr.

prœtērĭtŭs, ă, ŭm, *the pass. partic. of* prœtereo. Ŏ mĭhī prœtĕrĭtōs, Virg.

prœtērlābŏr, ĕrĭs, lāpsŭs, *to slide by.* Prœtērlābărĕ nĕcēsse ēst, Virg. SYN. Prœtĕrĕo; prœtērflŭo.

|| prœtērmĕo, ās, *to pass beyond.* Prœtērquĕ mĕāntŭm, Lucr.

prœtērmĭtto, īsī, *to pass over.* Tĕ prœtērmĭsĕrĭt ūndă, Hor.

|| prœtērrādo, sī, *to scrape.* Prœtērrādĭt ĕnĭm, Lucr.

prœtērvĕhŏr, ĕrĭs, vēctŭs, *to be carried by.* Prœtērvĕhŏr ōstĭă sāxŏ, Virg. SYN. Prœtĕrĕo, trānsvĕhŏr. ·

prœtērvŏlo, ās, *to fly over, outstrip.* Prœtērvŏlăt aŭrās, Sil.

prœtēxo, ĭs, ŭī, xtŭm, *to cover.* Prœtēxĭt ărūndĭnĕ rīpās, Virg. SYN. Prœtēndo.

prœtēxtă, œ, f., *a gown worn by the Roman children till seventeen years old.* Cēssĭt prœtēxtă mărĭtĭs, Prop.

prœtēxtātŭs, ă, ŭm, *clothed in the prœtexta.* Prœtēxtātĕ pŭĕr, Ov.

prætīnctŭs, ă, ŭm, *the pass. partic. of the obsol.* prætingo, *tinged beforehand.*
Vălĭdo prætīnctă vĕnēnō, Ov.

prætŏr, ōrĭs, m., *a Roman magistrate.* Prætŏr, ĕquō, Ov.

prætŏrĭānŭs, ĭtĭŭs *or* ĭŭs, ă, ŭm, *of a Prætor.* Dē prætŏrĭtĭā, Mart. Brūtī prætōrĭă pŭppĭs, Lucan.

prætōrĭŭm, ĭĭ, n., *the Prætor's tribunal.* Ipsa ād prætōrĭă dēnsæ, Virg. SYN.
Cūrĭă, Palătĭŭm.

|| prætrĕpĭdāns, ntĭs, *and* dŭs, ă, ŭm, *agitated with fear.* Jām mēns prætrĕpĭdāns,
Cat. Prætrĕpĭdŭm cor, Pers.

prætŭmĭdŭs, ă, ŭm, *very much swelled.* Ĕffĕră prætŭmĭdō, Claud.

prævălĕo, ēs, *to prevail, exceed.* Prævălĕt ārcŭ, Stat. SYN. Præsto, ēxcēllo.

prævălĭdŭs, ă, ŭm, *very powerful.* Neŭ sē prævălĭdŭm, Virg. SYN. Vălĭdŭs;
fīrmĭŏr.

prævallo, ās, *to fortify before.* Dōmĭbŭs prævāllĕt ămœnīs, Claud.

prævĕho, xī, *to carry before.* Prævēctŭs ĕquō, Virg.

prævēlo, ās, *to veil.* Prævēlātūră pŭdōrĕm.

prævĕnĭo, ĭs, *to arrive before.* Prævĕnĭēntĕ dĭēs, Ov. SYN. Prævērto, prægrĕdĭŏr, ōccŭpo, præcūrro, præēo.

prævĕrro, ĭs, *to sweep before.* Prævērrŭnt lātās, Ov.

prævērto, ĭs, *and* tŏr, ĕrĭs, *to go before, outstrip.* Cūrsŭquĕ pĕdŭm prævērtĕrĕ
vēntōs, Virg. Vŏlŭcrēmquĕ fŭgā prævērtĭtŭr Hēbrŭm, Id.

prævĕtĭtŭs, ă, ŭm, *forbidden before.* Prævĕtĭtŭm nāmquĕ, Sil.

prævĭdĕo, vīdī, vīsŭm, *to foresee.* Prævĭdĕt īllă, Ov. SYN. Prōspĭcĭo, vĭdĕo
āntĕ, præsēntĭo, præsāgĭo, vătĭcĭnŏr, aŭgŭrŏr, prædīco.

prævĭtĭo, ās, *to spoil before.* Hūnc Dĕă prævĭtĭăt, Cat.

prævĭŭs, ă, ŭm, *going before.* Prævĭŭs ānteĭt, Ov. SYN. Prægrēssŭs, āntĕvŏlāns.

præŭstŭs, ă, ŭm, *burnt at the end.* Sŭdĭbŭsvĕ præŭstīs, Virg. SYN. Ŭstŭs,
ădūstŭs, ēxūstŭs.

prāgmătĭcŭs, ă, ŭm, *skilful in law.* Fœdĕrĕ prāgmătĭcōrŭm, Juv.

prāndĕo, ēs, dī, *to dine.* Impēnsō prāndĕrĕ cŏēmtās, Hor. SYN. Prānsĭto.

prāndĭŭm, ĭĭ, n., *a repast at noon.* Prāndĭă mōrĭs, Hor. EPITH. Laŭtŭm,
pīnguĕ, ŏpīmŭm. V. Convivium.

prāsĭnŭs, ă, ŭm, *green.* Sī Vĕnĕtō prāsĭnŏvĕ, Mart.

prātēnsĭs, ĕ, *of meadows.* Prātēnsĭbŭs ŏptĭmă fūngĭs, Hor.

prātŭm, ī, n., *a meadow.* Prātă rĕcēntĭă rīvīs, Virg. EPITH. Flōrēns, flōrĭdŭm,
vĭrĭdĕ, vērnāns, pīctŭm, mōllĕ, gēmmāns, īrrĭgŭŭm, hērbōsŭm, hērbĭdŭm, grāmĭnĕŭm, lætŭm, hūmĭdŭm, ūdŭm, ămœnŭm; cŭltŭm, rīdēns, frăgrāns, hālāns,
ŏdōrŭm. V. Gramen.

prāvē, adv., *wickedly.* Pŭdēns prāvē, quăm, Hor.

prāvŭs, ă, ŭm, *crooked, bad.* Fĭçtī prāvĭquĕ tĕnāx, Virg. SYN. Dīstōrtŭs, pērvērsŭs, mălŭs. V. Sceleratus.

Prāxĭtĕlēs, ĭs, m., *the famous sculptor.* Prāxĭtĕlēm Părĭŭs, Prop.

prĕcārĭŭs, ă, ŭm, *precarious.* Fōrmă prĕcārĭă cēlăt, Ov.

* prĕcātĭo, ōnĭs, f., *and* tŭs, ūs, m., *an entreating.* Nōstrō rēddī tē pōssĕ prĕcātĭs,
Aus. SYN. Prĕcēs, vōtă. V. Preces.

prĕcātŏr, ōrĭs, m., *one that prays.* Vŏlŭcrŭmquĕ prĕcātŏr Ibўcŭs, Stat.

prĕcēs, ŭm, f. pl., *and* in sing. prĕcĕ, prĕcī, prĕcĕm, f., *prayers.* Āccĭpĭmŭsquĕ
prĕcēs, Ov. Prīmŭm prĕcĕ nūmĕn, ădōră. SYN. Prĕcātĭo, vōtă. EPITH.
Blāndæ, pĭæ, hŭmĭlēs, bĕnīgnæ, āttēntæ, ārdēntēs, īmpōrtūnæ, āssĭdŭæ, cōntĭ-
nŭæ, rĕpĕtītæ, ĭtĕrātæ, sōllĭcĭtæ, flēxănĭmæ, crēbræ, pŏtēntēs, ĭnānēs, īrrĭtæ,
cāssæ, vānæ, flēbĭlēs, sŭpplĭcēs, jūstæ, tĭmĭdæ, sōlēnnēs. V. Precor.

prĕcĭŭs, ă, ŭm, *early ripe.* Pŭrpŭrĕæ prĕcĭæquĕ, Virg.

prĕcŏr, ārĭs, *to pray.* Sīnt prĕcŏr īllă, Tibull. SYN. Oro, ōbtēstŏr, obsecro, rŏgo,
dĕprĕcŏr, īnvŏco, īmplōro, pōsco, pĕto, pōstŭlo, sŭpplĭco, sŭpplēx pĕto. V.
Oro.

prĕhendo, *and* prēndo, ĭs, *to seize.* Dēxtrāmquĕ prĕhēndĭt, Ov. SYN. Căpĭo.

prĕmo, ĭs, ssī, *to press.* Dĭtĭōnĕ prĕmēbăt, Virg. SYN. Cōmprĭmo, cōnstrīngo,
cālco, prōtĕro, ōpprĭmo, ūrgĕo, īnsto, vēxo.

prēsso, ās, *the frequent. of* premo. Et nŏvă prēssāntēs, Prop.

prĕtĭōsŭs, ă, ŭm, *precious.* Fŭlvŏ prĕtĭōsĭŏr ærĕ, Ov. Syn. Cārŭs, măgnī prĕtĭī, sūmptŭōsŭs, sŭpĕrbŭs, mūnĭfĭcŭs, ĕxĭmĭŭs, ĕxcēllēns, præstāns, ĕxquīsītŭs, præclārŭs.

prĕtĭŭm, ĭī, n., *a price, reward.* Mōrs prĕtĭŭm, Ov. Syn. Mērcēs; præmĭŭm. V. Præmium.

Prĭămēĭs, ĭdĭs, f., *the daughter of Priam.* Prĭămēĭdă vīdĕrăt īpsăm, Ov.

Prĭămēĭŭs, ă, ŭm, *of Priam.* Prĭămēĭă vīrgo, Virg.

Prĭămĭdēs, æ, m., *the son of Priam.* Prĭămĭdēs mūltīs, Virg.

Prĭămŭs, ī, m., *the king of Troy.* Vīx Prĭămŭs tāntī, Ov. Syn. Lăŏmĕdōntĭădēs.

Epithᴛ. Dārdănĭŭs, Trōjānŭs, dīvēs, pŏtēns, Mārtĭŭs, īnfēlīx, mĭsĕr.

Prĭāpŭs, ī, m., *the son of Bacchus and Venus, the God of gardens.* Tūrpĭŭs ēst nĭhĭl Prĭāpō, (Phal.) Mart. Syn. Lāmpsăcĭdēs. Epith. Tūrpĭs, lāscīvŭs, īnfāmĭs, sălāx, prŏtērvŭs, rŭbĭcūndŭs; rūrĭcŏlă, frūgĭfĕr, pōmĭfĕr.

prīdĕm, adv., *lately, long ago.* Nōn ĭtă prīdĕm, Hor. Syn. Dūdŭm, jāmdūdŭm, jāmprīdĕm.

prīmævŭs, ă, ŭm, *first-born.* Quōrŭm prīmævŭs Hĕlēnŏr, Virg. Syn. Sĕnĭŏr; lōngævŭs, sĕnēx.

prīmātēs, ŭm, m. pl., *primates, or chief personages.* Dīscĭtĕ, prīmātēs, Mart. V. Proceres.

prīmĭgĕnŭs, ă, ŭm, *first-born.* Prīmĭgĕnŭm mărĭs, Lucr.

prīmĭpīlŭs, ī, m., *the captain of the van of a legion.*

prīmĭtĭæ, ārŭm, f. pl., *the first-fruits of the year.* Mĭttĕrĕ prīmĭtĭās, Tib. Syn. Prīmă dōnă, mūnĕră, prīmōrdĭă, ēxŏrsă, ōrŭm. Epith. Faūstæ, nŏvæ.

prīmĭtĭŭs, ă, ŭm, *the first, principal.* Prīmĭtĭŭm tōrrĕm, Ov

prīmĭtŭs, adv., *at the first.* Prīmĭtŭs īnsĭnŭāntŭr, Lucr.

prīmō, *and* ŭm, adv., *at first.* Ět sī quīs prīmō, Tib. Mŏdōs prīmŭm dĕdĭt, Virg. Syn. Prīncĭpĭŏ.

prīmōrdĭŭm, ĭī, n., *the beginning.* Vĕtĕrŭm prīmōrdĭă rērŭm, Lucr. Syn. Ēxōrdĭŭm, prīncĭpĭŭm, ēxōrsă, -ōrŭm, ŏrīgo; rŭdīmēntŭm, tўrōcĭnĭŭm.

prīmōrēs, ŭm, m. pl., *nobles.* Prīmōrŭm mănŭs ād pōrtās, Virg.

prīmŭs, ă, ŭm, *first.* Vīx prīmī prælĭă tēntānt, Virg. Syn. Prĭŏr, prīncēps, præcĭpŭŭs.

prīncēps, ĭpĭs, *chief, principal.* Prīncĭpĭs īngĕnĭŭm, Mart. Syn. Prīmŭs, præsēs; rēx, dūx. Epith. Inclўtŭs, bēllĭgĕr, illūstrĭs, mītĭs, jūstŭs, pŏtēns, fōrtĭs. V. Rex, dux.

prīncĭpĭālĭs, ĕ, *original.* Prīncĭpĭăle ălĭquŏd, Lucr.

prīncĭpĭŏ, adv., *at the beginning.* Prīncĭpĭŏ dēlūbră, Virg

prīncĭpĭŭm, ĭī, n., *the beginning.* Ab Jŏvĕ prīncĭpĭŭm, Virg. Syn. Inĭtĭŭm, prīmōrdĭŭm, ŏrīgo, fōns, căpŭt, aūctŏr, caūsă; cœptŭm, īncēptŭm. V. Initium, primordium.

prĭŏr, ŭs, ōrĭs, *former, best.* Rōmă prĭōrĭbŭs, Mart. Syn. Prīmŭs; præstāntĭŏr, mĕlĭŏr.

prīsĕŭs, ă, ŭm, *old.* Cōgēbāt prīscōs, Prop. Syn. Āntīquŭs, vĕtŭs, vĕtūstŭs, lōngævŭs, ānnōsŭs, sĕnēx.

prīstĭnŭs, ă, ŭm, *ancient.* Prīstĭnŭs īllī, Virg. Syn. Prīmŭs, prĭŏr.

prīstĭs, *or* pīstrĭs, ĭs, *and* trīx, ĭcĭs, f., *a whale, a sort of ship.* Immānī cōrpŏrĕ prīstĭs, Virg.

prīvātŭs, ă, ŭm, *the pass. partic. of* privo. Prīvātās ūt quærăt, Hor.—2. *peculiar, private.* Syn. Prŏprĭŭs, sīngŭlārĭs; mūnĕrĭs ēxpērs, prīvātăm vītam ăgĕns.

Prīvērnŭm, ī, n., *a city of the Volscians.* Prīvērno āntīquă, Virg.

prīvīgnŭs, ī, m., *and* ă, æ, f., *a son or daughter-in-law.* Prīvīgnī mātrĕ cărēntēs, Hor. Prīvīgnæ nōmĭnĕ dīgnŭm, Ov.

prīvo, ās, *to deprive.* Fōrmīdĭnĕ prīvĕt, Hor. Syn. Spŏlĭo, ēxspŏlĭo, ōrbo, nūdo, dēnūdo, ērĭpĭo, aūfĕro, ădĭmo.

prĭŭs, adv., *sooner.* Syn. Āntĕ, cĭtĭŭs.

prīvŭs, ă, ŭm, *peculiar to.* Prīvă trīrēmĭs, Hor. Syn. Prīvātŭs.

prŏ, interj., *oh!* Cōmās, prŏ Jŭpĭtĕr! ĭbĭt, Virg.

prō, præp., *for.* Prō pūrpŭrĕŏ nārcīssŏ, Virg. Syn. Lŏcō, vĭcĕ; prōptĕr, jūxtā.

prŏăvītŭs, ă, ŭm, *of a great-grandfather.* Prŏăvītæ īnsīgnĭă, Sil.

prŏăvŭs, ī, m., *a great-grandfather.* Prŏăvīs īngēns, M. V. Avus.

prŏbābĭlĭs, ĕ, *likely.* Hīs prŏbābĭlī fĭdĕ, (Iamb. pur.) Avien.

prŏbātŏr, ōrĭs, m., *an approver.* Sæpĕ prŏbātŏr ĕrās, Ov.

prŏbĭtās, ātĭs, f., *probity.* Ēst ănĭmī prŏbĭtās, ōrīsquĕ, Mart. Syn. Bŏnĭtās, īntegrĭtās, pĭĕtās, vīrtūs. Epith. Gĕnĕrōsă, dūlcĭs, mītĭs, lēnĭs, īngĕnŭă, hŏnēstă, vĕnĕrāndă, īncŭlpātă, laūdāndă, īnsōns, īnnŏxĭă, sīmplēx. V. Virtus, pietas.

prŏbo, ās, *to approve, prove.* Ænĕæ, prŏbăt aūctŏr, Virg. Syn. Āpprŏbo, cōmprŏbo, laūdo, cōmmĕndo, āpplaūdo, āssēntĭŏr; dēmōnstro, suādĕo, cōnfīrmo, tēnto, ēxpĕrĭŏr.

|| prŏbŏscĭs, ĭdĭs, f., *an elephant's or insect's trunk.* Cŭlĭcīsvĕ prŏbŏscĭdĕ vēxŏr, Grat.

probrōsŭs, ă, ŭm, *shameful.* Cārthāgō prŏbrōsĭs, (Iamb.) Hor. Syn. Pŭdēndŭs, īnhŏnēstŭs, īgnōmĭnĭōsŭs, tūrpĭs, īnfāmĭs.

probrŭm, ī, n., *disgrace.* Mēntem īnhĭbērĕ prŏbrō, Cat. Syn. Ōpprobrĭŭm, īnfāmĭă, dēdĕcŭs, īgnōmĭnĭă, cōnvīcĭŭm.

prŏbŭs, ă, ŭm, *honest.* Jūstŭs, prŏbŭs, īnnŏcēns, (Phal.) Mart. Syn. Bŏnŭs, pĭŭs, jūstŭs, æquŭs. V. Pius.

prŏcācĭtās, ātĭs, f., *insolence.* Quī stŏlĭdă prŏcācĭtātĕ, (Phal.) Mart. Syn. Prŏtērvĭă, pĕtŭlāntĭă, lāscīvĭă. Epith. Stŏlĭdă, lĕpĭdă, īmprŏbă, tūrpĭs, fœdă, īnhŏnēstă, hĭlărĭs, lāscīvă.

Prŏcās, *and* că, æ, m., *a king of Alba.* Prōxĭmŭs īllĕ, Prŏcās, Virg. Prŏcă nātŭs īn īllīs, Ov.

prŏcāx, ācĭs, *insolent.* Pēnĭtūsquĕ prŏcācĭbŭs aūstrīs, Virg. Syn. Prŏtērvŭs, pĕtŭlāns, lāscīvŭs, īmprŏbŭs.

prŏcēdo, ssī, *to go on.* Ænēās prōcēdĕrĕ lōngĭŭs, Virg. Syn. Prōgrĕdĭŏr.

prŏcēllă, æ, f., *a storm.* Antēnnă prŏcēllās, Ov. Syn. Tēmpēstās, tūrbo, nīmbŭs, īmbĕr. V. Tempestas.

|| prŏcēllo, ĭs, *to throw down.* Ātquĕ prŏcēllĭt, Lucr.

prŏcēllōsŭs, ă, ŭm, *stormy.* Ālbă prŏcēllōsŏs, Ov. Syn. Nīmbōsŭs, vēntōsŭs.

prŏcērēs, ŭm, m. pl., *nobles.* Ēt mīssō prŏcĕrēs, Juv. Syn. Māgnātēs, nōbĭlēs, patrĭcĭī, prī̄nōrēs, prīncĭpēs, prīmī, prīmātēs, dŭcēs, dūctōrēs, præcĭpŭī, lēctī, dēlēctī, lēctīssĭmī.

prŏcērŭs, ă, ŭm, *tall.* Prŏcērōs ŏdīssĕ lŭpōs, Hor. Syn. Māgnŭs, āltŭs, ēxcēlsŭs, īngēns. V. Altus.

prŏcēssŭs, ūs, m., *a process.* Sīc tŭă prŏcēssŭs, Ov.

Prŏchȳtă, æ, *and* tē, ēs, f., *a small island in the gulf of Naples.* Sŏnĭtū Prŏchȳta āltă trĕmĭt, Virg. Inărĭmēn Prŏchȳtēnquĕ lĕgĭt, Ov.

prŏcĭdo, ĭs, ĭdī, (*from* cado,) *to fall forward.* Eūrō prŏcĭdĭt lātē, Hor. Syn. Prōlābŏr, prōcumbo, cădo.

prŏcĭdŭŭs, ă, ŭm, *falling prostrate.* Cōrpŏră prŏcĭdŭæ, Stat. Syn. Cădŭcŭs, lābĭlĭs.

prŏclāmo, ās, *to proclaim.* Māgnă prŏclāmāt vōcĕ Dĭōrēs, Virg. Syn. Ēxclāmo, clāmo.

prŏclīno, ās, *to bend downwards.* Tū prŏclīnātās, Ov. V. Inclino.

prŏclīvĭs, ĕ, *and* vŭs, ă, ŭm, *bending downwards.* Vĭă lābēndī prŏclīvĭŏr, ŭt, Paul. E. Ūndārŭm prŏclīvŭs, Lucr. Syn. Prōpēnsŭs, īnclīnātŭs, ācclīvĭs.

Prŏcnē. V. Progne.

* prōcrāstĭno, ās, *to defer.* Cic. Syn. Dīffĕro, cūnctŏr, tārdo, mŏrŏr. V. Piger, festino.

prŏcrĕo, ās, *to engender.* Prŏcrĕăt ēx sē, Lucr. Syn. Gĕnĕro, crĕo, prōdūco, părĭo.

prŏcrēsco, ĭs, *to increase, grow.* Ănĭmă prŏcrēscĕre, ĕt īmbrī, Lucr. V. Cresco.

Prŏcrĭs, ĭs, f., *a daughter of Erechtheus, unwittingly slain by her husband Cephalus.* Pēctŏrĕ Prŏcrĭs ĕrăt, Ov.

Procrūstēs, æ, m., *a robber slain by Theseus.* Cēphēsĭăs ōră Prŏcrūstēn, Ov.

prŏcŭbo, ās, ŭī, *to lie down.* Prŏcŭbŭīt sācrăm, Virg.

prŏcūdo, dī, sŭm, *to hammer, to stamp.* Dūrŭm prŏcūdĭt ărātŏr, Virg. Syn. Cūdo, ēxcūdo.

prŏcŭl, adv., *far off.* I prŏcŭl, hīnc, Ov. Syn. Lōngē, lōngĭŭs, rĕmōtē, prōtĕnŭs.

prŏcūlco, ās, *to trample under foot.* Sĕgĕtēs prŏcŭlcăt īn hērbă, Ov. Syn. Cālco, cōncūlco, prōtĕro, āttĕro, cōntĕro, tĕro, cālcĕ tĕro; spērno, cōntēmno.

Prŏcŭlēĭŭs, ī, m., *the name of a man.* Ēxtēntō Prŏcŭlēĭŭs ævŏ, Hor.

PRO 329

procŭmbo, cŭbŭï, *to lie along.* Pŏplĭtēsquĕ prŏcŭmbŭnt, Lucr. Trĕmēns prŏcŭmbĭt hŭmī bōs, Virg. Syn. Prŏcĭdo, prōstērnŏr, lăbŏr, dēcĭdo, rŭo, cōrrŭo, cădo.

procūrātŏr, ōrĭs, m., *a manager.* Indĕ prŏcūrātŏr, Ov.

procūro, ās, *to take care of.* Prŏcūrătĕ, vĭrī, Virg. Ipsĕ prŏcūrāvī, Tib. Syn. Cūro, gĕro, trācto, ādmĭnĭstro, rĕgo, gŭbērno, mŏdĕrŏr.

prŏcūrro, cūrrī, *to run before.* Mănum ēt prŏcūrrĕrĕ, Virg. Syn. Cūrro, ēxcūrro.

prŏcūrsŭs, ūs, m., *a sally.* Ēt prŏcūrsū cōncĭtŭs āxĭs, Virg.

prŏcūrvo, ās, *to bend before.* Cēlsūm prŏcūrvăt Ăgȳllēă Tȳdeūs, Stat.

prŏcūrvŭs, ă, ŭm, *crooked.* Ēxŏrĭtŭr prŏcūrva īngēns, Virg. Syn. Cūrvŭs, īncūrvŭs.

prŏcŭs, ī, m., *a lover.* Lūxŭrĭōsă, prŏcī, Ov. Syn. Ămātŏr. Epith. Blāndŭs, vĭgĭl, cŭpĭdŭs, lūxŭrĭōsŭs, īmpŏrtūnŭs, mĭsĕr, dŭbĭŭs, sōllĭcĭtŭs, pērvĭgĭl, īnsŏmnĭs, pāllēns, tĕnēllŭs, tĕnĕr. V. Amans.

Prŏcȳon, m., *a constellation which appeared before the dog-star.* Jăm Prŏcȳon fŭrĭt, Hor. Syn. Āntĕcănĭs. V. Canicula.

prōdĕo, īs, īvī *or* ĭī, *to go forth.* Prōdĭt ăquĭs, Prop. Syn. Ēo, prŏcēdo ; ēxĕo.

prōdēst, *it is useful.* Quīd prōdēst, sī tē, Mart. Syn. Jŭvăt. V. Prosum.

‖ prōdĭgālĭtās, ātĭs, f., *prodigality.* Syn. Prŏfūsĭo, ēffūsĭo. V. Luxuria.

prōdĭgĭālĕ, ĭtĕr, *or* ĭōsē, adv., *wonderfully.* Prōdĭgĭālĕ rŭbēns, Cl. Prōdĭgĭālĭtĕr ūnăm, Hor.

prōdĭgĭālĭs, ĕ, *and* ōsŭs, ă, ŭm, *wonderful.* Prōdĭgĭālĕ nĕmŭs, Stat. Prōdĭgĭōsă lŏquŏr, Ov. Syn. Pŏrtēntōsŭs, mōnstrōsŭs.

prōdĭgĭŭm, ĭī, n., *a prodigy.* Prōdĭgĭīs, ēn, Virg. Syn. Pŏrtēntŭm, mōnstrŭm. V. Monstrum.

prōdĭgo, ĭs, *to squander away.* Bēllōquĕ părātă Prōdĭgĕrĕ, Stat. Syn. Ēffūndo, prŏfūndo, &c.

prōdĭgŭs, ă, ŭm, *prodigal.* Prōdĭgŭs ātquĕ, (Phal.) Mart. Syn. Prŏfūsŭs, ēffūsŭs, dĭssŏlūtŭs ; nĕpōs. V. Liberalis, gulosus.

prōdĭtĭo, ōnĭs, f., *treachery.* Prōdĭtĭōnĕ Pĕlāsgī, Virg. Syn. Fraūs, dŏlŭs, pērfĭdĭă. Epith. Pērfĭdă, īmpĭă, scĕlĕrātă, ārcānă, ŏccūltă, sēcrētă, lătēns.

prōdĭtŏr, ōrĭs, m., *a traitor.* Prōdĭtŏr īntĭmō, (Alcaic.) Hor. Epith. Pērfĭdŭs, īmpĭŭs, scĕlĕrātŭs, īnfĭdŭs, īnsĭdĭōsŭs, caūtŭs, fāllāx, dŏlōsŭs, cāllĭdŭs, āstūtŭs, văfĕr, mēndāx, vērsūtŭs, mālŭs, mĕtŭēndŭs, dētēstāndŭs, pērnĭcĭōsŭs. V. Perfidus.

prōdĭtŭs, ă, ŭm, *the pass. partic. of* prodo. Prōdĭtă sōmnō, Virg.

prōdo, prōdĭdī, *to disclose, to betray.* Prōdĕrĕ fŭrĕm? Juv. Syn. Ōstēndo, pāndo, ăpĕrĭo ; māndo, scrībo, ēdo ; trādo ; dēstĭtŭo, dēsĕro.

prōdŏcĕo, ēs, ŭī, *to teach eagerly.* Sūmmŭs ăb īmŏ Prōdŏcĕt, Hor.

prōdūco, ūxī, ctŭm, *to lead out.* Ălĭŭs prōdūcĭtŭr ægĕr, Stat. Syn. Gĕnĕro, părĭo, pōrtēndo, prōtrăho, prŏfĕro ; prōrŏgo ; dīffĕro, tārdo ; prŏvĕho, prōmŏvĕo.

Prœtĭdĕs, ŭm, f. pl., *the three daughters of Prœtus, cured of madness by Melampus.* Prœtĭdĕs īmplērūnt, Virg.

Prœtŭs, ī, m., *a usurper of the throne of Argus, changed into a stone by Perseus.* Ăcrīsĭōnæās Prœtŭs pōssēdĕrăt ārcēs, Ov.

prŏfāno, ās, *to profane.* Mōrs īmpŏrtūnă prŏfānăt, Ov. Syn. Rēs sacrās vĭŏlo, pōllŭo, tĕmĕro.

prŏfānŭs, ă, ŭm, *profane.* Flāmmă prŏfānă pĭæ, Ov. ˙Syn. Nōn săcĕr, īmpĭŭs, scĕlĕrātŭs.

prŏfārī, *to speak.* Dēmīssă prŏfātŭr, Virg. Syn. Fārī, lŏquī. V. Loquor.

psŏfātŭs, ūs, m., *utterance.* Æquārĕ prŏfātū, Stat.

prŏfēctō, adv., *certainly.* Illĕ prŏfēctō, Hor. Syn. Cērtĕ, ĕquĭdĕm.

prŏfēctŭs, ūs, m., *success, advantage.* Vērbŭquĕ prŏfēctū, Ov. Syn. Ēffēctŭs, ūtĭlĭtās.

prŏfĕro, tŭlī, lātŭm, *to relate, to carry forth.* Prōfĕrăt īmpĕrĭŭm, Virg. Syn. Prōnūncĭo, cōmmĕmŏro, dīco, rĕfĕro, rĕcēnsĕo ; ōstēndo, mōnstro, pătĕfăcĭo ; prōdūco.

prŏfēssŭs, ă, ŭm, *the part. of* profiteor. Præbĕrĕ, prŏfēssŭs, Hor.

prŏfēstŭs, ă, ŭm, *not holy or solemn.* Fēstă prŏfēstĭs, Aus.

prŏfĭcĭo, fēcī, *to profit.* Prŏfĭcĭt ūsŭ, Prop. Syn. Prōgrĕdĭŏr ; prōsŭm.

prŏfĭcīscŏr, ĕrĭs, *to depart.* Ut prŏfĭcīscēntĕm, Hor. Syn. Ēo, vādo, prōcēdo, dīscēdo, ăbĕo, ēxĕo, tēndo, cōntēndo. V. Eo, abeo, navem solvo, peregrinor.

prŏfīndo, fīdī, *to break up.* Prŏfīndūnt ĭnărātă dĭū, Stat.

prŏfĭtĕŏr, ērĭs, fēssŭs, *to acknowledge freely.* Tĭmĭdē prŏfĭtētŭr ămōrēs, Ov. Syn. Cōnfĭtĕŏr, fătĕŏr ; dēnūncĭo, tēstŏr, sĭgnĭfĭco ; ēxērcĕo ; ēdŏcĕo.

prŏflātŭs, ūs, m., *a blowing or breathing.* Prŏflātū tērrēbăt ĕquōs, Stat. V. Ronchus.

prŏflīgo, ās, *to throw down.* Prŏflīgārētŭr pŏpŭlī, Mart. Syn. Afflīgo, stērno, prōstērno, dējĭcĭo, cædo, cōncīdo, dīssĭpo, fūndo, fūgo, vīnco, dŏmo.

prŏflo, ās, *to blow.* Tōtō prŏflābāt pēctŏrē, Virg. Syn. Ēfflo, flō.

prŏflŭo, ūxī, *to flow out.* Prŏflŭēt hūmŏr, Virg. Syn. Flŭo, māno, prōmāno, lābŏr, ēfflŭo, dēflŭo, dēlābŏr, fŭgĭo, fĕrŏr, cŭrro, dēcŭrro. V. Fluo.

prŏflŭvĭum, ĭī, n., *a flux.* Prŏflŭvĭum pōrrō, Lucr.

prŏflŭŭs, ă, ŭm, *flowing towards.* Prŏflŭă sȳlvăs, Ov. Syn. Rĭgŭŭs. V. Fluo.

prŏfŏrĕ, *the inf. fut. of* prosum. Quæ prŏfŏrĕ crēdăm, Hor.

prŏfŭgĭo, ūgī, *to flee.* Sīc fātă, prŏfŭgĭt, Val. Fl.

prŏfŭgŭs, ă, ŭm, *fugitive.* Scȳthĭcŭm prŏfŭgā, Ov. Syn. Fŭgĭtīvŭs, ēxŭl. V. Exul.

profŭndo, fūdī, fūsŭm, *to pour out.* Jūtūrnă prŏfŭdĭt, Virg. Æquŏră prŏfŭdĭt, Manil. Syn. Fūndo, ēffŭndo ; dīspērdo, dīssĭpo, prōdĭgo.

prŏfŭndŭs, ă, ŭm, *deep.* Ĭntŏnŭērĕ prŏfŭndæ, Virg. Syn. Altŭs, căvŭs, dēprēssŭs, īmŭs.

prŏfŭsŭs, ă, ŭm, *the pass. partic. of* profundor. Sŭpĕr ōră prŏfŭsŭs, Ov. Ītălō prŏfūsŭs ăcētō, Hor.

prŏgĕnĕr, ĕrī, m., *the grand-daughter's husband.* Gĕnĕrīque ēt prŏgĕnĕrī, Aus.

prŏgĕnĕro, ās, *to beget.* Prŏgĕnĕrānt ăquĭlæ, Hor. Syn. Gĕnĕro.

prŏgĕnĭēs, ĭēī, f., *offspring.* Prŏgĕnĭēm sēd ĕnĭm, Virg. Syn. Prōlēs, sŏbŏlēs. V. Genus.

prŏgĕnĭtŏr, ōrĭs, m., *a father, an ancestor.* Prŏgĕnĭtōrĕ Tŏnāntĕ, Ov. Syn. Gĕnĭtŏr, părēns, pătĕr.

prŏgĕnĭtŭs, ă, ŭm, *the pass. partic. of* progigno. Prŏgĕnĭtōs fulcīssĕ, Sedul.

prōgīgno, gĕnŭī, *to engender.* Sēnsŭm prŏgīgnĕre ăcērbŭm, Lucr. V. Gigno.

prōgnātŭs, ă, ŭm, *born, produced.* Ŏvō prōgnātŭs ĕōdĕm, Hor.

Prognē, ēs, f., *the daughter of Pandion, changed into a swallow.* Et mănĭbūs Prŏgnē, Virg. Ad mandātă Prŏgnēs, Ov. Epith. Quĕrŭlă, ĭmpĭā, Daūlĭăs ; Pāndĭŏnĭă, Thrācĭă, Thrēĭcĭă, Rhŏdŏpēĭă, Gĕtĭcă, sævă, dūră, Attĭcă, Cecrŏpĭs, crŭēntă, ăcērbă. V. Hirundo.

prŏgrĕdĭŏr, ĕrĭs, grēssŭs, *to proceed.* Prŏgrĕdĭŏr pōrtū. Syn. Prōcēdo, prōdĕo, ēgrĕdĭŏr.

prŏh, *or* prō, interj. V. Pro.

prŏhĭbĕo, ēs, ŭī, *to forbid, hinder.* Lūdō prŏhĭbēbĭs ĭnānī, Virg. Syn. Vĕto, ĭmpĕdĭo, obsŭm, ōbsto, ōbsīsto, tārdo, rĕtārdo, mŏrŏr, dīstĭnĕo ; ārcĕo, ēxclūdo, rĕpēllo, sūmmŏvĕo. V. Impedio.

prōjēctĭtĭŭs, ă, ŭm, *cast out, abandoned.* Prŏjēctĭtĭam īllăm, Plaut.

prōjēctŭs, ŭs, m., *a casting out.* Immānĭs prŏjēctŭs, Lucr.

prōjēctŭs, ă, ŭm, *the pass. partic. of* projicio. Caūtĕs, prōjēctăquĕ sāxă, Virg.

prōjĭcĭo, jēcī, jēctŭm, *to cast out.* Prŏjĭcĕ tēlă, Virg. Syn. Jăcĭo, cōnjĭcĭo, jăcŭlŏr ; ăbjĭcĭo, afflīgo, prōstērno.

prŏĭn, *or* proĭn, prŏīndĕ, *or* proīndĕ, adv., *therefore, as if.* Prŏīn, vĭātŏr, Catul. Proīndĕ tŏna, Virg. Prŏīndĕ ŏmīsī rĕgīmĕn, (Iamb.) Sen. Syn. Ĭdĕo, ērgo, prŏptĕrĕā, pĕrīndĕ.

prōlābŏr, ĕrĭs, lāpsŭs, *to fall down.* Intēntī prōlābĭtŭr æquŏrĭs ūndă, Avien. Syn. Lābŏr, rŭo, cădo, prōcŭmbo, prōcĭdo.

prōlāpsŭs, ă, ŭm, *the part. of* prolabor. Prōlāpsŭm lĕvĭtĕr, Prop.

prōlāto, ās, *to extend, prolong, lengthen.* Prōlātărĕ dĭēm, Sil.

prōlātŭs, ă, ŭm, *the pass. partic. of* profero. Nōn deēst prōlātō, L.

prōlēcto, ās, *to allure.* Ănĭmōs prōlēctăt ĭnānĭs, Ov. Syn. Allĭcĭo, pēllĭcĭo.

prōlēs, ĭs, f., *progeny.* Prōlĕ părēntĕm, Virg. Syn. Prōgĕnĭēs, sŏbŏlēs, propāgo, lībērī, nātī, fīlĭŭs, fīlĭă. Epith. Cără, dīlēctă, dūlcĭs, ămātă, ĕgrĕgĭă, inclȳtă, gĕnĕrōsă, māscŭlă, vīrīlĭs, tĕnĕră.

prōlixŭs, ă, ŭm, *long, large.* Squālĭdă prōlixīs, Ov. Syn. Lōngŭs, prŏdŭctŭs, ēxtēnsŭs.

prōlŏgŭs, ī, m., *a prologue.* Invĕnīrĕ prŏlŏgŭm, (Iamb.) Tcr. Ōrnātŭ prōlŏgī, (Iamb.) Id.

prōlŏquŏr, ĕrĭs, lŏcūtŭs, *to speak at length, to preface.* Prōlŏquăr, ătque, Prop. Syn. Lŏquŏr, cōllŏquŏr.

prōlūdo, ĭs, sī, sŭm, *to prelude.* Ăd pūgnām prōlūdĭt, Virg. Syn. Præludo.

prōlŭo, ĭs, lŭī, lūtŭm, *to wash.* Prōlŭĭt aūrō, Virg. Syn. Lăvo, ābĭŭo; hūmēcto, ĭrrĭgo.

prōlŭtŭs, ă, ŭm, *the pass. partic. of* proluo. Prōlūtŭs vāppā, Hor.

prōlŭvĭēs, ĭeī, f., *and* ĭŭm, ĭī, n., *filth washed off.* Vēntrĭs prōlŭvĭēs, Virg. Syn. Ēlŭvĭēs, sōrdēs.

prōmĕrĕo, ēs, *or* ĕŏr, ĕrĭs, *to deserve.* Prōmĕrŭērĕ bŏnōs, Prop. Syn. Mĕrĕo, mĕrĕŏr.

prōmĕrĭtŭs, ă, ŭm, *the partic. of* promereor. Prōmĕrĭtām, nēc mē, Virg.

Prŏmēthĕŭs, ĕŏs, ĕī *or* eī, m., *the son of Japetus, chained to a rock by Jupiter for stealing the vivifying fire from heaven.* Ārtēmquĕ Prōmētheī, Virg. Rŭpĕ Prōmēthĕă rōdăt, Man. Syn. Iăpĕtĭŏnĭdēs, Jāpĕtĭdēs. Epith. Cāllĭdŭs, ĭngĕnĭōsŭs, răptŏr, prōvĭdŭs, prūdēns, cōnsūltŭs, sŭbdŏlŭs, ĭgnĭfĕr, mĭsĕr, ĭnfēlīx, lānguēns, vīnctŭs, ĭrrĕquĭētŭs, sōllĭcĭtŭs, ĭnsōmnĭs, Caūcăsĕŭs.

Prŏmēthĕŭs, ă, ŭm, *of Prometheus.* Eccĕ Prōmēthĕæ, Mart.

Prŏmēthĭdēs, æ, m., *the son of Prometheus, Deucalion.* Indĕ Prŏmēthĭdēs, Ov.

prōmĭnĕo, ēs, *to project.* Prōmĭnĕt īn pōntŭm, Ov. Syn. Ēmĭnĕo, ăssūrgo, āppārĕo.

prōmīscŭŭs, ă, ŭm, *promiscuous.* Chŏrōs prōmīscŭă fāmă, Mart. Syn. Cōnfūsŭs, mīxtŭs, īncērtŭs.

prōmīssŏr, ōrĭs, m., *a promiser.* Hĭc prōmīssŏr hĭātŭ, Hor.

prōmīssŭm, ī, n., *a promise.* Vīrō prōmīssă jŭbēbānt, Virg. Syn. Prōmīssĭo, pōllĭcĭtŭm. Epith. Grātŭm, māgnĭfĭcŭm, prĕtĭōsŭm, ămīcŭm, jūcūndŭm, lĕvĕ, īncērtŭm, āncēps, dŭbĭŭm, fāllāx, dŏlōsŭm, mēndāx.

prōmīssŭs, ă, ŭm, *the pass. partic. of* promitto. Cĭnĕrī prōmīssă Sĭchæō, Virg.

prōmītto, sī, ssŭm, *to promise.* Pōssŭm prōmīttĕrĕ cūræ, Virg. Syn. Pōllĭcĕŏr, spōndĕo, rĕcĭpĭo; pōllĭcĭtŏr, păcīscŏr. V. Promissum.

prōmo, ĭs, prōmpsī, prōmptŭm, *to draw out.* Prōmĕrĕ mēllă, Mart. Syn. Exprōmo, dēprōmo; ēdūco, ĭs; ēxtrăho.

Prŏmŭlŭs, ī, m., *the name of a warrior.* Virg.

prōmōntŏrĭŭm, ĭī, n., *a cape, a promontory.* Căprĕăs prōmōntŏrĭŭmquĕ (*quadrisyl.*) Mĭnērvæ, Ov.

prōmŏvĕo, mŏvī, mōtŭm, *to move forward.* Aūdītŏr prōmŏvĕātŭr, Prop. Syn. Prŏvĕho, prŏdūco.

prōmptŭ, *abl. of the obsol.* prōmptŭs, ŭs; īn prōmptŭ, *at hand, easy.* Dŏctŭs, ĕt īn prōmptŭ, Ov. Syn. Ăd mănŭm, īn mănū, præstō; prōmptŭm, făcĭlĕ, prōnŭm.

prōmptŭs, ă, ŭm, *quick, ready.* Prōmptŭs, ĕt Isæō, Juv. Syn. Ălăcĕr, hĭlărĭs, părātŭs, ārdēns, vēlōx.

• prōmŭlgo, ās, *to divulge.* Syn. Prŏvŭlgo, vŭlgo, ēdīco, prōdo, mănĭfēsto, ăpĕrĭo, rĕtĕgo. V. Manifesto.

prōmŭs, ī, m., *a purveyor, steward.* Quŏd nūnc prōmŭs ăĭt, Aus. Syn. Cōndŭs, cēllărĭŭs.

prōnēcto, ās, *to spin out.* Prōnēctānt tĭbī cāndĭdæ sŏrōrēs, Stat.

prōnĕpōs, ōtĭs, m., *a great-grandchild.* Prōnĕpōs ĕgŏ rēgĭs, Ov. Syn. Nĕpōs.

prōnēptĭs, ĭs, f., *a great-granddaughter.* Nūllă prōnēptĭs, Pers.

prōnŭbă, æ, f., *presiding over nuptials, a title of Juno.* Tē, prōnŭbă; nēc făcĕ tāntŭm, Virg. V. Juno.

prōnŭbŭs, ă, ŭm, *of marriage.* Prōnŭbă flāmmă, Cl.

prōnūncĭo, ās, *to pronounce.* Sānctō prōnūncĭăt ōrĕ, Prud. Syn. Prōfĕro, dīco; nūncĭo.

prōnŭrŭs, ūs, f., *a grandson's wife.* Prōnŭrŭs ĕt māgnī, Ov.

prōnŭs, ă, ŭm, *bent downwards, inclined.* Prōnŭs ĕt aūrătăm, Juv. Syn. Prōpēnsŭs, prōclīvĭs; īnclīnātŭs, cūrvŭs, īncūrvŭs; īnclīnārī făcĭlĭs, părātŭs.

prŏœmĭŭm, ĭī, n., *a preface.* Cōgnōscĕ prŏœmĭă rīxæ, Juv. SYN. Êxōrdĭŭm, prīncĭpĭŭm.

prŏpāgēs, ĭs, f., *race.* Mēllŏrĕ prŏpāgĕ cōlēndŭs, Aus.

propāgo, ās, *to spread, propagate.* Sēclă prŏpāgēnt, Lucr. Prŏpāgārĕ gĕnŭs, Id. SYN. Prŏdūco, prŏfĕro, prŏtēndo, prŏtrāho, ămplĭfĭco, dīlăto, ēxtēndo, aŭgĕo. V. Imperium.

propāgo, ĭnĭs, f., *race, a tendril.* Vīrtūtĕ prŏpāgo, Virg. Prēssōs prŏpāgĭnĭs ārcŭs, Virg. SYN. Gĕnŭs, stīrps, prŏgĕnĭēs, sŏbŏlēs; vītĭs pālmēs, sārmēntŭm. V. Soboles.

prŏpălăm, adv., *openly, publicly.* Prŏpălăm laŭdāvĕrĭs, Aus. V. Palam.

prŏpĕ, prep., *near.* Cŭbăt ĭs prŏpĕ, Hor. SYN. Jŭxtă. prŏptĕr, sĕcūndŭm, nōn prŏcŭl.—2. adv., *near, nearly.* SYN. Fĕre, pænĕ, fērmē.

propĕllo, pŭlī, pŭlsŭm, *to thrust forward.* Cōrpŭs prŏpēllĭt ĕt ĭcĭt, Lucr. Åtquĕ prŏpēllăt, Id. SYN. Propŭlso, pēllo, ārcĕo. V. Pello.

prŏpēnsŭs, ă, ŭm, *hanging down.* Spēctā prŏpēnsĭŏr, aŭrī, Prop. SYN. Prŏclīvĭs, prŏnŭs.

prŏpĕrāntĕr, comp. tĭŭs, adv., *and prŏpĕrē, with haste, rapidly.* Ŭsque ădĕo prŏpĕrāntĕr, Lucr. Dĭēm prŏpĕrāntĭŭs īrĕ, Ov. Ê cāstrĭs prŏpĕrē cŏĭt ōmnĭs ĭn ŭnŭm, Virg.

prŏpĕro, ās, *to hasten.* Cōnsōrtĕm prŏpĕrēs ēvādĕrĕ, Prop. SYN. Fēstīno, mātūro, cĕlĕro, ăccĕlĕro. V. Festino, curro.

Prŏpērtĭŭs, ĭī, m., *the Roman poet.* Lāscīvĕ Prŏpērtī, Ov. EPITH. Ŭmbĕr; blāndŭs, tĕnĕr, fācūndŭs, dŏctŭs, ĭngĕnĭōsŭs.

prŏpĕrŭs; ă, ŭm, *hasty.* Sĕquī, prŏpĕrōsquĕ jŭbĕt, Val. Fl. SYN. Prŏpĕrāns, cĕlĕr, vēlōx, cītŭs, pērnīx, ăgĭlĭs. V. Celer.

prŏpēxŭs, ă, ŭm, *combed.* Mŭlcēns prŏpēxăm, Ov.

|| Prŏphĕtă, *and* tēs, æ, m., *a prophet.* Fōrtĕ Prŏphētārŭm, Prud. SYN. Săcĕr, vātēs, Dĕī ĭntērprēs. EPITH. Prænūncĭŭs, fātĭdĭcŭs, vērĭdĭcŭs, săcĕr, jŭstŭs, præscĭŭs, præsāgŭs, prŏvĭdŭs, săgāx, ōbscūrŭs, lōngævŭs, vĕnĕrābĭlĭs. V. Prædico, is.

propīnātŏr, ōrĭs, m., *he who drinks to another.* Ĭndĕ prŏpīnātŏr, Ov.

propīno, ās, *to drink to.* Nēmŏ prŏpīnābĭt, Mart. Prŏpīnābĭs ĭn ĭstĭs, Id. SYN. Vīnŭm, crātĕră pōrrĭgo.

prŏpīnquo, ās, *to approach.* Jāmquĕ prŏpīnquābānt, Virg.

prŏpīnquŭs, ă, ŭm, *near, a relation.* Lūcĕ prŏpīnquōrŭm, Mart. SYN. Prŏpĭŏr, prŏxĭmŭs, vīcīnŭs, fīnītĭmŭs, cōntērmĭnŭs; cōnsānguĭnĕŭs, āffīnĭs. V. Vicinus.

prŏpĭo, ās, *to approach.* Nēc dŏmĭbŭs nōstrĭs prŏpĭent mălă, Prop.

prŏpĭŏr, ōrĭs, *nearer.* Jām prŏpĭŏrĭs ăquās, Pris. SYN. Vīcīnĭŏr, prŏpīnquĭŏr.

prŏpĭtĭŭs, ă, ŭm, *favourable.* Et sī prŏpĭtĭŏs, (Iamb.) Sen. Prŏpĭtĭōsquĕ dĕōs, Claud. SYN. Fāvēns, sĕcūndŭs, dēxtĕr, făcĭlĭs, mītĭs, ămīcŭs, bĕnīgnŭs, clēmēns.

prŏpĭŭs, adv., *nearer, more closely.* Prŏpĭŭs rēs ādspĭcĕ nōstrās, Virg.

Prŏpœtĭdēs, ŭm, f. pl., *the daughters of Amathon, who, for having slighted Venus, were changed into stones.* Vĕnĕrēm Prŏpœtĭdēs aŭsæ, Virg.

prŏpōlă, æ, m., *a retailer.* Fīcŭs prŏpōlă rĕcēntēs, Lucil. EPITH. Åvĭdŭs, sōlērs, caŭtŭs.

prŏpōno, pŏsŭī, pŏsĭtŭm, *to propose.* Pŭgnæ prŏpōnĭt, Virg. SYN. Expōno, ōbjĭcĭo.

Prŏpōntĭăcŭs, ă, ŭm, *of the Propontis.* Hīncquĕ Prŏpōntĭăcĭs, Ov.

Prŏpōntĭs, ĭdĭs, f., *the sea of Marmora.* Lōngæquĕ Prŏpōntĭdĭs, Ov. EPITH. Lătă, āltă, lōngă, sævă, mĭnāx, hōrrĭdă, fūrēns.

prŏpŏsĭtŭm, ī, n., *a purpose.* Prŏpŏsĭtĭquĕ tĕnāx, Ov. SYN. Cōnsĭlĭŭm, sēntēntĭă. EPITH. Fīrmŭm, prūdēns, prŏvĭdŭm. V. Consilium, sentio.

prŏpŏsĭtŭs, ă, ŭm, *the pass. partic. of* propono. Åmbŏ prŏpŏsĭtŭm pĕrăgŭnt ĭtĕr, Hor.

proprĭē, adv., *properly.* Dĭffĭcĭle ēst prŏprĭē, Hor.

proprĭŭs, ă, ŭm, *peculiar.* Prŏprĭāmquĕ dĭcăbo, Virg. Hæc prŏprĭă vīrtŭs, Corn. Sev. SYN. Sŭŭs; pērpĕtŭŭs.

proptĕr, prep., *for, on account of.* Prŏptĕr mē mōta ēst, Virg.

prŏptĕrēă, adv., *therefore.* Prŏptĕrēă, sĕd, Mart. SYN. Idĕō, ĭdcīrcō, quārē, quāprŏptĕr

prŏpūgnăcŭlŭm, ī, n., *a bulwark.* Prŏpūgnăcŭlă bĕllō, Virg. SYN. Præsĭdĭŭm, mūnīmĕn, mūnīmēntŭm, vāllŭm, ăggĕr, mūrī, tūrrēs, fŏssœ, ārx. EPITH. Vălĭdŭm, lōngŭm, tūrrĭgĕrŭm, sēcūrŭm, tūtŭm, fŏrtĕ, mūnītŭm, ĭnēxpūgnăbĭlĕ. V. Munimen.

prŏpūgno, ās, *to defend.* Prŏpūgnăt nūgīs, Hor. SYN. Tŭĕŏr, tūtŏr, dēfēndo. V. Munio.

prŏpūlso, ās, *the freq. of* propello. Prŏpūlsābĭmŭs hŏstĕm, Lucr.

prŏră, æ, f., *the prow of a ship.* Ēt prŏrās ăd lĭttŏră tōrquēnt, Virg. EPITH. Ærĕă, fērrātă, cūrvă, ădūncă, ăcūtă, rĕcūrvă, cūrvātă, vălĭdă, ærātă. V. Navis.

prŏrēpo, psī, *to creep out.* Cŭm prŏrēpsērūnt, Hor. V. Repo.

prŏrētă, æ, *or* prŏreūs, ĕī, m., *a steersman.* Cȳmbæ prŏrētă fŭīstī. Pŏnĕ mĕtūm, prŏreūs, ēt, Ŏv.

prŏrĭpĭo, ŭī, *to take away by force.* Prŏrĭpĭs, ĭnquĭt, Virg. SYN. Ērĭpĭo. V. Rapio.

prŏrīto, ās, *to excite, provoke.* Prŏrītēt pōcŭlă Zȳthī, Colum.

prŏrŏgo, ās, *to defer.* Prŏrŏgăt ævŭm, Hor. SYN. Prōdūco, prŏtrăho, dĭffĕro.

prŏrsŭm, *and* sŭs, adv., *directly, quite.* Prŏrsŭs hăbĕrĕ, Ov. SYN. Ōmnīnō, plānĕ.

prŏrūmpo, rūpī, *to break forth.* Dēnsōs prŏrūmpĭt ĭn hŏstēs, Virg. SYN. Rūmpo, ĭrrŭmpo.

prŏrŭo, ĭs, rŭtŭm, *to throw or fall down.* Mōlēm prŏrŭĕre, Lucan.

prŏrūptŭs, ă, ŭm, *the pass. partic. of* prorumpo. Prŏrūptŭs cŏrpŏrĕ sŭdŏr, Virg.

prŏrŭtŭs, ă, ŭm, *the pass. partic. of* proruo. Dīscūssīs prŏrŭtă mūrīs, Luc.

* prŏsă, æ, f., *prose.* Quint.

prŏsătŭs, ă, ŭm, *the pass. partic. of* prosero, *born, descended.* Stīrpe ēt lărĕ prŏsătă Rhēnŭm, Aus.

prŏscēnĭŭm, ĭī, n., *the front of the stage.* Quāntōs prŏscēnĭă plausŭs, Claud.

prŏscīndo, cĭdī, cīssŭm, *to cleave.* Fērrō prŏscīndĕrĕ quērcŭm, Lucan. V. Scindo.

prŏscrībo, scrīpsī, ptŭm, *to banish.* Prŏscrīptī rĕgĭs, Hor. SYN. Vēnālĕ prŏpōno ; dāmno ēxĭlĭō, mōrti āddīco, dēvŏvĕo, dēstĭno.

prŏsĕco, ās, ŭī, *to cut, to lash.* Vĕtŭri ēxtă prŏsĕcārĭĕr, Pl.

prŏsēctŭs, ă, ŭm, *the pass. partic. of* proseco. Prŏsēctăquĕ pāssĭm Pēctŏră, V. Fl.—2. -tă, ōrŭm, n. pl., (sub. ēxtă,) *a portion of the entrails burnt in honour of the Gods.* Impŏsŭī prŏsēctă călēntĭbŭs ārīs, Ov.

prŏsĕquŏr, ĕrĭs, sĕcūtŭs, *to pursue.* Prŏsĕquĭtūr sūrgēns, Virg. SYN. Insĕquŏr, sĕquŏr.

prŏsĕro, ĭs, ēvī, ătŭm, *to sow, produce.* Nŏn prŏsērĭt ŭllăm, Luc.

prŏsĕro, ĭs, ĕrŭī, ērtŭm, *to put out, project.* Prŏsērĭt ĭn Cēltās, Sil.

Prŏsērpĭnă, æ, f., *the daughter of Ceres, and consort of Pluto.* Cūrēt Prŏsērpĭnă mātrĕm, Virg. SYN. Pērsĕphŏnĕ, Hĕcătĕ. EPITH. Infērnă, sævă, prŏfūndă, ĭnfĕră, ūmbrōsă, nĭgră, ĭnvĭdă, sĕvĕră, ăcērbă, dūră, fĕră, tŏrvă, dīră, trĭfŏrmĭs, ĭnēxōrābĭlĭs, ĭmmītĭs ; Sĭcŭlă, Trīnacrĭă, Ætnĕă ; Stȳgĭă, Lēthœă, Tārtărĕă. V. Hecate.

|| prŏseūchă, æ, f., *a place where beggars stood to ask alms.* Quærŏ prŏseūchă, Juv.

prŏsĭlĭo, ŭī *or* ĭī, *to leap out.* Prŏsĭlŭĕrĕ sŭīs, Virg. SYN. Sălĭo, ēxĭlĭo.

prŏsŏcĕr, ĕrī, m., *a wife's father's father.* Prŏsŏcĕr ēssĕ, Ov.

prŏspēcto, ās, *to descry afar off.* Ēt prŏspēctăt ĕūntĕm, Virg.

prŏspēctŭs, ūs, m., *a distant view.* Pāscăt prŏspēctŭs ĭnănĕm, Virg.

prŏspĕr, ĕră, ĕrŭm, *lucky, happy.* Prŏspĕră dīxĭt, Virg. SYN. Fēlīx, fŏrtūnātŭs, faustŭs, sĕcūndŭs. V. Felix.

prŏspĕrĭtās, ātĭs, f., *success.* Prŏspĕrĭtātĕ jŭvăt, Pr. SYN. Fēlīcĭtās ; sōrs prŏspĕră ; fŏrtūnă sĕcūndă, făvēns, ămīcă, rīdēns ; rēs sĕcūndæ, prŏspĕræ. EPITH. Ŏptātă, sĕcūndă, blāndă, sĕcūră, jūcūndă, grātă, bĕātă, plăcĭdă, ămīcă, sēgnĭs, ĭnērs, ōtĭōsă, pĭgră, dēsĭdĭōsă, flūxă, cădūcă, fŭgāx, fŭgĭtīvă, lūbrĭcă, fāllāx, ĭncōnstāns, pĕrĭtūră, ĭnstăbĭlĭs.

prŏspĭcĭo, spēxī, spēctŭm, *to see afar off, to foresee.* Prŏspĭcĭs āntĕ thrŏnŭm, Mart. Syn. Ăspĭcĭo, prævĭdĕo.

prŏspĭcŭŭs, ă, ŭm, *seen from afar.* Prŏspĭcŭæ scāndēntēm līmĭnā tūrrĭs, Stat.

prŏstērno, strāvī, strātŭm, *to throw down.* Et prŏstērnĭt hŭmī, Ov. Syn. Hŭmī stērno, āfflīgo, ābjĭcĭo, dēprĭmo, ēvērto, dīrŭo, dējĭcĭo, prŏtēro.

prŏstĭbŭlŭm, ī, n., *a prostitute.* Lŭpă prŏstĭbŭlŭmquĕ, Lucil. V. Lupanar.

prŏstĭtŭo, ĭs, *to prostitute.* Prŏstĭtŭīssĕ sŭăm, Ov.

prŏsto, ās, stĭtī, *to jut out, to be exposed for sale.* Prŏstĭtĭt īllă, Ov.

prŏstrātŭs, ă, ŭm, *overthrown, prostrated.* Pāssīs prŏstrātā căpīllīs, Ov.

prŏsŭbĭgo, ēgī, āctŭm, *to beat down.* Et pĕdĕ prŏsŭbĭgĭt, Virg.

prŏsŭm, prŏdĕs, prŏfŭī, *to be useful to.* Sānāvĭt, prŏsŭnt, Ser. Syn. Jŭvo, ūtĭlĭs sŭm.

prŏsŭs, ă, ŭm, *in prose, prosaic.* Prŏsīs sōlvĕrĭt ōră mŏdīs, Aus.

prŏtēctŭs, ă, ŭm, *the pass. partic. of* protego. Pārmā prŏtēctŭs, Virg.

prŏtēgo, tēxī, tēctŭm, *to cover over, to protect.* Prŏtĕgĭt īllĕ, Ov. Syn. Tĕgo, cōntĕgo; tŭĕŏr, tŭtŏr, dēfēndo.

prŏtēlŭm, ī, n., *a continual effort.* Et quăsī prŏtēlō, Lucr.

prŏtēndo, tēndī, tēntŭm, *to stretch forth.* Prŏtēndūnt lōngē, Virg. Syn. Prŏdūco, prŏfĕro, prŏtrăho, ēxtēndo, pŏrrĭgo.

Prŏtēnŏr, ŏrĭs, m., *the name of a warrior.* Prŏtēnŏră pērcŭtĭt Hÿpseūs, Ov.

prŏtēntŭs, ă, ŭm, *the pass. partic. of* protendo. Tēmō prŏtēntŭs īn ōctō, Virg.

prŏtĕnŭs, adv., *far off.* Prŏtĕnŭs æyĕr, Virg.

prŏtĕro, trīvī, trītŭm, *to trample upon.* Prŏtĕrĭs ūmbrăm! Ov. Syn. Prŏcūlco, cālco, tĕro; călcĕ tĕro. V. Concutio.

prŏtērrĕo, rŭī, *to frighten.* Prŏtērrēbăt ăgēns, Virg. V. Terreo.

prŏtērvē, adv., *frowardly.* Mūltă prŏtērvē, Ov.

prŏtērvĭă, æ, *and* ĭtăs, ātĭs, f., *frowardness, wantonness.* Lătă prŏtērvĭă Pānăs, Aus. Grătă prŏtērvĭtăs, (Glyc.) Hor. Syn. Pĕtŭlāntĭă, prŏcācĭtās, aūdācĭă, lāscīvĭă.

prŏtērvŭs, ă, ŭm, *boisterous, wanton.* Istĕ prŏtērvŭs, Prop. Syn. Pĕtŭlāns, prŏcăx, īmpŭdēns, tĕmĕrārĭŭs, aūdāx, lāscīvŭs, sălāx.

Prŏtēsĭlāŭs, ī, m., *the son of Iphiclus, slain by Hector.* Āmplēxū, Prŏtēsĭlāĕ, tŭō, Ov.

Prŏteūs, ĕī *or* cī, *or* ŏs; *acc.* ĕă; m., *a god of the sea, who had the power of transforming himself into all kinds of forms.* Hæc Prŏteūs, ēt sē, Virg. Prŏtĕă nōdō? Hor. Syn. Vērtūmnŭs. Epith. Cærŭlĕŭs, sūrdŭs, æquŏrĕŭs, mărīnŭs, āmbĭgŭŭs, mūtābĭlĭs, īncōnstāns, īnstābĭlĭs, ŏdīōsŭs, cāllĭdŭs, văfĕr.

prŏtĭnŭs, adv., *instantly.* Prŏtĭnŭs hīnc, Virg. Syn. Cōntĭnŭō; cōnfēstĭm, īllĭco, sŭbĭtō, stătĭm.

prŏtŏno, ās, ŭī, *to thunder loudly.* Prŏtŏnăt īrā, V. Fl.

prŏtŏllo, ĭs, *to prolong, put off.* Prŏtŏllĕrĕ fīnēs, Lucr.

prŏtŏtŏmŭs, ă, ŭm, *first cut.* Prŏtŏtŏmīquĕ rŭdēs, Mart.

prŏtrăho, āxī, āctŭm, *to drag forth.* Prŏtrăhĭtūr, nĕquĕūnt, Virg. Syn. Ēxtrăho; prŏfĕro, prŏtēndo, ēxtēndo, pŏrrĭgo.

prŏtrūdo, sī, sŭm, *to thrust forward.* Ŏnĕrīs prŏtrūdĕrĕ nōstrī, Lucr. Syn. Trūdo.

prŏtūbĕro, ās, *to be protuberant.* Nĕ quĭd prŏtūbĕrĕt āngŭlŭs æquīs, Stat.

prŏtūrbo, ās, *to disturb, expel.* Prŏtūrbāntque ēmĭnŭs, Virg.

prŏvēctŭs, ă, ŭm, *the pass. partic. of* proveho. Cŭm prŏvēctŭs ĕquō, Virg.

prŏvĕho, ēxī, ēctŭm, *to carry on.* Prŏvĕhăt ēt fēlīx, Nem. Syn. Vĕho, īnvĕho; prŏmŏvĕo.

prŏvĕnĭo, vēnī, vēntŭm, *to come forth.* Lānăquĕ prŏvĕnĭăt, Ov. Syn. Ēvĕnĭo, vĕnĭo.

prŏvēntŭs, ūs, m., *an income, abundance.* Vărĭīs prŏvēntĭbŭs ānnōs, Prop. Syn. Rēdĭtŭs; cōpĭă.

prŏvērbĭŭm, ĭī, n., *a proverb.* Tĕ prŏvērbĭā tāngūnt, Ov. Syn. Ădăgĭŭm. Epith. Vĕtŭs, cōmmŭnĕ, vŭlgārĕ, brĕvĕ, vērŭm, cērtŭm, āntĭquŭm.

prŏvĭdēntĭă, æ, f., *prudence, foresight, providence.* Quōndăm prŏvĭdēntĭă Dĕī, (Iamb.) Paulin. Syn. Prūdēntĭă, săpĭēntĭă, cūră.

prŏvĭdĕo, vĭdī, vīsŭm, *to foresee, prepare.* Prŏvīdīssĕt ĕŭm, Hor. Syn. Prŏspĭcĭo, căvĕo.

prŏvĭdŭs, ă, ŭm, *provident.*   Prŏvĭdŭs ūrbēs, Hor.   Syn. Prūdēns, săpĭēns, prŏspĭcĭēns, cаūtŭs.

prŏvīncĭă, æ, f., *a province.*   Pŏpŭlō prŏvīncĭă nŏstrō, Ov.   Syn. Rĕgĭo; mūnŭs.

prŏvīsŏr, ōrĭs, m., *a purveyor.*   Tārdŭs prŏvīsŏr, Hor.   Syn. Cōnsŭltŏr.

prŏvīsŭs, ŭ, ŭm, *the pass. partic. of* provideo.   Ĕt prŏvīsæ frŭgĭs ĭn ānnŭm, Hor.

prŏvŏco, ās, *to incite.*   Prŏvŏcăt hōră, Lucan.

prŏvŏlo, ās, *to fly on.*   Prŏvŏlăt ĭn mĕdĭŏs, Ov.   V. Volo, ruo.

prŏvŏlvo, ĭs, ŏlŭtŭm, *to roll along.*   Prŏvŏlvēns tērræ, Virg.

prŏvŏmo, ĭs, *to vomit forth,*   Vĭm prŏvŏmĭt ātquĕ prŏcēllæ, Lucr.

prout, *and* prŏŭt, conj., *as.*   Dăpĭbŭs, proŭt cuīquĕ lĭbĭdo ēst, Hor.   Vēllēm, proŭt ĭpsŏ rŏgābās, Ov.   Syn. Ŭt, sīcŭt.

|| prŏxĕnētă, æ, m., *a broker, a proxy.*   Prŏxĕnētă frāctōrŭm, (Scaz.) Mart.   Syn. Ĭnstĭtŏr.

prŏxĭmĭtās, ātĭs, f., *proximity.*   Prŏxĭmĭtătĕ bŏnī, Ov.   Syn. Vīcīnĭă.

prŏxĭmŭs, ă, ŭm, *the nearest.*   Prŏxĭmŭs huĭc.   Syn. Vīcīnŭs, fīnĭtĭmŭs, prŏpīnquŭs, prŏpĭŏr.

prūdēns, ntĭs, *prudent.*   Dēfĭcĭŏr prūdēns, Ov.   Syn. Prŏvĭdŭs, săpĭēns, cаūtŭs, sŏlērs, cāllĭdŭs, săgāx, cīrcŭmspēctŭs, prŏspĭcĭēns, ĭndūstrĭŭs, pĕrītŭs.   V. Adolescens, sapiens.

prūdēntĭă, æ, f., *prudence.*   Fātŏ prūdēntĭă mājŏr, Virg.   Syn. Săpĭēntĭă, sŏlērtĭă, săgācĭtās, cōnsĭlĭŭm, pĕrītĭă, āstūtĭă, cāllĭdĭtās.   Epith. Vĭgĭl, vĭgĭlāns, sŏnĭlĭs, præscĭă, cаūtă, săgāx, sŏlērs, cāllĭdă, dīvīnă.

prūīnă, æ, f., *a hoar-frost.*   Vĭdŭătă prūīnĭs, Virg.   Syn. Gĕlū, glăcĭēs.   V. Gelu.

prūīnōsŭs, ă, ŭm, *frosty.*   Lōngă prūīnōsă, Ov.   Syn. Gĕlĭdŭs, glăcĭālĭs, hўbērnŭs.

prūnă, æ, f., *a burning coal.*   Sŭbjĭcĭŭnt vĕrŭbŭs prūnās, Virg.   Syn. Cārbo.   Epith. Ardēns, āccēnsă, rŭbēns, tōrrēns, călēns.   V. Ignis.

prūnŭm, ĭ, n., *a plum.*   Prūnă fĕrēntēs, Virg.   Syn. Dūlcĕ, cĕrĕŭm, cānŭm, Dămāscēnŭm.

prūnŭs, ī, f., *a plum-tree.*   Ĕt prūnīs lăpĭdōsă, Virg.   Epith. Vĭrēns, vĭrĭdĭs, rāmōsă, frŏndēns.   V. Arbor.

prūrīgo, ĭnĭs, f., *an itching.*   Mŏrōsă prūrīgĭnĕ vĕrmĭnăt, Mart.   Syn. Prūrītŭs.   Epith. Impătĭēns, ĭmpōrtūnă, mŏlēstă, ūrēns, mŏrdāx, ŏbscœnă.   V. Desiderium, libido.

prūrĭo, ĭs, īvī *and* ĭī, *to itch.*   Incĭpĭăt prūrīrĕ chŏrō, Juv.

Prўtănĭs, ĭs, m., *the name of a warrior.*   Nŏēmŏnăquĕ Prўtănīnquĕ, Ov.

psăllo, psāllī, *to sing and play upon an instrument.*   Psāllĭmŭs, ĕt, Hor.   Syn. Căno; hўmnōs cōncĭno; fĭdĭbŭs căno.

Psămăthē, ēs, f., *the daughter of Crotopus, loved by Apollo.*   Ŭtquĕ pătrēm Psămăthēs, Ov.

Psĕcăs, ădĭs, f., *the name of a waiting-maid.*   Ĕt Psĕcăs ēt Phĭălē, Ov.

psĭlōthrŭm, ĭ, n., *white vine.*   Psĭlōthrō făcĭĕm, Mart.

psŷthĭă, *or* psŷthĭă, æ, f., *a sort of vine.*   Ĕt pāssō psŷthĭа ūtĭlĭŏr, Virg.

psīttăcŭs, ĭ, m., *a parrot.*   Psīttăcŭs ā vōbīs, Mart.   Epith. Lŏquāx, gārrŭlŭs, cănōrŭs, vōcālĭs, pĕrēgrīnŭs, Eōŭs, Indĭcŭs, vērsĭcŏlŏr, vĭrĭdĭs, pīctŭs.

Psŏphăĭcŭs, ă, ŭm, *of Psophis.*   Cūm Psŏphăĭcō Ĕrўmānthō, Ov.

Psŏphĭs, ĭdĭs, f., *a city of Arcadia.*   Psŏphĭdăquĕ Cўllēnŭmquĕ, Ov.

Ptĕrĕlās, æ, m., *a king of the Taphians.*   Quăm tĭbĭ vēl, Ptĕrĕlă, Ov.

ptĭsănă, æ, f., *and* nărĭŭm, ĭĭ, n., *barley.*   Ptĭsănāmquĕ făbāmquĕ, Mart.   Hŏc ptĭsănārĭum ŏrўzæ, Hor.

Ptŏlĕmæŭs, ī, m., *a captain-general in Alexander's army, and king of Egypt.*   Cūm Ptŏlĕmæōrŭm, Lucan.   Epith. Nīlĭăcŭs, Phărĭŭs, Pēllæŭs.

pūbĕo, ēs, *and* ēsco, ĭs, *to bloom, to begin to have a beard, to grow.*   Pūbēntēs hērbæ, Virg.   Lārgō pūbēscĭt, Id.   Syn. Crēsco, jŭvĕnēsco.

pūbĕr, *and* bĭs, ĕrĭs, *ripe of age.*   Pūbĕrĭs ævī, Nem.   Syn. Pūbēns, ădūltŭs; flōrēns.

pūbērtās, ātĭs, f., *ripeness, puberty.*   Pūbērtătĕ vălēnt, Mart.   V. Juventus.

pūbēs, ĭs, f., *first beard, youth.*   Cĕrĕrēm pūbēs ăgrēstĭs, Virg.   Syn. Lānūgo, flōs ætātĭs; jŭvēntūs.   V. Juventus.

Pŭblĭcĭŭs, ĭī, m., *the name of two brothers who were ædiles at Rome.*   Lĭcēntĭă tālĭs Pŭblĭcĭōs, Ov.

Pūblĭcŏlă. V. Poplicola.

pūblĭcŭs, ă, ŭm, *public*. Pūblĭcŭs ūsŭs Hor. Syn. Cōmmūnĭs, vŭlgārĭs.

Pūblĭŭs, ĭi, m., *a Roman prænomen*. Quīntĕ, pŭtă, aūt Pūblĭ, Hor.

pŭdēndŭs, ă, ŭm, *shameful*. Ēvāndrĕ, pŭdēndĭs, Virg. Syn. Tūrpĭs, probrōsŭs, ĭnfāmĭs.

pŭdēns, ēntĭs, *modest, reserved*. Vūltŭs sĭnĕ rūstĭcĭtātĕ pŭdēntēs, Ov.

pŭdēntĕr, adv., *bashfully*. Sūmāsnĕ pŭdēntĕr, Hor.

pŭdĕo, ēs, ērĕ, ŭī, *to cause shame, make ashamed*. Quēm sævă pŭdēbūnt, Luc.—2. *to be ashamed*. Ĭtă nūnc pŭdĕo, Pl.

‖ pŭdēsco, ĭs, *to begin to be ashamed*. Fērrĕ pŭdēscĭt, Prud. V. Pudet.

pŭdĕt, dŭĭt, *to be ashamed*. Āh! pŭdĕt īngrātæ, Mart. Syn. Vĕrēcūndŏr, ērŭ-bēsco. V. Pudor.

pŭdĭbūndŭs, ă, ŭm, *bashful*. Paūlūm pŭdĭbūndă prŏtērvīs, Hor. Syn. Vĕrē-cūndŭs, pŭdēns, pŭdīcŭs, mŏdēstŭs.

pŭdīcē, adv., *bashfully*. Āctūmquĕ pŭdīcē, Ov.

pŭdīcĭtĭă, æ, f., *chastity*. Læsă pŭdīcĭtĭa ēst, Ov. Syn. Cāstĭtās, vīrgĭnĭtās, īntegrĭtās, pūrĭtās, pŭdŏr. V. Castitas.

pŭdīcŭs, ă, ŭm, *chaste*. Vĕlĭt pŭdīcĭŏrĕm, (Phal.) Mart. Syn. Cāstŭs, pūrŭs, īntĕgĕr, pŭdēns, vĕrēcūndŭs, hŏnēstŭs.

pŭdŏr, ōrĭs, m., *chastity*. Plūs īllĕ pŭdōrĭs, Mart. Syn. Vĕrēcūndĭă, rŭbŏr ; mŏdēstĭă, pŭdīcĭtĭă. Epith. Tĭmĭdŭs, sŭbĭtŭs, rĕpēntīnŭs, rŏsĕŭs, mŏdēstŭs, hŏnēstŭs, vĕrēcūndŭs, cāstŭs, vīrgĭnĕŭs, tācĭtŭs, tĕnĕr, sōllĭcĭtŭs, trīstŭs, ægĕr, cōnscĭŭs, pāllĭdŭs ; īmpōllūtŭs, rŭbēscēns, nĭvĕŭs, pūlchĕr, īnnŏcŭŭs. V. Eru-besco.

pŭĕllă, æ, f., *a young girl*. Quēm sī pŭĕllārūm, (Alcaic.) Syn. Vīrgo. Epith. Fōrmōsă, tĕnĕră, vĕnūstă, cāndĭdă, nĭvĕă, cūltă, vĕrēcūndă, ĭngĕnŭă, īntāctă, cāstă, pŭdĭcă, hŏnēstă, crēdŭlă, tĭmĭdă, īmbēllĭs, cōmptă, īnnūbă, nūbĭlĭs.

pŭĕllārĭs, ĕ, *of a young girl*. Prædă pŭĕllārēs ănĭmōs, Ov. Syn. Vīrgĭnĕŭs.

pŭĕllŭlă, æ, f., *the dimin. of* puella. Sŏcĭī pŭĕllŭlārūm, Catul.

pŭĕllŭs, *and* ĕrŭlŭs, ī, m., *a little boy*. Cic. Lucr.

pŭĕr, ĕrī, m., *a boy*. Dīffĕrāt īn pŭĕrōs, Prop. Syn. Jŭvĕnĭs, īmpūbēs. Epith. Tĕnĕr, blāndŭs, īmbēllĭs, fōrmōsŭs, cāndĭdŭs, vĕnūstŭs, cōmptŭs, īngĕnŭŭs, vĕrēcūndŭs, īntōnsŭs, mōllĭs, lĕvĭs, rŭdĭs, dĕcōrŭs, prŏtērvŭs, īmbērbĭs, caūtŭs, lāscīvŭs. V. Infans, adolescens.

pŭĕrāsco, ĭs, *to become boyish*. Făcĭēs pŭĕrāscĕrĕ sēnsŭs, Aus.

pŭĕrīlĭs, ĕ, *of a boy*. Pŭĕrīlĭă tōrsĭt, Virg.

pŭĕrīlĭtĕr, adv., *childishly*. Tĕnĕrō pŭĕrīlĭtĕr ūnguī, Prop.

pŭĕrĭtĭă, *and* ērtĭă, æ, *and* ĭtĭēs, ēī, f., *childhood*. Rēgĕ pŭĕrtĭæ, Hor. Crēdĭtă pŭĕrĭtĭēs, Aus. Epith. Infīrmă, mōllĭs, tĕnĕră, īmbēllĭs, rŭdĭs, dēbĭlĭs, gārrŭlă, vĕnūstă.

puērpĕră, æ, f., *a woman lately delivered*. Prōlĕ pŭĕrpĕræ, (Asclep.) Hor.

pŭĕrpĕrĭŭm, ĭi, n., *a woman's delivery*. Crūdă pŭĕrpĕria, Stat. Syn. Pārtŭs. V. Pario.

pūgĭl, ĭlĭs, m., *a boxer, an athlete*. Aūt ūrsum aūt pŭgĭlēs, Hor. Syn. Lŭctātŏr, āthlētă, glădĭātŏr.

pūgĭllārēs, ĭn. pl., *and* rĭă, ĭum, n. pl., *a pair of writing tablets*. Rēddĭtūrām pūgĭllārĭă, (Phal.) Cat.

pūgĭo, ōnĭs, m., *a poniard*. Pŭgĭŏ quēm cūrvĭs, Mart. Syn. Sīcă, glădĭŭs, ēnsĭs.

pūgnă, æ, f., *a combat*. Æquēmŭs pūgnās, Virg. Syn. Cērtāmĕn, prælĭŭm ; cōnflīctŭs. Epith. Āncĕps, īnīquă, ācrĭs, fĕrōx, āspĕră, dūră, sævă, cæcă, crŭēntă, atrōx, sānguĭnĕă, flagrāns, crūdēlĭs. V. Pugno.

pūgnātŏr, ōrĭs, m., *a combatant*. Pūgnātōri ŏpĕrĭt, Virg. Syn. Pūgnāns, mīlĕs, bēllātŏr.

pŭgnāx, ācĭs, *fond of fighting*. Cēnsŭs pūgnācĭs ĕt Ancī, Juv. Syn. Bēllātŏr, bēllĭcōsŭs, fōrtĭs.

pūgno, ās, *to fight*. Fŏrī pūgnāmŭs ărēnă, Juv. Syn. Cērto, dēcērto, cōnflīgo, cōngrĕdĭŏr, prælĭŏr, dīmĭco. V. Luctor.

pūgnŭs, ī, m., *the fist*. Gūttŭră pūgnō, Ov.

pūlchĕr, chră, chrŭm, *handsome*. Pūlchĕr Āvēntīnŭs, Virg. Syn. Fōrmōsŭs, vĕnūstŭs, dĕcōrŭs, spĕcĭōsŭs. V. Forma.

pūlchrē, adv., *well, gallantly*. Ēst pūlchrē tĭbi, Cat.

• pŭlchrĭtūdo, ĭnĭs, f., *beauty.* Cic. Syn. Fŏrmă, vĕnŭstās, dĕcŏr, spĕcĭēs.

pūleĭŭm, *or* ējŭm, ī, n., *a plant, pennyroyal.* Cŏrōnă pūlējī, Mart.

pūlĕx, ĭcĭs, m., *a flea.* Pārvŭlŭs aūt pūlĕx, Col. Epith. Pārvŭlŭs, īnfēstŭs, mŏlēstŭs, lĕvĭs, mōrdāx, mōrdēns, pūngēns.

pŭllārĭŭs, ă. ŭm, *pertaining to young ones.* Nŭpĕr pŭllārĭă dīctŭs, Aus.

pŭllātŭs, ă, ŭm, *clothed in black.* Pŭllātī prŏcērēs, Juv. Syn. Ātrātŭs.

pŭllŭlo, ās, *to spring, to increase.* Pŭllŭlăt ātrā, Virg. Syn. Gērmĭno, frŭtĭco, sŭccrēsco.

pŭllŭs, ă, ŭm, *black.* Pŭllī cērvīcĕ căpĭllī, Ov. V. Niger.

pŭllŭs, ī, m., *a chicken, the young of any animal.* Implŭmĭbŭs pŭllīs ăvĭs, (Iamb.) Hor. Epith. Tĕnĕr, īmplūmĭs, ēxĭgŭŭs, mōllĭs, ēxīlĭs, tĕnēllŭs, lŏquāx, gārrŭlŭs, trĕpĭdŭs, fŭgāx.

pŭlmēntārĭă, ōrŭm, n. pl., *chopped meat.* Tūnc pŭlmēntārĭă lābrīs, Pers.

pŭlmēntŭm, ī, n., *pottage.* Mĭnūăs pŭlmēntă nĕcēsse ēst, Hor. V. Cibus.

pŭlmo, ōnĭs, m., *the lungs.* Rīsū pŭlmōnem ăgĭtārĕ, Juv. Epith. Mōllĭs, tŭmĭdŭs, tŭmēscēns, īnflātŭs, tŭmēns, īrrĕquĭētŭs, spīrāns, sīccŭs, ārĭdŭs, ārēns.

pūlpă, æ, f., *the pulp, fleshy part.* Ēt pŭlpām dŭbĭŏ, Mart.

pŭlpĭtŭm, ī, n., *a pulpit or desk to recite in.* Pŭlpĭtă sŏlēmnēs, Prop.

pŭls, pŭltĭs, f., *a kind of pottage.* Pŭltĭbŭs ōllæ, Juv. Epith. Cāndĭdă, lāctĕă, dēnsă, tĕpĭdă, călēns, rĕcēns.

pŭlsātŏr, ōrĭs, m., *he who strikes.* Cĭthāræ pŭlsātŏr Ăpōllo, V. Fl.

pŭlso, ās, *the freq. of* pello. Ōstĭă pŭlsăt, Hor. Syn. Pēllo, īmpēllo, prŏpŭlso. V. Pello, quatio.

pŭlsŭs, ă, ŭm, *the pass. partic. of* pello. Rēgnō pŭlsŭs fŭĭt, Hor.

pŭlsŭs, ūs, m., *a striking.* Pŭlsūquĕ pĕdŭm, Virg. Syn. Impŭlsŭs, Impĕtŭs, īctŭs.

pŭlvĕrĕŭs, *and* rŭlēntŭs, ă, ŭm, *dusty.* Pŭlvĕrēăm nūbĕm, Virg. Pŭlvĕrŭlēntă fŭgā, Virg.

pŭlvīllŭs, *and* īnŭs, ī, m., *and* īnăr, ārĭs, n., *a pillow, a cushion.* Intĕr sērĭcōs jăcērĕ pŭlvīllōs, Hor. Ēt dē pŭlvīnō sūrgăt, Juv. Ad pŭlvīnăr ŏdōrĕm, Id. Syn. Cērvīcăl, cūlcitră, cŭbĭtăl, fūlcrŭm. Epith. Mōllĕ, tĕnĕrŭm, plūmĕŭm, pūrpŭrĕŭm, aūrātŭm, sŭpērbŭm, sŭppŏsĭtŭm, tŭmēns, tŭmēscēns, tūrgēscēns.

pŭlvĭs, ĕrĭs, m., *dust.* Pŭlvĕrĭs ēxĭgŭī jāctū, Virg. Syn. Sīccŭs, ārĭdŭs, lĕvĭs, tĕnŭĭs, vŏlĭtāns, crāssŭs, ōbscūrŭs, ŏpācŭs, glŏmĕrātŭs, nĭgĕr, cæcŭs, ātĕr, sōrdĭdŭs, putrĭs, īmmūndŭs, tūrpĭs, lŭtĕŭs, æstīvŭs, bĭbŭlŭs, sĭtĭēns; nōbĭlĭs, Ōlўmpĭcŭs.

pūmĕx, ĭcĭs, m., *a pumice-stone.* In pūmĭcĕ pāstŏr, Virg. Epith. Lātĕbrōsŭs, căvŭs, mŭltĭcăvŭs, ēxēsŭs, frăgĭlĭs, ārĭdŭs, sīccŭs, cāndĭdŭs, āspĕr, scăbĕr, mūscōsŭs.

pūmĭcātŭs, ă, ŭm, *the pass. partic. of* pumico. Ēt pūmĭcātă paūpĕrēs, (Scaz.) Mart.

pūmĭcĕŭs, ă, ŭm, *of the pumice-stone.* Ēt quæ pūmĭcĕĭs, Mart. Syn. Ex pūmĭcĕ; ārĭdŭs, sīccŭs.

pūmĭco, ās, *to polish with a pumice-stone.* Pūmĭcĕt ēt cānās, Tib.

pūmĭlĭo, ĭōnĭs; lĭŭs, lī; lo, ōnĭs; *and* pŭmĭllŭs, ī, m., *a dwarf.* Pūmīllĭōnĭs ĕrăt, Mart. Ōrdŏ pūmĭlōnŭm, Stat. Mĭrāntŭr pūmĭlōs, Id.

pŭnctŭm, ī, n., *a point.* Tēmpŏrĭs īn pŭnctŏ, Lucr.

pūngo, pūnxī *or* pŭpŭgī, *to prick.* Quōs nūnquăm pūngŭnt, Prop. Syn. Cōmpūngo, stĭmŭlo, lāncĭno, fŏdĭco.

pūnĭcĕŭs, *and* cŭs, ă, ŭm, *red.* Pūnĭcĕŭs dē mŏlĕ, Ov. Pūnĭcă rōstră crŏcō, Id. Syn. Rŭbĕŭs, rŭbĕr, rŭbĭcŭndŭs.

Pūnĭcŭs, ă, ŭm, *Carthaginian.* Pūnĭcă rēgnă vĭdēs, Virg.

pūnĭo, īs, ītŭm, *to punish.* Pūnĭŏr ĭpsā, Ov. Syn. Cāstīgo, mŭlcto, plēcto, ănĭmādvērto īn. V. Ulciscor.

pūpă, æ, f., *a little girl.* Pūpăm sē dīcĭt, Mart.

pūpīlla *and* pŭlă, æ, f., *the ball of the eye.* Pērtērgĕt pūpīllās, Lucr. V. Oculus.

pūpīllŭs, ī, m., *and* lă, æ, f., *an orphan under ward.* Pūpīllīs quŏs, Hor.

Pūpĭŭs, *or* Pŭppĭŭs, ĭī, m., *the name of a poet.* Lăcrўmōsă pŏēmătă Pūpī, Hor.

pŭppĭs, ĭs, f., *the stern of a ship.* Pŏrtŭs pŭppĭbŭs āptŏs, Ov. V. Navis.

pŭpŭs, *and* ŭlŭs, ī, m., *a young boy.* Dēprēndī mŏdŏ pŭpŭlŭm, (Phal.) Cat.

pūrē, *and* pūrĭtĕr, adv., *purely, clearly.* Āppārēt tĭbĭ pūrē, Hor. Pūrĭtĕr ēgī, Cat.

pūrgāmĕn, ĭnĭs, *and* mēntŭm, ī, n., *a cleansing; expiation.* Æmŏnĭœ pūrgāmĭnă cædĭs, Ov. V. Piamen.

pūrgo, ās, *to clean.* Pūrgāmŭs ăgrēstĕs, Tib. Syn. Expūrgo, mūndo, ēmūndo, ēlŭo, āblŭo, ābstērgo, pĭo, ēxpĭo; ēxcūso, cūlpa ēxĭmo. V. Abluo, lavo.

pūrpŭră, æ, f., *purple, scarlet.* Pūrpŭră Mæāndrō, Virg. Syn. Mūrēx, ōstrŭm; cŏccŭs. Epith. Ārdēns, fūlgēns, rŭtĭlă, ĭgnĕă, rŭtĭlāns, pŭnĭcĕă, pĭctă, rŭbēns, cŏrūscă, fŭlgĭdă, splēndēns, mĭcāns, sānguĭnĕă, māgnĭfĭcă, sŭpērbă, rēgĭă, rēgālĭs, nŏbĭlĭs, trĭŭmphālĭs, īnsĭgnĭs; Tӯrĭă, Sārrānă, Sīdonĭă, Phœnĭcĕă; Āssӯrĭă, Œbālĭă, Spārtānă, Mēlĭbœă, Pœnă, Cŏă.

pūrpŭrĕŭs, ă, ŭm, *of purple.* Pūrpŭrĕŭm pēnnĭs, Virg. Syn. Pūrpŭrātŭs, cŏccĭnĕŭs, cŏnchӯlĭātŭs; rŭbĕr, rŭbĕŭs, rŭbēns, rŭbĭcūndŭs, pŭnĭcĕŭs, rŏsĕŭs. V. Purpura.

pūrŭs, ă, ŭm, *pure.* Pūrĭŏr ēlēctrō, Virg. Syn. Mūndŭs, cāstŭs, īntĕgĕr, īntĕmĕrātŭs; tērsŭs, lautŭs, pŏlītŭs, nĭtĭdŭs, cŭltŭs, līmpĭdŭs.

pŭs, ūrĭs, n., *corrupt matter which comes out from a sore.* Rŭpĭlī pūs ātquĕ vēnēnŭm, Hor. Syn. Tābŭm, sănĭēs, vīrŭs. V. Sanies.

* pŭsĭllănĭmĭs, ĕ, *or* ŭs, ă, ŭm, *cowardly.* Cic. Syn. Tĭmĭdŭs, ĭgnāvŭs, īmbēllĭs.

pŭsĭllŭs, ă, ŭm, *very small.* Ātquĕ pŭsĭllŏs, Juv.

pŭsĭo, ōnĭs, *and* sŭs, ī, m., *a little boy.* Pŭsī sæpĕ lăcŭm, Lucr.

pūstŭlă, æ, f., *a blister.* Pūstŭlă rūptă, Tibull. Syn. Tŭbĕr, āmpūllă.

pŭtă, adv., *suppose, for instance.* Hōc pŭtă nōn, Pers. Syn. Scīlĭcĕt, quīppĕ.

pŭtāmĕn; ĭnĭs, n., *a nut-shell.* Dēfēnsă pŭtāmĭnĕ quīnquāgēnŭs nŭx, Aus.

pŭtātŏr, ōrĭs, m., *a pruner.* Vītĭsquĕ pŭtātŏr, Ov. Syn. Frōndātŏr.

pŭtĕāl, ālĭs, n., *a circular area in the forum, where the money-changers and usurers met.* Fŏrŭm pŭtĕālquĕ Lĭbōnĭs, Hor.

pŭtĕālĭs, ĕ, *of a well.* Mērsīt pŭtĕālĭbŭs ūndĭs, Ov. Syn. Pŭtĕānŭs.

pŭtĕo, ēs, *to stink.* Mĕrō pŭtĕrē dĭūrnō, Hor. Syn. Fœtĕo; mălĕ ŏlĕo. V. Fœteo.

pŭtĕŭs, ī, m., *a well.* Ād pŭtĕōs, aŭt, Virg. Epith. Āltŭs, prŏfūndŭs, căvŭs, pătēns, hĭāns, ăpērtŭs, cōncăvŭs, pătŭlŭs. V. Fossa, fons.

pŭtĭdŭlŭs, ă, ŭm, *the dimin. of* putidus. Āltĕră pŭtĭdŭlă.

pŭtĭdŭs, ă, ŭm, *stinking.* Pŭtĭdŭs mūltō, Hor. Syn. Fœtĭdŭs, mălĕ ŏlēns, grăvĭs.

pŭto, ās, *to think; to prune.* Ipsĕ pŭtāvĭt, Mart. Syn. Ārbĭtrŏr, ŏpīnŏr, cēnsĕo, sēntĭo, ēxīstĭmo, rĕpŭto, rĕŏr, autŭmo, jūdĭco; āmpŭto, rĕsĕco. V. Sentio.

pŭtŏr, ōrĭs, m., *a stink.* Pŭtōrĕm nāctă ēst, Lucr. Syn. Fœtŏr, ŏdŏr grăvĭs. Epith. Fœtĭdŭs, sōrdĭdŭs, tētĕr, tūrpĭs, pēstĭfĕr, grăvĭs, mŏlēstŭs.

putrēdo, ĭnĭs, f., *rottenness.* Vĭtĭātă pŭtrēdĭnĕ nāvĭs, Ov. Syn. Cărĭēs, cŏrrūptĭo, tābŭm. Epith. Cŏrrūptă, sōrdĭdă, tētră, pēstĭfĕră, īmmūndă, fœtĭdă, tūrpĭs. V. Tabum.

putrēfĭo, ĭs, fāctŭs sŭm; ĕo, ēs, ŭī; *and* ēsco, scĭs, scĕrĕ, *to grow rotten.* Pŭtrēfācta ēst spīnă sĕpūlcrō, Ov. Pŭtrŭĭt ōrcă, Hor. Pŭtrēscăt ĭn ārcă, Hor.

putrĭdŭs, ă, ŭm, *rotten.* Pŭtrĭdă mūltĭvăgĭs, Cl. Syn. Pŭtrĭs, pŭtrĕfāctŭs, pŭtrēscēns, cŏrrūptŭs, cărĭōsŭs, tābĭdŭs.

putrĭs, ĕ, *rotten, putrid.* Ēxāmĭnă pŭtrī Dē bŏvĕ, Ov. Quădrŭpĕdāntĕ pŭtrĕm, Virg. V. Putridus.

putrŏr, ōrĭs, m., *a state of putrefaction.* Quŭm pūtrŏr cēpĭt ŏb īmbrēs, Lucr.

pūtŭs, ă, ŭm, *fined, made pure.* Juv.

pӯgă, *or* pūgă, æ, f., *the buttock.* Nē nūmmī pĕrĕănt aŭt pӯgæ, Hor.

pӯgārgŭs, ī, m., *a bird of prey.—*2. *a species of antelope.* Ātque ăpĕr ēt pӯgārgŭs, Juv.

Pӯgmæī, ōrŭm, m. pl., *a people of Thrace, very small in size.* Vĭrgĭnĕ Pӯgmæā, Juv. Epith. Pārvī, brĕvēs, ēxĭgŭī, pūgnācēs, ārmĭgĕrī, māgnănĭmī.

Pӯgmălĭōn, ōnĭs, m., *the king of Tyre, and brother to Dido.* Pӯgmălĭōn scĕlĕrĕ, Virg. Epith. Ăvārŭs, crūdēlĭs, īmmītĭs, bārbărŭs, sævŭs, dīrŭs, fĕrŭs, săcrīlĕgŭs.

Pȳlădēs, Is, m., *the friend of Orestes.* Æmŏnĭŭm Pȳlădĕm, Stat.   V. Orestes.
Epith. Strŏphĭŭs, Æmŏnĭŭs, Thĕssălŭs, Phŏcæŭs, fīdŭs, fīdēlĭs.
Pȳlĭŭs, ă, ŭm, *of Pylos, of Nestor.* Incūstōdītæ Pȳlĭŏs, Ov.
Pȳlŏs, *or* lŭs, ī, f., *the name of three cities of the Peloponnesus, which disputed the honour of being the birth-place of Nestor.* Nōn Pȳlŏs aūt Ithăcē, Tib.   Nŏs Pȳlŏn, āntīquī, Ov.
pȳră, æ, f., *a funeral pile.* Innŭmĕrās strūxĕrĕ pȳrās, Virg.   Syn. Rŏgŭs, būstŭm, sĕpūlcrŭm.   V. Rogus, sepulcrum.
Pȳrācmōn, ŏnĭs, m., *one of Vulcan's Cyclops.* Mĕmbră Pȳrācmōn, Virg.   Epith. Flāmmĕŭs, īgnĕŭs, dūrŭs, fĕrrūgĭnĕŭs.   Syn. Acmŏnĭdēs.   V. Brontes.
pȳrămĭs, ĭdĭs, f., *a pyramid.* Nōn mĭhī pȳrămĭdŭm, Lucan.   Syn. Obĕlīscŭs.
Epith. Altă, ārdŭă, excēlsă, āĕrĭă, Phărĭă, Ægȳptĭă, nŏbĭlĭs, sŭpērbă, prĕtĭŏsă, mārmŏrĕă, rēgĭă, mīră.
Pȳrămŭs, ī, m., *a young Babylonian, the lover of Thisbe.* Pȳrămŭs ēt Thīsbē, jŭvĕnūm pūlchērrĭmŭs āltĕr, Ov.
Pȳrēnē, ēs, f., *a fountain sacred to the Muses.* Pȳrēnē lārgōs, Stat.—2. *one of the mountains that divide Spain from France.* Epith. Āĕrĭă, ārdŭă, excēlsă, sūblĭmĭs, āltă, cēlsă, nĭvōsă, gĕlĭdă, glăcĭālĭs, fĕră, fĕrōx, rĭgĭdă, āspĕră, ŏccĭdŭă, pāllĭdă.
Pȳrēnēŭs, *and* Pȳrēnăĭcŭs, ă, ŭm, *of the Pyrenees.* Quā Pȳrēnăĭcīs, Claud.
Pȳrēnēŭs, ĕŏs, ĕī *or* eī, m., *a king of Thrace, who shut up the Muses in his palace. Apollo gave them wings to fly away with ; and Pyreneus, endeavouring to pursue them, fell from the top of a tower.* Impĕtŭs īrĕ fŭĭt ; claūdīt sŭă tēctă Pȳrēnĕŭs, Ov.
pȳrĕthrŭm, ī, n., *feverfew, a plant.* Flāvă pȳrĕthră mĕrō, Ov.
Pȳrĕtŭs, ī, m., *one of the Centaurs.* Gĕmīnī Pērĭphāntă Pȳrētī, Ov.
Pȳrgī, ōrŭm, m. pl., *a city of Etruria.* Ět Pȳrgī vĕtĕrēs, Virg.
Pȳrgō, ūs, f., *the name of a woman.* Pȳrgō, tōt Prĭāmī nātōrŭm rēgĭă nūtrīx, Virg.
Pȳrŏĭs, ēntĭs, *and* ŏŭs, ī, m., *a horse of the Sun.* Intĕrĕă vŏlūcrēs Pȳrŏĭs, Ov.
Epith. Rŭtĭlŭs, īgnĕŭs, flāmmĕŭs, ārdēns, cŏrūscŭs, mĭcāns, rŭbēns.   V. Æthon.
pȳrōpŭs, ī, m., *a carbuncle.* Imĭtāntĕ pȳrōpō, Ov.   Syn. Cārbūncŭlŭs.   Epith. Clārŭs, mĭcāns, rŭbĕr, īgnĕŭs, īgnĭvŏmŭs, flāmmĭvŏmŭs, ārdēns, splēndēns, rŭbēns, rŭbĕŭs, rŭbēscēns, flāmmās ĭmĭtāns.   V. Carbunculus, gemma.
Pȳrrhă, æ, f., *the wife of Deucalion.* Ită Pȳrrham āffātŭr, Ov.   Epith. Epĭmēthĭs, hŏmĭnūm rĕpărātrīx.
Pȳrrhĭă, æ, f., *the name of a woman.* Fūrtīvæ Pȳrrhĭă lānæ, Hor.
Pȳrrhĭăs, ădĭs, f., *of Pyrrha, a town of Lesbos.* Nōn mē Pȳrrhĭădĕs, Ov.
Pȳrrhŭs, ī, m., *the son of Achilles.* Pȳrrhŭs Achīllīdēs, Ov.   Epith. Nĕŏptŏlĕmŭs, Achīllīdēs, Pēlīdēs, Æăcĭdēs.   Epith. Fōrtĭs, gĕnĕrōsŭs, fĕrōx, īmpăvĭdŭs, īnvīctŭs, aūdāx.
pȳrŭm, ī, n., *a pear.* Nōn pȳră quæ, Mart.
pȳrŭs, ī, f., *a pear-tree.* Sȳrĭĭsquĕ pȳrĭs, Virg.   Epith. Lăpĭdōsă, sȳlvēstrĭs, grăvĭdă, vĭrēns, vĭrĭdĭs, ŏpācă, āltă, āĕrĭă.
Pȳthăgŏræŭs, ă, ŭm, *of Pythagoras.* Ex Pȳthăgŏræō, Pers.
Pȳthăgŏrās, æ, m., *the Samian philosopher.* Pȳthăgŏrān, Ănȳtīquĕ rĕŭm, Hor.
Epith. Sămĭŭs, prūdēns, dōctŭs, cĕlĕbĕr, dīvīnŭs.
Pȳthĭă, æ, f., *the priestess of Apollo.* Pȳthĭă, quæ trĭpŏdĕ, Lucr.
Pȳthĭă, ōrŭm, n. pl., *the Pythian games, celebrated in honour of Apollo.* Lūdōs, Pȳthĭă dē dŏmĭtæ sērpēntĭs nōmĭnĕ dīctōs, Ov.
Pȳthĭăs, ădĭs, f., *the name of a female servant.* Pȳthĭăs ēmūnctō, Hor.
Pȳthĭŭs, ă, ŭm, *of Apollo, Pythian.* Pȳthĭă rēgnă, Prop.
Pȳthĭŭs, ĭī, m., *Apollo.* Pȳthĭŭs īn lōngā, Prop.   Pȳthĭă quæ, Lucr.
Pȳthōn, ŏnĭs, m., *a serpent slain by Apollo.* Tūmĭdŭm Pȳthōnă săgīttīs, Ov.
Epith. Tūmēns, tūmĭdŭs, vĕnēnātŭs, tērrĭbĭlĭs, īmmānĭs, stŭpēndŭs, Deūcălĭōnĕŭs, vĭrĭdĭs, cærŭlĕŭs, atrōx, sānguĭnŏlēntŭs.
* Pȳxăgăthŭs, i, m., *a good boxer.* Pȳxăgăthŭs fŭĕrĭt, Mart.
pȳxĭs, ĭdĭs, f., *a box.* Cōndĭtă pȳxĭdĭbŭs, Mart.   Epith. Căvă, pārvă, ŏpērtă ; naūtĭcă.

q 2

Q.

QUA, adv., *which way.* Quā făcĕre ĭd, Virg. SYN. Quī, quŏmŏdŏ.
qui˜cūnquĕ, adv., *wherever.* Tūrnŏ, quācūnquĕ vĭăm, Virg.
quādrā, æ, f., *a table.* Vīvĕrĕ quādrā, Hor.
quadrāgīntă, (indecl.) *forty.* Quādrāgīntā tĭbi, Mart.
quadrāns, ntĭs, m., *a Roman coin.* Mĭhī quādrāntēs, Mart.
quadrāntăl, ālĭs, n., *a large vessel for wine.* Hīnc brŏmĭī quādrāntăl, Aus.
quadrātŭs, ă, ŭm, *square.* Mūtăt quādrātā rŏtūndĭs, Hor.
quādrĭfĭdŭs, ă, ŭm, *cleft into four parts.* Quādrĭfĭdāsquĕ sūdēs, Virg.
|| quādrĭflŭŭs, ă, ŭm, *flowing into four channels.* Quādrĭflŭŏ cĕlĕr, Prud.
quadrīgæ, ārŭm, f. pl., *a chariot drawn by four horses.* In dīvērsā quādrīgæ, Virg.
   Quādrīgīs pĕtĭmŭs, Hor. SYN. Quadrĭjŭgēs ĕquī, cūrrūs. EPITH. Vēlōcēs, pĕr-
   nīcēs, vŏlucrēs, præcĭpĭtēs, răpĭdæ, cĕlĕrēs, cītæ, cōncĭtæ, fālcātæ. V. Currus.
quādrĭjŭgēs, ŭm, m. pl., *four horses harnessed together.* Quādrĭjŭgēs spătĭŭm, Ov.
quādrĭjŭgŭs, ă, ŭm, *drawn by four horses.* Quādrĭjŭgō vēhĭtŭr, Virg. V.
   Quadrigæ.
quadrīmŭs, ă, ŭm, *four years old.* Dēprōmĕ quādrīmŭm, (Archil.) Hor.
quadrīngēntī, æ, ă, *four hundred.* Quādrīngēntōrŭm nūllæ, Mart.
quadrĭvĭŭm, ĭī, n., *a place where four ways meet.* Juv.
quadro, ās, *to make square.* Quādrĕt ăcērvŭm, Hor.
quadrŭpēs, ĕdĭs, *and* pĕdāns, ntĭs, m., *any beast with four feet.* Arrēctŭm quādrŭpēs, ĕt, Virg. Quādrŭpēdēs, ēt frænă, Id. Quādrŭpĕdāntĕ pŭtrĕm, Id. SYN.
   Ēquŭs, sŏnĭpēs, cōrnĭpēs. V. Equus.
quadruplēx, ĭcĭs, *fourfold.* Quæ mŏdŏ quādrŭplĭcēs, Aus.
quadrŭs, *and* drŭŭs, ă, ŭm, *square.* Quādrŭă mūrōrŭm spĕcĭēs, Aus.
quæro, quæsīvī *and* ĭī, ītŭm; *and* rĭto, ās, *to seek for.* In lēvī quæsīssĕt, Virg.
   Quærĭtăt ŏbscūrōs, Cat. SYN. Vēstīgo, īnvēstīgo, scrūtŏr, pērscrūtŏr, īndāgo,
   rīmŏr, ēxquīro, rĕquīro, īnquīro, pērquīro, dīsquīro; scīscĭtŏr, pērcōntŏr, rŏgo,
   pēto; ăcquīro.
quæsītŏr, ōrĭs, m., *an examiner, a judge.* Quæsītŏr Mīnōs, Virg. V. Judex.
quæsītŭs, ă, ŭm, *the pass. partic. of* quæro. Quæsītās ād săcră, Virg.
quæso, *I pray you.* Quæsō mīsĕrĕrĕ, Prop.
Quæstŏr, ōrĭs, m., *a Roman magistrate.* Quæstŏr ăvŭs, Hor. EPITH. Ærārĭŭs,
   fīdŭs, fĭdēlĭs, īncōrrūptŭs.
quæstŭs, ūs, m., *gain.* Quæstŭs ăcērbæ, Hor. SYN. Lucrŭm, cōmmŏdŭm, ūtĭlĭtās.
   V. Lucrum.
quālĭbĕt, adv., *where you will.* Quālĭbĕt ēxŭlēs, Hor.
quālĭs, ĕ, *what, of what kind.* Quālĭs ĕt ārēntēs, Tib.
quālīscūnquĕ, lĕcūnquĕ, *whatever.* Sīnt quālĭăcūnquĕ, Hor.
quālĭtĕr, *how, as.* Quālĭtĕr ūt vīvăm, Hor.
quālŭm, ī, n., *and* lŭs, ī, m., *a basket.* Mūndīssĭmă quālă, Col. Pōndĕrĕ
   quālōs, Id.
quăm, conj., *how! than, as.* Quăm măgĭs ēffūsŏ, Virg.
quămdĭŭ, *how long! as long as.* Quāmdĭŭ sălūtătŏr, (Scaz.) Mart.
quămlĭbĕt, adv., *as much as you will, howsoever.* Quāmlĭbĕt īnfīrmăs, Ov.
quămprīmŭm, adv., *as soon as possible.* Quærēns quămprĭmum, Virg. SYN.
   Stătĭm, īllĭcŏ, prŏtĭnŭs, sŭbĭtŏ, cĭto.
quămvīs, *though.* Quāmvīs Ēlÿsĭōs, Virg. SYN. Quănquăm, ētsī, lĭcĕt.
quăndo, adv., *when.* Quāndō paūpĕrĭĕm, Hor. Quāndŏ mŏræ dūlcēs, Mart.
   SYN. Cŭm.
quăndōcūnquĕ, adv., *whenever.* Quāndōcūnquĕ trāhŭnt.
quăndŏquĭdĕm, conj., *since.* Dīcĭtĕ, quāndŏquĭdem, Virg. SYN. Quăndo, sĭquĭ-
   dem, cŭm.
quănquăm, conj., *though.* Quănquam ănĭmŭs, Virg. SYN. Quămvīs.
quăntī, adv., *how much.* Quăntī sĭbĭ gaūdĭă cōnstēnt, Juv.
quăntŏ, adv., *by how much.* Āt quăntŏ mēlĭŏră, Hor. SYN. Quō; quăm.
quăntŭlŭs, ă, ŭm, *how little.* Quăntŭlă sīnt, Juv. SYN. Quăntĭllŭs.
quăntŭlŭscūnquĕ, ă, ŭm, *how little soever.* Quăntŭlăcūnquĕ grăvĭs, Mart.
quăntŭm, adv., *as much as, how much.* Quăntum ănĭmĭs, Virg.

quăntŭmvīs, adv., *although*. Quăntŭmvīs rŭstĭcŭs, ĭbĭt, Hor. Syn. Quămvīs.

quăntŭs, ă, ŭm, *how great*. Quăntās ōstēntēnt, Virg. Syn. Quālĭs.

quăntŭscŭnquĕ, lĭbĕt, *and* vīs, (ă, ŭm,) *how great soever*. Quăntĭcŭnquĕ dŏmŭs, Juv. Quăntōvīs ōrĭs hŏnōrĕ, Lucr. Quăntōlĭbĕt ōrdĭnĕ, Ov.

quārĕ, adv., *why*. Accēndīs quārĕ cŭpĭăm, Hor. Syn. Cūr, quĭănăm, ēccūr, cūrnăm, quāprōptĕr.

quārtănă, æ, f., *a quartan ague*. Sāltēm quārtănă fŭĭssĕt, Mart.

quārtō, *and* tŭm, adv., *the fourth time*. Tēr dēstĭtĭt; aūsăquĕ quārtō, Ov.

quārtŭs, ă, ŭm, *the fourth*. Exāctīs ŭbĭ quārtă, Virg.

quāsi, conj., *as if*. Ēt dēvīctă quăsī, Lucr. Sēd quăsī naūfrăgĭīs, Lucr. Syn. Vĕlŭtī, vĕlŭt; fērĕ, pœnĕ.

quăsīllŭm, ī, n., *and* lŭs, ī, m., *a little basket*. Prēssŭmquĕ quăsīllŭm, Tib. V. Canistrum.

quăssābĭlĭs, ĕ, *that may be shaken*. Nūllō quăssābĭlĕ fērrō, Lucan.

quăssātŭs, ă, ŭm, *the pass. partic. of* quasso. Quăssātām vēntīs, Virg.

quăsso, ās, *the freq. of* quatio. Vīsū quăssābăt Ētrūscăm, Virg.

quătĕnŭs, adv., *so far as*. Quătĕnŭs īmă, Hor.

quătĕr, adv., *four times*. Sŏnĭtŭm quătĕr ārmă, Virg.

quătērdĕnī, æ, ă, *forty*. Āntĕ quătērdĕnōs, Ov.

quătērnī, æ, ă, *four by four*. Cœnārĕ quătērnōs, Hor.

quătĭo, ĭs, ssī, *to shake*. Trĕmŭlă quătĭēbăt, Prop. Syn. Cōncŭtĭo, mŏvĕo, quăsso, sŭccŭtĭo, ăgĭto, cōmmŏvĕo, pŭlso, ēxcŭtĭo; frăngo; vēxo, mŏlēsto.

quătŭŏr, *four*. Quătŭŏr ārās, Virg. Tēr quătuŏr dĕ, Ennius. Syn. Bis dŭo, quătērnī.

quătŭŏrdĕcĭm, *fourteen*. In quătŭŏrdĕcĭm sĕdēs, Aus.

quĕ, conj., *and, too*. Ārmă vĭrŭmquĕ cănō, Virg. Syn. Ēt, ătquĕ, nēcnōn.

queīs, *or* quīs, *the old dat. pl. of* quī. Queīs āntĕ ōra pătrŭm, Virg.

quĕo, quīs, quīvī, *to be able*. Dīc ăgĕ, nōn quīs, Hor. V. Possum.

Quērcēns, ēntīs, m., *the name of a warrior*. Cōntĭnŭō Quērcēns, Virg.

quērcētŭm, ī, n., *a grove of oaks*. Rōrābānt quērcētă făvīs, Claud.

quērcŭs, ūs, f., *an oak*. Quērcŭs hăbēbĭt, Virg. Syn. Ilēx, rōbŭr, æscŭlŭs. Epith. Dūră, rĭgĭdă, ŭmbrōsă, aprĭcă, vĭrĭdĭs, dēnsă, āltă, ārdŭă, prōcēră, āĕrĭă, sŭblīmĭs, glāndĭfĕră, pătŭlă, ānnōsă, căvă, sўlvēstrĭs, frōndōsă, nōdōsă, Dōdōnĭă, Dōdōnæă, Chāŏnĭă.

quĕrēlă, æ, f., *a complaint*. Nōstră quĕrēlă tŭō, Ov. Syn. Quēstŭs, quĕrĭmōnĭă, lāmēntŭm, plānctŭs. Epith. Mœstă, mĭsĕră, lūgubrĭs, flēbĭlĭs, fūrālĭs, trīstĭs, ægră, lacrўmōsă, lōngă, āssĭdŭă, sŭpplēx, mŭlĭebrĭs, fœmĭnĕă, īnsānă, vēsānă, grăvĭs, atrōx, vānă, ĭnānĭs. V. Fletus, gemitus, lacryma, queror.

quĕrĭbūndŭs, ă, ŭm, *complaining*. Hīc quĕrĭbūndă sĕnēctŭs, Sil. Syn. Quĕrŭlŭs.

quĕrĭmōnĭă, æ, f., *a complaint*. Jūnctīs quĕrĭmōnĭă prīmŭm, Hor. V. Querela.

quērnŭs, ă, ŭm, *of oak*. Ēt quērnās glāndēs, Virg.

quĕrŏr, rĕrĭs, quēstŭs, *to complain*. Amīssōs quĕrĭtŭr fœtŭs, Virg. Syn. Cōnquĕrŏr; lāmēntŏr, plāngo. V. Gemo, suspiro.

quĕrŭlŭs, ă, ŭm, *querulous, croaking*. Rēttŭlĭt ēt quĕrŭlō, Prop. Syn. Quĕrĭbūndŭs; sŏnōrŭs.

quēstŭs, ūs, m., *a complaint*. Quēstĭbŭs īmplĕt, Virg. V. Querela.

quī, quæ, quŏd *or* quĭd, *who, which*. Sēd vōs, quī tāndĕm, Virg. Dīc quĭbŭs īn tērrīs, Id. Queīs āntĕ ōră pătrŭm, Id. Quōs īntĕr, Id. Nēscĭō quā dūlcēdĭnĕ, Id.

quī, adv., *how*. Quī fīt Mæcēnās, Hor. Syn. Quōmŏdŏ, quā rătĭōnĕ.

quĭă, conj., *because*. Nēc quĭă dēspērēs, Hor. Syn. Quŏnĭăm, quŏd, năm, nāmquĕ, ĕnĭm, ĕtĕnĭm.

quĭănăm, adv., *why*. Heū quĭănăm tāntī, Virg. Syn. Cūr, quārĕ, ŭndĕ.

quīcŭnquĕ, æ, ŏd, *whosoever*. Seū quīcŭnquĕ fŭrŏr, Virg. Syn. Quīvīs, quīlĭbĕt.

quĭd, n., *why, which*. Dāphnī, quĭd āntīquōs, Virg. Syn. Ecquĭd; cūr, quārĕ.

quĭdăm, æ, ŏd, *some*. Id făcĭt, ŭt quĭdăm, Hor. Syn. Ālĭquĭs, nōnnŭllŭs.

quĭdĕm, adv., *indeed*. Id quĭdem ăgo, Virg. Syn. Cērtĕ, ĕquĭdĕm.

quĭdnī, adv., *why not?* Fīngĕrĕ; quĭdnī? Hor.

quĭdquĭd, n., *whatever*. Quĭdquĭd ĭd ēst, Virg.

quidvīs, n., *what you please.* Et vŏlŏ quīdvīs, Hor.

quĭes, ētĭs, f., *quietness.* Plăcĭdām cēpīssĕ quĭētĕm, Ov. Syn. Rĕquĭēs; ōtĭŭm; sōmnŭs; pāx; mŏră. Epith. Sēcūră, blāndă, jūcūndă, dūlcĭs, trānquīllă, suāvĭs, ămīcă, rāră, pācātă, ōptātă, tăcĭtă, nōctūrnă, pigră, mŏllĭs, ignāvă, sēgnĭs, ĭnērs, lānguēns, dēsĭdĭŏsă, dēsĕs; sōmnĭfĕră, sŏpŏră, sŏpŏrĭfĕră. V. Somnus, otium, quiesco.

quĭesco, quĭēvī, *to rest.* Tūtă quĭēvĕrăt, (Chor.) Syn. Rĕquĭesco, ōtĭŏr. V. Otior, cesso, dormio.

quĭētŭs, ă, ŭm, *at rest.* Sēdēs ŭbĭ fātă quĭētăs, Virg. Syn. Quĭēscēns, rĕquĭ-ēscēns, ōtĭŏsŭs; trānquīllŭs, plăcĭdŭs, pācātŭs, sēdātŭs; sēcūrŭs.

quīlĭbĕt, æ, ōd *or* ĭd, *whosoever.* Quīlĭbĕt āltĕr ăgăt, Ov. Quĭdlĭbĕt īllĕ, Mart. Syn. Quīvīs, quīsquĕ.

quĭn, adv., conj., *why not, but that.* Dĕdī, quĭn āspĕră Jūno, Virg. Syn. Cūr nōn, quīdnī; quōmĭnŭs, īmo; quī nōn.

quīncūnx, ūncĭs, f., *five ounces, a figure like the five in cards.* Dē quīncūncĕ rĕmōta ēst, Hor.

quīncŭplēx, ĭcĭs, *divided into five.* Quīncŭplĭcī cēră, Mart.

quīndĕcĭēs, adv., *five times.* Quīndĕcĭēs pŏtĕrăm, Mart.

quīndĕcĭm, *fifteen.* Quīndĕcīm Dĭānă, (Sapph.) Hor. Syn. Tĕr quīnquĕ, tĕr quīnī.

quīndĕcīmvĭrī, ōrŭm, m. pl., *quindecemvirs, magistrates appointed to take care of the Sibylline books.* Sōlēnnī prĕcĕ quīndĕcĭm vĭrōrŭm, Stat.

quīnĕtĭăm, adv., *moreover.* Quīnĕtĭăm cœlī, Virg. Syn. Imo ĕtĭăm; īmo; quīn.

quīngēnī *or* gēntī, æ, ă, *five hundred.* Quīngēntĭs ēmptō, Hor.

quīnī, æ, ă, *five by five.* Quīnās hīc căpĭtī, Hor.

quīnquāgēnī, æ, ă, *fifty.* Et quīnquāgēnās, Mart.

quīnquāgĕnŭs, ă, ŭm, *of five kinds.* Pŭtāmĭnĕ quīnquāgĕnŭs nūx, Aus.

quīnquāgēsĭmŭs, ă, ŭm, *fiftieth.* Quīnquāgēsĭmă lĭbă, Mart.

quīnquāgīntă, (*indecl.*) *fifty.* Quīnquāgīntă dēdīstī, Mart.

Quīnquātrĭă, ĭŭm, n. pl., *and* ŭŭm, f. pl., *festivals in honour of Minerva.* Tōtĭs Quīnquātrĭbŭs ōptăt, Juv. Et jām Quīnquātrŭs, Ov.

quīnquĕ, (*indecl.*) *five.* Quīnquĕ tĕr īmplēbās, Ov. Syn. Quīnī.

quīnquēnnĭs, ĕ, *done every five years, five years old.* Quīnquēnnĭs Ŏlȳmpĭăs, Ov.

quīnquēnnĭŭm, ĭī, n., *a space of five years.* Pĕr quīnquēnnĭă bēllō, Ov.

quīnquĕvĭr, ī, m., *one of the quinqueviri, or commission of five members for the administration of affairs.* Scrība ēx quīnquĕvĭrō, Hor.

quīnquĭēs, adv., *five times.* Quīnquĭēs dūcĕnă, Mart.

Quīntă, *and* Quīntĭă, æ, f., *names of women.* Claudĭă Quīntă gĕnŭs, Hor.

Quīntĭānŭs, ī, m., *the name of a man.* Quīntĭānĕ, lĭbĕrālĭs, Mart.

Quīntĭlĭānŭs, *or* ctĭlĭānŭs, ī, m., *a celebrated rhetorician.* Quīntĭlĭānĕ, văgæ, Mart.

quīntĭlĭs, *or* ctĭlĭs, īs, m. *the month of July, afterwards called Julius.* Fŭĕrāt quīn-tĭlĭs, ĕt īndĕ, Ov. Syn. Julius.

Quīntĭlĭŭs, *or* ctĭlĭŭs, ĭī, m., *a man's name.* Vīncĕrĕ Quīntĭlĭōs, Ov.

Quīntĭŭs, *or* Quīnctĭŭs, ĭī, m., *a man's name.* Ŏptĭmĕ Quīntī, Hor.

quīntŭs, ă, ŭm, *the fifth.* Quīntăm fūgĕ, Hor.

quĭpŏtĕ, *how is it possible ?* Quĭpŏtĕ vīs, Pers.

quĭppĕ, conj., *for, because.* Quĭppĕ fĕrānt, Virg. Syn. Nām, quĭă.

Quĭrīnālĭs, ĕ, *of the Romans or Sabines.* Inquĕ Quĭrīnālī, Ov.

Quĭrīnŭs, ī, m., *a name of Romulus.* Cūm frātrĕ Quĭrīnŭs, Virg. V. Romulus.

Quĭrītēs, ĭŭm *or* ŭm, pl., *the Romans.* Bēllĭcōsīs fātă Quĭrītĭbŭs, (Alc.) Hor. Syn. Rōmānī, Rŏmŭlĭdæ.

quĭs, æ, ŏd *or* ĭd, *who, what ?* Sĕd quĭs Ŏlȳmpō, Virg. Syn. Quīsnăm.

quīsnăm, quænăm, quŏdnăm *and* quīdnăm, *who ?* Quīsnam ĭgĭtŭr lĭbĕr, Hor.

quīspĭăm, quæpĭăm, quīdpĭăm *or* quīppĭăm, *any one, any thing.* Nē vĕl īmŭs quīspĭăm, Aus.

quīsquăm, æ, ŏd *or* ĭd, *any one, who ?* Mātūrīs quīsquăm, Virg.

quīsquĕ, æ, ŏd *or* ĭd, *every one.* Sĭbĭ quīsquĕ tĭmēbăt, Virg. Syn. Quīlĭbĕt, quīvīs.

quīsquĭllīæ, ārŭm, f. pl., *trĭstes*. Būrrās quīsquĭllīāsquĕ, Aus.
quīsquĭs, quæquæ, quĭdquĭd *or* quĭcquĭd, *whosoever, whatsoever*. Quīsquĭs ĕs, Virg.
 Quĭdquĭd ĕrĭs, Id.
quīvīs, æ, ŏd *or* ĭd, *whosoever*. Invĭdĕāt quīvīs ĭtă, Hor. Syn. Quĭlĭbĕt.
quŏ, adv., conj., *whither*. Quō fŭgĭs, Ænĕā ? Virg.
quŏăd, *or* quoăd (*monosyll.*), *as much, as long, as far as*. Nōs quŏăd ĭllĕ, Ov.
 Quoăd pŏtŭĭt, Id.
quŏcīrcā, adv., *wherefore*. Quōcīrcā căpĕrc, Virg. Syn. Quāprŏptĕr, quārĕ,
 īdcīrco.
quŏcūnquĕ, adv., *wherever*. Quō mē cūnquĕ vŏcānt, Virg.
quŏd, n., *what, which*. Prīmă quŏd ād Trōjăm, Virg.
quŏlĭbĕt, adv., *whithersoever*. Nēc mē quŏlĭbĕt īră fĕrăt, Ov. V. Quocunque.
quŏmĭnŭs, adv., *that not*. Quōmĭnŭs ēst, Virg.
quŏmŏdŏ, adv., *how*. Quōmŏdŏ tēcŭm ? Hor. Syn. Quī, quā rătĭōnĕ, quā.
quŏnăm, adv., *whither*. Aŭt quŏnăm nōstrī, Virg. Syn. Quō.
quŏndăm, adv., *formerly*. Quī grăcĭlī quŏndăm, Virg.
quŏnĭăm, adv., *since*. Aŭt quŏnĭam ăgrĕstĕm, Pr. Syn. Sīquĭdĕm, quĭă,
 quŏd.
quŏquăm, adv., *into any place*. Nēc cēdĕrĕ quŏquăm, Lucr. Syn. Ălĭquō.
quŏquĕ, conj., *also*. Tū quŏquĕ vōtĭs, Virg. Syn. Ětĭăm, părĭtĕr.
quŏquō, adv., *whithersoever*. Quōquō vēstīgĭă flēctĭs, Tib.
quŏrsŭm, adv., *whither, to what purpose ?* Quōrsum hæc tăm pūtĭdă ? Hor.
quŏt, adv., *how many*. Ět quŏt Achāĭă fōrmās, Prop.
quŏtānnīs, adv., *every year*. Mĕllĭbœĕ, quŏtānnīs, Virg.
quŏtcūnquĕ, adv., *how many soever*. Năm quŏtcūnquĕ fĕrūnt cămpī, Catul.
quŏtīdĭānŭs, ă, ŭm, *daily*. Tū quŏtīdĭānō, (Phal.) Mart. Flāgrāvīt quŏtīdĭānā,
 Cat.
quŏtīdĭē, *every day*. Quŏtīdĭē mŏrīmŭr, Mant.
quŏtĭēs, adv., *how often*. O quŏtĭēs, ēt quæ, Virg.
quŏtquŏt, *how many soever*. Quŏtquŏt ĕŭnt dĭēs, (Alcaic.) Hor.
quŏtŭs, ă, ŭm, *of what number or quantity*. Ět quŏtă fōrtūnæ, Ov.
quŏtŭscūnquĕ, ă, ŭm, *how few soever*. Pārs quŏtăcūnquĕ dĕōs, Tib.
quŭm, *or* cŭm, conj., *when ?* V. Cum.

R.

RĂBĬLŬS, ă, ŭm, *mad*. Quī răbĭdārŭm mōrĕ, Stat. Syn. Fŭrĭōsŭs, fŭrēns,
 fŭrĭbūndŭs, īnsānŭs. V. Iratus, furens.
răbĭēs, ĭēī, f., *madness*. Bēllī răbĭēs, ĕt ămŏr, Virg. Syn. Fŭrŏr, īră, vĭŏlēntĭă,
 vēsānĭă. Epitii. Imprŏbă, mĭsĕrāndă, dīră, præcēps, īndŏmĭtă, hōrrēndă,
 trūx, pērvĭcāx, nōxĭă, fŭrĭōsă, sævă, fĕră, crŭēntă, tŭmĭdă, fŭrēns, fœdă, īnfāndă,
 pēstĭfĕră, pērnĭcĭōsă, hōstīlĭs, cæcă, fĕrīnă, ācrĭs, īmmītĭs, īnfēstă, mălĕsānă,
 ēffĕră, cōncĭtă, īnīquă, ămără, īnfrēndēns, īnfrēnis, vīrōsă, fĕrōx. V. Ira,
 furor.
răbĭōsŭs, ă, ŭm, *mad*. Hāc răbĭōsă fŭgĭt, Hor. Syn. Răbĭdŭs.
Răbīrĭŭs, ĭī, m., *a Latin epic poet*. Māgnīquĕ Răbīrĭŭs ōrĭs, Ov.
răbŭlă, æ, m., *a prating wrangler*. Hīs tānquăm răbŭlăm, Cl.
răcēmĭfĕr, ă, ŭm, *bearing grapes*. Bācchĕ, răcēmĭfĕrōs, Ov.
răcēmŭs, ī, m., *a bunch of grapes*. Būmāstĕ, răcēmĭs, Virg. Syn. Ūvă, botrŭs.
 Epitii. Tŭmĭdŭs, dūlcĭs, rŭbēns, pāmpĭnĕŭs, prædūlcĭs, sūspēnsŭs, rōrāns,
 mātūrŭs, rŭbĭcūndŭs, tūrgĭdŭs, pēndŭlŭs. V. Uva.
rădĭāns, āntĭs, *radiant, luminous, bright*. Aŭt rădĭāntĭs ĭmāgĭnĕ lūnæ, Virg.
rădĭātŭs, ă, ŭm, *receiving rays*. Phœbī rādĭātŭs ăb īctŭ, Luc.
rādīcĭtŭs, adv., *from the root*. Vīvōs rādīcĭtŭs ābstŭlĭt, Prop. Syn. Stīrpĭtŭs ; ā
 rādĭcĕ, ā stīrpĕ.
rădĭo, ās, *to shine, to glitter*. Bĭfŏrēs rădĭābānt, Ov. Syn. Irrădĭo, rŭtĭlo,
 cŏrūsco, splēndĕo, mĭco, fūlgĕo, lūcĕo, fūlgŭro, scīntīllo. V. Luceo, splendeo.
rădĭŭs, ĭī, m., *a ray*. Nōn rādĭī sōlĭs, Lucr. Syn. Lūx, lūmĕn, jŭbăr, splēndŏr.
 Epitii. Mĭcāns, cŏrūscŭs, trĕmŭlŭs, īgnĭtŭs, aŭrātŭs, aŭrĕŭs, ārdēns, Phœbĕŭs,
 Ăpōllĭnĕŭs, fūlgēns, clārŭs, ăcūtŭs, pūrŭs, sĕrēnŭs, flāmmāns, lūcĭdŭs, nĭtēns,

Illūstrǐs, lūbrǐcǔs, văgāns, flāmnǐſĕr, sīdĕrĕǔs, mōbǐlǐs, rŭbēscēns, sōlārǐs, pĕnetrāns, sǐtǐēns, ārēns. V. Pecten.

rādǐx, ǐcǐs, f., *a root*. Ŏdōrātō rādīcēs īncŏquĕ Bācchō, Virg. Syn. Stǐrps, fībrǎ. Epith. Prŏfŭndǎ, īmǎ, dēmǐssǎ, āltǔ, vǎgǎ, ērrāns, tĕnĕrǎ, īnflēxǎ, rāmōsǎ, fīxǎ, vālǐdǎ, tĕnāx.

rādo, rāsī, sǔm, *to scrape*. Rādǐt ǐtĕr, Virg. Syn. Abrādo, ērādo, dērādo, cōmplāno, sēco, rĕsēco.

rāmālĕ, ǐs, n., *a dry branch*. Fǎcēs rāmālǐǎque ārǐdǎ, Ov.

rāmēntǔm, ī, n., *a scraping, filing, chip*. Et rāmēntǎ sǐmǔl fĕrrī, Lucr. Syn. Pārtǐcǔlǎ, frāgmēntǔm.

rāmĕǔs, ǎ, ǔm, *of branches*. Rāmĕǎ cōstǐs, Virg.

rāmōsǔs, ǎ, ǔm, *having many branches*. Cērnās rāmōsǐs pālmās frŭtǐcǎrĕ lǎcērtǐs, Sid.

rāmǔs, *and* ǔlǔs, ī, m., *a branch*. Quǐs prŏcǔl īlle aūtēm rāmǐs, Virg. Syn. Rāmǔscǔlǔs, tērmĕs, rāmālĕ, pālmĕs. Epith. Tĕnĕr, nŏvǔs, frăgǐlǐs, pǎtǔlǔs, lēntǔs, cōmāns, vǐrǐdǐs, vǐrēns, vērnāns, pēndēns, pēndǔlǔs, ŏpācǔs, pāndǔs, cūrvǔs, cūrvātǔs, nūtāns, trĕmǔlǔs, grǎvǐdǔs, frōndēns, frōndōsǔs, ūmbrōsǔs, ūmbrǐſĕr, crīspāns, flōrǐdǔs, frūctǐſĕr, āmœnǔs, fĕrāx, ēxcēlsǔs, rĕnāscēns, tōrtǐlǐs, ārǐdǔs, sǐccǔs, ārēns, ārēscēns. V. Frutico, germino.

rānǎ, æ, f., *a frog*. In līmō rānæ cĕcǐnĕrĕ, Virg. Epith. Lŏquāx, gārrǔlǎ, quĕrǔlǎ, vǐrēns, vǐrǐdǐs, raūcǎ, cǎnōrǎ, crĕpǐtāns, cŏāxāns, clāmōsǎ, īmpōrtūnǎ, mŏlēstǎ, fœdǎ, līmōsǎ, sōrdǐdǎ, lǔtǔlēntǎ, tūrpǐs, pǎlūstrǐs, ăquātǐcǎ, lūrǐdǎ, stāgnǐcǒlǎ.

rāncēns, ntǐs; *and* cǐdǔs, ǎ, ǔm, *rank*. Ūndĕ cādāvĕrǎ rāncēntī, Lucr. Rāncǐdum āprǔm, Hor.

rāncǐdǔlǔs, ǎ, ǔm, *somewhat rank*. Rāncǐdǔlǔm quǐddǎm, Pers.

rāpǎ, ǔlǎ, æ, f., *and* pǔm, ǔlǔm, ī, n., *a turnip*. Frīgŏrĕ rāpǎ, Mart. Cǔm rāpǔlǎ plēnǔs, Hor.

rǎpācǐtās, ātǐs, f., *rapacity*. Fīlǐǔs ēst rǎpācǐtātǐs, (Phal.) Mart. Syn. Fŭrācǐtās; rǎpīnǎ.

rǎpāx, ācǐs, *ravenous*. Innǎrĕ rǎpācēs, Virg. Syn. Fŭrǐōsǔs; rǎpǐdǔs.

Rǎphǎēl, ēlǐs, m., *the Archangel*. Aūt Rǎphǎēl ŏccūrsǔm, Fort. Epith. Cœlēstǐs, fīdǔs, cǔstōs.

rǎphǎnǔs, ī, m., *a radish*. Pērcūrrēnt rǎphǎnǐquĕ, Catull. Syn. Rǎpǎ, rāpǔm. Epith. Agrēstǐs, sǎtīvǔs, ācĕr.

rǎpǐdǔs, ǎ, ǔm, *swift*. Nūnc mǎnǐhǔs rǎpǐdǐs, Virg. Syn. Cĕlĕr, cǐtǔs, cǐtātǔs, vēlōx, præcēps, vǐŏlēntǔs, vĕhĕmēns.

rǎpīnǎ, æ, f., *rapine*. Sūbstrūctǎ rǎpīnæ, Ov. Syn. Rāptǔm, prædǎ, fūrtǔm. Epith. Hōstīlǐs, trīstǐs, ăvǐdǎ, cǔpǐdǎ, dīrǎ, īnfāndǎ, vǐŏlēntǎ, sævǎ, tūrpǐs, prŏtērvǎ, īmmānǐs, aūdāx, crūdēlǐs, īmprŏbǎ, nĕfāndǎ. V. Furtum.

rǎpǐo, rǎpǔī, rāptǔm, *to take, to carry off*. Rǎpǐt ālvĕǔs āmnī, Virg. Syn. Ērǐpǐo, ăbrǐpǐo, dīrǐpǐo, præ
rǐpǐo, sūrrǐpǐo, aūſĕro, ābdūco, sūbdūco, tōllo, ădǐmo, ēxtōrquĕo, fŭrōr, prædōr. V. Prædor.

rāptǐm, adv., *hastily*. Plānī rāptǐm pĕtǐt, Lucr. Syn. Cǐto, rǎpǐdĕ, vēlōcǐtĕr.

rāpto, ās, *the freq. of* rapio. Ilǐǎcōs rāptāvĕrǎt Hēctŏrǎ, Virg.

rāptǒr, ōrǐs, m., *a plunderer*. Rāptōrǐsquĕ tǔlǐt, Ov. V. Latro, prædo.

rāptǔm, ī, n., *plunder, rapine*. Et vīvĕrĕ rāptō, Virg.

rāptǔs, ūs, m., *ravishment*. It Vĕnǔs ēt rāptǔs, Cl.

rārĕſǎcǐo, ǐs, ēcī, *to rarify*. Et rārēfēcǐt cǎlǐdō, Lucr.

rārēfīo, īs; *and* sco, ǐs, *to be rarified*. Nēc rārēfǐĕrī, Lucr. Āngūstī rārēscūnt, Virg. Syn. Ēxtĕnǔŏr, lāxŏr.

rārō, adv., *rarely*. Stŏmǎchǔs rārō vūlgārǐǎ, Hor. Syn. Rārē.

rārǔs, ǎ, ǔm, *rare, excellent*. Rārǔs ĕrǐt, Mart. Syn. Infrĕquēns, īnsuētǔs, paūcǔs; ēxquǐsǐtǔs, ēxcēllēns, ēxǐmǐǔs.

rāsǐlǐs, ĕ, *polished*. Rāsǐlǐbǔs cǎlǎthǐs, Ov.

rāstrǔm, ī, n.; rāstrǎ, n., *or* trī, m., ōrǔm, pl., *a harrow*, Virg. Quǐd rāstrǎ, quǐd ūsǔs ǎrātrī, Ov. Nēc rāstrōs pǎtǐĕtǔr hūmǔs, Virg. Epith. Mōrdāx, dēntātǔm, tĕnāx, rǐgǐdǔm, dūrǔm, fĕrrĕǔm, grǎvĕ, cūrvǔm. V. Aratrum.

rāsǔs, ǎ, ǔm, *the pass. partic. of* rado. Rāsǎ rĕcēntī, Mart.

rǎtǐo, ōnǐs, f., *reason*. Sǎt rǎtǐōnǐs ǐn ārmǐs, Virg. Syn. Mēns, ănǐmǔs, jūdǐcĭŭm, cōnsĭlĭŭm; ārgūmēntŭm; mŏdŭs, vĭă; rĕspēctŭs.   Epitii. Săpĭēns, prŏvĭdă, sōlērs, prūdēns, cœlēstĭs.   V. Animus.

rātĭs, ĭs, f., *a ship.*   Ēt pāndās rătĭbŭs, Virg.   Syn. Căvă trăbs, nāvĭs, nāvĭgĭŭm.   V. Navis.

rătŭs, ă, ŭm, *the partic. of* reor.   Sŭm rătŭs ēssĕ, Ov.   Syn. Arbĭtrātŭs, pŭtāns; fīrmŭs, fīxŭs, stătūtŭs, cōnstāns.

raūcĭsŏnŭs, ă, ŭm, *hoarse-sounding.*   Mūltī raūcĭsŏnĭs, Ov.

raūcŭs, ă, ŭm, *hoarse.*   Vŏlŭcrŭm raūcārum ăd līttŏră, Virg.

rāvŭlŭs, ă, ŭm, *the dimin. of* ravus.   Dătĕ rāvŭlōs chŏraūlās, Sil.

rāvŭs, *and* vĭdŭs, ă, ŭm, *hoarse; of a colour between grey and yellow.*   Rāvă dēcūrrēns, (Sapph.) Hor.

rĕātŭs, ă, ŭm, *the being arraigned.*   Fōrtūnă rĕātŭm, Mart.   V. Reus.

rĕbēllĭs, ĕ, *and* ātŏr, ōrĭs, m., ātrīx, īcĭs, f., *rebellious.*   Tŭquĕ rĕbēllātrīx, tăndēm, Gērmānĭă, Ov.   Nĕc ārmă rĕbēllēs, Virg.   Syn. Sēdĭtĭōsŭs, ĭndŏmĭtŭs, ĭndŏcĭlĭs, sŭpērbŭs.

rĕbēllo, ās, *to rebel.*   Pŏtŭĕrĕ rĕbēllēnt, Lucan.

rĕbŏo, ās, *to resound.*   Cŭm gēmĭtū rĕbŏănt, Virg.   Syn. Rĕmūgĭo; rĕsŏno, re-clāmo.   V. Mugio.

rĕcālcitro, ās, *to kick with the heel.*   Pālpĕrĕ, rĕcālcĭtrăt ŭndĭquĕ, Hor.

rĕcālĕo, ēs, *and* ēsco, ĭs, *to grow warm again.*   Rĕcălēnt nōstrō, Virg.

rĕcālfăcĭo, ĭs, ēcī, *to make warm again.*   Cædĕ rĕcālfēcĭt, Ov.

rĕcāndĕo, ēs, ŭī, *to wax white.*   Pērcŭssă rĕcāndŭĭt ŭndă, Ov.

rĕcăno, cĭnŭī, *or* rĕcānto, āvī, *to sing again, disenchant.*   Nūllă rĕcāntātăs, Ov.

rĕcēdo, rĕcēssī, *to retire.*   Mūltă rĕcēdēntēs, Hor.   Syn. Rēgrĕdĭŏr, cēdo, ēxcēdo, dēcēdo, cōncēdo, dīscēdo, ăbĕo, ābscēdo.   V. Abeo, fugio.

rĕcello, ĭs, *to draw back.*   Rētrōquĕ rĕcēllĭt, Lucr.

rĕcēns, nĭs, *new.*   Fīdēnsquĕ rĕcēntĭbŭs ārmīs, Ov.   Syn. Nŏvŭs; ĭnaūdītŭs, ĭnsŏlĭtŭs.

rĕcēns, *adv., recently.*   Ēccĕ rĕcēns, Ov.

rĕcēnsĕo, ŭī, *to recount.*   Fōrtĕ rĕcēnsēbăt, Virg.   Syn. Nārro, rĕfĕro, rĕcĭto, nŭmĕro.   V. Numero.

rĕcēpto, ās, *the frequent. of* recipio.   Nātūră rĕcēptăt, Luc.

rĕcēptŭs, ūs, m., *a retreat.*   Tūtĭquĕ rĕcēptŭs, Virg.   Syn. Rĕcēssŭs, sĕcēssŭs.

rĕcēptŭs, ă, ŭm, *the pass. partic. of* recipio.   Rēgĕ rĕcēptō, Virg.   Syn. Āccēptŭs; prŏmīssŭs.

rĕcēssŭs, ūs, m., *a retreat.*   Ōbtēctă rĕcēssŭ, Cl.   Syn. Dīscēssŭs, ăbĭtŭs, ēxĭtŭs ; sĕcēssŭs, lătĕbræ, sōlĭtūdo; pĕnĕtrālĕ, ădŷtŭm.   Epitii. Arcānŭs, ōccŭltŭs, ăbdĭtŭs, ābstrūsŭs, ōbscūrŭs, căvērnōsŭs, cālĭgāns, dŭlcĭs, grātŭs.

rĕcĭdīvŭs, ă, ŭm, *falling back.*   Ēt rĕcĭdīvă mănŭ, Virg.

rĕcĭdo, ĭs, (*from* cado,) *to fall back.*   Rēcĭdĭt, ŭt mālŭm, Juv.   Syn. Rĕlābŏr.   V. Cado.

rĕcĭdo, ĭs, (*from* cædo,) *to cut down.*   Phœbĕ, rĕcīdĕ cŏmās, Mart.   Syn. Incĭdo, rĕsĕco, sĕco.

rĕcīnctŭs, ă, ŭm, *the partic. of* recingor.   Vēstĕ rĕcīnctă, Virg.

rĕcīngŏr, ĕrĭs, *to be untied.*   Sūmptŭmquĕ rĕcīngĭtŭr ānguĕm, Ov.

rĕcĭno, ĭs, *to sing again.*   Hæc rĕcĭnŭnt jŭvēnĕs, Hor.   Syn. Rĕpĕto.

rĕcĭpĭo, rŏcēpī, ptŭm, *to receive, take, promise.*   Rĕcĭpĭtque ŭd lĭmĭnă, Virg.   Syn. Āccĭpĭo, căpĭo, sūmo, āssūmo, ādmītto ; pōllĭcĕŏr, prōmītto.

rĕcĭprŏcŭs, ă, ŭm, *mutual, ebbing.*   Sĕquĭtŭrquĕ rĕcĭprŏcă Tēthŷs, Virg.   Syn. Āltērnŭs, mūtŭŭs, āltērnātŭs; rĕflŭŭs.

rĕcīsŭs, ă, ŭm, *the pass. partic. of* recido.

rĕcĭtātŏr, ōrĭs, m., *a reciter.*   Rĕcĭtātŏr ăcērbŭs, Hor.

rĕcĭto, ās, *to recite, to read aloud.*   Mĭhī rĕcĭtāvĕrĭt ĭllĕ, Juv.   Syn. Rĕnārro, nārro, dīco, rĕfĕro.

reclāmo, ās, *to cry out against, to resound.*   Illīsă rŏclāmānt, Virg.   Syn. Clāmo; rĕsŏno, rĕbŏo.

reclīnĭs *and* vĭs, ĕ, *bent back, reclined.*   Vĭrĭdīquĕ rĕclīnĭs ĭn āntrō, Calph.   Pŏsĭtă cērvīcĕ rĕclīvĭs.

reclīno, ās, *to bend, incline.*   Hāstās āc scūtă rĕclīnānt, Virg.   Syn. Inclīno, ĭnflēcto, rĕflēcto.

reclūdo, ĭs, *to open.*   Ōpērtă rĕclūdĭt, Hor.   Syn. Ăpĕrĭo, pătĕfăcĭo, rĕsĕro.

reclūsŭs, ă, ŭm, *the pass. partic. of* recludo. Spēctārĕ rĕclūsīs, Lucr.

rĕcōgnōsco, ōvī, ītŭm, *to recognise.* Dōnă rĕcōgnōscīt, Virg. SYN. Agnōsco; rĕcēnsĕo.

rĕcōllĭgo, ēgī, *to gather up.* Prīmōsquĕ rĕcōllĭgăt ănnōs, Ov. SYN. Cōllĭgo; rĕsūmo.

rĕcōlo, ĭs, ŭī, *to cultivate again.* Lūstrābăt stŭdĭō rĕcŏlēns, Virg. SYN. Ītĕrŭm cōlo; mĕdĭtŏr, cōgĭto.

rĕcōmpŏsĭtŭs, ă, ŭm, *set in order again.* Pōnĕ rĕcōmpŏsĭtăs, Ov.

rĕcōncĭlĭo, ās, *to reconcile.* Plaut. SYN. Cōncĭlĭo, plăco, fœdŭs făcĭo.

rĕcōndo, dĭdī, dĭtŭm, *to conceal.* Sēdĕ rĕcōndăm, Virg. SYN. Abscōndo, cōndo, ăbdo, tēgo, cōntēgo; ōccŭlto. V. Occulto.

rĕcōnflŏr, ārĭs, *to be forged anew, to be repaired.* Ūndĕ rĕcōnflārī sēnsŭs, Lucr.

rĕcŏquo, ĭs, ctŭm, *to boil again.* Cēssĭt ămōr; rĕcŏquŭnt, Virg. SYN. Ītĕrŭm, rūrsŭs cŏquo.

rĕcōrdātŭs, ă, ŭm, *the partic. of* recordor. Indĕ rĕcōrdātī, Ov.

rĕcōrdŏr, ārĭs, *to remember.* Vūltŭmquĕ rĕcōrdŏr, Virg. SYN. Rĕmĭnīscŏr, mĕmĭnī; sŭm mĕmŏr; nōn sŭm īmmĕmŏr; nōn ōblītŭs sŭm. V. Memini.

recrĕo, ās, *to refresh, to repair.* Pŏtĕrŭnt rĕcrĕārĕ lĭbēllō, Hor. SYN. Rĕlāxo, rĕfĭcĭo, lĕvo, sūblĕvo, rĕlĕvo, sōlŏr, ēxcĭto, ōblēcto, dēlēcto, hĭlăro, ēxhĭlăro.

recrĕpo, ās, *to resound.* Cȳmbălă rĕcrĕpănt, Cat. V. Resono.

recrēsco, ēvī, *to grow again.* Ōrbĕ rĕcrēvīt, Ov. SYN. Rĕnāscŏr; rūrsŭs crēsco.

recrūdēsco, dŭī, *to grow sore again.* Ac rĕcrūdēscīt nĕfās, (Iamb.) Sen. SYN. Ingrăvēsco, ægrēsco, aŭgēsco, aŭgĕŏr.

rēctă *and* ē, adv., *rightly.* Tū rēctē vīvĭs, Hor.

rēctŏr, ōrĭs, m., *a governor, director.* Rēctōrēm văcŭŏ, Mart. SYN. Gŭbērnātŏr, dŭx, dŭctŏr, mŏdĕrātŏr, dŏmĭnŭs, măgĭstĕr, præsĕs, rēx.

rēctŭm, ī, n., *that which is right.* Cōnscĭă rēctī, Virg. SYN. Jūstŭm, æquŭm, bŏnŭm, jūs. V. Jus.

rĕcŭbo, ās, *to lie down.* Crōcĕō rĕcŭbārĕ cŭbīlī, Ped. V. Recumbo.

rĕcŭmbo, ŭbŭī, *to recline.* Cōnvīvă rĕcŭmbĕrĕ clīvō, Mart. SYN. Rĕcŭbo, dēcūmbo, prōcŭmbo, dīscŭmbo, jăcĕo, quĭēsco. V. Jaceo, accumbo.

rĕcŭpĕro, ās, *to regain.* Ŭt nātŭm rĕcŭpĕrĕt, (Iamb.) Pl. SYN. Rĕcĭpĭo, rĕpăro, rĕdĭmo, sārcĭo, rĕsārcĭo.

rĕcūro, ās, *to cure.* Mĕ rĕcūrāvī, Cat. SYN. Recrĕo, rĕfĭcĭo.

rĕcūrro, ĭs, *to return.* Cŭm rĕcūrrĭt ăd cœnăm, (Scaz.) Mart. SYN. Rĕcūrso, rĕdĕo, rĕvērtŏr.

rĕcūrso, ās, *the frequent. of* recurro. Mŭltŭsquĕ rĕcūrsăt, Virg. SYN. Rĕcūrro.

rĕcūrsŭs, ŭs, m., *a return.* Alĭōsquĕ rĕcūrsŭs, Virg. Dănt fătă rĕcūrsŭm, Ov. SYN. Rĕdĭtŭs.

rĕcūrvātŭs, ă, ŭm, *the pass. partic. of* recurvo. Quīquĕ rĕcūrvātīs, Ov.

rĕcūrvo, ās, *to crook.* Sævă rĕcūrvānt, Stat.

rĕcūrvŭs, ă, ŭm, *crooked.* Cōrnŭquĕ rĕcūrvō, Virg. SYN. Rĕcūrvātŭs, īncūrvŭs, cūrvŭs, reflēxŭs, īnflēxŭs.

rĕcūso, ās, *to refuse.* Irĕ rĕcūso, Virg. SYN. Dētrēcto, rĕfŭgĭo, ăbnĕgo, rĕnŭo, grăvŏr, īndīgnŏr. V. Nego, abnego.

rĕcūssŭs, ă, ŭm, *struck.* Ūtĕrōquĕ rĕcūssō, Virg.

rĕcūssŭs, ŭs, m., *a. shock.* Nŏcŭērŭnt tēlă rĕcūssŭ, Luc.

rĕcŭtītŭs, ă, ŭm, *circumcised.* Fērt rĕcŭtītōrŭm, Mart. SYN. Apēllă, vērpŭs.

rĕdāctŭs, ă, ŭm, *reduced.* Dēlēctāndŭmquĕ rĕdāctī, Hor.

rĕdămo, ās, *to love in return.* Quō rĕdămētŭr ămāns, Prud.

rĕdārdēsco, ĭs, *to be kindled again.* Flāmmă rĕdārdēscīt, Ov.

rĕdārgŭo, ŭī, *to blame, refute.* Vērbă rĕdārgŭĕrĕt, Virg. SYN. Argŭo, īncrĕpo, īncrĕpĭto, reprĕhēndo, ōbjūrgo; rĕfēllo, rĕfŭto, cōnfŭto.

rĕddĭtŭs, ă, ŭm, *the pass. partic. of* reddo. Rēddĭtŭs ārtĕ, Mart.

rēddo, dĭdī, dĭtŭm, *to render, restore.* Rēddĭdĭt ĭstĕ, Mart. SYN. Rēstĭtŭo, rĕpōno, rĕpōrto, rĕfĕro, sōlvo, pērsōlvo, ēxsōlvo, rĕmūndĕro; dō, trādo, trĭbŭo.

rĕdēmptŏr, ōrĭs, m., *a farmer, an undertaker; the Redeemer.* Sæpĕ rĕdēmptōrĭs, Mart. V. Jesus.

rĕdĕo, īvī *or* ĭī, *to return.* Tītȳrĕ, dŭm rĕdĕo, Virg. SYN. Rēgrĕdĭŏr, rĕvērtŏr, rĕvērto, rĕmĕo, rĕmĭgro, mĕ rĕcĭpĭo. V. Patria.

rĕdĭgo, ēgī, āctŭm, *to bring back.* Rĕdĭgătŭr ăd āssĕm, Hor. SYN. Adĭgo, cōgo, īmpēllo.

rĕdĭmĭcŭlŭm, ī, n., *an ornament for the head.* Hăbent rĕdĭmĭcŭlă mītræ, Virg.

rĕdĭmĭo, ĭvī, ĭtŭm, *to encircle.* Rĕdĭmībăt tēmpŏră vīttă, Virg. SYN. Cŏrŏnă cĭngo, præcĭngo. V. Corono.

rĕdĭmītŭs, ă, ŭm, *the pass. partic. of* redimio. Tŏrtă rĕdĭmītŭs, Virg.

rĕdĭmo, ēmī, ēmptŭm, *to buy again.* Prĕtĭŏ rĕdĭmēndă fŭissĕm, Ov. SYN. Lĭbĕro prĕtĭŏ, āssĕro ; rĕcŭpĕro, rĕpăro, rĕsārcĭo, sārcĭo. V. Salvo.

rĕdīntegro, ās, *to renew.* Pŏsĭtāsquĕ rĕdīntĕgrăt īrās, Juv. SYN. Ĭntegro, ĭnstaŭro, rĕnŏvo, rĕpăro.

rĕdĭtŭs, ŭs, m., *return.* Prŏ rĕdĭtū sīmŭlānt, Virg. SYN. Regrēssŭs ; prŏvēntŭs. EPITH. Fēlīx, ŏptātŭs, sŭbĭtŭs, rĕpēntĭnŭs, īmprŏvīsŭs, ĭnēxpēctātŭs.

rĕdĭvīvŭs, ă, ŭm, *revived.* Ēxhaŭstă rĕdĭvīvŭs, Juv. V. Resuscito.

rēdo, ōnĭs, f., *a sort of gudgeon.* Nŏcĭtūrŭs ăcūmĭnĕ rēdo, Aus.

rĕdŏlĕo, ēs, *to cast a smell.* Fērvĕt ŏpŭs, rĕdŏlēnt, Virg. SYN. Ŏlĕo, hālo, spīro. V. Oleo.

rĕdōno, ās, *to give back.* Rĕdōnāvīt Quĭrītĕm, Hor. SYN. Rĕddo.

rĕdūco, xī, ctŭm, *to bring back.* Lōngă rĕdūcĭtĕ vītæ, Calph. SYN. Rĕfĕro, rĕvĕho ; rĕvŏco, retrăho, retrŏ dūco.

rĕdūctŭs, ă, ŭm, *the pass. partic. of* reduco. Ūtrīnquĕ rĕdūctŭm, Hor.

rĕdŭncŭs, ă, ŭm, *crooked.* Rōstrŏquĕ rĕdŭncŏ, Ov. SYN. Reflēxŭs, rĕcūrvŭs, ădūncŭs.

rĕdŭndo, ās, *to overflow.* Pœnă rĕdūndĕt, Ov. SYN. Ēxŭndo, ēfflŭo, ăbūndo.

rĕdūndāns, āntĭs, *and* rĕdūndātŭs, ă, ŭm, *partic. of* redundo. Amnĕ rĕdūndāntī, Ov. Sīvĕ rĕdūndātās, Id.

rĕdūx, ŭcĭs, *come again.* Nāmquĕ tĭbī rĕdŭcēs, Virg.

rĕfēllo, fēllī, *to refute.* Cōmmŭnĕ rĕfēllăm, Virg. SYN. Rĕfūto, cōnfŭto ; rējĭcĭo, ēxplōdo, dīlŭo, īnfīrmo, cŏārgŭo, dīssōlvo, frāngo.

rĕfērcĭo, īs, rsī, rtŭm, *to fill.* Dōnīsquĕ rĕfērsĭt ŏpīmĭs, Sil. SYN. Implĕo, rĕplĕo, cŭmŭlo.

rĕfērĭo, īs, *to strike again.* Spĕcŭlī rĕfĕrītŭr ĭmāgĭnĕ, Ov.

rĕfĕro, tŭlī, *to bring back.* Pălătīnī rĕfĕrāmŭs Apōllĭnĭs, Prop. Dătĭs rĕfĕrūntŭr hăbēnĭs, Virg. SYN. Rĕvĕho, rĕpōrto ; rĕnūncĭo ; prŏfĕro ; rĕpōno, rēddo ; rēspōndĕo.

rĕfert, *it concerns.* Cōmprēndĕrĕ rĕfērt, Virg. SYN. Ĭntĕrēst, āttĭnĕt, pērtĭnĕt, spēctăt.

rĕfērtŭs, ă, ŭm, *full.* Cēră rĕfērtă nŏtĭs, Ov. V. Plenus.

rĕfĭcĭo, fēcī, fēctŭm, *to repair.* Fŭrĭōsă rĕfēcī, Ov. SYN. Rĕlāxo, recrĕo ; rĕpăro.

rĕfībŭlo, ās, *to unclasp.* Mart.

rĕfīgo, xī, xŭm, *to fasten again; to pull down.* Rēgnă rĕfīgŭnt, Virg. SYN. Fīgo ; rĕvēllo.

rĕfīngo, ĭs, *to fashion anew, repair.* Ĕt cērĕă tēctă rĕfīngūnt, Virg.

reflāgĭto, ās, *to implore again.* Pērsĕquāmŭr ĕam ēt rĕflāgĭtēmŭs, Cat.

reflēcto, flēxī, xŭm, *to turn back, to bend.* Cōllă rĕflēctŭnt, Virg. SYN. Rĕcūrso, rĕtōrquĕo, replĭco, reclīno, rĕpērcŭtĭo.

reflēxŭs, ă, ŭm, *the pass. partic. of* reflecto. Ĕt rĕflēxă prŏpĕ, Lucr. Cērvīcĕ rĕflēxăm, Virg.

reflo, ās, *to blow back.* Ātquĕ rĕflātŭr, Lucr.

reflōrĕo, ēs, *and* esco, ĭs, *to bloom afresh.* Stat.

reflŭo, ĭs, xī, xŭm, *to flow back.* Cŭm rĕflŭĭt cāmpĭs, Virg. SYN. Rĕcūrro, rĕlābŏr, rĕdĕo.

reflŭŭs, ă, ŭm, *ebbing and flowing.* Sīve ălĭŏ, rĕflŭŭs, Rutil. SYN. Reflŭēns, rĕlābēns, rĕfūsŭs.

|| reflŭxŭs, ŭs, m., *the ebb.* SYN. Rĕcūrsŭs. V. Fluxus.

rŭfŏdĭo, ĭs, ōdī, ōssŭm, *to dig up.* Tēllūrĕ rĕfōssă Occūltōs lătĭcēs quærŭnt, Luc.

rĕfōrmīdo, ās, *to fear much.* Antĕ rĕfōrmīdānt, Virg. SYN. Fōrmīdo, mĕtŭo, hōrrĕo. V. Timeo.

rĕfōrmo, ās, *to renew.* Antĕ rĕfōrmĕt, Ov. SYN. Instaŭro, rĕstaŭro, rĕpăro.

rĕfŏvĕo, ēs, *to renew, to warm.* Āstrīctōs rĕfŏvĕt, Lucr.

refrœno, ās, *to bridle, to check.* Sŭīs rĕfrœnāt vīrĭbŭs, Lucr. SYN. Frœno, cŏērcĕo, cŏhĭbĕo, reprĭmo, cōntĭnĕo.

refrăgŏr, ārĭs, *to resist.* Mănū rĕfrăgāntĕm, (Scaz.) SYN. Rĕlūctŏr, rĕsĭsto, rĕpūgno.

Q 6

rĕfrīco, ās, cŭī, *to rub again and again, revive.* Admŏnĭtū rĕfrĭcātŭr ămŏr, Ov.

refrīgĕo, ēs, ērĕ, *and* ēsco, ĕrĕ, xī, *to grow cold, to grow fresher.* Rĕfrīgēscĭt ĕnĭm, Lucr. Ēdūctă rĕfrīxĭt, Ov. SYN. Dēfrīgēsco, rĕfrīgĕrŏr, frĭgēfīo ; dēfĕrvĕo *or* -ēsco.

refrīgĕrĭŭm, ĭī, n., *a cooling, refreshing.* Gŭttă rĕfrīgĕrĭī, Paul. SYN. Frīgŭs ; sōlātĭŭm.

rĕfrīgĕro, ās, *to cool, refresh.* Mēmbră rĕfrīgĕrăt ūndă, Ov. SYN. Frīgĕfăcĭo.

refrīngo, rēgī, *to break.* Rōmă rĕfrīngăt ŏpēs, Prop. V. Frango.

rĕfŭgĭo, rĕfūgī, *to fly back.* Nī rĕfŭgĭs, Virg. SYN. Aūfŭgĭo, fŭgĭo ; āvērsŏr, rĕcūso, dētrēcto.

rĕfŭgŭs, ă, ŭm, *fugitive.* Cŭm rĕfŭgīs sē, Lucr. SYN. Rĕdĭēns, reflŭŭs, rĕjēctŭs.

rĕfŭlgĕo, sī, *to shine.* Fāmă rĕfŭlgĕt, Prop. SYN. Rĕnĭtĕo, rĕnĭdĕo, rŭtĭlo, mĭco, fŭlgĕo, cŏrūsco, rădĭo.

rĕfŭndo, īs, fūdī, fūsŭm, *to pour out.* Illīsă rĕfūndĭtŭr ālgă, Virg. SYN. Rĕgĕro, rējĭcĭo, ēffŭndo.

rĕfūsŭs, ă, ŭm, *the pass. partic. of* refundo. Stāgnă rĕfūsă vădĭs, Virg.

rĕfūtātŭs, ūs, m., *refutation.* Ancĭpĭtīquĕ rĕfūtātū, Lucr.

rĕfūto, ās, *to refute.* Dīctă rĕfūtĕt, Virg. SYN. Rĕfēllo, rĕdārgŭo, cōnfūto. V. Confuto, refello.

rēgālīs, ĕ, *kingly.* Intĕrĭŏr rēgālī, Virg. SYN. Rēgĭŭs, rēgĭfĭcŭs.

rēgālĭtĕr, rēgĭĕ, *and* ĭfĭcĕ, adv., *royally.* Mīnās rēgālĭtĕr ăddĭt, Ov. Rēgĭfĭce ēxstrūctīs, Stat.

rēgĕlo, ās, *to thaw.* Zĕphȳrŭs rēgĕlāvĕrĭt aūră, Col.

rēgĕmo, īs, uī, *to re-echo a groan or noise.* Tūnc rēgĕmŭnt pīgrīquĕ lăcŭs, Stat.

rēgēns, ntĭs, *partic. of* rego. Cæcă rēgēns fīlō, Virg.—Subst. m., *a ruler, chief sovereign.* Prēssŭs grăvĭtātĕ rēgēntĭs, Ov.

rĕȷĕro, gēssī, gēstŭm, *to reject.* Rēgĕrĕt īn fōntēm cĭtās, (Iamb.) Sen. SYN. Rējĭcĭo, rĕfĕro, rēddo.

rēgĭă, æ, f., *a palace.* Rēgĭă, Cæsăr, Virg. SYN. Palātĭŭm. EPITH. Dīvĕs, māgnĭfĭcă, sŭpērbă, mārmŏrĕă, aūrātă, pīctă, splēndēns, illūstrĭs, nōbĭlĭs, spătĭōsă, āmplă, ārdŭă, cēlsă, āntīquă, văstă, ēxĭmĭă, mīrābĭlĭs, sūblīmĭs.

rēgĭfĭcŭs, ă, ŭm, *royal.* Rēgĭfĭcō lūxŭ, Virg. SYN. Rēgālīs, rēgĭŭs.

rēgĭfūgĭŭm, ĭī, n., *an anniversary festival, to commemorate the exclusion of the Tarquins.* Nēc rēgĭfŭgĭŭm, pŭlsīs ēx ūrbĕ tȳrānnīs, Aus.

rēgĭgno, gĕnŭī, *to reproduce.* Cōnsūmptă rēgĭgnī, Lucr.

rēgĭmĕn, ĭnĭs, n., *government.* Hīc rēgĭmĕn nātūră, Manil. SYN. Mŏdĕrāmĕn ; īmpĕrĭŭm.

rēgĭnă, æ, f., *a queen.* Rēgīnāsquĕ părĭt, Cl. SYN. Rēgnātrīx, dŏmĭnātrīx. EPITH. Pŏtēns, aūgūstă, fōrmōsă, vĕnūstă, prūdēns, æquă, clēmēns, bĕnīgnă, pĭă, mītĭs.

rēgĭo, ōnĭs, f., *a country.* Sĭcŭlĭs rēgĭōnĭbŭs ūrbĕs, Virg. SYN. Plăgă, tērră, tēllūs, ōră, trāctŭs, fīnēs.

rēgĭŭs, ă, ŭm, *royal.* Rēgĭŭs āccītŭ, Virg. SYN. Rēgālĭs, rēgĭfĭcŭs, māgnĭfĭcŭs, splēndĭdŭs.

rēglūtĭno, ās, *to unglue.* Ab ūnguĭbŭs rēglŭtĭnā, Aus.

rēgnātŏr, ōrĭs, m., *a governor.* Rēgnātōrem Āsĭæ, Virg. SYN. Dŏmĭnātŏr, rēx.

rēgno, ās, *to reign.* Graīās rēgnārĕ pĕr ūrbēs, Virg. SYN. Impĕro, dŏmĭnŏr, præsŭm. V. Impero.

rēgnŭm, ī, n., *a kingdom.* Ēt rēgnīs ēxŭl, Virg. SYN. Dĭtĭo, īmpĕrĭŭm, dŏmĭnātŭs; scēptrŭm. EPITH. Ŏpŭlēntŭm, pŏtēns, dīvĕs, flōrēns, fēlīx, āmplŭm, spătĭōsŭm, cĕlĕbrĕ, nōbĭlĕ, āntīquŭm, ăvītŭm, pătērnŭm, patrĭŭm. V. Imperium.

rēgo, rēxī, ctŭm, *to govern.* Ætērnīs rēgĭs impĕrĭīs, Virg. SYN. Gŭbērno, mŏdĕrŏr, dīrĭgo, dŏmĭnŏr, īmpĕro, īmpĕrĭto.

regrĕdĭor, ĕrĭs, regrēssŭs, *to return.* Plaut. V. Redeo.

regrēssŭs, ūs, m., *a return.* Fōrtūnă rēgrēssŭm, Virg. SYN. Rĕdĭtŭs.

rēgŭlă, æ, f., *a rule.* Rēgŭlă pēccātīs, Hor. SYN. Nōrmă, lēx, ēxēmplŭm, rēgĭmĕn. EPITH. Rēctă, jūstă, cērtă, cōnstāns, fāllāx.

Rēgŭlŭs, ī, m., *a Roman general.* Prōvĭdă Rēgŭlī, Hor. EPITH. Fōrtĭs, fīdŭs, ămāns patrĭæ, gĕnĕrōsŭs, māgnănĭmŭs, cōnstāns.

rēgŭsto, ās, *to taste again.* Bărō, rēgŭstātŭm, Pers.

rĕhālo, ās, *to breathe back again.* Tōtă rĕhālăt, Lucr.

reīcĭo, ĭs, *the same as* rejicio. Ā flūmĭnĕ reīcĕ căpēllās, Virg.

rējĕcto, ās, *the frequent. of* rejicio. Ictī rējĕctănt vōcēs, Lucr.

rējĕctŭs, ă, ŭm, *the pass. partic. of* rejicio. Bīs rējĕcti ārmīs, Virg.

rējĭcĭo, rējĕcī, ctŭm, *to throw back, to reject.* Rējĭcĕt ārvīs, Virg. SYN. Abjĭcĭo, rĕpĕllo, rĕmŏvĕo ; rĕcūso, rēspŭo ; cōntēmno, āspērnŏr.

rĕlābŏr, ĕrĭs, lāpsŭs, *to fall back.* Fōrmōsĕ, rĕlābĕrĕ nōstrōs, Ov. SYN. Recīdo; reflŭo.

rĕlānguĕo, ēs, gŭī, *to languish.* Mŏrĭbūndă rĕlānguīt ŏrĕ, Ov. SYN. Lānguĕo; dēfĭcĭo.

rĕlātŭs, ă, ŭm, *the pass. partic. of* refero. Rĕfĕrētquĕ dĭēm, cōndĕtque rĕlātŭm, Virg.

|| rĕlātŭs, ūs, m., *a recital, discourse.* Vārĭōquĕ trăhănt ēvēntă rĕlātū, Aus.

rĕlāxo, ās, *to relax.* Vīnclă rĕlāxānt, Lucr.

rĕlēgātŭs, ă, ŭm, *the pass. partic. of* relego. Sēxtă rĕlēgātŭm, Ov.

rĕlēgo, ās, *to remove, banish.* Sōlă rĕlēgānt, Virg. SYN. Ablēgo, āmāndo, rējĭcĭo, rĕmŏvĕo, pēllo. V. Pello.

rĕlĕgo, ĭs, lēgī, ctŭm, *to read over again.* Cŭm rĕlĕgō, Ov.

rĕlēntēsco, cĭs, *to grow soft.* Nĕvĕ rĕlēntēscăt, Ov.

rĕlĕvo, ās, *to lift up again.* Cōrpŭs rĕlĕvārĕ, Ov.

rĕlīctŭs, ă, ŭm, *the pass. partic. of* relinquo. Sōlŭs rĕlīctŭs īllĕ, (Iamb.) Sen. SYN. Dēsērtŭs ; ōmīssŭs.

|| rĕlīdo, ĭs, īsī, *to overthrow, refute.* Aūt īnfīrmātă rĕlīdūnt, Aus.

rĕlĭgĭo, *or* rēllĭgĭo, ōnĭs, f., *religion.* Rēllĭgĭŏnĕ tŭērī, Virg. SYN. Pĭĕtās, dīvīnŭs cūltŭs. EPITH. Sacră, sānctă, ădōrāndă, vĕnĕrāndă, vĕrēndă, vēră, cērtă, pĭă, pūră, cāndĭdă, dīvīnă. V. Pietas.

rĕlĭgĭōsŭs, *or* rēllĭgĭōsŭs, ă, ŭm, *religious.* Rēllĭgĭōsă dĕōrŭm, Virg. SYN. Pĭŭs. V. Pius.

rĕlĭgo, ās, *to tie back.* Cuī flāvām rĕlĭgās cŏmăm, Hor. Rĕlĭgāvĭt ăb āggĕrĕ clāssĕm, Virg. SYN. Lĭgo, rĕvīncĭo, vīncĭo. V. Vincio.

rĕlīno, ĭs, ēvī *or* īvī, ĭtŭm, *to uncork, open.* Thēsaurīs rĕlīnēs, Virg.

rĕlīnquo, līquī, līctŭm, *to leave.* . Sērmōnĕ rĕlīquīt, Virg. SYN. Līnquo, dēsĕro, dēstĭtŭo, ōmītto, mītto, dīmītto.

rēllĭquĭæ, *or* rĕlĭquĭæ, ārŭm, f. pl., *remains.* Rēllĭquĭās Dănăŭm, Virg. Jūssīt rĕlĭquĭās pōnī, (Iamb.) Phædr. EPITH. Trīstēs, mĭsĕræ ; fēlīcēs, grātæ.

rēllĭquŭs, ă, ŭm, *remaining.* Tēxāntŭr rĕlĭquă, Mart. SYN. Sŭpērstĕs ; ălĭŭs.

rĕlūcĕo, ēs, *to shine.* Lătă rĕlūcēnt, Virg. SYN. Rĕfulgĕo, rĕnīdĕo, rēsplēndĕo.

rĕlūctŏr, ārĭs, *to resist.* Mūltă rĕlūctāntī, Virg. V. Resisto.

rĕmānĕo, mānsī, *to remain.* Ēt cŭbĭtō rĕmānētĕ, Hor. SYN. Mănĕo, sŭpērsŭm.

rĕmāno, ās, *to flow back.* Rētrōquĕ rĕmānăt, Lucr.

rĕmĕābĭlĭs, ĕ, *from which one can return.* Ūnī rĕmĕābĭlĕ bēllŭm, Stat.

rĕmĕdĭŭm, ĭī, n., *a remedy.* Dōlōrī rĕmĕdĭum ēst, (Iamb.) V. Medicamen.

rĕmĕo, ās, *to return.* Ūnquăm rĕmĕāssĕm, Virg. SYN. Rĕdĕo, rĕvērtŏr.

rĕmĭpēs, pĕdĭs, *going by means of oars.* Rĕmĭpĕdēs mĕdĭō, Aus.

rĕmētĭŏr, īrĭs, *to measure again.* Sērvātă rĕmētĭŏr āstră, Virg. SYN. Itĕrŭm mētĭŏr ; rĕpĕto.

rēmēx, ĭgĭs, m., *a rower.* Rēmĭgĕ cārpĭt, Ov. EPITH. Rōbūstŭs, vălĭdŭs, fōrtĭs, dēxtĕr. V. Nauta, remigo.

rēmĭgĭŭm, ĭī, n., *a rowing.* Rēmĭgĭīs sŭbĭgĭt, Virg. SYN. Rēmī ; rēmĭgēs.

rēmĭgo, ās, *to row.* Clāssĭs quŏd rēmĭgăt ālĭs, Prop. V. Navigo, remus.

rĕmĭgro, ās, *to return.* Inquĕ lŏcŭm quāndō rĕmĭgrănt, Lucr.

rĕmĭnīscŏr, ĕrĭs, *to remember.* Mŏrĭēns rĕmĭnīscĭtŭr Argōs, Virg. SYN. Rĕcōrdŏr, mĕmĭnī. V. Memini.

rĕmīscĕo, ēs, *to mingle together.* Fūlsă rĕmīscĕt, Hor. V. Misceo.

rĕmīssŭs, ă, ŭm, *the pass. partic. of* remitto. Ăchĕrōntĕ rĕmīssōs, Virg. SYN. Mīssŭs ; lāxātŭs.

rĕmītto, rĕmīsī, *to send back.* Pērsæpĕ rĕmīttĭt, Hor. V. Mitto, relaxo.

rĕmōlĭŏr, īrĭs, *to put from his place.* Sæpĕ rĕmōlīrī, Ov. V. Repello

rĕmōllēsco, ĭs, *to grow softer.* Cĕră rĕmōllēscĭt, Ov.

rĕmŏllĭo, īs, *to make softer.* Tāctōsquĕ rĕmŏllῑăt ārtūs, Ov.

rĕmŏră, æ, f., *a sea-lamprey.* Plin. SYN. Ĕchĕnēïs. EPITH. Pārvă, tĕnŭῐs, tῐmēndă.—2. *a hindrance.* Rĕmŏrāmquĕ făcῐŭnt, (Iamb.) Plaut.

rĕmŏrāmĕn, ῐnῐs, n., *a hindrance, obstacle.* Rĕmŏrāmῐnăque ῑpsă nŏcēbānt, Ov.

rĕmŏrdĕo, ēs, *to gnaw.* Cūră rĕmŏrdĕt, Virg.

rĕmŏrŏr, ārῐs, *to delay.* Paūlŭm rĕmŏrātŭr ĕt āltŭm, Sil. SYN. Mŏrŏr, rĕtārdo, tārdo.

rĕmōtŭs, ă, ŭm, *the pass. partic. of* removeo. Tῑthōnŭsquĕ rĕmōtŭs, Hor.

rĕmŏvĕo, mōvī, mōtŭm, *to remove, to withdraw.* Tē rĕmŏvērĕ mĕmēnto, Hor. SYN. Ădmŏvĕo, dῑmŏvĕo, sŭmmŏvĕo, ābdūco, āvērto, ārcĕo, dētōrquĕo, āmāndo, aūfĕro, sūbdūco, rējῐcῐo, rĕpēllo.

rĕmūgῐo, ῑi, *to answer with lowing.* Cœlūmquĕ rĕmūgῐt, Virg. SYN. Rĕbŏo, reclāmo ; rĕsŏno. V. Echo.

rĕmūlcĕo, ēs, *to appease ; to fold.* Caūdāmquĕ rĕmūlcēns, Virg.

rĕmūlcŭm, ī, n., *and* ūs, ῑ, m., *a rope for towing boats.* Nūsquăm cēssāntĕ rĕmūlcō, Aus.

Rĕmūlŭs, ī, m., *a king of the Latins, struck with lightning for his impiety.* Nātŭm Rĕmūlūmquĕ pŏtēnῐĕm, Ov.

rĕmūnĕro, ās, *and* ŏr, ārῐs, *to recompense.* Sūpplῐcῐῑs rĕmūnĕrābŏr, (Phal.) Cat. SYN. Cŏmpēnso, pēnso. V. Gratias ago.

Rĕmūrῐă, *or* Lĕmūrῐă, ōrŭm, n. pl., *festivals in honour of Remus.* Lūcēmquĕ Rĕmūrῐă dῑxῐt.

rĕmūrmŭro, ās, *to answer with a murmur.* Frāctă rĕmūrmŭrăt ūndă, Virg. SYN. Ŏbmūrmŭro ; rĕsŏno ; ŏblŏquŏr.

Rĕmŭs, ī, m., *the brother of Romulus.* Ūtquĕ Rĕmō, Virg. EPITH. Mārtῐgĕnă, Illῐădēs. V. Romulus.

rēmŭs, ī, m., *an oar.* Ăgmῐnĕ rēmōrŭm, Virg. SYN. Tōnsæ, ārbŏr ; rēmῐgῐŭm. EPITH. Lōngŭs, spūmāns, æquŏrĕŭs, vălῐdŭs, lūctāns, hūmēns ; ūdŭs, dēmῑssŭs, lĕvῐs, vēlōx, ærātŭs. V. Remigo.

rĕnārro, ās, *to tell over again.* Fātă rĕnārrābăt, Virg. V. Narro.

rĕnāscŏr, ĕrῐs, nātŭs, *to grow again.* Cōrdĕ rĕnāscῐtŭr ārdŏr, Stat. V. Nascor.

rēnēs, ŭm, m. pl., *the reins.* Quŏd lătŭs, aūt rēnēs, Hor. SYN. Lūmbī.

rĕnῑdĕo, ēs, ēsco, ῐs, *and* rĕnῑtĕo, ēs, *to shine.* Ærĕ rĕnῑdēntī, Virg. Ærĕ rĕnῑdēscῐt, Lucr. Ăt sōlī rĕnῐtĕt, Prisc. SYN. Rĕfūlgĕo, rĕlūcĕo, rĕsplēndĕo, cŏrūsco. V. Luceo.

rĕno, ās, *to swim back again.* Ŭmbră rĕnāvῐt ăquăs, Ov.

rĕnōdo, ās, *to tie again.* Lōngām rĕnōdāntῐs cŏmăm, Hor. V. Nodo.

rĕnŏvāmĕu, ῐnῐs, n., *a renewal.* Ῐn hŏc rĕnŏvāmῐnĕ mānsῐt, Ov.

rĕnŏvo, ās, *to renew.* Jăm rĕnŏvābăt hŭmŭm, Mart. SYN. Rĕpăro, ῐnstaūro, rĕstaūro, rĕfῐcῐo, ῐntegro, rĕdῑntegro, ῐtĕro.

rĕnūncῐo, ās, *to declare, to relate.* Nōn rĕnūncῐātă sīnt hæc, (Iamb.) SYN. Nūncῐo, nārro, rĕfĕro.

rĕnŭo, ῐs, ŭῑ, *to deny by a nod.* Ăn rĕnŭῐs? vīs tū, Pers. SYN. Ābnŭo, rĕcūso, nĕgo. V. Abnego.

rĕnūto, ās, *the frequent. of* renuo. Sῐmŭlācră rĕnūtānt, Lucr.

rĕŏr, rērῐs, *to judge, to deem.* Jăm rĕŏr hoc, Tib. SYN. Pŭto, cēnsĕo, ŏpῑnŏr, jūdῐco, ēxῑstῐmo.

rĕpāgŭlŭm, ī, n., *a rail, a bar.* Pĕdῐbūsquĕ rĕpāgŭlă pūlsănt, Ov. SYN. Ŏbēx. V. Obex.

rĕpāndŭs, ă, ŭm, *bent backward.* Trūncŏquĕ rĕpāndŭs, Ov. V. Curvus.

rĕpărābῐlῐs, ĕ, *which may be repaired.* Nūllă rĕpărābῐlῐs ārtĕ, Ov.

rĕpărātŏr, ōrῐs, m., *a repairer.* Ῐmmēnsī rĕpărătŏr, Sil.

rĕpăro, ās, *to repair.* Tămĕn cĕlĕrēs rĕpărānt, Hor. SYN. Rĕfῐcῐo, rĕnŏvo, rĕstaūro, ῐntegro, rĕdῑntegro, sārcῐo, rĕsārcῐo, rĕcŭpĕro.

rĕpēcto, pēxŭī *and* pēxī, *to comb again.* Stāntēsquĕ rĕpēctῐt, Stat. Crῑnēmquĕ rĕpēxī, Claud. V. Pecto.

rĕpēllo, pŭlī *or* rēppŭlī, pūlsŭm, *to repel.* Prĕcēsquĕ rĕpēllῐt, Ov. SYN. Rĕjῐcῐo, rĕmŏvĕo, ārcĕo, prŏhῐbĕo, pēllo, propēllo, propūlso, ēxpēllo, dēpēllo, āmŏlῐŏr, āmŏvĕo ; āmāndo. V. Pello.

rĕpēndo, pēndī, *to weigh, to pay back.* Fātă rĕpēndēns, Virg. SYN. Rēddo, rĕtrῐbŭo, sōlvo, pērsōlvo, rĕpōno, rĕfĕro, rĕmūnĕro. V. Remunero.

rĕpēns, ēntǐs, *sudden.* Quōve īstă rĕpēns dīscōrdǐǎ sūrgǐt, Virg

rĕpēns, *and* rĕpēntĕ, adv., *suddenly.* Bǐnǎ rĕpēns ŏcǔlǐs, Ov. Vīnctǎ rĕpēntĕ gĕlū, Mārt. Syn. Sŭbǐtō, stătǐm, ēxtēmplō, cōnfēstǐm, āctūtǔm, prōtǐnǔs, cōntǐnǔō, illǐco. V. Statim.

rĕpēntīnǔs, ǎ, ǔm, *sudden.* Sūmquĕ rĕpēntīnās, Ov. Syn. Rĕpēns, sŭbǐtǔs, īmprŏvīsǔs, ǐnŏpīnǔs.

rĕpērcŭtǐo, ūssī, ūssǔm, *to strike back.* Aūrōrǎ rĕpērcǔtǐt Indōs, Alc. Syn. Rĕvērbĕro, reflēcto.

rĕpērcŭssǔs, ǎ, ǔm, *the pass. partic. of* repercutio. Sōlĕ rĕpērcŭssum aūt, Virg. Syn. Rĕflēxǔs, rĕsūltāns.

rĕpĕrǐo, rĕpĕrī, *to find.* Nūllǎ fŭgām rĕpĕrǐt, Virg. Syn. Invĕnǐo, nāncīscor, cōmpĕrǐo, dēprēndo.

rĕpĕtēntǐǎ, æ, f., *recollection, memory.* Quūm sīt rĕpĕtēntǐǎ nōstrǎ, Lucr.

rĕpērtǒr, ōrǐs, m., *a discoverer.* Mĕdǐcæquĕ rĕpērtǒr, Ov.

rĕpērtǔs, ǎ, ǔm, *the pass. partic. of* reperio. Ingĕmŭǐtquĕ rĕpērtā, Virg.

rĕpĕtītǒr, ōrǐs, m., *he who requires a thing back.* Nūptæ rĕpĕtītǒr ădēmptæ, Ov.

rĕpĕto, ǐs, pĕtītǔm, *to demand back again.* Sī rĕpĕtās, ĕt, Mart. Syn. Ĭtĕro, ĭngĕmǐno, rĕsūmo; rĕpōsco, pĕto; rĕdĕo. V. Echo.

replĕo, plēvī, plētǔm, *to fill again.* Fōssǎ rĕplētǔr, Ov. Syn. Implĕo, cōmplĕo, ădīmplĕo, cǔmǔlo.

replētǔs, ǎ, ǔm, *the pass. partic. of* repleo. Ipsĕ rĕplētǔs, Lucr

replǐco, ās, *to fold again, fold.* Lĭgnī rĕplǐcētǔr ǐn ōrbĕm, Aus.

rēpo, rēpsī, *to crawl.* Infāntǐǎ rēpǐt, Prud. Syn. Rēpto, ādrēpto, sērpo.

rĕpōno, pŏsǔī, pŏsǐtǔm, *to replace.* Ārīsquĕ rĕpōnǐmǔs ǐgnĕm, Virg. V. Pono, reddo.

rĕpōrto, ās, *to bring again.* In vēstĕ rĕpōrtǎt, Virg. Syn. Rĕfĕro, rĕvĕho; ōbtǐnĕo, ācquīro, cōmpǎro.

rĕpōsco, pŏpōscī, *to ask again.* Orĕ rĕpōsco, Virg. Syn. Rĕpĕto, pĕto, pōsco. V. Pĕto, posco.

rĕpŏsǐtǔs, *and* pōstǔs, ǎ, ǔm, *the pass. partic. of* repono. Ālvōquĕ rĕpōstǎ, Lucr.

rĕpōtǐǎ, ōrǔm, n. pl., *a feast on the day after marriage.* Illĕ rĕpōtǐǎ, nātālēs, ălǐōsvĕ dǐērǔm, Hor.

repræsēnto, ās, *to show, exhibit.* Vīrtūtēmnĕ rĕpræsēntĕt, Hor. Syn. Exhǐbĕo, ōstēndo, mōnstro.

rĕprĕhēndo, *and* prēndo, dī, sǔm, *to blame, to take again.* Vērsǔs rĕprĕhēndĕt īnērtēs, Hor. Syn. Ārgǔo, ōbjūrgo, īncūso, īncrĕpǐto. V. Objurgo, redarguo.

rĕprĕhēnsǒr, ōrǐs, m., *a reprover.* Idēm rĕprĕhēnsǒr ĕt āctǒr, Ov. Syn. Cēnsǒr.

rĕprēssǔs, ǎ, ǔm, *the pass. partic. of* reprimo. Tālī rĕprēssǔs cōgnǐtǒr, (Iamb.) Prud.

reprǐmo, prēssī, sǔm, *to repress.* Ět rĕprǐmǐt flŭǐdōs, Sed. Syn. Cōmprǐmo, cŏhǐbĕo, cōntǐnĕo, cōmpēsco, cŏērcĕo, fræno, refræno, sīsto, tĕnĕo, rĕtārdo. V. Fræno.

rĕprŏbo, ās, *to reject.* Hūnc rĕprŏbāvǐt, Sed. Syn. Imprŏbo, rējǐcǐo, ābjǐcǐo, dāmno.

rēpto, ās, *the frequent. of* repo. Ět tăcǐtǔm sȳlvās īntĕr rēptārĕ sălūbrēs, Hor.

rĕpŭdǐo, ās, *to divorce.* Sǔm hōspĕs, rĕpŭdǐo, (Iamb.) Plaut. Syn. Rĕcūso, rēspǔo, ābjǐcǐo, rējǐcǐo, rĕpēllo; āspērnǒr.

rĕpŭdǐǔm, ǐī, n., *a refusal, a divorce.* Hæc sūnt rĕpŭdǐǎ! nĕc, (Iamb.) Sen. Syn. Rĕpūlsǎ; dǐvōrtǐǔm.

rĕpūgno, ās, *to resist.* Illĕ rĕpūgnāns, Virg. Syn. Ādvērsǒr, cōntrādīco, reclāmo. V. Resisto.

rĕpūlsǎ, æ, f., *a refusal.* Tūrpēmquĕ rĕpūlsām, Hor. Epith. Ācērbǎ, mŏlēstǎ, trīstǐs, dūrǎ, atrŏx, crūdēlǐs, āspĕrǎ, ǐnǐmīcǎ, īnjūstǎ, ǐnǐquǎ, fœdǎ, tūrpǐs.

rĕpūlso, ās, *the frequent. of* repello. Vērbǎ rĕpūlsāntĕs, Lucr.

rĕpūlsǔs, ǎ, ǔm, *the pass. partic. of* repello. Ærǎ rĕpūlsǎ mănū, Tib.

rĕpūlsǔs, ūs, m., *repulsion, reverberation.* Āssǐdǔō crēbrŏquĕ rĕpūlsū, Lucr.

rĕpūrgo, ās, *to clean anew.* Dūmquĕ rĕpūrgǎt, Ov. Syn. Pūrgo, mūndo, ēxpūrgo.

rĕpŭto, ās, *to consider.* Sĕd ĕnīm rĕpŭtā tēcǔm, Sil. Syn. Pŭto; mĕdǐtǒr. V. Cogito.

rĕquǐēs, ēī, f., *rest.* Āltērnā rĕquǐē, Ov. Syn. Quǐēs; ōtǐǔm; sōmnǔs.

rĕquĭesco, ēvī, *to rest.* Rĕquĭescĕ sŭb ŭmbrā, Virg. Syn. Quĭesco, ōtĭŏr, dōrmĭo.

rĕquīro, sīvī *and* ĭī, sītŭm, *to demand.* Pōrtūsquĕ rĕquīrĕ, Virg. Syn. Exquīro, quæro.

rēs, rĕī, f., *a thing, an affair, money, a state.* Incērtæquĕ rĕī, Juv. Quī pŏtŭīt rērŭm, Virg. Syn. Nĕgōtĭŭm, ŏpŭs, ŏpĕră; fāctŭm, fācĭnŭs; bŏnă, dīvĭtĭæ, ŏpēs.

rĕsævĭo, īs, *to grow furious.* Mōtă rĕsævĭăt īrā, Ov.

rĕsălūto, ās, *to salute again.* Nūllŭm rĕsălūtās, Mart.

rĕsārcĭo, īs, īvī *and* ĭī, ĭtŭm, *to repair.* Dīscĭdĭt vēstēm; rĕsārcĭētŭr, Ter. Syn. Sārcĭo, rĕfĭcĭo, rĕpăro, rĕnŏvo, rēstaūro. V. Reparo.

rēscĭndo, scĭdī, scĭssŭm, *to cut off.* Rēscĭdĭt ēnsĕ, Rut. Syn. Rĕsĕco, sĕco, āmpŭto, scĭndo, ābscĭndo; dīssōlvo, sōlvo, rĕvēllo; ăbŏlĕo, ābrŏgo, āntīquo, īrrīto, īnfīrmo, dēstrŭo. V. Scindo.

rēscĭo, īs, *and* scĭsco, īs, *to know, to learn.* Rēscĭērīs nōs, Hor.

rēscrībo, psī, ptŭm, *to write back or again.* Etĭam rēscrībĕrĕ, sī tĭbi, Hor.

rĕsĕco, ās, *to cut off.* Lōngōs rĕsĕcārĕ căpĭllōs, Ov. V. Rescindo.

rĕsēctŭs, ă, ŭm, *the pass. partic. of* reseco. Fārră rĕsēctă dăbānt, Ov.

rĕsēmĭno, ās, *to sow again.* Ipsă rĕsēmĭnĕt, ălĕs, Ov.

rĕsĕquŏr, ĕrĭs, *to follow.* Est rĕsĕcūtă rŏgāntĕm, Ov.

rĕsĕro, ās, *to open, to discover.* Insīgnĭs, rĕsĕrăt, Virg. Syn. Apĕrĭo, reclūdo, rĕsīgno, pāndo; rĕtĕgo, dēclāro, mānĭfēsto, ōstēndo.

rĕsērvo, ās, *to preserve.* Fātă rĕsērvānt, Virg. Syn. Sērvo, āssērvo; rĕcōndo.

rĕsĕs, ĭdĭs, *idle.* Jāmprĭdĕm rĕsīdĕs ănĭmōs, Virg. Syn. Dēsĕs, ōtĭōsŭs, pĭgĕr.

rĕsīdĕo, ēdī, *and* sīdo, ī, *to rest, remain.* Tŭm rĕsīdĕrĕt ŏpĕm, Avien. Ipsă rĕsīdānt, Virg. Syn. Sĕdĕo; rĕquĭesco, quĭesco, plăcĕo.

rĕsīgno, ās, *to unseal, to close up.* Mōrtĕ rĕsīgnăt, Virg. Syn. Apĕrĭo; claūdo.

rĕsĭlĭo, īī *or* ŭī, *to leap back.* Nōn sĕcŭs hæc rĕsīlĭt, Ov. In gĕlĭdōs rĕsĭlīrĕ lăcŭs, Id. Syn. Rĕsūlto, reflēctŏr, rĕtōrquĕŏr, rĕpērcŭtĭŏr, rĕpēllŏr, retrō ēxĭlĭo, sālĭo, fĕrŏr. V. Echo.

rēsīnă, æ, f., *rosin.* Rēsīnā, Vĕnĕtō, Mart.

rēsīnātŭs, ă, ŭm, *rosined.* Rēsīnātă jŭvēntŭs, Juv.

rĕsĭpīsco, īs, pŭī, *to return to a right understanding.* Fēssī rĕsĭp˙scĭmŭs æstŭ, Prop.

rĕsīsto, rēstĭtī, *to resist.* Mārtĕ rĕsīstūnt, Virg. Syn. Rĕpūgno, rĕlūctŏr, rĕnītŏr, ŏbnītŏr, ādvērsŏr, ōbsīsto, ōbsto, ōbsŭm.

|| rĕsŏlūbĭlĭs, ĕ, *that may be dissolved.* Strŭxīt rĕsŏlūbĭlĕ jūrĕ, Prud.

rĕsōlvo, sōlvī, sŏlūtŭm, *to dissolve.* Glēbă rĕsōlvĭt, Virg. Syn. Sōlvo; dīssōlvo; rēscĭndo, vĭŏlo; rĕmītto, rĕlāxo.

rĕsŏlūtŭs, ă, ŭm, *the pass. partic. of* resolvo. Ac rĕsōlūtă rĕfērrī, Virg.

rĕsŏnābĭlĭs, ĕ, *resounding.* Rĕsŏnābĭlĭs Echō, Ov.

rĕsŏno, ās, *to resound.* Fōrmōsām rĕsŏnārĕ dŏcēs, Virg. Syn. Cōnsŏno, pērsŏno, āssŏno, īnsŏno, sŏno; rĕbŏo, rĕmūgĭo. V. Echo.

rĕsŏnŭs, ă, ŭm, *resounding.* Lūdēbānt rĕsŏno mēdĭtāntēs, Prud. Syn. Rĕsŏnāns. sŏnōrŭs.

rĕsōrbĕo, psī, ptŭm, *to swallow again.* Rĕvŏlūtă rĕsōrbēns, Virg.

rēspēcto, ās, *the frequent. of* respicio. Armīs rēspēctānt, Virg.

rēspēctŭs, ūs, m., *a looking back, respect.* Vērī rēspēctŭs ĕt æquī, Mart. Syn. Cūră.

rēspērgo, sī, sŭm, *to besprinkle.* Ut taūrī rēspērgās, Cat. Syn. Pērfŭndo, āspērgo, spārgo.

rēspĭcĭo, rēspēxī, *to look behind.* Rēspĭcĕ; cuī rēgnŭm, Virg. Syn. Aspĭcĭo, cōnspĭcĭo, spēcto, āspĕcto, tŭĕŏr; īntŭĕŏr, spĕcŭlŏr, cērno, vĭdĕo, ī..sj.˙cĭo, sŭspĭcĭo, dēspĭcĭo, dēspēcto, cīrcŭmspĭcĭo, prōspĭcĭo. V. Aspicio.

rēspīrāmĕn, ĭnĭs, n., *the passage for the breath.* Rēspīrāmĭnă claūsĭt, Ov.

rēspīro, ās, *to breathe.* Nĕc rēspīrārĕ pŏtēstās, Virg. V. Refrigero.

rēsplēndĕo, ēs, *to shine.* Fūlvā rēsplēndēnt, Ov. V. Luceo.

rēspōndĕo, pōndī, *to answer.* Et rēspōndērĕ părātī, Virg. Syn. Rēspōnso. V Colloquor, loquor.

rēspōnsĭo, ōnĭs, f., *and* sŭm, ī, n., *an answer.* Nĕc rēspōnsă pŏtēst, Virg.

rēspōnso, ās, *the frequent. of* respondeo. Rēspōnsānt cīrcŭm, Virg.

rēspōnsŏr, ōrĭs, m., *a counsellor in law.* Quō rēspōnsōrĕ ĕt quō, Hor.

rēspŭo, ŭī, *to spit out, to reject.* Rēspŭĕrīs ĕtĭăm, Tib. SYN. Rējĭcĭo, rĕcūso, rĕnŭo, āspērnŏr, fāstīdĭo. V. Aspernor.

rēstāgno, ās, *to overflow.* Altō rēstāgnānt, Luc. V. Inundo.

* rēstaūro, ās, *to renew.* Tac. SYN. Instaūro, rĕpăro, rĕsārcĭo. V. Reparo.

rēstīnguo, ĭs, *to extinguish.* Rēstīnguĕrĕ fōntĭbŭs īgnēs, Virg.

rēstĭs, ĭs, m., *a rope.* Rēstĭbŭs üllăm, Juv. V. Funis.

rēstĭtŭo, ŭī, ūtŭm, *to restore.* Rēstĭtŭātŭr hŏnōs, Mart. SYN. Rĕddo, rĕfĕro; rĕpăro, rĕnŏvo.

rēstĭtūtŭs, ă, ŭm, *the pass. partic. of* restituo.

rēsto, tĭtī, *to stay behind.* Nŭnc ĕgŏ rēsto, Hor. SYN. Sŭpērsŭm.

rēstrīngo, strīnxī, strīctŭm, *to tie up.* SYN. Āstrīngo, lĭgo; rĕllĭgo, rĕvīncĭo; cŏērcĕo, cŏhĭbĕo, cōmprĭmo.

rēsūlto, ās, *to rebound.* Ōffēnsă rĕsūltăt ĭmāgo, Virg. SYN. Rĕsĭlĭo. V. Resilio.

rēsūmo, ĭs, sūmpsī, ptŭm, *to resume.* Prŏhĭbētquĕ rĕsūmĕrĕ vīrēs, Ov. SYN. Rĕcĭpĭo.

rēsŭpīnātŭs, *and* nŭs, ă, ŭm, *lying on his back.* Et rĕsŭpīnātī, Juv. Spēctăt rĕsŭpīnō, Mart. SYN. Sŭpīnŭs, reclīnĭs; rĕcūmbēns, jăcēns. V. Recumbens.

rēsŭpīno, ās, *to lay on the back, throw down.* Quŭm tōtăs rĕsŭpīnăt, Prop.

rēsūrgo, ĭs, *to rise again.* Rēgnă rĕsūrgĕrĕ Trōjæ, Virg. SYN. Assūrgo, sūrgo; īnstaūrōr, rĕnŏvōr, rĕpărōr. V. Resuscitor.

rēsūscĭto, ās, *to rouse.* Pōsĭtāmquĕ rĕsūscĭtăt īrăm, Ov. SYN. Ēxcĭto, sūscĭto.

rĕtārdo, ās, *to delay.* Tŭă nē rĕtārdĕt, (Sapph.) Hor. SYN. Tārdo, mŏrŏr, rĕmŏrŏr, dēmŏrŏr; rĕtĭnĕo, dĕtĭnĕo, sīsto. V. Moror.

rētĕ, ĭs, n., *a net.* Rētĭă sērvo, Virg. SYN. Lăquĕī, cāssēs, līnă, tēndĭcŭlă, pēdĭcæ, īndăgo. EPITH. Rārŭm, nēxĭlĕ, sĭnŭōsŭm, nōdōsŭm, ēxtēnsŭm, fāllāx, dōlōsŭm, sūbdŏlŭm, lătēns, ōccūltŭm, īnsĭdĭōsŭm, ābdĭtŭm, căvŭm, lătĭtāns, ĭnĭmīcŭm, părātŭm, pōsĭtŭm, āppŏsĭtŭm, dīspŏsĭtŭm. V. Venor, aucupor.

rētĕgo, ĭs, tēxī, ctŭm, *to uncover.* Cōnsĭlĭŭm rĕtĕgĭs, (Dactyl. Troch.) Hor. SYN. Ăpĕrĭo, dētĕgo, reclūdo, rĕsĕro, pāndo, ēxplĭco; nŭdo, dēnŭdo.

rētēndo, ĭs, *to unbend.* Lēntōsquĕ rĕtēndĭt, Ov.

rĕtēnto, ās, *to try again.* Īntērmīssă rĕtēntăt, Ov.

rĕtēntŭs, ūs, m., *a retaining, holding back.* Ĭmĭtātă rĕtēntŭs, Claud.

rĕtēxo, ĭs, xŭī, xtŭm, *to unweave.* Tōtĭdēmquĕ rĕtēxŭnt, Virg. SYN. Dīssōlvo, rĕsōlvo.

rĕtĭcĕo, ēs, ŭī, *to be silent.* Nōstrō rĕtĭcērĕ sĕpūlcrō, Prop. SYN. Tăcĕo, cōntĭcēsco, ŏbmūtēsco, sŭbtĭcĕo; sūpprĭmo. V. Obmutesco.

rĕtĭcŭlŭm, ī, n., *a little net.* Rētĭcŭlŭmquĕ cŏmīs, Juv.

rĕtĭnācŭlŭm, ī, n., *any check or stay.* Lēntæ rĕtĭnācŭlă vītī, Virg. Nē rĕtĭnāclīs, Prud. SYN. Vīncŭlŭm; lōrŭm, hăbēnă; fūnĭs.

rĕtĭnēntĭă, æ, f., *remembrance.* Ēxcĭdĕrīt rĕtĭnēntĭă rērŭm, Lucr.

rĕtĭnĕo, nŭī, rĕtēntŭm, *to hold back, detain.* Pōssūnt rĕtĭnērĕ măgīstrī, Virg. SYN. Tĕnĕo, cōntĭnĕo; tārdo, rĕtārdo, mŏrŏr, rĕmŏrŏr, dēmŏrŏr.

rĕtīngo, ĭs, xī, *to dip again.* Fērrŭmquĕ rĕtīngī, Stat.

rĕtōno, ās, ŭī, *to resound.* Frĕmĭtū lŏcă rĕtŏnēnt, Catul.

rĕtōrquĕo, rsī, rtŭm, *to twist back.* Jŭtūrnă rĕtōrsĭt, Virg. SYN. Reflēcto, rĕpēllo, flēcto.

‖ rĕtōrrĭdŭs, ă, ŭm, *parched with heat.* Vēnĭt ēt rĕtōrrĭdŭs, Phæd.

rĕtōrtŭs, ă, ŭm, *the pass. partic. of* retorqueo. Rĕtōrtă tērgō, Hor.

retrācto, ās, *to handle again.* Fērrŭmquĕ rĕtrāctānt, Virg. SYN. Ĭtĕrŭm trācto, rĕsūmo.

retrăho, āxī, āctŭm, *to draw back.* Ĭmpĕdĭūnt rĕtrāhĭtquĕ, Virg. SYN. Rĕdūco, āttrăho, trăho.

retrĭbŭo, ĭs, *to give back, recompense.* Cōrpŏră rĕtrĭbŭăt, Lucr. SYN. Rĕddo, rĕfĕro. Remunero.

retrō, trōrsŭm *and* trōrsŭs, adv., *backward, behind.* Abdūxĕrĕ rĕtrō, Virg. Ădrĭācās rĕtrō fŭgĭt, Virg. Nūllă rĕtrōrsŭm, Hor. SYN. Ā tērgo, pŏnĕ, pōst tērgă.

* retrōcēdo, ĭs, ssī; Liv.; grĕdĭŏr, dĕrĭs; Plin.; *(and* ‖ ĕo, īvī *or* ĭī,) *to go back.*

‖ retrōvērsŭs, ă, ŭm, *the pass. partic. of* retroverto, *turned backward.* Ipsĕ rĕtrōvērsŭs, Ov.

rĕtūndo, tŭdī, tūsŭm, *to blunt.* Vīrtŭtĕ rĕtŭndĕrĕ mēntēs, Fill. Syn. Reprĭmo; hĕbĕto, ŏbtūndo.

rĕtūsŭs, ă, ŭm, *the pass. partic. of* retundo. Lædĕ rĕtūsō, Virg.

rĕvălĕo, ēs, ŭī, *and* ēsco, ĭs, *to be well again.* Quā rĕvălēscĕrĕ pŏssĭs, Ov. Syn. Cōnvălēsco.

rĕvānēsco, ĭs, *to vanish again.* Ănĭmīquĕ rĕvānŭĭt ārdŏr, Ov.

rĕvĕho, vēxī, ctŭm, *to bring back.* Quī rĕvĕhĭs nŏbĭs, Virg. Syn. Rĕfĕro, rĕdūco.

rĕvĕllo, vĕllī, vūlsŭm, *to tear away.* Ūrbĕ rĕvĕllī, Virg. Syn. Āvĕllo, ābstrăho.

rĕvĕlo, ās, *to unveil.* Ārcănă rĕvēlăt, Vict. Syn. Ăpĕrĭo, dētĕgo, reclūdo, rĕsĕro, dēclāro, pāndo, ēxplĭco, mănĭfēsto, pătĕfăcĭo, prōdo, ĭndĭco. V. Manifesto.

rĕvĕrbĕro, ās, *to beat back.* Vălĭdōquĕ rĕvĕrbĕrăt īctū, Prop. V. Verbero.

rĕvĕrēndŭs, ă, ŭm, *to be revered, venerable.* Istŭd rĕvĕrēndă vĭrōrŭm, Aus.

rĕvĕrēntĕr, adv., *respectfully.* Fōrtūnăm rĕvĕrēntĕr hăbē, Aus.

rĕvĕrēntĭă, æ, f., *respect.* Ēst rĕvĕrēntĭă dāndī, Man. Syn. Vĕnĕrātĭo, ōbsērvāntĭă, cūltŭs, hŏnŏr.

rĕvĕrĕŏr, ērĭs, *to respect.* Lēctŭm rĕvĕrērĕ părēntĭs, Ov. Syn. Vĕnĕrŏr, cŏlo, hŏnōro. V. Veneror.

rĕvērto, *and* tŏr, sŭs, *to come back.* Lūnă rĕvērtēntēs, Virg. Cōnsūltă rĕvērtŏr, Virg. Syn. Rĕdĕo, rĕmĕo. V. Redeo.

rĕvīncĭo. ĭnxī, ĭnctŭm, *to bind.* Cēlsā Gўărōquĕ rĕvīnxĭt, Virg. Syn. Vīncĭo, lĭgo, rĕlĭgo. V. Vincio.

rĕvīnctŭs, ă, ŭm, *the pass. partic. of* revincio. Tērgă rĕvīnctŭm, Virg.

rĕvĭrēsco, ĭs, rŭī, *to be green again.* Părĭlī rĕvĭrēscĕrĕ pŏssĕ, Ov. Syn. Rūrsŭs vĭrēsco, rĕnŏvŏr.

rĕvīso, ĭs, sī, *to revisit.* Dūlcēsquĕ rĕvīsĕrĕ nātŏs, Virg.

rĕvīvo, *and* rĕvīvĭsco, vīxī, *to revive.* Cārnĕ rĕvīvēnt, P. Nol. Illĕ rĕvīvīscĕt, Ter. Mŏrĭbūndă rĕvīxĭt, Ov. Syn. Rĕsūrgo ād vītăm, rĕsūscĭtŏr; recrĕŏr. V. Resuscitor.

rĕvŏcābĭlĭs, ĕ, *that may be recalled.* Ēst rĕvŏcābĭlĭs īllĭs, Ov.

rĕvŏcāmĕn, ĭnĭs, n., *a recal.* Āccĭpĭō rĕvŏcāmĕn, ăĭt, Ov.

rĕvŏco, ās, *to recal.* Sēd rĕvŏcărĕ grădŭm, Virg. Syn. Rĕdūco, ābdūco, āvŏco, retrăho, āvērto, ābstrăho, āmŏvĕo.

rĕvŏlo, ās, *to fly back.* Cĕlĕrēs rĕvŏlănt ēx, Virg.

rĕvŏlūbĭlĭs, ĕ, *that may be rolled back.* Cōrpŭs rĕvŏlūbĭlĕ vōlvēns, Virg. Syn. Vŏlūbĭlĭs.

rĕvōlvo, vōlvī, vŏlūtŭm, *to roll back or again.* Ĭtĕrūmquĕ rĕvōlvĕrĕ cāsŭs, Virg. Syn. Ĭtĕrŭm *or* retrō vōlvo.

rĕvŏlūtŭs, ă, ŭm, *the pass. partic. of* revolvo. Jăcŭĭt rĕvŏlūtŭs ărēnă, Virg.

rĕvŏmŏ, ĭs, ŭī, *to vomit.* Rĭdēnt rĕvŏmēntĕm, Virg. Syn. Ēvŏmo, rējĭcĭo, ērūcto.

rĕŭs, ă, ŭm, *arraigned.* Bārbă rĕōrŭm, Mart. Syn. Sōns, nŏcēns, nŏxĭŭs, āccūsātŭs. Epith. Trīstĭs, pāllēns, păvĭdŭs, pāllĭdŭs, sōllĭcĭtŭs, ăttŏnĭtŭs, trĕpĭdŭs, squālĭdŭs, mĭsĕr. V. Accuso, sceleratus.

rĕvŭlsŭs, ă, ŭm, *the pass. partic. of* revello. Pārtĕ rĕvŭlsă, Virg.

rēx, rēgĭs, m., *a king.* Rēgĭbŭs ēssĕ, Ov. Syn. Prīncēps, ĭmpĕrātŏr, rēgnātŏr, rēctŏr. Epith. Fōrtĭs, māgnănĭmŭs, pŏtēns, gĕnĕrōsŭs, īnvīctŭs, bēllĭgĕr; Mārtĭŭs, Māvōrtĭŭs, māgnĭfĭcŭs, trĕmēndŭs, īnclўtŭs, īllūstrĭs, ārmĭpŏtēns, prūdēns, săpĭēns, prŏvĭdŭs, clārŭs, mŏdĕrātŭs, lēnĭs, jūstŭs, æquŭs. V. Princeps.

Rhădămānthŭs, ī, m., *one of the infernal judges.* Hæc Rhădămānthŭs hăbĕt, Virg. Syn. Ăgēnŏrĭdēs. Epith. Gnōssĭăcŭs, Gnōssĭŭs, lēgĭfĕr, sĕvĕrŭs, īmmītĭs, tōrvŭs, īnēxōrābĭlĭs, dūrŭs, trĕmēndŭs. V. Minos, Æacus.

rhădănŭs, ī, m., *a sort of fish.* Ov.

Rhætī, ōrŭm, m., *the inhabitants of Rhætia.* Vĭdērĕ Rhætī bēllă, Hor.

Rhætĭă, æ, f., *a part of ancient Italy, bordering on the eastern Alps.* Rhētĭă sўlvæ, Cl.

Rhætĭcŭs, ă, ŭm, *of Rhætia.* Rhætĭcă nūnc præbēnt, Ov.

Rhāmnēs *or* Rāmnēs, n. pl., *one of the three centuries of Roman knights.* Aūstĕră pŏēmătă Rhāmnēs, Hor.

Rhāmnēs, ētĭs, m., *the name of a Rutulian warrior.* Rhāmnētem āggrĕdĭtŭr, Virg.

rhămnŏs, *or* ŭs, m., *a sort of shrub.* Jăm rhămnī spŏntĕ vǐrēscŭnt, Colum.

Rhămnŭsĭă, æ, f., *the goddess of revenge.* Ŭltrīx Rhămnŭsĭă pœnās. Syn.
Nĕmĕsĭs. Epitu. Dūră, dīră, fŭrēns, fĕrŏx, ĭnīquă, crūdēlĭs, vīndēx, ĭuvīsă,
ăcĕrbă, ĭnĭmīcă.

Rhănĭs, ĭs, f., *one of the nymphs of Diana.* Hȳălēquĕ Rhănīsquĕ, Ov.

Rheă, æ, *or* ĕ̆e, ēs, f., *Rhea, Ops or Cybele.* Rhĕă quæ Lătīis Ŏps, Aus. Sæpĕ
Rhĕă quĕsta ĕst, Ov.—2. *Rhea Sylvia or Ilia.* Quĕm Rhĕă săcĕrdŏs, Virg.

Rhēbās, æ, m., *a river of Bithynia.* Ĕxīrĕnt flūmĭnă Rhēbæ, Virg.

rhēdă, æ, f., *a light chariot.* Mŏrbī, rhēdārŭm, Juv. V. Currus.

Rhēgĭŭm, *or* Ĭŏn, ĭī, n., *a city of Calabria.* Ădvērsăquĕ mœnĭă Rhēgī, Ov.
Rhēgĭŏn ĭngrēdĭtŭr, Id.

Rhēnŭs, ī, m., *a river which separates Germany from France.* Rhēnŭs ĭn ūrbĕm,
Mart. Epith. Bĭcŏrnĭs, trĭcŏrnĭs, spūmāns, gĕlĭdŭs, tŭmēns, fĕrŏx, flāvŭs,
tŭmĭdŭs, cĭtātŭs, præcēps, răpāx, răpĭdŭs, văgŭs, tūrgĭdŭs, aūdāx ; Teūtŏnĭcŭs,
cŏrnĭgĕr, lātŭs, spūmĕŭs, ūndĭsŏnŭs, Gāllĭcŭs. V. Fluvius.

Rhēsŭs, ī, m., *a king of Thrace, who came to the assistance of Priam, and was slain
on the night of his arrival by Ulysses and Diomed.* Hīnc Rhēsī nĭvĕĭs, Virg.

Rhētēnŏr, ŏrĭs, m., *one of the companions of Diomed.* Ĕt cūm Rhētēnŏrĕ Nȳcteŭs,
Ov.

rhētŏr, ŏrĭs, m., *a rhetorician.* Rhētŏrĭbŭsquĕ mĭhi, Mart. Syn. Ŏrātŏr.

rhētŏrĭcŭs, ă, ŭm, *of rhetoric.* Rhētŏrĭcă dēscēndĭt, Juv.

rhīnŏcĕrŏs, ŏtĭs, m., *a rhinoceros.* Rhīnŏcĕrŏtă măgĭstrī, Juv.

Rhīpæŭs, Rhīphæŭs *or* Rīphæŭs, ă, ŭm, *of the Riphæan mountains.* Rhīpæāsque
ārdŭŭs ārcēs, Virg.

Rhīpeŭs *or* Rhīpheŭs, ĕŏs, m., *the name of a Centaur.* Ĕxtāntēm Rhīpĕă sȳlvīs,
Ov.

Rhŏdănŭs, ī, m., *a river in France.* Ărār, Rhŏdănŭs, Mŏsă, Sid. Epith.
Tŭmĭdŭs, ĭncĭtŭs, fŭrēns, præcēps, spūmāns, spūmĕŭs, cĕlĕr, vēlŏx, răpĭdŭs.

Rhŏdĕ, ēs, f., *the name of a woman.* Tĕmpēstīvă pĕtĭt Rhŏdĕ, Hor.

Rhŏdĭŭs, ă, ŭm, *of Rhodes.* Ŏ Rhŏdĭæ dūctŏr fŏrtĭssĭmĕ clāssĭs, Ov.

Rhŏdŏpē, ēs, f., *a mountain of Thrace.* Lūstrātām Rhŏdŏpēn, Hor. Epith.
Thrēĭcĭă, ăĕrĭă, cānă, glăcĭālĭs, nĭmbŏsă, Thrēssă, gĕlĭdă, āltă, nĭvālĭs, præ-'
rŭptă, sŭblīmĭs, ārdŭă. V. Hæmus.

Rhŏdŏpēĭŭs, ă, ŭm, *of mount Rhodope.* Rhŏdŏpēĭŭs āccĭpĭt Ŏrpheŭs, Ov.

Rhŏdŭs, *or* dŏs, f., *an island of Asia.* Clārām Rhŏdŏn, aūt Mĭtȳlēnēn, Hor.
Epith. Phœbēĭă, clāră, īrrĭgŭă, aūrĕă, pūlchră, fērtĭlĭs, nōbĭlĭs, fœcūndă,
fĕrāx.

Rhœbŭs, ī, m., *the name of a horse.* Virg.

Rhœtēĭŭs *and* tēŭs, ă, ŭm, *of the promontory of Rhœteum, Trojan.* Rhœtēo ĭn lĭt-
tŏre ĭnānĕm, Virg. Rhœtēĭŭs hŏstĭs, Id.

Rhœteŭs, ĕŏs, ĕī *or* eī, m., *the name of a warrior.* Fŭgĭēntēm Rhœtĕă prætĕr,
Virg.

Rhœtŭs *or* cŭs, ī, m., *one of the Giants.*—2. *one of the Centaurs.* Rhœtūm rĕtŏrsĭstī,
Hor.

rhŏmbŭs, ī, m., *a wheel used by witches ; a turbot.* Cŏncĭtă rhŏmbō, Ov.

rhŏncbŭs, ī, m., *a snoring, a scoff.* Mājŏrēs nūsquăm rhŏncī, Mart. V. Sterto.

Rhȳndăcŭs, ī, m., *a river of Mysia.* Flāvēntēm, Rhȳndăcĕ, pŏntō, Virg

rhȳtĭŭm, ĭī, n., *a drinking vessel.* Ĭn rhȳtĭō pŏtĕrās, Mart.

rĭctŭs, ŭs, m., *and* ŭm, ī, n., *a gaping.* Sāngŭĭnĕ rĭctŭs, Ov. Mŏllĭă rīctă frĕmūnt, Lucr. Epith. Hīāns, hĭūlcŭs, ăpērtŭs, pătēns, pătŭlŭs, ĭmmānĭs, vŏrāx,
ăvĭdŭs, spūmāns, tērrĭbĭlĭs.

rĭdēndŭs, ă, ŭm, *ridiculous.* Pĕccĕt ăd ĕxtrēmŭm rĭdēndŭs, Hor.

rĭdĕo, ēs, rīsī, rīsŭm, *to laugh.* Rĭdĕt ămātŏrĕm, Ov. Syn. Căchĭnnŏr. V. Risus.

rĭdĭcŭlŭs, ă, ŭm, *merry, ridiculous.* Ŏ rēm rĭdĭcŭlăm ! Cat.

rĭgĕo, ēs, *and* ēsco, ĭs, *to grow stiff.* Fērrŏquĕ rĭgēbānt, Virg. Vēstēsquĕ
rĭgēscūnt, Ov. Syn. Ălgĕo, frīgĕo, hŏrrĕo. V. Frigeo, horreo.

rĭgĭdŭlŭs, ă, ŭm, *the dimin. of rigidus, shivering.* Pāllĭdŭlă, rĭgĭdŭlă, nūdŭlă,
Adrian.

rĭgĭdŭs, ă, ŭm, *stiff, frozen.* Rĭgĭdūm fūlcēs, Virg. Syn. Ăspĕr, dūrŭs ;
frĭgĭdŭs.

rĭgo, ās, *to water.* Lātē rĭgăt ārmă, Virg. Syn. Irrĭgo, īrrōro, hūmēcto.

rĭgŏr, ŏrĭs, m., *stiffness.* Pòstrēmă rĭgòrĭs, Lucr. Syn. Ăspĕrĭtās, dūrĭtĭēs ; frĭgŭs. Epith. Dūrŭs, āspĕr, mărmŏrĕŭs, ĭnflēxŭs, sævŭs, ĭmmnĭtĭs, ĭmmānĭs, bārbărŭs, trŭx, mĕtŭēndŭs.

rĭgŭŭs, ă, ŭm, *moist, watering.* Rūră mĭhi ēt rĭgŭī, Virg. Syn. Irrĭgŭŭs, ūdŭs, mădĭdŭs, hūmĭdŭs.

rīmă, æ, f., *a chink.* Imbrēm, rĭmĭsquĕ fătĭscūnt, Virg. Syn. Hĭātŭs, fĭssūră, scĭssūră, spĭrāmēntŭm, mĕātŭs, fŏrāmĕn. Epith. Pătēns, ăpērtă, āngŭstă, tĕnŭĭs, lātă, hĭŭlcă, hĭāns, căvă, mūrālĭs. V. Rimosus.

rīmātŭs, ă, ŭm, *the partic. of* rimor, *having searched.* Rīmātŭs lōngē, Stat.

rīmŏr, ārĭs, *to search into.* In stāgnĭs rīmāntŭr, Virg. Syn. Quæro, scrūtŏr. V. Quæro.

rīmōsŭs, ă, ŭm, *full of chinks.* Lævī rīmōsă cŭbĭlĭă līmō, Virg. Syn. Dĕhĭscēns, hĭāns ; pătēns, ăpērtŭs, hĭŭlcŭs.

rīmŭlă, æ, f., *a dimin. of* rima. Rīmŭlă quæ, Mant.

rīngŏr, ĕrĭs, *to be enraged.* Quăm săpĕre ĕt rīngī, Hor.

rīpă, æ, f., *the bank of a river.* Rīpārūmquĕ tŏrōs, Virg. Syn. Lĭttŭs ; ōră, āctă, mārgo. Epith. Grāmĭnĕă, vĭrĭdĭs, hūmēns, hūmĭdă, ūdă, mădĭdă, ămœnă, rīdēns, bĭbŭlă, hērbĭdă, mūscōsă, ŏpācă, frĭgĭdă, gēlĭdă, frŏndēns, vĭrēns, vērnāns, aprīcă, spūmāns, spūmōsă, ūndāns, dēclīvĭs, oblīquă, gārrŭlă, strĕpēns, flŭvĭālĭs. V. Littus.

rīsŏr, ŏrĭs, m., *a mocker.* Vērum ĭtă rīsōrēs, Hor. Syn. Dērīsŏr.

rīsŭs, ūs, m., *laughter.* Pārvĕ pŭĕr, rīsŭ, Virg. Syn. Căchĭnnŭs. Epith. Lætŭs, hĭlărĭs, jūcŭndŭs, blāndĭēns, tĕnĕr, trĕmŭlŭs, mōllĭs, dūlcĭs, sĕrēnŭs, ūrbānŭs, vĕnŭstŭs, ēffūsŭs, sŏlūtŭs, prŏtērvŭs, prŏcāx.

rītĕ, adv., *in due form.* Ergō rītĕ sŭŭm, Virg. Syn. Dē mŏrĕ, ĕx mŏrĕ, rēctē, ūt dĕcĕt.

rītŭs, ūs, *and* tēs, ĭs, m., *a rite, a custom.* Hīnc pŏpŭlī rītŭs, Ov. Syn. Mōs, cōnsuētūdo, rătĭo, mŏdŭs. Epith. Sōlēnnĭs, pĭŭs, vĕrēndŭs, vĕtūstŭs, prīscŭs, āntīquŭs, vĕtŭs, patrĭŭs, nŏvŭs.

rīvālĭs, ĕ, *rival.* Quĭn sĭnĕ rīvālī, Hor. Syn. Æmŭlŭs.

rīvŭs, *and* vŭlŭs, ī. m., *a river, a brook.* Pĕr grāmĭnă rīvŭs, Virg. Rīvŭlŭs ūndăs, Arat. Epith. Irrĭgŭŭs, rūgĭēns. ērrāns, sērpēns, lŏquāx, gārrŭlŭs, sŭsūrrāns, vitrĕŭs, nĭtĭdŭs, lĭmpĭdŭs, pēllūcĭdŭs, ārgēntĕŭs, crỹstāllĭnŭs, jūgĭs, pĕrēnnĭs, præcēps, flŭēns, lēvĭs, strĕpĭtāns, strĕpēns, prōnŭs, oblīquŭs, cĕlĕr, gēlĭdŭs, liquĭdŭs, raūcŭs, ārgūtŭs, ūndāns, sŏnāns, crĕpĭtāns, dūctĭlĭs, cădēns, văgŭs. V. Fluvius, fons, torrens.

rīxă, æ, f., *a quarrel.* Excĭtārĕ rīxăm, (Phal.) Syn. Jūrgĭŭm, āltērcātĭo, cōntēntĭo, dīscōrdĭă, dīssĭdĭŭm, līs, pūgnă. Epith. Clāmōsă, īnsānă, vēsānă, răbĭōsă, īmprŏbă, ĭnĭquă, dīră, ĭnĭmĭcă, fŭrēns, probrōsă, tŭrpĭs, ăcērbă, mŏlēstă, āspĕră, fērvĭdă, sānguĭnĕă, crŭēntă. V. Convicium, injuria.

rīxātŏr, ŏrĭs, m., *a quarreller.* Quint.

rīxŏr, ārĭs, *to quarrel.* Āltĕr rīxātŭr, Hor. Syn. Āltērcŏr, jūrgŏr, cōntēndo, lītĭgo, dīscēpto, pūgno, cērto.

Rōbīgo, ĭnĭs, f., *a goddess invoked against mildew.* Lūcūm Rōbīgĭnĭs ībăt, Ov.

rŏbŏrĕŭs, ă, ŭm, *of oak.* Mīttĕrĕ rŏbŏrĕō, Ov. Syn. Quērnĕŭs, quērnŭs, ĭlĭgnŭs.

rŏbŏro, ās, *to fortify.* Rŏbŏrăt ĭctŭm, Lucr. Syn. Cŏrrŏbŏro, fīrmo, cōnfīrmo.

rŏbŭr, ŏrĭs, n., *strength, fortitude.* Stānt rŏbŏrĕ vīrēs, Virg. Syn. Vīs, vīrtŭs, vĭgŏr, nērvī, lăcērtī; cōnstāntĭă, fōrtĭtūdo. Epith. Fīrmŭm, vălĭdŭm, ēxĭmĭŭm, īngēns, præstāns. jŭvĕnīlĕ, sŏlĭdŭm, fōrtĕ, prævălĭdŭm, dūrŭm, rĭgĭdŭm, īnsīgnĕ, lăcērtōsŭm, Hērcŭlĕŭm, Gĭgāntĕŭm, īnvīctŭm, īnfrāctŭm, īndŏmĭtŭm, ĭnēxpŭgnābĭlĕ, fūlmĭnĕŭm, ĭnclỹtŭm.—2. *an oak.* Illī rŏbŭr ĕt æs, Hor. Syn. Quērcŭs, ĭlēx. Epith. Sỹlvēstrĕ, nōdōsŭm, dūrŭm, fĭssĭlĕ, īmpĕnĕtrābĭlĕ. V. Quercus.

rŏbūstŭs, ă, ŭm, *robust.* Inde ŭbī rōbūstĭs, Lucr. Syn. Fōrtĭs, vălēns, vălĭdŭs, lăcērtōsŭs, nērvōsŭs. V. Fortis.

rŭdo, rūsī, rōsŭm, *to gnaw.* Rōdĕrĕt ūnguēs, Hor. Syn. Cōrrōdo, ārrōdo, cīrcŭmrōdo, ēxĕdo, cōnsŭmo, tŭndo, tōndĕo.

rŏgālĭs, ĕ, *of a funeral.* Flāmmæquĕ rŏgālēs, Ov.

rŏgātŏr, ŏrĭs, m., *he who asks.* Ăd lăcŭs rŏgătŏr, (Phal.) Mart.

rŏgĭto, ăs, *the frequent. of* rogo. Prĭāmō rŏgĭtāns, Virg. Syn. Rŏgo ; pĕto, ĭntērrŏgo.

rŏgo, ăs, *to intreat.* Sæpĕ rŏgēs ălĭquĭd, Prop. Syn. Oro, ōbsecro, prĕcŏr ; pĕto. V. Precor, oro.

rŏgŭs, ī, m., *a funeral pile.* Cōnscēndĭt fūrĭbūndă rŏgōs, Virg. Syn. Pўră, būstŭm ; sĕpŭlcrŭm. Epith. Ărdēns, flăgrāns, ăccēnsŭs, crĕpĭtāns, fūnĕrĕŭs, lūgubrĭs, trĭstĭs, mœstŭs, ēxcēlsŭs, sūblīmĭs, ŏdŏrŭs, ŏdŏrĭfĕr, ŏdŏrātŭs, strūctŭs, ēxstrūctŭs, ērēctŭs. V. Ignis.

Rōmă, æ, f., *Rome.* Rōmă, tūŭm nōmĕn, Tĭb. Epith. Inclўtă, fĕrōx, pŏtēns, bellīcă, bellātrīx, ārdŭă, āntīquă, vĕtūstă, prīscă, clără, nōbĭlĭs, cĕlebrĭs, splēndĭdă, vĭctrīx, trĭūmphātrīx, sŭpērbă, dīvĕs, sēptēmgĕmĭnă, pĭă, sānctă ; Rōmŭlă, Rōmŭlĕă, Mārtĭă, Māvōrtĭă. Quĭrīnālĭs ; Sāturnĭă ; Aŭsŏnĭă ; Dārdănă, Dārdănĭă.

Rōmānī, ōrŭm, m. pl., *the Romans.* Ĭtălās, Rōmānōrŭmquĕ trĭūmphōs, Virg. Syn. Rōmŭlĭdæ, Quĭrītēs, Ænĕădæ, Trōjŭgĕnæ, Dārdănĭdæ. Epith. Māgnănĭmī, bellācēs, aŭdācēs, fōrtēs, gĕnĕrōsī, īmpăvĭdī, ārmĭgĕrī, invīctī, fĕrōcēs, indŏmĭtī.

Rōmānŭs, ŭlĕŭs, *and* ŭlŭs, ă, ŭm, *Roman.* Avērtĭs Rōmānĭs ārcĭbŭs, Virg. Ět quæ Rōmŭlĕŭs, Mart. Rōmŭlă quōndăm, Virg.

Rōmŭlĭdæ, ārŭm *and* dŭm, m. pl., *the Romans.* Cōnsūrgĕrĕ bēllŭm Rōmŭlĭdīs, Virg.

Rōmŭlŭs, ī, m., *the founder of Rome.* Rōmŭlŭs, Assărăcī, Virg. Syn. Quĭrīnŭs, Ilĭădēs. Epith. Mārtĭgĕnă, Mārtĭŭs, Māvōrtĭŭs, Aŭsŏnĭŭs, aŭdāx, māgnănĭmŭs, fōrtĭs, frātrĭcīdă, fĕrōx, īmpăvĭdŭs, bellĭgĕr, ārmĭpŏtēns, vīctŏr, pŏtēns, aŭgŭr. V. Quirinus.

rōrālĭs, ĕ, *dewy.* Vīrgăquĕ rōrālēs, Ov.

rōrēsco, ĭs, *to dissolve in dew.* In lĭquĭdăs rōrēscĭt ăquăs, Ov.

rōrĭfĕr, ă, ŭm, *dewy.* Rōrĭfĕrĭs tērrăm, Lucr. Syn. Rĭgŭŭs, īrrĭgŭŭs.

rōro, ăs, *to bedew.* Spārsī rōrābānt, Virg. Syn. Irrōro, rĭgo, īrrĭgo, āspērgo, hūmēcto, rōrĕ pērfūndo ; rōrēsco, stīllo, rōrĕ difflŭo ; rōrĕm ēmītto, spārgo.

rōs, rōrĭs, m., *dew.* Rōrĭbŭs ārbŏr, Lucan. Epith. Mātūtīnŭs, frīgĭdŭs, gēlĭdŭs, nōctūrnŭs, liquĭdŭs, vitrĕŭs, tĕnŭĭs, hūmĭdŭs, ŭdŭs, hūmēns, ārgēntĕŭs, aĕrĭŭs, gēmĭnĕŭs, gēmmāns, cădēns, plŭvĭŭs, stīllāns, lacrўmōsŭs, fœcūndŭs, dūlcĭs, grātŭs.

rōsă, æ, f., *a rose.* Ullă rŏsæ, Ov. Epith. Vērnāns, flōrēns, rŭbēns, mĭcāns, rŭbēscēns, pūrpŭrĕă, lūtĕŏlă, sānguĭnĕă, pūnĭcĕă, pīctă, tĕnĕră, mōllĭs, rōscĭdă, ŏdŏră, bĕnĕ ŏlēns, hălāns ; Cўprĭă, Cўthērææ, Cўthērēĭă, Idălĭă, Pāphĭă.

rōsācĕŭs, ă, ŭm, *of a rose.* Undă rōsācĕă, Saut.

rōsārĭŭm, ĭī, n., *a place where roses grow.* Gaŭdērĕ rŏsārĭă cūltū, Aus. Epith. Amœnŭm, vĭrēns, vĭrĭdĕ, ŏdŏrŭm, ŏdŏrātŭm, grātŭm, pīctŭm, pūnĭcĕŭm, rŭbĭcūndŭm, Pæstānŭm.

rōscĭdŭs, ă, ŭm, *bedewed.* Rōscĭdă pēnnĭs, Virg. Syn. Rōrātŭs.

Rōscĭŭs, ĭī, m., *a comedian, the friend of Cicero.* Quæ dōctŭs Rōscĭŭs ăgĭt, Hor.

rōsētŭm, ī, n., *a place planted with rose-trees.* Sălĭŭncă rŏsētĭs, Virg.

rŏsĕŭs, ă, ŭm, *of a rose colour.* Avērtēns rŏsĕă, Virg. Syn. Rŭbēns, rŭbĕŭs, pūrpŭrĕŭs, rŭbĭcūndŭs.

Rŏsĕŭs cāmpŭs, m., *a district of the Sabines.* Quī Rŏsĕă rūră Vĕlīnī, Virg.

rōstră, ōrŭm, n. pl., *the tribunals at Rome.* Rōstră pŭsīllī, Juv.

rŏstrātŭs, ă, ŭm, *beaked.* Grăvī Rōstrātă dūcī pōndĕrĕ, Hor.

rŏstrŭm, ī, n., *a beak of a ship.* Ăttŏnĭtŭs rōstrĭs, Virg. Epith. Ūncŭm, ădūncŭm, rĕdūncŭm, ăcūtŭm, mōrdāx, pōrrēctŭm, cūrvŭm, ĭncūrvŭm, dūrŭm, rĭgĭdŭm, mĭnāx, ærātŭm.

rŏtă, æ, f., *a wheel.* Mētă tĕrēndă rŏtă, Ov. Syn. Ŏrbĭs, ōrbĭtă. Epith. Rŏtūndă, cūrvă, ăgĭlĭs, lĕvĭs, īnstăbĭlĭs, vēlōx, prŏpĕrāns, cĕlĕrĭs, vŏlūbĭlĭs, cĭtă, præcēps, fērvĭdă, fērvēns, fērrātă, strīdēns. V. Currus, gyrus.

rŏtātĭlĭs, ĕ, *turning like a wheel.* Ět rŏtātĭlēs trōchæōs, (Iamb. pur.) Prud. Syn. Vŏlūbĭlĭs, rŏtātŭs.

rŏtātŏr, ōrĭs, m., *a whirler round.* Bāssărĭdŭm rŏtātŏr Ēvān, Stat.

rŏtātŭs, ūs, m., *a turning or whirling round.* Pæŏnēs ārmă rŏtātū, Stat.

rŏto, ăs, *to whirl about.* Ăc rŏtăt ēnsĕm, Virg. Syn. Vērto, vērso, cīrcŭmăgo, cīrcŭmvōlvo, gўro. V. Gyrus.

rŏtŭlă, æ, f., *the dimin. of* rota. Quĭd rŏtŭlæ īnsīstĭs ? Aus.

rŏtūndo, ăs, *to make round.* Tălēntă rŏtūndēntŭr, Hor.

rŏtŭndŭs, ă, ŭm, *round.* Ōrĕ rŏtŭndō, Hor. SYN. Glŏbōsŭs, sphærĭcŭs, ŏrbĭcŭlātŭs, tĕrĕs.
rŭbĕfăcĭo, fēcī, făctŭm, *to make red.* Rŭbĕfēcĕrăt ōră, Sil.
rŭbēllŭs, ă, ŭm, *the dimin. of* ruber. Subst. -ŭm, ī, n., *rosy wine.* Fæx crāssă rŭbēllī, Mart.
rŭbĕo, ŭī, *to be red.* Aūrōră rŭbēbăt, Virg. SYN. Rŭbēsco. V. Erubesco.
rŭbĕr, ubră, brŭm, *red.* Flāvăquĕ dē rŭbrō, Ov. SYN. Rŭbĕŭs, rŭbēns, rŭbĭcŭndŭs, rŭbēscēns, rŏsĕŭs, pūnĭcĕŭs, pŭrpŭrĕŭs, sānguĭnĕŭs, īgnĕŭs.
rŭbēsco, ĭs, *to grow red.* Jāmquĕ rŭbēscēbăt, Virg.
rŭbētă, æ, f., *a toad.* Sĭtĭēntĕ rŭbētăm, Juv.
rŭbētŭm, ī, n., *a bushy place.* Mōră rŭbētīs, Ov. SYN. Spīnētŭm, dūmētŭm. V. Spinetum.
rŭbĕŭs, ă, ŭm, *red.* Nūnc făcĭlīs rŭbĕā, Virg. V. Ruber.
Rŭbī, ōrŭm, m. pl., *a city of Apulia.* Īndĕ Rŭbōs fēssī, Hor.
Rŭbĭcōn, ōnĭs, m., *a river in Italy.* Rŭbĭcōnĭs ăd ūndās, Lucan. EPITH. Părvŭs, Ălpīnŭs, ămœnŭs, grātŭs, vitrĕŭs, līmpĭdŭs, sŏnāns, cănōrŭs, lēnĭs, mītĭs, plăcĭdŭs, cærŭlĕŭs, vĭrēns, grāmĭnĕŭs. V. Fluvius.
rŭbĭcŭndŭlŭs, ă, ŭm, *the dimin. of* rubicundus. Īllă vĕnĭt rŭbĭcŭndŭlă, tōtŭm, Juv.
rŭbĭcŭndŭs, ă, ŭm, *red.* Cōnjūx rŭbĭcŭndă mărītī, Ov. SYN. Rŭbĕŭs.
rubīgĭnōsŭs, ă, ŭm, *rusty.* Rŭbīgĭnōsī dēntēs, Mart.
rubīgo, ĭnĭs, f., *rust.* Tēctă rŭbīgo, Prud. Ēssēt rŭbīgo, Virg. SYN. Ærūgo, fērrūgo, sĭtŭs. EPITH. Ātră, nigră, āspĕră, scabră, rĭgĭdă, fœdă, tūrpĭs, tētră, mōrdāx, ĕdāx.
rŭbŏr, ōrĭs, m., *redness.* Fāmă rŭbōrĕ, Mart. EPITH. Pŭrpŭrĕŭs, pūnĭcĕŭs, rŏsĕŭs, īgnĕŭs, flāmmĕŭs, dĕcōrŭs, splēndēns, cŏrŭscŭs, rŭtĭlŭs, mĭcāns. V. Pudor.
rubrīcă, æ, f., *red earth.* Prælĭă rŭbrīcā, Hor.
rŭbŭm, ī, n., *a bramble berry.* Plēnă cănīstră rŭbīs, Prop.
rŭbŭs, ī, m., *a bramble.* Īntĕrĭērĕ rŭbī, Ov. SYN. Sēntĭs, veprĭs, spīnă. EPITH. Āspĕr, hōrrēns, pīnguĭs, dūrŭs, ăcūtŭs, rĭgĭdŭs, vŭlnĭfĭcŭs, hāmātŭs, vĭlĭs, pūnĭcĕŭs, hīrsūtŭs. V. Spina.
rūctātrīx, īcĭs, f., *that rises on the stomach.* Nēc deēst rūctātrīx mēnthă, Mart.
rūcto, ās, *and* ŏr, ārĭs, *to belch.* Sī bĕnĕ rūctāvĭt, Juv.
rūctŭs, ūs, m., *a belch.* Pēctŏrĕ rūctūs, Lucil.
rŭdēns, ntĭs, m., *a cable.* Strīdōrquĕ rŭdēntŭm, Virg. SYN. Fūnĭs, rĕtĭnăcŭlŭm. EPITH. Naūtĭcŭs; grăvĭs, rĭgĭdŭs, tēnsŭs, lāxŭs, lōngŭs, īngēns, tōrtŭs, īntōrtŭs, mărīnŭs, ēxtēnsŭs, cōntēntŭs, nōdōsŭs. V. Funis.
rŭdīmēntŭm, ī, n., *a rudiment or principle.* Dūră rŭdīmēntă, Virg. SYN. Tȳrōcĭnĭŭm; prīmĭtĭæ.
rŭdĭs, ĕ, *rough, ignorant.* Ūllă rŭdēs, Ov. SYN. Īgnārŭs, tȳro; hĕbĕs, tārdŭs, stŭpĭdŭs.
rŭdĭs, ĭs, f., *a rod given to gladiators as a mark of their discharge.* Dōnārī jām rŭdĕ, Hor.
rudo, ĭs, dī, *to bray.* Rŭdĕrĕ crēdās, Pers. Ūt rŭdĭt ā scăbrā, Ov.—2. *To roar.* Sævā sūb nōctĕ rŭdēntŭm, Virg.
rŭdŭs, ĕrĭs, n., *rubbish.* Rŭdĕrĭbŭs lātĭs. SYN. Cæmēntŭm; părĭĕtīnă.
Rŭfīllŭs, ī, m., *the name of a man.* Pāstīllōs Rŭfīllŭs ŏlĕt, Hor.
Rŭfīnŭs, ī, m., *the name of a man.* Mĭttĭt, Rŭfīnĕ, sălūtĕm, Ov.
Rŭfræ, ārŭm, f. pl., *a city of Campania.* Quīquĕ Rŭfrās Bătŭlūmquĕ tĕnēnt, Virg.
rūfŭs, ă, ŭm, *reddish.* Gāllĭă rūfĭs, Mart. SYN. Flāvŭs, crŏcĕŭs, lūtĕŭs, flāvēns, rŭtĭlŭs, aūrĕŭs.
rūgă, æ, f., *a wrinkle.* Jām vĕnĭēnt rūgæ, Ov. EPITH. Rĭgĭdă, tūrpĭs, īnfōrmĭs, dēfōrmĭs, cōntrāctă, sĕvēră, fūnēstă, ănīlĭs, sĕnīlĭs.
rŭgĭo, īs, ĭī *or* īvī, *to roar.* Nōrānt rŭgīrĕ lĕōnēs, Tib.
rŭgītŭs, ūs, m., *a roaring.* Cūm fĕră rŭgītū, Mart. EPITH. Hōrrēndŭs, hōrrĭdŭs, tērrĭbĭlĭs, rĕsŏnāns, frĕmēns. V. Clamor.
rūgōsŭs, ă, ŭm, *wrinkled.* Rūgōsĭōrēm cūm gĕrās, (Scaz.) Mart. SYN. Rūgĭs āspĕr, fœdŭs. V. Ruga.
rŭīnă, æ, f., *a fall, destruction, misfortune.* Vāstā cōnvŭlsă rŭīnā, Virg. SYN.

Cāsŭs, lāpsŭs, prōlāpsĭo, ēxcĭdĭŭm; pērnĭcĭēs, ēxĭtĭŭm, clādēs, īnfōrtūnĭŭm. EPITH. Sŭbĭtă, rĕpēntīnă, ĭnōpīnă, hōrrēndă, īngēns, grăvĭs, īnfaŭstă, trīstĭs, mœstă, flēbĭlĭs, īmmānĭs, dīră, răpĭdă, tērrĭfĭcă, lēthĭfĕră, ĭrrĕpărăbĭlĭs. V. Rudus, ruo, cado.

rūīnōsŭs, ă, ŭm, *ruinous, decayed.* Vītă rūīnōsīs, Aus. SYN. Rŭēns, cădūcŭs, lābāns; rŭptŭs. V. Labans.

Rūmĭnă fĭcŭs, f., *the fig-tree under which Romulus and Remus were suckled.* Rū-mĭnă nūnc fĭcŭs, Ov.

rūmĭno, ās, *to chew the cud.* Rūmĭnăt hērbās, Virg.

rūmŏr, ōrĭs, m., *a rumour.* Rūmŏr ăcērbĕ, Tib. SYN. Fāmă, mūrmŭr, sērmo. EPITH. Văgŭs, vŏlāns, āncēps, dŭbĭŭs, īncērtŭs, lŏquāx, gārrŭlŭs, tūrbĭdŭs, vēlōx, pērnīx, prŏcāx, prŏtērvŭs, sŭbĭtŭs, rĕpēntīnŭs. V. Fama.

rūmpo, rūpī, rūptŭm, *to break.* Vīncŭlă rūpī, Virg. SYN. Pērrūmpo, dīsrūmpo, frāngo, ēffrīngo, refrīngo, dīscīndo, dīssōlvo. V. Frango.

rūnco, ās, *to extirpate bad plants.* Pers.

rŭo, ĭs, *to fall down.* Quō rŭĭtĭs quævĕ, Virg. SYN. Cădo, cōncĭdo, dēcĭdo, prŏcĭdo; lābŏr, dēlābŏr, cōllābŏr, prŏlābŏr, cōrrŭo, præcĭpĭto, prŏcŭmbo. V. Cado.

rūpēs, ĭs, f., *a rock.* Pĕlăgī rūpēs īmmōtă, Virg. SYN. Caŭtēs, scŏpŭlŭs, sāxŭm, sīlēx. EPITH. Ardŭă, ābrūptă, prærūptă, ăcrĭă, præcēps, ĭnăccēssă, īnvĭă, ĭn-hōspĭtă, hōrrēndă, hōrrĭdă, scŏpŭlōsă, sāxōsă, sāxĕă, scrŭpĕă, dūră, īmmānĭs, īmmōtă, æquŏrĕă, căvă, ēxēsă, dūmōsă, mūscōsă, frŭtĭcōsă, nĕmŏrōsă, sȳlvēstrĭs, ăcūtă, frōndēns, āspĕră, ŏpācă, aprīcă. V. Saxum, mons.

Rūpĭlĭŭs, iī, m., *the name of a man.* Rēgĭs Rūpĭlī pŭs ātquĕ vĕnēnŭm, Hor.

rūrālĭs, ĕ, *of the country.* Cārpēns rūrālĭs Ăpōllo, Nem. V. Rusticus.

rūrĭcŏlă, æ, m. f., *one who lives in the country, a tiller of the ground.* Tēmpŏrĕ rūrĭcŏlæ, Ov. SYN. Ăgrĭcŏlă, rūstĭcŭs.

rūrĭgĕnă, œ, m. f., *one born in the country.* Rūrĭgĕnæ pāvērĕ, Ov.

rūrsŭs, adv., *anew, again.* Rūrsŭs ĭn ārmă, Virg. SYN. Rūrsŭm, ĭtĕrŭm, dēnŭo, ăb īntegrō.

rūs, rūrĭs, n., *the country.* Rūrĭs ărātŏr, Man. SYN. Ăgĕr, cāmpŭs; vīllă. EPITH. Ămœnŭm, vĭrĭdāns, gĕnĭālĕ, nĕmŏrōsŭm, lætŭm, fērtĭlĕ, fĕrāx, ŏpācŭm, aprīcŭm, flōrĭdŭm, frōndēns, flōrĭfĕrŭm, vīrēns, spătĭōsŭm, flōrēns, Cĕrēălĕ, cāmpēstrĕ, rōscĭdŭm, pātēns, frāgrāns, vērnāns, ăquătĭcŭm. V. Ager, hortus.

rūssŭs, ă, ŭm, *of a deep red.* Lūtĕă rūssăquĕ vēlă, Lucr.

rūstĭcē, adv., *rustically.* Rūstĭcĭŭs tōnsō, Hor.

rūstĭcĭtās, ātĭs, f., *rusticity.* Rūstĭcĭtătĕ trŭcĕm, Mart. SYN. Ăspĕrĭtās mōrŭm, fĕrĭtās. EPITH. Incūltă, agrēstĭs, hōrrĭdă, dūră, īmmītĭs, īndōctă.

rūstĭcŭs, *and* cŭlŭs, ă, ŭm, *rustic.* Rūstĭcă cōrdă, Prop. SYN. Agrēstĭs, sȳlvēs-trĭs; ĭnūrbānŭs, īncūltŭs, hōrrĭdŭs, īncōndĭtŭs, rŭdĭs, trūx, fĕrŭs, bārbărŭs.

rūstĭcŭs, ī, m., *a husbandman, countryman.* Rūstĭcŭs ūrbĕm, Hor. SYN. Ăgrĭcŏlă, rūrĭcŏlă, cŏlōnŭs, vīllĭcŭs.

rūtă, æ, f., *the herb rue.* EPITH. Rĭgēns, vĭrĭdĭs, ămāră, mūltĭcŏmă, sălūbrĭs, sălūtărĭs, flōrēns, flōrĭdă.

rūtātŭs, ă, ŭm, *seasoned with rue.* Rūtātōs ŏvă lăcērtōs, Mart.

Rūtĭlĭŭs, iī, m., *a Roman consul who devoted himself in a war against the Marsi.* Rōbūr mīrārĕ Rūtĭlī, Ov.

rŭtĭlo, ās, *to shine.* Pĕr sūdŭm rŭtĭlārĕ, Virg. SYN. Mĭco, cŏrŭsco, splēndĕo. V. Splendeo, luceo.

rŭtĭlŭs, ă, ŭm, *shining.* Addĭdĕrānt rŭtĭlī, Virg. SYN. Rŭtĭlāns, splēndēns, mĭcāns, cŏrŭscŭs, rădĭāns, fūlgĭdŭs, splēndĭdŭs. V. Splendidus.

rūtrŭm, ī, n., *a spade.* Trānsĭlŭĭt: rūtrō, Ov.

Rŭtŭbă, æ, f., *a river of Liguria.* Făcĭt Rŭtŭbāmquĕ căvŭm, Luc.

Rŭtŭlī, ōrŭm, m. pl., *a people of Italy.* Trōs Rŭtŭlŭsvĕ fŭĭt, Virg. EPITH. Āntī-quī, fōrtēs, aŭdācēs, bēllĭgĕrī.

S.

SÁBÁ, æ, f., *and* Sǎbæ, ārǔm, f. pl., *a country of Arabia Felix.* Gūttǎ bĕātǎ
Sǎbæ. Cūm gēntĕ Sǎbārǔm, Prisc. EPITH. Thūrǐfĕrǎ, ŏdōrǎ, ŏdōrātǎ, frāgrāus,
rĕdŏlēns, fōrtǐs, pŏtēns, ĭnvīctǎ. V. Meroë.
Sǎbœǎ, æ, f., *Arabia Felix.* Dēvīctǐs Sǎbæææ Rēgǐbǔs, Hor.
Sǎbæī, ōrǔm, m. pl, *the inhabitants of Arabia Felix.* Thūrǎ Sǎbæī, Virg. EPITH.
Mōllēs, ŏdōrǐfĕrī, dītēs, thūrǐfĕrī, ūnctī, thūrǐlēgī, lĕvēs.
Sǎbbǎtǎrǐǔs, ǎ, ǔm, *of the Sabbath, observing the Sabbath.* Quōd jējūnǐǎ Sǎbbǎtǎ-
rǐōrǔm, Mart.
Sǎbbǎtǔm, ī, n., *and* tǎ, ōrǔm, n. pl., *the Sabbath.* Nēc tĕ pĕrĕgrīnǎ mŏrēntǔr
Sǎbbǎtǎ, Ov. EPITH. Fēstǔm, sānctǔm, sacrǔm, cŏlēndǔm, sōlēnnĕ, dīvīnǔm,
hŏnōrāndǔm, vĕnĕrāndǔm. V. Festum.
Sǎbēllǐcǔs, llǔs, *and* bīnǔs, ǎ, ǔm, *Sabine.* Dēntēsquĕ Sǎbēllǐcǔs, Virg. Pūbēm-
quĕ Sǎbēllǎm, Id. Mŏdǐcīs Sǎbīnǔm, (Sapph.) Hor.
Sǎbīnī, ōrǔm, m. pl., *and* næ, ārǔm, f. pl., *the Sabines.* Vĕtĕrēs cŏlŭĕrĕ
Sǎbīnī, Virg. Mŏrĕ Sǎbīnās, Id. EPITH. Prīscī, rǐgǐdī, vĕtĕrēs, fōrtēs.
sǎbǔlǔm, ī, n., *gravel.* Hǔmī sǎbǔlīquĕ fīmō, Lucil. SYN. Ărēnǎ, glārĕǎ.
sǎbūrrǎ, æ, f., *ballast.* Jāctāntĕ sǎbūrrǎm, Virg. EPITH. Crāssǎ, grǎvǐs.
sǎccātǔs, ǎ, ǔm, *strained through a bag.* Hǔmōrēm sǎccātum ǔt, Lucr.
sǎccǔs, *and* ǔlǔs, ī, m., *a bag.* Ondǐquĕ sǎccīs, Hor. Sǎccǔlǔs ŏrĕ, Prop. SYN.
Pērǎ, crǔmēnǎ, lŏcǔlǔs.
sǎcēllǔm, ī, n., *a chapel.* Vŏvĕāsquĕ sǎcēllīs, Juv. V. Templum.
sǎcĕr, acrǎ, rǔm, *holy.* Ārtǔs sǎcĕr ǐgnǐs, Virg. SYN. Sacrātǔs, cōnsecrātǔs,
rēlǐgǐōsǔs, aūgūstǔs.
sǎcērdōs, ōtǐs, m. f., *a priest.* Āntĕ sǎcērdōs, Ser. SYN. Prēsbўtĕr, Mȳstǎ;
flāmĕn, sacrǐfǐcǔs, Pōntǐfēx. EPITH. Pūrǔs, sānctǔs, ĭntĕgĕr, pǐǔs, rēlǐgǐōs s,
cāstǔs, cœlēbs, ālmǔs, vĕnĕrābǐlǐs, vĕrēndǔs, vĕnĕrāndǔs, sĕnēx, lōngævǔs,
vīttātǔs, ĭnfǔlātǔs, dīǔs, dīvīnǔs. V. Pontifex.
Sǎcēs, æ, m., *the name of a Rutulian warrior.* Virg.
sacrāmēntǔm, ī, n., *an oath.* Sǎcrāmēntǎ dīīs, Sil. Dīxī sǎcrāmēntǔm, Hor.
Sacrānī, ōrǔm, m. pl., *a people of Latium.* Ēt Sǎcrānæ ǎcǐēs, Virg.
sacrārǐǔm, ǐī, n., *a chapel.* Dīrī sǎcrārǐǎ Dītǐs, Virg. SYN. Sǎcēllǔm, tēmplǔm.
Sǎcrātor, orǐs, m., *the name of a warrior.* Obtrūncāt Sǎcrātŏr Hȳdāspēn, Virg.
sǎcrǐcŏlǎ, æ, m., f., *a sacrificer.* Sǎcrǐcŏlæ sūmmī, Prud. V. Sacerdos.
sacrǐfĕr, ǎ, ǔm, *bearing holy things.* Ēst Dĕǎ sǎcrǐfĕrās, Ov.
* sacrǐfǐcǐǔm, ǐī, n., *a sacrifice.* SYN. Sacrǔm lībāmĕn, vīctǐmǎ, hōstǐǎ, pǐācǔlǔm.
EPITH. Pǐǔm, aūgūstǔm, sōlēnnĕ, thūrǐfĕrǔm, ŏdōrātǔm, frāgrāns, pīnguĕ, ōb-
lātǔm, grātǔm, sānctǔm, cāstǔm, cælēstĕ, dīvīnǔm. V. Victima.
sacrǐfīco, ās, *to sacrifice.* Sǎcrǐfǐcārĕ Dĕæ, Ov. SYN. Līto, lǐbo; fǎcǐo, (fǎcǐǎm
vǐtǔlǎ;) ŏpĕrŏr, (ŏpĕrāntǔr ĭn hērbīs.) V. Adoleo, adoro, victimam macto.
sacrǐfǐcǔs, ǎ, ǔm, *sacrificial.* Sǎcrǐfǐcōs dŏcǔīt rītǔs, Ov.
sacrǐfǐcǔs, ī, m, *a priest.* Mārtǐǎ sǎcrǐfīco, Ov. V. Sacerdos.
sacrǐlĕgǐǔm, ǐī, n., *a sacrilege.* Ōnūstǔs quī sǎcrǐlēgǐō, Phæd.
sacrǐlĕgǔs, ǎ, ǔm, *sacrilegious.* Nēc nōs sǎcrǐlĕgōs, Tibull. SYN. Impǐǔs, nĕfāndǔs.
sacro, ās, *to consecrate.* Vĕtĕrēs sǎcrāssĕ Pĕlāsgōs, Virg. SYN. Cōnsecro, dǐco,
ās ; dēdǐco.
sacrǔm, ī, n., *a sacrifice.* Sǎcrǎ Jŏvī, Virg. V. Sacrificium.
sæcǔlǔm, *and* clǔm, ī, n., *an age.* Sæcǔlǎ bēllǐs, Virg. SYN. Ævǔm, ætās.
EPITH. Lōngǔm, fēlix, prǐǔs, fǔtūrǔm, vēntūrǔm. V. Tempus.
sæpĕ, adv., *often.* Sæpĕ tĕnĕr nōstrīs, Virg. SYN. Sæpǐǔs, crēbrō, frĕquēntĕr,
nōn rāro.
sævǐo, īs, *to rage.* Sævībāt, lĕvǐtĕrquĕ, Lucr. SYN. Fĕrōcǐo, fǔro, bācchŏr,
ĭnsānǐo ; īrāscŏr. V. Irascor.
sævǐtǐǎ, æ, *or* īēs, ǐēī, f., *cruelty.* Sævǐtǐam ēt vīrēs, Ov. SYN. Fĕrǐtās, bārbǎrǐēs ;
crūdēlǐtās. EPITH. Nĕfāndǎ, ĭnēxōrābǐlǐs, ātrōx, fǔrēns, bārbǎrǎ, prŏcāx. V.
Crudelitas.
sævǔs, ǎ, ǔm, *cruel.* Sævǐŏr ǔllǎ, Virg. SYN. Crūdēlǐs, fĕrōx, ēffĕrǔs. V. Crudelitas.

sāgă, æ, f., *a witch*. Dūm mĭhĭ sāgă tŭās, Mart. Syn. Mgăgă, ĭncāntātrīx, vĕnēfĭcă, lāmĭă, præstĭgĭātrīx. Epitu. Præsāgă, fātĭdĭcă, impĭă, scĕlĕrātă, fāllāx, ĭnfērnă. V. Maga, venefica.

Sāgănă, æ, f., *the name of a sorceress*. Cūm Sāgănā mājōre ŭlŭlāntĕm, Hor.

Sāgărĭs, ĭs, m., *a river of Phrygia*. Hūc Sāgărĭs, Pĕnĭūsquĕ, Ov.—2. *a man's name*. Et Sāgărim, ēt sūmmīs, Virg.

Sāgărītĭs, ĭdĭs, f., *of the river Sagaris*. In nȳmphā Sāgărītĭdĕ, Ov.

sāgātŭs, ă, ŭm, *cloked*. Mārcĕ, sāgātŭs, Mart.

sāgāx, ācĭs, *sagacious*. Cătŭlō sēctārĕ sāgācī, Ov. Syn. Sōlērs, prūdēns, cāllĭdŭs, ĭndūstrĭŭs; pērspĭcāx, ācūtŭs.

Sāgēs, ĭs or æ, m., *the name of a warrior*. Vēctŭs ĕquō spūmāntĕ Sāgēs, Virg.

sāgīnă, æ, f., *a stuffing, fatness*. Stŏmăchŭm lāxārĕ sāgīnīs, Juv. Syn. Adĕps, pīnguēdo; pīnguĭs cĭbŭs.

sāgīno, ās, *to fatten*. Pārvă sāgīnātī, Prop.

sāgĭttă, æ, f., *an arrow*. Impūlsă sāgĭttă, Virg. Syn. Tēlŭm, spīcŭlŭm; jăcŭlŭm, ărūndo, călămŭs. Epitu. Cĕlĕr, vŏlucrĭs, răpĭdă, pērnīx, præpĕs, vēlōx, vŏlāns, lĕvĭs, ācūtă, spīcātă, tĕrĕs, ālātă, pennĭgĕră, pennātă, fātālĭs, lēthĭfĕră, lēthālĭs, sævă, scĕlĕrātă, ūltrīx, ĭnfēstă, vĕnēnātă, ĭrrĕvŏcābĭlĭs, strīdŭlă, Thrēĭcĭă, Pārthĭcă, Gĕtĭcă, Scȳthĭcă, Ĭtȳræă, Cȳdōnĭs, Cȳdōnĭă, Crēssĭă, Gōrtȳnĭă, Gnōssĭă, Gnōssĭăcă. V. Sagitto.

Sāgĭttārĭŭs, ī, m., *an archer*. Syn. Jăcŭlātŏr. Epitu. Dēxtĕr, ĭndūstrĭŭs, pĕrĭtŭs, ācĕr.—2. *a sign of the zodiac*. Syn. Arcĭtĕnēns, sāgĭttĭfĕr. Epitu. Bĭfōrmĭs, nĭmbōsŭs, nĭmbĭfĕr, hūmĭdŭs, ūdŭs, ĭmbrĭfĕr, Æmŏnĭŭs. V. Chiron.

sāgĭttĭfĕr, ĕră, ŭm, *bearing arrows*. Cārāsquĕ sāgĭttĭfĕrōsquĕ Gĕlōnōs, Virg.

Sāgĭttĭpŏtēns, ēntĭs, m., *the sign Sagittarius*. Pīgră Sāgĭttĭpŏtēns, Aus.

* sāgĭtto, ās, *to shoot from a bow*. Curt. V. Jaculor, arcus, sagitta.

sāgŭm, *and* ŭlŭm, ī, n., *a cassock*. Mūtāvīt sāgŭm, Hor. Vīrgātīs lūcēnt sāgŭlĭs, Virg. Epitu. Cāstrēnsĕ, sērĭcŭm, vīrgātŭm, pīctŭm.

Sāgūntŭs, f., *and* tŭm, n, ī, *a town of Spain*. Tōtă Sāgūntŭs, Sil. Epitu. Anĭmōsă, mĭsĕră, Hīspānă, Mārtĭă, fīdă, fīdēlĭs.

sāgŭs, ă, ŭm, *giving omens*. Nūnc sāgās āffātŭr ăvēs, Stat.

sāl, sălĭs, n., *salt*. Et sălĕ tābēntēs, Virg. Epitu. Acrĕ, mōrdāx, ālbŭm, ālbēns, cāndĭdŭm, æquŏrĕŭm, mărīnŭm, săpĭdŭm, sălōrŭm.

sălămāndră, æ, f., *an animal fabled to exist in fire withou injury*. Seū sălămăndră pŏtēns, Ser.

Sălămīnĭăcŭs, ă, ŭm, *of Salamis*. Ut Sălămīnĭăcŭm, Virg.

Sălămĭs *or* mīn, ĭnĭs, *or* mīnă, æ, f., *a town in the island of Cyprus*. Teūcēr Sălămīnă pătrēmquĕ, Hor. Epitu. Antīquă, nōbĭlĭs, Cyprĭă.

Sălānŭs, ī, m., *a friend of Ovid*. Egŏ Nāsŏ Sălānō, Ov.

sălăr, ărĭs, m., *a young salmon*. Nēc jām sălăr, ămbĭgŭūsquĕ, Aus.

Sălārĭă, æ, f. vĭă, *one of the roads of Rome*. Flāmĭnĭæ Sălārĭæquĕ, Mart.

sălārĭŭm, ĭī, n., *a salary*. Jām sălārĭŭm dāndŭm, (Scaz.) Mart.

sălārĭŭs, ĭī, m., *a dealer in salt*. Pŭĕrī sălārĭōrŭm, (Scaz.) Mart.

sălāx, ācĭs, *lustful*. Vītārĕ sălācēs, Ov. Syn. Lāscīvŭs, lūxŭrĭōsŭs. V. Luxuriosus.

sălebræ, ārŭm, f. pl., *rugged and dangerous places*. Pēr sălĕbră, art. Epitu. Præcĭpĭtēs, āspĕræ, ĭnæquālēs, dĭffĭcĭlēs.

sălebrōsŭs, ă, ŭm, *rugged*. Tĕtrĭcī sălĕbrōsŭm, Mart.

Sālēntīnī, *or* Sāllentīnī, ōrŭm, m. pl., *the inhabitants of Sallentum, a city near the gulf of Tarentum.*—Adj., ŭs, ă, ŭm, *of Salentum*. Et Sāllēntīnōs ōbsēdīt mīlĭtĕ cāmpōs, Virg.

sălēs, ĭŭm, m. pl., *witticisms*. Et sălĭbŭs vărĭārĕ, Sulpit. Syn. Jŏcī, scōmmătă, făcētĭæ, ārgūtĭæ. Epitu. Făcĕtī, ārgūtī, jŏcōsī, ĭngĕnĭōsī, ūrbānī, dōctī, sūbtīlēs, vĕnūstī, hŏnēstī, ĭnnŏcŭī, lætī, blāndī, jūcūndī, fēstīvī, hĭlārēs, rīdĭcŭlī, prŏtērvī, mōrdācēs, āmārī, scūrrīlēs. V. Jocus.

sālgămă, ōrŭm, n. pl., *garden-fruit in jars, preserves*. Sālgămă nōn hōc sūnt, Aus.

Sălĭārĭs, ĕ, *of the Salii*. Jām Sălĭārĕ Nŭmæ cārmĕn, Hor.

sălĭctŭm, ī, n., *a grove of willows*. Dēpāstă sălĭctī, Virg. Syn. Sălĭcētŭm.

sălĭgnŭs, *and* nĕŭs, ă, ŭm, *of willow*. Dūmquĕ săcērdōtēs vĕrŭbŭs, dēfīxă sălĭgnīs, Ov. Clără sălĭgnĕă, Col.

R

Sălĭī, ōrŭm, m. pl., *priests of Mars.* Sīc ēxŭltāntēs Sălĭōs, Virg.

sălīnæ, ārŭm, f. pl., *salt-pits.* Pălūs vīcīnă sălīnīs, Colum.

sălīnŭm, *dimin.* īllŭm, ī, n., *a salt-cellar.* Plăcŭērŭnt fărră sălīnō, Stat.   Pŭrĭŏr sălīllō, Catul.

sălĭo, īs, sălĭī, *to jump, to dance.* Ăquæ sălĭēntĕ sītĭm, Virg. V. Salto.—2. *to salt.* Mīcæ sălĭēntīs, Ov.

sălīvă, æ, f., *spittle.* Mēmbră sălīvă, Lucan. Epith. Mōllĭs, dūlcĭs, putrĭs, lăbēns, lūstrālĭs, spūrcă, vĕnēnōsă. V. Sputum.

sălĭŭncă, æ, f., *lavender.* Quāntŭm sălĭŭncă rōsētĭs, Virg. Epith. Hŭmĭlĭs vīrēns, frōndēns, ŏpăcă, suāvĭs, ŏdōră.

sălīvōsŭs, ă, ŭm, *resembling spittle, thick.* Ēt sălīvōsīs ăquīs, Virg.

sălīx, ĭcĭs, f., *a willow.* Mēcum īntēr sălīcēs, Virg. Syn. Sălīctŭm. Epith. Ămără, pāllĭdă, pāllēns, glaŭcă, ŏpăcă, ūmbrōsă, tĕnĕră, vĭrĭdĭs, lēntă, flēxĭlĭs, flŭvĭālĭs, flūmĭnĕă.

·Sāllūstĭŭs, īī, m., *a celebrated Roman historian.* Ōrsă Sāllūstī brĕvĭs, Stat.

Sālmăcĭs, ĭdĭs, f., *a nymph and fountain of Caria.* Sālmăcīs ēnērvĕt, Ov.

sālmo, ōnĭs, m., *a salmon.* Pūnĭcĕō vīscĕrĕ, sālmo, Aus.

Sālmōneūs, ĕŏs, ĕī or eī, *a king of Elis, struck with thunder by Jupiter, for vaunting himself as a god.* Dāntēm Sālmōnĕă pœnās, Virg. Syn. Æŏlĭdēs. Epith. Aūdāx, sŭpērbŭs, tĕmĕrārĭŭs, īmpĭŭs, īnfēlīx.

Sālmōnĭs, ĭdĭs, f., *the daughter of Salmoneus.* Flāgrāns Sālmōnĭs Ēnīpeō, Prop.

Sălōmōn, ōnĭs, m., *a king of Judea.* Ūt Sălōmōnă pĭŭm, Juvenc.

sālpă, æ, f., *a stock-fish.* Vīlīssĭmă sālpă, Ov. Epith. Immūndă, vīlĭs, tūrpĭs, ōbscœnă.

sālpūgă, *or* sōlpūgă, æ, f., *a venomous serpent.* Mĕtŭăt, sālpūgă, tĕnēbrās, Luc.

‖ * sālsēdo, ĭnĭs, f., *saltness.* Spārgēns sālsēdĭnĕ, Fill. Syn. Sāl; sālīs săpŏr.

‖ * sālsūgo, ĭnĭs, f., *salt water.* Ōrītŭr sālsūgĭnĕ ălūmēn, F.

sālsŭs, ă, ŭm, *salt, briny; keen, satirical.* Sālsōs rĕvōmēntēm pēctŏrĕ flūctŭs, Virg. Syn. Ămārŭs, ăcērbŭs; fēstīvŭs, lĕpĭdŭs, făcētŭs, ārgūtŭs.

sāltātĭo, ōnĭs, f., *and* tătŭs, ūs, m., *the action of jumping or dancing.* Sāltātĭbŭs āptă, Ov. Syn. Sāltŭs. V. Chorea.

sāltĕm, adv., *at least.* Hūnc sāltĕm, Virg.

sālto, ūs, *to dance, jump.* Pāstōrēm sāltărĕt ŭtī, Hor. Syn. Sălĭo; trĭpūdĭo. V. Salio.

sāltŭs, ūs, m., *a leap.* Nōn sāltŭ sŭpĕrārĕ, Virg. Epith. Cĕlĕr, vŏlŭcĕr, ăgĭlĭs, præcēps, răpĭdŭs, lĕvĭs, pērnīx, cōncĭtŭs, cōmpŏsĭtŭs, trĕmŭlŭs.—2. *a wood, a thicket.* Sāltŭs vēnāntĭbŭs āptōs, Ov. Syn. Sȳlvă, nĕmŭs, lūcŭs. Epith. Prŏfūndŭs, vāstŭs, sȳlvēstĕr, vĭrĭdĭs, sēcrētŭs, ŏpăcŭs, rĭgŭŭs, fĕrŭs, īnāccēssŭs, dūmōsŭs, ūmbrōsŭs, ōccūltŭs, quĭētŭs, gĕlĭdŭs, fœcūndŭs, hērbōsŭs, sȳlvōsŭs, āvĭŭs, dēvĭŭs, īnvĭŭs, văgŭs, ēxcēlsŭs, ōbscūrŭs, sīlēns, īncūltŭs, ūmbrĭfĕr, rĕcōndĭtŭs. V. Sylva.

sălūbĕr *and* ŭbrĭs, ĭs, ĕ, *healthful.* Sānārĕ sălūbrĭbŭs hērbīs, Tib. Syn. Sălūtārĭs, sălūtĭfĕr, sānŭs, sānāns.

sălūbrĭtās, ātĭs, f., *healthfulness.* Pŏtēns sălūbrĭtătĕ, (Phal.) Sidon. Syn. Sănĭtās; īntegrĭtās.

sălūbrĭtĕr, adv., *healthfully.* Rūrsŭsquĕ sălūbrĭtĕr īnfīt, Ar. Syn. Ŭtĭlĭtĕr.

sălūtātŏr, ōrĭs, m., *and* trīx, ĭcĭs, f., *one who salutes.* Istă sălūtātŏr, Mart. Tōtă sălūtātrīx, Juv.

sālvē, (*imper.*) *hail, farewell.* Sālvē, sānctĕ părēns, Virg. Syn. Ăvĕ. V. Saluto.

sālvĕo, ēs, *to be well.* Sālvērĕ jŭbēmŭs, Hor.

sălŭm, ī, n., *the sea.* Spūmāntĕ sălō, Virg. Epith. Spūmĕŭm, cānŭm, tūrbĭdŭm, fĕrŭm. V. Mare.

sālvo, ās, *to save.* Syn. Sērvo, lībĕro.

sălūs, ūtĭs, f., *health, safety.* Fōrtūnă sălūtĭs, Virg. Syn. Incŏlŭmĭtās, īntegrĭtās, sēcūrĭtās, sănĭtās. Epith. Spērātă, dūlcĭs, grātă, ŏptātă, quæsītă, ēxpēctātă, cērtă, sēcūră, tūtă, dēspērātă, ăbjēctă.

sălūtārĭs, ĕ; tĭfĕr *and* tĭgĕr, ă, ŭm, *healthful.* Quī sălūtārī lĕvăt, (Sapph.) Hor. Ūtquĕ sălūtĭfĕră, Ov. Crēdĕ, sălūtĭgĕrōs, Prod. Syn. Sălūbrĭs; sānŭs.

·sălūto, ās, *to salute.* Antĕ sălūtābăt, Mart.

sălvŭs, ă, ŭm, *safe.* Sălvŭs ĕt hœdī, Virg. Syn. Incŏlŭmĭs, illæsŭs, intĕgĕr, sŏspĕs, tūtŭs, sĕcūrŭs, sānŭs.

sămbūcă, æ, f., *a harp.* Sămbūcām cĭtĭŭs, Pers. Syn. Cĭthără̆.

Sămē, ēs, f., *a city and harbour of Cephalenia.* Dŭlĭchĭŭmquĕ, Sămēquĕ, Virg.

Sămĭŭs, ă, ŭm, *of Samos, Samian.* Nōn ălĭtĕr Sămĭŏ, Hor.

Sămnīs, ĭtĭs, m., Sămnītēs, ŭm, ni. pl., *the inhabitants of Samnium in the south of Italy.* Lēntō Sămnītēs, Hor.

Sămŏs, ī, f., *an island of the Archipelago.* Pŏsthăbĭtă cŏlŭīssĕ Sămŏ, Virg. Epith. Jūnōnĭă, vĕtŭs, fœcūndă, pŭlchră, ĭllūstrĭs ; Thrēĭcĭă.

Sămŏthrăcĕs, ŭm, m. pl., *divinities worshipped in the mysteries of Samothrace.* Ĕt Sămŏthrăcŭm Ĕt nŏstrōrŭm ārăs, Juv.

Sămŏthrăcĭă, æ, f., *an island in the Ægean sea at the mouth of the Hebrus.* Quœ nūnc Sămŏthrăcĭă fĕrtŭr, Virg.

sānăbĭlĭs, ĕ, *which may be cured.* Prīmō sānăbĭlĕ vŭlnŭs, Ov.

sāncĭo, īvī and ĭī, ītŭm, *to consecrate, to enact.* Cŭpĭēns sāncīrĕ sălūtĕm, Prud. Syn. Dēcērno, stătŭo, dēfīnĭo.

sāncītŭs, ă, ŭm, *the pass. partic. of* sancio. Sāncītŭs quăndŏquĭ̆dĕm, Sed. || Sānctī, ōrŭm, m. pl., *the Saints,* Eccl. Syn. Cŏelĭtēs, Cœlĭcŏlæ, Dīvī, Sŭpĕrī. V. Cœlites.

sānctĭtās, ātĭs, f., *holiness.* Sānctĭtātī dīsplĭcĕt, (Iamb.) Syn. Pĭĕtās, rēl-ligĭo.

sānctŭs, ă, ŭm, *holy.* Ingrĕdĭŏr, sānctŏs aŭsŭs, Virg. Syn. Rēllĭgĭōsŭs, pĭŭs, innŏcēns.

Sāncŭs, ī, m., *the Hercules of the Sabines.* Nōnās Sāncō Fĭdĭŏnĕ̆ rĕfĕrrĕm, Ov

sāndălĭŭm, ĭī, n., *a sandal.* Ĕtĭăm sāndālĭă tālŏs, Virg.

sāndăpĭlă, æ, f., *a coffin.* Fābrōs sāndăpĭlārŭm, Juv.

sāndīx, ĭcĭs and ĭcĭs, m. f., *a red colour.* Spōntĕ sŭă sāndīx, Virg. Vēl sīt sān-dīcĭs āmīctŭ, Prop.

sānē, adv., *certainly.* Quō sānē pŏpŭlŭs, Hor. Syn. Cērtē, prŏfēctō, quī-dĕm.

sānguĕn, ĭnĭs, m., *the same as* sanguis. Ĕt sānguĕn ĕt ŏssă, Lucr.

sānguĭnārĭŭs and nĕŭs, ă, ŭm, *bloody.* Sānguĭnēĭs ĕbŭlī, Virg. Syn. Crŭēntŭs, rŭbĕŭs, pūrpŭrĕŭs.

sānguĭnŏlēntŭs, ă, ŭm, *bloody.* Sānguĭnŏlēntŭs hŭmŭm, Ov. Syn. Sānguĭnĕŭs, crŭēntŭs, crŭēntātŭs. V. Sanguis.

sānguĭs, ĭnĭs, m., *blood.* Sānguĭnĭs Ilĭă mātĕr, Virg. Syn. Crŭŏr. Epith. Pūnĭcĕŭs, rŏsĕŭs, rŭbĕŭs, fūmāns, tĕpēns, fērvēns, tĕpĭdŭs, călĭdŭs, cōn-crētŭs, fœdŭs, pīgĕr, fūsŭs, ēffūsŭs, flŭēns, flŭĭdŭs, bŭllĭēns, ūndāns. V. Cruor.

sānĭēs, ĭĕī, f., *corrupt blood.* Ĕt sānĭē tăbōquĕ, Virg. Syn. Tābŭm, tābēs, crŭŏr. Epith. Crāssă, pīnguĭs, crŭēntă, putrĭdă, putrĭs, concrētă, nigră, ātră, tētră, fœdă, sōrdĭdă, cōrrūptă, fœtĭdă, lūrĭdă, pēstĭfĕră, hōrrĭdă, flŭĭdă, stīllāns. V. Sanguis.

sānĭtās, ātĭs, f., *good health.* Pārs sānĭtātĭs, (Iamb.) Sen. Syn. Vălētūdo, vĭgŏr, incŏlŭmĭtās, sălūbrĭtās, sălūs. Epith. Integră, fīrmă, ōptātă, ĕxpēctātă, blāndă, dūlcĭs, ămābĭlĭs, vīvĭdă, pērpĕtŭă, cōnstāns. V. Robur.

sānnă, æ, f., *scoffing.* Aĕră sānnă, Juv.

sāno, ās, *to cure.* Fūncră, sānăbŭnt, Prop. V. Medeor.

sānŭs, ă, ŭm, *healthy.* Sānĭŏr āc sī, Hor. Syn. Vălēns, intĕgĕr, incŏlŭmĭs, sŏspĕs. V. Robustus, incolumis.

săpă, æ, f., *boiled wine.* Pūrpŭrĕāmquĕ săpăm, Ov.

Săpæī, ōrŭm, m. pl., *a people of Thrace.* Trĭvĭæ lībārĕ Săpæōs, Ov.

săpērdă, æ, f., *a kind of fish.* Pers.

săpĭēns, ntĭs, *wise.* Allŭm săpĭēntĕ bŏnōquĕ, Hor. Syn. Prūdēns ; dŏctŭs, ĕrŭdītŭs, pĕrītŭs. V. Prudens.

săpĭēntĕr, adv., *wisely.* Mŭnĕrĭbŭs săpĭēntĕr ūtī, (Dactyl. Troch.) Hor. Syn. Prūdēntĕr ; dŏctē.

săpĭēntĭă, æ, f., *wisdom.* Hæc săpĭēntĭă quōndăm, Hor. Syn. Prūdēntĭă, dŏc-trīnă, scĭēntĭă. V. Prudentia.

săpĭo, ĭs, ŭī, *to taste, to be wise.* Quŭm săpĭmŭs pătrŭŏs, Pers. Syn. Gūsto ; rĕdŏlĕo, ɪncŭdĭtŏr, cōgĭto.

|| sāpc, ōnĭs, m., *soap*. Āttrītō sāpōně gěnās, Ser.

sǎpǒr, ōrĭs, m., *flavour*. Āspērgě sǎpōrēs, Virg. Syn. Gūstǔs. Epith. Dūlcĭs, grātǔs, jūcūndǔs, suāvĭs, nēctǎrěǔs, āmbrŏsĭǔs, ĭngrātǔs, ĭnjūcūndǔs, āmārǔs, ǎspěr, ĭnsuāvĭs.

sǎpōrǔs, ǎ, ǔm, *savoury*. Mǎgĭs sǎpōrǔm, (Phal.) Prud. Syn. Sǎpĭdǔs.

* sǎpphīrǔs, ī, f., *a sapphire*. Plin. Epith. Cœrǔlěǎ, cœrǔlǎ, mǐcāns, aūrō vǎrǐātǎ.

Sǎppho, ūs, f., *a Greek poetess*. Mǎscǔlǎ Sǎpphŏ, Hor. Epith. Pŏětǐcǎ, Pělāsgĭs, Graǐǎ, Lēsbǐǎ, Lēsbĭs, Æōlǐǎ, Æōlĭs.

sārcĭnǎ, æ, f., *and* cīnǔlæ, ārǔm, f. pl., *baggage*. Sārcĭnǎ chārtæ, Hor. Cōllĭgě sārcĭnǔlās, Juv. Syn. Ŏnǔs, pōndǔs; fāscĭs. Epith. Grǎvĭs, ŏněrōsǎ, mŏlēstǎ, ĭngēns, grāndĭs, ĭnīquǎ, prěmēns. V. Onus.

sārcĭo, ĭs, īvī, ītǔm, *to repair*. Lāpsī sārcīrě rǔīnǎs, Virg. Syn. Rěsārcĭo, rěpǎro, pēnso, cōmpēnso. V. Reparo.

sārcŏphǎgǔs, ī, m., *a tomb, a coffin*. Sārcŏphǎgō cōntēntǔs, Juv.

* sārcǔlo, ās, *to weed*. Col.

sārcǔlǔm, n., *and* ǔs, m., ī, *a weeding-hook*. Fīnděrě sārcǔlō, Hor.

sārdǎ, æ, f., *a pilchard*. Ět nārdum ět sārdās ēssě sǎpōrě pǎrī, Aus.

Sārdǎnǎpǎlǔs, ī, m., *the last king of Assyria*. Plūmǎ Sārdǎnǎpǎlī, Juv. Epith. Mōllĭs, tūrpĭs, lāscīvǔs, ĭněrs, ĭmbēllĭs, Āssўrĭǔs, ĭnfāmĭs, lūxǔrĭōsǔs.

Sārdēs, ĭǔm, f. pl., *and* Sārdĭs, ĭs, f., *the capital city of Lydia*. Vīcīnūm Sārdĭbǔs āmněm, Ov.

Sārdĭnĭǎ, æ, f., *an island in the Mediterranean sea*. Insǔlǎ, Sārdĭnĭǎm, Claud. Epith. Dīvěs, fěrāx, pēstĭfěrǎ, fērtĭlĭs, fœcūndǎ, ŏpǔlēntǎ, pēstĭlēns, nōxĭǎ, fāmōsǎ.

Sārdŏnĭcǔs, nĭǔs, *and* ŏǔs, ǎ, ǔm, *Sardinian*. Nēc quæ Sārdŏnĭcō, Rutil. Sārdŏnĭǔm jūxtǎ, Prud. Sārdōĭs vĭděǎr, Virg. V. Sardinia.

sārdŏnўchātǔs, ǎ, ǔm, *adorned with sardonyx-stones*. Sārdŏnўchātǎ mǎnǔs, Mart.

sārdŏnўchǔs, ī, *and* ўx, ўchĭs, m., *a precious stone*. Sārdŏnўchǔs lŏcǔlĭs, Juv. V. Onyx.

Sārdǔs, ī, m., Sārdī, ōrǔm, m. pl., *the inhabitants of Sardinia*. Sārdǔs hǎbēbǎt, Hor.—Adj., -ǔs, ǎ, ǔm, *Sardinian*. Sārdō cūm mēllě pǎpāvěr, Id. V. Sardous.

sǎrgǔs, ī, m., *a sort of mallet*. Insīgnĭs sǎrgūsquě nŏtĭs, Ov.

sǎrĭo, *or* sārrĭo, ĭs, *to weed*. Quĭd sǎrīrě sī vēlĭt sǎxǔm, Mart.

sǎrīssǎ, æ, f., *a Macedonian pike*. Mǎcēdōnĭǎquě sǎrīssǎ, Ov. Epith. Pēllæǎ; Æmŏnĭǎ, lěvĭs, lōngǎ, fērrātǎ, vǎlĭdǎ.

Sārmǎtǎ, Saūrŏmǎtǎ, *and* Saūrŏmǎtēs, æ, m., Sārmǎtæ, *or* Saūrŏmǎtæ, ārǔm, m. pl., *a people of Scythia*. Sārmǎtǎ pāstǔs, Ov. Epith. Vělōcēs, trǔcēs, vǎgī, flāvī, ĭntōnsī, fōrtēs, frīgĭdī, gělĭdī, fěrī, crūdī, hīrtī, bēllācēs.

Sārmǎtĭcē, adv., *like a Sarmatian*. Sārmǎtĭcēquě lŏquī, Ov.

Sārmǎtĭcǔs, ǎ, ǔm, *and* mǎtĭs, ĭdĭs, f., *Sarmatian*. Sārmǎtĭcōsquě sĭnǔs, Ov. Sārmǎtĭs ōrǎ Gětĭs, Id.

sārmēntǔm, ī, n., *a twig*. Sārmēntǎ, ět vāllōs, Virg.

Sārmēntǔs, ī, m., *the name of a man*. Sārmēntī scūrræ pūgnǎm, Hor.

Sārnǔs, ī, m., *a river in Italy*. Sārnī mītĭs ōpēs, Sil. Epith. Cāmpānǔs, vĭtrěǔs, ǎmœnǔs, vělōx.

Sārpēdōn, ŏnĭs, m., *the son of Jupiter, and king of Lydia, slain by Patroclus at the siege of Troy*. Sārpēdōn; ŭbī tōt Sĭmŏĭs, Virg.

sārrācǔm, ī, n., *a cart*. Pĭgrī sārrācǎ Bŏŏtæ, Juv. Syn. Plaūstrǔm. Epith. Grǎvě, strīdēns, rŏbūstǔm, tārdǔm, sŏnōrǔm, gěmēns.

Sārrānǔs, ǎ, ǔm, *Syrian*. Sārrānō dōrmĭǎt ōstrō, Virg. Syn. Tўrĭǔs; pūrpǔrěǔs.

Sārrāstēs, ǔm, m. pl., *a people of Campania*. Sārrāstēs pŏpǔlōs, Virg.

sārtāgo, ĭnĭs, f., *a frying-pan*. Pēlvēs, sārtāgō, pǎtēllǎ, Juv.

sǎt, adv., *enough*. Hæc sǎt ěrĭt, Virg. Syn. Sǎtĭs, ǎbūndǎ.

sǎtǎ, ōrǔm, n. pl., *corn-fields*. Ingēntī sǎtǎ lætǎ, Virg. Syn. Sěgěs; ǎgěr; cūltǎ, ōrǔm. V. Ager, seges.

sǎtēllěs, ĭtĭs, m., *a guard, an officer*. Illě sǎtēllěs ěrǎt, Ov. Syn. Stīpātŏr, cūstōs, mīlěs, mĭnĭstěr. Epith. Armātǔs, rŏbūstǔs, vǎlĭdǔs, fōrtĭs, strěnǔǔs; audāx, sēdǔlǔs, ĭmpĭgěr, ĭnsōmnĭs, vǐgĭl, fĭdēlĭs, fīdǔs, trǔx, bārbǎrǔs, fěrōx.

sătăgo, ĭs, *to be busy, be occupied about a thing.*   Vīx ănno ēxēgī; nūnc sătăgĭt, Plaut.

Sătīcŭlŭs, ī, m., *a colony of Samnium.*   Părītērquĕ Sătīcŭlŭs āspĕr, Virg.

sătĭĕtās or sătĭās, ătĭs, f., *satiety.*   Sătĭs sătĭĕtās ēst, Ter.   Syn. Sătŭrătĭo; făstīdĭŭm, tædĭŭm, naūsĕă.   Epitii. Mŏlēstă, grăvĭs, fāstīdĭōsă.

sătĭo, ās, *to satiate.*   Cōrquĕ fērūin sătĭă, Ov.   V. Saturo.

sătĭo, ōnĭs, f., *sowing, planting.*   Vērĕ făbīs sătĭo ēst, Virg.

sătĭs, adv., *enough.*   Pŭĕrī, sătĭs ēst, Virg.   Syn. Săt, ăbŭndē.

sătĭsfăcĭo, fēcī, *to satisfy.*   Mălŏ sătĭsfăcĕrĕ, Mart.   Syn. Făcĭo sătĭs ; plăcĕo ; dĕbĭtŭm sōlvo, ēxsōlvo, pērsōlvo.

sătĭŭs, adv., *rather.*   Fŭĭt sătĭŭs trīstēs, Virg.   Syn. Pŏtĭŭs, mĕlĭŭs.

sătŏr, ōrĭs, m., *a sower.*   Nĭtĭdīquĕ sătŏr, Mart.

sătŭr, ă, ŭm, *full fed.*   Ărīēs sătŭrās īpsĕ, Prop.   Syn. Sătŭrātŭs, sătĭātŭs, rĕfēctŭs, ēxplētŭs, replētŭs.

Sătūræ pălūs, f., *a part of the Pontine marsh.*   Quā Sătūræ jăcĕt ātră pălūs, Virg.

sătŭrĕĭă, or ējă, æ, f., *and eīŭm, ī, n., the plant savory.*   Hērbăs sătŭrĕĭă nŏcēntēs, Ov.   V. Thymbra.

Sătŭrĕĭānŭs, ă, ŭm, *of Saturium, a town of Apulia.*   Mĕ Sătŭrĕĭānō, Hor.

Sătūrnālĭă, ŭm, n. pl., *feasts of Saturn.*   Sătūrnālĭbŭs āmbŭlăt, Mart.

Sătūrnālĭtĭŭs, ă, ŭm, *of the Saturnalia.*   Sătūrnālĭtĭās mĭttĭmŭs, Mart.

Sătūrnĭă, æ, f., *the daughter of Saturn, Juno.*   Vĕtĕrīsquĕ mĕmŏr Sătūrnĭă bēllī, Virg.

Sătūrnĭŭs, ă, ŭm, *of Saturn.*   Nēc Sătūrnĭŭs hæc, Virg.

Sătūrnŭs, ī, m., *the son of Cœlus and Terra.*   Sătūrnŭs rēgnĭs, Ov.   Epith. Antīquŭs, prīscŭs, sĕnēx, cānŭs, ānnōsŭs, ēxŭl, fŭgăx, prŏfŭgŭs, fŭgĭtīvŭs, aūrĕŭs, crūdēlĭs, ĭmmītĭs, trīstĭs, fălcĭtĕnēns, fălcātŭs, fălcĭgĕr.—2. *a planet.*   Ět grăvĕ Sătūrnī, Prop.

sătŭro, ās, *to satiate.*   Mĕlĭŭs sătŭrātŭr, Prud.   Syn. Sătĭo, ēxsătŭro, ēxsătĭo, ēxplĕo, replĕo.   V. Manduco, edo, epulor.

sătŭs, ă, ŭm, *the pass. partic. of sero.*   Vātēs, sătĕ sānguĭnĕ, Virg.

sătŭs, ūs, m., *generation, birth, origin.*   Ŏccŭltōsquĕ sătŭs, Aus.   V. Ortus.

sătўră, æ, f., *a satire.*   Sūnt quĭbŭs īn sătўră, Hor.   Epith. Mŏrdāx, dēntātă, līvēns, aūdāx, prŏcāx, pĕtŭlāns.

Sătўrī, ōrŭm, m. pl., *Satyrs.*   Cōnvēnĭĕt Sătўrōs, Hor.   Syn. Faūnī, Sўlvānī, Pănēs.   Epith. Agrēstēs, sўlvēstrēs, cōrnĭgĕrī, hīrsūtī, bĭcōrnēs, bĭfōrmēs, caprĭpĕdēs, prŏtērvī, prŏcăcēs, lāscīvī, pĕtŭlāntēs, sălăcēs, văgī, lĕvēs, cĕlĕrēs, vēlōcēs, ălăcrēs, sāltāntēs, fŭgăcēs, rūrĭcŏlæ, mōntĭcŏlæ.

saŭcĭo, ās, *to wound.*   Saŭcĭăt ūnguĕ, Ov.   V. Vulnero.

saŭcĭŭs, ă, ŭm, *wounded.*   Quŭm saŭcĭŭs ārăm Taŭrŭs, Virg.   Syn. Saŭcĭātŭs, vūlnĕrātŭs, læsŭs, ŏffēnsŭs, īctŭs, pērcūssŭs, cōnfōssŭs.

Saŭrŏmătæ, ārŭm, m. pl., *Sarmatians.*   Saŭrŏmătæquĕ trŭcēs, Juv.   V. Sarmatæ.

săxătĭlĭs pĭscĭs, *a fish that lives among the rocks.*   Pārvō săxătĭlĭs ōrĕ, Ov.

săxētānŭs, ă, ŭm, *living among the rocks.*   Cūm săxētānī, Mart.   Syn. Săxātĭlĭs.

săxĕŭs, ă, ŭm, *stony.*   Săxĕŭs īmbĕr, Sil.

săxĭfĭcŭs, ă, ŭm, *turning into stone.*   Săxĭfĭcōs vŭltŭs, Ov.

Săxo, ōnĭs, m., Săxŏnēs, ŭm, m. pl., *Saxons.*   Săxŏnĕ Tēthўs, Claud.   Epith. Dūrī, rĭgĭdī, fōrtēs, māgnănĭmī, bēllăcēs, fĕrōcēs.

săxōsŭs, ă, ŭm, *stony.*   Stĕrĭlēs săxōsĭs, Virg.   Syn. Lăpĭdōsŭs, petrōsŭs, scrūpĕŭs, sălebrōsŭs, scŏpŭlōsŭs.

săxŭm, ī, n., *a stone.*   Exsŭpĕrăbĭlĕ săxŭm, Virg.   Syn. Sīlēx, lăpĭs, rūpēs, scŏpŭlŭs.   Epitii. Dūrŭm, sŏlĭdŭm, āspĕrŭm, gĕlĭdŭm, hūmĭdŭm, hōrrēns, fĕrŭm, lătebrōsŭm, præruptŭm, cōncăvŭm, hōrrĭdŭm, frīgĭdŭm, hīrtŭm, rĭgēns, scabrŭm, crūdŭm, ūndĭsŏnŭm, ĭnhōspĭtŭm, mōntānŭm, ădēsŭm, sălebrōsŭm, dūmōsŭm, mūscōsŭm, scrŭpĕŭm.   V. Rupes.

• scăbēllŭm, ī, n., *a low bench.*   Syn. Scāmnŭm, sĕdĭlĕ, sēdēs.   V. Sedile.

scăbĕr, bră, brŭm, *rough.*   Ět tŏphŭs scăbĕr, ĕt, Virg.   Syn. Āspĕr, rĭgĭdŭs, rŭdĭs, scabrōsŭs.   V. Scabies.

scăbĭēs, ĭēī, f., *a scab.*   Quĕm scăbĭēs aŭt, Hor.   Syn. Pōrrĭgo, scabrĭtĭēs.   Epitii. Mălă, mŏlēstă, ĕdāx, tŭrpĭs, ĭmmŭndă, fœtĭdă, ōbscœnă, āspĕră.

scăbĭōsŭs, ă, ŭm, *scabby.* Ēst scăbĭōsŭs, ĕt ācrī, Pers. SYN. Scăbĕr; scăbĭē īnfēctŭs. V. Scabies.

scăbo, scăbī, *to scratch.* Sæpĕ căpūt scăbĕrĕt, Hor. SYN. Frīco.

scabrĭtĭēs, ĭēī, f., *roughness, scab.* Scăbrĭtĭēmque ănĭmī, Mart. SYN. Āspĕrĭtās; scăbĭēs. EPITH. Dūră, rĭgĭdă, āspĕră, rŭdĭs, īmpŏlītă, īngrātă.

Scœă pŏrtă, f., Scœæ pŏrtæ, f. pl., *the Scœan gate of Troy.* Scœās sævīssĭmă pŏrtās, Virg.

scălæ, ārŭm, f. pl., *a ladder.* Părĭĕtĭbŭs scălæ, pōstēs, Virg. EPITH. Ārdŭæ, āltæ, tĕrĕtēs, făcĭlēs, ērēctæ, pēnsĭlēs.

scălmŭs, ī, m., *a piece of wood, to fasten to the oars.* Ādvērsūm, scălmīs stīpāntĭbŭs. V. Remus.

scălpo, ĭs, psī, *to scratch.* Dĭgĭtō scălpūnt ūnō, Juv. SYN. Scăbo.

scālprŭm, ī, n., *a graving tool.* Sī scālpra ĕt fōrmās, Hor. SYN. Cælŭm. EPITH. Ăcūtŭm, ădūncŭm, dūrŭm, tĕnŭĕ, ēxĭlĕ. V. Cælum.

Scămāndĕr, drī, m., *a river of the Troad.* Fīndūnt Scămāndrī flūmĭnă, Hor. EPITH. Fātālĭs, Phrȳgĭŭs, Dārdănŭs, Trōjānŭs, præcēps, ămœnŭs, sŏnāns, rĕsŏnāns.

scămnŭm, ī, n., *a bench.* Scămnă dēdīssĕ, Ov. SYN. Sĕdīlĕ, sēdēs.

scāndălŭm, ī, n., *scandal.* Scāndălă prōcūlcăt, Prud. EPITH. Nōxĭŭm, mălŭm, ēxĭtĭōsŭm.

scāndo, scāndī, *to climb.* Scāndĕrĕt īmpĭă, (Alcaic.) Hor. V. Ascendo.

Scāntĭnĭă lēx, *a law passed against the corruptors of youth, proposed by the tribune Scantinius.* Ānte ōmnēs dēbēt Scāntīnĭă, Juv. Scāntĭnĭăm mĕtŭēns, Aus.

scăphă, æ, f., *a small boat.* Præsĭdĭō scăphæ, (Alcaic.) Hor. SYN. Cȳmbă, lēmbŭs. EPITH. Lĕvĭs, văgă, ăgĭlĭs, vŏlucrĭs, pārvă, bĭrēmĭs, tĕnŭĭs. V. Cymba.

scăphĭŭm, ĭī, n., *a cap, a chamber-pot.* Ēt rĭdĕ, scăphĭŭm pŏsĭtĭs, Juv. EPITH. Ǣrĕŭm, ăhēnŭm ; tūrpĕ, fœdŭm.

scăpŭlæ, ārŭm, f. pl., *the shoulders.* Tĕnŭēs scăpŭlĭs ănălēctrĭdĕs āltīs, Ov. SYN. Ārmī.

scāpŭs, ī, m., *the cross-piece of a weaver's loom.* Rădĭī scăpīquĕ sŏnāntēs, Lucr.

scărăbĕŭs, *or* bæŭs, ī, m., *a beetle, an insect sacred among the Egyptians.* Sēd scărăbēŭs ĕrĭt, Aus.

scărŭs, ī, m., *the char, a fish.* Ēt scărŭs ārtĕ, Ov. EPITH. Ŏbēsŭs, æquŏrĕŭs, Cārpăthĭŭs, mōllĭs, ăvĭdŭs.

scătebră, æ, f., *a spring.* Sāxă cĭēt scătĕbrīsque, Virg.

scătĕo, ēs, *to burst.* Quī scătĕt ĕt sālsās, Lucr. V. Scaturio.

• scătūrīgo, ĭnĭs, f., *a spring.* Col. SYN. Scătĕbră, fōns ; ŏrīgo. EPITH. Lătēns, ŏccūltă, cæcă, īmă, āltă, līmpĭdă, sŏnāns, pĕrēnnĭs, săllēns. V. Fons.

scătūrĭo, ĭs, ĭī, *to gush out.* Vērmĭcŭlīs scătūrĭēntēs, (Phal.) Prud. SYN. Scătĕo, ēfflŭo, ēmāno ; ērūmpo, ēxĭlĭo, dērīvŏr, ŏrĭŏr, ēbūllĭo.

scaŭrŭs, ă, ŭm, *club-footed.* Bālbūtĭt scaŭrŭm, Hor.—2. subst., m., *a Roman surname.* Rēgŭlum ēt Scaŭrōs, Id.

scĕlĕrātŭs, ă, ŭm, *wicked, abominable.* Ēt scĕlĕrātŭs ĕŏdĕm, Ov. SYN. Scĕlēstŭs, nĕfārĭŭs, nĕfāndŭs, īmprŏbŭs, flāgĭtĭōsŭs, nēquăm, pērdĭtŭs, mălīgnŭs, nōxĭŭs, īmpĭŭs. V. Impius.

scĕlĕro, ās, *to defile by a crime.* Scĕlĕrārĕ pĕnātēs, Cat. V. Polluo.

scĕlĕrōsŭs, *and* stŭs, ă, ŭm, *criminal.* Illŭm scĕlĕrōsŭm, Ter. Āntĕcēdēntēm scĕlēstŭm, (Dact. Troch.) Hor.

scĕlŭs, ĕrĭs, n., *a crime, a villain.* Mănēnt scĕlĕrĭs vēstīgĭă nōstrī, Virg. SYN. Crīmĕn, făcĭnŭs, flāgĭtĭŭm, nōxă, cūlpă, dēlīctŭm, nĕfās, pĭācŭlŭm. EPITH. Īnfāndŭm, nĕfāndŭm, ēxĭtĭălĕ, sævŭm, īmmānĕ, nĕfārĭŭm, hōrrĭdŭm, īmprŏbŭm, crūdēlĕ, ĭnaŭdītŭm, ātrŭm, fœdŭm, pĕtŭlcŭm, pŭdēndŭm, tētrŭm, mūlctābĭlĕ, ĭnīquŭm, sānguĭnĕŭm, mĭsĕrŭm, īnfēlīx, mōrtĭfĕrŭm.

scēnă, æ, f., *a bower, a stage.* Scēnă cŏrūscĭs, Virg. SYN. Ŭmbrācŭlŭm ; thĕātrŭm. EPITH. Ŭmbrōsă, frōndēns, grātă, vĭrēns, vĭrĭdĭs, ămœnă, lūdĭcră.

scēnālĭs, ĕ, *and* ĭcŭs, ă, ŭm, *of the stage.* Scēnālĭs spĕcĭĕ, Lucr. Scēnĭcŭs ārtĕ, Mart. SYN. Thĕātrĭcŭs, thĕātrālĭs.

Scēpsĭŭs, ĭī, m., *Metrodorus of Scepsis, a Greek writer.* Scēpsĭŭs Aŭsŏnĭŏs, Ov.

scēptrĭfĕr, *and* gĕr, ă, ŭm, *bearing a sceptre.* Scēptrĭfĕrās ārctă, Sil. Scēptrĭgĕrō cūm rēgĕ, Id. V. Rex.

scēptrŭm, ī, n., *a sceptre.* Scēptră mănū, Ov. EPITH. Aŭrātŭm, ĕbūrnĕŭm, Ĭnsīgnŏ, splēndĭdŭm, sŭpērbŭm, dĕcōrŭm, cŏrŭscŭm, prĕtĭōsŭm, gēmmāns, fūlgēns, vĕnĕrāndŭm, vĕrēndŭm, mĭnāx, ĭmpĕrĭōsŭm, rēgālĕ Scētānĭŭs, ĭī, or ānŭs, ī, m., *the name of a man.* Scētānī dīssĭmĭlīs sīs, Hor.

schĕdă, *or* ŭlă, æ, f., *a little scroll, a sheet.* Sūmmā pŏtĕs īn schĕdā, Mart.

schēmă, ătīs, n., *form, figure, costume.* Cōnfēr nūnc schēmă, Jŭvēncī, Mart.

Schĭnĭs, *or* Scĭnĭs, ĭs, m., *a robber, punished by Theseus.* Occĭdĭt ĭllĕ Schĭnĭs, Ov.

Epith. Sānguĭnĕŭs, sævŭs, trŭx, ĭmmītĭs, dīrŭs, atrōx.

Schœnēĭs, *and* Schœnĭs, ĭdĭs, f., *the daughter of Schœneus, Atalanta.* Schœnēĭdă præmĭă cūrsūs, Ov. Schœnĭdă tēr cădēntĕ pōmŏ, Sid.

Schœnēĭŭs, ă, ŭm, *of Schœneus, king of Arcadia, and father of Atalanta.* Vīrgō măgĭs hīs Schœnēĭă dīctūs, Ov.—2. subst., -ă, æ, f., *Atalanta.* Mōllī Schœnēĭă vŭltū, Id.

Schœnŏbătēs, æ, m., *a rope-dancer.* Aŭgŭr, schœnŏbătēs, mĕdĭcŭs, Juv.

schŏlă, æ, f., *a school.* Ět schŏlă cūltæ, Aus. Syn. Gȳmnăsĭŭm, pălœstră, lūdŭs. Epith. Dōctă, cĕlĕbrĭs, clără, īnsĭgnĭs.

* schŏlăstĭcŭs, ī, m., *a scholar.* Plin. Epith. Pĕrītŭs, ĭngĕnĭōsŭs, dōctŭs, fācūn-dŭs, dīsērtŭs, ĭngĕnŭŭs, vĭgĭl, ānxĭŭs. V. Doctus.

scĭēntĭă, æ, f., *science, knowledge.* Dō mănūs scĭēntĭæ, (Iamb. Dim.) Hor. Syn. Nŏtĭtĭă, cōgnĭtĭŏ; dīscĭplīnă, ārs, stŭdĭŭm; dōctrīnă. V. Doctrina, eloquentia, studia, artes.

scīlĭcĕt, adv., *truly, to wit.* Scīlĭcĕt hōc ūnŭm, Ov. Syn. Vĭdēlĭcĕt, nīmīrŭm, nēmpĕ, quīppĕ, năm, ĕnĭm.

scīllă, æ, f., *a sea onion.* Scīllāmque hēllĕbŏrōsquĕ grăvēs, Virg. V. Bulbus.

scīndo, scīdī, scīssŭm, *to slash, to rend.* Ăt scīdĭt, ēt mĕdĭō, L. Syn. Ăbscīndo, dīscīndo, rēscīndo, prōscīndo, sĕco, rĕsĕco, sūbsĕco, ēxsĕco, dīssĕco, ēxcīdo, ĭncīdo, rĕcīdo, āmpŭto; trūnco, mŭtĭlo, lăcĕro, dīlăcĕro; cædo, fĕrĭo. V. Lacero.

scīntīllă, æ, f., *a spark.* Cūjūs scīntīllās, Juv. Epith. Ignĭtă, ārdēns, rŭbēns, cŏrŭscāns, tĕnŭĭs, pārvă, vŏlāns, vŏlătĭlĭs. V. Ignis.

scīntīllo, ās, *to sparkle.* Scīntīllāre ŏlĕŭm, Virg.

scĭo, scīs, scīvī, *to know.* Tāntī scĭăt ĭllă, Virg. Syn. Nōvī, tĕnĕo, cōgnōsco, nōsco, cāllĕo, īntēllĭgo.

scĭŏlŭs, ī, m., *a smatterer in knowledge.* Ět scĭŏlō quīcquăm, Mart. Syn. Sēmĭ-dŏctŭs.

Scīpĭădæ, ārŭm, m. pl., *the two Scipios.* Dŭŏ fūlmĭnă bēllī, Scīpĭădās, Virg.

Scīpĭo, ōnĭs, m., *Africanus and Æmilianus, two great Roman generals.* Syn. Scīpĭădēs. Epith. Aŭsŏnĭŭs, Rōmŭlĕŭs, trŭcŭlēntŭs, fōrtĭs, aŭdāx, Mārtĭŭs, măgnănĭmŭs, gĕnĕrōsŭs, ănĭmōsŭs, Māvōrtĭŭs, ĭmpērtērrĭtŭs, tērrĭfĭcŭs, strē-nŭŭs.

scīpĭo, ōnĭs, m., *a staff.* Tăbērnæ scīpĭōnĭbŭs scrībăm, Catul.

Scīrōn, ōnĭs, m., *a robber killed by Theseus.* Ět Scīrōn ēt cŭm, Ov.

scīrpĕă, æ, f., *and* pĭcŭlŭs, ī, m., *a basket.* Scīrpĕă lătă, Ov. Scīrpĭcŭlīs mĕdĭŏ, Prop.

scīrpĕŭs, ă, ŭm, *of rushes.* Scīrpĕă prō dŏmĭnŏ Tĭbĕrī jāctētŭr ĭmāgo, Ov. Syn. Jūncĕŭs.

scīrpŭs, ī, m., *a rush.* Quærŭnt ĭn scīrpō, Enn. Epith. Ēnōdĭs, frăgĭlĭs, pălūstrĭs, līmōsŭs, stĕrĭlĭs, tĕnĕr, flēxĭlĭs. V. Juncus.

scīscĭtŏr, *and* scītŏr, ārĭs, *to inquire.* Istă scīscĭtārētŭr, (Scaz.) Eŭrȳpȳlum scī-tātŭm, Virg. Syn. Pērcōntŏr, pĕto, quæro, pōstŭlo, īntērrŏgo.

|| * scīssĭlĭs, ĕ, *easy to be cleft.* Syn. Fīssĭlĭs.

scītē, adv., *learnedly.* Sĕpŭlchrālēs scīte ĭncāntārĕ făvīllās, Prud. Syn. Dōctē; vĕnŭstē; ārgūtē.

scītŭm, ī, n, *doctrine, precept.* Quī scītă Plătōnĭs, Aus.

scītŭs, ă, ŭm, *learned.* Vălēns, scītŭsquĕ vădōrŭm, Ov. Syn. Scĭēns, dōctŭs; ārgūtŭs, vĕnŭstŭs.

scĭūrŭs, ī, m., *a squirrel.* Ĭnămĭăbĭlĭs scĭŭrŭs, Mart.

scŏbs, ŏbĭs, f., *saw-dust.* In scŏbĕ quāntŭs, Hor.

scōmbĕr, brī, m., *a sea-fish.* Ět lāxās scŏmbrīs, Catul.

Scŏpās, æ, m., *a famous statuary.* Aŭt Pārrhăsĭŭs prōtŭlĭt aŭt Scŏpās, Hor.

scōpæ, *or* ŭlœ, ārŭm, f. pl., *a broom.* In prĕtĭŏ scŏpās, Mart.

scŏpŭlōsŭs, ă, ŭm, *rocky.* Mŏntēs scŏpŭlōsæ, Lucan. V. Saxosus.

scŏpŭlŭs, ī, m., *a rock.* Dēdūcĭt scŏpŭlōs, Juv. SYN. Săxŭm, caūtēs, sīlēx, rūpēs. EPITH. Immānĭs, ădēsŭs, frŏndōsŭs, mĭnāx, scăbĕr, dūrŭs, mŭscōsŭs, ăcūtŭs, tŭmĭdŭs. V. Rupes.

scŏpŭs, ī, m., *the end.* Sĭt scŏpŭs, ēt vītæ, Alcim. SYN. Mētă, ĭndēx, fīnĭs ; prŏpŏsĭtŭm. EPITH. Prŏpŏsĭtŭs, dēsĭgnātŭs, sĭgnātŭs, stătūtŭs, cērtŭs. V. Jaculor.

scŏrpĭo, ōnĭs, *and* ĭŭs, ĭī, m., *a scorpion.* SYN. Nĕpă. EPITH. Vĕnĕnōsŭs, lē-thĭfĕr, dīrŭs, nŏcēns, mōrtĭfĕr, ĭnfēstŭs, mĭnāx, ācĕr.—2. *One of the twelve signs.* Scōrpĭŭs, ēt cœlī, Virg. EPITH. Mĭnāx, vĭŏlēntŭs, ācĕr, ārdēns, hŏr-rēns, dīrŭs.

scōrtātŏr, ōrĭs, m., *a fornicator.* Laūdātō scōrtātŏr ĕrĭt, Hor. SYN. Mœ-chŭs.

scōrtĕŭs, ă, ŭm, *leathern.* Scōrtĕă dēsĭt, Mart.

scōrtŏr, ārĭs, *to fornicate.* Ser. SYN. Mœchŏr. V. Adultero.

scōrtŭm *and* ĭllŭm, ī, n., *a harlot.* Ŏffĭcĭŭm scōrtō, Hor. V. Meretrix.

Scōtī, ōrŭm, m. pl., *Scotchmen.* Quæ Scōtō dăt, Claud.

scrība, æ, m., *a writer, a secretary.* Scrība quŏd ēssĕt, Mart. EPITH. Dēxtĕr, cĭtŭs, sōlērs, pĕrītŭs.

Scrībæ, ārŭm, m. pl., *doctors among the Jews,* Eccl.

scrīblĭtă, æ, f., *light pastry.* Mēnsĭs scrīblĭtă sĕcŭndĭs, Mart.

scrībo, ĭs, psī, *to write.* Scrībēbāmŭs ĕpŏs, cœpīstī scrībĕrĕ, cēssī, Mart. SYN. Pērscrībo, cōnscrībo, ĭnscrībo, pīngo, ēxāro.

scrīnĭŭm, ĭī, n., *an escritoire.* Scrīnĭăque ād tēctī, Prop.

scrīptŏr, ōrĭs, m., *a writer, an author.* Scrīptŏr hŏnōrātŭm, Hor.

scrīptŭm, ī, n., *a writing.* Scrīptă fĕrŭnt ānnŏs, Ov.

scrīptūră, æ, f, *writing, a writing, a manuscript.* Scrīptūră quāntī, (Scaz.) Mart. SYN. Scrīptŭm, scrīptă.

scrīpŭlŭm, scrīptŭlŭm, *and* scrŭpŭlŭm, ī, n., *a weight equal to the twenty-fourth part of an ounce.* Quīnquĕ trăhănt mărăthī scrŭpŭlă, Ov.—2. *a kind of game.* Scrīptŭlă quŏt mēnsēs, Id.

scrōbs, scrōbĭs, f., *a ditch.* Aūt scrōbĭbŭs māndĕt, Virg. SYN. Fōssă, fŏvĕă. EPITH. Ātră, căvă, cōncăvă, ōbscœnă, fœdă, tūrpĭs, hūmĭdă, ūdă, prŏfūndă. V. Spelunca

scrŭpĕŭs, ană pōsŭs, ă, ŭm, *stony.* Scrŭpĕă tūtă, Virg. Scrŭpōsĭs āngūstă văcānt, Luc. SYN. Lăpĭdōsŭs, sălebrōsŭs, săxōsŭs.

scrŭpŭs, ī, m., *a small stone.* Hŏrrēscĭt scrŭpŭs, Ov. SYN. Lăpĭllŭs, scrŭpŭlŭs, călcŭlŭs.

scrūtă, ōrŭm, n. pl., *old rubbish.* Scrūtă pŏpēllō, Hor.

scrūtātŏr, ōrĭs, m., *a searcher.* Ănĭmī scrūtātŏr ŏpērtī, Alc. SYN. Vēstĭgātŏr, quæsītŏr.

scrūtŏr, ārĭs, *to search carefully.* Tū scrūtābērĭs ūllĭŭs, Hor. SYN. Pērscrūtŏr, rīmŏr, quæro, ĭnquīro, ĭnvēstĭgo.

scūlpo, psī, ptŭm, *to engrave.* Scūlpĭt ĕbŭr, Ov. SYN. Scălpo, ĭncīdo, cælo. V. Simulacrum.

scūlptĭlĭs, ĕ, *that may be engraved.* Scūlptĭlĕ dēntĭs, Ov. SYN. Scūlptŭs, cælātŭs, ĭncīsŭs.

* scūlptŏr, ōrĭs, m., *an engraver, a sculptor.* Plin. SYN. Cælātŏr, stătŭārĭŭs.
* scūlptūră, æ, f., *sculpture, engraving.* Plin. SYN. Cælātūră, stătŭārĭă.

scūrră, æ, m., *a buffoon.* Infīdō scūrræ, Hor. EPITH. Tūrpĭs, prŏcāx, lŏquāx, gărrŭlŭs, făcētŭs.

scūrrĭlĭs, ĕ, *of a jester.* Scūrrĭlī strĕpĭtŭ, Ov. SYN. Jŏcōsŭs, făcētŭs, jŏcŭ-lārĭs.

scūrrĭlĭtăs, ātĭs, f., *drollery.* Scūrrĭlĭtāte āc gārrŭlĭtātĕ, (Iamb.) Alc. SYN. Jŏcī; prŏcācĭtăs.

scūrrŏr, ārĭs, *to play the jester.* Scūrrŏr ĕgo ĭpsĕ, Hor. SYN. Jŏcŏr.

scūtātŭs, ă, ŭm, *wearing a shield.* Tēr cēntŭm scūtātī, Virg. SYN. Clỹ-pĕātŭs.

scūtēllă, *and* ŭlă, æ, f., *a saucer.* Et lævēs scūtŭlās, Mart

scŭtĭcă, æ, f., *a scourge.* Nē scŭtĭcā dīgnŭm, Hor.

scŭtŭlātŭs, ă, ŭm, *wrought in needlework.* Ĭndūtŭs scŭtŭlātă, Juv.

scŭtŭm, ī, n., *a buckler.* Scūtă vīrum, Virg. Syn. Clўpĕŭs, ŭmbo, parmă. V. Clypeus.

Scўlăcēŏn, *and* ŭm, ī, n., *a promontory of Calabria.* Ět nāvīfrăgūm Scўlăcēŭm, Virg.—Adj. ŭs, ă, ŭm. Scўlăcēăquĕ līttŏră fērtŭr, Ov.

Scўllă, æ, f, *a rock, opposite to Messina, fabulously represented as a hideous monster.* Quīd Sўrtēs aūt Scўllă mīhi, Virg. Epitii. Fĕrŏx, vŏrāx, mĕtŭēndă, latrāns, răpāx, impĭă, īnfōrmīs, īnmānīs, trŭcŭlēntă, trīfōrmīs, Sĭcŭlă, Phŏrcīs, Phŏrcīnīs; Nērēĭă, Nēptūnĭă.—2. *the daughter of Nisus; she was changed into a* lark. Scўllă căpīllō, Virg. Syn. Nīsēïs. Epith. Impĭă, pērfĭdă, scĕlĕrătă, nĕfārĭă.

Scўllēĭŭs, *and* æŭs, ă, ŭm, *of Scylla.* Pōstquăm Scўllēĭă lēgĭt, Pedo. Vōs ět Scўllæām răbĭĕm, Virg.

scўmnŭs, ī, m., *a lion's whelp.* Scўmnīquĕ lĕōnŭm, Lucr. Syn. Cătŭlŭs.

scўphŭs, ī, m., *a cup.* Dēxtrām scўphŭs; ŏcўŭs ōmnēs, Virg. Syn. Călīx, crātēr, pōcŭlŭm. V. Calyx.

Scўrĭăs, ădīs, *and* rœïs, ĭdīs, f., *of Scyros, Scyrian.* Scўrĭăs Æmŏnĭō, Ov.

Scўrĭŭs, ă, ŭm, *of Scyros, Scyrian.* Ŏmnīs Scўrĭă pūbēs, Virg.

Scўrŏs, *or* rŭs, ī, m., *an island in the Ægean sea, where Lycomedes reigned, and Achilles was brought up.* Phthĭam hæc Scўrŏnvĕ fĕrāntŭr, Ov.

scўtălă, æ, *and* lē, ēs, f., *a kind of serpent.* Ět scўtălæ spārsīs, Lucan.

Scўthă, *and* ēs, æ, m., Scўthæ, ārŭm, m. pl., *a Scythian, Scythians.* Nōn Scўthă nŏn fīxŏ, Luc. Tē prŏfŭgŭs Scўthēs, Hor. Cāmpēstrēs mĕlĭŭs Scўthæ, Hor. Epitii. Ērrāntēs, prŏfŭgī, cāmpēstrēs, gĕlĭdī, ăcērbī, văgī, īndŏmĭtī, sævī, ærīsŏnī, bēllācēs, bēllĭgĕrī, īnvīctī.

Scўthĭă, æ, f., *the country of the Scythians.* Mūndŭs ŭt ād Scўthĭăm, Virg.

Scўthĭcŭs, *and* ĭŭs, ă, ŭm, *Scythian.* Nōmĕn ămā; Scўthĭcŭs, Ov. Quā Scўthĭæ gēntēs, Virg.

Scўthīs, ĭdīs, f., *Scythian.* Ārtēs Scўthĭdēs mĕmŏrāntŭr ĕāsdĕm, Ov.

sē, acc., *himself, herself.* Ænēās sē mātūtīnŭs ăgēbăt, Virg. Syn. Sēsē.

Sēbēthŏs, *or* ŭs, ī, m., *a river of Campania, discharging itself into the gulf of Naples.* Sēbēthŏs ălŭmnā, Stat.—Adj., -thīs, ĭdīs, f., *of Sebethos.* Sēbēthĭdĕ nўmphā, Virg.

sēbŭm, *or* vŭm, ī, n., *grease, fat.* Ālbēntēs sēbī glŏbŭlōs, Aus.

sĕcābĭlīs, ĕ, *that may be cut.* Nūllīquĕ sĕcābĭlĕ sēgmĕn, Aus.

sēcēdo, ssī, ssŭm, *to retire.* Văcŭōs sēcēdĕre īn hŏrtōs, Ov. Syn. Rĕcēdo, dīscēdo, ābscēdo.

sēcērno, ĭs, crēvī, crētŭm, *to separate, discern.* Jūstō sēcērnĕre īnīquŭm, Hor. Syn. Dīvĭdo, sēpăro, dīscērno, sēgrēgo.

sēcēssŭs, ūs, m., *retirement.* Ēst īn sēcēssū, Virg. Syn. Rĕcēssŭs. Epith. Tūtŭs, sēcūrŭs.

sēcĭŭs, adv., *less, otherwise.* Sēcĭŭs āĕrĕ nīngĭt, Virg. Syn. Mĭnŭs; sĕcŭs, ălītĕr; sērĭŭs.

sēclŭdo, sī, sŭm, *to separate.* Teŭcrī, sēclŭdĭtĕ cūrās, Virg. Syn. Sējŭngo; ēxclŭdo.

sēco, ās, cŭī, sēctŭm, *to cut.* Vēntōsquĕ sĕcābăt, Virg. V. Scindo.

sēcrētō, adv., *in secret.* Mē quŏquĕ sēcrētō, Ov. Syn. Ārcānō. V. Clam.

sēcrētŭm, ī, n., *a retired place, retreat; secret.* Sēcrētă Sĭbўllæ, Virg. Syn. Sēcēssŭs, rĕcēssŭs, pĕnetrālĕ; ārcānŭm. Epith. Abdĭtŭm, ōccŭltŭm; tăcēndŭm, sĭlēndŭm.

sēcrētŭs, ă, ŭm, *secret, retired.* Īn sōlā sēcrētæ, Virg. Syn. Ārcānŭs, ābstrūsŭs, ōccŭltŭs, lătēns, mўstĭcŭs. V. Arcanus.

sēctă, æ, f., *a sect.* Sēctārŭm caūsās, Mart. Syn. Hærēsĭs, ŏpĭnĭo, schŏlă, dōctrīnă, rēlĭgĭo.

sēctĭlīs, ĕ, *and* īvŭs, ă, ŭm, *easy to cleave or cut.* Sēctĭlĕ pōrrŭm, Juv. Fīlăquĕ sēctīvī, Id. Syn. Scīssĭlīs.

sēctŏr, ōrīs, m., *one that cuts.* Sēctōrquĕ făvōrīs, Luc.

sēctŏr, ārīs, *the frequent. of* sequor. Săpĭēns sēctābĭtŭr ārmōs, Hor.

sēcŭbĭtŭs, ūs, m., *a lying or sleeping alone.* Tōrmēntīs sēcŭbĭtūquĕ cŏlī, Ov.

sēcŭbo, ās, ŭī, *to sleep alone.* Sēcŭbăt īn văcŭō, Ov. V. Cubo.

sēcŭm, *by or with one's self.* Īn sīccā sēcŭm spătĭātŭr ărēnă, Virg.

sĕcŭndo, ās, *to favour, to aid.* Aūră sĕcŭndăt ĭtĕr, Prop. Syn. Adjŭvo, făvĕo prōspĕro. V. Auxilior.

sĕcŭndŭm, prep., *near ; after.* Plēnă sĕcŭndŭm, Virg. Syn. Jŭxtā ; prŏpĕ ; pŏst.

sĕcŭndŭs, ă, ŭm, *the second ; favourable.* Sācră sĕcŭndŭs, Virg. Syn. Altĕr ; prŏspĕr, faŭstŭs. V. Felix.

sĕcūrĭfĕr, *and* gĕr, ă, ŭm, *bearing an axe.* Hĕllĭmūmquĕ, sĕcūrĭfĕrūmquĕ, Ov. Mŏrĕ sĕcūrĭgĕrā, Sil.

sĕcūrĭs, ĭs, f., *an axe.* Ictă sĕcūrĭbŭs īlĕx, Virg. Syn. Bĭpĕnnĭs, āscĭā. Epith. Ǣrātă, fĕrrĕă, grăvĭs, dūră, ăcūtă, cūrvă, rĭgĭdă, sævă, crŭēntă, strīctă, Scўthĭcă, Ămāzŏnĭă, laŭrĭgĕră, cōnsŭlārĭs. V. Fasces, scindo.

sĕcūrĭtās, ātĭs, f., *safety, quietness.* Mĭhi ēst sĕcūrĭtās, (Iamb.) Sen. Syn. Quĭēs. Epith. Tŭtă, quĭētă, trānquĭllă, plăcĭdă.

sĕcūrŭs, ă, ŭm, *safe.* Mŏllĭă sĕcūræ, Ov. Syn. Tūtŭs, quĭētŭs, trānquĭllŭs, ĭmpăvĭdŭs, ĭntĕrrĭtŭs, ĭmpērtĕrrĭtŭs, fīdēns, cōnfīdēns, cōnfīdēntĭssĭmŭs.

sĕcŭs, adv., *otherwise.* Haŭd sĕcŭs āc, Virg. Ălĭtĕr ; jŭxtā, prŏpĕ, sĕcŭndŭm.

sĕcŭs, n., indecl., *sex.* Vēstă, Cĕrēs ēt Jūnō, sĕcŭs mŭlĭĕbrĕ, Aus. V. Sexus.

sĕcūtŏr, ōrĭs, m., *the gladiator who combated with the retiarius.* Jūssŭs pūgnārĕ sĕcūtŏr, Juv.

sĕcūtŭs, ă, ŭm, *the pass. partic. of* sequor. Ipsĕ sĕcūtŭs, Mart.

sĕd, conj., *but.* Ipsĕ sĕd hōrrĭfĭcĭs, Virg. Syn. Ăt, āst, vērŭm, sĕd ĕnĭm, ăt ĕnĭm.

sĕdātŭs, ă, ŭm, *the pass. partic. of* sedo. Ōllī sĕdātō, Virg.

sĕdĕnĭm, conj., *but, for.* Mĕtū, sĕdĕnĭm gĕlĭdŭs, Virg. Syn. Sĕd, ăt ; năm, ĕnĭm.

sĕdĕo, sĕdī, *to sit.* Pēndēnt : sĕdĕt, ætērnŭmquĕ sĕdēbĭt, Virg. Syn. Sīdo, cōnsĭdĕo, ăssĭdĕo, rĕsĭdĕo, āssīdo, rĕsīdo, cōnsīdo.

sĕdēs, ĭs, f., *a seat, an abode.* Sĕdĭbŭs ōptātĭs, Virg. Syn. Sĕdīlĕ, scăbēllŭm, sēllă, scămnŭm, sŭbsēllĭă, căthĕdră, sŭggēstŭm, sŏlĭŭm ; stătĭo, sēssĭo, lŏcŭs. Epith. Lignĕă, aŭrĕă, ĕburnă, pīctă, dĕcŏră, ōrnātă, āltă, cŭrūlĭs. V. Sedeo.

sĕdīlĕ, ĭs, n., *a seat.* Vīvōquĕ sĕdīlĭă sāxō, Virg. V. Sedes.

sĕdĭtĭo, ōnĭs, f., *sedition, discord.* Sĕdĭtĭō sævĭt, Virg. Syn. Dīssĭdĭŭm, dīscōrdĭă, dīssēnsĭo, tūrbă, mōtŭs, tŭmŭltŭs, fāctĭo. Epith. Tŭrbĭdă, clāmōsă, rĕbēllĭs, pŏpŭlārĭs, cīvīlĭs, rĕpēntīnă, sŭbĭtă, fŭrēns, crŭēntă, ēxĭtĭōsă, pērnĭcĭōsă, trūx, hōrrĭbĭlĭs, īnsānă, cœcă, sævă, nĕfārĭă, īntēstīnă, mĭsĕră. V. Discordia.

* sĕdĭtĭōsŭs, ă, ŭm, *factious.* Cic. Syn. Tŭrbŭlēntŭs, tŭrbĭdŭs.

sĕdo, ās, *to appease.* Immŏdĭcōs sĕdārăt īn ārcĕ, Pr. Syn. Mītĭgo, plāco, lēnĭo. V. Placo.

sĕdūco, ĭs, xī, ctŭm, *to draw apart.* Hūncquĕ mănū blāndă sĕdūxĭt, Ov. Syn. Sĕvōco, sēpăro ; dēcĭpĭo.

sĕdŭlĭtās, ātĭs, f., *diligence.* Sĕdŭlĭtătĕ lăbŏr, Ov. Syn. Vĭgĭlāntĭă, stŭdĭŭm, īndūstrĭă. Epith. Gnāvă, vĭgĭl, prŏvĭdă. V. Diligentia.

sĕdŭlŭs, ă, ŭm, *diligent.* Sĕdŭlŭs īnflăt, Hor. Syn. Dīlĭgēns, ĭmpĭgĕr, āssĭdŭŭs, vĭgĭlāns, stŭdĭōsŭs, āttēntŭs, gnāvŭs, īndūstrĭŭs. V. Diligens.

sĕdŭm, ī, n., *houseleek.* Mŭltŏquĕ sĕdī cōntĭngĕrĕ sŭccō, Aus. Epith. Sēmpērvīvŭm.

sĕgĕs, ĕtĭs, f., *corn.* Neū sĕgĕs ēlūdăt, Tib. Hīc sĕgĕtēs, ĭllīc, Virg. Syn. Sătă, frūgēs, ārīstæ, spīcæ, frūmēntŭm, trītĭcŭm, Cĕrēs. Epith. Spīcĕă, trītĭcĕă, Cĕrēālĭs, tĕnĕră, vĭrĭdĭs, lætă, fœcūndă, fērtĭlĭs, fĕrāx, ŭbĕr, ŏpīmă, frūgĭfĕră, grăvĭdă, dīvĕs, lārgă, āmplă, ăbūndāns, aŭrĕă, flāvēscēns, mātūră, ŏptātă, ēxpēctātă, cōllēctă. V. Messis, meto, fruges.

sĕgmēn, ĭnĭs, *or* mēntŭm, ī, n., *a shred.* Jăm sĕgmēntă rĕquīro, Ov. V. Frustum.

sĕgmēntă, ōrŭm, n. pl., *a collar.* Sĕgmēnta ēt lōngōs, Juv.

sĕgmēntātŭs, ă, ŭm, *made of many pieces.* Ēt sĕgmēntātĭs, Juv.

sĕgnĭpēs, ĕdĭs, *slow-paced.* Sĕgnĭpēdēs, dīgnĭquĕ, Juv. Syn. Tārdŭs.

sĕgnĭs, ĕ, *dull, slow.* Sĕgnĭŏr īnstăt, Virg. Syn. Tārdŭs, ĭgnāvŭs, pĭgĕr. V. Piger.

sĕgnĭtĕr, adv., *slothfully.* Sĕgnĭtĕr ārcŭs, Stat. Syn. Ignāvĕ.

sĕgnĭtĭă, æ, *and* ĭēs, ĕī, f., *sloth.* Sĕgnĭtĭēs ălĭī, Virg. Syn. Ignāvĭă, dēsĭdĭă, pĭgrĭtĭă. Epith. Sĕră, ĭnērs, trīstĭs. V. Pigritia.

sĕgrĕgo, ās, *to separate.* Sĕgrĕgăt ĭpsă, Prud. Syn. Sēpăro, sēpōno, dīsgrĕgo, sējūngo.

Sĕjānŭs, ī, m., *the favourite of Tiberius.* Sĕjānō dūcĭtŭr ūncō, Juv.

sējūngo, xī, ctŭm, *to separate, divide.* Pŏtĭs ēst sējūngī, Lucr.

sēlēctŭs, ă, ŭm, *the pass. partic. of* seligo. Jūdĭcĭbŭs sēlēctīs, Hor.

sēlībră, æ, f., *half a pound.* Trēs sēlībrās, (Phal.) Mart.

sēlĭgo, ĭs, lēgī, lēctŭm, *to select.* Sēlĭgĕ tāntŭm, Ov. Syn. Ēlĭgo, dēlĭgo, lĕgo.

Sēlīnūs, ūntĭs, f., *a city of Sicily.* Pālmōsā Sēlīnūs, Virg.

sēllă, æ, f., *a seat, a throne.* Ēt sēllām rēgnī, Virg. Syn. Sĕdēs, sĕdīlĕ, sŏlĭŭm.

sēmāmbūstŭs, ă, ŭm, *half burnt.* Sēmāmbūstă rŏtăt, Sil.

sĕmĕl, adv., *once.* Quō sĕmĕl ēst, Hor.

Sĕmĕlē, ēs, f., *the mother of Bacchus.* Ōbsĕquĭō Sĕmĕlē, Ov. Epith. Cādmēĭs, Thēbānă, pūlchră.

Sĕmĕlēĭŭs, *and* lœŭs *or* lēŭs, ă, ŭm, *of Semele.* Sĕmĕlēĭŭs Ēvān, Stat. Sĕmĕlœăquĕ būstă tĕnēntŭr, Ov.

sēmĕn, ĭnĭs, n., *seed.* Sēmĕn hūmŭm, Ov. Syn. Sēmēntĭs, sēmēntŭm. Epith. Fœcūndŭm, gĕnĭtālĕ, frūctĭfĕrŭm, fērtĭlĕ, fĕräx, spārsŭm. V. Grainen, sero.

sēmēntīnŭs, ă, ŭm, *belonging to seed-time.* Nēc sēmēntīna ēst, Ov.

sēmēntĭs, ĭs, f., *seed-time.* Ād mĕdĭăs sēmēntĕm, Ov.

sēmēstrĭs, ĕ, *of six months.* Sēmēstrī vātŭm, Juv.

sĕmēsŭs, ă, ŭm, *half eaten.* Sēmēsōs pīscēs, Hor.

sēmiănĭmĭs, ĕ, *and* ŭs, ă, ŭm, *half dead.* Sēmiănĭmēs vōlvūntŭr, Virg. Syn. Sēmiănīmātŭs.

sēmĭăpērtŭs, ă, ŭm, *half open.* Sēmĭăpērtă lătŭs, Ov.

sēmĭbōs, ŏvĭs, m., *half an ox.* Sēmĭbōvēmquĕ vĭrŭm, Ov.

sēmĭcăpĕr, prī, m., *half a goat, a satyr.* Sēmĭcăpēr cōlĕrĭs, Ov.

sēmĭcrēmātŭs, *and* mŭs, ă, ŭm, *half burnt.* Sēmĭcrēmātă fŏcō, Ov. Sēmĭcrēmŏquĕ nŏvăt, Id. Syn. Sēmūstŭs.

sēmĭcrūdŭs, ă, ŭm, *half raw.* Mānē sēmĭcrūdŭs, Stat.

sēmĭdĕŭs, ēī, m., *and* ă, æ, f., *a demi-god, demi-goddess.* Sēmĭdĕūmquĕ gĕnŭs, Ov. Aūt quās sēmĭdĕæ Drўădēs, Id.

sēmĭdĭēs, ēī, m., *half a day.* Sēmĭdĭēmquĕ, dŭōsquĕ dĭēs, Aus.

sēmĭdōctŭs, ă, ŭm, *half taught.* Ēt sēmĭdōctā vīllĭcī mănū, Mart.

sēmĭfĕr, *and* ĕrŭs, ă, ŭm, *half a beast.* Sēmĭfĕræ spĕcĭēs, Lucr.

sēmĭfūltŭs, ă, ŭm, *half propped up.* Sēmĭfūltŭs ēxtrēmō, (Scaz.) Mart.

sēmĭhĭāns, ntĭs, *half open.* Sēmĭhĭāntĕ lăbēllō, Cat.

sēmĭhŏmo, ĭnĭs, m., *half man.* Sēmĭhŏmĭnĭs Cācī, Virg. Syn. Sēmĭvĭr.

sēmĭlăcĕr, ĕră, ĕrŭm, *half torn.* Sēmĭlăcērquĕ tŏrō, Ov.

sēmĭlaūtŭs, ă, ŭm, *half washed.* Sēmĭlaūtă crūră, Catul.

sēmĭmărīnŭs, ă, ŭm, *half marine.* Sūccīnctăs sēmĭmărīnĭs, Lucr.

sēmĭmās, ărĭs, m., *half male, an eunuch.* Sēmĭmărēm fēcīssĕ, Ov.

sēmĭmōrtŭŭs, ă, ŭm, *half dead.* Sēmĭmōrtŭă lēctŭlō jăcēbănt, Catul. V. Semianimis.

sēmĭnēx, nĕcĭs, *half dead.* Sēmĭnĕcēs pārtĭm, Ov. Syn. Sēmiănĭmĭs.

sēmĭnĭŭm, ĭī, n., *a seed, a breed.* Sēmĭnĭŏquĕ, Lucr.

sēmĭno, ās, *to sow.* Sēmĭnăt ārbōs, Virg. Syn. Sēro, īnsēro, cōnsēro, īnsēmĭno, plānto. V. Semen.

sēmĭpāgānŭs, ă, ŭm, *half rustic.* Ipsĕ sēmĭpāgānŭs, (Scaz.) Pers.

sēmĭpătĕr, trĭs, m., *half father.* An tĭbī sēmĭpătĕr, Ov.

sēmĭpēs, pĕdĭs, m., *half a foot in verse.* Ēt pōst sēmĭpĕdĕm, Aus.

sēmĭpŭēllă, æ, f., *having half the body of a young woman.* Trēs sēmĭdĕæ, trēs sēmĭpŭēllæ, Aus.

sēmĭpŭtātŭs, ă, ŭm, *half cut.* Sēmĭpŭtătă tĭbī, Virg.

Sĕmīrămĭs, ĭs *and* ĭdĭs, f., *the wife of Ninus.* Băbўlōnā Sĕmīrămĭs ūrbĕm, Pr. Epith. Fōrmōsă, Mārtĭă, fōrtĭs, lāscīvă, tūrpĭs, phăretrātă, bēllātrīx, ārmĭpŏtēns.

Sĕmīrămĭŭs, ă, ŭm, *of Semiramis.* Nōstră Sĕmīrămĭæ, Claud.

sēmĭrāsŭs, ă, ŭm, *half shaved.* Ā sēmĭrāsō tūndĕrētŭr, Cat.

sēmĭrēdūctŭs, ă, ŭm, *half retired.* Sēmĭrēdūctă mănū, Ov.

sēmĭrēfēctŭs, ă, ŭm, *half repaired.* Sēmĭrēfēctă mŏrās, Ov.

sēmĭrŭtŭs, ă, ŭm, *half demolished.* Sēmĭrŭtīs pēndēnt, Luc.

sēmĭs, (*indecl.*) *or* sēmĭs, īssĭs, m., *half.* Quĭd fīt? Sēmĭs, Hor. V. Semissis.

sēmĭsĕpūltŭs, ă, ŭm, *half buried.* Sēmĭsĕpūltă vĭrŭm, Ov.

sēmĭsŏpītŭs, ă, ŭm, *half asleep.* Sēmĭsŏpītă tŏrō, Ov. Syn. Sēmĭsōmnĭs.

sēmīssĭs, ĭs, m , *half an as.* Sāltĕm sēmīssĕm, Mart. V. Semis.
sēīnĭsŭpīnŭs, ă, ŭm, *half turned upon the back.* Sēmĭsŭpīnă lătŭs, Ov.
sēmītă, æ, f., *a path.* Sēmītă cāllēs, Virg. Syn. Cāllĭs, trāmēs, vĭă, ītĕr. V. Via.
sēmītālĭs, ĕ, *of streets, of cross-ways.* Sēmītālĭbūs dīīs, Virg. Catal. Syn. Vĭālĭs.
sēmītārĭŭs, ă, ŭm, *of by-ways. of alleys.* Ĕt sēmītārīī mœchī, Catul.
sēmĭvĭr, vĭrī, m., *half man.* Cŭm sēmĭvĭrō cŏmĭtātū, Virg. Syn. Sēmihŏmo; īmbēllĭs, īgnāvŭs.
sēmiūstŭs, ă, ŭm, *half burnt.* Sŏcĭōs, sēmiūstăquĕ sērvānt, Virg. Syn. Sēmicrēmātŭs, sēmicrēmŭs.
sēmŏdĭŭs, īī, m., *half a bushel.* Sēmŏdĭūsquĕ făbæ, Mart.
sēmōtŭs, ă, ŭm, *the pass. partic. of* semoveo. Cūrā sēmōtă mĕtūquĕ, Lucr.
sēmŏvĕo, mŏvī, mōtŭm, *to put aside.* Sēmŏvĕōquĕ mălī, Ov. Syn. Rĕmŏvĕo, āmŏvĕo, sēpōno.
sēmpĕr, adv., *always.* Sēmpĕr ĕgo audītŏr, Juv. Syn. Ætērnŭm, ūsquĕ, pērpĕtŭō, nūnquăm nōn, cōntĭnŭō, āssĭdŭē. V. Immortalis, æťernus.
sēmpĭtērnŭs, ă, ŭm, *eternal.* Ōlīm sēmpĭtērnō jūdĭcī, (Iamb.) Prud. Syn. Pērpĕtŭŭs, ætērnŭs.
sēmūncĭă, æ, f., *half an ounce.* Sēmūncĭă rēctī, Pers.
sēnārĭŭs, ă, ŭm, *of six.—*Vērsŭs, *lines of six feet.* Vērsĭbūs sēnārĭīs, (Iamb.) Phæd.
sēnātŏr, ōrĭs, m.. *a senator.* Ipsĕ sēnātŏr ŏvēs, Ov. Syn. Jūdēx. Epith. Lōngævŭs, cānŭs, ānnōsŭs, prūdēns, grāvĭs, sŏlērs, sāgāx, prŏvĭdŭs, săpĭēns, jūstŭs, æquŭs, pūrpŭrĕŭs, vĕrēndŭs, vĕnĕrāndŭs, sānctŭs, īntĕgĕr, īllūstrĭs.
sēnātŭs, ŭs, m., *the senate.* Rōmă sĕnātū, Claud. Syn. Cūrĭă; sĕnātōrēs. Epith. Prūdēns, grāvĭs, jūstŭs, augūstŭs, æquŭs, săcĕr, sānctŭs, pūrpŭrĕŭs.
Sĕnĕcă, æ, m., *the Roman philosopher.* Ā Sĕnĕcă quæ Pīsŏ bŏnŭs, Juv. Epith. Dōctŭs, sĕvērŭs, pĭŭs.
sĕnēctă, æ, *and* tŭs, ūtĭs, f., *old age.* Ĕffœtă sĕnēctŭs, Virg. Syn. Sĕnĭŭm, cānĭtĭēs, vĕtūstās. Epith. Cānă, cānēns, ālbă, rūgōsă, frīgĭdă, gĕlĭdă, trĕmēns, trĕmŭlă, trĕmēbūndă, cūrvă, īncūrvă, ănhēlă, trīstĭs, ĕffœtă, grāvĭs, vĕtŭs, sĕră, lōngæva, tārdă, mātūră, ānnōsă, pigră, quĕrĕbūndă, īnfīrmă, ĭnērs, īgnāvă, lānguĭdă, squālĭdă, tĕtrĭcă, mōrōsă, ăvără, mĭsĕră, īnfēlīx, ærūmnōsă, fœdă, tūrpĭs, dēlīră, īngrātă, īnjūcūndă, crūdă, vĭrĭdĭs, rŏbūstă, prūdēns, săpĭēns, prŏvĭdă. V. Canities, senex.
sĕnēctŭs, ă, ŭm, *the old partic. of* seneo. Mēmbrīs ēxīrĕ sĕnēctĭs, Lucr.
sĕnĕo, ēs, *and* ēsco, ĭs, nŭī, *to grow old.* Rĕcōndĭtă Sēnēt quĭĕtĕ, Catul. Ĕt āmŏrĕ sĕnēscĭt, Hor. Syn. Cōnsĕnēsco, sĕnēx fīo.
sĕnēx, sĕnĭs, m., *an old man.* Ĕt sĕnĭbūs mĕdĭcāntŭr, Virg. Syn. Sĕnĭŏr, lōngævŭs, ānnōsŭs, grāndævŭs, vĕtŭlŭs, dēcrĕpĭtŭs. Epith. Fēssŭs, sĕvērŭs, squālĭdŭs, mūcōsŭs, dēlīrŭs, sāgāx, sŏlērs, pārcŭs, īmbēllĭs, īnfīrmŭs, ănhēlŭs, īnvālĭdŭs, trĕmēns, ĕffœtŭs, ægĕr, tārdŭs, ĭnērs, mātūrŭs, lōngævŭs, ānnōsŭs, grāndævŭs, dēcrĕpĭtŭs, căpŭlārĭs, ăvārŭs, sōrdĭdŭs, mĭsĕr, sĕvērŭs, mōrōsŭs, dēbĭlĭs, frāctŭs, ēxhaūstŭs, cānŭs, cānēns, ālbŭs, rūgōsŭs, frĭgĭdŭs.
sēnī, æ, ă, *six.* Bīs sēnōs, Virg.
sĕnīlĭs, ĕ, *of old age.* Rūgă sĕnīlĭs ĕrăt, Ov.
sēnīo, ōnĭs, m.. *the side of the die marked six.* Quīd dēxtēr sēnĭŏ fērrĕt, Pers.
sĕnĭŏr, ōrĭs, *older.* Cŭm sĕnĭŏrĕ sĕnēx, Mart.
sēnĭpēs, pĕdĭs, *having six feet.* Hīc quŭm sēnĭpĕdĕm, Sid.
sĕnĭŭm, īī, n., *old age.* Dēfōrmīs sĕnīī, (Alcaic.) V. Senectus
Sĕnŏnēs, ŭm, m. pl., *a people of Gaul.* Infāndī Sĕnŏnēs, Stat.
sēnsĭbĭlĭs, *or* sīlĭs, ĕ, *perceivable by the senses.* Sēnsĭbĭlī quŏvīs, Lucr. Sēnsĭlĕ gignī, Lucr.
sēnsĭfĕr, ă, ŭm, *causing sensation.* Lōngĕ ā sēnsĭfĕrīs, Lucr.
sēnsĭm, adv., *by degrees.* Līttŏrĕ sēnsĭm. Syn. Paūlātĭm, pĕdĕtēntĭm.
sēnsŭs, ūs, m., *sense.* Vărĭōs sēnsŭs ēxprōmĕrĕ, Lucr. Epith. Ācūtŭs, vĭgĭl, vīvŭs, tĕnŭĭs, sŭbtīlĭs, mōllĭs.
sēntēntĭă, æ, f., *sentiment, opinion.* Sēntēntĭārŭm nōtŭs, (Alcaic.) Hor. Syn. Cōnsĭlĭŭm, mēns, ănĭmŭs, sēnsŭs, ŏpīnĭŏ; jūdĭcĭŭm, dēcrētŭm. Epith. Cērtă, fīrmă, fīxă, dŭbĭă, vărĭă, cōnstāns, īncērtă. V. Dubius.
sēntēs, ŭm, m. pl., *brambles.* Ūndĭquĕ sēntēs, Virg. Syn. Spīnæ, rŭbī, veprēs. Epith. Incūltī, rĭgĭdī, hāmātī, ācūtī, mōrdācēs. V. Spina.

sĕntīnă, æ, f., *a sink, a pump.* Tŭnc sĕntīnă grăvĭs, Juv. EPITH. Fœdă, ŏlĭdă, ŏlēns, putrĭdă, tŭrpĭs, putrĭs. V. Cloaca.

sĕntĭo, sī, sŭm, *to feel, to think.* Sĕntĭt ĕt ĭllĕ, Mart. SYN. Sŭnsŭ pĕrcĭpĭo; vĭdĕo, aūdĕo, ŏdōrŏr, gŭsto, tāngo; ĭntĕllĭgo, căpĭo; jūdĭco, cēnsĕo, pŭto, ārbĭtrŏr, ēxīstĭmo, ŏpīnŏr, rĕŏr, aūtŭmo.

sĕntĭs, ĭs, m., *a bramble.* Sĕntĭbŭs ūvă, Virg. V. Sentes.

sĕntīsco, ĭs, ĕrĕ, *to begin to feel.* Lātē sĕntīscĕrĕ, quŭm Pān, Lucr.

sĕntŭs, ă, ŭm, *thorny, horrid.* Pĕr lŏcă sĕntă sĭtŭ, Virg.

sĕōrsĭm, or seōrsĭm, *(dissyl.)* adv., *separately.* Nārēsvĕ sĕōrsĭm, Lucr. Ĕt seōrsĭm vărĭōs, Id. SYN. Sĕōrsŭm, sĕōrsŭs.

sĕōrsŭs, or seōrsŭs, ă, ŭm, *separated, divided.* Sæpĕ sĕōrsĭs Ōbsīstūnt stŭdĭĭs, Aus.

sēpār, ărĭs, *divided.* Nĕc sēpărĕ cōntĕgăt ūrnă, V. Fl.

sēpăro, ās, *to separate.* Sēpărŏr ā dŏmĭnă, Ov. SYN. Sēcĕrno, sēgrĕgo, sēpŏno, rĕmŏvĕo; dīsjūngo, dīstrăho, dīvĕllo, dīstērmĭno, dīscrīmĭno, dīvĭdo, dīspērtĭo, dīssĕco, dīstīnguo.

sēpĕlĭo, īvī, sĕpūltŭm, *to bury.* Vīvō sĕpĕlīrī, Lucr. SYN. Hŭmo, ĭnhŭmo, tŭmŭlo, cōntŭmŭlo. V. Parento, funus, exequiæ.

sēpēs, ĭs, f., *a hedge.* Sēpĭbŭs īn nōstrĭs, Virg. SYN. Sēptŭm, vāllŭm. EPITH. Āltă, lōngă, sȳlvēstrĭs, spīnōsă, frŭtĭcōsă, hīrsūtă, ăcūtă; sēntĭbŭs, spīnīs hōrrēns.

sēpĭă, æ, f., *a cuttle-fish.* Sēpĭă tārdă fŭgœ, Ov.

sēpĭo, sēpīvī, sēpĭī, or sēpsī, *to hedge in.* Cēcrŏpĭī sēpĭt. SYN. Ŏbsēpĭo, vāllo, ās.

sēpōno, ĭs, sŭī, sĭtŭm, *to put aside.* Lĕpĭdō sēpŏnĕrĕ dīctō, Hor. SYN. Sēmŏvĕo, rĕmŏvĕo, āmŏvĕo.

sēpŏsĭtŭs, ă, ŭm, *the pass. partic. of* sepono. Sēpŏsĭtī cĭcĕrĭs, Hor.

sēps, sēpĭs, m., *a kind of serpent.* Tābĭfĭcŭs sēps, Lucan. V. Serpens.

sēptĕm, *seven.* Ŏblŏquĭtŭr nŭmĕrĭs sēptĕm, Virg. SYN. Sēptēnī.

Sēptēmbĕr, brĭs, m., *the ninth month.* Sēptēmbĕr ŏpīmăt, Aus. EPITH. Frūctĭfĕr, grăvĭdŭs, ŏnĕrātŭs, pōmĭfĕr, răcēmĭfĕr.—*Adj., of September.* Sēptēmbrĭbŭs hōrīs, Hor.

sēptēmflŭŭs, ă, ŭm, *flowing in seven channels.* Sēptēmflŭă flūmĭnă Nīlī, Ov.

sēptēmgĕmĭnŭs, ă, ŭm, *divided into seven.* Ĕt sēptēmgĕmīnī, Virg. SYN. Sēptēmplēx.

sēptēmplēx, ĭcĭs, *sevenfold.* Sēmtēmplĭcĭs ōrbēs, Virg.

sēptēmvĭr, ĭrī, m., *a member of the commission of seven magistrates, who regulated the religious festivals.* Sēptēmvĭrque ĕpŭlīs fēstīs, Lucr. SYN. Ĕpŭlo.

sēptēnārĭŭs, ă, ŭm, *belonging to seven.* Sēptēnārĭă sȳnthĕsĭs, (Phal.) Mart.

sēptēnī, m. pl., *seven.* Inquĕ dĭĕm sēptēnīs, Juv.

Sēptēntrĭo, ōnĭs, m., *the north.* Sēptĕm sūbjĕctă trĭōnī, Virg. V. Arctos.

sēptĭcĭānŭs, ă, ŭm, (nummus, libra, argentum,) *base coin put into circulation during the second Punic war.* Sēptĭcĭānă: quĭd ēst, Mart.

Sēptĭcĭŭs, ĭī, m., *the name of a man.* Būtrăm tĭbī Sēptĭcĭūmquĕ, Hor.

|| sēptĭfŏrĭs, ĕ, *having seven holes.* Sēptĭfŏrĕm vūltŭm, Alcim.

Sēptĭmĭŭs, ĭī, m., *a lyric and tragic poet, the friend of Horace.* Sēptĭmĭŭs, Claūdī, Hor.

sēptĭmŭs, ă, ŭm, *seventh.* Sēptĭmŭs ōctăvō, Hor.

sēptīngēntī, æ, ă, *seven hundred.* Sēptīngēntă Tītō, Mart.

sēptŭm, ī, n., *an enclosure.* Vīctĭmă sēptīs, Virg. SYN. Sēpīmĕn, cōnsēptŭm.

sēptūnx, ūncĭs, m., *a weight of seven ounces.* Pārs sēptĭmă sēptūnx, Aus.—2. *a measure of liquids, containing the seventh part of a sextarius.* Sēptūncĕ mūltō, Mart.

sēptŭs, ă, ŭm, *the pass. partic. of* sepio, *enclosed, enveloped.* Īnfĕrt sē sēptŭs nĕbŭlă, Virg.

sĕpūlcrālĭs, ĕ, *of a tomb.* Āntĕ sĕpūlcrālēs, Ov. SYN. Fūnĕrĕŭs.

sĕpūlcrētŭm, ī, n., *a church-yard.* Quam īn sĕpūlcrētīs, (Scaz.) Cat.

sĕpūlcrŭm, ī, n., *a tomb.* Cōndĕ sĕpūlcrō, Virg. SYN. Tŭmŭlŭs, mŏnŭmēntŭm, būstŭm. EPITH. Trīstĕ, mœstŭm, flēbĭlĕ, fătālĕ, fūnĕrĕŭm, lūgubrĕ, ātrŭm, ōbscūrŭm, gĕlĭdŭm, frīgēns, căvŭm, īmŭm, quĭētŭm, mārmŏrĕŭm, măgnĭfĭcŭm, sŭp⁴rbŭm, prĕtĭōsŭm, rēgālĕ, ēxstrūctŭm. V. Sepelio.

sĕpŭltūră, æ, f., *burial*. Pŏstquĕ sĕpŭltūrăm, Fil. Syn. Tŭmŭlī, sĕpŭlcrī hŏnŏr, tŭmŭlī dĕcŭs. V. Sepulcrum.

sĕpŭltŭs, ă, ŭm, *the pass. partic. of* sepelio. Crēdīs cūrārĕ sĕpŭltōs, Virg. Syn. Hŭmātŭs, tŭmŭlātŭs, cŏndītŭs, cŏmpŏsĭtŭs.

Sēquănă, æ, m., *a river in France*. Sēquănă, Lēdŭs, Sid.

Sēquănĭcŭs, ă, ŭm, *of the Seine*. Sēquănĭcæ pīnguĕm, Mart.

sĕquăx, ācĭs, *following*. Prætēndĕ sĕquācēs, Virg. Syn. Sĕquēns; dŭctĭlĭs, flēxĭlĭs.

sĕquēstĕr, ră, rŭm, *of an umpire*. Pācĕ sĕquēstrā, Virg.

sĕquēstĕr, trĭs, m., *an umpire*. Pācīsquĕ sĕquēstrĕm, Sil. Epith. Æquŭs, fīdŭs.

sĕquŏr, ĕrĭs, sĕcūtŭs, *to follow*. Sĕ sĕquĭtūrquĕ, Ov. Syn. Sēctŏr, sŭbsĕquŏr, īnsĕquŏr, īnsto.

sĕră, æ, f., *a lock*. Pŏstĕ sĕrăm, Ov. Syn. Claŭstrŭm, ŏbĕx, fērrŭm. Epith. Fērrĕă, fērrātă, ærātă, strīdēns, fīrmă, vălĭdă, fīdă, tūtă, sēcūră, āffīxă, āppŏsĭtă. V. Janua.

Sĕrāpĭs, ĭs *or* ĭdĭs, m., *an Egyptian god*. Tūrbă Sĕrāpĭn ămăt, Mart. Syn. Apĭs, Osīrĭs. V. Osiris, Apis.

sĕrēno, ās, *to clear up*. Tēmpēstātēsquĕ sĕrēnăt, Virg. Syn. Trānquĭllo; plāco, ● sĕrēnĭtās, ātĭs, f., *calmness*. Cic. Syn. Sĕrēnŭm, sūdŭm. Epith. Trānquĭllă, pācātă, plācĭdă, quĭētă, ămīcă, blāndă, ămœnă, ōptātă, făvēns. V. Mare tranquillum.

sĕrēnŭm, ī, n., *and* nă, ōrŭm, n. pl., *serenity, clear sky*. Clārō fŭlsērŭnt plūră sĕrēnō, Virg. Sōlēs ĕt ăpērtă sĕrēnă, Id. Syn. Sūdŭm, sĕrēnĭtās. V. Serenitas.

sĕrēnŭs, ă, ŭm, *calm*. Īnfĕrĭŏrĕ tŏnĕt nūbĕ sĕrēnŭs ăpēx, Mart. Syn. Sĕrēnātŭs, īnnūbĭlŭs; nŏn nūbĭlŭs, nŏn tūrbĭdŭs.

Sērĕs, ŭm, m. pl., *a people of Asia*. Tēnuĭă Sĕrĕs, Virg. Epith. Eōī, cŏlōrātī, flāvī, lōngīnquī, ēxtrēmī, bĕnīgnī, mītĕs.

sĕrēsco, ĭs, *to become dry*. Sōlĕ sĕrēscŭnt, Lucr. Syn. Sīccŏr.

Sĕrēstŭs, *and* Sērgēstŭs, ī, m., *companions of Æneas*. Lævāquĕ Sĕrēstŭm, Virg. Mnēsthĕă Sērgēstŭmquĕ vŏcăt, Id.

Sērgĭŭs, ĭī, m., gĭă, æ, f., *the name of a noble Roman family*. Tĕnĕt ā quō Sērgĭă nōmĕn, Virg.

sērĭă, *or* ŏlă, æ, f., *a wine-vessel*. Sērĭă dēxtrō, Pers. Sērĭŏlæ vĕtĕrĭs, Id.

sērĭcŭm, ī, n., *silk*. Sērĭcă tēxtĭlĭbŭs, Prop. Syn. Bōmbȳcĭnŭm, Sērĭcă, bōmbȳcĭnă -ōrŭm. Epith. Dīvĕs, nōbĭlĕ, prĕtĭōsŭm. V. Stamen.

sērĭcŭs, ă, ŭm, *of silk, of the Seres*. Tēndĕrĕ Sērĭcăs, Hor.

sērĭēs, ĭēī, f., *a concatenation, an order*. Jūnō, sērĭēsque, Ov. Syn. Ōrdo. Epith. Lōngă, īmmēnsă, cōntĭnŭă.

sērĭĕtās, ātĭs, f., *a serious air, gravity*. Lætăquĕ sērĭĕtās, Aus. Syn. Grăvĭtās.

Sērĭphŏs, *or* ŭs, ī, f. V. Seryphus.

sērĭŭs, ă, ŭm, *serious*. Sērĭă lūdō, Virg.

sērĭŭs, comp. adv., *later, too late*. Sērĭŭs ēgrĕdĭtŭr, Ov.

sērmo, ōnĭs, m., *discourse*. Pŏpŭlōs sērmōnĕ rĕplēbăt, Virg. Syn. Ōrātĭo; vōcēs, vērbă, dīctă, lŏquēlæ, cōllŏquĭŭm, āllŏquĭŭm. Epith. Cūltŭs, grăvĭs, ămœnŭs, văgŭs, lĕpĭdŭs, blāndŭs, mītĭs, dīsērtŭs, pŏlītŭs, dōctĭlŏquŭs, pūrŭs, cŏmĭs, cănōrŭs, prōmptŭs, fēstīvŭs, suāvĭs, pŏtēns, cōncīnnŭs, cōmptŭs, ōrnātŭs, mōllĭs, flēxănĭmŭs, nŭmĕrōsŭs, fācūndŭs, jējūnŭs, ārĭdŭs, ēxīlĭs, tĕnŭĭs, hŭmĭlĭs. V. Loquor, eloquium, eloquens.

sĕro, sĕvī, sătŭm, *to sow, to plant*. Tēctă sĕrăt lātē, Virg. Syn. Sēmĭno, īnsĕro, cōnsĕro. V. Semino.

sēro, adv., *late*. Heŭ sērō rĕvŏcātŭr, Tib. Sērō mĕmŏr, Stat. Syn. Tārdē, sērĭŭs, tārdĭŭs.

sĕro, ĭs, ŭī, ērtŭm, *to plait, interweave, mingle*. Quĭd sĕrīs fāndō mŏrās, Sen. Syn. Nēcto, tēxo, jūngo, cōnnēcto.

sērōtĭnŭs, ă, ŭm, *of the evening*. Prĕmĕrĕt sērōtĭnă nŏctĕ, Hilar. Syn. Sērŭs, vēspērtīnŭs.

sērpēns, ntĭs, m., *a serpent*. Gĕrĭt sērpēntĭbŭs hȳdrăm, Virg. Syn. Angŭĭs, drāco, cŏlŭbĕr, cŏlubră, hȳdrŭs, hȳdră, ăspĭs, chĕlȳdrŭs, vīpĕră. Epith. Vĕnēnōsŭs, lēthĭfĕr, lēthālĭs, āspĕr, nŏxĭŭs, nŏcŭŭs, tŭmĭdŭs, squālĭdŭs, squālēns, hŏrrēns, hŏrrĭbĭlĭs, hŏrrĭdŭs, mĭnāx, tērrĭbĭlĭs, lătēns, sĭnŭōsŭs, tŏrtŭs, tŏrtĭlĭs, ĭntŏrtŭs, ĭmplĭcĭtŭs, lūbrĭcŭs, squāmōsŭs, crĭstātŭs, pēnnātŭs, vĕnēnĭfĕr, līvĭdŭs, līvēns, fĕrōx, sævŭs, atrōx, vĭrēns, cærŭlĕŭs, vērsĭcŏlōr, cŏrŭscŭs, sībĭlŭs, ĭmmānĭs, vĭpĕrĕŭs, Gōrgŏnĕŭs, Lĭbўcŭs.

sērpēntĭgĕnă, æ, m. f., *born of a serpent.* Vōs sērpēntĭgĕnĭs, Ov.

sērpēntĭgĕr, ă, ŭm, *bearing a serpent.* Sērpēntĭgĕrōsquĕ gĭgāntŭs, Sil.

sērpēntĭpēs, pĕdĭs, *serpent-footed.* Sērpēntĭpĕdēsquĕ gĭgāntŭs, Ov.

sērpo, psī, *to creep.* Sērpĕrĕ laūrōs, Virg. Syn. Rēpo, rēpto, ādrēpo, ĭnsērpo. V. Repo.

sĕrpўllĭfĕr, ă, ŭm, *producing betony.* Quā sĕrpўllĭfĕrĭs, Sid.

sērpўllŭm, ī, n., *betony.* Lātē Sērpўlla, Virg. Epith. Ŏdōrĭfĕrŭm, ŏdōrŭm, frāgrāns, grātŭm, jūcūndŭm, suāvĕ, ămœnŭm, vĭrēns, vĭrĭdĕ, lūxŭrĭāns.

sērră, *and* rŭlă, æ, f., *a saw.* Sērră sĕcārĕ, Mart. Epith. Ărgūtă, fērrĕă, ăcūtă, strīdēns, dēntātă, raūcă, lōngă; Dædālĕă.

Sērrānŭs, ī, m., *the name of a man.* Et jŭvĕnēm Sērrānŭm, Virg.

sērro, ās, *to saw.* Sērrăvīt rāmōs, Sil. V. Seco.

sērtŭm, ī, n., *a garland of flowers.* Tēxtĭlĭbŭs sērtĭs, Mart. Syn. Cŏrōnă, cŏrōllă. Epith. Flōrēns, ŏdōrŭm, rĕdŏlēns, nēxĭlĕ, tēxtĭlĕ, pīctŭm, gĕnĭālĕ, fēstŭm, lūtĕŭm, ōlēns, spīcĕŭm, flōrĭdŭm, cærŭlĕŭm, grāmĭnĕŭm, flōrĕŭm, flāvēns, stēllāns, frāgrāns, rŏsĕŭm, pīctūrātŭm, hālāns, ĭnsīgnĕ, ămărānthæŭm, vĭrĭdĕ, cŏlōrātŭm, pūnĭcĕŭm, rădĭōsŭm, ĭntŏrtŭm, frōndĕŭm, rŏscĭdŭm. V. Corona.

sērtŭs, ă, ŭm, *pass. partic. of* sero, *to plait.* Sērtās nārdō flōrēntĕ cŏrōnās, Luc.

sērvă, æ, f., *a woman-servant.* Sērvă lăbōrĕ, Cat. Syn. Āncīllă, fămŭlă, mĭnīstră. .V. Servus.

sērvābĭlĭs, ĕ, *that may be preserved.* Nūllī sērvābĭlĕ, Ov.

sērvātŏr, ōrĭs, m., *and* trīx, īcĭs, f., *a preserver.* Sērvātŏrēmquĕ fŭtētŭr, Ov. Sērvātrīx ūrbēs, Id.

sērvīlĭs, ĕ, *slavish.* Stābāt sērvīlĭbŭs, ātquĕ, Hor.

sērvĭo, īs, *to be a slave, to obey.* Dēdĭtă sērvĭt, Tibull. Syn. Fămŭlŏr, mĭnīstro ; ŏbēdĭo, pārĕo, ŏbsĕquŏr.

sērvĭtĭŭm, ĭī, n., *and* vĭtŭs, ūtĭs, f., *slavery, service.* Sērvĭtĭō prĕmĕt, Virg. Quūm sērvĭtūtĕm, Pl. Syn. Fămŭlātŭs, mĭnīstĕrĭŭm, jŭgŭm. Epith. Grăvĕ, ægrŭm, trīstĕ, tūrpĕ, dūrŭm, nĕfāndŭm, ĭmʌnītĕ, ăcrĕ, mālīgnŭm, mĭsĕrŭm, mĭsĕrābĭlĕ, ĭnfāmĕ, mŏlēstŭm, ŏnĕrōsŭm, hŭmĭlĕ, ăbjēctŭm, vīlĕ.

Sērvĭŭs, ĭī *or* ĭ, m., *Servius Tullius, the sixth king of Rome.* Scēptrĭfĕrās Sērvī, Ov.

sĕrŭm, ī, n., *whey.* Pāscĕ sĕrō pīnguī, Virg.

sērvo, ās, *to preserve.* Mŏnĭtĭs sērvābĭs ămōrēs, Prop. Syn. Āssērvo, cōnsērvo, .cŭstōdĭo, tūtŏr, sālvo. V. Custodio, salvo.

sĕrŭs, ă, ŭm, *late.* Sĕrŭs ĭn ŏffēnsăm, Tib. Syn. Tārdŭs.

sērvŭs, *and* ŭlŭs, ī, m., *a slave.* Fŭgās sērvōrŭm, Hor. Sērvŭlŭs ĭnfēlīx, Juv. Syn. Fămŭlŭs, mĭnīstĕr, vērnă, māncĭpĭŭm, pŭĕr; cāptĭvŭs. Epith. Fĭdŭs, fĭdēlĭs, sēdŭlŭs, strēnŭŭs, vĭgĭl, ăcĕr, ŏffĭcĭōsŭs, ăgĭlĭs, sōlērs, ĭmpĭgĕr, gnārŭs, prōmptŭs, ĭnōps, mĭsĕr, ĭnfēlīx, ēgĕnŭs, vĭlĭs, ăbjēctŭs, hŭmĭlĭs, sōrdĭdŭs. V. Captivus.

Scŏrūphŭs, ī, f., *one of the Cyclades.* Plānămquĕ Scŭrўphŏn, Ov. Epith. Pārvă, hŭmĭlĭs, brĕvĭs, ĭncūltă.

Sĕsōstrĭs, ĭs *or* ĭdĭs, m., *an Egyptian king and lawgiver.* Mūndīquĕ ēxtrēmă Sĕsōstrĭs, Luc.

sēsquĭpĕdālĭs, ĕ, *a foot and a half long.* Sēsquĭpĕdālĭă vērbă, Hor.

sēsquĭpēs, pĕdĭs, m., *a foot and a half.* Brĕvĭŏr, Claudĭă, sēsquĭpĕdĕ, Mart.

sēssĭlĭs, ĕ, *low, dwarfish, that one may sit upon.* Sēssĭlĕ tērgŭm, Ov.

sēssŏr, ōrĭs, m., *he who sits.* In văcŭō lætŭs sēssŏr, Hor.

sēstērtĭŭm, *and* ĭŏlŭm, ī, n., *Roman money.* Quĕrĕrĭs sēstērtĭă fraūdĕ, Juv. Cuī sēstērtĭŏlŭm, Mart.

Sēstĭăs, ădĭs, *and* tĭs, ĭdĭs, f., *of Sestos.* Sēstĭăs ōră, Sid. Sēstĭ pŭēllă, tĭbi, Ov.

Sēstŏs, ī, f., *a promontory of Thrace, opposite Abydos.* Sēstŏs Abўdō, Virg.

sētæ, ārŭm, f. pl., *bristles, hair.* Hōrrēntĭ sētĭs, Ov. Syn. Pĭlī. Epith. Cŏmāntĕs, rĭgĭdæ, dūræ, hĭrtæ, fĕræ, trĕmŭlæ, hŏrrĭdæ, hŏrrēntĕs, hīspĭdæ.

Sētĭă, æ, f., *a town of Campania, famous for its wines.* Quă spēctăt Sētĭă cāmpōs, Mart.

sētĭgĕr, ă, ŭm, *hairy, bristly.* Sētĭgĕrōsquĕ sŭes, Ov.—2. subst., m., *a boar.* Mĕtŭēndŭs sētĭgĕr āgrĭs, Mart.

Sētīnŭs, ă, ŭm, *of Setia.* Clīvī spēctăt ūvă Sētīnī, Mart.—2. subst., -ŭm, ī, n., *Setian wine.* Et lātō Sētīnŭm, Juv.

sētōsŭs, ă, ŭm, *full of bristles.* Sētōsī căpŭt hōc, Virg. SYN. Sētĭgĕr.

seū, disj., *or.* Seū dŏlŏr, Ov. SYN. Sīvĕ, vĕl.

sĕvērĭtās, ātĭs, f., *severity.* Dēpŏsĭtā sĕvērĭtātĕ, (Phal.) Mart. SYN. Aūstērĭtās, ăcērbĭtās, āspĕrĭtās, dūrĭtĭēs, atrōcĭtās, īnclēmēntĭă, saevĭtĭă, fĕrōcĭă, crūdēlĭtās, tetrĭcĭtās, mōrōsĭtās; grăvĭtās. EPITH. Ăcērbă, dūră, mŏlēstă, īntŏlĕrābĭlĭs, aūstēră. V. Crudelitas, gravitas.

sĕvērŭs, ă, ŭm, *severe.* Cūrĭbūsquĕ sĕvērĭs, Virg. SYN. Aūstērŭs, ăcērbŭs, rĭgĭdŭs, āspĕr, dūrŭs, atrōx, īnclēmēns, saevŭs, fĕrōx, īmmītĭs, crūdēlĭs, tetrĭcŭs, mōrōsŭs; grăvĭs. V. Gravis, crudelis.

Sĕvērŭs, ī, m., *a Roman emperor.* Ārmă Sĕvērŭs ăb Istrō, Aus.—2. *a mountain of the Sabines.* Mōntēmquĕ Sĕvērŭm, Virg.

sĕvōco, ās, *to call aside.* Sĕvōcăt hūnc gĕnĭtŏr, Ov. SYN. Sējŭngo; āvōco.

sēx, *six.* Bīs sēx lēctīssĭmă, Virg. SYN. Sēnī.

sēxāgēsĭmŭs, ă, ŭm, *the sixtieth.* Sēxāgēsĭmă mēssĭs, Mart.

sēxāgīnta, n. pl., indecl., *sixty.* Cūm sēxāgīntă nŭmĕrĕt, Mart. Sēxāgīntă tĕrăs, Id.

sēxāngŭlŭs, ă, ŭm, *having six angles.* Tĕgĭt sēxāngŭlă foetūs, Mart.

sēxcēntī, ae, ă, *six hundred.* Sēxcēntōs īllī dĕdĕrăt, Virg.

sēxdĕcĭm *or* sēdĕcĭm, *sixteen.* Cōlĭphĭă sēxdĕcĭm cŏmēdĭt, Mart.

sēxtāns, āntĭs, m., *a weight, the sixth part of a libra.* Sēxtāntēmquĕ trăhăt, Ov.—2. *a measure of liquids.* Sēxtāntēs, Cāllīstĕ, Mart.

sēxtārĭŭs, ĭī, m., *a Roman measure.* Vīnī sēxtārĭŭs; āddĕ, Hor.

sēxtīlĭs, ĭs, m., *the month of August.* Tўbĕrĭs, sēxtīlī mēnsĕ, Hor.

Sēxtĭŭs *or* Sēstĭŭs, ĭī, m., *the name of a man.* Est Sēxtĭŭs·īllĕ, Mart.

sēxtŭlă, ae, f., *the sixth part of an ounce.* Sēxtŭlāsquĕ dīcĭt, Mart.

Sēxtŭs, ī, m., *a Roman praenomen and surname.* Sēxtĕ, cūrārŭm, Virg.

sēxtŭs, ă, ŭm, *the sixth.* Sēxtă rĕsūrgēbănt, Ov.

sēxŭs, ŭs, m., *sex.* Dīscrīmĭnă sēxŭs, Cl. SYN. Vĭrīlĭs, mŭlĭebrĭs, āmbĭgŭŭs, hērmaphrŏdītŭs; mēntĭtŭs, nĕgātŭs.

sī, conj., *if.* Sī pŏ:ŭĭt Mānēs, Virg.

sĭbi, *to himself, or herself.* Tēquĕ sĭbī gĕnĕrŭm, Virg. Pōnĭtĕ spēs sĭbi, Id.

sībĭlo, ās, *to hiss.* Sībĭlăt hўdrĭs, Virg. SYN. Assībĭlo. V. Serpens.

sībĭlŭm, n.; *and* ŭs, ī, m.; *a hissing.* Sībĭlă mōntēs, Ov. Sībĭlŭs Aūstrī, Virg. EPITH. Strīdŭlŭs, strīdēns, hōrrēns, hōrrĭdŭs, raūcŭs, ăcūtŭs, īngēns, tērrĭbĭlĭs, răbĭdŭs, quĕrŭlŭs, rĕpĕtītŭs, ĭtĕrātŭs, frĕquēns. V. Serpens.

sībĭlŭs, ă, ŭm, *hissing.* Sībĭlă cōllă, Virg.

Sībўllă, ae, f., *a Sibyl, a name applied to several celebrated prophetesses of different countries.* Sēcrētā Sībўllae, Virg. SYN. Phoebăs. EPITH. Cāstă, vĕtŭs, lōngaevă, ānnōsă, vīvāx, fătĭdĭcă, praesāgă, praenūncĭă, Phoebĕă, Cūmaeă, Dēlphĭcă. V. Vates.

Sībўllīnŭs, ă, ŭm, *of a Sibyl.* Quōd Sībўllīnī mŏnŭĕrĕ, (Sapph.) Hor.

sīc, adv., *so.* Sīc ăĭt, ĕt, Virg. SYN. Ĭtă, haud sĕcŭs, haud ălĭtĕr; hāc vĭā, hāc rătĭōnĕ, hōc pāctō, hōccĕ mŏdō.

sīcă, ae, f., *a poniard.* Rēstānt sīcīs Sўbĭnīsquĕ, Ennius. SYN. Pūgĭo, glădĭŭs, ēnsĭs.

Sīcāmbrĭ, ōrŭm, m. pl., *an ancient people of Germany.* Gaūdēntēs Sīcāmbrĭ, Hor. EPITH. Fĕrōcēs, flāvī, īndŏmĭtĭ, saevī, dūrī, fōrtēs, crīnītĭ, īntōnsī.

Sīcānī, ōrŭm, m. pl., *Sicanians, an Iberian people settled in Latium and Sicily; Sicilians.* Rŭtŭlī vĕtĕrēsquĕ Sīcānī, Virg. Teūcrī mīxtīquĕ Sīcānī, Id. SYN. Sīcŭlī.

Sīcānĭă, ae, f., *Sicily.* Sīcănĭăm rĕpĕtēns, Ov.

Sicanŭs, *or* Sīcānĭŭs, ă, ŭm, *Sicilian.* Sūbtĕr lābĕrĕ Sīcānōs, Virg. Gēns Sīcănă vōtīs, Sil. Hīnc Sīcānă mĕdīmnă, Aus. Insŭlă Sīcānĭŭm, Virg. SYN. Sīcŭlŭs, Sicĕlĭs, Trīnacrĭŭs. V. Sicilia.

sīcārĭŭs, ĭī, m., *an assassin.* Aūt sīcārĭŭs, aūt, Hor. EPITH. Fĕrŭs, ŏccūltŭs.

sǐccǐně ? *is it so ?* Sǐccǐně Thěssǎlǐcœ, Luc.   SYN. Sǐccě, ǐtǎně.

* sǐccǐtǎs, ātǐs, f., *dryness.* Cic.   SYN. Ārǐdǐtās.   EPITH. Fěrvǐdǎ, fěrvēns, tŏrrēns, vǎlǐdǎ, flǎmmāns, ǐgnāvǎ, sēgnǐs, ǐnērs, lēthǐfěrǎ.   V. Calor, œstus.

sǐcco, ās, *to make dry.* Anǐmī sǐccǎvěrǎt ārdŏr, Ov.   SYN. Exsǐcco, ārěfǎcǐo ; ēxhaŭrǐo, ēbǐbo ; ūro, ǎdūro, pērūro.   V. Siccitas.

sǐccǔm, ǐ, n., *a dry place.* Rŏstrǎ těnēnt sǐccǔm, Virg.   SYN. Lǐttǔs, tērrǎ, ǎrēnǎ.

sǐccǔs, ǎ, ǔm, *dry.* Sǐccǔs ǎd ūnctǔm, Hor.   SYN. Ārǐdǔs, ārēns, ārēscēns, sǐccǎtǔs, ēxsǐccǎtǔs, sǐtǐēns, sǐtǐbūndǔs, ūstǔs, ǎdūstǔs, pěrūstǔs.   V. Sitio ; siccitas.

Sicělǐs, ǐdǐs, f., *of Sicily.* Sǐcělǐdēs mūsœ, Virg.

Sichæǔs, ǐ, m., *the husband of Dido, killed by Pygmalion.* Huǐc cŏnjūx Sǐchæǔs ěrǎt, Virg.   Fǎtǎ Sǐchæī, Id.   EPITH. Sǐdonǐǔs, dīvěs, sǎcěr.

Sǐcǐlǐǎ, œ, f., *Sicily.* Sǐcǐlǐæ, drāchmæ, Fann.   SYN. Sǐcǎnǐǎ, Trīnacrǐs, Trīnacrǐǎ.   EPITH. Fērtǐlǐs, frūgǐfěrǎ, fěrāx, fœcūndǎ, dīvěs, trǐfǐdǎ, æquŏrěǎ.

sǐcǔbi, conj., *if any where.* Sicǔbǐ māgnǎ, Virg.

Sǐcǔlǔs, ǎ, ǔm, *Sicilian.* Ět Sǐcǔlǐs rěgǐŏnǐbǔs, Virg.   SYN. Sǐcǎnǐǔs, Sicanǔs, Trīnacrǐǔs, Ætnœǔs.   V. Sicilia.

sǐcǔt, *or* ǔti, conj., *as.* Sǐcǔt ǎquœ, Virg.   Sǐcǔtǐ quǎdrǔpědǔm, Lucr.   SYN. Ǔt, ǔti, vělǔti.

Sǐcўōn, ōnǐs, f., *a town of Peloponnesus.* Ōlǐvǐfěræ Sǐcўōnǐs, Stat.   SYN. Ægǐǎlŏs.   EPITH. Ǎltǎ, ārdǔǎ, prīscǎ, větǔs, āntīquǎ, Graǐǎ.

Sǐcўōnǐǔs, ǎ, ǔm, *of Sicyon.* Těrǐtǔr Sǐcўōnǐǎ bāccǎ, Virg.

sīděrěǔs, ǎ, ǔm, *and* sīděrālǐs, ě, *of the stars.* Sīděrěŏ flǎgrāns, Virg.   Ět sīděrāli īnscǐtǐǎ, Aus.   SYN. Stēllǎtǔs.

Sǐdǐcīnǔs, ǎ, ǔm, *of Sidicinum, a town of Campania.* Sǐdǐcīnǎquě jūxtǎ Æquŏrǎ, Virg.

sīdo, ǐs, sēdī, *to perch, settle.* Sēdǐbǔs ōptǎtǐs gěmǐnǎ sǔpěr ārbŏrě sīdǔnt, Virg.   SYN. Sěděo ; sǔbsīdo.

Sīdōn, onǐs, f., *a town of Syria.* Měmǐnī Sīdōnǎ věnīrě, Virg.   Něc Sīdōně vǐlǐŏr Aŭlōn, Stat.   EPITH. Pīscōsǎ, větǔs, pŏtēns, prīscǎ, ēlǎtǎ, nōbǐlǐs, īnclўtǎ, Tўrǐǎ, prětǐōsǎ, Cādmæǎ.

Sǐdonǐǔs, ǎ, ǔm, *and* onǐs, ǐs, f., *Sidonian.* Sǐdōnǐǎsque ōstēntǎt, Virg.   Aspēctū Sǐdōnǐǎ Dīdō, Virg.   Cōnchā Sǐdōnǐdě tīnctǐs, Ov.   Sǐdŏnǐs īntěrěǎ, Id.

sīdǔs, ěrǐs, n., *a star.* Sīděrǎ pāscět, Virg.   SYN. Astrǔm, stēllǎ, sǐděrǐs ǐgnēs.   V. Astrum.

Sīgěǔs *and* gēǐǔs, ǎ, ǔm, *of Sigeum, a promontory in Troas, Trojan.* Ūcǎlěgōn ; Sīgěa ǐgnī, Virg.   Hīc ēst Sīgěǐǎ tēllǔs, Ov.

sīgǐllǎtǐm, *or* sīngǐllǎtǐm, adv., *severally.* Něc sīngǐllǎtǐm, Lucr.   SYN. Sěōrsǐm.

sīgǐllǔm, ǐ, n., *a seal.* Grātǎ sīgǐllǎ, Hor.   SYN. Sǐgnǔm.   EPITH. Imprēssǔm, ǎppŏsǐtǔm.

sīgnǎcǔlǔm, ǐ, n., *a mark.* Frōntǐs sīgnǎcǔlǎ pěr quæ, Prud.   V. Signum.

sīgnǎtŏr, ōrǐs, m., *he who signs a will, contract, &c.* Sǐgnātŏrǐbǔs aŭspēx, Juv.

* sīgnǐfěr, ǎ, ǔm, *embossed.* Sīgnǐfěrō crātěrě, Val. Fl.—2. -fěr, ěrī, m., *a standard-bearer.* Sīgnǐfěr hōstǐs, Ov.

sīgnǐfǐco, ās, *to make signs, to intimate.* Sīgnǐfǐcātquě mǎnū, Virg.   SYN. Indǐco, nŏto, cōnnŏto, ādnŏto, dēnŏto, ōstēndo, mōnstro, sīgnǔm dŏ.   V. Ostendo, manifesto.

Sīgnǐǎ, œ, f., *a town of the Volscians.* Ǐmmǐtī Sīgnǐǎ mūstŏ, Sil.

Sīgnīnǔs, ǎ, ǔm, *of Signia.* Sīgnīnǔm Sўrǐǔmquě pǐrǔm, Juv.—Subst., ǔm, ǐ, (sub. vinum), n., *Signian wine.* Sīgnīnǎ mŏrāntǐǎ věntrěm, Mart.

sīgno, ās, *to mark, to impress.* Ablǔtǎs sīgnāvǐt ŏvěs, Arator.   SYN. Dēsīgno ; īmprīmo ; ōbsīgno sīgǐllo ; nŏto ; sīgnǐfǐco.

sīgnǔm, ǐ, n., *a mark, an omen, a statue, a standard.* Āntīquōs sīgnōrǔm, Virg.   SYN. Indǐcǐǔm, ārgǔmēntǔm, mǒnǔmēntǔm, tēstǐmōnǐǔm, nŏtǎ, īnsǐgně, spěcǐměn, vēstǐgǐǔm ; ōměn, aŭgǔrǐǔm, mīrǎcǔlǔm, prŏdǐgǐǔm ; sǐgnǎcǔlǔm, sǐgǐllǔm, vēxǐllǔm ; ǐmāgo, ēffǐgǐēs, sǐmǔlācrǔm.   EPITH. Mǎnǐfēstǔm, clǎrǔm, ǎpērtǔm ; ōccūltǔm, ōbscūrǔm, lǎtēns, ārcānǔm, ǐgnōtǔm, cērtǔm, dǔbǐǔm, īncērtǔm, āmbǐguǔm, prōspěrǔm, sěcūndǔm, ǎmīcǔm, ōptǎtǔm, īnfēlīx, prŏdǐgǐǎlě, mīrāndǔm, spěctǎbǐlě, stǔpēndǔm.

Sīlă, æ, f., *a mountain in Bruttium.* Ingĕntī Sīlă, sŭmmŏvĕ Tăbūrnŏ, Virg.

Sīlānŭs, ī, m., *a senator betrothed to Octavia.* Seū tū Sīlānŭs, Juv.

sīlānŭs, ī, m., *a conduit-pipe.* Cōrpŏră sīlānŏs, Lucr.

Sīlărŭs, ī ; rīs, īs ; *and* lĕr, ĕrīs, m., *a river near Naples, which changed leaves and branches into stones.* Nŭnc Sīlărŭs quŏs, Sil. Tĕctă Sīlĕr, Luc.

sīlĕntĭŭm, ĭī, n., *silence.* Āmīcă sīlĕntĭă Lūnæ, Virg. SYN. Rĕtĭcēntĭă, tăcĭtūrnĭtās. EPITH. Tăcĭtūrnŭm, mūtŭm, tăcĭtŭm, sēcrētŭm, ārcānŭm, fīdēlĕ, āmīcŭm, fīdŭm ; trānquĭllŭm, plăcĭdŭm, āltŭm, nōctūrnŭm, sōmnĭfĕrŭm, ŏpācŭm, ŏppōrtūnŭm, lōngŭm.

Sīlēnŭs, ī, m., *the foster-father of Bacchus.* Pāndŏ Sīlēnŭs ăsēllŏ, Ov. EPITH. Ēbrĭŭs ; Arcădĭŭs ; sĕnēx, spūmāns, mădĭdŭs, vĕtŭlŭs.

sīlĕo, ēs, *to be silent.* Cŭm sīlŭĕrĕ lŏcī, Mart. SYN. Tăcĕo, rĕtĭcĕo, cōntĭcĕo ; ōbmūtēsco ; ŏmĭtto, prætĕrĕo.

sīlĕr, ĕrīs, n., *osier.* Mōllĕ sīlĕr, Virg.

sīlēsco, īs, lŭī, *to be silent, to be quiet.* Āltă sīlēscĭt, Virg.

sīlēx, ĭcīs, m. f., *a flint.* Stābăt ăcūtă sīlēx, Virg. SYN. Caūtēs, rūpēs, sāxŭm. EPITH. Dūrŭs, rĭgĭdŭs, grăvĭs. V. Rupes.

sīlĭgĭnĕŭs, ă, ŭm, *of fine flour.* Īllă sīlĭgĭnĕīs, Mart.

sīlĭgo, ĭnīs, f., *fine flour.* Cōctæquĕ sīlĭgĭnīs ŏfăs, Juv. SYN. Trītĭcŭm, fār ; sēcălĕ.

sīlĭquă, æ, f., *the pod of a bean, &c.* Lætŭm sīlĭquā, Virg. EPITH. Quāssă, quāssāns, mōllĭs, plēnă, tŭmēns.

Sīlĭŭs, ĭī, m., *Silius Italicus, a consul and poet in the reign of Nero.* Sīlĭŭs hæc māgnī, Mart.

sīlvă, -vānŭs, -vēstrĭs, &c. V. Sylva, &c.

sĭmĭlă, æ, *and* lāgo, ĭnĭs, f., *fine flour.* Nēc pŏtĕrīs sĭmĭlæ, Mart.

sĭmĭlĭs, ĕ, *like.* Dĕŏ sĭmĭlĭs, nāmquĕ, Virg. SYN. Cōnsĭmĭlĭs, părĭlĭs, æquālĭs, æquŭs, pār, nōn īmpār, nōn dīssĭmĭlĭs, haūd ābsĭmĭlĭs, sĭmĭllĭmŭs.

* sĭmĭlĭtĕr, adv., *similarly.* Ciz. SYN. Părĭtĕr, æquē, æquālĭtĕr.

sĭmĭlo, ās, *to be like.* Crūră tĭbī, sĭmĭlĕnt, Mart.

sĭmĭŭs, ī, m., *and* ĭă, æ, f., *an ape.* Sīmĭŭs hāstās, Mart. EPITH. Cāllĭdŭs, āstūtŭs, văfĕr, caūtŭs, vērsūtŭs, sĭmŭlātŏr, ĭmĭtātŏr, dēfōrmĭs, hīrsūtŭs, tūrpĭs, prŏtērvŭs.

Sīmo, ōnĭs, m., *the name of a personage in comedy.* Lūcrātă Sĭmōnĕ tălĕntŭm, Hor.

Sīmŏīs, ēntĭs, m., *a river of the Troad.* Nōn Sīmŏīs tĭbi, Virg. EPITH. Răpĭdŭs, pĭnĭgĕr, Ilĭăcŭs, Phrўgĭŭs, Idæŭs.

simplēx, ĭcĭs, *simple, honest.* Sĭmplĭcĭŏrĕ mănū, Mart. SYN. Pūrŭs, nūdŭs, haūd cōncrētŭs ; sīncērŭs, cāndĭdŭs ; crēdŭlŭs, īncaūtŭs, hĕbĕs.

sĭmplĭcĭtās, ātĭs, f., *simplicity, sincerity.* Nūdăquĕ sĭmplĭcĭtās, Ov. SYN. Sīncērĭtās, cāndŏr ; crēdŭlĭtās, hĕbĕtūdo. EPITH. Nūdă, vēră, prūdēns, pūră, pŭēllārĭs, vīrgĭnĕă, īnnŏcŭă, īnsōns. V. Syncerus.

sĭmplĭcĭtĕr, adv., *simply, without art.* Frōndēs Sĭmplĭcĭtĕr pŏsĭtæ, Ov.

sĭmpŭvĭŭm, ĭī, n., *a small earthen cup.* Sīmpŭvĭŭm rīdērĕ, Juv. SYN. Sĭmpŭlŭm.

sĭmŭl, adv., *together.* Sĭmŭl ōblĭgāstī, Hor. SYN. Īnsĭmŭl, ūnā, ĭn ūnŭm, părĭtĕr.

sĭmŭl āc, sĭmŭl ātquĕ, *as soon as.* Quăm sĭmŭl āc, Virg. Sĭmŭl ātque aūdīvĭt, Hor. SYN. Stătĭm āc. V. Statim ac.

sĭmŭlācrŭm, ī, n., *a figure, a statue.* Īnfēlīx sĭmŭlācrŭm, Virg. SYN. Ēffĭgĭēs, sīgnŭm, ĭmāgo, stătŭă ; ūmbră, spēctrŭm, lārvă. V. Statua, larva.

sĭmŭlāmēn, ĭnĭs, *and* mēntŭm, ī, n., *a representation, a resemblance.* Pĕrāgĕt sĭmŭlāmĭnă nōstrī, Ov. V. Imago.

sĭmŭlātĭo, ōnĭs, f., *a feigning.* Āllŭd sĭmŭlātĭŏ vērī, Hor. SYN. Fīctĭo ; fāllācĭă, mēndācĭŭm. V. Fallacia, mendacium.

sĭmŭlātŏr, ōrĭs, m., *and* trīx, īcĭs, f., *a feigner.* Cōmpŏsĭtŭs sĭmŭlātŏr ăĭt, Sed. Ææŏ sĭmŭlātrīx lĭttŏrĕ Cīrcē, Stat. SYN. Dīssĭmŭlātŏr, fāllāx, mēndāx.

sĭmŭlo, ās, *to feign.* Spēm vūltū sĭmŭlăt, Virg. SYN. Fīngo, mēntĭŏr, ĭmĭtŏr, āssĭmŭlo ; cēlo, tĕgo, ōccūlto. V. Dissimulo.

sĭmūltās, ātĭs, f., *a secret hatred.* Āntīquă sĭmūltās, Juv. SYN. Ĭnĭmīcĭtĭă, dīssīdĭŭm, ŏdĭŭm.

sīmŭs, *and* ŭlŭs, ă, ŭm, *flat-nosed.* Āttōndēnt sīmæ, Virg. SYN. Cămŭrŭs.

sĭn, *but if.* Sĭn ābsūmptă sălūs, Virg. Syn. At sī, aūtĕm.

Sĭnă, *or* năī, f., *the mountain on which Moses received the divine law.* Syn. Hōrĕb.
Epith. Pălmĭfĕră, ārdŭă, āltă, āĕrĭă, lēgĭfĕră.

sĭnāpĭs, ĭs, f.; ĕ, ĭs, n.; *or* sĭnāpī, (*indecl.*) n.; *mustard.* Făctūră sĭnāpĭs, Col.
Mōrdāx haūrīrĕ sĭnāpī, Ser. Sam. Epith. Călēns, cǎlĭdă, ūrēns, ācrĭs, sălūbrĭs,
ōlēns, lacrȳmōsă, trīstĭs.

sĭncērĭtās. V. Synceritas.

sĭncērŭs. V. Syncerus.

sĭncĭpŭt, Ĭtĭs, n., *the forepart of the head.* Sĭncĭpŭt aūrĕ, Pers.

sīndōn, ŏnĭs, f., *fine linen.* Sīndŏnĕ tēctŭs, Mart.

sĭnĕ, prep., *without.* Mē sĭnĕ sōlă, Virg. Syn. Absquĕ.

sīngŭlārĭs, ĕ, *alone, extraordinary.* Rătĕ sīngŭlārī, (Sapph.) Sen. Syn. Sōlŭs,
sīngŭlŭs; ēxĭmĭŭs, ēxcēllēns, īnsīgnĭs, sūmmŭs, rārŭs, īnfrĕquēns, īnaūdītŭs.

sīngūltĭm, adv., *sobbingly.* Sīngūltĭm paŭcă, Hor.

sīngūlto, āvī, *to sob.* Ēt sīngūltătĭs, Ov. Syn. Sīngūltĭo.

sīngūltŭs, ūs, m., *a sob.* Sīngūltĭbŭs īlĭă pūlsăt, Virg. Epith. Ācĕr, āspĕr,
dūrŭs, frīgĭdŭlŭs, ămārŭs, nōxĭŭs, lēthālĭs.

sīngŭlŭs, ă, ŭm, *or (better)* ī, æ, ă, *one by one.* Sīngŭlă dē nōbĭs, Hor. Syn.
Quĭsquĕ, ūnūsquĭsquĕ.

Sĭnĭs, *or* Schĭnĭs, ĭs, m., *a robber, slain by Theseus.* Ōccĭdĭt īllĕ Sĭnĭs, Ov.

sĭnīstĕr, tră, trŭm, *on the left, unlucky.* Sæpĕ sĭnīstră căvă, Virg. Syn. Lævŭs;
īnfaūstŭs, īnfōrtūnātŭs, īnfēlīx. V. Infelix.

sĭnīstră, æ, f., *the left hand.* Īnfīrmă sĭnīstră, Ov. Syn. Lævă. V. Manus.

sĭnīstrē, adv., *unluckily.* Excēptūmquĕ sĭnīstrē, Hor.

sĭnīstrōrsŭm, adv., *on the left hand.* Īllĕ sĭnīstrōrsŭm, Hor.

sĭno, sĭvī, *to allow.* Tū sĭnĭs ēssĕ, Prop. Syn. Pērmītto, pătĭŏr, cōncēdo, dō.
V. Permitto.

Sĭnōn, ŏnĭs, m., *a Greek, who artfully persuaded the Trojans to draw the wooden
horse into Troy.* Claūstră Sĭnōn, Virg. Epith. Fāllāx, caūtŭs, cāllĭdŭs, văfĕr,
dŏlōsŭs.

Sĭnōpē, ēs, f., *a city of Paphlagonia on the Euxine sea, the birth-place of Diogenes.*
Stăt ōpĭmă Sĭnōpē. V. Fl.

Sĭnōpeŭs, ĕōs, ĕī *or* eī, m., *of Sinope.* Cȳnĭcŭs prŏcŭl ēssĕ Sĭnōpeŭs, Ov. Syn.
Sĭnōpēnsĭs.

Sĭnŭēssă, æ, f., *a city of Campania on the frontiers of Latium.* Frĕquēns Sĭnŭēssă
cŏlŭmbĭs, Ov.

Sĭnŭēssānŭs, ă, ŭm, *of Sinuessa.* Sĭnŭēssānūmquĕ Pĕtrīnŭm, Hor.

sĭnŭm, ī, n., *a milk-pail.* Sīnŭm lāctĭs, ĕt hæc, Virg

sĭnŭo, ās, *to twist, to bend.* Pătŭlōs sĭnŭāvĕrăt ārcŭs, Ov. V. Flecto.

sĭnŭōsŭs, ă, ŭm, *crooked, twisted.* Sĭnŭōsă vŏlŭmĭnă vērsăt, Virg. Syn. Inflēxŭs, cūrvŭs, flēxŭs, īncūrvŭs, cūrvātŭs, rĕvŏlūtŭs.

sĭnŭs, ūs, m., *the breast, a winding, a port.* Mōllĭs ămĭcă sĭnū, Ov. Syn. Grĕmĭŭm, pēctŭs, cōmplēxŭs, ūlnæ; spīră, flēxŭs, gȳrŭs, sĭnŭāmĕn, āmbāgēs,
mœāndrī; frĕtŭm, cūrvātŭm līttŭs. V. Gyrus, portus, fretum. Epith. Lāctĕŭs,
nĭvĕŭs, cāndĭdŭs, tĕnĕr, mātērnŭs, cǎlĭdŭs, dūlcĭs, ămĭcŭs.

Sĭōn, f., (*indecl.*) *the mountain where Solomon's temple was erected.* Pēctŏrĕ Sĭōn,
Prud.

sīpărĭum, ĭī, n., *a curtain.* Sīpărĭŏ clāmōsŭm, Juv.

sĭpho, *and* ōn, ōnĭs, m., *a tube, a pipe.* Lōngĭs sĭphōnĭbŭs īmplēnt, Juv.

Sĭpȳlŭs, ī, m., *a son of Niobe.* Frænă dăbāt Sĭpȳlŭs, Ov.—*2. a mountain in Lydia.*
Vīrgō Sĭpȳlūmquĕ cŏlĕbăt, Id.

sĭquĭdĕm, conj., *since, for.* Vēntūra ēst sĭquĭdĕm, Ov. Syn. Quŏnĭăm, quĭă,
năm, ĕnĭm.

Sīrēn, ēnĭs, f., Sīrēnĕs, ŭm, f. pl., *sea-monsters, mermaids, Sirens.* Imprŏbă Sīrēn,
Hor. Ădĕō scŏpŭlōs Sīrēnŭm, Virg. Syn. Āchĕlōĭdĕs, Āchĕlōĭădĕs. Epith.
Āchĕlōĭæ, Sĭcŭlæ, Tȳrrhēnæ; blāndæ, fāllācēs, dŏlōsæ, mārīnæ, æquŏrĕæ, glaūcæ,
cærŭlĕæ, dōctæ, cănōræ, lĕvēs, nătāntēs.

Sīrĭŭs, ĭī, m., *the dog-star.* Sīrĭŭs āstrō, Stat. Syn. Cănĭcŭlă. Epith. Ardēns,
sĭccŭs, răpĭdŭs, tōrrēns. V. Canicula.

Sīsēnnă, æ, m., *a Roman poet and historian.* Vērtĭt Ārīstīdēm Sīsēnnă, Ov.

sĭsĕr, ĕrĭs, n., *a parsnip.* Stŏmāchŭm sĭsĕr, ălēc, Hor.

sīsto, stĭtī, *to stop, to stand still.* Sīstĕrĕ cōntrā, Virg. Syn. Dĕtĭnĕo, rĕtĭnĕo, dīstĭnĕo, cŏhĭbĕo, mŏrŏr; rĕsīsto; ēxhĭbĕo; fīrmo, fūlcĭo, stăbĭlĭo.

sīstrātŭs, ă, ŭm, *carrying a timbrel.* Sīstrātăquĕ tūrbă, Mart.

sīstrŭm, ī, n., *a brazen timbrel.* Agmĭnă sīstrŏ, Virg. Epith. Tĭnnŭlŭm, mūltĭsŏnŭm, gārrŭlŭm, Isĭăcŭm, Phărĭŭm; bēllĭcŭm, ærĭsŏnŭm, ærĕŭm, crēpĭtāns, ārgūtŭm, strĭdŭlŭm, pērsŏnŭm, rĕsŏnāns, dūlcĕ.

sīsymbrĭŭm, ĭī, n., *a kind of mint.* Grătă sīsymbrĭă, Ov.

Sīsyphĭdēs, æ, m., *the descendant of Sisyphus, Ulysses.* Hīs sŭă Sīsyphĭdēs, Ov.

Sīsyphĭŭs, ă, ŭm, *of Sisyphus.* Sĕd tū Sīsyphĭŏs, Prop.

Sīsyphŭs, ī, m., *the son of Æolus. He infested Attica with his robberies, and was slain by Theseus.* Sīsyphĕ, nūpsĭt, Ov. Syn. Æŏlĭdēs. Epith. Infēlīx, mĭsĕr, ĭrrēquĭētŭs, lāssŭs, dēfēssŭs, Æŏlĭŭs.

Sīthōn, ŏnĭs, m., *the name of an hermaphrodite.* Mŏdŏ vīr fŭĕrīt, mŏdŏ fēmĭnă Sīthōn, Ov.

Sīthŏnĕs, ŭm, m. pl., *the Thracians.—Adj., Thracian.* Sīthŏnăs ēt Scythĭcōs, Ov. V. Thracius.

Sīthŏnĭŭs, ă, ŭm, *and* nĭs, ĭdĭs, f., *Thracian.* Sīthŏnĭāsquĕ nĭvēs, Virg. Sīthŏnĭs ŭndă rătēs, Ov. V. Thracius.

sĭtĭbūndŭs, ă, ŭm, *very thirsty.* Plaut. V. Sitiens.

sĭtĭcŭlōsŭs, ă, ŭm; *and* ĭens, ntĭs, *thirsty.* Sĭtĭcŭlōsæ Appŭlĭæ, Hor. Hīnc ălĭī sĭtĭēntēs, Virg. Syn. Sĭtĭbūndŭs; ārĭdŭs, ārēscēns, sīccŭs. V. Sitio.

sĭtĭo, īs, īvī, *to be thirsty.* Ipsĕ sĭtīrĕ, căpĕr, Mart.

sĭtĭs, ĭs, f., *thirst.* Sĭtĭs ŭssĕrăt hērbăs, Ov. Syn. Cŭpīdo, ārdŏr. Epith. Ignĕă, flāmmătă, fērvĭdă, fērvēns, ārdēns, ănhēlă, ārĭdă, sīccă, ārēns, āspĕră, dīră, ăvĭdă, răbĭdă, æstĭvă, vĕhĕmēns, vĭŏlēntă, īmpōrtūnă, mŏlēstă, ānxĭă, vēsānă, īnsătĭābĭlĭs, ĭnēxplēbĭlĭs, ĭntŏlĕrābĭlĭs, Tāntălĕă. V. Sitio.

sĭtītŏr, ŏrĭs, m., *that thirsts for.* Stēllă sĭtītŏr ăquæ, Mart.

sĭtŭlă, *or* tēllă, æ, f., *a bucket to draw water in.* Sĭtŭlam hūc, Plaut.

sĭtŭs, ă, ŭm, *placed, situated.* Mēllŭs sĭtŭm, (Alc.) V. Positus.

sĭtŭs, ūs, m., *situation, filth.* Nēc rĕvŏcărĕ sĭtŭs, Virg. Syn. Pŏsĭtŭs, lŏcŭs; squālŏr; vĕtūstās. Epith. Pāllēns, īnfōrmĭs, ĭnērs, īmmūndŭs.

sīvĕ, disj., *or.* Sīvĕ quĭs Antĭlŏchŭm, Ov. Syn. Seū, aūt, vĕl.

smărăgdŭs, ī, m., *an emerald.* Hĕbĕtărĕ smărăgdōs, Ov. Epith. Vĭrĭdĭs, clārŭs, rădĭāns, lætŭs, Ērythræŭs. V. Gemma.

smărĭs, ĭs, f., *a sea-fish.* Lămyrūsquĕ smărīsquĕ, Ov.

Smĭlāx, ăcĭs, f., *a young girl changed into the plant bind-weed.* Cūm Smĭlăcĕ flōrĕm, Ov.

Smīnthеūs, ĕŏs, ĕī *or* eī, m., *of Smynthe, a city of Phrygia; a name of Apollo.* Cōmpēllāt Smīnthĕă dīctĭs, Ov.

Smyrnă, æ, f., *a city of Ionia.* Smyrnă vīrŭm tĕnŭĭt, Ov.—2. *Myrrh, a perfume.* Ēt cōntēmptŭs ŏdŏr Smyrnæ, Lucr. V. Myrrha.

sŏbŏlēs, ĭs, f., *a race, progeny.* Dīgnātŭr sŏbŏlēs, (Chor.) Hor. Syn. Prōlēs, prōgĕnĭēs, prōpāgo, nātī. V. Proles.

sōbrĭĕtās, ātĭs, f., *gravity, temperance.* Sōbrĭĕtās ĕt, Prud. Syn. Mŏdĕrātĭo, tēmpĕrāntĭă, ābstĭnēntĭă, pārcĭtās. V. Temperantia.

sōbrĭŭs, ă, ŭm, *temperate.* Sōbrĭŭs ērgo, Hor. Syn. Mŏdĕrātŭs, ābstĭnēns, pārcŭs. V. Temperans.

sŏccŭs, ī, m., *a kind of sandal, worn by the Roman women and comic actors.* Hūnc sŏccī, Hor. Epith. Hŭmĭlĭs, lĕvĭs, tĕnŭĭs, lĕpĭdŭs, mŭlĭĕbrĭs.

sŏcĕr, ĕrī, m., *a father-in-law.* Nēc sŏcĕr ŭllŭs ĕrăt, Ov.

sŏcĭālĭs, ĕ, *pertaining to allies, confederates, or associates.* Bēllĭs sŏcĭālĭbŭs ŭvăm, Juv. Syn. Sŏcĭŭs.

sŏcĭālĭtĕr, adv., *sociably.* Aūt quārtă sŏcĭālĭtĕr, Hor.

sŏcĭātŏr, ŏrĭs, m., *and* trĭx, ĭcĭs, f., *one who joins or associates others.* Mĕdĭī sŏcĭātrīx, V. Fl.

sŏcĭĕtās, ātĭs, f., *partnership, confederacy.* Cic. Syn. Sŏdālĭtās, sŏdālĭtĭŭm, cōnvīctŭs, cŏmĭtātŭs, cōmmērcĭŭm, cōllĕgĭŭm. V. Communitas.

sŏcĭo, ās, *to join.* Vēllēm sŏcĭārĕ jŭgālī, Virg. Syn. Jūngo, cōnjūngo, ăssŏcĭo.

sŏcĭŭs, ă, ŭm, *associate, helping.* Exērcēnt ĭllī sŏcĭæ, Ov. Syn. Sŏcĭātŭs, jūnctŭs, cōnjūnctŭs; cŏmēs, āssĕclă, sŏdālĭs, ămīcŭs; cōnsŏrs, pārtĭcēps, cōnscĭŭs. Epith. Ŭnănĭmĭs, fīdēlĭs, fīdŭs, sīncĕrŭs, cāndĭdŭs, ămīcŭs, grātŭs.

sŏcĭŭs, ĭī, m., *and* ĭă, æ, f., *a companion, a confederate.* Mēne ĭgĭtūr sŏcĭŭm, Virg. Addĭt sē sŏcĭăm, Id.

sŏcŏrdĭă, æ, f., *sloth.* Făcĭāt sŏcŏrdĭă lēntŭm, M. Syn. Stŭpĭdĭtās, stŭpŏr, hĕbĕtūdo. V. Pigritia.

sŏcŏrs, rdĭs, *slothful.* Vītæ sŏcŏrdĭs ŏpprĭmăt, (Iamb. Dim.) Prud. Syn. Stŭpĭdŭs, hĕbĕs; ĭgnāvŭs, pĭgĕr.

Sŏcrătēs, ĭs, m., *the Athenian philosopher.* Sŏcrătĭs ŏră, Mart. Epith. Săpĭēns, īnclўtŭs; Actæŭs, Āttĭcŭs, īngĕnĭŏsŭs, cōnstāns, īmmōtŭs.

Sŏcrătĭcŭs, ă, ŭm, *of Socrates.* Sŏcrătĭcæ pŏtĕrŭnt, Hor.

sŏcrŭs, ūs, f., *a mother-in-law.* Invīsām sŏcrŭs ĭnīquă nŭrŭm, Ov.

sŏdālĭs, ĭs, m. f., *a companion.* Pārvīsquĕ sŏdālĭbŭs, ĕt, Hor. Syn. Sŏcĭŭs, cŏmĕs. V. Socius.

sŏdālĭtĭŭm, ĭī, n., *a fraternity, a company.* Dūlcĕ sŏdālĭtĭŭm, Catull. Syn. Cōnsortĭŭm. V. Societas.

sōdēs, interj., *I beseech you.* Aūt sōdēs mĭhi, Catull.

Sōl, sōlĭs, m., *the sun.* Mūndĭ Sōl aūrĕŭs āstră, Virg. Syn. Phœbŭs; Tītān, Hўpĕrīōn; Cўnthĭŭs; Dēlĭŭs; Ăpōllo. Epith. Ignĕŭs, cŏrŭscŭs, cŏrŭscāns, splēndĭdŭs, rădĭāns, rŭtĭlāns, mĭcāns, lūcĭdŭs, fūlgēns, aūrĭcŏmŭs, æthĕrĕŭs, crŏcĕŭs, răpĭdŭs, văgŭs, ŏrĭēns, nŏvŭs, blāndŭs, clārŭs, sĕrēnŭs, ālmŭs, cāndĭdŭs, rŭbēns, pūrpŭrĕŭs, æstīvŭs, flagrāns, fērvĭdŭs, flāmmĭfĕr, ĭgnĭvŏmŭs, ăcūtŭs, cālēns, cālĭdŭs, tĕpēns, ōccĭdŭŭs, prŏnŭs, cădēns, pūnĭcĕŭs, nūbĭlŭs, tĕnĕbrŏsŭs. V. Mane, oriens, occidens, meridies.

sōlāmĕn, ĭnĭs, n., *comfort.* Hōc sōlāmĕn ĕrăt, Virg. V. Solatium.

sōlārĭs, ĕ, *of the sun.* Lūmĕn sōlārĕ vĭdĕbo, Ov. Syn. Phœbēŭs, Tītānĭŭs, Ăpōllĭnĕŭs.

sōlārĭŭm, ĭī, n., *a sun-dial.* Hĭc sōlārĭŭm, (Iamb.) Plaut.

sōlātĭŭm, ĭī, dimin. ĭŏlŭm, ĭ, n., *consolation.* Āvēs sōlātĭă rūrĭs, Ov. Ŭt sōlātĭŏlŭm sŭī, Catul. Syn. Sōlāmĕn, lēnĭmĕn, lĕvāmĕn, aŭxĭlĭŭm. Epith. Dūlcĕ, mītĕ, blāndŭm, grātŭm, ămīcŭm, mōllĕ, lēnĕ, ŏptātŭm, spērātŭm, lēntŭm, tārdŭm, sŭbĭtŭm, ĭnŏpīnŭm. V. Solor.

sōlātŏr, ōrĭs, m., *a comforter.* Ipse ĕgŏ sōlātŏr, Tib.

sŏldŭm, ĭ, n., *a piece of money.* Fūndĭsquĕ trĭcĭēs sōldŭm, Mart.

sŏlĕă, æ, f., *a sandal.* Cōnstĭtĭt īn sŏlĕă, Cat.

sŏlĕātŭs, ă, ŭm, *shod with slippers.* Jām sŏlĕātŭs ĕrĭt, Mart.

sŏlēnnĭă, ĭŭm, n. pl., *solemnities, festivals.* Tŭmŭlō sŏlēnnĭă mīttēnt, Virg.

sŏlēnnĭs, ĕ, *annual, customary.* Impĕrĭŭm sŏlēnnĕ sŏcĕr, Virg.

sŏlĕo, sŏlĭtŭs sŭm, *to be accustomed.* Ŭtquĕ sŏlēbāmŭs, Ov. Syn. Āssŏlĕo, āssuēsco. V. Assuesco.

sŏlērs, rtĭs, *clever, diligent.* Cūstŏdĭă sōlērs, Virg. Syn. Săgāx, sūbtīlĭs, prūdēns, īngĕnĭŏsŭs, īndŭstrĭŭs. V. Prudens, ingeniosus.

sŏlērtĕr, adv., *cleverly, shrewdly.* Jūssōs sŏlērtĭŭs āltĕr, Ov. Syn. Pĕrītē.

sŏlērtĭă, æ, f., *cleverness, adroitness.* Părĭāt sŏlērtĭă, nūtrĭăt ūsŭs, Claud. Syn. Industrĭă, dēxtĕrĭtās. Epith. Ăcūtă, sūbtīlĭs, vīvāx, vīvĭdă, prūdēns, dŏcĭlĭs, vĭgĭl, pērvĭgĭl, īngĕnĭŏsă. V. Prudentia.

sŏlĭdo, ās, *to strengthen.* Crētā sŏlĭdāndă tĕnācĭ, Virg. Syn. Fīrmo, stăbĭlĭo.

sŏlĭdŭs, ă, ŭm, *solid, firm.* Sŏlĭdōque ădămāntĕ, Virg. Syn. Fīrmŭs; īntĕgĕr.

sŏlĭfĕr, ă, ŭm, *carrying the sun.* Sen.

sŏlĭgĕnă, æ, m. f., *born of the sun.* Sōlĭgĕnam Æētēn, V. Fl.

* sŏlĭtārĭŭs, ă, ŭm, *solitary, retired.* Syn. Sōlŭs; mŏnăchŭs.

sŏlĭtūdo, ĭnĭs, f., *solitude, a desert.* Cŏvĭnĕ, sōlĭtŭdo, (Phal.) Mart. Syn. Ērēmŭs, dēsērtŭm, sēcēssŭs, rĕcēssŭs. Epith. Vāstă, văcŭă, tăcĭtă, sīlēns, trānquīllă, sānctă, ūmbrŏsă, ŏpăcă, cæcă, stĕrīlĭs, dēsērtă, īnhōspĭtă, āvĭă, īmpērvĭă, sēcrētă, ĭgnōtă, rĕmōtă, dīssĭtă. V. Desertum.

sŏlĭtŭs, ă, ŭm, *the partic. of* soleo.

sŏlĭŭm, ĭī, n., *a throne.* Dīvōs, sŏlĭŏ rēx, Virg. Syn. Thrŏnŭs. Epith. Rēgālĕ, aūrĕŭm, ĕbūrnŭm, sŭpērbŭm, ĕbūrnĕŭm, aūrātŭm, rēgĭŭm, māgnĭfĭcŭm, fūlgēns, splēndēns, mĭcāns, cŏrŭscŭm, gēmmĭfĕrŭm, īnsīgnĕ, cōnspĭcŭŭm, āltŭm, ēxcēlsŭm.

sōllĭcĭtē, adv., *carefully, earnestly.* Sōllĭcĭtē mălă nōstră, Ov. Syn. Dīlĭgēntĕr, strēnŭĕ.

sōllĭcĭto, or sōlĭcĭto, ās, *to disquiet, torment.* Sōllĭcĭtābăt ŏpēs, Mart. Syn. Ango, pŭngo, tōrquĕo, vēxo, crŭcĭo; īnstīgo, ĭmpēllo, ĭncĭto, ūrgĕo, stĭmŭlo. V. Curis angor.

sōllĭcĭtūdo, ĭnĭs, f., *care, solicitude.* Sōllĭcĭtūdĭnĕ dīstrīctŭm, Hor. Syn. Cūră, ānxĭĕtās. Epith. Mōrdāx, dūră, mŏlēstă, trīstĭs, īnsŏmnĭs, ægră, īrrĕqŭĭĕtă, grăvĭs, ātrōx. V. Cura.

sōllĭcĭtŭs, ă, ŭm, *anxious, agitated.* Sōllĭcĭtĭs ănĭmīs, Hor. Syn. Anxĭŭs, āncēps, dŭbĭŭs, sūspēnsŭs; cōmmōtŭs, ăgĭtātŭs. V. Curis angor, dubius.

sōlo, ās, *to desolate.* Ănĭmŭs sōlārĕ dŏmōs, Stat.

sōlœcīsmŭs, ī, m., *a solecism.* Ātquĕ sōlœcīsmūm lĭcĕăt, Juv.

Sŏlōn, ōnĭs, m., *the Athenian legislator.* Ærūmnōsīquĕ Sŏlōnēs, Pers. Epith. Jūstŭs, Actæŭs, Āttĭcŭs, Cecrŏpĭŭs; săpĭēns, dōctŭs, īngĕnĭōsŭs, lēgĭfĕr.

sōlŏr, ārĭs, *to console.* Cūrās sōlābăr ănĭlēs, Virg. Syn. Cōnsōlŏr.

sōlstĭtĭālĭs, ĕ, *of the solstice.* Tēmpŭs sōlstĭtĭālĕ, Ov.

sōlstĭtĭŭm, ĭī, n., *the solstice.* Hūmĭdă sōlstĭtĭa ātque, Virg.

sōlŭm, ī, n., *the ground.* Inquĕ sōlō quŏd, Ov. Syn. Tērră, tēllŭs, hŭmŭs. V. Terra.

sōlŭm, adv., *only.* Nĕc călămīs sōlŭm, Virg. Syn. Tāntŭm.

sōlvo, sōlvī, sōlūtŭm, *to pay, to loose, to acquit.* Sōlvĕrĕ mēntēs, Virg. Syn. Pērsōlvo, pēndo, rēddo, nŭmĕro; lībĕro, ēxpĕdĭo; dīssōlvo, rĕsōlvo, rĕvēllo; liquĕfăcĭo; ĕuŏdo, ēxplĭco.

sōlŭs, ă, ŭm, *alone.* Syn. Incŏmĭtātŭs; ūnŭs, ūnĭcŭs; dēsērtŭs.

sōlūtŭs, ă, ŭm, *untied, discharged.* Lānguōrĕ sōlūtĭs, Ov. Syn. Pērsōlūtŭs; lībĕrātŭs; lībĕr, īmmūnĭs; rĕsōlūtŭs, dīssōlūtŭs.

Sōlўmă. V. Hierusalem.

Sōlўmŭs, ă, ŭm, *of Jerusalem.* Intērprēs lēgūm Sōlўmārŭm, Juv.—2. Subst., -ŭs, ī, m., *one of Æneas' companions, who founded a colony at Sulmo.* Hūjŭs ĕrăt Sōlўmŭs, Ov.

sōmnĭcŭlōsŭs, ă, ŭm, *drowsy.* Sōmnĭcŭlōsōs ĭllĕ, (Scaz.) Mart. Syn. Sōmnŏlēntŭs.

sōmnĭfĕr, ĕră, ĕrŭm, *causing sleep.* Sōmnĭfĕri ēt Mārsīs, Virg. Syn. Sŏpōrĭfĕr, sŏpōrŭs.

sōmnĭo, ās, *to dream.* Sōmnĭāssĕ Pārnāssō, (Scaz.) Pers. Syn. Pēr sōmnūm vĭdĕo; dēlīro, ĭnēptĭo, fīngo. V. Somnium.

sōmnĭŭm, ĭī, n., *a dream.* Sōmnĭă fīngŭnt, Virg. Syn. Insōmnĭŭm, vīsŭm. Epith. Nōctūrnŭm, nigrŭm, cæcŭm, văgŭm, ĭnānĕ, sōllĭcĭtŭm, vānŭm, lĕvĕ, fāllāx, mēndāx, hōrrēndŭm, tērrĭfĭcŭm. V. Somnus.

|| sōmnŏlēntĭă, æ, f., *drowsiness.* Ēxpēllĕ sōmnŏlēntĭăm, (Iamb. Dim.) Ambr. Syn. Sŏpōr, tōrpŏr, sōmnŭs.

|| sōmnŏlēntŭs, ă, ŭm, *drowsy.* Ēt sōmnŏlēntōs, (Iamb. Dim.) Ambr. Syn. Sōmnĭcŭlōsŭs; ĭgnāvŭs.

Sōmnŭs, ī, m., *the god of sleep, sleep.* In sōmnīs ŏcŭlōs, Virg. Syn. Sŏpŏr, rĕquĭēs, quĭēs. Epith. Nōctūrnŭs, lēnĭs, blāndŭs, jūcūndŭs, dūlcĭs, mōllĭs, plăcĭdŭs, trānquīllŭs, quĭētŭs, lānguĭdŭs, pĭgĕr, lēntŭs, grăvĭs, lĕvĭs, āltŭs, sēcūrŭs, īmpăvĭdŭs, tăcĭtŭs, īrrĭgŭŭs, sălŭbĕr, mātūtīnŭs.

sŏnābĭlĭs, ĕ, *sounding shrill.* Crĕpŭītquĕ sŏnābĭlĕ sīstrŭm, Ov. V. Resonus.

sŏnĭpēs, ĕdĭs, m., *a horse.* Stăt sŏnĭpēs, āc, Virg. Syn. Quadrŭpēs, cōrnĭpēs, ĕquŭs. V. Equus.

sŏnĭtŭs, ūs, m., *a sound.* Ārmōrŭm sŏnĭtŭm, Virg. Syn. Sŏnŭs, strĕpĭtŭs, clāmŏr, mūrmŭr, frăgŏr, strīdŏr. Epith. Ăcūtŭs, raŭcŭs, hōrrēndŭs, tērrĭfĭcŭs, dīssŏnŭs, hōrrĭsŏnŭs, ābsŏnŭs, văgŭs, strĕpēns, strīdŭlŭs. V. Murmuro, clamor, sonus.

sŏno, ās, ŭī, *to sound.* Ingēntī sŏnŭērŭnt, Virg. Syn. Rĕsŏno, pērsŏno, strĕpo. V. Resono, murmuro, clamor, sonitus.

sŏnŏr, ōrĭs, m., *a great noise.* Flāmmă sŏnŏrĕ, Virg. V. Sonus.

sŏnŏrŭs, ă, ŭm, *loud.* Tēmpēstātēsquĕ sŏnōrās, Virg. Syn. Rĕsŏnŭs, sŏnāns, strĕpēns, strīdēns, strīdŭlŭs, cănōrŭs.

sōns, ntĭs, *culpable, guilty.* Cōntĭnŭō sōntēs, Virg. Syn. Nŏcēns, nŏxĭŭs, rĕŭs.

sŏnŭs, ī, m., *a sound.* Mēntĕ sŏnūm, Virg. Syn. Sŏnĭtŭs, sŏnŏr, strĕpĭtŭs, mūrmŭr, clāngŏr, tīnnītŭs, clāmŏr, vōx. Epith. Strīdŭlŭs, ăcūtŭs, lætŭs, raŭcŭs, cōnfūsŭs, vōcālĭs. V. Sonitus.

sŏphĭă, æ, f., *wisdom.* Sīt sŏphĭæ pār, Mart.

sŏphĭsmă, ătĭs, n., *sophistry.* Cœcă sŏphĭsmătă sŏlvĭs, Pamphil.
sŏphĭstă, æ, m., *a sophist, philosopher.* Ūnō cōnclāmănt ŏrĕ sŏphĭstæ, Juv.
Sŏphŏclēs, ĭs, m., *the Greek tragic poet.* Quĭd Sŏphŏclēs, quĭd, Hor.
Sŏphŏclēŭs, ă, ŭm, *of Sophocles.* Sŏlă Sŏphŏclēō, Virg.
sŏphōs, n. indecl., *applause.* Quĭd tăm grăndĕ sŏphōs clāmăt, Mart.
sŏphús, ĭ, m., *a wise man.* Tē sŏphŭs ŏmnĭs, Mart. V. Sapiens.
sōpĭo, ĭs, ĭvĭ or ĭi, ĭtŭm, *to lull asleep.* Hērbĭs sŏpīrĕ drăcōnĕm, Ov. Syn.
  Sŏpōro.
sŏpītŭs, ă, ŭm, *the pass. partic. of* sopio. Ět sŏpītŏrŭm, Pub. Ep. V. Somnus,
  dormio.
sŏpŏr, ōrĭs, m., *sound sleep.* Sŏpŏr āltŭs hăbēbăt, Virg. V. Somnus.
sŏpōrātŭs, ă, ŭm, *asleep, dead.* Ět sæpĕ sŏpōrātōs, Ov.
sŏpōrĭfĕr, *and* pōrŭs, ă, ŭm, *causing sleep.* Mēllă, sŏpōrĭfĕrŭm, Virg. Nŏctĭsquĕ
  sŏpōræ, Virg. Syn. Sŏmnĭfĕr.
sŏpōro, ās, *to lull to sleep.* Anguēs nĭmĭa āstră sŏpōrănt, Stat. Syn. Sōpĭo.
Sŏrāctĕ, *or* ācĭēs, ĭs, m., *a mountain of Italy.* Cŭstŏs Sŏrāctĭs Ăpōllo, Virg.
sŏrbĕo, psĭ, ptŭm, *to suck in.* Părĭtĕr sŏrbērĕ nĕcēsse ēst, Lucr. Syn. Ābsŏrbĕo,
  dēglŭtĭo, vŏro, haŭrĭo. V. Haurio, voro, hiatus.
sŏrbĭllo, ās, *to sip often.* Cўāthōs sŏrbĭllāns, Ter.
sŏrbĭtĭo, ōnĭs, f., *a draught.* Sŏrbĭtĭō tōllĭt, Pers.
sŏrbŭm, ĭ, n., *the sorb-apple.* Vĭtĕă sŏrbĭs, Virg.
sŏrdĕo, ēs, *and* ēsco, ĭs, *to be filthy.* Quŏnĭăm sŏrdēnt tĭbi, Virg. Syn. Squālĕo.
  V. Sordidus.
sŏrdēs, ĭŭm, f. pl., *filth.* Sĭnĕ sŏrdĭbŭs ēxtrŭĕ, Hor. Syn. Fæx, fæcēs, ĭmmūn-
  dĭtĭă *or* ēs ; ĭmmūndĭtĭæ, lŭtŭm, cœnŭm, ĭllŭvĭēs, cōllŭvĭēs, spŭrcĭtĭēs, squālŏr,
  pædŏr, sĭtŭs, fœdĭtās ; măcŭlă, lābēs ; dēdĕcŭs. V. Cloaca.
sŏrdĭdātŭs, ă, ŭm, *dirtily dressed.* Nōn sŏrdĭdāti, (Iamb. Dim.) Prud.
sŏrdĭdŭs, *and* ŭlŭs, ă, ŭm, *dirty.* Sŏrdĭdŭs ēx hŭmĕrĭs, Virg. Syn. Ŏbscœnŭs,
  squālĭdŭs, squālēns, tŭrpĭs, fœdŭs, fœdātŭs, ĭmmūndŭs, spŭrcŭs. V. Turpis.
sŏrŏr, ōrĭs, f., *a sister.* Sŭrrēptă sŏrōrĭbŭs Āfrĭs, Juv. Syn. Gērmānă. Epith.
  Cără, dīlēctă, ămātă, cāstă, fīdă, pĭă.
sŏrōrĭŭs, ă, ŭm, *of a sister.* Lăcrўmānsquĕ sŏrōrĭă lĭnquĭt, Ov.
sŏrs, sŏrtĭs, f., *fate.* Sŏrtĭbŭs ūrnă, Virg. Syn. Fŏrtūnă, fātŭm, cāsŭs. Epith.
  Āmbĭgŭă, vărĭă, ĭnfīdă, cæcă, fāllāx, văgă, ĭnīquă, lūbrĭcă, ĭnstăbĭlĭs, mălīgnă,
  ĭrrĕquĭētă, ĭncērtă. V. Fortuna, fatum, sortior.
sŏrtĭlĕgŭs, ĭ, m., *and* ă, ŭm, f., *a fortune-teller.* Sŏrtĭlĕgĭs nōn, Hor.
sŏrtĭŏr, ĭrĭs, ĭtŭs, *to cast or draw lots, to gain by chance.* Ārmēntō sŏrtīrĕ quŏt-
  ānnĭs, Virg.
sŏrtĭto, adv., *by chance.* Sŏrtīto ōbtĭgĭt, Hor. Syn. Sŏrtĕ, sŏrtī, fŏrtŭĭtō.
sŏrtĭtŏr, ōrĭs, m., *he who casts lots.* Sŏrtĭtŏr ūrnæ, Sen.
sŏrtītŭs, ūs, m., *a casting of lots.* Quæ sŏrtītŭs nōn, Virg. V. Sortior.
Sŏsĭi, ōrŭm, m. pl., *Roman booksellers in the reign of Augustus.* Æră lĭbĕr Sŏsĭĭs,
  Hor.
sŏspĕs, ĭtĭs, *safe, whole.* Sŏspĭtĕ nūnquăm, Virg. Syn. Sālvŭs, ĭncŏlŭmĭs, ĭntĕgĕr, sŭpērstĕs. V. Incolumis.
Sŏspĭtă, æ, f., *a preserver, a title of Juno.* Sŏspĭtă dēlūbrĭs, Ov.
sŏspĭto, ās, *to save.* Sŏspĭtēs ŏpĕ gēntĕm, Catul.
sŏtērĭă, ōrŭm, n. pl., *presents sent to a friend recovered from sickness or escaped
  from danger,* Mart. Sūrgĭs, sŏtērĭă pŏscĭs, Mart.
spādīx, ĭcĭs, m., *a light red colour.* Spădīcēs glaŭcīquĕ, Virg.
spădo, ōnĭs, m., *a eunuch.* Mīlĕs ēt spădōnĭbŭs, Hor. Syn. Eūnūchŭs.
  Epith. Rūgōsŭs, tĕnĕr, flŭxŭs.
spărgo, sĭ, sŭm, *to spread.* Nŏvō spărgēbăt lūmĭnĕ, Virg. Syn. Dīspērgo,
  dĭffŭndo, fŭndo, ēffŭndo, dĭssēmĭno, ēxtēndo, prōjĭcĭo, ēmītto, āspērgo, cōnspērgo.
spărsĭo, ōnĭs, f., *a distribution among the people.* Dīvēs spărsĭō quŏs ăgĭt tŭmŭltŭs, Stat.
Spārtă, æ, *and* tē, ēs, f., *Lacedæmon.* Vēlōcēs Spārtæ, Virg. Syn. Lăcēdæmōn.
  Epith. Clără, Hērcŭlĕă, ănĭmōsă, vĕtŭs, āntīquă, prīscă, ĭnclўtă, pŏtēns.
Spārtăcŭs, ĭ, m., *a slave who headed a rebellion against the Romans.* Nĕc Spārtăcŭs ācĕr, Hor. Epith. Ācĕr, aŭdāx, ănĭmōsŭs, tĕmĕrārĭŭs, vīlĭs.

Spārtānŭs, ă, ŭm, *Spartan.* Vīrgĭnĭs ārmă Spārtānæ, Virg. Syn. Lăcĕdæmŏ-nĭŭs, Lăcōn, Œbălĭŭs, Amўclæŭs, Thĕrāpnæŭs, Lăcōnĭŭs, Lēdæŭs.

spărūlŭs, ī, m., *a species of sea-fish.* Aūrātā spărŭlŭs, Ov.

spărŭm, n., *or* ŭs, m., ī, *a dart.* Ārmāt spărŭs, īpsĕ, Virg.

spătĭŏr, ārĭs, *to pacĕ up and down.* Āprīcō spătĭārī, Hor. V. Ambulo.

spătĭōsē, adv., *spaciously.* Vōs spătĭōsĭŭs, Prop. Syn. Lātē.

spătĭōsŭs, ă, ŭm, *spacious, ample.* Dĕdĕrĭs spătĭōsŭm, Ov. Syn. Amplŭs, vāstŭs, căpăx, ĭngēns, lātŭs, ĭmmēnsŭs, pătŭlŭs.

spătĭŭm, ĭī, n., *a space, extent.* Ādvērsīs spătĭĭs, Virg. Syn. Ĭntērvāllŭm, lŏcŭs; dīscrīmĕn; cūrrĭcŭlŭm. Epith. Āmplŭm, vāstŭm, lātŭm, ĭmmēnsŭm, căpăx, ĭngēns, pārvŭm, āngŭstŭm, brĕvĕ.

spĕcĭēs, ĭēī, f., *a form, figure.* Vērtūntŭr spĕcĭēs, Virg. Syn. Fōrmă, fĭgūră; ĭmāgo; spēctrŭm, lārvă, pērsōnă; vŭltŭs, ōs; pŭlchrĭtūdo, vĕnūstās; āspēctŭs, cōnspēctŭs.

spĕcĭmĕn, ĭnĭs, n., *a pattern, an instance.* Tŭ spĕcĭmĕn cēnsūræ, Prop. Syn. Ĭndĭcĭŭm, sīgnŭm, nŏtă, ēxēmplŭm. V. Signum.

spĕcĭōsē, adv., *magnificently.* Quŏd spĕcĭōsĭŭs ārmă, Hor.

spĕcĭōsŭs, ă, ŭm, *beautiful, remarkable.* Quāntŭm spĕcĭōsĭŏr ēssĕt, Arat. Syn. Pŭl-chĕr, vĕnūstŭs, dĕcōrŭs; spēctābĭlĭs, cōnspĭcŭŭs, ĭllūstrĭs, ēxĭmĭŭs. V. Pulcher.

spēctābĭlĭs, ĕ, *remarkable.* Plăcĭdō spēctābĭlĭs ŏrĕ, Ov. Syn. Cōnspĭcŭŭs, spēc-tātŭs, ĭllūstrĭs.

spēctăcŭlă, ōrŭm, n. pl., *public shows.* Quīs spēctăcŭlă nōn, Mart. Syn. Lūdī. Epith. Pūblĭcă, fēstīvă, ādmīrāndă, sōlēnnĭă. V. Ludi.

spēctātŏr, ōrĭs, m., *and* trīx, īcĭs, f., *a beholder.* Quŏd spēctātōrĕm, Mart. Spēc-tātrīx ănĭmōs, Ov. Epith. Āttēntŭs, āvĭdŭs, frĕquēns.

spēctātŭs, ă, ŭm, *the pass partic. of* specto. Rēbŭs spēctātă jŭvēntŭs, Virg. Syn. Nōbĭlĭs, ĭllūstrĭs, ĭnsĭgnĭs, cĕlebrĭs, spēctābĭlĭs.

spēcto, ās, *to behold.* Ĭn cīrcō spēctātŭr, Mart. Syn. Aspēcto, cōnsīdĕro, cōntēmplŏr, ĭntŭĕŏr, āspĭcĭo, cērno, vĭdĕo, rēspĭcĭo. V. Respicio, video, aspicio.

* spēctră, ōrŭm, n. pl., *fantasies, ghosts.* Cic. Syn. Sĭmŭlācră, ŭmbræ, lārvæ; Mānēs, Lĕmŭrēs; Sōmnĭă. Epith. Hōrrēndă, ātră, nōctūrnă, pāllēntĭă, tērrĭfĭcă, ĭnfēstă, ĭnānĭă, vānă, prōdĭgĭōsă, mōnstrōsă. V. Somnium, manes.

spĕcŭlă, æ, f., *a beacon.* Aĕrĭī spĕcŭlă dē, Virg. Epith. Cēlsă, āltă, sūblīmĭs, ārdŭă, ēxcēlsă. V. Turris.

spĕcŭlābĭlĭs, ĕ, *to be seen.* Lōngē spĕcŭlābĭlĕ prōrĭs, Stat.

spĕcŭlārĕ, ĭs, n., *a piece of glass to reflect light.* Lātĭs spĕcŭlārĭbŭs aūrō, Juv.

spĕcŭlātĭo, ōnĭs, f., *a viewing, prospect.* Dīvēs spĕcŭlātĭō tērrĭs, Aus.

spĕcŭlātŏr, ōrĭs, m., *and* trīx, īcĭs, f., *a beholder.* Tŭmŭlō spĕcŭlātŏr ăb āltō, Ov. Spĕcŭlātrīx vīllă prŏfūndī, Stat.

spĕcŭlŏr, ārĭs, *to keep watch, to espy.* Ōbĭtŭs spĕcŭlāmŭr ĕt ōrtŭs, Virg. Syn. Cōntēmplŏr, cōnsīdĕro, spēcto, ĭntŭĕŏr, rēspĭcĭo, ōbsērvo, ēxplōro. V. Perspicio, aspicio.

spĕcŭlŭm, ī, n., *a mirror.* Ēlĭgăt ēt spĕcŭlŭm, Ov. Epith. Pŏlītŭm, lūcĭdŭm, pēllūcĭdŭm, mĭcāns, cŏrūscŭm, splēndĭdŭm, nĭtĭdŭm, nĭtēns, frăgĭlĕ, vĭtrĕŭm, crŷstāllĭnŭm, fāllāx, mēndāx, fĭdŭm, fĭdēlĕ, mŭlĭebrĕ, aūrātŭm, ārgēntĕŭm.

spĕcŭs, ŭs, m. f., (n. *indecl.* ;) spĕlæŭm, ī, n.; *and* spĕlūncă, æ, f., *a den, a cave, a grotto.* Hīc spĕcŭs hōrrēndŭm, Virg. Ĭntēr spĕlæă fĕrārŭm, Virg. Spĕlūnca āltă fŭīt, Virg. Syn. Căvērnă, āntrŭm. Spĕlūncæ rĕcēssŭs, claūstră, lătebræ, cōncăvă, āmbĭtŭs. V. Caverna, antrum.

Spērchēĭs *or* chĭĭs, ĭdĭs, f., *of the Sperchius.* Nĕc nōn Spērchēĭdēs ūndæ, Ov.

Spērchĭōnĭdēs, æ, m., *dwelling near or a son of the Sperchius.* Spērchĭōnĭdēmquŏ Lŷcētŭm, Ov.

Spērchĭŏs, *or* ŭs, ī, m., *a river of Thessaly.* Spērchĭōsque ēt vīrgĭnĭbŭs, Virg. Pŏpŭlĭfĕr Spērchĭŭs ĕt, Ov.

spērnāx, ācĭs, *slighting.* Spērnācēs mōrtĭs, Sil.

spērno, sprēvī, sprētŭm, *to despise.* Spērnĕ vŏlŭptātēs, Hor. Syn. Aspērnŏr, tēmno, cōntēmno. V. Contemno, aspernor.

spēro, ās, *to hope.* Spērābānt nŭnc ārmă, Virg. Syn. Expēcto, cōnfīdo. V. Despero.

spēs, spĕī, f., *hope.* Vānā spē lūsĭt, Virg. Syn. Expēctātĭo, fīdūcĭă, vōtă.
Epith. Crēdŭlă, ānxĭă, dŭbĭă, ĭncērtă, sŭspēnsă, pēndŭlă, āmbĭgŭă, āncēps, lūbrĭcă, sōllĭcĭtă, māgnă, ārrēctă, ĭmmŏdĭcă, ăvĭdă, tŭmĭdă, ăvără, dīvĕs, tĕnŭĭs, lĕvĭs, ēxĭgŭă, āngūstă, tĭmĭdă. blāndă, lœtă, stŭltă, nĕfāndă, scĕlĕrātă, vānă, ĭnānĭs, frăgĭlĭs, cădūcă, fālsă, fāllāx, ĭrrĭtă, sŭblāpsă, dēcēptă, văcŭă, cōncēptă, cērtă, cōnstāns. V. Spero.
* sphœră, æ, f., *a sphere, a globe.* Cic.
Sphīnx, gĭs, f., *a monster who proposed enigmas to passengers, and killed those who could not unriddle them.* Vīctă cădīt Sphīnx, Stat. Epith. Trĭcōrpŏr, cāllĭdă, vafră, vērsūtă, hōrrĭdă, ĭmmānĭs, sævă, āspĕră, vŏlucrĭs, ĭnfāndă, Thēbānă, Œdĭpŏdĭōnĭă, hōrrēndă, dīră, ĭmplēxă, crŭēntă.
spīcă, æ, f., *an ear of corn.* Et Cĕrĕrem ĭn spīcĭs, Ov. V. Arista, seges, messis.
spīcĕŭs, ă, ŭm, *of corn.* Spīcĕă jăm, Virg.
spīcĭfĕr, ĕră, ĕrŭm, *bearing corn.* Mē spīcĭfĕr căpĭt, (Scaz.) Mart.
spīcŭlŭm, ī, n., *a dart, a sling.* Spīcŭlă cōnvērsō, Virg. Syn. Jăcŭlŭm, tēlŭm, săgĭttă; ărūndo. Epith. Acūtŭm, sævŭm, tōrtŭm, pēnnātŭm, vēlōx, dūrŭm, fērrĕŭm, dīrŭm, lēthālĕ, fĕrŭm, rĭgĭdŭm, ĭmpĭŭm, vŏlĭtāns, ĭntōrtŭm, flāmmĕŭm, rŭtĭlāns, crūdŭm. V. Sagitta, jaculum.
spīnă, æ, f., *a thorn.* Tētră tŭŭm spīnĭs, Prop. Syn. Rŭbī, sēntēs, veprēs, Epith. Sўlvēstrĭs, stĕrĭlĭs, āspĕră, mōrdāx, pūngēns, vŭlnĭfĭcă, mĭcāns, hămātă, rĭgĭdă, dūră, hīrtă, hōrrēns, hīrsūtă, dēnsă, spārsă. V. Spinosus.
spīnētŭm, ī, n., *a thorny place.* Occŭltānt spīnētă lăcērtōs, Virg. Syn. Dūmē-tŭm, veprētŭm, rŭbētŭm. Epith. Dēnsŭm, āspĕrŭm, ăvĭŭm, ĭmpērvĭŭm, rĭgĭdŭm, sўlvēstrĕ. V. Spinosus.
spīnĕŭs, ă, ŭm, *thorny.* Spīnĕă sўlvă, Prud.
spīnĭfĕr, ă, ŭm, *bearing thorns.* Spīnĭfĕrăm sŭbtĕr, Cic. Syn. Spīnōsŭs.
spīnōsŭs, ă, ŭm, *thorny, rough.* Spīnōsās Erўcīnă, Cat. Syn. Spīnĭfĕr; dĭffĭcĭlĭs, dūrŭs, āspĕr.
spīnŭs, ī, f., *a sloe-tree.* Et spīnōs jăm, Virg. Epith. Aspĕră, agrēstĭs.
spīră, æ, f., *a winding, a circle.* Spīră gălĕrō, Juv. Syn. Gўrŭs, sĭnŭs, ōrbĭs. Epith. Cūrvă, ĭncūrvă, cūrvātă, sĭnŭōsă, ōblĭquă, mŭltĭplēx. V. Gyrus.
spīrābĭlĭs, ĕ, *that may be breathed.* Cœlī spīrābĭlĕ lūmĕn, Virg.
spīrācŭlŭm, ī, n., *a breathing hole.* Sævī spīrācŭlă Dītĭs, Virg. Syn. Mĕātŭs, spīrāmĕn, spīrāmēntŭm.
spīrāmĕn, ĭnĭs, *and* mēntŭm, ī, n., *a vent, an aperture.* Spīrāmĭnă nārĭs, Lucr. Spīrāmēntă lĭnŭnt, Virg. Syn. Fŏrāmĕn, spīrācŭlŭm.
spīrĭtŭs, ūs, *breath, life.* Spīrĭtŭs āltō, Virg. Syn. Aŭră, flāmĕn, flātŭs; hālĭtŭs, rēspīrātĭo, spīrātĭo, spīrāmĕn, rēspīrāmĕn, āfflātŭs, ānhēlĭtŭs, ănĭmă.
spīro, ās, *to breathe.* Spīrāvĕrĕ, pĕdēs, Virg. Syn. Flō, pērflo, āspīro, ēxpīro, ēxhālo, ĭnspīro, āfflo, ĭnhālo, hālo; ŏlĕo, rĕdŏlĕo; rēspīro, ănhēlo; ănĭmŭm, spīrĭtŭm trăho, vīvo.
spīssēsco, ĭs, *to grow thick.* Dŏcŭī spīssēscĕrĕ nŭbĕm, Lucr.
spīsso, ās, *to make thick.* Dēnsŭm spīssātŭs ĭn āĕră, Ov. Syn. Dēnso, cōndēnso, cōgo, āgglŏmĕro.
spīssŭs, ă, ŭm, *thick.* Nē spīssæ rīsŭm, Hor. Syn. Spīssātŭs, dēnsŭs.
splēn, ēnĭs, m., *the spleen.* Splēnĕ căchĭnno, Pers.
splēndĕo, ēs, *and* ēsco, ĭs, *to shine.* Tērrīs splēndĕrĕ cŏlōrĕ, Lucr. Splēndēscĕrĕ vōmĕr, Virg. Syn. Rēsplēndĕo, fŭlgĕo, ēffŭlgĕo, rĕfŭlgĕo, cŏrŭsco, nĭtĕo, nĭtēsco, rŭtĭlo, mĭco, ēmĭco, rădĭo, īrrădĭo, fŭlgŭro, scīntīllo, lūcĕo, rĕlūcĕo, cōllūcĕo. V. Luceo, illumino.
splēndĭdē, adv., *brightly.* Splēndĭdē mēndāx, Hor. Splēndĭdĭŭs mŭltō, Id.
splēndĭdŭs, ă, ŭm, *bright.* Splēndĭdă lūxū, Virg. Syn. Splēndēns, fŭlgēns; fŭlgĭdŭs, cŏrŭscŭs, nĭtĭdŭs, rŭtĭlŭs, lūcĭdŭs, pēllūcĭdŭs, clārŭs. V. Splendeo, lucidus.
splēndŏr, ōrĭs, m., *brightness.* Părŭm splēndōrĭs hăbēbŭnt, Hor. Syn. Fŭlgŏr, nĭtŏr, lūx, lūmĕn, rădĭī, jŭbăr. Epith. Nĭtĭdŭs, fŭlgĭdŭs, clārŭs, flāmmĕŭs, ĭgnĕŭs, aŭrĕŭs, trĕmŭlŭs, nĭvĕŭs, cāndĭdŭs, rŏsĕŭs, vīvŭs, ārdēns, pūrŭs, fŭlgēns, cŏrŭscāns, nĭtēns. V. Splendeo, lux.
splēnĭātŭs, ă, ŭm, *covered with a plaster.* Cŭr splēnĭātō, Mart.
splēnĭŭm, ĭī, n., *a plaster, a patch.* Splēnĭă frŏntĕm, Mart.

S

spŏlĭātŏr, ōrĭs, m., *and* trix, ĭcĭs, f., *a spoiler.* Hīc spŏlĭātŏr, Juv. Sīc spŏlĭātrīcĕm, Mart.

spŏlĭātŭs, ă, ŭm, *the pass. partic. of* spolio. Cŏrpūs spŏlĭātūm, Virg.

spŏlĭo, ās, *to spoil.* Quĭbŭs spŏlĭāvĕrăt hŏstĕm, Virg. SYN. Exspŏlĭo, nūdo, dēnūdo, exŭo, prīvo, ōrbo, prædŏr, fŭrŏr, răpĭo, aūfĕro. V. Prædor, nudo.

spŏlĭum, ĭī, n., spŏlĭă, ōrŭm, n. pl., *spoil.* Spŏlĭum mĕmŏrābĭlĕ mōnstrī, Ov. Et spŏlĭīs ĭgĭtŭr, Juv. SYN. Exŭvĭæ, prædă. EPITH. Bĕllĭcă, hŏstīlĭă, ŏpŭlēntă, crŭēntă, răptă. V. Præda.

spōndă, æ, f., *a bedstead, a couch.* In spōndă cŭbĕt, Hor. EPITH. Rŏtūndă, tĕrĕs, nĭtēns, clără, lūcĭdă, mūndă, cūltă, hŏnēstă, dĕcŏră.

spōndĕo, spŏpōndī, spōnsŭm, *to promise.* Spōndĕt fŏrtūnă sălūtĕm, Virg. SYN. Pŏllĭcĕŏr, prōmĭtto; rĕcĭpĭo. V. Promitto.

spōndēŭs, ī, m., *a foot of this quantity* (- -). Spōndēōs stăbĭlēs, Hor.

spōndўlŭs, ī, m., *a sort of shell-fish.* Tĕpēntī spōndўlōs sĭnū cōndĭt, Mart.

spūngĭă, æ, f., *a sponge.* Spōngĭă mēnsĭs, Mart. EPITH. Lēvĭs, tŭmēns, tūmĭdă, tūrgĭdă, bĭbŭlă, mōllĭs, ūdă, hūmēns, hūmĭdă, mădĭdă.

spōnsă, æ, f., *a bride.* Quĕm spōnsæ tūrpēs, Juv. EPITH. Vĕnŭstă, dĕcŏră, ōrnātă, măgnĭfĭcă, splēndĭdă, cōmptă, cōncīnnă, sŭpērbă. V. Uxor.

spōnsālĭă, ōrŭm, n. pl., *espousals.* Et spōnsālĭă nōstră, Juv. V. Conjugium.

spōnsālĭs, ĕ, *of marriage.* Vōtīs spōnsālĭbŭs ōmnēs, Juven.

spōnsĭo, ōnĭs, f., *a contract.* Spōnsĭō fīăt, Juv.

spōnsŏr, ōrĭs, m., *a surety.* Spōnsŏr cōnjŭgĭī, Ov.

spōnsŭs, ī, m., *a bridegroom.* Impĭæ spōnsōs pŏtŭĕrĕ dūrō, Hor. SYN. Cōnjūx, mărītŭs, vĭr. EPITH. Cārŭs, pūlchĕr, dīlēctŭs. V. Maritus.

spōntĕ, adv., *willingly.* Spōntĕ sŭă sāndĭx, Virg. SYN. Ultro, lĭbēntĕr; lĭbēns, vŏlēns. V. Ultro.

spōrtă, æ, f., *a basket, pannier.* Rĕdĭt spōrtă pĭscătŏr ĭnānī, Mart.

spōrtŭlă, æ, f., *a little basket.* Spōrtŭlă cēntŭm, Mart.

sprētŏr, ōrĭs, m., *a despiser.* Sēnsŭs, sprētōrquĕ mŏrārŭm, Nem. SYN. Cōntēmptŏr.

sprētŭs, ă, ŭm, *the pass. partic. of* sperno. Părĭdīs, sprētæquĕ, Virg.

spūmă, æ, f., *foam.* Et spūmās ăgĕt, Virg. EPITH. Albă, cāndĭdă, ālbēscēns, cānă, cāndēns, ālbēns, ālbĭdă, pīnguĭs, nătāns, fērvĭdă, vīrĭdĭs, crŭēntă.

spūmēsco, ĭs, *to foam.* Nōstră tŭŏ spūmēscānt, Virg. V. Spumo.

spūmĕŭs, ă, ŭm, *foamy.* Spūmĕŭs ĭn lōngā, Mart. SYN. Spūmōsŭs, spūmĭfĕr, spūmāns.

spūmĭfĕr, ă, ŭm, *bearing foam.* Illī spūmĭfĕrōs, Stat. SYN. Spūmĭgĕr, spūmĕŭs.

spūmo, ās, *to foam.* Sālsă spūmānt āspērgĭnĕ, Virg. SYN. Spūmēsco.

spūmōsŭs, ă, ŭm, *foamy.* Vĭrūm spūmōsa ĭmmĭsĕrăt, Virg.

spŭo, ĭs, *to spit.* Sĭccŏ spŭĭt ōrĕ, Virg. SYN. Spŭto, ēxcrĕo.

spūrcĭtĭă, æ, *and* ēs, ēī, f., *filthiness.* Spūrcĭtĭa āc pĕtŭlāntĭă, Lucr. Spūrcĭtĭēs ĕādĕm, Id. SYN. Fœdĭtās, măcŭlæ, sōrdēs, vĭtĭŭm.

spūrco, ās, *to defile.* Spūrcătă sĕnēctŭs, Cat. SYN. Fœdo, măcŭlo, vĭtĭo, cōntămĭno. V. Maculo.

spūrcŭs, ă, ŭm, *dirty.* Abscōndūnt spūrcās, Mart.

spūrĭŭs, ă, ŭm, *spurious.* Spūrĭīs vērsĭbŭs, Aus.

spŭto, ās, *the frequent. of* spuo, *to spit often.* Spūtāntĕm sāuguĭnĕ dēntēs, Ov.

spŭtŭm, ī, n., *and* tŭs, ūs, m., *spittle.* Spŭtă sŭbĭndĕ, Mart. SYN. Sălīvă. EPITH. Sōrdĭdŭm, tūrpĕ, fœtĭdŭm, fœdŭm, cāndĭdŭm, ālbēns, crāssŭm, ĭmmūndŭm.

squălĕo, ēs, *to be filthy.* Dīgnŭs hŏnŏr, squălēnt, Virg. SYN. Sōrdĕo, sōrdēsco. V. Sordeo, squalor.

squālĭdŭs, ă, ŭm, *filthy.* Squālĭdŭs ĭn rīpā, Ov. SYN. Squălēns, sōrdĭdŭs. V. Sordidus, macer, squalor.

squălŏr, *and* llŏr, ōrĭs, m., *filthiness.* Tērrĭbĭlī squălōrĕ Chărōn, Virg. SYN. Sōrdēs, sĭtŭs, pædŏr; mœrŏr, trīstĭtĭă, lūctŭs. EPITH. Tūrpĭs, fœdŭs, dēfōrmĭs, sōrdĭtŭs, ātĕr, hōrrĭdŭs. V. Sordes.

squālŭs, ī, m., *a sea-dog.* Et squālŭs tĕnŭī, Ov.

squāmă, *or* mmă, æ, f., *a scale of a fish, serpent, &c.* In plūmām squămĭs, Virg. EPITH. Dūră, āspĕră, nēxĭlĭs, crĕpĭtāns, nĭtĭdă, rŭtĭlă, fūlgēns, mĭcāns, splēndēns. V. Squamosus.

squāmĕŭs, ă, ŭm, *scaly.* Squāmĕŭs īn spīrām, Virg.

squāmĭfĕr, gĕr, *and* ōsŭs, ă, ŭm, *having scales.* Squāmĭfĕrōs īngēns, Luc. Squānĭgĕrūm gĕnŭs, Lucr. Squāmōsŭsquĕ drāco, Virg. Syn. Squāmĕŭs.

squĭllă, æ, f., *a sea-fish of the lobster kind.* Hīnc squĭllæ māxĭmă tūrbă sŭmŭs, Mart.

Stăbĕrĭŭs, ĭī, m., *the name of a man.* Hērēdĕs Stăbĕrī, Hor.

Stăbĭæ, ārŭm, f. pl., *a city of Campania.* Hērcŭlĕāmquĕ ūrbēm, Stăbĭāsquĕ, Ov.

stăbĭlĭo, īvī, ītŭm, *to make firm.* Quăssās stăbĭlīrĕ tūrĕs, (Sapph.) Sen. Syn. Firmo, cōnfĭrmo, cōrrōbŏro ; stătŭo, cōnstĭtŭo ; fīgo.

stăbĭlĭs, ĕ, *firm.* Quă mănĕăt stăbĭlī, Ov. Syn. Fīrmŭs, cōnstāns, fīrmātŭs, cōnfīrmātŭs, īmmūtābĭlĭs, īmmōbĭlĭs, īmmōtŭs, cērtŭs, pĕrēnnĭs, pĕrpĕtŭŭs, ætērnŭs, īmmōrtālĭs. V. Constans, immortalis.

stăbŭlŭm, ī, n., *a stable.* Ipsĕ vēlŭt stăbŭlī cūstŏs, Virg. Syn. Sĕptŭm, præsēpĕ ; ĕquīlĕ ; bŭbīlĕ ; ŏvīlĕ ; caŭlă ; sŭīlĕ ; hără, vŏlūtābrŭm ; hædīlĕ. Epith. Ingēns, āmplŭm, lātŭm, spătĭōsŭm, pătēns, ăpērtŭm, claūsŭm, mūnītŭm, tūtŭm, tĕpĭdŭm, tĕpēns, fūmāns, tūrpĕ, īnmūndŭm, sōrdĭdŭm, pīnguĕ.

stăbŭlo, ās, *and* ŏr, ārĭs, *to put in a stable.* Ūnă stăbŭlārĕ, sĕd āltĕr, Virg.

stāctă, æ, *and* tē, ēs, f., *essence of myrrh.* Blāndŭm stāctæquĕ līquŏrĕm, Lucr.

stădĭŭm, ĭī, n., *a place for running, a race-course.* Căptŭs ĕs īn stădĭō, Aus. Epith. Amplŭm, plānŭm, lātŭm, spătĭōsŭm, Ōlympĭăcŭm, Ōlympĭcŭm.

stăgno, ās, *to be stagnant.* Infūsō stăgnāntĕm, Virg.

stăgnōsŭs, ă, ŭm, *overflown.* Stăgnōsī spēctăt, Sil.

stăgnŭm, ī, n., *a pool.* Stăgnă vīrēntĭă, Virg. Syn. Lăcŭs, pălŭs. Epith. Rĕfūsŭm, mītĕ, hūmĭdŭm, tōrpēns, lēntŭm, cærŭlĕŭm, liquēns, rŭtĭlŭm, splēndĭdŭm, pīscōsŭm, căvŭm, īrrĭgŭŭm. V. Palus, lacus.

stāmĕn, ĭnĭs, n., *the woof, flax on a distaff.* Stāmĭnĕ tēlās, Ov. Syn. Fīlŭm, līcĭŭm, sŭbtēgmĕn. Epith. Tĕnŭĕ, sŭbtīlĕ, ēxĭgŭŭm, lĕvĕ, tĕnĕrŭm, tĕrĕs, tōrtŭm, īntōrtŭm, ŏpĕrōsŭm, nōdōsŭm, nĭvĕŭm, cāndĭdŭm, pūrpŭrĕŭm, aūrĕŭm, sērĭcŭm, līnĕŭm. V. Filum, neo.

stāmĭnĕŭs, ă, ŭm, *thready.* Stāmĭnĕă rhōmbī, Prop.

stătĕră, æ, f., *a balance, a scale.* Quādrŭpēs stătĕră, (Phal.) Stat. Syn. Lībră, trŭtīnă, lānx. V. Libra, lanx.

stătĭm, adv., *immediately.* Quīn stătĭm rēm gĕrăt, (Iamb.) Plaut. Syn. Cōntĭnŭō, rĕpēntĕ, sŭbĭtō, īllĭco, prōtĭnŭs, ēxtēmplo, ācŭtŭm, cĭto, cōnfēstĭm, ōcyŭs, īllĭcĕt, quāmprīmŭm, mōx, jāmjăm.—2. Stătim āc, *as soon as.* Syn. Sĭmŭl āc, sĭmŭl ātquĕ, ŭbi, ŭt prīmŭm, ŭbī prīmŭm, cŭm prīmŭm.

stătĭo, ōnĭs, f., *a station, a sentry.* Vĭcēs, stătĭōnĕ rĕlĭctă, Virg. Syn. Ātrĭŭm ; pōrtŭs ; ēxcŭbĭæ.

Stătĭŭs, ĭī, m., *an epic poet.* Quŭm Stătĭŭs ūrbĕm, Juv.

Stătŏr, ōrĭs, m., *a name of Jupiter.* Hīc Stătŏr, hōc prīmō, Ov.

stătŭă, æ, f., *a statue.* Infāntēs stătŭās, Hor. Syn. Ēffĭgĭēs, sĭmŭlācrŭm, sīgnŭm, spĕcĭēs, ĭmāgo. Epith. Aūrātă, mārmŏrĕă, ærĕă, ălĭĕnĕă, ārgēntĕă, ĕbūrnă, ĕbūrnĕă, līgnĕă, sāxĕă, cĕrĕă, mŭtă, sūrdă, ēxsānguĭs, ērēctă, sŭblīmĭs, ārdŭă, ĭnaūrātă, ēxĭmĭă, pŭlchră, dĕcŏră, ēxcūltă, sŭpērbă, āntīquă, scŭlptĭlĭs, scŭlptă, fīctĭlĭs, ēxprēssă, vīvă, spīrāns. V. Simulacrum.

* stătŭārĭă, æ, f., *the art of sculpture.* Plin. Syn. Cælātūră, scŭlptūră.

* stătŭārĭŭs, ĭī, m., *a statuary.* Quint. Syn. Cælātŏr, scŭlptŏr.

stătŭo, tŭī, tūtŭm, *to appoint, set up.* Ūrbĕm præclārăm stătŭī, Virg. Syn. Cōnstĭtŭo, dēcērno ; pōno, lŏco, cōllŏco, fīgo, fīrmo, stăbĭlĭo.

stătūrŭs, ă, ŭm, *the fut. partic. of sto, about to stand or remain.* Hīnc ăcĭēs stătūră dŭcŭm, Luc.

stătŭs, ă, ŭm, *the pass. partic. of sisto, stated, fixed.* Ad stătă sīgnă dĭēs, Ov. Syn. Cērtŭs, fīxŭs, sŏlēnnĭs, fīrmŭs, rătŭs.

stătŭs, ūs, m., *position, condition.* Hīc stătŭs, īn mēdĭō, Ov. Syn. Cōndĭtĭo, fōrtūnă, ōrdo, grădŭs, lŏcŭs. Epith. Fēlīx, faūstŭs, īnfēlīx, īnfaūstŭs, trānquīllŭs, flōrēns, plācĭdŭs, quĭĕtŭs, āptŭs, hōnēstŭs, dĕcōrŭs, mĭsĕr, tūrpĭs.

stēllă, æ, f., *a star.* Cŭm prīmō stēllās, Virg. Syn. Sīdŭs, āstrŭm. Epith. Cœlēstĭs, mĭcāns, ārdēns, lūcĭdă, cŏrŭscă, splēndĭdă, rădĭāns. V. Astrum.—2. *a Latin poet.* Stēllă pĕnātēs, Mart. Epith. Dūlcĭs, Pĭĕrĭŭs, Aŏnĭŭs, dĭsērtŭs, cănōrŭs.

stĕllătŭs, ĭfĕr, *and* ĭgĕr, ă, ŭm, *full of stars.* Illī stĕllătŭs ĭäspĭdĕ, Virg. Stĕllĭfĕrī jŭbăr, Mart. Stĕllĭgĕr äxĭs, Stat.

stĕllĭo, ōnĭs, m., *a lizard.* Ignōtŭs ădĕdĭt Stĕllĭo, Virg. V. Lacertus.

stĕllo, ās, *to cover with stars, to shine as stars.* Stĕllāntĭs rēgĭă cœlī, Virg.

stĕmĭnă, ătĭs, n., *a stem, a badge, a pedigree.* Stĕmmătĕ tōtă, Mart. Syn. Insĭgnĕ. Epith. Clārŭm, pŭlchrŭm, ĭllŭstrĕ, dĕcōrŭm, sŭpĕrbŭm, cĕlebrĕ, gĕnĕrōsŭm, patrĭŭm, ăvītŭm. V. Nobilitas.

Stĕntŏr, ŏrĭs, m., *a hero of the Iliad, who had a very loud voice.* Ŭt Stĕntŏră vīncĕrĕ pŏssĭs, Juv.

Stĕphănŭs, ī. m., *a man's name.* Quăm sīnt Stĕphănī bālnĕă, Mart.

* stĕrcŏro, ās, *to manure.* Cic.

stĕrcŭs, ŏrĭs, n, *dung.* Stĕrcŏrĕ fŭcātŭs, Hor. Syn. Fīmŭs. Epith. Tĕtrŭm, ŏlĭdŭm, ĭmmūndŭm, fœtēns.

stĕrĭlĭs, ĕ, *barren.* Ĕt stĕrĭlēs dŏmĭnāntŭr, Virg. Syn. Infœcŭndŭs, nŏn fœcŭndŭs, mălĕ fœcŭndŭs, ĕffœtŭs, ārĭdŭs.

* stĕrĭlĭtās, ātĭs, f., *sterility.* Col.

stĕrĭlŭs, ă, ŭm, *destitute of.* Ĕt sŏnĭtū stĕrĭlă, Lucr.

stĕrnāx, ācĭs, *casting down.* Ĕt stĕrnācĭs ĕquī, Virg.

stĕrno, strāvī, strătŭm, *to cast down.* Stĕrnĕrĕ cædĕ vīrōs, Virg. Syn. Prōstĕrno, ăfflīgo, dējĭcĭo, ĕxcŭtĭo. V. Dejicio.

stĕrnŭo, ĭs, *and* ŭto, ās, *to sneeze.* Stĕrnŭĭt ōmĕn, Prop.

Stĕrŏpē, ēs, f., *the daughter of Atlas, changed into one of the Pleiads.* Sæpĕ mĭnāx Stĕrŏpēs, Ov.

Stĕrŏpēs, æ, m., *one of the Cyclopes.* Brōntēsquĕ Stĕrŏpēsquĕ, Virg.

Stĕrtĭnĭŭs, ĭī, m., *a stoic philosopher.* Sī quĭd Stĕrtĭnĭŭs, Hor.—Adj.-ŭs, ă, ŭm, Stĕrtĭnĭŭm dēlīrāt ăcūmĕn, Id.

stĕrto, ĭs, ŭī, *to snore.* Stĕrtĭmŭs ĭndŏmĭtŭm, Pers.

Stēsĭchŏrŭs, ī, m., *a lyric poet of Sicily.* Stēsĭchŏrīquĕ grăvēs, Hor.

Sthĕnĕlēĭs, ĭdĭs, f., *of Sthenelus.* Nātī Sthĕnĕlēĭdă vērsŭm, Ov.

Sthĕnĕlēĭŭs, ă, ŭm, *of Sthenelus.* Prōlēs Sthĕnĕlēĭă Cўcnŭs, Ov.

Sthĕnĕlŭs, ī, m., *the son of Capaneus, one of the Grecian chiefs at the siege of Troy.* Thĕssāndrŭs Sthĕnĕlŭsquĕ dŭcēs, Virg.

Sthĕnŏbœă, œ, f., *wife of Prœtus, king of Argos.* Nēc Sthĕnŏbœă mĭnŭs, Virg. V. Bellerophon.

Stĭctĕ, ēs, f., *the name of a dog.* Ov.

stīgmă, ătĭs, n., *a mark of disgrace.* Stīgmătĕ dīgnŭm, Juv. Epith. Rĭgĭdŭm, dŭrŭm, flāmmāns, prēssŭm, fœdŭm, tŭrpĕ.

Stīlbōn, ōnĭs, m., *the planet Mercury.* Quæ Stīlbōn vŏlvăt, Aus.

stīllă, æ, f., *a drop.* Ātque ōlĕī stīllăm, Mart. V. Gutta.

stīllāns, āntĭs, *falling in drops, trickling.* Stīllāntī rōrĕ căpīllōs, Ov.

stīllātŭs, ă, ŭm, *fallen in drops.* Stīllātăquĕ sōlĕ rĭgēscŭnt, Ov.

stīllĭcĭdĭŭm, dĭī *or* dī, n., *a dropping, a little gutter.* Stīllĭcĭdī cāsŭs, Lucr.

stīllo, ās, *to let fall in drops.* Sānguĭnĕĭs stīllāvĭt, Lucan. Syn. Flŭo, ĕfflŭo.

Stĭmĭcōn, ōnĭs, m., *the name of a shepherd.* Jāmprĭdĕm Stĭmĭcōn, Virg.

Stĭmŭlă, æ, f., *a divinity worshipped at Rome.* Sĕmĕlæ Stĭmŭlænĕ vŏcĕtŭr, Ov.

stĭmŭlātŏr, ŏrĭs, m., *an instigator.* Arctŏī stĭmŭlātŏr, Claud.

stĭmŭlo, ās, *to excite.* Stĭmŭlānt Trĭĕtĕrĭcă, Virg. Syn. Pŭngo, lāncĭno, fŏdĭco, ĕxstĭmŭlo, ĕxcĭto, cōncĭto. V. Stimulus.

stĭmŭlŭs, ī, m., *a prick, a goad.* Et cæcī stĭmŭlōs, Virg. Syn. Ăcŭlĕŭs, cālcăr. Epith. Ăcĕr, ăcĕrbŭs, ăcūtŭs, pŭngēns, trūx, dīrŭs, fĕrrĕŭs, sævŭs, prĕmēns. V. Calcar.

stīnguo, ĭs, *to extinguish.* Paūlātĭm stīnguī, Lucr. V. Extinguo.

stīpātŏr, ŏrĭs, m., *an attendant.* Nĕquĕ tĕ quīsquăm stīpātŏr, ĭnĕptŭm, Hor.

|| stĭpendĭālĭs, ĕ, *pertaining to tribute.* Sŭb stĭpĕndĭālī, Sed.

stĭpēndĭŭm, ĭī, n., *wages.* Fĕrēns stĭpēndĭă taŭrō, Cat. Syn. Mērcēs.

stĭpēs, ĭtĭs, m., *a trunk, a log.* Stĭpĭtĭbŭs dŭrīs, Virg. Syn. Trŭncŭs, sŭdēs, pālŭs. Epith. Dūrŭs, nōdōsŭs, rāmōsŭs, tĕrēs, rŏtŭndŭs, prŏcĕrŭs, ĭmmōtŭs, ĭmmōbĭlĭs, rŏbŏrĕŭs, vĕtŭstŭs, ārĭdŭs, ārēns. V. Palus.

stīpo, ās, *to surround, to cram.* Dēnsō stīpāntquĕ, Virg. Syn. Ămbĭo, cīngo, cīrcŭmsto, sēpĭo ; dēnso ; ōbstrŭo.

stīps, Ῑpῐs, f., *a small piece of money.* Pārvā cūr stῑpĕ quærăt ŏpēs, Ov. Epith. Pārvā, tĕnŭῑs. V. Mendico.

stῑpŭlă, æ, f., *straw.* Strῑdēntῑ mῑsĕrūm stῑpŭlā, Virg. Syn. Cūlmŭs, călămŭs, pălĕă, strāmĕn. Epith. Trῑtῑcĕă, flāvă, agrēstῑs, vŏlāns, ārῑdă, sῑccă, frăgῑlῑs, crĕpῑtāns, gĕmēns, grăcῑlῑs. V. Culmus, palea.

stῑpŭlŏr, ārῑs, *to stipulate.* Quānῑvῑs stῑpŭlāre ĕt, Juv.

stῑrῑă, æ, f., *au icicle.* Stῑrῑă nāsō, Mart. Epith. Pēndēns, dēpēndēns, lōngă, rῑgῑdă, ăspĕră, dūră, pēndŭlă, rῑgēns, gĕlῑdă, frăgῑlῑs.

stῑrpῑtŭs, adv., *to the root.* Stῑrpῑtŭs ātquĕ, Fill. Syn. Rădῑcῑtŭs, ā stῑrpĕ, ā rădῑcĕ.

stῑrps, stῑrpῑs, m. f., *a root, lineage.* Hῑc stῑrpēs ŏbrŭῑt, Virg. Syn. Rădῑx; ŏrῑgo, gĕnŭs. V. Genus, radix.

stῑvă, æ, f., *the plough-tail.* Stῑvăquĕ, quæ, Virg.

stlātă, æ, f., *a cruising vessel, brigantine.* Lῑntrῑbŭs, stlātῑs, Aus.

stlātārῑŭs, ă, ŭm, *imported by a corsair, foreign.* Stlātārῑă pūrpŭră fῑlō, Juv.

stlŏpŭs, ῑ, m., *the sound produced in blowing up the cheeks.* Nĕc stlŏpō tŭmῑdās, Pers.

stō, stĕtῑ, *to stand.* Stăbῑt Ῑnērs, Virg. Syn. Cōnsῑsto, cōnsto; pērmănĕo, pēr-dūro; vῑgĕo, flŏrĕo.

Stŏῑcῑ, ōrŭm, m. pl., *Stoics, philosophers of the portico.* Stŏῑcŭs hās pārtēs, Aus.

Stŏῑcῑdæ, ārŭm, m. pl., *Stoics.* Mănῑfēstă cărēntĕm Stŏῑcῑdæ, Juv.

Stŏῑcŭs, ă, ŭm, *Stoic.* Stŏῑcă tūrbă, Mart.

stŏlă, æ, f., *a gown.* Ăd tālōs stŏlă dēmῑssă, Hor. Epith. Lōngă, fœmῑnĕă. V. Vestis.

stŏlātŭs, ă, ŭm, *wearing the stola, matronly.* Vēstῑt ēt stŏlātŭm, Mart.

stŏlῑdŭs, ă, ŭm, *stupid.* Dŏmῑnō stŏlῑdæ præcŏrdῑă, Ov. Syn. Stŭpῑdŭs, hĕbĕs, tārdŭs. V. Stupidus, hebes.

stŏmăchŏr, ārῑs, *to be in a passion.* Stŏmăchērῑs ŏb ŭnguĕm, Hor. V. Irascor.

stŏmăchōsŭs, ă, ŭm, *passionate, irascible.* Lævă stŏmăchōsŭs hăbēnă, Hor.

stŏmăchŭs, ῑ, m., *the stomach, indignation.* Lātrāntēm stŏmăchŭm, Hor. Syn. Pēctŭs; ῑră. Epith. Ăvῑdŭs, hῑāns, căpāx, văcŭŭs, jējūnŭs, Ῑnānῑs, plēnŭs, rĕfērtŭs.

străbo, ōnῑs, m., *squint-eyed.* Fāstῑdῑrĕ: străbōnĕm, Hor.

străgēs, ῑs, f., *destruction.* Tāntās străgēs ῑmpūnĕ, Virg. Syn. Clādēs, cædēs, ŏccῑsῑo, rŭῑnă, pērnῑcῑēs, ēxῑtῑŭm. Epith. Crŭēntă, ăcērbă, ῑmplă, fĕrōx, ῑn-făndă, nĕfāndă, hŏrrῑdă, hŏrrēndă, sănguῑnĕă, dĕfōrmῑs. V. Occisio, cædes.

străgŭlă, æ, *and* ŭm, ῑ, n., *the coverlet of a bed, a horse-cloth.* Străgŭlă pῑctă, Mart. Epith. Vῑllōsŭm, pūrpŭrĕŭm, prĕtῑōsŭm, aūrātŭm, dĕcōrŭm, hŏnēstŭm.

strāmĕn, ῑnῑs, *or* ēntŭm, ῑ, n., *a spreading, straw, litter.* Strāmῑnĕ pŏnūnt, Virg. Ět strāmēntῑs ῑncŭbĕt, Hor. Syn. Stῑpŭlă, pălĕă. Epith. Mŏllĕ, dūrŭm, ārῑdŭm, rῑgῑdŭm, sῑccŭm.

strāmῑnĕŭs, ă, ŭm, *of straw.* Strāmῑnĕă pŏssĕt, Prop.

strāngŭlo, ās, *to choke.* Strāngŭlăt, ĕt, Juv. Syn. Sŭffŏco, sŭspēndo.

strătāgēmă, ătῑs, n., *a stratagem.* Bĕlgῑcæ strătāgēmă, (Scaz.)

Strătoclēs, ῑs, m., *a man's name.* Aūt Strătoclēs, Juv.

strātŭm, ῑ, n., *any thing strewed; a couch.* Mŏllῑbŭs ē strātῑs, Virg. Syn. Lēc-tŭs, cŭbῑlĕ, thălămŭs. V. Lectus, stragulum.

strātŭs, ă, ŭm, *the pass. partic. of* sterno. Strătă jăcēnt, Virg.

strēnæ, ārŭm, f. pl., *new year's gifts.* Cūrăm prō strēnῑs, Aus. Epith. Lætæ, fēstæ, ămῑcæ, sŏlēnnēs, dῑtēs, mūnῑfῑcæ. V. Xenium.

strēnŭῑtās, ātῑs, f., *valour, adroitness.* Strēnŭῑtās āntῑquă, Ov. Syn. Fōrtῑtūdo; Ῑndūstrῑă.

strēnŭŭs, ă, ŭm, *active, valiant.* Strēnŭă jŭssῑs, Ov. Syn. Dῑlῑgēns, ῑmpῑgĕr, gnāvŭs, Ῑndūstrῑŭs; fōrtῑs.

strĕpῑto, ās, *and* po, ῑs, ŭῑ, *to make a noise.* Fŏllῑs strĕpῑtānt, Virg. Fūndūntŭr, strĕpῑt ōmnῑs, Virg. Syn. Sŭsūrro, mūrmŭro. V. Murmuro.

strĕpῑtŭs, ūs, m., *a noise.* Fῑt strĕpῑtŭs tēctῑs, Virg. Syn. Mūrmŭr, sŏnŭs, strῑdŏr. V. Sonitus.

strῑctūră, æ, f., *a spark flying from red-hot iron.* Strῑctūræ chălўbŭm, Virg.

strīdĕo, ēs, *and* do, ĭs, *to crack, shriek.* Sŏllĭcĭtūm strīdĕt rĕflŭēntĭbŭs, Virg. Strīdĕrĕ sēcrētā, Hor. Syn. Crĕpĭto, frĕmo. V. Murmuro.

strīdŏr, ōrĭs, m., *a sharp noise.* Māgnō strīdōrĕ pĕr aūrās, Virg. Syn. Strĕpĭtŭs, mūrmŭr. Epith. Acūtŭs, quĕrŭlŭs, raūcŭs, fĕrŭs, hŏrrĭsŏnŭs, tĕrrĭfĭcŭs, hŏr- rēndŭs, ācĕr, tĕrrĭbĭlĭs, sŏnāns, hŏrrĭbĭlĭs, hŏrrĭfĕr. V. Strideo.

strīdŭlŭs, ă, ŭm, *creaking.* Strīdŭlă Saūrŏmātēs, Ov. Syn. Strīdēns, strĕpĭtāns, sŏnŏrŭs.

strigĭl, *and* ĭlĭs, ĭs, m. f., *a horse-comb ; an instrument used by the Romans at the baths to scrape their bodies with.* Strīgĭlĭbŭs plēnō, Juv. I pŭĕr, ĕt strĭgĭlēs, Pers. Epith. Dēntātă, fērrĕă, dūră, rĭgĭdă.

strīngo, strīnxī, strīctŭm, *to grasp.* Strīngĕrĕt ēnsēs, Virg. Syn. Astrīngo, cōnstrīngo, cōmprĭmo, ārcto ; ĭn ārctŭm cōgo, cŏārcto, lĭgo, vīncĭo ; dīstrīngo, nŭdo, ē vāgīnā ēxtrāho ; ēdūco, ĭs ; dīrĭpĭo, ērĭpĭo.

strīngŏr, ōrĭs, m., *a congealing.* Strīngŏr ăquāī, Lucr.

strīx, strĭgĭs, f., *a screech-owl.* Quŏd strīx nōctŭrnă, Luc. Ēst īllīs strĭgĭbŭs nŏmĕn, Ov. Epith. Nŏctŭrnă, īnfaūstă, īmprŏbă, raūcă, nŏxĭă, trīstĭs, sĭnīstră, mœstă, fērālĭs, nĕfāndă, dīră, īnfēlīx, præsāgă.

strŏphă, æ, f., *evasion, subtlety.* Jām strŏphā tālĭs, Mart. Syn. Ārtēs, dŏlŭs, fāllācĭă.

Strŏphădĕs, ŭm, f. pl., *islands in the Ionian sea.* Accĭpĭunt : Strŏphădĕs, Virg.

Strŏphĭŭs, ĭī, m., *a king of Phocis, father of Pylades.* Vīxērūnt Strŏphĭŏ, Ov.

strŏphĭŭm, ĭī, n., *a coronet, a twisted girdle.* Nōn tĕrĕtī strŏphĭŏ, Cat.

strūctĭlĭs, ĕ, *made of divers pieces.* Strūctĭlīvĕ cēmēntŏ, (Scaz.) Mart. Syn. Strūctŭs, ēxstrūctŭs.

strūctŏr, ōrĭs, m., *a builder.* Strūctōrĭs, ŏfēllæ, Mart.

strūctūră, æ, f., *structure.* Ēt strūctūrā mĕī, Ov. Syn. Ædĭfĭcĭŭm ; ōrdo.

strŭēs, ĭs, f., *a heap.* Cūm strŭē fārră, Ov. Syn. Cōngĕrĭēs, āggĕ⬤ĭmŭlŭs, cōngēstŭs āggĕr.

strūmōsŭs, ă, ŭm, *having a wen.* Strūmōsum ātque ŭtĕrō, Juv.

strŭo, strūxī, ctŭm, *to build.* Sācrĭlĕgŭm strŭĕrĕt, Mart. Syn. Mōlĭŏr, cōn- strŭo, ēxstrŭo, ædĭfĭco ; pāro, āppāro, īnstrŭo.

Strȳmōn, ŏnĭs, m., *a river of Thracia.* Strȳmōnĭs ūndăm, Virg. Epith. Gĕlĭdŭs, Thrācĭŭs, Gĕtĭcŭs, răpĭdŭs, præcĕps, cĭtŭs, cōncĭtŭs, vēlōx, pērnīx.

Strȳmŏnĕŭs, ă, ŭm, *of the Strymon.* Strȳmŏncæquĕ grŭēs, Virg.

stŭdĕo, ēs, *to be fond of, to study.* Quī stŭdĕt ōptātăm, Hor.

stŭdĭă, ōrŭm, n. pl., *literary pursuits.* Quŏndăm stŭdĭōrŭm, Ov. Syn. Lĭtĕræ, ārtēs. Epith. Dōctă, īngĕnŭă, Pāllādĭă, Pĭĕrĭă, sacră, jūcūndă, hŏnēstă.

stŭdĭōsŭs, ă, ŭm, *eager, careful ; studious.* Ārbŏrĕī stŭdĭōsĭŏr, Ov. Syn. Amāns, cŭpĭdŭs, ōbsērvāns ; stŭdĭīs āddĭctŭs, āssĭdŭŭs, īnvĭgĭlāns, āssuētŭs. V. Doctus.

stŭdĭŭm, ĭī, n., *study, application.* Aūstērŭm stŭdĭŏ, Hor. Syn. Amŏr ; lăbŏr, cŭră, cōntēntĭo, ŏpĕră. V. Amor, labor.

stūltē, adv., *foolishly.* Dūm stūltē mĕdĭtŏr, Ov. Syn. Ĭnēptē, stŏlĭdē.

stūltĭtĭă, æ, f., *foolishness.* Mīscē stūltĭtĭăm, Hor. Syn. Īnsānĭă, āmēntĭă, dēmēntĭă, vēcordĭă, vēsānĭă ; dēlīrĭă, *in plur. ;* tĕmĕrĭtŭs. Epith. Pĕtŭlāns, præcĕps, cæcă, tĕmĕrārĭă, văgă, vēsānă, fŭrĭbūndă. V. Furor, stultus.

stūltŭs, ă, ŭm, *foolish.* Ēt stūltă pŏpŭlōs, Ov. Syn. Īnsānŭs, āmēns, dēmēns, fătŭŭs, dēlīrŭs, mălĕsānŭs, vēcōrs, tĕmĕrārĭŭs. V. Furens, furo.

stūpă, æ, f., *the coarse part of flax.* Stūpā vŏmēns, Virg.

stŭpĕfāctŭs, ă, ŭm, *astonished.* Mōtū stŭpĕfāctŭs ăquārŭm, Virg. Syn. Stŭ- pēns, ōbstŭpĕfāctŭs, āttŏnĭtŭs, pērcūlsŭs, tĕrrĭtŭs. V. Stupeo, territus, ob- stupefactus.

stŭpĕfĭo, fāctŭs, *to be astonished.* Nōstrō stŭpĕfĭăt, Prop. Syn. Ōbstŭpēsco. stŭpēsco, stŭpĕo.

stŭpēndŭs, ă, ŭm, *astonishing.* Mĕtrō stŭpēndĕ psāltēs, Sid.

stŭpĕo, *and* ēsco, ĭs, *to be stupefied.* Tĕrræ stŭpĕănt lūcēscĕrĕ, Virg. Syn. Ōb- stŭpēsco. V. Obstupeo.

stŭpĕŭs, ă, ŭm, *of tow.* Stŭpĕă flāmmă, Virg.

stŭpĭdŭs, ă, ŭm, *astonished, stupid.* Jām cērtē stŭpĭdŏ, Mart. Syn. Stŭpĕ- fāctŭs, stŏlĭdŭs, hĕbĕs, tārdŭs, bārdŭs, sōcŏrs ; īgnārŭs, īndōctŭs. V. Hebes, indoctus.

stŭpŏr, ōrĭs, m., *dulness, astonishment.* Ŏcŭlōs stŭpŏr ūrgĕt, Virg. Syn.
Stŭpĭdĭtās, tōrpŏr, hĕbĕtūdo; īngēns ādmīrātĭo; tērrŏr, păvŏr, fōrmīdo, mĕtŭs.
stupro, ās, *to ravish.* Īntĕgrām stŭprăvĕrĭt, (Iamb.) Sen. Syn. Cōnstupro,
vĭōlo, cōrrūmpo, vĭtĭo.
stuprŭm, ī, n., *a rape.* Cāstă dŏmŭs stŭprīs, (Chor.) Hor. Syn. Adŭltĕrĭŭm.
Epith. Tŭrpĕ, ŏbscœnŭm, īnfāmĕ, nĕfāndŭm, scĕlĕrātŭm, ēxecrāndŭm, ārcānŭm, lāscīvŭm.
stūrnŭs, ī, m., *a starling.* Nūnc stūrnōs ĭnŏpēs, Mart.
Stȳgĭŭs, ă, ŭm, *of the Styx.* Dētŭr ĭtĕr, Stȳgĭās, Ov. Syn. Tārtărĕŭs, īnfērnŭs,
Āvērnālĭs. V. Styx.
stȳlŭs, ī, m., *a pencil, style.* Sæpĕ stȳlŭm vērtās, Hor. Syn. Grăphĭŭm; ăcū-
mĕn; pēnnă, călămŭs, ărūndo; dīcēndī fōrmă, mŏdŭs, rătĭo.
Stȳmphălĭdĕs, ŭm, f. pl., *birds of the Stymphalian lake, killed by Hercules.* Stȳm-
phālĭdăs ūndīs, Mart.
Stȳmphālĭŭs, ă, ŭm, *and* ālĭs, ĭdĭs, f., *Stymphalian.* Stȳmphālĭă mōnstră, Catul.
Stȳmphālĭdĕs ūndæ, Ov.
Stȳmphālŭm, ī, n., *and* ălă, ōrŭm, n. pl., *a lake in Arcadia.* Ærĭsŏnŭm Stȳm-
phālŏn, Stat. Vōlŭcrēs Stȳmphălă cōlēntēs, Lucr.
Stȳphĕlŭs, ī, m., *one of the Centaurs.* Ov.
Stȳrāx *or* Stŏrāx, ăcĭs, m., *a tree growing in Syria; a fragrant gum that exudes*
from it. Nōn Stȳrăce Idæō, Virg.
Stȳx, Stȳgĭs, f., *a river of Hell.* Cūm Stȳgĕ vīnă bĭbās, Ov. Epith. Tārtărĕă, īnfērnă, ātră, nigră, ĭnērs, tōrpēns, pigră, lēntă, stāgnāns, trīstĭs, hōrrīdă,
hōrrēns, hōrrēndă, pāllĭdă, pāllēns, prŏfūndă, īmă, ĭnămābĭlĭs, īnnăbĭlĭs, īrrĕ-
mēăbĭlĭs. V. Acheron, Phlegethon, Lethe, Cocytus, Infernus.
Suādă, *and* dēlă, æ, f., *the goddess of persuasion.* Pŏpŭlī Suādæquĕ mĕdŭllă,
Enni~~us~~. Dĕcŏrāt Suādēlă, Vēnŭsquĕ, Hor. Syn. Pīthō. Epith. Dŏctă,
pŏtēns, făcūndă, dĭsērtă, flēxănĭmă, dŏctĭlŏquă, mēllītă, mēllĭflŭă, nēctărĕă,
suāvĭs, dŭlcĭs.
suādĕo, *or* suādĕo, (*trisyl.*) suāsī, suāsŭm, *to persuade.* Suādĕt ĕnĭm, Virg.
Vēstēm mūtārĕ suāsĭt, Anthol. Syn. Pērsuādĕo, hōrtŏr; īndūco, īnvīto, īncĭto,
īmpēllo, aūctŏr sŭm. V. Hortor.
suādŭs, ă, ŭm, *advising or persuading.* Suādŭmquĕ crŭōrēm, Stat.
suāptĕ, *of his, her, or its own accord.* Ipsĕ suāptĕ, Lucr.
suāsŏr, ōrĭs, m., *an adviser.* Suāsōrem Āntēnŏră pācĭs, Ov. Syn. Aūctŏr, hōrtātŏr, īmpūlsŏr, suādēndī ārtĭfēx.
suāvĕ, adv., *sweetly.* Suāvĕ rŭbēns, Virg.
suāveŏlēns, ēntĭs, *sweet-smelling.* Suāveŏlēntĭs ămărăcī, Catul. V. Odorus.
suāvĭdĭcŭs, ă, ŭm, suāvĭlŏquēns, ntĭs. *or* quŭs, ă, ŭm, *speaking sweetly.* Suāvĭdĭcīs
pŏtĭŭs, Lucr. Tĭbĭ suāvĭlŏquēntĕ, Id. Suāvĭlŏquī vērsūs, Id.
suāvĭŏr, ārĭs, *to kiss.* Ŏcŭlōsquĕ suāvĭābŏr, (Phal.) Cat. V. Osculor.
suāvĭs *or* suāvĭs, (*dissyl.*) *sweet, agreeable.* Īntēxēns suāvĭbŭs hērbīs, Virg.
Pēr pōmă suāvĭs ĭn ūmbrā, Fort. Syn. Grātŭs, dŭlcĭs, jūcūndŭs, āccēptŭs,
blāndŭs, lætŭs; bĕnīgnŭs, cōmĭs, ūrbānŭs.
suāvĭtĕr, adv., *sweetly.* Suāvĭtĕr āttĭngŭnt, Lucr.
suāvĭŭm *and* ĭŏlŭm, ī, n., *a kiss.* Suāvĭă cōnjūnxĭt, Cat. Syn. Ōscŭlŭm. V.
Osculum.
sŭb, prep., *under.* Ārmă sŭb ādvērsă, Virg. Syn. Sŭbtĕr; jūxtă, cīrcā.
sŭbāctŭs, ă, ŭm, *the pass. partic. of* subigo. Hȳbērnă sŭbāctĭs, Virg.
sŭbærātŭs, ă, ŭm, *of brass in the inside.* Nĕ quă sŭbærātō, Pers.
sŭbcăvŭs, ă, ŭm, *hollow within.* Sŭbcăvă mōntĭs, Lucr.
sŭbdĭto, ās, *the frequent. of* subdo. Sŭbdĭtăt hūnc stĭmŭlŭm, Lucr.
sŭbdĭtŭs, ă, ŭm, *the pass. partic. of* subdo. Sūbdĭtă flāmmă, Virg.
sŭbdo, dĭdĭ, dĭtŭm, *to put under, to supply.* Sŭbdĭdĕrātquĕ rŏtās, Virg. Syn.
Sŭbjĭcĭo, sŭppōno; sŭbjūngo; sŭbstĭtŭo, sūffĭcĭo.
sŭbdŏlŭs, ă, ŭm, *cunning.* Sŭbdŏlă līnguă, Ov. Syn. Dŏlōsŭs, āstūtŭs, cāllĭdŭs,
fāllāx. V. Fallax.
sŭbdūco, xī, ctŭm, *to withdraw.* Līcĕāt sŭbdūcĕrĕ clāssēm, Virg. Syn. Sŭb
trăho, aūfĕro, tōllo, rĕmŏvĕo.
sŭbĕdo, ĭs, *to eat under.* Rāncă sŭbēdĕrāt ūndă, Ov.
sŭbĕo, sŭbīvī *or* sŭbĭī, *to go under.* Prōgrēssī sŭbĕūnt, Virg. Syn. Ingrĕdĭŏr,

pĕnetro, ĭntro, pĕrvādo, pĕrmĕo ; ŏbĕo, āggrĕdĭŏr, sŭscĭpĭo ; sūstĭnĕo, fĕro, tŏlĕro, pătĭŏr.

sŭbĕr, ĕrĭs, n., *cork.* Sŭbĕrĕ cōrtĕx, Virg. EPITH. Sўlvēstrĕ ; lĕvĕ ; mūltĭfŏrŭm.

sŭbērĭgo, ĭs, ēxī, *to rouse.* Sŭblīmĕ sŭbērĭgĭt ūndā, Sil.

sŭbērro, ās, *to wander.* Quīcūnquĕ sŭbērrānt, Cl.

sŭbĭcĭo, ĭs, *the same as* sŭbjĭcĭo. Ipsĕ mănū sŭbĭcīt glădĭŏs, Lucr.

sŭbjăcĕo, ēs, *to lie under.* Sŭbjăcŭīt quăm, Prud. SYN. Sŭbjĭcĭŏr, sŭbstērnŏr.

sŭbjēcto, ās, *to throw up.* Sāxă sŭbjēctārĕ, Lucr.

sŭbīgo, ēgī, āctŭm, *to subdue.* Ārvīnā pīnguī sŭbĭgŭnt, Virg. SYN. Sŭbjĭcĭo, sŭbjŭgo, dŏmo ; cōgo, ădĭgo ; tĕro, āttĕro, cōntĕro, ēxtĕnŭo, mĭnŭo ; mōllĭo, ēmōllĭo.

sŭbjĭcĭo, jēcī, jēctŭm, *to put under, to rear.* Sŭbjĭcĭt ālnŭs, Virg. SYN. Sŭbstērno, sŭbmītto, sŭbdo, sŭppōno, sŭbjŭngo, sŭbĭgo ; sŭrrĭgo, ērĭgo.

sŭbīndĕ, adv., *afterwards, often.* Gaūdērĕ, sŭbīndĕ, Hor. SYN. Dĕīndĕ ; saepĭŭs.

sŭbĭtō, adv., *suddenly.* In pārvæ sŭbĭtō, Virg. SYN. Stătĭm, rĕpēntĕ, prōtĭnŭs, cōnfēstĭm, ēxtēmplō. V. Statim.

sŭbĭtŭs, ă, ŭm, *sudden.* Ænēās sŭbĭtĭs, Virg. SYN. Rĕpēntīnŭs, īmprōvīsŭs, ĭnŏpīnŭs, cĕlĕr, vēlōx, fēstīnŭs, cĭtŭs.

sŭbjŭgo, ās, *to subdue.* Sŭbjŭgăt hōstēs, Claud. SYN. Vīnco, dēvīnco, dēbēllo, dŏmo, sŭbĭgo, sŭpĕro. V. Debello.

sŭbjūngo, ĭs, *to put under the yoke ; to submit.* Cūrrū sŭbjūngĕrĕ tīgrēs, Virg.

sŭblābŏr, ĕrĭs, psŭs, *to recede silently ; to steal into.* Ūdō sŭblāpsā vĕnēnō, Virg.

sŭblātŭs, ă, ŭm, *the pass. partic. of* sŭffĕro. Ēt sŭblātŭs ăd, Virg.

sŭblēgo, ĭs, lēgī, ctŭm, *to steal, to pick up softly.* Vēl quæ sŭblēgī, Ⅴirg. V. Rapio.

sŭblēvo, ās, *to help, to raise up.* Sŭblēvăt ĭpsŭm, Virg. SYN. Lĕvo, āllĕvo, jŭvo, ădjŭvo ; sŭrrĭgo, ērĭgo ; mĭnŭo, ĭmmĭnŭo.

sŭblĭgăr, ārĭs, n., *trowsers.* Sŭblĭgăr Accī, Juv. SYN. Sŭblĭgăcŭlŭm.

sŭblĭgo, ās, *to tie under.* Sŭblĭgăt ēnsĕm, Virg.

sŭblīmĕ, *or* ĭtĕr, adv., *on high.* Cāntāntēs sŭblīmĕ fĕrēnt, Virg.

sŭblīmĭs, ĕ, *and* mŭs, ă, ŭm, *sublime, lofty.* Sŭblīmēs ĭn ĕquĭs, Virg. Sŭblīmăque cœlī, Lucr. SYN. Āltŭs, ēxcēlsŭs ; ērēctŭs, īngēns, prōcĕrŭs. V. Altus.

sŭblūcĕo, ūs, xī, *to shine faintly.* Quālĭă sŭblūcēnt, Ov.

sŭblŭo, ĭs, ŭī, *to bathe under.* Cæs.

sŭblūstrĭs, ĕ, *glimmering.* Eūrўălŭm sŭblūstrī, Virg.

sŭbmērgo, mērsī, sŭm, *to plunge under water.* Căvă sŭbmērgĕrĕ mēmbră, Ov. SYN. Mērgo, ĭnmērgo, dēmērgo. V. Mergo.

sŭbmĭssŭs, ă, ŭm, *low, humble, submissive.* Ăc sŭbmīssā prĕcătŭr, Virg.

sŭbmītto, īsī, īssŭm, *to put under.* Ănĭmōs sŭbmīttĕre ămōrī, Virg. SYN. Sŭbjĭcĭo, sŭbdo ; ăbjĭcĭo, dēprĭmo ; sŭbjŭgo, dŏmo, sŭpĕro.

sŭbmōtŭs, ă, ŭm, *the pass. partic. of* submoveo. Vāstō sŭbmōtă rĕcēssŭ, Virg.

sŭbmŏvĕo, mŏvī, mōtŭm, *to remove.* Sŭbmŏvĕt ŏcĕănō, Virg. SYN. Rĕmŏvĕo ; dēpēllo.

sŭbnāscŏr, ĕrĭs, nātŭs, *to spring up, or grow under.* Nŭm vădă sŭbnātĭs, Ov.

sŭbnăto, ās, *to swim under.* Sŭbnătăt ūndā, Sil.

sŭbnēcto, ĭs, xŭī, *to fasten.* Sŭbnēctīt fībŭlă gēmmā, Virg.

sŭbnītŏr, ĕrĭs, *to lean upon.* Sŭbnīxă rĕsēdĭt, Virg.

sŭbnŏto, ās, *to observe tacitly.* Dĭgĭtŏquĕ sŭbnŏtāssĕt, (Phal.) Mart.

sŭbnūbĭlŭs, ă, ŭm, *rather obscure.* Sŭbnūbĭlŭs ūmbră, Ov.

sŭbŏlĕo, ēs, *to smell a little.* Sīvĕ vĭrŭm sŭbŏlēs, Lucr.

sŭbŏrĭŏr, ĭrĭs, *to rise up.* Īnfīnītō sŭbŏrītŭr, Lucr.

sŭbōrno, ās, *to instruct privily, to suborn.* Sŭbōrnăt, căpĭtŭr īllĕ, (Iamb.) SYN. Īnstrŭo, păro ; ōrno ; cōrrŭmpo, sōllĭcĭto.

sŭbōrtŭs, ŭs, m., *birth, the rising of the stars.* Lūcēm jāctārĕ sŭbōrtū, Lucr.

sŭbrēmĭgo, ās, *to row.* Tăcĭtĭs sŭbrēmĭgăt ūndĭs, Virg.

sŭbrēpo, rēpsī, *to creep upon by degrees.* Sŭbrēpĭt ŏcĕllĭs, Ov. SYN. Īrrēpo, īllābŏr, me īnsĭnŭo.

sŭbrīdĕo, sī, *to smile*. Ad quēm sŭbrīdēns, Virg. Syn. Arrīdĕo. V. Rideo.

sŭbrīgo, ĭs, ēxī, *to lift*. Sŭbrīgĭt aŭrēs, Virg.

sŭbrīpĭo, ŭī, rēptŭm, *to take away*. Sŭbrīpĭēndă pătrĭs, Ov. Syn. Fūrŏr, răpĭo.

sŭbrŭbĕo, ēs, *to be rather red*. Sŭbrŭbĕt ūvă, Ov.

sŭbrŭo, ĭs, *to cast down*. Sŭbrŭĕt ārcēs, Prop.

sŭbrŭtŭs, ă, ŭm, *the pass. partic. of* subruo. Sŭbrŭtă fāllācī, Stat.

sŭbscrībo, ĭs, psī, *to subscribe, to favour*. Sŭbscrībĭtĕ Cæsărĭs īræ, Ov. Syn. Sŭbsīgno; ānnŭo, cōncēdo; āssēntĭŏr, prŏbo, cōmprŏbo, āpprŏbo.

sŭbsĕco, ās, *to cut under*. Sŭbsĕcăt ūnguĕ, Ov.

sŭbsēllĭŭm, ĭī, n., *a bench*. Pĕr sŭbsēllĭă lævĭs, Pers.

sŭbsĕquŏr, ĕrĭs, *to follow*. Sŭbsĕquŏr, īllĕ, Mart. Syn. Insĕquŏr, cōnsĕquŏr, sĕquŏr. V. Sequor.

sŭbsīdĕo, ēs, sēdī, *to rest upon*. Imă sŭbsēdĭt Acēstēs, Virg.

sŭbsīdĭŭm, ĭī, n., *help*. Sŭbsīdĭīs aūctī, Juv. Syn. Aūxĭlĭŭm, lĕvāmĕn, jŭvāmĕn, sŭppĕtĭæ, præsĭdĭŭm. V. Auxilium.

sŭbsīdo, sēdī, *to sink down*. Sŭbsīdūnt ūndæ, Virg. Syn. Rĕsīdo, mē sŭbdūco, dētŭmēsco.

sŭbsĭlĭo, ŭī, *and* ūlto, ās, *to start up*. Sŭbsĭlĭūnt īgnēs, Lucr. Syn. Exĭlĭo, ĕrĭgŏr, āttōllŏr.

sŭbsīsto, stĭtī, *to stay*. Sŭbstĭtĭt ūndă, Virg. Syn. Sŭbsto, rĕsīsto. V. Moror.

sŭbstērno, strāvī, *to strew under, stretch under*. Fŭlvā sŭbstrāvĭt, Ov.

sŭbstĭtŭo, ĭs, *to set before, substitute*. Sŭbstĭtŭīssĕ mĕīs, Ov.

sŭbstrāmĕn, ĭnĭs, n., *something strewed under, litter*. Sŭbstrāmĭnă plaūstrīs, Sil.

sŭbstrātŭs, ă, ŭm, *the pass. partic. of* substerno. Lăcŭs sŭbstrātŭs Ăvērnō, Lucr. Syn. Sŭppŏsĭtŭs.

sŭbstrīngo, ĭs, xī, *to bind up*. Sŭbstrīngĕrĕ cārbăsă, Mart.

sŭbstrŭo, ĭs, *to lay the foundations, build*. Sŭbstrŭctă crĕpīdĭnĕ fŭmānt, Aus.

sŭbsŭm, sŭbĕs, ēssĕ, *to be under*. Nātūră sŭbēst, Virg.

sŭbsŭo, ĭs, *to sew under*. Sŭbsūtă tālōs tĕgăt, Hor.

sŭbtēmĕn, ĭnĭs, n., *the woof*. Rădĭīs sŭbtēmĕn ăcūtīs, Ov.

sŭbtĕr, prep., *under*. Ēgīssĕ vĭās sŭbtĕr mărĕ, Virg.—adv., *underneath*. Tŏt vĭgĭlēs ŏcŭlī sŭbtĕr, Id.

sŭbtĕrfŭgĭo, fŭgī, *to escape, avoid*. Nē sŭbtĕrfŭgĭās, (Phal.) Syn. Vīto, ēvīto, dēvīto, dēclīno, dētrēcto, fŭgĭo, ēffŭgĭo.

sŭbtĕrlābŏr, ĕrĭs, psŭs, *to-flow under*. Sŭbtĕrlābĕrĕ Sĭcānōs, Virg.

sŭbtĕrmĕo, ās, *to flow under*. Pōntēs sŭbtĕrmĕăt æstū, Cl. V. Subeo.

sŭbtĕrrānĕŭs, ă, ŭm, *under-ground*. Sŭbtĕrrānĕă rēgnă, Juv. Syn. Infērnŭs.

sŭbtĕrtĕnŭo, ās, *to wear thin below*. Sŭbtĕrtĕnŭătŭr hăbēndo, Lucr.

sŭbtĕrvŏlo, ās, *to fly under*. Sŭbtĕrvŏlăt āstră, Stat.

sŭbtĕxo, ĭs, ŭī, *to weave, to cover*. Cœlŭm sŭbtēxĕrĕ fŭmō, Virg.

sŭbtīlĭs, ĕ, *thin; artful, ingenious*. Nōbīs sŭbtīlīs ĭmāgo, Lucr. Syn. Tĕnŭĭs; pērspĭcāx, săgāx, sōlērs, īngĕnĭōsŭs, īndūstrĭŭs, ăcūtŭs, gnārŭs, caūtŭs, cāllĭdŭs, prūdēns. V. Ingeniosus, prudens.

sŭbtīlĭtĕr, adv., *nicely, artfully*. Lucr.

sŭbtrăho, trāxī, trāctŭm, *to subtract, withdraw*. Sŭbtrăhĕ nōstrō, Virg. Syn. Sŭbdūco, sŭbrĭpĭo, sŭffŭrŏr, aūfĕro, răpĭo, ērĭpĭo.

sŭbtūndo, ĭs, ŭdī, *to strike lightly*. Tĕnĕrās sŭbtūsă gĕnās, Tib.

sŭbtŭs, adv., *under, underneath*. Sŭbtūs frīgēscĭt, Lucr. Syn. Sŭb, sŭbtĕr.

sŭbūcŭlă, æ, f., *a shirt, a shift*. Fŏrtĕ sŭbūcŭlă pēxæ, Hor.

sŭbvĕho, ĭs, xī *and* vēcto, ās, *to carry up*. Sŭbvēctăt cōrpŏră, Virg.

sŭbvĕnĭo, vēnī, *to succour*. Sŭbvĕnĭūnt ŏcŭlīs, Seren. Syn. Sŭccŭrro, aūxĭlĭŏ sŭbĕo, aūxĭlĭŏr.

sŭbvērto, tī, sŭm, *to overturn, to upset*. Ŏpĕrŭm sŭbvērtĕrĕ mōlēs, Ov. Syn. Dēstrŭo, ēvērto, tōllo, dēlĕo, sŭbvērto. V. Everto.

sŭbŭlă, æ, f., *a bodkin*. Sŭbŭlă, sīcă, Mart.

sŭbūlcŭs, ī, m., *a swineherd*. Vĕnĕrĕ sŭbŭlcī, Virg. Epith. Sōrdĭdŭs, mĭsĕr, ĕgēnŭs, lăcĕr, fœtĭdŭs, tārdŭs.

sŭbvŏlo, ās, *to fly up from under*. Ex ōrdĭnĕ mājŏr Sŭbvŏlăt, Ov. V. Volo.

sŭbvōlvo, ĭs, *to roll up*. Sŭbvōlvĕrĕ sāxă, Virg.

s 5

sŭbŭrbānŭs, ă, ŭm, *of the suburbs.* Rūră sŭbŭrbāna, Hor.

sŭbŭrgĕo, ēs, *to thrust forward.* Săxă sŭbŭrgĕt, Virg.

Sŭbūrră, *or* ūră, æ, f., *a district of Rome.* Vĕxĭllŭm pŏnŏ Sŭbūrră, Juv.

Sŭbūrrānŭs, ă, ŭm, *of the Suburra.* Ergŏ Sŭbūrrānæ, Mart.

sŭccēdo, cēssī, *to go under, to succeed.* Nōstrīs sŭccēdĕ pĕnātĭbŭs, Virg. Syn. Sŭbĕo; sŭbstĭtŭŏr, ăltĕrīŭs īn lŏcŭm sŭbmĭttŏr, ăltĕrīŭs lŏcum ŏccŭpo; ăccīdo, ēvēnīo, cōntĭngo, cădo.

sŭccēndo, īs, *to set on fire.* Sŭccēnsŭs ămōrĕ, Ov.

sŭccēnsĕo, ēs, *to be angry.* Sŭccēnsēt quŏd ădhŭc, Ov. V. Irascor.

sŭccēssŏr, ōrīs, m., *a successor.* Lŏquĕrīs sŭccēssŏr, Mart.

sŭccēssŭs, ūs, m., *issue, success.* Sŭccēssŭque ācrīŏr īpsŏ, Virg. Syn. Ēvēntŭs, ēxĭtŭs, cāsŭs; ēvēntă, ōrŭm. Epith. Fēlīx, prŏspĕr, faūstŭs, ōptātŭs, spērātŭs, ēxpēctātŭs, īnfēlīx.

sŭccīdo, īs, (*from* cădo,) *to fall down.* Sŭccīdīmŭs, nōn, Virg. Syn. Cădo, sŭccŭmbo.

sŭccīdo, īs, (*from* cædo,) *to cut down.* Mĕdīŏ sŭccīdĭtŭr æstū, Virg. V. Cædo.

sŭccīdŭs, ă, ŭm, *juicy.* Sŭccĭdă nōlĭt, Juv.

sŭccīdŭŭs, ă, ŭm, *tottering, bent.* Sŭccīdŭŏ dīcŏr, Ov. Syn. Lăbāns, tĭtŭbāns, cădēns.

sŭccīngo, īs, xī, *to gird.* Sŭccīngĭtŭr ālvŭm, Ov.

sŭccīno, īs. *to sing or speak after.* Sŭccĭnīs āmbāgēs, Pers.

sŭccĭnŭm, ī, n., *amber.* Sŭccĭnă trītăs, Juv. Syn. Ēlēctrŭm. Epith. Pīnguĕ, flăvŭm, pāllēns, pāllĭdŭm. V. Electrum.

sŭccĭnŭs, ă, ŭm, *of amber.* Sŭccĭnă gŭttă, Mart.

sŭccīsŭs, ă, ŭm, *the pass. partic.* of succido. Flōs sŭccīsŭs ărātrŏ, Virg.

sŭccrēsco, ēvī, *to grow up.* Vĭdēnt sŭccrēscĕrĕ vīnă, Ov.

sŭccŭbă, æ, m. f., *an adulterer, or adulteress.* Sŭccŭbă nōstrī, Ov.

sŭccŭmbo, cŭbŭī, *to fall down.* Sŭccŭbŭīssĕ sĭbi, Tib. Syn. Sŭccīdo, prŏcīdo, cădo, rŭo, ŏpprĭmŏr, ŏbrŭŏr. V. Ruo.

sŭccŭrro, rrī, *to help, succour.* Rēgīs sŭccŭrrĕrĕ tēctīs, Virg. Syn. Sŭbvĕnīo, sŭblĕvo, aŭxĭlĭŏr. V. Auxilior.

sŭccŭs, ī, m., *juice.* Sŭccŭs īn hērbās, Virg. Syn. Hūmŏr, liquŏr. Epith. Pīnguĭs, vălĭdŭs, sūdāns, dūlcĭs, liquĭdŭs.

sŭccŭtĭo, ŭssī, ŭssŭm, *to shake.* Sŭccŭtĭt ōrbēs, Lucr. Syn. Cōncŭtĭo, quătĭo, quăsso.

Sŭcro, ōnĭs, m., *the name of a warrior.* Rŭtŭlŭm Sŭcrōnĕm, Virg.

sūdābŭndŭs, ă, ŭm, *sweating.* Sŭdābŭndă rĕlīnquĭt, Ov.

sūdārĭŭm, ĭī, n., *a handkerchief or napkin.* Tōnsă sŭdārĭă bārbă, Mart.

sūdātŏr, ōrĭs, m., *trix, tricĭs,* f., *that causes perspiration.* Sŭdātrīx tŏgă, Mart.

sūdēs, īs, f., *a thick stake.* Quădrĭfĭdāsquĕ sŭdēs, Virg. Syn. Trŭncŭs, stīpēs; pālŭs, ī; vāllŭs. Epith. Ăcūtă, lōngă, tĕrēs, dūră, præŭstă, frāxĭnĕă, rōbŏrĕă.

sūdo, ās, *to perspire.* Pŭĕr, sŭdăvĭt ĕt ālsĭt, Hor. Syn. Dēsūdo, ēxsūdo.

sūdŏr, ōrĭs, m, *sweat.* Phălĕrās sūdŏrĕ rĕcēptăs, Virg. Epith. Sālsŭs, mădĭdŭs, gĕlĭdŭs, frīgĭdŭs, călĭdŭs, tĕpēns, pīnguĭs; fūmāns, stīllāns, flŭēns, æstīvŭs, sŭbĭtŭs, rĕpēntīnŭs, ănhēlŭs, ĭmmūndŭs, ĭllōtŭs, lārgŭs. V. Sudo.

sūdŭm, ī, n., *fine weather.* Pĕr sūdŭm rŭtĭlārĕ, Virg. Syn. Sĕrēnŭm. V. Serenus.

sūdŭs, ă, ŭm, *serene.* Ŭbĭ vēr nāctæ sūdŭm, Virg. Syn. Sĕrēnŭs.

suēsco, suēvī, suētŭm, *to grow accustomed.* Cīngĕrĕ suēvērăt ērrŏr, Prud. V. Soleo, assuesco.

Suētōnĭŭs, ĭī, m., *a Roman historian.* Suētōnĭŭs ōlĭm, Aus.

suētŭs, ă, ŭm, *the pass. partic.* of suesco. Părŭt suētŭs cīvīlĭbŭs ārmīs, Lucan.

sŭffĕro, ērs, *to sustain.* Cūstŏdēs sŭffērrĕ vălēnt, Virg.

sŭffĭcĭo, fēcī, *to suffice, to supply.* Sŭffĭcĭēt Bācchŏ, Virg. Syn. Sătĭs ēst, săt ēst, ăbŭnde ēst; sŭbstĭtŭo, sŭpplĕo, sŭppĕdĭto, præbĕo, mĭnīstro.

sŭffīgo, īs, xī, *to fasten.* In crŭcĕ sŭffīgăt, Hor.

sŭffīmĕn, ĭnīs, n., *perfume.* Vīrgĭnĕă sŭffīmĕn ăb ārā, Ov. Syn. Sŭffīmēntŭm, sŭffītŭs.

sŭffīo, īs, ītŭm, *to perfume.* Tērrās sŭffīrĕ fĕrācēs, Lucr. Syn. Fūmĭgo, ĭnŏdōro V. Odoro.

* sŭffītŭs, ūs, m., *perfume.* Plin. Syn. Sŭffīmĕn, sŭffīmĕntŭm, ŏdŏrāmĕn, ŏdŏrāmĕntŭm, ŏdŏrēs ; fūsŭs, ĭncēnsŭs ŏdŏr.

sŭfflāmĕn, ĭnĭs, n., *the lock of a wheel.* Mŭltō sŭfflāmĭnĕ cōnsŭl, Juv.

sŭfflo, ās, *to inflate.* Sŭfflāvĭt būccīs, Mart.

sŭffōco, ās, *to suffocate.* Sŭffōcĕnt ănĭmăm, Ov. Syn. Præfōco, ănĭmam ĭntĕrclūdo. V. Strangulo.

sŭffŏdĭo, ĭs, *to dig under.* Sŭffōssō rĕvŏlūtŭs, Virg.

sŭffrāgĭŭm, ĭī, n , *suffrage, favour.* Gĕmĭnæ sŭffrāgĭă tērræ, Stat. Syn. Jūdĭcĭŭm ; cōnsēnsŭs ; fŭvŏr.

sŭffrāgŏr, ārĭs, *to favour.* Quæquĕ sŭffrāgābĭtŭr, (Iamb.) Capell. Syn. Făvĕo ; fĕro sŭffrāgĭă.

sŭffūgĭo, ĭs, ūgī, *to steal away.* Hīnc ŭbī sŭffūgĭt, Lucr.

sŭffūgĭŭm, ĭī, n., *a refuge.* Sŭffūgĭŭm nĭmbōs, Ov.

sŭffŭlcĭo, ĭs, *to prop up.* Părĭbŭs sŭffŭltă cŏlŭmnĭs, Hor.

sŭffūndo, ūdī, ūsŭm, *to pour over.* Ōmnĭă sŭffūndēns, Lucr. Syn. Infūndo, ĭnspĕrgo, pērfūndo.

sŭffūsŭs, ă, ŭm, *the pass. partic. of* suffundo. Ŏcŭlōs sŭffūsă nĭtēntēs, Virg.

sŭggĕro, gēssī, gēstŭm, *to supply, to suggest.* Vĭrgĕă sŭggĕrĭtŭr, Virg. Syn. Sŭbjĭcĭo ; sŭppĕdĭto, sŭffĭcĭo.

sŭgo, sūxī, *to suck.* Ŭbĕră sūgŭnt, Ov. Syn. Exsūgo.

sŭī, *of himself, &c.* Pīgnŏră cără sŭī, Virg.

Sŭīllĭŭs, ĭī, m., *the name of a man.* Stŭdĭīs ēxcŭltĕ Sŭīllī, Ov.

sŭīllŭs, ă, ŭm, *of swine.* Hūmānă cārnĕ sŭīllăm, Juv.

sŭlcātŏr, ōrĭs, m., *he who makes furrows.* Sŭlcātŏr nāvĭtă pōntī, Sil.

Sŭlcĭŭs, ĭī, m., *the name of a man.* Sŭlcĭŭs ācĕr, Hor.

sŭlco, ās, *to plough.* Sŭlcārĕ tērrăm, (Iamb.) Sen. Syn. Prōscīndo.

sŭlcŭs, ī, m., *a furrow.* Dēpŏsŭĭt sŭlcĭs, Virg. Epith. Lōngŭs, rēctŭs, prŏfūndŭs, cŭrvŭs, dūctŭs, fĭssĭlĭs, dīvĭdŭŭs, Cĕrēālĭs. V. Aro.

Sŭlmo, ōnĭs, m., *a town in the kingdom of Naples.* Hōspēs Sŭlmōnĭs, Ov. Epith. Rĭgŭŭs, ăquōsŭs, ūdŭs.

sŭlphŭr, ŭrĭs, n., *brimstone.* Sŭlphŭrĕ fūmānt, Virg. Epith. Vīvŭm, ārdēns, fūmāns, ŏdōrŭm, grăvĕŏlēns (*trisyll.*), flāvŭm, pĭnguĕ.

sŭlphŭrātŭm, ī, n., *a match.* Pāllēntĭă sŭlphŭrātă, Mart.

sŭlphŭrātŭs, ă, ŭm, *impregnated with brimstone.* Nĕc sŭlphŭrātæ, (Scaz.) Mart.

sŭlphŭrĕŭs, ă, ŭm, *of brimstone.* Sŭlphŭrĕă Nār, Virg.

Sŭlpĭcĭŭs, ĭī, m., *the name of a man.—Adj.,* -ŭs, ă, ŭm, *of Sulpicius.* Sŭlpĭcĭīs āccŭbăt hŏrrēĭs, Hor.

sŭm, ĕs, fŭī, ēssĕ, *to be.* Sŭm pĭŭs Ænēās, Virg. Quīsquĭs ĕs, āmīssŭs, Id. Nōs nŭmĕrŭs sŭmŭs, Hor. Nōn fŭĭt Ænĕădŭm, Virg. Syn. Exīsto, ēxsto, vīvo ; hăbĭto, vērsŏr, mŏrŏr, dēgo, mănĕo.

sŭmĕn, ĭnĭs, n., *the pap of a sow.* Pŭtēs nōndŭm sŭmĕn, Mart.

sŭmmă, æ, f., *a sum of money, the sum or total.* Sŭmmă brĕvĭs, Hor.

Sŭmmānŭs, ī, m., *a name of Pluto.* Quīsquĭs ĭs ēst, Sŭmmānō, Ov. V. Pluto.

sŭmmātĭm, adv., *compendiously.* Lucr.

sŭmmātŭs, ūs, m., *sovereignty.* Sŭmmātŭĭn quīsquĕ pĕtēbăt, Lucr.

sŭmmœnĭānŭs, ă, ŭm, *living in the suburbs.* Sŭmmœnĭānăs cănĕt, (Scaz.) Mart.

sŭmmœnĭŭm, ĭī, n., *suburbs.* Nŭllăquĕ sŭmmœnī, Mart.

sŭmmŏpĕrĕ, adv., *extremely.* Ōmnĭă sŭmmŏpĕrĕ, Lucr.

sŭmmŭlă, æ, f., *the dimin. of* summa, *a small sum.* Sŭmmŭlă nĕ pĕrĕăt, Juv.

sŭmmŭs, ă, ŭm, *the highest.* Sŭmmă dĭēs, Virg. Syn. Māxĭmŭs ; ăltīssĭmŭs, sŭprēmŭs ; ēxtrēmŭs.

sŭmo, sŭmpsī, ptŭm, *to take.* Sŭmĕt hŏnēstī, Hor. Syn. Căpĭo, ăssūmo, āccĭpĭo ; lĕgo, ēlĭgo ; ārrŏgo, vĭndĭco, āttrĭbŭo.

sŭmptŭōsĕ, adv., *sumptuously.* Māgnă sŭmptŭōsĕ, (Phal.) Cat.

sŭmptŭōsŭs, ă, ŭm, *sumptuous.* Nōn sŭmptŭōsā, (Alcaic.) Hor. Syn. Māgnĭfĭcŭs, splēndĭdŭs, sŭpērbŭs.

sŭmptŭs, ūs, m., *expense.* Pўrămĭdŭm sŭmptŭs, Prop. Syn. Impēnsă, æ ; impēndĭŭm. Epith. Profūsŭs, māgnŭs, dīvēs, prŏdĭgŭs, ĭmmēnsŭs, ĭngēns, ĭnfīnītŭs, māgnĭfĭcŭs, sŭpērbŭs, tĕnŭĭs, pārvŭs, ēxĭgŭŭs.

Sūnĭŏn, *or* ŭm, ĭī, n., *a promontory of Attica.* Sūnĭŏn ēxpŏsĭtŭm, Ov.

sŭo, ĭs, ŭī, *to sew.* Sŭtă căvātĭs, Virg. Syn. Assŭo.

sŭpĕllēx, ēctĭlĭs, f., *furniture*. Spĕcĭōsă sŭpĕllēx, Mart. Epith. Prĕtĭōsă, splēn-dĭdă, dīvĕs, ŏpŭlēntă, sŭpērbă, măgnĭfĭcă, pūlchră, vīlĭs, cūrtă, sōrdĭdă, laūtă, mūndă, ēxcūltă.

sŭpĕr, prep., *above*. Sŭpĕr æthĕră nōtŭs, Virg. Syn. Suprā, dēsŭpĕr, sŭ-pērne ; dē.

sŭpĕră, ōrŭm, n. pl., *heaven*. Sŭpĕra ārdŭă līnquēns, Virg. V. Cœlum.

sŭpĕrābĭlĭs, ĕ, *that may be overcome*. Sŭpĕrābĭlĭs ūllī, Ov. Syn. Sŭpĕrāndŭs.

sŭpĕrāddĭtŭs, ă, ŭm, *the pass. partic. of* superaddo. Sŭpĕrāddĭtă vītĭs, Virg.

sŭpĕrāddo, ĭs, dĭdī, *to add to*. Tŭmŭlō sŭpĕrāddĭtĕ cārmĕn, Virg. V. Addo.

sŭpĕrādsto, ās, *to stand above*. Sŭpĕrādstĭtĭt ārcĕ, Virg.

sŭpĕrātŏr, ōrĭs, m., *a conqueror*. Pērseŭs sŭpĕrātŏr, Ov.

sŭpērbĭă, æ, f., *pride*. Sĕquĭtŭrquĕ sŭpērbĭă fōrmăm, Ov. Syn. Fāstŭs, āmbĭtĭo. Epith. Ēlātă, tŭmĭdă, tŭmēns, tūrgĭdă, vēntōsă, vānă, ĭnānĭs, trŭcŭlēntă, prŏ-tērvă, ĭnīquă, mălīgnă, grăvĭs, īmpĕrĭōsă, vĭŏlēntă, īnsānă, vēsānă, stŏlĭdă, dē-mēns, īnvīsă, dāmnōsă, ārrŏgāns, īmpŭdēns, tĕmĕrārĭă, aŭdāx. V. Ambitio, superbio.

sŭpērbĭo, ĭs, *to be proud*. Tŭmĕfāctă sŭpērbĭăt Ūmbrĭă, Prop. Syn. Insŏlēsco, glōrĭŏr.

sŭpērbŭs, ă, ŭm, *proud*. Ēgĕrĕ sŭpērbō, Virg. Syn. Ārrŏgāns, īmpĕrĭōsŭs, ām-bĭtĭōsŭs. V. Superbia, ambitiosus.

sŭpērcĭlĭŭm, ĭī, n., *the eye-brow, pride*. Hīrsūtūmquĕ sŭpērcĭlĭŭm, Virg. Epith. Hīrsūtŭm, trīstĕ, sĕvērŭm, grăvĕ, sŭpērbŭm, cōntrāctŭm, mĭnāx, ēlātŭm, tērrĭ-bĭlĕ, ārdŭŭm, trŭx.

sŭpĕrēdĭtŭs, ă, ŭm, *exalted*. Ējūs sŭpĕrēdĭtă vīdĭt, Lucr.

sŭpĕrēmĭnĕo, ēs, *to be above, to surpass*. Dĕās sŭpĕrēmĭnĕt ōmnēs, Virg. Syn. Sŭpērēmĭco, ēxsŭpĕro, sŭpĕro, ēmĭco, sŭm suprā ; ēxcēllo.

sŭpĕrēnăto, ās, *to swim over*. Sŭpĕrēnătăt āmnĕm, Lucan.

sŭpĕrēvŏlo, ās, *to soar above*. Sŭpĕrēvŏlăt Ālpĕm, Lucan.

sŭpērflŭo, ĭs, *to overflow, to abound*. Sŭpērbŭs ēt sŭpērflŭēns, Catul.

sŭpērflŭŭs, ă, ŭm, *overflowing, superfluous*. Vērbă sŭpērflŭă, Ov.

sŭpērfūgĭo, ĭs, *to fly over*. Ipsĕ sŭpērflŭĭt ūndās, V. Fl.

sŭpērfūlgĕo, ēs, *to shine above*. Tēmplă sŭpērfūlgēs, Stat.

sŭpērfūndo, ĭs, ūdī, *to spread over*. Nŭdă sŭpērfūsĭs, Ov.

sŭpērgrĕdĭŏr, ĕrĭs, *to walk over*. Ōră sŭpērgrēssŭs, Stat.

sŭpĕrī, ōrŭm, m. pl., *the gods*. Sī nĕquĕō sŭpĕrōs, Virg. Syn. Dū, dī, dīvī, cœlĭcŏlæ, cœlĭtēs.

sŭpĕrīmmĭnĕo, ēs, *to hang over, to threaten*. Sŭpĕrīmmĭnĕt īllĕ, Virg.

sŭpĕrīmpēndēns, ēntĭs, *overhanging*. Sўlvæ āugŭnt sŭpĕrīmpēndēntēs, Catul.

sŭpĕrīncēndo, ĭs, *to inflame moreover*. Hānc sŭpĕrīncēndĭt, V. Fl.

sŭpĕrīncūmbo, ĭs, *to lie down upon*. Quŭm sŭpĕrīncūmbēns, Ov.

sŭpĕrīngĕro, ĭs, *to pile upon*. Quæ sŭpĕrīngēsū, Stat.

sŭpĕrīnjĭcĭo, ērjăcĭo, and jĭcĭo, ēcī, *to cast over*. Sŭpĕrīnjĭcĕ frōndēs, Virg. Scŏ-pūlīsquĕ sŭpĕrjācĭt ūndăm, Virg.

sŭpĕrīnsĭdĕo, ēs, *to remain*. Sŭpĕrīnsĭdĕt ūnā, Lucr.

sŭpĕrīnstērno, ĭs, *to strew or cover over*. Quī sŭpĕrīnstrātōs, Sil.

sŭpĕrīnstrĕpo, ĭs, *to cry aloud upon*. Sŭpĕrīnstrĕpĭt ăcĕr, Sil.

sŭpĕrīnsūlto, ās, *to leap upon*. Tŭm sŭpĕrīnsūltāns, Virg.

sŭpĕrīntŏno, ās, *to thunder above*. Clўpĕŭm sŭpĕrīntŏnăt īngēns, Virg.

sŭpĕrīnvērgo, ĭs, *to pour upon*. Tŭm sŭpĕrīnvērgēns, Ov.

sŭpērne, adv., *from above*. Tēctă sŭpērnĕ tĭmēnt, Lucr. Syn. Dēsŭpĕr.

sŭpērnŭs, ă, ŭm, *coming from above*. Frōntĕ sŭpērnī, Stat. V. Superus.

sŭpĕro, ās, *to overcome*. Pālmă sŭpĕrābăt Ācēstēs, Virg. Syn. Vīnco, sŭbĭgo ; præsto, ēxcēllo ; āscēndo, cōnscēndo ; rēsto, sŭpērsŭm. V. Vinco, excello.

sŭpĕrōbrŭo, ĭs, *to overwhelm*. Ingēstĭs sŭpĕrōbrŭĭt ārmĭs, Prop.

sŭpērpŏsĭtŭs, ă, ŭm, *set upon, placed over*. Ægră sŭpērpŏsĭtă, Ov. Syn. Im-pŏsĭtŭs, āggēstŭs, āddĭtŭs.

sŭpērstĕs, stĭtĭs, *surviving*. Pārtĕ sŭpērstĕs ĕrĭs, Mart. Syn. Sālvŭs, īncŏlŭmĭs, sōspĕs ; rēlĭquŭs.

sŭpērstĭtĭo, ōnĭs, f., *superstition*. Vānă sŭpērstĭtĭo, Virg. Epith. Ănīlĭs, rīdēndă, āmēns, cæcă, īnsānă ; ĭnānĭs, stŭltă, īmprŏbă. V. Idololatria.

* sŭpērstĭtĭōsŭs, ă, ŭm, *superstitious*. Cic.

sŭpērsto, ās, *to stand upon.* Ŏssā sŭpērstābūnt vŏlŭcrēs, Ov.

sŭpērsŭm, pĕrĕs, rēst, fŭĭt, *to remain.* Ĭ'ŏpŭlīquĕ sŭpērsŭnt, Virg. Syn. Sŭm sŭpĕr, sŭpĕro, rēsto, sŭm rēlĭquŭs, sŭm sŭpērstĕs.

sŭpērvăcŭŭs, ă, ŭm, *superfluous.* Mĭttĕ sŭpērvăcŭŏs, (Dactyl. Troch.) Hor. Syn. Ĭnūtĭlĭs, ĭnānĭs, vānŭs.

sŭpērvĕnĭo, vēnī, *to come upon suddenly.* Grātā sŭpērvĕnĭŏt, Hor.

sŭpērvŏlĭto, ās, *to fly over often.* Tēctă sŭpērvŏlĭtāvĕrĭt ālīs, Virg.

sŭpērvŏlo, ās, *to fly over.* Trĕmĕbūndă sŭpērvŏlăt hāstă, Virg. Syn. Sŭpērvŏlĭto.

sŭpĕrŭs, ă, ŭm, *above, on high, of heaven.* Sŭpĕrīsquĕ Jŏvĕm dētrūdĕrĕ rēgnīs, Virg. Syn. Sŭpērnŭs; cœlēstĭs, æthĕrĕŭs.

sŭpīno, ās, *to lie on the back.* Tērgă sŭpīnăt, Hor.

sŭpīnŭs, ă, ŭm, *lying on the back.* Deĭndĕ sŭpīnŭs, Juv. Syn. Rĕsŭpīnŭs, reclīnĭs, rĕsŭpīnātŭs, prōstrātŭs, rĕcūmbēns, ĭnvērsŭs.

sŭppăr, ărĭs, *nearly equal.* Năm sŭppărĭs ævī, Aus.

sŭppărŭm, ī, n., *the smallest sail of a vessel, a mantle.* Sŭppără nūdātōs, Lucr.

sŭppĕdĭto, ās, *to give, to furnish.* Sŭppĕdĭtă mĭhi, Sil. Syn. Sŭffĭcĭo, sŭggĕro, præbĕo, mĭnīstro.

sŭppērnātŭs, ă, ŭm, *ham-strung.* Jăcēt sŭppērnātă sĕcūrī, Catul.

sŭppĕtĭæ, ārŭm, f. pl., *aid, supplies.* Sŭppĕtĭās mŏdŏ, Alcim. Syn. Sŭbsĭdĭŭm, aŭxĭlĭŭm. V. Auxilium.

sŭppĕto, ĭs, *to be sufficient, to supply.* Sŭppĕtĭt ūsŭs, Hor. Syn. Præsto sŭm, ădsŭm, sŭffĭcĭo.

sŭpplānto, ās, *to trip up ; to clip, pronounce only half.* Sŭpplāntāt vērbă pălātō, Pers.

sŭpplĕo, ēs, ēvī, *to fill up, to supply.* Sēd nĕquĕ sŭpplētĭs, Prop.

sŭpplēx, ĭcĭs, adj., *suppliant.* Sŭpplĭcĭbūs sŭpĕră, Virg. Syn. Abjēctŭs, jăcēns, prōstrātŭs, sŭbmīssŭs ; ōrāns, rŏgāns.

sŭpplĭcĭtĕr, adv., *suppliantly.* Sŭpplĭcĭtĕr vĕnĕrāns, Virg. Syn. Abjēctĕ, dēmīssĕ.

sŭpplĭcĭŭm, ĭī, n., *punishment.* Sŭpplĭcĭă haūsūrŭm, Virg. Syn. Tŏrmēntŭm, pœnă, crŭcĭātŭs. Epith. Ăcērbŭm, sŭmmŭm, sŭprēmŭm, dēbĭtŭm, jūstŭm, ĭnīquŭm, fĕrŭm, crūdēlĕ, dīrŭm, dūrŭm, sævŭm, ătrōx, ĭmmānĕ, hōrrēndŭm, ĭntŏlĕrābĭlĕ, grăvĕ, trīstĕ, āspĕrŭm, ēxquīsītŭm, īnfāmĕ, fŭnēstŭm, fĕrālĕ, lēthālĕ, ācrĕ, vĭŏlēntŭm, ĭnaūdītŭm. V. Pœna.

sŭpplĭco, ās, *to beseech.* Sŭpplĭcăt hērbă, Tib. Syn. Dēprĕcŏr, sŭpplēx āccēdo, ōro, rŏgo, prĕcŏr. V. Precor, genua flecto.

sŭppōno, pŏsŭī, pŏsĭtŭm, *to put below, to substitute.* Quīsquăm sŭppōnăt ărīstĭs, Virg. Syn. Pōno ; sŭbmītto.

sŭppŏsĭtĭtĭŭs, ă, ŭm, *substituted.* Hērmēs sŭppŏsĭtĭtĭŭs, Mart.

sŭppŏsĭtŭs, *and* ōstŭs, ă, ŭm, *the pass. partic. of* suppono. Āc vīx sŭppŏsĭtī, Virg. Trānsĕŏ sŭppŏsĭtōs, Juv. Syn. Sŭbjēctŭs, sŭbdĭtŭs.

sŭpprīmo, prēssī, prēssŭm, *to suppress.* Sŭpprĭmĕ, Mūsă, Ov. Syn. Ŏccūlto, ābdo, sūbdo, sŭbdūco ; cŏērcĕo, sēdo, plāco. V. Abdo.

† sŭppŭs, ă, ŭm, *the same as* sŭpīnŭs. Ănĭmālĭă sŭppă văgāri, Lucr.

sŭppŭto, ās, *to compute.* Sŭppŭtăt ārtĭcŭlīs, Ov.

sŭprā, prep., *above.* Cœrŭlĕŭs sŭprā căpŭt, Virg. Tērră sŭprū quæ, Lucr. Syn. Sŭpĕr ; dēsŭpĕr.

sŭprādīctŭs, ă, ŭm, *aforesaid.* Āddĕ sŭprādīctĭs, Hor.

sŭprēmo, *and* ŭm, adv., *lastly.* Ēt māgnā sŭprēmŭm, Virg.

sŭprēmŭs, ă, ŭm, *last.* Īllā sŭprēmā fŭĭt, Ov. Ĭngrātō sŭprēmă fĕrēbānt, Virg. Syn. Sŭmmŭs, ūltĭmŭs, ēxtrēmŭs.

sūră, æ, f., *the calf of the leg.* Sŭccēdĕrĕ sūrās, Ov.

sūræ, ārŭm, f. pl., *a kind of boots.* Ād sŭbsēllĭā sūræ, Juv.

sūrcŭlŭs, ī, m., *a shoot.* Sūrcŭlŭs ĭdĕm, Virg. Syn. Rāmŭlŭs, frŭtĭcēs, gērmĕn. V. Ramus.

* sūrdĭtās, ātĭs, f., *deafness.* Cic.

sūrdŭs, ă, ŭm, *deaf.* Sūrdāquĕ blāndĭtĭĭs, Ov.

sūrgo, sūrrēxī, *to rise.* Prīmō sūrgēbăt Ēŏō, Virg. Syn. Assūrgo, cōnsūrgo, ĭnsūrgo. V. Somnum excutio, lecto surgo.

Sūrrēntīnŭs, ă, ŭm, *of Surrentum.* Ēt Sūrrēntīnō.—Subst. -ŭm, ī, n., *Surrentine wine.* Sūrrēntīnă bĭbĭs, Mart.

Sūrrēntŭm, ī, n., *a town of Campania famous for its vineyards.* Et zĕphўrō Sūr-rēntŭm, Sil.

sūrr**ī**go, **ī**s, *to lift up.* Sūrr**ī**g**ī**t aūrēs, Virg. SYN. Er**ī**go, ēxtōllo, āttōllo.

sūrr**ī**p**ī**o, ŭī. ēptŭm, *to take away.* Sūrr**ī**pŭĕrĕ v**ī**rōs, Pet. Arb. SYN. Fûrŏr, răp**ī**o, ēr**ī**p**ī**o, sūbdūco.

sūrsŭm, *and* ŭs, adv., *above.* Adsp**ī**c**ī**t n**ī**h**ī**l sūrsŭm, Mart. SYN. Sŭpērne.

sūs, sŭ**ī**s, m., *a pig.* Sŭb**ī**tō sūs hŏrr**ī**dŭs, Virg. SYN. Pōrcŭs, pōrcă. EPITH. Immūndŭs, fœdŭs, tūrp**ī**s, sōrd**ī**dŭs, lŭtŭlēntŭs, cœnōsŭs, ōbscœnŭs, p**ī**ngu**ī**s, tārdŭs, īgnāvŭs, lēntŭs, grāv**ī**s, sētōsŭs, sēt**ī**gĕr, h**ī**sp**ī**dŭs. V. Porcus.

sūscēptŭm, ī, n., *an enterprise.* Sūscēptŭquĕ māgnă, Ov. SYN. Incēptŭm, cœptŭm, ōrsă.

sūsc**ī**p**ī**o, sūscēpī, pt**ī**m, *to undertake.* Sŭsc**ī**pĕ caŭsăm, Ov. SYN. Ĕxc**ī**p**ī**o, rĕ-c**ī**p**ī**o, ădmītto ; āggrĕd**ī**ŏr, ădŏr**ī**ŏr, ōrd**ī**ŏr, **ī**nc**ī**p**ī**o. V. Aggredior, incipio.

sūsc**ī**to, ās, *to rouse.* Sūsc**ī**tăt īgnēs, Virg. SYN. Ĕxc**ī**to. V. Somnus, excito.

sŭspēctŭs, ă, ŭm, *suspected.* Hōc m**ī**h**ī** sŭspēctum ēst, Mart.

sŭspēctŭs, ŭs, m., *a look upwards.* Mēntēs sŭspēctŭs hŏnōr**ī**s, Ov.

sŭspēnd**ī**ŭm, **ī**ī, n., *a hanging.* M**ī**sĕrō sŭspēnd**ī**ă cōllō, Ov.

sŭspēndo, dī, sŭm, *to hang up.* Sŭspēndĕrĕ vēstēs, Virg. SYN. Fūnĕ **ī**n āltŭm tōllo, ēr**ī**go, ĕffĕro ; străngŭlo. V. Strangulo.

sŭspēnsŭs, ă, ŭm, *the pass. partic. of* suspendo. Dŭb**ī**ō sŭspēnsă mĕtŭ, Stat.

sŭsp**ī**c**ī**o, ēxī, ēctŭm, *and* ēcto, ās, *to look upwards.* Sŭsp**ī**c**ī**t ūrb**ī**s, Virg. Ŏcŭlīs sŭspēctāns, Mart. SYN. Sūrsŭm āsp**ī**c**ī**o. V. Aspicio, admiror.

sŭsp**ī**c**ī**o, ōn**ī**s, f., *suspicion.* Sī qua ēst sŭsp**ī**c**ī**ō r**ī**mæ, Martial. SYN. Cōnjēc-tūră, ŏp**ī**n**ī**o, dŭb**ī**ŭm. EPITH. Fălsă, fāllāx, **ī**ncērtă, vĕră, cērtă, tăc**ī**tă, prūdēns.

sŭsp**ī**co, *and* ŏr, ār**ī**s, *to suspect.* Sŭsp**ī**cŏr ēssĕ, Mart. SYN. Aŭgŭrŏr, cōnj**ī**c**ī**o ŏp**ī**nŏr, ārbitrŏr.

sŭspīrātŭs, ŭs, m., *breathing.* Sŭspīrāt**ī**bŭs haŭstīs, Ov. SYN. Sŭspīr**ī**ŭm.

sŭspīr**ī**ŭm, **ī**ī, n., *a sigh.* Tōtă sŭspīr**ī**ă nōctĕ, Tib. SYN. Gĕm**ī**tŭs, sīngūltŭs, lŭctŭs, lāmēntŭm. EPITH. Ægrŭm, ānx**ī**ŭm, trīstĕ, fœdŭm, gĕmēbūndŭm, sēdŭ-lŭm, mœstŭm, strīdŭlŭm. V. Suspiro, gemitus, fletus.

sŭspīro, ās, *to sigh.* Äl**ī**ōs sŭspīrăt ămōrēs, Tib. SYN. Gĕmo. V. Gemo.

sŭstēnto, ās, *to support.* Ter. SYN. Ălo, nūtr**ī**o, pāsco. V. Nutrio.

sŭst**ī**nĕo, ēs, ŭī, *to sustain.* Sŭst**ī**nĕt ōrbēs, Virg. SYN. Fĕro, gĕro ; fūlc**ī**o, sŭs-tēnto ; tŭĕŏr, dĕfēndo, prōpūgno ; tŏlĕro, păt**ī**ŏr.

sŭstōllo, ŭlī, sŭblātŭm, *to lift up.* Sŭstŭl**ī**t ēxūtăs, Virg. SYN. Sŭblĕvo, āttōllo, ēr**ī**go.

sŭsūrro, ās, *to whisper.* Trāct**ī**mquĕ sŭsūrrānt, Virg. SYN. Mūrmŭro, strĕp**ī**to, crĕp**ī**to.

sŭsūrrŭs, ī, m., *and* ŭm, ī, n., *a murmuring.* Aŭrĕ sŭsūrrōs, Hor. SYN. Mūrmŭr, strĕp**ī**tŭs, sŏn**ī**tŭs, sŏnŭs. EPITH. Lēn**ī**s, lĕv**ī**s, mōllīs, blāndŭs, grātŭs, plăc**ī**dŭs, tĕnŭ**ī**s, sŏmn**ī**fĕr, sŏpōr**ī**fĕr, gārrŭlŭs, ārgūtŭs, quĕrŭlŭs, raŭcŭs, flŭv**ī**āl**ī**s. V. Murmur, susurro.

sŭsūrrŭs, ă, ŭm, *whispering softly.* Aŭdīrĕ sŭsūrră, Ov.

sūt**ī**l**ī**s, ĕ, *stitched.* Sūt**ī**l**ī**s āptĕtŭr, Mart. SYN. Sŭtŭs, cōnsūtŭs.

sŭtŏr, ōr**ī**s, m., *a shoemaker.* Sī dărĕ sŭtōrī, Mart.

sŭŭs, ă, ŭm, *his, her, its.* Cūr sŭŭs hæc, Ov. SYN. Propr**ī**ŭs.

Sўbăr**ī**s, **ī**s, f., *a town in Italy.*

Sўbăr**ī**t**ī**cŭs, ă, ŭm, *of Sybaris.* Sўbăr**ī**t**ī**cīs l**ī**bēllīs, Mart.

Sўbăr**ī**t**ī**s, **ī**d**ī**s, f., *a Sybaritan woman ; the title of a poem.* Nŭpēr Sўbăr**ī**t**ī**dă fŭg**ī**t, Ov.

sўdŭs, *or* sīdŭs, ĕr**ī**s, n., *a constellation.* Sўdĕră pāscĕt, Virg. SYN. Āstrŭm, stēllă. V. Astra.

Sўēnĕ, ēs, f., *a town of Egypt.* Et mūltă Sўēnĕ, Stat. EPITH. Ĕxūstă, căl**ī**dă, N**ī**l**ī**ăcă, Phăr**ī**ă, fūscă, æstīvă, s**ī**t**ī**būndă, ūstă, cōmbūstă, æst**ī**fĕră.

Sўēn**ī**tēs, æ, m., *of Syene.* Eccĕ Sўēn**ī**tēs, Ov.

Sўllă, æ, m., *a Roman general, of the family of the Scipios.* Et dōcīl**ī**s Sўllăm, Lucan. EPITH. Pŏtēns, sævŭs, trūx, crŭēntŭs, atrōx, fĕrōx, fācūndŭs, ācĕr.

sўllăbă, æ, f., *a syllable.* Sўllăbă pārtĕ, Ov.

Sўllānŭs, ă, ŭm, *of Sylla.* Sўllānŭm sōl**ī**tō, Lucan.

sўlvă, æ, f., *a forest.* Sўlvārŭmquĕ trĕmŏr, Mart. SYN. Nĕmŭs, sāltŭs, lūcŭs.

Epith. Nĕmŏrōsă, vĭrĭdĭs, vĭrēns, vĭrĭdāns, frŏndōsă, frŏndĕă, frŏndĕns, cŏmāns, ūmbrōsă, ūmbrīfĕră, ŏbscūră, ŏpācă, nigră, nigrāns, cæcă, ātră, prŏfūndă, tăcĭtă, sĭlēns, sēcrētă, ārcānă, auxĭă, dēnsă, spătĭōsă, āmplă, vāstă, incĭdŭă, dēsērtă, hŏrrēndă, sacră, āntīquă, vĕtŭs, vĕtūstă, sāxōsă, incūltă, āspĕră, frăgōsă, ămœnă, jūcūndă, ŏdōrātă, myrtĕă, laūrĕă.
Sўlvānī, ōrŭm, m. pl., gods of the woods. Căpĭtīs Sўlvānŭs hŏnōrĕ, Virg.   V. Satyrus.
sўlvēstrĭs, ĕ, rural, of the woods. Băcŭlŭs sўlvēstrĭs ŏlīvæ, Ov. Syn. Agrēstĭs, rūstĭcŭs; nĕmŏrōsŭs, sўlvōsŭs.
Sўlvĭă, æ, f., a daughter of Tyrrhenus. Sўlvĭă prīmă sŏrŏr, Virg.
sўlvĭcŏlă, æ, m. f., living in the woods. Sўlvĭcŏlæ Faūnō, Virg. Syn. Sўlvēstrĭs, sўlvās cŏlēns.
sўlvĭfrăgŭs, ă, ŭm, breaking down the forests. Sўlvĭfrăgīs vēxăt, Lucr.
Sўlvĭŭs, ī, m, the son or grandson of Æneas. Sўlvĭŭs, Albānŭm, Virg.
Sўmæthēŭs, and ĭŭs, ă, ŭm, and ĭs, ĭdĭs, f., of the Symæthus. Quăquĕ Sўmæthēās, Ov. Sўmæthĭă cīrcŭm, Virg. Nўmphāquĕ Sўmæthĭdĕ crētŭs, Ov.
Sўmæthŭm, ī, n., and ŭs, ī, m., a river of Sicily. Vădă flāvă Sўmæthī, Sil.
sўmbŏlă, æ, f.; and ŭm, ī, n., one's share in a reckoning. Sўmbŏlām dăbo, Plaut.
sўmphōnĭă, æ, f., harmony. Mēnsās sўmphōnĭă dīscōrs, Hor. Syn. Cōncēntŭs. V. Musica.
Sўmplēgăs, ădĭs, f., plēgădŭs, ŭm, f. pl., islands opposite the Thracian Bosporus. Spārsās Sўmplēgădăs ēlīsārŭm, Ov. Sўmplēgăs ĭnānĕm, Luc.
* sўncērĭtās, or sīncērĭtās, ātĭs, f., sincerity. Plin. Syn. Cāndŏr, sĭmplĭcĭtās, prŏbĭtās, īntegrĭtās. Epith. Vĕră, nūdă, ăpĕrtă, cāndĭdă, innŏcŭă, īnsōns, innŏcēns, bĕnīgnă, prūdēns.
sўncērŭs, or sīncērŭs, ă, ŭm, sincere, honest. Nēc sўncērĭŏr āltĕr, Mart. Syn. Cāndĭdŭs, sĭmplēx, ăpērtŭs. V. Synceritas.
sўnthĕsĭs, ĭs, f., a collection. Sўnthĕsĭs Săgūntī, Mart.
Sўphāx, ācĭs, m., a king of the Numidians. Sŭpĕrāt Măsĭnīssă Sўphācĕm, Ov.
Sўrācŏsĭŭs, and ŭsĭŭs, ă, ŭm, of Syracuse. Prīmă Sўrācŏsĭŏ, Virg.
Sўrācūsæ, ārŭm, f. pl., the principal city of Sicily. Utquĕ Sўrācūsās, Ov.
Sўrēn. V. Siren.
Sўrĭă, æ, f., a country in Asia. Āccēdŭnt Sўrĭæ, Luc. Epith. Āmplă, pŏtēns, dīvĕs, pīnguĭs, fæcūndă, fĕrāx, mōllĭs, bĕnīgnă.
Sўrĭăcŭs, rĭcŭs, rĭŭs, and rŭs, ă, ŭm, Syrian. Vīnă Sўră, Hor. Sўrĭŏ mūnĕrĕ, Prop.
Sўrīnx, ngĭs, f., a nymph changed into a reed. Jām Sўrīngă pŭtārĕt, Ov.
sўrmă, ătĭs, n., a long train. Sўrmătĕ nōstră, Mart. Syn. Cyclăs. Epith. Trăgĭcŭm, lōngŭm, flŭēns, măgnĭfĭcŭm, pūrpŭrĕŭm.
Sўrŏs, ī, f., one of the Cyclades. Ēt Sўrōn cēpīssĕ, Ov.
Sўrtĭcŭs, ă, ŭm, of the Syrtes. Sўrtĭcŭs ŏbstĭtĭt, Lucan.
Sўrtĭs, ĭs, f., the name of two dangerous quicksands in Africa. Sўrtĭbŭs ūsī, Virg. Epith. Naūfrăgă, ĭnhōspĭtă, æquŏrĕă, īnfĭdă, vădōsă, æstŭōsă, hŏrrēndă, mĕtŭēndă, sævă, Lĭbўcă, Gētūlă, Āfră.

T.

TĂBĂCŬM, and ăccŭm, ī, n., tobacco. Istĕ tăbāccŭm, Owen.
tăbĕfăcĭo, fēcī, făctŭm, to cause to waste away. Syn. Ēxtăbĕfăcĭo.
tăbēllă, æ, f., a picture. Vērbă tăbēllĭs, Ov. V. Tabula.
tăbĕo, ēs, and ēsco, ĭs, bŭī, to pine away, to be rotten. Tăbēscăt, nĕquĕ sē, Hor. Syn. Tăbĕo, cōntăbēsco, ēxtăbēsco, lānguēsco, lānguĕo, pĕrēdŏr, cōnfĭcĭŏr. V. Tabefacio.
tăbērnă, æ, f., a shop, an inn. Sĭlŭĭt cōmpăgŏ tăbērnæ, Juv. Syn. Caūpōnă, pŏpīnă. Epith. Fāmōsă, ŏbscūră, ăpērtă, pătēns, sōrdĭdă, ēbrĭă, lāscīvă, mădĭdă, bĭbŭlă, ārcānă, ūnctă, pīnguĭs

tābēs, Ĭs, f., *a corruption, u consumption.* Tābĕ pĕrēdĭt, Virg. Syn. Măcĭēs ; tābŭm. Epith. Pāllĭdă, lĭvĭdă, hŏrrēndă, tŭrpĭs, dēfŏrmĭs, nigră, dīră, pēstĭfĕră, crŭēntă, lūrĭdă, flŭēns, flŭĭdă.

tābĭdŭlūs, ă, ŭm, *the dimin. of* tabidus. Tābĭdŭlāmquĕ vĭdĕt, Virg.

tābĭdŭs, *and* fīcŭs, ă, ŭm, *wasting away.* Tābĭdă mēmbrĭs, Virg. Tābĭfĭcam ēxpīrăt, Sil. Syn. Măcĕr, măcĭlēntŭs. V. Macer.

tăbŭlă, æ, f., *a plank, a picture.* Exĭgŭĭs tăbŭlĭs, Juv. Epith. Sēctĭlĭs, pīctă, ōrnātă, dĕcōră, pŏlītă, mūndă, splēndĭdă, pēndŭlă, Ăpēllæă.

tăbŭlārĭă, ōrŭm, n. pl., *a registry office.* Rērŭm tăbŭlārĭă fērrō, Ov.

tăbŭlātŭm, ī, n., *a story of a building, a scaffold.* Jūnctūrās tăbŭlātă dăbănt, Virg.

tăbŭlātŭs, ă, ŭm, *of planks, boarded.* Scēnăm tăbŭlātăm, Aus.

tābŭm, ī, n., *corrupted blood.* Sānĭē tăbōquĕ, Virg. Syn. Sănĭēs, tābēs. Epith. Cŏrrūptŭm, putrĕ, fœdŭm, crāssŭm, crŭēntŭm, ātrŭm, tūrpĕ, nigrŭm, flŭĭdŭm, trīstĕ, cŏncrētŭm, lūrĭdŭm, pēstĭfĕrŭm, putrĭdŭm, stīllāns. V. Sanies.

Tăbūrnŭs, ī, m., *a mountain of Italy.* Vēstīrĕ Tăbūrnŭm, Virg. Epith. Altŭs, āĕrĭŭs, pīnguĭs, vĭrĭdĭs, māgnŭs, ēxcēlsŭs ; ŏlīvĭfĕr.

tăcēndŭs, ă, ŭm, *not to be mentioned.* Dīcēndă, tăcēndă lŏcūtŭs, Hor.

tăcĕo, ŭī, *to be silent ; not to mention.* Cōmmīssă tăcērĕ, Hor. Nūllōquĕ tăcēbĭtŭr ævō, Ov. Syn. Sĭlĕo, cōntĭcĕo, ŏbmūtēsco. V. Sileo.

Tăcĭtă, æ, f., *the goddess of silence.* Sācră făcĭt Tăcĭtæ, Ov.

tăcĭtē, adv., *silently, in silence.* Quēstŭs tăcĭtē, Luc.

tăcĭtŭm, ī, n., *a secret.* Mĕdĭĭs tăcĭtī vūlgātŏr ĭn ūndĭs, Ov. V. Arcanum.

tăcĭtūrnĭtăs, ātĭs, f., *taciturnity.* Sī tăcĭtūrnĭtăs, Hor.

tăcĭtūrnŭs, ă, ŭm, *silent.* Plăcĕt, tăcĭtūrnă sĭlēntĭă, Ov. Syn. Mūtŭs, tăcēns, sĭlēns, tăcĭtŭs ; trānquĭllŭs, plăcĭdŭs.

Tăcĭtŭs, ī, m., *a Roman historian.* Cōrnēlī Tăcĭte ēs, Sid.

tăcĭtŭs, ă, ŭm, *silent, obscure.* Mōnstrāvĭt tăcĭtăs, Mart. Syn. Tăcēns, sĭlēns, mūtŭs, tăcĭtūrnŭs ; ōbscūrŭs, lătĭtāns, ābdĭtŭs, sēcrētŭs, ārcānŭs ; ōmīssŭs, prætērmīssŭs.

tāctĭlĭs, ĕ, *palpable, capable of being touched.* Tāctĭlĕ nīl nōbĭs, Lucr.

tāctŭs, ūs, m., *the sense of touch.* Saŭcĭă tāctŭm, Ov.

tædă, æ, f., *a torch.* Ārdēntēs tædās, Virg. Syn. Fāx, lāmpăs, 'lychnŭs, fūnālĕ. Epith. Pīnguĭs, cērĕă, lŭcĭdă, pīnĕă, cērātă, fūmāns, cŏrūscă, tĕrēs. V. Fax.

tædĕt, *to be tiresome.* Mōrtcm ōrāt, tædĕt, Virg. Syn. Pĭgĕt, pērtæsum ēst.

tædĭfĕr, ă, ŭm, *bearing a torch.* Ēt pĕr tædĭfĕræ, Ov.

tædĭŭm, ĭī, n., *weariness.* Tædĭă laūdĭs, Virg. Syn. Fāstĭdĭŭm, sătĭĕtās, mœrŏr, mœstĭtĭă. Epith. Lōngŭm, ĭnērs, ĭgnāvŭm, lānguĭdŭm, lānguēns, ăcērbŭm, grāvĕ, trīstĕ, mŏlēstŭm.

Tænărĭdēs, æ, m, *of Tænarus, or Laconia.* Tōllĕrĕ Tænărĭdēs, Ov.

Tænărĭŭs, ă, ŭm, *and* rĭs, ĭdĭs, f., *of Tænarus.* Tænărĭās ĕtĭăm, Virg. Tænărĭs ūrbĕ sŏrŏr, Ov.

Tænărŭs, ī, m., *and* ă, ōrŭm, n. pl., *a town in Laconia, near the fabled entrance of hell.* Tænără gēntēs, Stat. V. Infernus.

tænĭă, æ, f., *a ribbon.* Tænĭă vīttæ, Virg. Syn. Rĕdĭmīcŭlŭm ; vīttă. Epith. Tĕnŭĭs, lōngă. V. Vittă.

Tāgēs, ĭs, m., *the son of Genius, and the first who taught the Etrurians the art of divination.* Indĭgĕnæ dīxĕrĕ Tăgēm, Ov. Epith. Thūscŭs, Etrūscŭs, Tyrrhēnŭs ; ărūspēx, sŏlērs, săgāx, prŏvĭdŭs, pĕrĭtŭs, prænūncĭŭs.

Tăgŭs, ī, m., *a river in Spain.* Quă Tăgŭs aūrĭfĕrĭs, Sil. Epith. Aūrĕŭs, aūrātŭs, aūrĭfĕr, aūrĭflŭŭs, dīvēs, prĕtĭōsŭs ; Hēspĕrĭŭs, Ibērŭs ; Tārtēssĭăcŭs ; mĭcāns, clārŭs, impĭgĕr, pūrpŭrĕŭs, aūrĭcŏlŏr, invĭdĭōsŭs, lŏcuplēs, ŏpācŭs, mĕtāllĭfĕr. V. Pactolus.

Tălăĭōnĭŭs, ă, ŭm, *of Talaus.* Tălăĭōnĭæ Ērĭphylēs, Ov.

tălārĭă, ĭŭm, n. pl., *wings at the heels.* Pĕdĭbŭs tālārĭă nēctĭt, Virg. Epith. Lĕvĭă, ālătă, aŭrĕă.

Tălāssĭo, ōnĭs ; ĭŭs, ĭī ; *and* ŭs, ī, m., *the god of espousals.* Mē jŭbĕās Tălāssĭōnĕm, (Phal.) Vērbă, Tălāssĕ, tĭbi, Mart. V. Hymen.

Tălăŭs, ĭ, m., *the father of Adrastus, Eurydice, and Eriphyle.* Cōnjŭgĕ, quám
Tălăī, Ov.

tălēntŭm, ĭ, n., *a sum of money, which varied in value in different places.* Sĭmōnĕ
tălēntŭm, Hor. Epith. Măgnŭm, īngēns. V. Aurum.

tālĭo, ōnĭs, f., *a requital.* Tāllŏ pœnās, Scr.

tālĭpĕdo, ās, *to walk staggering.* Tālĭpĕdāns prīmŭm, Lucr.

tālĭs, ĕ, *such.* Ĕt tālēs ăspĭcĕ, Juv. Syn. Hic, ĭs ; tāntŭs.

tālĭtĕr, adv., *in such a manner.* Tālĭtĕr ēxūta ēst, Mart.

tālpă, œ, m. f., *a mole.* Fōdĕrĕ cŭbīlĭă tālpæ, Virg. Epith. Cæcŭs, nĭgĕr, ătĕr,
văgŭs, ērrāns, tĭmĭdŭs, nūrītŭs.

Tālthўbĭŭs, ĭī, m., *a Grecian herald at the siege of Troy.* Tālthўbĭōquĕ cōmĕs, Ov.

tālŭs, ĭ, m., *the heel.* Căndĭdŭs, ēt tālōs, Hor.

tăm, adv., *so much, so.* Tăm fēlīx, Ov.

tămărīcĕ, ēs, *and* rīx, īcĭs, f., *a tamarind.* Ĕt tămărīx nōn lætă, Luc. Syn.
Mўrīcă.

Tămăsēŭs, ă, ŭm, *of Tamasus, a city of Cyprus.* Indĭgēnæ Tămăsēŭm, Ov.

tŭmĕn, adv., *still, however.* Hĭc tămĕn īlle, Virg. Syn. Attămĕn, vērŭm.

Tănăgĕr, grī, m., *a river of Lucania.* Sĭccī rīpă Tănăgrī, Virg.

Tănăĭs, ĭs, m., *a river between Asia and Europe.* Glăcĭēs, Tănăīmquĕ, Virg.
Epith. Gĕlĭdŭs, frīgĭdŭs, præcēps, răpĭdŭs, ālgēns, rĭgēns, glăcĭālĭs, Scўthĭcŭs.
V. Fluvius.

Tănăquĭl, indecl., *the wife of Tarquinius Priscus.* Fătōrŭm Tănăquĭl, Cl.

tāndĕm, adv., *at least.* Tāndem ĭn ĕōdĕm, Lucr. Syn. Pōstrēmō, dēnĭquĕ, dēmŭm ; pērpĕtŭō.

tāngo, tĕtĭgī, tāctŭm, *to touch.* Tămēn tĕtĭgĕrĕ Dĕōs, Ov. Syn. Ăttīngo, trācto,
ăttrācto, cōntīngo ; strīctĭm, lĕvĭtĕr ăttīngo, pērstrīngo, dēlĭbo ; mŏvĕo, cōmmŏvĕo.

tānquăm, adv., *us.* Mănănt tānquăm dē, Ov. Syn. Ŭt, quăsĭ, sĭcŭt.

Tāntălĕŭs, *and* lĭcŭs, ă, ŭm, *of Tantalus.* Tāntălĕă pŏtĕrĭt, Prop.

Tāntălĭdēs, æ, m., *the son or descendant of Tantalus.* Quĭd ?´nŭm Tāntălĭdēs, Ov.

Tāntălĭs, ĭdĭs, f., *the daughter or grand-daughter of Tantalus.* Tāntălĭdēs mātrēs,
Ov.

Tāntălŭs, ĭ, m., *the son of Jupiter, condemned in hell to an eternal thirst and hunger.*
Tāntălŭs, ŭt, Ov. Epith. Sĭtĭēns, sĭtībūndŭs, īnfēlīx, mĭsĕr, fămēlĭcŭs, bārbărŭs,
crūdēlĭs, fĕrŭs, gārrŭlŭs, prōdĭtŏr, īnfīdŭs, īmmītĭs, atrōx ; Phrўgĭŭs, Phrўx.

tāntīllŭm, adv., *ever so little.* Tāntīllŭm vēstræ, Cat.

tāntīspĕr, adv., *for a little time.* Hæc tĭbĭ tāntīspĕr, Ov.

tāntō, adv., *so much.* Tāntō, nătĕ, măgĭs, Virg.

tāntŏpĕrĕ, adv., *so much, so.* Mōbĭlĕ tāntŏpĕre ēst, Lucr.

tāntŭlŭs, *and* īllŭs, ă, ŭm, *so little.* Quī tāntŭli ēgĕt, Hor. Tāntīllō mōmĭnĕ
flūtăt, Lucr.

tāntŭm, adv., *so much, only.* Sērtă prŏcŭl tāntŭm, Virg.

tāntŭmdĕm, adv., *as much, the same.* Tāntŭmdem ēst, fĕrĭūnt, Juv.

tāntŭmmŏdŏ, adv., *only, alone.* Tāntŭmmŏdŏ vītă rēlīcta ēst, Ov.

tăpēs, ētĭs, m., ētĕ, ĭs ; ētĭŭm, ĭī, *and* ētŭm, ĭ, n., *tapestry.* Infērrĕ tăpētăs, Sil.
Pīctĭsquĕ tăpētĭs, Virg. Fōrtĕ tăpētĭbŭs āltĭs, Id. Syn. Aŭlæă, pĕristrōmătă,
străgŭlă, strătă. Epith. Pŭrpŭrĕĭ, ĕxquīsītī, pŭlchrī, prĕtĭōsī, măgnĭfĭcī, splēn-
dĭdĭ, vărĭātī, Assўrĭī, Băbўlōnĭcĭ, Bārbărĭcĭ ; Phrўgĭī ; Tўrĭī ; Attălĭcĭ ; Bēlgĭcĭ,
Flāndrĭăcĭ.

Tăprŏbănĕ, ēs, f., *an island of the Indian ocean, Ceylon.* Aŭt ŭbĭ Tăprŏbănēn, Ov.

tārdē, adv., *slowly.* Tārdĭŭs hōspēs, Hor.

tārdĕo, ēs, *and* ēsco, ĭs, *to grow slow.* Tārdēscīt līnguă, Lucr.

tārdĭpēs, ĕdĭs, *walking slowly.* Scrīptās tārdĭpĕdī, (Phal.) Cat. Syn. Tārdŭs,
lēntŭs.

tārdo, ās, *to stay, to delay.* Tārdātŭr, cārō, Virg. Syn. Mŏrŏr, rĕtārdo, rĕmŏrŏr ;
mŏram āffĕro.

tārdŭs, ă, ŭm, *slow.* Dēsĭdĭă tārdōs, Juv. Syn. Lēntŭs ; pĭgĕr, īgnāvŭs ; hĕbĕs,
stŭpĭdŭs.

Tărēntīnŭs, ă, ŭm, *of Tarentum.* Lānă Tărēntīnō, Hor.

Tărēntŭm, ĭ, n., *and* tŭs, ĭ, f., *a city of Magna Græcia.* Mōllĕ Tărēntŭm, Hor.
Cōnătă Tărēntŭs, Sil.

Tārpă, æ, m., *a Roman critic.* Jŭdĭcĕ Tārpā, Hor.

Tārpēĭā, æ, f., *a vestal who betrayed the citadel of Rome to the Sabines.* Vĭā Tārpēĭā rĕclūsā, Ov.

Tārpēĭŭs, ă, ŭm, *of the Tarpeian rock.* Tārpēĭā dē rūpĕ, Lucan. V. Capitolium.

Tārquĭnĭŭs, ĭī, m., *the name of two kings of Rome.* Tārquĭnĭŭs rēgnō, Hor. EPITH. Sŭpērbŭs, īnjūstŭs, dīrŭs, īmpĭŭs, fōrtĭs, gĕnĕrōsŭs, aŭdāx, māgnănĭmŭs.

Tārtărĕŭs, ă, ŭm, *of Tartarus.* Tārtărĕās ĕtĭăm, Virg. SYN. Infērnŭs, Tænărĭŭs. V. Infernus.

Tārtărŭs, ī, m., *and* rā, ōrŭm, n. pl., *the deepest part of hell.* Tārtărŭs hōrrĭfĕrōs, Lucr. Tārtără tēndĭt, Virg.

Tārtēssĭăcŭs, *and* ēssĭŭs, ă, ŭm, *of Tartessus.* Ēt Tārtēssĭăcā, Mart. Tārtēssĭă lĭttŏră Phœbŭs, Ov.

Tārtēssŏs, *and* ŭs, ī, m., *a city of Spain, near the pillars of Hercules.* Tūrtēssŏs stăbŭlāntī, Sil.

Tătĭēnsēs, ŭm, m. pl., *one of the centuries of Roman knights.* Tŏtĭdēm Tătĭēnsĭbŭs īllĕ, Ov.

Tătĭŭs, ĭī, m., *a king of the Sabines, who shared the supreme power with Romulus.* Tătĭŭmque āccēdĕrĕ rēgnō, Ov.

taŭrĕă, æ, f., *a leathern whip.* Taŭrĕă pūnĭt, Juv.

taŭrĕŭs, ă, ŭm, *of a bull.* Taŭrĕā tērgā, Ov.

Taŭrĭcŭs, ă, ŭm, *of the Tauri, or inhabitants of the Tauric Chersonesus.* Taŭrĭcă dīrā, Ov.

taŭrĭfĕr, ă, ŭm, *producing bulls.* Taŭrĭfĕrīs ŭbĭ, Luc.

taŭrĭfōrmĭs, ĕ, *like a bull.* Sīc taŭrĭfōrmĭs, (Alc.) Hor.

taŭrīnŭs, ă, ŭm, *of a bull.* Taŭrīnō quāntŭm, Virg. SYN. Taŭrĕŭs.

taŭrŭs, ī, m., *a bull.* Taŭrŭs ĭn ārvō, Virg. SYN. Jŭvēncŭs, bōs. EPITH. Indŏmĭtŭs, fŭrĭōsŭs, fĕrōx, ācĕr, bēllātŏr, fōrtĭs, trŭx, vălĭdŭs, tōrvŭs, fŭrĭbūndŭs, cōrnĭgĕr, fŭrēns, răpĭdŭs, tūrbĭdŭs, tŭmēns, dūrŭs, sēgnĭs, hōrrĭdŭs, fŭgāx, agrēstĭs. V. Bos.—2. *a mountain of Asia.* EPITH. Scȳthĭcŭs, frīgĭdŭs, gĕlĭdŭs, nĭvālĭs, āltŭs, āĕrĭŭs, cēlsŭs, ēxcēlsŭs, sŭblīmĭs, ārdŭŭs. V. Mons.—3. *a constellation.* Taŭrŭs ĕt aŭrātĭs. EPITH. Mĭcāns, rădĭāns.

tāxĕŭs, ă, ŭm, *of the yew-tree.* Ēn tāxĕā mārcēt Sȳlvă, Stat.

tāxŭs, ī, f., *the yew-tree.* EPITH. Nŏxĭă, fŭnēstă, lēthĭfĕră, lēthālĭs, fĕrālĭs, fŭnĕrĕā, trīstĭs, vĕnēnōsă, ămāră, ĭnĭmĭcă, bāccĭfĕră.

Tāȳgĕtĕ, ēs, f., *one of the Pleiades.* Tāȳgĕtē sĭmŭl ōs, Virg. Tāȳgĕtēnque Hȳădāsquĕ, Ov.

Tāȳgĕtŭs, ī, *and* ŭm, ī, *and* tă, ōrŭm, n. pl., *a mountain in Laconia.* Tāȳgĕtīquĕ cănēs, Virg. EPITH. Gĕlĭdŭs, ālgēns, vĭrēns, vĭrĭdĭs, ārdŭŭs, sūmmŭs.

tē, *acc. of* tu, *thee.* Tĕ vĕnĭēntĕ dĭĕ, tē, Virg.

tēchnă, æ, f., *a trick.* Tē sīnās tēchnĭs, (Iamb.) Ter.

Tecmēssă, æ, f., *the wife of Ajax.* Mœstŭs: Tēcmēssăm, Ov. Dŏmĭnŭm Tēcmēssæ, Hor.

tēctē, adv., *secretly.* Tēctĭŭs īllă, Ov.

tēctōrĭŭm, ĭī, n., *plaister, dissimulation.* Ēt tēctōrĭă prīmă, Juv.

tēctŭm, ī, n, *a roof, a house.* Tēctă vĭdēnt, Virg. EPITH. Ārdŭŭm, cēlsŭm, āltŭm, sŭblīmĕ, ēxcēlsŭm, lăquĕātŭm. V. Domus.

tēctŭs, ă, ŭm, *the pass. partic. of* tego. Cālĭgĭnĕ tēctŭs, Ov.

tēcŭm, *with thee.* Nēc tēcŭm tālĭā gēssī, Virg.

tĕgĕs, ĕtĭs, f., *a mat.* Tĕgĕtēm præfērrĕ cŭbĭlī, Juv. EPITH. Jūncĕă, spārtĕă.

tĕgĕtĭcŭlă, æ, f., *a dimin. of* teges. Vīlĭs tĕgĕtĭcŭlā sōmnōs, Mart.

tĕgmĕn, tĕgŭmĕn, ĭmĕn, -ĭnĭs, *and* mēntŭm, ĭ, n., *a covering.* Tĕgmĭnă tūtă, Virg. SYN. Vēlāmĕn, vēlāmēntŭm, vēstĭs, ămīctŭs, īnvŏlucrŭm, ŏpērcŭlŭm. V. Vestis.

tĕgo, tēxī, ctŭm, *to cover.* Mōllīquĕ tĕgārĭs, Mart. SYN. Obtĕgo, cōntĕgo, ŏpĕrĭo, ădŏpĕrĭo, cŏŏpĕrĭo, vēlo, ōbdūco, vēstĭo; ōccūlto; prōtĕgo, tŭĕor, ēxcūso.

tēgŭlă, æ, f., *a tile.* Tēgŭlā sōlă, Juv. EPITH. Cŏctă, dūră, lĕvĭs, căvă, cōncăvă, cŏctĭlĭs.

Tēĭŭs, ă, ŭm, *of Teos, a city of Ionia.* Ănăcrĕōntă Tēĭŭm, Hor.

tēlă, æ, f., *a web.* Pēndŭlă tēlă, Ov. EPITH. Tēxtĭlĭs, sŭbtīlĭs; Phărĭă, Mēmphĭtĭcă, Mēmphĭtĭs; Achæmĕnĭă; Băbȳlōnĭă, Assȳrĭă, Lȳdĭă; Pāllădĭă. V. Texo.

Tĕlămōn, ōnĭs, m., *the son of Æacus, and father of Ajax.* Ăjācēm Tĕlămōnŭ nātŭm, Hor.

Tĕlămōnĭădēs, æ, m., *the son of Telamon, Ajax.* Nēc Tĕlămōnĭădēs, Ov.

Tĕlămōnĭŭs, ă, ŭm, *of Telamon, Ajax.* Tĕlămōnĭŭs ārmīs, Ov.

Tĕlĕbŏæ, ārŭm *and* ŭm, m. pl., *a piratical people of Acarnania.* Tĕlĕbŏūm Căprĕās, Virg.

Tĕlĕgŏnŭs, ī, m., *the son of Ulysses and Circe.* Fāctăquĕ Tĕlĕgŏnī, Ov.

Tĕlĕmăchŭs, ī, m., *the son of Ulysses and Penelope.* Tĕlĕmăchŭs prōlēs, Hor.

Tĕlĕmŭs, ī, m., *a Cyclops and soothsayer.* Tĕlĕmŭs Eūrȳmĕdēs, Ov.

Tĕlĕphŭs, ī, m., *the son of Hercules and Auge.* Tĕlĕphōn hāstā, Ov.

Tĕlēstēs, æ, *or* ĭs, m., *a Cretan, the father of Ianthe.* Dīctæō nātă Tĕlēstĕ, Ov.

Tĕlĕthŭsă, æ, f., *the wife of Lygdus and mother of Iphis.* Vānīs Tĕlĕthŭsă, Ov.

tēlĭfĕr, ă, ŭm, *bearing arrows.* Sen.

tēllūs, ūrĭs, f., *the earth.* Sĭcŭlæ tēllūrĭs ĭn āltŭm, Virg. SYN. Tērră, hŭmŭs. V. Terra.

Telōn, ōnĭs, m., *a chief of the Teleboæ.* Ŏră Tĕlōnĭs, Sil. Tēlōn quŭm rēgnă, Virg.

Tĕlōnŭm, ī, m., *a river of the Marsi.* Flūmēnquĕ Tĕlōnŭm.

tēlŭm, ī, n., *an arrow, a dart.* Cōrrĭpŭĭt fīdŭs quæ tēlă gĕrēbăt Achātēs, Virg. SYN. Mīssĭlĕ, spīcŭlŭm, jăcŭlŭm, hāstă, hāstīlĕ, phălārĭcă, săgĭttă, fērrŭm, frāxĭnŭs, pīnŭs, cōrnŭs, ăbĭēs. EPITH. Mīssĭlĕ, pĕnetrābĭlĕ, vōlātĭlĕ, vōlāns, vibrātŭm, ēmīssŭm, cōntōrtŭm, strīdēns, răpĭdŭm, ăcūtŭm, ĭmmĕdĭcābĭlĕ, sævŭm, īnfēstŭm, fătālĕ, vūlnĭfĭcŭm, vĕnēnătŭm, ĭnĭmīcŭm, lēthālĕ, lēthĭfĕrŭm, hāmātŭm, pennātŭm, vēlōx, pērnīx, bēllĭcŭm, Mārtĭŭm, vălĭdŭm, crŭēntŭm, sănguĭnĕŭm, fērrĕŭm, frāxĭnĕŭm. V. Spiculum, hasta, jaculum.

tĕmĕrārĭŭs, ă, ŭm, *rash.* Jŭvēnĭs tĕmĕrārĭŭs, ēssĕ, Ov. SYN. Imprūdēns, īncōnsūltŭs, præcēps, cæcŭs, aūdāx, īncaūtŭs.

tĕmĕrĕ, adv., *rashly.* Fămŭlōs, tĕmĕre īntēr tēlă jăcēntēs, Virg. SYN. Incaūtē; lĕvĭtĕr.

tĕmĕrĭtās, ātĭs, f., *rashness.* Hīnc tĕmĕrĭtătĕ fērtŭr, (Iamb.) Sen. SYN. Imprūdēntĭă, aūdācĭă. EPITH. Cæcă, stūltă, dēmēns, nōxĭă, nōcēns.

tĕmĕro, ās, *to violate, to defile.* Flŭvĭōs tĕmĕrāssĕ vĕnēnĭs, Ov. SYN. Cōrrŭmpo, cōĭnquĭno, cōntămĭno. V. Maculo.

Tĕmĕsă, æ; sĕ, ēs, f. *and* sæ, ārŭm, f. pl., *a city in Bruttium, celebrated for its copper mines.* Thūrīnōsquĕ sīnŭs, Tĕmĕsāsquĕ, Ov.

Tĕmĕsæŭs, ă, ŭm, *of Temesa.* Tĕmĕsæăquĕ cōncrĕpăt æră, Ov.

tĕmētŭm, ī, n., *wine.* Tēmētŭm dūxĕrăt ūvă, Juv.

tēmno, ĭs, psĭ, *to despise.* Rārō vūlgārĭă tēmnĭt, Hor. SYN. Cōntēmno, nēglĭgo, dēspĭcĭo, rēspŭo. V. Aspernor.

tēmo, ōnĭs, n., *the beam of a waggon or carriage.* Lāpsŭm tēmōnĕ rĕlīnquĭt, Virg. V. Currus.

Tēmpē, indecl. n. pl., *a valley of Thessaly.* Fŭgĭēns Pēnēĭă Tēmpē, Virg. EPITH. Grātă, ŭmbrōsă, nĕmŏrōsă, ŏpācă, flōrĭdă, ămœnă, frīgĭdă, Pēnēĭă, Thēssălă, vĭrēntĭă.

* tĕmpĕrāns, ntĭs, *temperate.* Cic. SYN. Sōbrĭŭs, mŏdĕrātŭs, ăbstĭnēns, pārcŭs, tĕmpĕrātŭs. V. Abstinens.

* tĕmpĕrāntĭă, æ, f., *temperance.* Cic. SYN. Sōbrĭĕtās, mŏdĕrātĭo, ăbstĭnēntĭă, pārcĭtās. EPITH. Rēctă, hŏnēstă, ūtĭlĭs, cāstă, pārcă, sānctă, pĭă. V. Abstinentia, castitas.

tĕmpĕrātŏr, ōrĭs, m., *a moderator, a ruler.* Sălŏ tĕmpĕrătŏr, Mart.

tĕmpĕrātŭs, ă, ŭm, *the pass. partic. of* tempero. Nĭsĭ tĕmpĕrātŏ, (Sapph.) Hor. V. Temperies.

tĕmpĕrĭes, ēī, f., *temperate weather, gentleness.* Nēc mŏră tĕmpĕrĭē, Ov. EPITH. Mŏdĕrātă, vērnă, bĕnīgnă, lœtă, jūcūndă, sălūbrĭs, grātă. V. Serenitas.

tĕmpĕro, ās, *to moderate.* Tēmpĕrăt æquŏr, Virg. SYN. Mŏdĕrŏr; ăbstĭnĕo.

tĕmpēstās, ātĭs, f., *a storm.* Quĭd tĕmpēstātēs, Virg. SYN. Prŏcēllă, nīmbŭs, tūrbo, hўēms. EPITH. Strīdēns, sŏnŏră, āspĕră, hōrrēndă, nīmbōsă, pĭcĕă, ŏbscūră, ātră, ŏpācă, rĕpēntīnă, ĭnŏpīnă, tērrĭbĭlĭs, mīnāx, mĭnĭtāns, īnsānă, hўbērnă, præcēps, ādvērsă, īmmītĭs, sævă, ēffūsă, trīstĭs, fūrēns, æquŏrĕă.

tĕmpēstīvŭs, ă, ŭm, *seasonable.* Ēt tēmpēstīvŭm pŭĕrĭs, Hor. SYN. Mātūrŭs; cŏmmŏdŭs, ŏppōrtūnŭs.

tēmplŭm, ī, n., *a temple.* Ēssĕ ălĭquŏd nūmēn tēmplĭs, Juv. SYN. Dēlūbrŭm, fānŭnı, ædēs, sacrārĭŭm, săcēllŭm, ădўtŭm. EPITH. Rēllĭgĭōsŭm, sacrŭm, sānctŭm, pĭŭm, nōbĭlĕ, lăquĕātŭm, aūrăıŭm, fūlgēns, mărmŏrĕŭm, ēxcēlsŭm, āltŭm, ārdŭŭm, sūblīmĕ, īnclўtŭm, aūgūstŭm, vĕnĕrābĭlĕ, īngēns, pīctŭm, māgnĭfĭcŭm, pūlchrŭm, ŏpĕrōsŭm, cĕlĕbrĕ, āmplŭm, spătĭōsŭm, īmmānĕ, dīvĕs, vĕtūstŭm, āntīquŭm.

tĕmpŏră, ŭm, n. pl., *the temples of the head.*

tĕmpŏrĭŭs, adv., *prematurely.* Tĕmpŏrĭŭs cœlō, Ov.

tĕmpŭs, ŏrĭs, n., *time.* Tĕmpŏrĭbŭs dēfūnctă vĭdĕt, Hor. SYN. Ætās, ævŭm. EPITH. Fŭgĭēns, fūgāx, fŭgĭtĭvŭm, vŏlŭbĭlĕ, lābēns, vēlōx, sŭbĭtŭm, cĭtŭm, prœcēps, mŏbĭlĕ, răpĭdŭm, īnstābĭlĕ, lōngŭm, brĕvĕ, dĭŭtūrnŭm, cērtŭm, īrrĕvŏcābĭlĕ.

Tĕmpўră, ŏrŭm, n. pl., *a city of Thrace.* Tĕmpўră pĕtēntī, Ov.

tēmŭlēntŭs, ă, ŭm, *drunken.* Illĕ tēmŭlēntŭs, (Phal.) SYN. Ēbrĭōsŭs. V. Ebrius.

tĕnācĭtĕr, adv., *tenaciously.* Fōrtūnă tĕnācĭtĕr ŭrgĕt, Ov. V. Firmiter.

tĕnāx, ācĭs, *tenacious.* Mēllă tĕnācĭă fīngŭnt, Virg. SYN. Ădhærēns, hærēns, vīx sĕpărābĭlĭs; ăvārŭs, ŏbstĭnātŭs, pērtĭnāx, prŏpŏsĭtī tĕnāx.

tēndo, tĕtēndī, tĕnsŭm or tŭm, *to stretch.* Cŭm vŏcĕ tĕtēndĭt, Virg. SYN. Extēndo, pŏrrĭgo, īntēndo, cōntēndo ; ĕo, vādo, prŏfĭcīscŏr.

tĕnĕbræ, ārŭm, f. pl., *darkness.* Fūlgĕt tĕnēbrĭs, Ov. Ignĕ tĕnēbrĭs, Virg. SYN. Cālīgo, nōx, ŭmbră. EPITH. Ŏpācæ, cæcæ, nŏctūrnæ, ātræ, prŏfūndæ, nigræ, nigrāntēs, ōbscūræ, pĭcĕæ, crāssæ, hōrrēndæ, tăcĭtæ, sĭlēntēs, dēnsæ, sōmnĭfĕræ, squālĭdæ, dēfōrmĕs, Cīmmĕrĭæ; Infērnæ, Stўgĭæ, Tārtărĕæ. V. Nox, noctis tempore, fumus, nubes, umbra.

tĕnĕbrĭcōsŭs, *and* brōsŭs, ă, ŭm, *dark.* Ĭtĕr tĕnēbrĭcōsŭm, (Phal.) Cat. Dīcĭtŭr ēt tĕnĕbrōsă, Virg. Pīnguĕ tĕnēbrōsă, Ov. SYN. Ōbscūrŭs, nĭgĕr, nigrāns, ātĕr, cālīgĭnōsŭs, ŏpācŭs, cæcŭs, nūbĭlŭs. V. Nubilus, obscurus.

Tĕnĕdŏs, *or* ŭs, ī, m., *a small island in the Ægean sea.* Ēst īn cōnspēctū Tĕnĕdŏs, Virg.

tĕnēllŭs, *and* ŭlŭs, ă, ŭm, *very tender.* Pŭēllă tĕnēllŭlō, Cat.

tĕnĕo, ŭī, *to hold, restrain, possess.* Fūgăm tĕnŭīssĕ pĕr hōstēs, Virg. SYN. Rĕtĭnĕo, cōntĭnĕo, cŏērcĕo, cōmprĭmo, cŏhĭbĕo; trācto mănĭbŭs; pōssĭdĕo, ōbtĭnĕo; mŏrŏr, rĕtārdo, dīsıĭnĕo.

tĕnĕr, ră, ŭm, *tender, young.* Nŭm tŏnĕrās, Virg. SYN. Tĕnēllŭs, mōllĭs, flēxĭbĭlĭs, trāctābĭlĭs, făcĭlĭs, lēntŭs, flēxĭlĭs.

tĕnĕrāsco, ĭs, *to grow tender.* In tĕnĕrŏ tĕnĕrāscĕrĕ, Lucr.

tĕnŏr, ŏrĭs, m., *continuity, order.* Crŭēntă tĕnōrĕm, Virg. SYN. Tŏnŭs; sĕrĭēs, ōrdo.

Tĕnŏs, ī, f., *one of the Cyclades.* Ēt Tēnŏs ĕt Āndrŏs, Ov.

tēntāmĕn, ĭnĭs, *and* mēntŭm, ī, n., *an essay.* Tēntāmĭnă pārvă, Juv. Tēntāmēntă nĭhĭl, Ov. V. Conatus.

tēntātŏr, ŏrĭs, m., *he who tries or proves.* Tēntātŏr Ōrīŏn, Hor.

tēnto, ās, *to try.* Tēntāmŭsquĕ vĭam, Virg. SYN. Expĕrĭŏr, prŏbo, ēxplōro, pĕrīcŭlŭm făcĭo; cŏnŏr, mōlĭŏr; pērtēndo, tāngo, āttīngo.

tēntŏrĭŭm, iī, n., *a tent.* Intrā tēntŏrĭă sōmnŏs, Lucan. SYN. Tăbērnācŭlŭm. EPITH. Fīxŭm, āltŭm.

Tēntўră, æ, f., *a city of upper Egypt.* Ūmbrōsæ Tēntўră pālmæ, Juv.

tĕnŭĭs, *and* tĕnuĭs, ĕ, *slender.* Cŭm tĕnŭĕs hāmōs, Tibull. Tĕnŭĭă fērrī, Virg. SYN. Mĭnūtŭs, ēxīlĭs, grăcĭlĭs, āngūstŭs, pārvŭs, ēxĭgŭŭs; sūbtīlĭs, pūrŭs, lĕvĭs, rārŭs, āttĕnŭātŭs; ăcūtŭs, ăcĕr; paūpĕr, hūmĭlĭs, ābjēctŭs.

tĕnŭo, ās, *to diminish.* Vūltŭm tĕnŭāssĕ, sēd ŏpto, Prop. SYN. Ēxtĕnŭo, mĭnŭo, īmmĭnŭo, rărĕfăcĭo.

tĕnŭs, prep., *as far as.* Căpŭlō tĕnŭs ābdĭdĭt, Virg. SYN. Ūsque ăd.

tĕpĕfăcĭo, fēcī, făctŭm, *to warm.* Tĕnĕrīs tĕpĕfāctŭs ĭn ōssĭbŭs, Virg. V. Calefacio.

tĕpĕo, ēs, *to be warm.* Cædĕ tĕpēbăt hŭmŭs, Virg.

tĕpēsco, ĭs, pŭī, *to grow warm.* Sī tĕpŭĕrĕ, dĭēs, Mart. SYN. Tĕpĕo, tĕpĕfĭo.

tĕpĭdŭs, ă, ŭm, *warm.* Indĕ căvæ tĕpĭdō, Virg. SYN. Tĕpēns, tĕpĕfāctŭs, călĭdŭs.

tĕpŏr, ŏrĭs, m., *warmth.* Lēnĭquĕ tĕpŏrĕ, Ov. V. Calor.

tĕpŏrŭs, ă, ŭm, *warm.* Ā tĕpŏrō vērĭs æquĭnōctĭō, Aus. V. Tepidus.

tĕr, adv., *three times.* Ipsĕ tĕr ăddŭctā, Virg.

tĕrcēntēnī, ōrŭm, m. pl., *three hundred.* Tĕrcēntēnā quĭdĕm, Mart.

tĕrcēntŭm, adv., *three hundred.* Tĕrcēntŭm nĭvĕī, Virg.

tŭrdēnī, æ, ă, *thirty.* Tŭrdēnīs nāvĭbŭs ībānt, Virg.

tĕrĕbĭnthŭs, ī, f., *a turpentine tree.* Ōrīcīā tĕrĕbīnthō, Virg.

tĕrebro, ās, *to bore.* Tĕlō tĕrĕbrāmŭs ăcūtō, Virg. SYN. Pĕrfŏro, pĕrfŏdĭo.

tĕrĕdo, ĭnĭs, f., *a small worm.* Vĭtĭātā tĕrēdĭnĕ, Ov.

Tĕrĕīdĕs, æ, m., *the son of Tantalus, Itys.* Tĕrĕīdĕsquĕ pŭĕr, Ov.

Tĕrēntĭŭs, ĭī, m., *a Latin comic writer.* Grăvĭtātĕ, Tĕrēntĭŭs ārtĕ, Hor.

Tĕrēntŭs, ī, m., *a place in the Campus Martius.* Vādā jŭnctā Tărēntī, Ov.

tĕrĕs, ĕtĭs, *polished, round.* Incūmbēns tĕrĕtī Dāmōn, Virg. SYN. Ōblōngŭs, īn lōngŭm rŏtūndŭs ; pŏlītŭs.

Tĕreūs, (*dissyl.*) ĕŏs, ĕī *or* eī, acc. ĕă, m., *a king of Thrace, who committed violence upon his sister-in-law Philomela.* Mūtātōs Tĕreī, Virg. EPITH. Sævŭs, īncēstŭs, Thrĕīcĭŭs, Thrācĭŭs, Thrāx, Ōdrўsĭŭs, Ismărĭŭs, Bīstōnĭŭs, Gĕtĭcŭs; fĕrŭs, ĭnīquŭs, dīrŭs, īnfīdŭs, īmmītĭs, Mārtĭgĕnā. V. Progne, Philomela.

tĕrgĕmĭnŭs, ă, ŭm, *threefold.* Tĕrgĕmĭnī nĕcĕ, Virg. SYN. Trĭplĕx ; māxĭmŭs.

tĕrgĕnŭs, ă, ŭm, *of three kinds.* Tĕrgĕnŭs ārtēs, Aus.

tĕrgĕo, ēs, *or* tĕrgo, ĭs, tĕrsī, tĕrsŭm, *to clean.* Nĕc tĕrgĕrĕ săcrās, Sedul. SYN. Pūrgo, mūndo, ăblŭo, ăbstĕrgo, dētĕrgo. V. Abluo.

tĕrgŭm, ī, *or* gŭs, ŏrĭs, n., *the back.* Tĕrgŏrā dīrĭpĭūnt, Virg. Pōst tĕrgā rĕvīnctŭm, Id. SYN. Dōrsŭm, pōstĕrĭōrā, pārs pōstĕrĭŏr ; cŏrĭŭm, pēllĭs.

tĕrjūgŭs, ă, ŭm, *triple.* Vēl tĕrjūgā mīllĭā, Aus.

tĕrmĕs, ĭtĭs, m., *a branch.* Tĕrmĭtĕ gaūdēns, Grat. SYN. Rāmŭs, pālmĕs.

Tĕrmĭnālĭā, ŭm, n. pl., *festivals in honour of the god Terminus.* Cæsā Tĕrmĭnālĭbŭs, Hor.

tĕrmĭno, ās, *to set bounds, to limit.* Tĕrmĭnĕt āstrīs, Virg. SYN. Fīnĭo, līmĭto, ăbsōlvo, claūdo. V. Limito, finio.

Tĕrmĭnŭs, ī, m., *the god of boundaries, a boundary.* Tĕrmĭnŭs hærĕt, Virg. SYN. Fīnĭs, līmĕs, mētă, ōrā, rĕgĭo. V. Finis, limes.

tĕrnŭs, ă, ŭm, *three by three.* Tĕrnō cōnsūrgūnt, Virg.

tĕro, trīvī, trītŭm, *to rub, to bruise.* Dūrō tĕrăt ĭpsĕ, Virg. SYN. Āttĕro, cōntĕro, mŏlo ; īnsūmo, pērdo.

Tĕrpsĭchŏrē, ēs, f., *one of the Muses.* Tĕrpsĭchŏrē āffēctŭs, Virg. EPITH. Lætā, blāndā, hĭlărĭs, jŭcūndā. V. Musa.

tĕrrā, æ, f., *the earth.* Tĕrrārŭm dŏmĭnŭm, Mart. SYN. Tēllŭs, hŭmŭs, sŏlŭm, cāmpŭs, ăgĕr, ārvŭm ; ōrbĭs, tĕrræ ōrbĭs. EPITH. Frūgĭfĕrā, fĕrāx, fērtĭlĭs, fœcūndā, stĕrĭlĭs, vērnāns, vĭrēns, vĭrĭdĭs, flōrēns, pīctā, lætā, flōrĭdā, hērbĭdā, grāmĭnĕā, dīvĕs, āltrīx, ūbĕr, pīnguĭs, hūmĭdā, mădĭdā, ārĭdā, sīccā, sĭtĭēns, ārēns, ĭrrĭgŭā, tŭrrĭgĕrā, nĕmŏrōsā, ărēnōsā, cūltā, dĕsērtā, īncūltā, ĭnărātā, ĭgnōtā, dūlcĭs, mōllĭs, glēbōsā. līmōsā, lŭtōsā, īmmūndā, pătēns, glōbōsā, rŏtūndā, jăcēns, pēndŭlā, Dædălā ; ōmnĭpărēns. V. Ager, aro.

tĕrrēnŭs, *and* ĕŭs, ă, ŭm, *earthly.* Tĕrrēnĭs ŏcŭlĭs, Pr. SYN. Tĕrrēstrĭs, tĕrrĭgĕnā.

tĕrrĕo, ēs, *to frighten.* Tĕrrĕăt ū mbrās, Virg. SYN. Tĕrrĭto, cōntĕrrĕo, ēxtĕrrĕo, tĕrrĭfĭco, tŭrbo, cōntŭrbo. V. Timeo.

tĕrrēstrĭs, ĕ, *earthly.* Tĕrrēstrĭbŭs ārmĭs, Ov.

tĕrrĭbĭlĭs, ĕ, *and* fĭcŭs, ă, ŭm, *dreadful.* Tĕrrĭbĭlēm crĭstĭs, Virg. Sĕrăquĕ tĕrrĭfĭcī, Virg. SYN. Hŏrrĭdŭs, hŏrrēndŭs, hŏrrĭbĭlĭs, hŏrrĭfĭcŭs, trĕmēndŭs, mĕtŭēndŭs, stŭpēndŭs, tĭmēndŭs, fōrmīdābĭlĭs ; mĭnāx, sævŭs, crūdēlĭs. V. Horridus.

tĕrrĭfĭco, ās, *to terrify, frighten.* Tĕrrĭfĭcānt ănĭmōs, Virg. V. Terreo.

tĕrrĭgĕnă, æ, m. f., *earth-born.* Aūt sī tĕrrĭgĕnæ, Lucan. SYN. Tĕrrā gĕnĭtŭs, tĕrrēnŭs, tĕrrēstrĭs.

tĕrrĭlŏquŭs, ă, ŭm, *speaking dreadfully.* Tĕrrĭlŏquĭs vīctŭs, Hor.

tĕrrĭsŏnŭs, ă, ŭm, *making a dreadful noise.* Tĕrrĭsŏnŭs strīdŏr, Claud.

tĕrrĭtŭs, ă, ŭm, *the pass. partic. of* terreo. Tĕrrĭtā vīsū, Ov.

tĕrrŏr, ōrĭs, m., *fear.* Dĕŭm tĕrrōrĭbŭs ōbstānt, Virg. V. Timor.

tĕrtĭŭs, ă, ŭm, *the third.* Tĕrtĭā jām lūnæ, Virg.

tĕsquă, ōrŭm, n. pl., *rough woody places.* Inhŏspĭtă tĕsquă, Hor. Epitu. Nĕmŏrōsă, hŏrrĭdă, frŏndōsă, dūmōsă, ăspĕră, incŭltă.

tĕssĕllă, æ, f., *a small piece of wood for chequer-work.* Nēc tĕssĕllæ, Juv.

tĕssĕră, æ, f., *a die.* Tĕssĕră sīgnŭm, Virg. V. Talus, signum.

tĕssĕrŭlă, æ, f., *the dimin. of* tĕssĕră. Tĕssĕrŭlă făr, Pers.

tĕstă, æ, f., *an earthen vase.* Tĕstă dĭŭ, Hor. Syn. Amphŏră, cădŭs. Epitu Frăgĭlĭs, fīctĭlĭs, dūră, lūbrĭcă, Sămĭă.

tĕstāmēntŭm, ī, n, *a will.* Tĕstāmēntă sĕnŭm, Hor.

tĕstĭmōnĭŭm, ĭĭ, n., *testimony.* Syn. Tĕstātĭo; indĭcĭŭm, sīgnŭm.

tōstĭs, ĭs, m. f., *a witness.* Tĕstĭbŭs illĭs, Virg. Syn. Spĕctātŏr, ārbĭtĕr; cōnscĭŭs. Epitu. Vērāx, vērŭs, incōrrūptŭs, intĕgĕr, fālsŭs, sŭspēctŭs, cōrrūptŭs, ŏcŭlātŭs, fīdŭs, fĭdēlĭs, vŏcātŭs, cĭtātŭs.

tĕstŏr, *and* ĭfīcŏr, ārĭs, *to witness, to call to witness.* Tĕstātŭr mŏrĭtŭră, Virg. Syn. Tĕstēs dŏ, prŏfĕro, āddūco, prŏdūco; tĕstēs vŏco, āppēllo, invŏco. V. Juro.

tĕstūdĭnĕŭs, ă, ŭm, *of the tortoise, or tortoise-shell.* Aŭt tĕstūdĭnĕæ, Prop.

tĕstūdo, ĭnĭs, f., *a lyre, a vault.* Sŏnŏ tĕstūdĭnĭs, ēt prēcĕ, Hor. Syn. Lўră, chĕlўs, cĭthără; cămĕră, fōrnīx, ārcŭs. V. Fornix, cithara; fides, ium.—*2. a tortoise.* Epitu. Tărdă, lēntă, sēgnĭs, pigră, ignāvă, ĭnērs, tărdigrădă, squāmmĭgĕră, dūră, rēptĭlĭs, rēpēns.

tĕtĕr, tră, trŭm, *foul, cruel.* Tĕtĕr ŭt immūndæ, Mart. Syn. Fœdŭs, tŭrpĭs; sævŭs, scĕlĕrātŭs, dīrŭs.

Tēthys, ўŏs, f., *the daughter of Vesta, and wife of Neptune.* Tēthўs ŏt ēxtrēmŏ, Ov. Epitu. Tītănĭs, Nĕreĭs, ŏcĕănĕĭă, cœrŭlĕă, mărīnă, ăquŏsă, æquŏrĕă, văgă, fŭgāx, cānă, rĕcĭprŏcă, vĭrĭdĭs, sālsă, fœcūndă, ūndōsă, lōngævă, ūndĭvăgă, infūsă, stăgnāns, rĭgēns, spūmāns, Sātūrnĭă; gĕlĭdă, lĭquĭdă, cīrcūmflŭă, prŏfūndă, rĕfŭgă. V. Mare.

tĕtrārchă, *and* chēs, æ, m., *the governor of the fourth part of a kingdom.* Atquĕ tĕtrārchās, Hor.

tĕtrāstĭchŏn, *or* chŭm, ī, n., *a stanza of four lines.* Scrībĭs tĕtrāstĭchă quædăm, Mart.

Tetrĭcă, æ, f., *a mountain of the Sabines.* Quī Tĕtrĭcæ hŏrrēntĭs, Virg.

tetrĭcĭtās, ātĭs, f., *harshness.* Tĕtrĭcĭtātĕ dĕŏrŭm, Ov. Syn. Grăvĭtās, ŭspĕrĭtās, sĕvĕrĭtās.

tetrĭcŭs, ă, ŭm, *harsh.* Nŏn tĕtrĭcŭs, quăm, Mart. Syn. Sĕvērŭs, aŭstērŭs, rūstĭcŭs.

Tĕucĕr, *and* crŭs, crī, m., *a king of Troas.* Tĕucrŭs Rhœtēās, Virg.—*2. the son of Telamon, and brother of Ajax.* Prīmūsvĕ Tĕucĕr, Hor.

Tĕucrī, ōrŭm, m. pl., *the Trojans.* Tĕucrōrum āvērtĕrĕ rēgĕm, Virg. V. Trojani.—Adj. -cĕr *or* crŭs, ă, ŭm, *Trojan.* Tĕucrās fŭĕrāt, Ov.

Tĕucrĭă, æ, f, *Troas.* Sē Tĕucrĭă lŭctŭ, Virg. Syn. Troas.

Tĕucrĭs, ĭdĭs, f., *a Trojan woman.* Căptīvās Tĕucrĭdăs intĕr, Ov.

Tĕuthrāntĕŭs, *and* tĭŭs, ă, ŭm, *of Teuthras, Mysian.* Tĕuthrāntĕūsquĕ Cāīcŭs, Ov. Tĕuthrāntĭă tūrbă, Id.

Tĕuthrās, āntĭs, m., *a king of Mysia.* Tĕuthrāntĭs hŏc fātĕtŭr, Sen.

Tĕutŏnĕs, ŭm, *and* nī, ōrŭm, m. pl., *a people of Germany.* Mĕ, Tĕutŏnĕ jūnctŏ, Sid.

tĕxo, xŭī, xtŭm, *to weave.* Tēxĭtŭr ēt cōstĭs, Ov. Syn. Intēxo, cōntēxo, insērto, insĕro, intērtēxo, nēcto.

tēxtĭlĭs, ĕ, *woven.* Tēxtĭlĭbŭsque ŏnĕrāt, Virg. Syn. Tēxtŭs, intēxtŭs.

tēxtŏr, ōrĭs, m., *and* trīx, īcĭs, f., *a weaver.* Pērcūssās tēxtōrĭs, Juv. Tēxtrīx ŏpĕrātă, Tib.

tēxtŭm, ī, n., ŭs, ūs, m., *and* ūră, æ, f., *a web or woof.* Tēxtă dăbūntŭr, Ov. Tēxtūră Mĭnērvæ, Prop. Epitu. Sōlērs, tĕnŭĭs.

thălămŭs, ī, m., *a bed.* Jām thălămĭs sē, Virg. V. Lectus.

thălāssĭcŭs, ă, ŭm, *of the colour of sea-water, of the sea.* Tĕrĭtūrquĕ thălāssĭcă, Lucr. Syn. Thălāssĭnŭs.

Thălāssĭo, ōnĭs, *or* sĭŭs, ĭĭ, m., *a name repeated in nuptial ceremonies.* Nŏn Thălāssĭōnĭs, Mart. Sērvīrĕ Thălāssĭŏ, Cat.

Thălēs, ētĭs, m., *a Milesian, one of the seven wise men of Greece.* Nŏn mĭtĕ Thălētĭs, Juv.

Thălĭă, æ, f., *one of the Muses.* Sȳlvās hăbĭtărĕ Thălĭă, Virg. V. Musa, Charites.

Thălĭārchŭs, ī, m., *the name of a man.* Ŏ Thălĭārchĕ, mĕrŭm, Hor.

Thămȳrās, æ, *and* rĭs, ĭs, m., *a Thessalian poet, deprived of sight by the Muses.* Quĭd mĭsĕrŭm Thămȳrān, Ov.

Thăpsŏs, *or* ŭs, ī, m., *a peninsula of Sicily, near Syracuse.* Thăpsŭmquĕ jăcēntĕm, Virg.

Thăsĭŭs, ă, ŭm, *of Thasos.* Sūnt Thăsĭæ vītēs, Virg.

Thăsŏs, ī, f., *an island in the Ægean sea.* Sāxă Thăsīquĕ, Sil.

Thaūmāntĕŭs, ă, ŭm, *of Thaumas.* Cŭm vīrgĭnĕ Thaūmāntĕā, Ov.

Thaūmāntĭăs, ădĭs, *and* ĭs, ĭdŏs, f., *a name of Isis.* Rŏsĕŏ Thaūmāntĭăs ōrĕ, Virg.

Thaūmās, āntĭs, m., *a son of Oceanus.*—2. *one of the Centaurs,* Ov.

Thĕānŏ, ūs, f., *a Trojan female.* Quēm nŏctĕ Thĕānŏ, Virg.

thĕātrālĭs, ĕ, *of a theatre.* Jūră thĕātrālĭs, Mart. SYN. Thĕātrĭcŭs.

thĕātrŭm, ī, n., *a theatre.* Spēctāndă thĕātrīs, Hor. SYN. Căvĕă, cīrcŭs, spēctăcŭlŭm, scēnă, sūggēstŭm. EPITH. Mārmŏrĕŭm, ōrnātŭm, āltŭm, ēxcēlsŭm, īngēns, āmplŭm, spătĭōsŭm, căpāx, fēstŭm, sŏlēnnĕ, clāmōsŭm.

Thēbă, æ, *and* bē, ēs, f., *or* bæ, ārŭm, f. pl., *a city of Egypt.* Ātquĕ vĕtŭs Thēbæ, Juv. EPITH. Pālmĭfĕră.—2. *a city of Bœotia.* Cĭthærōnĭs Thēbās ăgĭtātă, Prop. EPITH. Cādmæă, Ăgēnŏrĕă, Tȳrĭă, Sīdonĭă; Ōgȳgĭă, Āmphĭōnĭă; Hērcŭlĕă, Ēchĭōnĭă, Œdĭpŏdĭōnĭă; Āŏnĭă; vĕtŭs, clāră, nŏbĭlĭs, āntīquă, cĕlĕbrĭs, fāmōsă, sēptēmgĕmĭnă.—3. *the name of several other towns.*

Thēbānŭs, ă, ŭm, *and* aĭs, ĭdĭs, f., *Theban.* Thēbānŏs āptārĕ mŏdōs, Hor. Thēbăĭdĕs jūssĭs, Ov.

thĕcă, æ, f., *a sheath, a case.* Mart.

Thĕmĭs, ĭs, ĭdŏs, *or* īstŏs, f., *the goddess of Justice.* Fātĭdĭcămquĕ Thĕmĭn, Ov. EPITH. Æquă, jūstă, īncōrrūptă, īntēgră, sĕvēră, ālmă, fātĭdĭcă, sacră. V. Justitia.

Thĕocrĭtŭs, ī, m., *the inventor of Bucolic poetry.*

Thĕŏdŏtŭs, *or* Theūdŏtŭs, ī, m., *the name of a man.* Sævŏ Theūdŏtŭs hŏstĕ, Ov.

Thĕōn, ōnĭs, m., *a Greek sophist.* Sālvērĕ Thĕōnĕm, Aus.

Thĕōnīnŭs, ă, ŭm, *of Theon, satirical.* Dēntĕ Thĕōnīnŏ, Hor.

Thĕrāpnē, ēs, f., *and* pnæ, ārŭm, f. pl., *a town of Laconia.* Cŏlŭĕrĕ Thĕrāpnæ, Stat. EPITH. Ŭmbrōsæ, vĭrĭdēs, Tȳndărĕæ.

Thĕrāpnĕŭs, ă, ŭm, *of Therapne.* Īstă Thĕrāpnĕīs, Mart.

Thĕrĭdāmās, āntĭs, m., *the name of a dog.* Ov.

thērmæ, *and* ŭlæ, ārŭm, f. pl., *warm baths.* Mārmŏrĕ thērmās, Mart. Thērmŭlīs lăvērĭs, (Phal.) Id. EPITH. Călēntēs, călĭdæ, sălŭtārēs. V. Balneum.

Thērmōdōn, ōntĭs, m., *a river of Cappadocia.* Flūmĭnă Thērmōdōntĭs, Virg.

Thērŏdāmās, āntĭs, m., *a king of Scythia.* Nōn tĭbĭ Thērŏdāmās.

Thērōn, ōnĭs, m., *the name of a warrior.* Ōccīsŏ Thērōnĕ, Virg.

Thērsāndĕr, *and* drŭs, drī, m., *the son of Polynices.* Thērsāndrŭs Sthĕnĕlŭsquĕ, Virg.

Thērsĭlŏchŭs, ī, m., *the son of Antenor.* Mĕdōntăquĕ Thērsĭlŏchŭmquĕ, Ov.

Thērsītēs, æ, m., *a Greek at the siege of Troy.* Tăm mălă Thērsītēn, Ov.

thēsaūrŭs, ī, m., *a treasure.* Thēsaūrōs ĭgnōtŭm, Virg. SYN. Gāză, dīvĭtĭæ, ŏpēs, pĕcūnĭă. EPITH. Lătēns, dēfōssŭs, ābdĭtŭs, ābscōndĭtŭs, ōccūltŭs, rĕcōndĭtŭs. V. Divitiæ.

Thēseūs, (*dissyl.*) eĭ *or* ĕŏs, acc. ĕă, m., *the son of Ægeus.* Īnfēlīx Thēseūs, Virg. SYN. Ægīdēs. EPITH. Fōrtĭs, sŭpērbŭs, fĕrōx, bēllātŏr, pērfĭdŭs, pērjūrŭs, Trœzēnĭŭs, Āttĭcŭs, Nēptūnĭŭs, īnclȳtŭs, hōrrĭdŭs, fīdŭs, prŏfūgŭs, crūdēlĭs, ārmĭgĕr, īngrātŭs.

Thēseŭs, *and* ēĭŭs, ă, ŭm, *of Theseus.* Ŏ mĭhĭ Thēseă, Ov. SYN. Thēsēĭŭs hērōs.

Thēsīdēs, æ, m., *the son or descendant of Theseus, Hippolytus.* Thēsīdēs Thēseŭsquĕ, Ov.

Thēspĭă, ădĭs, f., *of Thespiæ, a city of Bœotia : the Muses honoured there.* Thēspĭădēs cērtātĕ dĕæ, Ov.

Thēspĭs, ĭs, m., *an Attic poet, the inventor of tragedy.* Pŏēmătă Thēspĭs, Hor.

Thēssălĭă, æ, f., *a part of Epirus.* Thēssălĭæ rĕdūcī, Ov.

Thĕssălĭcŭs, lĭŭs, and lŭs, ă, ŭm, and lĭs, ĭdĭs, f., Thessalian. Pŭlsūm Thĕssălĭcīs, Ov. Vōcĕ Thĕssălā, Hor. Thĕssălĭs ārā mĕō, Ov.

Thĕstĭădēs, æ, m., the son or grandson of Thestius. Rĕspĭcĕ Thĕstĭădēn, Ov.

Thĕstĭăs, ădĭs, f., the daughter of Thestias, Althæa. Thĕstĭăs haŭd ălĭtĕr, Ov.

Thĕstĭŭs, ĭī, m., the father of Leda, Althæa, &c. Thĕstĭŭs ōrbŭs ĕrăt, Ov.

Thĕstŏrĭdēs, æ, m., the son of Thestor, Calchas. Aŭgūr Thĕstŏrĭdēs, Ov.

Thĕstȳlĭs, ĭs, f., the name of a woman. Thĕstȳlĭs ōrăt, Virg.

Thĕtĭs, ĭdĭs, f., the mother of Achilles. Lūsŭs hōs Thĕtĭs, aŭt, Mart. SYN. Nērīnĕ. EPITH. Nērĕĭs, æquŏrĕā. V. Tethys.

Thĭsbæŭs, ă, ŭm, of Thisbe, in Bœotia. Quæ nūnc Thĭsbæās, Ov.

Thĭsbē, ēs, f., a city of Bœotia.—2. a young Babylonian female loved by Pyramus. Pȳrămŭs ĕt Thĭsbē, Ov.

Thŏāctēs, æ, or ĭs, m., the name of a man. Rĕgīsquĕ Thŏāctēs, Ov.

Thŏāntēŭs, ă, ŭm, of Thoas, of Tauris. Quīquĕ Thŏāntēæ, Ov.

Thŏāntĭăs, ădĭs, and tĭs, ĭdĭs, f., the daughter of Thoas, Hypsipyle. Fraŭdātă Thŏāntĭăs ōro, Ov. Cōmĭtātă Thŏāntĭs, Stat.

Thŏās, āntĭs, m., a king of Tauris, who charged Iphigenia with the bloody worship of Diana. Rĕgnă Thŏās hăbŭĭt, Ov.—2. a son of Bacchus and king of Lemnos. Răpŭī dĕ cædĕ Thŏāntă, Id.

thŏlŭs, ī, m., a dome. Sŭspĕndĭvĕ thŏlo, Virg. EPITH. Altŭs, cūrvŭs, săcĕr.

Thŏōn, ŏnĭs, m., the name of a warrior. Cūm Chĕrsĭdămāntĕ Thŏōnă, Ov.

thŏrāx, ācĭs, m., a breastplate. Sŭmmī thŏrācĭs ĕt ōrās, Virg. SYN. Lōrīcă. EPITH. Ăhēnŭs, mŭltĭplēx, rŭtĭlŭs, flāmmĕŭs, ænĕŭs, pŏlītŭs, lævĭs, pīctŭs, ārdēns, ærĭsŏnŭs, squāmĭfĕr, fĕrrĕŭs. V. Lorica.

Thrācēs, ŭm, m. pl., Thracians. Thrācēs ărănt, ācrī, Virg. SYN. Bĭstŏnĭī, Ismărĭī, Ŏdrȳsĭī. V. Thracia. EPITH. Armĭgĕrī, indŏmĭtī, fōrtēs, gĕnĕrōsī, bĕllĭgĕrī, fĕrōcēs, crūdēlēs, ĭnmītēs, trŭcēs, aŭdācēs, Mārtĭī.

Thrācĭă, or că, æ, or cē, ēs, f., a part of Epirus. Hōrrĭdāmvĕ Thrācĭăm, Cat. Gĕmĭt ŭltĭmă pŭlsŭ Thrācă pĕdŭm, Virg. Bĕllō fŭrĭōsă Thrācē, Hor. EPITH. Gĕlĭdă, ārmĭfĕră, sævă, bārbără, hōrrĭdă, Māvōrtĭă, nĭvōsă, glăcĭālĭs, frĭgĭdă, āspĕră, incūltă.

Thrācĭŭs, Thrēĭcĭŭs, and Thrācŭs, ă, ŭm, Thracian. Nōn Thrācĭŭs Ōrpheŭs, Virg. Nĕc nōn Thrēĭcĭŭs, Id. Thrācă pălŭs, V. Fl. SYN. Thrāx, Bĭstŏnĭŭs, Sīthŏnĭŭs, Ismărĭŭs, Œagrĭŭs, Ŏdrȳsĭŭs, Rhīpœŭs, Rhŏdŏpĕŭs, Rhŏdŏpēĭŭs, Strȳmŏnĭŭs, Ēdŏnŭs; Arctōŭs, hȳpĕrbŏrĕŭs.

Thrăsĭŭs, ĭī, m., the name of a soothsayer. Quŭm Thrăsĭŭs Būsĭrĭn, Ov.

Thrāx, ācĭs, m., Thracian, a Thracian. Nĕquĕ Sārmătă nĕc Thrāx, Juv. Thrācĭs ĕt exĭtĭŭm Lȳcūrgī, Hor. V. Thraces.

Thrēcĭŭs, ă, ŭm, the same as Thracius. Ŭt Thrēcĭă Bācchē, Ov.

Thrēĭssă, and Thrēssă, æ, f., a Thracian woman. Ĕquās Thrēĭssā fătīgăt Hārpălȳcē, Virg. Thrēssă gĕnŭs, Id. SYN. Bĭstŏnĭs, Sīthŏnĭs, Ēdŏnĭs, Thrācĭă, Thrēĭcĭă.

thrēnŏs, or ŭs, ī, m., a funeral dirge. Nōmĭnĕ thrēnŭm, Aus. SYN. Næ) nĭă.

Thrēx, ēcĭs, or Thræx, Thrāx, m., a gladiator of the heaviest armour. Thrēx ēst Gāllĭnă Sȳrō păr, Hor.

Thrŏnĭŭs, ĭī, m., the name of a warrior. Dējĭcĭt, āt Thrŏnĭŭm, Virg.

* thrŏnŭs, ī, m., a throne. SYN. Sŏlĭŭm. EPITH. Rēgālĭs, rēgĭŭs, aŭrĕŭs, ĕbūrnĕŭs, ĕbūrnŭs, aŭrātŭs, sŭblīmĭs, altŭs, ēxcēlsŭs, insĭgnĭs, cōnspĭcŭŭs, cŏrūscŭs, mĭcāns, splēndēns, māgnĭfĭcŭs, fūlgēns. V. Solium.

Thūcȳdĭdēs, æ, m., a celebrated Greek historian. Attĭcŭs Thūcȳdĭdēs, Avien.

Thūlē, ēs, f., [it is not precisely ascertained what island the ancients designated by this name.] Ŭltĭmă Thūlē, Virg. EPITH. Hēspĕrĭă, nĭgră, inhōspĭtă, impĕrvĭă, rĕmōtă, gĕlĭdă, glăcĭālĭs.

thŭnnŭs, or ȳnnŭs, ī, m., a tunny-fish. Ădnābŭnt thŭnnī, Hor. Caŭdă nătăt thȳnnī, Pers.

thŭrĕŭs, ă, ŭm, of incense. Thūrĕā grānă, Ov.

thŭrībŭlŭm, ī, n., a censer. Thūrĭbŭlo, ĕt pătĕræ, Aus. SYN. Ăcēĭră. V. Acerra.

thŭrĭcrĕmŭs, ă, ŭm, burning incense. Thūrĭcrĕmīs cŭm, Virg.

thŭrĭfĕr, ĕră, rŭm, bearing incense. Tōtăquĕ thūrĭfĕrīs, Virg.

thŭrĭlĕgŭs, ă, ŭm, gathering incense. Nām mŏdŏ thūrĭlĕgōs, Ov.

Thŭrīnŭs, *and* rĭŭs, ă, ŭm, *of Thurium, a city of Magna Græcia.* Thŭrīnōsquĕ sīnŭs, Ov.

thŭs, thŭrĭs, n., *incense.* Ĕt thŭs ōcўŭs ūvæ, Hor. EPITH. Săbæŭm; Eōŭm, Nābăthæŭm, Pānchæŭm, Pānchăĭcŭm; mäscŭlŭm, pīnguĕ, pĭŭm, ŏdŏrĭfĕrŭm, ŏlēns, rĕdŏlēns, sacrŭm, frăgrāns, fūmāns, văpōrŭm, vōtīvŭm. V. Sacrifico, adoleo.

Thўăs, *or* Thyĭăs, ădĭs, f., *a bacchante.* Thўăs cōmmōtīs, Virg.

thўăsŭs, ī, m., *a dance in honour of Bacchus.* Instĭtŭĭt Dăphnīs thўăsōs, Virg. EPITH. Lĕvĭs, tĕrrĭbĭlĭs, raŭcŭs, fŭrēns.

Thўēnē, ēs, f., *one of the Hyades.* Dōdōnĭ Thўēnē, Ov.

Thўēstēs, ĭs *or* æ, m., *the son of Pelops.* Crūdĕ Thўēstă, tŭăm, Mart. SYN. Tāntălĭdēs. EPITH. Pĕlŏpĕĭŭs, ădŭltĕr, scĕlĕrătŭs, īnfēlīx, dīrŭs, mĭsĕrāndŭs, mĭsĕr.

Thўēstēŭs, ă, ŭm, *of Thyestes.* Nĕvĕ Thўēstēĭs, Ov.

Thўēstĭădēs, æ, m., *the son of Thyestes.* Indĕ Thўēstĭădēn, Ov.

thyĭă, æ, f., *a fragrant shrub.* Sĕd thyĭæ thălămō, Prop.

Thўmbĕr, *and* brŭs, brī, m.   Nōn tĭbĭ, Thўmbrĕ, căpŭt, Virg.

thўmbră, æ, f., *savory, a plant.* Cōpĭă thўmbræ, Virg.

Thўmbræŭs, ă, ŭm, *of Thymbra, a city of Troas; an epithet of Apollo.* Dā prŏprĭŭm, Thўmbræĕ, dŏmŭm, Virg.

Thўmœtēs, æ, m., *a son of Priam.* Prīmŭsquĕ Thўmœtēs, Virg.

thўmŭm, ī, n., *or* ŭs, ī, m., *thyme.* Rĕdŏlēntquĕ thўmō, Virg. EPITH. Ŏdōrŭm, ŏdōrātŭm, rĕdŏlēns, ŏlēns, frăgrāns, Āttĭcŭm, suāvĕ, dŭlcĕ, Cecrŏpĭŭm, Hўblæŭm, grātŭm, mōllĕ.

Thўnĭăcŭs, nĭcŭs, *and* nŭs, ă, ŭm, *of Bithynia.* Thўnĭăcōsquĕ sīnŭs, Ov. V. Bithynus.

Thўōneŭs, ĕŏs, ĕĭ *or* eī, m., *one of the names of Bacchus.* Indētōnsŭsquĕ Thўōneŭs, Ov.

Thўrēĭs, ĭdĭs, f., *of Thyre, a city of Messenia.* Thўrēĭdă tērrăm, Ov.

thўrsŭs, ī, m., *the stem of plants.* Thўrsī frŏndĕ vĭrēntēs, Ov.—2. *a sort of lance, covered at the end with ivy-leaves, and carried in the Bacchic processions.* Grăvĭ mĕtŭēndĕ thўrsō, Hor. EPITH. Bācchĭcŭs, Bācchēŭs, pāmpĭnĕŭs, frŏndēns.

tĭără, æ, f., *or* răs, æ, m., *a turban, a mitre.* Săcērquĕ tĭārăs, Virg. SYN. Mitră, gălērŭs. EPITH. Lūnătă, sacră, gēmmătă, fŭlgēns, mĭcāns, Eŏă; Pērsĭcă, Phrўgĭă. V. Mitra.

Tĭbĕrīnĭs, ĭdĭs, f., *of the Tiber.* Nўmphæ Tĭbĕrīnĭdēs, Ov.

Tĭbĕrīnŭs, *and* Tibrīnŭs, ă, ŭm, *of the Tiber.* Tĭbĕrīnī flŭmĭnĭs ūndă, Virg. Clœlĭă Tĭbrīnăs, Cl.

Tĭbĕrĭs, ĭs, Tibrĭs, ĭdĭs, *and* Tĭbĕrīnŭs, ī, m., *the river which flows through Rome.* Cōgnōmĭnĕ Tĭbrĭm, Virg.   Quēm Tĭbĕrĭm mērsŭs, Ov. SYN. Albŭlă. EPITH. Aŭsŏnĭŭs, răpāx, Tўrrhēnŭs, Thŭscŭs; cœrŭlŭs, cœrŭlĕŭs, cōrnĭgĕr, tŭmĭdŭs, Rōmŭlĕŭs, Rōmānŭs, Itălŭs, præcēps, lĭmpĭdŭs.

Tĭbĕrĭŭs, ĭī, m., *the Roman emperor.* Prænōmēn Tĭbĕrĭī, Aus.—2. *others.* Tē, Tībĕrī, nŭmĕrārĕ, Hor.

tĭbĭ, *the dat. of* tu.   Nŭcēs, tĭbĭ dĕsĕrĭt, Virg.   Cūnctă tĭbĭ Cĕrĕrĕm, Id.

tībĭă, æ, f., *a pipe.* Mĕă tībĭă, vērsŭs, Virg. SYN. Fīstŭlă, călămŭs, ărŭndo, būxŭs. V. Fistula.

tibĭālĭs, ĕ, *of the flute or pipe.* Gĕmĭt aŭră tībĭālĭs, Sid.

tībīcĕn, ĭnĭs, n., *a piper.* Tībīcĕn, trāxĭtquĕ, Hor. EPITH. Cănōrŭs, pĕrītŭs, blāndŭs, lætŭs, rūstĭcŭs, hĭlărĭs. V. Citharœdus.

tībīcĭnă, æ, f., *a female piper.* Rūmpĭt tībīcĭnă bŭccĭs, Mart.

Tĭbŭllŭs, ī, m., *a Roman poet.* Fāmă, Tĭbŭllŭs, Ov. EPITH. Argŭtŭs, cŭltŭs, tērsŭs, īnsĭgnĭs, săcĕr, tĕnĕr, făcĭlĭs.

Tĭbŭr, ŭrĭs, n., *a town near Rome.* Rōmæ Tĭbŭr ămēm vēntōsŭs, Tĭbŭrĕ Rōmăm, Hor.

Tĭbŭrnŭs, ī, m., *one of the founders of Tibur.* Rĕcŭbāt Tĭbŭrnŭs ĭn ūmbrā, Hor. —Adj., -ŭs, ă, ŭm, *of Tibur.* Hīc, Ănĭŏ Tĭbŭrnĕ, flŭĭs, Prop

Tĭbŭrs, ŭrtĭs, *and* Tĭbŭrtīnŭs, ă, ŭm, *of Tibur.* Quŭm Tĭbŭrtĕ vĭā, Hor. Tĭbŭrtĭă mœnĭă līnquŭnt, Virg.   Nŭnc Tĭbŭrtīnĭs, Mart.

Tĭbŭrtēs, ŭm, m. pl., *the inhabitants of Tibur.* Prædăm Tĭbŭrtŭm, Virg.

                                                                T

Tĭcĭdă, *or* Tĭcĭdās, æ, m., *a Latin poet.* Quĭd rĕfĕrăm Tĭcĭdæ, Ov.

Tĭcīnŭs, ĭ, m., *a river of Italy.* Tŭæ, Tĭcīnĕ, cădāvĕră rīpæ, Sil.

Tĭfātă, æ, m., *a mountain of Campania.* Tŭĭs, Tĭfātă, Tĕātĕ, Stat.

Tĭgēllĭŭs, ĭī, m., *a singer in the time of Augustus.* Cāntōrĭs mŏrtĕ Tĭgēllī, Hor.

tĭgnŭm, ıı., ŭs, m., ĭ, *and* tĭgīllŭm, (*dim.*) ĭ, n., *a beam.* Pŭlpĭtă tĭgnĭs, Hor. Sŭf-fīxă tĭgīllō, Cat. Syn. Trābs.

Tĭgrānēs, ĭs, m., *the name of several kings of Armenia.* Tĭgrānēmquĕ mĕŭm, Luc.

Tĭgrĭs, ĭdĭs *or* ĭs, m., *a river in Asia.* Tĭgrĭs ĕt Eŭphrātēs, Prop. Ēt Tĭgrĭs, ēt Rūbrī, Man. Epith. Răpĭdŭs, răpāx, vēlōx, cĭtŭs, præcĕps, Ăchæmĕnĭŭs, vĭŏ-lēntŭs, tĕpĭdŭs, văgŭs, cĕlĕr, cœrŭlĕŭs, lĭmpĭdŭs, vĭtrĕŭs, clārŭs.—2. f., *a tiger.* Tĭgrĭdĭs ēxŭvĭæ, Virg. Ūbĕră tĭgrēs, Id. Ărmĕnĭæquĕ tĭgrēs, Ov. Epith. Ărmĕnĭă, Pārthĭcă, Indă, Gāngētĭcă; Cāspĭă, Caŭcāsĕa; āspĕră, ĭmmānĭs, mă-cŭlōsă, sævă, răbĭdă, trūx, fūrēns, ēffĕră, fĕrōx, cĭtă, vēlōx, pērnīx, cĕlĕr, fūrĭōsă, răpāx, Indĭcă, tērrĭbĭlĭs, hōrrĭdă, prædātrīx.

tĭlĭă, æ, f., *a linden-tree.* Nēc tĭlĭæ lævēs, Virg.

Tĭllĭŭs, ĭī, m., *the name of a man.* Quō tĭbĭ, Tĭllī, Hor.

Tĭmāgĕnēs, ĭs, m., *the name of an orator and historian.* Tĭmāgĕnĭs æmŭlă lĭnguă, Hor.

Tĭmāvŭs, ĭ, m., *a river of Austria.* Sāxă Tĭmāvī, Virg. Epith. Aŭsŏnĭŭs, Vĕnĕtŭs, mūltĭfĭdŭs. V. Fluvius, timeo.

tĭmĕfāctŭs, ă, ŭm, *terrified.* Tŭm rēbŭs tĭmĕfāctæ, Lucr.

tĭmĕo, ēs, *to fear.* Nēc tĭmuī dē, Ov. Syn. Fōrmīdo, vĕrĕŏr, mĕtŭo, ēxtĭmēsco, pērtĭmēsco, păvĕo, trĕmo, trĕmīsco, cōntrĕmīsco, trĕpĭdo, rĕfōrmīdo, hōrrĕo, pērhōrrēsco.

tĭmĭdē, adv., *fearfully.* Nēc tĭmĭdĕ prōmīttĕ, Ov.

tĭmĭdŭs, ă, ŭm, *timid.* Illæsŭm tĭmĭdĭs, Mart. Syn. Trĕpĭdŭs, păvĭdŭs; ĭm-bēllĭs, ĭgnāvŭs. V. Timens.

tĭmŏr, ōrĭs, m., *fear.* Plēnă tĭmōrĭs, Ov. Syn. Mĕtŭs, fōrmīdo, păvŏr, tērrŏr, trĕmŏr, hōrrŏr. Epith. Āncĕps, dŭbĭŭs, trĕpĭdŭs, păvĭdŭs, gēlĭdŭs, ēxānguĭs, hōrrĭdŭs, pāllĭdŭs, frĭgĭdŭs, păvēns, sōllĭcĭtŭs, trīstĭs, mœstŭs, ăcērbŭs, vĭgĭl, ĭnsōmnĭs, lānguēns, mōlēstŭs, dīrŭs, sævŭs, præcĕps, rĕpēntīnŭs, sŭbĭtŭs, ĭn-quĭĕtŭs, tŭrpĭs, sērvīlĭs, sēgnĭs, hōrrēndŭs, ānxĭŭs, sŭspēnsŭs, ĭmbēllĭs, ĭgnāvŭs, āmēns, mălŭs, tăcĭtŭs, ēlĭnguĭs, fœmĭnĕŭs. V. Timeo, metus.

tīncă, æ, f., *tench, a fish.* Sōlātĭă, tīncās, Aus.

tīnctĭlĭs, ĕ, *fit to dye with.* Tīnctĭlĕ vīrŭs, Ov.

* tīnctūră, æ, f., *and* ŭs, ŭs, m., *tincture.* Plin.

tĭnĕă, æ, f., *a moth, a worm.* Aŭt tĭnĕās pāscēs, Hor. Epith. Agrēstĭs, ĕdāx, hōrrĭdă, fœdă, tūrpĭs.

tīngo, nxĭ, ctŭm, *to dye, tinge.* Tīngĕrĕt æquŏrĕ plāntŭs, Virg. Syn. Imbŭo, fūco, cŏlōro; cŏlōrĕ ĭnfĭcĭo, sătŭro, līno, ĭllĭno, mĕdĭcŏr, vĭtĭo; mădĕfăcĭo, ĭm-mērgo.

tĭnnĭo, īs, ĭī, *to jingle.* Aŭrēs tĭnnĭŭnt sŏnĭtŭ, Cat. Syn. Tĭntĭno.

tĭnnītŭs, ūs, m., *a jingling.* Tĭnnītŭsquĕ cĭĕ, Virg. Epith. Ăcūtŭs, ārgūtŭs, sŏnāns, raŭcŭs, cōnfūsŭs, rĕpĕtītŭs, crēbĕr.

tĭnnŭlŭs, ă, ŭm, *tinkling.* Tĭnnŭlă tăm frăgĭlī, Calph. Syn. Sŏnōrŭs, strīdēns, rĕsŏnāns, ārgūtŭs.

tīntĭnnābŭlŭm, ĭ, n., *a bell.* Tīntĭnnābŭlă dīcās, Juv.

tĭnŭs, ĭ, f., *a sort of wild laurel.* Cŭltăquĕ tĭnŭs ăbēst, Ov.

Tĭphÿs, ÿĭs *or* ÿŏs, m., *the pilot of the Argonauts, and inventor of the rudder.* Tĭphÿs ĭn Æmŏnĭă, Ov. Syn. Thēspĭădēs.

Tĭrĕsĭās, æ, m., *a famous diviner.* Tīrĕsĭās āspēxĭt, Prop. Epith. Lōngævŭs, cāllĭdŭs, prōvĭdŭs, Thēbānŭs.

Tĭrĭdātēs, ĭs, ın., *a king of the Parthians.* Quĭd Tīrĭdātēm tērrĕăt, Hor.

tīro, ōnĭs, *and* rūncŭlŭs, ĭ, m., *a novice.* Mŭltăquĕ tīrōnī, Ov. Nŏstēr tīrūn-cŭlŭs, Juv. Syn. Nŏvĭtĭŭs, nŏvŭs, rŭdĭs, ĭmpērītŭs. Epith. Ĭgnārŭs, ĭnscĭŭs, ĭnēxpērtŭs, āttēntŭs, dīlĭgēns, vĭgĭl, pērvĭgĭl, sēdŭlŭs, stŭdĭōsŭs.

tīrōcĭnĭŭm, ĭī, n., *a noviciate.* Nēc tīrōcĭnĭŭm, Man. Syn. Rŭdīmēntŭm, ĕlĕmēntŭm.

Tīrÿns, ÿnthĭs, f., *a city of Argolis.* Āntīquăm Tīrÿnthă dĕŭs, Stat.

Tīrynthĭŭs, ă, ŭm, *of Tiryns, Tirynthian.* Tīrynthĭŭs hērōs, Ov.—Subst., -ŭs, ī, m., *Hercules.* Extīnctō Tīrynthĭŭs āttĭgĭt ārvă, Virg.

Tīsămĕnŭs, ī, m., *a king of Argos, the son of Orestes.* Tīsămĕnīquĕ pătrī, Ov.

Tīsĭphŏnē, ēs, f., *one of the Furies.* Tīsĭphŏnēs ātrō, Prop. EPITH. Sœvă, fĕrōx, atrōx, ĭmmītĭs. V. Furiæ.

Tīsĭphŏnēŭs, ă, ŭm, *of Tisiphone.* Tēmpŏră, sī possīs, Tīsĭphŏnĕă tŭœ, Ov.

Tītān, ānĭs, m., *a Titan; the sun.* Ăn Tītān, ŭt ălēntēs, Lucan. SYN. Sōl, Phœbŭs. V. Sol.

Tītānēs, ŭm, m. pl., *Titans.* Tītānăs ĭmmānēmquĕ, (Iamb.) Hor. V. Gigantes.

Tītānĭă, œ, and nĭs, ĭdĭs, f., *the moon.* Sōlĭtă Tītānĭă lympha, Ov.

Tītānĭăcŭs, and Tītānĭŭs, ă, ŭm, *Titan; of the sun.* Hinc Tītānĭăcīs, Ov. Tītā- nĭŭs āfflăt, Av.

Tīthōnēŭs, and nĭŭs, ă, ŭm, *of Tithonus.* Lăcrymīs Tīthōnĭă flēctĕrĕ cōnjŭx, Virg.

Tīthōnĭs, ĭdĭs, and nĭă, œ, f., *Aurora, the wife of Tithonus.* Cĭtĭŭs Tīthōnĭdă mœstī, Stat.

Tīthōnŭs, ī, m., *the son of Laomedon, loved by Aurora.* Tīthōnī crŏcĕŭm, Virg. EPITH. Mȳgdŏnĭŭs, Phrȳgĭŭs, sĕnēx.

Tītĭēnsēs. V. Tātĭēnsēs.

tītĭllo, ās, *to tickle.* Tītĭllārĕ măgĭs, Lucr. SYN. Mūlcĕo, dēmūlcĕo, pērmūlcĕo, ōbjĕcto, dēlēcto, dēlīnĭo, āllĭcĭo, āllēcto.

tītĭo, ōnĭs, m., *a firebrand.* Stŭltīs tĭtĭōnĭbŭs ĭgnĭs, Buch. SYN. Tōrrĭs.

tītŭbo, ās, *to stagger.* Grăvīs tĭtŭbārĕ vĭdētŭr, Ov. SYN. Văcīllo, lăbo, nūto, lăbāsco, hæsĭto. V. Nuto, ebrius.

tītŭlŭs, ī, m., *a title, a mark of honour.* Tītŭlīs īnsĭgnĭs, Lucan. SYN. Nōmĕn, laŭs, hŏnŏr, mŏnŭmēntŭm. EPITH. Illūstrĭs, īnsĭgnĭs, cĕlebrĭs, sŭpērbŭs, grāndĭlŏquŭs. V. Nobilitas.

Tītŭs, ī, m., *a Roman name and surname.* Cōgĭt mē Tītŭs āctĭtārĕ, Mart.

Tītȳrŭs, ī, m., *the name of a shepherd.* Tītȳrĕ, tū pătŭlœ, Virg.

Tītȳŭs, ī, m., *a giant, punished in hell for his crimes.* Nŏvēm Tītȳŭs pĕr, Tib. EPITH. Tērrĭgĕnă, tĕmĕrārĭŭs, aŭdāx, fœdŭs, tūrpĭs, lāscīvŭs, ĭmmānĭs, īngēns, mĭsĕr, īnfēlīx.

Tlēpŏlĕmŭs, ī, m., *the leader of the Rhodians at the siege of Troy.* Sānguĭnĕ Tlēpŏlĕmŭs, Ov.

Tmōlĭŭs, ă, ŭm, *of Tmolus, Lydian.* Quŏt Tmōlĭă tērră răcēmōs, Virg.

Tmōlŭs, or Tīmōlŭs, ī, m., *a mountain of Lydia.* Tmōlŭs ŏdōrēs, Virg. EPITH. Dīvĕs, fĕrāx, fœcūndŭs, fērtĭlĭs, ārdŭŭs, āltŭs, sŭblīmĭs, aērĭŭs, vĭrēns, vĭrĭdĭs, grātŭs, ămœnŭs.

tōfŭs, ī, m., *a kind of gravel.* Et tōfŭs scăbĕr, Virg.

tŏgă, œ, f., *a Roman garment.* Cuī tŏgă lāxă, Tib. EPITH. Rōmānă, Aŭsŏnĭă, Lătĭă, lōngă, flŭēns, pācĭfĭcă, ūrbānă. V. Vestis.

tŏgātŭs, and ŭlŭs, ă, ŭm, *dressed in the toga.* Gēntēmquĕ tŏgātăm, Virg. Nŭ- mĕrŭs tŏgātŭlōrŭm, (Phal.) Mart.

tŏgŭlă, œ, f., *the dimin. of* toga. Nōbĭs tŏgŭla ēst vīlīsquĕ pŭtrīsquĕ, Mart.

tŏlĕrābĭlĭs, ĕ, *that may be endured.* Nōn tŏlĕrābĭlĕ nōmĕn, Virg.

tŏlĕro, ās, *to endure.* Tē tŏlĕrārĕ măgīstrō, Virg. SYN. Fĕro, pērfĕro, pătĭŏr, pērpĕtĭŏr, sŭstĭnĕo, sŭbĕo, ēxhaŭrĭo, ēxāntlo.

tōllo, sūstŭlī, sūblātŭm, *to lift, to take away.* Tōllēmŭs ĭn āstră, Virg. SYN. Evĕho, ēxtōllo, ēffĕro, ērĭgo, āttōllo; aŭfĕro, dētrăho.

Tŏlōsă, œ, f., *a town of France.* Dōctă Tŏlōsœ, Aus. EPITH. Māgnă, pŏpŭlōsă, splēndĭdă, cĕlebrĭs, īnclўtă, dīvĕs, pŏtēns, dōctă, fācūndă. V. Urbs.

Tŏlūmnĭŭs, ī, m., *the name of an ancient augur.* Fēlīxquĕ Tŏlūmnĭŭs, ēt quŏs, Virg.

tŏlūtĭm, adv., *with an ambling pace.* Acclīvĕ tŏlūtĭm, Lucil.

tŏmăcēllă, cīnă, œ, f., cŭlŭm *and* clŭm, ī, n., *a sausage.* Dīvīnă tŏmăcŭlă pōscī, Juv. Quī tŏmăclă raŭcŭs, (Phal.) Mart.

tŏmēntŭm, ī, n., *stuffing, as wool, feathers, &c.* Tōmēntŭm cōncīsă pălŭs, Mart.

Tŏmī, ōrŭm, m. pl., Tŏmŏs, ī, m., *and* Tŏmĭs, ĭs, f., *a town on the Euxine sea at the mouth of the Danube, where Ovid died in exile.* Vĕtĕrēsquĕ Tŏmī, Claud. Indĕ Tŏmĭs dīctŭs lŏcŭs ēst, Ov.

Tŏmītœ, ārŭm, m. pl., *the inhabitants of Tomis.* Pŏsĭtōs ăd lævă Tŏmītăs, Ov.

tŏmŭs, ī, m., *a volume.* Et tŏmŭs vīlĭs, Mart. SYN. Lĭbĕr, vŏlūmĕn.

Tŏmȳrĭs, ĭs, f., *a queen of the Massagetæ. who defeated Cyrus and put him to death.* Rēgnă vāgō Tŏmȳrīs fīnīvĭt Ărāxĕ, Tib.

Tŏnāns, ntĭs, m., *the Thunderer, a name of Jupiter.* Nūrūs Tŏnāntĭs, (Iamb.) Sen. V. Jupiter.

tŏndĕo, tŏtŏndī, tŏnsŭm, *to clip.* Tŏndēbĭt pŭĕrōs, Mart. Syn. Attŏndĕo, dĕtŏndĕo.

tŏnĭtrālĭs, ĕ, *thundering.* Cœlī tŏnĭtrālĭă tēmplă, Lucr

tŏnĭtrū, n., (*indecl.*) trŭs, ūs, m., *and* trŭŭm, ī, n., *thunder.* Et tŏnĭtrū cœlŭm, Virg. Epith. Grăvĕ, raŭcŭm, sŏnŏrŭm, tērrĭfĭcŭm, cŏrŭscŭm, văgŭm, sŭbĭtŭm, hŏrrĭsŏnŭm, tērrĭbĭlĕ, rĕbŏāns, cŏmmŏtŭm. V. Fulmen, fulgor.

tŏno, ās, āvī *or* ŭī, *to thunder.* Pŏrtă tŏnăt, Virg. V. Fulgur, tempestas.

tŏnsæ, ārŭm, f. pl., *oars.* Mārmŏrĕ tŏnsæ, Virg.

tŏnsĭlĭs, ĕ, *clipped, shaved.* Tŏnsĭlĭquĕ bŭxētō, (Scaz.) Mart.

tŏnsŏr, ōrĭs, m., *and* strĭx, ĭcĭs, f., *a barber.* Tŏnsōrĕm căpĭtī, Mart. Et tŏnsōrĭbŭs ēssĕ, Hor. Sĕd ĭstă tŏnstrĭx, (Scaz.) Mart. Epith. Fĭdŭs, fĭdēlĭs, dŏctŭs, sŏlērs, vĭgĭl, ĭndŭstrĭŭs, cŭltŭs.

tŏnsūră, æ, f., *a clipping.* Rĭgĭdōs tŏnsūră căpĭllōs, Ov.

tŏnŭs, ī, m., *tone.* Illă tŏnĭs, Cap. Epith. Dŭlcĭs, suāvĭs, grătŭs, Aŏnĭŭs, flēbĭlĭs, lŭgubrĭs.

tŏpăzŭs, ī, f., *and* zĭŭm, ĭī, n., *a topaz.* Clără tŏpăzŭs ĭnēst, Fort. Epith. Vĭrĭdĭs, vĭrēns, mĭcāns. V. Gemma.

tŏrāl, ālĭs, n., *bed-clothes.* Tŭrpĕ tŏrāl, nĕ, Virg.

tŏrcŭlăr, ārĭs, n., *a press for wine.* Tŏrcŭlārĭă sŏlŭs, Fort. Syn. Prælŭm. Epith. Strīdēns, prĕmēns, strĕpēns, ūdŭm, mădĭdŭm. V. Prælum.

tŏreŭmă, ătĭs, n., *any embossed work.* Tĕpĭdĭquĕ tŏreŭmătă Nīlī, Mart. Epith. Cœlātŭm, mārmŏrĕŭm, aŭrĕŭm.

tŏrmēntŭm, ī, n., *a torment.* Tŏrmēntō fŏrtĭŭs. Syn. Pœnă, sŭpplĭcĭŭm, crŭcĭātŭs. V. Pœna.—2. *an engine of war.* Mājūs tŏrmēntŭm, Hor. Syn. Măchĭnă bēllĭcă, bălīstă. Epith. Mŭrālĕ, fŭlmĭnĕŭm, ænĕŭm, ĭmmānĕ, strĕpēns, tŏnāns, Vŭlcānĭŭm, Māvŏrtĭŭm. V. Balista, machina.

tŏrno, ās, *to work with a wheel, as a turner.* Et mălĕ tŏrnātōs, Hor.

tŏrnŭs, ī, m., *a turner's wheel.* Făcĭlī tŏrnō sŭpĕrāddĭtă, Virg.

tŏrōsŭs, ă, ŭm, *brawny.* Mŭltŭmquĕ tŏrōsă jŭvēntŭs, Pers. Syn. Lăcērtōsŭs, nērvōsŭs.

tŏrpēdo, ĭnĭs, f., *numbness, idleness.* Mīræ tŏrpēdĭnĭs ārtĕm, Clem.

tŏrpĕo, ēs, *and* ēsco, ĭs, *to be benumbed.* Mēmbră gĕlū tŏrpēscŭnt, Sen. Nēc tŏrpērĕ grăvī, Virg. Syn. Stŭpĕo, stŭpēsco.

tŏrpŏr, ōrĭs, m., *numbness.* Fŏrmīdĭnĕ tŏrpŏr, Virg. Syn. Stŭpŏr; lānguŏr. V. Stupor, pigritia.

tŏrpĭdŭs, ă, ŭm, *benumbed, torpid.* Tŏrpĭdă sŭprēmōs, Aus.

tŏrquātŭs, ă, ŭm, *wearing a collar.* Tŏrquātă cŏlŭbrĭs, Ov.

tŏrquĕo, sī, tŭm, *to twist.* Tŏrquĕt hūmō, Prop. Syn. Intŏrquĕo, flēcto, ĭnflēcto; crŭcĭo, vēxo, ēxcrŭcĭo, ango, pūngo; vibro, jăcŭlōr.

tŏrquēs *or* ĭs, ĭs, m., *a collar.* Tŏrquĭbŭs āræ, Virg. Epith. Dīvĕs, mĭcāns, aŭrĕŭs. V. Monile.

tŏrrēns, ntĭs, m., *a torrent.* Intŭlĕrāt tŏrrēns, Virg. Epith. Răpāx, præcēps, vēlōx, vĭŏlēntŭs, ăquŏsŭs, tŭrbĭdŭs, spūmāns, hȳbērnŭs, fŭrēns, cădēns, rŭēns, lābēns, sŏnōrŭs, sŭbĭtŭs, mōntānŭs. V. Pluvius, inundatio.—2. ntĭs, adj., *rapid, violent.* Tŏrrēntem ūndăm, Virg.

tŏrrĕo, ēs, *to roast, to burn.* Et tŏrrērĕ părānt, Virg. Syn. Asso; ūro, crĕmo, ădūro, pĕrūro, ēxūro. V. Uro.

tŏrrēsco, ĭs, *to be burnt.* Călĭdĭs tŏrrēscĕrĕ flămmĭs, Lucr.

tŏrrĭdŭs, ă, ŭm, *burnt.* Tŏrrĭdă sēmpĕr, Virg. Syn. Ustŭs, ēxūstŭs, pĕrūstŭs; ārĭdŭs, sĭccŭs, ărēns.

tŏrrĭs, ĭs, m., *a firebrand.* Fŭnĕrĕŭm tŏrrĕm, Ov. Syn. Tĭtĭo. Epith. Ardēns, fūmāns, āmbūstŭs, āccēnsŭs, flāmmāns, flāmmĭfĕr, Ignītŭs, Ignĕŭs, rŭbēns, ĭgnĭfĕr

tŏrtĕ, adv., *crookedly.* Tŏrtĕ pĕnĭtŭsquĕ, Ov.

tŏrtĭlĭs, ĕ, *crooked, twisted.* Tŏrtĭlĭbŭs vībrātă, Lucan. Syn. Tŏrtŭs, ĭntŏrtŭs.

tŏrtŏr, ōrĭs, m., *an executioner.* Ălĭquĭs tŏrtŏrĕ vŏcātō, Juv. V. Carnifex.

tŏrtŭs, ūs, m., *a twisting.* Dăt cŏrpŏrĕ tŏrtŭs, Virg.

tŏrŭs, ī, m., *a bed, muscles.* Vĭrĭdāntĕ tŏrō, Virg. Syn. Lēctŭs, cŭbĭlĕ; lăcērtŭs, nĕrvŭs.

tŏrvă, ē, *or* ŭm, adv., *sternly.* Tŏrvă tŭēntĕm, Virg. Mē tŏrve āspēctās, Plaut. Tŏrvūmquĕ rĕpēntĕ, Ov.

tŏrvŭs, ă, ŭm, *fierce.* Ŏptĭmă tŏrvæ, Virg.

tŏt, indecl., *so many.* Vĭrūm, tŏt ădīrĕ, Virg.

tŏtĭdĕm, *so many.* Pĕlăgō tŏtĭdĕm sĭnĕ, Virg.

tŏtĭes, adv., *so often.* Extrēmū tŏtĭēs ēxōrĕt, Hor.

tōtŭs, ă, ŭm, *all.* Instūbāt tōtā cuī, Tib. Syn. Ōmnĭs, cūnctŭs, ūnĭvērsŭs, īntĕgĕr, pērfēctŭs, plēnŭs, sōlĭdŭs.

Tŏxcūs, ĕŏs, ĕī *or* eī, m., *the son of Œneus, and brother of Althœa.* Tŏxĕă, quīd făcĭăt, Ov

tŏxĭcŭm, ī, n., *poison.* Tŏxĭcă Thēssălĭă, Prop. V. Venenum.

trăbālĭs, ĕ, *of or like a beam.* Mūltă trăbālī, Virg.

trăbĕă, æ, f., *a robe worn by kings, consuls, and augurs.* Sŭccīnctŭs trăbĕā, Virg. Epitii. Rŏmŭlĕă, Quĭrīnālĭs; pūrpŭrĕă, sacră. V. Vestis.

trăbĕātŭs, ă, ŭm, *wearing the trabea.* Vīdīt trăbĕātī, Ov.

trăbs, trăbĭs, *and* bēcŭlă, æ, f. *timber, a beam of a house.* Hīc trăbĭbŭs cōntēxtŭs, Virg. Syn. Tīgnŭm, tĭgīllŭm, rōbŭr. Epitii. Lōngă, fīrmă, sŏlĭdă, vălĭdă, ārbŏrĕă, frăxĭnĕă, quērnă, ăcērnă, sēctă, cōntēxtă, cōmpāctĭlĭs.

Trăchās, æ, f., *another name of Anxur.* Trăchāsque ōbsēssă pălūdĕ, Ov.

Trăchȳn, ȳnĭs, *or* chīn, īnĭs, f., *a city of Thessaly.* Hērcŭlĕă Trăchīnĕ jŭbē, Ov.

Trăchȳnĭŭs, *or* īnĭŭs, ă, ŭm, *of Trachin.* Trăchīnĭŭs hērōs, Ov

trāctă, æ, f., *and* tă, ōrŭm, n. pl., *carded wool.* Trāctăquĕ dē nĭvĕō, Tibul.

trāctābĭlĭs, ĕ, *tractable, gentle.* Nōn trāctābĭlĕ cœlŭm, Virg. Syn. Dŏcĭlĭs, făcĭlĭs, mānsuētŭs, bĕnignŭs. V. Comis.

trāctātŏr, ōrĭs, m., *and* trīx, īcĭs, f., *a handler, one employed to rub the body.* Trāctātŏr īgnĭs, Sen. Ārtĕ trāctātrīx, (Scaz.) Mart.

trāctĭm, adv., *continually.* Trāctĭmquĕ sŭsūrrānt, Virg. Syn. Jūgĭtĕr, cōntĭnŭō, lōngō trāctū.

trācto, ās, *to handle.* Trāctānt făbrīlĭă, Hor. Syn. Āttrācto, cōntrēcto, tāngo; mănĭbŭs pērtēnto, vērso, vŏlūto; mūlcĕo, dēmūlcĕo, lēnĭo, dēlīnĭo; dīspŭto, dīssĕro; dŏcĕo.

trāctŭs, ūs, m., *a drawing, dragging.* Trāctūquĕ gĕmēntĕm, Virg.—2. *a country, a tract.* Trāctū sūrgēns ŏlĕăstĕr, Id. Syn. Ōră, plăgă, rĕgĭo, tēllūs, tērră, sŏlŭm.

* trādĭtŏr, ōrĭs, m., *a traitor.* Trādĭtŏr īmmītĭs, Sed.

trādĭtŭs, ă, ŭm, *the pass. partic. of* trado. Trādĭtum ăb āntīquīs, Hor.

trādo, trādĭdī, dĭtŭm, *to deliver, give.* Trādĭdīt Ægōn, Virg. Syn. Prōdo; dō, praebĕo, trībŭo; dŏcĕo, dīco, rĕfĕro, nārro, mĕmŏro, cōmmĕmŏro.

trādūco, xī, ctŭm, *to transfer.* Vīdī trādūcĕrĕ mēssēs, Virg. Syn. Trānsfĕro, ābdūco, cōnvērto, rĕfĕro, cōnfĕro; prōdūco, prōtrăho, ăgo, dūco, cōnsūmo; trājĭcĭo, trānsvĕho.

trăgĭcŭs, ă, ŭm, *tragic.* Quī trăgĭcō vīlĕm, Hor. Syn. Trīstĭs, fătālĭs, fūnēstŭs.

trăgœdĭă, æ, f., *tragedy.* Indīgnă trăgœdĭă vērsŭs, Hor. Epitii. Trīstĭs, mœstă, flēbĭlĭs, lacrȳmōsă, grăvĭs, sĕvēră. V. Cothurnus.

trăgœdŭs, ī, m., *a tragic actor.* Hĭāndă trăgœdō, Pers. Epitii. Grăvĭs, vōcĭfĕrāns, mœstŭs.

trăgŭlă, æ, f., *a kind of javelin.* Trăgŭlă sēmpĕr, Sil.

trăgŭs, ī, m., *a kind of fish.* Pērcæquĕ trăgĭquĕ, Ov.

trăhă *and* ĕă, æ, f., *a dray.* Trībŭlăquĕ trăhĕæquĕ.

trăho, trāxī, ctŭm, *to drag, attract.* Nē trăhăt ēt mēnsæ, Tib. Syn. Ēxtrăho, āttrăho, haūrĭo; răpĭo, dūco, ābdūco; āllĭcĭo, āllēcto, īmpēllo.

Trājānŭs, ī, m., *the Roman emperor.* Prīncēps Trājānĕ, mĕrŭrĭs, Mart.

trājĭcĭo, trājēcī, ctŭm, *to cast across, transport, trans er, pierce, cross, pass over.* Cūrsū trājēcĕrăt āxēm, Virg. Syn. Trānsĕo, trānsgrĕdĭor; trānsmītto, trādūco, trānsfĕro, trānsvĕho; trānsfīgo, trānsădĭgo.

trămă, æ, f., *the woof.* Trāmă lĭgūræ, Pers.

T 3

trāmĕs, ĭtĭs, m., *a cross-way.* Trāmĭtĕ vŭlgŭs, Prop. V. Collis, via.
trāno, ās, *to swim across.* Ĕrĕbī trănāvĭmŭs āmnēs, Virg. Syn. Trānsno, trāns-nǎto ; trānsĕo, trānsmĕo. V. Nato.
* trănquīllĭtās, ātĭs, f., *quietness.* Cic. Syn. Pāx, quĭēs. V. Quies, pax.
trānquīllo, ās, *to calm.* Quīd pūrē trānquīllĕt hŏnōs, Hor. Syn. Pāco, sēdo, lēnĭo, tēmpĕro.
trānquīllŭs, ǎ, ŭm, *quiet.* Trānquīllā sĕnēctūs, Hor. Syn. Quĭētŭs, plǎcĭdŭs, pācātŭs.
trāns, prep., *beyond.* Trāns mǎrĕ, Hor.
trānsăbĕo, īs, ĭī, *to go beyond.* Lōngē trānsăbĭīt, V. Fl.
trānsădĭgo, ēgī, āctŭm, *to pierce through.* Trānsădĭgīt cōstās, Virg. Syn. Trāns-vērbĕro, trānsfīgo, trānsfŏdĭo. V. Transfigo.
trānscēndo, dī, *to surmount.* Fīnēs trānscēndĕrĕ jūrĭs, Lucr. Syn. Sŭpĕro, trānsgrĕdĭŏr, āscēndo. V. Ascendo.
trānscrībo, psī, ptŭm, *to transcribe.* Dārdănĭīs trānscrībī, Virg. Syn. Exscrībo, dēscrībo ; trānsfĕro.
trānscŭrro, ĭs, *to run across.* Cœlŭm trānscŭrrĕrĕ, Virg.
ꞅrānsĕo, īvī, *to go beyond.* Trānsĭĕrāt, sōlĭtō, Ov. Syn. Trānsgrĕdĭŏr, trānsmĕo, trānsmigro, trājĭcĭo, pērmĕo, trānscēndo, trānsmītto, pĕnetro, pērvādo, rūmpo, pērrūmpo, trānsĭlĭo ; ŏmītto, prætĕrĕo. V. Eo.
trānsērtŭs, ǎ, ŭm, *engrafted.* Vīdi ĕgŏ trānsērtōs, Stat. Syn. Insĭtŭs.
trānsfĕro, tŭlī, lātŭm, *to carry over.* Trānsfĕrĕt ĕt, Virg. Syn. Trānsvĕho, trānspōrto, trājĭcĭo, trānsmītto, trādūco.
trānsfīgo, fīxī, xŭm, *to pierce through.* Trānsfīgĕrĕ fērrō, Mart. Syn. Trāns-ădĭgo, trānsfŏdĭo, trājĭcĭo, trānsvērbĕro, cōnfŏdĭo.
trānsfĭgūro, ās, *to change, transform.* Cōrpŏrǎ prīmǎ trānsfĭgūrānt, Stat.
trānsflŭo, īs, *to flow past, pass by.* Trānsflūxĕrĕ dĭēs, Claud.
trānsfŏdĭo, fōdī, fōssŭm, *to thrust through.* Gĕmĭnŏ trānsfōdīt vūlnĕrĕ, Ov. V. Transfigo.
trānsfōrmĭs, ĕ, *changing the form.* Trānsfōrmĭs ădŭltĕrăt ārtĕ, Ov.
trānsfōrmo, ās, *to transform.* Ōmnĭǎ trānsfōrmăt, Virg. Syn. Mūto, ĭmmūto, vărĭo. V. Metamorphosis.
trānsfŏro, ās, *to transpierce.* Pēctŭs trāns☞ōrăt, Sil.
trānsfŭgǎ, æ, m. f., *a deserter.* Trānsfūgǎ dīvĭtŭm, (Chor.) Hor. Syn. Pērfūgǎ, dēsērtŏr.
trānsfŭmo, ās, *to smoke through.* Trānsfūmăt ănhēlĭtŭs, Stat.
trānsfŭndo, ĭs, *to pour from one vessel into another.* Mǎnū trānsfūndĕt ĭn ūrnǎm, Lucr.
trānsgrĕdĭŏr, ĕrĭs, *to go beyond.* Pōstrēmī trānsgrĕdĭēntŭr, Juv. Syn. Trānsĕo, -ăbĕo, -scēndo.
trānsĭgo, ēgī, āctŭm, *to transact, to pierce through.* Jūstō trānsēgĭt Achīllĕǎ, Lucan. Syn. Trādūco, pĕrăgo, dūco, ăgo.
trānsĭlĭo, ĭī, *to jump over.* Trānsĭlĭt ūmbrās, Virg. Syn. Trānsĕo, trājĭcĭo, pērmĕo, pĕnetro, pērvādo, pērrūmpo, prætĕrĕo.
trānsĭtĭo, ōnĭs, f., *and* ĭtŭs, ūs, m., *a passage.* Trānsĭtĭŏnĕ nŏcēnt, Ov. Trānsĭtŭs īpsĕ, Ov. Epith. Brĕvĭs, făcĭlĭs. V. Via.
trānslābŏr, ĕrĭs, *to slide over.* Trānslāpsǎ vŏlātū, Cl.
trānslātŭs, ǎ, ŭm, *the pass. partic. of* transfero. Ēheū trānslātōs, Hor.
trānslūcĕo, ēs, *to be transparent.* In lĭquĭdīs trānslūcĕt ăquĭs, Ov. V. Per-luceo.
trānslūcĭdŭs, ǎ, ŭm, *transparent.* Trānslūcĭdŭs ūndǎ, Sil.
* trānsmigro, ās, *to change a dwelling.* Liv. V. Transeo.
trānsmītto, ĭs, *to send over.* Trānsmīttŭnt cūrsū, Virg.
trānsmŏvĕo, ēs, mōvī, *to remove.* In sē trānsmŏvĕt, Ter.
trānsmŭto, ās, *to change.* Imǎ lŏcāns, trānsmūtāns, Lucr. Syn. Immūto, cōm-mūto, mūto.
trānsnăto, ās, *and* no, ās, *to swim over,* Sil. Trānsnāntŏ Tībĕrĭm, Hor. Syn. Ēnăto, trānsmĕo. V. Trano.
trānspēctŭs, ūs, m., *a looking through.* Pēr sē trānspēctŭm, Lucr.
trānspĭcĭo, ĭs, *to see through.* Vērē trānspĭcĭūntŭr, Lucr.
trānspōrto, ās, *to carry over.* Trānspōrtărĕ dǎtŭr, Virg. V. Trajicio.

trānstră. ōrŭm, n. pl., *seats for rowers.* Cōnsĭdĕrĕ trŭnstrīs, Virg

trānsvĕho, ĭs, *to transport.* Quæ trānsvĕhăt ăgmĭnă, Stat.

trānsūmo, ĭs, msĭ, *to take from one to another.* Lævă trānsūmĭt ĕt ălto, Stat.

trānsŭo, ĭs, *to pierce with a needle.* Vĕrŭbŭs trānsŭtă, Ov.

trānsvĕrbĕro, ās, *to pierce through.* Clўpĕī trānsvĕrbĕrăt æră, Virg. Syn. Trānsfŏdĭo, trānsfīgo. V. Transfīgo.

trānsvērsŭs, ă, ŭm, *across, crosswise.* Trānsvĕraō călămō, Hor. Syn. Ōblīquŭs.

trānsvŏlĭto, *and* lo, ās, *to fly over.* Trānsvŏlăt īn mĕdĭō, Hor.

trăpētŭm, ī, n., *or* pēs, ĕtĭs, m.. *an oil-press.* Băccă trăpētĭs, Virg. Epith. Ŭnctŭm, mădĭdŭm, Pāllădĭŭm, dūrŭm, mărmŏrĕŭm, rŭdĕ.

Trăsĭmēnŭs, ī, m., *a lake in Italy, near which Hannibal defeated the Romans.* Et Trăsĭmēnī nōmĭnă, Sil.

trăvĭo, ās, *to pass through.* Trăvĭăt ōmnĭs, Lucr. Syn. Trānsmĕo.

Traūsĭŭs, ĭī, m., *the name of a man.* Traūsĭŭs īstĭs, Hor.

Trĕbūtĭŭs, ĭī, m., *a celebrated jurisconsult in the time of Cicero.* Pōssĕ, Trĕbātī, Hor.

Trĕbĭă, æ, f., *a river of Italy, near which Hannibal defeated the Romans.* Cănnārŭm Trĕbĭæquĕ, Luc.

Trĕbōnĭŭs, ĭī, m., *the name of a man.* Fāmă Trĕbōnī, Hor.

trĕcĕnī, *or* ĕntī, æ, ă, *three hundred.* Nōn sī trĕcēnĭs, (Alc.) Hor. Ilvă trĕcēntōs, Virg. Syn. Tĕr cēntŭm.

trĕcēntĭēs, adv., *three hundred times.* Aūt trĕcēntĭēs, (Iamb.) Cat.

trĕmĕbŭndŭs, ă, ŭm, *trembling with fear.* Prīmă trĕmĕbŭndŭs, Mart. Syn. Trĕmĕfāctŭs, trĕmēns, păvĭdŭs.

trĕmĕfăcĭo, ĭs, *to cause to tremble.* Nūtū trĕmĕfēcĭt Ŏlȳmpŭm, Virg. Syn. Tērrĕo, ēxtērrĕo; trĕmōrĕ cōncŭtĭo.

trĕmēndŭs, ă, ŭm, *the gerund. partic. of* tremo. Ădȳtūquĕ trĕmēndŭs, Stat.

trĕmīsco, ĭs, *to begin to tremble.* Tōnĭtrūquĕ trĕmīscunt, Virg.

trĕmo, ŭī, *to tremble.* Pīctă trĕmēbăt ăquă, Prop. Syn. Trĕmīsco, cōntrĕmīsco, trĕpĭdo, hōrrĕo; văcīllo, nūto, lăbo. V. Timeo.

trĕmŏr, ōrĭs, m., *a trembling.* Trĕmŏr ōccŭpăt, Virg. Syn. Trĕpĭdătĭo; hōrrŏr, păvŏr, tĭmŏr. V. Timor.

trĕmŭlŭs, ă, ŭm, *trembling.* Trĕmŭlŏquĕ grădū, Ov. Syn. Trĕmēns, trĕmĕfāctŭs, trĕpĭdāns, trĕpĭdŭs, trĕmĕbŭndŭs, păvĭdŭs, tĭmĭdŭs, tērrĭtŭs, cōntērrĭtŭs. V. Timens.

trĕpĭdo, ās, *to tremble, shake.* Ĭngēntī trĕpĭdārĕ mĕtū, Virg. Syn. Trĕmo, hōrrĕo.

trĕpĭdŭs, ă, ŭm, *trembling, alarmed.* Accēpĭt trĕpĭdōs, āc, Virg. Syn. Trĕmēns, trĕmĕfāctŭs, trĕpĭdāns, trĕmĕbŭndŭs, păvĭdŭs, tĭmĭdŭs, tērrĭtŭs, ēxtērrĭtŭs, cōncŭssŭs, văcīllāns. V. Timens.

trēs, ĭă, ĭŭm, trĭbŭs, *three.* Nēctĕ trĭbŭs, Virg. Trēs Eŭrŭs, Id.

trēssĭs, ĭs, m., *of the value of three asses; of small value.* Nōn trēssĭs ăgāso, Pers.

trĭbŭlă, æ, f., *and* ŭm, ī, n., *a dray to thresh corn.* Trĭbŭlăquĕ trăhĕæque, Virg.

trĭbŭlĭs, ĕ, *of the same tribe.* Accĭpĭĕndă trĭbŭlī, Mart.

trĭbŭlŭs, ī, m., *a thistle.* Lōlĭŭm trĭbŭlīquĕ, Ov. Epith. Ăcūtŭs, āspĕr, hōrrĭdŭs, mōrdāx, scăbĕr, rĭgĭdŭs. V. Carduus.

trĭbūnāl, ālĭs, n., *a tribunal.* Lēctĭcă, trĭbūnăl, Juv. Syn. Thrŏnŭs, sŏlĭŭm. Epith. Sŭblīmĕ; jūrĭdĭcŭm, æquŭm, jūstŭm.

trĭbūnātŭs, ūs, m., *the office of tribune.* Nōn trĭbūnātŭs, Mart.

trĭbūnĭtĭŭs, ă, ŭm, *of a tribune.* Armă trĭbūnĭtĭŭm, Mart.

trĭbūnŭs, ī, m., *a tribune.* Fĭĕrĭquĕ trĭbūnŭm, Hor. Epith. Pŏtēns, plēbĕĭŭs, tūrbŭlēntŭs, āmbĭtĭōsŭs.

trĭbŭo, ŭī, ūtŭm, *to grant, to give.* Ēt trĭbŭĕrĕ Dĕī, Mart. Syn. Dŏ, præbĕo, trădo, lārgĭŏr, īmpērtĭo; dēfĕro, cōncēdo; ārrŏgo, ādscrībo.

trĭbŭs, ūs, m., *a tribe.* Ēt trĭbŭs ēt gēns, Virg.

trĭbūtĭm, adv., *by tribes.* Pŏpŭlŭmquĕ trĭbūtĭm.

trĭbūtŭm, ī, n., *a tribute.* Gēntĕ trĭbūtă pĕtăt, Ov. Syn. Vēctīgăl, pōrtōrĭŭm. V. Vectigal.

trīcæ, ārŭm, f. pl., *trifles.* Sūnt ăpĭnæ, trīcæquĕ, Mart.

trīcēnī, æ, ă, *thirty.* Bĭs tĭbĭ trīcēnī sūlmŭs, Mart. Syn. Trīgīnta.

trĭcēsĭmŭs, ă, ŭm, *the thirtieth*. Plŭs trĭcēsĭmă lŭx ēst, Mart.

trĭcĕps, cĭpĭtĭs, *having three heads*. Tŭquĕ trĭcĕps, Ov. Syn. Tērgĕmĭnŭs, trĭfŏrmĭs.

trĭchĭlă, æ, f., *and* lŭm, ĭ, n., *an arbour, bower*. At quī sŭb trŭchĭlă, Colum.

trĭchōrŭm, ĭ, n., *a building divided into three dwellings*. Tēctă trĭchōrĭs, Stat.

trĭcĭēs, adv., *thirty times*. Tĭbĭ trĭcĭēs ĭn ānnŭm, Mart.

trĭclīnĭŭm, ĭĭ, *a dining-room*. Cīngānt trĭclīnĭă Baĭās, Mart. Syn. Cœnācŭlŭm.

trĭcōrpŏr, ŏrĭs, *having three bodies*. Lōngă trĭcōrpŏrĭs ārvă, Sil. Syn. Trĭfōrmĭs, tērgĕmĭnŭs.

trĭcŭspĭs, ĭdĭs, *having three points*. Pōsĭtōquĕ trĭcŭspĭdĕ, Ov. Syn. Trĭdēns, trĭfĭdŭs, trĭsŭlcŭs.

trĭdēns, ntĭs, m., *a trident*. Pērcŭssă trĭdēntĭ, Virg. Syn. Fŭscĭnă. Epith. Sævŭs, æquŏrĕŭs, mĭnăx, trĭfĭdŭs, ŭncŭs, ădŭncŭs, vălĭdŭs, tērrĭfĭcŭs, Nĕptūnĭŭs.

Trĭdēntĭfĕr, *and* gĕr, ă, ŭm, *bearing a trident*. Sŏrtītĕ Trĭdēntĭfĕr ŭndæ, Ov. Cŭmquĕ Trĭdēntĭgĕrō, Id. V. Neptunus.

Trĭdēntĭpŏtēns, ēntĭs, m., *lord of the trident*. Dīvĕ Trĭdēntĭpŏtēns, Sil.

trĭdŭŭm, ĭ, n., *three days*. Tĭbĭ trĭdŭŏ lĕgătŭr, (Phal.) Mart. V. Dies.

trĭēnnĭŭm, ĭĭ, n., *three years*. Rĕpĕtītă trĭēnnĭă, Ov. Syn. Trĭĕtērĭs.

trĭēns, ntĭs, *the third part*. Cālĭdŭmquĕ trĭēntĕm, Pers.

trĭĕtērĭcŭs, ă, ŭm, *done every three years*. Trĭĕtērĭcă Bācchī.

trĭĕtērĭs, ĭdĭs, f., *three years*. Trĭĕtērĭdĕ mēnsēs, Hor. Syn. Trĭēnnĭŭm.

trĭfaŭx, aŭcĭs, *having three mouths*. Rēgnă trĭfaŭcī, Virg. V. Cerberus.

trĭfĭdŭs, ă, ŭm, *cleft into three parts*. Hēspĕrĭæ trĭfĭdă, Ov. Syn. Trĭsŭlcŭs, trĭcŭspĭs.

trĭfōrmĭs, ĕ, *having three forms*. Dīvă trĭfōrmĭs, Hor.

trĭgēsĭmŭs, ă, ŭm, *the thirtieth*. Cōnsŭl trĭgēsĭmŭs ĭnstăt, Mart. Syn. Tĕr dĕnŭs.

trĭgīnta, indecl., *thirty*. Tĕr trĭgīntă quădrŭm, Man. Trĭgīntă māgnōs, Virg.

trĭgōn, ōnĭs, m., *a ball to play with*. Lævāquĕ trĭgōnĕm, Mart.

trĭgōnŭs, ă, ŭm, *having three corners*. Līgnă trĭgōnă, Man.

trĭhōrĭŭm, ĭĭ, n., *a period of three hours*. Pōst bīnă trĭhōrĭă cērvī, Aus.

trĭjŭgĭs, ĕ, *drawn by three horses*. Vĕl cĭsĭō trĭjŭgī, Aus.

trĭlībrĭs, ĕ, *of three pounds weight*. Insānĕ trĭlībrĕm, Hor.

trĭlĭnguĭs, ĕ, *having three tongues*. Rĕcēdēntĭs trĭlĭnguī, (Iamb.) Hor.

trĭlīx, īcĭs, *made of three threads*. Pārtēmquĕ trĭlīcĕm, Val. Fl.

trĭmēstrĭs, ĕ, *of three months*. Trīmēstrēs Annōrŭm, Aus.

trĭmĕtĕr, *or* trŭm, ī, *an Iambic verse of six feet*. Nōbĭlĭbŭs trĭmĕtrĭs, Hor.

trĭmŭs, ă, ŭm, *three years old*. Equă trīmă cāmpĭs, Hor.

Trīnacrĭă, æ, f., *Sicily*. Quăm tŭă Trīnăcrĭa ēst, Ov. V. Sicilia.

Trīnacrĭs, ĭdĭs, f., *Sicilian ; Sicily*. Trīnăcrĭs ēst ŏcŭlĭs, Ov.

* SS. Trīnĭtās, ātĭs, f., *the Holy Trinity*. Eccl. Hŏnōrĕm Trīnĭtātĭs hōspĭtæ, (Iamb.) Prud. Syn. Trĭās. Epith. Sānctă, ălmă, vĕnĕrāndă, ădōrāndă. V. Deus.

Trīnacrĭŭs, ă, ŭm, *Sicilian*. Præstăt Trīnăcrĭī, Virg. V. Siculus.

trĭnōctĭālĭs, ĕ, *of three nights*. Gĕnĭtŏr trĭnōctĭālī, Mart.

trĭnōctĭŭm, ĭĭ, n., *the space of three nights*. Cĕlĕbrātă trĭnōctĭă lūdō, Aus.

trĭnōdĭs, ĕ, *having three knots*. Pērfrāctă trĭnōdī, Ov.

trīnŭs, ă, ŭm, *bearing three*. Quæ trīnō jŭvĕnĭs, (Phal.) Stat.

Trĭōnēs, ŭm, m. pl., *a constellation*. Gĕmĭnōsquĕ Trĭōnēs, Virg. Epith. Hўpĕr bŏrĕī, gĕlĭdī, glăcĭālēs, nĭvōsī. V. Arctos.

Trĭŏpēĭs, ĭdĭs, f., *Metra, the grand-daughter of Triopas*. Pătĕr Trĭŏpēĭdă vēndĭt, Ov.

Trĭŏpēĭŭs, ĭĭ, m., *the son of Triopas, Erisichthon*. Fērrŭm Trĭŏpēĭŭs ĭllă, Ov.

trĭpēctŏrŭs, ă, ŭm, *having three bodies*. Quĭdvĕ trĭpēctŏră, Lucr.

trĭpēs, ĕdĭs, *having three feet*. Ibăt trĭpēs grăbātŭs, (Scaz.) Mart.

triplēx, ĭcĭs, *and* plŭs, ă, ŭm, *treble*. Nĕc vānī trĭplĭcēs, (Phal.) Mart. Syn. Tērgĕmĭnŭs.

trĭplĭco, ās, *to treble*. Trĭplĭcābĭt Äquārĭŭs ānnōs, Man.

Trĭptōlĕmŭs, ī, m , *the son of Celeus, whom Ceres suckled and instructed in agriculture*. Trĭptōlĕmŭm grĕmĭō, Ov.

trĭpŭdĭo, ās, *to dance, to caper.* Trĭpŭdĭārĕ grădū, Fort. Syn. Exsŭlto, sălto. V. Salto, chorea.
trĭpŭdĭŭm, ĭī, n., *a caper.* Cĕlĕbrārĕ trĭpŭdĭīs, Cat.
trĭpŭs, ŏdĭs, m., *a tripod, a three-footed stool.* Et trĭpŏdäs sĕptĕm, Ov. Syn. Cŏrtīnă. Epith. Săcĕr, fŭtĭdĭcŭs, præsăgŭs, cĕlĕbrĭs, Delphĭcŭs, Apŏllĭnĕŭs, Phœbĕŭs.
Trĭquetră, æ, f., *Sicily.* Prōmīssă Trĭquĕtrā, Hor.
trĭquetrŭs, ă, ŭm, *triangular.* Quĕm trĭquĕtrĭs, Lucr.
trĭrēmĭs, ĭs, f., *a galley with three oars.* Prīvă trĭrēmĭs, Hor. Syn. Nāvĭs, rătĭs. V. Navis.
trīscŭrrĭă, ōrŭm, n. pl., *buffooneries.* Trīscŭrrĭă pātrĭcĭōrŭm, Juv.
trīstĭs, ĕ, *sorrowful.* Trīstĭs ĕt āspĕr, Tib. Syn. Mœstŭs, mœrēns, dŏlēns, āfflīctŭs, ānxĭŭs, sŏllĭcĭtŭs, cōntrīstātŭs. V. Doleo, tristitia.
trīstĭtĭă, æ, f., *grief.* Pēctŏră trīstĭtĭæ, Tib. Syn. Mœrŏr, mœstĭtĭă, dŏlŏr, āngŏr, squālŏr, lūctŭs, ærūmnă, ānxĭĕtās. Epith. Grăvĭs, ăcŭrbă, mŏlēstă, quĕrŭlă, ăcūtă, ăcrĭs, ĭntŏlĕrābĭlĭs, sŭmmă, vĭŏlēntă, īnfāndă, īnsānă, sævă, ŏdĭōsă, fīctă, ŏccūltă, pērpĕtŭă, dĭūtūrnă, lāuguēns, squālēns, āuxĭă, sŏllĭcĭtă, īngēns, atrōx. V. Dolor.
‖ trīstŏr, ārĭs, *to be sorrowful.* Syn. Mœrĕo, cōntrīstŏr, dŏlĕo, gĕmo. V. Dolor, gemo, queror, tristis.
trĭsūlcŭs, ă, ŭm, *with three points.* Ōrĕ trĭsūlcīs, Virg. Syn. Trĭfĭdŭs, trĭcūspĭs, trĭdēns.
trītĭcĕŭs, ă, ŭm, *of wheat.* Āt sī trītĭcĕăm, Virg. Syn. Cĕrĕālĭs.
* trītĭcŭm, ī, n., *wheat.* Syn. Fār, frūmēntŭm, trītĭcĕă sĕgĕs. V. Frumentum, seges.
Trītōn, ōnĭs, m., *a sea-god.* Trītōnēsquĕ cĭtī, Virg. Epith. Cœrŭlĕŭs, cœrŭlŭs, æquŏrĕŭs, mărīnŭs, glaūcŭs, sēmĭfĕr, squāmōsŭs, squāmĕŭs, flŭctĭvăgŭs, hūmĭdŭs, ŭdŭs, hūmēns, mădĭdŭs, răpĭdŭs, lēvĭs, cĕlĕr, vēlōx.
Trītōnĭă, æ, *and* nĭs, ĭdĭs, f., *a name of Minerva.* Dēdīt Trītōnĭă mōnstrīs, Virg. Trītōnĭdĭs ālmæ, Lucr. V. Minerva.
Trītōnĭăcŭs, ă, ŭm, *of Minerva.* Quēm Trītōnĭăcă, Ov.
trītūră, æ, f., *a grinding.* Vĕnĭĕt trītūră călōrĕ, Virg.
trītŭs, ă, ŭm, *the pass. partic. of* tero. Trītŭs ĕt ē, Juv.
Trĭvĭă, æ, f., *a name of Diana.* Sŭbĕŭnt Trĭvĭæ lūcōs, Virg. V. Diana, Proserpina.
trĭvĭālĭs, ĕ, *common, vulgar.* Cārmēn trĭvĭălĕ, Juv.
Trĭvĭcŭs, ī, m., *a town of Italy.* Vīllā Trĭvĭcī, Hor.
trĭvĭŭm, ī, n., *a place where three roads meet.* Ōmnĭbŭs īn trĭvĭīs, Cat.
trĭŭmphālĭs, ĕ, *of a triumph.* Sāxă trĭŭmphālēs, Prop.
trĭŭmphātŏr, ōrĭs, m., *one who obtains triumphal honours.* Ergŏ trĭŭmphātŏr, Prud. Syn. Trĭŭmphāns, ŏvāns, vīctŏr. V. Victor.
trĭŭmphātŭs, ă, ŭm, *the pass. partic. of* triumpho. Illĕ trĭŭmphātā, Virg.
trĭŭmpho, ās, *to triumph.* Mūsă trĭŭmphăt ĕquĭs, Prop. Syn. Ovo ; ĕxŭlto, lætĭtĭā gēstĭo. V. Victor, triumphus.
trĭŭmphŭs, ī, m., *a triumph.* Rēgĭnă trĭŭmphō, Virg. Syn. Ovătĭo. Epith. Clārŭs, īnsīgnĭs, cĕlebrĭs, sŭpērbŭs, lætŭs, fēstŭs, fēstīvŭs, săcĕr, aūgŭstŭs, laūrĭgĕr, sŭblīmĭs, dĕcōrŭs, āmbĭtĭōsŭs.
trĭŭmvĭr, ī, m., trĭŭmvĭrī, ōrŭm, m. pl., *Roman magistrates.* Ov.
trĭŭmvĭrālĭs, ĕ, *of the triumvirs.* Flăgēllīs hīc trĭŭmvĭrālĭbŭs, Hor.
Trōäs, ădĭs, f., *the Troad ; or a Trojan woman.* Trōădĕs āctā, Virg. Syn. Teūcrĭs, Dārdănĭs, Ilĭăs, Trōjānă.
trochlĕă, ĕæ, f., *a pulley.* Pēr trŏchlĕās, Lucr.
trŏchŭs, ī, m., *a top.* Dīscĭvĕ trŏchĭvĕ, Hor. Syn. Tūrbo. Epith. Vērsātĭlĭs, vŏlūbĭlĭs, ăgĭtābĭlĭs, cĕlĕr, lēvĭs.
Trōĕs, ŭm, n. pl. V. Trojani.
Trœzēu, ēnĭs, f., *a city of the Peloponnesus.* Cŭrrū Trœzēuă pĕtēbăm, Ov.
Trœzēnĭŭs, ă, ŭm, *of Trœzen.* Trœzēnĭŭs hērōs, Ov.
Trōĭădĕs, ŭm, f. pl., *Trojan women.* Pŏlўdāmās ēt Trōĭădĕs Lăbĕōnĕm, Pers.
Trōĭcŭs, ĭŭs, *and* jānŭs, ă, ŭm, *Trojan.* Trōĭcă quī prŏfŭgĭs, Tib. Trōĭă gāză, Virg. Trōjānās ŭt ŏpĕs, Id.
Trōĭlŭs, ī, m., *a son of Priam, slain by Achilles.* Āmīssīs Trōĭlŭs ārmīs, Virg.

Trōjă, æ, f., *Troy.* Trōjăquĕ nūnc stārēs, Virg. Syn. Ĭlĭŭm, Ĭlĭŏn ; Pĕrgămă, ōrŭm. Epith. Nĕptūnĭă, Phœbēă, Ăpŏllĭnĕă, Lāŏmĕdōntĕă, Lāŏmĕdōntĭă, Dārdănă, Dārdănĭă, Ĭlĭăcă, Teūcrĭă, Prĭămĕĭă, Hēctŏrĕă, Phrўgĭă, Idæă, Rhœtēĭă, Sīgēă ; Mărtĭă, Māvōrtĭă, āntīquă, vĕtŭs, tŭrrītă, bēllĭcă, ārdŭă, sŭpērbă, pŏtēns, dĭvēs, pērjūră, pērfĭdă, mĭsĕră, ĭnfēlĭx, vāstātă ; dīrŭtă, dēlētă, crĕmātă, īncēnsă.
Trōjānī, ōrŭm ; jŭgĕnæ, ārŭm, *and* ĕs, ŭm, m. pl., *Trojans.* Trōjānĭs Pĕrgămă pārtū, Lucr. Trōjŭgĕnās āc tēlă, Virg. Trōĕs ărēnă, Id. Syn. Lāŏmĕdōntĭădæ, Dārdănĭdæ, Teūcrī, Hēctŏrĭdæ, Ænĕădæ ; Trōădēs, Ĭlĭădēs. Epith. Fōrtēs, māgnănĭmī, bēllĭgĕrī, ĭmpăvĭdī, aūdācēs, gĕnĕrōsī, trŭcēs, dūrī, Mărtĭī, āntīquī.
trŏphæŭm, *and* pæŭm, ī, n., *a monument of victory.* Tĭbĭ, māgnĕ, trŏphæŭm, Virg. Syn. Spŏlĭă, ĕxŭvĭæ. Epith. Lætŭm, clārŭm, fēstŭm, nōbĭlĕ, dĭvēs, īnsīgnĕ, sōlēnnĕ, sŭpērbŭm, ĭllūstrĕ, māgnĭfĭcŭm, hōstīlĕ.
trŏpĭcŭs, ī, m., *the tropic.* Idcīrcō trŏpĭcĭs, Man.
trŏpĭs, ĭs, f., *bad wine.* Ipsă trŏpĭn, Mart.
Trōs, ōĭs, m., *a Trojan.* Trōs ăĭt, Virg. V. Troicus.
Trōsmĭs, ĭs, f., *a city of Mœsia.* Cāotăm Trōsmĭn cĕlĕrī, Ov.
trōssŭlŭs, ă, ŭm, *spruce, foppish.* Trōssŭlŭs ēxsūltăt, Pers.
trŭcīdo, ās, *to slaughter.* Prīmōsquĕ trŭcīdānt, Virg. Syn. Intērfĭcĭo, intēr-ĭmo, jŭgŭlo, cædo, ōbtrūnco, nĕco, ōccīdo. V. Occido.
trŭcŭlēntŭs, ă, ŭm, *ferocious.* Sŭĭs trŭcŭlēntĭŏr Eūrĭs, Ov. Syn. Trŭx, fĕrŭs, atrōx, fĕrōx, crŭdēlĭs, īmmānĭs, bārbărŭs, ēffĕrŭs, sævŭs, tērrĭbĭlĭs, ĭnhūmānŭs, īmmītĭs, āspēr. V. Crudelis.
trŭdĭs, ĭs, f., *a hook, pole.* Fērrātāsquĕ trŭdēs, Virg.
trūdo, sī, sŭm, *to thrust.* Trūdĭt ĭnērmĕm, Hor. Syn. Pēllo, ĭmpēllo, cōmpēllo, ădĭgo.
trūllă, æ, f. *a vase, basin, pot.* Cāmpānă sōlĭtŭs trūllă, Hor.
trūnco, ās, *to chop off.* Trūncăvītquĕ căpŭt, Lucan. Syn. Ōbtrūnco, āmpŭto, mŭtĭlo, scīndo, ābscīndo.
trūncŭs, ī, m., *a stump.* Trūncōs hōstīlĭbŭs ārmĭs, Virg. Syn. Stĭpĕs. Epith. Dūrŭs, vălĭdŭs, fīrmŭs, stăbĭlĭs, prŏcērŭs, īngēns, tĕrēs, rŏtūndŭs, nōdōsŭs, fāmōsŭs ; stŭpĭdŭs, hĕbĕs, tārdŭs.
trūncŭs, ă, ŭm, *maimed.* Et trūncăs ĭnhŏnēstō, Virg. Syn. Trūncātŭs, ōbtrūn-cātŭs, āmpŭtātŭs, mŭtĭlŭs, scīssŭs, ābscīssŭs.
trŭtĭnă, æ, f., *scales.* In trŭtĭnā pōnētŭr, Hor. Syn. Lībră, stătēră, bĭlānx, lānx. V. Libra.
trŭtĭnŏr, ārĭs, *to weigh.* Ēxpōrrēctō trŭtĭnāntŭr, Pers. Syn. Lībro, pōndĕro, pēndo. V. Libro.
trūx, ŭcĭs, *cruel, frightful.* Īră trŭcēs ĭnĭmīcĭtĭăs, Hor. V. Truculentus.
Trўphĕrŭs, ī, m., *the name of a man.* Dīscĭpŭlŭs Trўphĕrī dōctōrĭs, Juv.
Trўphōn, ōnĭs, m., *the name of a man.* Nĕgāt Trўphōnĭs æmŭlī dŏmŭs, Virg.
tū, *thou.* Tū mĭhĭ quōdcūnque, Virg.
tŭbă, æ, f., *a trumpet.* At tŭbă tērrĭbĭlĕm, Virg. Syn. Clāssĭcŭm, lĭtŭŭs, cōrnŭ, būccĭnă. Epith. Clără, fĕră, cănōră, clāngēns, sŏnāns, īnflātă, ănĭmāns, rĕsŏ-nāns, tōrtĭlĭs, bēllĭcă, clāssĭcă, lūctĭsŏnă, strĭdēns, raūcă, căvă, ænĕă, aūdāx, trŭcŭlēntă, trĕmēndă, flēxĭlĭs, tērrĭbĭlĭs, vōcālĭs, grāndĭsŏnă, ūndĭsŏnă, māgnĭfĭcă, bēllĭgĕră, trīstĭs, Mărtĭă, sŭpērbă, tērrĭfĭcă, crĕpĭtāns, āltĭsŏnă, hōrrĭbĭlĭs, quĕ-rŭlă, hōrrĭdă, sānguĭnĕă, fūnēstă.
tŭbĕr, ĕrĭs, n., *a swelling.* Tūbĕrĕ tālī, Ov.
tŭbĕr, ĕrĭs, m., *jujub, a fruit.* Dē Lĭbўcĭs tŭbĕrēs, Mart.
tŭbĭcĕn, ĭnĭs, m., *a trumpeter.* Et Trōjæ tŭbĭcĕn, Prop.
tŭbĭlūstrĭă, ōrŭm, n. pl., *feasts wherein the trumpets used in sacrifices were purified.* Tŭbĭlūstrĭă dīcūnt, Ov.
tŭbŭs, *and* ŭlŭs, ī, m., *a pipe.* Tŭbōs ĭbăt, (Scaz.) Mart. Syn. Fīstŭlă, că-nālĭs.
tŭcētŭm, ī, n. *a kind of chopped meat.* Pătĭnæ, tŭcētăquĕ, Pers.
tŭdīto, ās, *to strike with a hammer.* Nēc tŭdĭtāntĭă, Lucr.
tŭĕŏr, ĕrĭs, *to defend, to behold.* Hæc ără tŭēbĭtŭr ōmnēs, Virg. Syn. Tūtŏr, dēfēndo, cŭstōdĭo, tĕgo, prŏtĕgo, sērvo, cōnsērvo, āssērvo ; Intŭĕŏr. V. De-fendo, video.

tŭgŭrĭŭm, ĭ, n., *a cottage.* Paŭpĕrĭs ĕt tŭgŭrī, Virg.   V. Casa.

Tŭllĭă, æ, f., *the daughter of Servius Tullius, the instigator of her father's murder.*
Cūm Tārquĭnĭŏ Tŭllĭă cŏnjūx, Sen.

Tŭllĭŭs, ĭī, m., *Servius Tullius, the sixth king of Rome.*   Nāmquĕ pătĕr Tŭllĭī,
Ov.   Syn. Sĕrvĭŭs.—2. *the family name of Cicero.*   Tŭllĭŭs ŏlĭm, Mart.   V.
Cicero.

Tŭllŭs, ĭ, m., *a Roman prænomen.*—2. *Tullus Hostilius, the third king of Rome.*
Tŭllŭs ĭn ārmă vīrōs, Virg.

tŭm, *then.*   Tŭm dēmŭm mŏvĕt, Virg.   Syn. Tŭnc, deĭndĕ, prætĕrĕă.

tŭmĕfăcĭo, fēcī, fāctŭm, *to cause to swell.*   Extēntăm tŭmĕfēcĭt, Ov.   Syn. Inflo;
tŭmŏrĕ replĕo.

tŭmĕo, ēs, *and* ēsco, ĭs, *to swell.*   Vēlă tŭmĕrĕ sĭnū, Mart.   Syn. Tŭrgĕsco,
tŭrgĕo, ĭntŭmēsco, īnflŏr, ēxtŭbĕro, prōtŭbĕro.

tŭmĭdŭs, ă, ŭm, *swelled.*   Clāmābăt tŭmĭdĭs, Mart.   Syn. Tŭmēns, tŭmĕfāctŭs,
tŭrgĭdŭs, īnflătŭs, ēxtŭbĕrāns, prōtŭbĕrāns.

tŭmŏr, ōrĭs, m., *a swelling.*   Sēptă tŭmŏrĕ plăcĕt, Prop.   Syn. Inflătĭo, tŭbĕr.

tŭmŭlo, ās, *to bury.*   Tellūs tŭmŭlābĭt ărēnă.   Syn. Sĕpĕlĭo, cŏntŭmŭlo.   V.
Sepelio.

* tŭmŭltŭo, ās, *and* ŏr, ārĭs, *to excite tumult.*   Suet.

tŭmŭltŭōsŭs, ă, ŭm, *tumultuous.*   Tŭmŭltŭōsŭm sŏllĭcĭtăt, (Alcaic.) Hor.   Syn.
Tŭrbātŭs, tŭrbĭdŭs; tŭrbŭlēntŭs, sēdĭtĭōsŭs.

tŭmŭltŭs, ūs, m., *tumult.*   Tŭrbāntĕ tŭmŭltū, Virg.   Syn. Strĕpĭtŭs, mŭrmŭr,
frăgŏr; sēdĭtĭo, tŭrbă, mōtŭs.   Epith. Pŏpŭlārĭs, cīvīlĭs, rĕbēllĭs, clāmōsŭs,
sævŭs, vēsānŭs, cæcŭs, īnsānŭs, sŭbĭtŭs, rĕpēntīnŭs, hŏrrĭbĭlĭs, crŭēntŭs.

tŭmŭlŭs, ĭ, m., *a hillock, a tomb.*   Sībĭlĕt ĭn tŭmŭlĭs, Prop.   Syn. Ăggĕr, cŏllĭs;
sĕpŭlcrŭm.   V. Sepulcrum.

tŭnc, adv., *then.*   Tŭnc dĕcŭĭt, Virg.   Syn. Tŭm; ĭllō tēmpŏrĕ, ĭllīs dĭēbŭs.

tŭndo, tŭtŭdī, tŭnsŭm, *to strike, grind.*   Tŭndĭtŭr Eŭrō, Virg.   Syn. Cŏntŭndo,
cædo, vērbĕro, fĕrĭo, pĕrcŭtĭo, pūlso; tĕro, āttĕro, cŏntĕro, frāngo.

tŭnĭcă, æ, f., *a tunic.*   In tŭnĭcās ĕăt, Juv.   Epith. Mōllĭs, rădĭāns, lāxă, ōstrīnă,
sŏlūtă.   V. Vestis.

tŭnĭcātŭs, ă, ŭm, *dressed in a tunic.*   Vēndēntēm tŭnĭcātō, Hor.

tŭŏr, ĕrĭs, *to see, behold.*   Cālĭdōs æstŭs tŭĭmŭr, nĕc frĭgŏră, Lucr.

tŭrbă, æ, f., *a crowd.*   Ōmnĭs tŭrba ād rīpās, Virg.   Syn. Cătērvă, cŏhŏrs, phălānx,
āgmĕn, glŏbŭs, mănŭs, frĕquēntĭă, mŭltĭtūdo, cŏpĭă, vīs, nŭmĕrŭs, cŏrōnă; cœtŭs, cŏnvēntŭs, cŏncĭo; plēbs; tŭmŭltŭs.   Epith. Nŭmĕrōsă, cŏnfūsă, plūrĭmă,
mŭltă, īngēns, dēnsă, cĕlĕbrĭs, frĕquēns, gārrŭlă, lŏquāx.   V. Seditio.

tŭrbātŏr, ōrĭs, m., *and* trīx, īcĭs, f., *a disturber.*   Crēbrōs tŭrbātrīx, Stat.

tŭrbĭdŭs, ă, ŭm, *disturbed.*   Tŭrbĭdĭŏrĕ nŏtās, Mart.   Syn. Tŭrbātŭs, mīstŭs,
cŏnfūsŭs; īmpŭrŭs, sōrdĭdŭs; tērrĭtŭs, trĕpĭdŭs; āmēns; īrātŭs, īrā cŏmmōtŭs.

tŭrbĭnĕŭs, ă, ŭm, *whirling round.*   Cōrpŏră tŭrbĭnĕō, Ov.

tŭrbo, ĭnĭs, m, *a whirlwind.*   Tŭrbĭnĭs īnstăr, Virg.   Epith. Nĭgĕr, răpāx, vĭo-
lēntŭs, vērsābūndŭs, nīmbōsŭs, cæcŭs, strīdŭlŭs, ĭnŏpīnŭs, īmmānĭs, pĭcĕŭs,
fŭrĭālĭs, răpĭdŭs, dēmēns, pŭlvĕrĕŭs, cĕlĕr, ŏbscūrŭs, fŭlmĭnĕŭs, hŏrrĭsŏnŭs, ăcĕr,
prŏcēllōsŭs, tērrĭfĭcŭs, īndŏmĭtŭs.   V. Ventus, tempestas.—2. *a top.*   Sŭb vērbĕrĕ
tŭrbo, Virg.

tŭrbo, ās, *to disturb.*   Ūsquĕ ădĕŏ tŭrbātŭr, Virg.   Syn. Cŏntŭrbo, pērtŭrbo,
mīscĕo, īmmīscĕo, pērmīscĕo, cŏnfūndo.

Tŭrbo, ŏnĭs, m., *the name of a man.*   Rīdēs Tŭrbŏnĭs ĭn ārmĭs, Hor.

tŭrbŭlēntŭs, ă, ŭm, *turbulent.*   Tŭrbŭlēntăm fēcīstī, Phæd.   Syn. Tŭrbĭdŭs;
sēdĭtĭōsŭs.

Tŭrcæ, ārŭm, m. pl., *the Turks.*   Syn. Ŏtŏmānī; Ŏttŏmănī, Măhŏmētĭgĕnæ.
Epith. Infĭdī, pērfĭdī, īmmānēs, īmprŏbī, atrōcēs, īmmītēs, fĕrōcēs, fŏrtēs,
pŏtēntēs, ārmĭpŏtēntēs, phăretrātī, mĭnācēs, aŭdācēs, hŏrrĭbĭlēs, trŭcēs.

tŭrdŭs, ĭ, m., *and* dă, æ, f., *a thrush.*   Nīl mēlĭŭs tŭrdō, Hor.   Epith. Ēdāx,
ŏbēsŭs, crāssŭs, ăvĭdŭs, văgŭs, ădvĕnă.

tŭrgĕo, ēs, *and* ēsco, ĭs, *to swell.*   Jăm lætō tŭrgĕnt, Virg.   Syn. Inflŏr.   V.
Tumeo.

tŭrgĭdŭs, *and* ŭlŭs, ă, ŭm, *swelled.*   Tŭrgĭdŭs Alpīnŭs, Hor.   Flēndō tŭrgĭdŭlī,
Cat.   Syn. Tŭmēns, tŭmĭdŭs, tŭmĕfāctŭs, īnflātŭs.

Tŭrĭŭs, ĭī, m., *the name of a man.* Grăndĕ mălŭm Tŭrĭŭs, Hor.

tŭrmă, æ, f., *a troop of horse.* Tŭrmāsquĕ fĕrōcēs, Virg. SYN. Cŏhōrs, phălānx, cătērvă. EPITH. Mĭnāx, aŭdāx, răpĭdă, ārmătă, mĭnāns, ærātă, tĕrrĭfĭcă, vălĭdă, hŏstĭlĭs, fŭrēns, pūgnāx, sēquāx, nŭmĕrōsă, fōrtĭs.

tŭrmālĭs, ĕ, *belonging to horsemen.* Excĭtĕt īnfēstōs tŭrmālĭs, Claud. SYN. Équēstrĭs ; bēllĭcŭs.

tŭrmātĭm, adv., *by troops.* Ēdĕrĕ tŭrmātĭm, Lucr. SYN. Ūnā, sĭmŭl.

Tŭrnŭs, ī, m., *the king of the Rutuli, vanquished by Æneas.* Tŭrnŭs ŭt īnfrāctōs, Virg. EPITH. Aŭdāx, fōrtĭs, gĕnĕrōsŭs, ĭmpăvĭdŭs, Mārtĭŭs, măgnănĭmŭs.

tŭrpĭs, ĕ, *and* ĭcŭlŭs, ă, ŭm, *ugly, shameful.* Tŭrpĭs ĭn ārcānā, Prop. Illă tŭrpĭcŭlō, (Phal.) Cat. SYN. Fœdŭs, dēfōrmĭs, īnfōrmĭs, tētĕr ; squālĭdŭs, sōrdĭdŭs ; īnhōnēstŭs, ĭmpūrŭs ; īnfāmĭs, probrōsŭs, pŭdēndŭs ; ĭnhŏnōrŭs, ăbjēctŭs, vīlĭs, īnglōrĭŭs, īndĕcōrŭs, īgnōbĭlĭs. V. Sordidus.

tŭrpĭtĕr, adv., *basely.* Tŭrpĭtĕr ōbtĭcŭĭt, Hor. SYN. Fœdē, dēfōrmĭtĕr ; probrōsē.

tŭrpĭtūdo, ĭnĭs, f., *ugliness, baseness.* Bŏnă tŭrpĭtūdo ēst, (Iamb.) Pub. Ser. SYN. Dēfōrmĭtās, fœdĭtās ; măcŭlă, lābēs, sōrdēs ; dēdĕcŭs, īnfāmĭă, nŏtă ; ĭnhŏnēstās, vītĭŭm. V. Macula, sordes.

tŭrpo, ās, *to defile.* Tŭrpārūnt hŭmĕrōs, (Chor.) Hor. SYN. Dētūrpo, fœdo. V. Maculo, infamo.

Tŭrrānĭŭs, ī, m., *the name of a tragic poet, and others.* Mŭsăquĕ Tŭrrānī, Ov.

tŭrrĭfĕr, *and* gĕr, ĕră, ĕrŭm, *bearing a tower.* Ăt cūr tŭrrĭfĕră, Ov. Tŭrrĭgĕræque ūrbēs, Virg.

tŭrrĭs, ĭs, f., *a tower.* Rōmānæ tŭrrēs, ĕt, Prop. SYN. Ărx, cāstēllŭm, spĕcŭlă, cāstrŭm, prōpūgnăcŭlŭm ; mūnīmĕn. EPITH. Aĕrĭă, ārdŭă, ēxcēlsă, sūblīmĭs, ēdĭtă, īngēns, vāstă, căvă, sŭpērbă, mārmŏrĕă, ĭnēxpūgnābĭlĭs, īnāccēssă, tūtă, sēcūră, mĭnāx, ămbĭtĭōsă, vălĭdă, mūnītă, vāllātă.

tŭrrītŭs, ă, ŭm, *turreted.* Mōlĕ vĭrī tŭrrītĭs, Virg. SYN. Tŭrrĭbŭs mūnītŭs, ārdŭŭs, cīnctŭs.

tŭrtŭr, ŭrĭs, m., *a turtle.* Tŭrtŭr ăb ŭlmō, Virg. EPITH. Pŭdīcŭs, cāstŭs, gĕmēns, gĕmĕbūndŭs, raŭcŭs, fĭdēlĭs, fĭdŭs, quĕrŭlŭs, mœrēns, lŏquāx.

Tūscī, ōrŭm, m. pl., *Tuscans, Etrurians.* Aŭt Tūscī tĭbi, Mart.

Tūscŭlānŭs, *and* ŭlŭs, ă, ŭm, *of Tusculum, Tusculan.* Nĕc Tūscŭlānōs, Mart. Tūscŭlă prōtĕgĭt ūmbră, Stat.

Tūscŭlī, ōrŭm, m. pl., *the inhabitants of Tusculum.* Tūscŭlīvĕ mĭttūnt, Mart.

Tūscŭlŭm, ī, n., *a town of Latium.* Vīllă cāndēns Tūscŭlī, Hor.

Tūscŭs, ă, ŭm, *Tuscan.* Nĕc Tūscŭs plăcĭdĭs, Ov. SYN. Etrūscŭs, Tўrrhēnŭs.

tŭssĭo, ĭs, *to cough.* Tōtĭs tŭssĭrĕ dĭēbŭs, Mart.

tŭssĭs, ĭs, f., *a cough.* Tŭssĭs ĕt ūnă, Mart. SYN. Tŭssēdo. EPITH. Frĕquēns, ăspĕră, mălă, ægră, vĭŏlēntă.

tūtāmĕn, ĭnĭs, n., *and* tēlă, æ, f., *a defence.* Ēt tūtāmĕn ĭn ārmīs, Virg. Rērŭm tŭtēlă mĕārŭm, Hor. SYN. Dēfēnsĭo, cūstōdĭă, patrōcĭnĭŭm, præsĭdĭŭm. EPITH. Fĭdēlĭs, fĭdă, ămīcă, blāndă. V. Auxilium.

tūtō, adv., *safely.* Aŭdēnt sē grāmĭnă tūtō, Virg. SYN. Tūtē.

tūtŏr, ārĭs, *to protect.* Prīmūm tūtārĕ dŏmŭm, Virg. SYN. Tŭĕŏr, dēfēndo, prōtĕgo. V. Defendo.

tūtŏr, ōrĭs, m., *a defender.* Tūtŏr ŏpŭm, Prisc. SYN. Cūrātŏr, patrōnŭs, dēfēnsŏr.

tūtŭs, ă, ŭm, *safe.* Tūtŭs ĕro, Prop. SYN. Sĕcūrŭs, tēctŭs. V. Securus.

tŭŭs, ă, ŭm, *thine.* Nĕc tŭŭs hīc, Virg.

Tўănēĭŭs, ă, ŭm, *of Tyane, a city of Cappadocia.* Ădhūc Tўănēĭŭs īllīc, Ov.

Tўchĭŭs, ĭī, m., *a Bœotian said to have invented shoemaking.* Sīt Tўchĭō dōctĭŏr, Ov.

Tўdeŭs, ĕŏs, ĕĭ *or* eī, m., *the son of Œneus, and father of Diomed.* Illi ōccūrrīt Tўdeŭs, Virg. SYN. Œnīdēs.

Tўdīdēs, æ, m., *the son of Tydeus, Diomed.* Tўdīdēs mūltă, Virg. V. Diomedes.

tўmpănŭm, ī, n., *a drum.* Tўmpănă vōs, Virg. EPITH. Taŭrīnŭm, căvŭm, tĕrrĭfĭcŭm, sŏnōrŭm, bēllĭcŭm, Mārtĭŭm.

Tўndărĕŭs, *and* rŭs, ī, m., *the king of Laconia, and husband of Leda.* Tўndărēĭquĕ gĕnĕr, Ov.

Tўndărĭdæ, ārŭm, m. pl., *Castor and Pollux, reputed sons of Tyndarus.* Fīnēs Tўndărĭdārŭm, Prop. SYN. Cāstŏr ĕt Pōllūx ; Tўndărĕī, Œbălĭdæ, Œbălĭī, Lēdæī,

Amyclœi; Thĕrāpnœī frātrēs; Tўndărĕī gĕmĭnī *vel* Dīī. Epith. Gĕmĭnī, gĕmēllī, gĕnĕrōsī, clārī, īmmōrtālēs. V. Gemini.

Tўndărĭs, ĭdĭs, f., *the daughter of Tyndarus, Helen or Clytemnestra.* Tўndărĭdōsquĕ lĕgĭs, Ov.

Tўndărĭus, ă, ŭm, *of Tyndarus; Lacedemonian.* Tўndărĭūsquĕ pŭĕr, V. Fl.

Tўphŏeūs, ŏĕŏs, ŏĕī, *or* ŏeī, *acc.* Tўphŏĕă, m., *a giant.* Impōstă Tўphŏeō, Virg. Ŏră Tўphŏĕŏs Ætnē, Ov. Epith. Sævŭs, ārdŭŭs, cēntĭmănŭs. V. Gigas.

Tўphŏĕŭs, *or* ŏĭŭs, ă, ŭm, *and* Tўphŏĭs, ĭdŏs, f., *of Typhoeus.* Tĕlă Tўphŏĕă, Ov. Dīvērsă Tўphŏĭdŏs Ætnœ, Id.

Tўphōn, ōnĭs, m., *a giant, perhaps the same as Typhoeus.* Fūgĭēns Tўphōnă Dĭōnĕ, Ov.—2. *a whirlwind mingled with lightning.* Ăb æthĕrĕ tўphōn, Virg.

Tўră, *or* rās, æ, m., *a river of Sarmatia.* Tārdĭŏr āmnĕ Tўrās, Ov.

tўrănnĭcŭs, ă, ŭm, *tyrannical, cruel.* Ēt tўrănnĭcārŭm, (Phal.) Sidon. Syn. Sŭpērbŭs, crūdēlĭs.

tўrănnĭs, ĭdĭs, f., *tyranny.* Crūdāquĕ tўrănnĭdĕ fēcĭt, Juv. Epith. Sævă, bār-bără, ĭnīquă, īnjūstă, īnvīsă, īnfēstă, īmpĭă, vĭŏlēntă, fĕră, īmmītĭs, dīră, ēffĕră, īmmānĭs, sŭpērbă, dūră, āmbĭtĭōsă, fĕrōx, atrōx, grăvĭs, ăcērbă, īntŏlĕrābĭlĭs, mōlēstă, hōrrēndă, nĕfāndă, fătālĭs.

tўrănnŭs, ī, m., *a tyrant.* Tĕtĭgīssĕ tўrănnī, Virg. Epith. Crūdēlĭs, īmpĭŭs, sānguĭnĕŭs, crŭēntŭs, īnhūmānŭs, tērrĭbĭlĭs, fūrĭōsŭs, sŭpērbŭs, ĭnĭquŭs, ĭnēxōrā-bĭlĭs, īnsānŭs, īnvīsŭs, īmmītĭs, fătālĭs, dīrŭs, īmmānĭs, īnfēstŭs, fĕrōx, atrōx, dūrŭs, sævŭs, ăcĕr, īmprŏbŭs, ēffĕrŭs, rĭgĭdŭs, trūx, bārbărŭs, fĕrŭs, īnjūstŭs.

Tўrĭānthĭnŭs, ă, ŭm, *hue of the purple violet.* Ŭrbĭcă Līngŏnĭcūs Tўrĭānthĭnă, Mart.

Tўrĭī, ōrŭm, m. pl., *Tyrians.* Ŭt Tўrĭŭs, Luc.

Tўrĭŭs, ă, ŭm, *of Tyre.* Aūdĭĕrāt, Tўrĭās, Virg. Syn. Sīdonĭŭs, Sārrānŭs.

tўro, *and* rōcĭnĭŭm. V. Tiro, &c.

Tўrŏs, *or* ŭs, ī, f., *a celebrated city of Phœnicia.* Dōctă Tўrŏs, Tib.

Tўrrhēnĭă, æ, f., *Tuscany.* Tўrrhēnĭă tŏtă, Ov.

Tўrrhēnŭs, ă, ŭm, *of Tuscany.* Gēns ĭnĭmīcă mĭhī Tўrrhēnŭm, Virg.

Tўrrhīdœ, ārŭm, m. pl., *the sons of Tyrrhus.* Tўrrhīdæ pŭĕrī, Virg.

Tўrrhŭs, ī, m., *the herdsman of king Latinus.* Tўrrhūsquĕ pătĕr, Virg.

Tўrtæŭs, ī, m., *a Greek elegiac poet.* Tўrtæūsquĕ mărēs, Hor.

U, V.

VĂCĀTIO, ōnĭs, f., *a vacant place.* Brĕvĭs văcātĭōnĕm, Sid.

Văccă, æ, f., *a cow.* Văccă părēntĭs, Ov. Syn. Bōs, būcŭlă, jŭvēncă, vĭtŭlă, jŭvēncŭlă. Epith. Tĕnĕră, pīnguĭs, pĕtŭlāns, pĕtŭlcă, lāctĭfĕră, cōrnĭgĕră, fœcūndă. V. Bos.

văccīnĭŭm, ĭī, n., *a blackberry.* Cădūnt, văccīnĭă nĭgră, Virg. Epith. Nigrŭm, mōllĕ, pŭllŭm, pūrpŭrĕŭm.

văccŭlă, æ, f., *the dimin. of* vacca, *a heifer.* Văccŭlă nōn ūnquăm, Catul.

văcēfīo, īs, *to become void.* Mūltŭsquĕ văcēfīt, Lucr. Syn. Văcŭŏr.

văcīllo, ās, *to stagger.* Tŏtă văcīllăt, Lucr. Syn. Tĭtŭbo, nūto, lăbo, lābāsco, hæsĭto. V. Titubo.

văco, ās, *to be empty, to be at leisure, to be intent upon.* Hŏstĕ văcărĕ dŏmōs, Virg. Syn. Cărĕo, sūni văcŭŭs; ŏtĭŏr, cēsso, fĕrĭŏr; stŭdĕo, īnvĭgĭlo, īnsūdo, incŭmbo, ŏpĕrăm dō.

Văcūnă, æ, f., *the goddess of repose and leisure.* Pūtrĕ Văcūnæ, Hor.

Văcūnālĭs, ĕ, *sacred to Vacuna.* Āntĕ Văcūnālēs, Ov.

văcŭo, ās, *to empty.* Sī văcŭārĕ nĕmŭs, Mart. Syn. Ēvăcŭo, ēxhaūrĭo; căvo, ēxcăvo.

văcŭŭs, ă, ŭm, *empty.* Dŏmōs Dītĭs văcŭās, Virg. Syn. Ĭnānĭs, văcŭātŭs, ēx-haūstŭs; jējūnŭs; ēxpērs, ĭnŏps, cărēns, ĕgēns; căvŭs, căvātŭs.

vădĭmōnĭŭm, ĭī, n., *bond for appearance.* Vădĭmōnĭă cūrrŭnt, Lucr.

vādo, ĭs, *to go.* Vādĭmŭs īmmīstī, Virg. Syn. Eo, tēndo, cōntēndo. V. Eo, proficiscor.

vădŏr, ārĭs, *to give bail.* Rēspōndĕrĕ vădātō, Hor.

vădōsŭs, ă, ŭm, *full of shallows.* Sĭnŭātă vădōsās.

vădŭm, ī, n., *a ford, a shallow.* Illīdītquĕ vădīs, Virg. Syn. Brĕvĭă, ŭm; Syrtĕs, Yŭm; ăggĕr ărēnæ; flūmĕn, flŭvYŭs, rīvŭs, ămnĭs. V. Fluvius, Syrtes. væ, interj., *alas! woe!* Măntŭā væ! mĭsēræ, Virg.

văfĕr, afră, ŭm, *cunning.* Sī văfĕr ūnŭs, Hor. Syn. Ăstūtŭs, cāllYdŭs, caūtŭs, dŏlōsŭs, vērsYpĕllYs, vērsūtŭs.

* vafrĭtĭēs, Yēī, f., *craftiness.* Sen. Syn. ĂstūtYă, cāllYdYtās, dŏlŭs. V. Calliditas.

* văgābūndŭs, ă, ŭm, *wandering.* Syn. Văgŭs, văgāns, ērro, ērrāns, ērrātYcŭs, ĕrrābūndŭs, pălāns, ăbĕrrāns, fŭgYtīvŭs, prŏfŭgŭs.

văgīnă, æ, f., *a scabbard.* HăbYlēm văgīna āptārăt, Virg. Epitii. Pēndēns, pĕndŭlă, ĕbūrnĕă, căvă.

văgYo, Ys, Yī, Ytŭm, *to cry like a child.* VāgYĕrānt āmbo, Ov. Syn. Vūgīto, flĕo, plōro, lacrYmŏr. V. Lacrymor.

văgītŭs, ūs, m., *the crying of children, wailing.* Vōcēs, văgītŭs ĕt īngēns, Virg. Epitii. Tĕnĕr, ăcūtŭs, nōctūrnŭs, flēbYlYs, quĕrŭlŭs, lūgubrYs. V. Lacrymæ, fletus, gemitus.

văgo, ās, *the same as* vagor. Achĕrōntĕ văgărĕ, Lucr.

văgŏr, ōrYs, m., *wailing.* Mīscētūr fūnĕrĕ văgŏr, Lucr.

văgŏr, ārYs, *to wander.* Fāmă văgātŭr, Virg. Syn. Ērro, ŏbērro; pālŏr, ārYs. V. Exulo, aberro.

văgŭlŭs, ă, ŭm, *the dimin. of* vagus. ĂnYmŭlă văgŭlă, blāndŭlă, Hadrian.

văgŭs, ă, ŭm, *wandering.* Jām văgă prōsYlYĕt, Hor. Syn. Văgāns, văgābūndŭs, dīspĕrsŭs.

văh! interj., *oh! ah!* Văh! cāllYdŭm cōnsYlYŭm, Ter.

Vălă, æ, m., *the name of a man.* Vălă, Sălērnī, Hor.

vāldē, adv., *much, very.* Hōc vāldē vYtYŭm, (Phal.) Syn. Mŭltŭm, vălYdē.

văle, vălētă, adieu. Fōrmōsĕ vălē, vălĕ, Virg. Sīgnă, vălētĕ, fŏrēs, Ov.

vălĕdīco, Ys, xī, *to bid farewell.* Vălĕdīcĕrĕ sāltĕm, Ov.

vălēntĕr, adv., *strongly.* Spīrārĕ vălēntYŭs, Ov. Syn. VălYdē, vĕhĕmēntĕr.

vălĕo, ēs, *to be able, to be in good health.* Artĕ vălēs, ōpĭă, Virg. Syn. Pŏssŭm, quĕo; pŏllĕo; vīgĕo, sŭm sānŭs, IncŏlŭmYs; ætYmŏr.

VălĕrYŭs, Yī, sync. ī, m., *the name of an illustrious Roman family.* Lævīnŭm, Vălĕrī gĕnŭs, Hor.

Vălĕrŭs, ī, m., *a Rutulian warrior.* Haŭd ēxpērs Vălĕrŭs, Virg.

vălēsco, Ys, *to get strength.* Rĕcrĕātă vălēscăt, Lucr.

vălētūdo, Ynīs, f., *good health; illness.* Fāmă, vălētūdō cōntīngăt, Hor. Syn. SānYtās, sălūbrYtās, sălŭs; mōrbŭs.

VălgYŭs, Yī, m., *a poet of the Augustan age.* Ămīcĕ Vălgī, Hor.

vălYdŭs, ă, ŭm, *strong.* Neū pătrYæ vălYdās, Virg. Syn. Vălēns, rōbŭstŭs, fīrmŭs, fōrtYs. V. Robustus.

vāllēs *and* Ys, Ys, f., *a valley.* In vāllYbŭs ūmnēs, Virg. Syn. CōnvāllYs. Epitii. Căvă, cōncăvă, īmă, cūrvă, prōnă, præcēps, ābrŭptă, prŏfūndă, rĕdūctă, dēprēssă, āltă, ōbscūră, ōccŭltă, ŏpācă, sēcrētă, sylvōsă, nĕmŏrōsă, frōndōsă, vYrēns, vYrYdYs, vYrYdāns, dūmōsă, dēnsă, hērbōsă, īrrYgŭă, frīgYdă, gĕlYdă, rĕsŏnāns.

vāllo, ās, *to fortify.* Ynŏpēm vāllăvĕrYt ūndYs, Flacc. Syn. Ōbvāllo, cīngo, āmbYo, cīrcŭmdo, sĕpYo, stīpo. V. Munimen.

vāllŭm, ī, n., *a trench, a fence.* Ænĕădŭm vāllīs, Virg. Syn. Prōpūgnācŭlŭm, ăggĕr, mūnīmĕn. V. Munimen.

vāllŭs, ī, m., *a stake.* Vāllŭs ĕrăt, Tib. Syn. Pālŭs, stīpĕs, sŭdēs. Epitii. Fīrmŭs, ăcūtŭs, rōbŏrĕŭs, dūrŭs.

vălvæ, ārŭm, f. pl., *folding-doors.* Vālvārŭm strĕpYtŭs, Hor. Syn. Pōrtă. Epitii. BYfŏrēs, ĕbūrnĕæ, pătēntēs, ăpērtæ, dĕcōræ. V. Janua.

vănesco, Ys, *to vanish.* StĕrYlēs vănēscYt Yn hērbās, Ov. Syn. Ēvānēsco, ăbĕo Yn aūrās. V. Evanesco.

vănYdYcŭs, *or* lŏquŭs, ă, ŭm, *prating, chattering.* VānYlŏquŭm Cĕltæ, Sil.

vănYtās, ātYs. f., *folly, pride.* PērsuāsYōnĭs vānYtās, (Iamb. Dim.) Prud. Syn. InānYtās, lĕvYtās, fāllācYă, mēndācYŭm, fābŭlă; sŭpērbYă, āmbYtYo.

vānnŭs, ī, f., *a winnowing fan.* MystYcă vānnŭs Yācchī, Virg. Syn. VēntYlābrŭm.

vānŭs, ă, ŭm, *vain, useless, false.* Sĕgēs vānīs ēlūsYt ărīstīs, Virg. Syn. YnānYs, futĭlĭs, lĕvĭs, cădūcŭs, fŭgāx, irrĭtŭs ; fĭctŭs, fŭcātŭs, sĭmŭlātŭs,'mĕntītŭs, falsŭs, făbŭlōsŭs.

văpĭdŭs, ă, ŭm, *ill-tasted.* Āstūtăm văpĭdō, Pers.

văpŏr, ōrĭs, m., *vapour.* Tŏlĕrărĕ văpōrēs, Lucan. Syn. Hūmŏr, hālĭtŭs,fūmŭs, călŏr. Epith. Nĕbŭlōsŭs, pĭcĕŭs, nĭgĕr, ŏbscūrŭs, cæcŭs, āĕrĭŭs, ūdŭs, hūmĭdŭs, ĭgnĕŭs, æstīvŭs, călĭdŭs, tĕpĭdŭs, tōrrēns, tĕnŭĭs, fĕrvĭdŭs, tĕtĕr, spūmĕŭs, ĭgnĭfĕr. V. Fumus.

văpōrĭfĕr, ă, ŭm, *exhaling vapours.* Sīvĕ văpōrĭfĕrās, Stat. Syn. Fūmĭdŭs.

văpōro, ās, *to exhale vapours.* Fŭgĭēntĕ văpōrĕt, Hor. Fūmĭgo, sŭfflo, călĕfăcĭo, călfăcĭo.

* || văpōrōsŭs, *and* rŭs, ă, ŭm, *vaporous.* Dēfŭgĕrĕt văpōrŭs ārdŏr, (Phal.) Prud.

văppă, æ, f., *bad wine.* Prōlūtŭs văppā, Hor. Syn. Vīllŭm.—2. *a libertine.* Tĕ fĭĕrī văppăm, Hor.

văpŭlo, ās, *to be scourged.* Văpŭlăt ŭmbră, Prop. Syn. Vērbĕrŏr, fĕrĭŏr, pĕrcŭtĭŏr, cœdŏr.

vārī, ōrŭm, m. pl., *forks to set up nets.* Rĕtĭă vārĭs, Luc.   •

Vărĭă, æ, f., *a city of the Æqui.* Sŏlĭtūm Vărĭam dīmĭttĕrĕ, Hor.

|| vărĭāntĭă, æ, f., *variety.* Ŏrĭtūr vărĭāntĭă rērŭm, Lucr.

* vārĭco, ās, *and* ŏr, ārĭs, *to straddle.* Juv.

vărĭcōsŭs, ă, ŭm, *dropsical.* Vŏlĕt, vărĭcōsŭs, Juv.

vărĭcŭs, ă, ŭm, *straddling.* Vārĭcă fērtquĕ, Ov.

vārĭo, ās, *to diversify.* Măcŭlīs vărĭāvĕrĭt ŏrbĕm, Virg. Syn. Mūto, cōmmūto, dīstīnguo ; dīscrĕpo, dīffĕro ; tĭtŭbo, văcīllo, hæsĭto, nūto, sūm dŭbĭŭs, āncēps, incōnstāns.

Vărĭŭs, ĭī, m., *a tragic poet of the Augustan age.* Scrībĕrĭs Vărĭō, Hor.

vărĭŭs, ă, ŭm, *various.* Tūm vărĭæ vĕnĕrĕ, Virg. Syn. Mŭltĭplēx, dīvērsŭs, mŭltŭs ; ăltērnŭs ; dīssĭmĭlĭs, dīspār ; ămbĭgŭŭs, āncēps, incĕrtŭs, mŭtābĭlĭs, īnstăbĭlĭs, incōnstāns.

vārīx, ĭcĭs, f., *a swelled vein.* Vārĭcĕ sŭccīsō, Hor.

Vārro, ōnĭs, m., *the name of a celebrated plebeian family.* Vārrōnem ād bēllă vŏcāstī, Sil. Arquĭtĭquĕ Vārrōquĕ, Virg. Catal.

Vārŭs, ī, m., *a friend of Virgil and Horace.* Vārĕ, tŭūm nōmĕn, Virg.

văs, vădĭs, m., *a surety.* Illĕ dătĭs vădĭbŭs, Hor. Syn. Spōnsŏr, præs, ŏbsĕs.

văs, vāsĭs, n., *a vase, vessel.* Sīncērŭm ēst nĭsĭ văs, Hor. Syn. Vāscŭlŭm, ūrcĕŭs, hydrĭă, ăquālĭs, pōcŭlŭm, pătĕră, cўăthŭs, ămphŏră, călīx, crātēr, crătēră, scўphŭs ; călăthŭs, cănĭstrŭm, cīstă, quălŭs. Epith. Ænĕŭm, ærĕŭm, cōncăvŭm, căvŭm, ămplŭm, căpāx, fūmāns, pūlchrŭm, prĕtĭōsŭm, aūrātŭm, aūrĕŭm, ārgēntĕŭm, ăhēnŭm, būxĕŭm, splēndĭdŭm, nĭtēns, gēmmĕŭm, cælātŭm, fīctĭlĕ, vitrĕŭm, crŷstāllĭnŭm, ŏdōrŭm, spīrāns. V. Pocula.

Vāscōnĕs, ŭm, m. pl., *a people of Spain, near the Pyrenees.* Vāscōnĕs ūt.fūma ēst, Juv.

vāscŭlŭm, ī, n., *a dimin. of* vas. Vāscŭlă pūrī, Juv.

vāstātŏr, ōrĭs, m., *a ravager.* Ārcădĭæ vāstātŏr ăpĕr, Juv. V. Vasto.

vāstĭtās, ātĭs, f., *immensity, devastation.* Vāstĭtās squālĕt sŏlī, (Iamb.) Sen. Syn. Immēnsĭtās ; sōlĭtūdo ; vāstātĭo, pŏpŭlātĭo, rŭīnă, pērnĭcĭēs, ēxĭtĭŭm.

vāsto, ās, *to lay waste, destroy.* Mŭltă vāstābăt cædĕ, Virg. Syn. Pŏpŭlŏr, pŏpŭlo, dēpŏpŭlŏr, ēxpĭlo, dīrŭo, ēvērto. V. Everto, prædor.

vāstŭs, ă, ŭm, *immense, laid waste.* Fūndĭtŭr ēt vāstōs, Virg. Syn. Immēnsŭs, ĭngēns, prōcērŭs,'immānĭs ; vāstātŭs, dēsērtŭs.

vātēs, ĭs, m., *a prophet, a poet.* Inspīrăt vātēs, Virg. Syn. Pŏĕtă. V. Poeta.

Aūgŭr, ărŭspēx. V. Augur, Propheta. Epith. Săcĕr, sānctŭs, dīvīnŭs, fătĭdĭcŭs, prænūncĭŭs, præscĭŭs, præsāgŭs, prōvĭdŭs, săgāx, vērŭs, āncēps, incērtŭs, ŏbscūrŭs, vānŭs, fāllāx, mēndāx, tērrĭfĭcŭs, sĭnĭstĕr, lōngævŭs, vĕnĕrābĭlĭs. V. Augur, prædico.

Vātĭcānŭs, ī, m., *one of the seven hills of Rome.* Tĭbĭ Vātĭcānī, Hor. In Vātĭcānĭs, Mart.

vātĭcĭnātŏr, ōrĭs, m., *a soothsayer.* Vātĭcĭnātŏr hăbĕt, Ov.

vātĭcĭnŏr, ārĭs, *to prophesy.* Vātĭcĭnātă sŏrŏr, Ov. Syn. Dīvīno, aūgŭrŏr, prædīco. V. Prædico, is.

vātĭcĭnŭs, ă, ŭm, *prophetic.* Hæc ŭbĭ vātĭcĭnōs, Ov.

✝ ūbĕr, ĕrĭs, n., *the pap.* Ălĭt ūbĕrĕ fœtūs, Virg. SYN. Mămmă. V. Mamma.—
2. n., *abundance.* Ūbĕrĕ glēbœ, Virg. V. Fertilitas.—3. adj., *abundant.* Ūbĕrĭŏrā
fĕrăm, Claud. SYN. Fĕrtĭlĭs, fœcūndŭs, ăbūndāns.

ūbĕrĭŭs, ūbērrĭmē, adv., *comp. and superl. of the obsol.* ūbĕrĭtĕr, *more, very abundantly.* Ūbĕrĭŭs nūllī, Ov. Sŭccrērūnt ūbērrĭmē, Pl.

ūbērtās, ātĭs, f., *fertility.* Ōpum ūbērtātĕ Săgūntŭm, -Sil. SYN. Ūbĕr (*subst.*);
fĕrtĭlĭtās; ăbūndāntĭă, cōpĭă.

ūbērtĭm, adv., *abundantly.* Ūbērtĭm lăcrўmæ, Ov. SYN. Ăbūndē, ūffŭēntĕr,
cōpĭōsĕ.

ūbĭ, adv., *where, when.* Hæc ūbĭ dīctă, Virg. Laŭrŭs ūbī, Tibul.

ūbĭcūnquĕ, *wherever.* Aŭdīte ūbĭcūnquĕ Lătīnæ, Virg. Sērvŏr ūbīcūnque ēst,
Ov.

ūbĭquĕ, *everywhere.* Quīcquĭd ūbĭque ēst, Virg. SYN. Pāssĭm.

ūbĭvīs, *anywhere.* Nōn ūbĭvĭs, cōrămvĕ, Hor. SYN. Ūbĭquĕ.

Ūcălĕgōn, ōntĭs, m., *a Trojan noble; a conflagration.* Prōxĭmŭs ārdĕt Ūcălĕgōn,
Virg.

✝ ūdŭs, ă, ŭm, *damp.* Nīgră sŭbēst ūdō, Virg. SYN. Hūmĭdŭs, mădĭdŭs, mădēns,
mădĕfāctŭs.

vĕ, conj., *or.* Căsūsvĕ Dĕūsvĕ, Virg. SYN. Vĕl, aŭt, sīvĕ, seū.

vēcōrdĭă, æ, f., *madness, dotage.* Quœ tē vēcōrdĭă, Thēseū, Ov. SYN. Stŭltĭtĭă;
īgnāvĭă.

vēcōrs, ōrdĭs, *furious, mad.* Cārmĭnă vēcōrs, Hor. SYN. Stŭltŭs, āmēns; īgnāvŭs, dēsĕs.

vēctīgăl, ālĭs, n., *a tribute, a revenue.* Ēgŏ vēctīgālĭă măgnă, Hor. SYN. Trĭbūtŭm, pōrtōrĭŭm; rēdĭtŭs, prōvēntŭs. EPITH. Dēbĭtŭm, grāndĕ, ānnŭŭm, pārvŭm, tĕnŭĕ, nŏvŭm, īnīquŭm, īnjūstŭm, mŏlēstŭm.

vēctĭs, ĭs, m., *a bar.* Cēntum ærēī claŭdūnt vēctēs, Virg. EPITH. Fērrātŭs,
fērrĕŭs, ăhēnŭs, dūrŭs, rĭgĭdŭs, rŏbŭstŭs.

vēcto, ās, *the frequent. of* veho. Stўgĭă vēctărĕ cărīnā, Virg.

vēctŏr, ōrĭs, m., *that carries.* Sīlēnī vēctŏr ăsēllŭs, Ov.

vēctŭs, ă, ŭm, *the pass. partic. of* veho. Vēctŭs Ăbās, Virg.

‖ vĕgĕo, ēs, *to excite, animate.* Frēnĭs dēxtrāquŏ vĕgĕrĕ, Lucr.

‖ vĕgĕtātŏr, ōrĭs, m., *that gives motion.* Vĕgĕtātŏr ĭnērtŭm, Aus.

‖ * vĕgĕto, ās, *to refresh.* Intĕmĕrātă sālŭs vĕgĕtăt, Juvenc. SYN. Recrĕo, cōrrōbŏro.

vĕgĕtŭs, ă, ŭm, *vigorous.* Mēmbră dĕdĭt vĕgĕtŭs, Hor. SYN. Fīrmŭs, vălĭdŭs,
vălēns, rŏbŭstŭs, fōrtĭs, sānŭs.

vēgrāndĭs, ĕ, *great and ill-proportioned.* Vēgrāndĭă fārră, Ov.

vĕhĕmēns, tĭs, *impetuous.* Ōpĕră vĕhĕmēntĕ mĭnīstĕr, Hor. SYN. Ăcĕr, vălĭdŭs,
grăvĭs; răpĭdŭs, præcēps, cītŭs, īncĭtātŭs; fĕrōx; īmmŏdĕrātŭs, ēffrænĭs.

vĕhĕmēntĕr, *impetuously.* Vĭtĭŭm vĕhĕmēntĕr ĭnēsto, Luc. SYN. Ăcrĭtĕr, grăvĭtĕr; ăcērbĕ, fĕrōcĭtĕr; ĭnmēnsē, vāldē, mūltŭm.

vĕhĭcŭlŭm, ī, n., *a vehicle.* Cōmĕs prō vĕhĭcŭlo ēst, P. Mim. SYN. Cŭrrŭs,
plaŭstrŭm, rhēdă, cārpēntŭm. V. Plaustrum, currus.

vĕho, vēxī, vēctŭm, *to carry.* Clāssĕ vĕhō mēcŭm, Virg. SYN. Vĕcto, ĭnvĕho,
sūbvĕho, fĕro, dēfĕro, ēffĕro, pōrto, dēpōrto, gĕro, gēsto, dŭco, trăho.

Veĭă, æ, f., *the name of a woman.* Nūllă Veĭă cōnscĭēntĭă, Hor.

Veĭānĭŭs, ĭī, m., *the name of a man.* Veĭānĭŭs ārmĭs, Hor.

Veĭēns, ēntĭs, *of Veii.* Ēmptŏr ăgrī Veĭēntĭs, Hor.

Veĭēntānŭs, ă, ŭm, *of Veii.* Ēt Veĭēntānī, Mart.—2. Subst., -nŭm, ī, n., (sub.
vinum.) Veĭēntānŭm fēstĭs pōtărĕ dĭēbŭs, Hor.

Veĭī, ōrŭm, m. pl., *an ancient and flourishing city of Etruria.* Ēt Veĭī vĕtĕrēs,
Prop.—2. Adj., Veĭŭs, ă, ŭm, *of Veii.* Dūx Veĭŭs, Id.

Vējŏvĭs, ĭs, m., *the name under which the Romans worshipped the god of evil.* Lūcōs
Vējŏvĭs āntĕ dŭōs, Ov.

vĕl, disj., *or.* Illă vĕl ĭntāctæ, Virg. SYN. Aŭt, vĕ; sīvĕ, seū.

Vēlābrŭm, ī, n., *and* bră, ōrŭm, n. pl., *a district of Rome at the base of the Aventine
hill.* Quā Vēlābră sŏlēnt, Ov. Quā Vēlābrī rēgĭō, Tib.

vēlāmēn, ĭnĭs, *and* mēntŭm, ī, n., *a veil.* Crŏcĕō vēlāmĕn ăcānthō, Virg. Vēlā-
mēntă mănū, Ov. SYN. Tēgmĕn, ămīctŭs, tĕgūmēntŭm. V. Vestis.

vēlārĭă, ōrŭm, n. pl., *sail-cloths over the theatres.* Ăd vēlārĭă răptōs, Juv.

vēlĕs, Ĭtĭs, m., *a soldier of the light troops.* Vēlĭtĭs ēnsĕ, Ov.

Vēlĭă, æ, f., *a city of Lucania.* Quæ sĭt hĭēms Vēlĭæ, Hor.

vēlĭfĕr, ă, ŭm, *having sails.* Hūc ŭbĭ vēlĭfĕrăm, Ov.

vēlĭfĭco, ās, *to set sail.* Vēlĭfĭcābăt ăquās, Prop. Syn. Vēlă dō, făcĭo. V. Navigo.

Vēlīnŭs, ă, ŭm, *of Velia.* Pŏrtūsquĕ rĕquīrĕ Vēlīnŏs, Virg.—2. Subst., -ŭs, ī, m., *a lake on the confines of the Sabines.* Fōntēsquĕ Vēlīnī, Virg.—3. -ă, æ, f., *one of the thirty-five tribes of Rome.* In Făbĭă vălĕt, īllĕ Vēlīnā, Hor.

vēlĭvŏlŭs, ă, ŭm, *sailed upon, moving with sails.* Dēspĭcĭēns mărĕ vēlĭvŏlŭm, Virg. Vēlĭvŏlās nŏn hăbĭtūră rătēs, Ov.

vēllĭco, ās, *to pinch.* Vēllĭcĕt ābsēntĕm, Hor. Syn. Vēllo; lăcĕro.

vēllo, vēllī *and* ŭlsī, ŭlsŭm, *to tear.* Vēllĭtŭr, huĭc ātrō, Virg. Syn. Avēllo, rĕvēllo, cōnvēllo, ābstrăho, ēxtĭrpo, ēxtrăho, ērŭo, aūfĕro.

vēllŭs, ĕrĭs, n., *a skin, a fleece.* Vēllŭs ŏvĭs, Tib. V. Lana.

vēlo, ās, *to veil.* Pūrpŭrĕō vēlărĕ cŏmās, Virg. Syn. Ōbvēlo, tĕgo, ămĭcĭo, ōc-cŭlto, ōbdūco, ŏpĕrĭo. V. Abscondo.

vēlōcĭtĕr, adv., *swiftly.* Tĕrĕrēt vēlōcĭtĕr hŷdrăm, Ped. Syn. Cĭto, ōcўŭs, sŭbĭtō, rĕpēntĕ, quāmprīmŭm. V. Statim, celeriter.

vēlōx, ōcĭs, *swift.* Vēlōcēs Spártæ, Virg. Syn. Cĕlĕr, vŏlŭcĕr, cĭtŭs, pērnīx, præpēs, lēvĭs, răpĭdŭs, prŏpĕrŭs, præcēps, prōmptŭs, vŏlāns. V. Celer.

vēlŭm, ī, n., *a veil.* Vēlă thĕātrō, Prop. Syn. Tĕgŭmĕn, vēlāmĕn, ămĭctŭs. V. Vestis.—2. *a sail.* Ov. Syn. Cārbăsă, līntĕă, līnă, sĭnūs. Epith. Tūrgĭdŭm, tŭmĭdŭm, tŭmēns, īnflātŭm, naūtĭcŭm, hŭmĭdŭm, lĕvĕ, cĭtŭm, pătēns, lāxŭm, cūrvŭm, sĭnŭōsŭm, vŏlĭtāns, fŭgāx, cōncăvŭm.

vēlŭt, *and* ŭtī, adv., *as.* Vĕlŭt ăgmĭnĕ făctō, Virg. Ăc vĕlŭtī lēntīs, Virg. Syn. Ŭt, sīcŭt, nōn sĕcŭs āc, haŭd ălĭtĕr.

vēnă, æ, f., *a vein.* Saŭcĭă vēnă mĕrō, Mart. Epith. Tūrgĭdă, tŭmĭdă, sălĭēns, trĕpĭdă, trĕmēns, tĕnĕră, săngŭĭnĕă, plēnă, tŭmens, tĕnŭĭs, ēxīlĭs, grăcĭlĭs, călēns. V. Fodina.

vēnābŭlŭm, ī, n., *a hunter's pole.* Lātō vēnābŭlă fērrō, Virg. Syn. Spīcŭlŭm. Epith. Lātŭm, ăcūtŭm, vŭlnĭfĭcŭm, fŭlgēns. V. Telum, hasta.

Vĕnāfrănŭs, ă, ŭm, *of Venafrum.* Prēssā Vĕnāfrănæ, Hor.

Vĕnāfrŭm, ī, n., *a city of Campania.* Băccā Vĕnāfrī, Mart.

vēnālĭs, ĕ, *to be sold.* Lĭbĭs vēnālĭbŭs, accĭpĕ, Juv. Syn. Vēnālĭtĭŭs, ēxpŏsĭtŭs.

vēnātĭcŭs, *and* tōrĭŭs, ă, ŭm, *of the chase.* Ĕquēs, vēnātĭcŭs ēx quō, Hor.

vēnātĭo, ōnĭs, f., *and* tŭs, tŭs, m., *a chase, hunting.* Mĭttĭ vēnātĭŏ dēbĕt, Mart. Vēnātu īnvĭgĭlānt pŭĕrī, Virg. Epith. Lætă, grātă, blāndă, jūcŭndă, dĭffĭ-cĭlĭs, dūră, pĕrīcŭlōsă. V. Venor.

vēnātŏr, ōrĭs, m., *and* trīx, īcĭs, f., *a hunter, huntress.* Ēt ĕquō vēnātŏr ĭăpўgĕ, Virg. Sŭspēndĕrăt ărcŭm Vēnātrīx, Id. Syn. Vēnāns. Epith. Vĭgĭl, mă-tūtīnŭs, sēdŭlŭs, pērnōx, pērvĭgĭl, pērnīx, vēlōx, præcēps, cĕlĕr, ăvĭdŭs, săgĭt-tĭfĕr, phăretrātŭs, sŷlvēstrĭs, ērrăbŭndŭs. V. Venor.

vēndĭbĭlĭs, ĕ, *to be sold.* Vēndĭbĭlĭs nĕc, Hor.

vēndĭco, ās, *to claim.* Nĕc vēndĭcābĭt, (Scaz.) Mart. Syn. Adscrībo, āttrĭbŭo, ārrŏgo, āssŭmo; āssĕro, lībĕro, ēxĭmo.

vēndĭto, ās, *to sell, to brag.* Ūrbĕ vēndĭtābăt, (Phal.) Fur. Syn. Jăcto, jăctĭto, ōstēnto.

vēndĭtŭs, ă, ŭm, *the pass. partic. of* vendo. Vēndĭtă sæpĕ, M.

vēndo, vēndĭdĭ, *to sell.* Vēndĭdĭt hīc aūrō, Virg. Syn. Ălĭēno, dīstrăho, vēnŭndo.

vĕnēfĭcă, æ, f., *a sorceress.* Vēnīssĕ vĕnēfĭcă tēcŭm, Ov. Syn. Măgă, săgă, īncāntātrix. Epith. Īmpūră, īmpĭă, scĕlĕrātă, tūrpĭs, īmprŏbă, dīră, Thēssălă. V. Maga.

vĕnēfĭcĭŭm, ĭī, n., *sorcery.* Quōsquĕ vĕnēfĭcĭīs, Ov. Syn. Măgĭă, præstĭgĭæ, cārmĕn, īncāntātĭo. Epith. Măgĭcŭm, Thēssălŭm, Thēssălĭcŭm, Æmŏnĭŭm, Cōlchĭcŭm, Ægæŭm, Circæŭm, Mēdæŭm; scĕlĕrātŭm, dīrŭm, īnfāndŭm, nĕfān-dŭm, īmpĭŭm, fāllāx, dŏlōsŭm, vānŭm, ĭnānĕ, īnvālĭdŭm, ēxĭtĭōsŭm, Tārtărĕŭm, Stŷgĭŭm. V. Venefica, Circe, transformo, magia.

vĕnēfĭcŭs, ī, m., *a sorcerer.* Syn. Măgŭs, īncāntātŏr, præstĭgĭātŏr. V. Magus, venefica.

vĕnēnātŭs, ĭfĕr, *and* ōsŭs, ă, ŭm, *poisonous.* Nēvĕ vĕnēnātō, Ov. Jāmquĕ vĕnē-nĭfĕrō, Ov.

vĕnēnŭm, ī, n., *poison.* Lānă vĕnēnō, Virg. Syn. Virŭs, tŏxĭcŭm, ăcŏnītă, tābŭm. Epith. Tābĭfĭcŭm, măgĭcŭm, Thĕssălĭcŭm ; Lērnæŭm, Gŏrgŏnĕŭm ; lūrĭdŭm, ātrŭm, tētrŭm, nĭgrŭm, vīpĕrĕŭm, dīrŭm, crāssŭm, līvēns, sŏmnĭfĕrŭm, sŏpŏrĭfĕrŭm, lēthālĕ, lēthĭfĕrŭm, fătălĕ, fūnēstŭm, ēxĭtĭālĕ, īmmĕdĭcābĭlĕ, īnsānā-bĭlĕ, ācrĕ, præsēns, nŏxĭŭm, hŏrrēndŭm, vĭŏlēntŭm, pēstĭfĕrŭm, fūrtīvŭm, lătēns, ārcānŭm, sērpēns, spūmāns, Tārtărĕŭm, Stўgĭŭm.

vēnĕo, ĭī, *to be sold.* Vēnĕăt aūrō, Hor. Syn. Vēndŏr.

vĕnĕrābĭlĭs, ĕ, *and* āndŭs, ă, ŭm, *venerable.* Ēt vĕnĕrābĭlĕ nōmĕn, Ov. Vīrgă vĕnĕrāndĕ pŏtēntī, Id. Syn. Vĕrēndŭs, rĕvĕrēndŭs, cŏlēndŭs, ădōrāndŭs, aūgūstŭs.

vĕnĕrātĭo, ōnĭs, f., *respect.* Vīvīs vĕnĕrātĭŏ rēgĭbŭs, Prud. Syn. Rĕvĕrēntĭă, ŏbsērvāntĭă, cūltŭs, hŏnŏr.

vĕnĕrātŏr, ōrĭs, m., *a worshipper, an adorer.* Prīmīs vĕnĕrātŏr ăb ānnīs, Ov.

vĕnĕrŏr, ārĭs, *to venerate.* Dĕōs vĕnĕrābĕrĕ sērīs, Virg. Syn. Hŏnōro, ŏbsērvo, rĕvĕrĕŏr, vĕrĕŏr, ădōro. V. Honoro, adoro.

Vĕnĕtĭæ, ārŭm, f. pl., *Venice.* Epith. Māgnæ, īllūstrēs, īnclўtæ, cĕlebrēs, fōrtēs, pŏtēntēs, īndŏmĭtæ, īnvīctæ; æquŏrĕæ.

Vĕnĕtŭs, ī, m., *a Venetian.* Sīc Vĕnĕtŭs, Luc.—Adj. -ŭs, ă, ŭm, *Venetian.* Vĕnĕtō dīssĭdĕt Erĭdănō, Prop. Syn. Āntēnŏrĕŭs, Eūgănĕŭs.—2. *azure, sea-green.* Illīc vĕnĕtō dūrŏquĕ cŭcŭllō, Juv.

vĕnĭă, æ, f., *pardon.* Ōrāntēs vĕnĭam, ĕt, Virg. Syn. Lĭcēntĭă, cōpĭă, pŏtēstās, făcūltās, lībērtās; īndūlgēntĭă, īmpūnĭtās, cōndōnātĭo. V. Pax, parco.

Vĕnīlĭă, æ, f., *the name of several nymphs of Latium.* Dīvă Vĕnīlĭă mātĕr, Virg.

vĕnĭo, ĭs, vēnī, vēntŭm, *to come.* Cĭtă mōrs vēnĭt, aŭt, Hor. Syn. Advēnĭo, ādvĕnĭo, āccēdo, prŏpīnquo, dēvĕnĭo, pērvĕnĭo; ădĕo, pĕto; āccĕlĕro, ādvŏlo, āpprŏpĕro; rĕdĕo, rĕvērtŏr; īnsto, īmmĭnĕo. V. Advenio.

vēnŏr, ārĭs, *to hunt.* Cănĭbŭs vēnābĕrĕ dāmās, Virg.

vēnōsŭs, ă, ŭm, *full of veins.* Vēnōsŭs lībĕr, Pers.

vēntĕr, trĭs, m., *the belly.* Vēntĕr ăpērtŭs ĕquī, Prop. Syn. Ālvŭs, ūtĕrŭs, vīscĕră, īlĭă. Epith. Jējūnŭs, īmprŏbŭs, vŏrāx, văcŭŭs, ĭnānĭs, fămēlĭcŭs, ăvĭdŭs, căvŭs, căpāx, tūrgēns, tūrgĭdŭs, tŭmēns, tŭmĭdŭs, grăvĭs, fœtŭs; ĕpŭlīs īnflātŭs.

vēntĭgĕnŭs, ă, ŭm, *producing wind.* Vēntĭgĕnī crātērēs, Lucr.

vēntĭlo, ās, *to winnow.* Vēntĭlātŭr ēbrĭō, (Iamb.) Pr. Syn. Ēvēntĭlo; vērso, ăgĭto.

vēntĭto, ās, *to go to and fro.* Cŭm vēnĭtābŭs, quō pŭēllă dūcēbăt, (Scaz.) Cat.

vēntōsŭs, ă, ŭm, *full of wind, light, vain.* Āspĭcĕ, vēntōsī, Virg. Syn. Vēntō plēnŭs, fœtŭs, grăvĭdŭs, tŭmēns; lĕvĭs, ĭnānĭs, vānŭs, fūtĭlĭs, tŭmĭdŭs, tŭmēns, tūrgēns, tūrgĭdŭs, īnflātŭs; sŭpērbŭs.

vēntrĭcŭlŭs, ī, m., *the dim. of* venter. Vēntrĭcŭlŭs, nĕc, Scæv.

vēntrōsŭs, ă, ŭm, *corpulent.* Vēntrōsă cŭcŭrbĭtă, Van.

vēntŭs, *and* ŭlŭs, ī, m., *wind.* Vēntŭs ĕŭntēs, Virg. Vēntŭlum huĭc făcĭto, Ter. Syn. Aūră, spīrĭtŭs, flāmĕn, flātŭs, flābrŭm; Aūstĕr, Ăquĭlo, Bŏrĕās, Āfrĭcŭs, Eūrŭs, Zĕphўrŭs, Făvōnĭŭs; tūrbo, prŏcēllă. Epith. Lēnĭs, spīrāns, mōllĭs, plăcĭdŭs, lĕvĭs, tĕnŭĭs, sĕcūndŭs, văgŭs, răpĭdŭs, præcēps, fūrēns, vălĭdŭs, vĭŏlēntŭs, sævŭs, vŏlūcĕr, cĕlĕr, raūcŭs, trūx, sŏnāns, sŏnōrŭs, frĕmēns, fūlmĭnĕŭs, strīdēns, tūrbĭdŭs, glăcĭālĭs, īmmītĭs, īnsānŭs, frīgĭdŭs, nūbĭlŭs, plŭvĭŭs, ūdŭs, mădĭdŭs, gĕlĭdŭs, ăspĕr, hўbērnŭs, brūmālĭs, dīscŏrs, lŭctāns, prŏcēllōsŭs, nīmbōsŭs, hŏrrĭsŏnŭs, fŭrĭbūndŭs, ĭnĭmīcŭs, ādvērsŭs, īnfēstŭs, Æŏlĭŭs. V. Tempestas, Aquilo, Boreas, Notus, Zephyrus, Eurus, Auster, Aura.

vēnŭcŭlă, æ, f., *a sort of raisin.* Vēnŭcŭlă cōnvĕnĭt ōllĭs, Hor.

Vĕnŭlŭs, ī, m., *a Rutulian warrior.* Ēt māgnăm Vĕnŭlŭs, Virg.

vēnŭmdo, dĕdī, *to sell.* Vēnŭm cūnctă dărī, Cl.

Vĕnŭs, ĕrĭs, f., *the Goddess of love, beauty, gracefulness, and mirth.* Sīc Vĕnŭs : āt Vĕnĕrĭs, Virg. Syn. Cўthĕrĕă, Cўthĕrēĭă, Cўthĕrēĭs, Cyprĭs. Epith. Păphĭă, Idălĭă, Ăcīdălĭă, Ērўcīnă, Dĭōnæă, Cўthĕrĕă, Cўthĕrēĭă, Cyprĭă, ālmă, pŏtēns, pūlchră, fōrmōsă, cāndĭdă, blāndă, lætă, ădūltĕră, prŏtērvă, lāscīvă, īnfāmĭs, dīvă, fœcūndă, lāctĕă, dūlcĭs, tūrpĭs, Vūlcānĭă, cōmptă, bĕnīgnă, plăcĭdă, dĕcōră, pērnĭcĭōsă, jūcūndă, rīdēns, fāllāx, īncēstă, īngĕnĭōsă, īgnĕă, fœdă, pĕtŭlāns, sălāx, vĕnŭstă, sŏlŭtă, īnsānă, īgnĭpŏtēns. V. Libido.

Vĕnŭsīnŭs, ă, ŭm, *of Venusia, the native place of Horace.* Năm Vĕnŭsīnŭs ărăt, Hor.

věnŭstās, ātĭs, f., *beauty.* Sēxtă věnŭstātĭs, Prop. Nūllă věnŭstās, Cat. V. Pulchritudo, lepor, forma.

věnŭstŭs, ă, ŭm, *handsome, graceful.* Flōrě věnŭstĭŏr ōmnī, Prud. Syn. Pŭlchěr, děcŏrŭs, fōrmōsŭs. V. Pulcher.

veprēs, *or* prĭs, ĭs, m., *a bramble.* Cōrnă věprēs ět, Hor. Věprě lătēns, Ov. Syn. Rŭbŭs, spīnă. V. Spina.

věr, ĭs, n., *the Spring.* Věr ădĕŏ frŏndī, Virg. Epith. Nŏvŭm, nāscēns, blăn-dŭm, plăcĭdŭm, sūdŭm, sěrēnŭm, těpĭdŭm, běnīgnŭm, flŏrĭdŭm, pŭrpŭrěŭm, flŏrēns, gěnĭālě, grātŭm, jūcŭndŭm, ămīcŭm, vĭrēns, ămœnŭm, ŏdōrŭm, frăgrāns, rīdēns, lūxŭrĭāns, fœcŭndŭm, fērtĭlě, ūtĭlě, mădĭdŭm, ūdŭm, nĭmbōsŭm, ĭmbrĭ-fěrŭm. V. Floreo, flos, frondeo, gramen, herba, arbor, serenitas.

věrātrŭm, ī, n., *hellebore.* Nōbīs věrātrum ēst, Lucr.

věrāx, ācĭs, *sincere.* Fīgăt, ěrăt věrāx, Ov. Syn. Vērŭs, sīncērŭs.

věrbēnă, œ, f., *vervain.* Vērbēnās ădŏlē, Virg.

věrbĕr. ěrĭs, n., *a whip.* Vērbĕră pēndēnt, Virg. Syn. Flăgēllŭm, vīrgă; băcŭlŭs, fūstĭs. Epith. Tōrtŭm, sævŭm, cōntōrtŭm, crūdēlě, crŭēntŭm, crū-dŭm, īntōrtŭm, vĭŏlēntŭm, trīstě, nōdōsŭm, crěpĭtāns, ăcērbŭm, īnsānŭm, nēfăndŭm, fērrěŭm, sānguĭněŭm, ārdēns, mĭnāx, mōrtĭfěrŭm. V. Flagellum.

věrbĕro, ās, *to whip.* Vērbĕrăt ūndă, Virg. Syn. Cædo, tŭndo, fěrĭo, pērcŭtĭo, dīvērbĕro, pūlso. V. Flagello, ictus.

|| věrbōsĭtās, ātĭs, f., *verbosity, talkativeness.* Vērbōsĭtātĭs īpsě, Prud. Syn. Gār-rŭlĭtās, lŏquācĭtās.

věrbōsŭs, ă, ŭm, *talkative.* Cēdŭnt vērbōsī, Ov. Syn. Lŏquāx, gārrŭlŭs, mūltĭ-lŏquŭs. V. Garrulus.

věrbŭm, ī, n., *a word.* Ūt præcēptōrī, vērbōrŭm, Juv. Syn. Vōx, dīctĭo, dīctŭm, vŏcābŭlŭm, sŏnŭs, lŏquēlă, sērmo. V. Vox, loquor, sermo.

vērē, adv., *truly.* Ō vērē Phrўgĭm, Virg.

věrēcūndŏr, ārĭs, *to be ashamed, to be bashful.* Věrēcūndārī němĭněm, (Iamb.) Pl. Syn. Pŭdět mē, ērŭbēsco. V. Erubesco.

věrēcūndŭs, ă, ŭm, *ashamed.* Illă věrēcūndĭs lūx ēst, Ov. Syn. Pŭdēns, pŭdĭ-būndŭs, mŏdēstŭs.

věrēdŭs, ī, m., *a post-horse.* Sūmě věrēdī, Mart.

věrěŏr, ērĭs, věrĭtŭs, *to fear.* Nĭl tālě věrēbăr, Virg. Syn. Tĭmĕo, mĕtŭo, fōr-mīdo, hōrrěo; V. Timeo. Ōbsērvo, cŏlo, hŏnōro, věněrŏr, rěvěrěŏr. V. Honoro.

Vērgĭlĭœ, ārŭm; f. pl., *the Pleiads.* Nāvĭtă Vērgĭlĭīs, Pr. V. Pleiades.

vērgo, sī, sŭm, *to incline towards.* Vērgēbānt, nūnc dānt, Lucr. Syn. Prōpēndĕo, īnclīno, pēndĕo, īnclīnŏr, dēclīno; tēndo, spēcto.

vērĭdĭcŭs, ă, ŭm, *speaking truth.* Vērĭdĭcæ dīcŭnt, Mart. Syn. Vērŭs.

vērĭtās, ātĭs, f., *truth.* Nūdăquě vērĭtās, Hor. Syn. Vērŭm. Epith. Cāndĭdă, ăpērtă, nūdă, sīmplēx, sīncēră. sānctă, æquă, fīdēlĭs, fīdă, cōncors.

vērmĭcŭlātŭs, ă, ŭm, *chequer-worked.* Ēmblēmătě vērmĭcŭlātŏ, Lucil.

vērmĭnă, æ, f., *the worms in the bowels.* Vērmĭnă sævă, Lucr.

vērmĭno, ās, *to itch.* Prūrīgĭně vērmĭnăt aurĭs, Mart.

vērmĭs, ĭs, *and* ĭcŭlŭs, ī, m., *a worm.* Vērmĭbŭs, ēt prīvās, Lucr. Vērmĭcŭlōs părĭŭnt, Id. Syn. Lūmbrīcŭs. Epith. Exĭgŭŭs, těnŭĭs, ēxĭlĭs, grăcĭlĭs, pārvŭs, lōngŭs, tērrěnŭs, tērrēstrĭs, fœdŭs, sōrdĭdŭs, īnfēstŭs.

vērnă, *and* ūlă, æ, f., *a slave.* Vērnāsquě prŏcācēs, Hor. Vērnŭlă pēndět, Mart. Syn. Fămŭlŭs, sērvŭs, mĭnīstěr, māncĭpĭŭm. V. Servus.

vērnăcŭlŭs, ī, m., *a slave.* Vērnăcŭlōrŭm dīctă, Mart.

vērnālĭtěr, adv., *as a slave.* Vērnālĭtěr īpsĭs, Hor.

vērno, ās, *to bud, to be verdant.* Vērnăt hŭmŭs, Ov.

vērnŭs, ă, ŭm, *of the spring.* Nīx vērnō sŏlě sŏlūtă, Ov.

vērō, adv., *truly.* Ēgrěgĭăm vērō laudĕm, Virg. Syn. Sānē; autěm.

Vērōnă, æ, f., *a town of Italy.* Dēbět Vērōnă Cătŭllō, Ov. Epith. Fērtĭlĭs, fěrāx, ămœnă, cūltă, grātă, pārvă.

vērpŭs, ă, ŭm, *circumcised.* Dēdūcěrě věrpōs, Juv. Syn. Ăpēllă, rěcŭtītŭs. V. Judœus.

vērrēs, ĭs, m., *a pig.* Vērrĭs ōblīquŭm, (Sapph.) Hor. V. Porcus, sus.

vērro, ĭs, *to sweep, to scour.* Vērrĕ păvīmēntŭm, Juv.

vĕrrūcă, æ, f., *a wart.* Ignōscăt vĕrrūcĭs, Hor.

vĕrrūcōsŭs, ă, ŭm, *rough, full of warts.*

vĕrsătĭlĭs, ĕ, *and* bŭndŭs, ă, ŭm, *easily turned.* Et vĕrsătĭlĕ tĕmplŭm, Lucr
Vĕrsābŭndŭs ĕnĭm. SYN. Vŏlūbĭlĭs.

vĕrsātŭs, ă, ŭm, *the pass. partic. of* verso. Tĕnŭĭ vĕrsātă făvĭllā, Mart.

vĕrsĭcŏlŏr, ōrĭs, *of many colours.* Vĕrsĭcŏlōrĭbŭs ārmĭs, Virg. SYN. Mūltĭcŏlŏr,
dĭscŏlŏr, vărĭŭs.

vĕrsĭcŭlŭs, ī, m., *the dimin. of* versus. Vĕrsĭcŭlōs fēcī, Virg.

vĕrso, ās, *the frequent. of* verto. Seŭ vĕrsărĕ dŏlōs, Virg. SYN. Trācto, tăngo;
cōnvĕrto, vŏlvo, flēcto, cōnvŏlvo; ăgĭto, mŏvĕo, tōrquĕo.

vĕrsŏr, ārĭs, *to stay in, to be engaged in.* Vĕrsātŭr Ātreŭs, (Iamb.) Sen. SYN.
Mănĕo, mŏrŏr, hăbĭto, sŭm, hærĕo; stŭdĕo, īncŭmbo, īnvĭgĭlo, īnsūdo, ŏpĕrăm do.

vĕrsŭs, ūs, m., *a line, verse.* Vĕrsĭbŭs īncōmptĭs, Virg. SYN. Cārmĕn, mŏdĭ.
EPITH. Cănōrŭs, făcūndŭs. V. Carmen.

vĕrsūtĭă, æ, f., *cunningness.* Chrīstūm vĕrsūtĭă fāllāx, Juvcnc. V. Astutia,
fallacia.

vĕrsūtŭs, ă, ŭm, *crafty, cunning.* Tōllāt vĕrsūtă sālīvās, Prop. SYN. Văfĕr,
cāllĭdŭs, āstūtŭs, dŏlōsŭs, mălīgnŭs.

vērtăgŭs, ī, m., *a hound.* Vērtăgŭs ācĕr, Mart. V. Canis.

vērtēx, ĭcĭs, m., *a summit.* Vērtĭcĕ pēndēnt, Virg. SYN. Căcūmĕn, cūlmĕn,
fāstīgĭŭm, ăpēx. V. Cacumen, vertex.

vērtīgo, ĭnĭs, f., *a whirling, giddiness.* Răpĭtŭr vērtīgĭnĕ cœlŭm, Ov.

vērto, tī, sŭm, *to turn.* Vērtĭtĕ vīrēs, Virg. SYN. Cōnvērto, flēcto, tōrquĕo,
vŏlvo, vērso; vărĭo, mūto, cōmmūto; ēvērto, dīrŭo.

Vērtūunŭs, ī, m., *the god of gardens and fruit.* Vērtūmnūm Jānūmquĕ, Ov.

vĕrū, n., indecl., *a spit.* Mūcrŏnĕ, vĕrūquĕ, Virg. EPITH. Lōngŭm, tĕrĕs,
fĕrrĕŭm.

vērvēcĕŭs, *or* vērvēcīnŭs, ă, ŭm, *of a sheep.* Plaut.

vērvēx, ēcĭs, m., *a sheep.* Ēlīxī vērvēcĭs mĕmbră, Juv. V. Aries.

vērŭm, adv., *but.* Vērum ĕtĭăm, Virg. SYN. Sĕd, ăt, āst.

vērūntămĕn, conj., *yet, notwithstanding.* Vērūntămĕn æstŭăt īntŭs, Ov.

vērŭs, ă, ŭm, *true.* Ac vērās aŭdīrĕ, Virg. SYN. Gērmānŭs, sīncērŭs; vērăx,
īngĕnŭŭs, cāndĭdŭs.

vērŭtŭm, ī, n., *a sort of dart.* Sæpĕ vĕrūtī, Lucr.

vĕrūtŭs, ă, ŭm, *armed with a dart.* Vōlscōsquĕ vĕrūtōs, Ov.

vēsānĭă, æ, f., *madness.* Ăgĕrĕt vēsānĭă dīscōrs, Hor. SYN. Insānĭă; fŭrŏr. V.
Stultitia, furor.

vūsānŭs, ă, ŭm, *mad.* Enĭm vēsānă fămēs, Virg. SYN. Stūltŭs; fŭrĭōsŭs.

vēscŏr, ĕrĭs, *to live upon.* Pārcŭs vēscātŭr ămārĭs, Hor. SYN. Pāscŏr, ălŏr,
nūtrĭŏr, sūstēntŏr, vīvo. V. Edo.

vēscŭs, ă, ŭm, *corrosive; edible.* Vēscūmquĕ păpāvĕr, Virg.

Vĕsēvŭs, ī, m., *a volcano near Naples.* Vīcīnă Vĕsēvō, Virg. SYN. Vĕsūvĭŭs,
Vĕsvĭŭs. EPITH. Prærūptŭs, fĕrāx, vĭrĭdĭs, vĭrēns, fērtĭlĭs, ārdēns, flāmmĭvŏmŭs, īgnĭvŏmŭs.

vēsīcă, *and* cūlă, æ, f., *a bladder.* Quāntūm vēsīcă, pĕpēdī, Hor. Anĭmæ vēsī-
cŭlă pārvă, Lucr.

vēspă, æ, f., *a wasp.* Vēspā jūdĭcĕ, Phæd. EPITH. Strīdŭlă, strīdēns, strĕpēns,
strĕpĭtāns.

Vēspāsĭānŭs, ī, m., *the Roman emperor.* Ādscītŭs Vēspāsĭānŭs, Aus.

Vēspĕr, ĕrĭs; *and* ĕrŭs, ī, m., *the evening, the evening star.* Vēspĕre ăb ātrō,
Virg. SYN. Vēspĕră, vēspĕrūgo, Hēspĕrŭs; vēspĕrtīnŭm tēmpŭs. EPITH.
Nōctĭfĕr, ōccĭdŭŭs, ūmbrĭfĕr, ŏpācŭs, sērŭs, frīgĭdŭs, rōscĭdŭs, ūdŭs, rŭbēns,
pĭgĕr.

vēspĕrĕ, *or* rī, adv., *in the evening.* Cic. SYN. Sērō. V. Noctesco, crepus-
culum.

vēspērtīlĭo, ōnĭs, m., *a bat.* Et vēspērtĭlĭŏ strīdŭnt, Ov.

vēspērtīnŭs, ă, ŭm, *of the evening.* Nēc vēspērtīnŭs cīrcŭm, Ov.

vēspīllo, ōnĭs, m., *one who carried dead bodies out in the night to be buried.* Făs-
tīdĭă vēspĭllōnŭm, Mart.

Vēstă, æ, f., *the goddess of fire, and patroness of chastity.* Pĕnĕtrālĭă Vēstæ,

Virg. Epith. Căstă, sānctă, pŭdīcă, sacră, vĕnĕrāndă, pŏtēns.—2. *earth.* Vĕstă vŏcātŭr, Ov. Epith. Antīquă, prīmævă, sĕnēx, vĕtŭs.

Vĕstālĭs, ĭs, f., *a virgin sacred to Vesta.* Quŏnĭam Vĕstālĭs ŏrīgo, Pr. Epith. Căstă, pŭdīcă, īnnŭbă, cœlēbs, īntegră, sacră, sānctă, vĕnĕrăbĭlĭs, vĕnĕrāndă, rĕlĭgĭōsă, Rōmānă.

vĕstĕr, tră, trŭm, *yours.* Vĕstrōs āccēdĕt, Ov.

vĕstĭbŭlŭm, ī, n., *a porch.* Vĕstĭbŭlĭs ăbĕŭnt, Juv. Syn. Pŏrtĭcŭs, ātrĭŭm. Epith. Mārmŏrĕŭm, sŭpērbŭm, māgnĭfĭcŭm, pīctŭm, lātŭm.

vĕstĭcēps, ĭpĭs, m., *a stripling.* Vĕstĭcĭpēs mōtū, Aus.

vĕstĭflŭŭs, ă, ŭm, *wearing loose flowing garments.* Vĕstĭflŭŭs Sēr, Aus.

vĕstĭgĭŭm, ĭī, n., *a trace, a footstep.* Vĕtĕrĭs vĕstīgĭă flāmmæ, Virg. Syn. Sīgnă pĕdŭm; sīgnŭm, relĭquĭæ; pēs, plāntă, pāssŭs, grădŭs. Epith. Imprēssŭm, sīgnātŭm, fīxŭm, rĕcēns, mănĭfēstŭm.

vĕstīgo, ās, *to trace, to search.* Vĕstīgēmŭs ĕt ā, Virg. Syn. Invēstīgo, īnquīro, quæro. V. Quæro.

vĕstīmēntŭm, ī, n., *a garment.* Vĕstīmēntă dăbăt, Hor. V. Vestis.

vĕstĭo, īvī *and* ĭī, ītŭm, *to dress, clothe.* Vĕstĭĕt āgnōs, Virg. Syn. Indŭo, ŏpĕrĭo, tĕgo, vēlo, ōrno, ēxōrno, dĕcōro, īnsīgnĭo.

vĕstĭs, ĭs, f., *a garment.* Ēt Tўrĭæ vĕstēs, Tib. Syn. Vĕstīmēntŭm, vĕstītŭs, tĕgmĕn, ămīctŭs, vēlāmĕn, vēlāmēntŭm, chlămўs, tŭnĭcă, tŏgă, pāllĭŭm; cārbăsŭs, līnŭm, pēplŭm. Epith. Prĕtĭōsă, pŭrpŭrĕă, cŏccĭnĕă, pīctă, līnĕă, sērĭcă, māgnĭfĭcă, rēgĭă, vērsĭcŏlŏr, lōngă, flŭēns, ūndāns, nĭtēns, splēndĭdă, dĕcōră, cāndĭdă, nĭvĕă, ālbă, vĭrĭdĭs, vĭrēns, rŭbĕă, rubră, rŭbēns, lūtĕă, crŏcĕă, cœrŭlĕă, nigră, pūllă, ātră, mœstă, lŭgŭbrĭs, fūnĕrĕă, fĕrālĭs, lăcĕră, squālēns, dēmīssă, sĭnŭōsă.

vĕstītŭs, ă, ŭm, *the pass. partic. of* vestio. Ætērnō vĕstītōs, Cl. Syn. Indūtŭs, ămīctŭs, tŭnĭcātŭs.

vĕstītŭs, ūs, m., *clothing.* Mēmbrăquĕ vĕstītū, Claud. V. Vestis.

Vĕsŭlŭs, ī, m., *a mountain of Liguria.* Vĕsŭlŭs quēm pīnĭfĕr ānnōs, Virg.

Vĕsŭvĭŭs, *or* Vĕsvĭŭs. V. Vesevus.

vĕtĕr, ĕrĭs, *old.* Jūxtāquĕ vĕtĕrrĭmă laūrŭs, Virg. V. Vetus.

vĕtĕrānŭs, ă, ŭm, *old.* Quæ nōstĕr vĕtĕrānŭs ārĕt, Lucan.—2. ī, m., *an old soldier.*

* vĕtĕrāsco, ĭs, *to grow old.* Col.

vĕtĕrīnŭs, ă, ŭm, *that carries burdens.* Ēst vĕtĕrīnō, Lucr.

vĕtĕrnŭs, ī, m., *sluggishness.* Rēgnă vĕtĕrnō, Virg. V. Pigritia.

vĕtĭtŭs, ă, ŭm, *the pass. partic. of* veto. Nĭtĭmŭr īn vĕtĭtŭm, Cl.

vĕto, ās, vĕtŭī, vĕtĭtŭm, *to forbid, hinder.* Rĕlĭgĭō vĕtŭĭt, Virg. Syn. Prŏhĭbĕo; īmpĕdĭo, ōbsto; ōbsŭm.

vĕtŭlă, æ, f., *an old woman.* Omnēs aūt vĕtŭlæ, (Phal.) Mart. Syn. Ănŭs. Epith. Frīgĭdă, trĕmēns, cūrvă, sĕgnĭs, mārcĭdă, rŭgōsă, mōrbōsă, ægră, lānguĭdă, dēlīrāns, dēfōrmĭs, sōrdĭdă, mōrōsă, trīstĭs.

vĕtŭlŭs, ī, m., *an old man.* Sī vĕtŭlō jŭvĕnĭs, Juv. V. Senex.

vĕtŭs, ĕrĭs; ŭlŭs, *and* ūstŭs, ă, ŭm, *old.* Vĕtŭs Ālbŭlă, Virg. Cōrnīcĭs vĕtŭlæ, Hor. Tēmplŭmquĕ vĕtŭstŭm, Cat. Syn. Antīquŭs, prīscŭs; sĕnēx, ānnōsŭs, lōngævŭs.

vĕtŭstās, ātĭs, f., *antiquity, old age.* Invĭdĭōsă vĕtŭstās, Ov. Syn. Antīquĭtās; sĕnēctŭs. Epith. Lōngīnquă, tārdă, ānnōsă, cānă, vĕnĕrāndă, sĕră.

vēxātĭo, ōnĭs, f., *grief, vexation.* Adĭmĕt vēxātĭō rēbŭs, Mart.

vēxīllŭm, ī, n., *a standard.* Vēxīllŭm nāvālĕ, Claud. Syn. Sīgnŭm, īnsīgnĕ bēllī. Epith. Mārtĭŭm, Māvōrtĭŭm, bēllĭcŭm, pīctŭm, vŏlāns, flŭĭtāns, vŏlĭtāns, ēxpānsŭm, ēxplĭcĭtŭm, ūndāns, lĕvĕ, mĭnāx, tērrĭfĭcŭm.

vēxo, ās, *to agitate, vex.* Vēxĕt īnērtĕs, Hor. Syn. Tōrquĕo, crŭcĭo, ēxcrŭcĭo, dīscrŭcĭo, āngo, ăgĭto, ēxăgĭto, āfflīgo, āfflīcto.

Ŭfēns, ēntĭs, m., *a river of Italy.* Vŏlvĭtŭr Ŭfēns, Virg.—2. *the name of a warrior.* Ŭfēns īnsīgnĭs, Id.

vĭă, æ, f., *a way.* Quŏ vĭă dŭcĭt, Virg. Syn. Ĭtĕr, cāllĭs, trāmĕs, sēmĭtă; cōmpĭtă, bĭvĭŭm, trĭvĭŭm, quādrĭvĭŭm. Epith. Trītă, frĕquēns, rēctă, plānă, făcĭlĭs, lūbrĭcă, dŭbĭă, āmbĭgŭă, fāllāx, ōccūltă, fūrtīvă, lātă, pătŭlă, pătēns, tūtă, pūblĭcă, spătĭōsă, ăpērtă, rēgĭă, āngūstă, ōblīquă, sălĕbrōsă, lŭtŭlēntă, cœnōsă, sāxōsă, sĭnŭōsă, īnvĭă.

vĭātĭcŭm, ĭ, n., *things necessary for a journey.* Sŭbdūctă vĭātĭcă plōrăt, Hor. SYN. Cĭbŭs; aŭxĭlĭŭm vĭæ.

vĭātŏr, ōrĭs, m., *a traveller.* Ārcĕ vĭātŏr, Virg. SYN. Pĕregrīnŭs; ādvĕnă. EPITH. Lăssŭs, fěssŭs, dēfěssŭs, fătĭgātŭs, sĭtĭěns, prŏpĕrāns, ěrrāns, văgābūndŭs, ĭgnōtŭs, pūlvĕrŭlēntŭs, mĭsěr.

vĭbĕx, ĭcĭs, m., *the mark of a stripe.* Caŭtŭs vĭbĭcĕ flăgěllās, Pers.

Vībĭdĭŭs, ĭī, m., *the name of a man.* Vībĭdĭūs quōs, Hor.

vibrābĭlĭs, ĕ, *that can be brandished.* Vībrābĭlĭs ōrnŭs, Aus.

vibro, ās, *to shake, to dart.* Tūtă vĭbrăbăt ămōr, Gal. Com. Jăcŭlŭm vībrārĕ lăcērtō, Ov. SYN. Quătĭo, cōrŭsco, tōrquĕo, ĭntōrquĕo, cōntōrquĕo, nĭĭtto, jăcŭlŏr, jăcĭo, cōnjĭcĭo; trĕmo, mĭco. V. Jaculor, luceo.

vĭcārĭŭs, ă, ŭm, *in the place of.* Sōrtĕ vĭcārĭŭs, Hor.

vĭcātĭm, adv., *from street to street, from village to village.* Tūrbă vĭcātim hĭnc ět hĭnc, Hor.

vĭcěm, *the acc. of* vĭcĭs, ĭs, f., *change, succession.* Vĭcěm nōn pĕrăgĭt, Ov. SYN. Fōrtūnăm, sōrtěm; pārtěm.—2. Vĭcĕ, *the abl. of* vicis. Hăc vĭcĕ, Virg. Fūngăr vĭcĕ cōtĭs, Hor. SYN. Lŏcō, prō.—3. Vĭcēs, *the nom. and acc. plur. of* vicis. Āltērnārĕ vĭcēs, Ov. SYN. Pārtēs, mūnŭs, ōffĭcĭŭm.—4. Vĭcĭbŭs, *the abl. plur. of* vicis. Ārmōrūm vĭcĭbŭs, Col.

vĭcēnī, æ, ă, *twenty.* Bĭs, vĭcēnōs tēr, pŭtŏ, nūmmōs, Mart. SYN. Vīgīntī.

vĭcēsĭmŭs, ă, ŭm, *the twentieth.* Nōndūm vĭcēsĭmă vēnĕrĭt, Ov. SYN. Vīgēsĭmŭs.

vĭcĭă, æ, f., *pulse.* Těnŭēs vĭcĭæ, Virg.

vĭcĭēs, adv., *twenty times.* Mŏdŏ vĭcĭēs hăbēbās, (Phal.) Mart.

vīcīnĭă, æ, f., *neighbourhood.* Pĕrēgrīnūm, vīcīnĭă raŭcă, Hor. SYN. Vīcīnĭtās; vīcīuī.

vīcīnŭs, ă, ŭm, *neighbouring.* Vīcīnūmquĕ pĕcŭs, Ov. SYN. Prōxĭmŭs, prŏpīnquŭs, cōntĭgŭŭs, cōntěrmĭnŭs, fīnĭtĭmŭs, prŏpĭŏr, āffĭnĭs.

vĭcīssĭm, adv., *by turns.* Utěrquĕ vĭcīssĭm, Virg. SYN. Pěr vĭcēs, ĭn vĭcěm, āltērnātĭm, pārĭtěr, mūtŭō, āltērnā vĭcĕ, āltērnĭs vĭcĭbŭs. V. Alternatim, certatim.

vĭcīssĭtūdo, ĭnĭs, f., *succession, change.* Ter. SYN. Vĭcēs.

victĭmă, æ, f., *a victim.* Vĭctĭmă quæ, Ov. SYN. Hōstĭă, plācŭlŭm. EPITH. Ŏpīmă, pīnguĭs, sacră, pĭă, plācābĭlĭs, īnfēlīx, īnsōns, mŷstĭcă, sōlēnnĭs. V. Sacrifico.

* victĭto, ās, *the freq. of* vivo.

victŏr, ōrĭs, m., *and* trīx, ĭcĭs, f., *a conqueror.* Vĭctŏr ěrăt, Prop. Quă vĭctrīx rědĭt, Virg. SYN. Trĭūmphātŏr, trĭūmphāns, ŏvāns. EPITH. Cělebrĭs, clārŭs, īllūstrĭs, fōrtĭs, māgnănĭmŭs, sŭpērbŭs. V. Vinco.

vĭctōrĭă, æ, f., *victory.* Vĭăm vĭctōrĭă pāndĭt, Virg. SYN. Pālmă, trĭūmphŭs, trŏphæŭm. EPITH. Nōbĭlĭs, clără, měmŏrāndă, cělebrĭs, īllūstrĭs, sŭpērbă, lætă, sānguĭněă, crŭēntă. V. Triumphus.

vĭctŭs, ă, ŭm, *the pass. partic. of* vinco. Vĭctŭs ăbĭt, Virg. V. Vinco.

victŭs, ūs, m., *nourishment.* Tūnc vĭctŭs ăbĭěrĕ, Tib. SYN. Ălĭmēntŭm, cĭbī.

vĭcŭs, ĭ, m., *a hamlet.* Vīcŭs hăbět, Mart. SYN. Pāgŭs; vĭă.

vĭdēlĭcět, adv., *forsooth, to wit.* Sīc īllă vĭdēlĭcět, Man. SYN. Scīlĭcět, nĭmĭrŭm, němpĕ.

vĭděn', *do you see?* Ědūcīt: vĭděn', ŭt, Virg. SYN. Vĭdēsnĕ, nōnnĕ vĭdēs.

vĭdĕo, ēs, vīdī, vīsŭm, *to see.* Aŭt vĭdět, aŭt vīdīssĕ pŭtăt, Virg. SYN. Aspĭcĭo, cērno, īntŭěŏr; sēntĭo, īntēllĭgo, āgnōsco, ādvērto. V. Aspicio. Pass. vĭdĕŏr, ěrĭs, vīsŭs sŭm, vĭdĕrī, *to be seen, to appear, to seem.* Ět sĕ cŭpĭt āntĕ vĭdērī, Virg. Sārdōīs vĭdĕăr tĭbĭ āmărĭŏr hērbīs, Ov. SYN. Aspĭcĭŏr; hăbĕŏr, dūcŏr.

vĭdēsĭs, *(for* vĭdē sī vīs,*) take care.* Vĭdēsĭs nĕ, Pers.

vĭdŭă, æ, f., *a widow.* Vĭdŭās vēnēntŭr, Hor. EPITH. Mĭsěră, sprētă, rělĭctă, cōntēmptă, dēsērtă, mœstă, trīstĭs, āfflīctă, lūgēns.

vĭdŭo, ās, *to deprive, bereave.* Gěmĭnā vĭdŭāvěrăt, Sed. SYN. Ōrbo; spŏlĭo.

vĭdŭŭs, ă, ŭm, *bereft, widowed.* Lăcŭs vĭdŭŏs, Vict. SYN. Vĭdŭātŭs, ōrbŭs, ōrbātŭs; spŏlĭātŭs.

vĭētŭs, *or* viētŭs (*dissyl.*). ă, ŭm, *withered.* Cěcĭdīssĕ vĭētŭm, Lucr. Quĭs sudŏr viētīs, Hor. SYN. Mārcēns, mārcĭdŭs.

vĭgĕo, ŭī, *to be strong.* Mōbĭlĭtātĕ vĭgět, Virg. SYN. Vĭgēsco, vălĕo; flōrĕo, flōrēscŏ, vĭrĕo.

vĭgēsco, ĭs, *to grow vigorous.* Pĕdēs vĭgēscŭnt, Cat.

vĭgēsĭmŭs, ă, ŭm, *the twentieth.* Stĕtĕrăt vĭgēsĭmŭs ănnŭs, Prop. Syn. Vīcēsĭmŭs.

vĭgēssĭs, ĭs, f., *a piece of Roman money.* Amphŏră vĭgēssī, Mart.

vĭgĭl, ĭlĭs, *awake, vigilant.* Pŏrtārŭm vĭgĭlēs, Virg. Syn. Pērvĭgĭl, vĭgĭlāns, īnsŏmnĭs, īnsōpītŭs, pērnŏx ; dīlĭgēns, ācĕr, sēdŭlŭs, ăttēntŭs. V. Vigilo.

vĭgĭlāntĭă, æ, f., *vigilance.* Vĭrōs vĭgĭlāntĭă fūgĭt, Virg. Syn. Vĭgĭlēs sēnsŭs; vĭgĭl cūră, stŭdĭŭm ; dīlĭgēntĭă, cūră, sēdŭlĭtăs.

vĭgĭlātŭs, ă, ŭm, *sleepless.* Vĭgĭlātæ cŏrpŏră nōctēs, Ov. Syn. Vĭgĭl, īnsōmnĭs.
—2. *performed with night-watchings.* Vĭgĭlātōrŭmquĕ lăbōrŭm, Id. Syn. Lūcŭbrātŭs.

vĭgĭlāx, ācĭs, *wakeful.* Vĭgĭlācĭbŭs ēxcĭtă cūrĭs, Ov. V. Vigil.

vĭgĭlēs, ŭm, m. pl., *sentinels.* Tērtĭă jăm vĭgĭlēs, Lucan.

vĭgĭlĭă, æ, f., *a watch, a sentry.* Plaut. Syn. Īnsōmnĭă ; ēxcŭbĭæ.

vĭgĭlo, ās, *to watch, to be awake.* Præcĭpĭtēs vĭgĭlātĕ vĭrī, Virg. Syn. Pērvĭgĭlo, ēvĭgĭlo ; ēxcŭbo, ēxcŭbĭās ăgo ; īnvĭgĭlo, īncŭmbo.

vĭgĭntī, (*indecl.*) *twenty.* Vĭgĭntī taūrōs, Virg. Syn. Bis dēnī.

vĭgŏr, ōrĭs, m , *strength.* Mŭtātquĕ vĭgōrĕm, Virg. Syn. Vīs, vīrēs, rōbŭr.
Epith. Ignĕŭs, ălăcĕr, ăgĭlĭs, mōbĭlĭs, ănĭmōsŭs, vīvŭs, ignĭfĕr, flagrāns, vīvĭfĭcŭs.

vīlēsco, lŭī, *to grow cheap.* Ŏcŭlīs vīlēscĭt hŏnōrĕ, Prud. Syn. Sōrdēsco, sŏrdĕo.

vīlĭs, ĕ, *base, contemptible.* Vīlĭŭs ārgēntŭm, Hor. Syn. Abjēctŭs, dēspēctŭs, cōntēmptŭs, nēglēctŭs, hŭmĭlĭs. sōrdĭdŭs.

vīllă, *and* ŭlă, æ, f., *a country-house.* Prŏcŭl vīllārŭm cŭlmĭnă, Virg. Syn. Prædĭŭm, dŏmŭs rūstĭcă. V. Ager, hortus.

vīllĭcor, ārĭs, *to manage a farm.* Quī vīllĭcātŭs prædĭĭs, Aus.

vīllĭcŭs, ī, m., *and* æ, f., *a farmer, a steward.* Vīllĭcŭs āptās, Hor. Syn. Cŏlōnŭs, ăgrĭcŏlă, rūstĭcŭs. V. Agricola.

Vīllĭŭs, ĭī, m., *the name of a man.* Vīllĭŭs īn Faūstā, Hor.

vīllōsŭs, ă, ŭm, *hairy.* Ŏssææ vīllōsĭs, Ov. Syn. Pĭlōsŭs, sētōsŭs.

vīllŭlŭs, ī, m., *the dimin. of* villus. Sōrdēbānt tĭbĭ vīllŭlī, Cat.

vīllŭs, ī, m., *wool, hair.* Ĭnēst, vīllōrŭm, Mart. Syn. Pĭlŭs, sētă. Epith. Hōrrēns, crīspŭs, crīspātŭs, lōngŭs, impēxŭs, ēffŭsŭs. V. Juba.

vīmĕn, ĭnĭs, n., *a twig, osier.* Vīmĭnĕ quērnō, Virg. Epith. Lēntŭm, flēxĭlĕ, tōrtŭm, īntōrtŭm, vĭrēns, vĭrĭdĕ, lēvĕ, tĕnŭĕ, frŭtĭcōsŭm, pălūstrĕ, ăcūtŭm.

vīmĭnĕŭs, ă, ŭm, *of osier.* Vīmĭnĕāsquĕ trăhĭt, Virg. Syn. Ēx vīmĭnĕ; ārbŭtĕŭs.

Vīnālĭă, ōrŭm *or* ĭŭm, n. pl., *festivals at the close of the vintage.* Fēstŭm Vīnālĭă dīcŭnt, Ov.

vīnārĭŭm, ĭī, n., *a vessel for wine.* Vīnārĭă tōtă, Hor.

vīncĭo, vīnxī, vīnctŭm, *to tie.·* Cērtō vīncĭtŭr fœdĕrĕ, Prop. Syn. Dēvīncĭo, rĕvīncĭo, lĭgo, āllĭgo, cōllĭgo, rĕlĭgo, rĕdĭmĭo, strīngo, ŏbstrīngo, āstrīngo, cōnstrīngo, nēcto, ādnēcto, cōnnēcto. V. Nodo.

vīnco, vīcī, vīctŭm, *to vanquish.* Vīvēndō vīcī, Virg. Syn. Dēvīnco, dēbēllo, sŭpĕro, sŭbĭgo, dŏmo, ēxpŭgno, fūndo, stērno. V. Victor, triumpho.

vīncŭlŭm, *and* clŭm, ī, n., *a chain, a bond.* Vīncŭlă pālmās, Virg. Vīnclă rŏsā, Ov. Syn. Cătēnă, nēxŭs, lĭgāmēn, lăquĕŭs, mănĭcă, cōmpāgēs, cōmpăgo, nōdŭs, cōmpēs, rĕtĭnācŭlŭm, fūnĭs, rēstĭs, lōră. Epith. Fīrmŭm, ārctŭm, īnēxtrĭcābĭlĕ, tĕnāx, vălĭdŭm, dūrŭm, sævŭm, īntōrtŭm, tōrtŭm, nēxŭm, nōdōsŭm, fōrtĕ, strīdēns, ădămāntæŭm, fērrĕŭm, fērrātŭm, ăhēnŭm. V. Catena, solvo.

Vīndĕlĭcī, ōrŭm, m. pl., *a people between the Alps and the Danube.* Vīndĕlĭcī dĭdĭcērĕ, Hor.

vīndēmĭă, æ, f., *vintage.* Plēnīs vīndēmĭă lăbrīs, Virg. Syn. Ūvæ, ūvārŭm mēssĭs. Epith. Fērāx, spūmāns, fœcūndă, mītĭs. V. Vinca, Autumnus.

Vīndēmĭātŏr, dēmĭātŏr (*quadr.*). mĭtŏr, ōrĭs, *the keeper of a vineyard.* Vīndēmĭātŏr ĕt īnvīctŭs, Hor. Effŭgĭēt vīndēmĭtŏr, Ov. V. Vinitor.

vīndēx, ĭcĭs, m., *an avenger.* Vīndĭcĭs ēssĕ, Mart. Syn. Ŭltŏr, pūnītŏr ; dēfēnsŏr, āssērtŏr. Epith. Ăcĕr, ĭrātŭs, grăvĭs, īnfēnsŭs, jŭstŭs, æquŭs.

vīndĭco, ās, *to avenge, to assume.* Vīndĭcăt ārmĭs, Virg. Syn. Ulcīscŏr ; **lúžľbŕo**, āssĕro, dēfēndo ; ārrŏgo. Attrĭbŭo, āssūmo, vēndĭco. V. Ulciscor.

vīndĭctă, æ, f., *revenge.* Lēgĭs vĭndĭctă sĕvēræ, Ov. Syn. Ŭltĭo, pœnă, sŭpplĭcĭum. Epith. Jŭstă, ĭnīquă, sævă, crūdēlīs, atrōx, dīră, tĕrrĭbĭlīs, sĕvēră, tărdă, hŏrrēndă, fūnēstă. V. Ultio.

vīnĕă, æ, f., *a vine.* Vīnĕă fălcĕm, Virg. Syn. Vīnētŭm; vītĭs, pālmĕs, pāmpĭnŭs. Epith. Fērtĭlĭs, fĕrāx, cūltă, ālmă, fœcūndă, lūxŭrĭāns, lætă, pūrpŭrĕă, grăvĭdă, frŏndōsă, ūmbrōsă, mōntānă, rŭbĭcūndă, vīnĭfĕră. V. Vitis.

vīnētŭm, ī, n., *a vineyard.* Cūrvæ vīnētă cărīnæ, Ov. Epith. Lætŭm, dūlcĕ, cūltŭm, fœcūndŭm.

vīnĭtŏr, ōrĭs, m., *a vine-dresser.* Vīnĭtŏr ūvæ, Virg. Epith. Vĭgĭl, mădĭdŭs, cūrvŭs.

Vīnnĭŭs, ī, m., *the name of a man.* Vŏlūmĭnă, Vīnnī.

vīnŏlēntŭs, ă, ŭm, *drunken.* Quās vīnŏlēntæ, (Iamb.) Prud. Syn. Tēmŭlēntŭs, ēbrĭōsŭs, vīnōsŭs. V. Ebrius.

vīnōsŭs, ă, ŭm, *fond of wine.* Vīnōsŭs Hŏmērŭs, Hor.

vīnŭm, ī, n., *wine.* Vīnă nŏvŭm, Virg. Syn. Mĕrŭm, mūstŭm, ūvă, vītĭs, Bācchŭs, Iacchŭs, Fălērnŭm. Epith. Dūlcĕ, suāvĕ, lætŭm, liquēns, gĕnĕrōsŭm, grātŭm, jūcūndŭm, vĭŏlēntŭm, fūmāns, spūmāns, cālĭdŭm, rŭbēns, rŭbĭcūndŭm, frăgrāns, ŏdōrātŭm, pūrŭm, fōrtĕ, vălĭdŭm, Mässĭcŭm, Fălērnŭm, Cæcŭbŭm, Sūrrēntīnŭm; Mărĕōtĭcŭm, Chĭŭm, Lēsbĭŭm. V. Epulor, ebrius.

vĭŏlă, æ, f., *a violet.* Pāllēntēs vĭŏlās, Virg. Epith. Pūrpŭrĕă, pāllēns, mōllĭs, flōrēns, tĕnĕră, suāvĭs, vērnă, lætă, āmœnă, ŏdōrĭfĕră, ŏdōrātă, ŏdōră, frăgrāns, hālāns, spīrāns, fōrmōsă. V. Flo.

vĭŏlābĭlĭs, ĕ, *that may be violated.* Nōn vĭŏlābĭlĕ nūmĕn, Virg.

vĭŏlārĭă, ōrŭm, n. pl., *violet-beds.* Vĭŏlārĭă fōntĕm, Virg. Epith. Mōllĭă, blāndă, rōscĭdă, grātă, dūlcĭă, suāvĭă.

vĭŏlātŏr, ōrĭs, m., *a polluter, a violator.* Tēmplī vĭŏlātŏr ăd ārās, Ov.

vĭŏlēntĕr, adv., *violently.* Vĭŏlēntĕr ūndīs, (Sapph.) Hor. Syn. Vī, pĕr vīm, impĕtū.

vĭŏlēntĭă, æ, f., *violence.* Vĭŏlēntĭă vīncăt, Virg. Syn. Vīs, impĕtŭs. Epith. Răbĭdă, sœvă, atrōx, aūdāx, cæcă, ĭnīquă, præcēps, răpĭdă, mĭnāx, fŭrĭōsă, fĕră, hŏstīlĭs. V. Impetus, ira, invado.

vĭŏlēntŭs, ă, ŭm, *violent.* Tăm vĭŏlēntŭs ĕās, Mart. Syn. Vĕhĕmēns, ācĕr; præcēps, tĕmĕrārĭŭs, impătĭēns, fĕrōx, īrātŭs, vĭŏlēns.

vĭŏlo, ās, *to violate.* Fērrō vĭŏlāvĭmŭs ăgrōs, Virg. Syn. Tĕmĕro, lædo, ōffēndo, cōntāmĭno, măcŭlo, fœdo; rūmpo, ăbrūmpo, pērfrīngo, rēscīndo, dīssōlvo, rēvēllo, lăbĕfācto; stuprum īnfĕro, cōnstupro.

vīpĕră, æ, f., *a viper.* Vīpĕră dēlĭtŭĭt, Virg. Syn. Mălă, īnsĭdĭōsă, ātră, mōrtĭfĕră, vĕnēnōsă. V. Serpens.

vīpĕrĕŭs, *and* īnŭs, ă, ŭm, *of a viper.* Tēlăquĕ vīpĕrĕō, Ov. Cŏērcēs vīpĕrīnō, Hor.

vĭr, vĭrī, m., *a man, a husband.* Hīc vĭr, hīc ēst, Virg. Præsēntēmquĕ vĭrīs, Virg. Syn. Mās, māscŭlŭs; hŏmo; cōnjūx, spōnsŭs, mărītŭs. Epith. Fōrtĭs, māgnănĭmŭs, gĕnĕrōsŭs, īnipăvĭdŭs, jūstŭs, prūdēns, săgāx, sōlērs, præstāns. īllūstrĭs.

vĭrāgo, ĭnĭs, f, *a heroine.* Jūtūrnă vĭrāgo, Virg.

Vīrbĭŭs, ĭī, m., *the name under which the Latins worshipped Hippolytus, restored to life.* Vīrbĭŭs ēssĕt, Virg.

vĭrĕo, ēs, *to be green, to flourish.* Frōndĕ vĭrērĕ nŏvă, Virg. Syn. Vĭrēsco, vērno, rĕvĭrēsco, flōrĕo, frōndēsco.

vĭrēs, ĭŭm, f. pl., *strength.* Vīrĭbŭs hāstăm, Virg. Syn. Rōbŭr, vīrtŭs, vĭgŏr, vīs; pŏtēntĭă. Epith. Vălĭdæ, fīrmæ, īngēntēs, īnvīctæ, īnfrāctæ, īndŏmĭtæ; ălăcrēs, Hērcŭlĕæ, Gĭgāntĕæ. V. Robur, fortis.

vĭrēsco, ĭs, *to grow green.* Injūssă vĭrēscŭnt, Virg. V. Vireo.

vĭrētŭm, ī, n., *a grass-plat.* Amœnă vĭrētă, Virg. Syn. Vĭrĭdārĭŭm, prātŭm, hōrtŭs. Epith. Ămœnŭm, fōrmōsŭm, pătēns, ūmbrōsŭm, lātŭm, ŏpācŭm, cūltŭm, flōrĭdŭm, dūlcĕ, mōllĕ, hērbōsŭm. V. Hortus.

vīrgă, æ, f., *a twig, a rod.* Tēxŭnt vīrgīs ĕt, Virg. Syn. Băcĭllŭs; flăgēllŭm, vērbĕr; vīmĕn, vīrgūltŭm, rāmŭscŭlŭs. V. Flagellum, vimen, ramus.

vīrgātŭs, *and* gĕŭs, ă, ŭm, *made of osiers.* Vīrgātī călăthīscī, Catull. Vīrgĕă sūggĕrĭtŭr, Virg. Syn. Vīmĭnĕŭs.

Vīrgĭlĭŭs, ĭī, m., *the most esteemed of the Roman Poets.* Illō Vīrgĭlĭŭm, Virg. Syn. Măro. Epith. Dōctŭs, īngĕnĭōsŭs, fācūndŭs, dīvīnŭs, ætērnŭs.

virgĭnĕŭs, ă, ŭm, *of a virgin.* Hæsĭt, vĭrgĭnĕŭm, Virg. Syn. Pŭĕllārĭs.

virgĭnĭtās, ātĭs, f., *virginity.* Vĭrgĭnĭtās ăvĭbŭs, Ov. Syn. Cāstĭtās, pŭdŏr, pŭdīcĭtĭă. Epitu. Cāstă, sānctă, cāndĭdă, ĭnnŭbă, intĕgră, illæsă. V. Pudicitia, castitas.

virgo, ĭnĭs, f., *a virgin.* Syn. Pŭĕllă. Epith. Innūptă, ĭnnŭbă, cāstă, intĕmĕrātă, incūlpātă, pūră, intāctă, illĭbātă, pŭdĭcă.—2. *one of the twelve signs.* Rĕdĭt ĕt vĭrgo, Virg. Syn. Astræă; Erĭgŏnē. Epitu. Clără, mĭcāns.

virgūltŭm, ĭ, n., *a bush.* Ăvĭbŭs vĭrgūltă cănŏrĭs, Virg. Syn. Frŭtĕx; ārbūstŭm. Epitu. Tĕnĕrŭm, sўlvēstrĕ, sŏnāns, implĭcĭtŭm, āvĭŭm, cōrnĕŭm, tūrgēscēns, vērnŭm, frŭtĭcōsŭm. V. Frutex.

virgūncŭlă, æ, f., *the dimin. of* virgo. Vĭrgūncŭlă Jūno, Juv.

vĭrĭdārĭŭm, ĭĭ, n., *a green.* Vĭrĭdārĭă, quĭd jŭvăt, Mart. Syn. Vĭrētŭm, prātŭm, hōrtŭs. V. Viretum.

vĭrĭdĭs, ĕ, *green.* Nŭnc vĭrĭdēs ĕtĭăm, Virg. Syn. Vĭrēns, vĭrĭdāns, vĭrēscēns, flōrēns, frŏndēns.

vĭrĭdo, ās, *to make green.* Vĭrĭdēntŭr ăb hērbĭs, Ov. V. Viresco.

vĭrīlĭs, ĕ, *manly.* Grădīvĕ, vĭrīlĭbŭs āptŭs, Ov. Syn. Māscŭlŭs, rōbūstŭs, fōrtĭs, Mārtĭŭs, gĕnĕrōsŭs, aŭdāx, intrĕpĭdŭs, intērrĭtŭs, cōnstāns.

vĭrīlĭtās, ātĭs, f., *manliness.* Vĭrīlĭātĭs dāmnă, (Scaz.) Mart.

vĭrīlĭtĕr, adv., *manfully.* Fēcĭtnĕ vĭrīlĭtĕr? ātquī, Hor. Syn. Fōrtĭtĕr, gĕnĕrōsē, aŭdāctĕr.

vĭrītĭm, adv., *man by man.* Tĕrĕrētquĕ vĭrītĭm, Hor.

vĭrōsŭs, ă, ŭm, *venomous, stinking.* Vĭrōsăquĕ Pōntŭs Cāstŏrĕă, Virg.

vĭrtūs, ūtĭs, f., *virtue, valour.* Vĭrtūtēs hăbĕăt, Hor. Syn. Prŏbĭtās, intĕgrĭtās, pĭĕtās, æquĭtās, māgnănĭmĭtās, prūdēntĭă; vīs, vīrēs, rŏbŭr; ārs, făcūltās. Epitu. Vĭvĭdă, māscŭlă, inclўtă, mĕmŏrāndă, gĕnĕrōsă, splēndĭdă, illūstrĭs, nōbĭlĭs, incōncūssă, impăvĭdă, præstāns, ēxcēllēns, invĭctă, intērrĭtă, cōnstāns, fīrmă, pĭă, pătĭēns, rără, ignĕă, vīvāx, pĕrēnnĭs, laŭdātă, cĕlĕbrĭs, ingēns, ămābĭlĭs, mīrāndă. V. Pietas, patientia, castitas, modestia, clementia, prudentia, justitia, generositas, temperantia, &c.

vĭrŭs, n., indecl., *venom.* Vīrŭs hăbē, Mart. V. Venenum.

vīs, īs, f., *strength.* Ûtrăquĕ vīs ăpĭbŭs, Virg. Syn. Vĭŏlēntĭă; rŏbŭr. V. Vires.

visco, ās, *to glue.* Vīscāntŭr lābră, Juv.

vīscōsŭs, ă, ŭm, *glutinous.* Mūltās vīscōsŭs ĭnēscăt, Prop. Syn. Glūtĭnĕŭs; vīscātŭs, vīsco illĭtŭs, ōbdūctŭs.

viscŭs, ĕrĭs, n., *and* ĕră, ŭm, n. pl., *bowels.* Pūtrī vīscĕrĕ pāssĭm, Ov. Vīscĕră fĕbrĭs, Mart. Syn. Intēstīnă, ĭlĭă, ēxtă, præcōrdĭă. Epith. Intĭmă, mōllĭă, pīnguĭă, lūbrĭcă, spīrāntĭă, fūmāntĭă, tĕpĭdă, tĕpēntĭă, călĭdă, fērvēntĭă.

viscŭs, ĭ, m., *or* ŭm, ĭ, n., *glue.* Fāllĕrĕ vīscō, Virg. Syn. Glūtēn, glūtĭnŭm. Epitu. Pīnguĭs, tēnāx, lēntŭs, sēquāx, strĭngēns, vălĭdŭs.

Vīsēllĭŭs, ĭĭ, m., *the name of a man.* Sŏcĕrŭmquĕ Vīsēllī, Hor.

vīsĭbĭlĭs, ĕ, *visible.* In quā vīsĭbĭlĭs, (Chor.) Prud.

vīso, ĭs, vīsī, *to visit.* Vīsĕrĕ tēctă, Mart. Syn. Cōnvĕnĭo, ădĕo, invīso, vīsĭto.

vīsŭm, ĭ, n., *a dream.* Ăttŏnĭtŭs vīsĭs, Virg. V. Somnium.

vīsŭs, ă, ŭm, *the pass. partic. of* video. Quī vīsŭs, ĕŭm, Virg.

vīsŭs, ūs, m., *sight.* Sĕcūndārēnt vīsŭs ōmēnquĕ, Virg. Syn. Ăspēctŭs. V Aspectus.

vītă, æ, f., *life.* Vītăquĕ māncĭpĭŏ, Lucr. Syn. Spīrĭtŭs, lūx. Epitu. Fŭgĭēns, răpĭdă, brĕvĭs, cădŭcă, flŭēns, āngūstă, ārctă, fāllāx, mĭsĕră, lānguĭdă, infaŭstă, infēlīx, ærūmnōsă.

vītābĭlĭs, ĕ, *that may be avoided.* Vītābĭlĭs Ascră, Ov.

vītālĭs, ĕ, *of life.* Vēscī vītālĭbŭs aūrĭs, Lucr. Syn. Vīvĭfĭcŭs.

vītēllŭs, ĭ, m, *the yellow of an egg.* Ûndă vĭtēllōs, Mart. Epith. Lūtĕŭs, rŭbĕr.

vītĕŭs, ă, ŭm, *of the vine.* Ĭmĭtāntŭr vītĕă sōrbĭs, Virg. V. Vitigenus.

vītĭcŏlă, æ, m., *cultivator of the vine.* Vītĭcŏlæ nōmĕn, Sil.

vītĭfĕr, ĕră, ĕrŭm, *vine-bearing.* Hæc dē vītĭfĕră, Mart.

vītĭgĕnŭs, ă, ŭm, *produced from the vine.* Vītĭgēnī lătĭcĕm, Lucr.

vītĭlĭgo, ĭnĭs, f., *the leprosy.* Mĭhī vītĭlĭgo ēst, Lucil.

U

vĭtĭo, ās, *to defile.* Vĭtĭāntŭr ŏdōrĭbŭs, Ov. Syn. Cŏrrŭmpo, vĭŏlo, dēprāvo.

vĭtĭōsŭs, ă, ŭm, *rotten.* Nōn vĭtĭōsŭs hŏmo, Mart. Syn. Imprŏbŭs, flāgĭtĭōsŭs, pērdĭtŭs, cŏrrŭptŭs. V. Sceleratus, libidinosus.

vītĭs, ĭs, f., *a vine.* Vītĭbŭs ūvæ, Virg. Syn. Ŭvă, vīnĕă, pālmĕs, pāmpĭnŭs. Epith. Flēxă, ōblīquă, grăvĭdă, fĕrāx, rŭbēns, pūrpŭrĕă, pĭctă, lætă, grātă. V. Vinea.

vĭtĭsătŏr, ōrĭs, m., *a planter of vines, an epithet of Saturn.* Vĭtĭsātŏr cūrvăm, Virg.

vĭtĭŭm, ĭī, n., *vice.* Tū vĭtĭīs hŏmĭnŭm, Prop. Syn. Dēfēctŭs, lābēs; crīmĕn, cūlpă, nōxă, scĕlŭs, flāgĭtĭŭm. Epith. Tūrpĕ, īnfāmĕ, fœdŭm, dēfōrmĕ, fŭgĭēndŭm, dētēstāndŭm, ēxecrāndŭm, pērnĭcĭōsŭm, ēxĭtĭălĕ, nĕfāndŭm, īnfāndŭm, īmpĭŭm. V. Scelus.

vīto, ās, *to avoid.* Vĭtĭŭm vĭtāvĕrĭs īllŭd, Hor. Syn. Ēvīto, dēvīto, fŭgĭo, ēffŭgĭo, dēclīno, dētrēcto.

vitrĕŭs, ă, ŭm, *glassy.* Vĭtrĕĭsquĕ sēdīlĭbŭs, Virg. Syn. Ēx vitrō crўstāllĭnŭs; clārŭs, nĭtĭdŭs, līmpĭdŭs, pēllūcĭdŭs.

vītrĭcŭs, ĭ, m., *a step-father.* Vĭtrĭcŭs ĭpsĕ, Ov.

vitrŭm, ĭ, n., *glass.* Ăd cўăthōs, vĭtrĭquĕ, Prop. Splēndĭdĭōr vĭtrō, (Asclep.) Hor. Syn. Crўstāllĭnŭs. Epith. Clārŭm, nĭtĭdŭm, lūcĭdŭm, pēllūcĭdŭm, splēndēns, splēndĭdŭm, mĭcāns, pūrŭm, tĕnŭĕ, frăgĭlĕ, pērspĭcŭŭm.

vĭttă, æ, f., *a ribbon, head-band.* Pērfūsŭs sănĭē vĭttăs, Virg. Syn. Tænĭă, fāscĭă, tænă. Epith. Tōrtă, lānĕă, pēndēns, pēndŭlă, pūrpŭrĕă, nĭvĕă, ālbēns, mōllĭs, lĭnĕă, crīnālĭs.

vĭttātŭs, ă, ŭm, *bound with fillets.* Pāllădă vĭttātæ, Ov.

vĭtŭlŭs, ĭ, m., *and ă, æ, f., a calf, a heifer.* Tŭm vĭtŭlŭs bīnă, Virg. Cūm făcĭăm vĭtŭlā, Virg. V. Juvenca, us; taurus, vacca.

vĭtŭpĕro, ās, *to blame.* Istŭd vĭtŭpĕrānt, Ter. Syn. Dāmno, cŭlpo, īmprŏbo, ārgŭo. V. Redarguo.

vīvārĭŭm, ĭī, n., *a park, a warren.* In vīvārĭă mīttŭnt, Hor.

vīvāx, ācĭs, *long-lived.* Sўlvă vīvācĭs ŏlīvæ, Virg. Syn. Vīvĭdŭs; lōngævŭs, īmmōrtālĭs.

vīvĕ, vīvĭtĕ, *farewell.* Vīvĕ, vălēquĕ, Hor. Vīvĭtĕ, sўlvæ, Virg.

vīvēsco, *and* īsco, ĭs, *to gain strength.* Ŭlcŭs ĕnīm vīvēscĭt, Lucr.

vīvĭdŭs, ă, ŭm, *lively, strong.* Vīvĭdŭs Ŭmbĕr, Virg. Syn. Vīvāx, vĕgĕtŭs, vălĭdŭs, ănĭmōsŭs, vĭgēns, fōrtĭs, rōbūstŭs.

vīvĭfĭco, ās, *to give life.* Vīvĭfĭcāntĕm, Prud. Syn. Ănĭmo, vītăm dŏ; rōbŏro, vīrēs dŏ.

vīvĭfĭcŭs, ă, ŭm, *giving life.* Cūnctăquĕ vīvĭfĭcĭs, Vict. Syn. Vītālĭs, vĕgĕtāns.

vīvo, xī, ctŭm, *to live.* Vīvĭt ĭmāgo, Juv. Syn. Spīro, rēspīro.

vīvŭs, ă, ŭm, *living.* Vīvŭs ĕt hērbă, Mart. Syn. Vīvēns, ănĭmātŭs, spīrāns, sŭpērstĕs.

vīx, adv., *hardly.* Vīx Prĭămŭs, Virg. Syn. Ægrĕ, dĭffĭcŭltĕr.

ŭlcĕro, ās, *to wound.* Ŭlcĕrĕt ātquĕ, Hor.

ŭlcĕrōsŭs, ă, ŭm, *full of sores.* Jĕcŭr ŭlcĕrōsŭm, (Sapph.) Hor.

ŭlcīscŏr, ĕrĭs, ŭltŭs, *to revenge.* Gēntēmque ŭlcīscăr īnīquăm, Vict. Syn. Vīndĭco; pūnĭo. V. Punio.

ŭlcŭs, ĕrĭs, n., *a sore, a wound.* Ŭlcĕrĭs ōs, Virg. Epith. Stīllāns, putrĕ, putrĭdŭm, putrĕfāctŭm, tētrŭm, squālēns, fœdŭm, tābĭfĭcŭm, hūmĭdŭm, sōrdĭdŭm, ācrĕ, ŭndāns, dīrŭm. V. Vulnus.

ūlīgo, ĭnĭs, f., *dampness.* Dūlcīque ūlīgĭnĕ lætă, Virg. Epith. Dūlcĭs, lætă.

ūllŭs, ă, ŭm, gen. ūllĭŭs, dat. ūllī, *any, any one.* Amnĕs ūllī rūmpūntŭr, Virg. Nĕ te ūllīŭs vĭŏlēntĭă, Id. Scrūtābĕrĭs ūllīŭs ūnquăm, Id.

ūlmĕŭs, ă, ŭm, *of elm-wood.* Sŏnăt ūlmĕă cœnă, Juv.

ūlmŭs, ĭ, f., *an elm.* Vītĭbŭs ūlmī, Ov. Epith. Frōndōsă, āltă, ŏpācă, dēnsă, pătŭlă; prōcērā, ŭmbrōsă, ārdŭă, vĭrĭdĭs, aĕrĭă, fōrtĭs, mōntōsă, rāmōsă, vĭrēns, mōllĭs, pāmpĭnĕă, vītĭcōmă, tēxtĭlĭs, dūră, frōndēns.

ūlnă, æ, f., *an arm.* Cōmplēctĭtŭr ūlnĭs, Claud. Syn. Brāchĭŭm. Epith. Mōllĭs, blāndă, cŭpĭdă, ăvĭdă, tĕnĕră, căpāx. V. Amplector.

ūltĕrĭŏr, ōrĭs, *further.* Ŭltĕrĭōrĭs ămōrĕ, Virg.

ūltĕrĭŭs, adv., *further.* Ăbĭt ūltĕrĭŭs, Ov.

ŭltĭmŭs, ă, ŭm, *the last.* Oltĭmŭs Æthĭŏpŭm, Virg. Syn. Pŏstrēmŭs, ēxtrēmŭs, nŏvĭssĭmŭs.

|| ŭltĭo, ōnĭs, f., *revenge.* Infĭrmi ēst ĕxĭgŭĭquĕ vŏlŭptās Oltĭo, Juv. Syn. Vĭndĭctă, pœnă, sŭpplĭcĭŭm. Sævă, crŭdēlĭs, atrōx, sĕvĕră, dīră, tĕrrĭbĭlĭs, fŭnēstă, hōrrēndă, ĭnīquă, ĭmpĭă, jūstă, mĕrĭtă. V. Sŭpplĭcium, Nemesis.

ŭltŏr, ōrĭs, m., *and* trīx, īcĭs, f., *a revenger.* Oltŏr ĕrĭs, Virg. Oltrīcēsquĕ sĕdēnt, Id. Syn. Vĭndēx,' pūnĭtŏr. Epitii. Irātŭs, īnfēnsŭs, grăvĭs, ācĕr, sĕvĕrŭs, crŭdēlĭs, atrōx, æquŭs, jŭstŭs, ĭnīquŭs. V. Ulciscor.

ŭltrā, *beyond.* Quŏs ŭltrā cītrāquĕ, Hor.

ŭltrō, adv., *willingly.* Oltrō cōntēmptŭs, Prop. Syn. Spōntĕ, lĭbēntĕr, vŏlēns, lĭbēns. V. Spoute.

ŭlvă, æ, f., *a reed.* Prŏcŭmbĭt ĭn ŭlvā, Virg.

Ŭlubræ, ārŭm, f. pl., *a town of Latium.* Ēst Ŭlŭbrĭs, sī tē, Hor. Văcŭĭs ædĭlĭs Ŭlūbrĭs, Juv.

ŭlŭlă, æ, f., *an owl.* Ēt cȳgnĭs ŭlŭlæ, Virg. Syn. Nōctŭă. Epitii. Trīstĭs, nōctūrnă.

ŭlŭlātŭs, ūs, m., *howling.* Quĕrŭlĭs ŭlŭlātĭbŭs Idăm, Ov. Syn. Clămŏr, quēstŭs, gēmĭtŭs. Epitii. Trĕmŭlŭs, mœstŭs, fœmĭnĕŭs, lŭgubrĭs, clāmōsŭs, quĕrŭlŭs, hōrrĭsŏnŭs, ăttŏnĭtŭs, flēbĭlĭs, tĕrrĭbĭlĭs, īnsānŭs, Tārtărĕŭs, tĕrrĭfĭcŭs, ăcūtŭs.

ŭlŭlo, ās, *to howl.* Cănēs ŭlŭlărĕ pĕr ūmbrăm, Virg. Syn. Ēxŭlŭlo, vōcĭfĕrŏr. V. Gemo, clamo, queror.

Ŭlȳssēs, *or* Olīxēs, ĭs; Ŭlȳsseŭs, ĕī, eī, *or* ī, m., *the king of Ithaca, and father of Telemachus.* Mŭtāvĭt Ŭlȳssī, Virg. Syn. Ithăcŭs, Lāertĭădēs, Æŏlīdēs. Epitii. Callĭdŭs, ăstūtŭs, prūdēns, văfĕr, fāllāx, dīsērtŭs, fācūndŭs, săgāx, sōlērs, văgŭs, ērrāns, Grājŭs, Pĕlāsgŭs.

ūmbēllă, æ, f., *the dim. of* umbra. Tŭ vĭrĭdem ūmbēllăm, Juv.

Ŭmbĕr, brĭ, m.; Ŭmbrĭ, ŏrŭm, m. pl., *Umbrian; an inhabitant of Umbria.* Ŭmbri rŭbĭcūndă mărītĭ, Ov.—2. *a sort of dog.* At vīvĭdŭs Ŭmbĕr, Virg.—3. adj., -bĕr, bră, brŭm, *Umbrian.* Lăcŭs æstīvĭs īntĕpĕt Ŭmbĕr äquĭs, Prop.

ūmbĭlīcŭs, ī, m., *the navel, a boss, the end of the ancient volumes.* Ŏsque ăd ŭmbĭlīcŏs, (Phal.) Mart.

ūmbo, ōnĭs, m., *the boss of a shield.* Nēquĭcquam ŭmbōnĕ pĕpēndĭt, Virg. Syn. Clȳpĕŭs, scūtŭm. V. Clypeus.

ūmbră, æ, f., *a shade, a shadow.* Ētĭăm pĕcŭdēs ūmbrās, Virg. Syn. Ŏmbrācŭlă; cālīgo, tĕnebræ. Epitii. Ŏpācă, dēnsă, ōbscūră, nĭgrāns, nĕmŏrālĭs, sȳlvēstrĭs, vĭrĭdĭs, vĭrēns, vĭrĭdāns, hērbōsă, frŏndōsă, ārbŏrĕă, flūmĭnĕă, frīgĭdă, gĕlĭdă, mōllĭs, grātă, dūlcĭs, ămœnă, sĭlēns, pāllēns, hōrrēns, căvă, spĭssă, hūmēns, cæcă, ĭnānĭs, nĭgră, grăcĭlĭs, nōctūrnă, trĕmŭlă, nōctĭvăgă, pĭcĕă, sŏpōrĭfĕră, tĕnŭĭs, rĕfŭgă, ātră, pătŭlă, lābĭlĭs, īnfōrmĭs, văgă, vŏlātĭlĭs, tĕrrĭfĭcă, tĕnebrōsă, trĭstĭs, mĭsĕră, sōmnĭfĕră. V. Refrigero, Manes.

ūmbrācŭlŭm, ī, n., *a place which affords shade.* Tēxŭnt ūmbrācŭlă vītēs, Virg. Syn. Ŏmbră; ūmbēllă.

ūmbrātĭcŭs, ă, ŭm, *and* ĭlĭs, ĕ, *in the shade, private, effeminate.* Vērĭs ūmbrătĭlĕ spēctrŭm, Mant.

Ŭmbrēnŭs, ī, m., *the name of a man.* Nŭnc ăgĕr Ŭmbrēnī, Hor.

Ŭmbrĭă, æ, f., *a country of Italy.* Ŭmbrĭă Rōmānī, Prop.

Ŭmbrĭcĭŭs, ĭī, m., *the name of a man.* Hīc tūnc Ŭmbrĭcĭŭs, Juv.

ūmbrĭfĕr, ĕră, ĕrŭm, *giving shade.* Ŭmbrĭfĕrŭm cōnjūx, Virg. Syn. Ŏmbrōsŭs, ŏpācŭs; ūmbrātĭlĭs; ūmbrās præbēns.

ūmbro, ās, *to shade.* Mōntēs ūmbrāntŭr ŏpācī, Virg. Syn. Inŭmbro, ŏbŭmbro, ŏpāco, tĕgo. V. Refrigero.

Ŭmbro, ōnĭs, m., *the name of a Marrhubian pontiff.* Fōrtissĭmŭs Ŭmbro, Virg.

ūmbrōsŭs, ă, ŭm, *shadowy.* Ŭmbrōsă căcūmĭnă, Virg. Syn. Ŭmbrĭfĕr, ūmbrātĭlĭs, ŏpācŭs, ūmbrās præbēns.

Ommĭdĭŭs, ĭī, m., *the name of a man.* Ŏmmĭdĭŭs quĭdăm, Hor.

ūnā, adv., *together.* Incēptūmque ūnā, Virg Syn. Sĭmŭl, părĭtĕr.

ŭnănĭmĭs, ĕ, *and* ŭs, ă, ŭm, *of the same sentiments.* Ŏnānĭmem āllŏquĭtŭr, Virg. Syn. Cōncōrs; cōncŏrdi ănĭmō.

ūncĭă, *and* ĭŏlă, æ, f., *an ounce.* Ŏncĭă pōndŭs ĕrĭt, Ov. Ŏncĭŏlăm Prŏcŭlēĭŭ, Juv.

ūnctŏr, ōrĭs, m., *an anointer.* Ŭnctŏr ŏpĕs, Mart.
ūncŭs, ī, m., *a hook.* Ŭncŭs ăbēst, Hor. Syn. Hārpăgo, ŭncīnŭs, hāmŭs.
Epith. Tĕnāx, fērrĕŭs, ăcūtŭs, cūrvŭs, trĭdēns. V. Harpago, hamus.
ūncŭs, ă, ŭm, *hooked.* Dēntĕ rĕclūdĭtŭr ūncō, Virg. Syn. Ădūncŭs, rĕdūncŭs,
rĕcūrvŭs, īncūrvŭs, īnflēxŭs.
ūndă, æ, f., *a wave, water.* Ignĭpŏtēns ūndīs, Virg. Syn. Ăquă, lўmphă, lătēx,
flūmĕn, flŭvĭŭs, rīvŭs, fōns ; flŭctŭs, æstŭs. Epith. Dūlcĭs, sălĭēns, liquĭdă,
pūră, lūcĭdă, līmpĭdă, quĭētă, vīvă, prŏpĕrāns, cĕlĕrĭs, frīgĭdă, gĕlĭdă, sŏnōră,
răpĭdă, īrrĭgŭă, cœnōsă, lŭtōsă, sŏrdĭdă, lĭmōsă, dēsĕs, pălūstrĭs, fōntānă, tōrrēns, flŭvĭālĭs, stăgnāns, plŭvĭālĭs, æquŏrĕă, mărīnă, spūmāns, văgă, tŭmēns,
tŭmĭdă. V. Fluvius, fons, mare, aqua.
ūndātĭm, adv., *like waves.* Nīmbŭs ūndātĭm nīgrō, (Iamb.) Prud.
ūndĕ, adv., *whence.* Ŭndĕ dŏmō, Virg.
ūndĕcĭēs, *eleven times.* Ŭndĕcĭēs ūnā, Mart.
ūndĕcĭm, indecl., *eleven.* Ŭndĕcĭm Phĭlētō, Mart.
ūndĕcĭmŭs, ă, ŭm, *the eleventh.* Ăltĕr ăb ūndĕcĭmō, Virg.
ūndĕcūnquĕ, adv., *whencesoever, from what part soever.* Ŭndĕ văcēfĭt Cūmquĕ
lŏcŭs, Lucr.
ūndēnī, æ, ă, *eleven.* Mūsă pĕr ūndēnōs, Ov.
ūndĭquĕ, adv., *on all sides.* Flŭĭt ūndĭquĕ rīvĭs, Virg.
ūndĭsŏnŭs, ă, ŭm, *sounding like waves.* Cōgŏr ĕt ūndĭsŏnōs, Prop. Syn. Flūctĭsŏnŭs.
ūndĭvăgŭs, ă, ŭm, *wandering on the waves, sailing.* Ŭrĭtŭr ūndĭvăgŭs Pўthōn,
ūndo, ās, *to undulate.* Cōstīs ūndāntĭs ăhēnī, Virg. Syn. Flūctŭo, æstŭo, Sil.
ĭnūndo. V. Fluctus.
ūndōsŭs, ă, ŭm, *full of waves, agitated.* Trōjă pĕr ūndōsăm, Virg. Syn. Ŭndāns, flūctŭāns, æstŭōsŭs, ūndĭvŏmŭs.
ūngo, xī, ctŭm, *to anoint.* Ŭngĕrĕ tēlă, Virg. Syn. Ĭnūngo, pĕrūngo, lĭno, ŏblĭno, tīngo, īmbŭo.
ūnguĕn, ĭnĭs, *and* tŭm, ī, n., *ointment, perfume.* Ŏnguĭnĕ cērās. Virg. Et
crāssŭm ūnguēntŭm, Hor. Syn. Ărōmătă; mĕdĭcāmēntŭm. Epith. Frāgrāns, ŏdōrātŭm, ūtĭlĕ. V. Odor, medicamen.
ūnguēntārĭŭs, ĭī, m., *a perfumer.* Ŏnguēntārĭŭs āc Thūscī, Hor.
ūnguēntātŭs, ă, ŭm, *perfumed.* Ŏnguēntātŭs mărītŭs, Cat. Syn. Ŭnctŭs.
ūnguĭs, ĭs, *and* ĭcŭlŭs, ī, m., *a nail, a claw.* Ŏnguĭbŭs ōră, Virg. Ŏnguĭcŭ-
lōsquĕ, Lucr. Epith. Ădūncŭs, cūrvŭs, īncūrvŭs, rĕcūrvŭs, tĕnĕr, cāndĭdŭs,
nĭtĭdŭs, ăcūtŭs, vūlnĭfĭcŭs, rĭgĭdŭs, rĭgēns, tĕnāx, hōrrĭdŭs. hāmātŭs, ūncŭs.
ūngŭlă, æ, f., *a hoof.* Ŭngŭlă cāmpŭm, Virg. Syn. Ŭnguĭs. Epith. Cōrnĕă,
dūră, sŏlĭdă, fīssă, bĭsŭlcă, hāmătă, ădūncă.
ūnĭcē, adv., *alone, particularly.* Ŭnĭcē Sĕcūrŭs, Hor.
ūnĭcŏlŏr, ōrĭs, *of one colour.* Ŏnĭcŏlŏr pūlĭō, Ov.
ūnĭcŭs, ă, ŭm, *one, alone.* Ŏnĭcŭs, ūt Pŏlўphēmī, Juv. Syn. Ŭnŭs, sōlŭs.
ūnĭo, ōnĭs, m., *a pearl.* Sēd pĕr ūnĭōnĕs, (Phal.) Mart. Syn. Mārgărītă,
băccă, gēmmă. Epith. Prĕtĭōsŭs, nĭtēns, cŏrūscŭs, Gāngĕtĭcŭs. V. Bacca,
gemma.
* || ūnĭo, īs, īvī *and* ĭī, ītŭm, *to unite.* Tālĭs ĕt ūnītī, Juv. Syn. Jūngo, ādjūngo,
cōnjūngo, cōnnēcto, cōllĭgo, āllĭgo, (ās,) cōpŭlo.
ūnĭtās, ātĭs, f., *unity.* Ŭnĭtātĭs īnvĭdŭs, (Iamb. pur.) Prud.
ūnĭtĕr, adv., *together, in one.* Ŭnĭtĕr āptăm, Lucr. Syn. Ŭnĭmŏdĕ, æquă-
bĭlĭtĕr.
ūnĭvērsŭs, ă, ŭm, *universal.* Mārtĭs ūnĭvērsī, (Phal.) Mart. Syn. Tōtŭs,
ōmnĭs, cūnctŭs.
ūnquăm, adv., *at any time, ever.* Sī pătrĭōs ūnquăm, Virg. Syn. Ălĭquāndo *or*
quāndo, ŏlĭm.
ūnŭs, ă, ŭm, *gen.* ūnīŭs, *dat.* ūnī, *one.* Ŏnŭs ĕrăt, Ov. Ŏnĭŭs ōb nŏxăm, Virg.
Ŏnīŭs ŏb īrăm, Id. Syn. Ŏnĭcŭs, sōlŭs.
ūnŭsquĭsquĕ, *every one.* Ŭnĭcuĭquĕ sŭŭs, Hor.
vŏbīs, *dat. and abl. of* vos. Ŭtĭnam ēx vŏbīs, Virg.
vŏbīscŭm, *with you.* Stānt mĭhĭ vŏbīscŭm, Ov.
vŏcābŭlŭm, ī, *and* cāmĕn, ĭnĭs, n., *a word, name.* Ĭn hŏnōrĕ vŏcābŭlă, Hor.
Prŏprĭŭm prŏfērrĕ vŏcāmĕn, Lucr. Syn. Nōmĕn, vērbŭm, vōx.

vŏcālĭs, ĕ, *having a voice, sounding.* Nŭnc tē vŏcālēs, Tib. Syn. Sŏnŏrŭs, sŏnāns; lŏquāx.

vŏcātĭo, ōnĭs. f., *a summoning, an invitation.* In trĭvĭŏ vŏcātĭōnēs, (Phal.) Cat. Syn. Invītātĭo.

vŏcātŏr, ōrĭs, m., *an inviter.* Vāpŭlēt vŏcātŏr, Mart.

vŏcātŭs, ă, ŭm, *the pass. partic. of* voco. Quāndŏ vŏcātŭs ădēst? Juv.

vŏcātŭs, ūs, m., *invocation, prayer.* Frūstrātă vŏcātŭs Hāstă mĕŏs, Virg.

vŏcĭfĕro, ās, *and* rŏr, ārĭs, *to cry out.* Tāllă vŏcĭfĕrāns, Virg. Cœpīt vŏcĭfĕrārī, Lucr. Syn. Clāmo, ēxclāmo, cōnclāmo. V. Clamo.

vŏco, *and* ĭto, ās, *to call.* In rēgnă vŏcēmŭs, Virg. Syn. Appēllo, ădvŏco, cōmpēllo, āccērso, āccĭŏo, āccĭo, vŏcĕ vŏco; ĭnvĭto, āddūco; āppēllo, nōmĭno, nūncŭpo. V. Accerso, nomino.

vŏcŭlă, æ, f., *the dim. of* vox. Vŏcŭlă rīmă, Prop.

Vŏgĕsŭs, ī, m., *a hill in France.* Cāstrăquĕ quæ Vŏgĕsī, Lucan. Epith. Altŭs, ārdŭŭs. V. Mons.

vŏlă, æ, f., *the palm of the hand.* Nŭmquīd vŏlă! Prud.

Vŏlānĕrĭŭs, ĭī, m., *the name of a man.* Scŭrră Vŏlānĕrĭŭs, Hor.

vŏlātĭlĭs, ĕ, *flying, flitting.* Līquītquĕ vŏlātĭlĕ fērrŭm, Virg. Syn. Vŏlāns, vŏlucrĭs; flūxŭs.

vŏlātŭs, ūs, m., *flight of birds.* Vēntūră vŏlātŭ, Mart. Syn. Vŏlātūră. Epith. Cĕlĕr, cĭtŭs, cōncĭtŭs, īncĭtŭs, cĭtātŭs, pērnīx, răpĭdŭs, sŭbĭtŭs, vēlōx, ăgĭlĭs, prŏpĕrŭs, prŏpĕrāns, præpĕs, ălăcĕr, lĕvĭs, trĕpĭdŭs, sŭblīmĭs, cēlsŭs, aŭdāx, văgŭs, ēffūsŭs, fŭlmĭnĕŭs, strīdēns, fŭgāx, āĕrĭŭs.

vŏlēmŭm, ī, n., *a large pear.* Grăvībŭsquĕ vŏlēmīs, Virg.

Vŏlĕsŭs, ī, m., *a powerful Sabine, the founder of the family Valeria.* Quōs Vŏlĕsūs pătrīī, Ov.

vŏlo, *and* ĭto, ās, *to fly.* Arcērēt, vŏlăt īllĕ, Virg. Pācātăm vŏlĭtăt, Hor.

vŏlo, vīs, vŏlŭī, *to be willing.* Mĕmĭnīssĕ vŏlēbānt, Virg. Syn. Cŭpĭo,ŏpto, ăvĕo, ārdĕo; plăcĕt; jŭbĕo, īmpĕro. V. Placet, desidero, voluntas.

Vŏlscēns, ēntĭs, m., *the name of a warrior.* Vŏlscēntĕ pĕrēmptŏ, Virg.

Vŏlscī, ōrŭm, m. pl., *a people of Latium.* Vŏlscōsquĕ vĕrūtōs, Virg.—2. Adj., -ŭs, ă, ŭm, *Volscian.* Vŏlscă dē gēntĕ Cămīllă, Id.

vŏlsēllæ, ārŭm, f. pl., *tweezers.* Cănă lābră vŏlsēllæ, Mart.

Vŏlsĭnĭī, ōrŭm, m. pl., *a city of Etruria.* Intĕr jŭgă Vŏlsĭnĭīs, Juv.

vŏlūbĭlĭs, ĕ, *easy to be turned.* Mīrătă vŏlūbĭlĕ būxŭm, Virg. Syn. Vērsātĭlĭs, lĕvĭs, mōbĭlĭs, mūtābĭlĭs, īnstābĭlĭs, īncōnstāns.

vŏlūbĭlĭtās, ātĭs, f., *aptness to roll, volubility.* Frāctă vŏlūbĭlĭtās, Ov. Syn. Mōbĭlĭtās, lĕvĭtās.

vŏlŭcĕr, crĭs, ĕ, *light, swift, winged.* Intĕrĕă vŏlŭcĕr, Pet. Arb. Syn. Vŏlāns, cĕlĕr, vēlōx, cĭtŭs, cōncĭtŭs, ălăcĕr, pērnīx. V. Celer.

vŏlucrĭpēs, pĕdĭs, *light-footed.* Præpĕs ēt vŏlucrĭpēs, Aus.

vŏlucrĭs, ĭs, f., *a bird.* Sĭmĭlĭs vŏlŭcrī, mōx vēră vŏlŭcrĭs, Ov. Syn. Ăvĭs, ālĕs. V. Avis.

vŏlūmĕn, ĭnĭs, n., *a volume, a winding.* Immēnsă vŏlŭmĭnĕ tērgă, Virg. Syn. Lĭbĕr, cōdēx, lĭbēllŭs; gȳrŭs, spīră, ōrbĭs, glŏmĕrāmĕn, rŏtātŭs. Epith. Sĭnŭōsŭm, glŏmĕrātŭm, flēxŭm. V. Gyrus, liber.

vŏlūmĭnōsŭs, ă, ŭm, *sinuous, tortuous.* Cŏrpŏrĭbŭs vŏlŭmĭnōsīs, Sid.

vŏlūntās, ātĭs, f., *will.* Cērtă vŏlūntās, Virg. Syn. Ārbĭtrĭŭm; mēns, ănĭmŭs, ārdŏr, stŭdĭŭm; cŭpĭdo; dēsĭdĕrĭŭm, vōtŭm, ōptātŭm; cōnsĭlĭŭm, prŏpŏsĭtŭm, sēntēntĭă. Epith. Ŏffĭcĭōsă, prŏpēnsă, lībĕră, prōnă, ămīcă, hŏnēstă. V. Desiderium, cupido.

vŏlvo, vŏlvī, vŏlūtŭm, *to roll.* Vŏlvĭtŭr Ixīōn, Ov. Syn. Vŏlūto, vērto, vērso, mŏvĕo, ăgĭto; cōnvōlvo, tōrquĕo, rŏto; ēvōlvo, pērvōlvo.

vŏlūp, *and* ŭpĕ, n., *indecl., agreeable.* Vŏlŭp făcĭlĕ, Plaut. Vŏlŭpĕ mĭhi ēst, Ter. Syn. Grātŭm, plăcĭtŭm, suāvĕ.

vŏlūptās, ātĭs, f., *pleasure, sensuality.* Sīgnă vŏlūptātĭs, Prop. Syn. Lætĭtĭă, gaŭdĭŭm; lĭbīdo, lūxŭrĭēs, lūxŭs, dēlĭcĭæ, lāscīvĭă. Epith. Blāndă, fāllāx, nōxĭă, īnfāmĭs, mĭsĕrāndă, tūrpĭs; prŏdĭgă, scĕlĕrātă, dāmnōsă, dūlcĭs, lætă, grātă, ămīcă, jūcūndă, suāvĭs; īnānĭs, īnsĭdĭōsă, dēsĭdĭōsă, ōbscœnă, mălĕsānă. V. Gaudium, libido, luxuries.

Vŏlŭsŭs, ī, m., *the name of a warrior.* Tū, Vŏlūse, ārmārī, Virg.

vŏlūtābrŭm, ī, n., *mud.* Sæpĕ vŏlūtābrīs, Virg. Epith. Fœdŭm, tūrpĕ, sōrdēns, sōrdĭdŭm.

vŏlūto, ās, *the frequent. of* volvo. Sēcūm Dĕă cōrdĕ vŏlūtāns, Virg.

vŏlūtŭs, ă, ŭm, *the pass. partic. of* volvo. Intĕr tăbŭlātă vŏlūtŭs, Virg.

vŏmĕr, *and* ĭs, ĕrĭs, m., *a coulter.* Vŏmĕrĭs ŏbtūsī, Virg. Epith. Ŭncŭs, fērrĕŭs, prēssŭs, rĕtūsŭs, ŏbtūsŭs, dūrŭs. V. Aratrum.

vŏmĭcă, æ, f., *an abscess.* Ět vŏmĭcæ pŭtrēs, Juv.

vŏmo, *and* ĭto, ās, *to vomit.* Vŏmĭt īlle ănĭmăm, Virg. Syn. Ēvŏmo, rĕvŏmo, vŏmĭto, ējĭcĭo, ējĕcto, ēgĕro, ērūcto, rējĭcĭo, rĕjĕcto; rĕmĭtto, ēfflo.

vŏrāgĭnōsŭs, ă, ŭm, *full of gulfs.* Aūt vŏrāgĭnōsō, Sid.

vŏrāgo, ĭnĭs, f., *a gulf.* Vāstāquĕ vŏrāgĭnĕ gūrgĕs, Virg. Syn. Bărathrŭm, ăbўssŭs, gūrgĕs, tēllūrĭs hĭātŭs. Epith. Immānĭs, tētră, ŏbscūră, ŏpācă, cālīgăns, cæcă, prŏfūndă, īmă, āltă, īngēns, stŭpēndă, hŏrrĭdă, hŏrrēndă, hŏrrĭbĭlĭs. V. Hiatus, gurges, Charybdis, barathrum.

Vŏrānŭs, ī, m., *the name of a man.* Fūrquĕ Vŏrānŭs, Hor.

vŏrāx, ācĭs, *ravenous.* Hīnc ūsūră vŏrāx, Lucan. Syn. Ēdāx, hēllŭo; gŭlōsŭs. V. Gulosus.

vŏro, ās, *to devour.* Vŏrăt æquŏrĕ vōrtēx, Virg. Syn. Dēvŏro, sōrbĕo, ābsōrbĕo, dēglūtĭo, ĕdo, ēxĕdo, pĕrĕdo, cŏmĕdo, māndo, dēpāscŏr, hēllŭŏr, cŏnsūmo. V. Absorbeo.

vōrtēx, ĭcĭs, m., *a whirlpool.* Cōntōrquēns vōrtĭcĕ sўlvās, Virg. Syn. Tūrbo; gūrgĕs; vŏrāgo. Epith. Vĭŏlēntŭs, răpĭdŭs, præcēps, răpāx, tōrtŭs, cōntōrtŭs, īntōrtŭs, sĭnŭōsŭs, tūrbĭnĕŭs, sŏnōrŭs. V. Gurges, Charybdis.

vōs, *you.* Vōs ăcŭăt, Ov.

vōtĭfĕr, ă, ŭm, *bearing something devoted to a deity.* Vŏtĭfĕra ārbōs, Stat.

vōtīvŭs, ă, ŭm, *devoted.* Vōtīvō sānguĭnĕ tīngĭt, Ov. Syn. Vŏtŭs; săcĕr.

vōtŭm, ī, n., *a vow, a wish.* Rŏmŭlŭs, ĕt vŏtĭs, Prop. Syn. Prŏmīssŭm; dōnārĭŭm; ŏptātŭm, dēsīdĕrĭŭm. Epith. Pĭŭm, sŏlēnnĕ, sacrŭm, sānctŭm, īrrĕvŏcābĭlĕ, īnvĭŏlābĭlĕ, sŭpplēx, lūstrālĕ; cŭpĭdŭm, păvĭdŭm, ăvārŭm. V. Oro, desiderium.

vōtŭs, ă, ŭm, *the pass. partic. of* voveo. Ět vōtās sŭspēndĕrĕ vēstēs, Virg.

vŏvĕo, vōvī, vōtŭm, *to vote, to pray for, to devote.* Quĭd vŏvĕăt dūlcī, Hor. Syn. Prōmĭtto; ōpto, dēsīdĕro; dēvŏvĕo, cōnsecro; dīco, ās.

vōx, vōcĭs, f., *voice.* Sŭprēmŭm vŏcĕ cĭĕmŭs, Virg. Syn. Vērbŭm, sŏnŭs, vŏcābŭlŭm, lŏquēlă, sērmo, ōrātĭo. Epith. Cănōră, ăcūtă, trĕmŭlă, rĕsŏnă, tĕnŭĭs; blāndă, suāvĭs, clāră, āltă, raūcă, sŭmmīssă, fūscă, cōntēntă, grăvĭs, āspĕră, īntērmīssă, īnclīnātă, mŭllĕbrĭs, lānguēns, vīrĭlĭs, fācūndă, dīsērtă, fēstīvă; mĭnāx, trūx, rĭgĭdă, fĕrōx, atrōx, sŭpērbă, tĕnĕrārĭă, īnsānă, ēffĕră, mŏlēstă, tūrpĭs, flēbĭlĭs, quĕrŭlă, mœstă, trĕmēns, tĭmĭdă, lācrўmōsă, lūgubrĭs, dēmīssă, mĭsĕrāndă, sŭpplēx. V. Loquor.

— ūpĭlĭo, ōnĭs, m., *a shepherd.* Vēnĭt ĕt ūpĭlĭo, Virg. Syn. Pāstŏr.

Ŭrănĭă, æ, *or* ē, ēs, f., *one of the Muses.* Excĭpĭt Ŭrănĭē, Ov. Epith. Dŏctă, cœlēstĭs. V. Musa.

ūrbānŭs, ă, ŭm, *dwelling in a city, polite.* Hīc tĭbī cōmĭs, ĕt ūrbānŭs, Hor. Syn. Cīvīlĭs, cīvĭcŭs; ūrbĭs īncŏlă; lĕpĭdŭs, mītĭs, āffābĭlĭs, bĕnīgnŭs.

ūrbĭcŭs, ă, ŭm, *of the city.* Ŏrbĭcă Līngŏnĭcŭs, Mart. Syn. Ŭrbānŭs.—2. *an author of Atellane verses.* Ŏrbĭcŭs ēxŏdĭō, Juv.

ūrbs, ūrbĭs, f., *a city.* Aūt ūrbĭbŭs ērrăt, Virg. Syn. Ŏppĭdŭm, cīvĭtās; mœnĭă, ārcēs. Epith. Tūrrĭgĕră, tūrrītă; clāră, āntīquă, nōbĭlĭs, dīvĕs, flōrēns, sŭpērbă, pŏtēns, cĕlĕbrĭs, īnsīgnĭs, măgnĭfĭcă, splēndĭdă, ămœnă, bēllĭcă, Mārtĭă, Māvōrtĭă, bēllātrīx, īnēxpŭgnābĭlĭs, īnāccēssă, īndŏmĭtă, īnvīctă.

ūrcĕŭs, *or* ŏlŭs, ī, m., *a pitcher.* Făcĭt ūrcĕŭs ānsă, Mart. Syn. Vās, pŏcŭlŭm.

ūrēdo, ĭnĭs, f., *an itching.* Sŭbĭtāque ūrēdĭnĕ tōrquēs, Mart. V. Rubigo.

ūrgĕo, ēs, *to press on.* Ūrgēbam ĕt tēlă, Virg. Syn. Prĕmo, īnsĕquŏr, īnsēctŏr, īnsto; cōmprĭmo; īmpēllo, ădĭgo, cōgo; ēxăgĭto, vēxo.

ūrīnă, æ, f., *urine.* Cōncēpta ūrīnă mŏvētŭr, Juv. Syn. Lōtĭŭm. Epith. Fœdă, tūrpĭs, grăvĕŏlēns, ŏlēns.

ūrnă, æ, f., *an urn, a vase.* Vēstālēsque ūrnās, Pers. Syn. Ŭrcĕŭs, nydrĭă, ăquālĭs, āmphŏră, vās. Epith. Fĭctĭlĭs, aūrĕă, căpāx, pătēns.—2. *an urn to contain the ballots of suffrage.* Epith. Fătālĭs, tĭmēndă, jūstă, ĭnĭquă.—3. *an urn for the ashes of the dead.* Epith. Fūnebrĭs, pĭă, frĭgĭdă, mœstă, trīstĭs.

ūro, ūssī, ūstŭm, *to burn.* Ŭrĭt ĕnĭm, Virg. Syn. Ĕxūro, ădūro, cŏmbūro, pĕrūro, crĕmo, tŏrrĕo, ĭnflāmmo, ĭncēndo, sŭccēndo, cōncrĕmŏr. V. Incendo, flammesco, ignis, ardeo.

ŭrŏpўgĭŭm, ĭĭ, n., *rump.* Hăbĕās ŭrŏpўgĭŭm, Mart.

Ŭrsă, æ, f., *a constellation.* Pŏrtītŏr Ŭrsæ, Stat. Syn. Arctŭs, Pārrhăsĭs, Cўnŏsūră, Hĕlĭcē. Epith. Pārrhăsĭă, Ĕrўmānthĭs, Mœnălĭs, Lўcăŏnĭă, Hўpērbŏrĕă, Scўthĭcă, glăcĭālĭs, gĕlĭdă, nĭvōsă. frīgĭdă, hўbērnă. V. Arctos.

ūrsŭs, ī, m., *and* ă, œ, f., *a bear.* Ŭrsŭs ŏvīlĕ, Hor. Căpŭt āspĕrăt ūrsæ, Stat. Epith. Ĭnfōrmĭs, trūx, răbĭdŭs, tērrĭbĭlĭs, sævŭs, fĕrŭs, fĕrōx, ĭnmānĭs, ăvĭdŭs, vŏrāx, răpāx, vīllōsŭs, ūnguĭbŭs ārmātŭs, mĭnāx.

ūrtīcă, æ, f., *a nettle.* Tŭōs ūrtīcă nĕpōtēs, Juv. Epith. Mōrdāx, āspĕră, ăcūtă, pūngēns, ācrĭs.

ūrŭs, ī, m., *a wild animal like a bull.* Sўlvēstrēs ūri, Virg.

ūsĭtātŭs, ă, ŭm, *usual.* Nōn ūsĭtātĭs, Vārē, (Iamb.) Hor. Syn. Sŏlĭtŭs.

ūspĭăm, *or* quăm, *any where.* Ŭsquăm jūstĭtĭæ ēst, Virg.

ūsquĕ, prep., *till.* Ŭsquĕ sŭb ēxtrēmŭm, Virg. Syn. Ad.—2. adv., *always.*

ūsquĕquāquĕ, adv., *every where.* Ŭsquĕquāquĕ quācūmquĕ, (Scaz.) Mart.

ūsquĕquō, *how long, until.* Quō tē spēctābĭmŭs ūsquĕ? Mart.

Ŭstĭcă, æ, f., *a mountain and valley in the country of the Sabines.* Vāllēs ĕt Ŭstĭcæ, Hor.

ūstŏr, ōrĭs, m., *one who burnt dead bodies.* Ŭstŏrquĕ tædās, (Scaz.) Mart.

ūstŭlo, ās, *the dimin. of* uro. Ĭnfēlīcĭbŭs ūstŭlāndă lĭgnĭs, (Phal.) Catull.

ūsūră, æ, f., *use, usury.* Hīnc ūsūră vŏrāx, Lucan. Syn. Ŭsŭs; fœnŭs. V. Fœnus.

ūsūrārĭŭs, ă, ŭm, *of which we have the use.* Cēpĭt ūsūrārĭăm, (Iamb.) Plaut. V. Fœnerator.

ūsūrpo, ās, *to use often, to usurp.* Ŭsūrpāre ŏcŭlĭs, Lucr. Syn. Ŭtŏr, frĕquēntĕr ūtŏr; ĭnvādo; ŏccŭpo.

ūsŭs, ūs, m., *use.* Dīspēnsānt ūsŭs, ēt tēmpŏră, Pedo. Syn. Mŏs, cōnsuētūdo; ēxpĕrĭēntĭă; ūtĭlĭtās.

ŭt, conj., *that, as.* Trōjānăs ŭt ŏpēs, Virg. Syn. Ŭti; vĕlŭtī.

ŭtcūnquĕ, *howsoever.* Ŭtcŭnquĕ fĕrēnt, Virg.

ŭtĕr, ŭtrĭs, m., *a bladder, a bottle.* Ŭnctōs sălĭērĕ pĕr ūtrēs, Virg. Epith. Ŭnctŭs, plēnŭs.

ŭtĕr, ă, ŭm, *which of the two.* Dīc ŭtĕr ēx, Mart.

* ŭtĕrlĭbĕt, (tră, ŭm,) *which you please.* Cic. Syn. Ŭtērvĭs.

ŭtērnăm, *which of the two?* Hor.

ŭtērquĕ, (tră, ŭm,) *both.* Quĭd pōssĭt ŭtērquĕ, Virg. Syn. Ămbo.

* ŭtērvĭs, (tră, ŭm,) *either of the two.* Syn. Ŭtērlĭbĕt.

ŭtĕrŭs, ī, m., *the womb, stomach.* Sēmĭnă fērt ŭtĕrō, Ov. Syn. Vēntĕr, ālvŭs, vīscĕră, īlĭă. V. Venter.

ŭti, conj., *that, as.* Tū quŏque ŭtī fĭĕrēs, Prop. Cĕrēs ŭtī cūlmō, Hor. Syn. Ŭt.

Ŭtĭcă, æ, f., *a maritime town of Africa.* Aŭt fūgĭās Ŭtĭcăm, Hor.

ūtĭlĭs, ĕ, *useful.* Vēr ūtĭlĕ sўlvĭs, Virg. Syn. Cŏmmŏdŭs, ŏppōrtūnŭs, āptŭs, ĭdŏnĕŭs, sălūtārĭs, sălūtĭfĕr.

ūtĭlĭtās, ātĭs, f., *utility, advantage.* Ātque ĭpsa ūtĭlĭtās, Hor. Syn. Cŏmmŏdĭtās, cŏmmŏdŭm, ŏppōrtūnĭtās, ūsŭs, frūctŭs, lucrŭm, quæstŭs, ēmŏlŭmēntŭm. Epith. Māgnă, īngēns, pārvă, ēxĭgŭă, tĕnŭĭa, prīvātă, pūblĭcă, cŏmmūnĭs.

ūtĭlĭtĕr, adv., *usefully.* Sērvĭĕt ūtĭlĭtĕr, Hor.

ŭtĭnăm! opt., *O that!* Ō ŭtĭnăm, Ov. Syn. Ō sī! quăm vēllĕm! Dī făcĭănt!

ūtŏr, ĕrĭs, ūsŭs, *to use.* Ŭtĭmŭr ēxēmplĭs, Juv. Syn. Ŭsūrpo, ădhĭbĕo; pŏssĭdĕo, ŏbtĭnĕo.

ŭtpŏtĕ, *inasmuch as.* Ŭtpŏtĕ fāllācĭ, Cat.

ūtprīmŭm, conj., *as soon as.* Ŭtprīmŭm lūx ālmă, Virg. Syn. Cŭm prīmŭm, ŭbi prīmŭm, sĭmŭl āc. V. Statim ac.

utrīnquĕ, adv., *on both sides.* Ĭnguēn ŭtrīnquĕ lĕvātă, Mart. Syn. Hīnc, ĭllīnc.

utrŏbī, adv., *in which of the two places.* Aŭt ŭtrŏbī fŭĕrĭs, Aus.

utrōquĕ ˣ bīquĕ, *on both sides.* Jāctāntēmque ūtrōquĕ căpŭt, Virg.

utrŭm, conj., *whether.* Dīcĭs ūtrŭm, Mart. Syn. Nŭm; ăn.

ūvă, æ, f., *a grape.* Ĭn cōllȳbŭs ūvă cŏlōrĕm, Virg. SYN. Răcēmŭs, botrŭs, *figur.* vītĭs, vīnĕă, vĭndēmĭă, vīnŭm. EPITH. Răcēmĭfĕră, rŭbēns, rŭbĭcūndă, pūrpŭrĕă, ātră, nigră, dūlcĭs, mītĭs, săpōră, lætă, grătă, tĕnĕră, tŭmēns, tŭmĭdă, tūrgĭdă, tūrgēns, grăvĭdă, sūspēnsă, pēndŭlă, pēndēns. V. Vindemia.

ūvēsco, ĭs, *to grow damp.* Ŭvēscūnt cădĕm, Lucr.

ūvĭdŭlŭs, ă, ŭm, *the dimin. of* uvidus. Ŭvĭdŭlam ā flūctū, Catul.

ūvĭdŭs, ă, ŭm, *damp.* Ŭvĭdŭs hȳbērnā, Virg. SYN. Mădĭdŭs, mădēns.

ūvĭfĕr, ă, ŭm, *bearing grapes.* Ŭvīfĕr rēmīttĭt, (Phal.) Stat.

Vūlcānĭŭs, ă, ŭm, *of Vulcan.* Ăcĭēs Vūlcānĭā cămpōs, Virg. SYN. Ignĕŭs, flāmmĕŭs.

Vūlcānŭs, ī, m., *the God of fire.* Ĭmmīssĭs Vūlcānŭs hăbēnĭs, Virg. SYN. Mūlcĭbĕr, Ignĭpŏtēns. EPITH. Lēmnĭŭs, Lēmnĭăcŭs; claudŭs; Ætnæŭs, Sĭcŭlŭs; Lȳpărēĭŭs; claudŭs, tārdŭs, tārdĭpēs, nūdŭs, nĭgĕr, ātĕr, flāmmĕŭs, rŭbēns. V. Ignis.

vūlgārĭs, ĕ, *common, vulgar.* Vūlgārĭā tēmnĭt, Hor. SYN. Pŏpŭlārĭs, plēbēiŭs, cōmmūnĭs, trītŭs, frĕquēns, quŏtĭdĭānŭs, pērvăgātŭs, nōn rārŭs.

vūlgātŏr, ōrĭs, m., *a divulger.* Tăcĭtī vūlgātŏr ĭn ūndĭs, Ov.

vūlgĭvăgŭs, ă, ŭm, *wandering among the people, common.* Vūlgĭvăgō vītăm, Lucr. V. Vulgaris.

vūlgo, ās, *to divulge.* Vērbĭs vūlgărĕ dŏlōrĕm, Virg. SYN. Dīvūlgo, ēvūlgo, pērvūlgo, dīspērgo, dīssēmĭno, spārgo, dīssĭpo.

vūlgō, adv., *every where, commonly.* Vūlgō nāscētŭr ămōmŭm, Virg. SYN. Pāssĭm, ūbĭquĕ; pălăm, ăpērtĕ; sæpĕ, sæpĭŭs, plērŭmquĕ, crēbrō, frĕquēntĕr.

vūlgŭs, ī, n., *also* m., *the commonalty.* Vūlgŭs ĭnērmŭm, Virg. Spārgĕrĕ vōcēs Ĭn vūlgum āmbĭgŭās, Id. SYN. Tūrbă, plēbs, pŏpŭlŭs. EPITH. Incautŭm, stŏlĭdŭm, ĭgnōbĭlĕ, mĭsĕrăbĭlĕ, ĭnērs, mĭsĕrŭm, īnfīdŭm, mălīgnŭm, prŏfānŭm, īndōctŭm, rŭdĕ, mōbĭlĕ, dēmēns, ăncēps, mūtābĭlĕ, vīlĕ, ĭnīquŭm, hŭmĭlĕ, īnstābĭlĕ, prŏcāx, vărĭābĭlĕ, fŭtĭlĕ, vānŭm, lĕvĕ, ĭgnārŭm, trĕpĭdŭm, īncōnstāns, rĕbēllĕ. V. Plebs.

vūlnĕrātŭs, ă, ŭm, *the pass. partic. of* vulnero. Sēd vūlnĕrātŭs ănguĭs, (Iamb.) Prud.

vūlnĕro, ās, *to wound.* Vūlnĕrăt ēnsĕ căpŭt, Ov. SYN. Saucĭo, lædo, vĭŏlo. V. Vulnus, transfigo, lacero; occido.

vūlnĭfĭcŭs, ă, ŭm, *wounding.* Vūlnĭfĭcūsquĕ chălўbs, Virg.

vūlnŭs, ĕrĭs, n., *a wound.* Ănĭmāsque ĭn vūlnĕrĕ pōnŭnt, Virg. SYN. Plāgă, īctŭs; vībēx; ūlcŭs; cĭcātrīx. EPITH. Ĭmmĕdĭcābĭlĕ, mōrtĭfĕrŭm, lēthālĕ, crūdēlĕ, ăcērbŭm, trīstĕ, atrōx, ĭmmānĕ, ēxĭtĭālĕ, īnfēstŭm, sānguĭnĕŭm, crūēntŭm, ātrŭm, fœdŭm, sævŭm, dīrŭm, līvēns, căvŭm, ăpērtŭm, pătēns, hĭāns, hĭūlcŭm, grāndĕ, īngēns, grăvĕ, vĭŏlēntŭm, ĭnhŏnēstŭm, nōbĭlĕ, clārŭm, Mārtĭŭm, īnflīctŭm. V. Vulnero.

vūlpēs, ĭs, *and* ēcŭlă, æ, f., *a fox.* Vūlpēs ĭmĭtātā lĕōnĕm, Hor. Fāllāx vūlpēcŭlă gānnĭt, Ov. EPITH. Astūtă, dŏlōsă, caută, vafră, cāllĭdă, vērsūtă, fāllāx, săgāx, sōlērs, īnsĭdĭātrīx, sævă, prædātrīx, ăvĭdă, răpāx.

vūlpīnŭs, ă, ŭm, *of a fox.* Vūlpīnŭs ănĭmŭs, (Iamb.) Plaut.

Vūlteĭŭs, ī, m., *the name of a man.* Dūrŭs, ăĭt, Vūlteī, Hor.

vūltŭr, ŭrĭs, m., *a vulture.* Ĭmmānĭs vūltŭr ŏbūncō, Virg. SYN. Vūltŭrĭŭs. EPITH. Ēdāx, ăvĭdŭs, răpāx, prædāx, prædātŏr, vŏrāx, obscœnŭs, dīrŭs, sævŭs, vēlōx, mōntānŭs, Caucăsĕŭs, Prōmēthæŭs.

Vūltŭr, ŭrĭs, m., *a mountain of Apulia.* Vūltŭre ĭn Appŭlō, Hor.

Vūltūrnŭs, ī, m., *a river of Campania.* Āccŏlă Vūltūrnī, Virg.

vūltŭs, ūs, m., *the face, countenance.* Cārmĭnĕ vūltŭs ērĭt, Mart. SYN. Făcĭēs; ōs, ōră; frōns; āspēctŭs. EPITH. Dĕcōrŭs, vĕnūstŭs, fōrmōsŭs, pūlchĕr, īnsĭgnĭs, rŏsĕŭs, nĭtēns, lætŭs, hĭlārĭs, sĕrēnŭs, blāndŭs, mŏdēstŭs, hŏnēstŭs, īngĕnŭŭs, bĕnīgnŭs, dēfōrmĭs, fœdŭs, tūrpĭs, hŏrrēndŭs, mĕtŭēndŭs, mĭnāx, sĕvērŭs, tōrvŭs, fĕrŭs, tērrĭfĭcŭs, īrātŭs, sānguĭnĕŭs, ārdēns, ĭgnītŭs, trīstĭs, mœstŭs, jŭvĕnīlĭs, vĕrēcūndŭs. V. Facies, frons frontis, os oris.

vūlvă, æ, f., *a sow's paunch.* Nīl vūlvă pūlchrĭŭs āmplă, Hor.

ūxŏr, ōrĭs, f., *a wife.* Ŏxŏrī nūbĕrĕ nōlŏ mĕæ, Mart. SYN. Cōnjūx, spōnsă. EPITH. Cără, ămīcă, ămātă, dīlēctă, vĕnūstă, fōrmōsă, cāstă, pŭdīcă, fĭdēlĭs.

ūxŏrĭŭs, ă, ŭm, *of a wife; uxorious.* Ŏxŏrĭŭs ūrbĕm, Virg

X.

XANTHIAS, æ, m., *the name of a man.* Xānthĭä Phōceŭ, Hor.
Xănthō, ūs, f., *the name of a Nereid.* Drȳmōquĕ Xănthōquĕ, Virg.
Xănthŭs, ī, m., *a river of the Troad.* Xănthīquĕ flŭēntă, Virg. Syn. Scămāndĕr.
Epith. Phrȳgĭŭs, flāvŭs. V. Scamander.
xĕnĭŭm, ī, n., *a present, a token.* Xĕnĭōrŭm tūrbă lĭbēllō, Mart. Syn. Mūnŭs,
dōnŭm; strēnă. Epith. Lætŭm, fēstīvŭm, ămīcŭm, dīvĕs, lārgŭm, sōlēnnĕ. V.
Donum.
xĕrāmpĕlĭnŭs, ă, ŭm, *of the colour of a dry leaf.* Ĕt xĕrāmpĕlĭnās, Juv.
Xērxēs, ĭs, m., *the son of Darius, king of Persia.* Sŭpĕr æquŏră Xērxĕm, Lucan.
Epith. Mēdŭs, sŭpērbŭs, tŭmĭdŭs, īnfēlīx, păvĭdŭs, Pērsĭcŭs, rēfŭgŭs.
xĭphĭās, æ, m., *a sword-fish.* Dūrŭs xĭphĭās īctŭ, Ov.
* xȳlĭnŭm, ī, n., *a kind of cotton.* Epith. Mōllĕ, nĭvĕŭm, tēxtĭlĕ, tīnctŭm.
xȳstŭs, ī, m., *or* tŭm, ī, n., *a walking-place, a gallery.* Alĭum īn xȳstŭm, Phæd.
Syn. Ambŭlācrŭm. Epith. Lætŭs, lōngŭs, ămœnŭs.

Z.

ZĂCȲNTHŎS, *or* thŭs, ī, m., *an island in the Ionian sea.* Nĕmŏrōsă Zăcȳnthŏs,
Virg.
Zānclæŭs, *and* ēĭŭs, ă, ŭm, *of Messina, Sicilian.* Zānclæā clāssĭs .ărēnă, Ov.
Cōntră Zānclēĭă sāxă, Id.
Zānclē, ēs, f., *Sicily, Messina.* Zānclē quŏquĕ jūnctă, Ov.
zēlŏtȳpŭs, ă, ŭm, *jealous.* Pōnĕrĕ zēlŏtȳpō, Juv. Syn. Æmŭlŭs, ĭnvĭdŭs.
zēlŭs, ī, m., *zeal.* Jūnctŭs quĭă zēlŭs ămōri ēst, Aus. Syn. Æmŭlŭs ārdŏr;
ĭnvĭdĭă; ămŏr; pĭĕtās.
Zēno, ōnĭs, m., *a philosopher, the chief of the Stoic sect.* Nōs Zēnōnĭs præcēptă,
Juv.
Zĕphȳrītĭs, ĭdĭs, f., *a name of Flora.* Zĕphȳrītĭs ĕō fămŭlŭm, Catull. V. Flora.
Zĕphȳrŭs, ī, m., *the west wind.* Zĕphȳrīs mōtāntĭbŭs ūmbrās, Virg. Syn. Fă-
vōnĭŭs. Epith. Ŏccĭdŭŭs, tĕpēns, plăcĭdŭs, grātŭs. lēnĭs, mōllĭs, blāndŭs,
mītĭs, sĕrēnŭs: gĕnĭtālĭs, gĕnĭtābĭlĭs, fœcūndŭs, fēlīx, făvēns, lēnĕ spīrāns. V.
Favonius.
Zērȳnthĭŭs, ă, ŭm, *of Zerynthos, a city of Samothrace.* Vēntō Zērȳnthĭă līttŏră,
Ov.
Zētēs, *or* Zēthēs, æ, m., *a son of Boreas, and king of Thrace.* Călăĭsquĕ pŭĕr
Zētēsquĕ, Ov.
Zēthŭs, ī, m., *the son of Jupiter and Antiope.* Āmphĭōnĭs ātquĕ Zēthī, Hor.
Zeūxĭs, ĭdĭs, m., *a Grecian painter.* Fāllĭt ăvēs Zeūxĭs, L. Lippus. Epith.
Clārŭs, sōlērs, īnsĭgnĭs, cĕlĕbrĭs. V. Pictor.
Zōdĭăcŭs, ī, m., *the Zodiac.* Sīdĕră Zōdĭăcī, Aus.
Zŏĭlŭs, ī, m., *an envious critic.* Zŏĭlĕ, nōmĕn hăbēs, Ov. Epith. Ĭnvĭdŭs, mă-
lĭgnŭs. V. Invidus.
zōnă, æ, f:, *a girdle.* Zōnă rĕcīnctă mănū, Ov. Syn. Cīngŭlŭm, cīnctŭs, bŭl-
thĕŭs; fāscĭă. Epith. Aūrĕă, aūrātă, dĕcōră, pīctă, fŭlgēns, gēmmātă, tĕrĕs.—
2. *a zone of the earth.* Zōnă nĭvālĭs, Luc. Zōnă rŭbēns, Id.
zōnŭlă, æ, f., *the dimin. of zona.* Zōnŭlă sōlŭūnt sĭnŭs, Catul.
zȳthŭm, ī, n., *and* ŭs, ī, m., *beer.* Pōcŭlă zȳthī, Col. Syn. Cērvīsĭă; cĕrĕvīsĭă.
Epith. Fŏrtĕ, suāvĕ, vălĭdŭm, liquĭdŭm, pūrŭm, Pēlūsĭăcŭm.

DIFFERENT KINDS

OF

VERSE AND METRE.

There are twenty-eight feet used in verse; of which some are simple, others compound.

The Simple feet are those which are not compounded of others, and are twelve in number; four dissyllabic, and eight trisyllabic.

The Compound feet are those which consist of dissyllabic feet, and are sixteen in number, of four syllables each.

Simple Dissyllabic Feet.

A Pyrrhic consists of two short syllables; as, ... Dĕŭs.
A Spondee, of two long; as, ... Mūsæ.
An Iambus, of one short and one long; as, ... Dĭēs.
A Trochee, or Choree, of one long and one short; as, . . Pānĭs.

Simple Trisyllabic Feet.

A Tribrach consists of three short syllables; as, . . . Dŏmĭnŭs.
A Molossus, of three long; as, ... Dōctōrēs.
An Anapest, of two short and one long; as, ... Spĕcĭēs.
A Dactyl, of one long and two short; as, ... Cārmĭnă.
An Amphibrach, of a long between two short syllables; as, . Vĭdētĕ.
An Amphimacer, of a short between two long syllables; as, Cāstĭtās.
A Bacchius, of one short and two long; as, ... Hŏnēstās.
An Antibacchius, of two long and one short; as, . . . Lūgērĕ.

Compound Feet.

A Proceleusmaticus, of two Pyrrhics; as, ... Hŏmĭnĭbŭs.
A Dispondee, of two Spondees; as, ... Ōrātōrēs.
A Diiambus, of two Iambs; as, ... Āmœnĭtās.
A Ditrochee, of two Trochees; as, ... Cāntĭlēnă.

Mixed Feet.

An Antispast, of an Iambus and a Trochee; as, . . . Rĕcūsārĕ.
A Choriambus, of a Trochee and an Iambus; as, . . . Pōntĭfĭcēs.
An Ionic major, of a Spondee and a Pyrrhic; as, . . Fōrtĭssĭmŭs.
An Ionic minor, of a Pyrrhic and a Spondee; as, . . Dĭŏmēdēs.

A Pæon consists of one long and three short syllables, variously placed.

The First Pæon consists of a Trochee and a Pyrrhic; as, . Lætĭtĭă.
The Second Pæon, of an Iambus and a Pyrrhic; as, . . Pŏtēntĭă.
The Third Pæon, of a Pyrrhic and a Trochee; as, . . Ălĭēnŭs.
The Fourth Pæon, of a Pyrrhic and an Iambus; as, . . Cĕlĕrĭtās.

An Epitrite consists of one short and three long syllables, variously placed.

The First Epitrite consists of an Iambus and a Spondee; as, . Săcērdōtēs.
The Second Epitrite, of a Trochee and a Spondee; as, . . Pērmănēbānt.
The Third Epitrite, of a Spondee and an Iambus; as, . . Dīscōrdĭæ.
The Fourth Epitrite, of a Spondee and a Trochee; as, . . Ādvēntārĕ.

TABLES

OF THE

QUANTITIES OF FINAL SYLLABLES IN DECLENSION AND CONJUGATION.

TERMINATIONS IN DECLENSION.

SINGULAR.

Case.	1. Declens.	2. Declens.	3. Declens.	4. Declens.	5. Declens.
Nom.	ă ē ās ēs	ŭs, *s.times* ŏs ĭŭs ĕr eūs ŭm ŏn		ŭs ū	ĭēs ēs
Gen.	āē ēs *old form* āī, ās	ī ĕī, eī *or* ĕŏs	ĭs ŏs	ūs ū	ĭēī ĕī *old form* ē
Dat.	āē	ō ĕō *or* eō	ī	ŭī *or* ū ū	*same as geni-tive.*
Accus.	ăm ēn ān, *s.times* ăn	ŭm ĕŭm ĕă *m. n.* ŏn	ĕm ĭm ĭn ă	ŭm ū	ĕm
Vocat.	ă ē ā (*from* as) *s.times* ă (*from* es)	ĕ ī ĕr eū	*as the nomina-tive.* *s.times* ĭ ē	*as the nomina-tive.*	*as the nomina-tive.*
Ablat.	ă ē	ō ĕō *or* eō	ĕ ī	ū	ē

PLURAL.

Case.	1. Declens.	2. Declens.	3. Declens.	4. Declens.	5. Declens.
Nom. & Voc.	āē	ī ă	*m. f.* ēs (*Gr. words*) ĕs *n.* ă	*m. f.* ūs *n.* ŭă	ēs
Gen.	ārŭm	ōrŭm	ŭm	ŭŭm	ērŭm
Dat & Abl.	īs *s.times* ābŭs	īs	ĭbŭs *s.times* sĭ, sĭn	ĭbŭs ŭbŭs	ēbŭs
Accus.	ās	ōs ă	*m. f.* ēs ăs *n.* ă	*m. f.* ūs *n.* ŭă	ēs

PRONOUNS.

	1st Person.		2nd Person.		3rd Person.
	Sing.	Plur.	Sing.	Plur.	Sing. & Plur.
Nom. & Voc.	Ĕgo	Nōs	Tū	Vōs	
Gen.	Mĕī	Nŏstrūm, Nŏstrī	Tŭī	Vēstrūm, Vēstrī	Sŭī
Dat.	Mĭhi	Nōbīs	Tĭbi	Vōbīs	Sĭbi
Acc.	Mē	Nōs	Tē	Vōs	Sē
Abl.	Mē	Nōbīs	Tē	Vōbīs	Sē

DEMONSTRATIVE PRONOUNS.

SINGULAR.

Nom.	s, ĕă, ĭd	Hic, hæc, hōc	Illĕ, illă, illŭd
Gen.	Ĕjŭs	Hūjŭs	Illĭŭs or illĭŭs
Dat.	Ĕī	Huīc	Illī.
Acc.	Ĕŭm	Hūnc, hănc, hōc	Illŭm, illăm, illŭd
Abl.	Ĕō, ĕā, ĕō	Hōc, hāc, hōc	Illō, illā, illō

PLURAL.

Nom.	Ĕī or īī, ĕæ, ĕă	Hī, hæ, hæc	Illī, illæ, illă [rŭm
Gen.	Ĕŏrŭm, ĕārŭm, ĕōrŭm	Hōrŭm, hārŭm, hōrŭm	Illōrŭm, illārŭm, illō-
Dat.	Ĕīs or īīs	Hīs	Illīs
Acc.	Ĕōs, ĕās, ĕă	Hōs, hās, hæc	Illōs, illās, illă
Abl.	Ĕīs or īīs	Hīs	Illīs

The quantity of Illu in declension is followed by Ipse, Unus, Ullus, Solus, Totus, Uter, Alter, Alius. Only the gen. of Alter is always Alterĭŭs, and that of Alius always Alĭŭs.

PRONOUN *IDEM*.

SINGULAR.

Nom.	Idĕm, ĕădĕm, ĭdĕm.
Gen.	Ĕjūsdĕm.
Dat.	Ĕīdĕm or eīdĕm.
Acc.	Ĕŭndĕm, ĕāndĕm, ĭdĕm.
Abl.	Ĕōdĕm, ĕādĕm, ĕōdĕm, or Ĕōdĕm, eādĕm, eōdĕm.

RELATIVE PRONOUN.

Quī, quæ, quŏd and quĭd.
Cūjŭs.
Cuī, s.times cŭi.
Quĕm, quăm, quŏd and quĭd.
Quō, quā, quō.

PLURAL.

Nom.	Ĕīdĕm, īīdĕm or īdĕm, ĕædĕm, ĕādĕm.
Gen.	Ĕōrūndĕm.
Dat.	Ĕīsdĕm, īīsdĕm or īsdĕm.
Acc.	Ĕōsdĕm, ĕāsdĕm, ĕādĕm.
Abl.	Ĕīsdĕm, īīsdĕm or īsdĕm.

Quī, quæ, quæ.
Quōrŭm, quārŭm, quōrŭm.
Quĭbŭs, queīs or quīs.
Quōs, quās, quæ.
Quĭbŭs, queīs or quīs.

CONJUGATION OF THE VERB-SUBSTANTIVE
SUM.

INDICATIVE.

Present.
Sŭm, ĕs, ēst, sŭmŭs, ēstĭs, sŭnt.

Imperfect.
Ĕrăm, ĕrās, ĕrăt, ĕrāmŭs, ĕrātĭs, ĕrānt.

Perfect.
Fŭī, fŭīstī, fŭĭt, fŭĭmŭs, fŭīstĭs, fŭērŭnt or fŭērĕ.

Pluperfect.
Fŭĕrăm, fŭĕrās, fŭĕrăt, fŭĕrāmŭs, fŭĕrātĭs, fŭĕrānt.

Future.
Ĕro, ĕrĭs, ĕrĭt, ĕrĭmŭs, ĕrĭtĭs, ĕrŭnt.

Future Perfect.
Fŭĕro, fŭĕris, fŭĕrĭt, fŭĕrĭmŭs, fŭĕrĭtĭs, fŭĕrĭnt.

IMPERATIVE.

Present.
Ĕs, ēstĕ.

Future.
Ēsto, ēstōtĕ, sūnto.

SUBJUNCTIVE.

Present.
Sĭm, sīs, sĭt, sīmŭs, sītĭs, sīnt.

Imperfect.
Essĕm, ēssēs, ēssĕt, ēssēmŭs, ēssētĭs, ēssēnt, or Fŏrĕm, fŏrēs, fŏrĕt, fŏrēmŭs, fŏrētĭs, fŏrēnt.

Perfect.
Fŭĕrĭm, fŭĕrĭs, fŭĕrĭt, fŭĕrĭmŭs, fŭĕrĭtĭs, fŭĕrĭut.

Pluperfect.
Fŭīssĕm, fŭīssēs, fŭīssĕt, fŭīssēmŭs, fŭīssētĭs, fŭīssēnt.

INFINITIVE.
Present, Essĕ. **Perfect,** Fŭīssĕ.

Future, Fŭtūrŭm ēssĕ or Fŏrĕ.

PARTICIPLE.
Future.
Fŭtūrŭs, ă, ŭm.

The compounds of Sum, as Absum, Adsum, Intersum, Supersum, Possum, and even Præsum, shorten the vowel or syllable placed before this verb in all instances, where it begins with a vowel: e. g., Ăbest, Ădesto, Intĕrerit, Pŏtĕs, Prǣest.

The verb Prosum alone retains the first syllable long in all its tenses, inserting a d whenever the primitive begins with a vowel: e. g., Prōdest, Prōdesse.

TERMINATIONS OF VERBS.
ACTIVE VOICE.

INDICATIVE.
Conj. **Present.**
1. o, ās, ăt, āmŭs, ātĭs, ānt.
2. ĕo, ēs, ĕt, ēmŭs, ētĭs, ēnt.
3. o / ĭo } ĭs, ĭt, ĭmŭs, ĭtĭs, ūnt.
4. ĭo, īs, ĭt, īmŭs, ītĭs, ĭŭnt.

Conj. **Imperfect.**
1. ābăm, ābās, ābăt, ābāmŭs, ābātĭs, ābānt.
2. ēbăm, ēbās, ēbăt, ēbāmŭs, ēbātĭs, ēbānt.
3. ēbăm, ēbās, ēbăt, &c., ĭēbăm, ĭēbās, ĭēbăt, &c.
4. ĭēbăm, ĭēbās, ĭēbăt, ĭēbāmŭs, ĭēbātĭs, ĭēbānt.
sync. ībăm, ībās, ībăt, &c.

Conj.   *Perfect.*

1. āvī, āvistī, āvĭt, āvĭmŭs, āvistĭs, āvē-
rŭnt *or* āvērĕ, *sync.* ārŭnt.
2. ēvī, ēvistī, ēvĭt, ēvĭmŭs, ēvistĭs, ēvē-
rŭnt *or* ēvērĕ, *sync.* ērŭnt.
or ŭī, ŭistī, ŭĭt, ŭĭmŭs, ŭistĭs, ŭērŭnt
or ŭērĕ.
3. ī, istī, ĭt, ĭmŭs, istĭs, ērŭnt *or* ērĕ,
s.times ērŭnt.
4. īvī, īvistī, īvĭt, īvĭmŭs, īvistĭs, īvē-
rŭnt *or* īvērĕ.
sync. īī, īistī, īĭt, īĭmŭs, īistĭs, īērŭnt
or īērĕ.
synær. ī, istī, ĭt, ĭmŭs, istĭs.

Conj.   *Pluperfect.*

1. āvĕrăm, āvĕrās, āvĕrăt, āvĕrāmŭs,
āvĕrătĭs, āvĕrānt.
sync. ārăm, ārās, ārăt,   ārānt.
2. ēvĕrăm, ēvĕrās, ēvĕrăt, ēvĕrāmŭs,
ēvĕrătĭs, ēvĕrānt.
or ŭĕrăm, ŭĕrās, ŭĕrăt, &c.
3. ĕrăm, ĕrās, ĕrăt, ĕrāmŭs, ĕrătĭs,
ĕrānt; *or* īĕrăm, īĕrās, īĕrăt, īĕrāmŭs, īĕrătĭs, īĕrānt.
4. īvĕrăm, īvĕrās, īvĕrăt, īvĕrāmŭs,
īvĕrătĭs, īvĕrānt.
sync. īĕrăm, īĕrās, īĕrăt, īĕrāmŭs, &c.

Conj.   *Future.*

1. ābo, ābĭs, ābĭt, ābĭmŭs, ābĭtĭs, ābŭnt.
2. ēbo, ēbĭs, ēbĭt, ēbĭmŭs, ēbĭtĭs, ēbŭnt.
3. ăm, ēs, ĕt, ēmŭs, ētĭs, ēnt ; *or* īăm,
īēs, īĕt, īēmŭs, &c.
4. īăm, īēs, īĕt, īēmŭs, īētĭs, īĕnt.
old form, ībo, ībĭs, ībĭt, ībĭmŭs, ībĭtĭs,
ībŭnt.

Conj.   *Future Perfect.*

1. āvĕro, āvĕris, āvĕrĭt, āvĕrĭmŭs, āvĕri-
tĭs, āvĕrīnt.
sync. āro, āris, ārĭt   ārīnt.
2. ēvĕro, ēvĕris, ēvĕrĭt, ēvĕrĭmŭs, ēvĕ-
ritĭs, ēvĕrīnt.
sync. ēro, ēris, ērĭt   ērīnt.
or ŭĕro, ŭĕris, ŭĕrĭt, ŭĕrimŭs, &c.
3. ĕro, ĕris, ĕrĭt, ĕrimŭs, ĕritĭs, ĕrīnt.
4. īvĕro, īvĕris, īvĕrĭt, īvĕrimŭs, īvĕri-
tĭs, īvĕrīnt.
sync. īĕro, īĕris, īĕrĭt, īĕrimŭs, &c.

IMPERATIVE.

Conj.   *Present.*

1. ā, ātĕ.
2. ē, ētĕ.
3. ĕ, ĭtĕ.
4. ī, ītĕ.

Conj.   *Future.*

1. āto, ātŏtĕ, ānto.
2. ēto, ētŏtĕ, ēnto.
3. ĭto, ĭtŏtĕ, ūnto *or* ĭunto.
4. īto, ītŏtĕ, ĭunto.

SUBJUNCTIVE.

Conj.   *Present.*

1. ĕm, ēs, ĕt, ēĭmŭs, ētĭs, ēnt.
2. ĕăm, ĕās, ĕăt, ĕāmŭs, ĕātĭs, ĕānt.
3. ăm, ās, ăt, āmŭs, ātĭs, ănt ; *or* īăm,
īās, īăt, īāmŭs, &c.
4. īăm, īās, īăt, īāmŭs, īātĭs, īănt.

Conj.   *Imperfect.*

1. ārĕm, ārēs, ārĕt, ārēmŭs, ārētĭs, ārĕnt.
2. ērĕm, ērēs, ērĕt, ērēmŭs, ērētĭs, ērĕnt.
3. ĕrĕm, ĕrēs, ĕrĕt, ĕrēmŭs, ĕrētĭs, ĕrĕnt.
4. īrĕm, īrēs, īrĕt, īrēmŭs, īrētĭs, īrĕnt.

Conj.   *Perfect.*

1. āvĕrĭm, āvĕris, *sync.*
ārĭm, &c.
2. ēvĕrĭm, ēvĕris, *or*   } *Like the*
ŭĕrĭm, ŭĕris,
3. ĕrĭm, ĕris,   *Future Perfect.*
4. īvĕrĭm, īvĕris, *sync.*
īĕrĭm, īĕris,

Conj.   *Pluperfect.*

1. āvīssĕm, āvīssēs, āvīssĕt, āvīssēmŭs,
āvīssĕtĭs, āvīssēnt.
sync. āssĕm, āssēs, &c.
2. ēvīssĕm, ēvīssēs, ēvīssĕt, ēvīssēmŭs,
ēvīssĕnt.
3. īssĕm, īssēs, īssĕt, īssēmŭs, īssētĭs,
īssĕnt.
4. īvīssĕm, īvīssēs, īvīssĕt, īvīssēmŭs,
īvīssctĭs, īvīssĕnt.
sync. īīssĕm, īīssēs, īīssĕt, īīssēmŭs, &c.
synær. īssĕm, īssēs, īssĕt, &c.

INFINITIVE.

Conj.   *Present.*

1. ārĕ.
2. ērĕ.
3. ĕrĕ.
4. īrĕ.

Conj.   *Perfect.*

1. āvīssĕ, *sync.* āssĕ.
2. ēvīssĕ, *sync.* ēssĕ ; *or* ŭīssĕ.
3. īssĕ.
4. īvīssĕ, *sync.* īīssĕ ; *synær.* īssĕ.

GERUND.

Conj.

1. āndī, āndo, āndŭm.
2.
3. } ēndī, ēndo, ēndŭm; *old form*, ūndī, &c.
4. ĭēndī, ĭēndo, ĭēndŭm.
   old form, ĭūndī, &c.

PARTICIPLES.

Conj.   *Present.*

1. āns, āntĭs.
2. ēns, ēntĭs.
3. ēns *or* ĭēns, ēntĭs, &c.
4. ĭēns, ĭēntĭs.

Conj.   *Future.*

1. ātūrŭs.
2. ētūrŭs, ĭtūrŭs *or* tūrŭs.
3. tūrŭs.
4. ĭtūrŭs.

SUPINE.

Conj.

1. ātŭm.
2. ētŭm, ĭtŭm *or* tŭm.
3. tŭm.
4. ĭtŭm.

PASSIVE VOICE.

INDICATIVE.

Conj.   *Present.*

1. ŏr, ārĭs *or* ārĕ, ūtŭr, āmŭr, āmĭnī, āntŭr.
2. ĕŏr, ērĭs *or* ērĕ, ētŭr, ēmŭr, ēmĭnī, ēntŭr.
3. ŏr *or* ĭŏr, ĕrĭs *or* ĕrĕ, ĭtŭr, ĭmŭr, ĭmĭnī, ūntŭr *or* ĭūntŭr.
4. ĭŏr, īrĭs *or* īrĕ, ītŭr, īmŭr, īmĭnī, ĭūntŭr.

Conj.   *Imperfect.*

1. ābăr, ābārĭs *or* ābărĕ, ābātŭr, ābāmŭr, ābānĭnī, ābāntŭr.
2.
3. } ēbăr, ēbārĭs *or* ēbărĕ, ēbātŭr, ēbāmŭr, ēbāmĭnī, ēbāntŭr.
4. ĭēbăr, ĭēbārĭs *or* ĭēbārĕ, ĭēbātŭr, ĭēbāmŭr, &c.

Conj.   *Perfect.*

1. ātŭs
2. ētŭs, ĭtŭs, *or* tŭs
3. tŭs
4. ītŭs
} sŭm, ĕs, ēst, &c.

Conj.   *Pluperfect.*

1. ātŭs
2. ētŭs, ĭtŭs, *or* tŭs
3. tŭs
4. ītŭs
} ĕrăm, ĕrās, &c.

Conj.   *Future.*

1. ābŏr, ābĕrĭs *or* ābĕrĕ, ābĭtŭr, ābĭmŭr, ābĭmĭnī, ābūntŭr.
2. ēbŏr, ēbĕrĭs *or* ēbĕrĕ, ēbĭtŭr, ēbĭmŭr, ēbĭmĭnī, ēbūntŭr.
3. ăr, ērĭs *or* ērĕ, ētŭr, ēmŭr, ēmĭnī, ēntŭr; *or* ĭăr, ĭērĭs *or* ĭērĕ, ĭētŭr, &c.
4. ĭăr, ĭērĭs *or* ĭērĕ, ĭētŭr, ĭēmŭr, ĭēmĭnī, ĭēntŭr.

Conj.   *Future Perfect.*

1. ātŭs
2. ētŭs, ĭtŭs, *or* tŭs
3. tŭs
4. ītŭs
} ĕro, ĕrĭs, &c.

IMPERATIVE.

Conj.   *Present.*

1. ārĕ, ētŭr, ēmŭr, ēmĭnī, ēntŭr.
2. ērĕ, ĕātŭr, ĕāmŭr, ĕāmĭnī, ĕāntŭr.
3. ĕrĕ, ātŭr, āmŭr, āmĭnī, āntŭr.
4. īrĕ, ĭātŭr, ĭāmŭr, ĭāmĭnī, ĭāntŭr.

Conj.   *Future.*

1. ātŏr, āmĭnŏr, āntŏr.
2. ētŏr, ĕāmĭnŏr, ĕāntŏr.
3. ĭtŏr, ĭmĭnŏr, ūntŏr *or* ĭūntŏr
4. ītŏr, īmĭnŏr, ĭūntŏr.

SUBJUNCTIVE.

Conj. *Present.*

1. ĕr, ērĭs *or* ērĕ, ētŭr, ēmŭr, ēmĭnī, ēntŭr.
2. ĕăr, ĕărĭs *or* ĕărĕ, ĕātŭr, ĕāmŭr, ĕāmĭnī, ĕāntŭr.
3. ăr, ārĭs *or* ārĕ, ātŭr, āmŭr, āmĭnī, āntŭr; *or* ĭăr, ĭărĭs, &c.
4. ĭăr, ĭārĭs *or* ĭārĕ, ĭātŭr, ĭāmŭr, ĭāmĭnī, ĭāntŭr.

Conj. *Imperfect.*

1. ārĕr, ārērĭs *or* ārērĕ, ārētŭr, ārēmŭr, ārēmĭnī, ārēntŭr.
2. ĕrĕr, ĕrērĭs *or* ĕrērĕ, ĕrētŭr, ĕrēmŭr, ĕrēmĭnī, ĕrēntŭr.
3. ĕrĕr, ĕrērĭs *or* ĕrērĕ, ĕrētŭr, ĕrēmŭr, ĕrēmĭnī, ĕrēntŭr.
4. īrĕr, īrērĭs *or* īrērĕ, īrētŭr, īrēmŭr, īrēmĭnī, īrēntŭr.

Conj. *Perfect.*

1. ātŭs
2. ētŭs, ĭtŭs, *or* tŭs
3. tŭs
4. ĭtŭs
} sīm, sīs, sĭt, &c.

Conj. *Pluperfect.*

1. ātŭs
2. ētŭs, ĭtŭs, *or* tŭs
3. tŭs
4. ĭtŭs
} ēssĕm, ēssēs, &c.

INFINITIVE.

Conj. *Present.*

1. ārī, *old form* ārĭĕr.
2. ērī, ērĭĕr.
3. ī, ĭĕr.
4. īrī, īrĭĕr.

PARTICIPLES.

Conj. *Perfect.*

1. ātŭs, ă, ŭm.
2. ētŭs, ĭtŭs *or* tŭs, ă, ŭm.
3. tŭs, ă, ŭm.
4. ītŭs, ă, ŭm.

Conj *Future.*

1. āndŭs.
2. ēndŭs.
3. ēndŭs *or* ĭēndŭs, *old form* ūndŭs.
4. ĭēndŭs, *old form* ĭūndŭs.

SUPINE.

Conj.

1. ātū.
2. ētū, ĭtū *or* tū.
3. tū.
4. ītū.

IRREGULAR VERBS.

DO.

Active Voice.   *Passive Voice.*

INDICATIVE.

Present.

Dŏ, dās, dăt, dămŭs, dătĭs, dănt. | Dŏr, ărĭs, ătŭr, ămŭr, ămĭnī, ăntŭr.

Imperfect.

Dăbăm, dăbās, dăbăt, dăbāmŭs, &c. | Dăbăr, bārĭs, bātŭr, bāmŭr, &c

Perfect.

Dĕdī, ĭstī, ĭt, ĭmŭs, ĭstĭs, ērŭnt *or* ērĕ. | Dătŭs sŭm *or* fŭī, &c.

Pluperfect.

Dĕdĕrăm, dĕdĕrās, dĕdĕrăt, &c. | Dătŭs ĕrăm, &c.

Active Voice.	*Passive Voice.*

First Future.

Dăbo, dăbĭs, dăbĭt, dăbĭmŭs, &c. | Dăbŏr, ĕrĭs, ĭtŭr, ĭmŭr, ĭmĭnĭ, ŭntŭr.

Second Future.

Dĕdĕro, ĕris, ĕrĭt, ĕrimŭs, ĕritĭs, ĕrīnt. | Dătŭs ĕro, &c.

IMPERATIVE.

Present.

Dă, dătĕ. | Dărĕ, dēmĭnĭ, dēntŭr.

Future.

Dăto, dānto. | Dătŏr, dămĭnŏr, dāntŏr.

SUBJUNCTIVE.

Present.

Dĕm, dēs, dĕt, dēmŭs, dētĭs, dēnt. | Dĕr, ĕrĭs *or* ĕrĕ, ētŭr, ēmŭr, ēmĭnĭ, ēntŭr

Imperfect.

Dărĕm, ărēs, ărĕt, ărēmŭs, ărētĭs, ărēnt. | Dărĕr, ērĭs, ētŭr, ēmŭr, &c.

Perfect.

Dĕdĕrĭm, is, ĭt, imŭs, itĭs, ĕrīnt. | Dătŭs sīm, &c.

Pluperfect.

Dĕdīssĕm, ēs, ĕt, ēmŭs, ētĭs, ēnt. | Dătŭs ēssĕm, &c.

INFINITIVE.

Present.

Dărĕ. | Dărī.

Perfect.

Dĕdīssĕ. | Dătŭm ēssĕ.

Future.

Dătūrŭm. | Dătŭm īrī.

PARTICIPLES.

Present.

Dāns, dāntĭs. |

Perfect.

| Dătŭs.

Future.

Dătūrŭs. | Dāndŭs.

SUPINE.

Dătŭm. | Dătū.

GERUND.

Dāndī, dāndo, dāndŭm. |

EO.

Active Voice.

INDICATIVE.

Present.

Ěo, īs, ĭt, īmŭs, ītĭs, ěūnt. | Ĭtŭr.

Imperfect.

Ībăm, ās, ăt, āmŭs, ātĭs, ānt. | Ībātŭr.

Perfect.

Ivī, īvīstī, īvĭt, īvĭmŭs, īvīstĭs, īvērūnt | Ĭtŭm ēst.
    or īvērě.
sync. Ĭi, īistī, ĭit, ĭimŭs, ĭistĭs, ĭěrūnt *or*
    ĭěrě.
syncær. I, īstī, īt, īmŭs, īstĭs.

Pluperfect.

Ivěrăm, *sync.* ĭěrăm, ās, ăt, āmŭs, &c. | Ĭtŭm ěrăt.

First Future.

Ībo, ībĭs, ībĭt, ībĭmŭs, ībĭtĭs, ībūnt. | Ībĭtŭr.

Second Future.

Ivěro, īvěris, īvěrĭt, īvěrimŭs, īvěritĭs,
    īvěrīnt ; *sync.* ĭěro, ĭěris, &c. |

IMPERATIVE.

Present.

I, ītě. |

Future.

Ito, ĭtōtě, ěūnto. |

SUBJUNCTIVE.

Present.

Ěăm, ěās, ěăt, ěāmŭs, ěātĭs, ěānt. | Ěātŭr.

Imperfect.

Irěm, īrēs, īrět, īrēmŭs, īrētĭs, īrēnt. | Irētŭr.

Perfect.

Ivěrĭm, īvěris, īvěrĭt, &c. | Ĭtŭm sĭt.
sync. ĭěrĭm, &c. |

Pluperfect.

Ivīssěm, īvīssēs, īvīssět, &c. | Ĭtŭm ěssĕt.
sync. ĭissěm, ĭissēs, ĭissět, &c.
syncær. Issěm, īssēs, īssět. |

INFINITIVE.

Present.

Irě. | Irī.

Active Voice.	*Passive Voice.*
	Perfect.
Ivīssĕ, *sync.* Iīssĕ, *synær.* Issĕ.	Itŭm essĕ.
	Future.
Itūrŭm.	

PARTICIPLES

	Present.
Iēns, ĕūntĭs.	
	Perfect.
	Itŭs, ă, ŭm, (*whence* Inĭtŭs, Öbĭtŭs, &c.)
	Future.
Itūrŭs, ă, ŭm.	Eūndŭs, ă, ŭm, (*whence* Incŭndŭs, Öb-ĕūndŭs, &c.)

SUPINE.

Itŭm.	Itū.

GERUND.

Eūndī, ĕūndo, ĕūndŭm.	

VOLO.   FIO.

INDICATIVE.

Present.

Vŏlo, vīs, vūlt, vŏlŭmŭs, vūltĭs, vŏlŭnt. | Fīo, fīs, fīt, fīmŭs, fītĭs, fīunt.

Imperfect.

Vŏlēbăm, ēbās, ēbăt, ēbāmŭs, ēbātĭs, ēbūnt. | Fīēbăm, ēbās, ēbăt, ēbāmŭs, ēbātĭs, ēbūnt.

Perfect.

Vŏlŭī, īstī, ĭt, ĭmŭs, īstĭs, ērūnt *or* ērĕ. | Fāctŭs sŭm, ĕs, ēst, &c.

Pluperfect.

Vŏlŭĕrăm, ĕrās, ĕrăt, ĕrāmŭs, ĕrātĭs, ĕrānt. | Fāctŭs ĕrăm, ĕrās, ĕrăt, &c.

First Future.

Vŏlăm, ēs, ĕt, ēmŭs, ētĭs, ēnt. | Fīăm, fīēs, fīĕt, fīēmŭs, fīētĭs, fīēnt.

Second Future.

Vŏlŭĕro, ĕris, ĕrĭt, ĕrimus, ĕritĭs, ĕrĭnt. | Fāctŭs ĕro, ĕrĭs, ĕrĭt, &c.

IMPERATIVE.

| Fī, fītĕ ; *and* fīto, fītōtĕ.

SUBJUNCTIVE.

Present.

Vĕlĭm, īs, ĭt, īmŭs, ıtĭs, īnt. | Fīăm, fīās, fīăt, fīāmŭs, &c.

Active Voice.	Passive Voice.

Imperfect.

Vĕllĕm, ēs, ĕt, ēmŭs, ētīs, ēnt. | Fĭĕrĕm, fĭĕrēs, fĭĕrĕt, fĭĕrēmŭs, &c.

Perfect.

Vŏlŭĕrĭm, ĕris, ĕrĭt, ĕrimŭs, ĕritīs, ĕrīnt. | Fāctŭs sīm, &c.

Pluperfect.

Vŏlŭīssĕm, és, ĕt, ēmŭs, ētīs, ēnt. | Fāctŭs ēssĕm, &c

INFINITIVE.

Present.

Vĕllĕ. | Fĭĕrī.

Perfect.

Vŏlŭīssĕ. | Fāctŭm ēssĕ.

PARTICIPLES.

Present.

Vŏlēns, ēntīs. |

Perfect.

| Fāctŭs, ă, ŭm.

Future.

| Făcĭēndŭs, ă, ŭm, *old form* Făcĭŭndŭs.

THE END.

GILBERT & RIVINGTON, Printers, St. John's Square, London.

www.ingramcontent.com/pod-product-compliance
Lightning Source LLC
Chambersburg PA
CBHW022025110726
47901CB00006B/1657